LATIN MOON
IN MANHATTAN

Books by Jaime Manrique

FICTION
El cadáver de papá
Columbian Gold
Latin Moon in Manhattan
Twilight at the Equator

POETRY
Los adoradores de la luna
Scarecrow (chapbook)
My Night with Federico García Lorca
Tarzan, My Body, Christopher Columbus

CRITICISM
Notas de cine: Confesiones de un crítico amateur

MEMOIR
Eminent Maricones: Arenas, Lorca, Puig, and Me

LATIN MOON
IN MANHATTAN

A Novel

JAIME MANRIQUE

The University of Wisconsin Press

The University of Wisconsin Press
1930 Monroe Street
Madison, Wisconsin 53711

www.wisc.edu/wisconsinpress/

3 Henrietta Street
London WC2E 8LU, England

5   4   3   2   1

Printed in the United States of America

Library of Congress Cataloging-in-Publication Data
Manrique Ardila, Jaime, 1949–
Latin moon in Manhattan : a novel / Jaime Manrique
p.   cm.
ISBN 0-299-18754-3 (paper)
1. New York (N.Y.)—Fiction. 2. Hispanic Americans—Fiction.
3. Manhattan (New York, N.Y.)—Fiction. I. Title.
PS3563.A573 L38   2003
813'.54—dc21   2002075666

Acknowledgments

My thanks to The Virginia Center for the Creative Arts for a residency in which this novel evolved into its final shape; to Laura Segal for helping me translate the tango lyrics and, most importantly, for the gift of Mr. O'Donnell; to Bill Sullivan for his unflagging enthusiasm; to the Ash Wednesday group, where I first workshopped the manuscript; and, most respectfully, to Helen O'Donnell, in memoriam.

For Tom and Elaine Colchie

LATIN MOON
IN MANHATTAN

PART ONE

AND IT WAS A LONG, LONE
SHADOW.

José Asunción Silva

1

Little Colombia, Jackson Heights

After it leaves Manhattan, the number seven train becomes an elevated, and crosses a landscape of abandoned railroad tracks, dilapidated buildings and, later, a conglomerate of ugly factories that blow serpentine plumes of gaudy poisonous smoke. As the train journeys deeper into Queens, the Manhattan skyscrapers in the distance resemble monuments of an enchanted place—ancient Baghdad, or even the Land of Oz. The sun, setting behind the towers of the World Trade Center, burnishes the sky with a warm orange glow and the windows of the towers look like gold-leafed entrances to huge hives bursting with honey.

Riding the number seven train to Jackson Heights, I thought of our immigration to the United States eighteen years ago. But "immigration" is too big a word to describe what happened. Let's just say we moved from Bogotá, Colombia, to Jackson Heights, Queens—from one cocaine capital to another, the main difference being that the former sits ten thousand feet up in the Andes, while the latter is a mere twenty-minute train ride from Manhattan.

I finished high school and college in Queens and it wasn't until years later, when I settled in Times Square, that I finally felt I was living in a foreign country. What I had observed through the years was that while Queens became more prosperous and upscale, the city of New York more and more resembled a third world capital; there was a wide—and ever widening—gap between rich and poor, and the streets teemed with crazies, junkies, homeless people, street urchins, hustlers, hookers, and pickpockets, just like in Bogotá. Since I had arrived in America, the human traffic on the number seven train had also changed; there were still a few blacks going to Queens, but now the Asians were just as numerous as the South Americans. The nicely dressed, well-scrubbed people riding in my car looked like solid, hard-working, law-abiding Republicans. That, plus the lack of graffiti, made the Queens-bound trains different from the Brooklyn and Bronx lines.

I was so engrossed in my observations that I almost missed my stop. Ninetieth Street, with its garish shops, vegetable and root stands, and South American eateries—everything in a small, Lilliputian scale—looks unreal, like a movie set. All the signs are in Spanish, and the pedestrians talk in the various regional accents of Colombia.

I walked under the elevated, and turned right at Eighty-seventh Street. I began to metamorphose; the closer I got to my mother's house, the more Colombian I became. Intense cravings for foods that were unavailable to me in the city—such as *ajiaco, arepa de huevo, morcillas, chicharrones*—awoke in me. The tree-shaded street was getting dark and, although this was hardly the country, I felt light-years away from the overheated cement of Forty-second Street. I passed pretty two-story houses with attics and gabled roofs, cypresses on their lawns, rose gardens in bloom, and sidewalks spattered with dog shit. It was hard to believe that just a few blocks away there was a world of drugs and crime in which coke-crazed Colombians iced each other in the most vicious, post-modern ways.

My mother's house was in darkness, except for the light above the side entrance that led to the kitchen. This was the house that Victor, my mother's present husband, gave her as a wedding present. Victor, a Sicilian who worked all his life for the mob and Queens politicians, had supported my mother nicely by running numbers until he developed Alzheimer's disease and was put in an institution. Now my mother lives alone, except for the periods when my nephew Eugene runs away from my sister's apartment.

I climbed the steps to the landing outside the kitchen and was about to open the door—which my mother still left open after all these years—when I felt something rubbing against my ankles. It was Puss, one of Mother's cats. Since her cats were not allowed inside the house, I sat on the steps to play with him. Puss was old and had lost a lot of his thick, tawny coat, but his tail was still beautiful and soft, like an ostrich feather.

"Hi, Puss. How're you doing, you old cat? Where is Me-shu?" I said, looking around for Mother's other cat, who was shy. Although Puss had lived all his life outside—maybe because of it—he craved human affection. He purred and purred, lying at my feet, while I scratched him behind the ears. He was wearing the flea collar I had given him a couple of months ago, but he had fleas, and his hair was so matted in places that he looked like a Rastafarian.

It was dark now, and the pertinacious mosquitoes were determined to get their evening meal. I got up, and as I turned the doorknob, I could hear Simón Bolívar screeching inside, "Who is it?" I tensed up; I intensely dislike my mother's parrot. Turning on the kitchen light, I saw to my relief that Simón Bolívar was caged. "Hello, hello, hello," he shrieked stupidly.

"Hi, Simón," I acknowledged him so he would shut up.

On the kitchen table Mother had left me a note: "I went to play bingo. Will be back late. Your dinner is on the stove. Love, Mother."

I was hungry so I uncovered the pans: Mother had cooked tongue stew, coconut rice with raisins, and fried ripe plantains. Everything was still warm. Serving myself, I sat down to eat. I picked up *El Espectador,* a Bogotá newspaper Mother bought every day, and began to peruse the headlines. Although I no longer feel very connected to Colombian life, I still read the newspapers and magazines Mother buys because, invariably, the first question I'm always asked by people I meet is, "How are things in Colombia?" Consequently, even though I'm an American citizen now, I keep abreast of the latest developments in the war against drugs and guerrilla insurgency down home.

There was a pitcher full of *peto* on the table, a Colombian corn drink; I poured myself a glass and started sipping it, tasting the cinnamon and nutmeg with which my mother peppered the drink.

Suddenly Simón Bolívar said in Spanish, "Long live the Liberal party!" He sat on his perch, staring at me uncannily with his bright yellow eyes.

"Shut up," I said, and threatened to fling the remnants of my *peto* at him. This created pandemonium. Thinking he was about to get a bath, Simón started flapping his brightly colored wings.

At my grandmother's death, my mother had inherited two ancestral avocado trees and a parrot. Simón had thus immigrated to the States ten years ago and I used to tease my mother that he was the only Colombian in Jackson Heights with a green card.

Imitating Flaubert's Felicité, my mother fell in love with the parrot. Some years back, in early spring, she placed his cage out in the backyard to give the bird some sun, and somehow Simón Bolívar managed to escape. Mother was sure he had been stolen, though why anyone would have wanted to steal such an obstreperous animal is beyond my understanding. Mother cried and cried and stopped eating and when these measures didn't bring Simón back, she built a shrine to San Martín de Porres in her living room and prayed to the Peruvian saint for the return of her parrot. Months later, a storm awakened her late at night. She claims she saw light streaming through the curtains of her bedroom window. She knew San Martín had answered her prayer, and when she opened the windows she found Simón Bolívar seeking shelter from the rain in the cypress tree. Since that time, Mother has declared him a holy parrot who has been to heaven and back. It was hard for me to believe that this was God's envoy as he sat on his perch screaming the sickeningly hackneyed words of some Julio Iglesias song.

I looked away, ignoring his nonsense. I had lost my appetite; it was too warm in the kitchen to eat. I set aside the newspaper. Simón Bolívar had quieted down, but suddenly I heard him screech, "Who's there?" I heard noises outside. The doorknob turned, the door opened, and a pair of huge decomposing Reeboks burst into the kitchen.

"Sammy, dude, what's happening?" my nephew Gene greeted me.

"Hi, Gene," I replied.

Gene sat at the table, lit a Marlboro and started whiffling clouds of smoke. He was seventeen and already six foot two, with the face of a baby Gulliver. Gene glanced suspiciously at the food on my plate. "Is that tongue?" He indicated the stew on my plate, making a face.

"It's better than hamburger, which is probably all you eat."

"Look, Sammy, I'm an American, not a Colombian, and Americans don't eat tongue."

"That just shows what a hick you are. In French cuisine tongue is considered a great delicacy."

"Oh, yeah? But we're in America not in France."

"We're in Jackson Heights, Colombia," I said.

"But don't let me spoil your chow," he added magnanimously. "It's cool with me, man. If you want to eat tongue, go right ahead."

"I've had enough. So you're living here now?"

"I guess so. School's out."

"Are you getting along with Wilbrajan?"

"Oh yeah, everything's cool."

"Is she working?"

"She's singing tangos at the Rose Saigon. The Japanese love tangos."

"But Saigon is not in Japan."

Gene shrugged. "What do I know; I just finished the tenth grade. I like to come here to keep grandma company. She's lonely, and she's getting old."

Guiltily, I said, "That's really nice of you."

"She nags like hell, though."

"You know what the French say: 'If you can't send them the devil, send them an old woman.' "

Gene smiled. "You're so mean."

I got up to turn on the air conditioner.

"Better not," Gene warned. "Grandma doesn't like it on unless it's above one hundred degrees. She's pretty nuts about conserving energy."

"You want to go outside and sit in the garden?"

As we were getting ready to leave the kitchen, Simón Bolívar, pissed off that were leaving him behind, started a racket.

"Shut up, asshole," Gene ordered him.

"Asshole, asshole, asshole," Simón Bolívar echoed as we stepped outside.

"Maybe I should leave the door open and let the cats in. I'm sure they'd love him for dinner. What do you think?" I asked, grinning.

"The cats are scared shitless of him. That parrot could scare a Colombian pusher away. He's the meanest mother I know."

We walked to the back of the house where Mother had her vegetable and flower gardens and sat down on the wooden chairs next to the barbecue grill. Above us was a patch of open sky. The night was clear and cool, and we could see a spattering of stars and a crescent moon. Pointing to the sky, I said, "That's the North Star over there, see it? If you ever get lost at sea just follow it and you'll reach land."

"You know the weirdest shit," Gene snorted. "Thanks for the tip, but I hate the sea. All that activity makes me crazy." There was a pause, which Gene broke by saying, "I haven't seen you in a long time. What's up?"

"Everything's okay," I said, not wanting to sound too pessimistic in front of a teenager. "I've been thinking about going back to school to finish my Ph.D."

Gene chortled. "Sammy, you have more degrees than a thermometer. Why don't you finish your book? That'd make you feel better." He referred to my Christopher Columbus epic, which I had been writing for some years.

"I haven't written anything new in some time. You know, one day it occurred to me that I couldn't go on writing it until I saw one of the caravels in which Columbus traveled."

"What's that?"

"You know, one of the ships he sailed to the New World in. There's a replica of one in the Barcelona harbor and somehow I feel I have to go see it before I can finish the poem," I concluded.

"And when are you going?"

"Soon," I said cryptically.

"Sammy, why don't you write something good?"

I bristled at his criticism. "What do you mean 'something good?' I want to write a great epic poem."

"That's what I mean. When was the last time there was a best-seller epic poem? Write something like . . . like . . . a story about teenagers. In English. You know, I could help you with it. What you have to do is write something that English teachers like so that they recommend it to the students. I'll guarantee you it'll make a million bucks."

"You write the teenager story, okay, and I'll write whatever I want to write."

"No need to get sore, man. I'm not gonna write anything. I just want to be an actor."

"Like Rocky Rambo, I suppose."

"Fuck no. Like Marlon Brando. Man, he's neat as shit. Did you see him in *The Wild One*? You haven't? I've seen it thirty-seven times. The way he rides that motorcycle all dressed up in black leather and chains. He's so cool, so radical—a real bad dude. He's awesome," Gene sighed, his face glowing in the dark. "I'm gonna buy me a motorcycle," he vowed.

"I wish you wouldn't; motorcycles are extremely dangerous. People get killed on those things all the time."

"You're so uncool; you don't know anything. More people get killed going to the post office, at least here in Jackson Heights."

"Who's giving you the money to buy a motorcycle?"

"I got a summer job. I'm going to save all the money I make, and in the fall I'll buy it."

"What kind of a job?"

"Making . . . deliveries . . . here in Queens. Hey, you want to get high?" Gene pulled a fat joint from his pack of Marlboros.

"I quit smoking," I said. Recently I had come to the sudden realization that it was because of drugs and alcohol that I had dropped out of graduate school and the reason why in the past ten years I had accomplished so little.

Gene lit the joint and inhaled deeply. "You want to smoke this," he said melodramatically, holding the smoke in his lungs. "This is great Colombian shit; this kind of thing never hits the streets of Manhattan. The Colombians smoke it all as soon as it comes in."

"Well, a puff won't do me any harm, I suppose."

Gene was right; this was great pot. It was like pouring hot water in a glass full of ice—I melted right away. Yet the sense of guilt gnawed at my conscience. I said, "Gene, I hope you're not into heavy drugs."

"No, man. Rusty and the Boners—you've got to meet them sometime; they're my best friends—do all kinds of shit. I just smoke pot, and drink beer on the weekends and do a line of coke once in a while."

I was horrified. "Gene, I didn't start doing anything until I was twenty-one."

"Yeah, well, that was a long time ago, right? You're old, Sammy; you know that."

"If you're lucky, some day you'll be my age," I said, pissed off, as if I were putting a curse on him. "Promise me you'll never do crack."

"You think I'm fucking crazy? I don't wanna get fucked up; I wanna be a famous actor."

Let's hope his thespian instincts will win out in the long run, I thought. We finished smoking the joint; I felt as if I were tripping.

"What are you doing tonight?" Gene asked.

"Nothing; just hanging out. Want to go see a movie?"

"Maybe tomorrow. I'm going to a party. Want to come along?"

"What's the occasion?" I asked, although I had no intention of going to a party with a bunch of drug-addicted teenagers.

"You know, girls, beer. We smoke jays and listen to Sinead O'Connor." Gene stood up. "Okay, Sammy, I've got to go. I promised the Boners I'd be there by now."

"What kind of name is that—the Boners?"

"They're twins. You have to meet them. They're real sleaze balls, but I know you'll like them. They're cool and neat as hell. They've done so many drugs they're all skin and bones. The Boners, you got it now?"

"I got it."

"If you get bored, just go by the Rose Saigon. Mom goes on around midnight. Okay, catch you later."

"Have a nice time and don't get too wasted," I said, feeling old. Gene disappeared into the darkness, and I was left by myself, pleasantly stoned. I thought about uncles and nephews, and, specifically, I thought about my Uncle Hernán, whom I worshiped in my adolescence. Twelve years before, he had died in a plane accident. In the sixties, he became mixed up with radical politics in Colombia and fled to Venezuela when the military got on his case. There, he go a job working in the diamond mines near Ciudad Bolívar. One Christmas, he was on his way to visit my grandparents when a bomb went off in the plane, blowing it to pieces and all that they could find of him was his arm.

The last time I had seen Uncle Hernán I was around Gene's age. That was the year my mother came to New York to see about settling here. She had dismantled our home in Bogotá and my sister and I were sent to stay with our maternal grandparents in the country. Uncle Hernán was twenty-two then, the youngest of my uncles. Although I had many cousins, he felt a special kinship for me. Every day after lunch he'd pack his rifle and I my fishing gear and we'd ride to Las Marías, my grandfather's farm a few miles outside of town. Uncle Hernán taught me to ride horses, burros and mules, to lasso cows and milk them, to fish and swim in the ponds of the Magdalena and César rivers. He read books about Marxism and the Cuban and Russian revolutions and was passionate about radical politics. Yet hunting was his favorite occupation. Every afternoon, he'd hunt ducks and other birds, and each night after supper he'd drive the jeep down to the savannah, where enormous termite colonies loomed, spectral and lunar in the darkness. There he'd hunt deer, tigers, armadillos, and wild boar.

My male cousins made fun of how clumsy I was at all the country activities for boys, but Uncle Hernán was patient. Sometimes, he'd take a break from tracking prey and, finding a shady tree on the plain, he'd read to me about Lenin or Trotsky. But that December, I had turned sixteen, and he informed me that the time had come for me to visit the town's whorehouse. The particular afternoon I remember so vividly, he had been looking for game without success and we had wandered far away from the farmhouse, arriving at the foothills of the Sierra Nevada. It was getting late, and in the mountains it was much cooler than in the town. The brooks and streams we waded through were cold and clear, and their sandy beds glittered with gold. In my grandfather's youth, this had been a gold-mining region and there was still gold to be found, but not in quantities sufficient to exploit commercially. The hills we ascended were paved with the palest green grass; the mango and ciruela trees, upon which fed flocks of parrots, macaws, and parakeets, and bands of boisterous monkeys, were now below us in the plain surrounding the river. Occasionally we ran into stray cows and menacing bulls and shy wild horses, but Uncle Hernán seemed pretty sure of the direction in which we were heading.

I was beginning to get tired of carrying his heavy rifle, as I always did, but I felt it would be unmanly to complain. Now we had an unobstructed view of the snowy peaks of the Sierra Nevada as they caught the reflection of the setting sun. The world was growing still, hushed. We started descending into an open *potrero* of verdant pastures with high hills on all sides fencing it in. At its center was a shallow pond where scores of burros were drinking and playing in the water. Above them, rainbow-colored dragonflies darted about. The burros seemed young, but tame and friendly. Uncle Hernán approached them cautiously, talking to them in low, silky tones, patting their backs and stroking their long ears. *"Burra, burrita,"* he said, separating two of them and patting their behinds until they had wandered meters away from the rest of the herd. Then Uncle Hernán stood behind one of the burras and lifted her tail, putting his fingers inside her vulva. He motioned me to do the same with the other donkey which stood still, expectantly. When I lifted her tail, little white gnats flew into the saffron light of sunset. It was smelly down there. The rims of the vulva were pinkish and ivory, and the tips of my fingers felt warm and gluey. A few inches inside the vagina a flexible but resistant membrane stopped my fingers from exploring further. Even though the animal seemed to enjoy it, I was afraid of pursuing this activity. I saw Uncle Hernán unzip his pants. With his huge dick sticking out, he approached me. Not understanding what was happening, I was seized with terror and started to shake. He motioned for me to move aside, and penetrated the burra once, twice, rocking back and forth. The burra stamped one of her hind hoofs on the ground and grunted, as if she were pleased. Uncle Hernán grinned. "Okay, Sammy, she's all yours: a virgin no more."

He hurried over to the other burra, which had stood motionless, waiting for him, and penetrated her. I imitated his bumping motions and was about to get an erection when several male burros with their black, baseball-bat-sized members, began circling the herd at a gallop and braying hysterically. I was afraid that they were angry and were getting ready to attack us. My cock kept falling out of the enormous vagina. Soon, Uncle Hernán was in a frenzy, eyes closed, his buttocks pushing in and out, in and out; he moaned and cried in pleasure when he finished. Then he rested his head on the burra's rump and embraced her around her haunches. He remained that way, panting, until he stepped backward and collapsed on the grass, his penis limp but still large, his pants tangled around his boots. I walked over to the burra he had just fucked, and what seemed like large quantities of semen oozed out of her vagina. Becoming aroused, I put my hard cock inside her.

A car door slamming brought me back to reality. Mother was back home from her bingo game.

"Buenas noches, mi amor," Mother called out to her friend as the car pulled away.

2

Volver

I had locked up Mr. O'Donnell in the bathroom by mistake. At first, he sat behind the door, patiently waiting for me to realize it. As time passed, he became anxious and started scratching the door and pacing the room restlessly. Getting frantic, he jumped from the bathtub to the sink, and, losing his balance, fell into the toilet, which automatically flushed. Tail first, Mr. O'Donnell began to disappear. . . . I woke up panting, the palms of my hands clammy. I sat in bed. It was true I was worried about my cat, Mr. O'Donnell, but I was sure the nightmare had been caused by my mother's Colombian cuisine.

A gentle breeze blew through the white lace curtains and through them I caught a glimpse of a sunny day and a cloudless sky. After many months in Manhattan where I had only seen concrete and glass, the deep green branches of the tree by my window had a soothing effect on me.

Although I had left home over ten years ago, nothing had changed in my room. The old Janis Joplin poster hung over my desk, the colors faded, Janis looking more ghostly than ever. The black Olivetti typewriter I had brought with me from Colombia now prehistoric. No new books had been added to the bookshelves, but the volumes were dustless and neatly arranged. Becoming nostalgic for my adolescence, I longed to be sick, to surrender to an asthma attack and to have the course of my life stopped. I longed for the freedom I had experienced during those times: no school, no duties, long stays in bed reading *Crime and Punishment, Wuthering Heights,* and other morbid books, and having my mother make baby pigeon soup for me and feed me spoonfuls of hot, buttery carrots and potatoes puree.

I could have stayed in bed indulging myself with these reveries, but the smells of *arepas, chicharrones* and *tostones* traveled up from the kitchen, their potent aromas luring me like a siren's song. I had decided to visit my friend Bobby. Perhaps this was the main reason for my trip to Queens this weekend. Bobby was deteriorating very fast and he was dying. I got out of bed, showered and shaved before going downstairs to meet my mother.

In the kitchen, a Spanish radio station was playing a Gardel program. I could hear my mother, singing along with Gardel, the lyrics of *"Yira, Yira"*:

> When luck is rotten
> Laughing and laughing
> While you lie in the streets.
> When you're down in the gutter
> Lost, in despair;
> When you've lost even hope
> And you're drinking the dregs,
> When your last cent is gone
> And you're looking for crumbs
> To keep you alive
> The world couldn't care less.
> Yira, yira.

It wasn't exactly the most cheerful music to listen to first thing in the morning, and Simón Bolívar, who was particularly excited by Mother's tango renditions, squealed along, *"Yira, yira, yira, yira."* On the other hand, it was better to listen to such existential angst in the morning. I could see how listening to these tangos late at night could drive one to suicide. My mother and Gardel were reaching a crescendo:

> Even if life breaks you up
> And the pain doesn't end
> Don't wait for a handout, or a favor,
> or friends.

"Sammy," Mother cried, stopping her singing. "Did you sleep well?" she added in Spanish, rushing over to kiss me. "I've been making your breakfast."

There was enough food on the table for a baseball team. "How are you, Mother?" I asked, sitting at the table and pouring myself a cup of chocolate. The pile of *arepas* in a straw basket was warm and tender.

"I'm as good as could be expected, considering everything. How's Mr. MacDonald?" she asked.

It was nice of her to inquire after my cat, but it mortified me that after many years she hadn't taken the trouble to get his name correctly. "His name is Mr. O'Donnell. He's the same, I guess."

"No wonder he's sick, cooped up in that apartment all the time. Look at my cats, they've lived all their lives outside and they're as healthy as can be."

"Mother," I said calmly, concentrating on my breathing, trying to muster a serenity I never had when we conversed. "First, I cannot let him out in Manhattan; he'd be killed in a minute. Second, he has an enlarged heart, and that's a congenital condition." As I finished saying this, I realized the absurdity of trying to explain anything rationally to a Colombian.

"Anyway, it's unnatural to love a cat that way," Mother said, baiting me. "That's what happens to men when they don't get married and have a family."

I felt like saying, Oh yeah? And why is it more *natural* to love a stupid parrot? But I held back. I didn't want to get upset before breakfast. Besides, I had been in her presence barely five minutes and had the rest of the weekend to fight.

She placed a tray of pork *chicharrones* on the table. "It's been fifty years since Gardel died," she said dreamily, changing the subject, "but for my money he sings better every day."

I cut open an *arepa* and buttered it. "Ummm, it's delicious," I commented, since I didn't feel like discussing Gardel. Half-closing her eyes, Mother hummed to herself the last bars of *"Yira, Yira."*

Waiting for the song to end, I picked up one of the *chicharrones* and bit off a juicy piece of pork meat. As I chewed, I studied my mother who was sitting next to me, her legs crossed. Even this early in the morning she wore a ton of jewelry, Colombian style: her wedding band, her heart-shaped emerald ring, gold bracelets, a gold chain with an emerald and diamond crucifix, plus her diamond earrings. I wondered if she ever took these things off. As usual, her auburn hair was made up and lacquered, her fingernails manicured and painted a transparent pink. She wore a Mexican cotton blouse with short sleeves, khaki bermudas, and open-toed blue cotton slippers. She had turned seventy in the spring, but with the years she had grown svelte. It bothered me that I got a kick out of how nice she still looked.

Mother selected a *chicharrón* and took a dainty bite. Her wonderfully lustrous maple sugar skin was smooth, unwrinkled, and the only places her age showed were on the back of her hands, and her neck and thighs, where her flesh sagged a bit. When she married Victor, over ten years ago, mother had the bags under her eyes removed and this procedure had considerably enlarged her marvelous hazel eyes so that at first she looked spooked, as if she had just seen a ghost. But with the passage of time, the eyes became more natural-looking and attractive. The Gardel program came to an end and Mother got up to turn off the radio. Then she got a pitcher of *guanabana* juice out of the refrigerator and poured me a glassful. I realized these gargantuan breakfasts Mother subjected me to were a continuation of my grandparents' breakfast table, where meat, fish, wild game, *suero,* butter and cheese, breads, *arepas,* and *empanadas,* fried plantains and *yucca,* papaya, mango, pineapple juice, coffee, chocolate, and *kumis* were the fare.

I was finishing my first cup of deliciously brewed Colombian coffee, when the phone rang.

"You'd better get it; it's for you," Mother informed me.

"*Lorito real, lorito real,*" Simón Bolívar twaddled, excited by the phone.

"It's Carmen Elvira," Mother went on. "I told her you'd be up by eleven and to call you then."

"Why is Carmen Elvira calling me?"

"She wants to invite you to become a member of their literary society, The Colombian Parnassus. Please, Santiago, don't humiliate me. She's one of my best friends. So please accept her invitation. It's a great honor."

The phone kept ringing and Simón Bolívar continued screaming his nonsense and flapping his wings.

"Please, Santiago, it will be the last thing I'll ever ask of you. She knows you're here. If you don't pick up, she'll come over."

"This is blackmail," I protested, picking up the receiver. "Hello," I said with great trepidation.

"*Hola, Sammy. Es Carmen Elvira.*"

"Hello, Carmen Elvira. How are you?"

"Fine, thank you, honey, and you?" she said in her polite *cachaco* manner. "I'm calling to give you great news; you're being invited to become a member of The Colombian Parnassus. *Enhorabuena!* Congratulations," she added in English.

I couldn't feign surprise, or happiness for that matter. But I saw Mother getting up and approaching me, so I said, "Thank you very much; I'm honored." Mother smiled at me.

"I thought you'd be. Anyway, we plan to induct you this afternoon. We're meeting at Olga's home around 12:30, American time. You know where she lives, don't you?"

"Yes," I said grimly.

"Well, *cariño,* it's been a real pleasure talking to you. Say hello to Lucy," she said, referring to my mother.

"Thank you very much. I will."

After I hung up, Mother rushed over and kissed me on both cheeks. Taking advantage of the proximity, Simón Bolívar bit me on the shoulder.

"Ouch," I complained. "Mother, he bit me."

"God, you're sensitive," she said. "He pecked you affectionately, that's all."

19

"Jesus, Mother!" I burst out. "What have you made me do? And the gall of that woman! She expects me to show up at 12:30 and I just found out about it. What if I had made plans?" Feeling all sorts of emotions welling up, I picked up an *arepa* and started gobbling it down.

"What plans? People in Queens don't make plans. And don't stuff yourself. They're making a delicious lunch just for you. So, please, Sammy, please be a gentleman and eat everything they serve you. Show them I've taught you some manners."

"I refuse to eat iguana stew!"

"I don't know when you became such a squeamish gringo; you used to love iguana eggs, and you ate plenty of iguana when you visited your grandparents in the country."

"I never ate iguana," I protested. "I loathe iguana eggs. They smell worse than a skunk's fart."

"Iguana stew," Mother said sadistically, "and rattlesnake *sancocho,* and barbecued sloth, and alligator tail fricasse. You ate all those things. And monkey brains soufflé."

"I'm going to puke if you don't stop."

Simón Bolívar leaped off my mother's shoulder onto the table and scurried toward me. I hopped off my seat. "Get that fucking bird away from me before I wring his neck!"

"Don't you dare use that language in front of me, Santiago! And don't talk about him like that. He understands you. He speaks."

"He doesn't speak; he imitates sounds."

"He's bilingual," Mother said. Looking dejected she stood up. "Come here, Simón. He wants you in prison. Come here, my darling," she purred, offering him her wrist. "What's going to happen to you after I'm gone?" Tenderly she stroked his feathers. "I only pray to God that when my time's up, he'll take you with me. Who's going to take care of you after I'm gone, my love?"

I shuddered. I knew that parrots lived to be a hundred years or more, so in all likelihood he'd outlive my mother and, with my luck, probably me too. "Mother, cut it out," I begged her. "Put that bird in his cage. You know he hates me and is going to bite me first chance he gets."

"*Lorito real, lorito real,*" the cunning parrot protested, looking like an innocent.

When the parrot was safely behind bars, I sat down to the table to finish my *guanabana* juice.

"It would be nice if you went to the nursing home to see Victor," Mother said, referring to my stepfather. "I told him you were coming this weekend, and you know he likes you very much. He'd be so happy to see you."

"I don't know. It's so depressing. The last time I was there he didn't recognize me at all."

"I think the doctors are wrong," she said. "Just because he can't talk doesn't mean he doesn't know who we are. I see how his eyes light up when I visit him and tell him stories. And you should feel grateful to Victor. It was he who put you through college. I couldn't have done it on my own."

"I know that, Mother, and I like him a lot, but what's the point? He's a vegetable; I'm going to skip visiting him this time. I have other plans."

"Like what?" she asked, displeased.

"I want to visit Bobby."

Mother stared at me. I realized that Bobby too was a vegetable. On my last visit, he hadn't recognized me either.

"I visit him at least once a week."

"That's very nice of you, Mother."

"It could happen in my own family, too, so I'm getting prepared. But it breaks my heart, Santiago. You know I've loved Bobby since the two of you met in Colegio Americano in Barranquilla. He always called me his second mother. By the way, Leticia finally came."

"When?"

"About a week ago. I guess all those letters I wrote her worked. Did you know she refuses to touch him? She won't even go into his room. She stands by the door, with her hands behind her back, and talks to him as if he were a baby, but she won't touch him with a ten-foot pole."

"What a hideous woman; that's horrible."

"I tried to explain to her that AIDS can't be caught by casual contact. To show her, I sat on Bobby's bed and combed his hair and arranged his pillows. Santiago," Mother said beseechingly, "why don't you get married? Why don't you marry Claudia? She's always been in love with you. I know. Paulina told me so. And she's rich," Mother threw in to tempt me.

Although Mother knows perfectly well what my sexual preference is, ever since Bobby had come down with AIDS she started an insane campaign to try to get me married to my childhood friend Claudia Urrutia, hoping perhaps I'd be spared Bobby's fate.

Deciding to ignore the marriage talk, I said, "Sure, I'd be rich like them if I were in the drug trade."

Mother made an angry face. "They're not in the drug business. How can you say that about Paulina? She's my best friend; she's practically my sister," she said, sincerely outraged.

"Mother, come off it. How can you be so naïve? Okay, so they're not in the drug trade. Then how did they make all those millions?"

"Working, of course. How else?"

"I never heard of anyone in that family working. Besides, nobody makes that kind of dough working. They own mansions all over the world, and planes and yachts and Mercedes Benzes and . . ."

"Are you saying Paulina and Claudia are in the mafia? Is that what you're saying?"

"Maybe they aren't personally," I relented. "But all the men in the family sure are. Everyone in Jackson Heights—except you, of course—knows that."

"Claudia is an architect, Santiago. She went to jail."

"Yale, Mother," I corrected her for the millionth time. "Anyway, she's never practiced, and she lives like a queen. . . ."

"She loves you, and that ought to be enough for you."

"Mother, Claudia is a . . ." dyke, I was going to add, but I knew this would just make matters worse. "I think she's nuts."

"Well, she's a little odd."

"A little odd, ha! That's got to be the understatement of the millennium. Is that what you call a girl who rides a motorcycle and wears a helmet all the time? She'd be the perfect wife for Gene," I chuckled. "He'd love to get a hold of her motorcycles."

"You and your sister are going to kill me," Mother said pathetically. "Maybe God is punishing me for having been such a bad mother. But Santiago, you're intelligent and you should know better." She paused, in pain, looking like a Greek tragedienne. "You won't marry, and your sister goes through men like through a box of Kleenex. And that poor boy, your nephew. What's going to happen to him after I'm gone?"

And don't forget Simón Bolívar, I was going to say but refrained myself. I started to shake, so I got up. I had to get away from that kitchen as soon as possible.

Mother got up and approached me. "Where are you going? Isn't it too early to leave now?"

I backed away. "I want to go for a walk; I want to see the roses in bloom," I lied.

"Make sure you go by Romelda's house. Her yellow roses this year are divine."

"Okay, I will."

"Don't be too late for dinner. Don't have any snacks after lunch and spoil your appetite. I'm making your favorite tonight."

"What's that?"

"Pigs feet and chick peas."

"Oh, great."

"Sammy," mother began sweetly, "if you don't have plans for tonight, why don't you take Claudia to the Saigon Rose to hear Wilbrajan."

"I hadn't thought about it."

"Well, think about it. I would love to go too; that is, if you don't mind."

"I got to go, Mother. I'll see you later," I said, and left the kitchen.

It was a lovely summer day. I put on my sunglasses and stood still, taking a whiff of the crisp, balmy air. Suddenly, in a flash, I saw myself as a child, walking with my mother along the beach at Puerto Colombia, digging for coquinas. Even here in Queens, the air smelled strongly of that ocean, because it wasn't New York's Atlantic I smelled, but Barranquilla's Caribbean: salty, dry, scorching, charged with the scent of honeysuckle. I descended the steps to the driveway and started walking toward the street. Feeling ornery yet amused, I said to myself, "I can't believe my luck. Here I am, on my way to becoming an immortal."

3

Colombian Queens

I had known Carmen Elvira and Olga since our immigration to Jackson Heights; but Irma, the other member of the Colombian Parnassus, was a more recent acquaintance. They published *Colombian Queens,* a monthly magazine that my mother always saved for me. It was distributed free, financed through ads taken out by Colombian restaurants, travel agencies, and grocery stores in the Jackson Heights area. Carmen Elvira wrote the gossip column; Olga was in charge of the horoscope and the Colombian recipes, and Irma, who worked as a teller in a Wall Street bank, wrote the business column. The rest of the articles were reprints, exclusively about Colombia. The middle section of the magazine—which was the bulk of it—was packed with photographs of Colombian show biz personalities in the New York area (the women usually in bathing suits), and pictures of people recently deceased and girls in their *quinces,* etc.

On more than one occasion, Carmen Elvira had invited me to submit a section of my Columbus poem for consideration, but I had repeatedly turned down her request. Without consulting me, five poems of my book *Lirio del Alba* had been reprinted with many typographical mistakes. For a long time after that, I forbade Mother to mention Carmen Elvira's name in my presence.

I was about to ring the bell of Olga's home when the door opened and the hostess greeted me with kisses on both cheeks. The pleasant smell of burnt eucalyptus hit my nostrils. Walking down the wide-planked hall carpeted with cowhides, I experienced déjà vu: I felt as if I were in a house in Bogotá. Every detail was Colombian— the furniture, the pictures on the walls, even the plastic flowers.

I greeted Carmen Elvira and Irma, who were sitting on a couch drinking *tinto,* the espresso-like demitasse that Colombians swill nonstop. The air-conditioning was on and the curtains drawn, so that the room was in semidarkness, giving the scene a vaguely conspiratorial atmosphere. The three women, who ranged in age from their late forties to midfifties, differed sharply in appearance: Carmen Elvira, who was from the Cauca Valley, was tall and her complexion and features Mediterranean in color and shape; Irma, who was from Pasto, was on the short side, stocky, and her features were Incan. She wore her hair in a crew cut and was dressed in bermudas and sandals.

Olga, who was from Bogotá, was extremely petite and a natural blond. She was dressed in a sleeveless white cotton dress and wore high heels. It was spooky how, because of their close association, they seemed, at least in spirit, three weird sisters.

I was offered, and accepted, a *tinto.* Without asking for my preference, the hostess put two heaping spoonfuls of sugar in the inch-and-a-half cup. I decided to be gracious and drink it this way for fear of being labeled a gringo. The three women looked at me with curious but benign expressions.

"May I smoke a cigarette?" I asked in Spanish.

"Sí, sí, por supuesto," Olga said in her tinny voice, pushing an ashtray on the coffee table in my direction. It was made of red clay and had the Colombian flag painted on it.

"We don't smoke anymore," Carmen Elvira said. "The group's New Year's resolution was to give up smoking."

"Thank God and the Holy Virgin," Irma said, and crossed herself.

Feeling like a criminal, I puffed on my Newport.

"How's Lucy?" Olga asked.

"She's fine, thank you," I said. Then, remembering I was among Colombians, I asked, "And how's your husband?"

For the next five minutes we inquired about each other's parents, husbands, brothers and sisters, children, and even pets. By then I had finished my cigarette and the sickeningly sweet *tinto*. It occurred to me that good manners required that I acknowledge the dubious honor of being elected a member of The Colombian Parnassus.

"Don't mention it," beamed Carmen Elvira as the unacknowledged spokesperson of the group. "We have to move with the times, and welcome the new generation."

"Personally, I'm not very fond of modern poetry. I prefer the old poets like Carranza. Ah, those sonnets. Do you love Carranza?" Irma asked me.

"Yes, I do." Like all Colombian children I had learned Carranza's poems in school, and did, indeed, favor his exuberant romanticism.

"The Sonnet to Teresa," Olga sighed, full of nostalgia for the poetry of the past.

Olga and Carmen Elvira looked at Irma beseechingly. Her expression becoming devout, Irma began reciting the sonnet:

> *Teresa, en cuya frente el cielo empieza,*
> *como el aroma en la sien de la flor.*
> *Teresa, la del suave desamor*
> *y el arroyuelo azul en la cabeza.*

Her eyes closed, her hands resting on her considerable breasts, Irma finished reciting the famous sonnet, which I will not endeavor to translate for you because its beautiful rhymes and music demand a greater translator than I could ever hope to be. When she finished, the women sighed and burst into applause. I joined them.

"That's poetry," Olga pronounced.

Carmen Elvira pontificated, "That's what I call great poetry."

"That's what I call love," elaborated Olga. "It's not enough to be a great poet. Oh, no. That's too easy. To write poetry like that, one must love very deeply and be a great lover. Like . . . like . . .

Petrarch. I hope some day you'll write a sonnet like that to your girlfriend, Sammy."

Unsure of how to respond, I said, "I hope so too."

"By the way," Irma interjected, "do you have a girlfriend?"

I assumed a blank expression and said nothing. It was one thing to join the Parnassus, but to have my life scrutinized by these ladies was out of the question.

"Yes, he does," Carmen Elvira said, to my astonishment. "Lucy told me all about it, Sammy."

"All about what?" I said.

Carmen Elvira flashed a maternal, approving smile. "About you and Claudia."

"Claudia!" I exclaimed, for the second time that day.

"Claudia Urrutia?" asked Irma in disbelief, giving me a long, searching look. "She's so . . ."

"So wealthy," said Carmen Elvira to settle the issue.

"Hey, look," I said, to no one in particular. "I—"

"I hope you don't mind my mentioning it," Carmen Elvira interrupted me, "but Lucy told me you're practically engaged, that you're proposing tonight at the Saigon Rose."

"Congratulations, honey!" exclaimed Olga, leaping from the couch. "This calls for a celebration. I have an *aguardiente* bottle I've been saving for a special occasion. Excuse me, I'll be right back."

"I'll help you with the glasses," Carmen Elvira offered, getting up too.

"We might as well have our lunch after the toast," Irma threw in. "I'll serve the *pasteles*. You do like *pasteles*, don't you?" And, without waiting for confirmation, she followed the rest of the Parnassus into the kitchen.

I could have killed my mother. I reached for the telephone, but in the middle of dialing her number, I changed my mind. "Maybe I'm dreaming," I blurted out. I shook my head in an effort to wake myself up. But dreams are odorless and I could smell the *pasteles*. The situation reminded me of something; I couldn't, though, tell quite what. *Rosemary's Baby, Macbeth,* and *The Trial* all came to mind. I wondered if Claudia had been let into this plot, or whether we were both just random bystanders snarled in the machinations of a bunch of crazed Queens matrons.

Toasting my induction to the Parnassus, we drank the *aguardiente* Colombian style—a small glass filled to the top, followed by a quarter of a lime soaked in salt, which I chewed until my teeth felt as if they would fall out. Tears choked my vision. Carmen Elvira proposed another toast to my imminent engagement. I figured it would be better to play along than to go into long explanations about my and Claudia's sexuality. We drank to love and happiness. I had never seen Colombian women drink *aguardiente:* it is essentially a man's drink, but then, I reasoned, I was among intellectuals, not conventional housewives.

My body temperature had shot up at least ten degrees. The ladies produced their fans and proceeded to cool themselves, their mouths open and blowing air as if to take off the sting of the *aguardiente* on their gums.

"How about another *aguardientico,* Sammy?" Olga said.

"No, no, thanks. Maybe later." I felt the insides of my stomach cooking.

Irma started giggling. Carmen Elvira and Olga joined in, and together they became hysterical.

"What?" I asked, feeling uncomfortable. "What is it?" They were certainly not being very polite.

"You should see the color of your face," Irma cackled. "It looks red like . . . guava paste."

"Like a brick out of the oven," Carmen Elvira chuckled, pouring herself another *aguardiente.*

I realized I had to put an end to the alcohol consumption before they became uncontrollable.

"I'm hungry," I said, pointing at the tray of aluminum foil-wrapped *pasteles* on the coffee table.

Irma unwrapped a *pastel* and served it to me on a plate, with a napkin and fork. It looked delicious; a steam cloud heavy with the aroma of vegetables and meats and corn traveled up my nostrils.

"Dig in, honey," Carmen Elvira said. "Don't wait for us; we made them just for you."

"I love corn *pasteles*," I said, putting a piece of moist chicken in my mouth. "Ummm, it's wonderful." Closing my eyes, I chewed slowly. When I opened my eyes, the three women were leaning over the table, serving themselves.

"Ah," Olga exclaimed, setting her plate on the table and pressing her lips on the napkin. "I forgot the drinks. Now, Sammy, since you're the guest of honor, what would you like to drink with your lunch?"

"I don't know," I said, wondering what kind of exotic Colombian fruit juice or brew she had to offer. "What do you have?"

Opening her eyes wide and looking at the ceiling, she counted with her fingers. "Let's see: Diet Coke . . . ginger ale, Tab, Perrier, grapefruit juice, and beer."

I asked for a Classic Coke.

Carmen Elvira ordered a Heineken.

"For me too," said Irma. "Nothing goes better with a *pastel* than a Heineken."

While the hostess went to get the refreshments, I made small talk, asking, "Who made the *pasteles?*"

"I did," Irma said proudly.

"I never thought it would be possible to make a *pastel* taste like they do in Colombia. But they taste just as if you had cooked them in banana leaves," Carmen Elvira said.

"This is the best *pastel* I've had in a long time," I complimented the cook.

"Thank you, *su merced.* Have another."

"I will, when I finish this one. It's so big."

"Yes, Irma makes the most generous portions," Carmen Elvira said. "I follow your recipe, my dear, but they just don't taste the same."

"There must be something you're leaving out."

"Obviously. But I wonder what it is. I cook the pork with the chicken in the scallions and tomato sauce."

"Do you use fresh or dry coriander? That makes a big difference."

"Fresh. And I sprinkle the coriander on the meat just before I wrap the *pastel* in the aluminum foil."

"Maybe you don't use enough *guascas.*"

"That's it. The *guascas*! Why didn't I think of it before? But it's impossible to get *guascas* in Jackson Heights."

"I bring it from Colombia. But you know they don't allow fruits or vegetables or spices into the country. I have to hide it in my panties. Once, I had to eat an *anón* at JFK because they were going to confiscate it. So, I said, 'Please, let me eat it.' And I did."

"I remember you told me. It was an *anón* from your mother's yard. I wish I had the guts to do something like that. Nerves of steel, that's what you have."

"In your panties?" I asked.

"Sure, sweetie. It was thrilling; I felt like a drug smuggler."

"Well, lucky you," Carmen Elvira complained. "The last time I went to Colombia, when I came back they made me take off my panties. I was furious."

"That's right. You wrote that marvelous column about it. It created an international uproar, Sammy. It was reprinted in two Colombian newspapers."

"That's the power of the press for you," Carmen Elvira said solemnly, looking at me.

"What's *guascas*?" I asked. It seemed to me that I was at least two steps behind in the conversation, but since I had never heard of this herb or spice or whatever it was, I had to ask.

Olga had returned from the kitchen, and was setting a tray with drinks on the table. "What's what, honey?" she asked, handing me my Coke.

"*Guascas*," said Carmen Elvira.

I realized that as the culinary expert of the group, it was up to Olga to explain the mystery. "*Guascas*," she repeated, as she distributed the drinks. With an air of authority, she sat down and smoothed her dress. "In pre-Columbian times, the Indians used it as an aphrodisiac. It's rare because it only grows in the *páramo*. I, for one, think that if we could cultivate and export it commercially, Western cuisine as we know it would be revolutionized overnight."

"I'll be damned," I said.

Carmen Elvira said, "Sammy, you're such a gentleman. Lucy is so lucky to have a son who appreciates our national dishes." Then, making a tragic face, she confessed, "My children only eat hamburgers and pizza."

"Mine too," Irma said. "I don't know what I did wrong."

Olga said, "I cook my *arepas, frijoles,* and *sobrebarriga,* and all the things I love to eat. If they don't like it, then they can go eat at MacDonald's. I cook to please myself; I'm not their servant."

"Right on," Irma cheered, making a fist.

"The last time I was in Colombia, everyone was eating hamburgers and pizza," I said. "Though Chinese takeout hadn't gotten there yet," I added.

"You were always so special," Carmen Elvira said to me. "From the time you were a boy you were so different from all the other children. That must be your poetic nature. You know, I used to say to my husband, 'If God had blessed me with a son, instead of five daughters, I wish he had been like Sammy.' "

I felt my face flush. "Thank you," I said.

"You have changed so much," Olga reminisced. "Irma," she said seriously, "you should have seen what huge ears he had when he was a boy."

"His ears look fine to me," Irma said in her curt, martinet manner.

"That's because you didn't know him back then. I have a picture of Sammy that now is of historic importance. Remind me to show it to you some day. His ears were not to be believed."

I had finished my *pastel* and was feeling terribly uncomfortable.

"Here, honey, have another one," Olga said.

"Thank you, very much. Not now." Seeing how disappointed she looked, I added, "Maybe later."

She said, "I promised Lucy I'd send her a couple of *pasteles* with you."

"She'll be so happy. She loves your *pasteles.* And I do too, but I had breakfast just a couple of hours ago. Maybe I'll take mine to Manhattan and have them later in the week."

"They taste better a few days later. Just freeze it, and when you want to eat it, warm it up in a *baño de María.*"

Carmen Elvira asked, "Do you cook all your meals?"

I noted that, as the gossip columnist, Carmen Elvira mainly asked questions. "Yes," I informed her, "though not much in the summer; it gets too hot in the kitchen."

Olga said, "He'll make such a perfect husband for Claudia."

The other women nodded in agreement; they had finished their *pasteles*.

Olga said to Irma, *"Mijita,* will you help me clear the table and bring dessert? Then we can discuss the details of Sammy's induction over coffee and a cordial."

I watched Olga and Irma clear the table and disappear in the direction of the kitchen. I'd just set down my napkin when I noticed Carmen Elvira reaching for her handbag and pulling out a small tape recorder. I lit another cigarette.

"Testing, testing. One, two, three," she spoke into the contraption. "Sammy," Carmen Elvira said, winking at me, crossing her legs and exposing her knees, "why don't you come over here and sit next to me?"

Thinking she was about to make a pass at me, I said, "What? You want to interview me?"

"Yes, honey. I'm going to ask you a few questions for *Colombian Queens,"* she explained, smiling.

"You know, Carmen Elvira, maybe this is not such a good time. I mean," I said, looking toward the kitchen door, "Irma and Olga will be coming back any minute."

"No, honey. They won't. They're doing the dishes and getting dessert ready while I interview you."

I realized I had been set up and that, as the guest of honor, it would be rude to decline the interview.

She interpreted my silence as acquiescence. "Here," she said pouring another *aguardiente* and handing me the little glass. "This will loosen you up."

I downed the *aguardiente.*

Patting the sofa, she said, "Come over here, Sammy. I'm not going to bite you. We'll just chat like two good old friends."

I sat next to her, feeling my forehead break into a sweat. "What kind of interview is this?"

She laughed. "You look as if you were facing a firing squad. Lighten up, honey. I'm just going to ask you a couple of questions, okay?"

"Okay." I put out my cigarette and lit another one.

"Ready?"

I nodded.

"We're here today with the award-winning poet Santiago Martínez Ardila, whose first book of poems *Lirio del Alba* (which, by the way, remains his only published title) will be remembered fondly by many poetry lovers, I'm sure. Today, however, we'll be talking to Santiago about other matters. Santiago, who has a Ph.D. in Medieval Studies from Queens College, and is a resident of Times Square, Manhattan, has announced today his plans to marry Claudia Urrutia."

"Wait a minute," I protested.

"Not now, honey," Carmen Elvira cut me off. "Claudia Urrutia, the import/export heiress of Barranquilla, Colombia; Jackson Heights, Queens; Miami, Florida; and Monte Carlo. Our Claudia, who trained in architecture at Yale, is also a great beauty and an accomplished . . ." Here Carmen Elvira looked lost. She motioned with her hand in front of my mouth, coaxing me to produce the word she wanted.

"Athlete," I ventured, remembering Claudia's fondness for motorcycles.

"Athlete. Yes. Athlete. Now, Santiago," she went on, pushing the machine against my nose, "tell us how you and Claudia met."

"This is preposterous. I'm not marrying Claudia Urrutia."

Carmen Elvira turned off the machine. She glared at me for a second and then broke into a big, fake smile. Her thin scarlet lips stretched taut over her big white teeth. "You're such a naughty boy, Sammy. It's a well-known fact in the Colombian community that you and Claudia are tying the knot very soon. Both your mother and Claudia's have confirmed the news. I understand how you want to protect your privacy, but honey, you're our foremost poet in the United States and this is news to our readers."

She must have thought that by flattering me I would simply

acquiesce as I had, after all, been doing all afternoon. Making an effort not to blow up (my mother would never have forgiven me if I offended her friends), I said, "Look, Carmen Elvira, I have no plans to get married at the moment. . . . But when I do, your readers will be the first to know. I promise. Cross my heart. Okay?"

Ignoring my speech, Carmen Elvira said, "Okay, Sammy. Don't you fret about it. I will fill out the details of the wedding. I know men don't like to talk about this sort of thing." Then she pushed the ON button and said, "Today, Santiago Martínez Ardila has been inducted as a member of The Colombian Parnassus, thus becoming the first male member of our society. Santiago, dear, we know that for the past ten years you've been working on a book of poems about Christopher Columbus."

"An epic poem, to be precise."

"We understand that this great . . . masterpiece, which will add glory to our national poetry, is almost finished. Is that so?"

"Not at all."

Totally unperturbed, she asked, "And is it in free verse or in rhyme?"

"Free verse, of course. I'm a modern poet."

"How innovative," Carmen Elvira said. "How avant-garde. May I ask what drew you to the subject of the Admiral of the Seven Seas?"

This was the first legitimate question she had asked. However, I had been writing the poem for such a long time that I could no longer remember why I had been drawn to Columbus originally.

"Could it have been his liaison with Queen Isabella?" Carmen Elvira (quick to dish everyone) came to my rescue.

"Certainly not."

She looked disappointed. "What is your opinion about the recent theory that Columbus was a woman?"

My jaw must have fallen open. In any case, Carmen Elvira did not wait for an answer. "We hope this long-awaited poem will be finished by 1992, the 500th anniversary of the discovery of America. We wish you great luck, both with it and with your forthcoming marriage." She turned off the machine and thanked me for the interview.

I was about to let her have a piece of my mind, when Olga and Irma burst into the room with dessert. Olga carried a tray with cheese, *obleas,* guava paste, stuffed figs and *arequipe,* and Irma the *tinto* service. While the sweets were being served on the saucers, I noticed Olga stealing glances at Carmen Elvira as if to find out how the interview had turned out. But the latter pretended to fuss with her glasses, ignoring Olga. We tasted the sweets in silence, making sounds of approval and sipping our *tintos.*

Olga said, "Tell us, Sammy, how does it feel to be a brand new member of The Parnassus? It's been so many years since I became a member. But I remember how honored I felt. I envy the way you feel right now."

"Yes," I said politely. "And what do I have to do now?"

"It's very simple," Carmen Elvira informed me. "We meet on the last Saturday of every month, except during August. It is suggested that all members attend the monthly meeting. Also, there are no dues or annual fees."

"Oh, good," I said, relieved.

"But to become a member there is a three hundred fifty dollar fee. Considering that it covers lifetime membership, it's a steal."

They offered me the perfect excuse, and I jumped at it. "I'm very honored to have been invited to join The Parnassus, but the truth is, I'm not solvent at the moment and three hundred fifty bucks is a lot of money for me. So maybe next year."

"Don't worry about it, sweetie," Olga reassured me. "Lucy was well aware of this and she has offered to take care of it."

"What? My mother is going to pay the fee?" I asked in disbelief, considering the many occasions she had denied me loans for small amounts.

"That's a mother's love for you, Sammy," Olga said.

"Treasure your mother while she's alive, and make her happy," Irma said. "I didn't know how lucky I was while my mom was alive, and I'll never get over it now."

"You just don't know how much you'll miss her when she's gone," Carmen Elvira prophesised.

"Let me explain a bit more in depth what is required to be a member," Olga said, taking a dainty bite of cheese and then licking her fingers. "A new member has to do some group service to join in."

"What kind of service?"

Carmen Elvira said, "Since you're a translator—"

"An interpreter," I corrected her.

"Well, it's the same thing, honey, isn't it?"

"Absolutely not," I said, setting down my saucer and glaring at her.

"It's almost the same thing," Olga said, "so why quibble?"

"Anyway," Carmen Elvira went on, "since you're an interpreter, we thought you'd be perfect for this. As you know, we are all poets. Not award-winning poets like you, but nonetheless serious poets."

"I've been writing poetry since I was seven," Olga said.

Carmen Elvira stared at me, waiting for me to certify their bona fides. "I didn't start quite that early," I said.

"In any case, I'm sure you've read our poems in *Colombian Queens*. We all publish quite regularly."

"Oh, yes," I lied. I had glanced at their gibberish on occasion to please my mother.

"I especially recommend this issue's selection," Olga said. "Carmen Elvira wrote the loveliest poem about the volcano disaster in Manizales, you remember? It's unbearably moving; Homeric in its ambition. If you encourage her, maybe Carmen Elvira will be gracious enough to recite it for you now."

Carmen Elvira was smiling and fluttering her hands and eyelids, so I hastened to say, "Thank you very much, but I promise you I'll read it tonight, in bed. That's how I read poetry. I never go to readings; I don't like people reading at me."

"How peculiar," Irma said.

"How un-Colombian," Olga added.

"What is it that you want me to translate?" I asked.

"Sammy, we've decided to go legit and to publish our poems in a collection," Olga said, clasping her hands. "And we've chosen you to translate them into English since you're such a talented poet, from our own country, and perfectly bilingual."

"What?" I croaked.

"And we'd love it if you could write an introduction. It doesn't have to be very long. We leave it entirely up to you, as long as it's written from the heart."

"But I've never translated any poetry into English. I think you've got the wrong guy for this project," I stammered.

"Your modesty is so appealing," Olga squealed flirtatiously, like a superannuated Lolita. "You'll do beautifully. We already have the title for you: *Muses of Queens*. Do you like it?"

"Can I have an *aguardiente*?" was my response.

"Of course, honey. You're right; this calls for a toast."

Once more we chugged down our drinks, toasting to poetry. It occurred to me that by joining the toast I was accepting their proposition just as I had already tacitly confirmed my engagement to Claudia. "Let me explain something," I said. "I have to think about this. I mean, as much as I'd like to do it, I don't know if I have the time right now."

"We understand, don't we, girls?" Carmen Elvira said.

"Take your time," added Olga.

"There's absolutely no hurry," Irma said. "What with your wedding and everything else, we don't want to put any extra pressure on you. When we meet again in September, we can discuss the details."

"What's more," Olga intervened, "we'd really love to pay you, but we have children going to college, so we live pretty close to what we make."

"We can't pay you in cash, that's true. But we have something much more valuable to offer you."

Shuddering, I asked, "Like what?"

"Power," she said. "That's right, honey, power! As a new member of The Parnassus you automatically become a contributing editor to *Colombian Queens*. You are aware of what that means, aren't you?"

"No. What does it mean?"

"It means you can reach one million compatriots in the greater

New York area. Our magazine reaches practically every member of this community. Think of the great audience you'll have for your poetry and your ideas."

"Did you know that the future of the next presidential election in Colombia is in our hands?" Olga giggled.

"No kidding!"

"We're a political force; we're a crucial element in the next presidential election. The candidates we endorse will receive about one hundred thousand votes, which is almost as many votes as there will be cast in all Colombia. You know our people are abstentionists, and only government employees go to the polls."

"Gee whiz," I said, genuinely impressed by their reasoning, though doubtful of their statistics.

Carmen Elvira said, "Your vote is of historical significance, Sammy."

"But I've never voted."

"Why not?" asked Olga, looking concerned.

"I don't know very much about Colombian politics."

She sighed with obvious relief. "That's all right. I thought it was something worse. Well, sweetie, this is your chance to learn. You couldn't ask for better teachers. We're all seasoned political campaigners."

"Do you always vote?" I asked stupidly.

"I can't vote," Carmen Elvira stated somberly.

This was interesting. "Why not?"

"She's an American citizen," Irma said.

"So are you," Carmen Elvira counterattacked angrily. "And you too, Olga."

"I don't deny it, *mijita*," a dejected Olga corroborated. "But I'm a Colombian at heart and will die Colombian."

"Me too," Carmen Elvira said, full of patriotic fervor. "I just did it so that my children could have a better chance in this country."

"I was practically forced to do it," Olga said. "In my ignorance, I thought I had to become a citizen in order to keep my federal job."

"Save your speeches; this is not the inquisition," Carmen Elvira said cattily. "We did it, and that's that. Period."

To cheer them up, I said, "My mother is an American citizen, too."

"Don't you ever become one," Carmen Elvira ordered me. "It would be disgraceful, a real tragedy of the first magnitude if our leading poet in the States became an American."

"I wonder if García Márquez is a Mexican," Olga pondered. "I think I read somewhere that he became a Mexican citizen a few years ago."

"I don't believe it for a second," snapped Carmen Elvira, slapping her knee. "Gabo would never do that. He'd never betray his country; he's one hundred fifty percent Colombian."

"But he's lived in Mexico for thirty years," Olga insisted.

"So what?"

"His children were born in Mexico," Olga expatiated.

"I don't care what the *National Enquirer* prints," Carmen Elvira scoffed, chugging down another *aguardiente*. Her speech was becoming slurred. "Gabo and Colombia will always be one, indivisible."

"Yes," Irma seconded her. "Like the Father, the Son, and the Holy Ghost."

The theological turn of the conversation warned me it was time to split. "I got to go," I said. "I have to go visit a friend."

Always the gossip, Carmen Elvira inquired, "Claudia?"

"No, my friend Bobby."

"Bobby Castro? Is it true he has AIDS?"

I stood up. "Yes, he's dying. Thank you for the delicious lunch. It was . . . nice to see you all," I said. Now that I was standing, I realized the *aguardiente* had gone to my head; my feet were wobbly, and the ladies and the room swam in front of my eyes. "And I'm really . . . pleased to be a member of The Parnassus."

"Wait," Olga said. "I promised Lucy a couple of *pasteles*."

Irma said, "Send her some figs. They're really fresh. My cousin brought them from Bogotá yesterday. These are Buga figs, Sammy. Be sure to tell that to your mother; she adores Buga figs. Actually, take all of them. I have plenty more at home," she finished magnanimously.

Minutes later, after another *aguardiente* for the road, and carrying a supermarket bag filled with Colombian delicacies, I staggered into the afternoon sun.

4

Mothers and Sons

It was a ten-block walk from Olga's home to Bobby's apartment. The scene with The Parnassus women had unsettled me; memories that I had suppressed long ago were becoming exposed. Or maybe it was just the *aguardiente,* or the fact that I was ambling down the shady streets of Jackson Heights on a placid summer afternoon, going to see my oldest friend who was dying of a disease that seemed the product of a science fiction horror fantasy. At any rate, all kinds of freaky thoughts crept into my head.

Colombia is known as—among Colombians—The Country of Poets. Any Colombian worth his salt is at least a closet poet. It was our love of some poets—and our hatred of the Spanish Nobel Laureate Juan Ramón Jiménez (whose "Platero and I" we ridiculed cruelly)—that had brought Bobby and me together.

There are a couple of things I ought to clarify. I was born in the town of Barranquilla and, at age seven, after Father ditched us, we moved to Bogotá. However, four years later, in pursuit of a man she had the hots for, Mother moved back to Barranquilla. That's where Bobby and I met, at Colegio Americano, an American Baptist school that took all the rejects of the Catholic schools, in the hope that we'd all become militant Baptists. Bobby and I were chubby, unathletic, and loved movies and books. I was convinced that Bobby was a genius. While I barely managed to pass, Bobby made straight A's. He was a brilliant mathematician, and wanted to be a writer or a painter. He read books in both English and French.

On Saturdays, and during school vacations when I remained in the city, I'd go to spend the day at Bobby's house. I'd arrive early in the morning, and we'd usually play chess until lunchtime. Then we'd go to the patio, where we sat under the guava trees and read books aloud, especially *Hamlet,* which we never tired of rereading. It was at that time that Bobby encouraged me to enter a declamation contest, which I won. For the next few years, I entered, and won, many of these events. Bobby served as my coach. We favored the poetry of José Asunción Silva, a romantic, morbid suicide; and also the poetry of Porfirio Barba Jacob, Colombia's *poet maudit.*

Bobby and I came from different social backgrounds. His mother was an executive secretary for Cola Román, a soda pop company, and they lived in a modest house in a blue-collar neighborhood. I, on the contrary, was the son of a wealthy man. After Father left us, he had been generous with Mother, so we didn't have to worry about money. Also, Mother's lover was a high-ranking official in local government; he was director of the state brewery. We enjoyed luxuries such as a limousine and a uniformed driver. Most adolescences are unhappy, but mine was particularly miserable. I hated school, my classmates, and the town of Barranquilla. Books and movies were my only refuge; and Bobby, Claudia Urrutia, and my sister were the only young people I felt close to.

As I walked into a section of Jackson Heights that consisted mainly of small apartment buildings, I could feel the supermarket bag shaking in my hand. The closer I got to Bobby's home, the more upset I became. My last visit with Bobby had been at the hospital in May. Then, I thought he'd never leave the hospital alive. What was left of Bobby was in a respirator, so he couldn't talk. He looked like an extraterrestrial creature, with a big head and a shrunken body. His eyes, which had sunk a couple of inches into his face, were open, but unfocused. It was obvious to me that they were not looking at anything. I sat for what seemed like an eternity, staring at the bouquet of yellow roses I had brought him, aware of the noises of the different machines and of the nurses in white gowns and white gloves who entered and exited the room.

By the time I arrived in front of the brick apartment building where Bobby had moved over a year ago, I was feeling pretty frazzled. I lit a cigarette and stood at the entrance, wondering whether I should go in or postpone the visit. But I knew that Bobby wasn't going to be sticking around much longer. The possibility that he would again not recognize me at all upset me still further. I felt guilty that over the long period of his illness, I hadn't been by his side more often. I climbed the steps that led to the buzzer system. I was about to press the button for his apartment when a voice behind my back called, "Hey, Sammy."

Turning around, I saw my nephew on his bike.

"Gene, what are you doing here?" I demanded.

"I went by the crazy ladies' house and they told me you were coming here. Man, those women are a trip and a half."

"Anything wrong?" I asked, walking down to his bike.

"What's that smell? Are you loaded?"

"I had a couple of *aguardientes*. That's all."

"Yeah? Well, it smells like a couple hundred to me. You smell like . . . like . . . like . . ."

"It's the *pasteles*," I said, pointing to my bag.

"Oh, okay. Can I ask you a favor? I'm working until late tonight, and I rented a couple of movies. Could you take them home for me? I could lose them, going around on the bike." He reached into the basket on the bike's handles and handed me two plastic cassettes.

"Rocky Rambo Dumbo," I teased him.

"Man, I told you. I hate that shit." Suddenly, there was a loud metallic beep. "Got to beat it, man. That's my beeper."

"What kind of deliveries you make, anyway?" I asked, noticing a bunch of white envelopes in his basket.

"Can't talk now. I'm late. Thanks for taking the movies home for me." He lowered his sunglasses and put on his headphones. Grabbing the bike's handles, he shouted, "See you tonight at Saigon Rose. It's the big night, eh? Congratulations. Claudia's a cool chick.

Take care. Say hi to Bobby," he called out, and zoomed off, pedaling furiously.

The Claudia situation, I realized, was seriously out of control. However, there was nothing I could do about it now. Putting the movies in the shopping bag, I rang the buzzer.

I rode the elevator to the fourth floor. After years of visiting Bobby in swank lofts and apartments, coming here felt like going back ten years in time, to when Bobby still lived in Queens, working during the day and going to school at night.

A new nurse opened the door. I explained who I was. She informed me that there was nobody at home, except Bobby, who was asleep. "Mr. Martínez," she said as I headed toward Bobby's room, "Mr. Weisberg [Bobby's lover] called to say he won't be back until six o'clock, and I really have to go home. Would you mind taking over for me until he arrives?"

Being alone with a dying person made me nervous, but I said I would gladly stay. We went into the bedroom where Bobby was sleeping. The room was tidy and cool, and Bobby's body was covered with light blue sheets. On a wardrobe was a vase with red roses. The shades were open, and the afternoon light streamed into the room. And yet, there was something icy about it. Death had Bobby in its bony grasp already, as the French would say. On Bobby's night table was a large tray crammed with medicine bottles. However, I was relieved to see that he wasn't on a respirator. The nurse pointed to a card with phone numbers I should call in case of an emergency. Then, matter-of-factly, in the calm, blank manner of people who deal with death on a daily basis, she removed her plastic gloves, gathered her things, and left. I took a chair and sat next to the head of the bed. Three machines were hooked to him. One to his nose, one to an arm, and the last one (which leaked a greenish liquid that looked like mint liqueur) attached to a patch on his skeletal chest. The patch itself looked rotten, like putrid flesh. Bobby's hair was longish and had obviously gone unwashed for several days. I sat a foot or so away from his face and now I could study it in detail, something which on prior occasions, when he had been awake, I had been too self-conscious to do. He was beginning to look like a recently excavated mummy. The skin between the eyebrows and eyelashes had sunken even further than the last time I had seen him, so that even in repose his eyes bulged like golf balls. The skin that covered them seemed translucent and thin like a spider's web. The eyes remained open a third of an inch, so that only the whites of his eyes showed. His entire face, including his parched lips, was peeling off in white, crispy flakes. He had become a monster.

Bobby's faint, irregular breathing frightened me; I felt sad, depressed. It was hard for me to believe that this was the Bobby I had known since childhood. For a while I had hoped that a miracle would happen, but now it was clear that Bobby was going to die. What disturbed me most about it was how quiet, how undramatic it all seemed.

At his death, Bobby would be taking with him a big chunk of my life's memories. Even when we had been apart, we always kept up a correspondence. After I moved to America, I didn't see him for four years, until one morning when he showed up unexpectedly at our home in Jackson Heights. I hardly recognized him; he had grown tall, willowy, extroverted. He stayed with us for several weeks. Right away he informed me that he was gay—this was in the late seventies—and that he couldn't stand living in Colombia as a homosexual. He had come to the United States, he announced, to be "a free fag." I was still struggling to come out of the closet but when Bobby appeared again in my life I understood that I had to move out of my mother's house if I was ever going to accept my sexuality. His example was very important to me in this respect.

He got a job working in a factory that made plastic ashtrays, moved into an attic not far away from us, and enrolled at Hunter College, where he took evening and weekend classes. His main goal at that time was to move into Manhattan as soon as possible.

After I finished my B.A., I decided to return to Colombia, where I hoped to settle permanently. Bobby warned me that as a gay man I wouldn't be able to adjust. He was right: two years later, I returned to the States. By then, Bobby's fortunes had changed. He was now the manager of the plastic ashtray factory and a partner as well, had finished his B.A. with honors and enrolled in the N.Y.U. Graduate Business Program. He moved into a loft in SoHo. The building had gone co-op and he purchased the loft, which he converted into a beautiful place decorated with art and antiques, his new hobbies. He was also involved in a multitude of business enterprises, and was beginning to become extremely successful in his investments. He bragged his portfolio was worth almost a million dollars. Bobby became infatuated with the American dream. His goal was to be a millionaire by age twenty-five.

I resented his material success, his handsome and successful boyfriend, his possessions, his trips all over the world. Ironically, the freedom he had sought and enjoyed in America was the very thing that was killing him. Bobby was proud of my writing and encouraged me, but he disliked the fact that I was a poor poet.

In the early 1980s, he was on his way to becoming a Wall Street tycoon. He purchased a luxurious condo behind the World Trade Center, became thinner, more polished and elegant, took elocution lessons, and was the very image of the immigrant made good. Sitting next to him, it occurred to me that we were the first generation of immigrants who had skipped the ghettos altogether, who had been able to go directly to the suburbs and to college, who could return to our homelands for weekend trips. Our homelands were so near, by jet, that in spite of our adaptability and American ways, we did not feel the need to shed our Colombianness.

I decided to turn on the TV, hoping to catch an afternoon baseball game. Remembering the two movies Gene had asked me to take home for him, I took out the two plastic cases. They had no labels on them, which was peculiar. I turned on the TV set and opened one of the plastic containers. Inside I found a plastic bag full of a white substance. I unzipped the bag, stuck my finger inside, and tasted. It was pure, uncut cocaine. A bag of cocaine that was worth a fortune. "Shit," I uttered.

"What?" a voice said behind my back. I turned around.

"Sammy, are you all right?" Bobby said in English.

I was astonished to see him speaking. "Bobby, I thought . . ." The words choked in my throat. I hurried to his side and sat on the edge of the bed. I felt overjoyed: I thought I'd never see Bobby conscious again.

"Oh, how nice. You brought me a present," he said pulling his hands from under the blanket and touching the bag in my hands. His smile was like an open fan. "You brought me cocaine. But I could never snort all that coke even if I lived to be a hundred years old," he said, examining the bag. "Are you trying to become a yuppie overnight?"

I explained how I had come into possession of the cocaine. I pulled out the other plastic box. It contained only Marlon Brando's *Last Tango in Paris.*

"So he makes home deliveries," I said.

"This is Jackson Heights, you gringo. Not Times Square. I'm constantly getting flyers under my door. If I weren't about to croak, I'd love to take a hit. But go ahead; don't let my deathbed scene stop you from getting high."

"I gave up drugs, Bobby."

"Good for you. It only took me ten years of lecturing you before you finally caught on. I see you haven't given up alcohol. What's that smell—*aguardiente?*"

I gave him an abridged version of my induction into The Parnassus. Bobby looked amused, and struggled to pull himself up in bed, coughing like a lawnmower cranking without oil. His face became cherry red. I looked in the direction of the tray of medicines. "Is there anything I can get you?" I asked, when his breathing had settled a bit.

"Actually, yes. Here, help me to remove this thing," he said pulling out the plastic tube in his nose. He handed it to me and asked me to turn off the oxygen tank.

"Should you be doing this?" I was alarmed.

"Sammy, it's just oxygen. But I'm breathing okay without it, aren't I?"

I did as he told me. I was fidgeting and a tic began to twitch under my left eye. I wished that Bobby's lover would show up; I didn't want to be alone with Bobby in case his condition deteriorated suddenly. He asked me to help him sit up on the bed with some pillows behind his back. I was astonished at his weightlessness, and when I placed my hands under his armpits, his arms were thin and light, like breadsticks. Settling in his new position, Bobby said, "What does this remind you of?"

I was too muddled to think; I shrugged.

"Camille, you dummy. Remember how we used to play Camille during religion class?"

"We did?"

"Ave María Purísima pues," he said, affecting a Medellín accent. "I don't know how you can be a writer with such a lousy memory. I sure hope you're not planning to write anything about me after I'm gone. Don't you remember we used to play Marguerite Gautier? We'd take turns coughing, and we'd imagine we were dying of consumption. Remember how Profesor Rincón—I swear he had a crush on me—for the most part ignored us. But one afternoon we must have pissed him off more than usual because he called on you. In that wonderful baritone voice of his he said, 'Mr. Martínez, since you seem to know so much about this subject that you don't even have to pay any attention to what I've been saying, would you be kind enough to explain to the slower students in class the meaning of Jesus Christ's immaculate conception?' I thought you were gonna shit in your pants; you looked whiter than chalk but you said, 'I hate to say it, sir. But in my opinion it means that St. Joseph was a cuckold, the Virgin a whore, and Jesus a son of a bitch.' Sammy, you used to be incredibly funny. I don't know what happened to your sense of humor." Bobby cackled, slapping his hands on the bed. I laughed too, until I remembered that my wisecrack had gotten me expelled from school for fifteen days.

"And who was our heroine?" He continued with his nostalgic vein.

"Vanessa Redgrave," I offered, remembering how we loved her in the life of Isadora Duncan.

"No, no, no, no, no, no," he chanted. "Close, but not quite right. Maybe this will help." He made a V with his arms; the pajama sleeves dropped to his elbows, revealing his emaciated extremities. "Now you remember?"

I shook my head.

"Diana Ross, you fool."

It might have been funny if he hadn't looked like a death camp survivor. It was a horrible sight. The only part left of the Bobby I had known was his humor.

"Okay, it's like this," he said. "I'm scared shitless of dying, but

I keep telling myself that it's important to die with a good attitude. You know what I mean? If there is an afterlife (and I sure as hell hope there isn't; one life is enough for me, thank you), I don't want to start it feeling sorry for myself."

In our adolescence, when we went through our existentialist period, we had become atheists. "Do you think there is an afterlife . . . now?" I asked.

"I haven't gotten any previews of it, if that's what you want to know. When I was in a coma, I saw myself walking down a dark, endless tunnel, and at the end of it, yes, there was the proverbial you-know-what beckoning me. But I resisted it. I dragged my feet. I refused to continue walking and sat down and just stared at it, without budging. I'm pretty sure it was death calling me. But I'll be damned if I go before I'm ready. I wanted to be conscious once more, so I could see Joel and even you, if you can believe that. Seriously now," he went on, "I had a good life. I sure got away from Barranquilla. I remember how I used to despair thinking I would never get away from that dreadful macho town. I knew I had to get away from there and become the gorgeous queen I was meant to be."

"You sure did," I said.

"And I had a good time with Joel these past five years so actually I don't give a flying fuck about all the other stuff. And you know, I'm glad that it's been such a long illness. This has been the first time since childhood that I've had time to think about spiritual matters. I became so wrapped up in making money that I thought only money and success could make me happy, but secretly I've always envied your freedom."

"Sure. Come on, Bobby. Get real. You wouldn't have liked Eighth Avenue all these years," I said referring to my place of residence.

"You'll be able to move now that you're marrying Claudia. Lucy told me all about it the last time she was here. Now you'll live in mansions for the rest of your life."

"Bobby, I can't believe you're talking such nonsense!"

"Hey, why not? Many of my fag friends are marrying women. And look at all the famous queens who've gone back into the closet.

Besides, it might save your life. Although, since you never have sex, you must be HIV negative. Tell the truth, have you had any in the last ten years since you came out?"

The uneventfulness of my sex life had always been a source of great amusement to Bobby. The truth is that other than the occasional vertical sex, I had practiced a single-handed celibacy for many years. Only recently had I realized that it wasn't so much AIDS I was afraid of, but of being sexually intimate with another person.

"Anyway," Bobby went on, "we were crazy about Claudia when we were kids; we had such great times. And she adores you. Plus she's rich. What more do you want? A true match made in heaven. A fag who's afraid of sex and a dyke who won't ask you for any! If she asked me to marry her—fat chance—I'd marry her in a second."

"Bullshit. You wouldn't. Just because you think you're dying I'm not going to let you take advantage of me. Is that your idea of having the last laugh?"

"No, it's not, *cariño.* I always said we were like Miriam Hopkins and Bette Davis in *Old Acquaintance.* You know me, a drama queen to the last. I really believe we were their modern-day incarnation. But the movie is over, Sammy. You've won the bet. This queen is dead."

It pleased me to see Bobby in such good spirits. Ironically, our most intimate times together since childhood had been during the past two years of his illness when we had been able to talk honestly and at leisure.

I said, "This is just like old times when I used to go by your house on Saturdays. Your grandmother cooked lunch for us. God, she was such a terrific cook. I loved her *plátano pícaro* and her *carne asada.* I can almost smell it now."

"The way you reminisce about food! You should have been a food critic instead of a poet. Maybe you should try to be a Colombian M.F.K. Fisher. This conversation is making me hungry. I'd give anything to eat something yummy."

"Are you still on your macrobiotic diet?"

"No, I went off it two weeks ago when the doctor told me I should get ready to die any minute. Since then I've been gobbling down pounds of ice cream, and chocolate, all the things I deprived myself of in my quest to be fashionably thin."

"I have a couple of *pasteles* in the bag. And Buga figs and *obleas*."

"My, my, you really go out well-prepared these days. Cocaine and *pasteles* and Buga figs. What else do you have in that bag?"

"The Parnassus women sent all that food to my mother."

Bobby perked up. "But Lucy will never forgive me if I eat her *pasteles*. Will she?"

"She might, eventually," I hypothesized.

"And what if she doesn't?" Bobby said mischievously. "I'll be dead anyway."

I touched the aluminum-wrapped *pasteles* inside the bag. "I think they're still warm, but I can heat them up if you want."

"This is perfect. It's now or never. I can't eat anything hot. Santiago, be a darling and go to the kitchen and get everything we need, and bring out a bottle of red wine. I've been dying to have a glass of wine."

I returned with the implements and cleared the medicine tray off the night table. Then I uncorked the bottle of wine and Bobby served the *pasteles*.

Bobby raised his glass to toast. "Here's a toast to . . . to all the good times I ever had; all the cocks I ever sucked. My only regret is that I never made it with an Albanian, but maybe it's not too late."

"Who was the best?" I asked with envy.

"Let's see . . . I know. The Belgian married count who sucked a bottled with baby formula while I whipped him."

I started to laugh; this was the Bobby I had known most of my life and loved like a twin.

Bobby began to chew the *pasteles* slowly and his face lit up with pleasure. "Superb. What a good idea this was!"

"It's the *guascas*," I informed him.

"But that's a sex drug. How interesting—a pornographic *pastel*."

"This is my second *pastel* of the day," I said.

Bobby smiled. I could see that although he was in great spirits he was also in pain. "Maybe tonight you'll pork Claudia."

"Cut it out, Bobby. Now, I wouldn't mind marrying one of her brothers. Those killers really turn me on."

"You know how Colombian men are, Sammy. If you marry the sister, you'll probably fuck all those hunky mafioso assassins."

Laughing, Bobby raised his glass, "This calls for another toast: To my last meal on earth."

"To our friendship," I said.

"I take back what I said earlier," Bobby said thoughtfully. "I'm not terrified of dying anymore. I mean, not hysterically so. As I told you, I've had a long time to think about spiritual matters during this illness. I know that you find the subject of religion fairly revolting, and I don't blame you. I haven't forgotten the pact we made at thirteen to be atheists forever. But I'm not an atheist anymore, Sammy. Sorry to disappoint you, old pal. Think what you want. Maybe my brain has gone soft because of this disease. I don't doubt it and I don't care. But the only way I can reconcile myself to dying is by believing in God. Otherwise, I would be terrrified of sinking into a bottomless void, for all eternity." He stopped to chew a chunk of *pastel.* Then he went on. "This way I know my spirit will find rest when my body goes. In these past two years, I've had a lot of time to study different religions and philosophies. Finally, only Christianity interested me because the Christian God sent his son to be one of us, and to suffer like all of us, and he knew how consuming and powerful love can be." He paused. There was a faraway look in his eyes, as if he saw something I couldn't see. "You know what my favorite passage in the Bible is? The Sermon on the Mount. Remember how it goes? 'Blessed are they that mourn: for they shall be comforted. Blessed are the meek: for they shall inherit the earth.' And it goes on and on. It's called the Beatitudes, and it's found only, I think, in the Gospel of St. Matthew." He took another bite of *pastel* and chewed slowly, munching and catching his breath at the same time. He handed me the plate. "This is delicious. Now I can die."

To distract him from his gloom, I said, "Would you like a Buga fig or an *oblea?*"

"An *oblea* would be lovely."

As I reached for the *obleas* wrapped in wax paper, a horrible burp erupted from Bobby's throat. The violent sound startled me.

I sat up very still, wondering what I should do next. I was struggling to dissemble my feelings. Bobby's face flushed crimson. With great desperation he sucked the air around him, as if he couldn't find it. His eyes opened wider, the light in them sparkled, and he stared at me with an enormous intensity and longing. Back in my childhood in Bogotá, when my mother went out at night, she would put belladonna in her eyes, and her pupils would enlarge and glisten so that they were both exciting and frightening to me—that was the look in Bobby's eyes, which were dilated, submerged in a face death had already claimed. And yet, his eyes were the only part of him that was still alive. It was as if his ravaged body had been dying bit by bit, but *life* had concentrated in that blazing, scorching stare. The light that sparked in his eyes was that of the supernatural, the other-worldly, a light that saw and bespoke of things to which the rest of us are not privy, and never glimpse until we approach the next world, if there is any such thing. By degrees, his face relaxed, becoming softer, fuller. Now that he was out of pain, a serene expression came over his features as if he had fallen into a deep, blissful sleep. He was dead. Just to make sure, I tried to take his pulse, holding his wrist until I realized I didn't know what I was looking for. Bobby's hand jerked spastically in my shaking hand. Spooked, I dropped his arm and put my palm on Bobby's chest, near the filthy patch. He was still as a board. Soon I started shaking all over. Oddly enough, I could accept the fact that Bobby was dead. But the fact that the IV and the other machine attached to his chest kept pumping liquids into his corpse really disturbed me. I turned off both machines. I wondered whether I should call the doctor or the hospital first. I dreaded the thought of a troop of paramedics bursting into the room and carrying away Bobby's corpse in a wailing ambulance. Yet I felt peaceful; now that Bobby was dead, there was nothing more that could happen to him. I called Joel at his office, and was informed he had already left for the day—it was, after all, Saturday afternoon. Next, I called the number I had for Bobby's mother (Doña Leticia was staying at a friend's house because she was afraid of catching AIDS) and told her she should come over as soon as possible—I didn't want to give her the news over the phone. The last call I made was to my mother; I told her not expect me back any time soon and the reason why. I sat on Bobby's bed and waited, staring at the ravaged corpse. I didn't cry or get hysterical or get down on my knees to pray for Bobby's soul. Afraid that the police might arrive and find the coke, I hid the shopping bag in the kitchen, under the sink. Then I cleared the dishes and put everything in the dishwasher. I was in the kitchen when the door opened and Joel came in. Speechless, I looked at him. He instantly knew because he froze on the spot, closed his eyes and clenched his fists. I walked up to him and we embraced and burst out sobbing aloud, clutching at one another, saying nothing.

Later, in the bedroom, I was recounting to Joel my last conversation with Bobby and how he had died, when the bell rang. I let Bobby's mother in. "How are you Doña Leticia?" I said. "I'm so glad you're here."

We had never liked one another. She was the stereotypical "stage mother." All her adult life she had worked extremely hard to give her son everything she had lacked—including great ambition. But this sacrifice had dehumanized her; she seemed more like Bobby's trainer than his mother. He loved her, but had been afraid of her and courted success desperately to make his mother proud.

She walked to the bedroom door and looked in. When she saw Joel sobbing quietly, she turned to me. "Santiago, what's the matter? Tell me!"

Lowering my eyes, I said, "He's dead."

Doña Leticia remained by the door, but she started banging her fists and her forehead against the door frame. She cried loudly, pulling her hair as if she were *Juana la loca*. Doña Leticia, who was a bilingual secretary in Colombia, spoke English well enough. Pointing a finger at Joel, she screamed shrilly, "You killed my son. *Murderer, murderer.* You killed my son. Goddamn you for turning Bobby into a homosexual. Bobby was no *maricón*. Not my son! I hate all homosexuals!" she screamed, turning to face me accusingly. "I hate them all! I hope they all die of this plague! I hate New York!"

After venting her hatred of homosexuals, she turned to Joel. "Where are the papers?" she demanded. "I want those papers! Don't think you're going to steal Bobby's money. I know my son left me a lot of money and I'm not going to let you steal it, you dirty Jew.

I'll hire the best lawyer in New York and you'll go to jail, you crook. That's where you belong, you degenerate corrupter. My son was a millionaire," she ranted. "I know that. Don't think I'm a stupid Colombian. I'll have my brothers come here and they'll kill you. Give me the papers!" Like an angry lioness protecting her prey, she paced back and forth in front of the door, growling. Joel ignored her. I took a chair in the living room, beginning to get really pissed. I felt that Bobby deserved much better, especially from his mother. Maybe this was the only way Doña Leticia could express her grief, but even now that her son was dead, she refused to enter his room. I thought about how heartbreaking it must have been for Bobby that his own mother would shun him when he was dying. All of a sudden, I could feel no compassion for her. I was angry. I was about to grab Doña Leticia by the shoulders and give her a good shaking when the bell rang. It was my mother.

"Lucy, Lucy!" Doña Leticia screamed, throwing herself into my mother's arms. They cried for a while. Mother kept saying, "Calm down, Leti. Calm down. The worst is over, Leti. Bobby is finally resting." When Doña Leticia quieted down, Mother went into the bedroom and, crossing herself, knelt at the foot of Bobby's bed and prayed silently, with her eyes closed and her hands clasped. When she finished, she kissed Bobby on the forehead and stroked Joel's head. Seeing this, perhaps wanting to do likewise but still afraid of disease, Doña Leticia resumed her histrionics. "You need a good cup of cammomile tea," Mother said with authority and, taking Doña Leticia's hand, dragged her in the direction of the kitchen.

I walked into the bedroom and closed the door. I sat on the chair and watched Joel, who seemed almost catatonic. Trying to collect my emotions, I breathed in and out deeply. A while later there was a knock at the door. Doña Leticia summoned Joel to the kitchen. She had calmed down now. For the next hour or so she worked Joel over about Bobby's will, insurance, holdings, etc. Mother watched all this with an expression of distaste. There was some ugly squabbling over Bobby's corpse. Doña Leticia claimed that it "belonged" to her, and that she wanted to take it back to Barranquilla and bury it there. Fortunately, in his will Bobby had been very specific about this matter; his last wish was to be cremated and have his ashes scattered in the Hudson. Joel must have seen all this coming, because he had all the papers ready and produced copies of all the documents. Bobby had left his mother his life insurance and real estate he owned in Colombia. The truth is that in the two years he had been stricken with AIDS, many of his businesses had fallen through and, except for the condo on Wall Street, which he had purchased with Joel, his art collection and antiques, plus some stock, he had lost most of his money. Again Doña Leticia accused Joel of being a crook and threatened to have her relatives in Colombia come over to fry him unless he gave her *everything*. Finally, she agreed to let Joel dispose of the corpse. Then she grabbed some papers, stood at the entrance to Bobby's room, announced that she was ready to go and once more began shrieking, cursing Joel, New York, and all homosexuals.

Mother offered to drop her off. I ordered a taxi, took my shopping bag from under the sink, and embraced Joel, telling him to call me if he needed anything. Joel stood by the door, waving good-bye, looking devastated, utterly lost, as we left him alone in the apartment with the corpse of his lover.

When the taxi arrived at Doña Leticia's address, Mother said, "If you'd like to have dinner before you go back to Colombia, I'd love to have you over."

Doña Leticia thanked Mother, and said that she would call her soon. As the taxi drove off, I said, "I hate that woman so much. I can't believe you're going to have dinner with her."

"It's more than just being polite," Mother said, staring at me. "I'm not crazy about her either. But Bobby was her only son, and I know how she must feel. Don't be too quick to judge harshly what you don't understand. If you ever have your own children, you may come to understand her a bit better."

Mother and I remained silent on the way home. Inside her kitchen, I removed the cartridges from the shopping bag. "The *obleas* and figs are for you. Irma wants you to know that the figs are from Buga." I paused. "They sent *pasteles,* but Bobby and I ate them."

Mother smiled. Eagerly, she asked, "Were they good? Were

they corn or rice *pasteles?* Did Bobby like them? He used to love my *pasteles."*

"He ate all of it," I said, which for Mother was the highest compliment one could pay to a dish.

"I remember how he used to come by on Saturday afternoon; I can almost see him now. He'd say, *'Tía'*—he always called me auntie—'what goodies do you have for me today?' He loved my *picadillo,* too."

"I'm going upstairs to take a nap," I said. "I feel beat."

I plodded upstairs. Spread out on my bed was a beautiful white Italian suit, a pink silk shirt, white Brazilian shoes, socks, and a gold designer tie. They were gorgeous. I hid the coke behind some books on the shelves and went back downstairs.

Mother was busy making pig's feet and chick-peas. Simón Bolívar greeted me, screeching, "Hello, stranger. Hello, stranger. Hello, hello."

Mother, who hadn't heard me coming downstairs, turned around to face me. There was an anxious look on her face, as if she had been worried I disliked her choice of clothes.

Regressing to my childish self, I said, "Thank you for the clothes, mommie. The suit is beautiful." I knew she wanted a hug, but I held back—it was very difficult for me to have any kind of physical contact with her.

"I'm so happy you like them. I know you don't have a nice summer suit. Anyway," she said, as she continued chopping scallions and tomatoes, "I want you to look nice tonight. You know Paulina and Claudia are such clothes horses."

"I really don't feel like going anywhere tonight, if you don't mind," I said, surprised that she still planned to go to the Saigon Rose.

"I don't feel so hot myself," she said. "But Paulina and Claudia will be disappointed if we don't show up. Paulina had a dress made just for the occasion. Anyway," she sighed, "I know Bobby would have wanted us to go out and enjoy ourselves. And I hope you do the same when I die, okay?"

The timing was wrong to confront her about the Claudia plot.

Chopping vegetables on the cutting board, all of a sudden she looked old, shrunken, defeated. The sorrow and weariness painted on her face deterred me from bringing it up. I thanked her again for the suit, and told her I wanted to nap for a couple of hours. As I climbed the stairs, I thought about how, for years, Mother had wished I had been a successful businessman like Bobby. His successes had made Mother proud of him. It was no wonder she took Bobby's death so badly. In my bedroom, I hung the suit, cleared the bed, set the alarm clock, and lay down, burying my face under the pillows. Immediately, I fell asleep. I began to dream about painful moments of my adolescence. I felt as if I were walking with a stick, using it to uncover the cobwebs that had accumulated on top of still-living and bleeding wounds. I dreamed I was in Colegio Americano, where Bobby and I had been classmates. I dreamed the principal called me into his office and for the millionth time asked me to bring my birth certificate to school. I promised to bring it soon, knowing deep down that it was impossible because my father had refused to acknowledge me legally and thus there was no legal record of my birth. The scene played and replayed in my mind, and with each new rehearsal the principal would get angrier until he threatened to expel me from school. In the dream, I experienced the acute feeling of inadequacy and rejection I felt at that time. At the first school I attended, the Jewish school, I saw the circumcised boys in the showers after gym class and I thought I was a freak. I saw myself during school recess, sitting at my desk, sobbing hysterically, while the other children were out in the yard playing. In the next sequence of dreams, I was eleven or twelve. I saw myself naked, holding my uncircumcised penis, trying to remove my foreskin with a razor. I made an incision and started bleeding. Afraid to call for help, I bled until I passed out in the bathroom where my mother found me. She wrapped a towel around my private parts and took me to her bed and applied Mercurochrome to my almost severed penis, then kissed me and hugged me, reassuring me that everything was all right, that I was not a freak, that a doctor would see me the next day and circumcise me if that's what I wanted. That night, I slept on mother's bed, embracing her, and when I woke up, I was kissing her, and we were both naked, panting and sweating and my penis was erect as if I had just stopped making love to her and I began to cry. I woke up, quaking. Was that what had really happened? Had I made love to my mother? Or was this just an incestuous dream of unfulfilled passion? Perhaps I would never find out and even if I did, what good would it do me to know the truth?

5

Nostalgias

It was nearly midnight when mother and I arrived at the Saigon Rose. Red-carpeted steps led to a landing where we were greeted by a woman attired in a glittering scarlet gown and lots of costume jewelry. Upon giving our names, we were admitted, but not before two beetle-browed men, with gold canines, frisked us.

The interior of the nightclub looked like a set out of *Scarface*—the remake. Hot yellows and reds predominated; from the ceiling hung baroque chandeliers all ablaze. A conga was in progress. The long line snaked around the dance floor and the tables surrounding it. The shimmering gowns of the women, plus the substantial rocks they flashed, made the line look like a Chinese dragon. We stood by the bar, waiting for the conga to finish. Although the Saigon Rose is owned by Asians, Saturday night is Colombian night. It was a prosperous, plastic-looking clientele; the women, heavily made up and dressed in elaborate gowns; the men dressed mostly Caribbean style—in white and mauve suits.

When the conga was over and the exhausted but excited couples dispersed, a tuxedoed waiter escorted us to our table. I was impressed by Mother's numerous acquaintances. She glided around the tables, waving and calling names and blowing kisses, as if she were the queen of the ball. Much to the annoyance of the waiter, she stopped to introduce me to several "businessmen."

Near the back of the dance floor, Paulina and Claudia were sitting across from one another, at a round table for eight. Claudia stood up, stretching her arms. "Lucy, Sammy," she called out, laughing her deep, nervous, raucous laugh. She looked like a Latin Grace Jones: spiked orange hair, boa-constrictor pants and jacket, and diamonds, rubies, and emeralds cascading from various extremities and orifices. We exchanged kisses and embraces. As I sat down, I noticed two grim-looking men at the next table who must have been Claudia's and Paulina's bodyguards. Mother and Paulina engaged in a heated and giggly tête-à-tête. Claudia's French perfume made her smell like a voluptuous Barranquilla flower.

"Sammy, *viejo* man. It's good to see you. I'm so sad tonight," she said, putting her arm over my shoulder. Her long purple fingernails were pierced by thin gold chains with tiny diamond stars at their tips. If I had to use an adjective to describe her, I would have to say . . . unique. She seemed a bit sauced already, but her agate eyes shone like movie projectors in the dark. Claudia poured me a glass of Dom Perignon and we toasted Bobby. Since her arrival in America, Claudia and I had seen one another only intermittently. All I know is that her family arrived in Miami penniless immigrants, and a couple of years later they were millionaires. When Paulina purchased a house in Jackson Heights our mothers became fast friends. During her years at Yale, I saw Claudia infrequently. After graduation, she seemed to spend most of her time traveling to distant places and residing at her many homes on three continents. A few years ago, she had had a motorcycle accident, from which she escaped unharmed, but the friend riding with her, her lover, I assumed, had been killed. Since that time, Claudia developed her peculiar laughter which reminded me of Tallulah Bankhead's. In the late eighties, she had come to visit me on Eighth Avenue, and she had taken me to rock concerts and punk clubs on the Lower East Side. But she must have sensed that they were not my idea of fun because, much to my relief, she stopped asking me out.

"Sammy, *qué vaina. No joda*," she moaned, swilling her champagne. "I always thought of us as the three musketeers, and now is over and I feel old as hell."

I thought it was disarming that, in spite of her Ivy League education, Claudia retained the macho Spanish working-class argot of the Caribbean coast of Colombia. We began to reminisce about our adolescence, which seemed to be our favorite topic of conversation.

"I remember so clearly the first time I met you," she said. "I was playing with my toy soldiers in the backyard when I heard you over the wall. Even then your voice was so deep and spectral," she said, laughing and slapping my back. "Although Mother had told me she'd kill my ass if she caught me climbing the wall, I had to find out what was going on. I climbed the wall and I saw you with your eyes closed and your arms stretched to one side, reciting Silva's *Nocturno:*

> *Y era una sola sombra larga*
> and it was a long, lone shadow,
> and it was a long, lone shadow.

"Oh, man," she went on. "You sounded like Anna Magnani on valium."

"Yeah," I said. "I remember Bobby called you down and you climbed down the guava tree, and although you were nine or ten all you had on was a pair of shorts. And you had a Mohawk haircut even then; I thought you were a boy," I said, to get even.

"It was a mango tree, not a guava tree, man. How can you have forgotten such a crucial detail?"

"Are you sure? I always thought it was a guava tree. Sour guavas, if I remember correctly."

"Man, it must be all that LSD you did that fried your brains. I tell you, Sammy, it was a *mango de azúcar* tree. Don't you remember how during mango season we'd spend whole afternoons eating ripe mangoes? We'd only stop when Bobby's grandmother, Doña Guillermina, would come out in the backyard screaming, 'Boys, if you don't stop eating mangoes you're gonna grow hairs on your tongues.'" She was laughing hard, although the anecdote did not seem all that hilarious to me. I could see Claudia was lit.

We continued reminiscing about Bobby, gossiping about Joel (whom we both liked), and Doña Leticia (whom we both detested). The conversation was interrupted when the set of boleros was over and the dancing couples returned to their seats. The emcee came out and commanded the attention of the audience. *"Damas y caballeros,* ladies and gentlemen, the moment we've been anxiously waiting for: I give you the artist we all came to see, the heiress to Gardel's immortal throne, the supreme interpreter of the tango in our time, the incomparable international superstar, Lucinda de las Estrellas."

I looked at Mother, but she was already in another galaxy—all her concentration was directed at the stage. Five Japanese men in tuxedos appeared, bowed, and took their seats. They tuned their instruments, as all eyes riveted on the golden circle of light the spotlight made on the curtains. Lucinda de las Estrellas, a.k.a. Wilbrajan, flung the curtains aside and strutted onto the stage. All loud conversation ended, although I heard whispers and titters. My sister scanned the audience with an arrogant, defiant nod, as if she were displeased to find an audience in the nightclub. She smiled at our table, though. I hadn't seen Wilbrajan in several months, and I was struck how every time I saw her, she seemed to have grown more beautiful. She was wearing a simple, tight, white silk dress, cut several inches above the knees. She wore her hair in a tress, which she kept over her breasts. Wilbrajan walked toward the musicians with the grace of a mother swan. While she chatted inaudibly with them, she turned her back to the audience, showing the low cut of her dress, which exposed her back and carnal shoulder blades. In her fleshiness, she reminded me of Ingres's Odalisque. I realized that years after her metamorphosis, I still kept looking for the "grasshopper" of my childhood.

Wilbrajan had started her career singing boleros, *cuplés,* and *rancheras,* in disreputable dives all over the United States, wherever there was a Latin population that supported her act. Once a year, she traveled to Mexico and South America, where she claimed she was famous. She had cut an album in Colombia. In the early 80s, she became a *tanguera.* God knows her lifestyle suited her stage persona;

she had had many boyfriends and a few ex-husbands, whose only trait in common was their shadiness.

She approached the mike slowly, fussing with her tress. All in white, she seemed a moon goddess. She wore a gold chain around her neck and a single large pearl dangled from it. The hand that held the mike had a tattoo of a purple dagger.

"*Buenas noches,* ladies and gentlemen," she said in her husky voice. "I'm honored to have in the audience the person to whom I owe everything, my mother." The spotlight fell on us, and Mother, playing the moment for all it was worth, took a bow and then blew a kiss at Wilbrajan. I was miffed that the entrancing chanteuse had ignored me, while acknowledging our mother, with whom she didn't get along at all. The spotlight returned to Wilbrajan, who now was hugging the mike with both hands. "I'm happy to be back at the Saigon Rose, in front of this public I adore," she purred, stretching her exquisitely dramatic arms and opening her expressive hands. The audience applauded, responding to her fakery. "Tonight," she went on, "is a very sad night for me. A fellow compatriot, and dear friend of the soul, Bobby Castro, died this afternoon. To his memory, I shall sing 'Volver.' " She signaled to her musicians, and the violins began rippling waves of melancholy notes throughout the nightclub. Closing her eyes, the way Gardel did it, she recited the first few lines of the famous tango:

> *Volver* . . . I can guess the city lights
> blinking in the distance,
> are marking my return.

Opening her eyes, she crooned:

> They are the same one that lit
> with their pale reflections,
> deep hours of pain;

She sang mournfully, as if delivering a dirge. But as the song progressed, her voice blossomed, taking dark, tragic tones:

And though I didn't want to return
one always returns to one's first love.
The old street that once echoed:
'Her life is yours, her love is yours,'
under the mocking glance of the stars
today indifferently watches my return.

Making a fist, Wilbrajan hit her breasts, as if she were stabbing herself. It was a most operatic effect. Then she ran her fingertips across her forehead:

To return
with a wilted brow
my hair silvered by the snows of time.
To feel
that life is just a sigh;
that twenty years are nothing,
that my feverish eyes
wandering in the dark
look for you and call your name.

Suddenly, the utter bleakness of the lyrics got to me, and watching my sister doing this striptease of her soul became unbearable. As I looked away, I caught Mother's profile and her beatific expression. Obviously, Wilbrajan had inherited her love of tango from our mother. To me, Mother was now just an old woman, but in her youth her story hadn't been much different from Wilbrajan's. The reason there was so much animosity between them was that they were like two different images of the same person: in Mother, Wilbrajan saw herself in old age. In my sister, Mother saw the woman she had been in her youth.

Vivir
con el alma aferrada
in sweet remembrance
that still makes me cry.

Wilbrajan paused, and, as if she were a latter-day but more glamorous and haunted Janis Joplin, she screamed at the top of her lungs:

I'm afraid of the appointed hour
when my past returns to confront my life
I'm afraid of the nights
alive with memories
that shackle my dreams.
But the wanderer who flees
sooner or later stops on his path
and though oblivion, smashing it all,
has killed my old dream,
I hide a flickering hope,
the only fortune left in my heart.

Wilbrajan's voice was barely adequate, but I had never heard anyone blast a tango in quite that way. She shook, and shivered, and shuddered, as she delivered her song in spasms of pain and despair, and I finally understood the old saying that tango was not sung but lived. When she finished, the entire audience leaped to its feet, and, banging tables, clinking glasses, it shouted: *"Viva el tango, Viva Gardel!"* Everyone clamored: *"Nostalgias, Nostalgias."* Smiling like a generous goddess, Wilbrajan obliged her fans. A few couples took to the dance floor.

"Come on, let's rip up the floor," Claudia said, standing and taking my hand.

"I can't dance the tango," I protested.

"Sure you can. Keep your crotch against mine, and push me around," she ordered me.

Ignoring the couples pirouetting around us in the lewdest manner, we danced, getting closer to Wilbrajan; the whiteness of her makeup made her look like a Kabuki performer. When we were about twenty feet away from her, we stopped and stood to the side, watching my sister's performance.

I hadn't lived until I heard Wilbrajan sing *"Nostalgias."* Standing with her feet apart, she raised her arms toward the ceiling, and with her hands open, palms up, as if she were worshiping in front of a pagan altar, begging to be sacrificed, she wailed:

> *Bandoneón,* howl out your tango blues.
> Perhaps you too have been wounded
> by a sentimental love.
> My clown's soul cries out
> sad and lonely tonight
> black night without stars.
> If drinking brings consolation
> then here I'm keeping vigil
> to drown my sorrow once and for all.
> I want my heart to get drunk
> so that later I can toast to
> the failures of love.

"Nostalgias" brought the house down, and Claudia and I returned to our table to listen to Wilbrajan interpret three more tangos. After taking innumerable curtain calls, she joined us, while the Japanese *tangueros* played their instruments to the total indifference of the audience who had come to drink, dance, and listen to Lucinda.

Aware of being the center of attention, Wilbrajan embraced and kissed Mother first, then she gave me a polite, cool peck; next she embraced and kissed the Urrutias. Although it was true that over the years my sister and I had grown distant, occasionally I missed the closeness of our early years. Mother proposed a toast to her great success. A bouquet of pink orchids, compliments of the management, arrived at our table. Wilbrajan pinned an orchid on Mother's dress. Mother purred and purred, calling Wilbrajan *"Mi chinita adorada.* My little angel." Several bottles of Dom Perignon, with cards, arrived. When the waiter pointed to the sender, Wilbrajan acknowledged him with a drop-dead stare.

"Mijita linda," mother said to Wilbrajan. "I can't tell you how proud you've made me. Now I can die; you've become a great singer. I know that, in heaven, Gardel is watching over you and approves."

"Thank you, Mommie," Wilbrajan said, giving Mother a tiny smile.

"Next you'll have to sing in Radio Music Hall," Paulina elaborated. "I wonder if we could rent it for one night. I promise you, *cariño*, I'll fly all my family from Barranquilla for the occasion."

Mother kissed Paulina profusely on her cheeks to thank her for her generous, if far fetched, offer.

"You don't have to thank me," Paulina said, holding Mother's face. "More than friends, we're family. You know, I'll do anything for your children, *mi amiga adorada*."

"Right on," Claudia said, watching our mothers carrying on. "Lucinda, that's a heck of an act you've put together. Man, you're awesome singing that stuff."

Getting carried away, Mother said, "Maybe Carnegie Hall. Why not? I think you're better than Liza Minnelli, anyway."

Wilbrajan stared at me. I realized I was the only one who hadn't complimented her yet.

"That was good, Sister," I said. "I really enjoyed it."

She continued staring at me, fishing for more compliments.

"I especially liked 'Volver,' " I said sincerely.

"It was so sweet of you to dedicate it to Bobby's memory," Paulina said.

"I was practically in tears," Mother added.

"It was freaking great," Claudia opined.

"I shall always think of Bobby when I sing 'Volver,' " Wilbrajan said. "Tango is about pain." She gulped down a glass of champagne.

We continued praising her performance and swilling the bottles of Dom Perignon that Claudia kept uncorking. I noticed a tall, tanned, muscular blond in safari clothes. He approached our table, smiling. Jumping off my chair, I cried, "I'll be damned! Stick Luster!"

It was my friend Stick, with whom I used to play hide-and-seek in the morgue in Bogotá. We hadn't seen one another in over twenty years, but I recognized him instantly. We embraced, and then Stick hugged and kissed my female relatives and was introduced to Paulina and Claudia. It was a happy occasion and there were many toasts.

"Stick, *mijito*, how did you know we'd be here tonight?" Mother asked.

"Well, you do see, Mrs. Lucy. It was a most fortuitous coincidence," he said in something that was almost Spanish. His Spanish had deteriorated a great deal, but now he spoke it with a musicality that was Brazilian. He went on. "I go to visit my client in Queens today and they have a poster for tonight on the table, and there was a picture of Will and I thought, Aha, I think I know this singer. And you know, my friends, never once in all past years did I lose hope we'd meet again."

"Stick, are you a devotee of the *Virgen de la Macarena?*" my mother asked.

"No, Doña Lucy. I'm Protestant. If you must remember."

"The reason I ask, my dear," Mother explained, "is that la *Virgen de la Macarena,* if we pray to her with all our hearts, will reunite us with long lost friends."

"Most useful piece of information to know," Stick said thoughtfully. "I do remember *Virgen de la Macaroni, Virgen del Chilindrina, Señor Nuestro de Monsterate,*" he said, mangling the names of the most popular saints in Colombia.

Unable to restrain herself, Claudia burst into loud squeals.

"Claudia, *muchacha,* behave yourself," Paulina admonished her daughter.

Disregarding Claudia, Stick said, "And since when did you come to America, my friends? I see you're a very beautiful artist, Will, and a famous singer. I'm very happy about your success. But what about you, Señora Lucy, and you Sammy?"

"Sammy's famous, too," Mother said. "He won the most important poetry award in Colombia. And now he's writing a long book about Christopher Columbus."

"Ah, like me, a lover of high adventure. I always knew you'd be a famous writer, Sammy. You always had lots of imagination. Since you were a little boy. Remember how you read to me from *The Adventures of Dick Turpin?*" he said to my embarrassment. "And you, Señora Lucy?"

"I got married to the nicest man, Stick. I wish you could have met him a few years ago. But he has Alzheimer's now," she concluded with sadness in her voice.

"I'm so sorry to hear that."

"We choose neither our blessings nor our curses, my dear," she sighed. "And what about you? What have you been up to all these years?"

"Well, you see, Señora Lucy," Stick began, clearing his throat. "Afterward we leave Bogotá we go to Brazil. Ah, Brazil, land of the samba. What a beautiful country. But poor Papa had to go put telephone cables not in Rio or Sao Paulo or Bahia but in jungle. Ah, it was most exciting and wondrous experience for a child. Too many mosquitoes and bugs, snakes and tigers and alligators for Mother. But not for me. We live with tribes who do not talk anything we speak. I learned to hunt and fish with spears, and weave. I do love the life very, very much. But, since we move here and there, poor Papa catches deadly virus and after four years in jungle we go back to Sweden."

"Tarzan of the Amazon," Claudia cried, breaking into shrill peals of laughter.

"You must excuse my daughter," Paulina said. "Too much Dom Perignon."

Oblivious to Claudia's guffaws, Stick continued. "Back in Sweden, my soul was not Swedish but Amazon. But I could not go back, as I was only a boy. So after I finished college (I study archaeology), I return to Brazil. Ah, Brazil. I make my living traveling to remote tribes in deepest jungle—some of them I'm first blond they've seen—and I bring back pottery and weaving of most artistic tribes. I sell these in America and in Europe. And I will show you some whenever you want."

"We have an apartment in Trump Tower," Paulina said. "Do you think we could decorate it with jungle things, Mr. Stick?"

"Oh, yes, madam. Jungle motifs will look most beautiful there."

Wilbrajan, who had remained silent all this time, and looked bored out of her mind with the conversation, finally said, "Stick, come over here and talk to me."

Pretty much the same way she had hogged him all to herself when we were children, she drew him into an intimate conversation that excluded the rest of the party. I must admit that they looked stunningly sexy together. Mother and Paulina returned with renewed vigor to their interrupted tête-à-tête.

Seeing them all cozy and romantic, Claudia remarked, "Isn't it wonderful? They look great together, don't you agree, Sammy?" I nodded my approval even though I was quite pissed with Wilbrajan for taking Stick hostage. After all, as children, he had been my best friend, not hers. I was dying to have a long conversation with him, alone. Could it be possible, I wondered, that now that we had grown up, he preferred her company to mine?

"I predict they will fall in love," Claudia said. "Look at them, Sammy. *Qué cheveridad.*"

"God, I hope not," I said crankily. "Not the way she goes through men."

"You're pretty snippy tonight, aren't you? It must be Bobby's death that's affected you so much. You're not usually like this," she said, taking my hand. "Anyway, since it's getting late I might as well remind you that you're supposed to propose to me tonight."

I pulled away my hand. I had thought all along that the marriage plot had been concocted by our mothers unbeknownst to both of us.

"Sammy, I'm hurt," Claudia said, looking teary-eyed. "Here I'm proposing to you and you recoil from me as if I were a green mamba."

"You're joking, aren't you?" I asked, although something told me she was serious.

Claudia laughed hysterically, slapping my back. When she had collected herself she said, "No, Sammy. I think it's a marvelous idea. I think it'd be neat to marry you. I've been waiting for you to propose to me for years. It'd be so cool to have your child."

I chugged down a glass of champagne. I might as well take this with a grain of salt, I thought.

"Don't you love me at all?" Claudia asked pathetically.

I patted her shoulder as if she were a big dog. "You know I love you, but not like that. You're like my sister. I wish you were my sister and not Wilbrajan."

"So? You love me; I love you. It's perfect, man. Think of it. Have we ever had an argument? Have I ever been pissed at you? Never."

"But Claudia," I said gently. "You're a dyke; I'm a fag."

"Big fucking deal. Look at our mothers. Don't they look like a couple of sweet old dykes? I've never seen such devotion. I mean, this thing runs in our families?"

"Are you saying my mother is a dyke?" I said, outraged.

"Just forget it, will you? Anyway, don't you think dykes want to get married too? You're thinking about the dykes in the 60s. Now we want children just like all other women. Plus I'm going through changes. I'm sick of blowing heaps of money on mean bulldykes who just take advantage of me. And I've known you for so long. There aren't going to be any nasty surprises coming from you. I know you as I know the palm of my hand. Better. And the way you love that cat of yours. That tells me you have good parental instincts. When we get married you'll have your own child to love instead of a pet."

"You don't understand. I don't think I could love anyone more than I love Mr. O'Donnell. Nobody could ever need me that much." I could see this marriage thing wasn't going to work. If she couldn't understand something as obvious as my love for Mr. O'Donnell, what about my other dreams? For example, what about Christopher Columbus? "Mr. O'Donnell isn't just a cat," I said.

"Okay, he's not just a cat. He's a Bengal tiger, whatever you want. I'm not allergic to him. I'll be a nice mother. I'll buy him lots of nice, juicy mice to eat."

"That's so gross."

"Sammy, I will *not* let Mr. O'Donnell stand in the way of our happiness. In any case, as I was saying before, it's true you looked a bit weird when you were a boy, but not now." Claudia smiled her killer smile. "I really dig your looks, man. You've grown so tall and slender, just my type, if I were straight. And you have such beautiful cow eyes and your wonderful curly hair," she purred, running her fingers through my hair. "And even your ears, which were so peculiar back then, now make such a punk statement. And those nice, pink, fleshy lips of yours . . . I just want to bite them."

Before I understood what was happening, I saw her black, painted lips approaching mine and we kissed. It wasn't disgusting like I thought it would be: it was different. For the first time I had kissed a woman and not felt as if I were kissing my mother or sister.

In other words, it didn't feel incestuous. It must have been the *guascas* in the *pasteles,* and the champagne certainly must have helped. Suddenly I melted and found myself feeling chummy and mushy toward Claudia and her untold riches. I took both her hands in mine and she rested her orange hair on my shoulder.

"Listen to me, Sammy," she began after awhile. "This is very serious. Right now I'm footloose and fancy free. But not for much longer. My family is determined to marry me. They don't want an unmarried dyke in the family. And if you don't marry me, they'll make me marry some horrible mafioso. You know my brothers. Now, I know you wouldn't like that happening to me, would you? Besides, I promise to take good care of you."

"Oh, oh," I said, remembering her unpleasant brothers. "I wouldn't want to join 'the family,' you know what I mean? I disapprove of the drug trade. I think it's evil."

"I do too. I've nothing to do with that business. Mother and I just get the revenues, that's all. But they'll leave us alone. They know you're a poet. You know Colombians respect poetry so much."

"I'll have to think about it, okay?" I said, letting go of her hands. I noticed that Mother and Paulina were looking at us, smiling. If this were an early Dickens novel, I would conclude it now by saying that my sister and Stick and Claudia and I got married and lived happily in Jackson Heights ever after. But this is what happened next: the romantic, plaintive notes of the violin and the *bandoneón* in the background were drowned out by loud complaints and harsh, "Hey, you animal, watch where you're going, will you?"

Out of the corner of my eye, I saw my nephew rushing toward us. When he was a few tables away, I spotted two men with drawn pistols hot on his trail, pushing aside the seated customers, overturning chairs and tables, weaving through the crowd to catch up with Gene. People screamed and ducked as Claudia's bodyguards sprang forth and bullets were exchanged generously all over the nightclub. Gene's pursuers, with their faces, chests, and stomachs looking like bloody graters, fell dead on top of some freaked out customers. Several women fainted, and the ladies and gentlemen in the audience crawled and hid under tables, summoning their own bodyguards to protect them. Brandishing guns, Claudia's bodyguards fired at the chandeliers, and, for a moment, the room sparkled with a shower of glass. Yelling, "The Urrutias are leaving; nobody move," the bodyguards surrounded our party and herded us out of the Saigon Rose and into Claudia's limousine. And just like it's been done in a million Hollywood thrillers, the driver peeled rubber into the night.

Paulina was the first person to speak a coherent sentence. *"Qué taquicardia,"* she said, beating her breasts lightly with her closed fan. "Isn't it terrible how decent folk can't go anywhere these days?"

"It was worth the price of admission," Claudia said. "I haven't had so much fun since Carnival in Rio."

"How providential those nice gentlemen were there to help us out," Paulina said referring to her bodyguards. "Claudia, please remind me to have them over for coffee."

"Qué horror! Qué horror!" Mother exclaimed. Then, addressing Wilbrajan, "Cookie, I'll never come to hear you again as long as you sing in that place."

"Oh, Mother, get real," Wilbrajan said. "I'm used to it; it's like singing in Colombia all the time."

While the limo scudded down the dark Queens streets, Gene sat sullenly in a corner, staring out the window, his knees jerking up and down. To me, he looked guilty as hell; I would have to confront him later that night, I decided, but not in the car. I was sure the men had been after him, and I thought I knew why.

Checking her watch Mother said, "It's still early. Why don't we all go home and have supper? I made the most delicious pig's feet and *garbanzos.* There's plenty for all."

It was agreed we'd continue the party at Mother's house and we proceeded in that direction. As soon as we arrived, Mother and Paulina busied themselves in the kitchen, while the rest of us settled in the living room to get sloshed and chat with Colombian music in the background. Stick had just finished telling a gruesome tale about a young woman with her period who had been devoured by piranhas in a jungle river, when Gene excused himself. I took the opportunity to follow him upstairs. Wilbrajan and Claudia were so riveted by Stick's tales and hunky looks, that they couldn't have cared less if we had excused ourselves to go to Siberia.

Gene was lying on his bed, listening to the Grateful Dead, or the Dead Kennedys, or some such necrophiliac group. He looked scared as hell when he saw me come in. I asked him to turn down the damned music and sat down on his bed. "You got to return that coke," I said. "You almost got all of us killed. Do you realize that?"

He pretended not to know what I was talking about.

"The coke in the cartridge," I snorted. "You stole it."

"Oh that," he said, lying on his bed, closing his eyes. "I just want to buy a bike."

"There is enough coke in that package to buy a Honda dealership. Are you out of your mind?"

"Okay, so I did," he said, sitting up. "What do you want me to do now? They don't know who stole the coke, but I can't return it just like that," he said, snapping his fingers.

"Cut the crap. They know who did it. Those men were out to kill you."

"Where do you get your information? From the *Reader's Digest*? You're so wrong. Those men weren't after me; they were after Claudia's ass."

"Bullshit."

"Sammy, don't you know shit? There's a fucking drug war going on, and those men were out to fry Claudia and her mother to get back at the Urrutia brothers for some drug squealing or something. The Urrutias have been snitching to the DEA about Pablo Escobar."

"What episode of 'Miami Vice' was that? Do you think I'm an idiot?"

"I don't give a fuck what you think, Mr. Geraldo Rivera."

I sat there staring at him. If he weren't taller than me, I would have slapped his insolent mouth. To my utter astonishment, he started rapping:

"I'm just a boy
from Jackson Heights,
I ain't no criminal
All I want's a bike."

Then he burst out sobbing. "Oh, Sammy, I'm scared shitless." This had the intended effect on me. "Okay," I said, patting his shoulder. "I don't mean to make it worse. We'll just have to think of something," I finished, feeling sorry for this pathetic boy who had no father (Wilbrajan wasn't sure who his father was), and a mother who carried on as the torch singer in *Blue Velvet*.

"You know, Uncle," he said. "Besides the Boners, you're the only friend I have in the world."

I knew he wanted something out of me—otherwise he'd never have called me Uncle. "What do you want me to do?"

He stopped crying. "You will help me? You're not shitting me?" he asked, smiling his killer smile.

"Of course I will. I said so, didn't I? You're my nephew and I care about you. I don't want to see you get fucked up."

"That's right. Because you know what they'll do to me? They'll chop me like *ropa vieja*," he said, referring to Cuban brisket of beef dish. "So please, uncle Sammy, take the coke with you to Manhattan until I can think of something. Is that cool, dude?"

I vehemently refused. Gene cried some more, and like the sucker I am, I fell for it.

I went downstairs to join the party, which went on for hours. We munched on delicious Colombian *pasabocas*, until the pig's feet were served. After supper, Mother and Paulina, accompanied by Wilbrajan at the guitar and Gene on the drums, entertained us singing their favorite *rancheras*. We danced *cumbias, pasodobles,* and *merengues*, and consumed several bottles of *aguardiente* and *Ron Medellín*. It was the wee hours when I went upstairs quite tipsy. Although I was exhausted, I couldn't fall asleep. I tossed on my bed until my room spun like a roulette wheel and the bed tilted like a raft on the high seas. Feeling nauseous, I got up and sat on the sill of my open window. The branches of the cypress in front of the window were so thick they blocked the street. Looking up, through the leaves, I saw a handful of stars and maybe a planet. The sky was a milky black color that belonged neither to night nor day, but rather to a state of mind. I thought about the times I used to go to my grandfather's farm by the river: The motorboat would come to pick us up around 4:00 A.M., so we'd wake up after midnight and sit by a bonfire near the shore to wait for it. The mosquitoes were merciless at that hour, and my only consolation was the rococo sky and the hundreds of wishing stars that dropped from midnight until dawn. Grandpa would say that some of the stars were witches on their night errands, and he'd entertain us recounting the many times he had been bewitched, and how he had broken the spells and captured the witches. These stories terrified me, and even when I returned to the city after my vacations, they would haunt me at night. This line of thinking always weirded me out, and presently I thought I saw Bobby's ghost standing a few feet away from me. I don't believe in ghosts, so I immediately remembered I was sloshed. And yet, I could almost see it—this shape that was like Bobby's outline etched in mercury. I looked out the window and toward the sky and after awhile I looked back into the room, and it was still there. But there was no reason for me to be frightened of Bobby—not even his ghost. "What is it?" I asked, feeling quite batty for talking aloud to a would-be ghost. "What do you want?" As I spoke these words, the outline contracted until it became a little red dot that flickered before it went out. Now I was sure I had imagined all this. With the kind of day I had had, it was probably the d.t.'s.

A lovely, cool breeze caressed my face and I looked again at the night sky. I closed my eyes and in the camera obscura of my brain an old reel began to play. I saw myself and Stick and my sister when we were children. It was late in the afternoon and we were on our way to play hide-and-seek. We were ascending a long, steep street that led to the mountains above Bogotá; crossing *Carrera Séptima,* we entered the grounds of Javeriana University. Instead of walking across campus, we hiked up a mossy, unpaved trail that led to the shantytowns above the city. It was dusk. The sky above Bogotá was charcoal-colored, and the pallid sun had sunk in the horizon, buried behind the clouds. Beneath us, the city lights were beginning to go on, and, in the distance, the tall downtown buildings lit their skinny silhouettes against the ashen background of the mountains in the south. The mountain peaks were swathed in fog, and the ground was moist and cold. We walked until we reached a promontory, at the bottom of which rose the back of the building of the school of medicine; it looked deserted. Since the previous year, when the government had ordered a curfew, all evening classes had been canceled. We made sure that there were no guards around, and then raced down the pebbly hill. One of the windows on the ground floor was ajar. I went in first and Stick helped Wilbrajan. Inside it was dark, cold, damp, and reeking of the strong chemicals used for embalming. This was the morgue, a big, high-ceilinged room with four rows of slabs crossing it, whose walls were fitted with refrigerators stuffed with fresh corpses and loose organs in plastic bags.

"I hate this game," Wilbrajan whispered.

"Then why don't you go home," I said. "Nobody invited you."

We sat on the cold tiles with our backs against the wall.

"Okay, let's play now," Stick said. "Who will hide first?"

"I will," I said.

Wilbrajan offered to count.

"You count too fast. Let Stick count."

"He can't count in Spanish."

"You're the one who doesn't know the numbers," I said.

Wilbrajan and Stick turned to the wall, covering their eyes with their hands. Stick began to count to a hundred. I tiptoed down the aisles. Most of the corpses were covered with yellowing, stained sheets. Usually I'd climb onto an empty slab and cover myself with a sheet, or I'd lie next to a corpse and hide. There weren't too many hiding places. I heard the count of sixty-eight; I'd better hurry. I decided to try something new; I opened one of the huge refrigerators in the back of the room and stepped in. The door closed behind me. I realized it couldn't be opened from the inside. A small frosted lightbulb lit the interior of the icebox, revealing two corpses hanging from hooks, one male, the other female. In the dim light, their skins looked greenish. The man's body was old, skinny, its flesh corrugated; the woman's was young. Her face was smashed and caked with blood, and her red teeth appeared in a horrifying grin. Her eyelids were opened and she had no eyeballs. Her skin was taut, translucent, and her fingers stretched out, as if she were ready to jump on me. Seized with terror, I lunged against the door, and started banging on it and kicking it. I slipped on the icy floor and, as I fell backward, I grabbed the woman by a leg, knocking her off the hook. The corpse landed on me. Her breasts were on my face.

I put my hands on them to push her away from me—her breasts were hard, cold, sticky like ice cubes. I realized I was running out of air, that I was beginning to freeze. I screamed: white smoke came out of my mouth. The echo of my scream ricocheted off the walls of the refrigerator. "Oh, God, I promise to be good," I said. "I promise to make my mother baptize me and I'll have my first communion and I'll go to mass every Sunday. I promise to obey my mother." I felt dizzy, slipping into unconsciousness. I couldn't get the woman's breasts off my face. When I touched her, it felt as if I were being glued to her corpse. Now I saw that her throat had been slit, and the insides were brownish-red, like guava paste, and the edges blackish, rotting. Her face grinned inches away from mine. I tried to remember what I knew of the Lord's Prayer. It was useless; I didn't know it. Suddenly, I heard a tremendous pop; the door of the refrigerator opened, and I heard voices calling my name, and hands pulling me by my sneakers, and I knew the devil that my mother had threatened me with so often was finally here to drag me to hell.

6

Just Say It

I woke up Sunday afternoon with a major hangover. I showered, shaved, dressed, and took a couple of Tylenols before going downstairs. I had decided to leave that afternoon. I was quite worried about Mr. O'Donnell.

"Buenos días," Mother greeted me. Then correcting herself, "Good afternoon. I just woke up myself. What a rumba. Have a cup of coffee," she said pouring me a full cup of *tinto.*

"Good morning, good morning," Simón Bolívar screeched as I sat down.

"Mother, make him shut up, will you," I said, giving Simón Bolívar a nasty look.

"I can't," she said flatly, sitting at the table. "He loves to talk for breakfast."

I had never seen Mother so dishevelled. She had no makeup on her face, and her hair was completely out of shape.

"Have you seen Gene?" I asked.

"He left just right before you came down. He got tired of waiting for you. He seemed in a hurry. He said he was going by his job to quit. Why couldn't he wait till tomorrow, it beats me. I was happier with him working. I don't know what he's going to do if he's free all the time. That boy needs a father, Sammy." Mother frowned and finished her coffee. She left the kitchen, and while I was having my second cup of coffee and beginning to feel the effects of the Tylenol, I heard strange chanting in the other room. Mother entered the kitchen holding a burning stick of *palo santo,* singing in some ancestral African dialect. She seemed in a trance, as she walked to the counter where she opened the jar that contained my grandmother's ashes. Next she painted a cross on the floor. Since Mother had been into *santería* ever since I can remember, there was nothing odd about this, although I wished she had waited until after I had left for Manhattan. She lit a bunch of aromatic crystals in the incense burner and placed the burner at the center of the cross; with the smoking *palo santo,* she approached me and made the sign of the cross over my head. Mother grabbed my hand. "Walk over the incense," she ordered me, "and make the sign of the cross."

"What the hell is going on?" I snapped.

"It's a *despojo.* You need to cleanse your aura. Bad spirits are following you."

"What?" I yelled. "Are you exorcising me? I refuse to go along with this bullshit. Stop it right this minute, Mother."

Simón Bolívar mimicked me, "Mother, Mother, Mother."

When I refused to walk over the incense burner, Mother started zigzagging around the kitchen as if she were having an epileptic seizure, and began chanting, *"Yemayá, Yemayá, Quimba, quimba, quimbará."*

"He, he, he, he," Simón Bolívar giggled hysterically, flapping his wings. Too hungover to do anything, I sat down to wait until she finished.

This was the first time she had tried to exorcise me. I was too flabbergasted to comment on her performance. My feelings toward her were very antagonistic. I knew that some kind of breakthrough psychological unraveling had taken place this weekend and I wanted to run away and confront her about it, all at the same time. She was an old woman now and she was actually getting to the point where she would be needing my support to help her navigate through the passages of her old age. And yet, I was angry not at the old woman she was, but at the beautiful Gaugin goddess that had given birth to me; the first and only woman I had ever loved.

"I'm really pissed," I said, feeling the plug that held my feelings removed and a lot of steam beginning to blow out uncontrollably.

"What? What have I done wrong this time?"

"Mother, this whole Claudia thing is . . . insane. I'm not going to marry Claudia now or ever, is that clear?"

"But why, Sammy?"

"Because I'm homosexual and Claudia is a lesbian, that's why. Because I'll never love a woman that way." I couldn't believe I had actually said those words. I was shaking. For many years now I knew Mother knew, as she had known about Bobby since we had been kids; as she had always accepted our friendship, even when as boys we were probably in love with each other; when it had been adolescent romance. But the word homosexual had never been spoken, never been said in her presence, nor in connection with me. It was as if as long as it was unspoken there was still room for things to change some day, to declare that everything had been a passing fancy. As long as I didn't admit to it, there was hope that I would eventually marry like all good Colombian boys. Bobby used to say that the main difference between Colombian and American men was that all Colombians were gay until they married, whereas most Americans first married and then came out.

Mother looked crushed, deeply hurt. She seemed to be shrinking in front of my eyes. She began to cry, softly, delicately. "I just don't want you to die like Bobby. That's all, Sammy. I'm not stupid. I know about you and I don't care." The pain she felt must have been so severe that it left no room for histrionics. The moment was actually quite peaceful, serene. I wanted to put my arms around her shoulders; I wanted to say to her that I, too, loved her; and that I wanted to forget the past and to forgive. And yet, I couldn't. Perhaps in the future, I thought. Perhaps one day when all these feelings and revelations have been sorted out, I will be able to embrace you as a son, Mother, I thought.

An hour later, I found myself at the train station waiting for the number seven to take me back to Times Square. Clutching the shopping bags with clothes and food, and the valuable cache of cocaine I was smuggling into Manhattan, I thought about everything that had happened that weekend. As ridiculous as it sounded, I had come out to my mother in my mid-thirties. Perhaps because of this I felt freer, more liberated, than I had just a couple of days before. I was reeling with new knowledge that I trusted would lead me with clarity into the mature years of my life. Looking into the direction of the skyscrapers of Manhattan, I realized that for the first time they didn't look to me as the land of dreams, but the place where reality awaited me, at long last.

PART TWO

THE CAT, THOUGH IT HAS
NEVER READ KANT, IS, PER-
HAPS, A METAPHYSICAL ANI-
MAL.

Philosopher or Dog?
Machado de Assis——

7

The Cat Who Loved *La Traviata*

Nothing seemed to have changed in Times Square, and I found the familiar squalor somehow reassuring. As usual at this time of day, shoeless Muslims knelt on green towels, praying to Mecca in front of subway posters for Broadway shows. Squatting on the stairs leading to the street, begging aggressively for quarters, was the same woman I had seen for months, with the same shrinking baby, wrapped in a bunch of grimy rags. Nearby, bored cops chatted idly, petting their police dogs.

Forty-second Street was thick with a Sunday crowd of black and Latino teenagers looking for cheap thrills. Mormon-looking tourists with cameras strolled, sticking close together while taking in the scene. They were offered sex of all kinds, pot, Colombian coke, smack, hash, ecstasy, uppers and downers, designer drugs and, of course, crack.

It was one of those rare, mild late afternoons at the end of July when the air was like silk and Manhattan felt like an island. The multicolored neon marquees of the movie theaters advertised life-sized photographs of seminude porno stars in sexy poses. A naked man, looking stoned out of his mind, wandered out of a peep show. Halfway down the block, a young woman dressed in Salvation Army uniform and armed with a megaphone, was stationed under the awning of a sex palace, preaching to the depraved and indifferent denizens of Times Square. Two preppies stopped in front of her, swayed, twirled, wobbled on their feet and collapsed, overdosing on the sidewalk.

"You don't have to get high on drugs," the woman blared. "Jesus will get you high. You'll be so high on Jesus you'll never want to come down."

Waiting for the light to change at the corner of Forty-second and Eighth, I looked over my shoulder: the skyscrapers of midtown had bloomed. The Chrysler building caught the reflection of the setting sun; its silver top reminded me of a minaret crowned with a long, shimmering sword. Crossing Eighth, I saw the sky beyond the Hudson, which looked as if all the nuclear reactors from Hoboken to Key West had exploded, setting the air afire. Yet the color was not that of natural combustion, but synthetic, like the orange of a hot burner on an electric stove.

I live on the west side of Eighth Avenue, above O'Donnell's Bar, between Forty-third and Forty-fourth Streets, an address formerly nicknamed The Minnesota Strip. The good old days had ended when the famous Greek restaurant The Pantheon closed due to lease problems. Since that time the short block—which comprises a Citibank at the corner of Forty-third, O'Donnell's Bar, the Pantheon building, a porno joint (Paradise Alley), a Gyro coffee shop, the Cameo (a beautiful old theater now turned XXX movie house), and a four-story building at the corner of Forty-fourth, formerly a whorehouse and now a shooting gallery—had been taken over by crack addicts, who conducted their business on the premises of Paradise Alley. Now I looked back with nostalgia to the days when young hookers (for all tastes) decorated the block around the clock. . . . But wait a minute, not *that* young, I thought, standing on the east corner of Forty-third, as I spotted a tiny hooker standing in front of the door of my building. She looked about seven years old, maybe seven and a half. I had seen teenage hookers and hustlers, but this was a child. This was real depravity and decadence—no doubt a product of the crack epidemic. In spite of her spike heels, she barely reached the doorknob. She wore a vinyl miniskirt and red satin tank top. A pink plastic purse was strapped across her shoulder and her belly button was plugged with a blue stone. Her hair was streaked gold and punked-out. Long rhinestone earrings framed her cheeks and above the false eyelashes her eyelids were painted purple and sprinkled with gold glitter. Her tiny crimson lips were done in the shape of a heart. I stood in front of my door, open-mouthed, dangling the keys, waiting for her to move.

In her childish voice she said, "Want a date?"

I recoiled, aghast. Now she placed her baby hand on her hip and crossing one leg behind her knee she reclined lewdly against the wall. "Cheap blow job," she offered. I noticed now that her voice, though squeaky and reedy, had a sultry timbre. She was not a child—she was a midget hooker. I breathed a sigh of relief, "No, thank you," I said. "I live here."

She gave me a blank look, but made enough room for me to open the door. I ran up the stairs to my apartment on the fourth floor. I was worried about Mr. O'Donnell. The six months the vet had given him to live were over and even though Mr. O'Donnell seemed fine, I felt anxious when he was alone. Inside the apartment I set down my shopping bag and went to the closet to hang up my new suit. I was walking toward the living room calling Mr. O'Donnell's name when the phone rang.

"Santiago, is that you upstairs?" said Rebecca, my downstairs neighbor.

I picked up. "Hi, Rebecca. I just got here but I can't find Mr. O'Donnell."

"I'm so relieved it's you. I thought it might be a burglar. Mr. O'Donnell is down here with me."

"I'm coming down to get him. Is that okay?"

"Come on over. I'm so glad you're back."

Rebecca met me at her door. Her eyes were wide open, as if she had just had a major fright. Locking the door after I came in, she said, "Can I offer you a beer, iced tea, a glass of lemonade?"

"The lemonade sounds delish, but no thanks. Where's Mr. O'Donnell?" I looked around the room for him.

"I don't know whether we ought to disturb him right now. He's in my bedroom listening to side two of *La Traviata*."

Rebecca had discovered that Mr. O'Donnell would revive from

his periodic bouts of listlessness by listening to Monserrat Caballe's rendition of Violeta. He'd lie still, smiling, his ears pricked up until the opera was over.

"Is he in bad shape?"

"I didn't want to call you at Lucy's, but when I went upstairs Saturday morning to feed him, he was more dead than alive. He refused his Kal Kan, so naturally I was worried. I went to Barkin' Fish for some catfish since he likes it so much. I practically had to force feed him, but he ate one fillet, a teensy bitty bit at a time."

"Should I take him to the hospital right now?" I said.

"Goodness gracious, Santiago. You're making me more nervous, and I'm already a shitty mess. I called the hospital and was told there's nothing we can do except make sure he takes his medicine with his meals. Today he's much better. He's been listening to *La Traviata* all day. This morning he refused to eat fish, so I gave him a container of pineapple yogurt. Wait till this side of the record is over and you can take him upstairs. He's as good as new, thanks to my ingenuity."

"I shouldn't have left him alone, but thank you so much, Rebecca."

"Will you stop feeling guilty about everything. I swear, Santiago, I'm going to start calling you the Honorary Jew. I took real good care of the kitty; Florence Nightingale couldn't have nursed him better. So, how's Lucy? Did you have a nice weekend?"

I gave Rebecca a much abridged and sanitized version of what transpired in Jackson Heights.

"Honey, it sounds like a Flannery O'Connor novel set in Queens," she observed. "It's the planets," she added philosophically. "As long as Pluto is aligned with Scorpio it's going to be bad."

Willing to blame it all on the stars, I said, "Oh yeah, and exactly how long is that going to last?"

"Seven years."

"Rebecca, I couldn't take seven years of this!"

"That's why I'm going away. I might as well enjoy myself while there's a chance."

Thinking she meant her upcoming vacation, I said, "I'd love to get away from here, if I could."

"Santiago, darling, I'm beginning to doubt this area is ever going to get any better. All this time I bought your theory that it was just a matter of time before Donald Trump moved in to redevelop Times Square."

"I agree with you, Rebecca," I said, conceding defeat. "Donald Trump can't solve his own problems nowadays, much less ours. If only they closed Paradise Alley it would be okay. It wasn't all that bad when it was just hookers."

"The hookers were like girl scouts selling cookies compared to what's going on now," Rebecca said. "But I'm getting tired of calling the mayor's office and the midtown precinct and signing petitions. Somebody is getting paid a lot of money to keep that business open."

"Maybe we ought to go to the press with the story," I suggested. "A front page story in the *Post* would do it, I'm sure."

"Honey, I'm afraid nothing will get done until there's a massacre down there. By then I'll be a basket case. I tell you, if Francisco asks me to marry him, I'm saying *sí, sí.*" She fanned herself with a letter.

"Is it a letter from Francisco?" I asked.

"Santiago," she said, "would you be a dear and do a little translating for me?"

"In that case I'll have some lemonade." I sat down and Rebecca went to the kitchen. Some months back, in a bookstore in Greenwich Village, Rebecca had met Francisco, a Venezuelan tourist and a hairdresser. Although she did not speak Spanish, nor Francisco English, they became lovers. After he returned to Caracas, I became the official translator of their correspondence. She entered the room and handed me a glass of cold lemonade.

"The weather's been so terrible, and the situation downstairs seems to be getting so much worse," she said in her melodramatic Alabamian twang, "that I declare I was ready to hang myself if something mighty good didn't happen to me soon. But there it was, in the mailbox, a letter from my beloved."

I took a sip of lemonade, cleared my throat and toasted to love. Striking a Cyrano de Bergerac pose, I pulled out the letter. It was written in Francisco's tiny gothic handwriting, which I had come to know so well. Rebecca sat very still and upright, holding in her lap her glass of lemonade. Her head thrust forward, her lips quivering, her aquamarine eyes wide open and gleaming; the intensity of her expression was almost frightening. I could have read the first paragraph blindfolded since it was always the same. "Dear Rebecca," I read. "I hope this finds you and your loved ones enjoying good health. God willing."

"Santiago, is that a South American convention of letter writing? He always says the same thing."

I ignored her and went on. "I was so happy to receive your last letter and to find out that you're doing well."

"Goodness gracious. He's so formal."

"Rebecca, my sweet, in case you haven't noticed, we South Americans are formal people. And now, shall I go on?" I asked, somewhat irked by her interruptions. She smiled for an answer. I continued with my translation. "I'm doing very well, thank God."

"Is that a South American thing, Santiago, to punctuate every sentence with God?"

I sipped my lemonade to control my temper. "Rebecca, don't be ridiculous."

"Well, better to have a Christian for a boyfriend than a druggie," she sighed.

Her reasoning escaped me, so I resumed my translation. "I've been incredibly busy lately, and I get to my apartment late at night, and I'm usually so tired that even though I want to sit down and write to you every night I fall asleep in spite of my good intentions." God is merciful, I thought. If he wrote to her like this every day, translating would become excruciating. May God keep him very, very busy.

"What is it? Bad news?"

"It's nothing," I said, and continued translating. "I have the most exciting piece of news. One of my clients has been elected Miss Caracas and she'll be representing our city in the Miss Venezuela competition. The girl is too divine for words, and very intelligent and has lots of personality, and I'm positively sure that she'll be elected Miss Venezuela and go on to represent our country in the

Miss Universe Pageant. Can you imagine what that will do for my business?"

"I smell a franchise," Rebecca exclaimed.

I looked up in disbelief. "I didn't know you were into beauty pageants."

"Beauty pageants are one of the interests Francisco and I share. Is that the end of the letter?"

I shook my head and continued. " 'In your last letter you mentioned wanting to visit me during your vacation. My humble abode is at your service, and I would be glad to receive you in my home.' "

"Glad? Is that what he says, Santiago? Are you sure?"

"Sorry. I would be *happy* to receive you in my home," I corrected myself.

"You know, Santiago, there is a difference. That's what's called a nuance of the English language."

"Even in the best translations something gets lost," I remarked, annoyed with her.

"Don't mind me, honey. Go on with the letter. You're doing beautifully. It always amazes me how well you do this sort of thing."

Predictably, the third paragraph referred to me. "All this part is about me, Rebecca. Do you want me to translate it also?"

"Would you, honey? I don't want to miss a single one of his words."

"Okay, here it goes: 'Please thank our dear friend Santiago for translating my letters. I hope everything is going well with him, and that he and Mr. O'Donnell are enjoying good health, God willing. I always include Mr. O'Donnell in my prayers and ask José Gregorio Hernández for a miracle.' "

"Who's that? Is it voodoo?"

"He may as well pray to Donald Duck," I said. "It might be more effective. José Gregorio isn't canonized, but he's Venezuela's national saint because he introduced the microscope to the country. And you want to know how smart he was? He was killed by the only automobile in Caracas at that time."

Rebecca frowned. "Well, it's real sweet and thoughtful of him, in any case."

"Yeah," I said. "It's real sweet of him. Now let me finish: 'I look forward to hearing from you soon, and I hope you're following my beauty tips and are taking good care of your hair and your lovely complexion. It's midnight now, and through my window I can see the moon illuminating the city below, and everything—the sensual breeze that comes from the Caribbean, the stars in the sky, the fires twinkling in the mountains—reminds me of you, my adored Rebecca. Love, Francisco.' "

"He's a poet," Rebecca said.

Folding the letter and handing it to her, I said, "He's a hairdresser."

"A hair stylist and a makeup artist," she corrected me, and started bragging about what a great lover Francisco was and how she had never met a man who cared so much about a woman's needs.

I studied her, marvelling at the change in her appearance since she had met this paragon. Before, she dressed like a receptionist in a funeral parlor. Tonight, she wore stone studded sandals and her toenails were painted a lurid purple. She had on khaki shorts and a Banana Republic shirt that depicted lush vegetation in an apocalyptic red. She wore too much glossy lipstick and mascara and green eyeshadow, but her gold-streaked, new wave haircut was becoming. I was alarmed, though, by all the gold and silver loops marching up her ears. I closed my eyes and saw Rebecca going all the way, like the Orinoco Indians in Venezuela, and piercing her lips, her nostrils, her . . .

"Santiago," she said, awakening me from my reverie, "is it very hot down there in August?"

"I don't know. I told you, I was there in November. It was pleasant during the day and cool at night. You might want to take a couple of sweaters."

"It sounds heavenly," she purred.

"So you've made up your mind to go?"

"I got to get away from these crack people downstairs before I crack up myself. Besides, I'm ready for adventure. Of course, I'm mighty apprehensive to be going there alone. I don't know what I'll do without you," she said, referring, I think, to my services as a translator.

I tried to reassure her. "Caracas is a cosmopolitan city. You'll have no problems communicating with the people."

"But, you know, Santiago. The truth is, when Francisco and I are together, we understand each other perfectly. Isn't that incredible?"

"I'll say. But you could learn Spanish too. It's an easy language to learn, unlike English."

"I purchased a dictionary, and I'm learning useful expressions: *Buenos días. Cómo está usted?*"

"Your accent is perfect," I lied.

"Thanks, honey. When I come back to New York (that is, if Francisco doesn't ask me to marry him), I'll take some lessons. Thank you so much for translating the letter. You're an angel, Santiago."

"Anything for love," I said.

"I hope it happens to you too. You'll be transformed, sugar." Rebecca sat with the letter on her breasts, blissed out. I could read love printed large over her face. Her happiness was becoming too painful to bear. I noticed side two of *La Traviata* was over and got up. "The opera is over," I said. "I'm exhausted and I have to get up early in the morning."

Rebecca followed me into her bedroom. Mr. O'Donnell was hiding under the blankets. "Uh-oh, Rebecca," I uttered in mock alarm, playing one of his favorite games. "Where's the kitty? I don't see him! He escaped again! Help!"

Mr. O'Donnell remained still. I sat on the bed and touched the bulge he made under the sheets, quickly pulling my hand away. In the winter this game was safe, because he was covered by heavy blankets; but in the summer his teeth and nails would poke through the sheets. I placed one hand on his head and the other on his thigh, immobilizing him. He struggled a bit to free himself but then started to purr loudly.

"It's a wonder to me how he can purr and be vicious at the same time," Rebecca said.

I uncovered him—Mr. O'Donnell was now on his back, smiling.

"Hello, kitty," I said, scratching him under his ears. "It's time to go home." As I picked him up, he felt lighter, bonier, as if he had lost weight over the weekend. On the spot where he had been lying remained thick chunks of his hair. In the summer Mr. O'Donnell shed copiously, but the way he was shedding lately he'd soon go bald. As I ran my fingers over his stomach, I noticed his coat of hair had lost all luster. Overnight, Mr. O'Donnell had become old.

I thanked Rebecca for everything and said good night. Upstairs, I stored the *pasteles* in the fridge. The cassette with the coke was harder to dispose of. Since I didn't own a TV, much less a VCR, its presence anywhere in the apartment was conspicuous. I threw the plastic case in the trash and then emptied the cocaine into a glass jar. I left it next to the salt, sugar, flour, oats, etc.

Setting the alarm for 6 A.M., I undressed, lay down, and turned off the overhead light. Although I was exhausted by the events of the past few days, I could not fall asleep. I was well aware of the strange turns and twists my otherwise dull existence was taking. I had in my possession what looked like a pound of cocaine. My brain went into overdrive. I needed to get some sleep, though. I turned on the air conditioner and tried to relax. I said to myself, "Your brain is out to kill you, Santiago. Stop thinking; remember your brain wants you dead." As the room cooled, I started to drift off. My eyelids felt heavy, as if they were glued. I thought of Caracas. Of huge, prehistoric leaves. And stars that had auras, like the moon. Of parks in which exquisite orchids nested in gigantic, emerald trees. And the smells: the tropical breeze scented with a million gardenias. And the Caribbean in the moonlight, silvery and smooth, and in the distance, riding shimmering seahorses, a chorus of mermaids serenading me with sensual, heartbreaking boleros.

I was hungry when I woke up around midnight. But I wanted something light, like yogurt or fruit, and there was nothing like that in the fridge. I splashed cold water on my face, combed my hair and went downstairs.

Both sides of Forty-third Street were lined with garbage bags, and the homeless huddled in front of the shops closed for the night. The after-theater crowd had dispersed and was replaced by the usual junkies, transvestites, and habitués of porno palaces.

I crossed Eighth Avenue and went into the *New York Times*

building to get today's newspaper. Then I walked to the Korean fruit stand at the corner of Forty-third and Eighth. I picked a piece of watermelon, oranges, carrots, and yogurt. I pulled out a twenty dollar bill. The woman rang the items as she placed them in a bag.

"Twelve-fifty," she said.

For some time I had suspected this woman of overcharging me. Tonight I decided to confront her.

"How's that possible?" I asked, grabbing the twenty from her hand.

"Pay, please. Next," she said, staring at me impassively.

Looking over my shoulder, I saw other customers in the store but no one behind me. I began pulling the items out of the bag. "Let's add them up one by one," I said.

"Four oranges, two dollars," she said, a flash of anger or annoyance sparkling in her eyes.

"Four oranges at fifty cents a piece, that's two dollars—if my math is correct."

"Watermelon," she paused, then looking directly into my eyes, "three dollars."

"It sounds like a lot for a small piece of watermelon, but it's too hot, okay, and I don't feel like arguing. So that's a total of five dollars."

With one sweep of her hand she grouped together the remaining items. "Carrots and yogurt, five dollars. Ten dollars total. Sorry for mistake. Pay, please."

"This is outrageous," I exploded, realizing my suspicions had been correct all along. "Yogurt is ninety cents at the supermarket, and a bag of carrots forty cents."

"Then go to supermarket."

I found it unnecessary to inform her that supermarkets in our neighborhood closed well before midnight.

"No want to pay price, no take," was her fortune cookie advice.

"Fine," I said. "I'll just take the oranges. And the yogurt."

She rang these items. I gave her the twenty dollar bill.

"Sorry, no change."

"You had change just a minute ago."

The woman said something in Korean, I guess. Wondering

which member of my family had been insulted, I prepared to call her a few names myself in Spanish when she turned and looked toward the back of the store. A man in a stained apron, looking like a cross between Gertrude Stein and a Sumo wrestler, emerged from behind a bamboo curtain holding a head of lettuce in one hand and a butcher knife in the other. They engaged in an animated conversation, and the man gave me a scorching look. Now Santiago, I said to myself, you don't want to engage in combat with that creature. I put my hand in my pocket and found a ten dollar bill. "Here," I said, looking at the man. "I'm sorry. It's this heat."

It was cooler now, but the humidity was unchanged and the sky looked cottony and gray. Feeling crappy, I dragged my feet on the sidewalk as I noticed several crack addicts milling excitedly in front of Paradise Alley, like hyenas around carrion. I unlocked the door and was about to go in, when a sharp object hit the middle of my spine.

"Don't move," a man's voice ordered me. "Just give me your money." His hand went into my right pocket, then into the left one where my money was. Thinking, This is where he busts my head and runs away, I closed my eyes.

"Give him back the dough," another voice screeched.

I turned around; the mugger's face was inches away from mine—these were eyes that hadn't seen straight in years. I grabbed the gun and snatched the bills. Out of the corner of my eye, I saw the midget hooker pressing a huge sparkling blade against the man's crotch.

"Now beat it, fuckface, before the cops get your stupid ass," she ordered him.

The man reeled backward until he reached the street curb. Pointing a finger at my rescuer he yelled, "You're dead, you fucking freak!"

I pointed the gun at the mugger. "You heard the lady! Piss off!"

The man ran across the street dodging the oncoming Eighth Avenue traffic. At the corner of Forty-third, he stopped and screamed a bunch of obscenities and threats. People were looking in our direction.

The gun shook violently in my hand; I felt dizzy. "I don't know how to thank you," I said.

"Don't mention it," she said, folding the blade and hooking it to a garter under her skirt.

"Here," I said, offering her the gun.

She shuddered as if I had offered her a cobra. "Are you crazy? I don't want that thing, man. It's yours. Who knows how many dudes he's killed with it."

Passersby were approaching. Like a gangster, I stuck the gun between my pants and my belly.

"See you around. I got to try to score tonight." She started to walk away.

"Hey, listen," I called after her, feeling that I hadn't thanked her enough. "What's your name?"

"Hot Sauce," she said. "And yours?"

I told her.

"Well, San-ti-a-go, it's been fun meeting you. Any time you want it, I'll give you a good deal, babe," she said, pouting and blowing me a kiss before she swaggered into the surrounding nocturnal sleaze. From behind, she looked like a child playing femme fatale.

The gun burning against my skin, I shut the door and dashed up the stairs. I locked the door and paced the length of the apartment looking for a niche to hide the gun in. Finally, I settled for the toilet water tank. Tomorrow I'll wipe off the fingerprints before I ditch it in the Hudson, I thought. I was still shaking and feeling slightly hysterical but it was too late to call anyone, even Rebecca. I lay in bed and tried to read the *Times,* but my eyes wouldn't focus. I ate an orange. Tonight, I wished I had a TV set. My mother was right—it was un-American not to own a television. Mr. O'Donnell jumped onto my bed. I set the paper aside. "You don't know how lucky you are to be a cat," I said. His face was on top of mine, and his breath stank, but I remained still. One half of his face was white and the other half gray, and he had the long pinkish nose of a tropical rat. I stared into his eyes. The black pupils were surrounded by a greenish circle that grew agate toward the edges. His whiskers were long and thick like plastic toothpicks stuck on his snout. I scratched him between his ears and he started to purr. "Yes, yes, I know," I said. Burying his nose under my chin, he went to sleep lying on my chest, his enlarged heart thumping against mine.

8

Mrs. O'Donnell and Moby Dick

The alarm rang at six. I had to be at the Social Security office by eight. Consoling myself that I would be home before noon, I got up. Curled up on a corner of the bed, Mr. O'Donnell pricked up his ears.

After I showered, I put on some water for coffee and gulped my vitamins. While waiting for the coffee, I sat by the window that overlooks the alley behind my apartment building. On the far side of the alley is another building with an entrance on Forty-third Street between Eighth and Ninth avenues; the other half of the block is taken up by a parking garage several stories high. The alley is active day and night because it's used as blow-job alley by many office workers on their way to Port Authority. But in the early morning, looking out through the screen and my gate, all I saw was a family of alley cats playing below. These cats seldom came up the fire escape, but each day Mr. O'Donnell would spend many hours by the window watching their antics.

In April, he had broken an old window screen and escaped. He was lost for eleven days. I thought he had reverted to his old alley cat life and I searched for him in vain. My friend, the painter Harry Hagin, did a drawing of him and we posted hundreds of copies around the neighborhood. Since he was a sick cat and needed his medicine to survive, the story caught the attention of a *Daily News* reporter, and a picture of me, displaying Harry's drawing, appeared in the "Manhattan" section that Friday. My line was swamped by callers offering me other cats and animals; others claimed Mr. O'Donnell was their lost cat; I also received obscene letters and phone calls from heavy breathers, but no information as to the cat's whereabouts. I had given up hope he was still alive when, one morning, with one of his ears chewed up and his muzzle so badly scratched that I hardly recognized him, he came up the fire escape, looking guilty and tired. That same week I took him to the Humane Society to have him fixed.

The coffee was ready. I poured myself a big cup and looked out the kitchen window. The handsome flasher who lived in one of the studio apartments across the alley was sitting by the window in his underwear. I had gotten used to seeing him dancing and playing with himself. Mr. O'Donnell zigzagged into the room and, eyes still half-closed, started to beg. He did not meow, but instead made a weird noise that reminded me of the cry of a toucan. I fixed his breakfast, which he ate half asleep and then went back to bed.

As I went downstairs at seven, there was already a long line of applicants at Mike's, the employment agency on the second floor of my building. The men were Mike's usual crop of shabbily dressed Hindu and Arabic types, chattering in exotic languages. Sometimes they came to the agency with their cardboard suitcases, as if they had just arrived from Baghdad or Sri Lanka or wherever they came from. I always wondered what kinds of jobs Mike got for them.

Outside, Eighth Avenue reeked of uncollected garbage. Masses of stone-faced commuters wearing suits and carrying briefcases poured out of the Port Authority Terminal. The humidity was thick and oppressive but the A train was prompt, although crowded. Minutes later I resurfaced at Chambers Street.

To kill time I sat on a bench outside the Federal Plaza Building, under a rachitic maple. I lit a cigarette and watched the usually frantic Wall Streeters dawdle, struggling with the prevailing mugginess. For a few years I had been working as an interpreter in different boroughs of New York City, for the Department of Social Security, a trove of stories and characters. I found it hard to believe that in New York, the Mecca of the twentieth century, there were people whose squalid lives seemed as horrifying as anything one could find in the novels of Gorky. I was uptight about having to interpret for Judge Warpick, who was the most detestable person I had ever met. I felt reassured that my hatred was shared by the other department employees as well as all the claimants who came before her. On many occasions, I had felt like leaping from my seat and twisting her neck. To ward off these thoughts, I reminded myself that I was just the interpreter, a vessel of language, the invisible man, a passive and disinterested nonparticipant.

At five to eight I took the elevator to the twenty-ninth floor.

"Hi, Jeff, how's it going?" I greeted the security guard.

"Hey, Santiago. Good to see you, man. You up for a game?"

Jeff and I played chess while we waited between hearings. Although we had played hundreds of times, he still managed to beat me in the first dozen moves.

"I'd like to. But I have Judge Warpick, you know. And she's always on time."

"Good luck. She's in a foul mood. If you ask me, what she needs is a good fuck. But I'd rather go to the electric chair," he said smiling. "Here," he added, handing me the claimant's file. "She don't have an attorney. Maybe we can play when you get out."

"Okay."

The room was empty but for a couple of women sitting way in the back, near a tall fan which made a lot of noise all right, but blew no air.

I approached the women. Smiling, I said to the older woman, "Good morning. I'm your Spanish interpreter."

The women exchanged puzzled looks as if I had spoken in Chinese. The older woman said, "Thank you."

I sat next to her. Reading her name on the file, I asked, "Are you Guadalupe Rama?"

She nodded.

"Señora, why don't you have a lawyer?"

"Nobody told me nothing about getting a lawyer."

"Señora Rama, the letter you received with the date of your

hearing had a list of places where you can get free legal services. It's your right under the law."

"It would take someone with a very black soul to deny me help," she said.

That sounded to me like the perfect description of Judge Warpick. "The judge is not here to defend you, Señora Rama, but to interpret the law," I warned her, as I leafed through the thick file. "This folder contains all the documents that the judge is going to review to reach a decision about your case. There are twenty-eight documents here." I pointed to the list on the first page. "They go as far back as 1978, and the most recent entry pertains to your visit to Dr. Miller on June of this year. I also see that your claim has been denied four times."

"And if I lose this time, I will reappeal," she said, waving her crutches.

"If you had had an attorney, you might have succeeded the first time."

When I had explained the file, I informed Jeff that we were ready to go before the judge. We were led to Judge Warpick's chambers by her assistant. I indicated to the women where to sit, and sat down next to them. While the judge's assistant fiddled with the tape recorder and the mikes, I studied Señora Rama's daughter. A teenager of medium height, she was incredibly thin. Her complexion was caramel-colored and her hair shiny ebony. She seemed withdrawn and avoided my eyes. When our eyes finally met, I noticed that hers were dark and moist like a canna flower in the moonlight.

Judge Warpick entered the room, followed by the doctor. I rose, indicating to Señora Rama to follow me. She rose with great difficulty.

"Please be seated." The judge motioned with her hands without looking at any of us. The doctor sat next to me.

"Mr. Interpreter, have you explained to the claimant that under the law she has the right to obtain legal counsel?"

"Yes, your honor, I have."

"And she still wants to go on with the hearing?"

"Yes, your honor. She does."

"Very well, Señora Rama. I advise you to go ahead with the hearing; it will be to your benefit."

I started interpreting. Judge Warpick interrupted me, "You don't have to translate that," she growled. "This is not the United Nations. Please stand up, Mr. Interpreter, and raise your right hand. Do you"—she read my name on a piece of paper—"solemnly swear to interpret faithfully the questions posed from English into Spanish and Spanish into English to the best of your ability so help you God?"

I already wanted to strangle her. "I do."

Señora Rama was sworn, we were seated, and Judge Warpick began, "Guadalupe Rama, when did you come to the mainland United States for the first time."

"October 4th, 1964, your honor."

This was something I had noticed about all immigrants I had ever interpreted for: they remembered the exact date when they had first arrived in the United States.

"What was the highest grade of education you completed in Puerto Rico?"

"I never went to school."

"Never?"

"That's right."

"Do you speak any English?"

"I know a few words."

"Can you read or write in Spanish?"

"No, ma'am."

"Who do you live with?"

"My children."

"How many children do you have?"

"Four."

"Give their names and ages."

"Dorcas Antioco, twenty-five; Hennil Rangel, twenty; Sonya Altagracia, eighteen and Raisa Cocecielo, here present, fifteen," she said, indicating her daughter.

The girl squirmed in her seat, and mumbled, "Sixteen."

"How many times have you been married?"

"Twice. My first husband died; my second husband divorced

105

me. The others, I didn't marry. I'm a useless woman. Men don't want me."

"Señora, just answer my questions. I don't want to hear long stories about your life. Is that understood?" She paused. Obviously she wasn't getting anywhere with this claimant. "Do you still live on Avenue A and First Street?"

"In the projects."

"On what floor?"

"Number four."

"Do you walk up the stairs or take the elevator?"

"I take the elevator when it's working, which is never. Otherwise, I walk the stairs one step at a time," she said, holding her crutches. Her hands shook violently now. There was a strange expression on her face, as if she were trying to smile. I noticed it was a grimace of pain; she was about to start crying.

"Señora Rama," the judge said, staring at her papers, "tell me about your present complaints."

Señora Rama's eyes were wet, but no tears came out of them. Eagerly, she extended her arms in front of her and opened her hands. It looked as if she were making an offering to the judge. "First, I had an operation on this hand," she said, looking at her right palm. "Then (shaking her left palm), I had an operation on this one."

I saw on each hand an S-shaped, wide, deep scar that ran from the joint of the middle finger to the wrist area. Now I noticed her gnarled fingers. "These hands are useless. I can't do anything with them."

"Who does the house chores?"

"Raisa," she said, nodding in the direction of the girl, who stared at her hands in her lap and sank lower in the chair.

"Don't you cook anything at all?"

Señora Rama shook her head; she squinted, as if trying to remember something. "I can boil two eggs and some potatoes. But I cannot peel them. That's all."

"Can you carry a five pound bag of potatoes?"

"I can't do nothing."

"Answer my question: Can you carry a five pound bag of potatoes?"

"If I hold it between my arms," she said, crossing her arms across her breasts.

"Do you have any other complaints?"

Señora Rama rose from her chair and, on her crutches, hopped to the side of the table.

"I have trouble with my feet. See? I have pins in my ankles." She pointed to scars the size of brown quarters on both ankles. "I had two operations," she explained.

The doctor rose and leaned over the table and took a look at the scars.

"You can sit down," the judge ordered her, looking very uncomfortable.

"And my knees, too," she said, refusing to sit down.

"What's the matter with your knees?"

"When I walk, the bones come out of joint, so I have to wear these braces all the time." She began to pull at her pants.

"That's enough. You can sit down." Visibly rattled, the judge waited until the claimant sat down and then went on. "And other than your hands and your knees, do you have any other physical complaints?"

Señora Rama lifted her blouse and showed three pink, corrugated scars that looked like scaly worms stretched across the width of her stomach.

"Please, señora," Judge Warpick screamed, hitting her desk with the palm of her hands. "You don't have to show us your scars. Please."

I took a good look at the judge. In her youth, she must have been a pretty woman. Now her still abundant hair was gray and cut short. Although her features were regular and firm, she was so skinny that she almost looked desiccated. But it was her expression of utter contempt and disgust—as if she hated her post, the world and its people, and maybe even herself—that I found so disturbing. Furiously, she scribbled on her pad.

Señora Rama went on. "I have to go back to the hospital for another operation."

In a voice filled with apprehension Judge Warpick asked, "In your stomach?"

"No, here," and she indicated behind her right ear.

"Can you bend?"

"No. I had an operation here." She turned sideways on the chair and pointed to her lower back. "The doctor gave me a shot in my spine."

"How many doctors do you see?"

I looked at Dr. McDowell, who all this time had been going over the woman's medical file. His beautiful green eyes darted back and forth between the claimant and myself.

Señora Rama asked her daughter for the handbag. She took out a stack of cards and handed them to me. I removed the rubber band. "Mr. Interpreter," the judge said, indicating that I should read the names on the cards.

"Dr. Bajit," I read.

"He's for my ankles," Señora Rama explained.

I handed the card to Dr. McDowell, who examined it on both sides. "Dr. Ramin Badrinthajanmon something," I read.

"He's for my stomach in Brooklyn."

"Dr. Dallon," I read.

"He's for my eyes."

"Do you have problems with your eyes?"

"If I didn't have problems with my eyes, I wouldn't see a doctor. I have great pain inside my eyes."

I read the names of at least twenty doctors. "Dr. Ramírez," I read the last card.

"Is he a psychiatrist?"

"Yes."

"And how long have you been seeing Dr. Ramírez?"

"Since 1969, when my son died." Suddenly, Señora Rama's eyes glistened and tears popped out.

"Do you want to take a break? Would you like to go to the ladies' room?"

She wiped her tears with the back of her trembling hand. "No, I want to finish this thing as soon as possible. I'm in a lot of pain."

"You can stand up if you'd like."

"It's worse when I stand up."

"So, Señora Rama," the judge said, breathing heavily. "Tell me, what do you do all day?"

"I sit by the window and look out. And I hear voices."

"What kind of voices?"

"Horrible voices; dirty voices. They tell me to jump off."

"And why don't you jump?" Warpick asked. "What prevents you from jumping?"

"I prevent her," Raisa said. "I have to watch her all the time."

"If you want to testify in your mother's behalf, I'll have to swear you in."

The claimant burst into loud sobs and stretched out her arms in her daughter's direction. In Spanish she said, *"No me dejes sola; no me dejes sola."*

"Silence," Judge Warpick yelled. "Silence. Mr. Interpreter, what's she saying?"

"Don't leave me alone; don't leave me alone."

"Señora Rama, listen to me," Judge Warpick said. "Forget about the voices. Nobody is going to do anything to you. We're all here to help you."

I noticed that my palms were sweating and my heart was pumping fast. I, too, was out of breath. I wanted to get up and run out of that room. I placed a hand on the claimant's arm—her flesh was very cold.

"So tell me, what else do you do?" the judge asked.

Señora Rama had stopped crying. "Well, on Monday mornings I go to see Dr. Bajit at Manhattan Eye and Ear. On Tuesday I go to see Dr. Ramírez in the afternoon. On Wednesdays I go to see two doctors. In the morning . . ."

"Okay, okay, okay," Judge Warpick interrupted. "I believe it." She paused, looked at the papers on her desk, and then asked, "Do you have any friends? Do any family members ever come to visit you?"

"I don't have any family here, just my children. There is a woman upstairs who used to come to visit me. She's so nice. But she's a sick woman . . . she's in a wheelchair. She had a stroke and . . ."

"I see," Warpick cut her off.

Señora Rama looked at me. I put a finger to my lips to indicate that she should shut up.

"Dr. McDowell," Judge Warpick said, looking exasperated. "I'm going to swear you in. Please stand up."

I could see the doctor didn't like having to stand up to be sworn in. He was tall like a basketball player and maybe a few years older than me. He wore a light brown summer jacket and a pale tie and a yellow shirt. When he was seated, the judge said, "Dr. McDowell, you have had an opportunity to hear Señora Rama's testimony. Have you gone over her medical file as well?"

"Yes, your honor," he said, turning to look at me.

"And could you tell me what you've found out?"

Dr. McDowell's handsome face turned red. He cleared his throat. "Based on my review of the documents, I've found no evidence, your honor, of severe physical impairment. According to Dr. Cummings, she can lift a twenty five pound bag of potatoes on an occasional basis. Furthermore, under article 11, 876, section B, rider H, paragraph 16," he read from a book, "Mrs. Rama doesn't meet the requirements for supplementary income. Moreover, it says here that . . ."

Señora Rama looked intently at the doctor, then at me, but I wasn't supposed to interpret his testimony. I observed Raisa, who did speak English and when I saw the expression of outrage on her face, I looked out the window, away from her anger. In the distance, I saw the Hudson and the Jersey shore, and tiny buildings billowing gray smoke. In the morning haze, this part of the world looked muted, ghostly, like an old painting whose colors are fading.

Señora Rama left in tears, but vowing to reappeal the decision in case it was unfavorable. I had the judge's assistant sign my form so I could get paid. Then I went to say good-bye to Jeff, who was disappointed I wasn't staying to play a game. Waiting for the elevator, I ran into the claimant and her daughter.

"Thank you, *guapo*," she said, opening her purse and pulling out a five dollar bill.

"No, no," I said, embarrassed but touched. "I get paid by the court," I explained. "You don't have to give me anything."

"Just for the cigarettes and coffee," she insisted.

"Thank you, but no," I said firmly. "Goodbye, Señora Rama; bye, Raisa," I said, heading for the restroom to escape them. When I returned, they were gone.

It was mornings like this that I wished I had kept my job as a reporter for *Modern Grocer.* Sure, it was dangerous and at least a couple of times I had come close to getting shot; but the lives and problems of *bodega* owners were glamorous Judith Krantz stuff compared to the plights of the social security claimants. And how could I change careers at thirty-three years of age? Wasn't that the age of Christ when he was crucified, anyway? I hadn't one skill necessary to do well in the Age of Libra, in which everything had its weight in gold. I hadn't learned to use a word processor—the most complicated machine I knew how to work was my answering machine. I cursed the fate that had made me be born in Colombia. If only I had been born somewhere in the California Valley, I thought, I would have been perfectly attuned to the needs of this age.

I was crossing the street, automatically heading for the subway entrance, when I heard someone call, "Yo, Santiago, are you ashamed of your old friends?" I turned sideways and saw my friend, the painter Harry Hagin, dressed in a white uniform and hat, standing on the curb next to an ice-cream cart.

"Don't you want to talk to me?" he called.

"Harry, I'll be damned. When did you start selling ice cream? Did you quit your job unloading fruit?"

"Yeah, man. I was becoming a hunchback. And it's not ice cream but ices, natural ices. Hey, you know, I figured there's no escape being a Rockefeller slave in America, so I decided to take it easy. I love being on my own; nobody gives me orders. I have delusions of being free: I go home in the evening, take a shower, drink a beer, eat something and paint for a few hours. So, how are you doing? How's old Mr. O'Donnell? Did you frame my drawing yet? Some day it's gonna be worth big bucks, you know."

Harry and I had met as students at Queens College, where he majored in arts and business, and I had majored in medieval Spanish studies. After graduation we had remained good friends.

"Mr. O'Donnell is living overtime. I took him to the vet a few weeks ago, and he says that he wished he had made a mistake diagnosing his condition, but Mr. O'Donnell is going to croak any day."

"That's rotten, you know. Such a nice cat. After all that trouble we went through trying to find him when he ran away. Sorry to hear that. That's a damned shame, you know."

"I know," I agreed, and shook my head, making an effort to push away the gloomy subject of death, which of late seemed to follow me everywhere. A customer approached to buy an ice. I stood thinking of how Harry, while still in college, had settled into a gutted building in the Lower East Side. It had taken him years to rebuild it, but now it was a hot piece of property. Besides, I knew he had invested successfully in the stock market and gotten out while it was still good.

"First sale of the day," he said, pocketing his change, when the customer wandered away.

"Harry, you're worth a lot of money. Why do you get these crazy jobs?"

"Look, Santiago," he said, becoming very excited, his big blue eyes dancing wildly. "It's heartbreaking, man. It took me ten years of heavy shit to fix my building and then, you know, I make a terrible mistake, all because I'm such a good-hearted asshole. Instead of renting the apartments to yuppies, I rented to Puerto Ricans. And you know, these Puerto Ricans, no offense, man (and you know I'm not racist!), will kill their mothers, fry their babies, jump out of windows to break every bone in their bodies, so they can sue the landlord. I'm involved in three litigations right now, you know. So I have to work to pay the lawyers to keep my building. And these fucking lawyers . . . man, the vermin capitalism produces! Santiago, let me tell you, never have anything to do with a lawyer."

If Harry had been a racist he wouldn't be my friend, but I was becoming alarmed. "Harry," I said, looking around nervously, "there could be a Puerto Rican going by."

He chortled. "Puerto Ricans on Wall Street? That's a hoot, man." He paused. "Hey, do you subscribe to *Business Monthly*?"

I shook my head.

"See, man, that's the problem with you. You're probably still subscribing to *The Tierra del Fuego Literary Review*, right? In any case,

I read this article that says that a guy who sells joints in Battery Park during lunch hour makes $125,000 a year, tax free. Weekends off, you know, plus ninety-day vacations in the can. And a hot dog seller makes twice as much. Of course, I wouldn't sell hot dogs. I'm sure they make them out of cancerous cats, no offense (you know I'm crazy about Mr. O'Donnell). So I says to myself, it's hot in the summer, you know. And what do people want when it's hot? Ices. Besides, if I want to play the market, if I get a hunch, I just push my cart to the stock exchange."

"It sounds good," I said.

"It sounds better than it is. Yet these capitalists warmongers love joints and crack and hot dogs. But ices, which are made of natural fruit—forget it! If I were selling diet drinks and other carcinogenic products, I'd be loaded. Even when it's 100 degrees they'll think twice before buying an ice. If it keeps going like this, I'm going to have to diversify. You know, Coca Cola or some degenerate capitalist product."

I didn't feel like getting involved in an argument about the final stages of the collapse of the capitalist state. So I said, "Harry, it just dawned on me. Why don't you bring your easel and paint when business is slow. You know, maybe a reporter from the *Wall Street Journal* will notice you and write an article, and you'll be taken by Castelli or somebody." I paused, remembering Harry's subject matter. "Are you still painting skeletons exclusively?"

"Santiago, that's a great idea. You know, just take a look at these people. Wouldn't you say they look like walking skeletons dressed in expensive suits? How about an ice? It's on the house. Maybe if they see you sucking on it they'll get the idea. Sheep!" he yelled at the passersby.

It was hot; an ice sounded like a wonderful idea. "What flavors do you have?"

"Tamarind. That's all I have this week. I make it myself."

"Tamarind? Are you crazy? No wonder you don't sell your ices! People buy watermelon, cherry, lemon ices. But tamarind is not a Wall Street fruit, Harry. It's not a Wasp fruit, or an oriental fruit, or a black fruit, either. It's for Colombians and Hindus—for brown people."

"The way you talk about colors you should have been a painter, you know. Anyway, I'm trying to give them something good. Tamarind is medicinal and it's also a laxative. I wanted to offer my customers an alternative, something unusual, you know. It's just that it hasn't caught on yet, you know." He filled a paper cup with two scoops of a shit-colored substance. I tasted it.

"Well?" Harry said, frowning and twitching his red Fu Manchu mustache.

"It's refreshing. Maybe a bit too acid."

"I don't want to use sugar, you know. Listen, Santiago, do you have any connections with the coffee crops in Colombia? You should invest in coffee commodities and make a pile of money that way. Isn't that where you grew up? A coffee plantation?"

"My father had a banana plantation."

"Hum, bananas. That's a thought. Banana ices, what do you think? Perhaps we can play the banana market. The market is very hot again, you know. And what I say is, let's make a killing before it collapses again. I don't see why Rockefeller has to be the only person who makes money in this country."

"I've got to go. I'm worried about Mr. O'Donnell."

"It's great to see you, man. I'll give you a call next week, you know. Maybe we can catch a flick, okay? Take care of yourself, and my regards to Mr. O'Donnell." He patted me on the shoulder and looking toward Broadway, he started yelling, "Natural tamarind ices. Treat yourselves to the fruit of Buddha and Montezuma."

It was noon by the time I arrived home. During the day, when the front door was open because of the employment agency, I'd go in and out quickly to avoid running into my landlady. But there were several items in the mailbox and I had to stop briefly to get them before the crack heads broke into the mailbox as they did almost on a daily basis.

One of the envelopes was from Unlimited Languages and it contained a check for $350. This was a lucky break. I had been hounding the agency to pay me for several jobs I had done for them back in June. For a second or two I stood there wondering whether I should run to the bank to deposit it and make a withdrawal. This interval of indecision was long enough for Mrs. O'Donnell to open the door leading to the bar. She grabbed me by the arm, as if I were a thief caught in flagrante delicto.

"Santiago, why haven't you answered my calls? Come in."

"Hi, Mrs. O'Donnell," I said, trying to fake a smile.

With her free hand, Mrs. O'Donnell indicated that I should go into the bar. Many alkies sat at the counter, and several of the booths were already taken up by the lunch crowd. We marched toward an empty booth in the back, near the kitchen. I said hi to Pete, Mrs. O'Donnell's oldest son, who was the head bartender; and to Sean, Pete's son. Both nodded, acknowledging me. I smiled to a couple of waitresses—they were Mrs. O'Donnell's relatives too. Need I add that the entire operation was run by Mrs. O'Donnell's many retainers? I wanted to become invisible. I knew they were all familiar with my situation, and although each and every one of them was always nice to me, I was under the impression they regarded me as the guy who ripped off the matriarch of the clan.

We sat at a booth. With her mass of auburn hair, and a map-lined face, Mrs. O'Donnell was the exact replica of Lillian Hellman. She also had the writer's whiskey-honed voice. "Well, Santiago, where's the rent?"

"I'm so sorry I haven't answered your phone calls, Mrs. O'Donnell," I said, trying to distract her from her one-track mind. "But I was planning to come to see you today."

"You're here now, so where's the rent?"

After eight years of being perpetually behind in my rent, I was hard up for excuses. "Mrs. O'Donnell, I was hoping I could give you one thousand dollars like you want, but I don't have that much in the bank. I haven't been working much lately. If it keeps going like this, I'm going to have to get a full-time job."

She had heard this argument so many times before that my words seemed to have no effect whatsoever on her. "I give you twenty-four hours to pack your things and move out. And don't make me evict you by force. That's final."

"Mrs. O'Donnell," I remonstrated, "you don't really mean that. You wouldn't do anything like that, would you?"

"What's to prevent me?"

So much anger flashed in her almond eyes that I became afraid of her. "Because . . . because you're a good woman," I said. "You know how fond I am of you."

"I'm a good person, that's true. But I'm not an idiot, Santiago. That's why you've been taking advantage of me all these years. My family thinks I'm crazy. My lawyer can't believe I've let this situation go on for years. I could rent that apartment for $1,500, even right now. You know I would've never let you move in if I had known you were Colombian. I thought you came from Venezuela, like Ben Burztyn," she said, referring to my friend Ben Ami who had lived in the downstairs apartment before Rebecca moved in.

Now that she had insulted my nationality, Mrs. O'Donnell softened. "I need some money today. Con Ed is turning off the electric if I don't pay the bill. You must have some money you can give me. Otherwise, I'll have to call Lucy. The poor thing; with all her problems with her husband, I hate to do this to her."

"Please, Mrs. O'Donnell, whatever you do, don't call my mother. I'll give you money right now. Here," I said, handing her the check from Unlimited Languages.

Instead of thanking me for the check, she became irate. "So you do have money! You must take me for the greatest jerk that ever lived."

"I swear to you that's all the money I have. But take it; it's all yours." I signed the check over to her.

She folded the check and pocketed it in her apron. "Here," she said, flinging some bills on the table. "I don't want you to go hungry."

I counted five twenties. "Thanks," I said.

"You now owe me $14,760 in back rent."

I couldn't repress a chuckle. "Mrs. O'Donnell, you do love to exaggerate; it must be your Irish temperament."

She cringed again. I should have never smiled; she was only forgiving when I acted remorseful. Maybe I should burst into tears, I thought. Or better yet, beg her for a job washing dishes.

"Santiago, you can't go on living like this. You're a young, bright guy. When are you going to get your act together?"

I wish I had a mother who owned a bar, I was going to say,

pointing at her children. But that was inappropriate, so I said, "When I finish my Columbus poem. Then I'll get a full-time job. I promise you."

Mrs. O'Donnell held her head between her hands. "Santiago, wake up. This is New York. People here don't care about poetry. If you must be a writer, for God's sake write a book that can be made into a miniseries. Why don't you write about," she stretched her arms toward the front of the bar, "Forty-second Street. Write about the crack people; how they're ruining my business, my family's way of life. That's what you should write about. That'll make money. Everybody already read about Columbus in high school."

I was sick and tired of people telling me what to write about, but I knew better than to argue with her.

"I fully agree with you," I said. "I hate those creeps. They're driving me insane, too."

"Whatever you do, don't do it."

"Mrs. O'Donnell, of course not."

"Santiago, I have an idea. This is also a good way for you to pay some back rent. We'll paint a sign, an anticrack sign, and you'll parade in front of the porno shop. A few hours every day. Maybe that'll get somebody's attention."

"No way," I said, getting up. "I'd rather become a homeless person, do you hear me?"

She got up too. "How about standing outside the Times building with the sign? Maybe we'll get them to write an exposé about it."

I was rendered inarticulate by her ridiculous proposition. I was infuriated too, and if it weren't that she was my landlady and I owed her some respect and a lot of money, I would have blown up. "I got to go," I said. "I'm worried . . ." about Mr. O'Donnell, I was going to add, but luckily caught myself in time. I lived in terror that she would find out I had named my cat after her late husband.

Reading my mind, she asked, "How's the cat?"

"He's fading quickly. I'm afraid this is the end."

"I know how it is. I had a cat like that; I had to crush his medicine and mix it with his food."

It seemed highly impossible that she had ever loved a cat; nevertheless, I said, "I'm sorry to hear that."

"Mind you, it was a long time ago. Before I married. I loved that cat so much I never had another one after him."

"Well, like I said, I have to go."

"How about a cheeseburger on the house? When was the last time you had a hot meal?"

I was hungry, but not hungry enough to stand the torture of having her whole family stare at me while I ate. "Gee, thanks a lot. But not today. I'm really in a hurry."

She pointed a finger at me. "I expect you to come with some more rent by Friday. Remember, you owe me $14,760."

"How could I ever forget it, Mrs. O'Donnell? Have a nice day. It's nice to see you."

As I slunk off down the aisle, she called out, "Santiago, pray for me that I can pay the Con Ed bill."

Mr. O'Donnell was in the kitchen in a carnivorous mood. He stood frozen by the refrigerator waiting for a mythic mouse to show up. He was so engrossed in his hunt that he glanced at me long enough to make eye contact, but that was all. "Suit yourself, ingrate, if you prefer dead mouse meat to my company," I said, somewhat hurt. I went to check my messages. No one had called. I sat down at my desk and went through the mail. It was all trash, except for an envelope that contained a newsletter with the ominous title the *Colombian Report*. It was eighty-eight pages long and written in English. I leafed through it; every item in it was about guerilla warfare in Colombia. Oh great, I thought, this is just what I need, to get on the mailing list of a terrorist group. What if the police raided my apartment and found subversive literature in my possession? I shook my head to expel these paranoid thoughts from my brain. This is New York, not Colombia, I reminded myself. My conscience was clear, I thought. And yet, regular guys did not keep pounds of cocaine stashed in their kitchens or illegal guns in their toilet tanks.

I started pacing the apartment. It was so hot and humid that I felt as if I were swimming against the current in a huge river of lukewarm pea soup. I thought about going to the park, to spend the afternoon cooling off under a tree. But Central Park in July is dustier than a ghost town in a western. At least Mr. O'Donnell seems okay,

I thought. Otherwise he would not be so intent upon catching that mouse. The phone rang.

"Santiago, pick up. I know you're there," said the sonorous voice of Ben Ami Burztyn.

"Hi, Ben," I said, picking up. "When did you get back in town?"

"Screening your calls, ha?" he said gruffly. "Hiding from Mrs. O'Donnell."

"Oh, man. I wish I could hide from that woman. I just saw her. So what's happening?"

"I'm calling to invite you to dine with me, on the off chance," he said sarcastically, "that you're free tonight."

"Sure," I said, delighted at the prospect since Ben Ami only ate at the very best restaurants.

"Meet me at Rupert's at seven-thirty." He gave me the address. "And look nice, will you? Wear a jacket and tie. Do you have a presentable tie?"

"Wait till you see me in the suit Mother gave me. I look like a million bucks."

"Humm," Ben said. "Anyway, please don't be late."

"Not a second late, I promise."

Benjamin chuckled at the other end. "See you tonight, *chico.*"

"Ciao."

Ben's call had put me in a good mood. I knew it would be a great dinner. Besides, I hadn't seen Ben in a few months. Suddenly feeling energized, I changed into my shorts and a T-shirt. I decided to go to the pier on Forty-third Street to catch some rays, read, and maybe work on my Columbus poem. The river always made me feel as if I were in one of the caravels. I was just going out the door when the phone rang. It was Tim Colby, my literary agent.

"Santiago, I'm at the corner with coffee and doughnuts. Are you home?"

I told him where I was heading and invited him to come along.

"I'm game," Tim said.

Tim was waiting for me downstairs, perspiring, as if he had been doing a lot of walking. He was loaded with a briefcase, shopping bags, and large manila envelopes.

"You look like a Caribbean surfer," he said smiling.

"You can leave all that stuff upstairs if you want," I said, referring to the portable stationery store he was saddled with.

"That's okay. Just help me with the coffee and doughnuts."

Taking the paper bags from him, I said, "Let's get the hell out of here before the crack people see me going out of the building dressed like this."

Tim glanced in the direction of Paradise Alley. "They're taking over my neighborhood too. These people reproduce quicker than roaches."

At the corner of Forty-third, we turned west, heading for the Hudson.

"Are those books you're carrying in the envelopes?" I asked, watching him struggle with the bulky packages, although it occurred to me that dressed in sandals, khaki pants, and a red shirt depicting macaws and coconut trees, he did not look like he was coming from the staid world of publishing.

"No, I'm making deliveries for a friend of mine who works on Wall Street. But I'll deliver these tomorrow morning."

"Are you working as a messenger?"

"A couple of days a week to make some extra cash. I work for a friend I met at Princeton. Now he's a big shot on Wall Street and he helps me out this way. How are you doing?" he asked as we crossed Ninth Avenue. "Getting any writing done?"

"Not in a few weeks. I'm rethinking the whole concept."

Tim smiled broadly. "I've got good news for you."

"Oh, yeah?"

"I met an editor who's interested in you."

"In me? Are you kidding? Did he read *Lirio del Alba*?" I asked, although that sounded improbable.

"She doesn't read Spanish."

"How can she be interested in me if she doesn't read Spanish?"

"I told her I knew an up-and-coming Latin American writer. I told her I was giving her the chance to publish the next great Latin American sensation."

That hardly sounded like me, but I was flattered nonetheless.

"Gee, Tim, thanks. So she wants to publish Christopher Columbus?"

"I said you were writing an exciting book."

My high spirits sank a bit. "Did you tell her I was writing an epic poem?"

"No. But nobody calls Nabokov's *Pale Fire* a poem. It's called a novel. Anyway," Tim went on, "we were talking at a reception and she said that she had never read a South American thriller. She said she'd love to publish one."

"You mean, you want me to turn *Christopher Columbus on his Death Bed* into a thriller?" I sputtered. "It riles me up how everyone wants me to write what they don't have the guts to write themselves."

"Not me, Santiago. I want you to write *Christopher Columbus*. I really dig that poem. I told you I'll translate it into English when you finish it."

Tim's promise made me feel better since he was such a highly regarded translator. "What's the editor's name?" I asked in a conciliatory mood.

He told me her name and the name of the house, both of which meant nothing to me.

Becoming uptight again, I said, "I'm not even sure what a thriller is."

"You've seen thrillers at the movies."

"But she wants a book, not a movie. You mean, a thriller like Graham Greene's *The Third Man*?"

"Yeah."

I shook my head. "I just don't think I can turn the discovery of America into a thriller. I don't think Graham Greene could either."

"All I'm saying is that she's keen on publishing a young, unknown, Latin American author. Preferably somebody who's writing a thriller. You're kind of young and you're Latin, so that's two out of three. Just think about it. Don't get all worked up. Maybe the two of you could meet, and if you hit it off, who knows?"

We had reached the corner of Eleventh Avenue. A warm marine breeze engulfed us. I breathed in deeply, holding it in my lungs before exhaling. We crossed the avenue and entered the pier through the open gate.

Until quite recently there had been three wonderful old piers. Two were demolished and only Pier 43 remained, although an open-air summer concert hall had been built on it. Fortunately, half of the pier was still open to the public. It was extremely overcast yet there were a few men in tiny swimming trunks out sunning. The weather was only fit to be cursed but hardcore joggers trotted in slow motion. At the end of the pier a bunch of boys dove into the river and fished for eels; several Chinese men dressed in black, who lived at the Chinese mission on Eleventh Avenue, stood at the edge of the pier, exchanging looks I could not read, looking like conspirators about to blow up the Statue of Liberty or invade New Jersey.

We sat at the edge of the pier, our legs hanging in the air. It was windless and the Hudson seemed static, like a river of glue, but I was happy to be away from the stench of midtown Manhattan in midsummer. Here, at least, the city did not stink like a drunkard's breath. Tim opened the box of doughnuts and we sipped our warm coffees. Whenever Tim came to visit, he brought me doughnuts and pastries and we indulged in an orgy of sweets. I complimented the freshness of the doughnuts.

"Wall Street doughnuts. Only decent thing about the place," Tim said.

In the oppressive heat the tepid coffee was refreshing. Watching the excited boys diving into the river, climbing back up onto the platform and diving off repeatedly, made me think cool thoughts. We chewed and drank in silence. Tim seemed mesmerized by the eel fishers. Amidst much shrieking, the boys killed the eels with their shoes, bricks, or smashing them against the cement. Grossed out, I concentrated on the different crafts going up and down the Hudson. Yet the river's murky waters made me think of a channel of eel soup. I looked up and saw rain was imminent. I hoped for heavy rain to wash off the thick coat of dust and garbage that had settled upon the city like icing on a cake. The sky was a luminous milky opal, oppressively metallic and hazy. A filmy mist enveloped the world. An ocean liner floating by blew its horn, sounding like a gigantic, moaning cow. This melancholy mood made me want to jump aboard the ship and go off to an exotic island far, far away, a place where I could spend the rest of my life being a beach bum, sipping purple daiquiris at sunset.

"This is really nice," Tim said, lazily stretching his torso and arms. "You come here often?"

"In the summer I do. I read or write or just look at the boats. It's like going to the country."

"It must make you think of Christopher Columbus."

"Water always reminds me of him."

"You know what Melville says in *Moby Dick*?"

"It's a big book, Tim. He says a mouthful about everything."

"Melville says that the flood has not subsided; that two-thirds of the world is still under water. Did you know that?"

As it headed toward the sea, the ocean liner made the river heave with ripples that lapped the pillars of the pier, producing a gentle, caressing music.

"So Columbus knew how important it was to discover new land," I said.

"You make him sound like a land speculator. I'm sure there's more to it than that. Oh, wow," Tim exclaimed, "see the Statue of Liberty down there?"

In the distance, emerging from the shroud of gray that wrapped around the landscape, the statue was tiny, like a lit match.

"Did you know that when the French gave it to us it was the highest structure in New York? At that time, because there were no elevators yet, the tallest buildings in the city were only six floors high."

"So the statue was the first skyscraper."

"Yeah, that's right," Tim said, biting into a jelly doughnut. "Santiago, do you think Americans are naïve?" he asked me out of the blue.

I studied him. His tawny hair was longish and he needed to shampoo it and get a haircut. He was in his late thirties, but because of his intense, gleaming eyes and sunny disposition, he looked like a philosopher-child. I was going to say the polite thing. Such as, "Well, no more so than other people." But I said, "Yes, definitely."

"Why is that?"

"Who knows, Tim? You'd better ask Octavio Paz or one of those French deconstructionists who know everything. I haven't got a clue. But what I can't get over is how the pursuit of happiness is written in the Bill of Rights. I think that's why Americans are so miserable a lot of the time. They believe happiness is one of their inalienable rights. And, essentially, I agree with Freud that happiness was not written into the contract. You know, momentary happiness yes," I went on, totally unashamed of my clichés. "Like I'm happy right this minute with you. But if we ever tried to duplicate it . . . forget it. I think it's unrepeatable. But happiness as a way of life? How can one be happy in the face of death surrounding us?" I said, thinking about Bobby's death and the approaching demise of Mr. O'Donnell. "How can one pursue happiness as a main goal in life when there's so much pain and suffering everywhere? It makes for a nation of blind people. People who search for what doesn't exist."

"Shit," Tim exclaimed. "It's raining." There was no place to run for shelter on the pier. He bunched his envelopes and bags and sat on them. The boys swimming and fishing went berserk with joy. It was not rain, but the fireboat going by. It had started a practice drill in front of us, drenching the pier with a cool, abundant spray. The Chinese men ran away screaming as if they were demons being sprayed with holy water. The boat's many spouts shot sheets of very fine mist. It looked unspeakably beautiful, like a mythological benevolent beast that had risen from the depths of the Hudson to cool and delight us.

Always the man of letters, Tim said, "It looks like . . . like . . . like . . . Moby Dick. Like a white whale with a hundred spouts."

Indeed, the monumental, splashy ghost going down the swelling river looked as if it were heading out for the open ocean, ready to put out all the fires of the world.

9

The Interpreter

I hailed a cab in front of the Port Authority building and directed the driver to Rupert's. Dressed in a snazzy suit, on my way to a fine restaurant, I suddenly felt grand, rich, glamorous. Being around Ben Ami Burztyn led me to fantasize like this. I had met Ben some nine years ago, standing in line to see Todd Browning's *Freaks*. A gigantic bearded man of ursine countenance wearing a red aviator's scarf and a green beret had wheeled around, almost knocking me off the line with his leviathan belly. Abruptly he demanded, "How many times have you seen *Freaks*?" I told him this was my first time and looked away, not eager to engage in conversations with a stranger. Tapping me on the shoulder, he informed me that he had seen *Freaks* twenty-eight times. I made up my mind to get away from this weirdo as soon as we entered the theater. I looked away. Ben Ami tapped my shoulder and said, "Is your schedule too busy to talk to me?" I decided to be polite. I said, "No, not really. . . ."

"I detect an accent. Where are you from?" he asked.

We discovered we had originated in neighboring countries. Ben's family had arrived in Venezuela from Russia after the revolution. We struck up a rapport and sat together during the film. Ben quoted entire sequences of dialogue as the actors spoke the lines. After the show, he invited me to his apartment for a glass of champagne. Although he looked freaky and acted like a nut, I accepted the invitation—I had few friends in Manhattan and fewer who loved the movies and were South American.

It turned out Ben lived on the third floor above O'Donnell's bar. At that time, he was the only tenant in the building. Ben opened the door into a pitch dark room and flicked his lighter. He lit a gas lamp on a table, and proceeded to light dozens of candles in an elaborate candelabra.

"What happened to the electricity?" I asked with some apprehension.

"I hate electricity," was Ben's curt reply.

The electricity was on in the apartment, but for illumination Ben preferred candles and gas lamps. He pulled a bottle of champagne out of the refrigerator. We sat on a huge bed by one of the windows overlooking Eighth Avenue and drank the champagne. Ben was going through his Edgar Allan Poe period at that time. He produced a couple of first editions of Poe's poetry and prose, a tattered manuscript of a letter and old, sepia-toned photographs of the author. Over champagne and caviar, Ben told me a bit about his background. His family was in oil and textiles. Among his childhood friends had been the children of the Kuwaiti royal family. Ben's parents had wanted him to pursue a business-related career, but he had dropped out of the London School of Economics and moved to New York to write the definitive biography of Poe. He had chosen to reside in Times Square because he felt that was the closest he could get to Poe's world. When I was about to leave, Ben told me he wanted me to meet his great-grandfather. From under one of the pillows, he removed a human bone. "This is my great-grandfather's femur," he said. "He was a general in the Russian army." I said hello to the bone. Ben kissed it and placed it under a pillow.

We became best friends. It was through Ben that I met Mrs. O'Donnell and moved into the apartment on the fourth floor. A year or so later one of Ben's maiden aunts died and he came into a large inheritance. He quit researching his Poe biography and moved to Paris, a city he preferred to New York. Over the next few years I saw him during his visits to Manhattan. The nineteenth-century French writer Gerard de Nerval had replaced Poe in his affection.

And now that he had lots of dough, he had become a great gourmand who traveled all over the world, eating at the best restaurants. He purchased a duplex at the Museum Tower, where he stayed during his overnight visits to the city. His most recent companion was a belly dancer named Scheherazade, who would break into dance whenever Ben was bored.

The taxi came to a stop; I had arrived at my destination. I gave the driver a three dollar tip. This was the danger of being around Ben—I, too, began to act as if I were rich. The restaurant was rather small and unpretentious in its decor. Inside the door the hostess greeted me. The woman sized me up from the tips of my shoes to the length of my sideburns and deciding, perhaps, that I was a wealthy South American or a coke kingpin (which is what I looked like in the clothes Mother had given me), she greeted me with a hale handshake and a cinemascope smile.

"I'm joining Mr. Benjamin Burztyn's party," I informed her.

Hastily, the woman withdrew her hand, as if I had just said, "I have the bubonic plague and want to kiss you on the mouth." Her fake smile transmogrified into a cold, unfriendly stare. "Follow me," she said.

The restaurant was sparsely attended and I assumed this was due to the fact that in late July its habitués were far, far away from New York or in the Hamptons. Ben was talking to a waiter.

"Hi, Ben," I said.

Ben looked up from the menu. "Hi, Santiago. Please sit down." Then he turned to the waiter. "I told you already," he said in the rotund tone of a pissed-off monarch, "bring me a bottle of what you personally think is the best champagne in the house."

The waiter's face reddened. "But sir . . ."

Ben crossed his hands, palms open, and pushed them toward the waiter's face. "I told you what I want. Now leave me alone." Flustered, the waiter headed for the bar, looking as if he couldn't make up his mind whether to curse aloud or kill Ben.

"Goodness gracious, Ben. What's going on?" I said.

"Santiago, my friend," Ben said smiling, as if he had just noticed me. He put his hand on my shoulder. "You certainly look dapper today. How are you?"

"Fine. But . . ." I was dying to find out why there was so much tension in the air, but now that I had a chance to see him in his full glory, my breath was taken away. He wore a magnificent white suit and a gold-leafed tie. Although he was a couple of years younger than I, recently his hair and his beard had grayed. Now he might have been mistaken for a sultan incognito, somebody who had been conceived in a womb of gold.

"Why is everyone acting so weird?" I asked.

Ben's eyes narrowed, his lips pursed and with hatred in his voice he growled as he looked toward the bar, "I'm about to sue this place for fifty thousand dollars."

"Why?"

Ben put a finger to his lips. The terrified waiter approached us with the champagne.

"Let me see what you have there," Ben said.

The waiter pulled out of the bucket a bottle of Dom Perignon.

"Dom Perignon!" Ben exclaimed. "Americans think that's the only champagne in the world."

"Sir, you told me I should choose the champagne," the deeply mortified waiter complained.

I was becoming embarrassed by the way Ben was bullying the waiter.

With the air of a grand lord who's grown up surrounded by servants at his beck and call, Ben said, "Well, what are you waiting for? The least you can do is open the bottle."

The waiter complied with Ben's wishes and we toasted to each other's health.

When we were left alone, Ben said, *"Chico,* I'm suing these people because the last time I was here they lost my umbrella, which was also my cane."

"I'm sorry to hear that," I said, full of sympathy, knowing that Ben had only the best of everything. "But there's no need to take it out on the poor waiter. Did he personally lose the umbrella?"

"But it was made in Paris," Ben said, with the total indifference of rich South Americans toward their inferiors. "It was especially designed for me. The knob was solid gold. It was unique. I haven't been able to replace it yet."

A few years ago, Ben had had a malignant tumor removed from one of his legs. The operation had been so severe that he ended up with a limp and thus needed a cane to get around.

"And you know how Americans are," he went on. "They don't take you seriously unless you threaten to sue them. As soon as my lawyer called the management they started listening to me. Anyway, they've promised to have the cane replaced. Exactly like the one I lost. They're having it made in Paris. But to mellow me, they invited me to a dinner, with three guests, everything on the house, including the drinks. I swear to you, Santiago, if anything goes wrong tonight, I'll put them out of business."

"I'm sure everything is going to be perfect," I said, feeling like I was going to break into a sweat, a knot forming in the pit of my stomach. I opened the menu and studied the appetizers and main courses and desserts. "Everything sounds delicious."

"I recommend the wild boar," Ben said. "The rabbit breast and the broiled snapper are good too."

The waiter approached us. We ordered the appetizers and main courses, and Ben asked the waiter to recommend the wine. Alone again, I said, "Where is Scheherazade?"

"She stayed in Chile. I just don't know about women anymore. I give them everything, take them everywhere, and there isn't one who understands what makes me happy. I went to a singles bar the other night just to try something different. So there is this beautiful woman sitting next to me—perfect-looking in that horrid Cher style—not exactly my type. Anyway, suddenly she turns to me and says, 'If you don't stop looking at me, I'll stub my cigarette in your eyeball.' "

"But Ben, you shouldn't go to those places. I'm sure there are plenty of women who'd give anything to make you happy."

Ben patted my hand. "That's the most romantic thing anybody has ever said to me. I wish there was a woman who talked to me the way you do."

"I had no idea you were in Chile," I said, to change this line of dialogue. "Why did you go there? I thought you hated Pinochet and had sworn never to return until Pinochet was shot."

Ben's rubicund face saddened. *"Chico,* one day I was walking down the beach in Macuto with Scheherazade and suddenly, Santiago, something in the air, a smell, you know, like Proust's madeleine . . . it hit me so strong and took possession of me. And I remembered the great meat *empanadas* I used to eat in Santiago when I was a child and my father was ambassador. I don't know what came over me. Before I knew it, I was landing at the airport in Santiago." He fell silent, wolfed down a glass of champagne and looked devastated.

The suspense was so unbearable, I had forgotten to breathe. "So what happened?"

"Oh, Santiago. I have never been so disappointed in my life. The restaurant was still there, and they still made meat *empanadas,* but the old cook had died, and the new *empanadas* tasted plastic, like McDonald's food." Ben took out his pipe, filled it and lit it, creating a huge cloud of aromatic smoke. I sipped my champagne in silence. I didn't want to talk; I didn't want to spoil his moment of perfect dejection. Finally, he said, *"Chico,* I had traveled thousands of miles to recapture the *empanadas* of my childhood, and they had become plastic, like everything else." He finished, his voice quivering with grief. "They had become a fraud. I had a fit. The police were called and I was arrested and taken away. Fortunately, Scheherazade called the Venezuelan ambassador, who called the President and threatened to cut off all oil supplies to Chile unless I was released on the spot," Ben was saying as the artichokes arrived.

A gleaming white limousine was waiting for Ben when we got out of the restaurant. The air was so muggy and swamplike that I gladly accepted his offer to give me a lift home.

Although Ben Ami had found fault with the waiter's choice of wine, and had found the artichokes tough, the wild boar bitter, the rabbit overcooked, and the desserts mediocre, the dinner had been a success—the lawsuit had been averted, at least for tonight. I was pleased with my mediating role; for a moment I considered offering my services to Rupert's to placate their irate, displeased rich South American customers. I was feeling great—riding a limo on a night like this beats taking the grimy subway back home. And since I did not have Ben Ami's excruciatingly high gourmand's standard, the meal for me had been excellent, if not sublime.

We were seated comfortably, Ben puffing on his pipe, I smoking a Newport Light, when Ben said, "I'd rather be a *clochard* in Paris than a rich man in New York. You have to move out of this city, Santiago. You can stay at my place in Paris anytime."

"I'd love to," I said, wishing he would extend the open invitation to his empty place at the Museum Tower. I remembered Paris fondly yet vaguely. Ben had flown me there for a weekend expressly to show me Gerard de Nerval's grave. "But what would I do there? Here I can make a living, kind of. Besides, I'd feel more displaced there than here. By now, I feel kind of a New Yorker, you know."

"Marry my cousin Edna," he ordered me. "She's just as rich as I am. And she doesn't have parents or brothers or sisters. It's all her money. Plus she's a fag hag."

"Ben, you make it sound like I'm a fortune hunter." I had met Edna, a doctoral candidate for a degree in Divinity. I had found her nice, quiet, thoughtful, scholarly, and a lady to boot. She worshiped Ben, and I knew she would have married me just to please him.

"Anyway," I added, "if I haven't married a woman it's not for a lack of candidates. There's always Claudia. Come to think of it," I said, picturing close-ups of Claudia and Edna in my mind's eye, "I'd much rather marry Edna."

The limo had stopped at a red light on Forty-second Street and Eighth. "And to think I used to love Times Square," Ben said, denigrating his old neighborhood. "I don't know how you can stand living here with all that," he said, waving his hand in the direction of the porno palaces, the junkies and criminals outside the window. "*Chico,* that's the Reagan–Bush legacy. If you don't make $100,000 a year, and you haven't sold your soul to a multinational, you don't belong in Manhattan. You're supposed to live here in Times Square or move to the South Bronx and fuck yourself into extinction smoking crack."

"Gee, Ben," I said, "money has really made you wise. Do all rich people have your political savvy?"

"All rich people are assholes. I'm different because I'm an artist; I have the soul of a poet. With the right woman in Paris, I wouldn't mind being poor," he sighed.

I wondered if God, in his infinite inventiveness, had ever

conceived of such a creature. The limo stopped in front of O'Donnell's bar. "Ah, the abode of my bohemian youth," Ben waxed
philosophic, his voice tinged with nostalgia. I knew that deep down
Ben yearned to turn the high places where he lived into the gutter.

I gave him a hug. He smiled and nodded but sat very still. As
I opened the door to let myself out, I saw, standing in front of my
door, Hot Sauce's tiny figure. I waved at her, but she was so busy
trying to lure customers that she didn't see me. Out of the blue, a
brilliant idea came over me. This is indeed providential, I thought.
"Ben, I think I have the answer to all your prayers." I turned toward
the street. "Hot Sauce," I called out, "come here. There's somebody
I want you to meet."

She recognized me. "Hi, Santiago," she said as she slithered
toward the limo exuding carnality and lust. "How're you doing, you
latino hunk?"

Sitting in the limo, with my feet on the pavement, my eyes met
her eyes. "I want you to meet an old friend," I said.

Suspiciously, she checked the figure of Ben Ami nesting in the
deep recesses of the limo. "He ain't a weirdo, is he?"

"Come on, Hot Sauce," I protested. "Would I introduce you to
a freak?"

"Hot Sauce," Ben exclaimed, his eyes dancing with excitement.
"Would you care to join me for dinner?"

"Delighted," she screeched.

I got out, helped her in and closed the door behind her. Ben
and Hot Sauce took off into the mysteries of the scorching summer
night.

Mr. O'Donnell was glued to his spot in front of the refrigerator. It was early for his midnight snack, but usually he'd start begging
for it hours earlier. Tonight, however, he was oblivious to food, to
me, and to the heat that usually knocked him out.

"You silly cat; you're gonna give yourself a heart attack waiting
for that mouse to show up," I said. His tail wagged, as if to brush
off my concern, but he did not even bother to cast a glance in my
direction.

"Either that or you're gonna die a crazy cat," I went on as the phone rang. There was no message. Picking up the receiver I said, "Hello, hello." A click was the only response, and I was left there standing like a fool holding a dead telephone to my ear. Suddenly, I heard a deafening, abrupt noise as if a truck had crashed on the roof. The building did not crumble, though; the ceiling did not cave in. It occurred to me that maybe the refrigerator had fallen on top of Mr. O'Donnell. I burst into the kitchen screaming, "Kitty, are you okay?" Mr. O'Donnell repaid my concern by giving me a quizzical look as if to say, "What's the matter with you?" A flash of effulgence lit the kitchen, and looking up at the window that overlooks the alley, I saw lightning paint platinum slivers in the obsidian sky. Raging thunder made the glass of the windowpanes rattle. My eyes wandered down from the sky to the building across the alley. The flasher was standing by his window, dancing for me. I noticed he had shorts on and wasn't playing with himself. He was crisscrossing his arms to call my attention. I stood there, transfixed. He leaned out of the window holding a large piece of cardboard that read PHONE #. "No way, José," I replied, giving him the finger, and was about to turn away from the window when he started shaking the cardboard frantically, and his desperation—he seemed about to fall out of the window—held me enthralled. Something was amiss, I thought. Or maybe he's just very horny, a voice said in my head; everyone is oversexed in the summer. But what if he was trying to tell me something else? And if he just wants sex, what would I do? Nothing ventured, nothing gained. With my fingers, I gave him the phone number. He signed it back to me and I nodded in confirmation and disappeared from the window. I ran to my telephone to turn off the machine. The phone rang and I picked up.

"Is that you?" a voice with an European accent said.

"Your neighbor across the alley," I said, choosing my words carefully, in case he was recording me.

"Listen, I want you to know," he said in an accent I couldn't quite pin down, "about a couple of hours ago, I caught two men trying to break into your apartment from the fire escape."

"What?"

"Yes, I saw them trying to break in. They had tools and were beginning to remove the screens on the window, so I started screaming, saying I was going to call the cops. One of them pointed a gun at me, but I ducked and continued screaming until they left."

"Did you recognize them? Are they crack people from downstairs?"

There was a pause. "Hum, let me think. No. Actually, they look more like you: slightly Oriental."

"I'm not Oriental," I remonstrated. "I'm Colombian."

"Oh, so I see. I knew you were a foreigner too because of the way you signed your phone number."

I didn't know whether to hang up, grab Mr. O'Donnell and run away from the apartment, or to call the police. In any case, it felt good to be talking to someone. I realized although I didn't even know his name, I felt almost close to this man; I knew more about his deepest sexual secrets than I knew about most of my friends.

"I'm German," he informed me. This did not surprise me at all. "What's your name?" he asked.

I told him, absentmindedly, aware that I was talking to him but was totally freaked out about the prospect of the Colombians breaking into my apartment.

"My name is Reinhardt," he said.

It occurred to me that the polite thing was to thank him for driving the burglars away. "Thank you so much, Reinhardt. I'm really grateful to you for what you've done. My cat could have escaped, and he's a sick cat. It would have been tragic."

"Now you know," he said. "It's better to be prepared."

"What do you mean?"

"You know: leave the radio and the lights on when you go out. Stuff like that."

"That's right. Thank you for reminding me."

"I wouldn't want anything to happen to you, handsome—or to your cat . . . maybe we can get together sometime."

A part of me wanted to say, "Sure. Why not." Instead, I mumbled, "Oh, oh, well, I . . ."

He interrupted me. "I don't mean sex," he said. "It's too dangerous nowadays. But we can go see a film."

"Sure," I said. "I go to the movies all the time."

"Well, then give me a call, Santiago. My phone number is

. . ." I took it down, thinking it might come in handy sometime. And, who knows, maybe some night . . . The truth was that I was extremely attracted to this tall slender blond Nibelung. And now that I knew he was Nordic I felt doubly turned on.

"Bye, Reinhardt," I said by way of conclusion. "Thanks a lot again."

"Don't mention it. Sweet dreams."

Sweet dreams? I shook my head. Rebecca was probably still awake, but what was the point of upsetting her? After all, the Colombians were out to get me, not her. It was my apartment they wanted to break into. Nevertheless, she should be aware of the danger. What if I got killed? Rebecca could help the police in tracking down my murderers. What did I care if justice was served when I was dead? Nothing was going to bring me back! At times like this, when I was afraid, restless, cracking up all over the place, I'd pick up Mr. O'Donnell and bury my face in his fur and smother him with kisses until the contact with a living thing calmed me down. Yet tonight something told me that if I distracted him from his ridiculous hunting, I was going to get badly scratched.

"I'll fight back; I'm not going down like a wimp," I said through clenched teeth. Feeling like Gary Cooper in *High Noon,* I removed the gun from the tank of the toilet and wrapped it in a towel to dry. I wondered if the bullets would still go off after having the gun soaked in water for two days. The Colombians did not know that, though. I was sure they would be scared shitless if I met them by the window aiming a gun at their balls. I decided to sleep on the couch by the window. If they returned, I would hear them coming up the creaky fire escape. Now that I was ready for a showdown with my persecutors, I stopped to reflect whom they might be. If they were indeed Gene's employers, should I call the police, the FBI, the CIA? Why couldn't they just be crack people trying to break in to steal anything valuable they could turn into quick cash? No. All they had to do was peek through the window to see that everything I owned was rubbish. Obviously, they were Colombian mafiosi who knew I had in my possession the coke Gene had stolen.

Even though it was only eleven o'clock, it was too late to call my mother's house. Tomorrow, I'll get in touch with Gene, I thought. You cannot afford to freak out, Santiago. Put away the bazooka; it's only a mosquito. You must muster all your wherewithal and clarity to control the situation. Tomorrow you can have an alarm system installed. I could borrow the money from Ben Ami. He'd always said he'd come to my rescue if I really needed him. Well, the time had finally come. Or should I take the money and move to Paris with Mr. O'Donnell until all this passed? I felt crazier than a shithouse rat. Perhaps the heat wave had done permanent damage to my brain.

I sat on the couch perspiring, the towel and gun in my lap; I looked down into the dark alley. Were they watching me? Were they at this moment aiming the gun and about to pull the trigger? I closed my eyes, took a deep breath and held it for a while and then, pumping my lungs as hard as I could, I puffed it all out. I heard a *clack, pop, clack*—the weapon had been fired, I thought. I'm a dead man. I felt as if I were falling off the face of the earth. Before it was too late, I opened my eyes to see Mr. O'Donnell for the last time. I seemed to be all right. I touched my head, and examined my chest, searching for the wound. They had missed me. I looked out into the alley again.

The rain had burst; a heavy wind blew fat drops through the window screens. I remained still, enjoying the refreshing wind. It was pouring with the violence of a typhoon. I hoped it would turn into a hurricane that would sweep away the killers down there in the alley, the crack heads outside the building, all the dirt and the grime of New York. There was nothing I loved better than a good summer shower. I flashed back to my adolescence in Barranquilla, when the rains were so heavy during the rainy season that the city became paralyzed and school was canceled.

My adolescence—roughly from my twelfth to my fifteenth birthday—had been the unhappiest period of my life. And yet, out of masochism, or the futile need to exorcise ghosts that would always haunt me—I kept regressing to those years over and over, with an insistence that was disturbing. We had moved from Bogotá back to Barranquilla, and I hated just about everything about my native city, except the rainy season when apocalyptic, violent downpours fed my fantasies of natural catastrophes of such severity that school would be shut down for weeks, months, years, and I would be left alone in my bedroom, forgotten, reading Dostoyevsky, Kierkegaard, Camus.

Barranquilla is situated below sea level. *Barranca,* from which its name derives, means gorge, ravine. The city did not have then—and does not have now—a sewer system. When it pours—the way it does in Jean Harlow's *Red Dust*—the city floods, and the streets and avenues become raging *arroyos* that sweep away people, cars, houses, and buses full of passengers. Enterprising *Barranquilleros* make their living during this time of the year by installing over the street wooden planks a foot wide, so that the citizens can get across the streets without having to wade through the muddy, treacherous and filthy waters.

Whenever the rains would burst after lunch, I knew there'd be no school that afternoon. Wilbrajan and I would change into our bathing suits and go out on the patio to play in the rain. Our patio—which was planted with banana and plantain trees—overflowed, and our domestic ducks and turtles came out. We chased them, running among the trees, splashing in the water that came up to our knees. At night, the patio became a swamp full of thick clouds of mosquitoes, and scores of frogs that honked and croaked a cacophonous music. Then the huge orange moon of the tropics would appear, casting its reflection on the onyx waters, like a golden spotlight.

After our return from Bogotá, Mother had lived with Don Miguel, her lover, for five years. Don Miguel had a high post in local government and was a married man. He came every night for supper and slept with Mother until midnight, when he went home to his wife and family. This situation, though fairly common in Colombian society, was nonetheless painful for my sister and me. It was especially hard to explain to my school friends, though all the neighbors knew and understood. Don Miguel was kind and gentle with children, and was crazy about Mother, so Wilbrajan and I treated him as a favorite uncle. At night, when he and Mother closed the door of their bedroom, I would sneak out of my room and go through the kitchen to the patio and around the back of the house to watch them make love through the windows that opened onto the patio. Night after night I watched, discovering my own sexual appetites as I saw them go at it with a voraciousness and passion that to me was exciting, frightening, exhausting.

That must be why I'm still a voyeur, I said to myself, thinking of Reinhardt. I shook my head to stop this reverie. Yet I was drowsy, and I had to get up early the next morning to go interpret again for Judge Warpick. I decided to sleep on the couch by the window with the gun under my mattress. I changed into my pajamas and set the alarm clock in the kitchen. Soon, a heaviness descended upon me, and I felt sinking, parachuting down a pitch-dark, airless well. Before I surrendered wakefulness, the last image I saw was the golden eyes of Mr. O'Donnell, shining in the dark: feral, deracinated, like the eyes of Blake's tiger.

Mr. O'Donnell walking on my chest woke me up. His head hovered above mine. In the dark I was aware of something caressing my nose; I looked harder and I saw he had a squirming mouse in his mouth, hanging by the head. "Aggghhh!" I screamed in disgust, sitting up. With the mouse in his teeth, Mr. O'Donnell flew twenty feet and landed in the next room. My heart threatened to erupt in my mouth. I got up and turned on the lights. I was having an attack of *pavor nocturnus*. I knew I was cracking up and ran through the different rooms turning all the lights on. I poured myself half a glass of scotch, guzzled it and then sat by the windows overlooking the alley to cool off. It was 4:20 A.M. Mr. O'Donnell entered the room with his prey. With the broom I tried to coax him into surrendering it. Angered, Mr. O'Donnell dropped the unconscious mouse, and, like a rabid jungle beast, bared his teeth, growling, and then scratched my legs and bit me to defend his catch. I raced to my room and shut the door and threw myself on the bed. After a while, collecting half of myself and getting up, I turned on the light over my bed, and the air-conditioning. I didn't care whether anyone broke in or not; I would not get out of my room for a few hours, until the mouse was dead and devoured. Lighting a cigarette, I propped myself on the pillows and wondered whether I should try to go back to sleep or whether I should make an effort to stay awake. I began to daydream; I saw Christopher Columbus, on his fourth voyage, sick, crazed, broken, his caravel arriving at the coast of Paria. In the distance, he saw a pear-shaped mountain which he mistook for a huge breast, the huge breast of earth, reaching all the way to heaven.

10

Ay Luna! Ay Luna!

"What's going down, dude?" Jeff greeted me as I walked into the Social Security office the next morning.

"Good morning, Jeff," I said, standing in front of his desk. He had his chess set out and a chair drawn to the side of his desk as a lure.

Jeff put the *New York Post* aside. "So how come you don't wanna play with me no more?"

"It's discouraging; you're too good for me," I said.

"Thanks. But you'll never improve unless you play good players. That's how I learned."

At that moment, Judge Warpick's assistant, who looked like a senior citizen version of Betty Boop, entered the room. "Are you ready, Mr. Martínez?" she asked me, batting her mile-long eyelashes.

I turned to Jeff. "Is the claimant here?"

"She was here before I arrived," Jeff informed me. "She's sitting way in the back of the room. Her name is," he winced, "Fridania Moquette. I wonder where these people get those names."

I called out the name. Today the room was packed with claimants, their relatives and friends, interpreters, lawyers and paralegals. In the back of the room a young woman got up with some difficulty. My heart sank a bit when she started walking toward us without a lawyer. The young woman pushed a baby carriage and moved with the help of a cane. As she lurched toward the front of the room, I saw that she used a golf club as a cane, and that she had braces on her legs.

Jeff tapped me on my thigh with the claimant's folder.

When the claimant reached the door, I accosted her with my usual introduction, "My name is Santiago. I'm your Spanish interpreter."

The girl stared blankly at me as if looking into a mirror. Slowly, we wended our way to the judge's chambers. The claimant stationed the baby carriage (which was covered by a cotton blanket) next to her chair and sat down, placing the golf club on the table.

I was feeling drowsy from lack of sleep. Presently, Judge Warpick entered the room swathed in her black robe, her gargoyle features truly frightening. She asked me to explain to the claimant her rights. We were sworn in and the hearing began. The first two questions—name and address—were asked and answered.

"Is it Miss or Mrs. Moquette?" Warpick asked.

"Miss," the girl said, blushing. I saw now that she was very young. She wore her black hair in two pigtails held with white and blue ribbons. Her eyes were decorated with gobs of purple eyeshadow and her nails were painted an aquamarine hue and dotted with silver stars.

"Where were you born?" Warpick asked with some disgust, as if she were sick to death of asking the same question over and over.

"In a hospital, I guess."

I couldn't repress a smile. Warpick looked at me as if she wanted to disintegrate me with her stare.

"The country, I mean."

"Puerto Rico."

"And when did you come to the United States?"

Fridania shrugged. "I don't remember; a long time ago."

"How come you haven't learned English if you came here so young?" the judge asked in disbelief.

A little voice chimed in, "Hi."

Smiling, Fridania tapped the blanket over the baby carriage.

Craning her flamingo neck, Warpick focused her eyes on the carriage.

"That's the baby," Fridania said, pulling off the blanket as if she were a magician about to produce a dove or a rabbit. A little boy's head was exposed. With his mop of black curls, he looked like a miniature Yanick Noah and was grabbing the side of the carriage with his hands. He smiled at us. There was something odd about him; although he seemed tiny, his face looked older.

"Hi," the boy greeted me, and reached over to touch me with his hand. I sat still. The judge's assistant sat up, snapping out of her usual torpor and put a finger on the tape recorder, ready to turn it off in case there was extraneous colloquy. The judge stretched an arm, opening her gnarled, knobby fingers to indicate to the assistant not to turn off the machine. "Miss Moquette, are you ready to continue?" Warpick asked.

I could see that by now she was on the warpath.

"Just a minute," Fridania said. She opened her bag, pulled out a milk bottle and gave it to the baby, who snatched it, squealing, before disappearing to the bottom of the carriage.

As if realizing for the first time the anomaly of the situation, Judge Warpick asked, "Miss Moquette, when were you born?"

"In 1974."

"So you are . . ."

Seventeen, I thought to myself, and took a real good look at the claimant. Then how old was she when she had the boy? That was Judge Warpick's next question.

"Thirteen and a half," Fridania said.

"So the boy is four and a half now?"

"He'll be five for Christmas."

"Isn't he a bit too old to be in a baby carriage?"

"No, ma'am. He can't walk."

"Why not?"

"Because he was born without legs."

"Why?"

"How should I know?" Fridania retorted angrily. "Ask God. He made him that way."

Warpick snarled back. "Miss Moquette, if you want to go on

with the hearing I advise you to control your temper. I will not put up with any tantrums from you or anybody else. Is that clear?"

Lowering my head, I interpreted all this in almost a whisper. I wanted to close my eyes and—

"Mr. Interpreter," Warpick shouted at me. "You have to speak up, otherwise the machine will not pick up your interpretation."

"I'm sorry, your honor," I said, giving her a look of hatred. Fortunately for me, she was staring at the claimant.

"Hi," the little boy said again. *"Ya terminé el tete, mami,"* he said. His head appeared again, and he handed his mother the empty bottle. For a moment, the judge, the assistant, and myself forgot about the hearing in process, and watched, galvanized, the interaction between mother and son. Fridania put the bottle in her bag and, taking the boy by his armpits, hoisted him out of the carriage. He was a perfectly developed boy from his head to his buttocks. The boy wore a red T-shirt with an image of Madonna grossly imitating Marilyn Monroe; his private parts were wrapped in diapers and covered with blue plastic. Fridania put the boy on her lap. Then she pulled a pad and crayons out of her bag, which she set on the table. The boy started to draw immediately.

"What's his name?" Warpick asked.

"Claus Pericles."

"Claus Pericles?"

"Claus after Santa Claus, because he was born around Christmas, and Pericles after my father."

"Where's Claus's father?"

"I don't know."

"What's his name?"

Impassively, the girl said, "I don't know that, either. I was raped by a gang of boys."

"Why didn't you have an abortion?" Warpick asked, to my utter astonishment. "I know why," she went on, "because you wanted to get on welfare as soon as possible."

"That's right," Claus answered in English for his mother, and resumed drawing fantastic beasts with red eyes.

"You have to tell the boy to keep quiet; otherwise he'll have to leave the room."

Claus set down his crayon and sat up straight, staring at Warpick.

"Tell me why you are asking for additional supplementary income."

"Because I don't have enough money to live on."

"But you get Medicare."

"Yes, ma'am."

"And food stamps."

"Sometimes," said Claus.

I sat on my hands as if this would somehow help me not to break into laughter.

Judge Warpick was becoming rattled; her features hardened as if set in cement. "What's wrong with Claus . . . I mean, besides the fact he was born without legs?"

Claus turned around to look at his mother, *"Dile, mami,"* he ordered.

Fridania ran her fingers through her son's black silky curls. "When Claus was born," she began, "he weighed four pounds; he had a bump on his back the size of a grapefruit and . . ." She paused; this part was obviously very painful to her. "He was born without a penis. So the doctors told me it would be easier to turn him into a girl than to make a penis for him. They said I should raise him as a girl."

"Why didn't you?" Warpick asked. "Why didn't you follow the doctors' advice?"

Fridania slapped the table; Claus imitated her. "Because if God had wanted Claus to be a girl, he would have made him a girl."

"I'm a boy," Claus shouted. "A boy, not a girl. Isn't that right, Mommy?"

"Sí, Clauscito," his mother reassured him. Then she continued. "The worst part is that because he was born without a penis, his urine and excrement come from the same place. They've done two operations but haven't been able to fix the problem."

"No more operations," Claus said. He turned to me. *"Mijo,* no more operations."

"Why don't you live with your parents, Miss Moquette?"

"Because I have my own family now."

"You are a child, Miss Moquette. And an invalid. You seem to have a severe impediment with your legs; you should live at home with your parents. Maybe Claus would be more comfortable in a rehabilitation center. As he grows up, you won't be able to care for him. He seems like an intelligent child. He will have to go to school. Maybe he can learn a trade and be a useful citizen."

"I will not put Claus in an institution!" Fridania shrieked, the veins in her neck swelling, her features becoming distorted by rage.

"It's not up to you to decide that, Miss Moquette," snarled Warpick. "A higher court will have to deal with this matter. I certainly will recommend that the boy go to a rehab."

"Never!" Fridania shouted in English. "Over my dead body, you hear me?" she went on in accentless English.

"Never, never, never, never!" shrieked Claus, leaping onto the table and hopping all over it like a rabbit. The judge's assistant sprang off her chair and backed off against the wall.

"Miss Moquette, the hearing is over," the judge said. "Take the boy and leave."

Fridania stood up. Grabbing the golf club, she looked at me and raised it. I cowered, covering my head with my arms. But Fridania, inching her way toward the bench, started jabbing the club into the air, whipping it back and forth. Warpick stood up horrified, croaking hysterically.

Still hopping on the table, Claus started to sing, *"Bamba, bamba. Bamba, bamba."*

"Mr. Interpreter," Warpick called out imploringly. "Please stop her. You must stop her!"

I realized Fridania meant no harm to me and I had no wish to get in the way of her avenging club.

The judge's assistant, who was across the room from Fridania, ran out of the room wailing. Warpick began to pitch the objects on her desk at the approaching claimant, who batted them with her club.

"Mr. Interpreter," Warpick screamed again. "Stop her! I tell you to stop her. If you don't, you'll be fired. You'll never work again."

I got up and took a good look at Fridania, who moved as fast as a convalescing snail, and decided that Judge Warpick could protect herself without my help. I turned around to exit the room.

"You'll never work again!" Warpick's voice trailed after me as I traipsed down the hall. I walked into the office to say good-bye to Jeff. I found the judge's assistant collapsed on Jeff's chair, blubbering as she tried to explain what was going on in the judge's office.

"Hey, man, what the hell is going on?" Jeff asked.

"The judge needs you," I said.

"Oh, yeah. Well, I'm busy right now," Jeff said.

I offered to shake Jeff's hand, which he took with a questioning look.

"I'm quitting," I informed him. "I'll miss you, though."

"Man, you can't do that. You're my chess partner." Realizing I was serious, he said, "What are you going to do?"

"I don't know," I shrugged. "Write a thriller, I guess."

"No shit."

"Bye," I said, feeling a lump rise in my throat.

As I exited the Federal Plaza building, I knew that I would never reenter it again as an interpreter. I knew Unlimited Languages would never call me again and this was the only agency that sent me out to interpret in Social Security and Welfare cases. I wished I felt exhilarated and free, like heroes do in movies and novels when they stand up for themselves—although in my case, Fridania had done the standing up for me. What I experienced was terror. I told myself it was unlikely that Judge Warpick would call all the agencies in town to ruin my interpreting career.

Outside, the day was sunny. After last night's rain, the city looked spic and span; the air was crisp, invigorating. We had just entered the dreaded month of August, but today there was a touch of autumn in the air. Usually, after leaving work I rushed back home. Today I wanted to linger in the streets. The men who had tried to break into my apartment were still present in my mind. Today I longed to sit down with a friend, to chew the fat for hours. I'll pay a visit to Harry Hagin, I thought. He always brightens my day. I put on my sunglasses and started walking in the direction of the corner where Harry had been selling ices the last time I had seen him. Harry was not at his corner. I walked east for a few blocks, thinking maybe he had moved deeper into the financial district.

I found hot dogs, pretzels, books, sunglasses, and fruit ice vendors, but no trace of Harry. It's not like Harry to take Monday off, I thought. I began to feel depressed. I felt as if a huge hippopotamus were being lowered on my head, squashing me onto the pavement. It was time to go home. I couldn't walk through Wall Street feeling like that. My life was in crisis and I was reacting to it like an ostrich.

Think positive, Santiago, I said to myself. Do something; buy the *New York Times* and study the classified section under jobs. I started to perspire remembering how many times in the past years I had done this, and after reading the first column given up in despair, realizing how few marketable skills I had. The heck with the past, I mumbled—I have to change all that. I was talking aloud to myself and the Wall Streeters were eyeing me suspiciously. Obviously, whether I ended up writing a thriller or not, I had to support myself somehow. Moving back to Mother's house in Queens was no longer an alternative. To prove to myself my new-found seriousness, I purchased a copy of the *Wall Street Journal* and, tucking it under my arm, I bolted for the subway. The E train was empty at that hour, and I sat down to read the paper and to enjoy the air-conditioning. I opened the *Journal* to the classified—my heart sank; it looked forbidding, like the obituary page of the *Times* without the photographs. I shut the paper in haste as if I had just seen a picture of the devil inside. At home, drinking a cold beer, maybe I could stand reading it. But the train was taking so long to fill up at the Chambers Street station that to escape my screaming thoughts I opened the *Journal* again, hoping against hope to find an article that would vaguely interest me. I flipped through the pages and glanced at most of the headlines until the E train arrived at Times Square.

I felt excited, manic. As I approached the corner of Eighth Avenue and Forty-third Street I saw many people bunched at the corner. Besides the riffraff and the crack people milling around, there were policemen and firemen. Police officers were setting up safety nets and pumping to inflate a safety cushion on the street. Was it a fire at the hotel? Now I noticed priests, nuns, and, of course, photographers. I knew an event of major proportions was going on in Times Square. Soon the TV people would be arriving. Everyone was looking up. No smoke came out of the building, but a man on a high floor was sitting on a window ledge threatening to jump. Brandishing a crucifix, a priest started to climb up the fire engine's ladder. A couple of nuns were praying on their knees. The crack heads watched the scene as if they were in an action movie. The whole thing was a turn-on to them. Looking like angry, demented demons just expelled from hell, they began to chant: "Jump! Jump! Jump!"

I gotta get the hell out of here, I thought; I don't want to see this. I was about to start crossing the street when the crowd broke up in a shrill roar and the man on the window ledge dove headfirst to the pavement. I froze; I didn't know whether to shit or go blind. The suicide landed inches away from me with a dull thump. The top of his head opened and shot some blood like a fire hydrant. The man was naked, except for a T-shirt and his legs looked brilliant as if they were waxed. One of my arms was red, as if spattered with ketchup. Touching my face and my head, I discovered I was drenched with blood. I howled, shutting my eyes. The crack heads screamed and tittered and giggled demonically.

Momentarily insane, I darted across the street, barely escaping the oncoming traffic. Sprinting up the stairs of my building, I stumbled upon a figure sitting on the steps.

"Jesus fucking Christ, Sammy," my nephew Gene screamed. "What happened to you, man? Is that paint or what?"

"It's blood," I blubbered, breaking into loud sobs and collapsing on the steps.

"Sammy, did you just kill someone? Did you? Why? Why? Oh man, why?" Gene shouted hysterically.

A couple of clients of George's employment agency were coming down the stairs. I nudged against the wall, turning my face away from them, but making enough room so they could go by. When the men reached the door, I said, "A man just jumped out of a building and almost fell on top of me."

"Oh, man. What a trip! I gotta go see that!"

"No, you're not," I said. "Come on, let's go upstairs."

Inside the apartment, I asked Gene to lock the door after us as I ran into the bathroom. Turning on the lights, I was so shocked by my bloody reflection in the mirror I became dizzy and had to sit on the toilet. I managed to remove my shirt and undershirt and used the latter to towel off my hair, face, and hands. Feeling stronger, I took off my shoes and pants. I leaned my back against the cool water tank and closed my eyes.

"Sammy, are you okay?" Gene asked, coming into the bathroom.

I opened my eyes. He was carrying Mr. O'Donnell, the cat's face against his cheeks.

"Hi, kitty," I said. "Gene, will you do me a favor? Take all these bloody clothes and put them in a plastic bag and get rid of them."

Gene made a face and handed Mr. O'Donnell to me. I set the cat on my knees, feeling his back paws clawing into my thighs. Gene made all sorts of disgusting sounds as he carried the clothes away. I noticed Mr. O'Donnell looked better, almost rejuvenated. "It must be the protein in that mouse you ate," I said. At that moment, a black, shiny, metallic-sounding fly—the size of a bumblebee—hurtled into the bathroom. Mr. O'Donnell sprang off my lap, caught the insect in midair and alighted at the bottom of the bathtub where he proceeded to chew on his catch. He made scratchy, dry sounds and, sticking out his tongue, started to lick his chops, as if he had just finished a gourmet meal.

"Get out of my sight, you disgusting beast," I muttered, rising and chasing him out of the room with the towel. I sat down again; I was shaking badly when loud music began to blast in the kitchen. Gene was playing one of his incomprehensible tapes. Without knocking, Gene entered the bathroom almost running, awkward and impetuous, like a wild horse. He had two glasses with him and handed me one. "Here, I think you might need this," he said. I took a swig of the scotch and shuddered as the alcohol sizzled down my throat.

"Why don't you take a nice bath?" Gene suggested. "I can make it for you."

I was touched by his concern, whether real or fake. This was one of the few occasions ever he had offered to do anything for me.

He began to fill the bathtub with steaming water. He left the water running and came back with a bottle of extract of vanilla, which he poured into the tub. I was too upset to argue. Before he left the room, I said, "Gene, how about turning down the volume of the music?"

"It's the Beastie Boys," he said, looking hurt, as if I had asked him to shut off a sublime Brahms symphony. "I'm going up front to listen, is that cool?"

I nodded. Gene shut the door with a whack that made me jump. I took off my underwear and got into the scalding water. With the water up to my neck, I sat there taking deep breaths and wriggling my toes. The room looked foggy and mysterious in the rising steam. I bean to fantasize: This was not my bathroom but an ancient Inca bath. Instead of the pleasant, mild scent of vanilla, what I smelled was *palo santo* and burnt eucalyptus; instead of laying in tap water, I was floating in a pool of hot mineral springs emanating from a sacred volcano. I was beginning to unwind when, against my will, a babel of voices started having a conference in my head. What was Gene doing here? He seldom came to visit me, and never unannounced. He'd come to get the coke, of course! I could picture him now ransacking the apartment, turning everything upside down. That's why he had suggested my bath. It was not concern on his part but sly, devious thinking, and I had fallen for it, giving in to my avuncular sentiments that always made me act against my best interest. "Give the kid a break," protested the even-tempered voice of reason. "He's not bad, he's just scared." "Oh yeah," interjected the scoffing voice of paranoia, stepping up to the mike, "Keep thinking like a Miss Pollyanna suppository and soon you'll lie in the gutter with your head blown off by nice Colombian bullets." I was freaking out again.

I was about to leap out of the bathtub when the phone rang. I heard Gene's caveman footsteps galloping for the phone. I sat still. Maybe it was one of his friends calling to chat. Now the thumping steps approached the bathroom door. I reached for the towel as the door opened and Gene stuck his head in. "It's the United Nations, Sammy."

"The United Nations? Are you sure?"

"Yeah, something about the United Nations."

"Wait, I'll take it," I said, getting up, wrapping the towel around my waist, and rushing to the telephone.

"Hello," I said, slightly out of breath.

"San-tiaaaaaa-gooooo, San-tiaaaaaa-go," sang Virginia, from the Language Workshop, one of the interpreting agencies I worked for. "I've got a jooob for youuuuuu, at the Uniiii-ted Nations. It's a lunnnnn-cheon. Do youuuuu want it?" she finished in her cracked quasisoprano voice. Virginia was a Viennese opera nut. She was in her seventies and still ran her own agency. I had run into her once at the Met when Rebecca had taken me for my birthday to see a performance of *La Traviata*. Since then, she was convinced that I went to the opera all the time.

"The United Nations, huh," I said very impressed. "Sure I'll take it."

"They asked me for my best interpreter, and of course I thought about you," she said, now in her normal speaking voice. Then she gave me all the information, which I took with great difficulty considering I was dripping wet and Gene stood next to me watching intently everything I said and did.

"Are you going to translate tomorrow at the U.N.?" Gene asked, visibly impressed, after I hung up.

"Yeah," I said, affecting a blasé tone as if I were used to interpreting at the U.N., when in fact I had never been there before.

"That's where you should get a full-time job, Sammy, instead of that welfare shit you do."

Gene's advice was undoubtedly not malicious, but I did not appreciate his tacit criticism of how I conducted my interpreting career. To punish him I said, "Will you make some coffee while I get dressed?"

"Can I use the Mr. Coffee I gave you last Christmas?"

"Sure. Do it any way you want."

He marched to the kitchen with the resolute, indelicate stride of a teenage Ollie Oop. In the bedroom, I toweled slowly, musing on the kind of day I was having. Just an hour ago, for all practical purposes, I had thought my interpreting career was over. And now, tomorrow I was going to work at the U.N. Who knows where that might lead? What if I screw up, though? I wondered. No, no, no, Santiago, I said, shutting off the negative tapes before they started running. I'm an excellent interpreter, I reminded myself. There are no coincidences; the U.N. is where I belong. I'll do beautifully tomorrow and they'll be so impressed I'll end up getting lots of assignments. My money situation will improve, and I won't have to interpret the squalid and horrifying lives of social security and welfare claimants anymore. Even my mother will be impressed, I thought, as I put on shorts, T-shirt, and sneakers. From now on, I would only interpret for statesmen and politicians. It occurred to me that the social security claimants were more admirable and honest than the corrupt politicians of the world—especially the ones from Latin America—for whom I no doubt would be interpreting. What's more, as grim as the lives of the claimants were, they were probably a more cheerful subject matter than Nazi criminals, famine, torture, genocide, and everything the U.N. had to deal with.

A plastic bag on my pillows distracted me from this line of thinking. I emptied its contents on the bedspread; Mother had sent the Colombian newspapers of the past few days with Gene. Wrongly, she assumed that I was interested in reading these newspapers; that I continued to be interested in whatever went on in Colombia. And yet, perhaps she understood something about myself that I denied; I always diligently perused the newspapers and found at least a couple of articles that interested me. I studied the front page of *El Espectador,* and read the headlines absentmindedly. I set the paper aside and let the back of my head sink into the pillows. Gene came into the room with two cups of steaming coffee. Mr. O'Donnell trotted after him and jumped on my bed while Gene set the cup of coffee on the night table and sat on my desk.

"How are you feeling?" he asked.

Mr. O'Donnell walked up the length of my legs and stretched out on my crotch. I sat up, brushing the cat aside. As he moved away, he stuck his back paws on my shorts. "Ouch," I uttered, covering my genitalia. I gave Mr. O'Donnell a hard look and tasted the sickeningly sweet coffee.

"How's the coffee?" Gene asked eagerly.

"It's very good. Thanks, Gene."

"You look awful, Sammy. I've never seen you look so shitty. It's like . . . it's like you need to relax or something."

I wasn't quite sure that whatever way I felt Gene wasn't at least partially responsible for it.

"Anyway, what are you doing in Manhattan?" I queried him, becoming suspicious of his motives for visiting me.

He shrugged. "Nothing." He ogled Mr. O'Donnell and sipped his coffee. "What a big cat," he said in admiration, as if he were praising Mr. O'Donnell for his genius or his poetic nature.

"Don't change the subject. You came to get the coke, didn't you?"

"No, man. I just wanted to get the hell out of Queens for a day. And I wanted to talk to you. You're like my only uncle. And you're my friend, aren't you?" he finished, looking hurt.

"I guess so," I mumbled, not being too thrilled at the prospect of being related to a future Al Capone. "I think your friends are after me," I said, giving him an accusing look. "We have to get rid of that coke. Last night there were two guys on my fire escape trying to break in."

"I just love the way you jump to conclusions," he said, exasperated. "How do you know they were Colombians? They were probably crack heads from the neighborhood. It's not like you live on Park Avenue, you know," Gene finished, with the cruelty of youth.

"Oh, yeah. I've lived here for many years and nobody ever tried to break into my apartment."

"Sammy, will you get off that horse? How would my . . . ex-boss know you have the coke? That's like so paranoid of you."

"If they didn't know before, they know now. I'm sure they followed you into the city."

"I can't believe this shit," Gene said, getting up and wringing his hands. "My own uncle trying to do me in. I'm gonna go and I'm never, ever no more coming back to see you."

"Not until you've learned to speak English properly," I snapped back. "Okay, okay, okay," I said. "I guess you're right. I'm overwrought by all the shit that's been raining on me lately. Please stay, okay?"

"Really, Sammy? You're not pissed off at me? How would you like to go to the park?" Gene proposed enthusiastically. Seeing me demur, he went on. "When was the last time you went to the park? You need the inspiration of nature."

"Sure, Mr. Wordsworth," I said, knowing full well that my allusion was completely wasted on him.

"We can have a picnic," Gene went on, "and spend the afternoon hanging out. I can chase the girls and you . . . can do whatever you want. How about that?"

"I just want to take it easy," I said.

"Remember how you used to take me to the park when I was little?" Gene said, waxing nostalgic as I wondered what had ever happened to the cute, lovable toddler I had known. "You used to say to me, 'Gene, want to go to the *patico* park?' That was so cute, the way you called the duck pond the *patico* park."

"Okay," I said, blushing. "That's enough. We'll go to the park for the afternoon."

"I'm raring to go," Gene said.

Now that I had agreed to do it, I got cold feet. "Wait, Gene. I can't go to the park just like that. Just cool it for a minute. Let me think about what we need to take with us, okay?"

Gene sat down again on the desk, although he looked like a race horse ready to take off. Mr. O'Donnell was now aware that we were leaving. He gave me the pitiful, longing, reproachful look he always used when he saw me getting ready to go out. Gene picked up on it.

"Let's take O'Donnell, too." He lifted the cat off the bed and started kissing his face.

"Put him down; he doesn't like to be mauled. It's not a good idea; forget it." As I said this, it occurred to me that the mafiosi might return, break in, and Mr. O'Donnell could escape. "Okay, we'll take him to the park," I said. "Let me get his box."

As soon as I said "box," Mr. O'Donnell torpedoed off Gene's arms and hid under the bed.

"What's come over him?" Gene asked, puzzled by the cat's bewildering reaction.

"He thinks I'm taking him to the ASPCA. He only sees the box when he has to go to the vet."

We tried to coax Mr. O'Donnell from under the bed—but to no avail.

"Wait," I said. "I know what will do it. Kal Kan," I cried out like a fool and started walking toward the kitchen. "Kal Kan, Kal Kan," I sang.

I opened the refrigerator and pretended to fetch the Kal Kan. As Mr. O'Donnell started rubbing against me, I grabbed him. Gene brought out the box and between the two of us we managed to put him inside it. Now I was afraid that the trauma of the skirmish might give him a heart attack. I was so exhausted by the ordeal that I didn't feel like going out anymore. But I knew Gene would be disappointed if I changed my mind.

In a duffle bag we packed blankets, cushions, paper dishes, insect repellent, suntan lotion, etc., and left the apartment as though we were going on a safari. In the street, Mr. O'Donnell started to bleat pathetically. We strolled up Eighth Avenue and stopped at a Korean grocery store to buy food for the picnic.

"It's been days since I ate anything that stuck to my ribs," Gene said. Living at my mother's house as he did, I wondered how that could be possible.

I reassured him. "Don't worry, we'll buy lots of food."

"I don't want to eat peaches and carrot sticks," Gene remonstrated. "You buy whatever you want to eat and I'll buy whatever I want."

That sounded fair enough. We marched up different aisles—I, carrying the cat box, he, the duffle bag. I bought a six-pack of beer, oranges, pears, rice cakes, and yogurt, and walked to the cash register to pay for my items. Gene had disappeared behind the aisles, so I waited, setting the box on the floor. Mr. O'Donnell was making blood-curdling sounds, as if he were possessed by the same demon that had gotten hold of Linda Blair in *The Exorcist*. The people in the store began to eye the box with alarm. I was getting uptight and restless when Gene appeared carrying three Hershey bars, a large Coke, a box of buttered popcorn, a bag of Chee-tohs, and two large containers of Pringle's Potato Chips. I was going to reprimand him on the junk he ate, but I decided it was wrong to begin arguing before the picnic started.

It was a cool, dry, golden afternoon crowned with an aquamarine sky. We dawdled all the way to Columbus Circle, where, in front of the statue at the edge of the park, a black trumpet player blasted to a large but hushed audience the melancholy notes of The Beatles' "Yesterday." The piercing notes of the melody felt like slivers stuck under my skin. I motioned Gene to move on. It was past noon and the park was alive with joggers and people having their lunches and smoking joints. We trekked away from the crowds until we reached a field where a baseball game was in progress. The teams wore uniforms and the players were young but serious. We chose a spot under a tree that was far enough from the action, but close enough that we could enjoy the game. We spread out our blanket and pulled out the cushions and emptied the shopping bags. Mr. O'Donnell had grown so strangely quiet that I wondered if he was all right. He was sitting up when I opened the box, and jumped out before I could reach in to pull him out. His eyes, like open yellow tulips, took in the scene, shining with the excitement of finding that he was someplace other than the Humane Society. He was ready to start exploring the surroundings.

"Oh, no," I said, "I'm afraid this is not going to work out. I forgot to bring some kind of leash. He could run away."

But, as if to purposefully contradict me, Mr. O'Donnell stretched out languidly and then collapsed on his side, facing the baseball field.

"Check that out," Gene exclaimed. "He likes baseball."

"No, no. He likes opera."

"He likes baseball, too. Don't you, O'Donnell?"

Mr. O'Donnell twitched his tail to indicate that he was both watching the game and listening to our conversation.

Gene opened one of the beers and took a long swig; with his teeth, he tore open one of the bags and stuffed his mouth, making loud, crunchy noises as he chewed. "Isn't this the ultimate?" he said with the fake sincerity of a budding thespian. "Nature," he expostulated, "summer, baseball, beer, everything. If I could choose one way to spend the rest of my life, I would choose this. Wouldn't you?" He finished as if he had just recited an immortal Shakespearean soliloquy. His face looked so enraptured that I wondered if he was already drunk from the beer. "Wouldn't you, too?" he insisted. Obviously I was not going to be allowed to brush off the silly question. I knew he was serious. I remembered how at fifteen I had been obsessed with the meaning of life, love, God, existence, the universe.

"I don't know," I said. "I don't think so," although I couldn't think of anything better. Perhaps the mountains, I thought; maybe the ocean. Life at a marina, sailing the pellucid sea. But I realized that "the ultimate"—Gene and I in harmony; Mr. O'Donnell happy, serene; the cool beer, the radiant afternoon; the guys hitting the ball—was very nice indeed, and despite my messy life, for the moment I could afford to be happy.

Gene and I became engrossed in the game. Mr. O'Donnell fell asleep, his snoring sounding like a pigeon cooing. After a while we got to know the names of the players, and when their teammates cheered them on, we'd join them. This was better than professional baseball, where I always rooted for the Mets. Here, I just wanted to see brilliant pitches, great hits, dazzling catches, no matter from whom. Whenever we'd scream too loud, Mr. O'Donnell would jerk awake, turn around and cast reproachful glances at us before going back to sleep.

We watched the game and drank and munched throughout the afternoon. At one point, Mr. O'Donnell woke up and begged for food. He ate an entire container of blueberry yogurt and a couple of Gene's Chee-tohs before he resumed his nap. By the time the game was over, maybe owing to the beers I'd had, maybe owing to the languid afternoon we were having, I felt relaxed and drowsy.

"Gene," I said, "I'm going to take a nap. Is that okay?"

"Go right ahead, man. Whatever makes you happy."

"I wonder if I should put Mr. O'Donnell in his box."

"Sammy, don't do that to the poor cat. He's so happy where he is."

"But I'm afraid he could run away."

"Not to worry. I'll watch over him. Just go to sleep, all right?"

"Thanks, Gene. I appreciate it. But don't let me sleep too long. Wake me up before dark, okay?"

"Okay."

I stretched out, my head on a cushion, and closed my eyes. In the darkness, I could hear the many sounds of the park; the twittering of different birds, traffic noises so far away that they almost sounded pleasant, bits and pieces of conversations of the people who walked near us. I began to dream of myself in Barranquilla when I was thirteen or fourteen years old.

In the afternoons, during vacation time or on weekends, I'd go for long walks in the best neighborhoods in town. I would pass all the great mansions, wishing I lived in one of them. I'd sit on a street curb, and then I'd proceed to create an entire fantasy about my life inside that particular house, complete with parents, pets, brothers and sisters I liked. Around the time I was Gene's age, I longed to escape my life. I wanted to go far away from everything that surrounded me, although the thought of leaving behind my dog, Spartacus, and my sister saddened me. Then my dream took on a different turn; it was nighttime. The moon was out and the sky was a rich, enamelled blue. I was on a farm with my mother, and we were strolling in a hilly, rolling landscape bereft of vegetation except for the grass we walked on. Spartacus appeared at the top of a hill, looking like a wolf. He stood erect, tough, vigilant, like a warrior. With his black and white markings, he looked as if he were dressed for a ball. I called him by his nickname, *Pita,* and he plunged down the hill to meet me. I patted his head and said to my mother, "Spartacus doesn't bark anymore," to which she replied, "It's because he's so fat, like you." Then a lovely and pure tenor's voice sang, *"Ay, luna que brillas; Ay, luna."*

When I woke up the afternoon was quite advanced; it was six-thirty but still very light. Another baseball game with different teams was in progress. I opened Mr. O'Donnell's box, thinking Gene had put him inside before going off by himself. The box was empty; my heart stopped. I refused to believe that the worst had happened, that Mr. O'Donnell had run away and now Gene was desperately roaming the park trying to find him. I was about to get up to start looking for them, when I saw Gene approaching. He carried a shopping bag but no cat.

"Where's Mr. O'Donnell?" I screamed.

"He's in the bag. I took him for a ride; we had a great time. He's so kickass bad. You should have seen him in the woods trying to get those birds and the squirrels and . . ."

"Asshole," I interrupted him. "You could have given me a fucking heart attack."

"Didn't you see my note?"

"What note?" I grumbled.

"Next to your pillow. See it?"

Indeed, next to my pillow there was a piece of paper bag with something scribbled on it. "Sorry, Gene," I apologized, feeling ashamed of myself. "I guess I woke up in a state."

Gene dumped Mr. O'Donnell out of the bag. As if to cheer me up, O'Donnell sat on my lap and began to purr. Gene sat next to me.

"Where you having a nightmare?"

"Not really. I was dreaming about when I was your age," I said, scratching the cat under his chin. "Lately I've been dreaming a lot about my childhood. I wonder what it means. All I know is that I had an unhappy childhood and adolescence."

"Sammy, you didn't have a bad childhood, just a long one," Gene said.

"In the past couple of weeks, though, I've felt as if my life were going from monochrome into color."

"Sure. Your best friend died, you got engaged . . ."

"I'm not getting married to Claudia, is that clear?"

"Why not?"

"Because I'm gay. And because . . . it's none of your business." I lit a cigarette and took several quick, furious drags like Bette Davis in *Dark Victory*. I looked up; the sun had traveled three-quarters of its way from sunrise, and now it hovered above the gothic, malignant structure of the Dakota, where God knew what Satanic ritual was taking place. The sun's rays fell obliquely; they felt warm and gentle. The treetops swayed in the tranquil breeze, and a flock of noisy geese flew northward. The sky was still immaculately blue, but the light was golden, like twilight in a luminist painting. The nippy air promised a crisp evening.

"You wanna go home now or you wanna stay a bit longer?" Gene asked.

"What do you want to do? Want to stay? I don't mind catching some of this game," I said, nodding in the direction of the players. "Those guys look really good."

"That's cool with me," Gene said.

I construed this to mean we were staying. I looked toward the baseball field and began to space out again. This time of day made me think of my grandparents' town. The air became charged with the acrid smell of cow manure. It was my favorite time of day. If I didn't go by the quay to watch the sunset, I'd sit on a rocking chair outside the house and watch the young girls carrying baskets loaded with fresh fish, returning to their homes before nightfall. Then, as the sun sank, vapors rose from the muddy river bed, where litters of squealing pigs rolled and vultures searched for carrion. Later, as dusk set in, the smell of ripe *ciruelas,* mangoes, *nísperos,* and cashew fruit turned the evening into an aphrodisiac. My grandfathers and uncles approached the house, riding their horses after an afternoon at the farm. They rode up the mossy street, which was decorated with huge white boulders set in the middle of the road like fossilized dinosaur eggs. Barefoot, almost naked, children led their family burros back into their corrals. The African-looking *palenqueras,* advertising their coconut sweets, sashayed their way up the street singing in their soprano voices, *"Alegría, alegría con coco y maní."* As night fell, the mosquitoes arrived, myriads of bats took over the sky, fireflies glowed on the patios, and the sweet smell of honeysuckle spread all over town, like an elixir, mixing with the dinners being prepared in the open-air kitchens.

"Want a hit of this?" Gene asked, waking me up from my reverie; he was smoking a fat joint.

"No, it makes me paranoid." I took the opportunity to scold him. "You should quit drugs; they're not good for you," I said sternly, aware that I sounded like the detestable Nancy Reagan.

"I'm gonna quit soon. I promise you."

"The trick is to quit while you're alive."

"I know you want to have a hit of this. This is the best pot in Queens, man."

I took a long drag and felt the marijuana resin singe the insides of my lungs; I also felt pleasantly stoned.

"What did you do in Colombia all those years after college— besides being a garbage head?" Gene asked.

"I can't remember a lot of it."

"It sounds to me like you were fucking vegged out on drugs," Gene said.

"It was like being in a spiritual coma, if you know what I mean. I'm only beginning to wake up from it now," I said.

"I think you should still get hammered once in a while, before you're too old."

"Gene, when I was your age, cigarettes were the strongest stuff I did."

"Mr. O'Donnell looks so happy on your lap," Gene said, changing the subject. "What do you think he's dreaming about? Look, he's smiling."

"Whatever cats dream about: a fat mouse, perhaps. A saucer heaped with Kal Kan, pigeons, juicy flies. Maybe he's dreaming of Monserrat Caballe singing Violeta."

"He really likes opera? That's like so fucking bizarre, man."

"He likes Monserrat Caballe singing *La Traviata*. I don't know that he likes anything else."

"You shouldda seen him in the woods; he was awesome. He was one happy cat. Sammy, do you think cats have like a last wish? You know, like prisoners before they die?"

I thought about it. "It's different, I think. Prisoners know they're going to die; I don't think cats know."

"How do you now? You're not a cat." Gene paused. "I think I know what his last wish is."

"What?"

"To be free."

"What do you mean?"

"To be free in the park. To be loose. To go wild killing pigeons and squirrels and birds. I'd bet you anything that's what he wants. Before you got him, wasn't he an alley cat, anyway?"

"Just because all you think about is guns and killing doesn't mean my cat wants to decimate the endangered fauna of Central Park."

"I'd bet you anything he'd rather have his last heart attack while munching on a pigeon or something."

This vision made me shudder. I lifted up Mr. O'Donnell in my arms and kissed his cold nose.

"When is he supposed to croak, anyway?"

"Any minute," I said, "but I'd rather not talk about it, if you don't mind."

"Sammy, if you really loved him, you'd rather let him go. You'd let him die a free cat."

"Hell, no," I boomed, nettled by his insistence. "When you have your own cat you can do that, if you want. I could never forgive myself if I did anything that stupid."

"You should have been in the woods with me. You shouldda seen how his eyes shone when he spotted the wild animals, especially the squirrels. He'd die a happy cat, that's all I'm saying to you."

Maybe there was something to what he was saying, although it sounded suspiciously like pseudo-hippy new age talk. "Mr. O'Donnell," I said, poking him gently to wake him up. "Is that what you'd prefer? Do you want to be set loose in the park?"

"Sure, man," Gene answered for the cat. "If you were dying wouldn't you rather die in nature than in Times Square or in a hospital?"

"Let him speak for himself," I said, setting Mr. O'Donnell on the blanket. I got up. "Let's go," I said. "Help me pack." I began to pick up the garbage without looking at Mr. O'Donnell. When we finished packing, Mr. O'Donnell's box remained open. He sat next to it, looking up into the trees.

"Okay, Mr. O'Donnell," I said. "This is good-bye, old man. You are a free cat; you can go."

Mr. O'Donnell turned around to look at me. He stared me in the eyes, sprang to his feet and jumped into his box, without any coaxing on my part.

I slapped Gene on his back. "You see? He prefers me to squirrels and rabbits. He loves me as I love him."

163

Gene's jaw fell open. There was a look of total perplexity on his face. "Man, what a cat! That's so fucking unbelievable."

I scratched Mr. O'Donnell between his ears and closed his box. It was the perfect way to end the day. It almost made up for the horrible morning I had had. Shadows were taking over the park. A couple of stars and a planet gleamed in the cobalt sky.

11

This Island, This Kingdom

The alarm woke me at eight. I had to be at the U.N. at noon but I wanted to have plenty of time to get ready. Gene was sleeping on the couch in the living room. In his underwear, he looked gigantic, fleshy and amorphous like a pale sea lion. The sheets were on the floor, and he had fallen asleep reading *Rolling Stone*. Mr. O'Donnell, who was sleeping on a pillow, leaped out of bed when he saw me enter the kitchen. I fed him, put on the water for coffee, and went into the bathroom to wash my face and brush my teeth.

Around ten o'clock I got dressed. Since Gene was still asleep and I had to tiptoe around the apartment, I decided to leave early. For some months now, I had been thinking about taking my type-writer to be cleaned. I put the machine in its case and left. I walked to a repair shop on Fortieth Street, between Seventh and Eighth avenues. The store was empty, except for the clerk behind the counter.

"What can I do for you?" the man greeted me.

I told him several of the typewriter's keys were stuck and I wanted to give the machine a complete overhaul. The man asked me to open the case. I hadn't finished removing the top when he diagnosed, "We can't help you."

"Why?"

"Because we don't carry parts for that kind of machine anymore."

Ha, I thought. He's trying to sell me a machine; I know this trick.

"Well, do you know of another place where they might repair it, since I can't afford to buy a new machine?"

"There's a store up the block, on the other side of the street. You can try them, but I doubt it. The manufacturer doesn't make parts for that model anymore."

"What do you mean?" I asked in disbelief. "It's almost a new machine."

"It's about ten years old, right?"

I nodded.

"You can see for yourself," he said, making a sweep with his arm around the store, "we don't carry typewriters that old."

I glanced at the different models on display, and I observed that all the machines for sale had a high-tech look unrelated to my primitive-looking electric typewriter. I thanked the man and headed for the other store. It was a replay of the same story. What's more, the salesman told me I should throw the machine in the garbage. Something told me these men were right. At the corner of Broadway and Fortieth, as I lowered my machine slowly into a trash receptacle, I also felt as if I were unburdening myself of a different kind of weight—my Rip van Winkling of the past decade. Where had I been all these years? How had I gotten so out of touch with everything? Was it possible that the typewriter was a symbol of everything I had to get rid of? By what process had I become an anachronism at age thirty-three? Was it in any way related to all the memories that I had been having in the past few weeks about my childhood and adolescence? I shook my head. I knew this was not the most cheerful line of thinking to be engaged in before starting my interpreting career at the U.N. I would concentrate on the sunny morning. We were having a spell of gorgeous days, which for New York City, in August, amounted to a miracle. As I walked in the direction of the East River, it dawned on me that I had lived half of my life in New York and I had never passed, much less gone inside, the U.N. building. Instead of getting depressed over this fact, I told myself I should look at the positive side of it; today was a new beginning. Feeling much better, I strode to Forty-third and Lexington, where the Language Workshop was located and I had to get my admission pass to the U.N.

I had seen the U.N. building in the movies, so that in a way it was déjà vu. I flashed the blue pass on my lapel to the guards at the main entrance. I was an hour early, so I decided to take a stroll in the expansive, well-kept grounds. Hundreds of colorful flags made snapping sounds high in the wind. Variegated groups of tourists headed excitedly in all directions. I walked east down a series of steps that cut through rows of what looked like cherry trees, leading to a promenade above the East River. The industrial, ugly carcasses of buildings on the other side of the river contrasted unfavorably with the gleaming structures of the U.N. The only sign of beauty across the river was provided by the pink, white, and blue neon Pepsi Cola sign, which was lit even though it was nearly noon. The chartreuse waters of the East River teemed with sailing vessels, small motor boats, yachts, and even a monumental tugboat. To the north loomed the imposing structure of the Queensboro Bridge. All this was very scenic, but I was nervous; the palms of my hands were clammy and I felt an uncomfortable tightness in the pit of my stomach.

I could have stayed on the promenade another twenty minutes, but I decided the sooner I stepped inside the building and reached my destination the less there was to fear. I took several deep breaths, taking in the seemingly fresh but undoubtedly polluted air. After wending my way through a maze and further scrutiny and frisking, I walked into the cathedral-sized lobby. This is what being inside the Tower of Babel must have felt like, I thought, as I overheard the well-dressed herds of tourists speaking in exotic languages, darting excitedly from display to display, led by the tour guides. At the Language Workshop I had been given the details of where I had to report to; I was going to interpret for the annual luncheon of the meeting of Parliamentarians for Global Disarmament. As I moved deeper into the inner chambers of the U.N., the security outposts became more thorough, the crowds thinned, and only diplomats and U.N. employees were visible. I felt more and more like a character in a Hitchcock thriller—*The Man Who Knew Too Much* or something like that. I took an elevator to the second floor. It dropped me off inside a small reception room. A security guard in a blue blazer promptly demanded to know my business. He gave me brief and precise instructions where to go. I stepped into a spacious dining room. It was barely noon, but there were people having lunch already. All the tables had arrangements of orange and yellow flowers and through the twelve-foot glass windows streamed the silvery noon light. Heavenly smells hit my nostrils and I felt envious of the elegantly dressed people sipping aromatic wines and conversing in hushed tones. I turned left down a corridor that led into a small dining room. The tables were arranged in a U shape, the bottom of the U against the south wall. The people catering the affair gave me inquiring glances. I informed them I was the interpreter, which was acknowledged by blank stares. Since none of the world parliamentarians or the U.N. officials had arrived, I stood by the huge windows watching the multifarious crafts going up and down the East River.

The waiters were putting the finishing touches on the luncheon; more flowers were brought in, French rolls were distributed around the table, a shrimp and lobster salad on a bed of wonderfully fresh Romaine lettuce was served, wines were uncorked. I had forgotten to eat anything for breakfast and the smells perfuming the room made me feel faint with hunger. I decided to concentrate on matters other than food; I had to get a new typewriter. Because of the expense, a word processor was out of the question. I needed a machine if I was going to finish my Columbus poem, or start my thriller. This purchase would severely deplete my nest egg. Perhaps my mother would give me a loan—although I was aware how hard it was to squeeze a penny out of her CDs.

Suddenly, a rising murmur of voices approached and the delegates entered the room. I had been instructed to introduce myself to Mr. McClanahan, who had contracted my services from the Language Workshop. I approached a thin man in his early thirties, quintessentially the executive type: clean-cut, efficient-looking and impeccably and conservatively dressed. McClanahan gave me the tiniest smile possible and absentmindedly shook my hand and told me to hang around until all the delegates had taken their places.

When everyone had sat down in a hurry—they all looked as hungry as I was—I saw there was no seat left for me. McClanahan motioned to a waiter to produce a chair, and a place was made for me near the window, at the tip of the upside-down U. Quickly, plates, bread, salad, and wine appeared. A pink-looking man in his midfifties sat to my right. He nodded, smiling, and asked me where I was from. I told him. Then he introduced himself as the delegate from Botswana. I wasn't sure where Botswana was, so I was speechless.

Mistaking me for a delegate, the man said, "I didn't see you this morning at the sessions. Did you just get here? Have you met the other members of the Latin delegation?"

I told him I was the interpreter.

"Oh," the man said frowning, and immediately turned to talk to the woman on his right.

Racist creep, I thought to myself, bunching together Botswanians and South Africans. I imitated the people buttering their rolls and sipping their wines and was about to take my first bite when a very Ivy Leaguey, lean man, stood up and introduced himself as the vice prime minister of New Zealand or something like that.

"Good afternoon, ladies and gentlemen," he said, beginning the session. "Welcome to the annual luncheon of the Third International Congress of the Security Commission of the Parliamentarians for Global Disarmament," and he extended his open palm in my direction to indicate I should start interpreting his introductory remarks. Much to my dismay I had to put down my roll and begin to interpret. "The U.N. has provided us with the services of an excellent interpreter for the members of the Latin delegation who do not speak English," he said. Everyone stared at me; I tried to smile the best I could.

The vice prime minister launched on a long and convoluted explanation of what the Parliamentarians for Global Disarmament stood for. I realized I wasn't being paid to have lunch; nonetheless the man's explanation struck me as an utter waste of time designed to prevent me from enjoying my lunch. The vice prime minister then went on to talk about the recent origins of the organization, the main resolutions of the past congresses, and the goals of the current summit. While the man pontificated, and I interpreted, the delegates gobbled their salads, bread, and wine. The vice prime minister was still talking about the importance of the organization, how necessary it was in order to keep the world from self-destructing with nuclear weapons, when the salad plates were removed and replaced by large, juicy salmon steaks and done-to-perfection steamed vegetables. The aromas of the fish, broiled in a light butter and lime sauce, and the vegetables made me dizzy. The vice prime minister concluded his peroration hyperbolically, though in a dispassionate tone: "World Parliamentarians for Global Disarmament, remember that the future of mankind is in your hands."

The delegates stopped chewing in order to clap. I reached for a glass of wine and took a long sip. I was perspiring; I had been interpreting nonstop for twenty minutes and my throat was dry. I was about to cut into my salmon steak when the vice prime minister stood up again and said, "If there are any questions, I would be delighted to answer them." I put the chunk of salmon in my mouth, praying that there'd be no questions and I could have my lunch in peace. I washed it down with a little more wine. To my enormous displeasure, the Malaysian delegate raised his hand.

"Mr. Frost," he addressed the New Zealander, "the Malaysian delegation was wondering who funds the Security Commission of the Parliamentarians for Global Disarmament."

Disgusted, I put my fork down and averted my gaze from the scrumptious lunch. Something told me that to justify their having been flown to New York for the session, some of the members felt compelled to ask all sorts of inane questions.

Looking poleaxed, Frost fidgeted before answering. "Our main backers are the Rockefeller family and the MacArthur Foundation."

"*Los Rockefellers,*" exclaimed a delegate in Spanish.

"The Rockefellers," I echoed in English, forgetting my lunch and becoming interested in the proceedings. It was the Peruvian delegate who had extrapolated thus. Who's this nut? I wondered. A member of the Shining Path?

"Had we known the imperialist Rockefeller family funded this congress, Peru would have abstained from attending," I interpreted for him, both amused and embarrassed at what I was saying. I noticed the Colombian delegate next to him. He was dressed in an

English three-piece gray suit and a red tie and he looked like an Andean cousin of Peter Lorre. The man reminded me of one of my mother's Colombian "businessmen" friends in Jackson Heights.

"The Rockefeller family," I caught Mr. Frost saying, "is very interested in nuclear disarmament, yes, sir."

The Latin delegates turned to me for an interpretation. I interpreted the last words I had heard. Then, in Spanish, I said to the delegates, "I'm sorry, but I couldn't hear what he was saying; he was talking too softly."

A Central American delegate raised her hand. Oh, my God, I thought, she's going to complain about me.

"Sir," she said, "will you please speak up so that the interpreter can hear you?"

I wanted to die right then and there. My incipient career as a U.N. interpreter was certainly over.

"Mr. Interpreter," Frost said.

"What?" I cried, jumping from my seat.

"Please, sit down, sir," Frost ordered me in his even, computer manner. "If you have trouble hearing me, please let me know."

I sat down as the marvelous salmon was being removed from my field of vision.

"What the Latin delegates want to know," said the Peruvian representative, "is what the Parliamentarians for Global Disarmament plan to do about the difficult situation in Central America."

Luscious strawberries and aromatic coffee made their appearance at the table.

"The Parliamentarians for Global Disarmament deals exclusively with the subject of nuclear disarmament. There are many other committees at the U.N. where you can bring up the concerns of Central America for discussion."

"But Mr. Chairman," the testy delegate went on, "none of the nations here present have nuclear weapons. In Latin America the threat of nuclear war is not perceived as one of our more pressing problems."

Good question, I thought, realizing that none of the nations present had the economic might to create or purchase nuclear weapons. So what were they doing here?

"Perhaps I should stress to all delegates the fact that the Parliamentarians for Global Disarmament is a nonpartisan organization. Our only concern is how to contain the spread of nuclear weapons and the threat it represents to all of mankind, not just the industrial nations. This afternoon," he said by way of concluding, "there will be many interesting sessions that all of you will find enlightening. On behalf of the United Nations, once more I extend my welcome to the third congress and I wish you all a pleasant and fruitful stay in the Big Apple."

He smiled, sat down, and attacked his dessert. Frost was obviously as hungry as I was. Although he did not live on my starvation budget, I was sure he, too, mourned the sumptuous lunch.

I ate my dessert slowly and relished the marvelously brewed Colombian coffee, second only to my mother's coffee in Queens. An hour later, after many cordials of which I did not partake, the delegates rose to leave the room. I got up to follow them and was about to exit when Frost approached me, smiling.

"Mr. Interpreter," he said in the oily, insincere manner of all politicians, "thank you very much for doing a difficult job so well."

I must have blushed, I'm sure. "Oh, thank you, sir," I said politely, thinking I should be nice to this cold fish, who in a few years would undoubtedly be ruling over a big chunk of the world.

"I will certainly recommend you to your superiors," he finished and shook my hand. Then he turned to greet a bunch of delegates from faraway countries.

As I walked back home thoughts tossed in my head like wet clothes in a tumble dryer: Had I done well? Would I be hired by the United Nations? Did I want to spend the rest of my life interpreting for those people? Interpreting at all? Being an interpreter for the rest of my life, in every aspect of my life?

In this unserene frame of mind, I arrived at the east corner of Forty-third Street and Eighth Avenue. As I looked up I shuddered, remembering the man who had killed himself yesterday. On the spot where he had landed there was still a moist black stain. As I waited for the light to change, all I could see on the other side of the street were scores of crack heads panhandling outside Paradise Alley. I felt incredible anger rise up in my throat; I was thankful at that moment

I did not own a machine gun, because otherwise I would have sprayed thousands of bullets on these vermin. Maybe I should burn the porno place one night, I thought as I crossed the street. Late at night, I would douse the premises with gasoline and light it up. Thinking these incendiary thoughts I reached my front door. I was about to go in when something pulled at the sleeve of my jacket. I swung around ready to strike whoever it was.

"Santiago, what's the matter? Are you okay?" Hot Sauce said.

"Hot Sauce," I exclaimed, breaking out of my mood and smiling. "You don't know how glad I'm to see you. If you only knew the kind of days I've been having lately."

"Man, you tell me. I'm gonna have to move my business; this block has gone to hell. Anyway," she chortled, "thanks for introducing me to Ben Ami."

"Did you hit it off? I haven't talked to him since that night."

"He's in Paris. He wanted me to go with him. He'll be back tonight, I think. Yeah, he's nice. Thanks, Santiago."

"Don't mention it. Anyway, I'd love to chat more with you but I'm anxious to get upstairs. Maybe we can get together soon, all of us."

"Wait. I don't know if I should mention this to you. But a couple of minutes ago I saw some real sleazeballs go in."

All kinds of alarms went off. To reassure myself I said, "Maybe they were George's customers."

"They didn't look Pakistani to me, if you know what I mean."

"Were they crack heads?"

"No. They looked like . . . like . . . like . . ."

"Colombians," I offered.

"Yeah, man. No offense."

"Jesus, I gotta go! This could be serious."

"If you need help, just yell."

"Thanks." I raced up the stairs; the partition door at the second floor was ajar. I went in and left it open in case I had to leave my apartment in a hurry. I sprinted up the remaining sets of steps. As I put the key in, the door caved in. "Gene, Mr. O'Donnell," I screamed, bursting into the living room.

A not-too-distant relative of the apes stood a few feet away, pointing a nasty-looking gun at me.

"Entra, pues," he said in what I recognized as a Medellín accent. "Close the door," he ordered me. Extending my arm behind my back, I slammed the door.

Jerking the gun, the man motioned me to go into the next room where I found Gene sitting at the table, still in his underwear, puffing frantically at a Marlboro, and looking scared shitless. Next to him, also armed with another revolver, sat another *paisa,* as people from Medellín are called.

I looked anxiously around the room trying to spot Mr. O'Donnell but I couldn't find him.

"Qué pasa?" was all I could say.

The seated killer, who was small, razor-thin, dark, with swarthy hands and puffy eyebags, barked, *"Este vergajo* stole a pound of cocaine. Just hand it back and nobody will be hurt. Otherwise . . ." He put the gun against Gene's temple and something told me he wasn't kidding.

"Sammy, tell them . . . I don't have it," Gene said, whining like a child about to burst into tears.

"Okay, okay," I said, knowing I had to act quickly before the electric saw appeared and our limbs started painting red spots all over the place. Yet I knew that if I gave these men the cocaine, we would be killed afterward. "Señores," I said diplomatically, trying to disguise my fear and distaste, "we'll give you back the coke. Just relax, *por favor?"*

Gene's eyes seemed about to pop out. He shook his head ever so imperceptibly as if to say no.

"The coke is in the bathroom," I said.

"Dónde?" hissed the seated simian.

"Just follow me and I'll show you."

"Get up." The killer slapped Gene's cheek with the gun's muzzle.

I went in first; the Colombian who had greeted me at the door poked the end of his gun against my tailbone. The four of us crammed into the tiny bathroom.

"It's in the water tank of the toilet." I informed them. I

removed the top of the water tank and was about to put my hand in, when the mafioso who had Gene at gunpoint hissed, *"Cuídado, it could be a trap. Dario, you get it."*

"Not me, *ave María purísima*," Dario hissed back. "There could be a snake in there."

"Okay, you get it out," the nameless man said to me.

As I put my hand in, I heard Mr. O'Donnell galloping in the other room, making quite a racket.

"What's that?" the man yelled, turning to look in the direction of the living room. Quickly, I grabbed the gun at the bottom of the tank, and, in one motion, hooked the man's neck with my left arm and stuck the dripping gun's muzzle into his mouth. "If you try anything, I'll blow your fucking brains out," I barked in my best Jimmy Cagney manner.

The other mafioso placed the gun on Gene's temple. "Drop the gun before I count to three or I'll kill the boy. One . . . two . . ."

I had no choice but to aim at the man's head and pull the trigger. The gun went *clack;* I pulled again and nothing happened.

The man I had been grabbing struggled free. *"Mátalo,"* he said, spitting on my face.

"If you kill him," Gene interjected, "I'll never tell you where the coke is, no matter what you do to me."

"What's a pound of coke?" the man said with hatred. "Kill the son of a bitch."

Well, this is it, folks, I thought, when a shrill scream pierced my ears and I heard Hot Sauce say, "Cool your bones, motherfuckers, or you're dead fish." And two shots were fired in succession at the men's feet. Gene and I jumped on top of the astonished killers and disarmed them. We herded them out of the bathroom.

"Put them hands up against the wall," Hot Sauce said, jerking the gun from man to man.

I began to frisk one man when I heard a loud stampede of heavy shoes come up the stairs. "Oh God," I said, "their friends are coming."

"Nothing doing," Hot Sauce reassured me. "It's the cops. I sent word before I came up."

"You sent for the cops?"

"Santiago, I'm an undercover agent," she explained and pulled a walkie-talkie out from under her skirt. "Hot Sauce speaking. Reinforcements have arrived at 687. Thanks. Over." She smiled at me.

Gene and I exchanged flabbergasted looks. "You should get dressed," I said to Gene as three gun-happy cops arrived on the scene. I recognized Lieutenant McGavin, with whom I had had many conversations concerning the crack heads downstairs.

"Hi, Santiago," he said, giving Gene an inquisitive stare.

"Lieutenant, this is my nephew Gene. He's staying with me for a couple of days," I said.

McGavin and the other cops were panting from the exertion of making it up to the fourth floor in a hurry. He addressed the Colombians, "Hi, fellows. You'd better have your green cards in order."

My fellow countrymen betrayed no emotions; they looked at each other as though in a daze, as if this new development was the last thing they had expected. The men were handcuffed, their rights were explained to them in English and translated by me into Spanish. Seldom had I enjoyed my role as interpreter as much as I did on this occasion.

Gene excused himself to go into the bathroom to get dressed. While the cops checked the killers' IDs and reported their findings back to headquarters, I sat anxiously, wondering what would happen next. Would I, too, be charged with illegal possession of a firearm? No, I thought; Hot Sauce saw how I got that gun. And what if the mafiosi talked? What if they snitched on Gene? Should I turn in the coke before the killers implicated me?

The report from headquarters threw the cops into a loud celebration. These men were on all sorts of most wanted lists, and had been identified as important links in one of the most powerful cocaine rings in Queens.

"Lieutenant," Hot Sauce said, "take them away and lock 'em in the can. I'll stay here with Santiago and Gene to write the report of the break-in."

As they were about to depart, Lieutenant McGavin stopped to

ponder and said, "The one question I have is why did they break in here? What were they hoping to get here?"

Confess, a voice screamed in my head. "Well, Lieutenant, I hope you . . ."

"Oh, no, no," McGavin interrupted me. "We're very aware of your efforts to try to clean up this block; you've helped us to smash one of the most vicious drug rings in America. We've been trying to catch these guys for a long time, but it's impossible if they remain in Queens. You and your nephew will have to come to the midtown precinct tomorrow or the next day and we'll have a press conference. I'm going to recommend that the mayor's office awards you the medal of civic service. You and your nephew are heroes. I wish there were more concerned citizens like you. Now, amigos," he said to the downcast drug fiends, *"vamos."*

We shook hands, expressed our thanks and said good-bye. Gene, Hot Sauce, and I were left alone in the apartment.

Hot Sauce and I lounged on the couch and Gene sat around the table. Gene, who had just now met Hot Sauce, could not get his eyes off her. Mr. O'Donnell walked into the room cautiously to make sure the commotion was over. Then he jumped on the couch, sniffed Hot Sauce, and crouched on my lap. I looked around me and saw a teenage mafioso, a Times Square hooker, and a dying alley cat, and wondered at the principals in my life.

"You have to write a report now?" I asked, still amazed she was an undercover agent.

"Oh, no. I can do that later. I just said that so I could stay here to chat with you."

"That's nice," I said. "Oh, God, I'm about to croak from hunger."

"Me too," Gene said.

"How about going out for lunch?" Hot Sauce said. "I'll treat you guys."

"Thanks a lot, but I'm too tired; I don't think I could make it down the stairs."

"We could order Chinese takeout; how's that?"

"I hate Chinese food," Gene said.

I sighed. "Well, as I said before, I'm starving."

"I know what," Gene said getting up. "I'll make lunch while you two guys talk."

I shuddered at the prospect but had no choice but to accept the offer. "I don't think there's much in the fridge."

"That's cool," Gene said. "Just leave it to me, man. I'll improvise. Lunch will be ready in five minutes. In the meantime, how about a cup of coffee? I had just made some coffee before my . . . before the *paisas* broke in."

"A cup of coffee would be lovely," Hot Sauce said. "Black, no sugar, please."

"The same for me. Thanks, Gene."

Gene served the coffee and disappeared in the kitchen. Mr. O'Donnell, who was always a persistent beggar when there was any activity in the kitchen, followed him.

"I can't get over that you're a cop, not a hooker," I said.

"Yeah, undercover agent. That's my job. We're conducting an investigation. You know, gathering enough evidence so we can shut down the crack den downstairs. But it ain't easy, Santiago. First, the place belongs to the mob so there are big bucks involved. Second, since it is a porno place, we're dealing with freedom of speech. And that's the law."

"But your real name is not Hot Sauce, is it?"

"No," she blushed. "My real name is Rosita. Rosita Levine."

"Are you Latin?"

"Do I look Latin to you? I'm a Jewish girl from Brooklyn. When I was born, my mother's best friend was from Cuba. Her name was Rosita Matamoros; so my mother named me after her best friend. Rosita means Little Rose, as you know, being an interpreter and all that. So I came up with Hot Sauce, which is a compound name, you get it now?"

"Oh, oh," I uttered, feeling more and more discombobulated all the time. In the kitchen, Gene had turned on the radio very, very loud, but through the heavy pounding of the rock music I heard the blender going on, and what sounded like a machine gun firing hundreds of bullets. The toxic fumes of hot dogs invaded the room.

"I wanted to talk to you about something else."

"Shoot," I said.

"It's about Ben. You know the way he is so . . . like romantic, you know. I'm worried that when he finds out I'm a cop instead of a hooker he won't like me no more. Watcha think?"

"Well, yeah, I don't know," I said. "I'm sure the hooker part probably seemed very . . . interesting to him. On the other hand," I said, recalling Ben's fondness for the leading lady in *Freaks*, "I also think he likes the fact that you are . . ." I didn't quite know how to put it.

"A little person."

"That's right. A little person."

"You mean there's hope? You really don't think it's over?"

"Do you like him that much?"

"I'm crazy about the guy, Santiago. He's the nicest person I've ever met. A girl like me doesn't meet too many guys like that."

Gene stuck his head out of the kitchen. "Lunch is ready. Please sit down at the table."

"Gene, hon, can I help you?" Hot Sauce offered, for the first time showing her motherly instincts.

"That's cool; it's under control."

We sat at the table while Gene brought out the place mats, dishes, silverware, napkins, and glasses. First, he produced a tray heaped with steaming hot dogs plastered with mayonnaise. Next, he brought out a pitcher of chocolate milk shake. "And the chef's masterpiece," he announced, producing a huge bowl of popcorn swimming in melted butter.

"Well?" he said, beaming, standing in front of us, fishing for compliments.

"You'll make a good husband," Hot Sauce said.

This compliment didn't go over very well with Gene. "It looks just . . . great," I lied, digging into the popcorn.

After lunch, when Hot Sauce announced she had to go, Gene informed me he was going to walk Hot Sauce back to the precinct and then was going back to Queens. I was tired and feeling so muddled that it didn't occur to me to stop him.

When I was alone in the apartment, I remembered the cocaine was still in the kitchen, so I decided to wash it down the toilet. The glass container on the shelf was empty; it had been rinsed not too long ago because the inside glass was still wet.

I had been experiencing so many contradictory emotions for the past week or so that, instead of getting frantic, I merely shrugged it off. Later, when Gene had had enough time to get back to Jackson Heights, I would call him to straighten out the situation. I felt drained; I felt as if I were dragging a dead horse behind me. I decided to lie down for a while. I picked up Mr. O'Donnell and closed the door of my bedroom and turned on the air conditioner. Mr. O'Donnell went into the closet to investigate God knows what and remained there.

This was perhaps the first moment of quiet and solitude I had had in days. I thought of Bobby, and I thought of how he was dead and it was almost as if he had never existed and that somehow did not seem right. It occurred to me that I had known Bobby for most of my life, and I had no tangible memento of him, not even a photograph, just memories, which time would eventually distort and flatten out. I made a mental note to call Joel and ask him for a picture of Bobby. Then I felt Bobby's presence next to my bed. I was sober today, not like the last time I thought I had seen him. It was invisible, whatever it was, but it felt like a warm spot in the air, throbbing to express itself. I closed my eyes. "I surrender," I said. "You can talk to me, Bobby, if that's what you want." Then I fell asleep.

In my dream, I saw Paradise Alley in flames, and hundreds of wailing crack heads trapped inside. Standing on the street curb, I watched. There were no other witnesses: no cops, no firemen, no gawking New Yorkers, nothing, nobody except myself watching them as if they were on a window display of a chamber of hell. As I watched, I started to shrink, growing smaller and smaller until I was a boy of seven or so. The scene in front of me changed: the chamber of hell turned into our house in Barranquilla, after my parents separated, but before we moved to Bogotá. I was wearing short pants, sneakers, and a cotton shirt. It was nighttime. Mother and a stranger, a foreigner, were in the living room, sitting very close. Mother wore a tight, white dress, and her hair was done and she had makeup on. She radiated sensuality. She had sent for me to introduce me to this man, who was obviously drunk. The stranger was tall, blond, heavyset, and he was sweating. His pink face revolted me. The man spoke in English and gave me some sticks of bubble gum. I accepted the gum out of politeness, but then changing my mind flung the sticks at Mother's lap and stormed out of the living room. I hid in the garden, behind some leafy *yucca* plants, where I crouched, crying. The dark night frightened me, but I was too upset to go back inside the house, and no one, not even my nanny, came out to look for me. Bolero music played and Mother's laughter rippled in rich, high-pitched notes through the tropical night, reaching me. I hated my mother for bringing this man to the house; I hated my father for abandoning us. I longed to run away to another city to become a gamin. I wished a kindly couple without children would adopt me and take me far, far away to another country.

I crouched there for what seemed an eternity, alternately feeling hungry and cold. Finally, the music and the laughing died out and lights were turned off inside. I entered the house unobserved. On the way to my bedroom I had to pass by the door of my mother's alcove. Loud moans and writhing sounds reached me and I peeked in and saw my mother and the stranger making love. Shaking with anger, I went into the next room, where Eduardito, my little brother, slept. He was nearly a year old, and had been born with a defective heart and was not expected to make it to adulthood. In a corner of the room, there was a shrine to St. Jude Thadeus, with several votive candles lit. Irrationally, I flung myself at the shrine, smashing the saint's statue on the floor and with my arms I swept the votive candles aside. Before I realized what had happened, the curtains caught on fire. Terrified at what I had done I ran out of the room and into the next bedroom, where Wilbrajan slept, and I woke her up and told her there was a fire and we left the house, Wilbrajan still half asleep. Wilbrajan started crying when she saw smoke coming out of the house and she knew that Mother and Eduardito were still inside. The maids ran out of the house coughing and crying; the neighbors woke up; and curious people stood on the street watching the house go up in flames and there were many screams and Wilbrajan cried, "Mommy, mommy, mommy," and then it struck me that my little brother was probably dead and I, too, started screaming and

. . . I woke up, Mr. O'Donnell's nose nuzzling me as if to wake me from my nightmare. I squeezed him tight against my chest. "Kitty, I'm so happy you're here," I said. "I don't know what I'd do without you." Realizing he was uncomfortable I let go of him. Mr. O'Donnell jumped onto the night table and then leaped into the air, doing a flip-flop before he plopped to the floor. He was having a horrible seizure.

The moment I had been dreading for so long had finally arrived. Mr. O'Donnell's eyes looked as if they were about to pop out of their sockets; he was foaming at the mouth, baring his teeth like a feline with rabies; his chest swelled and collapsed, gasping for air; his tail curled, and his hind legs kicked the air as if it were an invisible yet solid wall.

"Kitty," I screamed, unsure of what step to take next. I was afraid he'd bite me if I touched him. Mr. O'Donnell did not seem pathetic, broken, but phenomenally angry, as if he were locked in a fierce confrontation with death and he was unwilling to go like a wimp. I ran to the telephone and dialed Rebecca's number and got her machine. She was out; nevertheless, I left a message. "Rebecca, Mr. O'Donnell is dying. Please, come upstairs if you get home soon." I hung up and returned to my bedroom. Mr. O'Donnell's eyes had turned emerald, but the violence of the convulsions had diminished. "Mr. O'Donnell, kitty, please don't die," I said to encourage him. It occurred to me that perhaps he might be saved if I took him to the hospital; he might survive for a few days or weeks or who knows. I pulled his box out of the closet but I still didn't dare pick him up. I looked for a beach towel and covered him with it and placed him inside the box. I wrote down the hospital's address, made sure I had enough cash to pay for the taxi, and slowly made my way down the stairs, making sure the box did not rock too much. Pandora's box couldn't have made more horrifying noises.

The taxi ride to the hospital seemed interminable, as I remembered other taxi rides when I had taken him to the Humane Society to be neutered, for his shots and checkups. He'd always cry pathetically and I'd have to talk to him, sticking my fingers through the holes of the box to reassure him that I was with him and there was nothing to fear. On this taxi ride, once or twice he made shrill, piercing noises, and his paws scratched the insides of the box violently.

Arriving at the hospital, the size of the building surprised me—it seemed like a real hospital, not a toy one like the Humane Society. The woman at the reception desk took down my name, address, a brief medical history of the pet, and then gave me directions to the elevators. I went to the fifth floor where I stepped into the waiting room. A man with manic eyes approached me and told me his cat had jumped from the living room into the street seven floors below and broken two legs. Two hospital vets in white uniforms came rushing from behind glass walls and asked me to turn Mr. O'Donnell over to them so they could place him inside an oxygen tent. The man opened the box and pulled him out. My hands reached out, as if to wrestle Mr. O'Donnell away from the doctor. Mr. O'Donnell's eyes and mine met, and he gave me a look I had never seen before. He was saying at the same time, "I love you; I'm scared; don't leave me alone; good-bye." His eyes were very yellow, like lighted lanterns, and they expressed horror. I thought of Bobby, of the last look he had given me, and at that moment I understood one of the differences between man and cat: man knows he's going to die, so he can get ready and be willing, even eager, to go. A cat knows the end is near, but that's all. He can't accept death: he can't trust in it; cats are perhaps too metaphysical an entity to need to believe in the idea of a beyond; a cat is his own god and man his creation.

I sat there, numb, staring at my hands, listening to the crazy man tell me stories about his cat, the many times he had jumped before. I was grateful when the nurse came out and told me that Mr. O'Donnell was on a respirator and to call the hospital tomorrow to inquire about his condition. She was sympathetic, I thought, but it sounded like a mere formality. Downstairs, before I left the hospital, I had to finish filling out the forms. Outside I lit a cigarette and walked to the nearest subway station. It was 10:00 P.M. and the station was almost deserted. I waited, leaning against the wall of the station. As the train rumbled in, I moved forward and stared at the tracks which, as the train neared me, became conduits for rushing gold rills that were almost an invitation to jump in front of the oncoming car. I had known all along that Mr. O'Donnell's days were numbered, but now that the moment had come the notion of joining him in death was appealing.

I got off the train at Times Square, and was about to turn west on Forty-third when loud music coming from the island on Broadway between Forty-sixth and Forty-seventh streets reached my ears. I really didn't want to go home to be alone with my feelings. Welcoming any distraction, I headed for the little island where a big crowd had gathered. As I approached it, the music got louder and brassier along this stretch of Broadway. It was hard to find an inch of cement to stand on on the island. The band had stationed itself in the middle of it, between the statues of George M. Cohan and Father Duffy. Six players blew on huge instruments. It was crazy, happy honky-tonk music that could have resurrected the dead. As the players puffed their shiny cheeks and stomped their feet, swaying with their tubas and trombones, the crowd rocked sideways. Most of the spectators looked like summer tourists and suburban theatergoers, but there were also many regulars of Times Square, including myself. Black kids climbed on the large cement pots where scraggly trees grew. Everybody was smiling, and many people were clapping, surrendering to the rambunctious sounds.

Behind the band rose the red Coca Cola sign displaying geometric combinations of lines and colors; and the blazing lights of Broadway, the legendary White Way that was anything but white, had never seemed so beautiful, so glittering, so inviting, so dazzling. It was one of those rare moments when a mass of people surrender to the city, embracing everything that gets pressured out of us as we grow up and become responsible citizens and assume obligations and conform. I turned to look behind me and, to the east, a full ivory moon was poised on top of the red tip of the antenna of the Empire State Building. I stood with my back to the crowd, feeling the music surge through my veins, and rush to my head, and I thought about this island, this city, where the homeless and the rich, the powerful and the powerless, the radiant and the sick, the lovely and the hideous, the arrogant and the humble, and the crazed and the hopeful, where Blacks, Asiatics, Hispanics, WASPs, Europeans, their descendants, refugees, exiles, where people from all over the world came to, as if this were their Mecca, a Byzantium throbbing with thieves, and hookers and hustlers and murderers and suicides, and cops and tourists and stockbrokers, and the rootless and great stars and beggars, all commingling, coming together for a slice of the elusive dream these neon signs promised, for moments like this one, when the night was like red wine and it was summertime and for a moment we could forget all our wounds, all our pains.

I looked up and saw the Times Square zipper going round and round, flashing news about the weather, bankruptcies, murders, and catastrophes from all over the globe, and then, at the tail end of it, just for me, to show me that I, too, belonged here, in gold letters, against a black velvety background, through the tears that clouded my vision, I read: MR. O'DONNELL, THE MOST WONDERFUL CAT OF FORTY-SECOND STREET, DIED TONIGHT, AUGUST 2, 1990.

12

Everyone Happy in Manhattan and Mr. O'Donnell Enters Heaven

I didn't set the alarm clock for the next morning because I didn't have to work that day. I thought I would sleep at least until noon, but I awoke by ten o'clock. I realized things were different as soon as I opened my eyes; for the past two years I had gotten used to seeing Mr. O'Donnell upon waking up.

I went to the kitchen to make coffee, and the saucers on the floor, the steel comb hanging on a nail, the bag of dry food, and the cans of Kal Kan in the cupboard reminded me of him. Although I knew Mr. O'Donnell was dead, I called the hospital to make it official. The woman who gave me the news was nice and gentle; she informed me that Mr. O'Donnell had passed away last night, shortly after I had brought him in. I thanked her and hung up. I was about to return to the kitchen when the phone rang. It was Rebecca; I gave her the news.

"Actually," I said calmly, but feeling a big hole open up inside my chest, "would you like to come upstairs for a cup of coffee?"

"I'd love to."

I opened the door and waited for Rebecca to come up the stairs. She was dressed to go to work. We embraced, patting each other's backs. As the person who had found Mr. O'Donnell in the alley, she had taken the role of adoptive mother and she too had grown to love him.

We sat on the couch sipping our coffees. She was giving me such a look of commiseration that just to break up the silence, I said, "Aren't you late for work?"

"I start at noon today, but I'm going to call in sick."

"I'm okay. Really," I said, assuming she was doing this for my sake.

"I'm just sick and tired of that place. Thank God I'm going to Caracas next week." She paused. "Santiago, I have an idea. I think we should have a memorial service for Mr. O'Donnell tonight."

"Rebecca, you've got to be kidding!"

"Not at all. We owe it to him. We ought to celebrate the fact that he's gone to kitty heaven. Because I have no doubts whatsoever that that's where he is. Any old how, his friends should all get together to reminisce."

"You mean, we should have a wake?" I asked, totally astonished and wondering if Rebecca's elevator was ever going to make it to the top floor. "Anyway, what friends are you talking about?"

"Mr. O'Donnell had legions of adoring fans. He was absolutely beloved by everyone who ever came into contact with him. He was the most perfect bundle of joy that ever drew breath."

"We could invite Harry Hagin," I said, remembering the drawing he had made of Mr. O'Donnell when he had run away in the spring.

"And Francisco would come too if he were in New York," Rebecca said, not missing the opportunity to bring in her paramour. "He always said hello to the kitty in his letters, didn't he? But there are lots of other people," she prattled on. "It'll be a lovely gathering. A wake for Mr. O'Donnell as well as my bon voyage soirée. After all, I may not see you all for a long, long, long time."

"For goodness sake, Rebecca, you make it sound like you're going to Jupiter. But anyway, maybe a party is not a bad idea. It's very Colombian to celebrate someone's passing."

"Leave the details to me. I once organized the loveliest *fête champêtre* for Aunt Annabel back in Jackson. Is seven o'clock okay with you?"

I shrugged.

"You *poor* darling, you've been through so much lately. You don't have to lift a finger; I'll take care of everything. All you have to do is straighten up the place a little bit."

"I'll be here all day, if you need anything," I offered just in case.

She finished her coffee. "Thank you, doll face. Now I've got to run. There are a million pressing details that need to be attended to."

We embraced again. As soon as she left the room, I felt the full weight of my aloneness. When Mr. O'Donnell was alive, I'd always felt as if I shared the apartment with a roommate. I became aware of an uncanny silence creeping all over the house. Feeling spooked, I decided to get busy tidying up the place. I got the broom and duster out of the kitchen, but realizing how much I would have to work before the place looked decent, I was overwhelmed by the task ahead of me. I headed back for the security of the bedroom and threw myself on the bed where I tossed around despondently. I found myself staring at the spot where Mr. O'Donnell had collapsed the night before. To my horror, the image of him contorting and gasping for breath replayed in my mind's eye. I closed my eyes and when I opened them, I noticed one of his whiskers on the floor. I picked it up. It wasn't a particularly long or beautiful whisker, but I decided to put it in the box where I kept all the whiskers I had saved in the past couple of years. I ran the end of it up and down my cheeks and then I pressed it between my lips. I took all the whiskers out and spread them on my open palm, fingering them. I realized that unless I found another whisker lying around somewhere, this was the end of the collection; these were all the mortal reminders I had of my cat. I closed my fist, clutching the white, prickly things, and I broke down crying.

I spent the rest of the day tidying up the apartment, which was no small chore. I was mopping the floors when Mr. O'Donnell's loss hit me again; he loved to see the mop in action, and always attacked it as if it were a wild animal to be conquered.

Around six o'clock I was so exhausted all I wanted to do was take a nap, but Rebecca asked me to come downstairs. I could barely walk around her living room; she had bought many large arrangements of assorted flowers, a baked ham, two cases of white wine, half gallons of vodka, scotch, gin, rum, hundreds of candles, huge breads, three or four kinds of olives, what looked like an entire farmers' market of vegetables and fruits, dips, club soda, Coca Cola, diet drinks, juices, Perrier. . . .

"Have you gone crazy?" I said. "You must have spent a fortune."

"I may never get another chance to give a party in New York, so I'm gonna go hog-wild."

"I'd say. You could feed all the homeless people of New York with that spread. I thought you were just going to invite Harry Hagin."

"Wherever did you get that notion, sweetie? It's going to be a bacchanal, an authentic, honest-to-goodness hoedown. Everybody accepted, of course. And I asked everyone to bring something. I'm so excited I can barely breathe."

I was too astonished to say anything.

"Honey, are you okay? You must start taking everything upstairs," she said. "We have not a minute to waste. I have to attend to my toilette. I want to look lovelier than a catalpa tree in May."

"Who's coming besides Harry?" I managed to ask with great apprehension.

"Lucy is coming, and she's bringing some friends. And I invited Tim, and Ben, and he's bringing his new girlfriend and lots of other people are coming. The list of guests is too long to mention them all."

"My mother is coming! She hated Mr. O'Donnell, Rebecca."

"No one hated Mr. O'Donnell, Santiago. Your mother is just partial to Simón Bolívar. Besides, this is the time to let bygones be bygones."

"And what friends is she talking about?" I asked, horrified, thinking of what my mother and the matrons of Queens would make of Hot Sauce. Boy, was I ever ready to get on my high horse and fly away from Times Square! I felt so dizzy I had to sit down.

Rebecca crossed her arms and stared at me. "Santiago, honey, please don't be a party pooper and spoil my bon voyage revelry. Oh, before I forget. Let me go get it," she said leaving the room.

Now what, I thought. My life sentence?

Rebecca came back with a large plastic frame. "This is for that superb drawing Harry Hagin did of Mr. O'Donnell. Later we'll have to frame it right, but for tonight this will do, I'm afraid," she said, handing it to me. "We must have it prominently displayed in a place of honor. Now be an angel and start taking the goodies upstairs. As your cohostess I have to be ready when the first guest arrives. I wonder who will be the first person to arrive?" she said aloud, but it was obvious she was talking to herself.

My mother, of course, arrived first. And she didn't arrive with friends but with a wrapped cage that contained Simón Bolívar.

"Ay, Dios mio, virgen santísima," Mother said as we met her at the door. "Those stairs are murderous. I have to sit down before I get chest pains. Rebecca, you look divine."

Using all the Spanish at her command, Rebecca said, *"Muchas gracias,* Lucy."

"Santiago, *mijito,* I left two bags downstairs. Please get them before the junkies steal them. I don't know how you can live in this neighborhood." Realizing that Rebecca too lived in the building, she added, "It does have its advantages, of course. It's so central and so close to Broadway."

Downstairs I found two large bags which I carried up the stairs. I found Rebecca and mother lounging on the couch.

"Sammy, the place looks wonderful; the flowers make a big difference," Mother commented.

Setting the bags down, I said, "Rebecca purchased everything."

"Thank you so much, Rebecca. You're too nice to Sammy. He needs a wife soon, now that you're going to be married."

"Keep your fingers crossed. He hasn't proposed yet."

"He will, he will, trust me. If I know everything about man, this trip means wedding," she said in her highly peculiar English.

"I hope you're right."

"I never mistaken about such things, my dear. Never. Always I'm right. Plus Francisco is so nice: nobody did my hair better than he did. And we are devouts to the same saints. You make good choice, Rebecca. Now you learn Spanish. Tell you this," she added, getting carried away, "to celebrate you wedding, Sammy and I will fly to Caracas for the church ceremony. And I can visit my sister

Aurora that I had not seen in many years. I will kill two birds with one rock."

"I would be so honored if you came down for my wedding. If you do, you have to promise me right now you'll be my maid of honor."

"Of course, I will be the maid of honor! Thank you for asking, my dear." Mother turned to me. "Well, Sammy, what are you doing standing there? Take the bags to the kitchen and start unpacking. And make me an *aguardiente*. Stiff. And one for Rebecca. And one for you if you want," she added grandly, as if I were her maid.

As I unpacked the victuals, I heard Mother and Rebecca giggling in the other room. Mother had brought half a gallon of *Aguardiente Cristal,* two pineapple flans, a large plastic container full of *frijoles antioqueños* with pork, a large *jamón,* a five pound moist white Colombian cheese, guava paste, *arequipe,* stuffed figs, many odds and ends, and tapes of cumbias, *vallenatos,* and folkloric music of the Atlantic coast of Colombia.

I poured three generous shots of *aguardiente* and distributed them.

"I propose a toast to Mr. O'Donnell," Rebecca said.

Giving me a small smile, Mother said, "And not to forget your future marriage."

"Who's there?" a third voice said.

"Dios mio, mi pobrecito, Simón Bolívar," Mother said, setting down her drink to unwrap the cage, while Rebecca and I stood with our glasses raised.

With his nasty little eyes, Simón Bolívar glanced at me, then at Rebecca, and then he started looking around the room.

"You better, *cuchi cuchi?"* Mother asked.

"Lorito real, lorito real," the hideous parrot cheered.

"Now we can finish our toasts," Mother said.

"To Mr. O'Donnell," I repeated.

We had finished downing our drinks when the bell rang.

"I can't stand the excitement," Rebecca said. "I haven't had so much fun in years. Who could it be?"

It was the entire Colombian Parnassus, the muses of Queens. Olga, the shortest, carried the flowers; Carmen Elvira, the tallest, carried two boxes—one containing a cake, the other one full of cookies; and Irma, the stockiest, carried two large Balducci's bags.

"Welcome," I said at the door. "What a nice surprise to see you."

I had to bend to receive Olga's kiss. "Please, Sammy," she said, handing me the flowers. "Put them in water before they wilt."

"I'll take care of the flowers," Rebecca offered. I handed her the bunches of roses and relieved Carmen Elvira of the boxes. None of the ladies had ever met Rebecca, but Carmen Elvira, in particular, couldn't hide her curiosity.

"This is Rebecca Allevant, my neighbor," I added, so there would be no misunderstandings.

Carmen Elvira, who undoubtedly had assumed Rebecca was a secret romantic attachment of mine, immediately lost interest. The women exchanged names and pleasantries as we wandered into the living room. Mother rushed to kiss her friends. Then they settled down on the couch.

"Sammy, where are your manners?" Mother said. "Aren't you going to offer your friends a drink?"

"Yes, of course, Mother," I said, irritated at her bossy manner. "There is *aguardiente,* and Coca—"

"*Aguardiente,*" they all cried out at once.

"Sammy, I have to go downstairs to get the vases for the flowers. I don't know if I have anything appropriate for such lovely flowers. I'll be right back," Rebecca said.

I went into the kitchen with the bags. While I was unpacking the viands, I heard Mother say, "If I had known you were going to arrive so early, I would have waited for you. I had to take a taxi all the way from Jackson Heights. There was no way I could carry the food and Simón Bolívar in the subway. We could have split the ride."

In her practical banker's style Irma commented, "It's called poor planning. How typically Colombian."

"*Sí, mijita,* but you forget we are professional women and housewives, too," I recognized Olga babbling. "I had to go home straight from work so I could take the pizza out of the fridge. Pizza and Coca Cola, that's what they'll have for dinner; the cook is on strike today."

I was surprised by the contents of the bag; I had expected *pasteles, arepas, buñuelos*. But the Balducci's bags actually contained Balducci's staples: pickled salmon, black caviar, soft French cheeses, quail eggs, artichoke hearts.

"If we hadn't just been invited this morning," Irma said, "we could have chipped in to cook a terrific Colombian meal. There's nothing like our own food."

"Well, *cariño,*" Mother said. "The cat just died last night, so we cannot to plan it in advance."

I poured the *aguardiente* in the cups and brought them out on the tray.

Crossing her legs and exposing her knees, and showing both rows of teeth, Olga said, "Thank you, handsome."

"Thanks, hon," Irma said in her laconic Wall Street manner.

Always the fake, Carmen Elvira said, "Thank you so much, Sammy. You're an adoration."

Rebecca arrived with four empty bottles that would serve as vases.

"Well, Sammy," Mother said. "Don't just stand there. Show my friends you know how to be a good host. Bring out the Colombian cheese. Nothing goes better with *aguardiente* than nice white cheese."

"I'm so hungry I could eat an entire suckling pig," Irma said.

"*Ay, mujer,* all you can think about is eating. That's what comes from having such a high pressure job," Olga said. "Look at me; I keep my doll figure because I eat *poquito, poquito* and I'm happy just being a secretary. While you look positively like a *Botero,*" Olga finished cattily.

The phone rang. I asked Rebecca, who was emerging out of the kitchen with the flower arrangements, to get it. "I have to get the cheese," I told her.

I was in the kitchen cutting the cheese into tiny pieces (Colombian style), when Rebecca arrived at a run. "Santiago, it's for you," she said, flinging her hands, her eyes dancing with excitement. "It's the *New York Post.*"

Carmen Elvira, who obviously had been eavesdropping, exclaimed from the other room, "The *New York Post!* Is it Suzy? Is it Page Six?"

"I don't know," I said, coming out of the kitchen and setting the cheese down. "Please, excuse me. I'll be right back."

"Hello," I said, sure that they were calling to sell me a subscription or that this was a mistake.

"Mr. Santiago Martínez?"

I noticed that Carmen Elvira had wandered into the room and was practically breathing in my ears. "This is he."

"We'd like to send a photographer to take your picture. Tomorrow we're running the story of how you helped the police to break into the ring of Colombian drug smugglers."

I was speechless.

"We're running a story about it and we'd like to illustrate it with your picture."

"Why?"

"You're a hero, Mr. Martínez. Is it okay if we send a photographer?"

"When?"

"Now. We need the picture tonight before the paper goes to press."

Carmen Elvira's nosiness was so intense that I was afraid she'd wrestle the receiver from me if I didn't hang up. "Okay," I said. I gave the man my address and hung up.

Carmen Elvira and I locked gazes. I lit a cigarette and walked back to the living room where the guests were as silent as if they were in church. Never in my life had there been so many people eagerly waiting to hear the next words out of my mouth. Relishing my moment of triumph, I cleared my throat. "The *New York Post* is sending a photographer to take my picture. Tonight," I added for more effect.

"Yes, but why?" Carmen Elvira demanded to know.

"The *New York Post!*" exclaimed Irma.

I chose my words carefully. "Well, yesterday, two men broke into the apartment. Gene and I were here and we caught them. It turns out the police had been after these criminals for a long time."

"I declare, Santiago," Rebecca said peevishly. "This all happened yesterday, under my very own roof, and I just find out about it by a mere fluke. Some friend you are."

"Sammy was saving surprise for us to celebrate," Mother interjected. "But I know about it. Gene tells everything to his grandma last night. Of course, I didn't believe him quite completely. That boy has such imaginative head."

"We'll have to run a big article about it in *Colombian Queens*," Irma said. "It will have to be the lead article in the upcoming issue."

"But, *mijita*, the material has already gone to the printers," Olga reminded her.

"We'll just have to can something, *cariño*. Maybe the poetry," Irma said.

"Not my 'Ode to My Mother'!" Olga said. "I promised *mami* her birthday poem would be coming out in the next issue."

Carmen Elvira pulled out her tape recorder. "Sammy, buttercup, a journalist's work is never done. You must answer a few questions for me before the guests arrive."

The bell rang.

"The *New York Post* is here," Rebecca screamed.

"Oh, *virgen santísima*," Mother said, "is my hair all right?"

Trying to establish some semblance of order in the proceedings, I said, "It can't be the *Post;* it's too soon."

I was right. Ben Ami and Hot Sauce made their entrance. Ben leaned against the wall, heaving like a beached whale. He carried a large tray wrapped in aluminum foil.

"Here, Santiago, I brought a leg of wild boar," he said by way of greeting me.

I took the leg and moved aside to let him in—he was so wide he had to enter sideways. Hot Sauce walked in behind him, carrying two bottles of champagne. She wore a cotton skirt and blouse instead of her regular uniform, and her makeup was subdued, but she still looked like a Times Square hooker. I took a low bow to receive a peck on my cheek.

"*Chico*, I had forgotten about those stairs. Now I remember why I moved from here," Ben said inching forward into the living room. "*Doña Lucy, qué alegría*," he shouted to my mother. "I'm so happy to see you."

"Ben, *querido,*" Mother said, getting up and rushing over. They exchanged kisses.

"Ben brought a leg of wild boar and champagne," I said.

"That's class for you," Mother editorialized to the other guests. Then she spotted Hot Sauce.

"Allow me to make the introductions," I said, standing with the leg of wild boar in my arms, "my old friend Ben Ami Burztyn and his . . . girlfriend Rosita Levine."

"I hate Rosita. I told her she could keep Hot Sauce," Ben corrected me.

"Salsa picante," translated Olga, and mother and the Parnassus ladies started giggling. Hot Sauce looked nonplussed.

"Hi, Rebecca," Ben said, as she came out of the kitchen with a tray of hors d'oeuvres.

"Hi, Ben. I'll be in Caracas next week," she said, offering him a morsel.

"She's getting married," Mother informed him.

"Felicitaciones, Rebecca," Ben said, hugging her and the tray against his belly. "Hot Sauce," he said, letting go of Rebecca, "hand me those bottles. This calls for a toast. Champagne for everyone. This is," he shouted the name in French, "and it costs one thousand dollars per bottle," he boasted in typical nouveau riche Venezuelan manner.

Always the southern belle, Rebecca said to me, "But we don't have champagne glasses."

Hot Sauce came to my rescue. "Paper cups will do."

I set the leg of wild boar on the table and went into the kitchen to get the cups. The corks were popped, the champagne poured and all glasses were raised. "To Rebecca's happiness," Ben proposed.

"To Rebecca's happiness," we all chimed in.

"And I have an announcement to make," Ben said, passing the bottles around once more. "Hot Sauce and I got engaged tonight. Show them the ring, Hot Sauce."

Extending her arm, Hot Sauce flashed a diamond ring the size of a sugar cube.

"Oh, oh, ah, my, oh, ah," shrieked the ladies like excited teenyboppers.

We toasted their engagement.

The toasts finished, Ben asked me to carve the leg of wild boar. I was on my way to the kitchen when Carmen Elvira approached Ben.

"Your engagement is big news to the readers of *Colombian Queens,*" she said. "I wonder if you'd be so kind as to answer a few questions for me."

When I came out of the kitchen, mother, Rebecca, Olga, Irma, and Hot Sauce were all snuggled on the couch in animated conversation. Ben and Carmen Elvira were seated at the table. As I began to serve the wild boar, Carmen Elvira, talking to her tape recorder, said, "Ben Ami Burztyn, the peripatetic scion of our sister Republic of Venezuela, has announced his engagement tonight at a reception given by his great pal, Colombia's poet laureate, Santiago Martínez Ardila."

The bell rang and, much to my disappointment, I had to stop eavesdropping to go meet the arriving guests.

"Yeah, I haven't been up these stairs since I was a young girl." I recognized the familiar basso voice of Mrs. O'Donnell coming up the stairs. And she was not alone! Mrs. O'Donnell's medusa head appeared at the landing of the third floor. I took two steps back. My God, I thought, she's coming with her sons and the cops to evict me.

I was about to run back into the apartment and shut the door, when I heard her boom, "Santiago, come down here and give me a hand."

I lurched forward. Mrs. O'Donnell was carrying a heavy tray. Behind her, I spotted Tim Colby. I felt my legs shake as I went down the stairs to meet them.

"Here," Mrs. O'Donnell said, handing me a heavy, warm tray. "It's chili con carne; I made it this afternoon. Sorry to hear about the cat."

It occurred to me that she had been the first person to offer her condolences. "Thank you," I mumbled, feeling my face blush. "It's nice to see you."

"Well, yeah. I know if Lucy hadn't called me about the wake, you'd never have invited me. Is she here?"

"Oh, yes. She'll be so glad to see you. Hi, Tim," I said to my agent.

Mrs. O'Donnell added, "I had to ask this nice gentleman to help me bring up the beer. Now move aside so I can get upstairs."

I smiled at Tim. Slowly, Mrs. O'Donnell made her way to the top of the landing. I waited until she had gone through the door before I let out a loud sigh.

"Tim, she gave me the scare of my life. I thought she was coming upstairs with eviction papers."

"Nah," Tim said. "She likes you. By the way, sorry to hear about," he whispered Mr. O'Donnell's name. "But cheer up. I have great news for you."

"What?" I said as I started walking up the stairs with the hot chili.

"The editor I told you about is crazy about the idea."

"What idea?"

"Writing a thriller about Christopher Columbus. She pointed out that 1992 is around the corner, so there'll be a big hoopla about it. We're talking big bucks, my friend."

We had arrived at the landing. "Well, I hope so," I said. "I'm tired of Eighth Avenue."

"You'll never have a better landlady," Tim said. "When I ran into her at the door she asked me if I was coming to the wake and then she asked me who I was. When I told her I was your agent she asked me if I could pay your back rent. I said, 'Don't worry. He's going to be rich soon.' And I told her the story of García Márquez and his landlady in Paris. She said, 'García who?' And I said, 'You know, the guy who wrote *One Hundred Years of Solitude*.' And she says to me, get a load of this Santiago, she says, 'If it hasn't been made into a miniseries, I don't know it. I'm too busy to read books.'" Tim broke up laughing. "Oh, man, that's a story for an anthology."

It was a mildly amusing story, I thought. But I wondered if he would have found it so funny if she had been his landlady. "I need an *aguardiente*," I said to Tim.

As I walked into the apartment, the phone rang. "Tim, please take the beer to the kitchen and make yourself at home. I have to answer the phone."

I set down the chili and picked up the receiver. "Hello," I said.

"Is this Santiago Martínez?" the unmistakable voice of the overseas operator asked.

"Speaking."

"A call from Caracas."

"Okay, go ahead."

"Santiago, es Francisco."

"Hola, Francisco."

"I'm sorry to hear about Mr. O'Donnell."

Between the long distance static and the raucous noises coming from the living room, I was having a lot of trouble hearing him. "It's very sweet of you to call," I screamed.

"I lit a candle for him," Francisco said.

"Thanks, Francisco," I said, sincerely touched.

"I loved that cat; he was so special. *Qué gato, chico. Qué gato.*"

This conversation was making me sad. "Rebecca is here. Would you like to talk to her?"

"Yes, please. If you don't mind."

I placed my hand on the receiver. "Rebecca," I shouted, "long distance from Caracas."

Like a drive-in waitress on roller skates, Rebecca sailed into the room with a tray heaped with delicacies. "Is it Francisco? Is it?" she asked.

"Do you know anybody else in Caracas, silly?"

"Francisco, Francisco, *mi amor,*" she cooed, dropping the tray on the desk and yanking the phone from me.

I grabbed Rebecca by the hand and led her into my bedroom, where I closed the door. I picked up the extension phone and we sat on the bed.

"Palomita adorada," Francisco said. "I have great news," I interpreted. "My client has been elected Miss Venezuela."

"Felicitaciones," I said, overstepping my boundaries as interpreter. I interpreted for Rebecca.

"I'm going to be very, very successful," Francisco said. "Now I can offer you the life you deserve, *mi reina.* Will you marry me?"

"I'm faint," Rebecca exclaimed, placing the receiver on her breasts and closing her eyes.

"Rebecca, qué pasa?" asked Francisco.

"I think she's fainting," I said. "But I'm sure that means yes," I interpreted.

"Sí, sí, sí, mi amor," Rebecca gushed, opening her eyes. Then she threw herself at me and started kissing me.

"She's kissing me," I informed Francisco.

"Oh, I'm not jealous, Santiago. Will you be our best man? *Chico,*" he added, "you can move to Caracas and live with us."

The idea of being an interpreter indefinitely to the lovey-doves was not very enticing. "That's very kind of you," I said. "But I think you should learn a language in common first."

"Rebecca," Francisco said, ignoring my suggestion, "I'm counting the minutes till you arrive."

"Okay, I'd better go now," Francisco said. *"Adiós,* Santiago. Sorry to hear about Mr. O'Donnell. Bye, Rebecca my love."

"Adiós," she sighed.

"Ciao," I threw in to break the linguistic monotony.

Rebecca leaped off her feet, took the tray and rushed in the direction of the living room. I trotted after her.

"He proposed," Rebecca screamed upon entering the room.

"See, I know everything about man," Mother screamed back, running over to kiss Rebecca.

The guests cheered and clapped and toasted. I noticed Carmen Elvira was still interviewing Ben, but had lost interest in him and was now eyeing Tim. "One last question," she said. "Are you still on friendly terms with Bianca Jagger?"

I was dying to hear Ben's answer, when Mother shouted, "Santiago, bring out the *aguardiente* bottle."

As I came out of the kitchen with the booze, Carmen Elvira approached me.

"Sammy, darling," she said in her most ingratiating manner. "I want you to know that everything is just hunky-dory." Now that she had flattered me she came out with what was really on her mind. "Will you please introduce me to your agent?" Seeing my resistance, she added, "I want to interview him for the magazine. Besides," she argued further, "now that we're about to publish our book of poems (with your translations, of course), we need representation. I hear it's very difficult to crack the American market without an agent."

"Sammy, the *aguardiente*," Mother called.

"Sure," I said, and walked over to where Ben and Tim were chatting. Ben made a face as he saw Carmen Elvira approach, but nonetheless I made the introduction and refreshed their drinks. I walked over to where Mother and Hot Sauce were merrily gabbing away. "Here, Mother," I said, handing her the *aguardiente* bottle. "You can keep the bottle by your side, okay?"

"Okeydokey," she said, and I could see she was completely sauced.

The bell rang. I went to the door to receive my guests. I heard Gene's thunderous steps coming up the stairs. Good, I thought, I have quite a few questions to ask him. Looking down, I saw Gene and behind him Wilbrajan and Stick Luster's golden curls. Behind Stick trudged Harry Hagin, carrying a wrapped package.

"Hi, Sammy," Gene greeted me. Giving me a crushing hug, he whispered in my ear, "I washed the coke down the drain. So be cool." Then he went through the living room door.

Much to my surprise, Wilbrajan looked radiant and happy. She offered me her cheek to kiss, though reticently, as if I had the flu, or worse.

"Hi, Sister," I said.

"Sammy, Sammy," Stick Luster said, giving me a bear hug. "I'm so happy to see you, my friend."

"Come, Stick," Wilbrajan said haughtily, taking Stick by his arm and dragging away my childhood friend before I could say anything to him.

"Man, do I have a surprise for you," said a beaming Harry Hagin as he reached the top of the stairs.

"Oh, yeah. What is it?"

"You got to wait, okay?"

Knowing that it would please him, I said, "I finally framed Mr. O'Donnell's drawing."

"You're catching on."

Two vaguely familiar women arrived at the landing downstairs. "Who are those women?" I asked.

Harry gave them a quick inspection, and with his artist's intuition pronounced, "You know, they're . . . up to something." He went in and left me to deal with the strangers.

Are they old acquaintances of my mother I've forgotten? I wondered as they climbed the stairs.

"We fooled you," cried out Claudia, laughing and clapping her hands. She and Paulina were in disguise! They wore matching outfits: black skirts, white cotton blouses, and sneakers. Claudia hid behind black-rimmed glasses, a short brown wig, no makeup and no jewelry except for a modest gold chain with a cheap trinket.

Mother and daughter looked like Latin Jehovah's Witness missionaries. "Where's the Bible?" I kidded them.

"Man, I knew you'd get it," Claudia roared, slapping my shoulder. Her appearance had changed, but not her manner.

"Mijito, they're after us," Paulina whispered, looking behind her back. "We came because we know how much this means to you."

"We're getting the fuck out of this town tonight," Claudia elaborated. "You're welcome to come with us."

"I told Lucy that now that the cat's dead nothing is holding you here in New York. *Virgen del Carmen,* the joint is jumping. Come, Claudia, let's go in. *Muchacha,* don't get out of my sight for a minute. You hear me?"

Claudia winked and blew me a kiss as they went in. I closed the door behind them.

Mother's *cumbia* tapes were blaring, and Gene was lighting dozens of candles on the table. Ben and Tim chatted on the couch, and all the ladies surrounded Harry Hagin, who stood in front of Mr. O'Donnell's framed drawing which now hung in the living room.

"Here, have an *aguardiente,*" Rebecca said solicitously to Harry.

"Mr. Hagin, would you be so gracious as to answer just a few questions for the readers of our magazine?" asked Carmen Elvira.

Seeing Harry hesitate, Irma threw in, "We'll put you on the cover. We print fifty thousand copies of *Colombian Queens.* A profile in our magazine guarantees instant celebrity."

"I don't know if you're aware of the fact that there are many important Colombian art collectors," Olga said, referring no doubt to the coke kingpins who buy all the trendiest painters.

Paulina said, "Mr. Hagin, we just bought an apartment at Trump Tower. We already have a Salle, a Schnabel, a Keifer, and all the Italians, but we'd love to have a large painting of yours."

"I'll have to dip seriously into my savings," Mother said, "but I can pay a good price for a painting of Simón Bolívar."

"Thank you, Lucy. You can have my paintings for nothing. But I just don't paint parrots."

"Two thousand dollars," Mother insisted.

"Actually, I brought Santiago a present," Harry said.

"What? What is it?" asked Carmen Elvira.

"It's an oil painting. An homage to Mr. O'Donnell."

Everyone present looked in the direction of Mrs. O'Donnell. Her eyes widened thinking a portrait of her late husband was going to be unveiled. Then everyone looked at me.

"Ben, Tim, Gene," Rebecca called to break up the tension. "Harry is going to unveil his latest masterpiece."

"We have to toast to the unveiling," Mother said, pouring a big shot of *aguardiente* into Mrs. O'Donnell's glass.

"Watch it, Grandma," Gene said. "You're gonna get everybody shitfaced."

Harry finished unwrapping the painting. All the ladies, including Mrs. O'Donnell, looked at me with envious eyes.

"Oh, oh," Mother opined, "it's just beautiful."

"Pure Edgar Allan Poe," boomed Ben Ami.

"It's, like, so downtown," said Claudia.

"That's the baddest painting I've seen," Gene said.

"It's a masterpiece," sighed Paulina. "We want one just like that for Trump Tower." Maybe she realized I wasn't going to marry Claudia, and she thought perhaps this way she could get Harry to solve her problem.

"It's definitely appearing on our cover," said Olga. "We'll print seventy-five thousand copies."

The canvas was an expressionistic rendition of Mr. O'Donnell wearing some kind of crown, and with a real rat's skeleton glued to his mouth.

"What does the crown mean?" asked Mrs. O'Donnell.

"It's a halo," Harry explained. "The painting is called *Mr.*

O'Donnell Enters Heaven. I hope it'll always keep Sammy's memory green."

"But Harry," I demurred, "it must be very valuable."

"Someday it will hang in the Museum of Modern Art," Harry said.

Squealing and jumping up and down, Olga announced, "We have a tribute to Mr. O'Donnell, too."

"Irma will recite the elegy," Carmen Elvira said.

"How poetic," Mother mused aloud.

"Oh, God," I heard Wilbrajan snort.

"Colombians are most poetic people," Stick pronounced.

Harry put the painting on the table, leaning against the wall. Some of the guests sat down, Mother turned off the *cumbias,* and the rest of the audience stood with their backs against the walls.

Standing in the middle of the room, Irma began. "Ladies and gentlemen, this is the first collaborative effort of The Colombian Parnassus in Shakespeare's mother tongue. Also, please excuse my pronunciation." She closed her eyes, placed her hands on her Rubenesque breasts, and began:

> For we will honor Santiago's cat Mr. O'Donnell.
> For he was the best cat in Times Square.
> For he was from the alley but loved opera.
> For he was a foe to rats and mice.
> For he loved his owner and was loved in return.
> For his heart was too big.

"It has a familiar sound," I whispered to Tim, who was standing next to me.

"It's a rip-off of Christopher Smart's 'Rejoice in the Lamb,' " Tim informed me.

Fortunately, the elegy was shorter than Smart's original, and Irma was now bringing it to a conclusion with:

> For he's alive in Heaven.
> For God loves Mr. O'Donnell.
> For now he's been immortalized by Art.

The applause was thunderous. After receiving and giving zillions of kisses and hugs, Irma approached Tim. "What do you think, Mr. Colby?" she asked, obviously eager for his approval.

Always the gentleman and the diplomat, Tim said, "It's very appropriate. Congratulations."

"Tim loved it," Irma announced loudly to her fellow muses.

Rebecca was going around the room distributing printed matter. "This is a memento of the occasion," she said to me, handing me a sheet with an engraved photograph of Mr. O'Donnell. Under it were the dates Summer 1988 (when she had found him in the alley) and August 1990. Beneath the dates, in gothic calligraphy, was Albert Schweitzer's "A Prayer to Animals."

Rebecca asked for a moment of silence so she could read her farewell prayer to Mr. O'Donnell.

"Wait a minute," Mother said. "I always pray on my knees."

Gene gave her a hand and she kneeled, setting a lighted candle in front of her. Paulina and Mrs. O'Donnell joined her.

We all read: "Hear our humble prayer, O God, for our friends the animals." Rebecca read beautifully. We finished with, "Make us, ourselves, to be true friends to animals and so to share the blessings of the merciful."

A moment of silence followed. Still on her knees, Mother was the first to speak. "I can't get over we have a wake to Mr. O'Donnell and not to Bobby who died a few days past and now is like he never was alive. For my very own part," she went on, getting up, "I think it's a useless thing to try to impress a cat. I love my two cats because they killed mouses, and they in return put up with me because I open cans for them, I'm sure."

Striking a melodramatic pose, Wilbrajan stepped forward. Oh, my God, I thought, she's going to sing one of her gloomy tangos. Instead, she said, "Let's have a minute of silence for Bobby who can't be physically here, although he's with us in spirit." Even those who had never met Bobby bowed their heads. In the reigning silence I heard stifled sobs. I was about to raise my head and wipe the tears when the bell rang. "Who could it be?" I pondered aloud. "Everyone is here."

"It's the *Post*," Rebecca screamed.

"The *Post*," parroted Paulina, horrified, "Why?"

"For Sammy and Gene help to smash the ring of drugs," Mother told her.

"Claudia, *muchacha*," Paulina screamed. "We cannot have our pictures in the papers."

"I don't know what the big deal is," Wilbrajan sneered. "My picture has been in the *Post* and the *Daily News*."

I said to the Urrutias, "You can hide in my bedroom while they take the pictures. Just close the door and it will be fine."

Mother and daughter left the scene, and I opened the door. Two *New York Post* photographers shot their flashes at me.

"Please, come in," I said.

"You're Santiago Martínez, right?" a photographer queried. "Is your nephew here, too? We'd like to get a picture of the two of you if possible."

"Don't forget the cat," the other photographer added. "What's going on here anyway, a party?"

"The cat's dead; we're having a wake for him," I said.

"That's a real human interest story. Is that a Colombian custom? Wow! What a story." The man began to fiddle with his cameras.

Carmen Elvira handed two drinks to the men.

"What is it?" asked a photographer, taking his glass and examining the contents.

"*Aguardiente Cristal,*" Carmen Elvira told them.

"Firewater," uttered one photographer. "It's like tequila or something like that, right?" He wolfed down his drink. "Thanks, lady," he said to a flirtatious Carmen Elvira.

We entered the living room where silence reigned, and everyone was on their best behavior, with the exception of Wilbrajan, who somehow had managed to get everyone off the couch where she lounged seductively like one of Goya's *majas.*

"I'm Gene," my nephew introduced himself to the photographers. "I helped Sammy catch the drug smugglers. It was like this. I was here all alone . . . like really alone with the cat. You know what I mean?"

"I hear you. You were here alone," the man said. "Now please stand up against the wall," he ordered Gene and me. Then, noticing Harry's painting, he said, "What's that? A painting of the cat? Maybe you should hold the painting between the two of you."

"Great shot," agreed his partner.

"Watch it, man. Handle with care. That painting is still wet," Harry said.

"Is that the painter?" the photographer inquired.

"That's right," I said.

The photographers took a couple of photos of Harry and his painting.

"I wish my mom were still alive to see this," Harry commented.

Now the men turned to Gene and me. We positioned ourselves at either side of the painting.

"Be sure you like print my full name and everything," Gene told the men. "And like don't forget to say I'm an actor. Is that cool?"

When the picture was taken, the photographers were rewarded with another round of drinks. Ben commissioned the men to take a group photograph. Although Wilbrajan was quite miffed she had not been asked to pose for the men, she graciously consented to be part of the group composition. Saying they had to rush to have the pictures developed for the morning edition, the *Post* men exited.

As soon as the strangers left, Claudia and Paulina emerged from the bedroom and Mother began to play her *cumbia* tapes again, and the party went into full swing. Taking Simón Bolívar out of his cage, she perched him on a finger and, grabbing a lit candle with the other hand, she began circling the room, singing along with the tape, *"La cumbia cienaguera que se baila sabrosona."* Mother was totally lit but happy. Grabbing a candle (Colombian style), Gene became her partner and, bending his knees, he started circling around her like a rooster courting a hen. Paulina was the next guest to grab a candle, and she chose as her partner Mrs. O'Donnell, who, to my utter astonishment, needed no prodding to join in. Saying that he hadn't danced *cumbia* since he was a child, Stick took my reluctant sister by the hand and they attached themselves to the end of the line that, led by Mother and Gene, was heading toward the front of the apartment. Ben Ami and Hot Sauce, Olga and Irma, Harry and Rebecca, Tim Colby and Carmen Elvira eventually tagged in. Finally, only Claudia and myself were left alone in the room.

I was standing with my back to the windows when Claudia approached me. It occurred to me I should ask her to dance.

"No, man. *Cumbia* is so corny. I'd rather talk to you. What's out there?" She pointed to the alley.

"The fire escape," I said. "Want to go out?"

"Yeah, let's do that."

I opened the gates and went out first; then I gave her my hand to help her come through the window. We stood close together on the platform of the fire escape, looking into the dark alley and a patch of black-coated sky. The air reeked of the uncollected garbage in the alley, but it was cooler than in the apartment where the lit candles created a lot of heat. We sat down in silence and Claudia rested her head on my shoulder. I was feeling a bit uncomfortable with the closeness of this forced intimacy when Claudia said, "Hey, look at that." She pointed to the building opposite the fire escape. Reinhardt, wearing tiny red bikini underwear, stood in front of his window waving at us.

"Do you know him?" she said.

"We've talked once."

"Oh, so you're friends."

"Not really. I told you: We spoke once. That's all."

"I knew you were kinky."

"Oh, come on, Claudia," I protested. "It's not at all what you're thinking of."

"Anyway, Sammy. What are your plans now that the cat is dead? Rebecca is going away. You just can't live above O'Donnell's bar for the rest of your life," she said. "Now there's nothing standing between you and me. Why don't you come with us to Europe?"

"Oh, thanks a lot . . . but just because Mr. O'Donnell is dead, doesn't mean anything's changed."

"That's what you think. Nothing ever remains the same for

more than a minute. It's some law of physics or something. Yay!"
she cheered abruptly. A show of strobe lights and rock music went
on in Reinhardt's apartment as he danced seductively for us, with a
hand inside his bikini underwear.

"He's humpy," Claudia said, putting an arm around my shoulders. "Oh, what a turn-on, Santiago. I just feel like jumping your
bones and smoking."

Actually, out of her punk costume, I found her appealing, less
intimidating. I was pondering this when I saw her parted lips approaching my face. We kissed on the mouth, lips closed. Yet nothing
happened: it felt like when I used to kiss Mr. O'Donnell on his cold
nose. I turned to look inside the apartment—Carmen Elvira stood
behind the window smiling at us and scribbling furiously on her pad.

The last guest left well past midnight. I started to clean up right
away but was too exhausted. I sat on the couch by the window. I
looked across the valley. Reinhardt appeared at his window, completely naked and with a hard-on. He stood there without gesticulating, looking in my direction with great concentration. I got up, went
to the phone and dialed his number.

"Reinhardt, it's Santiago," I said, feeling a hot wave come over
me. "If you want to, you can come over tonight."

Something crawling across my chest woke me up. In my
half-awake state, I brushed it aside thinking it was Mr. O'Donnell.
Then I remembered Mr. O'Donnell was dead and I opened my
eyes completely: the lean and long body of Reinhardt lay next to
mine. He breathed gently, like a child. I moved my nose within
inches of his, to drink in the air he exhaled. It smelled sweet—
like rose water. The room was cool from the air-conditioning and
he was deep in his sleep. All of a sudden, seeing this stranger on
my bed, I wanted to run away and to be by myself. I covered his
body with a sheet, pressed my lips on his and went to the kitchen
where I put on the Mr. Coffee. While I was leaning against the
sink, waiting for the coffee, I spotted Mr. O'Donnell's china on
the floor and decided to put it away. I emptied the saucers in the
trash can and stacked the dishes in the sink. Next, I decided to

get rid of the contents of his litter box. I put the empty box in the bathtub so I could wash it later.

Sitting on the couch, I savored a couple of cups of coffee. In true August form, the weather had turned warm and sticky again. I didn't have any jobs lined up for the day, so I was free to go back to bed or to do anything I wanted. I wondered whether I should wake up Reinhardt or let him sleep for as long as he wanted; or whether I should go back and get in bed with him. This I wanted to do: to hold his warm body in mine, to exchange a kiss like the night before, which seemed to last for half an hour. It was the wildest and the tenderest act I had ever engaged in. Of course I had had sexual contacts off and on with anonymous men. But this was quite different. Reinhardt was my neighbor and, after teasing each other for a long time, I felt I knew him intimately—even though I didn't know the first thing about him. Did the fact that we had been to bed mean that he was now my boyfriend? Would we ever do it again? I didn't have a clue about any of these things. I wished Bobby were still alive and I could call him and ask him these questions. Rebecca was not homophobic, but did she know anything about gay men? What was very clear to me this morning was that after all the revelations of the past few days, my life was about to change. I didn't know what any of it meant; but for the first time ever, I felt grown up, ready to leave behind the shackles of the past.

A scratching noise distracted me from my galloping thoughts. I looked around the room but didn't see anything. I decided to remove the screens on the windows. Now that Mr. O'Donnell was dead, there was no need for them. As I approached a window, I thought I spotted something on the fire escape: a pigeon, a rat? I removed the screen to see what it was. A small, gray-and-white cat, looking very scared, stared at me with large, curious green eyes. We both froze. When I could breathe again, I said, very gently, "Hi, kitty. Come in. It's okay." His shyness disappeared and, in one motion, he jumped through the open window and landed on the couch. "Meow," he said. "Meow." It occurred to me that perhaps when Mr. O'Donnell had escaped in the spring he had mated with one of the cats in the alley, and this was part of the litter. I leaned forward and offered him my open palm. He sniffed the tips of my fingers and, smelling his father, tapped my hand with his paws before stepping onto it. Bringing the little furry purring machine to my face, I said, "Your name is . . . Christopher Columbus." Then I kissed his face. He purred and purred shamelessly, just like his father.

NVI
SANTA
BIBLIA

[La Biblia para todos]

Contenido

TABLA DE PESAS, MEDIDAS Y MONEDAS

Las equivalencias son aproximadas.

ANTIGUO TESTAMENTO

No se incluye aquí una tabla de unidades monetarias porque los hebreos no acuñaron monedas antes del exilio. Cuando la NVI usa la palabra «moneda», se trata de una unidad de peso, principalmente el *siclo*. (Nótese también que en el libro de Ezequiel las relaciones entre las medidas son un poco diferentes.)

Medidas de peso

talento (= 60 minas)	33 Kg.
mina (= 50 siclos)	550 gr.
siclo (= 2 becás)	11 gr.
pim (= 2/3 siclos)	7 gr.
becá (= 10 guerás)	5,5 gr.
guerá	0,5 gr.

Medidas de longitud

caña/vara (= 6 codos)	2,70 m.
codo (= 2 palmos)	45 cm.
palmo (= 3 palmos menores)	22,5 cm.
palmo menor (= 4 dedos)	7,5 cm.
dedo	1,9 cm.

Medidas de capacidad: áridos

coro = jómer (= 2 létec)	220 litros
létec (= 5 efas)	110 litros
efa (= 3 seah)	22 litros
seah (= 1/3 de efa)	7,3 litros
gómer	2,2 litros
cab (= 1/18 de efa)	1,2 litros

Medidas de capacidad: líquidos

coro (= 10 batos)	220 litros
bato (= 6 hin)	22 litros
hin (= 12 log)	3,7 litros
log	0,3 litros

NUEVO TESTAMENTO

La única unidad de peso que se usa en el Nuevo Testamento es la *litra* (= la libra romana), con una equivalencia aproximada de 327 gr.

Medidas de longitud

milla (= 8.3 estadios)	1.500 m.
estadio (= 100 brazas)	180 m.
braza (= 4 codos)	1,80 m.
codo	45 cm.

Medidas de capacidad: áridos

coro	370 litros
sata	22 litros
joinix	1 litro

Medidas de capacidad: líquidos

metreta	39 litros
bato	37 litros

Monedas

Es extremadamente difícil dar el valor de las monedas antiguas con equivalencias modernas. Un denario era el salario de un obrero por un día de trabajo.

talento	60 minas
mina	100 denarios
dracma	denario
denario	10 asaria
asarion	4 cuadrantes
cuadrante	2 lepta
lepton	1/80 de denario

Prefacio

La **Nueva Versión Internacional** es una traducción de las Sagradas Escrituras elaborada por un grupo de expertos biblistas que representan a una docena de países de habla española, y que pertenecen a un buen número de denominaciones cristianas evangélicas. La traducción se hizo directamente de los textos hebreos, arameos y griegos en sus mejores ediciones disponibles. Se aprovechó, en buena medida, el trabajo de investigación y exégesis que antes efectuaron los traductores de la *New International Version*, traducción de la Biblia al inglés, ampliamente conocida.

Claridad, fidelidad, dignidad y elegancia son las características de esta nueva versión de la Biblia, cualidades que están garantizadas por la cuidadosa labor de los traductores, reconocidos expertos en los diferentes campos del saber bíblico. Muchos de ellos son pastores o ejercen la docencia en seminarios e institutos bíblicos a lo largo y ancho de nuestro continente. Más importante aun, son todos fervientes creyentes en el valor infinito de la Palabra, como revelación infalible de la verdad divina y única regla de fe y de vida para todos.

La alta calidad de esta **Nueva Versión Internacional** está, además, garantizada por el minucioso proceso de traducción en el que se invirtieron miles de horas de trabajo de los traductores a quienes se asignaron determinados libros; de los revisores, que cuidadosamente cotejaron los primeros borradores producidos por los traductores; de los diferentes comités que, a su vez, revisaron frase por frase y palabra por palabra el trabajo de los traductores y revisores; y de los lectores que enviaron sus observaciones al comité de estilo. A este comité le correspondió, en última instancia, velar para que la versión final no solamente fuera exacta, clara y fiel a los originales, sino digna y elegante, en conformidad con los cánones del mejor estilo de nuestra lengua.

Claridad y exactitud en la traducción y fidelidad al sentido y mensaje de los escritores originales fueron la preocupación fundamental de los traductores. Una traducción es clara, exacta y fiel cuando reproduce en la lengua de los lectores de hoy lo que el autor quiso transmitir a la gente de su tiempo, en su propia lengua. Claridad, exactitud y fidelidad no significan necesariamente traducir palabra por palabra o, como se dice ordinariamente, hacer una traducción literal del texto. Las estructuras fonológicas, sintácticas y semánticas varían de una lengua a otra. Por eso una traducción fiel y exacta no solamente tiene que tomar en cuenta la lengua original, sino también la lengua receptora. Esto significa vaciar el contenido total del mensaje en las nuevas formas gramaticales de la lengua receptora, cuidando de que no se pierda «ni una letra ni una tilde» de ese mensaje (Mt 5:18). Para lograrlo los traductores de esta **Nueva Versión Internacional** han procurado emplear el lenguaje más fresco y contemporáneo posible, a fin de que el mensaje de la Palabra divina sea tan claro, sencillo y natural como lo fue cuando el Espíritu Santo inspiró el texto original. A la vez han cuidado de que el lenguaje de esta **Nueva Versión Internacional** conserve la dignidad y belleza que se merece la Palabra inspirada. Términos y expresiones que ya han hecho carrera entre el pueblo cristiano evangélico, y que son bien entendidos por los lectores familiarizados con la Biblia, se han dejado en lo posible intactos. Se han buscado al mismo tiempo nuevos giros y expresiones para comunicar lo que en otras versiones no parecía tan evidente. Se ha añadido además un **glosario** que explica el significado de términos que en el texto están precedidos por un asterisco; se trata de términos poco conocidos o difíciles de traducir. Esperamos que todo esto, más un buen número de notas explicativas al pie de página, sea de gran ayuda al lector.

En las notas al pie de página aparecen las siguientes abreviaturas:

Lit. (traducción literal): indica una posible representación más exacta, aunque no necesariamente más clara, del texto original, la cual puede ser de ayuda para algunos lectores.

Alt. (traducción alterna): indica que existen otras posibles traducciones o interpretaciones del texto, las cuales cuentan con el apoyo de otras versiones o de otros eruditos.

Var. (variante textual): se usa solamente en el Nuevo Testamento, e indica que hay diferencias entre los manuscritos neotestamentarios. La traducción se basa en el **texto crítico griego** actual, que da preferencia a los manuscritos más antiguos. Cuando se dan diferencias sustanciales entre este texto crítico y el texto tradicional conocido como *Textus Receptus*, la lectura tradicional se incluye en una nota, como variante textual. Otras variantes importantes también se incluyen en esta clase de notas.

En el Antiguo Testamento, las diferencias textuales se indican de otro modo. La base de la traducción es el *Texto Masorético* (TM), pero en algunos pasajes se ha aceptado una lectura diferente. En estos casos, la nota incluye entre paréntesis la evidencia textual (principalmente en las versiones antiguas) que apoya tal lectura; luego se indica lo que dice el TM.

Además, en el Antiguo Testamento se ha usado el vocablo SEÑOR para representar las cuatro consonantes hebreas que constituyen el nombre de Dios, es decir, *YHVH*, que posiblemente se pronunciaba *Yahvé*. La combinación de estas cuatro consonantes con la forma reverencial *Adonay* («Señor» sin versalitas) dieron como resultado el nombre «Jehová», que se ha usado en las versiones tradicionales. En pasajes donde *YHVH* y *Adonay* aparecen juntos, se ha variado la traducción (p.ej. «SEÑOR mi Dios»).

Otra diferencia entre la **Nueva Versión Internacional** y las versiones tradicionales tiene que ver con la onomástica hebrea. En el caso de nombres propios bien conocidos, esta versión ha mantenido las formas tradicionales, aun cuando no correspondan con las del hebreo (p.ej. *Jeremías*, aunque el hebreo es *Yirmeyahu*). En otros casos se ha hecho una revisión moderada para que los nombres no solamente reflejen con mayor exactitud el texto original (p.ej., la consonante *jet* se ha representado con *j* en vez de *h*), sino también para que se ajusten a la fonología castellana (p.ej., se ha evitado usar la consonante *m* en posición final).

Como todas las traducciones de la Biblia, la **Nueva Versión Internacional** que hoy colocamos en manos de nuestros lectores es susceptible de perfeccionarse. Y seguiremos trabajando para que así ocurra en sucesivas ediciones de la misma. Con todo, estamos muy agradecidos al Señor por el gran trabajo que nos ha permitido realizar, en el cual todos los integrantes del comité de traducción bíblica de la Sociedad Bíblica Internacional hemos puesto el mayor empeño, amor y fe, a fin de entregar a los lectores de este siglo la mejor versión posible del texto bíblico. Que todo sea para la mayor gloria de Dios y el más amplio conocimiento de su Palabra. Dedicamos este trabajo a Aquel, cuyo nombre debe ser honrado por todos los que lean su Palabra. Y oramos para que, a través de esta edición de la **Nueva Versión Internacional**, muchos puedan entender, asimilar y aceptar el mensaje de salvación que, por medio de Jesucristo, tiene el Dios de la Biblia para cada uno de ellos.

Comité de Traducción Bíblica
Bíblica Internacional
P.O. Box 522241
Miami, Florida 33152-2241
EE.UU.

Septiembre de 1998

Antiguo Testamento

GÉNESIS

La creación

1 Dios, en el principio,
　　creó los cielos y la tierra.
2La tierra era un caos total,
　　las tinieblas cubrían el abismo,
　y el Espírituª de Dios iba y venía
　　sobre la superficie de las aguas.
3Y dijo Dios: «¡Que exista la luz!»
　　Y la luz llegó a existir.
4Dios consideró que la luz era buena
　　y la separó de las tinieblas.
5A la luz la llamó «día»,
　　y a las tinieblas, «noche».
　Y vino la noche, y llegó la mañana:
　　ése fue el primer día.

6Y dijo Dios: «¡Que exista el firmamento
　　en medio de las aguas, y que las separe!»
7Y así sucedió: Dios hizo el firmamento
　　y separó las aguas que están abajo,
　de las aguas que están arriba.
8Al firmamento Dios lo llamó «cielo».
　　Y vino la noche, y llegó la mañana:
　　ése fue el segundo día.

9Y dijo Dios: «¡Que las aguas debajo del cielo
　　se reúnan en un solo lugar,
　y que aparezca lo seco!»
　Y así sucedió. **10**A lo seco Dios lo llamó «tierra»,
　y al conjunto de aguas lo llamó «mar».
　Y Dios consideró que esto era bueno.
11Y dijo Dios: «¡Que haya vegetación sobre la
　　tierra;
　　que ésta produzca hierbas que den semilla,
　y árboles que den su fruto con semilla,
　　todos según su especie!»
　Y así sucedió. **12**Comenzó a brotar la
　　vegetación:
　　hierbas que dan semilla,
　y árboles que dan su fruto con semilla,
　　todos según su especie.
　Y Dios consideró que esto era bueno.
13 Y vino la noche, y llegó la mañana:
　　ése fue el tercer día.

14Y dijo Dios: «¡Que haya luces en el firmamento
　　que separen el día de la noche;
　que sirvan como señales de las estaciones,
　de los días y de los años,
15y que brillen en el firmamento
　　para iluminar la tierra!»
　Y sucedió así. **16**Dios hizo los dos grandes astros:
　　el astro mayor para gobernar el día,
　y el menor para gobernar la noche.
　　También hizo las estrellas.
17Dios colocó en el firmamento
　　los astros para alumbrar la tierra.
18Los hizo para gobernar el día y la noche,
　　y para separar la luz de las tinieblas.
　Y Dios consideró que esto era bueno.
19Y vino la noche, y llegó la mañana:
　　ése fue el cuarto día.

20Y dijo Dios: «¡Que rebosen de seres vivientes
　　las aguas,
　y que vuelen las aves sobre la tierra
　　a lo largo del firmamento!»

21Y creó Dios los grandes animales marinos,
　　y todos los seres vivientes
　　que se mueven y pululan en las aguas
　y todas las aves,
　　según su especie.
　Y Dios consideró que esto era bueno,
22y los bendijo con estas palabras:
　　«Sean fructíferos y multiplíquense;
　　llenen las aguas de los mares.
　　¡Que las aves se multipliquen sobre la
　　　tierra!»
23Y vino la noche, y llegó la mañana:
　　ése fue el quinto día.

24Y dijo Dios: «¡Que produzca la tierra seres
　　vivientes:
　　animales domésticos, animales salvajes,
　y reptiles, según su especie!»
　Y sucedió así. **25**Dios hizo los animales
　　domésticos,
　　los animales salvajes, y todos los reptiles,
　　según su especie.
　Y Dios consideró que esto era bueno,
26y dijo: «Hagamos al *ser humano
　　a nuestra imagen y semejanza.
　Que tenga dominio sobre los peces del mar,
　　y sobre las aves del cielo;
　sobre los animales domésticos,
　　sobre los animales salvajes,b
　y sobre todos los reptiles
　　que se arrastran por el suelo.»
27Y Dios creó al ser humano a su imagen;
　　lo creó a imagen de Dios.
　　*Hombre y mujer los creó.
28 y los bendijo con estas palabras:
　　«Sean fructíferos y multiplíquense;
　　llenen la tierra y sométanla;
　dominen a los peces del mar y a las aves del
　　cielo,
　y a todos los reptiles que se arrastran por el
　　suelo.»
29También les dijo: «Yo les doy de la tierra
　　todas las plantas que producen semilla
　y todos los árboles que dan fruto con semilla;
　todo esto les servirá de alimento.
30Y doy la hierba verde como alimento
　　a todas las fieras de la tierra,
　a todas las aves del cielo
　y a todos los seres vivientes
　　que se arrastran por la tierra.»
　Y así sucedió. **31**Dios miró todo lo que había
　　hecho,
　　y consideró que era muy bueno.
　Y vino la noche, y llegó la mañana:
　　ése fue el sexto día.

2 Así quedaron terminados los cielos y la tierra,
　　y todo lo que hay en ellos.
2Al llegar el séptimo día, Dios descansó
　　porque había terminado la obra que había
　　　emprendido.
3Dios bendijo el séptimo día, y lo *santificó,
　　porque en ese día descansó de toda su obra
　　　creadora.
4Ésta es la historiac de la creación
　　de los cielos y la tierra.

---

a **1:2** *Espíritu.* Alt. *viento o soplo.* b **1:26** *los animales salvajes* (Siríaca); *toda la tierra* (TM). c **2:4** *Ésta es la historia.* Lit. *Éstas son las generaciones;* véanse 6:9; 10:1; 11:10,27; 25:12,19; 36:1,9; 37:2; véase también 5:1.

Adán y Eva

Cuando Dios el SEÑOR hizo la tierra y los cielos, [5]aún no había ningún arbusto del campo sobre la tierra, ni había brotado la hierba, porque Dios el SEÑOR todavía no había hecho llover sobre la tierra ni existía el *hombre para que la cultivara. [6]No obstante, salía de la tierra un manantial que regaba toda la superficie del suelo. [7]Y Dios el SEÑOR formó al hombre[d] del polvo de la tierra, y sopló en su nariz hálito de vida, y el hombre se convirtió en un ser viviente.

[8]Dios el SEÑOR plantó un jardín al oriente del Edén, y allí puso al hombre que había formado. [9]Dios el SEÑOR hizo que creciera toda clase de árboles hermosos, los cuales daban frutos buenos y apetecibles. En medio del jardín hizo crecer el árbol de la vida, y también el árbol del conocimiento del bien y del mal.

[10]Del Edén nacía un río que regaba el jardín, y que desde allí se dividía en cuatro ríos menores. [11]El primero se llamaba Pisón, y recorría toda la región de Javilá, donde había oro. [12]El oro de esa región era fino, y también había allí resina muy buena y piedra de ónice. [13]El segundo se llamaba Guijón, que recorría toda la región de Cus.[e] [14]El tercero se llamaba Tigris, que corría al este de Asiria. El cuarto era el Éufrates.

[15]Dios el SEÑOR tomó al hombre y lo puso en el jardín del Edén para que lo cultivara y lo cuidara, [16]y le dio este mandato: «Puedes comer de todos los árboles del jardín, [17]pero del árbol del conocimiento del bien y del mal no deberás comer. El día que de él comas, ciertamente morirás.»

[18]Luego Dios el SEÑOR dijo: «No es bueno que el hombre esté solo. Voy a hacerle una ayuda adecuada.» [19]Entonces Dios el SEÑOR formó de la tierra toda ave del cielo y todo animal del campo, y se los llevó al hombre para ver qué *nombre les pondría. El hombre les puso nombre a todos los seres vivos, y con ese nombre se les conoce. [20]Así el hombre fue poniéndoles nombre a todos los animales domésticos, a todas las aves del cielo y a todos los animales del campo. Sin embargo, no se encontró entre ellos la ayuda adecuada para el hombre.

[21]Entonces Dios el SEÑOR hizo que el hombre cayera en un sueño profundo y, mientras éste dormía, le sacó una costilla y le cerró la herida. [22]De la costilla que le había quitado al hombre, Dios el SEÑOR hizo una mujer y se la presentó al hombre, [23]el cual exclamó:

«Ésta sí es hueso de mis huesos
    y carne de mi carne.
Se llamará "mujer"[f]
    porque del hombre fue sacada.»

[24]Por eso el hombre deja a su padre y a su madre, y se une a su mujer, y los dos se funden en un solo ser.[g] [25]En ese tiempo el hombre y la mujer estaban desnudos, pero ninguno de los dos sentía vergüenza.

La caída del ser humano

3 La serpiente era más astuta que todos los animales del campo que Dios el SEÑOR había hecho, así que le preguntó a la mujer:

—¿Es verdad que Dios les dijo que no comieran de ningún árbol del jardín?

[2]—Podemos comer del fruto de todos los árboles —respondió la mujer—. [3]Pero, en cuanto al fruto del árbol que está en medio del jardín, Dios nos ha dicho: "No coman de ese árbol, ni lo toquen; de lo contrario, morirán."

[4]Pero la serpiente le dijo a la mujer:

—¡No es cierto, no van a morir! [5]Dios sabe muy bien que, cuando coman de ese árbol, se les abrirán los ojos y llegarán a ser como Dios, conocedores del bien y del mal.

[6]La mujer vio que el fruto del árbol era bueno para comer, y que tenía buen aspecto y era deseable para adquirir sabiduría, así que tomó de su fruto y comió. Luego le dio a su esposo, y también él comió. [7]En ese momento se les abrieron los ojos, y tomaron conciencia de su desnudez. Por eso, para cubrirse entretejieron hojas de higuera.

[8]Cuando el día comenzó a refrescar, oyeron el *hombre y la mujer que Dios andaba recorriendo el jardín; entonces corrieron a esconderse entre los árboles, para que Dios no los viera. [9]Pero Dios el SEÑOR llamó al hombre y le dijo:

—¿Dónde estás?

[10]El hombre contestó:

—Escuché que andabas por el jardín, y tuve miedo porque estoy desnudo. Por eso me escondí.

[11]—¿Y quién te ha dicho que estás desnudo? —le preguntó Dios—. ¿Acaso has comido del fruto del árbol que yo te prohibí comer?

[12]Él respondió:

—La mujer que me diste por compañera me dio de ese fruto, y yo lo comí.

[13]Entonces Dios el SEÑOR le preguntó a la mujer:

—¿Qué es lo que has hecho?

—La serpiente me engañó, y comí —contestó ella.

[14]Dios el SEÑOR dijo entonces a la serpiente:

«Por causa de lo que has hecho,
    ¡maldita serás entre todos los animales,
    tanto domésticos como salvajes!
Te arrastrarás sobre tu vientre,
    y comerás polvo todos los días de tu vida.
[15]Pondré enemistad entre tú y la mujer,
    y entre tu simiente y la de ella;
su simiente te aplastará la cabeza,
    pero tú le morderás el talón.»

[16]A la mujer le dijo:

«Multiplicaré tus dolores en el parto,
    y darás a luz a tus hijos con dolor.
Desearás a tu marido,
    y él te dominará.»

[17]Al hombre le dijo:

«Por cuanto le hiciste caso a tu mujer,
    y comiste del árbol del que te prohibí
    comer,
    ¡maldita será la tierra por tu culpa!
Con penosos trabajos comerás de ella
    todos los días de tu vida.
[18]La tierra te producirá cardos y espinas,
    y comerás hierbas silvestres.
[19]Te ganarás el pan con el sudor de tu frente,
    hasta que vuelvas a la misma tierra
    de la cual fuiste sacado.
Porque polvo eres,
    y al polvo volverás.»

---

d 2:7 El término hebreo que significa *hombre* (*adam*) está relacionado con el que significa *tierra* (*adamá*). Además, el mismo término *adam* corresponde al nombre propio *Adán* (véase 4:25).   **e** 2:13 *Cus.* Posiblemente la región sudeste de Mesopotamia.   **f** 2:23 En hebreo, la palabra que significa *mujer* (*'ishah*) suena como la palabra que significa *hombre* (*'ish*).   **g** 2:24 *se funden en un solo ser.* Lit. *llegar a ser una sola carne.*

20El hombre llamó Evah a su mujer, porque ella sería la madre de todo ser viviente.

21Dios el SEÑOR hizo ropa de pieles para el hombre y su mujer, y los vistió. 22Y dijo: «El *ser humano ha llegado a ser como uno de nosotros, pues tiene conocimiento del bien y del mal. No vaya a ser que extienda su mano y también tome del fruto del árbol de la vida, y lo coma y viva para siempre.» 23Entonces Dios el SEÑOR expulsó al ser humano del jardín del Edén, para que trabajara la tierra de la cual había sido hecho. 24Luego de expulsarlo, puso al oriente del jardín del Edén a los *querubines, y una espada ardiente que se movía por todos lados, para custodiar el camino que lleva al árbol de la vida.

Caín y Abel

4 El *hombre se unió a su mujer Eva, y ella concibió y dio a luz a Caín.i Y dijo: «¡Con la ayuda del SEÑOR, he tenido un hijo varón!» 2Después dio a luz a Abel, hermano de Caín. Abel se dedicó a pastorear ovejas, mientras que Caín se dedicó a trabajar la tierra. 3Tiempo después, Caín presentó al SEÑOR una ofrenda del fruto de la tierra. 4Abel también presentó al SEÑOR lo mejor de su rebaño, es decir, los primogénitos con su grasa. Y el SEÑOR miró con agrado a Abel y a su ofrenda, 5pero no miró así a Caín ni a su ofrenda. Por eso Caín se enfureció y andaba cabizbajo.

6Entonces el SEÑOR le dijo: «¿Por qué estás tan enojado? ¿Por qué andas cabizbajo? 7Si hicieras lo bueno, podrías andar con la frente en alto. Pero si haces lo malo, el pecado te acecha, como una fiera lista para atraparte. No obstante, tú puedes dominarlo.»

8Caín habló con su hermano Abel. Mientras estaban en el campo, Caín atacó a su hermano y lo mató.

9El SEÑOR le preguntó a Caín:

—¿Dónde está tu hermano Abel?

—No lo sé —respondió—. ¿Acaso soy yo el que debe cuidar a mi hermano?

10—¡Qué has hecho! —exclamó el SEÑOR—. Desde la tierra, la sangre de tu hermano reclama justicia. 11Por eso, ahora quedarás bajo la maldición de la tierra, la cual ha abierto sus fauces para recibir la sangre de tu hermano, que tú has derramado. 12Cuando cultives la tierra, no te dará sus frutos, y en el mundo serás un fugitivo errante.

13—Este castigo es más de lo que puedo soportar —le dijo Caín al SEÑOR—. 14Hoy me condenas al destierro, y nunca más podré estar en tu presencia. Andaré por el mundo errante como un fugitivo, y cualquiera que me encuentre me matará.

15—No será asíj —replicó el SEÑOR—. El que mate a Caín, será castigado siete veces.

Entonces el SEÑOR le puso una marca a Caín, para que no fuera a matarlo quien lo hallara. 16Así Caín se alejó de la presencia del SEÑOR y se fue a vivir a la región llamada Nod,k al este del Edén.

17Caín se unió a su mujer, la cual concibió y dio a luz a Enoc. Caín había estado construyendo una ciudad, a la que le puso el *nombre de su hijo Enoc. 18Luego Enoc tuvo un hijo llamado Irad, que fue el padre de Mejuyael. Éste, a su vez, fue el padre de Metusael, y Metusael fue el padre de Lamec. 19Lamec tuvo dos mujeres. Una de ellas se llamaba Ada, y la otra Zila. 20Ada dio a luz a Jabal, quien a su vez fue el antepasado de los que viven en tiendas de campaña y crían ganado. 21Jabal tuvo un hermano llamado Jubal, quien fue el antepasado de los que tocan el arpa y la flauta. 22Por su parte, Zila dio a luz a Tubal Caín, que fue herrero y forjador de toda clase de herramientas de bronce y de hierro. Tubal Caín tuvo una hermana que se llamaba Noamá.

23Lamec dijo a sus mujeres Ada y Zila:

«¡Escuchen bien, mujeres de Lamec!
¡Escuchen mis palabras!
Maté a un hombre por haberme herido,
　y a un muchacho por golpearme.
24Si Caín será vengado siete veces,
　setenta y siete veces será vengado Lamec.»

25Adán volvió a unirse a su mujer, y ella tuvo un hijo al que llamó Set,l porque dijo: «Dios me ha concedido otro hijo en lugar de Abel, al que mató Caín.» 26También Set tuvo un hijo, a quien llamó Enós. Desde entonces se comenzó a invocar el nombre del SEÑOR.

Descendientes de Adán

5 Ésta es la lista de los descendientes de Adán. Cuando Dios creó al *ser humano, lo hizo a semejanza de Dios mismo. 2Los creó *hombre y mujer, y los bendijo. El día que fueron creados los llamó «seres humanos».m

3Cuando Adán llegó a la edad de ciento treinta años, tuvo un hijo a su imagen y semejanza, y lo llamó Set. 4Después del nacimiento de Set, Adán vivió ochocientos años más, y tuvo otros hijos y otras hijas. 5De modo que Adán murió a los novecientos treinta años de edad.

6Set tenía ciento cinco años cuando fue padre den Enós. 7Después del nacimiento de Enós, Set vivió ochocientos siete años más, y tuvo otros hijos y otras hijas. 8De modo que Set murió a los novecientos doce años de edad.

9Enós tenía noventa años cuando fue padre de Cainán. 10Después del nacimiento de Cainán, Enós vivió ochocientos quince años más, y tuvo otros hijos y otras hijas. 11De modo que Enós murió a los novecientos cinco años de edad.

12Cainán tenía setenta años cuando fue padre de Malalel. 13Después del nacimiento de Malalel, Cainán vivió ochocientos cuarenta años más, y tuvo otros hijos y otras hijas. 14De modo que Cainán murió a los novecientos diez años de edad.

15Malalel tenía sesenta y cinco años cuando fue padre de Jared. 16Después del nacimiento de Jared, Malalel vivió ochocientos treinta años más, y tuvo otros hijos y otras hijas. 17De modo que Malalel murió a los ochocientos noventa y cinco años de edad.

18Jared tenía ciento sesenta y dos años cuando fue padre de Enoc. 19Después del nacimiento de Enoc, Jared vivió ochocientos años más, y tuvo otros hijos y otras hijas. 20De modo que Jared murió a los novecientos sesenta y dos años de edad.

21Enoc tenía sesenta y cinco años cuando fue padre de Matusalén. 22Después del nacimiento de Matusalén, Enoc anduvo fielmente con Dios trescientos años más, y tuvo otros hijos y otras hijas. 23En total, Enoc vivió trescientos sesenta y cinco años, 24y como anduvo fielmente con Dios, un día desapareció porque Dios se lo llevó.

---

h 3:20 En hebreo, Eva significa Vida.　i 4:1 En hebreo, Caín suena como el verbo que significa llegar a tener, adquirir. j 4:15 No será así (LXX, Vulgata y Siríaca); Por tanto (TM).　k 4:16 En hebreo, Nod significa errante (véanse vv. 12 y 14). l 4:25 En hebreo, Set significa concedido.　m 5:2 seres humanos. Lit. Adán. El término hebreo también significa hombre en el sentido genérico de humanidad.　n 5:6 fue padre de. Lit. engendró a; y así sucesivamente en el resto de esta genealogía. En este contexto, padre puede significar antepasado; también en vv. 7-26.

²⁵Matusalén tenía ciento ochenta y siete años cuando fue padre de Lamec. ²⁶Después del nacimiento de Lamec, Matusalén vivió setecientos ochenta y dos años más, y tuvo otros hijos y otras hijas. ²⁷De modo que Matusalén murió a los novecientos sesenta y nueve años de edad.

²⁸Lamec tenía ciento ochenta y dos años cuando fue padre de Noé.ñ ²⁹Le dio ese *nombre porque dijo: «Este niño nos dará descanso en nuestra tarea y penosos trabajos, en esta tierra que maldijo el SEÑOR.» ³⁰Después del nacimiento de Noé, Lamec vivió quinientos noventa y cinco años más, y tuvo otros hijos y otras hijas. ³¹De modo que Lamec murió a los setecientos setenta y siete años de edad.

³²Noé ya había cumplido quinientos años cuando fue padre de Sem, Cam y Jafet.

La maldad humana

6 Cuando los *seres humanos comenzaron a multiplicarse sobre la tierra y tuvieron hijas, ²los hijos de Dios vieron que las hijas de los seres humanos eran hermosas. Entonces tomaron como mujeres a todas las que desearon. ³Pero el SEÑOR dijo: «Mi espíritu no permanecerá en el *ser humano para siempre, porque no es más que un simple *mortal; por eso vivirá solamente ciento veinte años.»

⁴Al unirse los hijos de Dios con las hijas de los seres humanos y tener hijos con ellas, nacieron gigantes, que fueron los famosos héroes de antaño. A partir de entonces hubo gigantes en la tierra.

⁵Al ver el SEÑOR que la maldad del ser humano en la tierra era muy grande, y que todos sus pensamientos tendían siempre hacia el mal, ⁶se arrepintió de haber hecho al ser humano en la tierra, y le dolió en el corazón. ⁷Entonces dijo: «Voy a borrar de la tierra al ser humano que he creado. Y haré lo mismo con los animales, los reptiles y las aves del cielo. ¡Me arrepiento de haberlos creado!» ⁸Pero Noé contaba con el favor del SEÑOR.

El diluvio

⁹Ésta es la historia de Noé.

Noé era un hombre justo y honrado entre su gente. Siempre anduvo fielmente con Dios. ¹⁰Tuvo tres hijos: Sem, Cam y Jafet. ¹¹Pero Dios vio que la tierra estaba corrompida y llena de violencia. ¹²Al ver Dios tanta corrupción en la tierra, y tanta perversión en la gente, ¹³le dijo a Noé: «He decidido acabar con toda la gente, pues por causa de ella la tierra está llena de violencia. Así que voy a destruir a la gente junto con la tierra. ¹⁴Constrúyete un arca de madera resinosa,º hazle compartimentos, y cúbrela con brea por dentro y por fuera. ¹⁵Dale las siguientes medidas: ciento cuarenta metros de largo, veintitrés de ancho y catorce de alto.p ¹⁶Hazla de tres pisos, con una abertura a medio metroq del techo y con una puerta en uno de sus costados. ¹⁷Porque voy a enviar un diluvio sobre la tierra, para destruir a todos los seres vivientes bajo el cielo. Todo lo que existe en la tierra morirá. ¹⁸Pero contigo estableceré mi *pacto, y entrarán en el arca tú y tus hijos, tu esposa y tus nueras. ¹⁹Haz que entre en el arca una pareja de todos los seres vivientes, es decir, un macho y una hembra de cada especie, para que sobrevivan contigo. ²⁰Contigo entrará también una pareja de cada especie de aves, de ganado y de reptiles, para que puedan sobrevivir. ²¹Recoge además toda clase de alimento, y almacénalo, para que a ti y a ellos les

sirva de comida.» ²²Y Noé hizo todo según lo que Dios le había mandado.

7 El SEÑOR le dijo a Noé: «Entra en el arca con toda tu familia, porque tú eres el único *hombre justo que he encontrado en esta generación. ²De todos los animales puros, lleva siete machos y siete hembras; pero de los impuros, sólo un macho y una hembra. ³Lleva también siete machos y siete hembras de las aves del cielo, para conservar su especie sobre la tierra. ⁴Porque dentro de siete días haré que llueva sobre la tierra durante cuarenta días y cuarenta noches, y así borraré de la faz de la tierra a todo ser viviente que hice.»

⁵Noé hizo todo de acuerdo con lo que el SEÑOR le había mandado. ⁶Tenía Noé seiscientos años de edad cuando las aguas del diluvio inundaron la tierra. ⁷Entonces entró en el arca junto con sus hijos, su esposa y sus nueras, para salvarse de las aguas del diluvio. ⁸De los animales puros e impuros, de las aves y de todos los seres que se arrastran por el suelo, ⁹entraron con Noé por parejas, el macho y su hembra, tal como Dios se lo había mandado. ¹⁰Al cabo de siete días, las aguas del diluvio comenzaron a caer sobre la tierra.

¹¹Cuando Noé tenía seiscientos años, precisamente en el día diecisiete del mes segundo, se reventaron las fuentes del mar profundo y se abrieron las compuertas del cielo. ¹²Cuarenta días y cuarenta noches llovió sobre la tierra. ¹³Ese mismo día entraron en el arca Noé, sus hijos Sem, Cam y Jafet, su esposa y sus tres nueras. ¹⁴Junto con ellos entró toda clase de animales salvajes y domésticos, de animales que se arrastran por el suelo, y de aves. ¹⁵Así entraron en el arca con Noé parejas de todos los seres vivientes; ¹⁶entraron un macho y una hembra de cada especie, tal como Dios se lo había mandado a Noé. Luego el SEÑOR cerró la puerta del arca.

¹⁷El diluvio cayó sobre la tierra durante cuarenta días. Cuando crecieron las aguas, elevaron el arca por encima de la tierra. ¹⁸Las aguas crecían y aumentaban cada vez más, pero el arca se mantenía a flote sobre ellas. ¹⁹Tanto crecieron las aguas, que cubrieron las montañas más altas que hay debajo de los cielos. ²⁰El nivel del agua subió más de siete metrosr por encima de las montañas. ²¹Así murió todo *ser viviente que se movía sobre la tierra: las aves, los animales salvajes y domésticos, todo tipo de animal que se arrastraba por el suelo, y todo ser humano. ²²Pereció todo ser que habitaba la tierra firme y tenía aliento de vida. ²³Dios borró de la faz de la tierra a todo ser viviente, desde los seres humanos hasta los ganados, los reptiles y las aves del cielo. Todos fueron borrados de la faz de la tierra. Sólo quedaron Noé y los que estaban con él en el arca. ²⁴Y la tierra quedó inundada ciento cincuenta días.

8 Dios se acordó entonces de Noé y de todos los animales salvajes y domésticos que estaban con él en el arca. Hizo que soplara un fuerte viento sobre la tierra, y las aguas comenzaron a bajar. ²Se cerraron las fuentes del mar profundo y las compuertas del cielo, y dejó de llover. ³Poco a poco las aguas se fueron retirando de la tierra. Al cabo de ciento cincuenta días las aguas habían disminuido. ⁴El día diecisiete del mes séptimo el arca se detuvo sobre las montañas de Ararat, ⁵y las aguas siguieron bajando hasta que el primer día del mes décimo pudieron verse las cimas de las montañas.

ñ **5:28** En hebreo, el nombre propio *Noé* suena como la palabra que significa *descanso.* o **6:14** *resinosa.* Palabra de difícil traducción. p **6:15** *ciento cuarenta metros de largo, veintitrés de ancho y catorce de alto.* Lit. *300 *codos de largo, 50 codos de ancho y 30 codos de alto.* q **6:16** *medio metro.* Lit. *un codo.* r **7:20** *siete metros.* Lit. *quince *codos.*

⁶Después de cuarenta días, Noé abrió la ventana del arca que había hecho ⁷y soltó un cuervo, el cual estuvo volando de un lado a otro, esperando a que se secara la tierra. ⁸Luego soltó una paloma, para ver si las aguas que cubrían la tierra ya se habían retirado. ⁹Pero la paloma no encontró un lugar donde posarse, y volvió al arca porque las aguas aún cubrían la tierra. Noé extendió la mano, tomó la paloma y la metió consigo en el arca. ¹⁰Esperó siete días más y volvió a soltar la paloma fuera del arca. ¹¹Caía la noche cuando la paloma regresó, trayendo en su pico una ramita de olivo recién cortada. Así Noé se dio cuenta de que las aguas habían bajado hasta dejar la tierra al descubierto. ¹²Esperó siete días más y volvió a soltar la paloma, pero esta vez la paloma ya no regresó.

¹³Noé tenía seiscientos un años cuando las aguas se secaron. El primer día del primer mes de ese año, Noé quitó la cubierta del arca y vio que la tierra estaba seca. ¹⁴Para el día veintisiete del segundo mes, la tierra estaba ya completamente seca. ¹⁵Entonces Dios le dijo a Noé: ¹⁶«Sal del arca junto con tus hijos, tu esposa y tus nueras. ¹⁷Saca también a todos los seres vivientes que están contigo: las aves, el ganado y todos los animales que se arrastran por el suelo. ¡Que sean fecundos! ¡Que se multipliquen y llenen la tierra!»

¹⁸Salieron, pues, del arca Noé y sus hijos, su esposa y sus nueras. ¹⁹Salieron también todos los animales: el ganado, las aves, y todos los reptiles que se mueven sobre la tierra, cada uno según su especie. ²⁰Luego Noé construyó un altar al SEÑOR, y sobre ese altar ofreció como *holocausto animales puros y aves puras. ²¹Cuando el SEÑOR percibió el grato aroma, se dijo a sí mismo: «Aunque las intenciones del *ser humano son perversas desde su juventud, nunca más volveré a maldecir la tierra por culpa suya. Tampoco volveré a destruir a todos los seres vivientes, como acabo de hacerlo.

²²»Mientras la tierra exista,
      habrá siembra y cosecha,
frío y calor,
      verano e invierno,
      y días y noches.»

El pacto de Dios con Noé

9 Dios bendijo a Noé y a sus hijos con estas palabras: «Sean fecundos, multiplíquense y llenen la tierra. ²Todos los animales de la tierra sentirán temor y respeto ante ustedes: las aves, las bestias salvajes, los animales que se arrastran por el suelo, y los peces del mar. Todos estarán bajo su dominio. ³Todo lo que se mueve y tiene vida, al igual que las verduras, les servirá de alimento. Yo les doy todo esto. ⁴Pero no deberán comer carne con su *vida, es decir, con su sangre. ⁵Por cierto, de la sangre de ustedes yo habré de pedirles cuentas. A todos los animales y a todos los seres humanos les pediré cuentas de la vida de sus semejantes.

⁶»Si alguien derrama la sangre de un *ser
      humano,
   otro ser humano derramará la suya,
porque el ser humano ha sido creado
   a imagen de Dios mismo.

⁷»En cuanto a ustedes, sean fecundos y multiplíquense; sí, multiplíquense y llenen la tierra.»

⁸Dios les habló otra vez a Noé y a sus hijos, y les dijo: ⁹«Yo establezco mi *pacto con ustedes, con sus descendientes, ¹⁰y con todos los seres vivientes que están con ustedes, es decir, con todos los seres vivientes de la tierra que salieron del arca: las aves, y los animales domésticos y salvajes. ¹¹Éste es mi pacto con ustedes: Nunca más serán exterminados los seres humanos por un diluvio; nunca más habrá un diluvio que destruya la tierra.»

¹²Y Dios añadió: «Ésta es la señal del pacto que establezco para siempre con ustedes y con todos los seres vivientes que los acompañan: ¹³He colocado mi arco iris en las nubes, el cual servirá como señal de mi pacto con la tierra. ¹⁴Cuando yo cubra la tierra de nubes, y en ellas aparezca el arco iris, ¹⁵me acordaré del pacto que he establecido con ustedes y con todos los seres vivientes. Nunca más las aguas se convertirán en un diluvio para destruir a todos los mortales. ¹⁶Cada vez que aparezca el arco iris entre las nubes, yo lo veré y me acordaré del pacto que establecí para siempre con todos los seres vivientes que hay sobre la tierra.»

¹⁷Dios concluyó diciéndole a Noé: «Éste es el pacto que establezco con todos los seres vivientes que hay en la tierra.»

Los hijos de Noé

¹⁸Los hijos de Noé que salieron del arca fueron Sem, Cam, que fue el padre de Canaán, y Jafet. ¹⁹Éstos fueron los tres hijos de Noé que con su descendencia poblaron toda la tierra.

²⁰Noé se dedicó a cultivar la tierra, y plantó una viña. ²¹Un día, bebió vino y se embriagó, quedándose desnudo dentro de su carpa. ²²Cam, el padre de Canaán, vio a su padre desnudo y fue a contárselo a sus hermanos, que estaban afuera. ²³Entonces Sem y Jafet tomaron un manto, se lo echaron sobre los hombros, y caminando hacia atrás, cubrieron la desnudez de su padre. Como miraban en dirección opuesta, no lo vieron desnudo.

²⁴Cuando Noé despertó de su borrachera y se enteró de lo que su hijo menor le había hecho, ²⁵declaró:

   «¡Maldito sea Canaán!
      Será de sus dos hermanos
      el más bajo de sus esclavos.»

²⁶Y agregó:

   «¡Bendito sea el SEÑOR, Dios de Sem!
      ¡Que Canaán sea su esclavo!
²⁷¡Que Dios extienda el territorio de Jafet!ˢ
      ¡Que habite Jafet en los campamentos de
      Sem,
   y que Canaán sea su esclavo!»

²⁸Después del diluvio Noé vivió trescientos cincuenta años más, ²⁹de modo que murió a la edad de novecientos cincuenta años.

Las naciones de la tierra
10:2-31 — 1Cr 1:5-27
10:21-31 — Gn 11:10-27

10 Ésta es la historia de Sem, Cam y Jafet, hijos de Noé, quienes después del diluvio tuvieron sus propios hijos.

² Los hijosᵗ de Jafet fueron Gómer, Magog, Maday, Javán, Tubal, Mésec y Tirás.

³ Los hijos de Gómer fueron Asquenaz, Rifat y Togarma.

⁴ Los hijos de Javán fueron Elisá, Tarsis, Quitín y Rodanín.ᵘ

ˢ **9:27** En hebreo, el nombre propio *Jafet* suena como el verbo que significa *extender*. ᵗ **10:2** En este contexto *hijos* puede significar *descendientes*; así en el resto de este capítulo. ᵘ **10:4** *Rodanín* (varios mss. hebreos y 1Cr 1:7); *Dodanín* (TM).

5Algunos de ellos, que poblaron las costas, formaron naciones y clanes en sus respectivos territorios y con sus propios idiomas.

6 Los hijos de Cam fueron Cus, Misrayin, Fut y Canaán.

7 Los hijos de Cus fueron Seba, Javilá, Sabtá, Ragama y Sabteca.

Los hijos de Ragama fueron Sabá y Dedán.

8Cus fue el padre de Nimrod, conocido como el primer hombre fuerte de la tierra, 9quien llegó a ser un valiente cazador ante el SEÑOR. Por eso se dice: «Como Nimrod, valiente cazador ante el SEÑOR.» 10Las principales ciudades de su reino fueron Babel, Érec, Acad y Calné, en la región de Sinar.

11Desde esa región Nimrod salió hacia Asur, donde construyó,v las ciudades de Nínive, Rejobot Ir,w Cala 12y Resén, la gran ciudad que está entre Nínive y Cala.

13 Misrayin fue el antepasado de los ludeos, los anameos, los leabitas, los naftuitas, 14los patruseos, los caslujitas y los caftoritas, de quienes descienden los filisteos.

15 Canaán fue el padre de Sidón, su primogénito, y de Het, 16y el antepasado de los jebuseos, los amorreos, los gergeseos, 17los heveos, los araceos, los sineos, 18los arvadeos, los zemareos y los jamatitas.

Luego, estos clanes cananeos se dispersaron, 19y su territorio se extendió desde Sidón hasta Guerar y Gaza, y en dirección de Sodoma, Gomorra, Admá y Zeboyín, hasta Lasa.

20Éstos fueron los descendientes de Cam, según sus clanes e idiomas, territorios y naciones.

21Sem, antepasado de todos los hijos de Éber, y hermano mayor de Jafet, también tuvo hijos.

22 Los hijos de Sem fueron Elam, Asur, Arfaxad, Lud y Aram.

23 Los hijos de Aram fueron Uz, Hul, Guéter y Mas.

24 Arfaxad fue el padre de Selaj.

Selaj fue el padre de Éber.

25 Éber tuvo dos hijos: el primero se llamó Péleg,x porque en su tiempo se dividió la tierra; su hermano se llamó Joctán.

26 Joctán fue el padre de Almodad, Sélef, Jazar Mávet, Yeraj, 27Hadorán, Uzal, Diclá, 28Obal, Abimael, Sabá, 29Ofir, Javilá y Jobab. Todos éstos fueron hijos de Joctán, 30y vivieron en la región que va desde Mesá hasta Sefar, en la región montañosa oriental.

31Éstos fueron los hijos de Sem, según sus clanes y sus idiomas, sus territorios y naciones.

32Éstos son los clanes de los hijos de Noé, según sus genealogías y sus naciones. A partir de estos clanes, las naciones se extendieron sobre la tierra después del diluvio.

La torre de Babel

11 En ese entonces se hablaba un solo idioma en toda la tierra. 2Al emigrar al oriente, la gente encontró una llanura en la región de Sinar, y allí se asentaron. 3Un día se dijeron unos a otros: «Vamos a hacer ladrillos, y a cocerlos al fuego.» Fue así como usaron ladrillos en vez de piedras, y asfalto en vez de mezcla. 4Luego dijeron: «Construyamos una ciudad con una torre que llegue hasta el cielo.

De ese modo nos haremos famosos y evitaremos ser dispersados por toda la tierra.»

5Pero el SEÑOR bajó para observar la ciudad y la torre que los *hombres estaban construyendo, 6y se dijo: «Todos forman un solo pueblo y hablan un solo idioma; esto es sólo el comienzo de sus obras, y todo lo que se propongan lo podrán lograr. 7Será mejor que bajemos a confundir su idioma, para que ya no se entiendan entre ellos mismos.»

8De esta manera el SEÑOR los dispersó desde allí por toda la tierra, y por lo tanto dejaron de construir la ciudad. 9Por eso a la ciudad se le llamó Babel,y porque fue allí donde el SEÑOR confundió el idioma de toda la gente de la tierra, y de donde los dispersó por todo el mundo.

Descendientes de Sem
11:10-27 — Gn 10:21-31; 1Cr 1:17-27

10Ésta es la historia de Sem:

Dos años después del diluvio, cuando Sem tenía cien años, nació su hijo Arfaxad. 11Después del nacimiento de Arfaxad, Sem vivió quinientos años más, y tuvo otros hijos y otras hijas.

12Cuando Arfaxad tenía treinta y cinco años, nació su hijo Selaj. 13Después del nacimiento de Selaj, Arfaxad vivió cuatrocientos tres años más, y tuvo otros hijos y otras hijas.

14Cuando Selaj tenía treinta años, nació su hijo Éber. 15Después del nacimiento de Éber, Selaj vivió cuatrocientos tres años más, y tuvo otros hijos y otras hijas.

16Cuando Éber tenía treinta y cuatro años, nació su hijo Péleg. 17Después del nacimiento de Péleg, Éber vivió cuatrocientos treinta años más, y tuvo otros hijos y otras hijas.

18Cuando Péleg tenía treinta años, nació su hijo Reú. 19Después del nacimiento de Reú, Péleg vivió doscientos nueve años más, y tuvo otros hijos y otras hijas.

20Cuando Reú tenía treinta y dos años, nació su hijo Serug. 21Después del nacimiento de Serug, Reú vivió doscientos siete años más, y tuvo otros hijos y otras hijas.

22Cuando Serug tenía treinta años, nació su hijo Najor. 23Después del nacimiento de Najor, Serug vivió doscientos años más, y tuvo otros hijos y otras hijas.

24Cuando Najor tenía veintinueve años, nació su hijo Téraj. 25Después del nacimiento de Téraj, Najor vivió ciento diecinueve años más, y tuvo otros hijos y otras hijas.

26Cuando Téraj tenía setenta años, ya habían nacido sus hijos Abram, Najor y Jarán.

Descendientes de Téraj

27Ésta es la historia de Téraj, el padre de Abram, Najor y Jarán.

Jarán fue el padre de Lot, 28y murió en Ur de los *caldeos, su tierra natal, cuando su padre Téraj aún vivía. 29Abram se casó con Saray, y Najor se casó con Milca, la hija de Jarán, el cual tuvo otra hija llamada Iscá. 30Pero Saray era estéril; no podía tener hijos.

31Téraj salió de Ur de los caldeos rumbo a Canaán. Se fue con su hijo Abram, su nieto Lot y su nuera Saray, la esposa de Abram. Sin embargo, al llegar a la ciudad de Jarán, se quedaron a vivir en aquel lugar,

---

v **10:11** *Desde esa región Nimrod salió hacia Asur, donde construyó.* Alt. *Desde esa región salió Asur, quien construyó.*

w **10:11** *Rejobot Ir.* Alt. *con sus plazas urbanas.* x **10:25** En hebreo, *Péleg* significa *división.* y **11:9** En hebreo, *Babel* suena como el verbo que significa *confundir.*

³²y allí mismo murió Téraj a los doscientos años de edad.

Llamamiento de Abram

12 El SEÑOR le dijo a Abram: «Deja tu tierra, tus parientes y la casa de tu padre, y vete a la tierra que te mostraré.

²»Haré de ti una nación grande,
    y te bendeciré;
haré famoso tu *nombre,
    y serás una bendición.
³Bendeciré a los que te bendigan
    y maldeciré a los que te maldigan;
¡por medio de ti serán bendecidas
    todas las familias de la tierra!»

⁴Abram partió, tal como el SEÑOR se lo había ordenado, y Lot se fue con él. Abram tenía setenta y cinco años cuando salió de Jarán. ⁵Al encaminarse hacia la tierra de Canaán, Abram se llevó a su esposa Saray, a su sobrino Lot, a toda la gente que habían adquirido en Jarán, y todos los bienes que habían acumulado. Cuando llegaron a Canaán, ⁶Abram atravesó toda esa región hasta llegar a Siquén, donde se encuentra la encina sagrada de Moré. En aquella época, los cananeos vivían en esa región. ⁷Allí el SEÑOR se le apareció a Abram y le dijo: «Yo le daré esta tierra a tu descendencia.» Entonces Abram erigió un altar al SEÑOR, porque se le había aparecido. ⁸De allí se dirigió a la región montañosa que está al este de Betel, donde armó su campamento, teniendo a Betel al oeste y Hai al este. También en ese lugar erigió un altar al SEÑOR e invocó su nombre. ⁹Después, Abram siguió su viaje por etapas hasta llegar a la región del Néguev.

Abram en Egipto

¹⁰En ese entonces, hubo tanta hambre en aquella región que Abram se fue a vivir a Egipto. ¹¹Cuando estaba por entrar a Egipto, le dijo a su esposa Saray: «Yo sé que eres una mujer muy hermosa. ¹²Estoy seguro que en cuanto te vean los egipcios, dirán: "Es su esposa"; entonces a mí me matarán, pero a ti te dejarán con vida. ¹³Por favor, di que eres mi hermana, para que gracias a ti me vaya bien y me dejen con vida.»

¹⁴Cuando Abram llegó a Egipto, los egipcios vieron que Saray era muy hermosa. ¹⁵También los funcionarios del faraón la vieron, y fueron a contarle al faraón lo hermosa que era. Entonces la llevaron al palacio real. ¹⁶Gracias a ella trataron muy bien a Abram. Le dieron ovejas, vacas, esclavos y esclavas, asnos y asnas, y camellos. ¹⁷Pero por causa de Saray, la esposa de Abram, el SEÑOR castigó al faraón y a su familia con grandes plagas. ¹⁸Entonces el faraón llamó a Abram y le dijo: «¿Qué me has hecho? ¿Por qué no me dijiste que era tu esposa? ¹⁹¿Por qué dijiste que era tu hermana? ¡Yo pude haberla tomado por esposa! ¡Anda, toma a tu esposa y vete!» ²⁰Y el faraón ordenó a sus hombres que expulsaran a Abram y a su esposa, junto con todos sus bienes.

Abram y Lot se separan

13 Abram salió de Egipto con su esposa, con Lot y con todos sus bienes, en dirección a la región del Néguev. ²Abram se había hecho muy rico en ganado, plata y oro. ³Desde el Néguev, Abram regresó por etapas hasta Betel, es decir, hasta el lugar donde había acampado al principio, entre Betel y Hai. ⁴En ese lugar había erigido antes un altar, y allí invocó Abram el *nombre del SEÑOR.

⁵También Lot, que iba acompañando a Abram, tenía rebaños, ganado y tiendas de campaña. ⁶La región donde estaban no daba abasto para mantener a los dos, porque tenían demasiado como para vivir juntos. ⁷Por eso comenzaron las fricciones entre los pastores de los rebaños de Abram y los que cuidaban los ganados de Lot. Además, los cananeos y los ferezeos también habitaban allí en aquel tiempo.

⁸Así que Abram le dijo a Lot: «No debe haber pleitos entre nosotros, ni entre nuestros pastores, porque somos parientes. ⁹Allí tienes toda la tierra a tu disposición. Por favor, aléjate de mí. Si te vas a la izquierda, yo me iré a la derecha, y si te vas a la derecha, yo me iré a la izquierda.»

¹⁰Lot levantó la vista y observó que todo el valle del Jordán, hasta Zoar, era tierra de regadío, como el jardín del SEÑOR o como la tierra de Egipto. Así era antes de que el SEÑOR destruyera a Sodoma y a Gomorra. ¹¹Entonces Lot escogió para sí todo el valle del Jordán, y partió hacia el oriente. Fue así como Abram y Lot se separaron. ¹²Abram se quedó a vivir en la tierra de Canaán, mientras que Lot se fue a vivir entre las ciudades del valle, estableciendo su campamento cerca de la ciudad de Sodoma. ¹³Los habitantes de Sodoma eran malvados y cometían muy graves pecados contra el SEÑOR.

¹⁴Después de que Lot se separó de Abram, el SEÑOR le dijo: «Abram, levanta la vista desde el lugar donde estás, y mira hacia el norte y hacia el sur, hacia el este y hacia el oeste. ¹⁵Yo te daré a ti y a tu descendencia, para siempre, toda la tierra que abarca tu mirada. ¹⁶Multiplicaré tu descendencia como el polvo de la tierra. Si alguien puede contar el polvo de la tierra, también podrá contar tus descendientes. ¹⁷¡Ve y recorre el país a lo largo y a lo ancho, porque a ti te la daré!»

¹⁸Entonces Abram levantó su campamento y se fue a vivir cerca de Hebrón, junto al encinar de Mamré. Allí erigió un altar al SEÑOR.

Abram rescata a Lot

14 En aquel tiempo los reyes Amrafel de Sinar,ᶻ Arioc de Elasar, Quedorlaómer de Elam, y Tidal de Goyim ²estuvieron en guerra contra los reyes Bera de Sodoma, Birsá de Gomorra, Sinab de Admá, Semeber de Zeboyín, y el rey de Bela, es decir, de Zoar. ³Estos dos últimos aunaron fuerzas en el valle de Sidín, conocido como el Mar Muerto. ⁴Durante doce años habían estado bajo el dominio de Quedorlaómer, pero en el año trece se rebelaron contra él.

⁵Al año siguiente, Quedorlaómer y los reyes que estaban con él salieron y derrotaron a los refaítas en la región de Astarot Carnayin; luego derrotaron a los zuzitas en Jam, a los emitas en Save Quiriatayin, ⁶y a los horeos en los montes de Seír, hasta El Parán, que está cerca del desierto. ⁷Al volver, llegaron hasta Enmispat, es decir, Cades, y conquistaron todo el territorio de los amalecitas, y también en el Edén los amorreos que vivían en la región de Jazezón Tamar.

⁸Entonces los reyes de Sodoma, Gomorra, Admá, Zeboyín y Bela, es decir, Zoar, salieron al valle de Sidín y presentaron batalla ⁹a los reyes Quedorlaómer de Elam, Tidal de Goyim, Amrafel de Sinar, y Arioc de Elasar. Eran cuatro reyes contra cinco. ¹⁰El valle de Sidín estaba lleno de pozos de asfalto, y cuando los reyes de Sodoma y Gomorra huyeron, se cayeron en ellos, pero los demás lograron escapar hacia los mon-

---

ᶻ **14:1** *Sinar*. Es decir, Babilonia; también en v. 9.

tes. **11**Los vencedores saquearon todos los bienes de Sodoma y de Gomorra, junto con todos los alimentos, y luego se retiraron. **12**Y como Lot, el sobrino de Abram, habitaba en Sodoma, también se lo llevaron a él, con todas sus posesiones.

13Uno de los que habían escapado le informó todo esto a Abram el hebreo, que estaba acampando junto al encinar de Mamré el amorreo. Mamré era hermano^a de Escol y de Aner, y éstos eran aliados de Abram. **14**En cuanto Abram supo que su sobrino estaba cautivo, convocó a trescientos dieciocho hombres adiestrados que habían nacido en su casa, y persiguió a los invasores hasta Dan. **15**Durante la noche Abram y sus siervos desplegaron sus fuerzas y los derrotaron, persiguiéndolos hasta Hobá, que está al norte de Damasco. **16**Así recuperó todos los bienes, y también rescató a su sobrino Lot, junto con sus posesiones, las mujeres y la demás gente.

17Cuando Abram volvía de derrotar a Quedorlaómer y a los reyes que estaban con él, el rey de Sodoma salió a su encuentro en el valle de Save, es decir, en el valle del Rey.

18Y Melquisedec, rey de *Salén y sacerdote del Dios *altísimo, le ofreció pan y vino. **19**Luego bendijo a Abram con estas palabras:

> «¡Que el Dios altísimo,
> creador^b del cielo y de la tierra,
> bendiga a Abram!
> **20**¡Bendito sea el Dios altísimo,
> que entregó en tus manos a tus enemigos!»

Entonces Abram le dio el diezmo de todo.

21El rey de Sodoma le dijo a Abram:

—Dame las personas y quédate con los bienes.

22Pero Abram le contestó:

—He jurado por el SEÑOR, el Dios altísimo, creador del cielo y de la tierra, **23**que no tomaré nada de lo que es tuyo, ni siquiera un hilo ni la correa de una sandalia. Así nunca podrás decir: "Yo hice rico a Abram." **24**No quiero nada para mí, salvo lo que mis hombres ya han comido. En cuanto a los hombres que me acompañaron, es decir, Aner, Escol y Mamré, que tomen ellos su parte.

Dios hace un pacto con Abram

15 Después de esto, la palabra del SEÑOR vino a Abram en una visión:

> «No temas, Abram.
> Yo soy tu escudo,
> y muy grande será tu recompensa.»

2Pero Abram le respondió:

—SEÑOR y Dios, ¿para qué vas a darme algo, si aún sigo sin tener hijos, y el heredero^c de mis bienes será Eliezer de Damasco? **3**Como no me has dado ningún hijo, mi herencia la recibirá uno de mis criados.

4—¡No! Ese hombre no ha de ser tu heredero —le contestó el SEÑOR—. Tu heredero será tu propio hijo.

5Luego el SEÑOR lo llevó afuera y le dijo:

—Mira hacia el cielo y cuenta las estrellas, a ver si puedes. ¡Así de numerosa será tu descendencia!

6Abram creyó al SEÑOR, y el SEÑOR lo reconoció a él como justo. **7**Además, le dijo:

—Yo soy el SEÑOR, que te hice salir de Ur de los *caldeos para darte en posesión esta tierra.

8Pero Abram le preguntó:

—SEÑOR y Dios, ¿cómo sabré que voy a poseerla?

9El SEÑOR le respondió:

—Tráeme una ternera, una cabra y un carnero, todos ellos de tres años, y también una tórtola y un pichón de paloma.

10Abram llevó todos estos animales, los partió por la mitad, y puso una mitad frente a la otra, pero a las aves no las partió. **11**Y las aves de rapiña comenzaron a lanzarse sobre los animales muertos, pero Abram las espantaba.

12Al anochecer, Abram cayó en un profundo sueño, y lo envolvió una oscuridad aterradora. **13**El SEÑOR le dijo:

—Debes saber que tus descendientes vivirán como extranjeros en tierra extraña, donde serán esclavizados y maltratados durante cuatrocientos años. **14**Pero yo castigaré a la nación que los esclavizará, y luego tus descendientes saldrán en libertad y con grandes riquezas. **15**Tú, en cambio, te reunirás en *paz con tus antepasados, y te enterrarán cuando ya seas muy anciano. **16**Cuatro generaciones después tus descendientes volverán a este lugar, porque antes de eso no habrá llegado al colmo la iniquidad de los amorreos.

17Cuando el sol se puso y cayó la noche, aparecieron una hornilla humeante y una antorcha encendida, las cuales pasaban entre los animales descuartizados. **18**En aquel día el SEÑOR hizo un *pacto con Abram. Le dijo:

—A tus descendientes les daré esta tierra, desde el río de Egipto hasta el gran río, el Éufrates. **19**Me refiero a la tierra de los quenitas, los quenizitas, los cadmoneos, **20**los hititas, los ferezeos, los refaítas, **21**los amorreos, los cananeos, los gergeseos y los jebuseos.

Agar e Ismael

16 Saray, la esposa de Abram, no le había dado hijos. Pero como tenía una esclava egipcia llamada Agar, **2**Saray le dijo a Abram:

—El SEÑOR me ha hecho estéril. Por lo tanto, ve y acuéstate con mi esclava Agar. Tal vez por medio de ella podré tener hijos.

Abram aceptó la propuesta que le hizo Saray.

3Entonces ella tomó a Agar, la esclava egipcia, y se la entregó a Abram como mujer. Esto ocurrió cuando ya hacía diez años que Abram vivía en Canaán.

4Abram tuvo relaciones con Agar, y ella concibió un hijo. Al darse cuenta Agar de que estaba embarazada, comenzó a mirar con desprecio a su dueña. **5**Entonces Saray le dijo a Abram:

—¡Tú tienes la culpa de mi afrenta! Yo puse a mi esclava en tus brazos, y ahora que se ve embarazada me mira con desprecio. ¡Que el SEÑOR juzgue entre tú y yo!

6—Tu esclava está en tus manos —contestó Abram—; haz con ella lo que bien te parezca.

Y de tal manera comenzó Saray a maltratar a Agar, que ésta huyó al desierto. **7**Allí, junto a un manantial que está en el camino a la región de Sur, la encontró el ángel del SEÑOR **8**y le preguntó:

—Agar, esclava de Saray, ¿de dónde vienes y a dónde vas?

—Estoy huyendo de mi dueña Saray —respondió ella.

9—Vuelve junto a ella y sométete a su autoridad —le dijo el ángel—. **10**De tal manera multiplicaré tu descendencia, que no se podrá contar.

---

^a **14:13** *hermano*. Alt. *pariente* o *un aliado*. ^b **14:19** *creador*. Alt. *dueño*; también en v. 22. ^c **15:2** *heredero*. Palabra de difícil traducción.

¹¹»Estás embarazada, y darás a luz un hijo,
　y le pondrás por *nombre Ismael,ᵈ
porque el SEÑOR ha escuchado tu aflicción.
¹²Será un hombre indómito como asno salvaje.
　Luchará contra todos, y todos lucharán
　　contra él;
　y vivirá en conflicto con todos sus
　　hermanos.

¹³Como el SEÑOR le había hablado, Agar le puso por nombre «El Dios que me ve»,ᵉ pues se decía: «Ahora he visto alf que me ve.» ¹⁴Por eso también el pozo que está entre Cades y Béred se conoce con el nombre de «Pozo del Viviente que me ve».ᵍ

¹⁵Agar le dio a Abram un hijo, a quien Abram llamó Ismael. ¹⁶Abram tenía ochenta y seis años cuando nació Ismael.

El pacto y la circuncisión

17 Cuando Abram tenía noventa y nueve años, el SEÑOR se le apareció y le dijo:

—Yo soy el Dios *Todopoderoso. Vive en mi presencia y sé intachable. ²Así confirmaré mi *pacto contigo, y multiplicaré tu descendencia en gran manera.

³Al oír que Dios le hablaba, Abram cayó rostro en tierra, y Dios continuó:

⁴—Éste es el pacto que establezco contigo: Tú serás el padre de una multitud de naciones. ⁵Ya no te llamarás Abram,ʰ sino que de ahora en adelante tu *nombre será Abraham,ⁱ porque te he confirmado como padre de una multitud de naciones. ⁶Te haré tan fecundo que de ti saldrán reyes y naciones. ⁷Estableceré mi pacto contigo y con tu descendencia, como pacto perpetuo, por todas las generaciones. Yo seré tu Dios, y el Dios de tus descendientes. ⁸A ti y a tu descendencia les daré, en posesión perpetua, toda la tierra de Canaán, donde ahora andan peregrinando. Y yo seré su Dios.

⁹Dios también le dijo a Abraham:

—Cumple con mi pacto, tú y toda tu descendencia, por todas las generaciones. ¹⁰Y éste es el pacto que establezco contigo y con tu descendencia, y que todos deberán cumplir: Todos los varones entre ustedes deberán ser circuncidados. ¹¹Circuncidarán la carne de su prepucio, y ésa será la señal del pacto entre nosotros. ¹²Todos los varones de cada generación deberán ser circuncidados a los ocho días de nacidos, tanto los niños nacidos en casa como los que hayan sido comprados por dinero a un extranjero y que, por lo tanto, no sean de la estirpe de ustedes. ¹³Todos sin excepción, tanto el nacido en casa como el que haya sido comprado por dinero, deberán ser circuncidados. De esta manera mi pacto quedará como una marca indeleble en la carne de ustedes, como un pacto perpetuo. ¹⁴Pero el varón incircunciso, al que no se le haya cortado la carne del prepucio, será eliminado de su pueblo por quebrantar mi pacto.

¹⁵También le dijo Dios a Abraham:

—A Saray, tu esposa, ya no la llamarás Saray, sino que su nombre será Sara.ʲ ¹⁶Yo la bendeciré, y por medio de ella te daré un hijo. Tanto la bendeciré, que será madre de naciones, y de ella surgirán reyes de pueblos.

¹⁷Entonces Abraham inclinó el rostro hasta el suelo y se rió de pensar: «¿Acaso puede un hombre tener un hijo a los cien años, y ser madre Sara a los noventa?» ¹⁸Por eso le dijo a Dios:

—¡Concédele a Ismael vivir bajo tu bendición!

¹⁹A lo que Dios contestó:

—¡Pero es Sara, tu esposa, la que te dará un hijo, al que llamarás Isaac!ᵏ Yo estableceré mi pacto con él y con sus descendientes, como pacto perpetuo. ²⁰En cuanto a Ismael, ya te he escuchado. Yo lo bendeciré, lo haré fecundo y le daré una descendencia numerosa. Él será el padre de doce príncipes. Haré de él una nación muy grande. ²¹Pero mi pacto lo estableceré con Isaac, el hijo que te dará Sara de aquí a un año, por estos días.

²²Cuando Dios terminó de hablar con Abraham, se retiró de su presencia. ²³Ese mismo día Abraham tomó a su hijo Ismael, a los criados nacidos en su casa, a los que había comprado con su dinero y a todos los otros varones que había en su casa, y los circuncidó, tal como Dios se lo había mandado. ²⁴Abraham tenía noventa y nueve años cuando fue circuncidado, ²⁵mientras que su hijo Ismael tenía trece. ²⁶Así que ambos fueron circuncidados el mismo día ²⁷junto con todos los varones de su casa, tanto los nacidos en ella como los comprados a extranjeros.

La visita del SEÑOR

18 El SEÑOR se le apareció a Abraham junto al encinar de Mamré, cuando Abraham estaba sentado a la entrada de su carpa, a la hora más calurosa del día. ²Abraham alzó la vista, y vio a tres hombres de pie cerca de él. Al verlos, corrió desde la entrada de la carpa a saludarlos. Inclinándose hasta el suelo, ³dijo:

—Mi señor, si este servidor suyo cuenta con su favor, le ruego que no me pase de largo. ⁴Haré que les traigan un poco de agua para que ustedes se laven los pies, y luego podrán descansar bajo el árbol. ⁵Ya que han pasado por donde está su servidor, déjenme traerles algo de comer para que se sientan mejor antes de seguir su camino.

—¡Está bien —respondieron ellos—, hazlo así!

⁶Abraham fue rápidamente a la carpa donde estaba Sara, y le dijo:

—¡Date prisa! Toma unos veinte kilosˡ de harina fina, amásalos y haz unos panes.

⁷Después Abraham fue corriendo adonde estaba el ganado, eligió un ternero bueno y tierno, y se lo dio a su sirviente, quien a toda prisa se puso a prepararlo. ⁸Luego les sirvió requesón y leche con el ternero que estaba preparado. Mientras comían, Abraham se quedó de pie junto a ellos, debajo del árbol.

⁹Entonces ellos le preguntaron:

—¿Dónde está Sara, tu esposa?

—Allí en la carpa —les respondió.

¹⁰—Dentro de un año volveré a verte —dijo uno de ellos—, y para entonces tu esposa Sara tendrá un hijo.

Sara estaba escuchando a la entrada de la carpa, a espaldas del que hablaba. ¹¹Abraham y Sara eran ya bastante ancianos, y Sara ya había dejado de menstruar. ¹²Por eso, Sara se rió y pensó: «¿Acaso voy a tener este placer, ahora que ya estoy consumida y mi esposo es tan viejo?» ¹³Pero el SEÑOR le dijo a Abraham:

—¿Por qué se ríe Sara? ¿No cree que podrá tener un hijo en su vejez? ¹⁴¿Acaso hay algo imposible para

---

ᵈ **16:11** En hebreo, *Ismael* significa *Dios escucha*. ᵉ **16:13** *El Dios que me ve*. Lit. *El Roí*. f **16:13** *he visto al*. Lit. *he visto la espalda del*. ᵍ **16:14** *Pozo del Viviente que me ve*. Lit. *Ber Lajay Roí*. ʰ **17:5** En hebreo, *Abram* significa *padre enaltecido*. ⁱ **17:5** En hebreo, *Abraham* puede significar *padre de muchos* o *padre de misericordia*. ʲ **17:15** En hebreo, *Sara* significa *princesa*. ᵏ **17:19** En hebreo, *Isaac* significa *él se ríe*. ˡ **18:6** *unos veinte kilos*. Lit. *tres *seah*.

el SEÑOR? El año que viene volveré a visitarte en esta fecha, y para entonces Sara habrá tenido un hijo.

15Sara, por su parte, tuvo miedo y mintió al decirle:

—Yo no me estaba riendo.

Pero el SEÑOR le replicó:

—Sí te reíste.

Abraham intercede en favor de Sodoma

16Luego aquellos visitantes se levantaron y partieron de allí en dirección a Sodoma. Abraham los acompañó para despedirlos. 17Pero el SEÑOR estaba pensando: «¿Le ocultaré a Abraham lo que estoy por hacer? 18Es un hecho que Abraham se convertirá en una nación grande y poderosa, y en él serán bendecidas todas las naciones de la tierra. 19Yo lo he elegido para que instruya a sus hijos y a su familia, a fin de que se mantengan en el *camino del SEÑOR y pongan en práctica lo que es justo y recto. Así el SEÑOR cumplirá lo que le ha prometido.»

20Entonces el SEÑOR le dijo a Abraham:

—El clamor contra Sodoma y Gomorra resulta ya insoportable, y su pecado es gravísimo. 21Por eso bajaré, a ver si realmente sus acciones son tan malas como el clamor contra ellas me lo indica; y si no, he de saberlo.

22Dos de los visitantes partieron de allí y se encaminaron a Sodoma, pero Abraham se quedó de pie frente al SEÑOR. 23Entonces se acercó al SEÑOR y le dijo:

—¿De veras vas a exterminar al justo junto con el malvado? 24Quizá haya cincuenta justos en la ciudad. ¿Exterminarás a todos, y no perdonarás a ese lugar por amor a los cincuenta justos que allí hay? 25¡Lejos de ti el hacer tal cosa! ¿Matar al justo junto con el malvado, y que ambos sean tratados de la misma manera? ¡Jamás hagas tal cosa! Tú, que eres el Juez de toda la tierra, ¿no harás justicia?

26El SEÑOR le respondió:

—Si encuentro cincuenta justos en Sodoma, por ellos perdonaré a toda la ciudad.

27Abraham le dijo:

—Reconozco que he sido muy atrevido al dirigirme a mi SEÑOR, yo, que apenas soy polvo y ceniza. 28Pero tal vez falten cinco justos para completar los cincuenta. ¿Destruirás a toda la ciudad si faltan esos cinco?

—Si encuentro cuarenta y cinco justos no la destruiré —contestó el SEÑOR.

29Pero Abraham insistió:

—Tal vez se encuentren sólo cuarenta.

—Por esos cuarenta justos, no destruiré la ciudad —respondió el SEÑOR.

30Abraham volvió a insistir:

—No se enoje mi SEÑOR, pero permítame seguir hablando. Tal vez se encuentren sólo treinta.

—No lo haré si encuentro allí a esos treinta —contestó el SEÑOR.

31Abraham siguió insistiendo:

—Sé que he sido muy atrevido en hablarle así a mi SEÑOR, pero tal vez se encuentren sólo veinte.

—Por esos veinte no la destruiré.

32Abraham volvió a decir:

—No se enoje mi SEÑOR, pero permítame hablar una vez más. Tal vez se encuentren sólo diez…

—Aun por esos diez no la destruiré —respondió el SEÑOR por última vez.

33Cuando el SEÑOR terminó de hablar con Abraham, se fue de allí, y Abraham regresó a su carpa.

Destrucción de Sodoma y Gomorra

19 Caía la tarde cuando los dos ángeles llegaron a Sodoma. Lot estaba sentado a la entrada de la ciudad. Al verlos, se levantó para recibirlos y se postró rostro en tierra. 2Les dijo:

—Por favor, señores, les ruego que pasen la noche en la casa de este servidor suyo. Allí podrán lavarse los pies, y mañana al amanecer seguirán su camino.

—No, gracias —respondieron ellos—. Pasaremos la noche en la plaza.

3Pero tanto les insistió Lot que fueron con él y entraron en su casa. Allí Lot les preparó una buena comida y coció panes sin levadura, y ellos comieron.

4Aún no se habían acostado cuando los hombres de la ciudad de Sodoma rodearon la casa. Todo el pueblo sin excepción, tanto jóvenes como ancianos, estaba allí presente. 5Llamaron a Lot y le dijeron:

—¿Dónde están los hombres que vinieron a pasar la noche en tu casa? ¡Échalos afuera! ¡Queremos acostarnos con ellos!

6Lot salió a la puerta y, cerrándola detrás de sí, 7les dijo:

—Por favor, amigos míos, no cometan tal perversidad. 8Tengo dos hijas que todavía son vírgenes; voy a traérselas para que hagan con ellas lo que les plazca, pero a estos hombres no les hagan nada, pues han venido a hospedarse bajo mi techo.

9—¡Quítate de ahí! —le contestaron, y añadieron—: Éste ni siquiera es de aquí, y ahora nos quiere mandar. ¡Pues ahora te vamos a tratar peor que a ellos!

Entonces se lanzaron contra Lot y se acercaron a la puerta con intenciones de derribarla. 10Pero los dos hombres extendieron los brazos, metieron a Lot en la casa y cerraron la puerta. 11Luego, a los jóvenes y ancianos que se agolparon contra la puerta de la casa los dejaron ciegos, de modo que ya no podían encontrar la puerta. 12Luego le advirtieron a Lot:

—¿Tienes otros familiares aquí? Saca de esta ciudad a tus yernos, hijos, hijas, y a todos los que te pertenezcan, 13porque vamos a destruirla. El clamor contra esta gente ha llegado hasta el SEÑOR, y ya resulta insoportable. Por eso nos ha enviado a destruirla.

14Lot salió para hablar con sus futuros yernos, es decir, con los prometidos de sus hijas.

—¡Apúrense! —les dijo—. ¡Abandonen la ciudad, porque el SEÑOR está por destruirla!

Pero ellos creían que Lot estaba bromeando, 15así que al amanecer los ángeles insistieron con Lot. Exclamaron:

—¡Apúrate! Llévate a tu esposa y a tus dos hijas que están aquí, para que no perezcan cuando la ciudad sea castigada.

16Como Lot titubeaba, los hombres lo tomaron de la mano, lo mismo que a su esposa y a sus dos hijas, y los sacaron de la ciudad, porque el SEÑOR los tuvo compasión. 17Cuando ya los habían sacado de la ciudad, uno de los ángeles le dijo:

—¡Escápate! No mires hacia atrás, ni te detengas en ninguna parte del valle. Huye hacia las montañas, no sea que perezcas.

18—¡No, señor mío, por favor! —respondió Lot—. 19Tú has visto con buenos ojos a este siervo tuyo, y tu lealtad ha sido grande al salvarme la *vida. Pero yo no puedo escaparme a las montañas, no sea que la destrucción me alcance y pierda yo la vida. 20Cerca de aquí hay una ciudad pequeña, en la que podría refugiarme. ¿Por qué no dejan que me escape hacia allá? Es una ciudad muy pequeña, y en ella me pondré a salvo.

21—Está bien —le respondió—; también esta petición te la concederé. No destruiré la ciudad de que hablas. 22Pero date prisa y huye de una vez, porque no puedo hacer nada hasta que llegues allí.

Por eso aquella ciudad recibió el *nombre de Zoar.m

23Lot llegó a Zoar cuando estaba amaneciendo. 24Entonces el SEÑOR hizo que cayera del cielo una lluvia de fuego y azufre sobre Sodoma y Gomorra. 25Así destruyó a esas ciudades y a todos sus habitantes, junto con toda la llanura y la vegetación del suelo. 26Pero la esposa de Lot miró hacia atrás, y se quedó convertida en estatua de sal.

27Al día siguiente Abraham madrugó y regresó al lugar donde se había encontrado con el SEÑOR. 28Volvió la mirada hacia Sodoma y Gomorra, y hacia toda la llanura, y vio que de la tierra subía humo, como de un horno.

29Así arrasó Dios a las ciudades de la llanura, pero se acordó de Abraham y sacó a Lot de en medio de la catástrofe que destruyó a las ciudades en que había habitado.

Lot y sus hijas

30Luego, por miedo a quedarse en Zoar, Lot se fue con sus dos hijas a vivir en la región montañosa. Allí vivió con ellas en una cueva. 31Un día, la hija mayor le dijo a la menor:

—Nuestro padre ya está viejo, y no quedan hombres en esta región para que se casen con nosotras, como es la costumbre de todo el mundo. 32Ven, vamos a emborracharlo, y nos acostaremos con él; y así, por medio de él tendremos descendencia.

33Esa misma noche emborracharon a su padre y, sin que éste se diera cuenta de nada, la hija mayor fue y se acostó con él. 34A la mañana siguiente, la mayor le dijo a la menor:

—Mira, anoche me acosté con mi padre. Vamos a emborracharlo de nuevo esta noche, y ahora tú te acostarás con él; y así, por medio de él tendremos descendencia.

35Esa misma noche volvieron a emborrachar a su padre y, sin que éste se diera cuenta de nada, la hija menor fue y se acostó con él. 36Así las dos hijas de Lot quedaron embarazadas de su padre. 37La mayor tuvo un hijo, a quien llamó Moab,n padre de los actuales moabitas. 38La hija menor también tuvo un hijo, a quien llamó Ben Amí,ñ padre de los actuales amonitas.

Abraham y Abimélec

20 Abraham partió desde allí en dirección a la región del Néguev, y se quedó a vivir entre Cades y Sur. Mientras vivía en Guerar, 2Abraham decía que Sara, su esposa, era su hermana. Entonces Abimélec, rey de Guerar, mandó llamar a Sara y la tomó por esposa. 3Pero aquella noche Dios se le apareció a Abimélec en sueños y le dijo:

—Puedes darte por muerto a causa de la mujer que has tomado, porque ella es casada.

4Pero como Abimélec todavía no se había acostado con ella, le contestó:

—Señor, ¿acaso vas a matar al inocente?o 5Como Abraham me dijo que ella era su hermana, y ella me lo confirmó, yo hice todo esto de buena fe y sin mala intención.

6—Sí, ya sé que has hecho todo esto de buena fe —le respondió Dios en el sueño—; por eso no te permití tocarla, para que no pecaras contra mí. 7Pero ahora devuelve esa mujer a su esposo, porque él es profeta y va a interceder por ti para que vivas. Si no lo haces, ten por seguro que morirás junto con todos los tuyos.

8En la madrugada del día siguiente, Abimélec se levantó y llamó a todos sus servidores para contarles en detalle lo que había ocurrido, y un gran temor se apoderó de ellos. 9Entonces Abimélec llamó a Abraham y le reclamó:

—¡Qué nos has hecho! ¿En qué te he ofendido, que has traído un pecado tan grande sobre mí y sobre mi reino? ¡Lo que me has hecho no tiene nombre! 10¿Qué pretendías conseguir con todo esto?

Al reclamo de Abimélec, 11Abraham contestó:

—Yo pensé que en este lugar no había temor de Dios, y que por causa de mi esposa me matarían. 12Pero en realidad ella es mi hermana, porque es hija de mi padre aunque no de mi madre; y además es mi esposa. 13Cuando Dios me mandó dejar la casa de mi padre y andar errante, yo le dije a mi esposa: "Te pido que me hagas este favor: Dondequiera que vayamos, di siempre que soy tu hermano."

14Abimélec tomó entonces ovejas y vacas, esclavos y esclavas, y se los regaló a Abraham. Al mismo tiempo, le devolvió a Sara, su esposa, 15y le dijo:

—Mira, ahí está todo mi territorio; quédate a vivir donde mejor te parezca.

16A Sara le dijo:

—Le he dado a tu hermano mil monedas de plata, que servirán de compensación por todo lo que te ha pasado; así quedarás vindicada ante todos los que están contigo.p

17Entonces Abraham oró a Dios, y Dios sanó a Abimélec y permitió que su esposa y sus siervas volvieran a tener hijos, 18porque a causa de lo ocurrido con Sara, la esposa de Abraham, el SEÑOR había hecho que todas las mujeres en la casa de Abimélec quedaran estériles.

Nacimiento de Isaac

21 Tal como el SEÑOR lo había dicho, se ocupó de Sara y cumplió con la promesa que le había hecho. 2Sara quedó embarazada y le dio un hijo a Abraham en su vejez. Esto sucedió en el tiempo anunciado por Dios. 3Al hijo que Sara le dio, Abraham le puso por *nombre Isaac.q 4Cuando su hijo Isaac cumplió ocho días de nacido, Abraham lo circuncidó, tal como Dios se lo había ordenado. 5Abraham tenía ya cien años cuando nació su hijo Isaac. 6Sara dijo entonces: «Dios me ha hecho reír, y todos los que se enteren de que he tenido un hijo, se reirán conmigo. 7¿Quién le hubiera dicho a Abraham que Sara amamantaría hijos? Sin embargo, le he dado un hijo en su vejez.»

Expulsión de Agar e Ismael

8El niño Isaac creció y fue destetado. Ese mismo día, Abraham hizo un gran banquete. 9Pero Sara se dio cuenta de que el hijo que Agar la egipcia le había dado a Abraham se burlaba de su hijo Isaac.r 10Por eso le dijo a Abraham:

—¡Echa de aquí a esa esclava y a su hijo! El hijo de esa esclava jamás tendrá parte en la herencia con mi hijo Isaac.

---

m 19:22 En hebreo, Zoar significa pequeña. n 19:37 En hebreo, Moab suena como la palabra que significa por parte del padre. ñ 19:38 En hebreo, Ben Amí suena como la palabra que significa hijo de mi pueblo. o 20:4 al inocente. Lit. a una nación justa. p 20:16 que servirán ... contigo. Texto de difícil traducción. q 21:3 En hebreo, Isaac significa él se ríe. r 21:9 de su hijo Isaac (LXX); TM no incluye estas palabras.

11Este asunto angustió mucho a Abraham porque se trataba de su propio hijo. 12Pero Dios le dijo a Abraham: «No te angusties por el muchacho ni por la esclava. Hazle caso a Sara, porque tu descendencia se establecerá por medio de Isaac. 13Pero también del hijo de la esclava haré una gran nación, porque es hijo tuyo.»

14Al día siguiente, Abraham se levantó de madrugada, tomó un pan y un odre de agua, y se los dio a Agar, poniéndoselos sobre el hombro. Luego le entregó a su hijo y la despidió. Agar partió y anduvo errante por el desierto de Berseba. 15Cuando se acabó el agua del odre, puso al niño debajo de un arbusto 16y fue a sentarse sola a cierta distancia,s pues pensaba: «No quiero ver morir al niño.» En cuanto ella se sentó, comenzó a llorar desconsoladamente.

17Cuando Dios oyó al niño sollozar, el ángel de Dios llamó a Agar desde el cielo y le dijo: «¿Qué te pasa, Agar? No temas, pues Dios ha escuchado los sollozos del niño. 18Levántate y tómalo de la mano, que yo haré de él una gran nación.»

19En ese momento Dios le abrió a Agar los ojos, y ella vio un pozo de agua. En seguida fue a llenar el odre y le dio de beber al niño. 20Dios acompañó al niño, y éste fue creciendo; vivió en el desierto y se convirtió en un experto arquero; 21habitó en el desierto de Parán y su madre lo casó con una egipcia.

Pacto entre Abraham y Abimélec

22En aquel tiempo Abimélec, que estaba acompañado por Ficol, jefe de su ejército, le dijo a Abraham:

—Dios está contigo en todo lo que haces. 23Júrame ahora, por Dios mismo, que no me tratarás a mí con falsedad, ni tampoco a mis hijos ni a mis descendientes. Júrame que a mí y al país que te ha recibido como extranjero nos tratarás con la misma lealtad con que yo te he tratado.

24—¡Lo juro! —respondió Abraham.

25Luego Abraham se quejó ante Abimélec por causa de un pozo de agua del cual los siervos de Abimélec se habían apropiado. 26Pero Abimélec dijo:

—No sé quién pudo haberlo hecho. Me acabo de enterar, pues tú no me lo habías dicho.

27Entonces Abraham llevó ovejas y vacas, y se las dio a Abimélec, y los dos hicieron un pacto. 28Pero Abraham apartó siete corderas del rebaño, 29por lo que Abimélec le preguntó:

—¿Qué pasa? ¿Por qué has apartado estas siete corderas?

30—Acepta estas siete corderas —le contestó Abraham—. Ellas servirán de prueba de que yo cavé este pozo.

31Por eso a aquel lugar le dieron el nombre de Berseba,t porque allí los dos hicieron un juramento.

32Después de haber hecho el pacto en Berseba, Abimélec y Ficol, el jefe de su ejército, volvieron al país de los filisteos. 33Abraham plantó un tamarisco en Berseba, y en ese lugar invocó el *nombre del SEÑOR, el Dios eterno. 34Y se quedó en el país de los filisteos durante mucho tiempo.

Dios prueba a Abraham

22 Pasado cierto tiempo, Dios puso a prueba a Abraham y le dijo:

—¡Abraham!

—Aquí estoy —respondió.

2Y Dios le ordenó:

—Toma a tu hijo, el único que tienes y al que tanto amas, y ve a la región de Moria. Una vez allí, ofrécelo como *holocausto en el monte que yo te indicaré.

3Abraham se levantó de madrugada y ensilló su asno. También cortó leña para el holocausto y, junto con dos de sus criados y su hijo Isaac, se encaminó hacia el lugar que Dios le había indicado. 4Al tercer día, Abraham alzó los ojos y a lo lejos vio el lugar. 5Entonces le dijo a sus criados:

—Quédense aquí con el asno. El muchacho y yo seguiremos adelante para adorar a Dios, y luego regresaremos junto a ustedes.

6Abraham tomó la leña del holocausto y la puso sobre Isaac, su hijo; él, por su parte, cargó con el fuego y el cuchillo. Y los dos siguieron caminando juntos.

7Isaac le dijo a Abraham:

—¡Padre!

—Dime, hijo mío.

—Aquí tenemos el fuego y la leña —continuó Isaac—; pero, ¿dónde está el cordero para el holocausto?

8—El cordero, hijo mío, lo proveerá Dios —le respondió Abraham.

Y siguieron caminando juntos.

9Cuando llegaron al lugar señalado por Dios, Abraham construyó un altar y preparó la leña. Después ató a su hijo Isaac y lo puso sobre el altar, encima de la leña. 10Entonces tomó el cuchillo para sacrificar a su hijo, 11pero en ese momento el ángel del SEÑOR le gritó desde el cielo:

—¡Abraham! ¡Abraham!

—Aquí estoy —respondió.

12—No pongas tu mano sobre el muchacho, ni le hagas ningún daño —le dijo el ángel—. Ahora sé que temes a Dios, porque ni siquiera te has negado a darme a tu único hijo.

13Abraham alzó la vista y, en un matorral, vio un carnero enredado por los cuernos. Fue entonces, tomó el carnero y lo ofreció como holocausto, en lugar de su hijo. 14A ese sitio Abraham le puso por *nombre: «El SEÑOR provee.» Por eso hasta el día de hoy se dice: «En un monte provee el SEÑOR.»

15El ángel del SEÑOR llamó a Abraham por segunda vez desde el cielo, 16y le dijo:

—Como has hecho esto, y no me has negado a tu único hijo, juro por mí mismo —afirma el SEÑOR— 17que te bendeciré en gran manera, y que multiplicaré tu descendencia como las estrellas del cielo y como la arena del mar. Además, tus descendientes conquistarán las ciudades de sus enemigos. 18Puesto que me has obedecido, todas las naciones del mundo serán bendecidas por medio de tu descendencia.

19Abraham regresó al lugar donde estaban sus criados, y juntos partieron hacia Berseba, donde Abraham se quedó a vivir.

Los hijos de Najor

20Pasado cierto tiempo, Abraham recibió la noticia de que también Milca le había dado hijos a su hermano Najor. 21Su hijo primogénito fue Uz; luego nacieron sus hermanos Buz y Quemuel. Este último fue el padre de Aram. 22Después siguieron Quésed, Jazó, Pildás, Yidlaf y Betuel, 23que fue el padre de Rebeca. Éstos fueron los ocho hijos que Milca le dio a Najor, hermano de Abraham. 24Najor también tuvo hijos con Reumá, su concubina. Ellos fueron Tébaj, Gaján, Tajás y Macá.

s 21:16 a cierta distancia. Lit. a la distancia de un tiro de arco.   t 21:31 En hebreo, Berseba significa pozo de los siete, o pozo del juramento.

Muerte de Sara

23 Sara vivió ciento veintisiete años, ²y murió en Quiriat Arbá, es decir, en la ciudad de Hebrón, en la tierra de Canaán. Abraham hizo duelo y lloró por ella. ³Luego se retiró de donde estaba la difunta y fue a proponer a los hititas lo siguiente:

⁴—Entre ustedes yo soy un extranjero; no obstante, quiero pedirles que me vendan un sepulcro para enterrar a mi esposa.

⁵Los hititas le respondieron:

⁶—Escúchenos, señor; usted es un príncipe poderoso entre nosotros. Sepulte a su esposa en el mejor de nuestros sepulcros. Ninguno de nosotros le negará su tumba para que pueda sepultar a su esposa.

⁷Abraham se levantó, hizo una reverencia ante los hititas del lugar, ⁸y les dijo:

—Si les parece bien que yo entierre aquí a mi difunta, les ruego que intercedan ante Efrón hijo de Zojar ⁹para que me venda la cueva de Macpela, que está en los linderos de su campo. Dígale que me la venda en su justo precio, y así tendré entre ustedes un sepulcro para mi familia.

¹⁰Efrón el hitita, que estaba sentado allí entre su gente, le respondió a Abraham en presencia de todos ellos y de los que pasaban por la *puerta de su ciudad:

¹¹—No, señor mío, escúcheme bien: yo le regalo el campo, y también la cueva que está en él. Los hijos de mi pueblo son testigos de que yo se los regalo. Entierre usted a su esposa.

¹²Una vez más, Abraham hizo una reverencia ante la gente de ese lugar, ¹³y en presencia de los que allí estaban le dijo a Efrón:

—Escúcheme, por favor. Yo insisto en pagarle el precio justo del campo. Acéptelo usted, y así yo podré enterrar allí a mi esposa.

¹⁴Efrón le contestó a Abraham:

¹⁵—Señor mío, escúcheme. El campo vale cuatrocientas monedas^u de plata. ¿Qué es eso entre nosotros? Vaya tranquilo y entierre a su esposa.

¹⁶Abraham se puso de acuerdo con Efrón, y en presencia de los hititas le pagó lo convenido: cuatrocientas monedas de plata, moneda corriente entre los comerciantes.

¹⁷Así fue como el campo de Efrón, que estaba en Macpela, cerca de Mamré, pasó a ser propiedad de Abraham, junto con la cueva y todos los árboles que estaban dentro de los límites del campo. ¹⁸La transacción se hizo en presencia de los hititas y de los que pasaban por la puerta de su ciudad. ¹⁹Luego Abraham sepultó a su esposa Sara en la cueva del campo de Macpela que está cerca de Mamré, es decir, en Hebrón, en la tierra de Canaán. ²⁰De esta manera, el campo y la cueva que estaba en él dejó de ser de los hititas y pasó a ser propiedad de Abraham para sepultura.

Isaac y Rebeca

24 Abraham estaba ya entrado en años, y el SEÑOR lo había bendecido en todo. ²Un día, Abraham le dijo al criado más antiguo de su casa, que era quien le administraba todos sus bienes:

—Pon tu mano debajo de mi muslo, ³y júrame por el SEÑOR, el Dios del cielo y de la tierra, que no tomarás de esta tierra de Canaán, donde yo habito, una mujer para mi hijo ⁴Isaac, sino que irás a mi tierra, donde vive mi familia, y de allí le escogerás una esposa.

⁵—¿Qué pasa si la mujer no está dispuesta a venir conmigo a esta tierra? —respondió el criado—. ¿Debo entonces llevar a su hijo hasta la tierra de donde usted vino?

⁶—¡De ninguna manera debes llevar a mi hijo hasta allá! —le replicó Abraham—. ⁷El SEÑOR, el Dios del cielo, que me sacó de la casa de mi padre y de la tierra de mis familiares, y que bajo juramento me prometió dar esta tierra a mis descendientes, enviará su ángel delante de ti para que puedas traer de allá una mujer para mi hijo. ⁸Si la mujer no está dispuesta a venir contigo, quedarás libre de este juramento; pero ¡en ningún caso llevarás a mi hijo hasta allá!

⁹El criado puso la mano debajo del muslo de Abraham, su amo, y le juró que cumpliría con su encargo. ¹⁰Luego tomó diez camellos de su amo, y toda clase de regalos, y partió hacia la ciudad de Najor en Aram Najarayin.^{v} ¹¹Allí hizo que los camellos se arrodillaran junto al pozo de agua que estaba en las afueras de la ciudad. Caía la tarde, que es cuando las mujeres salen a buscar agua. ¹²Entonces comenzó a orar: «SEÑOR, Dios de mi amo Abraham, te ruego que hoy me vaya bien, y que demuestres el amor que le tienes a mi amo. ¹³Aquí me tienes, a la espera junto a la fuente, mientras las jóvenes de esta ciudad vienen a sacar agua. ¹⁴Permite que la joven a quien le diga: "Por favor, baje usted su cántaro para que tome yo un poco de agua", y que me conteste: "Tome usted, y además les daré agua a sus camellos", sea la que tú has elegido para tu siervo Isaac. Así estaré seguro de que tú has demostrado el amor que le tienes a mi amo.»

¹⁵Aún no había terminado de orar cuando vio que se acercaba Rebeca, con su cántaro al hombro. Rebeca era hija de Betuel, que a su vez era hijo de Milca y Najor, el hermano de Abraham. ¹⁶La joven era muy hermosa, y además virgen, pues no había tenido relaciones sexuales con ningún hombre. Bajó hacia la fuente y llenó su cántaro. Ya se preparaba para subir ¹⁷cuando el criado corrió a su encuentro y le dijo:

—¿Podría usted darme un poco de agua de su cántaro?

¹⁸—Sírvase, mi señor —le respondió.

Y en seguida bajó el cántaro y, sosteniéndolo entre sus manos, le dio de beber.

¹⁹Cuando ya el criado había bebido, ella le dijo:

—Voy también a sacar agua para que sus camellos beban todo lo que quieran.

²⁰De inmediato vació su cántaro en el bebedero, y volvió corriendo al pozo para buscar más agua, repitiendo la acción hasta que hubo suficiente agua para todos los camellos. ²¹Mientras tanto, el criado de Abraham la observaba en silencio, para ver si el SEÑOR había coronado su viaje con el éxito.

²²Cuando los camellos terminaron de beber, el criado tomó un anillo de oro que pesaba seis gramos, y se lo puso a la joven en la nariz;^{w} también le colocó en los brazos dos pulseras de oro que pesaban más de cien gramos,^{x} y le preguntó:

²³—¿Podría usted decirme de quién es hija, y si habrá lugar en la casa de su padre para hospedarnos?

²⁴—Soy hija de Betuel, el hijo de Milca y Najor —respondió ella, ²⁵a lo que agregó—: No sólo tenemos lugar para ustedes, sino que también tenemos paja y forraje en abundancia para los camellos.

u 23:15 *monedas*. Lit. *siclos*. **v 24:10** *Aram Najarayin*. Es decir, el noroeste de Mesopotamia. **w 24:22** *se lo puso a la joven en la nariz* (Pentateuco Samaritano). TM no incluye esta frase; véase v. 47. **x 24:22** *seis gramos ... más de cien gramos*. Lit. *un *becá ... diez *siclos*.

²⁶Entonces el criado de Abraham se arrodilló y adoró al SEÑOR ²⁷con estas palabras: «Bendito sea el SEÑOR, el Dios de mi amo Abraham, que no ha dejado de manifestarle su amor y fidelidad, y que a mí me ha guiado a la casa de sus parientes.»

²⁸La joven corrió hasta la casa de su madre, y allí contó lo que le había sucedido. ²⁹Tenía Rebeca un hermano llamado Labán, que salió corriendo al encuentro del criado, quien seguía junto a la fuente. ³⁰Labán se había fijado en el anillo y las pulseras en los brazos de su hermana, y también la había escuchado contar lo que el criado le había dicho. Por eso salió en busca del criado, y lo encontró junto a la fuente, con sus camellos.

³¹—¡Ven, bendito del SEÑOR! —le dijo—. ¿Por qué te quedas afuera? ¡Ya he preparado la casa y un lugar para los camellos!

³²El criado entró en la casa. En seguida Labán desaparejó los camellos, les dio paja y forraje, y llevó agua para que el criado y sus acompañantes se lavaran los pies. ³³Cuando le sirvieron de comer, el criado dijo:

—No comeré hasta haberles dicho lo que tengo que decir.

—Habla con toda confianza —respondió Labán.

³⁴—Yo soy criado de Abraham —comenzó él—. ³⁵El SEÑOR ha bendecido mucho a mi amo y lo ha prosperado. Le ha dado ovejas y ganado, oro y plata, siervos y siervas, camellos y asnos. ³⁶Sara, la esposa de mi amo, le dio en su vejez un hijo, al que mi amo le ha dejado todo lo que tiene. ³⁷Mi amo me hizo jurar, y me dijo: "No tomarás para mi hijo una mujer de entre las hijas de los cananeos, en cuyo país habito. ³⁸Al contrario, irás a la familia de mi padre, y le buscarás una esposa entre las mujeres de mis parientes." ³⁹Yo le pregunté a mi amo: "¿Y si la mujer no acepta venir conmigo?" ⁴⁰Él me respondió: "El SEÑOR, en cuya presencia he caminado, enviará su ángel contigo, y él hará prosperar tu viaje para que consigas para mi hijo una esposa que pertenezca a la familia de mi padre. ⁴¹Sólo quedarás libre del juramento si vas a ver a mi familia y ellos no te conceden a la joven."

⁴²»Todavía no había terminado yo de orar cuando vi que Rebeca se acercaba con un cántaro sobre el hombro. Bajó a la fuente para sacar agua, y yo le dije: "Por favor, déme usted de beber." ⁴³Aquí me tienes, a la espera junto a la fuente. Si una joven sale a buscar agua, y yo le digo: 'Por favor, déjeme usted beber un poco de agua de su cántaro', ⁴⁴y ella me contesta: 'Beba usted, y también le daré agua a sus camellos', que sea ella la mujer que tú, SEÑOR, has escogido para el hijo de mi amo."

⁴⁵»Todavía no había terminado yo de orar cuando vi que Rebeca se acercaba con un cántaro sobre el hombro. Bajó a la fuente para sacar agua, y yo le dije: "Por favor, déme usted de beber." ⁴⁶En seguida bajó ella su cántaro y me dijo: "Beba usted, y también les daré de beber a sus camellos." Mientras yo bebía, ella les dio agua a los camellos. ⁴⁷Luego le pregunté: "¿Hija de quién es usted?" Y cuando ella me respondió: "Soy hija de Betuel, el hijo de Najor y de Milca", yo le puse un anillo en la nariz y pulseras en los brazos, ⁴⁸y me incliné para adorar al SEÑOR. Bendije al SEÑOR, el Dios de Abraham, que me guió por el camino correcto para llevarle al hijo de mi amo una parienta cercana suya. ⁴⁹Y ahora, si desean mostrarle lealtad y fidelidad a mi amo, díganmelo; y si no, díganmelo también. Así yo sabré qué hacer.

⁵⁰Labán y Betuel respondieron:

—Sin duda todo esto proviene del SEÑOR, y nosotros no podemos decir ni que sí ni que no. ⁵¹Aquí está Rebeca; tómela usted y llévesela para que sea la esposa del hijo de su amo, tal como el SEÑOR lo ha dispuesto.

⁵²Al escuchar esto, el criado de Abraham se postró en tierra delante del SEÑOR. ⁵³Luego sacó joyas de oro y de plata, y vestidos, y se los dio a Rebeca. También entregó regalos a su hermano y a su madre. ⁵⁴Más tarde, él y sus acompañantes comieron y bebieron, y pasaron allí la noche.

A la mañana siguiente, cuando se levantaron, el criado de Abraham dijo:

—Déjenme ir a la casa de mi amo.

⁵⁵Pero el hermano y la madre de Rebeca le respondieron:

—Que se quede la joven con nosotros unos diez días, y luego podrás irte.

⁵⁶—No me detengan —repuso el criado—. El SEÑOR ha prosperado mi viaje, así que déjenme ir a la casa de mi amo.

⁵⁷—Llamemos a la joven, a ver qué piensa ella —respondieron.

⁵⁸Así que llamaron a Rebeca y le preguntaron:

—¿Quieres irte con este hombre?

—Sí —respondió ella.

⁵⁹Entonces dejaron ir a su hermana Rebeca y a su nodriza con el criado de Abraham y sus acompañantes. ⁶⁰Y bendijeron a Rebeca con estas palabras:

«Hermana nuestra:
¡que seas madre de millares!
¡Que dominen tus descendientes
las ciudades de sus enemigos!»

⁶¹Luego Rebeca y sus criadas se prepararon, montaron en los camellos y siguieron al criado de Abraham. Así fue como él tomó a Rebeca y se marchó de allí.

⁶²Ahora bien, Isaac había vuelto del pozo de Lajay Roí, porque vivía en la región del Néguev. ⁶³Una tarde, salió a dar un paseoʸ por el campo. De pronto, al levantar la vista, vio que se acercaban unos camellos. ⁶⁴También Rebeca levantó la vista y, al ver a Isaac, se bajó del camello ⁶⁵ y le preguntó al criado:

—¿Quién es ese hombre que viene por el campo a nuestro encuentro?

—Es mi amo —contestó el criado.

Entonces ella tomó el velo y se cubrió.

⁶⁶El criado le contó a Isaac todo lo que había hecho. ⁶⁷Luego Isaac llevó a Rebeca a la carpa de Sara, su madre, y la tomó por esposa. Isaac amó a Rebeca, y así se consoló de la muerte de su madre.

Muerte de Abraham
25:1-4 — 1Cr 1:32-33

25 Abraham volvió a casarse, esta vez con una mujer llamada Cetura. ²Los hijos que tuvo con ella fueron: Zimrán, Jocsán, Medán, Madián, Isbac y Súaj.

³Jocsán fue el padre de Sabá y Dedán.

Los descendientes de Dedán fueron los asureos, los letuseos y los leumeos.

⁴Los hijos de Madián fueron Efá, Éfer, Janoc, Abidá y Eldá. Todos éstos fueron hijos de Cetura.

⁵Abraham entregó todos sus bienes a Isaac. ⁶A los hijos de sus concubinas les hizo regalos y, mientras él todavía estaba con vida, los separó de su hijo Isaac, enviándolos a las regiones orientales.

ʸ 24:63 *a dar un paseo.* Texto de difícil traducción.

7Abraham vivió ciento setenta y cinco años, 8y murió en buena vejez, luego de haber vivido muchos años, y fue a reunirse con sus antepasados. 9Sus hijos Isaac e Ismael lo sepultaron en la cueva de Macpela, que está cerca de Mamré, es decir, en el campo del hitita Efrón hijo de Zojar. 10Éste era el campo que Abraham les había comprado a los hititas. Allí lo enterraron, junto a su esposa Sara. 11Luego de la muerte de Abraham, Dios bendijo a Isaac, hijo de Abraham, quien se quedó a vivir cerca del pozo de Lajay Roí.

Descendientes de Ismael
25:12-16 — 1Cr 1:29-31

12Ésta es la descendencia de Ismael, el hijo que Abraham tuvo con Agar, la criada egipcia de Sara. 13Éstos son los nombres de los hijos de Ismael, comenzando por el primogénito: Nebayot, Cedar, Adbel, Mibsán, 14Mismá, Dumá, Masá, 15Hadar, Temá, Jetur, Nafis y Cedema. 16Éstos fueron los hijos de Ismael, y éstos los nombres de los doce jefes de tribus, según sus propios territorios y campamentos.

17Ismael vivió ciento treinta y siete años. Al morir, fue a reunirse con sus antepasados. 18Sus descendientes se quedaron a vivir en la región que está entre Javilá y Sur, cerca de Egipto, en la ruta que conduce a Asiria. Allí se establecieron en franca oposición a todos sus hermanos.

Nacimiento de Jacob y de Esaú

19Ésta es la historia de Isaac, el hijo que tuvo Abraham. 20Isaac tenía cuarenta años cuando se casó con Rebeca, que era hija de Betuel y hermana de Labán. Betuel y Labán eran *arameos de Padán Aram.z 21Isaac oró al SEÑOR en favor de su esposa, porque era estéril. El SEÑOR oyó su oración, y ella quedó embarazada. 22Pero como los niños luchaban dentro de su seno, ella se preguntó: «Si esto va a seguir así, ¿para qué sigo viviendo?» Entonces fue a consultar al SEÑOR, 23y él le contestó:

«Dos naciones hay en tu seno;
    dos pueblos se dividen desde tus entrañas.
Uno será más fuerte que el otro,
    y el mayor servirá al menor.»

24Cuando le llegó el momento de dar a luz, resultó que en su seno había mellizos. 25El primero en nacer era pelirrojo, y tenía todo el cuerpo cubierto de vello. A éste lo llamaron Esaú.a 26Luego nació su hermano, agarrado con una mano del talón de Esaú. A éste lo llamaron Jacob.b Cuando nacieron los mellizos, Isaac tenía sesenta años.

27Los niños crecieron. Esaú era un hombre de campo y se convirtió en un excelente cazador, mientras que Jacob era un hombre tranquilo que prefería quedarse en el campamento. 28Isaac quería más a Esaú, porque le gustaba comer de lo que él cazaba; pero Rebeca quería más a Jacob.

29Un día, cuando Jacob estaba preparando un guiso, Esaú llegó agotado del campo y le dijo:

30—Dame de comer de ese guiso rojizo, porque estoy muy cansado. (Por eso a Esaú se le llamó Edom.)c

31—Véndeme primero tus derechos de hijo mayor —le respondió Jacob.

32—Me estoy muriendo de hambre —contestó Esaú—, así que ¿de qué me sirven los derechos de primogénito?

33—Véndeme entonces los derechos bajo juramento —insistió Jacob.

Esaú se lo juró, y fue así como le vendió a Jacob sus derechos de primogénito. 34Jacob, por su parte, le dio a Esaú pan y guiso de lentejas.

Luego de comer y beber, Esaú se levantó y se fue. De esta manera menospreció sus derechos de hijo mayor.

Isaac y Abimélec

26 En ese tiempo hubo mucha hambre en aquella región, además de la que hubo en tiempos de Abraham. Por eso Isaac se fue a Guerar, donde se encontraba Abimélec, rey de los filisteos. 2Allí el SEÑOR se le apareció y le dijo: «No vayas a Egipto. Quédate en la región de la que te he hablado. 3Vive en ese lugar por un tiempo. Yo estaré contigo y te bendeciré, porque a ti y a tu descendencia les daré todas esas tierras. Así confirmaré el juramento que le hice a tu padre Abraham. 4Multiplicaré a tus descendientes como las estrellas del cielo, y les daré todas esas tierras. Por medio de tu descendencia todas las naciones de la tierra serán bendecidas, 5porque Abraham me obedeció y cumplió mis preceptos y mis mandamientos, mis normas y mis enseñanzas.»

6Isaac se quedó en Guerar. 7Y cuando la gente del lugar le preguntaba a Isaac acerca de su esposa, él respondía que ella era su hermana. Tan bella era Rebeca que Isaac tenía miedo de decir que era su esposa, pues pensaba que por causa de ella podrían matarlo.

8Algún tiempo después, mientras Abimélec, el rey de los filisteos, miraba por una ventana, vio a Isaac acariciando a su esposa Rebeca. 9Entonces mandó llamar a Isaac y le dijo:

—¡Conque ella es tu esposa! ¿Por qué dijiste que era tu hermana?

—Yo pensé que por causa de ella podrían matarme —contestó Isaac.

10—¿Por qué nos hiciste esto? —replicó Abimélec—. Alguno de nosotros podría haberse acostado con tu esposa, ¡y tú nos habrías hecho a todos culpables de ese pecado!

11Por eso Abimélec envió esta orden a todo el pueblo:

—Si alguien molesta a este hombre o a su esposa, será condenado a muerte.

12Isaac sembró en aquella región, y ese año cosechó al ciento por uno, porque el SEÑOR lo había bendecido. 13Así Isaac fue acumulando riquezas, hasta que llegó a ser muy rico. 14Esto causó que los filisteos comenzaran a tenerle envidia, pues llegó a tener muchas ovejas, vacas y siervos. 15Ahora bien, los filisteos habían cegado todos los pozos de agua que los siervos del padre de Isaac habían cavado. 16Así que Abimélec le dijo a Isaac:

—Aléjate de nosotros, pues ya eres más poderoso que nosotros.

17Isaac se fue de allí, y acampó en el valle de Guerar, donde se quedó a vivir. 18Abrió nuevamente los pozos de agua que habían sido cavados en tiempos de su padre Abraham, y que los filisteos habían tapado después de su muerte, y les puso los mismos *nombres que su padre les había dado.

19Cierta vez, cuando los siervos de Isaac estaban cavando en el valle, encontraron un manantial. 20Pero los pastores de Guerar discutieron acaloradamente con los pastores de Isaac, alegando que el agua era de

z 25:20 Padán Aram. Es decir, el noroeste de Mesopotamia. a 25:25 En hebreo, Esaú puede significar velludo; véase también v. 30. b 25:26 En hebreo, Jacob significa él agarra el talón. c 25:30 En hebreo, Edom significa rojo.

ellos. Por eso Isaac llamó a ese pozo Pleito,ᵈ porque habían peleado con él. ²¹Después sus siervos cavaron otro pozo, por el cual también se pelearon. Por eso Isaac lo llamó Enemistad.ᵉ ²²Entonces Isaac se fue de allí y cavó otro pozo, pero esta vez no hubo ninguna disputa. A este pozo lo llamó Espacios libres,ᶠ y dijo: «El SEÑOR nos ha dado espacio para que prosperemos en esta región.»

²³De allí Isaac se dirigió a Berseba. ²⁴Esa noche se le apareció el SEÑOR, y le dijo:

«Yo soy el Dios de tu padre Abraham.
No temas, que yo estoy contigo.
Por amor a mi siervo Abraham,
te bendeciré y multiplicaré tu descendencia.»

²⁵Allí Isaac construyó un altar e invocó el nombre del SEÑOR. Acampó en ese lugar, y sus siervos cavaron un pozo. ²⁶Cierto día, Abimélec fue a ver a Isaac desde Guerar. Llegó acompañado de su consejero Ajuzat, y de Ficol, el jefe de su ejército. ²⁷Isaac les preguntó:

—Si tanto me odian, que hasta me echaron de su tierra, ¿para qué vienen a verme?

²⁸—Nos hemos dado cuenta de que el SEÑOR está contigo —respondieron—. Hemos pensado que tú y nosotros debiéramos hacer un pacto, respaldado por un juramento. Ese pacto será el siguiente: ²⁹Tú no nos harás ningún daño, ya que nosotros no te hemos perjudicado, sino que te hemos tratado bien y te hemos dejado ir en *paz. ¡Ahora el bendecido del SEÑOR eres tú!

³⁰Isaac les preparó un banquete, y comieron y bebieron. ³¹A la mañana siguiente se levantaron muy temprano, e hicieron un compromiso mutuo. Luego Isaac los despidió, y ellos se fueron en calidad de amigos.

³²Aquel mismo día, los siervos de Isaac fueron y le informaron acerca de un pozo que habían cavado, y le dijeron:

—¡Hemos encontrado agua!

³³Isaac llamó a ese pozo Juramento.ᵍ Por eso la ciudad se llama Bersebaʰ hasta el día de hoy.

Isaac bendice a Jacob

³⁴Esaú tenía cuarenta años de edad cuando se casó con Judit hija de Beerí, el hitita. También se casó con Basemat, hija de un hitita llamado Elón. ³⁵Estas dos mujeres les causaron mucha amargura a Isaac y a Rebeca.

27 Isaac había llegado a viejo y se había quedado ciego. Un día llamó a Esaú, su hijo mayor.

—¡Hijo mío! —le dijo.

—Aquí estoy —le contestó Esaú.

—Como te darás cuenta, ya estoy muy viejo y en cualquier momento puedo morirme. ³Toma, pues, tus armas, tu arco y tus flechas, y ve al campo a cazarme algún animal. ⁴Prepárame luego un buen guiso, como a mí me gusta, y tráemelo para que me lo coma. Entonces te bendeciré antes de que muera.

⁵Como Rebeca había estado escuchando mientras Isaac le hablaba a su hijo Esaú, en cuanto éste se fue al campo a cazar un animal para su padre, ⁶ella le dijo a su hijo Jacob:

—Según acabo de escuchar, tu padre le ha pedido a tu hermano Esaú ⁷que cace un animal y se lo traiga para hacerle un guiso como a él le gusta. También le ha prometido que antes de morirse lo va a bendecir, poniendo al SEÑOR como testigo. ⁸Ahora

bien, hijo mío, escúchame bien, y haz lo que te mando. ⁹Ve al rebaño y tráeme de allí dos de los mejores cabritos, para que yo le prepare a tu padre un guiso como a él le gusta. ¹⁰Tú se lo llevarás para que se lo coma, y así él te dará su bendición antes de morirse.

¹¹Pero Jacob le dijo a su madre:

—Hay un problema: mi hermano Esaú es muy velludo, y yo soy lampiño. ¹²Si mi padre me toca, se dará cuenta de que quiero engañarlo, y esto hará que me maldiga en vez de bendecirme.

¹³—Hijo mío, ¡que esa maldición caiga sobre mí! —le contestó su madre—. Tan sólo haz lo que te pido, y ve a buscarme esos cabritos.

¹⁴Jacob fue a buscar los cabritos, se los llevó a su madre, y ella preparó el guiso tal como le gustaba a su padre. ¹⁵Luego sacó la mejor ropa de su hijo mayor Esaú, la cual tenía en casa, y con ella vistió a su hijo menor Jacob. ¹⁶Con la piel de los cabritos le cubrió los brazos y la parte lampiña del cuello, ¹⁷y le entregó a Jacob el guiso y el pan que había preparado.

¹⁸Jacob se presentó ante su padre y le dijo:

—¡Padre!

—Dime, hijo mío, ¿quién eres tú? —preguntó Isaac.

¹⁹—Soy Esaú, tu primogénito —le contestó Jacob—. Ya hice todo lo que me pediste. Ven, por favor, y siéntate a comer de lo que he cazado; así podrás darme tu bendición.

²⁰Pero Isaac le preguntó a su hijo:

—¿Cómo fue que lo encontraste tan pronto, hijo mío?

—El SEÑOR tu Dios me ayudó —respondió Jacob.

²¹Isaac le dijo:

—Acércate, hijo mío, para que pueda tocarte y saber si de veras eres o no mi hijo Esaú.

²²Jacob se acercó a su padre, quien al tocarlo dijo:

—La voz es la de Jacob, pero las manos son las de Esaú.

²³Así que no lo reconoció, porque sus manos eran velludas como las de Esaú. Ya se disponía a bendecirlo ²⁴cuando volvió a preguntarle:

—¿En serio eres mi hijo Esaú?

—Claro que sí —respondió Jacob.

²⁵Entonces su padre le dijo:

—Tráeme lo que has cazado, para que lo coma, y te daré mi bendición.

Jacob le sirvió, y su padre comió. También le llevó vino, y su padre lo bebió.

²⁶Luego le dijo su padre:

—Acércate ahora, hijo mío, y dame un beso.

²⁷Jacob se acercó y lo besó. Cuando Isaac olió su ropa, lo bendijo con estas palabras:

«El olor de mi hijo es como el de un campo
bendecido por el SEÑOR.
²⁸Que Dios te conceda el rocío del cielo;
que de la riqueza de la tierra
te dé trigo y vino en abundancia.
²⁹Que te sirvan los pueblos;
que ante ti se inclinen las naciones.
Que seas señor de tus hermanos;
que ante ti se inclinen los hijos de tu
madre.
Maldito sea el que te maldiga,
y bendito el que te bendiga.»

³⁰No bien había terminado Isaac de bendecir a Jacob, y éste de salir de la presencia de su padre,

---

ᵈ **26:20** *Pleito.* Hebreo *Esek.*   ᵉ **26:21** *Enemistad.* Hebreo *Sitna.*   ᶠ **26:22** *Espacios libres.* Hebreo *Rejobot.*   ᵍ **26:33** *Juramento.* Alt. *Siete.*   ʰ **26:33** En hebreo, *Berseba* puede significar *Pozo del Juramento* o *Pozo de los Siete.*

cuando Esaú volvió de cazar. ³¹También él preparó un guiso, se lo llevó a su padre y le dijo:

—Levántate, padre mío, y come de lo que ha cazado tu hijo. Luego podrás darme tu bendición.

³²Pero Isaac lo interrumpió:

—¿Quién eres tú?

—Soy Esaú, tu hijo primogénito —respondió.

³³Isaac comenzó a temblar y, muy sobresaltado, dijo:

—¿Quién fue el que ya me trajo lo que había cazado? Poco antes de que llegaras, yo me lo comí todo. Le di mi bendición, y bendecido quedará.

³⁴Al escuchar Esaú las palabras de su padre, lanzó un grito aterrador y, lleno de amargura, le dijo:

—¡Padre mío, te ruego que también a mí me bendigas!

³⁵Pero Isaac le respondió:

—Tu hermano vino y me engañó, y se llevó la bendición que a ti te correspondía.

³⁶—¡Con toda razón le pusieron Jacob!ⁱ —replicó Esaú—. Ya van dos veces que me engaña: primero me quita mis derechos de primogénito, y ahora se lleva mi bendición. ¿No te queda ninguna bendición para mí?

³⁷Isaac le respondió:

—Ya lo he puesto por señor tuyo: todos sus hermanos serán siervos suyos; lo he sustentado con trigo y con vino. ¿Qué puedo hacer ahora por ti, hijo mío?

³⁸Pero Esaú insistió:

—¿Acaso tienes una sola bendición, padre mío? ¡Bendíceme también a mí!

Y se echó a llorar. ³⁹Entonces su padre le dijo:

«Vivirás lejos de las riquezas de la tierra,
　　lejos del rocío que cae del cielo.
⁴⁰Gracias a tu espada,
　　vivirás y servirás a tu hermano.
Pero cuando te impacientes,
　　te librarás de su opresión.»

Jacob huye de Esaú

⁴¹A partir de ese momento, Esaú guardó un profundo rencor hacia su hermano por causa de la bendición que le había dado su padre, y pensaba: «Ya falta poco para que hagamos duelo por mi padre; después de eso, mataré a mi hermano Jacob.»

⁴²Cuando Rebeca se enteró de lo que estaba pensando Esaú, mandó llamar a Jacob, y le dijo:

—Mira, tu hermano Esaú está planeando matarte para vengarse de ti. ⁴³Por eso, hijo mío, obedéceme: Prepárate y huye en seguida a Jarán, a la casa de mi hermano Labán, ⁴⁴y quédate con él por un tiempo, hasta que se calme el enojo de tu hermano. ⁴⁵Cuando ya se haya tranquilizado, y olvide lo que le has hecho, yo enviaré a buscarte. ¿Por qué voy a perder a mis dos hijos en un solo día?

⁴⁶Luego Rebeca le dijo a Isaac:

—Estas mujeres hititas me tienen harta. Me han quitado las ganas de vivir. Si Jacob se llega a casar con una de las hititas que viven en este país, ¡más me valdría morir!

28 Isaac llamó a Jacob, lo bendijo y le ordenó:
—No te cases con ninguna mujer de aquí de Canaán. ²Vete ahora mismo a Padán Aram,ʲ a la casa de Betuel, tu abuelo materno, y cásate allá con una de las hijas de tu tío Labán. ³Que el Dios *Todopoderoso te bendiga, te haga fecundo y haga

que salgan de ti numerosas naciones. ⁴Que también te dé, a ti y a tu descendencia, la bendición de Abraham, para que puedan poseer esta tierra donde ahora vives como extranjero, esta tierra que Dios le prometió a Abraham.

⁵Así envió Isaac a Jacob a Padán Aram, a la casa de Labán, quien era hijo de Betuel el *arameo, y hermano de Rebeca, la madre de Jacob y de Esaú.

⁶Esaú supo que Isaac había bendecido a Jacob, y que lo había enviado a Padán Aram para casarse allá. También se enteró de que, al bendecirlo, le dio la orden de no casarse con ninguna cananea, ⁷y de que Jacob había partido hacia Padán Aram en obediencia a su padre y a su madre. ⁸Entonces Esaú se dio cuenta de la antipatía de su padre por las cananeas. ⁹Por eso, aunque ya tenía otras esposas cananeas, Esaú fue hasta donde vivía Ismael hijo de Abraham y se casó con su hija Majalat, que era hermana de Nebayot.

El sueño de Jacob en Betel

¹⁰Jacob partió de Berseba y se encaminó hacia Jarán. ¹¹Cuando llegó a cierto lugar, se detuvo para pasar la noche, porque ya estaba anocheciendo. Tomó una piedra, la usó como almohada, y se acostó a dormir en ese lugar. ¹²Allí soñó que había una escalinata apoyada en la tierra, y cuyo extremo superior llegaba hasta el cielo. Por ella subían y bajaban los ángeles de Dios. ¹³En el sueño, el SEÑOR estaba de pie junto a él y le decía: «Yo soy el SEÑOR, el Dios de tu abuelo Abraham y de tu padre Isaac. A ti y a tu descendencia les daré la tierra sobre la que estás acostado. ¹⁴Tu descendencia será tan numerosa como el polvo de la tierra. Te extenderás de norte a sur, y de oriente a occidente, y todas las familias de la tierra serán bendecidas por medio de ti y de tu descendencia. ¹⁵Yo estoy contigo. Te protegeré por dondequiera que vayas, y te traeré de vuelta a esta tierra. No te abandonaré hasta cumplir con todo lo que te he prometido.»

¹⁶Al despertar Jacob de su sueño, pensó: «En realidad, el SEÑOR está en este lugar, y yo no me había dado cuenta.» ¹⁷Y con mucho temor, añadió: «¡Qué asombroso es este lugar! Es nada menos que la casa de Dios; ¡es la puerta del cielo!»

¹⁸A la mañana siguiente Jacob se levantó temprano, tomó la piedra que había usado como almohada, la erigió como una *estela y derramó aceite sobre ella. ¹⁹En aquel lugar había una ciudad que se llamaba Luz, pero Jacob le cambió el *nombre y le puso Betel.ᵏ

²⁰Luego Jacob hizo esta promesa: «Si Dios me acompaña y me protege en este viaje que estoy haciendo, y si me da alimento y ropa para vestirme, ²¹y si regreso sano y salvo a la casa de mi padre, entonces el SEÑOR será mi Dios. ²²Y esta piedra que yo erigí como pilar será casa de Dios, y de todo lo que Dios me dé, le daré la décima parte.»

Jacob llega a Padán Aram

29 Jacob continuó su viaje y llegó a la tierra de los orientales. ²Al llegar vio, en medio del campo, un pozo donde descansaban tres rebaños de ovejas, ya que éstas bebían agua de allí. Sobre la boca del pozo había una piedra muy grande. ³Por eso los pastores corrían la piedra sólo cuando estaban juntos todos los rebaños, y luego de abrevar a las ovejas volvían a colocarla en su lugar, sobre la boca del pozo.

⁴Jacob les preguntó a los pastores:

ⁱ **27:36** En hebreo, *Jacob* significa *él agarra el talón* (en sentido figurado: *él suplanta* o *engaña*). ʲ **28:2** *Padán Aram*. Es decir, el noroeste de Mesopotamia; también en vv. 5,6 y 7. ᵏ **28:19** En hebreo, *Betel* significa *casa de Dios*.

—¿De dónde son ustedes?
—Somos de Jarán —respondieron.
5—¿Conocen a Labán, el hijo de Najor? —volvió
a preguntar Jacob.
—Claro que sí —respondieron.
6Jacob siguió preguntando:
—¿Se encuentra bien de salud?
—Sí, está bien —le contestaron—. A propósito,
ahí viene su hija Raquel con las ovejas.
7Entonces Jacob les dijo:
—Todavía estamos en pleno día, y es muy temprano para encerrar el rebaño. ¿Por qué no les dan
de beber a las ovejas y las llevan a pastar?
8Y ellos respondieron:
—No podemos hacerlo hasta que se junten todos los rebaños y los pastores quiten la piedra que
está sobre la boca del pozo. Sólo entonces podremos
dar de beber a las ovejas.
9Todavía estaba Jacob hablando con ellos, cuando Raquel llegó con las ovejas de su padre, pues era
ella quien las cuidaba. 10En cuanto Jacob vio a Raquel,
hija de su tío Labán, con las ovejas de éste, se acercó y
quitó la piedra que estaba sobre la boca del pozo, y les
dio de beber a las ovejas. 11Luego besó a Raquel, rompió en llanto, 12y le contó que era pariente de Labán,
por ser hijo de su hermana Rebeca. Raquel salió entonces corriendo a contárselo a su padre.
13Al oír Labán las noticias acerca de su sobrino
Jacob, salió a recibirlo y, entre abrazos y besos, lo llevó a su casa. Allí Jacob le contó todo lo que había sucedido, 14y Labán le dijo: «Realmente, tú eres de mi
propia sangre.»

Jacob se casa con Lea y Raquel

Jacob había estado ya un mes con Labán 15cuan-
do éste le dijo:
—Por más que seas mi pariente, no vas a trabajar
para mí gratis. Dime cuánto quieres ganar.
16Labán tenía dos hijas. La mayor se llamaba
Lea, y la menor, Raquel. 17Lea tenía ojos apagados,[l]
mientras que Raquel era una mujer muy hermosa.
18Como Jacob se había enamorado de Raquel, le dijo
a su tío:
—Me ofrezco a trabajar para ti siete años, a cambio de Raquel, tu hija menor.
19Labán le contestó:
—Es mejor que te la entregue a ti, y no a un extraño. Quédate conmigo.
20Así que Jacob trabajó siete años para poder casarse con Raquel, pero como estaba muy enamorado
de ella le pareció poco tiempo. 21Entonces Jacob le
dijo a Labán:
—Ya he cumplido con el tiempo pactado. Dame
mi mujer para que me case con ella.
22Labán reunió a toda la gente del lugar y ofreció
una gran fiesta. 23Pero cuando llegó la noche, tomó a
su hija Lea y se la entregó a Jacob, y Jacob se acostó
con ella. 24Además, como Lea tenía una criada que se
llamaba Zilpá, Labán se la dio, para que la atendiera.
25A la mañana siguiente, Jacob se dio cuenta
de que había estado con Lea, y le reclamó a Labán:
—¿Qué me has hecho? ¿Acaso no trabajé contigo
para casarme con Raquel? ¿Por qué me has engañado?
26Labán le contestó:
—La costumbre en nuestro país es casar primero
a la mayor y luego a la menor. 27Por eso, cumple ahora con la semana nupcial de ésta, y por siete años más
de trabajo te daré la otra.
28Así lo hizo Jacob, y cuando terminó la semana
nupcial de la primera, Labán le entregó a Raquel por
esposa. 29También Raquel tenía una criada, llamada
Bilhá, y Labán se la dio para que la atendiera. 30Jacob
entonces se acostó con Raquel, y la amó mucho más
que a Lea, aunque tuvo que trabajar para Labán siete
años más.

Los hijos de Jacob

31Cuando el SEÑOR vio que Lea no era amada, le
concedió hijos. Mientras tanto, Raquel permaneció estéril. 32Lea quedó embarazada y dio a luz un hijo, al
que llamó Rubén,[m] porque dijo: «El SEÑOR ha visto mi
aflicción; ahora sí me amará mi esposo.» 33Lea volvió a
quedar embarazada y dio a luz otro hijo, al que llamó
Simeón,[n] porque dijo: «Llegó a oídos del SEÑOR que
no soy amada, y por eso me dio también este hijo.»
34Luego quedó embarazada de nuevo y dio a luz
un tercer hijo, al que llamó Leví,[ñ] porque dijo: «Ahora
sí me amará mi esposo, porque le he dado tres hijos.»
35Lea volvió a quedar embarazada, y dio a luz un
cuarto hijo, al que llamó Judá[o] porque dijo: «Esta vez
alabaré al SEÑOR.» Después de esto, dejó de dar a luz.

30 Cuando Raquel se dio cuenta de que no le
podía dar hijos a Jacob, tuvo envidia de su
hermana y le dijo a Jacob:
—¡Dame hijos! Si no me los das, ¡me muero!
2Pero Jacob se enojó muchísimo con ella y le
dijo:
—¿Acaso crees que soy Dios? ¡Es él quien te ha
hecho estéril!
3—Aquí tienes a mi criada Bilhá —propuso Raquel—. Acuéstate con ella. Así ella dará a luz sobre
mis rodillas, y por medio de ella también yo podré
formar una familia.
4Entonces Raquel le dio a Jacob por mujer su
criada Bilhá, y Jacob se acostó con ella. 5Bilhá quedó
embarazada y le dio un hijo a Jacob. 6Y Raquel exclamó: «¡Dios me ha hecho justicia! ¡Escuchó mi plegaria y me ha dado un hijo!» Por eso Raquel le puso por
*nombre Dan.[p]
7Después Bilhá, la criada de Raquel, quedó embarazada otra vez y dio a luz un segundo hijo de Jacob. 8Y Raquel dijo: «He tenido una lucha muy
grande con mi hermana, pero he vencido.» Por eso
Raquel lo llamó Neftalí.[q]
9Lea, al ver que ya no podía tener hijos, tomó a
su criada Zilpá y se la entregó a Jacob por mujer, 10y
ésta le dio a Jacob un hijo. 11Entonces Lea exclamó:
«¡Qué suerte!» Por eso lo llamó Gad.[r]
12Zilpá, la criada de Lea, le dio un segundo hijo a
Jacob. 13Lea volvió a exclamar: «¡Qué feliz soy! Las
mujeres me dirán que soy feliz.» Por eso lo llamó
Aser.[s]
14Durante los días de la cosecha de trigo, Rubén
salió al campo. Allí encontró unas frutas llamadas
mandrágoras, y se las llevó a Lea, su madre. Entonces Raquel le dijo a Lea:
—Por favor, dame algunas mandrágoras de las
que te trajo tu hijo.
15Pero Lea le contestó:

[l] **29:17** *apagados.* Alt. *tiernos.* [m] **29:32** En hebreo, *Rubén* suena como las palabras que significan *miren, un hijo,* y también *él vio mi aflicción.* [n] **29:33** En hebreo, *Simeón* probablemente significa *el que oye.* [ñ] **29:34** En hebreo, *Leví* suena parecido al verbo que significa *unir, amar.* [o] **29:35** En hebreo, *Judá* tiene un sonido parecido al verbo que significa *alabar.* [p] **30:6** En hebreo, *Dan* significa *él hizo justicia.* [q] **30:8** En hebreo, *Neftalí* significa *mi lucha.* [r] **30:11** En hebreo, *Gad* puede significar *suerte, buena fortuna.* [s] **30:13** En hebreo, *Aser* significa *feliz, dichoso.*

—¿Te parece poco el haberme quitado a mi marido, que ahora quieres también quitarme las mandrágoras de mi hijo?

—Bueno —contestó Raquel—, te propongo que, a cambio de las mandrágoras de tu hijo, Jacob duerma contigo esta noche.

¹⁶Al anochecer, cuando Jacob volvía del campo, Lea salió a su encuentro y le dijo:

—Hoy te acostarás conmigo, porque te he alquilado a cambio de las mandrágoras de mi hijo.

Y Jacob durmió con ella esa noche.

¹⁷Dios escuchó a Lea, y ella quedó embarazada y le dio a Jacob un quinto hijo. ¹⁸Entonces dijo Lea: «Dios me ha recompensado, porque yo le entregué mi criada a mi esposo.» Por eso lo llamó Isacar.ᵗ

¹⁹Lea quedó embarazada de nuevo, y le dio a Jacob un sexto hijo. ²⁰«Dios me ha favorecido con un buen regalo —dijo Lea—. Esta vez mi esposo se quedará conmigo,ᵘ porque le he dado seis hijos.» Por eso lo llamó Zabulón.ᵛ

²¹Luego Lea dio a luz una hija, a la cual llamó Dina. ²²Pero Dios también se acordó de Raquel; la escuchó y le quitó la esterilidad. ²³Fue así como ella quedó embarazada y dio a luz un hijo. Entonces exclamó: «Dios ha borrado mi desgracia.» ²⁴Por eso lo llamó José, y dijo: «Quiera el SEÑOR darme otro hijo.»

Jacob se enriquece

²⁵Después de que Raquel dio a luz a José, Jacob le dijo a Labán:

—Déjame regresar a mi hogar y a mi propia tierra. ²⁶Dame las mujeres por las que te he servido, y mis hijos, y déjame ir. Tú bien sabes cómo he trabajado para ti.

²⁷Pero Labán le contestó:

—Por favor, quédate. He sabido por adivinación que, gracias a ti, el SEÑOR me ha bendecido.

²⁸Y le propuso:

—Fija tú mismo el salario que quieras ganar, y yo te lo pagaré.

²⁹Jacob le respondió:

—Tú bien sabes cómo he trabajado, y cómo gracias a mis desvelos han mejorado tus animales. ³⁰Lo que tenías antes de mi venida, que era muy poco, se ha multiplicado enormemente. Gracias a mí, el SEÑOR te ha bendecido. Ahora quiero hacer algo por mi propia familia.

³¹—¿Cuánto quieres que te pague? —preguntó Labán.

—No tienes que pagarme nada —respondió Jacob—. Si aceptas lo que estoy por proponerte, seguiré cuidando tus ovejas. ³²Hoy, cuando pase yo con todo tu rebaño, tú irás apartando toda oveja manchada o moteada, y todos los corderos negros, y todos los cabritos manchados o moteados. Ellos serán mi salario. ³³Así, el día de mañana, cuando vengas a controlar lo que he ganado, mi honradez responderá por mí: si encuentras alguna oveja o cabrito que no sea manchado o moteado, o algún cordero que no sea negro, será que te lo he robado.

³⁴—Está bien —acordó Labán—, acepto tu propuesta.

³⁵Ese mismo día Labán apartó todos los chivos rayados y moteados, todas las cabras manchadas y moteadas, todas las que tenían alguna mancha blanca, y todos los corderos negros, y los puso al cuidado de sus hijos. ³⁶Después de eso, puso una

distancia de tres días de viaje entre él y Jacob. Mientras tanto, Jacob seguía cuidando las otras ovejas de Labán.

³⁷Jacob cortó ramas verdes de álamo, de almendro y de plátano, y las peló de tal manera que quedaran franjas blancas al descubierto. ³⁸Luego tomó las ramas que había pelado, y las puso en todos los abrevaderos para que el rebaño las tuviera enfrente cuando se acercara a beber agua. Cuando las ovejas estaban en celo y llegaban a los abrevaderos, ³⁹los machos se unían con las hembras frente a las ramas, y así tenían crías rayadas, moteadas o manchadas. ⁴⁰Entonces Jacob apartaba estos corderos y los ponía frente a los animales rayados y negros del rebaño de Labán. De esta manera logró crear su propio rebaño, diferente al de Labán. ⁴¹Además, cuando las hembras más robustas estaban en celo, Jacob colocaba las ramas en los bebederos, frente a los animales, para que se unieran mirando hacia las ramas. ⁴²Pero cuando llegaban los animales más débiles, no colocaba las ramas. Así los animales débiles eran para Labán y los robustos eran para Jacob. ⁴³De esta manera Jacob prosperó muchísimo y llegó a tener muchos rebaños, criados y criadas, camellos y asnos.

Jacob huye de Labán

31 Pero Jacob se enteró de que los hijos de Labán andaban diciendo: «Jacob se ha ido apoderando de todo lo que le pertenecía a nuestro padre, y se ha enriquecido a costa suya.» ²También notó que Labán ya no lo trataba como antes. ³Entonces el SEÑOR le dijo a Jacob: «Vuélvete a la tierra de tus padres, donde están tus parientes, que yo estaré contigo.»

⁴Jacob mandó llamar a Raquel y a Lea al campo donde estaba el rebaño, ⁵y les dijo:

—Me he dado cuenta de que su padre ya no me trata como antes. ¡Pero el Dios de mi padre ha estado conmigo! ⁶Ustedes saben muy bien que yo he trabajado para su padre Labán con todas mis fuerzas. ⁷No obstante, él me ha engañado y me ha cambiado el salario muchas veces.ʷ Pero Dios no le ha permitido causarme ningún daño. ⁸Si él acordaba conmigo: "Los animales manchados serán tu salario", todas las hembras tenían crías manchadas; y si él acordaba: "Los animales rayados serán tu salario", todas las hembras tenían crías rayadas. ⁹Así Dios le ha quitado el ganado al padre de ustedes, y me lo ha dado a mí.

¹⁰»En cierta ocasión, durante la época en que los animales estaban en celo, tuve un sueño. En ese sueño veía que los chivos que cubrían a las cabras eran rayados, manchados o moteados. ¹¹En ese mismo sueño, el ángel de Dios me llamó: "¡Jacob!" Y yo le respondí: "Aquí estoy." ¹²Entonces él me dijo: "Fíjate bien, y te darás cuenta de que todos los chivos que cubren a las cabras son rayados, manchados o moteados. Yo he visto todo lo que te ha hecho Labán. ¹³Yo soy el Dios de Betel, donde ungiste una *estela y me hiciste una promesa. Vete ahora de esta tierra, y vuelve a la tierra de tu origen."

¹⁴Raquel y Lea le respondieron:

—Ya no tenemos ninguna parte ni herencia en la casa de nuestro padre. ¹⁵Al contrario, nos ha tratado como si fuéramos extranjeras. Nos ha vendido, y se ha gastado todo lo que recibió por nosotras. ¹⁶Lo cierto es que toda la riqueza que Dios le ha quitado a nuestro padre es

---

ᵗ **30:18** En hebreo, *Isacar* tiene un sonido parecido a las palabras que significan *premiar* y *alquilar*. ᵘ **30:20** *se quedará conmigo*. Lit. *me honrará*. ᵛ **30:20** En hebreo, *Zabulón* suena como el verbo que significa *honrar*. ʷ **31:7** *muchas veces*. Lit. *diez veces*.

nuestra y de nuestros hijos. Por eso, haz ahora todo lo que Dios te ha ordenado.

17Entonces Jacob se preparó y montó a sus hijos y a sus esposas en los camellos, 18puso en marcha todo su ganado, junto con todos los bienes que había acumulado en Padán Aram,x y se dirigió hacia la tierra de Canaán, donde vivía su padre Isaac.

19Mientras Labán estaba ausente esquilando sus ovejas, Raquel aprovechó el momento para robarse los ídolos familiares. 20Fue así como Jacob engañó a Labán el *arameo y huyó sin decirle nada. 21Jacob se escapó con todo lo que tenía. Una vez que cruzó el río Éufrates, se encaminó hacia la región montañosa de Galaad.

Labán persigue a Jacob

22Al tercer día le informaron a Labán que Jacob se había escapado. 23Entonces Labán reunió a sus parientes y lo persiguió durante siete días, hasta que lo alcanzó en los montes de Galaad. 24Pero esa misma noche Dios se le apareció en un sueño a Labán el *arameo, y le dijo: «¡Cuidado con amenazar a Jacob!»

25Labán alcanzó a Jacob en los montes de Galaad, donde éste había acampado. También Labán acampó allí, junto con sus parientes, 26y le reclamó a Jacob:

—¿Qué has hecho? ¡Me has engañado, y te has llevado a mis hijas como si fueran prisioneras de guerra! 27¿Por qué has huido en secreto, con engaños y sin decirme nada? Yo te habría despedido con alegría, y con música de tambores y de arpa. 28Ni siquiera me dejaste besar a mis hijas y a mis nietos. ¡Te has comportado como un necio! 29Mi poder es más que suficiente para hacerles daño, pero anoche el Dios de tu padre me habló y me dijo: "¡Cuidado con amenazar a Jacob!" 30Ahora bien, entiendo que hayas querido irte porque añoras la casa de tu padre, pero, ¿por qué me robaste mis dioses?

31Jacob le respondió:

—La verdad es que me entró mucho miedo, porque pensé que podrías quitarme a tus hijas por la fuerza. 32Pero si encuentras tus dioses en poder de alguno de los que están aquí, tal persona no quedará con vida. Pongo a nuestros parientes como testigos: busca lo que sea tuyo, y llévatelo.

Pero Jacob no sabía que Raquel se había robado los ídolos de Labán, 33así que Labán entró en la carpa de Jacob, luego en la de Lea y en la de las dos criadas, pero no encontró lo que buscaba. Cuando salió de la carpa de Lea, entró en la de Raquel. 34Pero Raquel, luego de tomar los ídolos y esconderlos bajo la montura del camello, se sentó sobre ellos. Labán los buscó por toda la carpa, pero no los encontró. 35Entonces Raquel le dijo a su padre:

—Por favor, no se enoje mi padre si no puedo levantarme ante usted, pero es que estoy en mi período de menstruación.

Labán buscó los ídolos, pero no logró encontrarlos.

36Entonces Jacob se enojó con Labán, e indignado le reclamó:

—¿Qué crimen o pecado he cometido, para que me acoses de esta manera? 37Ya has registrado todas mis cosas, ¿y acaso has encontrado algo que te pertenezca? Si algo has encontrado, ponlo aquí, frente a nuestros parientes, y que ellos determinen quién de los dos tiene la razón. 38Durante los veinte años que estuve contigo, nunca abortaron tus ove-

jas ni tus cabras, ni jamás me comí un carnero de tus rebaños. 39Nunca te traje un animal despedazado por las fieras, ya que yo mismo me hacía cargo de esa pérdida. Además, lo que se robaban de día o de noche, tú me lo reclamabas. 40De día me consumía el calor, y de noche me moría de frío, y ni dormir podía. 41De los veinte años que estuve en tu casa, catorce te serví por tus dos hijas, y seis por tu ganado, y muchas vecesy me cambiaste el salario. 42Si no hubiera estado conmigo el Dios de mi padre, el Dios de Abraham, el Dios a quien Isaac temía, seguramente me habrías despedido con las manos vacías. Pero Dios vio mi aflicción y el trabajo de mis manos, y anoche me hizo justicia.

43Labán le replicó a Jacob:

—Estas mujeres son mis hijas, y estos muchachos son mis nietos; mías también son las ovejas; todo lo que ves me pertenece. Pero, ¿qué podría hacerles ahora a mis hijas y a mis nietos? 44Hagamos un pacto tú y yo, y que ese pacto nos sirva como testimonio.

45Entonces Jacob tomó una piedra, la levantó como una *estela, 46y les dijo a sus parientes:

—¡Junten piedras!

Ellos juntaron piedras, las amontonaron, y comieron allí, junto al montón de piedras. 47A ese lugar Labán le puso por *nombre Yegar Saduta, mientras que Jacob lo llamó Galaad.z

48—Este montón de piedras —declaró Labán— nos servirá de testimonio.

Por eso se le llamó Galaad a ese lugar, 49y también se le llamó Mizpa, porque Labán juró:

—Que el SEÑOR nos vigile cuando ya estemos lejos el uno del otro. 50Si tú maltratas a mis hijas, o tomas otras mujeres aún no sean ellas, recuerda que Dios es nuestro testigo, aunque no haya ningún otro testigo entre nosotros. 51Mira este montón de piedras y la estela que he levantado entre nosotros —señaló Labán—. 52Ambos serán testigos de que ni tú ni yo cruzaremos esta línea con el propósito de hacernos daño. 53¡Que el Dios de Abraham y el Dios de Najor sea nuestro juez!

Entonces Jacob juró por el Dios a quien temía su padre Isaac. 54Luego ofreció un sacrificio en lo alto de un monte, e invitó a sus parientes a participar en la comida. Después de que todos comieron, pasaron la noche allí.

55A la madrugada del día siguiente Labán se levantó, besó y bendijo a sus nietos y a sus hijas, y regresó a su casa.

Jacob envía mensajeros a Esaú

32 Jacob también siguió su camino, pero unos ángeles de Dios salieron a su encuentro. 2Al verlos, exclamó: «¡Éste es el campamento de Dios!» Por eso llamó a ese lugar Majanayin.a

3Luego Jacob envió mensajeros a su hermano Esaú, que estaba en la tierra de Seír, en la región de Edom. 4Y les ordenó que le dijeran: «Mi señor Esaú, su siervo Jacob nos ha enviado a decirle que él ha vivido en la casa de Labán todo este tiempo, 5y que ahora tiene vacas, asnos, ovejas, esclavos y esclavas. Le manda este mensaje, con la esperanza de ganarse su favor.»

6Cuando los mensajeros regresaron, le dijeron a Jacob: «Fuimos a hablar con su hermano Esaú, y ahora viene al encuentro de usted, acompañado de cuatrocientos hombres.»

---

x **31:18** *Padán Aram.* Es decir, el noroeste de Mesopotamia. y **31:41** *muchas veces.* Lit. *diez veces.* z **31:47** *Yegar Saduta* en arameo, y *Galaad* en hebreo, significan *montículo del testimonio.* a **32:2** En hebreo, *Majanayin* significa *dos campamentos.*

7Jacob sintió mucho miedo, y se puso muy angustiado. Por eso dividió en dos grupos a la gente que lo acompañaba, y lo mismo hizo con las ovejas, las vacas y los camellos, 8pues pensó: «Si Esaú ataca a un grupo, el otro grupo podrá escapar.»

9Entonces Jacob se puso a orar: «SEÑOR, Dios de mi abuelo Abraham y de mi padre Isaac, que me dijiste que regresara a mi tierra y a mis familiares, y que me harías prosperar: 10realmente yo, tu siervo, no soy digno de la bondad y fidelidad con que me has privilegiado. Cuando crucé este río Jordán, no tenía más que mi bastón; pero ahora he llegado a formar dos campamentos. 11¡Líbrame del poder de mi hermano Esaú, pues tengo miedo de que venga a matarme a mí y a las madres y a los niños! 12Tú mismo afirmaste que me harías prosperar, y que mis descendientes serían tan numerosos como la arena del mar, que no se puede contar.»

13Jacob pasó la noche en aquel lugar, y de lo que tenía consigo escogió, como regalo para su hermano Esaú, 14doscientas cabras, veinte chivos, doscientas ovejas, veinte carneros, 15treinta camellas con sus crías, cuarenta vacas, diez novillos, veinte asnas y diez asnos. 16Luego los puso a cargo de sus siervos, cada manada por separado, y les dijo: «Vayan adelante, pero dejen un buen espacio entre manada y manada.»

17Al que iba al frente, le ordenó: «Cuando te encuentres con mi hermano Esaú y te pregunte de quién eres, a dónde te diriges y de quién es el ganado que llevas, 18le contestarás: "Es un regalo para usted, mi señor Esaú, que de sus ganados le manda su siervo Jacob. Además, él mismo viene detrás de nosotros." »

19Jacob les dio la misma orden al segundo y al tercer grupo, y a todos los demás que iban detrás del ganado. Les dijo: «Cuando se encuentren con Esaú, le dirán todo esto, 20y añadirán: "Su siervo Jacob viene detrás de nosotros." »

Jacob pensaba: «Lo apaciguaré con los regalos que le llegarán primero, y luego me presentaré ante él; tal vez así me reciba bien.» 21De esta manera los regalos lo precedieron, pero Jacob se quedó esa noche en el campamento.

Jacob lucha con un ángel

22Aquella misma noche Jacob se levantó, tomó a sus dos esposas, a sus dos esclavas y a sus once hijos, y cruzó el vado del río Jaboc. 23Una vez que lo habían cruzado, hizo pasar también todas sus posesiones, 24quedándose solo. Entonces un hombre luchó con él hasta el amanecer. 25Cuando ese hombre se dio cuenta de que no podía vencer a Jacob, lo tocó en la coyuntura de la cadera, y ésta se le dislocó mientras luchaban. 26Entonces el hombre le dijo:

—¡Suéltame, que ya está por amanecer!

—¡No te soltaré hasta que me bendigas! —respondió Jacob.

27—¿Cómo te llamas? —le preguntó el hombre.

—Me llamo Jacob —respondió.

28Entonces el hombre le dijo:

—Ya no te llamarás Jacob, sino Israelb, porque has luchado con Dios y con los *hombres, y has vencido.

29—Y tú, ¿cómo te llamas? —le preguntó Jacob.

—¿Por qué preguntas cómo me llamo? —le respondió el hombre.

Y en ese mismo lugar lo bendijo. 30Jacob llamó a ese lugar Penuel,b porque dijo: «He visto a Dios cara a cara, y todavía sigo con *vida.»

31Cruzaba Jacob por el lugar llamado Penuel, cuando salió el sol. A causa de su cadera dislocada iba rengueando. 32Por esa razón los israelitas no comen el tendón que está en la coyuntura de la cadera, porque a Jacob se le tocó en dicho tendón.

Encuentro de Jacob con Esaú

33 Cuando Jacob alzó la vista y vio que Esaú se acercaba con cuatrocientos hombres, repartió a los niños entre Lea, Raquel y las dos esclavas. 2Al frente de todos colocó a las criadas con sus hijos, luego a Lea con sus hijos, y por último a Raquel con José. 3Jacob, por su parte, se adelantó a ellos, inclinándose hasta el suelo siete veces mientras se iba acercando a su hermano. 4Pero Esaú corrió a su encuentro y, echándole los brazos al cuello, lo abrazó y lo besó. Entonces los dos se pusieron a llorar. 5Luego Esaú alzó la vista y, al ver a las mujeres y a los niños, preguntó:

—¿Quiénes son estos que te acompañan?

—Son los hijos que Dios le ha concedido a tu siervo —respondió Jacob.

6Las esclavas y sus hijos se acercaron y se inclinaron ante Esaú. 7Luego, Lea y sus hijos hicieron lo mismo y, por último, también se inclinaron José y Raquel.

8—¿Qué significan todas estas manadas que han salido a mi encuentro? —preguntó Esaú.

—Intentaba con ellas ganarme tu confianza —contestó Jacob.

9—Hermano mío —repuso Esaú—, ya tengo más que suficiente. Quédate con lo que te pertenece.

10—No, por favor —insistió Jacob—; si me he ganado tu confianza, acepta este presente que te ofrezco. Ya que me has recibido tan bien, ¡ver tu rostro es como ver a Dios mismo! 11Acéptame el regalo que he traído. Dios ha sido muy bueno conmigo, y tengo más de lo que necesito.

Fue tanta la insistencia de Jacob que, finalmente, Esaú aceptó. 12Más tarde, Esaú le dijo:

—Sigamos nuestro viaje; yo te acompañaré.

13Pero Jacob se disculpó:

—Mi hermano y señor debe saber que los niños son todavía muy débiles, y que las ovejas y las vacas acaban de tener cría, y debo cuidarlas. Si les exijo demasiado, en un solo día se me puede morir todo el rebaño. 14Es mejor que mi señor se adelante a su siervo, que yo seguiré al paso de la manada y de los niños, hasta que nos encontremos en Seír.

15—Está bien —accedió Esaú—, pero permíteme dejarte algunos de mis hombres para que te acompañen.

—¿Para qué te vas a molestar? —contestó Jacob—. Lo importante es que me he ganado tu confianza.

16Aquel mismo día, Esaú regresó a Seír. 17Jacob, en cambio, se fue hacia Sucot, y allí se hizo una casa para él y cobertizos para su ganado. Por eso a ese lugar se le llamó Sucot.c

18Cuando Jacob volvió de Padán Aram,d llegó sano y salvo a la ciudad de Siquén, en Canaán, y acampó frente a ella. 19Luego, por cien monedas de plata les compró una parcela a los hijos de Jamor, el padre de Siquén, y allí instaló su carpa. 20También construyó un altar, y lo llamó El Elohé Israel.e

---

b **32:28** En hebreo, *Israel* significa *él lucha con Dios.* b **32:30** En hebreo, *Penuel* significa *cara de Dios.* c **33:17** En hebreo, *Sucot* significa *cobertizos, enramadas o cabañas.* d **33:18** Padán Aram. Es decir, el noroeste de Mesopotamia. e **33:20** En hebreo, *El Elohé Israel* puede significar *Dios, el Dios de Israel,* o *poderoso es el Dios de Israel.*

Rapto y violación de Dina

34 En cierta ocasión Dina, la hija que Jacob tuvo con Lea, salió a visitar a las mujeres del lugar. 2Cuando la vio Siquén, que era hijo de Jamor el heveo, jefe del lugar, la agarró por la fuerza, se acostó con ella y la violó. 3Pero luego se enamoró de ella y trató de ganarse su afecto. 4Entonces le dijo a su padre: «Consígueme a esta muchacha para que sea mi esposa.»

5Jacob se enteró de que Siquén había violado a su hija Dina pero, como sus hijos estaban en el campo cuidando el ganado, no dijo nada hasta que ellos regresaron. 6Mientras tanto Jamor, el padre de Siquén, salió en busca de Jacob para hablar con él. 7Cuando los hijos de Jacob volvieron del campo y se enteraron de lo sucedido, quedaron muy dolidos y, a la vez, llenos de ira. Siquén había cometido una ofensa muy grande contra Israel al abusar de su hija; era algo que nunca debió haber hecho. 8Pero Jamor les dijo:

—Mi hijo Siquén está enamorado de la hermana de ustedes. Por favor, permitan que ella se case con él. 9Háganse parientes nuestros. Intercambiemos nuestras hijas en casamiento. 10Así ustedes podrán vivir entre nosotros y el país quedará a su disposición para que lo habiten, hagan negocios*f* y adquieran terrenos.

11Siquén, por su parte, les dijo al padre y a los hermanos de Dina:

—Si ustedes me hallan digno de su favor, yo les daré lo que me pidan. 12Pueden pedirme cuanta dote quieran, y exigirme muchos regalos, pero permitan que la muchacha se case conmigo.

13Sin embargo, por el hecho de que su hermana Dina había sido deshonrada, los hijos de Jacob les respondieron con engaños a Siquén y a su padre Jamor.

14—Nosotros no podemos hacer algo así —les explicaron—. Sería una vergüenza para todos nosotros entregarle nuestra hermana a un hombre que no está circuncidado. 15Sólo aceptaremos con esta condición: que todos los varones entre ustedes se circunciden para que sean como nosotros. 16Entonces sí intercambiaremos nuestras hijas con las de ustedes en casamiento, y viviremos entre ustedes y formaremos un solo pueblo. 17Pero si no aceptan nuestra condición de circuncidarse, nos llevaremos a nuestra hermana*g* y nos iremos de aquí.

18Jamor y Siquén estuvieron de acuerdo con la propuesta; 19y tan enamorado estaba Siquén de la hija de Jacob que no demoró en circuncidarse.

Como Siquén era el hombre más respetado en la familia, 20su padre Jamor lo acompañó hasta la entrada de la ciudad, y allí hablaron con todos sus conciudadanos. Les dijeron:

21—Estos hombres se han portado como amigos. Dejen que se establezcan en nuestro país, y que lleven a cabo sus negocios aquí, ya que hay suficiente espacio para ellos. Además, nosotros nos podremos casar con sus hijas, y ellos con las nuestras. 22Pero ellos aceptan quedarse entre nosotros y formar un solo pueblo, con una sola condición: que todos nuestros varones se circunciden, como lo hacen ellos. 23Aceptemos su condición, para que se queden a vivir entre nosotros. De esta manera su ganado, sus propiedades y todos sus animales serán nuestros.

24Todos los que se reunían a la entrada de la ciudad estuvieron de acuerdo con Jamor y con su hijo Siquén, y fue así como todos los varones fueron circuncidados. 25Al tercer día, cuando los varones todavía estaban muy adoloridos, dos de los hijos de Jacob, Simeón y Leví, hermanos de Dina, empuñaron cada uno su espada y fueron a la ciudad, donde los varones se encontraban desprevenidos, y los mataron a todos. 26También mataron a filo de espada a Jamor y a su hijo Siquén, sacaron a Dina de la casa de Siquén y se retiraron. 27Luego los otros hijos de Jacob llegaron y, pasando sobre los cadáveres, saquearon la ciudad en venganza por la deshonra que había sufrido su hermana. 28Se apropiaron de sus ovejas, ganado y asnos, y de todo lo que había en la ciudad y en el campo. 29Se llevaron todos sus bienes, y sus hijos y mujeres, y saquearon todo lo que encontraron en las casas.

30Entonces Jacob les dijo a Simeón y Leví:

—Me han provocado un problema muy serio. De ahora en adelante los cananeos y ferezeos, habitantes de este lugar, me van a odiar. Si ellos se unen contra mí y me atacan, me matarán a mí y a toda mi familia, pues cuento con muy pocos hombres.

31Pero ellos replicaron:

—¿Acaso podíamos dejar que él tratara a nuestra hermana como a una prostituta?

Jacob vuelve a Betel

35 Dios le dijo a Jacob: «Ponte en marcha, y vete a vivir a Betel. Erige allí un altar al Dios que se te apareció cuando escapabas de tu hermano Esaú.»

2Entonces Jacob dijo a su familia y a quienes lo acompañaban: «Desháganse de todos los dioses extraños que tengan con ustedes, purifíquense y cámbiense de ropa. 3Vámonos a Betel. Allí construiré un altar al Dios que me socorrió cuando estaba yo en peligro, y que me ha acompañado en mi camino.»

4Así que le entregaron a Jacob todos los dioses extraños que tenían, junto con los aretes que llevaban en las orejas, y Jacob los enterró a la sombra de la encina que estaba cerca de Siquén. 5Cuando partieron, nadie persiguió a la familia de Jacob, porque un terror divino se apoderó de las ciudades vecinas.

6Fue así como Jacob y quienes lo acompañaban llegaron a Luz, es decir, Betel, en la tierra de Canaán. 7Erigió un altar y llamó a ese lugar El Betel,*h* porque allí se le había revelado Dios cuando escapaba de su hermano Esaú.

8Por esos días murió Débora, la nodriza de Rebeca, y la sepultaron a la sombra de la encina que se encuentra cerca de Betel. Por eso Jacob llamó a ese lugar Elón Bacut.*i*

9Cuando Jacob regresó de Padán Aram*j*, Dios se le apareció otra vez y lo bendijo 10con estas palabras: «Tu *nombre es Jacob,*k* pero ya no te llamarás así. De aquí en adelante te llamarás Israel.»*l* Y, en efecto, ese fue el nombre que le puso.

11Luego Dios añadió: «Yo soy el Dios *Todopoderoso. Sé fecundo y multiplícate. De ti nacerá una nación y una comunidad de naciones, y habrá reyes entre tus vástagos. 12La tierra que les di a Abraham y a Isaac te la doy a ti, y también a tus descendientes.»

13Y Dios se alejó del lugar donde había hablado con Jacob.

---

f 34:10 *hagan negocios.* Alt. *se muevan con libertad.*   g 34:17 *hermana.* Lit. *Hija.*   h 35:7 En hebreo, *El Betel* significa *Dios de Betel.*   i 35:8 En hebreo, *Elón Bacut* significa *encina del llanto.*   j 35:9 *Padán Aram.* Es decir, el noroeste de Mesopotamia; también en v. 26.   k 35:10 En hebreo, *Jacob* significa *él agarra el talón* (en sentido figurado: *él suplanta* o *engaña*).   l 35:10 En hebreo, *Israel* significa *él lucha con Dios.*

14Jacob erigió una *estela de piedra en el lugar donde Dios le había hablado. Vertió sobre ella una libación, y la ungió con aceite, 15y al lugar donde Dios le había hablado lo llamó Betel.m

Muerte de Raquel y de Isaac
35:23-26 — 1Cr 2:1-2

16Después partieron de Betel. Cuando todavía estaban lejos de Efrata, Raquel dio a luz, pero tuvo un parto muy difícil. 17En el momento más difícil del parto, la partera le dijo: «¡No temas; estás por tener otro varón!» 18No obstante, ella se estaba muriendo, y en sus últimos suspiros alcanzó a llamar a su hijo Benoní,n pero Jacob, su padre, le puso por *nombre Benjamín.ñ

19Así murió Raquel, y la sepultaron en el camino que va hacia Efrata, que es Belén. 20Sobre la tumba Jacob erigió una estela, que hasta el día de hoy señala el lugar donde Raquel fue sepultada.

21Israel siguió su camino y acampó más allá de Migdal Edar. 22Mientras vivía en esa región, Rubén fue y se acostó con Bilhá, la concubina de su padre. Cuando Israel se enteró de esto, se enojó muchísimo.o

Jacob tuvo doce hijos:

23 Los hijos de Lea fueron Rubén, que era el primogénito de Jacob, Simeón, Leví, Judá, Isacar y Zabulón.
24 Los hijos de Raquel fueron José y Benjamín.
25 Los hijos de Bilhá, la esclava de Raquel, fueron Dan y Neftalí.
26 Los hijos de Zilpá, la esclava de Lea, fueron Gad y Aser.

Éstos fueron los hijos que tuvo Jacob en Padán Aram.

27Jacob volvió a la casa de su padre Isaac en Mamré, cerca de Quiriat Arbá, es decir, Hebrón, donde también habían vivido Abraham e Isaac. 28Isaac tenía ciento ochenta años 29cuando se reunió con sus antepasados. Era ya muy anciano cuando murió, y lo sepultaron sus hijos Esaú y Jacob.

Descendientes de Esaú
36:10-14 — 1Cr 1:35-37
36:20-28 — 1Cr 1:38-42

36 Éstos son los descendientes de Esaú, o sea Edom.

2Esaú se casó con mujeres cananeas: con Ada, hija de Elón el hitita; con Aholibama, hija de Aná y nieta de Zibeón el heveo; 3y con Basemat, hija de Ismael y hermana de Nebayot.

4Esaú tuvo estos hijos: con Ada tuvo a Elifaz; con Basemat, a Reuel; 5con Aholibama, a Jeús, Jalán y Coré. Éstos fueron los hijos que tuvo Esaú mientras vivía en la tierra de Canaán.

6Después Esaú tomó a sus esposas, hijos e hijas, y a todas las personas que lo acompañaban, junto con su ganado y todos sus animales, y todos los bienes que había adquirido en la tierra de Canaán, y se trasladó a otra región para alejarse de su hermano Jacob. 7Los dos habían acumulado tantos bienes que no podían estar juntos; la tierra donde vivían no bastaba para alimentar al ganado de ambos. 8Fue así como Esaú, o sea Edom, se asentó en la región montañosa de Seír.

9Éstos son los descendientes de Esaú, padre de los edomitas, que habitaron en la región montañosa de Seír. 10Los nombres de sus hijos son éstos:

Elifaz hijo de Ada, esposa de Esaú; y Reuel hijo de Basemat, esposa de Esaú.
11 Los hijos de Elifaz fueron Temán, Omar, Zefo, Gatán y Quenaz.
12Elifaz tuvo un hijo con una concubina suya, llamada Timná, al que llamó Amalec.
Todos éstos fueron nietos de Ada, esposa de Esaú.
13 Los hijos de Reuel fueron Najat, Zera, Sama y Mizá. Éstos fueron los nietos de Basemat, esposa de Esaú.
14 Los hijos de la otra esposa de Esaú, Aholibama, que era hija de Aná y nieta de Zibeón fueron Jeús, Jalán y Coré.

15Éstos fueron los jefes de los descendientes de Esaú:

De los hijos de Elifaz, primogénito de Esaú, los jefes fueron Temán, Omar, Zefo, Quenaz, 16Coré, Gatán y Amalec. Éstos fueron los jefes de los descendientes de Elifaz en la tierra de Edom, y todos ellos fueron nietos de Ada.
17 De los hijos de Reuel hijo de Esaú, los jefes fueron Najat, Zera, Sama y Mizá.
Éstos fueron los jefes de los descendientes de Reuel en la tierra de Edom, y todos ellos fueron nietos de Basemat, esposa de Esaú.
18 De los hijos de Aholibama, hija de Aná y esposa de Esaú, los jefes fueron Jeús, Jalán y Coré.
19Éstos fueron descendientes de Esaú, también llamado Edom, y a su vez jefes de sus respectivas tribus.

20Éstos fueron los descendientes de Seír el horeo, que habitaban en aquella región:

Lotán, Sobal, Zibeón, Aná, 21Disón, Ezer y Disán. Estos descendientes de Seír fueron los jefes de los horeos en la tierra de Edom.
22 Los hijos de Lotán fueron Horí y Homán. Lotán tenía una hermana llamada Timná.
23 Los hijos de Sobal fueron: Alván, Manajat, Ebal, Sefó y Onam.
24 Los hijos de Zibeón fueron Ayá y Aná. Este último es el mismo que encontró las aguas termalesp en el desierto mientras cuidaba los asnos de su padre Zibeón.
25 Los hijos de Aná fueron: Disón y Aholibama, hija de Aná.
26 Los hijos de Disón fueron Hemdán, Esbán, Itrán y Querán.
27 Los hijos de Ezer fueron Bilán, Zaván y Acán.
28 Los hijos de Disán fueron Uz y Arán.
29 Los jefes de los horeos fueron Lotán, Sobal, Zibeón, Aná, 30Disón, Ezer y Disán. Cada uno de ellos fue jefe de su tribu en la región de Seír.

Los reyes de Edom
36:31-43 — 1Cr 1:43-54

31Antes de que los israelitas tuvieran rey, éstos fueron los reyes que reinaron en el país de Edom:

32 Bela hijo de Beor, reinó en Edom. El nombre de su ciudad era Dinaba.
33 Cuando murió Bela, reinó en su lugar Jobab hijo de Zera, que provenía de Bosra.

---

m 35:15 En hebreo, Betel significa casa de Dios.   n 35:18 En hebreo, Benoní significa hijo de mi aflicción o hijo de mi tristeza.
ñ 35:18 En hebreo, Benjamín significa hijo de mi mano derecha.   o 35:22 Cuando Israel se enteró, se enojó muchísimo (LXX); Israel se enteró (TM).   p 36:24 aguas termales. Texto de difícil traducción.

34 Cuando murió Jobab, reinó en su lugar Jusán, que venía de la región de Temán.

35 Cuando murió Jusán, reinó en su lugar Hadad hijo de Bedad. Éste derrotó a Madián en el campo de Moab. El nombre de su ciudad era Avit.

36 Cuando murió Hadad, reinó en su lugar Samla, que era del pueblo de Masreca.

37 Cuando murió Samla, reinó en su lugar Saúl de Rejobot del Río.

38 Cuando murió Saúl, reinó en su lugar Baal Janán hijo de Acbor.

39 Cuando murió Baal Janán hijo de Acbor, reinó en su lugar Hadad.^q El nombre de su ciudad era Pau. Su esposa se llamaba Mehitabel, y era hija de Matred y nieta de Mezab.

40 Éstos son los nombres de los jefes que descendieron de Esaú, cada uno según su clan y región: Timná, Alvá, Jetet, **41**Aholibama, Elá, Pinón, **42**Quenaz, Temán, Mibzar, **43**Magdiel e Iram. Éstos fueron los jefes de Edom, según los lugares que habitaron.

Éste fue Esaú, padre de los edomitas.

Los sueños de José

37 Jacob se estableció en la tierra de Canaán, donde su padre había residido como extranjero.

2Ésta es la historia de Jacob y su familia.

Cuando José tenía diecisiete años, apacentaba el rebaño junto a sus hermanos, los hijos de Bilhá y de Zilpá, que eran concubinas de su padre. El joven José solía informar a su padre de la mala fama que tenían estos hermanos suyos.

3Israel amaba a José más que a sus otros hijos, porque lo había tenido en su vejez. Por eso mandó que le confeccionaran una túnica especial de mangas largas.^r **4**Viendo sus hermanos que su padre amaba más a José que a ellos, comenzaron a odiarlo y ni siquiera lo saludaban.

5Cierto día José tuvo un sueño y, cuando se lo contó a sus hermanos, éstos le tuvieron más odio todavía, **6**pues les dijo:

—Préstenme atención, que les voy a contar lo que he soñado. **7**Resulta que estábamos todos nosotros en el campo atando gavillas. De pronto, mi gavilla se levantó y quedó erguida, mientras que las de ustedes se juntaron alrededor de la mía y le hicieron reverencias.

8Sus hermanos replicaron:

—¿De veras crees que vas a reinar sobre nosotros, y que nos vas a someter?

Y lo odiaron aún más por los sueños que él les contaba.

9Después José tuvo otro sueño, y se lo contó a sus hermanos. Les dijo:

—Tuve otro sueño, en el que veía que el sol, la luna y once estrellas me hacían reverencias.

10Cuando se lo contó a su padre y a sus hermanos, su padre lo reprendió:

—¿Qué quieres decirnos con este sueño que has tenido? —le preguntó—. ¿Acaso tu madre, tus hermanos y yo vendremos a hacerte reverencias?

11Sus hermanos le tenían envidia, pero su padre meditaba en todo esto.

José es vendido por sus hermanos

12En cierta ocasión, los hermanos de José se fueron a Siquén para apacentar las ovejas de su padre. **13**Israel le dijo a José:

—Tus hermanos están en Siquén apacentando las ovejas. Quiero que vayas a verlos.

—Está bien —contestó José.

14Israel continuó:

—Vete a ver cómo están tus hermanos y el rebaño, y tráeme noticias frescas.

Y lo envió desde el valle de Hebrón. Cuando José llegó a Siquén, **15**un hombre lo encontró perdido en el campo y le preguntó:

—¿Qué andas buscando?

16—Ando buscando a mis hermanos —contestó José—. ¿Podría usted indicarme dónde están apacentando el rebaño?

17—Ya se han marchado de aquí —le informó el hombre—. Les oí decir que se dirigían a Dotán.

José siguió buscando a sus hermanos, y los encontró cerca de Dotán. **18**Como ellos alcanzaron a verlo desde lejos, antes de que se acercara tramaron un plan para matarlo. **19**Se dijeron unos a otros:

—Ahí viene ese soñador. **20**Ahora sí que le llegó la hora. Vamos a matarlo y echarlo en una de estas cisternas, y diremos que lo devoró un animal salvaje. ¡Y a ver si se cumplen sus sueños!

21Cuando Rubén escuchó esto, intentó librarlo de las garras de sus hermanos, así que les propuso:

—No lo matemos. **22**No derramen sangre. Arrójenlo en esta cisterna en el desierto, pero no le pongan la mano encima.

Rubén dijo esto porque su intención era rescatar a José y devolverlo a su padre.

23Cuando José llegó adonde estaban sus hermanos, le arrancaron la túnica especial de mangas largas, **24**lo agarraron y lo echaron en una cisterna que estaba vacía y seca. **25**Luego se sentaron a comer. En eso, al levantar la vista, divisaron una caravana de ismaelitas que venía de Galaad. Sus camellos estaban cargados de perfumes, bálsamo y mirra, que llevaban a Egipto. **26**Entonces Judá les propuso a sus hermanos:

—¿Qué ganamos con matar a nuestro hermano y ocultar su muerte? **27**En vez de eliminarlo, vendámoslo a los ismaelitas; al fin de cuentas, es nuestro propio hermano.

Sus hermanos estuvieron de acuerdo con él, **28**así que cuando los mercaderes madianitas se acercaron, sacaron a José de la cisterna y se lo vendieron a los ismaelitas por veinte monedas de plata. Fue así como se llevaron a José a Egipto.

29Cuando Rubén volvió a la cisterna y José ya no estaba allí, se rasgó las vestiduras en señal de duelo. **30**Regresó entonces adonde estaban sus hermanos, y les reclamó:

—¡Ya no está ese mocoso! Y ahora, ¿qué hago?

31En seguida los hermanos tomaron la túnica especial de José, degollaron un cabrito, y con la sangre empaparon la túnica. **32**Luego la mandaron a su padre con el siguiente mensaje: «Encontramos esto. Fíjate bien si es o no la túnica de tu hijo.»

33En cuanto Jacob la reconoció, exclamó: «¡Sí, es la túnica de mi hijo! ¡Seguro que un animal salvaje se lo devoró y lo hizo pedazos!» **34**Y Jacob se rasgó las vestiduras y se vistió de luto, y por mucho tiempo hizo duelo por su hijo. **35**Todos sus hijos y sus hijas intentaban calmarlo, pero él no se dejaba consolar, sino que decía: «No. Guardaré luto hasta que des-

q **36:39** *Hadad* (mss. hebreos, Pentateuco Samaritano y Siríaca; véase 1Cr 1:50); *Hadar* (TM). r **37:3** *de mangas largas*. Frase de difícil traducción; también en vv. 23 y 32.

cienda al *sepulcro para reunirme con mi hijo.» Así Jacob siguió llorando la muerte de José.

36En Egipto, los madianitass lo vendieron a un tal Potifar, funcionario del faraón y capitán de la guardia.

Judá y Tamar

38 Por esos días, Judá se apartó de sus hermanos y se fue a vivir a la casa de un hombre llamado Hirá, residente del pueblo de Adulán. 2Allí Judá conoció a una mujer, hija de un cananeo llamado Súa, y se casó con ella. Luego de tener relaciones con él, 3ella concibió y dio a luz un hijo, al que llamó Er. 4Tiempo después volvió a concebir, y dio a luz otro hijo, al que llamó Onán. 5Pasado el tiempo tuvo otro hijo, al que llamó Selá, el cual nació en Quezib.

6Judá consiguió para Er, su hijo mayor, una esposa que se llamaba Tamar. 7Pero al SEÑOR no le agradó la conducta del primogénito de Judá, y le quitó la vida. 8Entonces Judá le dijo a Onán: «Cásate con la viuda de tu hermano y cumple con tu deber de cuñado; así le darás descendencia a tu hermano.» 9Pero Onán sabía que los hijos que nacieran no serían reconocidos como suyos. Por eso, cada vez que tenía relaciones con ella, derramaba el semen en el suelo, y así evitaba que su hermano tuviera descendencia. 10Esta conducta ofendió mucho al SEÑOR, así que también a él le quitó la vida. 11Entonces Judá le dijo a su nuera Tamar: «Quédate como viuda en la casa de tu padre, hasta que mi hijo Selá tenga edad de casarse.» Pero en realidad Judá pensaba que Selá podría morirse, lo mismo que sus hermanos. Así que Tamar se fue a vivir a la casa de su padre.

12Después de mucho tiempo, murió la esposa de Judá, la hija de Súa. Al concluir el tiempo de duelo, Judá fue al pueblo de Timnat para esquilar sus ovejas. Lo acompañó su amigo Hirá, el adulanita. 13Cuando Tamar se enteró de que su suegro se dirigía hacia Timnat para esquilar sus ovejas, 14se quitó el vestido de viuda, se cubrió con un velo para que nadie la reconociera, y se sentó a la entrada del pueblo de Enayin, que está en el camino a Timnat. Esto lo hizo porque se dio cuenta de que Selá ya tenía edad de casarse y aún no se lo daban a ella por esposo.

15Cuando Judá la vio con el rostro cubierto, la tomó por una prostituta. 16No sabiendo que era su nuera, se acercó a la orilla del camino y le dijo:

—Deja que me acueste contigo.

—¿Qué me das si te digo que sí? —le preguntó ella.

17—Te mandaré uno de los cabritos de mi rebaño —respondió Judá.

—Está bien —respondió ella—, pero déjame algo en garantía hasta que me lo mandes.

18—¿Qué prenda quieres que te deje? —preguntó Judá.

—Dame tu sello y su cordón, y el bastón que llevas en la mano —respondió Tamar.

Judá se los entregó, se acostó con ella y la dejó embarazada. 19Cuando ella se levantó, se fue inmediatamente de allí, se quitó el velo y volvió a ponerse la ropa de viuda.

20Más tarde, Judá envió el cabrito por medio de su amigo adulanita, para recuperar las prendas que había dejado con la mujer; pero su amigo no dio con ella. 21Entonces le preguntó a la gente del lugar:

—¿Dónde está la prostitutat de Enayin, la que se sentaba junto al camino?

—Aquí nunca ha habido una prostituta así —le contestaron.

22El amigo regresó adonde estaba Judá y le dijo:

—No la pude encontrar. Además, la gente del lugar me informó que allí nunca había estado una prostituta como ésa.

23—Que se quede con las prendas —replicó Judá—; no es cuestión de que hagamos el ridículo. Pero que quede claro: yo le envié el cabrito, y tú no la encontraste.

24Como tres meses después, le informaron a Judá lo siguiente:

—Tu nuera Tamar se ha prostituido, y como resultado de sus andanzas ha quedado embarazada.

—¡Sáquenla y quémenla! —exclamó Judá.

25Pero cuando la estaban sacando, ella mandó este mensaje a su suegro: «El dueño de estas prendas fue quien me embarazó. A ver si reconoce usted de quién son este sello, el cordón del sello, y este bastón.»

26Judá los reconoció y declaró: «Su conducta es más justa que la mía, pues yo no la di por esposa a mi hijo Selá.» Y no volvió a acostarse con ella.

27Cuando llegó el tiempo de que Tamar diera a luz, resultó que tenía mellizos en su seno. 28En el momento de nacer, uno de los mellizos sacó la mano; la partera le ató un hilo rojo en la mano, y dijo: «Éste salió primero.» 29Pero en ese momento el niño metió la mano, y salió primero el otro. Entonces la partera dijo: «¡Cómo te abriste paso!» Por eso al niño lo llamaron Fares.u 30Luego salió su hermano, con el hilo rojo atado en la mano, y lo llamaron Zera.v

José y la esposa de Potifar

39 Cuando José fue llevado a Egipto, los ismaelitas que lo habían trasladado allá lo vendieron a Potifar, un egipcio que era funcionario del faraón y capitán de su guardia. 2Ahora bien, el SEÑOR estaba con José y las cosas le salían muy bien. Mientras José vivía en la casa de su patrón egipcio, 3éste se dio cuenta de que el SEÑOR estaba con José y lo hacía prosperar en todo. 4José se ganó la confianza de Potifar, y éste lo nombró mayordomo de toda su casa y le confió la administración de todos sus bienes 5Por causa de José, el SEÑOR bendijo la casa del egipcio Potifar a partir del momento en que puso a José a cargo de su casa y de todos sus bienes. La bendición del SEÑOR se extendió sobre todo lo que tenía el egipcio, tanto en la casa como en el campo. 6Por esto Potifar dejó todo a cargo de José, y tan sólo se preocupaba por lo que tenía que comer.

José tenía muy buen físico y era muy atractivo. 7Después de algún tiempo, la esposa de su patrón empezó a echarle el ojo y le propuso:

—Acuéstate conmigo.

8Pero José no quiso saber nada, sino que le contestó:

—Mire, señora: mi patrón ya no tiene que preocuparse de nada en la casa, porque todo me lo ha confiado a mí. 9En esta casa no hay nadie más importante que yo. Mi patrón no me ha negado nada, excepto meterme con usted, que es su esposa. ¿Cómo podría yo cometer tal maldad y pecar así contra Dios?

---

s 37:36 madianitas (Pentateuco Samaritano, LXX, Vulgata y Siríaca; véase v. 28); medanitas (TM). t 38:21 prostituta. Lit. consagrada; es decir, una prostituta consagrada al culto. u 38:29 En hebreo, Fares significa abertura, brecha. v 38:30 En hebreo, Zera puede significar rojo, brillo o resplandor.

¹⁰Y por más que ella lo acosaba día tras día para que se acostara con ella y le hiciera compañía, José se mantuvo firme ante su rechazo.

¹¹Un día, en un momento en que todo el personal de servicio se encontraba ausente, José entró en la casa para cumplir con sus responsabilidades. ¹²Entonces la mujer de Potifar lo agarró del manto y le rogó: «¡Acuéstate conmigo!»

Pero José, dejando el manto en manos de ella, salió corriendo de la casa. ¹³Al ver ella que él había dejado el manto en sus manos y había salido corriendo, ¹⁴llamó a los siervos de la casa y les dijo: «¡Miren!, el hebreo que nos trajo mi esposo sólo ha venido a burlarse de nosotros. Entró a la casa con la intención de acostarse conmigo, pero yo grité con todas mis fuerzas. ¹⁵En cuanto me oyó gritar, salió corriendo y dejó su manto a mi lado.»

¹⁶La mujer guardó el manto de José hasta que su marido volvió a su casa. ¹⁷Entonces le contó la misma historia: «El esclavo hebreo que nos trajiste quiso aprovecharse de mí. ¹⁸Pero en cuanto grité con todas mis fuerzas, salió corriendo y dejó su manto a mi lado.»

¹⁹Cuando el patrón de José escuchó de labios de su mujer cómo la había tratado el esclavo, se enfureció ²⁰y mandó que echaran a José en la cárcel donde estaban los presos del rey.

Pero aun en la cárcel ²¹el SEÑOR estaba con él y no dejó de mostrarle su amor. Hizo que se ganara la confianza del guardia de la cárcel, ²²el cual puso a José a cargo de todos los prisioneros y de todo lo que allí se hacía. ²³Como el SEÑOR estaba con José y hacía prosperar todo lo que él hacía, el guardia de la cárcel no se preocupaba de nada de lo que dejaba en sus manos.

El copero y el panadero

40 Tiempo después, el copero y el panadero del rey de Egipto ofendieron a su señor. ²El faraón se enojó contra estos dos funcionarios suyos, es decir, contra el jefe de los coperos y el jefe de los panaderos, ³así que los mandó presos a la casa del capitán de la guardia, que era la misma cárcel donde estaba preso José. ⁴Allí el capitán de la guardia le encargó a José que atendiera a estos funcionarios.

Después de haber estado algún tiempo en la cárcel, ⁵una noche los dos funcionarios, es decir, el copero y el panadero, tuvieron cada uno un sueño, cada sueño con su propio significado. ⁶A la mañana siguiente, cuando José fue a verlos, los encontró muy preocupados, ⁷y por eso les preguntó:

—¿Por qué andan hoy tan cabizbajos?

⁸—Los dos tuvimos un sueño —respondieron—, y no hay nadie que nos lo interprete.

—¿Acaso no es Dios quien da la interpretación? —preguntó José—. ¿Por qué no me cuentan lo que soñaron?

⁹Entonces el jefe de los coperos le contó a José el sueño que había tenido:

—Soñé que frente a mí había una vid, ¹⁰la cual tenía tres ramas. En cuanto la vid echó brotes, floreció; y maduraron las uvas en los racimos. ¹¹Yo tenía la copa del faraón en la mano. Tomé las uvas, las exprimí en la copa, y luego puse la copa en manos del faraón.

¹²Entonces José le dijo:

—Ésta es la interpretación de su sueño: Las tres ramas son tres días. ¹³Dentro de los próximos tres días el faraón lo indultará a usted y volverá a colocarlo en su cargo. Usted volverá a poner la copa del faraón en su mano, tal como lo hacía antes, cuando era su copero. ¹⁴Yo le ruego que no se olvide de mí. Por favor, cuando todo se haya arreglado, háblele usted de mí al faraón para que me saque de esta cárcel. ¹⁵A mí me trajeron por la fuerza, de la tierra de los hebreos. ¡Yo no hice nada aquí para que me echaran en la cárcel!

¹⁶Al ver que la interpretación había sido favorable, el jefe de los panaderos le dijo a José:

—Yo también tuve un sueño. En ese sueño, llevaba yo tres canastas de panʷ sobre la cabeza. ¹⁷En la canasta de arriba había un gran surtido de repostería para el faraón, pero las aves venían a comer de la canasta que llevaba sobre la cabeza.

¹⁸José le respondió:

—Ésta es la interpretación de su sueño: Las tres canastas son tres días. ¹⁹Dentro de los próximos tres días, el faraón mandará que a usted lo decapiten y lo cuelguen de un árbol, y las aves devorarán su cuerpo.

²⁰En efecto, tres días después el faraón celebró su cumpleaños y ofreció una gran fiesta para todos sus funcionarios. En presencia de éstos, mandó sacar de la cárcel al jefe de los coperos y al jefe de los panaderos. ²¹Al jefe de los coperos lo restituyó en su cargo para que, una vez más, pusiera la copa en manos del faraón. ²²Pero, tal como lo había predicho José, al jefe de los panaderos mandó que lo ahorcaran. ²³Sin embargo, el jefe de los coperos no se acordó de José, sino que se olvidó de él por completo.

Los sueños del faraón

41 Dos años más tarde, el faraón tuvo un sueño: Estaba de pie junto al río Nilo ²cuando, de pronto, del río salieron siete vacas hermosas y gordas que se pusieron a pastar entre los juncos. ³Detrás de ellas salieron otras siete vacas, feas y flacas, que se pararon a orillas del Nilo, junto a las primeras. ⁴¡Y las vacas feas y flacas se comieron a las vacas hermosas y gordas!

En ese momento el faraón se despertó. ⁵Pero volvió a dormirse, y tuvo otro sueño: Siete espigas de trigo, grandes y hermosas, crecían de un solo tallo. ⁶Tras ellas brotaron otras siete espigas, delgadas y quemadas por el viento solano. ⁷¡Y las siete espigas delgadas se comieron a las espigas grandes y hermosas!

En eso el faraón se despertó y se dio cuenta de que sólo era un sueño. ⁸Sin embargo, a la mañana siguiente se levantó muy preocupado, mandó llamar a todos los magos y sabios de Egipto, y les contó los dos sueños. Pero nadie se los pudo interpretar. ⁹Entonces el jefe de los coperos le dijo al faraón: «Ahora me doy cuenta del grave error que he cometido. ¹⁰Cuando el faraón se enojó con sus servidores, es decir, conmigo y con el jefe de los panaderos, nos mandó a la cárcel, bajo la custodia del capitán de la guardia. ¹¹Una misma noche, los dos tuvimos un sueño, cada sueño con su propio significado. ¹²Allí, con nosotros, había un joven hebreo, esclavo del capitán de la guardia. Le contamos nuestros sueños, y a cada uno nos interpretó el sueño. ¹³¡Y todo sucedió tal como él lo había interpretado! A mí me restituyeron mi cargo, y al jefe de los panaderos lo ahorcaron.»

¹⁴El faraón mandó llamar a José, y en seguida lo sacaron de la cárcel. Luego de afeitarse y cambiarse de ropa, José se presentó ante el faraón, ¹⁵quien le dijo:

ʷ **40:16** *pan.* Alt. *mimbre.*

—Tuve un sueño que nadie ha podido interpretar. Pero me he enterado de que, cuando tú oyes un sueño, eres capaz de interpretarlo.

16—No soy yo quien puede hacerlo —respondió José—, sino que es Dios quien le dará al faraón una respuesta favorable.

17El faraón le contó a José lo siguiente:

—En mi sueño, estaba yo de pie a orillas del río Nilo. 18De pronto, salieron del río siete vacas gordas y hermosas, y se pusieron a pastar entre los juncos. 19Detrás de ellas salieron otras siete vacas, feas y flacas. ¡Jamás se habían visto vacas tan raquíticas en toda la tierra de Egipto! 20Y las siete vacas feas y flacas se comieron a las siete vacas gordas. 21Pero, después de habérselas comido, no se les notaba en lo más mínimo, porque seguían tan feas como antes. Entonces me desperté.

22»Después tuve otro sueño: Siete espigas de trigo, grandes y hermosas, crecían de un solo tallo. 23Tras ellas brotaron otras siete espigas marchitas, delgadas y quemadas por el viento solano. 24Las siete espigas delgadas se comieron las espigas grandes y hermosas. Todo esto se lo conté a los magos, pero ninguno de ellos me lo pudo interpretar.

25José le explicó al faraón:

—En realidad, los dos sueños del faraón son uno solo. Dios le ha anunciado lo que está por hacer. 26Las siete vacas hermosas y las siete espigas hermosas son siete años. Se trata del mismo sueño. 27Y las siete vacas flacas y feas, que salieron detrás de las otras, y las siete espigas delgadas y quemadas por el viento solano, son también siete años. Pero éstos serán siete años de hambre.

28»Tal como le he dicho al faraón, Dios le está mostrando lo que está por hacer. 29Están por venir siete años de mucha abundancia en todo Egipto, 30a los que les seguirán siete años de hambre, que harán olvidar toda la abundancia que antes hubo. ¡El hambre acabará con Egipto! 31Tan terrible será el hambre, que nadie se acordará de la abundancia que antes hubo en el país. 32El faraón tuvo el mismo sueño dos veces porque Dios ha resuelto firmemente hacer esto, y lo llevará a cabo muy pronto.

33»Por todo esto, el faraón debería buscar un hombre competente y sabio, para que se haga cargo de la tierra de Egipto. 34Además, el faraón debería nombrar inspectores en todo Egipto, para que durante los siete años de abundancia recauden la quinta parte de la cosecha en todo el país. 35Bajo el control del faraón, esos inspectores deberán juntar el grano de los años buenos que vienen y almacenarlo en las ciudades, para que haya una reserva de alimento. 36Este alimento almacenado le servirá a Egipto para los siete años de hambre que sufrirá, y así la gente del país no morirá de hambre.

37Al faraón y a sus servidores les pareció bueno el plan. 38Entonces el faraón les preguntó a sus servidores:

—¿Podremos encontrar una persona así, en quien repose el espíritu de Dios?

39Luego le dijo a José:

—Puesto que Dios te ha revelado todo esto, no hay nadie más competente y sabio que tú. 40Quedarás a cargo de mi palacio, y todo mi pueblo cumplirá tus órdenes. Sólo yo tendré más autoridad que tú, porque soy el rey.

José, gobernador de Egipto

41Así que el faraón le informó a José:

—Mira, yo te pongo a cargo de todo el territorio de Egipto.

42De inmediato, el faraón se quitó el anillo oficial y se lo puso a José. Hizo que lo vistieran con ropas de lino fino, y que le pusieran un collar de oro en el cuello. 43Después lo invitó a subirse al carro reservado para el segundo en autoridad, y ordenó que gritaran: «¡Abran paso!»x Fue así como el faraón puso a José al frente de todo el territorio de Egipto.

44Entonces el faraón le dijo:

—Yo soy el faraón, pero nadie en todo Egipto podrá hacer nada sin tu permiso.

45Y le cambió el *nombre a José, y lo llamó Zafenat Panea; además, le dio por esposa a Asenat, hija de Potifera, sacerdote de la ciudad de On.y De este modo quedó José a cargo de Egipto. 46Tenía treinta años cuando comenzó a trabajar al servicio del faraón, rey de Egipto.

Tan pronto como se retiró José de la presencia del faraón, se dedicó a recorrer todo el territorio de Egipto. 47Durante los siete años de abundancia la tierra produjo grandes cosechas, 48así que José fue recogiendo todo el alimento que se produjo en Egipto durante esos siete años, y lo almacenó en las ciudades. 49Juntó alimento como quien junta arena del mar, y fue tanto lo que recogió que dejó de contabilizarlo. ¡Ya no había forma de mantener el control!

50Antes de comenzar el primer año de hambre, José tuvo dos hijos con su esposa Asenat, la hija de Potifera, sacerdote de On. 51Al primero lo llamó Manasés, porque dijo: «Dios ha hecho que me olvide de todos mis problemas, y de mi casa paterna.» 52Al segundo lo llamó Efraín, porque dijo: «Dios me ha hecho fecundo en esta tierra donde he sufrido.»

53Los siete años de abundancia en Egipto llegaron a su fin 54y, tal como José lo había anunciado, comenzaron los siete años de hambre, la cual se extendió por todos los países. Pero a lo largo y a lo ancho del territorio de Egipto había alimento. 55Cuando también en Egipto comenzó a sentirse el hambre, el pueblo clamó al faraón pidiéndole comida. Entonces el faraón le dijo a todo el pueblo de Egipto: «Vayan a ver a José, y hagan lo que él les diga.»

56Cuando ya el hambre se había extendido por todo el territorio, y había arreciado, José abrió los graneros para vender alimento a los egipcios. 57Además, de todos los países llegaban a Egipto para comprarle alimento a José, porque el hambre cundía ya por todo el mundo.

Los hermanos de José van a Egipto

42 Cuando Jacob se enteró de que había alimento en Egipto, les dijo a sus hijos: «¿Qué hacen ahí parados, mirándose unos a otros? 2He sabido que hay alimento en Egipto. Vayan allá y compren comida para nosotros, para que no muramos, sino que podamos sobrevivir.»

3Diez de los hermanos de José fueron a Egipto a comprar alimento. 4Pero Jacob no dejó que Benjamín, el hermano de José, se fuera con ellos porque pensó que podría sucederle alguna desgracia. 5Fue así como los hijos de Israel fueron a comprar alimento, al igual que otros, porque el hambre se había apoderado de Canaán.

6José era el gobernador del país, y el que vendía trigo a todo el mundo. Cuando sus hermanos llegaron ante él, se postraron rostro en tierra. 7En cuanto

---

x 41:43 «¡Abran paso!» Alt. «¡Inclínense!» y 41:45 On. Es decir, Heliópolis (Ciudad del Sol); también en v. 50.

José vio a sus hermanos, los reconoció; pero, fingiendo no conocerlos, les habló con rudeza:

—¡Y ustedes!, ¿de dónde vienen?

—Venimos de Canaán, para comprar alimento —contestaron.

8Aunque José los había reconocido, sus hermanos no lo reconocieron a él. 9En ese momento se acordó José de los sueños que había tenido acerca de ellos, y les dijo:

—¡De seguro ustedes son espías, y han venido para investigar las zonas desprotegidas del país!

10—¡No, señor! —respondieron—. Sus siervos hemos venido a comprar alimento. 11Todos nosotros somos hijos de un mismo padre, y además somos gente honrada. ¡Sus siervos no somos espías!

12—¡No es verdad! —insistió José—. Ustedes han venido para investigar las zonas desprotegidas del país.

13Pero ellos volvieron a responder:

—Nosotros, sus siervos, éramos doce hermanos, todos hijos de un mismo padre que vive en Canaán. El menor se ha quedado con nuestro padre, y el otro ya no vive.

14Pero José los increpó una vez más:

—Es tal como les he dicho. ¡Ustedes son espías! 15Y con esto lo vamos a comprobar: Les juro por la vida del faraón, que de aquí no saldrán con vida a menos que traigan a su hermano menor. 16Manden a uno de ustedes a buscar a su hermano; los demás se quedarán en la cárcel. Así sabremos si es verdad lo que dicen. Y si no es así, ¡por la vida del faraón, ustedes son espías!

17José los encerró en la cárcel durante tres días. 18Al tercer día les dijo:

—Yo soy un hombre temeroso de Dios. Hagan lo siguiente y salvarán su vida. 19Si en verdad son honrados, quédese uno de ustedes bajo custodia, y vayan los demás y lleven alimento para calmar el hambre de sus familias. 20Pero tráiganme a su hermano menor y pruébenme que dicen la verdad. Así no morirán.

Ellos aceptaron la propuesta, 21pero se decían unos a otros:

—Sin duda estamos sufriendo las consecuencias de lo que hicimos con nuestro hermano. Aunque vimos su angustia cuando nos suplicaba que lo tuviéramos compasión, no le hicimos caso. Por eso ahora nos vemos en aprietos.

22Entonces habló Rubén:

—Yo les advertí que no le hicieran daño al muchacho, pero no me hicieron caso. ¡Ahora tenemos que pagar el precio de su sangre!

23Como José les hablaba por medio de un intérprete, ellos no sabían que él entendía todo lo que estaban diciendo. 24José se apartó de ellos y se echó a llorar. Luego, cuando se controló y pudo hablarles, apartó a Simeón y ordenó que lo ataran en presencia de ellos.

25José dio también la orden de que llenaran de alimentos sus costales, que repusieran en cada una de sus bolsas el dinero que habían pagado, y que les dieran provisiones para el viaje. Y así se hizo. 26Entonces ellos cargaron el alimento sobre sus asnos y emprendieron el viaje de vuelta.

27Cuando llegaron al lugar donde acamparían esa noche, uno de ellos abrió su bolsa para darle de comer a su asno, ¡y allí en la abertura descubrió su dinero! 28Entonces les dijo a sus hermanos:

—¡Me devolvieron el dinero! Miren, ¡aquí está, en mi bolsa!

Los otros se asustaron mucho, y temblando se decían unos a otros:

—¿Qué es lo que Dios nos ha hecho?

29Al llegar a Canaán, donde estaba su padre Jacob, le contaron todo lo que les había sucedido:

30—El hombre que gobierna aquel país nos trató con rudeza, a tal grado que nos acusó de ser espías. 31Nosotros le dijimos: "Somos gente honrada. No somos espías." 32Además, le dijimos: "Somos doce hermanos, hijos de un mismo padre. Uno ya no vive, y el menor se ha quedado con nuestro padre en Canaán."

33»Entonces el hombre que gobierna aquel país nos dijo: "Con esto voy a comprobar si en verdad son gente honrada. Dejen aquí conmigo a uno de sus hermanos, y vayan a llevar alimento para calmar el hambre de sus familias. 34Pero a la vuelta tráiganme a su hermano menor. Así comprobaré que no son espías, y que en verdad son gente honrada. Luego les entregaré de vuelta a su hermano, y podrán moverse^z con libertad por el país."

35Cuando comenzaron a vaciar sus costales, se encontraron con que la bolsa de dinero de cada uno estaba allí. Esto hizo que ellos y su padre se llenaran de temor. 36Entonces Jacob, su padre, les dijo:

—¡Ustedes me van a dejar sin hijos! José ya no está con nosotros, Simeón tampoco está aquí, ¡y ahora se quieren llevar a Benjamín! ¡Todo esto me perjudica!

37Pero Rubén le dijo a su padre:

—Yo me hago cargo de Benjamín. Si no te lo devuelvo, podrás matar a mis dos hijos.

38—¡Mi hijo no se irá con ustedes! —replicó Jacob—. Su hermano José ya está muerto, y ahora sólo él me queda. Si le llega a pasar una desgracia en el viaje que van a emprender, ustedes tendrán la culpa de que este pobre viejo se muera de tristeza.

Los hermanos de José vuelven a Egipto

43 El hambre seguía aumentando en aquel país. 2Llegó el momento en que se les acabó el alimento que habían llevado de Egipto. Entonces su padre les dijo:

—Vuelvan a Egipto y compren un poco más de alimento para nosotros.

3Pero Judá le recordó:

—Aquel hombre nos advirtió claramente que no nos presentáramos ante él, a menos que lo hiciéramos con nuestro hermano menor. 4Si tú nos permites llevar a nuestro hermano menor, iremos a comprarte alimento. 5De lo contrario, no tiene objeto que vayamos. Aquel hombre fue muy claro en cuanto a no presentarnos ante él sin nuestro hermano menor.

6—¿Por qué me han causado este mal? —inquirió Israel—. ¿Por qué le dijeron a ese hombre que tenían otro hermano?

7—Porque aquel hombre nos preguntó específicamente acerca de nuestra familia —respondieron ellos—. "¿Vive todavía su padre de ustedes? —nos preguntó—. ¿Tienen algún otro hermano?" Lo único que hicimos fue responder a sus preguntas. ¿Cómo íbamos a saber que nos pediría llevar a nuestro hermano menor?

8Judá le dijo a su padre Israel:

—Bajo mi responsabilidad, envía al muchacho y nos iremos ahora mismo, para que nosotros y nuestros hijos podamos seguir viviendo. 9Yo te respondo por su seguridad; a mí me pedirás cuentas. Si no te lo devuelvo sano y salvo, yo seré el culpable ante ti para toda la

^z 42:34 *moverse.* Alt. *comerciar.*

vida. 10Si no nos hubiéramos demorado tanto, iya habríamos ido y vuelto dos veces!

11Entonces Israel, su padre, les dijo:

—Ya que no hay más remedio, hagan lo siguiente: Echen en sus costales los mejores productos de esta región, y llévenselos de regalo a ese hombre: un poco de bálsamo, un poco de miel, perfumes, mirra, nueces, almendras. 12Lleven también el doble del dinero, pues deben devolver el que estaba en sus bolsas, ya que seguramente fue un error. 13Vayan con su hermano menor y preséntense ante ese hombre. 14iQue el Dios *Todopoderoso permita que ese hombre les tenga compasión y deje libre a su otro hermano, y además vuelvan con Benjamín! En cuanto a mí, si he de perder a mis hijos, iqué le voy a hacer! iLos perderé!

15Ellos tomaron los regalos, el doble del dinero, y a Benjamín, y emprendieron el viaje a Egipto. Allí se presentaron ante José. 16Cuando éste vio a Benjamín con ellos, le dijo a su mayordomo: «Lleva a estos hombres a mi casa. Luego, mata un animal y prepáralo, pues estos hombres comerán conmigo al mediodía.»

17El mayordomo cumplió la orden y los llevó a la casa de José. 18Al ver ellos que los llevaban a la casa de José, se asustaron mucho y se dijeron: «Nos llevan por causa del dinero que se puso en nuestras bolsas la vez pasada. Ahora nos atacarán, nos acusarán, y hasta nos harán sus esclavos, con nuestros animales y todo.»

19Entonces se acercaron al mayordomo de la casa de José, y antes de entrar le dijeron:

20—Perdón, señor: nosotros ya vinimos antes para comprar alimento; 21pero a nuestro regreso, cuando acampamos para pasar la noche, descubrimos que en cada una de nuestras bolsas estaba el dinero que habíamos pagado. iPero lo hemos traído para devolverlo! 22También hemos traído más dinero para comprar alimento. iNo sabemos quién puso el dinero de vuelta en nuestras bolsas!

23—Está bien, no tengan miedo —contestó aquel hombre—. El Dios de ustedes y de su padre habrá puesto ese tesoro en sus bolsas. A mí me consta que recibí el dinero que ustedes pagaron.

El mayordomo les llevó a Simeón, 24y a todos los hizo pasar a la casa de José. Allí les dio agua para que se lavaran los pies, y les dio de comer a sus asnos. 25Ellos, por su parte, prepararon los regalos, mientras esperaban que José llegara al mediodía, pues habían oído que comerían allí.

26Cuando José entró en su casa, le entregaron los regalos que le habían llevado, y rostro en tierra se postraron ante él. 27José les preguntó cómo estaban, y añadió:

—¿Cómo está su padre, el anciano del cual me hablaron? ¿Vive todavía?

28—Nuestro padre, su siervo, se encuentra bien, y todavía vive —respondieron ellos.

Y en seguida le hicieron una reverencia para honrarlo. 29José miró a su alrededor y, al ver a Benjamín, su hermano de padre y madre, les preguntó:

—¿Es éste su hermano menor, del cual me habían hablado? iQue Dios te guarde, hijo mío!

30Conmovido por la presencia de su hermano, y no pudiendo contener el llanto, José salió de prisa. Entró en su habitación, y allí se echó a llorar desconsoladamente. 31Después se lavó la cara y, ya más calmado, salió y ordenó: «iSirvan la comida!»

32A José le sirvieron en un sector, a los hermanos en otro, y en otro más a los egipcios que comían con José. Los egipcios no comían con los hebreos porque, para los habitantes de Egipto, era una abominación. 33Los hermanos de José estaban sentados frente a él, de mayor a menor, y unos a otros se miraban con asombro. 34Las porciones les eran servidas desde la mesa de José, pero a Benjamín se le servían porciones mucho más grandes que a los demás. En compañía de José, todos bebieron y se alegraron.

La copa de José

44 Más tarde, José ordenó al mayordomo de su casa: «Llena con todo el alimento que les quepa los costales de estos hombres, y pon en sus bolsas el dinero de cada uno de ellos. 2Luego mete mi copa de plata en la bolsa del hermano menor, junto con el dinero que pagó por el alimento.» Y el mayordomo hizo todo lo que José le ordenó.

3A la mañana siguiente, muy temprano, los hermanos de José fueron enviados de vuelta, junto con sus asnos. 4Todavía no estaban muy lejos de la ciudad cuando José le dijo al mayordomo de su casa: «iAnda! iPersigue a esos hombres! Cuando los alcances, diles: "¿Por qué me han pagado mal por bien? 5¿Por qué han robado la copa que usa mi señor para beber y para adivinar? iEsto que han hecho está muy mal!" »

6Cuando el mayordomo los alcanzó, les repitió esas mismas palabras. 7Pero ellos respondieron:

—¿Por qué dice usted tales cosas, mi señor? iLejos sea de nosotros actuar de esa manera! 8Es más, nosotros le trajimos de vuelta de Canaán el dinero que habíamos pagado, pero que encontramos en nuestras bolsas. ¿Por qué, entonces, habríamos de robar oro o plata de la casa de su señor? 9Si se encuentra la copa en poder de alguno de nosotros, que muera el que la tenga, y el resto de nosotros seremos esclavos de mi señor.

10—Está bien —respondió el mayordomo—, se hará como ustedes dicen, pero sólo el que tenga la copa en su poder será mi esclavo; el resto de ustedes quedará libre de todo cargo.

11En seguida cada uno de ellos bajó al suelo su bolsa y la abrió. 12El mayordomo revisó cada bolsa, comenzando con la del hermano mayor y terminando con la del menor. iY encontró la copa en la bolsa de Benjamín! 13Al ver esto, los hermanos de José se rasgaron las vestiduras en señal de duelo y, luego de cargar sus asnos, volvieron a la ciudad.

14Todavía estaba José en su casa cuando llegaron Judá y sus hermanos. Entonces se postraron rostro en tierra, 15y José les dijo:

—¿Qué manera de portarse es ésta? ¿Acaso no saben que un hombre como yo puede adivinar?

16—iNo sabemos qué decirle, mi señor! —contestó Judá—. iNo hay excusa que valga! ¿Cómo podemos demostrar nuestra inocencia? Dios ha puesto al descubierto la maldad de sus siervos. Aquí nos tiene usted: somos sus esclavos, nosotros y el que tenía la copa.

17—iJamás podría yo actuar de ese modo! —respondió José—. Sólo será mi esclavo el que tenía la copa en su poder. En cuanto a ustedes, regresen tranquilos a la casa de su padre.

18Entonces Judá se acercó a José para decirle:

—Mi señor, no se enoje usted conmigo, pero le ruego que me permita hablarle en privado. Para mí, usted es tan importante como el faraón. 19Cuando mi señor nos preguntó si todavía teníamos un padre o algún otro hermano, 20nosotros le contestamos que teníamos un padre anciano, y un hermano que le nació a nuestro padre en su vejez. Nuestro padre quiere muchísimo a este último porque es el único que le queda de la misma madre, ya que el otro murió. 21Entonces usted nos obligó a traer a este hermano menor para conocerlo. 22Nosotros le dijimos que el joven no podía dejar a su padre porque, si lo hacía, seguramente su padre moriría. 23Pero usted insistió y nos advirtió que, si no traíamos a nuestro hermano menor, nunca más seríamos recibidos en su presencia. 24Entonces regresamos adonde vive mi padre, su siervo, y le informamos de todo lo que usted nos había dicho. 25Tiempo después nuestro padre nos dijo: "Vuelvan otra vez a comprar un poco de alimento." 26Nosotros le contestamos: "No podemos ir si nuestro hermano menor no va con nosotros. No podremos presentarnos ante hombre tan importante, a menos que nuestro hermano menor nos acompañe." 27Mi padre, su siervo, respondió: "Ustedes saben que mi esposa me dio dos hijos. 28Uno desapareció de mi lado, y no he vuelto a verlo. Con toda seguridad fue despedazado por las fieras. 29Si también se llevan a éste, y le pasa alguna desgracia, ¡ustedes tendrán la culpa de este pobre viejo se muera de tristeza!"

30»Así que, si yo regreso a mi padre, su siervo, y el joven, cuya *vida está tan unida a la de mi padre, no regresa con nosotros, 31seguramente mi padre, al no verlo, morirá, y nosotros seremos los culpables de que nuestro padre se muera de tristeza. 32Este siervo suyo quedó ante mi padre como responsable del joven. Le dije: "Si no te lo devuelvo, padre mío, seré culpable ante ti toda mi vida." 33Por eso, permita usted que yo me quede como esclavo suyo en lugar de mi hermano menor, y que él regrese con sus hermanos. 34¿Cómo podré volver junto a mi padre si mi hermano menor no está conmigo? ¡No soy capaz de ver la desgracia que le sobrevendrá a mi padre!

José se da a conocer

45 José ya no pudo controlarse delante de sus servidores, así que ordenó: «¡Que salgan todos de mi presencia!» Y ninguno de ellos quedó con él. Cuando se dio a conocer a sus hermanos, 2comenzó a llorar tan fuerte que los egipcios se enteraron, y la noticia llegó hasta la casa del faraón.

3—Yo soy José —les declaró a sus hermanos—. ¿Vive todavía mi padre?

Pero ellos estaban tan pasmados que no atinaban a contestarle. 4No obstante, José insistió:

—¡Acérquense!

Cuando ellos se acercaron, él añadió:

—Yo soy José, el hermano de ustedes, a quien vendieron a Egipto. 5Pero ahora, por favor no se aflijan más ni se reprochen el haberme vendido, pues en realidad fue Dios quien me mandó delante de ustedes para salvar vidas. 6Desde hace dos años la región está sufriendo de hambre, y todavía faltan cinco años más en que no habrá siembras ni cosechas. 7Por eso Dios me envió delante de ustedes: para salvarles la vida de manera extraordinariaa y de ese modo asegurarles descendencia sobre la tierra. 8Fue Dios quien me envió aquí, y no ustedes. Él me ha puesto como asesorb del faraón y administrador de su casa, y como gobernador de todo Egipto. 9¡Vamos, apúrense! Vuelvan a la casa de mi padre y díganle: "Así dice tu hijo José: 'Dios me ha hecho gobernador de todo Egipto. Ven a verme. No te demores. 10Vivirás en la región de Gosén, cerca de mí, con tus hijos y tus nietos, y con tus ovejas, y vacas y todas tus posesiones. 11Yo les proveeré alimento allí, porque aún quedan cinco años más de hambre. De lo contrario, tú y tu familia, y todo lo que te pertenece, caerán en la miseria.' " 12Además, ustedes y mi hermano Benjamín son testigos de que yo mismo lo he dicho. 13Cuéntenle a mi padre del

prestigio que tengo en Egipto, y de todo lo que han visto. ¡Pero apúrense y tráiganlo ya!

14Y abrazó José a su hermano Benjamín, y comenzó a llorar. Benjamín, a su vez, también lloró abrazado a su hermano José. 15Luego José, bañado en lágrimas, besó a todos sus hermanos. Sólo entonces se animaron ellos a hablarle.

16Cuando llegó al palacio del faraón la noticia de que habían llegado los hermanos de José, tanto el faraón como sus funcionarios se alegraron. 17Y el faraón le dijo a José: «Ordena a tus hermanos que carguen sus animales y vuelvan a Canaán. 18Que me traigan a su padre y a sus familias. Yo les daré lo mejor de Egipto, y comerán de la abundancia de este país. 19Diles, además, que se lleven carros de Egipto para traer a sus niños y mujeres, y también al padre de ustedes, 20y que no se preocupen por las cosas que tengan que dejar, porque lo mejor de todo Egipto será para ustedes.»

21Así lo hicieron los hijos de Israel. José les proporcionó los carros, conforme al mandato del faraón, y también les dio provisiones para el viaje. 22Además, a cada uno le dio ropa nueva, y a Benjamín le entregó trescientas monedas de plata y cinco mudas de ropa. 23A su padre le envió lo siguiente: diez asnos cargados con lo mejor de Egipto, diez asnas cargadas de cereales, y pan y otras provisiones para el viaje de su padre. 24Al despedirse de sus hermanos, José les recomendó: «¡No se vayan peleando por el camino!»

25Los hermanos de José salieron de Egipto y llegaron a Canaán, donde residía su padre Jacob. 26Al llegar le dijeron: «¡José vive, José vive! ¡Es el gobernador de todo Egipto!» Jacob quedó atónito y no les creía, 27pero ellos le repetían una y otra vez todo lo que José les había dicho. Y cuando su padre Jacob vio los carros que José había enviado para llevarlo, se reanimó. 28Entonces exclamó: «¡Con esto me basta! ¡Mi hijo José aún vive! Iré a verlo antes de morirme.»

Jacob viaja a Egipto

46 Israel emprendió el viaje con todas sus pertenencias. Al llegar a Berseba, ofreció sacrificios al Dios de su padre Isaac. 2Esa noche Dios le habló a Israel en una visión:

—¡Jacob! ¡Jacob!

—Aquí estoy —respondió.

3—Yo soy Dios, el Dios de tu padre —le dijo—. No tengas temor de ir a Egipto, porque allí haré de ti una gran nación. 4Yo te acompañaré a Egipto, y yo mismo haré que vuelvas. Además, cuando mueras, será José quien te cierre los ojos.

5Luego Jacob salió de Berseba, y los hijos de Israel hicieron con su padre Jacob, y sus hijos y sus mujeres, subieran en los carros que el faraón había enviado para trasladarlos. 6También se llevaron el ganado y las posesiones que habían adquirido en Canaán. Fue así como Jacob y sus descendientes llegaron a Egipto. 7Con él se llevó a todos sus hijos, hijas, nietos y nietas, es decir, a todos sus descendientes.

8Éstos son los nombres de los israelitas que fueron a Egipto, es decir, Jacob y sus hijos:

Rubén, el primogénito de Jacob.

9 Los hijos de Rubén: Janoc, Falú, Jezrón y Carmí.

10 Los hijos de Simeón: Jemuel, Jamín, Oad, Jaquín, Zojar y Saúl, hijo de una cananea.

11 Los hijos de Leví: Guersón, Coat y Merari.

---

a **45:7** *salvarles ... extraordinaria.* Alt. *salvarlos como un gran número de sobrevivientes.*　b **45:8** *asesor.* Lit. *padre.*

12 Los hijos de Judá: Er, Onán, Selá, Fares y Zera. (Er y Onán habían muerto en Canaán).

Los hijos de Fares: Jezrón y Jamul.

13 Los hijos de Isacar: Tola, Fuvá, Job y Simrón.

14 Los hijos de Zabulón: Séred, Elón y Yalel.

15 Éstos fueron los hijos que Jacob tuvo con Lea en Padán Aram,c además de su hija Dina. En total, entre hombres y mujeres eran treinta y tres personas.

16 Los hijos de Gad: Zefón, Jaguí, Esbón, Suni, Erí, Arodí y Arelí.

17 Los hijos de Aser: Imná, Isvá, Isví, Beriá, y su hermana que se llamaba Sera.

Los hijos de Beriá: Héber y Malquiel.

18 Éstos fueron los hijos que Zilpá tuvo con Jacob. Zilpá era la esclava que Labán le había regalado a su hija Lea. Sus descendientes eran en total dieciséis personas.

19 Los hijos de Raquel, la esposa de Jacob: José y Benjamín.

20 En Egipto, José tuvo los siguientes hijos con Asenat, hija de Potifera, sacerdote de On: Manasés y Efraín.

21 Los hijos de Benjamín: Bela, Béquer, Asbel, Guerá, Naamán, Ehí, Ros, Mupín, Jupín y Ard.

22 Éstos fueron los descendientes de Jacob y Raquel, en total catorce personas.

23 El hijo de Dan: Jusín.

24 Los hijos de Neftalí: Yazel, Guní, Jéser y Silén.

25 Éstos fueron los hijos que Jacob tuvo con Bilhá. Ella era la esclava que Labán le regaló a su hija Raquel. El total de sus descendientes fue de siete personas.

26 Todos los familiares de Jacob que llegaron a Egipto, y que eran de su misma sangre, fueron sesenta y seis, sin contar a las nueras. 27 José tenía dos hijos que le nacieron en Egipto. En total los familiares de Jacob que llegaron a Egipto fueron setenta.

28 Jacob mandó a Judá que se adelantara para que le anunciara a José su llegada y éste lo recibiera en Gosén. Cuando llegaron a esa región, 29 José hizo que prepararan su carruaje, y salió a Gosén para recibir a su padre Israel. Cuando se encontraron, José se fundió con su padre en un abrazo, y durante un largo rato lloró sobre su hombro. 30 Entonces Israel le dijo a José:

—¡Ya me puedo morir! ¡Te he visto y aún estás con vida!

31 José les dijo a sus hermanos y a la familia de su padre:

—Voy a informarle al faraón que mis hermanos y la familia de mi padre, quienes vivían en Canaán, han venido a quedarse conmigo. 32 Le diré que ustedes son pastores que cuidan ganado, y que han traído sus ovejas y sus vacas, y todo cuanto tenían. 33 Por eso, cuando el faraón los llame y les pregunte a qué se dedican, 34 díganle que siempre se han ocupado de cuidar ganado, al igual que sus antepasados. Así podrán establecerse en la región de Gosén, pues los egipcios detestan el oficio de pastor.

47 José fue a informarle al faraón, y le dijo:
—Mi padre y mis hermanos han venido desde Canaán con sus ovejas y sus vacas y todas sus pertenencias. Ya se encuentran en la región de Gosén.

2 Además, José había elegido a cinco de sus hermanos para presentárselos al faraón. 3 Y éste les preguntó:

—¿En qué trabajan ustedes?

—Nosotros, sus siervos, somos pastores, al igual que nuestros antepasados —respondieron ellos—. 4 Hemos venido a vivir en este país porque en Canaán ya no hay pastos para nuestros rebaños. ¡Es terrible el hambre que acosa a ese país! Por eso le rogamos a usted nos permita vivir en la región de Gosén.

5 Entonces el faraón le dijo a José:

—Tu padre y tus hermanos han venido a estar contigo. 6 La tierra de Egipto está a tu disposición. Haz que se asienten en lo mejor de la tierra; que residan en la región de Gosén. Y si sabes que hay entre ellos hombres capaces, ponlos a cargo de mi propio ganado.

7 Luego José llevó a Jacob, su padre, y se lo presentó al faraón. Jacob saludó al faraón con reverencia,d 8 y el faraón le preguntó:

—¿Cuántos años tienes?

9 —Ya tengo ciento treinta años —respondió Jacob—. Mis años de andar peregrinando de un lado a otro han sido pocos y difíciles, pero no se comparan con los años de peregrinaje de mis antepasados.

10 Luego Jacob se despidió del faraón con sumo respeto,e y se retiró de su presencia.

11 José instaló a su padre y a sus hermanos, y les entregó terrenos en la mejor región de Egipto, es decir, en el distrito de Ramsés, tal como lo había ordenado el faraón. 12 José también proveyó de alimentos a su padre y a sus hermanos, y a todos sus familiares, según las necesidades de cada uno.

La administración de José

13 El hambre en Egipto y en Canaán era terrible. No había alimento en ninguna parte, y la gente estaba a punto de morir. 14 Todo el dinero que los habitantes de Egipto y de Canaán habían pagado por el alimento, José lo recaudó para depositarlo en el palacio del faraón. 15 Cuando a egipcios y cananeos se les acabó el dinero, los egipcios fueron a ver a José y le reclamaron:

—¡Dénos de comer! ¿Hemos de morir en su presencia sólo porque no tenemos más dinero?

16 Y les contestó:

—Si ya se les acabó el dinero, traigan su ganado y, a cambio, les daré alimento.

17 Los egipcios llevaron a José su ganado, es decir, sus caballos, vacas, ovejas y asnos, y a cambio de ellos José les dio alimento durante todo ese año. 18 Al año siguiente fueron a decirle a José:

—Señor, no podemos ocultar el hecho de que ya no tenemos más dinero, y de que todo nuestro ganado ya es suyo. Ya no tenemos nada que ofrecerle, de no ser nuestros propios cuerpos y nuestras tierras. 19 ¿Va usted a permitir que nos muramos junto con nuestras tierras? Cómprenos usted a nosotros y a nuestras tierras, a cambio de alimento. Así seremos esclavos del faraón junto con nuestras tierras. ¡Pero dénos usted semilla, para que podamos vivir y la tierra no quede desolada!

20 De esta manera José adquirió para el faraón todas las tierras de Egipto, porque los egipcios, obligados por el hambre, le vendieron todos sus terrenos. Fue así como todo el país llegó a ser propiedad del faraón, 21 y todos quedaron reducidos a la esclavitud.f 22 Los únicos terrenos que José no compró fueron los que pertenecían a los sacerdotes. Éstos no tuvieron que vender sus terrenos porque recibían una ración de alimento de parte del faraón.

c 46:15 Padán Aram. Es decir, el noroeste de Mesopotamia. d 47:7 saludó al faraón con reverencia. Lit. bendijo al faraón.
e 47:10 se despidió del faraón con sumo respeto. Lit. bendijo al farón. f 47:21 quedaron reducidos a la esclavitud (Pentateuco Samaritano, LXX; véase también Vulgata); fueron trasladados a las ciudades (TM).

23Luego José le informó al pueblo:

—Desde ahora ustedes y sus tierras pertenecen al faraón, porque yo los he comprado. Aquí tienen semilla. Siembren la tierra. 24Cuando llegue la cosecha, deberán entregarle al faraón la quinta parte de lo cosechado. Las otras cuatro partes serán para la siembra de los campos, y para alimentarlos a ustedes, a sus hijos y a sus familiares.

25—¡Usted nos ha salvado la vida, y hemos contado con su favor! —respondieron ellos—. ¡Seremos esclavos del faraón!

26José estableció esta ley en toda la tierra de Egipto, que hasta el día de hoy sigue vigente: la quinta parte de la cosecha le pertenece al faraón. Sólo las tierras de los sacerdotes no llegaron a ser del faraón.

27Los israelitas se asentaron en Egipto, en la región de Gosén. Allí adquirieron propiedades, prosperaron y llegaron a ser muy numerosos. 28Jacob residió diecisiete años en Egipto, y llegó a vivir un total de ciento cuarenta y siete años. 29Cuando Israel estaba a punto de morir, mandó llamar a su hijo José y le dijo:

—Si de veras me quieres, pon tu mano debajo de mi muslo y prométeme amor y lealtad. ¡Por favor, no me entierres en Egipto! 30Cuando vaya a descansar junto a mis antepasados, sácame de Egipto y entiérrame en el sepulcro de ellos.

—Haré lo que me pides —contestó José.

31—¡Júramelo! —insistió su padre.

José se lo juró, e Israel se reclinó sobre la cabecera de la cama.

Bendición de Efraín y Manasés

48 Poco tiempo después le informaron a José que su padre estaba enfermo. Entonces fue a visitarlo y llevó consigo a sus dos hijos, Manasés y Efraín. 2Cuando le avisaron a Jacob que su hijo venía a verlo, hizo un esfuerzo, se sentó en la cama 3y le dijo a José:

—El Dios *Todopoderoso se me apareció en Luz, en la tierra de Canaán, y me bendijo 4con esta promesa: "Te haré fecundo, te multiplicaré, y haré que tus descendientes formen una comunidad de naciones. Además, a tu descendencia le daré esta tierra como su posesión perpetua." 5Ahora bien, los dos hijos que te nacieron aquí en Egipto, antes de que me reuniera contigo, serán considerados míos. Efraín y Manasés serán tan míos como lo son Rubén y Simeón. 6Los hijos que tengas después de ellos serán tuyos, y a través de sus hermanos recibirán su herencia. 7Cuando yo regresaba de Padán Aram,g tu madre murió cerca de Efrata, en tierra de Canaán, y allí la sepulté junto al camino de Efrata, es decir, Belén.

8Al ver a los hijos de José, Israel preguntó:

—Y estos chicos, ¿quiénes son?

9—Son los hijos que Dios me ha concedido aquí —le respondió José a su padre.

Entonces Israel le dijo:

—Acércalos, por favor, para que les dé mi bendición.

10Israel ya era muy anciano, y por su avanzada edad casi no podía ver; por eso José los acercó, y su padre los besó y abrazó. 11Luego le dijo a José:

—Ya había perdido la esperanza de volver a verte, ¡y ahora Dios me ha concedido ver también a tus hijos!

12José los retiró de las rodillas de Israel y se postró rostro en tierra. 13Luego tomó a sus dos hijos, a Efraín con la *derecha y a Manasés con la izquierda, y se los presentó a su padre. De esta manera Efraín quedó a la izquierda de Israel y Manasés a su derecha. 14Pero Israel, al extender las manos, las entrecruzó y puso su derecha sobre la cabeza de Efraín, aunque era el menor, y su izquierda sobre la cabeza de Manasés, aunque era el mayor. 15Y los bendijo con estas palabras:

«Que el Dios en cuya presencia
   caminaron mis padres, Abraham e Isaac,
el Dios que me ha guiado
   desde el día en que nací hasta hoy,
16el ángel que me ha rescatado de todo mal,
   bendiga a estos jóvenes.
Que por medio de ellos sea recordado
   mi *nombre y el de mis padres, Abraham e
   Isaac.
Que crezcan y se multipliquen
   sobre la tierra.»

17A José no le agradó ver que su padre pusiera su mano derecha sobre la cabeza de Efraín, así que tomando la mano de su padre, la pasó de la cabeza de Efraín a la de Manasés, 18mientras le reclamaba:

—¡Así no, padre mío! ¡Pon tu mano derecha sobre la cabeza de éste, que es el primogénito!

19Pero su padre se resistió, y le contestó:

—¡Ya lo sé, hijo, ya lo sé! También él gestará a un pueblo, y llegará a ser importante. Pero su hermano menor será aún más importante, y su descendencia dará origen a muchas naciones.

20Aquel día Jacob los bendijo así:

«Ésta será la bendición
   que en Israel se habrá de pronunciar:
   "Que Dios cuide de ti
   como cuidó de Efraín y de Manasés."»

De este modo, Israel dio a Efraín la primacía sobre Manasés.

21Finalmente, Israel le dijo a José:

—Yo estoy a punto de morir; pero Dios estará con ustedes y los hará volver a la tierra de sus antepasados. 22Y a ti, que estás por encima de tus hermanos, te doy Siquén,h tierra que luchando a brazo partidoi arrebaté a los amorreos.

Jacob bendice a sus hijos

49 Jacob llamó a sus hijos y les dijo: «Reúnanse, que voy a declararles lo que les va a suceder en el futuro:

2»Hijos de Jacob: acérquense y escuchen;
   presten atención a su padre Israel.

3»Tú, Rubén, eres mi primogénito,
   primer fruto de mi fuerza y virilidad,
   primero en honor y en poder.
4Impetuoso como un torrente,
   ya no serás el primero:
te acostaste en mi cama;
   profanaste la cama de tu propio padre.

5»Simeón y Leví son chacales;j
   sus espadask son instrumentos de
   violencia.
6No quiero participar de sus reuniones,
   ni arriesgar mi honor en sus asambleas!

---

g 48:7 *Padán Aram.* Es decir, el noroeste de Mesopotamia. h 48:22 *Siquén.* Alt. *una franja de tierra.* Palabra de difícil traducción. i 48:22 *luchando ... partido.* Lit. *con mi espada y con mi arco.* j 49:5 *chacales* (lectura probable); *hermanos* (TM). k 49:5 *espadas.* Palabra de difícil traducción.

En su furor mataron *hombres,
y por capricho mutilaron toros.
7¡Malditas sean la violencia de su enojo
y la crueldad de su furor!
Los dispersaré en el país de Jacob,
los desparramaré en la tierra de Israel.

8»Tú, Judá, serás alabadol por tus hermanos;
dominarás a tus enemigos,
y tus propios hermanos se inclinarán ante ti.
9Mi hijo Judá es como un cachorro de león
que se ha nutrido de la presa.
Se tiende al acecho como león,
como leona que nadie se atreve a molestar.
10El cetro no se apartará de Judá,
ni de entre sus pies el bastón de mando,
hasta que llegue el verdadero rey,m
quien merece la obediencia de los pueblos.
11Judá amarra su asno a la vid,
y la cría de su asno a la mejor cepa;
lava su ropa en vino;
su manto, en la sangre de las uvas.
12Sus ojos son más oscuros que el vino;
sus dientes, más blancos que la leche.n

13»Zabulón vivirá a la orilla del mar;
será puerto seguro para las naves,
y sus fronteras llegarán hasta Sidón.

14»Isacar es un asno fuerte
echado entre dos alforjas.
15Al ver que el establo era bueno
y que la tierra era agradable,
agachó el hombro para llevar la carga
y se sometió a la esclavitud.

16»Dan hará justicia en su pueblo,
como una de las tribus de Israel.
17Dan es una serpiente junto al camino,
una víbora junto al sendero,
que muerde los talones del caballo
y hace caer de espaldas al jinete.

18»¡SEÑOR, espero tu *salvación!

19»Las hordas atacan a Gad,
pero él las atacará por la espalda.

20»Aser disfrutará de comidas deliciosas;
ofrecerá manjares de reyes.

21»Neftalí es una gacela libre,
que tiene hermosos cervatillos.ñ

22»José es un retoño fértil,
fértil retoño junto al agua,
cuyas ramas trepan por el muro.
23Los arqueros lo atacaron sin piedad;
le tiraron flechas, lo hostigaron.
24Pero su arco se mantuvo firme,
porque sus brazos son fuertes.
¡Gracias al Dios fuerte de Jacob,
al Pastor y Roca de Israel!
25¡Gracias al Dios de tu padre, que te ayuda!
¡Gracias al *Todopoderoso, que te bendice!
¡Con bendiciones de lo alto!
¡Con bendiciones del abismo!
¡Con bendiciones de los pechos y del seno
materno!

26Son mejores las bendiciones de tu padre
que las de los montes de antaño,
que la abundancia de las colinas eternas.
¡Que descansen estas bendiciones
sobre la cabeza de José,
sobre la frente del escogido entre sus
hermanos!

27»Benjamín es un lobo rapaz
que en la mañana devora la presa
y en la tarde reparte los despojos.»

28Éstas son las doce tribus de Israel, y esto es lo
que su padre les dijo cuando impartió a cada una de
ellas su bendición.

Muerte de Jacob

29Además, Jacob les dio estas instrucciones: «Ya
estoy a punto de reunirme con los míos. Entiérrenme junto a mis antepasados, en la cueva que está en
el campo de Efrón el hitita. 30Se trata de la cueva de
Macpela, frente a Mamré, en la tierra de Canaán.
Está en el campo que Abraham le compró a Efrón el
hitita, para que fuera el sepulcro de la familia. 31Allí
fueron sepultados Abraham y su esposa Sara, Isaac y
su esposa Rebeca, y allí también enterré a Lea. 32Ese
campo y su cueva se les compró a los hititas.»

33Cuando Jacob terminó de dar estas instrucciones a sus hijos, volvió a acostarse, exhaló el último suspiro, y fue a reunirse con sus antepasados.

50 Entonces José se abrazó al cuerpo de su padre y, llorando, lo besó. 2Luego ordenó a los
médicos a su servicio que embalsamaran el cuerpo, y
así lo hicieron. 3El proceso para embalsamarlo tardó
unos cuarenta días, que es el tiempo requerido. Los
egipcios, por su parte, guardaron luto por Israel durante setenta días.

4Pasados los días de duelo, José se dirigió así a
los miembros de la corte del faraón:

—Si me he ganado el respeto de la corte, díganle
por favor al faraón 5que mi padre, antes de morirse,
me hizo jurar que yo lo sepultaría en la tumba que él
mismo se preparó en la tierra de Canaán. Por eso le
ruego encarecidamente me permita ir a sepultar a mi
padre, y luego volveré.

6El faraón le respondió:

—Ve a sepultar a tu padre, conforme a la promesa que te pidió hacerle.

7José fue a sepultar a su padre, y lo acompañaron los servidores del faraón, es decir, los ancianos
de su corte y todos los ancianos de Egipto. 8A éstos se
sumaron todos los familiares de José, es decir, sus
hermanos y los de la casa de Jacob. En la región de
Gosén dejaron únicamente a los niños y a los animales. 9También salieron con él carros y jinetes, formando así un cortejo muy grande.

10Al llegar a la era de Hatad, que está cerca del río
Jordán, hicieron grandes y solemnes lamentaciones.
Allí José guardó luto por su padre durante siete días.
11Cuando los cananeos que vivían en esa región vieron en la era de Hatad aquellas manifestaciones de
duelo, dijeron: «Los egipcios están haciendo un duelo
muy solemne.» Por eso al lugar, que está cerca del Jordán, lo llamaron Abel Misrayin.o
12Los hijos de Jacob hicieron con su padre lo que
él les había pedido: 13lo llevaron a la tierra de Canaán

---

l 49:8 En hebreo, Judá suena como el verbo que significa alabar. m 49:10 el verdadero rey. Alt. Siló. Texto de difícil traducción. n 49:12 Sus ojos ... la leche. Alt. Sus ojos están oscurecidos por el vino; sus dientes, blanqueados por la leche.
ñ 49:21 que ... cervatillos. Alt. que pronuncia hermosas palabras. o 50:11 En hebreo, Abel Misrayin significa luto de los
egipcios.

y lo sepultaron en la cueva que está en el campo de Macpela, frente a Mamré, en el mismo campo que Abraham le había comprado a Efrón el hitita para sepultura de la familia. **14**Luego de haber sepultado a su padre, José regresó a Egipto junto con sus hermanos y con toda la gente que lo había acompañado.

La promesa de José a sus hermanos

15Al reflexionar sobre la muerte de su padre, los hermanos de José concluyeron: «Tal vez José nos guarde rencor, y ahora quiera vengarse de todo el mal que le hicimos.» **16**Por eso le mandaron a decir: «Antes de morir tu padre, dejó estas instrucciones: **17**"Díganle a José que perdone, por favor, la terrible maldad que sus hermanos cometieron contra él." Así que, por favor, perdona la maldad de los siervos del Dios de tu padre.»

Cuando José escuchó estas palabras, se echó a llorar. **18**Luego sus hermanos se presentaron ante José, se inclinaron delante de él y le dijeron:

—Aquí nos tienes; somos tus esclavos.

19—No tengan miedo —les contestó José—. ¿Puedo acaso tomar el lugar de Dios? **20**Es verdad que ustedes pensaron hacerme mal, pero Dios transformó ese mal en bien para lograr lo que hoy estamos viendo: salvar la vida de mucha gente. **21**Así que, ¡no tengan miedo! Yo cuidaré de ustedes y de sus hijos.

Y así, con el corazón en la mano, José los reconfortó.

Muerte de José

22José y la familia de su padre permanecieron en Egipto. Alcanzó la edad de ciento diez años, **23**y llegó a ver nacer a los hijos de Efraín hasta la tercera generación. Además, cuando nacieron los hijos de Maquir, hijo de Manasés, él los recibió sobre sus rodillas.p

24Tiempo después, José les dijo a sus hermanos: «Yo estoy a punto de morir, pero sin duda Dios vendrá a ayudarlos, y los llevará de este país a la tierra que prometió a Abraham, Isaac y Jacob.» **25**Entonces José hizo que sus hijos le prestaran juramento. Les dijo: «Sin duda Dios vendrá a ayudarlos. Cuando esto ocurra, ustedes deberán llevarse de aquí mis huesos.»

26José murió en Egipto a los ciento diez años de edad. Una vez que lo embalsamaron, lo pusieron en un ataúd.

---

p **50:23** *él recibió sobre sus rodillas.* Es decir, fueron considerados como suyos.

ÉXODO

Los egipcios oprimen a los israelitas

1 Éstos son los nombres de los hijos de Israel que, acompañados de sus familias, llegaron con Jacob a Egipto: 2Rubén, Simeón, Leví, Judá, 3Isacar, Zabulón, Benjamín, 4Dan, Neftalí, Gad y Aser. 5En total, los descendientes de Jacob eran setenta. José ya estaba en Egipto.

6Murieron José y sus hermanos y toda aquella generación. 7Sin embargo, los israelitas tuvieron muchos hijos, y a tal grado se multiplicaron que fueron haciéndose más y más poderosos. El país se fue llenando de ellos.

8Pero llegó al poder en Egipto otro rey que no había conocido a José, 9y le dijo a su pueblo: «¡Cuidado con los israelitas, que ya son más fuertes y numerosos que nosotros! 10Vamos a tener que manejarlos con mucha astucia; de lo contrario, seguirán aumentando y, si estalla una guerra, se unirán a nuestros enemigos, nos combatirán y se irán del país.»

11Fue así como los egipcios pusieron capataces para que oprimieran a los israelitas. Les impusieron trabajos forzados, tales como los de edificar para el faraón las ciudades de almacenaje Pitón y Ramsés. 12Pero cuanto más los oprimían, más se multiplicaban y se extendían, de modo que los egipcios llegaron a tenerles miedo; 13por eso les imponían trabajos pesados y los trataban con crueldad. 14Les amargaban la vida obligándolos a hacer mezcla y ladrillos, y todas las labores del campo. En todos los trabajos de esclavos que los israelitas realizaban, los egipcios los trataban con crueldad.

15Había dos parteras hebreas, llamadas Sifrá y Fuvá, a las que el rey de Egipto ordenó:

16—Cuando ayuden a las hebreas en sus partos, fíjense en el sexo:a si es niño, mátenlo; pero si es niña, déjenla con vida.

17Sin embargo, las parteras temían a Dios, así que no siguieron las órdenes del rey de Egipto sino que dejaron con vida a los varones. 18Entonces el rey de Egipto mandó llamar a las parteras, y les preguntó:

—¿Por qué han hecho esto? ¿Por qué han dejado con vida a los varones?

19Las parteras respondieron:

—Resulta que las hebreas no son como las egipcias, sino que están llenas de vida y dan a luz antes de que lleguemos.

20De este modo los israelitas se hicieron más fuertes y más numerosos. Además, Dios trató muy bien a las parteras 21y, por haberse mostrado temerosas de Dios, les concedió tener muchos hijos. 22El faraón, por su parte, dio esta orden a todo su pueblo:

—¡Tiren al río a todos los niños hebreos que nazcan! A las niñas, déjenlas con vida.

Nacimiento de Moisés

2 Hubo un levita que tomó por esposa a una mujer de su propia tribu. 2La mujer quedó embarazada y tuvo un hijo, y al verlo tan hermoso lo escondió durante tres meses. 3Cuando ya no pudo seguir ocultándolo, preparó una cesta de papiro, la embadurnó con brea y asfalto y, poniendo en ella al niño, fue a dejar la cesta entre los juncos que había a la orilla del Nilo. 4Pero la hermana del niño se quedó a cierta distancia para ver qué pasaría con él.

5En eso, la hija del faraón bajó a bañarse en el Nilo. Sus doncellas, mientras tanto, se paseaban por la orilla del río. De pronto la hija del faraón vio la cesta entre los juncos, y ordenó a una de sus esclavas que fuera por ella. 6Cuando la hija del faraón abrió la cesta y vio allí dentro un niño que lloraba, le tuvo compasión, pero aclaró que se trataba de un niño hebreo.

7La hermana del niño preguntó entonces a la hija del faraón:

—¿Quiere usted que vaya y llame a una nodriza hebrea, para que críe al niño por usted?

8—Ve a llamarla —contestó.

La muchacha fue y trajo a la madre del niño, 9y la hija del faraón le dijo:

—Llévate a este niño y críamelo. Yo te pagaré por hacerlo.

Fue así como la madre del niño se lo llevó y lo crió. 10Ya crecido el niño, se lo llevó a la hija del faraón, y ella lo adoptó como hijo suyo; además, le puso por *nombre Moisés,b pues dijo: «¡Yo lo saqué del río!»

Huida de Moisés a Madián

11Un día, cuando ya Moisés era mayor de edad, fue a ver a sus hermanos de sangre y pudo observar sus penurias. De pronto, vio que un egipcio golpeaba a uno de sus hermanos, es decir, a un hebreo. 12Miró entonces a uno y otro lado y, al no ver a nadie, mató al egipcio y lo escondió en la arena. 13Al día siguiente volvió a salir y, al ver que dos hebreos peleaban entre sí, le preguntó al culpable:

—¿Por qué golpeas a tu compañero?

14—¿Y quién te nombró a ti gobernante y juez sobre nosotros? —respondió aquél—. ¿Acaso piensas matarme a mí, como mataste al egipcio?

Esto le causó temor a Moisés, pues pensó: «¡Ya supo lo que hice!» 15Y, en efecto, el faraón se enteró de lo sucedido y trató de matar a Moisés; pero Moisés huyó del faraón y se fue a la tierra de Madián, donde se quedó a vivirc junto al pozo.

16El sacerdote de Madián tenía siete hijas, las cuales solían ir a sacar agua para llenar los abrevaderos y dar de beber a las ovejas de su padre. 17Pero los pastores llegaban y las echaban de allí. Un día, Moisés intervino en favor de ellas: las puso a salvo de los pastores y dio de beber a sus ovejas. 18Cuando las muchachas volvieron a la casa de Reuel, su padre, éste les preguntó:

—¿Por qué volvieron hoy tan temprano?

19—Porque un egipcio nos libró de los pastores —le respondieron—. ¡Hasta sacó el agua del pozo y dio de beber al rebaño!

20—¿Y dónde está ese hombre? —les contestó—. ¿Por qué lo dejaron solo? ¡Invítenlo a comer!

21Moisés convino en quedarse a vivir en casa de aquel hombre, quien le dio por esposa a su hija Séfora. 22Ella tuvo un hijo, y Moisés le puso por *nombre Guersón,d pues razonó: «Soy un extranjero en tierra extraña.»

23Mucho tiempo después murió el rey de Egipto. Los israelitas, sin embargo, seguían lamentando su condición de esclavos y clamaban pidiendo ayuda. Sus gritos desesperados llegaron a oídos de Dios, 24quien al oír sus quejas se acordó del *pacto que ha-

---

a 1:16 el sexo. Lit. las dos piedras. b 2:10 En hebreo, Moisés suena como el verbo que significa sacar. c 2:15 donde se quedó a vivir. Alt. y se sentó. d 2:22 En hebreo, Guersón suena como la frase que significa extranjero allí.

bía hecho con Abraham, Isaac y Jacob. 25Fue así como Dios se fijó en los israelitas y los tomó en cuenta.

Moisés y la zarza ardiente

3 Un día en que Moisés estaba cuidando el rebaño de Jetro, su suegro, que era sacerdote de Madián, llevó las ovejas hasta el otro extremo del desierto y llegó a Horeb, la montaña de Dios. 2Estando allí, el ángel del SEÑOR se le apareció entre las llamas de una zarza ardiente. Moisés notó que la zarza estaba envuelta en llamas, pero que no se consumía, 3así que pensó: «¡Qué increíble! Voy a ver por qué no se consume la zarza.»

4Cuando el SEÑOR vio que Moisés se acercaba a mirar, lo llamó desde la zarza:

—¡Moisés, Moisés!

—Aquí me tienes —respondió.

5—No te acerques más —le dijo Dios—. Quítate las sandalias, porque estás pisando tierra santa. 6Yo soy el Dios de tu padre. Soy el Dios de Abraham, de Isaac y de Jacob.

Al oír esto, Moisés se cubrió el rostro, pues tuvo miedo de mirar a Dios. 7Pero el SEÑOR siguió diciendo:

—Ciertamente he visto la opresión que sufre mi pueblo en Egipto. Los he escuchado quejarse de sus capataces, y conozco bien sus penurias. 8Así que he descendido para librarlos del poder de los egipcios y sacarlos de ese país, para llevarlos a una tierra buena y espaciosa, tierra donde abundan la leche y la miel. Me refiero al país de los cananeos, hititas, amorreos, ferezeos, heveos y jebuseos. 9Han llegado a mis oídos los gritos desesperados de los israelitas, y he visto también cómo los oprimen los egipcios. 10Así que disponte a partir. Voy a enviarte al faraón para que saques de Egipto a los israelitas, que son mi pueblo.

11Pero Moisés le dijo a Dios:

—¿Y quién soy yo para presentarme ante el faraón y sacar de Egipto a los israelitas?

12—Yo estaré contigo —le respondió Dios—. Y te voy a dar una señal de que soy yo quien te envía: Cuando hayas sacado de Egipto a mi pueblo, todos ustedes me rendirán culto[e] en esta montaña.

13Pero Moisés insistió:

—Supongamos que me presento ante los israelitas y les digo: "El Dios de sus antepasados me ha enviado a ustedes." ¿Qué les respondo si me preguntan: "¿Y cómo se llama?"

14—YO SOY EL QUE SOY[f] —respondió Dios a Moisés—. Y esto es lo que tienes que decirles a los israelitas: "YO SOY me ha enviado a ustedes."

15Además, Dios le dijo a Moisés:

—Diles esto a los israelitas: "El SEÑOR,[g] el Dios de sus antepasados, el Dios de Abraham, de Isaac y de Jacob, me ha enviado a ustedes. Éste es mi *nombre eterno; éste es mi nombre por todas las generaciones." 16Y tú, anda y reúne a los *ancianos de Israel, y diles: "El SEÑOR, el Dios de sus antepasados, el Dios de Abraham, de Isaac y de Jacob, se me apareció y me dijo: 'Yo he estado pendiente de ustedes. He visto cómo los han maltratado en Egipto. 17Por eso me propongo sacarlos de su opresión en Egipto y llevarlos al país de los cananeos, hititas, amorreos, ferezeos, heveos y jebuseos. ¡Es una tierra donde abundan la leche y la miel!'" 18Los ancianos de Israel te harán caso. Entonces ellos y tú se presentarán ante el rey de Egipto y le dirán: "El SEÑOR, Dios de los hebreos, ha venido a nuestro encuentro. Déjanos hacer un viaje de tres días al desierto, para ofrecerle sacrificios al SEÑOR nuestro Dios." 19Yo sé bien que el rey de Egipto no va a dejarlos ir, a no ser por la fuerza. 20Entonces manifestaré mi poder y heriré de muerte a los egipcios con todas las maravillas que realizaré entre ellos. Después de eso el faraón los dejará ir. 21Pero yo haré que este pueblo se gane la simpatía de los egipcios, de modo que cuando ustedes salgan de Egipto no se vayan con las manos vacías. 22Toda mujer israelita le pedirá a su vecina, y a cualquier otra mujer que viva en su casa, objetos de oro y de plata, y ropa para vestir a sus hijos y a sus hijas. Así despojarán ustedes a los egipcios.

Señales para Moisés

4 Moisés volvió a preguntar:

—¿Y qué hago si no me creen ni me hacen caso? ¿Qué hago si me dicen: "El SEÑOR no se te ha aparecido"?

2—¿Qué tienes en la mano? —preguntó el SEÑOR.

—Una vara —respondió Moisés.

3—Déjala caer al suelo —ordenó el SEÑOR.

Moisés la dejó caer al suelo, y la vara se convirtió en una serpiente. Moisés trató de huir de ella, 4pero el SEÑOR le mandó que la agarrara por la cola. En cuanto Moisés agarró la serpiente, ésta se convirtió en una vara en sus propias manos.

5—Esto es para que crean que yo el SEÑOR, Dios de sus padres, Dios de Abraham, de Isaac y de Jacob, me ha aparecido a ti. 6Y ahora —ordenó el SEÑOR—, ¡llévate la mano al pecho!

Moisés se llevó la mano al pecho y, cuando la sacó, la tenía toda cubierta de *lepra y blanca como la nieve.

7—¡Llévatela otra vez al pecho! —insistió el Señor.

Moisés se llevó de nuevo la mano al pecho y, cuando la sacó, la tenía tan sana como el resto de su cuerpo.

8—Si con la primera señal milagrosa no te creen ni te hacen caso —dijo el SEÑOR—, tal vez te crean con la segunda. 9Pero si no te creen ni te hacen caso después de estas dos señales, toma agua del Nilo y derrámala en el suelo. En cuanto el agua del río toque el suelo, se convertirá en sangre.

10—SEÑOR, yo nunca me he distinguido por mi facilidad de palabra —objetó Moisés—. Y esto no es algo que haya comenzado ayer ni anteayer, ni hoy que te diriges a este servidor tuyo. Francamente, me cuesta mucho trabajo hablar.

11—¿Y quién le puso la boca al *hombre? —le respondió el SEÑOR—. ¿Acaso no soy yo, el SEÑOR, quien lo hace sordo o mudo, quien le da la vista o se la quita? 12Anda, ponte en marcha, que yo te ayudaré a hablar y te diré lo que debas decir.

13—SEÑOR —insistió Moisés—, te ruego que envíes a alguna otra persona.

14Entonces el SEÑOR ardió en ira contra Moisés y le dijo:

—¿Y qué hay de tu hermano Aarón, el levita? Yo sé que él es muy elocuente. Además, ya ha salido a tu encuentro, y cuando te vea se le alegrará el *co-

---

[e] 3:12 me rendirán culto. Lit. me servirán. Aquí y en el resto de este libro, el texto hebreo usa el mismo verbo servir para indicar el servicio al faraón como esclavos, y el servir a Dios rindiéndole culto. [f] 3:14 YO SOY EL QUE SOY. Alt. YO SERÉ EL QUE SERÉ. [g] 3:15 La palabra hebrea que se traduce como SEÑOR suena como la forma verbal que en el v. 14 se ha traducido como YO SOY.

razón. 15Tú hablarás con él y le pondrás las palabras en la boca; yo los ayudaré a hablar, a ti y a él, y les enseñaré lo que tienen que hacer. 16Él hablará por ti al pueblo, como si tú mismo le hablaras, y tú le hablarás a él por mí, como si le hablara yo mismo. 17Pero no te olvides de llevar contigo esta vara, porque con ella harás señales milagrosas.

Moisés regresa a Egipto

18Moisés se fue de allí y volvió a la casa de Jetro, su suegro. Al llegar le dijo:

—Debo marcharme. Quiero volver a Egipto, donde están mis hermanos de sangre. Voy a ver si todavía viven.

—Anda, pues; que te vaya bien —le contestó Jetro.

19Ya en Madián el SEÑOR le había dicho a Moisés: «Vuelve a Egipto, que ya han muerto todos los que querían matarte.» 20Así que Moisés tomó a su mujer y a sus hijos, los montó en un asno y volvió a Egipto. En la mano llevaba la vara de Dios.

21El SEÑOR le había advertido a Moisés: «Cuando vuelvas a Egipto, no dejes de hacer ante el faraón todos los prodigios que te he dado el poder de realizar. Yo, por mi parte, endureceré su *corazón para que no deje ir al pueblo. 22Entonces tú le dirás de mi parte al faraón: "Israel es mi primogénito. 23Ya te he dicho que dejes ir a mi hijo para que me rinda culto, pero tú no has querido dejarlo ir. Por lo tanto, voy a quitarle la vida a tu primogénito." »

24Ya en el camino, el SEÑOR salió al encuentro de Moisésh en una posada y estuvo a punto de matarlo. 25Pero Séfora, tomando un cuchillo de pedernal, le cortó el prepucio a su hijo; luego tocó los piesi de Moisés con el prepucio y le dijo: «No hay duda. Tú eres para mí un esposo de sangre.» 26Después de eso, el SEÑOR se apartó de Moisés. Pero Séfora había llamado a Moisés «esposo de sangre» por causa de la circuncisión.

27El SEÑOR le dijo a Aarón: «Anda a recibir a Moisés en el desierto.» Aarón fue y se encontró con Moisés en la montaña de Dios, y lo besó. 28Entonces Moisés le comunicó a Aarón todo lo que el SEÑOR le había ordenado decir y todas las señales milagrosas que le mandaba realizar. 29Luego Moisés y Aarón reunieron a todos los *ancianos israelitas, 30y Aarón, además de repetirles todo lo que el SEÑOR le había dicho a Moisés, realizó también las señales a la vista del pueblo, 31con lo que el pueblo creyó. Y al oír que el SEÑOR había estado pendiente de ellos y había visto su aflicción, los israelitas se inclinaron y adoraron al SEÑOR.

Primer encuentro con el faraón

5 Después de eso, Moisés y Aarón se presentaron ante el faraón y le dijeron:

—Así dice el SEÑOR, Dios de Israel: "Deja ir a mi pueblo para que celebre en el desierto una fiesta en mi honor."

2—¿Y quién es el SEÑOR —respondió el faraón— para que yo le obedezca y deje ir a Israel? ¡Ni conozco al SEÑOR, ni voy a dejar que Israel se vaya!

3—El Dios de los hebreos nos ha salido al encuentro —contestaron—. Así que debemos hacer un viaje de tres días, hasta el desierto, para ofrecer sacrificios al SEÑOR nuestro Dios. De lo contrario, podría castigarnos con plagas o matarnos a filo de espada.

4—Moisés y Aarón —replicó el rey de Egipto—, ¿por qué distraen al pueblo de sus quehaceres?

¡Vuelvan a sus obligaciones! 5Dense cuenta de que es mucha la gente de este país, y ustedes no la dejan trabajar.

6Ese mismo día el faraón les ordenó a los capataces y a los jefes de cuadrilla: 7«Ya no le den paja a la gente para hacer ladrillos. ¡Que vayan ellos mismos a recogerla! 8Pero sigan exigiéndoles la misma cantidad de ladrillos que han estado haciendo. ¡No les reduzcan la cuota! Son unos holgazanes, y por eso me ruegan: "Déjanos ir a ofrecerle sacrificios a nuestro Dios." 9Impónganles tareas más pesadas. Manténganlos ocupados. Así no harán caso de mentiras.»

10Los capataces y los jefes de cuadrilla salieron de allí y fueron a decirle al pueblo: «Así dice el faraón: "Ya no voy a darles paja. 11Vayan ustedes mismos a recogerla donde la encuentren. Pero eso sí, ¡en nada se les rebajará la tarea!" »

12Fue así como el pueblo se esparció por todo Egipto para recoger rastrojo y usarlo en lugar de paja. 13Los capataces no dejaban de apremiarlos y decirles: «Cumplan con su tarea diaria, como cuando se les daba paja.» 14Además, esos mismos capataces del faraón golpeaban a los jefes de cuadrilla israelitas que ellos mismos habían nombrado, y les preguntaban: «¿Por qué ni ayer ni hoy cumplieron con su cuota de ladrillos, como antes lo hacían?»

15Los jefes de cuadrilla israelitas fueron entonces a quejarse ante el faraón. Le dijeron:

—¿Por qué Su Majestad trata así a sus siervos? 16¡Ya ni paja recibimos! A pesar de eso, ¡se nos exige hacer ladrillos y, como si fuera poco, se nos golpea! ¡La gente de Su Majestad no está actuando bien!

17—¡Haraganes, haraganes! —exclamó el faraón—. ¡Eso es lo que son! Por eso andan diciendo: "Déjanos ir a ofrecerle sacrificios al SEÑOR." 18Ahora, ¡vayan a trabajar! No se les va a dar paja, pero tienen que entregar su cuota de ladrillos.

19Los jefes de cuadrilla israelitas se dieron cuenta de que estaban en un aprieto cuando se les dijo que la cuota diaria de ladrillos no se les iba a rebajar. 20Al encontrarse con Moisés y Aarón, que los estaban esperando a la salida, 21les dijeron: «¡Que el SEÑOR los examine y los juzgue! ¡Por culpa de ustedes somos unos apestados ante el faraón y sus siervos! ¡Ustedes mismos les han puesto la espada en la mano, para que nos maten!»

Dios promete liberación

22Moisés se volvió al SEÑOR y le dijo:

—¡Ay, SEÑOR! ¿Por qué tratas tan mal a este pueblo? ¿Para esto me enviaste? 23Desde que me presenté ante el faraón y le hablé en tu *nombre, no ha hecho más que maltratar a este pueblo, que es tu pueblo. ¡Y tú no has hecho nada para librarlo!

6 El SEÑOR le respondió:

—Ahora verás lo que voy a hacer con el faraón. Realmente, sólo por mi mano poderosa va a dejar que se vayan; sólo por mi mano poderosa va a echarlos de su país.

2En otra ocasión, Dios habló con Moisés y le dijo: «Yo soy el SEÑOR. 3Me aparecí a Abraham, a Isaac y a Jacob bajo el nombre de Dios *Todopoderoso, pero no les revelé mi verdadero nombre, que es el SEÑOR.j 4También con ellos confirmé mi *pacto de darles la tierra de Canaán, donde residieron como forasteros. 5He oído además el gemir de los israelitas, a quienes los egipcios han esclavizado, y he recordado mi pacto. 6Así que ve y diles a los israelitas: "Yo soy el

---

h 4:24 Moisés. Lit. él; también en vv. 25-26. i 4:25 los pies. Puede ser un eufemismo para referirse a los órganos sexuales. j 6:3 Véase nota en 3:15.

SEÑOR, y voy a quitarles de encima la opresión de los egipcios. Voy a librarlos de su esclavitud; voy a liberarlos con gran despliegue de poder y con grandes actos de *justicia. [7]Haré de ustedes mi pueblo; y yo seré su Dios. Así sabrán que yo soy el SEÑOR su Dios, que los libró de la opresión de los egipcios. [8]Y los llevaré a la tierra que bajo juramento prometí darles a Abraham, Isaac y Jacob. Yo, el SEÑOR, les daré a ustedes posesión de ella." »

[9]Moisés les dio a conocer esto a los israelitas, pero por su desánimo y las penurias de su esclavitud ellos no le hicieron caso. [10]Entonces el SEÑOR habló con Moisés y le dijo:

[11]—Ve y habla con el faraón, el rey de Egipto. Dile que deje salir de su país a los israelitas.

[12]Pero Moisés se enfrentó al SEÑOR y le dijo:

—¿Y cómo va a hacerme caso el faraón, si ni siquiera los israelitas me creen? Además, no tengo facilidad de palabra.[k]

[13]En otra ocasión el SEÑOR habló con Moisés y Aarón acerca de los israelitas y del faraón, rey egipcio, y les ordenó sacar de Egipto a los israelitas.

Antepasados de Moisés y de Aarón

[14]Éstos fueron los jefes de las familias patriarcales:

Los hijos de Rubén, primogénito de Israel: Janoc, Falú, Jezrón y Carmí. Éstos fueron los clanes de Rubén.

[15]Los hijos de Simeón: Jemuel, Jamín, Oad, Jaquín, Zojar y Saúl, hijo de la cananea. Éstos fueron los clanes de Simeón.

[16]Según los registros familiares, éstos son los nombres de los hijos de Leví, quien vivió ciento treinta y siete años: Guersón, Coat y Merari.

[17]Los hijos de Guersón, según sus clanes: Libní y Simí.

[18]Los hijos de Coat, quien vivió ciento treinta y tres años: Amirán, Izar, Hebrón y Uziel.

[19]Los hijos de Merari: Majlí y Musí.

Éstos fueron los clanes de Leví, según sus registros familiares. [20]Amirán, que vivió ciento treinta y siete años, se casó con su tía Jocabed, la cual le dio dos hijos, Aarón y Moisés.

[21]Los hijos de Izar: Coré, Néfeg y Zicrí.

[22]Los hijos de Uziel: Misael, Elzafán y Sitri.

[23]Aarón se casó con Elisabet, hija de Aminadab y hermana de Naasón, y ella le dio cuatro hijos: Nadab, Abiú, Eleazar e Itamar.

[24]Los hijos de Coré: Asir, Elcaná y Abiasaf. Éstos fueron los clanes de Coré.

[25]Eleazar hijo de Aarón se casó con una de las hijas de Futiel, la cual le dio un hijo, Finés.

Éstos fueron los jefes de los clanes levitas, en orden de familias.

[26]Aarón y Moisés son los mismos a quienes el SEÑOR mandó que sacaran de Egipto a los israelitas, ordenados en escuadrones. [27]Son ellos quienes hablaron con el faraón, rey egipcio, en cuanto a sacar de Egipto a los israelitas.

Aarón, vocero de Moisés

[28]Cuando el SEÑOR habló con Moisés en Egipto, [29]le dijo:

—Yo soy el SEÑOR. Habla con el faraón, rey de Egipto, y comunícale todo lo que yo te diga.

[30]Pero Moisés se enfrentó al SEÑOR y le dijo:

—¿Y cómo va a hacerme caso el faraón, si yo no tengo facilidad de palabra?

7 —Toma en cuenta —le dijo el SEÑOR a Moisés— que te pongo por Dios ante el faraón. Tu hermano Aarón será tu profeta. [2]Tu obligación es decir todo lo que yo te ordene que digas; tu hermano Aarón, por su parte, le pedirá al faraón que deje salir de su país a los israelitas. [3]Yo voy a endurecer el *corazón del faraón, y aunque haré muchas señales milagrosas y prodigios en Egipto, [4]él no les hará caso. Entonces descargaré mi poder sobre Egipto; ¡con grandes actos de *justicia sacaré de allí a los escuadrones de mi pueblo, los israelitas! [5]Y cuando yo despliegue mi poder contra Egipto y saque de allí a los israelitas, sabrán los egipcios que yo soy el SEÑOR.

La vara de Moisés

[6]Moisés y Aarón cumplieron al pie de la letra las órdenes del SEÑOR. [7]Cuando hablaron con el faraón, Moisés tenía ochenta años y Aarón ochenta y tres.

[8]El SEÑOR les dijo a Moisés y a Aarón: [9]«Cuando el faraón les pida que hagan un milagro, le dirás a Aarón que tome la vara y la arroje al suelo ante el faraón. Así la vara se convertirá en serpiente.»

[10]Moisés y Aarón fueron a ver al faraón y cumplieron las órdenes del SEÑOR. Aarón arrojó su vara al suelo ante el faraón y sus funcionarios, y la vara se convirtió en serpiente. [11]Pero el faraón llamó a los sabios y hechiceros y, mediante sus artes secretas, también los magos egipcios hicieron lo mismo: [12]Cada uno de ellos arrojó su vara al suelo, y cada vara se convirtió en una serpiente. Sin embargo, la vara de Aarón se tragó las varas de todos ellos. [13]A pesar de esto, y tal como lo había advertido el SEÑOR, el faraón endureció su *corazón y no les hizo caso.

La plaga de sangre

[14]El SEÑOR le dijo a Moisés: «El *corazón del faraón se ha obstinado, y se niega a dejar salir al pueblo. [15]Anda a verlo por la mañana, cuando salga a bañarse. Espéralo a orillas del río Nilo, y sal luego a su encuentro. No dejes de llevar la vara que se convirtió en serpiente. [16]Dile allí: "El SEÑOR, el Dios de los hebreos, me ha enviado a decirte: 'iDeja ir a mi pueblo para que me rinda culto en el desierto!' Como no has querido obedecer, [17]el SEÑOR dice: 'iAhora vas a saber que yo soy el SEÑOR!' Con esta vara que llevo en la mano voy a golpear las aguas del Nilo, y el río se convertirá en sangre. [18]Morirán los peces que hay en el río, y el río apestará y los egipcios no podrán beber agua de allí." »

[19]Dijo también el SEÑOR a Moisés: «Dile a Aarón que tome su vara y extienda el brazo sobre las aguas de Egipto, para que se conviertan en sangre sus arroyos y canales, y sus lagunas y depósitos de agua. Habrá sangre por todo el territorio de Egipto, ihasta en las vasijas de madera y de piedra!»

[20]Moisés y Aarón cumplieron las órdenes del SEÑOR. En presencia del faraón y de sus funcionarios, Aarón levantó su vara y golpeó las aguas del Nilo. ¡Y toda el agua del río se convirtió en sangre! [21]Murieron los peces que había en el Nilo, y tan mal olía el río que los egipcios no podían beber agua de allí. Por todo Egipto se veía sangre.

[22]Sin embargo, mediante sus artes secretas los magos egipcios hicieron lo mismo, de modo que el faraón endureció su corazón y, tal como el SEÑOR lo había advertido, no les hizo caso ni a Aarón ni a Moisés. [23]Como si nada hubiera pasado, se dio media vuelta y regresó a su palacio. [24]Mientras tanto, todos los egip-

---

[k] **6:12** *no tengo facilidad de palabra.* Lit. *soy incircunciso de labios;* también en v. 30.

cios hacían pozos a la orilla del Nilo en busca de agua potable, porque no podían beber el agua del río.

La plaga de ranas

25Siete días pasaron después de que el SEÑOR golpeó el Nilo.

8 El SEÑOR le ordenó a Moisés: «Ve a advertirle al faraón que así dice el SEÑOR: "Deja ir a mi pueblo para que me rinda culto. 2Si no los dejas ir, infestaré de ranas todo tu país. 3El Nilo hervirá de ranas, y se meterán en tu palacio, y hasta en tu alcoba y en tu cama, y en las casas de tus funcionarios y de tu pueblo, y en tus hornos y artesas. 4Se treparán sobre ti, sobre tu pueblo y sobre tus funcionarios."»

5Luego el SEÑOR le dijo a Moisés: «Dile a Aarón que extienda su vara sobre ríos, arroyos y lagunas, para que todo Egipto se llene de ranas.»

6Aarón extendió su brazo sobre las aguas de Egipto, y las ranas llegaron a cubrir todo el país. 7Pero, mediante sus artes secretas, los magos hicieron lo mismo, de modo que hicieron venir ranas sobre todo Egipto. 8Entonces el faraón mandó llamar a Moisés y a Aarón, y les dijo:

—Ruéguenle al SEÑOR que aleje las ranas de mí y de mi pueblo, y yo dejaré ir al pueblo para que le ofrezca sacrificios.

9Moisés le respondió:

—Dime cuándo quieres que ruegue al SEÑOR por ti, por tus funcionarios y por tu pueblo. Las ranas se quedarán sólo en el Nilo, y tú y tus casas se librarán de ellas.

10—Mañana mismo —contestó el faraón.

—Así se hará —respondió Moisés—, y sabrás que no hay dios como el SEÑOR, nuestro Dios. 11Las ranas se apartarán de ti y de tus casas, de tus funcionarios y de tu pueblo, y se quedarán únicamente en el Nilo.

12Tan pronto como salieron Moisés y Aarón de hablar con el faraón, Moisés clamó al SEÑOR en cuanto a las ranas que había mandado sobre el faraón. 13El SEÑOR atendió a los ruegos de Moisés, y las ranas comenzaron a morirse en las casas, en los patios y en los campos. 14La gente las recogía y las amontonaba, y el hedor de las ranas llenaba el país. 15Pero en cuanto el faraón experimentó alivio, endureció su *corazón, y tal como el SEÑOR lo había advertido, ya no quiso saber nada de Moisés ni de Aarón.

La plaga de mosquitos

16El SEÑOR le ordenó a Moisés que le dijera a Aarón: «Extiende tu vara y golpea el suelo, para que en todo Egipto el polvo se convierta en mosquitos.» 17Así lo hizo. Y Aarón extendió su brazo, golpeó el suelo con la vara, y del polvo salieron mosquitos que picaban a *hombres y animales. En todo Egipto el polvo se convirtió en mosquitos.

18Los magos, recurriendo a sus artes secretas, trataron también de producir mosquitos, pero no pudieron. Mientras tanto, los mosquitos picaban a hombres y animales. 19«En todo esto anda la mano de Dios», admitieron los magos ante el faraón, pero éste había endurecido su *corazón, así que no les hizo caso, tal como el SEÑOR lo había advertido.

La plaga de tábanos

20El SEÑOR le dijo a Moisés: «Mañana vas a madrugar. Le saldrás al paso al faraón cuando baje al río, y le advertirás: "Así dice el SEÑOR: 'Deja ir a mi pueblo para que me rinda culto. 21Si no lo dejas ir, enviaré enjambres de tábanos sobre ti y sobre tus funcionarios, sobre tu pueblo y sobre tus casas. Todas las casas egipcias, y aun el suelo que pisan, se llenarán de tábanos. 22Cuando eso suceda, la única región donde no habrá tábanos será la de Gosén, porque allí vive mi pueblo. Así sabrás que yo, el SEÑOR, estoy en este país. 23Haré distinción[1] entre mi pueblo y tu pueblo. Esta señal milagrosa tendrá lugar mañana.'"»

24Y así lo hizo el SEÑOR. Densas nubes de tábanos irrumpieron en el palacio del faraón y en las casas de sus funcionarios, y por todo Egipto. Por causa de los tábanos, el país quedó arruinado. 25Llamó entonces el faraón a Moisés y a Aarón, y les dijo:

—Vayan y ofrezcan sacrificios a su Dios aquí en el país.

26—No estaría bien hacerlo así —contestó Moisés—, porque los sacrificios que ofrecemos al SEÑOR nuestro Dios resultan ofensivos para los egipcios. Si a la vista de ellos ofrecemos sacrificios que les son ofensivos, seguramente nos apedrearán. 27Tenemos que hacer un viaje de tres días, hasta el desierto, para ofrecerle sacrificios al SEÑOR nuestro Dios, pues así nos lo ha ordenado.

28El faraón respondió:

—Voy a dejarlos ir para que ofrezcan sacrificios al SEÑOR su Dios en el desierto, con tal de que no se vayan muy lejos y de que rueguen a Dios por mí.

29—En cuanto salga yo de aquí —le aseguró Moisés al faraón—, rogaré por ti al SEÑOR, y de aquí a mañana los tábanos se habrán apartado de ti, de tus funcionarios y de tu pueblo. Pero tú no debes seguir engañándonos ni impidiendo que el pueblo vaya a ofrecerle sacrificios al SEÑOR.

30Así que Moisés salió y le rogó al SEÑOR por el faraón. 31El SEÑOR accedió a los ruegos de Moisés y apartó los tábanos del faraón, de sus funcionarios y de su pueblo. No quedó un solo tábano. 32Pero una vez más el faraón endureció su *corazón y no dejó que el pueblo se fuera.

La plaga en el ganado

9 El SEÑOR le ordenó a Moisés que fuera a hablar con el faraón y le advirtiera: «Así dice el SEÑOR, Dios de los hebreos: "Deja ir a mi pueblo para que me rinda culto. 2Si te niegas a dejarlos ir y sigues reteniéndolos, 3la mano del SEÑOR provocará una terrible plaga entre los ganados que tienes en el campo, y entre tus caballos, asnos, camellos, vacas y ovejas. 4Pero el SEÑOR hará distinción entre el ganado de Israel y el de Egipto, de modo que no morirá un solo animal que pertenezca a los israelitas."»

5Además, el SEÑOR fijó un plazo y dijo: «Mañana yo, el SEÑOR, haré esto en el país.» 6En efecto, al día siguiente murió todo el ganado de los egipcios, pero del ganado de los israelitas no murió ni un solo animal. 7Envió el faraón gente a ver los ganados de los israelitas, y se encontraron con que ni un solo animal había muerto. Sin embargo, el faraón endureció su *corazón y no quiso dejar ir al pueblo.

La plaga de úlceras

8Entonces el SEÑOR les dijo a Moisés y a Aarón: «Tomen de algún horno puñados de ceniza, y que la arroje Moisés al aire en presencia del faraón. 9La ceniza se convertirá en polvo fino, y caerá sobre todo Egipto y abrirá úlceras en personas y animales en todo el país.»

10Moisés y Aarón tomaron ceniza de un horno y se plantaron ante el faraón. Allí Moisés la arrojó al

[1] 8:23 *distinción* (LXX, Siríaca y Vulgata); *liberación* (TM).

aire, y se abrieron úlceras purulentas en personas y animales. 11Los magos no pudieron enfrentarse a Moisés, pues ellos y todos los egipcios tenían úlceras. 12Pero el SEÑOR endureció el *corazón del faraón y, tal como el SEÑOR se lo había advertido a Moisés, no quiso el faraón saber nada de Moisés ni de Aarón.

La plaga de granizo

13El SEÑOR le ordenó a Moisés madrugar al día siguiente, y salirle al paso al faraón para advertirle: «Así dice el SEÑOR y Dios de los hebreos: "Deja ir a mi pueblo para que me rinda culto. 14Porque esta vez voy a enviar el grueso de mis plagas contra ti, y contra tus funcionarios y tu pueblo, para que sepas que no hay en toda la tierra nadie como yo. 15Si en este momento desplegara yo mi poder, y a ti y a tu pueblo los azotara con una plaga, desaparecerían de la tierra. 16Pero te he dejado con vida precisamente para mostrarte mi poder, y para que mi *nombre sea proclamado por toda la tierra. 17Tú, sin embargo, sigues enfrentándote a mi pueblo y no quieres dejarlo ir. 18Por eso mañana a esta hora enviaré la peor granizada que haya caído en Egipto desde su fundación. 19Ordena inmediatamente que se pongan bajo techo tus ganados y todo lo que tengas en el campo, lo mismo personas que animales, porque el granizo caerá sobre los que anden al aire libre y los matará."»

20Algunos funcionarios del faraón temieron la palabra del SEÑOR y se apresuraron a poner bajo techo a sus esclavos y ganados, 21pero otros no hicieron caso de la palabra de Dios y dejaron en el campo a sus esclavos y ganados.

22Entonces el SEÑOR le dijo a Moisés: «Levanta los brazos al cielo, para que en todo Egipto caiga granizo sobre la *gente y los animales, y sobre todo lo que crece en el campo.»

23Moisés levantó su vara hacia el cielo, y el SEÑOR hizo que cayera granizo sobre todo Egipto: envió truenos, granizo y rayos sobre toda la tierra. 24Llovió granizo, y con el granizo caían rayos zigzagueantes. Nunca en toda la historia de Egipto como nación hubo una tormenta peor que ésta. 25El granizo arrasó con todo lo que había en los campos de Egipto, y con personas y animales; acabó con todos los cultivos y derribó todos los árboles. 26El único lugar en donde no granizó fue en la tierra de Gosén, donde estaban los israelitas.

27Entonces el faraón mandó llamar a Moisés y a Aarón, y les dijo:

—Esta vez reconozco mi pecado. El SEÑOR ha actuado con justicia, mientras que yo y mi pueblo hemos actuado mal. 28No voy a detenerlos más tiempo; voy a dejarlos ir. Pero rueguen por mí al SEÑOR, que truenos y granizo los hemos tenido de sobra.

29—En cuanto yo salga de la ciudad —le contestó Moisés—, elevaré mis manos en oración al SEÑOR, y cesarán los truenos y dejará de granizar. Así sabrás que la tierra es del SEÑOR. 30Sin embargo, yo sé que tú y tus funcionarios aún no tienen temor de Dios.

31El lino y la cebada fueron destruidos, ya que la cebada estaba en espiga, y el lino en flor. 32Sin embargo, el trigo y la espelta no se echaron a perder porque maduran más tarde.

33Tan pronto como Moisés dejó al faraón y salió de la ciudad, elevó sus manos en oración al SEÑOR y, en seguida, cesaron los truenos y dejó de granizar y de llover sobre la tierra. 34Pero en cuanto vio que el faraón habían cesado la lluvia, el gra-

nizo y los truenos, reincidió en su pecado, y tanto él como sus funcionarios endurecieron su *corazón. 35Tal como el SEÑOR lo había advertido por medio de Moisés, el faraón endureció su corazón y ya no dejó que los israelitas se fueran.

La plaga de langostas

10 El SEÑOR le dijo a Moisés: «Ve a hablar con el faraón. En realidad, soy yo quien ha endurecido su *corazón y el de sus funcionarios, para realizar entre ellos mis señales milagrosas. 2Lo hice para que puedas contarles a tus hijos y a tus nietos la dureza con que traté a los egipcios,m y las señales que realicé entre ellos. Así sabrán que yo soy el SEÑOR.»

3Moisés y Aarón se presentaron ante el faraón, y le advirtieron: «Así dice el SEÑOR y Dios de los hebreos: "¿Hasta cuándo te opondrás a humillarte en mi presencia? Deja ir a mi pueblo para que me rinda culto. 4Si te niegas a dejarlo ir, mañana mismo traeré langostas sobre tu país. 5De tal manera cubrirán la superficie de la tierra que no podrá verse el suelo. Se comerán lo poco que haya quedado después del granizo, y acabarán con todos los árboles que haya en los campos. 6Infestarán tus casas, y las de tus funcionarios y las de todos los egipcios. ¡Será algo que ni tus padres ni tus antepasados vieron jamás, desde el día en que se establecieron en este país hasta la fecha!"»

Dicho esto, Moisés se dio media vuelta y se retiró de la presencia del faraón. 7Entonces los funcionarios le dijeron al faraón:

—¿Hasta cuándo este individuo será una trampa para nosotros? ¡Deja que el pueblo se vaya y que rinda culto al SEÑOR su Dios! ¿Acaso no sabes que Egipto está arruinado?

8El faraón mandó llamar a Moisés y a Aarón, y les dijo:

—Vayan y rindan culto al SEÑOR su Dios. Tan sólo díganme quiénes van a ir.

9—Nos van a acompañar nuestros jóvenes y nuestros ancianos —respondió Moisés—. También nos acompañarán nuestros hijos y nuestras hijas, y nuestros rebaños y nuestros ganados, pues vamos a celebrar la fiesta del SEÑOR.

10—Que el SEÑOR los acompañe —repuso el faraón—, isi es que yo dejo que se vayan con sus mujeres y sus hijos! ¡Claramente se ven sus malas intenciones!n 11¡Pero no será como ustedes quieren! Si lo que quieren es rendirle culto al SEÑOR, ivayan sólo ustedes los hombres!

Y Moisés y Aarón fueron arrojados de la presencia del faraón. 12Entonces el SEÑOR le dijo a Moisés: «Extiende los brazos sobre todo Egipto, para que vengan langostas y cubran todo el país, y se coman todo lo que crece en los campos y todo lo que dejó el granizo.»

13Moisés extendió su vara sobre Egipto, y el SEÑOR hizo que todo ese día y toda esa noche un viento del este soplara sobre el país. A la mañana siguiente, el viento del este había traído las langostas, 14las cuales invadieron todo Egipto y se asentaron en gran número por todos los rincones del país. ¡Nunca antes hubo semejante plaga de langostas, ni la habrá después! 15Eran tantas las langostas que cubrían la superficie de la tierra, que ni el suelo podía verse. Se comieron todas las plantas del campo y todos los frutos de los árboles que dejó el granizo. En todo Egipto no quedó nada verde, ni en los árboles ni en las plantas.

m **10:2** *la dureza con que traté a los egipcios.* Alt. *cómo me burlé de los egipcios.* n **10:10** *¡Claramente se ven sus malas intenciones!.* Alt. *¡Tengan cuidado; los espera la aflicción!*

16A toda prisa mandó llamar el faraón a Moisés y a Aarón, y admitió: «He pecado contra el SEÑOR su Dios y contra ustedes. 17Yo les pido que perdonen mi pecado una vez más, y que rueguen por mí al SEÑOR su Dios, para que por lo menos aleje de donde yo estoy esta plaga mortal.»

18En cuanto Moisés salió de la presencia del faraón, rogó al SEÑOR por el faraón. 19El SEÑOR hizo entonces que el viento cambiara, y que un fuerte viento del oeste se llevara las langostas y las echara al *Mar Rojo. En todo Egipto no quedó una sola langosta. 20Pero el SEÑOR endureció el corazón del faraón, y éste no dejó que los israelitas se fueran.

La plaga de tinieblas

21El SEÑOR le dijo a Moisés: «Levanta los brazos al cielo, para que todo Egipto se cubra de tinieblas, ¡tinieblas tan densas que se puedan palpar!» 22Moisés levantó los brazos al cielo, y durante tres días todo Egipto quedó envuelto en densas tinieblas. 23Durante ese tiempo los egipcios no podían verse unos a otros, ni moverse de su sitio. Sin embargo, en todos los hogares israelitas había luz.

24Entonces el faraón mandó llamar a Moisés y le dijo:

—Vayan y rindan culto al SEÑOR. Llévense también a sus hijos, pero dejen atrás sus rebaños y sus ganados.

25A esto replicó Moisés:

—¡Al contrario!, tú vas a darnos los sacrificios y *holocaustos que hemos de presentar al SEÑOR nuestro Dios, 26y además nuestro ganado tiene que ir con nosotros. ¡No puede quedarse aquí ni una sola pezuña! Para rendirle culto al SEÑOR nuestro Dios tendremos que tomar algunos de nuestros animales, y no sabremos cuáles debemos presentar como ofrenda hasta que lleguemos allá.

27Pero el SEÑOR endureció el *corazón del faraón, y éste no quiso dejarlos ir, 28sino que le gritó a Moisés:

—¡Largo de aquí! ¡Y cuidado con volver a presentarte ante mí! El día que vuelvas a verme, puedes darte por muerto.

29—¡Bien dicho! —le respondió Moisés—. ¡Jamás volveré a verte!

La plaga contra los primogénitos

11 El SEÑOR le dijo a Moisés: «Voy a traer una plaga más sobre el faraón y sobre Egipto. Después de eso, dejará que se vayan. Y cuando lo haga, los echará de aquí para siempre. 2Habla con el pueblo y diles que todos ellos, hombres y mujeres, deben pedirles a sus vecinos y vecinas objetos de oro y de plata.»

3El SEÑOR hizo que los egipcios vieran con buenos ojos a los israelitas. Además, en todo Egipto Moisés mismo era altamente respetado por los funcionarios del faraón y por el pueblo.

4Moisés anunció: «Así dice el SEÑOR: "Hacia la medianoche pasaré por todo Egipto, 5y todo primogénito egipcio morirá: desde el primogénito del faraón que ahora ocupa el trono hasta el primogénito de la esclava que trabaja en el molino, lo mismo que todo primogénito del ganado. 6En todo Egipto habrá grandes lamentos, como no los ha habido ni volverá a haberlos. 7Pero entre los israelitas, no los perros le ladrarán a persona o animal alguno. Así sabrán que el SEÑOR hace distinción entre Egipto e Israel. 8Todos estos funcionarios tuyos vendrán a verme, y de

rodillas me suplicarán: '¡Vete ya, con todo el pueblo que te sigue!' Cuando esto suceda, me iré."»

Y ardiendo de ira, salió Moisés de la presencia del faraón, 9aunque ya el SEÑOR le había advertido a Moisés que el faraón no les iba a hacer caso, y que tenía que ser así para que las maravillas del SEÑOR se multiplicaran en Egipto.

10Moisés y Aarón realizaron ante el faraón todas estas maravillas; pero el SEÑOR endureció el *corazón del faraón, y éste no dejó salir de su país a los israelitas.

La Pascua
12:14-20 – Lv 23:4-8; Nm 28:16-25; Dt 16:1-8

12 En Egipto el SEÑOR habló con Moisés y Aarón. Les dijo: 2«Este mes será para ustedes el más importante, pues será el primer mes del año. 3Hablen con toda la comunidad de Israel, y díganles que el día décimo de este mes todos ustedes tomarán un corderoñ por familia, uno por cada casa. 4Si alguna familia es demasiado pequeña para comerse un cordero entero, deberá compartirlo con sus vecinos más cercanos, teniendo en cuenta el número de personas que sean y las raciones de cordero que se necesiten, según lo que cada persona haya de comer. 5El animal que se escoja puede ser un cordero o un cabrito de un año y sin defecto, 6al que cuidarán hasta el catorce del mes, día en que la comunidad de Israel en pleno lo sacrificará al caer la noche. 7Tomarán luego un poco de sangre y la untarán en los dos postes y en el dintel de la puerta de la casa donde coman el cordero. 8Deberán comer la carne esa misma noche, asada al fuego y acompañada de hierbas amargas y pan sin levadura. 9No deberán comerla cruda ni hervida, sino asada al fuego, junto con la cabeza, las patas y los intestinos. 10Y no deben dejar nada. En caso de que algo quede, lo quemarán al día siguiente. 11Comerán el cordero de este modo: con el manto ceñido a la cintura, con las sandalias puestas, con la vara en la mano, y de prisa. Se trata de la Pascua del SEÑOR.

12»Esa misma noche pasaré por todo Egipto y heriré de muerte a todos los primogénitos, tanto de personas como de animales, y ejecutaré mi sentencia contra todos los dioses de Egipto. Yo soy el SEÑOR. 13La sangre servirá para señalar las casas donde ustedes se encuentren, pues al verla pasaré de largo. Así, cuando hiera yo de muerte a los egipcios, no los tocará a ustedes ninguna plaga destructora.

14»Éste es un día que por ley deberán conmemorar siempre. Es una fiesta en honor del SEÑOR, y las generaciones futuras deberán celebrarla. 15Durante siete días comerán pan sin levadura, de modo que deben retirar de sus casas la levadura el primer día. Todo el que coma algo con levadura desde el día primero hasta el séptimo será eliminado de Israel. 16Celebrarán una reunión solemne el día primero, y otra el día séptimo. En todo ese tiempo no harán ningún trabajo, excepto preparar los alimentos que cada uno haya de comer. Sólo eso podrán hacer.

17»Celebrarán la fiesta de los Panes sin levadura, porque fue ese día cuando los saqué de Egipto formados en escuadrones. Por ley, las generaciones futuras siempre deberán celebrar ese día. 18Comerán pan sin levadura desde la tarde del día catorce del mes primero hasta la tarde del día veintiuno del mismo mes. 19Durante siete días se abstendrán de tener levadura en sus casas. Todo el que coma algo con levadura, sea extranjero o israelita, será eliminado de

---

ñ 12:3 *cordero*. Alt. *cabrito*; también en v. 4.

la comunidad de Israel. 20No coman nada que tenga levadura. Dondequiera que vivan ustedes, comerán pan sin levadura.»

21Convocó entonces Moisés a todos los *ancianos israelitas, y les dijo: «Vayan en seguida a sus rebaños, escojan el cordero para sus respectivas familias, y mátenlo para celebrar la Pascua. 22Tomen luego un manojo de *hisopo, mójenlo en la sangre recogida en la palangana, unten de sangre el dintel y los dos postes de la puerta, iy no salga ninguno de ustedes de su casa hasta la mañana siguiente! 23Cuando el SEÑOR pase por el país para herir de muerte a los egipcios, verá la sangre en el dintel y en los postes de la puerta, y pasará de largo por esa casa. No permitirá el SEÑOR que el ángel exterminador entre en las casas de ustedes y los hiera.

24»Obedezcan estas instrucciones. Será una ley perpetua para ustedes y para sus hijos.

25Cuando entren en la tierra que el SEÑOR ha prometido darles, ustedes seguirán celebrando esta ceremonia. 26Y cuando sus hijos les pregunten: "¿Qué significa para ustedes esta ceremonia?", 27les responderán: "Este sacrificio es la Pascua del SEÑOR, que en Egipto pasó de largo por las casas israelitas. Hirió de muerte a los egipcios, pero a nuestras familias les salvó la vida."»

Al oír esto, los israelitas se inclinaron y adoraron al SEÑOR, 28y fueron y cumplieron al pie de la letra lo que el SEÑOR les había ordenado a Moisés y a Aarón.

Muerte de los primogénitos egipcios

29A medianoche el SEÑOR hirió de muerte a todos los primogénitos egipcios, desde el primogénito del faraón en el trono hasta el primogénito del preso en la cárcel, así como a las primeras crías de todo el ganado. 30Todos en Egipto se levantaron esa noche, lo mismo el faraón que sus funcionarios, y hubo grandes lamentos en el país. No había una sola casa egipcia donde no hubiera algún muerto.

31Esa misma noche mandó llamar el faraón a Moisés y a Aarón, y les ordenó: ¡Largo de aquí! ¡Aléjense de mi pueblo ustedes y los israelitas! ¡Vayan a adorar al SEÑOR, como lo han estado pidiendo! 32Llévense también sus rebaños y sus ganados, como lo han pedido, ipero váyanse ya, que para mí será una bendición!

33El pueblo egipcio, por su parte, instaba a los israelitas a que abandonaran pronto el país. «De lo contrario —decían—, ipodemos darnos por muertos!» 34Entonces los israelitas tomaron las artesas de masa todavía sin leudar y, luego de envolverlas en sus ropas, se las echaron al hombro. 35Después, siguiendo las instrucciones que Moisés les había dado, pidieron a los egipcios que les dieran objetos de oro y de plata, y también ropa. 36El SEÑOR hizo que los egipcios vieran con buenos ojos a los israelitas, así que les dieron todo lo que les pedían. De este modo los israelitas despojaron por completo a los egipcios.

El éxodo

37Los israelitas partieron de Ramsés, en dirección a Sucot. Sin contar a las mujeres y a los niños, eran unos seiscientos mil hombres de a pie. 38Con ellos salió también gente de toda laya, y grandes manadas de ganado, tanto de ovejas como de vacas. 39Con la masa que sacaron de Egipto cocieron panes sin levadura, pues la masa aún no había fermentado.

Como los echaron de Egipto, no tuvieron tiempo de preparar comida.

40Los israelitas habían vivido en Egipto cuatrocientos treinta años. 41Precisamente el día en que se cumplían los cuatrocientos treinta años, todos los escuadrones del SEÑOR salieron de Egipto. 42Aquella noche el SEÑOR la pasó en vela para sacar de Egipto a los israelitas. Por eso también las generaciones futuras de israelitas deben pasar esa noche en vela, en honor del SEÑOR.

Restricciones para la Pascua

43El SEÑOR les dijo a Moisés y a Aarón: «Éstas son las normas para la Pascua:

»Ningún extranjero podrá participar de ella.

44»Podrán participar de ella todos los esclavos que hayas comprado con tu dinero, siempre y cuando los hayas circuncidado antes.

45»Ningún residente temporal ni trabajador a sueldo podrá participar de ella.

46»La Pascua deberá comerse en casa, y de allí no se sacará ni un solo pedazo de carne. Tampoco se le quebrará ningún hueso al animal sacrificado.

47»Toda la comunidad de Israel debe celebrar la Pascua.

48»Todo extranjero que viva entre ustedes y quiera celebrar la Pascua del SEÑOR, deberá primero circuncidar a todos los varones de su familia; sólo entonces podrá participar de la Pascua como si fuera nativo del país.

»Ningún incircunciso podrá participar de ella.

49»La misma ley se aplicará al nativo y al extranjero que viva entre ustedes.»

50Todos los israelitas cumplieron al pie de la letra lo que el SEÑOR les había ordenado a Moisés y a Aarón. 51Ese mismo día el SEÑOR sacó de Egipto a los israelitas, escuadrón por escuadrón.

Consagración de los primogénitos israelitas

13 El SEÑOR habló con Moisés y le dijo: 2«Conságrame el primogénito de todo vientre. Míos son los primogénitos israelitas y todos los primeros machos de sus animales.»

3Moisés le dijo al pueblo: «Acuérdense de este día en que salen de Egipto, país donde han sido esclavos y de donde el SEÑOR los saca desplegando su poder. No coman pan con levadura. 4Ustedes salen hoy, en el mes de *aviv, 5y en este mismo mes deberán celebrar esta ceremonia, cuando ya el SEÑOR los haya hecho entrar en la tierra que prometió dar a los antepasados de ustedes. Se trata de la tierra de los cananeos, hititas, amorreos, heveos y jebuseos: itierra donde abundan la leche y la miel! 6Durante siete días comerán pan sin levadura, y el día séptimo celebrarán una fiesta en honor al SEÑOR. 7En ningún lugar de su territorio debe haber nada que contenga levadura. No habrá levadura entre ustedes. Comerán pan sin levadura durante esos siete días.

8»Ese día ustedes les dirán a sus hijos:o "Esto lo hacemos por lo que hizo el SEÑOR por nosotros cuando salimos de Egipto." 9Y será para ustedes como una marca distintiva en la mano o en la frente, que les hará recordar que la *ley del SEÑOR debe estar en sus labios, porque el SEÑOR los sacó de Egipto desplegando su poder. 10Año tras año, en la misma fecha, cumplirán con esta ley.

11»Una vez que el SEÑOR los haga entrar en la tierra de los cananeos y se la haya dado, conforme al juramento que les hizo a ustedes y a sus antepasa-

---

o **13:8** *ustedes les dirán a sus hijos.* Lit. *le dirás a tu hijo.* En vv. 8-16 el texto hebreo usa el singular en sentido colectivo.

dos, 12le dedicarán al SEÑOR el primogénito de todo vientre, y todo primer macho de su ganado, pues éstos le pertenecen al SEÑOR. 13El primogénito de una asna podrá ser rescatado a cambio de un cordero; pero si no se rescata, se le quebrará el cuello. Todos los primogénitos de ustedes o de sus descendientes deberán ser rescatados.

14»El día de mañana, cuando sus hijos les pregunten: "¿Y esto qué significa?", les dirán: "El SEÑOR, desplegando su poder, nos sacó de Egipto, país donde fuimos esclavos. 15Cuando el faraón se empeñó en no dejarnos ir, el SEÑOR les quitó la vida a todos los primogénitos de Egipto, tanto de *hombres como de animales. Por eso le ofrecemos al SEÑOR en sacrificio el primer macho que nace, y rescatamos a nuestros primogénitos." 16Esto será para ustedes como una marca distintiva en la mano o en la frente, de que el SEÑOR nos sacó de Egipto desplegando su poder.

El paso del Mar Rojo

17Cuando el faraón dejó salir a los israelitas, Dios no los llevó por el camino que atraviesa la tierra de los filisteos, que era el más corto, pues pensó: «Si se les presentara batalla, podrían cambiar de idea y regresar a Egipto.» 18Por eso les hizo dar un rodeo por el camino del desierto, en dirección al *Mar Rojo.

Los israelitas salieron de Egipto en formación de combate. 19Moisés se llevó consigo los restos de José, según éste se lo había pedido a los israelitas bajo juramento. Éstas habían sido las palabras de José: «Pueden contar ustedes con que Dios vendrá en su ayuda. Cuando eso suceda, llévense de aquí mis restos.»

20Los israelitas partieron de Sucot y acamparon en Etam, donde comienza el desierto. 21De día, el SEÑOR iba al frente de ellos en una columna de nube para indicarles el camino; de noche, los alumbraba con una columna de fuego. De ese modo podían viajar de día y de noche. 22Jamás la columna de nube dejaba de guiar al pueblo durante el día, ni la columna de fuego durante la noche.

14 El SEÑOR habló con Moisés y le dijo: 2«Ordénales a los israelitas que regresen y acampen frente a Pi Ajirot, entre Migdol y el mar. Que acampen junto al mar, frente a Baal Zefón. 3El faraón va a pensar: "Los israelitas andan perdidos en esa tierra. ¡El desierto los tiene acorralados!" 4Yo, por mi parte, endureceré el *corazón del faraón para que los persiga. Voy a cubrirme de gloria, a costa del faraón y de todo su ejército. ¡Y los egipcios sabrán que yo soy el SEÑOR!»

Así lo hicieron los israelitas. 5Y cuando el rey de Egipto se enteró de que el pueblo se había escapado, tanto él como sus funcionarios cambiaron de parecer en cuanto a los israelitas y dijeron: «¡Pero qué hemos hecho! ¿Cómo pudimos dejar que se fueran los israelitas y abandonaran su trabajo?» 6Al momento ordenó el faraón que le prepararan su carro y, echando mano de su ejército, 7se llevó consigo seiscientos de los mejores carros y todos los demás carros de Egipto, cada uno de ellos bajo el mando de un oficial.

8El SEÑOR endureció el corazón del faraón, rey de Egipto, para que saliera en persecución de los israelitas, los cuales marchaban con aire triunfal. 9Todo el ejército del faraón —caballos, carros, jinetesp y tropas de Egipto— salió tras los israelitas y los dio alcance cuando éstos acampaban junto al mar, cerca de Pi Ajirot y frente a Baal Zefón.

10El faraón iba acercándose. Cuando los israelitas se fijaron y vieron a los egipcios pisándoles los talones, sintieron mucho miedo y clamaron al SEÑOR. 11Entonces le reclamaron a Moisés:

—¿Acaso no había sepulcros en Egipto, que nos sacaste de allá para morir en el desierto? ¿Qué has hecho con nosotros? ¿Para qué nos sacaste de Egipto? 12Ya en Egipto te decíamos: "¡Déjanos en paz! ¡Preferimos servir a los egipcios!" ¡Mejor nos hubiera sido servir a los egipcios que morir en el desierto!

13—No tengan miedo —les respondió Moisés—. Mantengan sus posiciones, que hoy mismo serán testigos de la *salvación que el SEÑOR realizará en favor de ustedes. A esos egipcios que hoy ven, ¡jamás volverán a verlos! 14Ustedes quédense quietos, que el SEÑOR presentará batalla por ustedes.

15Pero el SEÑOR le dijo a Moisés: «¿Por qué clamas a mí? ¡Ordena a los israelitas que se pongan en marcha! 16Y tú, levanta tu vara, extiende tu brazo sobre el mar y divide las aguas, para que los israelitas lo crucen sobre terreno seco. 17Yo voy a endurecer el corazón de los egipcios, para que los persigan. ¡Voy a cubrirme de gloria a costa del faraón y de su ejército, y de sus carros y jinetes! 18Y cuando me haya cubierto de gloria a costa de ellos, los egipcios sabrán que yo soy el SEÑOR.»

19Entonces el ángel de Dios, que marchaba al frente del ejército israelita, se dio vuelta y fue a situarse detrás de éste. Lo mismo sucedió con la columna de nube, que dejó su puesto de vanguardia y se desplazó hacia la retaguardia, 20quedando entre los egipcios y los israelitas. Durante toda la noche, la nube dio oscuridad para unos y luz para otros, así que en toda esa noche no pudieron acercarse los unos a los otros.

21Moisés extendió su brazo sobre el mar, y toda la noche el SEÑOR envió sobre el mar un recio viento del este que lo hizo retroceder, convirtiéndolo en tierra seca. Las aguas del mar se dividieron, 22y los israelitas lo cruzaron sobre tierra seca. El mar era para ellos una muralla de agua a la derecha y otra a la izquierda.

23Los egipcios los persiguieron. Todos los caballos y carros del faraón, y todos sus jinetes, entraron en el mar tras ellos. 24Cuando ya estaba por amanecer, el SEÑOR miró al ejército egipcio desde la columna de fuego y de nube, y sembró la confusión entre ellos: 25hizo que las ruedas de sus carros se atascaran, de modo que se les hacía muy difícil avanzar. Entonces exclamaron los egipcios: «¡Alejémonos de los israelitas, pues el SEÑOR está peleando por ellos y contra nosotros!»

26Entonces el SEÑOR le dijo a Moisés: «Extiende tu brazo sobre el mar, para que las aguas se vuelvan contra los egipcios y contra sus carros y jinetes.» 27Moisés extendió su brazo sobre el mar y, al despuntar el alba, éste volvió a su estado normal. Los egipcios, en su huida, se toparon con el mar, y así el SEÑOR los hundió en el fondo del mar. 28Al recobrar las aguas su estado normal, se tragaron a todos los carros y jinetes del faraón, y a todo el ejército que había entrado al mar para perseguir a los israelitas. Ninguno de ellos quedó con vida. 29Los israelitas, sin embargo, cruzaron el mar sobre tierra seca, pues para ellos el mar formó una muralla de agua a la derecha y otra a la izquierda.

30En ese día el SEÑOR salvó a Israel del poder de Egipto. Los israelitas vieron los cadáveres de los egipcios tendidos a la orilla del mar. 31Y al ver los is-

---

p **14:9** *jinetes.* Alt. *aurigas;* también en vv. 17,23,26 y 28.

raelitas el gran poder que el SEÑOR había desplegado en contra de los egipcios, temieron al SEÑOR y
creyeron en él y en su siervo Moisés.

El cántico de Moisés

15 Entonces Moisés y los israelitas entonaron
un cántico en honor del SEÑOR, que a la letra
decía:

Cantaré al SEÑOR, que se ha coronado de
*triunfo
arrojando al mar caballos y jinetes.
2El SEÑOR es mi fuerza y mi cántico;
él es mi *salvación.
Él es mi Dios, y lo alabaré;
es el Dios de mi padre, y lo enalteceré.
3El SEÑOR es un guerrero;
su *nombre es el SEÑOR.
4El SEÑOR arrojó al mar
los carros y el ejército del faraón.
Los mejores oficiales egipcios
se ahogaron en el *Mar Rojo.
5Las aguas profundas se los tragaron;
¡como piedras se hundieron en los abismos!

6Tu diestra, SEÑOR, reveló su gran poder;
tu diestra, SEÑOR, despedazó al enemigo.
7Fue tan grande tu *victoria
que derribaste a tus oponentes;
diste rienda suelta a tu ardiente ira,
y fueron consumidos como rastrojo.
8Bastó un soplo de tu nariz
para que se amontonaran las aguas.
Las olas se irguieron como murallas;
¡se inmovilizaron las aguas en el fondo del
mar!

9«Iré tras ellos y les daré alcance
—alardeaba el enemigo—.
Repartiré sus despojos
hasta quedar hastiado.
¡Desenvainaré la espada
y los destruiré con mi propia mano!»
10Pero con un soplo tuyo se los tragó el mar;
¡se hundieron como plomo en las aguas
turbulentas!

11¿Quién, SEÑOR, se te compara entre los
dioses?
¿Quién se te compara en grandeza y
*santidad?
Tú, hacedor de maravillas,
nos impresionas con tus portentos.
12Extendiste tu brazo derecho,
¡y se los tragó la tierra!

13Por tu gran amor guías al pueblo que has
rescatado;
por tu fuerza los llevas a tu santa morada.
14Las naciones temblarán al escucharlo;
la angustia dominará a los filisteos.
15Los jefes edomitas se llenarán de terror;
temblarán de miedo los caudillos de Moab.
Los cananeos perderán el ánimo,
16pues caerá sobre ellos pavor y espanto.
Por tu gran poder, SEÑOR,
quedarán mudos como piedras
hasta que haya pasado tu pueblo,
el pueblo que adquiriste para ti.
17Tú los harás entrar, y los plantarás,
en el monte que te pertenece;
en el lugar donde tú, SEÑOR, habitas;
en el santuario que tú, Señor, te hiciste.

18¡El SEÑOR reina por siempre y para siempre!

El cántico de Miriam

19Cuando los caballos y los carros del faraón entraron en el mar con sus jinetes,[q] el SEÑOR hizo que
las aguas se les vinieran encima. Los israelitas, sin
embargo, cruzaron el mar sobre tierra seca. 20Enton-
ces Miriam la profetisa, hermana de Aarón, tomó
una pandereta, y mientras todas las mujeres la seguían danzando y tocando panderetas, 21Miriam les
cantaba así:

Canten al SEÑOR, que se ha coronado de
*triunfo
arrojando al mar caballos y jinetes.

Las aguas de Mara y de Elim

22Moisés les ordenó a los israelitas que partieran
del *Mar Rojo y se internaran en el desierto de Sur. Y
los israelitas anduvieron tres días por el desierto sin
hallar agua. 23Llegaron a Mara,[r] lugar que se llama
así porque sus aguas son amargas, y no pudieron
apagar su sed allí. 24Comenzaron entonces a murmurar en contra de Moisés, y preguntaban: «¿Qué
vamos a beber?» 25Moisés clamó al SEÑOR, y él le
mostró un pedazo de madera, el cual echó Moisés al
agua, y al instante el agua se volvió dulce.

En ese lugar el SEÑOR los puso a prueba y les dio
una *ley como norma de conducta. 26Les dijo: «Yo
soy el SEÑOR su Dios. Si escuchan mi voz y hacen lo
que yo considero justo, y si cumplen mis leyes y
mandamientos, no traeré sobre ustedes ninguna de
las enfermedades que traje sobre los egipcios. Yo soy
el SEÑOR, que les devuelve la salud.»

27Después los israelitas llegaron a Elim, donde
había doce manantiales y setenta palmeras, y acamparon allí, cerca del agua.

El maná y las codornices

16 Toda la comunidad israelita partió de Elim y
llegó al desierto de Sin, que está entre Elim y
el Sinaí. Esto ocurrió a los quince días del mes segundo, contados a partir de su salida de Egipto. 2Allí, en
el desierto, toda la comunidad murmuró contra Moisés y Aarón:

3—¡Cómo quisiéramos que el SEÑOR nos hubiera quitado la vida en Egipto! —les decían los israelitas—. Allá nos sentábamos en torno a las ollas de
carne y comíamos pan hasta saciarnos. ¡Ustedes han
traído nuestra comunidad a este desierto para matarnos de hambre a todos!

4Entonces el SEÑOR le dijo a Moisés: «Voy a hacer que les llueva pan del cielo. El pueblo deberá salir
todos los días a recoger su ración diaria. Voy a ponerlos a prueba, para ver si cumplen o no mis instrucciones. 5El día sexto recogerán una doble porción, y
todo esto lo dejarán preparado.»

6Moisés y Aarón les dijeron a todos los israelitas:
—Esta tarde sabrán que fue el SEÑOR quien los
sacó de Egipto, 7y mañana por la mañana verán la
gloria del SEÑOR. Ya él sabe que ustedes andan murmurando contra él. Nosotros no somos nadie, para
que ustedes murmuren contra nosotros.

8Y añadió Moisés:
—Esta tarde el SEÑOR les dará a comer carne, y
mañana los saciará de pan, pues ya los oyó murmurar contra él. Porque ¿quiénes somos nosotros?

[q] **15:19** *jinetes* Alt. *Aurigas* [r] **15:23** En hebreo, *Mara* significa *amarga.*

¡Ustedes no están murmurando contra nosotros sino contra el SEÑOR!

⁹Luego se dirigió Moisés a Aarón:

—Dile a toda la comunidad israelita que se acerque al SEÑOR, pues los ha oído murmurar contra él.

¹⁰Mientras Aarón hablaba con toda la comunidad israelita, volvieron la mirada hacia el desierto, y vieron que la gloria del SEÑOR se hacía presente en una nube.

¹¹El SEÑOR habló con Moisés y le dijo: ¹²«Han llegado a mis oídos las murmuraciones de los israelitas. Diles que antes de que caiga la noche comerán carne, y que mañana por la mañana se hartarán de pan. Así sabrán que yo soy el SEÑOR su Dios.»

¹³Esa misma tarde el campamento se llenó de codornices, y por la mañana una capa de rocío rodeaba el campamento. ¹⁴Al desaparecer el rocío, sobre el desierto quedaron unos copos muy finos, semejantes a la escarcha que cae sobre la tierra. ¹⁵Como los israelitas no sabían lo que era, al verlo se preguntaban unos a otros: «¿Y esto qué es?» Moisés les respondió:

—Es el pan que el SEÑOR les da para comer. ¹⁶Y éstas son las órdenes que el SEÑOR me ha dado: "Recoja cada uno de ustedes la cantidad necesaria para toda la familia, calculando dos litros^s por persona."

¹⁷Así lo hicieron los israelitas. Algunos recogieron mucho; otros recogieron poco. ¹⁸Pero cuando lo midieron por litros, ni al que recogió mucho le sobraba, ni al que recogió poco le faltaba: cada uno recogió la cantidad necesaria. ¹⁹Entonces Moisés les dijo:

—Nadie debe guardar nada para el día siguiente.

²⁰Hubo algunos que no le hicieron caso a Moisés y guardaron algo para el día siguiente, pero lo guardado se llenó de gusanos y comenzó a apestar. Entonces Moisés se enojó contra ellos.

²¹Todas las mañanas cada uno recogía la cantidad que necesitaba, porque se derretía en cuanto calentaba el sol. ²²Pero el día sexto recogieron el doble, es decir, cuatro litros^t por persona, así que los jefes de la comunidad fueron a informar de esto a Moisés.

²³—Esto es lo que el SEÑOR ha ordenado —les contestó—. Mañana *sábado es día de reposo consagrado al SEÑOR. Así que cuezan lo que tengan que cocer, y hiervan lo que tengan que hervir. Lo que sobre, apártenlo y guárdenlo para mañana.

²⁴Los israelitas cumplieron las órdenes de Moisés y guardaron para el día siguiente lo que les sobró, ¡y no se pudrió ni se agusanó!

²⁵—Cómanlo hoy sábado —les dijo Moisés—, que es el día de reposo consagrado al SEÑOR. Hoy no encontrarán nada en el campo. ²⁶Deben recogerlo durante seis días, porque el día séptimo, que es sábado, no encontrarán nada.

²⁷Algunos israelitas salieron a recogerlo el día séptimo, pero no encontraron nada. ²⁸Así que el SEÑOR le dijo a Moisés: «¿Hasta cuándo seguirán desobedeciendo mis *leyes y mandamientos? ²⁹Tomen en cuenta que yo, el SEÑOR, les he dado el sábado. Por eso en el día sexto les doy pan para dos días. El día séptimo nadie debe salir. Todos deben quedarse donde estén.»

³⁰Fue así como los israelitas descansaron el día séptimo. ³¹Y llamaron al pan «maná».^u Era blanco como la semilla de cilantro, y dulce como las tortas con miel.

³²—Esto es lo que ha ordenado el SEÑOR —dijo Moisés—: "Tomen unos dos litros^v de maná, y guárdenlos para que las generaciones futuras puedan ver el pan que yo les di a comer en el desierto, cuando los saqué de Egipto."

³³Luego Moisés le dijo a Aarón:

—Toma una vasija y pon en ella unos dos litros de maná. Colócala después en la presencia del SEÑOR, a fin de conservarla para las generaciones futuras.

³⁴Aarón puso el maná ante el arca del *pacto, para que fuera conservado como se lo ordenó el SEÑOR a Moisés. ³⁵Comieron los israelitas maná cuarenta años, hasta que llegaron a los límites de la tierra de Canaán, que fue su país de residencia.

³⁶La medida de dos litros, a la que llamaban *gómer*, era la décima parte de la medida a la que llamaban *efa.^w

El agua de la roca

17 Toda la comunidad israelita partió del desierto de Sin por etapas, según lo había ordenado el SEÑOR. Acamparon en Refidín, pero no había allí agua para que bebieran, ²así que altercaron con Moisés.

—Danos agua para beber —le exigieron.

—¿Por qué pelean conmigo? —se defendió Moisés—. ¿Por qué provocan al SEÑOR?

³Pero los israelitas estaban sedientos, y murmuraron contra Moisés.

—¿Para qué nos sacaste de Egipto? —reclamaban—. ¿Sólo para matarnos de sed a nosotros, a nuestros hijos y a nuestro ganado?

⁴Clamó entonces Moisés al SEÑOR, y le dijo:

—¿Qué voy a hacer con este pueblo? ¡Sólo falta que me maten a pedradas!

⁵—Adelántate al pueblo —le aconsejó el SEÑOR— y llévate contigo a algunos *ancianos de Israel, pero lleva también la vara con que golpeaste el Nilo. Ponte en marcha, ⁶que yo estaré esperándote junto a la *roca que está en Horeb. Aséstale un golpe a la roca, y de ella brotará agua para que beba el pueblo.

Así lo hizo Moisés, a la vista de los ancianos de Israel. ⁷Además, a ese lugar lo llamó Masá,^x y también Meribá,^y porque los israelitas habían altercado con él y provocado al SEÑOR al decir: «¿Está o no está el SEÑOR entre nosotros?»

Derrota de los amalecitas

⁸Los amalecitas vinieron a Refidín y atacaron a los israelitas. ⁹Entonces Moisés le ordenó a Josué: «Escoge algunos de nuestros hombres y sal a combatir a los amalecitas. Mañana yo estaré en la cima de la colina con la vara de Dios^z en la mano.»

¹⁰Josué siguió las órdenes de Moisés y les presentó batalla a los amalecitas. Por su parte, Moisés, Aarón y Jur subieron a la cima de la colina. ¹¹Mientras Moisés mantenía los brazos^a en alto, la batalla se inclinaba en favor de los israelitas; pero cuando los bajaba, se inclinaba en favor de los amalecitas. ¹²Cuando a Moisés se le cansaron los brazos, tomaron una piedra y se la pusieron debajo para que se sentara en ella; luego Aarón y Jur le sostuvieron los brazos, uno el izquierdo y otro el derecho, y así Moisés pudo mantenerlos firmes hasta la puesta del sol. ¹³Fue así como Josué derrotó al ejército amalecita a filo de espada.

---

^s **16:16** *dos litros*. Lit. *un *gómer*; también en vv. 18 y 36. ^t **16:22** *cuatro litros*. Lit. *dos gómer*. ^u **16:31** En hebreo, *maná* significa *¿Qué es?* (Véase v. 15.) ^v **16:32** *unos dos litros*. Lit. *un gómer*; también en v. 33. ^w **16:36** *La medida ... efa*. Lit. *Un gómer es la décima parte de un efa.* ^x **17:7** En hebreo, *Masá* significa *prueba* o *provocación.* ^y **17:7** En hebreo, *Meribá* significa *altercado.* ^z **17:9** *vara de Dios.* Alt. *vara milagrosa.* ^a **17:11** *los brazos* (las versiones antiguas); *el brazo* (TM).

14Entonces el SEÑOR le dijo a Moisés: «Pon esto por escrito en un rollo de cuero, para que se recuerde, y que lo oiga Josué: Yo borraré por completo, bajo el cielo, todo rastro de los amalecitas.»

15Moisés edificó un altar y lo llamó «El SEÑOR es mi estandarte». **16**Y exclamó: «¡Echa mano al estandarte[b] del SEÑOR! ¡La guerra del SEÑOR contra Amalec será de generación en generación!»

Jetro visita a Moisés

18 Todo lo que Dios había hecho por Moisés y por su pueblo Israel, y la manera como el SEÑOR había sacado a Israel de Egipto, llegó a oídos de Jetro, sacerdote de Madián y suegro de Moisés. **2**Cuando Moisés despidió a Séfora, su esposa, Jetro la recibió a ella **3**y a sus dos hijos. Uno de ellos se llamaba Guersón,[c] porque dijo Moisés: «Soy un extranjero en tierra extraña»; **4**el otro se llamaba Eliezer,[d] porque dijo: «El Dios de mi padre me ayudó y me salvó de la espada del faraón.»

5Jetro fue al desierto para ver a Moisés, que estaba acampando junto a la montaña de Dios. Lo acompañaban la esposa y los hijos de Moisés. **6**Jetro le había avisado: «Yo, tu suegro Jetro, voy a verte. Me acompañan tu esposa y tus dos hijos.»

7Moisés salió al encuentro de su suegro, se inclinó delante de él y lo besó. Luego de intercambiar saludos y desearse lo mejor, entraron en la tienda de campaña. **8**Allí Moisés le contó a su suegro todo lo que el SEÑOR les había hecho al faraón y a los egipcios en favor de Israel, todas las dificultades con que se habían encontrado en el camino, y cómo el SEÑOR los había salvado.

9Jetro se alegró de saber que el SEÑOR había tratado bien a Israel y lo había rescatado del poder de los egipcios, **10**y exclamó: «¡Alabado sea el SEÑOR, que los salvó a ustedes del poder de los egipcios! ¡Alabado sea el que salvó a los israelitas del poder opresor del faraón! **11**Ahora sé que el SEÑOR es más grande que todos los dioses, por lo que hizo a quienes trataron a Israel con arrogancia.» **12**Dicho esto, Jetro le presentó a Dios un *holocausto y otros sacrificios, y Aarón y todos los *ancianos de Israel se sentaron a comer con el suegro de Moisés en presencia de Dios.

13Al día siguiente, Moisés ocupó su lugar como juez del pueblo, y los israelitas estuvieron de pie ante Moisés desde la mañana hasta la noche. **14**Cuando su suegro vio cómo procedía Moisés con el pueblo, le dijo:

—¡Pero qué es lo que haces con esta gente! ¿Cómo es que sólo tú te sientas, mientras todo este pueblo se queda de pie ante ti desde la mañana hasta la noche?

15—Es que el pueblo viene a verme para consultar a Dios —le contestó Moisés—. **16**Cuando tienen algún problema, me lo traen a mí para que yo dicte sentencia entre las dos partes. Además, les doy a conocer las *leyes y las enseñanzas de Dios.

17—No está bien lo que estás haciendo —le respondió su suegro—, **18**pues te cansas tú y se cansa la gente que te acompaña. La tarea es demasiado pesada para ti; no la puedes desempeñar tú solo. **19**Oye bien el consejo que voy a darte, y que Dios te ayude. Tú debes representar al pueblo ante Dios y presentarle los problemas que ellos tienen. **20**A ellos los debes instruir en las leyes y en las enseñanzas de Dios, y darles a conocer la conducta que deben llevar y las

obligaciones que deben cumplir. **21**Elige tú mismo entre el pueblo hombres capaces y temerosos de Dios, que amen la verdad y aborrezcan las ganancias mal habidas, y desígnalos jefes de mil, de cien, de cincuenta y de diez personas. **22**Serán ellos los que funjan como jueces de tiempo completo, atendiendo los casos sencillos, y los casos difíciles te los traerán a ti. Eso te aligerará la carga, porque te ayudarán a llevarla. **23**Si pones esto en práctica y Dios así te lo ordena, podrás aguantar; el pueblo, por su parte, se irá a casa satisfecho.

24Moisés atendió a la voz de su suegro y siguió sus sugerencias. **25**Escogió entre todos los israelitas hombres capaces, y los puso al frente de los israelitas como jefes de mil, cien, cincuenta y diez personas. **26**Estos jefes fungían como jueces de tiempo completo, atendiendo los casos sencillos pero remitiendo a Moisés los casos difíciles.

27Más tarde Moisés despidió a su suegro, quien volvió entonces a su país.

Los israelitas en el Sinaí

19 Los israelitas llegaron al desierto de Sinaí a los tres meses de haber salido de Egipto. **2**Después de partir de Refidín, se internaron en el desierto de Sinaí, y allí en el desierto acamparon, frente al monte. Y desde allí lo llamó el SEÑOR y le dijo:

«Anúnciale esto al pueblo de Jacob;
　　declárale esto al pueblo de Israel:
4"Ustedes son testigos de lo que hice con
　　Egipto,
y de que los he traído hacia mí
　　como sobre alas de águila.
5Si ahora ustedes me son del todo obedientes,
　　y cumplen mi *pacto,
serán mi propiedad exclusiva
　　entre todas las naciones.
Aunque toda la tierra me pertenece,
6ustedes serán para mí un reino de sacerdotes
　　y una nación santa."

»Comunícales todo esto a los israelitas.»

7Moisés volvió y convocó a los *ancianos del pueblo para exponerles todas estas palabras que el SEÑOR le había ordenado comunicarles, **8**y todo el pueblo respondió a una sola voz: «Cumpliremos con todo lo que el SEÑOR nos ha ordenado.»

Así que Moisés le llevó al SEÑOR la respuesta del pueblo, **9**y el SEÑOR le dijo:

—Voy a presentarme ante ti en medio de una densa nube, para que el pueblo me oiga hablar contigo y así tenga siempre confianza en ti.

Moisés refirió al SEÑOR lo que el pueblo le había dicho, **10**y el SEÑOR le dijo:

—Ve y consagra al pueblo hoy y mañana. Diles que laven sus ropas **11**y que se preparen para el tercer día, porque en ese mismo día yo descenderé sobre el monte Sinaí, a la vista de todo el pueblo. **12**Pon un cerco alrededor del monte para que el pueblo no pase. Diles que no suban al monte, y que ni siquiera pongan un pie en él, pues cualquiera que lo toque será condenado a muerte. **13**Sea *hombre o animal, no quedará con vida. Quien se atreva a tocarlo, morirá a pedradas o a flechazos. Sólo podrán subir al monte cuando se oiga el toque largo de la trompeta.

---

b 17:16 *estandarte*. Lit. *Trono.*　　**c** 18:3 En hebreo, *Guersón* suena como la frase que significa *extranjero allí.*　　**d** 18:4 En hebreo, *Eliezer* significa *mi Dios es mi ayuda.*

14En cuanto Moisés bajó del monte, consagró al pueblo; ellos, por su parte, lavaron sus ropas. 15Luego Moisés les dijo: «Prepárense para el tercer día, y absténganse de relaciones sexuales.»

16En la madrugada del tercer día hubo truenos y relámpagos, y una densa nube se posó sobre el monte. Un toque muy fuerte de trompeta puso a temblar a todos los que estaban en el campamento. 17Entonces Moisés sacó del campamento al pueblo para que fuera a su encuentro con Dios, y ellos se detuvieron al pie del monte Sinaí. 18El monte estaba cubierto de humo, porque el SEÑOR había descendido sobre él en medio de fuego. Era tanto el humo que salía del monte, que parecía un horno; todo el monte se sacudía violentamente, 19y el sonido de la trompeta era cada vez más fuerte. Entonces habló Moisés, y Dios le respondió en el trueno.e

20El SEÑOR descendió a la cumbre del monte Sinaí, y desde allí llamó a Moisés para que subiera. Cuando Moisés llegó a la cumbre, 21el SEÑOR le dijo:

—Baja y advierte al pueblo que no intenten ir más allá del cerco para verme, no sea que muchos de ellos pierdan la vida. 22Hasta los sacerdotes que se acercan a mí deben consagrarse; de lo contrario, yo arremeteré contra ellos.

23Moisés le dijo al SEÑOR:

—El pueblo no puede subir al monte Sinaí, pues tú mismo nos has advertido: "Pon un cerco alrededor del monte, y conságramelo."

24El SEÑOR le respondió:

—Baja y dile a Aarón que suba contigo. Pero ni los sacerdotes ni el pueblo deben intentar subir adonde estoy, pues de lo contrario, yo arremeteré contra ellos.

25Moisés bajó y repitió eso mismo al pueblo.

Los Diez Mandamientos
20:1-17 — Dt 5:6-21

20 Dios habló, y dio a conocer todos estos mandamientos:

2 «Yo soy el SEÑOR tu Dios. Yo te saqué de Egipto, del país donde eras esclavo.

3 »No tengas otros dioses además de mí.f

4 »No te hagas ningún ídolo, ni nada que guarde semejanza con lo que hay arriba en el cielo, ni con lo que hay abajo en la tierra, ni con lo que hay en las aguas debajo de la tierra. 5No te inclines delante de ellos ni los adores. Yo, el SEÑOR tu Dios, soy un Dios celoso. Cuando los padres son malvados y me odian, yo castigo a sus hijos hasta la tercera y cuarta generación. 6Por el contrario, cuando me aman y cumplen mis mandamientos, les muestro mi amor por mil generaciones.

7 »No pronuncies el *nombre del SEÑOR tu Dios a la ligera. Yo, el SEÑOR, no tendré por inocente a quien se atreva a pronunciar mi nombre a la ligera.

8 »Acuérdate del *sábado, para consagrarlo. 9Trabaja seis días, y haz en ellos todo lo que tengas que hacer, 10pero el día séptimo será un día de reposo para honrar al SEÑOR tu Dios. No hagas en ese día ningún trabajo, ni tampoco tu hijo, ni tu hija, ni tu esclavo, ni tu esclava, ni tus animales, ni tampoco los extranjeros que vivan en tus ciudades.g 11Acuérdate de que en seis días hizo el SEÑOR los cielos y la tierra,

el mar y todo lo que hay en ellos, y que descansó el séptimo día. Por eso el SEÑOR bendijo y consagró el día de reposo.

12 »Honra a tu padre y a tu madre, para que disfrutes de una larga vida en la tierra que te da el SEÑOR tu Dios.

13 »No mates.

14 »No cometas adulterio.

15 »No robes.

16 »No des falso testimonio en contra de tu prójimo.

17 »No codicies la casa de tu prójimo: No codicies su esposa, ni su esclavo, ni su esclava, ni su buey, ni su burro, ni nada que le pertenezca.»

Reacción temerosa de los israelitas

18Ante ese espectáculo de truenos y relámpagos, de sonidos de trompeta y de la montaña envuelta en humo, los israelitas temblaban de miedo y se mantenían a distancia. 19Así que le suplicaron a Moisés:

—Háblanos tú, y te escucharemos. Si Dios nos habla, seguramente moriremos.

20—No tengan miedo —les respondió Moisés—. Dios ha venido a ponerlos a prueba, para que sientan temor de él y no pequen.

21Entonces Moisés se acercó a la densa oscuridad en la que estaba Dios, pero los israelitas se mantuvieron a distancia.

El altar de piedra

22El SEÑOR le ordenó a Moisés:

«Diles lo siguiente a los israelitas: "Ustedes mismos han oído que les he hablado desde el cielo. 23No me ofendan; no se hagan dioses de plata o de oro, ni los adoren. 24Háganme un altar de tierra, y ofrézcanme sobre él sus *holocaustos y sacrificios de *comunión, sus ovejas y sus toros. Yo vendré al lugar donde les pida invocar mi *nombre, y los bendeciré. 25Si me hacen un altar de piedra, no lo construyan con piedras labradas, pues las herramientas profanan la piedra. 26Y no le pongan escalones a mi altar, no sea que al subir se les vean los genitales."

Esclavos hebreos
21:2-6 — Dt 15:12-18

21 »Éstas son las leyes que tú les expondrás:

2»Si alguien compra un esclavo hebreo, éste le servirá durante seis años, pero en el séptimo año recobrará su libertad sin pagar nada a cambio.

3»Si el esclavo llega soltero, soltero se irá.

»Si llega casado, su esposa se irá con él.

4»Si el amo le da mujer al esclavo, como ella es propiedad del amo, serán también del amo los hijos o hijas que el esclavo tenga con ella. Así que el esclavo se irá solo.

5»Si el esclavo llega a declarar: "Yo no quiero recobrar mi libertad, pues les tengo cariño a mi amo, a mi mujer y a mis hijos", 6el amo lo hará comparecer ante los jueces,h luego lo llevará a una puerta, o al marco de una puerta, y allí le horadará la oreja con un punzón. Así el esclavo se quedará de por vida con su amo.

7»Si alguien vende a su hija como esclava, la muchacha no se podrá ir como los esclavos varones.

8»Si el amo no toma a la muchacha como mujer por no ser ella de su agrado, deberá permitir que sea rescatada. Como la rechazó, no podrá vendérsela a ningún extranjero.

---

e 19:19 en el trueno. Lit. con su voz.   f 20:3 además de mí. Lit. junto a mí.   g 20:10 en tus ciudades. Lit. dentro de tus puertas.
h 21:6 ante los jueces. Alt. ante Dios.

⁹»Si el amo entrega la muchacha a su hijo, deberá tratarla con todos los derechos de una hija.

¹⁰»Si toma como esposa a otra mujer, no podrá privar a su primera esposa de sus derechos conyugales, ni de alimentación y vestido.

¹¹»Si no le provee esas tres cosas, la mujer podrá irse sin que se pague nada por ella.

Injurias personales

¹²»El que hiera a otro y lo mate será condenado a muerte.

¹³»Si el homicidio no fue intencional, pues ya estaba de Dios que ocurriera, el asesino podrá huir al lugar que yo designaré.

¹⁴»Si el homicidio es premeditado, el asesino será condenado a muerte aun cuando busque refugio en mi altar.

¹⁵»El que mate a su padre o a su madre será condenado a muerte.

¹⁶»El que secuestre a otro y lo venda, o al ser descubierto lo tenga aún en su poder, será condenado a muerte.

¹⁷»El que maldiga a su padre o a su madre será condenado a muerte.

¹⁸»Si en una riña alguien golpea a otro con una piedra, o con el puño,ⁱ y el herido no muere pero se ve obligado a guardar cama, ¹⁹el agresor deberá indemnizar al herido por daños y perjuicios. Sin embargo, quedará libre de culpa si el herido se levanta y puede caminar por sí mismo o con la ayuda de un bastón.

²⁰»Si alguien golpea con un palo a su esclavo o a su esclava, y como resultado del golpe él o ella muere, su crimen será castigado. ²¹Pero si después de uno o dos días el esclavo se recupera, el agresor no será castigado porque el esclavo era de su propiedad.

²²»Si en una riña los contendientes golpean a una mujer encinta, y la hacen abortar pero sin poner en peligro su *vida, se les impondrá la multa que el marido de la mujer exija y que en justicia le corresponda.

²³»Si se pone en peligro la vida de la mujer, ésta será la indemnización: vida por vida, ²⁴ojo por ojo, diente por diente, mano por mano, pie por pie, ²⁵quemadura por quemadura, golpe por golpe, herida por herida.

²⁶»Si alguien golpea en el ojo a su esclavo o a su esclava, y se lo saca, en compensación por el ojo los pondrá en libertad.

²⁷»Si alguien le rompe un diente a su esclavo o a su esclava, en compensación por el diente los pondrá en libertad.

²⁸»Si un toro cornea y mata a un hombre o a una mujer, se matará al toro a pedradas y no se comerá su carne. En tal caso, no se hará responsable al dueño del toro.

²⁹»Si el toro tiene la costumbre de cornear, se le matará a pedradas si llega a matar a un hombre o a una mujer. Si su dueño sabía de la costumbre del toro, pero no lo mantuvo sujeto, también será condenado a muerte.

³⁰»Si a cambio de su vida se le exige algún pago, deberá pagarlo.

³¹»Esta misma ley se aplicará en caso de que el toro cornee a un muchacho o a una muchacha.

³²»Si el toro cornea a un esclavo o a una esclava, el dueño del toro deberá pagarle treinta monedasʲ de plata al amo del esclavo o de la esclava. El toro será apedreado.

³³»Si alguien deja abierto un pozo, o cava un pozo y no lo tapa, y llegan a caerse en él un buey o un asno, ³⁴el dueño del pozo indemnizará al dueño del animal, y podrá quedarse con el animal muerto.

³⁵»Si un toro cornea a otro toro, y el toro corneado muere, se venderá el toro vivo, y los dos dueños se repartirán por partes iguales el dinero y el animal muerto.

³⁶»Si el toro tenía la maña de cornear, y su dueño le conocía esta maña pero no lo mantuvo amarrado, tendrá que pagar por el animal muerto con un animal vivo, pero podrá quedarse con el animal muerto.

Protección de la propiedad

22 »Si alguien roba un toro o una oveja, y lo mata o lo vende, deberá devolver cinco cabezas de ganado por el toro, y cuatro ovejas por la oveja.

²»Si a alguien se le sorprende robando, y se le mata, su muerte no se considerará homicidio.

³»Si se mata al ladrón a plena luz del día, su muerte se considerará homicidio.

»El ladrón está obligado a restituir lo robado. Si no tiene con qué hacerlo, será vendido para restituir lo robado.

⁴»Si el animal robado se halla en su poder y todavía con vida, deberá restituirlo doble, ya sea que se trate de un toro, un asno o una oveja.

⁵»Si alguien apacienta su ganado en un campo o en una viña, y por dejar a sus animales sueltos ellos pastan en campo ajeno, el dueño del animal deberá reparar el daño con lo mejor de su cosecha.

⁶»Si se prende fuego en pasto seco, y el fuego se propaga y quema algún trigal, o el trigo ya apilado, o algún campo sembrado, el que haya comenzado el fuego deberá reparar el daño.

⁷»Si alguien deja dinero o bienes en la casa de un amigo, y esos bienes le son robados, el ladrón deberá devolver el doble, en caso de que lo atrapen.

⁸»Si no se atrapa al ladrón, el dueño de la casa deberá comparecer ante los juecesᵏ para que se determine si no dispuso de los bienes del otro.

⁹»En todos los casos de posesión ilegal, las dos partes deberán llevar el asunto ante los jueces. El que sea declarado culpable deberá restituir el doble a su prójimo, ya sea que se trate de un toro, o de un asno, o de una oveja, o de ropa, o de cualquier otra cosa perdida que alguien reclame como de su propiedad.

¹⁰»Si alguien deja al cuidado de algún amigo suyo un asno, un toro, una oveja, o cualquier otro animal, y el animal muere, o sufre algún daño, o es robado sin que lo vea, ¹¹el amigo del dueño jurará ante el SEÑOR no haberse adueñado de la propiedad de su amigo. El dueño deberá aceptar ese juramento, y el amigo no deberá restituirle nada.

¹²»Si el animal le fue robado al amigo, éste deberá indemnizar al dueño.

¹³»Si el animal fue despedazado por una fiera, el amigo no tendrá que indemnizar al dueño si presenta como evidencia los restos del animal.

¹⁴»Si alguien pide prestado un animal de algún amigo suyo, y el animal sufre algún daño, o muere, no estando presente su dueño, el que lo pidió prestado deberá restituirlo.

¹⁵»Si el dueño del animal estaba presente, el que pidió prestado el animal no tendrá que pagar nada.

»Si el animal fue alquilado, el precio del alquiler cubrirá la pérdida.

ⁱ **21:18** *el puño* Alt. *alguna herramienta.*   ʲ **21:32** *monedas.* Lit. **Siclos.*   ᵏ **22:8** *ante los jueces.* Alt. *ante Dios;* también en v. 9.

Responsabilidades sociales

16»Si alguien seduce a una mujer virgen que no esté comprometida para casarse, y se acuesta con ella, deberá pagarle su precio al padre y tomarla por esposa. 17Aun si el padre se niega a entregársela, el seductor deberá pagar el precio establecido para las vírgenes.

18»No dejes con vida a ninguna hechicera.

19»Todo el que tenga relaciones sexuales con un animal será condenado a muerte.

20»Todo el que ofrezca sacrificios a otros dioses, en vez de ofrecérselos al SEÑOR, será condenado a muerte.

21»No maltrates ni oprimas a los extranjeros, pues también tú y tu pueblo fueron extranjeros en Egipto.

22»No explotes a las viudas ni a los huérfanos, 23porque si tú y tu pueblo lo hacen, y ellos me piden ayuda, yo te aseguro que atenderé a su clamor: 24arderá mi furor y los mataré a ustedes a filo de espada. ¡Y sus mujeres se quedarán viudas, y sus hijos se quedarán huérfanos!

25»Si uno de ustedes presta dinero a algún necesitado de mi pueblo, no deberá tratarlo como los prestamistas ni le cobrará intereses.

26»Si alguien toma en prenda el manto de su prójimo, deberá devolvérselo al caer la noche. 27Ese manto es lo único que tiene para abrigarse; no tiene otra cosa sobre la cual dormir. Si se queja ante mí, yo atenderé a su clamor, pues soy un Dios compasivo.

28»No blasfemes nunca contra Dios,[l] ni maldigas al jefe de tu pueblo.

29»No te demores en presentarme las ofrendas de tus graneros y de tus lagares.[m]

»Tus hijos primogénitos serán para mí.

30»También serán para mí tus toros y tus ovejas. Los dejarás con sus madres siete días, pero al octavo día me los entregarás.

31»Ustedes serán mi pueblo *santo.

»No comerán la carne de ningún animal que haya sido despedazado por las fieras. Esa carne se la echarán a los perros.

Leyes de justicia y de misericordia

23 »No divulgues informes falsos.

»No te hagas cómplice del malvado ni apoyes los testimonios del violento.

2»No imites la maldad de las mayorías.

»No te dejes llevar por la mayoría en un proceso legal.

»No perviertas la justicia tomando partido con la mayoría.

3»No seas parcial con el pobre en sus demandas legales.

4»Si encuentras un toro o un asno perdido, devuélvelo, aunque sea de tu enemigo.

5»Si ves un asno caído bajo el peso de su carga, no lo dejes así; ayúdalo, aunque sea de tu enemigo.

6»No tuerzas la justicia contra los pobres de tu pueblo en sus demandas legales.

7»Mantente al margen de cuestiones fraudulentas.

»No le quites la vida al que es inocente y honrado, porque yo no absolveré al malvado.

8»No aceptes soborno, porque nubla la vista y tuerce las sentencias justas.

9»No opriman al extranjero, pues ya lo han experimentado en carne propia: ustedes mismos fueron extranjeros en Egipto.

Leyes sabáticas

10»Seis años sembrarás tus campos y recogerás tus cosechas, 11pero al séptimo año no cultivarás la tierra. Déjala descansar, para que la gente pobre del pueblo obtenga de ella su alimento, y para que los animales del campo se coman lo que la gente deje.

»Haz lo mismo con tus viñas y con tus olivares.

12»Seis días trabajarás, pero el día séptimo descansarán tus bueyes y tus asnos, y recobrarán sus fuerzas los esclavos nacidos en casa y los extranjeros.

13»Cumplan con todo lo que les he ordenado.

»No invoquen los *nombres de otros dioses. Jamás los pronuncien.

Las tres fiestas anuales

14»Tres veces al año harás fiesta en mi honor.

15»La fiesta de los Panes sin levadura la celebrarás en el mes de *aviv, que es la fecha establecida. Fue en ese mes cuando ustedes salieron de Egipto. De acuerdo con mis instrucciones, siete días comerán pan sin levadura.

»Nadie se presentará ante mí con las manos vacías.

16»La fiesta de la cosecha la celebrarás cuando recojas las *primicias de tus siembras.

»La fiesta de recolección de fin de año la celebrarás cuando recojas tus cosechas.

17»Tres veces al año todo varón se presentará ante mí, su SEÑOR y Dios.

18»No mezcles con levadura la sangre del sacrificio que me ofrezcas.

»No guardes hasta el día siguiente la grasa que me ofreces en las fiestas.

19»Llevarás a la casa del SEÑOR tu Dios lo mejor de tus primicias.

»No cocerás ningún cabrito en la leche de su madre.

El ángel del SEÑOR

20»Date cuenta, Israel, que yo envío mi ángel delante de ti, para que te proteja en el camino y te lleve al lugar que te he preparado. 21Préstale atención y obedécelo. No te rebeles contra él, porque va en representación mía y no perdonará tu rebelión. 22Si lo obedeces y cumples con todas mis instrucciones, seré enemigo de tus enemigos y me opondré a quienes se te opongan. 23Mi ángel te guiará y te introducirá en la tierra de estos pueblos que voy a exterminar: tierra de amorreos, hititas, ferezeos, cananeos, heveos y jebuseos.

24»No te inclines ante los dioses de esos pueblos. No les rindas culto ni imites sus prácticas. Más bien, derriba sus ídolos y haz pedazos sus piedras sagradas.

25»Adora al SEÑOR tu Dios, y él bendecirá tu pan y tu agua.

»Yo apartaré de ustedes toda enfermedad.

26»En tu país ninguna mujer abortará ni será estéril. ¡Yo te concederé larga vida!

27»En toda nación donde pongas el pie haré que tus enemigos te tengan miedo, se turben y huyan de ti.

28»Delante de ti enviaré avispas, para que ahuyenten a los heveos, cananeos e hititas. 29Sin embargo, no los desalojaré en un solo año, no sea que, al quedarse desolada la tierra, aumente el número de animales salvajes y te ataquen. 30Los desalojaré poco a poco, hasta que seas lo bastante fuerte para tomar posesión de la tierra.

---

l **22:28** *No blasfemes nunca contra Dios.* Alt. *Nunca desprecies a los jueces.* m **22:29** *las ofrendas ... lagares.* Frase de difícil traducción.

31»Extenderé las fronteras de tu país, desde el *Mar Rojo hasta el mar Mediterráneo,n y desde el desierto hasta el río Éufrates. Pondré bajo tu dominio a los que habitan allí, y tú los desalojarás.

32»No hagas ningún *pacto con ellos ni con sus dioses.

33»Si los dejas vivir en tu tierra, te pondrán una trampa para que adores a sus dioses, y acabarás pecando contra mí.»

Ratificación del pacto

24 También le dijo el SEÑOR a Moisés: «Sube al monte a verme, junto con Aarón, Nadab y Abiú, y setenta de los ancianos de Israel. Ellos podrán arrodillarse a cierta distancia, 2pero sólo tú, Moisés, podrás acercarte a mí. El resto del pueblo no deberá acercarse ni subir contigo.»

3Moisés fue y refirió al pueblo todas las palabras y disposiciones del SEÑOR, y ellos respondieron a una voz: «Haremos todo lo que el SEÑOR ha dicho.» 4Moisés puso entonces por escrito lo que el SEÑOR había dicho.

A la mañana siguiente, madrugó y levantó un altar al pie del monte, y en representación de las doce tribus de Israel consagró doce piedras. 5Luego envió a unos jóvenes israelitas para que ofrecieran al SEÑOR novillos como *holocaustos y sacrificios de *comunión. 6La mitad de la sangre la echó Moisés en unos tazones, y la otra mitad la roció sobre el altar. 7Después tomó el libro del *pacto y lo leyó ante el pueblo, y ellos respondieron:

—Haremos todo lo que el SEÑOR ha dicho, y le obedeceremos.

8Moisés tomó la sangre, roció al pueblo con ella y dijo:

—Ésta es la sangre del pacto que, con base en estas palabras, el SEÑOR ha hecho con ustedes.

9Moisés y Aarón, Nadab y Abiú, y los setenta ancianos de Israel subieron 10y vieron al Dios de Israel. Bajo sus pies había una especie de pavimento de zafiro, tan claro como el cielo mismo. 11Y a pesar de que estos jefes de los israelitas vieron a Dios, siguieron con vida,ñ pues Dios no alzó su mano contra ellos.

12El SEÑOR le dijo a Moisés: «Sube a encontrarte conmigo en el monte, y quédate allí. Voy a darte las tablas con la *ley y los mandamientos que he escrito para guiarlos en la vida.»

13Moisés subió al monte de Dios, acompañado por su asistente Josué, 14pero a los ancianos les dijo: «Esperen aquí hasta que volvamos. Aarón y Jur se quedarán aquí con ustedes. Si alguno tiene un problema, que acuda a ellos.»

15En cuanto Moisés subió, una nube cubrió el monte, 16y la gloria del SEÑOR se posó sobre el Sinaí. Seis días la nube cubrió el monte. Al séptimo día, desde el interior de la nube el SEÑOR llamó a Moisés. 17A los ojos de los israelitas, la gloria del SEÑOR en la cumbre del monte parecía un fuego consumidor. 18Moisés se internó en la nube y subió al monte, y allí permaneció cuarenta días y cuarenta noches.

Las ofrendas para el santuario
25:1-7 — Éx 35:4-9

25 El SEÑOR habló con Moisés y le dijo: 2«Ordénales a los israelitas que me traigan una ofrenda. La deben presentar todos los que sientan deseos de traérmela. 3Como ofrenda se les aceptará lo siguiente: oro, plata, bronce, 4lana teñida de púrpura, carmesí y escarlata; lino fino, pelo de cabra, 5pieles de carnero teñidas de rojo, pieles de delfín, madera de acacia, 6aceite para las lámparas, especias para aromatizar el aceite de la unción y el incienso, 7y piedras de ónice y otras piedras preciosas para adornar el *efod y el pectoral del sacerdote. 8Después me harán un santuario, para que yo habite entre ustedes. 9El santuario y todo su mobiliario deberán ser una réplica exacta del modelo que yo te mostraré.

El arca
25:10-20 — Éx 37:1-9

10»Hazo un arca de madera de acacia, de un metro con diez centímetros de largo, setenta centímetros de ancho y setenta centímetros de alto.p 11Recúbrela de oro puro por dentro y por fuera, y ponle su derredor una moldura de oro. 12Funde cuatro anillos de oro para colocarlos en sus cuatro patas, dos en cada costado. 13Prepara luego unas varas de madera de acacia, y recúbrelas de oro. 14Introduce las varas en los anillos que van a los costados del arca, para transportarla. 15Deja las varas en los anillos del arca, y no las saques de allí, 16y pon dentro del arca la *ley que voy a entregarte.

17»Haz un *propiciatorio de oro puro, de un metro con diez centímetros de largo por setenta centímetros de ancho,q 18y también dos *querubines de oro labrado a martillo, para los dos extremos del propiciatorio. 19En cada uno de los extremos irá un querubín. Hazlos de modo que formen una sola pieza con el propiciatorio.

20»Los querubines deberán tener las alas extendidas por encima del propiciatorio, y cubrirlo con ellas. Quedarán el uno frente al otro, mirando hacia el propiciatorio.

21»Coloca el propiciatorio encima del arca, y pon dentro de ella la ley que voy a entregarte. 22Yo me reuniré allí contigo en medio de los dos querubines que están sobre el arca del *pacto. Desde la parte superior del propiciatorio te daré todas las instrucciones que habrás de comunicarles a los israelitas.

La mesa
25:23-29 — Éx 37:10-16

23»Haz una mesa de madera de acacia, de noventa centímetros de largo por cuarenta y cinco de ancho y setenta de alto.r 24Recúbrela de oro puro, y ponle su derredor una moldura de oro. 25Haz también un reborde de veinte centímetros de ancho, y una moldura de oro para ponerla alrededor del reborde.

26»Haz cuatro anillos de oro para la mesa, y sújetalos a sus cuatro esquinas, donde van las cuatro patas. 27Los anillos deben quedar junto al reborde, a fin de que por ellos pasen las varas para transportar la mesa.

28»Esas varas deben ser de madera de acacia, y estar recubiertas de oro. 29También deben ser de oro puro sus platos y sus bandejas, así como sus jarras y tazones para verter las ofrendas. 30Sobre la mesa

---

n 23:31 mar Mediterráneo. Lit. mar de los filisteos.   ñ 24:11 siguieron con vida. Lit. comieron y bebieron.   o 25:10 Haz (LXX y Pentateuco Samaritano); Hagan ustedes (TM).   p 25:10 de un metro ... de alto. Lit. de dos *codos y medio de largo, de un codo y medio de ancho y de un codo y medio de alto.   q 25:17 de un metro ... de ancho. Lit. de dos codos y medio de largo por un codo y medio de ancho.   r 25:23 de noventa ... de alto. Lit. de dos codos de largo por un codo de ancho, y un codo y medio de alto.   s 25:25 veinte centímetros. Lit. un *palmo.

pondrás el *pan de la Presencia, para que esté ante mí siempre.

El candelabro
25:31-39 — Éx 37:17-24

31»Haz un candelabro de oro puro labrado a martillo. Su base, su tallo y sus copas, cálices y flores, formarán una sola pieza. 32Seis de sus brazos se abrirán a los costados, tres de un lado y tres del otro. 33Cada uno de los seis brazos del candelabro tendrá tres copas en forma de flor de almendro, con cálices y pétalos. 34El candelabro mismo tendrá cuatro copas en forma de flor de almendro, con cálices y pétalos. 35Cada uno de los tres pares de brazos tendrá un cáliz en la parte inferior, donde se unen con el tallo del candelabro. 36Los cálices y los brazos deben formar una sola pieza con el candelabro, y ser de oro puro, labrado a martillo.

37»Hazle también sus siete lámparas, y colócalas de tal modo que alumbren hacia el frente. 38Sus cortapabilos y braseros deben ser de oro puro. 39Para hacer el candelabro y todos estos accesorios se usarán treinta y tres kilos de oro puro.

40»Procura que todo esto sea una réplica exacta de lo que se te mostró en el monte.

El santuario
26:1-37 — Éx 36:8-38

26 »Haz el santuario con diez cortinas de lino fino y de lana teñida de púrpura, carmesí y escarlata, con dos *querubines artísticamente bordados en ellas. 2Todas las cortinas deben medir lo mismo, es decir, doce metros y medio de largo por un metro con ochenta centímetros de ancho.u

3»Cose cinco cortinas, uniendo la una con la otra por el borde, y haz lo mismo con las otras cinco. 4En el borde superior del primer conjunto de cortinas pon unas presillas de lana teñida de púrpura, lo mismo que en el borde del otro conjunto de cortinas. 5En las cortinas del primer conjunto pon cincuenta presillas, lo mismo que en las cortinas del otro conjunto, de modo que cada presilla tenga su pareja. 6Haz luego cincuenta ganchos de oro para que las cortinas queden enganchadas una con otra, de modo que el santuario tenga unidad de conjunto.

7»Haz once cortinas de pelo de cabra para cubrir el santuario a la manera de una tienda de campaña. 8Todas ellas deben medir lo mismo, es decir, trece metros y medio de largo por un metro con ochenta centímetros de ancho.v 9Cose cinco cortinas en un conjunto, y las otras seis en otro conjunto, doblando la sexta cortina en la parte frontal del santuario.

10»Haz cincuenta presillas en el borde de la cortina con que termina el primer conjunto, y otras cincuenta presillas en el borde de la cortina con que termina el segundo. 11Haz luego cincuenta ganchos de bronce y mételos en las presillas para formar el santuario, de modo que éste tenga unidad de conjunto. 12Las diez cortinas tendrán una cortina restante, que quedará colgando a espaldas del santuario. 13A esta cortina le sobrarán cincuenta centímetrosw en cada extremo, y con esa parte sobrante se cerrará el santuario.

14»Haz para el santuario un toldo de piel de carnero, teñido de rojo, y para la parte superior un toldo de piel de delfín. 15Prepara para el santuario

unos tablones de acacia, para que sirvan de pilares. 16Cada tablón debe medir cuatro metros y medio de largo por setenta centímetros de ancho,x 17y contar con dos ranuras para que cada tablón encaje con el otro. Todos los tablones para el santuario los harás así. 18Serán veinte los tablones para el lado sur del santuario.

19»Haz también cuarenta bases de plata para colocarlas debajo de los tablones, dos bases por tablón, para que las dos ranuras de cada tablón encajen en cada base. 20Para el lado opuesto, es decir, para el lado norte del santuario, prepararás también veinte tablones 21y cuarenta bases de plata, y pondrás dos bases debajo de cada tablón. 22Pondrás seis tablones en el lado posterior, que es el lado occidental del santuario, 23y dos tablones más en las esquinas de ese mismo lado. 24Estos dos tablones deben ser dobles en la base, quedando unidos por un solo anillo en la parte superior. Haz lo mismo en ambas esquinas, 25de modo que haya ocho tablones y dieciséis bases de plata, es decir, dos bases debajo de cada tablón.

26»Prepara también unos travesaños de acacia: cinco para los tablones de un costado del santuario, 27cinco para los del costado opuesto, y cinco para los del costado occidental, es decir, para la parte posterior. 28El travesaño central deberá pasar de uno a otro extremo, a media altura de los tablones. 29Recubre de oro los tablones, y haz unos anillos de oro para que los travesaños pasen por ellos. También debes recubrir de oro los travesaños. 30Erige el santuario ciñéndote al modelo que se te mostró en el monte.

31»Haz una cortina de púrpura, carmesí, escarlata y lino fino, con querubines artísticamente bordados en ella. 32Cuélgala con ganchos de oro en cuatro postes de madera de acacia recubiertos de oro, los cuales levantarás sobre cuatro bases de plata. 33Cuelga de los ganchos la cortina, la cual separará el Lugar Santo del Lugar Santísimo, y coloca el arca del *pacto detrás de la cortina. 34Pon el *propiciatorio sobre el arca del pacto, dentro del Lugar Santísimo, 35y coloca la mesa fuera de la cortina, en el lado norte del santuario. El candelabro lo pondrás frente a la mesa, en el lado sur.

36»Haz para la entrada del santuario una cortina de púrpura, carmesí, escarlata y lino fino, recamada artísticamente. 37Para esta cortina prepara cinco postes de acacia recubiertos de oro, con sus respectivos ganchos de oro, y funde para los postes cinco bases de bronce.

El altar de los holocaustos
27:1-8 — Éx 38:1-7

27 »Haz un altar de madera de acacia, cuadrado, de dos metros con treinta centímetrosy por lado, y de un metro con treinta centímetrosz de alto. 2Ponle un cuerno en cada una de sus cuatro esquinas, de manera que los cuernos y el altar formen una sola pieza, y recúbre de bronce el altar. 3Haz de bronce todos sus utensilios, es decir, sus portacenizas, sus tenazas, sus aspersorios, sus tridentes y sus braseros. 4Hazle también un enrejado de bronce, con un anillo del mismo metal en cada una de sus cuatro esquinas. 5El anillo irá bajo el reborde del altar, de modo que quede a media altura del mismo. 6Prepara para el altar varas de madera de acacia, y

---

t 25:39 treinta y tres kilos. Lit. un *talento. u 26:2 doce metros ... de ancho. Lit. veintiocho *codos de largo por cuatro codos de ancho. v 26:8 trece metros ... de ancho. Lit. treinta codos de largo por cuatro codos de ancho. w 26:13 cincuenta centímetros. Lit. un codo. x 26:16 cuatro metros ... de ancho. Lit. diez codos de largo por un codo y medio de ancho. y 27:1 dos metros con treinta centímetros. Lit. cinco *codos. z 27:1 un metro con treinta centímetros. Lit. tres codos.

recúbrelas de bronce. 7Las varas deberán pasar por los anillos, de modo que sobresalgan en los dos extremos del altar para que éste pueda ser transportado. 8El altar lo harás hueco y de tablas, exactamente como el que se te mostró en el monte.

El atrio
27:9-19 — Éx 38:9-20

9»Haz un atrio para el santuario. El lado sur debe medir cuarenta y cinco metrosᵃ de largo, y tener cortinas de lino fino, 10veinte postes y veinte bases de bronce. Los postes deben contar con empalmes y ganchos de plata. 11También el lado norte debe medir cuarenta y cinco metros de largo y tener cortinas, veinte postes y veinte bases de bronce. Los postes deben también contar con empalmes y ganchos de plata.

12»A todo lo ancho del lado occidental del atrio, que debe medir veintidós metros y medio,ᵇ habrá cortinas, diez postes y diez bases. 13El lado oriental del atrio, que da hacia la salida del sol, también deberá medir veintidós metros de largo. 14Habrá cortinas de siete metrosᶜ de largo, y tres postes y tres bases a un lado de la entrada, 15lo mismo que del otro lado.

16»A la entrada del atrio habrá una cortina de nueve metrosᵈ de largo, de púrpura, carmesí, escarlata y lino fino, recamada artísticamente, y además cuatro postes y cuatro bases. 17Todos los postes alrededor del atrio deben tener empalmes y ganchos de plata, y bases de bronce. 18El atrio medirá cuarenta y cinco metros de largo por veintidós metros y medio de ancho,ᵉ con cortinas de lino fino de dos metros con treinta centímetrosᶠ de alto, y con bases de bronce. 19Todas las estacas y los demás utensilios para el servicio del santuario serán de bronce, incluyendo las estacas del atrio.

El aceite para el candelabro
27:20-21 — Lv 24:1-3

20»Ordénales a los israelitas que te traigan aceite puro de oliva, para que las lámparas estén siempre encendidas. 21Aarón y sus hijos deberán mantenerlas encendidas toda la noche en presencia del SEÑOR, en la *Tienda de reunión, fuera de la cortina que está ante el arca del *pacto. Esta ley deberá cumplirse entre los israelitas siempre, por todas las generaciones.

Las vestiduras sacerdotales

28 »Haz que comparezcan ante ti tu hermano Aarón y sus hijos Nadab, Abiú, Eleazar e Itamar. De entre todos los israelitas, ellos me servirán como sacerdotes. 2Hazle a tu hermano Aarón vestiduras sagradas que le confieran honra y dignidad. 3Habla con todos los expertos a quienes he dado habilidades especiales, para que hagan las vestiduras de Aarón, y así lo consagre yo como mi sacerdote. 4»Las vestiduras que le harás son las siguientes: un pectoral, un *efod, un manto, una túnica bordada, un turbante y una faja. Estas vestiduras sagradas se harán para tu hermano Aarón y para sus hijos, a fin de que me sirvan como sacerdotes. 5Al efecto se usará oro, púrpura, carmesí, escarlata y lino.

El efod
28:6-14 — Éx 39:2-7

6»El *efod se bordará artísticamente con oro, púrpura, carmesí, escarlata y lino fino. 7En sus dos extremos tendrá hombreras con cintas, para que pueda sujetarse. 8El cinturón bordado con el que se sujeta el efod deberá ser del mismo material, es decir, de oro, púrpura, carmesí, escarlata y lino fino, y formará con el efod una sola pieza.

9»Toma dos piedras de ónice, y graba en ellas los *nombres de los doce hijos de Israel 10por orden de nacimiento, seis nombres en una piedra, y seis en la otra. 11Un joyero grabará los nombres en las piedras, como los orfebres graban sellos: engarzará las piedras en filigrana de oro 12y las sujetará a las hombreras del efod. Así Aarón llevará en sus hombros los nombres de los hijos de Israel, para recordarlos ante el SEÑOR. 13Haz también engastes en filigrana de oro, 14y dos cadenillas de oro puro, a manera de cordón, para fijar las cadenillas en los engastes.

El pectoral
28:15-28 — Éx 39:8-21

15»El pectoral para impartir justicia lo bordarás artísticamente con oro, púrpura, carmesí, escarlata y lino fino, como hiciste con el *efod. 16Será doble y cuadrado, de veinte centímetrosᵍ de largo por veinte de ancho. 17Engarzarás en él cuatro hileras de piedras preciosas. En la primera pondrás un rubí, un crisólito y una esmeralda; 18en la segunda, una turquesa, un zafiro y un jade; 19en la tercera, un jacinto, un ágata y una amatista, 20y en la cuarta, un topacio, un ónice y un jaspe.ʰ Engárzalas en filigrana de oro. 21Deben ser doce piedras, una por cada uno de los doce hijos de Israel. Cada una de las piedras llevará grabada como un sello el *nombre de una de las doce tribus.

22»Haz unas cadenillas de oro puro, en forma de cordón, para el pectoral. 23Ponle al pectoral dos anillos de oro, y sujétalos a sus dos extremos. 24Sujeta las cadenillas de oro a los anillos del pectoral, 25y une los extremos de las cadenillas a los dos engastes, para fijarlos por la parte delantera a las hombreras del efod.

26»Haz otros dos anillos de oro, y fíjalos en los extremos del pectoral, en su borde interno cercano al efod. 27Haz dos anillos más, también de oro, para fijarlos por el frente del efod, pero por debajo de las hombreras, cerca de la costura que va justamente arriba del cinturón. 28Los anillos del pectoral deberán sujetarse a los anillos del efod con un cordón azul, trabándolo con el cinturón para que el pectoral y el efod queden unidos. 29De este modo, siempre que Aarón entre en el Lugar Santo llevará sobre su *corazón, en el pectoral para impartir justicia, los nombres de los hijos de Israel para recordarlos siempre ante el SEÑOR. 30Sobre el pectoral para impartir justicia pondrás el *urim y el tumim. De esta manera, siempre que Aarón se presente ante el SEÑOR, llevará en el pecho la causa de los israelitas.

ᵃ 27:9 cuarenta y cinco metros. Lit. cien codos; también en v. 11. ᵇ 27:12 veintidós metros y medio. Lit. cincuenta codos; también en v. 13. ᶜ 27:14 siete metros. Lit. quince codos; también en v. 15. ᵈ 27:16 nueve metros. Lit. veinte codos. ᵉ 27:18 cuarenta y cinco...de ancho. Lit. cien codos de largo por cincuenta codos de ancho. ᶠ 27:18 dos metros con treinta centímetros. Lit. cinco codos. ᵍ 28:16 veinte centímetros. Lit. un *palmo. ʰ 28:20 La identificación de algunas de estas piedras preciosas no ha podido establecerse con precisión.

Otras vestiduras sacerdotales
28:31-43 — Éx 39:22-31

31»Haz de púrpura todo el manto del *efod, 32con una abertura en el centro para meter la cabeza. Alrededor de la abertura le pondrás un refuerzo, como el que se pone a los chalecos,i para que no se desgarre. 33En torno al borde inferior del manto pondrás granadas de púrpura, carmesí y escarlata, alternándolas con campanillas de oro. 34Por todo el borde del manto pondrás primero una campanilla y luego una granada. 35Aarón debe llevar puesto el manto mientras esté ejerciendo su ministerio, para que el tintineo de las campanillas se oiga todo el tiempo que él esté ante el SEÑOR en el Lugar Santo, y así él no muera.

36»Haz una placa de oro puro, y graba en ella, a manera de sello: CONSAGRADO AL SEÑOR. 37Sujétala al turbante con un cordón púrpura, de modo que quede fija a éste por la parte delantera. 38Esta placa estará siempre sobre la frente de Aarón, para que el SEÑOR acepte todas las ofrendas de los israelitas, ya que Aarón llevará sobre sí el pecado en que ellos incurran al dedicar sus ofrendas sagradas.

39»La túnica y el turbante los harás de lino. El cinturón deberá estar recamado artísticamente. 40A los hijos de Aarón les harás túnicas, cinturones y mitras, para conferirles honra y dignidad. 41Una vez que hayas vestido a tu hermano Aarón y a sus hijos, los ungirás para conferirles autoridadj y consagrarlos como mis sacerdotes.

42»Hazles también calzoncillos de lino que les cubran el cuerpo desde la cintura hasta el muslo. 43Aarón y sus hijos deberán ponérselos siempre que entren en la *Tienda de reunión, o cuando se acerquen al altar para ejercer su ministerio en el Lugar Santo, a fin de que no incurran en pecado y mueran. Ésta es una ley perpetua para Aarón y sus descendientes.

Consagración de los sacerdotes
29:1-37 — Lv 8:1-36

29 »Para consagrarlos como sacerdotes a mi servicio, harás lo siguiente: Tomarás un novillo y dos carneros sin defecto, 2y con harina fina de trigo harás panes y tortas sin levadura amasadas con aceite, y obleas sin levadura untadas con aceite. 3Pondrás los panes, las tortas y las obleas en un canastillo, y me los presentarás junto con el novillo y los dos carneros. 4Luego llevarás a Aarón y a sus hijos a la entrada de la *Tienda de reunión, y los bañarás. 5Tomarás las vestiduras y le pondrás a Aarón la túnica, el *efod con su manto, y el pectoral. El efod se lo sujetarás con el cinturón. 6Le pondrás el turbante en la cabeza, y sobre el turbante, la tiara sagrada. 7Luego lo ungirás derramando el aceite de la unción sobre su cabeza. 8Acercarás entonces a sus hijos y les pondrás las túnicas 9y las mitras; a continuación, les ceñirás los cinturones a Aarón y a sus hijos. Así les conferirás autoridad, y el sacerdocio será para ellos una ley perpetua.

10»Arrimarás el novillo a la entrada de la Tienda de reunión para que Aarón y sus hijos le pongan las manos sobre la cabeza, 11y allí, en presencia del SEÑOR, sacrificarás al novillo. 12Con el dedo tomarás un poco de la sangre del novillo y la untarás en los cuernos del altar, y al pie del altar derramarás la sangre restante. 13Al hígado y a los dos riñones les quitarás la grasa que los recubre, y la quemarás sobre el

altar; 14pero la carne del novillo, su piel y su excremento los quemarás fuera del campamento, pues se trata de un sacrificio por el pecado.

15»Tomarás luego uno de los carneros para que Aarón y sus hijos le pongan las manos sobre la cabeza; 16lo sacrificarás, y con la sangre rociarás el altar y sus cuatro costados. 17Destazarás el carnero y, luego de lavarle los intestinos y las piernas, los pondrás sobre los pedazos y la cabeza del carnero, 18y quemarás todo el carnero sobre el altar. Se trata de un *holocausto, de una ofrenda presentada por fuego, de aroma grato al SEÑOR.

19»Tomarás entonces el otro carnero para que Aarón y sus hijos le pongan las manos sobre la cabeza, 20y lo sacrificarás, poniendo un poco de su sangre en el lóbulo de la oreja derecha de Aarón y de sus hijos, lo mismo que en el pulgar derecho y en el dedo gordo derecho. Después de eso rociarás el altar y sus cuatro costados con la sangre, 21y rociarás también un poco de esa sangre y del aceite de la unción sobre Aarón y sus hijos, y sobre sus vestiduras. Así Aarón y sus hijos y sus vestiduras quedarán consagrados.

22»De este carnero, que representa la autoridad conferida a los sacerdotes, tomarás la cola, la grasa que recubre las vísceras, el hígado, los dos riñones y el muslo derecho. 23Del canastillo del pan sin levadura que está ante el SEÑOR, tomarás uno de los panes, una torta hecha con aceite y una oblea, 24y meciéndolos ante el SEÑOR los pondrás en las manos de Aarón y de sus hijos. Se trata de una ofrenda mecida. 25Luego esto les deberán devolver esto para que tú, en presencia del SEÑOR, lo quemes sobre el altar, junto con el holocausto de aroma grato. Ésta es una ofrenda presentada por fuego en honor del SEÑOR. 26Después de eso, tomarás el pecho del carnero que representa la autoridad conferida a Aarón, y lo mecerás ante el SEÑOR, pues se trata de una ofrenda mecida. Esa porción será la tuya.

27»Aparta el pecho del carnero que fue mecido para conferirles autoridad a Aarón y a sus hijos, y también el muslo que fue presentado como ofrenda, pues son las porciones que a ellos les corresponden. 28Éstas son las porciones que, de sus sacrificios de *comunión al SEÑOR, les darán siempre los israelitas a Aarón y a sus hijos como contribución.

29»Las vestiduras sagradas de Aarón pasarán a ser de sus descendientes, para que sean ungidos y ordenados con ellas. 30Cualquiera de los sacerdotes descendientes de Aarón que se presente en la Tienda de reunión para ministrar en el Lugar Santo, deberá llevar puestas esas vestiduras durante siete días.

31»Toma el carnero con que se les confirió autoridad, y cuece su carne en el lugar sagrado. 32A la entrada de la Tienda de reunión, Aarón y sus hijos comerán la carne del carnero y el pan que está en el canastillo. 33Con esas ofrendas se hizo *expiación por ellos, se les confirió autoridad y se les consagró; sólo ellos podrán comerlas, y nadie más, porque son ofrendas sagradas. 34Si hasta el otro día queda algo del carnero con que se les confirió autoridad, o algo del pan, quémalo. No debe comerse, porque es parte de las ofrendas sagradas.

35»Haz con Aarón y con sus hijos todo lo que te he ordenado. Dedica siete días a conferirles autoridad. 36Para hacer expiación, cada día ofrecerás un novillo como ofrenda por el pecado. Purificarás el altar haciendo expiación por él y ungiéndolo para consagrar-

---

i **28:32** *como el que se pone a los chalecos*. Frase de difícil traducción. j **28:41** *para conferirles autoridad*. Lit. *y llenarás sus manos;* también en 29:9.

lo. **37**Esto lo harás durante siete días. Así el altar y cualquier cosa que lo toque quedarán consagrados.

38»Todos los días ofrecerás sobre el altar dos corderos de un año. **39**Al despuntar el día, ofrecerás uno de ellos, y al caer la tarde, el otro. **40**Con el primer cordero ofrecerás, como ofrenda de libación, dos kilosk de harina fina mezclada con un litro de aceite de oliva, y un litrol de vino. **41**El otro cordero lo sacrificarás al caer la tarde, como ofrenda presentada por fuego de aroma grato al SEÑOR, junto con una ofrenda de libación como la presentada en la mañana.

42»Las generaciones futuras deberán ofrecer siempre este holocausto al SEÑOR. Lo harán a la entrada de la Tienda de reunión, donde yo me reuniré contigo y te hablaré, **43**y donde también me reuniré con los israelitas. Mi gloriosa presencia *santificará ese lugar.

44»Consagraré la Tienda de reunión y el altar, y consagraré también a Aarón y a sus hijos para que me sirvan como sacerdotes. **45**Habitaré entre los israelitas, y seré su Dios. **46**Así sabrán que yo soy el SEÑOR su Dios, que los sacó de Egipto para habitar entre ellos. Yo soy el SEÑOR su Dios.

El altar del incienso
30:1-5 — Éx 37:25-28

30 »Haz un altar de madera de acacia para quemar incienso. **2**Hazlo cuadrado, de cuarenta y cinco centímetros de largo por cuarenta y cinco centímetros de ancho y noventa centímetros de alto.m Sus cuernos deben formar una pieza con el altar. **3**Recubre de oro puro su parte superior, sus cuatro costados y los cuernos, y ponle una moldura de oro alrededor. **4**Ponle también dos anillos de oro en cada uno de sus costados, debajo de la moldura, para que pasen por ellos las varas para transportarlo. **5**Prepara las varas de madera de acacia, y recúbrelas de oro. **6**Pon el altar frente a la cortina que está ante el arca del *pacto, es decir, ante el *propiciatorio que está sobre el arca, que es donde me reuniré contigo.

7»Cada mañana, cuando Aarón prepare las lámparas, quemará incienso aromático sobre el altar, **8**y también al caer la tarde, cuando las encienda. Las generaciones futuras deberán quemar siempre incienso ante el SEÑOR. **9**No ofrezcas sobre ese altar ningún otro incienso, ni *holocausto ni ofrenda de grano, ni derrames sobre él libación alguna. **10**Cada año Aarón hará *expiación por el pecado de las generaciones futuras. Lo hará poniendo la sangre de la ofrenda de expiación sobre los cuernos del altar. Este altar estará completamente consagrado al SEÑOR.»

Dinero para la expiación

11El SEÑOR habló con Moisés y le dijo: **12**«Cuando hagas el censo y cuentes a los israelitas, cada uno deberá pagar al SEÑOR rescate por su *vida, para que no le sobrevenga ninguna plaga durante el censo. **13**Cada uno de los censados deberá pagar como ofrenda al SEÑOR seis gramosn de plata, que es la mitad de la tasación oficial del santuario.ñ **14**Todos los censados mayores de veinte años deberán entregar esta ofrenda al SEÑOR. **15**Al pagar su rescate, ni el rico dará más ni el pobre dará menos. **16**Tú mismo recibirás esta plata de manos de los israelitas, y la entregarás para el servicio de la *Tienda de reunión. De esta manera el SEÑOR tendrá presente que los israelitas pagaron su rescate.»

El lavamanos

17El SEÑOR habló con Moisés y le dijo: **18**«Haz un lavamanos de bronce, con un pedestal también de bronce, y colócalo entre la *Tienda de reunión y el altar. Échale agua, **19**pues con ella deben lavarse Aarón y sus hijos las manos y los pies. **20**Siempre que entren en la Tienda de reunión, o cuando se acerquen al altar y presenten al SEÑOR alguna ofrenda por fuego, deberán lavarse con agua **21**las manos y los pies para que no mueran. Ésta será una ley perpetua para Aarón y sus descendientes por todas las generaciones.»

El aceite de la unción

22El SEÑOR habló con Moisés y le dijo: **23**«Toma las siguientes especias finas: seis kilos de mirra líquida, tres kilos de canela aromática, tres kilos de caña aromática, **24**seis kiloso de casia, y cuatro litrosp de aceite de oliva, según la tasación oficialq del santuario. **25**Con estos ingredientes harás un aceite, es decir, una mezcla aromática como las de los fabricantes de perfumes. Éste será el aceite de la unción sagrada. **26**Con él deberás ungir la *Tienda de reunión, el arca del *pacto, **27**la mesa y todos sus utensilios, el candelabro y sus accesorios, el altar del incienso, **28**el altar de los *holocaustos y todos sus utensilios, y el lavamanos con su pedestal. **29**De este modo los consagrarás, y serán objetos santísimos; cualquier cosa que toque esos objetos quedará también consagrada.

30»Unge a Aarón y a sus hijos, y conságralos para que me sirvan como sacerdotes. **31**A los israelitas les darás las siguientes instrucciones: "De aquí en adelante, éste será mi aceite de la unción sagrada. **32**No lo derramen sobre el cuerpo de cualquier hombre, ni preparen otro aceite con la misma fórmula. Es un aceite sagrado, y así deberán considerarlo. **33**Cualquiera que haga un perfume como éste, y cualquiera que unja con él a alguien que no sea sacerdote, será eliminado de su pueblo." »

El incienso

34El SEÑOR le dijo a Moisés: «Toma una misma cantidad de resina, ámbar, gálbano e incienso puro, **35**y mezcla todo esto para hacer un incienso aromático, como lo hacen los fabricantes de perfumes. Agrégale sal a la mezcla, para que sea un incienso puro y sagrado. **36**Muele parte de la mezcla hasta hacerla polvo, y colócala en la *Tienda de reunión, frente al arca del *pacto, donde yo me reuniré contigo. Este incienso será para ustedes algo muy sagrado, **37**y no deberá hacerse ningún otro incienso con la misma fórmula, pues le pertenece al SEÑOR. Ustedes deberán considerarlo como algo sagrado. **38**Quien haga otro incienso parecido para disfrutar de su fragancia, será eliminado de su pueblo.»

Bezalel y Aholiab
31:2-6 — Éx 35:30-35

31 El SEÑOR habló con Moisés y le dijo: **2**«Toma en cuenta que he escogido a Bezalel, hijo de Uri y nieto de Jur, de la tribu de Judá, **3**y lo he llenado del Espíritu de Dios, de sabiduría, inteligencia y capacidad creativa **4**para hacer trabajos artísticos en oro, plata y bronce, **5**para cortar y engastar piedras

---

k **29:40** dos kilos. Lit. un *efa. l **29:40** un litro ... un litro. Lit. un cuarto de *hin ... un cuarto de *hin. m **30:2** cuarenta y cinco ... de alto. Lit. un *codo de largo por un codo de ancho y dos codos de alto. n **30:13** seis gramos. Lit. medio *siclo; también en v. 15. ñ **30:13** que es la mitad de la tasación oficial del santuario. Lit. según el siclo del santuario, que es de veinte *guerás. o **30:23** seis kilos ... tres kilos ... tres kilos ... seis kilos. Lit. quinientos siclos ... doscientos cincuenta siclos ... doscientos cincuenta siclos ... quinientos siclos. p **30:24** cuatro litros. Lit. un hin. q **30:24** la tasación oficial. Lit. el siclo.

preciosas, para hacer tallados en madera y para realizar toda clase de artesanías.

6»Además, he designado como su ayudante a Aholiab hijo de Ajisamac, de la tribu de Dan, y he dotado de habilidad a todos los artesanos para que hagan todo lo que te he mandado hacer, es decir:

7 la *Tienda de reunión,
    el arca del *pacto,
    el *propiciatorio que va encima de ella,
    el resto del mobiliario de la Tienda,
8 la mesa y sus utensilios,
    el candelabro de oro puro y todos sus accesorios,
    el altar del incienso,
9 el altar de los *holocaustos y todos sus utensilios,
    el lavamanos con su pedestal,
10 las vestiduras tejidas, tanto las vestiduras sagradas para Aarón el sacerdote como las vestiduras sacerdotales de sus hijos,
11 el aceite de la unción,
    y el incienso aromático para el Lugar Santo.
»Todo deberán hacerlo tal como te he mandado que lo hagas.»

El sábado

12El SEÑOR le ordenó a Moisés:
13«Diles lo siguiente a los israelitas: "Ustedes deberán observar mis *sábados. En todas las generaciones venideras, el sábado será una señal entre ustedes y yo, para que sepan que yo, el SEÑOR, los he consagrado para que me sirvan.r

14 »"El sábado será para ustedes un día sagrado. Obsérvenlo.
»"Quien no lo observe será condenado a muerte.
»"Quien haga algún trabajo en sábado será eliminado de su pueblo.

15 »"Durante seis días se podrá trabajar, pero el día séptimo, el sábado, será de reposo consagrado al SEÑOR.
»"Quien haga algún trabajo en sábado será condenado a muerte."

16»Los israelitas deberán observar el sábado. En todas las generaciones futuras será para ellos un *pacto perpetuo, 17una señal eterna entre ellos y yo.
»En efecto, en seis días hizo el SEÑOR los cielos y la tierra, y el séptimo día descansó.»

18Y cuando terminó de hablar con Moisés en el monte Sinaí, le dio las dos tablas de la *ley, que eran dos lajas escritas por el dedo mismo de Dios.

El becerro de oro

32 Al ver los israelitas que Moisés tardaba en bajar del monte, fueron a reunirse con Aarón y le dijeron:
—Tienes que hacernos dioses que marchen al frente de nosotros, porque a ese Moisés que nos sacó de Egipto, ¡no sabemos qué pudo haberle pasado!

2Aarón les respondió:
—Quítenles a sus mujeres los aretes de oro, y también a sus hijos e hijas, y tráiganmelos.

3Todos los israelitas se quitaron los aretes de oro que llevaban puestos, y se los llevaron a Aarón, 4quien los recibió y los fundió; luego cinceló el oro fundido e hizo un ídolo en forma de becerro. Entonces exclamó el pueblo: «Israel, ¡aquí tienes a tu dios que te sacó de Egipto!»

5Cuando Aarón vio esto, construyó un altar enfrente del becerro y anunció:
—Mañana haremos fiesta en honor del SEÑOR.

6En efecto, al día siguiente los israelitas madrugaron y presentaron *holocaustos y sacrificios de *comunión. Luego el pueblo se sentó a comer y a beber, y se entregó al desenfreno. 7Entonces el SEÑOR le dijo a Moisés:
—Baja, porque ya se ha corrompido el pueblo que sacaste de Egipto. 8Demasiado pronto se han apartado del *camino que les ordené seguir, pues no sólo han fundido oro y se han hecho un ídolo en forma de becerro, sino que se han inclinado ante él, le han ofrecido sacrificios, y han declarado: "Israel, ¡aquí tienes a tu dios que te sacó de Egipto!"

9»Ya me he dado cuenta de que éste es un pueblo terco —añadió el SEÑOR, dirigiéndose a Moisés—. 10Tú no te metas. Yo voy a descargar mi ira sobre ellos, y los voy a destruir. Pero de ti haré una gran nación.

11Moisés intentó apaciguar al SEÑOR su Dios, y le suplicó:
—SEÑOR, ¿por qué ha de encenderse tu ira contra este pueblo tuyo, que sacaste de Egipto con gran poder y con mano poderosa? 12¿Por qué dar pie a que los egipcios digan que nos sacaste de su país con la intención de matarnos en las montañas y borrarnos de la faz de la tierra? ¡Calma ya tu enojo! ¡Aplácate y no traigas sobre tu pueblo esa desgracia! 13Acuérdate de tus siervos Abraham, Isaac e Israel. Tú mismo les juraste que harías a sus descendientes tan numerosos como las estrellas del cielo; ¡tú les prometiste que a sus descendientes les darías toda esta tierra como su herencia eterna!

14Entonces el SEÑOR se calmó y desistió de hacerle a su pueblo el daño que le había sentenciado.

15Moisés volvió entonces del monte. Cuando bajó, traía en sus manos las dos tablas de la *ley, las cuales estaban escritas por sus dos lados. 16Tanto las tablas como la escritura grabada en ellas eran obra de Dios.

17Cuando Josué oyó el ruido y los gritos del pueblo, le dijo a Moisés:
—Se oyen en el campamento gritos de guerra.

18Pero Moisés respondió:
«Lo que escucho no son gritos de victoria,
ni tampoco lamentos de derrota;
más bien, lo que escucho son canciones.»

19Cuando Moisés se acercó al campamento y vio el becerro y las danzas, ardió en ira y arrojó de sus manos las tablas de la ley, haciéndolas pedazos al pie del monte. 20Tomó entonces el becerro que habían hecho, lo arrojó al fuego y, luego de machacarlo hasta hacerlo polvo, lo esparció en el agua y se la dio a beber a los israelitas. 21A Aarón le dijo:
—¿Qué te hizo este pueblo? ¿Por qué lo has hecho cometer semejante pecado?

22—Hermano mío,t no te enojes —contestó Aarón—. Tú bien sabes cuán inclinado al mal es este pueblo. 23Ellos me dijeron: "Tienes que hacernos dioses que marchen al frente de nosotros, porque a ese Moisés que nos sacó de Egipto, ¡no sabemos qué pudo haberle pasado!" 24Yo les contesté que todo el que tuviera joyas de oro se desprendiera de ellas. Ellos me dieron el oro, yo lo eché al fuego, ¡y lo que salió fue este becerro!

25Al ver Moisés que el pueblo estaba desenfrenado y que Aarón le había permitido desmandarse y convertirse en el hazmerreír de sus enemigos, 26se puso a la entrada del campamento y dijo: «Todo el

---

r **31:13** los he consagrado para que me sirvan. Alt. los he separado como santos.   s **32:1** dioses que marchen. Alt. un dios que marche; también en v. 23.   t **32:22** Hermano mío. Lit. Señor mío.

que esté de parte del SEÑOR, que se pase de mi lado.» Y se le unieron todos los levitas.

²⁷Entonces les dijo Moisés: «El SEÑOR, Dios de Israel, ordena lo siguiente: "Cíñase cada uno la espada y recorra todo el campamento de un extremo al otro, y mate al que se le ponga enfrente, sea hermano, amigo o vecino." » ²⁸Los levitas hicieron lo que les mandó Moisés, y aquel día mataron como a tres mil israelitas. ²⁹Entonces dijo Moisés: «Hoy han recibido ustedes plena autoridad de parte del SEÑOR; él los ha bendecido este día, pues se pusieron en contra de sus propios hijos y hermanos.»

³⁰Al día siguiente, Moisés les dijo a los israelitas: «Ustedes han cometido un gran pecado. Pero voy a subir ahora a reunirme con el SEÑOR, y tal vez logre yo que Dios les perdone su pecado.»

³¹Volvió entonces Moisés para hablar con el SEÑOR, y le dijo:

—¡Qué pecado tan grande ha cometido este pueblo al hacerse dioses^u de oro! ³²Sin embargo, yo te ruego que les perdones su pecado. Pero si no vas a perdonarlos, ¡bórrame del libro que has escrito!

³³El SEÑOR le respondió a Moisés:

—Sólo borraré de mi libro a quien haya pecado contra mí. ³⁴Tú ve y lleva al pueblo al lugar del que te hablé. Delante de ti irá mi ángel. Llegará el día en que deba castigarlos por su pecado, y entonces los castigaré.

³⁵Fue así como, por causa del becerro que había hecho Aarón, el SEÑOR lanzó una plaga sobre el pueblo.

33 El SEÑOR le dijo a Moisés: «Anda, vete de este lugar, junto con el pueblo que sacaste de Egipto, y dirígete a la tierra que bajo juramento prometí a Abraham, Isaac y Jacob que les daría a sus descendientes. ²Enviaré un ángel delante de ti, y desalojaré a cananeos, amorreos, hititas, ferezeos, heveos y jebuseos. ³Ve a la tierra donde abundan la leche y la miel. Yo no los acompañaré, porque ustedes son un pueblo terco, y podría yo destruirlos en el camino.»

⁴Cuando los israelitas oyeron estas palabras tan demoledoras, comenzaron a llorar y nadie volvió a ponerse sus joyas, ⁵pues el SEÑOR le había dicho a Moisés: «Diles a los israelitas que son un pueblo terco. Si aun por un momento tuviera que acompañarlos, podría destruirlos. Diles que se quiten esas joyas, que ya decidiré qué hacer con ellos.» ⁶Por eso, a partir del monte Horeb los israelitas no volvieron a ponerse joyas.

La Tienda de reunión

⁷Moisés tomó una tienda de campaña y la armó a cierta distancia fuera del campamento. La llamó «la *Tienda de la reunión con el SEÑOR.» Cuando alguien quería consultar al SEÑOR, tenía que salir del campamento e ir a esa tienda. ⁸Siempre que Moisés se dirigía a ella, todo el pueblo se quedaba de pie a la entrada de su carpa y seguía a Moisés con la mirada, hasta que éste entraba en la Tienda de reunión. ⁹En cuanto Moisés entraba en ella, la columna de nube descendía y tapaba la entrada, mientras el SEÑOR hablaba con Moisés. ¹⁰Cuando los israelitas veían que la columna de nube se detenía a la entrada de la Tienda de reunión, todos ellos se inclinaban a la entrada de su carpa y adoraban al SEÑOR. ¹¹Y hablaba el SEÑOR con Moisés cara a cara, como quien habla con un amigo. Después de eso, Moisés regresaba al campamento; pero Josué, su joven asistente, nunca se apartaba de la Tienda de reunión.

La gloria del SEÑOR

¹²Moisés le dijo al SEÑOR:

—Tú insistes en que yo debo guiar a este pueblo, pero no me has dicho a quién enviarás conmigo. También me has dicho que soy tu amigo^v y que cuento con tu favor. ¹³Pues si realmente es así, dime qué quieres que haga. Así sabré que en verdad cuento con tu favor. Ten presente que los israelitas son tu pueblo.

¹⁴—Yo mismo iré contigo y te daré descanso —respondió el SEÑOR.

¹⁵—O vas con todos nosotros —replicó Moisés—, o mejor no nos hagas salir de aquí. ¹⁶Si no vienes con nosotros, ¿cómo vamos a saber, tu pueblo y yo, que contamos con tu favor? ¿En qué seríamos diferentes de los demás pueblos de la tierra?

¹⁷—Está bien, haré lo que me pides —le dijo el SEÑOR a Moisés—, pues cuentas con mi favor y te considero mi amigo.^{w}

¹⁸—Déjame verte en todo tu esplendor —insistió Moisés.

¹⁹Y el SEÑOR le respondió:

—Voy a darte pruebas de mi bondad, y te daré a conocer mi *nombre. Y verás que tengo clemencia de quien quiero tenerla, y soy compasivo con quien quiero serlo. ²⁰Pero debo aclararte que no podrás ver mi rostro, porque nadie puede verme y seguir con vida.

²¹»Cerca de mí hay un lugar sobre una *roca —añadió el SEÑOR—. Puedes quedarte allí. ²²Cuando yo pase en todo mi esplendor, te pondré en una hendidura de la roca y te cubriré con mi mano, hasta que haya pasado. ²³Luego, retiraré la mano y podrás verme la espalda. Pero mi rostro no lo verás.

Las nuevas tablas de piedra

34 El SEÑOR le dijo a Moisés: «Labra dos tablas de piedra semejantes a las primeras que rompiste. Voy a escribir en ellas lo mismo que estaba escrito en las primeras. ²Prepárate para subir mañana a la cumbre del monte Sinaí, y presentarte allí ante mí. ³Nadie debe acompañarte, ni debe verse a nadie en ninguna parte del monte. Ni siquiera las ovejas y las vacas deben pastar frente al monte.»

⁴Moisés labró dos tablas de piedra semejantes a las primeras, y muy de mañana subió con ellas al monte Sinaí, como se lo había ordenado el SEÑOR. ⁵El SEÑOR descendió en la nube y se puso junto a Moisés. Luego le dio a conocer su *nombre: ⁶pasando delante de él, proclamó:

—El SEÑOR, el SEÑOR, Dios clemente y compasivo, lento para la ira y grande en amor y fidelidad, ⁷que mantiene su amor hasta mil generaciones después, y que perdona la iniquidad, la rebelión y el pecado; pero que no deja sin castigo al culpable, sino que castiga la maldad de los padres en los hijos y en los nietos, hasta la tercera y la cuarta generación.

⁸En seguida Moisés se inclinó hasta el suelo, y oró al Señor ⁹de la siguiente manera:

—Señor, si realmente cuento con tu favor, ven y quédate entre nosotros. Reconozco que éste es un pueblo terco, pero perdona nuestra iniquidad y nuestro pecado, y adóptanos como tu herencia.

¹⁰—Mira el *pacto que hago contigo —respondió el SEÑOR—. A la vista de todo tu pueblo haré ma-

---

^{u} **32:31** dioses. Alt. *un dios.* ^{v} **33:12** *me has dicho que soy tu amigo.* Lit. *has dicho: «Te conozco por nombre».* ^{w} **33:17** *te considero mi amigo.* Lit. *te conozco por nombre.*

ravillas que ante ninguna nación del mundo han sido realizadas. El pueblo en medio del cual vives verá las imponentes obras que yo, el SEÑOR, haré por ti. [11]Por lo que a ti toca, cumple con lo que hoy te mando. Echaré de tu presencia a los amorreos, cananeos, hititas, ferezeos, heveos y jebuseos. [12]Ten mucho cuidado de no hacer ningún pacto con los habitantes de la tierra que vas a ocupar, pues de lo contrario serán para ti una trampa. [13]Derriba sus altares, y haz pedazos sus piedras sagradas y sus imágenes de la diosa Aserá. [14]No adores a otros dioses, porque el SEÑOR es muy celoso. Su nombre es Dios celoso.

[15]»No hagas ningún pacto con los habitantes de esta tierra, porque se prostituyen por ir tras sus dioses, y cuando les ofrezcan sacrificios a esos dioses, te invitarán a participar de ellos. [16]Y si casas a tu hijo con una de sus mujeres, cuando ella se prostituya por ir tras sus dioses, inducirá a tu hijo a hacer lo mismo.

[17]»No te hagas ídolos de metal fundido.

[18]»Celebra la fiesta de los Panes sin levadura, y come de ese pan durante siete días, como te lo he ordenado. Celebra esa fiesta en el mes de *aviv*, que es la fecha señalada, pues en ese mes saliste de Egipto.

[19]»Todo hijo primogénito me pertenece, incluyendo las primeras crías de tus vacas y de tus ovejas. [20]Deberás rescatar a todos tus primogénitos. Al asno primogénito podrás rescatarlo a cambio de un cordero; pero si no lo rescatas, tendrás que romperle el cuello.

»Nadie se presentará ante mí con las manos vacías.

[21]»Trabaja durante seis días, pero descansa el séptimo. Ese día deberás descansar, incluso en el tiempo de arar y cosechar.

[22]»Celebra con las *primicias la fiesta de las Semanas, y también la fiesta de la cosecha de fin de año.x

[23]»Todos tus varones deberán presentarse ante mí, su SEÑOR y Dios, el Dios de Israel, tres veces al año. [24]Entonces yo echaré de tu presencia a las naciones, ensancharé tu territorio y nadie codiciará tu tierra.

[25]»Cuando me ofrezcas un animal, no mezcles con levadura su sangre.

»Del animal que se ofrece en la fiesta de la Pascua no debe quedar nada para el día siguiente.

[26]»Lleva tus mejores primicias a la casa del SEÑOR tu Dios.

»No cuezas ningún cabrito en la leche de su madre.

[27]El SEÑOR le dijo a Moisés:

—Pon estas palabras por escrito, pues en ellas se basa el pacto que ahora hago contigo y con Israel.

[28]Y Moisés se quedó en el monte, con el SEÑOR, cuarenta días y cuarenta noches, sin comer ni beber nada. Allí, en las tablas, escribió los términos del pacto, es decir, los diez mandamientos.

El rostro radiante de Moisés

[29]Cuando Moisés descendió del monte Sinaí, traía en sus manos las dos tablas de la *ley. Pero no sabía que, por haberle hablado el SEÑOR, de su rostro salía un haz de luz. [30]Al ver Aarón y todos los israelitas el rostro resplandeciente de Moisés, tuvieron miedo de acercársele; [31]pero Moisés llamó a Aarón y a todos los jefes, y ellos regresaron para hablar con él. [32]Luego se le acercaron todos los israelitas, y Moisés les ordenó acatar todo lo que el SEÑOR le había dicho en el monte Sinaí.

[33]En cuanto Moisés terminó de hablar con ellos, se cubrió el rostro con un velo. [34]Siempre que entraba a la presencia del SEÑOR para hablar con él, se quitaba el velo mientras no salía. Al salir, les comunicaba a los israelitas lo que el Señor le había ordenado decir. [35]Y como los israelitas veían que su rostro resplandecía, Moisés se cubría de nuevo el rostro, hasta que entraba a hablar otra vez con el SEÑOR.

Normas para el sábado

35 Moisés reunió a toda la comunidad israelita, y les dijo: «Éstas son las órdenes que el SEÑOR les manda cumplir: [2]Trabajen durante seis días, pero el séptimo día, el *sábado, será para ustedes un día de reposo consagrado al SEÑOR. Quien haga algún trabajo en él será condenado a muerte. [3]En sábado no se encenderá ningún fuego en ninguna de sus casas.»

Materiales para el santuario
35:4-9 — Éx 25:1-7
35:10-19 — Éx 39:32-41

[4]Moisés le dijo a toda la comunidad israelita: «Esto es lo que el SEÑOR les ordena: [5]Tomen de entre sus pertenencias una ofrenda para el SEÑOR. Todo el que se sienta movido a hacerlo, presente al SEÑOR una ofrenda de oro, plata y bronce; [6]lana púrpura, carmesí y escarlata; lino, pelo de cabra, [7]pieles de carnero teñidas de rojo y pieles de delfín, madera de acacia, [8]aceite de oliva para el alumbrado, especias para el aceite de la unción y para el incienso aromático, [9]y piedras de ónice y otras piedras preciosas para engastarlas en el *efod y en el pectoral.

[10]»Todos los artesanos hábiles que haya entre ustedes deben venir y hacer todo lo que el SEÑOR ha ordenado que se haga: [11]el santuario, con su tienda y su toldo, sus ganchos, sus tablones, sus travesaños, sus postes y sus bases; [12]el arca con sus varas, el *propiciatorio y la cortina que resguarda el arca; [13]la mesa con sus varas y todos sus utensilios, y el *pan de la Presencia; [14]el candelabro para el alumbrado y sus accesorios, las lámparas y el aceite para el alumbrado; [15]el altar del incienso con sus varas, el aceite de la unción y el incienso aromático, la cortina para la puerta a la entrada del santuario; [16]el altar del los *holocaustos con su enrejado de bronce, sus varas y todos sus utensilios, el lavamanos de bronce con su pedestal, [17]las cortinas del atrio con sus postes y bases, la cortina para la entrada del atrio, [18]las estacas del toldo para el santuario y para el atrio, y sus cuerdas; [19]y las vestiduras tejidas que deben llevar los sacerdotes para ministrar en el santuario, tanto las vestiduras sagradas para Aarón como las vestiduras para sus hijos.»

[20]Toda la comunidad israelita se retiró de la presencia de Moisés, [21]y todos los que en su interior se sintieron movidos a hacerlo llevaron una ofrenda al SEÑOR para las obras en la *Tienda de reunión, para todo su servicio, y para las vestiduras sagradas. [22]Así mismo, todos los que se sintieron movidos a hacerlo, tanto hombres como mujeres, llevaron como ofrenda toda clase de joyas de oro: broches, pendientes, anillos, y otros adornos de oro. Todos ellos presentaron su oro como ofrenda mecida al SEÑOR, [23]o bien llevaron lo que tenían: lana púrpura, carmesí y escarlata, lino, pelo de cabra, pieles de carnero teñidas de rojo, y pieles de delfín. [24]Los que tenían plata o bronce lo presentaron como ofrenda al SEÑOR, lo mismo que quienes tenían madera de acacia, contri-

---

x **34:22** El fin de año caía en otoño.

buyendo así con algo para la obra. 25Las mujeres expertas en artes manuales presentaron los hilos de lana púrpura, carmesí o escarlata que habían torcido, y lino. 26Otras, que conocían bien el oficio y se sintieron movidas a hacerlo, torcieron hilo de pelo de cabra. 27Los jefes llevaron piedras de ónice y otras piedras preciosas, para que se engastaran en el efod y en el pectoral. 28También llevaron especias y aceite de oliva para el alumbrado, el aceite de la unción y el incienso aromático. 29Todos los israelitas que se sintieron movidos a hacerlo, lo mismo hombres que mujeres, presentaron al SEÑOR ofrendas voluntarias para toda la obra que el SEÑOR, por medio de Moisés, les había mandado hacer.

Bezalel y Aholiab
35:30-35 — Éx 31:2-6

30Moisés les dijo a los israelitas: «Tomen en cuenta que el SEÑOR ha escogido expresamente a Bezalel, hijo de Uri y nieto de Jur, de la tribu de Judá, 31y lo ha llenado del Espíritu de Dios, de sabiduría, inteligencia y capacidad creativa 32para hacer trabajos artísticos en oro, plata y bronce, 33para cortar y engastar piedras preciosas, para hacer tallados en madera y realizar toda clase de diseños artísticos y artesanías.

34Dios les ha dado a él y a Aholiab hijo de Ajisamac, de la tribu de Dan, la habilidad de enseñar a otros. 35Los ha llenado de gran sabiduría para realizar toda clase de artesanías, diseños y recamados en lana púrpura, carmesí y escarlata, y lino. Son expertos tejedores y hábiles artesanos en toda clase de labores y diseños.

36 »Así, pues, Bezalel y Aholiab llevarán a cabo los trabajos para el servicio del santuario, tal y como el SEÑOR lo ha ordenado, junto con todos los que tengan ese mismo espíritu artístico, a quienes el SEÑOR haya dado pericia y habilidad para realizar toda la obra del servicio del santuario.»

2Moisés llamó a Bezalel y a Aholiab, y a todos los que tenían el mismo espíritu artístico, y a quienes el SEÑOR había dado pericia y habilidad y se sentían movidos a venir y hacer el trabajo, 3y les entregó todas las ofrendas que los israelitas habían llevado para realizar la obra del servicio del santuario. Pero como día tras día el pueblo seguía llevando ofrendas voluntarias, 4todos los artesanos y expertos que estaban ocupados en la obra del santuario suspendieron su trabajo 5para ir a decirle a Moisés: «La gente está trayendo más de lo que se necesita para llevar a cabo la obra que el SEÑOR mandó hacer.»

6Entonces Moisés ordenó que corriera la voz por todo el campamento: «¡Que nadie, ni hombre ni mujer, haga más labores ni traiga más ofrendas para el santuario!» De ese modo los israelitas dejaron de llevar más ofrendas, 7pues lo que ya habían hecho era más que suficiente para llevar a cabo toda la obra.

El santuario
36:8-38 — Éx 26:1-37

8Todos los obreros con espíritu artístico hicieron el santuario con diez cortinas de lino fino y de lana púrpura, carmesí y escarlata, con *querubines artísticamente bordados en ellas.

9Todas las cortinas medían lo mismo, es decir, doce metros y medio de largo por un metro con ochenta centímetros de ancho.y 10Cosieron cinco cortinas una con otra, e hicieron lo mismo con las otras cinco. 11En el borde de la cortina, en el extremo del primer conjunto, hicieron presillas de lana púrpura; lo mismo hicieron con la cortina que estaba en el extremo del otro conjunto. 12También hicieron cincuenta presillas en una cortina, y otras cincuenta presillas en la cortina del extremo del otro conjunto, quedando las presillas unas frente a las otras. 13Después hicieron cincuenta ganchos de oro y los usaron para sujetar los dos conjuntos de cortinas, de modo que el santuario tenía unidad de conjunto.

14Hicieron un total de once cortinas de pelo de cabra para cubrir el santuario a la manera de una tienda de campaña. 15Las once cortinas tenían las mismas medidas, es decir, trece metros y medio de largo por un metro con ochenta centímetros de ancho.z 16Cosieron dos conjuntos de cortinas, uno de cinco y otro de seis; 17hicieron cincuenta presillas en el borde de la cortina del extremo de uno de los conjuntos, y también en el borde de la cortina del extremo del otro conjunto, 18e hicieron cincuenta ganchos de bronce para unir la tienda en un solo conjunto. 19Luego hicieron para la tienda un toldo de pieles de carnero teñidas de rojo, y sobre ese toldo pusieron de pieles de delfín.

20Hicieron tablones de madera de acacia para el santuario, y los colocaron en posición vertical. 21Cada tablón medía cuatro metros y medio de largo por setenta centímetros de ancho,a 22con dos ranuras paralelas entre sí. Todos los tablones del santuario los hicieron así:

23Veinte tablones para el lado sur del santuario, 24con cuarenta bases de plata que iban debajo de ellos, dos por cada tablón, una debajo de cada ranura;

25veinte tablones para el lado opuesto, el lado norte del santuario, 26con cuarenta bases de plata que iban debajo de ellos, dos por cada tablón, una debajo de cada ranura;

27seis tablones para el extremo occidental del santuario, que era el más distante, y

28dos tablones más para las esquinas del santuario en el extremo opuesto.

29En estas esquinas los tablones eran dobles de abajo hacia arriba, pero quedaban unidos por un solo anillo. En ambas esquinas se hizo lo mismo, 30de modo que había ocho tablones y dieciséis bases de plata, dos debajo de cada tablón.

31También hicieron travesaños de madera de acacia: cinco para los tablones de un costado del santuario, 32cinco para los tablones del costado opuesto, y cinco para los tablones del costado occidental, en la parte posterior del santuario. 33El travesaño central lo hicieron de tal modo que pasaba de uno a otro extremo, a media altura de los tablones. 34Recubrieron de oro los tablones, e hicieron unos anillos de oro para que los travesaños pasaran por ellos. También recubrieron de oro los travesaños.

35La cortina la hicieron de lana púrpura, carmesí y escarlata, y de lino fino, con querubines artísticamente bordados en ella. 36Le hicieron cuatro postes de madera de acacia y los recubrieron de oro, les pusieron ganchos de oro, y fundieron para ellos cuatro bases de plata. 37Para la entrada de la tienda hicieron una cortina de lana teñida de púrpura, carmesí y escarlata, y de lino fino, recamada artísticamente, 38y cinco postes con ganchos, para los que hicieron cinco bases de bronce; también recubrieron de oro los capiteles y los empalmes de los postes.

---

y **36:9** doce metros ... de ancho. Lit. veintiocho *codos de largo por cuatro de ancho. z **36:15** trece metros ... de ancho. Lit. treinta codos de largo por cuatro de ancho. a **36:21** cuatro metros ... de ancho. Lit. diez codos de largo por un codo y medio de ancho.

El arca
37:1-9 — Éx 25:10-20

37 Bezalel hizo el arca de madera de acacia, de un metro con diez centímetros de largo por setenta centímetros de ancho y setenta centímetros de alto.b 2La recubrió de oro puro por dentro y por fuera, y puso en su derredor una moldura de oro. 3Fundió cuatro anillos de oro para el arca, y se los ajustó a sus cuatro patas, colocando dos anillos en un lado y dos en el otro. 4Hizo luego unas varas de madera de acacia, las recubrió de oro, 5y las pasó a través de los anillos en los costados del arca para poder transportarla.

6El *propiciatorio lo hizo de oro puro, de un metro con diez centímetros de largo por setenta centímetros de ancho.c 7Para los dos extremos del propiciatorio hizo dos *querubines de oro trabajado a martillo. 8Uno de ellos iba en uno de los extremos, y el otro iba en el otro extremo; los hizo de modo que en ambos extremos los dos querubines formaran una sola pieza con el propiciatorio. 9Los querubines tenían las alas extendidas por encima del propiciatorio, y con ellas lo cubrían. Quedaban el uno frente al otro, mirando hacia el propiciatorio.

La mesa
37:10-16 — Éx 25:23-29

10Bezalel hizo la mesa de madera de acacia, de noventa centímetros de largo por cuarenta y cinco centímetros de ancho y setenta centímetros de alto.d 11La recubrió de oro puro y le puso en derredor una moldura de oro. 12También le hizo un reborde de veinte centímetrose de ancho, y alrededor del reborde le puso una moldura de oro. 13Fundió cuatro anillos de oro para la mesa y se los sujetó a las cuatro esquinas, donde iban las cuatro patas. 14Los anillos fueron colocados cerca del reborde para pasar por ellos las varas empleadas para transportar la mesa. 15Esas varas eran de madera de acacia y estaban recubiertas de oro. 16Los utensilios para la mesa, y sus platos, bandejas, tazones, y jarras para derramar las ofrendas de libación, los hizo de oro puro.

El candelabro
37:17-24 — Éx 25:31-39

17Bezalel hizo el candelabro de oro puro labrado a martillo. Su base y su tallo, y sus copas, cálices y flores formaban una sola pieza con él. 18De los costados del candelabro salían seis brazos, tres de un lado y tres del otro. 19En cada uno de los seis brazos del candelabro había tres copas en forma de flores de almendro, con cálices y pétalos. 20El candelabro mismo tenía cuatro copas en forma de flor de almendro, con cálices y pétalos. 21Debajo del primer par de brazos que salía del candelabro había un cáliz; debajo del segundo par de brazos había un segundo cáliz, y debajo del tercer par de brazos había un tercer cáliz. 22Los cálices y los brazos formaban una sola pieza con el candelabro, el cual era de oro puro labrado a martillo.

23Hizo también de oro puro sus siete lámparas, lo mismo que sus cortapabilos y braseros. 24Para hacer el candelabro y todos sus accesorios, usó treinta y tres kilosf de oro puro.

El altar del incienso
37:25-28 — Éx 30:1-5

25Bezalel hizo de madera de acacia el altar del incienso. Era cuadrado, de cuarenta y cinco centímetros de largo por cuarenta y cinco centímetros de ancho y noventa centímetros de alto.g Sus cuernos formaban una sola pieza con el altar. 26Recubrió de oro puro su parte superior, sus cuatro costados y sus cuernos, y en su derredor le puso una moldura de oro. 27Debajo de la moldura le puso dos anillos de oro, es decir, dos en cada uno de sus costados, para pasar por ellos las varas empleadas para transportarlo. 28Las varas eran de madera de acacia, y las recubrió de oro.

29Bezalel hizo también el aceite de la unción sagrada y el incienso puro y aromático, como lo hacen los fabricantes de perfumes.

El altar de los holocaustos
38:1-7 — Éx 27:1-8

38 Bezalel hizo de madera de acacia el altar de los *holocaustos. Era cuadrado, de dos metros con treinta centímetros por lado, y de un metro con treinta centímetros de alto.h 2Puso un cuerno en cada una de sus cuatro esquinas, los cuales formaban una sola pieza con el altar, y el altar lo recubrió de bronce. 3Hizo de bronce todos sus utensilios: sus portacenizas, sus tenazas, sus aspersorios, sus tridentes y sus braseros. 4Hizo también un enrejado para el altar —una rejilla de bronce—, y la puso bajo el reborde inferior del altar, a media altura del mismo. 5Fundió cuatro anillos de bronce para las cuatro esquinas del enrejado de bronce, para pasar por ellos las varas; 6hizo las varas de madera de acacia, las recubrió de bronce 7y las introdujo en los anillos, de modo que quedaron a los dos costados del altar para poder transportarlo. El altar lo hizo hueco y de tablas. 8Además, con el bronce de los espejos de las mujeres que servían a la entrada de la *Tienda de reunión, hizo el lavamanos y su pedestal.

El atrio
38:9-20 — Éx 27:9-19

9Después hicieron el atrio. El lado sur medía cuarenta y cinco metrosi de largo, y tenía cortinas de lino fino, 10veinte postes y veinte bases de bronce, con ganchos y empalmes de plata en los postes. 11El lado norte medía también cuarenta y cinco metros de largo, y tenía veinte postes y veinte bases de bronce, con ganchos y empalmes de plata en los postes.

12El lado occidental medía veintidós metros y medioj de ancho, y tenía cortinas y diez postes y diez bases, con ganchos y empalmes de plata en los postes. 13Por el lado oriental, hacia la salida del sol, medía también veintidós metros y medio de ancho. 14A un lado de la entrada había cortinas de siete metrosk de largo, tres postes y tres bases, 15y al otro lado de la entrada había también cortinas de siete metros de largo, tres postes y tres bases. 16Todas las cortinas que rodeaban el atrio eran de lino fino. 17Las bases para los

b **37:1** *un metro ... de alto*. Lit. *dos *codos y medio de largo por un codo y medio de ancho y un codo y medio de alto*. c **37:6** *un metro ... de ancho*. Lit. *dos codos y medio de largo por un codo y medio de ancho*. d **37:10** *noventa ... de alto*. Lit. *dos codos de largo por un codo de ancho y un codo y medio de alto*. e **37:12** *veinte centímetros*. Lit. *un *palmo*. f **37:24** *treinta y tres kilos*. Lit. *un *talento*. g **37:25** *cuarenta y cinco ... de alto*. Lit. *un codo de largo por un codo de ancho y dos codos de alto*. h **38:1** *dos metros ... de alto*. Lit. *cinco *codos de largo por cinco codos de ancho y tres codos de alto*. i **38:9** *cuarenta y cinco metros*. Lit. *cien codos; también en v. 11. j **38:12** *veintidós metros y medio*. Lit. *cincuenta codos; también en v. 13. k **38:14** *siete metros*. Lit. *quince codos; también en v. 15.

postes eran de bronce, los ganchos y los empalmes en los postes eran de plata, y sus capiteles estaban recubiertos de plata. Todos los postes del atrio tenían empalmes de plata.

[18]La cortina a la entrada del atrio era de lana teñida de púrpura, carmesí y escarlata, y de lino fino, recamada artísticamente. Medía nueve metros[l] de largo por dos metros con treinta centímetros[m] de alto, como las cortinas del atrio, [19]y tenía cuatro postes y cuatro bases de bronce. Sus ganchos y sus empalmes eran de plata, y sus capiteles estaban recubiertos de plata. [20]Todas las estacas del toldo para el santuario y del atrio que lo rodeaba eran de bronce.

Los materiales usados

[21]Éstas son las cantidades de los materiales usados para el santuario del *pacto. Los levitas hicieron este registro por orden de Moisés y bajo la dirección de Itamar, hijo del sacerdote Aarón. [22]Bezalel, hijo de Uri y nieto de Jur, de la tribu de Judá, hizo todo lo que el SEÑOR le ordenó a Moisés. [23]Con él estaba Aholiab hijo de Ajisamac, de la tribu de Dan, que era artesano, diseñador y recamador en lana teñida de púrpura, carmesí y escarlata, y en lino.

[24]El total del oro dado como ofrenda y empleado en toda la obra del santuario era de una tonelada,[n] según la tasación oficial del santuario.

[25]La plata entregada por los miembros de la comunidad contados en el censo llegó a tres toneladas y media,[o] según la tasación oficial del santuario. [26]Todos los mayores de veinte años de edad que fueron censados llegaron a un total de seiscientos tres mil quinientos cincuenta, y cada uno de ellos dio seis gramos[p] de plata, según la tasación oficial del santuario. [27]Tres mil trescientos kilos[q] de plata se emplearon en las cien bases fundidas para el santuario y para la cortina, de modo que cada base pesaba treinta y tres kilos.[r] [28]La plata restante[s] se empleó en hacer los ganchos para los postes y recubrir los capiteles de los postes, y para hacer sus empalmes.

[29]El total del bronce dado como ofrenda fue de dos mil trescientos cuarenta kilos,[t] [30]y se empleó en las bases para la entrada de la *Tienda de reunión, en el altar de bronce con su enrejado de bronce y todos sus utensilios, [31]en las bases para el atrio y la entrada al atrio, y en todas las estacas del toldo para el santuario y para el atrio que lo rodeaba.

Las vestiduras sacerdotales

39 Las vestiduras tejidas para ministrar en el santuario se hicieron de lana teñida de púrpura, carmesí y escarlata. También se hicieron vestiduras sagradas para Aarón, como se lo mandó el SEÑOR a Moisés.

El efod
39:2-7 — Éx 28:6-14

[2]El *efod lo hizo Bezalel de oro, lana teñida de púrpura, carmesí y escarlata, y lino fino. [3]Martillaron finas láminas de oro, y las cortaron en hebras para entretejerlas artísticamente con la lana teñida de púrpura, carmesí y escarlata, y con el lino. [4]Se hicieron hombreras para el efod, las cuales se sujetaron a sus dos extremos. [5]Su cinturón tenía la misma hechura que el efod, y formaba una sola pieza con él; estaba hecho de oro, lana teñida de púrpura, carmesí y escarlata, y lino fino, como se lo mandó el SEÑOR a Moisés.

[6]Las piedras de ónice se engarzaron en los engastes de filigrana de oro, y en ellas se grabaron, a manera de sello, los *nombres de los hijos de Israel. [7]Luego las sujetaron a las hombreras del efod para recordar a los hijos de Israel, como se lo mandó el SEÑOR a Moisés.

El pectoral
39:8-21 — Éx 28:15-28

[8]Bezalel hizo también el pectoral, bordado artísticamente, como el *efod, con hilo de oro, lana teñida de púrpura, carmesí y escarlata, y lino fino, [9]doble y cuadrado, de veinte centímetros por lado.[u] [10]En él se engastaron cuatro filas de piedras preciosas. En la primera fila había un rubí, un crisólito y una esmeralda; [11]en la segunda hilera, una turquesa, un zafiro y un jade; [12]en la tercera hilera, un jacinto, un ágata y una amatista; [13]en la cuarta hilera, un topacio, un ónice y un jaspe.[v] Estaban engarzadas en engastes de filigrana de oro, [14]y eran doce piedras, una por cada uno de los hijos de Israel, grabada a manera de sello con el *nombre de cada una de las doce tribus.

[15]Para el pectoral se hicieron cadenillas de oro puro, a manera de cordón. [16]Se hicieron dos engastes en filigrana de oro y dos anillos de oro, y se sujetaron los anillos en los dos extremos del pectoral; [17]luego se sujetaron las dos cadenillas de oro en los anillos a los extremos del pectoral, [18]y los otros dos extremos de las cadenillas en los dos engastes, asegurándolos a las hombreras del efod por la parte delantera. [19]Se hicieron otros dos anillos de oro, y los sujetaron a los otros dos extremos del pectoral, en el borde interior, junto al efod. [20]Además, se hicieron otros dos anillos de oro, los cuales sujetaron la parte inferior de las hombreras, por delante del efod y junto a la costura, exactamente encima del cinturón del efod. [21]Con un cordón de lana púrpura ataron los anillos del pectoral a los anillos del efod, a fin de unir el pectoral al cinturón para que no se desprendiera del efod, como se lo mandó el SEÑOR a Moisés.

Otras vestiduras sacerdotales
39:22-31 — Éx 28:31-43

[22]Bezalel hizo de lana teñida de púrpura, y tejido artísticamente, todo el manto del *efod. [23]Lo hizo con una abertura en el centro, como abertura para la cabeza,[w] y con un refuerzo alrededor de la abertura, para que no se rasgara. [24]En todo el borde inferior del manto se hicieron granadas de lana púrpura, carmesí y escarlata, y de lino fino, [25]lo mismo que campanillas de oro puro, las cuales se colocaron en todo el borde inferior, entre las granadas. [26]Las campanillas y las granadas se colocaron, en forma alternada, en todo el borde inferior del manto que debía llevarse para ejercer el ministerio, como se lo mandó el SEÑOR a Moisés.

---

[l] **38:18** *nueve metros.* Lit. *veinte codos.* [m] **38:18** *dos metros con treinta centímetros.* Lit. *cinco codos.* [n] **38:24** *era de una tonelada.* Lit. *fue de veintinueve *talentos y setecientos treinta *siclos.* [ñ] **38:24** *la tasación oficial.* Lit. *el siclo;* también en vv. 25,26. [o] **38:25** *tres toneladas y media.* Lit. *cien talentos y mil setecientos setenta y cinco siclos.* [p] **38:26** *seis gramos.* Lit. *un becá, o* decir, medio siclo. [q] **38:27** *tres mil trescientos kilos.* Lit. *cien talentos.* [r] **38:27** *treinta y tres kilos.* Lit. *un talento.* [s] **38:28** *La plata restante.* Lit. *Los mil setecientos setenta y cinco siclos.* [t] **38:29** *dos mil trescientos cuarenta kilos.* Lit. *setenta talentos y dos mil trescientos cuarenta siclos.* [u] **39:9** *veinte centímetros por lado.* Lit. *un *palmo de largo y un palmo de ancho.* [v] **39:13** La identificación de algunas de estas piedras preciosas no ha podido establecerse con precisión.

[w] **39:23** *cabeza.* Palabra de difícil traducción.

27Para Aarón y sus hijos se hicieron túnicas de lino tejidas artísticamente, 28las mitras y el turbante de lino, y la ropa interior de lino fino. 29La faja era de lino fino y de lana teñida de púrpura, carmesí y escarlata, recamada artísticamente, como se lo mandó el SEÑOR a Moisés.

30La placa sagrada se hizo de oro puro, y se grabó en ella, a manera de sello, *SANTO PARA EL SEÑOR. 31Luego se le ató un cordón de lana teñida de púrpura para sujetarla al turbante, como se lo mandó el SEÑOR a Moisés.

Moisés inspecciona el santuario
39:32-41 — Éx 35:10-19

32Toda la obra del santuario, es decir, la *Tienda de reunión, quedó terminada. Los israelitas lo hicieron todo tal y como el SEÑOR se lo mandó a Moisés, 33y le presentaron a Moisés el santuario, la tienda y todos sus utensilios, sus ganchos, tablones, travesaños, postes y bases, 34el toldo de pieles de carnero teñidas de rojo, el toldo de pieles de delfín y la cortina que resguardaba el arca, 35el arca del *pacto con sus varas y el *propiciatorio, 36la mesa con todos sus utensilios y el *pan de la Presencia, 37el candelabro de oro puro con su hilera de lámparas y todos sus utensilios, y el aceite para el alumbrado; 38el altar de oro, el aceite de la unción, el incienso aromático y la cortina para la entrada de la tienda, 39el altar de bronce con su enrejado de bronce, sus varas y todos sus utensilios; el lavamanos y su pedestal, 40las cortinas del atrio con sus postes y bases, y la cortina para la entrada del atrio; las cuerdas y las estacas del toldo para el atrio; todos los utensilios para el santuario, la Tienda de reunión, 41y las vestiduras tejidas para ministrar en el santuario, tanto las vestiduras sagradas para el sacerdote Aarón como las vestiduras sacerdotales para sus hijos.

42Los israelitas hicieron toda la obra tal y como el SEÑOR se lo había ordenado a Moisés. 43Moisés, por su parte, inspeccionó la obra y, al ver que la habían hecho tal y como el SEÑOR se lo había ordenado, los bendijo.

Se levanta el santuario

40 El SEÑOR habló con Moisés y le dijo: 2«En el día primero del mes primero, levanta el santuario, es decir, la *Tienda de reunión. 3Pon en su interior el arca del *pacto, y cúbrela con la cortina. 4Lleva adentro la mesa y ponla en orden. Pon también dentro del santuario el candelabro, y enciende sus lámparas. 5Coloca el altar del incienso frente al arca del pacto, y cuelga la cortina a la entrada del santuario.

6»Coloca el altar de los *holocaustos frente a la entrada del santuario, la Tienda de reunión; 7coloca el lavamanos entre la Tienda de reunión y el altar, y pon agua en él. 8Levanta el atrio en su derredor, y coloca la cortina a la entrada del atrio.

9»Toma el aceite de la unción, y unge el santuario y todo lo que haya en él; conságralo, junto con todos sus utensilios, para que sea un objeto sagrado. 10Unge también el altar de los holocaustos y todos sus utensilios; conságralo, para que sea un objeto

muy sagrado. 11Unge además, y consagra, el lavamanos y su pedestal.

12»Lleva luego a Aarón y a sus hijos a la entrada de la Tienda de reunión, haz que se bañen, 13y ponle a Aarón sus vestiduras sagradas. Úngelo y conságralo, para que ministre como sacerdote mío. 14Acerca entonces a sus hijos, ponles sus túnicas, 15y úngelos como ungiste a su padre, para que ministren como mis sacerdotes. La unción les conferirá un sacerdocio válido para todas las generaciones venideras.»

16Moisés hizo todo tal y como el SEÑOR se lo mandó. 17Fue así como el santuario se instaló el día primero del mes primero del año segundo. 18Al instalar el santuario, Moisés puso en su lugar las bases, levantó los tablones, los insertó en los travesaños, y levantó los postes; 19luego extendió la tienda de campaña sobre el santuario, y encima de ésta puso el toldo, tal y como el SEÑOR se lo mandó.

20A continuación, tomó el documento del pacto y lo puso en el arca; luego ajustó las varas al arca, y sobre ella puso el *propiciatorio. 21Llevó el arca al interior del santuario, y colgó la cortina para resguardarla. De este modo protegió el arca del pacto, tal y como el SEÑOR se lo había ordenado.

22Moisés puso la mesa en la Tienda de reunión, en el lado norte del santuario, fuera de la cortina, 23y puso el pan en orden ante el SEÑOR, como el SEÑOR se lo había ordenado. 24Colocó luego el candelabro en la Tienda de reunión, frente a la mesa, en el lado sur del santuario, 25y encendió las lámparas ante el SEÑOR, como el SEÑOR se lo había ordenado. 26Puso también el altar de oro en la Tienda de reunión, frente a la cortina, 27y sobre él quemó incienso aromático, tal y como el SEÑOR se lo había ordenado. 28Después de eso colgó la cortina a la entrada del santuario.

29Moisés puso también el altar de los holocaustos a la entrada del santuario, la Tienda de reunión, y sobre él ofreció holocaustos y ofrendas de grano, tal y como el SEÑOR se lo había ordenado. 30Colocó luego el lavamanos entre la Tienda de reunión y el altar, y echó en ella agua para lavarse, 31y Moisés, Aarón y sus hijos se lavaron allí las manos y los pies. 32Siempre que entraban en la Tienda de reunión o se acercaban al altar se lavaban, tal y como el SEÑOR se lo había ordenado.

33Después levantó Moisés el atrio en torno al santuario y al altar, y colgó la cortina a la entrada del atrio. Así terminó Moisés la obra.

La gloria del SEÑOR

34En ese instante la nube cubrió la *Tienda de reunión, y la gloria del SEÑOR llenó el santuario. 35Moisés no podía entrar en la Tienda de reunión porque la nube se había posado en ella y la gloria del SEÑOR llenaba el santuario.

36Siempre que la nube se levantaba y se apartaba del santuario, los israelitas levantaban campamento y se ponían en marcha. 37Si la nube no se levantaba, ellos no se ponían en marcha. 38Durante todas las marchas de los israelitas, la nube del SEÑOR reposaba sobre el santuario durante el día, pero durante la noche había fuego en la nube, a la vista de todo el pueblo de Israel.

LEVÍTICO

El holocausto

1 El SEÑOR llamó a Moisés y le habló desde la *Tienda de reunión. Le ordenó 2que les dijera a los israelitas: «Cuando alguno de ustedes traiga una ofrenda al SEÑOR, deberá presentar un animal de ganado vacuno u ovino.

3»Si el animal que ofrece en *holocausto es de ganado vacuno, deberá presentar un macho sin defecto, a la entrada de la Tienda de reunión. Así será aceptable al SEÑOR. 4Pondrá su mano sobre la cabeza de la víctima, la cual le será aceptada en su lugar y le servirá de *propiciación. 5Después degollará el novillo ante el SEÑOR, y los hijos de Aarón, los sacerdotes, tomarán la sangre y la derramarán alrededor del altar que está a la entrada de la Tienda de reunión. 6Luego desollará la víctima del holocausto y la cortará en trozos. 7Los hijos de Aarón, los sacerdotes, harán fuego sobre el altar y le echarán leña; 8después acomodarán los trozos sobre la leña encendida del altar, junto con la cabeza y el sebo. 9Las entrañas y las patas se lavarán con agua, y el sacerdote lo quemará todo en el altar. Es un holocausto, una ofrenda presentada por fuego de aroma grato al SEÑOR.

10»Si alguien ofrece un holocausto de ganado ovino, sea de corderos o de cabras, deberá presentar un macho sin defecto. 11Lo degollará ante el SEÑOR, en el costado norte del altar, y los hijos de Aarón, los sacerdotes, derramarán la sangre alrededor del altar. 12Luego lo cortará en trozos, los cuales el sacerdote acomodará sobre la leña encendida del altar, junto con la cabeza y el sebo. 13Las entrañas y las patas se lavarán con agua, y el sacerdote lo tomará todo y lo quemará en el altar. Es un holocausto, una ofrenda presentada por fuego de aroma grato al SEÑOR.

14»Si alguien ofrece al SEÑOR un holocausto de ave, deberá presentar una tórtola o un pichón de paloma. 15El sacerdote llevará el ave al altar y le arrancará la cabeza, y luego la quemará en el altar. Después exprimirá la sangre en un costado del altar, 16y le quitará también el buche y las entrañas, y los arrojará hacia el costado oriental del altar, donde se echa la ceniza. 17Después la desgarrará por las alas, pero sin arrancárselas. Entonces el sacerdote la quemará en el altar, sobre la leña encendida. Es un holocausto, una ofrenda presentada por fuego de aroma grato al SEÑOR.

La ofrenda de cereal

2 »Si alguien presenta al SEÑOR una ofrenda de cereal, ésta será de flor de harina, sobre la cual pondrá aceite e incienso. 2Luego la llevará a los hijos de Aarón, los sacerdotes; allí tomará un puñado de flor de harina con aceite, junto con todo el incienso, y el sacerdote quemará esa ofrenda memorial en el altar. Es una ofrenda presentada por fuego de aroma grato al SEÑOR. 3El resto de la ofrenda de cereal será para Aarón y sus hijos. Entre las ofrendas por fuego que se presentan al SEÑOR, ésta es sumamente sagrada.

4»Si presentas una ofrenda de cereal cocida al horno, ésta será de panes de flor de harina sin levadura, amasados con aceite, o de obleas sin levadura untadas con aceite.

5»Si presentas una ofrenda de cereal cocida en la sartén, la ofrenda será de flor de harina sin levadura, amasada con aceite. 6La partirás en pedazos y le echarás aceite. Es una ofrenda de cereal.

7»Si presentas una ofrenda de cereal cocida a la olla, la ofrenda será de flor de harina con aceite. 8Así preparada la ofrenda de cereal, se la llevarás al SEÑOR, es decir, se la llevarás al sacerdote, quien la presentará en el altar. 9El sacerdote, luego de tomar una parte como ofrenda memorial, la quemará en el altar. Es una ofrenda presentada por fuego de aroma grato al SEÑOR. 10El resto de la ofrenda de cereal será para Aarón y sus hijos. Entre las ofrendas por fuego que se presentan al SEÑOR, ésta es sumamente sagrada.

11»Ninguna ofrenda de cereal que ustedes presenten al SEÑOR se hará de masa fermentada, porque en una ofrenda al Señor presentada por fuego no se deben quemar ni miel ni levadura. 12Llevarán al SEÑOR levadura y miel como ofrenda de *primicias, pero no las pondrán sobre el altar como aroma grato. 13Todas las ofrendas de cereal las sazonarán con sal, y no dejarán que les falte la sal del *pacto de su Dios. A todas las ofrendas deberán ponerles sal.

14»Si le presentas al SEÑOR una ofrenda de las primicias de tus cereales, ésta será de trigo nuevo, molido y tostado al fuego. Es la ofrenda de cereal de tus primicias. 15Le pondrás aceite e incienso; es una ofrenda de cereal. 16El sacerdote quemará parte del trigo nuevo y molido como ofrenda memorial, junto con todo el incienso y el aceite. Es una ofrenda al SEÑOR presentada por fuego.

El sacrificio de comunión

3 »Si alguien ofrece ganado vacuno al SEÑOR como sacrificio de *comunión, deberá presentarle un animal sin defecto, sea macho o hembra. 2Pondrá su mano sobre la cabeza del animal, al que degollará a la entrada de la *Tienda de reunión. Luego los hijos de Aarón, los sacerdotes, derramarán la sangre alrededor del altar. 3El oferente le presentará al SEÑOR, como ofrenda por fuego, las siguientes partes del sacrificio de comunión: la grasa que recubre los intestinos y la que se adhiere a éstos, 4los dos riñones y la grasa que los recubre, la grasa que recubre los lomos, y también el lóbulo del hígado, el cual extraerá junto con los riñones. 5Entonces los hijos de Aarón quemarán todo esto en el altar, encima del *holocausto que está sobre la leña encendida. Es una ofrenda presentada por fuego de aroma grato al SEÑOR.

6»Si el sacrificio de comunión es de ganado ovino, el oferente deberá presentarle al SEÑOR un animal sin defecto, sea macho o hembra. 7Si la ofrenda es un cordero, lo presentará ante el SEÑOR 8y le impondrá la mano sobre la cabeza, degollando luego al animal ante la Tienda de reunión. Luego los hijos de Aarón derramarán la sangre alrededor del altar. 9El oferente le presentará al SEÑOR, como ofrenda por fuego, las siguientes partes de este sacrificio: la grasa, la cola entera (la cual cortará desde el espinazo), la grasa que recubre los intestinos y la que se adhiere a éstos, 10los dos riñones y la grasa que los recubre, la grasa que recubre los lomos, y también el lóbulo del hígado, el cual extraerá junto con los riñones. 11Entonces el sacerdote quemará todo esto en el altar. Es una comida, una ofrenda presentada por fuego al SEÑOR.

12»Si la ofrenda es una cabra, la presentará ante el SEÑOR 13poniendo la mano sobre la cabeza del animal, al que degollará ante la Tienda de reunión. Luego los hijos de Aarón derramarán la sangre alrededor del altar. 14El oferente le presentará al SEÑOR, como ofrenda por fuego, las siguientes partes del animal: la grasa que recubre los intestinos y la que se adhiere a éstos, 15los dos riñones y la grasa que los recubre, la grasa que recubre los lomos, y también el lóbulo del hígado, el cual se extraerá junto con los riñones. 16Entonces el sacerdote quemará todo esto en el altar. Es una comida, una ofrenda presentada por fuego de aroma grato. Toda la grasa pertenece al SEÑOR.

17»Éste será un estatuto perpetuo para los descendientes de ustedes, dondequiera que habiten: No se comerán la grasa ni la sangre.»

El sacrificio expiatorio

4 El SEÑOR le ordenó a Moisés 2que les dijera a los israelitas: «Cuando alguien viole inadvertidamente cualquiera de los mandamientos del SEÑOR, e incurra en algo que esté prohibido, se procederá de la siguiente manera:

El sacrificio expiatorio por el pecado del sacerdote

3»Si el que peca es el sacerdote ungido, haciendo con ello culpable al pueblo, deberá ofrecer al SEÑOR, como sacrificio *expiatorio por su pecado, un novillo sin defecto. 4Llevará el novillo ante el SEÑOR, a la entrada de la *Tienda de reunión, e impondrá la mano sobre la cabeza del novillo, al que degollará en presencia del SEÑOR. 5El sacerdote ungido tomará un poco de la sangre del novillo y la llevará a la Tienda de reunión. 6Mojará el dedo en la sangre, y rociará con ella siete veces en dirección a la cortina del santuario, en presencia del SEÑOR. 7Después el sacerdote untará un poco de la sangre en los cuernos del altar del incienso aromático, que está ante el SEÑOR, en la Tienda de reunión. El resto de la sangre del novillo la derramará al pie del altar de la *holocausto, que está a la entrada de la Tienda de reunión. 8Luego, al novillo del sacrificio expiatorio le sacará toda la grasa que recubre los intestinos, y la que se adhiere a éstos, 9los dos riñones y la grasa que los recubre, la grasa que recubre los lomos, y también el lóbulo del hígado, el cual se extraerá junto con los riñones. 10Esto se hará tal y como se saca la grasa de la res para el sacrificio de *comunión. Entonces el sacerdote quemará todo esto en el altar del holocausto, 11pero sacará del campamento la piel y toda la carne del novillo, junto con la cabeza, las patas, los intestinos y el excremento. 12Todo esto, es decir, el resto del novillo, lo sacará del campamento y lo llevará a un lugar ritualmente *puro, al vertedero de la ceniza, y dejará que se consuma sobre la leña encendida. Sobre el vertedero de la ceniza se consumirá.

El sacrificio expiatorio por el pecado de la comunidad

13»Si la que peca inadvertidamente es toda la comunidad de Israel, toda la asamblea será culpable de haber hecho algo que los mandamientos del SEÑOR prohíben. 14Cuando la asamblea se dé cuenta del pecado que ha cometido, deberá ofrecer un novillo como sacrificio *expiatorio. Lo llevarán a la *Tienda de reunión, 15y allí, en presencia del SEÑOR, los *ancianos de la comunidad impondrán las manos sobre la cabeza del novillo y lo degollarán. 16Luego el sacerdote ungido tomará un poco de la sangre del novillo y la llevará a la Tienda de reunión. 17Mojará el dedo en la sangre, y rociará con ella siete veces en dirección a la cortina en presencia del SEÑOR. 18Después untará un poco de la sangre en los cuernos del altar, que está ante el SEÑOR, en la Tienda de reunión. El resto de la sangre la derramará al pie del altar del *holocausto, que está a la entrada de la

Tienda de reunión, 19y sacará del animal toda la grasa, quemándola en el altar. 20Se hará con este novillo lo mismo que se hace con el de la ofrenda expiatoria. Así el sacerdote hará expiación por ellos, y serán perdonados. 21Luego sacará del campamento el resto del novillo y dejará que se consuma en el fuego, como el otro. Éste es el sacrificio expiatorio por la asamblea.

El sacrificio expiatorio por el pecado de un gobernante

22»Si el que peca inadvertidamente es uno de los gobernantes, e incurre en algo que los mandamientos del SEÑOR su Dios prohíben, será culpable. 23Cuando se le haga saber que ha cometido un pecado, llevará como ofrenda un macho cabrío sin defecto, 24pondrá la mano sobre la cabeza del macho cabrío, y lo degollará en presencia del SEÑOR, en el mismo lugar donde se degüellan los animales para el *holocausto. Es un sacrificio *expiatorio. 25Entonces el sacerdote tomará con el dedo un poco de la sangre del sacrificio expiatorio y la untará en los cuernos del altar del holocausto, después de lo cual derramará al pie del altar del holocausto el resto de la sangre.

26Toda la grasa del animal la quemará en el altar, tal como se hace con el sacrificio de *comunión. Así el sacerdote hará expiación por el pecado del gobernante, y su pecado le será perdonado.

El sacrificio expiatorio por el pecado de un miembro del pueblo

27»Si el que peca inadvertidamente es alguien del pueblo, e incurre en algo que los mandamientos del SEÑOR prohíben, será culpable. 28Cuando se le haga saber que ha cometido un pecado, llevará como ofrenda por su pecado una cabra sin defecto. 29Pondrá la mano sobre la cabeza del animal, y lo degollará en el lugar donde se degüellan los animales para el *holocausto. 30Entonces el sacerdote tomará con el dedo un poco de la sangre y la untará en los cuernos del altar del holocausto, después de lo cual derramará el resto de la sangre al pie del altar. 31Luego le sacará al animal toda la grasa, tal y como se le saca la grasa al sacrificio de *comunión, y el sacerdote la quemará toda en el altar, como aroma grato al SEÑOR. Así el sacerdote hará *expiación por él, y su pecado le será perdonado.

32»Si la persona ofrece como sacrificio expiatorio un cordero, deberá presentar una hembra sin defecto. 33Pondrá la mano sobre la cabeza del animal, y lo degollará como sacrificio expiatorio en el lugar donde se degüellan los animales para el holocausto. 34Entonces el sacerdote tomará con el dedo un poco de la sangre del sacrificio expiatorio y la untará en los cuernos del altar del holocausto, después de lo cual derramará al pie del altar el resto de la sangre. 35Luego le sacará al animal toda la grasa, tal y como se le saca la grasa al cordero del sacrificio de comunión, y el sacerdote la quemará en el altar sobre la ofrenda presentada por fuego al SEÑOR. Así el sacerdote hará expiación por esa persona, y el pecado que haya cometido le será perdonado.

El sacrificio expiatorio por diversos pecados

5 »Si alguien peca por negarse a declarar bajo juramento lo que vio o escuchó, sufrirá las consecuencias de su pecado.

2»Si alguien sin darse cuenta toca alguna cosa ritualmente *impura, tal como el cadáver de un animal impuro, sea o no doméstico, o el cadáver de un reptil impuro, se vuelve impuro él mismo y es culpable.

3»Si alguien sin darse cuenta toca alguna impureza humana, cualquiera que ésta sea, se vuelve impuro él mismo. Pero al darse cuenta, será culpable.

4»Si alguien hace uno de esos juramentos que se acostumbra hacer a la ligera, y si en saberlo jura hacer bien o mal, ha pecado. Pero al darse cuenta, será culpable de haber hecho ese juramento.

5»Si alguien resulta culpable de alguna de estas cosas, deberá reconocer que ha pecado 6y llevarle al SEÑOR en sacrificio *expiatorio por la culpa del pecado cometido, una hembra del rebaño, que podrá ser una oveja o una cabra. Así el sacerdote hará expiación por ese pecado.

El caso del pobre

7»Si a alguien no le alcanza para comprar ganado menor, entonces le llevará al SEÑOR, como sacrificio por la culpa del pecado cometido, dos tórtolas o dos pichones de paloma, uno de las aves como sacrificio por el pecado y la otra como *holocausto. 8Se las llevará al sacerdote, quien primero ofrecerá el ave para el sacrificio *expiatorio. Para esto, le retorcerá el cuello, pero sin desprenderle del todo la cabeza. 9Luego rociará un poco de la sangre del sacrificio expiatorio en un costado del altar, y al pie del altar exprimirá el resto de la sangre. Es un sacrificio expiatorio. 10Con la segunda ave hará un holocausto, como ya ha sido prescrito. Así el sacerdote hará expiación por el pecado cometido, y ese pecado le será perdonado.

11»Si a esa persona tampoco le alcanza para comprar dos tórtolas o dos pichones, presentará entonces en sacrificio expiatorio, como ofrenda por el pecado cometido, dos litros[a] de flor de harina. Como se trata de un sacrificio expiatorio, no se le pondrá aceite ni incienso. 12Llevará este sacrificio al sacerdote, quien tomará un puñado de la ofrenda memorial y lo quemará en el altar junto con los sacrificios presentados por fuego al SEÑOR. Es un sacrificio expiatorio. 13Así el sacerdote hará expiación por el pecado cometido en alguna de estas cosas, y ese pecado le será perdonado. El resto de la ofrenda será para el sacerdote, como sucede con la ofrenda de cereal.»

El sacrificio por la culpa

14El SEÑOR le dijo a Moisés: 15«Si alguien comete una falta y peca inadvertidamente contra lo que ha sido consagrado al SEÑOR, le llevará al SEÑOR un carnero sin defecto como sacrificio por la culpa. Su precio será tasado en plata, según la tasación oficial del santuario. Es un sacrificio por la culpa. 16Además, el culpable hará restitución por haber pecado contra lo consagrado, añadiendo la quinta parte, la cual entregará al sacerdote. Así el sacerdote hará *expiación por él mediante el carnero del sacrificio por la culpa, y ese pecado le será perdonado.

17»Si alguien peca inadvertidamente e incurre en algo que los mandamientos del SEÑOR prohíben, es culpable y sufrirá las consecuencias de su pecado. 18Le llevará al sacerdote un carnero sin defecto, cuyo precio será fijado como sacrificio por la culpa. Así el sacerdote hará expiación por el pecado que esa persona cometió inadvertidamente, y ese pecado le será perdonado. 19Es un sacrificio por la culpa, de la que se hizo acreedor por pecar contra el SEÑOR.»

6 El SEÑOR le dijo a Moisés: 2«Si alguien comete una falta y peca contra el SEÑOR al defraudar a su prójimo en algo que se dejó a su cuidado, o si roba u oprime a su prójimo despojándolo de lo que es suyo, 3o si se encuentra algo que se perdió y niega tenerlo, o si comete perjurio en alguna de las cosas en que se acostumbra pecar, 4será culpable y deberá devolver lo que haya robado, o quitado, o si se haya dado a guardar, o el objeto perdido que niega tener, 5o cualquier otra cosa por la que haya cometido perjurio. Así que deberá restituirlo íntegramente y añadir la quinta parte de su valor. Todo esto lo entregará a su dueño el día que presente su sacrificio por la culpa. 6Le llevará al SEÑOR un carnero sin defecto, cuyo precio será fijado como sacrificio por la culpa. Lo presentará al sacerdote, 7quien hará *expiación ante el SEÑOR por esa persona, y cualquier cosa por la que se haya hecho culpable le será perdonada.»

El holocausto

8El SEÑOR le dijo a Moisés 9que les ordenara a Aarón y a sus hijos: «Ésta es la ley respecto al *holocausto: El holocausto se dejará arder sobre el altar toda la noche hasta el amanecer, y el fuego del altar se mantendrá encendido. 10El sacerdote, vestido con su túnica de lino y su ropa interior de lino, removerá las cenizas del holocausto consumido por el fuego sobre el altar, y las echará a un lado del altar. 11Luego se cambiará de ropa y sacará del campamento las cenizas, llevándolas a un lugar ritualmente *puro. 12Mientras tanto, el fuego se mantendrá encendido sobre el altar; no deberá apagarse. Cada mañana el sacerdote pondrá más leña sobre el altar, y encima de éste colocará el holocausto para quemar en él la grasa del sacrificio de *comunión. 13El fuego sobre el altar no deberá apagarse nunca; siempre deberá estar encendido.

La ofrenda de cereal

14»Ésta es la ley respecto a la ofrenda de cereal: Los hijos de Aarón la presentarán ante el SEÑOR, delante del altar. 15El sacerdote tomará de la ofrenda un puñado de flor de harina con aceite, así como todo el incienso que está sobre la ofrenda de cereal. Todo esto lo quemará en el altar, como ofrenda memorial de aroma grato al SEÑOR. 16Aarón y sus hijos se comerán el resto de la ofrenda, pero sin levadura y en un lugar *santo, que podrá ser el atrio de la *Tienda de reunión. 17No se cocerá con levadura, porque esa es la porción que les doy de mis sacrificios presentados por fuego. Es una porción sumamente sagrada, como lo son el sacrificio *expiatorio y el sacrificio por la culpa. 18Todos los hijos varones de Aarón podrán comer de ella. Es un estatuto[b] perpetuo para los descendientes de ustedes, respecto a los sacrificios presentados por fuego al SEÑOR. Cualquier cosa que toque los sacrificios quedará consagrada.»

La ofrenda de los sacerdotes

19El SEÑOR le dijo a Moisés: 20«Ésta es la ofrenda que Aarón y sus hijos deben presentar al SEÑOR el día en que sean ungidos: dos kilos[c] de flor de harina, como ofrenda regular de cereal. Una mitad de la ofrenda se presentará por la mañana, y la otra mitad por la tarde. 21Se preparará con aceite en una sartén, y se llevará amasada y se presentará en porciones, como una ofrenda de cereal de aroma grato al SEÑOR. 22La preparará el hijo de Aarón que lo suceda como sacerdote ungido. Éste es el estatuto perpetuo del SEÑOR: La ofrenda se quemará completamente. 23No

---

a 5:11 dos litros. Lit. una décima de *efa.   b 6:18 estatuto. Alt. derecho; también en vv. 22 y 36.   c 6:20 dos kilos. Lit. una décima de efa.

se comerá ninguna de las ofrendas que presenten los sacerdotes; todas deberán quemarse por completo.»

El sacrificio expiatorio

24El SEÑOR le ordenó a Moisés 25que les dijera a Aarón y a sus hijos: «Ésta es la ley respecto al sacrificio *expiatorio: La víctima deberá ser degollada ante el SEÑOR, en el mismo lugar donde se degüellan los animales para el *holocausto. Es algo sumamente sagrado. 26El mismo sacerdote que ofrezca el sacrificio expiatorio deberá comérselo. Se lo comerá en un lugar *santo, que podrá ser el atrio de la *Tienda de reunión. 27Cualquier cosa que toque la carne del sacrificio quedará consagrada. Si su sangre llega a salpicar algún vestido, éste deberá lavarse en un lugar santo. 28Además, deberá romperse la vasija de barro en que se haya cocido el sacrificio; pero si se cuece en una vasija de bronce, ésta se restregará y se enjuagará con agua. 29Todo varón entre los sacerdotes podrá comer del sacrificio. Es algo sumamente sagrado. 30Pero no se comerá ningún sacrificio expiatorio cuya sangre haya sido llevada a la Tienda de reunión para hacer *propiciación en el santuario; este sacrificio se consumirá en el fuego.

El sacrificio por la culpa

7 »Ésta es la ley respecto al sacrificio por la culpa, el cual es sumamente sagrado: 2La víctima deberá ser degollada en el mismo lugar donde se degüellan los animales para el *holocausto, y su sangre será derramada alrededor del altar. 3Luego se ofrecerá toda su grasa: la cola, la grasa que recubre los intestinos, 4los dos riñones y la grasa que los recubre, la grasa que recubre los lomos, y también el lóbulo del hígado, el cual se extraerá junto con los riñones. 5El sacerdote quemará todo esto en el altar como ofrenda presentada por fuego al SEÑOR. Es un sacrificio por la culpa. 6Todo varón entre los sacerdotes podrá comer del sacrificio, pero deberá comerlo en un lugar *santo. Es algo sumamente sagrado.

Derechos de los sacerdotes

7»La misma ley se aplica tanto al sacrificio *expiatorio como al sacrificio por la culpa: El animal pertenecerá al sacerdote que haga *propiciación con él. 8La piel de la víctima del holocausto también será para el sacerdote que la ofrezca. 9Así mismo, toda ofrenda de cereal cocida al horno, a la olla o a la sartén, será del sacerdote que la ofrezca. 10Toda ofrenda de cereal, ya sea seca o amasada con aceite, pertenecerá a todos los hijos de Aarón, por partes iguales.

Diversos sacrificios de comunión

11»Ésta es la ley respecto al sacrificio de *comunión que se ofrece al SEÑOR: 12Si se ofrece en acción de gracias, entonces se ofrecerán también panes sin levadura amasados con aceite, obleas sin levadura untadas con aceite, o panes de flor de harina amasados con aceite. 13Junto con el sacrificio de comunión en acción de gracias, se deberá presentar una ofrenda de pan con levadura. 14De toda ofrenda deberá presentarse una parte como contribución al SEÑOR, y se destinará al sacerdote a quien le corresponda derramar la sangre del sacrificio de comunión. 15La carne de este sacrificio deberá comerse el día en que se ofrezca, sin dejar nada para el día siguiente.

16»Si el sacrificio tiene que ver con un voto, o si se trata de una ofrenda voluntaria, no sólo se comerá en el día que se ofrezca el sacrificio, sino que podrá comerse el resto del día siguiente. 17Pero toda

la carne que quede hasta el tercer día se quemará en el fuego.

18»Si alguna carne del sacrificio de comunión llega a comerse al tercer día, tal sacrificio no será válido ni se tomará en cuenta, porque la carne ya está descompuesta. El que la coma sufrirá las consecuencias de su pecado.

19»No deberá comerse la carne que haya tocado alguna cosa ritualmente *impura, sino que se quemará en el fuego. En cuanto a otra carne, toda persona pura podrá comerla.

20»Si una persona impura come la carne ofrecida al SEÑOR en el sacrificio de comunión, será eliminada de su pueblo.

21»Si alguien toca cualquier clase de impureza humana, o de animal o de algo detestable, y luego come la carne ofrecida al SEÑOR en el sacrificio de comunión, será eliminado de su pueblo.»

Prohibiciones acerca de la grasa y de la sangre

22El SEÑOR le ordenó a Moisés 23que les dijera a los israelitas: «Ustedes no comerán grasa de ganado vacuno, ovino o cabrío. 24La grasa de un animal muerto o destrozado podrá usarse con cualquier otro fin, menos para comerla. 25Todo el que coma grasa de animales presentados como ofrenda por fuego al SEÑOR, será eliminado de su pueblo. 26Vivan donde vivan, ustedes no comerán grasa ni sangre alguna, sea de ave o de otro animal. 27Todo el que coma cualquier clase de sangre, será eliminado de su pueblo.»

La porción de los sacerdotes

28El SEÑOR le ordenó a Moisés 29que les dijera a los israelitas: «El que ofrezca al SEÑOR un sacrificio de *comunión deberá presentar al SEÑOR parte de ese sacrificio, 30y presentarle también una ofrenda por fuego. Llevará la grasa y el pecho, y mecerá ante el SEÑOR el pecho de la víctima como ofrenda mecida. 31El sacerdote quemará la grasa en el altar, pero el pecho será para Aarón y sus hijos. 32Al sacerdote se le dará, como contribución, el muslo derecho del sacrificio de comunión. 33El muslo derecho será la porción del sacerdoted a quien le toque ofrecer la sangre y la grasa del sacrificio. 34Porque de los sacrificios de comunión que ofrecen los israelitas, yo he tomado el pecho mecido y el muslo para dárselos, como contribución, al sacerdote Aarón y a sus hijos. Éste será un estatutoe perpetuo entre los israelitas.»

35De las ofrendas presentadas por fuego al SEÑOR, ésa es la porción consagrada para Aarón y sus hijos desde el día en que Moisés se los presentó al SEÑOR como sacerdotes. 36El día en que fueron ungidos, el SEÑOR ordenó a los israelitas darles esa porción. Es un estatuto perpetuo para sus descendientes.

37Ésta es la ley respecto a los *holocaustos, las ofrendas de cereales, los sacrificios *expiatorios, los sacrificios por la culpa, los sacrificios de ordenación y los sacrificios de comunión. 38El SEÑOR se la dio a Moisés en el monte Sinaí el día en que mandó a los israelitas presentarle ofrendas en el desierto de Sinaí.

La ordenación de Aarón y sus hijos
8:1-36 — Éx 29:1-37

8 El SEÑOR le dijo a Moisés: 2«Toma a Aarón y a sus hijos, junto con sus vestiduras, el aceite de la unción, el novillo para el sacrificio *expiatorio, los dos carneros y el canastillo de los panes sin levadura, 3y congrega a toda la comunidad a la entrada de la *Tienda de reunión.»

---

d 7:33 del sacerdote. Lit. de entre los hijos de Aarón.   e 7:34 estatuto. Alt. derecho; también en v. 36.

⁴Moisés llevó a cabo la orden del SEÑOR, y congregó a la comunidad a la entrada de la Tienda de reunión. ⁵Allí Moisés les dijo: «Esto es lo que el SEÑOR nos ha ordenado hacer.» ⁶Acto seguido, Moisés hizo que se acercaran Aarón y sus hijos, y los lavó con agua. ⁷A Aarón le puso la túnica y se la ciñó con la faja; luego lo cubrió con el manto, y encima le puso el *efod, ciñéndoselo con la cinta del mismo. ⁸En seguida, le colocó el pectoral, y sobre éste puso el *urim y el tumim. ⁹Por último, le colocó la tiara en la cabeza, y en la parte delantera puso la placa de oro, símbolo de su consagración, tal como el SEÑOR se lo había mandado.

¹⁰Después Moisés tomó el aceite de la unción, y ungió el santuario y todo lo que había en él, para consagrarlos. ¹¹Siete veces roció el aceite sobre el altar, para ungirlo y consagrarlo junto con el lavamanos y su base, y todos sus utensilios. ¹²Luego, para consagrar a Aarón, lo ungió derramando sobre su cabeza el aceite de la unción.

¹³Acto seguido, Moisés hizo que los hijos de Aarón se acercaran, y los vistió con las túnicas; se las ciñó con la faja, y les sujetó las mitras, tal como el SEÑOR se lo había mandado. ¹⁴Luego hizo traer el novillo del sacrificio expiatorio, y Aarón y sus hijos pusieron las manos sobre la cabeza del novillo. ¹⁵Después Moisés lo degolló, y tomando un poco de sangre con el dedo, la untó en los cuernos alrededor del altar para *purificarlo. El resto de la sangre la derramó al pie del altar, y así lo consagró e hizo *propiciación por él. ¹⁶Luego Moisés tomó toda la grasa que recubre los intestinos, el lóbulo del hígado, los dos riñones y su grasa, y los quemó en el altar. ¹⁷Pero el resto del novillo, es decir, la piel, la carne y el excremento, lo quemó en el fuego, fuera del campamento, tal como el SEÑOR se lo había mandado.

¹⁸Moisés mandó traer el carnero del *holocausto, y Aarón y sus hijos pusieron las manos sobre la cabeza del carnero. ¹⁹Moisés lo degolló, y derramó la sangre alrededor del altar. ²⁰Cortó luego el carnero en trozos, y quemó la cabeza, los trozos y el sebo. ²¹Lavó con agua los intestinos y las patas, y luego quemó todo el carnero en el altar como holocausto de aroma grato, como ofrenda presentada por fuego al SEÑOR, tal como el SEÑOR se lo había mandado.

²²Después Moisés mandó traer el otro carnero, el del sacrificio de ordenación, y Aarón y sus hijos pusieron las manos sobre la cabeza del carnero. ²³Moisés lo degolló, y tomando un poco de la sangre, se la untó a Aarón en el lóbulo de la oreja derecha, en el pulgar de la mano derecha y en el dedo gordo del pie derecho. ²⁴Además, hizo que los hijos de Aarón se acercaran, y les untó sangre en el lóbulo de la oreja derecha, en el pulgar de la mano derecha y en el dedo gordo del pie derecho. Luego derramó la sangre alrededor del altar. ²⁵Tomó la grasa y la cola, y toda la grasa que recubre los intestinos, el lóbulo del hígado, los dos riñones y su grasa, y el muslo derecho, ²⁶y tomando del canastillo que estaba colocado ante el SEÑOR un pan sin levadura, una oblea y una torta de pan amasada con aceite, lo puso todo sobre la grasa y el muslo derecho. ²⁷Todo esto lo puso sobre las manos de Aarón y de sus hijos, y Aarón lo ofreció ante el SEÑOR como ofrenda mecida. ²⁸Después se lo entregaron a Moisés, quien lo quemó en el altar, junto con el holocausto, como un sacrificio de ordenación de aroma grato, como una ofrenda presentada por fuego al SEÑOR. ²⁹Luego, de la parte de la ofrenda que le pertenecía, Moisés tomó el pecho de la víctima y se lo presentó al SEÑOR como ofrenda mecida, tal como el SEÑOR se lo había mandado.

³⁰Moisés tomó un poco del aceite de la unción y de la sangre del altar, y roció a Aarón y a sus hijos, junto con sus vestiduras. Así consagró a Moisés a Aarón y a sus hijos, junto con sus vestiduras.

³¹Luego les dijo Moisés a Aarón y a sus hijos: «Cuezan la carne a la entrada de la Tienda de reunión, y cómanla allí junto con el pan del sacrificio de ordenación, tal como lo ordené cuando dije: "Aarón y sus hijos se lo comerán." ³²Quemen después en el fuego el resto de la carne y del pan. ³³Quédense siete días a la entrada de la Tienda de reunión, hasta que se complete el rito de su ordenación, que dura siete días. ³⁴El SEÑOR mandó que se hiciera propiciación por ustedes, tal como se ha hecho hoy. ³⁵Así que siete días con sus noches se quedarán a la entrada de la Tienda de reunión, cumpliendo con lo que el SEÑOR ha prescrito, para que no mueran. Así me lo ha mandado el SEÑOR.» ³⁶Y Aarón y sus hijos hicieron todo lo que el SEÑOR había mandado por medio de Moisés.

Los sacerdotes inician su ministerio

9 Al octavo día Moisés llamó a Aarón y a sus hijos, y a los *ancianos de Israel. ²A Aarón le dijo: «Toma un becerro para el sacrificio *expiatorio y un carnero para el *holocausto, ambos sin defecto, y preséntaselos al SEÑOR. ³Diles después a los israelitas: "Traigan un macho cabrío para el sacrificio expiatorio, y un becerro y un cordero para el holocausto, ambos de un año y sin defecto. ⁴Traigan también un toro y un carnero para ofrecérselos al SEÑOR como sacrificio de *comunión; y traigan una ofrenda de cereal amasada con aceite. El SEÑOR se manifestará hoy ante ustedes."»

⁵Los israelitas llevaron hasta la *Tienda de reunión lo que Moisés había mandado; y toda la comunidad se acercó y se quedó de pie ante el SEÑOR. ⁶Y Moisés les dijo: «Esto es lo que el SEÑOR les manda hacer, para que la gloria del SEÑOR se manifieste ante ustedes.»

⁷Después Moisés le dijo a Aarón: «Acércate al altar, y ofrece tu sacrificio expiatorio y tu holocausto. Haz *propiciación por ti y por el pueblo. Presenta la ofrenda por el pueblo y haz propiciación por ellos, tal como el SEÑOR lo ha mandado.»

⁸Aarón se acercó al altar y degolló el becerro como sacrificio expiatorio por sí mismo. ⁹Sus hijos le llevaron la sangre, y él mojó el dedo en la sangre y la untó en los cuernos del altar, derramando luego la sangre al pie del altar. ¹⁰Luego quemó en el altar la grasa, los riñones y el lóbulo del hígado del animal sacrificado, tal como el SEÑOR se lo había mandado a Moisés. ¹¹La carne y la piel las quemó fuera del campamento.

¹²Después Aarón degolló la víctima del holocausto. Sus hijos le llevaron la sangre, y él la derramó alrededor del altar. ¹³También le fueron pasando los trozos del animal y la cabeza, y él lo quemó todo en el altar. ¹⁴Lavó los intestinos y las patas, y luego quemó todo esto en el altar, junto con el holocausto.

¹⁵Entonces Aarón presentó la ofrenda del pueblo, es decir, el macho cabrío del sacrificio expiatorio. Lo tomó y lo degolló, ofreciéndolo como sacrificio expiatorio, como hizo con el primero.

¹⁶Luego presentó la víctima del holocausto, la cual sacrificó en la forma prescrita. ¹⁷También presentó la ofrenda de cereal, y tomando un puñado de lo que quemó en el altar, además del holocausto de la mañana.

¹⁸Después degolló el toro y el carnero como sacrificio de comunión del pueblo. Sus hijos le llevaron la sangre, y él la derramó alrededor del altar. ¹⁹Pero tomó la grasa del toro y del carnero, es decir, la cola, el sebo que recubre los intestinos, los riñones

y el lóbulo del hígado, 20y lo puso todo sobre el pecho de las víctimas para quemarlo en el altar. 21Aarón meció ante el SEÑOR el pecho y el muslo derecho de las víctimas. Fue una ofrenda mecida, tal como Moisés se lo había mandado.

22Aarón levantó las manos hacia el pueblo, y los bendijo. Una vez que terminó de ofrecer el sacrificio expiatorio, el holocausto y el sacrificio de comunión, se retiró del altar.

23Moisés y Aarón entraron en la Tienda de reunión. Al salir, bendijeron al pueblo, y la gloria del SEÑOR se manifestó a todo el pueblo. 24De la presencia del SEÑOR salió un fuego, que consumió el holocausto y la grasa que estaban sobre el altar. Al ver esto, todo el pueblo prorrumpió en gritos de júbilo y cayó rostro en tierra.

Muerte de Nadab y Abiú

10 Pero Nadab y Abiú, hijos de Aarón, tomaron cada uno su incensario y, poniendo en ellos fuego e incienso, ofrecieron ante el SEÑOR un fuego que no tenían por qué ofrecer, pues él no se lo había mandado. 2Entonces salió de la presencia del SEÑOR un fuego que los consumió, y murieron ante él. 3Moisés le dijo a Aarón: «De esto hablaba el SEÑOR cuando dijo:

» "Entre los que se acercan a mí
manifestaré mi *santidad,
y ante todo el pueblo
manifestaré mi gloria." »

Y Aarón guardó silencio.

4Moisés mandó llamar a Misael y a Elzafán, hijos de Uziel, tío de Aarón, y les dijo: «Vengan acá y retiren del santuario a sus hermanos. ¡Sáquenlos del campamento!» 5Ellos se acercaron y, tomándolos por las túnicas, se los llevaron fuera del campamento, tal como Moisés lo había ordenado.

Ley sobre el duelo sacerdotal

6Luego Moisés les dijo a Aarón y a sus hijos Eleazar e Itamar: «No anden ustedes con el pelo despeinado, ni se rasguen los vestidos. Así no morirán ustedes ni se irritará el SEÑOR contra toda la comunidad. Sus hermanos israelitas harán duelo por el incendio que produjo el SEÑOR, 7pero ustedes no vayan a salir de la *Tienda de reunión, no sea que mueran, porque el aceite de la unción del SEÑOR está sobre ustedes.» Y ellos hicieron lo que Moisés les dijo.

Ley sobre el culto y el licor

8El SEÑOR le dijo a Aarón: 9«Ni tú ni tus hijos deben beber vino ni licor cuando entren en la Tienda de reunión, pues de lo contrario morirán. Éste es un estatuto perpetuo para tus descendientes, 10para que puedan distinguir entre lo *santo y lo profano, y entre lo *puro y lo impuro, 11y puedan también enseñar a los israelitas todos los estatutos que el SEÑOR les ha dado a conocer por medio de Moisés.»

La porción de los sacerdotes

12Moisés le dijo a Aarón, y también a Eleazar e Itamar, los hijos que le quedaban a Aarón: «Tomen el resto de la ofrenda de cereal presentada al SEÑOR, y cómanla sin levadura, junto al altar, porque es sumamente sagrada. 13Cómanla en un lugar *santo, porque así se me ha mandado. Es un estatuto^f para ti y

para tus hijos con respecto a la ofrenda presentada por fuego al SEÑOR.

14»Tú y tus hijos e hijas podrán comer también, en un lugar *puro, el pecho que es ofrenda mecida y el muslo dado como contribución. Ambos son parte de los sacrificios de *comunión de los israelitas, y ti y a tus hijos se les han dado como estatuto. 15Tanto el muslo como el pecho serán presentados junto con la ofrenda de la grasa, para ofrecérselos al SEÑOR como ofrenda mecida. Será un estatuto perpetuo para ti y para tus hijos, tal como lo ha mandado el SEÑOR.»

Un caso especial

16Moisés pidió con insistencia el macho cabrío del sacrificio *expiatorio, pero éste ya había sido quemado en el fuego. Irritado con Eleazar e Itamar, los hijos sobrevivientes de Aarón, les preguntó:

17—¿Por qué no comieron el sacrificio expiatorio dentro del santuario? Es un sacrificio sumamente sagrado; se les dio para quitar la culpa de la comunidad y hacer *propiciación por ellos ante el SEÑOR. 18Si no se introdujo en el Lugar Santo la sangre del macho cabrío, ustedes debieron haberse comido el animal en el área del santuario, tal como se lo mandé.

19Entonces Aarón le respondió a Moisés:

—Hoy mis hijos ofrecieron ante el SEÑOR su sacrificio expiatorio y su *holocausto, iy es cuando tenía que sucederme semejante desgracia! Si hoy hubiera yo comido del sacrificio expiatorio, ¿le habría parecido correcto al SEÑOR?

20Al oír esto, Moisés quedó satisfecho con la respuesta.

Leyes sobre animales puros e impuros^g
11:1-23 — Dt 14:3-20

11 El SEÑOR les ordenó a Moisés y a Aarón 2que les dijeran a los israelitas: «De todas las bestias que hay en tierra firme, éstos son los animales que ustedes podrán comer: 3los rumiantes que tienen la pezuña partida en dos. 4Hay, sin embargo, rumiantes que no tienen la pezuña partida. De esos animales no podrán comer los siguientes:

»El camello, porque es rumiante pero no tiene la pezuña partida; este animal será *impuro para ustedes.

5»El conejo, porque es rumiante pero no tiene la pezuña partida; este animal será impuro para ustedes.

6»La liebre, porque es rumiante^h pero no tiene la pezuña partida; este animal será impuro para ustedes.

7»El cerdo, porque tiene la pezuña partida en dos pero no es rumiante; este animal será impuro para ustedes.

8»No comerán la carne ni tocarán el cadáver de estos animales. Ustedes los considerarán animales impuros.

9»De los animales que hay en las aguas, es decir, en los mares y en los ríos, ustedes podrán comer los que tengan aletas y escamas. 10En cambio, considerarán inmundos a todos los animales de los mares y de los ríos que no tengan aletas ni escamas, sean reptiles u otros animales acuáticos. 11No comerán su carne, y rechazarán su cadáver, porque ustedes los considerarán animales inmundos. 12Todo animal acuático que no tenga aletas ni escamas será para ustedes un animal inmundo.

---

f **10:13** *estatuto.* Alt. *derecho;* también en vv. 14 y 15. g **11:1** tít. La identificación de algunos animales, aves e insectos de este capítulo no ha podido establecerse con precisión. h **11:5,6** *rumiante ... rumiante.* Así percibían los hebreos al conejo y a la liebre.

13»Las siguientes aves ustedes las rechazarán y no las comerán, porque las considerarán animales inmundos: el águila, el quebrantahuesos, el águila marina, 14toda clase de milanos y gavilanes, 15toda clase de cuervos, 16el avestruz, la lechuza, toda clase de gaviotas, 17el búho, el avetoro, el cisne, 18la lechuza nocturna, el pelícano, el buitre, 19la cigüeña, toda clase de garzas, la abubilla y el murciélago.

20»A todo insecto alado que camina en cuatro patas lo considerarán ustedes un animal inmundo. 21Hay, sin embargo, algunos insectos alados que caminan en cuatro patas y que ustedes podrán comer: los que además de sus patas tienen zancas para saltar, 22y también toda clase de langostas, grillos y saltamontes. 23Pero a los demás insectos alados que caminan en cuatro patas ustedes los considerarán animales inmundos.

Leyes sobre la impureza por tocar un animal impuro

24»Ustedes quedarán *impuros por lo siguiente:

»Todo el que toque el cadáver de esos animales quedará impuro hasta el anochecer.

25»Todo el que recoja alguno de esos cadáveres deberá lavarse la ropa, y quedará impuro hasta el anochecer.

26»Considerarán impuro a todo animal que no tenga la pezuña partida ni sea rumiante. Cualquiera que lo toque quedará impuro.

27»De los animales de cuatro patas, tendrán por impuro a todo el que se apoya sobre sus plantas. Cualquiera que toque su cadáver quedará impuro hasta el anochecer, 28y todo el que lo recoja deberá lavarse la ropa, y quedará impuro hasta el anochecer. A estos animales ustedes los considerarán impuros.

29»Entre los animales que se arrastran, ustedes considerarán impuros a la comadreja, al ratón, a toda clase de lagartos, 30a la salamanquesa, a la iguana, al camaleón y a la salamandra. 31Éstos son los animales que ustedes considerarán impuros entre los que se arrastran. Todo el que toque el cadáver de esos animales quedará impuro hasta el anochecer.

Otras leyes sobre el contacto con animales impuros

32»Cuando el cadáver de algún animal *impuro toque algún objeto de madera, o ropa, o piel, o un saco o cualquier utensilio de uso cotidiano, tal objeto quedará impuro. Deberá lavarse con agua, y quedará impuro hasta el anochecer. Entonces volverá a ser puro.

33»Si el cadáver de alguno de estos animales cae dentro de una vasija de barro, todo lo que la vasija contenga quedará impuro, y habrá que romperla. 34Todo alimento sobre el que caiga agua de dicha vasija quedará impuro; lo mismo sucederá con todo líquido que haya en esa vasija. 35Cualquier cosa sobre la que caiga parte de estos cadáveres quedará impura, y habrá que destruir los hornos y los fogones con los que haya entrado en contacto. Los cadáveres son impuros, y así deberán considerarlos. 36Sólo las fuentes o las cisternas que recogen agua permanecerán puras; cualquier otra cosa que toque un cadáver quedará impura.

37»Si alguno de esos cadáveres cae sobre la semilla destinada a la siembra, la semilla permanecerá pura. 38Pero si la semilla se remoja en agua, y alguno

de esos cadáveres cae sobre ella, deberán considerarla impura.

39»Si muere algún animal de los que está permitido comer, quien toque su cadáver quedará impuro hasta el anochecer. 40Quien coma carne de ese cadáver se lavará la ropa y quedará impuro hasta el anochecer. Quien lo recoja se lavará la ropa y quedará impuro hasta el anochecer.

Resumen sobre los reptiles y la santidad

41»No comerán ustedes ninguno de los animales que se arrastran, porque son inmundos. 42No comerán ningún animal que se arrastre sobre su vientre, o que se apoye sobre sus plantas, o que tenga más de cuatro patas. En resumen, no comerán ustedes ningún animal que se arrastra, porque es inmundo; 43es decir, no se *contaminen por causa de su inmundicia, pues son animales inmundos. 44Yo soy el SEÑOR su Dios, así que *santifíquense y manténganse santos, porque yo soy santo. No se hagan *impuros por causa de los animales que se arrastran. 45Yo soy el SEÑOR, que los sacó de la tierra de Egipto, para ser su Dios. Sean, pues, santos, porque yo soy santo.

Conclusión

46»Ésta es la ley acerca de los animales y de las aves, y de todo ser que se mueve dentro de las aguas o que se arrastra por el suelo, 47para que así puedan distinguir entre lo puro y lo impuro, y entre lo que se puede comer y lo que no se debe comer.»

Purificación después del alumbramiento

12 El SEÑOR le ordenó a Moisés 2que les dijera a los israelitas: «Cuando una mujer conciba y dé a luz un niño, quedará *impura durante siete días, como lo es en el tiempo de su menstruación. 3Al octavo día, el niño será circuncidado.

4La madre deberá permanecer treinta y tres días más purificándose de su flujo de sangre. No tocará ninguna cosa *santa, ni irá al santuario, hasta que termine su período de purificación.

5»Si da a luz una niña, la madre quedará impura durante dos semanas, como lo es en el tiempo de su menstruación, y permanecerá sesenta y seis días más purificándose de su flujo de sangre.

6»Una vez cumplido su período de purificación, sea que haya tenido un niño o una niña, tomará un cordero de un año como *holocausto, y un pichón de paloma o una tórtola como sacrificio *expiatorio, y los llevará al sacerdote, a la entrada de la *Tienda de reunión, y los ofrecerá ante el SEÑOR. 7Así el sacerdote hará *propiciación por la mujer, y la purificará de su flujo de sangre.

»Ésta es la ley concerniente a la mujer que dé a luz un niño o una niña. 8Pero si no le alcanza para comprar un cordero, tomará dos tórtolas o dos pichones de paloma, uno como holocausto y el otro como sacrificio expiatorio. Así el sacerdote hará propiciación por la mujer, y ella quedará purificada.»

Leyes sobre enfermedades cutáneas

13 El SEÑOR les dijo a Moisés y a Aarón: 2«Cuando a una persona le salga en la piel alguna inflamación, erupción o mancha blancuzca que pueda convertirse en infección,[i] se le llevará al sacerdote Aarón, o a alguno de sus descendientes los sacerdotes. 3El sacerdote examinará la llaga. Si el vello en la parte afectada se ha puesto blanco y la llaga se ve más hundida que la piel, entonces se trata de

---

i **13:2** *infección*. Tradicionalmente *lepra*; así en el resto de este capítulo y en el siguiente.

una enfermedad infecciosa. Después de examinar a la persona, el sacerdote la declarará *impura.

4»Si la mancha blancuzca no se ve más hundida que la piel, ni el vello se le ha puesto blanco, el sacerdote aislará a la persona enferma durante siete días, 5y al séptimo día la examinará de nuevo. Si juzga que la infección no ha seguido extendiéndose sobre la piel, aislará a esa persona otros siete días. 6Cumplidos los siete días, el sacerdote la examinará otra vez, y si el mal no se ha extendido sobre la piel sino que ha disminuido, la declarará pura. No era más que una erupción, así que la persona enferma se lavará la ropa y quedará pura.

7»Si la erupción se le sigue extendiendo sobre la piel luego de haberse presentado ante el sacerdote para su purificación, la persona enferma tendrá que volver a presentarse ante él. 8El sacerdote la examinará, y si la erupción se ha extendido sobre la piel, declarará impura a esa persona, pues se trata de una enfermedad infecciosa.

Leyes sobre enfermedades infecciosas

9»Cuando una persona tenga una infección en la piel, deberá ser llevada ante el sacerdote, 10quien la examinará. Si ocurre que la inflamación y el vello se han puesto blancos, y se ve la carne viva, 11se trata de una infección crónica. El sacerdote declarará *impura a tal persona. No hará falta aislarla otra vez, porque ya se sabe que es impura.

12»Si la infección se ha extendido sobre la piel de tal manera que, hasta donde el sacerdote pueda ver, cubre toda la piel de la persona enferma, 13entonces el sacerdote la examinará. Si ve que la infección le cubre todo el cuerpo, la declarará pura. Esa persona es pura porque todo el cuerpo se le ha puesto blanco. 14Pero será impura en el momento en que le aparezca una llaga ulcerosa. 15Cuando el sacerdote examine la carne viva, declarará impura a esa persona. La carne viva es impura, pues se trata de una enfermedad infecciosa. 16Pero si la llaga ulcerosa se le pone blanca, la persona enferma deberá ir al sacerdote 17para que la examine. Si la llaga se le ha puesto blanca, el sacerdote declarará pura a esa persona, y en efecto lo será.

Leyes sobre los abscesos

18»Si alguien ha tenido un absceso en la piel, y luego sana 19pero en el sitio del absceso le aparece una inflamación blancuzca, o una mancha rojiza, deberá presentarse ante el sacerdote 20para que lo examine. Si la inflamación se ve más hundida que la piel y el vello se le ha puesto blanco, el sacerdote lo declarará *impuro. Se trata de una enfermedad infecciosa que ha brotado en el sitio donde estaba el absceso. 21Pero si, al examinar al enfermo, encuentra el sacerdote que el vello no se le ha puesto blanco, y que el absceso no se ve más hundido que la piel sino que ha disminuido, entonces aislará al enfermo durante siete días. 22Si el absceso se extiende sobre la piel, declarará impuro al enfermo, pues se trata de una enfermedad. 23Si el absceso no se desarrolla ni la mancha blanca se extiende sino que ha cicatrizado, declarará puro al enfermo.

Leyes sobre las quemaduras

24»Si alguien se quema, y sobre la quemadura aparece una mancha blancuzca o rojiza, 25el sacerdote deberá examinarla. Si el vello de la mancha se le ha puesto blanco, y la mancha misma se ve más hundida que la piel, se trata de una enfermedad infecciosa que brotó en el sitio de la quemadura. El sacerdote declarará *impuro al enfermo, pues se trata de una infección.

26»Si al examinar la quemadura encuentra el sacerdote que el vello no se ha puesto blanco ni la mancha se ve más hundida que la piel, sino que ha disminuido, entonces aislará al enfermo durante siete días. 27Al séptimo día el sacerdote volverá a examinarlo, y si observa que la mancha se ha extendido sobre la piel, lo declarará impuro, pues se trata de una infección. 28En cambio, si la mancha blancuzca no ha seguido extendiéndose sobre la piel, se trata sólo de la inflamación de la quemadura. Entonces el sacerdote lo declarará puro, ya que se trata sólo de una quemadura cicatrizada.

Leyes sobre enfermedades del cuero cabelludo y de la barba

29»Si a un hombre o a una mujer les sale una llaga en la cabeza o en el mentón, 30el sacerdote deberá examinar la llaga. Si ésta se ve más hundida que la piel, y el pelo se ve amarillento y delgado, declarará *impuro al enfermo. Se trata de tiña, que es una infección en la cabeza o en el mentón. 31Pero si al examinar la llaga tiñosa el sacerdote ve que no está más hundida que la piel ni tiene pelo negro, aislará al enfermo de tiña durante siete días. 32Al séptimo día el sacerdote deberá examinar otra vez al enfermo; si la tiña no se ha extendido, ni tiene pelo amarillento ni se ve más hundida que la piel, 33entonces el enfermo se afeitará el pelo, pero no la parte afectada, y el sacerdote lo aislará otros siete días. 34Al séptimo día el sacerdote volverá a examinar al enfermo; si la tiña no se ha extendido por la piel ni se ve más hundida que ésta, lo declarará puro. Entonces el enfermo se lavará la ropa y quedará puro.

35»Si después de su purificación la tiña se extiende por toda la piel, 36el sacerdote deberá examinarlo. Si la tiña se ha extendido por toda la piel, ya no hará falta que el sacerdote busque pelo amarillento, porque el enfermo es impuro. 37En cambio, si considera que la tiña no se ha desarrollado y nota que le ha crecido pelo negro, entonces el enfermo ha sanado. Es puro, y así deberá declararlo el sacerdote.

Afecciones cutáneas benignas

38»Si a un hombre o a una mujer les salen manchas blancuzcas en la piel, 39el sacerdote deberá examinarlas. Si las manchas resultan ser blancuzcas, se trata sólo de una erupción cutánea, de modo que la persona es *pura.

Leyes sobre la calvicie

40»Si a alguien se le cae el pelo de la nuca, y se queda calvo, es puro. 41Si se le cae el pelo de las sienes y se queda calvo, también es puro. 42Pero si en su calvicie de la nuca o de las sienes le aparece una llaga rojiza, se trata de una infección que le ha brotado en la parte calva. 43El sacerdote deberá examinarlo. Si la inflamación es rojiza, parecida a las infecciones de la piel, 44se trata entonces de una persona infectada e impura. El sacerdote la declarará impura por esa llaga en la cabeza.

Ley sobre las infecciones

45»La persona que contraiga una infección se vestirá de harapos y no se peinará; con el rostro semicubierto irá gritando: "¡*Impuro! ¡Impuro!", 46y será impuro todo el tiempo que le dure la enfermedad. Es impuro, así que deberá vivir aislado y fuera del campamento.

Leyes sobre el moho

47»Cuando la ropa de lana o de lino se llene de moho, 48o éste aparezca en la urdimbre o trama del lino o de la lana, o en algún cuero o artículo de piel,

⁴⁹y su color sea verdusco o rojizo, se trata de una infección de moho, y deberá mostrársele al sacerdote, ⁵⁰quien examinará la mancha y aislará durante siete días el objeto infectado. ⁵¹Al séptimo día el sacerdote examinará la mancha. Si ésta se ha extendido en la ropa o en la urdimbre, trama, o en el cuero o en cualquier artículo de piel, se trata de un moho corrosivo. Tal objeto es *impuro. ⁵²Se le prenderá fuego a la ropa o a la urdimbre, trama, lana, lino o cualquier artículo de piel que haya sido infectado, porque se trata de un moho corrosivo. El objeto deberá ser quemado.

⁵³»Si al examinar el objeto, el sacerdote observa que la mancha no se ha extendido sobre el vestido, ni sobre la urdimbre, trama, lana, lino, o cualquier artículo de cuero, ⁵⁴entonces mandará lavar el objeto infectado y lo aislará otros siete días. ⁵⁵Una vez lavado el objeto, el sacerdote procederá a examinarlo. Si observa que la mancha no ha cambiado de aspecto, dicho objeto será considerado impuro aun cuando la mancha no se haya extendido. El objeto será quemado por estar corroído, sea por dentro o por fuera.

⁵⁶»Si después de lavado el objeto, el sacerdote lo examina y observa que la mancha ha disminuido, deberá arrancar la parte manchada del vestido, del cuero, de la urdimbre o de la trama. ⁵⁷Si la mancha reaparece en la ropa, en la urdimbre, en la trama o en cualquier artículo de piel, significa que ha vuelto a brotar. La parte infectada será quemada, ⁵⁸pero toda ropa, urdimbre, trama o artículo de piel que al lavarse pierda la mancha, se volverá a lavar, y el objeto quedará puro.»

⁵⁹Ésta es la ley respecto al moho que infecta la ropa, la lana, el lino, la urdimbre, la trama o cualquier artículo de piel, para poder declararlos puros o impuros.

Purificación de las enfermedades cutáneas

14 El SEÑOR le dijo a Moisés: ²«Ésta es la ley que se aplicará para declarar *pura a una persona infectada. Será presentada ante el sacerdote, ³quien la examinará fuera del campamento. Si el sacerdote comprueba que la persona infectada se ha sanado de su enfermedad, ⁴mandará traer para la purificación de esa persona dos aves vivas y puras, un pedazo de madera de cedro, un paño escarlata y una rama de *hisopo. ⁵Después el sacerdote mandará degollar la primera ave sobre una vasija de barro llena de agua de manantial. ⁶Tomará la otra ave viva, la madera de cedro, el paño escarlata y la rama de hisopo, y mojará todo esto junto con el ave viva en la sangre del ave que fue degollada sobre el agua de manantial. ⁷Luego rociará siete veces a quien va a ser purificado de la infección, y lo declarará puro. Entonces dejará libre a campo abierto el ave viva.

⁸»El que se purifica deberá lavarse la ropa, afeitarse todo el pelo y bañarse. Así quedará puro. Después de esto podrá entrar en el campamento, pero se quedará fuera de su carpa durante siete días. ⁹Al séptimo día se rapará por completo el cabello, la barba y las cejas; se lavará la ropa y se bañará. Así quedará puro.

¹⁰»Al octavo día, el que se purifica deberá traer dos corderos sin defecto y una cordera de un año, también sin defecto; como ofrenda de cereal traerá seis kilosʲ de flor de harina amasada con aceite, junto con un tercio de litroᵏ de aceite. ¹¹El sacerdote que oficia en la purificación presentará ante el SEÑOR, a la entrada de la *Tienda de reunión, al que se purifi-

ca y a sus ofrendas. ¹²Después el sacerdote tomará uno de los corderos y, junto con el aceite, lo ofrecerá como sacrificio por la culpa. Lo mecerá ante el SEÑOR, pues se trata de una ofrenda mecida. ¹³Después degollará al cordero en el lugar *santo, donde se degüellan las víctimas del sacrificio *expiatorio y del *holocausto, porque el sacrificio por la culpa, al igual que el sacrificio expiatorio, pertenecen al sacerdote. Se trata de algo sumamente sagrado. ¹⁴Luego tomará el sacerdote un poco de sangre del sacrificio por la culpa y la untará en el lóbulo de la oreja derecha, en el pulgar de la mano derecha y en el dedo gordo del pie derecho del que se purifica. ¹⁵El sacerdote tomará un poco de aceite y se lo echará en la palma de la mano izquierda. ¹⁶Mojará el índice de la mano derecha en el aceite que tiene en la palma izquierda, y rociará el aceite siete veces ante el SEÑOR. ¹⁷Luego, del aceite que le quede en la mano, el sacerdote untará un poco en el lóbulo de la oreja derecha, en el pulgar de la mano derecha y en el dedo gordo del pie derecho del que se purifica, sobre la sangre del sacrificio por la culpa. ¹⁸El sacerdote derramará sobre la cabeza del que se purifica el aceite que le quede en la mano. De este modo celebrará ante el SEÑOR el rito de *propiciación por él. ¹⁹A continuación, el sacerdote ofrecerá el sacrificio expiatorio, haciendo propiciación por el que se purifica de su impureza. Hecho esto, degollará la víctima del holocausto, ²⁰y la ofrecerá en el altar junto con la ofrenda de cereal. Así hará propiciación por él, y lo declarará puro.

²¹»Si el que se purifica es pobre y no tiene para comprar lo requerido, tomará como sacrificio por la culpa un solo cordero, el cual será mecido para hacer propiciación por él. También llevará como ofrenda de cereal dos kilosˡ de flor de harina amasada con aceite, y un cuarto de litro de aceite, ²²junto con dos tórtolas o dos pichones de paloma, según lo que pueda pagar, uno como sacrificio expiatorio y otro como holocausto. ²³Al octavo día los llevará a la entrada de la Tienda de reunión, ante el sacerdote, para su purificación en presencia del SEÑOR. ²⁴El sacerdote tomará el cordero del sacrificio por la culpa, junto con el aceite, y los mecerá ante el SEÑOR, pues se trata de una ofrenda mecida. ²⁵Después degollará al cordero del sacrificio por la culpa, tomará un poco de sangre y la untará en el lóbulo de la oreja derecha, en el pulgar de la mano derecha y en el dedo gordo del pie derecho del que se purifica. ²⁶El sacerdote se echará aceite en la palma de la mano izquierda, ²⁷y con el índice de la mano derecha lo rociará siete veces ante el SEÑOR. ²⁸Luego, al que se purifica, el sacerdote le untará un poco del aceite que le quede en la mano. Se lo untará en el lóbulo de la oreja derecha, en el pulgar de la mano derecha y en el dedo gordo del pie derecho, allí donde puso la sangre del sacrificio por la culpa. ²⁹El aceite que le quede en la mano lo untará el sacerdote en la cabeza del que se purifica, y así hará propiciación por él ante el SEÑOR. ³⁰Luego ofrecerá las tórtolas o los pichones de paloma, según lo que pueda pagar el oferente, ³¹uno como sacrificio expiatorio y otro como holocausto, junto con la ofrenda de cereal. Así hará el sacerdote propiciación ante el SEÑOR en favor del que se purifica.»

³²Esta ley se aplicará a la persona que haya contraído una infección cutánea y no tenga para pagar las ofrendas regulares de su purificación.

ʲ **14:10** *seis kilos*. Lit. *tres décimas* (de *efa).   ᵏ **14:10** *un tercio de litro*. Lit. *un *log*; también en v. 21.   ˡ **14:21** *dos kilos*. Lit. *una décima* (de efa).

Purificación de casas infectadas

33El SEÑOR les dijo a Moisés y a Aarón: **34**«Si al entrar ustedes en la tierra de Canaán, la cual les doy en propiedad, yo pongo moho infeccioso en alguna de sus casas, **35**el dueño de la casa deberá decirle al sacerdote: "En mi casa ha aparecido una especie de moho." **36**Entonces el sacerdote, antes de entrar para examinar el moho, mandará que desocupen la casa para que no se *contamine todo lo que haya en ella. Hecho esto, el sacerdote entrará a examinarla. **37**Si el moho de las paredes forma cavidades verduscas o rojizas que parezcan hundirse en la pared, **38**el sacerdote saldrá de la casa y la clausurará durante siete días. **39**Al séptimo día regresará y la examinará. Si el moho se ha extendido por las paredes de la casa, **40**mandará quitar las piedras mohosas y tirarlas fuera de la ciudad, en un lugar *impuro. **41**También mandará raspar todo el interior de la casa, y el material raspado lo arrojará fuera de la ciudad, en un lugar impuro.

42Después se repondrán las antiguas piedras con otras nuevas, y se resanará la casa con estuco nuevo.

43»Si después de haber quitado las piedras infectadas y de haber raspado y resanado la casa, vuelve a aparecer el moho y se extiende por toda ella, **44**el sacerdote irá a examinarla. Si el moho se ha extendido por toda la casa, se trata de moho corrosivo. Por lo tanto, la casa es impura **45**y deberán demolerla y arrojar, en un lugar impuro fuera de la ciudad, las piedras, el maderamen y el estuco.

46»Cualquiera que entre en la casa mientras esté clausurada quedará impuro hasta el anochecer, **47**y todo el que duerma o coma en dicha casa deberá lavarse la ropa.

48»Si después de haber sido resanada la casa, el sacerdote la examina y el moho no se ha extendido, la declarará pura, porque la infección ha desaparecido.

49»Para purificar la casa, el sacerdote deberá tomar dos aves, pedazos de madera de cedro, ramas de *hisopo y un paño escarlata. **50**Degollará una de las aves sobre una vasija de barro llena de agua de manantial; **51**tomará la madera de cedro, las ramas de hisopo, el paño escarlata y la otra ave viva, y mojará todo esto en la sangre del ave degollada y en el agua de manantial. **52**Luego rociará la casa siete veces, y así la purificará con la sangre del ave, con el agua de manantial y con el ave viva, la madera de cedro, las ramas de hisopo y el paño escarlata. **53**Soltará entonces el ave viva a campo abierto. Así hará *propiciación por la casa, y ésta quedará pura.

54»Ésta es la ley respecto a cualquier tipo de infección cutánea o de tiña, **55**o de moho, ya sea en la ropa o en una casa, **56**o de inflamación, o erupción o mancha blancuzca **57**para así poder enseñar al pueblo cuándo algo es puro o impuro. Ésta es la ley respecto a las infecciones.»

Impurezas sexuales en el hombre

15 El SEÑOR les ordenó a Moisés y a Aarón **2**que les dijeran a los israelitas: «Si algún hombre tiene un derrame seminal, tal derrame es *impuro, **3**lo mismo que el hombre, ya sea que su órgano sexual emita el flujo o que el flujo obstruya el órgano.

»El flujo causa impureza en los siguientes casos:

4»Será impura toda cama donde se acueste el afectado por el flujo, lo mismo que todo objeto sobre el que se siente.

5»Todo el que toque la cama del afectado por el flujo deberá lavarse la ropa y bañarse, y quedará impuro hasta el anochecer.

6»Todo el que se siente donde se haya sentado el afectado por el flujo deberá lavarse la ropa y bañarse, y quedará impuro hasta el anochecer.

7»Todo el que toque el cuerpo del afectado por el flujo deberá lavarse la ropa y bañarse con agua, y quedará impuro hasta el anochecer.

8»Si el afectado por el flujo escupe sobre alguien no *contaminado, éste deberá lavarse la ropa y bañarse, y quedará impuro hasta el anochecer.

9»Toda montura sobre la que cabalgue el afectado por el flujo quedará impura.

10»Todo el que toque algún objeto que haya estado debajo del afectado por el flujo quedará impuro hasta el anochecer; el que transporte dicho objeto deberá lavarse la ropa y bañarse, y quedará impuro hasta el anochecer.

11»Si el afectado por el flujo toca a alguien sin haberse lavado las manos con agua, el que fue tocado deberá lavarse la ropa y bañarse, y quedará impuro hasta el anochecer.

12»Si el afectado por el flujo toca alguna vasija de barro, se romperá la vasija; si toca algún utensilio de madera, éste deberá lavarse con agua.

13»Si al afectado le cesa el flujo, deberá esperar siete días para el rito de su purificación. Se lavará la ropa y se bañará con agua de manantial, y así quedará puro. **14**Al octavo día tomará dos tórtolas o dos pichones de paloma, y se presentará ante el SEÑOR, a la entrada de la *Tienda de reunión. Allí entregará las aves al sacerdote, **15**quien ofrecerá una como sacrificio *expiatorio y la otra como *holocausto. Así, en presencia del SEÑOR, el sacerdote hará *propiciación por el afectado a causa de su flujo.

16»Cuando un hombre tenga una eyaculación, deberá bañarse todo el cuerpo, y quedará impuro hasta el anochecer. **17**Toda ropa o piel sobre la que haya caído semen deberá lavarse con agua, y quedará impura hasta el anochecer.

18»Cuando un hombre y una mujer tengan relaciones sexuales con eyaculación, ambos deberán bañarse, y quedarán impuros hasta el anochecer.

Impurezas sexuales en la mujer

19»Cuando a una mujer le llegue su menstruación, quedará *impura durante siete días.

»Todo el que la toque quedará impuro hasta el anochecer.

20»Todo aquello sobre lo que ella se acueste mientras dure su período menstrual quedará impuro.

»Todo aquello sobre lo que ella se siente durante su período menstrual quedará impuro.

21»Todo el que toque la cama de esa mujer deberá lavarse la ropa y bañarse, y quedará impuro hasta el anochecer.

22»Todo el que toque algún objeto donde ella se haya sentado, deberá lavarse la ropa y bañarse, y quedará impuro hasta el anochecer.

23»Si alguien toca algún objeto que estuvo sobre su cama o en el lugar donde ella se sentó, quedará impuro hasta el anochecer.

24»Si un hombre tiene relaciones sexuales con esa mujer, se *contaminará con su menstruación y quedará impuro durante siete días. Además, toda cama en la que él se acueste quedará también impura.

25»Cuando una mujer tenga flujo continuo de sangre fuera de su período menstrual, o cuando se le prolongue el flujo, quedará impura todo el tiempo que le dure, como durante su período.

26»Toda cama en la que se acueste mientras dure su flujo quedará impura, como durante su período.

»Todo aquello sobre lo que se siente quedará impuro, como durante su período.

27»Todo el que toque cualquiera de estos objetos quedará impuro. Deberá lavarse la ropa y bañarse, y quedará impuro hasta el anochecer.

28»Cuando ella sane de su flujo, deberá esperar siete días para el rito de su purificación. 29Al octavo día tomará las tórtolas o dos pichones de paloma, y los llevará a la entrada de la *Tienda de reunión, donde se los entregará al sacerdote, 30quien ofrecerá uno como sacrificio *expiatorio y el otro como *holocausto. Así, en presencia del SEÑOR, el sacerdote hará *propiciación por ella a causa de su flujo.

31»Ustedes deben mantener apartados de la impureza a los israelitas. Así evitarán que ellos mueran por haber contaminado mi santuario, que está en medio de ellos.

32»Esta ley se aplicará a quien quede impuro por derrame seminal, 33a la que tenga flujo menstrual, al hombre y a la mujer que tenga relaciones sexuales con eyaculación, y a quien tenga relaciones sexuales con una mujer impura.»

Leyes para la expiación de pecados
16:2-34 — Lv 23:26-32; Nm 29:7-11

16 El SEÑOR le habló a Moisés después de la muerte de los dos hijos de Aarón, quienes murieron al acercarse imprudentemente al SEÑOR. 2Le dijo el SEÑOR a Moisés: «Dile a tu hermano Aarón que no entre a cualquier hora en la parte del santuario que está detrás de la cortina, es decir, delante del *propiciatorio que está sobre el arca, no sea que muera cuando yo aparezca en la nube por encima del propiciatorio.

3»Aarón deberá entrar en el santuario con un novillo para el sacrificio *expiatorio y un carnero para el *holocausto. 4Se pondrá la túnica sagrada de lino y la ropa interior de lino. Se ceñirá con la faja de lino y se pondrá la tiara de lino. Éstas son las vestiduras sagradas que se pondrá después de haberse bañado con agua.

5»De la comunidad de los israelitas, Aarón tomará dos machos cabríos para el sacrificio expiatorio y un carnero para el holocausto. 6Después de que haya ofrecido el novillo del sacrificio expiatorio como propiciación por él y por su familia, 7tomará los dos machos cabríos y los presentará ante el SEÑOR, a la entrada de la *Tienda de reunión. 8Entonces Aarón echará suertes sobre los dos machos cabríos, uno para el SEÑOR y otro para soltarlo en el desierto.m 9Aarón ofrecerá como sacrificio expiatorio el macho cabrío que le tocó al SEÑOR, 10pero presentará vivo ante el SEÑOR, como propiciación, el macho cabrío que soltará en el desierto; es decir, lo enviará a Azazel.

11»Aarón presentará el novillo para su propio sacrificio expiatorio, y hará propiciación por él y por su familia. Degollará el novillo para su propio sacrificio expiatorio; 12luego tomará del altar que está ante el SEÑOR un incensario lleno de brasas, junto con dos puñados llenos de incienso aromático en polvo, y los llevará tras la cortina; 13colocará entonces el incienso sobre el fuego, en presencia del SEÑOR, para que la nube de incienso cubra el propiciatorio que está sobre el arca del pacto. De esa manera Aarón no morirá. 14Después tomará un poco de la sangre del novillo y la rociará con su dedo al costado oriental del propiciatorio; la rociará delante del propiciatorio siete veces.

15»Luego degollará el macho cabrío del sacrificio expiatorio en favor del pueblo. Llevará su sangre detrás de la cortina, y hará con esa sangre lo mismo que hizo con la del novillo: la rociará sobre y delante del propiciatorio. 16Así hará propiciación por el santuario para *purificarlo de las impurezas y transgresiones de los israelitas, cualesquiera que hayan sido sus pecados. Hará lo mismo por la Tienda de reunión, que está entre ellos en medio de sus impurezas. 17Nadie deberá estar en la Tienda de reunión desde el momento en que Aarón entre para hacer propiciación en el santuario hasta que salga, es decir, mientras esté haciendo propiciación por sí mismo, por su familia y por toda la asamblea de Israel.

18»Aarón saldrá luego para hacer propiciación por el altar que está delante del SEÑOR. Tomará sangre del novillo y del macho cabrío, y la untará sobre cada uno de los cuernos del altar, 19y con el dedo rociará con sangre el altar siete veces. Así lo *santificará y lo purificará de las impurezas de los israelitas.

20»Cuando Aarón haya terminado de hacer propiciación por el santuario, la Tienda de reunión y el altar, presentará el macho cabrío vivo, 21y le impondrá las manos sobre la cabeza. Confesará entonces todas las iniquidades y transgresiones de los israelitas, cualesquiera que hayan sido sus pecados. Así el macho cabrío cargará con ellos, y será enviado al desierto por medio de un hombre designado para esto. 22El hombre soltará en el desierto al macho cabrío, y éste se llevará a tierra árida todas las iniquidades.

23»Entonces Aarón entrará en la Tienda de reunión, se quitará los vestidos de lino que se puso antes de entrar en el santuario, y allí los dejará. 24Se bañará con agua en un lugar *santo y se volverá a vestir. Después saldrá y ofrecerá su propio holocausto y el del pueblo. Hará propiciación por sí mismo y por el pueblo. 25Además, quemará sobre el altar la grasa del sacrificio expiatorio.

26»El encargado de soltar el macho cabrío en el desierto deberá lavarse la ropa y bañarse con agua. Sólo después de hacer esto podrá volver al campamento.

27»El novillo del sacrificio expiatorio y el macho cabrío del sacrificio expiatorio, cuya sangre se llevó para hacer propiciación por el santuario, se sacarán del campamento; a la piel, la carne y el excremento se quemarán. 28El que les prenda fuego deberá lavarse la ropa y bañarse. Sólo después de hacer esto podrá volver al campamento.

29»Éste será para ustedes un estatuto perpetuo, tanto para el nativo como para el extranjero: El día diez del mes séptimo ayunarán y no realizarán ningún tipo de trabajo. 30En dicho día se hará propiciación por ustedes para purificarlos, y delante del SEÑOR serán purificados de todos sus pecados. 31Será para ustedes un día de completo reposo, en el cual ayunarán. Es un estatuto perpetuo.

32»La propiciación la realizará el sacerdote que haya sido ungido y ordenado como sucesor de su padre. Se pondrá las vestiduras sagradas de lino, 33y hará propiciación por el lugar santísimo, por la Tienda de reunión y por el altar. También hará propiciación por los sacerdotes y por toda la comunidad allí reunida.

34»Éste les será un estatuto perpetuo: Una vez al año se deberá hacer propiciación por todos los israelitas a causa de todos sus pecados.»

Y se hizo tal como el SEÑOR se lo había mandado a Moisés.

---

m 16:8 *para soltarlo en el desierto.* Lit. *para Azazel* (que puede significar un lugar árido); también en v. 26.

Prohibición de comer sangre

17 El SEÑOR le ordenó a Moisés [2]que les dijera a Aarón y a sus hijos, y a todos los israelitas: «Esto es lo que ha mandado el SEÑOR:

[3]»Cuando algún israelita sacrifique una res, un cordero o una cabra dentro o fuera del campamento, [4]será considerado culpable de haber derramado sangre si no lleva el animal a la entrada de la *Tienda de reunión y lo presenta como ofrenda al SEÑOR ante su santuario. Por lo tanto, ese israelita será eliminado de su pueblo. [5]El propósito de este mandamiento es que los israelitas lleven al SEÑOR los sacrificios que suelen hacer en el campo. Deberán llevarlos al sacerdote, a la entrada de la Tienda de reunión, y ofrecérselos al SEÑOR como sacrificios de *comunión. [6]El sacerdote derramará la sangre sobre el altar del SEÑOR, a la entrada de la Tienda de reunión, y quemará la grasa como aroma grato al SEÑOR. [7]Y nunca más volverán a ofrecer ningún sacrificio a sus ídolos que tienen forma de machos cabríos,[n] con los que se han prostituido. Éste es un estatuto perpetuo para ellos y para sus descendientes.

[8]»Cuando algún israelita o extranjero que viva entre ustedes ofrezca un *holocausto o sacrificio [9]y no lo lleve a la entrada de la Tienda de reunión para ofrecerlo al SEÑOR, el tal será eliminado de su pueblo.

[10]»Cuando algún israelita o extranjero que viva entre ustedes coma cualquier clase de sangre, yo me pondré en su contra y lo eliminaré de su pueblo. [11]Porque la *vida de toda criatura está en la sangre. Yo mismo se la he dado a ustedes sobre el altar, para que hagan *propiciación por ustedes mismos, ya que la propiciación se hace por medio de la sangre. [12]Por eso les digo: Ninguno de ustedes deberá comer sangre, ni tampoco deberá comerla el extranjero que viva entre ustedes.

[13]»Cuando un israelita o algún extranjero que viva entre ustedes cace algún animal o ave que sea lícito comer, le extraerá la sangre y la cubrirá con tierra, [14]pues la vida de toda criatura está en su sangre. Por eso les he dicho: No coman la sangre de ninguna criatura, porque la vida de toda criatura está en la sangre; cualquiera que la coma será eliminado.

[15]»Todo nativo o extranjero que coma la carne de un animal que las fieras hayan matado o despedazado, deberá lavarse la ropa y bañarse con agua, y quedará *impuro hasta el anochecer; después de eso quedará puro. [16]Pero si no se lava la ropa ni se baña, sufrirá las consecuencias de su pecado.»

Relaciones sexuales ilícitas

18 El SEÑOR le ordenó a Moisés [2]que les dijera a los israelitas: «Yo soy el SEÑOR su Dios. [3]No imitarán ustedes las costumbres de Egipto, donde antes habitaban, ni tampoco las de Canaán, adonde los llevo. No se conducirán según sus estatutos, [4]sino que pondrán en práctica mis preceptos y observarán atentamente mis leyes. Yo soy el SEÑOR su Dios. [5]Observen mis estatutos y mis preceptos, pues todo el que los practique vivirá por ellos. Yo soy el SEÑOR.

Relaciones no permitidas

[6]»Nadie se acercará a ningún pariente cercano para tener relaciones sexuales con él o con ella. Yo soy el SEÑOR.

[7]»No deshonrarás a tu padre, teniendo relaciones sexuales con tu madre. No lo hagas, porque es tu madre.

[8]»No tendrás relaciones sexuales con la esposa de tu padre, porque sería como tenerlas con él.

[9]»No tendrás relaciones sexuales con tu hermana por parte de padre o de madre, ya sea nacida en la misma casa o en otro lugar.

[10]»No tendrás relaciones sexuales con la hija de tu hijo, ni con la hija de tu hija, porque sería deshonrarte a ti mismo.

[11]»No tendrás relaciones sexuales con la hija que tu padre haya tenido con su mujer. No la deshonres, porque es tu hermana.

[12]»No tendrás relaciones sexuales con la hermana de tu padre, porque sería como tenerlas con tu padre.

[13]»No tendrás relaciones sexuales con la hermana de tu madre, porque sería como tenerlas con tu madre.

[14]»No deshonrarás al hermano de tu padre, teniendo relaciones sexuales con su mujer, porque es tu tía.

[15]»No tendrás relaciones sexuales con tu nuera. No las tendrás, porque sería como tenerlas con tu hijo.

[16]»No tendrás relaciones sexuales con la mujer de tu hermano, porque sería como tenerlas con él mismo.

[17]»No tendrás relaciones sexuales con dos mujeres que sean madre e hija, ni con las nietas de ellas, ya sea por parte de un hijo o de una hija de las mismas. Son parientes cercanas, de modo que eso sería una perversión.

[18]»No te casarás con la hermana de tu esposa, ni tendrás relaciones sexuales con ella mientras tu esposa viva, para no crear rivalidades entre ellas.

Otras relaciones ilícitas

[19]»No tendrás relaciones sexuales con ninguna mujer durante su período de *impureza menstrual.

[20]»No tendrás trato sexual con la mujer de tu prójimo, para que no te hagas impuro por causa de ella.

[21]»No profanarás el *nombre de tu Dios, entregando a tus hijos para que sean quemados como sacrificio a Moloc. Yo soy el SEÑOR.

[22]»No te acostarás con un hombre como quien se acuesta con una mujer. Eso es una abominación.

[23]»No tendrás trato sexual con ningún animal. No te hagas impuro por causa de él.

»Ninguna mujer tendrá trato sexual con ningún animal. Eso es una depravación.

[24]»No se *contaminen con estas prácticas, porque así se contaminaron las naciones que por amor a ustedes estoy por arrojar, [25]y aun la tierra misma se contaminó. Por eso la castigué por su perversidad, y ella vomitó a sus habitantes. [26]Ustedes obedezcan mis estatutos y preceptos. Ni los nativos ni los extranjeros que vivan entre ustedes deben practicar ninguna de estas abominaciones, [27]pues las practicaron los que vivían en esta tierra antes que ustedes, y la tierra se contaminó. [28]Si ustedes contaminan la tierra, ella los vomitará como vomitó a las naciones que la habitaron antes que ustedes.

[29]»Cualquiera que practique alguna de estas abominaciones será eliminado de su pueblo. [30]Ustedes observen mis mandamientos y absténganse de seguir las abominables costumbres que se practicaban en la tierra antes de que ustedes llegaran. No se contaminen por causa de ellas. Yo soy el SEÑOR su Dios.»

---

n 17:7 ídolos que tienen forma de machos cabríos. Alt. demonios.

Llamado a la santidad

19 El SEÑOR le ordenó a Moisés ²que hablara con toda la asamblea de los israelitas y les dijera: «Sean *santos, porque yo, el SEÑOR su Dios, soy santo.

³»Respeten todos ustedes a su madre y a su padre, y observen mis *sábados. Yo soy el SEÑOR su Dios.

⁴»No se vuelvan a los ídolos inútiles, ni se hagan dioses de metal fundido. Yo soy el SEÑOR su Dios.

⁵»Cuando le ofrezcan al SEÑOR un sacrificio de *comunión, háganlo de tal manera que el SEÑOR lo acepte de buen grado. ⁶Cómanselo el día en que lo sacrifiquen, o al día siguiente. Lo que sobre para el tercer día deberán quemarlo. ⁷Si alguien lo come al tercer día, tal sacrificio no le será válido, pues la carne ya se habrá descompuesto. ⁸Cualquiera que lo coma sufrirá las consecuencias de su pecado por profanar lo que ha sido consagrado al SEÑOR. Tal persona será eliminada de su pueblo.

Relaciones sociales

⁹»Cuando llegue el tiempo de la cosecha, no sieguen hasta el último rincón de sus campos ni recojan todas las espigas que allí queden.

¹⁰»No rebusquen hasta el último racimo de sus viñas, ni recojan las uvas que se hayan caído. Déjenlas para los pobres y los extranjeros. Yo soy el SEÑOR su Dios.

¹¹»No roben.

»No mientan.

»No engañen a su prójimo.

¹²»No juren en mi *nombre sólo por jurar, ni profanen el nombre de su Dios. Yo soy el SEÑOR.

¹³»No explotes a tu prójimo, ni lo despojes de nada.

»No retengas el salario de tu jornalero hasta el día siguiente.

¹⁴»No maldigas al sordo, ni le pongas tropiezos al ciego, sino teme a tu Dios. Yo soy el SEÑOR.

¹⁵»No perviertas la justicia, ni te muestres parcial en favor del pobre o del rico, sino juzga a todos con justicia.

¹⁶»No andes difundiendo calumnias entre tu pueblo, ni expongas la vida de tu prójimo con falsos testimonios. Yo soy el SEÑOR.

¹⁷»No alimentes odios secretos contra tu hermano, sino reprende con franqueza a tu prójimo para que no sufras las consecuencias de su pecado.

¹⁸»No seas vengativo con tu prójimo, ni le guardes rencor. Ama a tu prójimo como a ti mismo.ñ Yo soy el SEÑOR.

Otras exigencias de la santidad

¹⁹»Cumplan mis estatutos:

»No crucen animales de especies diferentes.

»No planten en su campo dos clases distintas de semilla.

»No usen ropa tejida con dos clases distintas de hilo.

²⁰»Si un hombre se acuesta con una esclava prometida a otro en matrimonio, pero que aún no ha sido rescatada ni declarada libre, a los dos se les impondrá el castigo debido,º pero no se les condenará a muerte porque ella aún no ha sido declarada libre. ²¹No obstante, el hombre deberá ofrecer al SEÑOR un carnero como ofrenda por su culpa. Lo llevará a la entrada de la *Tienda de reunión, ²²y el sacerdote

hará *expiación ante el SEÑOR por el pecado cometido. De este modo su pecado le será perdonado.

²³»Cuando ustedes entren en la tierra y planten cualquier clase de árboles frutales, durante tres años no comerán su fruto, sino que lo considerarán inmundo.ᵖ ²⁴En el cuarto año todo su fruto será consagrado como una ofrenda de alabanza al SEÑOR, ²⁵y en el quinto año ya podrán comer de su fruto. De este modo aumentarán sus cosechas. Yo soy el SEÑOR su Dios.

²⁶»No coman nada que tenga sangre.

»No practiquen la adivinación ni los sortilegios.

²⁷»No se corten el cabello en redondo ni se despunten la barba.

²⁸»No se hagan heridas en el cuerpo por causa de los muertos, ni tatuajes en la piel. Yo soy el SEÑOR.

²⁹»No degraden a su hija haciendo de ella una prostituta, para que tampoco se prostituya la tierra ni se llene de perversidad.

Otros deberes

³⁰»Observen mis *sábados, y tengan reverencia por mi santuario. Yo soy el SEÑOR.

³¹»No acudan a la nigromancia, ni busquen a los espiritistas, porque se harán *impuros por causa de ellos. Yo soy el SEÑOR su Dios.

³²»Ponte de pie en presencia de los mayores.

»Respeta a los *ancianos.

»Teme a tu Dios. Yo soy el SEÑOR.

³³»Cuando algún extranjero se establezca en el país de ustedes, no lo traten mal. ³⁴Al recibirlo, trátenlo como si fuera uno de ustedes. Ámenlo como a ustedes mismos, porque también ustedes fueron extranjeros en Egipto. Yo soy el SEÑOR y Dios de Israel.

³⁵»No cometan injusticias falseando las medidas de longitud, de peso y de capacidad. ³⁶Usen balanzas, pesas y medidas justas. Yo soy el SEÑOR su Dios, que los saqué de Egipto.

³⁷»Obedezcan todos mis estatutos. Pongan por obra todos mis preceptos. Yo soy el SEÑOR.»

Castigos por el pecado

20 El SEÑOR le ordenó a Moisés ²que les dijera a los israelitas: «Todo israelita o extranjero residente en Israel que entregue a uno de sus hijos para quemarlo como sacrificio a Moloc, será condenado a muerte. Los miembros de la comunidad lo matarán a pedradas. ³Yo mismo me pondré en contra de ese hombre y lo eliminaré de su pueblo porque, al entregar a uno de sus hijos para quemarlo como sacrificio a Moloc, profana mi santuario y mi *santo nombre.

⁴»Si los miembros de la comunidad hacen caso omiso del hombre que haya entregado alguno de sus hijos a Moloc, y no lo condenan a muerte, ⁵yo mismo me pondré en contra de él y de su familia; eliminaré del pueblo a ese hombre y a todos los que se hayan prostituido con él, siguiendo a Moloc.

⁶»También me pondré en contra de quien acuda a la nigromancia y a los espiritistas, y por seguirlos se prostituya. Lo eliminaré de su pueblo.

⁷»Conságrense a mí, y sean santos, porque yo soy el SEÑOR su Dios.

⁸»Obedezcan mis estatutos y pónganlos por obra. Yo soy el SEÑOR, que los santifica.

ñ **19:18** *como a ti mismo.* Alt. *que es como tú.*   º **19:20** *a los dos se les impondrá el castigo debido.* Alt. *los dos deberán ser investigados.*   ᵖ **19:23** *inmundo.* Lit. *Incircunciso.*   ᑫ **19:36** *medidas.* Lit. *efas e *hins.*

9»Si alguien maldice a su padre o a su madre, será condenado a muerte: ha maldecido a su padre o a su madre, y será responsable de su propia muerte.

10»Si alguien comete adulterio con la mujer de su prójimo, tanto el adúltero como la adúltera serán condenados a muerte.

11»Si alguien se acuesta con la mujer de su padre, deshonra a su padre. Tanto el hombre como la mujer serán condenados a muerte, de la cual ellos mismos serán responsables.

12»Si alguien se acuesta con su nuera, hombre y mujer serán condenados a muerte. Han cometido un acto depravado, y ellos mismos serán responsables de su propia muerte.

13»Si alguien se acuesta con otro hombre como quien se acuesta con una mujer, comete un acto abominable y los dos serán condenados a muerte, de la cual ellos mismos serán responsables.

14»Si alguien tiene relaciones sexuales con hija y madre, comete un acto depravado. Tanto él como ellas morirán quemados, para que no haya tal depravación entre ustedes.

15»Si alguien tiene trato sexual con un animal, será condenado a muerte, y se matará también al animal.

16»Si una mujer tiene trato sexual con un animal, se les dará muerte a ambos, y ellos serán responsables de su muerte.

17»Si alguien tiene relaciones sexuales con una hermana suya, comete un acto vergonzoso y los dos serán ejecutados en público. Ha deshonrado a su hermana, y sufrirá las consecuencias de su pecado.

18»Si alguien se acuesta con una mujer y tiene relaciones sexuales con ella durante su período menstrual, pone al descubierto su flujo, y tanto ella expone el flujo de su sangre. Los dos serán eliminados de su pueblo.

19»No tendrás relaciones sexuales ni con tu tía materna ni con tu tía paterna, pues eso significaría la deshonra de un pariente cercano y los dos sufrirían las consecuencias de su pecado.

20»Si alguien se acuesta con su tía, deshonra a su tío, y los dos sufrirán las consecuencias de su pecado: morirán sin tener descendencia.

21»Si alguien viola a la esposa de su hermano, comete un acto de *impureza: ha deshonrado a su hermano, y los dos se quedarán sin descendencia.

22»Cumplan todos mis estatutos y preceptos; pónganlos por obra, para que no los vomite la tierra adonde los llevo a vivir. 23No vivan según las costumbres de las naciones que por amor a ustedes voy a expulsar. Porque ellas hicieron todas estas cosas, y yo las aborrecí. 24Pero a ustedes les digo: "Poseerán la tierra que perteneció a esas naciones, tierra donde abundan la leche y la miel. Yo mismo se la daré a ustedes como herencia."

»Yo soy el SEÑOR su Dios, que los he distinguido entre las demás naciones. 25Por consiguiente, también ustedes deben distinguir entre los animales puros y los impuros, y entre las aves puras y las impuras. No se hagan detestables ustedes mismos por causa de animales, de aves o de cualquier alimaña que se arrastra por el suelo, pues yo se los he señalado como impuros. 26Sean ustedes santos, porque yo, el SEÑOR, soy santo, y los he distinguido entre las demás naciones, para que sean míos.

27»Cualquiera de ustedes, hombre o mujer, que sea nigromante o espiritista, será condenado a muerte. Morirá apedreado, y será responsable de su propia muerte.»

La santidad de los sacerdotes

21 El SEÑOR le ordenó a Moisés que les dijera a los sacerdotes, hijos de Aarón: «No se *contaminen tocando el cadáver de alguien de su pueblo, 2excepto en el caso de un pariente cercano, como su madre, su padre, su hijo, su hija, su hermano 3o una hermana soltera que, por no tener marido, dependa de él. 4Como jefes de su pueblo, no deben hacerse *impuros ni contaminarse.

5»Los sacerdotes no se raparán la cabeza, ni se despuntarán la barba ni se harán heridas en el cuerpo. 6Deben ser *santos para su Dios, y no profanar su *nombre. Son ellos los que presentan al SEÑOR las ofrendas por fuego, que son como el pan de su Dios. Por eso deben ser santos.

7»Ningún sacerdote se casará con una prostituta, ni con una divorciada, ni con una mujer que no sea virgen, porque está consagrado a su Dios. 8Considéralo santo, porque él ofrece el pan de tu Dios. Santo será para ti, porque santo soy yo, el SEÑOR que los santifico a ustedes.

9»La hija de un sacerdote que se hace prostituta se profana a sí misma y profana a su padre. Deberá ser quemada viva.

Santidad del sumo sacerdote

10»Aquel que sea elegido sumo sacerdote entre sus hermanos, y sobre cuya cabeza se haya derramado el aceite de la unción, a quien se le haya conferido autoridadr para llevar las vestiduras sacerdotales, no deberá andar despeinado ni rasgarse las vestiduras.

11»No entrará en ningún lugar donde haya un cadáver.

»No deberá *contaminarse, ni siquiera por su padre o por su madre.

12»No saldrá del santuario, para no profanar el santuario de su Dios, porque ha sido consagrado mediante el aceite de la unción divina. Yo soy el SEÑOR.

13»La mujer que tome por esposa debe ser virgen. 14No debe casarse con una viuda, ni con una divorciada ni con una prostituta. Debe casarse con una virgen de su mismo pueblo, 15para que no profane su descendencia entre su pueblo. Yo soy el SEÑOR, que lo *santifica.»

Impedimentos para ejercer el sacerdocio

16El SEÑOR le ordenó a Moisés 17que le dijera a Aarón: «Ninguno de tus descendientes que tenga defecto físico deberá acercarse jamás a su Dios para presentar la ofrenda de pan. 18En efecto, no deberá acercarse nadie que tenga algún defecto físico: ninguno que sea ciego, cojo, mutilado, deforme, 19lisiado de pies o manos, 20jorobado o enano; o que tenga sarna o tiña, o cataratas en los ojos, o que haya sido castrado. 21Ningún descendiente del sacerdote Aarón que tenga algún defecto podrá acercarse a presentar al SEÑOR las ofrendas por fuego. No podrá acercarse para presentarle a su Dios la ofrenda de pan por tener un defecto. 22Podrá comer de la ofrenda de pan, tanto del alimento *santo como del santísimo, 23pero por causa de su defecto no pasará más allá de la cortina ni se acercará al altar, para no profanar mi santuario. Yo soy el SEÑOR, que santifico a los sacerdotes.»

---

r **21:10** y a quien se le haya conferido autoridad. Lit. y quien llenó sus manos.   s **22:4** alguna enfermedad infecciosa en la piel. Tradicionalmente *lepra.

24Y Moisés les comunicó todo esto a Aarón y a sus hijos, y a todos los israelitas.

Las ofrendas del SEÑOR

22 El SEÑOR le ordenó a Moisés 2que les dijera a Aarón y a sus hijos: «Traten con mucho respeto las ofrendas sagradas que me consagran los israelitas, para no profanar mi *santo *nombre. Yo soy el SEÑOR.»

3También le ordenó decirles: «Si alguno de los descendientes de Aarón está ritualmente *impuro y se acerca a las ofrendas que los israelitas consagran al SEÑOR, será eliminado de mi presencia. Yo soy el SEÑOR.

4»Si un descendiente de Aarón padece de alguna enfermedad infecciosa en la piel,ˢ o de derrame seminal, deberá abstenerse de comer de las ofrendas sagradas, hasta que se purifique. Cualquiera que toque un objeto *contaminado por el contacto con un cadáver, o que tenga derrame de semen, 5o que toque algún animal u *hombre impuros, cualquiera que sea la impureza, 6quedará impuro hasta el anochecer. Por tanto, se abstendrá de comer de las ofrendas sagradas. Lavará su cuerpo con agua, 7y al ponerse el sol quedará puro. Después de esto podrá comer de las ofrendas sagradas, porque son su alimento. 8No deberá comer nada que sea hallado muerto o despedazado por las fieras, pues de lo contrario quedará impuro. Yo soy el SEÑOR.

9»Los sacerdotes cumplirán con mis instrucciones, y así no pecarán ni sufrirán la muerte por haber profanado las ofrendas. Yo soy el SEÑOR, que santifico a los sacerdotes.

10»Nadie ajeno a la familia sacerdotal comerá de las ofrendas sagradas, ni tampoco comerá de ellas ningún huésped del sacerdote, ni su jornalero. 11Pero sí podrá comer de ellas el esclavo comprado por un sacerdote, y el esclavo nacido en casa del mismo. 12Si la hija de un sacerdote se casa con alguien que no sea sacerdote, no podrá comer de las ofrendas recibidas como contribución. 13Pero si queda viuda o divorciada y, sin haber tenido hijos, regresa a la casa de su padre como cuando era soltera, entonces sí podrá comer del alimento de su padre. Pero nadie ajeno a la familia sacerdotal está autorizado para comerlo.

14»Si inadvertidamente alguien come de una ofrenda sagrada, deberá restituir la ofrenda al sacerdote y añadirle una quinta parte de su valor. 15»No deberán los sacerdotes profanar las ofrendas sagradas que los israelitas presentan al SEÑOR, 16porque al permitir que las coman harán recaer sobre sí mismos un pecado que requiere un sacrificio por la culpa. Yo soy el SEÑOR, que los santifico.»

Sacrificios inaceptables

17El SEÑOR le ordenó a Moisés 18que les dijera a Aarón y a sus hijos, y a todos los israelitas: «Si alguno de ustedes, sea israelita o extranjero residente en Israel, presenta un *holocausto al SEÑOR para cumplir un voto, o como ofrenda voluntaria, 19para que le sea aceptado deberá presentar un macho sin defecto de entre el ganado vacuno, ovino o caprío. 20No presenten ningún animal que tenga algún defecto, porque no se les aceptará.

21»Si alguien, para cumplir un voto especial o como ofrenda voluntaria, le presenta al SEÑOR ganado vacuno u ovino como sacrificio de *comunión, para que el animal le sea aceptado no deberá tener ningún defecto. 22No deberán presentarle al SEÑOR,

como ofrenda por fuego, animales ciegos, cojos, mutilados, llagados, sarnosos ni tiñosos. No ofrecerán en el altar ningún animal así. 23Podrán presentar como ofrenda voluntaria una res o una oveja deforme o enana, pero tal ofrenda no será aceptada en cumplimiento de un voto.

24»No ofrecerán al SEÑOR ningún animal con los testículos lastimados, magullados, cortados o arrancados. No harán esto en su tierra. 25No recibirán de manos de un extranjero animales así, para ofrecerlos como alimento del Dios de ustedes. No se les aceptarán porque son deformes y tienen defectos.»

26El SEÑOR le dijo a Moisés: 27«Cuando nazca un ternero, un cordero o un cabrito, quedará con su madre durante siete días. Del octavo día en adelante será aceptable al SEÑOR como ofrenda por fuego.

28»No degollarán el mismo día una vaca o una oveja con su cría.

29»Cuando sacrifiquen una ofrenda de acción de gracias al SEÑOR, háganlo de tal modo que les sea aceptada. 30Deberá comerse ese mismo día, sin dejar nada para el siguiente. Yo soy el SEÑOR.

31»Obedezcan mis mandamientos y pónganlos por obra. Yo soy el SEÑOR.

32»No profanen mi *santo *nombre sino reconózcanme como santo en medio de los israelitas. Yo soy el SEÑOR, que los santifica. 33Yo los saqué de Egipto para ser su Dios. Yo soy el SEÑOR.»

Calendario de fiestas solemnes

23 El SEÑOR le ordenó a Moisés 2que les dijera a los israelitas: «Éstas son las fiestas que yo he establecido, y a las que ustedes han de convocar como fiestas solemnes en mi honor. Yo, el SEÑOR, las establecí.

Celebración del sábado

3»Trabajarán ustedes durante seis días, pero el séptimo día es de reposo, es un día de fiesta solemne en mi honor, en el que no harán ningún trabajo. Dondequiera que ustedes vivan, será *sábado consagrado al SEÑOR.

Fiesta de la Pascua
23:4-8 — Éx 12:14-20; Nm 28:16-25; Dt 16:1-8

4»Éstas son las fiestas que el SEÑOR ha establecido, las fiestas solemnes en su honor que ustedes deberán convocar en las fechas señaladas para ellas:

5»La Pascua del SEÑOR comienza el día catorce del mes primero, a la hora del crepúsculo. 6El día quince del mismo mes comienza la fiesta de los Panes sin levadura en honor al SEÑOR. Durante siete días comerán pan sin levadura. 7El primer día celebrarán una fiesta solemne en su honor; ese día no harán ningún trabajo. 8Durante siete días presentarán al SEÑOR ofrendas por fuego, y el séptimo día celebrarán una fiesta solemne en su honor; ese día no harán ningún trabajo.»

Fiesta de las Primicias

9El SEÑOR le ordenó a Moisés 10que les dijera a los israelitas: «Cuando ustedes hayan entrado en la tierra que les voy a dar, y sieguen la mies, deberán llevar al sacerdote una gavilla de las primeras espigas que cosechen. 11El sacerdote mecerá la gavilla ante el SEÑOR para que les sea aceptada. La mecerá a la mañana siguiente del *sábado. 12Ese mismo día sacrificarán ustedes un cordero de un año, sin defecto, como *holocausto al SEÑOR. 13También presentarán cuatro kilosᵗ de harina fina mezclada con aceite,

---

ᵗ 23:13 cuatro kilos. Lit. dos décimas (de *efa); también en v. 17.

como ofrenda de cereal, ofrenda por fuego, de aroma grato al SEÑOR, y un litrou de vino como ofrenda de libación. ¹⁴No comerán pan, ni grano tostado o nuevo, hasta el día en que traigan esta ofrenda a su Dios. Éste será un estatuto perpetuo para todos tus descendientes, dondequiera que habiten.

Fiesta de las Semanas
23:15-22 — Nm 28:26-31; Dt 16:9-12

¹⁵»A partir del día siguiente al *sábado, es decir, a partir del día en que traigan la gavilla de la ofrenda mecida, contarán siete semanas completas. ¹⁶En otras palabras, contarán cincuenta días incluyendo la mañana siguiente al séptimo sábado; entonces presentarán al SEÑOR una ofrenda de grano nuevo. ¹⁷Desde su lugar de residencia le llevarán al SEÑOR, como ofrenda mecida de las *primicias, dos panes hechos con cuatro kilos de flor de harina, cocidos con levadura. ¹⁸Junto con el pan deberán presentar siete corderos de un año, sin defecto, un novillo y dos carneros. Serán, junto con sus ofrendas de cereal y sus ofrendas de libación, un *holocausto al SEÑOR, una ofrenda presentada por fuego, de aroma grato al SEÑOR. ¹⁹Luego sacrificarán un macho cabrío como ofrenda por el pecado, y dos corderos de un año como sacrificio de *comunión. ²⁰El sacerdote mecerá los dos corderos, junto con el pan de las primicias. Son una ofrenda mecida ante el SEÑOR, una ofrenda consagrada al SEÑOR y reservada para el sacerdote. ²¹Ese mismo día convocarán ustedes a una fiesta solemne en honor al SEÑOR, y en ese día no harán ningún trabajo. Éste será un estatuto perpetuo para todos tus descendientes, dondequiera que habiten.

²²»Cuando llegue el tiempo de la cosecha, no sieguen hasta el último rincón del campo ni recojan todas las espigas que queden de la mies. Déjenlas para los pobres y los extranjeros. Yo soy el SEÑOR su Dios.»

Fiesta de las Trompetas
23:23-25 — Nm 29:1-6

²³El SEÑOR le ordenó a Moisés ²⁴que les dijera a los israelitas: «El primer día del mes séptimo será para ustedes un día de reposo, una conmemoración con toques de trompeta, una fiesta solemne en honor al SEÑOR. ²⁵Ese día no harán ningún trabajo, sino que presentarán al SEÑOR ofrendas por fuego.»

El día del Perdón
23:26-32 — Lv 16:2-34; Nm 29:7-11

²⁶El SEÑOR le dijo a Moisés: ²⁷«El día diez del mes séptimo es el día del Perdón. Celebrarán una fiesta solemne en honor al SEÑOR, y ayunarán y le presentarán ofrendas por fuego. ²⁸En ese día no harán ningún tipo de trabajo, porque es el día del Perdón, cuando se hace *expiación por ustedes ante el SEÑOR su Dios. ²⁹Cualquiera que no observe el ayuno será eliminado de su pueblo. ³⁰Si alguien hace algún trabajo en ese día, yo mismo lo eliminaré de su pueblo. ³¹Por tanto, no harán ustedes ningún trabajo. Éste será un estatuto perpetuo para todos sus descendientes, dondequiera que habiten. ³²Será para ustedes un *sábado de solemne reposo, y deberán observar el ayuno. Este sábado lo observarán desde la tarde del día nueve del mes hasta la tarde siguiente.»

Fiesta de las Enramadas
23:33-43 — Nm 29:12-39; Dt 16:13-17

³³El SEÑOR le ordenó a Moisés ³⁴que les dijera a los israelitas: «El día quince del mes séptimo comienza la fiesta de las *Enramadas en honor al SEÑOR, la cual durará siete días. ³⁵El primer día se celebrará una fiesta solemne en honor al SEÑOR. Ese día no harán ningún trabajo. ³⁶Durante siete días le presentarán al SEÑOR ofrendas por fuego. Al octavo día celebrarán una fiesta solemne en honor al SEÑOR y volverán a presentarle ofrendas por fuego. Es una fiesta solemne; ese día no harán ningún trabajo.

³⁷»Éstas son las fiestas que el SEÑOR ha establecido, y a las que ustedes habrán de convocar como fiestas solemnes en su honor, para presentarle ofrendas por fuego, *holocaustos, ofrendas de cereal, y sacrificios y ofrendas de libación, tal como está prescrito para cada día. ³⁸Todas estas fiestas son adicionales a los *sábados del SEÑOR y a los tributos y ofrendas votivas o voluntarias que ustedes le presenten.

³⁹»A partir del día quince del mes séptimo, luego de que hayan recogido los frutos de la tierra, celebrarán durante siete días la fiesta del SEÑOR. El primer día y el octavo serán de descanso especial. ⁴⁰El primer día tomarán frutos de los mejores árboles, ramas de palmera, de árboles frondosos y de sauces de los arroyos, y durante siete días se regocijarán en presencia del SEÑOR su Dios. ⁴¹Cada año, durante siete días, celebrarán esta fiesta en honor al SEÑOR. La celebrarán en el mes séptimo. Éste será un estatuto perpetuo para las generaciones venideras. ⁴²Durante siete días vivirán bajo enramadas. Todos los israelitas nativos vivirán bajo enramadas, ⁴³para que sus descendientes sepan que yo hice vivir así a los israelitas cuando los saqué de Egipto. Yo soy el SEÑOR su Dios.»

⁴⁴Así anunció Moisés a los israelitas las fiestas establecidas por el SEÑOR.

Iluminación del santuario
24:1-3 — Éx 27:20-21

24 El SEÑOR le dijo a Moisés: ²«Manda a los israelitas que te traigan aceite *puro de olivas prensadas, para la iluminación del santuario. Las lámparas se mantendrán siempre encendidas. ³Aarón preparará las lámparas en la *Tienda de reunión, fuera de la cortina del *pacto, para que ardan delante del SEÑOR toda la noche. Éste será un estatuto perpetuo para las generaciones venideras. ⁴Las lámparas que están sobre el candelabro de oro puro se mantendrán siempre encendidas delante del SEÑOR.

Los panes ofrecidos al SEÑOR

⁵»Toma flor de harina y hornea doce tortas de pan. Cada torta debe pesar cuatro kilos.ᵛ ⁶Ponlas ante el SEÑOR sobre la mesa de oro puro, en dos hileras de seis tortas cada una. ⁷En cada hilera pondrás incienso puro. Así el pan será una ofrenda memorial presentada por fuego al SEÑOR. ⁸Este pan se dispondrá regularmente ante el SEÑOR todos los *sábados. Éste es un *pacto perpetuo de los israelitas. ⁹El pan les pertenece a Aarón y a sus hijos, quienes lo comerán en un lugar *santo. Es una parte sumamente sagrada de las ofrendas que se presentan por fuego al SEÑOR. Es un estatuto perpetuo.»

---

u 23:13 un litro. Lit. un cuarto de *hin. v 24:5 pesar cuatro kilos. Lit. tener dos décimas (de *efa).

Lapidación de un blasfemo

10Entre los israelitas vivía un hombre, hijo de madre israelita y de padre egipcio. Y sucedió que un día este hombre y un israelita iniciaron un pleito en el campamento. 11Pero el hijo de la mujer israelita, al lanzar una maldición, pronunció el *nombre del SEÑOR; así que se lo llevaron a Moisés. (El nombre de su madre era Selomit hija de Dibrí, de la tribu de Dan.) 12Y lo pusieron bajo arresto hasta que el SEÑOR les dijera qué hacer con él.

13Entonces el SEÑOR le dijo a Moisés: 14«Saca al blasfemo fuera del campamento. Quienes lo hayan oído impondrán las manos sobre su cabeza, y toda la asamblea lo apedreará. 15Diles a los israelitas: "Todo el que *blasfeme contra su Dios sufrirá las consecuencias de su pecado." 16Además, todo el que pronuncie el nombre del SEÑOR al maldecir a su prójimo será condenado a muerte. Toda la asamblea lo apedreará. Sea extranjero o nativo, si pronuncia el nombre del SEÑOR al maldecir a su prójimo, será condenado a muerte.

La ley del talión

17»El que le quite la *vida a otro *ser humano será condenado a muerte.

18»El que le quite la vida a algún animal ajeno, reparará el daño con otro animal.

19»Al que lesione a su prójimo se le infligirá el mismo daño que haya causado: 20fractura por fractura, ojo por ojo, diente por diente. Sufrirá en carne propia el mismo daño que haya causado.

21»Todo el que mate un animal reparará el daño, pero el que mate a un *hombre será condenado a muerte. 22Una sola ley regirá, tanto para el nativo como para el extranjero. Yo soy el SEÑOR su Dios.»

23Moisés les comunicó todo esto a los israelitas, y ellos sacaron al blasfemo fuera del campamento, y allí lo apedrearon. Los israelitas procedieron tal como el SEÑOR se lo ordenó a Moisés.

El año sabático

25 En el monte Sinaí el SEÑOR le ordenó a Moisés 2que les dijera a los israelitas: «Cuando ustedes hayan entrado en la tierra que les voy a dar, la tierra misma deberá observar un año de reposow en honor al SEÑOR. 3Durante seis años sembrarás tus campos, podarás tus viñas y cosecharás tus productos; 4pero llegado el séptimo año la tierra gozará de un año de reposo en honor al SEÑOR. No sembrarás tus campos ni podarás tus viñas; 5no segarás lo que haya brotado por sí mismo ni vendimiarás las uvas de tus viñas no cultivadas. La tierra gozará de un año completo de reposo. 6Sin embargo, de todo lo que la tierra produzca durante ese año sabático, podrán comer no sólo tú sino también tu siervo y tu sierva, el jornalero y el residente transitorio entre ustedes. 7También podrán alimentarse tu ganado y los animales que haya en el país. Todo lo que la tierra produzca ese año será sólo para el consumo diario.

El año del jubileo

8»Siete veces contarás siete años sabáticos, de modo que los siete años sabáticos sumen cuarenta y nueve años, 9y el día diez del mes séptimo, es decir, el día del Perdón, harás resonar la trompeta por todo el país. 10El año cincuenta será declarado *santo, y se proclamará en el país la liberación de todos sus habitantes. Será para ustedes un jubileo, y cada uno volverá a su heredad familiar y a su propio clan. 11El año

cincuenta será para ustedes un jubileo: ese año no sembrarán ni cosecharán lo que haya brotado por sí mismo, ni tampoco vendimiarán las viñas no cultivadas. 12Ese año es jubileo y será santo para ustedes. Comerán solamente lo que los campos produzcan por sí mismos.

13»En el año de jubileo cada uno volverá a su heredad familiar.

14»Si entre ustedes se realizan transacciones de compraventa, no se exploten los unos a los otros. 15Tú comprarás de tu prójimo a un precio proporcional al número de años que falten para el próximo jubileo, y él te venderá a un precio proporcional al número de años que queden por cosechar. 16Si aún faltan muchos años para el jubileo, aumentarás el precio en la misma proporción; pero si faltan pocos, rebajarás el precio proporcionalmente, porque lo que se te está vendiendo es sólo el número de cosechas. 17No se explotarán los unos a los otros, sino que temerán a su Dios. Yo soy el SEÑOR su Dios.

Consecuencias de la obediencia

18»Pongan en práctica mis estatutos y observen mis preceptos, y habitarán seguros en la tierra. 19La tierra dará su fruto, y comerán hasta saciarse, y allí vivirán seguros.

20»Si acaso se preguntan: "¿Qué comeremos en el séptimo año, si no plantamos ni cosechamos nuestros productos?", 21déjenme decirles que en el sexto año les enviaré una bendición tan grande que la tierra producirá como para tres años. 22Cuando ustedes siembren durante el octavo año, todavía estarán comiendo de la cosecha anterior, y continuarán comiendo de ella hasta la cosecha del año siguiente.

Leyes sobre el rescate de propiedades

23»La tierra no se venderá a perpetuidad, porque la tierra es mía y ustedes no son aquí más que forasteros y huéspedes. 24Por tanto, en el país habrá la posibilidad de recobrar todo terreno que haya sido heredad familiar.

25»En el caso de que uno de tus compatriotas se empobrezca y tenga que vender parte de su heredad familiar, su pariente más cercano rescatará lo que su hermano haya vendido. 26Si el hombre no tiene a nadie que pague el rescate a su favor, pero él mismo llega a prosperar y consigue lo suficiente para rescatar su propiedad, 27deberá calcular el número de años transcurridos desde la venta y reembolsar el saldo a quien se la haya comprado. Así podrá volver a su propiedad. 28Pero si no consigue lo suficiente para rescatarla, la tierra quedará en posesión del comprador hasta el año del jubileo, cuando el que la vendió la recobrará, y ésta volverá a su heredad familiar.

29»Si alguno vende una casa en una ciudad amurallada, tendrá derecho a rescatarla durante un año completo a partir de la fecha de venta. Ése es el tiempo que dura su derecho a rescatarla. 30Si no rescata la casa antes de cumplirse el año, no se le devolverá en el jubileo sino que pasará a ser propiedad perpetua del comprador y de sus descendientes. 31»Las casas que estén en aldeas sin murallas se considerarán campo abierto, pero podrán rescatarse y se devolverán en el jubileo.

32»Los levitas tendrán siempre el derecho de rescatar sus casas en las ciudades de su propiedad. 33Si alguno de los levitas hace valer su derecho, la casa que vendió en una de sus ciudades se le devolverá en el jubileo, porque las casas en las ciudades de los levitas son su heredad familiar entre los israelitas. ³⁴Pero los campos alrededor de sus ciudades no se venderán, pues son su propiedad inalienable.

³⁵»Si alguno de tus compatriotas se empobrece y no tiene cómo sostenerse, ayúdale como lo harías con el extranjero o con el residente transitorio; así podrá seguir viviendo entre ustedes. ³⁶No le exigirás interés cuando le prestes dinero o víveres, sino que temerás a tu Dios; así tu compatriota podrá seguir viviendo entre ustedes. ³⁷Tampoco le prestarás dinero con intereses ni le impondrás recargo a los víveres que le fíes. ³⁸Yo soy el SEÑOR su Dios, que los saqué de Egipto para darles la tierra de Canaán y para ser su Dios.

³⁹»Si alguno de tus compatriotas se empobrece y se ve obligado a venderse a ti, no lo hagas trabajar como esclavo. ⁴⁰Trátalo como al jornalero o como al residente transitorio que vive entre ustedes. Trabajará para ti, sólo hasta el año del jubileo. ⁴¹Entonces lo pondrás en libertad junto con sus hijos, y podrán volver a su propia familia y a la heredad de sus antepasados. ⁴²Todos los israelitas son mis siervos. Yo los saqué de Egipto, así que no serán vendidos como esclavos. ⁴³No serás un amo cruel, sino que temerás a tu Dios.

⁴⁴»Asegúrate de que tus esclavos y esclavas provengan de las naciones vecinas; allí podrás comprarlos. ⁴⁵También podrás comprar esclavos nacidos en tu país, siempre y cuando sean de las familias extranjeras que vivan en medio de ustedes. Ellos serán propiedad de ustedes, ⁴⁶y podrán dejárselos a sus hijos como herencia para que les sirvan de por vida. En lo que respecta a tus compatriotas, no serás un amo cruel.

⁴⁷»Si un extranjero o un residente transitorio entre ustedes se enriquece, y uno de tus compatriotas se empobrece y tiene que venderse a un extranjero o a un familiar de ese extranjero, ⁴⁸no perderá su derecho a ser rescatado después de haberse vendido. Podrá rescatarlo cualquiera de sus parientes: ⁴⁹un tío, un primo o cualquier otro de sus parientes. Y si llegara a prosperar, él mismo podrá pagar su rescate. ⁵⁰Él y su dueño calcularán el tiempo transcurrido, desde el año en que se vendió hasta el año del jubileo. El precio de su liberación se determinará en proporción al sueldo de un jornalero por ese número de años. ⁵¹Si aún faltan muchos años, pagará por su rescate una suma proporcional a la que se pagó por él. ⁵²Si sólo faltan pocos años para el jubileo, calculará y pagará por su rescate en proporción a esos años. ⁵³Ustedes vigilarán que su dueño lo trate como a los que trabajan por contrato anual, y que no lo trate con crueldad.

⁵⁴»Si tu compatriota no es rescatado por ninguno de esos medios, tanto él como sus hijos quedarán en libertad en el año del jubileo. ⁵⁵»Los israelitas son mis siervos. Yo los saqué de Egipto. Yo soy el SEÑOR su Dios.

Bendiciones de la obediencia

26 »No se hagan ídolos, ni levanten imágenes ni piedras sagradas. No coloquen en su territorio piedras esculpidas ni se inclinen ante ellas. Yo soy el SEÑOR su Dios.

²»Observen mis *sábados y muestren reverencia por mi santuario. Yo soy el SEÑOR.

³»Si se conducen según mis estatutos, y obedecen fielmente mis mandamientos, ⁴yo les enviaré lluvia a su tiempo, y la tierra y los árboles del campo darán sus frutos; ⁵la trilla durará hasta la vendimia, y la vendimia durará hasta la siembra. Comerán hasta saciarse y vivirán seguros en su tierra.

⁶»Yo traeré *paz al país, y ustedes podrán dormir sin ningún temor. Quitaré de la tierra las bestias salvajes, y no habrá guerra en su territorio. ⁷Perseguirán a sus enemigos, y ante ustedes caerán a filo de espada. ⁸Cinco de ustedes perseguirán a cien, y cien de ustedes perseguirán a diez mil, y ante ustedes sus enemigos caerán a filo de espada.

⁹»Yo les mostraré mi favor. Yo los haré fecundos. Los multiplicaré, y mantendré mi *pacto con ustedes. ¹⁰Todavía estarán comiendo de la cosecha del año anterior cuando saldrá para dar lugar a la nueva. ¹¹Estableceré mi morada en medio de ustedes, y no los aborreceré. ¹²Caminaré entre ustedes. Yo seré su Dios, y ustedes serán mi pueblo. ¹³Yo soy el SEÑOR su Dios, que los saqué de Egipto para que dejaran de ser esclavos. Yo rompí las coyundas de su yugo y los hice caminar con la cabeza erguida.

Maldiciones de la desobediencia

¹⁴»Si ustedes no me obedecen ni ponen por obra todos estos mandamientos, ¹⁵sino que desprecian mis estatutos y aborrecen mis preceptos, y dejan de poner por obra todos mis mandamientos, violando así mi *pacto, ¹⁶entonces yo mismo los castigaré con un terror repentino, con enfermedades y con fiebre que les harán perder la vista y acabarán con su *vida. En vano sembrarán su semilla, porque se la comerán sus enemigos. ¹⁷Yo les negaré mi favor, y sus adversarios los derrotarán. Sus enemigos los dominarán, y ustedes huirán sin que nadie los persiga.

¹⁸»Si después de todo esto siguen sin obedecerme, siete veces los castigaré por sus pecados. ¹⁹Yo quebrantaré su orgullo y terquedad. Endureceré el cielo como el hierro y la tierra como el bronce, ²⁰por lo que en vano agotarán sus fuerzas, y ni el suelo ni los árboles del campo les darán sus frutos.

²¹»Si a pesar de esto siguen oponiéndose a mí, y se niegan a obedecerme, siete veces los castigaré por sus pecados. ²²Lanzaré sobre ustedes fieras salvajes, que les arrebatarán sus hijos y destruirán su ganado. De tal manera los diezmarán, que sus caminos quedarán desiertos.

²³»Si a pesar de todo esto no aceptan mi disciplina, sino que continúan oponiéndose a mí, ²⁴yo también seguiré oponiéndome a ustedes. Yo mismo los heriré siete veces por sus pecados. ²⁵Dejaré caer sobre ustedes la espada de la venganza prescrita en el pacto. Cuando se retiren a sus ciudades, les enviaré una plaga, y caerán en poder del enemigo. ²⁶Cuando yo destruya sus trigales, diez mujeres hornearán para ustedes pan en un solo horno. Y lo distribuirán racionado, de tal manera que comerán pero no se saciarán.

²⁷»Si a pesar de esto todavía no me obedecen, sino que continúan oponiéndose a mí, ²⁸entonces yo también me pondré definitivamente en su contra. Siete veces los castigaré por sus pecados, ²⁹y tendrán que comerse la carne de sus hijos y de sus hijas. ³⁰Destruiré sus *santuarios paganos, demoleré sus altares de incienso, y amontonaré sus cadáveres sobre las figuras sin vida de sus ídolos. Volcaré mi odio sobre ustedes; ³¹convertiré en ruinas sus ciudades, y asolaré sus santuarios. No me complaceré más en el aroma de sus ofrendas, que me era grato. ³²De tal manera asolaré al país, que sus enemigos que vengan a ocuparlo quedarán atónitos. ³³Los dispersaré entre las naciones: desenvainaré la espada, y los perseguiré hasta dejar desolada su tierra, y en ruinas sus ciudades. ³⁴Entonces la tierra disfrutará de sus años sabáticos todo el tiempo que permanezca desolada, mientras ustedes vivan en el país de sus enemigos. Así la tierra descan-

26:34

...los. ³⁵Mientras la tierra
...án dor-
...bestias
...erse-
...lo de
...cien
...sus
...nso que no tuvo duran-
...e ustedes la habitaran.

...que sobrevivan, tan profundo
...nfundiré en tierra de sus ene-
...usurro de una hoja movida por
...rá en fuga. Correrán como quien
...y caerán sin que nadie los persiga.

...eran de la espada, tropezarán unos
...que nadie los persiga, y no podrán ha-
...e a sus enemigos. ³⁸Perecerán en medio
...iones; el país de sus enemigos los devorará.
...tos de ustedes que sobrevivan serán abatidos
...s enemigo, porque a sus pecados se añadirá la
...sus padres.

⁴⁰»Pero si confiesan su maldad y la maldad de
sus padres, y su traición y constante rebeldía contra
mí, ⁴¹las cuales me han obligado a enviarlos al país
de sus enemigos, y si su obstinado *corazón se humilla y reconoce su pecado, ⁴²entonces me acordaré de
mi pacto con Jacob, Isaac y Abraham, y también me
acordaré de la tierra. ⁴³Al abandonar ellos la tierra,
ésta disfrutará de sus sábados mientras permanezca
deshabitada. Pero tendrán que reconocer sus pecados, por cuanto rechazaron mis preceptos y aborrecieron mis estatutos.

⁴⁴»A pesar de todo, y aunque estén en la tierra de
sus enemigos, no los rechazaré ni los aborreceré hasta el punto de exterminarlos, ni romperé tampoco mi
pacto con ellos. Yo soy el SEÑOR su Dios. ⁴⁵Antes
bien, recordaré en su favor el pacto que hice con sus
antepasados, a quienes, a la vista de las naciones, saqué de Egipto para ser su Dios. Yo soy el SEÑOR».

⁴⁶Éstos son los estatutos, preceptos y leyes que,
por medio de Moisés, estableció el SEÑOR en el monte
Sinaí entre él y los israelitas.

Rescate de las ofrendas al SEÑOR

27 El SEÑOR le ordenó a Moisés ²que les dijera a
los israelitas: «Cuando alguien quiera hacerle al SEÑOR un voto especial equivalente al valor de
una persona, ³se aplicará el siguiente cálculo:

»Por los varones de veinte a sesenta años de
edad se pagarán cincuenta monedasˣ de plata, según la tasación oficial del santuario.

⁴»Por las mujeres se pagarán treinta monedas de
plata.

⁵»Por los varones de cinco a veinte años de edad
se pagarán veinte monedas, y diez monedas por las
mujeres de la misma edad.

⁶»Por los niños de un mes a cinco años se pagarán cinco monedas, y tres monedas por las niñas de
la misma edad.

⁷»Por los varones mayores de sesenta años se pagarán quince monedas, y diez monedas por las mujeres de la misma edad.

⁸»Si quien hace el voto es tan pobre que ni el precio estipulado puede pagar, se le hará comparecer
ante el sacerdote, el cual fijará el valor a pagar, según
los recursos de quien haga el voto.

⁹»Si lo que se presenta como ofrenda al SEÑOR es
un animal, éste quedará consagrado por haber sido
ofrecido al SEÑOR. ¹⁰No podrá cambiarse ni sustituir-
se un animal bueno por uno malo, ni un animal malo
por uno bueno. Si se cambia un animal por otro, ambos quedarán consagrados.

¹¹»Si lo que se presenta como ofrenda al SEÑOR
es un animal *impuro, se llevará el animal ante el sacerdote, ¹²quien determinará el valor del animal. El
cálculo aplicado por el sacerdote deberá aceptarse,
cualquiera que éste sea. ¹³Si el dueño quiere rescatar
el animal, deberá añadir una quinta parte al valor
que haya fijado el sacerdote.

¹⁴»Si alguno consagra su casa al SEÑOR, el sacerdote determinará su valor. El cálculo aplicado por el
sacerdote deberá aceptarse, cualquiera que éste sea.
¹⁵Si el que la consagró su casa quiere rescatarla, deberá
añadir una quinta parte al valor que haya fijado el sacerdote, y la casa volverá a ser suya.

¹⁶»Si alguno consagra al SEÑOR parte del campo
de su heredad familiar, su precio se determinará según la cantidad de semilla que se requiera para sem-
brarlo, a razón de cincuenta monedas de plata por
cada doscientos veinte litrosᶻ de semilla de cebada.
¹⁷Si consagra su campo a partir del año del jubileo,
dicho precio se mantendrá; ¹⁸pero si lo consagra después del jubileo, el sacerdote hará el cálculo según el
número de años que falten para el próximo jubileo,
con el descuento correspondiente.

¹⁹»Si el que consagra su campo realmente quiere
rescatarlo, deberá añadir una quinta parte al valor que
haya fijado el sacerdote, y el campo volverá a ser
suyo. ²⁰Pero si no lo rescata, o se lo vende a otro, ya no
podrá rescatarlo. ²¹Cuando en el jubileo el campo
quede libre, será consagrado como campo reservado
para el SEÑOR, y pasará a ser propiedad del sacerdote.

²²»Si alguno compra un campo que no sea parte
de su heredad familiar, y lo consagra al SEÑOR, ²³el
sacerdote determinará su precio según el tiempo que
falte para el año del jubileo. Ese mismo día, el que
consagra el campo pagará el monto de su valor. Es
algo consagrado al SEÑOR. ²⁴En el año del jubileo, el
campo volverá a ser parte de la heredad familiar de
su dueño anterior.

²⁵»Todo precio se fijará según la tasación oficial
del santuario, que es de diez gramosª por moneda.

²⁶»Sin embargo, nadie podrá consagrar la primera cría de su ganado, sea de res o de oveja, pues por
derecho las primeras crías le pertenecen al SEÑOR.
²⁷Si se trata de animales impuros, se podrán rescatar
pagando el valor fijado por el sacerdote, más una
quinta parte. Si no se rescata, se venderá en el precio
que el sacerdote haya fijado.

²⁸»Nadie podrá vender ni rescatar sus bienes,
sean *hombres, animales o campos, si los ha consagrado como propiedad exclusiva del SEÑOR. Todo
cuanto se consagra como propiedad exclusiva del
SEÑOR, es cosa *santísima. ²⁹Ninguna persona así
consagrada podrá ser rescatada, sino que será *con-
denada a muerte.

³⁰»El diezmo de todo producto del campo, ya sea
grano de los sembrados o fruto de los árboles, pertenece al SEÑOR, pues le está consagrado. ³¹Si alguien
desea rescatar algo de su diezmo, deberá añadir a su
valor una quinta parte. ³²En cuanto al diezmo del ganado mayor y menor, uno de cada diez animales con-
tadosᵇ será consagrado al SEÑOR. ³³El pastor no hará
distinción entre animales buenos y malos, ni hará sustitución alguna. En caso de cambiar un animal por
otro, los dos quedarán consagrados y no se les podrá
rescatar.»

³⁴Éstos son los mandamientos que el SEÑOR le
dio a Moisés para los israelitas, en el monte Sinaí.

ˣ 27:3 monedas. Lit. *siclos; así en el resto de este capítulo. ʸ 27:3 la tasación oficial. Lit. el *siclo; también en v. 25. ᶻ
27:16 cada doscientos veinte litros. Lit. cada *jómer. ª 27:25 diez gramos. Lit. veinte *guerás. ᵇ 27:32 contados. Lit. que pasen
bajo la vara del pastor.

NÚMEROS

Censo de las tribus de Israel

1 El SEÑOR le habló a Moisés en el desierto de Sinaí, en la *Tienda de reunión, el día primero del mes segundo, en el segundo año después de que los israelitas salieron de Egipto. Le dijo: 2«Hagan un censo de toda la comunidad de Israel por clanes y por familias patriarcales, anotando uno por uno los nombres de todos los varones. 3Tú y Aarón reclutarán por escuadrones a todos los varones israelitas mayores de veinte años que sean aptos para el servicio militar. 4Para esto contarán con la colaboración de un hombre de cada tribu, que sea jefe de una familia patriarcal.

Los encargados del censo

5»Éstos son los nombres de quienes habrán de ayudarles:

por la tribu de Rubén, Elisur hijo de Sedeúr;
6 por la de Simeón, Selumiel hijo de Zurisaday;
7 por la de Judá, Naasón hijo de Aminadab;
8 por la de Isacar, Natanael hijo de Zuar;
9 por la de Zabulón, Eliab hijo de Helón;
10 por las tribus de los hijos de José: Elisama hijo de Amiud por la tribu de Efraín, y Gamaliel hijo de Pedasur por la de Manasés;
11 por la tribu de Benjamín, Abidán hijo de Gedeoni;
12 por la de Dan, Ajiezer hijo de Amisaday;
13 por la de Aser, Paguiel hijo de Ocrán;
14 por la de Gad, Eliasaf hijo de Deuel;
15 por la de Neftalí, Ajirá hijo de Enán.»

16A éstos la comunidad los nombró jefes de las tribus patriarcales y comandantes de los escuadrones de Israel.

El censo y sus resultados

17Moisés y Aarón tomaron consigo a los hombres que habían sido designados por nombre, 18y el día primero del mes segundo reunieron a toda la comunidad. Uno por uno fueron empadronados por clanes y por familias patriarcales. De este modo quedaron anotados los nombres de todos los varones mayores de veinte años, 19tal como el SEÑOR se lo había mandado a Moisés. Este censo lo hizo Moisés en el desierto de Sinaí.

20 Los descendientes de Rubén, primogénito de Israel, quedaron registrados por clanes y por familias patriarcales, según su genealogía. Uno por uno fueron empadronados todos los varones mayores de veinte años que eran aptos para el servicio militar. 21El número de la tribu de Rubén llegó a cuarenta y seis mil quinientos hombres.

22 Los descendientes de Simeón quedaron registrados por clanes y por familias patriarcales según su genealogía. Uno por uno fueron empadronados todos los varones mayores de veinte años que eran aptos para el servicio militar. 23El número de la tribu de Simeón llegó a cincuenta y nueve mil trescientos hombres.

24 Los descendientes de Gad quedaron registrados por clanes y por familias patriarcales según su genealogía. Uno por uno fueron empadronados todos los varones mayores de veinte años que eran aptos para el servicio militar. 25El número de la tribu de Gad llegó a cuarenta y cinco mil seiscientos cincuenta hombres.

26 Los descendientes de Judá quedaron registrados por clanes y por familias patriarcales según su genealogía. Uno por uno fueron empadronados todos los varones mayores de veinte años que eran aptos para el servicio militar. 27El número de la tribu de Judá llegó a setenta y cuatro mil seiscientos hombres.

28 Los descendientes de Isacar quedaron registrados por clanes y por familias patriarcales según su genealogía. Uno por uno fueron empadronados todos los varones mayores de veinte años que eran aptos para el servicio militar. 29El número de la tribu de Isacar llegó a cincuenta y cuatro mil cuatrocientos hombres.

30 Los descendientes de Zabulón quedaron registrados por clanes y por familias patriarcales según su genealogía. Uno por uno fueron empadronados todos los varones mayores de veinte años que eran aptos para el servicio militar. 31El número de la tribu de Zabulón llegó a cincuenta y siete mil cuatrocientos hombres.

32Los descendientes de José:
Los descendientes de Efraín quedaron registrados por clanes y por familias patriarcales según su genealogía. Uno por uno fueron empadronados todos los varones mayores de veinte años que eran aptos para el servicio militar. 33El número de la tribu de Efraín llegó a cuarenta mil quinientos hombres.

34 Los descendientes de Manasés quedaron registrados por clanes y por familias patriarcales según su genealogía. Uno por uno fueron empadronados todos los varones mayores de veinte años que eran aptos para el servicio militar. 35El número de la tribu de Manasés llegó a treinta y dos mil doscientos hombres.

36 Los descendientes de Benjamín quedaron registrados por clanes y por familias patriarcales según su genealogía. Uno por uno fueron empadronados todos los varones mayores de veinte años que eran aptos para el servicio militar. 37El número de la tribu de Benjamín llegó a treinta y cinco mil cuatrocientos hombres.

38 Los descendientes de Dan quedaron registrados por clanes y por familias patriarcales según su genealogía. Uno por uno fueron empadronados todos los varones mayores de veinte años que eran aptos para el servicio militar. 39El número de la tribu de Dan llegó a sesenta y dos mil setecientos hombres.

40 Los descendientes de Aser quedaron registrados por clanes y por familias patriarcales según su genealogía. Uno por uno fueron empadronados todos los varones mayores de veinte años que eran aptos para el servicio militar. 41El número de la tribu de Aser llegó a cuarenta y un mil quinientos hombres.

42 Los descendientes de Neftalí quedaron registrados por clanes y por familias patriarcales según su genealogía. Uno por uno fueron

empadronados todos los varones mayores de veinte años que eran aptos para el servicio militar. 43El número de la tribu de Neftalí llegó a cincuenta y tres mil cuatrocientos hombres.

44Éste es el resultado del censo que hicieron Moisés y Aarón, con la ayuda de los doce jefes de Israel, cada uno en representación de su familia patriarcal. 45Todos los israelitas mayores de veinte años que eran aptos para el servicio militar fueron anotados, según su familia patriarcal. 46El total llegó a seiscientos tres mil quinientos cincuenta israelitas censados.

Los levitas

47Los levitas no fueron censados con los demás, 48porque el SEÑOR le había dicho a Moisés: 49«A la tribu de Leví no la incluirás en el censo de los hijos de Israel. 50Más bien, tú mismo los pondrás a cargo del santuario del *pacto, de todos sus utensilios y de todo lo relacionado con él. Los levitas transportarán el santuario y todos sus utensilios. Además, serán los ministros del santuario y acamparán a su alrededor. 51Cuando haya que trasladar el santuario, los levitas se encargarán de desarmarlo; cuando haya que instalarlo, serán ellos quienes lo armen. Pero cualquiera que se acerque al santuario y no sea sacerdote, morirá. 52Todos los israelitas acamparán bajo su propio estandarte y en su propio campamento, según sus escuadrones. 53En cambio, los levitas acamparán alrededor del santuario del pacto, para evitar que Dios descargue su ira sobre la comunidad de Israel. Serán, pues, los levitas los encargados de cuidar el santuario del pacto.»

54Los israelitas hicieron todo conforme a lo que el SEÑOR le había mandado a Moisés.

Disposición de las tribus en el campamento

2 El SEÑOR les dijo a Moisés y a Aarón: 2«Los israelitas acamparán alrededor de la *Tienda de reunión, mirando hacia ella, cada cual bajo el estandarte de su propia familia patriarcal.

3»Al este, por donde sale el sol, acamparán los que se agrupan bajo el estandarte del campamento de Judá, según sus escuadrones. Su jefe es Naasón hijo de Aminadab. 4Su ejército está integrado por setenta y cuatro mil seiscientos hombres.

5»A un lado de Judá acampará la tribu de Isacar. Su jefe es Natanael hijo de Zuar. 6Su ejército está integrado por cincuenta y cuatro mil cuatrocientos hombres.

7»Al otro lado acampará la tribu de Zabulón. Su jefe es Eliab hijo de Helón. 8Su ejército está integrado por cincuenta y siete mil cuatrocientos hombres.

9»Todos los reclutas del campamento de Judá, según sus escuadrones, suman ciento ochenta y seis mil cuatrocientos hombres, los cuales marcharán a la cabeza.

10»Al sur acamparán los que se agrupan bajo el estandarte del campamento de Rubén, según sus escuadrones. Su jefe es Elisur hijo de Sedeúr. 11Su ejército está integrado por cuarenta y seis mil quinientos hombres.

12»A un lado de Rubén acampará la tribu de Simeón. Su jefe es Selumiel hijo de Zurisaday. 13Su

ejército está integrado por cincuenta y nueve mil trescientos hombres.

14»Al otro lado acampará la tribu de Gad. Su jefe es Eliasaf hijo de Reuel.a 15Su ejército está integrado por cuarenta y cinco mil seiscientos cincuenta hombres.

16»Todos los reclutas del campamento de Rubén, según sus escuadrones, suman ciento cincuenta y un mil cuatrocientos cincuenta hombres, los cuales marcharán en segundo lugar.

17»Entonces se pondrá en marcha la Tienda de reunión junto con el campamento de los levitas que está situado en medio de los demás campamentos. Partirán en el mismo orden en que hayan acampado, cada uno en su lugar y bajo su estandarte.

18»Al oeste acamparán los que se agrupan bajo el estandarte del campamento de Efraín, según sus escuadrones. Su jefe es Elisama hijo de Amiud. 19Su ejército está integrado por cuarenta mil quinientos hombres.

20»A un lado de Efraín acampará la tribu de Manasés. Su jefe es Gamaliel hijo de Pedasur. 21Su ejército está integrado por treinta y dos mil doscientos hombres.

22»Al otro lado acampará la tribu de Benjamín. Su jefe es Abidán hijo de Gedeoni. 23Su ejército está integrado por treinta y cinco mil cuatrocientos hombres.

24»Todos los reclutas del campamento de Efraín, según sus escuadrones, suman ciento ocho mil cien hombres, los cuales marcharán en tercer lugar.

25»Al norte, acamparán los que se agrupan bajo el estandarte del campamento de Dan, según sus escuadrones. Su jefe es Ajiezer hijo de Amisaday. 26Su ejército está integrado por sesenta y dos mil setecientos hombres.

27»A un lado de Dan acampará la tribu de Aser. Su jefe es Paguiel hijo de Ocrán. 28Su escuadrón está integrado por cuarenta y un mil quinientos hombres.

29»Al otro lado acampará la tribu de Neftalí. Su jefe es Ajirá hijo de Enán. 30Su escuadrón está integrado por cincuenta y tres mil cuatrocientos hombres.

31»Todos los reclutas del campamento de Dan, según sus escuadrones, suman ciento cincuenta y siete mil seiscientos hombres, los cuales marcharán en último lugar, según sus estandartes.»

32Éstos son los israelitas reclutados de entre las familias patriarcales. El total de reclutas por escuadrones suma seiscientos tres mil quinientos cincuenta hombres. 33Pero los levitas no están incluidos con los demás israelitas, conforme a lo que el SEÑOR le había mandado a Moisés.

34Los israelitas hicieron todo lo que el SEÑOR le mandó a Moisés: acampaban bajo sus propios estandartes, y se ponían en marcha, según sus clanes y familias patriarcales.

La tribu de Leví

3 Así quedó registrada la familia de Aarón y Moisés cuando el SEÑOR habló con Moisés en el monte Sinaí.

---

a **2:14** *Reuel* (mss. hebreos, Pentateuco Samaritano y Vulgata); *Deuel* (TM).

Los sacerdotes

2Los nombres de los hijos de Aarón son los siguientes: Nadab el primogénito, Abiú, Eleazar e Itamar. 3Ellos fueron los aaronitas ungidos, ordenados al sacerdocio. 4Nadab y Abiú murieron en presencia del SEÑOR cuando, en el desierto de Sinaí, le ofrecieron sacrificios con fuego profano. Como Nadab y Abiú no tuvieron hijos, sólo Eleazar e Itamar ejercieron el sacerdocio en vida de su padre Aarón.

Ministerio de los levitas

5El SEÑOR le dijo a Moisés: 6«Trae a la tribu de Leví y preséntasela a Aarón. Los levitas le ayudarán en el ministerio. 7Desempeñarán sus funciones en lugar de Aarón y de toda la comunidad, encargándose del servicio del santuario en la *Tienda de reunión. 8Cuidarán allí de todos los utensilios de la Tienda de reunión y desempeñarán sus funciones en lugar de los israelitas, encargándose del servicio del santuario. 9Pondrás a los levitas a las órdenes de Aarón y de sus hijos. Entre los israelitas, serán ellos los que estén totalmente dedicados a mí.b 10A Aarón y a sus hijos les asignarás el ministerio sacerdotal. Pero cualquiera que se acerque al santuario y no sea sacerdote, será condenado a muerte.»

Elección de los levitas

11El SEÑOR le dijo a Moisés: 12«Yo mismo he escogido a los levitas de entre los israelitas, como sustitutos de todo primogénito. Los levitas son míos, 13porque míos son todos los primogénitos. Cuando exterminé a todos los primogénitos de Egipto, consagré para mí a todo primogénito de Israel, tanto de *hombres como de animales. Por lo tanto, son míos. Yo soy el SEÑOR.»

Censo de la tribu de Leví

14El SEÑOR le dijo a Moisés en el desierto de Sinaí: 15«Haz un censo de los levitas por clanes y por familias patriarcales, tomando en cuenta a todo varón mayor de un mes.»

16Moisés llevó a cabo el censo, tal como el SEÑOR mismo se lo había ordenado.

17 Hijos de Leví:
　　Guersón, Coat y Merari.
18 Clanes guersonitas:
　　Libní y Simí.
19 Clanes coatitas:
　　Amirán, Izar, Hebrón y Uziel.
20 Clanes meraritas:
　　Majlí y Musí.

Éstos son los clanes levitas, según sus familias patriarcales.

Los clanes guersonitas

21De Guersón procedían los clanes de Libní y de Simí. Éstos eran los clanes guersonitas. 22El total de los varones censados mayores de un mes llegó a siete mil quinientos. 23Los clanes guersonitas acampaban al oeste, detrás del santuario. 24El jefe de la familia patriarcal de los guersonitas era Eliasaf hijo de Lael. 25En lo que atañe a la *Tienda de reunión, los guersonitas tenían a su cargo la tienda que cubría el santuario, su toldo, la cortina que estaba a la entrada, 26el cortinaje del atrio y la cortina a la entrada del atrio que rodea el santuario y el altar, como también las cuerdas y todo lo necesario para su servicio.

Los clanes coatitas

27De Coat procedían los clanes de Amirán, Izar, Hebrón y Uziel. Éstos eran los clanes coatitas, 28que tenían a su cargo el santuario. El total de los varones mayores de un mes llegó a ocho mil seiscientos. 29Los clanes coatitas acampaban al sur del santuario. 30El jefe de la familia patriarcal de los coatitas era Elizafán hijo de Uziel. 31Tenían a su cargo el arca, la mesa, el candelabro, los altares, los utensilios del santuario con los que ministraban, y la cortina de la entrada, como también todo lo necesario para su servicio.

32El jefe principal de los levitas era Eleazar, hijo de Aarón el sacerdote, a quien se designó como jefe de los que tenían a su cargo el santuario.

Los clanes meraritas

33De Merari procedían los clanes de Majlí y Musí. Éstos eran los clanes meraritas. 34El total de los varones censados mayores de un mes llegó a seis mil doscientos. 35El jefe de la familia patriarcal de los meraritas era Zuriel hijo de Abijaíl. Los clanes meraritas acampaban al norte del santuario. 36Tenían a su cargo el armazón del santuario, es decir, sus travesaños, postes y bases, junto con todos sus utensilios y todo lo necesario para su servicio. 37También cuidaban de los postes que estaban alrededor del atrio, junto con sus bases, estacas y cuerdas.

La tribu de Leví

38Moisés, Aarón y sus hijos acampaban delante del santuario, es decir, al este de la *Tienda de reunión, por donde sale el sol, ya que tenían a su cargo el santuario en representación de los israelitas. Pero cualquiera que, sin ser sacerdote, se acercaba al santuario, era condenado a muerte.

39Moisés y Aarón censaron a los levitas, tal como el SEÑOR mismo se lo había ordenado. El total de los levitas mayores de un mes censados por clanes llegó a veintidós mil.

Los levitas y los primogénitos

40El SEÑOR le dijo a Moisés: «Haz un censo de todos los primogénitos israelitas mayores de un mes, y registra sus nombres. 41Apártame a los levitas en sustitución de todos los primogénitos israelitas, así como el ganado de los levitas en sustitución de todas las primeras crías del ganado de los israelitas. Yo soy el SEÑOR.»

42Moisés hizo el censo de todos los primogénitos israelitas, conforme a lo que el SEÑOR le había mandado. 43El total de los primogénitos mayores de un mes, anotados por nombre, llegó a veintidós mil doscientos setenta y tres.

44El SEÑOR le dijo a Moisés: 45«Apártame a los levitas en sustitución de todos los primogénitos de los israelitas, así como el ganado de los levitas en sustitución del ganado de los israelitas. Los levitas son míos. Yo soy el SEÑOR.

46»Para rescatar a los doscientos setenta y tres primogénitos israelitas que exceden al número de levitas, 47recaudarás cinco monedas de plata por cabeza, según la moneda oficial del santuario, que pesa once gramos.c 48Esa suma se la entregarás a Aarón y a sus hijos, como rescate por los israelitas que exceden a su número.»

49Moisés recaudó el dinero del rescate de los israelitas que excedían al número de los rescatados por los levitas. 50En total recaudó mil trescientas sesenta y cinco monedas de plata, según la moneda

b 3:9 a mí (mss. hebreos, LXX y Pentateuco Samaritano); a él (TM).　c 3:47 cinco monedas ... once gramos. Lit. cinco *siclos por cabeza, según el siclo del santuario, que pesa veinte *guerás.

oficial del santuario.ᵈ ⁵¹Luego entregó ese dinero a Aarón y a sus hijos, tal como el SEÑOR mismo se lo había ordenado.

Ministerio de los coatitas

4 El SEÑOR les dijo a Moisés y a Aarón: ²«Hagan un censo, por clanes y por familias patriarcales, de los levitas que descienden de Coat. ³Incluye en él a todos los varones de treinta a cincuenta años de edad que sean aptos para trabajar en la *Tienda de reunión.

⁴»El ministerio de los coatitas en la Tienda de reunión consiste en cuidar de las cosas más sagradas. ⁵Cuando los israelitas deban ponerse en marcha, Aarón y sus hijos entrarán en el santuario y descolgarán la cortina que lo resguarda, y con ella cubrirán el arca del *pacto. ⁶Después la cubrirán con piel de delfín y con un paño púrpura, y le colocarán las varas para transportarla.

⁷»Sobre la mesa de la presencia del SEÑOR extenderán un paño púrpura y colocarán los platos, las bandejas, los tazones y las jarras para las libaciones. También estará allí el pan de la ofrenda permanente. ⁸Sobre todo esto extenderán un paño escarlata. Luego cubrirán la mesa con piel de delfín y le colocarán las varas para transportarla.

⁹»Con un paño púrpura cubrirán el candelabro y sus lámparas, cortapabilos, ceniceros y utensilios que sirven para suministrarle aceite. ¹⁰Después cubrirán el candelabro y todos sus accesorios con piel de delfín, y lo colocarán sobre las andas.

¹¹»Extenderán un paño púrpura sobre el altar de oro, lo cubrirán con piel de delfín y le colocarán las varas para transportarlo.

¹²»Envolverán en un paño púrpura todos los utensilios con los que ministran en el santuario, los cubrirán con piel de delfín, y luego los colocarán sobre las andas.

¹³»Al altar del *holocausto le quitarán las cenizas y lo cubrirán con un paño carmesí. ¹⁴Sobre el altar pondrán todos los utensilios que usan en su ministerio: ceniceros, tenedores, tenazas, aspersorios y todos los utensilios del altar. Luego lo cubrirán con piel de delfín y le colocarán las varas para transportarlo.

¹⁵»Cuando Aarón y sus hijos hayan terminado de cubrir el santuario y todos sus accesorios, los israelitas podrán ponerse en marcha. Entonces vendrán los coatitas para transportar el santuario, pero sin tocarlo para que no mueran. También transportarán los objetos que están en la Tienda de reunión.

¹⁶»En cambio, Eleazar hijo de Aarón estará a cargo del aceite para el candelabro, del incienso aromático, de la ofrenda permanente de cereal y del aceite de la unción. Además, cuidará del santuario y de todos sus utensilios.»

¹⁷El SEÑOR les dijo a Moisés y a Aarón: ¹⁸«Asegúrense de que los clanes de Coat no vayan a ser eliminados de la tribu de Leví. ¹⁹Para que no mueran cuando se acerquen a las cosas más sagradas, deberán hacer lo siguiente: Aarón y sus hijos asignarán a cada uno lo que deba hacer y transportar. ²⁰Pero los coatitas no mirarán ni por un momento las cosas sagradas; de lo contrario, morirán.»

Ministerio de los guersonitas

²¹El SEÑOR les dijo a Moisés y a Aarón: ²²«Hagan también un censo de los guersonitas por clanes y por familias patriarcales. ²³Incluyan a todos los varones

de treinta a cincuenta años que sean aptos para servir en la *Tienda de reunión.

²⁴»El ministerio de los clanes guersonitas consiste en encargarse del transporte. ²⁵Llevarán las cortinas del santuario, la Tienda de reunión, su toldo, la cubierta de piel de delfín que va encima, y la cortina de la entrada a la Tienda de reunión. ²⁶También transportarán el cortinaje del atrio y la cortina que está a la entrada del atrio que rodea el santuario y el altar, junto con las cuerdas y todos los utensilios necesarios para su servicio. Deberán ocuparse de todo lo relacionado con éstos. ²⁷Todo su trabajo, ya sea transportando los utensilios o sirviendo en la Tienda, deberán hacerlo bajo la dirección de Aarón y de sus hijos. De ellos será la responsabilidad de todo el transporte. ²⁸El servicio de los clanes de Guersón en la Tienda de reunión será supervisado por Itamar, hijo del sacerdote Aarón.

Ministerio de los meraritas

²⁹»Haz un censo de los meraritas por clanes y por familias patriarcales. ³⁰Incluye a todos los varones de treinta a cincuenta años que sean aptos para servir en la *Tienda de reunión. ³¹Su trabajo en la Tienda de reunión consistirá en transportar el armazón del santuario, es decir, sus travesaños, postes y bases, ³²lo mismo que los postes que están alrededor del atrio, sus bases, estacas y cuerdas, como también todos los utensilios necesarios para su servicio. Asígnale a cada uno los objetos que deberá transportar. ³³El servicio de los clanes de Merari en la Tienda de reunión será supervisado por Itamar, hijo del sacerdote Aarón.»

Censo del clan de Coat

³⁴Moisés, Aarón y los líderes de la comunidad hicieron un censo de los coatitas por clanes y por familias patriarcales. ³⁵El censo incluía a todos los varones de treinta a cincuenta años que eran aptos para servir en la *Tienda de reunión. ³⁶El total de los censados por clanes llegó a dos mil setecientos cincuenta hombres. ³⁷Éste fue el total de los censados entre los clanes de Coat para servir en la Tienda de reunión, según el recuento que hicieron Moisés y Aarón, conforme al mandato del SEÑOR por medio de Moisés.

Censo del clan de Guersón

³⁸Se hizo un censo de guersonitas por clanes y por familias patriarcales. ³⁹El censo incluía a todos los varones de treinta a cincuenta años que eran aptos para servir en la *Tienda de reunión. ⁴⁰El total de los censados por familias patriarcales llegó a dos mil seiscientos treinta hombres. ⁴¹Éste fue el total de los censados entre los clanes de Guersón para servir en la Tienda de reunión, según el recuento que hicieron Moisés y Aarón, conforme al mandato del SEÑOR.

Censo del clan de Merari

⁴²Se hizo un censo de los meraritas por clanes y por familias patriarcales. ⁴³El censo incluía a todos los varones de treinta a cincuenta años que eran aptos para servir en la *Tienda de reunión. ⁴⁴El total de los censados por clanes llegó a tres mil doscientos hombres. ⁴⁵Éste fue el total de los censados entre los clanes de Merari, según el recuento que hicieron Moisés y Aarón, conforme al mandato del SEÑOR por medio de Moisés.

ᵈ **3:50** *monedas ... santuario.* Lit. *siclos, según el siclo del santuario.*

Conclusión

⁴⁶Moisés, Aarón y los líderes de Israel hicieron un censo de todos los levitas por clanes y por familias patriarcales. ⁴⁷El total de los varones de treinta a cincuenta años, que eran aptos para servir en la *Tienda de reunión y transportarla, ⁴⁸llegó a ocho mil quinientos ochenta. ⁴⁹Conforme al mandato del SEÑOR por medio de Moisés, a cada uno se le asignó lo que tenía que hacer y transportar.

Así fueron censados, según el mandato que Moisés recibió del SEÑOR.

La pureza del campamento

5 El SEÑOR le dijo a Moisés: ²«Ordénales a los israelitas que expulsen del campamento a cualquiera que tenga una infección en la piel,ᵉ o padezca de flujo venéreo, o haya quedado ritualmente *impuro por haber tocado un cadáver. ³Ya sea que se trate de hombres o de mujeres, los expulsarás del campamento para que no *contaminen el lugar donde habito en medio de mi pueblo.» ⁴Y los israelitas los expulsaron del campamento, tal como el SEÑOR se lo había mandado a Moisés.

Restitución por daños

⁵El SEÑOR le ordenó a Moisés ⁶que les dijera a los israelitas: «El hombre o la mujer que peque contra su prójimo, traiciona al SEÑOR y tendrá que responder por ello. ⁷Deberá confesar su pecado y pagarle a la persona perjudicada una compensación por el daño causado, con un recargo del veinte por ciento. ⁸Pero si la persona perjudicada no tiene ningún pariente, la compensación será para el SEÑOR y se le entregará al sacerdote, junto con el carnero para *expiación del culpable. ⁹Toda contribución que los israelitas consagren para dársela al sacerdote, será del sacerdote. ¹⁰Lo que cada uno consagra es suyo, pero lo que se da al sacerdote es del sacerdote.»

Ley sobre los celos

¹¹El SEÑOR le ordenó a Moisés ¹²que les dijera a los israelitas: «Supongamos que una mujer se desvía del buen *camino y le es infiel a su esposo ¹³acostándose con otro; supongamos también que el asunto se mantiene oculto, ya que ella se mancilló en secreto, y no hubo testigos ni fue sorprendida en el acto. ¹⁴Si el esposo le da un ataque de celos y sospecha que ella está mancillada, o le da un ataque de celos y sospecha de ella, aunque no esté mancillada, ¹⁵entonces la llevará ante el sacerdote y ofrecerá por ella dos kilosᶠ de harina de cebada. No derramará aceite sobre la ofrenda ni le pondrá incienso, puesto que se trata de una ofrenda por causa de celos, una ofrenda memorial de cereal para señalar un pecado.

¹⁶»El sacerdote llevará a la mujer ante el SEÑOR, ¹⁷pondrá agua pura en un recipiente de barro, y le echará un poco de tierra del suelo del santuario. ¹⁸Luego llevará a la mujer ante el SEÑOR, le soltará el cabello y pondrá en sus manos la ofrenda memorial por los celos, mientras él sostiene la vasija con las aguas amargas de la maldición. ¹⁹Entonces el sacerdote pondrá a la mujer bajo juramento, y le dirá: "Si estando bajo la potestad de tu esposo no te has acostado con otro hombre, ni te has desviado hacia la *impureza, estas aguas amargas de la maldición no te dañarán. ²⁰Pero si estando bajo la potestad de tu esposo te has desviado, mancillándote y acostándote con otro hombre ²¹—aquí el sacerdote pondrá a la mujer bajo el juramento del voto de maldición—,

que el SEÑOR haga recaer sobre ti la maldición y el juramento en medio de tu pueblo, que te haga estéril, y que el vientre se te hinche. ²²Cuando estas aguas de la maldición entren en tu cuerpo, que te hinchen el vientre y te hagan estéril." Y la mujer responderá: "¡Amén! ¡Que así sea!"

²³»El sacerdote escribirá estas maldiciones en un documento, que lavará con las aguas amargas. ²⁴Después hará que la mujer se beba las aguas amargas de la maldición, que entrarán en ella para causarle amargura.

²⁵»El sacerdote recibirá de ella la ofrenda por los celos. Procederá a mecer ante el SEÑOR la ofrenda de cereal, la cual presentará sobre el altar; ²⁶tomará de la ofrenda un puñado de cereal como memorial, y lo quemará en el altar. Después hará que la mujer se beba las aguas. ²⁷Cuando ella se haya bebido las aguas de la maldición, y éstas entren en ella para causarle amargura, si le fue infiel a su esposo y se mancilló, se le hinchará el vientre y quedará estéril. Así esa mujer caerá bajo maldición en medio de su pueblo. ²⁸Pero si no se mancilló, sino que se mantuvo pura, entonces no sufrirá daño alguno y será fértil.

²⁹»Ésta es la ley en cuanto a los celos, cuando se dé el caso de que una mujer, estando bajo la potestad de su esposo, se desvíe del buen camino y se mancille a sí misma, ³⁰o cuando al esposo le dé un ataque de celos y sospeche de su esposa. El sacerdote llevará a la mujer a la presencia del SEÑOR y le aplicará esta ley al pie de la letra. ³¹El esposo quedará exento de culpa, pero la mujer sufrirá las consecuencias de su pecado.»

Los nazareos

6 El SEÑOR le ordenó a Moisés ²que les dijera a los israelitas: «Cuando un hombre o una mujer haga un voto especial, un voto para consagrarse al SEÑOR como nazareo, ³deberá abstenerse de vino y de otras bebidas fermentadas. No beberá vinagre de vino ni de otra bebida fermentada; tampoco beberá jugo de uvas ni comerá uvas ni pasas. ⁴Mientras dure su voto de nazareo, no comerá ningún producto de la vid, desde la semilla hasta la cáscara.

⁵»Mientras dure el tiempo de su consagración al SEÑOR, es decir, mientras dure su voto de nazareo, tampoco se cortará el cabello, sino que se lo dejará crecer y se mantendrá *santo.

⁶»Mientras dure el tiempo de su consagración al SEÑOR, no podrá acercarse a ningún cadáver, ⁷ni siquiera en caso de que muera su padre, su madre, su hermano o su hermana. No deberá hacerse ritualmente *impuro a causa de ellos, porque lleva sobre la cabeza el símbolo de su consagración al SEÑOR. ⁸Mientras dure el tiempo de su consagración al SEÑOR, se mantendrá santo.

⁹»Si de improviso muere alguien junto a él, la consagración de su cabeza quedará anulada; así que al cabo de siete días, en el día de su purificación, deberá rasurarse la cabeza. ¹⁰Al octavo día llevará dos palomas o dos tórtolas, y se las entregará al sacerdote a la entrada de la *Tienda de reunión. ¹¹El sacerdote ofrecerá una de ellas como sacrificio *expiatorio, y la otra como *holocausto. Así el sacerdote hará expiación por el nazareo, ya que éste pecó al entrar en contacto con un cadáver. Ese mismo día el nazareo volverá a santificarse la cabeza, ¹²consagrando al SEÑOR el tiempo de su nazareato y llevando un cordero de un año como sacrificio por la culpa. No se le

---

ᵉ **5:2** *una infección en la piel.* Tradicionalmente *lepra.*   ᶠ **5:15** *dos kilos.* Lit. *una décima de *efa.*

tomará en cuenta el tiempo anterior, porque su consagración quedó anulada.

13»Esta ley se aplicará al nazareo al cumplir su período de consagración. Será llevado a la entrada de la Tienda de reunión, 14y allí ofrecerá como holocausto al SEÑOR un cordero de un año, sin defecto; como sacrificio expiatorio una oveja de un año, sin defecto; y como sacrificio de *comunión un carnero sin defecto. 15Ofrecerá además un canastillo de panes sin levadura, panes de flor de harina amasados con aceite, obleas sin levadura untadas con aceite, y también ofrendas de cereal y de libación.

16»Entonces el sacerdote las presentará al SEÑOR y ofrecerá el sacrificio expiatorio y el holocausto en favor del nazareo. 17Ofrecerá el carnero al SEÑOR como sacrificio de comunión, junto con el canastillo de panes sin levadura. También presentará las ofrendas de cereal y de libación.

18»Luego, a la entrada de la Tienda de reunión, el nazareo se rapará la cabeza. Tomará el cabello que consagró, y lo echará al fuego que arde bajo el sacrificio de comunión.

19»Una vez que el nazareo se haya rapado la cabeza, el sacerdote tomará del canastillo un pan sin levadura y una oblea sin levadura, más la pierna cocida del carnero, y pondrá todo esto en manos del nazareo, 20después de lo cual mecerá todo esto ante el SEÑOR como una ofrenda. Todo esto es santo y le pertenece al sacerdote, lo mismo que el pecho mecido y el muslo ofrecido como contribución. Finalizado este rito, el nazareo podrá beber vino.

21»Esta ley se aplicará al nazareo que haga un voto. Ésta es la ofrenda que presentará al SEÑOR por su nazareato, aparte de lo que pueda dar según sus recursos. Según la ley del nazareato, deberá cumplir el voto que hizo.»

Bendición sacerdotal

22El SEÑOR le ordenó a Moisés: 23«Diles a Aarón y a sus hijos que impartan la bendición a los israelitas con estas palabras:

24»"El SEÑOR te bendiga
    y te guarde;
25el SEÑOR te mire con agradog
    y te extienda su amor;
26el SEÑOR te muestre su favor
    y te conceda la *paz."

27»Así invocarán mi *nombre sobre los israelitas, para que yo los bendiga.»

Ofrendas para la consagración del santuario

7 Cuando Moisés terminó de levantar el santuario, lo consagró ungiéndolo junto con todos sus utensilios. También ungió y consagró el altar y sus utensilios. 2Entonces los jefes de Israel, es decir, los jefes de las familias patriarcales y de las tribus, que habían presidido el censo, hicieron una ofrenda 3y la llevaron al santuario para presentarla ante el SEÑOR. La ofrenda consistía en una carreta por cada dos jefes, y un buey por cada uno de ellos; eran, en total, seis carretas cubiertas y doce bueyes.

4El SEÑOR le dijo a Moisés: 5«Recibe estas ofrendas que te entregan, para que sean usadas en el ministerio de la *Tienda de reunión. Tú se las entregarás a los levitas, según lo requiera el trabajo de cada uno.»

6Moisés recibió las carretas y los bueyes, y se los entregó a los levitas. 7A los guersonitas les dio dos carretas y cuatro bueyes, como lo requería su ministerio. 8A los meraritas les dio cuatro carretas y ocho bueyes, como lo requería su ministerio. Todos ellos estaban bajo las órdenes de Itamar, hijo del sacerdote Aarón. 9A los coatitas no les dio nada, porque la responsabilidad de ellos era llevar las cosas sagradas sobre sus propios hombros.

Ofrendas para la dedicación del altar

10Cuando el altar fue consagrado, los jefes llevaron una ofrenda de dedicación y la presentaron ante el altar, 11porque el SEÑOR le había dicho a Moisés: «Para presentar su ofrenda de dedicación del altar, cada jefe tendrá su propio día.»

La ofrenda de Judá

12El primer día le tocó presentar su ofrenda a Naasón hijo de Aminadab, de la tribu de Judá.

13Para la ofrenda de cereal, presentó una fuente de plata y un aspersorio de plata, llenos de flor de harina amasada con aceite. Según la tasación oficial del santuario, la fuente pesaba un kilo y medio, y el aspersorio pesaba ochocientos gramos.h

14También presentó una bandeja de oro de ciento diez gramos,i llena de incienso.

15Para el *holocausto, presentó un novillo, un carnero y un cordero de un año.

16Para el sacrificio *expiatorio, presentó un macho cabrío.

17Para el sacrificio de *comunión, presentó dos bueyes, cinco carneros, cinco machos cabríos y cinco corderos de un año.

Ésta fue la ofrenda de Naasón hijo de Aminadab.

La ofrenda de Isacar

18El segundo día le tocó presentar su ofrenda a Natanael hijo de Zuar, jefe de la tribu de Isacar.

19Para la ofrenda de cereal, presentó una fuente de plata y un aspersorio de plata, llenos de flor de harina amasada con aceite. Según la tasación oficial del santuario, la fuente pesaba un kilo y medio, y el aspersorio pesaba ochocientos gramos.

20También presentó una bandeja de oro de ciento diez gramos, llena de incienso.

21Para el holocausto, presentó un novillo, un carnero y un cordero de un año.

22Para el sacrificio expiatorio, presentó un macho cabrío.

23Para el sacrificio de comunión, presentó dos bueyes, cinco carneros, cinco machos cabríos y cinco corderos de un año.

Ésta fue la ofrenda de Natanael hijo de Zuar.

La ofrenda de Zabulón

24El tercer día le tocó presentar su ofrenda a Eliab hijo de Helón, jefe de la tribu de Zabulón.

25Para la ofrenda de cereal, presentó una fuente de plata y un aspersorio de plata, llenos de flor de harina amasada con aceite. Según la tasación oficial del santuario, la fuente pesaba un kilo y medio, y el aspersorio pesaba ochocientos gramos.

26También presentó una bandeja de oro de ciento diez gramos, llena de incienso.

27Para el holocausto, presentó un novillo, un carnero y un cordero de un año.

28Para el sacrificio expiatorio, presentó un macho cabrío.

---

g 6:25 *te mire con agrado.* Lit. *haga resplandecer su rostro sobre ti.* h 7:13 *la tasación oficial ... un kilo y medio ... ochocientos gramos.* Lit. *el *siclo ... ciento treinta siclos ... setenta siclos;* así en el resto de este capítulo. i 7:14 *ciento diez gramos.* Lit. *diez siclos;* así en el resto de este capítulo.

²⁹Para el sacrificio de comunión, presentó dos bueyes, cinco carneros, cinco machos cabríos, y cinco corderos de un año.

Ésta fue la ofrenda de Eliab hijo de Helón.

La ofrenda de Rubén

³⁰El cuarto día le tocó presentar su ofrenda a Elisur hijo de Sedeúr, jefe de la tribu de Rubén.

³¹Para la ofrenda de cereal, presentó una fuente de plata y un aspersorio de plata, llenos de flor de harina amasada con aceite. Según la tasación oficial del santuario, la fuente pesaba un kilo y medio, y el aspersorio pesaba ochocientos gramos.

³²También presentó una bandeja de oro de ciento diez gramos, llena de incienso.

³³Para el holocausto, presentó un novillo, un carnero y un cordero de un año.

³⁴Para el sacrificio expiatorio, presentó un macho cabrío.

³⁵Para el sacrificio de comunión, presentó dos bueyes, cinco carneros, cinco machos cabríos, y cinco corderos de un año.

Ésta fue la ofrenda de Elisur hijo de Sedeúr.

La ofrenda de Simeón

³⁶El quinto día le tocó presentar su ofrenda a Selumiel hijo de Zurisaday, jefe de la tribu de Simeón.

³⁷Para la ofrenda de cereal, presentó una fuente de plata y un aspersorio de plata, llenos de flor de harina amasada con aceite. Según la tasación oficial del santuario, la fuente pesaba un kilo y medio, y el aspersorio pesaba ochocientos gramos.

³⁸También presentó una bandeja de oro de ciento diez gramos, llena de incienso.

³⁹Para el holocausto, presentó un novillo, un carnero y un cordero de un año.

⁴⁰Para el sacrificio expiatorio, presentó un macho cabrío.

⁴¹Para el sacrificio de comunión, presentó dos bueyes, cinco carneros, cinco machos cabríos, y cinco corderos de un año.

Ésta fue la ofrenda de Selumiel hijo de Zurisaday.

La ofrenda de Gad

⁴²El sexto día le tocó presentar su ofrenda a Eliasaf hijo de Deuel, jefe de la tribu de Gad.

⁴³Para la ofrenda de cereal, presentó una fuente de plata y un aspersorio de plata, llenos de flor de harina amasada con aceite. Según la tasación oficial del santuario, la fuente pesaba un kilo y medio, y el aspersorio pesaba ochocientos gramos.

⁴⁴También presentó una bandeja de oro de ciento diez gramos, llena de incienso.

⁴⁵Para el holocausto, presentó un novillo, un carnero y un cordero de un año.

⁴⁶Para el sacrificio expiatorio, presentó un macho cabrío.

⁴⁷Para el sacrificio de comunión, presentó dos bueyes, cinco carneros, cinco machos cabríos, y cinco corderos de un año.

Ésta fue la ofrenda de Eliasaf hijo de Deuel.

La ofrenda de Efraín

⁴⁸El séptimo día le tocó presentar su ofrenda a Elisama hijo de Amiud, jefe de la tribu de Efraín.

⁴⁹Para la ofrenda de cereal, presentó una fuente de plata y un aspersorio de plata, llenos de flor de harina amasada con aceite. Según la tasación oficial del santuario, la fuente pesaba un kilo y medio, y el aspersorio pesaba ochocientos gramos.

⁵⁰También presentó una bandeja de oro de ciento diez gramos, llena de incienso.

⁵¹Para el holocausto, presentó un novillo, un carnero y un cordero de un año.

⁵²Para el sacrificio expiatorio, presentó un macho cabrío.

⁵³Para el sacrificio de comunión, presentó dos bueyes, cinco carneros, cinco machos cabríos, y cinco corderos de un año.

Ésta fue la ofrenda de Elisama hijo de Amiud.

La ofrenda de Manasés

⁵⁴El octavo día le tocó presentar su ofrenda a Gamaliel hijo de Pedasur, jefe de la tribu de Manasés.

⁵⁵Para la ofrenda de cereal, presentó una fuente de plata y un aspersorio de plata, llenos de flor de harina amasada con aceite. Según la tasación oficial del santuario, la fuente pesaba un kilo y medio, y el aspersorio pesaba ochocientos gramos.

⁵⁶También presentó una bandeja de oro de ciento diez gramos, llena de incienso.

⁵⁷Para el holocausto, presentó un novillo, un carnero y un cordero de un año.

⁵⁸Para el sacrificio expiatorio, presentó un macho cabrío.

⁵⁹Para el sacrificio de comunión, presentó dos bueyes, cinco carneros, cinco machos cabríos, y cinco corderos de un año.

Ésta fue la ofrenda de Gamaliel hijo de Pedasur.

La ofrenda de Benjamín

⁶⁰El noveno día le tocó presentar su ofrenda a Abidán hijo de Gedeoni, jefe de la tribu de Benjamín.

⁶¹Para la ofrenda de cereal, presentó una fuente de plata y un aspersorio de plata, llenos de flor de harina amasada con aceite. Según la tasación oficial del santuario, la fuente pesaba un kilo y medio, y el aspersorio pesaba ochocientos gramos.

⁶²También presentó una bandeja de oro de ciento diez gramos, llena de incienso.

⁶³Para el holocausto, presentó un novillo, un carnero y un cordero de un año.

⁶⁴Para el sacrificio expiatorio, presentó un macho cabrío.

⁶⁵Para el sacrificio de comunión, presentó dos bueyes, cinco carneros, cinco machos cabríos, y cinco corderos de un año.

Ésta fue la ofrenda de Abidán hijo de Gedeoni.

La ofrenda de Dan

⁶⁶El décimo día le tocó presentar su ofrenda a Ajiezer hijo de Amisaday, jefe de la tribu de Dan.

⁶⁷Para la ofrenda de cereal, presentó una fuente de plata y un aspersorio de plata, llenos de flor de harina amasada con aceite. Según la tasación oficial del santuario, la fuente pesaba un kilo y medio, y el aspersorio pesaba ochocientos gramos.

⁶⁸También presentó una bandeja de oro de ciento diez gramos, llena de incienso.

⁶⁹Para el holocausto, presentó un novillo, un carnero y un cordero de un año.

⁷⁰Para el sacrificio expiatorio, presentó un macho cabrío.

⁷¹Para el sacrificio de comunión, presentó dos bueyes, cinco carneros, cinco machos cabríos, y cinco corderos de un año.

Ésta fue la ofrenda de Ajiezer hijo de Amisaday.

La ofrenda de Aser

⁷²El undécimo día le tocó presentar su ofrenda a Paguiel hijo de Ocrán, jefe de la tribu de Aser.

⁷³Para la ofrenda de cereal, presentó una fuente de plata y un aspersorio de plata, llenos de flor de harina amasada con aceite. Según la tasación oficial del

santuario, la fuente pesaba un kilo y medio, y el aspersorio pesaba ochocientos gramos.

74También presentó una bandeja de oro de ciento diez gramos, llena de incienso.

75Para el holocausto, presentó un novillo, un carnero y un cordero de un año.

76Para el sacrificio expiatorio, presentó un macho cabrío.

77Para el sacrificio de comunión, presentó dos bueyes, cinco carneros, cinco machos cabríos, y cinco corderos de un año.

Ésta fue la ofrenda de Paguiel hijo de Ocrán.

La ofrenda de Neftalí

78El duodécimo día le tocó presentar su ofrenda a Ajirá hijo de Enán, jefe de la tribu de Neftalí.

79Para la ofrenda de cereal, presentó una fuente de plata y un aspersorio de plata, llenos de flor de harina amasada con aceite. Según la tasación oficial del santuario, la fuente pesaba un kilo y medio, y el aspersorio pesaba ochocientos gramos.

80También presentó una bandeja de oro de ciento diez gramos, llena de incienso.

81Para el holocausto, presentó un novillo, un carnero y un cordero de un año.

82Para el sacrificio expiatorio, presentó un macho cabrío.

83Para el sacrificio de comunión, presentó dos bueyes, cinco carneros, cinco machos cabríos, y cinco corderos de un año.

Ésta fue la ofrenda de Ajirá hijo de Enán.

Conclusión

84Las ofrendas de dedicación que los jefes de Israel presentaron cuando se consagró el altar fueron las siguientes: doce fuentes de plata, doce aspersorios de plata y doce bandejas de oro. 85Cada fuente de plata pesaba un kilo y medio, y cada aspersorio, ochocientos gramos. El peso total de los objetos de plata llegaba a veintisiete kilos,j según la tasación oficialk del santuario. 86Las doce bandejas de oro llenas de incienso pesaban ciento diez gramos cada una, según la tasación oficial del santuario. El peso total de las bandejas de oro era de un kilo con cuatrocientos gramos.l 87Los animales para el *holocausto fueron en total doce novillos, doce carneros, doce corderos de un año, y doce machos cabríos para el sacrificio *expiatorio, más las ofrendas de cereal. 88Los animales para el sacrificio de *comunión fueron en total veinticuatro bueyes, sesenta carneros, sesenta machos cabríos y sesenta corderos de un año. Éstas fueron las ofrendas para la dedicación del altar después de haber sido consagrado.

Dios se revela en medio del pueblo

89Cuando Moisés entró en la *Tienda de reunión para hablar con el SEÑOR, escuchó su voz de entre los dos *querubines, desde la cubierta del *propiciatorio que estaba sobre el arca del *pacto. Así hablaba el SEÑOR con Moisés.

Las lámparas del candelabro

8 El SEÑOR le dijo a Moisés: 2«Dile a Aarón: "Cuando instales las siete lámparas, éstas deberán alumbrar hacia la parte delantera del candelabro."»

3Así lo hizo Aarón. Instaló las lámparas de modo que alumbraran hacia la parte delantera del candelabro, tal como el SEÑOR se lo había ordenado a Moi-

sés. 4Desde la base hasta las flores, el candelabro estaba hecho de oro labrado, según el modelo que el SEÑOR le había revelado a Moisés.

Consagración de los levitas

5El SEÑOR le dijo a Moisés: 6«Toma a los levitas de entre los israelitas, y *purifícalos. 7Para purificarlos, rocíales agua *expiatoria, y haz que se afeiten todo el cuerpo y se laven los vestidos. Así quedarán purificados. 8Luego tomarán un novillo y una ofrenda de flor de harina amasada con aceite. Tú, por tu parte, tomarás otro novillo para el sacrificio expiatorio. 9Llevarás a los levitas a la *Tienda de reunión y congregarás a toda la comunidad israelita. 10Presentarás a los levitas ante el SEÑOR, y los israelitas les impondrán las manos. 11Entonces Aarón presentará a los levitas ante el SEÑOR, como ofrenda mecida de parte de los israelitas. Así quedarán consagrados al servicio del SEÑOR.

12»Los levitas pondrán las manos sobre la cabeza de los novillos, y tú harás *propiciación por ellos ofreciendo un novillo como sacrificio expiatorio y otro como *holocausto para el SEÑOR. 13Harás que los levitas se pongan de pie frente a Aarón y sus hijos, y los presentarás al SEÑOR como ofrenda mecida. 14De este modo apartarás a los levitas del resto de los israelitas, para que sean míos.

15»Después de que hayas purificado a los levitas y los hayas presentado como ofrenda mecida, ellos irán a ministrar en la Tienda de reunión. 16De todos los israelitas, ellos me pertenecen por completo; son mi regalo especial. Los he apartado para mí en lugar de todos los primogénitos de Israel. 17Porque mío es todo primogénito de Israel, ya sea *hombre o animal. Los aparté para mí cuando herí de muerte a todos los primogénitos de Egipto. 18Sin embargo, he tomado a los levitas en lugar de todos los primogénitos de los israelitas, 19y se los he entregado a Aarón y a sus hijos como un regalo. Los levitas ministrarán en la Tienda de reunión en favor de los israelitas, y harán propiciación por ellos, para que no sufran una desgracia al acercarse al santuario.»

20Así lo hicieron Moisés y Aarón, y toda la comunidad de Israel. Los israelitas hicieron todo lo que el SEÑOR le había mandado a Moisés en cuanto a los levitas, 21los cuales se purificaron y lavaron sus vestidos. Aarón los presentó ante el SEÑOR como ofrenda mecida, e hizo propiciación por ellos para purificarlos. 22Después de esto los levitas fueron a la Tienda de reunión, para ministrar allí bajo la supervisión de Aarón y de sus hijos. De este modo se cumplió todo lo que el SEÑOR le había mandado a Moisés en cuanto a los levitas.

23El SEÑOR le dijo a Moisés: 24«Esta ley se aplicará a los levitas: Para el servicio de la Tienda de reunión se inscribirá a los que tengan veinticinco años o más; 25pero cesarán en sus funciones y se jubilarán cuando cumplan los cincuenta, 26después de lo cual podrán seguir ayudando a sus hermanos en el ejercicio de sus deberes en la Tienda de reunión, pero no estarán ya a cargo del ministerio. Éstas son las obligaciones que asignarás a los levitas.»

La fecha de la Pascua

9 El SEÑOR le habló a Moisés en el desierto de Sinaí, en el primer mes del segundo año después de la salida de Egipto. Le dijo: 2«Los israelitas cele-

---

j 7:85 kilo y medio ... ochocientos gramos ... veintisiete kilos. Lit. ciento treinta siclos...setenta siclos...dos mil cuatrocientos siclos. k 7:85 la tasación oficial. Lit. el siclo; también en v. 86. l 7:86 ciento diez gramos ... un kilo con cuatrocientos gramos. Lit. diez siclos ... ciento veinte siclos.

brarán la Pascua en la fecha señalada. ³La celebrarán al atardecer del día catorce del mes, que es la fecha señalada. La celebrarán ciñéndose a todos sus estatutos y preceptos.»

⁴Moisés mandó que los israelitas celebraran la Pascua, ⁵y ellos la celebraron en el desierto de Sinaí, al atardecer del día catorce del mes primero. Los israelitas hicieron todo lo que el SEÑOR le había mandado a Moisés.

Casos excepcionales

⁶Pero algunos no pudieron celebrar la Pascua en aquel día, pues estaban ritualmente *impuros por haber tocado un cadáver. Ese mismo día se acercaron a Moisés y a Aarón, ⁷y les dijeron:

—Hemos tocado un cadáver, así que estamos impuros. Ahora bien, ésa no es razón para que no presentemos nuestras ofrendas al SEÑOR en la fecha establecida, junto con los demás israelitas.

⁸Moisés les respondió:

—Esperen a que averigüe lo que el SEÑOR dispone con relación a ustedes.

⁹Entonces el SEÑOR le ordenó a Moisés ¹⁰que les dijera a los israelitas: «Cuando alguno de ustedes o de sus descendientes esté ritualmente impuro por haber tocado un cadáver, o se encuentre fuera del país, aun así podrá celebrar la Pascua del SEÑOR. ¹¹Sólo que, en ese caso, la celebrará al atardecer del día catorce del mes segundo. Comerá el cordero con pan sin levadura y hierbas amargas, ¹²y no dejará nada del cordero para el día siguiente ni le quebrará un solo hueso. Cuando celebre la Pascua, lo hará según las disposiciones al respecto.

¹³»Si alguien deja de celebrar la Pascua no estando impuro ni fuera del país, será eliminado de su pueblo por no haber presentado sus ofrendas al SEÑOR en la fecha establecida. Así que sufrirá las consecuencias de su pecado.

¹⁴»Si el extranjero que vive entre ustedes quiere celebrar la Pascua del SEÑOR, deberá hacerlo ciñéndose a sus estatutos y preceptos. Las mismas disposiciones se aplicarán tanto a nativos como a extranjeros.»

La nube sobre el santuario

¹⁵El día en que se armó el santuario, es decir, la Tienda del *pacto, la nube lo cubrió, y durante toda la noche cobró apariencia de fuego. ¹⁶Así sucedía siempre: de día la nube cubría el santuario, mientras que de noche cobraba apariencia de fuego. ¹⁷Cada vez que se levantaba de la Tienda, los israelitas se ponían en marcha; y donde la nube se detenía, allí acampaban. ¹⁸Dependiendo de lo que el SEÑOR les indicara, los israelitas se ponían en marcha o acampaban; y todo el tiempo que la nube reposaba sobre el santuario, se quedaban allí. ¹⁹No importaba que se quedara muchos días sobre el santuario; los israelitas obedecían el mandamiento del SEÑOR y no abandonaban el lugar. ²⁰Lo mismo ocurría cuando la nube reposaba poco tiempo sobre el santuario: cuando el SEÑOR así lo indicaba, los israelitas acampaban o se ponían en marcha. ²¹A veces la nube se quedaba una sola noche; pero ya fuera de día o de noche, cuando la nube se levantaba, los israelitas se ponían en marcha. ²²Aunque la nube reposara sobre el santuario un par de días, un mes o más tiempo, los israelitas se quedaban en el campamento y no partían; pero cuando se levantaba, se ponían en marcha. ²³Cuando el SEÑOR así lo indicaba, los israelitas acampaban o se ponían en marcha. Así obedecían el mandamiento del SEÑOR, según lo que el SEÑOR les había dicho por medio de Moisés.

La señal de las trompetas

10 El SEÑOR le dijo a Moisés: ²«Hazte dos trompetas de plata labrada, y úsalas para reunir al pueblo acampado y para dar la señal de ponerse en marcha. ³Cuando ambas trompetas den el toque de reunión, toda la comunidad se reunirá contigo a la entrada de la *Tienda de reunión. ⁴Cuando sólo una de ellas dé el toque, se reunirán contigo únicamente los jefes de las tribus de Israel. ⁵Al primer toque de avance, se pondrán en marcha las tribus que acampan al este, ⁶y al segundo, las que acampan al sur. Es decir, la señal de partida será el toque de avance. ⁷Cuando se quiera reunir a la comunidad, el toque de reunión que se dé será diferente.

⁸»Las trompetas las tocarán los sacerdotes aaronitas. Esto será un estatuto perpetuo para ustedes y sus descendientes.

⁹»Cuando estén ya en su propia tierra y tengan que salir a la guerra contra el enemigo opresor, las trompetas darán la señal de combate. Entonces el SEÑOR se acordará de ustedes y los salvará de sus enemigos.

¹⁰»Cuando celebren fiestas en fechas solemnes o en novilunios, también tocarán trompetas para anunciar los *holocaustos y los sacrificios de *comunión. Así Dios se acordará de ustedes. Yo soy el SEÑOR tu Dios.»

Desde el Sinaí hasta Parán

¹¹El día veinte del segundo mes del año segundo, la nube se levantó del santuario del *pacto. ¹²Entonces los israelitas avanzaron desde el desierto de Sinaí hasta el desierto de Parán, donde la nube se detuvo. ¹³A la orden que el SEÑOR dio por medio de Moisés, los israelitas emprendieron la marcha por primera vez.

¹⁴Los primeros en partir fueron los escuadrones que marchaban bajo el estandarte del campamento de Judá. Los comandaba Naasón hijo de Aminadab. ¹⁵Natanael hijo de Zuar comandaba el escuadrón de la tribu de Isacar. ¹⁶Eliab hijo de Helón comandaba el escuadrón de la tribu de Zabulón.

¹⁷Entonces se desmontó el santuario, y los guersonitas y meraritas que lo transportaban se pusieron en marcha.

¹⁸Les siguieron los escuadrones que marchaban bajo el estandarte del campamento de Rubén. Los comandaba Elisur hijo de Sedeúr. ¹⁹Selumiel hijo de Zurisaday comandaba el escuadrón de la tribu de Simeón, ²⁰y Eliasaf hijo de Deuel comandaba el escuadrón de la tribu de Gad. ²¹Luego partieron los coatitas, que llevaban las cosas sagradas. El santuario se levantaba antes de que ellos llegaran al próximo lugar de campamento.

²²Les siguieron los escuadrones que marchaban bajo el estandarte del campamento de Efraín. Los comandaba Elisama hijo de Amiud. ²³Gamaliel hijo de Pedasur comandaba el escuadrón de la tribu de Manasés, ²⁴y Abidán hijo de Gedeoni comandaba el escuadrón de la tribu de Benjamín.

²⁵Por último, a la retaguardia de todos los campamentos, partieron los escuadrones que marchaban bajo el estandarte del campamento de Dan. Los comandaba Ajiezer hijo de Amisaday. ²⁶Paguiel hijo de Ocrán comandaba el escuadrón de la tribu de Aser, ²⁷y Ajirá hijo de Enán comandaba el escuadrón de la tribu de Neftalí. ²⁸Éste era el orden de los escuadrones israelitas, cuando se ponían en marcha.

Moisés invita a Hobab

²⁹Entonces Moisés le dijo al madianita Hobab hijo de Reuel, que era su suegro:

—Estamos por partir hacia la tierra que el SEÑOR prometió darnos. Ven con nosotros. Seremos generosos contigo, ya que el SEÑOR ha prometido ser generoso con Israel.

30—No, no iré —respondió Hobab—; quiero regresar a mi tierra y a mi familia.

31—Por favor, no nos dejes —insistió Moisés—. Tú conoces bien los lugares del desierto donde debemos acampar. Tú serás nuestro guía. 32Si vienes con nosotros, compartiremos contigo todo lo bueno que el SEÑOR nos dé.

Israel se pone en marcha

33Los israelitas partieron de la montaña del SEÑOR y anduvieron por espacio de tres días, durante los cuales el arca del *pacto del SEÑOR marchaba al frente de ellos para buscarles un lugar donde acampar. 34Cuando partían, la nube del SEÑOR permanecía sobre ellos todo el día. 35Cada vez que el arca se ponía en marcha, Moisés decía:

«¡Levántate, SEÑOR!
Sean dispersados tus enemigos;
huyan de tu presencia los que te odian.»

36Pero cada vez que el arca se detenía, Moisés decía:

«¡Regresa, SEÑOR,
a la incontable muchedumbre de Israel!»

El fuego del SEÑOR en Taberá

11 Un día, el pueblo se quejó de sus penalidades que estaba sufriendo. Al oírlas el SEÑOR, ardió en ira y su fuego consumió los alrededores del campamento. 2Entonces el pueblo clamó a Moisés, y éste oró al SEÑOR por ellos y el fuego se apagó. 3Por eso aquel lugar llegó a ser conocido como Taberá,m pues el fuego del SEÑOR ardió entre ellos.

Queja del pueblo en Quibrot Hatavá

4Al populacho que iba con ellos le vino un apetito voraz. Y también los israelitas volvieron a llorar, y dijeron: «¡Quién nos diera carne! 5¡Cómo echamos de menos el pescado que comíamos gratis en Egipto! ¡También comíamos pepinos y melones, y puerros, cebollas y ajos! 6Pero ahora, tenemos reseca la garganta; ¡no vemos nada que no sea este maná!»

7A propósito, el maná se parecía a la semilla del cilantro y brillaba como la resina. 8El pueblo salía a recogerlo, y lo molía entre dos piedras, o bien lo machacaba en morteros, y lo cocía en una olla o hacía pan con él. Sabía a pan amasado con aceite. 9Por la noche, cuando el rocío caía sobre el campamento, también caía el maná.

Queja de Moisés en Quibrot Hatavá

10Moisés escuchó que las familias del pueblo lloraban, cada una a la entrada de su tienda, con lo cual hacían que la ira del SEÑOR se encendiera en extremo. Entonces, muy disgustado, 11Moisés oró al SEÑOR:

—Si yo soy tu siervo, ¿por qué me perjudicas? ¿Por qué me niegas tu favor y me obligas a cargar con todo este pueblo? 12¿Acaso yo lo concebí, o lo di a luz, para que me exijas que lo lleve en mi regazo, como si fuera su nodriza, y lo lleve hasta la tierra que les prometiste a sus antepasados? 13Todo este pueblo viene llorando a pedirme carne. ¿De dónde voy a sacarla? 14Yo solo no puedo con todo este pueblo. ¡Es una carga demasiado pesada para mí! 15Si éste es el trato que

vas a darme, ¡me harás un favor si me quitas la vida! ¡Así me veré libre de mi desgracia!

El SEÑOR le responde a Moisés

16El SEÑOR le respondió a Moisés:

—Tráeme a setenta *ancianos de Israel, y asegúrate de que sean ancianos y gobernantes del pueblo. Llévalos a la *Tienda de reunión, y haz que esperen allí contigo. 17Yo descenderé para hablar contigo, y compartiré con ellos el Espíritu que está sobre ti, para que te ayuden a llevar la carga que te significa este pueblo. Así no tendrás que llevarla tú solo.

18»Al pueblo sólo le dirás lo siguiente: "*Santifíquense para mañana, pues van a comer carne. Ustedes lloraron ante el SEÑOR, y le dijeron: '¡Quién nos diera carne! ¡En Egipto la pasábamos mejor!' Pues bien, el SEÑOR les dará carne, y tendrán que comérsela. 19No la comerán un solo día, ni dos, ni cinco, ni diez, ni veinte, 20sino todo un mes, hasta que les salga por las narices y les provoque náuseas. Y esto, por haber despreciado al SEÑOR, que está en medio de ustedes, y por haberle llorado, diciendo: '¿Por qué tuvimos que salir de Egipto?' "

La palabra de Dios se cumple

21Moisés replicó:

—Me encuentro en medio de un ejército de seiscientos mil hombres, ¿y tú hablas de darles carne todo un mes? 22Aunque se les degollaran rebaños y manadas completas, ¿les alcanzaría? Y aunque se les pescaran todos los peces del mar, ¿eso les bastaría?

23El SEÑOR le respondió a Moisés:

—¿Acaso el poder del SEÑOR es limitado? ¡Pues ahora verás si te cumplo o no mi palabra!

24Moisés fue y le comunicó al pueblo lo que el SEÑOR le había dicho. Después juntó a setenta *ancianos del pueblo, y se quedó esperando con ellos alrededor de la *Tienda de reunión. 25El SEÑOR descendió en la nube y habló con Moisés, y compartió con los setenta ancianos el Espíritu que estaba sobre él. Cuando el Espíritu descansó sobre ellos, se pusieron a profetizar. Pero esto no se volvió a repetirse.

26Dos de los ancianos se habían quedado en el campamento. Uno se llamaba Eldad y el otro Medad. Aunque habían sido elegidos, no acudieron a la Tienda de reunión. Sin embargo, el Espíritu descansó sobre ellos y se pusieron a profetizar dentro del campamento. 27Entonces un muchacho corrió a contárselo a Moisés:

—¡Eldad y Medad están profetizando dentro del campamento!

28Josué hijo de Nun, uno de los siervos escogidos de Moisés, exclamó:

—¡Moisés, señor mío, detenlos!

29Pero Moisés le respondió:

—¿Estás celoso por mí? ¡Cómo quisiera que todo el pueblo del SEÑOR profetizara, y que el SEÑOR pusiera su Espíritu en todos ellos!

30Entonces Moisés y los ancianos regresaron al campamento.

Las codornices

31El SEÑOR desató un viento que trajo codornices del mar y las dejó caer sobre el campamento. Las codornices cubrieron los alrededores del campamento, en una superficie de casi un día de camino a una altura de casi un metron sobre la superficie del suelo. 32El pueblo estuvo recogiendo codornices todo ese día y toda esa noche, y todo el día siguiente.

---

m 11:3 En hebreo, *Taberá* significa *arder*. n 11:31 *casi un metro.* Lit. *dos* *codos.*

¡Ninguno recogió menos de dos toneladas!ñ Después las distribuyeron por todo el campamento.

33Ni siquiera habían empezado a masticar la carne que tenían en la boca cuando la ira del SEÑOR se encendió contra el pueblo y los hirió con gran mortandad. 34Por eso llamaron a ese lugar Quibrot Hatavá,o porque allí fue sepultado el pueblo glotón.

35Desde Quibrot Hatavá el pueblo partió rumbo a Jazerot, y allí se quedó.

Quejas de Miriam y de Aarón

12 Moisés había tomado por esposa a una egipcia,p así que Miriam y Aarón empezaron a murmurar contra él por causa de ella. 2Decían: «¿Acaso no ha hablado el SEÑOR con otro que no sea Moisés? ¿No nos ha hablado también a nosotros?» Y el SEÑOR oyó sus murmuraciones.

3A propósito, Moisés era muy humilde, más humilde que cualquier otro sobre la tierra.

4De pronto el SEÑOR les dijo a Moisés, Aarón y Miriam: «Salgan los tres de la *Tienda de reunión.» Y los tres salieron. 5Entonces el SEÑOR descendió en una columna de nube y se detuvo a la entrada de la Tienda. Llamó a Aarón y a Miriam, y cuando ambos se acercaron, 6el SEÑOR les dijo: «Escuchen lo que voy a decirles:

»Cuando un profeta del SEÑOR
　　se levanta entre ustedes,
yo le hablo en visiones
　　y me revelo a él en sueños.
7Pero esto no ocurre así
　　con mi siervo Moisés,
porque en toda mi casa
　　él es mi hombre de confianza.
8Con él hablo cara a cara,
　　claramente y sin enigmas.
Él contempla la imagen del SEÑOR.
¿Cómo se atreven a murmurar
　　contra mi siervo Moisés?»

9Entonces la ira del SEÑOR se encendió contra ellos, y el SEÑOR se marchó. 10Tan pronto como la nube se apartó de la Tienda, a Miriam se le puso la piel blancaq como la nieve. Cuando Aarón se volvió hacia ella, vio que tenía una enfermedad infecciosa. 11Entonces le dijo a Moisés: «Te suplico, mi señor, que no nos tomes en cuenta este pecado que neciamente hemos cometido. 12No la dejes como un abortivo, que sale del vientre de su madre con el cuerpo medio deshecho.»

Moisés intercede por Miriam

13Moisés le rogó al SEÑOR: «¡Oh Dios, te ruego que la sanes!»

14El SEÑOR le respondió a Moisés: «Si su padre le hubiera escupido el rostro, ¿no habría durado su humillación siete días? Que se le confine siete días fuera del campamento, y después de eso será readmitida.»

15Así que Miriam quedó confinada siete días fuera del campamento. El pueblo no se puso en marcha hasta que ella se reintegró. 16Después el pueblo partió de Jazerot y acampó en el desierto de Parán.

Los israelitas exploran Canaán

13 El SEÑOR le dijo a Moisés: 2«Quiero que envíes a algunos de tus hombres a explorar la tierra que estoy por entregar a los israelitas. De cada tribu enviarás a un líder que la represente.»

3De acuerdo con la orden del SEÑOR, Moisés los envió desde el desierto de Parán. Todos ellos eran jefes en Israel, 4y éstos son sus nombres:

Samúa hijo de Zacur, de la tribu de Rubén;
5Safat hijo de Horí, de la tribu de Simeón;
6Caleb hijo de Jefone, de la tribu de Judá;
7Igal hijo de José, de la tribu de Isacar;
8Oseas hijo de Nun, de la tribu de Efraín;
9Palti hijo de Rafú, de la tribu de Benjamín;
10Gadiel hijo de Sodi, de la tribu de Zabulón;
11Gadí hijo de Susi, de la tribu de Manasés (una de las tribus de José);
12Amiel hijo de Guemalí, de la tribu de Dan;
13Setur hijo de Micael, de la tribu de Aser;
14Najbí hijo de Vapsi, de la tribu de Neftalí;
15Geuel hijo de Maquí, de la tribu de Gad.

16Éstos son los *nombres de los líderes que Moisés envió a explorar la tierra. (A Oseas hijo de Nun, Moisés le cambió el nombre y le puso Josué.)

17Cuando Moisés los envió a explorar la tierra de Canaán, les dijo: «Suban por el Néguev, hasta llegar a la montaña. 18Exploren el país, y fíjense cómo son sus habitantes, si son fuertes o débiles, muchos o pocos. 19Averigüen si la tierra en que viven es buena o mala, y si sus ciudades son abiertas o amuralladas. 20Examinen el terreno, y vean si es fértil o estéril, y si tiene árboles o no. ¡Adelante! Traigan algunos frutos del país.»

Ésa era la temporada en que maduran las primeras uvas.

21Los doce hombres se fueron y exploraron la tierra, desde el desierto de Zin hasta Rejob, cerca de Lebó Jamat.r 22Subieron por el Néguev y llegaron a Hebrón, donde vivían Ajimán, Sesay y Talmay, descendientes de Anac. (Hebrón había sido fundada siete años antes que la ciudad egipcia de Zoán.) 23Cuando llegaron al valle del arroyo Escol,s cortaron un sarmiento que tenía un solo racimo de uvas, y entre dos lo llevaron colgado de una vara. También cortaron granadas e higos. 24Por el racimo que estos israelitas cortaron, a ese lugar se le llamó Valle de Escol.

Informe de los exploradores

25Al cabo de cuarenta días los doce hombres regresaron de explorar aquella tierra. 26Volvieron a Cades, en el desierto de Parán, que era donde estaban Moisés, Aarón y toda la comunidad israelita, y les presentaron a todos ellos un informe, y les mostraron los frutos de esa tierra. 27Éste fue el informe:

—Fuimos al país al que nos enviaste, ¡y por cierto que allí abundan la leche y la miel! Aquí pueden ver sus frutos. 28Pero el pueblo que allí habita es poderoso, y sus ciudades son enormes y están fortificadas. Hasta vimos *anaquitas allí. 29Los amalecitas habitan en el Néguev; los hititas, jebuseos y amorreos viven en la montaña, y los cananeos ocupan la zona costera y la ribera del río Jordán.

30Caleb hizo callar al pueblo ante Moisés, y dijo:

—Subamos a conquistar esa tierra. Estoy seguro de que podremos hacerlo.

31Pero los que habían ido con él respondieron:

—No podremos combatir contra esa gente. ¡Son más fuertes que nosotros!

ñ 11:32 dos toneladas. Lit. diez *jómer. o 11:34 En hebreo, Quibrot Hatavá significa sepultura de la glotonería. p 12:1 egipcia. Lit. *Cusita. q 12:10 blanca. Lit. Leprosa r 13:21 Lebó Jamat. Alt. la entrada de Jamat. s 13:23 En hebreo, Escol significa racimo; también en v. 24.

³²Y comenzaron a esparcir entre los israelitas falsos rumores acerca de la tierra que habían explorado. Decían:

—La tierra que hemos explorado se traga a sus habitantes, y los hombres que allí vimos son enormes. ³³¡Hasta vimos *anaquitas! Comparados con ellos, parecíamos langostas, y así nos veían ellos a nosotros.

El pueblo se rebela

14 Aquella noche toda la comunidad israelita se puso a gritar y a llorar. ²En sus murmuraciones contra Moisés y Aarón, la comunidad decía: «¡Cómo quisiéramos haber muerto en Egipto! ¡Más nos valdría morir en este desierto! ³¿Para qué nos ha traído el SEÑOR a esta tierra? ¿Para morir atravesados por la espada, y que nuestras esposas y nuestros niños se conviertan en botín de guerra? ¿No sería mejor que volviéramos a Egipto?» ⁴Y unos a otros se decían: «¡Escojamos un cabecilla que nos lleve a Egipto!»

⁵Entonces Moisés y Aarón cayeron rostro en tierra ante toda la comunidad israelita. ⁶Allí estaban también Josué hijo de Nun y Caleb hijo de Jefone, los cuales habían participado en la exploración de la tierra. Ambos se rasgaron las vestiduras en señal de duelo ⁷y le dijeron a toda la comunidad israelita:

—La tierra que recorrimos y exploramos es increíblemente buena. ⁸Si el SEÑOR se agrada de nosotros, nos hará entrar en ella. ¡Nos va a dar una tierra donde abundan la leche y la miel! ⁹Así que no se rebelen contra el SEÑOR ni tengan miedo de la gente que habita en esa tierra. ¡Ya son pan comido! No tienen quién los proteja, porque el SEÑOR está de parte nuestra. Así que, ¡no les tengan miedo!

¹⁰Pero como toda la comunidad hablaba de apedrearlos, la gloria del SEÑOR se manifestó en la Tienda, frente a todos los israelitas. ¹¹Entonces el SEÑOR le dijo a Moisés:

—¿Hasta cuándo esta gente me seguirá menospreciando? ¿Hasta cuándo se negarán a creer en mí, a pesar de todas las maravillas que he hecho entre ellos? ¹²Voy a enviarles una plaga que los destruya, pero de ti haré un pueblo más grande y fuerte que ellos.

¹³Moisés le argumentó al SEÑOR:

—¡Recuerda que fuiste tú quien con tu poder sacaste de Egipto a este pueblo! Cuando los egipcios se enteren de lo ocurrido, ¹⁴se lo contarán a los habitantes de este país, quienes ya saben que tú, SEÑOR, estás en medio de este pueblo. También saben que a ti, SEÑOR, se te ha visto cara a cara; que tu nube reposa sobre tu pueblo, y que eres tú quien los guía, de día con la columna de nube y de noche con la columna de fuego. ¹⁵De manera que, si matas a todo este pueblo, las naciones que han oído hablar de tu fama dirán: ¹⁶"El SEÑOR no fue capaz de llevar a este pueblo a la tierra que juró darles, ¡y acabó matándolos en el desierto!"

¹⁷»Ahora, Señor, ¡deja sentir tu poder! Tú mismo has dicho ¹⁸que eres lento para la ira y grande en amor, y que aunque perdonas la maldad y la rebeldía, jamás dejas impune al culpable, sino que castigas la maldad de los padres en sus hijos, nietos, bisnietos y tataranietos. ¹⁹Por tu gran amor, te suplico que perdones la maldad de este pueblo, tal como lo has venido perdonando desde que salió de Egipto.

²⁰El SEÑOR le respondió:

—Me pides que los perdone, y los perdono. ²¹Pero juro por mí mismo, y por mi gloria que llena[t] toda la tierra, ²²que aunque vieron mi gloria y las maravillas que hice en Egipto y en el desierto, ninguno de los que me desobedecieron y me pusieron a prueba repetidas veces ²³verá jamás la tierra que, bajo juramento, prometí dar a sus padres. ¡Ninguno de los que me despreciaron la verá jamás! ²⁴En cambio, a mi siervo Caleb, que ha mostrado una actitud diferente y me ha sido fiel, le daré posesión de la tierra que exploró, y su descendencia la heredará. ²⁵Pero regresen mañana al desierto por la ruta del *Mar Rojo, puesto que los amalecitas y los cananeos viven en el valle.

²⁶El SEÑOR les dijo a Moisés y a Aarón:

²⁷—¿Hasta cuándo ha de murmurar contra mí esta perversa comunidad? Ya he escuchado cómo se quejan contra mí los israelitas. ²⁸Así que diles de parte mía: "Juro por mí mismo, que haré que se les cumplan sus deseos. ²⁹Los cadáveres de todos ustedes quedarán tirados en este desierto. Ninguno de los censados mayores de veinte años, que murmuraron contra mí, ³⁰tomará posesión de la tierra que les prometí. Sólo entrarán en ella Caleb hijo de Jefone y Josué hijo de Nun. ³¹También entrarán a la tierra los niños que ustedes dijeron que serían botín de guerra. Y serán ellos los que gocen de la tierra que ustedes rechazaron. ³²Pero los cadáveres de todos ustedes quedarán tirados en este desierto. ³³Durante cuarenta años los hijos de ustedes andarán errantes por el desierto. Cargarán con esta infidelidad, hasta que el último de ustedes caiga muerto en el desierto. ³⁴La exploración del país duró cuarenta días, así que ustedes sufrirán un año por cada día. Cuarenta años llevarán a cuestas su maldad, y sabrán lo que es tenerme por enemigo." ³⁵Yo soy el SEÑOR, y cumpliré al pie de la letra todo lo que anuncié contra esta perversa comunidad que se atrevió a desafiarme. En este desierto perecerán. ¡Morirán aquí mismo!

³⁶Los hombres que Moisés había enviado a explorar el país fueron los que, al volver, difundieron la falsa información de que la tierra era mala. Con esto hicieron que toda la comunidad murmurara. ³⁷Por eso los responsables de haber difundido este falso informe acerca de aquella tierra murieron delante del SEÑOR, víctimas de una plaga. ³⁸De todos los hombres que fueron a explorar el país, sólo sobrevivieron Josué hijo de Nun y Caleb hijo de Jefone.

El pueblo intenta conquistar la tierra

³⁹Cuando Moisés terminó de decirles esto, todos los israelitas se pusieron a llorar amargamente. ⁴⁰Al otro día, muy de mañana, el pueblo empezó a subir a la parte alta de la zona montañosa, diciendo:

—Subamos al lugar que el SEÑOR nos ha prometido, pues reconocemos que hemos pecado.

⁴¹Pero Moisés les dijo:

—¿Por qué han vuelto a desobedecer la orden del SEÑOR? ¡Esto no les va a dar resultado! ⁴²Si suben los derrotarán sus enemigos, porque el SEÑOR no está entre ustedes. ⁴³Tendrán que enfrentarse a los amalecitas y a los cananeos, que los matarán a filo de espada. Como ustedes se han alejado del SEÑOR, él no los ayudará.

⁴⁴Pero ellos se empecinaron en subir a la zona montañosa, a pesar de que ni Moisés ni el arca del *pacto del SEÑOR salieron del campamento. ⁴⁵Entonces los amalecitas y los cananeos que vivían en esa

---

t **14:21** *juro por mí mismo, y por mi gloria que llena.* Lit. *vivo yo y la gloria del SEÑOR llena.*

zona descendieron y los derrotaron, haciéndolos retroceder hasta Jormá.

Leyes adicionales sobre las ofrendas

15 El SEÑOR le ordenó a Moisés 2que les dijera a los israelitas: «Después de que hayan entrado en la tierra que les doy para que la habiten, 3tal vez alguno quiera ofrecerle al SEÑOR una vaca o una oveja, ya sea como ofrenda presentada por fuego, o como *holocausto, o como sacrificio para cumplir un voto, o como ofrenda voluntaria, o para celebrar una fiesta solemne. Para que esa ofrenda sea un aroma grato al SEÑOR, 4el que presente su ofrenda deberá añadirle, como ofrenda de cereal, dos kilos de flor de harina mezclada con un litrou de aceite. 5A cada cordero que se le ofrezca al SEÑOR como holocausto o sacrificio se le añadirá como libación un litrov de vino.

6»Si se trata de un carnero, se preparará una ofrenda de cereal de cuatro kilosw de flor de harina, mezclada con un litro y mediox de aceite. 7Como libación ofrecerás también un litro y medio de vino. Así será una ofrenda de aroma grato al SEÑOR.

8»Si ofreces un novillo como holocausto o sacrificio, a fin de cumplir un voto o hacer un sacrificio de *comunión para el SEÑOR, 9junto con el novillo presentarás, como ofrenda de cereal, seis kilosy de flor de harina mezclada con dos litrosz de aceite. 10Presentarás también, como libación, dos litros de vino. Será una ofrenda presentada por fuego, de aroma grato al SEÑOR. 11Cada novillo, carnero, cordero o cabrito deberá prepararse de la manera indicada. 12Procederás así con cada uno de ellos, sin que importe el número de animales que ofrezcas.

13»Cada vez que un israelita presente una ofrenda por fuego, de aroma grato al SEÑOR, se ceñirá a estas instrucciones. 14Si un extranjero que viva entre ustedes desea presentar una ofrenda por fuego, de aroma grato al SEÑOR, se ceñirá a estas mismas instrucciones, 15porque en la comunidad regirá un solo estatuto para ti y para el extranjero que viva en tus ciudades. Será un estatuto perpetuo para todos tus descendientes. Tú y el extranjero son iguales ante el SEÑOR, 16así que la misma ley y el mismo derecho regirán, tanto para ti como para el extranjero que viva contigo.»

Ofrenda de los primeros frutos

17El SEÑOR le ordenó a Moisés 18que les dijera a los israelitas: «Cuando entren en la tierra adonde los llevo, 19y coman de lo que ella produce, ofrecerán una contribución al SEÑOR. 20De tu primera horneada presentarás, como contribución, una torta de flor de harina. 21Todos tus descendientes ofrecerán perpetuamente al SEÑOR una contribución de la primera horneada.

Ofrendas por pecados inadvertidos

22»Podría ocurrir que ustedes pecaran inadvertidamente, y que no cumplieran con todos los mandamientos que el SEÑOR entregó a Moisés, 23es decir, con todos los mandamientos que el Señor les dio a ustedes por medio de Moisés, desde el día en que los promulgó para todos sus descendientes. 24Si el pecado de la comunidad pasa inadvertido, ésta ofrecerá un novillo como *holocausto de aroma grato al SEÑOR, junto con la libación, la ofrenda de cereal y un macho cabrío como sacrificio *expiatorio, tal

como está prescrito. 25El sacerdote hará *propiciación en favor de toda la comunidad israelita, y serán perdonados porque fue un pecado inadvertido y porque presentaron al SEÑOR una ofrenda por fuego y un sacrificio expiatorio por el pecado inadvertido que cometieron. 26Toda la comunidad israelita será perdonada, junto con los extranjeros, porque todo el pueblo pecó inadvertidamente.

27»Si es una persona la que peca inadvertidamente, deberá presentar, como sacrificio expiatorio, una cabra de un año. 28El sacerdote hará propiciación ante el SEÑOR en favor de la persona que inadvertidamente haya pecado. El sacerdote hará propiciación, y la persona que pecó será perdonada. 29Una sola ley se aplicará para todo el que peque inadvertidamente, tanto para el israelita como para el extranjero residente.

30»Pero el que peque deliberadamente, sea nativo o extranjero, ofende al SEÑOR. Tal persona será eliminada de la comunidad, 31y cargará con su culpa, por haber despreciado la palabra del SEÑOR y quebrantado su mandamiento.»

Quebrantamiento del día de reposo

32Un *sábado, durante la estadía de los israelitas en el desierto, un hombre fue sorprendido recogiendo leña. 33Quienes lo sorprendieron lo llevaron ante Moisés y Aarón, y ante toda la comunidad. 34Al principio sólo quedó detenido, porque no estaba claro qué se debía hacer con él. 35Entonces el SEÑOR le dijo a Moisés: «Ese hombre debe morir. Que toda la comunidad lo apedree fuera del campamento.» 36Así que la comunidad lo llevó fuera del campamento y lo apedreó hasta matarlo, tal como el SEÑOR se lo ordenó a Moisés.

Flecos recordatorios

37El SEÑOR le ordenó a Moisés 38que les dijera a los israelitas: «Ustedes y todos sus descendientes deberán confeccionarse flecos, y coserlos sobre sus vestidos con hilo de color púrpura. 39Estos flecos los ayudarán a recordar que deben cumplir con todos los mandamientos del SEÑOR, y que no deben prostituirse ni dejarse llevar por los impulsos de su *corazón ni por los deseos de sus ojos. 40Tendrán presentes todos mis mandamientos, y los pondrán por obra. Así serán mi pueblo consagrado. 41Yo soy el SEÑOR su Dios, que los sacó de Egipto para ser su Dios. ¡Yo soy el SEÑOR!»

La rebelión de Coré, Datán y Abirán

16 Coré, que era hijo de Izar, nieto de Coat y bisnieto de Leví, y los rubenitas Datán y Abirán, hijos de Eliab, y On hijo de Pélet, 2se atrevieron a sublevarse contra Moisés, con el apoyo de doscientos cincuenta israelitas. Todos ellos eran personas de renombre y líderes que la comunidad misma había escogido. 3Se reunieron para oponerse a Moisés y a Aarón, y les dijeron:

—¡Ustedes han ido ya demasiado lejos! Si toda la comunidad es *santa, lo mismo que sus miembros, ¿por qué se creen ustedes los dueños de la comunidad del SEÑOR?

4Cuando Moisés escuchó lo que le decían, se inclinó ante ellos 5y les respondió a Coré y a todo su grupo:

—Mañana el SEÑOR dirá quién es quién. Será él quien declare quién es su escogido, y hará que se le

---

u 15:4 dos kilos ... un litro. Lit. una décima (de *efa) ... un cuarto de *hin. v 15:5 un litro. Lit. un cuarto de hin. w 15:6 cuatro kilos. Lit. dos décimas (de efa). x 15:6 litro y medio. Lit. un tercio de hin; también en v. 7. y 15:9 seis kilos. Lit. tres décimas (de efa). z 15:9 dos litros. Lit. medio hin; también en v. 10.

acerque. 6Coré, esto es lo que tú y tu gente harán mañana: tomarán incensarios, 7y les pondrán fuego e incienso en la presencia del SEÑOR. El escogido del SEÑOR será aquel a quien él elija. ¡Son ustedes, hijos de Leví, los que han ido demasiado lejos!

8Moisés le dijo a Coré:

—¡Escúchenme ahora, levitas! 9¿Les parece poco que el Dios de Israel los haya separado del resto de la comunidad para que estén cerca de él, ministren en el santuario del SEÑOR, y se distingan como servidores de la comunidad? 10Dios mismo los ha puesto a su lado, a ti y a todos los levitas, ¿y ahora quieren también el sacerdocio? 11Tú y tu gente se han reunido para oponerse al SEÑOR, porque ¿quién es Aarón para que murmuren contra él?

12Moisés mandó llamar a Datán y Abirán, hijos de Eliab, pero ellos contestaron:

—¡No iremos! 13¿Te parece poco habernos sacado de la tierra donde abundan la leche y la miel, para que ahora quieras matarnos en este desierto y dártelas de gobernante con nosotros? 14Lo cierto es que tú no has logrado llevarnos todavía a esa tierra donde abundan la leche y la miel, ni nos has dado posesión de campos y viñas. Lo único que quieres es seguir engatusandoᵃ a este pueblo. ¡Pues no iremos!

15Entonces Moisés, sumamente enojado, le dijo al SEÑOR:

—No aceptes la ofrenda que te traigan, que yo de ellos no he tomado ni siquiera un asno, ni les he hecho ningún daño.

16A Coré, Moisés le dijo:

—Tú y tu gente y Aarón se presentarán mañana ante el SEÑOR. 17Cada uno de ustedes se acercará al SEÑOR con su incensario lleno de incienso, es decir, se acercarán con doscientos cincuenta incensarios. También tú y Aarón llevarán los suyos.

18Así que cada uno, con su incensario lleno de fuego e incienso, se puso de pie a la entrada de la *Tienda de reunión, junto con Moisés y Aarón. 19Cuando Coré hubo reunido a toda su gente en contra de Moisés y Aarón a la entrada de la Tienda de reunión, la gloria del SEÑOR se apareció ante todos ellos. 20Entonces el SEÑOR les dijo a Moisés y a Aarón:

21—Apártense de esta gente, para que yo la consuma de una vez por todas.

22Pero Moisés y Aarón se postraron rostro en tierra, y exclamaron:

—SEÑOR, Dios de toda la humanidad:ᵇ un solo hombre ha pecado, ¿y vas tú a enojarte con todos ellos?

23Entonces el SEÑOR le dijo a Moisés:

24—Ordénales que se alejen de las tiendas de Coré, Datán y Abirán.

25Moisés y los *ancianos de Israel fueron adonde estaban Datán y Abirán. 26Entonces Moisés le advirtió a la gente:

—¡Aléjense de las tiendas de estos impíos! No toquen ninguna de sus pertenencias, para que ustedes no sean castigados por los pecados de ellos.

27El pueblo se alejó de las tiendas de Coré, Datán y Abirán. Los dos últimos habían salido a la entrada de sus tiendas, y estaban allí, de pie, con sus esposas y todos sus hijos.

28Moisés siguió diciendo:

—Ahora van a saber si el SEÑOR me ha enviado a hacer todas estas cosas, o si estoy actuando por mi cuenta. 29Si estos hombres mueren de muerte natural, como es el destino de todos los hombres, eso querrá decir que el SEÑOR no me ha enviado. 30Pero si el SEÑOR crea algo nuevo, y hace que la tierra se abra y se los trague con todas sus pertenencias, de tal forma que desciendan vivos al *sepulcro, entonces sabrán que estos hombres menospreciaron al SEÑOR.

31Tan pronto como Moisés terminó de hablar, la tierra se abrió debajo de ellos; 32se abrió y se los tragó, a ellos y a sus familias, junto con la gente y las posesiones de Coré. 33Bajaron vivos al sepulcro, junto con todo lo que tenían, y la tierra se cerró sobre ellos. De este modo fueron eliminados de la comunidad. 34Al oírlos gritar, todos los israelitas huyeron de allí exclamando:

—¡Corramos, no sea que la tierra nos trague también a nosotros!

35Y los doscientos cincuenta hombres que ofrecían incienso fueron consumidos por el fuego del SEÑOR.

Los incensarios

36El SEÑOR le dijo a Moisés: 37«Ya que ahora los incensarios son *santos, ordena a Eleazar, hijo del sacerdote Aarón, que los retire del rescoldo y que esparza las brasas. 38Toma los incensarios de aquellos que pecaron a costa de su *vida, y haz con ellos láminas para recubrir el altar. Ahora son santos, porque fueron presentados ante el SEÑOR, y serán así una señal para los israelitas.»

39Entonces el sacerdote Eleazar recogió esos incensarios, y con ellos mandó hacer láminas para recubrir el altar. 40Las láminas quedaron allí, como advertencia a los israelitas, para que ninguno que no fuera descendiente de Aarón ni estuviera autorizado se atreviera a ofrecer incienso ante el SEÑOR; de lo contrario, le sucedería lo mismo que a Coré y su gente, tal como el SEÑOR se lo había advertido por medio de Moisés.

Aarón intercede por el pueblo

41Al día siguiente, toda la congregación de los israelitas volvió a murmurar contra Moisés y Aarón, alegando:

—Ustedes mataron al pueblo del SEÑOR.

42Como la congregación empezó a amotinarse contra Moisés y Aarón, éstos se dirigieron a la *Tienda de reunión. De repente la nube cubrió la Tienda, y apareció la gloria del SEÑOR. 43Entonces Moisés y Aarón se detuvieron frente a la Tienda de reunión, 44y el SEÑOR le dijo a Moisés:

45—Apártate de esta gente, para que yo la consuma de una vez por todas.

Ellos se postraron rostro en tierra, 46y Moisés le dijo a Aarón:

—Toma tu incensario y pon en él algunas brasas del altar; agrégale incienso, y vete corriendo adonde está la congregación, para hacer *propiciación por ellos, porque la ira del SEÑOR se ha desbordado y el azote divino ha caído sobre ellos.

47Aarón hizo lo que Moisés le dijo, y corrió a ponerse en medio de la asamblea. El azote divino ya se había desatado entre el pueblo, así que Aarón ofreció incienso y hizo propiciación por el pueblo. 48Se puso entre los vivos y los muertos, y así detuvo la mortandad. 49Con todo, catorce mil setecientas personas murieron, sin contar las que se perdieron la vida por causa de Coré. 50Una vez que cesó la mortandad, Aarón volvió a la entrada de la Tienda de reunión, donde estaba Moisés.

ᵃ 16:14 seguir engatusando. Lit. sacarle los ojos.　ᵇ 16:22 toda la humanidad. Lit. los espíritus de toda carne.

La vara de Aarón

17 El SEÑOR le ordenó a Moisés: ²«Diles a los israelitas que traigan doce varas, una por cada familia patriarcal, es decir, una por cada uno de los jefes de las familias patriarcales. Escribe el *nombre de cada uno de ellos sobre su propia vara. ³Sobre la vara de Leví escribe el nombre de Aarón, pues cada jefe de familia patriarcal debe tener su vara. ⁴Colócalas frente al arca del *pacto, en la Tienda donde me reúno con ustedes. ⁵La vara que retoñe será la de mi elegido. De ese modo me quitaré de encima las constantes quejas que los israelitas levantan contra ustedes.»

⁶Moisés se lo comunicó a los israelitas, y los jefes le entregaron doce varas, una por cada jefe de su familia patriarcal. Entre ellas estaba la vara de Aarón. ⁷Moisés colocó las varas delante del SEÑOR, en la Tienda del pacto.

⁸Al día siguiente, Moisés entró en la Tienda del pacto y, al fijarse en la vara que representaba a la familia de Leví, vio que la vara de Aarón no sólo había retoñado, sino que también tenía botones, flores y almendras. ⁹Sacó entonces de la presencia del SEÑOR todas las varas, y las puso delante de los israelitas, para que por sí mismos vieran lo que había ocurrido, y cada jefe tomó su propia vara.

¹⁰El SEÑOR le dijo a Moisés: «Vuelve a colocar la vara de Aarón frente al arca del pacto, para que sirva de advertencia a los rebeldes. Así terminarás con las quejas en contra mía, y evitarás que mueran los israelitas.»

¹¹Moisés hizo todo tal como el SEÑOR se lo ordenó. ¹²Entonces los israelitas le dijeron a Moisés: «¡Estamos perdidos, totalmente perdidos! ¡Vamos a morir! ¹³Todo el que se acerca al santuario del SEÑOR muere, ¡así que todos moriremos!»

Deberes de sacerdotes y levitas

18 El SEÑOR le dijo a Aarón: «Todos los de la tribu de Leví se expondrán a sufrir las consecuencias de acercarse a las cosas sagradas, pero de entre ellos sólo tú y tus hijos se expondrán a las consecuencias de ejercer el sacerdocio. ²Cuando tú y tus hijos estén ministrando delante de la Tienda del *pacto, tendrán como ayudantes a sus hermanos de la tribu de Leví. ³Ellos te ayudarán en tus deberes y estarán a cargo de la *Tienda de reunión, pero no se acercarán a los objetos sagrados ni al altar, para que no mueran. ⁴Ellos serán tus ayudantes, y estarán a cargo de la Tienda de reunión y de todo su servicio. Así que, cuando ustedes ministren, nadie que no esté autorizado se les acercará.

⁵»Sólo ustedes estarán a cargo de las cosas sagradas y del altar, para que no se vuelva a derramar mi ira sobre los israelitas. ⁶Considera que yo mismo he escogido, de entre la comunidad, a tus hermanos los levitas, para dártelos como un regalo. Ellos han sido dedicados al SEÑOR para que sirvan en la Tienda de reunión. ⁷Pero sólo tú y tus hijos se harán cargo del sacerdocio, es decir, de todo lo referente al altar y a lo que está detrás de la cortina. A ustedes les doy de regalo el sacerdocio, pero cualquier otro que se acerque a las cosas sagradas será condenado a muerte.»

Privilegios de los sacerdotes

⁸El SEÑOR le dijo a Aarón: «Yo mismo te he puesto a cargo de todas las cosas sagradas que los israelitas me traen como contribución. A ti y a tus hijos se las he entregado como su porción consagrada, como estatuto perpetuo. ⁹Te corresponderán las cosas más sagradas, que no se queman en el altar. Tuya será toda ofrenda que presenten los israelitas, junto con las ofrendas de cereal, los sacrificios *expiatorios y los sacrificios por la culpa. Todo esto que ellos me traen será algo muy *santo para ti y para tus hijos. ¹⁰Comerás de las cosas más sagradas, y las considerarás santas. Todo varón comerá de ellas.

¹¹»También te corresponderán las contribuciones de todas las ofrendas mecidas que me presenten los israelitas. A ti y a tus hijos y a tus hijas se las he dado, como estatuto perpetuo.

¹²»De las *primicias que ellos traen al SEÑOR te doy también lo mejor del aceite, del vino nuevo y de los cereales. ¹³Ellos traerán al SEÑOR las primicias de todo lo que la tierra produce, y yo te las entregaré a ti. Toda persona que esté ritualmente *pura podrá comer de ellas.

¹⁴»Todo lo que en Israel haya sido dedicado por completo al SEÑOR, será tuyo. ¹⁵Todo primogénito presentado al SEÑOR será tuyo, ya sea de *hombre o de animal. Pero rescatarás al primogénito nacido de hombre y al de animales impuros. ¹⁶El rescate tendrá lugar cuando el primogénito tenga un mes de edad. El precio del rescate será de cinco monedas de plata, según la moneda oficial del santuario, que pesa once gramos.ᶜ

¹⁷»Pero no podrás rescatar al primogénito de un toro, de una oveja o de un macho cabrío, pues son santos. Rociarás su sangre en el altar, y quemarás su grasa como ofrenda presentada por fuego, de aroma grato al SEÑOR. ¹⁸Pero la carne será tuya, lo mismo que el pecho de la ofrenda mecida y el muslo derecho. ¹⁹Yo, el SEÑOR, te entrego todas las contribuciones sagradas que los israelitas me presentan. Son tuyas, y de tus hijos y de tus hijas, como estatuto perpetuo. Éste es un *pacto perpetuo, sellado en mi presencia, con sal. Es un pacto que hago contigo y con tus descendientes.»

Privilegios de los levitas

²⁰El SEÑOR le dijo a Aarón: «Tú no tendrás herencia en el país, ni recibirás ninguna porción de tierra, porque yo soy tu porción; yo soy tu herencia entre los israelitas.

²¹»A los levitas les doy como herencia, y en pago por su servicio en la *Tienda de reunión, todos los diezmos de Israel. ²²Si los israelitas volvieran a cometer el pecado de acercarse a la Tienda de reunión, morirían. ²³Por eso únicamente los levitas servirán en la Tienda de reunión y cargarán con la culpa de los israelitas. El siguiente es un estatuto perpetuo para todas las generaciones venideras: Los levitas no recibirán herencia entre los israelitas, ²⁴porque yo les he dado como herencia los diezmos que los israelitas ofrecen al SEÑOR como contribución. Por eso he decidido que no tengan herencia entre los israelitas.»

El diezmo de los diezmos

²⁵El SEÑOR le ordenó a Moisés ²⁶que les dijera a los levitas: «Cuando reciban de los israelitas los diezmos que les he dado a ustedes como herencia, ofrézcanme, como contribución, el diezmo de esos diezmos. ²⁷La contribución que ustedes me presenten les será contada como si fuera trigo de la era o mosto del lagar. ²⁸Así que reservarán para mí, como su contribución, el diezmo de todos los diezmos que reciban de los israelitas, y se lo entregarán al sacerdote Aarón. ²⁹De todos los dones que reciban, reserva-

---

ᶜ **18:16** *monedas ... gramos.* Lit. *siclos, según el siclo del santuario, que pesa veinte *guerás.*

rán para mí una contribución. Y me consagrarán lo mejor.

³⁰»Cuando me hayan presentado la mejor parte, se les tomará en cuenta como si fuera vino o grano. ³¹Lo que sobre, ustedes y sus familias podrán comerlo donde quieran. Ése será el pago por su ministerio en la *Tienda de reunión. ³²Después de presentarme el diezmo de los diezmos, ya no será pecado que coman lo que sobre.

»No profanen las ofrendas sagradas de los israelitas, porque de lo contrario morirán.»

Purificación de los impuros

19 El SEÑOR les dijo a Moisés y a Aarón: ²«El siguiente estatuto forma parte de la ley que yo, el SEÑOR, he promulgado: Los israelitas traerán una vaca de piel rojiza, sin defecto, y que nunca haya llevado yugo. ³La entregarán al sacerdote Eleazar, quien ordenará que la saquen fuera del campamento y que en su presencia la degüellen. ⁴Después el sacerdote Eleazar mojará el dedo en la sangre y rociará siete veces en dirección a la *Tienda de reunión. ⁵Hará también que la vaca sea incinerada en su presencia. Se quemará la piel, la carne y la sangre, junto con el excremento. ⁶Luego el sacerdote tomará ramas de cedro y de *hisopo, y un paño escarlata, y lo echará al fuego donde se incinere la vaca. ⁷Finalmente, el sacerdote lavará sus vestidos y se bañará. Después de eso podrá volver al campamento, pero quedará *impuro hasta el anochecer. ⁸El que incinere la vaca lavará también sus vestidos y se bañará, y quedará impuro hasta el anochecer.

⁹»Un hombre ritualmente puro recogerá las cenizas de la vaca, y las llevará a un lugar puro fuera del campamento. Allí se depositarán las cenizas para que la comunidad israelita las use como sacrificio *expiatorio, junto con el agua de purificación. ¹⁰El que recoja las cenizas de la vaca lavará también sus vestidos, y quedará impuro hasta el anochecer. Éste será un estatuto perpetuo para los israelitas y para los extranjeros que vivan entre ellos.

El uso del agua de la purificación

¹¹»Quien toque el cadáver de alguna persona, quedará *impuro siete días. ¹²Para purificarse, los días tercero y séptimo usará el agua de la purificación, y así quedará puro. Pero si no se purifica durante esos días, quedará impuro.

¹³»Quien toque el cadáver de alguna persona, y no se purifique, contamina el santuario del SEÑOR. Tal persona será eliminada de Israel, pues habrá quedado impura por no haber recibido las aguas de purificación.

¹⁴»Ésta es la ley que se aplicará cuando alguien muera en alguna de las tiendas: Todo el que entre en la tienda, y todo el que se encuentre en ella, quedará impuro siete días. ¹⁵Toda vasija que no haya estado bien tapada también quedará impura.

¹⁶»Quien al pasar por un campo toque el cadáver de alguien que haya sido asesinado o que haya muerto de muerte natural, o toque huesos *humanos o un sepulcro, quedará impuro siete días.

¹⁷»Para purificar a la persona que quedó impura, en una vasija se pondrá un poco de la ceniza del sacrificio *expiatorio, y se le echará agua fresca. ¹⁸Después de eso, alguien ritualmente puro tomará *hisopo, lo mojará en el agua, y rociará la tienda y todos sus utensilios, y a todos los que estén allí. También se rociará al que haya tocado los huesos

humanos, el sepulcro o el cadáver de alguien que haya sido asesinado o que haya muerto de muerte natural. ¹⁹El hombre ritualmente puro rociará a la persona impura los días tercero y séptimo. Al séptimo día, purificará a la persona impura, la cual lavará sus vestidos y se bañará. Así quedará purificada al anochecer. ²⁰Pero si la persona impura no se purifica, será eliminada de la comunidad por haber contaminado el santuario del SEÑOR. Tal persona habrá quedado impura por no haber recibido las aguas de purificación. ²¹Éste es un estatuto perpetuo para Israel.

»El que rocía con las aguas de purificación también lavará sus vestidos, y quien toque el agua de purificación quedará impuro hasta el anochecer. ²²Todo lo que el impuro toque quedará impuro, y quien lo toque a él, también quedará impuro.»

El agua de la roca

20 Toda la comunidad israelita llegó al desierto de Zin el mes primero, y acampó en Cades. Fue allí donde Miriam murió y fue sepultada.

²Como hubo una gran escasez de agua, los israelitas se amotinaron contra Moisés y Aarón, ³y le reclamaron a Moisés: «¡Ojalá el SEÑOR nos hubiera dejado morir junto con nuestros hermanos! ⁴¿No somos acaso la asamblea del SEÑOR? ¿Para qué nos trajiste a este desierto, a morir con nuestro ganado? ⁵¿Para qué nos sacaste de Egipto y nos metiste en este horrible lugar? Aquí no hay semillas, ni higueras, ni viñas, ni granados, ¡y ni siquiera hay agua!»

⁶Moisés y Aarón se apartaron de la asamblea y fueron a la entrada de la *Tienda de reunión, donde se postraron rostro en tierra. Entonces la gloria del SEÑOR se manifestó ante ellos, ⁷y el SEÑOR le dijo a Moisés: ⁸«Toma la vara y reúne a la asamblea. En presencia de ésta, tú y tu hermano le ordenarán a la *roca que dé agua. Así harán que de ella brote agua, y darán de beber a la asamblea y a su ganado.»

⁹Tal como el SEÑOR se lo había ordenado, Moisés tomó la vara que estaba ante el SEÑOR. ¹⁰Luego Moisés y Aarón reunieron a la asamblea frente a la roca, y Moisés dijo: «¡Escuchen, rebeldes! ¿Acaso tenemos que sacarles agua de esta roca?» ¹¹Dicho esto, levantó la mano y dos veces golpeó la roca con la vara, ¡y brotó agua en abundancia, de la cual bebieron la asamblea y su ganado!

¹²El SEÑOR les dijo a Moisés y a Aarón: «Por no haber confiado en mí, ni haber reconocido mi *santidad en presencia de los israelitas, no serán ustedes los que lleven a esta comunidad a la tierra que les he dado.»

¹³A estas aguas se les conoce como la fuente de Meribá,ᵉ porque fue allí donde los israelitas le hicieron reclamaciones al SEÑOR, y donde él manifestó su santidad.

Edom le niega el paso a Israel

¹⁴Desde Cades, Moisés envió emisarios al rey de Edom, con este mensaje:

«Así dice tu hermano Israel: "Tú conoces bien todos los sufrimientos que hemos padecido. ¹⁵Sabes que nuestros antepasados fueron a Egipto, donde durante muchos años vivimos, y que los egipcios nos maltrataron a nosotros y a nuestros padres. ¹⁶También sabes que clamamos al SEÑOR, y que él escuchó nuestra súplica y nos envió a un ángel que nos sacó de Egipto.

ᵈ 19:14 *el que.* Alt. *lo que.*   ᵉ 20:13 En hebreo, *Meribá* significa *reclamación.*

»"Ya estamos en Cades, población que está en las inmediaciones de tu territorio. 17Sólo te pedimos que nos dejes cruzar por tus dominios. Te prometo que no entraremos en ningún campo ni viña, ni beberemos agua de ningún pozo. Nos limitaremos a pasar por el camino real, sin apartarnos de él para nada, hasta que salgamos de tu territorio."»

18Pero el rey de Edom le mandó a decir:

«Ni siquiera intenten cruzar por mis dominios; de lo contrario, saldré con mi ejército y los atacaré.»

19Los israelitas insistieron:

«Sólo pasaremos por el camino principal, y si nosotros o nuestro ganado llegamos a beber agua de tus pozos, lo te pagaremos. Lo único que pedimos es que nos permitas pasar por él.»

20El rey fue tajante en su respuesta:

«¡Por aquí no pasarán!»

Y salió contra ellos con un poderoso ejército, 21resuelto a no dejarlos cruzar por su territorio. Así que los israelitas se vieron obligados a ir por otro camino.

Muerte de Aarón

22Toda la comunidad israelita partió de Cades y llegó al monte Hor, 23cerca de la frontera de Edom. Allí el SEÑOR les dijo a Moisés y a Aarón: 24«Pronto Aarón partirá de este mundo, de modo que no entrará en la tierra que les he dado a los israelitas porque ustedes dos no obedecieron la orden que les di en la fuente de Meribá. 25Así que lleva a Aarón y a su hijo al monte Hor. 26Allí le quitarás a Aarón sus vestiduras sacerdotales, y se las pondrás a su hijo Eleazar, pues allí Aarón se reunirá con sus antepasados.»

27Moisés llevó a cabo lo que el SEÑOR le ordenó. A la vista de todo el pueblo, los tres subieron al monte Hor. 28Moisés le quitó a Aarón las vestiduras sacerdotales, y se las puso a Eleazar. Allí, en la cumbre del monte, murió Aarón. Luego Moisés y Eleazar descendieron del monte. 29Y cuando el pueblo se enteró de que Aarón había muerto, lo lloró treinta días.

Derrota de Arad

21 Cuando el cananeo que reinaba en la ciudad de Arad y vivía en el Néguev se enteró de que los israelitas venían por el camino de Atarín, los atacó y capturó a algunos de ellos. 2Entonces el pueblo de Israel hizo este voto al SEÑOR: «Si tú nos aseguras la victoria sobre este enemigo, *destruiremos por completo sus ciudades.» 3El SEÑOR atendió a la súplica de los israelitas y les concedió la victoria sobre los cananeos, a los que destruyeron por completo, junto con sus ciudades. Por eso a aquel lugar se le llamó Jormá.f

La serpiente de bronce

4Los israelitas salieron del monte Hor por la ruta del *Mar Rojo, bordeando el territorio de Edom. En el camino se impacientaron 5y comenzaron a hablar contra Dios y contra Moisés:

—¿Para qué nos trajeron ustedes de Egipto a morir en este desierto? ¡Aquí no hay pan ni agua! ¡Ya estamos hartos de esta pésima comida!

6Por eso el SEÑOR mandó contra ellos serpientes venenosas, para que los mordieran, y muchos israelitas murieron. 7El pueblo se acercó entonces a Moisés, y le dijo:

—Hemos pecado al hablar contra el SEÑOR y contra ti. Ruégale al SEÑOR que nos quite esas serpientes.

Moisés intercedió por el pueblo, 8y el SEÑOR le dijo:

—Hazte una serpiente, y ponla en un asta. Todos los que sean mordidos y la miren, vivirán.

9Moisés hizo una serpiente de bronce y la puso en un asta. Los que eran mordidos, miraban a la serpiente de bronce y vivían.

En camino a Moab

10Los israelitas se pusieron en marcha y acamparon en Obot. 11De allí partieron y acamparon en Iyé Abarín, que está en el desierto, al oriente de Moab. 12De allí partieron y acamparon en el valle de Zéred. 13De allí partieron y acamparon al otro lado del río Arnón, que está en el desierto que se extiende desde el territorio de los amorreos. El río Arnón sirve de frontera entre el territorio de los moabitas y el de los amorreos. 14Por eso puede leerse en el libro de las guerras del SEÑOR:

«... hacia el Mar Rojo,g los valles y el Arnón.
15La ladera de los valles que se extienden
hasta la región de Ar y la frontera de
Moab.»

16De allí continuaron hasta Ber, el pozo donde el SEÑOR le dijo a Moisés: «Reúne al pueblo, y les daré agua.» 17En esa ocasión Israel entonó este cántico:

«¡Que brote el agua!
¡Que cante el pozo!
18¡Pozo que el gobernante cavó con su cetro
y que el noble abrió con su vara!»

Desde el desierto se dirigieron a Matana; 19de Matana a Najaliel, de Najaliel a Bamot, 20y de Bamot al valle que está en la región de Moab, hasta la cumbre del monte Pisgá, desde donde puede verse el desierto de Jesimón.

Victoria sobre Sijón

21Israel envió emisarios a Sijón, rey de los amorreos, con este mensaje:

22«Te pido que nos dejes pasar por tus dominios. Te prometo que no entraremos en ningún campo ni viña, ni beberemos agua de ningún pozo. Nos limitaremos a pasar por el camino real, hasta que salgamos de tu territorio.»

23Pero Sijón no dejó que los israelitas pasaran por sus dominios. Más bien, reunió a sus tropas y salió a hacerles frente en el desierto. Cuando llegó a Yahaza, los atacó. 24Pero los israelitas lo derrotaron y se apoderaron de su territorio, desde el río Arnón hasta el río Jaboc, es decir, hasta la frontera de los amonitas, la cual estaba fortificada. 25Israel se apoderó de todas las ciudades amorreas y se estableció en ellas, incluso en Hesbón y en todas sus aldeas. 26Hesbón era la ciudad capital de Sijón, rey de los amorreos, quien había luchado en contra del anterior rey de Moab, conquistando todo su territorio, hasta el río Arnón.

27Por eso dicen los poetas:

«Vengan a Hesbón, la ciudad de Sijón.
¡Reconstrúyanla! ¡Restáurenla!
28Porque de Hesbón ha salido fuego;
de la ciudad de Sijón salieron llamas.

---

f 21:3 En hebreo, Jormá significa destrucción. g 21:14 hacia el Mar Rojo. Texto de difícil traducción.

¡Y consumieron las ciudades de Moab
y las alturas que dominan el Arnón!
²⁹¡Ay de ti, Moab!
¡Estás destruido, pueblo de Quemós!
Tu dios convirtió a tus hijos en fugitivos
y a tus hijas en prisioneras de Sijón,
rey de los amorreos.

³⁰»Los hemos destruido por completo,
desde Hesbón hasta Dibón.
Los devastamos hasta Nofa,
¡los destruimos hasta Medeba!»

³¹Así fue como Israel se estableció en la tierra de
los amorreos.

Victoria sobre el rey Og de Basán

³²Moisés también envió a explorar Jazer, y los israelitas se apoderaron de sus aldeas, expulsando a
los amorreos que vivían allí. ³³Al volver, tomaron el
camino de Basán. Fue allí donde Og, el rey de Basán,
salió con su ejército para hacerles frente en Edrey.
³⁴Pero el SEÑOR le dijo a Moisés: «No le tengas
miedo, porque voy a entregar en tus manos a Og, a
su ejército, y a su territorio. Harás con él lo mismo
que hiciste con Sijón, el rey de los amorreos que vivía
en Hesbón.»
³⁵Así fue como los israelitas mataron a Og, a sus
hijos y a todo su ejército, hasta no dejar sobreviviente, y se apoderaron de su territorio.

Balac manda llamar a Balán

22 Los israelitas se pusieron otra vez en marcha,
y acamparon en las estepas de Moab, al otro
lado del Jordán, a la altura de Jericó.
²Cuando Balac hijo de Zipor se dio cuenta de
todo lo que Israel había hecho con los amorreos, ³los
moabitas sintieron mucho miedo de los israelitas.
Estaban verdaderamente aterrorizados de ellos, porque eran un ejército muy numeroso.
⁴Entonces dijeron los moabitas a los *ancianos
de Madián: «¡Esta muchedumbre barrerá con todo lo
que hay a nuestro alrededor, como cuando el ganado barre con la hierba del campo!»
En aquel tiempo, Balac hijo de Zipor era rey de
Moab, ⁵así que mandó llamar a Balán hijo de Beor,
quien vivía en Petor, a orillas del río Éufrates, en la
tierra de los amavitas.ʰ Balac mandó a decirle:

«Hay un pueblo que salió de Egipto, y que
ahora cubre toda la tierra y ha venido a asentar-
se cerca de mí. ⁶Te ruego que vengas y maldigas
por mí a este pueblo, porque es más poderoso
que yo. Tal vez así pueda yo vencerlos y echarlos
fuera del país. Yo sé que a quien tú bendices,
queda bendito, y a quien tú maldices, queda
maldito.»

⁷Los ancianos de Moab y de Madián fueron a
darle a Balán el mensaje que Balac le enviaba, y llevaron consigo dinero para pagarle sus conjuros.
⁸Balán los invitó a pasar allí la noche, prometien-
do comunicarles después lo que el SEÑOR le dijera. Y
los gobernantes se alojaron con él.
⁹Dios se le apareció a Balán, y le dijo:
—¿Quiénes son estos hombres que se alojan
contigo?
¹⁰Balán le respondió:
—Son los mensajeros que envió Balac hijo de Zipor, que es el rey de Moab. Los envió a decirme:
¹¹"Un pueblo que salió de Egipto cubre ahora toda la

tierra. Ven y échales una maldición por mí. Tal vez
así pueda yo luchar contra ellos y echarlos fuera de
mi territorio."
¹²Pero Dios le dijo a Balán:
—No irás con ellos, ni pronunciarás ninguna
maldición sobre los israelitas, porque son un pueblo
bendito.
¹³Al otro día Balán se levantó y les dijo a los gobernantes enviados por Balac: «Regresen a su tierra,
porque el SEÑOR no quiere que yo vaya con ustedes.»
¹⁴Los gobernantes moabitas regresaron adonde
estaba Balac y le dijeron: «Balán no quiere venir con
nosotros.»
¹⁵Balac envió entonces a otros gobernantes,
más numerosos y distinguidos que los primeros,
¹⁶quienes fueron y le dijeron a Balán:
—Esto es lo que dice Balac hijo de Zipor:

"No permitas que nada te impida venir a verme, ¹⁷porque yo te recompensaré con creces
y haré todo lo que tú me pidas. Te ruego que
vengas y maldigas por mí a este pueblo."

¹⁸Pero Balán le respondió:
—Aun si Balac me diera su palacio lleno de oro y
de plata, yo no podría hacer nada grande ni pequeño, sino ajustarme al mandamiento del SEÑOR mi
Dios. ¹⁹Ustedes pueden también alojarse aquí esta
noche, mientras yo averiguo si el SEÑOR quiere decirme alguna otra cosa.
²⁰Aquella noche Dios se le apareció a Balán y le
dijo: «Ya que estos hombres han venido a llamarte,
ve con ellos, pero sólo harás lo que yo te ordene.»

Balán y su burra

²¹Balán se levantó por la mañana, ensilló su burra, y partió con los gobernantes de Moab. ²²Mientras iba con ellos, la ira de Dios se encendió y en el
camino el ángel del SEÑOR se hizo presente, dispuesto a no dejarlo pasar. Balán iba montado en su burra,
y sus dos criados lo acompañaban. ²³Cuando la burra vio al ángel del SEÑOR en medio del camino, con
la espada desenvainada, se apartó del camino para
meterse en el campo. Pero Balán la golpeó para hacerla volver al camino.
²⁴El ángel del SEÑOR se detuvo en un sendero estrecho que estaba entre dos viñas, con cercos de piedra en ambos lados. ²⁵Cuando la burra vio al ángel del
SEÑOR, se arrimó contra la pared, con lo que lastimó el
pie de Balán. Entonces Balán volvió a pegarle.
²⁶El ángel del SEÑOR se les adelantó y se detuvo
en un lugar más estrecho, donde ya no había hacia
dónde volverse. ²⁷Cuando la burra vio al ángel del
SEÑOR, se echó al suelo con Balán encima. Entonces
se encendió la ira de Balán y golpeó a la burra con un
palo. ²⁸Pero el SEÑOR hizo hablar a la burra, y ella le
dijo a Balán:
—¿Se puede saber qué te he hecho, para que me
hayas pegado tres veces?
²⁹Balán le respondió:
—¡Te has venido burlando de mí! Si hubiera tenido una espada en la mano, te habría matado de
inmediato.
³⁰La burra le contestó a Balán:
—¿Acaso no soy la burra sobre la que siempre
has montado, hasta el día de hoy? ¿Alguna vez te
hice algo así?
—No —respondió Balán.
³¹El SEÑOR abrió los ojos de Balán, y éste pudo
ver al ángel del SEÑOR en el camino y empuñando la

ʰ **22:5** *de los amavitas.* Alt. *de los hijos de su pueblo.*

espada. Balán se inclinó entonces y se postró rostro en tierra.

³²El ángel del SEÑOR le preguntó:

—¿Por qué golpeaste tres veces a tu burra? ¿No te das cuenta de que vengo dispuesto a no dejarte pasar porque he visto que tus *caminos son malos?ⁱ ³³Cuando la burra me vio, se apartó de mí tres veces. De no haber sido por ella, tú estarías ya muerto y ella seguiría con vida.

³⁴Balán le dijo al ángel del SEÑOR:

—He pecado. No me di cuenta de tu presencia en el camino para cerrarme el paso. Ahora bien, como esto te parece mal, voy a regresar.

³⁵Pero el ángel del SEÑOR le dijo a Balán:

—Ve con ellos, pero limítate a decir sólo lo que yo te mande.

Y Balán se fue con los jefes que Balac había enviado.

Balac se encuentra con Balán

³⁶Cuando Balac se enteró de que Balán venía, salió a recibirlo en una ciudad moabita que está en la frontera del río Arnón. ³⁷Balac le dijo a Balán:

—¿Acaso no te mandé llamar? ¿Por qué no viniste a mí? ¿Crees que no soy capaz de recompensarte?

³⁸—¡Bueno, ya estoy aquí! —contestó Balán—. Sólo que no podré decir nada que Dios no ponga en mi boca.

³⁹De allí se fueron Balán y Balac a Quiriat Jusot. ⁴⁰Balac ofreció en sacrificio vacas y ovejas, y las compartió con Balán y los gobernantes que estaban con él. ⁴¹A la mañana siguiente, Balac llevó a Balán a Bamot Baal, desde donde Balán pudo ver parte del campamento israelita.

Primer oráculo de Balán

23 Balán le dijo a Balac: «Edifícame siete altares en este lugar, y prepárame siete novillos y siete carneros.» ²Balac hizo lo que Balán le pidió, y juntos ofrecieron un novillo y un carnero en cada altar.

³Entonces Balán le dijo a Balac: «Quédate aquí, al lado de tu *holocausto, mientras yo voy a ver si el SEÑOR quiere reunirse conmigo. Luego te comunicaré lo que él me revele.» Y se fue a un cerro desierto.

⁴Dios vino a su encuentro, y Balán le dijo:

—He preparado siete altares, y en cada altar he ofrecido un novillo y un carnero.

⁵Entonces el SEÑOR puso su palabra en boca de Balán, y le dijo:

—Vuelve adonde está Balac, y repítele lo que te voy a decir.

⁶Balán regresó y encontró a Balac de pie, al lado de su holocausto, en compañía de todos los jefes de Moab. ⁷Y Balán pronunció su oráculo:

«De Aram, de las montañas de Oriente,
　me trajo Balac, el rey de Moab.
"Ven —me dijo—, maldice por mí a Jacob;
　ven, deséale el mal a Israel."
⁸¿Pero cómo podré echar maldiciones
　sobre quien Dios no ha maldecido?
¿Cómo podré desearle el mal
　a quien el SEÑOR no se lo desea?
⁹Desde la cima de las peñas lo veo;
　desde las colinas lo contemplo:
es un pueblo que vive apartado,
　que no se cuenta entre las naciones.
¹⁰¿Quién puede calcular la descendencia de Jacob,

tan numerosa como el polvo,
o contar siquiera la cuarta parte de Israel?
¡Sea mi muerte como la del justo!
¡Sea mi fin semejante al suyo!»

¹¹Entonces Balac le reclamó a Balán:

—¿Qué me has hecho? Te traje para que lanzaras una maldición sobre mis enemigos, ¡y resulta que no has hecho más que bendecirlos!

¹²Pero Balán le respondió:

—¿Acaso no debo decir lo que el SEÑOR me pide que diga?

Segundo oráculo de Balán

¹³Entonces Balac le dijo:

—Por favor, ven conmigo a otro lugar. Desde allí podrás ver sólo a una parte del pueblo, y no a todos ellos,ʲ y les desearás el mal.

¹⁴Así que lo llevó al campo de Zofín en la cumbre del monte Pisgá. Allí edificó siete altares, y en cada uno de ellos ofreció un novillo y un carnero. ¹⁵Allí Balán le dijo a Balac: «Quédate aquí, al lado de tu *holocausto, mientras yo voy a reunirme con Dios.»ᵏ

¹⁶El SEÑOR se reunió con Balán y puso en boca de éste su palabra. Le dijo: «Vuelve adonde está Balac, y repite lo que te voy a decir.»

¹⁷Balán se fue adonde estaba Balac, y lo encontró de pie, al lado de su holocausto, en compañía de los jefes de Moab. Balac le preguntó:

—¿Qué dijo el SEÑOR?

¹⁸Entonces Balán pronunció su oráculo:

«Levántate, Balac, y escucha;
　óyeme, hijo de Zipor.
¹⁹Dios no es un simple *mortal
　para mentir y cambiar de parecer.
¿Acaso no cumple lo que promete
　ni lleva a cabo lo que dice?
²⁰Se me ha ordenado bendecir,
　y si eso es lo que Dios quiere,
　yo no puedo hacer otra cosa.

²¹»Dios no se ha fijado en la maldad de Jacob
　ni ha reparado en la violencia de Israel.
El SEÑOR su Dios está con ellos;
　y entre ellos se le aclama como rey.
²²Dios los sacó de Egipto
　con la fuerza de un toro salvaje.
²³Contra Jacob no hay brujería que valga,
　ni valen las hechicerías contra Israel.
De Jacob y de Israel se dirá:
　"¡Miren lo que Dios ha hecho!"
²⁴Un pueblo se alza como leona;
　se levanta como león.
No descansará hasta haber devorado su presa
　y bebido la sangre de sus víctimas.»

²⁵Balac le dijo entonces a Balán:

—¡Si no los vas a maldecir, tampoco los bendigas!

²⁶Balán le respondió:

—¿Acaso no te advertí que yo repetiría todo lo que el SEÑOR me ordenara decir?

Tercer oráculo de Balán

²⁷Balac le dijo a Balán:

—Por favor, ven conmigo, que te llevaré a otro lugar. Tal vez a Dios le parezca bien que los maldigas desde allí.

ⁱ **22:32** *son malos* (véase LXX y Vulgata). Texto de difícil traducción.　ʲ **23:13** *podrás ver sólo a una parte del pueblo, y no a todos ellos*. Alt. *podrás ver al pueblo, ya que ahora sólo ves parte de él*.　ᵏ **23:15** *con Dios* (LXX); *allí* (TM).

28Así que llevó a Balán hasta la cumbre del monte Peor, desde donde puede verse el desierto de Jesimón. 29Allí Balán le dijo:

—Edifícame siete altares en este lugar, y prepárame siete novillos y siete carneros.

30Balac hizo lo que Balán le pidió, y en cada altar ofreció un novillo y un carnero.

24 Pero cuando Balán se dio cuenta de que al SEÑOR le complacía que se bendijera a Israel, no recurrió a la hechicería, como otras veces, sino que volvió su rostro hacia el desierto. 2Cuando Balán alzó la vista y vio a Israel acampando por tribus, el Espíritu del SEÑOR vino sobre él; 3entonces pronunció su oráculo:

«Palabras de Balán hijo de Beor;
    palabras del varón clarividente.
4Palabras del que oye las palabras de Dios,
    del que contempla la visión del
        *Todopoderoso,
    del que cae en trance y tiene visiones.

5»¡Cuán hermosas son tus tiendas, Jacob!
    ¡Qué bello es tu campamento, Israel!
6Son como arroyos que se ensanchan,
    como jardines a la orilla del río,
    como áloes plantados por el SEÑOR,
    como cedros junto a las aguas.
7Sus cántaros rebosan de agua;
    su semilla goza de agua abundante.
Su rey es más grande que Agag;
    su reinado se engrandece.

8»Dios los sacó de Egipto
    con la fuerza de un toro salvaje.
Israel devora a las naciones hostiles
    y les parte los huesos;
    ¡las atraviesa con sus flechas!
9Se agacha como un león,
    se tiende como una leona:
    ¿quién se atreverá a molestarlo?
¡Benditos sean los que te bendigan!
    ¡Malditos sean los que te maldigan!»

10Entonces la ira de Balac se encendió contra Balán, y chasqueando los dedos le dijo:

—Te mandé llamar para que echaras una maldición sobre mis enemigos, ¡y estas tres veces no has hecho sino bendecirlos! 11¡Más te vale volver a tu tierra! Prometí que te recompensaría, pero esa recompensa te la ha negado el SEÑOR.

12Balán le contestó:

—Yo les dije a tus mensajeros que me enviaste: 13"Aun si Balac me diera su palacio lleno de oro y de plata, yo no podría hacer nada bueno ni malo, sino ajustarme al mandamiento del SEÑOR mi Dios. Lo que el SEÑOR me ordene decir, eso diré." 14Ahora que vuelvo a mi pueblo, voy a advertirte en cuanto a lo que este pueblo hará con tu pueblo en los días postreros.

Cuarto oráculo de Balán

15Entonces Balán pronunció su oráculo:

«Palabras de Balán hijo de Beor,
    palabras del varón clarividente.
16Palabras del que oye las palabras de Dios
    y conoce el pensamiento del *Altísimo;
    del que contempla la visión del
        *Todopoderoso,
    del que cae en trance y tiene visiones:

17»Lo veo, pero no ahora;
    lo contemplo, pero no de cerca.
Una estrella saldrá de Jacob;
    un rey surgirá en Israel.
Aplastará las sienes de Moab
    y el cráneo de todos los hijos de Set.
18Edom será conquistado;
    Seír, su enemigo, será dominado,
    mientras que Israel hará proezas.
19De Jacob saldrá un soberano,
    y destruirá a los sobrevivientes de Ar.»

Últimos oráculos de Balán

20Balán miró a Amalec y pronunció este oráculo:

«Amalec fue el primero entre las naciones,
    pero su fin será la destrucción total.»

21Luego miró Balán al quenita y pronunció este oráculo:

«Aunque tienes una morada segura
    y tu nido está sobre las rocas,
22tú, Caín, estás destinado al fuego,
    y Asiria te llevará cautivo.»

23Entonces Balán pronunció este oráculo:

«¡Ay!, ¿quién seguirá con vida
    cuando Dios determine hacer esto?
24Vendrán barcos desde las costas de Chipre,
    que oprimirán a Asiria y a Éber,
    pues ellos también serán destruidos.»

25Después de esto Balán se levantó y volvió a su tierra, y también Balac se fue por su camino.

Infidelidad de Israel

25 Mientras los israelitas acampaban en Sitín, comenzaron a prostituirse con las mujeres moabitas, 2las cuales los invitaban a participar en los sacrificios a sus dioses. Los israelitas comían delante de esos dioses y se inclinaban a adorarlos. 3Esto los llevó a unirse al culto de Baal Peor. Por tanto, la ira del SEÑOR se encendió contra ellos.

4Entonces el SEÑOR le dijo a Moisés: «Toma a todos los jefes del pueblo y ahórcalos en mi presencia a plena luz del día, para que el furor de mi ira se aparte de Israel.»

5Moisés les ordenó a los jueces de Israel: «Maten a los hombres bajo su mando que se hayan unido al culto de Baal Peor.»

6Mientras el pueblo lloraba a la entrada de la *Tienda de reunión, un israelita trajo a una madianita y, en presencia de Moisés y de toda la comunidad israelita, tuvo el descaro de presentársela a su familia. 7De esto se dio cuenta el sacerdote Finés, que era hijo de Eleazar y nieto del sacerdote Aarón. Finés abandonó la asamblea y, lanza en mano, 8siguió al hombre, entró en su tienda y atravesó al israelita y a la mujer.[1] De este modo cesó la mortandad que se había desatado contra los israelitas. 9Con todo, los que murieron a causa de la plaga fueron veinticuatro mil.

10El SEÑOR le dijo a Moisés: 11«Finés, hijo de Eleazar y nieto del sacerdote Aarón, ha hecho que mi ira se aparte de los israelitas, pues ha actuado con el mismo celo que yo habría tenido por mi honor. Por eso no destruí a los israelitas con el furor de mi celo. 12Dile, pues, a Finés que yo le concedo mi *pacto de comunión, 13por medio del cual él y sus descendientes gozarán de un sacerdocio eterno, ya que defen-

---

[1] 25:8 mujer (lectura probable); mujer, por el vientre de ella (TM).

dió celosamente mi honor e hizo *expiación por los israelitas.»

14El hombre que fue atravesado junto con la madianita se llamaba Zimri hijo de Salu, y era jefe de una familia de la tribu de Simeón. **15**La madianita se llamaba Cozbí, y era hija de Zur, jefe de una familia de Madián.

16El SEÑOR le dijo a Moisés: **17**«Ataca a los madianitas y mátalos, **18**porque ellos también los atacaron a ustedes con sus artimañas, pues en Baal Peor los sedujeron, con eso en el caso de Cozbí, la hija del jefe madianita que fue muerta el día de la mortandad en Baal Peor.»

Segundo censo de las tribus de Israel

26 Después de la mortandad, el SEÑOR les dijo a Moisés y al sacerdote Eleazar hijo de Aarón: **2**«Hagan un censo de toda la comunidad israelita por sus familias patriarcales. Enlisten a los varones mayores de veinte años, que sean aptos para el servicio militar en Israel.»

3Moisés y el sacerdote Eleazar hablaron con el pueblo en las llanuras de Moab, cerca del Jordán, a la altura de Jericó, y le ordenaron **4**levantar un censo de todos los varones mayores de veinte años, tal como el SEÑOR se lo había mandado a Moisés.

Los israelitas que salieron de Egipto fueron los siguientes:

5-6 De Enoc, Falú, Jezrón y Carmí, hijos de Rubén, el primogénito de Israel, proceden los siguientes clanes: los enoquitas, los faluitas, los jezronitas y los carmitas. **7**Éstos son los clanes de la tribu de Rubén. Su número llegó a cuarenta y tres mil setecientos treinta hombres.

8Eliab fue el único hijo de Falú. **9**Los hijos de Eliab fueron Nemuel, Datán y Abirán. Éstos son los mismos Datán y Abirán que, no obstante haber sido escogidos por la comunidad como oficiales, se rebelaron contra Moisés y Aarón junto con la facción de Coré cuando este último se rebeló contra el SEÑOR. **10**En esa ocasión, la tierra abrió sus fauces y se los tragó junto con Coré, muriendo también sus seguidores. El fuego devoró a doscientos cincuenta hombres, y este hecho los convirtió en una señal de advertencia. **11**Sin embargo, los hijos de Coré no perecieron.

12-13 De Nemuel, Jamín, Zera y Saúl, hijos de Simeón, proceden los siguientes clanes: los nemuelitas, los jaminitas, los zeraítas y los saulitas. **14**Éstos son los clanes de la tribu de Simeón. Su número llegó a veintidós mil doscientos hombres.

15-17 De Zefón, Jaguí, Suni, Ozni, Erí, Arodí y Arelí, hijos de Gad, proceden los siguientes clanes: los zefonitas, los jaguitas, los sunitas, los oznitas, los eritas, los aroditas y los arelitas. **18**Éstos son los clanes de la tribu de Gad. Su número llegó a cuarenta mil quinientos hombres.

19-20 Er y Onán eran hijos de Judá, pero ambos murieron en Canaán. De sus hijos Selá, Fares y Zera proceden los siguientes clanes: los selaítas, los faresitas y los zeraítas.

21De Jezrón y de Jamul, hijos de Fares, proceden los clanes jezronitas y jamulitas. **22**Éstos son los clanes de la tribu de Judá. Su número llegó a setenta y seis mil quinientos hombres.

23-24 De Tola, Fuvá, Yasub y Simrón, hijos de Isacar, proceden los siguientes clanes: los tolaítas, los fuvitas, los yasubitas y los simronitas. **25**Éstos son los clanes de la tribu de Isacar. Su número llegó a sesenta y cuatro mil trescientos hombres.

26De Séred, Elón y Yalel, hijos de Zabulón, proceden los siguientes clanes: los sereditas, los elonitas y los yalelitas. **27**Éstos son los clanes de la tribu de Zabulón. Su número llegó a sesenta mil quinientos hombres.

28De Manasés y Efraín, hijos de José, proceden los siguientes clanes:

29De Maquir hijo de Manasés y de Galaad hijo de Maquir proceden el clan maquirita y el clan galaadita.

30-32 De Jezer, Jélec, Asriel, Siquén, Semidá y Héfer, hijos de Galaad, proceden los siguientes clanes: los jezeritas, los jelequitas, los asrielitas, los siquenitas, los semidaítas y los heferitas. **33**Zelofejad hijo de Héfer no tuvo hijos sino sólo hijas, cuyos nombres eran Majlá, Noa, Joglá, Milca y Tirsá. **34**Éstos son los clanes de la tribu de Manasés. Su número llegó a cincuenta y dos mil setecientos hombres.

35De Sutela, Béquer y Taján, hijos de Efraín, proceden los siguientes clanes: los sutelaítas, los bequeritas y los tajanitas. **36**De Erán hijo de Sutela procede el clan de los eranitas. **37**Éstos son los clanes de la tribu de Efraín. Su número llegó a treinta y dos mil quinientos hombres.
Todos estos clanes descendieron de José.

38-39 De Bela, Asbel, Ajirán, Sufán y Jufán, hijos de Benjamín, proceden los siguientes clanes: los belaítas, los asbelitas, los ajiranitas, los sufanitas y los jufanitas.

40De Ard y Naamán, hijos de Bela, proceden los clanes de los arditas y de los naamanitas. **41**Éstos son los clanes de la tribu de Benjamín. Su número llegó a cuarenta y cinco mil seiscientos hombres.

42De Suján hijo de Dan procede el clan de los sujanitas, que fueron los únicos clanes danitas. **43**Su número llegó a sesenta y cuatro mil cuatrocientos hombres.

44De Imná, Isví y Beriá, hijos de Aser, proceden los siguientes clanes: los imnaítas, los isvitas y los beriaítas.

45De Héber y Malquiel, hijos de Beriá, proceden los clanes de los heberitas y de los malquielitas. **46**Aser tuvo una hija llamada Sera. **47**Éstos son los clanes de la tribu de Aser. Su número llegó a cincuenta y tres mil cuatrocientos hombres.

48-49 De Yazel, Guní, Jéser y Silén, hijos de Neftalí, proceden los siguientes clanes: los yazelitas, los gunitas, los jeseritas y los silenitas. **50**Éstos son los clanes de la tribu de Neftalí. Su número llegó a cuarenta y cinco mil cuatrocientos hombres.

51Los hombres de Israel eran en total seiscientos un mil setecientos treinta.

Instrucciones para el reparto de la tierra

52El SEÑOR le dijo a Moisés: **53**«Reparte la tierra entre estas tribus para que sea su heredad. Hazlo según el número de nombres registrados. **54**A la tribu más numerosa le darás la heredad más grande, y a la tribu menos numerosa le darás la heredad más pequeña. Cada tribu recibirá su heredad en proporción al número de censados. **55**La tierra deberá repartirse por sorteo, según el nombre de las tribus patriarcales. **56**El sorteo se hará entre todas las tribus, grandes y pequeñas.»

Censo de los levitas

57De los levitas Guersón, Coat y Merari proceden los clanes guersonitas, coatitas y meraritas.

58De los levitas proceden también los siguientes clanes: los libnitas, los hebronitas, los majlitas, los musitas y los coreítas. Coat fue el padre de Amirán. 59La esposa de Amirán se llamaba Jocabed hija de Leví, y había nacido en Egipto. Los hijos que ella tuvo de Amirán fueron Aarón y Moisés, y su hermana Miriam. 60Aarón fue el padre de Nadab, Abiú, Eleazar e Itamar, 61pero Nadab y Abiú murieron bajo el juicio del SEÑOR por haberle ofrecido fuego profano.

62Los levitas mayores de un mes de edad fueron en total veintitrés mil. Pero no fueron censados junto con los demás israelitas porque no habrían de recibir heredad entre ellos.

63Éstos fueron los israelitas censados por Moisés y el sacerdote Eleazar, cuando los contaron en las llanuras de Moab, cerca del río Jordán, a la altura de Jericó. 64Entre los censados no figuraba ninguno de los registrados en el censo que Moisés y Aarón habían hecho antes en el desierto del Sinaí, 65porque el SEÑOR había dicho que todos morirían en el desierto. Con la excepción de Caleb hijo de Jefone y de Josué hijo de Nun, ninguno de ellos quedó con vida.

Las hijas de Zelofejad
27:1-11 — Nm 36:1-12

27 Majlá, Noa, Joglá, Milca y Tirsá pertenecían a los clanes de Manasés hijo de José, pues eran hijas de Zelofejad hijo de Héfer, hijo de Galaad, hijo de Maquir, hijo de Manasés. Las cinco se acercaron 2a la entrada de la *Tienda de reunión, para hablar con Moisés y el sacerdote Eleazar, y con los jefes de toda la comunidad. Les dijeron: 3«Nuestro padre murió sin dejar hijos, pero no por haber participado en la rebelión de Coré contra el SEÑOR. Murió en el desierto por su propio pecado. 4¿Será borrado de su clan el *nombre de nuestro padre por el solo hecho de no haber dejado hijos varones? Nosotras somos sus hijas. ¡Danos una heredad entre los parientes de nuestro padre!»

5Moisés le presentó al SEÑOR el caso de ellas, 6y el SEÑOR le respondió: 7«Lo que piden las hijas de Zelofejad es algo justo, así que debes darles una propiedad entre los parientes de su padre. Traspásales a ellas la heredad de su padre.

8»Además, diles a los israelitas: "Cuando un hombre muera sin dejar hijos, su heredad será traspasada a su hija. 9Si no tiene hija, sus hermanos recibirán la herencia. 10Si no tiene hermanos, se entregará la herencia a los hermanos de su padre. 11Si su padre no tiene hermanos, se entregará la herencia al pariente más cercano de su clan, para que tome posesión de ella. Éste será el procedimiento legal que seguirán los israelitas, tal como yo se lo ordené a Moisés."»

Anuncio de la muerte de Moisés

12El SEÑOR le dijo a Moisés:

—Sube al monte Abarín y contempla desde allí la tierra que les he dado a los israelitas. 13Después de que la hayas contemplado, partirás de este mundo para reunirte con tus antepasados, como tu hermano Aarón. 14En el desierto de Zin, cuando la comunidad se puso a reclamar, ustedes dos me desobedecieron, pues al sacar agua de la *roca no reconocieron ante el pueblo mi santidad.

Esas aguas de Meribá están en Cades, en el desierto de Zin.

Moisés pide un líder para Israel

15Moisés le respondió al SEÑOR:

16—Dígnate, SEÑOR, Dios de toda la *humanidad,m nombrar un jefe sobre esta comunidad, 17uno que los dirija en sus campañas, que los lleve a la guerra y los traiga de vuelta a casa. Así el pueblo del SEÑOR no se quedará como rebaño sin pastor.

18El SEÑOR le dijo a Moisés:

—Toma a Josué hijo de Nun, que es un hombre de gran espíritu.n Pon tus manos sobre él, 19y haz que se presente ante el sacerdote Eleazar y ante toda la comunidad. En presencia de ellos le entregarás el mando. 20Lo investirás con algunas de tus atribuciones, para que toda la comunidad israelita le obedezca. 21Se presentará ante el sacerdote Eleazar, quien mediante el *urim consultará al SEÑOR. Cuando Josué ordene ir a la guerra, la comunidad entera saldrá con él, y cuando le ordene volver, volverá.

22Moisés hizo lo que el SEÑOR le ordenó. Tomó a Josué y lo puso delante del sacerdote Eleazar y de toda la comunidad. 23Luego le impuso las manos y le entregó el cargo, tal como el SEÑOR lo había mandado.

Calendario litúrgico

28 El SEÑOR le dijo a Moisés: 2«Ordénale al pueblo de Israel que se asegure de que se me presente mi ofrenda en el día señalado. Esa ofrenda de aroma grato presentada por fuego es mi comida.

Sacrificio diario

3»Dile también al pueblo que, como ofrenda presentada por fuego, todos los días me deben traer para el *holocausto continuo dos corderos de un año y sin defecto. 4Uno de ellos lo ofrecerás en la mañana, y el otro al atardecer, 5junto con dos kilosñ de flor de harina mezclada con un litroo de aceite de oliva. 6Éste es el holocausto diario, instituido en el monte Sinaí como ofrenda presentada por fuego, de aroma grato al SEÑOR. 7Con cada cordero ofrecerás un litro de vino, como ofrenda de libación, la cual derramarás en el santuario en honor del SEÑOR. 8El segundo cordero lo ofrecerás al atardecer, junto con una ofrenda de cereales y una libación semejantes a las que presentaste en la mañana. Es una ofrenda presentada por fuego, de aroma grato al SEÑOR.

Ofrendas del sábado

9»Cada *sábado ofrecerás dos corderos de un año y sin defecto, junto con una libación y una ofrenda de cuatro kilos y mediop de flor de harina mezclada con aceite. 10Éste es el *holocausto de cada sábado, además del holocausto que cada día se ofrece con su libación.

Ofrenda mensual

11»Cada primer día del mes presentarás, como tu holocausto al SEÑOR, dos novillos, un carnero y siete corderos de un año y sin defecto. 12Con cada novillo presentarás también una ofrenda de seis kilos y medioq de flor de harina mezclada con aceite; con el carnero, cuatro kilos y medio de flor de harina mezclada con aceite; 13y con cada cordero, dos kilos de flor de harina mezclada con aceite. Éste será un holocausto, una ofrenda presentada por fuego, de aroma grato al SEÑOR. 14Las libaciones serán las siguientes: Con cada novillo presentarás dos litrosr de vino; con el carnero, un litro y un cuartos de vino; y con cada cordero, un litro de vino. Éste es el holocausto que debes presentar durante todo el año, una vez al mes, en el día de luna nueva. 15Además del holocausto diario y su libación, también presentarás al SEÑOR, como sacrificio *expiatorio, un macho cabrío.

La Pascua

16»La Pascua del SEÑOR se celebrará el día catorce del mes primero. 17El día quince del mismo mes celebrarás una fiesta, y durante siete días comerás pan sin levadura. 18El primer día celebrarás una fiesta solemne, y nadie realizará ningún tipo de trabajo. 19Presentarás al SEÑOR una ofrenda por fuego, un *holocausto que consistirá en dos novillos, un carnero y siete corderos de un año. Asegúrate de que los animales no tengan defecto. 20Con cada novillo presentarás una ofrenda de seis kilos y medio de flor de harina mezclada con aceite; con el carnero, cuatro kilos y medio; 21y con cada uno de los siete corderos, dos kilos. 22También incluirás un macho cabrío como sacrificio *expiatorio para hacer *propiciación en tu favor. 23Presentarás estas ofrendas, además del holocausto diario de cada mañana. 24De igual manera las ofrecerás cada día, durante siete días consecutivos; es un alimento que consiste en una ofrenda presentada por fuego, de aroma grato al SEÑOR. Todo esto se ofrecerá, además del holocausto diario y su libación. 25Al séptimo día celebrarás una fiesta solemne, y nadie realizará ningún tipo de trabajo.

Fiesta de las Semanas
28:26-31 — Lv 23:15-22; Dt 16:9-12

26»Durante la fiesta de las Semanas, presentarás al SEÑOR una ofrenda de grano nuevo en el día de las *primicias, y celebrarás también una fiesta solemne. Ese día nadie realizará ningún tipo de trabajo. 27Ofrecerás dos novillos, un carnero y siete machos cabríos de un año, como *holocausto de aroma grato al SEÑOR. 28Con cada novillo presentarás una ofrenda de seis kilos y medio de flor de harina mezclada con aceite; con el carnero, cuatro kilos y medio de esa misma harina; 29y con cada uno de los siete corderos, dos kilos. 30Incluirás también un macho cabrío para hacer *propiciación en tu favor. 31Presentarás todo esto junto con sus libaciones, además del holocausto diario y su libación. Los animales no deben tener ningún defecto.

Fiesta de las Trompetas
29:1-6 — Lv 23:23-25

29 »El día primero del mes séptimo celebrarás una fiesta solemne, y nadie realizará ningún tipo de trabajo. Ese día se anunciará con toque de trompetas. 2Como *holocausto de aroma grato al SEÑOR, ofrecerás un novillo, un carnero, y siete corderos de un año y sin defecto. 3Con el novillo presentarás seis kilos y medio de flor de harina mezclada con aceite; con el carnero, cuatro kilos y medio† de esa misma harina; 4y con cada uno de los siete corderos, dos kilos.u 5Incluirás también un macho cabrío como sacrificio *expiatorio, para hacer *propiciación en tu favor. 6Todo esto se ofrecerá junto con las ofrendas de cereales y las libaciones, además del holocausto mensual y del holocausto diario. Tal como está estipulado, todo esto lo presentarás como ofrenda por fuego, de aroma grato al SEÑOR.

El día del Perdón
29:7-11 — Lv 16:2-34; 23:26-32

7»El día diez del mes séptimo celebrarás una fiesta solemne. En ese día se ayunará, y nadie realizará ningún tipo de trabajo. 8Como *holocausto de aroma grato al SEÑOR presentarás un novillo, un carnero y siete corderos de un año. Los animales no deben tener ningún defecto. 9Con el novillo ofrecerás seis kilos y medio de flor de harina mezclada con aceite; con el carnero, cuatro kilos y medio de esa misma harina; 10y con cada uno de los siete corderos, dos kilos. 11Incluirás también un macho cabrío como sacrificio *expiatorio, además del sacrificio expiatorio para la *propiciación y del holocausto diario con su ofrenda de cereales y su libación.

Fiesta de las *Enramadas
29:12-39 — Lv 23:33-43; Dt 16:13-17

12»El día quince del mes séptimo celebrarás una fiesta solemne, y nadie realizará ningún tipo de trabajo. Durante siete días celebrarás una fiesta en honor del SEÑOR. 13Como *holocausto presentado por fuego, de aroma grato al SEÑOR, ofrecerás trece novillos, dos carneros y catorce corderos de un año, que no tengan defecto. 14Con cada uno de los trece novillos presentarás seis kilos y medio de flor de harina mezclada con aceite; con cada uno de los dos carneros, cuatro kilos y medio de esa misma harina; 15y con cada uno de los catorce corderos, dos kilos. 16Incluirás también un macho cabrío como sacrificio *expiatorio, además del holocausto diario con su ofrenda de cereales y su libación.

17»El segundo día prepararás doce novillos, dos carneros y catorce corderos de un año y sin defecto. 18Con los novillos, carneros y corderos presentarás ofrendas de cereales y libaciones, según lo que se especifica para cada número. 19Incluirás también un macho cabrío como sacrificio expiatorio, además del holocausto diario con su ofrenda de cereales y su libación.

20»El tercer día prepararás once novillos, dos carneros y catorce corderos de un año y sin defecto. 21Con los novillos, carneros y corderos presentarás ofrendas de cereales y libaciones, según lo que se especifica para cada número. 22Incluirás también un macho cabrío como sacrificio expiatorio, además del holocausto diario con su ofrenda de cereales y su libación.

23»El cuarto día prepararás diez novillos, dos carneros y catorce corderos de un año y sin defecto. 24Con los novillos, carneros y corderos presentarás ofrendas de cereales y libaciones, según lo que se especifica para cada número. 25Incluirás también un macho cabrío como sacrificio expiatorio, además del holocausto diario con su ofrenda de cereales y su libación.

26»El quinto día prepararás nueve novillos, dos carneros y catorce corderos de un año y sin defecto. 27Con los novillos, carneros y corderos presentarás ofrendas de cereales y libaciones, según lo que se especifica para cada número. 28Incluirás también un macho cabrío como sacrificio expiatorio, además

---

m 27:16 *toda la humanidad.* Lit. *los espíritus de toda carne.* n 27:18 *de gran espíritu.* Alt. *en quien mora el Espíritu.* ñ 28:5 *dos kilos.* Lit. *una décima de *efa;* también en vv. 13,21,29. o 28:5 *un litro.* Lit. *un cuarto de *hin;* también en vv. 7 y 14. p 28:9 *cuatro kilos y medio.* Lit. *dos décimas* (de efa); también en vv. 12,20,28. q 28:12 *seis kilos y medio.* Lit. *tres décimas* (de efa); también en vv. 20 y 28. r 28:14 *dos litros.* Lit. *la mitad de un hin.* s 28:14 *un litro y un cuarto.* Lit. *un tercio de hin.* t 29:3 *seis kilos y medio ... cuatro kilos y medio.* Lit. *tres décimas* (de *efa) *... dos décimas* (de efa); también en vv. 9 y 14. u 29:4 *dos kilos.* Lit. *una décima* (de efa); también en vv. 10 y 15.

del holocausto diario con su ofrenda de cereales y su libación.

29»El sexto día prepararás ocho novillos, dos carneros y catorce corderos de un año y sin defecto. **30**Con los novillos, carneros y corderos presentarás ofrendas de cereales y libaciones, según lo que se especifica para cada número. **31**Incluirás también un macho cabrío como sacrificio expiatorio, además del holocausto diario con su ofrenda de cereales y su libación.

32»El séptimo día prepararás siete novillos, dos carneros y catorce corderos de un año y sin defecto. **33**Con los novillos, carneros y corderos presentarás ofrendas de cereales y libaciones, según lo que se especifica para cada número. **34**Incluirás también un macho cabrío como sacrificio expiatorio, además del holocausto diario con su ofrenda de cereales y su libación.

35»El octavo día celebrarás una fiesta solemne, y nadie realizará ningún tipo de trabajo. **36**Como holocausto presentado por fuego, de aroma grato al SEÑOR, ofrecerás un novillo, un carnero y siete corderos de un año y sin defecto. **37**Con el novillo, el carnero y los corderos presentarás ofrendas de cereales y libaciones, según lo que se especifica para cada número. **38**Incluirás también un macho cabrío como sacrificio expiatorio, además del holocausto diario con su ofrenda de cereales y su libación.

39»Éstas son las ofrendas que presentarás al SEÑOR en las fiestas designadas, aparte de otros votos, ofrendas voluntarias, holocaustos, ofrendas de cereales, libaciones y sacrificios de *comunión que quieras presentarle.»

40Y Moisés les comunicó a los israelitas todo lo que el SEÑOR le había mandado.

Votos de las mujeres

30 Moisés les dijo a los jefes de las tribus de Israel: «El SEÑOR ha ordenado que **2**cuando un hombre haga un voto al SEÑOR, o bajo juramento haga un compromiso, no deberá faltar a su palabra sino que cumplirá con todo lo prometido.

3»Cuando una joven, que todavía vive en casa de su padre, haga un voto al SEÑOR y se comprometa en algo, **4**si su padre se entera de su voto y de su compromiso pero no le dice nada, entonces ella estará obligada a cumplir con todos sus votos y promesas. **5**Pero si su padre se entera y no lo aprueba, todos los votos y compromisos que la joven haya hecho quedarán anulados, y el SEÑOR la absolverá porque fue el padre quien los desaprobó.

6»Si la joven se casa después de haber hecho un voto o una promesa precipitada que la compromete, **7**y su esposo se entera pero no le dice nada, entonces ella estará obligada a cumplir sus votos y promesas. **8**Pero si su esposo se entera y no lo aprueba, el voto y la promesa que ella hizo en forma precipitada quedarán anulados, y el SEÑOR la absolverá.

9»La viuda o divorciada que haga un voto o compromiso estará obligada a cumplirlo.

10»Cuando una mujer casada haga un voto, o bajo juramento se comprometa en algo, **11**si su esposo se entera, pero se queda callado y no lo desaprueba, entonces ella estará obligada a cumplir todos sus votos y promesas. **12**Pero si su esposo se entera y los anula, entonces ninguno de los votos o promesas que haya hecho le serán obligatorios, pues su esposo los anuló. El SEÑOR la absolverá.

13»El esposo tiene la autoridad de confirmar o de anular cualquier voto o juramento de abstinencia que ella haya hecho. **14**En cambio, si los días pasan y el esposo se queda callado, su silencio

confirmará todos los votos y compromisos contraídos por ella. El esposo los confirmará por no haber dicho nada cuando se enteró. **15**Pero si llega a anularlos después de un tiempo de haberse enterado, entonces él cargará con la culpa de su esposa.»

16Éstos son los estatutos que el SEÑOR dio a Moisés en cuanto a la relación entre esposo y esposa, y entre el padre y la hija que todavía viva en su casa.

Guerra contra Madián

31 El SEÑOR le dijo a Moisés: **2**«Antes de partir de este mundo para reunirte con tus antepasados, en nombre de tu pueblo tienes que vengarte de los madianitas.»

3Moisés se dirigió al pueblo y le dijo: «Preparen a algunos de sus hombres para la guerra contra Madián. Vamos a descargar sobre ellos la venganza del SEÑOR. **4**Que cada una de las tribus de Israel envíe mil hombres a la guerra.»

5Los escuadrones de Israel proveyeron mil hombres por cada tribu, con lo que se reunieron doce mil hombres armados para la guerra. **6**Moisés envió a la guerra a los mil hombres de cada tribu. Con ellos iba Finés, hijo del sacerdote Eleazar, quien tenía a su cargo los utensilios del santuario y las trompetas que darían la señal de ataque.

7Tal como el SEÑOR se lo había ordenado a Moisés, los israelitas entraron en batalla y mataron a todos los madianitas. **8**Pasaron a espada a Eví, Requen, Zur, Jur y Reba, que eran los cinco reyes de Madián, y también a Balán hijo de Beor. **9**Capturaron a las mujeres y a los niños de los madianitas, y tomaron como botín de guerra todo su ganado, rebaños y bienes. **10**A todas las ciudades y campamentos donde vivían los madianitas les prendieron fuego, **11**y se apoderaron de *gente y de animales. Todos los despojos y el botín **12**se los llevaron a Moisés y al sacerdote Eleazar, y a toda la comunidad israelita. A los prisioneros, el botín y los despojos los llevaron hasta el campamento que estaba en las llanuras de Moab, cerca del Jordán, a la altura de Jericó.

13Moisés y el sacerdote Eleazar y todos los líderes de la comunidad salieron a recibirlos fuera del campamento. **14**Moisés estaba furioso con los jefes de mil y de cien soldados que regresaban de la batalla. **15**¿Cómo que dejaron con vida a las mujeres? —les preguntó—. **16**¡Si fueron ellas las que, aconsejadas por Balán, hicieron que los israelitas traicionaran al SEÑOR en Baal Peor! Por eso murieron tantos del pueblo del SEÑOR. **17**Maten a todos los niños, y también a todas las mujeres que hayan tenido relaciones sexuales, **18**pero quédense con todas las muchachas que jamás las hayan tenido.

Purificación de combatientes y de prisioneros

19»Todos los que hayan matado a alguien, o hayan tocado un cadáver, deberán quedarse fuera del campamento durante siete días. Al tercer día, y al séptimo, se *purificarán ustedes y sus prisioneros. **20**También deberán purificar toda la ropa, y todo artículo de cuero, de pelo de cabra, o de madera.»

21El sacerdote Eleazar les dijo a los soldados que habían ido a la guerra: «Esto es lo que manda la ley que el SEÑOR le entregó a Moisés: **22**Oro, plata, bronce, hierro, estaño, plomo **23**y todo lo que resista el fuego, deberá ser pasado por el fuego para purificarse, pero también deberá limpiarse con las aguas de la purificación. Todo lo que no resista el fuego deberá pasar por las aguas de la purificación. **24**Al séptimo día, lavarán ustedes sus vestidos y quedarán purificados. Entonces podrán reintegrarse al campamento.»

Reparto del botín

25El SEÑOR le dijo a Moisés: 26«Tú y el sacerdote Eleazar y los jefes de las familias patriarcales harán un recuento de toda la *gente y de todos los animales capturados. 27Dividirán el botín entre los soldados que fueron a la guerra y el resto de la comunidad. 28A los que fueron a la guerra les exigirás del botín una contribución para el SEÑOR. Tanto de la gente como de los asnos, vacas u ovejas, apartarás uno de cada quinientos. 29Los tomarás de la parte que les tocó a los soldados, y se los darás al sacerdote Eleazar como contribución al SEÑOR. 30De la parte que les toca a los israelitas, apartarás de la gente uno de cada cincuenta, lo mismo que de los asnos, vacas, ovejas y otros animales, y se los darás a los levitas, pues ellos son los responsables del cuidado de mi santuario.»

31Moisés y el sacerdote Eleazar hicieron tal como el SEÑOR se lo ordenó a Moisés.

32Sin tomar en cuenta los despojos que tomaron los soldados, el botín fue de seiscientas setenta y cinco mil ovejas, 33setenta y dos mil cabezas de ganado, 34sesenta y un mil asnos 35y treinta y dos mil mujeres que jamás habían tenido relaciones sexuales.

36A los que fueron a la guerra les tocó lo siguiente:

Trescientas treinta y siete mil quinientas ovejas, 37de las cuales se entregaron seiscientas setenta y cinco como contribución al SEÑOR.

38 Treinta y seis mil vacas, de las cuales se entregaron setenta y dos como contribución al SEÑOR.

39 Treinta mil quinientos asnos, de los cuales se entregaron sesenta y uno como contribución al SEÑOR.

40 Dieciséis mil mujeres, de las cuales se entregaron treinta y dos como contribución al SEÑOR.

41La parte que le correspondía al SEÑOR, se la entregó Moisés al sacerdote Eleazar, tal como el SEÑOR se lo había ordenado.

42Del botín que trajeron los soldados, Moisés tomó la mitad que les correspondía a los israelitas, 43de modo que a la comunidad le tocaron trescientas treinta y siete mil quinientas ovejas, 44treinta y seis mil vacas, 45treinta mil quinientos asnos 46y dieciséis mil mujeres. 47De la parte que les tocó a los israelitas, Moisés tomó una de cada cincuenta personas, y uno de cada cincuenta animales, tal como el SEÑOR se lo había ordenado, y todos ellos se los entregó a los levitas, que eran los responsables del cuidado del santuario del SEÑOR.

La ofrenda de los capitanes

48Entonces los oficiales que estaban a cargo de la tropa, es decir, los jefes de mil y de cien soldados, se acercaron a Moisés 49y le dijeron: «Tus siervos han pasado revista, y no falta ninguno de los soldados que estaban bajo nuestras órdenes. 50Por eso hemos traído, como ofrenda al SEÑOR, los artículos de oro que cada uno de nosotros encontró: brazaletes, cadenas, sortijas, pendientes y collares. Todo esto lo traemos para hacer *propiciación por nosotros ante el SEÑOR.»

51Moisés y el sacerdote Eleazar recibieron todos los artículos de oro. 52Todo el oro que los jefes de mil y de cien soldados presentaron como contribución al SEÑOR pesó ciento noventa kilos.v 53Cada soldado había tomado botín para sí mismo. 54Moisés y el sacerdote Eleazar recibieron el oro de manos de los jefes, y lo llevaron a la *Tienda de reunión para que el SEÑOR tuviera presentes a los israelitas.

Rubén y Gad se establecen en Transjordania

32 Las tribus de Rubén y Gad, que tenían mucho ganado, se dieron cuenta de que las tierras de Jazer y Galaad eran apropiadas para la ganadería. 2Así que fueron a decirles a Moisés, al sacerdote Eleazar y a los jefes de la comunidad:

3—Las tierras de Atarot, Dibón, Jazer, Nimrá, Hesbón, Elalé, Sebán, Nebo y Beón 4las conquistó el SEÑOR para el pueblo de Israel, y son apropiadas para la ganadería de tus siervos. 5Si nos hemos ganado tu favor, permítenos tomar esas tierras como heredad. No nos hagas cruzar el Jordán.

6Entonces Moisés les dijo a los rubenitas y a los gaditas:

—¿Les parece justo que sus hermanos vayan al combate mientras ustedes se quedan aquí sentados? 7Los israelitas se han propuesto conquistar la tierra que el SEÑOR les ha dado; ¿no se dan cuenta de que esto los desanimaría? 8¡Esto mismo hicieron los padres de ustedes cuando yo los envié a explorar la tierra de Cades Barnea! 9Fueron a inspeccionar la tierra en el valle de Escol y, cuando volvieron, desanimaron a los israelitas para que no entraran en la tierra que el SEÑOR les había dado. 10Ese día el SEÑOR se encendió en ira y juró: 11"Por no haberme seguido de todo *corazón, ninguno de los mayores de veinte años que salieron de Egipto verá la tierra que juré darles a Abraham, Isaac y Jacob. 12Ninguno de ellos la verá, con la sola excepción de Caleb hijo de Jefone, el quenizita, y Josué hijo de Nun, los cuales me siguieron de todo corazón." 13El SEÑOR se encendió en ira contra Israel, y los hizo vagar por el desierto cuarenta años, hasta que murió toda la generación que había pecado.

14»¡Y ahora ustedes, caterva de pecadores, vienen en lugar de sus padres para aumentar la ira del SEÑOR contra Israel! 15Si ustedes se niegan a seguir al SEÑOR, él volverá a dejar en el desierto a todo este pueblo, y ustedes serán la causa de su destrucción.

16Entonces ellos se acercaron otra vez a Moisés, y le dijeron:

—Vamos a construir corrales para el ganado, y a edificar ciudades para nuestros pequeños. 17Sin embargo, tomaremos las armas y marcharemos al frente de los israelitas hasta llevarlos a su lugar. Mientras tanto, nuestros pequeños vivirán en ciudades fortificadas que los protejan de los habitantes del país. 18No volveremos a nuestras casas hasta que cada uno de los israelitas haya recibido su heredad. 19Nosotros no queremos compartir con ellos ninguna heredad al otro lado del Jordán, porque nuestra heredad está aquí, en el lado oriental del río.

20Moisés les contestó:

—Si están dispuestos a hacerlo así, tomen las armas y marchen al combate. 21Crucen con sus armas el Jordán, y con la ayuda del SEÑOR luchen hasta que él haya quitado del camino a sus enemigos. 22Cuando a su paso el SEÑOR haya sometido la tierra, entonces podrán ustedes regresar a casa, pues habrán cumplido con su deber hacia el SEÑOR y hacia Israel. Y con la aprobación del SEÑOR esta tierra será de ustedes.

23»Pero si se niegan, estarán pecando contra el SEÑOR. Y pueden estar seguros de que no escaparán de su pecado. 24Edifiquen ciudades para sus peque-

---

v **31:52** *ciento noventa kilos.* Lit. *dieciséis mil setecientos cincuenta* *siclos.*

ños, y construyan corrales para su ganado, pero cumplan también lo que han prometido.

25Los gaditas y los rubenitas le dijeron a Moisés:

—Tus siervos harán tal como el Señor lo ha mandado. 26Aquí en las ciudades de Galaad se quedarán nuestros pequeños, y todos nuestros ganados y rebaños, 27pero tus siervos cruzarán con sus armas el Jordán para pelear a la vanguardia del SEÑOR, tal como él lo ha ordenado.

28Así que Moisés dio las siguientes instrucciones al sacerdote Eleazar, y a Josué hijo de Nun y a los jefes de las familias patriarcales de las tribus de Israel:

29—Si los gaditas y los rubenitas, armados para la guerra, cruzan el Jordán con ustedes y conquistan el país, como el SEÑOR quiere, ustedes les entregarán como heredad la tierra de Galaad. 30Pero si no lo cruzan, ellos recibirán su heredad entre ustedes en Canaán.

31Los gaditas y los rubenitas respondieron:

—Tus siervos harán lo que el SEÑOR ha mandado. 32Tal como él lo quiere, cruzaremos armados a la tierra de Canaán. Pero nuestra heredad estará a este lado del Jordán.

33Entonces Moisés entregó a los gaditas y rubenitas, y a la media tribu de Manasés hijo de José, el reino de Sijón, rey de los amorreos, y el reino de Og, rey de Basán. Les entregó la tierra con las ciudades que estaban dentro de sus fronteras, es decir, las ciudades de todo el país.

34Los gaditas edificaron las ciudades de Dibón, Atarot, Aroer, 35Atarot Sofán, Jazer, Yogbea, 36Bet Nimrá y Bet Arán. Las edificaron como ciudades fortificadas, y construyeron corrales para sus rebaños. 37También edificaron las ciudades de Hesbón, Elalé, Quiriatayin, 38Nebo, Baal Megón y Sibma, y les cambiaron de *nombre.

39Los descendientes de Maquir hijo de Manasés fueron a Galaad y la conquistaron, echando de allí a los amorreos que la habitaban. 40Entonces Moisés entregó Galaad a los maquiritas, que eran descendientes de Manasés, y ellos se establecieron allí. 41Yaír hijo de Manasés capturó algunas aldeas y les puso por nombre Javot Yaír. 42Noba capturó Quenat y sus aldeas, y a la región le dio su propio nombre.

Ruta de Israel por el desierto

33 Cuando los israelitas salieron de Egipto bajo la dirección de Moisés y de Aarón, marchaban ordenadamente, como un ejército. 2Por mandato del SEÑOR, Moisés anotaba cada uno de los lugares de donde partían y adonde llegaban. Ésta es la ruta que siguieron:

3El día quince del mes primero, un día después de la Pascua, los israelitas partieron de Ramsés. Marcharon desafiantes a la vista de todos los egipcios, 4mientras éstos sepultaban a sus primogénitos, a quienes el SEÑOR había herido de muerte. El SEÑOR también dictó sentencia contra los dioses egipcios.

5Los israelitas partieron de Ramsés y acamparon en Sucot.

6Partieron de Sucot y acamparon en Etam, en los límites del desierto.

7Partieron de Etam, pero volvieron a Pi Ajirot, al este de Baal Zefón, y acamparon cerca de Migdol.

8Partieron de Pi Ajirot y cruzaron el mar hasta llegar al desierto. Después de andar tres días por el desierto de Etam, acamparon en Mara.

9Partieron de Mara con dirección a Elim, donde había doce fuentes de agua y setenta palmeras, y acamparon allí.

10Partieron de Elim y acamparon cerca del *Mar Rojo.

11Partieron del Mar Rojo y acamparon en el desierto de Sin.

12Partieron del desierto de Sin y acamparon en Dofcá.

13Partieron de Dofcá y acamparon en Alús.

14Partieron de Alús y acamparon en Refidín, donde los israelitas no tenían agua para beber.

15Partieron de Refidín y acamparon en el desierto de Sinaí.

16Partieron del desierto de Sinaí y acamparon en Quibrot Hatavá.

17Partieron de Quibrot Hatavá y acamparon en Jazerot.

18Partieron de Jazerot y acamparon en Ritmá.

19Partieron de Ritmá y acamparon en Rimón Peres.

20Partieron de Rimón Peres y acamparon en Libná.

21Partieron de Libná y acamparon en Risá.

22Partieron de Risá y acamparon en Celata.

23Partieron de Celata y acamparon en el monte Séfer.

24Partieron del monte Séfer y acamparon en Jaradá.

25Partieron de Jaradá y acamparon en Maquelot.

26Partieron de Maquelot y acamparon en Tajat.

27Partieron de Tajat y acamparon en Téraj.

28Partieron de Téraj y acamparon en Mitca.

29Partieron de Mitca y acamparon en Jasmoná.

30Partieron de Jasmoná y acamparon en Moserot.

31Partieron de Moserot y acamparon en Bené Yacán.

32Partieron de Bené Yacán y acamparon en el monte Guidgad.

33Partieron del monte Guidgad y acamparon en Jotbata.

34Partieron de Jotbata y acamparon en Abroná.

35Partieron de Abroná y acamparon en Ezión Guéber.

36Partieron de Ezión Guéber y acamparon en Cades, en el desierto de Zin.

37Partieron de Cades y acamparon en el monte Hor, en la frontera con Edom. 38Al mandato del SEÑOR, el sacerdote Aarón subió al monte Hor, donde murió el día primero del mes quinto, cuarenta años después de que los israelitas habían salido de Egipto. 39Aarón murió en el monte Hor a la edad de ciento veintitrés años.

40El rey cananeo de Arad, que vivía en el Néguev de Canaán, se enteró de que los israelitas se acercaban.

41Partieron del monte Hor y acamparon en Zalmona.

42Partieron de Zalmona y acamparon en Punón.

43Partieron de Punón y acamparon en Obot.

44Partieron de Obot y acamparon en Iyé Abarín, en la frontera con Moab.

45Partieron de Iyé Abarín y acamparon en Dibón Gad.

46Partieron de Dibón Gad y acamparon en Almón Diblatayin.

⁴⁷Partieron de Almón Diblatayin y acamparon en los campos de Abarín, cerca de Nebo.

⁴⁸Partieron de los montes de Abarín y acamparon en las llanuras de Moab, cerca del Jordán, a la altura de Jericó. ⁴⁹Acamparon a lo largo del Jordán, desde Bet Yesimot hasta Abel Sitín, en las llanuras de Moab.

Instrucciones acerca de la tierra prometida

⁵⁰Allí en las llanuras de Moab, cerca del Jordán, a la altura de Jericó, el SEÑOR le dijo a Moisés: ⁵¹«Habla con los israelitas y diles que, una vez que crucen el Jordán y entren en Canaán, ⁵²deberán expulsar del país a todos sus habitantes y destruir a todos los ídolos e imágenes fundidas que ellos tienen. Ordénales que arrasen todos sus santuarios paganos ⁵³y conquisten la tierra y la habiten, porque yo se la he dado a ellos como heredad. ⁵⁴La tierra deberán repartirla por sorteo, según sus clanes. La tribu más numerosa recibirá la heredad más grande, mientras que la tribu menos numerosa recibirá la heredad más pequeña. Todo lo que les toque en el sorteo será de ellos, y recibirán su heredad según sus familias patriarcales.

⁵⁵»Pero si no expulsan a los habitantes de la tierra que ustedes van a poseer, sino que los dejan allí, esa gente les causará problemas, como si tuvieran clavadas astillas en los ojos y espinas en los costados. ⁵⁶Entonces yo haré con ustedes lo que había pensado hacer con ellos.»

Fronteras de Canaán

34 El SEÑOR le dijo a Moisés: ²«Hazles saber a los israelitas que las fronteras de Canaán, la tierra que van a recibir en heredad, serán las siguientes:

³»La frontera sur empezará en el desierto de Zin, en los límites con Edom. Por el este, la frontera sur estará donde termina el Mar Muerto. ⁴A partir de allí, la línea fronteriza avanzará hacia el sur, hacia la cuesta de los Alacranes, cruzará Zin hasta alcanzar Cades Barnea, y llegará hasta Jazar Adar y Asmón. ⁵De allí la frontera se volverá hacia el arroyo de Egipto, para terminar en el mar Mediterráneo.

⁶»La frontera occidental del país será la costa del mar Mediterráneo.

⁷»Para la frontera norte, la línea fronteriza correrá desde el mar Mediterráneo hasta el monte Hor, ⁸y desde el monte Hor hasta Lebó Jamat.ʷ De allí, esta línea seguirá hasta llegar a Zedad, ⁹para continuar hasta Zifrón y terminar en Jazar Enán. Ésta será la frontera norte del país.

¹⁰»Para la frontera oriental, la línea fronteriza correrá desde Jazar Enán hasta Sefán. ¹¹De Sefán bajará a Riblá, que está al este de Ayin; de allí descenderá al este, hasta encontrarse con la ribera del lago Quinéret,ˣ ¹²y de allí la línea bajará por el río Jordán, hasta el Mar Muerto.

»Ésas serán las cuatro fronteras del país.»

¹³Moisés les dio a los israelitas la siguiente orden: «Ésta es la tierra que se repartirá por sorteo. El SEÑOR ha ordenado que sea repartida sólo entre las nueve tribus y media, ¹⁴pues las familias patriarcales de las tribus de Rubén y de Gad, y la media tribu de Manasés, ya recibieron su heredad. ¹⁵Estas dos tribus y media ya tienen su heredad en el este, cerca del río Jordán, a la altura de Jericó, por donde sale el sol.»

Repartición de la tierra

¹⁶El SEÑOR le dijo a Moisés:

¹⁷«Éstos son los nombres de los encargados de repartir la tierra como heredad: el sacerdote Eleazar, y Josué hijo de Nun. ¹⁸Ustedes, por su parte, tomarán a un jefe de cada tribu para que les ayuden a repartir la tierra.»

¹⁹Los nombres de los jefes de tribu fueron los siguientes:

Caleb hijo de Jefone, de la tribu de Judá;
²⁰ Samuel hijo de Amiud, de la tribu de Simeón;
²¹ Elidad hijo de Quislón, de la tribu de Benjamín;
²² Buquí hijo de Joglí, jefe de la tribu de Dan;
²³ Janiel hijo de Efod, jefe de la tribu de Manasés hijo de José;
²⁴ Quemuel hijo de Siftán, jefe de la tribu de Efraín hijo de José;
²⁵ Elizafán hijo de Parnac, jefe de la tribu de Zabulón;
²⁶ Paltiel hijo de Azán, jefe de la tribu de Isacar;
²⁷ Ajiud hijo de Selomí, jefe de la tribu de Aser;
²⁸ Pedael hijo de Amiud, jefe de la tribu de Neftalí.

²⁹A éstos les encargó el SEÑOR repartir la heredad entre los israelitas, en la tierra de Canaán.

Ciudades levíticas

35 En las llanuras de Moab, cerca del Jordán, a la altura de Jericó, el SEÑOR le dijo a Moisés: ²«Ordénales a los israelitas que, de las heredades que reciban, entreguen a los levitas ciudades donde vivir, junto con las tierras que rodean esas ciudades. ³De esta manera los levitas tendrán ciudades donde vivir y tierras de pastoreo para su ganado, rebaños y animales.

⁴»Las tierras de pastoreo que entreguen a los levitas rodearán la ciudad, a quinientos metrosʸ de la muralla. ⁵A partir de los límites de la ciudad, ustedes medirán mil metrosᶻ hacia el este, mil hacia el sur, mil hacia el oeste y mil hacia el norte. La ciudad quedará en el centro. Éstas serán las tierras de pastoreo de sus ciudades.

⁶»De las ciudades que recibirán los levitas, seis serán ciudades de refugio. A ellas podrá huir cualquiera que haya matado a alguien. Además de estas seis ciudades, les entregarán otras cuarenta y dos. ⁷En total, les darán cuarenta y ocho ciudades con sus tierras de pastoreo. ⁸El número de ciudades que los israelitas entreguen a los levitas de la tierra que van a heredar, deberá ser proporcional a la heredad que le corresponda a cada tribu. Es decir, de una tribu numerosa se tomará un número mayor de ciudades, mientras que de una tribu pequeña se tomará un número menor de ciudades.»

Ciudades de refugio

⁹El SEÑOR le ordenó a Moisés ¹⁰que les dijera a los israelitas: «Cuando crucen el Jordán y entren a Canaán, ¹¹escojan ciudades de refugio adonde pueda huir quien inadvertidamente mate a alguien. ¹²Esa persona podrá huir a esas ciudades para protegerse del vengador. Así se evitará que se mate al homicida antes de ser juzgado por la comunidad.

¹³»Seis serán las ciudades que ustedes reservarán como ciudades de refugio. ¹⁴Tres de ellas estarán en el lado este del Jordán, y las otras tres en Canaán. ¹⁵Estas seis ciudades les servirán de refugio a los israelitas y a los extranjeros, sean éstos inmigrantes o residentes. Cualquiera que inadvertidamente dé muerte a alguien, podrá refugiarse en estas ciudades.

ʷ **34:8** *Lebó Jamat*. Alt. *la entrada de Jamat*. ˣ **34:11** *lago Quinéret*. Es decir, lago de Galilea. ʸ **35:4** *quinientos metros*. Lit. *mil *codos*. ᶻ **35:5** *mil metros*. Lit. *dos mil codos*.

16»Si alguien golpea a una persona con un objeto de hierro, y esa persona muere, el agresor es un asesino y será condenado a muerte.

17»Si alguien golpea a una persona con una piedra, y esa persona muere, el agresor es un asesino y será condenado a muerte.

18»Si alguien golpea a una persona con un pedazo de madera, y esa persona muere, el agresor es un asesino y será condenado a muerte. Cuando lo encuentre, lo matará.

20»Si alguien mata a una persona por haberla empujado con malas intenciones, o por haberle lanzado algo intencionalmente, **21**o por haberle dado un puñetazo por enemistad, el agresor es un asesino y será condenado a muerte. Cuando el vengador lo encuentre, lo matará.

22»Pero podría ocurrir que alguien sin querer empuje a una persona, o que sin mala intención le lance algún objeto, **23**o que sin darse cuenta le deje caer una piedra, y que esa persona muera. Como en este caso ellos no eran enemigos, ni hubo intención de hacer daño, **24**será la comunidad la que, de acuerdo con estas leyes, deberá arbitrar entre el acusado y el vengador. **25**La comunidad deberá proteger del vengador al acusado, dejando que el acusado regrese a la ciudad de refugio adonde huyó, y que se quede allí hasta la muerte del sumo sacerdote que fue ungido con el aceite sagrado.

26»Pero si el acusado sale de los límites de la ciudad de refugio adonde huyó, **27**el vengador podrá matarlo, y no será culpable de homicidio si lo encuentra fuera de la ciudad. **28**Así que el acusado debe permanecer en su ciudad de refugio hasta la muerte del sumo sacerdote. Después de eso podrá volver a su heredad.

29»Esta ley regirá siempre sobre todos tus descendientes, dondequiera que vivan.

30»Sólo por el testimonio de varios testigos se le podrá dar muerte a una persona acusada de homicidio. Nadie podrá ser condenado a muerte por el testimonio de un solo testigo.

31»No aceptarás rescate por la *vida de un asesino condenado a muerte. Tendrá que morir.

32»Tampoco aceptarás rescate para permitir que el refugiado regrese a vivir a su tierra antes de la muerte del sumo sacerdote.

33»No profanes la tierra que habitas. El derramamiento de sangre *contamina la tierra, y sólo con la sangre de aquel que la derramó es posible hacer *expiación en favor de la tierra.

34»No profanes la tierra donde vives, y donde yo también vivo, porque yo, el SEÑOR, habito entre los israelitas.»

Herencia de las mujeres

36:1-12 — Nm 27:1-11

36 Los jefes de las familias patriarcales de los clanes de Galaad fueron a hablar con Moisés y con los otros jefes de familias patriarcales israelitas. Galaad era hijo de Maquir y nieto de Manasés, por lo que sus clanes descendían de José. **2**Les dijeron:

—Cuando el SEÑOR te ordenó repartir por sorteo la tierra entre los israelitas, también te ordenó entregar la heredad de nuestro hermano Zelofejad a sus hijas. **3**Ahora bien, si ellas se casan con hombres de otras tribus, su heredad saldrá del círculo de nuestra familia patriarcal y será transferida a la tribu de aquellos con quienes ellas se casen. De este modo perderíamos parte de la heredad que nos tocó por sorteo. **4**Cuando los israelitas celebren el año del jubileo, esa heredad será incorporada a la tribu de sus esposos, y se perderá como propiedad de nuestra familia patriarcal.

5Entonces, por mandato del SEÑOR, Moisés entregó esta ley a los israelitas:

—La tribu de los descendientes de José tiene razón. **6**Respecto a las hijas de Zelofejad, el SEÑOR ordena lo siguiente: Ellas podrán casarse con quien quieran, con tal de que se casen dentro de la tribu de José. **7**Ninguna heredad en Israel podrá pasar de una tribu a otra, porque cada israelita tiene el derecho de conservar la tierra que su tribu heredó de sus antepasados. **8**Toda hija que herede tierras, en cualquiera de las tribus, deberá casarse con alguien que pertenezca a la familia patriarcal de sus antepasados. Así cada israelita podrá conservar la heredad de sus padres. **9**Ninguna heredad podrá pasar de una tribu a otra, porque cada tribu israelita debe conservar la tierra que heredó.

10Las hijas de Zelofejad hicieron lo que el SEÑOR le ordenó a Moisés. **11**Se llamaban Majlá, Tirsá, Joglá, Milca y Noa. Se casaron con sus primos, **12**dentro de los clanes de los descendientes de Manasés hijo de José, de modo que su heredad quedó dentro del clan y de la familia patriarcal de su padre.

13Éstos son los mandamientos y ordenanzas que, por medio de Moisés, dio el SEÑOR a los israelitas en las llanuras de Moab, cerca del Jordán, a la altura de Jericó.

DEUTERONOMIO

Moisés ordena salir de Horeb

1 Éstas son las palabras que Moisés dirigió a todo Israel en el desierto al este del Jordán, es decir, en el Arabá, frente a Suf, entre la ciudad de Parán y las ciudades de Tofel, Labán, Jazerot y Dizahab. 2Por la ruta del monte Seír hay once días de camino entre Horeb y Cades Barnea.

3El día primero del mes undécimo del año cuarenta, Moisés les declaró a los israelitas todo lo que el SEÑOR les había ordenado por medio de él. 4Poco antes, Moisés había derrotado a Sijón, rey de los amorreos, que reinaba en Hesbón, y a Og, rey de Basán, que reinaba en Astarot y en Edrey.

5Moisés comenzó a explicar esta *ley cuando todavía estaban los israelitas en el país de Moab, al este del Jordán. Les dijo:

6«Cuando estábamos en Horeb, el SEÑOR nuestro Dios nos ordenó: "Ustedes han permanecido ya demasiado tiempo en este monte. 7Pónganse en marcha y diríjanse a la región montañosa de los amorreos y a todas las zonas vecinas: el Arabá, las montañas, las llanuras occidentales, el Néguev y la costa, hasta la tierra de los cananeos, el Líbano y el gran río, el Éufrates. 8Yo les he entregado esta tierra; ¡adelante, tomen posesión de ella! El SEÑOR juró que se la daría a los antepasados de ustedes, es decir, a Abraham, Isaac y Jacob, y a sus descendientes.

Nombramiento de jefes

9»En aquel tiempo les dije: "Yo solo no puedo con todos ustedes. 10El SEÑOR su Dios los ha hecho tan numerosos que hoy son ustedes tantos como las estrellas del cielo. 11¡Que el SEÑOR, el Dios de sus antepasados, los multiplique mil veces más, y los bendiga tal como lo prometió! 12¿Cómo puedo seguir ocupándome de todos los problemas, las cargas y los pleitos de ustedes? 13Escojan de cada una de sus tribus a hombres sabios, inteligentes y experimentados, para que sean sus jefes."

14»Ustedes me respondieron: "Tu plan de acción nos parece excelente." 15Así que tomé a los líderes de sus tribus, hombres sabios y experimentados, y les di autoridad sobre ustedes. Los puse como jefes de grupos de mil, de cien, de cincuenta y de diez, y como funcionarios de las tribus. 16Además, en aquel tiempo les di a sus jueces la siguiente orden: "Atiendan todos los litigios entre sus hermanos, y juzguen con imparcialidad, tanto a los israelitas como a los extranjeros. 17No sean parciales en el juicio; consideren de igual manera la causa de los débiles y la de los poderosos. No se dejen intimidar por nadie, porque el juicio es de Dios. Los casos que no sean capaces de resolver, tráiganmelos, que yo los atenderé."

18»Fue en aquel tiempo cuando yo les ordené todo lo que ustedes debían hacer.

Misión de los espías

19»Obedecimos al SEÑOR nuestro Dios y salimos de Horeb rumbo a la región montañosa de los amorreos. Cruzamos todo aquel inmenso y terrible desierto que ustedes han visto, y así llegamos a Cades Barnea. 20Entonces les dije: "Han llegado a la región montañosa de los amorreos, la cual el SEÑOR nuestro Dios nos da. 21Miren, el SEÑOR su Dios les ha entregado la tierra. Vayan y tomen posesión de ella como les dijo el SEÑOR, el Dios de sus antepasados. No tengan miedo ni se desanimen."

22»Pero todos ustedes vinieron a decirme: "Enviemos antes algunos de los nuestros para que exploren la tierra y nos traigan un informe de la ruta que debemos seguir y de las ciudades en las que podremos entrar."

23»Su propuesta me pareció buena, así que escogí a doce de ustedes, uno por cada tribu. 24Los doce salieron en dirección a la región montañosa, y llegaron al valle de Escol y lo exploraron. 25Tomaron consigo algunos de los frutos de la tierra, nos los trajeron y nos informaron lo buena que es la tierra que nos da el SEÑOR nuestro Dios.

Rebelión contra el SEÑOR

26»Sin embargo, ustedes se negaron a subir y se rebelaron contra la orden del SEÑOR su Dios. 27Se pusieron a murmurar en sus carpas y dijeron: "El SEÑOR nos aborrece; nos hizo salir de Egipto para entregarnos a los amorreos y destruirnos. 28¿A dónde iremos? Nuestros hermanos nos han llenado de miedo, pues nos informan que la gente de allá es más fuerte y más alta que nosotros, y que las ciudades son grandes y tienen muros que llegan hasta el cielo. ¡Para colmo, nos dicen que allí vieron *anaquitas!"

29»Entonces les respondí: "No se asusten ni les tengan miedo. 30El SEÑOR su Dios marcha al frente y peleará por ustedes, como vieron que lo hizo en Egipto 31y en el desierto. Por todo el camino que han recorrido, hasta llegar a este lugar, ustedes han visto cómo el SEÑOR su Dios los ha guiado, como lo hace un padre con su hijo."

32»A pesar de eso, ninguno de ustedes confió en el SEÑOR su Dios, 33que se adelantaba a ustedes para buscarles dónde acampar. De noche lo hacía con fuego, para que vieran el camino a seguir, y de día los acompañaba con una nube.

34»Cuando el SEÑOR oyó lo que ustedes dijeron, se enojó e hizo este juramento: 35"Ni un solo *hombre de esta generación perversa verá la buena tierra que juré darles a sus antepasados. 36Sólo la verá Caleb hijo de Jefone. A él y a sus descendientes les daré la tierra que han tocado sus pies, porque fue fiel al SEÑOR."

37»Por causa de ustedes el SEÑOR se enojó también conmigo, y me dijo: "Tampoco tú entrarás en esa tierra. 38Quien sí entrará es tu asistente, Josué hijo de Nun. Infúndele ánimo, pues él hará que Israel posea la tierra. 39En cuanto a sus hijos pequeños, que todavía no saben distinguir entre el bien y el mal, y de quienes ustedes pensaron que servirían de botín, ellos sí entrarán en la tierra y la poseerán, porque yo se la he dado. 40Y ahora, ¡regresen al desierto! Sigan la ruta del *Mar Rojo."

41»Ustedes me respondieron: "Hemos pecado contra el SEÑOR. Pero iremos y pelearemos, como el SEÑOR nuestro Dios nos lo ha ordenado." Así que cada uno de ustedes se equipó para la guerra, pensando que era fácil subir a la región montañosa.

42»Pero el SEÑOR me dijo: "Diles que no suban ni peleen, porque yo no estaré con ellos. Si insisten, los derrotarán sus enemigos."

43»Yo les di la información, pero ustedes no obedecieron. Se rebelaron contra la orden del SEÑOR y temerariamente subieron a la región montañosa. 44Los amorreos que vivían en aquellas montañas les salieron al encuentro y los persiguieron como abejas, y los vencieron por completo desde Seír hasta Jormá. 45Entonces ustedes regresaron y lloraron ante el SEÑOR, pero él no prestó atención a su lamento ni les hizo caso. 46Por eso ustedes tuvieron que permanecer en Cades tanto tiempo.

Peregrinación por el desierto

2 »En seguida nos dirigimos hacia el desierto por la ruta del *Mar Rojo, como el SEÑOR me lo había ordenado. Nos llevó mucho tiempo rodear la región montañosa de Seír. 2Entonces el SEÑOR me dijo: 3"Dejen ya de andar rondando por estas montañas, y diríjanse al norte. 4Dale estas órdenes al pueblo: 'Pronto pasarán ustedes por el territorio de sus hermanos, los descendientes de Esaú, que viven en Seír. Aunque ellos les tienen miedo a ustedes, tengan mucho cuidado; 5no peleen con ellos, porque no les daré a ustedes ninguna porción de su territorio, ni siquiera el lugar donde ustedes planten el pie. A Esaú le he dado por herencia la región montañosa de Seír. 6Páguenles todo el alimento y el agua que ustedes consuman.'"

7»Bien saben que el SEÑOR su Dios los ha bendecido en todo lo que han emprendido, y los ha cuidado por todo este inmenso desierto. Durante estos cuarenta años, el SEÑOR su Dios ha estado con ustedes y no les ha faltado nada.

8»Así que bordeamos el territorio de nuestros hermanos, los descendientes de Esaú, que viven en Seír. Seguimos la ruta del Arabá, que viene desde Elat y Ezión Guéber. Luego dimos vuelta y viajamos por la ruta del desierto de Moab.

9»El SEÑOR también me dijo: "No ataquen a los moabitas, ni los provoquen a la guerra, porque yo les daré a ustedes ninguna porción de su territorio. A los descendientes de Lot les he dado por herencia la región de Ar."»

10Tiempo atrás vivió allí un pueblo fuerte y numeroso, el de los emitas, que eran tan altos como los *anaquitas. 11Tanto a ellos como a los anaquitas se les consideraba gigantes, pero los moabitas los llamaban emitas. 12Antiguamente los horeos vivieron en Seír, pero los descendientes de Esaú los desalojaron, los destruyeron y se establecieron en su lugar, tal como lo hará Israel en la tierra que el SEÑOR le va a dar en posesión.

13«El SEÑOR ordenó: "¡En marcha! ¡Crucen el arroyo Zéred!" Y así lo hicimos. 14Habían pasado treinta y ocho años desde que salimos de Cades Barnea hasta que cruzamos el arroyo Zéred. Para entonces ya había desaparecido del campamento toda la generación de guerreros, tal como el SEÑOR lo había jurado. 15El SEÑOR atacó al campamento hasta que los eliminó por completo.

16»Cuando ya no quedaba entre el pueblo ninguno de aquellos guerreros, 17el SEÑOR me dijo: 18"Hoy van a cruzar la frontera de Moab por la ciudad de Ar. 19Cuando lleguen a la frontera de los amonitas, no los ataquen ni los provoquen a la guerra, porque no les daré a ustedes ninguna porción de su territorio. Esa tierra se la he dado por herencia a los descendientes de Lot." 20Hace mucho tiempo, a esta región se le consideró tierra de gigantes, porque antiguamente ellos vivían allí. Los amonitas los llamaban zamzumitas. 21Eran fuertes y numerosos, y tan altos como los *anaquitas, pero el SEÑOR los destruyó por medio de los amonitas, quienes luego de desalojarlos se establecieron en su lugar. 22Lo mismo hizo el SEÑOR en favor de los descendientes de Esaú, que vivían en Seír, cuando por medio de ellos destruyó a los horeos. A éstos los desalojó para que los descendientes de Esaú se establecieran en su lugar, y hasta el día de hoy residen allí. 23Y en cuanto a los aveos que vivían en las aldeas cercanas a Gaza, los caftoritas procedentes de Creta los destruyeron y se establecieron en su lugar.

Derrota de Sijón, rey de Hesbón

24»Después nos dijo el SEÑOR: "Emprendan de nuevo el viaje y crucen el arroyo Arnón. Yo les entrego a Sijón el amorreo, rey de Hesbón, y su tierra. Láncense a la conquista. Declárenle la guerra. 25Hoy mismo comenzaré a infundir entre todas las naciones que hay debajo del cielo terror y espanto hacia ustedes. Cuando ellas escuchen hablar de ustedes, temblarán y se llenarán de pánico."

26»Desde el desierto de Cademot envié mensajeros a Sijón, rey de Hesbón, con esta oferta de paz: 27"Déjanos pasar por tu país; nos mantendremos en el camino principal, sin desviarnos ni a la derecha ni a la izquierda. 28Te pagaremos todo el alimento y toda el agua que consumamos. Sólo permítenos pasar, 29tal como nos lo permitieron los descendientes de Esaú, que viven en Seír, y los moabitas, que viven en Ar. Necesitamos cruzar el Jordán para entrar en la tierra que nos da el SEÑOR nuestro Dios."

30»Pero Sijón, rey de Hesbón, se negó a dejarnos pasar por allí, porque el SEÑOR nuestro Dios había ofuscado su espíritu y endurecido su *corazón, para hacerlo súbdito nuestro, como lo es hasta hoy. 31Entonces el SEÑOR me dijo: "Ahora mismo voy a entregarles a Sijón y su país. Láncense a conquistarlo, y tomen posesión de su territorio."

32»Cuando Sijón, acompañado de todo su ejército, salió a combatirnos en Yahaza, 33el SEÑOR nuestro Dios nos lo entregó y lo derrotamos, junto con sus hijos y todo su ejército. 34En aquella ocasión conquistamos todas sus ciudades y las *destruimos por completo; matamos a varones, mujeres y niños. ¡Nadie quedó con vida! 35Sólo nos llevamos el ganado y el botín de las ciudades que conquistamos. 36Desde Aroer, que está a la orilla del arroyo Arnón, hasta Galaad, no hubo ciudad que nos ofreciera resistencia; el SEÑOR nuestro Dios nos entregó las ciudades una a una. 37Sin embargo, conforme a la orden del SEÑOR nuestro Dios, no nos acercamos al territorio amonita, es decir, a toda la franja que se extiende a lo largo del arroyo Jaboc, ni a las ciudades de la región montañosa.

Derrota de Og, rey de Basán

3 »Cuando tomamos la ruta hacia Basán, el rey Og, que gobernaba ese país, nos salió al encuentro en Edrey. Iba acompañado de todo su ejército, dispuesto a pelear. 2Pero el SEÑOR me dijo: "No le tengan miedo, porque se lo he entregado a ustedes, con todo su ejército y su territorio. Hagan con él lo que hicieron con Sijón, rey de los amorreos, que reinaba en Hesbón."

3»Y así sucedió. El SEÑOR nuestro Dios también entregó en nuestras manos al rey de Basán y a todo su ejército. Los derrotamos, y nadie vivió para contarlo. 4En aquella ocasión conquistamos todas sus ciudades. Nos apoderamos de las sesenta ciudades que se encontraban en la región de Argob, del reino de Og en Basán. 5Todas esas ciudades estaban fortificadas con altos muros, y con portones y barras, sin contar las muchas aldeas no amuralladas. 6Tal como hicimos con Sijón, rey de Hesbón, *destruimos por completo las ciudades con sus varones, mujeres y niños, 7pero nos quedamos con todo el ganado y el botín de sus ciudades.

8»Fue así como en aquella ocasión nos apoderamos del territorio de esos dos reyes amorreos, es decir, de toda la porción al este del Jordán, desde el arroyo Arnón hasta el monte Hermón, 9al que los sidonios llaman Sirión y los amorreos Senir. 10También nos apoderamos de todas las ciudades de la meseta, todo Galaad y todo Basán, hasta Salcá y Edrey, ciudades del reino de Og en Basán. **11**Por cierto, el rey Og de Basán fue el último de los gigantes. Su cama[a] era de hierro y medía cuatro metros y medio de largo por dos de ancho.[b] Todavía se puede verla en Rabá de los amonitas.

División de la tierra

12»Una vez que nos apoderamos de esa tierra, a los rubenitas y a los gaditas les entregué el territorio que está al norte de Aroer y junto al arroyo Arnón, y también la mitad de la región montañosa de Galaad con sus ciudades. **13**El resto de Galaad y todo el reino de Og, es decir, Basán, se los entregué a la media tribu de Manasés.

»Ahora bien, a toda la región de Argob en Basán se le conoce como tierra de gigantes. **14**Yaír, uno de los descendientes de Manasés, se apoderó de toda la región de Argob hasta la frontera de los guesureos y los macateos, y a esa región de Basán le puso su propio *nombre, llamándola Javot Yaír,[c] nombre que retiene hasta el día de hoy. **15**A Maquir le entregué Galaad, **16**y a los rubenitas y a los gaditas les entregué el territorio que se extiende desde Galaad hasta el centro del arroyo Arnón, y hasta el río Jaboc, que marca la frontera de los amonitas. **17**Su frontera occidental era el Jordán en el Arabá, desde el lago Quinéret[d] hasta el mar del Arabá, que es el Mar Muerto, en las laderas del monte Pisgá.

18»En aquel tiempo les di esta orden: "El SEÑOR su Dios les ha dado posesión de esta tierra. Ustedes, los hombres fuertes y guerreros, pasen al otro lado al frente de sus hermanos israelitas. **19**En las ciudades que les he entregado permanecerán solamente sus mujeres, sus niños y el mucho ganado que yo sé que ustedes tienen. **20**No podrán volver al territorio que les he entregado hasta que el SEÑOR haya dado reposo a sus hermanos, como se lo ha dado a ustedes, y hasta que ellos hayan tomado posesión de la tierra que el SEÑOR su Dios les entregará al otro lado del Jordán."

Instrucciones a Josué

21»En aquel tiempo le ordené a Josué: "Con tus propios ojos has visto todo lo que el SEÑOR, el Dios de ustedes, ha hecho con esos dos reyes. Y lo mismo hará con todos los reinos por donde vas a pasar. **22**No les tengas miedo, que el SEÑOR tu Dios pelea por ti."

Dios le prohíbe a Moisés cruzar el Jordán

23»En aquella ocasión le supliqué al SEÑOR: **24**"Tú, SEÑOR y Dios, has comenzado a mostrarle a tu siervo tu grandeza y tu poder; pues ¿qué dios hay en el cielo o en la tierra capaz de hacer las obras y los prodigios que tú realizas? **25**Déjame pasar y ver la buena tierra al otro lado del Jordán, esa hermosa región montañosa y el Líbano." **26**Pero por causa de ustedes el SEÑOR se enojó conmigo y no me escuchó, sino que me dijo: "¡Basta ya! No me hables más de este asunto. **27**Sube hasta la cumbre del Pisgá y mira al norte, al sur, al este y al oeste. Contempla la tierra con tus propios ojos, porque no vas a cruzar este río Jordán. **28**Dale a Josué las debidas instrucciones; anímalo y fortalécelo, porque será él quien pasará al frente de este pueblo y quien le dará en posesión la tierra que vas a ver."

29»Y permanecimos en el valle, frente a Bet Peor.

Exhortación a la obediencia

4 »Ahora, israelitas, escuchen los preceptos y las normas que les enseñé, para que los pongan en práctica. Así vivirán y podrán entrar a la tierra que el SEÑOR, el Dios de sus antepasados, les da en posesión. **2**No añadan ni quiten palabra alguna a esto que yo les ordeno. Más bien, cumplan los mandamientos del SEÑOR su Dios.

3»Ustedes vieron con sus propios ojos lo que el SEÑOR hizo en Baal Peor, y cómo el SEÑOR su Dios destruyó de entre ustedes a todos los que siguieron al dios de ese lugar. **4**Pero ustedes, los que se mantuvieron fieles al SEÑOR su Dios, todavía están vivos.

5»Miren, yo les he enseñado los preceptos y las normas que me ordenó el SEÑOR mi Dios, para que ustedes los pongan en práctica en la tierra de la que ahora van a tomar posesión. **6**Obedézcanlos y pónganlos en práctica; así demostrarán su sabiduría e inteligencia ante las naciones. Ellas oirán todos estos preceptos, y dirán: "En verdad, éste es un pueblo sabio e inteligente; ¡ésta es una gran nación!" **7**¿Qué otra nación hay tan grande como la nuestra? ¿Qué nación tiene dioses tan cerca de ella como lo está de nosotros el SEÑOR nuestro Dios cada vez que lo invocamos? **8**¿Y qué nación hay tan grande que tenga normas y preceptos tan justos, como toda esta *ley que hoy les expongo?

9»¡Pero tengan cuidado! Presten atención y no olviden las cosas que han visto sus ojos, ni las aparten de su *corazón mientras vivan. Cuéntenselas a sus hijos y a sus nietos. **10**El día que ustedes estuvieron ante el SEÑOR su Dios en Horeb, él me dijo: "Convoca al pueblo para que se presente ante mí y oiga mis palabras, para que aprenda a temerme todo el tiempo que viva en la tierra, y para que enseñe esto mismo a sus hijos." **11**Ustedes se acercaron al pie de la montaña, y allí permanecieron, mientras la montaña ardía en llamas que llegaban hasta el cielo mismo, entre negros nubarrones y densa oscuridad. **12**Entonces el SEÑOR les habló desde el fuego, y ustedes oyeron el sonido de las palabras, pero no vieron forma alguna; sólo se oía una voz. **13**El SEÑOR les dio a conocer su *pacto, los diez mandamientos, los cuales escribió en dos tablas de piedra y les ordenó que los pusieran en práctica. **14**En aquel tiempo el SEÑOR me ordenó que les enseñara los preceptos y las normas que ustedes deberán poner en práctica en la tierra que van a poseer al cruzar el Jordán.

Prohibición de la idolatría

15»El día que el SEÑOR les habló en Horeb, en medio del fuego, ustedes no vieron ninguna figura. Por lo tanto, tengan mucho cuidado **16**de no corromperse haciendo ídolos o figuras que tengan alguna forma o imagen de hombre o de mujer, **17**o imágenes de animales terrestres o de aves que vuelan por el aire, **18**o imágenes de animales que se arrastran por la tierra, o peces que viven en las aguas debajo de la tierra. **19**De lo contrario, cuando levanten los ojos y vean todo el ejército del cielo —es decir, el sol, la luna y las estrellas—, pueden sentirse tentados a postrarse ante ellos y adorarlos. Esos astros los ha designado el SEÑOR, el Dios de ustedes, como dioses de todas las naciones que están debajo del cielo. **20**Pero a ustedes el SEÑOR los tomó y los sacó de Egipto, de ese horno donde se funde el hierro, para que fueran el pueblo de su propiedad, como lo son ahora.

---

a **3:11** *cama. Alt. Sarcófago.*   b **3:11** *cuatro ... ancho.* Lit. *nueve *codos de largo y cuatro codos de ancho según el codo de un hombre.*   c **3:14** *Javot Yaír. Alt. poblados de Yaír.*   d **3:17** *lago Quinéret. Es decir, lago de Galilea.*

21»Sin embargo, por culpa de ustedes el SEÑOR se enojó conmigo y juró que yo no cruzaría el Jordán ni entraría en la buena tierra que el SEÑOR su Dios les da en posesión. 22Yo moriré en esta tierra sin haber cruzado el Jordán, pero ustedes sí lo cruzarán y tomarán posesión de esa buena tierra. 23Tengan, pues, cuidado de no olvidar el *pacto que el SEÑOR su Dios ha hecho con ustedes. No se fabriquen ídolos de ninguna figura que el SEÑOR su Dios les haya prohibido, 24porque el SEÑOR su Dios es fuego consumidor y Dios celoso.

25»Si después de haber tenido hijos y nietos, y de haber vivido en la tierra mucho tiempo, ustedes se corrompen y se fabrican ídolos y toda clase de figuras, haciendo así lo malo ante el SEÑOR su Dios y provocándolo a ira, 26hoy pongo al cielo y a la tierra por testigos contra ustedes, de que muy pronto desaparecerán de la tierra que van a poseer al cruzar el Jordán. No vivirán allí mucho tiempo, sino que serán destruidos por completo. 27El SEÑOR los dispersará entre las naciones, y entre todas ellas sólo quedarán esparcidos unos pocos. 28Allí ustedes adorarán a dioses de madera y de piedra, hechos por *seres humanos: dioses que no pueden ver ni oír, ni comer ni oler.

29»Pero si desde allí buscas al SEÑOR tu Dios con todo tu *corazón y con toda tu alma, lo encontrarás. 30Y al cabo del tiempo, cuando hayas vivido en medio de todas esas angustias y dolores, volverás al SEÑOR tu Dios y escucharás su voz. 31Porque el SEÑOR tu Dios es un Dios compasivo, que no te abandonará ni te destruirá, ni se olvidará del pacto que mediante juramento hizo con tus antepasados.

El SEÑOR es Dios

32»Pregúntales ahora a los tiempos pasados que te precedieron, desde el día que Dios creó al *ser humano en la tierra, e investiga de un extremo a otro del cielo. ¿Ha sucedido algo así de grandioso, o se ha sabido alguna vez de algo semejante? 33¿Qué pueblo ha oído a Diose hablarle en medio del fuego, como lo has oído tú, y ha vivido para contarlo? 34¿Qué dios ha intentado entrar en una nación o tomarla para sí mediante pruebas, señales, milagros, guerras, actos portentosos y gran despliegue de fuerza y de poderf, como lo hizo por ti el SEÑOR tu Dios en Egipto, ante tus propios ojos?

35»A ti se te ha mostrado todo esto para que sepas que el SEÑOR es Dios, y que no hay otro fuera de él. 36Desde el cielo te permitió escuchar su voz, para instruirte. Y en la tierra te permitió ver su gran fuego, desde el cual te habló. 37El SEÑOR amó a tus antepasados y escogió a la descendencia de ellos; por eso te sacó de Egipto con su presencia y gran poder, 38y ante tus propios ojos desalojó a naciones más grandes y más fuertes que tú, para hacerte entrar en su tierra y dártela en posesión, como sucede hoy.

39»Reconoce y considera seriamente hoy que el SEÑOR es Dios arriba en el cielo y abajo en la tierra, y que no hay otro. 40Obedece sus preceptos y normas que hoy te mando cumplir. De este modo a ti y a tus descendientes les irá bien, y permanecerán mucho tiempo en la tierra que el SEÑOR su Dios les da para siempre.»

Ciudades de refugio

41Entonces Moisés reservó tres ciudades al este del Jordán, 42para que en alguna de ellas pudiera re-

fugiarse el que, sin premeditación ni rencor alguno, hubiera matado a su prójimo. De este modo tendría a dónde huir para ponerse a salvo. 43Para los rubenitas designó Béser en el desierto, en la planicie; para los gaditas, Ramot de Galaad; y para los manasesitas, Golán de Basán.

Introducción a la ley

44Ésta es la *ley que Moisés expuso a los israelitas. 45Éstos son los mandatos, preceptos y normas que Moisés les dictó después de que salieron de Egipto, 46cuando todavía estaban al este del Jordán, en el valle cercano a Bet Peor. Era la tierra de Sijón, rey de los amorreos, que vivía en Hesbón y que había sido derrotado por Moisés y los israelitas cuando salieron de Egipto. 47Los israelitas tomaron posesión de su tierra y de la tierra de Og, rey de Basán, es decir, de los dos reyes amorreos cuyos territorios estaban al este del Jordán. 48Este territorio se extendía desde Aroer, a la orilla del arroyo Arnón, hasta el monte Sirión,g es decir, el monte Hermón. 49Incluía además todo el Arabá al este del Jordán, hasta el mar del Arabá, en las laderas del monte Pisgá.

Los Diez Mandamientos
5:6-21 — Éx 20:1-17

5 Moisés convocó a todo Israel y dijo: «Escuchen, israelitas, los preceptos y las normas que yo les comunico hoy. Apréndanselos y procuren ponerlos en práctica. 2El SEÑOR nuestro Dios hizo un *pacto con nosotros en el monte Horeb. 3No fue con nuestros padres con quienes el SEÑOR hizo ese pacto, sino con nosotros, con todos los que hoy estamos vivos aquí. 4Desde el fuego el SEÑOR les habló cara a cara en la montaña. 5En aquel tiempo yo actué como intermediario entre el SEÑOR y ustedes, para declararles la palabra del SEÑOR, porque ustedes tenían miedo del fuego y no subieron a la montaña. El SEÑOR dijo:

6 »Yo soy el SEÑOR tu Dios. Yo te saqué de Egipto, país donde eras esclavo.

7 »No tengas otros dioses además de mí.h

8 »No hagas ningún ídolo ni nada que guarde semejanza con lo que hay arriba en el cielo, ni con lo que hay abajo en la tierra, ni con lo que hay en las aguas debajo de la tierra. 9No te inclines delante de ellos ni los adores. Yo, el SEÑOR tu Dios, soy un Dios celoso. Cuando los padres son malvados y me odian, yo castigo a sus hijos hasta la tercera y cuarta generación. 10Por el contrario, cuando me aman y cumplen mis mandamientos, les muestro mi amor por mil generaciones.

11 »No pronuncies el *nombre del SEÑOR tu Dios a la ligera. Yo, el SEÑOR, no tendré por inocente a quien se atreva a pronunciar mi nombre a la ligera.

12 »Observa el día *sábado, y conságraselo al SEÑOR tu Dios, tal como él te lo ha ordenado. 13Trabaja seis días, y haz en ellos todo lo que tengas que hacer, 14pero observa el séptimo día como día de reposo para honrar al SEÑOR tu Dios. No hagas en ese día ningún trabajo, ni tampoco tu hijo, ni tu hija, ni tu esclavo, ni tu esclava, ni tu buey, ni tu burro, ni ninguno de tus animales, ni tampoco los extranjeros que vivan en tus ciudades. De ese modo podrán

---

e 4:33 *a Dios*. Alt. *a un dios*. f 4:34 *gran despliegue de fuerza y de poder*. Lit. *mano fuerte y brazo extendido*; también en otros pasajes similares. g 4:48 *Sirión* (Siríaca; véase también 3:9); *Sión* (TM).

descansar tu esclavo y tu esclava, lo mismo que tú. 15Recuerda que fuiste esclavo en Egipto, y que el SEÑOR tu Dios te sacó de allí con gran despliegue de fuerza y de poder. Por eso el SEÑOR tu Dios te manda observar el día sábado.

16 »Honra a tu padre y a tu madre, como el SEÑOR tu Dios te lo ha ordenado, para que disfrutes de una larga vida y te vaya bien en la tierra que te da el SEÑOR tu Dios.

17 »No mates.

18 »No cometas adulterio.

19 »No robes.

20 »No des falso testimonio en contra de tu prójimo.

21 »No codicies la esposa de tu prójimo, ni desees su casa, ni su tierra, ni su esclavo, ni su esclava, ni su buey, ni su burro, ni nada que le pertenezca.

22»Éstas son las palabras que el SEÑOR pronunció con voz fuerte desde el fuego, la nube y la densa oscuridad, cuando ustedes estaban reunidos al pie de la montaña. No añadió nada más. Luego las escribió en dos tablas de piedra, y me las entregó.

23»Cuando ustedes oyeron la voz que salía de la oscuridad, mientras la montaña ardía en llamas, todos los jefes de sus tribus y sus *ancianos vinieron a mí 24y me dijeron: "El SEÑOR nuestro Dios nos ha mostrado su gloria y su majestad, y hemos oído su voz que salía del fuego. Hoy hemos visto que un simple *mortal puede seguir con vida aunque Dios hable con él. 25Pero, ¿por qué tenemos que morir? Este gran fuego nos consumirá, y moriremos, si seguimos oyendo la voz del SEÑOR nuestro Dios. 26Pues ¿qué mortal ha oído jamás la voz del Dios viviente hablarle desde el fuego, como la hemos oído nosotros, y ha vivido para contarlo? 27Acércate tú al SEÑOR nuestro Dios, y escucha todo lo que él te diga. Repítenos luego todo lo que te comunique, y nosotros escucharemos y obedeceremos."

28»El SEÑOR escuchó cuando ustedes me hablaban, y me dijo: "He oído lo que este pueblo te dijo. Todo lo que dijeron está bien. 29¡Ojalá su *corazón esté siempre dispuesto a temerme y a cumplir todos mis mandamientos, para que a ellos y a sus hijos siempre les vaya bien!

30» Ve y diles que vuelvan a sus carpas. 31Pero tú quédate aquí conmigo, que voy a darte todos los mandamientos, preceptos y normas que has de enseñarles, para que los pongan en práctica en la tierra que les daré como herencia."

32»Tengan, pues, cuidado de hacer lo que el SEÑOR su Dios les ha mandado; no se desvíen ni a la derecha ni a la izquierda. 33Sigan por el *camino que el SEÑOR su Dios les ha trazado, para que vivan, prosperen y disfruten de larga vida en la tierra que van a poseer.

El amor a Dios

6 »Éstos son los mandamientos, preceptos y normas que el SEÑOR tu Dios mandó que yo te enseñara, para que los pongas en práctica en la tierra de la que vas a tomar posesión, 2para que durante toda tu vida tú y tus hijos y tus nietos honren al SEÑOR tu Dios cumpliendo todos los preceptos y mandamientos que te doy, y para que disfrutes de larga vida. 3Escucha, Israel, y esfuérzate en obedecer. Así te irá bien y serás un pueblo muy numeroso en la tierra

donde abundan la leche y la miel, tal como te lo prometió el SEÑOR, el Dios de tus antepasados.

4»Escucha, Israel: El SEÑOR nuestro Dios es el único SEÑOR.i 5Ama al SEÑOR tu Dios con todo tu *corazón y con toda tu *alma y con todas tus fuerzas. 6Grábate en el corazón estas palabras que hoy te mando. 7Incúlcaselas continuamente a tus hijos. Háblales de ellas cuando estés en tu casa y cuando vayas por el camino, cuando te acuestes y cuando te levantes. 8Átalas a tus manos como un signo; llévalas en tu frente como una marca; 9escríbelas en los postes de tu casa y en los *portones de tus ciudades.

10»El SEÑOR tu Dios te hará entrar en la tierra que les juró a tus antepasados Abraham, Isaac y Jacob. Es una tierra con ciudades grandes y prósperas que tú no edificaste, 11con casas llenas de toda clase de bienes que tú no acumulaste, con cisternas que no cavaste, y con viñas y olivares que no plantaste. Cuando comas de ellas y te sacies, 12cuídate de no olvidarte del SEÑOR, que te sacó de Egipto, la tierra donde viviste en esclavitud.

13»Teme al SEÑOR tu Dios, sírvele solamente a él, y jura sólo en su *nombre. 14No sigas a esos dioses de los pueblos que te rodean, 15pues el SEÑOR tu Dios está contigo y es un Dios celoso; no vaya a ser que su ira se encienda contra ti y te borre de la faz de la tierra.

16»No pongas a prueba al SEÑOR tu Dios, como lo hiciste en Masá. 17Cumple cuidadosamente los mandamientos del SEÑOR tu Dios, y los mandatos y preceptos que te ha dado. 18Haz lo que es recto y bueno a los ojos del SEÑOR, para que te vaya bien y tomes posesión de la buena tierra que el SEÑOR les juró a tus antepasados. 19El SEÑOR arrojará a todos los enemigos que encuentres en tu camino, tal como te lo prometió.

20»En el futuro, cuando tu hijo te pregunte: "¿Qué significan los mandatos, preceptos y normas que el SEÑOR nuestro Dios les mandó?", 21le responderás: "En Egipto nosotros éramos esclavos del faraón, pero el SEÑOR nos sacó de allá con gran despliegue de fuerza. 22Ante nuestros propios ojos, el SEÑOR realizó grandes señales y terribles prodigios en contra de Egipto, del faraón y de toda su familia. 23Y nos sacó de allá para conducirnos a la tierra que a nuestros antepasados había jurado que nos daría. 24El SEÑOR nuestro Dios nos mandó temerle y obedecer estos preceptos, para que siempre nos vaya bien y sigamos con vida. Y así ha sido hasta hoy. 25Y si obedecemos fielmente todos estos mandamientos ante el SEÑOR nuestro Dios, tal como nos lo ha ordenado, entonces seremos justos."

Expulsión de las naciones

7 »El SEÑOR tu Dios te hará entrar en la tierra que vas a poseer, y expulsará de tu presencia a siete naciones más grandes y fuertes que tú, que son los hititas, los gergeseos, los amorreos, los cananeos, los ferezeos, los heveos y los jebuseos. 2Cuando el SEÑOR tu Dios te los haya entregado y tú las hayas derrotado, deberás *destruirlas por completo. No harás ningún pacto con ellas, ni les tendrás compasión. 3Tampoco te unirás en matrimonio con ninguna de esas naciones; no darás tus hijas a sus hijos ni tomarás sus hijas para tus hijos, 4porque ellas los apartarán del Señor y los harán servir a otros dioses. Entonces la ira del SEÑOR se encenderá contra ti y te destruirá de inmediato.

---

h 5:7 además de mí. Lit. junto a mí. i 6:4 el SEÑOR nuestro Dios es el único SEÑOR. Alt. el SEÑOR es nuestro Dios, el SEÑOR es uno.

5»Esto es lo que harás con esas naciones: Destruirás sus altares, romperás sus *piedras sagradas, derribarás sus imágenes de la diosa *Aserá y les prenderás fuego a sus ídolos. 6Porque para el SEÑOR tu Dios tú eres un pueblo *santo; él te eligió para que fueras su posesión exclusiva entre todos los pueblos de la tierra.

7»El SEÑOR se encariñó contigo y te eligió, aunque no eras el pueblo más numeroso sino el más insignificante de todos. 8Lo hizo porque te ama y quería cumplir su juramento a tus antepasados; por eso te rescató del poder del faraón, el rey de Egipto, y te sacó de la esclavitud con gran despliegue de fuerza.

9»Reconoce, por tanto, que el SEÑOR tu Dios es el Dios verdadero, el Dios fiel, que cumple su *pacto generación tras generación, y muestra su fiel amor a quienes lo aman y obedecen sus mandamientos, 10pero que destruye a quienes lo odian y no se tarda en darles su merecido. 11Por eso debes obedecer los mandamientos, los preceptos y las normas que hoy te mando que cumplas.

12»Si prestas atención a estas normas, y las cumples y las obedeces, entonces el SEÑOR tu Dios cumplirá el pacto que bajo juramento hizo con tus antepasados, y te mostrará su amor fiel. 13Te amará, te multiplicará y bendecirá el fruto de tu vientre, y también el fruto de la tierra que juró a tus antepasados que les daría. Es decir, bendecirá el trigo, el vino y el aceite, y las crías de tus ganados y los corderos de tus rebaños. 14Bendito serás, más que cualquier otro pueblo; no habrá entre los tuyos hombre ni mujer estéril, ni habrá un solo animal de tus ganados que se quede sin cría. 15El SEÑOR te mantendrá libre de toda enfermedad y alejará de ti las horribles enfermedades que conociste en Egipto; en cambio, las reservará para tus enemigos. 16Destruye a todos los pueblos que el SEÑOR tu Dios entregue en tus manos. No te apiades de ellos ni sirvas a sus dioses, para que no te sean una trampa mortal.

17»Tal vez te preguntes: "¿Cómo podré expulsar a estas naciones, si son más numerosas que yo?" 18Pero no les temas; recuerda bien lo que el SEÑOR tu Dios hizo contra el faraón y contra todo Egipto. 19Con tus propios ojos viste las grandes pruebas, señales y prodigios milagrosos que con gran despliegue de fuerza y de poder realizó el SEÑOR tu Dios para sacarte de Egipto, y lo mismo hará contra todos los pueblos a quienes ahora temes. 20Además, el SEÑOR tu Dios enviará contra ellos avispas, hasta que hayan perecido todos los sobrevivientes y aun los que intenten esconderse de ti. 21No te asustes ante ellos, pues el SEÑOR tu Dios, el grande y temible, está contigo. 22El SEÑOR tu Dios expulsará a las naciones que te salgan al paso, pero lo hará poco a poco. No las eliminarás a todas de una sola vez, para que los animales salvajes no se multipliquen ni invadan tu territorio. 23El SEÑOR tu Dios entregará a esas naciones en tus manos, y las llenará de gran confusión hasta destruirlas. 24Pondrá a sus reyes bajo tu poder, y de sus *nombres tú borrarás hasta el recuerdo. Ninguna de esas naciones podrá resistir tu presencia, porque tú las destruirás. 25Pero tú deberás quemar en el fuego las esculturas de sus dioses. No codicies la plata y el oro que las recubren, ni caigas en la trampa de quedarte con ellas, pues eso es algo que aborrece el SEÑOR tu Dios. 26No metas en tu casa nada que sea abominable. Todo eso debe ser *destruido. Recházalo y detéstalo por completo, para que no seas destruido tú también.

Recuerda al SEÑOR tu Dios

8 »Cumple fielmente todos los mandamientos que hoy te mando, para que vivas, te multipliques y tomes posesión de la tierra que el SEÑOR juró a tus antepasados. 2Recuerda que durante cuarenta años el SEÑOR tu Dios te llevó por todo el camino del desierto, y te humilló y te puso a prueba para conocer lo que había en tu *corazón y ver si cumplirías o no sus mandamientos. 3Te humilló y te hizo pasar hambre, pero luego te alimentó con maná, comida que ni tú ni tus antepasados habían conocido, con lo que te enseñó que no sólo de pan vive el *hombre, sino de todo lo que sale de la boca del SEÑOR. 4Durante esos cuarenta años no se te gastó la ropa que llevabas puesta, ni se te hincharon los pies. 5Reconoce en tu corazón que, así como un padre *disciplina a su hijo, también el SEÑOR tu Dios te disciplina a ti. 6Cumple los mandamientos del SEÑOR tu Dios; témelo y sigue sus *caminos. 7Porque el SEÑOR tu Dios te conduce a una tierra buena: tierra de arroyos y de fuentes de agua, con manantiales que fluyen en los valles y en las colinas; 8tierra de trigo y de cebada; de viñas, higueras y granados; de miel y de olivares; 9tierra donde no escaseará el pan y donde nada te faltará; tierra donde las rocas son de hierro y de cuyas colinas sacarás cobre.

10»Cuando hayas comido y estés satisfecho, alabarás al SEÑOR tu Dios por la tierra buena que te habrá dado. 11Pero ten cuidado de no olvidar al SEÑOR tu Dios. No dejes de cumplir sus mandamientos, normas y preceptos que yo te mando hoy. 12Y cuando hayas comido y te hayas saciado, cuando hayas edificado casas cómodas y las habites, 13cuando se hayan multiplicado tus ganados y tus rebaños, y hayan aumentado tu plata y tu oro y sean abundantes tus riquezas, 14no te vuelvas orgulloso ni olvides al SEÑOR tu Dios, quien te sacó de Egipto, la tierra donde viviste como esclavo. 15El SEÑOR te guió a través del vasto y horrible desierto, esa tierra reseca y sedienta, llena de serpientes venenosas y escorpiones; te dio el agua que hizo brotar de la más dura *roca; 16en el desierto te alimentó con maná, comida que jamás conocieron tus antepasados. Así te humilló y te puso a prueba, para que al fin de cuentas te fuera bien. 17No se te ocurra pensar: "Esta riqueza es fruto de mi poder y de la fuerza de mis manos." 18Recuerda al SEÑOR tu Dios, porque es él quien te da el poder para producir esa riqueza; así ha confirmado hoy el *pacto que bajo juramento hizo con tus antepasados.

19»Si llegas a olvidar al SEÑOR tu Dios, y sigues a otros dioses para adorarlos e inclinarte ante ellos, testifico hoy en contra tuya que ciertamente serás destruido. 20Si no obedeces al SEÑOR tu Dios, te sucederá lo mismo que a las naciones que el SEÑOR está destruyendo a tu paso.

El mérito no es de Israel

9 »Escucha, Israel: hoy vas a cruzar el Jordán para entrar y desposeer a naciones más grandes y fuertes que tú, que habitan en grandes ciudades con muros que llegan hasta el cielo. 2Esa gente es poderosa y de gran estatura; ¡son los *anaquitas! Tú ya los conoces y sabes que de ellos se dice: "¿Quién puede oponerse a los descendientes de Anac?" 3Pero tú, entiende bien hoy que el SEÑOR tu Dios avanzará al frente de ti, y que los destruirá como un fuego consumidor y los someterá a tu poder. Tú los expulsarás y los aniquilarás en seguida, tal como el SEÑOR te lo ha prometido.

4»Cuando el SEÑOR tu Dios los haya arrojado lejos de ti, no vayas a pensar: "El SEÑOR me ha traído hasta aquí, por mi propia justicia, para tomar posesión de esta tierra." ¡No! El SEÑOR expulsará a esas naciones por la maldad que las caracteriza. 5De modo que no es por tu justicia ni por tu rectitud por lo que vas a tomar posesión de su tierra. ¡No! La propia maldad de esas naciones hará que el SEÑOR tu Dios las arroje lejos de ti. Así cumplirá lo que juró a tus antepasados Abraham, Isaac y Jacob. 6Entiende bien que eres un pueblo terco, y tu justicia y tu rectitud no tienen nada que ver con que el SEÑOR tu Dios te dé en posesión esta buena tierra.

El becerro de oro

7»Recuerda esto, y nunca olvides cómo provocaste la ira del SEÑOR tu Dios en el desierto. Desde el día en que saliste de Egipto hasta tu llegada aquí, has sido rebelde contra él. 8A tal grado provocaste su enojo en Horeb, que estuvo a punto de destruirte. 9Cuando subí a la montaña para recibir las tablas de piedra, es decir, las tablas del *pacto que el SEÑOR había hecho contigo, me quedé en la montaña cuarenta días y cuarenta noches, y no comí pan ni bebí agua. 10Allí el SEÑOR me dio dos tablas de piedra, en las que él mismo escribió todas las palabras que proclamó desde la montaña, de en medio del fuego, el día de la asamblea.

11»Pasados los cuarenta días y las cuarenta noches, el SEÑOR me dio las dos tablas de piedra, es decir, las tablas del pacto, 12y me dijo: "Levántate y baja de aquí en seguida, porque ese pueblo tuyo, que sacaste de Egipto, se ha descarriado. Bien pronto se han apartado del *camino que les mandé seguir, y se han fabricado un ídolo de metal fundido."

13»También me dijo: "He visto a este pueblo, y ¡realmente es un pueblo terco! 14Déjame que lo destruya y borre hasta el recuerdo de su *nombre. De ti, en cambio, haré una nación más fuerte y numerosa que la de ellos."

15»Luego me di vuelta y bajé de la montaña que ardía en llamas. En las manos traía yo las dos tablas del pacto. 16Entonces vi que ustedes habían pecado contra el SEÑOR su Dios, pues se habían fabricado un ídolo fundido con forma de becerro. ¡Bien pronto se habían apartado del camino que el SEÑOR les había trazado! 17Así que tomé las dos tablas que traía en las manos y las arrojé al suelo, haciéndolas pedazos delante de ustedes.

18»Nuevamente me postré delante del SEÑOR cuarenta días y cuarenta noches, y no comí pan ni bebí agua. Lo hice por el gran pecado que ustedes habían cometido al hacer lo malo a los ojos del SEÑOR, provocando así su ira. 19Tuve verdadero miedo del enojo y de la ira del SEÑOR, pues a tal grado se indignó contra ustedes, que quiso destruirlos. Sin embargo, el SEÑOR me escuchó una vez más. 20Así mismo, tan enojado estaba el SEÑOR contra Aarón que quería destruirlo, y también en esa ocasión intercedí por él. 21Luego agarré el becerro que ustedes se fabricaron, ese ídolo que los hizo pecar, y lo quemé en el fuego; lo desmenucé y lo reduje a polvo fino, y arrojé el polvo al arroyo que baja de la montaña.

22»En Taberá, en Masá y en Quibrot Hatavá ustedes provocaron también la indignación del SEÑOR, 23lo mismo que cuando el SEÑOR los envió desde Cades Barnea y les dijo: "Vayan y tomen posesión de la tierra que les he dado." Ustedes se rebelaron contra la orden del SEÑOR su Dios; no confiaron en él ni le obedecieron. 24¡Desde que los conozco han sido rebeldes al SEÑOR!

25»Como el SEÑOR había dicho que los destruiría, yo me quedé postrado ante él esos cuarenta días y cuarenta noches. 26Oré al SEÑOR y le dije: "SEÑOR y Dios, ¡no destruyas tu propia heredad, el pueblo que por tu grandeza redimiste y sacaste de Egipto con gran despliegue de fuerza! 27¡Acuérdate de tus siervos Abraham, Isaac y Jacob! Pasa por alto la terquedad de este pueblo, y su maldad y su pecado, 28no sea que allá, en el país de donde nos sacaste, digan: 'El SEÑOR no pudo llevarlos a la tierra que les había prometido. Y como los aborrecía, los sacó para que murieran en el desierto.' 29Después de todo, ellos son tu propia heredad; son el pueblo que sacaste con gran despliegue de fuerza y de poder."

Las nuevas tablas de la ley

10 »En aquel tiempo el SEÑOR me dijo: "Talla dos tablas de piedra iguales a las primeras, y haz un arca de madera; después de eso, sube a la montaña para que te encuentres conmigo. 2Yo escribiré en esas tablas las mismas palabras que estaban escritas en las primeras, y después las guardarás en el arca."

3»Hice, pues, el arca de madera de acacia, y tallé dos tablas de piedra como las primeras; luego subí a la montaña llevando en las manos las dos tablas. 4En esas tablas, que luego me entregó, el SEÑOR escribió lo mismo que había escrito antes, es decir, los diez mandamientos que les dio a ustedes el día en que estábamos todos reunidos en asamblea, cuando habló desde el fuego en la montaña. 5En seguida bajé de la montaña y guardé las tablas en el arca que había hecho. Y allí permanecen, tal como me lo ordenó el SEÑOR.»

Ministerio de los levitas

6Después los israelitas se trasladaron de los pozos de Berot Bené Yacán a Moserá. Allí murió Aarón y fue sepultado, y su hijo Eleazar lo sucedió en el sacerdocio. 7De allí se fueron a Gudgoda, y siguieron hasta Jotbata, tierra con abundantes corrientes de agua. 8En aquel tiempo el SEÑOR designó a la tribu de Leví para llevar el arca del *pacto y estar en su presencia, y para ministrar y pronunciar bendiciones en su *nombre, como hasta hoy lo hace. 9Por eso los levitas no tienen patrimonio alguno entre sus hermanos, pues el SEÑOR es su herencia, como él mismo lo ha declarado.

Las demandas del SEÑOR

10«Yo me quedé en la montaña cuarenta días y cuarenta noches, como lo hice la primera vez, y también esta vez el SEÑOR me escuchó. Como no era su voluntad destruirlos, 11el SEÑOR me dijo: "Ve y guía al pueblo en su *camino, para que entren y tomen posesión de la tierra que juré a sus antepasados que les daría."

12»Y ahora, Israel, ¿qué te pide el SEÑOR tu Dios? Simplemente que le temas y andes en todos sus caminos, que lo ames y le sirvas con todo tu *corazón y con toda tu *alma, 13y que cumplas los mandamientos y los preceptos que hoy te manda cumplir, para que te vaya bien.

14»Al SEÑOR tu Dios le pertenecen los cielos y lo más alto de los cielos, la tierra y todo lo que hay en ella. 15Sin embargo, él se encariñó con tus antepasados y los amó; y a ti, que eres su descendencia, te eligió de entre todos los pueblos, como lo vemos hoy. 16Por eso, despójate de lo pagano que hay en tu corazón,j y ya no seas terco. 17Porque el SEÑOR tu Dios es

---

j **10:16** *despójate de lo pagano que hay en tu corazón.* Lit. *circuncídate el corazón.*

Dios de dioses y Señor de señores; él es el gran Dios, poderoso y terrible, que no actúa con parcialidad ni acepta sobornos. 18Él defiende la causa del huérfano y de la viuda, y muestra su amor por el extranjero, proveyéndole ropa y alimentos. 19Así mismo debes tú mostrar amor por los extranjeros, porque también tú fuiste extranjero en Egipto. 20Teme al SEÑOR tu Dios y sírvele. Aférrate a él y jura sólo por su *nombre. 21Él es el motivo de tu alabanza; él es tu Dios, el que hizo en tu favor las grandes y maravillosas hazañas que tú mismo presenciaste. 22Setenta eran los antepasados tuyos que bajaron a Egipto, y ahora el SEÑOR tu Dios te ha hecho un pueblo tan numeroso como las estrellas del cielo.

Amor y obediencia al SEÑOR

11 »Amen al SEÑOR su Dios y cumplan siempre sus ordenanzas, preceptos, normas y mandamientos. 2Recuerden hoy que fueron ustedes, y no sus hijos, los que vieron y experimentaron la *disciplina del SEÑOR su Dios. Ustedes vieron su gran despliegue de fuerza y de poder, 3y los hechos y señales que realizó en Egipto contra el faraón y contra todo su país. 4Ustedes vieron lo que hizo contra el ejército de los egipcios, y cómo desató las aguas del *Mar Rojo sobre sus caballos y carros de guerra, cuando éstos los perseguían a ustedes. El SEÑOR los destruyó para siempre.

5»Recuerden también lo que él hizo por ustedes en el desierto, hasta que llegaron a este lugar. 6Además, vieron lo que les hizo a Datán y Abirán, hijos de Eliab el rubenita, pues en presencia de todo el pueblo hizo que la tierra se abriera y se los tragara junto con sus familias, sus carpas y todo lo que les pertenecía. 7Ciertamente ustedes han visto con sus propios ojos todas las maravillas que el SEÑOR ha hecho.

8»Por eso, cumplan todos los mandamientos que hoy les mando, para que sean fuertes y puedan cruzar el Jordán y tomar posesión de la tierra, 9y para que vivan mucho tiempo en esa tierra que el SEÑOR juró dar a los antepasados de ustedes y a sus descendientes, tierra donde abundan la leche y la miel. 10Esa tierra, de la que van a tomar posesión, no es como la de Egipto, de donde salieron; allá ustedes plantaban sus semillas y tenían que regarlask como se riega un huerto. 11En cambio, la tierra que van a poseer es tierra de montañas y de valles, regada por la lluvia del cielo. 12El SEÑOR su Dios es quien la cuida; los ojos del SEÑOR su Dios están sobre ella todo el año, de principio a fin.

13»Si ustedes obedecen fielmente los mandamientos que hoy les doy, y si aman al SEÑOR su Dios y le sirven con todo el *corazón y con toda el *alma, 14entonces él enviarál la lluvia oportuna sobre su tierra, en otoño y en primaveram, para que obtengan el trigo, el vino y el aceite. 15También harán que crezca hierba en los campos para su ganado, y ustedes comerán y quedarán satisfechos.

16»¡Cuidado! No se dejen seducir. No se descarríen ni adoren a otros dioses, ni se inclinen ante ellos, 17porque entonces se encenderá la ira del SEÑOR contra ustedes, y cerrará los cielos para que no llueva; el suelo no dará sus frutos, y pronto ustedes desaparecerán de la buena tierra que les da el SEÑOR. 18Grábense estas palabras en el corazón y en la *mente; átenlas en sus manos como un signo, y llévenlas en su frente como una marca. 19Enséñenselas a sus hijos y repítan-

selas cuando estén en su casa y cuando anden por el camino, cuando se acuesten y cuando se levanten; 20escríbanlas en los postes de su casa y en los *portones de sus ciudades. 21Así, mientras existan los cielos sobre la tierra, ustedes y sus descendientes prolongarán su vida sobre la tierra que el SEÑOR juró a los antepasados de ustedes que les daría.

22»Si ustedes obedecen todos estos mandamientos que les doy, y aman al SEÑOR su Dios, y siguen por todos sus *caminos y le son fieles, 23entonces el SEÑOR expulsará del territorio de ustedes a todas esas naciones. Así podrán desposeerlas, aunque sean más grandes y más fuertes que ustedes. 24Todo lugar donde planten el pie será de ustedes; su territorio se extenderá desde el desierto hasta el monte Líbano, y desde el río Éufrates hasta el mar Mediterráneo. 25Nadie podrá hacerles frente. Por dondequiera que vayan, el SEÑOR su Dios hará que todo el mundo sienta miedo y terror ante ustedes, como se lo ha prometido.

26»Hoy les doy a elegir entre la bendición y la maldición: 27bendición, si obedecen los mandamientos que yo, el SEÑOR su Dios, hoy les mando obedecer; 28maldición, si desobedecen los mandamientos del SEÑOR su Dios y se apartan del camino que hoy les mando seguir, y se van tras dioses extraños que jamás han conocido. 29Cuando el SEÑOR su Dios los haya hecho entrar en la tierra que van a poseer, ustedes bendecirán al monte Guerizín y maldecirán al monte Ebal. 30Esos montes están al otro lado del Jordán, hacia el oeste, en el territorio de los cananeos que viven en el Arabá, en la vecindad de Guilgal, junto a las encinas de Moré.

31»Ustedes están a punto de cruzar el Jordán y entrar a tomar posesión de la tierra que les da el SEÑOR su Dios. Cuando la hayan tomado y ya estén viviendo allí, 32cuiden de obedecer todos los preceptos y las normas que les mando.

El lugar único de adoración

12 »Éstos son los preceptos y las normas que tendrán cuidado de poner en práctica mientras vivan en la tierra que el SEÑOR y Dios de sus antepasados les ha dado en posesión: 2Destruirán por completo todos los lugares donde adoran a sus dioses las naciones que ustedes van a desposeer, es decir, en las montañas, en las colinas y debajo de todo árbol frondoso.

3»Demolerán sus altares, harán pedazos sus *piedras sagradas, les prenderán fuego a sus imágenes de la diosa *Aserá, derribarán sus ídolos y borrarán de esos lugares los *nombres de sus dioses.

4»No harán lo mismo con el SEÑOR su Dios, 5sino que irán y lo buscarán en el lugar donde, de entre todas las tribus de ustedes, él decida habitar. 6Allí llevarán ustedes sus *holocaustos, sacrificios, diezmos, contribuciones, promesas, ofrendas voluntarias, y los primogénitos de sus ganados y rebaños. 7Allí, en la presencia del SEÑOR su Dios, ustedes y sus familias comerán y se regocijarán por los logros de su trabajo, porque el SEÑOR su Dios los habrá bendecido.

8»Ustedes no harán allí lo que ahora hacemos aquí, donde cada uno hace lo que mejor le parece, 9pues todavía no han entrado en el reposo ni en la herencia que les da el SEÑOR su Dios. 10Pero ustedes cruzarán el río Jordán y vivirán en la tierra que el SEÑOR su Dios les da en herencia; él los librará de sus enemigos que los rodean, y ustedes vivirán seguros.

---

k 11:10 tenían que regarlas. Lit. las regabas con tu pie. (Posiblemente se refiere a las ruedas que eran movidas con los pies para sacar el agua.) l 11:14 él enviará (LXX, Pentateuco Samaritano y Vulgata); yo enviaré (TM). m 11:14 en otoño y en primavera. Lit. la temprana y la tardía. n 11:15 hará (Pentateuco Samaritano y mss. de LXX); haré (TM).

11Y al lugar donde el SEÑOR su Dios decida habitar llevarán todo lo que les he ordenado: holocaustos, sacrificios, diezmos, contribuciones, y las ofrendas más selectas que le hayan prometido al SEÑOR. 12Y se regocijarán en la presencia del SEÑOR su Dios, junto con sus hijos e hijas, con sus esclavos y esclavas, y con los levitas que vivan en las ciudades de ustedes, pues ellos no tendrán ninguna posesión ni herencia.

13»Cuando ofrezcas holocaustos, cuídate de no hacerlo en el lugar que te plazca. 14Los ofrecerás sólo en el lugar que el SEÑOR elija en una de tus tribus, y allí harás todo lo que yo te ordeno. 15Sin embargo, siempre que lo desees podrás matar animales y comer su carne en cualquiera de tus ciudades, según el SEÑOR tu Dios te haya bendecido. Podrás comerla, estés o no ritualmente *puro, como si se tratara de carne de gacela o de ciervo. 16Pero no deberás comer la sangre, sino que la derramarás en la tierra como si fuera agua.

17»No podrás comer en tus ciudades el diezmo de tu trigo, de tu vino o de tu aceite, ni los primogénitos de tus ganados y de tus rebaños, ni lo que hayas prometido dar, ni tus ofrendas voluntarias ni tus contribuciones. 18Disfrutarás de ellos en presencia del SEÑOR tu Dios, en el lugar que él elija. Así también lo harán tu hijo y tu hija, tu esclavo y tu esclava, y los levitas que vivan en tus ciudades, y te alegrarás ante el SEÑOR tu Dios por los logros de tu trabajo. 19Cuídate de no abandonar al levita mientras vivas en tu tierra.

20»Cuando el SEÑOR tu Dios haya extendido tu territorio, según te lo ha prometido, y digas: "¡Cómo quisiera comer carne!", podrás comer toda la carne que quieras. 21Si queda demasiado lejos el lugar donde el SEÑOR tu Dios decida habitar, podrás sacrificar animales de tus ganados y rebaños, según mis instrucciones, y comer en tus pueblos todo lo que quieras. 22Come de su carne como si fuera carne de gacela o de ciervo. Estés o no ritualmente puro, podrás comerla. 23Pero asegúrate de no comer la sangre, porque la sangre es la *vida. No debes comer la vida con la carne. 24En lugar de comerla, derrámala en la tierra como si fuera agua. 25No comas la sangre, para que te vaya bien a ti y a tu descendencia, pues estarás haciendo lo recto a los ojos del SEÑOR.

26»Las cosas que hayas consagrado, y las ofrendas que hayas prometido, prepáralas y llévalas al lugar que el SEÑOR habrá de elegir. 27Tanto la carne como la sangre de tus holocaustos las ofrecerás sobre el altar del SEÑOR tu Dios. Derramarás la sangre sobre el altar, pero podrás comer la carne.

28»Ten cuidado de obedecer todos estos mandamientos que yo te he dado, para que siempre te vaya bien, lo mismo que a tu descendencia. Así habrás hecho lo bueno y lo recto a los ojos del SEÑOR tu Dios.

29»Ante tus propios ojos el SEÑOR tu Dios exterminará a las naciones que vas a invadir y desposeer. Cuando las hayas expulsado y te hayas establecido en su tierra, 30después de haberlas destruido cuídate de no seguir su ejemplo y caer en la trampa de inquirir acerca de sus dioses. No preguntes: "¿Cómo adoraban estas naciones a sus dioses, para que yo pueda hacer lo mismo?" 31No adorarás de esa manera al SEÑOR tu Dios, porque al SEÑOR le resulta abominable todo lo que ellos hacen para honrar a sus dioses. ¡Hasta quemaban a sus hijos e hijas en el fuego como sacrificios a sus dioses!

32»Cuídate de poner en práctica todo lo que te ordeno, sin añadir ni quitar nada.

Advertencia contra la idolatría

13 »Cuando en medio de ti aparezca algún profeta o visionario, y anuncie algún prodigio o señal milagrosa, 2si esa señal o prodigio se cumple y él te dice: "Vayamos a rendir culto a otros dioses", dioses que no has conocido, 3no prestes atención a las palabras de ese profeta o visionario. El SEÑOR tu Dios te estará probando para saber si lo amas con todo el *corazón y con toda tu *alma. 4Solamente al SEÑOR tu Dios debes seguir y rendir culto. Cumple sus mandamientos y obedécelo; sírvele y permanece fiel a él. 5Condenarás a muerte a ese profeta o visionario por haberte aconsejado rebelarte contra el SEÑOR tu Dios, que te sacó de Egipto y te rescató de la tierra de esclavitud. Así extirparás el mal que haya en medio de ti, porque tal profeta habrá intentado apartarte del *camino que el SEÑOR tu Dios te mandó que siguieras.

6»Si tu propio hermano, o tu hijo, o tu hija, o tu esposa amada, o tu amigo íntimo, trata de engañarte y en secreto te insinúa: "Vayamos a rendir culto a otros dioses", dioses que ni tú ni tus padres conocieron, 7dioses de pueblos cercanos o lejanos que abarcan toda la tierra, 8no te dejes engañar ni le hagas caso. Tampoco le tengas lástima. No le compadezcas de él ni lo encubras, 9ni dudes en matarlo. Al contrario, sé tú el primero en alzar la mano para matarlo, y que haga lo mismo todo el pueblo. 10Apedréalo hasta que muera, porque trató de apartarte del SEÑOR tu Dios, que te sacó de Egipto, la tierra donde eras esclavo. 11Entonces todos en Israel oirán esto y temblarán de miedo, y nadie intentará otra vez cometer semejante maldad.

12»Si de alguna de las ciudades que el SEÑOR tu Dios te da para que la habites llega el rumor de 13que han surgido hombres perversos que descarrían a la gente y le dicen: "Vayamos a rendir culto a otros dioses", dioses que ustedes no han conocido, 14entonces deberás inquirir e investigar todo con sumo cuidado. Si se comprueba que tal hecho abominable ha ocurrido en medio de ti, 15no dudes en matar a filo de espada a todos los habitantes de esa ciudad. *Destrúyelos junto con todo lo que haya en ella, incluyendo el ganado. 16Lleva todo el botín a la plaza pública, y préndele fuego a la ciudad y a todo el botín. Será una ofrenda totalmente quemada para el SEÑOR tu Dios. La ciudad se quedará para siempre en ruinas, y no volverá a ser reedificada. 17No te apropies de nada que haya sido consagrado a la *destrucción. De ese modo, el SEÑOR alejará de ti el furor de su ira, y te tratará con misericordia y compasión, y hará que te multipliques, tal como se lo juró a tus antepasados. 18Así será, siempre y cuando obedezcas todos estos mandamientos que te ordeno hoy, y hagas lo recto ante el SEÑOR tu Dios.

Alimentos puros e impuros
14:3-20 - Lv 11:1-23

14 »Eres hijo del SEÑOR tu Dios. No te hagas cortes en la piel ni te rapes la cabeza en honor de un muerto, 2porque eres pueblo consagrado al SEÑOR tu Dios. Él te eligió de entre todos los pueblos de la tierra, para que fueras su posesión exclusiva.

3»No comas ningún animal abominable. 4Los que podrás comer son los siguientes: el buey, la oveja, la cabra, 5el ciervo, la gacela, el venado, la cabra montés, el íbice, el antílope y el carnero montés.ñ 6Podrás comer cualquier animal rumiante que tenga

---

ñ 14:5 La identificación de algunas aves y animales de este capítulo no ha podido establecerse con precisión.

la pezuña hendida y partida en dos; 7pero no podrás comer camello, liebre ni tejón porque, aunque rumian, no tienen la pezuña hendida. Los tendrás por animales *impuros.

8»El cerdo es también impuro porque, aunque tiene la pezuña hendida, no rumia. No podrás comer su carne ni tocar su cadáver.

9»De todos los animales que viven en el agua podrás comer los que tienen aletas y escamas, 10pero no podrás comer los que no tienen aletas ni escamas, sino que los tendrás por animales impuros.

11»Podrás comer cualquier ave que sea pura, 12pero no podrás comer águila, quebrantahuesos, azor, 13gallinazo, ni especie alguna de milanos ni de halcones, 14ni especie alguna de cuervos, 15ni avestruz, lechuza o gaviota, ni especie alguna de gavilanes, 16ni búho, ibis, cisne, 17pelícano, buitre, cuervo marino 18o cigüeña, ni especie alguna de garzas, ni abubilla ni murciélago.

19»A los insectos voladores los tendrás por impuros, así que no los comas. 20Pero sí podrás comer cualquier animal alado que sea puro.

21»No comas nada que encuentres ya muerto. Podrás dárselo al extranjero que viva en cualquiera de tus ciudades; él sí podrá comérselo, o vendérselo a un forastero. Pero tú eres un pueblo consagrado al SEÑOR tu Dios.

»No cocines el cabrito en la leche de su madre.o

Los diezmos

22»Cada año, sin falta, apartarás la décima parte de todo lo que produzcan tus campos. 23En la presencia del SEÑOR tu Dios comerás la décima parte de tu trigo, tu vino y tu aceite, y de los primogénitos de tus manadas y rebaños; lo harás en el lugar donde él decida habitar. Así aprenderás a temer siempre al SEÑOR tu Dios. 24Pero si el SEÑOR tu Dios te ha bendecido y el lugar donde ha decidido habitar está demasiado distante, de modo que no puedes transportar tu diezmo hasta allá, 25entonces lo venderás y te presentarás con el dinero en el lugar que el SEÑOR tu Dios haya elegido. 26Con ese dinero podrás comprar lo que prefieras o más te guste: ganado, ovejas, vino u otra bebida fermentada, y allí, en presencia del SEÑOR tu Dios, tú y tu familia comerán y se regocijarán. 27Pero no tengas en cuenta a los levitas que vivan en tus ciudades. Recuerda que, a diferencia de ti, ellos no tienen patrimonio alguno.

28»Cada tres años reunirás los diezmos de todos tus productos de ese año, y los almacenarás en tus ciudades. 29Así los levitas que no tienen patrimonio alguno, y los extranjeros, los huérfanos y las viudas que viven en tus ciudades podrán comer y quedar satisfechos. Entonces el SEÑOR tu Dios bendecirá todo el trabajo de tus manos.

El año del perdón de las deudas

15 »Cada siete años perdonarás toda clase de deudas. 2Lo harás de la siguiente manera: Cada acreedor le perdonará a su prójimo o hermano que le pague la deuda, porque se habrá proclamado el año del perdón de las deudas en honor del SEÑOR. 3Podrás exigirle el pago de sus deudas al forastero, pero a tu hermano le perdonarás cualquier deuda que tenga contigo. 4Entre ustedes no deberá haber pobres, porque el SEÑOR tu Dios te colmará de bendiciones en la tierra que él mismo te da para que la poseas como herencia. 5Y así será,

siempre y cuando obedezcas al SEÑOR tu Dios y cumplas fielmente todos estos mandamientos que hoy te ordeno. 6El SEÑOR tu Dios te bendecirá, como lo ha prometido, y tú podrás darles prestado a muchas naciones, pero no tendrás que pedir prestado de ninguna. Dominarás a muchas naciones, pero ninguna te dominará a ti.

7»Cuando en alguna de las ciudades de la tierra que el SEÑOR tu Dios te da veas a un hermano hebreo pobre, no endurezcas tu *corazón ni le cierres tu mano. 8Antes bien, tiéndele la mano y préstale generosamente lo que necesite. 9No des cabida en tu corazón a la perversa idea de que, por acercarse el año séptimo, año del perdón de las deudas, puedes hacerle mala cara a tu hermano hebreo necesitado y no darle nada. De lo contrario, él podrá apelar al SEÑOR contra ti, y tú resultarás convicto de pecado. 10No seas mezquino sino generoso, y así el SEÑOR tu Dios bendecirá todos tus trabajos y todo lo que emprendas. 11Gente pobre en esta tierra, siempre la habrá; por eso te ordeno que seas generoso con tus hermanos hebreos y con los pobres y necesitados de tu tierra.

Liberación de los esclavos
15:12-18 — Éx 21:2-6

12»Si tu hermano hebreo, hombre o mujer, se vende a ti y te sirve durante seis años, en el séptimo año lo dejarás libre. 13Y cuando lo liberes, no lo despidas con las manos vacías. 14Abastécelo bien con regalos de tus rebaños, de tus cultivos y de tu lagar. Dale según el SEÑOR tu Dios te haya bendecido. 15Recuerda que fuiste esclavo en Egipto, y que el SEÑOR tu Dios te dio libertad. Por eso te doy ahora esta orden.

16»Pero si tu esclavo, porque te ama a ti y a tu familia y le va bien contigo, te dice: "No quiero dejarte", 17entonces tomarás un punzón y, apoyándole la oreja contra una puerta, le perforarás el lóbulo. Así se convertirá en tu esclavo de por vida. Lo mismo harás con la esclava. 18No te pese dejar en libertad a tu esclavo, porque sus servicios durante esos seis años te costaron apenas la mitad de lo que le habrías pagado a un empleado. Así el SEÑOR tu Dios te bendecirá en todo lo que hagas.

Los animales primogénitos

19»Apartarás para el SEÑOR tu Dios todo primogénito macho de tus manadas y rebaños. No pondrás a trabajar al primogénito de tus bueyes, ni esquilarás al primogénito de tus ovejas. 20Cada año, tú y tu familia los comerán en la presencia del SEÑOR tu Dios, en el lugar que él habrá de elegir. 21Si alguno de esos animales está cojo o ciego, o tiene algún otro defecto grave, no se lo presentarás en sacrificio al SEÑOR tu Dios. 22En tal caso, podrás comerlo en tu propia ciudad, como si fuera una gacela o un ciervo, estés o no ritualmente *puro. 23Pero no comerás la sangre, sino que la derramarás en la tierra, como si fuera agua.

Fiesta de la Pascua
16:1-8 — Éx 12:14-20; Lv 23:4-8; Nm 28:16-25

16 »Aparta el mes de *aviv para celebrar la *Pascua del SEÑOR tu Dios, porque fue en una noche del mes de aviv cuando el SEÑOR tu Dios te sacó de Egipto. 2En la Pascua del SEÑOR tu Dios sacrificarás de tus vacas y ovejas, en el lugar donde el SEÑOR decida habitar. 3No comerás la Pascua con

o 14:21 La última prohibición posiblemente alude a alguna práctica supersticiosa de los cananeos.

pan leudado, sino que durante siete días comerás pan sin levadura, pan de aflicción, pues de Egipto saliste de prisa. Lo harás así para que toda tu vida te acuerdes del día en que saliste de Egipto. 4Durante siete días no habrá levadura en todo el país. De la carne que sacrifiques al atardecer del primer día, no quedará nada para la mañana siguiente.

5»No ofrecerás el sacrificio de la Pascua en ninguna de las otras ciudades que te dé el SEÑOR tu Dios. 6Lo ofrecerás solamente en el lugar donde el SEÑOR decida habitar. Allí ofrecerás el sacrificio de la Pascua por la tarde, al ponerse el sol, que fue la hora en que saliste de Egipto. 7Cocerás y comerás el sacrificio de la Pascua en el lugar que el SEÑOR tu Dios haya elegido, y a la mañana siguiente regresarás a tu casa. 8Durante seis días comerás pan sin levadura, y el séptimo día convocarás una asamblea solemne para el SEÑOR tu Dios. Ese día no trabajarás.

Fiesta de las Semanas
16:9-12 — Lv 23:15-22; Nm 28:26-31

9»Contarás siete semanas a partir del día en que comience la cosecha del trigo. 10Entonces celebrarás en honor del SEÑOR tu Dios la fiesta solemne de las Semanas, en la que presentarás ofrendas voluntarias en proporción a las bendiciones que el SEÑOR tu Dios te haya dado. 11Y te alegrarás en presencia del SEÑOR tu Dios en el lugar donde él decida habitar, junto con tus hijos y tus hijas, tus esclavos y tus esclavas, los levitas de tus ciudades, los extranjeros, y los huérfanos y las viudas que vivan en medio de ti. 12Recuerda que fuiste esclavo en Egipto; cumple, pues, fielmente estos preceptos.

Fiesta de las Enramadas
16:13-17 — Lv 23:33-43; Nm 29:12-39

13»Al terminar la vendimia y la cosecha del trigo, celebrarás durante siete días la fiesta de las *Enramadas. 14Te alegrarás en la fiesta junto con tus hijos y tus hijas, tus esclavos y tus esclavas, y los levitas, extranjeros, huérfanos y viudas que vivan en tus ciudades. 15Durante siete días celebrarás esta fiesta en honor al SEÑOR tu Dios, en el lugar que él elija, pues el SEÑOR tu Dios bendecirá toda tu cosecha y todo el trabajo de tus manos. Y tu alegría será completa.

16»Tres veces al año todos tus varones se presentarán ante el SEÑOR tu Dios, en el lugar que él elija, para celebrar las fiestas de los Panes sin levadura, de las Semanas y de las Enramadas. Nadie se presentará ante el SEÑOR con las manos vacías. 17Cada uno llevará ofrendas, según lo haya bendecido el SEÑOR tu Dios.

Impartición de justicia

18»Nombrarás jueces y funcionarios que juzguen con justicia al pueblo, en cada una de las ciudades que el SEÑOR tu Dios entregará a tus tribus. 19No pervertirás la justicia ni actuarás con parcialidad. No aceptarás soborno, pues el soborno nubla los ojos del sabio y tuerce las palabras del justo. 20Seguirás la justicia y solamente la justicia, para que puedas vivir y poseer la tierra que te da el SEÑOR tu Dios.

Exhortación contra la idolatría

21»No levantarás ninguna imagen de la diosa *Aserá junto al altar que edifiques para el SEÑOR tu Dios; 22tampoco erigirás *piedras sagradas, porque el SEÑOR tu Dios las aborrece.

17 »No sacrificarás al SEÑOR tu Dios ninguna oveja ni buey que tenga algún defecto o imperfección, pues eso es abominable para el SEÑOR tu Dios.

2»Puede ser que a algún hombre o mujer entre los tuyos, habitante de una de las ciudades que el SEÑOR tu Dios te dará, se le sorprenda haciendo lo malo a los ojos de Dios. Tal persona habrá violado el *pacto 3y desobedecido mi orden, al adorar a otros dioses e inclinarse ante ellos o ante el sol, la luna o las estrellas del cielo. 4Tan pronto como lo sepas, deberás hacer una investigación escrupulosa. Si resulta verdad y se comprueba que algo tan abominable se ha cometido en Israel, 5llevarás al culpable, sea hombre o mujer, fuera de las *puertas de la ciudad, para que muera apedreado. 6Por el testimonio de dos o tres testigos se podrá condenar a muerte a una persona, pero nunca por el testimonio de uno solo. 7Los primeros en ejecutar el castigo serán los testigos, y luego todo el pueblo. Así extirparás el mal que esté en medio de ti.

Los tribunales

8»Si te enfrentas a casos demasiado difíciles de juzgar, tales como homicidios, pleitos, violencia y otros litigios que surjan en las ciudades, irás al lugar que el SEÑOR tu Dios elija 9y te presentarás ante los sacerdotes levitas y ante el juez en funciones. Los consultarás, y ellos te darán el veredicto. 10Actuarás conforme a la sentencia que ellos dicten en el lugar que el SEÑOR elija, y harás todo lo que te digan. 11Procederás según las instrucciones que te den y el veredicto que pronuncien, y seguirás al pie de la letra todas sus decisiones. 12El soberbio que muestre desacato al juez o al sacerdote en funciones, será condenado a muerte. Así extirparás de Israel el mal. 13Todo el pueblo lo sabrá, y tendrá temor y dejará de ser altivo.

El rey

14»Cuando tomes posesión de la tierra que te da el SEÑOR tu Dios, y te establezcas, si alguna vez dices: "Quiero tener sobre mí un rey que me gobierne, así como lo tienen todas las naciones que me rodean", 15asegúrate de nombrar como rey a uno de tu mismo pueblo, uno que el SEÑOR tu Dios elija. No aceptes como rey a ningún forastero ni extranjero.

16»El rey no deberá adquirir gran cantidad de caballos, ni hacer que el pueblo vuelva a Egipto con el pretexto de aumentar su caballería, pues el SEÑOR se ha dicho: "No vuelvas más por ese camino." 17El rey no tomará para sí muchas mujeres, no sea que se extravíe su *corazón, ni tampoco acumulará enormes cantidades de oro y plata.

18»Cuando el rey tome posesión de su reino, ordenará que le hagan una copia del libro de esta *ley, que está al cuidado de los sacerdotes levitas. 19Esta copia la tendrá siempre a su alcance y la leerá todos los días de su vida. Así aprenderá a temer al SEÑOR su Dios, cumplirá fielmente todas las palabras de esta ley y sus preceptos, 20no se creerá superior a sus hermanos ni se apartará de la ley en el más mínimo detalle, y junto con su descendencia reinará por mucho tiempo sobre Israel.

Ofrendas para los sacerdotes levitas

18 »La tribu de Leví, a la que pertenecen los sacerdotes levitas, no tendrá patrimonio alguno en Israel. Vivirán de las ofrendas presentadas por fuego y de la herencia que corresponde al SEÑOR. 2Los levitas no tendrán herencia entre sus hermanos; el SEÑOR mismo es su herencia, según les prometió.

3»Cuando alguien del pueblo sacrifique un buey o un cordero, los sacerdotes tendrán derecho a la espaldilla, las quijadas y los intestinos. 4También les darás las *primicias de tu trigo, de tu vino y de tu aceite, así como la primera lana que esquiles de tus ovejas. 5Porque el SEÑOR tu Dios los eligió a ellos y a su descendencia, de entre todas tus tribus, para que estuvieran siempre en su presencia, ministrando en su *nombre.

6»Si un levita que viva en alguna de las ciudades de Israel, respondiendo al impulso de su *corazón se traslada al lugar que el SEÑOR haya elegido, 7podrá ministrar en el nombre del SEÑOR su Dios como todos los otros levitas que sirvan allí, en la presencia del SEÑOR. 8Recibirá los mismos beneficios que ellos, además de su patrimonio familiar.

Costumbres abominables

9»Cuando entres en la tierra que te da el SEÑOR tu Dios, no imites las costumbres abominables de esas naciones. 10Nadie entre los tuyos deberá sacrificar a su hijo o hija en el fuego; ni practicar adivinación, brujería o hechicería; 11ni hacer conjuros, servir de médium espiritista o consultar a los muertos. 12Cualquiera que practique estas costumbres se hará abominable al SEÑOR, y por causa de ellas el SEÑOR tu Dios expulsará de tu presencia a esas naciones. 13A los ojos del SEÑOR tu Dios serás irreprensible.

El profeta

14»Las naciones cuyo territorio vas a poseer consultan a hechiceros y adivinos, pero a ti el SEÑOR tu Dios no te ha permitido hacer nada de eso. 15El SEÑOR tu Dios levantará de entre tus hermanos un profeta como yo. A él sólo escucharás. 16Eso fue lo que le pediste al SEÑOR tu Dios en Horeb, el día de la asamblea, cuando dijiste: "No quiero seguir escuchando la voz del SEÑOR mi Dios, ni volver a contemplar este enorme fuego, no sea que muera."

17»Y me dijo el SEÑOR: "Está bien lo que ellos dicen. 18Por eso levantaré entre sus hermanos un profeta como tú; pondré mis palabras en su boca, y él les dirá todo lo que yo le mande. 19Si alguien no presta oído a las palabras que el profeta proclame en mi nombre, yo mismo le pediré cuentas. 20Pero el profeta que se atreva a hablar en mi nombre y diga algo que yo no le haya mandado decir, morirá. La misma suerte correrá el profeta que hable en nombre de otros dioses."

21»Tal vez te preguntes: "¿Cómo podré reconocer un mensaje que no provenga del SEÑOR?" 22Si lo que el profeta proclame en nombre del SEÑOR no se cumple ni se realiza, será señal de que su mensaje no proviene del SEÑOR. Ese profeta habrá hablado con presunción. No le temas.

Las ciudades de refugio

19 »Cuando el SEÑOR tu Dios haya destruido a las naciones cuyo territorio va a entregarte, y tú las hayas expulsado y te hayas establecido en sus ciudades y en sus casas, 2apartarás tres ciudades centrales en la tierra que el SEÑOR tu Dios te da en posesión. 3Dividirás en tres partes la tierra que el SEÑOR tu Dios te da por herencia, y construirás caminos para que cualquiera que haya cometido un homicidio pueda ir a refugiarse en ellas.

4»En cuanto al homicida que llegue allí a refugiarse, sólo se salvará el que haya matado a su prójimo sin premeditación ni rencor alguno. 5Por ejemplo, si un *hombre va con su prójimo al bosque a cortar leña, y al dar el hachazo para cortar un árbol el hierro se desprende y golpea a su prójimo y lo mata, tal hombre podrá refugiarse en una de esas ciudades y ponerse a salvo. 6Es necesario evitar grandes distancias, para que el enfurecido vengador del delito de sangre no le dé alcance y lo mate; aquel hombre no merece la muerte, puesto que mató a su

prójimo sin premeditación. 7Por eso te ordeno apartar tres ciudades.

8»Si el SEÑOR tu Dios extiende tu territorio, como se lo juró a tus antepasados, y te da toda la tierra que te prometió, 9y si tú obedeces todos estos mandamientos que hoy te ordeno, y amas al SEÑOR tu Dios y andas siempre en sus *caminos, entonces apartarás tres ciudades más. 10De este modo no se derramará sangre inocente en la tierra que el SEÑOR tu Dios te da por herencia, y tú no serás culpable de homicidio.

11»Pero si un hombre odia a su prójimo y le prepara una emboscada, y lo asalta y lo mata, y luego busca refugio en una de esas ciudades, 12los *ancianos de su ciudad mandarán arrestarlo y lo entregarán al vengador para que lo mate. 13No le tendrás lástima, porque así evitarás que Israel sea culpable de que se derrame sangre inocente, y a ti te irá bien.

14»Cuando ocupes el territorio que el SEÑOR tu Dios te da como herencia, no reduzcas el límite de la propiedad de tu prójimo, que hace mucho tiempo le fue señalado.

Los testigos requeridos

15»Un solo testigo no bastará para condenar a un hombre acusado de cometer algún crimen o delito. Todo asunto se resolverá mediante el testimonio de dos o tres testigos.

16»Si un testigo falso acusa a alguien de un crimen, 17las dos personas involucradas en la disputa se presentarán ante el SEÑOR, en presencia de los sacerdotes y de los jueces que estén en funciones. 18Los jueces harán una investigación minuciosa, y si comprueban que el testigo miente y que es falsa la declaración que ha dado contra su hermano, 19entonces le harán a él lo mismo que se proponía hacerle a su hermano. Así extirparás el mal que haya en medio de ti. 20Y cuando todos los demás oigan esto, tendrán temor y nunca más se hará semejante maldad en el país. 21No le tengas consideración a nadie. Cobra *vida por vida, ojo por ojo, diente por diente, mano por mano, y pie por pie.

Instrucciones para la guerra

20 »Cuando salgas a pelear contra tus enemigos y veas un ejército superior al tuyo, con muchos caballos y carros de guerra, no les temas, porque el SEÑOR tu Dios, que te sacó de Egipto, estará contigo. 2Cuando estés a punto de entrar en batalla, el sacerdote pasará al frente y exhortará al ejército 3con estas palabras: "¡Escucha, Israel! Hoy vas a entrar en batalla contra tus enemigos. No te desanimes ni tengas miedo; no te acobardes ni te llenes de pavor ante ellos, 4porque el SEÑOR tu Dios está contigo; él peleará en favor tuyo y te dará la *victoria sobre tus enemigos."

5»Luego los oficiales le dirán al ejército: "Si alguno de ustedes ha construido una casa nueva y no la ha estrenado, que vuelva a su casa, no sea que muera en batalla y otro la estrene. 6Y si alguno ha plantado una viña y no ha disfrutado de las uvas, que vuelva a su finca, no sea que muera en batalla y sea otro el que disfrute de ellas. 7Y si alguno se ha comprometido con una mujer y no se ha casado, que regrese a su pueblo, no sea que muera en batalla y sea otro el que se case con ella." 8Y añadirán los oficiales: "Si alguno de ustedes es miedoso o cobarde, que vuelva a su casa, no sea que desanime también a sus hermanos." 9Cuando los oficiales hayan terminado de hablar, nombrarán capitanes que dirijan al ejército.

10»Cuando te acerques a una ciudad para atacarla, hazle primero una oferta de paz. 11Si acepta y abre las *puertas, todos los habitantes de esa ciudad quedarán bajo tu dominio y serán tus esclavos. 12Pero si la ciudad rechaza la paz y entra en batalla contra ti, la sitiarás; 13y cuando el SEÑOR tu Dios la entregue en tus manos, matarás a filo de espada a todos sus hombres. 14Como botín, podrás retener a las mujeres y a los niños, y el ganado y todo lo demás que haya en la ciudad. También podrás comer del botín de tus enemigos, que te entrega el SEÑOR tu Dios. 15Así tratarás a todas las ciudades lejanas que no pertenezcan a las naciones vecinas.

16»Sin embargo, a las ciudades de los pueblos que el SEÑOR tu Dios te da como herencia, no dejarás nada con vida. 17*Exterminarás del todo a hititas, amorreos, cananeos, ferezeos, heveos y jebuseos, tal como el SEÑOR tu Dios te lo ha mandado. 18De lo contrario, ellos te enseñarán a hacer todas las cosas abominables que hacen para adorar a sus dioses, y pecarás contra el SEÑOR tu Dios.

19»Si antes de conquistar una ciudad tienes que sitiarla por mucho tiempo, no derribes sus árboles a golpe de hacha, pues necesitarás alimentarte de sus frutos. No los derribes, pues no son hombres que puedan defenderse de ti sino sólo árboles del campo. 20Sin embargo, podrás derribar los árboles que no sean frutales y construir con ellos instrumentos de asedio contra la ciudad que tengas sitiada, hasta que caiga bajo tu dominio.

Un caso especial de homicidio

21 »Si en algún campo de la tierra que el SEÑOR tu Dios te da en posesión se halla un muerto, y no se sabe quién pudo haberlo matado, 2tus *ancianos y tus jueces irán y medirán la distancia que haya entre el cuerpo y las ciudades vecinas. 3Entonces los ancianos de la ciudad más cercana al muerto tomarán una becerra, a la cual nunca se le haya hecho trabajar ni se le haya puesto el yugo. 4La llevarán a algún valle donde no se haya arado ni plantado, y donde haya un arroyo de aguas continuas, y allí le romperán el cuello. 5Los sacerdotes levitas pasarán al frente para cumplir su tarea, porque el SEÑOR tu Dios los eligió para pronunciar bendiciones en su *nombre, y para ministrar y decidir en todos los casos de disputas y asaltos. 6Luego, todos los ancianos del pueblo más cercano al muerto se lavarán las manos sobre la becerra desnucada, 7y declararán: "No derramaron nuestras manos esta sangre, ni vieron nuestros ojos lo ocurrido. 8Perdona, SEÑOR, a tu pueblo Israel, al cual liberaste, y no lo culpes de esta sangre inocente." 9Así quitarás de en medio de ti la culpa de esa sangre inocente, y habrás hecho lo recto a los ojos del SEÑOR.

El matrimonio con prisioneras de guerra

10»Cuando salgas a la guerra contra tus enemigos, y el SEÑOR tu Dios los entregue en tus manos y los hagas prisioneros, 11si ves entre las cautivas alguna mujer hermosa que te atraiga, podrás tomarla por esposa. 12La llevarás a tu casa y harás que se rape la cabeza, se corte las uñas 13y se deshaga de su ropa de cautiva. Después de que haya vivido en tu casa y guardado luto por su padre y su madre durante todo un mes, podrás unirte a ella y serán marido y mujer. 14Pero si no resulta de tu agrado, la dejarás ir adonde ella lo desee. No deberás venderla ni tratarla como esclava, puesto que la habrás deshonrado.

El derecho del primogénito

15»Tomemos el caso de un hombre que tiene dos esposas, y que ama a una de ellas, pero no a la otra; ambas le dan hijos, y el primogénito es el hijo de la mujer a quien no ama. 16Cuando tal hombre reparta la herencia entre sus hijos, no dará los derechos de primogenitura al hijo de la esposa a quien ama, ni lo preferirá en perjuicio de su verdadero primogénito, es decir, el hijo de la esposa a quien no ama. 17Más bien, reconocerá a éste como el primogénito, y le dará el doble de las posesiones que le correspondan. Ese hijo es el primer fruto de su vigor, y a él le pertenece el derecho de primogenitura.

Un hijo rebelde

18»Si un hombre tiene un hijo obstinado y rebelde, que no escucha a su padre ni a su madre, ni los obedece cuando lo *disciplinan, 19su padre y su madre lo llevarán a la *puerta de la ciudad y lo presentarán ante los *ancianos. 20Y dirán los padres a los ancianos: "Este hijo nuestro es obstinado y rebelde, libertino y borracho. No nos obedece." 21Entonces todos los hombres de la ciudad lo apedrearán hasta matarlo. Así extirparás el mal que haya en medio de ti. Y todos en Israel lo sabrán, y tendrán temor.

Diversas leyes

22»Si alguien, por ser culpable de un delito, es condenado a la horca, 23no dejarás el cuerpo colgado del árbol durante la noche sino que lo sepultarás ese mismo día. Porque cualquiera que es colgado de un árbol está bajo la maldición de Dios. No *contaminarás la tierra que el SEÑOR tu Dios te da como herencia.

22 »Si ves que un buey o una oveja de tu hermano se ha extraviado, no te hagas el desentendido sino llévalo en seguida a su dueño. 2Si el dueño no es tu vecino, o no lo conoces, lleva el animal a tu casa y cuídalo hasta que el dueño te lo reclame; entonces se lo devolverás. 3Lo mismo harás si encuentras un burro, un manto, o cualquier otra cosa que se le haya perdido a tu hermano. No te portes con indiferencia.

4»Si en el camino encuentras caído un burro o un buey que pertenezca a tu hermano, no te hagas el desentendido: ayúdalo a levantarlo.

5»La mujer no se pondrá ropa de hombre, ni el hombre se pondrá ropa de mujer, porque el SEÑOR tu Dios detesta a cualquiera que hace tal cosa.

6»Si en el camino encuentras el nido de un ave en un árbol o en el suelo, y a la madre echada sobre los polluelos o sobre los huevos, no te quedes con la madre y con la cría. 7Quédate con los polluelos, pero deja ir a la madre. Así te irá bien y gozarás de larga vida.

8»Cuando edifiques una casa nueva, construye una baranda alrededor de la azotea, no sea que alguien se caiga de allí y sobre tu familia recaiga la culpa de su muerte.

9»Cuando plantes en tu viña, no mezcles diferentes clases de semilla; si lo haces, tendrás que consagrar a Dios tanto el producto de lo plantado como el fruto total de la viña.

10»No ares con una yunta compuesta de un buey y un burro.

11»No te vistas con ropa de lana mezclada con lino.

12»Pon cuatro borlas en las puntas del manto con que te cubres.

Violación de las reglas matrimoniales

13»Si un hombre se casa, y después de haberse acostado con su esposa le toma aversión, 14y falsamente la difama y la acusa, alegando: "Me casé con esta mujer, pero al tener relaciones con ella descubrí que no era virgen"; 15entonces el padre y la madre de la joven irán a la *puerta de la ciudad y entregarán a los *ancianos pruebas de que ella sí era virgen. 16El padre de la joven dirá a los ancianos: "A este hombre le entregué mi hija en matrimonio, pero él le tomó aversión. 17Ahora la difama y alega haber descubierto que no era virgen. ¡Pero aquí está la prueba de que sí lo era!" Entonces sus padres exhibirán la sábana a la vista de los ancianos del pueblo, 18y ellos tomarán preso al hombre y lo castigarán; 19además, le impondrán una multa de cien monedas de plata por haber difamado a una virgen israelita, y se las darán al padre de la joven. Ella seguirá siendo su esposa y, mientras él viva, no podrá divorciarse de ella.

20»Pero si la acusación es verdadera y no se demuestra la virginidad de la joven, 21la llevarán a la puerta de la casa de su padre, y allí los hombres de la ciudad la apedrearán hasta matarla. Esto le pasará por haber cometido una maldad en Israel y por deshonrar con su mala conducta la casa de su padre. Así extirparás el mal que haya en medio de ti.

22»Si un hombre es sorprendido durmiendo con la esposa de otro, los dos morirán, tanto el hombre que se acostó con ella como la mujer. Así extirparás el mal que haya en medio de Israel.

23»Si en una ciudad se encuentra casualmente un hombre con una joven virgen, ya comprometida para casarse, y se acuesta con ella, 24llevarán a ambos a la puerta de la ciudad y los apedrearán hasta matarlos; a la joven, por no gritar pidiendo ayuda a los de la ciudad, y al hombre, por deshonrar a la prometida de su prójimo. Así extirparás el mal que haya en medio de ti.

25»Pero si un hombre se encuentra en el campo con una joven comprometida para casarse, y la viola, sólo morirá el hombre que forzó a la joven a acostarse con él. 26A ella no le harás nada, pues ella no cometió ningún pecado que merezca la muerte. Este caso es como el de quien ataca y mata a su prójimo: 27el hombre encontró a la joven en el campo y, aunque ella hubiera gritado, no habría habido quien la rescatara.

28»Si un hombre se encuentra casualmente con una joven virgen que no esté comprometida para casarse, y la obliga a acostarse con él, y son sorprendidos, 29el hombre le pagará al padre de la joven cincuenta monedas de plata, y además se casará con la joven por haberla deshonrado. En toda su vida no podrá divorciarse de ella.

30»Ningún hombre tendrá relaciones íntimas con la esposa de su padre, ya que usurpa sus derechos de esposo.

Exclusión de la asamblea

23 »No podrá entrar en la asamblea del SEÑOR ningún hombre que tenga magullados los testículos o mutilado el pene.

2»No podrá entrar en la asamblea del SEÑOR quien haya nacido de una unión ilegítima; tampoco podrá hacerlo ninguno de sus descendientes, hasta la décima generación.

3»No podrán entrar en la asamblea del SEÑOR los amonitas ni los moabitas, ni ninguno de sus descendientes, hasta la décima generación. 4Porque no te ofrecieron pan y agua cuando cruzaste por su territorio, después de haber salido de Egipto. Además, emplearon a Balán hijo de Beor, originario de Petor en Aram Najarayin,p para que te maldijera. 5Sin embargo, por el amor que el SEÑOR tu Dios siente por ti, no quiso el SEÑOR escuchar a Balán, y cambió la maldición en bendición. 6Por eso, a lo largo de toda tu existencia no procurarás ni la *paz ni el bienestar de ellos.

7»No aborrecerás al edomita, pues es tu hermano. Tampoco aborrecerás al egipcio, porque viviste en su país como extranjero. 8La tercera generación de sus descendientes sí podrá estar en la asamblea del SEÑOR.

Higiene en el campamento

9»Cuando tengas que salir en campaña de guerra contra tus enemigos, te mantendrás alejado de *impurezas. 10Si alguno de tus hombres queda impuro por causa de una emisión nocturna, saldrá del campamento y se quedará afuera, 11pero se bañará al atardecer, y al ponerse el sol podrá volver al campamento.

12»Designarás un lugar fuera del campamento donde puedas ir a hacer tus necesidades. 13Como parte de tu equipo tendrás una estaca, con la que cavarás un hueco y, luego de hacer tu necesidad, cubrirás tu excremento. 14Porque el SEÑOR tu Dios anda por tu campamento para protegerte y para entregar a tus enemigos en tus manos. Por eso tu campamento debe ser un lugar *santo; si el Señor ve algo indecente, se apartará de ti.

Leyes misceláneas

15»Si un esclavo huye de su amo y te pide refugio, no se lo entregues a su amo 16sino déjalo que viva en medio de ti, en la ciudad que elija y donde se sienta a gusto. Y no lo oprimas.

17»Ningún hombre o mujer de Israel se dedicará a la prostitución ritual.

18»No lleves a la casa del SEÑOR tu Dios dineros ganados con estas prácticas, ni pagues con esos dineros ninguna ofrenda prometida, porque unos y otros son abominables al SEÑOR tu Dios.

19»No le cobres intereses a tu hermano sobre el dinero, los alimentos, o cualquier otra cosa que gane intereses. 20Cóbrale intereses a un extranjero, pero no a un hermano israelita. Así el SEÑOR tu Dios bendecirá todo el trabajo de tus manos en el territorio del que vas a tomar posesión.

21»Si le haces una promesa al SEÑOR tu Dios, no tardes en cumplirla, porque sin duda él demandará que se la cumplas; si no se la cumples, habrás cometido pecado. 22No serás culpable si evitas hacer una promesa. 23Pero, si por tu propia voluntad le haces una promesa al SEÑOR tu Dios, cumple fielmente lo que le prometiste.

24»Si entras a la viña de tu prójimo, podrás comer todas las uvas que quieras, pero no podrás llevarte nada en tu cesto.

25»Si entras al trigal de tu prójimo, podrás arrancar espigas con las manos pero no cortar el trigo con la hoz.

24 »Si un hombre se casa con una mujer, pero luego deja de quererla por haber encontrado en ella algo indecoroso, sólo podrá despedirla si le entrega un certificado de divorcio. 2Una vez que ella salga de la casa, podrá casarse con otro hombre.

3»Si ocurre que el segundo esposo le toma aversión, y también le extiende un certificado de divorcio y la despide de su casa, o si el segundo esposo muere, 4el primer esposo no podrá casarse con ella de nuevo, pues habrá quedado *impura. Eso sería abominable a los ojos del *SEÑOR.

»No perviertas la tierra que el SEÑOR tu Dios te da como herencia.

5»No envíes a la guerra a ningún hombre recién casado, ni le impongas ningún otro deber. Tendrá li-

p 23:4 Aram Najarayin. Es decir, el noroeste de Mesopotamia.

bre todo un año para atender su casa y hacer feliz a la mujer que tomó por esposa.

6»Si alguien se endeuda contigo, no tomes como prenda su molino de mano ni su piedra de moler, porque sería lo mismo que arrebatarle su propia subsistencia.

7»Si se descubre que alguien ha secuestrado a uno de sus hermanos israelitas, y lo trata como esclavo, o lo vende, el secuestrador morirá. Así extirparás el mal que haya en medio de ti.

8»Cuando se trate de una infección de la piel,q ten mucho cuidado de seguir las instrucciones de los sacerdotes levitas. Sigue al pie de la letra todo lo que te he mandado. 9Recuerda lo que el SEÑOR tu Dios hizo con Miriam mientras andaban peregrinando, después de que el pueblo salió de Egipto.

10»Cuando le hagas un préstamo a tu prójimo, no entres en su casa ni tomes lo que te ofrezca en prenda. 11Quédate afuera y deja que él mismo te entregue la prenda. 12Si es pobre y en prenda te ofrece su manto, no se lo retengas durante la noche. 13Devuélveselo antes de la puesta del sol, para que se cubra con él durante la noche. Así estará él agradecido contigo, y tú habrás actuado con justicia a los ojos del SEÑOR tu Dios.

14»No te aproveches del empleado pobre y necesitado, sea éste un compatriota israelita o un extranjero. 15Le pagarás su jornal cada día, antes de la puesta del sol, porque es pobre y cuenta sólo con ese dinero. De lo contrario, él clamará al SEÑOR contra ti y tú resultarás convicto de pecado.

16»No se dará muerte a los padres por la culpa de sus hijos, ni se dará muerte a los hijos por la culpa de sus padres. Cada uno morirá por su propio pecado.

17»No le niegues sus derechos al extranjero ni al huérfano, ni tomes en prenda el manto de la viuda. 18Recuerda que fuiste esclavo en Egipto, y que el SEÑOR tu Dios te sacó de allí. Por eso te ordeno que actúes con justicia.

19»Cuando recojas la cosecha de tu campo y olvides una gavilla, no vuelvas por ella. Déjala para el extranjero, el huérfano y la viuda. Así el SEÑOR tu Dios bendecirá todo el trabajo de tus manos.

20»Cuando sacudas tus olivos, no rebusques en las ramas; las aceitunas que queden, déjalas para el extranjero, el huérfano y la viuda.

21»Cuando coseches las uvas de tu viña, no repases las ramas; los racimos que queden, déjalos para el inmigrante, el huérfano y la viuda.

22»Recuerda que fuiste esclavo en Egipto. Por eso te ordeno que actúes con justicia.

25 »Cuando dos hombres tengan un pleito, se presentarán ante el tribunal y los jueces decidirán el caso, absolviendo al inocente y condenando al culpable. 2Si el culpable merece que lo azoten, el juez le ordenará tenderse en el suelo y hará que allí mismo le den el número de azotes que su crimen merezca. 3Pero no se le darán más de cuarenta azotes; más de eso sería humillante para tu hermano.

4»No le pongas bozal al buey mientras esté trillando.

5»Si dos hermanos viven en el mismo hogar, y uno muere sin dejar hijos, su viuda no se casará fuera de la familia. El hermano del esposo la tomará y se casará con ella, para cumplir con su deber de cuñado. 6El primer hijo que ella tenga llevará el *nombre del hermano muerto, para que su nombre no desaparezca de Israel.

7»Si tal hombre no quiere casarse con la viuda de su hermano, ella recurrirá a los *ancianos, a la *entrada de la ciudad, y les dirá: "Mi cuñado no quiere mantener vivo en Israel el nombre de su hermano. Se niega a cumplir conmigo su deber de cuñado." 8Entonces los ancianos lo llamarán y le hablarán. Si persiste en decir: "No quiero casarme con ella", 9la cuñada se acercará a él y, en presencia de los ancianos, le quitará una de las sandalias, le escupirá en la cara, y dirá: "Esto es lo que se hace con quien no quiere mantener viva la descendencia de su hermano." 10Y para siempre se conocerá en Israel a ese hombre y a su familia como "los descalzos".

11»Cuando dos hombres se estén peleando y la esposa de uno de ellos venga a rescatar a su esposo de manos de su atacante, si la mujer le hiere los genitales al otro hombre, 12tú le cortarás a ella la mano. No le tendrás compasión.

13»No tendrás en tu bolsa dos pesas diferentes, una más pesada que la otra. 14Tampoco tendrás en tu casa dos medidas diferentes, una más grande que la otra. 15Más bien, tendrás pesas y medidas precisas y justas, para que vivas mucho tiempo en la tierra que te da el SEÑOR tu Dios, 16porque él aborrece a quien comete tales actos de injusticia.

17»Recuerda lo que te hicieron los amalecitas después de que saliste de Egipto: 18cuando estabas cansado y fatigado, salieron a tu encuentro y atacaron por la espalda a todos los rezagados. ¡No tuvieron temor de Dios! 19Por eso, cuando el SEÑOR tu Dios te dé la victoria sobre todas las naciones enemigas que rodean la tierra que él te da como herencia, borrarás para siempre el recuerdo de los descendientes de Amalec. ¡No lo olvides!

Diezmos y primicias

26 »Cuando hayas entrado en la tierra que el SEÑOR tu Dios te da como herencia, y tomes posesión de ella y te establezcas allí, 2tomarás de las *primicias de todo lo que produzca la tierra que el SEÑOR tu Dios te da, y las pondrás en una canasta. Luego irás al lugar donde el SEÑOR tu Dios haya decidido habitar, 3y le dirás al sacerdote que esté oficiando: "Hoy declaro, ante el SEÑOR tu Dios, que he entrado en la tierra que él nos dio, tal como se lo juró a nuestros antepasados."

4»El sacerdote tomará de tus manos la canasta y la pondrá frente al altar del SEÑOR tu Dios. 5Entonces tú declararás ante el SEÑOR tu Dios:

"Mi padre fue un *arameo errante, y descendió a Egipto con poca gente. Vivió allí hasta llegar a ser una gran nación, fuerte y numerosa. 6Pero los egipcios nos maltrataron, nos hicieron sufrir y nos sometieron a trabajos forzados. 7Nosotros clamamos al SEÑOR, el Dios de nuestros padres, y él escuchó nuestro ruego y vio la miseria, el trabajo y la opresión que nos habían impuesto. 8Por eso el SEÑOR nos sacó de Egipto con actos portentosos y gran despliegue de poder, con señales, prodigios y milagros que provocaron gran terror. 9Nos trajo a este lugar, y nos dio esta tierra, donde abundan la leche y la miel. 10Por eso ahora traigo las primicias de la tierra que el SEÑOR tu Dios me ha dado."

»Acto seguido, pondrás la canasta delante del SEÑOR tu Dios, y te postrarás ante él. 11Y tú, los levitas y los extranjeros celebrarán contigo todo lo bueno que el SEÑOR tu Dios te ha dado a ti y a tu familia.

---

q **24:8** *una infección de la piel.* Tradicionalmente *lepra.*

¹²»Cuando ya hayas apartado la décima parte de todos tus productos del tercer año, que es el año del diezmo, se la darás al levita, al extranjero, al huérfano y a la viuda, para que coman y se sacien en tus ciudades. ¹³Entonces le dirás al SEÑOR tu Dios:

"Ya he retirado de mi casa la porción consagrada a ti, y se la he dado al levita, al extranjero, al huérfano y a la viuda, conforme a todo lo que tú me mandaste. No me he apartado de tus mandamientos ni los he olvidado. ¹⁴Mientras estuve de luto, no comí nada de esta porción consagrada; mientras estuve *impuro, no tomé nada de ella ni se la ofrecí a los muertos. SEÑOR mi Dios, yo te he obedecido y he hecho todo lo que me mandaste. ¹⁵Mira desde el cielo, desde el *santo lugar donde resides y, tal como se lo juraste a nuestros antepasados, bendice a tu pueblo Israel y a la tierra que nos has dado, tierra donde abundan la leche y la miel."

Exhortación a seguir los mandamientos del SEÑOR

¹⁶»Hoy el SEÑOR tu Dios te manda obedecer estos preceptos y normas. Pon todo lo que esté de tu parte para practicarlos con entusiasmo. ¹⁷Hoy has declarado que el SEÑOR es tu Dios y que andarás en sus *caminos, que prestarás oído a su voz y que cumplirás sus preceptos, mandamientos y normas. ¹⁸Por su parte, hoy mismo el SEÑOR ha declarado que tú eres su pueblo, tu posesión preciosa, tal como lo prometió. Obedece, pues, todos sus mandamientos. ¹⁹El SEÑOR ha declarado que te pondrá por encima de todas las naciones que ha formado, para que seas alabado y recibas fama y honra. Serás una nación consagrada al SEÑOR tu Dios.»

El altar sobre el monte Ebal

27 Moisés y los *ancianos de Israel le dieron al pueblo esta orden: «Cumple todos estos mandamientos que hoy te entrego. ²Después de cruzar el Jordán y de entrar en la tierra que el SEÑOR tu Dios te da, levantarás unas piedras grandes, las revocarás con cal, ³y escribirás sobre ellas todas las palabras de esta *ley. Esto lo harás después de cruzar el Jordán y de entrar en la tierra que el SEÑOR tu Dios te da, tierra donde abundan la leche y la miel, tal como el SEÑOR tu Dios se lo prometió a tus antepasados. ⁴Cuando hayas cruzado el Jordán, colocarás esas piedras sobre el monte Ebal y las revocarás con cal, tal como te lo ordeno hoy. ⁵Edificarás allí un altar de piedra en honor al SEÑOR tu Dios, pero no con piedras labradas con instrumentos de hierro, sino con piedras enteras, ⁶porque el altar del SEÑOR deberá construirse con piedras del campo. Quemarás sobre él ofrendas al SEÑOR tu Dios; ⁷ofrecerás allí sacrificios de *comunión, y los comerás y te regocijarás en la presencia del SEÑOR tu Dios. ⁸Sobre las piedras de ese altar escribirás claramente todas las palabras de esta ley.»

Maldiciones desde el monte Ebal

⁹Entonces Moisés y los sacerdotes levitas dijeron a todo Israel: «¡Guarda silencio, Israel, y escucha! Hoy te has convertido en el pueblo del SEÑOR tu Dios. ¹⁰Obedece al SEÑOR tu Dios y cumple los mandamientos y preceptos que hoy te mando.»

¹¹Ese mismo día Moisés le ordenó al pueblo:

¹²«Cuando hayan cruzado el Jordán, las siguientes tribus estarán sobre el monte Guerizín para bendecir al pueblo: Simeón, Leví, Judá, Isacar, José y Benjamín.

¹³»Sobre el monte Ebal estarán estas otras, para pronunciar las maldiciones: Rubén, Gad, Aser, Zabulón, Dan y Neftalí.

¹⁴»Los levitas tomarán la palabra, y en voz alta le dirán a todo el pueblo de Israel:

¹⁵"Maldito sea quien haga un ídolo, ya sea tallado en madera o fundido en metal, y lo ponga en un lugar secreto. Es creación de las manos de un artífice, y por lo tanto es detestable al SEÑOR."

Y todo el pueblo dirá: "¡Amén!"

¹⁶"Maldito sea quien deshonre a su padre o a su madre."

Y todo el pueblo dirá: "¡Amén!"

¹⁷"Maldito sea quien altere los límites de la propiedad de su prójimo."

Y todo el pueblo dirá: "¡Amén!"

¹⁸"Maldito sea quien desvíe de su camino a un ciego."

Y todo el pueblo dirá: "¡Amén!"

¹⁹"Maldito sea quien viole los derechos del extranjero, del huérfano o de la viuda."

Y todo el pueblo dirá: "¡Amén!"

²⁰"Maldito sea quien se acueste con la mujer de su padre, pues con tal acción deshonra el lecho de su padre."

Y todo el pueblo dirá: "¡Amén!"

²¹"Maldito sea quien tenga relaciones sexuales con un animal."

Y todo el pueblo dirá: "¡Amén!"

²²"Maldito sea quien se acueste con su hermana, hija de su padre o de su madre."

Y todo el pueblo dirá: "¡Amén!"

²³"Maldito sea quien se acueste con su suegra."

Y todo el pueblo dirá: "¡Amén!"

²⁴"Maldito sea quien mate a traición a su prójimo."

Y todo el pueblo dirá: "¡Amén!"

²⁵"Maldito sea quien acepte soborno para matar al inocente."

Y todo el pueblo dirá: "¡Amén!"

²⁶"Maldito sea quien no practique fielmente las palabras de esta *ley."

Y todo el pueblo dirá: "¡Amén!"

Bendiciones por la obediencia

28 »Si realmente escuchas al SEÑOR tu Dios, y cumples fielmente todos estos mandamientos que hoy te ordeno, el SEÑOR tu Dios te pondrá por encima de todas las naciones de la tierra. ²Si obedeces al SEÑOR tu Dios, todas estas bendiciones vendrán sobre ti y te acompañarán siempre:

³»Bendito serás en la ciudad,
    y bendito en el campo.

⁴»Benditos serán el fruto de tu vientre,
    tus cosechas, las crías de tu ganado,
    los terneritos de tus manadas
    y los corderitos de tus rebaños.

⁵»Benditas serán tu canasta
    y tu mesa de amasar.

⁶»Bendito serás en el hogar,
    y bendito en el camino.ʳ

ʳ **28:6** *en el hogar ... en el camino.* Lit. *en tu entrar ... en tu salir;* también en v. 19.

7»El SEÑOR te concederá la victoria sobre tus enemigos. Avanzarán contra ti en perfecta formación, pero huirán en desbandada.

8»El SEÑOR bendecirá tus graneros, y todo el trabajo de tus manos.

»El SEÑOR tu Dios te bendecirá en la tierra que te ha dado.

9»El SEÑOR te establecerá como su pueblo *santo, conforme a su juramento, si cumples sus mandamientos y andas en sus *caminos. 10Todas las naciones de la tierra te respetarán al reconocerte como el pueblo del SEÑOR.

11»El SEÑOR te concederá abundancia de bienes: multiplicará tus hijos, tu ganado y tus cosechas en la tierra que a tus antepasados juró que te daría.

12»El SEÑOR abrirá los cielos, su generoso tesoro, para derramar a su debido tiempo la lluvia sobre la tierra, y para bendecir todo el trabajo de tus manos. Tú les prestarás a muchas naciones, pero no tomarás prestado de nadie. 13El SEÑOR te pondrá a la cabeza, nunca en la cola. Siempre estarás en la cima, nunca en el fondo, con tal de que prestes atención a los mandamientos del SEÑOR tu Dios que hoy te mando, y los obedezcas con cuidado. 14Jamás te apartes de ninguna de las palabras que hoy te ordeno, para seguir y servir a otros dioses.

Maldiciones por la desobediencia

15»Pero debes saber que, si no obedeces al SEÑOR tu Dios ni cumples fielmente todos sus mandamientos y preceptos que hoy te ordeno, vendrán sobre ti y te alcanzarán todas estas maldiciones:

16»Maldito serás en la ciudad,
    y maldito en el campo.

17»Malditas serán tu canasta
    y tu mesa de amasar.

18»Malditos serán el fruto de tu vientre,
    tus cosechas,
    los terneritos de tus manadas
    y los corderitos de tus rebaños.

19»Maldito serás en el hogar,
    y maldito en el camino.

20»El SEÑOR enviará contra ti maldición, confusión y fracaso en toda la obra de tus manos, hasta que en un abrir y cerrar de ojos quedes arruinado y exterminado por tu mala conducta y por haberme abandonado.

21»El SEÑOR te infestará de plagas, hasta acabar contigo en la tierra de la que vas a tomar posesión. 22El SEÑOR te castigará con epidemias mortales, fiebres malignas e inflamaciones, con calor sofocante y sequía, y con plagas y pestes sobre tus cultivos. Te hostigará hasta que perezcas. 23Sobre tu cabeza, el cielo será como bronce; bajo tus pies, la tierra será como hierro. 24En lugar de lluvia, el SEÑOR enviará sobre tus campos polvo y arena; del cielo lloverá ceniza, hasta que seas aniquilado.

25»El SEÑOR hará que te derroten tus enemigos. Avanzarás contra ellos en perfecta formación, pero huirás en desbandada. ¡Todos los reinos de la tierra te humillarán! 26Tu cadáver servirá de alimento a las aves de los cielos y a las bestias de la tierra, y no habrá quien las espante.

27»El SEÑOR te afligirá con tumores y úlceras, como las de Egipto, y con sarna y comezón, y no podrás sanar.

28»El SEÑOR te hará sufrir de locura, ceguera y delirio. 29En pleno día andarás a tientas, como ciego en la oscuridad. Fracasarás en todo lo que hagas; día tras día serás oprimido; te robarán y no habrá nadie que te socorra. 30Estarás comprometido para casarte, pero otro tomará a tu prometida y la violará. Construirás una casa, y no podrás habitarla. Plantarás una viña, pero no podrás gozar de sus frutos. 31Ante tus propios ojos degollarán a tu buey, y no probarás su carne. Te quitarán tu burro a la fuerza y no te lo devolverán. Tus ovejas pasarán a manos de tus enemigos, y nadie te ayudará a rescatarlas. 32Tus hijos y tus hijas serán entregados a otra nación; te cansarás de buscarlos, y no los podrás encontrar. 33Un pueblo desconocido se comerá los frutos de tu tierra y todo el producto de tu trabajo; para ti sólo habrá opresión y malos tratos cada día. 34Tendrás visiones que te enloquecerán.

35»El SEÑOR te herirá en las rodillas y en las piernas, y con llagas malignas e incurables que te cubrirán todo el cuerpo, desde la planta del pie hasta la coronilla.

36»El SEÑOR hará que tú y el rey que hayas elegido para gobernarte sean deportados a un país que ni tú ni tus antepasados conocieron. Allí adorarás a otros dioses, dioses de madera y de piedra. 37Serás motivo de horror y objeto de burla y de ridículo en todas las naciones a las que el SEÑOR te conduzca.

38»Sembrarás en tus campos mucho, pero cosecharás poco, porque las langostas devorarán tus plantíos. 39Plantarás viñas y las cultivarás, pero no cosecharás las uvas ni beberás el vino, porque los gusanos se comerán tus vides. 40Tendrás olivares por todo tu territorio, pero no te ungirás con su aceite, porque se caerán las aceitunas. 41Tendrás hijos e hijas pero no podrás retenerlos, porque serán llevados al cautiverio. 42Enjambres de langostas devorarán todos tus árboles y las cosechas de tu tierra!

43»Los extranjeros que vivan contigo alcanzarán cada vez más poder sobre ti, mientras que tú te irás hundiendo más y más. 44Ellos serán tus acreedores, y tú serás su deudor. Ellos irán a la cabeza, y tú quedarás rezagado.

45»Todas estas maldiciones caerán sobre ti. Te perseguirán y te alcanzarán hasta destruirte, porque desobedeciste al SEÑOR tu Dios y no cumpliste sus mandamientos y preceptos. 46Ellos serán señal y advertencia permanente para ti y para tus descendientes. 47pues no serviste al SEÑOR tu Dios con gozo y alegría cuando tenías de todo en abundancia. 48Por eso sufrirás hambre y sed, desnudez y pobreza extrema, y serás esclavo de los enemigos que el SEÑOR enviará contra ti. Ellos te pondrán un yugo de hierro sobre el cuello, y te destruirán por completo.

49»El SEÑOR levantará contra ti una nación muy lejana, cuyo idioma no podrás entender; vendrá de los confines de la tierra, veloz como un águila. 50Esta nación tendrá un aspecto feroz y no respetará a los viejos ni se compadecerá de los jóvenes. 51Devorará las crías de tu ganado y las cosechas de tu tierra, hasta aniquilarte. No te dejará trigo, ni mosto ni aceite, ni terneras en las manadas, ni corderos en los rebaños. ¡Te dejará completamente arruinado! 52Te acorralará en todas las ciudades de tu tierra; te sitiará hasta que se derrumben esas murallas fortificadas en las que has confiado. ¡Te asediará en toda la tierra y en las ciudades que el SEÑOR tu Dios te ha dado!

53»Tal será tu sufrimiento durante el sitio de la ciudad, que acabarás comiéndote el fruto de tu vientre, ¡la carne misma de los hijos y las hijas que el SEÑOR tu Dios te ha dado! 54Aun el más tierno y sensible de tus hombres no tendrá compasión de su propio hermano, ni de la esposa que ama, ni de los hijos que todavía le queden, 55a tal grado que no compartirá con ellos nada de la carne de sus hijos que esté comiendo, pues será todo lo que le quede.

»Tal será la angustia que te hará sentir tu enemigo durante el asedio de todas tus ciudades, 56que aun la más tierna y sensible de tus mujeres, tan sensible y tierna que no se atrevería a rozar el suelo con la planta de los pies, no tendrá compasión de su propio esposo al que ama, ni de sus hijos ni de sus hijas. 57No compartirá el hijo que acaba de parir, ni su placenta, sino que se los comerá en secreto, pues será lo único que le quede. ¡Tal será la angustia que te hará sentir tu enemigo durante el asedio de todas tus ciudades!

58»Si no te empeñas en practicar todas las palabras de esta *ley, que están escritas en este libro, ni temes al SEÑOR tu Dios, ¡*nombre glorioso e imponente!, 59el SEÑOR enviará contra ti y contra tus descendientes plagas terribles y persistentes, y enfermedades malignas e incurables. 60Todas las plagas de Egipto, que tanto horror te causaron, vendrán sobre ti y no te darán respiro.

61»El SEÑOR también te enviará, hasta exterminarte, toda clase de enfermedades y desastres no registrados en este libro de la ley. 62Y tú, que como pueblo fuiste tan numeroso como las estrellas del cielo, quedarás reducido a unos cuantos por no haber obedecido al SEÑOR tu Dios. 63Así como al SEÑOR le agradó multiplicarte y hacerte prosperar, también le agradará arruinarte y destruirte. ¡Serás arrancado de raíz, de la misma tierra que ahora vas a poseer!

64»El SEÑOR te dispersará entre todas las naciones, de uno al otro extremo de la tierra. Allí adorarás a otros dioses, dioses de madera y de piedra, que ni tú ni tus antepasados conocieron. 65En esas naciones no hallarás *paz ni descanso. El SEÑOR mantendrá angustiado tu *corazón; tus ojos se cansarán de anhelar, y tu corazón perderá toda esperanza. 66Noche y día vivirás en constante zozobra, lleno de terror y nunca seguro de tu vida. 67Debido a las visiones que tendrás y al terror que se apoderará de ti, dirás en la mañana: "¡Si tan sólo fuera de noche!", y en la noche: "¡Si tan sólo fuera de día!" 68Y aunque el SEÑOR te prometió que jamás volverías por el camino de Egipto, te hará volver en barcos. Allá te ofrecerás a tus enemigos como esclavo, y no habrá nadie que quiera comprarte.»

La renovación del pacto

29 Éstos son los términos del *pacto que, por orden del SEÑOR, hizo Moisés en Moab con los israelitas, además del pacto que ya había hecho con ellos en Horeb. 2Moisés convocó a todos los israelitas y les dijo:

«Ustedes vieron todo lo que el SEÑOR hizo en Egipto con el faraón y sus funcionarios, y con todo su país. 3Con sus propios ojos vieron aquellas grandes pruebas, señales y maravillas. 4Pero hasta este día el SEÑOR no les ha dado *mente para entender, ni ojos para ver, ni oídos para oír. 5Durante los cuarenta años que los guié a través del desierto, no se les desgastó la ropa ni el calzado. 6No comieron pan ni bebieron vino ni ninguna bebida fermentada. Esto lo hice para que supieran que yo soy el SEÑOR su Dios.

7»Cuando llegamos a este lugar, Sijón, rey de Hesbón, y Og, rey de Basán, salieron a pelear contra nosotros, pero los derrotamos. 8Tomamos su territorio y se lo dimos como herencia a los rubenitas, a los gaditas y a la media tribu de Manasés.

9»Ahora, cumplan con cuidado las condiciones de este pacto para que prosperen en todo lo que hagan. 10Hoy están ante la presencia del SEÑOR su Dios

todos ustedes, sus líderes y sus jefes, sus *ancianos y sus oficiales, y todos los hombres de Israel, 11junto con sus hijos y sus esposas, y los extranjeros que viven en sus campamentos, desde dos que cortan la leña hasta los que acarrean el agua. 12Están aquí para hacer un pacto con el SEÑOR su Dios, quien hoy lo establece con ustedes y lo sella con su juramento. 13De esta manera confirma hoy que ustedes son su pueblo, y que él es su Dios, según lo prometió y juró a sus antepasados Abraham, Isaac y Jacob. 14El SEÑOR nuestro Dios afirma que no sólo hace su pacto y su juramento con los que ahora estamos en su presencia, 15sino también con los que todavía no se encuentran entre nosotros.

16»Ustedes saben cómo fue nuestra vida en Egipto, y cómo avanzamos en medio de las naciones que encontramos en nuestro camino hasta aquí. 17Ustedes vieron entre ellos sus detestables imágenes e ídolos de madera y de piedra, de plata y de oro. 18Asegúrense de que ningún hombre ni mujer, ni clan ni tribu entre ustedes, aparte hoy su *corazón del SEÑOR nuestro Dios para ir a adorar a los dioses de esas naciones. Tengan cuidado de que ninguno de ustedes sea como una raíz venenosa y amarga.

19»Si alguno de ustedes, al oír las palabras de este juramento, se cree bueno y piensa: "Todo me saldrá bien, aunque persista yo en hacer lo que me plazca", provocará la ruina de todos. 20El SEÑOR no lo perdonará. La ira y el celo de Dios arderán contra ese hombre. Todas las maldiciones escritas en este libro caerán sobre él, y el SEÑOR hará que desaparezca hasta el último de sus descendientes. 21El SEÑOR lo apartará de todas las tribus de Israel, para su desgracia, conforme a todas las maldiciones del pacto escritas en este libro de la *ley.

22»Sus hijos y las generaciones futuras, y los extranjeros que vengan de países lejanos, verán las calamidades y enfermedades con que el SEÑOR habrá azotado esta tierra. 23Toda ella será un desperdicio ardiente de sal y de azufre, donde nada podrá plantarse, nada germinará, y ni siquiera la hierba crecerá. Será como cuando el SEÑOR destruyó con su furor las ciudades de Sodoma y Gomorra, Admá y Zeboyín. 24Todas las naciones preguntarán: "¿Por qué trató así el SEÑOR a esta tierra? ¿Por qué derramó con tanto ardor su furia sobre ella?" 25Y la respuesta será: "Porque este pueblo abandonó el pacto del Dios de sus padres, pacto que el SEÑOR hizo con ellos cuando los sacó de Egipto. 26Se fueron y adoraron a otros dioses; se inclinaron ante dioses que no conocían, dioses que no tenían por qué adorar. 27Por eso se encendió la ira del SEÑOR contra esta tierra, y derramó sobre ella todas las maldiciones escritas en este libro. 28Y como ahora podemos ver, con mucha furia y enojo el SEÑOR los arrancó de raíz de su tierra, y los arrojó a otro país."

29»Lo secreto le pertenece al SEÑOR nuestro Dios, pero lo revelado nos pertenece a nosotros y a nuestros hijos para siempre, para que obedezcamos todas las palabras de esta ley.

Bendición a causa del arrepentimiento

30 »Cuando recibas todas estas bendiciones o sufras estas maldiciones de las que te he hablado, y las recuerdes en cualquier nación por donde el SEÑOR tu Dios te haya dispersado; 2y cuando tú y tus hijos se vuelvan al SEÑOR tu Dios y le obedezcan con todo el *corazón y con toda el *alma, tal como hoy te lo ordeno, 3entonces el SEÑOR tu Dios restaurará tu buena fortunas y se compadecerá de ti. ¡Vol-

---

s **30:3** *restaurará tu buena fortuna.* Alt. *te hará volver del destierro.*

verá a reunirte de todas las naciones por donde te haya dispersado! 4Aunque te encuentres desterrado en el lugar más distante de la tierra, desde allá el SEÑOR tu Dios te traerá de vuelta, y volverá a reunirte. 5Te hará volver a la tierra que perteneció a tus antepasados, y tomarás posesión de ella. Te hará prosperar, y tendrás más descendientes que los que tuvieron tus antepasados. 6El SEÑOR tu Dios quitará lo pagano que haya en tu corazón¹ y en el de tus descendientes, para que lo ames con todo tu corazón y con toda tu alma, y así tengas vida. 7Además, el SEÑOR tu Dios hará que todas estas maldiciones caigan sobre tus enemigos, los cuales te odian y persiguen. 8Y tú volverás a obedecer al SEÑOR y a cumplir todos sus mandamientos, tal como hoy te lo ordeno. 9Entonces el SEÑOR tu Dios te bendecirá con mucha prosperidad en todo el trabajo de tus manos y en el fruto de tu vientre, en las crías de tu ganado y en las cosechas de tus campos. El SEÑOR se complacerá de nuevo en tu bienestar, así como se deleitó en la prosperidad de tus antepasados, 10siempre y cuando obedezcas al SEÑOR tu Dios y cumplas sus mandamientos y preceptos, escritos en este libro de la *ley, y te vuelvas al SEÑOR tu Dios con todo tu corazón y con toda tu alma.

Elección entre la vida y la muerte

11»Este mandamiento que hoy te ordeno obedecer no es superior a tus fuerzas ni está fuera de tu alcance. 12No está arriba en el cielo, para que preguntes: "¿Quién subirá al cielo por nosotros, para que nos lo traiga, y así podamos escucharlo y obedecerlo?" 13Tampoco está más allá del océano, para que preguntes: "¿Quién cruzará por nosotros hasta el otro lado del océano, para que nos lo traiga, y así podamos escucharlo y obedecerlo?" 14¡No! La palabra está muy cerca de ti; la tienes en la boca y en el *corazón, para que la obedezcas.

15»Hoy te doy a elegir entre la vida y la muerte, entre el bien y el mal. 16Hoy te ordeno que ames al SEÑOR tu Dios, que andes en sus *caminos, y que cumplas sus mandamientos, preceptos y leyes. Así vivirás y te multiplicarás, y el SEÑOR tu Dios te bendecirá en la tierra de la que vas a tomar posesión. 17»Pero si tu corazón se rebela y no obedeces, sino que te desvías para adorar y servir a otros dioses, 18te advierto hoy que serás destruido sin remedio. No vivirás mucho tiempo en el territorio que vas a poseer luego de cruzar el Jordán.

19»Hoy pongo al cielo y a la tierra por testigos contra ti, de que te he dado a elegir entre la vida y la muerte, entre la bendición y la maldición. Elige, pues, la vida, para que vivan tú y tus descendientes. 20Ama al SEÑOR tu Dios, obedécelo y sé fiel a él, porque de él depende tu vida, y por él vivirás mucho tiempo en el territorio que juró dar a tus antepasados Abraham, Isaac y Jacob.»

Josué, sucesor de Moisés

31 De nuevo habló Moisés a todo el pueblo de Israel, y les dijo: 2«Ya tengo ciento veinte años de edad, y no puedo seguir siendo su líder. Además, el SEÑOR me ha dicho que no voy a cruzar el Jordán, 3pues ha ordenado que sea Josué quien lo cruce al frente de ustedes. El SEÑOR su Dios marchará al frente de ustedes para destruir a todas las naciones que encuentren a su paso, y ustedes se apoderarán de su territorio. 4El SEÑOR las arrasará como arrasó a Sijón y a Og, los reyes de los amorreos, junto con sus

países. 5Cuando el SEÑOR los entregue en sus manos, ustedes los tratarán según mis órdenes. 6Sean fuertes y valientes. No teman ni se asusten ante esas naciones, pues el SEÑOR su Dios siempre los acompañará; nunca los dejará ni los abandonará.»

7Llamó entonces Moisés a Josué, y en presencia de todo Israel le dijo: «Sé fuerte y valiente, porque tú entrarás con este pueblo al territorio que el SEÑOR juró darles a sus antepasados. Tú harás que ellos tomen posesión de su herencia. 8El SEÑOR mismo marchará al frente de ti y estará contigo; nunca te dejará ni te abandonará. No temas ni te desanimes.»

La lectura de la ley

9Moisés escribió esta *ley y se la entregó a los sacerdotes levitas que transportaban el arca del *pacto del SEÑOR, y a todos los *ancianos de Israel. 10Luego les ordenó: «Cada siete años, en el año de la cancelación de deudas, durante la fiesta de las *Enramadas, 11cuando tú, Israel, te presentes ante el SEÑOR tu Dios en el lugar que él habrá de elegir, leerás en voz alta esta ley en presencia de todo Israel. 12Reunirás a todos los hombres, mujeres y niños de tu pueblo, y a los extranjeros que vivan en tus ciudades, para que escuchen y aprendan a temer al SEÑOR tu Dios, y obedezcan fielmente todas las palabras de esta ley. 13Y los descendientes de ellos, para quienes esta ley será desconocida, la oirán y aprenderán a temer al SEÑOR tu Dios mientras vivan en el territorio que vas a poseer al otro lado del Jordán.»

Predicción de la rebeldía de Israel

14El SEÑOR le dijo a Moisés: «Ya se acerca el día de tu muerte. Llama a Josué, y preséntate con él en la *Tienda de reunión para que reciba mis órdenes.»

Fue así como Moisés y Josué se presentaron allí. 15Entonces el SEÑOR se apareció a la entrada de la Tienda de reunión, en una columna de nube, 16y le dijo a Moisés: «Tú irás a descansar con tus antepasados, y muy pronto esta gente me será infiel con los dioses extraños del territorio al que van a entrar. Me rechazarán y quebrantarán el *pacto que hice con ellos. 17Cuando esto haya sucedido, se encenderá mi ira contra ellos y los abandonaré; ocultaré mi rostro, y serán presa fácil. Entonces les sobrevendrán muchos desastres y adversidades, y se preguntarán: "¿No es verdad que todos estos desastres nos han sobrevenido porque nuestro Dios ya no está con nosotros?" 18Y ese día yo ocultaré aún más mi rostro, por haber cometido la maldad de irse tras otros dioses.

19»Escriban, pues, este cántico, y enséñenselo al pueblo para que lo cante y sirva también de testimonio contra ellos.

20»Cuando yo conduzca a los israelitas a la tierra que juré darles a sus antepasados, tierra donde abundan la leche y la miel, comerán hasta saciarse y engordarán; se irán tras otros dioses y los adorarán, despreciándome y quebrantando mi pacto. 21Y cuando les sobrevengan muchos desastres y adversidades, este cántico servirá de testimonio contra ellos, porque sus descendientes lo recordarán y lo cantarán. Yo sé lo que mi pueblo piensa hacer, aun antes de introducirlo en el territorio que juré darle.»

22Entonces Moisés escribió ese cántico aquel día, y se lo enseñó a los israelitas. 23Y el SEÑOR le dio a Josué hijo de Nun esta orden: «Esfuérzate y sé valiente, porque tú conducirás a los israelitas al territorio que juré darles, y yo mismo estaré contigo.»

---

† 30:6 quitará lo pagano que haya en tu corazón. Lit. circuncidará tu corazón.

²⁴Moisés terminó de escribir en un libro todas las palabras de esta *ley. ²⁵Luego dio esta orden a los levitas que transportaban el arca del pacto del SEÑOR: ²⁶«Tomen este libro de la ley, y pónganlo junto al arca del pacto del SEÑOR su Dios. Allí permanecerá como testigo contra ustedes los israelitas, ²⁷pues sé cuán tercos y rebeldes son. Si fueron rebeldes contra el SEÑOR mientras viví con ustedes, ¡cuánto más lo serán después de mi muerte! ²⁸Reúnan ante mí a todos los *ancianos y los líderes de sus tribus, para que yo pueda comunicarles estas palabras y las escuchen claramente. Pongo al cielo y a la tierra por testigos contra ustedes, ²⁹porque sé que después de mi muerte se pervertirán y se apartarán del *camino que les he mostrado. En días venideros les sobrevendrán calamidades, porque harán lo malo a los ojos del SEÑOR y con sus detestables actos provocarán su ira.»

El cántico de Moisés

³⁰Y éste fue el cántico que recitó Moisés de principio a fin, en presencia de toda la asamblea de Israel:

32 «Escuchen, cielos, y hablaré;
   oye, tierra, las palabras de mi boca.
²Que caiga mi enseñanza como lluvia
   y desciendan mis palabras como rocío,
como aguacero sobre el pasto nuevo,
   como lluvia abundante sobre plantas
      tiernas.
³Proclamaré el *nombre del SEÑOR.
   ¡Alaben la grandeza de nuestro Dios!
⁴Él es la *Roca, sus obras son perfectas,
   y todos sus *caminos son justos.
Dios es fiel; no practica la injusticia.
   Él es recto y justo.
⁵Actuaron contra él de manera corrupta;
   para vergüenza de ellos, ya no son sus
      hijos;
   ¡son una generación torcida y perversa!

⁶»¿Y así le pagas al SEÑOR,
   pueblo tonto y necio?
¿Acaso no es tu Padre, tu Creador,
   el que te hizo y te formó?
⁷Recuerda los días de antaño;
   considera las épocas del remoto pasado.
Pídele a tu padre que te lo diga,
   y a los ancianos que te lo expliquen.
⁸Cuando el *Altísimo dio su herencia a las
      naciones,
   cuando dividió a toda la *humanidad,
les puso límites a los pueblos
   según el número de los hijos de Israel.
⁹Porque la porción del SEÑOR es su pueblo;
   Jacob es su herencia asignada.
¹⁰Lo halló en una tierra desolada,
   en la rugiente soledad del yermo.
Lo protegió y lo cuidó;
   lo guardó como a la niña de sus ojos;
¹¹como un águila que agita el nido
   y revolotea sobre sus polluelos,
que despliega su plumaje
   y los lleva sobre sus alas.

¹²»Sólo el SEÑOR lo guiaba;
   ningún Dios extraño iba con él.
¹³Lo hizo cabalgar sobre las alturas de la tierra
   y lo alimentó con el fruto de los campos.
Lo nutrió con miel y aceite,
   que hizo brotar de la roca;

¹⁴con natas y leche de la manada y del rebaño,
   y con cebados corderos y cabritos;
con toros selectos de Basán
   y las mejores espigas del trigo.
   ¡Bebió la sangre espumosa de la uva!

¹⁵»Jesurúnᵘ engordó y pateó;
   se hartó de comida,
   y se puso corpulento y rollizo.
Abandonó al Dios que le dio vida
   y rechazó a la Roca, su Salvador.
¹⁶Lo provocó a celos con dioses extraños
   y lo hizo enojar con sus ídolos detestables.
¹⁷Ofreció sacrificios a los demonios,
   que no son Dios;
   dioses que no había conocido,
   dioses recién aparecidos,
   dioses no honrados por sus padres.
¹⁸¡Desertaste de la Roca que te engendró!
   ¡Olvidaste al Dios que te dio vida!

¹⁹»Al ver esto, el SEÑOR los rechazó
   porque sus hijos y sus hijas lo irritaron.
²⁰»Les voy a dar la espalda —dijo—,
   y a ver en qué terminan;
son una generación perversa,
   ¡son unos hijos infieles!
²¹Me provocaron a celos con quien no es Dios
      como yo,
   y me enojaron con sus ídolos indignos.
Pues yo haré que ustedes sientan envidia de
      los que no son pueblo;
   voy a irritarlos con una nación insensata.
²²Se ha encendido el fuego de mi ira,
   que quema hasta lo profundo del *abismo.
Devorará la tierra y sus cosechas,
   y consumirá la raíz de las montañas.

²³» "Amontonaré calamidades sobre ellos
   y gastaré mis flechas en su contra.
²⁴Enviaré a que los consuman el hambre,
   la pestilencia nauseabunda y la plaga
      mortal.
Lanzaré contra ellos los colmillos de las fieras
   y el veneno de las víboras que se arrastran
      por el polvo.
²⁵En la calle, la espada los dejará sin hijos,
   y en sus casas reinará el terror.
Perecerán los jóvenes y las doncellas,
   los que aún maman y los que peinan canas.
²⁶Me dije: 'Voy a dispersarlos;
   borraré de la tierra su memoria.'
²⁷Pero temí las provocaciones del enemigo;
   temí que el adversario no entendiera
y llegara a pensar: 'Hemos triunfado;
   nada de esto lo ha hecho el SEÑOR.' "

²⁸»Como nación, son unos insensatos;
   carecen de discernimiento.
²⁹¡Si tan sólo fueran sabios y entendieran esto,
   y comprendieran cuál será su fin!
³⁰¿Cómo podría un hombre perseguir a mil
   si su Roca no los hubiera vendido?
¿Cómo podrían dos hacer huir a diez mil
   si el SEÑOR no los hubiera entregado?
³¹Su roca no es como la nuestra.
   ¡Aun nuestros enemigos lo reconocen!
³²Su viña es un retoño de Sodoma,
   de los campos de Gomorra.
Sus uvas están llenas de veneno;

ᵘ **32:15** En hebreo, *Jesurún* significa *el justo*, es decir, Israel.

sus racimos, preñados de amargura.
33Su vino es veneno de víboras,
ponzoña mortal de serpientes.

34»"¿No he tenido esto en reserva,
y lo he sellado en mis archivos?
35Mía es la venganza; yo pagaré.
A su debido tiempo, su pie resbalará.
Se apresura su desastre,
y el día del juicio se avecina."

36»El SEÑOR defenderá a su pueblo
cuando lo vea sin fuerzas;
tendrá compasión de sus siervos
cuando ya no haya ni esclavos ni libres.
37Y les dirá: "¿Dónde están ahora sus dioses,
la roca en la cual se refugiaron?
38¿Dónde están los dioses
que comieron la gordura de sus sacrificios
y bebieron el vino de sus libaciones?
¡Que se levanten a ayudarles!
¡Que les den abrigo!

39» "¡Vean ahora que yo soy único!
No hay otro Dios fuera de mí.
Yo doy la muerte y devuelvo la vida,
causo heridas y doy sanidad.
Nadie puede librarse de mi poder.
40Levanto la mano al cielo y declaro:
Tan seguro como que vivo para siempre,
41cuando afile mi espada reluciente
y en el día del juicio la tome en mis manos,
me vengaré de mis adversarios;
¡les daré su merecido a los que me odian!
42Mis flechas se embriagarán de sangre,
y mi espada se hartará de carne:
sangre de heridos y de cautivos,
cabezas de caudillos enemigos."

43»Alégrense, naciones, con el pueblo de Dios;v
él vengará la sangre de sus siervos.
¡Sí! Dios se vengará de sus enemigos,
y hará *expiación por su tierra y por su
pueblo.»

44Acompañado de Josué hijo de Nun, Moisés fue
y recitó ante el pueblo todas las palabras de este cántico. 45Cuando terminó, les dijo a todos los israelitas:
46«Mediten bien en todo lo que les he declarado solemnemente este día, y díganles a sus hijos que obedezcan fielmente todas las palabras de esta *ley.
47Porque no son palabras vanas para ustedes, sino
que de ellas depende su vida; por ellas vivirán mucho tiempo en el territorio que van a poseer al otro
lado del Jordán.»

Anuncio de la muerte de Moisés

48Ese mismo día el SEÑOR le dijo a Moisés:
49«Sube a las montañas de Abarín, y contempla desde allí el monte Nebo, en el territorio de Moab, frente
a Jericó, y el territorio de Canaán, el cual voy a dar en
posesión a los israelitas. 50En el monte al que vas a
subir morirás, y te reunirás con los tuyos, así como tu
hermano Aarón murió y se reunió con sus antepasados en el monte Hor. 51Esto será así porque, a la vista
de todos los israelitas, ustedes dos me fueron infieles
en las aguas de Meribá Cades; en el desierto de Zin
no honraron mi *santidad. 52Por eso no entrarás en
el territorio que voy a darle al pueblo de Israel; solamente podrás verlo de lejos.»

Moisés bendice a las tribus

33 Antes de su muerte, Moisés, hombre de Dios,
bendijo así a los israelitas:

2«Vino el SEÑOR desde el Sinaí:
vino sobre su pueblo, como aurora, desde
Seír;
resplandeció desde el monte Parán,
y llegó desde Meribá Cades
con rayos de luz en su diestra.w
3Tú eres quien ama a su pueblo;
todos los *santos están en tu mano.
Por eso siguen tus pasos
y de ti reciben instrucción.
4Es la *ley que nos dio Moisés,
el tesoro de la asamblea de Jacob.
5El SEÑOR era rey sobre Jesurúnx
cuando los líderes del pueblo se reunieron,
junto con las tribus de Israel.

6»Que Rubén viva, y que no muera;
isean innumerables sus hombres!»

7Y esto dijo acerca de Judá:

«Oye, SEÑOR, el clamor de Judá;
hazlo volver a su pueblo.
Judá defiende su causa con sus propias
fuerzas.
¡Ayúdalo contra sus enemigos!»

8Acerca de Leví dijo:

«El *urim y el tumim, que son tuyos,
los has dado al hombre que favoreces.
Lo pusiste a prueba en Masá;
en las aguas de Meribá contendiste con él.
9Dijo de su padre y de su madre:
"No los tomo en cuenta."
No reconoció a sus hermanos,
y hasta desconoció a sus hijos,
pero tuvo en cuenta tu palabra
y obedeció tu *pacto.
10Le enseñó tus preceptos a Jacob
y tu ley a Israel.
Presentó ante ti, sobre tu altar,
el incienso y las ofrendas del todo
quemadas.
11Bendice, SEÑOR, sus logros
y acepta la obra de sus manos.
Destruye el poder de sus adversarios;
¡que nunca más se levanten sus enemigos!»

12Acerca de Benjamín dijo:

«Que el amado del SEÑOR repose seguro en él,
porque lo protege todo el día
y descansa tranquilo entre sus hombros.»

13Acerca de José dijo:

«El SEÑOR bendiga su tierra
con el rocío precioso del cielo
y con las aguas que brotan de la tierra;
14con las mejores cosechas del año
y los mejores frutos del mes;
15con lo más selecto de las montañas de
siempre
y la fertilidad de las colinas eternas;
16con lo mejor de lo que llena la tierra

---

v 32:43 *Alégrense, naciones, con el pueblo de Dios.* Alt. *Hagan regocijar al pueblo de Dios, naciones.* w 33:2 *con rayos de luz en su diestra.* Frase de difícil traducción. x 33:5 En hebreo, *Jesurún* significa *el justo,* es decir, Israel; también en v. 26.

y el favor del que mora en la zarza
ardiente.
Repose todo esto sobre la cabeza de José,
sobre la corona del elegido entre sus
hermanos.
17José es majestuoso como primogénito de toro;
¡poderoso como un búfalo!
Con sus cuernos atacará a las naciones,
hasta arrinconarlas en los confines del
mundo.
¡Tales son los millares de Manasés,
las decenas de millares de Efraín!»

18Acerca de Zabulón dijo:

«Tú, Zabulón, eres feliz emprendiendo viajes,
y tú, Isacar, quedándote en tu carpa.
19Invitarán a los pueblos a subir a la montaña,
para ofrecer allí sacrificios de justicia.
Disfrutarán de la abundancia del mar
y de los tesoros escondidos en la arena.»

20Acerca de Gad dijo:

«¡Bendito el que ensanche los dominios de
Gad!
Ahí habita Gad como león,
desgarrando brazos y cabezas.
21Escogió la mejor tierra para sí;
se guardó la porción del líder.
Cuando los jefes del pueblo se reunieron,
cumplió la justa voluntad del SEÑOR,
los decretos que había dado a su pueblo.»

22Acerca de Dan dijo:

«Dan es un cachorro de león,
que salta desde Basán.»

23Acerca de Neftalí dijo:

«Neftalí rebosa del favor del SEÑOR,
y está lleno de sus bendiciones;
sus dominios se extienden
desde el mar hasta el desierto.»

24Acerca de Aser dijo:

«Aser es el más bendito de los hijos;
que sea el favorito de sus hermanos,
y se empape en aceite los pies.
25Tus cerrojos serán de hierro y bronce;
¡que dure tu fuerza tanto como tus días!

26»No hay nadie como el Dios de Jesurún,
que para ayudarte cabalga en los cielos,
entre las nubes, con toda su majestad.
27El Dios sempiterno es tu refugio;
por siempre te sostiene entre sus brazos.
Expulsará de tu presencia al enemigo
y te ordenará que lo destruyas.
28¡Vive seguro, Israel!
¡Habita sin enemigos, fuente de Jacob!
Tu tierra está llena de trigo y de mosto;
tus cielos destilan rocío.
29¡Sonríele a la vida, Israel!
¿Quién como tú,
pueblo rescatado por el SEÑOR?
Él es tu escudo y tu ayuda;
él es tu espada victoriosa.
Tus enemigos se doblegarán ante ti;
sus espaldas te servirán de tapete.»y

Muerte de Moisés

34 Moisés ascendió de las llanuras de Moab al
monte Nebo, a la cima del monte Pisgá, frente a Jericó. Allí el SEÑOR le mostró todo el territorio
que se extiende desde Galaad hasta Dan, 2todo el territorio de Neftalí y de Efraín, Manasés y Judá, hasta
el mar Mediterráneo. 3Le mostró también la región
del Néguev y la del valle de Jericó, la ciudad de palmeras, hasta Zoar. 4Luego el SEÑOR le dijo: «Éste es
el territorio que juré a Abraham, Isaac y Jacob que
daría a sus descendientes. Te he permitido verlo con
tus propios ojos, pero no podrás entrar en él.»

5Allí en Moab murió Moisés, siervo del SEÑOR,
tal como el SEÑOR se lo había dicho. 6Y fue sepultado
en Moab, en el valle que está frente a Bet Peor, pero
hasta la fecha nadie sabe dónde está su sepultura.

7Moisés tenía ciento veinte años de edad cuando
murió. Con todo, no se había debilitado su vista ni
había perdido su vigor. 8Durante treinta días los israelitas lloraron a Moisés en las llanuras de Moab,
guardando así el tiempo de luto acostumbrado.

9Entonces Josué hijo de Nun fue lleno de espíritu de sabiduría, porque Moisés puso sus manos sobre él. Los israelitas, por su parte, obedecieron a
Josué e hicieron lo que el SEÑOR le había ordenado a
Moisés.

10Desde entonces no volvió a surgir en Israel
otro profeta como Moisés, con quien el SEÑOR tenía
trato directo. 11Sólo Moisés hizo todas aquellas señales y prodigios que el SEÑOR le mandó realizar en
Egipto ante el faraón, sus funcionarios y todo su país.
12Nadie ha demostrado jamás tener un poder tan extraordinario, ni ha sido capaz de realizar las proezas
que hizo Moisés ante todo Israel.

---

y **33:29** *sus espaldas te servirán de tapete.* Alt. *hollarás sus *santuarios paganos.*

JOSUÉ

Orden del SEÑOR a Josué

1 Después de la muerte de Moisés, siervo del SEÑOR, Dios le dijo a Josué hijo de Nun, asistente de Moisés: [2]«Mi siervo Moisés ha muerto. Por eso tú y todo este pueblo deberán prepararse para cruzar el río Jordán y entrar a la tierra que les daré a ustedes los israelitas. [3]Tal como le prometí a Moisés, yo les entregaré a ustedes todo lugar que toquen sus pies. [4]Su territorio se extenderá desde el desierto hasta el Líbano, y desde el gran río Éufrates, territorio de los hititas, hasta el mar Mediterráneo, que se encuentra al oeste. [5]Durante todos los días de tu vida, nadie será capaz de enfrentarse a ti. Así como estuve con Moisés, también estaré contigo; no te dejaré ni te abandonaré.

[6]»Sé fuerte y valiente, porque tú harás que este pueblo herede la tierra que les prometí a sus antepasados. [7]Sólo te pido que tengas mucho valor y firmeza para obedecer toda la *ley que mi siervo Moisés te mandó. No te apartes de ella para nada; sólo así tendrás éxito dondequiera que vayas. [8]Recita siempre el libro de la ley y medita en él de día y de noche; cumple con cuidado todo lo que en él está escrito. Así prosperarás y tendrás éxito. [9]Ya te lo he ordenado: ¡Sé fuerte y valiente! ¡No tengas miedo ni te desanimes! Porque el SEÑOR tu Dios te acompañará dondequiera que vayas.»

[10]Entonces Josué dio la siguiente orden a los jefes del pueblo: [11]«Vayan por todo el campamento y díganle al pueblo que prepare provisiones, porque dentro de tres días cruzará el río Jordán para tomar posesión del territorio que Dios el SEÑOR le da como herencia.»

[12]A los rubenitas, a los gaditas y a la media tribu de Manasés, Josué les mandó:

[13]—Recuerden la orden que les dio Moisés, siervo del SEÑOR: "Dios el SEÑOR les ha dado reposo y les ha entregado esta tierra." [14]Sus mujeres, sus niños y su ganado permanecerán en el territorio que Moisés les dio al este del Jordán. Pero ustedes, los hombres de guerra, cruzarán armados al frente de sus hermanos. Les prestarán ayuda [15]hasta que el SEÑOR les dé reposo, como lo ha hecho con ustedes, y hasta que ellos tomen posesión de la tierra que el SEÑOR su Dios les da. Sólo entonces podrán ustedes retornar a sus tierras y ocuparlas. Son las tierras que Moisés, siervo del SEÑOR, les dio al este del Jordán.

[16]Ellos le respondieron a Josué:

—Nosotros obedeceremos todo lo que nos has mandado, e iremos adondequiera que nos envíes. [17]Te obedeceremos en todo, tal como lo hicimos con Moisés. Lo único que pedimos es que el SEÑOR esté contigo como estuvo con Moisés. [18]Cualquiera que se rebele contra tus palabras o que no obedezca lo que tú ordenes, será condenado a muerte. Pero tú, ¡sé fuerte y valiente!

Rajab y los espías

2 Luego Josué hijo de Nun envió secretamente, desde Sitín, a dos espías con la siguiente orden: «Vayan a explorar la tierra, especialmente Jericó.» Cuando los espías llegaron a Jericó, se hospedaron en la casa de una prostituta llamada Rajab. [2]Pero el rey de Jericó se enteró de que dos espías israelitas habían entrado esa noche en la ciudad para reconocer el país. [3]Así que le envió a Rajab el siguiente mensaje: «Echa fuera a los hombres que han entrado en tu casa, pues vinieron a espiar nuestro país.»

[4]Pero la mujer, que ya había escondido a los espías, le respondió al rey: «Es cierto que unos hombres vinieron a mi casa, pero no sé quiénes eran ni de dónde venían. [5]Salieron cuando empezó a oscurecer, a la hora de cerrar las *puertas de la ciudad, y no sé a dónde se fueron. Vayan tras ellos; tal vez les den alcance.» [6](En realidad, la mujer había llevado a los hombres al techo de la casa y los había escondido entre los manojos de lino que allí secaba.) [7]Los hombres del rey fueron tras los espías, por el camino que lleva a los vados del río Jordán. En cuanto salieron, las puertas de Jericó se cerraron.

[8]Antes de que los espías se acostaran, Rajab subió al techo [9]y les dijo:

—Yo sé que el SEÑOR les ha dado esta tierra, y por eso estamos aterrorizados; todos los habitantes del país están muertos de miedo ante ustedes. [10]Tenemos noticias de cómo el SEÑOR secó las aguas del *Mar Rojo para que ustedes pasaran, después de haber salido de Egipto. También hemos oído cómo *destruyeron completamente a los reyes amorreos, Sijón y Og, al este del Jordán. [11]Por eso estamos todos tan amedrentados y descorazonados frente a ustedes. Yo sé que el SEÑOR y Dios es Dios de dioses tanto en el cielo como en la tierra. [12]Por lo tanto, les pido ahora mismo que juren en el *nombre del SEÑOR que serán bondadosos con mi familia, como yo lo he sido con ustedes. Quiero que me den como garantía una señal [13]de que perdonarán la vida de mis padres, de mis hermanos y de todos los que viven con ellos. ¡Juren que nos salvarán de la muerte!

[14]—¡Juramos por nuestra vida que la de ustedes no correrá peligro! —contestaron ellos—. Si no nos delatas, seremos bondadosos contigo y cumpliremos nuestra promesa cuando el SEÑOR nos entregue este país.

[15]Entonces Rajab los bajó por la ventana con una soga, pues la casa donde ella vivía estaba sobre la muralla de la ciudad. [16]Ya les había dicho previamente: «Huyan rumbo a las montañas para que sus perseguidores no los encuentren. Escóndanse allí por tres días, hasta que ellos regresen. Entonces podrán seguir su camino.»

[17]Los hombres le dijeron a Rajab:

—Quedaremos libres del juramento que te hemos hecho [18]si, cuando conquistemos la tierra, no vemos este cordón rojo atado a la ventana por la que nos bajas. Además, tus padres, tus hermanos y el resto de tu familia deberán estar reunidos en tu casa. [19]Quien salga de la casa en ese momento, será responsable de su propia vida, y nosotros seremos inocentes. Sólo nos haremos responsables de quienes permanezcan en la casa, si alguien se atreve a ponerles la mano encima. [20]Conste que si nos delatas, nosotros quedaremos libres del juramento que nos obligaste hacer.

[21]—De acuerdo —respondió Rajab—. Que sea tal como ustedes han dicho.

Luego los despidió; ellos partieron, y ella ató el cordón rojo a la ventana.

[22]Los hombres se dirigieron a las montañas y permanecieron allí tres días, hasta que sus perseguidores regresaron a la ciudad. Los habían buscado por todas partes, pero sin éxito. [23]Los dos hombres emprendieron el regreso; bajando de las montañas, vadearon el río y llegaron adonde estaba Josué hijo de Nun. Allí le relataron todo lo que les había sucedi-

do: 24«El SEÑOR ha entregado todo el país en nuestras manos. ¡Todos sus habitantes tiemblan de miedo ante nosotros!»

El cruce del río Jordán

3 Muy de mañana, Josué y todos los israelitas partieron de Sitín y se dirigieron hacia el río Jordán; pero antes de cruzarlo, acamparon a sus orillas. 2Al cabo de tres días, los jefes del pueblo recorrieron todo el campamento 3con la siguiente orden: «Cuando vean el arca del *pacto del SEÑOR su Dios, y a los sacerdotes levitas que la llevan, abandonen sus puestos y pónganse en marcha detrás de ella. 4Así sabrán por dónde ir, pues nunca antes han pasado por ese camino. Deberán, sin embargo, mantener como un kilómetroa de distancia entre ustedes y el arca; no se acerquen a ella.»

5Josué le ordenó al pueblo: «*Purifíquense, porque mañana el SEÑOR va a realizar grandes prodigios entre ustedes.» 6Y a los sacerdotes les dijo: «Carguen el arca del pacto y pónganse al frente del pueblo.» Los sacerdotes obedecieron y se pusieron al frente del pueblo.

7Luego el SEÑOR le dijo a Josué: «Este día comenzaré a engrandecerte ante el pueblo de Israel. Así sabrán que estoy contigo como estuve con Moisés. 8Dales la siguiente orden a los sacerdotes que llevan el arca del pacto: "Cuando lleguen a la orilla del Jordán, deténganse." »

9Entonces Josué les dijo a los israelitas: «Acérquense y escuchen lo que Dios el SEÑOR tiene que decirles.» 10Y añadió: «Ahora sabrán que el Dios viviente está en medio de ustedes, y que de seguro expulsará a los cananeos, los hititas, los heveos, los ferezeos, los gergeseos, los amorreos y los jebuseos. 11El arca del pacto, que pertenece al Soberano de toda la tierra, cruzará el Jordán al frente de ustedes. 12Ahora, pues, elijan doce hombres, uno por cada tribu de Israel. 13Tan pronto como los sacerdotes que llevan el arca del SEÑOR, soberano de toda la tierra, pongan pie en el Jordán, las aguas dejarán de correr y se detendrán formando un muro.»

14Cuando el pueblo levantó el campamento para cruzar el Jordán, los sacerdotes que llevaban el arca del pacto marcharon al frente de todos. 15Ahora bien, las aguas del Jordán se desbordan en el tiempo de la cosecha. A pesar de eso, tan pronto como los pies de los sacerdotes que portaban el arca tocaron las aguas, 16éstas dejaron de fluir y formaron un muro que se veía a la distancia, más o menos a la altura del pueblo de Adán, junto a la fortaleza de Saretán. A su vez, dejaron de correr las aguas que fluían en el mar del Arabá, es decir, el Mar Muerto, y así el pueblo pudo cruzar hasta quedar frente a Jericó. 17Por su parte, los sacerdotes que portaban el arca del pacto del SEÑOR permanecieron de pie en terreno seco, en medio del Jordán, mientras todo el pueblo de Israel terminaba de cruzar el río por el cauce totalmente seco.

Monumento conmemorativo

4 Cuando todo el pueblo terminó de cruzar el río Jordán, el SEÑOR le dijo a Josué: 2«Elijan a un hombre de cada una de las doce tribus de Israel, 3y ordénenles que tomen doce piedras del cauce, exactamente del lugar donde los sacerdotes permanecieron de pie. Díganles que las coloquen en el lugar donde hoy pasarán la noche.»

4Entonces Josué reunió a los doce hombres que había escogido de las doce tribus, 5y les dijo: «Vayan al centro del cauce del río, hasta donde está el arca del SEÑOR su Dios, y cada uno cargue al hombro una piedra. Serán doce piedras, una por cada tribu de Israel, 6y servirán como señal entre ustedes. En el futuro, cuando sus hijos les pregunten: "¿Por qué están estas piedras aquí?", 7ustedes les responderán: "El día en que el arca del *pacto del SEÑOR cruzó el Jordán, las aguas del río se dividieron frente a ella. Para nosotros los israelitas, estas piedras que están aquí son un recuerdo permanente de aquella gran hazaña."»

8Los israelitas hicieron lo que Josué les ordenó, según las instrucciones del SEÑOR. Tomaron las piedras del cauce del Jordán, conforme al número de las tribus, las llevaron hasta el campamento y las colocaron allí. 9Además, Josué colocó doce piedras en el cauce del río donde se detuvieron los sacerdotes que llevaban el arca del pacto. Esas piedras siguen allí hasta el día de hoy.

10Los sacerdotes que llevaban el arca permanecieron en medio del cauce hasta que los israelitas hicieron todo lo que el SEÑOR le había ordenado a Josué. Todo se hizo según las instrucciones que Josué había recibido de Moisés. El pueblo se apresuró a cruzar el río, 11y cuando todos lo habían hecho, el arca del SEÑOR y los sacerdotes cruzaron también en presencia del pueblo. 12Acompañaban al pueblo los guerreros de las tribus de Rubén, Gad y la media tribu de Manasés, según las órdenes que había dado Moisés. 13Unos cuarenta mil guerreros armados desfilaron en presencia del SEÑOR y se dirigieron a la planicie de Jericó, listos para la guerra.

14Aquel mismo día, el SEÑOR engrandeció a Josué ante todo Israel. El pueblo admiró a Josué todos los días de su vida, como lo había hecho con Moisés.

15Luego el SEÑOR le dijo a Josué: 16«Ordénales a los sacerdotes portadores del arca del pacto que salgan del Jordán.» 17Josué les ordenó a los sacerdotes que salieran, 18y al hacerlo, portando el arca del pacto. Tan pronto como sus pies tocaron tierra firme, las aguas del río regresaron a su lugar y se desbordaron como de costumbre. 19Así, el día diez del mes primero, el pueblo de Israel cruzó el Jordán y acampó en Guilgal, al este de Jericó. 20Entonces Josué erigió allí las piedras que habían tomado del cauce del Jordán, 21y se dirigió a los israelitas: «En el futuro, cuando sus hijos les pregunten: "¿Por qué están estas piedras aquí?", 22ustedes les responderán: "Porque el pueblo de Israel cruzó el río Jordán en seco." 23El SEÑOR, Dios de ustedes, hizo lo mismo que había hecho con el *Mar Rojo cuando lo mantuvo seco hasta que todos nosotros cruzamos. 24Esto sucedió para que todas las naciones de la tierra supieran que el SEÑOR es poderoso, y para que ustedes aprendieran a temerlo para siempre.»

5 En efecto, un gran pánico invadió a todos los reyes amorreos que estaban al oeste del Jordán y a los reyes cananeos de la costa del Mediterráneo, cuando se enteraron de que el SEÑOR había secado el Jordán para que los israelitas lo cruzaran. ¡No se atrevían a hacerles frente!

Liberación del oprobio egipcio

2En aquel tiempo, el SEÑOR le dijo a Josué: «Prepara cuchillos de pedernal, y vuelve a practicar la circuncisión entre los israelitas.» 3Así que Josué hizo los cuchillos y circuncidó a los varones israelitas en la colina de Aralot.b 4Realizó la ceremonia porque los israelitas en edad militar que habían salido de Egipto ya

---

a 3:4 un kilómetro. Lit. dos mil *codos.   b 5:3 En hebreo, Aralot significa prepucios.

habían muerto en el desierto. 5Todos ellos habían sido circuncidados, pero no los que nacieron en el desierto mientras el pueblo peregrinaba después de salir de Egipto. 6Dios les había prometido a sus antepasados que les daría una tierra donde abundan la leche y la miel. Pero los israelitas que salieron de Egipto no obedecieron al SEÑOR, y por ello él juró que no verían esa tierra. En consecuencia, deambularon por el desierto durante cuarenta años, hasta que murieron todos los varones en edad militar. 7A los hijos de éstos, a quienes Dios puso en lugar de ellos, los circuncidó Josué, pues no habían sido circuncidados durante el viaje. 8Una vez que todos fueron circuncidados, permanecieron en el campamento hasta que se recuperaron.

9Luego el SEÑOR le dijo a Josué: «Hoy les he quitado de encima el oprobio de Egipto.» Por esa razón, aquel lugar se llama Guilgalc hasta el día de hoy.

Celebración de la Pascua

10Al caer la tarde del día catorce del mes primero, mientras acampaban en la llanura de Jericó, los israelitas celebraron la Pascua. 11Al día siguiente, después de la Pascua, el pueblo empezó a alimentarse de los productos de la tierra, de panes sin levadura y de trigo tostado. 12Desde ese momento dejó de caer maná, y durante todo ese año el pueblo se alimentó de los frutos de la tierra.

El comandante del ejército del SEÑOR

13Cierto día Josué, que acampaba cerca de Jericó, levantó la vista y vio a un hombre de pie frente a él, espada en mano. Josué se le acercó y le preguntó:

—¿Es usted de los nuestros, o del enemigo?

14—¡De ninguno! —respondió—. Me presento ante ti como comandante del ejército del SEÑOR.

Entonces Josué se postró rostro en tierra y le preguntó:

—¿Qué órdenes trae usted, mi Señor, para este siervo suyo?

15El comandante del ejército del SEÑOR le contestó:

—Quítate las sandalias de los pies, porque el lugar que pisas es sagrado.

Y Josué le obedeció.

La conquista de Jericó

6 Las *puertas de Jericó estaban bien aseguradas por temor a los israelitas; nadie podía salir o entrar. 2Pero el SEÑOR le dijo a Josué: «¡He entregado en tus manos a Jericó, y a su rey con sus guerreros! 3Tú y tus soldados marcharán una vez alrededor de la ciudad; así lo harán durante seis días. 4Siete sacerdotes llevarán trompetas hechas de cuernos de carneros, y marcharán frente al arca. El séptimo día ustedes marcharán siete veces alrededor de la ciudad, mientras los sacerdotes tocan las trompetas. 5Cuando todos escuchen el toque de guerra, el pueblo deberá gritar a voz en cuello. Entonces los muros de la ciudad se derrumbarán, y cada uno entrará sin impedimento.»

6Josué hijo de Nun llamó a los sacerdotes y les ordenó: «Carguen el arca del *pacto, y que siete de ustedes lleven trompetas y marchen frente a ella.» 7Y le dijo al pueblo: «¡Adelante! ¡Marchen alrededor de la ciudad! Pero los hombres armados deben marchar al frente del arca del SEÑOR.»

8Cuando Josué terminó de dar las instrucciones al pueblo, los siete sacerdotes marcharon al frente del arca del pacto del SEÑOR tocando sus trompetas; y el arca del pacto les seguía. 9Los hombres armados

marchaban al frente de los sacerdotes que tocaban las trompetas, y tras el arca marchaba la retaguardia. Durante todo ese tiempo las trompetas no cesaron de sonar. 10Al resto del pueblo, en cambio, Josué le ordenó marchar en silencio, sin decir palabra alguna ni gritar hasta el día en que les diera la orden de gritar a voz en cuello.

11Josué hizo llevar el arca alrededor de Jericó una sola vez. Después, el pueblo regresó al campamento para pasar la noche. 12Al día siguiente, Josué se levantó temprano, y los sacerdotes cargaron el arca del SEÑOR. 13Los siete sacerdotes que llevaban las trompetas tomaron la delantera y marcharon al frente del arca mientras tocaban sus trompetas. Los hombres armados marchaban al frente de ellos, y tras el arca del SEÑOR marchaba la retaguardia. ¡Nunca dejaron de oírse las trompetas! 14También en este segundo día marcharon una sola vez alrededor de Jericó, y luego regresaron al campamento. Así hicieron durante seis días.

15El séptimo día, a la salida del sol, se levantaron y marcharon alrededor de la ciudad tal como lo habían hecho los días anteriores, sólo que en ese día repitieron la marcha siete veces. 16A la séptima vuelta, los sacerdotes tocaron las trompetas, y Josué le ordenó al ejército: «¡Empiecen a gritar! ¡El SEÑOR les ha entregado la ciudad! 17Jericó, con todo lo que hay en ella, será destinada al *exterminio como ofrenda al SEÑOR. Sólo se salvarán la prostituta Rajab y los que se encuentren en su casa, porque ella escondió a nuestros mensajeros. 18No vayan a tomar nada de lo que ha sido destinado al exterminio para que ni ustedes ni el campamento de Israel se pongan en peligro de exterminio y de desgracia. 19El oro y la plata y los utensilios de bronce y de hierro pertenecen al SEÑOR: colóquenlos en su tesoro.»

20Entonces los sacerdotes tocaron las trompetas, y la gente gritó a voz en cuello, ante lo cual las murallas de Jericó se derrumbaron. El pueblo avanzó, sin ceder ni un centímetro, y tomó la ciudad. 21Mataron a filo de espada a todo hombre y mujer, joven y anciano. Lo mismo hicieron con las vacas, las ovejas y los burros; destruyeron todo lo que tuviera aliento de vida. ¡La ciudad entera quedó *arrasada!

22Ahora bien, Josué les había dicho a los dos exploradores: «Vayan a casa de la prostituta, y tráiganla junto con sus parientes, tal como se lo juraron.» 23Así que los jóvenes exploradores entraron y sacaron a Rajab junto con sus padres y hermanos, y todas sus pertenencias, y llevaron a toda la familia a un lugar seguro, fuera del campamento israelita. 24Sólo entonces los israelitas incendiaron la ciudad con todo lo que había en ella, menos los objetos de plata, de oro, de bronce y de hierro, los cuales depositaron en el tesoro de la casa del SEÑOR. 25Así Josué salvó a la prostituta Rajab, a toda su familia y todas sus posesiones, por haber escondido a los mensajeros que él había enviado a Jericó. Y desde entonces, Rajab y su familia viven con el pueblo de Israel.

26En aquel tiempo, Josué hizo este juramento:

«¡Maldito sea en la presencia del SEÑOR
el que se atreva a reconstruir esta ciudad!
Que eche los cimientos
a costa de la vida de su hijo mayor.
Que ponga las puertas
a costa de la vida de su hijo menor.»

27El SEÑOR estuvo con Josué, y éste se hizo famoso por todo el país.

---

c 5:9 En hebreo, *Guilgal* suena como el verbo traducido *he quitado.*

El pecado de Acán

7 Sin embargo, los israelitas desobedecieron al SEÑOR conservando lo que él había decidido que fuera destinado a la *destrucción, pues Acán hijo de Carmí, nieto de Zabdí y bisnieto de Zera, guardó para sí parte del botín que Dios había destinado al *exterminio. Este hombre de la tribu de Judá provocó la ira del SEÑOR contra los israelitas.

La derrota en Hai

2Josué envió a unos hombres de Jericó hacia Hai, lugar cercano a Bet Avén, frente a Betel, y les dijo: «Vayan a explorar la tierra.» Fueron, pues, a explorar la ciudad de Hai. 3Poco después regresaron y le dieron el siguiente informe a Josué: «No es necesario que todo el pueblo vaya a la batalla. Dos o tres mil soldados serán suficientes para que tomemos Hai. Esa población tiene muy pocos hombres y no hay necesidad de cansar a todo el pueblo.» 4Por esa razón, sólo fueron a la batalla tres mil soldados, pero los de Hai los derrotaron. 5El ejército israelita sufrió treinta y seis bajas, y fue perseguido desde la *puerta de la ciudad hasta las canteras. Allí, en una pendiente, fueron vencidos. Como resultado, todo el pueblo se acobardó y se llenó de miedo.

6Ante esto, Josué se rasgó las vestiduras y se postró rostro en tierra ante el arca del *pacto del SEÑOR. Lo acompañaban los jefes de Israel, quienes también mostraban su dolor y estaban consternados. 7Josué le reclamó a Dios:

—SEÑOR y Dios, ¿por qué hiciste que este pueblo cruzara el Jordán, y luego lo entregaste en manos de los amorreos para que lo destruyeran? ¡Mejor nos hubiéramos quedado al otro lado del río! 8Dime, Señor, ¿qué puedo decir ahora que Israel ha huido de sus enemigos? 9Los cananeos se enterarán y llamarán a los pueblos de la región; entonces nos rodearán y nos exterminarán. ¡Qué será de tu gran prestigio!

10Y el SEÑOR le contestó:

—¡Levántate! ¿Qué haces allí postrado? 11Los israelitas han pecado y han violado la alianza que concerté con ellos. Se han apropiado del botín de guerra que debía ser *destruido y lo han escondido entre sus posesiones. 12Por eso los israelitas no podrán hacerles frente a sus enemigos, sino que tendrán que huir de sus adversarios. Ellos mismos se acarrearon su destrucción. Y si no destruyen ese botín que está en medio de ustedes, yo no seguiré a su lado. 13¡Levántate! ¡*Purifica al pueblo! Diles que se consagren para presentarse ante mí mañana, y que yo, el SEÑOR, Dios de Israel, declaro: "¡La destrucción está en medio de ti, Israel! No podrás resistir a tus enemigos hasta que hayas quitado el oprobio que está en el pueblo." 14Mañana por la mañana se presentarán por tribus. La tribu que yo señale por suertes presentará a sus clanes; el clan que el Señor señale presentará a sus familias; y la familia que el SEÑOR señale presentará a sus varones. 15El que sea sorprendido en posesión del botín de guerra destinado a la destrucción será quemado junto con su familia y sus posesiones, pues ha violado el pacto del SEÑOR y ha causado el oprobio a Israel.

El castigo de Acán

16Al día siguiente, muy de madrugada, Josué mandó llamar, una por una, las tribus de Israel; y la suerte cayó sobre Judá. 17Todos los clanes de Judá se acercaron, y la suerte cayó sobre el clan de Zera. Del clan de Zera la suerte cayó sobre la familia de Zabdí. 18Josué, entonces, hizo pasar a cada uno de los varones de la familia de Zabdí, y la suerte cayó sobre Acán hijo de Carmí, nieto de Zabdí y bisnieto de Zera. 19Entonces Josué lo interpeló:

—Hijo mío, honra y alaba al SEÑOR, Dios de Israel. Cuéntame lo que has hecho. ¡No me ocultes nada!

20Acán le replicó:

—Es cierto que he pecado contra el SEÑOR, Dios de Israel. Ésta es mi falta: 21Vi en el botín un hermoso manto de Babilonia, doscientas monedas de plata y una barra de oro de medio kilo.d Me deslumbraron y me apropié de ellos. Entonces los escondí en un hoyo que cavé en medio de mi carpa. La plata está también allí, debajo de todo.

22En seguida, Josué envió a unos mensajeros, los cuales fueron corriendo a la carpa de Acán. Allí encontraron todo lo que Acán había escondido, 23lo recogieron y se lo llevaron a Josué y a los israelitas, quienes se lo presentaron al SEÑOR. 24Y Josué y todos los israelitas tomaron a Acán, bisnieto de Zera, y lo llevaron al valle de Acor, junto con la plata, el manto y el oro; también llevaron a sus hijos, sus hijas, el ganado, su carpa y todas sus posesiones. Cuando llegaron al valle de Acor, 25Josué exclamó:

—¿Por qué has traído esta desgracia sobre nosotros? ¡Que el SEÑOR haga caer sobre ti esa misma desgracia!

Entonces todos los israelitas apedrearon a Acán y a los suyos, y los quemaron. 26Luego colocaron sobre ellos un gran montón de piedras que sigue en pie hasta el día de hoy. Por eso aquel lugar se llama valle de Acor.e Así aplacó el SEÑOR el ardor de su ira.

Obediencia y victoria

8 El SEÑOR exhortó a Josué: «¡No tengas miedo ni te acobardes! Toma contigo a todo el ejército, y ataquen la ciudad de Hai. Yo les daré la victoria sobre su rey y su ejército; se apropiarán de su ciudad y de todo el territorio que la rodea. 2Tratarás a esta ciudad y a su rey como hiciste con Jericó y con su rey. Sin embargo, podrán quedarse con el botín de guerra y todo el ganado. Prepara una emboscada en la parte posterior de la ciudad.»

3Se levantó Josué junto con su ejército y fueron a pelear contra Hai. Josué escogió treinta mil guerreros y los envió durante la noche 4con estas palabras: «Ustedes pondrán una emboscada en la parte posterior de la ciudad. No se alejen mucho de ella, y manténganse en sus posiciones. 5Yo me acercaré con mi tropa, y cuando los enemigos salgan a pelear contra nosotros, huiremos como la primera vez. 6Ellos nos perseguirán, pensando que estamos huyendo de nuevo, y así los alejaremos de la ciudad. 7Entonces ustedes saldrán de su escondite y se apoderarán de Hai. El SEÑOR les dará la victoria. 8Cuando hayan capturado la ciudad, quémenla tal como nos lo ordenó el SEÑOR. Éstas son mis órdenes.»

9Dicho esto, Josué envió a sus guerreros a preparar la emboscada, y ellos se apostaron entre Betel y Hai, al oeste de la ciudad mientras él, por su parte, pasaba esa noche con su ejército.

10Muy de mañana se levantó Josué, pasó revista al ejército y, junto con los jefes de Israel, se puso en marcha hacia Hai. 11Todos los guerreros que iban con Josué llegaron cerca de Hai y acamparon al norte de la ciudad. Sólo había un valle entre ellos y la ciu-

---

d **7:21** *doscientas ... medio kilo.* Lit. *doscientos* *siclos de plata* *y una barra de oro de cincuenta siclos.* e **7:26** En hebreo, *Acor* significa *desgracia.*

dad. 12Josué envió a cinco mil guerreros a preparar la emboscada, y ellos se escondieron entre Betel y Hai, al oeste de la ciudad. 13De esa manera, una tropa acampó al norte de la ciudad y la otra al oeste. Esa noche Josué avanzó hacia el medio del valle.

14Cuando el rey de Hai se dio cuenta de lo que pasaba, se apresuró a salir con toda su tropa a pelear contra Israel, en la pendiente que está frente al desierto, sin saber que le habían puesto una emboscada en la parte posterior de la ciudad. 15Josué y su tropa, fingiéndose derrotados, huyeron por el camino que lleva al desierto. 16Mientras tanto, todos los hombres que estaban en la ciudad recibieron el llamado de perseguir a los israelitas, alejándose así de Hai. 17No quedó ni un solo hombre en Hai o en Betel que no hubiera salido a perseguir a Israel, de modo que la ciudad de Hai quedó desprotegida.

18Entonces el SEÑOR le ordenó a Josué: «Apunta hacia Hai con la jabalina que llevas, pues en tus manos entregaré la ciudad.» Y así lo hizo Josué. 19Al ver esto, los que estaban en la emboscada salieron de inmediato de donde estaban y, entrando en la ciudad, la tomaron y la incendiaron.

20Cuando los hombres de Hai miraron hacia atrás, vieron que subía de la ciudad una nube de humo. Entonces se dieron cuenta de que no podían huir en ninguna dirección, porque la gente de Josué que antes huía hacia el desierto, ahora se lanzaba contra sus perseguidores. 21En efecto, tan pronto como Josué y todos los israelitas vieron que los que tendieron la emboscada habían tomado la ciudad y la habían incendiado, se volvieron y atacaron a los de Hai. 22Los de la emboscada salieron de la ciudad y persiguieron a los guerreros de Hai, y así éstos quedaron atrapados por todos lados. Los israelitas atacaron a sus enemigos hasta no dejar ni fugitivos ni sobrevivientes. 23Al rey de Hai lo capturaron vivo y se lo entregaron a Josué.

24Después de que los israelitas terminaron de matar a filo de espada, en el campo y el desierto, a todos los guerreros de Hai que habían salido a perseguirlos, regresaron a la ciudad y del mismo modo mataron a todos los que quedaban. 25Ese día murieron todos los habitantes de Hai, como doce mil hombres y mujeres. 26Josué mantuvo extendido el brazo con el que sostenía su jabalina, hasta que el ejército israelita *exterminó a todos los habitantes de Hai. 27Y tal como el SEÑOR había mandado, el pueblo se quedó con el botín de guerra y todo el ganado. 28Luego Josué incendió la ciudad, reduciéndola a escombros, que permanece hasta el día de hoy. 29También mandó ahorcar en un árbol al rey de Hai, y ordenó que dejaran su cuerpo colgando hasta la tarde. Al ponerse el sol, Josué mandó que bajaran el cuerpo del rey y lo arrojaran a la *entrada de la ciudad. Así mismo, pidió que se amontonaran piedras encima del cadáver. Y ese montón de piedras permanece hasta el día de hoy.

Lectura de la ley en el monte Ebal

30Entonces Josué levantó, en el monte Ebal, un altar al SEÑOR, Dios de Israel, 31tal como Moisés, siervo del SEÑOR, había ordenado a los israelitas. Lo levantó de acuerdo con lo que está escrito en el libro de la *ley de Moisés: un altar de piedras sin labrar, es decir, que no habían sido trabajadas con ninguna herramienta. En él ofrecieron *holocaustos y sacrificios de *comunión al SEÑOR.

32Allí, en presencia de los israelitas, Josué escribió en tablas de piedra una copia de la ley que Moisés había escrito. 33Todos los israelitas, con sus jefes, oficiales y jueces, estaban de pie a ambos lados del arca del *pacto, frente a los sacerdotes levitas que la cargaban en hombros. Tanto los israelitas como los inmigrantes tomaron sus posiciones, la mitad de ellos hacia el monte Guerizín y la otra mitad hacia el monte Ebal, tal como Moisés, siervo del SEÑOR, había mandado cuando bendijo por primera vez al pueblo de Israel.

34Luego Josué leyó todas las palabras de la ley, tanto las bendiciones como las maldiciones, según lo que estaba escrito en el libro de la ley. 35De esta lectura que hizo Josué ante toda la asamblea de los israelitas, incluyendo a las mujeres, a los niños y a los inmigrantes, no se omitió ninguna palabra de lo ordenado por Moisés.

Astucia de los gabaonitas

9 Había reyes que vivían en el lado occidental del Jordán, en la montaña, en la llanura y a lo largo de la costa del Mediterráneo, hasta el Líbano: hititas, amorreos, cananeos, ferezeos, heveos y jebuseos. Cuando estos monarcas se enteraron de lo sucedido, 2se aliaron bajo un solo mando para hacer frente a Josué y a los israelitas.

3Los gabaonitas, al darse cuenta de cómo Josué había tratado a las ciudades de Jericó y de Hai, 4maquinaron un plan. Enviaron unos mensajeros, cuyos asnos llevaban costales viejos, y odres para el vino, rotos y remendados. 5Iban vestidos con ropa vieja y tenían sandalias gastadas y remendadas. El pan que llevaban para comer estaba duro y hecho migas. 6Fueron al campamento de Guilgal, donde estaba Josué, y les dijeron a él y a los israelitas:

—Venimos de un país muy lejano. Queremos hacer un tratado con ustedes.

7Los israelitas replicaron:

—Tal vez ustedes son de por acá y, en ese caso, no podemos hacer ningún tratado con ustedes.

8Ellos le dijeron a Josué:

—Nosotros estamos dispuestos a servirles.

Y Josué les preguntó:

—¿Quiénes son ustedes y de dónde vienen?

9Ellos respondieron:

—Nosotros somos sus siervos, y hemos venido de un país muy distante, hasta donde ha llegado la fama del SEÑOR su Dios. Nos hemos enterado de todo lo que él hizo en Egipto 10y de lo que les hizo a los dos reyes amorreos al este del Jordán: Sijón, rey de Hesbón, y Og, rey de Basán, el que residía en Astarot. 11Por eso los habitantes de nuestro país, junto con nuestros *dirigentes, nos pidieron que nos preparáramos para el largo viaje y que les diéramos a ustedes el siguiente mensaje: "Deseamos ser siervos de ustedes; hagamos un tratado." 12Cuando salimos para acá, nuestro pan estaba fresco y caliente, pero ahora, ¡mírenlo! Está duro y hecho migas. 13Estos odres estaban nuevecitos y repletos de vino, y ahora, tal como pueden ver, están todos rotos. Y nuestra ropa y sandalias están gastadas por el largo viaje.

14Los *hombres de Israel participaron de las provisiones de los gabaonitas, pero no consultaron al SEÑOR. 15Entonces Josué hizo con ellos un tratado de ayuda mutua y se comprometió a perdonarles la vida. Y los jefes israelitas ratificaron el tratado.

16Tres días después de haber concluido el tratado con los gabaonitas, los israelitas se enteraron de que eran sus vecinos y vivían en las cercanías. 17Por eso se pusieron en marcha, y al tercer día llegaron a sus ciudades: Gabaón, Cafira, Berot y Quiriat Yearín. 18Pero los israelitas no los atacaron porque los jefes de la comunidad les habían jurado en *nombre del SEÑOR, Dios de Israel, perdonarles la vida. Y aunque toda la comunidad se quejó contra sus jefes, ¹⁹éstos contestaron:

—Hemos hecho un juramento en nombre del SEÑOR, y no podemos hacerles ningún daño. ²⁰Esto es lo que haremos con ellos: les perdonaremos la vida, para que no caiga sobre nosotros el castigo divino por quebrantar el juramento que hicimos.

²¹Luego añadieron:

—Se les permitirá vivir, pero a cambio de ser los leñadores y aguateros de la comunidad.

De ese modo, los jefes de la comunidad cumplieron su promesa.

²²Entonces Josué llamó a los gabaonitas y les reclamó:

—¿Por qué nos engañaron con el cuento de que eran de tierras lejanas, cuando en verdad son nuestros vecinos? ²³A partir de ahora, ésta será su maldición: serán por siempre sirvientes del templo de mi Dios, responsables de cortar la leña y de acarrear el agua.

²⁴Los gabaonitas contestaron:

—Nosotros, servidores suyos, fuimos bien informados de que el SEÑOR su Dios ordenó a su siervo Moisés que les diera toda esta tierra y que destruyera a todos sus habitantes. Temimos tanto por nuestra *vida que decidimos hacer lo que ya saben. ²⁵Estamos a merced de ustedes. Hagan con nosotros lo que les parezca justo y bueno.

²⁶Así salvó Josué a los gabaonitas de morir a manos del pueblo de Israel. ²⁷Ese mismo día Josué los hizo leñadores y aguateros de la asamblea israelita, especialmente del altar del SEÑOR que está en el lugar que él mismo eligió. Y así han permanecido hasta el día de hoy.

Ataque de los reyes amorreos

10 Adonisédec, rey de Jerusalén, se enteró de que Josué había tomado la ciudad de Hai y la había *destruido completamente, pues Josué hizo con Hai y su rey lo mismo que había hecho con Jericó y su rey. Adonisédec también supo que los habitantes de Gabaón habían hecho un tratado de ayuda mutua con los israelitas y se habían quedado a vivir con ellos. ²Esto, por supuesto, alarmó grandemente a Adonisédec y a su gente, porque Gabaón era más importante y más grande que la ciudad de Hai; era tan grande como las capitales reales, y tenía un ejército poderoso.

³Por eso Adonisédec envió un mensaje a los siguientes reyes: Hohán de Hebrón, Pirán de Jarmut, Jafía de Laquis, y Debir de Eglón. ⁴El mensaje decía: «Únanse a mí y conquistemos a Gabaón, porque ha hecho un tratado de ayuda mutua con Josué y los israelitas.»

⁵Entonces los cinco reyes amorreos de Jerusalén, Hebrón, Jarmut, Laquis y Eglón se unieron y marcharon con sus ejércitos para acampar frente a Gabaón y atacarla.

Derrota de los reyes amorreos

⁶Los gabaonitas, por su parte, enviaron el siguiente mensaje a Josué, que estaba en Guilgal: «No abandone usted a estos siervos suyos. ¡Venga de inmediato y sálvenos! Necesitamos su ayuda, porque todos los reyes amorreos de la región montañosa se han aliado contra nosotros.»

⁷Josué salió de Guilgal con todo su ejército, acompañados de su comando especial. ⁸Y el SEÑOR le dijo a Josué: «No tiembles ante ellos, pues yo te los entrego; ninguno de ellos podrá resistirte.»

⁹Después de marchar toda la noche desde Guilgal, Josué los atacó por sorpresa. ¹⁰A su vez, el SEÑOR llenó de pánico a los amorreos ante la presencia del ejército israelita, y éste les infligió una tremenda derrota en Gabaón. A los que huyeron los persiguieron por el camino de Bet Jorón, y acabaron con ellos por toda la vía que va a Azeca y Maquedá. ¹¹Mientras los amorreos huían de Israel, entre Bet Jorón y Azeca, el SEÑOR mandó del cielo una tremenda granizada que mató a más gente de la que el ejército israelita había matado a filo de espada.

¹²Ese día en que el SEÑOR entregó a los amorreos en manos de los israelitas, Josué le dijo al SEÑOR en presencia de todo el pueblo:

«Sol, detente en Gabaón,
luna, párate sobre Ayalón.»

¹³El sol se detuvo
y la luna se paró,
hasta que Israel
se vengó de sus adversarios.

Esto está escrito en el libro de Jaser. Y, en efecto, el sol se detuvo en el cenit y no se movió de allí por casi un día entero. ¹⁴Nunca antes ni después ha habido un día como aquél; fue el día en que el SEÑOR obedeció la orden de un *ser humano. ¡No cabe duda de que el SEÑOR estaba peleando por Israel!

¹⁵Al terminar todo, Josué regresó a Guilgal con todo el ejército israelita.

Muerte de los reyes amorreos

¹⁶Los cinco reyes habían huido y se habían refugiado en una cueva en Maquedá. ¹⁷Tan pronto como Josué supo que habían hallado a los cinco reyes en la cueva, ¹⁸dio la siguiente orden: «Coloquen rocas a la entrada de la cueva y pongan unos guardias para que la vigilen. ¹⁹¡Que nadie se detenga! Persigan a los enemigos y atáquenlos por la retaguardia. No les permitan llegar a sus ciudades. ¡El SEÑOR, Dios de ustedes, ya se los ha entregado!»

²⁰Josué y el ejército israelita *exterminaron a sus enemigos; muy pocos de éstos pudieron refugiarse en las ciudades amuralladas. ²¹Finalmente, todos los israelitas retornaron a Maquedá sanos y salvos. ¡Nadie en la comarca se atrevía a decir nada contra Israel!

²²Entonces Josué mandó que destaparan la entrada de la cueva y que le trajeran los cinco reyes amorreos. ²³De inmediato sacaron a los cinco reyes de la cueva: los reyes de Jerusalén, Hebrón, Jarmut, Laquis y Eglón. ²⁴Cuando se los trajeron, Josué convocó a todo el ejército israelita y les ordenó a todos los comandantes que lo habían acompañado: «Acérquense y písenles el cuello a estos reyes.» Los comandantes obedecieron al instante. ²⁵Entonces Josué les dijo: «No teman ni den un paso atrás; al contrario, sean fuertes y valientes. Esto es exactamente lo que el SEÑOR hará con todos los que ustedes enfrenten en batalla.»

²⁶Dicho esto, Josué mató a los reyes, los colgó en cinco árboles, y allí los dejó hasta el atardecer. ²⁷Cuando ya el sol estaba por ponerse, Josué mandó que los descolgaran de los árboles y los arrojaran en la misma cueva donde antes se habían escondido. Entonces taparon la cueva con unas enormes rocas, que permanecen allí hasta el día de hoy.

²⁸Ese mismo día Josué tomó Maquedá y mató a filo de espada a su rey y a todos sus habitantes; inadie quedó con vida! Y al rey de Maquedá le sucedió lo mismo que al rey de Jericó.

Conquista de las ciudades del sur

²⁹De Maquedá, Josué y todo Israel se dirigieron a Libná y la atacaron. ³⁰El SEÑOR entregó en manos de Israel al rey y a sus habitantes. Josué pasó a filo

de espada a todos sus habitantes; nadie quedó con vida. Y al rey de Libná le sucedió lo mismo que al rey de Jericó.

31De Libná, Josué y todo Israel se dirigieron a Laquis. El ejército la sitió y la atacó. 32El SEÑOR la entregó en manos de Israel, y al segundo día la conquistaron. Todos en Laquis murieron a filo de espada, tal como había sucedido con Libná. 33Además, Horán, rey de Guézer, que había salido a defender a Laquis, fue totalmente derrotado junto con su ejército; nadie sobrevivió a la espada de Josué.

34De Laquis, Josué y todo Israel se dirigieron a Eglón. Sitiaron la ciudad y la atacaron. 35En un solo día la conquistaron y *destruyeron a todos a filo de espada, tal como lo habían hecho con Laquis.

36De Eglón, Josué y todo Israel se dirigieron a Hebrón, y la atacaron. 37El ejército israelita tomó la ciudad y la pasó a filo de espada, de modo que nadie, ni el rey ni ninguno de los habitantes de la ciudad y de sus aldeas, escapó con vida. Y tal como sucedió en Eglón, Hebrón fue destruida completamente.

38De Hebrón, Josué y todo Israel se dirigieron a Debir y la atacaron. 39Se apoderaron de la ciudad, de su rey y de todas sus aldeas, y mataron a filo de espada a todos sus habitantes. Nadie quedó con vida; todo fue *arrasado. A Debir le sucedió lo mismo que les había sucedido a Libná, a Hebrón y a sus respectivos reyes.

40Así Josué conquistó toda aquella región: la cordillera, el Néguev, los llanos y las laderas. Derrotó a todos sus reyes, sin dejar ningún sobreviviente. ¡Todo cuanto tenía aliento de vida fue *destruido completamente! Esto lo hizo según el mandato del SEÑOR, Dios de Israel. 41Josué conquistó a todos, desde Cades Barnea hasta Gaza, y desde la región de Gosén hasta Gabaón. 42A todos esos reyes y sus territorios Josué los conquistó en una sola expedición, porque el SEÑOR, Dios de Israel, combatía por su pueblo.

43Después Josué regresó al campamento de Guilgal junto con todo el ejército israelita.

Conquista de los reinos del norte

11 Cuando Jabín, rey de Jazor, se enteró de todo lo ocurrido, convocó a Jobab, rey de Madón, y a los reyes de Simrón y de Acsaf. 2También llamó a los reyes de la región montañosa del norte; a los de la región al sur del lago Quinéret;f a los de los valles, y a los de Nafot Dor,g al occidente. 3Llamó además a los cananeos de oriente y occidente, a los amorreos, a los hititas, a los ferezeos, a los jebuseos de las montañas y a los heveos que viven en las laderas del monte Hermón en Mizpa.

4Todos ellos salieron con sus ejércitos, caballos y carros de guerra. Eran tan numerosos que parecían arena a la orilla del mar. 5Formaron un solo ejército y acamparon junto a las aguas de Merón para pelear contra Israel.

6Entonces el SEÑOR le dijo a Josué: «No le tengas miedo, porque mañana, a esta hora, yo le entregaré muerto a Israel todo ese ejército. Ustedes, por su parte, deberán desjarretar sus caballos e incendiar sus carros de guerra.»

7Así que Josué partió acompañado de sus guerreros y tomó por sorpresa a sus enemigos junto a las aguas de Merón. 8El SEÑOR los entregó en manos de los israelitas, quienes los atacaron y persiguieron hasta la gran ciudad de Sidón, y hasta Misrefot Ma-

yin y el valle de Mizpa al este, y no quedaron sobrevivientes. 9Josué cumplió con todo lo que el SEÑOR le había ordenado: desjarretó los caballos del enemigo e incendió sus carros de guerra.

10Al regreso Josué conquistó Jazor y mató a filo de espada a su rey, pues Jazor había sido cabecera de todos aquellos reinados. 11Los israelitas mataron a espada a todo cuanto tenía *vida. *Arrasaron la ciudad y le prendieron fuego. 12Josué conquistó todas las ciudades de aquellos reinos junto con sus reyes; a éstos mató a filo de espada, *destruyéndolos por completo. Así obedeció Josué todo lo que Moisés, siervo del SEÑOR, le había mandado. 13Las ciudades que estaban sobre los cerros fueron las únicas que los israelitas no quemaron, excepto Jazor. 14Tomaron como botín de guerra todas las pertenencias del enemigo y su ganado, y mataron a todos los hombres a filo de espada, de modo que ninguno quedó con vida. 15Así como el SEÑOR había ordenado a su siervo Moisés, también Moisés se lo ordenó a Josué. Y éste, por su parte, cumplió al pie de la letra todo lo que el SEÑOR le había ordenado a Moisés.

Síntesis de la conquista

16Josué logró conquistar toda aquella tierra: la región montañosa, todo el Néguev, toda la región de Gosén, el valle, el Arabá, la región montañosa de Israel y su valle. 17También se apoderó de todos los territorios, desde la región de Jalac que se eleva hacia Seír, hasta Baal Gad en el valle del Líbano, a las faldas del monte Hermón. Josué capturó a todos los reyes de esa región y los ejecutó, 18después de combatir con ellos por largo tiempo.

19Ninguna ciudad hizo tratado de ayuda mutua con los israelitas, excepto los heveos de Gabaón. A todas esas ciudades Josué las derrotó en el campo de batalla, 20porque el SEÑOR endureció el *corazón de los enemigos para que entablaran guerra con Israel. Así serían *exterminados sin compasión alguna, según el mandato que el SEÑOR le había dado a Moisés.

21En aquel tiempo Josué destruyó a los *anaquitas del monte Hebrón, de Debir, de Anab y de la región montañosa de Judá e Israel. Habitantes y ciudades fueron *arrasados por Josué. 22Ningún anaquita quedó con vida en la tierra que ocupó el pueblo de Israel. Su presencia se redujo sólo a Gaza, Gat y Asdod.

23Así logró Josué conquistar toda aquella tierra, conforme a la orden que el SEÑOR le había dado a Moisés, y se la entregó como herencia al pueblo de Israel, según la distribución tribal. Por fin, aquella región descansó de las guerras.

Reyes derrotados por Moisés

12 Los israelitas derrotaron a dos reyes cuyos territorios se extendían al este del río Jordán, desde el arroyo Arnón hasta el monte Hermón, y abarcaban el Arabá al oriente.

2Uno de ellos era Sijón, rey de los amorreos, cuyo trono estaba en Hesbón. Este rey gobernaba desde Aroer, ciudad asentada a orillas del arroyo Arnón, hasta el arroyo Jaboc, que era la frontera del territorio de los amonitas. El territorio de Sijón incluía la cuarta parte del valle y la mitad de Galaad. 3Abarcaba también la parte oriental del Arabá hasta el lago Quinéret,h y de allí al mar del sur, por la vía del Mar Muerto, hasta Bet Yesimot y, más al sur, hasta las laderas del monte Pisgá.

---

f 11:2 *lago Quinéret.* Es decir, lago de Galilea.   g 11:2 *Nafot Dor.* Alt. *las alturas de Dor.*   h 12:3 *lago Quinéret.* Es decir, lago de Galilea.

4El otro rey era Og, rey de Basán, uno de los últimos refaítas, que residía en Astarot y Edrey. 5Este rey gobernaba desde el monte Hermón, en Salcá, y en toda la región de Basán, hasta la frontera de Guesur y de Macá, y en la mitad de Galaad, hasta la frontera del territorio de Sijón, rey de Hesbón.

6Los israelitas bajo el mando de Moisés derrotaron a estos reyes. Y Moisés repartió aquel territorio entre los rubenitas, los gaditas y la media tribu de Manasés.

Reyes derrotados por Josué

7A continuación aparece la lista de los reyes que los israelitas derrotaron bajo el mando de Josué. Sus territorios se encontraban al lado occidental del río Jordán, y se extendían desde Baal Gad, en el valle del Líbano, hasta el monte Jalac, que asciende hacia Seír. Josué entregó las tierras de estos reyes como propiedad a las tribus de Israel, según las divisiones tribales. 8Tales territorios comprendían la región montañosa, los valles occidentales, el Arabá, las laderas, el desierto y el Néguev. Esas tierras habían pertenecido a los hititas, amorreos, cananeos, ferezeos, heveos y jebuseos. Ésta es la lista de reyes:

9　el rey de Jericó,
　　el rey de Hai, ciudad cercana a Betel,
10　el rey de Jerusalén,
　　el rey de Hebrón,
11　el rey de Jarmut,
　　el rey de Laquis,
12　el rey de Eglón,
　　el rey de Guézer,
13　el rey de Debir,
　　el rey de Guéder,
14　el rey de Jormá,
　　el rey de Arad,
15　el rey de Libná,
　　el rey de Adulán,
16　el rey de Maquedá,
　　el rey de Betel,
17　el rey de Tapúaj,
　　el rey de Héfer,
18　el rey de Afec,
　　el rey de Sarón,
19　el rey de Madón,
　　el rey de Jazor,
20　el rey de Simrón Merón,
　　el rey de Acsaf,
21　el rey de Tanac,
　　el rey de Meguido,
22　el rey de Cedes,
　　el rey de Jocneán que está en el Carmelo,
23　el rey de Dor que está en Nafot Dor,i
　　el rey Goyim de Guilgal
24　y el rey de Tirsá.
　　Eran treinta y un reyes en total.

El territorio no conquistado

13　Cuando Josué era ya bastante anciano, el SEÑOR le dijo: «Ya estás muy viejo, y todavía queda mucho territorio por conquistar. 2Me refiero a todo el territorio filisteo y guesureo, 3que se extiende desde el río Sijor, al este de Egipto, hasta la frontera de Ecrón al norte. A ése se le considera territorio cananeo, y en él se encuentran los cinco gobernantes filisteos: el de Gaza, el de Asdod, el de Ascalón, el de Gat y el de Ecrón. También queda sin conquistar el territorio de los aveos. 4Por el lado sur queda todo el territorio cananeo, desde Araj, tierra de los sidonios, hasta Afec, que está en la frontera de los amorreos. 5Además queda el territorio de los guiblitas y todo el Líbano oriental, desde Baal Gad, al pie del monte Hermón, hasta Lebó Jamat.j 6Yo mismo voy a echar de la presencia de los israelitas a todos los habitantes de Sidón y a cuantos viven en la región montañosa, desde el Líbano hasta Misrefot Mayin.

»Tú, por tu parte, repartirás y les darás por herencia esta tierra a los israelitas, tal como te lo he ordenado. 7Ya es tiempo de que repartas esta tierra entre las nueve tribus restantes y la otra media tribu de Manasés.»

División de los territorios al oriente del Jordán

8La otra media tribu de Manasés, los rubenitas y los gaditas ya habían recibido la herencia que Moisés, siervo del SEÑOR, les había asignado de antemano. 9Abarcaba desde Aroer, que estaba a orillas del arroyo Arnón, con la población ubicada en medio del valle. Incluía también toda la meseta de Medeba hasta Dibón, 10todas las ciudades de Sijón —rey de los amorreos que reinaba desde Hesbón—, hasta la frontera del país de los amonitas. 11Comprendía, además, Galaad, el territorio de la gente de Guesur y Macá, toda la montaña del Hermón y todo Basán hasta Salcá. 12Ésa era la tierra de Og, rey de Basán, que reinó en Astarot y Edrey; fue el último de los refaítas, a quienes Moisés había derrotado y arrojado de su territorio. 13Pero los israelitas no expulsaron de su territorio a los habitantes de Guesur y Macá, que hasta el día de hoy viven en territorio israelita.

14Sin embargo, a la tribu de Leví Moisés no le dio tierras por herencia, pues su herencia son las ofrendas del pueblo del SEÑOR, Dios de Israel, tal como él se lo había prometido.

15Éstas son las tierras que Moisés había entregado a cada uno de los clanes de la tribu de Rubén: 16abarcaban desde Aroer, que estaba a orillas del arroyo Arnón, con la población ubicada en medio del valle. Incluían también toda la meseta de Medeba 17hasta Hesbón y todas las poblaciones de la meseta: Dibón, Bamot Baal, Bet Baal Megón, 18Yahaza, Cademot, Mefat, 19Quiriatayin, Sibma, Zaret Sajar, que está en la colina del valle, 20Bet Peor, Bet Yesimot y las laderas del monte Pisgá; 21es decir, las ciudades y los pueblos de la meseta, y todos los dominios de Sijón, rey amorreo que gobernó en Hesbón. Moisés había derrotado a este rey y a los príncipes madianitas Eví, Requen, Zur, Jur y Reba, todos ellos aliados de Sijón y habitantes de la región. 22Los israelitas pasaron a filo de espada a muchos hombres en el campo de batalla, incluso al adivino Balán hijo de Beor. 23El río Jordán sirvió como frontera del territorio perteneciente a los rubenitas. Estas ciudades y pueblos fueron la herencia de la tribu de Rubén, según sus clanes.

24Moisés también había entregado a la tribu de Gad y a sus respectivos clanes los siguientes territorios: 25las tierras de Jazer, todas las poblaciones de la región de Galaad y la mitad del territorio amonita, hasta Aroer, que está frente a Rabá; 26y las tierras comprendidas entre Hesbón, Ramat Mizpé y Betonín, y entre Majanayin y la frontera de Debir. 27En el valle recibieron Bet Aram, Bet Nimrá, Sucot y Zafón, junto con lo que quedaba del reino de Sijón, rey de Hesbón. Así que su territorio se extendía desde el este del Jordán hasta el sur del lago Quinéret.k

---

i 12:23 Nafot Dor. Alt. las alturas de Dor. j 13:5 Lebó Jamat. Alt. la entrada de Jamat. k 13:27 lago Quinéret. Es decir, lago de Galilea.

²⁸Estas ciudades y pueblos fueron la herencia de la tribu de Gad, según sus clanes.

²⁹Éstas son las tierras que Moisés había entregado a la media tribu de Manasés y sus clanes: ³⁰el territorio que abarca Majanayin y toda la región de Basán, es decir, todo el reino de Og, incluyendo las sesenta poblaciones de Yaír. ³¹Además, la mitad de Galaad, y Astarot y Edrey, ciudades del reino de Og, les correspondieron a la mitad de los descendientes de Maquir hijo de Manasés, según sus clanes.

³²Ésta es la herencia que Moisés repartió cuando se encontraba en los llanos de Moab, al otro lado del río Jordán, al este de Jericó. ³³Sin embargo, a la tribu de Leví Moisés no le dio tierras por herencia, porque el SEÑOR, Dios de Israel, es su herencia, tal como él se lo había prometido.

División de los territorios al occidente del Jordán

14 Éstas son las tierras cananeas que el sacerdote Eleazar, Josué hijo de Nun y los jefes de los clanes entregaron a los israelitas como herencia. ²Esa herencia se les repartió por sorteo a las nueve tribus y media, tal como el SEÑOR había ordenado por medio de Moisés. ³⁻⁴Ya que éste les había dado por herencia la parte oriental del Jordán a las dos tribus y media, pues los descendientes de José se habían dividido en dos tribus, Manasés y Efraín. Pero a los levitas no les dio tierras, sino sólo algunas poblaciones con sus respectivos campos de cultivo y pastoreo. ⁵Así los israelitas dividieron el territorio tal como el SEÑOR se lo había ordenado a Moisés.

Caleb recibe Hebrón

⁶Los descendientes de Judá se acercaron a Josué en Guilgal. El quenizita Caleb hijo de Jefone le pidió a Josué: «Acuérdate de lo que el SEÑOR le dijo a Moisés, hombre de Dios, respecto a ti y a mí en Cades Barnea. ⁷Yo tenía cuarenta años cuando Moisés, siervo del SEÑOR, me envió desde Cades Barnea para explorar el país, y con toda franqueza le informé de lo que vi. ⁸Mis compañeros de viaje, por el contrario, desanimaron a la gente y le infundieron temor. Pero yo me mantuve fiel al SEÑOR mi Dios. ⁹Ese mismo día Moisés me hizo este juramento: "La tierra que toquen tus pies será herencia tuya y de tus descendientes para siempre, porque fuiste fiel al SEÑOR mi Dios."ˡ

¹⁰»Ya han pasado cuarenta y cinco años desde que el SEÑOR hizo la promesa por medio de Moisés, mientras Israel peregrinaba por el desierto; aquí estoy este día con mis ochenta y cinco años: ¡el SEÑOR me ha mantenido con vida! ¹¹Y todavía mantengo la misma fortaleza que tenía el día en que Moisés me envió. Para la batalla tengo las mismas energías que tenía entonces. ¹²Dame, pues, la región montañosa que el SEÑOR me prometió en esa ocasión. Desde ese día, tú bien sabes que los *anaquitas habitan allí, y que sus ciudades son enormes y fortificadas. Sin embargo, con la ayuda del SEÑOR los expulsaré de ese territorio, tal como él ha prometido.»

¹³Entonces Josué bendijo a Caleb y le dio por herencia el territorio de Hebrón. ¹⁴A partir de ese día Hebrón ha pertenecido al quenizita Caleb hijo de Jefone, porque fue fiel al SEÑOR, Dios de Israel. ¹⁵Hebrón se llamaba originalmente Quiriat Arbá, porque Arbá fue un importante antepasado de los anaquitas.

Después de todo esto el país se vio libre de guerras.

Los territorios de Judá
15:15-19—Jue 1:11-15

15 El territorio asignado a los clanes de la tribu de Judá abarcaba las tierras comprendidas hasta la frontera de Edom, incluyendo el desierto de Zin en el sur.

²La frontera sur, que partía de la bahía ubicada al extremo sur del Mar Muerto, ³salía hacia el sur de la cuesta de Acrabín, cruzaba hacia el desierto de Zin y continuaba hacia Cades Barnea, al sur. De allí seguía por Jezrón, subía hacia Adar, daba la vuelta hacia Carcá, ⁴continuaba por Asmón y salía hacia el arroyo de Egipto, para terminar en el Mediterráneo. Ésta es la frontera sur de Judá.ᵐ

⁵La frontera oriental la formaba el Mar Muerto hasta la desembocadura del río Jordán.

La frontera norte se iniciaba en la bahía de la desembocadura del Jordán ⁶y subía por Bet Joglá, continuando al norte de Bet Arabá, hasta la peña de Bohán hijo de Rubén. ⁷Subía luego hacia Debir desde el valle de Acor, y giraba hacia el norte en dirección a Guilgal, al frente de la pendiente de Adumín, al sur del valle. Seguía bordeando las aguas de Ensemes y llegaba a Enroguel. ⁸Continuaba hacia el valle de Ben Hinón al sur de la cuesta de la ciudad jebusea, es decir, Jerusalén. Ascendía a la cumbre de la loma al oeste del valle de Hinón, al norte del valle de Refayín. ⁹De aquella cumbre la frontera se dirigía hacia el manantial de Neftóaj, seguía por las ciudades del monte Efrón y descendía hacia Balá, también llamada Quiriat Yearín. ¹⁰De allí giraba al oeste de Balá y se dirigía hacia el monte Seír, bordeaba por el norte las laderas del monte Yearín, llamado también Quesalón, y descendía hacia Bet Semes, pasando por Timná. ¹¹Después seguía por la parte norte las cuestas de Ecrón, giraba hacia Sicrón, rodeaba el monte Balá y llegaba hasta Jabnel. La línea fronteriza terminaba en el mar Mediterráneo.

¹²La frontera occidental la formaba la costa del mar Mediterráneo.

Éstas son las fronteras de los territorios asignados a la tribu de Judá y sus clanes.

Caleb conquista Hebrón y Debir

¹³De acuerdo con lo ordenado por el SEÑOR, Josué le dio a Caleb hijo de Jefone una porción del territorio asignado a Judá. Esa porción es Quiriat Arbá, es decir, Hebrón (Arbá fue un ancestro de los *anaquitas). ¹⁴Caleb expulsó de Hebrón a tres descendientes de Anac: Sesay, Ajimán y Talmay. ¹⁵De allí subió para atacar a los habitantes de Debir, ciudad que antes se llamaba Quiriat Séfer. ¹⁶Y dijo: «Le daré mi hija Acsa como esposa al hombre que ataque y conquiste la ciudad de Quiriat Séfer.» ¹⁷Entonces Otoniel hijo de Quenaz y sobrino de Caleb capturó Quiriat Séfer y se casó con Acsa.

¹⁸Cuando ella llegó, Otoniel la convencióⁿ de que le pidiera un terreno a su padre. Al bajar Acsa del asno, Caleb le preguntó:

—¿Qué te pasa?

¹⁹—Concédeme un gran favor —respondió ella—. Ya que me has dado tierras en el Néguev, dame también manantiales.

Fue así como Caleb le dio a su hija manantiales en las zonas altas y en las bajas.

Ciudades de Judá

²⁰Ésta es la lista de los territorios que recibieron como herencia los clanes de la tribu de Judá:

ˡ **14:9** Dt 1:36   ᵐ **15:4** *Judá*. Lit. *Ustedes.*   ⁿ **15:18** *Otoniel la convenció* (mss. de LXX); *lo convenció* (TM).

²¹Las ciudades sureñas de la tribu, ubicadas en el Néguev, cerca de la frontera con Edom:

Cabsel, Edar, Jagur, ²²Quiná, Dimoná, Adadá, ²³Cedes, Jazor, Itnán, ²⁴Zif, Telén, Bealot, ²⁵Jazor Jadatá, Queriot, Jezrón (conocida también como Jazor), ²⁶Amán, Semá, Moladá, ²⁷Jazar Gadá, Hesmón, Bet Pelet, ²⁸Jazar Súal, Berseba, con sus poblados,ñ ²⁹Balá, Iyín, Esen, ³⁰Eltolad, Quesil, Jormá, ³¹Siclag, Madmana, Sansaná, ³²Lebaot, Siljín, Ayin y Rimón, es decir, un total de veintinueve ciudades con sus pueblos.

³³En la llanura:

Estaol, Zora, Asena, ³⁴Zanoa, Enganín, Tapúaj, Enam, ³⁵Jarmut, Adulán, Soco, Azeca, ³⁶Sajarayin, Aditayin, Guederá y Guederotayin, es decir, catorce ciudades con sus pueblos.

³⁷Zenán, Jadasá, Migdal Gad, ³⁸Dileán, Mizpa, Joctel, ³⁹Laquis, Boscat, Eglón, ⁴⁰Cabón, Lajmás, Quitlís, ⁴¹Guederot, Bet Dagón, Noamá y Maquedá, es decir, dieciséis ciudades con sus pueblos.

⁴²Libná, Éter, Asán, ⁴³Jifta, Asena, Nezib, ⁴⁴Queilá, Aczib y Maresá, es decir, nueve ciudades con sus pueblos.

⁴⁵Ecrón, con sus pueblos y aldeas; ⁴⁶de allí al mar, todo el territorio colindante con Asdod, junto con sus poblaciones; ⁴⁷Asdod, con sus pueblos y aldeas, y Gaza, con sus pueblos y aldeas, hasta el arroyo de Egipto y la costa del mar Mediterráneo.

⁴⁸En la región montañosa:

Samir, Jatir, Soco, ⁴⁹Daná, Quiriat Saná (conocida como Debir), ⁵⁰Anab, Estemoa, Anín, ⁵¹Gosén, Holón y Guiló, es decir, once ciudades con sus pueblos.

⁵²Arab, Dumá, Esán, ⁵³Yanún, Bet Tapúaj, Afecá, ⁵⁴Humtá, Quiriat Arbá (llamada también Hebrón) y Sior, es decir, nueve ciudades con sus pueblos.

⁵⁵Maón, Carmel, Zif, Yutá, ⁵⁶Jezrel, Jocdeán, Zanoa, ⁵⁷Caín, Guibeá y Timná, es decir, diez ciudades con sus pueblos.

⁵⁸Jaljul, Betsur, Guedor, ⁵⁹Marat, Bet Anot y Eltecón, es decir, seis ciudades con sus pueblos.

⁶⁰Quiriat Baal (o Quiriat Yearín) y Rabá, con sus pueblos.

⁶¹En el desierto:

Bet Arabá, Midín, Secacá, ⁶²Nibsán, la Ciudad de la sal y Engadi, es decir, seis ciudades con sus pueblos.

⁶³Los descendientes de Judá no pudieron expulsar de la ciudad de Jerusalén a los jebuseos, así que hasta el día de hoy éstos viven allí junto con los descendientes de Judá.

Los territorios de Efraín y Manasés

16 El territorio asignado a los descendientes de José comenzaba en el río Jordán,º al este de los manantiales de Jericó; y de allí ascendía hacia la región montañosa de Betel, a través del desierto. ²De Betel, es decir, Luz,ᴾ continuaba hacia el territorio de los arquitas hasta Astarot, ³descendía hacia el oeste al territorio de los jafletitas hasta la región de Bet Jorón de Abajo y Guézer, y terminaba en el mar Mediterráneo. ⁴Así fue como las tribus de Manasés y

Efraín, descendientes de José, recibieron como herencia sus territorios.

El territorio de Efraín

⁵Éste es el territorio que recibieron la tribu de Efraín y sus respectivos clanes:

En el lado oriental sus límites se extendían desde Atarot Adar hasta Bet Jorón de Arriba, ⁶y llegaban hasta el mar Mediterráneo. En Micmetat, que está al norte, hacían una curva hacia el oriente rumbo a Tanat Siló y de allí llegaban a Janoa. ⁷Descendían de Janoa hacia Atarot y Nará, pasando por Jericó hasta llegar al río Jordán. ⁸De Tapúaj la frontera seguía hacia el occidente rumbo al arroyo de Caná y terminaba en el mar Mediterráneo. Éste es el territorio que recibió como herencia la tribu de Efraín por sus clanes. ⁹El territorio también incluía las ciudades y sus respectivas aldeas que se encontraban en el territorio asignado a la tribu de Manasés.

¹⁰Los efraimitas no expulsaron a los cananeos que vivían en Guézer; les permitieron vivir entre ellos, como sucede hasta el día de hoy, pero los sometieron a trabajos forzados.

El territorio de Manasés

17 También a la tribu de Manasés se le asignó su propio territorio, porque él era el primogénito de José. A Maquir, primogénito de Manasés y antepasado de los galaaditas, se le concedió Galaad y Basán por ser hombre de guerra. ²Los demás clanes de la tribu de Manasés también recibieron sus territorios: Abiezer, Jélec, Asriel, Siquén, Héfer y Semidá. Éstos eran descendientes de Manasés hijo de José.

³Sucedió que Zelofejad hijo de Héfer, nieto de Galaad y bisnieto de Manasés, sólo tuvo hijas, cuyos nombres eran Majlá, Noa, Joglá, Milca y Tirsá. ⁴Ellas se presentaron ante Eleazar el sacerdote, ante Josué hijo de Nun y ante los jefes de Israel, y les dijeron: «El SEÑOR le ordenó a Moisés que nos diera tierras en los territorios asignados como herencia a nuestro clan.» Entonces Josué hizo tal como el SEÑOR le había ordenado.

⁵La tribu de Manasés recibió diez porciones de tierra, además de los territorios de Galaad y Basán, que están al lado oriental del Jordán. ⁶Esto se debió a que las hijas de Manasés recibieron tierras como herencia, además de las repartidas a los descendientes varones. Galaad fue asignada a los otros descendientes de Manasés.

⁷El territorio de Manasés abarcaba desde Aser hasta Micmetat, ubicada al este de Siquén. De allí la frontera seguía hacia el sur, hasta las tierras pertenecientes a Yasubᵠ En Tapúaj. ⁸A Manasés le pertenecían también las tierras de Tapúaj, pero la ciudad de Tapúaj, ubicada en los límites de Manasés, era de los descendientes de Efraín. ⁹La frontera continuaba hacia el sur, por el lado norte del arroyo de Caná, hasta llegar al mar Mediterráneo. En esa zona, varias ciudades de la tribu de Efraín se mezclaban con ciudades pertenecientes a Manasés. ¹⁰Los territorios del sur le pertenecían a Efraín, y los del norte, a Manasés. El territorio de Manasés llegaba hasta el mar Mediterráneo y bordeaba, por el norte, con la tribu de Aser, y por el este, con la de Isacar. ¹¹Dentro de las fronteras de Isacar y Aser, la tribu de Manasés tenía las siguientes ciudades con sus poblaciones: Betseán,

---

ñ **15:28** *con sus poblados* (LXX); *Biziotía* (TM). o **16:1** *en el río Jordán.* Lit. *en el Jordán de Jericó* (uno de los antiguos nombres asignados al río Jordán). p **16:2** *de Betel, es decir, Luz* (véase v. 1 de LXX); *de Betel hacia Luz* (TM). q **17:7** *Yasub* (lectura probable; véase LXX); *los habitantes de* (TM).

Ibleam, Dor, Endor, Tanac y Meguido. La tercera ciudad de la lista era Nafot.

¹²Los miembros de la tribu de Manasés no pudieron habitar estas ciudades, porque los cananeos persistieron en vivir en ellas. ¹³Cuando los israelitas se hicieron fuertes, redujeron a los cananeos a esclavitud, pero no los expulsaron totalmente de esas tierras.

¹⁴Las tribus de José le reprocharon a Josué:

—¿Por qué nos has dado sólo una parte del territorio? Nosotros somos numerosos, y el SEÑOR nos ha bendecido ricamente.

¹⁵Entonces Josué les respondió:

—Ya que son tan numerosos y encuentran que la región montañosa de Efraín es demasiado pequeña para ustedes, vayan a la zona de los bosques que están en territorio ferezeo y refaíta, y desmonten tierra para que habiten allá.

¹⁶Los descendientes de José replicaron:

—La región montañosa nos queda muy pequeña, y los cananeos que viven en el llano poseen carros de hierro, tanto los de Betsán y sus poblaciones como los del valle de Jezrel.

¹⁷Pero Josué animó a las tribus de Efraín y Manasés, descendientes de José:

—Ustedes son numerosos y tienen mucho poder. No se quedarán con un solo territorio, ¹⁸sino que poseerán la región de los bosques. Desmóntenla y ocúpenla hasta sus límites más lejanos. Y a pesar de que los cananeos tengan carros de hierro y sean muy fuertes, ustedes los podrán expulsar.

Los territorios de las otras tribus

18 Cuando el país quedó bajo el control de los israelitas, toda la asamblea israelita se reunió en Siló, donde habían establecido la *Tienda de reunión. ²Para entonces, todavía quedaban siete tribus que no habían recibido como herencia sus respectivos territorios.

³Así que Josué los desafió: «¿Hasta cuándo van a esperar para tomar posesión del territorio que les otorgó el SEÑOR, Dios de sus antepasados? ⁴Nombren a tres hombres de cada tribu para que yo los envíe a reconocer las tierras, y que hagan por escrito una reseña de cada territorio. A su regreso, ⁵dividan el resto del país en siete partes. Judá mantendrá sus territorios en el sur, y los descendientes de José, en el norte. ⁶Cuando hayan terminado la descripción de las siete regiones, tráiganmela, y yo las asignaré echando suertes en presencia del SEÑOR nuestro Dios. ⁷Los levitas, como ya saben, no recibirán ninguna porción de tierra, porque su herencia es su servicio sacerdotal ante el SEÑOR. Además, Gad, Rubén y la media tribu de Manasés ya han recibido sus respectivos territorios en el lado oriental del Jordán. Moisés, siervo del SEÑOR, se los entregó como herencia.»

⁸Cuando los hombres estaban listos para salir a hacer el reconocimiento del país, Josué les ordenó: «Exploren todo el país y tráiganme una descripción escrita de todos sus territorios. Cuando regresen aquí a Siló, yo haré el sorteo de tierras en presencia del SEÑOR.» ⁹Los hombres hicieron tal como Josué les ordenó, y regresaron a Siló con la descripción de todo el país, ciudad por ciudad, y su división en siete partes. ¹⁰Josué hizo allí el sorteo en presencia del SEÑOR, y repartió los territorios entre los israelitas, según sus divisiones tribales.

El territorio de Benjamín

¹¹A la tribu de Benjamín se le asignó su territorio según sus clanes. Ese territorio quedó ubicado entre las tribus de Judá y José.

¹²La frontera norte se iniciaba en el río Jordán, pasaba por las laderas al norte de Jericó y avanzaba en dirección occidental hacia la región montañosa, hasta llegar al desierto de Bet Avén. ¹³Continuaba hacia la ladera sureña de Luz, también llamada Betel, y descendía desde Atarot Adar hasta el cerro que está al sur de Bet Jorón de Abajo.

¹⁴De allí la frontera continuaba hacia el sur, por el lado occidental, hasta llegar a Quiriat Baal, llamada también Quiriat Yearín, una población perteneciente a Judá. Ésta era la frontera occidental.

¹⁵La frontera sur partía desde Quiriat Yearín, en el lado occidental, y continuaba hasta el manantial de Neftóaj. ¹⁶Descendía a las laderas del monte ubicado frente al valle de Ben Hinón, al norte del valle de Refayin. Seguía en descenso por el valle de Hinón, bordeando la cuesta de la ciudad de Jebús, hasta llegar a Enroguel. ¹⁷De allí giraba hacia el norte, rumbo a Ensemes, seguía por Guelilot, al frente de la cuesta de Adumín, y descendía a la peña de Bohán hijo de Rubén. ¹⁸La frontera continuaba hacia la cuesta norte de Bet Arabá,ʳ y descendía hasta el Arabá. ¹⁹De allí se dirigía a la cuesta norte de Bet Joglá y salía en la bahía norte del Mar Muerto, donde desemboca el río Jordán. Ésta era la frontera sur.

²⁰El río Jordán marcaba los límites del lado oriental.

Éstas eran las fronteras de las tierras asignadas como herencia a todos los clanes de la tribu de Benjamín.

²¹Los clanes de la tribu de Benjamín poseyeron las siguientes ciudades: Jericó, Bet Joglá, Émec Casís, ²²Bet Arabá, Zemarayin, Betel, ²³Avín, Pará, Ofra, ²⁴Quefar Amoní, Ofni y Gueba, es decir, doce ciudades con sus poblaciones; ²⁵y Gabaón, Ramá, Berot, ²⁶Mizpa, Cafira, Mozá, ²⁷Requen, Irpel, Taralá, ²⁸Zela, Élef, Jebús, llamada también Jerusalén, Guibeá y Quiriat, es decir, catorce ciudades con sus poblaciones.

Ésta fue la herencia que recibieron los clanes de la tribu de Benjamín.

El territorio de Simeón
19:2-10—1Cr 4:28-33

19 Simeón fue la segunda tribu que recibió sus territorios, según sus clanes. Su herencia estaba ubicada dentro del territorio de Judá. ²Le pertenecían las siguientes ciudades: Berseba (o Sabá), Moladá, ³Jazar Súal, Balá, Esen, ⁴Eltolad, Betul, Jormá, ⁵Siclag, Bet Marcabot, Jazar Susá, ⁶Bet Lebaot y Sarujén, es decir, trece ciudades con sus poblaciones; ⁷y Ayin, Rimón, Éter y Asán, es decir, cuatro ciudades con sus poblaciones. ⁸A estas ciudades se agregaban los pueblos que se contaban hasta los bordes de Balatber, ciudad de Ramat ubicada en el Néguev.

Éstos fueron los territorios asignados a los clanes de la tribu de Simeón. ⁹Como la tribu de Judá tenía más territorio de lo que sus clanes necesitaban, la tribu de Simeón recibió su porción del territorio asignado a Judá.

El territorio de Zabulón

¹⁰Zabulón fue la tercera tribu que recibió su territorio, según sus clanes. La frontera del territorio se extendía hasta Sarid. ¹¹Por el occidente, se dirigía hacia Maralá, y llegaba a Dabéset, hasta tocar el arroyo

---

ʳ **18:18** *de Bet Arabá* (LXX); *al frente del Arabá* (TM).

frente a Jocneán. 12De allí, giraba al este de Sarid, hacia la salida del sol, hasta el territorio de Quislot Tabor, luego continuaba hasta alcanzar Daberat y subía hasta Jafía. 13La frontera cruzaba por el oriente hacia Gat Jefer e Itacasín, hasta llegar a Rimón y girar hacia Negá. 14De allí la frontera giraba hacia el norte hasta llegar a Janatón, y terminaba en el valle de Jeftel. 15Ese territorio incluía doce ciudades y sus poblaciones, entre ellas Catat, Nalal, Simrón, Idalá y Belén. 16Éste es el territorio asignado como herencia a los clanes de la tribu de Zabulón, incluyendo sus ciudades y pueblos.

El territorio de Isacar

17Isacar fue la cuarta tribu que recibió su territorio, según sus clanes. 18Las ciudades que se encontraban dentro de ese territorio eran: Jezrel, Quesulot, Sunén, 19Jafarayin, Sijón, Anajarat, 20Rabit, Cisón, Abez, 21Rémet, Enganín, Enadá y Bet Pasés. 22La frontera llegaba a Tabor, Sajazimá y Bet Semes, y terminaba en el río Jordán. En total, dieciséis ciudades con sus poblaciones 23componían la herencia de los clanes de la tribu de Isacar.

El territorio de Aser

24Aser fue la quinta tribu que recibió su territorio, según sus clanes. 25En él se incluían las ciudades de Jelcat, Jalí, Betén, Acsaf, 26Alamélec, Amad y Miseal. La frontera tocaba, por el oeste, el monte Carmelo y Sijor Libnat. 27De allí giraba al este en dirección a Bet Dagón y llegaba a Zabulón, en el valle de Jeftel. Luego se dirigía al norte rumbo a Bet Émec y Neyel, bordeando, a la izquierda, Cabul. 28La frontera seguía hacia Abdón,s Rejob, Hamón y Caná, hasta tocar la gran ciudad de Sidón. 29Luego hacía un giro hacia Ramá, y de allí, hasta la ciudad fortificada de Tiro. Después giraba hacia Josá y salía al mar Mediterráneo. 30Las ciudades sumaban veintidós, entre ellas Majaleb, Aczib, Uma, Afec y Rejob.t 31Éste es el territorio asignado como herencia a los clanes de la tribu de Aser, incluyendo sus ciudades y pueblos.

El territorio de Neftalí

32Neftalí fue la sexta tribu que recibió su territorio, según sus clanes. 33Su territorio abarcaba desde Jélef y el gran árbol de Sananín hacia Adaminéqueb y Jabnel, y continuaba hacia Lacún, hasta el río Jordán. 34La frontera seguía por el occidente, pasando por Aznot Tabor, y proseguía en Hucoc. Bordeaba el territorio de la tribu de Zabulón por el sur, la de Aser por el occidente yu el río Jordán por el oriente. 35Las ciudades fortificadas eran: Sidín, Ser, Jamat, Racat, Quinéret, 36Adamá, Ramá, Jazor, 37Cedes, Edrey, Enjazor, 38Irón, Migdal El, Jorén, Bet Anat y Bet Semes. En total sumaban diecinueve ciudades con sus poblaciones. 39Éste es el territorio asignado como herencia a los clanes de la tribu de Neftalí, incluyendo sus ciudades y pueblos.

El territorio de Dan

40Dan fue la séptima tribu que recibió territorio, según sus clanes. 41Se incluían en el territorio Zora, Estaol, Ir Semes, 42Sagalbín, Ayalón, Jetlá, 43Elón, Timnat, Ecrón, 44Eltequé, Guibetón, Balat, 45Jehúd, Bené Berac, Gat Rimón, 46Mejarcón y Racón, con la región que estaba frente a Jope.

47Como a los danitas no les alcanzó el territorio que se les asignó, fueron a conquistar la ciudad de

Lesén. Después de que la tomaron, pasaron a filo de espada a todos sus habitantes. Luego los danitas la habitaron y le dieron por nombre Dan, en honor de su antepasado. 48Así quedó establecido el territorio de los clanes de la tribu de Dan, junto con sus ciudades y pueblos.

El territorio de Josué

49Cuando se terminó de asignarle a cada tribu el territorio que le correspondía, el pueblo de Israel le entregó a Josué hijo de Nun el territorio que le pertenecía a él como herencia. 50Así cumplieron con lo que el SEÑOR había ordenado. Josué recibió la ciudad de Timnat Sera, que estaba enclavada en la región montañosa de Efraín. Él la había solicitado, así que la reconstruyó y se estableció en ella.

51Este modo terminaron de dividir los territorios el sacerdote Eleazar, Josué y los jefes de las tribus de Israel. El sorteo lo realizaron en Siló, en presencia del SEÑOR, a la entrada de la *Tienda de reunión.

Ciudades de refugio

20 El SEÑOR le dijo a Josué: 2«Pídeles a los israelitas que designen algunas ciudades de refugio, tal como te lo ordené por medio de Moisés. 3Así cualquier persona que mate a otra accidentalmente o sin premeditación podrá huir a esas ciudades para refugiarse del vengador del delito de sangre.

4»Cuando tal persona huya a una de esas ciudades, se ubicará a la *entrada y allí presentará su caso ante los *ancianos de la ciudad. Acto seguido, los ancianos lo aceptarán en esa ciudad y le asignarán un lugar para vivir con ellos. 5Si el vengador del delito de sangre persigue a la persona hasta esa ciudad, los ancianos no deberán entregárselo, pues ya habrán aceptado al que mató sin premeditación ni rencor alguno. 6El acusado permanecerá en aquella ciudad hasta haber comparecido ante la asamblea del pueblo y hasta que el sumo sacerdote en funciones haya fallecido. Sólo después de esto el acusado podrá regresar a su hogar y al pueblo del cual huyó tiempo atrás.»

7En respuesta a la orden de Josué, los israelitas designaron Cedes en Galilea, en la región montañosa de Neftalí; Siquén, en la región montañosa de Efraín, y Quiriat Árbá, conocida como Hebrón, en la región montañosa de Judá. 8Al este del río Jordán,v escogieron las tres ciudades siguientes: Béser, en el desierto que está en la meseta perteneciente al territorio de la tribu de Rubén; Ramot de Galaad, en el territorio de la tribu de Gad, y Golán de Basán, en el territorio de la tribu de Manasés. 9Todo israelita o inmigrante que hubiera matado accidentalmente a alguien podría huir hacia una de esas ciudades para no morir por mano del vengador del delito de sangre, antes de ser juzgado por la asamblea.

Las poblaciones de los levitas
21:4-39—1Cr 6:54-80

21 Los jefes de familia de los levitas se acercaron al sacerdote Eleazar, a Josué hijo de Nun y a los representantes de los clanes israelitas, 2los cuales estaban en Siló, en la tierra de Canaán, y les dijeron: «El SEÑOR ordenó por medio de Moisés que ustedes nos asignaran pueblos donde vivir y tierras para nuestro ganado.»

---

s 19:28 Abdón (mss. hebreos; véase 21:30); Hebrón (TM).　t 19:29,30 Mediterráneo. 30 Las ciudades ... Rejob. Alt. Mediterráneo en la región de Aczib, 30 Uma, Afec y Rejob. Las ciudades sumaban veintidós.　u 19:34 y (LXX); y la de Judá (TM).
v 20:8 del río Jordán. Lit. del Jordán de Jericó (uno de los antiguos nombres asignados al río Jordán).

³Entonces, según el mandato del SEÑOR, los israelitas entregaron, de su propiedad, las siguientes poblaciones y campos de pastoreo a los levitas:

⁴Los primeros en recibir sus poblaciones, por sorteo, fueron los levitas descendientes de Coat. A estos descendientes del sacerdote Aarón se les entregaron trece poblaciones en los territorios de las tribus de Judá, Simeón y Benjamín. ⁵Al resto de los descendientes de Coat se les entregaron diez poblaciones en los territorios de las tribus de Efraín, Dan y la media tribu de Manasés.

⁶A los descendientes de Guersón se les entregaron, por sorteo, trece poblaciones en los territorios de las tribus de Isacar, Aser, Neftalí y la media tribu de Manasés en Basán.

⁷Los descendientes de Merari recibieron doce poblaciones en los territorios de las tribus de Rubén, Gad y Zabulón.

⁸De este modo los israelitas asignaron todas estas poblaciones con sus campos de pastoreo a los levitas, según el mandato del SEÑOR por medio de Moisés.

⁹Lo mismo se hizo con los territorios de las tribus de Judá y Simeón. ¹⁰Las poblaciones que se asignaron las recibieron los descendientes aaronitas del clan de Coat, porque ellos fueron los primeros que resultaron favorecidos en el sorteo. ¹¹A ellos se les asignó Quiriat Arbá, es decir, Hebrón, junto con sus campos de pastoreo, en la región montañosa de Judá (Arbá fue un ancestro de los *anaquitas). ¹²Pero las aldeas y los campos adyacentes a Hebrón no se asignaron a ningún levita, pues ya se habían asignado a Caleb hijo de Jefone.

¹³Además de Hebrón (ciudad de refugio para los acusados de homicidio), a los descendientes del sacerdote Aarón se les asignaron las siguientes poblaciones con sus campos de pastoreo: Libná, ¹⁴Jatir, Estemoa, ¹⁵Holón, Debir, ¹⁶Ayin, Yutá y Bet Semes, nueve poblaciones en total. ¹⁷Del territorio de la tribu de Benjamín se asignaron las siguientes poblaciones con sus campos de pastoreo: Gabaón, Gueba, ¹⁸Anatot y Almón, es decir, cuatro poblaciones. ¹⁹En total fueron trece poblaciones con sus campos de pastoreo las que se asignaron a los sacerdotes descendientes de Aarón.

²⁰Al resto de los levitas descendientes de Coat se les asignaron poblaciones en el territorio de la tribu de Efraín. ²¹En la región montañosa de Efraín se asignó la ciudad de Siquén, que fue una de las ciudades de refugio para los acusados de homicidio. También se les asignaron Guézer, ²²Quibsayin y Bet Jorón, es decir, cuatro poblaciones con sus campos de pastoreo. ²³De la tribu de Dan se les asignaron Eltequé, Guibetón, ²⁴Ayalón y Gat Rimón, es decir, cuatro poblaciones con sus campos de pastoreo. ²⁵De la media tribu de Manasés se les asignaron Tanac y Gat Rimón, es decir, dos poblaciones con sus campos de pastoreo. ²⁶En total fueron diez poblaciones con sus campos de pastoreo las que se asignaron al resto de los descendientes de los clanes de Coat.

²⁷A los levitas descendientes de Guersón se les asignaron dos poblaciones con sus campos de pastoreo en el territorio de la media tribu de Manasés: Golán en Basán (ciudad de refugio para los acusados de homicidio) y Besterá. ²⁸De la tribu de Isacar se les asignaron Cisón, Daberat, ²⁹Jarmut y Enganín, es decir, cuatro poblaciones con sus campos de pastoreo. ³⁰De la tribu de Aser se les asignaron Miseal, Abdón, ³¹Jelcat y Rejob, es decir, cuatro poblaciones con sus campos de pastoreo. ³²De la tribu de Neftalí se les asignaron tres poblaciones con sus campos de pastoreo: Cedes (ciudad de refugio en la región de Gali-

lea), y las poblaciones de Jamot Dor y Cartán. ³³En total fueron trece poblaciones con sus campos de pastoreo las que se asignaron a los levitas descendientes de los clanes de Guersón.

³⁴A los meraritas, uno de los clanes levitas, se les asignaron cuatro poblaciones de la tribu de Zabulón, con sus campos de pastoreo: Jocneán, Cartá, ³⁵Dimná y Nalal. ³⁶De la tribu de Rubén se les asignaron cuatro poblaciones con sus campos de pastoreo: Béser, Yahaza, ³⁷Cademot y Mefat. ³⁸De la tribu de Gad se les asignaron cuatro poblaciones con sus campos de pastoreo: Ramot de Galaad (ciudad de refugio), Majanayin, ³⁹Hesbón y Jazer. ⁴⁰Fue así como los clanes levitas descendientes de Merari, los últimos a quienes se les asignaron poblaciones, recibieron un total de doce.

⁴¹Los levitas recibieron en total cuarenta y ocho poblaciones con sus respectivos campos de pastoreo en territorio israelita. ⁴²Cada una de esas poblaciones estaba rodeada de campos de pastoreo.

⁴³Así fue como el SEÑOR les entregó a los israelitas todo el territorio que había prometido darles a sus antepasados; y el pueblo de Israel se estableció allí. ⁴⁴El SEÑOR les dio descanso en todo el territorio, cumpliendo así la promesa hecha años atrás a sus antepasados. Ninguno de sus enemigos pudo hacer frente a los israelitas, pues el SEÑOR entregó en sus manos a cada uno de los que se les oponían. ⁴⁵Y ni una sola de las buenas promesas del SEÑOR a favor de Israel dejó de cumplirse, sino que cada una se cumplió al pie de la letra.

Retorno de las tribus orientales

22 Luego Josué convocó a las tribus de Rubén y Gad, y a la media tribu de Manasés, ²y les dijo: «Ustedes han cumplido todas las órdenes que les dio Moisés, siervo del SEÑOR. Además, ustedes me han obedecido en cada mandato que les he dado. ³Durante todo el tiempo que ha pasado, hasta este mismo día, ustedes no han abandonado a sus hermanos los israelitas. Más bien, han cumplido todos los mandatos del SEÑOR. ⁴Y ahora que el SEÑOR su Dios ha cumplido lo que prometió y les ha dado descanso a sus hermanos, regresen ustedes a sus hogares y a sus tierras que Moisés, siervo del SEÑOR, les entregó al lado oriental del río Jordán. ⁵Y esfuércense por cumplir fielmente el mandamiento y la *ley que les ordenó Moisés, siervo del SEÑOR: amen al SEÑOR su Dios, condúzcanse de acuerdo con su voluntad, obedezcan sus mandamientos, manténganse unidos firmemente a él y sírvanle de todo *corazón y con todo su ser.»

⁶Dicho esto, Josué les dio su bendición y los envió a sus hogares. ⁷A la mitad de la tribu de Manasés, Moisés ya le había entregado el territorio de Basán; a la otra mitad Josué le entregó el territorio que está en el lado occidental del río Jordán, donde se estableció la mayoría de los israelitas. A los primeros, Josué los envió a sus hogares, junto con las tribus de Rubén y Gad, y los bendijo ⁸así: «Regresen a sus hogares repletos de bienes: oro, plata, bronce, hierro, gran cantidad de ropa y mucho ganado. Compartan con sus hermanos lo que le han arrebatado al enemigo.»

⁹Entonces los rubenitas, los gaditas y la media tribu de Manasés salieron de Siló en Canaán, donde estaban congregados todos los israelitas, y regresaron a Galaad, el territorio que habían adquirido según el mandato que el SEÑOR había dado por medio de Moisés.

¹⁰Cuando llegaron a Guelilot, a orillas del río Jordán, todavía en territorio cananeo, las dos tribus y media construyeron un enorme altar. ¹¹Los demás

israelitas se enteraron de que los rubenitas, los gaditas y la media tribu de Manasés habían construido aquel altar a orillas del Jordán, en pleno territorio israelita. 12Entonces toda la asamblea se reunió en Siló con la intención de combatir contra las dos tribus y media.

13Por tanto, los israelitas enviaron a Finés hijo del sacerdote Eleazar a la región de Galaad para hablar con esas tribus. 14Con él iban diez representantes de cada una de las tribus de Israel, jefes de clanes y tribus. 15Al llegar a Galaad, les dijeron a los de las dos tribus y media:

16—Toda la asamblea del SEÑOR quisiera saber por qué se han rebelado contra el Dios de Israel como lo han hecho. ¿Por qué le han dado la espalda al SEÑOR y se han rebelado contra él, construyéndose un altar? 17¿Acaso no hemos aprendido ninguna lección del pecado de Peor, del cual todavía no nos hemos *purificado? ¿Nada nos ha enseñado la muerte de tantos miembros de nuestro pueblo? 18¿Por qué insisten en darle la espalda al SEÑOR? ¡Si hoy se rebelan contra él, mañana su ira se descargará sobre todo Israel! 19Si la tierra que ustedes poseen es impura, crucen a esta tierra que le pertenece al SEÑOR, y en la cual se encuentra su santuario. ¡Vengan, habiten entre nosotros! Pero, por favor, no se rebelen contra él ni contra nosotros, erigiendo otro altar además del altar del SEÑOR nuestro Dios. 20¿No es verdad que cuando Acán hijo de Zera pecó al hurtar de lo que estaba destinado a la *destrucción, la ira de Dios se descargó sobre toda la comunidad de Israel? Recuerden que Acán no fue el único que murió por su pecado.

21Los de las tribus de Rubén, Gad y la media tribu de Manasés respondieron a los líderes israelitas:

22—¡El SEÑOR, Dios de dioses, sí, el SEÑOR, Dios de dioses, sabe bien que no hicimos esto por rebeldía o por infidelidad! Y que todo Israel también lo sepa. Si no es así, que no se nos perdone la vida. 23¡Que el SEÑOR mismo nos llame a cuenta si hemos construido nuestro propio altar para abandonarlo a él o para ofrecer alguno de los sacrificios ordenados por Moisés! 24En realidad lo construimos pensando en el futuro. Tememos que algún día los descendientes de ustedes les digan a los nuestros: "¡El SEÑOR, Dios de Israel, no tiene nada que ver con ustedes, 25descendientes de Rubén y de Gad! Entre ustedes y nosotros el SEÑOR ha puesto el río Jordán como barrera. ¡Ustedes no tienen nada que ver con el SEÑOR!" Si esto sucediera, sus descendientes serían culpables de que los nuestros dejen de adorar al SEÑOR.

26»Por eso decidimos construir este altar, no como altar de *holocaustos y sacrificios, 27sino como testimonio entre ustedes y nosotros y entre las generaciones futuras, de que también nosotros podemos servir al SEÑOR y ofrecerle los distintos sacrificios en su santuario. Así, en el futuro, los descendientes de ustedes nunca podrán decirles a los nuestros: "Ustedes no tienen nada que ver con el SEÑOR." 28Por tanto, convenimos que si algún día nos dijeran eso a nosotros o a nuestros descendientes, nosotros les contestaríamos: "Miren la réplica del altar del SEÑOR que nuestros antepasados construyeron, no para hacer sacrificios en él, sino como testimonio entre ustedes y nosotros." 29En fin, no tenemos intención alguna de rebelarnos contra el SEÑOR o de abandonarlo construyendo otro altar para holocaustos, ofrendas o sacrificios, además del que está construido a la entrada de su santuario.

30Cuando escucharon lo que los rubenitas, los gaditas y la media tribu de Manasés tenían que decir, Finés el sacerdote y los jefes de clanes y de la comunidad quedaron satisfechos. 31Entonces Finés hijo de Eleazar les contestó a los de esas tribus:

—Ahora estamos seguros de que el SEÑOR está en medio de nosotros, pues ustedes no pretendían serle infieles al SEÑOR; así que nos han salvado del castigo divino.

32Luego Finés, hijo del sacerdote Eleazar, y los jefes de la nación se despidieron de los gaditas y rubenitas, y abandonaron Galaad para regresar a la tierra de Canaán con el fin de rendir su informe al resto de los israelitas. 33Éstos recibieron el informe con agrado y alabaron a Dios, y no hablaron más de pelear con las tribus orientales ni de destruir sus tierras.

34Y los rubenitas y los gaditas le dieron al altar el nombre de «Testimonio», porque dijeron: «Entre nosotros servirá de testimonio de que el SEÑOR es Dios.»

Despedida de Josué

23 Mucho tiempo después de que el SEÑOR le diera a Israel *paz con sus enemigos cananeos, Josué, anciano y cansado, 2convocó a toda la nación, incluyendo a sus líderes, jefes, jueces y oficiales, y les dijo: «Yo ya estoy muy viejo, y los años me pesan. 3Ustedes han visto todo lo que el SEÑOR su Dios ha hecho con todas aquellas naciones a favor de ustedes, pues él peleó las batallas por ustedes. 4Yo repartí por sorteo, como herencia de sus tribus, tanto las tierras de las naciones que aún quedan entre ustedes como de aquellas que ya han sido conquistadas, entre el río Jordán y el mar Mediterráneo. 5El SEÑOR su Dios expulsará a esas naciones de estas tierras, y ustedes tomarán posesión de ellas, tal como él lo ha prometido.

6»Por lo tanto, esfuércense por cumplir todo lo que está escrito en el libro de la *ley de Moisés. No se aparten de esa ley para nada. 7No se mezclen con las naciones que aún quedan entre ustedes. No rindan culto a sus dioses ni juren por ellos. 8Permanezcan fieles a Dios, como lo han hecho hasta ahora. 9El SEÑOR ha expulsado a esas grandes naciones que se han enfrentado con ustedes, y hasta ahora ninguna de ellas ha podido resistírselo. 10Uno solo de ustedes hace huir a mil enemigos, porque el SEÑOR pelea por ustedes, tal como lo ha prometido. 11Hagan, pues, todo lo que está de su parte para amar al SEÑOR su Dios. 12Porque si ustedes le dan la espalda a Dios y se unen a las naciones que aún quedan entre ustedes, mezclándose y formando matrimonios con ellas, 13tengan por cierto que el SEÑOR su Dios no expulsará de entre ustedes a esas naciones. Por el contrario, ellas serán como red y trampa contra ustedes, como látigos en sus espaldas y espinas en sus ojos, hasta que ustedes desaparezcan de esta buena tierra que el SEÑOR su Dios les ha entregado.

14»Por mi parte, yo estoy a punto de ir por el camino que todo mortal transita. Ustedes bien saben que ninguna de las buenas promesas del SEÑOR su Dios ha dejado de cumplirse al pie de la letra. Todas se han hecho realidad, pues él no ha faltado a ninguna de ellas. 15Pero así como el SEÑOR su Dios ha cumplido sus buenas promesas, también descargará sobre ustedes todo tipo de calamidades, hasta que cada uno sea borrado de esta tierra que él les ha entregado. 16Si no cumplen con el *pacto que el SEÑOR su Dios les ha ordenado, sino que siguen a otros dioses, adorándolos e inclinándose ante ellos, tengan por seguro que la ira del SEÑOR se descargará sobre ustedes y que serán borrados de la buena tierra que el SEÑOR les ha entregado.»

Renovación del pacto en Siquén

24 Josué reunió a todas las tribus de Israel en Siquén. Allí convocó a todos los jefes, líderes, jueces y oficiales del pueblo. Todos se reunieron en presencia de Dios. ²Josué se dirigió a todo el pueblo, y le exhortó:

—Así dice el SEÑOR, Dios de Israel: "Hace mucho tiempo, sus antepasados, Téraj y sus hijos Abraham y Najor, vivían al otro lado del río Éufrates, y adoraban a otros dioses. ³Pero yo tomé de ese lugar a Abraham, antepasado de ustedes, lo conduje por toda la tierra de Canaán y le di una descendencia numerosa. Primero le di un hijo, Isaac; ⁴y a Isaac le di dos hijos, Jacob y Esaú. A Esaú le entregué la serranía de Seír, en tanto que Jacob y sus hijos descendieron a Egipto.

⁵» "Tiempo después, envié a Moisés y Aarón, y herí con plagas a Egipto hasta que los saqué a ustedes de allí. ⁶Cuando saqué de ese país a sus antepasados, ustedes llegaron al *Mar Rojo y los egipcios los persiguieron con sus carros de guerra y su caballería. ⁷Sus antepasados clamaron al SEÑOR, y él interpuso oscuridad entre ellos y los egipcios. El SEÑOR hizo que el mar cayera sobre éstos y los cubriera. Ustedes fueron testigos de lo que les hice a los egipcios. Después de esto, sus antepasados vivieron en el desierto durante mucho tiempo. ⁸A ustedes los traje a la tierra de los amorreos, los que vivían al este del río Jordán. Cuando ellos les hicieron la guerra, yo los entregué en sus manos; ustedes fueron testigos de cómo los destruí para que ustedes poseyeran su tierra. ⁹Y cuando Balac, hijo de Zipor y rey de Moab, se dispuso a presentarles combate, él envió al profeta Balán hijo de Beor para que los maldijera. ¹⁰Pero yo no quise escuchar a Balán, por lo cual él los bendijo una y otra vez, y así los salvé a ustedes de su poder. ¹¹Finalmente, cruzaron el río Jordán y llegaron a Jericó, cuyos habitantes pelearon contra ustedes. Lo mismo hicieron los amorreos, ferezeos, cananeos, hititas, gergeseos, heveos y jebuseos. Pero yo los entregué en sus manos. ¹²No fueron ustedes quienes, con sus espadas y arcos, derrotaron a los dos reyes amorreos; fui yo quien por causa de ustedes envié tábanos, para que expulsaran de la tierra a sus enemigos. ¹³A ustedes les entregué una tierra que no trabajaron y ciudades que no construyeron. Vivieron en ellas y se alimentaron de viñedos y olivares que no plantaron."

¹⁴»Por lo tanto, ahora ustedes entréguense al SEÑOR y sírvanle fielmente. Deshágase de los dioses que sus antepasados adoraron al otro lado del río Éufrates y en Egipto, y sirvan sólo al SEÑOR. ¹⁵Pero si a ustedes les parece mal servir al SEÑOR, elijan ustedes mismos a quiénes van a servir: a los dioses que sirvieron sus antepasados al otro lado del río Éufrates, o a los dioses de los amorreos, en cuya tierra ustedes ahora habitan. Por mi parte, mi familia y yo serviremos al SEÑOR.

¹⁶El pueblo respondió:

—¡Eso no pasará jamás! ¡Nosotros no abandonaremos al SEÑOR por servir a otros dioses! ¹⁷El SEÑOR nuestro Dios es quien nos sacó a nosotros y a nuestros antepasados del país de Egipto, aquella tierra de servidumbre. Él fue quien hizo aquellas grandes señales ante nuestros ojos. Nos protegió durante todo nuestro peregrinaje por el desierto y cuando pasamos entre tantas naciones. ¹⁸El SEÑOR expulsó a todas las que vivían en este país, incluso a los amorreos. Por esa razón, nosotros también serviremos al SEÑOR, porque él es nuestro Dios.

¹⁹Entonces Josué les dijo:

—Ustedes son incapaces de servir al SEÑOR, porque él es Dios *santo y Dios celoso. No les tolerará sus rebeliones y pecados. ²⁰Si ustedes lo abandonan y sirven a dioses ajenos, él se les echará encima y les traerá desastre; los *destruirá completamente, a pesar de haber sido bueno con ustedes.

²¹Pero el pueblo insistió:

—¡Eso no pasará jamás! Nosotros sólo serviremos al SEÑOR.

²²Y Josué les dijo una vez más:

—Ustedes son testigos contra ustedes mismos de que han decidido servir al SEÑOR.

—Sí, sí lo somos —respondió toda la asamblea.

²³Josué replicó:

—Deshágase de los dioses ajenos que todavía conservan. ¡Vuélvanse de todo *corazón al SEÑOR, Dios de Israel!

²⁴El pueblo respondió:

—Sólo al SEÑOR nuestro Dios serviremos, y sólo a él obedeceremos.

²⁵Aquel mismo día Josué renovó el *pacto con el pueblo de Israel. Allí mismo, en Siquén, les dio preceptos y normas, ²⁶y los registró en el libro de la *ley de Dios. Luego tomó una enorme piedra y la colocó bajo la encina que está cerca del santuario del SEÑOR. ²⁷Entonces le dijo a todo el pueblo:

—Esta piedra servirá de testigo contra ustedes. Ella ha escuchado todas las palabras que el SEÑOR nos ha dicho hoy. Testificará contra ustedes en caso de que ustedes digan falsedades contra su Dios.

²⁸Después de todo esto, Josué envió a todo el pueblo a sus respectivas propiedades.

Entierros en la tierra prometida
24:29-31—Jue 2:6-9

²⁹Tiempo después murió Josué hijo de Nun, siervo del SEÑOR, a la edad de ciento diez años. ³⁰Fue sepultado en la parcela que se le había dado como herencia, en el lugar conocido como Timnat Sera, en la región montañosa de Efraín, al norte del monte Gaas. ³¹Durante toda la vida de Josué, el pueblo de Israel había servido al SEÑOR. Así sucedió también durante el tiempo en que estuvieron al frente de Israel los jefes que habían compartido el liderazgo con Josué y que sabían todo lo que el SEÑOR había hecho a favor de su pueblo.

³²Los restos de José, que los israelitas habían traído de Egipto, fueron sepultados en Siquén, en un terreno que Jacob había comprado por cien monedas de plata a los hijos de Jamor, padre de Siquén. El terreno después llegó a ser propiedad de los descendientes de José.

³³Finalmente, Eleazar hijo de Aarón murió y fue sepultado en Guibeá, propiedad de su hijo Finés, en la región montañosa de Efraín.

JUECES

Israel continúa su lucha contra los cananeos
1:11-15—Jos 15:15-19

1 Después de la muerte de Josué, los israelitas le preguntaron al SEÑOR:

—¿Quién de nosotros será el primero en subir y pelear contra los cananeos?

[2]El SEÑOR respondió:

—Judá será el primero en subir, puesto que ya le he entregado el país en sus manos.

[3]Entonces los de la tribu de Judá dijeron a sus hermanos de la tribu de Simeón: «Suban con nosotros al territorio que nos ha tocado, y pelearemos contra los cananeos; después nosotros iremos con ustedes al territorio que les tocó.» Y los de la tribu de Simeón los acompañaron.

[4]Cuando Judá atacó, el SEÑOR entregó en sus manos a los cananeos y a los ferezeos. En Bézec derrotaron a diez mil hombres. [5]Allí se toparon con Adoní Bézec y pelearon contra él, y derrotaron a los cananeos y a los ferezeos. [6]Adoní Bézec logró escapar, pero lo persiguieron hasta que lo alcanzaron, y le cortaron los pulgares de las manos y los dedos gordos de los pies.

[7]Entonces Adoní Bézec exclamó: «¡Setenta reyes, cortados los pulgares de las manos y los dedos gordos de los pies, recogían migajas debajo de mi mesa! ¡Ahora Dios me ha pagado con la misma moneda!» Luego lo llevaron a Jerusalén, y allí murió.

[8]Los de la tribu de Judá también atacaron a Jerusalén; la capturaron, matando a todos a filo de espada, y luego incendiaron la ciudad.

[9]Después la tribu de Judá fue a pelear contra los cananeos que vivían en la región montañosa, en el Néguev y en la Sefelá. [10]Avanzaron contra los cananeos que vivían en Hebrón, ciudad que antes se llamaba Quiriat Arbá, y derrotaron a Sesay, Ajimán y Talmay.

[11]Desde allí, avanzaron contra los habitantes de Debir, ciudad que antes se llamaba Quiriat Séfer. [12]Entonces Caleb dijo: «A quien derrote a Quiriat Séfer y la conquiste, yo le daré por esposa a mi hija Acsa.» [13]Y fue Otoniel hijo de Quenaz, hermano menor de Caleb, quien la conquistó; así que Caleb le dio por esposa a su hija Acsa. [14]Cuando ella llegó, Otoniel la convenció[a] de que le pidiera un terreno a su padre. Al bajar Acsa del asno, Caleb le preguntó:

—¿Qué te pasa?

[15]—Concédeme un gran favor —respondió ella—. Ya que me has dado tierras en el Néguev, dame también manantiales.

Fue así como Caleb le dio a su hija manantiales en las zonas altas y en las bajas.

[16]Los descendientes de Hobab[b] el quenita, suegro de Moisés, acompañaron a la tribu de Judá desde la Ciudad de las Palmeras[c] hasta el desierto de Judá, que está en el Néguev, cerca de Arad. Allí habitaron con la gente del lugar.

[17]Después fueron los de la tribu de Judá con sus hermanos de la tribu de Simeón y derrotaron a los cananeos que vivían en Sefat, ciudad a la que *destruyeron por completo. Desde entonces Sefat fue llamada Jormá.[d] [18]Los hombres de Judá también conquistaron las ciudades de Gaza, Ascalón y Ecrón, cada una de ellas con su propio territorio.

[19]El SEÑOR estaba con los hombres de Judá. Éstos tomaron posesión de la región montañosa, pero no pudieron expulsar a los que vivían en las llanuras, porque esa gente contaba con carros de hierro. [20]Tal como lo había prometido Moisés, Caleb recibió Hebrón y expulsó de esa ciudad a los tres hijos de Anac. [21]En cambio, los de la tribu de Benjamín no lograron expulsar a los jebuseos, que vivían en Jerusalén. Por eso hasta el día de hoy los jebuseos viven con los benjaminitas en Jerusalén.

[22]Los de la tribu de José, por su parte, subieron contra Betel, y el SEÑOR estaba con ellos. [23]Enviaron espías a Betel, ciudad que antes se llamaba Luz, [24]y éstos, al ver que un hombre salía de la ciudad, le dijeron: «Muéstranos cómo entrar en la ciudad, y seremos bondadosos contigo.» [25]Aquel hombre les mostró cómo entrar en la ciudad, y ellos la conquistaron a filo de espada; pero al hombre y a toda su familia les perdonaron la vida. [26]Y ese hombre se fue a la tierra de los hititas, donde fundó una ciudad a la que llamó Luz, nombre que conserva hasta el día de hoy.

[27]Pero los de la tribu de Manasés no pudieron expulsar a los de Betseán y de Tanac con sus respectivas aldeas, ni tampoco a los habitantes de Dor, Ibleam y Meguido con sus respectivas aldeas, porque los cananeos estaban decididos a permanecer en esa tierra. [28]Sólo cuando Israel se hizo fuerte pudo someter a los cananeos a trabajos forzados, aunque nunca pudo expulsarlos del todo. [29]Los de la tribu de Efraín tampoco pudieron expulsar a los cananeos que vivían en Guézer, de modo que los cananeos siguieron viviendo entre ellos. [30]Los de la tribu de Zabulón, por su parte, tampoco pudieron expulsar a los cananeos que vivían en Quitrón y Nalol, y éstos siguieron viviendo entre ellos, aunque fueron sometidos a trabajos forzados. [31]Tampoco los de la tribu de Aser pudieron expulsar a los habitantes de Aco, Sidón, Ajlab, Aczib, Jelba, Afec y Rejob. [32]Por eso, como no pudieron expulsarlos, el pueblo de la tribu de Aser vivió entre los cananeos que habitaban en aquella región. [33]Tampoco los de la tribu de Neftalí pudieron expulsar a los habitantes de Bet Semes y Bet Anat, sino que vivieron entre los cananeos que habitaban en aquella región. Sin embargo, sometieron a trabajos forzados a los que vivían en Bet Semes y Bet Anat. [34]Los amorreos hicieron retroceder a los de la tribu de Dan hasta la región montañosa, y no les permitieron bajar a la llanura. [35]Los amorreos también estaban decididos a permanecer en el monte Heres, en Ayalón y en Salbín. Pero cuando se acrecentó el poder de la tribu de José, los amorreos también fueron sometidos a trabajos forzados. [36]La frontera de los amorreos iba desde la cuesta de los Escorpiones hasta Selá, e incluso más arriba.

El ángel del SEÑOR en Boquín

2 El ángel del SEÑOR subió de Guilgal a Boquín y dijo: «Yo los saqué a ustedes de Egipto y los hice entrar en la tierra que juré darles a sus antepasados. Dije: "Nunca quebrantaré mi *pacto con ustedes; [2]ustedes, por su parte, no harán ningún pacto con la gente de esta tierra, sino que derribarán sus altares." ¡Pero me han desobedecido! ¿Por qué han actuado así? [3]Pues quiero que sepan que no expulsaré de la

---

a 1:14 Otoniel la convenció (LXX y Vulgata); lo convenció (TM). b 1:16 Hobab. Véase 4:11. c 1:16 la Ciudad de las Palmeras. Es decir, Jericó. d 1:17 En hebreo, Jormá significa destrucción.

presencia de ustedes a esa gente; ellos les harán la vida imposible, y sus dioses les serán una trampa.»

⁴Cuando el ángel del SEÑOR les habló así a todos los israelitas, el pueblo lloró a gritos. ⁵Por eso llamaron a aquel lugar Boquín,ᵉ y allí ofrecieron sacrificios al SEÑOR.

Desobediencia y derrota
2:6-9—Jos 24:29-31

⁶Cuando Josué despidió al pueblo, los israelitas se fueron a tomar posesión de la tierra, cada uno a su propio territorio. ⁷El pueblo sirvió al SEÑOR mientras vivieron Josué y los ancianos que le sobrevivieron, los cuales habían visto todas las grandes obras que el SEÑOR había hecho por Israel.

⁸Josué hijo de Nun, siervo del SEÑOR, murió a la edad de ciento diez años, ⁹y lo sepultaron en Timnat Jeres,ᶠ tierra de su heredad, en la región montañosa de Efraín, al norte del monte de Gaas. ¹⁰También murió toda aquella generación, y surgió otra que no conocía al SEÑOR ni sabía lo que él había hecho por Israel. ¹¹Esos israelitas hicieron lo que ofende al SEÑOR y adoraron a los ídolos de *Baal. ¹²Abandonaron al SEÑOR, Dios de sus padres, que los había sacado de Egipto, y siguieron a otros dioses —dioses de los pueblos que los rodeaban—, y los adoraron, provocando así la ira del SEÑOR. ¹³Abandonaron al SEÑOR, y adoraron a Baal y a las imágenes de *Astarté. ¹⁴Entonces el SEÑOR se enfureció contra los israelitas y los entregó en manos de invasores que los saquearon. Los vendió a sus enemigos que tenían a su alrededor, a los que ya no pudieron hacerles frente. ¹⁵Cada vez que los israelitas salían a combatir, la mano del SEÑOR estaba en contra de ellos para su mal, tal como el SEÑOR se lo había dicho y jurado. Así llegaron a verse muy angustiados.

¹⁶Entonces el SEÑOR hizo surgir caudillosᵍ que los libraron del poder de esos invasores. ¹⁷Pero tampoco escucharon a esos caudillos, sino que se prostituyeron al entregarse a otros dioses y adorarlos. Muy pronto se apartaron del *camino que habían seguido sus antepasados, el camino de la obediencia a los mandamientos del SEÑOR. ¹⁸Cada vez que el SEÑOR levantaba entre ellos un caudillo, estaba con él. Mientras ese caudillo vivía, los libraba del poder de sus enemigos, porque el SEÑOR se compadecía de ellos al oírlos gemir por causa de quienes los oprimían y afligían. ¹⁹Pero cuando el caudillo moría, ellos volvían a corromperse aun más que sus antepasados, pues se iban tras otros dioses, a los que servían y adoraban. De este modo se negaban a abandonar sus malvadas costumbres y su obstinada conducta.

²⁰Por eso el SEÑOR se enfureció contra Israel y dijo: «Puesto que esta nación ha violado el *pacto que yo establecí con sus antepasados y no me ha obedecido, ²¹tampoco yo echaré de su presencia a ninguna de las naciones que Josué dejó al morir. ²²Las usaré para poner a prueba a Israel y ver si guarda mi camino y anda por él, como lo hicieron sus antepasados.» ²³Por eso el SEÑOR dejó en paz a esas naciones; no las echó en seguida ni las entregó en manos de Josué.

3 Las siguientes naciones son las que el SEÑOR dejó a salvo para poner a prueba a todos los is-raelitas que no habían participado en ninguna de las guerras de Canaán. ²Lo hizo solamente para que los descendientes de los israelitas, que no habían tenido experiencia en el campo de batalla, aprendieran a combatir. ³Quedaron los cinco príncipes de los filisteos, todos los cananeos, y los sidonios y heveos que vivían en los montes del Líbano, desde el monte de Baal Hermón hasta Lebó Jamat.ʰ ⁴Allí los dejó el SEÑOR para poner a prueba a los israelitas, a ver si obedecían sus mandamientos, que él había dado a sus antepasados por medio de Moisés.

⁵Los israelitas vivían entre cananeos, hititas, amorreos, ferezeos, heveos y jebuseos. ⁶Se casaron con las hijas de esos pueblos, y a sus propias hijas las casaron con ellos y adoraron a sus dioses.

Otoniel

⁷Los israelitas hicieron lo que ofende al SEÑOR; se olvidaron del SEÑOR su Dios, y adoraron a las imágenes de *Baal y de *Aserá. ⁸El SEÑOR se enfureció contra Israel a tal grado que los vendió a Cusán Risatayin, rey de Aram Najarayin,ⁱ a quien estuvieron sometidos durante ocho años. ⁹Pero clamaron al SEÑOR, y él hizo que surgiera un libertador, Otoniel hijo de Quenaz, hermano menor de Caleb. Y Otoniel liberó a los israelitas. ¹⁰El Espíritu del SEÑOR vino sobre Otoniel, y así Otoniel se convirtió en caudillo de Israel y salió a la guerra. El SEÑOR entregó a Cusán Risatayin, rey de *Aram, en manos de Otoniel, quien prevaleció sobre él. ¹¹El país tuvo *paz durante cuarenta años, hasta que murió Otoniel hijo de Quenaz.

Aod

¹²Una vez más los israelitas hicieron lo que ofende al SEÑOR, y por causa del mal que hicieron, el SEÑOR le dio poder sobre ellos a Eglón, rey de Moab. ¹³Luego de aliarse con los amonitas y los amalecitas, Eglón fue y atacó a Israel, y se apoderó de la Ciudad de las Palmeras.ʲ ¹⁴Los israelitas estuvieron sometidos a Eglón, rey de Moab, durante dieciocho años.

¹⁵Los israelitas volvieron a clamar al SEÑOR, y el SEÑOR les levantó un libertador, Aod hijo de Guerá, de la tribu de Benjamín, quien era zurdo. Por medio de él los israelitas enviaron tributo a Eglón, rey de Moab. ¹⁶Aod se había hecho una espada de doble filo y de medio metroᵏ de largo, la cual sujetó a su muslo derecho por debajo de la ropa. ¹⁷Le presentó el tributo a Eglón, rey de Moab, que era muy gordo. ¹⁸Cuando Aod terminó de presentárselo, se fue a despedir a los hombres que habían transportado el tributo. ¹⁹Pero luego se regresó desde las canteras que estaban cerca de Guilgal, y dijo:

—Majestad, tengo un mensaje secreto para usted.

—¡Silencio! —ordenó el rey.

Y todos sus servidores se retiraron de su presencia.

²⁰Entonces Aod se acercó al rey, que estaba sentado solo en la habitación del piso superior de su palacio de verano,ˡ y le dijo:

—Tengo un mensaje de Dios para usted.

Cuando el rey se levantó de su trono, ²¹Aod extendió la mano izquierda, sacó la espada que llevaba en el muslo derecho, y se la clavó al rey en el vientre. ²²La empuñadura se hundió tras la hoja, a tal punto que le salió por la espalda.ᵐ Además, Aod no le sacó la espada, ya que ésta quedó totalmente cubierta por la gordura. ²³Luego de cerrar y atrancar las puertas

---

ᵉ 2:5 En hebreo, *Boquín* significa *los que lloran.* ᶠ 2:9 *Timnat Jeres.* También conocida como *Timnat Sera* (véanse Jos 19:50 y 24:30). ᵍ 2:16 *caudillos.* Tradicionalmente *jueces;* así en el resto de este libro. ʰ 3:3 *Lebó Jamat.* Alt. *la entrada de Jamat.* ⁱ 3:8 *Aram Najarayin.* Es decir, el noroeste de Mesopotamia. ʲ 3:13 *la Ciudad de las Palmeras.* Es decir, Jericó. ᵏ 3:16 *medio metro.* Lit. *un codo.* ˡ 3:20 *palacio de verano.* Frase de difícil traducción. ᵐ 3:22 *la espalda.* Palabra de difícil traducción.

de la habitación del piso superior, Aod salió por la ventana.n 24Cuando ya Aod se había ido, llegaron los siervos del rey y, al ver atrancadas las puertas de la habitación del piso superior, dijeron: «Tal vez está haciendo sus necesidadesñ en el cuarto interior de la casa.» 25Y tanto esperaron que se sintieron desconcertados. Al ver que el rey no abría las puertas de la habitación, las abrieron con una llave. Allí encontraron a su señor tendido en el piso, ya muerto.

26Mientras esperaban, Aod se escapó. Pasó junto a las canteras y huyó a Seirat. 27Cuando llegó allí, tocó la trompeta en la región montañosa de Efraín, y los israelitas descendieron de la montaña, con él a la cabeza.

28«Síganme —les ordenó—, porque el SEÑOR ha entregado en manos de ustedes a sus enemigos los moabitas.» Bajaron con él y, tomando posesión de los vados del Jordán que conducían a Moab, no dejaron pasar a nadie. 29En aquella ocasión derrotaron a unos diez mil moabitas, todos robustos y aguerridos. No escapó ni un solo hombre. 30Aquel día Moab quedó sometido a Israel, y el país tuvo *paz durante ochenta años.

Samgar

31El sucesor de Aod fue Samgar hijo de Anat, quien derrotó a seiscientos filisteos con una vara para arrear bueyes. También él liberó a Israel.

Débora

4 Después de la muerte de Aod, los israelitas volvieron a hacer lo que ofende al SEÑOR. 2Así que el SEÑOR los vendió a Jabín, un rey cananeo que reinaba en Jazor. El jefe de su ejército era Sísara, que vivía en Jaroset Goyim. 3Los israelitas clamaron al SEÑOR porque Yabín tenía novecientos carros de hierro y, durante veinte años, había oprimido cruelmente a los israelitas.

4En aquel tiempo gobernaba a Israel una profetisa llamada Débora, que era esposa de Lapidot. 5Ella tenía su tribunal bajo la Palmera de Débora, entre Ramá y Betel, en la región montañosa de Efraín, y los israelitas acudían a ella para resolver sus disputas. 6Débora mandó llamar a Barac hijo de Abinoán, que vivía en Cedes de Neftalí, y le dijo:

—El SEÑOR, el Dios de Israel, ordena: "Ve y reúne en el monte Tabor a diez mil hombres de la tribu de Neftalí y de la tribu de Zabulón. 7Yo atraeré a Sísara, jefe del ejército de Jabín, con sus carros y sus tropas, hasta el arroyo Quisón. Allí lo entregaré en tus manos."

8Barac le dijo:

—Sólo iré si tú me acompañas; de lo contrario, no iré.

9—¡Está bien, iré contigo! —dijo Débora—. Pero, por la manera en que vas a encarar este asunto, la gloria no será tuya, ya que el SEÑOR entregará a Sísara en manos de una mujer.

Así que Débora fue con Barac hasta Cedes, 10donde él convocó a las tribus de Zabulón y Neftalí. Diez mil hombres se pusieron a sus órdenes, y también Débora lo acompañó.

11Héber el quenita se había separado de los otros quenitas que descendían de Hobab, el suegro de Moisés, y armó su campamento junto a la encina que está en Zanayin, cerca de Cedes.

12Cuando le informaron a Sísara que Barac hijo de Abinoán había subido al monte Tabor, 13Sísara convocó a sus novecientos carros de hierro, y a todos sus soldados, desde Jaroset Goyim hasta el arroyo Quisón.

14Entonces Débora le dijo a Barac:

—¡Adelante! Éste es el día en que el SEÑOR entregará a Sísara en tus manos. ¿Acaso no marcha el SEÑOR al frente de tu ejército?

Barac descendió del monte Tabor, seguido por los diez mil hombres. 15Ante el avance de Barac, el SEÑOR desbarató a Sísara a filo de espada, con todos sus carros y su ejército, a tal grado que Sísara saltó de su carro y huyó a pie. 16Barac persiguió a los carros y al ejército hasta Jaroset Goyim. Todo el ejército de Sísara cayó a filo de espada; no quedó nadie con vida.

17Mientras tanto, Sísara había huido a pie hasta la carpa de Jael, la esposa de Héber el quenita, pues había buenas relaciones entre Jabín, rey de Jazor, y el clan de Héber el quenita.

18Jael salió al encuentro de Sísara, y le dijo:

—¡Adelante, mi señor! Entre usted por aquí. No tenga miedo.

Sísara entró en la carpa, y ella lo cubrió con una manta.

19—Tengo sed —dijo él—. ¿Podrías darme un poco de agua?

Ella destapó un odre de leche, le dio de beber, y volvió a cubrirlo.

20—Párate a la entrada de la carpa —le dijo él—. Si alguien viene y te pregunta: "¿Hay alguien aquí?", contéstale que no.

21Pero Jael, esposa de Héber, tomó una estaca de la carpa y un martillo, y con todo sigilo se acercó a Sísara, quien agotado por el cansancio dormía profundamente. Entonces ella le clavó la estaca en la sien y se la atravesó, hasta clavarla en la tierra. Así murió Sísara.

22Barac pasó por allí persiguiendo a Sísara, y Jael salió a su encuentro. «Ven —le dijo ella—, y te mostraré al hombre que buscas.» Barac entró con ella, y allí estaba tendido Sísara, muerto y con la estaca atravesándole la sien.

23Aquel día Dios humilló en presencia de los israelitas a Jabín, el rey cananeo. 24Y el poder de los israelitas contra Jabín se consolidaba cada vez más, hasta que lo destruyeron.

La canción de Débora

5 Aquel día Débora y Barac hijo de Abinoán entonaron este canto:

2«Cuando los príncipes de Israel toman el
    mando,
    cuando el pueblo se ofrece
        voluntariamente,
    ¡bendito sea el SEÑOR!

3»¡Oigan, reyes! ¡Escuchen, gobernantes!
    Yo cantaré, cantaré al SEÑOR;
    tocaré música al SEÑOR, el Dios de Israel.

4»Oh SEÑOR, cuando saliste de Seír,
    cuando marchaste desde los campos de Edom,
    tembló la tierra,
    se estremecieron los cielos,
    las nubes derramaron agua.
5Temblaron las montañas
    al ver al SEÑOR, el Dios del Sinaí;
    al ver al SEÑOR, el Dios de Israel.

6»En los días de Samgar hijo de Anat,
    en los días de Jael,

---

n 3:23 la ventana. Palabra de difícil traducción. ñ 3:24 haciendo sus necesidades. Lit. cubriéndose los pies.

los viajeros abandonaron los caminos
y se fueron por sendas escabrosas.
7Los guerreros de Israel desaparecieron;
desaparecieron hasta que yo me levanté.
¡Yo, Débora, me levanté
como una madre en Israel!
8Cuando escogieron nuevos dioses,
llegó la guerra a las *puertas de la ciudad,
pero no se veía ni un escudo ni una lanza
entre cuarenta mil hombres de Israel.
9Mi *corazón está con los príncipes de Israel,
con los voluntarios del pueblo.
¡Bendito sea el SEÑOR!

10»Ustedes, los que montan asnas blancas
y se sientan sobre tapices,
y ustedes, los que andan por el camino,
¡pónganse a pensar!
11La voz de los que cantan en los abrevaderos
relata los actos de *justicia del SEÑOR,
los actos de justicia de sus guerreros en
Israel.
Entonces el ejército del SEÑOR
descendió a las puertas de la ciudad.

12»¡Despierta, despierta, Débora!
¡Despierta, despierta, y entona una canción!
¡Levántate, Barac!
Lleva cautivos a tus prisioneros,
oh hijo de Abinoán.

13»Los sobrevivientes
descendieron con los nobles;
el ejército del SEÑOR
vino a mí con los valientes.
14Algunos venían de Efraín,
cuyas raíces estaban en Amalec;
Benjamín estaba con el pueblo que te
seguía.
Desde Maquir bajaron capitanes;
desde Zabulón, los que llevan el bastón de
mando.
15Con Débora estaban los príncipes de Isacar;
Isacar estaba con Barac,
y tras él se lanzó hasta el valle.
En los distritos de Rubén
hay grandes resoluciones.
16¿Por qué permaneciste entre las fogatas
escuchando los silbidos para llamar a los
rebaños?
En los distritos de Rubén
hay grandes titubeos.
17Galaad habitó más allá del Jordán.
Y Dan, ¿por qué se quedó junto a los
barcos?
Aser se quedó en la costa del mar;
permaneció en sus ensenadas.
18El pueblo de Zabulón arriesgó la *vida
hasta la muerte misma,
a ejemplo de Neftalí
en las alturas del campo.

19»Los reyes vinieron y lucharon
junto a las aguas de Meguido;
los reyes de Canaán lucharon en Tanac,
pero no se llevaron plata ni botín.
20Desde los cielos lucharon las estrellas,
desde sus órbitas lucharon contra Sísara.
21El torrente Quisón los arrastró;
el torrente antiguo, el torrente Quisón.
¡Marcha, *alma mía, con vigor!
22Resonaron entonces los cascos equinos;
¡galopan, galopan sus briosos corceles!

23"Maldice a Meroz —dijo el ángel del
SEÑOR—.
Maldice a sus habitantes con dureza,
porque no vinieron en ayuda del SEÑOR,
en ayuda del SEÑOR y de sus valientes."

24»¡Sea Jael, esposa de Héber el quenita,
la más bendita entre las mujeres,
la más bendita entre las mujeres
que habitan en carpas!
25Sísara pidió agua, Jael le dio leche;
en taza de nobles le ofreció leche cuajada.
26Su mano izquierda tomó la estaca,
su mano derecha, el mazo de trabajo.
Golpeó a Sísara, le machacó la cabeza
y lo remató atravesándole las sienes.
27A los pies de ella se desplomó;
allí cayó y quedó tendido.
Cayó desplomado a sus pies;
allí donde cayó, quedó muerto.

28»Por la ventana se asoma la madre de Sísara;
tras la celosía clama a gritos:
"¿Por qué se demora su carro en venir?
¿Por qué se atrasa el estruendo de sus
carros?"
29Las más sabias de sus damas le responden;
y ella se repite a sí misma:
30"Seguramente se están repartiendo
el botín arrebatado al enemigo:
una muchacha o dos para cada guerrero;
telas de colores como botín para Sísara;
una tela, dos telas, de colores
bordadas para mi cuello.
¡Todo esto como botín!"

31»¡Así perezcan todos tus enemigos, oh SEÑOR!
Pero los que te aman sean como el sol
cuando sale en todo su esplendor.»

Entonces el país tuvo *paz durante cuarenta
años.

Gedeón

6 Los israelitas hicieron lo que ofende al SEÑOR, y
él los entregó en manos de los madianitas durante siete años. 2Era tal la tiranía de los madianitas que
los israelitas se hicieron escondites en las montañas y
en las cuevas, y en otros lugares donde pudieran defenderse. 3Siempre que los israelitas sembraban, los
madianitas, amalecitas y otros pueblos del oriente venían y los atacaban. 4Acampaban y arruinaban las cosechas por todo el territorio, hasta la región de Gaza.
No dejaban en Israel nada con vida: ni ovejas, ni bueyes ni asnos. 5Llegaban con su ganado y con sus carpas como plaga de langostas. Tanto ellos como sus
camellos eran incontables, e invadían el país para de-
vastarlo. 6Era tal la miseria de los israelitas por causa
de los madianitas, que clamaron al SEÑOR pidiendo
ayuda.

7Cuando los israelitas clamaron al SEÑOR a causa de los madianitas, 8el SEÑOR les envió un profeta
que dijo: «Así dice el Señor, Dios de Israel: "Yo los
saqué de Egipto, tierra de esclavitud, 9y los libré de
su poder. También los libré del poder de todos sus
opresores, a quienes expulsé de la presencia de ustedes para entregarles su tierra." 10Les dije: "Yo soy
el SEÑOR su Dios; no adoren a los dioses de los amorreos, en cuya tierra viven." Pero ustedes no me
obedecieron.»

11El ángel del SEÑOR vino y se sentó bajo la encina que estaba en Ofra, la cual pertenecía a Joás, del
clan de Abiezer. Su hijo Gedeón estaba trillando tri-

go en un lagar, para protegerlo de los madianitas. [12]Cuando el ángel del SEÑOR se le apareció a Gedeón, le dijo:

—¡El SEÑOR está contigo, guerrero valiente!

[13]—Pero, señor —replicó Gedeón—, si el SEÑOR está con nosotros, ¿cómo es que nos sucede todo esto? ¿Dónde están todas las maravillas que nos contaban nuestros padres, cuando decían: "¡El SEÑOR nos sacó de Egipto!"? ¡La verdad es que el SEÑOR nos ha desamparado y nos ha entregado en manos de Madián!

[14]El SEÑOR lo encaró y le dijo:

—Ve con la fuerza que tienes, y salvarás a Israel del poder de Madián. Yo soy quien te envía.

[15]—Pero, Señor —objetó Gedeón—, ¿cómo voy a salvar a Israel? Mi clan es el más débil de la tribu de Manasés, y yo soy el más insignificante de mi familia.

[16]El SEÑOR respondió:

—Tú derrotarás a los madianitas como si fueran un solo hombre, porque yo estaré contigo.

[17]—Si me he ganado tu favor, dame una señal de que en realidad eres tú quien habla conmigo —respondió Gedeón—. [18]Te ruego que no te vayas hasta que yo vuelva y traiga mi ofrenda y te ponga ante ti.

—Esperaré hasta que vuelvas —le dijo el SEÑOR.

[19]Gedeón se fue a preparar un cabrito; además, con una medida[o] de harina hizo panes sin levadura. Luego puso la carne en una canasta y el caldo en una olla, y los llevó y se los ofreció al ángel bajo la encina.

[20]El ángel de Dios le dijo:

—Toma la carne y el pan sin levadura, y ponlos sobre esta roca; y derrama el caldo.

Y así lo hizo Gedeón. [21]Entonces, con la punta del bastón que llevaba en la mano, el ángel del SEÑOR tocó la carne y el pan sin levadura, ¡y de la roca salió fuego, que consumió la carne y el pan! Luego el ángel del SEÑOR desapareció de su vista. [22]Cuando Gedeón se dio cuenta de que se trataba del ángel del SEÑOR, exclamó:

—¡Ay de mí, SEÑOR y Dios! ¡He visto al ángel del SEÑOR cara a cara!

[23]Pero el SEÑOR le dijo:

—¡Quédate tranquilo! No temas. No vas a morir.

[24]Entonces Gedeón construyó allí un altar al SEÑOR, y lo llamó «El SEÑOR es la *paz», el cual hasta el día de hoy se encuentra en Ofra de Abiezer.

[25]Aquella misma noche el SEÑOR le dijo: «Toma un toro del rebaño de tu padre; el segundo, el que tiene siete años.[p] Derriba el altar que tu padre ha dedicado a *Baal, y el poste con la imagen de la diosa *Aserá que está junto a él. [26]Luego, sobre la cima de este lugar de refugio, construye un altar apropiado[q] para el SEÑOR tu Dios. Toma entonces la leña del poste de Aserá que cortaste, y ofrece el segundo toro[r] como un *holocausto.»

[27]Gedeón llevó a diez de sus siervos e hizo lo que el SEÑOR le había ordenado. Pero en lugar de hacerlo de día lo hizo de noche, pues tenía miedo de su familia y de los hombres de la ciudad.

[28]Cuando los hombres de la ciudad se levantaron por la mañana, vieron que el altar de Baal estaba destruido, que el poste con la imagen de la diosa Aserá estaba cortado, y que el segundo toro había sido sacrificado sobre el altar recién construido.

[29]Entonces se preguntaban el uno al otro: «¿Quién habrá hecho esto?» Luego de investigar cuidadosamente, llegaron a la conclusión: «Gedeón hijo de Joás lo hizo.» [30]Entonces los hombres de la ciudad le exigieron a Joás:

—Saca a tu hijo, pues debe morir, porque destruyó el altar de Baal y derribó la imagen de Aserá que estaba junto a él.

[31]Pero Joás le respondió a todos los que lo amenazaban:

—¿Acaso van ustedes a defender a Baal? ¿Creen que lo van a salvar? ¡Cualquiera que defienda a Baal, que muera antes del amanecer! Si de veras Baal es un dios, debe poder defenderse de quien destruya su altar.

[32]Por eso aquel día llamaron a Gedeón «Yerubaal»,[s] diciendo: «Que Baal se defienda contra él», porque él destruyó su altar.

[33]Todos los madianitas y amalecitas, y otros pueblos del oriente, se aliaron y cruzaron el Jordán, acampando en el valle de Jezrel. [34]Entonces Gedeón, poseído por el Espíritu del SEÑOR, tocó la trompeta, y todos los del clan de Abiezer fueron convocados a seguirlo. [35]Envió mensajeros a toda la tribu de Manasés, convocándolos para que lo siguieran, y además los envió a Aser, Zabulón y Neftalí, de modo que también éstos se le unieron.

[36]Gedeón le dijo a Dios: «Si has de salvar a Israel por mi conducto, como has prometido, [37]mira, tenderé un vellón de lana en la era, sobre el suelo. Si el rocío cae sólo sobre el vellón y todo el suelo alrededor queda seco, entonces sabré que salvarás a Israel por mi conducto, como prometiste.»

[38]Y así sucedió. Al día siguiente Gedeón se levantó temprano, exprimió el vellón para sacarle el rocío, y llenó una taza de agua. [39]Entonces Gedeón le dijo a Dios: «No te enojes conmigo. Déjame hacer sólo una petición más. Permíteme hacer una prueba más con el vellón. Esta vez haz que sólo el vellón quede seco, y que todo el suelo quede cubierto de rocío.»

[40]Así lo hizo Dios aquella noche. Sólo el vellón quedó seco, mientras que todo el suelo estaba cubierto de rocío.

Gedeón derrota a los madianitas

7 Yerubaal —es decir, Gedeón— y todos sus hombres se levantaron de madrugada y acamparon en el manantial de Jarod. El campamento de los madianitas estaba al norte de ellos, en el valle que está al pie del monte de Moré. [2]El SEÑOR le dijo a Gedeón: «Tienes demasiada gente para que yo entregue a Madián en sus manos. A fin de que Israel no vaya a jactarse contra mí y diga que su propia fortaleza lo ha librado, [3]anúnciale ahora al pueblo: "¡Cualquiera que esté temblando de miedo, que se vuelva y se retire del monte de Galaad!"» Así que se volvieron veintidós mil hombres, y se quedaron diez mil.

[4]Pero el SEÑOR le dijo a Gedeón: «Todavía hay demasiada gente. Hazlos bajar al agua, y allí los seleccionaré por ti. Si digo: "Éste irá contigo", ése irá; pero si digo: "Éste no irá contigo", ése no irá.»

[5]Gedeón hizo que los hombres bajaran al agua. Allí el SEÑOR le dijo: «A los que laman el agua con la lengua, como los perros, sepáralos de los que se arrodillen a beber.»

[6]Trescientos hombres lamieron el agua llevándola de la mano a la boca. Todos los demás se arrodillaron para beber. [7]El SEÑOR le dijo a Gedeón: «Con los trescientos hombres que lamieron el agua, yo los

---

o 6:19 *una medida*. Lit. *un *efa, es decir, aprox. 22 litros. p 6:25 *Toma un toro ... siete años*. Alt. *Toma un toro crecido, plenamente desarrollado, del rebaño de tu padre*. q 6:26 *Construye un altar apropiado*. Alt. *Construye con capas de piedra un altar*. r 6:26 *el segundo toro*. Alt. *el toro crecido*; también en v. 28. s 6:32 En hebreo, *Yerubaal* significa *que Baal defienda*.

salvaré; y entregaré a los madianitas en tus manos. El resto, que se vaya a su casa.»

8Entonces Gedeón mandó a los demás israelitas a sus carpas, pero retuvo a los trescientos, los cuales se hicieron cargo de las provisiones y de las trompetas de los otros.

El campamento de Madián estaba situado en el valle, más abajo del de Gedeón. **9**Aquella noche el SEÑOR le dijo a Gedeón: «Levántate y baja al campamento, porque voy a entregar en tus manos a los madianitas. **10**Si temes atacar, baja primero al campamento, con tu criado Furá, **11**y escucha lo que digan. Después de eso cobrarás valor para atacar el campamento.»

Así que él y Furá, su criado, bajaron hasta los puestos de los centinelas, en las afueras del campamento. **12**Los madianitas, los amalecitas y todos los otros pueblos del oriente se habían establecido en el valle eran numerosos como langostas. Sus camellos eran incontables, como la arena a la orilla del mar. **13**llegó precisamente en el momento en que un hombre le contaba su sueño a un amigo.

—Tuve un sueño —decía—, en el que un pan de cebada llegaba rodando al campamento madianita, y con tal fuerza golpeaba una carpa que ésta se volteaba y se venía abajo.

14Su amigo le respondió:

—Esto no significa otra cosa que la espada del israelita Gedeón hijo de Joás. ¡Dios ha entregado en sus manos a los madianitas y a todo el campamento!

15Cuando Gedeón oyó el relato del sueño y su interpretación, se inclinó y adoró. Luego volvió al campamento de Israel y ordenó: «¡Levántense! El SEÑOR ha entregado en manos de ustedes el campamento madianita.»

16Gedeón dividió a los trescientos hombres en tres compañías y distribuyó entre todos ellos trompetas y cántaros vacíos, con antorchas dentro de los cántaros. **17**«Mírenme —les dijo—. Sigan mi ejemplo. Cuando llegue a las afueras del campamento, hagan exactamente lo mismo que me vean hacer. **18**Cuando yo y todos los que están conmigo toquemos nuestras trompetas, ustedes también toquen las suyas alrededor del campamento, y digan: "Por el SEÑOR y por Gedeón."»

19Gedeón y los cien hombres que iban con él llegaron a las afueras del campamento durante el cambio de guardia, cuando estaba por comenzar el relevo de medianoche. Tocaron las trompetas y estrellaron contra el suelo los cántaros que llevaban en sus manos. **20**Las tres compañías tocaron las trompetas y hicieron pedazos los cántaros. Tomaron las antorchas en la mano izquierda y, sosteniendo en la mano derecha las trompetas que iban a tocar, gritaron: «¡Desenvainen sus espadas, por el SEÑOR y por Gedeón!» **21**Como cada hombre se mantuvo en su puesto alrededor del campamento, todos los madianitas salieron corriendo y dando alaridos mientras huían.

22Al sonar las trescientas trompetas, el SEÑOR hizo que los hombres de todo el campamento se atacaran entre sí con sus espadas. El ejército huyó hasta Bet Sitá, en dirección a Zererá, hasta la frontera de Abel Mejolá, cerca de Tabat. **23**Entonces se convocó a los israelitas de Neftalí y Aser, y a toda la tribu de Manasés, y éstos persiguieron a los madianitas. **24**Por toda la región montañosa de Efraín, Gedeón envió mensajeros que decían: «Desciendan contra los madianitas, y apodérense antes que ellos de los vados del Jordán, hasta Bet Bará.»

Se convocó entonces a todos los hombres de Efraín, y éstos se apoderaron de los vados del Jordán, hasta Bet Bará. **25**También capturaron a Oreb y Zeb, los dos jefes madianitas. A Oreb lo mataron en la roca de Oreb, y a Zeb en el lagar de Zeb. Luego de perseguir a los madianitas, llevaron la cabeza de Oreb y de Zeb a Gedeón, que estaba al otro lado del Jordán.

Zeba y Zalmuna

8 Los de la tribu de Efraín le dijeron a Gedeón:
—¿Por qué nos has tratado así? ¿Por qué no nos llamaste cuando fuiste a luchar contra los madianitas?

Y se lo reprocharon severamente.

2—¿Qué hice yo, comparado con lo que hicieron ustedes? —replicó él—. ¿No valen más los rebuscos de las uvas de Efraín que toda la vendimia de Abiezer? **3**Dios entregó en manos de ustedes a Oreb y a Zeb, los jefes madianitas. Comparado con lo que hicieron ustedes, ¡lo que yo hice no fue nada!

Al oír la respuesta de Gedeón, se calmó el resentimiento de ellos contra él.

4Gedeón y sus trescientos hombres, agotados pero persistiendo en la persecución, llegaron al Jordán y lo cruzaron. **5**Allí Gedeón dijo a la *gente de Sucot:

—Denles pan a mis soldados; están agotados y todavía estoy persiguiendo a Zeba y a Zalmuna, los reyes de Madián.

6Pero los jefes de Sucot le respondieron:

—¿Acaso tienes ya en tu poder las manos de Zeba y Zalmuna? ¿Por qué tendríamos que darle pan a tu ejército?

7Gedeón contestó:

—¡Está bien! Cuando el SEÑOR haya entregado en mis manos a Zeba y a Zalmuna, les desgarraré a ustedes la carne con espinas y zarzas del desierto.

8Desde allí subió a Penielᵗ y les pidió lo mismo. Pero los de Peniel le dieron la misma respuesta que los hombres de Sucot. **9**Por eso les advirtió a los hombres de Peniel: «Cuando yo vuelva victorioso, derribaré esta torre.»

10Zeba y Zalmuna estaban en Carcor con una fuerza de quince mil guerreros, que era todo lo que quedaba de los ejércitos del oriente, pues habían caído en batalla ciento veinte mil soldados. **11**Gedeón subió por la ruta de los nómadas, al este de Noba y Yogbea, y atacó al ejército cuando éste se creía seguro. **12**Huyeron Zeba y Zalmuna, los dos reyes de Madián, pero él los persiguió y los capturó, aterrorizando a todo el ejército.

13Cuando Gedeón hijo de Joás volvió de la batalla por el paso de Jeres, **14**capturó a un joven de Sucot y lo interrogó. Entonces el joven le anotó los nombres de los setenta y siete jefes y *ancianos de Sucot. **15**Luego Gedeón fue y les dijo a los hombres de Sucot: «Aquí están Zeba y Zalmuna, por causa de quienes se burlaron de mí al decir: "¿Acaso tienes ya en tu poder las manos de Zeba y Zalmuna? ¿Por qué tendríamos que darles pan a tus hombres que están agotados?"» **16**Se apoderó de los ancianos de la ciudad, tomó espinos y zarzas del desierto, y castigando con ellos a los hombres de Sucot les enseñó quién era él. **17**También derribó la torre de Peniel y mató a los hombres de la ciudad.

18Entonces les preguntó a Zeba y a Zalmuna:

—¿Cómo eran los hombres que ustedes mataron en Tabor?

ᵗ **8:8** *Peniel*. Alt. *Penuel*; también en vv. 9 y 17.

—Parecidos a ti —respondieron ellos—; cada uno de ellos tenía el aspecto de un príncipe.

19—¡Eran mis hermanos —replicó Gedeón—, los hijos de mi propia madre! Tan cierto como que vive el SEÑOR, si les hubieran perdonado la vida, yo no los mataría a ustedes.

20Volviéndose a Jéter, su hijo mayor, le dijo:

—¡Vamos, mátalos!

Pero Jéter no sacó su espada, porque era apenas un muchacho y tenía miedo. 21Zeba y Zalmuna dijeron:

—Vamos, mátanos tú mismo. "¡Al hombre se le conoce por su valentía!"

Gedeón se levantó y mató a Zeba y Zalmuna, y les quitó a sus camellos los adornos que llevaban en el cuello.

El efod de Gedeón

22Entonces los israelitas le dijeron a Gedeón:

—Gobierna sobre nosotros, y después de ti, tu hijo y tu nieto; porque nos has librado del poder de los madianitas.

23Pero Gedeón les dijo:

—Yo no los gobernaré, ni tampoco mi hijo. Sólo el SEÑOR los gobernará. 24Pero tengo una petición —añadió—: que cada uno de ustedes me dé un anillo, de lo que les tocó del botín.

Era costumbre de los ismaelitas usar anillos de oro.

25—Con mucho gusto te los daremos —le contestaron.

Así que tendieron una manta, y cada hombre echó en ella un anillo de su botín. 26El peso de los anillos de oro que les pidió llegó a diecinueve kilos,u sin contar los adornos, los aros y los vestidos de púrpura que usaban los reyes madianitas, ni los collares que llevaban sus camellos. 27Con el oro Gedeón hizo un *efod, que puso en Ofra, su ciudad. Todo Israel se prostituyó al adorar allí el efod, el cual se convirtió en una trampa para Gedeón y su familia.

Muerte de Gedeón

28Los madianitas fueron sometidos delante de los israelitas, y no volvieron a levantar cabeza. Y durante cuarenta años, mientras vivió Gedeón, el país tuvo *paz.

29Yerubaal hijo de Joás regresó a vivir a su casa. 30Tuvo setenta hijos, pues eran muchas sus esposas. 31Su concubina que vivía en Siquén también le dio un hijo, a quien Gedeón llamó Abimélec. 32Gedeón hijo de Joás murió a una edad avanzada y fue sepultado en la tumba de Joás, su padre, en Ofra, pueblo del clan de Abiezer. 33En cuanto murió Gedeón, los israelitas volvieron a prostituirse ante los ídolos de *Baal. Erigieron a Baal Berit como su dios 34y se olvidaron del SEÑOR su Dios, que los había rescatado del poder de todos los enemigos que los rodeaban. 35También dejaron de mostrarse bondadosos con la familia de Yerubaal, es decir, Gedeón, no obstante todo lo bueno que él había hecho por Israel.

Abimélec

9 Abimélec hijo de Yerubaal fue a Siquén a ver a los hermanos de su madre, y les dijo a ellos y a todo el clan de su madre: 2«Pregúntenles a todos los señores de Siquén: "¿Qué les conviene más: que todos los setenta hijos de Yerubaal los gobiernen, o que los gobierne un solo hombre?" Acuérdense de que yo soy de la misma sangre que ustedes.»

3Cuando los hermanos de su madre comunicaron todo esto a los señores de Siquén, éstos se inclinaron a favor de Abimélec, porque dijeron: «Él es nuestro hermano.» 4Y le dieron setenta monedas de platav del templo de Baal Berit, con el cual Abimélec contrató a unos maleantes sin escrúpulos para que lo siguieran. 5Fue a Ofra, a la casa de su padre, y sobre una misma piedra asesinó a sus setenta hermanos, hijos de Yerubaal. Pero Jotán, el hijo menor de Yerubaal, se escondió y logró escaparse. 6Todos los señores de Siquén y Bet Miló se reunieron junto a la encina y la *piedra sagrada que están en Siquén, para coronar como rey a Abimélec.

7Cuando Jotán se enteró, subió a la cima del monte Guerizín y les gritó bien fuerte:

«¡Escúchenme, señores de Siquén,
y que Dios los escuche a ustedes!

8»Un día los árboles salieron
a ungir un rey para sí mismos.
Y le dijeron al olivo:
"Reina sobre nosotros."
9Pero el olivo les respondió:
"¿He de renunciar a dar mi aceite,
con el cual se honra a los dioses y a los
*hombres,
para ir a mecerme sobre los árboles?"

10»Después los árboles le dijeron a la higuera:
"Reina sobre nosotros."
11Pero la higuera les respondió:
"¿He de renunciar a mi fruto,
tan bueno y dulce,
para ir a mecerme sobre los árboles?"

12»Luego los árboles le dijeron a la vid:
"Reina sobre nosotros."
13Pero la vid les respondió:
"¿He de renunciar a mi vino,
que alegra a los dioses y a los hombres,
para ir a mecerme sobre los árboles?"

14»Por último, todos los árboles le dijeron al
espino:
"Reina sobre nosotros."
15Pero el espino respondió a los árboles:
"Si de veras quieren ungirme como su rey,
vengan y refúgiense bajo mi sombra;
pero si no, ¡que salga fuego del espino,
y que consuma los cedros del Líbano!"

16»Ahora bien, ¿han actuado ustedes con honradez y buena fe al coronar rey a Abimélec? ¿Han sido justos con Yerubaal y su familia, y lo han tratado como se merecía? 17Mi padre luchó por ustedes, y arriesgando su *vida los libró del poder de los madianitas. 18Pero hoy ustedes se han rebelado contra la familia de mi padre; han matado a sus setenta hijos sobre una misma piedra, y han hecho de Abimélec, hijo de su esclava, el rey de los señores de Siquén sólo porque él es pariente de ustedes. 19Si hoy han actuado con honradez y buena fe hacia Yerubaal y su familia, ¡que sean felices con Abimélec, y que también él lo sea con ustedes! 20Pero si no, ¡que salga fuego de Siquén y Bet Miló, ¡que salga fuego de Abimélec y los consuma, y que salga fuego de ustedes y consuma a Abimélec!»

21Luego Jotán escapó, huyendo hasta Ber. Allí se quedó a vivir porque le tenía miedo a su hermano Abimélec.

---

u **8:26** *diecinueve kilos.* Lit. *mil setecientos* *siclos.*　v **9:4** *setenta monedas de plata.* Lit. *setenta* { *siclos*} *de plata.*

²²Abimélec había ya gobernado a Israel tres años ²³cuando Dios interpuso un *espíritu maligno entre Abimélec y los señores de Siquén, quienes lo traicionaron. ²⁴Esto sucedió a fin de que la violencia contra los setenta hijos de Yerubaal, y el derramamiento de su sangre, recayera sobre su hermano Abimélec, que los había matado, y sobre los señores de Siquén, que habían sido sus cómplices en ese crimen. ²⁵Los señores de Siquén le tendían emboscadas en las cumbres de las colinas, y asaltaban a todos los que pasaban por allí. Pero Abimélec se enteró de todo esto.

²⁶Aconteció que Gaal hijo de Ébed llegó a Siquén, junto con sus hermanos, y los señores de aquella ciudad confiaron en él. ²⁷Después de haber salido a los campos y recogido y pisado las uvas, celebraron un festival en el templo de su dios. Mientras comían y bebían, maldijeron a Abimélec. ²⁸Gaal hijo de Ébed dijo: «¿Quién se cree Abimélec, y qué es Siquén, para que tengamos que estar sometidos a él? ¿No es acaso el hijo de Yerubaal, y no es Zebul su delegado? ¡Que sirvan a los hombres de Jamor, el padre de Siquén! ¿Por qué habremos de servir a Abimélec? ²⁹¡Si este pueblo estuviera bajo mis órdenes, yo echaría a Abimélec! Le diría:ʷ "¡Reúne a todo tu ejército y sal a pelear!"»

³⁰Zebul, el gobernador de la ciudad, se enfureció cuando oyó lo que decía Gaal hijo de Ébed. ³¹Entonces envió en secreto mensajeros a Abimélec, diciéndole: «Gaal hijo de Ébed y sus hermanos han llegado a Siquén y están instigando a la ciudad contra ti. ³²Ahora bien, levántense tú y tus hombres durante la noche, y pónganse al acecho en los campos. ³³Por la mañana, a la salida del sol, lánzate contra la ciudad. Cuando Gaal y sus hombres salgan contra ti, haz lo que más te convenga.»

³⁴Así que Abimélec y todo su ejército se levantaron de noche y se pusieron al acecho cerca de Siquén, divididos en cuatro compañías. ³⁵Gaal hijo de Ébed había salido, y estaba de pie a la entrada de la *puerta de la ciudad, precisamente cuando Abimélec y sus soldados salían de donde estaban al acecho. ³⁶Cuando Gaal los vio, le dijo a Zebul:

—¡Mira, viene bajando gente desde las cumbres de las colinas!

—Confundes con gente las sombras de las colinas —replicó Zebul.

³⁷Pero Gaal insistió, diciendo:

—Mira, viene bajando gente por la colina Ombligo de la Tierra, y otra compañía viene por el camino de la Encina de los Adivinos.

³⁸Zebul le dijo entonces:

—¿Dónde están ahora tus fanfarronerías, tú que decías: "¿Quién es Abimélec para que nos sometamos a él?" ¿No son ésos los hombres de los que tú te burlabas? ¡Sal y lucha contra ellos!

³⁹Gaal salió al frente de los señores de Siquén y peleó contra Abimélec; ⁴⁰pero éste los persiguió y, en la huida, muchos cayeron muertos por todo el camino, hasta la entrada de la puerta. ⁴¹Abimélec se quedó en Arumá, y Zebul expulsó de Siquén a Gaal y a sus hermanos.

⁴²Al día siguiente el pueblo de Siquén salió a los campos, y fueron a contárselo a Abimélec. ⁴³Entonces Abimélec tomó a sus hombres, los dividió en tres compañías, y se puso al acecho en los campos. Cuando vio que el ejército salía de la ciudad, se levantó para atacarlo. ⁴⁴Abimélec y las compañías que estaban con él se apresuraron a ocupar posiciones a la entrada de la puerta de la ciudad. Luego dos de las compañías arremetieron contra los que estaban en los campos y los derrotaron. ⁴⁵Abimélec combatió contra la ciudad durante todo aquel día, hasta que la conquistó matando a sus habitantes; arrasó la ciudad y esparció sal sobre ella.

⁴⁶Al saber esto, los señores que ocupaban la torre de Siquén entraron en la fortaleza del templo de El Berit. ⁴⁷Cuando Abimélec se enteró de que ellos se habían reunido allí, ⁴⁸él y todos sus hombres subieron al monte Zalmón. Tomó un hacha, cortó algunas ramas, y se las puso sobre los hombros. A los hombres que estaban con él les ordenó: «¡Rápido! ¡Hagan lo mismo que me han visto hacer!» ⁴⁹Todos los hombres cortaron ramas y siguieron a Abimélec hasta la fortaleza, donde amontonaron las ramas y les prendieron fuego. Así murió toda la gente que estaba dentro de la torre de Siquén, que eran como mil hombres y mujeres.

⁵⁰Después Abimélec fue a Tebes, la sitió y la capturó. ⁵¹Dentro de la ciudad había una torre fortificada, a la cual huyeron todos sus habitantes, hombres y mujeres. Se encerraron en la torre y subieron al techo. ⁵²Abimélec se dirigió a la torre y la atacó. Pero cuando se acercaba a la entrada para prenderle fuego, ⁵³una mujer le arrojó sobre la cabeza una piedra de moler y le partió el cráneo.

⁵⁴De inmediato llamó Abimélec a su escudero y le ordenó: «Saca tu espada y mátame, para que no se diga de mí: "¡Lo mató una mujer!"» Entonces su escudero le clavó la espada, y así murió. ⁵⁵Cuando los israelitas vieron que Abimélec estaba muerto, regresaron a sus casas.

⁵⁶Fue así como Dios le pagó a Abimélec con la misma moneda, por el crimen que había cometido contra su padre al matar a sus setenta hermanos. ⁵⁷Además, Dios hizo que los hombres de Siquén pagaran por toda su maldad. Así cayó sobre ellos la maldición de Jotán hijo de Yerubaal.

Tola

10 Después de Abimélec surgió un hombre de Isacar para salvar a Israel. Se llamaba Tola, y era hijo de Fuvá y nieto de Dodó. Vivía en Samir, en la región montañosa de Efraín, ²y gobernó a Israel durante veintitrés años; entonces murió, y fue sepultado en Samir.

Yaír

³A Tola lo sucedió Yaír de Galaad, que gobernó a Israel durante veintidós años. ⁴Tuvo treinta hijos, cada uno de los cuales montaba su propio asno y gobernaba su propia ciudad en Galaad. Hasta el día de hoy estas ciudades se conocen como «los poblados de Yaír».ˣ ⁵Cuando murió Yaír, fue sepultado en Camón.

Jefté

⁶Una vez más los israelitas hicieron lo que ofende al SEÑOR. Adoraron a los ídolos de *Baal y a las imágenes de *Astarté; a los dioses de *Aram, Sidón y Moab, y a los de los amonitas y los filisteos. Y como los israelitas abandonaron al SEÑOR y no le sirvieron más, ⁷él se enfureció contra ellos. Los vendió a los filisteos y a los amonitas, ⁸los cuales desde entonces y durante dieciocho años destrozaron y agobiaron a todos los israelitas que vivían en Galaad, un territorio amorreo, al otro lado del Jordán. ⁹También los amonitas cruzaron el Jordán para luchar contra las tribus de Judá, Benjamín y Efraín, por lo que Israel se encontró en una situación de extrema angustia. ¹⁰Entonces los israelitas clamaron al SEÑOR:

ʷ **9:29** *Le diría* (LXX); *Entonces él le dijo a Abimélec* (TM). ˣ **10:4** *los poblados de Yaír.* Alt. *Javot Yaír.*

—¡Hemos pecado contra ti, al abandonar a nuestro Dios y adorar a los ídolos de Baal!

11El SEÑOR respondió:

—Cuando los egipcios, los amorreos, los amonitas, los filisteos, 12los sidonios, los amalecitas y los madianitas* los oprimían y ustedes clamaron a mí para que los ayudara, ¿acaso no los libré de su dominio? 13Pero ustedes me han abandonado y han servido a otros dioses; por lo tanto, no los volveré a salvar. 14Vayan y clamen a los dioses que han escogido. ¡Que ellos los libren en tiempo de angustia!

15Pero los israelitas le contestaron al SEÑOR:

—Hemos pecado. Haz con nosotros lo que mejor te parezca, pero te rogamos que nos salves en este día.

16Entonces se deshicieron de los dioses extranjeros que había entre ellos y sirvieron al SEÑOR. Y el SEÑOR no pudo soportar más el sufrimiento de Israel.

17Cuando los amonitas fueron convocados y acamparon en Galaad, los israelitas se reunieron y acamparon en Mizpa. 18Los jefes y el pueblo de Galaad se dijeron el uno al otro: «El que inicie el ataque contra los amonitas será el caudillo de todos los que viven en Galaad.»

11 Jefté el galaadita era un guerrero valiente, hijo de Galaad y de una prostituta. 2Galaad también tuvo hijos con su esposa, quienes cuando crecieron echaron a Jefté. «No tendrás parte en la herencia de nuestra familia —le dijeron—, porque eres hijo de otra mujer.» 3Entonces Jefté huyó de sus hermanos y se fue a vivir en la región de Tob, donde se le juntaron unos hombres sin escrúpulos, que salían con él a cometer fechorías.

4Después de algún tiempo, cuando los amonitas hicieron la guerra contra Israel, 5los *ancianos de Galaad fueron a traer a Jefté de la tierra de Tob.

6—Ven —le dijeron—, sé nuestro jefe, para que podamos luchar contra los amonitas.

7Jefté les contestó:

—¿No eran ustedes los que me odiaban y me echaron de la casa de mi padre? ¿Por qué vienen a verme ahora, cuando están en apuros?

8Los ancianos de Galaad le dijeron:

—Por eso ahora venimos a verte. Ven con nosotros a luchar contra los amonitas, y serás el caudillo de todos los que vivimos en Galaad.

9Jefté respondió:

—Si me llevan con ustedes para luchar contra los amonitas y el SEÑOR me los entrega, entonces de veras seré el caudillo de ustedes.

10Los ancianos de Galaad le aseguraron:

—El SEÑOR es nuestro testigo: haremos lo que tú digas.

11Jefté fue con los ancianos de Galaad, y el pueblo lo puso como su caudillo y jefe. Y reiteró en Mizpa todas sus palabras en presencia del SEÑOR.

12Entonces Jefté envió unos mensajeros al rey de los amonitas, para que le preguntaran:

—¿Qué tienes contra mí, que has venido a hacerle la guerra a mi país?

13El rey de los amonitas respondió a los mensajeros de Jefté:

—Cuando Israel salió de Egipto, se apoderó de mi tierra desde el Arnón hasta el Jaboc, y aun hasta el Jordán. Ahora devuélvemela por las buenas.

14Jefté volvió a enviar mensajeros al rey amonita, 15diciéndole:

«Así dice Jefté: "Israel no se apoderó de la tierra de los moabitas ni de los amonitas. 16Cuando los israelitas salieron de Egipto, caminaron por el desierto hasta el *Mar Rojo y siguieron hasta Cades. 17Entonces enviaron mensajeros al rey de Edom, diciéndole: 'Danos permiso para pasar por tu país.' Pero el rey de Edom no les hizo caso. Le enviaron el mismo mensaje al rey de Moab, pero él tampoco aceptó. Así que Israel se quedó a vivir en Cades.

18» "Después anduvieron por el desierto, y bordeando los territorios de Edom y Moab, entraron en territorio moabita por la parte oriental, y acamparon al otro lado del río Arnón. No entraron en el territorio moabita, pues el Arnón era la frontera.

19» "Entonces Israel mandó mensajeros a Sijón, rey de los amorreos, que gobernaba en Hesbón, y le dijo: 'Permítenos pasar por tu país hasta nuestro territorio.' 20Pero Sijón desconfió de Israelz en cuanto a dejarlo pasar por su territorio, por lo que reunió a todo su ejército y acampó en Yahaza y luchó contra Israel.

21» "El SEÑOR, Dios de Israel, entregó a Sijón y a todo su ejército en manos de Israel, y los derrotó. Así tomó Israel posesión de toda la tierra de los amorreos que vivían en aquel país, 22ocupándolo todo, desde el Arnón hasta el Jaboc y desde el desierto hasta el Jordán.

23» "El SEÑOR, Dios de Israel, les quitó esta tierra a los amorreos para dársela a su pueblo Israel, ¿y tú nos la vas a quitar? 24¿Acaso no consideras tuyo lo que tu dios Quemós te da? Pues también nosotros consideramos nuestro lo que el SEÑOR nuestro Dios nos ha dado. 25¿Acaso te crees mejor que Balac hijo de Zipor, rey de Moab? ¿Acaso alguna vez entró él en litigio con Israel, o luchó contra ellos? 26Hace ya trescientos años que Israel ocupó a Hesbón y Aroer, con sus poblados y todas las ciudades en la ribera del Arnón. ¿Por qué no las recuperaron durante ese tiempo? 27Yo no te he hecho ningún mal. Tú, en cambio, obras mal conmigo al librar una guerra contra mí. Que el SEÑOR, el gran Juez, dicte hoy su sentencia en esta contienda entre israelitas y amonitas."»

28Sin embargo, el rey de los amonitas no prestó atención al mensaje que le envió Jefté.

29Entonces Jefté, poseído por el Espíritu del SEÑOR, recorrió Galaad y Manasés, pasó por Mizpa de Galaad, y desde allí avanzó contra los amonitas. 30Y Jefté le hizo un juramento solemne al SEÑOR: «Si verdaderamente entregas a los amonitas en mis manos, 31quien salga primero de la puerta de mi casa a recibirme, cuando yo vuelva de haber vencido a los amonitas, será del SEÑOR y lo ofreceré en *holocausto.»

32Jefté cruzó el río para luchar contra los amonitas, y el SEÑOR los entregó en sus manos. 33Derrotó veinte ciudades, desde Aroer hasta las inmediaciones de Minit, y hasta Abel Queramín. La derrota fue muy grande; así los amonitas quedaron sometidos a los israelitas.

34Cuando Jefté volvió a su hogar en Mizpa, salió a recibirlo su hija, bailando al son de las panderetas. Ella era hija única, pues Jefté no tenía otros hijos. 35Cuando Jefté la vio, se rasgó las vestiduras y exclamó:

---

y 10:12 madianitas (LXX); maonitas (TM).   z 11:20 desconfió de Israel. Alt. no acordó con Israel.

—¡Ay, hija mía, me has destrozado por completo! ¡Eres la causa de mi desgracia! Le juré algo al SEÑOR, y no puedo retractarme.

36—Padre mío —replicó ella—, le has dado tu palabra al SEÑOR. Haz conmigo conforme a tu juramento, ya que el SEÑOR te ha vengado de tus enemigos, los amonitas. **37**Pero concédeme esta sola petición —añadió—. Ya que nunca me casaré, dame un plazo de dos meses para retirarme a las montañas y llorar allí con mis amigas.

38—Está bien, puedes ir —le respondió él.

Y le permitió irse por dos meses. Ella y sus amigas se fueron a las montañas, y lloró porque nunca se casaría. **39**Cumplidos los dos meses volvió a su padre, y él hizo con ella conforme a su juramento. Ella era virgen.

De allí se originó la costumbre israelita **40**de que todos los años, durante cuatro días, las muchachas de Israel fueran a conmemorar la muerte de la hija de Jefté de Galaad.

Jefté y Efraín

12 Los hombres de Efraín se alistaron, y cruzaron el río hacia Zafón y le dijeron a Jefté:

—¿Por qué fuiste a luchar contra los amonitas sin llamarnos para ir contigo? ¡Ahora prenderemos fuego a tu casa, contigo adentro!

2Jefté respondió:

—Mi pueblo y yo estábamos librando una gran contienda con los amonitas y, aunque yo los llamé, ustedes no me libraron de su poder. **3**Cuando vi que ustedes no me ayudarían, arriesgué mi *vida, marché contra los amonitas, y el SEÑOR los entregó en mis manos. ¿Por qué, pues, han subido hoy a luchar contra mí?

4Entonces Jefté reunió a todos los hombres de Galaad y lucharon contra los de la tribu de Efraín. Los de Galaad derrotaron a los de Efraín porque éstos les habían dicho: «Ustedes los galaaditas son renegados de Efraín y Manasés.» **5**Los galaaditas ocuparon los vados del Jordán que conducen a Efraín, y cada vez que algún sobreviviente de Efraín decía: «Déjenme cruzar», los hombres de Galaad le preguntaban: «¿Eres de la tribu de Efraín?» Si él contestaba: «No», **6**ellos decían: «Muy bien, di "Shibolet".» Si decía: «Sibolet», porque no podía pronunciar la palabra correctamente, lo agarraban y allí mismo, en los vados del Jordán, lo degollaban. En aquella ocasión murieron cuarenta y dos mil hombres de la tribu de Efraín.

7Jefté gobernó a Israel durante seis años. Cuando murió Jefté el galaadita, fue sepultado en su puebloa de Galaad.

Ibsán, Elón y Abdón

8Después de Jefté, gobernó a Israel Ibsán de Belén. **9**Tuvo treinta hijos y treinta hijas. A sus hijas las dio en matrimonio a gente que no pertenecía a su clan, y para sus hijos trajo como esposas a treinta muchachas que no eran de su tribu. Ibsán gobernó a Israel por siete años. **10**Cuando murió, fue sepultado en Belén.

11Después de Ibsán gobernó a Israel Elón, de la tribu de Zabulón, durante diez años. **12**Cuando murió Elón el zabulonita, fue sepultado en Ayalón, en el territorio de Zabulón.

13Después de Elón gobernó a Israel Abdón hijo de Hilel, de Piratón. **14**Tuvo cuarenta hijos y treinta nietos, cada uno de los cuales montaba su propio

asno. Gobernó a Israel durante ocho años. **15**Cuando murió Abdón hijo de Hilel, fue sepultado en Piratón, que está en el territorio de Efraín, en la región montañosa de los amalecitas.

Nacimiento de Sansón

13 Una vez más los israelitas hicieron lo que ofende al SEÑOR. Por eso él los entregó en manos de los filisteos durante cuarenta años.

2Cierto hombre de Zora, llamado Manoa, de la tribu de Dan, tenía una esposa que no le había dado hijos porque era estéril. **3**Pero el ángel del SEÑOR se le apareció a ella y le dijo: «Eres estéril y no tienes hijos, pero vas a concebir y tendrás un hijo. **4**Cuídate de no beber vino ni ninguna otra bebida fuerte, ni tampoco comas nada *impuro, **5**porque concebirás y darás a luz un hijo. No pasará la navaja sobre su cabeza, porque el niño va a ser nazareo, consagrado a Dios desde antes de nacer. Él comenzará a librar a Israel del poder de los filisteos.»

6La mujer fue adonde estaba su esposo y le dijo: «Un hombre de Dios vino adonde yo estaba. Por su aspecto imponente, parecía un ángel de Dios. Ni yo le pregunté de dónde venía, ni él me dijo cómo se llamaba. **7**Pero me dijo: "Concebirás y darás a luz un hijo. Ahora bien, cuídate de no beber vino ni ninguna otra bebida fuerte, ni de comer nada impuro, porque el niño será nazareo, consagrado a Dios desde antes de nacer hasta el día de su muerte." »

8Entonces Manoa oró al SEÑOR: «Oh SEÑOR, te ruego que permitas que vuelva el hombre de Dios que nos enviaste, para que nos enseñe cómo criar al niño que va a nacer.»

9Dios escuchó a Manoa, y el ángel de Dios volvió a aparecerse a la mujer mientras ésta se hallaba en el campo; pero Manoa su esposo no estaba con ella. **10**La mujer corrió de inmediato a avisarle a su esposo: «¡Está aquí! ¡El hombre que se me apareció el otro día!»

11Manoa se levantó y siguió a su esposa. Cuando llegó adonde estaba el hombre, le dijo:

—¿Eres tú el que habló con mi esposa?

—Sí, soy yo —respondió él.

12Así que Manoa le preguntó:

—Cuando se cumplan tus palabras, ¿cómo debemos criar al niño? ¿Cómo deberá portarse?

13El ángel del SEÑOR contestó:

—Tu esposa debe cumplir con todo lo que le he dicho. **14**Ella no debe probar nada que proceda de la vid, ni beber ningún vino ni ninguna otra bebida fuerte; tampoco debe comer nada impuro. En definitiva, debe cumplir con todo lo que le he ordenado.

15Manoa le dijo al ángel del SEÑOR:

—Nos gustaría que te quedaras hasta que te preparemos un cabrito.

16Pero el ángel del SEÑOR respondió:

—Aunque me detengan, no probaré nada de tu comida. Pero si preparas un *holocausto, ofréceselo al SEÑOR.

Manoa no se había dado cuenta de que aquél era el ángel del SEÑOR. **17**Así que le preguntó:

—¿Cómo te llamas, para que podamos honrarte cuando se cumpla tu palabra?

18—¿Por qué me preguntas mi *nombre? —replicó él—. Es un misterio maravilloso.

19Entonces Manoa tomó un cabrito, junto con la ofrenda de cereales, y lo sacrificó sobre una roca al SEÑOR. Y mientras Manoa y su esposa observaban, el SEÑOR hizo algo maravilloso: **20**Mientras la llama su-

---

a **12:7** *su pueblo* (LXX); *las ciudades* (TM).

bía desde el altar hacia el cielo, el ángel del SEÑOR ascendía en la llama. Al ver eso, Manoa y su esposa se postraron en tierra sobre sus rostros. ²¹Y el ángel del SEÑOR no se volvió a aparecer a Manoa y a su esposa. Entonces Manoa se dio cuenta de que aquél era el ángel del SEÑOR.

²²—¡Estamos condenados a morir! —le dijo a su esposa—. ¡Hemos visto a Dios!

²³Pero su esposa respondió:

—Si el SEÑOR hubiera querido matarnos, no nos habría aceptado el holocausto ni la ofrenda de cereales de nuestras manos; tampoco nos habría mostrado todas esas cosas ni anunciado todo esto.

²⁴La mujer dio a luz un niño y lo llamó Sansón. El niño creció y el SEÑOR lo bendijo. ²⁵Y el Espíritu del SEÑOR comenzó a manifestarse en él mientras estaba en Majané Dan, entre Zora y Estaol.

Matrimonio de Sansón

14 Sansón descendió a Timnat y vio allí a una joven filistea. ²Cuando él volvió, les dijo a sus padres:

—He visto en Timnat a una joven filistea; pídanla para que sea mi esposa.

³Pero sus padres le dijeron:

—¿Acaso no hay ninguna mujer aceptable entre tus parientes, o en todo nuestro[b] pueblo, que tienes que ir a buscar una esposa entre esos filisteos incircuncisos?

Sansón le respondió a su padre:

—¡Pídeme a ésa, que es la que a mí me gusta!

⁴Sus padres no sabían que esto era de parte del SEÑOR, que buscaba la ocasión de confrontar a los filisteos; porque en aquel tiempo los filisteos dominaban a Israel. ⁵Así que Sansón descendió a Timnat junto con sus padres. De repente, al llegar a los viñedos de Timnat, un rugiente cachorro de león le salió al encuentro. ⁶Pero el Espíritu del SEÑOR vino con poder sobre Sansón, quien a mano limpia despedazó al león como quien despedaza a un cabrito. Pero no les contó a sus padres lo que había hecho. ⁷Luego fue y habló con la mujer que le gustaba.

⁸Pasado algún tiempo, cuando regresó para casarse con ella, se apartó del camino para mirar el león muerto, y vio que había en su cadáver un enjambre de abejas y un panal de miel. ⁹Tomó con las manos un poco de miel y comió, mientras proseguía su camino. Cuando se reunió con sus padres, les ofreció miel, y también ellos comieron, pero no les dijo que la había sacado del cadáver del león.

¹⁰Después de eso su padre fue a ver a la mujer. Allí Sansón ofreció un banquete, como era la costumbre entre los jóvenes. ¹¹Cuando los filisteos lo vieron, le dieron treinta compañeros para que estuvieran con él.

¹²—Permítanme proponerles una adivinanza —les dijo Sansón. Si me dan la solución dentro de los siete días que dura el banquete, yo les daré treinta vestidos de lino y treinta mudas de ropa de fiesta. ¹³Pero si no me la dan, serán ustedes quienes me darán los treinta vestidos de lino y treinta mudas de ropa de fiesta. —Dinos tu adivinanza —le respondieron—, que te estamos escuchando.

¹⁴Entonces les dijo:

«Del que come salió comida;
y del fuerte salió dulzura.»

Pasaron tres días y no lograron resolver la adivinanza. ¹⁵Al cuarto[c] día le dijeron a la esposa de Sansón: «Seduce a tu esposo para que nos revele la adivinanza; de lo contrario, te quemaremos a ti y a la familia de tu padre. ¿Acaso nos invitaron aquí para robarnos?»

¹⁶Entonces la esposa de Sansón se tiró sobre él llorando, y le dijo:

—¡Me odias! ¡En realidad no me amas! Le propusiste a mi pueblo una adivinanza, pero no me has dicho la solución.

—Ni siquiera se la he dado a mis padres —replicó él—; ¿por qué habría de dártela a ti?

¹⁷Pero ella le lloró los siete días que duró el banquete, hasta que al fin, el séptimo día, Sansón le dio la solución, porque ella seguía insistiéndole. A su vez ella fue y les reveló la solución a los de su pueblo.

¹⁸Antes de la puesta del sol del séptimo día los hombres de la ciudad le dijeron:

«¿Qué es más dulce que la miel?
¿Qué es más fuerte que un león?»

Sansón les respondió:

«Si no hubieran arado con mi ternera,
no habrían resuelto mi adivinanza.»

¹⁹Entonces el Espíritu del SEÑOR vino sobre Sansón con poder, y éste descendió a Ascalón y derrotó a treinta de sus hombres, les quitó sus pertenencias y les dio sus ropas a los que habían resuelto la adivinanza. Luego, enfurecido, regresó a la casa de su padre. ²⁰Entonces la esposa de Sansón fue entregada a uno de los que lo habían acompañado en su boda.

Sansón se venga de los filisteos

15 Pasado algún tiempo, durante la cosecha de trigo, Sansón tomó un cabrito y fue a visitar a su esposa.

—Voy a la habitación de mi esposa —dijo él.

Pero el padre de ella no le permitió entrar, ²sino que le dijo:

—Yo estaba tan seguro de que la odiabas, que se la di a tu amigo. ¿Pero acaso no es más atractiva su hermana menor? Tómala para ti, en lugar de la mayor.

³Sansón replicó:

—¡Esta vez sí que no respondo por el daño que les cause a los filisteos!

⁴Así que fue y cazó trescientas zorras, y las ató cola con cola en parejas, y a cada pareja le amarró una antorcha; ⁵luego les prendió fuego a las antorchas y soltó a las zorras por los sembrados de los filisteos. Así incendió el trigo que ya estaba en gavillas y el que todavía estaba en pie, junto con los viñedos y olivares.

⁶Cuando los filisteos preguntaron: «¿Quién hizo esto?», les dijeron: «Sansón, el yerno del timnateo, porque éste le quitó a su esposa y se la dio a su amigo.»

Por eso los filisteos fueron y la quemaron a ella y a su padre. ⁷Pero Sansón les dijo: «Puesto que actuaron de esa manera, ¡no pararé hasta que me haya vengado de ustedes!» ⁸Y los atacó tan furiosamente que causó entre ellos una tremenda masacre. Luego se fue a vivir a una cueva, que está en la peña de Etam.

⁹Los filisteos subieron y acamparon en Judá, incursionando cerca de Lehí. ¹⁰Los hombres de Judá preguntaron:

—¿Por qué han venido a luchar contra nosotros?

---

b **14:3** *nuestro.* Lit. *mi.* c **14:15** *cuarto* (mss. de LXX y Siríaca); *séptimo* (TM).

—Hemos venido a tomar prisionero a Sansón —les respondieron—, para hacerle lo mismo que nos hizo a nosotros.

11Entonces tres mil hombres de Judá descendieron a la cueva en la peña de Etam y le dijeron a Sansón:

—¿No te das cuenta de que los filisteos nos gobiernan? ¿Por qué nos haces esto?

—Simplemente les he hecho lo que ellos me hicieron a mí —contestó él.

12Ellos le dijeron:

—Hemos venido a atarte, para entregarte en manos de los filisteos.

—Júrenme que no me matarán ustedes mismos —dijo Sansón.

13—De acuerdo —respondieron ellos—. Sólo te ataremos y te entregaremos en sus manos. No te mataremos.

Entonces lo ataron con dos sogas nuevas y lo sacaron de la peña. 14Cuando se acercaba a Lehí, los filisteos salieron a su encuentro con gritos de victoria. En ese momento el Espíritu del SEÑOR vino sobre él con poder, y las sogas que ataban sus brazos se volvieron como fibra de lino quemada, y las ataduras de sus manos se deshicieron. 15Al encontrar una quijada de burro que todavía estaba fresca, la agarró y con ella mató a mil hombres.

16Entonces dijo Sansón:

«Con la quijada de un asno
    los he amontonado.d
Con una quijada de asno
    he matado a mil hombres.»

17Cuando terminó de hablar, arrojó la quijada y llamó a aquel lugar Ramat Lehí.e 18Como tenía mucha sed, clamó al SEÑOR: «Tú le has dado a tu siervo esta gran *victoria. ¿Acaso voy ahora a morir de sed, y a caer en manos de los incircuncisos?» 19Entonces Dios abrió la hondonada que hay en Lehí, y de allí brotó agua. Cuando Sansón la bebió, recobró sus fuerzas y se reanimó. Por eso al manantial que todavía hoy está en Lehí se le llamó Enacoré.f

20Y Sansón gobernó a Israel durante veinte años en tiempos de los filisteos.

Sansón y Dalila

16 Un día Sansón fue a Gaza, donde vio a una prostituta. Entonces entró para pasar la noche con ella. 2Al pueblo de Gaza se le anunció: «¡Sansón ha venido aquí!» Así que rodearon el lugar y toda la noche estuvieron al acecho junto a la *puerta de la ciudad. Se quedaron quietos durante toda la noche diciéndose: «Lo mataremos al amanecer.»

3Pero Sansón estuvo acostado allí hasta la medianoche; luego se levantó y arrancó las puertas de la entrada de la ciudad, junto con sus dos postes, con cerrojo y todo. Se las echó al hombro y las llevó hasta la cima del monte que está frente a Hebrón.

4Pasado algún tiempo, Sansón se enamoró de una mujer del valle de Sorec, que se llamaba Dalila. 5Los jefes de los filisteos fueron a verla y le dijeron: «Sedúcelo, para que te revele el secreto de su tremenda fuerza y cómo podemos vencerlo, de modo que lo atemos y lo tengamos sometido. Cada uno de nosotros te dará mil cien monedas de plata.»g

6Dalila le dijo a Sansón:

—Dime el secreto de tu tremenda fuerza, y cómo se te puede atar y dominar.

7Sansón le respondió:

—Si se me ata con siete cuerdas de arcoh que todavía no estén secas, me debilitaré y seré como cualquier otro hombre.

8Los jefes de los filisteos le trajeron a ella siete cuerdas de arco que aún no se habían secado, y Dalila lo ató con ellas. 9Estando unos hombres al acecho en el cuarto, ella le gritó:

—¡Sansón, los filisteos se lanzan sobre ti!

Pero él rompió las cuerdas como quien rompe un pedazo de cuerda chamuscada. De modo que no se descubrió el secreto de su fuerza.

10Dalila le dijo a Sansón:

—¡Te burlaste de mí! ¡Me dijiste mentiras! Vamos, dime cómo se te puede atar.

11—Si se me ata firmemente con sogas nuevas, sin usar —le dijo él—, me debilitaré y seré como cualquier otro hombre.

12Mientras algunos filisteos estaban al acecho en el cuarto, Dalila tomó sogas nuevas y lo ató, y luego le gritó:

—¡Sansón, los filisteos se lanzan sobre ti!

Pero él rompió las sogas que ataban sus brazos, como quien rompe un hilo.

13Entonces Dalila le dijo a Sansón:

—¡Hasta ahora te has burlado de mí, y me has dicho mentiras! Dime cómo se te puede atar.

—Si entretejes las siete trenzas de mi cabello con la tela del telar, y aseguras ésta con la clavija —respondió él—, me debilitaré y seré como cualquier otro hombre.

Entonces, mientras él dormía, Dalila tomó las siete trenzas de Sansón, las entretejió con la tela 14yi las aseguró con la clavija.

Una vez más ella le gritó: «¡Sansón, los filisteos se lanzan sobre ti!» Sansón despertó de su sueño y arrancó la clavija y el telar, junto con la tela.

15Entonces ella le dijo: «¿Cómo puedes decir que me amas, si no confías en mí? Ya van tres veces que te burlas de mí, y aún no me has dicho el secreto de tu tremenda fuerza.»

16Como todos los días lo presionaba con sus palabras, y lo acosaba hasta hacerlo sentirse harto de la vida, 17al fin se lo dijo todo. «Nunca ha pasado navaja por mi cabeza —le explicó—, porque soy nazareo, consagrado a Dios desde antes de nacer. Si se me afeitara la cabeza, perdería mi fuerza, y llegaría a ser tan débil como cualquier otro hombre.»

18Cuando Dalila se dio cuenta de que esta vez le había confiado todo, mandó llamar a los jefes de los filisteos, y les dijo: «Vuelvan una vez más, que él me lo ha confiado todo.» Entonces los gobernantes de los filisteos regresaron a ella con la plata que le habían ofrecido. 19Después de hacerlo dormir sobre sus rodillas, ella llamó a un hombre para que le cortara las siete trenzas de su cabello. Así comenzó a dominarlo. Y su fuerza lo abandonó.

20Luego ella gritó: «¡Sansón, los filisteos se lanzan sobre ti!»

Sansón despertó de su sueño y pensó: «Me escaparé como las otras veces, y me los quitaré de encima.» Pero no sabía que el SEÑOR lo había abandonado.

---

d 15:16 *los he amontonado.* Alt. *los he convertido en asnos;* en hebreo, las palabras que significan *asno* y *montón* son idénticas.   e 15:17 En hebreo, *Ramat Lehí* significa *colina de la quijada.*   f 15:19 En hebreo, *Enacoré* significa *manantial del que clama.*   g 16:5 *mil cien monedas de plata.* Lit. *mil cien {*siclos} de plata.*   h 16:7 *cuerdas de arco.* Alt. *correas nuevas;* también en vv. 8 y 9.   i 16:13,14 —*Si entretejes ... la tela* 14 y (algunos mss. de LXX) —*Hay que entretejer las siete trenzas de mi cabello en la tela del telar* —respondió él. / 14 *Así que ella* (TM).

21Entonces los filisteos lo capturaron, le arrancaron los ojos y lo llevaron a Gaza. Lo sujetaron con cadenas de bronce, y lo pusieron a moler en la cárcel. 22Pero en cuanto le cortaron el cabello, le comenzó a crecer de nuevo.

Muerte de Sansón

23Los jefes de los filisteos se reunieron para festejar y ofrecerle un gran sacrificio a Dagón, su dios, diciendo:

«Nuestro dios ha entregado en nuestras
    manos
a Sansón, nuestro enemigo.»

24Cuando el pueblo lo vio, todos alabaron a su dios diciendo:

«Nuestro dios ha entregado en nuestras
    manos
a nuestro enemigo,
al que asolaba nuestra tierra
y multiplicaba nuestras víctimas.»

25Cuando ya estaban muy alegres, gritaron: «¡Saquen a Sansón para que nos divierta!» Así que sacaron a Sansón de la cárcel, y él les sirvió de diversión.

Cuando lo pusieron de pie entre las columnas, 26Sansón le dijo al muchacho que lo llevaba de la mano: «Ponme donde pueda tocar las columnas que sostienen el templo, para que me pueda apoyar en ellas.» 27En ese momento el templo estaba lleno de hombres y mujeres; todos los jefes de los filisteos estaban allí, y en la parte alta había unos tres mil hombres y mujeres que se divertían a costa de Sansón. 28Entonces Sansón oró al SEÑOR: «Oh soberano SEÑOR, acuérdate de mí. Oh Dios, te ruego que me fortalezcas sólo una vez más, y déjame de una vez por todas vengarme de los filisteos por haberme sacado los ojos.» 29Luego Sansón palpó las dos columnas centrales que sostenían el templo y se apoyó contra ellas, la mano derecha sobre una y la izquierda sobre la otra. 30Y gritó: «¡Muera yo junto con los filisteos!» Luego empujó con toda su fuerza, y el templo se vino abajo sobre los jefes y sobre toda la gente que estaba allí. Fueron muchos más los que Sansón mató al morir, que los que había matado mientras vivía.

31Sus hermanos y toda la familia de su padre descendieron para recogerlo. Lo llevaron de regreso y lo sepultaron entre Zora y Estaol, en la tumba de su padre Manoa. Sansón había gobernado a Israel durante veinte años.

Los ídolos de Micaías

17 En la región montañosa de Efraín había un hombre llamado Micaías, 2quien le dijo a su madre:

—Con respecto a las mil cien monedas de plataj que te robaron y sobre las cuales te oí pronunciar una maldición, yo tengo esa plata; yo te la robé.

Su madre le dijo:

—¡Que el SEÑOR te bendiga, hijo mío!

3Cuando Micaías le devolvió a su madre las mil cien monedas de plata, ella dijo:

—Solemnemente consagro mi plata al SEÑOR para que mi hijo haga una imagen tallada y un ídolo de fundición.k Ahora pues, te la devuelvo.

4Cuando él le devolvió la plata a su madre, ella tomó doscientas monedas de platal y se las dio a un platero, quien hizo con ellas una imagen tallada y un ídolo de fundición, que fueron puestos en la casa de Micaías.

5Este Micaías tenía un santuario. Hizo un *efod y algunos ídolos domésticos, y consagró a uno de sus hijos como sacerdote. 6En aquella época no había rey en Israel; cada uno hacía lo que le parecía mejor.

7Un joven levita de Belén de Judá, que era forastero y de la tribu de Judá, 8salió de aquella ciudad en busca de algún otro lugar donde vivir. En el curso de su viajem llegó a la casa de Micaías en la región montañosa de Efraín.

9—¿De dónde vienes? —le preguntó Micaías.

—Soy levita, de Belén de Judá —contestó él—, y estoy buscando un lugar donde vivir.

10—Vive conmigo —le propuso Micaías—, y sé mi padre y sacerdote; yo te daré diez monedas de platan al año, además de ropa y comida.

11El joven levita aceptó quedarse a vivir con él, y fue para Micaías como uno de sus hijos. 12Luego Micaías invistió al levita, y así el joven se convirtió en su sacerdote y vivió en su casa. 13Y Micaías dijo: «Ahora sé que el SEÑOR me hará prosperar, porque tengo a un levita como sacerdote.»

La tribu de Dan se establece en Lais

18 En aquella época no había rey en Israel, y la tribu de Dan andaba buscando un territorio propio donde establecerse, porque hasta ese momento no había recibido la parte que le correspondía de entre las tribus de Israel. 2Desde Zora y Estaol los danitas enviaron a cinco de sus hombres más valientes, para que espiaran la tierra y la exploraran. Les dijeron: «Vayan, exploren la tierra.»

Los hombres entraron en la región montañosa de Efraín y llegaron hasta la casa de Micaías, donde pasaron la noche. 3Cuando estaban cerca de la casa de Micaías, reconocieron la voz del joven levita; así que entraron y le preguntaron:

—¿Quién te trajo aquí? ¿Qué haces en este lugar? ¿Qué buscas aquí?

4El joven les contó lo que Micaías había hecho por él, y dijo:

—Me ha contratado, y soy su sacerdote.

5Le dijeron:

—Te rogamos que consultes a Dios para que sepamos si vamos a tener éxito en nuestro viaje.

6El sacerdote les respondió:

—Vayan en *paz. Su viaje tiene la aprobación del SEÑOR.

7Los cinco hombres se fueron y llegaron a Lais, donde vieron que la gente vivía segura, tranquila y confiada, tal como vivían los sidonios. Gozaban de prosperidad y no les faltaba nada.ñ Además, vivían lejos de los sidonios y no se relacionaban con nadie más. 8Cuando volvieron a Zora y Estaol, sus hermanos les preguntaron:

—¿Cómo les fue?

9Ellos respondieron:

—¡Subamos, ataquémoslos! Hemos visto que la tierra es excelente. ¿Qué pasa? ¿Se van a quedar ahí, sin hacer nada? No duden un solo instante en marchar allí y apoderarse de ella. 10Cuando lleguen allí, encontrarán a un pueblo confiado y una tierra espa-

---

j 17:2 mil cien monedas de plata. Lit. mil cien {*siclos} de plata; también en v. 3.   k 17:3 una imagen tallada y un ídolo de fundición. Alt. una imagen tallada revestida de metal fundido; también en v. 4 y 18:14.   l 17:4 doscientas monedas de plata. Lit. doscientos {*siclos} de plata.   m 17:8 En el curso de su viaje. Alt. Para ejercer su oficio.   n 17:10 diez monedas de plata. Lit. diez {*siclos} de plata.   ñ 18:7 Gozaban ... nada. Frases de difícil traducción.

ciosa que Dios ha entregado en manos de ustedes. Sí, es una tierra donde no hace falta absolutamente nada.

[11]Entonces partieron de Zora y Estaol seiscientos danitas armados para la batalla. [12]Subieron y acamparon cerca de Quiriat Yearín en Judá. Por eso hasta el día de hoy el sector oeste de Quiriat Yearín se llama Majané Dan.o [13]Desde allí cruzaron hasta la región montañosa de Efraín, y llegaron a la casa de Micaías.

[14]Entonces los cinco hombres que habían explorado la tierra de Lais les dijeron a sus hermanos:

—¿Saben que una de esas casas tiene un *efod, algunos dioses domésticos, una imagen tallada y un ídolo de fundición? Ahora bien, ustedes sabrán qué hacer.

[15]Ellos se acercaron hasta allí, y entraron en la casa del joven levita, que era la misma de Micaías, y lo saludaron amablemente. [16]Los seiscientos danitas armados para la batalla se quedaron haciendo guardia en la entrada de la puerta. [17]Los cinco hombres que habían explorado la tierra entraron y tomaron la imagen tallada, el efod, los dioses domésticos y el ídolo de fundición. Mientras tanto, el sacerdote y los seiscientos hombres armados para la batalla permanecían a la entrada de la puerta.

[18]Cuando aquellos hombres entraron en la casa de Micaías y tomaron la imagen tallada, el efod, los dioses domésticos y el ídolo de fundición, el sacerdote les preguntó:

—¿Qué están haciendo?

[19]Ellos le respondieron:

—¡Silencio! No digas ni una sola palabra. Ven con nosotros, y serás nuestro padre y sacerdote. ¿No crees que es mejor ser sacerdote de toda una tribu y de un clan de Israel, que de la familia de un solo hombre?

[20]El sacerdote se alegró. Tomó el efod, los dioses domésticos y la imagen tallada, y se fue con esa gente. [21]Ellos, poniendo por delante a sus niños, su ganado y sus bienes, se volvieron y partieron.

[22]Cuando ya se habían alejado de la casa de Micaías, los hombres que vivían cerca de Micaías se reunieron y dieron alcance a los danitas. [23]Como gritaban tras ellos, los danitas se dieron vuelta y le preguntaron a Micaías:

—¿Qué te sucede, que has convocado a tu gente?

[24]Micaías les respondió:

—Ustedes se llevaron mis dioses, que yo mismo hice, y también se llevaron a mi sacerdote y luego se fueron. ¿Qué más me queda? ¡Y todavía se atreven a preguntarme qué me sucede!

[25]Los danitas respondieron:

—No nos levantes la voz, no sea que algunos de los nuestros pierdan la cabeza y los ataquen a ustedes, y tú y tu familia pierdan la *vida.

[26]Y así los danitas siguieron su camino. Micaías, viendo que eran demasiado fuertes para él, se dio la vuelta y regresó a su casa. [27]Así fue como los danitas se adueñaron de lo que había hecho Micaías, y también de su sacerdote, y marcharon contra Lais, un pueblo tranquilo y confiado; mataron a sus habitantes a filo de espada, y quemaron la ciudad. [28]No hubo nadie que los librara, porque vivían lejos de Sidón y no se relacionaban con nadie más. La ciudad estaba situada en un valle cercano a Bet Rejob.

Después los mismos danitas reconstruyeron la ciudad y se establecieron allí. [29]La llamaron Dan en honor a su antepasado del mismo nombre, que fue hijo de Israel, aunque antes la ciudad se llamaba Lais. [30]Allí erigieron para sí la imagen tallada, y Jonatán, hijo de Guersón y nieto de Moisés,p y sus hijos fueron sacerdotes de la tribu de Dan hasta el tiempo del exilio. [31]Instalaron la imagen tallada que había hecho Micaías, y allí quedó todo el tiempo que la casa de Dios estuvo en Siló.

El levita y su concubina

19 En la época en que no había rey en Israel, un levita que vivía en una zona remota de la región montañosa de Efraín tomó como concubina a una mujer de Belén de Judá. [2]Pero ella le fue infiel y lo dejó, volviéndose a la casa de su padre, en Belén de Judá. Había estado allí cuatro meses [3]cuando su esposo fue a verla para convencerla de que regresara. Con él llevó a un criado suyo y dos asnos. Ella lo hizo pasar a la casa de su propio padre, quien se alegró mucho de verlo. [4]Su suegro, padre de la muchacha, lo convenció de que se quedara, y él se quedó con él tres días, comiendo, bebiendo y durmiendo allí.

[5]Al cuarto día madrugaron y él se dispuso a salir, pero el padre de la muchacha le dijo a su yerno: «Repón tus fuerzas con algo de comida; luego podrás irte.» [6]Así que se sentaron a comer y a beber los dos juntos. Después el padre de la muchacha le pidió: «Por favor, quédate esta noche para pasarla bien.» [7]Cuando el levita se levantó para irse, su suegro le insistió de tal manera que se vio obligado a quedarse allí esa noche. [8]Al quinto día madrugó para irse, pero el padre de la muchacha le dijo: «Repón tus fuerzas. ¡Espera hasta la tarde!» Así que los dos comieron juntos.

[9]Cuando el hombre se levantó para irse con su concubina y su criado, su suegro, que era el padre de la muchacha, le dijo: «Mira, está a punto de oscurecer, y el día ya se termina. Pasa aquí la noche; quédate para pasarla bien. Mañana podrás madrugar y emprender tu camino a casa.» [10]No queriendo quedarse otra noche, el hombre salió y partió rumbo a Jebús, es decir, Jerusalén, con sus dos asnos ensillados y su concubina.

[11]Cuando estaban cerca de Jebús, y ya era casi de noche, el criado le dijo a su amo:

—Vamos, desviémonos hacia esta ciudad de los jebuseos y pasemos la noche en ella.

[12]Pero su amo le replicó:

—No. No nos desviaremos para entrar en una ciudad extranjera, cuyo pueblo no sea israelita. Seguiremos hasta Guibeá.

[13]Luego añadió:

—Ven, tratemos de acercarnos a Guibeá o a Ramá, y pasemos la noche en uno de esos lugares.

[14]Así que siguieron de largo, y al ponerse el sol estaban frente a Guibeá de Benjamín. [15]Entonces se desviaron para pasar la noche en Guibeá. El hombre fue y se sentó en la plaza de la ciudad, pero nadie les ofreció alojamiento para pasar la noche.

[16]Aquella noche volvía de trabajar en el campo un anciano de la región montañosa de Efraín, que vivía en Guibeá como forastero, pues los hombres del lugar eran benjaminitas. [17]Cuando el anciano miró y vio en la plaza de la ciudad al viajero, le preguntó:

—¿Adónde vas? ¿De dónde vienes?

[18]El viajero le respondió:

—Estamos de paso. Venimos de Belén de Judá, y vamos a una zona remota de la región montañosa de Efraín, donde yo vivo. He estado en Belén de Judá, y

---

o **18:12** En hebreo, *Majané Dan* significa *Campamento de Dan.* P **18:30** *Moisés* (una tradición rabínica, mss. de LXX y Vulgata); *Manasés* (TM).

ahora me dirijo a la casa del SEÑOR, pero nadie me ha ofrecido alojamiento. ¹⁹Tenemos paja y forraje para nuestros asnos, y también pan y vino para mí y para tu sierva, y para el joven que está conmigo. No nos hace falta nada.

²⁰—En mi casa serás bienvenido —le dijo el anciano—. Yo me encargo de todo lo que necesites. Pero no pases la noche en la plaza.

²¹Así que lo llevó a su casa y dio de comer a sus asnos, y después de lavarse los pies, comieron y bebieron.

²²Mientras pasaban un momento agradable, algunos hombres perversos de la ciudad rodearon la casa. Golpeando la puerta, le gritaban al anciano dueño de la casa:

—¡Saca al hombre que llegó a tu casa! ¡Queremos tener relaciones sexuales con él!

²³El dueño de la casa salió y les dijo:

—No, hermanos míos, no sean tan viles, pues este hombre es mi huésped. ¡No cometan con él tal infamia! ²⁴Miren, aquí está mi hija, que todavía es virgen, y la concubina de este hombre. Las voy a sacar ahora, para que las usen y hagan con ellas lo que bien les parezca. Pero con este hombre no cometan tal infamia.

²⁵Aquellos perversos no quisieron hacerle caso, así que el levita tomó a su concubina y la echó a la calle. Los hombres la violaron y la ultrajaron toda la noche, hasta el amanecer; ya en la madrugada la dejaron ir. ²⁶Despuntaba el alba cuando la mujer volvió, y se desplomó a la entrada de la casa donde estaba hospedado su marido. Allí se quedó hasta que amaneció.

²⁷Cuando por la mañana su marido se levantó y abrió la puerta de la casa, dispuesto a seguir su camino, vio allí a su concubina, tendida a la entrada de la casa y con las manos en el umbral. ²⁸«¡Levántate, vámonos!», le dijo, pero no obtuvo respuesta. Entonces el hombre la puso sobre su asno y partió hacia su casa.

²⁹Cuando llegó a su casa, tomó un cuchillo y descuartizó a su concubina en doce pedazos, después de lo cual distribuyó los pedazos por todas las regiones de Israel. ³⁰Todo el que veía esto decía: «Nunca se ha visto, ni se ha hecho semejante cosa, desde el día que los israelitas salieron de la tierra de Egipto. ¡Piensen en esto! ¡Considérenlo y díganos qué hacer!»

Los israelitas derrotan a los benjaminitas

20 Todos los israelitas desde Dan hasta Berseba, incluso de la tierra de Galaad, salieron como un solo *hombre y se reunieron ante el SEÑOR en Mizpa. ²Los jefes de todo el pueblo, es decir, de todas las tribus de Israel, tomaron sus puestos en la asamblea del pueblo de Dios. Eran cuatrocientos mil soldados armados con espadas. ³A su vez, los de la tribu de Benjamín se enteraron de que los israelitas habían subido a Mizpa. Entonces los israelitas le dijeron al levita:

—Cuéntanos cómo sucedió esta infamia.

⁴El levita, esposo de la mujer asesinada, respondió:

—Mi concubina y yo llegamos a Guibeá de Benjamín para pasar la noche. ⁵Durante la noche los hombres de Guibeá se levantaron contra mí y rodearon la casa, con la intención de matarme. Luego violaron a mi concubina de tal manera que murió. ⁶Entonces la tomé, la corté en pedazos, y envié un pedazo a cada tribu en el territorio israelita, porque

esa gente cometió un acto depravado e infame en Israel. ⁷Ahora, todos ustedes israelitas, opinen y tomen una decisión aquí mismo.

⁸Todo el pueblo se levantó como un solo hombre, y dijo:

—¡Ninguno de nosotros volverá a su carpa! ¡Nadie regresará a su casa! ⁹Y esto es lo que le haremos ahora a Guibeá: Echaremos suertes para ver quiénes subirán contra ella. ¹⁰De entre todas las tribus de Israel, tomaremos a diez hombres de cada cien, a cien de cada mil, y a mil de cada diez mil, para conseguir provisiones para el ejército. Cuando el ejército llegue a Guibeá de Benjamín, les dará su merecido por toda la infamia cometida en Israel.

¹¹Así que todos los israelitas, como un solo hombre, unieron sus fuerzas para atacar la ciudad. ¹²Las tribus de Israel enviaron mensajeros por toda la tribu de Benjamín, diciendo: «¿Qué les parece este crimen que se cometió entre ustedes? ¹³Entreguen ahora a esos malvados de Guibeá, para que los matemos y eliminemos así la maldad en Israel.»

Pero los de la tribu de Benjamín no quisieron hacerles caso a sus hermanos israelitas.

¹⁴Al contrario, gente de todas sus ciudades se reunió en Guibeá para luchar contra los israelitas. ¹⁵En aquel día los de Benjamín movilizaron de entre sus ciudades veintiséis mil soldados armados de espada, además de setecientos hombres escogidos de los que vivían en Guibeá. ¹⁶Entre todos ellos había setecientos soldados escogidos que eran zurdos, todos ellos capaces de lanzar con la honda una piedra contra un cabello, sin errar.

¹⁷Israel, sin contar a Benjamín, movilizó a cuatrocientos mil soldados armados de espada, todos ellos expertos guerreros.

¹⁸Los israelitas subieron a Betelq y consultaron a Dios. Le preguntaron:

—¿Cuál de nosotros será el primero en combatir a los de la tribu de Benjamín?

El SEÑOR respondió:

—Judá será el primero.

¹⁹Los israelitas se levantaron temprano y acamparon frente a Guibeá; ²⁰salieron a luchar contra los de Benjamín, y frente a Guibeá se dispusieron contra ellos en orden de batalla. ²¹Pero los de Benjamín salieron de Guibeá y abatieron aquel día a veintidós mil israelitas en el campo de batalla. ²²Los israelitas se animaron unos a otros, y volvieron a presentar batalla donde se habían apostado el primer día, ²³pues habían subido a llorar en presencia del SEÑOR hasta el anochecer, y le habían consultado:

—¿Debemos subir y volver a luchar contra los de Benjamín, nuestros hermanos?

Y el SEÑOR les había contestado:

—Suban contra ellos.

²⁴Fue así como los israelitas se acercaron a Benjamín el segundo día. ²⁵Los de Benjamín salieron de Guibeá para combatirlos, abatiendo esta vez a dieciocho mil israelitas más, todos ellos armados con espadas.

²⁶Entonces los israelitas, con todo el pueblo, subieron a Betel, y allí se sentaron y lloraron en presencia del SEÑOR. Ayunaron aquel día hasta el anochecer y presentaron al SEÑOR *holocaustos y sacrificios de *comunión. ²⁷Después consultaron al SEÑOR, pues en aquel tiempo estaba allí el arca del *pacto de Dios, ²⁸y Finés, hijo de Eleazar y nieto de Aarón, ministraba delante de ella. Preguntaron:

---

q **20:18** *Betel.* Alt. *la casa de Dios;* también en v. 26.   r **20:33** *oeste* (mss. de LXX y Vulgata); palabra de difícil traducción.

—¿Debemos subir y volver a luchar contra los de Benjamín, nuestros hermanos, o nos retiramos?

El SEÑOR respondió:

—Suban, porque mañana los entregaré en sus manos.

29Israel tendió una emboscada alrededor de Guibeá. 30Al tercer día subieron contra los de Benjamín y se pusieron en orden de batalla contra Guibeá, como lo habían hecho antes. 31Los de Benjamín salieron a su encuentro, y se vieron obligados a alejarse de la ciudad. Comenzaron a causar bajas entre los israelitas, como en las ocasiones anteriores, y alcanzaron a matar a unos treinta hombres en el campo abierto y por el camino que lleva a Betel, y también por el que lleva a Guibeá.

32Los benjaminitas decían: «Los estamos derrotando como antes», pero los israelitas decían: «Huyamos, para que se alejen de la ciudad hasta los caminos.»

33De pronto, los israelitas cambiaron de táctica y presentaron batalla en Baal Tamar, y los israelitas que estaban emboscados salieron a atacar al oeste[r] de Guibeá. 34Diez mil de los mejores guerreros de Israel lanzaron un ataque frontal contra Guibeá, y fue tan intenso el combate que los benjaminitas no se dieron cuenta de que la calamidad se les venía encima. 35El SEÑOR derrotó a Benjamín delante de Israel, y aquel día los israelitas mataron a veinticinco mil cien hombres de la tribu de Benjamín, todos ellos armados con espadas. 36Allí los de Benjamín cayeron en cuenta de que habían sido vencidos.

Los hombres de Israel habían cedido terreno delante de Benjamín, porque confiaban en la emboscada que habían tendido contra Guibeá. 37De repente los hombres que habían estado emboscados asaltaron a Guibeá, se desplegaron, y mataron a filo de espada a todos los habitantes de la ciudad. 38Los israelitas habían acordado con los que estaban emboscados que, cuando éstos levantaran una gran nube de humo desde la ciudad, 39los hombres de Israel volverían a la batalla.

Cuando los de Benjamín comenzaron a causar bajas entre los israelitas, matando a unos treinta, se decían: «¡Los estamos derrotando, como en la primera batalla!» 40Pero cuando la columna de humo comenzó a levantarse de la ciudad, los de Benjamín se dieron vuelta y vieron que el fuego de la ciudad entera subía al cielo. 41En ese momento atacaron los israelitas, y los hombres de Benjamín se aterrorizaron al darse cuenta de que la calamidad se les venía encima. 42Así que huyeron ante los israelitas por el camino del desierto; pero no pudieron escapar de la batalla, pues a los que salían de las ciudades los abatieron allí. 43Rodearon a los de Benjamín; los persiguieron y los aplastaron con facilidad[s] en las inmediaciones de Guibeá, hacia el lado oriental. 44Cayeron dieciocho mil de la tribu de Benjamín, todos ellos guerreros valientes. 45Cuando se volvieron y huyeron hacia el desierto, a la peña de Rimón, los israelitas abatieron a cinco mil hombres junto a los caminos. Continuaron persiguiéndolos hasta Guidón, y mataron a dos mil más.

46Aquel día cayeron en combate veinticinco mil soldados benjaminitas armados con espada, todos ellos guerreros valientes. 47Pero seiscientos hombres se volvieron y huyeron por el desierto hasta la peña de Rimón, donde permanecieron cuatro meses. 48Los israelitas se volvieron contra los de Benjamín y mataron a filo de espada a los habitantes de todas las ciudades, incluso a los animales, y destrozaron todo lo que encontraron a su paso. También les prendieron fuego a todas las ciudades.

Esposas para los benjaminitas

21 Los israelitas habían jurado en Mizpa: «Ninguno de nosotros dará su hija en matrimonio a un benjaminita.»

2El pueblo fue a Betel,[t] y allí permanecieron hasta el anochecer, clamando y llorando amargamente en presencia de Dios. 3«Oh SEÑOR, Dios de Israel —clamaban—, ¿por qué le ha sucedido esto a Israel? ¡Hoy ha desaparecido una de nuestras tribus!»

4Al día siguiente el pueblo se levantó de madrugada, construyó allí un altar, y presentaron *holocaustos y sacrificios de *comunión.

5Luego preguntaron los israelitas: «¿Quién de entre todas las tribus de Israel no se presentó a la asamblea del SEÑOR?» Porque habían pronunciado un juramento solemne contra cualquiera que no se presentara ante el SEÑOR en Mizpa, diciendo: «Tendrá que morir.»

6Los israelitas se afligieron por sus hermanos, los benjaminitas. «Hoy ha sido arrancada una tribu de Israel —dijeron ellos—. 7¿Cómo podemos proveerles esposas a los que quedan, si ya hemos jurado ante el SEÑOR no darles ninguna de nuestras hijas en matrimonio?» 8Entonces preguntaron: «¿Cuál de las tribus de Israel no se presentó ante el SEÑOR en Mizpa?» Y resultó que ninguno de Jabés Galaad había llegado al campamento para la asamblea, 9porque al pasar revista al pueblo notaron que de los habitantes de Jabés Galaad no había allí ninguno.

10Así que la asamblea envió doce mil de los mejores guerreros con la siguiente orden: «Vayan y maten a filo de espada a los habitantes de Jabés Galaad. Maten también a las mujeres y a los niños. 11Esto es lo que van a hacer: *Exterminarán a todos los hombres y a todas las mujeres que no sean vírgenes.» 12Entre los habitantes de Jabés Galaad encontraron a cuatrocientas muchachas que no habían tenido relaciones sexuales con ningún hombre, y las llevaron al campamento de Siló, que está en la tierra de Canaán.

13Entonces toda la comunidad envió una oferta de paz a los benjaminitas que estaban en la peña de Rimón. 14En esa ocasión regresaron los benjaminitas, y se les dieron las mujeres de Jabés Galaad que habían dejado con vida. Pero no hubo mujeres para todos.

15El pueblo todavía se afligía por Benjamín, porque el SEÑOR había dejado un vacío en las tribus de Israel. 16Y los *ancianos de la asamblea dijeron: «¿Cómo podemos darles mujeres a los hombres que quedaron, si las mujeres de Benjamín fueron exterminadas? 17¡Los sobrevivientes benjaminitas deben tener herederos —exclamaron—, para que no sea aniquilada una tribu de Israel! 18Pero nosotros no podemos darles nuestras hijas como esposas, porque hemos jurado diciendo: "Maldito sea el que dé una mujer a un benjaminita." 19Pero miren, se acerca la fiesta del SEÑOR que todos los años se celebra en Siló, al norte de Betel, y al este del camino que va de Betel a Siquén, y al sur de Leboná.»

20Así que dieron estas instrucciones a los de Benjamín: «Vayan, escóndanse en los viñedos 21y estén atentos. Cuando las muchachas de Siló salgan a bailar, salgan ustedes de los viñedos y róbese cada uno de ustedes una de esas muchachas para

---

s **20:43** *con facilidad.* Palabra de difícil traducción.　t **21:2** *Betel.* Alt. *la casa de Dios.*

esposa, y váyase a la tierra de Benjamín. ²²Y si sus padres o sus hermanos vienen a reclamarnos algo, les diremos: "Sean bondadosos con ellos, porque no conseguimos esposas para todos ellos durante la guerra. Además, ustedes son inocentes, ya que no les dieron sus hijas."»

²³Así lo hicieron los de la tribu de Benjamín. Mientras bailaban las muchachas, cada uno de ellos se robó una y se la llevó. Luego regresaron a sus propias tierras, reconstruyeron las ciudades y se establecieron en ellas.

²⁴Luego de eso los israelitas también se fueron de aquel lugar y regresaron a sus tribus y a sus clanes, cada uno a su propia tierra.

²⁵En aquella época no había rey en Israel; cada uno hacía lo que le parecía mejor.

RUT

Noemí y Rut

1 En el tiempo en que los caudillos[a] gobernaban el país, hubo allí una época de hambre. Entonces un hombre de Belén de Judá emigró a la tierra de Moab, junto con su esposa y sus dos hijos. [2]El hombre se llamaba Elimélec, su esposa se llamaba Noemí y sus dos hijos, Majlón y Quilión, todos ellos efrateos, de Belén de Judá. Cuando llegaron a la tierra de Moab, se quedaron a vivir allí.

[3]Pero murió Elimélec, esposo de Noemí, y ella se quedó sola con sus dos hijos. [4]Éstos se casaron con mujeres moabitas, la una llamada Orfa y la otra Rut. Después de haber vivido allí unos diez años, [5]murieron también Majlón y Quilión, y Noemí se quedó viuda y sin hijos.

[6]Noemí regresó de la tierra de Moab con sus dos nueras, porque allí se enteró de que el SEÑOR había acudido en ayuda de su pueblo al proveerle de alimento. [7]Salió, pues, con sus dos nueras del lugar donde había vivido, y juntas emprendieron el camino que las llevaría hasta la tierra de Judá.

[8]Entonces Noemí les dijo a sus dos nueras:

—¡Miren, vuelva cada una a la casa de su madre! Que el SEÑOR los trate a ustedes con el mismo amor y lealtad que ustedes han mostrado con los que murieron y conmigo. [9]Que el SEÑOR les conceda hallar seguridad en un nuevo hogar, al lado de un nuevo esposo.

Luego las besó. Pero ellas, deshechas en llanto, alzaron la voz [10]y exclamaron:

—¡No! Nosotras volveremos contigo a tu pueblo.

[11]—¡Vuelvan a su casa, hijas mías! —insistió Noemí—. ¿Para qué se van a ir conmigo? ¿Acaso voy a tener más hijos que pudieran casarse con ustedes? [12]¡Vuelvan a su casa, hijas mías! ¡Váyanse! Yo soy demasiado vieja para volver a casarme. Aun si abrigara esa esperanza, y esta misma noche me casara y llegara a tener hijos, [13]¿los esperarían ustedes hasta que crecieran? ¿Y por ellos se quedarían sin casarse? ¡No, hijas mías! Mi amargura es mayor que la de ustedes; ¡la mano del SEÑOR se ha levantado contra mí!

[14]Una vez más alzaron la voz, deshechas en llanto. Luego Orfa se despidió de su suegra con un beso, pero Rut se aferró a ella.

[15]—Mira —dijo Noemí—, tu cuñada se vuelve a su pueblo y a sus dioses. Vuélvete con ella.

[16]Pero Rut respondió:

—¡No insistas en que te abandone o en que me separe de ti!

»Porque iré adonde tú vayas,
    y viviré donde tú vivas.
Tu pueblo será mi pueblo,
    y tu Dios será mi Dios.
[17]Moriré donde tú mueras,
    y allí seré sepultada.
¡Que me castigue el SEÑOR con toda severidad
    si me separa de ti algo que no sea la muerte!

[18]Al ver Noemí que Rut estaba tan decidida a acompañarla, no le insistió más.

[19]Entonces las dos mujeres siguieron caminando hasta llegar a Belén. Apenas llegaron, hubo gran conmoción en todo el pueblo a causa de ellas.

—¿No es ésta Noemí? —se preguntaban las mujeres del pueblo.

[20]—Ya no me llamen Noemí[b] —repuso ella—. Llámenme Mara,[c] porque el *Todopoderoso ha colmado mi vida de amargura.

[21]»Me fui con las manos llenas,
    pero el SEÑOR me ha hecho volver sin
        nada.
¿Por qué me llaman Noemí
    si me ha afligido el SEÑOR,[d]
si me ha hecho desdichada el
        Todopoderoso?

[22]Así fue como Noemí volvió de la tierra de Moab acompañada por su nuera, Rut la moabita. Cuando llegaron a Belén, comenzaba la cosecha de cebada.

Encuentro de Rut con Booz

2 Noemí tenía, por parte de su esposo, un pariente que se llamaba Booz. Era un hombre rico e influyente de la familia de Elimélec.

[2]Y sucedió que Rut la moabita le dijo a Noemí:

—Permíteme ir al campo a recoger las espigas que vaya dejando alguien a quien yo le caiga bien.

—Anda, hija mía —le respondió su suegra.

[3]Rut salió y comenzó a recoger espigas en el campo, detrás de los segadores. Y dio la casualidad de que el campo donde estaba trabajando pertenecía a Booz, el pariente de Elimélec.

[4]En eso llegó Booz desde Belén y saludó a los segadores:

—¡Que el SEÑOR esté con ustedes!

—¡Que el SEÑOR lo bendiga! —respondieron ellos.

[5]—¿De quién es esa joven? —preguntó Booz al capataz de sus segadores.

[6]—Es una joven moabita que volvió de la tierra de Moab con Noemí —le contestó el capataz—. [7]Ella me rogó que la dejara recoger espigas de entre las gavillas, detrás de los segadores. No ha dejado de trabajar desde esta mañana que entró en el campo, hasta ahora que ha venido a descansar un rato en el cobertizo.[e]

[8]Entonces Booz le dijo a Rut:

—Escucha, hija mía. No vayas a recoger espigas a otro campo, ni te alejes de aquí; quédate junto a mis criadas, [9]fíjate bien en el campo donde se esté cosechando, y síguelas. Ya les ordené a los criados que no te molesten. Y cuando tengas sed, ve adonde están las vasijas y bebe del agua que los criados hayan sacado.

[10]Rut se inclinó hacia la tierra, se postró sobre su rostro y exclamó:

—¿Cómo es que le he caído tan bien a usted, hasta el punto de fijarse en mí, siendo sólo una extranjera?

[11]—Ya me han contado —le respondió Booz— todo lo que has hecho por tu suegra desde que murió tu esposo; cómo dejaste padre y madre, y la tierra donde naciste, y viniste a vivir con un pueblo que antes no conocías. [12]¡Que el SEÑOR te recompense por lo que has hecho! Que el SEÑOR, Dios de Israel,

---

a **1:1** *caudillos.* Véase Jue. 2:16. b **1:20** En hebreo, *Noemí* significa *placentera* o *dulce.* c **1:20** En hebreo, *Mara* significa *amarga.* d **1:21** *si me ha afligido el SEÑOR* Alt. *si el SEÑOR ha testificado contra mí.* e **2:7** *que ha venido ... cobertizo.* Frase de difícil traducción.

bajo cuyas alas has venido a refugiarte, te lo pague con creces.

13—¡Ojalá siga yo siendo de su agrado, mi señor! —contestó ella—. Usted me ha consolado y me ha hablado con cariño, aunque ni siquiera soy como una de sus servidoras.

14A la hora de comer, Booz le dijo:

—Ven acá. Sírvete pan y moja tu bocado en el vinagre.

Cuando Rut se sentó con los segadores, Booz le ofreció grano tostado. Ella comió, quedó satisfecha, y hasta le sobró. 15Después, cuando ella se levantó a recoger espigas, él dio estas órdenes a sus criados:

—Aun cuando saque espigas de las gavillas mismas, no la hagan pasar vergüenza. 16Más bien, dejen caer algunas espigas de los manojos para que ella las recoja, ¡y no la reprendan!

17Así que Rut recogió espigas en el campo hasta el atardecer. Luego desgranó la cebada que había recogido, la cual pesó más de veinte kilos.f 18La cargó de vuelta al pueblo, y su suegra vio cuánto traía. Además, Rut le entregó a su suegra lo que le había quedado después de haber comido hasta quedar satisfecha.

19Su suegra le preguntó:

—¿Dónde recogiste espigas hoy? ¿Dónde trabajaste? ¡Bendito sea el hombre que se fijó en ti!

Entonces Rut le contó a su suegra acerca del hombre con quien había estado trabajando. Le dijo:

—El hombre con quien hoy trabajé se llama Booz.

20—¡Que el SEÑOR lo bendiga! —exclamó Noemí delante de su nuera—. El SEÑOR no ha dejado de mostrar su fiel amor hacia los vivos y los muertos. Ese hombre es nuestro pariente cercano; es uno de los parientes que nos pueden redimir.

21Rut la moabita añadió:

—Incluso me dijo que me quede allí con sus criados hasta que terminen de recogerle toda la cosecha.

22—Hija mía, te conviene seguir con sus criadas —le dijo Noemí—, para que no se aprovechen de ti en otro campo.

23Así que Rut se quedó junto con las criadas de Booz para recoger espigas hasta que terminó la cosecha de la cebada y del trigo. Mientras tanto, vivía con su suegra.

Rut y Booz en la era

3 Un día su suegra Noemí le dijo:

—Hija mía, ¿no debiera yo buscarte un hogar seguro donde no te falte nada? 2Además, ¿acaso Booz, con cuyas criadas has estado, no es nuestro pariente? Pues bien, él va esta noche a la era para aventar la cebada. 3Báñate y perfúmate, y ponte tu mejor ropa. Baja luego a la era, pero no dejes que él se dé cuenta de que estás allí hasta que haya terminado de comer y beber. 4Cuando se vaya a dormir, te fijas dónde se acuesta. Luego vas, le destapas los pies, y te acuestas allí. Verás que él mismo te dice lo que tienes que hacer.

5—Haré todo lo que me has dicho —respondió Rut.

6Y bajó a la era e hizo todo lo que su suegra le había mandado.

7Booz comió y bebió, y se puso alegre. Luego se fue a dormir detrás del montón de grano. Más tarde Rut se acercó sigilosamente, le destapó los pies y se acostó allí. 8A medianoche Booz se despertó sobresaltado y, al darse vuelta, descubrió que había una mujer acostada a sus pies.

9—¿Quién eres? —le preguntó.

—Soy Rut, su sierva. Extienda sobre mí el borde de su manto,g ya que usted es un pariente que me puede redimir.

10—Que el SEÑOR te bendiga, hija mía. Esta nueva muestra de lealtad de tu parte supera la anterior, ya que no has ido en busca de hombres jóvenes, sean ricos o pobres. 11Y ahora, hija mía, no tengas miedo. Haré por ti todo lo que me pidas. Todo mi puebloh sabe que eres una mujer ejemplar. 12Ahora bien, aunque es cierto que soy un pariente que puede redimirte, hay otro más cercano que yo. 13Quédate aquí esta noche. Mañana, si él quiere redimirte, está bien que lo haga. Pero si no está dispuesto a hacerlo, ¡tan cierto como que el SEÑOR vive, te juro que yo te redimiré! Ahora acuéstate aquí hasta que amanezca.

14Así que se quedó acostada a sus pies hasta el amanecer, y se levantó cuando aún estaba oscuro; pues él había dicho: «Que no se sepa que una mujer vino a la era.»

15Luego Booz le dijo:

—Pásame el manto que llevas puesto y sostenlo firmemente.

Rut lo hizo así, y él echó en el manto veinte kilosi de cebada y puso la carga sobre ella. Luego él regresó al pueblo.

16Cuando Rut llegó adonde estaba su suegra, ésta le preguntó:

—¿Cómo te fue, hija mía?

Rut le contó todo lo que aquel hombre había hecho por ella, 17y añadió:

—Me dio estos veinte kilos de cebada, y me dijo: "No debes volver a tu suegra con las manos vacías."

18Entonces Noemí le dijo:

—Espérate, hija mía, a ver qué sucede. Porque este hombre no va a descansar hasta dejar resuelto este asunto hoy mismo.

Matrimonio de Booz y Rut

4 Booz, por su parte, subió hasta la *puerta de la ciudad y se sentó allí. En eso pasó el pariente redentor que él había mencionado.

—Ven acá, amigo mío, y siéntate —le dijo Booz.

El hombre fue y se sentó.

2Entonces Booz llamó a diez de los *ancianos de la ciudad, y les dijo:

—Siéntense aquí.

Y ellos se sentaron. 3Booz le dijo al pariente redentor:

—Noemí, que ha regresado de la tierra de Moab, está vendiendo el terreno que perteneció a nuestro hermano Elimélec. 4Consideré que debía informarte del asunto y sugerirte que lo compres en presencia de estos testigos y de los ancianos de mi pueblo. Si vas a redimir el terreno, hazlo. Pero si no vasj a redimirlo, házmelo saber, para que yo lo sepa. Porque ningún otro tiene el derecho de redimirlo sino tú, y después de ti, yo tengo ese derecho.

—Yo lo redimo —le contestó.

5Pero Booz le aclaró:

---

f 2:17 *más de veinte kilos.* Lit. *casi un* *efa.   g 3:9 *Extienda sobre mí el borde de su manto.* Esta acción implicaba una propuesta de matrimonio.   h 3:11 *Todo mi pueblo.* Lit. *Toda la* *puerta de mi pueblo.   i 3:15 *veinte kilos.* Lit. *seis (medidas);* también en v. 17.   j 4:4 *si no vas* (mss. hebreos, LXX, Vulgata y Siríaca); *si él no va* (TM).

—El día que adquieras el terreno de Noemí, adquieres también a Rut la moabita, viuda del difunto,k a fin de conservar su *nombre junto con su heredad.

6—Entonces no puedo redimirlo —respondió el pariente redentor—, porque podría perjudicar mi propia herencia. Redímelo tú; te cedo mi derecho. Yo no puedo ejercerlo.

7En aquellos tiempos, para ratificar la redención o el traspaso de una propiedad en Israel, una de las partes contratantes se quitaba la sandalia y se la daba a la otra. Así se acostumbraba legalizar los contratos en Israel. 8Por eso el pariente redentor le dijo a Booz:

—Cómpralo tú.

Y se quitó la sandalia.

9Entonces Booz proclamó ante los ancianos y ante todo el pueblo:

—Hoy son ustedes testigos de que le he comprado a Noemí toda la propiedad de Elimélec, Quilión y Majlón, 10y de que he tomado como esposa a Rut la moabita, viuda de Majlón, a fin de preservar el nombre del difunto con su heredad, para que su nombre no desaparezca de entre su familia ni de los registros del pueblo. ¡Hoy son ustedes testigos!

11Los ancianos y todos los que estaban en la puerta respondieron:

—Somos testigos.

»¡Que el SEÑOR haga que la mujer que va a formar parte de tu hogar sea como Raquel y Lea, quienes juntas edificaron el pueblo de Israel! »¡Que seas un hombre ilustre en Efrata, y que adquieras renombre en Belén!

12»¡Que por medio de esta joven el SEÑOR te conceda una descendencia tal que tu familia sea como la de Fares, el hijo que Tamar le dio a Judá!

Genealogía de David
4:18-22—1Cr 2:5-15; Mt 1:3-6; Lc 3:31-33

13Así que Booz tomó a Rut y se casó con ella. Cuando se unieron, el SEÑOR le concedió quedar embarazada, de modo que tuvo un hijo. 14Las mujeres le decían a Noemí: «¡Alabado sea el SEÑOR, que no te ha dejado hoy sin un redentor! ¡Que llegue a tener renombre en Israel! 15Este niño renovará tu *vida y te sustentará en la vejez, porque lo ha dado a luz tu nuera, que te ama y es para ti mejor que siete hijos.»

16Noemí tomó al niño, lo puso en su regazo y se encargó de criarlo. 17Las vecinas decían: «¡Noemí ha tenido un hijo!» Y lo llamaron Obed. Éste fue el padre de Isaí, padre de David.

18Así es éste es el linaje de Fares:

Fares fue el padre de Jezrón;
19Jezrón, el padre de Ram;
Ram, el padre de Aminadab;
20Aminadab, el padre de Naasón;
Naasón, el padre de Salmón;l
21Salmón, el padre de Booz;
Booz, el padre de Obed;
22Obed, el padre de Isaí;
e Isaí, el padre de David.

---

k **4:5** *de Noemí ... viuda* (Vulgata y Siríaca); *de Noemí y de Rut la moabita, tendrás que casarte con la viuda* (TM).　l **4:20** *Salmón* (mss. hebreos, mss. de LXX y Vulgata; véanse también v. 21 y LXX de 1Cr 2:11); *Salmá* (TM).

1 SAMUEL

Nacimiento de Samuel

1 En la sierra de Efraín había un hombre zufita de Ramatayin.ª Su nombre era Elcaná hijo de Jeroán, hijo de Eliú, hijo de Tohu, hijo de Zuf, efraimita. **2**Elcaná tenía dos esposas. Una de ellas se llamaba Ana, y la otra, Penina. Ésta tenía hijos, pero Ana no tenía ninguno.

3Cada año Elcaná salía de su pueblo para adorar al SEÑOR *Todopoderoso y ofrecerle sacrificios en Siló, donde Ofni y Finés, los dos hijos de Elí, oficiaban como sacerdotes del SEÑOR. **4**Cuando llegaba el día de ofrecer su sacrificio, Elcaná solía darles a Penina y a todos sus hijos e hijas la porción que les correspondía. **5**Pero a Ana le daba una porción especial,ᵇ pues la amaba a pesar de que el SEÑOR la había hecho estéril. **6**Penina, su rival, solía atormentarla para que se enojara, ya que el SEÑOR la había hecho estéril.

7Cada año, cuando iban a la casa del SEÑOR, sucedía lo mismo: Penina la atormentaba, hasta que Ana se ponía a llorar y ni comer quería. **8**Entonces Elcaná, su esposo, le decía: «Ana, ¿por qué lloras? ¿Por qué no comes? ¿Por qué estás resentida? ¿Acaso no soy para ti mejor que diez hijos?»

9Una vez, estando en Siló, Ana se levantó después de la comida. Y a la vista del sacerdote Elí, que estaba sentado en su silla junto a la puerta del santuario del SEÑOR, **10**con gran angustia comenzó a orar al SEÑOR y a llorar desconsoladamente. **11**Entonces hizo este voto: «SEÑOR Todopoderoso, si te dignas mirar la desdicha de esta sierva tuya, y, si en vez de olvidarme, te acuerdas de mí y me concedes un hijo varón, yo te lo entregaré para toda su vida, y nunca se le cortará el cabello.»

12Como Ana estuvo orando largo rato ante el SEÑOR, Elí se fijó en su boca. **13**Sus labios se movían pero, debido a que Ana oraba en voz baja, no se podía oír su voz. Elí pensó que estaba borracha, **14**así que le dijo:

—¿Hasta cuándo te va a durar la borrachera? ¡Deja ya el vino!

15—No, mi señor; no he bebido ni vino ni cerveza. Soy sólo una mujer angustiada que ha venido a desahogarse delante del SEÑOR. **16**No me tome usted por una mala mujer. He pasado este tiempo orando debido a mi angustia y aflicción.

17—Vete en *paz —respondió Elí—. Que el Dios de Israel te conceda lo que le has pedido.

18—Gracias. Ojalá favorezca usted siempre a esta sierva suya.

Con esto, Ana se despidió y se fue a comer. Desde ese momento, su semblante cambió. **19**Al día siguiente madrugaron y, después de adorar al SEÑOR, volvieron a su casa en Ramá. Luego Elcaná se unió a su esposa Ana, y el SEÑOR se acordó de ella. **20**Ana concibió y, pasado un año, dio a luz un hijo y le puso por nombre Samuel,ᶜ pues dijo: «Al SEÑOR se lo pedí.»

Ana dedica a Samuel

21Cuando Elcaná salió con toda su familia para cumplir su promesa y ofrecer su sacrificio anual al SEÑOR, **22**Ana no lo acompañó.

—No iré hasta que el niño sea destetado —le explicó a su esposo—. Entonces lo llevaré para dedicarlo al SEÑOR, y allí se quedará el resto de su vida.

23—Bien, haz lo que te parezca mejor —respondió su esposo Elcaná—. Quédate hasta que lo destetes, con tal de que el SEÑOR cumpla su palabra.

Así pues, Ana se quedó en su casa y crió a su hijo hasta que lo destetó.

24Cuando dejó de amamantarlo, salió con el niño, a pesar de ser tan pequeño, y lo llevó a la casa del SEÑOR en Siló. También llevó un becerro de tres años,ᵈ una medida de harina y un odre de vino. **25**Luego sacrificaron el becerro y presentaron el niño a Elí. **26**Dijo Ana: «Mi señor, tan cierto como que usted vive, le juro que yo soy la mujer que estuvo aquí a su lado orando al SEÑOR. **27**Éste es el niño que yo le pedí al SEÑOR, y él me lo concedió. **28**Ahora yo, por mi parte, se lo entrego al SEÑOR. Mientras el niño viva, estará dedicado a él.» Entonces Elíᵉ se postró allí ante el SEÑOR.

Oración de Ana

2 Ana elevó esta oración:

«Mi *corazón se alegra en el SEÑOR;
    en él radica mi poder.ᶠ
Puedo celebrar su *salvación
    y burlarme de mis enemigos.

2»Nadie es santo como el SEÑOR;
    no hay *roca como nuestro Dios.
    ¡No hay nadie como él!

3»Dejen de hablar con tanto orgullo y altivez;
    ¡no profieran palabras soberbias!
El SEÑOR es un Dios que todo lo sabe,
    y él es quien juzga las acciones.

4»El arco de los poderosos se quiebra,
    pero los débiles recobran las fuerzas.
5Los que antes tenían comida de sobra
    se venden por un pedazo de pan;
los que antes sufrían hambre
    ahora viven saciados.
La estéril ha dado a luz siete veces,
    pero la que tenía muchos hijos languidece.

6»Del SEÑOR vienen la muerte y la vida;
    él nos hace bajar al *sepulcro,
    pero también nos levanta.
7El SEÑOR da la riqueza y la pobreza;
    humilla, pero también enaltece.
8Levanta del polvo al desvalido
    y saca del basurero al pobre
para sentarlos en medio de príncipes
    y darles un trono esplendoroso.

»Del SEÑOR son los fundamentos de la tierra;
    ¡sobre ellos afianzó el mundo!
9Él guiará los pasos de sus fieles,
    pero los malvados se perderán entre las
      sombras.
    ¡Nadie triunfa por sus propias fuerzas!

10»El SEÑOR destrozará a sus enemigos;
    desde el cielo lanzará truenos contra ellos.

ª **1:1** *zufita de Ramatayin.* Lit. *de Ramatayin Zofín.* ᵇ **1:5** *especial.* Alt. *Doble.* ᶜ **1:20** En hebreo, el nombre *Samuel* suena como la expresión que significa *Dios oyó.* ᵈ **1:24** *un becerro de tres años* (Qumrán, LXX, Siríaca); *tres becerros* (TM). ᵉ **1:28** *Elí.* Lit. *Él.* ᶠ **2:1** *poder.* Lit. *cuerno;* también en v. 10.

El SEÑOR juzgará los confines de la tierra,
fortalecerá a su rey
y enaltecerá el poder de su *ungido.»

11Elcaná volvió a su casa en Ramá, pero el niño se quedó para servir al SEÑOR, bajo el cuidado del sacerdote Elí.

Perversidad de los hijos de Elí

12Los hijos de Elí eran unos perversos que no tomaban en cuenta al SEÑOR. 13La costumbre de estos sacerdotes era la siguiente: Cuando alguien ofrecía un sacrificio, el asistente del sacerdote se presentaba con un tenedor grande en la mano y, mientras se cocía la carne, 14metía el tenedor en la olla, en el caldero, en la cacerola o en la cazuela; y el sacerdote tomaba para sí mismo todo lo que se enganchaba en el tenedor. De este modo trataban a todos los israelitas que iban a Siló. 15Además, antes de quemarse la grasa, solía llegar el ayudante del sacerdote para decirle al que estaba por ofrecer el sacrificio: «Dame carne para el asado del sacerdote, pues no te la va a aceptar cocida, sino cruda.» 16Y si el hombre contestaba: «Espera a que se queme la grasa, como es debido; luego podrás tomar lo que desees», el asistente replicaba: «No, dámela ahora mismo; de lo contrario, te la quito por la fuerza.» 17Así que el pecado de estos jóvenes era gravísimo a los ojos del SEÑOR, pues trataban con desprecio las ofrendas que le pertenecían.

18El niño Samuel, por su parte, vestido con un *efod de lino, seguía sirviendo en la presencia del SEÑOR. 19Cada año su madre le hacía una pequeña túnica, y se la llevaba cuando iba con su esposo para ofrecer su sacrificio anual. 20Elí entonces bendecía a Elcaná y a su esposa, diciendo: «Que el SEÑOR te conceda hijos de esta mujer, a cambio del niño que ella pidió para dedicárselo al SEÑOR.» Luego regresaban a su casa.

21El SEÑOR bendijo a Ana, de manera que ella concibió y dio a luz tres hijos y dos hijas. Durante ese tiempo, Samuel crecía en la presencia del SEÑOR.

22Elí, que ya era muy anciano, se enteró de todo lo que sus hijos le estaban haciendo al pueblo de Israel, incluso de que se acostaban con las mujeres que servían a la entrada del santuario. 23Les dijo: «¿Por qué se comportan así? Todo el pueblo me habla de su mala conducta. 24No, hijos míos; no es nada bueno lo que se comenta en el pueblo del SEÑOR. 25Si alguien peca contra otra persona, Dios le servirá de árbitro; pero si peca contra el SEÑOR, ¿quién podrá interceder por él?» No obstante, ellos no le hicieron caso a la advertencia de su padre, pues la voluntad del SEÑOR era quitarles la vida.

26Por su parte, el niño Samuel seguía creciendo y ganándose el aprecio del SEÑOR y de la gente.

Profecía contra la familia de Elí

27Un hombre de Dios fue a ver a Elí, y le dijo:

«Así dice el SEÑOR: "Bien sabes que yo me manifesté a tus antepasados cuando estaban en Egipto bajo el poder del faraón. 28De entre todas las tribus de Israel, escogí a Aarón para que fuera mi sacerdote, es decir, para que en mi presencia se acercara a mi altar, quemara el incienso y se pusiera el *efod. Además, a su familia le concedí las ofrendas que los israelitas queman en mi honor. 29¿Por qué, pues, tratan ustedes con tanto desprecio los sacrificios y ofrendas que yo he ordenado que me traigan? ¿Por qué honras a tus

hijos más que a mí, y los engordas con lo mejor de todas las ofrendas de mi pueblo Israel?"

30»Por cuanto has hecho esto, de ninguna manera permitiré que tus parientes me sirvan, aun cuando yo había prometido que toda tu familia, tanto tus antepasados como tus descendientes, me servirían siempre. Yo, el SEÑOR, Dios de Israel, lo afirmo. Yo honro a los que me honran, y humillo a los que me desprecian. 31En efecto, se acerca el día en que acabaré con tu poder y con el de tu familia; ninguno de tus descendientes llegará a viejo. 32Mirarás con envidia el bien que se le hará a Israel, y ninguno de tus descendientes llegará a viejo. 33Si permito que alguno de los tuyos continúe sirviendo en mi altar, será para empañarte de lágrimas los ojos y abatirte el *alma; todos tus descendientes morirán en la flor de la vida. 34Y te doy esta señal: tus dos hijos, Ofni y Finés, morirán el mismo día.

35»Pero yo levantaré a un sacerdote fiel, que hará mi voluntad y cumplirá mis deseos. Jamás le faltará descendencia, y vivirá una larga vida en presencia de mi *ungido. 36Y los familiares tuyos que sobrevivan vendrán y de rodillas le rogarán que les regale una moneda de plata o un pedazo de pan. Le suplicarán: "¡Dame algún trabajo sacerdotal para mi sustento!"»

El SEÑOR llama a Samuel

3 Samuel, que todavía era joven, servía al SEÑOR bajo el cuidado de Elí. En esos tiempos no era común oír palabra del SEÑOR, ni eran frecuentes las visiones. 2Elí ya se estaba quedando ciego. Un día, mientras él descansaba en su habitación, 3Samuel dormía en el santuario, donde se encontraba el arca de Dios. La lámpara de Dios todavía estaba encendida. 4El SEÑOR llamó a Samuel, y éste respondió:

—Aquí estoy.

5Y en seguida fue corriendo a donde estaba Elí, y le dijo:

—Aquí estoy; ¿para qué me llamó usted?

—Yo no te he llamado —respondió Elí—. Vuelve a acostarte. Y Samuel volvió a su cama.

6Pero una vez más el SEÑOR lo llamó:

—¡Samuel!

Él se levantó, fue a donde estaba Elí y le dijo:

—Aquí estoy; ¿para qué me llamó usted?

—Hijo mío —respondió Elí—, yo no te he llamado. Vuelve a acostarte.

7Samuel todavía no conocía al SEÑOR, ni su palabra se le había revelado.

8Por tercera vez llamó el SEÑOR a Samuel. Él se levantó y fue a donde estaba Elí.

—Aquí estoy —le dijo—; ¿para qué me llamó usted?

Entonces Elí se dio cuenta de que el SEÑOR estaba llamando al muchacho.

9—Ve y acuéstate —le dijo Elí—. Si alguien vuelve a llamarte, dile: "Habla, SEÑOR, que tu siervo escucha."

Así que Samuel se fue y se acostó en su cama.

10Entonces el SEÑOR se le acercó y lo llamó de nuevo:

—¡Samuel! ¡Samuel!

—Habla, que tu siervo escucha —respondió Samuel.

11—Mira —le dijo el SEÑOR—, estoy por hacer en Israel algo que a todo el que lo oiga le quedará retumbando en los oídos. 12Ese día llevaré a cabo todo lo que he anunciado en contra de Elí y su familia.

---

g **2:32** *Mirarás ... y ninguno.* Alt. *Verás angustia en mi morada. Y aunque a Israel se le hará el bien, ninguno.*

13Ya le dije que por la maldad de sus hijos he condenado a su familia para siempre; él sabía que estaban *blasfemando contra Dios[h] y, sin embargo, no los refrenó. 14Por lo tanto, hago este juramento en contra de su familia: ¡Ningún sacrificio ni ofrenda podrá *expiar jamás el pecado de la familia de Elí!

15Samuel se acostó, y a la mañana siguiente abrió las puertas de la casa del SEÑOR, pero no se atrevía a contarle a Elí la visión. 16Así que Elí tuvo que llamarlo.

—¡Samuel, hijo mío!

—Aquí estoy —respondió Samuel.

17—¿Qué fue lo que te dijo el SEÑOR? —le preguntó Elí—. Te pido que no me lo ocultes. ¡Que Dios te castigue sin piedad, si me ocultas una sola palabra de todo lo que te ha dicho!

18Samuel se lo refirió todo, sin ocultarle nada, y Elí dijo:

—Él es el SEÑOR; que haga lo que mejor le parezca.

19Mientras Samuel crecía, el SEÑOR estuvo con él y confirmó todo lo que le había dicho.20Y todo Israel, desde Dan hasta Berseba, se dio cuenta de que el SEÑOR había confirmado a Samuel como su profeta. 21Además, el SEÑOR siguió manifestándose en Siló; allí se revelaba a Samuel y le comunicaba su palabra.

Los filisteos capturan el arca

4 La palabra de Samuel llegó a todo el pueblo de Israel. En aquellos días, los israelitas salieron a enfrentarse con los filisteos y acamparon cerca de Ebenezer. Los filisteos, que habían acampado en Afec,[a] 2desplegaron sus tropas para atacar a los israelitas. Se entabló la batalla, y los filisteos derrotaron a los israelitas, matando en el campo a unos cuatro mil de ellos. 3Cuando el ejército regresó al campamento, los *ancianos de Israel dijeron: «¿Por qué nos ha derrotado hoy el SEÑOR por medio de los filisteos? Traigamos el arca del *pacto del SEÑOR, que está en Siló, para que nos acompañe y nos salve del poder de nuestros enemigos.»

4Así que enviaron un destacamento a Siló para sacar de allá el arca del pacto del SEÑOR *Todopoderoso, que reina entre los *querubines. Los dos hijos de Elí, Ofni y Finés, estaban a cargo del arca del pacto de Dios. 5Cuando ésta llegó al campamento, los israelitas empezaron a gritar de tal manera que la tierra temblaba.

6Los filisteos oyeron el griterío y preguntaron: «¿A qué viene tanto alboroto en el campamento hebreo?» Y al oír que el arca del SEÑOR había llegado al campamento, 7los filisteos se acobardaron y dijeron: «Dios ha entrado en el campamento. ¡Ay de nosotros, que nunca nos ha pasado algo así! 8¡Ay de nosotros! ¿Quién nos va a librar de las manos de dioses tan poderosos, que en el desierto hirieron a los egipcios con toda clase de plagas? 9¡Ánimo, filisteos! Si no quieren llegar a ser esclavos de los hebreos, tal como ellos lo han sido de nosotros, ¡ármense de valor y luchen como hombres!»

10Entonces los filisteos se lanzaron al ataque y derrotaron a los israelitas, los cuales huyeron en desbandada. La matanza fue terrible, pues de los israelitas cayeron treinta mil soldados de infantería. 11Además, fue capturada el arca de Dios, y murieron Ofni y Finés, los dos hijos de Elí.

Muerte de Elí

12Un soldado que pertenecía a la tribu de Benjamín salió corriendo del frente de batalla, y ese mismo día llegó a Siló, con la ropa hecha pedazos y la cabeza cubierta de polvo. 13Allí se encontraba Elí, sentado en su silla y vigilando el camino, pues su *corazón le temblaba sólo de pensar en el arca de Dios.Cuando el soldado entró en el pueblo y contó lo que había sucedido, todos se pusieron a gritar.

14—¿A qué viene tanto alboroto? —preguntó Elí, al oír el griterío.

El hombre corrió para darle la noticia. 15(Elí ya tenía noventa y ocho años, y sus ojos ni se movían, de modo que no podía ver.)

16—Vengo del frente de batalla —le dijo a Elí—; huí de las filas hoy mismo.

—¿Qué pasó, hijo mío? —preguntó Elí.

17—Los israelitas han huido ante los filisteos —respondió el mensajero—; el ejército ha sufrido una derrota terrible. Además, tus dos hijos, Ofni y Finés, han muerto, y el arca de Dios ha sido capturada.

18Solamente de oír mencionar el arca de Dios, Elí se fue de espaldas, cayéndose de la silla junto a la puerta. Como era viejo y pesaba mucho, se rompió la nuca y murió. Durante cuarenta años había dirigido al pueblo de Israel.

19Su nuera, la esposa de Finés, estaba embarazada y próxima a dar a luz. Cuando supo que el arca de Dios había sido capturada, y que tanto su suegro como su esposo habían muerto, le vinieron los dolores de parto y tuvo un alumbramiento muy difícil. 20Al verla agonizante, las parteras que la atendían le dijeron: «Anímate, que has dado a luz un niño.» Ella no respondió; ni siquiera les hizo caso. 21Pero por causa de la captura del arca de Dios, y por la muerte de su suegro y de su esposo, le puso al niño el nombre de Icabod,[i] para indicar que la gloria de Israel había sido desterrada. 22Exclamó: «¡Se han llevado la gloria de Israel! ¡El arca de Dios ha sido capturada!»

El arca en Asdod y Ecrón

5 Después de capturar el arca de Dios, los filisteos la llevaron de Ebenezer a Asdod 2y la pusieron junto a la estatua de Dagón, en el templo de ese dios. 3Al día siguiente, cuando los habitantes de Asdod se levantaron, vieron que la estatua de Dagón estaba tirada en el suelo, boca abajo, frente al arca del SEÑOR. Así que la levantaron y la colocaron en su sitio. 4Pero al día siguiente, cuando se levantaron, volvieron a encontrar la estatua tirada en el suelo, boca abajo, frente al arca del SEÑOR. Sobre el umbral estaban su cabeza y sus dos manos, separadas del tronco. 5Por eso, hasta el día de hoy, ninguno de los que entran en el templo de Dagón en Asdod pisan el umbral, ¡ni siquiera los sacerdotes!

6El SEÑOR descargó su mano sobre la población de Asdod y sus alrededores, y los azotó con tumores. 7La gente de Asdod reconoció lo que estaba pasando, y declaró: «El arca del Dios de Israel no puede quedarse en medio nuestro, porque ese dios ha descargado su mano sobre nosotros y contra nuestro dios Dagón.»

8Así que convocaron a todos los jefes filisteos y les preguntaron:

—¿Qué vamos a hacer con el arca del Dios de Israel?

—Trasládenla a la ciudad de Gat —respondieron los jefes.

---

h 3:13 *contra Dios* (LXX y tradición rabínica); *por sí mismos* (TM). i 4:21 En hebreo, *Icabod* significa *sin gloria*.

Y así lo hicieron. 9Pero después de que la trasladaron, el SEÑOR castigó a esa ciudad, afligiendo con una erupción de tumores a sus habitantes, desde el más pequeño hasta el mayor. Eso provocó un pánico horrible. 10Entonces enviaron el arca del SEÑOR a Ecrón pero, tan pronto como entró el arca en la ciudad, sus habitantes se pusieron a gritar: «¡Nos han traído el arca del Dios de Israel para matarnos a todos!» 11Por eso convocaron a todos los jefes filisteos y protestaron: «¡Llévense el arca del Dios de Israel! ¡Devuélvanla a su lugar de origen, para que no nos mate a nosotros y a todos los nuestros!» Y es que el terror de la muerte se había apoderado de la ciudad, porque Dios había descargado su mano sobre ese lugar. 12Los que no murieron fueron azotados por tumores, de modo que los gritos de la ciudad llegaban hasta el cielo.

Los filisteos devuelven el arca a Israel

6 El arca del SEÑOR estuvo en territorio filisteo siete meses, 2y los filisteos convocaron a los sacerdotes y a los adivinos para preguntarles:

—¿Qué vamos a hacer con el arca del SEÑOR? Dígannos de qué modo hay que devolverla a su lugar.

3—Si piensan devolverla —contestaron—, no la manden sin nada; tienen que presentarle a Dios una ofrenda compensatoria. Entonces recobrarán la salud y sabrán por qué Dios no ha dejado de castigarlos.

4—¿Y qué le debemos ofrecer? —preguntaron los filisteos.

—Cinco figuras de oro en forma de tumor —respondieron aquéllos— y otras cinco en forma de rata, conforme al número de jefes filisteos, pues la misma plaga los ha azotado a ustedes y a sus jefes. 5Así que hagan imágenes de los tumores y de las ratas que han devastado el país, y den honra al Dios de Israel. Tal vez suavice su castigo contra ustedes, sus dioses y su tierra. 6¿Por qué se van a obstinar, como lo hicieron los egipcios bajo el faraón? ¿No es cierto que Dios tuvo que hacerles daño para que dejaran ir a los israelitas?

7»Ahora manden a construir una carreta nueva. Escojan también dos vacas con cría y que nunca hayan llevado yugo. Aten las vacas a la carreta, pero encierren los becerros en el establo. 8Tomen luego el arca del SEÑOR y pónganla en la carreta. Coloquen una caja junto al arca, con los objetos de oro que van a entregarle a Dios como ofrenda compensatoria. Luego dejen que la carreta se vaya sola, 9y obsérvenla. Si se va en dirección de Bet Semes, su propio territorio, eso quiere decir que el SEÑOR es quien nos ha causado esta calamidad tan terrible. Pero si la carreta se desvía para otro lugar, sabremos que no fue él quien nos hizo daño, sino que todo ha sido por casualidad.

10Así lo hicieron. Tomaron dos vacas con cría y las ataron a la carreta, pero encerraron los becerros en el establo. 11Además, en la carreta pusieron el arca del SEÑOR y la caja que contenía las figuras de ratas y de tumores de oro. 12Y las vacas se fueron mugiendo por todo el camino, directamente a Bet Semes! Siguieron esa ruta sin desviarse para ningún lado. Los jefes de los filisteos se fueron detrás de la carreta, hasta llegar al territorio de Bet Semes.

13Los habitantes de Bet Semes, que estaban en el valle cosechando el trigo, alzaron la vista y, al ver el arca, se llenaron de alegría. 14La carreta llegó hasta el campo de Josué de Bet Semes, donde había una gran piedra, y allí se detuvo. Entonces la gente del pueblo usó la madera de la carreta como leña, y ofreció las vacas en *holocausto al SEÑOR. 15Los levitas que habían descargado la carreta pusieron el arca del SEÑOR sobre la gran piedra, junto con la caja que contenía las figuras de oro. Aquel día los habitantes de Bet Semes ofrecieron holocaustos y sacrificios al SEÑOR. 16Los cinco jefes filisteos vieron todo esto, y regresaron a Ecrón ese mismo día.

17Las figuras de oro en forma de tumor, que los filisteos entregaron al SEÑOR como ofrenda compensatoria, correspondían a cada una de estas ciudades: Asdod, Gaza, Ascalón, Gat y Ecrón. 18Así mismo, el número de las ratas de oro correspondía a las ciudades filisteas que pertenecían a los cinco jefes, tanto las ciudades fortificadas como las aldeas sin murallas. Y la gran piedra donde depositaron el arca del SEÑOR permanece hasta el día de hoy, como testimonio, en el campo de Josué de Bet Semes.

19Algunos hombres de ese lugar se atrevieron a mirar dentro del arca del SEÑOR, y Dios los mató. Fueron setentaj los que perecieron. El pueblo hizo duelo por el terrible castigo que el SEÑOR había enviado, 20y los habitantes de Bet Semes dijeron: «El SEÑOR es un Dios *santo. ¿Quién podrá presentarse ante él? ¿Y adónde podremos enviar el arca para que no se quede entre nosotros?» 21Así que mandaron este mensaje a los habitantes de Quiriat Yearín: «Los filisteos han devuelto el arca del SEÑOR; vengan y llévensela.»

7 Los de Quiriat Yearín fueron a Bet Semes y se llevaron el arca del SEÑOR a la casa de Abinadab, que estaba en una loma. Luego consagraron a su hijo Eleazar para que estuviera a cargo de ella.

Samuel derrota a los filisteos en Mizpa

2El arca permaneció en Quiriat Yearín durante mucho tiempo. Pasaron veinte años, y todo el pueblo de Israel buscaba con ansiedad al SEÑOR. 3Por eso Samuel le dijo al pueblo: «Si ustedes desean volverse al SEÑOR de todo *corazón, desháganse de los dioses extranjeros y de las imágenes de *Astarté. Dedíquense totalmente a servir sólo al SEÑOR, y él los librará del poder de los filisteos.» 4Así que los israelitas echaron fuera a los ídolos de *Baal y a las imágenes de Astarté, y sirvieron sólo al SEÑOR.

5Luego Samuel ordenó: «Reúnan a todo Israel en Mizpa para que yo ruegue al SEÑOR por ustedes.» 6Cuando los israelitas se reunieron en Mizpa, sacaron agua y la derramaron ante el SEÑOR. También ayunaron durante el día, y públicamente confesaron: «Hemos pecado contra el SEÑOR.» Fue en Mizpa donde Samuel comenzó a gobernar a los israelitas.

7Cuando los filisteos se enteraron de que los israelitas se habían reunido en Mizpa, los jefes filisteos marcharon contra Israel. Al darse cuenta de esto, los israelitas tuvieron miedo de los filisteos 8y le dijeron a Samuel: «No dejes de clamar al SEÑOR por nosotros, para que nos salve del poder de los filisteos.» 9Samuel tomó entonces un cordero pequeño y lo ofreció en *holocausto al SEÑOR. Luego clamó al SEÑOR en favor de Israel, y el SEÑOR le respondió.

10Mientras Samuel ofrecía el sacrificio, los filisteos avanzaron para atacar a Israel. Pero aquel día el SEÑOR lanzó grandes truenos contra los filisteos. Esto creó confusión entre ellos, y cayeron derrotados ante los israelitas. 11Entonces los israelitas persiguieron a los filisteos desde Mizpa hasta más allá de Bet Car, matándolos por el camino. 12Después Samuel tomó una piedra, la colocó entre Mizpa y Sen, y la llamó Ebenezer,k «El Señor no ha dejado de ayudarnos.»

j 6:19 setenta (mss. hebreos); cincuenta mil setenta (TM). 	k 7:12 En hebreo, Ebenezer significa piedra de ayuda.

13Durante toda la vida de Samuel, el SEÑOR manifestó su poder sobre los filisteos. Éstos fueron subyugados por los israelitas y no volvieron a invadir su territorio. 14Fue así como los israelitas recuperaron las ciudades que los filisteos habían capturado anteriormente, desde Ecrón hasta Gat, y libraron todo ese territorio del dominio de los filisteos. También hubo paz entre Israel y los amorreos.

15Samuel siguió gobernando a Israel toda su vida. 16Todos los años recorría las ciudades de Betel, Guilgal y Mizpa, y atendía los asuntos del país en esas regiones. 17Luego regresaba a Ramá, donde residía, y desde allí gobernaba a Israel. También allí erigió un altar al SEÑOR.

Los israelitas piden un rey

8 Cuando Samuel entró en años, puso a sus hijos como gobernadores de Israel, 2con sede en Berseba. El hijo mayor se llamaba Joel, y el segundo, Abías. 3Pero ninguno de los dos siguió el ejemplo de su padre, sino que ambos se dejaron guiar por la avaricia, aceptando sobornos y pervirtiendo la justicia.

4Por eso se reunieron los *ancianos de Israel y fueron a Ramá para hablar con Samuel. 5Le dijeron: «Tú has envejecido ya, y tus hijos no siguen tu ejemplo. Mejor danos un rey que nos gobierne, como lo tienen las naciones.»

6Cuando le dijeron que querían tener un rey, Samuel se disgustó. Entonces se puso a orar al SEÑOR, 7pero el SEÑOR le dijo: «Considera seriamente todo lo que el pueblo te diga. En realidad, no te han rechazado a ti, sino a mí, pues no quieren que yo reine sobre ellos. 8Te están tratando del mismo modo que me han tratado a mí desde el día en que los saqué de Egipto hasta hoy. Me han abandonado para servir a otros dioses. 9Así que hazles caso, pero adviérteles claramente del poder que el rey va a ejercer sobre ellos.»

10Samuel comunicó entonces el mensaje del SEÑOR a la gente que le estaba pidiendo un rey. 11Les explicó:

—Esto es lo que hará el rey que va a ejercer el poder sobre ustedes: Les quitará a sus hijos para que se hagan cargo de los carros militares y de la caballería, y para que le abran paso al carro real. 12Los hará comandantes y capitanes,l y los pondrá a labrar y a cosechar, y a fabricar armamentos y pertrechos. 13También les quitará a sus hijas para emplearlas como perfumistas, cocineras y panaderas. 14Se apoderará de sus mejores campos, viñedos y olivares, y se los dará a sus ministros, 15y a ustedes les exigirá una décima parte de sus cosechas y vendimias para entregársela a sus funcionarios y ministros. 16Además, les quitará sus criados y criadas, y sus mejores bueyesm y asnos, de manera que trabajen para él. 17Les exigirá una décima parte de sus rebaños, y ustedes mismos le servirán como esclavos. 18Cuando llegue aquel día, clamarán por causa del rey que hayan escogido, pero el SEÑOR no les responderá.

19El pueblo, sin embargo, no le hizo caso a Samuel, sino que protestó:

—¡De ninguna manera! Queremos un rey que nos gobierne. 20Así seremos como las otras naciones, con un rey que nos gobierne y que marche al frente de nosotros cuando vayamos a la guerra.

21Después de oír lo que el pueblo quería, Samuel se lo comunicó al SEÑOR.

22—Hazles caso —respondió el SEÑOR—; dales un rey.

Entonces Samuel les dijo a los israelitas:
—¡Regresen a sus pueblos!

Samuel unge a Saúl

9 Había un hombre de la tribu de Benjamín, muy respetado, cuyo nombre era Quis hijo de Abiel, hijo de Zeror, hijo de Becorat, hijo de Afía, también benjaminita. 2Quis tenía un hijo llamado Saúl, que era buen mozo y apuesto como ningún otro israelita, tan alto que los demás apenas le llegaban al hombro.

3En cierta ocasión se extraviaron las burras de su padre Quis, y éste le dijo a Saúl: «Toma a uno de los criados y ve a buscar las burras.» 4Saúl y el criado se fueron y cruzaron la sierra de Efraín, hasta pasar por la región de Salisá, pero no las encontraron. Pasaron también por la región de Salín, y después por el territorio de Benjamín, pero tampoco allí las encontraron. 5Cuando llegaron al territorio de Zuf, Saúl le dijo al criado que lo acompañaba:

—Vámonos. Debemos regresar, no sea que mi padre comience a preocuparse más por nosotros que por las burras.

6El criado le contestó:
—En este pueblo vive un hombre de Dios que es muy famoso. Todo lo que dice se cumple sin falta. ¿Por qué no vamos allá? A lo mejor nos indica el camino que debemos seguir.

7—Pero si vamos, ¿qué le podemos llevar? —preguntó Saúl—. En las alforjas no nos queda nada de comer, ni tenemos ningún regalo que ofrecerle.

8—Aquí tengo casi tres gramosn de plata —respondió el criado—. Se los puedo dar al hombre de Dios para que nos indique el camino.

9(Antiguamente, cuando alguien en Israel iba a consultar a Dios, solía decir: «Vamos a ver al vidente», porque así se le llamaba entonces al que ahora se le llama profeta.)

10—Muy bien —dijo Saúl—, vamos.

Dicho esto, se dirigieron al pueblo donde vivía el hombre de Dios. 11Subían por la cuesta de la ciudad cuando se encontraron con unas jóvenes que iban a sacar agua. Les preguntaron:

—¿Se encuentra por aquí el vidente?

12—Sí, está más adelante —contestaron ellas—. Dense prisa, que acaba de llegar a la ciudad, y el pueblo va a ofrecer un sacrificio en el santuario del cerro. 13Cuando entren en la ciudad lo encontrarán, si llegan antes de que suba al santuario para comer. La gente no empezará a comer hasta que él llegue, pues primero tiene que bendecir el sacrificio, y luego los invitados comerán. Así que vayan de inmediato, que hoy mismo lo van a encontrar.

14Saúl y su criado se dirigieron entonces a la ciudad. Iban entrando cuando Samuel se encontró con ellos, camino al santuario del cerro.

15Un día antes de que Saúl llegara, el SEÑOR le había hecho esta revelación a Samuel: 16«Mañana, a esta hora, te voy a enviar un hombre de la tierra de Benjamín. Lo ungirás como gobernante de mi pueblo Israel, para que lo libre del poder de los filisteos. Me he compadecido de mi pueblo, pues sus gritos de angustia han llegado hasta mí.» 17Cuando Samuel vio a Saúl, el SEÑOR le dijo: «Ahí tienes al hombre de quien te hablé; él gobernará a mi pueblo.»

18Al llegar a la *puerta de la ciudad, Saúl se acercó a Samuel y le preguntó:

---

l 8:12 comandantes y capitanes. Lit. jefes de mil y jefes de cincuenta. m 8:16 bueyes (LXX); jóvenes (TM). n 9:8 casi tres gramos. Lit. un cuarto de *siclo.

—¿Podría usted indicarme dónde está la casa del vidente?

19—Yo soy el vidente —respondió Samuel—. Acompáñame al santuario del cerro, que hoy comerán ustedes conmigo. Ya mañana, cuando te deje partir, responderé a todas tus inquietudes. 20En cuanto a las burras que se te perdieron hace tres días, ni te preocupes, que ya las encontraron.

Y agregó:

—Lo que Israel más desea, ¿no tiene que ver contigo y con toda la familia de tu padre?

21—¿Por qué me dices eso? —respondió Saúl—. ¿No soy yo de la tribu de Benjamín, que es la más pequeña de Israel? ¿Y no es mi familia la más insignificante de la tribu de Benjamín?

22No obstante, Samuel tomó a Saúl y a su criado, los llevó al salón y les dio un lugar especial entre los invitados, que eran unos treinta. 23Luego Samuel le dijo al cocinero:

—Trae la ración de carne que te pedí que apartaras, y que yo mismo te entregué.

24El cocinero sacó un pernil entero, y se lo sirvió a Saúl. Entonces Samuel dijo:

—Ahí tienes lo que estaba reservado para ti. Come, pues antes de invitar a los otros, tu ración ya había sido apartada para esta ocasión.

Así fue como Saúl comió aquel día con Samuel. 25Luego bajaron del santuario a la ciudad, y Samuel conversó con Saúl en la azotea de su casa. 26Al amanecer, a la hora de levantarse, Samuel habló con Saúl en ese mismo lugar:

—¡Levántate! —le dijo—; ya debes partir.

Saúl se levantó, y salieron de la casa juntos. 27Mientras se dirigían a las afueras de la ciudad, Samuel le dijo a Saúl:

—Dile al criado que se adelante, pero tú quédate un momento, que te voy a dar un mensaje de parte de Dios.

El criado se adelantó.

10 Entonces Samuel tomó un frasco de aceite y lo derramó sobre la cabeza de Saúl. Luego lo besó y le dijo:

—¡Es el SEÑOR quien te ha ungido para que gobiernes a su pueblo!ñ 2Hoy mismo, cuando te alejes de mí y llegues a Selsa, en el territorio de Benjamín, cerca de la tumba de Raquel verás a dos hombres. Ellos te dirán: "Ya encontramos las burras que andabas buscando. Pero tu padre ya no piensa en las burras, sino que ahora está preocupado por ustedes y se pregunta: '¿Qué puedo hacer para encontrar a mi hijo?'"

3»Más adelante, cuando llegues a la encina de Tabor, te encontrarás con tres hombres que se dirigen a Betel para adorar a Dios. Uno de ellos lleva tres cabritos; otro, tres panes; el otro, un odre de vino. 4Después de saludarte, te entregarán dos panes. Acéptalos.

5»De ahí llegarás a Guibeá de Dios, donde hay una guarnición filistea. Al entrar en la ciudad te encontrarás con un grupo de profetas que bajan del santuario en el cerro. Vendrán profetizando, precedidos por músicos que tocan liras, panderetas, flautas y arpas. 6Entonces el Espíritu del SEÑOR vendrá sobre ti con poder, y tú profetizarás con ellos y serás una nueva persona. 7Cuando se cumplan estas señales que has recibido, podrás hacer todo lo que esté a tu alcance, pues Dios estará contigo.

8»Baja luego a Guilgal antes que yo. Allí me reuniré contigo para ofrecer *holocaustos y sacrificios de *comunión, y cuando llegue, te diré lo que tienes que hacer. Pero tú debes esperarme siete días.

Saúl es proclamado rey

9Cuando Saúl se dio vuelta para alejarse de Samuel, Dios le cambió el *corazón, y ese mismo día se cumplieron todas esas señales. 10En efecto, al llegar Saúl y su criado a Guibeá, un grupo de profetas les salió al encuentro. Entonces el Espíritu de Dios vino con poder sobre Saúl, quien cayó en trance profético junto con ellos. 11Los que desde antes lo conocían, al verlo profetizar junto con los profetas se preguntaban unos a otros:

—¿Qué le pasa a Saúl hijo de Quis? ¿Acaso él también es uno de los profetas?

12Alguien que vivía allí replicó:

—¿Y quién es el responsableo de ellos?

De ahí viene el dicho: «¿Acaso también Saúl es uno de los profetas?»

13Cuando Saúl acabó de profetizar, subió al santuario del cerro. 14Su tío les preguntó a él y a su criado:

—¿Y ustedes dónde estaban?

—Andábamos buscando las burras —respondió Saúl—; pero como no dábamos con ellas, fuimos a ver a Samuel.

15—Cuéntame lo que les dijo Samuel —pidió el tío de Saúl.

16—Nos aseguró que ya habían encontrado las burras.

Sin embargo, Saúl no le contó a su tío lo que Samuel le había dicho acerca del reino.

17Después de esto, Samuel convocó al pueblo de Israel para que se presentara ante el SEÑOR en Mizpa. 18Allí les dijo a los israelitas:

«Así dice el SEÑOR, Dios de Israel: "Yo saqué a Israel de Egipto. Yo los libré a ustedes del poder de los egipcios y de todos los reinos que los oprimían." 19Ahora, sin embargo, ustedes han rechazado a su Dios, quien los libra de todas las calamidades y aflicciones. Han dicho: "¡No! ¡Danos un rey que nos gobierne!" Por tanto, preséntense ahora ante el SEÑOR por tribus y por familias.»

20Dicho esto, Samuel hizo que se acercaran todas las tribus de Israel y, al echar la suerte, fue escogida la tribu de Benjamín. 21Luego mandó que se acercara la tribu de Benjamín, familia por familia, y la suerte cayó sobre la familia de Matri, y finalmente sobre Saúl hijo de Quis. Entonces fueron a buscar a Saúl, pero no lo encontraron, 22de modo que volvieron a consultar al SEÑOR:

—¿Ha venido aquí ese hombre?

—Sí —respondió el SEÑOR—, pero se ha escondido entre el equipaje.

23Fueron corriendo y lo sacaron de allí. Y cuando Saúl se puso en medio de la gente, vieron que era tan alto que nadie le llegaba al hombro. 24Dijo entonces Samuel a todo el pueblo:

—¡Miren al hombre que el SEÑOR ha escogido! ¡No hay nadie como él en todo el pueblo!

—¡Viva el rey! —exclamaron todos.

25A continuación, Samuel le explicó al pueblo las leyes del reino y las escribió en un libro que depositó ante el SEÑOR. Luego mandó que todos regresaran a sus casas.

ñ **10:1** *su pueblo.* Lit. *su heredad.*   o **10:12** *responsable.* Lit. *padre.*

²⁶También Saúl se fue a su casa en Guibeá, acompañado por un grupo de hombres leales, a quienes el SEÑOR les había movido el corazón. ²⁷Pero algunos insolentes protestaron: «¿Y éste es el que nos va a salvar?» Y fue tanto su desprecio por Saúl, que ni le ofrecieron regalos. Saúl, por su parte, no les hizo caso.

Saúl libera la ciudad de Jabés

11 Najás el amonita subió contra Jabés de Galaad y la sitió. Los habitantes de la ciudad le dijeron:

—Haz un pacto con nosotros, y seremos tus siervos.

²—Haré un pacto con ustedes —contestó Najás el amonita—, pero con una condición: que les saque a cada uno de ustedes el ojo derecho. Así dejaré en desgracia a todo Israel.

³—Danos siete días para que podamos enviar mensajeros por todo el territorio de Israel —respondieron los *ancianos de Jabés—. Si no hay quien nos libre de ustedes, nos rendiremos.

⁴Cuando los mensajeros llegaron a Guibeá, que era la ciudad de Saúl, y le comunicaron el mensaje al pueblo, todos se echaron a llorar. ⁵En esos momentos Saúl regresaba del campo arreando sus bueyes, y preguntó: «¿Qué le pasa a la gente? ¿Por qué están llorando?» Entonces le contaron lo que habían dicho los habitantes de Jabés.

⁶Cuando Saúl escuchó la noticia, el Espíritu de Dios vino sobre él con poder. Enfurecido, ⁷agarró dos bueyes y los descuartizó, y con los mensajeros envió los pedazos por todo el territorio de Israel, con esta advertencia: «Así se hará con los bueyes de todo el que no salga para unirse a Saúl y Samuel.»

El temor del SEÑOR se apoderó del pueblo, y todos ellos, como un solo *hombre, salieron a la guerra. ⁸Saúl los reunió en Bézec para pasar revista, y había trescientos mil soldados de Israel y treinta mil de Judá. ⁹Luego les dijo a los mensajeros que habían venido: «Vayan y díganles a los habitantes de Jabés de Galaad: "Mañana, cuando más calor haga, serán librados."»

Los mensajeros fueron y les comunicaron el mensaje a los de Jabés. Éstos se llenaron de alegría ¹⁰y les dijeron a los amonitas: «Mañana nos rendiremos, y podrán hacer con nosotros lo que bien les parezca.»

¹¹Al día siguiente, antes del amanecer, Saúl organizó a los soldados en tres columnas. Invadieron el campamento de los amonitas, e hicieron una masacre entre ellos hasta la hora más calurosa del día. Los que sobrevivieron fueron dispersados, así que no quedaron dos hombres juntos.

Saúl es confirmado como rey

¹²El pueblo le dijo entonces a Samuel:

—¿Quiénes son los que no querían que Saúl reinara sobre nosotros? Entréguenlos, que vamos a matarlos.

¹³—¡Nadie va a morir hoy! —intervino Saúl—. En este día el SEÑOR ha librado a Israel.

¹⁴—¡Vengan! —le dijo Samuel al pueblo—. Vamos a Guilgal para confirmar a Saúl como rey.

¹⁵Todos se fueron a Guilgal, y allí, ante el SEÑOR, confirmaron a Saúl como rey. También allí, ante el SEÑOR, ofrecieron sacrificios de *comunión, y Saúl y

todos los israelitas celebraron la ocasión con gran alegría.

Discurso de despedida de Samuel

12 Samuel le habló a todo Israel:

—¡Préstenme atención! Yo les he hecho caso en todo lo que me han pedido, y les he dado un rey que los gobierne. ²Ya tienen al rey que va a dirigirlos. En cuanto a mí, ya estoy viejo y lleno de canas, y mis hijos son parte del pueblo. Yo los he guiado a ustedes desde mi juventud hasta la fecha. ³Aquí me tienen. Pueden acusarme en la presencia del SEÑOR y de su *ungido. ¿A quién le he robado un buey o un asno? ¿A quién he defraudado? ¿A quién he oprimido? ¿Por quién me he dejado sobornar? Acúsenme, y pagaré lo que corresponda.

⁴—No nos has defraudado —respondieron—; tampoco nos has oprimido ni le has robado nada a nadie.

⁵Samuel insistió:

—¡Que el SEÑOR y su ungido sean hoy testigos de que ustedes no me han hallado culpable de nada!

—¡Que lo sean! —fue la respuesta del pueblo.

⁶Además Samuel les dijo:

—Testigo es el SEÑOR, que escogió a Moisés y a Aarón para sacar de Egipto a los antepasados de ustedes. ⁷Y ahora, préstenme atención. El SEÑOR los ha colmado de beneficios a ustedes y a sus antepasados, pero yo tengo una querella contra ustedes.

⁸»Después que Jacob entró en Egipto, sus descendientes clamaron al SEÑOR. Entonces el SEÑOR envió a Moisés y a Aarón para sacarlos de Egipto y establecerlos en este lugar. ⁹Pero como se olvidaron de su SEÑOR y Dios, él los entregó al poder de Sísara, comandante del ejército de Jazor, y al poder de los filisteos y del rey de Moab, y ellos les hicieron la guerra. ¹⁰Por eso ustedes clamaron al SEÑOR: "Hemos pecado al abandonar al SEÑOR y adorar a los ídolos de *Baal y a las imágenes de *Astarté. Pero ahora, si nos libras del poder de nuestros enemigos, sólo a ti te serviremos." ¹¹Entonces el SEÑOR envió a Yerubaal, Barac,ʳ Jefté y Samuel, y los libró a ustedes del poder de los enemigos que los rodeaban, para que vivieran seguros.

¹²»No obstante, cuando ustedes vieron que Najás, rey de los amonitas, los amenazaba, me dijeron: "¡No! ¡Queremos que nos gobierne un rey!" Y esto, a pesar de que el SEÑOR su Dios es el rey de ustedes. ¹³Pues bien, aquí tienen al rey que pidieron y que han escogido. Pero tengan en cuenta que es el SEÑOR quien les ha dado ese rey. ¹⁴Si ustedes y el rey que los gobierne temen al SEÑOR su Dios, y le sirven y le obedecen, acatando sus mandatos y manteniéndose fieles a él, ¡magnífico! ¹⁵En cambio, si lo desobedecen y no acatan sus mandatos, él descargará su mano sobre ustedes como la descargó contra sus antepasados.

¹⁶»Y ahora, préstenme atención y observen con sus propios ojos algo grandioso que el SEÑOR va a hacer. ¹⁷Ahora no es tiempo de lluvias sino de cosecha.ˢ Sin embargo, voy a invocar al SEÑOR, y él enviará truenos y lluvia; así se darán cuenta de la gran maldad que han cometido ante el SEÑOR al pedir un rey.

¹⁸Samuel invocó al SEÑOR, y ese mismo día el SEÑOR mandó truenos y lluvia. Todo el pueblo sintió un gran temor ante el SEÑOR y ante Samuel, ¹⁹y le dijeron a Samuel:

—Ora al SEÑOR tu Dios por nosotros, tus siervos, para que no nos quite la vida. A todos nuestros

---

p **11:9** les dijo. Lit. Dijeron. q **11:11** antes del amanecer. Lit. en la vigilia de la mañana. r **12:11** Barac (mss. de LXX y Siríaca); Bedán (TM). s **12:17** Ahora no es ... de cosecha. Lit. ¿Acaso no es la cosecha de trigo?

pecados hemos añadido la maldad de pedirle un rey. ²⁰—No teman —replicó Samuel—. Aunque ustedes han cometido una gran maldad, no se aparten del SEÑOR; más bien, sírvanle de todo *corazón. ²¹No se alejen de él por seguir a ídolos inútiles, que no los pueden ayudar ni rescatar, pues no sirven para nada. ²²Por amor a su gran *nombre, el SEÑOR no rechazará a su pueblo; de hecho él se ha dignado hacerlos a ustedes su propio pueblo. ²³En cuanto a mí, que el SEÑOR me libre de pecar contra él dejando de orar por ustedes. Yo seguiré enseñándoles el *camino bueno y recto. ²⁴Pero los exhorto a temer al SEÑOR y a servirle fielmente y de todo corazón, recordando los grandes beneficios que él ha hecho en favor de ustedes. ²⁵Si persisten en la maldad, tanto ustedes como su rey serán destruidos.

Samuel reprende a Saúl

13 Saúl tenía treinta años[t] cuando comenzó a reinar sobre Israel, y su reinado duró cuarenta y dos años.[u]

²De entre los israelitas, Saúl escogió tres mil soldados; dos mil estaban con él en Micmás y en los montes de Betel, y mil estaban con Jonatán en Guibeá de Benjamín. Al resto del ejército Saúl lo mandó a sus hogares.

³Jonatán atacó la guarnición filistea apostada en Gueba, y esto llegó a oídos de los filisteos. Entonces Saúl mandó que se tocara la trompeta por todo el país, pues dijo: «¡Que se enteren todos los hebreos!»

⁴Todo Israel se enteró de esta noticia: «Saúl ha atacado la guarnición filistea, así que los israelitas se han hecho odiosos a los filisteos.» Por tanto el pueblo se puso a las órdenes de Saúl en Guilgal.

⁵Los filisteos también se juntaron para hacerle la guerra a Israel. Contaban con tres mil[v] carros, seis mil jinetes, y un ejército tan numeroso como la arena a la orilla del mar. Avanzaron hacia Micmás, al este de Bet Avén, y allí acamparon. ⁶Los israelitas se dieron cuenta de que estaban en aprietos, pues todo el ejército se veía amenazado. Por eso tuvieron que esconderse en las cuevas, en los matorrales, entre las rocas, en las zanjas y en los pozos. ⁷Algunos hebreos incluso cruzaron el Jordán para huir al territorio de Gad, en Galaad.

Saúl se había quedado en Guilgal, y todo el ejército que lo acompañaba temblaba de miedo. ⁸Allí estuvo esperando siete días, según el plazo indicado por Samuel, pero éste no llegaba. Como los soldados comenzaban a desbandarse, ⁹Saúl ordenó: «Tráiganme el *holocausto y los sacrificios de *comunión»; y él mismo ofreció el holocausto. ¹⁰En el momento en que Saúl terminaba de celebrar el sacrificio, llegó Samuel. Saúl salió a recibirlo, y lo saludó. ¹¹Pero Samuel le reclamó:

—¿Qué has hecho?

Y Saúl le respondió:

—Pues como vi que la gente se desbandaba, que tú no llegabas en el plazo indicado, y que los filisteos se habían juntado en Micmás, ¹²pensé: "Los filisteos ya están por atacarme en Guilgal, y ni siquiera he implorado la ayuda del SEÑOR." Por eso me atreví a ofrecer el holocausto.

¹³—¡Eres un necio! —le replicó Samuel—. No has cumplido el mandato que te dio el SEÑOR tu Dios. El SEÑOR habría establecido tu reino sobre Israel para siempre, ¹⁴pero ahora te digo que tu reino no permanecerá. El SEÑOR ya está buscando un hombre más de su agrado, pues tú no has cumplido su mandato.

¹⁵Dicho esto, Samuel se fue de Guilgal hacia Guibeá de Benjamín.

Jonatán ataca a los filisteos

Saúl pasó revista de los soldados que estaban con él, y eran unos seiscientos hombres. ¹⁶Él y su hijo Jonatán, junto con sus soldados, se quedaron en Gueba de Benjamín, mientras que los filisteos seguían acampados en Micmás. ¹⁷Del campamento filisteo salió una tropa de asalto dividida en tres grupos: uno de ellos avanzó por el camino de Ofra, hacia el territorio de Súal; ¹⁸otro, por Bet Jorón; y el tercero, por la frontera del valle de Zeboyín, en dirección al desierto.

¹⁹En todo el territorio de Israel no había un solo herrero, pues los filisteos no permitían que los hebreos se forjaran espadas y lanzas. ²⁰Por tanto, todo Israel dependía de los filisteos para que les afilaran los arados, los azadones, las hachas y las hoces.[w] ²¹Por un arado o un azadón cobraban ocho gramos de plata, y cuatro gramos[x] por una horqueta o un hacha, o por arreglar las aguijadas. ²²Así que ninguno de los soldados israelitas tenía espada o lanza, excepto Saúl y Jonatán.

²³Un destacamento de filisteos avanzó hasta el paso de Micmás.

14 Cierto día, Jonatán hijo de Saúl, sin decirle nada a su padre, le ordenó a su escudero: «Ven acá. Vamos a cruzar al otro lado, donde está el destacamento de los filisteos.» ²Y es que Saúl estaba en las afueras de Guibeá, bajo un granado en Migrón, y tenía con él a unos seiscientos hombres. ³El *efod lo llevaba Abías hijo de Ajitob, que era hermano de Icabod, el hijo de Finés y nieto de Elí, sacerdote del SEÑOR en Siló.

Nadie sabía que Jonatán había salido, ⁴y para llegar a la guarnición filistea Jonatán tenía que cruzar un paso entre dos peñascos, llamados Bosés y Sene. ⁵El primero estaba al norte, frente a Micmás; el otro, al sur, frente a Gueba. ⁶Así que Jonatán le dijo a su escudero:

—Vamos a cruzar hacia la guarnición de esos paganos.[y] Espero que el SEÑOR nos ayude, pues para él no es difícil salvarnos, ya sea con muchos o con pocos.

⁷—¡Adelante! —respondió el escudero—. Haga usted todo lo que tenga pensado hacer, que cuenta con todo mi apoyo.

⁸—Bien —dijo Jonatán—; vamos a cruzar hasta donde están ellos, para que nos vean. ⁹Si nos dicen: "¡Esperen a que los alcancemos!", ahí nos quedaremos, en vez de avanzar. ¹⁰Pero si nos dicen: "¡Vengan acá!", avanzaremos, pues será señal de que el SEÑOR nos va a dar la *victoria.

¹¹Así pues, los dos se dejaron ver por la guarnición filistea.

—¡Miren! —exclamaron los filisteos—, los hebreos empiezan a salir de las cuevas donde estaban escondidos!

¹²Entonces los soldados de la guarnición les gritaron a Jonatán y a su escudero:

—¡Vengan acá! Tenemos algo que decirles.

---

[t] **13:1** *treinta años* (LXX). TM no incluye el número de años. [u] **13:1** *cuarenta y dos años* (texto probable; véase Hch 13:21); *dos años* (TM). [v] **13:5** *tres mil* (LXX y Siríaca); *treinta mil* (TM). [w] **13:20** *las hoces* (LXX); *los arados* (TM).

[x] **13:21** *ocho gramos de plata ... cuatro gramos.* Lit. *un *pim ... un tercio de *siclo.* [y] **14:6** *paganos.* Lit. *Incircuncisos*

—Ven conmigo —le dijo Jonatán a su escudero—, porque el SEÑOR le ha dado la victoria a Israel. [13]Jonatán trepó con pies y manos, seguido por su escudero. A los filisteos que eran derribados por Jonatán, el escudero los remataba. [14]En ese primer encuentro, que tuvo lugar en un espacio reducido, Jonatán y su escudero mataron a unos veinte hombres.

Israel derrota a los filisteos

[15]Cundió entonces el pánico en el campamento filisteo y entre el ejército que estaba en el campo abierto. Todos ellos se acobardaron, incluso los soldados de la guarnición y las tropas de asalto. Hasta la tierra tembló, y hubo un pánico extraordinario.[z] [16]Desde Guibeá de Benjamín, los centinelas de Saúl podían ver que el campamento huía en desbandada. [17]Saúl dijo entonces a sus soldados: «Pasen revista, a ver quién de los nuestros falta.» Así lo hicieron, y resultó que faltaban Jonatán y su escudero.

[18]Entonces Saúl le pidió a Ahías que trajera el arca de Dios. (En aquel tiempo el arca estaba con los israelitas.) [19]Pero mientras hablaban, el desconcierto en el campo filisteo se hizo peor, así que Saúl le dijo al sacerdote: «¡No lo hagas!»

[20]En seguida Saúl reunió a su ejército, y todos juntos se lanzaron a la batalla. Era tal la confusión entre los filisteos, que se mataban unos a otros. [21]Además, los hebreos que hacía tiempo se habían unido a los filisteos, y que estaban con ellos en el campamento, se pasaron a las filas de los israelitas que estaban con Saúl y Jonatán. [22]Y los israelitas que se habían escondido en los montes de Efraín, al oír que los filisteos huían, se unieron a la batalla para perseguirlos. [23]Así libró el SEÑOR a Israel aquel día, y la batalla se extendió más allá de Bet Avén.

El juramento de Saúl

[24]Los israelitas desfallecían de hambre, pues Saúl había puesto al ejército bajo este juramento: «¡Maldito el que coma algo antes del anochecer, antes de que pueda vengarme de mis enemigos!» Así que aquel día ninguno de los soldados había probado bocado.

[25]Al llegar a un bosque, notaron que había miel en el suelo. [26]Cuando el ejército entró en el bosque, vieron que la miel corría como agua, pero por miedo al juramento nadie se atrevió a probarla. [27]Sin embargo, Jonatán, que no había oído a su padre poner al ejército bajo juramento, alargó la vara que llevaba en la mano, hundió la punta en un panal de miel, y se la llevó a la boca. En seguida se le iluminó el rostro. [28]Pero uno de los soldados le advirtió:

—Tu padre puso al ejército bajo un juramento solemne, diciendo: "¡Maldito el que coma algo hoy!" Y por eso los soldados desfallecen.

[29]—Mi padre le ha causado un gran daño al país —respondió Jonatán—. Miren cómo me volvió el color al rostro cuando probé un poco de esta miel. [30]¡Imagínense si todo el ejército hubiera comido del botín que le arrebató al enemigo! ¡Cuánto mayor habría sido el estrago causado a los filisteos!

[31]Aquel día los israelitas mataron filisteos desde Micmás hasta Ayalón. Y como los soldados estaban exhaustos, [32]echaron mano del botín. Agarraron ovejas, vacas y terneros, los degollaron sobre el suelo, y se comieron la carne con todo y sangre. [33]Entonces le contaron a Saúl:

—Los soldados están pecando contra el SEÑOR, pues están comiendo carne junto con la sangre.

—¡Son unos traidores! —replicó Saúl—. Hagan rodar una piedra grande, y tráiganmela ahora mismo. [34]También les dijo:

—Vayan y díganle a la gente que cada uno me traiga su toro o su oveja para degollarlos y comerlos aquí; y que no coman ya carne junto con la sangre, para que no pequen contra el SEÑOR.

Esa misma noche cada uno llevó su toro, y lo degollaron allí. [35]Luego Saúl construyó un altar al SEÑOR. Éste fue el primer altar que levantó. [36]Y dijo:

—Vayamos esta noche tras los filisteos. Antes de que amanezca, quitémosles todo lo que tienen y no dejemos a nadie con vida.

—Haz lo que te parezca mejor —le respondieron.

—Primero debemos consultar a Dios —intervino el sacerdote.

[37]Saúl entonces le preguntó a Dios: «¿Debo perseguir a los filisteos? ¿Los entregarás en manos de Israel?» Pero Dios no le respondió aquel día. [38]Así que Saúl dijo:

—Todos ustedes, jefes del ejército, acérquense y averigüen cuál es el pecado que se ha cometido hoy. [39]El SEÑOR y Salvador de Israel me es testigo de que, aun si el culpable es mi hijo Jonatán, morirá sin remedio!

Nadie se atrevió a decirle nada. [40]Les dijo entonces a todos los israelitas:

—Pónganse ustedes de un lado, y yo y mi hijo Jonatán nos pondremos del otro.

—Haz lo que te parezca mejor —respondieron ellos.

[41]Luego le rogó Saúl al SEÑOR, Dios de Israel, que le diera una respuesta clara. La suerte cayó sobre Jonatán y Saúl, de modo que los demás quedaron libres. [42]Entonces dijo Saúl:

—Echen suertes entre mi hijo Jonatán y yo.

Y la suerte cayó sobre Jonatán, [43]así que Saúl le dijo:

—Cuéntame lo que has hecho.

—Es verdad que probé un poco de miel con la punta de mi vara —respondió Jonatán—. ¿Y por eso tengo que morir?

[44]—Jonatán, si tú no mueres, ¡que Dios me castigue sin piedad! —exclamó Saúl.

[45]Los soldados le replicaron:

—¡Cómo va a morir Jonatán, siendo que le ha dado esta gran victoria a Israel! ¡Jamás! Tan cierto como que el SEÑOR vive, que ni un pelo de su cabeza caerá al suelo, pues con la ayuda de Dios hizo esta proeza.

Así libraron a Jonatán de la muerte. [46]Saúl, a su vez, dejó de perseguir a los filisteos, los cuales regresaron a su tierra.

[47]Después de consolidar su reinado sobre Israel, Saúl luchó contra todos los enemigos que lo rodeaban, incluso contra los moabitas, los amonitas, los edomitas, los reyes de Sobá y los filisteos; y a todos los vencía [48]haciendo gala de valor. También derrotó a los amalecitas y libró a Israel de quienes lo saqueaban.

La familia de Saúl

[49]Saúl tuvo tres hijos: Jonatán, Isví y Malquisúa. También tuvo dos hijas: la mayor se llamaba Merab, y la menor, Mical. [50]Su esposa era Ajinoán hija de Ajimaz. El general de su ejército era Abner hijo de Ner, tío de Saúl. [51]Ner y Quis, el padre de Saúl, eran hermanos, y ambos eran hijos de Abiel.

---

[z] 14:15 *pánico extraordinario.* Lit. *pánico de Dios.*

⁵²Durante todo el reinado de Saúl se luchó sin cuartel contra los filisteos. Por eso, siempre que Saúl veía a alguien fuerte y valiente, lo alistaba en su ejército.

El SEÑOR rechaza a Saúl

15 Un día Samuel le dijo a Saúl: «El SEÑOR me envió a ungirte como rey sobre su pueblo Israel. Así que pon atención al mensaje del SEÑOR. ²Así dice el SEÑOR *Todopoderoso: "He decidido castigar a los amalecitas por lo que le hicieron a Israel, pues no lo dejaron pasar cuando salía de Egipto. ³Así que ve y ataca a los amalecitas ahora mismo. *Destruye por completo todo lo que les pertenezca; no les tengas compasión. Mátalos a todos, hombres y mujeres, niños y recién nacidos, toros y ovejas, camellos y asnos." »

⁴Saúl reunió al ejército y le pasó revista en Telayin: eran doscientos mil soldados de infantería más diez mil soldados de Judá. ⁵Luego se dirigió a la ciudad de Amalec y tendió una emboscada en el barranco. ⁶Los quenitas se apartaron de los amalecitas, pues Saúl les dijo: «¡Váyanse de aquí! Salgan y apártense de los amalecitas. Ustedes fueron bondadosos con todos los israelitas cuando ellos salieron de Egipto. Así que no quiero destruirlos a ustedes junto con ellos.»

⁷Saúl atacó a los amalecitas desde Javilá hasta Sur, que está cerca de la frontera de Egipto. ⁸A Agag, rey de Amalec, lo capturó vivo, pero a todos los habitantes los mató a filo de espada. ⁹Además de perdonar la vida al rey Agag, Saúl y su ejército preservaron las mejores ovejas y vacas, los terneros más gordos y, en fin, todo lo que era de valor. Nada de esto quisieron destruir; sólo destruyeron lo que era inútil y lo que no servía.

¹⁰La palabra del SEÑOR vino a Samuel: ¹¹«Me arrepiento de haber hecho rey a Saúl, pues se ha apartado de mí y no ha llevado a cabo mis instrucciones.» Tanto se alteró Samuel que pasó la noche clamando al SEÑOR. ¹²Por la mañana, muy temprano, se levantó y fue a encontrarse con Saúl, pero le dijeron: «Saúl se fue a Carmel, y allí se erigió un monumento. Luego dio una vuelta y continuó hacia Guilgal.»

¹³Cuando Samuel llegó, Saúl le dijo:

—¡Que el SEÑOR te bendiga! He cumplido las instrucciones del SEÑOR.

¹⁴—Y entonces, ¿qué significan esos balidos de oveja que me parece oír? —le reclamó Samuel—. ¿Y cómo es que oigo mugidos de vaca?

¹⁵—Son las que nuestras tropas trajeron del país de Amalec —respondió Saúl—. Dejaron con vida a las mejores ovejas y vacas para ofrecerlas al SEÑOR tu Dios, pero todo lo demás lo destruimos.

¹⁶¡Basta! —lo interrumpió Samuel—. Voy a comunicarte lo que el SEÑOR me dijo anoche.

—Te escucho —respondió Saúl.

¹⁷Entonces Samuel le dijo:

—¿No es cierto que, aunque te creías poca cosa, has llegado a ser jefe de las tribus de Israel? ¿No fue el SEÑOR quien te ungió como rey de Israel, ¹⁸y te envió a cumplir una misión? Él te dijo: "Ve y destruye a esos pecadores, los amalecitas. Atácalos hasta acabar con ellos." ¹⁹¿Por qué, entonces, no obedeciste al SEÑOR? ¿Por qué echaste mano del botín e hiciste lo que ofende al SEÑOR?

²⁰—¡Yo sí he obedecido al SEÑOR! —insistió Saúl—. He cumplido la misión que él me encomendó. Traje prisionero a Agag, rey de Amalec, pero destruí a los amalecitas. ²¹Y del botín, los soldados tomaron ovejas y vacas con el propósito de ofrecerlas en Guilgal al SEÑOR tu Dios.

²²Samuel respondió:

«¿Qué le agrada más al SEÑOR:
  que se le ofrezcan *holocaustos y sacrificios,
  o que se obedezca lo que él dice?
El obedecer vale más que el sacrificio,
  y el prestar atención, más que la grasa de
    carneros.
²³La rebeldía es tan grave como la adivinación,
  y la arrogancia, como el pecado de la
    idolatría.
Y como tú has rechazado la palabra del
    SEÑOR,
  él te ha rechazado como rey.»

²⁴—¡He pecado! —admitió Saúl—. He quebrantado el mandato del SEÑOR y tus instrucciones. Los soldados me intimidaron y les hice caso. ²⁵Pero te ruego que perdones mi pecado, y que regreses conmigo para adorar al SEÑOR.

²⁶—No voy a regresar contigo —le respondió Samuel—. Tú has rechazado la palabra del SEÑOR, y él te ha rechazado como rey de Israel.

²⁷Cuando Samuel se dio vuelta para irse, Saúl le agarró el borde del manto, y se lo arrancó. ²⁸Entonces Samuel le dijo:

—Hoy mismo el SEÑOR ha arrancado de tus manos el reino de Israel, y se lo ha entregado a otro más digno que tú. ²⁹En verdad, el que es la Gloria de Israel no miente ni cambia de parecer, pues no es *hombre para que se arrepienta.

³⁰—¡He pecado! —respondió Saúl—. Pero a pido que por ahora me sigas reconociendo ante los *ancianos de mi pueblo y ante todo Israel. Regresa conmigo para adorar al SEÑOR tu Dios.

³¹Samuel regresó con él, y Saúl adoró al SEÑOR. ³²Luego dijo Samuel:

—Tráiganme a Agag, rey de Amalec.

Agag se le acercó muy confiado, pues pensaba: «Sin duda que el trago amargo de la muerte ya pasó.»

³³Pero Samuel le dijo:

—Ya que tu espada dejó a tantas mujeres sin hijos, también sin su hijo se quedará tu madre.

Y allí en Guilgal, en presencia del SEÑOR, Samuel descuartizó a Agag. ³⁴Luego regresó a Ramá, mientras que Saúl se fue a su casa en Guibeá de Saúl. ³⁵Y como el SEÑOR se había arrepentido de haber hecho a Saúl rey de Israel, nunca más volvió Samuel a ver a Saúl, sino que hizo duelo por él.

Samuel unge a David

16 El SEÑOR le dijo a Samuel:

—¿Cuánto tiempo vas a quedarte llorando por Saúl, si ya lo he rechazado como rey de Israel? Mejor llena de aceite tu cuerno, y ponte en camino. Voy a enviarte a Belén, a la casa de Isaí, pues he escogido como rey a uno de sus hijos.

²—¿Y cómo voy a ir? —respondió Samuel—. Si Saúl llega a enterarse, me matará.

—Lleva una ternera —dijo el SEÑOR—, y diles que vas a ofrecerle al SEÑOR un sacrificio. ³Invita a Isaí al sacrificio, y entonces te explicaré lo que debes hacer, pues ungirás para mi servicio a quien yo te diga.

⁴Samuel hizo lo que le mandó el SEÑOR. Pero cuando llegó a Belén, los *ancianos del pueblo lo recibieron con mucho temor.

—¿Vienes en son de paz? —le preguntaron.

⁵—Claro que sí. He venido a ofrecerle al SEÑOR un sacrificio. Purifíquense y vengan conmigo para tomar parte en él.

Entonces Samuel *purificó a Isaí y a sus hijos, y los invitó al sacrificio. ⁶Cuando llegaron, Samuel se fijó en Eliab y pensó: «Sin duda que éste es el *ungido del SEÑOR.» ⁷Pero el SEÑOR le dijo a Samuel:

—No te dejes impresionar por su apariencia ni por su estatura, pues yo lo he rechazado. La gente se fija en las apariencias, pero yo me fijo en el *corazón.

⁸Entonces Isaí llamó a Abinadab para presentárselo a Samuel, pero Samuel dijo:

—A éste no lo ha escogido el SEÑOR.

⁹Luego le presentó a Sama, y Samuel repitió:

—Tampoco a éste lo ha escogido.

¹⁰Isaí le presentó a siete de sus hijos, pero Samuel le dijo:

—El SEÑOR no ha escogido a ninguno de ellos. ¹¹¿Son éstos todos tus hijos?

—Queda el más pequeño —respondió Isaí—, pero está cuidando el rebaño.

—Manda a buscarlo —insistió Samuel—, que no podemos continuar hasta que él llegue.

¹²Isaí mandó a buscarlo, y se lo trajeron. Era buen mozo, trigueño y de buena presencia. El SEÑOR le dijo a Samuel:

—Éste es; levántate y úngelo.

¹³Samuel tomó el cuerno de aceite y ungió al joven en presencia de sus hermanos. Entonces el Espíritu del SEÑOR vino con poder sobre David, y desde ese día estuvo con él. Luego Samuel regresó a Ramá.

David al servicio de Saúl

¹⁴El Espíritu del SEÑOR se apartó de Saúl, y en su lugar el SEÑOR le envió un espíritu maligno para que lo atormentara. ¹⁵Sus servidores le dijeron:

—Como usted se dará cuenta, un espíritu maligno de parte de Dios lo está atormentando. ¹⁶Así que ordene Su Majestad a estos siervos suyos que busquen a alguien que sepa tocar el arpa. Así, cuando lo ataque el espíritu maligno de parte de Dios, el músico tocará, y Su Majestad se sentirá mejor.

¹⁷—Bien —les respondió Saúl—, consíganme un buen músico y tráiganlo.

¹⁸Uno de los cortesanos sugirió:

—Conozco a un muchacho que sabe tocar el arpa. Es valiente, hábil guerrero, sabe expresarse y es de buena presencia. Además, el SEÑOR está con él. Su padre es Isaí, el de Belén.

¹⁹Entonces Saúl envió unos mensajeros a Isaí para decirle: «Mándame a tu hijo David, el que cuida del rebaño.» ²⁰Isaí tomó un asno, alimento, un odre de vino y un cabrito, y se los envió a Saúl por medio de su hijo David. ²¹Cuando David llegó, quedó al servicio de Saúl, quien lo llegó a apreciar mucho y lo hizo su escudero. ²²Luego Saúl le mandó este mensaje a Isaí: «Permite que David se quede a mi servicio, pues me ha causado muy buena impresión.»

²³Cada vez que el espíritu de parte de Dios atormentaba a Saúl, David tomaba su arpa y tocaba. La música calmaba a Saúl y lo hacía sentirse mejor, y el espíritu maligno se apartaba de él.

David y Goliat

17 Los filisteos reunieron sus ejércitos para la guerra, concentrando sus fuerzas en Soco, pueblo de Judá. Acamparon en Efesdamín, situado entre Soco y Azeca. ²Por su parte, Saúl y los israelitas

se reunieron también y, acampando en el valle de Elá, ordenaron sus filas para la batalla contra los filisteos. ³Con el valle de por medio, los filisteos y los israelitas tomaron posiciones en montes opuestos.

⁴Un famoso guerrero, oriundo de Gat, salió del campamento filisteo. Su nombre era Goliat, y tenía una estatura de casi tres metros.ᵃ ⁵Llevaba en la cabeza un casco de bronce, y su coraza, que pesaba cincuenta y cinco kilos,ᵇ también era de bronce, ⁶como lo eran las polainas que le protegían las piernas y la jabalina que llevaba al hombro. ⁷El asta de su lanza se parecía al rodillo de un telar, y tenía una punta de hierro que pesaba casi siete kilos.ᶜ Delante de él marchaba un escudero.

⁸Goliat se detuvo ante los soldados israelitas, los desafió: «¿Para qué están ordenando sus filas para la batalla? ¿No soy yo un filisteo? ¿Y no están ustedes al servicio de Saúl? ¿Por qué no escogen a alguien que se me enfrente? ⁹Si es capaz de hacerme frente y matarme, nosotros les serviremos a ustedes; pero si yo lo venzo y lo mato, ustedes serán nuestros esclavos y nos servirán.» ¹⁰Dijo además el filisteo: «¡Yo desafío hoy al ejército de Israel! ¡Elijan a un hombre que pelee conmigo!» ¹¹Al oír lo que decía el filisteo, Saúl y todos los israelitas se consternaron y tuvieron mucho miedo.

¹²David era hijo de Isaí, un efrateo que vivía en Belén de Judá. En tiempos de Saúl, Isaí era ya de edad muy avanzada, y tenía ocho hijos. ¹³Sus tres hijos mayores habían marchado a la guerra con Saúl. El primogénito se llamaba Eliab; el segundo, Abinadab; el tercero, Sama. ¹⁴Estos tres habían seguido a Saúl por ser los mayores. David, que era el menor, ¹⁵solía ir adonde estaba Saúl, pero regresaba a Belén para cuidar las ovejas de su padre.

¹⁶El filisteo salía mañana y tarde a desafiar a los israelitas, y así lo estuvo haciendo durante cuarenta días.

¹⁷Un día, Isaí le dijo a su hijo David: «Toma esta bolsaᵈ de trigo tostado y estos diez panes, y vete pronto al campamento para dárselos a tus hermanos. ¹⁸Lleva también estos tres quesos para el jefe del batallón. Averigua cómo les va a tus hermanos, y tráeme una prueba de que ellos están bien. ¹⁹Los encontrarás en el valle de Elá, con Saúl y todos los soldados israelitas, peleando contra los filisteos.»

²⁰David cumplió con las instrucciones de Isaí. Se levantó muy de mañana y, después de encargarle el rebaño a un pastor, tomó las provisiones y se puso en camino. Llegó al campamento en el momento en que los soldados, lanzando gritos de guerra, salían a tomar sus posiciones. ²¹Los israelitas y los filisteos se alinearon frente a frente. ²²David, por su parte, dejó su carga al cuidado del encargado de las provisiones, y corrió a las filas para saludar a sus hermanos. ²³Mientras conversaban, Goliat, el gran guerrero filisteo de Gat, salió de entre las filas para repetir su desafío, y David lo oyó. ²⁴Cuando los israelitas vieron a Goliat, huyeron despavoridos. ²⁵Algunos decían: «¿Ven a ese hombre que sale a desafiar a Israel? A quien lo venza y lo mate, el rey lo colmará de riquezas. Además, le dará su hija como esposa, y su familia quedará exenta de impuestos aquí en Israel.»

²⁶David preguntó a los que estaban con él:

—¿Qué dicen que le darán a quien mate a ese filisteo y salve del honor de Israel? ¿Quién se cree este filisteo pagano,ᵉ que se atreve a desafiar al ejército del Dios viviente?

ᵃ **17:4** *casi tres metros.* Lit. *seis *codos y un *palmo.* ᵇ **17:5** *cincuenta y cinco kilos.* Lit. *cinco mil *siclos.* ᶜ **17:7** *casi siete kilos.* Lit. *seiscientos siclos.* ᵈ **17:17** *esta bolsa.* Lit. *este *efa.* ᵉ **17:26** *pagano.* Lit. *incircunciso;* también en v. 36.

27—Al que lo mate —repitieron— se le dará la recompensa anunciada.

28Eliab, el hermano mayor de David, lo oyó hablar con los hombres y se puso furioso con él. Le reclamó:

—¿Qué has venido a hacer aquí? ¿Con quién has dejado esas pocas ovejas en el desierto? Yo te conozco. Eres un atrevido y mal intencionado. ¡Seguro que has venido para ver la batalla!

29—¿Y ahora qué hice? —protestó David—. ¡Si apenas he abierto la boca!

30Apartándose de su hermano, les preguntó a otros, quienes le dijeron lo mismo. **31**Algunos que oyeron lo que había dicho David, se lo contaron a Saúl, y éste mandó a llamarlo. **32**Entonces David le dijo a Saúl:

—¡Nadie tiene por qué desanimarse a causa de este filisteo! Yo mismo iré a pelear contra él.

33—¡Cómo vas a pelear tú solo contra este filisteo! —replicó Saúl—. No eres más que un muchacho, mientras que él ha sido un guerrero toda la vida.

34David le respondió:

—A mí me toca cuidar el rebaño de mi padre. Cuando un león o un oso viene y se lleva una oveja del rebaño, **35**yo lo persigo y lo golpeo hasta que suelta la presa. Y si el animal me ataca, lo sigo golpeando hasta matarlo. **36**Si este siervo de Su Majestad ha matado leones y osos, lo mismo puede hacer con ese filisteo pagano, porque está desafiando al ejército del Dios viviente. **37**El SEÑOR, que me libró de las garras del león y del oso, también me librará del poder de ese filisteo.

—Anda, pues —dijo Saúl—, y que el SEÑOR te acompañe.

38Luego Saúl vistió a David con su uniforme de campaña. Le entregó también un casco de bronce y le puso una coraza. **39**David se ciñó la espada sobre la armadura e intentó caminar, pero no pudo porque no estaba acostumbrado.

—No puedo andar con todo esto —le dijo a Saúl—; no estoy entrenado para ello.

De modo que se quitó todo aquello, **40**tomó su bastón, fue al río a escoger cinco piedras lisas, y las metió en su bolsa de pastor. Luego, honda en mano, se acercó al filisteo. **41**Éste, por su parte, también avanzaba hacia David detrás de su escudero. **42**Le echó una mirada a David y, al darse cuenta de que era apenas un muchacho, trigueño y buen mozo, con desprecio **43**le dijo:

—¿Soy acaso un perro para que vengas a atacarme con palos?

Y maldiciendo a David en *nombre de sus dioses, **44**añadió:

—¡Ven acá, que les voy a echar tu carne a las aves del cielo y a las fieras del campo!

45David le contestó:

—Tú vienes contra mí con espada, lanza y jabalina, pero yo vengo a ti en el nombre del SEÑOR *Todopoderoso, el Dios de los ejércitos de Israel, a los que has desafiado. **46**Hoy mismo el SEÑOR te entregará en mis manos; y yo te mataré y te cortaré la cabeza. Hoy mismo echaré los cadáveres del ejército filisteo a las aves del cielo y a las fieras del campo, y todo el mundo sabrá que hay un Dios en Israel. **47**Todos los que están aquí reconocerán que el SEÑOR salva sin necesidad de espada ni de lanza. La batalla es del SEÑOR, y él los entregará a ustedes en nuestras manos.

48En cuanto el filisteo avanzó para acercarse a David y enfrentarse con él, también éste corrió rápidamente hacia la línea de batalla para hacerle frente. **49**Metiendo la mano en su bolsa sacó una piedra, y con la honda se la lanzó al filisteo, hiriéndolo en la frente. Con la piedra incrustada entre ceja y ceja, el filisteo cayó de bruces al suelo. **50**Así fue como David triunfó sobre el filisteo: lo hirió de muerte con una honda y una piedra, y sin empuñar la espada. **51**Luego corrió adonde estaba el filisteo, le quitó la espada y, desenvainándola, lo remató con ella y le cortó la cabeza. Cuando los filisteos vieron que su héroe había muerto, salieron corriendo. **52**Entonces los soldados de Israel y de Judá, dando gritos de guerra, se lanzaron contra ellos y los persiguieron hasta la entrada de Gatf y hasta las *puertas de Ecrón. Todo el camino, desde Sajarayin hasta Gat y Ecrón, quedó regado de cadáveres de filisteos. **53**Cuando los israelitas dejaron de perseguir a los filisteos, regresaron para saquearles el campamento. **54**Luego David tomó la cabeza de Goliat y la llevó a Jerusalén, pero las armas las guardó en su tienda de campaña.

55Anteriormente Saúl, al ver a David enfrentarse con el filisteo, le había preguntado a Abner, general de su ejército:

—Abner, ¿quién es el padre de ese muchacho?

—Le aseguro, Su Majestad, que no lo sé.

56—Averíguame quién es —le había dicho el rey.

57Tan pronto como David regresó, después de haber matado a Goliat, y con la cabeza del filisteo todavía en la mano, Abner lo llevó ante Saúl.

58—¿De quién eres hijo, muchacho? —le preguntó Saúl.

—De Isaí de Belén, servidor de Su Majestad —respondió David.

Envidia de Saúl

18 **1-2**Una vez que David y Saúl terminaron de hablar, Saúl tomó a David a su servicio y, desde ese día, no lo dejó volver a la casa de su padre. Jonatán, por su parte, entabló con David una amistad entrañable y llegó a quererlo como a sí mismo. **3**Tanto lo quería, que hizo un pacto con él: **4**Se quitó el manto que llevaba puesto y se lo dio a David; también le dio su túnica, y aun su espada, su arco y su cinturón.

5Cualquier encargo que David recibía de Saúl, lo cumplía con éxito, de modo que Saúl lo puso al mando de todo su ejército, con la aprobación de los soldados de Saúl y hasta de sus oficiales.

6Ahora bien, cuando el ejército regresó, después de haber matado David al filisteo, de todos los pueblos de Israel salían mujeres a recibir al rey Saúl. Al son de liras y panderetas, cantaban y bailaban, **7**y exclamaban con gran regocijo:

«Saúl destruyó a un ejército,
¡pero David aniquiló a diez!»

8Disgustado por lo que decían, Saúl se enfureció y protestó: «A David le dan crédito por diez ejércitos, pero a mí por uno solo. ¡Lo único que falta es que le den el reino!» **9**Y a partir de esa ocasión, Saúl empezó a mirar a David con recelo.

10Al día siguiente, el espíritu maligno de parte de Dios se apoderó de Saúl, quien cayó en trance en su propio palacio. Andaba con una lanza en la mano y, mientras David tocaba el arpa, como era su costumbre, **11**Saúl se la arrojó, pensando: «¡A éste lo cla-

---

f **17:52** *Gat* (mss. de LXX); *un valle* (MT).

vo en la pared!» Dos veces lo intentó, pero David logró esquivar la lanza.

¹²Saúl sabía que el SEÑOR lo había abandonado, y que ahora estaba con David. Por eso tuvo temor de David ¹³y lo alejó de su presencia, nombrándolo jefe de mil soldados para que dirigiera al ejército en campaña. ¹⁴David tuvo éxito en todas sus expediciones, porque el SEÑOR estaba con él. ¹⁵Al ver el éxito de David, Saúl se llenó de temor. ¹⁶Pero todos en Israel y Judá sentían gran aprecio por David, porque él los dirigía en campaña.

¹⁷Un día Saúl le dijo a David:

—Aquí tienes a Merab, mi hija mayor. Te la entrego por esposa, con la condición de que me sirvas con valentía, peleando las batallas del SEÑOR.

Saúl pensaba: «Será mejor que no muera por mi mano, sino a mano de los filisteos.»

¹⁸Pero David le respondió:

—¿Quién soy yo? ¿Y quiénes son en Israel mis parientes, o la familia de mi padre, para que yo me convierta en yerno del rey?

¹⁹Sin embargo, cuando llegó la fecha en que Saúl había de casar a su hija Merab con David, Saúl se la entregó por esposa a Adriel de Mejolá.

²⁰Mical, la otra hija de Saúl, se enamoró de David. Cuando se lo dijeron a Saúl, le agradó la noticia ²¹y pensó: «Se la entregaré a él, como una trampa para que caiga en manos de los filisteos.» Así que volvió a decirle a David:

—Ahora sí vas a ser mi yerno.

²²Entonces Saúl ordenó a sus funcionarios:

—Hablen con David en privado y díganle: "Oye, el rey te aprecia, y todos sus funcionarios te quieren. Acepta ser su yerno."

²³Esto se lo repitieron a David, pero él respondió:

—¿Creen que es cosa fácil ser yerno del rey? ¡Yo no soy más que un plebeyo insignificante!

²⁴Los funcionarios le comunicaron a Saúl la reacción de David. ²⁵Pero Saúl insistió:

—Díganle a David: "Lo único que el rey quiere es vengarse de sus enemigos, y como dote por su hija pide cien prepucios de filisteos."

En realidad, lo que Saúl quería era que David cayera en manos de los filisteos.

²⁶Cuando los funcionarios de Saúl le dieron el mensaje a David, no le pareció mala la idea de convertirse en yerno del rey. Aún no se había cumplido el plazo ²⁷cuando David fue con sus soldados y mató a doscientos filisteos, cuyos prepucios entregó al rey para convertirse en su yerno. Así fue como Saúl le dio la mano de su hija Mical.

²⁸Saúl se dio cuenta de que, en efecto, el SEÑOR estaba con David, y de que su hija Mical lo amaba. ²⁹Por eso aumentó el temor que Saúl sentía por David, y se convirtió en su enemigo por el resto de su vida.

³⁰Además, cada vez que los jefes filisteos salían a campaña, David los enfrentaba con más éxito que los otros oficiales de Saúl. Por eso llegó a ser muy famoso.

Saúl intenta matar a David

19 Saúl les comunicó a su hijo Jonatán y a todos sus funcionarios su decisión de matar*g* a David. Pero como Jonatán le tenía tanto afecto a David, ²le advirtió: «Mi padre Saúl está buscando una oportunidad para matarte. Así que ten mucho cuidado mañana; escóndete en algún sitio seguro, y quédate allí. ³Yo saldré con mi padre al campo donde tú estés,

y le hablaré de ti. Cuando averigüe lo que pasa, te lo haré saber.»

⁴Jonatán le habló a su padre Saúl en favor de David:

—¡No vaya Su Majestad a hacerle daño a su siervo David! —le rogó—. Él no le ha hecho ningún mal; al contrario, lo que ha hecho ha sido de gran beneficio para Su Majestad. ⁵Para matar al filisteo arriesgó su propia *vida, y el SEÑOR le dio una gran *victoria a todo Israel. Su Majestad mismo lo vio y se alegró. ¿Por qué ha de hacerle daño a un inocente y matar a David sin motivo?

⁶Saúl le hizo caso a Jonatán, y exclamó:

—Tan cierto como que el SEÑOR vive, te juro que David no morirá.

⁷Entonces Jonatán llamó a David y, después de contarle toda la conversación, lo llevó ante Saúl para que estuviera a su servicio como antes.

⁸Volvió a estallar la guerra. David salió a pelear contra los filisteos, y los combatió con tal violencia que tuvieron que huir.

⁹Sin embargo, un espíritu maligno de parte del SEÑOR se apoderó de Saúl. Estaba sentado en el palacio, con una lanza en la mano. Mientras David tocaba el arpa, ¹⁰intentó clavarlo en la pared con la lanza, pero David esquivó el golpe de Saúl, de modo que la lanza quedó clavada en la pared. Esa misma noche David se dio a la fuga.

¹¹Entonces Saúl mandó a varios hombres a casa de David, para que lo vigilaran durante la noche y lo mataran al día siguiente. Pero Mical, la esposa de David, le advirtió: «Si no te pones a salvo esta noche, mañana serás hombre muerto.» ¹²En seguida ella descolgó a David por la ventana, y así él pudo escapar. ¹³Luego Mical tomó un ídolo*h* y lo puso en la cama con un tejido de pelo de cabra en la cabeza, y lo cubrió con una sábana.

¹⁴Cuando Saúl mandó a los hombres para apresar a David, Mical les dijo: «Está enfermo.» ¹⁵Pero Saúl los mandó de nuevo a buscar a David: «Aunque esté en cama, ¡tráiganmelo aquí para matarlo!» ¹⁶Al entrar en la casa, los hombres vieron que lo que estaba en la cama era un ídolo, con un tejido de pelo de cabra en la cabeza. ¹⁷Entonces Saúl le reclamó a Mical:

—¿Por qué me has engañado así? ¿Por qué dejaste escapar a mi enemigo?

Ella respondió:

—Él me amenazó con matarme si no lo dejaba escapar.

¹⁸Después de huir y ponerse a salvo, David fue a Ramá para ver a Samuel y contarle todo lo que le había hecho. Entonces los dos se fueron a vivir a Nayot. ¹⁹Cuando Saúl se enteró de que David estaba en Nayot de Ramá, ²⁰mandó a sus hombres para que lo apresaran. Pero se encontraron con un grupo de profetas, dirigidos por Samuel, que estaban profetizando. Entonces el Espíritu de Dios vino con poder sobre los hombres de Saúl, y también ellos cayeron en trance profético. ²¹Al oír la noticia, Saúl envió otro grupo, pero ellos también cayeron en trance. Luego mandó un tercer grupo, y les pasó lo mismo. ²²Por fin, Saúl en persona fue a Ramá y llegó al gran pozo que está en Secú.

—¿Dónde están Samuel y David? —preguntó.

—En Nayot de Ramá —alguien le respondió.

²³Saúl se dirigió entonces hacia allá, pero el Espíritu de Dios vino con poder también sobre él, y Saúl estuvo en trance profético por todo el camino, hasta llegar a Nayot de Ramá. ²⁴Luego se quitó la ropa y,

---

g **19:1** *comunicó ... su decisión de matar.* Alt. *ordenó ... que mataran.*   *h* **19:13** *un ídolo.* Lit. *los terafines*; también en v. 16.

desnudo y en el suelo, estuvo en trance en presencia de Samuel todo el día y toda la noche. De ahí viene el dicho: «¿Acaso también Saúl es uno de los profetas?»

David y Jonatán

20 David huyó de Nayot de Ramá y fue adonde estaba Jonatán.

—¿Qué he hecho yo? —le preguntó—. ¿Qué crimen o delito he cometido contra tu padre, para que él quiera matarme?

2 —¿Morir tú? ¡De ninguna manera! —respondió Jonatán—. Mi padre no hace nada, por insignificante que sea, sin que me lo diga. ¿Por qué me lo habría de ocultar? ¡Eso no es posible!

3 Pero David juró y perjuró:

—Tu padre sabe muy bien que tú me estimas, así que seguramente habrá pensado: "Jonatán no debe enterarse, para que no se disguste." Pero tan cierto como que el SEÑOR y tú viven, te aseguro que estoy a un paso de la muerte.

4 —Dime qué quieres que haga, y lo haré —le respondió Jonatán.

5 —Sabes —dijo David—, mañana es la fiesta de luna nueva, y se supone que yo debo sentarme a la mesa para comer con el rey. Pues bien, deja que me esconda en el campo hasta pasado mañana por la tarde. 6 Si tu padre me extraña, dile que yo insistí en que me dejaras ir en seguida a Belén, mi pueblo, pues toda mi familia estaba reunida allá para celebrar su sacrificio anual. 7 Si él responde que está bien, entonces no corro ningún peligro. Pero si se enfurece, con eso sabrás que ha decidido acabar conmigo. 8 Ya que en presencia del SEÑOR has hecho un pacto conmigo, que soy tu servidor, te ruego que me seas leal. Si me consideras culpable, no hace falta que me entregues a tu padre; ¡mátame tú mismo!

9 —¡No digas tal cosa! —exclamó Jonatán—. Si llegara a enterarme de que mi padre ha decidido hacerte algún daño, ¿no crees que te lo diría?

10 David le preguntó:

—Si tu padre te responde de mal modo, ¿quién me lo hará saber?

11 Por toda respuesta, Jonatán invitó a David a salir al campo. Una vez allí, 12 le dijo:

—David, te juro por el SEÑOR, Dios de Israel, que a más tardar pasado mañana a esta hora averiguaré lo que piensa mi padre. Si no corres peligro, de alguna manera te lo haré saber. 13 Pero si mi padre intenta hacerte daño, y yo no te aviso para que puedas escapar, ¡que el SEÑOR me castigue sin piedad, y que esté contigo como estuvo con mi padre! 14 Y si todavía estoy vivo cuando el SEÑOR te muestre su bondad, te pido que también tú seas bondadoso conmigo y no dejes que me maten. 15 ¡Nunca dejes de ser bondadoso con mi familia, aun cuando el SEÑOR borre de la faz de la tierra a todos tus enemigos! 16 ¡Que el SEÑOR pida cuentas de esto a tus enemigos!

De ese modo Jonatán hizo un pacto con la familia de David, 17 pues quería a David como a sí mismo. Por ese cariño que le tenía, le pidió a David confirmar el pacto bajo juramento. 18 Además le dijo:

—Mañana es la fiesta de luna nueva. Cuando vean tu asiento desocupado, te van a extrañar. 19 Pasado mañana, sin falta, ve adonde te escondiste la otra vez, y quédate junto a la piedra de Ézel. 20 Yo fingiré estar tirando al blanco y lanzaré tres flechas en esa dirección. 21 Entonces le diré a uno de mis criados que vaya a buscarlas. Si le digo: "Mira, las flechas están más acá, recógelas"; eso querrá decir que no hay

peligro y podrás salir sin ninguna preocupación. ¡Tan cierto como que el SEÑOR vive! 22 Pero si le digo: "Mira, las flechas están más allá", eso querrá decir que el SEÑOR quiere que te vayas, así que ¡escápate! 23 ¡Que el SEÑOR sea siempre testigo del juramento que tú y yo nos hemos hecho!

24 David se escondió en el campo. Cuando llegó la fiesta de luna nueva, el rey se sentó a la mesa para comer 25 ocupando, como de costumbre, el puesto junto a la pared. Jonatán se sentó enfrente,ⁱ mientras que Abner se acomodó a un lado de Saúl. El asiento de David quedó desocupado. 26 Ese día Saúl no dijo nada, pues pensó: «Algo le habrá pasado a David, que lo dejó ritualmente *impuro, y seguramente no pudo purificarse.» 27 Pero como al día siguiente, que era el segundo del mes, el puesto de David seguía desocupado, Saúl le preguntó a Jonatán:

—¿Cómo es que ni ayer ni hoy vino el hijo de Isaí a la comida?

28 Jonatán respondió:

—David me insistió en que le diera permiso para ir a Belén. 29 Me dijo: "Por favor, déjame ir. Mi familia va a celebrar el sacrificio anual en nuestro pueblo, y mi hermano me ha ordenado que vaya. Hazme este favor, y permite que me dé una escapada para ver a mis hermanos." Por eso es que David no se ha sentado a comer con Su Majestad.

30 Al oír esto, Saúl se enfureció con Jonatán.

—¡Hijo de mala madre! —exclamó—. ¿Crees que no sé que eres muy amigo del hijo de Isaí, para vergüenza tuya y de tu desgraciada madre? 31 Mientras el hijo de Isaí viva en esta tierra, ¡ni tú ni tu reino estarán seguros! Así que manda a buscarlo, y tráemelo, pues está condenado a morir.

32 —¿Y por qué ha de morir? —le reclamó Jonatán—. ¿Qué mal ha hecho?

33 Por toda respuesta, Saúl le arrojó su lanza para herirlo. Así Jonatán se convenció de que su padre estaba decidido a matar a David. 34 Enfurecido, Jonatán se levantó de la mesa y no quiso tomar parte en la comida del segundo día de la fiesta. Estaba muy afligido porque su padre había insultado a David.

35 Por la mañana Jonatán salió al campo para encontrarse con David. Uno de sus criados más jóvenes lo acompañaba. 36 Jonatán le dijo: «Corre a buscar las flechas que voy a lanzar.»

El criado se echó a correr, y Jonatán lanzó una flecha que lo sobrepasó. 37 Cuando el criado llegó al lugar donde la flecha había caído, Jonatán le gritó: «¡Más allá! ¡La flecha está más allá! 38 ¡Date prisa! ¡No te detengas!» Y así continuó gritándole Jonatán. Cuando el criado recogió la flecha y se la trajo a su amo, 39 lo hizo sin sospechar nada, pues sólo Jonatán y David sabían de qué se trataba. 40 Entonces Jonatán le dio sus armas al criado. «Vete —le dijo—; llévalas de vuelta a la ciudad.»

41 En cuanto el criado se fue, David salió de su escondite ʲ y, luego de inclinarse tres veces, se postró rostro en tierra. En seguida se besaron y lloraron juntos, hasta que David se desahogó.

42 «Puedes irte tranquilo —le dijo Jonatán a David—, pues los dos hemos hecho un juramento eterno en el *nombre del SEÑOR, pidiéndole que juzgue entre tú y yo, y entre tus descendientes y los míos.» Así que David se fue, y Jonatán regresó a la ciudad.

ⁱ **20:25** *se sentó enfrente* (LXX); *se levantó* (TM).   ʲ **20:41** *salió de su escondite.* Lit. *se levantó del lado del sur.*

David en Nob

21 Cuando David llegó a Nob, fue a ver al sacerdote Ajimélec, quien al encontrarse con David se puso nervioso.

—¿Por qué vienes solo? —le preguntó—. ¿Cómo es que nadie te acompaña?

²David le respondió:

—Vengo por orden del rey, pero nadie debe saber a qué me ha enviado ni cuál es esa orden. En cuanto a mis hombres, ya les he indicado dónde encontrarnos. ³¿Qué provisiones tienes a mano? Dame unos cinco panes, o algo más que tengas.

⁴—No tengo a la mano pan común y corriente —le contestó el sacerdote—. Podría darte del pan consagrado, si es que tus hombres se han abstenido por lo menos de estar con mujeres.

⁵David respondió:

—Te aseguro que, como es la costumbre cuando salimos en una expedición, no hemos tenido contacto con mujeres. Además, mis hombresᵏ se consagran incluso en expediciones ordinarias, así que con más razón están consagrados ahora.

⁶Por tanto, el sacerdote le entregó a David el pan consagrado, ya que no había otro. Era el *pan de la Presencia que había sido quitado de delante del SEÑOR y reemplazado por el pan caliente del día.

⁷Aquel día estaba allí uno de los oficiales de Saúl, que había tenido que quedarse en el santuario del SEÑOR. Se trataba de un edomita llamado Doeg, que era jefe de los pastores de Saúl.

⁸Más tarde, David le preguntó a Ajimélec:

—¿No tienes a la mano una lanza o una espada? Tan urgente era el encargo del rey que no alcancé a tomar mi espada ni mis otras armas.

⁹El sacerdote respondió:

—Aquí tengo la espada del filisteo Goliat, a quien mataste en el valle de Elá. Está detrás del *efod, envuelta en un paño. Puedes llevártela, si quieres. Otras armas no tengo.

—Dámela —dijo David—. ¡Es la mejor que podrías ofrecerme!

David en Gat

¹⁰Ese mismo día David, todavía huyendo de Saúl, se dirigió a Aquis, rey de Gat. ¹¹Los oficiales le dijeron a Aquis:

—¿No es éste David, el rey del país? ¿No es él por quien danzaban, y en los cantos decían:

«Saúl destruyó a un ejército,
pero David aniquiló a diez»?

¹²Al oír esto, David se preocupó y tuvo mucho miedo de Aquis, rey de Gat. ¹³Por lo tanto, cuando estaban por apresarlo, fingió perder la razón y, en público, comenzó a portarse como un loco, haciendo garabatos en las puertas y dejando que la saliva le corriera por la barba.

¹⁴Aquis dijo entonces a sus oficiales:

—¿Pero qué, no se fijan? ¡Ese hombre está loco! ¿Para qué me lo traen? ¹⁵¿Acaso me hacen falta más locos, que encima me traen a éste para hacer sus locuras en mi presencia? ¡Sáquenlo de mi palacio!

David huye a Adulán y a Mizpa

22 David se fue de Gat y huyó a la cueva de Adulán. Cuando sus hermanos y el resto de la familia se enteraron, fueron a verlo allí. ²Además, se le unieron muchos otros que estaban en apuros, cargados de deudas o amargados. Así, David llegó a tener bajo su mando a unos cuatrocientos hombres.

³De allí se dirigió a Mizpa, en Moab, y le pidió al rey de ese lugar: «Deja que mis padres vengan a vivir entre ustedes hasta que yo sepa lo que Dios quiere de mí.» ⁴Fue así como dejó a sus padres con el rey de Moab, y ellos se quedaron allí todo el tiempo que David permaneció en su refugio.

⁵Pero el profeta Gad le dijo a David: «No te quedes en el refugio. Es mejor que regreses a la tierra de Judá.» Entonces David se fue de allí, y se metió en el bosque de Jaret.

Saúl elimina a los sacerdotes de Nob

⁶Mientras Saúl estaba sentado a la sombra de un tamarisco que había en la colina de Guibeá, se enteró de que David y sus hombres habían sido localizados. Tenía Saúl su lanza en la mano, y lo rodeaban todos sus oficiales, ⁷a quienes les dijo:

—¡Pongan atención, hombres de Benjamín! ¿Creen ustedes que el hijo de Isaí les va a dar tierras y viñedos, y que a todos los va a nombrar jefes de mil y de cien soldados? ⁸¡Ahora veo por qué todos ustedes conspiran contra mí, y por qué nadie me informa del pacto que mi hijo ha hecho con el hijo de Isaí! Nadie se ha tomado la molestia de avisarme que mi propio hijo instiga a uno de mis súbditos a que se subleve y me aceche, como en realidad está pasando.

⁹Doeg el edomita, que se encontraba entre los oficiales de Saúl, le dijo:

—Yo vi al hijo de Isaí reunirse en Nob con Ajimélec hijo de Ajitob. ¹⁰Ajimélec consultó al SEÑOR por David y le dio provisiones, y hasta le entregó la espada de Goliat.

¹¹Entonces el rey mandó a llamar al sacerdote Ajimélec hijo de Ajitob, y a todos sus parientes, que eran sacerdotes en Nob. Cuando llegaron, ¹²Saúl le dijo:

—Escucha, hijo de Ajitob.

—Diga, mi señor —respondió Ajimélec.

¹³—¿Por qué tú y el hijo de Isaí conspiran contra mí? —le reclamó Saúl—. Le diste comida y una espada. También consultaste a Dios por él para que se subleve y me aceche, como en realidad está pasando.

¹⁴Ajimélec le respondió al rey:

—¿Quién entre todos los oficiales del rey es tan fiel como su yerno David, jefe de la guardia real y respetado en el palacio? ¹⁵¿Es acaso ésta la primera vez que consulto a Dios por él? ¡Claro que no! No debiera el rey acusarnos ni a mí ni a mi familia, pues de este asunto su servidor no sabe absolutamente nada.

¹⁶—¡Te llegó la hora, Ajimélec! —replicó el rey—. ¡Y no sólo a ti sino a toda tu familia!

¹⁷De inmediato el rey ordenó a los guardias que lo acompañaban:

—¡Maten a los sacerdotes del SEÑOR, que ellos también se han puesto de parte de David! Sabían que estaba huyendo, y sin embargo no me lo dijeron.

Pero los oficiales del rey no se atrevieron a levantar la mano en contra de los sacerdotes del SEÑOR. ¹⁸Así que el rey le ordenó a Doeg:

—¡Pues mátalos tú!

Entonces Doeg el edomita se lanzó contra ellos y los mató. Aquel día mató a ochenta y cinco hombres que tenían puesto el *efod de lino. ¹⁹Luego fue a Nob, el pueblo de los sacerdotes, y mató a filo de espada a hombres y mujeres, a niños y recién nacidos, y hasta a los bueyes, asnos y ovejas.

ᵏ **21:5** *mis hombres.* Lit. *los utensilios de los jóvenes.*

²⁰Sin embargo, un hijo de Ajimélec, llamado Abiatar, logró escapar y huyó hasta encontrarse con David. ²¹Cuando le informó que Saúl había matado a los sacerdotes del SEÑOR, ²²David le respondió:

—Ya desde aquel día, cuando vi a Doeg en Nob, sabía yo que él le avisaría a Saúl. Yo tengo la culpa de que hayan muerto todos tus parientes. ²³Pero no tengas miedo. Quédate conmigo, que aquí estarás a salvo. Quien quiera matarte tendrá que matarme a mí.

David libera la ciudad de Queilá

23 Los filisteos atacaron la ciudad de Queilá y saquearon los graneros. Cuando David se enteró de lo sucedido, ²consultó al SEÑOR:

—¿Debo ir a luchar contra los filisteos?

—Ve —respondió el SEÑOR—, lucha contra los filisteos y libera a Queilá.

³Pero los soldados le dijeron a David:

—Si aun aquí en Judá vivimos con miedo, ¡cuánto más si vamos a Queilá para atacar al ejército filisteo!

⁴David volvió a consultar al SEÑOR, y él le respondió:

—Ponte en camino y ve a Queilá, que voy a entregar en tus manos a los filisteos.

⁵Así que David y sus hombres fueron allá y lucharon contra los filisteos, derrotándolos por completo. David se apoderó de los ganados de los filisteos y rescató a los habitantes de la ciudad. ⁶Ahora bien, cuando Abiatar hijo de Ajimélec huyó a Queilá para refugiarse con David, se llevó consigo el *efod.

Saúl persigue a David

⁷Cuando le contaron a Saúl que David había ido a Queilá, exclamó: «¡Dios me lo ha entregado! David se ha metido en una ciudad con puertas y cerrojos, y no tiene escapatoria.» ⁸Entonces convocó a todo su ejército para ir a combatir a David y a sus hombres, y sitiar la ciudad de Queilá.

⁹David se enteró de que Saúl tramaba su destrucción. Por tanto, le ordenó a Abiatar que le llevara el *efod. ¹⁰Luego David oró:

—Oh SEÑOR, Dios de Israel, yo, tu siervo, sé muy bien que por mi culpa Saúl se propone venir a Queilá para destruirla. ¹¹¿Me entregarán los habitantes de esta ciudad en manos de Saúl? ¿Es verdad que Saúl vendrá, según me han dicho? Yo te ruego, SEÑOR, Dios de Israel, que me lo hagas saber.

—Sí, vendrá —le respondió el SEÑOR.

¹²David volvió a preguntarle:

—¿Me entregarán los habitantes de Queilá a mí y a mis hombres en manos de Saúl?

Y el SEÑOR le contestó:

—Sí, los entregarán.

¹³Entonces David y sus hombres, que eran como seiscientos, se fueron de Queilá y anduvieron de un lugar a otro. Cuando le contaron a Saúl que David había ido de Queilá, decidió suspender la campaña.

¹⁴David se estableció en los refugios del desierto, en los áridos cerros de Zif. Día tras día Saúl lo buscaba, pero Dios no lo entregó en sus manos.

¹⁵Estando David en Hores, en el desierto de Zif, se enteró de que Saúl había salido en su busca con la intención de matarlo. ¹⁶Jonatán hijo de Saúl fue a ver a David en Hores, y lo animó a seguir confiando en Dios. ¹⁷«No tengas miedo —le dijo—, que mi padre no podrá atraparte. Tú vas a ser el rey de Israel, y yo seré tu segundo. Esto, hasta mi padre lo sabe.» ¹⁸Entonces los dos hicieron un pacto en presencia del SEÑOR, después de lo cual Jonatán regresó a su casa y David se quedó en Hores.

¹⁹Los habitantes de Zif fueron a Guibeá y le dijeron a Saúl:

—¿No sabe Su Majestad que David se ha escondido en nuestro territorio? Está en el monte de Jaquilá, en los refugios de Hores, al sur del desierto. ²⁰Cuando Su Majestad tenga a bien venir, entregaremos a David en sus manos.

²¹—¡Que el SEÑOR los bendiga por tenerme tanta consideración! —respondió Saúl—. ²²Vayan y averigüen bien por dónde anda y quién lo ha visto, pues me han dicho que es muy astuto. ²³Infórmense bien de todos los lugares donde se esconde, y tráiganme datos precisos. Entonces yo iré con ustedes, y si es verdad que está en esa región, lo buscaré entre todos los clanes de Judá.

²⁴Los de Zif se despidieron de Saúl y volvieron a su tierra. Mientras tanto, David y sus hombres se encontraban en el desierto de Maón, en el Arabá, al sur del desierto. ²⁵Cuando le avisaron a David que Saúl y sus hombres venían en su búsqueda, bajó al peñasco del desierto de Maón. Al enterarse de esto, Saúl dirigió la persecución hacia ese lugar.

²⁶Saúl avanzaba por un costado del monte, mientras que David y sus hombres iban por el otro, apresurándose para escapar. Pero Saúl y sus hombres le tenían rodeado. Ya estaban a punto de atraparlo, ²⁷cuando un mensajero llegó y le dijo a Saúl: «¡Apresúrese, Su Majestad, que los filisteos están saqueando el país!» ²⁸Saúl dejó entonces de perseguir a David y volvió para enfrentarse con los filisteos. Por eso aquel sitio se llama Sela Hamajlecot.¹ ²⁹Luego David se fue de allí para establecerse en los refugios de Engadi.

David le perdona la vida a Saúl

24 Cuando Saúl regresó de perseguir a los filisteos, le informaron que David estaba en el desierto de Engadi. ²Entonces Saúl tomó consigo tres batallones de hombres escogidos de todo Israel, y se fue por los Peñascos de las Cabras, en busca de David y de sus hombres.

³Por el camino, llegó a un redil de ovejas; y como había una cueva en el lugar, entró allí para hacer sus necesidades.ᵐ David estaba escondido en el fondo de la cueva, con sus hombres, ⁴y éstos le dijeron:

—En verdad, hoy se cumple la promesa que te hizo el SEÑOR cuando te dijo: "Yo pondré a tu enemigo en tus manos, para que hagas con él lo que mejor te parezca."

David se levantó y, sin hacer ruido, cortó el borde del manto de Saúl. ⁵Pero le remordió la conciencia por lo que había hecho, ⁶y les dijo a sus hombres:

—¡Que el SEÑOR me libre de hacerle al rey lo que ustedes sugieren! No puedo alzar la mano contra él, porque es el *ungido del SEÑOR.

⁷De este modo David contuvo a sus hombres, y no les permitió que atacaran a Saúl. Pero una vez que éste salió de la cueva para proseguir su camino, ⁸David lo siguió, gritando:

—¡Majestad, Majestad!

Saúl miró hacia atrás, y David, postrándose rostro en tierra, se inclinó ⁹y le dijo:

—¿Por qué hace caso Su Majestad a los que dicen que yo quiero hacerle daño? ¹⁰Usted podrá ver con sus propios ojos que hoy mismo, en esta cueva, el SEÑOR lo había entregado en mis manos. Mis hombres me incitaban a que lo matara, pero yo res-

---

l **23:28** En hebreo, *Sela Hamajlecot* significa *peñasco de la despedida.*　m **24:3** *hacer sus necesidades.* Lit. *cubrirse los pies.*

peté su vida y dije: "No puedo alzar la mano contra
el rey, porque es el ungido del SEÑOR." 11 Padre mío,
mire usted el borde de su manto que tengo en la
mano. Yo corté este pedazo, pero a usted no lo maté.
Reconozca que yo no intento hacerle mal ni traicionarlo. Usted, sin embargo, me persigue para quitarme la *vida, aunque yo no le he hecho ningún
agravio. 12 ¡Que el SEÑOR juzgue entre nosotros dos!
¡Y que el SEÑOR me vengue de usted! Pero mi mano
no se alzará contra usted. 13 Como dice el antiguo refrán: "De los malos, la maldad"; por eso mi mano jamás se alzará contra usted.

14 »¿Contra quién ha salido el rey de Israel? ¿A
quién persigue? ¡A un perro muerto! ¡A una pulga!
15 ¡Que sea el SEÑOR quien juzgue y dicte la sentencia
entre nosotros dos! ¡Que examine mi causa, y me defienda y me libre de usted!

16 Cuando David terminó de hablar, Saúl le
preguntó:

—David, hijo mío, ¡pero si eres tú quien me habla!

Y alzando la voz, se echó a llorar.

17 —Has actuado mejor que yo —continuó
Saúl—. Me has devuelto bien por mal. 18 Hoy me
has hecho reconocer lo bien que me has tratado,
pues el SEÑOR me entregó en tus manos, y no me
mataste. 19 ¿Quién encuentra a su enemigo y le perdona la vida?[n] ¡Que el SEÑOR te recompense por lo
bien que me has tratado hoy! 20 Ahora caigo en
cuenta de que tú serás el rey, y de que consolidarás
el reino de Israel. 21 Júrame entonces, por el SEÑOR,
que no exterminarás mi descendencia ni borrarás el
*nombre de mi familia.

22 David se lo juró. Luego Saúl volvió a su palacio, y David y sus hombres subieron al refugio.

David, Nabal y Abigaíl

25 Samuel murió, y fue enterrado en Ramá,
donde había vivido. Todo Israel se reunió
para hacer duelo por él. Después de eso David bajó
al desierto de Maón.[ñ]

2 Había en Maón un hombre muy rico, dueño de
mil cabras y tres mil ovejas, las cuales esquilaba en
Carmel, donde tenía su hacienda. 3 Se llamaba Nabal
y pertenecía a la familia de Caleb. Su esposa, Abigaíl,
era una mujer bella e inteligente; Nabal, por el contrario, era insolente y de mala conducta.

4 Estando David en el desierto, se enteró de que
Nabal estaba esquilando sus ovejas. 5 Envió entonces
diez de sus hombres con este encargo: «Vayan a Carmel para llevarle a Nabal un saludo de mi parte. 6 Díganle: "¡Que tengan salud[o] y *paz tú y tu familia, y
todo lo que te pertenece! 7 Acabo de escuchar que estás esquilando tus ovejas. Como has de saber, cuando tus pastores estuvieron con nosotros, jamás los
molestamos. En todo el tiempo que se quedaron en
Carmel, nunca se les quitó nada. 8 Pregúntales a tus
criados, y ellos mismos te lo confirmarán. Por tanto,
te agradeceré que recibas bien a mis hombres, pues
este día hay que celebrarlo. Dales, por favor, a tus
siervos y a tu hijo David lo que tengas a la mano." »

9 Cuando los hombres de David llegaron, le dieron a Nabal este mensaje de parte de David y se quedaron esperando. 10 Pero Nabal les contestó:

—¿Y quién es ese tal David? ¿Quién es el hijo de
Isaí? Hoy día son muchos los esclavos que se escapan
de sus amos. 11 ¿Por qué he de compartir mi pan y mi
agua, y la carne que he reservado para mis esquiladores, con gente que ni siquiera sé de dónde viene?

12 Los hombres de David se dieron la vuelta y se
pusieron en camino. Cuando llegaron ante él, le comunicaron todo lo que Nabal había dicho. 13 Entonces David les ordenó: «¡Cíñanse todos la espada!» Y
todos, incluso él, se la ciñeron. Acompañaron a David unos cuatrocientos hombres, mientras que otros
doscientos se quedaron cuidando el bagaje.

14 Uno de los criados avisó a Abigaíl, la esposa de
Nabal: «David envió desde el desierto unos mensajeros para saludar a nuestro amo, pero él los trató mal.
15 Esos hombres se portaron muy bien con nosotros.
En todo el tiempo que anduvimos con ellos por el
campo, jamás nos molestaron ni nos quitaron nada.
16 Día y noche nos protegieron mientras cuidábamos
los rebaños cerca de ellos. 17 Piense usted bien lo que
debe hacer, pues la ruina está por caer sobre nuestro
amo y sobre toda su familia. Tiene tan mal genio que
ni hablar se puede con él.»

18 Sin perder tiempo, Abigaíl reunió doscientos
panes, dos odres de vino, cinco ovejas asadas, treinta
y cinco litros[p] de trigo tostado, cien tortas de uvas
pasas y doscientas tortas de higos. Después de car-
garlo todo sobre unos asnos, 19 les dijo a los criados:
«Adelántense, que yo los sigo.» Pero a Nabal, su esposo, no le dijo nada de esto.

20 Montada en un asno, Abigaíl bajaba por la ladera del monte cuando vio que David y sus hombres
venían en dirección opuesta, de manera que se encontraron. 21 David recién había comentado: «De balde estuve protegiendo en el desierto las propiedades
de ese tipo, para que no perdiera nada. Ahora resulta
que me paga mal por el bien que le hice. 22 ¡Que Dios
me castigue[q] sin piedad si antes del amanecer no
acabo con todos sus hombres!»

23 Cuando Abigaíl vio a David, se bajó rápidamente del asno y se inclinó ante él, postrándose rostro en tierra. 24 Se arrojó a sus pies y dijo:

—Señor mío, yo tengo la culpa. Deje que esta
sierva suya le hable; le ruego que me escuche. 25 No
haga usted caso de ese grosero de Nabal, pues le hace
honor a su *nombre, que significa "necio". La necedad lo acompaña por todas partes. Yo, por mi parte,
no vi a los mensajeros que usted, mi señor, envió.

26 »Pero ahora el SEÑOR le ha impedido a usted
derramar sangre y hacerse justicia con sus propias
manos. ¡Tan cierto como que el SEÑOR y usted viven!
Por eso, pido que a sus enemigos, y a todos los que
quieran hacerle daño, les pase lo mismo que a Nabal.
27 Acepte usted este regalo que su servidora le ha traído, y repártalo entre los criados que lo acompañan.
28 Yo le ruego que perdone la falta de esta servidora
suya. Ciertamente, el SEÑOR le dará a usted una dinastía que se mantendrá firme, y nunca nadie podrá
hacerle a usted ningún daño,[r] pues usted pelea las
batallas del SEÑOR. 29 Aun si alguien lo persigue con
la intención de matarlo, su *vida estará protegida[s]
por el SEÑOR su Dios, mientras que sus enemigos serán lanzados a la destrucción.[t] 30 Así que, cuando el
SEÑOR le haya hecho todo el bien que le ha prometido, y lo haya establecido como jefe de Israel, 31 no
tendrá usted que sufrir la pena y el remordimiento
de haberse vengado por sí mismo, ni de haber derra-

[n] **24:19** *le perdona la vida.* Lit. *lo envía por buen camino.* [ñ] **25:1** *Maón* (LXX); *Parán* (TM). [o] **25:6** *salud.* Palabra de difícil traducción. [p] **25:18** *treinta y cinco litros.* Lit. *cinco *seah.* [q] **25:22** *me castigue* (lit. *castigue a David;* LXX); *castigue a los enemigos de David* (TM). [r] **25:28** *nunca nadie ... ningún daño.* Alt. *nunca cometerá usted ningún mal.* [s] **25:29** *estará protegida.* Lit. *está embolsada en la bolsa de los vivos.* [t] **25:29** *sus enemigos ... destrucción.* Lit. *él lanzará la vida de sus enemigos de en medio de la palma de una honda.*

mado sangre inocente. Acuérdese usted de esta servidora suya cuando el SEÑOR le haya dado
prosperidad.

³²David le dijo entonces a Abigaíl:

—¡Bendito sea el SEÑOR, Dios de Israel, que te
ha enviado hoy a mi encuentro! ³³¡Y bendita seas tú
por tu buen juicio, pues me has impedido derramar
sangre y vengarme con mis propias manos! ³⁴El
SEÑOR, Dios de Israel, me ha impedido hacerte mal;
pero te digo que si no te hubieras dado prisa en venir
a mi encuentro, para mañana no le habría quedado
vivo a Nabal ni uno solo de sus hombres. ¡Tan cierto
como que el SEÑOR vive!

³⁵Dicho esto, David aceptó lo que ella le había
traído.

—Vuelve tranquila a tu casa —añadió—. Como
puedes ver, te he hecho caso: te concedo lo que me
has pedido.ᵘ

³⁶Cuando Abigaíl llegó a la casa, Nabal estaba
dando un regio banquete. Se encontraba alegre y
muy borracho, así que ella no le dijo nada hasta el día
siguiente. ³⁷Por la mañana, cuando a Nabal ya se le
había pasado la borrachera, su esposa le contó lo sucedido. Al oírlo, Nabal sufrió un ataque al corazón y
quedó paralizado. ³⁸Unos diez días después, el
SEÑOR hirió a Nabal, y así murió.

³⁹Cuando David se enteró de que Nabal había
muerto, exclamó: «¡Bendito sea el SEÑOR, que me ha
hecho *justicia por la afrenta que recibí de Nabal! El
SEÑOR libró a este siervo suyo de hacer mal, pero
hizo recaer sobre Nabal su propia maldad.»

Entonces David envió un mensaje a Abigaíl,
proponiéndole matrimonio. ⁴⁰Cuando los criados
llegaron a Carmel, hablaron con Abigaíl y le dijeron:

—David nos ha enviado para pedirle a usted
que se case con él.

⁴¹Ella se inclinó, y postrándose rostro en tierra
dijo:

—Soy la sierva de David, y estoy para servirle.
Incluso estoy dispuesta a lavarles los pies a sus
criados.

⁴²Sin perder tiempo, Abigaíl se dispuso a partir.
Se montó en un asno y, acompañada de cinco criadas, se fue con los mensajeros de David. Después se
casó con él.

⁴³David también se había casado con Ajinoán de
Jezrel, así que ambas fueron sus esposas. ⁴⁴Saúl, por
su parte, había entregado su hija Mical, esposa de
David, a Paltielᵛ hijo de Lais, oriundo de Galín.

David le perdona la vida a Saúl

26 Los habitantes de Zif fueron a Guibeá y le dijeron a Saúl:

—¿No sabe el rey que David está escondido en el
monte de Jaquilá, frente al desierto?

²Entonces Saúl se puso en marcha con los tres
batallones de hombres escogidos de Israel, y bajó al
desierto de Zif en busca de David. ³Acampó en el
monte de Jaquilá, que está frente al desierto, junto al
camino. Cuando David, que vivía en el desierto, se
dio cuenta de que Saúl venía tras él, ⁴envió espías
para averiguar dónde se encontraba. ⁵Luego se dirigió al campamento de Saúl, y observó el lugar donde
dormían Saúl y Abner hijo de Ner, jefe del ejército.
Saúl estaba dentro del campamento, y el ejército lo
rodeaba. ⁶David entonces les preguntó a Ajimélec el
hitita y a Abisay hijo de Sarvia, hermano de Joab:

—¿Quién quiere venir conmigo al campamento
de Saúl?

—Yo voy contigo —respondió Abisay.

⁷David y Abisay llegaron esa noche y vieron a
Saúl dormido en medio del campamento, con su lanza hincada en tierra a su cabecera. Abner y el ejército
estaban acostados a su alrededor.

⁸—Hoy ha puesto Dios en tus manos a tu enemigo —le dijo Abisay a David—. Déjame matarlo.
De un solo golpe de lanza lo dejaré clavado en el
suelo. ¡Y no tendré que rematarlo!

⁹—¡No lo mates! —exclamó David—. ¿Quién
puede impunemente alzar la mano contra el *ungido del SEÑOR?

¹⁰Y añadió:

—Tan cierto como que el SEÑOR vive, que él mismo lo herirá. O le llegará la hora de morir, o caerá en
batalla. ¹¹En cuanto a mí, ¡que el SEÑOR me libre de
alzar la mano contra su ungido! Sólo toma la lanza y
el jarro de agua que están a su cabecera, y vámonos
de aquí.

¹²David mismo tomó la lanza y el jarro de agua
que estaban a la cabecera de Saúl, y los dos se marcharon. Nadie los vio, ni se dio cuenta, pues todos estaban dormidos. No se despertaron, pues el SEÑOR
los había hecho caer en un sueño profundo. ¹³David
cruzó al otro lado y se detuvo en la cumbre del monte, de modo que había una buena distancia entre
ellos. ¹⁴Entonces llamó al ejército y a Abner hijo de
Ner:

—¡Abner! ¿Me oyes?

Abner replicó:

—¿Quién le está gritando al rey?

¹⁵David le contestó:

—¿No eres tú el valiente sin par en Israel?
¿Cómo es que no has protegido a tu señor el rey? Te
cuento que uno del pueblo entró con la intención
de matarlo. ¹⁶¡Lo que has hecho no tiene nombre!
Tan cierto como que el SEÑOR vive, que ustedes merecen la muerte por no haber protegido a su rey, el
ungido del SEÑOR. A ver, ¿dónde están la lanza del
rey y el jarro de agua que estaban a su cabecera?

¹⁷Saúl, que reconoció la voz de David, dijo:

—David, hijo mío, ¡pero si eres tú quien habla!

—Soy yo, mi señor y rey —respondió David—.
¹⁸¿Por qué persigue mi señor a este siervo suyo?
¿Qué le he hecho? ¿Qué delito he cometido? ¹⁹Le
ruego a Su Majestad que escuche mis palabras. Si
quien lo mueve a usted en mi contra es el SEÑOR,
una ofrenda bastará para aplacarlo. Pero si son los
hombres, ¡que el SEÑOR los maldiga! Hoy me expulsan de esta tierra, que es la herencia del SEÑOR, y me
dicen: "¡Vete a servir a otros dioses!" ²⁰Ahora bien,
no deje usted que mi sangre sea derramada lejos de
la presencia del SEÑOR. ¿Por qué ha salido el rey de
Israel en busca de una simple pulga? ¡Es como si estuviera cazando una perdiz en los montes!

²¹—¡He pecado! —exclamó Saúl—. Regresa, David, hijo mío. Ya no voy a hacerte daño. Tú has valo-
rado hoy mi vida; yo, en cambio, me he portado
como un necio.

²²David respondió:

—Su Majestad, aquí está su lanza. Mande usted
a uno de sus criados a recogerla. ²³Que el SEÑOR le
pague a cada uno según su rectitud y lealtad, pues
hoy él lo había puesto a usted en mis manos, pero yo
no me atreví a tocar siquiera al ungido del SEÑOR.
²⁴Sin embargo, así como hoy valoré la *vida de usted, quiera el SEÑOR valorar mi propia vida y librarme de toda angustia.

ᵘ **25:35** *te concedo lo que me has pedido.* Lit. *he levantado tu semblante.* ᵛ **25:44** *Paltiel.* Lit. *Paltí* (variante de este nombre).

25—¡Bendito seas, David, hijo mío! —respondió Saúl—. Tú harás grandes cosas, y en todo triunfarás.

Luego David siguió su camino, y Saúl regresó a su palacio.

David entre los filisteos

27 Con todo, David pensaba: «Un día de éstos voy a morir a manos de Saúl. Lo mejor que puedo hacer es huir a la tierra de los filisteos. Así Saúl se cansará de buscarme por el territorio de Israel, y podré escapar de sus manos.»

2Acompañado de sus seiscientos hombres, David se puso en marcha y se trasladó a la tierra de Gat, donde reinaba Aquis hijo de Maoc. 3Tanto David como sus hombres se establecieron allí, y quedaron bajo la protección de Aquis. Cada hombre había llevado a su familia, y David tenía consigo a sus dos esposas, Ajinoán la jezrelita y Abigaíl de Carmel, la viuda de Nabal. 4En efecto, cuando Saúl se enteró de que David había huido a Gat, dejó de perseguirlo.

5David le dijo a Aquis: «Si en verdad cuento con el favor de Su Majestad, le ruego que me conceda algún pueblo en el campo, y allí viviré. No tiene ningún sentido que este siervo suyo viva en la capital del reino.»

6Aquel mismo día Aquis le dio la ciudad de Siclag, la cual hasta hoy pertenece a los reyes de Judá.

7David vivió en territorio filisteo un año y cuatro meses. 8Acostumbraba salir en campaña con sus hombres para saquear a los guesureos, guirzitas y amalecitas, pueblos que durante mucho tiempo habían habitado la zona que se extiende hacia Sur y hasta el país de Egipto. 9Cada vez que David atacaba la región, no dejaba a nadie con vida, ni hombre ni mujer. Antes de regresar adonde estaba Aquis se apoderaba de ovejas, vacas, asnos o camellos, y hasta de la ropa que vestían. 10Si Aquis le preguntaba: «¿Qué región saqueaste hoy?», David le respondía: «La del sur de Judá»; o bien: «La del sur de Jeramel»; o «La del sur, donde viven los quenitas». 11David no dejaba con vida ni a hombre ni a mujer, pues pensaba que si llevaba prisioneros a Gat lo denunciarían por lo que estaba haciendo. Ésta fue su patrón de conducta todo el tiempo que estuvo en territorio filisteo. 12Aquis, por su parte, confiaba en David y se decía: «David se está haciendo odioso a los israelitas, su propia gente. Sin duda me servirá para siempre.»

Saúl y la adivina de Endor

28 Por aquel tiempo, los filisteos reunieron sus tropas para ir a la guerra contra Israel. Por lo tanto, Aquis le dijo a David:

—Quiero que sepas que tú y tus hombres saldrán conmigo a la guerra.

2—Está bien —respondió David—. Ya verá Su Majestad de lo que es capaz este siervo suyo.

—Si es así —añadió Aquis—, de ahora en adelante te nombro mi guardaespaldas.

3Ya Samuel había muerto. Todo Israel había hecho duelo por él, y lo habían enterrado en Ramá, que era su propio pueblo. Saúl, por su parte, había expulsado del país a los adivinos y a los hechiceros.

4Los filisteos concentraron sus fuerzas y fueron a Sunén, donde acamparon. Saúl reunió entonces a los israelitas, y armaron su campamento en Guilboa. 5Pero cuando vio Saúl al ejército filisteo, le entró tal miedo que se descorazonó por completo. 6Por eso consultó al SEÑOR, pero él no le respondió ni en sue-

ños, ni por el *urim ni por los profetas. 7Por eso Saúl les ordenó a sus oficiales:

—Búsquenme a una adivina, para que yo vaya a consultarla.

—Pues hay una en Endor —le respondieron.

8Saúl se disfrazó con otra ropa y, acompañado de dos hombres, se fue de noche a ver a la mujer.

—Quiero que evoques a un espíritu —le pidió Saúl—. Haz que se me aparezca el que yo te diga.

9—¿Acaso no sabe usted lo que ha hecho Saúl? —respondió la mujer—. ¡Ha expulsado del país a los adivinos y a los hechiceros! ¿Por qué viene usted a tenderme una trampa y exponerme a la muerte?

10—¡Tan cierto como que el SEÑOR vive, te juro que nadie te va a castigar por esto! —contestó Saúl.

11—¿A quién desea usted que yo haga aparecer? —preguntó la mujer.

—Evócame a Samuel —respondió Saúl.

12Al ver a Samuel, la mujer pegó un grito.

—¡Pero si usted es Saúl! ¿Por qué me ha engañado? —le reclamó.

13—No tienes nada que temer —dijo el rey—. Dime lo que has visto.

—Veo un espíritu que subew de la tierra —respondió ella.

14—¿Y qué aspecto tiene?

—El de un anciano, que sube envuelto en un manto.

Al darse cuenta Saúl de que era Samuel, se postró rostro en tierra.

15Samuel le dijo a Saúl:

—¿Por qué me molestas, haciéndome subir?

—Estoy muy angustiado —respondió Saúl—. Los filisteos me están atacando, y Dios me ha abandonado. Ya no me responde, ni en sueños ni por medio de profetas. Por eso decidí llamarte, para que me digas lo que debo hacer.

16Samuel le replicó:

—Pero si el SEÑOR se ha alejado de ti y se ha vuelto tu enemigo, ¿por qué me consultas a mí? 17El SEÑOR ha cumplido lo que había anunciado por medio de mí: él te ha arrebatado de las manos el reino, y se lo ha dado a tu compañero David. 18Tú no obedeciste al SEÑOR, pues no llevaste a cabo la furia de su castigo contra los amalecitas; por eso él te condena hoy. 19El SEÑOR te entregará a ti y a Israel en manos de los filisteos. Mañana tú y tus hijos se unirán a mí, y el campamento israelita caerá en poder de los filisteos.

20Al instante Saúl se desplomó. Y es que estaba lleno de miedo por lo que Samuel le había dicho, además de que se moría de hambre, pues en toda la noche y en todo el día no había comido nada. 21Al verlo tan asustado, la mujer se le acercó y le dijo:

—Yo, su servidora, le hice caso a usted y, por obedecer sus órdenes, me jugué la *vida. 22Ahora yo le pido que me haga caso a mí. Déjeme traerle algún alimento para que coma; así podrá recuperarse y seguir su camino.

23Pero Saúl se negó a comer. Sin embargo, sus oficiales insistieron al igual que la mujer, y por fin consintió. Se levantó del suelo y tomó asiento. 24La mujer tenía en su casa un ternero gordo, al que mató. También amasó harina y horneó unos panes sin levadura. 25Luego les sirvió a Saúl y a sus oficiales. Esa misma noche, después de comer, todos ellos emprendieron el camino.

---

w 28:13 *un espíritu que sube*. Lit. *dioses que suben*.

Los filisteos desconfían de David

29 Los filisteos reunieron a todas sus tropas en Afec. Los israelitas, por su parte, acamparon junto al manantial que está en Jezrel. 2Los jefes filisteos avanzaban en compañías de cien y de mil soldados, seguidos de Aquis y de David y sus hombres.

3—Y estos hebreos, ¿qué hacen aquí? —preguntaron los generales filisteos.

Aquis les respondió:

—¿No se dan cuenta de que éste es David, quien antes estuvo al servicio de Saúl, rey de Israel? Hace ya más de un año que está conmigo, y desde el primer día que se unió a nosotros no he visto nada que me haga desconfiar de él.

4Pero los generales filisteos, enojados con Aquis, le ordenaron:

—Despídelo; que regrese al lugar que le diste. No dejes que nos acompañe en la batalla, no sea que en medio del combate se vuelva contra nosotros. ¿Qué mejor manera tendría de reconciliarse con su señor, que llevándole las cabezas de estos soldados? 5¿Acaso no es éste el David por quien danzaban, y en sus cantos decían:

«Saúl mató a sus miles;
    pero David, a sus diez miles»?

6Ante esto, Aquis llamó a David y le dijo:

—Tan cierto como que el SEÑOR vive, que tú eres un hombre honrado y me gustaría que me acompañaras en esta campaña. Desde el día en que llegaste, no he visto nada que me haga desconfiar de ti. Pero los jefes filisteos te miran con recelo. 7Así que vete, con mis mejores deseos, vuélvete a tu casa y no hagas nada que les desagrade.

8—Pero, ¿qué es lo que he hecho? —reclamó David—. ¿Qué falla ha visto Su Majestad en este servidor suyo desde el día en que entré a su servicio hasta hoy? ¿Por qué no me permiten luchar contra los enemigos de mi señor y rey?

9—Ya lo sé —respondió Aquis—. Para mí tú eres como un ángel de Dios. Sin embargo, los generales filisteos han decidido que no vayas con nosotros a la batalla. 10Por lo tanto, levántense mañana temprano, tú y los siervos de tu señor que vinieron contigo, y váyanse con la primera luz del día.

11Así que al día siguiente David y sus hombres se levantaron temprano para regresar al país filisteo. Por su parte, los filisteos avanzaron hacia Jezrel.

David derrota a los amalecitas

30 Al tercer día David y sus hombres llegaron a Siclag, pero se encontraron con que los amalecitas habían invadido la región del Néguev y con que, luego de atacar e incendiar a Siclag, 2habían tomado cautivos a las mujeres y a todos los que estaban allí, desde el más grande hasta el más pequeño. Sin embargo, no habían matado a nadie.

3Cuando David y sus hombres llegaron, encontraron que la ciudad había sido quemada, y que sus esposas, hijos e hijas habían sido llevados cautivos. 4David y los que estaban con él se pusieron a llorar y a gritar hasta quedarse sin fuerzas. 5También habían caído prisioneras dos esposas de David, la jezrelita Ajinoán y Abigaíl, la viuda de Nabal de Carmel.

6David se alarmó, pues la tropa hablaba de apedrearlo; y es que todos se sentían amargados por la pérdida de sus hijos e hijas. Pero cobró ánimo y puso su confianza en el SEÑOR su Dios. 7Entonces le dijo al sacerdote Abiatar hijo de Ajimélec:

—Tráeme el *efod.

Tan pronto como Abiatar se lo trajo, 8David consultó al SEÑOR:

—¿Debo perseguir a esa banda? ¿Los voy a alcanzar?

—Persíguelos —le respondió el SEÑOR—. Vas a alcanzarlos, y rescatarás a los cautivos.

9David partió con sus seiscientos hombres hasta llegar al arroyo de Besor. Allí se quedaron rezagados 10doscientos hombres que estaban demasiado cansados para cruzar el arroyo. Así que David continuó la persecución con los cuatrocientos hombres restantes.

11Los hombres de David se encontraron en el campo con un egipcio, y se lo llevaron a David. Le dieron de comer y de beber, 12y le ofrecieron una torta de higo y dos tortas de uvas pasas, pues hacía tres días y tres noches que no había comido nada. En cuanto el egipcio comió, recobró las fuerzas.

13—¿A quién perteneces? —le preguntó David—. ¿De dónde vienes?

—Soy egipcio —le respondió—, esclavo de un amalecita. Hace tres días caí enfermo, y mi amo me abandonó. 14Habíamos invadido la región sur de los quereteos, de Judá y de Caleb; también incendiamos Siclag.

15—Guíanos adonde están esos bandidos —le dijo David.

—Júreme usted por Dios —suplicó el egipcio— que no me matará ni me entregará a mi amo. Con esa condición, lo llevo adonde está la banda.

16El egipcio los guió hasta los amalecitas, los cuales estaban dispersos por todo el campo, comiendo, bebiendo y festejando el gran botín que habían conseguido en el territorio filisteo y en el de Judá. 17David los atacó al amanecer y los combatió hasta la tarde del día siguiente. Los únicos que lograron escapar fueron cuatrocientos muchachos que huyeron en sus camellos. 18David pudo recobrar todo lo que los amalecitas se habían robado, y también rescató a sus dos esposas. 19Nada les faltó del botín, ni grande ni pequeño, ni hijos ni hijas, ni ninguna otra cosa de lo que les habían quitado. 20David también se apoderó de todas las ovejas y del ganado. La gente llevaba todo al frente y pregonaba: «¡Éste es el botín de David!»

21Luego David regresó al arroyo de Besor, donde se habían quedado los doscientos hombres que estaban demasiado cansados para seguirlo. Ellos salieron al encuentro de David y su gente, y David, por su parte, se acercó para saludarlos. 22Pero entre los que acompañaban a David había gente mala y perversa que reclamó:

—Éstos no vinieron con nosotros, así que no vamos a darles nada del botín que recobramos. Que tome cada uno a su esposa y a sus hijos, y que se vaya.

23—No hagan eso, mis hermanos —les respondió David—. Fue el SEÑOR quien nos lo dio todo, y quien nos protegió y puso en nuestras manos a esa banda de maleantes que nos había atacado. 24¿Quién va a estar de acuerdo con ustedes? Del botín participan tanto los que se quedan cuidando el bagaje como los que van a la batalla.

25Aquel día David estableció esa norma como ley en Israel, la cual sigue vigente hasta el día de hoy.

26Después de llegar a Siclag, David envió parte del botín a sus amigos que eran *ancianos de Judá, con este mensaje: «Aquí tienen un regalo del botín que rescatamos de los enemigos del SEÑOR.» 27Recibieron ese regalo los ancianos de Betel, Ramot del Néguev, Jatir, 28Aroer, Sifmot, Estemoa, 29Racal, las ciudades de Jeramel, las ciudades quenitas 30de Jormá, Corasán, Atac, 31y Hebrón, y los ancianos de todos los lugares donde David y sus hombres habían vivido.

Muerte de Saúl

31:1-13 — 2S 1:4-12; 1Cr 10:1-12

31 Los filisteos fueron a la guerra contra Israel, y los israelitas huyeron ante ellos. Muchos cayeron muertos en el monte Guilboa. ²Entonces los filisteos se fueron en persecución de Saúl, y lograron matar a sus hijos Jonatán, Abinadab y Malquisúa. ³La batalla se intensificó contra Saúl, y los arqueros lo alcanzaron con sus flechas. Al verse gravemente herido, ⁴Saúl le dijo a su escudero: «Saca la espada y mátame, no sea que lo hagan esos incircuncisos cuando lleguen, y se diviertan a costa mía.»

Pero el escudero estaba tan asustado que no quiso hacerlo, de modo que Saúl mismo tomó su espada y se dejó caer sobre ella. ⁵Cuando el escudero vio que Saúl caía muerto, también él se arrojó sobre su propia espada y murió con él. ⁶Así, en un mismo día murieron Saúl, sus tres hijos, su escudero y todos sus hombres.

⁷Cuando los israelitas que vivían al otro lado del valle y del Jordán vieron que el ejército de Israel había huido, y que Saúl y sus hijos habían muerto, también ellos abandonaron sus ciudades y se dieron a la fuga. Así fue como los filisteos las ocuparon.

⁸Al otro día, cuando los filisteos llegaron para despojar a los cadáveres, encontraron a Saúl y a sus hijos muertos en el monte Guilboa. ⁹Entonces lo decapitaron, le quitaron las armas, y enviaron mensajeros por todo el país filisteo para que proclamaran la noticia en el templo de sus ídolos y ante todo el pueblo. ¹⁰Sus armas las depositaron en el templo de la diosa *Astarté, y su cadáver lo colgaron en el muro de Betsán.

¹¹Cuando los habitantes de Jabés de Galaad se enteraron de lo que habían hecho los filisteos con Saúl, ¹²los más valientes de ellos caminaron toda la noche hacia Betsán, tomaron los cuerpos de Saúl y de sus hijos y, luego de bajarlos del muro, regresaron a Jabés. Allí los incineraron, ¹³y luego tomaron los huesos y los enterraron a la sombra del tamarisco de Jabés. Después de eso guardaron siete días de ayuno.

2 SAMUEL

Noticia de la muerte de Saúl
1:4-12 — 1S 31:1-13; 1Cr 10:1-12

1 Después de la muerte de Saúl, David se detuvo dos días en Siclag, luego de haber derrotado a los amalecitas. ²Al tercer día, llegó a Siclag un hombre que venía del campamento de Saúl. En señal de duelo se presentó ante David con la ropa rasgada y la cabeza cubierta de ceniza, y se postró rostro en tierra.

³—¿De dónde vienes? —le preguntó David.

—Vengo huyendo del campamento israelita —respondió.

⁴—Pero, ¿qué ha pasado? —exclamó David—. ¡Cuéntamelo todo!

—Pues resulta que nuestro ejército ha huido de la batalla, y muchos han caído muertos —contestó el mensajero—. Entre los caídos en combate se cuentan Saúl y su hijo Jonatán.

⁵—¿Y cómo sabes tú que Saúl y su hijo Jonatán han muerto? —le preguntó David al criado que le había traído la noticia.

⁶—Por casualidad me encontraba yo en el monte Guilboa. De pronto, vi a Saúl apoyado en su lanza y asediado por los carros y la caballería —respondió el criado—. ⁷Saúl se volvió y, al verme, me llamó. Yo me puse a sus órdenes. ⁸Me preguntó quién era yo, y le respondí que era amalecita. ⁹Entonces me pidió que me acercara y me ordenó: "¡Mátame de una vez, pues estoy agonizando y no acabo de morir!" ¹⁰Yo me acerqué y lo maté, pues me di cuenta de que no iba a sobrevivir al desastre. Luego le quité la diadema de la cabeza y el brazalete que llevaba en el brazo, para traérselos a usted, mi señor.

¹¹Al oírlo, David y los que estaban con él se rasgaron las vestiduras. ¹²Lloraron y ayunaron hasta el anochecer porque Saúl y su hijo Jonatán habían caído a filo de espada, y también por el ejército del SEÑOR y por la nación de Israel.

¹³Entonces David le preguntó al joven que le había traído la noticia:

—¿De dónde eres?

—Soy un extranjero amalecita —respondió.

¹⁴—¿Y cómo te atreviste a alzar la mano para matar al *ungido del SEÑOR? —le reclamó David.

¹⁵Y en seguida llamó a uno de sus hombres y le ordenó:

—¡Anda, mátalo!

Aquél cumplió la orden y lo mató. ¹⁶David, por su parte, dijo:

—¡Que tu sangre caiga sobre tu cabeza! Tu boca misma te condena al admitir que mataste al ungido del SEÑOR.

Lamento de David por Saúl y Jonatán

¹⁷David compuso este lamento en honor de Saúl y de su hijo Jonatán. ¹⁸Lo llamó el «Cántico del Arco» y ordenó que lo enseñaran a los habitantes de Judá. Así consta en el libro de Jaser:

¹⁹«¡Ay, Israel! Tu gloria yace herida
en las alturas de los montes.
¡Cómo han caído los valientes!

²⁰»No lo anuncien en Gat
ni lo pregonen en las calles de Ascalón,
para que no se alegren las filisteas

ni lo celebren esas paganas.ᵃ

²¹»¡Ay, montes de Guilboa,
que no caiga sobre ustedes lluvia ni rocío!
¡Que no crezca el trigo para las ofrendas!ᵇ
Porque allí deshonraron el escudo de Saúl:
¡allí quedó manchadoᶜ el escudo de los
valientes!

²²¡Jamás volvía el arco de Jonatán
sin haberse saciado con la sangre de los
heridos,
ni regresaba la espada de Saúl
sin haberse hartado con la grasa de sus
oponentes!

²³»¡Saúl! ¡Jonatán! ¡Nobles personas!
Fueron amados en la vida,
e inseparables en la muerte.
Más veloces eran que las águilas,
y más fuertes que los leones.

²⁴»¡Ay, mujeres de Israel! Lloren por Saúl,
que las vestía con lujosa seda carmesí
y las adornaba con joyas de oro.

²⁵»¡Cómo han caído los valientes en batalla!
Jonatán yace muerto en tus alturas.
²⁶¡Cuánto sufro por ti, Jonatán,
pues te quería como a un hermano!
Más preciosa fue para mí tu amistad
que el amor de las mujeres.

²⁷»¡Cómo han caído los valientes!
¡Las armas de guerra han perecido!»

David es ungido rey de Judá

2 Pasado algún tiempo, David consultó al SEÑOR:

—¿Debo ir a alguna de las ciudades de Judá?

—Sí, debes ir —le respondió el SEÑOR.

—¿Y a qué ciudad quieres que vaya?

—A Hebrón.

²Así que David fue allá con sus dos esposas, Ajinoán la jezrelita y Abigaíl, la viuda de Nabal de Carmel. ³Se llevó además a sus hombres, cada cual acompañado de su familia, y todos se establecieron en Hebrón y sus aldeas. ⁴Entonces los habitantes de Judá fueron a Hebrón, y allí ungieron a David como rey de su tribu. Además, le comunicaron que los habitantes de Jabés de Galaad habían sepultado a Saúl. ⁵Entonces David envió a los de Jabés el siguiente mensaje: «Que el SEÑOR los bendiga por haberle sido fieles a su señor Saúl, y por darle sepultura. ⁶Y ahora, que el SEÑOR les muestre a ustedes su amor y fidelidad, aunque yo también quiero recompensarlos por esto que han hecho. ⁷Cobren ánimo y sean valientes, pues aunque su señor Saúl ha muerto, la tribu de Judá me ha ungido como su rey.»

Guerra entre las tribus

⁸Entretanto, Abner hijo de Ner, general del ejército de Saúl, llevó a Isboset hijo de Saúl a la ciudad de Majanayin, ⁹y allí lo instauró rey de Galaad, de Guesurí,ᵈ de Jezrel, de Efraín, de Benjamín y de todo Israel.

¹⁰Isboset hijo de Saúl tenía cuarenta años cuando fue instaurado rey de Israel, y reinó dos años. La tribu de Judá, por su parte, reconoció a David,

---

ᵃ **1:20** esas paganas. Lit. hijas de incircuncisos. ᵇ **1:21** ¡Que no crezca el trigo para las ofrendas! Texto de difícil traducción. ᶜ **1:21** allí quedó manchado. Lit. sin ser ungido con aceite. ᵈ **2:9** Guesurí (Vulgata y Siríaca); Asurí o Aser (TM).

¹¹quien desde Hebrón reinó sobre la tribu de Judá durante siete años y seis meses.

¹²Abner hijo de Ner salió de Majanayin con las tropas de Isboset hijo de Saúl, y llegó a Gabaón. ¹³Joab hijo de Sarvia, por su parte, salió al frente de las tropas de David. Los dos ejércitos se encontraron en el estanque de Gabaón y tomaron posiciones en lados opuestos. ¹⁴Entonces Abner le dijo a Joab:

—Propongo que salgan unos cuantos jóvenes y midan sus armas en presencia de nosotros.

—De acuerdo —respondió Joab.

¹⁵Así que pasaron al frente doce jóvenes del ejército benjaminita de Isboset hijo de Saúl, y doce de los siervos de David. ¹⁶Cada soldado agarró a su rival por la cabeza y le clavó la espada en el costado, de modo que ambos combatientes murieron al mismo tiempo. Por eso a aquel lugar, que queda cerca de Gabaón, se le llama Jelcat Hazurín.ᵉ

¹⁷Aquel día la batalla fue muy dura, y los siervos de David derrotaron a Abner y a los soldados de Israel. ¹⁸Allí se encontraban Joab, Abisay y Asael, los tres hijos de Sarvia. Asael, que corría tan ligero como una gacela en campo abierto, ¹⁹se lanzó tras Abner y lo persiguió sin vacilar. ²⁰Al mirar hacia atrás, Abner preguntó:

—¿Acaso no eres tú, Asael?

—¡Claro que sí! —respondió.

²¹—¡Déjame tranquilo! —exclamó Abner—. Más te vale que agarres a algún otro y que te quedes con sus armas.

Pero Asael no le hizo caso, ²²así que Abner le advirtió una vez más:

—¡Deja ya de perseguirme, o me veré obligado a matarte! Y entonces, ¿cómo podría darle la cara a tu hermano Joab?

²³Como Asael no dejaba de perseguirlo, Abner le dio un golpe con la punta trasera de su lanza y le atravesó el vientre. La lanza le salió por la espalda, y ahí mismo Asael cayó muerto.

Todos los que pasaban por ahí se detenían a ver el cuerpo de Asael, ²⁴pero Joab y Abisay se lanzaron tras Abner. Ya se ponía el sol cuando llegaron al collado de Amá, frente a Guiaj, en el camino que lleva al desierto de Gabaón. ²⁵Entonces los soldados benjaminitas se reunieron para apoyar a Abner, y formando un grupo cerrado tomaron posiciones en lo alto de una colina. ²⁶Abner le gritó a Joab:

—¿Vamos a dejar que siga esta matanza? ¿No te das cuenta de que, al fin de cuentas, la victoria es amarga? ¿Qué esperas para ordenarles a tus soldados que dejen de perseguir a sus hermanos?

²⁷Joab respondió:

—Tan cierto como que Dios vive, que si no hubieras hablado, mis soldados habrían perseguido a sus hermanos hasta el amanecer.

²⁸En seguida Joab hizo tocar la trompeta, y todos los soldados, dejando de perseguir a los israelitas, se detuvieron y ya no pelearon más. ²⁹Toda esa noche Abner y sus hombres atravesaron el Arabá. Después de cruzar el Jordán, siguieron por todo el territorio de Bitrónᶠ hasta llegar a Majanayin.

³⁰Una vez que Joab dejó de perseguir a Abner, regresó y reunió a todo su ejército para contarlo. Además de Asael, faltaban diecinueve de los soldados de David. ³¹Sin embargo, los soldados de David habían matado a trescientos sesenta de los soldados benjaminitas de Abner. ³²Tomaron luego el cuerpo de Asael y lo sepultaron en Belén, en la tumba de su padre. Toda esa noche Joab y sus hombres marcharon, y llegaron a Hebrón al amanecer.

3 La guerra entre las familias de Saúl y David se prolongó durante mucho tiempo. David consolidaba más y más su reino, en tanto que el de Saúl se iba debilitando.

Hijos de David nacidos en Hebrón
3:2-5 — 1Cr 3:1-4

² Mientras estuvo en Hebrón, David tuvo los siguientes hijos:

Su *primogénito fue Amnón hijo de Ajinoán la jezrelita;

³ el segundo, Quileab hijo de Abigaíl, viuda de Nabal de Carmel;

el tercero, Absalón hijo de Macá, la hija del rey Talmay de Guesur;

⁴ el cuarto, Adonías hijo de Jaguit;

el quinto, Sefatías hijo de Abital;

⁵ el sexto, Itreán hijo de Eglá, que era otra esposa de David.

Éstos son los hijos que le nacieron a David mientras estuvo en Hebrón.

Abner hace un pacto con David

⁶Durante la guerra entre las familias de Saúl y David, Abner fue consolidando su posición en el reino de Saúl, ⁷aunque Isboset le reclamó a Abner el haberse acostado con Rizpa hija de Ayá, que había sido concubina de Saúl. ⁸A Abner le molestó mucho el reclamo, así que replicó:

—¿Acaso soy un *perro de Judá? Hasta el día de hoy me he mantenido fiel a la familia de tu padre Saúl, incluso a sus parientes y amigos, y conste que no te he entregado en manos de David. ¡Y ahora me sales con que he cometido una falta con esa mujer! ⁹Que Dios me castigue sin piedad si ahora yo no procedo con David conforme a lo que el SEÑOR le juró: ¹⁰Voy a quitarle el reino a la familia de Saúl y a establecer el trono de David sobre Israel y Judá, desde Dan hasta Berseba.

¹¹Isboset no se atrevió a responderle a Abner ni una sola palabra, pues le tenía miedo. ¹²Entonces Abner envió unos mensajeros a decirle a David: «¿A quién le pertenece la tierra, si no a usted? Haga un pacto conmigo, y yo lo apoyaré para hacer que todo Israel se ponga de su parte.»

¹³«Muy bien —respondió David—. Haré un pacto contigo, pero con esta condición: Cuando vengas a verme, trae contigo a Mical hija de Saúl. De lo contrario, no te recibiré.» ¹⁴Además, David envió unos mensajeros a decirle a Isboset hijo de Saúl: «Devuélveme a mi esposa Mical, por la que di a cambio cien prepucios de filisteos.»

¹⁵Por tanto, Isboset mandó que se la quitaran a Paltiel hijo de Lais, que era su esposo, ¹⁶pero Paltiel se fue tras ella, llorando por todo el camino hasta llegar a Bajurín. Allí Abner le ordenó que regresara, y Paltiel obedeció.

¹⁷Luego Abner habló con los *ancianos de Israel. «Hace tiempo que ustedes quieren hacer rey a David —les dijo—. ¹⁸Ya pueden hacerlo, pues el SEÑOR le ha prometido: "Por medio de ti, que eres mi siervo, libraré a mi pueblo Israel del poder de los filisteos y de todos sus enemigos."»

¹⁹Abner habló también con los de Benjamín, y más tarde fue a Hebrón para contarle a David todo lo que Israel y la tribu de Benjamín deseaban hacer.

ᵉ **2:16** En hebreo, *Jelcat Hazurín* probablemente significa *campo de dagas*.   ᶠ **2:29** *siguieron por todo el territorio de Bitrón.* Alt. *caminaron toda la mañana.*

²⁰Cuando Abner llegó a Hebrón, David preparó un banquete para él y los veinte hombres que lo acompañaban. ²¹Allí Abner le propuso a David: «Permítame Su Majestad convocar a todo Israel para que hagan un pacto con usted, y así su reino se extenderá a su gusto.» Con esto, David despidió a Abner, y éste se fue tranquilo.

Joab asesina a Abner

²²Ahora bien, los soldados de David regresaban con Joab de una de sus campañas, y traían un gran botín. Abner ya no estaba con David en Hebrón, pues David lo había despedido, y él se había ido tranquilo. ²³Cuando llegó Joab con la tropa que lo acompañaba, le notificaron que Abner hijo de Ner había visitado al rey, y que el rey lo había dejado ir en paz.

²⁴Por tanto, Joab fue a ver al rey y le dijo: «¡Así que Abner vino a ver a Su Majestad! ¿Y cómo se le ocurre dejar que se vaya tal como vino? ²⁵¡Y Su Majestad lo conoce! Lo más seguro es que haya venido con engaño para averiguar qué planes tiene usted, y para enterarse de todo lo que usted está haciendo.»

²⁶En cuanto Joab salió de hablar con David, envió mensajeros tras Abner, los cuales lo hicieron volver del pozo de Sirá. Pero de esto Joab no le dijo nada a David. ²⁷Cuando Abner regresó a Hebrón, Joab lo llevó aparte a la *entrada de la ciudad, como para hablar con él en privado. Allí lo apuñaló en el vientre, y Abner murió. Así Joab se vengó de la muerte de su hermano Asael.

²⁸Algún tiempo después, David se enteró de esto y declaró: «Hago constar ante el SEÑOR, que mi reino y yo somos totalmente inocentes de la muerte de Abner hijo de Ner. ²⁹¡Los responsables de su muerte son Joab y toda su familia! ¡Que nunca falte en la familia de Joab alguien que sufra de hemorragia o de *lepra, o que sea cojo, o que muera violentamente, o que pase hambre!»

³⁰Joab y su hermano Abisay asesinaron a Abner porque en la batalla de Gabaón él había matado a Asael, hermano de ellos. ³¹David ordenó a Joab y a todos los que estaban con él: «Rásguense las vestiduras, vístanse de luto, y hagan duelo por Abner.» El rey David en persona marchó detrás del féretro, ³²y Abner fue enterrado en Hebrón. Junto a la tumba, el rey lloró a gritos, y todo el pueblo lloró con él. ³³Entonces el rey compuso este lamento por Abner:

«¿Por qué tenía que morir Abner
    como mueren los canallas?
³⁴¡No tenías atadas las manos
    ni te habían encadenado los pies!
¡Caíste como el que cae
    en manos de criminales!»

Y el pueblo lloró aun más. ³⁵Todos se acercaron a David y le rogaron que comiera algo mientras todavía era de día, pero él hizo este juramento: «¡Que Dios me castigue sin piedad si pruebo pan o algún otro alimento antes de que se ponga el sol!»

³⁶La gente prestó atención, y a todos les pareció bien. En realidad, todo lo que hacía el rey les agradaba. ³⁷Aquel día todo el pueblo y todo Israel reconocieron que el rey no había sido responsable de la muerte de Abner hijo de Ner.

³⁸El rey también le dijo a su gente: «¿No se dan cuenta de que hoy ha muerto en Israel un hombre extraordinario? ³⁹En cuanto a mí, aunque me han ungido rey, soy todavía débil; no puedo hacerles frente a estos hijos de Sarvia. ¡Que el SEÑOR le pague al malhechor según sus malas obras!»

Asesinato de Isboset

4 Cuando Isboset hijo de Saúl se enteró de que Abner había muerto en Hebrón, se acobardó, y con él todos los israelitas. ²Isboset contaba con dos sujetos que comandaban bandas armadas. Uno de ellos se llamaba Baná, y el otro Recab, y ambos eran hijos de Rimón el berotita y pertenecían a la tribu de Benjamín. Berot se consideraba parte de Benjamín, ³pues los habitantes de Berot se habían refugiado en Guitayin, donde hasta la fecha residen.

⁴Por otra parte, Jonatán hijo de Saúl tenía un hijo de cinco años, llamado Mefiboset, que estaba tullido. Resulta que cuando de Jezrel llegó la noticia de la muerte de Saúl y Jonatán, su nodriza lo cargó para huir pero, con el apuro, se le cayó y por eso quedó cojo.

⁵Ahora bien, Recab y Baná, los hijos de Rimón el berotita, partieron para la casa de Isboset y llegaron a la hora más calurosa del día, cuando él dormía la siesta. ⁶Con el pretexto de sacar un poco de trigo, Recab y su hermano Baná entraron al interior de la casa, y allí mismo lo apuñalaron en el vientre. Después de eso, escaparon. ⁷Se habían metido en la casa mientras Isboset estaba en la alcoba, acostado en su cama. Lo mataron a puñaladas, y luego le cortaron la cabeza y se la llevaron. Caminaron toda la noche por el Arabá ⁸y, al llegar a Hebrón, le entregaron a David la cabeza de Isboset, diciendo:

—Mire, Su Majestad: aquí le traemos la cabeza de Isboset, hijo de su enemigo Saúl, que intentó matarlo a usted. El SEÑOR ha vengado hoy a Su Majestad por lo que Saúl y su descendencia le hicieron.

⁹Pero David les respondió a Recab y a Baná, los hijos de Rimón el berotita:

—Tan cierto como que vive el SEÑOR, quien me ha librado de todas mis angustias, ¹⁰les juro que quien me anunció la muerte de Saúl se imaginaba que me traía buenas noticias, ¡pero la recompensa que le di por tan "buenas noticias" fue apresarlo y matarlo en Siclag! ¹¹¡Y con mayor razón castigaré a los malvados que han dado muerte a un inocente mientras éste dormía en su propia cama! ¿Acaso no voy a vengar su muerte exterminándolos a ustedes de la tierra?

¹²Entonces David les ordenó a sus soldados que los mataran, y que además les cortaran las manos y los pies, y colgaran sus cuerpos junto al estanque de Hebrón. En cambio, la cabeza de Isboset la enterraron en Hebrón, en el sepulcro de Abner.

David es ungido rey de Israel
5:1-3 — 1Cr 11:1-3

5 Todas las tribus de Israel fueron a Hebrón para hablar con David. Le dijeron: «Su Majestad y nosotros somos de la misma sangre. ²Ya desde antes, cuando Saúl era nuestro rey, usted dirigía a Israel en sus campañas. El SEÑOR le dijo a Su Majestad: "Tú guiarás a mi pueblo Israel y lo gobernarás."» ³Así pues, todos los *ancianos de Israel fueron a Hebrón para hablar con el rey David, y allí el rey hizo un pacto con ellos en presencia del SEÑOR. Después de eso, ungieron a David para que fuera rey sobre Israel.

⁴David tenía treinta años cuando comenzó a reinar, y reinó cuarenta años. ⁵Durante siete años y seis meses fue rey de Judá en Hebrón; luego reinó en Jerusalén sobre todo Israel y Judá durante treinta y tres años.

David conquista Jerusalén
5:6-10 — 1Cr 11:4-9
5:11-16 — 1Cr 3:5-9; 14:1-7

6El rey y sus soldados marcharon sobre Jerusalén para atacar a los jebuseos, que vivían allí. Los jebuseos, pensando que David no podría entrar en la ciudad, le dijeron a David: «Aquí no entrarás; para ponerte en retirada, nos bastan los ciegos y los cojos.» 7Pero David logró capturar la fortaleza de *Sión, que ahora se llama la Ciudad de David. 8Aquel día David dijo: «Todo el que vaya a matar a los jebuseos, que suba por el acueducto, para alcanzar a los cojos y a los ciegos. ¡Los aborrezco!» De ahí viene el dicho: «Los ciegos y los cojos no entrarán en el palacio.»

9David se instaló en la fortaleza y la llamó Ciudad de David. También construyó una muralla alrededor, desde el terrapléng hasta el palacio, 10y se fortaleció más y más, porque el SEÑOR Dios *Todopoderoso estaba con él.

11Hiram, rey de Tiro, envió una embajada a David, y también le envió madera de cedro, carpinteros y canteros, para construirle un palacio. 12Con esto David se dio cuenta de que el SEÑOR, por amor a su pueblo, lo había establecido a él como rey sobre Israel y había engrandecido su reino.

13Cuando David se trasladó de Hebrón a Jerusalén, tomó más concubinas y esposas, con las cuales tuvo otros hijos y otras hijas. 14Los hijos que allí tuvo fueron Samúa, Sobab, Natán, Salomón, 15Ibjar, Elisúa, Néfeg, Jafía, 16Elisama, Eliadá y Elifelet.

David derrota a los filisteos
5:17-25 — 1Cr 14:8-17

17Al enterarse los filisteos de que David había sido ungido rey de Israel, subieron todos ellos contra él; pero David lo supo de antemano y bajó a la fortaleza. 18Los filisteos habían avanzado, desplegando sus fuerzas en el valle de Refayin, 19así que David consultó al SEÑOR:

—¿Debo atacar a los filisteos? ¿Los entregarás en mi poder?

—Atácalos —respondió el SEÑOR—; te aseguro que te los entregaré.

20Entonces David fue a Baal Perasín, y allí los derrotó. Por eso aquel lugar se llama Baal Perasín,h pues David dijo: «El SEÑOR ha abierto brechas a mi paso entre mis enemigos, así como se abren brechas en el agua.» 21Allí los filisteos dejaron abandonados sus ídolos, y David y sus soldados se los llevaron.

22Pero los filisteos volvieron a avanzar contra David, y desplegaron sus fuerzas en el valle de Refayin, 23así que David volvió a consultar al SEÑOR.

—No los ataques todavía —le respondió el SEÑOR—; rodéalos hasta llegar a los árboles de bálsamo, y entonces atácalos por la retaguardia. 24Tan pronto como oigas un ruido como de pasos sobre las copas de los árboles, lánzate al ataque, pues eso quiere decir que el SEÑOR va al frente de ti para derrotar al ejército filisteo.

25Así lo hizo David, tal como el SEÑOR se lo había ordenado, y derrotó a los filisteos desde Gabaóni hasta Guézer.

David lleva el arca a Jerusalén
6:1-11 — 1Cr 13:1-14
6:12-19 — 1Cr 15:25—16:3

6 Una vez más, David reunió los treinta batallones de soldados escogidos de Israel, 2y con todo su ejército partió hacia Balá de Judá para trasladar de allí el arca de Dios, sobre la que se invoca su *nombre, el nombre del SEÑOR *Todopoderoso que reina entre los *querubines. 3Colocaron el arca de Dios en una carreta nueva y se la llevaron de la casa de Abinadab, que estaba situada en una colina. Uza y Ajío, hijos de Abinadab, guiaban la carreta nueva 4que llevaba el arca de Dios.j Ajío iba delante del arca, 5mientras David y todo el pueblo de Israel danzaban ante el SEÑOR con gran entusiasmo y cantaban al son de arpas,k liras, panderetas, sistros y címbalos.

6Al llegar a la parcela de Nacón, los bueyes tropezaron; pero Uza, extendiendo las manos, sostuvo el arca de Dios. 7Con todo, la ira del SEÑOR se encendió contra Uza por su atrevimiento y lo hirió de muerte ahí mismo, de modo que Uza cayó fulminado junto al arca.

8David se enojó porque el SEÑOR había matado a Uza, así que llamó a aquel lugar Peres Uza,l nombre que conserva hasta el día de hoy. 9Aquel día David se sintió temeroso del SEÑOR y exclamó: «¡Es mejor que no me lleve el arca del SEÑOR!» 10Y como ya no quería llevarse el arca del SEÑOR a la Ciudad de David, ordenó que la trasladaran a la casa de Obed Edom, oriundo de Gat. 11Fue así como el arca del SEÑOR permaneció tres meses en la casa de Obed Edom de Gat, y el SEÑOR lo bendijo a él y a toda su familia.

12En cuanto le contaron al rey David que por causa del arca el SEÑOR había bendecido a la familia de Obed Edom y toda su hacienda, David fue a la casa de Obed Edom y, en medio de gran algarabía, trasladó el arca de Dios a la Ciudad de David. 13Apenas habían avanzado seis pasos los que llevaban el arca cuando David sacrificó un toro y un ternero engordado. 14Vestido tan sólo con un *efod de lino, se puso a bailar ante el SEÑOR con gran entusiasmo. 15Así que entre vítores y al son de cuernos de carnero, David y todo el pueblo de Israel llevaban el arca del SEÑOR.

16Sucedió que, al entrar el arca del SEÑOR a la Ciudad de David, Mical hija de Saúl se asomó a la ventana; y cuando vio que el rey David estaba saltando y bailando delante del SEÑOR, sintió por él un profundo desprecio.

17El arca del SEÑOR fue llevada a la tienda de campaña que David le había preparado. La instalaron en su sitio, y David ofreció *holocaustos y sacrificios de *comunión en presencia del SEÑOR. 18Después de ofrecer los holocaustos y los sacrificios de comunión, David bendijo al pueblo en el nombre del SEÑOR Todopoderoso, 19y a cada uno de los israelitas que estaban allí congregados, que eran toda una multitud de hombres y mujeres, les repartió pan, una torta de dátiles y una torta de uvas pasas. Después de eso, todos regresaron a sus casas.

20Cuando David volvió para bendecir a su familia, Mical, la hija de Saúl, le salió al encuentro y le reprochó:

---

g **5:9** terraplén. Alt. Milo. h **5:20** En hebreo, Baal Perasín significa el dueño de las brechas. i **5:25** Gabaón (LXX; véase 1Cr 14:16); Gueba (TM). j **6:4** que llevaba el arca de Dios (Qumrán y mss. de LXX); y se la llevaron de la casa de Abinadab, que estaba situada en una colina, con el arca de Dios (TM). k **6:5** danzaban … arpas (véanse Qumrán, LXX, 1Cr 13:8); danzaban ante el SEÑOR al son de todo instrumento de madera, arpas (TM). l **6:8** En hebreo, Peres Uza significa golpe de Uza o brecha en Uza.

—¡Qué distinguido se ha visto hoy el rey de Israel, desnudándose como un cualquiera en presencia de las esclavas de sus oficiales!

21David le respondió:

—Lo hice en presencia del SEÑOR, quien en vez de escoger a tu padre o a cualquier otro de su familia, me escogió a mí y me hizo gobernante de Israel, que es el pueblo del SEÑOR. De modo que seguiré bailando en presencia del SEÑOR, 22y me rebajaré más todavía, hasta humillarme completamente. Sin embargo, esas mismas esclavas de quienes hablas me rendirán honores.

23Y Mical hija de Saúl murió sin haber tenido hijos.

Promesa de Dios a David
7:1-17 — 1Cr 17:1-15

7 Una vez que el rey David se hubo establecido en su palacio, el SEÑOR le dio descanso de todos los enemigos que lo rodeaban. 2Entonces el rey le dijo al profeta Natán:

—Como puedes ver, yo habito en un palacio de cedro, mientras que el arca de Dios se encuentra bajo el toldo de una tienda de campaña.

3—Bien —respondió Natán—. Haga Su Majestad lo que su *corazón le dicte, pues el SEÑOR está con usted.

4Pero aquella misma noche la palabra del SEÑOR vino a Natán y le dijo:

5«Ve y dile a mi siervo David que así dice el SEÑOR: "¿Serás tú acaso quien me construya una casa para que yo la habite? 6Desde el día en que saqué a los israelitas de Egipto, y hasta el día de hoy, no he habitado en casa alguna, sino que he andado de acá para allá, en una tienda de campaña a manera de santuario. 7Todo el tiempo que anduve con los israelitas, cuando mandé a sus gobernantes que pastorearan a mi pueblo Israel, ¿acaso se reclamé a alguno de ellos el no haberme construido una casa de cedro?"

8»Pues bien, dile a mi siervo David que así dice el SEÑOR *Todopoderoso: "Yo te saqué del redil para que, en vez de cuidar ovejas, gobernaras a mi pueblo Israel. 9Yo he estado contigo por dondequiera que has ido, y por ti he aniquilado a todos tus enemigos. Y ahora voy a hacerte tan famoso como los más grandes de la tierra. 10También voy a designar un lugar para mi pueblo Israel, y allí los plantaré para que puedan vivir sin sobresaltos. Sus malvados enemigos no volverán a humillarlos como lo han hecho desde el principio, 11desde el día en que nombré gobernantes sobre mi pueblo Israel. Y a ti te daré descanso de todos tus enemigos."

»Pero ahora el SEÑOR te hace saber que será él quien te construya una casa. 12"Cuando tu vida llegue a su fin y vayas a descansar entre tus antepasados, yo pondré en el trono a uno de tus propios descendientes, y afirmaré su reino. 13Será él quien construya una casa en mi honor, y yo afirmaré su trono real para siempre. 14Yo seré su padre, y él será mi hijo. Así que, cuando haga lo malo, lo castigaré con varas y azotes, como lo haría un padre. 15Sin embargo, no le negaré mi amor, como se lo negué a Saúl, a quien abandoné

para abrirte paso. 16Tu casa y tu reino durarán para siempre delante de mí;m tu trono quedará establecido para siempre."»

17Natán le comunicó todo esto a David, tal como lo había recibido por revelación.

Oración de David
7:18-29 — 1Cr 17:16-27

18Luego el rey David se presentó ante el SEÑOR y le dijo:

«SEÑOR y Dios, ¿quién soy yo, y qué es mi familia, para que me hayas hecho llegar tan lejos? 19Como si esto fuera poco, SEÑOR y Dios, también has hecho promesas a este siervo tuyo en cuanto al futuro de su dinastía. ¡Tal es tu plan para con los *hombres, SEÑOR y Dios!n

20»¿Qué más te puede decir tu siervo David que tú no sepas, SEÑOR mi Dios? 21Has hecho estas maravillas en cumplimiento de tu palabra, según tu voluntad, y las has revelado a tu siervo.

22»¡Qué grande eres, SEÑOR omnipotente! Nosotros mismos hemos aprendido que no hay nadie como tú, y que aparte de ti no hay Dios. 23¿Y qué nación se puede comparar con tu pueblo Israel? Es la única nación en la tierra que tú has redimido, para hacerla tu propio pueblo y para dar a conocer tu *nombre. Hiciste prodigios y maravillas cuando al paso de tu pueblo, al cual redimiste de Egipto, expulsaste a las naciones y a sus dioses.ñ 24Estableciste a Israel para que fuera tu pueblo para siempre, y para que tú, SEÑOR, fueras su Dios.

25»Y ahora, SEÑOR y Dios, reafirma para siempre la promesa que les has hecho a tu siervo y a su dinastía. Cumple tu palabra 26para que tu nombre sea siempre exaltado, y para que todos digan: "¡El SEÑOR *Todopoderoso es Dios de Israel!" Entonces la dinastía de tu siervo David quedará establecida en tu presencia.

27»SEÑOR Todopoderoso, Dios de Israel, tú le has revelado a tu siervo el propósito de establecerle una dinastía, y por eso tu siervo se ha atrevido a hacerte esta súplica. 28SEÑOR mi Dios, tú que le has prometido tanta bondad a tu siervo, ¡tú eres Dios, y tus promesas son fieles! 29Dígnate entonces bendecir a la familia de tu siervo, de modo que bajo tu protección exista para siempre, pues tú mismo, SEÑOR omnipotente, lo has prometido. Si tú bendices a la dinastía de tu siervo, quedará bendita para siempre.»

Victorias de David
8:1-14 — 1Cr 18:1-13

8 Pasado algún tiempo, David derrotó a los filisteos y los subyugó, quitándoles el control de Méteg Amá. 2También derrotó a los moabitas, a quienes obligó a tenderse en el suelo y midió con un cordel; a los que cabían a lo largo de dos medidas los condenó a muerte, pero dejó con vida a los que quedaban dentro de la medida siguiente. Fue así como los moabitas pasaron a ser vasallos tributarios de David.

3Además, David derrotó a Hadad Ezer, hijo del rey Rejob de Sobá, cuando Hadad Ezer trató de restablecer su dominio sobre la región del río Éufrates. 4David le capturó mil carros, siete mil jinetesо y vein-

---

m 7:16 *mí* (mss. hebreos; véanse LXX y Siríaca); *ti* (TM). n 7:19 *¡Tal ... Dios!* Alt. *¿Así procedes con el hombre, SEÑOR y Dios?* o *¿Así actúa el hombre, SEÑOR y Dios?* ñ 7:23 *cuando al paso ... a sus dioses* (LXX; véase 1Cr 17:21); *por tu tierra al paso de tu pueblo, al cual redimiste de Egipto, de las naciones y sus dioses* (TM). o 8:4 *mil carros, siete mil jinetes* (LXX; véanse Qumrán y 1Cr 18:4); *mil setecientos jinetes* (TM).

te mil soldados de infantería; también desjarretó los caballos de tiro, aunque dejó los caballos suficientes para cien carros.

5Luego, cuando los *sirios de Damasco acudieron en auxilio de Hadad Ezer, rey de Sobá, David aniquiló a veintidós mil de ellos. 6También puso guarniciones en Damasco, de modo que los sirios pasaron a ser vasallos tributarios de David. En todas las campañas de David, el SEÑOR le daba la *victoria.

7En cuanto a los escudos de oro que llevaban los oficiales de Hadad Ezer, David se apropió de ellos y los trasladó a Jerusalén. 8Así mismo se apoderó de una gran cantidad de bronce que había en Tébajp y Berotay, poblaciones de Hadad Ezer.

9Tou,q rey de Jamat, se enteró de que David había derrotado por completo al ejército de Hadad Ezer. 10Como Tou también era enemigo de Hadad Ezer, envió a su hijo Joránr a desearle *bienestar al rey David, y a felicitarlo por haber derrotado a Hadad Ezer en batalla. Jorán llevó consigo objetos de plata, de oro y de bronce, 11los cuales el rey David consagró al SEÑOR, tal como lo había hecho con la plata y el oro de las otras naciones que él había subyugado: 12Edom,s Moab, los amonitas, los filisteos y los amalecitas. También consagró el botín que le había quitado a Hadad Ezer, hijo del rey Rejob de Sobá.

13La fama de David creció aún más cuando regresó victorioso del valle de la Sal, donde aniquiló a dieciocho mil edomitas. 14También puso guarniciones en Edom; las estableció por todo el país, de modo que los edomitas pasaron a ser vasallos tributarios de David. En todas sus campañas, el SEÑOR le daba la victoria.

Los oficiales de David
8:15-18 — 1Cr 18:14-17

15David reinó sobre todo Israel, gobernando al pueblo entero con justicia y rectitud. 16Joab hijo de Sarvia era general del ejército; Josafat hijo de Ajilud era el secretario; 17Sadoc hijo de Ajitob y Ajimélec hijo de Abiatar eran sacerdotes; Seraías era el cronista; 18Benaías hijo de Joyadá estaba al mando de los soldados quereteos y peleteos, y los hijos de David eran ministros.t

David y Mefiboset

9 El rey David averiguó si había alguien de la familia de Saúl a quien pudiera beneficiar en memoria de Jonatán, 2y como la familia de Saúl había tenido un administrador que se llamaba Siba, mandaron a llamarlo. Cuando Siba se presentó ante David, éste le preguntó:

—¿Tú eres Siba?

—A las órdenes de Su Majestad —respondió.

3—¿No queda nadie de la familia de Saúl a quien yo pueda beneficiar en el *nombre de Dios? —volvió a preguntar el rey.

—Sí, Su Majestad. Todavía le queda a Jonatán un hijo que está tullido de ambos pies —le respondió Siba.

4—¿Y dónde está?

—En Lo Debar; vive en casa de Maquir hijo de Amiel.

5Entonces el rey David mandó a buscarlo a casa de Maquir hijo de Amiel, en Lo Debar. 6Cuando Mefiboset, que era hijo de Jonatán y nieto de Saúl, estu-

vo en presencia de David, se inclinó ante él rostro en tierra. —¿Tú eres Mefiboset? —le preguntó David.

—A las órdenes de Su Majestad —respondió.

7—No temas, pues en memoria de tu padre Jonatán he decidido beneficiarte. Voy a devolverte todas las tierras que pertenecían a tu abuelo Saúl, y de ahora en adelante te sentarás a mi mesa.

8Mefiboset se inclinó y dijo:

—¿Y quién es este siervo suyo, para que Su Majestad se fije en él? ¡Si no valgo más que un *perro muerto!

9Pero David llamó a Siba, el administrador de Saúl, y le dijo: —Todo lo que pertenecía a tu amo Saúl y a su familia se lo entrego a su nieto Mefiboset. 10Te ordeno que cultives para él la tierra y guardes la cosecha para el sustento de su casa. Que le ayuden tus quince hijos y tus veinte criados. En cuanto al nieto de tu amo, siempre comerá en mi mesa.

11—Yo estoy para servir a Su Majestad. Haré todo lo que Su Majestad me mande —respondió Siba.

A partir de ese día Mefiboset se sentó a la mesa de Davidu como uno más de los hijos del rey. 12Toda la familia de Siba estaba al servicio de Mefiboset, quien tenía un hijo pequeño llamado Micaías. 13Tullido de ambos pies, Mefiboset vivía en Jerusalén, pues siempre se sentaba a la mesa del rey.

David derrota a los amonitas
10:1-19 — 1Cr 19:1-19

10 Pasado algún tiempo, murió el rey de los amonitas, y su hijo Janún lo sucedió en el trono. 2Entonces David pensó: «Debo ser leal con Janún hijo de Najás, tal como su padre lo fue conmigo.» Así que envió a unos mensajeros para darle el pésame por la muerte de su padre.

Cuando los mensajeros de David llegaron al país de los amonitas, 3los jefes de ese pueblo aconsejaron a Janún, su rey: «¿Y acaso cree Su Majestad que David ha enviado a estos mensajeros sólo para darle el pésame, y porque quiere honrar a su padre? ¿No será más bien que los ha enviado a espiar la ciudad para luego destruirla?» 4Entonces Janún mandó que apresaran a los mensajeros de David y que les afeitaran media barba y les rasgaran la ropa por la mitad, a la altura de las nalgas. Y así los despidió.

5Los hombres del rey David se sentían muy avergonzados. Cuando David se enteró de lo que les había pasado, mandó que los recibieran y les dieran este mensaje de su parte: «Quédense en Jericó, y no regresen hasta que les crezca la barba.»

6Al darse cuenta los amonitas de que habían ofendido a David, hicieron trámites para contratar mercenarios: de entre los *sirios de Bet Rejob y de Sobá, veinte mil soldados de infantería; del rey de Macá, mil hombres; y de Tob, doce mil hombres. 7Cuando David lo supo, despachó a Joab con todos los soldados del ejército. 8Los amonitas avanzaron hasta la *entrada de su ciudad y se alistaron para la batalla, mientras que los sirios de Sobá y Rejob se quedaron aparte, en campo abierto, junto con los hombres de Tob y de Macá.

9Joab se vio amenazado por el frente y por la retaguardia, así que escogió a las mejores tropas israelitas para pelear contra los sirios, 10y el resto de las tropas las puso al mando de su hermano Abisay,

p 8:8 Tébaj (Siríaca; véanse mss. de LXX y 1Cr 18:8); Beta (TM). q 8:9 Tou (véanse mss. de LXX, Vulgata, Siríaca, 1Cr 18:9-10); Toy (TM); también en v. 10. r 8:10 Jorán. También llamado Adorán (véase 1Cr 18:10). s 8:12 Edom (mss. hebreos, LXX y Siríaca; véase 1Cr 18:11); Aram (TM); también en v. 13 (edomitas). t 8:18 ministros. Lit. Sacerdotes. u 9:11 la mesa de David (LXX); mi mesa (TM).

para que enfrentaran a los amonitas. ¹¹A Abisay le ordenó: «Si los sirios pueden más que yo, tú vendrás a rescatarme; y si los amonitas pueden más que tú, yo iré a tu rescate. ¹²¡Ánimo! ¡Luchemos con valor por nuestro pueblo y por las ciudades de nuestro Dios! Y que el SEÑOR haga lo que bien le parezca.»

¹³En seguida Joab y sus tropas avanzaron para atacar a los sirios, y éstos huyeron de él. ¹⁴Al ver que los sirios se daban a la fuga, también los amonitas huyeron de Abisay y se refugiaron en la ciudad. Entonces Joab suspendió el ataque contra los amonitas y regresó a Jerusalén.

¹⁵Los sirios, al verse derrotados por Israel, volvieron a reunirse. ¹⁶Además, Hadad Ezer mandó movilizar a los sirios que estaban al otro lado del río Éufrates, los cuales fueron a Jelán bajo el mando de Sobac, general del ejército de Hadad Ezer.

¹⁷Cuando David se enteró de esto, reunió a todo Israel, cruzó el Jordán y marchó hacia Jelán. Los sirios se enfrentaron con David y lo atacaron, ¹⁸pero tuvieron que huir ante los israelitas. David mató a setecientos soldados sirios de caballería y cuarenta mil de infantería.ᵛ También hirió a Sobac, general del ejército sirio, quien murió allí mismo. ¹⁹Al ver que los sirios habían sido derrotados por los israelitas, todos los reyes vasallos de Hadad Ezer hicieron la paz con los israelitas y se sometieron a ellos. Y nunca más se atrevieron los sirios a ir en auxilio de los amonitas.

David y Betsabé

11 En la primavera, que era la época en que los reyesʷ salían de campaña, David mandó a Joab con la guardia real y todo el ejército de Israel para que aniquilara a los amonitas y sitiara la ciudad de Rabá. Pero David se quedó en Jerusalén.

²Una tarde, al levantarse David de la cama, comenzó a pasearse por la azotea del palacio, y desde allí vio a una mujer que se estaba bañando. La mujer era sumamente hermosa, ³por lo que David mandó que averiguaran quién era, y le informaron: «Se trata de Betsabé, que es hija de Elián y esposa de Urías el hitita.» ⁴Entonces David ordenó que la llevaran a su presencia, y cuando Betsabé llegó, él se acostó con ella. Después de eso, ella volvió a su casa. Hacía poco que Betsabé se había *purificado de su menstruación,ˣ ⁵así que quedó embarazada y se lo hizo saber a David.

⁶Entonces David le envió este mensaje a Joab: «Mándame aquí a Urías el hitita.» Y Joab así lo hizo. ⁷Cuando Urías llegó, David le preguntó cómo estaban Joab y los soldados, y cómo iba la campaña. ⁸Luego le dijo: «Vete a tu casa y acuéstate con tu mujer.»ʸ Tan pronto como salió del palacio, Urías recibió un regalo de parte del rey, ⁹pero en vez de irse a su propia casa, se acostó a la entrada del palacio, donde dormía la guardia real.

¹⁰David se enteró de que Urías no había ido a su casa, así que le preguntó:

—Has hecho un viaje largo; ¿por qué no fuiste a tu casa?

¹¹—En este momento —respondió Urías—, tanto el arca como los hombres de Israel y de Judá se guarecen en simples enramadas, y mi señor Joab y sus oficiales acampan al aire libre, ¿y yo voy a entrar en mi casa para darme un banquete y acostarme con mi esposa?

¡Tan cierto como que Su Majestad vive, que yo no puedo hacer tal cosa!

¹²—Bueno, entonces quédate hoy aquí, y mañana te enviaré de regreso —replicó David.

Urías se quedó ese día en Jerusalén. Pero al día siguiente ¹³David lo invitó a un banquete y logró emborracharlo. A pesar de eso, Urías no fue a su casa sino que volvió a pasar la noche donde dormía la guardia real. ¹⁴A la mañana siguiente, David le escribió una carta a Joab, y se la envió por medio de Urías. ¹⁵La carta decía: «Pongan a Urías al frente de la batalla, donde la lucha sea más dura. Luego déjenlo solo, para que lo hieran y lo maten.»

¹⁶Por tanto, cuando Joab ya había sitiado la ciudad, puso a Urías donde sabía que estaban los defensores más aguerridos. ¹⁷Los de la ciudad salieron para enfrentarse a Joab, y entre los oficiales de David que cayeron en batalla también perdió la vida Urías el hitita.

¹⁸Entonces Joab envió a David un informe con todos los detalles del combate, ¹⁹y le dio esta orden al mensajero: «Cuando hayas terminado de contarle al rey todos los pormenores del combate, ²⁰tal vez se enoje y te pregunte: "¿Por qué se acercaron tanto a la ciudad para atacarla? ¿Acaso no sabían que les dispararían desde la muralla? ²¹¿Quién mató a Abimélec hijo de Yerubéset?ᶻ ¿No fue acaso una mujer la que le arrojó una piedra de molino desde la muralla de Tebes y lo mató? ¿Por qué se acercaron tanto a la muralla?" Pues si te hace estas preguntas, respóndele: "También ha muerto Urías el hitita, siervo de Su Majestad."»

²²El mensajero partió, y al llegar le contó a David todo lo que Joab le había mandado decir.

²³—Los soldados enemigos nos estaban venciendo —dijo el mensajero—, pero cuando nos atacaron a campo abierto pudimos rechazarlos hasta la *entrada de la ciudad. ²⁴Entonces los arqueros dispararon desde la muralla a los soldados de Su Majestad, de modo que murieron varios de los nuestros. También ha muerto Urías el hitita, siervo de Su Majestad.

²⁵Entonces David le dijo al mensajero:

—Dile a Joab de mi parte que no se aflija tanto por lo que ha pasado, pues la espada devora sin discriminar. Dile también que reanude el ataque contra la ciudad, hasta destruirla.

²⁶Cuando Betsabé se enteró de que Urías, su esposo, había muerto, hizo duelo por él. ²⁷Después del luto, David mandó que se la llevaran al palacio y la tomó por esposa. Con el tiempo, ella le dio un hijo. Sin embargo, lo que David había hecho le desagradó al SEÑOR.

Natán reprende a David
11:1; 12:29-31 — 1Cr 20:1-3

12 El SEÑOR envió a Natán para que hablara con David. Cuando este profeta se presentó ante David, le dijo:

—Dos hombres vivían en un pueblo. El uno era rico, y el otro pobre. ²El rico tenía muchísimas ovejas y vacas; ³en cambio, el pobre no tenía más que una sola ovejita que él mismo había comprado y criado. La ovejita creció con él y con sus hijos: comía de su plato, bebía de su vaso y dormía en su regazo. Era para ese hombre como su propia hija. ⁴Pero sucedió

ᵛ **10:18** *de infantería* (mss. de LXX; véase también 1Cr 19:18); *jinetes* (TM). ʷ **11:1** *reyes* (LXX, Vulgata y varios mss. hebreos); *mensajeros* (TM). ˣ **11:4** *Hacía poco ... se había purificado de su menstruación.* Es decir, no había quedado embarazada por Urías, y era tiempo propicio para la concepción. ʸ **11:8** *acuéstate con tu mujer.* Lit. *lávate los pies.* ᶻ **11:21** *Yerubéset.* Es decir, Yerubaal o Gedeón (véanse Jue 8:35; 9:1,53).

que un viajero llegó de visita a casa del hombre rico, y como éste no quería matar ninguna de sus propias ovejas o vacas para darle de comer al huésped, le quitó al hombre pobre su única ovejita.

5Tan grande fue el enojo de David contra aquel hombre, que le respondió a Natán:

—¡Tan cierto como que el SEÑOR vive, que quien hizo esto merece la muerte! 6¿Cómo pudo hacer algo tan ruin? ¡Ahora pagará cuatro veces el valor de la oveja!

7Entonces Natán le dijo a David:

—¡Tú eres ese hombre! Así dice el SEÑOR, Dios de Israel: "Yo te ungí como rey sobre Israel, y te libré del poder de Saúl. 8Te di el palacio de tu amo, y puse sus mujeres en tus brazos. También te permití gobernar a Israel y a Judá. Y por si esto hubiera sido poco, te habría dado mucho más. 9¿Por qué, entonces, despreciaste la palabra del SEÑOR haciendo lo que me desagrada? ¡Asesinaste a Urías el hitita para apoderarte de su esposa! ¡Lo mataste con la espada de los amonitas! 10Por eso la espada jamás se apartará de tu familia, pues me despreciaste al tomar la esposa de Urías el hitita para hacerla tu mujer."

11»Pues bien, así dice el SEÑOR: "Yo haré que el desastre que mereces surja de tu propia familia, y ante tus propios ojos tomaré a tus mujeres y se las daré a otro, el cual se acostará con ellas en pleno día. 12Lo que tú hiciste a escondidas, yo lo haré a plena luz, a la vista de todo Israel."

13—¡He pecado contra el SEÑOR! —reconoció David ante Natán.

—El SEÑOR ha perdonado ya tu pecado, y no morirás —contestó Natán—.

14Sin embargo, tu hijo sí morirá, pues con tus acciones has ofendido al[a] SEÑOR.

15Dicho esto, Natán volvió a su casa. Y el SEÑOR hirió al hijo que la esposa de Urías le había dado a David, de modo que el niño cayó gravemente enfermo. 16David se puso a rogar a Dios por él; ayunaba y pasaba las noches tirado en el suelo. 17Los ancianos de su corte iban a verlo y le rogaban que se levantara, pero él se resistía, y aun se negaba a comer con ellos.

18Siete días después, el niño murió. Los oficiales de David tenían miedo de darle la noticia, pues decían: «Si cuando el niño estaba vivo, le hablábamos al rey y no nos hacía caso, ¿qué locura no hará ahora si le decimos que el niño ha muerto?» 19Pero David, al ver que sus oficiales estaban cuchicheando, se dio cuenta de lo que había pasado y les preguntó:

—¿Ha muerto el niño?

—Sí, ya ha muerto —le respondieron.

20Entonces David se levantó del suelo y en seguida se bañó y se perfumó; luego se vistió y fue a la casa del SEÑOR para adorar. Después regresó al palacio, pidió que le sirvieran alimentos, y comió.

21—¿Qué forma de actuar es ésta? —le preguntaron sus oficiales—. Cuando el niño estaba vivo, usted ayunaba y lloraba; pero ahora que se ha muerto, ¡usted se levanta y se pone a comer!

22David respondió:

—Es verdad que cuando el niño estaba vivo yo ayunaba y lloraba, pues pensaba: "¿Quién sabe? Tal vez el SEÑOR tenga compasión de mí y permita que el niño viva." 23Pero ahora que ha muerto, ¿qué razón tengo para ayunar? ¿Acaso puedo devolverle la

vida? Yo iré adonde él está, aunque él ya no volverá a mí.

24Luego David fue a consolar a su esposa y se unió a ella. Betsabé le dio un hijo, al que David llamó Salomón. El SEÑOR amó al niño 25y mandó a decir por medio del profeta Natán que le pusieran por *nombre Jedidías,[b] por disposición del SEÑOR.

26Mientras tanto, Joab había atacado la ciudad amonita de Rabá y capturado la fortaleza[c] real. 27Entonces envió unos mensajeros a decirle a David: «Acabo de atacar a Rabá y he capturado los depósitos[d] de agua. 28Ahora, pues, le pido a Su Majestad que movilice el resto de las tropas para sitiar y capturar la ciudad. Si no, lo haré yo mismo y le pondrán mi nombre.»

29Por tanto, David, movilizando todas las tropas, marchó contra Rabá, la atacó y la capturó. 30Al rey de los amonitas[e] le quitó la corona de oro que tenía puesta, la cual pesaba treinta y tres kilos[f] y estaba adornada con piedras preciosas. Luego se la pusieron a David. Además, David saqueó la ciudad y se llevó un botín inmenso. 31Expulsó de allí a sus habitantes y los puso a trabajar con sierras, trillos y hachas, y también los forzó a trabajar en los hornos de ladrillos. Lo mismo hizo con todos los pueblos amonitas, después de lo cual regresó a Jerusalén con todas sus tropas.

Amnón y Tamar

13 Pasado algún tiempo, sucedió lo siguiente. Absalón hijo de David tenía una hermana muy bella, que se llamaba Tamar; y Amnón, otro hijo de David, se enamoró de ella. 2Pero como Tamar era virgen, Amnón se enfermó de angustia al pensar que le sería muy difícil llevar a cabo sus intenciones con su hermana. 3Sin embargo, Amnón tenía un amigo muy astuto, que se llamaba Jonadab, y que era hijo de Simá y sobrino de David. Jonadab 4le preguntó a Amnón:

—¿Cómo es que tú, todo un príncipe, te ves cada día peor? ¿Por qué no me cuentas lo que te pasa?

—Es que estoy muy enamorado de mi hermana Tamar —respondió Amnón.

5Jonadab le sugirió:

—Acuéstate y finge que estás enfermo. Cuando tu padre vaya a verte, dile: "Por favor, que venga mi hermana Tamar a darme de comer. Quisiera verla preparar la comida aquí mismo, y que ella me la sirva."

6Así que Amnón se acostó y fingió estar enfermo. Y cuando el rey fue a verlo, Amnón le dijo:

—Por favor, que venga mi hermana Tamar a prepararme aquí mismo dos tortas, y que me las sirva.

7David envió un mensajero a la casa de Tamar, para que le diera este recado: «Ve a casa de tu hermano Amnón, y prepárale la comida.» 8Tamar fue a casa de su hermano Amnón y lo encontró acostado. Tomó harina, la amasó, preparó las tortas allí mismo, y las coció. 9Luego tomó la sartén para servirle, pero Amnón se negó a comer y ordenó:

—¡Fuera de aquí todos! ¡No quiero ver a nadie!

Una vez que todos salieron, 10Amnón le dijo a Tamar:

—Trae la comida a mi habitación, y dame de comer tú misma.

Ella tomó las tortas que había preparado y se las llevó a su hermano Amnón a la habitación, 11pero

a 12:14 al. Lit. a los enemigos del.   b 12:25 En hebreo, Jedidías significa amado por el SEÑOR.   c 12:26 fortaleza. Lit. Ciudad.   d 12:27 los depósitos. Lit. la ciudad.   e 12:30 al rey de los amonitas. Alt. a Milcón (es decir, el dios Moloc).   f 12:30 treinta y tres kilos. Lit. un *talento.

cuando se le acercó para darle de comer, él la agarró por la fuerza y le dijo:

—¡Ven, hermanita; acuéstate conmigo!

12Pero ella exclamó:

—¡No, hermano mío! No me humilles, que esto no se hace en Israel. ¡No cometas esta infamia! 13¿Adónde iría yo con mi vergüenza? ¿Y qué sería de ti? ¡Serías visto en Israel como un depravado! Yo te ruego que hables con el rey; con toda seguridad, no se opondrá a que yo sea tu esposa.

14Pero Amnón no le hizo caso sino que, aprovechándose de su fuerza, se acostó con ella y la violó. 15Pero el odio que sintió por ella después de violarla fue mayor que el amor que antes le había tenido. Así que le dijo:

—¡Levántate y vete!

16—¡No me eches de aquí! —replicó ella—. Después de lo que has hecho conmigo, ¡echarme de aquí sería una maldad aun más terrible!

Pero él no le hizo caso, 17sino que llamó a su criado y le ordenó:

—¡Echa de aquí a esta mujer! Y luego que la hayas echado, cierra bien la puerta.

18Así que el criado la echó de la casa, y luego cerró bien la puerta. Tamar llevaba puesta una túnica especial de mangas largas,g pues así se vestían las princesas solteras. 19Al salir, se echó ceniza en la cabeza, se rasgó la túnica y, llevándose las manos a la cabeza, se fue por el camino llorando a gritos. 20Entonces su hermano Absalón le dijo:

—¡Así que tu hermano Amnón ha estado contigo! Pues bien, hermana mía, cálmate y no digas nada. Al fin de cuentas, es tu hermano.

Desolada, Tamar se quedó a vivir en casa de su hermano Absalón. 21El rey David, al enterarse de todo lo que había pasado, se enfureció. 22Absalón, por su parte, no le dirigía la palabra a Amnón, pues lo odiaba por haber violado a su hermana Tamar.

Asesinato de Amnón

23Pasados dos años, Absalón convidó a todos los hijos del rey a un banquete en Baal Jazor, cerca de la frontera de Efraín, donde sus hombres estaban esquilando ovejas. 24Además, se presentó ante el rey y le dijo:

—Su Majestad, este siervo suyo tiene esquiladores trabajando. Le ruego venir con su corte.

25—No, hijo mío —le respondió el rey—. No debemos ir todos, pues te seríamos una carga.

Absalón insistió, pero el rey no quiso ir; sin embargo, le dio su bendición. 26Entonces Absalón le dijo:

—Ya que Su Majestad no viene, ¿por qué no permite que nos acompañe mi hermano Amnón?

—¿Y para qué va a ir contigo? —le preguntó el rey.

27Pero tanto insistió Absalón que el rey dejó que Amnón y sus otros hijos fueran con Absalón. 28Éste, por su parte, les había dado instrucciones a sus criados: «No pierdan de vista a Amnón. Y cuando se le haya subido el vino,h se la daré la señal de ataque, y ustedes lo matarán. No tengan miedo, pues soy yo quien les da la orden. Ánimo; sean valientes.»

29Los criados hicieron con Amnón tal como Absalón les había ordenado. Entonces los otros hijos

del rey se levantaron y, montando cada uno su mula, salieron huyendo.

30Todavía estaban en camino cuando llegó este rumor a oídos de David: «¡Absalón ha matado a todos los hijos del rey! ¡Ninguno de ellos ha quedado con vida!»

31El rey se levantó y, rasgándose las vestiduras en señal de duelo, se arrojó al suelo. También todos los oficiales que estaban con él se rasgaron las vestiduras. 32Pero Jonadab, el hijo de Simá y sobrino de David, intervino:

—No piense Su Majestad que todos los príncipes han sido asesinados, sino sólo Amnón. Absalón ya tenía decidido desde el día en que Amnón violó a su hermana Tamar. 33Su Majestad no debe dejarse llevar por el rumor de que han muerto todos sus hijos, pues el único que ha muerto es Amnón.

34El centinela de la ciudad alzó la vista y vio que del oeste, por la ladera del monte, venía bajando una gran multitud. Entonces fue a decirle al rey: «Veo venir gente por el camino de Joronayin, por la ladera del monte.»i Mientras tanto, Absalón había huido. 35Jonadab le comentó al rey:

—¿Ya ve Su Majestad? Aquí llegan sus hijos, tal como yo se lo había dicho.

36Apenas había terminado de hablar cuando entraron los hijos del rey, todos ellos llorando a voz en cuello, y también el rey y sus oficiales se pusieron a llorar desconsoladamente.

37-38Absalón, en su huida, fue a refugiarse con Talmay hijo de Amiud, rey de Guesur, y allí se quedó tres años. David, por su parte, lloraba todos los días por su hijo Amnón, 39y cuando se consoló por su muerte, comenzó a sentir grandes deseos de ver a Absalón.

Absalón regresa a Jerusalén

14 Joab hijo de Sarvia se dio cuenta de que el rey extrañaba mucho a Absalón. 2Por eso mandó traer a una mujer muy astuta, la cual vivía en Tecoa, y le dijo:

—Quiero que te vistas de luto, y que no te eches perfume, sino que finjas estar de duelo, como si llevaras mucho tiempo llorando la muerte de alguien.

3Luego Joab le ordenó presentarse ante el rey, explicándole antes lo que tenía que decirle. 4Cuando aquella mujer de Tecoa se presentó ante el rey,j le hizo una reverencia y se postró rostro en tierra.

—¡Ayúdeme, Su Majestad! —exclamó.

5—¿Qué te pasa? —le preguntó el rey.

—Soy una pobre viuda —respondió ella—; mi esposo ha muerto. 6Esta servidora de Su Majestad tenía dos hijos, los cuales se pusieron a pelear en el campo. Como no había nadie que los separara, uno de ellos le asestó un golpe al otro y lo mató. 7Pero ahora resulta que toda la familia se ha puesto en contra de esta servidora de Su Majestad. Me exigen que entregue al asesino para que lo maten, y así vengar la muerte de su hermano, aunque al hacerlo eliminen al heredero. La verdad es que de esa manera apagarían la última luz de esperanza que me queda, y dejarían a mi esposo sin *nombre ni descendencia sobre la tierra.

8—Regresa a tu casa, que yo me encargaré de este asunto —respondió el rey.

9Pero la mujer de Tecoa replicó:

---

g 13:18 de mangas largas. Frase de difícil traducción. Véase Gn 37:3.   h 13:28 se le haya subido el vino. Lit. se le alegre el corazón por el vino.   i 13:34 Entonces fue ... monte (LXX); TM no incluye esta oración.   j 14:4 se presentó ante el rey (muchos mss. hebreos, LXX, Vulgata y Siríaca); le habló al rey (TM).

—Su Majestad, que la culpa caiga sobre mí y sobre mi familia, y no sobre el rey ni su trono.

10—Si alguien te amenaza —insistió el rey—, tráemelo para que no vuelva a molestarte.

11Entonces ella le suplicó:

—¡Ruego a Su Majestad invocar al SEÑOR su Dios, para que quien deba vengar la muerte de mi hijo no aumente mi desgracia matando a mi otro hijo!

—¡Tan cierto como que el SEÑOR vive —respondió el rey—, juro que tu hijo no perderá ni un solo cabello!

12Pero la mujer siguió diciendo:

—Permita Su Majestad a esta servidora suya decir algo más.

—Habla.

13—¿Cómo es que Su Majestad intenta hacer lo mismo contra el pueblo de Dios? Al prometerme usted estas cosas, se declara culpable, pues no deja regresar a su hijo desterrado. 14Así como el agua que se derrama en tierra no se puede recoger, así también todos tenemos que morir. Pero Dios no nos arrebata la *vida, sino que provee los medios para que el desterrado no siga separado de él para siempre.

15»Yo he venido a hablar con Su Majestad porque hay gente que me ha infundido temor. He pensado: "Voy a hablarle al rey; tal vez me conceda lo que le pida, 16librándonos a mí y a mi hijo de quien quiere eliminarnos, para quedarse con la heredad que Dios nos ha dado."

17»Pensé, además, que su palabra me traería alivio, pues Su Majestad es como un ángel de Dios, que sabe distinguir entre lo bueno y lo malo. ¡Que el SEÑOR su Dios lo bendiga!

18Al llegar a este punto, el rey le dijo a la mujer:

—Voy a hacerte una pregunta, y te pido que no me ocultes nada.

—Dígame usted.

19—¿Acaso no está Joab detrás de todo esto?

La mujer respondió:

—Juro por la vida de Su Majestad que su pregunta ha dado en el blanco.k En efecto, fue su siervo Joab quien me instruyó y puso en mis labios todo lo que he dicho. 20Lo hizo para disimular el asunto,l pero Su Majestad tiene la sabiduría de un ángel de Dios, y sabe todo lo que sucede en el país.

21Entonces el rey llamó a Joab y le dijo:

—Estoy de acuerdo. Anda, haz que regrese el joven Absalón.

22Postrándose rostro en tierra, Joab le hizo una reverencia al rey y le dio las gracias, añadiendo:

—Hoy sé que cuento con el favor de mi señor y rey, pues usted ha accedido a mi petición.

23Dicho esto, Joab emprendió la marcha a Guesur, y regresó a Jerusalén con Absalón. 24Pero el rey dio esta orden: «Que se retire a su casa, y que nunca me visite.» Por tanto, Absalón tuvo que irse a su casa sin presentarse ante el rey.

25En todo Israel no había ningún hombre tan admirado como Absalón por su hermosura; era perfecto de pies a cabeza. 26Tenía una cabellera tan pesada que una vez al año tenía que cortársela; y según la medida oficial, el pelo cortado pesaba dos kilos.m 27Además, tuvo tres hijos y una hija. Su hija, que se llamaba Tamar, llegó a ser una mujer muy hermosa.

28Absalón vivió en Jerusalén durante dos años sin presentarse ante el rey. 29Un día, le pidió a Joab que fuera a ver al rey, pero Joab no quiso ir. Se lo volvió a pedir, pero Joab se negó a hacerlo. 30Así que Absalón dio esta orden a sus criados: «Miren, Joab ha sembrado cebada en el campo que tiene junto al mío. ¡Vayan y préndanle fuego!»

Los criados fueron e incendiaron el campo de Joab. 31Entonces éste fue en seguida a casa de Absalón y le reclamó:

—¿Por qué tus criados le han prendido fuego a mi campo?

32Y Absalón le respondió:

—Te pedí que fueras a ver al rey y le preguntaras para qué he vuelto de Guesur. ¡Más me habría valido quedarme allá! Voy a presentarme ante el rey, y si soy culpable de algo, ¡que me mate!

33Joab fue a comunicárselo al rey; éste, por su parte, mandó llamar a Absalón, el cual se presentó ante el rey y, postrándose rostro en tierra, le hizo una reverencia. A su vez, el rey recibió a Absalón con un beso.

Absalón conspira contra David

15 Pasado algún tiempo, Absalón consiguió carros de combate, algunos caballos y una escolta de cincuenta soldados. 2Se levantaba temprano y se ponía a la vera del camino, junto a la *entrada de la ciudad. Cuando pasaba alguien que iba a ver al rey para que le resolviera un pleito, Absalón lo llamaba y le preguntaba de qué pueblo venía. Aquél le decía de qué tribu israelita era, 3y Absalón le aseguraba: «Tu demanda es muy justa, pero no habrá quien te escuche de parte del rey.» 4En seguida añadía: «¡Ojalá me pusieran por juez en el país! Todo el que tuviera un pleito o una demanda vendría a mí, y yo le haría justicia.»

5Además de esto, si alguien se le acercaba para inclinarse ante él, Absalón le tendía los brazos, lo abrazaba y lo saludaba con un beso. 6Esto hacía Absalón con todos los israelitas que iban a ver al rey para que les resolviera algún asunto, y así fue ganándose el cariño del pueblo.

7Al cabo de cuatron años, Absalón le dijo al rey:

—Permítame Su Majestad ir a Hebrón, a cumplir un voto que le hice al SEÑOR. 8Cuando vivía en Guesur de *Aram, hice este voto: "Si el SEÑOR me concede volver a Jerusalén, le ofreceré un sacrificio."

9—Vete tranquilo —respondió el rey.

Absalón emprendió la marcha a Hebrón, 10pero al mismo tiempo envió mensajeros por todas las tribus de Israel con este mensaje: «Tan pronto como oigan el toque de trompeta, exclamen: "¡Absalón reina en Hebrón!"» 11Además, desde Jerusalén llevó Absalón a doscientos invitados, los cuales lo acompañaron de buena fe y sin sospechar nada. 12Luego, mientras celebraba los sacrificios, Absalón mandó llamar a un consejero de su padre David, el cual se llamaba Ajitofel y era del pueblo de Guiló. Así la conspiración fue tomando fuerza, y el número de los que seguían a Absalón crecía más y más.

13Un mensajero le llevó a David esta noticia: «Todos los israelitas se han puesto de parte de Absalón.»

14Entonces David les dijo a todos los oficiales que estaban con él en Jerusalén:

—¡Vámonos de aquí! Tenemos que huir, pues de otro modo no podremos escapar de Absalón. Démonos prisa, no sea que él se nos adelante. Si nos al-

---

k **14:19** *su pregunta ha dado en el blanco.* Lit. *nadie va a la derecha o a la izquierda de todo lo que mi señor el rey ha dicho.*
l **14:20** *para disimular el asunto.* Alt. *con el propósito de cambiar la situación.*　m **14:26** *dos kilos.* Lit. *doscientos *siclos.*
n **15:7** *cuatro* (Siríaca, Josefo y mss. de LXX); *cuarenta* (TM).

canza, nos traerá la ruina y pasará a toda la gente a filo de espada.

15—Como diga Su Majestad —respondieron los oficiales—; nosotros estamos para servirle.

16De inmediato partió el rey acompañado de toda la corte, con excepción de diez concubinas que dejó para cuidar el palacio. 17Habiendo salido del palacio con todo su séquito, se detuvo junto a la casa más lejana de la ciudad. 18Todos sus oficiales se pusieron a su lado. Entonces los quereteos y los peleteos, y seiscientos guititas que lo habían seguido desde Gat, desfilaron ante el rey.

19El rey se dirigió a Itay el guitita:

—¿Y tú por qué vienes con nosotros? Regresa y quédate con el rey Absalón, ya que eres extranjero y has sido desterrado de tu propio país. 20¿Cómo voy a dejar que nos acompañes, si acabas de llegar y ni yo mismo sé a dónde vamos? Regresa y llévate a tus paisanos. ¡Y que el amor y la fidelidad de Dios te acompañen!

21Pero Itay le respondió al rey:

—¡Tan cierto como que vive el SEÑOR y Su Majestad viven, juro que, para vida o para muerte, iré adondequiera que usted vaya!

22—Está bien —contestó el rey—, ven con nosotros.

Así que Itay el guitita marchó con todos los hombres de David y con las familias que lo acompañaban. 23Todo el pueblo lloraba a gritos mientras David pasaba con su gente, y cuando el rey cruzó el arroyo de Cedrón, toda la gente comenzó la marcha hacia el desierto. 24Entre ellos se encontraba también Sadoc, con los levitas que llevaban el arca del *pacto de Dios. Éstos hicieron descansar el arca en el suelo, y Abiatar ofreció sacrificiosñ hasta que toda la gente terminó de salir de la ciudad. 25Luego le dijo el rey al sacerdote Sadoc:

—Devuelve el arca de Dios a la ciudad. Si cuento con el favor del SEÑOR, él hará que yo regrese y vuelva a ver el arca y el lugar donde él reside. 26Pero si el SEÑOR me hace saber que no le agrado, quedo a su merced y puede hacer conmigo lo que mejor le parezca.

27También le dijo:

—Como tú eres vidente, puedes volver tranquilo a la ciudad con Abiatar, y llevarte contigo a tu hijo Ajimaz y a Jonatán hijo de Abiatar. 28Yo me quedaré en los llanos del desierto hasta que ustedes me informen de la situación.

29Entonces Sadoc y Abiatar volvieron a Jerusalén con el arca de Dios, y allí se quedaron. 30David, por su parte, subió al monte de los Olivos llorando, con la cabeza cubierta y los pies descalzos. También todos los que lo acompañaban se cubrieron la cabeza y subieron llorando. 31En eso le informaron a David que Ajitofel se había unido a la conspiración de Absalón. Entonces David oró: «SEÑOR, haz que fracasen los planes de Ajitofel.»

32Cuando David llegó a la cumbre del monte, donde se rendía culto a Dios, se encontró con Husay el arquita, que en señal de duelo llevaba las vestiduras rasgadas y la cabeza cubierta de ceniza. 33David le dijo:

—Si vienes conmigo, vas a serme una carga. 34Es mejor que regreses a la ciudad y le digas a Absalón: "Majestad, estoy a su servicio. Antes fui siervo de su padre, pero ahora lo soy de usted." De ese modo podrás ayudarme a desbaratar los planes de Ajitofel. 35Allí contarás con los sacerdotes Sadoc y Abiatar, así

que manténlos informados de todo lo que escuches en el palacio real. 36También contarás con Ajimaz hijo de Sadoc y con Jonatán hijo de Abiatar; comuníquenme ustedes por medio de ellos cualquier cosa que averigüen.

37Husay, que era amigo de David, llegó a Jerusalén en el momento en que Absalón entraba en la ciudad.

David y Siba

16 Un poco más allá de la cumbre del monte, David se encontró con Siba, el criado de Mefiboset, que llevaba un par de asnos aparejados y cargados con doscientos panes, cien tortas de uvas pasas, cien tortas de higos y un odre de vino.

2—¿Qué vas a hacer con todo esto? —le preguntó el rey.

Siba respondió:

—Los asnos son para que monte la familia de Su Majestad, el pan y la fruta son para que coman los soldados, y el vino es para que beban los que desfallezcan en el desierto.

3Entonces el rey le preguntó:

—¿Dónde está el nieto de tu amo?

—Se quedó en Jerusalén —respondió Siba—. Él se imagina que ahora la nación de Israel le va a devolver el reino de su abuelo.

4—Bueno —replicó el rey—, todo lo que antes fue de Mefiboset ahora es tuyo.

—¡A sus pies, mi señor y rey! —exclamó Siba—. ¡Que cuente yo siempre con el favor de Su Majestad!

Simí maldice a David

5Cuando el rey David llegó a Bajurín, salía de allí un hombre de la familia de Saúl, llamado Simí hijo de Guerá. Éste se puso a maldecir, 6y a tirarles piedras a David y a todos sus oficiales, a pesar de que las tropas y la guardia real rodeaban al rey. 7En sus insultos, Simí le decía al rey:

—¡Largo de aquí! ¡Asesino! ¡Canalla! 8El SEÑOR te está dando tu merecido por haber masacrado a la familia de Saúl para reinar en su lugar. Por eso el SEÑOR le ha entregado el reino a tu hijo Absalón. Has caído en desgracia, porque eres un asesino.

9Abisay hijo de Sarvia le dijo al rey:

—¿Cómo se atreve este *perro muerto a maldecir a Su Majestad? ¡Déjeme que vaya y le corte la cabeza!

10Pero el rey respondió:

—Esto no es asunto mío ni de ustedes, hijos de Sarvia. A lo mejor el SEÑOR le ha ordenado que me maldiga y, si es así, ¿quién se lo puede reclamar?

11Dirigiéndose a Abisay y a todos sus oficiales, David añadió:

—Si el hijo de mis entrañas intenta quitarme la *vida, ¡qué no puedo esperar de este benjaminita! Déjenlo que me maldiga, pues el SEÑOR se lo ha mandado. 12A lo mejor el SEÑOR toma en cuenta mi aflicción y me paga con bendiciones las maldiciones que estoy recibiendo.

13David y sus hombres reanudaron el viaje. Simí, por su parte, les seguía por la ladera del monte, maldiciendo a David, tirándole piedras y levantando polvo. 14El rey y quienes lo acompañaban llegaron agotados a su destino, así que descansaron allí.

El consejo de Husay y Ajitofel

15Mientras tanto, Absalón y todos los israelitas que lo seguían habían entrado en Jerusalén; también

---

ñ **15:24** *ofreció sacrificios.* Alt. *subió.*

Ajitofel lo acompañaba. 16Entonces Husay el arquita, amigo de David, fue a ver a Absalón y exclamó:

—¡Viva el rey! ¡Viva el rey!

17Absalón le preguntó:

—¿Así muestras tu lealtad a tu amigo? ¿Cómo es que no te fuiste con él?

18—De ningún modo —respondió Husay—. Soy más bien amigo del elegido del SEÑOR, elegido también por este pueblo y por todos los israelitas. Así que yo me quedo con usted. 19Además, ¿a quién voy a servir? Serviré al hijo, como antes serví al padre.

20Luego le dijo Absalón a Ajitofel:

—Pónganse a pensar en lo que debemos hacer.

21Ajitofel le respondió:

—Acuéstese usted con las concubinas que su padre dejó al cuidado del palacio. De ese modo todos los israelitas se darán cuenta de que Su Majestad ha roto con su padre, y quienes lo apoyan a usted se fortalecerán en el poder.

22Entonces instalaron una tienda de campaña en la azotea para que Absalón se acostara con las concubinas de su padre a la vista de todos los israelitas. 23En aquella época, recibir el consejo de Ajitofel era como oír la palabra misma de Dios, y esto era así tanto para David como para Absalón.

17 Además, Ajitofel le propuso a Absalón lo siguiente:

—Yo escogería doce mil soldados, y esta misma noche saldría en busca de David. 2Como él debe de estar cansado y sin ánimo, lo atacaría, le haría sentir mucho miedo y pondría en fuga al resto de la gente que está con él. Pero mataría solamente al rey, 3y los demás se los traería a Su Majestad. La muerte del hombre que usted busca dará por resultado el regreso de los otros,o y todo el pueblo quedará en *paz.

4La propuesta le pareció acertada a Absalón, lo mismo que a todos los *ancianos de Israel, 5pero Absalón dijo:

—Llamemos también a Husay el arquita, para ver cuál es su opinión.

6Cuando Husay llegó, Absalón le preguntó:

—¿Debemos adoptar el plan que Ajitofel nos ha propuesto? Si no, ¿qué propones tú?

7—Esta vez el plan de Ajitofel no es bueno —respondió Husay—. 8Usted conoce bien a su padre David y a sus soldados: son valientes, y deben estar furiosos como una osa salvaje a la que le han robado su cría. Además, su padre tiene mucha experiencia como hombre de guerra y no ha de pasar la noche con las tropas. 9Ya debe de estar escondido en alguna cueva o en otro lugar. Si él ataca primero,p cualquiera que se entere dirá: "Ha habido una matanza entre las tropas de Absalón." 10Entonces aun los soldados más valientes, que son tan bravos como un león, se van a acobardar, pues todos los israelitas saben que David, su padre, es un gran soldado y cuenta con hombres muy valientes.

11»El plan que yo propongo es el siguiente: Convoque Su Majestad a todos los israelitas que hay, desde Dan hasta Berseba. Son tan numerosos como la arena a la orilla del mar, y Su Majestad mismo debe dirigirlos en la batalla. 12Atacaremos a David, no importa dónde se encuentre; caeremos sobre él como el rocío que cae sobre la tierra. No quedarán vivos ni él ni ninguno de sus soldados. 13Y si llega a re-

fugiarse en algún pueblo, todos los israelitas llevaremos sogas a ese lugar, y juntos arrastraremos a ese pueblo hasta el arroyo, de modo que no quede allí ni una piedra.

14Absalón y todos los israelitas dijeron:

—El plan de Husay el arquita es mejor que el de Ajitofel.

Esto sucedió porque el SEÑOR había determinado hacer fracasar el consejo de Ajitofel, aunque era el más acertado, y de ese modo llevar a Absalón a la ruina.

15Entonces Husay les dijo a los sacerdotes Sadoc y Abiatar:

—Ajitofel les propuso tal y tal plan a Absalón y a los ancianos de Israel, pero yo les propuse este otro. 16Dense prisa y mándenle este mensaje a David: "No pase Su Majestad la noche en los llanos del desierto; más bien, cruce de inmediato al otro lado, no vaya a ser que Su Majestad y quienes lo acompañan sean aniquilados."

17Jonatán y Ajimaz se habían quedado en Enroguel. Como no se podían arriesgar a que los vieran entrar en la ciudad, una criada estaba encargada de darles la información para que ellos se la pasaran al rey David. 18Sin embargo, un joven los vio y se lo hizo saber a Absalón, así que ellos se fueron de allí en seguida. Cuando llegaron a la casa de cierto hombre en Bajurín, se metieron en un pozo que él tenía en el patio. 19La esposa de aquel hombre cubrió el pozo y esparció trigo sobre la tapa. De esto nadie se enteró. 20Al pasar los soldados de Absalón por la casa, le preguntaron a la mujer:

—¿Dónde están Jonatán y Ajimaz?

—Cruzaron el ríoq —respondió ella.

Los soldados salieron en busca de ellos, pero como no pudieron encontrarlos, regresaron a Jerusalén. 21Después de que los soldados se fueron, Jonatán y Ajimaz salieron del pozo y se dirigieron adonde estaba David para ponerlo sobre aviso. Le dijeron:

—Crucen el río a toda prisa, pues Ajitofel ha aconsejado que los ataquen.

22Por tanto, David y quienes lo acompañaban se fueron y cruzaron el Jordán antes de que amaneciera. Todos sin excepción lo cruzaron. 23Ajitofel, por su parte, al ver que Absalón no había seguido su consejo, aparejó el asno y se fue a su pueblo. Cuando llegó a su casa, luego de arreglar sus asuntos, fue y se ahorcó. Así murió, y fue enterrado en la tumba de su padre.

24David se dirigió a Majanayin, y Absalón lo siguió, cruzando el Jordán con todos los israelitas. 25Ahora bien, en lugar de Joab, Absalón había nombrado general de su ejército a Amasá, que era hijo de un hombre llamado Ítrá,r el cual era ismaelitas y se había casado con Abigaíl, hija de Najás y hermana de Sarvia, la madre de Joab. 26Los israelitas que estaban con Absalón acamparon en el territorio de Galaad.

27Cuando David llegó a Majanayin, allí estaban Sobí hijo de Najás, oriundo de Rabá, ciudad amonita; Maquir hijo de Amiel, que era de Lo Debar; y Barzilay el galaadita, habitante de Roguelín. 28Éstos habían llevado camas, vasijas y ollas de barro, y también trigo, cebada, harina, grano tostado, habas, lentejas,t 29miel, cuajada, queso de vaca y ovejas. Les ofrecieron esos alimentos a David y a su comitiva para que se los co-

---

o 17:3 *La muerte ... los otros.* Texto de difícil traducción. p 17:9 *Si él ataca primero.* Alt. *Cuando algunos de los hombres caigan en el primer ataque.* q 17:20 *Cruzaron el río.* Alt. *Pasaron por el redil hacia el agua.* r 17:25 *Itrá.* También llamado *Jeter* (véase 1Cr 2:17). s 17:25 *ismaelita* (mss. de LXX; véase 1Cr 2:17); *israelita* (TM). t 17:28 *lentejas* (LXX y Siríaca); *lentejas y grano tostado* (TM).

mieran, pues pensaban que en el desierto esta gente habría pasado hambre y sed, y estaría muy cansada.

Muerte de Absalón

18 David pasó revista a sus tropas y nombró jefes sobre grupos de mil y de cien soldados. ²Los dividió en tres unidades y los envió a la batalla. La primera unidad estaba bajo el mando de Joab, la segunda bajo el mando de Abisay, hijo de Sarvia y hermano de Joab, y la tercera bajo el mando de Itay el guitita.

—Yo los voy a acompañar —dijo el rey.

³Pero los soldados respondieron:

—No, Su Majestad no debe acompañarnos. Si tenemos que huir, el enemigo no se va a ocupar de nosotros. Y aun si la mitad de nosotros muere, a ellos no les va a importar. ¡Pero Su Majestad vale por diez mil de nosotros!ᵘ Así que es mejor que se quede y nos apoye desde la ciudad.

⁴—Bien —dijo el rey—, haré lo que les parezca más conveniente.

Dicho esto, se puso a un lado de la *entrada de la ciudad, mientras todos los soldados marchaban en grupos de cien y de mil. ⁵Además, el rey dio esta orden a Joab, Abisay e Itay:

—No me traten duro al joven Absalón.

Y todas las tropas oyeron las instrucciones que el rey le dio a cada uno de sus generales acerca de Absalón.

⁶El ejército marchó al campo para pelear contra Israel, y la batalla se libró en el bosque de Efraín. ⁷La lucha fue intensa aquel día: hubo veinte mil bajas. Sin embargo, los soldados de David derrotaron allí al ejército de Israel. ⁸La batalla se extendió por toda el área, de modo que el bosque causó más muertes que la espada misma.

⁹Absalón, que huía montado en una mula, se encontró con los soldados de David. La mula se metió por debajo de una gran encina, y a Absalón se le trabó la cabeza entre las ramas. Como la mula siguió de largo, Absalón quedó colgado en el aire. ¹⁰Un soldado que vio lo sucedido le dijo a Joab:

—Acabo de ver a Absalón colgado de una encina.

¹¹—¡Cómo! —exclamó Joab—. ¿Lo viste y no lo mataste ahí mismo? Te habría dado diez monedas de plataᵛ y un cinturón.

¹²Pero el hombre respondió:

—Aun si recibiera mil monedas, yo no alzaría la mano contra el hijo del rey. Todos oímos cuando el rey les ordenó a usted, a Abisay y a Itay que no le hicieran daño al joven Absalón. ¹³Si yo me hubiera arriesgado,ʷ me habrían descubierto, pues nada se le escapa al rey; y usted, por su parte, me habría abandonado.

¹⁴—No voy a malgastar mi tiempo contigo —replicó Joab.

Acto seguido, agarró tres lanzas y fue y se las clavó en el pecho a Absalón, que todavía estaba vivo en medio de la encina. ¹⁵Luego, diez de los escuderos de Joab rodearon a Absalón y lo remataron.

¹⁶Entonces Joab mandó tocar la trompeta para detener a las tropas, y dejaron de perseguir a los israelitas. ¹⁷Después tomaron el cuerpo de Absalón, lo tiraron en un hoyo grande que había en el bosque, y sobre su cadáver amontonaron muchísimas piedras. Mientras tanto, todos los israelitas huyeron a sus hogares.

¹⁸En vida, Absalón se había erigido una *estela en el valle del Rey, pues pensaba: «No tengo ningún hijo que conserve mi memoria.» Así que a esa estela le puso su propio *nombre, y por eso hasta la fecha se conoce como la Estela de Absalón.

David hace duelo

¹⁹Ajimaz hijo de Sadoc le propuso a Joab:

—Déjame ir corriendo para avisarle al rey que el SEÑOR lo ha librado del poder de sus enemigos.

²⁰—No le llevarás esta noticia hoy —le respondió Joab—. Podrás hacerlo en otra ocasión, pero no hoy, pues ha muerto el hijo del rey.

²¹Entonces Joab se dirigió a un soldado *cusita y le ordenó:

—Ve tú y dile al rey lo que has visto.

El cusita se inclinó ante Joab y salió corriendo. ²²Pero Ajimaz hijo de Sadoc insistió:

—Pase lo que pase, déjame correr con el cusita.

—Pero muchacho —respondió Joab—, ¿para qué quieres ir? ¡Ni pienses que te van a dar una recompensa por la noticia!

²³—Pase lo que pase, quiero ir.

—Anda, pues.

Ajimaz salió corriendo por la llanura y se adelantó al cusita. ²⁴Mientras tanto, David se hallaba sentado en el pasadizo que está entre las dos *puertas de la ciudad. El centinela, que había subido al muro de la puerta, alzó la vista y vio a un hombre que corría comentó:

—Si viene solo, debe de traer buenas noticias.

Pero mientras el hombre seguía corriendo y se acercaba, ²⁶el centinela se dio cuenta de que otro hombre corría detrás de él, así que le anunció al guarda de la puerta:

—¡Por ahí viene otro hombre corriendo solo!

—Ése también debe de traer buenas noticias —dijo el rey.

²⁷El centinela añadió:

—Me parece que el primero corre como Ajimaz hijo de Sadoc.

—Es un buen hombre —comentó el rey—; seguro que trae buenas noticias.

²⁸Ajimaz llegó y saludó al rey postrándose rostro en tierra, y le dijo:

—¡Bendito sea el SEÑOR, Dios de Su Majestad, pues nos ha entregado a los que se habían rebelado en contra suya!

²⁹—¿Y está bien el joven Absalón? —preguntó el rey.

Ajimaz respondió:

—En el momento en que tu siervo Joab me enviaba, vi que se armó un gran alboroto, pero no pude saber lo que pasaba.

³⁰—Pasa y quédate ahí —le dijo el rey.

Ajimaz se hizo a un lado. ³¹Entonces llegó el cusita y anunció:

—Le traigo buenas noticias a Su Majestad. El SEÑOR lo ha librado hoy de todos los que se habían rebelado en contra suya.

³²—¿Y está bien el joven Absalón? —preguntó el rey. El cusita contestó:

—¡Que sufran como ese joven los enemigos de Su Majestad, y todos los que intentan hacerle mal!

³³Al oír esto, el rey se estremeció; y mientras subía al cuarto que está encima de la puerta, lloraba y

---

ᵘ **18:3** *Su Majestad vale por diez mil de nosotros* (dos mss. hebreos; véanse también LXX y Vulgata); *ahora hay diez mil como nosotros* (TM).   ᵛ **18:11** *diez monedas de plata*. Lit. *diez* { *siclos* } *de plata*.   ʷ **18:13** *me hubiera arriesgado*. Alt. *lo hubiera traicionado*.

decía: «¡Ay, Absalón, hijo mío! ¡Hijo mío, Absalón, hijo mío! ¡Ojalá hubiera muerto yo en tu lugar! ¡Ay, Absalón, hijo mío, hijo mío!»

19 Avisaron a Joab que el rey estaba llorando amargamente por Absalón. 2Cuando las tropas se enteraron de que el rey estaba afligido por causa de su hijo, la victoria de aquel día se convirtió en duelo para todo el ejército. 3Por eso las tropas entraron en la ciudad furtivamente, como lo hace un ejército abochornado por haber huido del combate. 4Pero el rey, cubriéndose la cara, seguía gritando a voz en cuello: «¡Ay, Absalón, hijo mío! ¡Ay, Absalón, hijo mío, hijo mío!»

5Entonces Joab fue adonde estaba el rey y le dijo: «Hoy Su Majestad ha llenado de vergüenza a todos sus siervos que le salvaron la *vida, y la de sus hijos e hijas y esposas y concubinas. 6¡Usted ama a quienes lo odian, y odia a quienes lo aman! Hoy ha dejado muy en claro que nada le importan sus generales ni sus soldados. Ahora me doy cuenta de que usted preferiría que todos nosotros estuviéramos muertos, con tal de que Absalón siguiera con vida. 7¡Vamos! ¡Salga usted y anime a sus tropas! Si no lo hace, juro por el SEÑOR que para esta noche ni un solo soldado se quedará con usted. ¡Y eso sería peor que todas las calamidades que Su Majestad ha sufrido desde su juventud hasta ahora!»

8Ante esto, el rey se levantó y fue a sentarse junto a la puerta de la ciudad. Cuando los soldados lo supieron, fueron todos a presentarse ante él.

David regresa a Jerusalén

Los israelitas, mientras tanto, habían huido a sus hogares, 9y por todas las tribus de Israel se hablaba de la situación. Decían: «El rey nos rescató del poder de nuestros enemigos; él nos libró del dominio de los filisteos. Por causa de Absalón tuvo que huir del país. 10Pero ahora Absalón, al que habíamos ungido como rey, ha muerto en la batalla. ¿Qué nos impide pedirle al rey que vuelva?»

11Entonces el rey David mandó este mensaje a los sacerdotes Sadoc y Abiatar: «Hablen con los *ancianos de Judá y díganles: "El rey se ha enterado de lo que se habla por todo Israel. ¿Serán ustedes los últimos en pedirme a mí, el rey, que regrese a mi palacio? 12Ustedes son mis hermanos, ¡son de mi propia sangre! ¿Por qué han de ser los últimos en llamarme?" 13Díganle también a Amasá: "¿Acaso no eres de mi propia sangre? Tú serás de por vida el general de mi ejército, en lugar de Joab. ¡Que Dios me castigue sin piedad si no lo cumplo!" »

14Así el rey se ganó el aprecio de todos los de Judá, quienes a una voz le pidieron que regresara con todas sus tropas, 15de modo que el rey emprendió el viaje y llegó hasta el Jordán. Los de Judá se dirigieron entonces a Guilgal para encontrarse con el rey y acompañarlo a cruzar el río. 16Pero el benjaminita Simí hijo de Guerá, oriundo de Bajurín, se apresuró a bajar con los de Judá para recibir al rey David. 17Con él iban mil benjaminitas, e incluso Siba, que había sido administrador de la familia de Saúl, con sus quince hijos y veinte criados. Éstos llegaron al Jordán antes que el rey 18y vadearon el río para ponerse a las órdenes del rey y ayudar a la familia real a cruzar el Jordán. Cuando el rey estaba por cruzarlo, Simí hijo de Guerá se inclinó ante él 19y le dijo:

—Ruego a mi señor el rey que no tome en cuenta mi delito ni recuerde el mal que hizo este servidor suyo el día en que Su Majestad salió de Jerusalén. Le ruego a Su Majestad que olvide eso. 20Reconozco que he pecado, y por eso hoy, de toda la tribu de José, he sido el primero en salir a recibir a mi señor el rey.

21Pero Abisay hijo de Sarvia exclamó:

—¡Simí maldijo al *ungido del SEÑOR, y merece la muerte!

22David respondió:

—Hijos de Sarvia, esto no es asunto de ustedes, sino mío. Están actuando como si fueran mis adversarios. ¿Cómo va a morir hoy alguien del pueblo, cuando precisamente en este día vuelvo a ser rey de Israel?

23Y dirigiéndose a Simí, el rey le juró:

—¡No morirás!

24También Mefiboset, el nieto de Saúl, salió a recibir al rey. No se había lavado los pies ni la ropa, ni se había recortado el bigote, desde el día en que el rey tuvo que irse hasta que regresó sano y salvo. 25Cuando llegó de Jerusalén para recibir al rey, éste le preguntó:

—Mefiboset, ¿por qué no viniste conmigo?

26—Mi señor y rey, como este servidor suyo es cojo, yo quería que me aparejaran un asno para montar y así poder acompañarlo. Pero mi criado Siba me traicionó, 27y ahora me ha calumniado ante Su Majestad. Sin embargo, Su Majestad es como un ángel de Dios y puede hacer conmigo lo que mejor le parezca. 28No hay nadie en mi familia paterna que no merezca la muerte en presencia de mi señor el rey. A pesar de eso, Su Majestad le concedió a este servidor suyo comer en la mesa real. ¿Qué derecho tengo de pedirle algo más a Su Majestad?

29El rey le dijo:

—No tienes que dar más explicaciones. Ya he decidido que tú y Siba se repartan las tierras.

30—Él puede quedarse con todo —le respondió Mefiboset—; a mí me basta con que mi señor el rey haya regresado a su palacio sano y salvo.

31También Barzilay el galaadita bajó al Jordán. Había viajado desde Roguelín para escoltar al rey cuando cruzara el río. 32Barzilay, que ya era un anciano de ochenta años, le había proporcionado al rey todo lo necesario durante su estadía en Majanayin, pues era muy rico. 33El rey le dijo:

—Acompáñame. Quédate conmigo en Jerusalén, y yo me encargaré de todo lo que necesites.

34—Pero ¿cuántos años de vida me quedan? —respondió Barzilay—. ¿Para qué subir con el rey a Jerusalén? 35Ya tengo ochenta años, y apenas puedo distinguir lo bueno de lo malo, o saborear lo que como y bebo, o aun apreciar las voces de los cantores y las cantoras. ¿Por qué ha de ser este servidor una carga más para mi señor el rey? 36¿Y por qué quiere Su Majestad recompensarme de este modo, cuando tan sólo voy a acompañarlo a cruzar el Jordán? 37Déjeme usted regresar a mi propio pueblo, para que pueda morir allí y ser enterrado en la tumba de mis padres. Pero aquí le dejo a Quimán para que sirva a Su Majestad y lo acompañe a cruzar el río. Haga usted por él lo que haría por mí.

38—Está bien —respondió el rey—, Quimán irá conmigo, y haré por él lo que me pides. Y a ti te daré todo lo que quieras.

39La gente y el rey cruzaron el Jordán. Luego el rey le dio un beso a Barzilay y lo bendijo, y Barzilay volvió a su pueblo. 40El rey, acompañado de Quimán y escoltado por las tropas de Judá y la mitad de las tropas de Israel, siguió hasta Guilgal. 41Por eso los israelitas fueron a ver al rey y le reclamaron: —¿Cómo es que nuestros hermanos de Judá se han adueñado del rey al cruzar el Jordán, y lo han escoltado a él, a su familia y a todas sus tropas?

42Los de Judá respondieron:

—¿Y a qué viene ese enojo? ¡El rey es nuestro pariente cercano! ¿Acaso hemos vivido a costillas del rey? ¿Acaso nos hemos aprovechado de algo?

⁴³Pero los israelitas insistieron:

—¿Por qué nos tratan con tanto desprecio? ¡Nosotros tenemos diez veces más derecho que ustedes sobre el rey David! Además, ¿no fuimos nosotros los primeros en pedirle que volviera?

Entonces los de Judá les contestaron aun con más severidad.

Sabá se rebela contra David

20 Por allí se encontraba un malvado que se llamaba Sabá hijo de Bicrí, que era benjaminita. Dando un toque de trompeta, se puso a gritar:

«¡Pueblo de Israel, todos a sus casas,
    pues no tenemos parte con David,
    ni herencia con el hijo de Isaí!»

²Entonces todos los israelitas abandonaron a David y siguieron a Sabá hijo de Bicrí. Los de Judá, por su parte, se mantuvieron fieles a su rey y lo acompañaron desde el Jordán hasta Jerusalén. ³Cuando el rey David llegó a su palacio en Jerusalén, sacó a las diez concubinas que había dejado a cargo del palacio y las puso bajo vigilancia. Siguió manteniéndolas, pero no volvió a acostarse con ellas. Hasta el día de su muerte, quedaron encerradas y viviendo como si fueran viudas.

⁴Luego el rey le ordenó a Amasá: «Moviliza a las tropas de Judá, y preséntate aquí con ellas dentro de tres días.» ⁵Amasá salió para movilizar a las tropas, pero no cumplió con el plazo. ⁶Por eso David le dijo a Abisay: «Ahora Sabá hijo de Bicrí va a perjudicarnos más que Absalón. Así que hazte cargo de la guardia real, y sal a perseguirlo, no sea que llegue a alguna ciudad fortificada y se nos escape.»ˣ ⁷Entonces los soldados de Joab, junto con los quereteos, los peleteos y todos los oficiales, bajo el mando de Abisay salieron de Jerusalén para perseguir a Sabá hijo de Bicrí.

⁸Al llegar a la gran roca que está en Gabaón, Amasá les salió al encuentro. Joab tenía su uniforme ajustado con un cinturón, y ceñida al muslo llevaba una daga envainada. Pero al caminar, la daga se le cayó. ⁹Con la mano derecha, Joab tomó a Amasá por la barba para besarlo, mientras le preguntaba: «¿Cómo estás, hermano?» ¹⁰Amasá no se percató de que en la otra mano Joab llevaba la daga, así que Joab se la clavó en el vientre, y las entrañas de Amasá se derramaron por el suelo. Amasá murió de una sola puñalada, y luego Joab y su hermano Abisay persiguieron a Sabá hijo de Bicrí.

¹¹Uno de los soldados de Joab, deteniéndose junto al cuerpo de Amasá, exclamó: «¡Todos los que estén a favor de Joab y que apoyen a David, sigan a Joab!» ¹²Como el cuerpo de Amasá, bañado en sangre, había quedado en medio del camino, todas las tropas que pasaban se detenían para verlo. Cuando aquel soldado se dio cuenta de esto, retiró el cuerpo hacia el campo y lo cubrió con un manto. ¹³Luego que Amasá fue apartado del camino, todas las tropas fueron con Joab a perseguir a Sabá hijo de Bicrí.

¹⁴Sabá recorrió todas las tribus de Israel, hasta llegar a Abel Betmacá, y allí todos los del clan de Bicríy se le unieron. ¹⁵Las tropas de Joab llegaron a la ciudad de Abel Betmacá y la sitiaron. Construyeron una rampa contra la fortificación para atacar la ciudad, y cuando los soldados comenzaban a derribar la muralla, ¹⁶una astuta mujer de la ciudad les gritó:

—¡Escúchenme! ¡Escúchenme! Dígale a Joab que venga acá para que yo pueda hablar con él.

¹⁷Joab se le acercó.

—¿Es usted Joab? —le preguntó la mujer.

—Así es.

Entonces la mujer le dijo:

—Ponga atención a las palabras de esta servidora suya.

—Te escucho —respondió Joab.

¹⁸Ella continuó:

—Antiguamente, cuando había alguna discusión, la gente resolvía el asunto con este dicho: "Vayan y pregunten en Abel." ¹⁹Nuestra ciudad es la más pacífica y fiel del país, y muy importante en Israel; usted, sin embargo, intenta arrasarla. ¿Por qué quiere destruir la heredad del SEÑOR?

²⁰—¡Que Dios me libre! —replicó Joab—. ¡Que Dios me libre de arrasarla y destruirla! ²¹Yo no he venido a eso, sino a capturar a un hombre llamado Sabá hijo de Bicrí. Es de la sierra de Efraín y se ha sublevado contra el rey David. Si me entregan a ese hombre, me retiro de la ciudad.

—Muy bien —respondió la mujer—. Desde la muralla arrojaremos su cabeza.

²²Y fue tal la astucia con que la mujer habló con todo el pueblo, que le cortaron la cabeza a Sabá hijo de Bicrí y se la arrojaron a Joab. Entonces Joab hizo tocar la trompeta, y todos los soldados se retiraron de la ciudad y regresaron a sus casas. Joab, por su parte, volvió a Jerusalén para ver al rey.

²³Joab era general en jefe del ejército de Israel; Benaías hijo de Joyadá estaba al mando de los quereteos y los peleteos; ²⁴Adonirán supervisaba el trabajo forzado; Josafat hijo de Ajilud era el secretario; ²⁵Seva era el cronista; Sadoc y Abiatar eran los sacerdotes; ²⁶Ira el yairita era sacerdote personal de David.

Los gabaonitas se vengan

21 Durante el reinado de David hubo tres años consecutivos de hambre. David le pidió ayuda al SEÑOR, y él le contestó: «Esto sucede porque Saúl y su sanguinaria familia asesinaron a los gabaonitas.»

²Los gabaonitas no pertenecían a la nación de Israel, sino que eran un remanente de los amorreos. Los israelitas habían hecho un pacto con ellos, pero tanto era el celo de Saúl por Israel y Judá que trató de exterminarlos. Entonces David convocó a los gabaonitas ³y les preguntó:

—¿Qué quieren que haga por ustedes? ¿Cómo puedo reparar el mal que se les ha hecho, de modo que bendigan al pueblo que es herencia del SEÑOR?

⁴Los gabaonitas respondieron:

—No nos interesa el dinero de Saúl y de su familia, ni tampoco queremos que muera alguien en Israel.

—Entonces, ¿qué desean que haga por ustedes? —volvió a preguntar el rey.

⁵—Saúl quiso destruirnos —contestaron ellos—; se propuso exterminarnos y nos expulsó de todo el territorio israelita. ⁶Por eso pedimos que se nos entreguen siete de los descendientes de Saúl, a quien el SEÑOR escogió, para colgarlos en presencia del SEÑOR en Guibeá de Saúl.

—Se los entregaré —les prometió el rey.

ˣ **20:6** *se nos escape.* Lit. *libre nuestro ojo.* ʸ **20:14** *todos los del clan de Bicrí* (véase LXX); *todos los beritas* (TM).

7Sin embargo, por el juramento que David y Jonatán se habían hecho en presencia del SEÑOR, el rey tuvo compasión de Mefiboset, que era hijo de Jonatán y nieto de Saúl. 8Pero mandó apresar a Armoní y a Mefiboset, los dos hijos que Rizpa hija de Ayá había tenido con Saúl, y a los cinco hijos que Merabz hija de Saúl había tenido con Adriel hijo de Barzilay, el mejolatita. 9David se los entregó a los gabaonitas, y ellos los colgaron en un monte, en presencia del SEÑOR. Los siete murieron juntos, ajusticiados en los primeros días de la siega, cuando se comenzaba a recoger la cebada.

10Rizpa hija de Ayá tomó un saco y lo tendió para acostarse sobre la peña, y allí se quedó desde el comienzo de la siega hasta que llegaron las lluvias. No permitía que las aves en el día ni las fieras en la noche tocaran los cadáveres. 11Cuando le contaron a David lo que había hecho Rizpa hija de Ayá y concubina de Saúl, 12fue a recoger los huesos de Saúl y de su hijo Jonatán, que estaban en Jabés de Galaad. Los filisteos los habían colgado en la plaza de Betsán el día en que derrotaron a Saúl en Guilboa, pero los habitantes de la ciudad se los habían robado de allí. 13Así que David hizo que los trasladaran a Jerusalén, y que recogieran también los huesos de los siete hombres que habían sido colgados. 14Así fue como los huesos de Saúl y de su hijo Jonatán fueron enterrados en la tumba de Quis, el padre de Saúl, que está en Zela de Benjamín. Todo se hizo en cumplimiento de las órdenes del rey, y después de eso Dios tuvo piedad del país.

Hazañas de los oficiales de David
21:15-22 — 1Cr 20:4-8

15Los filisteos reanudaron la guerra contra Israel, y David salió con sus oficiales para hacerles frente. Pero David se quedó agotado, 16así que intentó matarlo un gigantea llamado Isbibenob, que iba armado con una espada nueva y una lanza de bronce que pesaba más de tres kilos.b 17Sin embargo, Abisay hijo de Sarvia fue en su ayuda e hirió al filisteo y lo mató. Allí los soldados de David le hicieron este juramento: «Nunca más saldrá Su Majestad con nosotros a la batalla, no sea que alguien lo mate y se apague la lámpara de Israel.»

18Algún tiempo después hubo en Gob otra batalla con los filisteos, y en esa ocasión Sibecay el jusatita mató al gigante Saf. 19En una tercera batalla, que también se libró en Gob, Eljanán hijo de Yaré Oreguín, oriundo de Belén, mató a Goliatc el guitita, cuya lanza tenía un asta tan grande como el rodillo de un telar. 20Hubo una batalla más en Gat. Allí había otro gigante, un hombre altísimo que tenía veinticuatro dedos, seis en cada mano y seis en cada pie. 21Éste se puso a desafiar a los israelitas, pero Jonatán hijo de Simá, que era hermano de David, lo mató.

22Esos cuatro gigantes, que eran descendientes de Rafá el guitita, cayeron a manos de David y de sus oficiales.

Salmo de David
22:1-51 — Sal 18:1-50

22 David dedicó al SEÑOR la letra de esta canción cuando el SEÑOR lo libró de Saúl y de todos sus enemigos. 2Dijo así:

«El SEÑOR es mi *roca, mi amparo, mi
　　libertador;
3es mi Dios, el peñasco en que me refugio.
Es mi escudo, el poder que me salva,d
　　imi más alto escondite!
Él es mi protector y mi salvador.
　　¡Tú me salvaste de la violencia!
4Invoco al SEÑOR, que es digno de alabanza,
　　y quedo a salvo de mis enemigos.

5»Las olas de la muerte me envolvieron;
　　los torrentes destructores me abrumaron.
6Me enredaron los lazos del *sepulcro,
　　y me encontré ante las trampas de la
　　muerte.
7En mi angustia invoqué al SEÑOR;
　　llamé a mi Dios,
y él me escuchó desde su templo;
　　imi clamor llegó a sus oídos!

8»La tierra tembló, se estremeció;
　　se sacudieron los cimientos de los cielos;
　　ise tambalearon a causa de su enojo!
9Por la nariz echaba humo,
　　por la boca, fuego consumidor;
　　ilanzaba carbones encendidos!

10»Rasgando el cielo, descendió,
　　pisando sobre oscuros nubarrones.
11Montando sobre un *querubín, surcó los
　　cielos
　　y se remontóe sobre las alas del viento.
12De las tinieblas y de los cargados nubarrones
　　hizo pabellones que lo rodeaban.
13De su radiante presencia
　　brotaron carbones encendidos.

14»Desde el cielo se oyó el trueno del SEÑOR,
　　resonó la voz del *Altísimo.
15Lanzó flechas y centellas contra mis
　　enemigos;
　　los dispersó y los puso en fuga.
16A causa de la reprensión del SEÑOR,
　　y por el resoplido de su enojo,f
las cuencas del mar quedaron a la vista;
　　ial descubierto quedaron los cimientos de
　　la tierra!

17»Extendiendo su mano desde lo alto,
　　tomó la mía y me sacó del mar profundo.
18Me libró de mi enemigo poderoso,
　　de aquellos que me odiaban
　　y que eran más fuertes que yo.
19En el día de mi desgracia
　　me salieron al encuentro,
　　pero mi apoyo fue el SEÑOR.
20Me sacó a un amplio espacio;
　　me libró porque se agradó de mí.

21»El SEÑOR me ha pagado conforme a mi
　　*justicia,
　　me ha premiado conforme a la *limpieza
　　de mis manos;
22pues he andado en los *caminos del SEÑOR;
　　no he cometido mal alguno
　　ni me he apartado de mi Dios.
23Presentes tengo todas sus sentencias;

---

z 21:8 Merab (Targum, Siríaca y algunos mss. hebreos y griegos; véase 1S 19:19); Mical (TM). a 21:16 un gigante. Lit. uno de los descendientes de Refa (también en vv. 18 y 20, con cierta variación). b 21:16 más de tres kilos. Lit. trescientos *siclos. c 21:19 Goliat. Es decir, el hermano de Goliat (véase 1Cr 20:5). d 22:3 el poder que me salva. Lit. el cuerno de mi salvación. e 22:11 se remontó (mss. hebreos; véanse Siríaca, Targum, Vulgata, Sal 18:10); apareció (TM). f 22:16 por ... su enojo. Lit. por el soplo del aliento de su nariz.

no me he alejado de sus *decretos.
24He sido íntegro ante él
y me he abstenido de pecar.
25El SEÑOR me ha recompensado conforme a
mi justicia,
conforme a mi limpieza delante de él.

26»Tú eres fiel con quien es fiel,
e irreprochable con quien es irreprochable;
27sincero eres con quien es sincero,
pero sagaz con el que es tramposo.
28Das la *victoria a los humildes,
pero tu mirada humilla a los altaneros.
29Tú, SEÑOR, eres mi lámpara;
tú, SEÑOR, iluminas mis tinieblas.
30Con tu apoyo me lanzaré contra un ejército;
contigo, Dios mío, podré asaltar murallas.

31»El camino de Dios es *perfecto;
la palabra del SEÑOR es intachable.
Escudo es Dios a los que en él se refugian.
32¿Pues quién es Dios, si no el SEÑOR?
¿Quién es la roca, si no nuestro Dios?
33Es él quien me arma de valor
y endereza mi camino;
34da a mis pies la ligereza del venado,
y me mantiene firme en las alturas;
35adiestra mis manos para la batalla,
y mis brazos para tensar arcos de bronce.
36Tú me cubres con el escudo de tu *salvación;
tu bondad me ha hecho prosperar.
37Me has despejado el camino,
por eso mis tobillos no flaquean.

38»Perseguí a mis enemigos y los destruí;
no retrocedí hasta verlos aniquilados.
39Los aplasté por completo. Ya no se levantan.
¡Cayeron debajo de mis pies!
40Tú me armaste de valor para el combate;
bajo mi planta sometiste a los rebeldes.
41Hiciste retroceder a mis enemigos,
y así exterminé a los que me odiaban.
42Pedían ayuda; no hubo quien los salvara.
Al SEÑOR clamaron, pero no les respondió.
43Los desmenucé. Parecían el polvo de la tierra.
¡Los pisoteé como al lodo de las calles!

44»Me has librado de una turba amotinada;
me has puesto por encima de los *paganos;
me sirve gente que yo no conocía.
45Son extranjeros, y me rinden homenaje;
apenas me oyen, me obedecen.
46¡Esos extraños se descorazonan,
y temblando salen de sus refugios!
47¡El SEÑOR vive! ¡Alabada sea mi roca!
¡Exaltado sea Dios mi Salvador!
48Él es el Dios que me vindica,
el que pone los pueblos a mis pies.
49Tú me libras de mis enemigos,
me exaltas por encima de mis adversarios,
me salvas de los hombres violentos.
50Por eso, SEÑOR, te alabo entre las naciones
y canto salmos a tu *nombre.

51»El SEÑOR da grandes victorias a su rey;
a su *ungido David y a sus descendientes
les muestra por siempre su gran amor.»

Últimas palabras de David

23 Éstas son las últimas palabras de David:

«Oráculo de David hijo de Isaí,
dulce cantor de Israel;
hombre exaltado por el *Altísimo
y ungido por el Dios de Jacob.

2»El Espíritu del SEÑOR habló por medio de mí;
puso sus palabras en mi lengua.
3El Dios de Israel habló,
la Roca de Israel me dijo:
"El que gobierne a la gente con justicia,
el que gobierne en el temor de Dios,
4será como la luz de la aurora
en un amanecer sin nubes,
que tras la lluvia resplandece
para que brote la hierba en la tierra."

5»Dios ha establecido mi casa;
ha hecho conmigo un *pacto eterno,
bien reglamentado y seguro.
Dios hará que brote mi *salvación
y que se cumpla todo mi deseo.
6Pero los malvados son como espinos que se
desechan;
nadie los toca con la mano.
7Se recogen con un hierro o con una lanza,
y ahí el fuego los consume.»

Héroes en el ejército de David
23:8-39 — 1Cr 11:10-41

8Éstos son los nombres de los soldados más valientes de David:
Joseb Basébet el tacmonita, que era el principal
de los tres más famosos, en una batalla mató con su
lanzag a ochocientos hombres.
9En segundo lugar estaba Eleazar hijo de Dodó
el ajojita, que también era uno de los tres más famosos. Estuvo con David cuando desafiaron a los filisteos que se habían concentrado en Pasdamính para
la batalla. Los israelitas se retiraron, 10pero Eleazar
se mantuvo firme y derrotó a tantos filisteos que,
por la fatiga, la mano se le quedó pegada a la espada. Aquel día el SEÑOR les dio una gran *victoria.
Las tropas regresaron adonde estaba Eleazar, pero
sólo para tomar los despojos.
11El tercer valiente era Sama hijo de Agué el ararita. En cierta ocasión, los filisteos formaron sus tro-
pasi en un campo sembrado de lentejas. El ejército
de Israel huyó ante ellos, 12pero Sama se plantó en
medio del campo y lo defendió, derrotando a los filisteos. El SEÑOR les dio una gran victoria.
13En otra ocasión, tres de los treinta más valientes
fueron a la cueva de Adulán, donde estaba David. Era
el comienzo de la siega, y una tropa filistea acampaba
en el valle de Refayin. 14David se encontraba en su fortaleza, y en ese tiempo había una guarnición filistea en
Belén. 15Como David tenía mucha sed, exclamó: «¡Ojalá pudiera yo beber agua del pozo que está a la *entrada de Belén!» 16Entonces los tres valientes se metieron
en el campamento filisteo, sacaron agua del pozo de
Belén, y se la llevaron a David. Pero él no quiso beberla,
sino que derramó el agua en honor al SEÑOR 17y declaró solemnemente: «¡Que el SEÑOR me libre de beberla!
¡Eso sería como beberme la sangre de hombres que se
han jugado la *vida!» Y no quiso beberla.
Tales hazañas hicieron esos tres héroes.
18Abisay, el hermano de Joab hijo de Sarvia, estaba al mando de los tres y ganó fama entre ellos. En
cierta ocasión, lanza en mano atacó y mató a trescientos hombres. 19Se destacó más que los tres valientes, y
llegó a ser su jefe, pero no fue contado entre ellos.

g **23:8** mató con su lanza (mss. de LXX; véase 1Cr 11:11); *Adino el eznita mató* (TM). h **23:9** en Pasdamín (texto probable;
véase 1Cr 11:13); *allí* (TM). i **23:11** formaron sus tropas. Alt. *se concentraron en Lehí*.

20Benaías hijo de Joyadá era un guerrero de Cabsel que realizó muchas hazañas. Derrotó a dos de los mejores hombresj de Moab, y en otra ocasión, cuando estaba nevando, se metió en una cisterna y mató un león. 21También derrotó a un egipcio de gran estatura. El egipcio empuñaba una lanza, pero Benaías, que no llevaba más que un palo, le arrebató la lanza y lo mató con ella. 22Tales hazañas hizo Benaías hijo de Joyadá, y también él ganó fama como los tres valientes, 23pero no fue contado entre ellos, aunque se destacó más que los treinta valientes. Además, David lo puso al mando de su guardia personal.

24Entre los treinta valientes estaban:
Asael hermano de Joab,
Eljanán hijo de Dodó, el de Belén,
25 Sama el jarodita,
Elicá el jarodita,
26 Heles el paltita,
Ira hijo de Iqués el tecoíta,
27 Abiezer el anatotita,
Mebunay el jusatita,
28 Zalmón el ajojita,
Maray el netofatita,
29 Jéledk hijo de Baná el netofatita,
Itay hijo de Ribay, el de Guibeá de los benjaminitas,
30 Benaías el piratonita,
Hiday, el de los arroyos de Gaas,
31 Abí Albón el arbatita,
Azmávet el bajurinita,
32 Elijaba el salbonita,
los hijos de Jasén,
Jonatán hijo del 33Sama el ararita,
Ahían hijo de Sarar el ararita,
34 Elifelet hijo de Ajasbay el macateo,
Elián hijo de Ajitofel el guilonita,
35 Jezró el de Carmel,
Paray el arbita,
36 Igal hijo de Natán, el de Sobá,
el hijo de Hagrí,m
37 Sélec el amonita,
Najaray el berotita, que fue escudero de Joab hijo de Sarvia,
38 Ira el itrita,
Gareb el itrita,
39 y Urías el hitita.
En total fueron treinta y siete.

David hace un censo militar
24:1-17 — 1Cr 21:1-17

24 Una vez más, la ira del SEÑOR se encendió contra Israel, así que el SEÑOR incitó a David contra el pueblo al decirle: «Haz un censo de Israel y de Judá.» 2Entonces el rey les ordenó a Joab y a los capitanes del ejército que lo acompañaban:n

—Vayan por todas las tribus de Israel, desde Dan hasta Berseba, y hagan un censo militar, para que yo sepa cuántos pueden servir en el ejército.

3Joab le respondió:

—¡Que el SEÑOR su Dios multiplique cien veces las tropas de Su Majestad, y le permita llegar a verlo con sus propios ojos! Pero, ¿qué lleva a Su Majestad a hacer tal cosa?

4Sin embargo, la orden del rey prevaleció sobre la opinión de Joab y de los capitanes del ejército, de modo que salieron de su audiencia con el rey para llevar a cabo el censo militar de Israel. 5Cruzaron el Jordán y acamparon cerca de Aroer, al sur del pueblo que está en el valle, después de lo cual siguieron hacia Gad y Jazer. 6Fueron por Galaad y por el territorio de Tajtín Jodsí, hasta llegar a Dan Jaán y a los alrededores de Sidón. 7Siguieron hacia la fortaleza de Tiro y recorrieron todas las ciudades de los heveos y los cananeos. Finalmente, llegaron a Berseba, en el Néguev de Judá.

8Al cabo de nueve meses y veinte días, y después de haber recorrido todo el país, regresaron a Jerusalén. 9Joab le entregó al rey los resultados del censo militar: en Israel había ochocientos mil hombres que podían servir en el ejército, y en Judá, quinientos mil.

10Entonces le remordió a David la conciencia por haber realizado este censo militar, y le dijo al SEÑOR: «He cometido un pecado muy grande. He actuado como un necio. Yo te ruego, SEÑOR, que perdones la maldad de tu siervo.»

11Por la mañana, antes de que David se levantara, la palabra del SEÑOR vino al profeta Gad, vidente de David, y le dio este mensaje: 12«Ve a decirle a David: "Así dice el SEÑOR: 'Te doy a escoger entre estos tres castigos; dime cuál de ellos quieres que te imponga.'"»

13Entonces Gad fue a ver a David y le preguntó:

—¿Qué prefieres: que vengan tresñ años de hambre en el país, o que tus enemigos te persigan durante tres meses, y tengas que huir de ellos, o que el país sufra tres días de peste? Piénsalo bien, y dime qué debo responderle al que me ha enviado.

14—¡Estoy entre la espada y la pared! —respondió David—. Pero es mejor que caigamos en las manos del SEÑOR, porque su amor es grande, y no que yo caiga en las manos de los *hombres.

15Por lo tanto, el SEÑOR mandó contra Israel una peste que duró desde esa mañana hasta el tiempo señalado; y en todo el país, desde Dan hasta Berseba, murieron setenta mil personas. 16Entonces el ángel del SEÑOR, que estaba junto a la parcela de Arauna el jebuseo, extendió su mano hacia Jerusalén para destruirla. Pero el SEÑOR se arrepintió del castigo que había enviado. «¡Basta! —le dijo al ángel que estaba hiriendo al pueblo—. ¡Detén tu mano!»

17David, al ver que el ángel destruía a la gente, oró al SEÑOR: «¿Qué culpa tienen estas ovejas? ¡Soy yo el que ha pecado! ¡Soy yo el que ha hecho mal! ¡Descarga tu mano sobre mí y sobre mi familia!»

David construye un altar
24:18-25 — 1Cr 21:18-26

18Ese mismo día, Gad volvió a donde estaba David y le dijo: «Sube y construye un altar al SEÑOR en la parcela de Arauna el jebuseo.»

19David se puso en camino, tal como el SEÑOR se lo había ordenado por medio de Gad. 20Arauna se asomó y, al ver que el rey y sus oficiales se acercaban, salió y rostro en tierra se postró delante de él.

21—Su Majestad —dijo Arauna—, ¿a qué debo el honor de su visita?

—Quiero comprarte la parcela —respondió David— y construir un altar al SEÑOR para que se detenga la plaga que está afligiendo al pueblo.

22—Tome Su Majestad y presente como ofrenda lo que mejor le parezca. Aquí hay bueyes para el *holocausto, y hay también trillos y yuntas que usted

---

j **23:20** *dos de los mejores hombres.* Alt. *los dos (hijos) de Ariel.*   k **23:29** *Jéled* (mss. hebreos; véase 1Cr 11:30); *Jéleb* (TM). l **23:32** *Jonatán hijo de* (mss. de LXX); *Jonatán* (TM). m **23:36** *el hijo de Hagrí* (mss. de LXX; véase 1Cr 11:38); *Baní el gadita* (TM). n **24:2** *les ordenó ... acompañaban* (LXX; véanse v. 4 y 1Cr 21:2); *le ordenó a Joab, capitán del ejército, que lo acompañaba* (TM). ñ **24:13** *tres* (LXX; véase 1Cr 21:12); *siete* (TM).

puede usar como leña. 23Todo esto se lo doy a usted. ¡Que el SEÑOR su Dios vea a Su Majestad con agrado!

24Pero el rey le respondió a Arauna:

—Eso no puede ser. No voy a ofrecer al SEÑOR mi Dios holocaustos que nada me cuesten. Te lo compraré todo por su precio justo.

o 24:24 *monedas*. Lit. **siclos*.

Fue así como David compró la parcela y los bueyes por cincuenta monedaso de plata. 25Allí construyó un altar al SEÑOR y ofreció holocaustos y sacrificios de *comunión. Entonces el SEÑOR tuvo piedad del país, y se detuvo la plaga que estaba afligiendo a Israel.

1 REYES

Adonías usurpa el trono

1 El rey David era ya tan anciano y tan entrado en años que, por más que lo abrigaban, no conseguía entrar en calor. 2Por eso sus servidores le dijeron: «Busquemos a una joven soltera para que atienda a Su Majestad y lo cuide, y se acueste a su lado para darle calor.» 3Así que fueron por todo Israel en busca de una muchacha hermosa, y encontraron a una sunamita llamada Abisag y se la llevaron al rey. 4La muchacha era realmente muy hermosa, y se dedicó a cuidar y a servir al rey, aunque el rey nunca tuvo relaciones sexuales con ella.

5Adonías, cuya madre fue Jaguit, ambicionaba ser rey, y por lo tanto se levantó en armas. Consiguió carros de combate, caballos[a] y cincuenta guardias de escolta. 6Adonías era más joven que Absalón, y muy bien parecido. Como David, su padre, nunca lo había contrariado ni le había pedido cuentas de lo que hacía, 7Adonías se confabuló con Joab hijo de Sarvia y con el sacerdote Abiatar, y éstos le dieron su apoyo. 8Quienes no lo apoyaron fueron el sacerdote Sadoc, Benaías hijo de Joyadá, el profeta Natán, Simí y Reguí, y la guardia personal de David.

9Cerca de Enroguel, junto a la peña de Zojélet, Adonías ofreció un sacrificio de ovejas, bueyes y terneros engordados. Invitó a todos sus hermanos, los hijos del rey, y a todos los funcionarios reales de Judá, 10pero no invitó al profeta Natán, ni a Benaías, ni a la guardia real ni a su hermano Salomón. 11Por eso Natán le preguntó a Betsabé, la madre de Salomón: «¿Ya sabes que Adonías, el hijo de Jaguit, se ha proclamado rey a espaldas de nuestro señor David? 12Pues si quieres salvar tu *vida y la de tu hijo Salomón, déjame darte un consejo: 13Ve a presentarte ante el rey David, y dile: "¿Acaso no le había jurado Su Majestad a esta servidora suya que mi hijo Salomón lo sucedería en el trono y que ahora el rey es Adonías?" 14Mientras tú estés allí, hablando con el rey, yo entraré para confirmar tus palabras.»

15Betsabé se dirigió entonces a la habitación del rey. Como éste ya era muy anciano, lo atendía Abisag la sunamita. 16Al llegar Betsabé, se arrodilló ante el rey, y éste le preguntó:

—¿Qué quieres?

17—Mi señor juró por el SEÑOR su Dios a esta servidora suya —contestó Betsabé—, que mi hijo Salomón sucedería en el trono a Su Majestad. 18Pero ahora resulta que Adonías se ha proclamado rey a espaldas de Su Majestad. 19Ha sacrificado una gran cantidad de toros, terneros engordados y ovejas, y ha invitado a todos los hijos del rey, al sacerdote Abiatar y a Joab, general del ejército; sin embargo, no invitó a Salomón, que es un fiel servidor de Su Majestad. 20Mi señor y rey, todo Israel está a la expectativa y quiere que le diga quién lo sucederá en el trono. 21De lo contrario, tan pronto como Su Majestad muera, mi hijo Salomón y yo seremos acusados de alta traición.

22Mientras Betsabé hablaba con el rey, llegó el profeta Natán, 23y el rey se enteró de su llegada. Entonces Natán se presentó ante el rey y, arrodillándose, 24le dijo:

—Mi señor y rey, ¿acaso ha decretado usted que Adonías lo suceda en el trono? 25Pregunto esto porque él ha ido hoy a sacrificar una gran cantidad de toros, terneros engordados y ovejas. Además, ha invitado a todos los hijos de Su Majestad, a los comandantes del ejército y al sacerdote Abiatar, y allí están todos ellos comiendo y bebiendo, y gritando en su presencia: "¡Viva el rey Adonías!" 26Sin embargo, no me invitó a mí, que estoy al servicio de Su Majestad, ni al sacerdote Sadoc, ni a Benaías hijo de Joyadá, ni a Salomón, que es un fiel servidor de Su Majestad. 27¿Será posible que mi señor y rey haya hecho esto sin dignarse comunicarles a sus servidores quién lo sucederá en el trono?

David proclama rey a Salomón
1:28-53 — 1Cr 29:21-25

28Al oír esto, el rey David ordenó:

—¡Llamen a Betsabé!

Ella entró y se quedó de pie ante el rey. 29Entonces el rey le hizo este juramento:

—Tan cierto como que vive el SEÑOR, que me ha librado de toda angustia, 30te aseguro que hoy cumpliré lo que te juré por el SEÑOR, el Dios de Israel. Yo te prometí que tu hijo Salomón me sucederá en el trono y reinará en mi lugar.

31Betsabé se inclinó ante el rey y, postrándose rostro en tierra, exclamó:

—¡Que viva para siempre mi señor el rey David!

32David ordenó:

—Llamen al sacerdote Sadoc, al profeta Natán y a Benaías hijo de Joyadá.

Cuando los tres se presentaron ante el rey, 33éste les dijo:

—Tomen con ustedes a los funcionarios de la corte, monten a mi hijo Salomón en mi propia mula, y llévenlo a Guijón 34para que el sacerdote Sadoc y el profeta Natán lo unjan como rey de Israel. Toquen luego la trompeta, y griten: "¡Viva el rey Salomón!" 35Después de eso, regresen con él para que ocupe el trono en mi lugar y me suceda como rey, pues he dispuesto que sea él quien gobierne a Israel y a Judá.

36—¡Que así sea! —le respondió Benaías hijo de Joyadá—. ¡Que así lo confirme el SEÑOR, Dios de Su Majestad! 37Que así como el SEÑOR estuvo con Su Majestad, esté también con Salomón; ¡y que engrandezca su trono aún más que el trono de mi señor el rey David!

38El sacerdote Sadoc, el profeta Natán y Benaías hijo de Joyadá, y los quereteos y los peleteos, montaron a Salomón en la mula del rey David y lo escoltaron mientras bajaban hasta Guijón. 39Allí el sacerdote Sadoc tomó el cuerno de aceite que estaba en el santuario, y ungió a Salomón. Tocaron entonces la trompeta, y todo el pueblo gritó: «¡Viva el rey Salomón!» 40Luego, todos subieron detrás de él, tocando flautas y lanzando gritos de alegría. Era tal el estruendo, que la tierra temblaba.

41Adonías y todos sus invitados estaban por terminar de comer cuando sintieron el estruendo. Al oír el sonido de la trompeta, Joab preguntó:

—¿Por qué habrá tanta bulla en la ciudad?

42Aún estaba hablando cuando llegó Jonatán, hijo del sacerdote Abiatar.

—¡Entra! —le dijo Adonías—. Un hombre respetable como tú debe traer buenas noticias.

43—¡No es así! —exclamó Jonatán—. Nuestro señor el rey David ha nombrado rey a Salomón. 44También ha ordenado que el sacerdote Sadoc, el profeta Natán y Benaías hijo de Joyadá, con los quereteos y los peleteos, monten a Salomón en la mula del rey. 45Sadoc y Natán lo han ungido como rey en Guijón. Desde allí han subido lanzando gritos de alegría, y la ciudad está alborotada. A eso se debe tanta bulla. 46Además, Salomón se ha sentado en el trono real, 47y los funcionarios de la corte han ido a felicitar a nuestro señor, el rey David. Hasta le desearon que su Dios hiciera el *nombre de Salomón más famoso todavía que el de David, y que engrandeciera el trono de Salomón más que el suyo. Ante eso, el rey se inclinó en su cama 48y dijo: "¡Alabado sea el SEÑOR, Dios de Israel, que hoy me ha concedido ver a mi sucesor sentarse en mi trono!"

49Al oír eso, todos los invitados de Adonías se levantaron llenos de miedo y se dispersaron. 50Adonías, por temor a Salomón, se refugió en el santuario, en donde se agarró de los cuernos del altar. 51No faltó quien fuera a decirle a Salomón:

—Adonías tiene miedo de Su Majestad y está agarrado de los cuernos del altar. Ha dicho: "¡Quiero que hoy mismo jure el rey Salomón que no condenará a muerte a este servidor suyo!"

52Salomón respondió:

—Si demuestra que es un hombre de honor, no perderá ni un cabello de su cabeza; pero si se le sorprende en alguna maldad, será condenado a muerte.

53Acto seguido, el rey Salomón mandó que lo trajeran. Cuando Adonías llegó, se inclinó ante el rey Salomón, y éste le ordenó que se fuera a su casa.

Últimas instrucciones de David
2:10-12 — 1Cr 29:26-28

2 David ya estaba próximo a morir, así que le dio estas instrucciones a su hijo Salomón:

2«Según el destino que a todos nos espera, pronto partiré de este mundo. ¡Cobra ánimo y pórtate como hombre! 3Cumple los mandatos del SEÑOR tu Dios; sigue sus sendas y obedece sus decretos, mandamientos, leyes y preceptos, los cuales están escritos en la *ley de Moisés. Así prosperarás en todo lo que hagas y por dondequiera que vayas, 4y el SEÑOR cumplirá esta promesa que me hizo: "Si tus descendientes cuidan su conducta y me son fieles con toda el *alma y de todo *corazón, nunca faltará un sucesor tuyo en el trono de Israel."

5»Ahora bien, tú mismo sabes que Joab hijo de Sarvia derramó sangre en tiempo de paz como si estuviera en guerra, y mató a Abner hijo de Ner y a Amasá hijo de Jéter, los dos comandantes de los ejércitos israelitas, manchándose así de sangre las manos.b 6Por tanto, usa la cabeza y no lo dejes llegar a viejo y morir en *paz.c 7En cambio, sé bondadoso con los hijos de Barzilay de Galaad y permíteles comer en tu mesa, pues ellos me ampararon cuando huía de tu hermano Absalón.

8»También encárgate de Simí hijo de Guerá, ese benjaminita de Bajurín que me lanzó terribles maldiciones cuando me dirigía a Majanayin. Es cierto que, cuando fue al Jordán a recibirme, le juré por el SEÑOR que no lo condenaría a muerte. 9Sin embargo, no tienes ya por qué perdonarle la vida. Tú eres inteligente, y sabrás qué hacer con él; aunque ya está viejo, hazlo sufrir una muerte sangrienta.»d

10David murió y fue sepultado en la ciudad que lleva su *nombre. 11Había reinado siete años en Hebrón y treinta y tres en Jerusalén, así que en total rei-

nó en Israel cuarenta años. 12Lo sucedió en el trono su hijo Salomón, y así se consolidó firmemente su reino.

Salomón consolida el reino

13Adonías hijo de Jaguit fue a ver a Betsabé, madre de Salomón, y Betsabé le preguntó:

—¿Vienes en son de *paz?

—Sí —respondió él—; 14tengo algo que comunicarle.

—Habla —contestó ella.

15—Como usted sabe —dijo Adonías—, el reino me pertenecía, y todos los israelitas esperaban que yo llegara a ser rey. Pero ahora el reino ha pasado a mi hermano, que lo ha recibido por voluntad del SEÑOR. 16Pues bien, tengo una petición que hacerle, y espero que me la conceda.

—Continúa —dijo ella.

17—Por favor, pídale usted al rey Salomón que me dé como esposa a Abisag la sunamita; a usted no se lo negará.

18—Muy bien —contestó Betsabé—; le hablaré al rey en tu favor.

19Betsabé fue a ver al rey Salomón para interceder en favor de Adonías. El rey se puso de pie para recibirla y se inclinó ante ella; luego se sentó en su trono y mandó que pusieran otro trono para su madre; y ella se sentó a la *derecha del rey.

20—Quiero pedirte un pequeño favor —dijo ella—. Te ruego que no me lo niegues.

—Dime de qué se trata, madre mía. A ti no puedo negarte nada.

21Ella continuó:

—Concédele a tu hermano Adonías casarse con Abisag la sunamita.

22—Pero ¿cómo puedes pedirme semejante cosa? —respondió el rey a su madre—. Es mi hermano mayor, y cuenta con el apoyo del sacerdote Abiatar y de Joab hijo de Sarvia. ¡Realmente me estás pidiendo que le ceda el trono!

23Dicho esto, el rey Salomón juró por el SEÑOR: «¡Que Dios me castigue sin piedad si no hago que Adonías pague con su *vida por esa petición! 24El SEÑOR me ha establecido firmemente en el trono de mi padre, y conforme a su promesa me ha dado una dinastía. Por tanto, tan cierto como que él vive, ¡juro que hoy mismo Adonías morirá!»

25En seguida, el rey Salomón le dio a Benaías hijo de Joyadá la orden de matar a Adonías. 26Al sacerdote Abiatar, el rey mismo le ordenó: «Regresa a tus tierras en Anatot. Mereces la muerte, pero por el momento no voy a quitarte la vida, pues compartiste con David mi padre todas sus penurias, y en su presencia llevaste el arca del SEÑOR omnipotente.» 27Fue así como, al destituir Salomón a Abiatar del sacerdocio del SEÑOR, se cumplió la palabra que el SEÑOR había pronunciado en Siló contra la familia de Elí.

28Joab había conspirado con Adonías, aunque no con Absalón, así que al oír que Adonías había muerto, fue a refugiarse en el santuario del SEÑOR, agarrándose de los cuernos del altar. 29Cuando le dijeron a Salomón que Joab había huido al santuario, y que estaba junto al altar, el rey le ordenó a Benaías hijo de Joyadá que fuera a matarlo. 30Benaías fue al santuario del SEÑOR y le dijo a Joab:

—El rey te ordena que salgas.

---

b 2:5 las manos. Lit. su cinturón y sus sandalias. c 2:6 no lo dejes llegar a viejo y morir en paz. Lit. no dejes que sus canas bajen en paz al *Seol. d 2:9 aunque ... sangrienta. Lit. haz que sus canas bajen con sangre al *Seol.

—¡No! —respondió Joab—. ¡De aquí sólo me sacarán muerto!

Benaías fue y le contó al rey lo que había dicho Joab.

³¹—¡Pues dale gusto! —ordenó el rey—. ¡Mátalo y entiérralo! De ese modo me absolverás a mí y a mi familia de la sangre inocente que derramó Joab. ³²El SEÑOR hará recaer sobre su cabeza la sangre que derramó, porque a espaldas de mi padre atacó Joab a Abner hijo de Ner, que era comandante del ejército de Israel, y a Amasá hijo de Jéter, que era comandante del ejército de Judá. Así mató a filo de espada a dos hombres que eran mejores y más justos que él. ³³¡Que la culpa de esas muertes recaiga para siempre sobre la cabeza de Joab y de sus descendientes! ¡Pero que la paz del SEÑOR esté por siempre con David y sus descendientes, y con su linaje y su trono!

³⁴Benaías hijo de Joyadá fue y mató a Joab, e hizo que lo sepultaran en su hacienda de la estepa. ³⁵Entonces el rey puso a Benaías hijo de Joyadá sobre el ejército en lugar de Joab, y al sacerdote Sadoc lo puso en lugar de Abiatar. ³⁶Luego mandó llamar a Simí y le dijo:

—Constrúyete una casa en Jerusalén, y quédate allí. No salgas a ninguna parte, ³⁷porque el día que salgas y cruces el arroyo de Cedrón, podrás darte por muerto. Y la culpa será tuya.

³⁸—De acuerdo —le respondió Simí al rey—. Yo estoy para servir a Su Majestad, y acataré sus órdenes.

Simí permaneció en Jerusalén por un buen tiempo, ³⁹pero tres años más tarde dos de sus esclavos escaparon a Gat, donde reinaba Aquis hijo de Macá. Cuando le avisaron a Simí que sus esclavos estaban en Gat, ⁴⁰aparejó su asno y se fue allá a buscarlos y traerlos de vuelta. Al oír Salomón que Simí había ido de Jerusalén a Gat y había regresado, ⁴²lo mandó llamar y le dijo:

—Yo te hice jurar por el SEÑOR, y te advertí: "El día que salgas a cualquier lugar, podrás darte por muerto." Y tú dijiste que estabas de acuerdo y que obedecerías. ⁴³¿Por qué, pues, no cumpliste con tu juramento al SEÑOR ni obedeciste la orden que te di?

⁴⁴El rey también le dijo a Simí:

—Tú bien sabes cuánto daño le hiciste a mi padre David; ahora el SEÑOR se vengará de ti por tu maldad. ⁴⁵En cambio, yo seré bendecido, y el trono de David permanecerá firme para siempre en presencia del SEÑOR.

⁴⁶Acto seguido, el rey le dio la orden a Benaías hijo de Joyadá, y éste fue y mató a Simí. Así se consolidó el reino en manos de Salomón.

Salomón pide sabiduría
3:4-15 — 2Cr 1:2-13

3 Salomón entró en alianza con el faraón, rey de Egipto, casándose con su hija, a la cual llevó a la Ciudad de David mientras terminaba de construir su palacio, el templo del SEÑOR y el muro alrededor de Jerusalén. ²Como aún no se había construido un templo en honor⁴ del SEÑOR, el pueblo seguía ofreciendo sacrificios en los *santuarios paganos. ³Salomón amaba al SEÑOR y cumplía los decretos de su padre David. Sin embargo, también iba a los santuarios paganos para ofrecer sacrificios y quemar incienso. ⁴Como en Gabaón estaba el santuario pagano más importante, Salomón acostumbraba ir allá para ofrecer sacrificios. Allí ofreció mil *holocaustos; ⁵y allí mismo se le apareció el SEÑOR en un sueño, y le dijo:

—Pídeme lo que quieras.

⁶Salomón respondió:

—Tú trataste con mucho amor a tu siervo David, mi padre, pues se condujo delante de ti con lealtad y justicia, y con un *corazón recto. Y, como hoy se puede ver, has reafirmado tu gran amor al concederle que un hijo suyo lo suceda en el trono.

⁷»Ahora, SEÑOR mi Dios, me has hecho rey en lugar de mi padre David. No soy más que un muchacho, y apenas sé cómo comportarme. ⁸Sin embargo, aquí me tienes, un siervo tuyo en medio del pueblo que has escogido, un pueblo tan numeroso que es imposible contarlo. ⁹Yo te ruego que le des a tu siervo discernimiento para gobernar a tu pueblo y para distinguir entre el bien y el mal. De lo contrario, ¿quién podrá gobernar a este gran pueblo tuyo?

¹⁰Al Señor le agradó que Salomón hubiera hecho esa petición, ¹¹de modo que le dijo:

—Como has pedido esto, y no larga vida ni riquezas para ti, ni has pedido la muerte de tus enemigos sino discernimiento para administrar justicia, ¹²voy a concederte lo que has pedido. Te daré un corazón sabio y prudente, como nadie antes de ti lo ha tenido ni lo tendrá después. ¹³Además, aunque no me lo has pedido, te daré tantas riquezas y esplendor que en toda tu vida ningún rey podrá compararse contigo. ¹⁴Si andas por mis sendas y obedeces mis decretos y mandamientos, como lo hizo tu padre David, te daré una larga vida.

¹⁵Cuando Salomón despertó y se dio cuenta del sueño que había tenido, regresó a Jerusalén. Se presentó ante el arca del *pacto del Señor y ofreció *holocaustos y sacrificios de *comunión. Luego ofreció un banquete para toda su corte.

Un gobernante sabio

¹⁶Tiempo después, dos prostitutas fueron a presentarse ante el rey. ¹⁷Una de ellas le dijo:

—Su Majestad, esta mujer y yo vivimos en la misma casa. Mientras ella estaba allí conmigo, yo di a luz, ¹⁸y a los tres días también ella dio a luz. No había en la casa nadie más que nosotras dos. ¹⁹Pues bien, una noche esta mujer se acostó encima de su hijo, y el niño murió. ²⁰Pero ella se levantó a medianoche, mientras yo dormía, y tomando a mi hijo, lo acostó junto a ella y puso a su hijo muerto a mi lado. ²¹Cuando amaneció, me levanté para amamantar a mi hijo, ¡y me di cuenta de que estaba muerto! Pero al clarear el día, lo observé bien y pude ver que no era el hijo que yo había dado a luz.

²²—¡No es cierto! —exclamó la otra mujer—. ¡El niño que está vivo es el mío, y el muerto es el tuyo!

—¡Mientes! —insistió la primera—. El niño muerto es el tuyo, y el vivo es el mío.

Y se pusieron a discutir delante del rey.

²³El rey deliberó: «Una dice: "El niño que está vivo es el mío, y el muerto es el tuyo." Y la otra dice: "¡No es cierto! El niño muerto es el tuyo, y el que está vivo es el mío."» ²⁴Entonces ordenó:

—Tráiganme una espada.

Cuando se la trajeron, ²⁵dijo:

—Partan en dos al niño que está vivo, y denle una mitad a ésta y la otra mitad a aquélla.

²⁶La verdadera madre, angustiada por su hijo, le dijo al rey:

—¡Por favor, Su Majestad! ¡Déle usted a ella el niño que está vivo, pero no lo mate!

En cambio, la otra exclamó:

—¡Ni para mí ni para ti! ¡Que lo partan!

²⁷Entonces el rey ordenó:

---

e **3:2** en honor. Lit. al nombre; así en el resto de este libro.

—No lo maten. Entréguenle a la primera el niño que está vivo, pues ella es la madre.

28Cuando todos los israelitas se enteraron de la sentencia que el rey había pronunciado, sintieron un gran respeto por él, pues vieron que tenía sabiduría de Dios para administrar justicia.

Administración del reino

4 Salomón reinó sobre todo Israel, 2y éstos fueron sus funcionarios:

Azarías, hijo del sacerdote Sadoc;
3 Elijoref y Ahías, hijos de Sisá, cronistas;
Josafat hijo de Ajilud, el secretario;
4 Benaías hijo de Joyadá, comandante en jefe;
Sadoc y Abiatar, sacerdotes;
5 Azarías hijo de Natán, encargado de los gobernadores;
Zabud hijo de Natán, sacerdote y consejero personal del rey;
6 Ajisar, encargado del palacio;
Adonirán hijo de Abdá, supervisor del trabajo forzado.

7Salomón tenía por todo Israel a doce gobernadores, cada uno de los cuales debía abastecer al rey y a su corte un mes al año. 8Éstos son sus nombres:

Ben Jur, en la región montañosa de Efraín;
9 Ben Decar, en Macaz, Salbín, Bet Semes y Elón Bet Janán;
10 Ben Jésed, en Arubot (Soco y toda la tierra de Héfer entraban en su jurisdicción);
11 Ben Abinadab, en Nafot Dorf (la esposa de Ben Abinadab fue Tafat hija de Salomón);
12 Baná hijo de Ajilud, en Tanac y Meguido, y en todo Betseán (junto a Saretán, más abajo de Jezrel, desde Betseán hasta Abel Mejolá, y todavía más allá de Jocmeán);
13 Ben Guéber, en Ramot de Galaad (los poblados de Yaír hijo de Manasés en Galaad entraban en su jurisdicción, así como también el distrito de Argob en Basán y sus sesenta grandes ciudades, amuralladas y con cerrojos de bronce);
14 Ajinadab hijo de Idó, en Majanayin;
15 Ajimaz, en Neftalí (Ajimaz estaba casado con Basemat hija de Salomón);
16 Baná hijo de Husay, en Aser y en Alot;
17 Josafat hijo de Parúaj, en Isacar;
18 Simí hijo de Elá, en Benjamín;
19 Guéber hijo de Uri, en Galaad (que era el país de Sijón, rey de los amorreos, y de Og, rey de Basán).

En la tierra de Judá había un solo gobernador.

Prosperidad de Salomón

20Los pueblos de Judá y de Israel eran tan numerosos como la arena que está a la orilla del mar; y abundaban la comida, la bebida y la alegría. 21Salomón gobernaba sobre todos los reinos desde el río Éufrates hasta la tierra de los filisteos y la frontera con Egipto. Mientras Salomón vivió, todos estos países fueron sus vasallos tributarios.

22La provisión diaria de Salomón era de seis mil seiscientos litros de flor de harina y trece mil doscientos litrosh de harina, 23diez bueyes engordados y veinte de pastoreo, y cien ovejas, así como venados,

gacelas, corzos y aves de corral. 24El dominio de Salomón se extendía sobre todos los reinos al oeste del río Éufrates, desde Tifsa hasta Gaza, y disfrutaba de *paz en todas sus fronteras. 25Durante el reinado de Salomón, todos los habitantes de Judá y de Israel, desde Dan hasta Berseba, vivieron seguros bajo su propia parra y su propia higuera.

26Salomón tenía doce mil caballos,i y cuatro mil establos para los caballos de sus carros de combate.

27Los gobernadores, cada uno en su mes, abastecían al rey Salomón y a todos los que se sentaban a su mesa, y se ocupaban de que no les faltara nada. 28Además, llevaban a los lugares indicados sus cuotas de cebada y de paja para los caballos de tiro y para el resto de la caballería.

La sabiduría de Salomón

29Dios le dio a Salomón sabiduría e inteligencia extraordinarias; sus conocimientos eran tan vastos como la arena que está a la orilla del mar. 30Sobrepasó en sabiduría a todos los sabios del Oriente y de Egipto. 31En efecto, fue más sabio que nadie: más que Etán el ezraíta, y más que Hemán, Calcol y Dardá, los hijos de Majol. Por eso la fama de Salomón se difundió por todas las naciones vecinas. 32Compuso tres mil proverbios y mil cinco canciones. 33Disertó acerca de las plantas, desde el cedro del Líbano hasta el *hisopo que crece en los muros. También enseñó acerca de las bestias y las aves, los reptiles y los peces. 34Los reyes de todas las naciones del mundo que se enteraron de la sabiduría de Salomón enviaron a sus representantes para que lo escucharan.

Preparativos para la construcción del templo
5:1-16 — 2Cr 2:1-18

5 El rey Hiram de Tiro siempre había tenido buenas relaciones con David, así que al saber que Salomón había sido ungido para suceder en el trono a su padre David, le mandó una embajada. 2En respuesta, Salomón le envió este mensaje:

3«Tú bien sabes que, debido a las guerras en que mi padre David se vio envuelto, no le fue posible construir un templo en honor del SEÑOR su Dios. Tuvo que esperar hasta que el SEÑOR sometiera a sus enemigos bajo su dominio. 4Pues bien, ahora el SEÑOR mi Dios me ha dado *paz por todas partes, de modo que no me amenazan ni adversarios ni calamidades. 5Por lo tanto me propongo construir un templo en honor del SEÑOR mi Dios, pues él le prometió a mi padre David: "Tu hijo, a quien pondré en el trono como sucesor tuyo, construirá el templo en mi honor."

6»Ahora, pues, ordena que se talen para mí cedros del Líbano. Mis obreros trabajarán con los tuyos, y te pagaré el salario que determines para tus obreros. Tú sabes que no hay entre nosotros quien sepa talar madera tan bien como los sidonios.»

7Cuando Hiram oyó el mensaje de Salomón, se alegró mucho y dijo: «¡Alabado sea hoy el SEÑOR, porque le ha dado a David un hijo sabio para gobernar a esta gran nación!» 8Entonces Hiram envió a Salomón este mensaje:

«He recibido tu petición. Yo te proporcionaré toda la madera de cedro y de pino que quie-

---

f 4:11 Nafot Dor. Alt. las alturas de Dor. g 4:19 tierra de Judá. Lit. Tierra. h 4:22 seis mil seiscientos litros ... trece mil doscientos litros. Lit. treinta *coros ... sesenta coros. i 4:26 caballos. Alt. Aurigas. j 4:26 cuatro mil (mss. de LXX; véase también 2Cr 9:25); cuarenta mil (TM).

ras. 9Mis obreros la transportarán desde el Líbano hasta el mar. Allí haré que la aten en forma de balsas para llevarla flotando hasta donde me indiques, y allí se desatará para que la recojas. Tú, por tu parte, tendrás a bien proporcionarle alimento a mi corte.»

10Así que Hiram le proveía a Salomón toda la madera de cedro y de pino que éste deseaba, 11y Salomón, por su parte, año tras año le entregaba a Hiram, como alimento para su corte, veinte mil cargas^k de trigo y veinte mil medidas^l de aceite de oliva. 12El SEÑOR, cumpliendo su palabra, le dio sabiduría a Salomón. Hiram y Salomón hicieron un tratado, y hubo paz entre ellos.

13El rey Salomón impuso trabajo forzado y reclutó a treinta mil obreros de todo Israel. 14Los envió al Líbano en relevos de diez mil al mes, de modo que pasaban un mes en el Líbano y dos meses en su casa. La supervisión del trabajo forzado estaba a cargo de Adonirán. 15Salomón tenía en las montañas setenta mil cargadores y ochenta mil canteros; 16había además tres mil trescientos capataces que estaban al frente de la obra y dirigían a los trabajadores. 17Para echar los cimientos del templo, el rey mandó que sacaran de la cantera grandes bloques de piedra de la mejor calidad. 18Los obreros de Salomón e Hiram, junto con los que habían llegado de Guebal,^m tallaron la madera y labraron la piedra para la construcción del templo.

Salomón construye el templo
6:1-29 — 2Cr 3:1-14

6 Salomón comenzó a construir el templo del SEÑOR en el cuarto año de su reinado en Israel, en el mes de *zif, que es el mes segundo. Habían transcurrido cuatrocientos ochenta años desde que los israelitas salieron de Egipto.

2El templo que el rey Salomón construyó para el SEÑOR medía veintisiete metros de largo por nueve metros de ancho y trece de ancho y medio de alto.^n 3El vestíbulo de la nave central del templo medía también nueve metros de ancho y por el frente del templo sobresalía cuatro metros y medio. 4Salomón también mandó colocar en el templo ventanales con celosías. 5Alrededor del edificio, y contra las paredes de la nave central y del santuario interior, construyó un anexo con celdas laterales. 6El piso inferior del anexo medía dos metros con veinticinco centímetros de ancho; el piso intermedio, dos metros con setenta centímetros, y el piso más alto, tres metros con quince centímetros. Salomón había mandado hacer salientes en el exterior del templo para que las vigas no se empotraran en la pared misma.

7En la construcción del templo sólo se emplearon piedras de cantera ya labradas, así que durante las obras no se oyó el ruido de martillos ni de piquetas, ni de ninguna otra herramienta.

8La entrada al piso inferior^ñ se hallaba en el lado sur del templo; una escalera de caracol conducía al nivel intermedio y a la planta alta. 9Salomón terminó de construir el templo techándolo con vigas y tablones de cedro. 10A lo largo del templo construyó el anexo, el cual tenía una altura de dos metros con veinticinco centímetros y quedaba unido a la pared del templo por medio de vigas de cedro.

11La palabra del SEÑOR vino a Salomón y le dio este mensaje: 12«Ya que estás construyendo este templo, quiero decirte que si andas según mis decretos, y obedeces mis leyes y todos mis mandamientos, yo cumpliré por medio de ti la promesa que le hice a tu padre David. 13Entonces viviré entre los israelitas, y no abandonaré a mi pueblo Israel.»

14Cuando Salomón terminó de construir la estructura del templo, 15revistió las paredes interiores con tablas de cedro, artesonándolas desde el piso hasta el techo; el piso lo recubrió con tablones de pino. 16En el santuario interior, al fondo del templo, acondicionó el Lugar Santísimo, recubriendo el espacio de nueve metros con tablas de cedro desde el piso hasta el techo. 17Junto al Lugar Santísimo estaba la nave central, la cual medía dieciocho metros de largo. 18El interior del templo lo recubrió de cedro tallado con figuras de calabazas y flores abiertas. No se veía una sola piedra, pues todo era de cedro.

19Salomón dispuso el Lugar Santísimo del templo para que se colocara allí el arca del *pacto del SEÑOR. 20El interior de este santuario, que medía nueve metros de largo por nueve metros de alto, lo recubrió de oro puro, y también recubrió de cedro el altar. 21Además, Salomón recubrió de oro puro el interior del templo, y tendió cadenas de oro a lo largo del frente del Lugar Santísimo, el cual estaba recubierto de oro. 22En efecto, recubrió de oro todo el santuario interior, y así mismo el altar que estaba delante de éste.

23Salomón mandó esculpir para el santuario interior dos *querubines de madera de olivo, cada uno de los cuales medía cuatro metros y medio de altura. 24De una punta a otra, las alas extendidas del primer querubín medían cuatro metros y medio, es decir, cada una de sus alas medía dos metros con veinticinco centímetros. 25Las del segundo querubín también medían cuatro metros y medio, pues los dos eran idénticos en tamaño y forma. 26Cada querubín medía cuatro metros y medio de altura. 27Salomón puso los querubines con sus alas extendidas en medio del recinto interior del templo. Con una de sus alas, cada querubín tocaba una pared, mientras que sus otras alas se tocaban en medio del santuario. 28Luego Salomón recubrió de oro los querubines.

29Sobre las paredes que rodeaban el templo, lo mismo por dentro que por fuera, talló figuras de querubines, palmeras y flores abiertas. 30Además, recubrió de oro los pisos de los cuartos interiores y exteriores del templo.

31Para la entrada del Lugar Santísimo, Salomón hizo puertas de madera de olivo, con jambas y postes pentagonales. 32Sobre las dos puertas de madera de olivo talló figuras de querubines, palmeras y flores abiertas, y todas ellas las recubrió de oro. 33Así mismo, para la entrada de la nave central hizo postes cuadrangulares de madera de olivo. 34También hizo dos puertas de pino, cada una con dos hojas giratorias. 35Sobre ellas talló figuras de querubines, palmeras y flores abiertas, y las recubrió de oro bien ajustado al relieve.

36Las paredes del atrio interior las construyó con tres hileras de piedra labrada por cada hilera de vigas de cedro.

37Los cimientos del templo del SEÑOR se habían echado en el mes de zif del cuarto año del reinado de

---

k **5:11** *veinte mil cargas*. Lit. *veinte mil* *coros (más de cuatro millones de litros). l **5:11** *veinte mil medidas* (lit. *veinte mil* *batos*, LXX; véase también 2Cr 2:10); *veinte coros* (TM). m **5:18** *Guebal*. Es decir, Byblos. n **6:2** En este capítulo las medidas de longitud se han convertido al sistema métrico, sin explicación en las notas. ñ **6:8** *inferior* (LXX y Targum); *intermedio* (TM).

Salomón, 38y en el mes de *bul del año undécimo, es decir, en el mes octavo de ese año, se terminó de construir el templo siguiendo al pie de la letra todos los detalles del diseño. Siete años le llevó a Salomón la construcción del templo.

Salomón construye su palacio

7 Salomón también terminó la construcción de su propio palacio, pero el proyecto le llevó trece años. 2Construyó el palacio «Bosque del Líbano», el cual medía cuarenta y cinco metros de largo por veintidós metros y medio de ancho y trece metros y medio de alto.º Cuatro hileras de columnas de cedro sostenían las vigas, las cuales también eran de cedro. 3Encima de las columnas había cuarenta y cinco celdas, quince en cada piso; y sobre las celdasp había un techo de cedro. 4Las ventanas estaban colocadas en tres filas, de tres en tres y unas frente a las otras. 5Todas las entradas tenían un marco rectangular y estaban colocadas de tres en tres, unas frente a las otras.

6Salomón también hizo un vestíbulo de columnas que medía veintidós metros y medio de largo por trece metros y medio de ancho. Al frente había otro vestíbulo con columnas, y un alero. 7Construyó además una sala para su trono, es decir, el tribunal donde impartía justicia. Esta sala la recubrió de cedro de arriba abajo. 8Su residencia personal estaba en un atrio aparte y tenía un modelo parecido. A la hija del faraón, con la cual se había casado, Salomón le construyó un palacio semejante.

9Desde los cimientos hasta las cornisas, y desde la parte exterior hasta el gran atrio, todo se hizo con bloques de piedra de buena calidad, cortados a la medida y aserrados por ambos lados. 10Para echar los cimientos se usaron piedras grandes y de buena calidad; unas medían más de cuatro metros, y otras, más de tres. 11Para la parte superior se usaron también piedras selectas, cortadas a la medida, y vigas de cedro. 12El muro que rodeaba el gran atrio tenía tres hileras de piedra labrada por cada hilera de vigas de cedro, lo mismo que el atrio interior y el vestíbulo del templo del SEÑOR.

Mobiliario del templo
7:23-26 — 2Cr 4:2-5
7:38-51 — 2Cr 4:6,10—5:1

13El rey Salomón mandó traer de Tiro a Hiram, 14que era hijo de una viuda de la tribu de Neftalí y de un nativo de Tiro que era artesano en bronce. Hiram era sumamente hábil e inteligente, experto en toda clase de trabajo en bronce, así que se presentó ante el rey Salomón y realizó todo el trabajo que se le asignó.

15Hiram fundió dos columnas de bronce, cada una de ocho metros de alto y cinco metros y medio de circunferencia, medidas a cordel. 16Las columnas que hizo remataban en dos capiteles de bronce fundido que medían dos metros con veinticinco centímetros de alto. 17Una red de cadenas trenzadas adornaba los capiteles en la parte superior de las columnas, y en cada capitel había siete trenzas. 18El capitel de cada columnaq lo cubrió con dos hileras de granadasr entrelazadas con las cadenas. 19Estos capiteles en que remataban las columnas del vestíbulo tenían forma de azucenas y medían un metro con ochenta centímetros. 20La parte más alta y más ancha de los capiteles de ambas columnas estaba rodeada por doscientas granadas, dispuestas en hileras junto a la red de cadenas. 21Cuando Hiram levantó las columnas en el vestíbulo de la nave central, llamó Jaquín a la columna de la derecha, y Boaz a la de la izquierda.s 22El trabajo de las columnas quedó terminado cuando se colocaron en la parte superior las figuras en forma de azucenas.

23Hizo también una fuentet circular de metal fundido, que medía cuatro metros y medio de diámetro y dos metros con veinticinco centímetros de alto. Su circunferencia, medida a cordel, era de trece metros y medio. 24Debajo del borde hizo dos hileras de figuras de calabazas, diez por cada medio metro, las cuales estaban fundidas en una sola pieza con la fuente.

25La fuente descansaba sobre doce bueyes, que tenían sus cuartos traseros hacia adentro. Tres bueyes miraban al norte, tres al oeste, tres al sur y tres al este. 26El grosor de la fuente era de ocho centímetros, y su borde, en forma de copa, se asemejaba a un capullo de azucena. Tenía una capacidad de cuarenta y cuatro mil litros.u

27También hizo diez bases de bronce, cada una de las cuales medía un metro con ochenta centímetros de largo y un metro con ochenta centímetros de ancho, por un metro con treinta y cinco centímetros de alto. 28Estaban revestidas con paneles entre los bordes, 29y en los paneles había figuras de leones, bueyes y *querubines, mientras que en los bordes, por encima y por debajo de los leones y los bueyes, había guirnaldas repujadas. 30Cada base tenía cuatro ruedas de bronce con ejes también de bronce, y por debajo de su lavamanos se apoyaba sobre cuatro soportes fundidos que tenían guirnaldas en cada lado. 31La boca del lavamanos estaba dentro de una corona, y sobresalía cuarenta y cinco centímetros; era redonda, y con su pedestal medía sesenta y siete centímetros. Alrededor de la boca había entalladuras, pero sus paneles eran cuadrados, no redondos. 32Las cuatro ruedas estaban debajo de los paneles, y los ejes de las ruedas estaban unidos a la base. Cada rueda medía sesenta y siete centímetros de diámetro 33y estaba hecha de metal fundido, como las ruedas de los carros, con sus ejes, aros, rayos y cubos.

34Cada base tenía cuatro soportes unidos a ella, uno en cada esquina. 35En la parte superior de la base había un marco redondo de veintidós centímetros. Los soportes y paneles formaban una misma pieza con la parte superior de la base. 36Sobre las superficies de los soportes y sobre los paneles Hiram grabó querubines, leones y palmeras, con guirnaldas alrededor, según el espacio disponible. 37De ese modo hizo las diez bases, las cuales fueron fundidas en los mismos moldes y eran idénticas en forma y tamaño.

38Hiram hizo también diez lavamanos de bronce, uno para cada base. Cada uno de ellos medía un metro con ochenta centímetros y tenía capacidad para ochocientos ochenta litros.v 39Colocó cinco de las bases al lado derecho del templo y cinco al lado izquierdo. La fuente de metal la colocó en la esquina

---

o 7:2 En este capítulo las medidas de longitud se han convertido al sistema métrico, sin explicación en las notas.
p 7:3 celdas, quince en cada piso; y sobre las celdas. Alt. vigas, quince en cada hilera; y sobre las vigas. q 7:18 de cada columna (muchos mss. hebreos, LXX y Siríaca); de las granadas (TM). r 7:18 con dos hileras de granadas (dos mss. hebreos y LXX); hizo las columnas y dos hileras (TM). s 7:21 Jaquín (que probablemente significa él establece) estaba al sur, y Boaz (probablemente en él hay fuerza) estaba al norte. t 7:23 una fuente. Lit. el mar; así en el resto de este pasaje. u 7:26 cuarenta y cuatro mil litros. Lit. dos mil *batos. v 7:38 ochocientos ochenta litros. Lit. cuarenta *batos.

del lado derecho, al sureste del templo. ⁴⁰También hizo las ollas,ʷ las tenazas y los aspersorios. Así Hiram terminó todo el trabajo que había emprendido para el rey Salomón en el templo del SEÑOR, es decir:

⁴¹ las dos columnas;

los dos capiteles en forma de tazón que coronaban las columnas;

las dos redes que decoraban los capiteles;

⁴² las cuatrocientas granadas, dispuestas en dos hileras para cada red;

⁴³ las diez bases con sus diez lavamanos;

⁴⁴ la fuente de metal y los doce bueyes que la sostenían;

⁴⁵ las ollas, las tenazas y los aspersorios.

Todos esos utensilios que Hiram le hizo al rey Salomón para el templo del SEÑOR eran de bronce bruñido. ⁴⁶El rey los hizo fundir en moldes de arcilla en la llanura del Jordán, entre Sucot y Saretán. ⁴⁷Eran tantos los utensilios que Salomón ni los pesó, así que no fue posible determinar el peso del bronce.

⁴⁸Salomón también mandó hacer los otros utensilios que estaban en el templo del SEÑOR, es decir:

el altar de oro;

la mesa de oro sobre la que se ponía el *pan de la Presencia;

⁴⁹ los candelabros de oro puro, cinco en el lado sur y cinco en el lado norte, en frente del Lugar Santísimo;

la obra floral, las lámparas y las tenazas, que también eran de oro;

⁵⁰ las copas, las despabiladeras, los aspersorios, la vajilla y los incensarios;

y los goznes de oro para las puertas del Lugar Santísimo, como también para las puertas de la nave central del templo.

⁵¹Una vez terminada toda la obra que el rey había mandado hacer para el templo del SEÑOR, Salomón hizo traer el oro, la plata y los utensilios que su padre David había consagrado, y los depositó en el tesoro del templo del SEÑOR.

Traslado del arca al templo
8:1-21 — 2Cr 5:2—6:11

8 Entonces el rey Salomón mandó que los *ancianos de Israel, y todos los jefes de las tribus y los patriarcas de las familias israelitas, se congregaran ante él en Jerusalén para trasladar el arca del *pacto del SEÑOR desde *Sión, la Ciudad de David. ²Así que en el mes de *etanim, durante la fiesta del mes séptimo, todos los israelitas se congregaron ante el rey Salomón. ³Cuando llegaron todos los ancianos de Israel, los sacerdotes alzaron el arca. ⁴Con la ayuda de los levitas, trasladaron el arca del SEÑOR junto con la *Tienda de reunión y con todos los utensilios sagrados que había en ella.

⁵El rey Salomón y toda la asamblea de Israel reunida con él delante del arca sacrificaron ovejas y bueyes en tal cantidad que fue imposible llevar la cuenta. ⁶Luego los sacerdotes llevaron el arca del pacto del SEÑOR a su lugar en el santuario interior del templo, que es el Lugar Santísimo, y la pusieron bajo las alas de los *querubines. ⁷Con sus alas extendidas sobre ese lugar, los querubines cubrían el arca y sus travesaños. ⁸Los travesaños eran tan largos que sus extremos se podían ver desde el Lugar Santo, delante del Lugar Santísimo, aunque no desde

afuera; y ahí han permanecido hasta hoy. ⁹En el arca sólo estaban las dos tablas de piedra que Moisés había colocado en ella en Horeb, donde el SEÑOR hizo un pacto con los israelitas después de que salieron de Egipto.

¹⁰Cuando los sacerdotes se retiraron del Lugar Santo, la nube llenó el templo del SEÑOR. ¹¹Y por causa de la nube, los sacerdotes no pudieron celebrar el culto, pues la gloria del SEÑOR había llenado el templo.

¹²Entonces Salomón declaró:

«SEÑOR, tú has dicho que habitarías en la oscuridad de una nube, ¹³y yo te he construido un excelso templo, un lugar donde habites para siempre.»

¹⁴Luego se puso de frente para bendecir a toda la asamblea de Israel que estaba allí de pie, ¹⁵y dijo:

«Bendito sea el SEÑOR, Dios de Israel, que con su mano ha cumplido ahora lo que con su boca le había prometido a mi padre David cuando le dijo: ¹⁶"Desde el día en que saqué de Egipto a mi pueblo Israel, no elegí ninguna ciudad de las tribus de Israel para que en ella se me construyera un templo donde yo habitara, sino que elegí a David para que gobernara a mi pueblo Israel."

¹⁷»Pues bien, mi padre David tuvo mucho interés en construir un templo en honor del SEÑOR, Dios de Israel, ¹⁸pero el SEÑOR le dijo: "Me agrada que te hayas interesado en construir un templo en mi honor. ¹⁹Sin embargo, no serás tú quien me lo construya, sino un hijo de tus entrañas; él será quien construya el templo en mi honor."

²⁰»Ahora el SEÑOR ha cumplido su promesa: Tal como lo prometió, he sucedido a mi padre David en el trono de Israel y he construido el templo en honor del SEÑOR, Dios de Israel. ²¹Allí he fijado un lugar para el arca, en la cual está el pacto que el SEÑOR hizo con nuestros antepasados cuando los sacó de Egipto.»

Oración de Salomón
8:22-53 — 2Cr 6:12-40

²²A continuación, Salomón se puso delante del altar del SEÑOR y, en presencia de toda la asamblea de Israel, extendió las manos hacia el cielo ²³y dijo:

«SEÑOR, Dios de Israel, no hay Dios como tú arriba en el cielo ni abajo en la tierra, pues tú cumples tu *pacto de amor con quienes te sirven y te siguen de todo *corazón. ²⁴Has llevado a cabo lo que le dijiste a tu siervo David, mi padre; y este día has cumplido con tu mano lo que con tu boca le prometiste.

²⁵»Ahora, SEÑOR, Dios de Israel, cumple también la promesa que le hiciste a tu siervo, mi padre David, cuando le dijiste: "Si tus hijos observan una buena conducta y me siguen como tú lo has hecho, nunca te faltará un descendiente que ocupe el trono de Israel en mi presencia." ²⁶Dios de Israel, ¡confirma ahora la promesa que le hiciste a mi padre David, tu siervo!

²⁷»Pero ¿será posible, Dios mío, que tú habites en la tierra? Si los cielos, por altos que sean, no pueden contenerte, ¡mucho menos este templo que he construido! ²⁸Sin embargo, SEÑOR mi Dios, atiende a la oración y a la súplica de este

---

ʷ **7:40** *las ollas* (muchos mss., LXX, Siríaca y Vulgata; véase v. 45); *los lavabos* (TM).

siervo tuyo. Oye el clamor y la oración que hoy elevo en tu presencia. 29¡Que tus ojos estén abiertos día y noche sobre este templo, el lugar donde decidiste habitar, para que oigas la oración que tu siervo te eleva aquí! 30Oye la súplica de tu siervo y de tu pueblo Israel cuando oren en este lugar. Oye desde el cielo, donde habitas; ¡escucha y perdona!

31»Si alguien peca contra su prójimo y se le exige venir a este templo para jurar ante tu altar, 32óyelo tú desde el cielo y juzga a tus siervos. Condena al culpable, y haz que reciba su merecido; absuelve al inocente, y vindícalo por su rectitud.

33»Cuando tu pueblo Israel sea derrotado por el enemigo por haber pecado contra ti, si luego se vuelve a ti para honrar tu *nombre, y ora y te suplica en este templo, 34óyelo tú desde el cielo, y perdona su pecado y hazlo regresar a la tierra que les diste a sus antepasados.

35»Cuando tu pueblo peque contra ti y tú lo aflijas cerrando el cielo para que no llueva, si luego ellos oran en este lugar y honran tu nombre y se *arrepienten de su pecado, 36óyelos tú desde el cielo y perdona el pecado de tus siervos, de tu pueblo Israel. Guíalos para que sigan el buen *camino, y envía la lluvia sobre esta tierra, que es tuya, pues tú se la diste a tu pueblo por herencia.

37»Cuando en el país haya hambre, peste, sequía, o plagas de langostas o saltamontes en los sembrados, o cuando el enemigo sitie alguna de nuestras ciudades; en fin, cuando venga cualquier calamidad o enfermedad, 38si luego cada israelita, consciente de su propia culpa,ˣ extiende sus manos hacia este templo, y ora y te suplica, 39óyelo tú desde el cielo, donde habitas, y perdónalo. Trata a cada uno según su conducta, la cual tú conoces, puesto que sólo tú escudriñas el corazón *humano. 40Así todos tendrán temor de ti mientras vivan en la tierra que les diste a nuestros antepasados.

41»Trata de igual manera al extranjero que no pertenece a tu pueblo Israel, pero que atraído por tu fama ha venido de lejanas tierras. 42(En efecto, los pueblos oirán hablar de tu gran nombre y de tus despliegues de fuerza y poder.) Cuando ese extranjero venga y ore en este templo, 43óyelo tú desde el cielo, donde habitas, y concédele cualquier petición que te haga. Así todos los pueblos de la tierra conocerán tu nombre y, al igual que tu pueblo Israel, tendrán temor de ti y comprenderán que en este templo que he construido se invoca tu nombre.

44»SEÑOR, cuando saques a tu pueblo para combatir a sus enemigos, sea donde sea, si el pueblo ora a ti y dirige la mirada hacia la ciudad que has escogido, hacia el templo que he construido en tu honor, 45oye tú desde el cielo su oración y su súplica, y defiende su causa.

46»Ya que no hay ser humano que no peque, si tu pueblo peca contra ti, y tú te enojas con ellos y los entregas al enemigo para que se los lleven cautivos a otro país, lejano o cercano, 47si en el destierro, en el país de los vencedores, se arrepienten y se vuelven a ti, y oran a ti diciendo: "Somos culpables, hemos pecado, hemos hecho lo malo", 48y allá en la tierra de sus enemigos que los tomaron cautivos se vuelven a ti de todo corazón y con toda el *alma, y oran a ti y dirigen la mirada hacia la tierra que les diste a sus antepasados, hacia la ciudad que has escogido y hacia el templo que he construido en tu honor, 49oye tú su oración y su súplica desde el cielo, donde habitas, y defiende su causa. 50Perdona a tu pueblo, que ha pecado contra ti; perdona todas las ofensas que te haya infligido. Haz que sus enemigos le muestren clemencia, 51pues Israel es tu pueblo y tu heredad; ¡tú lo sacaste de aquel horno de fundición que es Egipto!

52»¡Dígnate mantener atentos tus oídosy a la súplica de este siervo tuyo y de tu pueblo Israel! ¡Escúchalos cada vez que te invoquen! 53Tú los apartaste de todas las naciones del mundo para que fueran tu heredad. Así lo manifestaste por medio de tu siervo Moisés cuando tú, SEÑOR y Dios, sacaste de Egipto a nuestros antepasados.»

54Salomón había estado ante el altar del SEÑOR, de rodillas y con las manos extendidas hacia el cielo. Cuando terminó de orar y de hacer esta súplica al SEÑOR, se levantó 55y, puesto de pie, bendijo en voz alta a toda la asamblea de Israel, diciendo:

56»¡Bendito sea el SEÑOR, que conforme a sus promesas ha dado descanso a su pueblo Israel! No ha dejado de cumplir ni una sola de las gratas promesas que hizo por medio de su siervo Moisés. 57Que el SEÑOR nuestro Dios esté con nosotros, como estuvo con nuestros antepasados; que nunca nos deje ni nos abandone. 58Que incline nuestro corazón hacia él, para que sigamos todos sus caminos y cumplamos los mandamientos, decretos y leyes que les dio a nuestros antepasados. 59Y que día y noche el SEÑOR tenga presente todo lo que le he suplicado, para que defienda la causa de este siervo suyo y la de su pueblo Israel, según la necesidad de cada día. 60Así todos los pueblos de la tierra sabrán que el SEÑOR es Dios, y que no hay otro. 61Y ahora, dedíquense por completo al SEÑOR nuestro Dios; vivan según sus decretos y cumplan sus mandamientos, como ya lo hacen.»

Dedicación del templo
8:62-66 — 2Cr 7:1-10

62Entonces el rey, con todo Israel, ofreció sacrificios en presencia del SEÑOR. 63Como sacrificio de *comunión, Salomón ofreció al SEÑOR veintidós mil bueyes y ciento veinte mil ovejas. Así fue como el rey y todos los israelitas dedicaron el templo del SEÑOR.

64Aquel mismo día el rey consagró la parte central del atrio, que está frente al templo del SEÑOR, y allí presentó los *holocaustos, las ofrendas de cereales y la grasa de los sacrificios de comunión, ya que el altar de bronce que estaba ante el SEÑOR era pequeño y no había espacio para todos estos sacrificios y ofrendas.

65Y así, en presencia del SEÑOR, Salomón y todo Israel celebraron la fiesta durante siete días, extendiéndola luego siete días más: ¡catorce días de fiesta en total! A la fiesta llegó gente de todas partes, desde Lebó Jamatᶻ hasta el río de Egipto, y se formó una gran asamblea. 66Al final, Salomón despidió al pueblo, y ellos bendijeron al rey y regresaron a sus casas, contentos y llenos de alegría por todo el bien que el

---

ˣ **8:38** *de su propia culpa.* Lit. *de la plaga en su corazón.* ʸ **8:52** *atentos tus oídos* (véase 2Cr 6:40); *abiertos tus ojos* (TM).
ᶻ **8:65** *Lebó Jamat.* Alt. *la entrada de Jamat.*

SEÑOR había hecho en favor de su siervo David y de su pueblo Israel.

Pacto de Dios con Salomón
9:1-9 — 2Cr 7:11-22

9 Cuando Salomón terminó de construir el templo del SEÑOR y el palacio real, cumpliendo así todos sus propósitos y deseos, ²el SEÑOR se le apareció por segunda vez, como lo había hecho en Gabaón, ³y le dijo:

«He oído la oración y la súplica que me has hecho. Consagro este templo que tú has construido para que yo habite en él por siempre. Mis ojos y mi *corazón siempre estarán allí.

⁴»En cuanto a ti, si me sigues con integridad y rectitud de corazón, como lo hizo tu padre David, y me obedeces en todo lo que yo te ordene y cumples mis decretos y leyes, ⁵yo afirmaré para siempre tu trono en el reino de Israel, como le prometí a tu padre David cuando le dije: "Nunca te faltará un descendiente en el trono de Israel."

⁶»Pero si ustedes o sus hijos dejan de cumplir los mandamientos y decretos que les he dado, y se apartan de mí para servir y adorar a otros dioses, ⁷yo arrancaré a Israel de la tierra que le he dado y repudiaré el templo que he consagrado en mi honor. Entonces Israel será el hazmerreír de todos los pueblos. ⁸Y aunque ahora este templo es imponente, llegará el día en que todo el que pase frente a él quedará asombrado y, en son de burla, preguntará: "¿Por qué el SEÑOR ha tratado así a este país y a este templo?" ⁹Y le responderán: "Porque abandonaron al SEÑOR su Dios, que sacó de Egipto a sus antepasados, los israelitas, y se echaron en los brazos de otros dioses, a los cuales adoraron y sirvieron. Por eso el SEÑOR ha dejado que les sobrevenga tanto desastre."»

Otras actividades de Salomón
9:10-28 — 2Cr 8:1-18

¹⁰Veinte años tardó el rey Salomón en construir los dos edificios, es decir, el templo del SEÑOR y el palacio real, ¹¹después de lo cual le dio a Hiram, rey de Tiro, veinte ciudades en Galilea, porque Hiram lo había abastecido con todo el cedro, el pino y el oro que quiso. ¹²Sin embargo, cuando Hiram salió de Tiro y fue a ver las ciudades que Salomón le había dado, no quedó satisfecho con ellas. ¹³«Hermano mío —protestó Hiram—, ¿qué clase de ciudades son éstas que me has dado?» De modo que llamó a esa región Cabul,ᵃ nombre que conserva hasta hoy. ¹⁴Hiram, por su parte, le había enviado a Salomón tres mil novecientos sesenta kilosᵇ de oro. ¹⁵En cuanto al trabajo forzado, el rey Salomón reunió trabajadores para construir el templo del SEÑOR, su propio palacio, los terraplenes,ᶜ la muralla de Jerusalén, y Jazor, Meguido y Guézer. ¹⁶El faraón, rey de Egipto, había atacado y tomado Guézer a sangre y fuego, matando a sus habitantes cananeos. Luego, como regalo de bodas, le dio esta ciudad a su hija, la esposa de Salomón. ¹⁷Por eso Salomón reconstruyó las ciudades de Guézer, Bet Jorón la de abajo, ¹⁸Balat y Tadmor,ᵈ en el desierto del país, ¹⁹así como todos

sus lugares de almacenamiento, los cuarteles para sus carros de combate y para su caballería, y cuanto quiso construir en Jerusalén, en el Líbano y en todo el territorio bajo su dominio.

²⁰⁻²¹A los descendientes de los pueblos no israelitas (es decir, a los amorreos, hititas, ferezeos, heveos y jebuseos, pueblos que quedaron en el país porque los israelitas no pudieron *destruirlos), Salomón los sometió a trabajos forzados, y así continúan hasta el día de hoy. ²²Pero a los israelitas Salomón no los convirtió en esclavos, sino que le servían como soldados, ministros, comandantes, oficiales de carros de combate y jefes de caballería. ²³Salomón tenía además quinientos cincuenta capataces que supervisaban a sus trabajadores en la obra.

²⁴Los terraplenes se hicieron después de que la hija del faraón se trasladó de la Ciudad de David al palacio que Salomón le había construido.

²⁵Tres veces al año Salomón presentaba *holocaustos y sacrificios de *comunión sobre el altar que él había construido para el SEÑOR, y al mismo tiempo quemaba incienso en su presencia. Así cumplía con las obligaciones del templo.ᵉ

²⁶El rey Salomón también construyó una flota naviera en Ezión Guéber, cerca de Elat en Edom, a orillas del *Mar Rojo. ²⁷Hiram envió a algunos de sus oficiales, que eran marineros expertos, para servir en la flota con los oficiales de Salomón, ²⁸y ellos se hicieron a la mar y llegaron a Ofir, de donde volvieron con unos catorce mil kilosᶠ de oro, que le entregaron al rey Salomón.

La reina de Sabá visita a Salomón
10:1-13 — 2Cr 9:1-12

10 La reina de Sabá se enteró de la fama de Salomón, con la cual él honraba al SEÑOR, así que fue a verlo para ponerlo a prueba con preguntas difíciles. ²Llegó a Jerusalén con un séquito muy grande. Sus camellos llevaban perfumes y grandes cantidades de oro y piedras preciosas. Al presentarse ante Salomón, le preguntó todo lo que tenía pensado, ³y él respondió a todas sus preguntas. No hubo ningún asunto, por difícil que fuera, que el rey no pudiera resolver.

⁴⁻⁵La reina de Sabá se quedó atónita al ver la sabiduría de Salomón y el palacio que él había construido, los manjares de su mesa, los asientos que ocupaban sus funcionarios, el servicio y la ropa de los camareros, las bebidas, y los *holocaustos que ofrecía en el temploᵍ del SEÑOR. ⁶Entonces le dijo al rey: «¡Todo lo que escuché en mi país acerca de tus triunfos y de tu sabiduría es cierto! ⁷No podía creer nada de eso hasta que vine y lo vi con mis propios ojos. Pero en realidad, ¡no me habían contado ni siquiera la mitad! Tanto en sabiduría como en riqueza, superas todo lo que había oído decir. ⁸¡*Dichosos tus súbditos! ¡Dichosos estos servidores tuyos, que constantemente están en tu presencia bebiendo de tu sabiduría! ⁹¡Y alabado sea el SEÑOR tu Dios, que se ha deleitado en ti y te ha puesto en el trono de Israel! En su eterno amor por Israel, el SEÑOR te ha hecho rey para que gobiernes con justicia y rectitud.»

¹⁰Luego la reina le regaló a Salomón tres mil novecientos sesenta kilosʰ de oro, piedras preciosas y

---

ᵃ **9:13** El nombre *Cabul* parece ser un juego de palabras que sugiere que ésta era una región *inútil*. ᵇ **9:14** *tres mil novecientos sesenta kilos.* Lit. *ciento veinte *talentos.* ᶜ **9:15** *los terraplenes.* Alt. *el Milo;* también en v. 24. ᵈ **9:18** *Tadmor.* Alt. *Tamar.* ᵉ **9:25** *cumplía con las obligaciones del templo.* Lit. *completó el templo.* ᶠ **9:28** *catorce mil kilos.* Lit. *cuatrocientos veinte *talentos.* ᵍ **10:5** *los holocaustos ... templo.* Alt. *la escalinata por la cual él subía al templo.* ʰ **10:10** *tres mil novecientos sesenta kilos.* Lit. *ciento veinte *talentos.*

gran cantidad de perfumes. Nunca más llegaron a Israel tantos perfumes como los que la reina de Sabá le obsequió al rey Salomón.

11La flota de Hiram trajo desde Ofir, además del oro, grandes cargamentos de madera de sándalo y de piedras preciosas. 12Con la madera, el rey construyó escalonesⁱ para el templo del SEÑOR y para el palacio real, y también hizo arpas y liras para los músicos. Desde entonces, nunca más se ha importado, ni ha vuelto a verse, tanto sándalo como aquel día.

13El rey Salomón, por su parte, le dio a la reina de Sabá todo lo que a ella se le antojó pedirle, además de lo que él, en su magnanimidad, ya le había regalado. Después de eso, la reina regresó a su país con todos los que la atendían.

El esplendor de Salomón
10:14-29 — 2Cr 1:14-17; 9:13-28

14La cantidad de oro que Salomón recibía anualmente llegaba a los veintidós mil kilos,ʲ 15sin contar los impuestos aportados por los mercaderes, el tráfico comercial, y todos los reyes árabes y los gobernadores del país.

16El rey Salomón hizo doscientos escudos grandes de oro batido, en cada uno de los cuales se emplearon unos seis kilos y medioᵏ de oro. 17Hizo además trescientos escudos más pequeños, también de oro batido, empleando en cada uno de ellos un kilo y medioˡ de oro. Estos escudos los puso el rey en el palacio llamado «Bosque del Líbano».

18El rey hizo también un gran trono de marfil, recubierto de oro puro. 19El trono tenía seis peldaños, un espaldar redondo, brazos a cada lado del asiento, dos leones de pie junto a los brazos 20y doce leones de pie sobre los seis peldaños, uno en cada extremo. En ningún otro reino se había hecho algo semejante. 21Todas las copas del rey Salomón y toda la vajilla del palacio «Bosque del Líbano» eran de oro puro. Nada estaba hecho de plata, pues en tiempos de Salomón la plata era poco apreciada. 22Cada tres años, la flota comercial que el rey tenía en el mar, junto con la flota de Hiram, regresaba de Tarsis trayendo oro, plata y marfil, monos y mandriles.ᵐ

23Tanto en riquezas como en sabiduría, el rey Salomón sobrepasó a los demás reyes de la tierra. 24Todo el mundo procuraba visitarlo para oír la sabiduría que Dios le había dado, 25y año tras año le llevaban regalos: artículos de plata y de oro, vestidos, armas y perfumes, y caballos y mulas.

26Salomón multiplicó el número de sus carros de combate y sus caballos; llegó a tener mil cuatrocientos carros y doce mil caballos,ⁿ los cuales mantenía en las caballerizas y también en su palacio en Jerusalén. 27El rey hizo que en Jerusalén la plata fuera tan común y corriente como las piedras, y el cedro tan abundante como las higueras de la llanura. 28Los caballos de Salomón eran importados de Egipto y de Coa, que era donde los mercaderes de la corte los compraban. 29En Egipto compraban carros por seiscientas monedas de plata,ñ y caballos por ciento cincuenta, para luego vendérselos a todos los reyes hititas y *sirios.

Las mujeres de Salomón

11 Ahora bien, además de casarse con la hija del faraón, el rey Salomón tuvo amoríos con muchas mujeres moabitas, amonitas, edomitas, sidonias e hititas, todas ellas mujeres extranjeras, 2que procedían de naciones de las cuales el SEÑOR había dicho a los israelitas: «No se unan a ellas, ni ellas a ustedes, porque de seguro les desviarán el *corazón para que sigan a otros dioses.» Con tales mujeres se unió Salomón y tuvo amoríos. 3Tuvo setecientas esposas que eran princesas, y trescientas concubinas; todas estas mujeres hicieron que se pervirtiera su corazón. 4En efecto, cuando Salomón llegó a viejo, sus mujeres le pervirtieron el corazón de modo que él siguió a otros dioses, y no siempre fue fiel al SEÑOR su Dios como lo había sido su padre David. 5Por el contrario, Salomón siguió a *Astarté, diosa de los sidonios, y a Moloc,º el detestable dios de los amonitas. 6Así que Salomón hizo lo que ofende al SEÑOR y no permaneció fiel a él como su padre David. 7Fue en esa época cuando, en una montaña al este de Jerusalén, Salomón edificó un *altar pagano para Quemós, el detestable dios de Moab, y otro para Moloc, el despreciable dios de los amonitas. 8Lo mismo hizo en favor de sus mujeres extranjeras, para que éstas pudieran quemar incienso y ofrecer sacrificios a sus dioses.

9Entonces el SEÑOR, Dios de Israel, se enojó con Salomón porque su corazón se había apartado de él, a pesar de que en dos ocasiones se le había aparecido 10para prohibirle que siguiera a otros dioses. Como Salomón no había cumplido esa orden, 11el SEÑOR le dijo: «Ya que procedes de este modo, y no has cumplido con mi *pacto ni con los decretos que te he ordenado, puedes estar seguro de que te quitaré el reino y se lo daré a uno de tus siervos. 12No obstante, por consideración a tu padre David no lo haré mientras tú vivas, sino que lo arrancaré de la mano de tu hijo. 13Y a éste, también por consideración a mi siervo David y a Jerusalén, no le quitaré todo el reino, sino que le dejaré una sola tribu, la cual ya he escogido.»

Los adversarios de Salomón

14Por lo tanto, el SEÑOR hizo que Hadad el edomita, que pertenecía a la familia real de Edom, surgiera como adversario de Salomón. 15Ahora bien, durante la guerra entre David y los edomitas, Joab, el general del ejército, había ido a enterrar a los muertos de Israel y había aprovechado la ocasión para matar a todos los hombres de Edom. 16Joab y los israelitas que estaban con él se quedaron allí seis meses, hasta que exterminaron a todos los varones edomitas. 17Pero Hadad, que entonces era apenas un muchacho, huyó a Egipto con algunos oficiales edomitas que habían estado al servicio de su padre. 18Partieron de Madián y llegaron a Parán, donde se les unieron unos hombres de ese lugar. De allí siguieron hacia Egipto y se presentaron ante el faraón, rey del país, quien le regaló a Hadad una casa y se encargó de darle sustento y tierras.

19Hadad agradó tanto al faraón, que éste le dio por esposa a su cuñada, una hermana de la reina Tapenés. 20La hermana de Tapenés dio a luz un hijo, al que llamó Guenubat, y Tapenés lo educó en el palacio real. De modo que Guenubat creció junto con los hijos del faraón.

21Mientras Hadad estaba en Egipto, se enteró de que ya habían muerto David y Joab, general del ejército. Entonces Hadad le dijo al faraón:

—Déjeme usted regresar a mi país.

22—¿Y por qué quieres regresar a tu país? —le preguntó el faraón—. ¿Acaso te falta algo aquí?

—No —respondió Hadad—, ¡pero de todos modos déjeme ir!

²³Dios también incitó a Rezón hijo de Eliadá para que fuera adversario de Salomón. Rezón, que había huido de su amo Hadad Ezer, rey de Sobá, ²⁴formó una banda de rebeldes y se convirtió en su jefe. Cuando David destruyó a los *sirios, los rebeldes fueron a Damasco y allí establecieron su gobierno. ²⁵Así fue como Rezón llegó a ser rey de Siria. Mientras vivió Salomón, Rezón aborreció a Israel y fue su adversario, de modo que agravó el daño causado por Hadad.

Jeroboán se rebela contra Salomón

²⁶También se rebeló contra el rey Salomón uno de sus funcionarios, llamado Jeroboán hijo de Nabat. Este Jeroboán era efrateo, oriundo de Seredá; su madre se llamaba Zerúa, y era viuda. ²⁷La rebelión de Jeroboán tuvo lugar cuando Salomón estaba construyendo los terraplenesᵖ para cerrar la brecha en el muro de la ciudad de David, su padre. ²⁸Jeroboán se había ganado el respeto de todos, de modo que cuando Salomón vio su buen desempeño lo puso a supervisar todo el trabajo forzado que se realizaba entre los descendientes de José.

²⁹Un día en que Jeroboán salía de Jerusalén, se encontró en el camino con el profeta Ahías de Siló, quien llevaba puesto un manto nuevo. Los dos estaban solos en el campo. ³⁰Entonces Ahías tomó el manto nuevo que llevaba puesto y, rasgándolo en doce pedazos, ³¹le dijo a Jeroboán: «Toma diez pedazos para ti, porque así dice el SEÑOR, Dios de Israel: "Ahora voy a arrancarle de la mano a Salomón el reino, y a ti te voy a dar diez tribus. ³²A él le dejaré una sola tribu, y esto por consideración a mi siervo David y a Jerusalén, la ciudad que he escogido entre todas las tribus de Israel. ³³Voy a hacerlo así porque él me ha abandonadoᑫ y adora a *Astarté, diosa de los sidonios, a Quemós, dios de los moabitas, y a Moloc, dios de los amonitas. Salomón no ha seguido mis *caminos; no ha hecho lo que me agrada, ni ha cumplido mis decretos y leyes como lo hizo David, su padre.

³⁴» "Sin embargo, no le quitaré todo el reino a Salomón sino que lo dejaré gobernar todos los días de su vida, por consideración a David mi siervo, a quien escogí y quien cumplió mis mandamientos y decretos. ³⁵Le quitaré el reino a su hijo, y te daré a ti diez tribus. ³⁶Pero a su hijo le dejaré una sola tribu, para que en Jerusalén, la ciudad donde decidí habitar, la lámpara de mi siervo David se mantenga siempre encendida delante de mí. ³⁷En lo que a ti atañe, yo te haré rey de Israel, y extenderás tu reino a tu gusto. ³⁸Si haces todo lo que te ordeno, y sigues mis caminos, haciendo lo que me agrada y cumpliendo mis decretos y mandamientos, como lo hizo David mi siervo, estaré contigo. Estableceré para ti una dinastía tan firme como la que establecí para David,ʳ y te daré Israel. ³⁹Así que haré sufrir a la descendencia de David, aunque no para siempre."»

⁴⁰Salomón, por su parte, intentó matar a Jeroboán, pero éste huyó a Egipto y se quedó allí, bajo la protección del rey Sisac, hasta la muerte de Salomón.

Muerte de Salomón
11:41-43 — 2Cr 9:29-31

⁴¹Los demás acontecimientos del reinado de Salomón, y su sabiduría y todo lo que hizo, están escritos en el libro de las crónicas de Salomón, ⁴²quien durante cuarenta años reinó en Jerusalén sobre todo Israel. ⁴³Cuando murió, fue sepultado en la ciudad de David, su padre, y su hijo Roboán lo sucedió en el trono.

División del reino
12:1-24 — 2Cr 10:1—11:4

12 Roboán fue a Siquén porque todos los israelitas se habían reunido allí para proclamarlo rey. ²De esto se enteró Jeroboán hijo de Nabat, quien al huir del rey Salomón se había establecido en Egipto y aún vivía allí. ³Cuando lo mandaron a buscar, él y toda la asamblea de Israel fueron a ver a Roboán y le dijeron:

⁴—Su padre nos impuso un yugo pesado. Alívienos usted ahora el duro trabajo y el pesado yugo que él nos echó encima; así serviremos a Su Majestad.

⁵—Váyanse por ahora —respondió Roboán—, pero vuelvan a verme dentro de tres días.

Cuando el pueblo se fue, ⁶el rey Roboán consultó con los *ancianos que habían estado en vida de su padre Salomón habían estado a su servicio.

—¿Qué me aconsejan ustedes que le responda a este pueblo? —preguntó.

⁷—Si Su Majestad se pone hoy al servicio de este pueblo —respondieron ellos—, y condesciende con ellos y les responde con amabilidad, ellos le servirán para siempre.

⁸Pero Roboán rechazó el consejo que le dieron los ancianos, y consultó más bien con los jóvenes que se habían criado con él y que estaban a su servicio.

⁹—¿Ustedes qué me aconsejan? —les preguntó—. ¿Cómo debo responderle a este pueblo que me dice: "Alívienos el yugo que su padre nos echó encima"?

¹⁰Aquellos jóvenes, que se habían criado con él, le contestaron:

—Este pueblo le ha dicho a Su Majestad: "Su padre nos impuso un yugo pesado; hágalo usted más ligero". Pues bien, respóndales de este modo: "Mi dedo meñique es más grueso que la cintura de mi padre. ¹¹Si él les impuso un yugo pesado, ¡yo les aumentaré la carga! Y si él los castigaba a ustedes con una vara, ¡yo lo haré con un látigo!"ˢ

¹²Al tercer día, en la fecha que el rey Roboán había indicado, Jeroboán regresó con todo el pueblo para presentarse ante él. ¹³Pero el rey les respondió con brusquedad: rechazó el consejo que le habían dado los ancianos, ¹⁴y siguió más bien el de los jóvenes. Les dijo: «Si mi padre les impuso un yugo pesado, ¡yo les aumentaré la carga! Si él los castigaba a ustedes con una vara, ¡yo lo haré con un látigo!» ¹⁵De modo que el rey no le hizo caso al pueblo. Las cosas tomaron este rumbo por voluntad del SEÑOR, para que se cumpliera lo que ya él le había dicho a Jeroboán hijo de Nabat por medio de Ahías el silonita.

¹⁶Cuando se dieron cuenta de que el rey no iba a hacerles caso, todos los israelitas exclamaron a una:

«¡Pueblo de Israel, todos a sus casas!
¡Y tú, David, ocúpate de los tuyos!

ᵖ **11:27** *los terraplenes.* Alt. *el Milo.* ᑫ **11:33** *me ha abandonado* (LXX, Siríaca y mss. de Vulgata); *me han abandonado* (TM). El cambio del singular al plural se aplica igualmente a los otros verbos en el versículo. ʳ **11:38** *Estableceré ... David.* Lit. *Te construiré una casa firme como le construí a David.* ˢ **12:11** *con una vara ... con un látigo.* Lit. *con azotes ... con escorpiones;* también en v. 14.

¿Qué parte tenemos con David?
¿Qué herencia tenemos con el hijo de Isaí?»

Así que se fueron, cada uno a su casa. [17]Sin embargo, Roboán siguió reinando sobre los israelitas que vivían en las ciudades de Judá. [18]Más tarde, el rey Roboán envió a Adoniránt para que supervisara el trabajo forzado, pero todos los israelitas lo mataron a pedradas. ¡A duras penas logró el rey subir a su carro y escapar a Jerusalén! [19]Desde entonces Israel ha estado en rebelión contra la familia de David.

[20]Cuando los israelitas se enteraron de que Jeroboán había regresado, mandaron a llamarlo para que se presentara ante la asamblea, y lo proclamaron rey de todo Israel. No hubo quien se mantuviera leal a la familia de David, con la sola excepción de la tribu de Judá.

[21]Roboán hijo de Salomón llegó a Jerusalén y movilizó a todas las familias de Judá y a la tribu de Benjamín, ciento ochenta mil guerreros selectos en total, para hacer la guerra contra Israel y así recuperar el reino. [22]Pero la palabra de Dios vino a Semaías, hombre de Dios, y le dio este mensaje: [23]«Diles a Roboán hijo de Salomón y rey de Judá, a todas las familias de Judá y de Benjamín, y al resto del pueblo [24]que así dice el SEÑOR: "No vayan a luchar contra sus hermanos, los israelitas. Regrese cada uno a su casa, porque es mi voluntad que esto haya sucedido."» Y ellos obedecieron la palabra del SEÑOR y regresaron, tal como el SEÑOR lo había ordenado.

Los becerros de oro en Betel y Dan

[25]Jeroboán fortificó la ciudad de Siquén en la región montañosa de Efraín, y se estableció allí. Luego se fue de Siquén y fortificó Peniel.u [26]Pero reflexionó: «¿Y qué tal si ahora el reino vuelve a la familia de David? [27]Si la gente sigue subiendo a Jerusalén para ofrecer sacrificios en el templo del SEÑOR, acabará por reconciliarse con su señor Roboán, rey de Judá. Entonces a mí me matarán, y volverán a unirse a él.»

[28]Después de buscar consejo, el rey hizo dos becerros de oro, y le dijo al pueblo: «¡Israelitas, no es necesario que sigan subiendo a Jerusalén! Aquí están sus dioses, que los sacaron de Egipto.» [29]Así que colocó uno de los becerros en Betel, y el otro en Dan. [30]Y esto inició al pueblo a pecar; muchos incluso iban hasta Dan para adorar al becerro que estaba allí.

[31]Jeroboán construyó *santuarios paganos en los cerros, y puso como sacerdotes a toda clase de gente, hasta a quienes no eran levitas. [32]Decretó celebrar una fiesta el día quince del mes octavo, semejante a la que se celebraba en Judá. En el altar de Betel ofreció sacrificios a los becerros que había hecho, y estableció también sacerdotes para los santuarios paganos que había construido. [33]Así pues, el día quince del mes octavo Jeroboán subió al altar que había construido en Betel y quemó incienso.v Ése fue el día que arbitrariamente decretó como día de fiesta para los israelitas.

El hombre de Dios que llegó de Judá

13 Sucedió que un hombre de Dios fue desde Judá hasta Betel en obediencia a la palabra del SEÑOR. Cuando Jeroboán, de pie junto al altar, se disponía a quemar incienso,w [2]el hombre de Dios, en obediencia a la palabra del SEÑOR, gritó: «Altar, altar! Así dice el SEÑOR: "En la familia de David nacerá un hijo llamado Josías, el cual sacrificará sobre ti a estos sacerdotes de *altares paganos que aquí queman incienso. ¡Sobre ti se quemarán huesos *humanos!"»

[3]Aquel mismo día el hombre de Dios ofreció una señal: «Ésta es la señal que el SEÑOR les da: ¡El altar será derribado, y las cenizas se esparcirán!»

[4]Al oír la sentencia que el hombre de Dios pronunciaba contra el altar de Betel, el rey extendió el brazo desde el altar y dijo: «¡Agárrenlo!» Pero el brazo que había extendido contra el hombre se le paralizó, de modo que no podía contraerlo. [5]En ese momento el altar se vino abajo y las cenizas se esparcieron, según la señal que, en obediencia a la palabra del SEÑOR, les había dado el hombre de Dios. [6]Entonces el rey le dijo al hombre de Dios:

—¡Apacigua al SEÑOR tu Dios! ¡Ora por mí, para que se me cure el brazo!

El hombre de Dios suplicó al SEÑOR, y al rey se le curó el brazo, quedándole como antes. [7]Luego el rey le dijo al hombre de Dios:

—Ven a casa conmigo, y come algo; además, quiero hacerte un regalo.

[8]Pero el hombre de Dios le respondió al rey:

—Aunque usted me diera la mitad de sus posesiones, no iría a su casa. Aquí no comeré pan ni beberé agua, [9]porque así me lo ordenó el SEÑOR. Me dijo: "No comas pan, ni bebas agua, ni regreses por el mismo camino."

[10]De modo que tomó un camino diferente al que había tomado para ir a Betel.

[11]En ese tiempo vivía en Betel cierto profeta anciano. Sus hijos fueron a contarlex todo lo que el hombre de Dios había hecho allí aquel día, y lo que había dicho al rey. [12]Su padre les preguntó:

—¿Por dónde se fue?

Sus hijos le indicaron el camino que había tomado el hombre de Dios que había llegado de Judá, [13]y el padre les ordenó:

—Aparéjenme un asno, para que lo monte.

Cuando el asno estuvo listo, el profeta anciano lo montó [14]y se fue tras el hombre de Dios. Lo encontró sentado debajo de una encina, y le preguntó:

—¿Eres tú el hombre de Dios que vino de Judá?

—Sí, lo soy —respondió.

[15]Entonces el profeta le dijo:

—Ven a comer a mi casa.

[16]—No puedo volver contigo ni acompañarte —respondió el hombre de Dios—; tampoco puedo comer pan ni beber agua contigo en este lugar, [17]pues el SEÑOR me ha dado esta orden: "No comas pan ni bebas agua allí, ni regreses por el mismo camino."

[18]El anciano replicó:

—También yo soy profeta, como tú. Y un ángel, obedeciendo a la palabra del SEÑOR, me dijo: "Llévalo a tu casa para que coma pan y beba agua."

Así lo engañó, [19]y el hombre de Dios volvió con él, y comió y bebió en su casa. [20]Mientras estaban sentados a la mesa, la palabra del SEÑOR vino al profeta que lo había hecho volver. [21]Entonces el profeta le anunció al hombre de Dios que había llegado de Judá:

—Así dice el SEÑOR: "Has desafiado la palabra del SEÑOR y no has cumplido la orden que el SEÑOR tu Dios te dio. [22]Has vuelto para comer pan y beber agua en el lugar donde él te dijo que no lo hicieras. Por lo tanto, no será sepultado tu cuerpo en la tumba de tus antepasados."

---

t **12:18** Adonirán (mss. de LXX y Siríaca; véanse también 1R 4:6 y 5:14); Adorán (TM). u **12:25** Peniel. Lit. Penuel. v **12:33** incienso. Alt. Sacrificios. w **13:1** incienso. Alt. sacrificios; también en v. 2. x **13:11** Sus hijos fueron a contarle. Lit. Su hijo fue a contarle.

23Cuando el hombre de Dios terminó de comer y beber, el profeta que lo había hecho volver le aparejó un asno, 24y el hombre de Dios se puso en camino. Pero un león le salió al paso y lo mató, dejándolo tendido en el camino. Sin embargo, el león y el asno se quedaron junto al cuerpo. 25Al ver el cuerpo tendido, y al león cuidando el cuerpo, los que pasaban por el camino llevaron la noticia a la ciudad donde vivía el profeta anciano.

26Cuando el profeta que lo había hecho volver de su viaje se enteró de eso, dijo: «Ahí tienen al hombre de Dios que desafió la palabra del SEÑOR. Por eso el SEÑOR lo entregó al león, que lo ha matado y despedazado, como la palabra del SEÑOR se lo había advertido.»

27Luego el profeta les dijo a sus hijos: «Aparéjenme el asno.» En cuanto lo hicieron, 28el profeta salió y encontró el cuerpo tendido en el camino, con el asno y el león junto a él. El león no se había comido el cadáver, ni había despedazado al asno. 29Entonces el profeta levantó el cadáver del hombre de Dios, lo puso sobre el asno y se lo llevó de vuelta a la ciudad para hacer duelo por él y enterrarlo. 30Luego lo puso en la tumba de su propiedad, e hicieron duelo por él, clamando: ¡Ay, hermano mío!»

31Después de enterrarlo, el profeta les dijo a sus hijos: «Cuando yo muera, entiérrenme en la misma tumba donde está enterrado el hombre de Dios, y pongan mis huesos junto a los suyos. 32Porque ciertamente se cumplirá la sentencia que, en obediencia a la palabra del SEÑOR, él pronunció contra el altar de Betel y contra todos los santuarios paganos que están en los montes de las ciudades de Samaria.»

33Con todo, Jeroboán no cambió su mala conducta, sino que una vez más puso como sacerdotes para los santuarios paganos a toda clase de gente. A cualquiera que deseaba ser sacerdote de esos santuarios, él lo consagraba como tal. 34Esa conducta llevó a la dinastía de Jeroboán a pecar, y causó su caída y su desaparición de la faz de la tierra.

Profecía de Ahías contra Jeroboán

14 En aquel tiempo se enfermó Abías hijo de Jeroboán, 2y éste le dijo a su esposa: «Disfrázate para que nadie se dé cuenta de que eres mi esposa. Luego vete a Siló, donde está Ahías, el profeta que me anunció que yo sería rey de este pueblo. 3Llévate diez panes, algunas tortas y un jarro de miel. Cuando llegues, él te dirá lo que va a pasar con nuestro hijo.» 4Así que la esposa de Jeroboán emprendió el viaje a Siló y fue a casa de Ahías.

Debido a su edad, Ahías había perdido la vista y estaba ciego. 5Pero el SEÑOR le había dicho: «La esposa de Jeroboán, haciéndose pasar por otra, viene a pedirte información acerca de su hijo, que está enfermo. Quiero que le des tal y tal respuesta.» 6Así que cuando Ahías oyó el sonido de sus pasos, se dirigió a la puerta y dijo: «Esposa de Jeroboán, ¿por qué te haces pasar por otra? Entra, que tengo malas noticias para ti. 7Regresa a donde está Jeroboán y adviértele que así dice el SEÑOR, Dios de Israel: "Yo te levanté de entre mi pueblo Israel y te hice su gobernante. 8Le quité el reino a la familia de David para dártelo a ti. Tú, sin embargo, no has sido como mi siervo David, que cumplió mis mandamientos y me siguió con todo el *corazón, haciendo solamente lo que me agrada. 9Por el contrario, te has portado peor que todos los que vivieron antes de ti, al extremo de hacerte

otros dioses, ídolos de metal; esto me enfurece, pues me has dado la espalda.

10» "Por eso voy a enviarle una desgracia a la familia de Jeroboán. De sus descendientes en Israel exterminaré hasta el último varón,y esclavo o libre. Barreré la descendencia de Jeroboán como se barre el estiércol, hasta no dejar rastro. 11A los que mueran en la ciudad se los comerán los perros, y a los que mueran en el campo se los comerán las aves del cielo. ¡El SEÑOR lo ha dicho!"

12»En cuanto a ti, vuelve a tu casa, pues cuando llegues a la ciudad, morirá el muchacho. 13Entonces todos los israelitas harán duelo por él y lo sepultarán. De la familia de Jeroboán sólo él será sepultado, porque en esa familia sólo él ha complacido al SEÑOR, Dios de Israel.

14»El SEÑOR levantará para sí un rey en Israel que exterminará a la familia de Jeroboán. De ahora en adelantez 15el SEÑOR sacudirá a los israelitas como el agua sacude las cañas. Los desarraigará de esta buena tierra que les dio a sus antepasados y los dispersará más allá del río Éufrates, porque se hicieron imágenes de la diosa *Aserá y provocaron así la ira del SEÑOR. 16Y el SEÑOR abandonará a Israel por los pecados que Jeroboán cometió e hizo cometer a los israelitas.»

17Entonces la esposa de Jeroboán se puso en marcha y regresó a Tirsá. En el momento en que atravesó el umbral de la casa, el muchacho murió. 18Así que lo sepultaron, y todo Israel hizo duelo por él, según la palabra que el SEÑOR había anunciado por medio de su siervo, el profeta Ahías.

19Los demás acontecimientos del reinado de Jeroboán, sus batallas y su gobierno, están escritos en el libro de las crónicas de los reyes de Israel. 20Jeroboán reinó veintidós años. Cuando murió, su hijo Nadab lo sucedió en el trono.

Roboán, rey de Judá
14:21,25-31 — 2Cr 12:9-16

21Roboán hijo de Salomón fue rey de Judá. Tenía cuarenta y un años cuando ascendió al trono, y reinó diecisiete años en Jerusalén, la ciudad donde, de entre las tribus de Israel, el SEÑOR había decidido habitar. La madre de Roboán era una amonita llamada Noamá.

22Los habitantes de Judá hicieron lo que ofende al SEÑOR, y con sus pecados provocaron los celos del SEÑOR más que sus antepasados. 23Además, en todas las colinas y bajo todo árbol frondoso se construyeron *santuarios paganos, *piedras sagradas e imágenes de la diosa *Aserá. 24Incluso se practicaba en el país la prostitución sagrada. El pueblo participaba en todas las repugnantes ceremonias de las naciones que el SEÑOR había expulsado del territorio de los israelitas.

25Sisac, rey de Egipto, atacó a Jerusalén en el quinto año del reinado de Roboán, 26y saqueó los tesoros del templo del SEÑOR y del palacio real. Se lo llevó todo, aun los escudos de oro que Salomón había hecho. 27Para reemplazarlos, el rey Roboán mandó hacer escudos de bronce y los puso al cuidado de los jefes de la guardia que custodiaba la entrada del palacio real. 28Siempre que el rey iba al templo del SEÑOR, los guardias portaban los escudos, pero luego los devolvían a la sala de los centinelas.

29Los demás acontecimientos del reinado de Roboán, y todo lo que hizo, están escritos en el libro de las crónicas de los reyes de Judá. 30Durante su reina-

---

y **14:10** hasta el último varón. Lit. al que orina contra la pared; también en 1R 16:11; 21:21. z **14:14** De ahora en adelante. Lit. Éste es el día. ¿Y qué? Aun ahora.

do hubo guerra constante entre él y Jeroboán. [31]Cuando murió Roboán, hijo de la amonita llamada Noamá, fue sepultado con sus antepasados en la Ciudad de David, y su hijo Abías[a] lo sucedió en el trono.

Abías, rey de Judá
15:1-2,6-8 — 2Cr 13:1-2,22—14:1

15 En el año dieciocho del reinado de Jeroboán hijo de Nabat, Abías ascendió al trono de Judá, [2]y reinó en Jerusalén tres años. Su madre era Macá hija de Abisalón.

[3]Abías cometió todos los pecados que, antes de él, había cometido su padre, pues no siempre fue fiel al SEÑOR su Dios como lo había sido su antepasado David. [4]No obstante, por consideración a David, el SEÑOR su Dios mantuvo la lámpara de David encendida en Jerusalén, y le dio un hijo que lo sucediera, para fortalecer así a Jerusalén. [5]Porque David había hecho lo que agrada al SEÑOR, y en toda su vida no había dejado de cumplir ninguno de los mandamientos del SEÑOR, excepto en el caso de Urías el hitita.

[6]Durante toda la vida de Abías hubo guerra entre Roboán y Jeroboán. [7]Los demás acontecimientos del reinado de Abías, y todo lo que hizo, están escritos en el libro de las crónicas de los reyes de Judá. También hubo guerra entre Abías y Jeroboán. [8]Y Abías murió y fue sepultado en la Ciudad de David. Y su hijo Asá lo sucedió en el trono.

Asá, rey de Judá
15:9-22 — 2Cr 14:2-3; 15:16—16:6
15:23-24 — 2Cr 16:11—17:1

[9]En el año veinte de Jeroboán, rey de Israel, Asá ocupó el trono de Judá, [10]y reinó en Jerusalén cuarenta y un años. Su abuela[b] era Macá hija de Abisalón.

[11]Asá hizo lo que agrada al SEÑOR, como lo había hecho su antepasado David. [12]Expulsó del país a los que practicaban la prostitución sagrada y acabó con todos los ídolos que sus antepasados habían fabricado. [13]Hasta destituyó a su abuela Macá de su puesto como reina madre, porque ella se había hecho una escandalosa imagen de la diosa *Aserá. Asá derribó la imagen y la quemó en el arroyo de Cedrón. [14]Aunque no quitó los *santuarios paganos, Asá se mantuvo siempre fiel al SEÑOR. [15]Además, llevó al templo del SEÑOR el oro, la plata y los utensilios que él y su padre habían consagrado.

[16]Durante los reinados de Asá y Basá, rey de Israel, hubo guerra entre ellos. [17]Basá, rey de Israel, atacó a Judá y fortificó Ramá para aislar totalmente a Asá, rey de Judá. [18]Entonces Asá tomó todo el oro y la plata que habían quedado en los tesoros del templo del SEÑOR y de su propio palacio, y los encargó a sus funcionarios para que se los llevaran a Ben Adad, hijo de Tabrimón y nieto de Hezión, rey de *Siria, que estaba gobernando en Damasco. Y le envió este mensaje: [19]«Hagamos tú y yo un tratado como el que antes hicieron tu padre y el mío. Aquí te envío un presente de oro y plata. Anula tu tratado con Basá, rey de Israel, para que se marche de aquí.»

[20]Ben Adad estuvo de acuerdo con el rey Asá y mandó a los jefes de su ejército para que atacaran las ciudades de Israel. Así conquistó Iyón, Dan, Abel Betmacá y todo Quinéret, además de Neftalí. [21]Cuando Basá se enteró, dejó de fortificar Ramá y se retiró a Tirsá. [22]Entonces el rey Asá movilizó a todo Judá, sin eximir a nadie, y se llevaron de Ramá las piedras y la madera con que Basá había estado fortificando la ciudad. Con ellas el rey Asá fortificó Gueba de Benjamín, y también Mizpa.

[23]Los demás acontecimientos del reinado de Asá, y todo su poderío y todo lo que hizo, y lo que atañe a las ciudades que edificó, están escritos en el libro de las crónicas de los reyes de Judá. Sin embargo, en su vejez sufrió una enfermedad de los pies. [24]Luego Asá murió y fue sepultado con sus antepasados en la Ciudad de David. Y su hijo Josafat lo sucedió en el trono.

Nadab, rey de Israel

[25]En el segundo año de Asá, rey de Judá, Nadab hijo de Jeroboán ascendió al trono de Israel y reinó allí dos años. [26]Pero Nadab hizo lo que ofende al SEÑOR, pues siguió el mal ejemplo de su padre, persistiendo en el mismo pecado con que éste hizo pecar a Israel.

[27]Basá hijo de Ahías, de la tribu de Isacar, conspiró contra Nadab y lo derrotó en la ciudad filistea de Guibetón, a la que Nadab y todo Israel tenían sitiada. [28]En el tercer año de Asá, rey de Judá, Basá mató a Nadab y lo sucedió en el trono.

[29]Tan pronto como comenzó a reinar, Basá mató a toda la familia de Jeroboán. No dejó vivo a ninguno de sus descendientes, sino que los eliminó a todos, según la palabra que el SEÑOR dio a conocer por medio de su siervo Ahías el silonita. [30]Esto sucedió a raíz de los pecados que Jeroboán cometió e hizo cometer a los israelitas, con lo que provocó la ira del SEÑOR, Dios de Israel.

[31]Los demás acontecimientos del reinado de Nadab, y todo lo que hizo, están escritos en el libro de las crónicas de los reyes de Israel. [32]Durante los reinados de Asá de Judá y Basá de Israel, hubo guerra entre ellos.

Basá, rey de Israel

[33]En el tercer año de Asá, rey de Judá, Basá hijo de Ahías ascendió al trono, y durante veinticuatro años reinó en Tirsá sobre todo Israel. [34]Basá hizo lo que ofende al SEÑOR, pues siguió el mal ejemplo de Jeroboán, persistiendo en el mismo pecado con que éste hizo pecar a Israel.

16 En aquel tiempo la palabra del SEÑOR vino a Jehú hijo de Jananí y le dio este mensaje contra Basá: [2]«Yo te levanté del polvo y te hice gobernante de mi pueblo Israel, pero tú seguiste el mal ejemplo de Jeroboán e hiciste que mi pueblo Israel pecara y provocara así mi enojo. [3]Por eso estoy a punto de aniquilarte y de hacer con tu familia lo mismo que hice con la de Jeroboán hijo de Nabat. [4]A los que mueran en la ciudad se los comerán los perros, y a los que mueran en el campo se los comerán las aves del cielo.»

[5]Los demás acontecimientos del reinado de Basá, y lo que hizo y atañe a sus obras, están escritos en el libro de las crónicas de los reyes de Israel. [6]Basá murió y fue sepultado en Tirsá. Y su hijo Elá lo sucedió en el trono.

[7]Además, por medio del profeta Jehú hijo de Jananí la palabra del SEÑOR vino contra Basá y su familia, debido a todas las ofensas que éste había cometido contra el SEÑOR, provocando así su ira. Y aunque destruyó a la familia de Jeroboán, llegó a ser semejante a ésta por las obras que hizo.

Elá, rey de Israel

8En el año veintiséis de Asá, rey de Judá, Elá hijo de Basá ascendió al trono de Israel, y reinó dos años en Tirsá. 9Pero conspiró contra él Zimri, uno de sus funcionarios, que tenía el mando de la mitad de sus carros de combate. Estaba Elá en Tirsá, emborrachándose en la casa de Arsá, administrador de su palacio. 10En ese momento irrumpió Zimri y lo hirió de muerte, y lo suplantó en el trono. Era el año veintisiete de Asá, rey de Judá.

11Tan pronto como Zimri usurpó el trono, eliminó a toda la familia de Basá. Exterminó hasta el último varón, fuera pariente o amigo. 12Así aniquiló a toda la familia de Basá, conforme a la palabra que el SEÑOR había anunciado contra Basá por medio del profeta Jehú. 13Esto sucedió a raíz de todos los pecados que Basá y su hijo Elá cometieron e hicieron cometer a los israelitas, provocando con sus ídolos inútiles la ira del SEÑOR, Dios de Israel.

14Los demás acontecimientos del reinado de Elá, y todo lo que hizo, están escritos en el libro de las crónicas de los reyes de Israel.

Zimri, rey de Israel

15En el año veintisiete de Asá, rey de Judá, mientras el ejército estaba acampado contra la ciudad filistea de Guibetón, Zimri reinó en Tirsá siete días. 16El mismo día en que las tropas oyeron decir que Zimri había conspirado contra el rey y lo había asesinado, allí mismo en el campamento todo Israel proclamó como rey de Israel a Omrí, el jefe del ejército. 17Entonces Omrí y todos los israelitas que estaban con él se retiraron de Guibetón y sitiaron Tirsá. 18Cuando Zimri vio que la ciudad estaba a punto de caer, se metió en la torre del palacio real y le prendió fuego. Así murió 19por los pecados que había cometido, pues hizo lo que ofende al SEÑOR, siguiendo el mal ejemplo de Jeroboán y persistiendo en el mismo pecado con que éste hizo pecar a Israel.

20Los demás acontecimientos del reinado de Zimri, incluso lo que atañe a su rebelión, están escritos en el libro de las crónicas de los reyes de Israel.

Omrí, rey de Israel

21Entonces el pueblo de Israel se dividió en dos facciones: la mitad respaldaba como rey a Tibni hijo de Guinat, y la otra, a Omrí. 22Pero los partidarios de Omrí derrotaron a los de Tibni, el cual murió en la contienda. Así fue como Omrí ascendió al trono.

23En el año treinta y uno de Asá, rey de Judá, Omrí ascendió al trono de Israel, y reinó doce años, seis de ellos en Tirsá. 24A un cierto Sémer le compró el cerro de Samaria por sesenta y seis kilosc de plata, y allí construyó una ciudad. En honor a Sémer, nombre del anterior propietario del cerro, la llamó Samaria.

25Pero Omrí hizo lo que ofende al SEÑOR y pecó más que todos los reyes que lo precedieron. 26Siguió el mal ejemplo de Jeroboán hijo de Nabat, persistiendo en el mismo pecado con que éste hizo pecar a Israel y provocando con sus ídolos inútiles la ira del SEÑOR, Dios de Israel.

27Los demás acontecimientos del reinado de Omrí, incluso lo que atañe a las proezas que realizó, están escritos en el libro de las crónicas de los reyes de Israel. 28Omrí murió y fue sepultado en Samaria. Y su hijo Acab lo sucedió en el trono.

Acab, rey de Israel

29En el año treinta y ocho de Asá, rey de Judá, Acab hijo de Omrí ascendió al trono, y reinó sobre Israel en Samaria veintidós años. 30Acab hijo de Omrí hizo lo que ofende al SEÑOR, más que todos los reyes que lo precedieron. 31Como si hubiera sido poco el cometer los mismos pecados de Jeroboán hijo de Nabat, también se casó con Jezabel hija de Et Baal, rey de los sidonios, y se dedicó a servir a *Baal y a adorarlo. 32Le erigió un altar en el templo que le había construido en Samaria, 33y también fabricó una imagen de la diosa *Aserá. En fin, hizo más para provocar la ira del SEÑOR, Dios de Israel, que todos los reyes de Israel que lo precedieron.

34En tiempos de Acab, Jiel de Betel reconstruyó Jericó. Echó los cimientos al precio de la vida de Abirán, su hijo mayor, y puso las *puertas al precio de la vida de Segub, su hijo menor, según la palabra que el SEÑOR había dado a conocer por medio de Josué hijo de Nun.

Elías es alimentado por los cuervos

17 Ahora bien, Elías, el de Tisbéd de Galaad, fue a decirle a Acab: «Tan cierto como que vive el SEÑOR, Dios de Israel, a quien yo sirvo, te juro que no habrá rocío ni lluvia en los próximos años, hasta que yo lo ordene.»

2Entonces la palabra del SEÑOR vino a Elías y le dio este mensaje: 3«Sal de aquí hacia el oriente, y escóndete en el arroyo de Querit, al este del Jordán. 4Beberás agua del arroyo, y yo les ordenaré a los cuervos que te den de comer allí.» 5Así que Elías se fue al arroyo de Querit, al este del Jordán, y allí permaneció, conforme a la palabra del SEÑOR. 6Por la mañana y por la tarde los cuervos le llevaban pan y carne, y bebía agua del arroyo.

La viuda de Sarepta

7Algún tiempo después, se secó el arroyo porque no había llovido en el país. 8Entonces la palabra del SEÑOR vino a él y le dio este mensaje: 9«Ve ahora a Sarepta de Sidón, y permanece allí. A una viuda de ese lugar le he ordenado darte de comer.» 10Así que Elías se fue a Sarepta. Al llegar a la *puerta de la ciudad, encontró a una viuda que recogía leña. La llamó y le dijo:

—Por favor, tráeme una vasija con un poco de agua para beber.

11Mientras ella iba por el agua, él volvió a llamarla y le pidió:

—Tráeme también, por favor, un pedazo de pan.

12—Tan cierto como que vive el SEÑOR tu Dios —respondió ella—, no me queda ni un pedazo de pan; sólo tengo un puñado de harina en la tinaja y un poco de aceite en el jarro. Precisamente estaba recogiendo unos leños para llevármelos a casa y hacer una comida para mi hijo y para mí. ¡Será nuestra última comida antes de morirnos de hambre!

13—No temas —le dijo Elías—. Vuelve a casa y haz lo que pensabas hacer. Pero antes prepárame un panecillo con lo que tienes, y tráemelo; luego haz algo para ti y para tu hijo. 14Porque así dice el SEÑOR, Dios de Israel: "No se agotará la harina de la tinaja ni se acabará el aceite del jarro, hasta el día en que el SEÑOR haga llover sobre la tierra."

15Ella fue e hizo lo que le había dicho Elías, de modo que cada día hubo comida para ella y su hijo, como también para Elías. 16Y tal como la palabra del SEÑOR lo había anunciado por medio de Elías, no se agotó la harina de la tinaja ni se acabó el aceite del jarro.

---

c 16:24 sesenta y seis kilos. Lit. dos *talentos. d 17:1 de Tisbé. Alt. de los pobladores.

[17]Poco después se enfermó el hijo de aquella viuda, y tan grave se puso que finalmente expiró. [18]Entonces ella le reclamó a Elías:

—¿Por qué te entrometes, hombre de Dios? ¡Viniste a recordarme mi pecado y a matar a mi hijo!

[19]—Dame a tu hijo —contestó Elías.

Y arrebatándoselo del regazo, Elías lo llevó al cuarto de arriba, donde estaba alojado, y lo acostó en su propia cama. [20]Entonces clamó: «SEÑOR mi Dios, ¿también a esta viuda, que me ha dado alojamiento, la haces sufrir matándole a su hijo?» [21]Luego se tendió tres veces sobre el muchacho y clamó: «¡SEÑOR mi Dios, devuélvele la *vida a este muchacho!»

[22]El SEÑOR oyó el clamor de Elías, y el muchacho volvió a la vida. [23]Elías tomó al muchacho y lo llevó de su cuarto a la planta baja. Se lo entregó a su madre y le dijo:

—¡Tu hijo vive! ¡Aquí lo tienes!

[24]Entonces la mujer le dijo a Elías:

—Ahora sé que eres un hombre de Dios, y que lo que sale de tu boca es realmente la palabra del SEÑOR.

Elías y Abdías

18 Después de un largo tiempo, en el tercer año, la palabra del SEÑOR vino a Elías y le dio este mensaje: «Ve y preséntate ante Acab, que voy a enviar lluvia sobre la tierra.» [2]Así que Elías se puso en camino para presentarse ante Acab.

En Samaria había mucha hambre. [3]Por lo tanto, Acab mandó llamar a Abdías, quien administraba su palacio y veneraba al SEÑOR. [4]Como Jezabel estaba acabando con los profetas del SEÑOR, Abdías había tomado a cien de ellos y los había escondido en dos cuevas, cincuenta en cada una, y les había dado de comer y de beber. [5]Acab instruyó a Abdías: «Recorre todo el país en busca de fuentes y ríos. Tal vez encontremos pasto para mantener vivos los caballos y las mulas, y no perdamos nuestras bestias.» [6]Así que se dividieron la tierra que iban a recorrer: Acab se fue en una dirección, y Abdías en la otra.

[7]Abdías iba por su camino cuando Elías le salió al encuentro. Al reconocerlo, Abdías se postró rostro en tierra y le preguntó:

—Mi señor Elías, ¿de veras es usted?

[8]—Sí, soy yo —le respondió—. Ve a decirle a tu amo que aquí estoy.

[9]—¿Qué mal ha hecho este servidor suyo —preguntó Abdías—, para que usted me entregue a Acab y él me mate? [10]Tan cierto como que vive el SEÑOR su Dios, que no hay nación ni reino adonde mi amo no haya mandado a buscarlo. Y a quienes afirmaban que usted no estaba allí, él los hacía jurar que no lo habían encontrado. [11]¿Y ahora usted me ordena que vaya a mi amo y le diga que usted está aquí? [12]¡Qué sé yo a dónde lo va a llevar el Espíritu del SEÑOR cuando nos separemos! Si voy y le digo a Acab que usted está aquí, y luego él no lo encuentra, ¡me matará! Tenga usted en cuenta que yo, su servidor, he sido fiel al SEÑOR desde mi juventud. [13]¿No le han contado a mi señor lo que hice cuando Jezabel estaba matando a los profetas del SEÑOR? ¡Pues escondí a cien de los profetas del SEÑOR en dos cuevas, cincuenta en cada una, y les di de comer y de beber! [14]¡Y ahora usted me ordena que vaya a mi amo y le diga que usted está aquí! ¡De seguro me matará!

[15]Elías le respondió:

—Tan cierto como que vive el SEÑOR *Todopoderoso, a quien sirvo, te aseguro que hoy me presentaré ante Acab.

Elías en el monte Carmelo

[16]Abdías fue a buscar a Acab y le informó de lo sucedido, así que éste fue al encuentro de Elías [17]y, cuando lo vio, le preguntó:

—¿Eres tú el que le está causando problemas a Israel?

[18]—No soy yo quien le está causando problemas a Israel —respondió Elías—. Quienes se los causan son tú y tu familia, porque han abandonado los mandamientos del SEÑOR y se han ido tras los *baales. [19]Ahora convoca de todas partes al pueblo de Israel, para que se reúna conmigo en el monte Carmelo con los cuatrocientos cincuenta profetas de Baal y los cuatrocientos profetas de la diosa *Aserá que se sientan a la mesa de Jezabel.

[20]Acab convocó en el monte Carmelo a todos los israelitas y a los profetas. [21]Elías se presentó ante el pueblo y dijo:

—¿Hasta cuándo van a seguir indecisos?[e] Si el Dios verdadero es el SEÑOR, deben seguirlo; pero si es Baal, síganlo a él.

El pueblo no dijo una sola palabra. [22]Entonces Elías añadió:

—Yo soy el único que ha quedado de los profetas del SEÑOR; en cambio, Baal cuenta con cuatrocientos cincuenta profetas. [23]Tráigannos dos bueyes. Que escojan ellos uno, y lo descuarticen y pongan los pedazos sobre la leña, pero sin prenderle fuego. Yo prepararé el otro buey y lo pondré sobre la leña, pero tampoco le prenderé fuego. [24]Entonces invocarán ellos el *nombre de su dios, y yo invocaré el nombre del SEÑOR. ¡El que responda con fuego, ése es el Dios verdadero!

Y todo el pueblo estuvo de acuerdo.

[25]Entonces Elías les dijo a los profetas de Baal:

—Ya que ustedes son tantos, escojan uno de los bueyes y prepárenlo primero. Invoquen luego el nombre de su dios, pero no prendan fuego.

[26]Los profetas de Baal tomaron el buey que les dieron y lo prepararon, e invocaron el nombre de su dios desde la mañana hasta el mediodía.

—¡Baal, respóndenos! —gritaban, mientras daban brincos alrededor del altar que habían hecho.

Pero no se escuchó nada, pues nadie respondió. [27]Al mediodía Elías comenzó a burlarse de ellos:

—¡Griten más fuerte! —les decía—. Seguro que es un dios, pero tal vez esté meditando, o esté ocupado o de viaje. ¡A lo mejor se ha quedado dormido y hay que despertarlo!

[28]Comenzaron entonces a gritar más fuerte y, como era su costumbre, se cortaron con cuchillos y dagas hasta quedar bañados en sangre. [29]Pasó el mediodía, y siguieron con su espantosa algarabía hasta la hora del sacrificio vespertino. Pero no se escuchó nada, pues nadie respondió ni prestó atención.

[30]Entonces Elías le dijo a todo el pueblo:

—¡Acérquense!

Así lo hicieron. Como el altar del SEÑOR estaba en ruinas, Elías lo reparó. [31]Luego recogió doce piedras, una por cada tribu descendiente de Jacob, a quien el SEÑOR le había puesto por nombre Israel. [32]Con las piedras construyó un altar en honor del SEÑOR, y alrededor cavó una zanja en que cabían quince litros[f] de cereal. [33]Colocó la leña, descuartizó el buey, puso los pedazos sobre la leña [34]y dijo:

---

e **18:21** *seguir indecisos.* Lit. *estar cojeando con dos muletas.*   f **18:32** *quince litros.* Lit. *dos *seah.*

—Llenen de agua cuatro cántaros, y vacíenlos sobre el *holocausto y la leña.

Luego dijo:

—Vuelvan a hacerlo.

Y así lo hicieron.

—¡Háganlo una vez más! —les ordenó.

Y por tercera vez vaciaron los cántaros. **35**El agua corría alrededor del altar hasta llenar la zanja.

36A la hora del sacrificio vespertino, el profeta Elías dio un paso adelante y oró así: «SEÑOR, Dios de Abraham, de Isaac y de Israel, que todos sepan hoy que tú eres Dios en Israel, y que yo soy tu siervo y he hecho todo esto en obediencia a tu palabra. **37**¡Respóndeme, SEÑOR, respóndeme, para que esta gente reconozca que tú, SEÑOR, eres Dios, y que estás convirtiendo a ti su *corazón!»

38En ese momento cayó el fuego del SEÑOR y quemó el holocausto, la leña, las piedras y el suelo, y hasta lamió el agua de la zanja. **39**Cuando todo el pueblo vio esto, se postró y exclamó: «¡El SEÑOR es Dios, el Dios verdadero!»

40Luego Elías les ordenó:

—¡Agarren a los profetas de Baal! ¡Que no escape ninguno!

Tan pronto como los agarraron, Elías hizo que los bajaran al arroyo Quisón, y allí los ejecutó. **41**Entonces Elías le dijo a Acab:

—Anda a tu casa, y come y bebe, porque ya se oye el ruido de un torrentoso aguacero.

42Acab se fue a comer y beber, pero Elías subió a la cumbre del Carmelo, se inclinó hasta el suelo y puso el rostro entre las rodillas.

43—Ve y mira hacia el mar —le ordenó a su criado.

El criado fue y miró, y dijo:

—No se ve nada.

Siete veces le ordenó Elías que fuera a ver, **44**y la séptima vez el criado le informó:

—Desde el mar viene subiendo una nube. Es tan pequeña como una mano.

Entonces Elías le ordenó:

—Ve y dile a Acab: "Engancha el carro y vete antes de que la lluvia te detenga."

45Las nubes fueron oscureciendo el cielo; luego se levantó el viento y se desató una fuerte lluvia. Pero Acab se fue en su carro hacia Jezrel. **46**Entonces el poder del SEÑOR vino sobre Elías, quien ajustándose el manto con el cinturón, echó a correr y llegó a Jezrel antes que Acab.

Elías huye a Horeb

19 Acab le contó a Jezabel todo lo que Elías había hecho, y cómo había matado a todos los profetas a filo de espada. **2**Entonces Jezabel envió un mensajero a que le dijera a Elías: «¡Que los dioses me castiguen sin piedad si mañana a esta hora no te he quitado la *vida como tú se la quitaste a ellos!»

3Elías se asustó^g y huyó para ponerse a salvo. Cuando llegó a Berseba de Judá, dejó allí a su criado **4**y caminó todo un día por el desierto. Llegó a donde había un arbusto,^h y se sentó a su sombra con ganas de morirse. «¡Estoy harto, SEÑOR! —protestó—. Quítame la vida, pues no soy mejor que mis antepasados.» **5**Luego se acostó debajo del arbusto y se quedó dormido.

De repente, un ángel lo tocó y le dijo: «Levántate y come.» **6**Elías miró a su alrededor, y vio a su cabecera un panecillo cocido sobre carbones calientes, y un jarro de agua. Comió y bebió, y volvió a acostarse.

7El ángel del SEÑOR regresó y, tocándolo, le dijo: «Levántate y come, porque te espera un largo viaje.» **8**Elías se levantó, y comió y bebió. Una vez fortalecido por aquella comida, viajó cuarenta días y cuarenta noches hasta que llegó a Horeb, el monte de Dios. **9**Allí pasó la noche en una cueva.

El SEÑOR se le aparece a Elías

Más tarde, la palabra del SEÑOR vino a él.

—¿Qué haces aquí, Elías? —le preguntó.

10—Me consume mi amor^i por ti, SEÑOR Dios *Todopoderoso —respondió él—. Los israelitas han rechazado tu *pacto, han derribado tus altares, y a tus profetas los han matado a filo de espada. Yo soy el único que ha quedado con vida, ¡y ahora quieren matarme a mí también!

11El SEÑOR le ordenó:

—Sal y preséntate ante mí en la montaña, porque estoy a punto de pasar por allí.

Como heraldo del SEÑOR vino un viento recio, tan violento que partió las montañas e hizo añicos las rocas; pero el SEÑOR no estaba en el viento. Al viento lo siguió un terremoto, pero el SEÑOR tampoco estaba en el terremoto. **12**Tras el terremoto vino un fuego, pero el SEÑOR tampoco estaba en el fuego. Y después del fuego vino un suave murmullo. **13**Cuando Elías lo oyó, se cubrió el rostro con el manto y, saliendo, se puso a la entrada de la cueva.

Entonces oyó una voz que le dijo:

—¿Qué haces aquí, Elías?

14Él respondió:

—Me consume mi amor por ti, SEÑOR, Dios Todopoderoso. Los israelitas han rechazado tu pacto, han derribado tus altares, y a tus profetas los han matado a filo de espada. Yo soy el único que ha quedado con vida, ¡y ahora quieren matarme a mí también!

15El SEÑOR le dijo:

—Regresa por el mismo camino, y ve al desierto de Damasco. Cuando llegues allá, unge a Jazael como rey de *Siria, **16**y a Jehú hijo de Nimsi como rey de Israel; unge también a Eliseo hijo de Safat, de Abel Mejolá, para que te suceda como profeta. **17**Jehú dará muerte a cualquiera que escape de la espada de Jazael, y Eliseo dará muerte a cualquiera que escape de la espada de Jehú. **18**Sin embargo, yo preservaré a siete mil israelitas que no se han arrodillado ante *Baal ni lo han besado.

El llamamiento de Eliseo

19Elías salió de allí y encontró a Eliseo hijo de Safat, que estaba arando. Había doce yuntas de bueyes en fila, y él mismo conducía la última. Elías pasó junto a Eliseo y arrojó su manto sobre él. **20**Entonces Eliseo dejó sus bueyes y corrió tras Elías.

—Permítame usted despedirme de mi padre y de mi madre con un beso —dijo él—, y luego lo seguiré.

—Anda, ve —respondió Elías—. Yo no te lo voy a impedir.^j

21Eliseo lo dejó y regresó. Tomó su yunta de bueyes y los sacrificó. Quemando la madera de la yunta, asó la carne y se la dio al pueblo, y ellos comieron. Luego partió para seguir a Elías y se puso a su servicio.

Ben Adad ataca a Samaria

20 Entonces Ben Adad, rey de *Siria, reunió a todo su ejército, acompañado por treinta y dos reyes con sus caballos y carros de combate, salió a

---

^g **19:3** se asustó. Alt. Vio. ^h **19:4** un arbusto. Lit. una *retama; también en v. 5. ^i **19:10** amor. Alt. celo; también en v. 14. ^j **19:20** Yo no te lo voy a impedir. Alt. Pero recuerda lo que he hecho por ti.

hacerle guerra a Samaria, y la sitió. [2]Envió a la ciudad mensajeros para que le dijeran a Acab, rey de Israel: «Así dice Ben Adad: [3]"Tu oro y tu plata son míos, lo mismo que tus mujeres y tus hermosos hijos."»

[4]El rey de Israel envió esta respuesta: «Tal como dices, mi señor y rey, yo soy tuyo, con todo lo que tengo.»

[5]Los mensajeros volvieron a Acab y le dijeron: «Así dice Ben Adad: "Mandé a decirte que me entregaras tu oro y tu plata, tus esposas y tus hijos. [6]Por tanto, mañana como a esta hora voy a enviar a mis funcionarios a requisar tu palacio y las casas de tus funcionarios, y se apoderarán de todo lo que más valoras y se lo llevarán."»

[7]El rey de Israel mandó llamar a todos los *ancianos del país y les dijo:

—¡Miren cómo ese tipo nos quiere causar problemas! Cuando mandó que le entregara mis esposas y mis hijos, mi oro y mi plata, no se los negué.

[8]Los ancianos y todos los del pueblo respondieron:

—No le haga caso, Su Majestad, ni ceda a sus exigencias.

[9]Así que Acab les respondió a los mensajeros de Ben Adad:

—Díganle a mi señor y rey: "Yo, tu servidor, haré todo lo que me pediste la primera vez, pero no puedo satisfacer esta nueva exigencia."

Ellos regresaron a Ben Adad con esa respuesta. [10]Entonces Ben Adad le envió otro mensaje a Acab: «Que los dioses me castiguen sin piedad si queda en Samaria el polvo suficiente para que mis hombres se lleven un puñado.»

[11]Pero el rey de Israel respondió: «Díganle que no cante victoria antes de tiempo.»[k]

[12]Cuando Ben Adad recibió este mensaje, estaba bebiendo con los reyes en su campamento.[l] De inmediato les ordenó a sus tropas: «¡A las armas!» Así se prepararon para atacar la ciudad.

Acab derrota a Ben Adad

[13]Mientras tanto, un profeta se presentó ante Acab, rey de Israel, y le anunció:

—Así dice el SEÑOR: "¿Ves ese enorme ejército? Hoy lo entregaré en tus manos, y entonces sabrás que yo soy el SEÑOR."

[14]—¿Por medio de quién lo hará? —preguntó Acab.

—Así dice el SEÑOR —respondió el profeta—: "Lo haré por medio de los cadetes."[m]

—¿Y quién iniciará el combate? —insistió Acab.

—Tú mismo —respondió el profeta.

[15]Así que Acab pasó revista a los cadetes, que sumaban doscientos treinta y dos hombres. También pasó revista a las demás tropas israelitas: siete mil en total. [16]Se pusieron en marcha al mediodía, mientras Ben Adad y los treinta y dos reyes aliados que estaban con él seguían emborrachándose en su campamento.

[17]Los cadetes formaban la vanguardia. Cuando los exploradores que Ben Adad había enviado le informaron que unos soldados estaban avanzando desde Samaria, [18]ordenó: «¡Captúrenlos vivos, sea que vengan en son de paz o en son de guerra!»

[19]Los cadetes salieron de la ciudad al frente del ejército. [20]Cada soldado abatió a su adversario, y los

*sirios tuvieron que huir. Los israelitas los persiguieron, pero Ben Adad, rey de Siria, escapó a caballo con algunos de sus jinetes. [21]El rey de Israel avanzó y abatió a la caballería, de modo que los sirios sufrieron una gran derrota.

[22]Más tarde, el profeta se presentó ante el rey de Israel y le dijo: «No se duerma usted en sus laureles;[n] trace un buen plan, porque el año entrante el rey de Siria volverá a atacar.»

[23]Por otra parte, los funcionarios del rey de Siria le aconsejaron: «Los dioses de los israelitas son dioses de las montañas. Por eso son demasiado fuertes para nosotros. Pero si peleamos contra ellos en las llanuras, sin duda los venceremos. [24]Haga usted lo siguiente: Destituya a todos los reyes y reemplácelos por otros funcionarios. [25]Prepare usted también un ejército como el que perdió, caballo por caballo y carro por carro, para atacar a Israel en las llanuras. ¡Sin duda los venceremos!»

Ben Adad estuvo de acuerdo, y así lo hizo. [26]Al año siguiente, pasó revista a las tropas sirias y marchó a Afec para atacar a Israel. [27]Acab, por su parte, pasó revista a las tropas israelitas y las aprovisionó. Éstas se pusieron en marcha para salir al encuentro de los sirios, y acamparon frente a ellos. Parecían un pequeño rebaño de cabras, mientras que los sirios cubrían todo el campo.

[28]El hombre de Dios se presentó ante el rey de Israel y le dijo: «Así dice el SEÑOR: "Por cuanto los sirios piensan que el SEÑOR es un dios de las montañas y no un dios de los valles, yo te voy a entregar este enorme ejército en tus manos, y así sabrás que yo soy el SEÑOR."»

[29]Siete días estuvieron acampados los unos frente a los otros, y el séptimo día se desató el combate. En un solo día los israelitas le causaron cien mil bajas a la infantería siria. [30]Los demás soldados huyeron a Afec, pero la muralla de la ciudad se desplomó sobre veintisiete mil de ellos.

Ben Adad, que también se había escapado a la ciudad, andaba de escondite en escondite. [31]Entonces sus funcionarios le dijeron: «Hemos oído decir que los reyes del linaje de Israel son compasivos. Rindámonos ante el rey de Israel y pidámosle perdón.[ñ] Tal vez le perdone a usted la *vida.»

[32]Se presentaron ante el rey de Israel, se rindieron ante él y le rogaron:

—Su siervo Ben Adad dice: "Por favor, perdóname la vida."

—¿Todavía está vivo? —preguntó el rey—. ¡Pero si es mi hermano!

[33]Los hombres tomaron esa respuesta como un buen augurio, y aprovechando la ocasión, exclamaron:

—¡Claro que sí, Ben Adad es su hermano!

—Vayan por él —dijo el rey.

Cuando Ben Adad se presentó ante Acab, éste lo hizo subir a su carro de combate. Entonces Ben Adad le propuso:

[34]—Te devolveré las ciudades que mi padre le quitó al tuyo, y podrás establecer zonas de mercado en Damasco, como lo hizo mi padre en Samaria.

Acab le respondió:

—Sobre esa base, te dejaré en libertad.

Y así firmó un tratado con él, y lo dejó ir.

---

[k] **20:11** *que no cante ... de tiempo.* Lit. *no ha de jactarse el que se pone la armadura sino el que se la quita.* [l] **20:12** *en su campamento.* Alt. *en Sucot;* también en v. 16. [m] **20:14** *los cadetes.* Lit. *los jóvenes de los jefes provinciales;* también en vv. 15,17 y 19. [n] **20:22** *No se duerma usted en sus laureles.* Lit. *Vaya y fortalézcase.* [ñ] **20:31** *Rindámonos ... perdón.* Lit. *Pongámonos *cilicio en la cintura y sogas en la cabeza y vayamos al rey de Israel.*

Un profeta condena a Acab

35En obediencia a la palabra del SEÑOR, un miembro de la comunidad de profetas le dijo a otro:

—¡Golpéame!

Pero aquél se negó a hacerlo.

36Entonces el profeta dijo:

—Por cuanto no has obedecido al SEÑOR, tan pronto como nos separemos te matará un león.

Y después de que el profeta se fue, un león le salió al paso y lo mató.

37Más adelante, el mismo profeta encontró a otro hombre y le dijo: «¡Golpéame!» Así que el hombre lo golpeó y lo hirió. **38**Luego el profeta salió a esperar al rey a la vera del camino, cubierto el rostro con un antifaz. **39**Cuando pasaba el rey, el profeta le gritó:

—Este servidor de Su Majestad entró en lo más reñido de la batalla. Allí alguien se me presentó con un prisionero y me dijo: "Hazte cargo de este hombre. Si se te escapa, pagarás su *vida con la tuya, o con tres mil monedas° de plata." **40**Mientras este servidor de Su Majestad estaba ocupado en otras cosas, el hombre se escapó.

—¡Ésa es tu sentencia! —respondió el rey de Israel—. Tú mismo has tomado la decisión.

41En el acto, el profeta se quitó el antifaz, y el rey de Israel se dio cuenta de que era uno de los profetas. **42**Y el rey dijo:

—Así dice el SEÑOR: "Has dejado en libertad a un hombre que yo había condenado a muerte.ᴾ Por lo tanto, pagarás su vida con la tuya, y su pueblo con el tuyo."

43Entonces el rey de Israel, deprimido y malhumorado, volvió a su palacio en Samaria.

El viñedo de Nabot

21 Un tiempo después sucedió lo siguiente: Nabot el jezrelita tenía un viñedo en Jezrel, el cual colindaba con el palacio de Acab, rey de Samaria. **2**Éste le dijo a Nabot:

—Dame tu viñedo para hacerme una huerta de hortalizas, ya que está tan cerca de mi palacio. A cambio de él te daré un viñedo mejor o, si lo prefieres, te pagaré lo que valga.

3Pero Nabot le respondió:

—El SEÑOR prohíbe que yo le venda a Su Majestad lo que heredé de mis antepasados.

4Acab se fue a su casa deprimido y malhumorado porque Nabot el jezrelita le había dicho: «No puedo cederle a Su Majestad lo que heredé de mis antepasados.» De modo que se acostó de cara a la pared, y no quiso comer. **5**Su esposa Jezabel entró y le preguntó:

—¿Por qué estás tan deprimido que ni comer quieres?

6—Porque le dije a Nabot el jezrelita que me vendiera su viñedo o que, si lo prefería, se lo cambiaría por otro; pero él se negó.

7Ante esto, Jezabel su esposa le dijo:

—¿Y no eres tú quien manda en Israel? ¡Anda, levántate y come, que te hará bien! Yo te conseguiré el viñedo del tal Nabot.

8De inmediato escribió cartas en nombre de Acab, puso en ellas el sello del rey, y las envió a los *ancianos y nobles que vivían en la ciudad de Nabot. **9**En las cartas decía:

«Decreten un día de ayuno, y den a Nabot un lugar prominente en la asamblea del pueblo. **10**Pongan frente a él a dos sinvergüenzas y háganlos testificar que él ha maldecido tanto a Dios como al rey. Luego sáquenlo y mátenlo a pedradas.»

11Los ancianos y nobles que vivían en esa ciudad acataron lo que Jezabel había ordenado en sus cartas. **12**Decretaron un día de ayuno y le dieron a Nabot un lugar prominente en la asamblea. **13**Llegaron los dos sinvergüenzas, se sentaron frente a él y lo acusaron ante el pueblo, diciendo: «¡Nabot ha maldecido a Dios y al rey!» Como resultado, la gente lo llevó fuera de la ciudad y lo mató a pedradas. **14**Entonces le informaron a Jezabel: «Nabot ha sido apedreado, y está muerto.»

15Tan pronto como Jezabel se enteró de que Nabot había muerto a pedradas, le dijo a Acab: «¡Vamos! Toma posesión del viñedo que Nabot el jezrelita se negó a venderte. Ya no vive; está muerto.» **16**Cuando Acab se enteró de que Nabot había muerto, fue a tomar posesión del viñedo.

17Entonces la palabra del SEÑOR vino a Elías el tisbita y le dio este mensaje: **18**«Ve a encontrarte con Acab, rey de Israel, que gobierna en Samaria. En este momento se encuentra en el viñedo de Nabot, tomando posesión del mismo. **19**Dile que así dice el SEÑOR: "¿No has asesinado a un hombre, y encima te has adueñado de su propiedad?" Luego dile que así también dice el SEÑOR: "¡En el mismo lugar donde los perros lamieron la sangre de Nabot, lamerán también tu propia sangre!"»

20Acab le respondió a Elías:

—¡Mi enemigo! ¿Así que me has encontrado?

—Sí —contestó Elías—, te he encontrado porque te has vendido para hacer lo que ofende al SEÑOR, **21**quien ahora te dice: "Voy a enviarte una desgracia. Acabaré contigo, y de tus descendientes en Israel exterminaré hasta el último varón, esclavo o libre. **22**Haré con tu familia lo mismo que hice con la de Jeroboán hijo de Nabat y con la de Basá hijo de Ahías, porque me has provocado mi ira y has hecho que Israel peque." **23**Y en cuanto a Jezabel, el SEÑOR dice: "Los perros se la comerán junto al muroᵠ de Jezrel." **24**También a los familiares de Acab que mueran en la ciudad se los comerán los perros, y a los que mueran en el campo se los comerán las aves del cielo.

25Nunca hubo nadie como Acab que, animado por Jezabel su esposa, se prestara para hacer lo que ofende al SEÑOR. **26**Su conducta fue repugnante, pues siguió a los ídolos, como lo habían hecho los amorreos, a quienes el SEÑOR expulsó de la presencia de Israel.

27Cuando Acab escuchó estas palabras, se rasgó las vestiduras, se vistió de luto y ayunó. Dormía vestido así, y andaba deprimido. **28**Entonces la palabra del SEÑOR vino a Elías el tisbita y le dio este mensaje: **29**«¿Has notado cómo Acab se ha humillado ante mí? Por cuanto se ha humillado, no enviaré esta desgracia mientras él viva, sino que la enviaré a su familia durante el reinado de su hijo.»

Micaías profetiza contra Acab

22:1-28 — 2Cr 18:1-27

22 Durante tres años no hubo guerra entre *Siria e Israel. **2**Pero en el tercer año Josafat, rey de Judá, fue a ver al rey de Israel, **3**el cual dijo a sus

---

o 20:39 *tres mil monedas.* Lit. *un *talento.* **P 20:42** *un hombre ... muerte.* Lit. *al hombre de mi *destrucción.* **q 21:23** *muro* (mss. hebreos); *campo* (TM).

funcionarios: «¿No saben que Ramot de Galaad nos pertenece? ¡Y no hemos hecho nada para obligar al rey de Siria a que nos la devuelva!»

⁴Así que le preguntó a Josafat:

—¿Irías conmigo a pelear contra Ramot de Galaad?

Josafat le respondió al rey de Israel:

—Estoy a tu disposición, lo mismo que mi pueblo y mis caballos. ⁵Pero antes que nada, consultemos al SEÑOR —añadió.

⁶Así que el rey de Israel reunió a los profetas, que eran casi cuatrocientos, y les preguntó:

—¿Debo ir a la guerra contra Ramot de Galaad, o no?

—Vaya, Su Majestad —contestaron ellos—, porque el Señor la entregará en sus manos.

⁷Pero Josafat inquirió:

—¿No hay aquí un profeta del SEÑOR a quien podamos consultar?

⁸El rey de Israel le respondió:

—Todavía hay alguien por medio de quien podemos consultar al SEÑOR, pero me cae muy mal porque nunca me profetiza nada bueno; sólo me anuncia desastres. Se trata de Micaías hijo de Imlá.

—No digas eso —replicó Josafat.

⁹Entonces el rey de Israel llamó a uno de sus funcionarios y le ordenó:

—¡Traigan de inmediato a Micaías hijo de Imlá!

¹⁰El rey de Israel, y Josafat, rey de Judá, vestidos con su ropaje real y sentados en sus respectivos tronos, estaban en la plaza a la *entrada de Samaria, con todos los que profetizaban en presencia de ellos. ¹¹Sedequías hijo de Quenaná, que se había hecho unos cuernos de hierro, anunció: «Así dice el SEÑOR: "Con estos cuernos atacarás a los sirios hasta aniquilarlos."» ¹²Y los demás profetas vaticinaban lo mismo: «Ataque Su Majestad a Ramot de Galaad, y vencerá, porque el SEÑOR la entregará en sus manos.»

¹³Ahora bien, el mensajero que había ido a llamar a Micaías le advirtió:

—Mira, los demás profetas a una voz predicen el éxito del rey. Habla favorablemente, para que tu mensaje concuerde con el de ellos.

¹⁴Pero Micaías repuso:

—Tan cierto como que vive el SEÑOR, ten la seguridad de que yo le anunciaré al rey lo que el SEÑOR me diga.

¹⁵Cuando compareció ante el rey, éste le preguntó:

—Micaías, ¿debemos ir a la guerra contra Ramot de Galaad, o no?

—Ataque, Su Majestad, que vencerá —contestó él—, porque el SEÑOR la entregará en sus manos.

¹⁶El rey le reclamó:

—¿Cuántas veces debo hacerte jurar que no me digas nada más que la verdad en el *nombre del SEÑOR?

¹⁷Ante esto, Micaías concedió:

—Vi a todo Israel esparcido por las colinas, como ovejas sin *pastor. Y el SEÑOR dijo: "Esta gente no tiene amo. ¡Que cada cual se vaya a su casa en *paz!"

¹⁸El rey de Israel le dijo a Josafat:

—¿No te dije que jamás me profetiza nada bueno, y que sólo me anuncia desastres?

¹⁹Micaías prosiguió:

—Por lo tanto, oiga usted la palabra del SEÑOR: Vi al SEÑOR sentado en su trono con todo el ejército del cielo alrededor de él, a su derecha y a su izquier-

da. ²⁰Y el SEÑOR dijo: "¿Quién seducirá a Acab para que ataque a Ramot de Galaad y vaya a morir allí?" Uno sugería una cosa, y otro sugería otra. ²¹Por último, un espíritu se adelantó, se puso delante del SEÑOR y dijo: "Yo lo seduciré." ²²"¿Por qué medios?", preguntó el SEÑOR. Y aquel espíritu respondió: "Saldré y seré un espíritu mentiroso en la boca de todos sus profetas." Entonces el SEÑOR ordenó: "Ve y hazlo así, que tendrás éxito en seducirlo." ²³Así que ahora el SEÑOR ha puesto un espíritu mentiroso en la boca de todos estos profetas de Su Majestad. El SEÑOR ha decretado para usted la calamidad.

²⁴Al oír esto, Sedequías hijo de Quenaná se levantó y le dio una bofetada a Micaías.

—¿Por dónde se fue el espíritu[r] del SEÑOR cuando salió de mí para hablarte? —le preguntó.

²⁵Micaías contestó:

—Lo sabrás el día en que andes de escondite en escondite.

²⁶Entonces el rey de Israel ordenó:

—Tomen a Micaías y llévenselo a Amón, el gobernador de la ciudad, y a Joás, mi hijo. ²⁷Díganles que les ordeno echar en la cárcel a ese tipo, y no darle más que pan y agua, hasta que yo regrese sin contratiempos.

²⁸Micaías manifestó:

—Si regresas sin contratiempos, el SEÑOR no ha hablado por medio de mí. ¡Tomen nota todos ustedes de lo que estoy diciendo!

Muerte de Acab
22:29-36 — 2Cr 18:28-34

²⁹El rey de Israel, y Josafat, rey de Judá, marcharon juntos contra Ramot de Galaad. ³⁰Allí el rey de Israel le dijo a Josafat: «Yo entraré a la batalla disfrazado, pero tú te pondrás tu ropaje real.» Así que el rey de Israel se disfrazó y entró al combate.

³¹Pero el rey de *Siria les había ordenado a sus treinta y dos capitanes de los carros de combate: «No luchen contra nadie, grande o pequeño, salvo contra el rey de Israel.» ³²Cuando los capitanes de los carros vieron a Josafat, pensaron: «Sin duda, éste es el rey de Israel.» Así que se volvieron para atacarlo; pero Josafat gritó. ³³Entonces los capitanes de los carros vieron que no era el rey de Israel, y dejaron de perseguirlo.

³⁴Sin embargo, alguien disparó su arco al azar y hirió al rey de Israel entre las piezas de su armadura. El rey le ordenó al que conducía su carro: «Da la vuelta y sácame del campo de batalla, pues me han herido.» ³⁵Todo el día arreció la batalla, y al rey se le mantuvo de pie en su carro, frente a los sirios. Pero la sangre de su herida no dejaba de correr por el piso del carro, y esa misma tarde Acab murió. ³⁶Ya se ponía el sol cuando por todo el ejército se difundió un clamor: «Cada hombre a su ciudad; ¡todo el mundo a su tierra!»

³⁷Así que el rey murió, y fue llevado a Samaria, donde lo sepultaron. ³⁸Lavaron el carro en un estanque de Samaria, donde se bañaban las prostitutas, y los perros lamieron la sangre, tal como lo había declarado la palabra del SEÑOR.

³⁹Los demás acontecimientos del reinado de Acab, incluso todo lo que hizo, el palacio que construyó e incrustó de marfil, y las ciudades que fortificó, están escritos en el libro de las crónicas de los reyes de Israel. ⁴⁰Acab murió, y su hijo Ocozías lo sucedió en el trono.

ʳ 22:24 *espíritu.* Alt. *Espíritu.*

Josafat, rey de Judá
22:41-50 — 2Cr 20:31—21:1

⁴¹Josafat hijo de Asá ascendió al trono de Judá en el cuarto año de Acab, rey de Israel. ⁴²Josafat tenía treinta y cinco años cuando comenzó a reinar, y reinó en Jerusalén veinticinco años. El nombre de su madre era Azuba hija de Siljí. ⁴³Siempre siguió el buen ejemplo de su padre Asá, y nunca se desvió de él, sino que hizo lo que agrada al SEÑOR. Sin embargo, no se quitaron los *santuarios paganos, de modo que el pueblo siguió ofreciendo allí sacrificios e incienso quemado. ⁴⁴Josafat también estaba en paz con el rey de Israel.

⁴⁵Los demás acontecimientos del reinado de Josafat, lo que llevó a cabo y sus proezas militares, están escritos en el libro de las crónicas de los reyes de Judá. ⁴⁶Libró la tierra del resto de hombres que practicaban la prostitución en los santuarios, los cuales se habían quedado allí incluso después del reinado de su padre Asá. ⁴⁷En aquel tiempo no había rey en Edom, sino que gobernaba un regente.

⁴⁸Por esos días Josafat construyó una flota mercanteˢ para ir a Ofir por oro, pero nunca llegaron a zarpar, pues naufragaron en Ezión Guéber. ⁴⁹Entonces Ocozías hijo de Acab le dijo a Josafat: «Deja que mis hombres naveguen con tus hombres.» Pero Josafat no se lo permitió.

⁵⁰Josafat murió y fue sepultado con sus antepasados en la ciudad de su padre David. Y su hijo Jorán lo sucedió en el trono.

Ocozías, rey de Israel

⁵¹Ocozías hijo de Acab ascendió al trono de Israel en Samaria en el año diecisiete de Josafat, rey de Judá, y reinó dos años en Israel. ⁵²Pero hizo lo que ofende al SEÑOR, porque anduvo en los *caminos de su padre y de su madre, y en los caminos de Jeroboán hijo de Nabat, que hizo que Israel pecara. ⁵³Sirvió y adoró a *Baal, y provocó a ira al SEÑOR, Dios de Israel, tal como lo había hecho su padre.

ˢ **22:48** *una flota mercante.* Lit. *unos barcos de Tarsis.*

2 REYES

El juicio del Señor contra Ocozías

1 Después de la muerte de Acab, la nación de Moab se rebeló contra Israel. ²Ocozías, que se había herido al caerse por la ventana del piso superior de su palacio en Samaria, despachó a unos mensajeros con este encargo: «Vayan y consulten a *Baal Zebub, dios de Ecrón, para saber si voy a recuperarme de estas heridas.» ³Pero el ángel del SEÑOR le dijo a Elías el tisbita: «Levántate y sal al encuentro de los mensajeros del rey de Samaria. Diles: "Y ustedes, ¿por qué van a consultar a Baal Zebub, dios de Ecrón? ¿Acaso no hay Dios en Israel?" ⁴Pues bien, así dice el SEÑOR: "Ya no te levantarás de tu lecho de enfermo, sino que ciertamente morirás."»

Así lo hizo Elías, ⁵y cuando los mensajeros regresaron, el rey les preguntó:

—¿Cómo? ¿Ya están de regreso?

⁶Ellos respondieron:

—Es que un hombre nos salió al encuentro y nos dijo que regresáramos al rey que nos había enviado y le dijéramos: "Así dice el SEÑOR: '¿Por qué mandas a consultar a Baal Zebub, dios de Ecrón? ¿Acaso no hay Dios en Israel? Pues bien, ya no te levantarás de tu lecho de enfermo, sino que ciertamente morirás.'"

⁷El rey les preguntó:

—¿Qué aspecto tenía el hombre que les salió al encuentro y les habló de ese modo?

⁸—Llevaba puesto un manto de piel, y tenía un cinturón de cuero atado a la cintura —contestaron ellos.

—¡Ah! ¡Era Elías el tisbita! —exclamó el rey.

⁹Y en seguida envió a un oficial con cincuenta soldados a buscarlo. El oficial fue y encontró a Elías sentado en la cima de un monte.

—Hombre de Dios —le dijo—, el rey le ordena que baje.

¹⁰—Si soy hombre de Dios —replicó Elías—, ¡que caiga fuego del cielo y te consuma junto con tus cincuenta soldados!

Al instante cayó fuego del cielo, y consumió al oficial y a sus soldados. ¹¹Así que el rey envió a otro oficial con otros cincuenta soldados en busca de Elías.

—Hombre de Dios —le dijo—, el rey le ordena que baje inmediatamente.

¹²—Si soy hombre de Dios —repuso Elías—, ¡que caiga fuego del cielo y te consuma junto con tus cincuenta soldados!

Una vez más, fuego de Dios cayó del cielo y consumió al oficial y a sus soldados.

¹³Por tercera vez el rey envió a un oficial con otros cincuenta soldados. Cuando éste llegó hasta donde estaba Elías, se puso de rodillas delante de él y le imploró:

—Hombre de Dios, le ruego que respete mi *vida y la de estos cincuenta servidores suyos. ¹⁴Sé bien que cayó fuego del cielo y consumió a los dos primeros oficiales y a sus soldados. Por eso le pido ahora que respete mi vida.

¹⁵El ángel del SEÑOR le ordenó a Elías: «Baja con él; no le tengas miedo.» Así que Elías se levantó y bajó con el oficial para ver al rey, ¹⁶a quien le dijo:

—Así dice el SEÑOR: "Enviaste mensajeros a consultar a Baal Zebub, dios de Ecrón. ¿Acaso no hay Dios en Israel a quien puedas consultar? Puesto que

has actuado así, ya no te levantarás de tu lecho de enfermo, sino que ciertamente morirás."

¹⁷Así fue como murió el rey, según la palabra que el SEÑOR había anunciado por medio de Elías. Como Ocozías no llegó a tener hijos, Jorán lo sucedió en el trono. Esto aconteció en el segundo año de Jorán hijo de Josafat, rey de Judá. ¹⁸Los demás acontecimientos del reinado de Ocozías están escritos en el libro de las crónicas de los reyes de Israel.

Elías llevado al cielo

2 Cuando se acercaba la hora en que el SEÑOR se llevaría a Elías al cielo en un torbellino, Elías y Eliseo salieron de Guilgal. ²Entonces Elías le dijo a Eliseo:

—Quédate aquí, pues el SEÑOR me ha enviado a Betel.

Pero Eliseo le respondió:

—Tan cierto como que el SEÑOR y tú viven, te juro que no te dejaré solo.

Así que fueron juntos a Betel. ³Allí los miembros de la comunidad de profetas de Betel salieron a recibirlos, y le preguntaron a Eliseo:

—¿Sabes que hoy el SEÑOR va a quitarte a tu maestro, y a dejarte sin guía?

—Lo sé muy bien; ¡cállense!

⁴Elías, por su parte, volvió a decirle:

—Quédate aquí, Eliseo, pues el SEÑOR me ha enviado a Jericó.

Pero Eliseo le repitió:

—Tan cierto como que el SEÑOR y tú viven, te juro que no te dejaré solo.

Así que fueron juntos a Jericó. ⁵También allí los miembros de la comunidad de profetas de la ciudad se acercaron a Eliseo y le preguntaron:

—¿Sabes que hoy el SEÑOR va a quitarte a tu maestro, y a dejarte sin guía?

—Lo sé muy bien; ¡cállense!

⁶Una vez más Elías le dijo:

—Quédate aquí, pues el SEÑOR me ha enviado al Jordán.

Pero Eliseo insistió:

—Tan cierto como que el SEÑOR y tú viven, te juro que no te dejaré solo.

Así que los dos siguieron caminando ⁷y se detuvieron junto al río Jordán. Cincuenta miembros de la comunidad de profetas fueron también hasta ese lugar, pero se mantuvieron a cierta distancia, frente a ellos. ⁸Elías tomó su manto y, enrollándolo, golpeó el agua. El río se partió en dos, de modo que ambos lo cruzaron en seco. ⁹Al cruzar, Elías le preguntó a Eliseo:

—¿Qué quieres que haga por ti antes de que me separen de tu lado?

—Te pido que sea yo el heredero de tu espíritu por partida doble[a] —respondió Eliseo.

¹⁰—Has pedido algo difícil —le dijo Elías—, pero si logras verme cuando me separen de tu lado, te será concedido; de lo contrario, no.

¹¹Iban caminando y conversando cuando, de pronto, los separó un carro de fuego con caballos de fuego, y Elías subió al cielo en medio de un torbellino. ¹²Eliseo, viendo lo que pasaba, se puso a gritar: «¡Padre mío, padre mío, carro y fuerza conductora de Israel!» Pero no volvió a verlo.

---

a **2:9** *por partida doble*. Véase Dt 21:17.

Entonces agarró su ropa y la rasgó en dos. ¹³Luego recogió el manto que se le había caído a Elías y, regresando a la orilla del Jordán, ¹⁴golpeó el agua con el manto y exclamó: «¿Dónde está el SEÑOR, el Dios de Elías?» En cuanto golpeó el agua, el río se partió en dos, y Eliseo cruzó.

¹⁵Los profetas de Jericó, al verlo, exclamaron: «¡El espíritu de Elías se ha posado sobre Eliseo!» Entonces fueron a su encuentro y se postraron ante él, rostro en tierra.

¹⁶—Mira —le dijeron—, aquí se encuentran, entre nosotros tus servidores, cincuenta hombres muy capaces, que pueden ir a buscar a tu maestro. Quizás el Espíritu del SEÑOR lo tomó y lo arrojó en algún monte o en algún valle.

—No —respondió Eliseo—, no los manden.

¹⁷Pero ellos insistieron tanto que él se sintió incómodo[b] y por fin les dijo:

—Está bien, mándenlos.

Así que enviaron a cincuenta hombres, los cuales buscaron a Elías durante tres días, pero no lo encontraron. ¹⁸Cuando regresaron a Jericó, donde se había quedado Eliseo, él les reclamó:

—¿No les advertí que no fueran?

Eliseo purifica el agua

¹⁹Luego, los habitantes de la ciudad le dijeron a Eliseo:

—Señor, como usted puede ver, nuestra ciudad está bien ubicada, pero el agua es mala, y por eso la tierra ha quedado estéril.

²⁰—Tráiganme una vasija nueva, y échenle sal —les ordenó Eliseo.

Cuando se la entregaron, ²¹Eliseo fue al manantial y, arrojando allí la sal, exclamó:

—Así dice el SEÑOR: "¡Yo *purifico esta agua para que nunca más cause muerte ni esterilidad!"

²²A partir de ese momento, y hasta el día de hoy, el agua quedó purificada, según la palabra de Eliseo.

Eliseo maldice a los burlones

²³De Jericó, Eliseo se dirigió a Betel. Iba subiendo por el camino cuando unos muchachos salieron de la ciudad y empezaron a burlarse de él. «¡Anda, viejo calvo! —le gritaban—. ¡Anda, viejo calvo!» ²⁴Eliseo se volvió y, clavándoles la vista, los maldijo en el *nombre del SEÑOR. Al instante, dos osas salieron del bosque y despedazaron a cuarenta y dos muchachos. ²⁵De allí, Eliseo se fue al monte Carmelo; y luego regresó a Samaria.

Los moabitas se rebelan

3 En el año dieciocho de Josafat, rey de Judá, Jorán hijo de Acab ascendió al trono de Israel en Samaria, y reinó doce años. ²Jorán hizo lo que ofende al SEÑOR, aunque no tanto como su padre y su madre, pues mandó que se quitara una *piedra sagrada que su padre había erigido en honor de *Baal. ³Sin embargo, Jorán se aferró a los mismos pecados con que Jeroboán hijo de Nabat había hecho pecar a los israelitas, pues no se apartó de esos pecados.

⁴Ahora bien, Mesá, rey de Moab, criaba ovejas, y como tributo anual le entregaba al rey de Israel cien mil ovejas y la lana de cien mil corderos. ⁵Pero al morir Acab, el rey de Moab se rebeló contra el rey de Israel. ⁶Entonces el rey Jorán salió de Samaria, movilizó a todo el ejército de Israel, ⁷y le envió este mensaje a Josafat, rey de Judá:

—El rey de Moab se ha rebelado contra mí. ¿Irías conmigo a pelear contra Moab?

—Claro que sí —le respondió Josafat—. Estoy a tu disposición, lo mismo que mi ejército y mi caballería. ⁸¿Qué ruta tomaremos?

—La ruta del desierto de Edom —contestó Jorán.

⁹Fue así como los reyes de Israel, Judá y Edom se pusieron en marcha. Durante siete días anduvieron por el desierto, hasta que el ejército y los animales se quedaron sin agua.

¹⁰—¡Ay! —exclamó el rey de Israel—. ¡El SEÑOR ha reunido a tres reyes para entregarlos en manos de los moabitas!

¹¹Pero Josafat preguntó:

—¿Acaso no hay aquí un profeta del SEÑOR, para que consultemos al SEÑOR por medio de él?

Un oficial del rey de Israel contestó:

—Aquí cerca está Eliseo hijo de Safat, el que servía a Elías.[c]

¹²—Pues él puede darnos palabra del SEÑOR —comentó Josafat.

Así que el rey de Israel fue a ver a Eliseo, acompañado del rey Josafat y del rey de Edom. ¹³Pero Eliseo le dijo al rey de Israel:

—¿Qué tengo yo que ver con usted? Váyase a consultar a los profetas de su padre y de su madre.

—No —respondió el rey de Israel—, pues el SEÑOR nos ha reunido a los tres para entregarnos en manos de los moabitas.

¹⁴Eliseo replicó:

—Le juro que si no fuera por el respeto que le tengo a Josafat, rey de Judá, ni siquiera le daría a usted la cara. ¡Tan cierto como que vive el SEÑOR *Todopoderoso, a quien sirvo! ¹⁵En fin, ¡que me traigan un músico!

Mientras el músico tañía el arpa, la mano del SEÑOR vino sobre Eliseo, ¹⁶y éste dijo:

—Así dice el SEÑOR: "Abran zanjas por todo este valle, ¹⁷pues aunque no vean viento ni lluvia —dice el SEÑOR—, este valle se llenará de agua, de modo que podrán beber ustedes y todos sus animales." ¹⁸Esto es poca cosa para el SEÑOR, que además entregará a Moab en manos de ustedes. ¹⁹De hecho, ustedes destruirán todas las ciudades fortificadas y las otras ciudades principales. Cortarán los mejores árboles, cegarán los manantiales y sembrarán de piedras los campos fértiles.

²⁰A la mañana siguiente, a la hora de la ofrenda, toda el área se inundó con el agua que venía de la región de Edom. ²¹Ahora bien, cuando los moabitas se enteraron de que los reyes habían salido para atacarlos, movilizaron a todos los que podían servir en el ejército y tomaron posiciones en la frontera. ²²Al levantarse ellos por la mañana, el sol se reflejaba sobre el agua, y a los moabitas les pareció que estaba teñida en sangre. ²³«¡Es sangre de batalla! —exclamaron—. Esos reyes deben de haber peleado, y se han matado unos a otros. ¡Vamos, Moab, al saqueo!»

²⁴Cuando los moabitas llegaron al campamento de Israel, los israelitas les hicieron frente y los derrotaron. Aquéllos se dieron a la fuga, pero los israelitas los persiguieron y los aniquilaron, ²⁵y destruyeron sus ciudades. Cada uno tiró una piedra en los campos fértiles de Moab hasta llenarlos; además, cegaron los manantiales y cortaron los mejores árboles. Sólo Quir Jaréset quedó en pie, aunque los honderos la cercaron y también lograron conquistarla.

---

[b] 2:17 insistieron tanto que él se sintió incómodo. Alt. le insistieron por largo rato.   [c] 3:11 servía a Elías. Lit. echaba agua en manos de Elías.

²⁶El rey de Moab, al ver que perdía la batalla, se llevó consigo a setecientos guerreros con el propósito de abrirse paso hasta donde estaba el rey de Edom, pero no logró pasar. ²⁷Tomó entonces a su hijo *primogénito, que había de sucederlo en el trono, y lo ofreció en *holocausto sobre la muralla. A raíz de esto, se desató contra Israel una furia incontenible, de modo que los israelitas tuvieron que retirarse y volver a su país.

El aceite de la viuda

4 La viuda de un miembro de la comunidad de los profetas le suplicó a Eliseo:

—Mi esposo, su servidor, ha muerto, y usted sabe que él era fielᵈ al SEÑOR. Ahora resulta que el hombre con quien estamos endeudados ha venido para llevarse a mis dos hijos como esclavos.

²—¿Y qué puedo hacer por ti? —le preguntó Eliseo—. Dime, ¿qué tienes en casa?

—Su servidora no tiene nada en casa —le respondió—, excepto un poco de aceite.

³Eliseo le ordenó:

—Sal y pide a tus vecinos que te presten sus vasijas; consigue todas las que puedas. ⁴Luego entra en la casa con tus hijos y cierra la puerta. Echa aceite en todas las vasijas y, a medida que las llenes, ponlas aparte.

⁵En seguida la mujer dejó a Eliseo y se fue. Luego se encerró con sus hijos y empezó a llenar las vasijas que ellos le pasaban. ⁶Cuando ya todas estuvieron llenas, ella le pidió a uno de sus hijos que le pasara otra más, y él respondió: «Ya no hay.» En ese momento se acabó el aceite.

⁷La mujer fue y se lo contó al hombre de Dios, quien la mandó: «Ahora ve a vender el aceite, y paga tus deudas. Con el dinero que te sobre, podrán vivir tú y tus hijos.»

El hijo de la sunamita

⁸Un día, cuando Eliseo pasaba por Sunén, cierta mujer de buena posición le insistió que comiera en su casa. Desde entonces, siempre que pasaba por ese pueblo, comía allí. ⁹La mujer le dijo a su esposo: «Mira, yo estoy segura de que este hombre que siempre nos visita es un *santo hombre de Dios. ¹⁰Hagámosle un cuarto en la azotea, y pongámosle allí una cama, una mesa con una silla, y una lámpara. De ese modo, cuando nos visite, tendrá un lugar donde quedarse.»

¹¹En cierta ocasión Eliseo llegó, fue a su cuarto y se acostó. ¹²Luego le dijo a su criado Guiezi:

—Llama a la señora.ᵉ

El criado así lo hizo, y ella se presentó. ¹³Entonces Eliseo le dijo a Guiezi:

—Dile a la señora: "¡Te has tomado muchas molestias por nosotros! ¿Qué puedo hacer por ti? ¿Quieres que le hable al rey o al jefe del ejército en tu favor?"

Pero ella le respondió:

—Yo vivo segura en medio de mi pueblo.

¹⁴Eliseo le preguntó a Guiezi:

—¿Qué puedo hacer por ella?

—Bueno —contestó el siervo— ella no tiene hijos, y su esposo ya es anciano.

¹⁵—Llámala —ordenó Eliseo.

Guiezi la llamó, y ella se detuvo en la puerta. ¹⁶Entonces Eliseo le prometió:

—El año que viene, por esta fecha, estarás abrazando a un hijo.

—¡No, mi señor, hombre de Dios! —exclamó ella—. No engañe usted a su servidora.

¹⁷En efecto, la mujer quedó embarazada. Y al año siguiente, por esa misma fecha, dio a luz un hijo, tal como Eliseo se lo había dicho.

¹⁸El niño creció, y un día salió a ver a su padre, que estaba con los segadores. ¹⁹De pronto exclamó:

—¡Ay, mi cabeza! ¡Me duele la cabeza!

El padre le ordenó a un criado:

—¡Llévaselo a su madre!

²⁰El criado lo cargó y se lo llevó a la madre, la cual lo tuvo en sus rodillas hasta el mediodía. A esa hora, el niño murió. ²¹Entonces ella subió, lo puso en la cama del hombre de Dios y, cerrando la puerta, salió. ²²Después llamó a su esposo y le dijo:

—Préstame un criado y una burra; en seguida vuelvo. Voy de prisa a ver al hombre de Dios.

²³—¿Para qué vas a verlo hoy? —le preguntó su esposo—. No es día de luna nueva ni *sábado.

—No importa —respondió ella.

²⁴Entonces hizo aparejar la burra y le ordenó al criado: —¡Anda, vamos! No te detengas hasta que te lo diga.

²⁵La mujer se puso en marcha y llegó al monte Carmelo, donde estaba Eliseo, el hombre de Dios. Éste a la vio a lo lejos y le dijo a su criado Guiezi:

—¡Mira! Ahí viene la sunamita. ²⁶Corre a recibirla y pregúntale cómo está ella, y cómo están su esposo y el niño.

El criado fue, y ella respondió que todos estaban bien. ²⁷Pero luego fue a la montaña y se abrazó a los pies del hombre de Dios. Guiezi se acercó con el propósito de apartarla, pero el hombre de Dios intervino:

—¡Déjala! Está muy angustiada, y el SEÑOR me ha ocultado lo que pasa; no me ha dicho nada.

²⁸—Señor mío —le reclamó la mujer—, ¿acaso yo le pedí a usted un hijo? ¿No le rogué que no me engañara?

²⁹Eliseo le ordenó a Guiezi:

—Arréglate la ropa, toma mi bastón y ponte en camino. Si te encuentras con alguien, ni lo saludes; si alguien te saluda, no le respondas. Y cuando llegues, coloca el bastón sobre la cara del niño.

³⁰Pero la madre del niño exclamó:

—¡Le juro a usted que no lo dejaré solo! ¡Tan cierto como que el SEÑOR y usted viven!

Así que Eliseo se levantó y fue con ella. ³¹Guiezi, que se había adelantado, llegó y colocó el bastón sobre la cara del niño, pero éste no respondió ni dio ninguna señal de vida. Por tanto, Guiezi volvió para encontrarse con Eliseo y le dijo:

—El niño no despierta.

³²Cuando Eliseo llegó a la casa, encontró al niño muerto, tendido sobre su cama. ³³Entró al cuarto, cerró la puerta y oró al SEÑOR. ³⁴Luego subió a la cama y se tendió sobre el niño boca a boca, ojos a ojos y manos a manos, hasta que el cuerpo del niño empezó a entrar en calor. ³⁵Eliseo se levantó y se puso a caminar de un lado a otro del cuarto, y luego volvió a tenderse sobre el niño. Esto lo hizo siete veces, al cabo de las cuales el niño estornudó y abrió los ojos.ᶠ ³⁶Entonces Eliseo le dijo a Guiezi:

—Llama a la señora.

Guiezi así lo hizo, y cuando la mujer llegó, Eliseo le dijo:

—Puedes llevarte a tu hijo.

---

d **4:1** *era fiel.* Lit. *Temía.* e **4:12** *señora.* Lit. *sunamita*; también en v. 36. f **4:35** *Esto lo ... los ojos.* Alt. *El niño estornudó siete veces, y abrió los ojos.*

37Ella entró, se arrojó a los pies de Eliseo y se postró rostro en tierra. Entonces tomó a su hijo y salió.

El milagro de la comida

38Eliseo regresó a Guilgal y se encontró con que en esos días había mucha hambre en el país. Por tanto, se reunió con la comunidad de profetas y le ordenó a su criado: «Pon esa olla grande en el fogón y prepara un guisado para los profetas.»

39En eso, uno de ellos salió al campo para recoger hierbas; allí encontró una planta silvestre y arrancó varias frutas hasta llenar su manto. Al regresar, las cortó en pedazos y las echó en el guisado sin saber qué eran. 40Sirvieron el guisado, pero cuando los hombres empezaron a comerlo, gritaron:

—¡Hombre de Dios, esto es veneno!g

Así que no pudieron comer. 41Entonces Eliseo ordenó:

—Tráiganme harina.

Y luego de echar la harina en la olla, dijo:

—Sírvanle a la gente para que coma.

Y ya no hubo nada en la olla que les hiciera daño.

Alimentación de cien hombres

42De Baal Salisá llegó alguien que le llevaba al hombre de Dios pan de los *primeros frutos: veinte panes de cebada y espigas de trigo fresco.h Eliseo le dijo a su criado:

—Dale de comer a la gente.

43—¿Cómo voy a alimentar a cien personas con esto? —replicó el criado.

Pero Eliseo insistió:

—Dale de comer a la gente, pues así dice el SEÑOR: "Comerán y habrá de sobra."

44Entonces el criado les sirvió el pan y, conforme a la palabra del SEÑOR, la gente comió y hubo de sobra.

Eliseo sana a Naamán

5 Naamán, jefe del ejército del rey de *Siria, era un hombre de mucho prestigio y gozaba de favor de su rey porque, por medio de él, el SEÑOR le había dado victorias a su país. Era un soldado valiente, pero estaba enfermo de *lepra.

2En cierta ocasión los sirios, que salían a merodear, capturaron a una muchacha israelita y la hicieron criada de la esposa de Naamán. 3Un día la muchacha le dijo a su ama: «Ojalá el amo fuera a ver al profeta que hay en Samaria, porque él lo sanaría de su lepra.»

4Naamán fue a contarle al rey lo que la muchacha israelita había dicho. 5El rey de Siria le respondió:

—Bien, puedes ir; yo le mandaré una carta al rey de Israel.

Y así Naamán se fue, llevando treinta mil monedas de plata, seis mil monedas de oroi y diez mudas de ropa. 6La carta que le llevó al rey de Israel decía: «Cuando te llegue esta carta, verás que el portador es Naamán, uno de mis oficiales. Te lo envío para que lo sanes de su lepra.»

7Al leer la carta, el rey de Israel se rasgó las vestiduras y exclamó: «¿Y acaso soy Dios, capaz de dar vida o muerte, para que ese tipo me pida sanar a un leproso? ¡Fíjense bien que me está buscando pleito!»

8Cuando Eliseo, hombre de Dios, se enteró de que el rey de Israel se había rasgado las vestiduras, le

envió este mensaje: «¿Por qué está Su Majestad tan molesto?j ¡Mándeme usted a ese hombre, para que sepa que hay profeta en Israel!»

9Así que Naamán, con sus caballos y sus carros, fue a la casa de Eliseo y se detuvo ante la puerta. 10Entonces Eliseo envió un mensajero a que le dijera: «Ve y zambúllete siete veces en el río Jordán; así tu piel sanará, y quedarás limpio.»

11Naamán se enfureció y se fue, quejándose: «¡Yo creí que el profeta saldría a recibirme personalmente para invocar el *nombre del SEÑOR su Dios, y que con un movimiento de la mano me sanaría de la lepra! 12¿Acaso los ríos de Damasco, el Abaná y el Farfar, no son mejores que toda el agua de Israel? ¿Acaso no podría zambullirme en ellos y quedar limpio?» Furioso, dio media vuelta y se marchó.

13Entonces sus criados se le acercaron para aconsejarle: «Señor,k si el profeta le hubiera mandado hacer algo complicado, ¿usted no le habría hecho caso? ¡Con más razón si lo único que le dice a usted es que se zambulla, y así quedará limpio!» 14Así que Naamán bajó al Jordán y se sumergió siete veces, según se lo había ordenado el hombre de Dios. ¡Y su piel se volvió como la de un niño, y quedó limpio! 15Luego Naamán volvió con todos sus acompañantes y, presentándose ante el hombre de Dios, le dijo:

—Ahora reconozco que no hay Dios en todo el mundo, sino sólo en Israel. Le ruego a usted aceptar un regalo de su servidor.

16Pero Eliseo respondió:

—¡Tan cierto como que vive el SEÑOR, a quien yo sirvo, que no voy a aceptar nada!

Y por más que insistió Naamán, Eliseo no accedió.

17—En ese caso —persistió Naamán—, permítame usted llevarme dos cargas de esta tierra,l ya que de aquí en adelante su servidor no va a ofrecerle *holocaustos ni sacrificios a ningún otro dios, sino sólo al SEÑOR. 18Y cuando mi señor el rey vaya a adorar en el templo de Rimón y se apoye de mi brazo, y yo me vea obligado a inclinarme allí, desde ahora ruego al SEÑOR que me perdone por inclinarme en ese templo.

19—Puedes irte en *paz —respondió Eliseo.

Naamán se fue, y ya había recorrido cierta distancia 20cuando Guiezi, el criado de Eliseo, hombre de Dios, pensó: «Mi amo ha sido demasiado bondadoso con este sirio Naamán, pues no le aceptó nada de lo que había traído. Pero yo voy a correr tras él, a ver si me da algo. ¡Tan cierto como que el SEÑOR vive!»

21Así que Guiezi se fue para alcanzar a Naamán. Cuando éste lo vio correr tras él, se bajó de su carro para recibirlo y lo saludó. 22Respondiendo al saludo, Guiezi dijo:

—Mi amo me ha enviado con este mensaje: "Dos jóvenes de la comunidad de profetas acaban de llegar de la sierra de Efraín. Te pido que me des para ellos tres mil monedasm de plata y dos mudas de ropa."

23—Por favor, llévate seis mil —respondió Naamán, e insistió en que las aceptara.

Echó entonces las monedas en dos sacos, junto con las dos mudas de ropa, y todo esto se lo entregó a dos criados para que lo llevaran delante de Guiezi. 24Al llegar a la colina, Guiezi tomó los sacos y los guardó en la casa; después despidió a los hombres, y

g 4:40 esto es veneno. Lit. hay muerte en la olla.   h 4:42 espigas de trigo fresco. Alt. trigo fresco en su alforja.   i 5:5 treinta mil ... oro. Lit. diez *talentos de plata y seis mil {*siclos} de oro.   j 5:8 está Su Majestad tan molesto. Lit. se ha rasgado la ropa.   k 5:13 Señor. Lit. Padre mío.   l 5:17 dos cargas de esta tierra. Es decir, para construir un altar.   m 5:22 tres mil monedas. Lit. un *talento.

éstos se fueron. 25Entonces Guiezi se presentó ante su amo.

—¿De dónde vienes, Guiezi? —le preguntó Eliseo.

—Su servidor no ha ido a ninguna parte —respondió Guiezi.

26Eliseo replicó:

—¿No estaba yo presente en espíritu cuando aquel hombre se bajó de su carro para recibirte? ¿Acaso es éste el momento de recibir dinero y ropa, huertos y viñedos, ovejas y bueyes, criados y criadas? 27Ahora la lepra de Naamán se les pegará a ti y a tus descendientes para siempre.

No bien había salido Guiezi de la presencia de Eliseo cuando ya estaba blanco como la nieve por causa de la lepra.

El milagro del hacha

6 Un día, los miembros de la comunidad de los profetas le dijeron a Eliseo:

—Como puede ver, el lugar donde ahora vivimos con usted nos resulta pequeño. 2Es mejor que vayamos al Jordán. Allí podremos conseguir madera y construirn un albergue.

—Bien, vayan —respondió Eliseo.

3Pero uno de ellos le pidió:

—Acompañe usted, por favor, a sus servidores.

Eliseo consintió 4en acompañarlos, y cuando llegaron al Jordán empezaron a cortar árboles. 5De pronto, al cortar un tronco, a uno de los profetas se le zafó el hacha y se le cayó al río.

—¡Ay, maestro! —gritó—. ¡Esa hacha no era mía!

6—¿Dónde cayó? —preguntó el hombre de Dios.

Cuando se le indicó el lugar, Eliseo cortó un palo y, echándolo allí, hizo que el hacha saliera a flote.

7—Sácala —ordenó Eliseo.

Así que el hombre extendió el brazo y la sacó.

Eliseo captura una tropa siria

8El rey de *Siria, que estaba en guerra con Israel, deliberó con sus ministros y les dijo: «Vamos a acampar en tal lugar.» 9Pero el hombre de Dios le envió este mensaje al rey de Israel: «Procura no pasar por este sitio, pues los sirios se han tendido allí una emboscada.»ñ 10Así que el rey de Israel envió a reconocer el lugar que el hombre de Dios le había indicado. Y en varias otras ocasiones Eliseo le avisó al rey, de modo que éste tomó precauciones. 11El rey de Siria, enfurecido por lo que estaba pasando, llamó a sus ministros y les reclamó:

—¿Quieren decirme quién está informando al rey de Israel?

12—Nadie, mi señor y rey —respondió uno de ellos—. El responsable es Eliseo, el profeta que está en Israel. Es él quien le comunica todo al rey de Israel, aun lo que Su Majestad dice en su alcoba.

13—Pues entonces averigüen dónde está —ordenó el rey—, para que mande a capturarlo.

Cuando lo informaron que Eliseo estaba en Dotán, 14el rey envió allá un destacamento grande, con caballos y carros de combate. Llegaron de noche y cercaron la ciudad. 15Por la mañana, cuando el criado del hombre de Dios se levantó para salir, vio que un ejército con caballos y carros de combate rodeaba la ciudad.

—¡Ay, mi señor! —exclamó el criado—. ¿Qué vamos a hacer?

16—No tengas miedo —respondió Eliseo—. Los que están con nosotros son más que ellos.

17Entonces Eliseo oró: «SEÑOR, ábrele a Guiezi los ojos para que vea.» El SEÑOR así lo hizo, y el criado vio que la colina estaba llena de caballos y de carros de fuego alrededor de Eliseo. 18Como ya los sirios se acercaban a él, Eliseo volvió a orar: «SEÑOR, castiga a esta gente con ceguera.» Y el SEÑOR hizo lo que le pidió Eliseo.

19Luego Eliseo les dijo: «Ésta no es la ciudad adonde iban; han tomado un camino equivocado. Síganme, que yo los llevaré adonde está el hombre que buscan.» Pero los llevó a Samaria. 20Después de entrar en la ciudad, Eliseo dijo: «SEÑOR, ábreles los ojos, para que vean.» El SEÑOR así lo hizo, y ellos se dieron cuenta de que estaban dentro de Samaria. 21Cuando el rey de Israel los vio, le preguntó a Eliseo:

—¿Los mato, mi señor? ¿Los mato?

22—No, no los mates —contestó Eliseo—. ¿Acaso los has capturado con tu espada y tu arco, para que los mates? Mejor sírveles comida y agua para que coman y beban, y que luego vuelvan a su rey.

23Así que el rey de Israel les dio un tremendo banquete. Cuando terminaron de comer, los despidió, y ellos regresaron a su rey. Y las bandas de sirios no volvieron a invadir el territorio israelita.

Hambre en Samaria

24Algún tiempo después, Ben Adad, rey de *Siria, movilizó todo su ejército para ir a Samaria y sitiarla. 25El sitio duró tanto tiempo que provocó un hambre terrible en la ciudad, a tal grado que una cabeza de asno llegó a costar ochenta monedas de plata,o y un poco de algarroba,p cinco.

26Un día, mientras el rey recorría la muralla, una mujer le gritó:

—¡Sálvenos, Su Majestad!

27—Si el SEÑOR no te salva —respondió el rey—, ¿de dónde voy a sacar yo comida para salvarte? ¿Del granero? ¿Del lagar? 28¿Qué te pasa?

Ella se quejó:

—Esta mujer me propuso que le entregara mi hijo para que nos lo comiéramos hoy, y que mañana nos comeríamos el de ella. 29Pues bien, cocinamos a mi hijo y nos lo comimos, pero al día siguiente, cuando le pedí que entregara su hijo para que nos lo comiéramos, resulta que ya lo había escondido.

30Al oír la queja de la mujer, el rey se rasgó las vestiduras. Luego reanudó su recorrido por la muralla, y la gente pudo ver que bajo su túnica real iba vestido de luto. 31«¡Que el SEÑOR me castigue sin piedad —exclamó el rey— si hoy mismo no le corto la cabeza a Eliseo hijo de Safat!»

32Mientras Eliseo se encontraba en su casa, sentado con los *ancianos, el rey le envió un mensajero. Antes de que éste llegara, Eliseo les dijo a los ancianos:

—Ahora van a ver cómo ese asesino envía a alguien a cortarme la cabeza. Pues bien, cuando llegue el mensajero, atranquen la puerta para que no entre. ¡Ya oigo detrás de él los pasos de su señor!

33No había terminado de hablar cuando el mensajero llegó y dijo:

—Esta desgracia viene del SEÑOR; ¿qué más se puede esperar de él?

---

n 6:2 *podremos conseguir madera y construir*. Lit. *cada uno tomará una viga y construirá*. ñ 6:9 *te han tendido allí una emboscada*. Alt. *piensan acampar allí*. o 6:25 *ochenta monedas de plata*. Lit. *ochenta* (**siclos*) *de plata*. p 6:25 *un poco de algarroba*. Lit. *un cuarto de *cab de estiércol de paloma* (es decir, aprox. un tercio de litro de cierta legumbre no comestible).

7 Eliseo contestó:

—Oigan la palabra del SEÑOR, que dice así: "Mañana a estas horas, a la *entrada de Samaria, podrá comprarse una medida^q de flor de harina con una sola moneda de plata,^r y hasta una doble medida de cebada por el mismo precio."

²El ayudante personal del rey replicó:

—¡No me digas! Aun si el SEÑOR abriera las ventanas del cielo, ¡no podría suceder tal cosa!

—Pues lo verás con tus propios ojos —le advirtió Eliseo—, pero no llegarás a comerlo.

Liberación de Samaria

³Ese día, cuatro hombres que padecían de *lepra se hallaban a la *entrada de la ciudad.

—¿Qué ganamos con quedarnos aquí sentados, esperando la muerte? —se dijeron unos a otros—. ⁴No ganamos nada con entrar en la ciudad. Allí nos moriremos de hambre con todos los demás, pero si nos quedamos aquí, nos sucederá lo mismo. Vayamos, pues, al campamento de los *sirios, para rendirnos. Si nos perdonan la vida, viviremos; y si nos matan, de todos modos moriremos.

⁵Al anochecer se pusieron en camino, pero cuando llegaron a las afueras del campamento sirio, ¡ya no había nadie allí! ⁶Y era que el Señor había confundido a los sirios haciéndoles oír el ruido de carros de combate y de caballería, como si fuera un gran ejército. Entonces se dijeron unos a otros: «¡Seguro que el rey de Israel ha contratado a los reyes hititas y egipcios para atacarnos!» ⁷Por lo tanto, emprendieron la fuga al anochecer abandonando tiendas de campaña, caballos y asnos. Dejaron el campamento tal como estaba, para escapar y salvarse.

⁸Cuando los leprosos llegaron a las afueras del campamento, entraron en una de las tiendas de campaña. Después de comer y beber, se llevaron de allí plata, oro y ropa, y fueron a esconderlo. Luego regresaron, entraron en otra tienda, y también de allí tomaron varios objetos y los escondieron.

⁹Entonces se dijeron unos a otros:

—Esto no está bien. Hoy es un día de buenas noticias, y no las estamos dando a conocer. Si esperamos hasta que amanezca, resultaremos culpables. Vayamos ahora mismo al palacio, y demos aviso.

¹⁰Así que fueron a la puerta y llamaron a los centinelas. Les dijeron: «Fuimos al campamento de los sirios y ya no había nadie allí. Sólo se oía a los caballos y asnos, que estaban atados. Y las tiendas las dejaron tal como estaban.» ¹¹Los centinelas, a voz en cuello, hicieron llegar la noticia hasta el interior del palacio. ¹²Aunque era de noche, el rey se levantó y les dijo a sus ministros:

—Déjenme decirles lo que esos sirios están tramando contra nosotros. Como saben que estamos pasando hambre, han abandonado el campamento y se han escondido en el campo. Lo que quieren es que salgamos, para atraparnos vivos y entrar en la ciudad.

¹³Uno de sus ministros propuso:

—Que salgan algunos hombres con cinco de los caballos que aún quedan aquí. Si mueren, no les irá peor que a la multitud de israelitas que está por perecer. ¡Enviémoslos a ver qué pasa!

¹⁴De inmediato los hombres tomaron dos carros con caballos, y el rey los mandó al campamento del ejército sirio, con instrucciones de que investigaran. ¹⁵Llegaron hasta el Jordán, y vieron que todo el camino estaba lleno de ropa y de objetos que los sirios habían arrojado al huir precipitadamente. De modo que regresaron los mensajeros e informaron al rey, ¹⁶y el pueblo salió a saquear el campamento sirio. Y tal como la palabra del SEÑOR lo había dado a conocer, se pudo comprar una medida de flor de harina con una sola moneda de plata, y hasta una doble medida de cebada por el mismo precio.

¹⁷El rey le había ordenado a su ayudante personal que vigilara la entrada de la ciudad, pero el pueblo lo atropelló ahí mismo, y así se cumplió lo que había dicho el hombre de Dios cuando el rey fue a verlo. ¹⁸De hecho, cuando el hombre de Dios le dijo al rey: «Mañana a estas horas, a la entrada de Samaria, podrá comprarse una doble medida de cebada con una sola moneda de plata, y una medida de flor de harina por el mismo precio», ¹⁹ese oficial había replicado: «¡No me digas! Aun si el SEÑOR abriera las ventanas del cielo, ¡no podría suceder tal cosa!» De modo que el hombre de Dios respondió: «Pues lo verás con tus propios ojos, pero no llegarás a comerlo.» ²⁰En efecto, así ocurrió: el pueblo lo atropelló a la entrada de la ciudad, y allí murió.

La sunamita recupera su terreno

8 Ahora bien, Eliseo le había dicho a la mujer a cuyo hijo él había revivido: «Anda, vete con tu familia a vivir donde puedas, porque el SEÑOR ha ordenado que haya una gran hambre en el país, y que ésta dure siete años.» ²La mujer se dispuso a seguir las instrucciones del hombre de Dios y se fue con su familia al país de los filisteos, donde se quedó siete años.

³Al cabo de los siete años, cuando regresó del país de los filisteos, la mujer fue a rogarle al rey que le devolviera su casa y sus tierras. ⁴En esos momentos el rey estaba hablando con Guiezi, el criado del hombre de Dios, y le había dicho: «Cuéntame todas las maravillas que ha hecho Eliseo.» ⁵Y precisamente cuando Guiezi le contaba al rey que Eliseo había revivido al niño muerto, la madre llegó para rogarle al rey que le devolviera su casa y sus tierras. Así que Guiezi dijo:

—Mi señor y rey, ésta es la mujer, y éste es el hijo que Eliseo revivió.

⁶El rey le hizo preguntas a la mujer, y ella se lo contó todo. Entonces el rey le ordenó a un funcionario^s que se encargara de ella y le dijo:

—Devuélvele todo lo que le pertenecía, incluso todas las ganancias que hayan producido sus tierras, desde el día en que salió del país hasta hoy.

Jazael, rey de Siria

⁷Luego Eliseo se fue a Damasco. Ben Adad, rey de *Siria, estaba enfermo, y cuando le avisaron que el hombre de Dios había llegado, ⁸le ordenó a Jazael: «Llévale un regalo al hombre de Dios. Cuando lo veas, consulta al SEÑOR por medio de él para saber si me voy a recuperar de esta enfermedad.»

⁹Jazael fue a ver a Eliseo, y como regalo le llevó de las mejores mercancías de Damasco, cargadas en cuarenta camellos. Cuando llegó, se presentó ante él y le dijo:

—Ben Adad, rey de Siria, su servidor,^t me ha enviado para preguntarle si él se va a recuperar de su enfermedad.

¹⁰Eliseo respondió:

q **7:1** *una medida.* Lit. *un* *seah (aprox. siete litros); también en vv. 16 y 18.　r **7:1** *una sola moneda de plata.* Lit. *un* *siclo; también en vv. 16 y 18.　s **8:6** *funcionario.* Lit. *Eunuco.*　t **8:9** *servidor.* Lit. *Hijo.*

—Ve y dile que[u] sobrevivirá a esa enfermedad, aunque el SEÑOR me ha revelado que de todos modos va a morir.

11Luego Eliseo se quedó mirándolo fijamente, hasta que Jazael se sintió incómodo.[v] Entonces el hombre de Dios se echó a llorar.

12—¿Por qué llora mi señor? —le preguntó Jazael.

—Porque yo sé bien que vas a causarles mucho daño a los israelitas —respondió—. Vas a incendiar sus fortalezas, y a matar a sus jóvenes a filo de espada; despedazarás a los niños y les abrirás el vientre a las mujeres embarazadas.

13Jazael exclamó:

—¡Qué es este servidor de usted sino un pobre perro! ¿Cómo es posible que haga tal cosa?

Entonces Eliseo le declaró:

—El SEÑOR me ha revelado que vas a ser rey de Siria.

14Jazael se despidió de Eliseo y regresó para presentarse ante su rey. Cuando Ben Adad le preguntó qué le había dicho Eliseo, Jazael le respondió:

—Me dijo que usted sobrevivirá a su enfermedad.

15Pero al día siguiente tomó una colcha y, empapándola en agua, le tapó la cara al rey hasta asfixiarlo. Así fue como Jazael usurpó el trono.

Jorán, rey de Judá
8:16-24 — 2Cr 21:5-10,20

16En el quinto año del reinado de Jorán hijo de Acab, rey de Israel y contemporáneo de Josafat, rey de Judá, Jorán hijo de Josafat ascendió al trono de Judá. 17Tenía treinta y dos años cuando comenzó a reinar, y reinó en Jerusalén ocho años. 18Jorán hizo lo que ofende al SEÑOR, pues siguió el mal ejemplo de los reyes de Israel, como lo había hecho la familia de Acab, y llegó incluso a casarse con la hija de Acab. 19Pero el SEÑOR no quiso destruir a Judá por consideración a su siervo David, pues le había prometido mantener encendida para siempre una lámpara para él y sus descendientes.

20En tiempos de Jorán, los edomitas se sublevaron contra Judá y se nombraron su propio rey. 21Por lo tanto, Jorán marchó sobre Zaír con todos sus carros de combate. Los edomitas cercaron a Jorán y a los capitanes de los carros, pero durante la noche Jorán logró abrirse paso; sin embargo, su ejército se dispersó.[w] 22Desde entonces Edom ha estado en rebelión contra Judá, al igual que la ciudad de Libná, que en ese mismo tiempo se sublevó.

23Los demás acontecimientos del reinado de Jorán, y todo lo que hizo, están escritos en el libro de las crónicas de los reyes de Judá. 24Cuando murió, fue sepultado con sus antepasados en la Ciudad de David. Y su hijo Ocozías lo sucedió en el trono.

Ocozías, rey de Judá
8:25-29 — 2Cr 22:1-6

25En el año duodécimo de Jorán hijo de Acab, rey de Israel, Ocozías hijo de Jorán ascendió al trono de Judá. 26Tenía veintidós años cuando ascendió al trono, y reinó en Jerusalén un año. Su madre era Atalía, nieta[x] de Omrí, rey de Israel. 27Ocozías hizo lo que ofende al SEÑOR, pues siguió el mal ejemplo de la familia de Acab, con la que estaba emparentado.

28Ocozías, junto con Jorán hijo de Acab, marchó hacia Ramot de Galaad para hacerle guerra a Jazael,

rey de *Siria, pero en la batalla los sirios hirieron a Jorán. 29Por eso el rey Jorán tuvo que regresar a Jezrel, para reponerse de las heridas que había recibido de los sirios en Ramot,[y] cuando luchó contra Jazael, rey de Siria. Como Jorán hijo de Acab convalecía en Jezrel, Ocozías hijo de Jorán, rey de Judá, fue a visitarlo.

Jehú ungido rey de Israel

9 Un día, el profeta Eliseo llamó a un miembro de la comunidad de los profetas. «Arréglate la ropa para viajar —le ordenó—. Toma este frasco de aceite y ve a Ramot de Galaad. 2Cuando llegues, busca a Jehú, hijo de Josafat y nieto de Nimsi. Y adonde esté, apártalo de sus compañeros y llévalo a un cuarto. 3Toma entonces el frasco, derrama el aceite sobre su cabeza y declárale: "Así dice el SEÑOR: 'Ahora te unjo como rey de Israel.'" Luego abre la puerta y huye; ino te detengas!»

4Acto seguido, el joven profeta se fue a Ramot de Galaad. 5Cuando llegó, encontró reunidos a los capitanes del ejército y les dijo:

—Tengo un mensaje para el capitán.

—¿Para cuál de todos nosotros? —preguntó Jehú.

—Para usted, mi capitán —respondió.

6Jehú se levantó y entró en la casa. Entonces el profeta lo ungió con el aceite y declaró:

«Así dice el SEÑOR, Dios de Israel: "Ahora te unjo como rey sobre mi pueblo Israel. 7Destruirás a la familia de Acab, tu señor, y así me vengaré de la sangre de mis siervos los profetas; castigando a Jezabel, vengaré la sangre de todos mis siervos. 8Toda la familia de Acab perecerá, pues de sus descendientes en Israel exterminaré hasta el último varón,[z] esclavo o libre. 9Haré con ellos lo mismo que hice con la familia de Jeroboán hijo de Nabat y con la familia de Basá hijo de Ahías. 10Y en cuanto a Jezabel, los perros se la comerán en el campo de Jezrel, y nadie le dará sepultura."»

Acto seguido, el profeta abrió la puerta y huyó. 11Cuando Jehú salió para volver a reunirse con los capitanes, uno de ellos le preguntó:

—¿Todo bien? ¿Qué quería ese loco?

—Ustedes ya lo conocen —respondió—, y saben cómo habla.

12—¡Pamplinas! —replicaron—. Dinos la verdad.

Jehú admitió:

—Esto es lo que me declaró, palabra por palabra: "Así dice el SEÑOR: 'Ahora te unjo como rey de Israel.'"

13Dicho esto, todos se apresuraron a tender sus mantos sobre los escalones, a los pies de Jehú. Luego tocaron la trompeta y gritaron: «¡Viva el rey Jehú!»

Jehú asesina a Jorán y a Ocozías
9:21-29 — 2Cr 22:7-9

14Entonces Jehú, hijo de Josafat y nieto de Nimsi, conspiró contra Jorán. Sucedió que Jorán, con todo el ejército israelita, había estado defendiendo Ramot de Galaad contra Jazael, rey de *Siria, 15pero tuvo que regresar a Jezrel para reponerse de las heridas que había recibido de los sirios en la batalla. Así que Jehú les dijo a sus partidarios: «Si ustedes quieren que yo sea rey, no dejen que nadie salga de la ciudad para ir a Jezrel con el informe.» 16Luego se

---

u 8:10 dile que (mss. hebreos); di que no (TM).   v 8:11 se quedó ... se sintió incómodo. Alt. se quedó inmovilizado por largo rato.   w 8:21 Los edomitas ... dispersó. Texto de difícil traducción.   x 8:26 nieta. Lit. Hija.   y 8:29 Ramot. Lit. Ramá (variante de Ramot).   z 9:8 hasta el último varón. Lit. al que orina contra la pared.

montó en su carro de combate y fue a Jezrel, pues allí se estaba recuperando Jorán, a quien también Ocozías, rey de Judá, había ido a visitar.

17Cuando el centinela que vigilaba desde la torre de Jezrel vio que las tropas de Jehú se acercaban, gritó:

—¡Se acercan unas tropas!

En seguida Jorán ordenó:

—Llama a un jinete y mándalo al encuentro de las tropas para preguntarles si vienen en son de paz.

18El jinete se fue al encuentro de Jehú y le dijo:

—El rey quiere saber si vienen en son de paz.

—¿Y a ti qué te importa? —replicó Jehú—. Ponte allí atrás.

Entonces el centinela anunció:

—El mensajero ya llegó hasta ellos, pero no lo veo regresar.

19Por tanto, el rey mandó a otro jinete, el cual fue a ellos y repitió:

—El rey quiere saber si vienen en son de paz.

—Eso a ti no te importa —replicó Jehú—. Ponte allí atrás.

20El centinela informó de nuevo:

—Ya llegó el mensajero hasta ellos, pero a él tampoco lo veo regresar. Además, el que conduce el carro ha de ser Jehú hijo de Nimsi, pues lo hace como un loco.

21—¡Enganchen el carro! —exclamó Jorán.

Así lo hicieron. Y en seguida Jorán, rey de Israel, y Ocozías, rey de Judá, cada uno en su carro, salieron y se encontraron con Jehú en la propiedad que había pertenecido a Nabot el jezrelita. **22**Cuando Jorán vio a Jehú, le preguntó:

—Jehú, ¿vienes en son de paz?

—¿Cómo puede haber paz mientras haya tantas idolatrías*a* y hechicerías de tu madre Jezabel? —replicó Jehú.

23Jorán se dio la vuelta para huir, mientras gritaba:

—¡Traición, Ocozías!

24Pero Jehú, que ya había tensado su arco, le disparó a Jorán por la espalda, y la flecha le atravesó el corazón. Jorán se desplomó en el carro, **25**y Jehú le ordenó a su ayudante Bidcar:

—Saca el cadáver y tíralo en el terreno que fue propiedad de Nabot el jezrelita. Recuerda el día en que tú y yo conducíamos juntos detrás de Acab, padre de Jorán, y el SEÑOR pronunció contra él esta sentencia: **26**"Ayer vi aquí la sangre de Nabot y de sus hijos. Por lo tanto, juro que en este mismo terreno te haré pagar por ese crimen. Yo, el SEÑOR, lo afirmo."*b* Saca, pues, el cadáver y tíralo en el terreno, según la palabra que dio a conocer el SEÑOR.

27Cuando Ocozías, rey de Judá, vio lo que pasaba, huyó en dirección a Bet Hagán.*c* Pero Jehú lo persiguió, y ordenó:

—¡Mátenlo a él también!

Y lo hirieron*d* en su carro cuando iba por la cuesta de Gur, cerca de Ibleam, pero logró escapar y llegar a Meguido. Allí murió. **28**Luego sus siervos trasladaron el cuerpo a Jerusalén, la Ciudad de David, donde lo sepultaron en su tumba, junto a sus antepasados. **29**Ocozías había ascendido al trono en el undécimo año del reinado de Jorán hijo de Acab.

Muerte de Jezabel

30Cuando Jezabel se enteró de que Jehú estaba regresando a Jezrel, se sombreó los ojos, se arregló el cabello y se asomó a la ventana. **31**Al entrar Jehú por la *puerta de la ciudad, ella le preguntó:

—¿Cómo estás, Zimri, asesino de tu señor?*e*

32Levantando la vista hacia la ventana, Jehú gritó:

—¿Quién está de mi parte? ¿Quién?

Entonces se asomaron dos o tres oficiales,*f* **33**y Jehú les ordenó:

—¡Arrójenla de allí!

Así lo hicieron, y su sangre salpicó la pared y a los caballos que la pisotearon. **34**Luego Jehú se sentó a comer y beber, y dio esta orden:

—Ocúpense de esa maldita mujer; denle sepultura, pues era hija de un rey.

35Pero cuando fueron a enterrarla, no encontraron más que el cráneo, los pies y las manos. **36**Así que volvieron para informarle a Jehú, y éste comentó:

—Se ha cumplido la palabra que el SEÑOR dio a conocer por medio de su siervo Elías el tisbita, que dijo: "En el campo de Jezrel los perros se comerán a Jezabel."*g* **37**De hecho, el cadáver de Jezabel será como estiércol en el campo de Jezrel, y nadie podrá identificarla ni decir: "Ésta era Jezabel."

Jehú extermina a la familia de Acab

10 Acab tenía setenta hijos, los cuales vivían en Samaria. Por tanto, Jehú escribió cartas y las envió a Samaria, es decir, a las autoridades de la ciudad,*h* a los *ancianos y a los protectores de los hijos de Acab. En las cartas decía:

> **2**«Ustedes cuentan con los hijos de Acab,*i* y con los carros de combate y sus caballos, con una ciudad fortificada, y con un arsenal. Así que tan pronto como reciban esta carta, **3**escojan al más capaz y más noble de los hijos de Acab, y pónganlo en el trono de su padre. Pero prepárense para luchar por la familia de su rey.»

4Ellos se aterrorizaron y dijeron: «Si dos reyes no pudieron hacerle frente, ¿cómo podremos hacerlo nosotros?» **5**Por lo tanto, el administrador del palacio, el gobernador de la ciudad, los ancianos y los protectores le enviaron este mensaje a Jehú: «Nosotros somos sus servidores, y haremos lo que usted nos diga. No haremos rey a nadie. Haga usted lo que mejor le parezca.» **6**Entonces Jehú les escribió otra carta, en la que decía: «Si ustedes están de mi parte y de veras están dispuestos a obedecerme, vengan a Jezrel mañana a esta hora y tráiganme las cabezas de los hijos de Acab.»

Los setenta príncipes vivían con las familias más notables de la ciudad, pues éstas los criaban. **7**Cuando llegó la carta, prendieron a todos los príncipes y los decapitaron. Luego echaron las cabezas en unos cestos y se las enviaron a Jehú, que estaba en Jezrel. **8**Un mensajero llegó y le dijo a Jehú que habían traído las cabezas de los príncipes. Entonces Jehú ordenó que las pusieran en dos montones a la *entrada de la ciudad, y que las dejaran allí hasta el día siguiente.

9Por la mañana, Jehú salió y, presentándose ante todo el pueblo, confesó: «¡Ustedes son inocentes! ¡Yo fui el que conspiró contra mi señor! ¡Yo lo maté! Pero ¿quién ha matado a todos éstos? **10**Sepan, pues, que nada de lo que el SEÑOR ha dicho contra la familia de Acab dejará de cumplirse. En efecto, el SEÑOR ha hecho lo que había prometido por medio de su siervo

---

a **9:22** *idolatrías.* Lit. *Prostituciones.*   *b* **9:26** Véase 1R 21:19.   *c* **9:27** *en dirección a Bet Hagán.* Alt. *por el camino de la casa del huerto.*   *d* **9:27** *lo hirieron* (véanse LXX y Siríaca); TM no incluye esta frase.   *e* **9:31** *¿Cómo estás ... tu señor?* Alt. *¿Hay paz para Zimri, asesino de su señor?* (véase 1R 16:9-15).   *f* **9:32** *oficiales.* Lit. **Eunucos.*   *g* **9:36** Véase 1R 21:23.   *h* **10:1** *la ciudad* (mss. de LXX); *Jezrel* (TM).   *i* **10:2** *Acab.* Lit. *su señor;* también en vv. 3 y 6.

Elías.» 11Dicho esto, Jehú mató a todos los que quedaban de la familia de Acab en Jezrel, y a todos sus dignatarios, sus amigos íntimos y sus sacerdotes. No dejó a ninguno de ellos con vida.

12Después emprendió la marcha contra Samaria y, al llegar a Bet Équed de los Pastores, 13se encontró con unos parientes de Ocozías, rey de Judá.

—¿Quiénes son ustedes? —les preguntó.

—Somos parientes de Ocozías; hemos venido a visitar a la familia real.

14—¡Captúrenlos vivos! —ordenó Jehú.

Así lo hicieron, y después los degollaron junto al pozo de Bet Équed. Eran cuarenta y dos hombres; Jehú no dejó vivo a ninguno de ellos.

15Al dejar ese lugar, Jehú se encontró con Jonadab hijo de Recab, que había ido a verlo. Jehú lo saludó y le preguntó:

—¿Me eres leal, como yo lo soy contigo?

—Lo soy —respondió Jonadab.

Jehú replicó:

—Si es así, dame la mano.

Jonadab le dio la mano, y Jehú, haciéndolo subir con él a su carro, 16le dijo:

—Ven conmigo, para que veas el celo que tengo por el SEÑOR.

Y lo llevó en su carro. 17Tan pronto como Jehú llegó a Samaria, exterminó a la familia de Acab, matando a todos los que quedaban allí, según la palabra que el SEÑOR le había dado a conocer a Elías.

Jehú elimina a los adoradores de Baal

18Entonces Jehú reunió a todo el pueblo y dijo: «Acab adoró a *Baal con pocas ganas; Jehú lo hará con devoción. 19Llamen, pues, a todos los profetas de Baal, junto con todos sus ministros y sacerdotes. Que no falte ninguno de ellos, pues voy a ofrecerle a Baal un sacrificio grandioso. Todo el que falte, morirá.» En realidad, Jehú no era sincero, pues tenía el propósito de eliminar a los adoradores de Baal.

20Luego dio esta orden: «Convoquen una asamblea en honor de Baal.» Y así se hizo. 21Como Jehú envió mensajeros por todo Israel, vinieron todos los que servían a Baal, sin faltar ninguno. Eran tantos los que llegaron, que el templo de Baal se llenó de un extremo a otro. 22Jehú le ordenó al encargado del guardarropa que sacara las vestiduras para los adoradores de Baal, y así lo hizo.

23Cuando Jehú y Jonadab hijo de Recab entraron en el templo de Baal, Jehú les dijo a los congregados: «Asegúrense de que aquí entre ustedes no haya siervos del SEÑOR, sino sólo de Baal.» 24Entonces pasaron a ofrecer sacrificios y *holocaustos.

Ahora bien, Jehú había apostado una guardia de ochenta soldados a la entrada, con esta advertencia: «Ustedes me responden por estos hombres. El que deje escapar a uno solo de ellos, lo pagará con su *vida.» 25Así que tan pronto como terminó de ofrecer el holocausto, Jehú ordenó a los guardias y oficiales: «¡Entren y mátenlos! ¡Que no escape nadie!» Y los mataron a filo de espada y los echaron fuera. Luego los guardias y los oficiales entraron en el santuarioj del templo de Baal, 26sacaron la *piedra sagrada que estaba allí, y la quemaron. 27Además de tumbar la piedra sagrada, derribaron el templo de Baal y lo convirtieron en un muladar, y así ha quedado hasta el día de hoy.

28De este modo Jehú erradicó de Israel el culto a Baal. 29Sin embargo, no se apartó del pecado que Jeroboán hijo de Nabat hizo cometer a los israelitas, es decir, el de rendir culto a los becerros de oro en Betel y en Dan.

30El SEÑOR le dijo a Jehú: «Has actuado bien. Has hecho lo que me agrada, pues has llevado a cabo lo que yo me había propuesto hacer con la familia de Acab. Por lo tanto, durante cuatro generaciones tus descendientes ocuparán el trono de Israel.» 31Sin embargo, Jehú no cumplió con todo el *corazón la *ley del SEÑOR, Dios de Israel, pues no se apartó de los pecados con que Jeroboán hizo pecar a los israelitas.

32Por aquel tiempo, el SEÑOR comenzó a reducir el territorio israelita. Jazael atacó el país por todas las fronteras: 33desde el Jordán hacia el este, toda la región de Galaad, ocupada por las tribus de Gad, Rubén y Manasés; y desde la ciudad de Aroer, junto al arroyo Arnón, hasta las regiones de Galaad y Basán.

34Los demás acontecimientos del reinado de Jehú, y todo lo que hizo y todo su poderío, están escritos en el libro de las crónicas de los reyes de Israel. 35Jehú murió y fue sepultado en Samaria. Y su hijo Joacaz lo sucedió en el trono. 36Jehú reinó en Samaria sobre Israel durante veintiocho años.

Atalía y Joás
11:1-21 — 2Cr 22:10—23:21

11 Cuando Atalía, madre de Ocozías, vio que su hijo había muerto, tomó medidas para eliminar a toda la familia real. 2Pero Josaba, que era hija del rey Jorán y hermana de Ocozías, raptó a Joás hijo de Ocozías cuando los príncipes estaban a punto de ser asesinados. Metiéndolo en un dormitorio con su nodriza, logró esconderlo de Atalía, de modo que no lo mataron. 3Seis años estuvo Joás escondido con su nodriza en el templo del SEÑOR, mientras Atalía reinaba en el país.

4En el séptimo año, el sacerdote Joyadá mandó llamar a los capitanes,k a los quereteos y a los guardias, para que se presentaran ante él en el templo del SEÑOR. Allí en el templo hizo un pacto con ellos y les tomó juramento. Luego les mostró al hijo del rey, 5y les dio estas órdenes: «Hagan lo siguiente: Una tercera parte de los que están de servicio el *sábado vigilará el palacio real; 6otra tercera parte, la puerta de Sur; y la otra tercera parte, la puerta detrás del cuartel. Harán la guardia del templo por turnos. 7Los dos grupos que están libres el sábado protegerán al rey en el templo del SEÑOR. 8Arma en mano, rodeen por completo al rey; y si alguien se atreve a penetrar las filas,l mátenlo. ¡No dejen solo al rey, vaya donde vaya!»

9Los capitanes cumplieron con todo lo que el sacerdote Joyadá les había ordenado. Cada uno reunió a sus hombres, tanto a los que estaban de servicio el sábado como a los que estaban libres, y se presentaron ante Joyadá. 10Éste repartió entre los capitanes las lanzas y los escudos del rey David, que estaban guardados en el templo del SEÑOR. 11Arma en mano, los guardias tomaron sus puestos alrededor del rey, cerca del altar, y desde el lado sur hasta el lado norte del templo. 12Entonces Joyadá sacó al hijo del rey, le puso la corona y le entregó una copia del pacto.m Luego lo ungieron, y todos aplaudieron, gritando: «¡Viva el rey!»

13Cuando Atalía oyó la gritería de los guardias y de la tropa, fue al templo del SEÑOR, donde estaba la gente. 14Al ver que el rey estaba de pie junto a la co-

---

j 10:25 el santuario. Lit. la ciudad. k 11:4 capitanes. Lit. jefes de cien; también en vv. 9,10,15,19. l 11:8 las filas. Alt. los precintos; también en v. 15. m 11:12 le puso ... pacto. Alt. y le puso la corona y las insignias.

lumna, como era la costumbre, y que los capitanes y músicos estaban a su lado, y que toda la gente tocaba alegre las trompetas, Atalía se rasgó las vestiduras y gritó: «¡Traición! ¡Traición!»

15Entonces el sacerdote Joyadá, como no quería que la mataran en el templo del SEÑOR, ordenó a los capitanes que estaban al mando de las fuerzas: «Sáquenla de entre las filas; y si alguien se pone a su lado, imátenlo a filo de espada!» 16Así que la apresaron y la llevaron al palacio por la puerta de la caballería, y allí la mataron.

17Luego Joyadá hizo un *pacto entre el SEÑOR, el rey y la gente para que fueran el pueblo del SEÑOR; también hizo un pacto entre el rey y el pueblo. 18Entonces toda la gente fue al templo de *Baal y lo derribó. Destruyeron los altares y los ídolos, y enfrente de los altares degollaron a Matán, sacerdote de Baal.

El sacerdote Joyadá apostó guardias en el templo del SEÑOR 19y, acompañado de los capitanes y de los quereteos, los guardias y todo el pueblo, llevó al rey desde el templo del SEÑOR hasta el palacio real. Entraron juntos por la puerta del cuartel, y Joás se sentó en el trono real. 20Todo el pueblo estaba alegre, y tranquila la ciudad, pues habían matado a Atalía a filo de espada en el palacio.

21Joás tenía siete años cuando ascendió al trono.

Joás, rey de Judá
12:1-21 — 2Cr 24:1-14,23-27

12 En el año séptimo del reinado de Jehú, Joás comenzó a reinar, y reinó en Jerusalén cuarenta años. Su madre era Sibia, oriunda de Berseba. 2Joás hizo durante toda su vida lo que agrada al SEÑOR, pues siguió las enseñanzas del sacerdote Joyadá.n 3Sin embargo, no se quitaron los *altares paganos, sino que el pueblo continuó ofreciendo sacrificios y quemando incienso en ellos.

4Un día Joás ordenó a los sacerdotes: «Recojan todo el dinero que cada persona traiga al templo del SEÑOR como ofrenda sagrada, incluso el impuesto del censo, el dinero de votos personales y todas las ofrendas voluntarias. 5Cada sacerdote debe tomar el dinero de manos de su propio tesorero,ñ y usarlo para restaurar el templo y reparar todo lo que esté dañado.»

6En el año veintitrés del reinado de Joás sucedió que, como los sacerdotes no habían hecho reparaciones al templo, 7el rey llamó al sacerdote Joyadá y a los otros sacerdotes, y les recriminó: «¿Por qué no han comenzado la restauración del templo? De aquí en adelante, no recibirán dinero de manos de los tesoreros, y deberán entregar lo que tengan para que se repare el templo.»

8Los sacerdotes accedieron a no recibir más dinero del pueblo, y renunciaron al encargo de restaurar el templo. 9Sin embargo, el sacerdote Joyadá tomó un cofre y, después de hacer una ranura en la tapa, le puso junto al altar, a la derecha, según se entra en el templo del SEÑOR. Los sacerdotes que vigilaban la entrada comenzaron a poner en el cofre todo el dinero que la gente traía al templo del SEÑOR. 10Cuando veían que el cofre ya estaba lleno, subía el secretario real con el sumo sacerdote para vaciarloo y contar el dinero que había en el templo del SEÑOR. 11Una vez determinada la cantidad, entregaban el dinero a los que supervisaban la restau-

ración del templo. Éstos les pagaban a los que trabajaban allí en el templo: carpinteros, maestros de obra, 12albañiles y canteros. También compraban madera y piedras de cantería, y cubrían todos los gastos necesarios para restaurar el templo del SEÑOR.

13Sin embargo, del dinero que se traía al templo del SEÑOR, no se usaba nada para hacer copas, despabiladeras, aspersorios y trompetas, ni otros utensilios de plata y oro, 14sino que ese dinero se les entregaba a los trabajadores, que lo usaban para reparar el templo. 15A los que estaban encargados de pagar a los trabajadores no se les pedían cuentas, pues procedían con toda honradez. 16El dinero de los sacrificios *expiatorios y por la culpa no era para el templo del SEÑOR, pues pertenecía a los sacerdotes.

17Por aquel tiempo, Jazael, rey de *Siria, atacó la ciudad de Gat y la conquistó; luego se propuso atacar a Jerusalén. 18Por eso Joás, rey de Judá, recogió todos los objetos que habían consagrado sus antepasados Josafat, Jorán y Ocozías, reyes de Judá, junto con los que él mismo había consagrado, más todo el oro que pudo encontrar entre los tesoros del templo del SEÑOR y en el palacio real. Todo esto se lo envió a Jazael, rey de Siria, el cual se retiró de Jerusalén.

19Los demás acontecimientos del reinado de Joás, y todo lo que hizo, están escritos en el libro de las crónicas de los reyes de Israel. 20Sus propios ministros conspiraron contra él y lo asesinaron en Bet Miló,p camino a Sila. 21Quienes lo atacaron fueron Josacar hijo de Simat y Jozabad hijo de Semer. Así murió Joás, y fue sepultado con sus antepasados en la Ciudad de David. Y su hijo Amasías lo sucedió en el trono.

Joacaz, rey de Israel

13 En el año veintitrés del reinado de Joás hijo de Ocozías, rey de Judá, Joacaz hijo de Jehú ascendió al trono de Israel, y reinó en Samaria diecisiete años. 2Joás hizo lo que ofende al SEÑOR, pues siguió el mal ejemplo de Jeroboán hijo de Nabat y no se apartó del pecado con que éste hizo pecar a Israel. 3Por eso la ira del SEÑOR se encendió contra los israelitas y, por mucho tiempo, los puso bajo el poder de Jazael, rey de *Siria, y de su hijo Ben Adad.

4Entonces Joacaz clamó al SEÑOR, y él le escuchó, pues vio la gran opresión del rey de Siria sobre Israel. 5El SEÑOR les proveyó un libertador, de modo que los israelitas pudieron librarse del poder de los sirios y vivir tranquilos,q como antes. 6Sin embargo, siguieron el mal ejemplo de la familia de Jeroboán y no se apartaron de los pecados con que éstos hicieron pecar a Israel, y hasta dejaron en pie la imagen de la diosa *Aserá, que estaba en Samaria.

7Del ejército no le habían quedado a Joacaz más que cincuenta jinetes, diez carros de combate y diez mil soldados de infantería, pues el rey de Siria había destruido el ejército, aniquilándolo por completo.

8Los demás acontecimientos del reinado de Joacaz, y todo lo que hizo y su poderío, están escritos en el libro de las crónicas de los reyes de Israel. 9Joacaz murió y fue sepultado en Samaria. Y su hijo Joás lo sucedió en el trono.

Joás, rey de Israel

10En el año treinta y siete del reinado de Joás, rey de Judá, Joás hijo de Joacaz ascendió al trono de Israel,

---

n 12:2 Joás ... Joyadá. Alt. Joás hizo lo que agrada al SEÑOR durante todo el tiempo que el sacerdote Joyadá lo instruyó (véase 2Cr 24:2). ñ 12:5 tesorero. Palabra de difícil traducción; también en v. 7. o 12:10 vaciarlo. Palabra de difícil traducción. p 12:20 Bet Miló. Alt. el edificio del terraplén. q 13:5 tranquilos. Lit. en sus casas.

y reinó en Samaria dieciséis años. 11Joás hizo lo que ofende al SEÑOR, pues siguió el mal ejemplo de Jeroboán hijo de Nabat y no se apartó de ninguno de los pecados con que éste hizo pecar a Israel.

12Los demás acontecimientos del reinado de Joás, y todo lo que hizo y su poderío, incluso la guerra que sostuvo contra Amasías, rey de Judá, están escritos en el libro de las crónicas de los reyes de Israel. 13Joás murió y fue sepultado en Samaria con los reyes de Israel. Y Jeroboán lo sucedió en el trono.

Muerte de Eliseo

14Cuando Eliseo cayó enfermo de muerte, Joás, rey de Israel, fue a verlo. Echándose sobre él, lloró y exclamó:

—¡Padre mío, padre mío, carro y fuerza conductora de Israel!

15Eliseo le dijo:

—Consigue un arco y varias flechas.

Joás así lo hizo. 16Luego Eliseo le dijo:

—Empuña el arco.

Cuando el rey empuñó el arco, Eliseo puso las manos sobre las del rey 17y le dijo:

—Abre la ventana que da hacia el oriente.

Joás la abrió, y Eliseo le ordenó:

—¡Dispara!

Así lo hizo. Entonces Eliseo declaró:

—¡Flecha victoriosa del SEÑOR! ¡Flecha victoriosa contra *Siria! ¡Tú vas a derrotar a los sirios en Afec hasta acabar con ellos! 18Así que toma las flechas —añadió.

El rey las tomó, y Eliseo le ordenó:

—¡Golpea el suelo!

Joás golpeó el suelo tres veces, y se detuvo. 19Ante eso, el hombre de Dios se enojó y le dijo:

—Debiste haber golpeado el suelo cinco o seis veces; entonces habrías derrotado a los sirios hasta acabar con ellos. Pero ahora los derrotarás sólo tres veces.

20Después de esto, Eliseo murió y fue sepultado.

Cada año, bandas de guerrilleros moabitas invadían el país. 21En cierta ocasión, unos israelitas iban a enterrar a un muerto, pero de pronto vieron a esas bandas y echaron el cadáver en la tumba de Eliseo. Cuando el cadáver tocó los huesos de Eliseo, ¡el hombre recobró la vida y se puso de pie!

Jazael oprime a los israelitas

22Durante el reinado de Joacaz, Jazael, rey de *Siria, oprimió a los israelitas. 23Sin embargo, el SEÑOR tuvo misericordia de ellos. Por causa del *pacto que había hecho con Abraham, Isaac y Jacob, se compadeció de los israelitas y los preservó, y hasta el día de hoy no ha querido destruirlos ni arrojarlos de su presencia.

24Cuando murió Jazael, rey de Siria, lo sucedió en el trono su hijo Ben Adad. 25Entonces Joás hijo de Joacaz logró rescatar del poder de Ben Adad las ciudades que éste le había arrebatado a Joacaz. En tres ocasiones Joás logró derrotarlo, de modo que pudo recuperar las ciudades de Israel.

Amasías, rey de Judá
14:1-7 — 2Cr 25:1-4,11-12
14:8-22 — 2Cr 25:17—26:2

14 En el segundo año de Joás hijo de Joacaz, rey de Judá, Amasías hijo de Joás, rey de Judá, ascendió al trono. 2Tenía veinticinco años cuando comenzó a reinar, y reinó en Jerusalén veintinueve años. Su madre era Joadán, oriunda de Jerusalén. 3Amasías hizo lo que agrada al SEÑOR, aunque no como lo había hecho su antepasado David. En todo siguió el ejemplo de su padre Joás, 4pero no se quitaron los *altares paganos, sino que el pueblo siguió ofreciendo sacrificios y quemando incienso en ellos.

5Después de afianzarse en el poder, Amasías ajustició a los ministros que habían asesinado a su padre el rey. 6Sin embargo, según lo que ordenó el SEÑOR, no mató a los hijos de los asesinos, pues está escrito en el libro de la *ley de Moisés: «A los padres no se les dará muerte por la culpa de sus hijos, ni a los hijos se les dará muerte por la culpa de sus padres, sino que cada uno morirá por su propio pecado.»r

7Amasías derrotó a diez mil edomitas en el valle de la Sal; también conquistó la ciudad de Selá y le puso por nombre Joctel, que es como se conoce hasta el día de hoy.

8Por aquel tiempo, Amasías envió mensajeros a Joás, hijo de Joacaz y nieto de Jehú, rey de Israel, con este reto: «¡Sal para que nos enfrentemos!»

9Pero Joás, rey de Israel, le respondió a Amasías, rey de Judá: «El cardo del Líbano le mandó este mensaje al cedro: "Entrega a tu hija como esposa a mi hijo." Pero luego pasaron por allí las fieras del Líbano, y aplastaron al cardo. 10De hecho, has derrotado a los edomitas, y el éxito se te ha subido a la cabeza. Está bien, jáctate si quieres, pero quédate en casa. ¿Para qué provocas una desgracia que significará tu perdición y la de Judá?»

11Amasías no le hizo caso. Así que Joás, rey de Israel, marchó a Bet Semes, en Judá, para enfrentarse con él. 12Los israelitas batieron a los de Judá, y éstos huyeron a sus hogares. 13En Bet Semes, Joás, rey de Israel, capturó a Amasías, rey de Judá, hijo de Joás y nieto de Ocozías. Luego fue a Jerusalén y derribó ciento ochenta metross de la muralla, desde la puerta de Efraín hasta la puerta de la Esquina. 14Además, se apoderó de todo el oro, la plata y los utensilios que había en el templo del SEÑOR y en el tesoro del palacio real. También tomó rehenes, y regresó a Samaria.

15Los demás acontecimientos del reinado de Joás, y todo lo que hizo y su poderío, incluso la guerra que sostuvo contra Amasías, rey de Judá, están escritos en el libro de las crónicas de los reyes de Israel. 16Joás murió y fue sepultado en Samaria con los reyes de Israel. Y su hijo Jeroboán lo sucedió en el trono.

17Amasías hijo de Joás, rey de Judá, sobrevivió quince años a Joás hijo de Joacaz, rey de Israel. 18Los demás acontecimientos del reinado de Amasías están escritos en el libro de las crónicas de los reyes de Judá. 19Como se tramó una conspiración contra él en Jerusalén, Amasías huyó a Laquis; pero lo persiguieron y allí lo mataron. 20Luego lo llevaron a caballo hasta Jerusalén, la Ciudad de David, y allí fue sepultado con sus antepasados.

21Entonces todo el pueblo de Judá tomó a Azarías,t que tenía dieciséis años, y lo proclamó rey en lugar de su padre Amasías. 22Y fue Azarías quien, después de la muerte del rey Amasías, reconstruyó la ciudad de Elat y la reincorporó a Judá.

Jeroboán II, rey de Israel

23En el año quince del reinado de Amasías hijo de Joás, rey de Judá, Jeroboán hijo de Joás, rey de Israel, ascendió al trono, y reinó en Samaria cuarenta y un años. 24Jeroboán hizo lo que ofende al SEÑOR,

r 14:6 Dt 24:16   s 14:13 ciento ochenta metros. Lit. cuatrocientos *codos.   t 14:21 Azarías. Lit. Uzías.

pues no se apartó de ninguno de los pecados con que Jeroboán hijo de Nabat hizo pecar a Israel. 25Él fue quien restableció las fronteras de Israel desde Lebó Jamatu hasta el mar del Arabá, según la palabra que el SEÑOR, Dios de Israel, había dado a conocer por medio de su siervo Jonás hijo de Amitay, el profeta de Gat Jefer. 26Porque el SEÑOR había visto que todos los habitantes de Israel, esclavos o libres, sufrían amargamente, y que no había nadie que los ayudara. 27Pero el SEÑOR los salvó por medio de Jeroboán hijo de Joás, pues había dicho que no borraría de la tierra el *nombre de Israel.

28Los demás acontecimientos del reinado de Jeroboán, y todo lo que hizo y su poderío, incluso sus guerras en las que recuperó Damasco y Jamat para Israel,v están escritos en el libro de las crónicas de los reyes de Israel. 29Jeroboán murió y fue sepultado con sus antepasados, los reyes de Israel. Y su hijo Zacarías lo sucedió en el trono.

Azarías, rey de Judá
15:1-7 — 2Cr 26:3-4,21-23

15 En el año veintisiete del reinado de Jeroboán, rey de Israel, Azarías hijo de Amasías, rey de Judá, ascendió al trono. 2Tenía dieciséis años cuando comenzó a reinar, y reinó en Jerusalén cincuenta y dos años. Su madre era Jecolías, oriunda de Jerusalén. 3Azarías hizo lo que agrada al SEÑOR, pues en todo siguió el buen ejemplo de su padre Amasías; 4pero no se quitaron los *altares paganos, sino que el pueblo siguió ofreciendo sacrificios y quemando incienso en ellos.

5Sin embargo, el SEÑOR castigó al rey con *lepra hasta el día de su muerte. Y como el rey Azarías tuvo que vivir aislado en casa,w su hijo Jotán quedó a cargo del palacio y del gobierno del país.

6Los demás acontecimientos del reinado de Azarías, y todo lo que hizo, están escritos en el libro de las crónicas de los reyes de Israel. 7Azarías murió y fue sepultado con sus antepasados en la Ciudad de David. Y su hijo Jotán lo sucedió en el trono.

Zacarías, rey de Israel

8En el año treinta y ocho del reinado de Azarías, rey de Judá, Zacarías hijo de Jeroboán ascendió al trono de Israel, y reinó en Samaria seis meses. 9Zacarías hizo lo que ofende al SEÑOR, como lo hicieron sus antepasados, pues no se apartó de los pecados con que Jeroboán hijo de Nabat hizo pecar a Israel.

10Salún hijo de Jabés conspiró contra Zacarías. Lo atacó en Ibleamx y lo mató, usurpando así el trono. 11Los demás acontecimientos del reinado de Zacarías están escritos en el libro de las crónicas de los reyes de Israel. 12De este modo se cumplió la palabra que el SEÑOR le había dado a conocer a Jehú: «Durante cuatro generaciones tus descendientes ocuparán el trono de Israel.»y

Salún, rey de Israel

13Salún hijo de Jabés ascendió al trono en el año treinta y nueve de Uzías, rey de Judá, y reinó en Samaria un mes. 14Pero Menajem hijo de Gadí llegó de Tirsá a Samaria, y allí atacó a Salún hijo de Jabés y lo mató, usurpando así el trono.

15Los demás acontecimientos del reinado de Salún, incluso su conspiración, están escritos en el libro de las crónicas de los reyes de Israel.

16Por aquel tiempo, Menajem atacó la ciudad de Tifsa. Como no le abrieron las *puertas de la ciudad, mató a todos los que vivían allí y en los alrededores, comenzando por Tirsá, y les abrió el vientre a las mujeres embarazadas.

Menajem, rey de Israel

17En el año treinta y nueve del reinado de Azarías, rey de Judá, Menajem hijo de Gadí ascendió al trono de Israel, y reinó en Samaria diez años. 18Pero hizo lo que ofende al SEÑOR, pues durante toda su vida jamás se apartó de los pecados con que Jeroboán hijo de Nabat hizo pecar a Israel.

19Tiglat Piléser,z rey de Asiria, invadió el país, y Menajem le entregó treinta y tres mil kilosa de plata para ganarse su apoyo y mantenerse en el trono. 20Menajem les exigió este dinero a los israelitas: todos los ricos tenían que pagarle al rey de Asiria medio kilob de plata. Entonces el rey de Asiria se retiró y dejó de ocupar el país.

21Los demás acontecimientos del reinado de Menajem, y todo lo que hizo, están escritos en el libro de las crónicas de los reyes de Israel. 22Menajem murió, y su hijo Pecajías lo sucedió en el trono.

Pecajías, rey de Israel

23En el año cincuenta de Azarías, rey de Judá, Pecajías hijo de Menajem ascendió al trono de Israel, y reinó en Samaria dos años. 24Pero hizo lo que ofende al SEÑOR, pues no se apartó de los pecados con que Jeroboán hijo de Nabat hizo pecar a Israel. 25Uno de sus oficiales, que se llamaba Pecaj hijo de Remalías, conspiró contra él. Apoyado por cincuenta galaaditas, atacó a Pecajías, a Argob y a Arié, en la torre del palacio real en Samaria. Así fue como lo mató y usurpó el trono.

26Los demás acontecimientos del reinado de Pecajías, y todo lo que hizo, están escritos en el libro de las crónicas de los reyes de Israel.

Pecaj, rey de Israel

27En el año cincuenta y dos del reinado de Azarías, rey de Judá, Pecaj hijo de Remalías ascendió al trono de Israel, y reinó en Samaria veinte años. 28Pero hizo lo que ofende al SEÑOR, pues no se apartó de los pecados con que Jeroboán hijo de Nabat hizo pecar a Israel.

29En tiempos de Pecaj, rey de Israel, Tiglat Piléser, rey de Asiria, invadió el país y conquistó Iyón, Abel Betmacá, Janoa, Cedes, Jazor, Galaad y Galilea, incluyendo todo el territorio de Neftalí; además, deportó a los habitantes a Asiria. 30Entonces Oseas hijo de Elá conspiró contra Pecaj hijo de Remalías y lo atacó. Así fue como, en el año veinte de Jotán hijo de Uzías, lo mató y usurpó el trono.

31Los demás acontecimientos del reinado de Pecaj, y todo lo que hizo, están escritos en el libro de las crónicas de los reyes de Israel.

Jotán, rey de Judá
15:33-38 — 2Cr 27:1-4,7-9

32En el segundo año del reinado de Pecaj hijo de Remalías, rey de Israel, Jotán hijo de Uzías, rey de Judá, ascendió al trono. 33Tenía veinticinco años

---

u 14:25 Lebó Jamat. Alt. la entrada de Jamat.   v 14:28 para Israel (lectura probable; véase Siríaca); para Judá en Israel (TM). w 15:5 aislado en casa. Lit. en casa de libertad (es decir, libre de responsabilidad). x 15:10 en Ibleam (mss. de LXX); ante el pueblo (TM). y 15:12 2R 10:30 z 15:19 Tiglat Piléser. Lit. Pul. a 15:19 treinta y tres mil kilos. Lit. mil *talentos. b 15:20 medio kilo. Lit. cincuenta *siclos.

cuando comenzó a reinar, y reinó en Jerusalén dieciséis años. Su madre era Jerusa hija de Sadoc. 34Jotán hizo lo que agrada al SEÑOR, pues en todo siguió el buen ejemplo de su padre Uzías. 35Fue Jotán quien reconstruyó la puerta superior del templo del SEÑOR, pero no se quitaron los altares paganos, sino que el pueblo siguió ofreciendo sacrificios y quemando incienso en ellos.

36Los demás acontecimientos del reinado de Jotán están escritos en el libro de las crónicas de los reyes de Judá. 37Durante su reinado, el SEÑOR comenzó a enviar contra Judá a Rezín, rey de *Siria, y a Pecaj hijo de Remalías. 38Jotán murió y fue sepultado con sus antepasados en la Ciudad de David, su antecesor. Y su hijo Acaz lo sucedió en el trono.

Acaz, rey de Judá
16:1-20 — 2Cr 28:1-27

16 En el año diecisiete del reinado de Pecaj hijo de Remalías, Acaz hijo de Jotán ascendió al trono. 2Tenía veinte años cuando comenzó a reinar, y reinó en Jerusalén dieciséis años. Pero a diferencia de su antepasado David, Acaz no hizo lo que agradaba al SEÑOR su Dios. 3Al contrario, siguió el mal ejemplo de los reyes de Israel, y hasta sacrificó en el fuego a su hijo, según las repugnantes ceremonias de las naciones que el SEÑOR había expulsado delante de los israelitas. 4También ofrecía sacrificios y quemaba incienso en los *santuarios paganos, en las colinas y bajo todo árbol frondoso.

5En cierta ocasión, Rezín, rey de *Siria, y Pecaj hijo de Remalías, rey de Israel, marcharon hacia Jerusalén para hacerle guerra a Acaz, y sitiaron la ciudad, pero no lograron tomarla. 6Por aquel tiempo, Rezín, rey de Siria, había reconquistado la ciudad de Elat, desalojando a los de Judá que vivían allí. Posteriormente los edomitas se establecieron en Elat, y allí se han quedado hasta el día de hoy.

7Acaz envió entonces mensajeros a Tiglat Piléser, rey de Asiria, con este mensaje: «Ya que soy tu servidor y vasallo,c ven y líbrame del poder del rey de Siria y del rey de Israel, que se han puesto en mi contra.» 8Acaz también juntó la plata y el oro que había en el templo del SEÑOR y en el tesoro del palacio real, y se lo envió todo al rey de Asiria como un regalo. 9El rey de Asiria, accediendo a su petición, lanzó un ataque contra Damasco y conquistó la ciudad. Luego deportó a sus habitantes a Quir, y mató a Rezín.

10El rey Acaz fue entonces a Damasco para encontrarse con Tiglat Piléser, rey de Asiria. Cuando vio el altar que había en la ciudad, el rey Acaz le envió al sacerdote Urías un plano del altar, con un dibujo de todos los detalles. 11Entonces Urías construyó un altar según las instrucciones que el rey Acaz le había enviado desde Damasco, y lo terminó antes de que el rey regresara. 12Cuando éste llegó de Damasco y vio el altar, se acercó y presentó allí una ofrenda. 13Ofreció el *holocausto con la ofrenda, derramó su libación y roció sobre el altar la sangre de los sacrificios de *comunión. 14El altar de bronce, que estaba en la presencia del SEÑOR, lo retiró de la parte delantera del edificio y lo situó en el lado norte del nuevo altar, ya que ahora quedaba entre el nuevo altar y el templo del SEÑOR.

15Luego le dio estas órdenes al sacerdote Urías: «Ofrece en este gran altar el holocausto matutino y la ofrenda vespertina, así como el holocausto y la ofrenda del rey, y también los holocaustos, las ofren-

das y las libaciones del pueblo en general. Rocía sobre este altar la sangre de todos los holocaustos y sacrificios. Pero el altar de bronce lo usaré yo.» 16Y el sacerdote Urías hizo todo lo que el rey Acaz le ordenó.

17El rey desmontó los paneles de las bases y les quitó las lavamanos; además bajó la fuented que estaba encima de los bueyes de bronce y la instaló sobre un enlosado de piedra; 18y por deferencia al rey de Asiria, quitó del templo del SEÑOR el techado que se había construido allí para celebrar los *sábados,e así como la entrada exterior para el rey.

19Los demás acontecimientos del reinado de Acaz están escritos en el libro de las crónicas de los reyes de Judá. 20Acaz murió y fue sepultado con sus antepasados en la Ciudad de David. Y su hijo Ezequías lo sucedió en el trono.

Oseas, rey de Israel
17:3-7 — 2R 18:9-12

17 En el año duodécimo del reinado de Acaz, rey de Judá, Oseas hijo de Elá ascendió al trono de Israel, y reinó en Samaria nueve años. 2Hizo lo que ofende al SEÑOR, aunque no tanto como los reyes de Israel que lo habían precedido.

3Salmanasar, rey de Asiria, atacó a Oseas, lo hizo su vasallo y le impuso tributo. 4Más tarde, el rey de Asiria descubrió que Oseas lo traicionaba, pues éste había enviado emisarios a So, rey de Egipto, y además había dejado de pagarle el tributo anual. Por eso el rey de Asiria mandó arrestarlo y lo metió en la cárcel. 5Después invadió el país entero, marchó contra Samaria y sitió la ciudad durante tres años. 6En el año noveno del reinado de Oseas, el rey de Asiria, después de conquistar Samaria, deportó a los israelitas a Asiria y los instaló en Jalaj, en Gozán (que está junto al río Jabor) y en las ciudades de los medos.

El pecado de Israel

7Todo esto sucedió porque los israelitas habían pecado contra el SEÑOR su Dios, que los había sacado de Egipto, librándolos del poder del faraón, rey de Egipto. Adoraron a otros dioses 8y siguieron las costumbres de las naciones que el SEÑOR había expulsado delante de ellos, como también las prácticas que introdujeron los reyes de Israel. 9Además blasfemaronf contra el SEÑOR su Dios, y dondequiera que habitaban se construían *altares paganos. Desde las torres de vigilancia hasta las ciudades fortificadas, 10y en cada colina y bajo todo árbol frondoso, erigieron *piedras sagradas e imágenes de la diosa *Aserá; 11y en todos los altares paganos quemaron incienso, siguiendo el ejemplo de las naciones que el SEÑOR había desterrado delante de ellos. Fueron tantas las maldades que cometieron, que provocaron la ira del SEÑOR. 12Rindieron culto a los ídolos, aunque el SEÑOR se lo había prohibido categóricamente. 13Por eso el SEÑOR les dio esta advertencia a Israel y a Judá por medio de todos los profetas y videntes: «¡Vuélvanse de sus malos *caminos! Cumplan mis mandamientos y decretos, y obedezcan todas las leyes que ordené a sus antepasados, y que les di a conocer a ustedes por medio de mis siervos los profetas.»

14Con todo, no hicieron caso, sino que fueron tan tercos como lo habían sido sus antepasados, que no confiaron en el SEÑOR su Dios. 15Rechazaron los decretos y las advertencias del SEÑOR, y el *pacto que él había hecho con sus antepasados. Se fueron

---

tras ídolos inútiles, de modo que se volvieron inútiles ellos mismos; y aunque el SEÑOR lo había prohibido, siguieron las costumbres de las naciones vecinas. 16Abandonaron todos los mandamientos del SEÑOR su Dios, y se hicieron dos ídolos fundidos en forma de becerro y una imagen de la diosa Aserá. Se postraron ante todos los astros del cielo, y adoraron a *Baal; 17sacrificaron en el fuego a sus hijos e hijas; practicaron la adivinación y la hechicería; en fin, se entregaron a hacer lo que ofende al SEÑOR, provocando así su ira.

18Por lo tanto, el SEÑOR se enojó mucho contra Israel y lo arrojó de su presencia. Sólo quedó la tribu de Judá. 19Pero aun Judá dejó de cumplir los mandatos del SEÑOR su Dios, y siguió las costumbres que introdujo Israel. 20Por eso el SEÑOR rechazó a todos los israelitas: los afligió y los entregó en manos de invasores, y acabó por arrojarlos de su presencia.

21Cuando el SEÑOR arrancó de la familia de David a los israelitas, éstos hicieron rey a Jeroboán hijo de Nabat. Jeroboán, por su parte, los alejó del camino del SEÑOR y los hizo cometer un gran pecado. 22De hecho, los israelitas imitaron todos los pecados de Jeroboán y no se apartaron de ellos. 23Finalmente, el SEÑOR arrojó a Israel de su presencia, tal como lo había anunciado por medio de sus siervos los profetas. Así, pues, fueron desterrados y llevados cautivos a Asiria, donde hasta el día de hoy se han quedado.

Repoblación de Samaria

24Para reemplazar a los israelitas en los poblados de Samaria, el rey de Asiria trajo gente de Babilonia, Cuta, Ava, Jamat y Sefarvayin. Estos tomaron posesión de Samaria y habitaron en sus poblados. 25Al principio, cuando se establecieron, no adoraban al SEÑOR, de modo que el SEÑOR les envió leones que causaron estragos en la población. 26Entonces le dieron este informe al rey de Asiria: «La gente que Su Majestad deportó y estableció en los poblados de Samaria no sabe lo que requiere el dios de ese país. Por esta razón, él les ha enviado leones, para que los maten.»

27El rey de Asiria dio esta orden: «Hagan que regrese a vivir en Samaria uno de los sacerdotes que ustedes capturaron allí, y que le enseñe a la población lo que requiere el dios de ese país.» 28Así que uno de los sacerdotes que habían sido deportados de Samaria fue a vivir a Betel y comenzó a enseñarles cómo adorar al SEÑOR.

29Sin embargo, todos esos pueblos se fabricaron sus propios dioses en las ciudades donde vivían, y los colocaron en los *altares paganos que habían construido los samaritanos. 30Los de Babilonia hicieron al dios Sucot Benot; los de Cuta, a Nergal; los de Jamat, a Asimá, 31y los de Ava, a Nibjaz y a Tartac. Los de Sefarvayin quemaban a sus hijos como sacrificio a Adramélec y a Anamélec, dioses de Sefarvayin; 32adoraban también al SEÑOR, pero de entre ellos mismos nombraron sacerdotes a toda clase de gente para que oficiaran en los altares paganos. 33Aunque adoraban al SEÑOR, servían también a sus propios dioses, según las costumbres de las naciones de donde habían sido deportados.

34Hasta el día de hoy persisten en sus antiguas costumbres. No adoran al SEÑOR ni actúan según sus decretos y sus normas, ni según la *ley y el mandamiento que el SEÑOR ordenó a los descendientes de Jacob, a quien le dio el *nombre de Israel. 35Cuando el SEÑOR hizo un *pacto con los israelitas, les ordenó:

«No adoren a otros dioses ni se inclinen delante de ellos; no les sirvan ni les ofrezcan sacrificios. 36Adoren sólo al SEÑOR, que los sacó de Egipto con gran despliegue de fuerza y poder. Es a él a quien deben adorar y ofrecerle sacrificios. 37Tengan cuidado de cumplir siempre los decretos y ordenanzas, leyes y mandamientos que él les dio por escrito. No adoren a otros dioses. 38No olviden el pacto que él ha hecho con ustedes. Por tanto, no adoren a otros dioses, 39sino sólo al SEÑOR su Dios. Y él los librará del poder de sus enemigos.»

40Sin embargo, no hicieron caso, sino que persistieron en sus antiguas costumbres. 41Aquellos pueblos adoraban al SEÑOR, y al mismo tiempo servían a sus propios ídolos. Hasta el día de hoy sus hijos y sus descendientes siguen actuando como sus antepasados.

Ezequías, rey de Judá

18:2-4 — 2Cr 29:1-2; 31:1
18:5-7 — 2Cr 31:20-21
18:9-12 — 2R 17:3-7

18 En el tercer año de Oseas hijo de Elá, rey de Israel, Ezequías hijo de Acaz, rey de Judá, ascendió al trono. 2Tenía veinticinco años cuando ascendió al trono, y reinó en Jerusalén veintinueve años. Su madre era Abí hija de Zacarías. 3Ezequías hizo lo que agrada al SEÑOR, pues en todo siguió el ejemplo de su antepasado David. 4Quitó los *altares paganos, destrozó las *piedras sagradas y quebró las imágenes de la diosa *Aserá. Además, destruyó la serpiente de bronce que Moisés había hecho, pues los israelitas todavía le quemaban incienso, y la llamaban Nejustán.g

5Ezequías puso su confianza en el SEÑOR, Dios de Israel. No hubo otro como él entre todos los reyes de Judá, ni antes ni después. 6Se mantuvo fiel al SEÑOR y no se apartó de él, sino que cumplió los mandamientos que el SEÑOR le había dado a Moisés. 7El SEÑOR estaba con Ezequías, y por tanto éste tuvo éxito en todas sus empresas. Se rebeló contra el rey de Asiria y no se sometió a él. 8Y derrotó a los filisteos, tanto en las torres de vigilancia como en las ciudades fortificadas, hasta llegar a Gaza y sus alrededores.

9En el año cuarto del reinado de Ezequías, es decir, en el año séptimo del reinado de Oseas hijo de Elá, rey de Israel, Salmanasar, rey de Asiria, marchó contra Samaria y la sitió. 10Al cabo de tres años logró conquistarla. Era el año sexto del reinado de Ezequías, es decir, el año noveno del reinado de Oseas, rey de Israel. 11El rey de Asiria deportó a los israelitas a Asiria, y los estableció en Jalaj, en Gozán (que está junto al río Jabor) y en las ciudades de los medos. 12Esto sucedió porque no obedecieron al SEÑOR su Dios, sino que violaron su *pacto. No cumplieron ni pusieron en práctica lo que Moisés, siervo del SEÑOR, les había ordenado.

13En el año catorce del reinado de Ezequías, Senaquerib, rey de Asiria, atacó y tomó todas las ciudades fortificadas de Judá. 14Entonces Ezequías le envió este mensaje al rey de Asiria, que se encontraba en Laquis: «He actuado mal. Si te retiras, te paga-

---

g 18:4 *la llamaban Nejustán.* Alt. *la llamó Nejustán.* Este nombre suena como las palabras hebreas que significan *bronce* y *serpiente.*

ré cualquier tributo que me impongas.» El rey de Asiria le impuso a Ezequías, rey de Judá, un tributo de nueve mil novecientos kilos de plata y novecientos noventa kilos[h] de oro. 15Así que Ezequías le entregó a Senaquerib toda la plata que había en el templo del SEÑOR y en los tesoros del palacio real. 16Fue entonces cuando Ezequías, rey de Judá, les quitó a las puertas y los quiciales del templo del SEÑOR el oro con que él mismo los había cubierto, y se lo entregó al rey de Asiria.

Senaquerib amenaza a Jerusalén
18:13,17-37 — Is 36:1-22
18:17-35 — 2Cr 32:9-19

17Desde Laquis el rey de Asiria envió a su virrey, al funcionario[i] principal y a su comandante en jefe,[j] al frente de un gran ejército, para hablar con el rey Ezequías en Jerusalén. Marcharon hacia Jerusalén y, al llegar, se detuvieron junto al acueducto del estanque superior, en el camino que lleva al Campo del Lavandero. 18Entonces llamaron al rey, y salió a recibirlos Eliaquín hijo de Jilquías, que era el administrador del palacio, junto con el cronista Sebna y el secretario Joa hijo de Asaf.

19El comandante en jefe les dijo:

—Díganle a Ezequías que así dice el gran rey, el rey de Asiria: "¿En qué se basa tu confianza? 20Tú dices que tienes estrategia y fuerza militar, pero éstas no son más que palabras sin fundamento. ¿En quién confías, que te rebelas contra mí? 21Ahora bien, tú confías en Egipto, ¡ese bastón de caña astillada, que traspasa la mano y hiere al que se apoya en él! Porque eso es el faraón, el rey de Egipto, para todos los que en él confían. 22Y si ustedes me dicen: 'Nosotros confiamos en el SEÑOR, nuestro Dios', ¿no se trata acaso, Ezequías, del Dios cuyos altares y *santuarios paganos tú mismo quitaste, diciéndoles a Judá y a Jerusalén: 'Deben adorar solamente ante este altar en Jerusalén'?"

23»Ahora bien, Ezequías, haz este trato con mi señor, el rey de Asiria: Yo te doy dos mil caballos, si tú consigues otros tantos jinetes para montarlos. 24¿Cómo podrás rechazar el ataque de uno solo de los funcionarios más insignificantes de mi señor, si confías en obtener de Egipto carros de combate y jinetes? 25¿Acaso he venido a atacar y a destruir este lugar sin el apoyo del SEÑOR? ¡Si fue él mismo quien me ordenó: "Marcha contra este país y destrúyelo!"

26Eliaquín hijo de Jilquías, Sebna y Joa le dijeron al comandante en jefe:

—Por favor, hábleles usted a sus siervos en arameo, ya que lo entendemos. No nos hable en hebreo, que el pueblo que está sobre el muro nos escucha.

27Pero el comandante en jefe respondió:

—¿Acaso mi señor me envió a decirles estas cosas sólo a ti y a tu señor, y no a los que están sentados en el muro? ¡Si tanto ellos como ustedes tendrán que comerse su excremento y beberse su orina!

28Dicho esto, el comandante en jefe se puso de pie y a voz en cuello gritó en hebreo:

—¡Oigan las palabras del gran rey, el rey de Asiria! 29Así dice el rey: "No se dejen engañar por Ezequías. ¡Él no puede librarlos de mis manos! 30No dejen que Ezequías los persuada a confiar en el SEÑOR, diciendo: 'Sin duda el SEÑOR nos librará; ¡esta ciudad no caerá en manos del rey de Asiria!'"

31»No le hagan caso a Ezequías. Así dice el rey de Asiria: "Hagan las paces conmigo, y ríndanse. De este modo cada uno podrá comer de su vid y de su higuera, y beber agua de su propio pozo, 32hasta que yo venga y los lleve a un país como el de ustedes, país de grano y de mosto, de pan y de viñedos, de aceite de oliva y de miel. Así vivirán en vez de morir."

»No le hagan caso a Ezequías, que los quiere seducir cuando dice: "El SEÑOR nos librará." 33¿Acaso alguno de los dioses de las naciones pudo librar a su país de las manos del rey de Asiria? 34¿Dónde están los dioses de Jamat y de Arfad? ¿Dónde están los dioses de Sefarvayin, de Hená y de Ivá? ¿Acaso libraron a Samaria de mis manos?

35¿Cuál de todos los dioses de estos países ha podido salvar de mis manos a su país? ¿Cómo entonces podrá el SEÑOR librar de mis manos a Jerusalén?

36Pero el pueblo permaneció en silencio y no respondió ni una sola palabra, porque el rey había ordenado: «No le respondan.»

37Entonces Eliaquín hijo de Jilquías, administrador del palacio, el cronista Sebna, y el secretario Joa hijo de Asaf, con las vestiduras rasgadas en señal de duelo, fueron a ver a Ezequías y le contaron lo que había dicho el comandante en jefe.

Isaías profetiza la liberación de Jerusalén
19:1-13 — Is 37:1-13

19 Cuando el rey Ezequías escuchó esto, se rasgó las vestiduras, se vistió de luto y fue al templo del SEÑOR. 2Además, envió a Eliaquín, administrador del palacio, al cronista Sebna y a los sacerdotes más ancianos, todos vestidos de luto, para hablar con el profeta Isaías hijo de Amoz. 3Y le dijeron: «Así dice Ezequías: "Hoy es un día de angustia, castigo y deshonra, como cuando los hijos están a punto de nacer y no se tienen fuerzas para darlos a luz. 4Tal vez el SEÑOR tu Dios oiga todas las palabras del comandante en jefe, a quien su señor, el rey de Asiria, envió para insultar al Dios viviente. ¡Que el SEÑOR tu Dios lo castigue por las palabras que ha oído! Eleva, pues, una oración por el remanente del pueblo que aún sobrevive."»

5Cuando los funcionarios del rey Ezequías fueron a ver a Isaías, 6éste les dijo: «Díganle a su señor que así dice el SEÑOR: "No temas por las blasfemias que has oído, y las has pronunciado contra mí los subalternos del rey de Asiria. 7¡Mira! Voy a poner un espíritu en él, de manera que cuando oiga cierto rumor se regrese a su propio país. ¡Allí haré que lo maten a filo de espada!"»

8Cuando el comandante en jefe se enteró de que el rey de Asiria había salido de Laquis, se retiró y encontró al rey luchando contra Libná.

9Luego Senaquerib recibió el informe de que Tiracá, rey de *Cus, había salido para luchar contra él, así que una vez más envió mensajeros a Ezequías 10para que le dijeran: «Tú, Ezequías, rey de Judá: No dejes que tu Dios, en quien confías, te engañe cuando dice: "No caerá Jerusalén en manos del rey de Asiria." 11Sin duda te habrás enterado de lo que han hecho los reyes de Asiria en todos los países, *destruyéndolos por completo. ¿Y acaso vas tú a librarte? 12¿Libraron sus dioses a las naciones que mis antepasados han destruido: Gozán, Jarán, Résef y la gente de Edén que vivía en Telasar? 13¿Dónde están el rey

---

de Jamat, el rey de Arfad, el rey de la ciudad de Sefarvayin, o de Hená o Ivá?»

Oración de Ezequías
19:14-19 — Is 37:14-20

14Ezequías tomó la carta de mano de los mensajeros, y la leyó. Luego subió al templo del SEÑOR, la desplegó delante del SEÑOR, 15y en su presencia oró así: «SEÑOR, Dios de Israel, entronizado sobre los *querubines: sólo tú eres el Dios de todos los reinos de la tierra. Tú has hecho los cielos y la tierra. 16Presta atención, SEÑOR, y escucha; abre tus ojos, SEÑOR, y mira; escucha las palabras que Senaquerib ha mandado a decir para insultar al Dios viviente.

17»Es verdad, SEÑOR, que los reyes asirios han asolado todas estas naciones y sus tierras. 18Han arrojado al fuego sus dioses, y los han destruido, porque no eran dioses sino sólo madera y piedra, obra de manos *humanas. 19Ahora, pues, SEÑOR y Dios nuestro, por favor, sálvanos de su mano, para que todos los reinos de la tierra sepan que sólo tú, SEÑOR, eres Dios.»

Muerte de Senaquerib
19:20-37 — Is 37:21-38
19:35-37 — 2Cr 32:20-21

20Entonces Isaías hijo de Amoz le envió este mensaje a Ezequías: «Así dice el SEÑOR, Dios de Israel: "Por cuanto me has rogado respecto a Senaquerib, rey de Asiria, te he escuchado. 21Ésta es la palabra que yo, el SEÑOR, he pronunciado contra él:

»"La virginal hija de *Sión
  te desprecia y se burla de ti.
La hija de Jerusalén
  menea la cabeza al verte huir.
22¿A quién has insultado?
  ¿Contra quién has blasfemado?
¿Contra quién has alzado la voz
  y levantado los ojos con orgullo?
  ¡Contra el *Santo de Israel!
23Has enviado a tus mensajeros
  a insultar al Señor, diciendo:
'Con mis numerosos carros de combate
  escalé las cumbres de las montañas,
  ¡las laderas del Líbano!
Talé sus cedros más altos,
  sus cipreses más selectos.
Alcancé sus refugios más lejanos,
  y sus bosques más frondosos.
24Cavé pozos en tierras extranjeras,
  y en esas aguas apagué mi sed.
Con las plantas de mis pies
  sequé todos los ríos de Egipto.'

25»"¿No te has dado cuenta?
  ¡Hace mucho tiempo que lo he preparado!
Desde tiempo atrás lo vengo planeando,
  y ahora lo he llevado a cabo;
por eso tú has dejado en ruinas
  a las ciudades fortificadas.
26Sus habitantes, impotentes,
  están desalentados y avergonzados.
Son como plantas en el campo,
  como tiernos pastos verdes,
como hierba que brota sobre el techo
  y que se quema antes de crecer.

27»"Yo sé bien cuándo te sientas,
  cuándo sales, cuándo entras,
  y cuánto ruges contra mí.
28Porque has rugido contra mí
  y tu insolencia ha llegado a mis oídos,

te pondré una argolla en la nariz
  y un freno en la boca,
y por el mismo camino por donde viniste
  te haré regresar.

29»"Ésta será la señal para ti, Ezequías:

»"Este año comerán lo que crezca por sí solo,
  y el segundo año lo que de allí brote.
Pero al tercer año sembrarán y cosecharán,
  plantarán viñas y comerán su fruto.
30Una vez más los sobrevivientes de la tribu de Judá
  echarán raíces abajo, y arriba darán fruto.
31Porque de Jerusalén saldrá un remanente,
  del monte Sión un grupo de sobrevivientes.
Esto lo hará mi celo,
  celo del SEÑOR *Todopoderoso.

32»"Yo, el SEÑOR, declaro esto acerca del rey de Asiria:

»"No entrará en esta ciudad,
  ni lanzará contra ella una sola flecha.
No se enfrentará a ella con escudos,
  ni construirá contra ella una rampa de asalto.
33Volverá por el mismo camino que vino;
  ¡en esta ciudad no entrará!
  Yo, el SEÑOR, lo afirmo.
34Por mi causa, y por consideración a David mi siervo,
  defenderé esta ciudad y la salvaré."»

35Esa misma noche el ángel del SEÑOR salió y mató a ciento ochenta y cinco mil hombres del campamento asirio. A la mañana siguiente, cuando los demás se levantaron, ¡allí estaban tendidos todos los cadáveres! 36Así que Senaquerib, rey de Asiria, levantó el campamento y se retiró. Volvió a Nínive y permaneció allí. 37Pero un día, mientras adoraba en el templo de su dios Nisroc, sus hijos Adramélec y Sarézer lo mataron a espada y escaparon a la tierra de Ararat. Y su hijo Esarjadón lo sucedió en el trono.

Enfermedad de Ezequías
20:1-11 — 2Cr 32:24-26; Is 38:1-8

20 Por aquellos días Ezequías se enfermó gravemente y estuvo a punto de morir. El profeta Isaías hijo de Amoz fue a verlo y le dijo: «Así dice el SEÑOR: "Pon tu casa en orden, porque vas a morir; no te recuperarás."»

2Ezequías volvió el rostro hacia la pared y le rogó al SEÑOR: 3«Recuerda, SEÑOR, que yo me he conducido delante de ti con lealtad y con un *corazón íntegro, y que he hecho lo que te agrada.» Y Ezequías lloró amargamente.

4No había salido Isaías del patio central, cuando le llegó la palabra del SEÑOR: 5«Regresa y dile a Ezequías, gobernante de mi pueblo, que así dice el SEÑOR, Dios de su antepasado David: "He escuchado tu oración y he visto tus lágrimas. Voy a sanarte, y en tres días podrás subir al templo del SEÑOR. 6Voy a darte quince años más de vida. Y a ti y a esta ciudad los libraré de caer en manos del rey de Asiria. Yo defenderé esta ciudad por mi causa y por consideración a David mi siervo."»

7Entonces Isaías dijo: «Preparen una pasta de higos.» Así lo hicieron; luego se la aplicaron al rey en la llaga, y se recuperó.

8Ezequías le había preguntado al profeta:
—¿Qué señal recibiré de que el SEÑOR me sanará, y de que en tres días podré subir a su templo?

⁹Isaías le contestó:

—Ésta es la señal que te dará el SEÑOR para confirmar lo que te ha prometido: la sombra ha avanzado diez gradas; ¿podrá retroceder diez?

¹⁰—Es fácil que la sombra se alargue diez gradas —replicó Ezequías—, pero no que vuelva atrás.

¹¹Entonces el profeta Isaías invocó al SEÑOR, y el SEÑOR hizo que la sombra retrocediera diez gradas en la escala de Acaz.

Mensajeros de Babilonia
20:12-19 — Is 39:1-8
20:20-21 — 2Cr 32:32-33

¹²En aquel tiempo Merodac* Baladán hijo de Baladán, rey de Babilonia, le envió cartas y un regalo a Ezequías, porque supo que había estado enfermo. ¹³Ezequías se alegró* al recibir esto, y les mostró a los mensajeros todos sus tesoros: la plata, el oro, las especias, el aceite fino, su arsenal y todo lo que había en ellos. No hubo nada en su palacio ni en todo su reino que Ezequías no les mostrara.

¹⁴Entonces el profeta Isaías fue a ver al rey Ezequías y le preguntó:

—¿Qué querían esos hombres? ¿De dónde vinieron?

—De un país lejano —respondió Ezequías—. Vinieron a verme desde Babilonia.

¹⁵—¿Y qué vieron en tu palacio? —preguntó el profeta.

—Vieron todo lo que hay en él —contestó Ezequías—. No hay nada en mis tesoros que yo no les haya mostrado.

¹⁶Entonces Isaías le dijo:

—Oye la palabra del SEÑOR: ¹⁷Sin duda vendrán días en que todo lo que hay en tu palacio, y todo lo que tus antepasados atesoraron hasta el día de hoy, será llevado a Babilonia. No quedará nada —dice el SEÑOR—. ¹⁸Y algunos de tus hijos y de tus descendientes serán llevados para servir como *eunucos en el palacio del rey de Babilonia.

¹⁹—El mensaje del SEÑOR que tú me has traído es bueno —respondió Ezequías.

Y es que pensaba: «Al menos mientras yo viva, sin duda que habrá *paz y seguridad.»

²⁰Los demás acontecimientos del reinado de Ezequías, y todo lo que hizo, su poderío y cómo construyó el estanque y el acueducto que llevaba agua a la ciudad, están escritos en el libro de las crónicas de los reyes de Judá. ²¹Ezequías murió, y su hijo Manasés lo sucedió en el trono.

Manasés, rey de Judá
21:1-10 — 2Cr 33:1-10
21:17-18 — 2Cr 33:18-20

21 Manasés tenía doce años cuando ascendió al trono, y reinó en Jerusalén cincuenta y cinco años. Su madre era Hepsiba. ²Manasés hizo lo que ofende al SEÑOR, pues practicaba las repugnantes ceremonias de las naciones que el SEÑOR había expulsado delante de los israelitas. ³Reconstruyó los *altares paganos que su padre Ezequías había destruido; además, erigió otros altares en honor de *Baal e hizo una imagen de la diosa *Aserá, como lo había hecho Acab, rey de Israel. Se postró ante todos los astros del cielo y los adoró. ⁴Construyó altares en el templo del SEÑOR, lugar del cual el SEÑOR había dicho: «Jerusalén será el lugar donde yo habite.» ⁵En

ambos atrios del templo del SEÑOR construyó altares en honor de los astros del cielo. ⁶Sacrificó en el fuego a su propio hijo, practicó la magia y la hechicería, y consultó a nigromantes y a espiritistas. Hizo continuamente lo que ofende al SEÑOR, provocando así su ira.

⁷Tomó la imagen de la diosa Aserá que él había hecho, y la puso en el templo, lugar del cual el SEÑOR había dicho a David y a su hijo Salomón: «En este templo en Jerusalén, la ciudad que he escogido de entre todas las tribus de Israel, he decidido habitar para siempre. ⁸Nunca más dejaré que los israelitas anden perdidos fuera de la tierra que les di a sus antepasados, siempre y cuando tengan cuidado de cumplir todo lo que yo les he ordenado, es decir, toda la *ley que les dio mi siervo Moisés.» ⁹Pero no hicieron caso; Manasés los descarrió, de modo que se condujeron peor que las naciones que el SEÑOR destruyó delante de ellos.

¹⁰Por lo tanto, el SEÑOR dijo por medio de sus siervos los profetas: ¹¹«Como Manasés, rey de Judá, ha practicado estas repugnantes ceremonias y se ha conducido peor que los amorreos que lo precedieron, haciendo que los israelitas pequen con los ídolos que él hizo, ¹²así dice el SEÑOR, Dios de Israel: "Voy a enviar tal desgracia sobre Jerusalén y Judá, que a todo el que lo oiga le quedará retumbando en los oídos. ¹³Extenderé sobre Jerusalén el mismo cordel con que medí a Samaria, y la misma plomada con que señalé a la familia de Acab. Voy a tratar a Jerusalén como se hace con un plato que se restriega y se pone boca abajo. ¹⁴Abandonaré al resto de mi heredad, entregando a mi pueblo en manos de sus enemigos, que lo saquearán y lo despojarán. ¹⁵Porque los israelitas han hecho lo que me ofende, y desde el día en que sus antepasados salieron de Egipto hasta hoy me han provocado."»

¹⁶Además del pecado que hizo cometer a Judá, haciendo así lo que ofende al SEÑOR, Manasés derramó tanta sangre inocente que inundó a Jerusalén de un extremo a otro.

¹⁷Los demás acontecimientos del reinado de Manasés, y todo lo que hizo, incluso el pecado que cometió, están escritos en el libro de las crónicas de los reyes de Judá. ¹⁸Manasés murió y fue sepultado en su palacio, en el jardín de Uza. Y su hijo Amón lo sucedió en el trono.

Amón, rey de Judá
21:19-24 — 2Cr 33:21-25

¹⁹Amón tenía veintidós años cuando ascendió al trono, y reinó en Jerusalén dos años. Su madre era Mesulémet hija de Jaruz, oriunda de Jotba. ²⁰Amón hizo lo que ofende al SEÑOR, como lo había hecho su padre Manasés. ²¹En todo siguió el mal ejemplo de su padre, adorando e inclinándose ante los ídolos que éste había adorado. ²²Así que abandonó al SEÑOR, Dios de sus antepasados, y no anduvo en el *camino del SEÑOR.

²³Los ministros del rey Amón conspiraron contra él, y lo asesinaron en su palacio. ²⁴Entonces el pueblo mató a todos los que habían conspirado contra el rey Amón, y en su lugar proclamaron rey a su hijo Josías.

²⁵Los demás acontecimientos del reinado de Amón están escritos en el libro de las crónicas de los reyes de Judá. ²⁶Amón fue sepultado en su sepulcro,

---

k **20:12** *Merodac* (mss. hebreos, LXX y Siríaca; véase Is 39:1); *Berodac* (TM). l **20:13** *se alegró* (LXX, Vulgata, Siríaca y varios mss. hebreos; véase Is 39:2); *escuchó* (TM).

en el jardín de Uza. Y su hijo Josías lo sucedió en el trono.

Josías, rey de Judá
22:1-20 — 2Cr 34:1-2,8-28

22 Josías tenía ocho años cuando ascendió al trono, y reinó en Jerusalén treinta y un años. Su madre era Jedidá hija de Adaías, oriunda de Boscat. ²Josías hizo lo que agrada al SEÑOR, pues en todo siguió el buen ejemplo de su antepasado David; no se desvió de él en el más mínimo detalle.

³En el año dieciocho de su reinado, el rey Josías mandó a su cronista Safán, hijo de Asalías y nieto de Mesulán, que fuera al templo del SEÑOR. Le dijo: ⁴«Preséntate ante el sumo sacerdote Jilquías y encárgale que recoja el dinero que el pueblo ha llevado al templo del SEÑOR y ha entregado a los porteros. ⁵Ordena que ahora se les entregue el dinero a los que supervisan la restauración del templo del SEÑOR, para pagarles a los trabajadores que lo están reparando. ⁶Que les paguen a los carpinteros, a los maestros de obra y a los albañiles, y que compren madera y piedras de cantería para restaurar el templo. ⁷Pero no les pidan cuentas a los que están encargados de pagar, pues ellos proceden con toda honradez.»

⁸El sumo sacerdote Jilquías le dijo al cronista Safán: «He encontrado el libro de la *ley en el templo del SEÑOR.» Entonces se lo entregó a Safán, y éste, después de leerlo, ⁹fue y le informó al rey:

—Los ministros de Su Majestad han recogido el dinero[m] que estaba en el templo del SEÑOR, y se lo han entregado a los trabajadores y a los supervisores.

¹⁰El cronista Safán también le informó al rey que el sumo sacerdote Jilquías le había entregado un libro, el cual leyó en su presencia.

¹¹Cuando el rey oyó las palabras del libro de la ley, se rasgó las vestiduras ¹²y dio esta orden a Jilquías el sacerdote, a Ajicán hijo de Safán, a Acbor hijo de Micaías, a Safán el cronista, y a Asaías, su ministro personal:

¹³—Vayan a consultar al SEÑOR por mí, por el pueblo y por todo Judá con respecto a lo que dice este libro que se ha encontrado. Sin duda que la gran ira del SEÑOR arde contra nosotros, porque nuestros antepasados no obedecieron lo que dice este libro ni actuaron según lo que está prescrito para nosotros.

¹⁴Así que Jilquías el sacerdote, Ajicán, Acbor, Safán y Asaías fueron a consultar a la profetisa Huldá, que vivía en el barrio nuevo de Jerusalén. Huldá era la esposa de Salún, el encargado del vestuario, quien era hijo de Ticvá y nieto de Jarjás.

¹⁵Huldá les contestó: «Así dice el SEÑOR, Dios de Israel: "Díganle al que los ha enviado ¹⁶que yo, el SEÑOR, les advierto: 'Voy a enviar desgracia sobre este lugar y sus habitantes, según todo lo que dice el libro que ha leído el rey de Judá. ¹⁷Ellos me han abandonado; han quemado incienso a otros dioses y me han provocado a ira con todos sus ídolos.[n] Por eso mi ira arde contra este lugar, y no se apagará.' ¹⁸Pero al rey de Judá, que los envió para consultarme, díganle que en lo que atañe a las palabras que él ha oído, yo, el SEÑOR, Dios de Israel, afirmo: ¹⁹'Como te has conmovido y humillado ante el SEÑOR al escuchar lo que he anunciado contra este lugar y sus habitantes, que serían asolados y malditos; y como te has rasgado las vestiduras y has llorado en mi pre-

sencia, yo te he escuchado. Yo, el SEÑOR, lo afirmo. ²⁰Por lo tanto, te reuniré con tus antepasados, y serás sepultado en *paz. Tus ojos no verán la desgracia que enviaré sobre este lugar.' "»

Así que ellos regresaron para informar al rey.

Renovación del pacto
23:1-3 — 2Cr 34:29-32
23:21-23 — 2Cr 35:1,18-19
23:28-30 — 2Cr 35:20—36:1

23 Entonces el rey mandó convocar a todos los *ancianos de Judá y Jerusalén. ²Acompañado de toda la *gente de Judá, de los habitantes de Jerusalén, de los sacerdotes, de los profetas y, en fin, de la nación entera, desde el más pequeño hasta el más grande, el rey subió al templo del SEÑOR. Y en presencia de ellos leyó todo lo que está escrito en el libro del *pacto que fue hallado en el templo del SEÑOR. ³Después se puso de pie junto a la columna, y en presencia del SEÑOR renovó el pacto. Se comprometió a seguir al SEÑOR y a cumplir, de todo *corazón y con toda el *alma, sus mandamientos, sus preceptos y sus decretos, reafirmando así las palabras del pacto que están escritas en ese libro. Y todo el pueblo confirmó el pacto.

⁴Luego el rey ordenó al sumo sacerdote Jilquías, a los sacerdotes de segundo rango y a los porteros, que sacaran del templo del SEÑOR todos los objetos consagrados a *Baal, a *Aserá y a todos los astros del cielo. Hizo que los quemaran en los campos de Cedrón, a las afueras de Jerusalén, y que llevaran las cenizas a Betel. ⁵También destituyó a los sacerdotes idólatras que los reyes de Judá habían nombrado para quemar[ñ] incienso en los *altares paganos, tanto en las ciudades de Judá como en Jerusalén, los cuales quemaban incienso a Baal, al sol y a la luna, al zodíaco y a todos los astros del cielo. ⁶El rey sacó del templo del SEÑOR la imagen para el culto a Aserá y la llevó al arroyo de Cedrón, en las afueras de Jerusalén; allí la quemó hasta convertirla en cenizas, las cuales echó en la fosa común. ⁷Además, derrumbó en el templo del SEÑOR los cuartos dedicados a la prostitución sagrada, donde las mujeres tejían mantos[o] para la diosa Aserá.

⁸Josías trasladó a Jerusalén a todos los sacerdotes de las ciudades de Judá, y desde Gueba hasta Berseba eliminó[p] los *santuarios paganos donde ellos habían quemado incienso. También derribó los altares paganos junto a la puerta de Josué el gobernador, que está ubicada a la izquierda de la entrada a la ciudad. ⁹Aunque los sacerdotes que habían servido en los altares paganos no podían ministrar en el altar del SEÑOR en Jerusalén, participaban de las comidas sagradas junto con los otros sacerdotes.[q]

¹⁰El rey eliminó el santuario llamado Tofet, que estaba en el valle de Ben Hinón, para que nadie sacrificara en el fuego a su hijo o hija en honor de Moloc. ¹¹Se llevó los caballos que los reyes de Judá habían consagrado al sol y que se habían puesto en la entrada al templo del SEÑOR, junto a la habitación de Natán Mélec, el *eunuco encargado del recinto. Josías también quemó los carros consagrados al sol.

¹²Además, el rey derribó los altares que los reyes de Judá habían erigido en la azotea de la sala de Acaz, y los que Manasés había erigido en los dos atrios del templo del SEÑOR. Los hizo pedazos y

m 22:9 recogido el dinero. Lit. fundido la plata. n 22:17 todos sus ídolos. Lit. toda la obra de sus manos. ñ 23:5 para quemar (mss. de LXX, Siríaca y Vulgata); y quemó (TM). o 23:7 mantos. Palabra de difícil traducción. p 23:8 eliminó. Lit. profanó; también en vv. 10 y 13. q 23:9 participaban ... sacerdotes. Lit. comían panes sin levadura con sus hermanos.

echó los escombros en el arroyo de Cedrón. ¹³Eliminó los altares paganos que había al este de Jerusalén, en el lado sur de la Colina de la Destrucción,ʳ los cuales Salomón, rey de Israel, había construido para *Astarté, la despreciable diosa de los sidonios, para Quemós, el detestable dios de los moabitas, y para Moloc,ˢ el abominable dios de los amonitas.

¹⁴Josías hizo pedazos las *piedras sagradas y las imágenes de la diosa Aserá, y llenó con huesos *humanos los lugares donde se habían erigido. ¹⁵Derribó también el altar de Betel y el santuario pagano construidos por Jeroboán hijo de Nabat, que hizo pecar a Israel. Además, quemó el santuario pagano hasta convertirlo en cenizas, y le prendió fuego a la imagen de Aserá.

¹⁶De regreso, al ver los sepulcros que había en la colina, Josías mandó que recogieran los huesos y los quemaran en el altar para profanarlo, cumpliendo así la palabra del SEÑOR que el hombre de Dios había comunicado cuando anunció estas cosas. ¹⁷Luego el rey preguntó:

—¿De quién es ese monumento que veo allá?

Y los habitantes de la ciudad le contestaron:

—Es el sepulcro del hombre de Dios que vino desde Judá, y que pronunció contra el altar de Betel lo que Su Majestad acaba de hacer.

¹⁸—Déjenlo, pues —replicó el rey—; que nadie mueva sus huesos.

Fue así como se conservaron sus huesos junto con los del profeta que había venido de Samaria.

¹⁹Tal como lo hizo en Betel, Josías eliminó todos los santuarios paganos que los reyes de Israel habían construido en las ciudades de Samaria, con los que provocaron la ira del SEÑOR. ²⁰Finalmente, mató sobre los altares a todos los sacerdotes de aquellos santuarios, y encima de ellos quemó huesos humanos. Entonces regresó a Jerusalén.

²¹Después el rey dio esta orden al pueblo:

—Celebren la Pascua del SEÑOR su Dios, según está escrito en este libro del pacto.

²²Desde la época de los *jueces que gobernaron a Israel hasta la de los reyes de Israel y de Judá, no se había celebrado una Pascua semejante. ²³Pero en el año dieciocho del reinado del rey Josías, esta Pascua se celebró en Jerusalén en honor del SEÑOR.

²⁴Además, Josías expulsó a los adivinos y a los hechiceros, y eliminó toda clase de ídolos y el resto de las cosas detestables que se veían en el país de Judá y en Jerusalén. Lo hizo así para cumplir las instrucciones de la *ley, escritas en el libro que el sacerdote Jilquías encontró en el templo del SEÑOR. ²⁵Ni antes ni después de Josías hubo otro rey que, como él, se volviera al SEÑOR de todo corazón, con toda el alma y con todas sus fuerzas, siguiendo en todo la ley de Moisés.

²⁶A pesar de eso, el SEÑOR no apagó el gran fuego de su ira, que ardía contra Judá por todas las afrentas con que Manasés lo había provocado. ²⁷Por lo tanto, el SEÑOR declaró: «Voy a apartar de mi presencia a Judá, como lo hice con Israel; repudiaré a Jerusalén, la ciudad que escogí, y a este templo, del cual dije: "Ése será el lugar donde yo habite."»

²⁸Los demás acontecimientos del reinado de Josías, y todo lo que hizo, están escritos en el libro de las crónicas de los reyes de Judá. ²⁹En aquel tiempo el faraón Necao, rey de Egipto, fue a encontrarse con el rey de Asiria camino del río Éufrates. El rey Josías le salió al paso, pero Necao le hizo frente en Meguido y

lo mató. ³⁰Los oficiales de Josías llevaron su cadáver en un carro desde Meguido hasta Jerusalén y lo sepultaron en su tumba. Entonces el pueblo tomó a Joacaz hijo de Josías, lo ungió y lo proclamó rey en lugar de su padre.

Joacaz, rey de Judá
23:31-34 — 2Cr 36:2-4

³¹Joacaz tenía veintitrés años cuando ascendió al trono, y reinó en Jerusalén tres meses. Su madre era Jamutal hija de Jeremías, oriunda de Libná. ³²Joacaz hizo lo que ofende al SEÑOR, tal como lo habían hecho sus antepasados. ³³Para impedir que Joacaz reinara en Jerusalén, el faraón Necao lo encarceló en Riblá, en el territorio de Jamat, y además impuso sobre Judá un tributo de tres mil trescientos kilos de plata y treinta y tres kilosᵗ de oro. ³⁴Luego hizo rey a Eliaquín hijo de Josías en lugar de su padre, y le dio el nombre de Joacim. En cuanto a Joacaz, lo llevó a Egipto, donde murió.

³⁵Joacim le pagó al faraón Necao la plata y el oro que exigió, pero tuvo que establecer un impuesto sobre el país: reclamó de cada persona, según su tasación, la plata y el oro que se le debía entregar al faraón Necao.

Joacim, rey de Judá
23:36—24:6 — 2Cr 36:5-8

³⁶Joacim tenía veinticinco años cuando ascendió al trono, y reinó en Jerusalén once años. Su madre era Zebudá hija de Pedaías, oriunda de Rumá. ³⁷También este rey hizo lo que ofende al SEÑOR, tal como lo hicieron sus antepasados.

24 Durante el reinado de Joacim, lo atacó Nabucodonosor, rey de Babilonia, y lo sometió durante tres años, al cabo de los cuales Joacim decidió rebelarse. ²Entonces el SEÑOR envió contra Joacim bandas de guerrilleros *babilonios, *sirios, moabitas y amonitas. Las envió contra Judá para destruir el país, según la palabra que el SEÑOR había dado a conocer por medio de sus siervos los profetas. ³De hecho, esto le sucedió a Judá por orden del SEÑOR, para apartar al pueblo de su presencia por los pecados de Manasés y por todo lo que hizo, ⁴incluso por haber derramado sangre inocente, con la cual inundó a Jerusalén. Por lo tanto, el SEÑOR no quiso perdonar.

⁵Los demás acontecimientos del reinado de Joacim, y todo lo que hizo, están escritos en el libro de las crónicas de los reyes de Judá. ⁶Joacim murió, y su hijo Joaquín lo sucedió en el trono.

⁷El rey de Egipto no volvió a hacer campañas militares fuera de su país, pues el rey de Babilonia se había adueñado de todas sus posesiones, desde el río de Egipto hasta el río Éufrates.

Joaquín, rey de Judá
24:8-17 — 2Cr 36:9-10

⁸Joaquín tenía dieciocho años cuando ascendió al trono, y reinó en Jerusalén tres meses. Su madre era Nejustá hija de Elnatán, oriunda de Jerusalén. ⁹Joaquín hizo lo que ofende al SEÑOR, tal como lo había hecho su padre.

¹⁰En aquel tiempo, las tropas de Nabucodonosor, rey de Babilonia, marcharon contra Jerusalén y la sitiaron. ¹¹Cuando ya la tenían cercada, Nabucodonosor llegó a la ciudad. ¹²Joaquín, rey de Judá, se rindió, junto con su madre y sus funcionarios, gene-

---

rales y oficiales. Así, en el año octavo de su reinado, el rey de Babilonia capturó a Joaquín.

13Tal como le había anunciado, Nabucodonosor se llevó los tesoros del templo del SEÑOR y del palacio real, partiendo en pedazos todos los utensilios de oro que Salomón, rey de Israel, había hecho para el templo. 14Además, deportó a todo Jerusalén: a los generales y a los mejores soldados, a los artesanos y a los herreros, un total de diez mil personas. No quedó en el país más que la gente pobre.

15Nabucodonosor deportó a Joaquín a Babilonia, y también se llevó de Jerusalén a la reina madre, a las mujeres del rey, a sus oficiales y a la flor y nata del país. 16Deportó además a todos los guerreros, que eran siete mil, y a mil artesanos y herreros, todos aptos para la guerra. El rey de Babilonia se los llevó cautivos a Babilonia. 17Luego puso como rey a Matanías, tío de Joaquín, y le dio el nombre de Sedequías.

Sedequías, rey de Judá
24:18-20 — 2Cr 36:11-16; Jer 52:1-3

18Sedequías tenía veintiún años cuando ascendió al trono, y reinó en Jerusalén once años. Su madre se llamaba Jamutal hija de Jeremías, oriunda de Libná. 19Al igual que Joacim, Sedequías hizo lo que ofende al SEÑOR, 20a tal grado que el SEÑOR, en su ira, los echó de su presencia. Todo esto sucedió en Jerusalén y en Judá.

La caída de Jerusalén
25:1-12 — Jer 39:1-10
25:1-21 — 2Cr 36:17-20; Jer 52:4-27
25:22-26 — Jer 40:7-9; 41:1-3,16-18

25 Sedequías se rebeló contra el rey de Babilonia. 1En el año noveno del reinado de Sedequías, a los diez días del mes décimo, Nabucodonosor, rey de Babilonia, marchó con todo su ejército y atacó a Jerusalén. Acampó frente a la ciudad y construyó una rampa de asalto a su alrededor. 2La ciudad estuvo sitiada hasta el año undécimo del reinado de Sedequías.

3A los nueve días del mes cuarto,u cuando el hambre se agravó en la ciudad, y no había más alimento para el pueblo, 4se abrió una brecha en el muro de la ciudad, de modo que, aunque los *babilonios la tenían cercada, todo el ejército se escapó de noche por la puerta que estaba entre los dos muros, junto al jardín real. Huyeron camino al Arabá,v 5pero el ejército babilonio persiguió a Sedequías hasta alcanzarlo en la llanura de Jericó. Sus soldados se dispersaron, abandonándolo, 6y los babilonios lo capturaron. Entonces lo llevaron ante el rey de Babilonia, que estaba en Riblá. Allí Sedequías recibió su sentencia. 7Ante sus propios ojos degollaron a sus hijos, y después le sacaron los ojos, lo ataron con cadenas de bronce y lo llevaron a Babilonia.

8A los siete días del mes quinto del año diecinueve del reinado de Nabucodonosor, rey de Babilonia, su ministro Nabuzaradán, que era el comandante de la guardia, fue a Jerusalén 9y le prendió fuego al templo del SEÑOR, al palacio real y a todas las casas de Jerusalén, incluso a todos los edificios importantes. 10Entonces el ejército babilonio bajo su mando derribó las murallas que rodeaban la ciudad. 11Nabuzaradán además deportó a la gente que quedaba en la ciudad, es decir, al resto de la muchedumbre y a los que se habían aliado con el rey de Babilonia. 12Sin embargo, dejó a algunos de los más pobres para que se encargaran de los viñedos y de los campos.

13Los babilonios quebraron las columnas de bronce, las bases y la fuentew de bronce que estaban en el templo del SEÑOR, y se llevaron todo el bronce a Babilonia. 14También se llevaron las ollas, las tenazas, las despabiladeras, la vajilla y todos los utensilios de bronce que se usaban para el culto. 15Además, el comandante de la guardia se apoderó de los incensarios y de los aspersorios, todo lo cual era de oro y de plata.

16El bronce de las dos columnas, de la fuente y de las bases, que Salomón había hecho para el templo del SEÑOR, era tanto que no se podía pesar. 17Cada columna medía ocho metros de altura. El capitel de bronce que estaba encima de cada columna medía metro y mediox de altura y estaba decorado alrededor con una red y con granadas de bronce. Las dos columnas tenían el mismo adorno.

18El comandante de la guardia tomó presos a Seraías, sacerdote principal, a Sofonías, sacerdote de segundo rango, y a los tres porteros. 19De los que quedaban en la ciudad, apresó al oficial encargado de las tropas, a cinco de los servidores personales del rey, al cronista principal del ejército, encargado de reclutar soldados de entre el pueblo, y a sesenta ciudadanos que todavía estaban en la ciudad. 20Después de apresarlos, Nabuzaradán, comandante de la guardia, se los llevó al rey de Babilonia, que estaba en Riblá. 21Allí, en el territorio de Jamat, el rey los hizo ejecutar.

Así Judá fue desterrado y llevado cautivo.

22Nabucodonosor, rey de Babilonia, nombró a Guedalías, hijo de Ajicán y nieto de Safán, para que gobernara a la gente que había dejado en Judá. 23Cuando los oficiales del ejército de Judá y sus tropas se enteraron de que el rey de Babilonia había nombrado gobernador a Guedalías, fueron a ver a éste en Mizpa. Los oficiales eran Ismael hijo de Netanías, Johanán hijo de Carea, Seraías hijo de Tanjumet, oriundo de Netofa, y Jazanías, hijo de un hombre de Macá. 24Guedalías les hizo este juramento a ellos y a sus tropas: «No teman a los oficiales babilonios. Si ustedes se quedan en el país y sirven al rey de Babilonia, les aseguro que les irá bien.»

25Pero a los siete meses Ismael, hijo de Netanías y nieto de Elisama, que era de la estirpe real, y diez hombres que lo acompañaban, fueron y asesinaron a Guedalías; también mataron a los hombres de Judá y a los babilonios que formaban parte de su séquito en Mizpa. 26Acto seguido, todos huyeron a Egipto, grandes y pequeños, junto con los oficiales, pues temían a los babilonios.

Liberación del rey Joaquín
25:27-30 — Jer 52:31-34

27En el día veintisiete del mes duodécimo del año treinta y siete del exilio de Joaquín, rey de Judá, Evil Merodac, rey de Babilonia, en el año primero de su reinado, sacó a Joaquín de la cárcel. 28Lo trató amablemente y le dio una posición más alta que la de los otros reyes que estaban con él en Babilonia. 29Joaquín dejó su ropa de prisionero, y por el resto de su vida comió a la mesa del rey. 30Además, durante toda su vida Joaquín gozó de una pensión diaria que le proveía el rey de Babilonia.

---

u 25:3 cuarto. El texto hebreo no incluye esta palabra, pero véase Jer 52:6. v 25:4 Arabá. Alt. valle del Jordán. w 25:13 la fuente. Lit. el mar; también en v. 16. x 25:17 ocho metros ... metro y medio. Lit. dieciocho *codos ... tres codos.

1 CRÓNICAS

Descendientes de Adán

1 Adán, Set, Enós, 2Cainán, Malalel, Jared, 3Enoc, Matusalén, Lamec, 4Noé.

Descendientes de Noé
1:5-23 — Gn 10:2-31; 11:10-27

Hijos de Noé:a Sem, Cam y Jafet.

5 Hijos de Jafet: Gómer, Magog, Maday, Javán, Tubal, Mésec y Tirás.

6 Hijos de Gómer: Asquenaz, Rifat y Togarma.

7 Hijos de Javán: Elisá, Tarsis, Chipre y Rodanín.

8 Hijos de Cam: Cus, Misrayin, Fut y Canaán.

9 Hijos de Cus: Seba, Javilá, Sabtá, Ragama y Sabteca.

Hijos de Ragama: Sabá y Dedán.

10 Cus fue el padre de Nimrod, quien llegó a ser un notable guerrero en la tierra.

11 Misrayin fue el antepasado de los ludeos, los anameos, los leabitas, los naftuitas, 12los patruseos, los caslujitas y los caftoritas, de quienes descienden los filisteos.

13 Canaán fue el padre de Sidón, su primogénito, y de Het, 14y el antepasado de los jebuseos, los amorreos, los gergeseos, 15los heveos, los araceos, los sineos, 16los arvadeos, los zemareos y los jamatitas.

17 Hijos de Sem: Elam, Asur, Arfaxad, Lud y Aram.

Hijos de Aram:b Uz, Hul, Guéter y Mésec. 18Arfaxad fue el padre de Selá, y éste lo fue de Éber. 19Éber tuvo dos hijos; el primero se llamó Péleg, porque en su tiempo se dividió la tierra. El hermano de Péleg se llamó Joctán. 20Joctán fue el padre de Almodad, Sélef, Jazar Mávet, Yeraj, 21Hadorán, Uzal, Diclá, 22Obal,c Abimael, Sabá, 23Ofir, Javilá y Jobab. Todos éstos fueron hijos de Joctán.

Descendientes de Sem

24 Sem, Arfaxad, Selá, 25Éber, Péleg, Reú, 26Serug, Najor, Téraj 27y Abram, que es también Abraham.

Descendientes de Abraham
1:29-31 — Gn 25:12-16
1:32-33 — Gn 25:1-4

28 Hijos de Abraham: Isaac e Ismael.

29 Sus descendientes fueron Nebayot, primogénito de Ismael, Cedar, Adbel, Mibsán, 30Mismá, Dumá, Masá, Hadad, Temá, 31Jetur, Nafis y Cedema. Éstos fueron los hijos de Ismael.

32 Los hijos de Cetura, la concubina de Abraham, fueron Zimrán, Jocsán, Medán, Madián, Isbac y Súah.

Hijos de Jocsán: Sabá y Dedán.

33 Hijos de Madián: Efá, Éfer, Janoc, Abidá y Eldá. Todos éstos fueron hijos de Cetura.

34 Abraham también fue el padre de Isaac. Los hijos de Isaac fueron Esaú e Israel.

Descendientes de Esaú
1:35-42 — Gn 36:10-14,20-28

35 Hijos de Esaú: Elifaz, Reuel, Jeús, Jalán y Coré.

36 Hijos de Elifaz: Temán, Omar, Zefo, Gatán y Quenaz, Timná y Amalec.

37 Hijos de Reuel: Najat, Zera, Sama y Mizá.

38 Hijos de Seír:d Lotán, Sobal, Zibeón, Aná, Disón, Ezer y Disán.

39 Hijos de Lotán: Horí y Homán. Timná fue hermana de Lotán.

40 Hijos de Sobal: Alván, Manajat, Ebal, Sefó y Onam.

Hijos de Zibeón: Ayá y Aná.

41 El hijo de Aná fue Disón.

Hijos de Disón: Amirán, Esbán, Itrán y Querán.

42 Hijos de Ezer: Bilán, Zaván y Yacán.

Hijos de Disán: Uz y Arán.

Reyes de Edom
1:43-54 — Gn 36:31-43

43 Los reyes que a continuación se mencionan reinaron en la tierra de Edom antes de que los israelitas tuvieran rey:

Bela hijo de Beor; su ciudad se llamaba Dinaba.

44 Cuando Bela murió, lo sucedió en el trono Jobab hijo de Zera, que era de Bosra.

45 Cuando Jobab murió, lo sucedió en el trono Jusán, que era de la tierra de Temán.

46 Cuando Jusán murió, lo sucedió en el trono Hadad hijo de Bedad, quien derrotó a Madián en el campo de Moab. Su ciudad se llamaba Avit.

47 Cuando Hadad murió, lo sucedió en el trono Samla, que era de Masreca.

48 Cuando Samla murió, lo sucedió en el trono Saúl, que era de Rejobot a orillas del río Éufrates.

49 Cuando Saúl murió, lo sucedió en el trono Baal Janán hijo de Acbor.

50 Cuando Baal Janán murió, lo sucedió en el trono Hadad. Su ciudad se llamaba Pau,e y su esposa fue Mehitabel, hija de Matred y nieta de Mezab.

51 Después de que murió Hadad, gobernaron en Edom los siguientes caudillos: Timná, Alvá, Jetet, 52Aholibama, Elá, Pinón, 53Quenaz, Temán, Mibzar, 54Magdiel e Iram. Éstos fueron los caudillos de Edom.

Hijos de Israel
2:1-2 — Gn 35:23-26

2 Los hijos de Israel fueron Rubén, Simeón, Leví, Judá, Isacar, Zabulón, 2Dan, José, Benjamín, Neftalí, Gad y Aser.

Descendientes de Judá
2:5-15 — Rt 4:18-22; Mt 1:3-6

3 Hijos de Judá: Er, Onán y Selá. Estos tres le nacieron de una cananea que era hija de Súaj. Er, primogénito de Judá, hizo lo que ofende al SEÑOR, y el SEÑOR le quitó la vida. 4Y Tamar, nuera de Judá, le dio a éste dos hijos: Fares y Zera. En total, Judá tuvo cinco hijos.

5 Hijos de Fares: Jezrón y Jamul.

---

a 1:4 *Hijos de Noé* (LXX); TM no incluye esta frase.   b 1:17 *Hijos de Aram* (un ms. hebreo y mss. de LXX; véase Gn 10:23); TM no incluye esta frase.   c 1:22 *Obal* (mss. hebreos y Siríaca; véase Gn 10:28); *Ebal* (TM).   d 1:38 *Seír*. Es decir, Esaú.   e 1:50 *Pau* (mss. hebreos, mss. de LXX, Siríaca, Targum, Vulgata); véase Gn 36:39); *Pay* (TM).

⁶ Los hijos de Zera fueron cinco en total: Zimri, Etán, Hemán, Calcol y Dardá.ᶠ

⁷ El hijo de Carmí fue Acar,ᵍ quien provocó la desgracia sobre Israel por haber violado el mandato de Dios de *destruirlo todo.

⁸ El hijo de Etán fue Azarías.

⁹ Hijos de Jezrón: Jeramel, Ram y Quelubay.ʰ

¹⁰ Ram fue el padre de Aminadab, y éste lo fue de Naasón, príncipe de los judíos.

¹¹ Naasón fue el padre de Salmón,ⁱ y éste lo fue de Booz.

¹² Booz fue el padre de Obed, y éste lo fue de Isaí. ¹³El primer hijo de Isaí fue Eliab; el segundo, Abinadab; el tercero, Simá; ¹⁴el cuarto, Natanael; el quinto, Raday; ¹⁵el sexto, Ozén; y el séptimo, David. ¹⁶Las hermanas de ellos fueron Sarvia y Abigaíl. Los hijos de Sarvia fueron tres: Abisay, Joab y Asael. ¹⁷Abigaíl fue la madre de Amasá hijo de Jéter, el ismaelita.

¹⁸ Caleb hijo de Jezrón tuvo hijos con su esposa Azuba y con Jeriot. Éstos fueron sus hijos: Jéser, Sobab y Ardón. ¹⁹Cuando Azuba murió, Caleb tomó por esposa a Efrata, con la que tuvo a su hijo Jur.

²⁰ Jur fue el padre de Uri, y éste lo fue de Bezalel.

²¹ Cuando Jezrón tenía sesenta años, tomó por esposa a una hija de Maquir, padre de Galaad, y tuvo con ella a su hijo Segub. ²²Segub fue el padre de Yaír, y fue dueño de veintitrés ciudades en la tierra de Galaad. ²³Pero Guesur y Aram le quitaron los campamentos de Yaír y Quenat, y sus aldeas. En total, le quitaron sesenta pueblos. Todos éstos fueron los descendientes de Maquir, padre de Galaad.

²⁴ Después de que Jezrón murió en Caleb Efrata, Abías, la esposa de Jezrón, dio a luz a Asur, padreɩ de Tecoa.

²⁵ Los hijos de Jeramel, primogénito de Jezrón, fueron Ram, el mayor, Buná, Orén, Ozén y Ahías. ²⁶Jeramel tuvo otra esposa, la cual se llamaba Atará. Ésta fue la madre de Onam.

²⁷ Los hijos de Ram, primogénito de Jeramel, fueron Maaz, Jamín y Équer.

²⁸ Hijos de Onam: Samay y Yada.

Hijos de Samay: Nadab y Abisur. ²⁹La esposa de Abisur se llamaba Abijaíl, con la que tuvo a Ajbán y Molid.

³⁰ Hijos de Nadab: Séled y Apayin. Séled murió sin tener hijos.

³¹ El hijo de Apayin fue Isí, el hijo de Isí fue Sesán y el hijo de Sesán fue Ajlay.

³² Los hijos de Yada, hermano de Samay, fueron Jéter y Jonatán. Jéter murió sin tener hijos.

³³ Hijos de Jonatán: Pélet y Zazá.

Éstos fueron los descendientes de Jeramel.

³⁴ Sesán no tuvo hijos sino hijas, y tenía un esclavo egipcio llamado Yarjá. ³⁵A éste le dio por esposa una de sus hijas, la cual fue la madre de Atay.

³⁶ Atay fue el padre de Natán, Natán fue el padre de Zabad,

³⁷ Zabad fue el padre de Eflal, Eflal fue el padre de Obed,

³⁸ Obed fue el padre de Jehú, Jehú fue el padre de Azarías,

³⁹ Azarías fue el padre de Heles,

Heles fue el padre de Elasá,

⁴⁰ Elasá fue el padre de Sismay, Sismay fue el padre de Salún,

⁴¹ Salún fue el padre de Jecamías, y Jecamías fue el padre de Elisama.

Descendientes de Caleb

⁴² Los hijos de Caleb, hermano de Jeramel, fueron: Mesá, el primogénito, que fue el padre de Zif; y Maresá, que fue el padre de Hebrón.

⁴³ Hijos de Hebrón: Coré, Tapúaj, Requen y Semá.

⁴⁴ Semá fue el padre de Raham, que fue el padre de Jorcoán.

Requen fue el padre de Samay.

⁴⁵ Samay fue el padre de Maón. Maón fue el padre de Betsur.

⁴⁶ Efá, concubina de Caleb, fue la madre de Jarán, Mosá y Gazez. Jarán fue el padre de Gazez.

⁴⁷ Hijos de Yaday: Reguen, Jotán, Guesán, Pélet, Efá y Sagaf.

⁴⁸ Macá, concubina de Caleb, fue la madre de Séber y de Tirjaná, ⁴⁹y también de Sagaf, que fue el padre de Madmana; y de Seva, que fue el padre de Macbena y de Guibeá. Además, Caleb tuvo una hija llamada Acsa.

⁵⁰ Éstos fueron los descendientes de Caleb.

Los hijos de Jur, primogénito de Efrata, fueron: Sobal, padre de Quiriat Yearín, ⁵¹Salmá, padre de Belén, y Jaref, padre de Bet Gader.

⁵² Los hijos de Sobal, padre de Quiriat Yearín, fueron: Haroé, la mitad de los manajatitas, ⁵³las familias de Quiriat Yearín, los itritas, los futitas, los sumatitas y los misraítas, de quienes proceden los zoratitas y los estaolitas.

⁵⁴ Hijos de Salmá: Belén, los netofatitas, Aterot Bet Joab, la mitad de los manajatitas, los zoreítas, ⁵⁵y las familias de los escribas que vivían en Jabés, es decir, los tirateos, los simateos y los sucateos. Éstos fueron los quenitas, descendientes de Jamat, padre de la familia de Recab.

Hijos de David

3:1-4 — 2S 3:2-5

3:5-8 — 2S 5:14-16; 1Cr 14:4-7

3 Éstos fueron los hijos de David nacidos en Hebrón:

Su *primogénito fue Amón hijo de Ajinoán la jezrelita;

el segundo, Daniel hijo de Abigaíl de Carmel;

² el tercero, Absalón hijo de Macá, la hija del rey Talmay de Guesur;

el cuarto, Adonías hijo de Jaguit;

³ el quinto, Sefatías hijo de Abital;

y el sexto, Itreán hijo de Eglá, que era otra esposa de David.

⁴ Estos seis le nacieron en Hebrón, donde reinó siete años y seis meses. En Jerusalén reinó treinta y tres años. ⁵Allí le nacieron Simá, Sobab, Natán y Salomón, hijos de Betsabé,ᵏ la hija de Amiel. ⁶Tuvo también a Ibjar, Elisama, Elifelet, ⁷Noga, Néfeg, Jafía, ⁸Elisama, Eliadá y Elifelet; nueve en total. ⁹Todos éstos fueron hijos de David, sin contar los hijos que tuvo con sus concubinas. La hermana de ellos fue Tamar.

ᶠ **2:6** *Dardá* (mss. hebreos, mss. de LXX, Siríaca y Targum; véase 1R 4:31); *Dara* (TM). ᵍ **2:7** En hebreo, *Acar* significa *desgracia*. En el libro de Josué este nombre aparece como *Acán*. ʰ **2:9** *Quelubay*. Variante de *Caleb*. ⁱ **2:11** *Salmón* (LXX; véase Rt 4:20); *Salmá* (TM). ɩ **2:24** *padre*. Alt. *fundador*. ᵏ **3:5** *Betsabé* (un ms. hebreo, LXX y Vulgata; véase 2S 11:3); *Bet Súa* (TM).

Descendientes de Salomón

10 Éstos fueron los descendientes de Salomón en línea directa: Roboán, Abías, Asá, Josafat, 11Jorán, Ocozías, Joás, 12Amasías, Azarías, Jotán, 13Acaz, Ezequías, Manasés, 14Amón y Josías.

15 Los hijos de Josías fueron:

Johanán, el primero;
Joacim, el segundo;
Sedequías, el tercero,
y Salún, el cuarto.

16 Los hijos de Joacim fueron Jeconías y Sedequías.

17 Los hijos de Jeconías, el desterrado, fueron Salatiel, 18Malquirán, Pedaías, Senazar, Jecamías, Hosamá y Nedabías.

19 Los hijos de Pedaías fueron Zorobabel y Simí.

Los hijos de Zorobabel fueron Mesulán y Jananías; Selomit fue hermana de ellos. 20Tuvo también estos cinco: Jasubá, Ohel, Berequías, Jasadías y Yusab Jésed.

21 Los descendientes de Jananías fueron Pelatías e Isaías, y también los hijos de Refaías, los de Arnán, los de Abdías y los de Secanías.

22 Los descendientes de Secanías fueron Semaías y sus hijos Jatús, Igal, Barías, Nearías y Safat; seis en total.

23 Los hijos de Nearías fueron Elihoenay, Ezequías y Azricán; tres en total.

24 Los hijos de Elihoenay fueron Hodavías, Eliasib, Pelaías, Acub, Johanán, Delaías y Ananí; siete en total.

Descendientes de Judá

4 Los descendientes de Judá en línea directa fueron Fares, Jezrón, Carmí, Jur y Sobal. 2Reaías hijo de Sobal fue el padre de Yajat, y Yajat fue el padre de Ajumay y de Lajad. Éstas fueron las familias de los zoratitas.

3 Los hijosl de Etam fueron Jezrel, Ismá e Idbás. La hermana de ellos fue Jazelelponi. 4También fueron sus hijos Penuel, padre de Guedor, y Ezer, padre de Jusá. Éstos fueron los descendientes de Jur, primogénito de Efrata, padrem de Belén.

5 Asur, padre de Tecoa, tuvo dos esposas, Helá y Nara. 6Nara fue la madre de Ajusán, Héfer, Temení y Ajastarí. Éstos fueron los hijos de Nara.

7 Los hijos de Helá fueron Zéret, Yezojar y Etnán.

8 Cos fue el padre de Anub, de Zobebá y de las familias de Ajarjel hijo de Harún.

9Jabés fue más importante que sus hermanos. Cuando su madre le puso ese *nombre, dijo: «Con aflicción lo he dado a luz».n 10Jabés le rogó al Dios de Israel: «Bendíceme y ensancha mi territorio; ayúdame y líbrame del mal, para que no padezca aflicción.» Y Dios le concedió su petición.

11Quelub, hermano de Sujá, fue el padre de Mejir, y Mejir fue el padre de Estón; 12Estón fue el padre de Bet Rafá, de Paseaj y de Tejiná, padre de Ir Najás.ñ Éstos fueron los habitantes de Reca.

13 Los hijos de Quenaz fueron Otoniel y Seraías.

Los hijos de Otoniel fueron Jatat 14y Meonotay, padre de Ofra.

Seraías fue el padre de Joab, padre de Ge Carisín,o porque sus habitantes eran herreros.

15 Los hijos de Caleb hijo de Jefone fueron Ir, Elá y Noán. Elá fue el padre de Quenaz.

16 Los hijos de Yalelel fueron Zif, Zifá, Tirías y Asarel.

17 Los hijos de Esdras fueron Jéter, Méred, Éfer y Jalón. Una de las esposas de Méred —con la cual tuvo a Miriam, Samay e Isba, padre de Estemoa— 18era Bitiá, hija del faraón. La otra esposa de Méred era de la tribu de Judá, y con ella tuvo a Jéred, padre de Guedor, a Héber, padre de Soco, y a Jecutiel, padre de Zanoa.

19Queilá, el garmita, y Estemoa, el macateo, fueron hijos de la esposa de Hodías, es decir, de la hermana de Naján.

20 Los hijos de Simón fueron Amnón, Riná, Ben Janán y Tilón.

Los hijos de Isí fueron Zojet y Ben Zojet.

21 Los descendientes de Selá hijo de Judá fueron Er, padre de Lecá; Ladá, padre de Maresá y de las familias que trabajan el lino en Bet Asbea; 22también descendientes de Selá fueron Joaquín, y los habitantes de Cozebá, Joás y Saraf, quienes (según crónicas muy antiguas) antes de volver a Belénp se casaron con mujeres moabitas.q 23Éstos eran alfareros que habitaban en Netaín y Guederá, donde se quedaron al servicio del rey.

Descendientes de Simeón
4:28-33 — Jos 19:2-10

24 Los descendientes de Simeón fueron Nemuel, Jamín, Jarib, Zera y Saúl. 25El hijo de Saúl fue Salún, el de Salún, Mibsán, y el de Mibsán, Mismá.

26 Los descendientes de Mismá en línea directa fueron Jamuel, Zacur y Simí. 27Simí tuvo dieciséis hijos y seis hijas; pero sus hermanos tuvieron pocos hijos, por lo cual sus familias no fueron tan numerosas como las de los descendientes de Judá. 28Se establecieron en Berseba, Moladá, Jazar Súal, 29Bilhá, Esen, Tolad, 30Betuel, Jormá, Siclag, 31Bet Marcabot, Jazar Susín, Bet Biray y Sajarayin. Éstas fueron sus ciudades hasta el reinado de David. 32Sus aldeas fueron Etam, Ayin, Rimón, Toquén y Asán —cinco en total—, 33más todas las aldeas que estaban alrededor de aquellas ciudades hasta la región de Baal. Éstos fueron los lugares que habitaron, según sus registros genealógicos.

34 Mesobab, Jamlec, Josías hijo de Amasías, 35Joel, Jehú hijo de Josibías, hijo de Seraías, hijo de Asiel; 36Elihoenay, Jacoba, Yesojaías, Asaías, Adiel, Jesimiel, Benaías, 37Ziza hijo de Sifí, hijo de Alón, hijo de Jedaías, hijo de Simri, hijo de Semaías: 38todos éstos eran jefes de sus clanes. Como sus familias patriarcales llegaron a ser muy numerosas, 39fueron hasta la *entrada de Guedor, al este del valle, en busca de pastos para sus ganados. 40Allí encontraron pastos buenos y abundantes, y una tierra extensa, tranquila y pacífica. En ese lugar habían vivido los descendientes de

---

l 4:3 *Los hijos* (mss. de LXX); *El padre* (TM). m 4:4 *padre*. Alt. *fundador* (también en vv. 5,12,14,17,18,21). n 4:9 En hebreo, *Jabés* suena como la palabra que significa *dolor* o *aflicción*. ñ 4:12 *Ir Najás.* Alt. *la ciudad de Najás.* o 4:14 *de Ge Carisín.* Alt. *del valle de Carisín.* (La palabra *carisín* significa *herreros.*) p 4:22 *antes de volver a Belén* (véanse LXX y Vulgata); en TM, texto de difícil traducción. q 4:22 *se casaron con mujeres moabitas.* Alt. *dominaron en Moab.*

Cam. [41]Los jefes mencionados anteriormente llegaron en los días de Ezequías, rey de Judá. Atacaron los campamentos de los descendientes de Cam y las viviendas[r] que encontraron, y los *destruyeron por completo. Y como en esa región había pastos para sus ganados, se quedaron allí en lugar de ellos, donde habitan hasta el día de hoy. [42]Quinientos de sus soldados, que eran descendientes de Simeón y estaban bajo las órdenes de Pelatías, Nearías, Refaías y Uziel, hijos de Isí, fueron a la montaña de Seír. [43]Después de destruir a los fugitivos del pueblo de Amalec que habían quedado, se establecieron allí, donde habitan hasta el día de hoy.

Descendientes de Rubén

5 Descendencia de Rubén, primogénito de Israel. Rubén era el primogénito, pero en la genealogía no fue reconocido como tal por haber profanado el lecho de su padre. Su derecho de primogenitura pasó a los hijos de José hijo de Israel. [2]Y aunque es verdad que Judá fue más poderoso que sus hermanos, y hasta llegó a ser jefe de ellos, la primogenitura pasó a José. [3]Los hijos de Rubén, primogénito de Israel, fueron Janoc, Falú, Jezrón y Carmí.

[4] Los descendientes de Joel en línea directa fueron Semaías, Gog, Simí, [5]Micaías, Reaías, Baal [6]y Beerá, jefe de los rubenitas. A este último se lo llevó cautivo Tiglat Piléser, rey de Asiria.

[7] Éstos fueron los parientes de Beerá, según los registros genealógicos de sus familias: Jeyel el jefe, Zacarías [8]y Bela hijo de Azaz, hijo de Semá, hijo de Joel. Bela habitó en Aroer, y su territorio se extendía hasta Nebo y Baal Megón. [9]Por el oriente se extendía hasta el borde del desierto que colinda con el río Éufrates, pues sus ganados aumentaron mucho en la tierra de Galaad. [10]En el tiempo de Saúl le declararon la guerra a los agarenos y los derrotaron, y se establecieron en la región oriental de Galaad.

Descendientes de Gad

[11] Éstos fueron los hijos de Gad que habitaron frente a los rubenitas en la región de Basán, hasta llegar a Salcá: [12]Joel fue el jefe en Basán; el segundo, Safán; y luego Janay y Safat. [13]Sus parientes, según las familias patriarcales, fueron siete en total: Micael, Mesulán, Sabá, Joray, Jacán, Zía y Éber. [14]Éstos fueron los hijos de Abijaíl hijo de Jurí, hijo de Jaroa, hijo de Galaad, hijo de Micael, hijo de Jesisay, hijo de Yadó, hijo de Buz. [15]El jefe de sus familias era Ahí, hijo de Abdiel y nieto de Guní. [16]Éstos habitaron en Galaad, en Basán y sus aldeas, y en todos los campos de pastoreo de Sarón, hasta sus confines. [17]La genealogía de ellos se registró en el tiempo de Jotán, rey de Judá, y de Jeroboán, rey de Israel.

[18]Los rubenitas, los gaditas y los de la media tribu de Manasés contaban con un ejército de cuarenta y cuatro mil setecientos sesenta hombres valientes, armados de escudo y de espada, hábiles en el manejo del arco y diestros en la guerra. [19]Combatieron a los agarenos y a Jetur, Nafis y Nodab. [20]Por cuanto confiaban en Dios, clamaron a él en medio del combate, y Dios los ayudó a derrotar a los agarenos y a sus aliados. [21]Se apoderaron de su ganado (cincuenta mil camellos, doscientas cincuenta mil ovejas y dos mil burros) y capturaron a cien mil personas, [22]a muchas de las cuales mataron, porque Dios estaba con ellos. En ese lugar habitaron hasta el tiempo del exilio.

La media tribu de Manasés

[23]Los hijos de la media tribu de Manasés eran numerosos y se establecieron en el país, desde Basán hasta Baal Hermón, Senir y el monte Hermón. [24]Los jefes de sus familias patriarcales fueron Éfer, Isí, Eliel, Azriel, Jeremías, Hodavías y Yadiel. Todos ellos eran guerreros valientes, hombres importantes y jefes de sus respectivas familias patriarcales. [25]Pero pecaron contra el Dios de sus antepasados, pues se prostituyeron al adorar a los dioses de los pueblos de la región, a los cuales Dios había destruido delante de ellos. [26]Por eso el Dios de Israel incitó contra ellos a Pul, es decir, a Tiglat Piléser, rey de Asiria, quien deportó a los rubenitas, los gaditas y a la media tribu de Manasés, llevándolos a Jalaj, Jabor, Hará, y al río Gozán, donde permanecen hasta hoy.

Descendientes de Leví

6 Éstos fueron los hijos de Leví: Guersón, Coat y Merari.

[2] Hijos de Coat: Amirán, Izar, Hebrón y Uziel.

[3] Hijos de Amirán: Aarón, Moisés y Miriam.
Hijos de Aarón: Nadab, Abiú, Eleazar e Itamar.

[4] Eleazar fue el padre de Finés.
Finés fue el padre de Abisúa.

[5] Abisúa fue el padre de Buquí,
Buquí fue el padre de Uzi,

[6] Uzi fue el padre de Zeraías,
Zeraías fue el padre de Merayot,

[7] Merayot fue el padre de Amarías,
Amarías fue el padre de Ajitob,

[8] Ajitob fue el padre de Sadoc,
Sadoc fue el padre de Ajimaz,

[9] Ajimaz fue el padre de Azarías,
Azarías fue el padre de Johanán,

[10] Johanán fue el padre de Azarías, quien ejerció el sacerdocio en el templo que Salomón construyó en Jerusalén.

[11] Azarías fue el padre de Amarías,
Amarías fue el padre de Ajitob,

[12] Ajitob fue el padre de Sadoc,
Sadoc fue el padre de Salún,

[13] Salún fue el padre de Jilquías,
Jilquías fue el padre de Azarías,

[14] Azarías fue el padre de Seraías,
y Seraías fue el padre de Josadac.

[15] Josadac fue llevado al cautiverio cuando el SEÑOR deportó a Judá y a Jerusalén por medio de Nabucodonosor.

[16] Los hijos de Leví fueron Guersón, Coat y Merari.

[17] Hijos de Guersón: Libní y Simí.

[18] Hijos de Coat: Amirán, Izar, Hebrón y Uziel.

[19] Hijos de Merari: Majlí y Musí.
Éstos fueron los descendientes de los levitas por sus familias.

[20] Los descendientes de Guersón en línea directa fueron Libní, Yajat, Zimá, [21]Joa, Idó, Zera y Yatray.

[22] Los descendientes de Coat en línea directa fueron Aminadab, Coré, Asir, [23]Elcaná, Ebiasaf, Asir, [24]Tajat, Uriel, Uzías y Saúl.

25 Los hijos de Elcaná fueron Amasay y Ajimot.

26 Los descendientes de Ajimot en línea directa fueron Elcaná, Zofay, Najat, 27Eliab, Jeroán y Elcaná.

28 Los hijos de Samuel fueron Vasni, el primogénito, y Abías.

29 Los descendientes de Merari en línea directa fueron Majlí, Libní, Simí, Uza, 30Simá, Jaguías y Asaías.

Cantores del templo

31Éstos fueron los cantores que David nombró para el templo del SEÑOR, desde que se colocó allí el arca. 32Ellos ya cantaban en la *Tienda de reunión, delante del santuario, antes de que Salomón edificara el templo del SEÑOR en Jerusalén. Luego continuaron su ministerio según las normas establecidas.

33Éstos y sus hijos estuvieron a cargo del canto:

De los descendientes de Coat, el cantor Hemán fue hijo de Joel, descendiente en línea directa de Samuel, 34Elcaná, Jeroán, Eliel, Toa, 35Zuf, Elcaná, Mahat, Amasay, 36Elcaná, Joel, Azarías, Sofonías, 37Tajat, Asir, Ebiasaf, Coré, 38Izar, Coat, Leví e Israel.

39 A la derecha de Hemán se colocaba su pariente Asaf hijo de Berequías, descendiente en línea directa de Simá, 40Micael, Baseías, Malquías, 41Etni, Zera, Adaías, 42Etán, Zimá, Simí, 43Yajat, Guersón y Leví.

44 A la izquierda de Hemán se colocaba Etán hijo de Quisi, que era de sus parientes los meraritas y descendiente en línea directa de Abdí, Maluc, 45Jasabías, Amasías, Jilquías, 46Amsí, Baní, Sémer, 47Majlí, Musí, Merari y Leví.

48Sus hermanos los levitas estaban al servicio del santuario, en el templo de Dios. 49Aarón y sus hijos estaban encargados de quemar las ofrendas sobre el altar de los *holocaustos y sobre el altar del incienso. De acuerdo con lo ordenado por Moisés, siervo de Dios, eran también responsables de todo lo relacionado con el Lugar Santísimo y de hacer la *expiación por Israel.

50 Los descendientes de Aarón en línea directa fueron Eleazar, Finés, Abisúa, 51Buquí, Uzi, Zeraías, 52Merayot, Amarías, Ajitob, 53Sadoc y Ajimaz.

Ciudades de los levitas
6:54-80 — Jos 21:4-39

54Éstos fueron los territorios donde vivían los descendientes de Aarón.

A las familias de los coatitas se les adjudicó por sorteo 55Hebrón, en la tierra de Judá, con sus campos de pastoreo. 56A Caleb hijo de Jefone le tocaron el campo de la ciudad y sus aldeas. 57A los descendientes de Aarón les entregaron las siguientes ciudades de refugio: Hebrón, Libná, Jatir, Estemoa, 58Hilén, Debir, 59Asán y Bet Semes, con sus respectivos campos de pastoreo. 60De la tribu de Benjamín les dieron Gueba, Alemet y Anatot, con sus respectivos campos de pastoreo. En total les tocaron trece ciudades, distribuidas entre sus familias.

61Al resto de los descendientes de Coat les tocaron por sorteo diez ciudades de la media tribu de Manasés.

62A los descendientes de Guersón, según sus familias, les dieron trece ciudades de las tribus de Isacar, Aser y Neftalí, y de la tribu de Manasés que estaba en Basán.

63A los descendientes de Merari, según sus familias, les tocaron por sorteo doce ciudades de las tribus de Rubén, Gad y Zabulón.

64Fue así como los israelitas entregaron a los levitas estas ciudades con sus campos de pastoreo. 65Les adjudicaron por sorteo las ciudades de las tribus de Judá, Simeón y Benjamín, las cuales ya han sido mencionadas.

66Algunas de las familias descendientes de Coat recibieron por sorteo ciudades de la tribu de Efraín. 67Como ciudades de refugio les dieron Siquén, en los montes de Efraín, Guézer, 68Jocmeán, Bet Jorón, 69Ayalón y Gat Rimón, con sus respectivos campos de pastoreo. 70De la media tribu de Manasés les entregaron Aner y Bileán, con sus respectivos campos de pastoreo. Éstas fueron las ciudades asignadas al resto de las familias de Coat.

71Los descendientes de Guersón recibieron las siguientes ciudades de la media tribu de Manasés: Golán de Basán, y Astarot, con sus respectivos campos de pastoreo. 72De la tribu de Isacar recibieron Cedes, Daberat, 73Ramot y Anén, con sus respectivos campos de pastoreo. 74De la tribu de Aser recibieron Masal, Abdón, 75Hucoc y Rejob, con sus respectivos campos de pastoreo. 76De la tribu de Neftalí recibieron Cedes de Galilea, Hamón y Quiriatayin, con sus respectivos campos de pastoreo.

77Los demás descendientes de Merari recibieron las siguientes ciudades de la tribu de Zabulón: Rimón y Tabor, con sus respectivos campos de pastoreo. 78De la tribu de Rubén, que está en la ribera oriental del Jordán, frente a Jericó, recibieron Béser, que está en el desierto, Jaza, 79Cademot y Mefat, con sus respectivos campos de pastoreo. 80De la tribu de Gad recibieron Ramot de Galaad, Majanayin, 81Hesbón y Jazer, con sus respectivos campos de pastoreo.

Descendientes de Isacar

7 Los hijos de Isacar fueron cuatro en total: Tola, Fuvá, Yasub y Simrón.

2 Los hijos de Tola fueron Uzi, Refaías, Jeriel, Yamay, Ibsán y Samuel, todos ellos guerreros valientes y jefes de las familias patriarcales de Tola. Según sus registros genealógicos, en el tiempo de David eran veintidós mil seiscientos.

3 Israías fue el hijo de Uzi, y los hijos de Israías fueron Micael, Abdías, Joel e Isías, en total cinco jefes. 4Tan grande era el número de sus mujeres y niños que, según sus registros genealógicos, contaban con un ejército de treinta y seis mil hombres de guerra. 5El número total de todos sus parientes de las familias de Isacar ascendía a ochenta y siete mil guerreros valientes.

Descendientes de Benjamín

6 Los hijos de Benjamín fueron Bela, Béquer y Jediael, tres en total.

7 Los hijos de Bela fueron Esbón, Uzi, Uziel, Jerimot e Irí, cinco en total. Todos ellos eran jefes de las familias patriarcales y guerreros valientes, y sumaban veintidós mil treinta y cuatro.

8 Los hijos de Béquer fueron Zemirá, Joás, Eliezer, Elihoenay, Omrí, Jerimot, Abías, Anatot y Alamet. Todos ellos eran hijos de Béquer, 9jefes de sus familias patriarcales y guerreros valientes. Según sus registros genealógicos, eran veinte mil doscientos.

10Bilhán fue el hijo de Jediael, y los hijos de Bilán fueron Jeús, Benjamín, Áod, Quenaná, Zetán, Tarsis y Ajisajar. 11Todos ellos descendían de Jediael, y eran jefes de sus familias patriarcales y guerreros valientes. En total, eran diecisiete mil doscientos hombres aptos para la guerra. [12] Los hijos de Ir fueron Supín y Jupín. Jusín fue el hijo de Ajer.

Descendientes de Neftalí

[13] Los hijos de Neftalí fueron Yazel, Guní, Jéser y Salún. Éstos eran descendientes de Bilhá.

Descendientes de Manasés

[14] Los hijos que Manasés tuvo con su concubina *siria fueron Asriel y Maquir, este último, padre de Galaad. [15]Maquir tomó por esposa a Macá, de la familia de Jupín y Supín.

El segundo hijo se llamaba Zelofejad, quien solamente tuvo hijas. [16]Macá, la esposa de Maquir, dio a luz un hijo, al que llamó Peres. Éste fue hermano de Seres y padre de Ulán y Requen. [17]Bedán fue hijo de Ulán.

Éstos fueron los hijos de Galaad, hijo de Maquir, hijo de Manasés. [18]Su hermana Hamoléquet fue la madre de Isod, Abiezer y Majlá.

[19] Los hijos de Semidá fueron Ahián, Siquén, Liquejí y Anián.

Descendientes de Efraín

[20] Los descendientes de Efraín en línea directa fueron Sutela, Béred, Tajat, Eladá, Tajat, [21]Zabad, Sutela, Ezer y Elad. Los habitantes de Gad mataron a estos dos últimos porque bajaron a robarles sus ganados. [22]Durante mucho tiempo Efraín guardó luto por sus hijos, y sus parientes llegaron para consolarlo. [23]Luego se unió a su esposa, la cual concibió y le dio a luz un hijo, al que llamó Beriá por la desgracia[s] que su familia había sufrido.

[24] Su hija Será edificó Bet Jorón la de arriba y Bet Jorón la de abajo, y también Uzén Será.

[25] Los descendientes de Beriá en línea directa fueron Refa, Résef, Télaj, Taján, [26]Amiud, Elisama, [27]Nun y Josué. [28]Sus posesiones y lugares de residencia fueron Betel con sus aldeas; Narán, al este; Guézer con sus aldeas, al oeste; y Siquén con sus aldeas hasta Ayah con sus aldeas. [29]Los descendientes de Manasés tenían en su poder a Betseán, Tanac, Meguido y Dor, con sus respectivas aldeas. En estos lugares se asentaron los descendientes de José hijo de Israel.

Descendientes de Aser

[30] Los hijos de Aser fueron Imná, Isvá, Isví, Beriá y Sera, su hermana.

[31] Los hijos de Beriá fueron Héber y Malquiel, padre de Birzávit.

[32] Los hijos de Héber fueron Jaflet, Semer, Jotán y Suá, su hermana.

[33] Los hijos de Jaflet fueron Pasac, Bimal y Asvat.

[34] Los hijos de su hermano Semer fueron Rohegá, Yehubá y Aram.

[35] Los hijos de su hermano Hélem fueron Zofa, Imná, Seles y Amal.

[36] Los hijos de Zofa fueron Súaj, Harnéfer, Súal, Berí, Imrá, [37]Béser, Hod, Sama, Silsa, Itrán y Beerá.

[38] Los hijos de Jéter fueron Jefone, Pispa y Ará.

[39] Los hijos de Ula fueron Araj, Janiel y Risiyá.

[40]Todos ellos fueron descendientes de Aser, jefes de familias patriarcales, hombres selectos, guerreros valientes e importantes. Según sus registros genealógicos eran veintiséis mil hombres, aptos para la guerra.

Descendientes de Benjamín
8:28-38 — 1Cr 9:34-44

8 Los hijos de Benjamín fueron:
Bela, el primero;
Asbel, el segundo;
Ajará, el tercero;
[2] Noja, el cuarto,
y Rafá, el quinto.

[3] Los hijos de Bela fueron Adar, Guerá, Abiud, [4]Abisúa, Naamán, Ajoaj, [5]Guerá, Sefufán e Hiram.

[6] Los hijos de Aod, jefes de las familias patriarcales que habitaban en Gueba y que luego se trasladaron a Manajat, fueron [7]Naamán, Ahías y Guerá, padre de Uza y de Ajiud. Guerá fue el que los trasladó a Manajat.

[8] Después de que Sajarayin repudió a sus esposas Jusín y Bará, tuvo otros hijos en los campos de Moab. [9]Con su esposa Hodes tuvo a Jobab, Sibia, Mesá, Malcán, [10]Jeús, Saquías y Mirma. Estos hijos suyos fueron jefes de familias patriarcales.

[11] Con Jusín tuvo a Abitob y a Elpal.

[12] Los hijos de Elpal fueron Éber, Misán y Sémed. Sémed edificó las ciudades de Ono y Lod, con sus aldeas; [13]Beriá y Semá fueron jefes de las familias patriarcales de los habitantes de Ayalón, y expulsaron a los habitantes de Gat.

[14] Los hijos de Beriá fueron Ajío, Sasac, Jeremot, [15]Zebadías, Arad, Ader, [16]Micael, Ispá y Yojá.

[17] Zebadías, Mesulán, Hizqui, Éber, [18]Ismeray, Jezlías y Jobab fueron los hijos de Elpal.

[19] Yaquín, Zicrí, Zabdí, [20]Elienay, Ziletay, Eliel, [21]Adaías, Beraías y Simrat fueron los hijos de Simí.

[22] Ispán, Éber, Eliel, [23]Abdón, Zicrí, Janán, [24]Jananías, Elam, Anatotías, [25]Ifdaías y Peniel fueron los hijos de Sasac.

[26] Samseray, Seharías, Atalías, [27]Jaresías, Elías y Zicrí fueron los hijos de Jeroán. [28]Según sus registros genealógicos, éstos fueron jefes de familias patriarcales y habitaron en Jerusalén.

[29] Jehiel,[t] padre de Gabaón, vivía en Gabaón. Su esposa se llamaba Macá. [30]Sus hijos fueron Abdón, el primogénito; Zur, Quis, Baal, Ner,[u] Nadab, [31]Guedor, Ajío, Zéquer [32]y Miclot, padre de Simá. Éstos vivían también en Jerusalén con sus hermanos.

[33] Ner fue el padre de Quis, y éste fue padre de Saúl, quien fue padre de Jonatán, Malquisúa, Abinadab y Esbaal.[v]

[34] El hijo de Jonatán fue Meríbaal, padre de Micaías.

[35] Los hijos de Micaías fueron Pitón, Mélec, Tarea y Acaz.

[36] Acaz fue padre de Joada, y éste lo fue de Alemet, Azmávet y Zimri. Zimri fue el padre de

[s] 7:23 En hebreo, *Beriá* suena como la palabra que significa *desgracia*. [t] 8:29 *Jehiel* (mss. de LXX; véase 9:35); TM no incluye este nombre. [u] 8:30 *Ner* (mss. de LXX; véase 9:36); TM no incluye este nombre. [v] 8:33 *Esbaal*. Conocido también como *Isboset*; también en 9:39.

Mosá; 37Mosá fue el padre de Biná, y éste lo fue de Rafá; Rafá fue el padre de Elasá, y éste lo fue de Azel.

38Azel tuvo seis hijos, cuyos nombres fueron Azricán, Bocrú, Ismael, Searías, Abdías y Janán. Éstos fueron los hijos de Azel.

39Los hijos de su hermano Ésec fueron:

Ulán, el primero;

Jeús, el segundo,

y Elifelet, el tercero.

40Los hijos de Ulán fueron hombres guerreros valientes, diestros con el arco. Tuvieron muchos hijos y nietos: ciento cincuenta en total. Todos éstos fueron los descendientes de Benjamín.

9 Todos los israelitas fueron registrados en las listas genealógicas e inscritos en el libro de los reyes de Israel.

Los que regresaron a Jerusalén
9:1-17 — Neh 11:3-19

Por causa de su infidelidad a Dios, Judá fue llevado cautivo a Babilonia.

2Los primeros en ocupar nuevamente sus posesiones y ciudades fueron israelitas, sacerdotes, levitas y servidores del templo. 3Algunos de los descendientes de Judá, Benjamín, Efraín y Manasés habitaron en Jerusalén.

4 De los judíos: Utay hijo de Amiud, descendiente en línea directa de Omrí, Imrí, Baní y Fares hijo de Judá.

5 De los silonitas: Asaías, el primogénito, con sus hijos.

6 De los zeraítas: Jeuel y el resto de sus parientes; en total seiscientos noventa personas.

7 De los benjaminitas: Salú hijo de Mesulán, hijo de Hodavías, hijo de Senuá;w 8Ibneías hijo de Jeroán; Elá hijo de Uzi, hijo de Micri; Mesulán hijo de Sefatías, hijo de Reuel, hijo de Ibnías, 9con sus parientes. Según sus registros genealógicos, eran en total novecientos cincuenta y seis, todos ellos jefes de sus familias patriarcales.

10De los sacerdotes: Jedaías, Joyarib, Jaquín, 11Azarías hijo de Jilquías, que era descendiente en línea directa de Mesulán, Sadoc, Merayot y Ajitob, que fue jefe del templo de Dios; 12Adaías hijo de Jeroán, hijo de Pasur, hijo de Malquías; Masay hijo de Adiel, que era descendiente en línea directa de Jazera, Mesulán, Mesilemit e Imer, 13y sus parientes, en total mil setecientos sesenta jefes de familias patriarcales y hombres muy capacitados para el servicio en el templo de Dios.

14De los levitas: Semaías hijo de Jasub, que descendía en línea directa de Azricán, Jasabías y Merari; 15Bacbacar, Heres, Galal y Matanías hijo de Micaías, hijo de Zicrí, hijo de Asaf, 16Abdías hijo de Semaías, hijo de Galal, hijo de Jedutún; Berequías hijo de Asá, hijo de Elcaná, que habitó en las aldeas de los netofatitas.

17Los porteros: Salún, Acub, Talmón y Ajimán, y sus parientes; Salún era el jefe. 18Hasta ahora custodian la puerta del rey, que está al oriente, y han sido porteros de los campamentos levitas. 19Además, Salún hijo de Coré, hijo de Ebiasaf, hijo de Coré, y sus parientes coreítas de la misma familia patriarcal, estaban encargados de custodiar la entrada de la *Tienda de reunión, tal como sus antepasados habían custodiado la entrada del campamento del SEÑOR. 20En el pasado, Finés hijo de Eleazar fue su jefe, y el SEÑOR estuvo con él. 21Zacarías hijo de Meselemías era el portero de la Tienda de reunión.

22Los escogidos como porteros fueron un total de doscientos doce. En sus aldeas se encuentran sus registros genealógicos. David y Samuel el vidente les asignaron sus funciones. 23Los porteros y sus hijos estaban encargados de custodiar la entrada de la tienda de campaña que se usaba como templo del SEÑOR. 24Había porteros en los cuatro puntos cardinales. 25Cada siete días, sus parientes que vivían en las aldeas se turnaban para ayudarlos. 26Los cuatro porteros principales estaban en servicio permanente. Eran levitas y custodiaban las salas y los tesoros del templo de Dios. 27Durante la noche montaban guardia alrededor del templo, y en la mañana abrían sus puertas.

28Algunos de ellos estaban encargados de los utensilios que se usaban en el servicio del templo, y debían contarlos al sacarlos y al guardarlos. 29Otros estaban a cargo de los utensilios, de todos los vasos sagrados, de la harina, el vino, el aceite, el incienso y los perfumes. 30Algunos de los sacerdotes preparaban la mezcla de los perfumes. 31El levita Matatías, primogénito del coreíta Salún, estaba encargado de hacer las tortas para las ofrendas. 32Algunos de sus parientes coatitas preparaban los *panes sagrados para cada *sábado.

33También había cantores que eran jefes de familias patriarcales de los levitas, los cuales vivían en las habitaciones del templo. Éstos estaban exentos de cualquier otro servicio, porque de día y de noche tenían que ocuparse de su ministerio.

34Según sus registros genealógicos, éstos eran jefes de las familias patriarcales de los levitas y vivían en Jerusalén.

Genealogía de Saúl
9:34-44 — 1Cr 8:28-38

35En Gabaón vivía Jehiel, padre de Gabaón. Su esposa se llamaba Macá, 36y sus hijos fueron Abdón, el primogénito; Zur, Quis, Baal, Ner, Nadab, 37Guedor, Ajío, Zacarías y Miclot, 38que fue padre de Simán. Éstos también vivían en Jerusalén con sus parientes.

39Ner fue el padre de Quis, Quis lo fue de Saúl, y Saúl lo fue de Jonatán, Malquisúa, Abinadab y Esbaal. 40Jonatán fue el padre de Meribaal, y Meribaal lo fue de Micaías.

41Los hijos de Micaías fueron Pitón, Mélec, Tarea y Acaz.x 42Acaz fue el padre de Jará, y éste lo fue de Alemet, Azmávet y Zimri. Zimri fue el padre de Mosá; 43Mosá fue el padre de Biná, y éste lo fue de Refaías; Refaías fue el padre de Elasá, y éste lo fue de Azel.

44Azel tuvo seis hijos, cuyos nombres fueron Azricán, Bocrú, Ismael, Searías, Abdías y Janán. Éstos fueron los hijos de Azel.

Muerte de Saúl
10:1-12 — 1S 31:1-13; 2S 1:4-12

10 Los filisteos fueron a la guerra contra Israel, y los israelitas huyeron ante ellos. Muchos de ellos cayeron muertos en el monte Guilboa. 2Entonces los filisteos se fueron en persecución de Saúl, y lograron matar a sus hijos Jonatán, Abinadab y Malquisúa.

---

w 9:7 *Senuá.* Alt. *Hasenuá.* x 9:41 *y Acaz* (mss. de LXX, Siríaca, Targum y Vulgata; véase 8:35); TM no incluye esta frase.

³La batalla se intensificó contra Saúl, y los arqueros lo alcanzaron con sus flechas. Al verse herido, ⁴Saúl le dijo a su escudero: «Saca la espada y mátame, no sea que me maten esos incircuncisos cuando lleguen, y se diviertan a costa mía.»

Pero el escudero estaba tan asustado que no quiso hacerlo, de modo que Saúl mismo tomó su espada y se dejó caer sobre ella. ⁵Cuando el escudero vio que Saúl caía muerto, también él se arrojó sobre su propia espada y murió. ⁶Así murieron Saúl y sus tres hijos. Ese día pereció toda su familia.

⁷Cuando los israelitas que vivían en el valle vieron que el ejército había huido, y que Saúl y sus hijos habían muerto, también ellos abandonaron sus ciudades y se dieron a la fuga. Así fue como los filisteos las ocuparon.

⁸Al otro día, cuando los filisteos llegaron para despojar a los cadáveres, encontraron muertos a Saúl y a sus hijos en el monte Guilboa. ⁹Lo despojaron, tomaron su cabeza y sus armas, y enviaron mensajeros por todo el país filisteo para que proclamaran la noticia a sus ídolos y al pueblo. ¹⁰Después colocaron las armas en el templo de sus dioses y colgaron la cabeza en el templo de Dagón.

¹¹Cuando los de Jabés de Galaad se enteraron de lo que habían hecho los filisteos con Saúl, ¹²se levantaron todos los valientes y rescataron los cuerpos de Saúl y de sus hijos. Los llevaron a Jabés, sepultaron sus huesos debajo de la encina de Jabés y guardaron siete días de ayuno.

¹³⁻¹⁴Saúl murió por haberse rebelado contra el SEÑOR, pues en vez de consultarlo, desobedeció su palabra y buscó el consejo de una adivina. Por eso el SEÑOR le quitó la vida y entregó el reino a David hijo de Isaí.

Proclamación de David como rey de Israel
11:1-3 — 2S 5:1-3

11 Todos los israelitas se reunieron con David en Hebrón y le dijeron: «Su Majestad y nosotros somos de la misma sangre. ²Ya desde antes, cuando Saúl era rey, usted dirigía a Israel en sus campañas. Además, el SEÑOR su Dios le dijo a Su Majestad: "Tú guiarás a mi pueblo Israel y lo gobernarás."» ³Así pues, todos los *ancianos de Israel fueron a Hebrón para hablar con el rey, quien hizo allí un pacto con ellos en presencia del SEÑOR. Después de eso, ungieron a David para que fuera rey sobre Israel, conforme a lo que el SEÑOR había dicho por medio de Samuel.

David conquista Jerusalén
11:4-9 — 2S 5:6-10

⁴David y todos los israelitas marcharon contra Jebús (que es Jerusalén), la cual estaba habitada por los jebuseos. ⁵Éstos le dijeron a David: «No entrarás aquí!» Pero David se apoderó de la fortaleza de *Sión, que también se conoce como la Ciudad de David. ⁶Y es que había prometido: «Al primero que mate a un jebuseo lo nombraré comandante en jefe.»

El primero en matar a un jebuseo fue Joab hijo de Sarvia, por lo cual fue nombrado jefe. ⁷David se estableció en la fortaleza, y por eso la llamaron «Ciudad de David». ⁸Luego edificó la ciudad, desde el terraplén hasta sus alrededores, y Joab reparó el resto de la ciudad. ⁹Y David se fortaleció más y más, porque el SEÑOR *Todopoderoso estaba con él.

Jefes del ejército de David
11:10-41 — 2S 23:8-39

¹⁰Éstos fueron los jefes del ejército de David, quienes lo apoyaron durante su reinado y se unieron a todos los israelitas para proclamarlo rey, conforme a lo que el SEÑOR dijo acerca de Israel. ¹¹Esta es la lista de los soldados más valientes de David:

Yasobeán hijo de Jacmoní, que era el principal de los tres *más famosos, en una batalla mató con su lanza a trescientos hombres. ¹²En segundo lugar estaba Eleazar hijo de Dodó el ajoíta, que también era uno de los más famosos. ¹³Estuvo con David en Pasdamín, donde los filisteos se habían reunido para la batalla. Allí había un campo sembrado de cebada y, cuando el ejército huía ante los filisteos, ¹⁴los oficiales se plantaron en medio del campo y lo defendieron, matando a los filisteos. Así el SEÑOR los salvó y les dio una gran *victoria.

¹⁵En otra ocasión, tres de los treinta más valientes fueron a la roca, hasta la cueva de Adulán, donde estaba David; y el ejército filisteo acampaba en el valle de Refayin. ¹⁶David se encontraba en su fortaleza, y en ese tiempo había una guarnición filistea en Belén. ¹⁷Como David tenía mucha sed, exclamó: «¡Ojalá pudiera yo beber agua del pozo que está a la *entrada de Belén!» ¹⁸Entonces los tres valientes se metieron en el campamento filisteo, sacaron agua del pozo de Belén, y se la llevaron a David. Pero David no quiso beberla, sino que derramó el agua en honor al SEÑOR ¹⁹y declaró solemnemente: «¡Que Dios me libre de beberla! ¿Cómo podría yo beber la sangre de quienes han puesto su *vida en peligro? ¡Se jugaron la vida para traer el agua!» Y no quiso beberla.

Tales hazañas hicieron estos tres héroes.

²⁰Abisay, el hermano de Joab, estaba al mando de los tres y ganó fama entre ellos. En cierta ocasión, lanza en mano atacó y mató a trescientos hombres. ²¹Se destacó mucho más que los tres valientes, y llegó a ser su jefe, pero no fue contado entre ellos.

²²Benaías hijo de Joyadá era un guerrero de Cabsel que realizó muchas hazañas. Derrotó a dos de los mejores hombresᶻ de Moab, y en otra ocasión, cuando estaba nevando, se metió en una cisterna y mató un león. ²³También derrotó a un egipcio que medía como dos metros y medio,ᵃ y que empuñaba una lanza del tamaño de un rodillo de telar. Benaías, que no llevaba más que un palo, le arrebató la lanza y lo mató con ella. ²⁴Tales hazañas hizo Benaías hijo de Joyadá, y también él ganó fama como los tres valientes, ²⁵pero no fue contado entre ellos, aunque se destacó más que los treinta valientes. Además, David lo puso al mando de su guardia personal.

²⁶Los soldados más distinguidos eran:

Asael, hermano de Joab; Elhanán hijo de Dodó, de Belén; ²⁷Samot el harorita, Heles el pelonita, ²⁸Irá hijo de Iqués el tecoíta; Abiezer el anatotita; ²⁹Sibecay el jusatita, Ilay el ajoíta, ³⁰Maray el netofatita, Jéled hijo de Baná el netofatita; ³¹Itay hijo de Ribay, el de Guibeá de los benjaminitas; Benaías el piratonita; ³²Juray, del arroyo de Gaas; Abiel el arbatita; ³³Azmávet el bajurinita; Elijaba el salbonita; ³⁴los hijos de Jasén el guizonita; Jonatán hijo de Sague el ararita, ³⁵Ahían hijo de Sacar el ararita, Elifal hijo de Ur, ³⁶Héfer el mequeratita, Ahías el pelonita, ³⁷Jezró, de Carmel; Naray hijo de Ezbay, ³⁸Joel, herma-

y 11:11 *tres* (mss. de LXX); *treinta* (TM). ᶻ 11:22 *dos de los mejores hombres.* Alt. *los dos {hijos} de Ariel.* ᵃ 11:23 *dos metros y medio.* Lit. *cinco* *codos.*

no de Natán; Mibar hijo de Hagrí, [39]Sélec el amonita, Najaray el berotita, que fue escudero de Joab hijo de Sarvia; [40]Irá el itrita, Gareb el itrita, [41]Urías el hitita, Zabad hijo de Ajlay, [42]Adiná hijo de Sizá el rubenita, jefe de los rubenitas, y treinta hombres con él; [43]Janán hijo de Macá; Josafat el mitnita, [44]Uzías el astarotita, Sama y Jehiel, hijos de Jotán el aroerita; [45]Jediael hijo de Simri, y su hermano Yojá el tizita; [46]Eliel el majavita; Jerebay y Josavía, hijos de Elnán; Itmá el moabita, [47]Eliel, Obed y Jasiel, de Sobá.

Guerreros que se unieron a David

12 Éstos fueron los guerreros que se unieron a David en Siclag cuando éste se encontraba desterrado por causa de Saúl hijo de Quis. Ellos lo ayudaron en tiempos de guerra. [2]Eran arqueros que podían lanzar piedras y disparar flechas con ambas manos.

De los benjaminitas parientes de Saúl: [3]el jefe Ajiezer y Joás, que eran hijos de Semá de Guibeá; Jeziel y Pélet hijos de Azmávet; Beracá y Jehú, oriundos de Anatot; [4]Ismaías el gabaonita, que era uno de los treinta guerreros y jefe de ellos; Jeremías, Jahaziel, Johanán, Jozabad de Guederá, [5]Eluzay, Jerimot, Bealías, Semarías, Sefatías el harufita; [6]los coreítas Elcaná, Isías, Azarel, Joezer y Yasobeán, [7]Joelá y Zebadías, hijos de Jeroán, oriundos de Guedor.

[8]También algunos de los gaditas se unieron a David cuando se encontraba en la fortaleza del desierto. Eran guerreros valientes, preparados para la guerra, hábiles en el manejo del escudo y de la lanza, feroces como leones y veloces como gacelas monteses. [9]Se llamaban: Ezer, el primero; Abdías, el segundo; Eliab, el tercero; [10]Mismaná, el cuarto; Jeremías, el quinto; [11]Atay, el sexto; Eliel, el séptimo; [12]Johanán, el octavo; Élzabad, el noveno; [13]Jeremías, el décimo, y Macbanay, el undécimo. [14]Estos gaditas eran jefes del ejército; el menor de ellos valía por cien, y el mayor, por mil. [15]Fueron ellos quienes atravesaron el Jordán en el mes primero, cuando el río se desbordó por sus dos riberas, e hicieron huir a los habitantes de los valles hacia el este y el oeste.

[16]También algunos guerreros de las tribus de Benjamín y de Judá se unieron a David en la fortaleza. [17]David salió a su encuentro y les dijo:

—Si vienen en son de paz y para ayudarme, los aceptaré; pero si vienen para entregarme a mis enemigos, ¡que el Dios de nuestros padres lo vea y lo castigue, pues yo no soy ningún criminal!

[18]Y el Espíritu vino sobre Amasay, jefe de los treinta, y éste exclamó:

«¡Somos tuyos, David!
¡Estamos contigo, hijo de Isaí!
¡Tres veces deseamos la paz
a ti y a quien te brinde su ayuda!
¡Y quien te ayuda es tu Dios!»

David los recibió y los puso entre los jefes de la tropa.

[19]También algunos guerreros de Manasés se unieron a David cuando éste iba con los filisteos a luchar contra Saúl. Pero los príncipes de los filisteos se reunieron y decidieron rechazarlo, así que los filisteos se negaron a ayudarlo, pues dijeron: «David se pondrá de parte de su señor Saúl, y eso nos costará la cabeza.» [20]Éstos fueron los manasesitas que se unieron a David cuando éste fue a Siclag: Adnás, Jozabad, Jediael, Micael, Jozabad, Eliú y Ziletay, jefes manasesitas de escuadrones de mil hombres. [21]Ayudaban a David a combatir a las bandas de invasores, pues cada uno de ellos era un guerrero valiente y jefe del ejército. [22]Y cada día se le unían más soldados a David, hasta que llegó a tener un ejército grande y poderoso.

Los que se unieron a David en Hebrón

[23]Éste es el número de los guerreros diestros para la guerra que se presentaron ante David en Hebrón, para entregarle el reino de Saúl, conforme a la palabra del SEÑOR:

[24]De Judá: seis mil ochocientos hombres armados de lanza y escudo, diestros para la guerra.

[25]De Simeón: siete mil cien guerreros valientes.

[26]De Leví: cuatro mil seiscientos, [27]y tres mil setecientos aaronitas, con Joyadá, su jefe; [28]y Sadoc, joven guerrero muy valiente, con veintidós jefes de su familia patriarcal.

[29]De Benjamín, parientes de Saúl: tres mil hombres. La mayor parte de ellos había permanecido fiel a la familia de Saúl.

[30]De Efraín: veinte mil ochocientos hombres valientes, famosos en sus propias familias patriarcales.

[31]De la media tribu de Manasés: dieciocho mil hombres que fueron nombrados para ir a proclamar rey a David.

[32]De Isacar: doscientos jefes y todos sus parientes bajo sus órdenes. Eran hombres expertos en el conocimiento de los tiempos, que sabían lo que Israel tenía que hacer.

[33]De Zabulón: cincuenta mil hombres listos para tomar las armas, preparados para usar cualquier clase de armamento y dispuestos a luchar sin cuartel en favor de David.

[34]De Neftalí: mil jefes con treinta y siete mil hombres armados de escudos y lanzas.

[35]De Dan: veintiocho mil seiscientos guerreros listos para el combate.

[36]De Aser: cuarenta mil hombres aptos para la guerra.

[37]De las tribus al otro lado del Jordán, es decir, de Rubén, Gad y de la media tribu de Manasés: ciento veinte mil hombres equipados con todo tipo de armamento.

[38]Todos estos guerreros, preparados para el combate, fueron a Hebrón decididos a proclamar a David como rey de todo Israel. También los demás israelitas proclamaron de manera unánime a David como rey. [39]Todos se quedaron allí tres días, comiendo y bebiendo con David, ya que sus hermanos les dotaron de lo necesario. [40]Además, los que vivían cerca, y hasta de Isacar, Zabulón y Neftalí, traían burros, camellos, mulas y bueyes cargados con harina, tortas de higos, pasas, vino y aceite. También les llevaron toros y ovejas en abundancia, porque Israel rebosaba de alegría.

Traslado del arca a la casa de Obed Edom
13:1-14 — 2S 6:1-11

13 Después de consultar a los jefes de mil y de cien soldados, y a todos los oficiales, David [2]dijo a toda la asamblea de Israel: «Si les parece bien, y si es lo que el SEÑOR nuestro Dios desea, invitemos a nuestros hermanos que se han quedado por todo el territorio de Israel, y también a los sacerdotes y levitas que están en los pueblos y aldeas, a que se unan a nosotros [3]para traer de regreso el arca de nuestro

Dios. La verdad es que desde el tiempo de Saúl no la hemos consultado.»

⁴A la asamblea le agradó la propuesta, y acordó que se hiciera así.

⁵Entonces David reunió a todo el pueblo de Israel, desde Sijor en Egipto hasta Lebó Jamat,ᵇ para trasladar el arca que estaba en Quiriat Yearín. ⁶Luego David y todo Israel fueron a Balá, que es Quiriat Yearín de Judá, para trasladar de allí el arca de Dios, sobre la cual se invoca el *nombre del SEÑOR, que reina entre *querubines. ⁷Colocaron el arca de Dios en una carreta nueva y la sacaron de la casa de Abinadab. Uza y Ajío guiaban la carreta. ⁸David y todo Israel danzaban ante Dios con gran entusiasmo y cantaban al son de liras, arpas, panderos, címbalos y trompetas.

⁹Al llegar a la parcela de Quidón, los bueyes tropezaron; pero Uza, extendiendo las manos, sostuvo el arca. ¹⁰Con todo, la ira del SEÑOR se encendió contra Uza por haber tocado el arca, y allí en su presencia Dios lo hirió y le quitó la vida.

¹¹David se enojó porque el SEÑOR había matado a Uza. Por eso le puso a aquel lugar el nombre de Peres Uza,ᶜ nombre que conserva hasta hoy. ¹²Aquel día David se sintió temeroso de Dios y exclamó: «¡Es mejor que no me lleve el arca de Dios!» ¹³Por eso no se la llevó a la Ciudad de David, sino que ordenó que la trasladaran a la casa de Obed Edom, oriundo de Gat. ¹⁴Fue así como el arca de Dios permaneció tres meses en la casa de Obed Edom, y el SEÑOR bendijo a la familia de Obed Edom y todo lo que tenía.

Palacio y familia de David
14:1-7 — 2S 5:11-16; 1Cr 3:5-8

14 Hiram, rey de Tiro, envió a David una embajada que le llevó madera de cedro, albañiles y carpinteros para construirle un palacio. ²Con esto David se dio cuenta de que el SEÑOR, por amor a su pueblo, le había establecido a él como rey sobre Israel y había engrandecido su reino.

³En Jerusalén David tomó otras esposas, y tuvo más hijos e hijas. ⁴Los hijos que tuvo fueron Samúa, Sobab, Natán, Salomón, ⁵Ibjar, Elisúa, Elpélet, ⁶Noga, Néfeg, Jafía, ⁷Elisama, Belyadá y Elifelet.

David derrota a los filisteos
14:8-17 — 2S 5:17-25

⁸Al enterarse los filisteos de que David había sido ungido rey de todo Israel, subieron todos ellos contra él. Pero David lo supo y salió a su encuentro. ⁹Ya los filisteos habían incursionado en el valle de Refayin. ¹⁰Así que David consultó a Dios:

—¿Debo atacar a los filisteos? ¿Los entregarás en mi poder?

—Atácalos —le respondió el SEÑOR—, pues yo los entregaré en tus manos.

¹¹Fueron, pues, a Baal Perasín,ᵈ y allí David los derrotó. Entonces dijo: «Como brecha producida por las aguas, así Dios ha abierto brechas entre mis enemigos por medio de mí.» Por eso a aquel lugar lo llamaron Baal Perasín. ¹²Allí los filisteos abandonaron a sus dioses, y éstos fueron quemados por orden de David.

¹³Los filisteos hicieron una nueva incursión y se desplegaron por el valle. ¹⁴Así que David volvió a consultar a Dios, y él le contestó:

—No los ataques de frente, sino rodéalos hasta llegar a los árboles de bálsamo, y entonces atácalos

por la retaguardia. ¹⁵Tan pronto como oigas un ruido como de pasos sobre las copas de los árboles, atácalos, pues eso quiere decir que Dios va al frente de ti para derrotar al ejército filisteo.

¹⁶Así lo hizo David, tal como Dios se lo había ordenado, y derrotaron al ejército filisteo desde Gabaón hasta Guézer. ¹⁷La fama de David se extendió por todas las regiones, y el SEÑOR hizo que todos los pueblos le tuvieran miedo.

David lleva el arca a Jerusalén
15:25—16:3 — 2S 6:12-19

15 David construyó para sí casas en la Ciudad de David, dispuso un lugar para el arca de Dios y le levantó una tienda de campaña. ²Luego dijo: «Sólo los levitas pueden transportar el arca de Dios, pues el SEÑOR los eligió a ellos para este oficio y para que le sirvan por siempre.»

³Después David congregó a todo Israel en Jerusalén para trasladar el arca del SEÑOR al lugar que había dispuesto para ella. ⁴También reunió a los descendientes de Aarón y a los levitas. Convocó a los siguientes:

⁵ De los descendientes de Coat, a su jefe Uriel y a sus parientes; ciento veinte en total.

⁶ De los descendientes de Merari, a su jefe Asaías y a sus compañeros; doscientos veinte en total.

⁷ De los descendientes de Guersón, a su jefe Joel y a sus parientes; ciento treinta en total.

⁸ De los descendientes de Elizafán, a su jefe Semaías y a sus parientes; doscientos en total.

⁹ De los descendientes de Hebrón, a su jefe Eliel y a sus parientes; ochenta en total.

¹⁰ De los descendientes de Uziel, a su jefe Aminadab y a sus parientes; ciento doce en total.

¹¹Luego David llamó a los sacerdotes Sadoc y Abiatar, y a los levitas Uriel, Asaías, Joel, Semaías, Eliel y Aminadab, ¹²y les dijo: «Como ustedes son los jefes de las familias patriarcales de los levitas, *purifíquense y purifiquen a sus parientes para que puedan traer el arca del SEÑOR, Dios de Israel, al lugar que he dispuesto para ella. ¹³La primera vez ustedes no la transportaron, ni nosotros consultamos al SEÑOR nuestro Dios, como está establecido; por eso él se enfureció contra nosotros.»

¹⁴Entonces los sacerdotes y los levitas se purificaron para transportar el arca del SEÑOR, Dios de Israel. ¹⁵Luego los descendientes de los levitas, valiéndose de las varas, llevaron el arca de Dios sobre sus hombros, tal como el SEÑOR lo había ordenado por medio de Moisés.

¹⁶David les ordenó a los jefes de los levitas que nombraran cantores de entre sus parientes para que entonaran alegres cantos al son de arpas, liras y címbalos. ¹⁷Los levitas nombraron a Hemán hijo de Joel, a su pariente Asaf hijo de Berequías, y a Etán hijo de Cusaías, de los descendientes de Merari. ¹⁸Junto con ellos nombraron a sus parientes que les seguían en rango y que se desempeñaban como porteros: Zacarías hijo de Jaziel, Semiramot, Jehiel, Uni, Eliab, Benaías, Maseías, Matatías, Elifeleu, Micnías, Obed Edom y Jeyel.

¹⁹Los cantores Hemán, Asaf y Etán tocaban los címbalos de bronce. ²⁰Zacarías, Aziel, Semiramot, Jehiel, Uni, Eliab, Maseías y Benaías tenían arpas de tono agudo.ᵉ ²¹Matatías, Elifeleu, Micnías, Obed Edom, Jeyel y Azazías tenían arpas de ocho cuerdas para guiar el canto. ²²Quenanías, jefe de los levitas,

---

ᵇ **13:5** *Lebó Jamat.* Alt. *la entrada de Jamat.* ᶜ **13:11** En hebreo, *Peres Uza* significa *golpe de Uza* o *brecha en Uza.* ᵈ **14:11** En hebreo, *Baal Perasín* significa *el dueño de las brechas.* ᵉ **15:20** *de tono agudo.* Lit. *sobre *alamot.*

como experto que era, dirigía el canto. ²³Berequías y Elcaná eran porteros del arca. ²⁴Los sacerdotes Sebanías, Josafat, Natanael, Amasay, Zacarías, Benaías y Eliezer tocaban las trompetas delante del arca. Obed Edom y Jehías eran también porteros del arca.

²⁵Muy alegres, David, los *ancianos de Israel y los jefes de mil fueron a trasladar el arca del *pacto del SEÑOR desde la casa de Obed Edom. ²⁶Y como Dios ayudaba a los levitas que transportaban el arca del pacto del SEÑOR, se sacrificaron siete toros y siete carneros. ²⁷David estaba vestido con un manto de lino fino, lo mismo que todos los levitas que transportaban el arca, los cantores y Quenanías, director del canto. Además, David llevaba puesto un *efod de lino. ²⁸Así que entre vítores, y al son de cuernos de carnero, trompetas, címbalos, arpas y liras, todo Israel llevaba el arca del pacto del SEÑOR.

²⁹Sucedió que, al entrar el arca del pacto del SEÑOR a la Ciudad de David, Mical, la hija de Saúl, se asomó a la ventana; y cuando vio que el rey David saltaba y danzaba con alegría, sintió por él un profundo desprecio.

16 El arca de Dios fue llevada a la tienda de campaña que David le había preparado. Allí la instalaron, y luego presentaron *holocaustos y sacrificios de *comunión en presencia de Dios. ²Después de ofrecer los holocaustos y los sacrificios de comunión, David bendijo al pueblo en el *nombre del SEÑOR ³y dio a cada israelita, tanto a hombres como a mujeres, una porción de pan, una torta de dátiles y una torta de pasas.

⁴David puso a algunos levitas a cargo del arca del SEÑOR para que ministraran, dieran gracias y alabaran al SEÑOR, Dios de Israel. ⁵Los nombrados fueron: Asaf, el primero; Zacarías, el segundo; luego Jejiyel, Semiramot, Jehiel, Matatías, Eliab, Benaías, Obed Edom y Jeyel, los cuales tenían arpas y liras. Asaf tocaba los címbalos. ⁶Los sacerdotes Benaías y Jahaziel tocaban continuamente las trompetas delante del arca del pacto del SEÑOR.

Salmo de David
16:8-22 — Sal 105:1-15
16:23-33 — Sal 96:1-13
16:34-36 — Sal 106:1,47-48

⁷Ese mismo día, David ordenó, por primera vez, que Asaf y sus compañeros fueran los encargados de esta alabanza al SEÑOR:

⁸«¡Alaben al SEÑOR, proclamen su *nombre,
    testifiquen de sus proezas entre los
      pueblos!
⁹¡Cántenle, cántenle salmos!
    ¡Hablen de sus maravillosas obras!
¹⁰¡Gloríense en su nombre *santo!
    ¡Alégrense de veras los que buscan al
      SEÑOR!
¹¹¡Refúgiense en el SEÑOR y en su fuerza,
    busquen siempre su presencia!
¹²¡Recuerden las maravillas que ha realizado,
    los prodigios y los juicios que ha emitido!
¹³»Descendientes de Israel, su siervo,
    hijos de Jacob, sus elegidos:
¹⁴el SEÑOR es nuestro Dios,
    sus juicios rigen en toda la tierra.
¹⁵Él se acuerda siempre de su *pacto,
    de la palabra que dio a mil generaciones;
¹⁶del pacto que hizo con Abraham,
    y del juramento que le hizo a Isaac,
¹⁷que confirmó como estatuto para Jacob,
    como pacto eterno para Israel:

¹⁸"A ti te daré la tierra de Canaán
    como la herencia que te corresponde."
¹⁹Cuando apenas eran un puñado de vivientes,
    unos cuantos extranjeros en la tierra,
²⁰cuando iban de nación en nación
    y pasaban de reino en reino,
²¹Dios no permitió que los oprimieran;
    por amor a ellos advirtió a los reyes:
²²"¡No toquen a mis *ungidos!
    ¡No maltraten a mis profetas!"

²³¡Que toda la tierra cante al SEÑOR!
    ¡Proclamen su *salvación cada día!
²⁴Anuncien su gloria entre las naciones,
    y sus maravillas a todos los pueblos.
²⁵Porque el SEÑOR es grande,
    y digno de toda alabanza;
    ¡más temible que todos los dioses!
²⁶Nada son los dioses de los pueblos,
    pero el SEÑOR fue quien hizo los cielos;
²⁷esplendor y majestad hay en su presencia;
    poder y alegría hay en su santuario.

²⁸»Tributen al SEÑOR, familias de los pueblos,
    tributen al SEÑOR la gloria y el poder;
²⁹tributen al SEÑOR la gloria que corresponde a
    su nombre;
    preséntense ante él con ofrendas,
    adoren al SEÑOR en su hermoso santuario.
³⁰¡Que tiemble ante él toda la tierra!
    Él afirmó el mundo, y éste no se moverá.
³¹¡Alégrense los cielos, y regocíjese la tierra!
    Digan las naciones: "¡El SEÑOR reina!"

³²»¡Que resuene el mar y todo cuanto contiene!
    ¡Que salte de alegría el campo y lo que hay
      en él!
³³¡Que los árboles del campo canten de gozo
    ante el SEÑOR,
    porque él ha venido a juzgar a la tierra!
³⁴»¡Alaben al SEÑOR porque él es bueno,
    y su gran amor perdura para siempre!
³⁵Díganle: "¡Sálvanos, oh Dios, Salvador
    nuestro!
    Reúnenos y líbranos de entre los *paganos,
    y alabaremos tu santo nombre
    y nos regocijaremos en tu alabanza."
³⁶¡Bendito sea el SEÑOR, Dios de Israel,
    desde siempre y para siempre!»

Y todo el pueblo respondió: «Amén», y alabó al SEÑOR.

³⁷David dejó el arca del pacto del SEÑOR al cuidado de Asaf y sus hermanos, para que sirvieran continuamente delante de ella, de acuerdo con el ritual diario. ³⁸Como porteros nombró a Obed Edom y sus sesenta y ocho hermanos, junto con Obed Edom hijo de Jedutún y Josá. ³⁹Al sacerdote Sadoc y a sus hermanos sacerdotes los encargó del santuario del SEÑOR, que está en la cumbre de Gabaón, ⁴⁰para que sobre el altar ofrecieran constantemente los *holocaustos al SEÑOR, en la mañana y en la tarde, tal como está escrito en la *ley que el SEÑOR le dio a Israel. ⁴¹Con ellos nombró también a Hemán y a Jedutún, y a los demás que había escogido y designado por nombre para cantar al SEÑOR: «Su gran amor perdura para siempre.» ⁴²Hemán y Jedutún tenían trompetas, címbalos y otros instrumentos musicales para acompañar los cantos de Dios. Los hijos de Jedutún eran porteros.

⁴³Luego todos regresaron a su casa, y David se fue a bendecir a su familia.

Promesa de Dios a David
17:1-15 — 2S 7:1-17

17 Una vez instalado en su palacio, David le dijo al profeta Natán:

—¡Aquí me tienes, habitando un palacio de cedro, mientras que el arca del *pacto del SEÑOR se encuentra bajo una simple tienda de campaña!

²—Bien —respondió Natán—. Haga Su Majestad lo que su corazón le dicte, pues Dios está con usted.

³Pero aquella misma noche la palabra de Dios vino a Natán y le dijo:

⁴«Ve y dile a mi siervo David que así dice el SEÑOR: "No serás tú quien me construya una casa para que yo la habite. ⁵Desde el día en que liberé a Israel hasta el día de hoy, no he habitado en casa alguna, sino que he ido de campamento en campamento y de santuario en santuario. ⁶Todo el tiempo que anduve con Israel, cuando mandé a sus jueces que *pastorearan a mi pueblo, ¿acaso le reclamé a alguno de ellos el no haberme construido una casa de cedro?"

⁷»Pues bien, dile a mi siervo David que así dice el SEÑOR *Todopoderoso: "Yo te saqué del redil para que, en vez de cuidar ovejas, gobernaras a mi pueblo Israel. ⁸Yo he estado contigo por dondequiera que has ido, y he aniquilado a todos tus enemigos. Y ahora voy a hacerte tan famoso como los más grandes de la tierra. ⁹También voy a designar un lugar para mi pueblo Israel, y allí los plantaré para que puedan vivir sin sobresaltos. Sus malvados enemigos no volverán a oprimirlos como lo han hecho desde el principio, ¹⁰desde los días en que nombré jueces sobre mi pueblo Israel. Yo derrotaré a todos tus enemigos. Te anuncio, además, que yo, el SEÑOR, te edificaré una casa. ¹¹Cuando tu vida llegue a su fin y vayas a reunirte con tus antepasados, yo pondré en el trono a uno de tus descendientes, a uno de tus hijos, y afirmaré su reino. ¹²Será él quien construya una casa en mi honor, y yo afirmaré su trono para siempre. ¹³Yo seré su padre, y él será mi hijo. Jamás le negaré mi amor, como se lo negué a quien reinó antes que tú. ¹⁴Al contrario, para siempre lo estableceré en mi casa y en mi reino, y su trono será firme para siempre."»

¹⁵Natán le comunicó todo esto a David, tal como lo había recibido por revelación.

Oración de David
17:16-27 — 2S 7:18-29

¹⁶Luego el rey David se presentó ante el SEÑOR y le dijo:

«SEÑOR y Dios, ¿quién soy yo, y qué es mi familia, para que me hayas hecho llegar tan lejos? ¹⁷Como si esto fuera poco, SEÑOR y Dios, has hecho promesas a este siervo tuyo en cuanto al futuro de su dinastía. ¡Me has tratado como si fuera yo un hombre muy importante, SEÑOR y Dios! ¹⁸¿Qué más podría yo decir del honor que me has dado, si tú conoces a tu siervo? ¹⁹SEÑOR, tú has hecho todas estas grandes maravillas, por amor a tu siervo y según tu voluntad, y las has dado a conocer. ²⁰SEÑOR, nosotros mismos hemos aprendido que no hay nadie como tú, y que aparte de ti no hay Dios. ²¹¿Y qué nación se puede comparar con tu pueblo Israel? Es la única nación en la tierra que tú has redimido, para hacerla tu propio pueblo y para dar a conocer tu *nombre. Hiciste prodigios y maravillas cuando al paso de tu pueblo, al cual redimiste de Egipto, expulsaste a las naciones y a sus dioses. ²²Adoptaste a Israel para que fuera tu pueblo para siempre, y para que tú, SEÑOR, fueras su Dios.

²³»Y ahora, SEÑOR, mantén para siempre la promesa que le has hecho a tu siervo y a su dinastía. Cumple tu palabra ²⁴para que tu nombre permanezca y sea exaltado por siempre, y para que todos digan: "¡El SEÑOR *Todopoderoso es el Dios de Israel!" Entonces la dinastía de tu siervo David quedará establecida en tu presencia.

²⁵»Tú, Dios mío, le has revelado a tu siervo el propósito de establecerle una dinastía, y por eso tu siervo se ha atrevido a dirigirte esta súplica. ²⁶Oh SEÑOR, ¡tú eres Dios y has prometido este favor a tu siervo! ²⁷Te has dignado bendecir a la familia de tu siervo, de modo que bajo tu protección exista para siempre. Tú, SEÑOR, la has bendecido, y por eso quedará bendita para siempre.»

Victorias de David
18:1-13 — 2S 8:1-14

18 Pasado algún tiempo, David derrotó a los filisteos y los subyugó, quitándoles el control de la ciudad de Gat y de sus aldeas. ²También derrotó y sometió a los moabitas, los cuales pasaron a ser vasallos tributarios de David.

³Además, David derrotó en Jamat a Hadad Ezer, rey de Sobá, cuando éste se dirigía a establecer su dominio sobre la región del río Éufrates. ⁴David le capturó mil carros, siete mil jinetes y veinte mil soldados de infantería; también desjarretó los caballos de tiro, aunque dejó los caballos suficientes para cien carros.

⁵Luego, cuando los *sirios de Damasco acudieron en auxilio de Hadad Ezer, rey de Sobá, David aniquiló a veintidós mil de ellos. ⁶También puso guarniciones en Damasco, de modo que los sirios pasaron a ser vasallos tributarios de David. En todas las campañas de David, el SEÑOR le daba la *victoria.

⁷En cuanto a los escudos de oro que llevaban los oficiales de Hadad Ezer, David se apropió de ellos y los trasladó a Jerusalén. ⁸Así mismo se apoderó de una gran cantidad de bronce que había en las ciudades de Tébajᶠ y de Cun, poblaciones de Hadad Ezer. Ése fue el bronce que Salomón usó para hacer la fuente, las columnas y todos los utensilios de bronce.

⁹Tou, rey de Jamat, se enteró de que David había derrotado por completo al ejército de Hadad Ezer, rey de Sobá. ¹⁰Como Tou también era enemigo de Hadad Ezer, envió a su hijo Adorán a desearle *bienestar al rey David, y a felicitarlo por haber derrotado a Hadad Ezer en batalla. Y Tou envió toda clase de utensilios de oro, de plata y de bronce, ¹¹los cuales el rey David consagró al SEÑOR, tal como lo había hecho con toda la plata y el oro que había tomado de las naciones de Edom, Moab, Amón, Filistea y Amalec.

¹²Por su parte, Abisay hijo de Sarvia derrotó a los edomitas en el valle de la Sal, y aniquiló a dieciocho mil de ellos. ¹³También puso guarniciones en Edom, de modo que los edomitas pasaron a ser vasallos tributarios de David. En todas sus campañas, el SEÑOR le daba la victoria.

ᶠ **18:8** *Tébaj.* Lit. *Tibjat* (variante de este nombre).

Oficiales de David
18:14-17 — 2S 8:15-18

14David reinó sobre todo Israel, gobernando al pueblo entero con justicia y rectitud. 15Joab hijo de Sarvia era general del ejército; Josafat hijo de Ajilud era el secretario; 16Sadoc hijo de Ajitob y Ajimélec hijo de Abiatar eran sacerdotes; Savsa lea el cronista. 17Benaías hijo de Joyadá estaba al mando de los soldados quereteos y peleteos, y los hijos de David ocupaban los principales puestos junto al rey.

Guerra contra los amonitas
19:1-19 — 2S 10:1-19

19 Pasado algún tiempo, murió Najás, rey de los amonitas, y su hijo lo sucedió en el trono. 2Entonces David pensó: «Debo ser leal con Janún hijo de Najás, pues su padre lo fue conmigo.» Así que envió a unos mensajeros para darle el pésame por la muerte de su padre.

Cuando los mensajeros de David llegaron al país de los amonitas para darle el pésame a Janún, 3los jefes de ese pueblo le aconsejaron: «¿Y acaso cree Su Majestad que David ha enviado a estos mensajeros sólo para darle el pésame, y porque quiere honrar a su padre? ¿No será más bien que han venido a espiar y explorar el país para luego destruirlo?» 4Entonces Janún mandó que apresaran a los mensajeros de David y que les afeitaran la barba y les rasgaran la ropa por la mitad, a la altura de las nalgas. Y así los despidió.

5Los hombres de David se sentían muy avergonzados. Cuando David se enteró de lo que les había pasado, mandó que los recibieran y les dieran este mensaje de su parte: «Quédense en Jericó, y no regresen hasta que les crezca la barba.»

6Al darse cuenta Janún y los amonitas de que habían ofendido a David, enviaron treinta y tres mil kilosh de plata para contratar carros y jinetes en Aram Najarayin,i en Aram de Macá y en Sobá. 7Contrataron treinta y dos mil carros y al rey de Macá con su ejército, que acampó frente a Medeba. Por su parte, los amonitas salieron de sus ciudades y se dispusieron para el combate. 8Cuando David lo supo, despachó a Joab con todos los soldados del ejército. 9Los amonitas avanzaron hasta la *entrada de su ciudad, pero los reyes que habían venido a reforzarlos se quedaron aparte, en campo abierto.

10Joab se vio amenazado por el frente y por la retaguardia, así que escogió a las mejores tropas israelitas para pelear contra los *sirios, 11y el resto de las tropas las puso al mando de su hermano Abisay, para que enfrentaran a los amonitas. 12A Abisay le ordenó: «Si los sirios pueden más que yo, tú vendrás a rescatarme; y si los amonitas pueden más que tú, yo te rescataré. 13¡Ánimo! Luchemos con valor por nuestro pueblo y por las ciudades de nuestro Dios. ¡Y que el SEÑOR haga lo que bien le parezca!»

14En seguida Joab y sus tropas avanzaron contra los sirios, y éstos huyeron de él. 15Al ver que los sirios se daban a la fuga, también los amonitas huyeron de Abisay y se refugiaron en la ciudad. Entonces Joab regresó a Jerusalén.

16Los sirios, al verse derrotados por Israel, enviaron mensajeros para pedir ayuda a los sirios que vivían al otro lado del río Éufrates. Sofac, jefe del ejército de Hadad Ezer, se puso al frente de ellos. 17Cuando David se enteró de esto, reunió a todo Israel, cruzó el Jordán y tomó posición de batalla contra los sirios. Éstos lo atacaron, 18pero tuvieron que huir ante los israelitas. David mató a siete mil soldados sirios de caballería y cuarenta mil de infantería; también mató a Sofac, jefe del ejército. 19Al ver que los sirios habían sido derrotados por los israelitas, todos los vasallos de Hadad Ezer hicieron la paz con David y se sometieron a él. A partir de entonces, los sirios se negaron a ir en auxilio de los amonitas.

Conquista de Rabá
20:1-3 — 2S 11:1; 12:29-31

20 En la primavera, que era la época en que los reyes salían de campaña, Joab sacó el grueso del ejército y devastó el país de los amonitas. Llegó hasta Rabá, la atacó y la destruyó; pero David se quedó en Jerusalén. 2Al rey de los amonitasj David le quitó la corona de oro que tenía puesta, la cual pesaba treinta y tres kilosk y estaba adornada con piedras preciosas. Luego se la pusieron a David. Además, David saqueó la ciudad y se llevó un botín inmenso. 3Expulsó de allí a sus habitantes y los puso a trabajar con sierras, rastrillos y hachas. Lo mismo hizo con todos los pueblos de los amonitas, después de lo cual regresó a Jerusalén con todas sus tropas.

Guerra contra los filisteos
20:4-8 — 2S 21:15-22

4Después de esto, hubo una batalla contra los filisteos en Guézer. Fue en esa ocasión cuando Sibecay el jusatita mató a Sipay, descendiente de los gigantes. Así sometieron a los filisteos.

5Luego, en otra batalla que hubo contra los filisteos, Elján hijo de Yaír mató a Lajmí, hermano de Goliat el guitita, cuya lanza tenía un asta tan grande como el rodillo de un telar.

6Hubo una batalla más en Gat. Allí había otro gigante, un hombre altísimo que tenía seis dedos en cada mano y seis en cada pie, es decir, tenía veinticuatro dedos en total. 7Éste se puso a desafiar a los israelitas, pero Jonatán hijo de Simá, que era hermano de David, lo mató.

8Éstos fueron los descendientes de Rafá el guitita que cayeron a manos de David y de sus oficiales.

David hace un censo militar
21:1-17 — 2S 24:1-17

21 *Satanás conspiró contra Israel e indujo a David a hacer un censo del pueblo. 2Por eso David les dijo a Joab y a los jefes del pueblo:

—Vayan y hagan un censo militar que abarque desde Berseba hasta Dan, y tráiganme el informe para que yo sepa cuántos pueden servir en el ejército.

3Joab le respondió:

—¡Que el SEÑOR multiplique cien veces a su pueblo! Pero ¿acaso no son todos ellos servidores suyos? ¿Para qué quiere hacer esto Su Majestad? ¿Por qué ha de hacer algo que traiga la desgracia sobre Israel?

4Sin embargo, la orden del rey prevaleció sobre la opinión de Joab, de modo que éste salió a recorrer todo el territorio de Israel. Después regresó a Jerusalén 5y le entregó a David los resultados del censo militar: En Israel había un millón cien mil que podían servir en el ejército, y en Judá, cuatrocientos setenta mil. 6Pero Joab no contó a los de las tribus de Leví ni

g 18:16 Ajimélec (mss. hebreos, Vulgata y Siríaca); véase 2S 8:17); Abimélec (TM). h 19:6 treinta y tres mil kilos. Lit. mil *talentos. i 19:6 Aram Najarayin. Es decir, el noroeste de Mesopotamia. j 20:2 al rey de los amonitas. Alt. a Milcón (es decir, el dios Moloc). k 20:2 treinta y tres kilos. Lit. un *talento.

de Benjamín, porque para él era detestable la orden del rey. 7Dios también la consideró como algo malo, por lo cual castigó a Israel.

8Entonces David le dijo a Dios: «He cometido un pecado muy grande al hacer este censo. He actuado como un *necio. Yo te ruego que perdones la maldad de tu siervo.»

9El SEÑOR le dijo a Gad, el vidente de David: 10«Anda y dile a David que así dice el SEÑOR: "Te doy a escoger entre estos tres castigos: dime cuál de ellos quieres que te imponga."»

11Gad fue a donde estaba David y le dijo:

—Así dice el SEÑOR: "Elige una de estas tres cosas: 12tres años de hambre, o tres meses de persecución y derrota por la espada de tus enemigos, o tres días en los cuales el SEÑOR castigará con peste al país, y su ángel causará estragos en todos los rincones de Israel." Piénsalo bien y dime qué debo responderle al que me ha enviado.

13—¡Estoy entre la espada y la pared! —respondió David—. Pero es mejor que caiga en las manos del SEÑOR, porque su amor es muy grande, y no que caiga en las manos de los *hombres.

14Por lo tanto, el SEÑOR mandó contra Israel una peste, y murieron setenta mil israelitas. 15Luego envió un ángel a Jerusalén para destruirla. Y al ver el SEÑOR que el ángel la destruía, se arrepintió del castigo y le dijo al ángel destructor: ¡Basta! ¡Detén tu mano!» En ese momento, el ángel del SEÑOR se hallaba junto a la parcela de Ornán el jebuseo.

16David alzó la vista y vio que el ángel del SEÑOR estaba entre la tierra y el cielo, con una espada desenvainada en la mano que apuntaba hacia Jerusalén. Entonces David y los *ancianos, vestidos de luto, se postraron sobre su rostro. 17Y David le dijo a Dios: «SEÑOR y Dios mío, ¿acaso no fui yo el que dio la orden de censar al pueblo? ¿Qué culpa tienen estas ovejas? ¡Soy yo el que ha pecado! ¡He actuado muy mal! ¡Descarga tu mano sobre mí y sobre mi familia, pero no sigas hiriendo a tu pueblo!»

David construye un altar
21:18-26 — 2S 24:18-25

18Entonces el ángel del SEÑOR le dijo a Gad: «Dile a David que vaya y construya un altar para el SEÑOR en la parcela de Ornán el jebuseo.» 19David se puso en camino, conforme a la palabra que Gad le dio en *nombre del SEÑOR.

20Ornán se encontraba trillando y, al mirar hacia atrás, vio al ángel. Los cuatro hijos que estaban con él corrieron a esconderse. 21Al ver Ornán que David se acercaba a su parcela, salió a recibirlo y se postró delante de él. 22David le dijo:

—Véndeme una parte de esta parcela para construirle un altar al SEÑOR, a fin de que se detenga la plaga que está afligiendo al pueblo. Véndemela por su verdadero precio.

23Ornán le contestó a David:

—Su Majestad, yo se la regalo, para que haga usted en ella lo que mejor le parezca. Yo mismo le daré los bueyes para los *holocaustos, los trillos para la leña y el trigo para la ofrenda de cereal. Todo se lo regalo.

24Pero el rey David le respondió a Ornán:

—Eso no puede ser. No tomaré lo que es tuyo para dárselo al SEÑOR, ni le ofreceré un holocausto que nada me cueste. Te lo compraré todo por su verdadero precio.

25Fue así como David le dio a Ornán seiscientas monedasl de oro por aquel lugar. 26Allí construyó un altar al SEÑOR y le ofreció holocaustos y sacrificios de *comunión. Luego oró al SEÑOR, y en respuesta Dios envió fuego del cielo sobre el altar del holocausto.

27Entonces el SEÑOR le ordenó al ángel que envainara su espada. 28Al ver David que el SEÑOR le había respondido, le ofreció sacrificios. 29En aquel tiempo, tanto el santuario del SEÑOR que Moisés hizo en el desierto como el altar del holocausto se encontraban en el santuario de Gabaón. 30Pero David no fue a consultar al SEÑOR a ese lugar porque, por causa de la espada del ángel del SEÑOR, estaba aterrorizado.

22 Entonces dijo David: «Aquí se levantará el templo de Dios el SEÑOR, y también el altar donde Israel ofrecerá el holocausto.»

Preparativos para el templo

2Luego David ordenó que se reuniera a los extranjeros que vivían en territorio israelita. De entre ellos nombró canteros que labraran piedras para la construcción del templo de Dios. 3Además, David juntó mucho hierro para los clavos y las bisagras de las puertas, y bronce en abundancia. 4También amontonó mucha madera de cedro, pues los habitantes de Sidón y de Tiro le habían traído madera de cedro en abundancia.

5«Mi hijo Salomón —pensaba David— es muy joven e inexperto, y el templo que hay que construir para el SEÑOR debe ser el más grande y famoso de toda la tierra; por eso le dejaré todo listo.» Así que antes de morir, David dejó todo listo.

6Luego llamó a su hijo Salomón y le encargó construir el templo para el SEÑOR, Dios de Israel. 7David le dijo a Salomón: «Hijo mío, yo tenía la intención de construir un templo para honrar al SEÑOR mi Dios. 8Pero el SEÑOR me dijo: "Ante mis propios ojos has derramado mucha sangre y has hecho muchas guerras en la tierra; por eso no serás tú quien me construya un templo. 9Pero tendrás un hijo que será un hombre pacífico; yo haré que los países vecinos que sean sus enemigos lo dejen en *paz; por eso se llamará Salomón.m Durante su reinado, yo le daré a Israel paz y tranquilidad. 10Él será quien me construya un templo. Él será para mí como un hijo, y yo seré para él como un padre. Yo afirmaré para siempre el trono de su reino en Israel."

11»Ahora, hijo mío, que el SEÑOR tu Dios te ayude a construir su templo, tal como te lo ha prometido. 12Que te dé prudencia y sabiduría para que, cuando estés al frente de Israel, obedezcas su *ley. Él es el SEÑOR tu Dios. 13Si cumples las leyes y normas que el SEÑOR entregó a Israel por medio de Moisés, entonces te irá bien. ¡Sé fuerte y valiente! ¡No tengas miedo ni te desanimes!

14»Mira, con mucho esfuerzo he logrado conseguir para el templo del SEÑOR tres mil trescientas toneladas de oro, treinta y tres mil toneladas de platan y una incontable cantidad de bronce y de hierro. Además, he conseguido madera y piedra, pero tú debes adquirir más. 15También cuentas con una buena cantidad de obreros: canteros, albañiles, carpinteros, y expertos en toda clase de trabajos 16en oro, plata, bronce y hierro. Así que, ¡pon manos a la obra, y que el SEÑOR te acompañe!»

17Después David les ordenó a todos los jefes de Israel que colaboraran con su hijo Salomón. 18Les dijo: «El SEÑOR su Dios está con ustedes, y les ha

---

l 21:25 seiscientas monedas. Lit. seiscientos *siclos.   m 22:9 En hebreo, Salomón suena como la palabra que significa paz.   n 22:14 tres mil trescientas ... plata. Lit. cien mil *talentos de oro, un millón de talentos de plata.

dado paz en todo lugar. Él ha entregado en mi poder a los habitantes de la región, y éstos han quedado sometidos al SEÑOR y a su pueblo. 19Ahora, pues, busquen al SEÑOR su Dios de todo *corazón y con toda el *alma. Comiencen la construcción del santuario de Dios el SEÑOR, para que trasladen el arca del *pacto y los utensilios sagrados al templo que se construirá en su honor.»

Los levitas

23 David era muy anciano cuando declaró a su hijo Salomón rey de Israel. 2Reunió a todos los jefes de Israel, y a los sacerdotes y levitas. 3Entonces contaron a los levitas que tenían más de treinta años, y resultó que eran en total treinta y ocho mil hombres. 4De éstos, veinticuatro mil estaban a cargo del trabajo del templo del SEÑOR, seis mil eran oficiales y jueces, 5cuatro mil eran porteros, y los otros cuatro mil estaban encargados de alabar al SEÑOR con los instrumentos musicales que David había ordenado hacer[n] para ese propósito.

6David dividió a los levitas en grupos de acuerdo con el número de los hijos de Leví, que fueron Guersón, Coat y Merari.

Los guersonitas

7 De los guersonitas: Ladán y Simí.

8 Los hijos de Ladán fueron tres: Jehiel, el mayor, Zetán y Joel.

9 Simí también tuvo tres hijos: Selomit, Jaziel y Jarán. Éstos fueron los jefes de las familias patriarcales de Ladán.

10Los hijos de Simí fueron cuatro: Yajat, Ziza,[o] Jeús y Bería. Éstos fueron los hijos de Simí. 11Yajat era el mayor y Ziza, el segundo. Como Jeús y Bería no tuvieron muchos hijos, se les contó como una sola familia y se les dio un mismo cargo.

Los coatitas

12Los hijos de Coat fueron cuatro: Amirán, Izar, Hebrón y Uziel. 13Los hijos de Amirán fueron Aarón y Moisés. Aarón y sus descendientes fueron los escogidos para presentar las ofrendas *santas, quemar el incienso, servir al SEÑOR y pronunciar la bendición en su *nombre. 14A Moisés, hombre de Dios, y a sus hijos se les incluyó en la tribu de Leví.

15Los hijos de Moisés fueron Guersón y Eliezer. 16Sebuel fue el primero de los descendientes de Guersón.

17Eliezer no tuvo sino un solo hijo, que fue Rejabías, pero éste sí tuvo muchos hijos.

18El primer hijo de Izar fue Selomit.

19El primer hijo de Hebrón fue Jerías; el segundo, Amarías; el tercero, Jahaziel, y el cuarto, Jecamán.

20El primer hijo de Uziel fue Micaías, y el segundo, Isías.

Los meraritas

21Los hijos de Merari fueron Majlí y Musí. Los hijos de Majlí fueron Eleazar y Quis. 22Eleazar murió sin tener hijos: solamente tuvo hijas. Éstas se casaron con sus primos, los hijos de Quis. 23Musí tuvo tres hijos: Majlí, Edar y Jeremot.

24Éstos fueron los descendientes de Leví por sus familias patriarcales. El censo los registró por nombre como jefes de sus familias patriarcales. Éstos prestaban servicio en el templo del SEÑOR, y eran mayores de veinte años.

25David dijo: «Desde que el SEÑOR, Dios de Israel, estableció a su pueblo y estableció su residencia para siempre en Jerusalén, 26los levitas ya no tienen que cargar el santuario ni los utensilios que se usan en el culto.»

27De acuerdo con las últimas disposiciones de David, fueron censados los levitas mayores de veinte años, 28y su función consistía en ayudar a los descendientes de Aarón en el servicio del templo del SEÑOR. Eran los responsables de los atrios, de los cuartos y de la *purificación de todas las cosas *santas; en fin, de todo lo relacionado con el servicio del templo de Dios. 29También estaban encargados del *pan de la Presencia, de la harina para las ofrendas de cereales, de las hojuelas sin levadura, de las ofrendas fritas en sartén o cocidas, y de todas las medidas de capacidad y de longitud. 30Cada mañana y cada tarde debían estar presentes para agradecer y alabar al SEÑOR. 31Así mismo, debían ofrecer todos los *holocaustos que se presentaban al SEÑOR los *sábados y los días de luna nueva, y durante las otras fiestas. Así que siempre servían al SEÑOR, según el número y la función que se les asignaba. 32De modo que tenían a su cargo el cuidado de la *Tienda de reunión y del santuario. El servicio que realizaban en el templo del SEÑOR quedaba bajo las órdenes de sus hermanos, los descendientes de Aarón.

Organización del servicio sacerdotal

24 Los descendientes de Aarón se organizaron de la siguiente manera:

Los hijos de Aarón fueron Nadab, Abiú, Eleazar e Itamar. 2Nadab y Abiú murieron antes que su padre, y no tuvieron hijos, así que Eleazar e Itamar ejercieron el sacerdocio.

3Con la ayuda de Sadoc, descendiente de Eleazar, y de Ajimélec, descendiente de Itamar, David organizó a los sacerdotes por turnos para el desempeño de sus funciones. 4Como había más jefes entre los descendientes de Eleazar que entre los de Itamar, los organizaron así: dieciséis jefes de las familias patriarcales de los descendientes de Eleazar, y ocho jefes de los descendientes de Itamar. 5La distribución se hizo por sorteo, pues tanto los descendientes de Eleazar como los de Itamar tenían oficiales del santuario y oficiales de Dios. 6El cronista Semaías hijo de Natanael, que era levita, registró sus nombres en presencia del rey y de los oficiales, del sacerdote Sadoc, de Ajimélec hijo de Abiatar, de los jefes de las familias patriarcales de los sacerdotes y de los levitas. La suerte se echó dos veces por la familia de Eleazar y una vez por la familia de Itamar.

7 La primera suerte le tocó a Joyarib; la segunda, a Jedaías;

8 la tercera, a Jarín; la cuarta, a Seorín;

9 la quinta, a Malquías; la sexta, a Mijamín;

10la séptima, a Cos; la octava, a Abías;

11la novena, a Jesúa; la décima, a Secanías;

12la undécima, a Eliasib; la duodécima, a Yaquín;

13la decimotercera, a Hupá;

ñ 23:5 *que David había ordenado hacer*. Lit. *que yo hice*.   o 23:10 *Ziza* (un ms. hebreo, LXX y Vulgata; véase v. 11); *Ziná* (TM).

la decimocuarta, a Jesebab;
14 la decimoquinta, a Bilgá;
la decimosexta, a Imer;
15 la decimoséptima, a Hezir;
la decimoctava, a Afsés;
16 la decimonovena, a Petaías;
la vigésima, a Ezequiel;
17 la vigesimoprimera, a Jaquín;
la vigesimosegunda, a Gamul;
18 la vigesimotercera, a Delaías;
la vigesimocuarta, a Maazías.

19 Así fue como se organizaron los turnos para el servicio en el templo del SEÑOR, tal como el SEÑOR, Dios de Israel, lo había ordenado por medio de Aarón, antepasado de ellos.

El resto de los levitas

20 La siguiente es la lista del resto de los descendientes de Leví:
de los descendientes de Amirán, Subael;
de los descendientes de Subael, Jehedías;
21 de los descendientes de Rejabías, Isías, el hijo mayor;
22 de los descendientes de Izar, Selomot;
de los descendientes de Selomot, Yajat.
23 De los hijos de Hebrón: el primero,ᴾ Jerías; el segundo, Amarías; el tercero, Jahaziel, y el cuarto, Jecamán.
24 De los descendientes de Uziel, Micaías;
de los descendientes de Micaías, Samir;
25 Isías, hermano de Micaías;
de los descendientes de Isías, Zacarías;
26 de los descendientes de Merari, Majlí y Musí;
Benó, hijo de Jazías.
27 De entre los descendientes de Merari:
de Jazías: Benó, Soján, Zacur e Ibrí;
28 de Majlí: Eleazar, quien no tuvo hijos;
29 de Quis: su hijo Jeramel;
30 y los hijos de Musí: Majlí, Edar y Jeremot.

Éstos eran los hijos de los levitas por sus familias patriarcales. **31** Al igual que a sus hermanos los descendientes de Aarón, también a ellos les repartieron por sorteo en presencia del rey David y de Sadoc, de Ajimélec y de los jefes de las familias patriarcales de los sacerdotes y de los levitas. A las familias de los hermanos mayores las trataron de la misma manera que a las de los hermanos menores.

Organización de los músicos

25 Para el ministerio de la música, David y los comandantes del ejército apartaron a los hijos de Asaf, Hemán y Jedutún, los cuales profetizaban acompañándose de arpas, liras y címbalos. Ésta es la lista de los que fueron apartados para el servicio:

2 De los hijos de Asaf: Zacur, José, Netanías y Asarela. A éstos los dirigía Asaf, quien profetizaba bajo las órdenes del rey.
3 De Jedutún, sus seis hijos: Guedalías, Zeri, Isaías, Simí,�q Jasabías y Matatías. A éstos los dirigía su padre Jedutún, quien al son del arpa profetizaba para dar gracias y alabar al SEÑOR.
4 De los hijos de Hemán: Buquías, Matanías, Uziel, Sebuel, Jeremot, Jananías, Jananí, Eliatá, Guidalti, Romanti Ezer, Josbecasa, Malotí, Hotir y Mahaziot. **5** Todos éstos fueron hijos de Hemán, vidente del rey, y con la palabra de Dios

exaltaban su poder.ʳ Dios le dio a Hemán catorce hijos y tres hijas.

6 Su padre los dirigía en el culto del templo del SEÑOR, cuando cantaban acompañados de címbalos, liras y arpas. Asaf, Jedutún y Hemán estaban bajo las órdenes del rey. **7** Ellos eran en total doscientos ochenta y ocho, incluyendo a sus demás compañeros, y habían sido instruidos para cantarle al SEÑOR.

8 Para asignarles sus turnos se echaron suertes, sin hacer distinción entre menores y mayores, ni entre maestros y discípulos.

9 La primera suerte le tocó a José el asafita;
la segunda le tocó a Guedalías, junto con sus hermanos y sus hijos, doce en total.
10 La tercera, a Zacur, junto con sus hijos y hermanos, doce en total.
11 La cuarta, a Izri, junto con sus hijos y hermanos, doce en total.
12 La quinta, a Netanías, junto con sus hijos y hermanos, doce en total.
13 La sexta, a Buquías, junto con sus hijos y hermanos, doce en total.
14 La séptima, a Jesarela, junto con sus hijos y hermanos, doce en total.
15 La octava, a Isaías, junto con sus hijos y hermanos, doce en total.
16 La novena, a Matanías, junto con sus hijos y hermanos, doce en total.
17 La décima, a Simí, junto con sus hijos y hermanos, doce en total.
18 La undécima, a Azarel, junto con sus hijos y hermanos, doce en total.
19 La duodécima, a Jasabías, junto con sus hijos y hermanos, doce en total.
20 La decimotercera, a Subael, junto con sus hijos y hermanos, doce en total.
21 La decimocuarta, a Matatías, junto con sus hijos y hermanos, doce en total.
22 La decimoquinta, a Jeremot, junto con sus hijos y hermanos, doce en total.
23 La decimosexta, a Jananías, junto con sus hijos y hermanos, doce en total.
24 La decimoséptima, a Josbecasa, junto con sus hijos y hermanos, doce en total.
25 La decimoctava, a Jananí, junto con sus hijos y hermanos, doce en total.
26 La decimonovena, a Malotí, junto con sus hijos y hermanos, doce en total.
27 La vigésima, a Eliatá, junto con sus hijos y hermanos, doce en total.
28 La vigesimoprimera, a Hotir, junto con sus hijos y hermanos, doce en total.
29 La vigesimosegunda, a Guidalti, junto con sus hijos y hermanos, doce en total.
30 La vigesimotercera, a Mahaziot, junto con sus hijos y hermanos, doce en total.
31 La vigesimocuarta, a Romanti Ezer, junto con sus hijos y hermanos, doce en total.

Organización de los porteros

26 La organización de los porteros fue la siguiente:

De los coreítas: Meselemías hijo de Coré, descendiente de Asaf.
2 Los hijos de Meselemías fueron:
Zacarías, el primero;

---

p **24:23** *Hebrón: el primero* (2 mss. hebreos; véanse mss. de LXX y 1Cr 23:19); TM no incluye esta frase.

q **25:3** *Simí* (un ms. hebreo y mss. de LXX); TM no incluye este nombre. r **25:5** *su poder.* Lit. *el cuerno.*

Jediael, el segundo;
Zebadías, el tercero;
Jatniel, el cuarto;
3 Elam, el quinto;
Johanán, el sexto,
y Elihoenay, el séptimo.
4 Los hijos de Obed Edom fueron:
Semaías, el primero;
Jozabad, el segundo;
Joa, el tercero;
Sacar, el cuarto;
Natanael, el quinto;
5 Amiel, el sexto;
Isacar, el séptimo,
y el octavo, Peultay.
Dios bendijo a Obed Edom con muchos hijos.

6 Semaías hijo de Obed Edom también tuvo hijos, los cuales fueron jefes de sus familias patriarcales, pues eran hombres muy valientes. 7Los hijos de Semaías fueron Otni, Rafael, Obed, Elzabad, y sus hermanos Eliú y Samaquías, todos ellos hombres valientes. 8Todos éstos eran descendientes de Obed Edom. Tanto ellos como sus hijos y hermanos eran hombres muy valientes y fuertes para el trabajo. En total, los descendientes de Obed Edom fueron sesenta y dos.

9 Los hijos y hermanos de Meselemías fueron dieciocho, todos ellos hombres muy valientes.

10 Los hijos de Josá, descendiente de Merari, fueron Simri, el jefe (que en verdad no había sido el primero, pero su padre lo puso por jefe); 11el segundo fue Jilquías; el tercero, Tebalías; y el cuarto, Zacarías. En total, los hijos y hermanos de Josá fueron trece.

12Así fue como se organizó a los porteros, tanto a los jefes como a sus hermanos, para que sirvieran en el templo del SEÑOR. 13El cuidado de cada puerta se asignó echando suertes entre las familias, sin hacer distinción entre menores y mayores.

14Según el sorteo, a Selemías se le asignó la puerta del este, y a su hijo Zacarías, sabio consejero, la puerta del norte. 15A Obed Edom le correspondió la puerta del sur, y a sus hijos les correspondió el cuidado de los depósitos del templo. 16A Supín y a Josá les correspondió la puerta de Saléquet, que está al oeste, en el camino de la subida.

Los turnos se distribuyeron así: 17Cada día había seis levitas en el este, cuatro en el norte y cuatro en el sur, y dos en cada uno de los depósitos. 18En el patio del oeste había cuatro levitas para la calzada y dos para el patio mismo.

19Así fue como quedaron distribuidos los porteros descendientes de Coré y de Merari.

Los tesoreros y otros oficiales

20A los otros levitas se les puso al cuidado de los tesoros del templo y de los depósitos de los objetos sagrados. 21Los descendientes de Guersón por parte de Ladán tenían a los jehielitas como jefes de las familias de Ladán el guersonita. 22Zetán y su hermano Joel, hijos de Jehiel, quedaron a cargo de los tesoros del templo del SEÑOR.

23-24Sebuel, que era descendiente de Guersón hijo de Moisés, era el tesorero mayor de los amiranitas, izaritas, hebronitas y uzielitas.

25 Sus descendientes en línea directa por parte de Eliezer eran Rejabías, Isaías, Jorán, Zicrí y Selomit. 26Selomit y sus hermanos tenían a su cargo los depósitos de todos los objetos sagrados que habían sido obsequiados por

el rey David y por los jefes de familia, así como por los comandantes de mil y de cien soldados y por los demás oficiales del ejército. 27Ellos habían dedicado parte del botín de guerra para las reparaciones del templo del SEÑOR. 28Selomit y sus hermanos tenían bajo su cuidado todo lo que había sido obsequiado por el vidente Samuel, por Saúl hijo de Quis, y por Abner hijo de Ner y Joab hijo de Sarvia.

29Quenanías y sus hijos, que eran descendientes de Izar, estaban a cargo de los asuntos exteriores de Israel, y ejercían las funciones de oficiales y jueces.

30Jasabías y sus parientes, que descendían de Hebrón, eran mil setecientos hombres valientes. Ellos eran los que al sudoeste del Jordán administraban a Israel en todo lo referente al SEÑOR y al rey. 31El jefe de los hebronitas era Jerías. En el año cuarenta del reinado de David se investigó el registro genealógico de los descendientes de Hebrón, y se encontró que en Jazer de Galaad había entre ellos hombres valientes. 32El número de los jefes de familia de estos valientes era de dos mil setecientos. El rey David les asignó la administración de las tribus de Rubén y Gad y de la media tribu de Manasés, en todos los asuntos relacionados con Dios y con el rey.

Divisiones del ejército

27 La siguiente lista corresponde a los jefes patriarcales, a los comandantes de mil y de cien soldados, y a los oficiales de las divisiones militares de Israel. Cada división constaba de veinticuatro mil hombres, y se turnaban cada mes, durante todo el año, para prestar servicio al rey.

2 Al frente de la primera división de veinticuatro mil hombres, la cual prestaba su servicio en el primer mes, estaba Yasobeán hijo de Zabdiel, 3descendiente de Fares. Él era el jefe de todos los oficiales del ejército que hacían su turno el primer mes.

4 Al frente de la segunda división de veinticuatro mil, que prestaba su servicio en el segundo mes, estaba Doday el ajoíta. El jefe de esa división era Miclot.

5 La tercera división de veinticuatro mil, asignada para el tercer mes, tenía como jefe a Benaías, hijo del sumo sacerdote Joyadá. 6Este Benaías fue uno de los treinta valientes, y el jefe de ellos. En esa división estaba su hijo Amisabad.

7 La cuarta división de veinticuatro mil, asignada para el cuarto mes, tenía como jefe a Asael, hermano de Joab. Su sucesor fue su hijo Zebadías.

8 La quinta división de veinticuatro mil, asignada para el quinto mes, tenía como jefe a Samut el izraíta.

9 La sexta división de veinticuatro mil, asignada para el sexto mes, tenía como jefe a Irá hijo de Iqués el tecoíta.

10 La séptima división de veinticuatro mil, asignada para el séptimo mes, tenía como jefe a Heles el pelonita, de los descendientes de Efraín.

11 La octava división de veinticuatro mil, asignada para el octavo mes, tenía como jefe a Sibecay de Jusá, descendiente de los zeraítas.

12 La novena división de veinticuatro mil, asignada para el noveno mes, tenía como jefe a Abiezer de Anatot, descendiente de Benjamín.

13 La décima división de veinticuatro mil, asignada para el décimo mes, tenía como jefe a Maray de Netofa, descendiente de los zeraítas.

14 La undécima división de veinticuatro mil, asignada para el undécimo mes, tenía como jefe a Benaías de Piratón, descendiente de Efraín.

15 La duodécima división de veinticuatro mil, asignada para el duodécimo mes, tenía como jefe a Jelday de Netofa, descendiente de Otoniel.

Jefes de las tribus

16 Los siguientes fueron los jefes de las tribus de Israel:

de Rubén: Eliezer hijo de Zicrí;
de Simeón: Sefatías hijo de Macá;
17 de Leví: Jasabías hijo de Quemuel;
de Aarón: Sadoc;
18 de Judá: Eliú, hermano de David;
de Isacar: Omrí hijo de Micael;
19 de Zabulón: Ismaías hijo de Abdías;
de Neftalí: Jerimot hijo de Azriel;
20 de Efraín: Oseas hijo de Azazías;
de la media tribu de Manasés: Joel hijo de Pedaías;
21 de la otra media tribu de Manasés que estaba en Galaad: Idó hijo de Zacarías;
de Benjamín: Jasiel hijo de Abner;
22 de Dan: Azarel hijo de Jeroán.

Éstos eran los jefes de las tribus de Israel.

23 David no censó a los hombres que tenían menos de veinte años porque el SEÑOR había prometido que haría a Israel tan numeroso como las estrellas del cielo. 24 Joab hijo de Sarvia comenzó a hacer el censo, pero no lo terminó porque eso desató la ira de Dios sobre Israel. Por eso no quedó registrado el número en las crónicas del rey David.

Superintendentes del rey

25 El encargado de los tesoros del rey era Azmávet hijo de Adiel.

El encargado de los tesoros de los campos, y de ciudades, aldeas y fortalezas, era Jonatán hijo de Uzías.

26 Ezrí hijo de Quelub estaba al frente de los agricultores.

27 Simí de Ramat estaba a cargo de los viñedos. Zabdí de Sefán era el encargado de almacenar el vino en las bodegas.

28 Baal Janán de Guéder estaba a cargo de los olivares y de los bosques de sicómoros de la Sefelá.

Joás tenía a su cargo los depósitos de aceite.

29 Sitray de Sarón estaba a cargo del ganado que pastaba en Sarón.

Safat hijo de Adlay estaba a cargo del ganado de los valles.

30 Obil el ismaelita era el encargado de los camellos.

Jehedías de Meronot era el encargado de las burras.

31 Jaziz el agareno era el encargado de las ovejas.

Todos éstos eran los que administraban los bienes del rey.

32 Jonatán, tío de David, escriba inteligente, era consejero del rey. Jehiel hijo de Jacmoní cuidaba a los príncipes.

33 Ajitofel era otro consejero del rey. Husay el arquita era hombre de confianza del rey. 34 A Ajitofel lo sucedieron Joyadá hijo de Benaías, y Abiatar.

Joab era el jefe del ejército real.

Instrucciones para la construcción del templo

28 David reunió en Jerusalén a todos los jefes de Israel, es decir, a los jefes de las tribus, los jefes de las divisiones que por turno servían al rey, los jefes de mil y de cien soldados, los administradores de los bienes, del ganado y de los príncipes, los *eunucos del palacio, los guerreros, y todos los valientes.

2 Puesto de pie, el rey David dijo: «Hermanos de mi pueblo, escúchenme. Yo tenía el propósito de construir un templo para que en él reposara el arca del *pacto del SEÑOR nuestro Dios y sirviera como estrado de sus pies. Ya tenía todo listo para construirlo 3 cuando Dios me dijo: "Tú no me construirás ningún templo, porque eres hombre de guerra y has derramado sangre."

4 »Sin embargo, el SEÑOR, Dios de Israel, me escogió de entre mi familia para ponerme por rey de Israel para siempre. En efecto, él escogió a Judá como la tribu gobernante; de esta tribu escogió a mi familia, y de entre mis hermanos me escogió a mí, para ponerme por rey de Israel. 5 De entre los muchos hijos que el SEÑOR me ha dado, escogió a mi hijo Salomón para que se sentara en el trono real del SEÑOR y gobernara a Israel. 6 Dios me dijo: "Será tu hijo Salomón el que construya mi templo y mis atrios, pues lo he escogido como hijo, y seré para él como un padre. 7 Y si persevera en cumplir mis *leyes y mis normas, como lo hace hoy, entonces afirmaré su reino para siempre."

8 »En presencia de Dios que nos escucha, y de todo Israel, que es la congregación del SEÑOR, hoy les encarezco que obedezcan cumplidamente todos los mandamientos del SEÑOR su Dios. Así poseerán esta hermosa tierra y la dejarán en herencia perpetua a sus hijos.

9 »Y tú, Salomón, hijo mío, reconoce al Dios de tu padre, y sírvele de todo *corazón y con buena disposición, pues el SEÑOR escudriña todo corazón y discierne todo pensamiento. Si lo buscas, se permitirá que lo encuentres; si lo abandonas, te rechazará para siempre. 10 Ten presente que el SEÑOR te ha escogido para que le edifiques un templo como santuario suyo. Así que ¡anímate y pon manos a la obra!»

11 Luego David le entregó a Salomón el diseño del pórtico del templo, de sus edificios, de los almacenes, de las habitaciones superiores, de los cuartos interiores y del lugar del *propiciatorio. 12 También le entregó el diseño de todo lo que había planeado para los atrios del templo del SEÑOR, para los cuartos de alrededor, para los tesoros del templo de Dios y para los depósitos de las ofrendas sagradas. 13 Asimismo, le dio instrucciones en cuanto a la labor de los sacerdotes y levitas, y de todos los servicios del templo del SEÑOR y de todos los utensilios sagrados que se usarían en el servicio del templo. 14 Además, le entregó abundante oro y plata para todos los utensilios de oro y de plata que se debían usar en cada uno de los servicios en el templo. 15 También le pesó el oro y la plata para cada uno de los candelabros y sus lámparas, tanto los de oro como los de plata, según el uso de cada candelabro. 16 De igual manera, le pesó el oro y la plata para cada una de las mesas de los panes de la proposición, tanto las de oro como las de plata. 17 Le hizo entrega del oro puro para los tenedores, los tazones y las jarras. Le pesó oro y plata suficiente para cada una de las copas de oro y de plata. 18 Para el altar del incienso le entregó una cantidad suficiente

de oro refinado. También le dio el diseño de la carroza y de los *querubines que cubren con sus alas extendidas el arca del pacto del SEÑOR.

19«Todo esto —dijo David— ha sido escrito por revelación del SEÑOR, para darme a conocer el diseño de las obras.»

20Además, David le dijo a su hijo Salomón: «Sé fuerte y valiente, y pon manos a la obra! No tengas miedo ni te desanimes, porque Dios el SEÑOR, mi Dios, estará contigo. No te dejará ni te abandonará hasta que hayas terminado toda la obra del templo. 21Aquí tienes la organización de los sacerdotes y de los levitas para el servicio del templo de Dios. Además, contarás con la ayuda voluntaria de expertos en toda clase de trabajos. Los jefes y todo el pueblo estarán a tu disposición.»

Ofrendas para el templo

29 El rey David le dijo a toda la asamblea: «Dios ha escogido a mi hijo Salomón, pero para una obra de esta magnitud todavía le falta experiencia. El palacio no es para un *hombre sino para Dios el SEÑOR. 2Con mucho esfuerzo he hecho los preparativos para el templo de Dios. He conseguido oro para los objetos de oro, plata para los de plata, bronce para los de bronce, hierro para los de hierro, madera para los de madera, y piedras de ónice, piedras de engaste, piedras talladas de diversos colores, piedras preciosas de toda clase, y mármol en abundancia. 3Además, aparte de lo que ya he conseguido, por amor al templo de mi Dios entrego para su templo todo el oro y la plata que poseo: 4cien mil kilos de oro de Ofir y doscientos treinta mil kilos de plataˢ fínisima, para recubrir las paredes de los edificios, 5para todos los objetos de oro y de plata, y para toda clase de trabajo que hagan los orfebres. ¿Quién de ustedes quiere hoy dar una ofrenda al SEÑOR?»

6Entonces los jefes de familia, los jefes de las tribus de Israel, los jefes de mil y de cien soldados, y los encargados de las obras del rey hicieron sus ofrendas voluntarias. 7Donaron para las obras del templo de Dios ciento sesenta y cinco mil kilos y diez mil monedas de oro, trescientos treinta mil kilos de plata, y alrededor de seiscientos mil kilos de bronce y tres millones trescientos mil kilos de hierro.ᵗ 8Los que tenían piedras preciosas las entregaron a Jehiel el guersonita para el tesoro del templo del SEÑOR. 9El pueblo estaba muy contento de poder dar voluntariamente sus ofrendas al SEÑOR, y también el rey David se sentía muy feliz.

Oración de David

10Entonces David bendijo así al SEÑOR en presencia de toda la asamblea:

«¡Bendito seas, SEÑOR,
    Dios de nuestro padre Israel,
    desde siempre y para siempre!
11Tuyos son, SEÑOR,
    la grandeza y el poder,
    la gloria, la *victoria y la majestad.
Tuyo es todo cuanto hay
    en el cielo y en la tierra.
Tuyo también es el reino,
    y tú estás por encima de todo.
12De ti proceden la riqueza y el honor;
    tú lo gobiernas todo.
En tus manos están la fuerza y el poder,

y eres tú quien engrandece y fortalece a
    todos.
13Por eso, Dios nuestro, te damos gracias,
    y a tu glorioso *nombre tributamos
    alabanzas.

14»Pero, ¿quién soy yo, y quién es mi pueblo, para que podamos darte estas ofrendas voluntarias? En verdad, tú eres el dueño de todo, y lo que te hemos dado, de ti lo hemos recibido. 15Ante ti, somos extranjeros y peregrinos, como lo fueron nuestros antepasados. Nuestros días sobre la tierra son sólo una sombra sin esperanza. 16SEÑOR y Dios nuestro, de ti procede todo cuanto hemos conseguido para construir un templo a tu *santo nombre. ¡Todo es tuyo! 17Yo sé, mi Dios, que tú pruebas los corazones y amas la rectitud. Por eso, con rectitud de *corazón te he ofrecido voluntariamente todas estas cosas, y he visto con júbilo que tu pueblo, aquí presente, te ha traído sus ofrendas. 18SEÑOR, Dios de nuestros antepasados Abraham, Isaac e Israel, conserva por siempre estos pensamientos en el corazón de tu pueblo, y dirige su corazón hacia ti. 19Dale también a mi hijo Salomón un corazón íntegro, para que obedezca y ponga en práctica tus mandamientos, preceptos y *leyes. Permítele construir el templo para el cual he hecho esta provisión.»

20Luego David animó a toda la asamblea: «¡Alaben al SEÑOR su Dios!» Entonces toda la asamblea alabó al SEÑOR, Dios de sus antepasados, y se inclinó ante el SEÑOR y ante el rey.

Coronación de Salomón
29:21-25 — 1R 1:28-53

21Al día siguiente, ofrecieron sacrificios y *holocaustos al SEÑOR por todo Israel: mil becerros, mil carneros y mil corderos, con sus respectivas libaciones, y numerosos sacrificios. 22Ese día comieron y bebieron con gran regocijo en presencia del SEÑOR.

Luego, por segunda vez, proclamaron como rey a Salomón hijo de David, y lo consagraron ante el SEÑOR como rey, y a Sadoc lo ungieron como sacerdote. 23Y Salomón sucedió en el trono del SEÑOR a su padre David, y tuvo éxito. Todo Israel le obedeció. 24Todos los jefes, los guerreros y los hijos del rey David rindieron pleitesía al rey Salomón.

25El SEÑOR engrandeció en extremo a Salomón ante todo Israel, y le otorgó un reinado glorioso, como jamás lo tuvo ninguno de los reyes de Israel.

Muerte de David
29:26-28 — 1R 2:10-12

26David hijo de Isaí reinó sobre todo Israel. 27En total, reinó cuarenta años sobre Israel: siete años reinó en Hebrón, y treinta y tres en Jerusalén. 28Y murió muy anciano y entrado en años, en medio de grandes honores y riquezas, y su hijo Salomón lo sucedió en el trono.

29-30Todos los hechos del rey David, desde el primero hasta el último, y lo que tiene que ver con su reinado y su poder, y lo que les sucedió a él, a Israel y a los pueblos vecinos, están escritos en las crónicas del vidente Samuel, del profeta Natán y del vidente Gad.

ˢ 29:4 cien mil ... plata. Lit. tres mil *talentos de oro de Ofir y siete mil talentos de plata.   ᵗ 29:7 ciento sesenta ... hierro. Lit. cien mil talentos y diez mil *dracmas de oro, y diez mil talentos de plata, y dieciocho mil talentos de bronce, y cien mil talentos de hierro.

2 CRÓNICAS

Salomón pide sabiduría
1:2-13 — 1R 3:4-15
1:14-17 — 1R 10:26-29; 2Cr 9:25-28

1 Salomón hijo de David consolidó su reino, pues el SEÑOR su Dios estaba con él y lo hizo muy poderoso.

2Salomón habló con todos los israelitas, es decir, con los jefes de mil y de cien soldados, con los gobernantes y con todos los jefes de las familias patriarcales de Israel. 3Luego, él y toda la asamblea que lo acompañaba se dirigieron al santuario de Gabaón, porque allí se encontraba la *Tienda de la reunión con Dios que Moisés, siervo del SEÑOR, había hecho en el desierto. 4El arca de Dios se encontraba en Jerusalén, en la tienda que David le había preparado cuando la trasladó desde Quiriat Yearín, 5pero el altar de bronce que había hecho Bezalel, hijo de Uri y nieto de Jur, estaba en Gabaón, frente al santuario del SEÑOR. Por eso Salomón y los israelitas fueron a ese lugar para consultar al SEÑOR. 6Allí, en presencia del SEÑOR, Salomón subió al altar que estaba en la Tienda de reunión, y en él ofreció mil *holocaustos. 7Aquella noche Dios se le apareció a Salomón y le dijo: —Pídeme lo que quieras.

8Salomón respondió:

—Tú trataste con mucho amor a David mi padre, y a mí me has permitido reinar en su lugar. 9SEÑOR y Dios, cumple ahora la promesa que le hiciste a mi padre David, pues tú me has hecho rey de un pueblo tan numeroso como el polvo de la tierra. 10Yo te pido sabiduría y conocimiento para gobernar a este gran pueblo tuyo; de lo contrario, ¿quién podrá gobernarlo?

11Entonces Dios le dijo a Salomón:

—Ya que has pedido sabiduría y conocimiento para gobernar a mi pueblo, sobre el cual te he hecho rey, y no has pedido riquezas ni bienes ni esplendor, y ni siquiera la muerte de tus enemigos o una vida muy larga, 12te los otorgo. Pero además voy a darte riquezas, bienes y esplendor, como nunca los tuvieron los reyes que te precedieron ni los tendrán los que habrán de sucederte.

13Después de esto, Salomón bajó de la Tienda de reunión, que estaba en el santuario de Gabaón, y regresó a Jerusalén, desde donde reinó sobre Israel.

14Salomón multiplicó el número de sus caballos y de sus carros de combate; llegó a tener mil cuatrocientos carros y doce mil caballos, los cuales mantenía en las caballerizas y en su palacio de Jerusalén. 15El rey hizo que la plata y el oro fueran en Jerusalén tan comunes como las piedras, y que el cedro abundara como las higueras en la llanura. 16Los caballos de Salomón eran importados de Egipto y de Cilicia, donde los compraban los mercaderes de la corte. 17Un carro importado de Egipto costaba seiscientas monedas de plataa; un caballo, ciento cincuenta. Además, estos carros y caballos se los vendían a todos los reyes hititas y *sirios.

Preparativos para la construcción del templo
2:1-18 — 1R 5:1-16

2 Salomón decidió construir su palacio real y un templo en honor del SEÑOR. 2Con este fin reclutó a setenta mil cargadores y ochenta mil canteros, para que trabajaran en la montaña. Al frente de ellos puso a tres mil seiscientos capataces. 3Luego le envió este mensaje a Hiram, rey de Tiro:

«Envíame madera de cedro, tal como lo hiciste con mi padre David cuando se la enviaste para que se construyera un palacio. 4Voy a construir un templo en honor del SEÑOR mi Dios. Lo consagraré a él, para quemar incienso aromático en su presencia, colocar siempre el pan consagrado, y ofrecer allí los *holocaustos de la mañana y de la tarde, los sacrificios de los *sábados y de luna nueva, así como los de las otras fiestas del SEÑOR nuestro Dios. Esto se hará en Israel siempre.

5»Voy a edificar un templo majestuoso, pues nuestro Dios es el más grande de todos los dioses. 6Pero, ¿cómo edificarle un templo, si ni los cielos más altos pueden contenerlo? ¿Y quién soy yo para construirle un templo, aunque sólo sea para quemar incienso para él?

7»Envíame un experto para trabajar el oro y la plata, el bronce y el hierro, el carmesí, la escarlata y la púrpura, y que sepa hacer grabados, para que trabaje junto con los expertos que yo tengo en Judá y en Jerusalén, los cuales contrató mi padre David.

8»Envíame también del Líbano madera de cedro, de ciprés y de sándalo, pues yo sé que tus obreros son expertos en cortar estos árboles. Mis obreros trabajarán con los tuyos 9para prepararme mucha madera, porque el templo que voy a edificar será grande y maravilloso. 10A tus siervos que corten la madera les daré veinte mil cargas de trigo, veinte mil cargas de cebada, veinte mil medidas de vino, y veinte mil medidasb de aceite.»

11En respuesta, Hiram, rey de Tiro, le envió a Salomón la siguiente carta:

«El SEÑOR te ha hecho rey de su pueblo, porque te ama. 12¡Alabado sea el SEÑOR, Dios de Israel, que hizo el cielo y la tierra, porque le ha dado al rey David un hijo sabio, dotado de sabiduría e inteligencia, el cual construirá un palacio real y un templo para el SEÑOR!

13»Te envío, pues, a Hiram Abí, hombre sabio e inteligente, 14hijo de una mujer oriunda de Dan y de un nativo de Tiro. Sabe trabajar el oro y la plata, el bronce y el hierro, la piedra y la madera, el carmesí y la púrpura, el lino y la escarlata; también es experto en hacer toda clase de figuras y en realizar cualquier diseño que se le encargue. Hiram trabajará junto con tus expertos y con los de David, tu padre y mi señor.

15»Envíanos ahora el trigo, la cebada, el aceite y el vino que tan bondadosamente me has prometido. 16Nosotros cortaremos del Líbano la madera que necesites, y te la llevaremos

---

por mar hasta Jope, en forma de balsas. De allí tú la llevarás a Jerusalén.»

17Salomón hizo un censo de todos los extranjeros que vivían en Israel. Este censo, que fue posterior al que había hecho su padre David, arrojó la cifra de ciento cincuenta y tres mil seiscientos. 18A setenta mil de ellos los puso como cargadores; a ochenta mil, como canteros en las montañas; y a tres mil seiscientos, como capataces para dirigir a los trabajadores.

Construcción del templo
3:1-14 — 1R 6:1-29

3 Salomón comenzó a construir el templo del SEÑOR en el monte Moria, en Jerusalén, donde el SEÑOR se le había aparecido a su padre David. Lo construyó en el lugar que David había destinado, esto es, en la parcela de Arauna,c el jebuseo. 2La construcción la comenzó el día dos del mes segundo del cuarto año de su reinado.

3Salomón determinó que los cimientos del templo de Dios fueran de veintisiete metros de largo por nueve metros de ancho.d 4El vestíbulo de la nave medía lo mismo que el ancho del templo, es decir, también medía nueve metros de largo, y nueve metros de alto. Por dentro, Salomón lo recubrió de oro puro. 5Recubrió la nave central con paneles de madera de ciprés, sobre los cuales colocó figuras de palmeras y cadenas de oro fino. 6El templo lo adornó con piedras preciosas y con oro de Parvayin. 7En el interior del templo recubrió de oro las vigas, los umbrales, las paredes y las puertas, y en las paredes esculpió *querubines.

8Salomón hizo también el Lugar Santísimo, el cual medía lo mismo que el ancho del templo, es decir, nueve metros de largo y nueve metros de ancho. Lo recubrió por dentro con veintitrés toneladase de oro fino. 9Cada clavo de oro pesaba medio kilo.f También recubrió de oro las habitaciones superiores.

10En el Lugar Santísimo mandó tallar dos querubines, y los recubrió de oro. 11Las alas de los querubines medían nueve metros de largo. Cada una de las alas del primer querubín medía dos metros con veinticinco centímetros; una de ellas tocaba la pared interior de la habitación, y la otra rozaba el ala del segundo querubín. 12Cada una de las alas del segundo querubín también medía dos metros con veinticinco centímetros; una de ellas tocaba la pared interior de la habitación, y la otra rozaba el ala del primer querubín. 13Los querubines estaban de pie, con el rostro hacia la nave, y sus alas extendidas medían en total nueve metros.

14La cortina la hizo de púrpura, carmesí, escarlata y lino, y sobre ella mandó bordar querubines.

15En la fachada del templo levantó dos columnas de dieciséis metros de altura, y el capitel que coronaba cada columna medía más de dos metros; 16además, mandó hacer unas cadenas trenzadasg y las colocó en lo alto de las columnas; hizo también cien granadas, y las intercaló entre las cadenas. 17Levantó las columnas en la fachada del templo, una en el lado sur y otra en el lado norte. A la primera la nombró Jaquín, y a la segunda, Boaz.

Mobiliario del templo
4:2-6,10—5:1 — 1R 7:23-26,38-51

4 Salomón hizo un altar de bronce que medía nueve metros de largo por nueve de ancho y cuatro metros y medio de alto. 2Hizo también una fuenteh circular de metal fundido, que medía cuatro metros y medio de diámetro y dos metros con veinticinco centímetros de alto. Su circunferencia, medida a cordel, era de trece metros y medio. 3Bajo el borde hizo dos hileras de figuras de bueyes, diez por cada medio metro, las cuales estaban fundidas en una sola pieza con la fuente. 4La fuente descansaba sobre doce bueyes, que tenían sus cuartos traseros hacia adentro. Tres bueyes miraban al norte, tres al oeste, tres al sur y tres al este. 5El grosor de la fuente era de ocho centímetros, y su borde, en forma de copa, se asemejaba a un capullo de azucena. Tenía una capacidad de sesenta y seis mil litros.i

6Salomón hizo también diez lavamanos, y puso cinco en el lado sur y cinco en el lado norte. En ellos se lavaba todo el material de los *holocaustos, mientras que en la fuente se lavaban los sacerdotes.

7Hizo además diez candelabros de oro, según el modelo prescrito, y los colocó en el templo, cinco en el lado sur y cinco en el lado norte.

8Salomón hizo diez mesas y las colocó en el templo, cinco en el lado sur y cinco en el lado norte. También hizo cien aspersorios de oro. 9Edificó el atrio de los sacerdotes y el atrio mayor con sus puertas, las cuales recubrió de bronce. 10La fuente de metal la colocó en la esquina del lado derecho, que da al sureste. 11También hizo las ollas, las palas y los aspersorios. Así fue como Hiram terminó todo el trabajo que había emprendido para el rey Salomón en el templo de Dios, es decir:

12las dos columnas;
los dos capiteles en forma de tazón que coronaban las columnas;
las dos redes que decoraban los capiteles;
13las cuatrocientas granadas, dispuestas en dos hileras para cada red;
14las bases con sus lavamanos;
15la fuente de metal y los doce bueyes que la sostenían;
16las ollas, las tenazas y los tenedores.

Todos los utensilios que Hiram Abí le hizo al rey Salomón para el templo del SEÑOR eran de bronce pulido. 17El rey los hizo fundir en moldes de arcilla en la llanura del Jordán, entre Sucot y Saretán.j 18Eran tantos los utensilios que hizo Salomón, que no fue posible determinar el peso del bronce utilizado.

19Salomón también mandó hacer los otros utensilios que estaban en el templo de Dios, es decir:

el altar de oro;
las mesas sobre las cuales se ponía el *pan de la Presencia;
20los candelabros de oro puro con sus respectivas lámparas, para encenderlas en frente del Lugar Santísimo, tal como está prescrito;
21la obra floral, las lámparas y las tenazas, que también eran de oro puro;

---

c 3:1 *Arauna*. Lit. *Ornán* (variante de este nombre). d 3:3 En los capítulos 3 al 6, las medidas de longitud se han convertido al sistema métrico, sin explicación en las notas. e 3:8 *veintitrés toneladas*. Lit. *seiscientos *talentos*. f 3:9 *medio kilo*. Lit. *cincuenta *siclos*. g 3:16 *trenzadas*. Alt. *asociadas con el santuario*. h 4:2 *una fuente*. Lit. *el mar*; así en el resto de este pasaje. i 4:5 *sesenta y seis mil litros*. Lit. *tres mil *batos*. j 4:17 *Saretán* (véanse 1R 7:46 y Vetus Latina); *Seredata* (TM).

22 las despabiladeras, los aspersorios, la vajilla y los incensarios;

y la entrada del templo, es decir, las puertas interiores del Lugar Santísimo y las puertas de la nave central del templo, las cuales eran de oro.

5 Una vez terminada toda la obra que había mandado hacer para el templo del SEÑOR, Salomón hizo traer el oro, la plata y todos los utensilios que su padre David había consagrado, y los depositó en el tesoro del templo de Dios.

El arca del pacto
5:2—6:11 — 1R 8:1-21

2Entonces Salomón mandó que los *ancianos de Israel, y todos los jefes de las tribus y los patriarcas de las familias israelitas, se congregaran en Jerusalén para trasladar el arca del *pacto del SEÑOR desde *Sión, la Ciudad de David. 3Así que durante la fiesta del mes séptimo todos los israelitas se congregaron ante el rey. 4Cuando llegaron todos los ancianos de Israel, los levitas alzaron el arca. 5Los sacerdotes y los levitas la trasladaron junto con la *Tienda de reunión y con todos los utensilios sagrados que había en ella.

6El rey Salomón y toda la asamblea de Israel reunida delante del arca sacrificaron ovejas y bueyes en tal cantidad que fue imposible llevar la cuenta. 7Luego los sacerdotes llevaron el arca del pacto del SEÑOR a su lugar en el santuario interior del templo, que es el Lugar Santísimo, y la pusieron bajo las alas de los *querubines. 8Con sus alas extendidas sobre ese lugar, los querubines cubrían el arca y sus travesaños. 9Los travesaños eran tan largos que sus extremos se podían ver desde el arca delante del Lugar Santísimo, aunque no desde afuera; y ahí han permanecido hasta hoy. 10En el arca sólo estaban las dos tablas que Moisés había colocado en ella en Horeb, donde el SEÑOR hizo un pacto con los israelitas después de que ellos salieron de Egipto.

11Los sacerdotes se retiraron del Lugar Santo. Todos los sacerdotes allí presentes, sin distinción de clases, se habían *santificado. 12Todos los levitas cantores —es decir, Asaf, Hemán, Jedutún, sus hijos y sus parientes— estaban de pie en el lado este del altar, vestidos de lino fino y con címbalos, arpas y liras. Junto a ellos estaban ciento veinte sacerdotes que tocaban la trompeta.

13Los trompetistas y los cantores alababan y daban gracias al SEÑOR al son de trompetas, címbalos y otros instrumentos musicales. Y cuando tocaron y cantaron al unísono: «El SEÑOR es bueno; su gran amor perdura para siempre», una nube cubrió el templo del SEÑOR. 14Por causa de la nube, los sacerdotes no pudieron celebrar el culto, pues la gloria del SEÑOR había llenado el templo.

6 Entonces Salomón declaró:

«SEÑOR, tú has dicho que habitarías en la oscuridad de una nube, 2y yo te he construido un excelso templo, un lugar donde habites para siempre.»

3Luego se puso de frente para bendecir a toda la asamblea de Israel que estaba allí de pie, 4y dijo:

«Bendito sea el SEÑOR, Dios de Israel, que con su mano ha cumplido ahora lo que con su boca le había prometido a mi padre David cuando le dijo: 5"Desde el día en que saqué de la tierra de Egipto a mi pueblo, no elegí a ninguna ciudad de las tribus de Israel para que en ella se

me construyera un templo donde yo habitara, ni elegí a nadie para que gobernara a mi pueblo Israel. 6Más bien, elegí a Jerusalén para habitar en ella, y a David para que gobernara a mi pueblo Israel."

7»Pues bien, mi padre David tuvo mucho interés en construir un templo en honor del SEÑOR, Dios de Israel, 8pero el SEÑOR le dijo: "Me agrada que te hayas interesado en construir un templo en mi honor. 9Sin embargo, no serás tú quien me lo construya, sino un hijo de tus entrañas; él será quien construya el templo en mi honor."

10»Ahora el SEÑOR ha cumplido su promesa: Tal como lo prometió, he sucedido a mi padre David en el trono de Israel, y he construido el templo en honor del SEÑOR, Dios de Israel. 11Allí he colocado el arca, en la cual está el pacto que el SEÑOR hizo con los israelitas.»

Oración de Salomón
6:12-40 — 1R 8:22-53
6:41-42 — Sal 132:8-10

12A continuación, Salomón se puso ante el altar del SEÑOR y, en presencia de toda la asamblea de Israel, extendió las manos. 13Había mandado construir y colocar en medio del atrio una plataforma de bronce cuadrada, de dos metros con veinticinco centímetros por lado, y un metro con treinta y cinco centímetros de alto. Allí, sobre la plataforma, se arrodilló y, extendiendo las manos al cielo, 14oró así:

«SEÑOR, Dios de Israel, no hay Dios como tú en el cielo ni en la tierra, pues tú cumples tu *pacto de amor con quienes te sirven y te siguen de todo *corazón. 15Has llevado a cabo lo que le dijiste a tu siervo David, mi padre; y este día has cumplido con tu mano lo que con tu boca prometiste.

16»Y ahora, SEÑOR, Dios de Israel, cumple también la promesa que le hiciste a tu siervo, mi padre David, cuando le dijiste: "Si tus hijos observan una buena conducta, viviendo de acuerdo con mi *ley como tú lo has hecho, nunca te faltará un descendiente que ocupe el trono de Israel en mi presencia." 17SEÑOR, Dios de Israel, ¡confirma ahora esta promesa que le hiciste a tu siervo David!

18»Pero ¿será posible que tú, Dios mío, habites en la tierra con la *humanidad? Si los cielos, por altos que sean, no pueden contenerte, ¡mucho menos este templo que he construido! 19Sin embargo, SEÑOR mi Dios, atiende a la oración y a la súplica de este siervo tuyo. Oye el clamor y la oración que elevo en tu presencia. 20¡Que tus ojos estén abiertos día y noche sobre este templo, el lugar donde decidiste habitar, para que oigas la oración que tu siervo te eleva aquí! 21Oye las súplicas de tu siervo y de tu pueblo Israel cuando oren en este lugar. Oye desde el cielo, donde habitas; ¡escucha y perdona!

22»Si alguien peca contra su prójimo y se le exige venir a este templo para jurar delante de tu altar, 23óyelo tú desde el cielo y juzga a tus siervos. Condena al culpable, y haz que reciba su merecido; absuelve al inocente, y vindícalo por su rectitud.

24»Si tu pueblo Israel es derrotado por el enemigo por haber pecado contra ti, y luego se vuelve a ti para honrar tu *nombre, y ora y te suplica en este templo, 25óyelo tú desde el cielo, y perdona su pecado y hazlo regresar a la tierra que les diste a ellos y a sus antepasados.

26»Cuando tu pueblo peque contra ti y tú lo aflijas cerrando el cielo para que no llueva, si luego ellos oran en este lugar y honran tu nombre y se *arrepienten de su pecado, 27óyelos tú desde el cielo y perdona el pecado de tus siervos, de tu pueblo Israel. Guíalos para que sigan el buen *camino, y envía la lluvia sobre esta tierra, que es tuya, pues tú se la diste a tu pueblo por herencia.

28»Cuando en el país haya hambre, peste, sequía, o plagas de langostas o saltamontes en los sembrados, o cuando el enemigo sitie alguna de nuestras ciudades; en fin, cuando venga cualquier calamidad o enfermedad, 29si luego en su dolor cada israelita, consciente de su culpa^k extiende sus manos hacia este templo, y ora y te suplica, 30óyelo tú desde el cielo, donde habitas, y perdónalo. Págale a cada uno según su conducta, la cual tú conoces, puesto que sólo tú escudriñas el corazón humano. 31Así todos tendrán temor de ti y andarán en tus caminos mientras vivan en la tierra que les diste a nuestros antepasados.

32»Trata de igual manera al extranjero que no pertenece a tu pueblo Israel, pero que atraído por tu gran fama y por tus despliegues de fuerza y poder ha venido de lejanas tierras. Cuando ese extranjero venga y ore en este templo, 33óyelo tú desde el cielo, donde habitas, y concédele cualquier petición que te haga. Así todos los pueblos de la tierra conocerán tu nombre y, al igual que tu pueblo Israel, tendrán temor de ti y comprenderán que en este templo que he construido se invoca tu nombre.

34»Cuando saques a tu pueblo para combatir a sus enemigos, sea donde sea, si el pueblo ora a ti y dirige la mirada hacia esta ciudad que has escogido, hacia el templo que he construido en tu honor, 35oye tú desde el cielo su oración y su súplica, y defiende su causa.

36»Ya que no hay ser humano que no peque, si tu pueblo peca contra ti y tú te enojas con ellos y los entregas al enemigo para que se los lleven cautivos a otro país, lejano o cercano, 37si en el destierro, en el país de los vencedores, se arrepienten y se vuelven a ti, y oran a ti diciendo: "Somos culpables, hemos pecado, hemos hecho lo malo"; 38y en la tierra de sus captores se vuelven a ti de todo corazón y con toda el *alma, y oran y dirigen la mirada hacia la tierra que les diste a sus antepasados, hacia la ciudad que has escogido y el templo que he construido en tu honor, 39oye tú sus oraciones y súplicas desde el cielo, donde habitas, y defiende su causa. ¡Perdona a tu pueblo que ha pecado contra ti!

40»Ahora, Dios mío, te ruego que tus ojos se mantengan abiertos, y atentos tus oídos a las oraciones que se eleven en este lugar.

41»Levántate, SEÑOR y Dios;
    ven a descansar,
    tú y tu arca poderosa.
SEÑOR y Dios,
    ¡que tus sacerdotes se revistan de
        *salvación!
    ¡Que tus fieles se regocijen en tu bondad!
42SEÑOR y Dios,
    no le des la espalda a^l tu *ungido.

¡Recuerda tu fiel amor hacia David, tu siervo!»

Dedicación del templo
7:1-10 — 1R 8:62-66

7 Cuando Salomón terminó de orar, descendió fuego del cielo y consumió el *holocausto y los sacrificios, y la gloria del SEÑOR llenó el templo. 2Tan lleno de su gloria estaba el templo, que los sacerdotes no podían entrar en él. 3Al ver los israelitas que el fuego descendía y que la gloria del SEÑOR se posaba sobre el templo, cayeron de rodillas y, postrándose rostro en tierra, alabaron al SEÑOR diciendo: «El SEÑOR es bueno; su gran amor perdura para siempre.»

4Entonces el rey y todo el pueblo ofrecieron sacrificios en presencia del SEÑOR. 5El rey Salomón ofreció veintidós mil bueyes y ciento veinte mil ovejas. Así fue como el rey y todo el pueblo dedicaron el templo de Dios.

6Los sacerdotes estaban de pie en sus puestos. Los levitas tocaban los instrumentos musicales que el rey David había hecho para alabar al SEÑOR, y con los cuales cantaba: «Su gran amor perdura para siempre.» Los sacerdotes tocaban las trompetas frente a los levitas, y todo Israel permanecía de pie.

7Salomón también consagró la parte central del atrio, que está frente al templo del SEÑOR, y allí presentó los holocaustos y la grasa de los sacrificios de *comunión, ya que en el altar de bronce que hizo Salomón no había espacio para los holocaustos, la grasa y las ofrendas de cereales.

8En aquella ocasión Salomón y todo Israel celebraron la fiesta durante siete días. Era una inmensa asamblea que había acudido de todo lugar, desde Lebó Jamat^m hasta el río de Egipto. 9Al octavo día tuvieron una asamblea solemne, porque habían celebrado la consagración del altar durante siete días, y la fiesta durante siete días más. 10El día veintitrés del mes séptimo, Salomón envió al pueblo a sus casas, y ellos regresaron contentos y llenos de alegría por el bien que el SEÑOR había hecho en favor de David, de Salomón y de su pueblo Israel.

Pacto de Dios con Salomón
7:11-22 — 1R 9:1-9

11Cuando Salomón terminó el templo del SEÑOR y el palacio real, llevando a feliz término todo lo que se había propuesto hacer en ellos, 12el SEÑOR se le apareció una noche y le dijo:

«He escuchado tu oración, y he escogido este templo para que en él se me ofrezcan sacrificios. 13Cuando yo cierre los cielos para que no llueva, o le ordene a la langosta que devore la tierra, o envíe pestes sobre mi pueblo, 14si mi pueblo, que lleva mi *nombre, se humilla y ora, y me busca y abandona su mala conducta, yo lo escucharé desde el cielo, perdonaré su pecado y restauraré su tierra. 15Mantendré abiertos mis ojos, y atentos mis oídos a las oraciones que se eleven en este lugar. 16Desde ahora y para siempre escojo y consagro este templo para habitar en él. Mis ojos y mi *corazón siempre estarán allí.

17»En cuanto a ti, si me sigues como lo hizo tu padre David, y me obedeces en todo lo que yo te ordene y cumples mis decretos y *leyes, 18yo afirmaré tu trono real, como pacté con tu padre David cuando

---

k 6:29 culpa. Lit. plaga.   l 6:42 no le des la espalda a. Lit. no vuelvas el rostro de.   m 7:8 Lebó Jamat. Alt. la entrada de Jamat.

le dije: "Nunca te faltará un descendiente en el trono de Israel."

19»Pero si ustedes me abandonan, y desobedecen los decretos y mandamientos que les he dado, y se apartan de mí para servir y adorar a otros dioses, 20los desarraigaré de la tierra que les he dado y repudiaré este templo que he consagrado en mi honor. Entonces los convertiré en el hazmerreír de todos los pueblos. 21Y aunque ahora este templo es imponente, llegará el día en que todo el que pase frente a él quedará asombrado y preguntará: "¿Por qué el SEÑOR ha tratado así a este país y a este templo?" 22Y le responderán: "Porque abandonaron al SEÑOR, Dios de sus antepasados, que los sacó de Egipto, y se echaron en los brazos de otros dioses, a los cuales adoraron y sirvieron. Por eso el SEÑOR ha dejado que les sobrevenga tanto desastre."»

Otras actividades de Salomón
8:1-18 — 1R 9:10-28

8 Veinte años tardó el rey Salomón en construir el templo del SEÑOR y su propio palacio. 2Después de esto, reconstruyó las ciudades que le había entregado Hiram y las pobló con israelitas. 3Luego marchó contra la ciudad de Jamat de Sobá y la conquistó. 4Reconstruyó Tadmor, en el desierto, y todos los lugares de almacenamiento que había construido en Jamat. 5Reconstruyó como ciudades fortificadas Bet Jorón la de arriba y Bet Jorón la de abajo, y les puso murallas, *puertas y cerrojos. 6Lo mismo hizo con Balat y con todos los lugares de almacenamiento que tenía, con los cuarteles para sus carros de combate y para su caballería, y con todo cuanto quiso construir en Jerusalén, en el Líbano y en todo el territorio bajo su dominio.

7-8A los descendientes de los pueblos no israelitas (es decir, a los hititas, amorreos, ferezeos, heveos y jebuseos, pueblos que quedaron en el país porque los israelitas no pudieron *destruirlos), Salomón los sometió a trabajos forzados, y así continúan hasta el día de hoy. 9Pero a los israelitas Salomón no los hizo trabajar como esclavos, sino que se servían como soldados, comandantes, oficiales de carros de combate y jefes de caballería. 10El rey Salomón tenía además doscientos cincuenta capataces que supervisaban a los obreros.

11A la hija del faraón, Salomón la trasladó de la Ciudad de David al palacio que le había construido, pues dijo: «Mi esposa no debe vivir en el palacio de David, rey de Israel, porque los lugares donde ha estado el arca del SEÑOR son sagrados.»

12En el altar del SEÑOR que había construido frente al atrio, Salomón ofrecía *holocaustos al SEÑOR 13los días correspondientes, según lo ordenado por Moisés: los *sábados, las fiestas de luna nueva, y las tres fiestas anuales, es decir, la de los *Panes sin levadura, la de las Semanas y la de las *Enramadas.

14Conforme a lo dispuesto por su padre David, Salomón asignó turnos a los sacerdotes para prestar su servicio. A los levitas les estableció en sus cargos para entonar las alabanzas y para ayudar a los sacerdotes en los ritos diarios. También fijó turnos a los porteros en cada puerta, porque así lo había ordenado David, hombre de Dios. 15Y se obedecieron

todas las órdenes del rey en cuanto a los sacerdotes y levitas, y aun en lo referente a los tesoros.

16Toda la obra de Salomón se llevó a cabo, desde el día en que se echaron los cimientos del templo hasta que se terminó de construirlo. Así el templo del SEÑOR quedó perfectamente terminado.

17Luego Salomón se dirigió a Ezión Guéber y a Elat, en la costa de Edom. 18Hiram, por medio de sus oficiales, le envió a Salomón barcos y marineros expertos. Éstos y los oficiales de Salomón navegaron a Ofir y volvieron con unos quince mil kilosn de oro, que le entregaron al rey Salomón.

La reina de Sabá visita a Salomón
9:1-12 — 1R 10:1-13

9 La reina de Sabá se enteró de la fama de Salomón, así que fue a verlo en Jerusalén para ponerlo a prueba con preguntas difíciles. Llegó con un séquito muy grande; sus camellos llevaban perfumes, oro en abundancia y piedras preciosas. Al presentarse ante Salomón, le preguntó todo lo que tenía pensado, 2y él respondió a todas sus preguntas. No hubo ningún asunto, por difícil que fuera, que Salomón no pudiera resolver. 3-4La reina de Sabá se quedó atónita al ver la sabiduría de Salomón y el palacio que él había construido, los manjares de su mesa, los asientos que ocupaban sus funcionarios, el servicio y la ropa de sus criados y coperos, y los *holocaustos que ofrecía en el templon del SEÑOR. 5Entonces le dijo al rey: «¡Todo lo que escuché en mi país acerca de tus triunfos y de tu sabiduría es cierto! No podía creer nada de eso hasta que vine y lo vi con mis propios ojos. Pero en realidad, ¡no me habían contado ni siquiera la mitad de tu extraordinaria sabiduría! Tú superas todo lo que había oído decir de ti. 7¡*Dichosos tus súbditos! ¡Dichosos estos servidores tuyos, que constantemente están en tu presencia bebiendo de tu sabiduría! 8¡Y alabado sea el SEÑOR tu Dios, que se ha deleitado en ti y te ha puesto en su trono para que lo representes como rey! En su amor por Israel, tu Dios te ha hecho rey de ellos para que gobiernes con justicia y rectitud, pues él quiere consolidar a su pueblo para siempre.»

9Luego la reina le regaló a Salomón tres mil novecientos sesenta kiloso de oro, piedras preciosas y una gran cantidad de perfumes. Jamás volvió a haber perfumes como los que la reina de Sabá le obsequió al rey Salomón.

10Además del oro de Ofir, los oficiales de Hiram y los de Salomón trajeron madera de sándalo y piedras preciosas. 11Con la madera, el rey construyó escalinatas para el templo del SEÑOR y para el palacio real, y también hizo arpas y liras para los músicos. Nunca antes se había visto en Judá algo semejante.

12El rey Salomón, por su parte, le dio a la reina de Sabá todo lo que a ella se le antojó pedirle, lo cual fue más de lo que ella le dio al rey. Después de eso, la reina regresó a su país con todos los que la atendían.

El esplendor de Salomón
9:13-28 — 1R 10:14-29; 2Cr 1:14-17

13La cantidad de oro que Salomón recibía anualmente llegaba a los veintidós mil kilos,p 14sin contar los impuestos que pagaban los mercaderes y comerciantes. También los reyes de Arabia y los gobernadores del país le llevaban oro y plata a Salomón.

---

n 8:18 quince mil kilos. Lit. cuatrocientos cincuenta *talentos. ñ 9:4 los holocaustos ... templo. Alt. la escalinata por la cual él subía al templo. o 9:9 tres mil novecientos sesenta kilos. Lit. ciento veinte *talentos. p 9:13 veintidós mil kilos. Lit. seiscientos sesenta y seis talentos.

15El rey Salomón hizo doscientos escudos grandes de oro batido, en cada uno de los cuales se emplearon seis kilos y medio*q* de oro. 16Hizo además trescientos escudos más pequeños, también de oro batido, empleando en cada uno de ellos tres kilos*r* de oro. Estos escudos los puso el rey en el palacio llamado «Bosque del Líbano».

17El rey hizo también un gran trono de marfil, recubierto de oro puro. 18El trono tenía seis peldaños, un estrado de oro, brazos a cada lado del asiento, dos leones de pie junto a los brazos 19y doce leones de pie sobre los seis peldaños, uno en cada extremo. En ningún otro reino se había hecho algo semejante. 20Todas las copas del rey Salomón y toda la vajilla del palacio «Bosque del Líbano» eran de oro puro. Nada estaba hecho de plata, pues en tiempos de Salomón la plata era poco apreciada. 21Cada tres años, la flota comercial del rey, que era tripulada por los oficiales de Hiram, regresaba de Tarsis trayendo oro, plata y marfil, monos y mandriles.*s*

22Tanto en riquezas como en sabiduría, el rey Salomón sobrepasó a los demás reyes de la tierra. 23Todos ellos procuraban visitarlo para oír la sabiduría que Dios le había dado, 24y tras año le llevaban regalos: artículos de plata y de oro, vestidos, armas y perfumes, y caballos y mulas.

25Salomón tenía cuatro mil establos para sus caballos y sus carros de combate, y doce mil caballos que mantenía en las caballerizas y también en su palacio en Jerusalén.

26El rey Salomón extendió su dominio sobre todos los reyes, desde el río Éufrates hasta Filistea y la frontera de Egipto. 27Hizo que en Jerusalén la plata fuera tan común y corriente como las piedras, y el cedro tan abundante como las higueras de la llanura. 28Sus caballos eran importados de Egipto y de todos los otros países.

Muerte de Salomón
9:29-31 — 1R 11:41-43

29Los demás acontecimientos del reinado de Salomón, desde el primero hasta el último, están escritos en las crónicas del profeta Natán, en la profecía de Ahías el silonita, y en las visiones del vidente Idó acerca de Jeroboán hijo de Nabat. 30Salomón reinó en Jerusalén cuarenta años sobre todo Israel. 31Cuando murió, fue sepultado en la ciudad de David, su padre, y su hijo Roboán lo sucedió en el trono.

División del reino
10:1-11 — 1R 12:1-24

10 Roboán fue a Siquén porque todos los israelitas se habían reunido allí para proclamarlo rey. 2De esto se enteró Jeroboán hijo de Nabat, así que volvió de Egipto, que es adonde había huido del rey Salomón. 3Cuando lo mandaron a buscar, él y todo Israel fueron a ver a Roboán y le dijeron:

4—Su padre nos impuso un yugo pesado. Alívienos usted el duro trabajo y el pesado yugo que él nos echó encima; así serviremos a Su Majestad.

5—Váyanse por ahora —respondió Roboán—, pero vuelvan a verme dentro de tres días.

Cuando el pueblo se fue, 6el rey Roboán consultó con los *ancianos que en vida de su padre Salomón habían estado a su servicio.

—¿Qué me aconsejan ustedes que le responda a este pueblo? —preguntó.

7Ellos respondieron:

—Si Su Majestad trata con bondad a este pueblo, y condesciende con ellos y les responde con amabilidad, ellos le servirán para siempre.

8Pero Roboán rechazó el consejo que le dieron los ancianos, y consultó más bien con los jóvenes que se habían criado con él y que estaban a su servicio.

9—¿Ustedes qué me aconsejan? —les preguntó—. ¿Cómo debo responderle a este pueblo que me dice: "Alívienos el yugo que su padre nos echó encima"?

10Aquellos jóvenes, que se habían criado con él, le contestaron:

—El pueblo le ha dicho a Su Majestad: "Su padre nos impuso un yugo pesado; hágalo usted más ligero." Pues bien, respóndales de este modo: "Mi dedo meñique es más grueso que la cintura de mi padre. 11Si él les impuso un yugo pesado, ¡yo les aumentaré la carga! Y si él los castigaba a ustedes con una vara, ¡yo lo haré con un látigo!"*t*

12Al tercer día, en la fecha que el rey Roboán había indicado, Jeroboán regresó con todo el pueblo para presentarse ante él. 13Pero el rey Roboán les respondió con brusquedad: rechazó el consejo de los ancianos, 14y siguió más bien el de los jóvenes. Les dijo: «Si mi padre les impuso*u* un yugo pesado, ¡yo les aumentaré la carga! Si él los castigaba a ustedes con una vara, ¡yo lo haré con un látigo!»

15Y como el rey no escuchó al pueblo, las cosas tomaron este rumbo por voluntad de Dios. Así se cumplió la palabra que el SEÑOR le había comunicado a Jeroboán hijo de Nabat por medio de Ahías el silonita.

16Cuando se dieron cuenta de que el rey*v* no iba a hacerles caso, todos los israelitas exclamaron a una:

«¡Pueblo de Israel, todos a sus casas!
¡Y tú, David, ocúpate de los tuyos!
¿Qué parte tenemos con David?
¿Qué herencia tenemos con el hijo de Isaí?»

Así que se fueron, cada uno a su casa. 17Sin embargo, Roboán siguió reinando sobre los israelitas que vivían en las ciudades de Judá. 18Más tarde, el rey Roboán envió a Adonirán*w* para que supervisara el trabajo forzado, pero los israelitas lo mataron a pedradas. ¡A duras penas logró el rey subir a su carro y escapar a Jerusalén! 19Desde entonces Israel ha estado en rebelión contra la familia de David.

11 Roboán llegó a Jerusalén y movilizó a las familias de Judá y de Benjamín, ciento ochenta mil guerreros selectos en total, para hacer la guerra contra Israel y así recuperar el reino. 2Pero la palabra del SEÑOR vino a Semaías, hombre de Dios, y le dio este mensaje: 3«Diles a Roboán hijo de Salomón, rey de Judá, y a todos los israelitas que están en Judá y en Benjamín, 4que así dice el SEÑOR: "No vayan a luchar contra sus hermanos. Regrese cada uno a su casa, porque es mi voluntad que esto haya sucedido."» Y ellos obedecieron las palabras del SEÑOR y desistieron de marchar contra Jeroboán.

Roboán fortifica las ciudades de Judá

5Roboán se estableció en Jerusalén y fortificó las siguientes ciudades de Judá: 6Belén, Étam, Tecoa,

---

q **9:15** seis kilos y medio. Lit. seiscientos {*siclos}.   r **9:16** tres kilos. Lit. trescientos {*siclos}.   s **9:21** mandriles. Alt. pavos reales.   t **10:11** con una vara ... con un látigo. Lit. con azotes ... con escorpiones; también en v. 14.   u **10:14** Si mi padre les impuso (mss. hebreos y versiones antiguas); Yo les impondré (TM).   v **10:16** Cuando se dieron cuenta de que el rey (mss. hebreos y versiones antiguas); Como el rey (TM).   w **10:18** Adonirán. Lit. Adorán (variante de este nombre).

7Betsur, Soco, Adulán, 8Gat, Maresá, Zif, 9Adorayin, Laquis, Azeca, 10Zora, Ayalón y Hebrón. Estas ciudades fueron fortificadas en Judá y en Benjamín. 11Roboán nombró gobernantes, reforzó las fortificaciones, almacenó en ellas víveres, aceite y vino, 12y las armó a todas con escudos y lanzas. Así fortificó completamente todas las ciudades y quedó en posesión de Judá y de Benjamín.

Los sacerdotes y los levitas apoyan a Roboán

13De todas las regiones de Israel llegaron sacerdotes y levitas para unirse a Roboán. 14Los levitas abandonaron sus campos de pastoreo y demás posesiones para irse a Judá y a Jerusalén, ya que Jeroboán y sus hijos les habían impedido ejercer el sacerdocio del SEÑOR. 15En su lugar, Jeroboán había nombrado sacerdotes para los *santuarios paganos y para el culto a los machos cabríos y a los becerros que había mandado hacer. 16Tras los levitas se fue gente de todas las tribus de Israel que con todo el *corazón buscaba al SEÑOR, Dios de Israel. Llegaron a Jerusalén para ofrecer sacrificios al SEÑOR, Dios de sus antepasados. 17Así consolidaron el reino de Judá, y durante tres años apoyaron a Roboán hijo de Salomón y siguieron el buen ejemplo de David y Salomón.

Esposas e hijos de Roboán

18Roboán se casó con Majalat hija de Jerimot, el hijo de David y de Abijaíl, hija de Eliab y nieta de Isaí. 19Los hijos que ella le dio fueron Jeús, Semarías y Zaján. 20Después se casó con Macá hija de Absalón. Los hijos que ella le dio fueron Abías, Atay, Ziza y Selomit. 21Roboán amó a Macá hija de Absalón más que a sus otras esposas y concubinas. En total, tuvo dieciocho esposas y sesenta concubinas, y fue padre de veintiocho hijos y de sesenta hijas.

22Roboán puso como jefe de sus hermanos a Abías hijo de Macá, pues tenía la intención de hacerlo rey. 23Y actuó con astucia, pues a sus otros hijos les dio víveres en abundancia, les consiguió muchas esposas y los dispersó por todo el territorio de Judá y de Benjamín y por todas las ciudades fortificadas.

Sisac invade Jerusalén
12:9-16 — 1R 14:21,25-31

12 Después de que Roboán consolidó su reino y se afirmó en el trono, él y todo Israel abandonaron la *ley del SEÑOR 2y le fueron infieles. Por eso en el quinto año del reinado de Roboán, Sisac, rey de Egipto, atacó a Jerusalén. 3Con mil doscientos carros de combate, sesenta mil jinetes y una innumerable multitud de libios, suqueos y *cusitas procedentes de Egipto, 4Sisac conquistó las ciudades fortificadas de Judá y llegó hasta Jerusalén.

5Entonces el profeta Semaías se presentó ante Roboán y los jefes de Judá que por miedo a Sisac se habían reunido en Jerusalén, y les dijo:

—Así dice el SEÑOR: "Como ustedes me abandonaron, ahora yo también los abandono, para que caigan en manos de Sisac."

6Los jefes israelitas y el rey confesaron con humildad:

—¡El SEÑOR es justo!

7Cuando el SEÑOR vio que se habían humillado, le habló nuevamente a Semaías y le dijo: «Puesto que han mostrado humildad, ya no voy a destruirlos; dentro de poco tiempo los libraré. No voy a permitir que Sisac ejecute mi castigo sobre Jerusalén, 8aunque sí dejaré que los someta a su dominio, para que

aprendan la diferencia que hay entre servirme a mí y servir a los reyes de otros países.»

9Sisac, rey de Egipto, atacó a Jerusalén y se llevó los tesoros del templo del SEÑOR y del palacio real. Se lo llevó todo, aun los escudos de oro que Salomón había hecho. 10Para reemplazarlos, el rey Roboán mandó hacer escudos de bronce y los puso al cuidado de los jefes de la guardia que custodiaba la entrada del palacio real. 11Siempre que el rey iba al templo del SEÑOR, los guardias lo acompañaban portando los escudos, pero luego los devolvían a la sala de los centinelas.

12Por haberse humillado Roboán, y porque aún quedaba algo bueno en Judá, el SEÑOR apartó su ira de él y no lo destruyó por completo, 13así que el rey Roboán afirmó su trono y continuó reinando en Jerusalén. Su madre era una amonita llamada Noamá.

Roboán tenía cuarenta y un años cuando ascendió al trono, y reinó diecisiete años en Jerusalén, la ciudad donde, de entre todas las tribus de Israel, el SEÑOR había decidido habitar. 14Pero Roboán actuó mal, porque no tuvo el firme propósito de buscar al SEÑOR.

15Los acontecimientos del reinado de Roboán, desde el primero hasta el último, incluyendo las constantes guerras que hubo entre Jeroboán y él, están escritos en las crónicas del profeta Semaías y del vidente Idó.

16Cuando Roboán murió, fue sepultado en la Ciudad de David. Y su hijo Abías lo sucedió en el trono.

Abías, rey de Judá
13:1-2,22—14:1 — 1R 15:1-2,6-8

13 En el año dieciocho del reinado de Jeroboán, Abías ascendió al trono de Judá 2y reinó en Jerusalén tres años. Su madre era Micaías, hija de Uriel de Guibeá.

Hubo guerra entre Abías y Jeroboán. 3Para ir al combate, Abías escogió a cuatrocientos mil guerreros valientes; Jeroboán, por su parte, escogió a ochocientos mil y le hizo frente.

4Abías subió al monte Zemarayin, en la sierra de Efraín, y gritó: «¡Jeroboán! ¡Israelitas! ¡Escúchenme todos ustedes! 5¿No saben que el SEÑOR, Dios de Israel, concedió para siempre el reino de Israel a David y a sus descendientes mediante un *pacto inalterable?x 6Sin embargo, Jeroboán hijo de Nabat, oficial de Salomón hijo de David, se rebeló contra su señor. 7Unos hombres ociosos y malvados se unieron a Roboán hijo de Salomón, cuando éste era joven y débil de carácter, y se le impusieron, de modo que no pudo hacerles frente.

8»Ustedes piensan que ahora, por ser muy numerosos y por tener los becerros de oro, esos ídolos que Jeroboán les hizo pueden oponerse al reino del SEÑOR, aunque él se lo ha entregado a los hijos de David. 9¡Hasta expulsaron a los descendientes de Aarón, que son los sacerdotes del SEÑOR, y a los levitas! En su lugar han nombrado sacerdotes, y a cualquiera que trae un ternero y siete carneros se consagran como sacerdote de los dioses falsos, tal como lo hacen los pueblos *paganos.

10»Nosotros, en cambio, no hemos abandonado al SEÑOR, porque él es nuestro Dios. Los descendientes de Aarón siguen siendo nuestros sacerdotes que sirven al SEÑOR, y los levitas son los encargados del culto. 11Todos los días, por la mañana y por la tarde, ofrecen al SEÑOR los *holocaustos y queman el in-

---

x 13:5 inalterable. Lit. de sal; véase Nm 18:19.

cienso; además, todas las tardes colocan el pan consagrado sobre la mesa de oro puro, y encienden las lámparas del candelabro de oro. Dense cuenta de que nosotros sí mantenemos el culto al SEÑOR nuestro Dios, a quien ustedes han abandonado. 12Así que Dios, con sus sacerdotes, va al frente de nosotros. ¡Las trompetas están listas para dar la orden de ataque contra ustedes! ¡Israelitas, no peleen contra el SEÑOR, Dios de sus antepasados, pues no podrán vencerlo!»

13Para tenderle una emboscada a Abías, Jeroboán situó parte de sus tropas detrás del ejército de Judá, mientras que al resto de sus tropas lo mandó al frente. 14Cuando los de Judá miraron hacia atrás, se dieron cuenta de que los israelitas los atacaban también por la retaguardia. Entonces clamaron al SEÑOR, y los sacerdotes tocaron las trompetas. 15En el momento en que los de Judá lanzaron el grito de guerra, Dios derrotó a Jeroboán y a los israelitas, dándoles la *victoria a Abías y Judá. 16Los israelitas intentaron huir, pero Dios los entregó al poder de Judá. 17Abías y su ejército les ocasionaron una gran derrota, matando a quinientos mil soldados selectos de Israel. 18En esa ocasión fueron humillados los israelitas, mientras que los de Judá salieron victoriosos porque confiaron en el SEÑOR, Dios de sus antepasados.

19Abías persiguió a Jeroboán y le arrebató las ciudades de Betel, Jesaná y Efraín, con sus respectivas aldeas. 20Durante el reinado de Abías, Jeroboán no pudo recuperar su poderío. Al final, el SEÑOR lo hirió, y Jeroboán murió.

21Abías, en cambio, siguió afirmándose en el trono. Tuvo catorce esposas, veintidós hijos y dieciséis hijas. 22Los demás acontecimientos del reinado de Abías, y su conducta y sus obras, están escritos en el comentario del profeta Idó.

14 Abías murió y fue sepultado en la Ciudad de David, y su hijo Asá lo sucedió en el trono. Durante su reinado, el país disfrutó de diez años de *paz.

Asá, rey de Judá
14:2-3 — 1R 15:11-12

2Asá hizo lo que era bueno y agradable ante el SEÑOR su Dios. 3Se deshizo de los altares y *santuarios paganos, destrozó las piedras sagradas, y derribó las imágenes de la diosa *Aserá. 4Además, ordenó a los habitantes de Judá que acudieran al SEÑOR, Dios de sus antepasados, y que obedecieran su *ley y sus mandamientos. 5De este modo Asá se deshizo de los santuarios paganos y de los altares de incienso que había en todas las ciudades de Judá, y durante su reinado hubo tranquilidad. 6Asá construyó en Judá ciudades fortificadas, pues durante esos años el SEÑOR le dio descanso, y el país disfrutó de *paz y no estuvo en guerra con nadie.

7Asá les dijo a los de Judá: «Reconstruyamos esas ciudades, y levantemos a su alrededor murallas con torres, *puertas y cerrojos. El país todavía es nuestro, porque hemos buscado al SEÑOR nuestro Dios; como lo hemos buscado, él nos ha concedido estar en paz con nuestros vecinos.» Y tuvieron mucho éxito en la reconstrucción de las ciudades.

8Asá contaba con un ejército de trescientos mil soldados de Judá, los cuales portaban lanzas y escudos grandes, y de doscientos ochenta mil benjaminitas, los cuales portaban arcos y escudos pequeños. Todos ellos eran guerreros valientes.

9Zera el *cusita marchó contra ellos al frente de un ejército de un millón de soldados y trescientos carros de guerra, y llegó hasta Maresá. 10Asá le salió al encuentro en el valle de Sefata, y tomó posiciones cerca de Maresá. 11Allí Asá invocó al SEÑOR su Dios y le dijo: «SEÑOR, sólo tú puedes ayudar al débil y al poderoso. ¡Ayúdanos, SEÑOR y Dios nuestro, porque en ti confiamos, y en tu *nombre hemos venido contra esta multitud! ¡Tú, SEÑOR, eres nuestro Dios! ¡No permitas que ningún *mortal se alce contra ti!»

12El SEÑOR derrotó a los cusitas cuando éstos lucharon contra Asá y Judá. Los cusitas huyeron, 13pero Asá y su ejército los persiguieron hasta Guerar. Allí cayeron los cusitas, y ni uno de ellos quedó con vida, porque el SEÑOR y su ejército los aniquilaron. Los de Judá se llevaron un enorme botín, 14luego atacaron todas las ciudades que había alrededor de Guerar, las cuales estaban llenas de pánico ante el SEÑOR, y las saquearon, pues había en ellas un gran botín. 15Además, atacaron los campamentos, donde había mucho ganado, y se llevaron una gran cantidad de ovejas y camellos. Después de eso, regresaron a Jerusalén.

Reformas de Asá
15:16-19 — 1R 15:13-16

15 El Espíritu de Dios vino sobre Azarías hijo de Oded, 2y éste salió al encuentro de Asá y le dijo: «Asá, y gente de Judá y de Benjamín, ¡escúchenme! El SEÑOR estará con ustedes, siempre y cuando ustedes estén con él. Si lo buscan, él dejará que ustedes lo hallen; pero si lo abandonan, él los abandonará. 3Por mucho tiempo Israel estuvo sin el Dios verdadero y sin instrucción,z pues no había sacerdote que le enseñara. 4Pero cuando en su tribulación se volvieron al SEÑOR, Dios de Israel, y lo buscaron, él les permitió que lo hallaran. 5En aquellos tiempos no había seguridad para ningún viajero, sino que los habitantes de todos los países sufrían grandes calamidades. 6Las naciones y las ciudades se destrozaban unas a otras, porque Dios las castigaba con toda clase de calamidades. 7Pero ustedes, ¡manténganse firmes y no bajen la guardia, porque sus obras serán recompensadas!»

8Cuando Asá oyó este mensaje del profeta Azarías hijo de Oded,a se animó a eliminar los detestables ídolos que había en todo el territorio de Judá y Benjamín, y en las ciudades que había conquistado en los montes de Efraín. Además, restauró el altar del SEÑOR que estaba frente al atrio del templo del SEÑOR. 9Después convocó a los habitantes de Judá y de Benjamín, como también a los de Efraín, Manasés y Simeón que vivían entre ellos, pues muchos israelitas se habían unido a Asá, al ver que el SEÑOR su Dios estaba con él. 10Se reunieron en Jerusalén en el mes tercero del año quince del reinado de Asá. 11Ese día ofrecieron al SEÑOR setecientos bueyes y siete mil ovejas del botín que habían tomado. 12Luego hicieron un *pacto, mediante el cual se comprometieron a buscar de todo *corazón y con toda el *alma al SEÑOR, Dios de sus antepasados. 13Al que no buscara al SEÑOR, Dios de Israel, se le castigaría con la muerte, fuera grande o pequeño, hombre o mujer. 14Así lo juraron ante el SEÑOR, a voz en cuello y en medio de gritos y toques de trompetas y de cuernos. 15Todos los de Judá se alegraron de haber hecho este juramento, porque lo habían hecho de todo corazón y habían buscado al SEÑOR con voluntad sincera, y él

---

se había dejado hallar de ellos y les había concedido vivir en *paz con las naciones vecinas.

16Además, el rey Asá destituyó a su abuela Macá de su puesto como reina madre, porque ella había hecho una escandalosa imagen de la diosa *Aserá. Asá derribó la imagen, la redujo a polvo y la quemó en el arroyo de Cedrón. 17Aunque no quitó de Israel los *santuarios paganos, Asá se mantuvo siempre fielb al SEÑOR, 18y llevó al templo de Dios el oro, la plata y los utensilios que él y su padre habían consagrado.

19Durante los primeros treinta y cinco años del reinado de Asá no hubo guerra.

Pacto de Asá con Ben Adad
16:1-6 — 1R 15:17-22
16:11—17:1 — 1R 15:23-24

16 En el año treinta y seis del reinado de Asá, Basá, rey de Israel, atacó a Judá y fortificó Ramá para aislar totalmente a Asá, rey de Judá.

2Entonces Asá sacó plata y oro de los tesoros del templo del SEÑOR y del palacio real, y se los envió a Ben Adad, rey de *Siria, que gobernaba en Damasco. También le envió este mensaje: 3«Hagamos un pacto entre tú y yo, como el que hicieron tu padre y el mío. Aquí te envío oro y plata. Anula tu pacto con Basá, rey de Israel, para que se marche de aquí.»

4Ben Adad estuvo de acuerdo con el rey Asá y dio a los jefes de su ejército la orden de atacar las ciudades de Israel. Así conquistaron Iyón, Dan y Abel Mayin, y todos los depósitos que había en las ciudades de Neftalí.

5Cuando Basá se enteró, suspendió las obras de fortificación de Ramá. 6Entonces el rey Asá movilizó a todo Judá y se llevó de Ramá las piedras y la madera con que había estado fortificando aquella ciudad, y fortificó más bien Gueba y Mizpa.

7En esa ocasión el vidente Jananí se presentó ante Asá, rey de Judá, y le dijo: «Por cuanto pusiste tu confianza en el rey de Siria en vez de confiar en el SEÑOR tu Dios, el ejército sirio se te ha escapado de las manos. 8También los *cusitas y los libios formaban un ejército numeroso, y tenían muchos carros de combate y caballos, y sin embargo el SEÑOR los entregó en tus manos, porque en esa ocasión tú confiaste en él. 9El SEÑOR recorre con su mirada toda la tierra, y está listo para ayudar a quienes le son fieles.c Pero de ahora en adelante tendrás guerras, pues actuaste como un *necio.»

10Asá se enfureció contra el vidente por lo que éste le dijo, y lo mandó encarcelar. En ese tiempo, Asá oprimió también a una parte del pueblo. 11Los hechos de Asá, desde el primero hasta el último, están escritos en el libro de los reyes de Judá e Israel. 12En el año treinta y nueve de su reinado, Asá se enfermó de los pies; y aunque su enfermedad era grave, no buscó al SEÑOR, sino que recurrió a los médicos. 13En el año cuarenta y uno de su reinado, Asá murió y fue sepultado con sus antepasados. 14Lo sepultaron en la tumba que él había mandado cavar en la Ciudad de David, y lo colocaron sobre un lecho lleno de perfumes y diversas clases de especias aromáticas, muy bien preparadas. En su honor encendieron una enorme hoguera.

Josafat, rey de Judá

17 Al rey Asá lo sucedió en el trono su hijo Josafat, quien se impuso a la fuerza sobre

Israel. 2Colocó tropas en todas las ciudades fortificadas de Judá, y guarniciones en el territorio de Judá y en las ciudades de Efraín que su padre Asá había conquistado.

3El SEÑOR estuvo con Josafat porque siguió el ejemplo inicial de su padre,d pues no buscó a los *baales 4sino al Dios de su padre, obedeció los mandamientos de Dios, y no siguió las prácticas de los israelitas. 5Por eso el SEÑOR afirmó el reino en sus manos. Todo Judá le llevaba regalos, y Josafat llegó a tener muchas riquezas y recibió muchos honores. 6Anduvo con orgullo en los *caminos del SEÑOR, y hasta quitó de Judá los *santuarios paganos y las imágenes de la diosa *Aserá.

7En el año tercero de su reinado, Josafat envió a sus oficiales Ben Jayil, Abdías, Zacarías, Natanael y Micaías, para que instruyeran a la gente en las ciudades de Judá. 8Con ellos fueron los levitas Semaías, Netanías, Zebadías, Asael, Semiramot, Jonatán, Adonías, Tobías y Tobadonías, y también los sacerdotes Elisama y Jorán. 9Llevaron consigo el libro de la *ley del SEÑOR para instruir a los habitantes de Judá. Así que recorrieron todas las ciudades de Judá, enseñando al pueblo.

10Todos los reinos de las naciones vecinas de Judá sintieron un miedo profundo hacia el SEÑOR y no se atrevieron a declararle la guerra a Josafat. 11Aun algunos filisteos le llevaron a Josafat, como tributo, regalos y plata. Los árabes también le llevaron siete mil setecientos carneros y siete mil setecientos machos cabríos.

12Josafat se hizo cada vez más poderoso. Construyó en Judá fortalezas y lugares de almacenamiento, 13y tenía muchas provisiones en las ciudades. En Jerusalén contaba con un regimiento de soldados muy valientes, 14cuyo registro, según sus familias patriarcales, es el siguiente:

Jefes de mil soldados en Judá:
Adnás, el comandante, al frente de trescientos mil soldados.

15 Le seguía Johanán, al frente de doscientos ochenta mil soldados;

16 le seguía Amasías hijo de Zicrí, que se ofreció voluntariamente para servir al SEÑOR, y estaba al frente de doscientos mil soldados.

17 De Benjamín:
Eliadá, guerrero valiente, al frente de doscientos mil soldados que portaban arcos y escudos.

18 Le seguía Jozabad, al frente de ciento ochenta mil soldados adiestrados para la guerra.

19Todos ellos estaban al servicio del rey, sin contar los que éste había destinado para las ciudades fortificadas de todo Judá.

Micaías profetiza contra Acab
18:1-27 — 1R 22:1-28

18 Josafat se hizo muy rico y famoso, y como había emparentado con Acab, 2después de algún tiempo fue a visitarlo en Samaria. Allí Acab mató muchas ovejas y vacas para Josafat y sus acompañantes, y lo animó a marchar contra Ramot de Galaad.

3Acab, rey de Israel, le preguntó a Josafat, rey de Judá:

---

b **15:17** *Asá se mantuvo siempre fiel.* Lit. *el corazón de Asá fue* *perfecto.* c **16:9** *quienes le son fieles.* Lit. *los de corazón* *perfecto para él.* d **17:3** *de su padre* (mss. hebreos y LXX); *de su padre David* (TM).

—¿Irías conmigo a pelear contra Ramot de Galaad?

Josafat le respondió:

—Estoy a tu disposición, lo mismo que mi pueblo. Iremos contigo a la guerra. 4Pero antes que nada, consultemos al SEÑOR —añadió.

5Así que el rey de Israel reunió a los cuatrocientos profetas, y les preguntó:

—¿Debemos ir a la guerra contra Ramot de Galaad, o no?

—Vaya, Su Majestad —contestaron ellos—, porque Dios la entregará en sus manos.

6Pero Josafat inquirió:

—¿No hay aquí un profeta del SEÑOR a quien podamos consultar?

7El rey de Israel le respondió:

—Todavía hay alguien por medio de quien podemos consultar al SEÑOR, pero me cae muy mal porque nunca me profetiza nada bueno; sólo me anuncia desastres. Se trata de Micaías hijo de Imlá.

—No digas eso —replicó Josafat.

8Entonces el rey de Israel llamó a uno de sus funcionarios y le ordenó:

—¡Traigan de inmediato a Micaías hijo de Imlá!

9El rey de Israel, y Josafat, rey de Judá, vestidos con sus vestiduras reales y sentados en sus respectivos tronos, estaban en la plaza a la *entrada de Samaria, con todos los que profetizaban en su presencia. 10Sedequías hijo de Quenaná, que se había hecho unos cuernos de hierro, anunció: «Así dice el SEÑOR: "Con estos cuernos atacarás a los *sirios hasta aniquilarlos."» 11Y los demás profetas vaticinaban lo mismo. «Ataque Su Majestad a Ramot de Galaad, y vencerá, porque el SEÑOR la entregará en sus manos.»

12Ahora bien, el mensajero que había ido a llamar a Micaías le advirtió:

—Mira, los demás profetas a una voz predicen el éxito del rey. Habla favorablemente, para que tu mensaje concuerde con el de ellos.

13Pero Micaías repuso:

—Tan cierto como que el SEÑOR vive, te juro que yo le anunciaré al rey lo que Dios me diga.

14Cuando compareció ante el rey, éste le preguntó:

—Micaías, ¿debemos ir a la guerra contra Ramot de Galaad, o no?

—Ataquen y vencerán —contestó él—, porque les será entregada.

15El rey le reclamó:

—¿Cuántas veces debo hacerte jurar que no me digas nada más que la verdad en el *nombre del SEÑOR?

16Ante esto, Micaías concedió:

—Vi a todo Israel esparcido por las colinas, como ovejas sin *pastor. Y el SEÑOR dijo: "Esta gente no tiene amo. ¡Que cada cual se vaya a su casa en paz!"

17El rey de Israel le dijo a Josafat:

—¿No te dije que jamás me profetiza nada bueno, y que sólo me anuncia desastres?

18Micaías prosiguió:

—Por lo tanto, oigan la palabra del SEÑOR: Vi al SEÑOR sentado en su trono con todo el ejército del cielo alrededor de él, a su derecha y a su izquierda. 19Y el SEÑOR dijo: "¿Quién seducirá a Acab, rey de Israel, para que ataque a Ramot de Galaad y vaya a morir allí?" Uno sugería una cosa, y otro sugería otra. 20Por último, un espíritu se adelantó, se puso delante del SEÑOR y dijo: "Yo lo seduciré." "¿Por qué me-

dios?", preguntó el SEÑOR. 21Y aquel espíritu respondió: "Saldré y seré un espíritu mentiroso en la boca de sus profetas." Entonces el SEÑOR ordenó: "Ve y hazlo así, que tendrás éxito en seducirlo." 22Así que ahora el SEÑOR ha puesto un espíritu mentiroso en la boca de estos profetas de Su Majestad. El SEÑOR ha decretado para usted la calamidad.

23Al oír esto, Sedequías hijo de Quenaná se levantó y le dio una bofetada a Micaías.

—¿Por dónde se fue el espíritue del SEÑOR cuando salió de mí para hablarte? —le preguntó.

24Micaías contestó:

—Lo sabrás el día en que andes de escondite en escondite.

25Entonces el rey de Israel ordenó:

—Tomen a Micaías, y llévenselo a Amón, el gobernador de la ciudad, y a Joás, mi hijo. 26Díganles que les ordeno echar en la cárcel a ese tipo, y no darle más que pan y agua, hasta que yo regrese sin contratiempos.

27Micaías manifestó:

—Si regresas sin contratiempos, el SEÑOR no ha hablado por medio de mí. ¡Tomen nota todos ustedes de lo que estoy diciendo!

Muerte de Acab en Ramot de Galaad
18:28-34 — 1R 22:29-36

28El rey de Israel, y Josafat, rey de Judá, marcharon juntos contra Ramot de Galaad. 29Allí el rey de Israel le dijo a Josafat: «Yo entraré a la batalla disfrazado, pero tú te pondrás tus vestiduras reales.» Así que el rey de Israel se disfrazó y entró al combate.

30Pero el rey de *Siria les había ordenado a sus capitanes de los carros de combate: «No luchen contra nadie, grande o pequeño, salvo contra el rey de Israel.» 31Cuando los capitanes de los carros vieron a Josafat, pensaron: «Éste es el rey de Israel.» Así que se volvieron para atacarlo; pero Josafat gritó, y Dios el SEÑOR lo ayudó, haciendo que se apartaran de él. 32Entonces los capitanes de los carros vieron que no era el rey de Israel, y dejaron de perseguirlo.

33Sin embargo, alguien disparó su arco al azar y hirió al rey de Israel entre las piezas de su armadura. El rey le ordenó al que conducía su carro: «Da la vuelta y sácame del campo de batalla, pues me han herido.» 34Todo el día arreció la batalla, y al rey de Israel se le mantuvo de pie en su carro frente a los sirios, hasta el atardecer, y murió al ponerse el sol.

19 Cuando Josafat, rey de Judá, regresó sin ningún contratiempo a su palacio en Jerusalén, 2el vidente Jehú hijo de Jananí fue a visitarlo y le dijo: «¿Cómo te atreviste a ayudar a los malvados, haciendo alianza con los enemigos delf SEÑOR? Por haber hecho eso, la ira del SEÑOR ha caído sobre ti. 3Pero hay cosas buenas a tu favor, pues has quitado del país las imágenes de la diosa *Aserá, y has buscado a Dios de todo *corazón.»

Josafat nombra jueces

4Josafat se estableció en Jerusalén, pero volvió a visitar al pueblo, desde Berseba hasta los montes de Efraín, para hacerlo volver al SEÑOR, Dios de sus antepasados. 5En cada una de las ciudades fortificadas de Judá nombró jueces 6y les advirtió: «Tengan mucho cuidado con lo que hacen, pues su autoridad no proviene de un *hombre, sino del SEÑOR, que estará con ustedes cuando impartan justicia. 7Por eso, teman al SEÑOR y tengan cuidado con lo que hacen,

---

e 18:23 *espíritu.* Alt. *Espíritu.* f 19:2 *haciendo alianza con los enemigos del.* Lit. *y amas a los que odian al.*

porque el SEÑOR nuestro Dios no admite la injusticia ni la parcialidad ni el soborno.»

8En Jerusalén, Josafat designó también a levitas, sacerdotes y jefes de las familias patriarcales de Israel, para que administraran la *ley del SEÑOR y resolvieran pleitos. Éstos vivían en Jerusalén. 9Josafat les ordenó: «Ustedes actuarán con fidelidad e integridad, bajo el temor del SEÑOR. 10Cuando sus compatriotas vengan de las ciudades y sometan al juicio de ustedes casos de violencia, o algún otro asunto concerniente a la ley, los mandamientos, los estatutos y los juicios, ustedes les advertirán que no pequen contra el SEÑOR, para que su ira no caiga sobre ustedes y sobre ellos. Si así lo hacen, no serán culpables.

11»El sumo sacerdote Amarías los orientará en todo asunto de carácter religioso, mientras que Zebadías hijo de Ismael, que es el jefe de la tribu de Judá, lo hará en todo asunto de carácter civil.g También los levitas estarán al servicio de ustedes. ¡Anímense, y manos a la obra! El SEÑOR estará con los que actúen bien.»

Josafat derrota a Moab y Amón

20 Después de esto, los moabitas, los amonitas y algunos de los meunitash le declararon la guerra a Josafat, 2y alguien fue a informarle: «Del otro lado del Mar Muerto y de Edomi viene contra ti una gran multitud. Ahora están en Jazezón Tamar, es decir, en Engadi.» 3Atemorizado, Josafat decidió consultar al SEÑOR y proclamó un ayuno en todo Judá. 4Los habitantes de todas las ciudades de Judá llegaron para pedir juntos la ayuda del SEÑOR.

5En el templo del SEÑOR, frente al atrio nuevo, Josafat se puso de pie ante la asamblea de Judá y de Jerusalén, 6y dijo:

«SEÑOR, Dios de nuestros antepasados, ¿no eres tú el Dios del cielo, y el que gobierna a todas las naciones? ¡Es tal tu fuerza y tu poder que no hay quien pueda resistirte! 7¿No fuiste tú, Dios nuestro, quien a los ojos de tu pueblo Israel expulsó a los habitantes de esta tierra? ¿Y no fuiste tú quien les dio para siempre esta tierra a los descendientes de tu amigo Abraham? 8Ellos la habitaron y construyeron un santuario en tu honor, diciendo: 9"Cuando nos sobrevenga una calamidad, o un castigo por medio de la espada, la peste o el hambre, si nos congregamos ante ti, en este templo donde habitas, y clamamos a ti en medio de nuestra aflicción, tú nos escucharás y nos salvarás."

10»Cuando Israel salió de Egipto, tú no le permitiste que invadiera a los amonitas, ni a los moabitas ni a los del monte de Seír, sino que lo enviaste por otro camino para que no destruyera a esas naciones. 11¡Mira cómo nos pagan ahora, viniendo a arrojarnos de la tierra que tú nos diste como herencia! 12Dios nuestro, ¿acaso no vas a dictar sentencia contra ellos? Nosotros no podemos oponernos a esa gran multitud que viene a atacarnos. ¡No sabemos qué hacer! ¡En ti hemos puesto nuestra esperanza!»

13Todos los hombres de Judá estaban de pie delante del SEÑOR, junto con sus mujeres y sus hijos, aun los más pequeños. 14Entonces el Espíritu del SEÑOR vino sobre Jahaziel, hijo de Zacarías y descendiente en línea directa de Benaías, Jeyel y Matanías. Este último era un levita de los hijos de Asaf que se encontraba en la asamblea. 15Y dijo Jahaziel: «Escuchen, habitantes de Judá y de Jerusalén, y escuche también Su Majestad. Así dice el SEÑOR: "No tengan miedo ni se acobarden cuando vean ese gran ejército, porque la batalla no es de ustedes sino mía. 16Mañana, cuando ellos suban por la cuesta de Sis, ustedes saldrán contra ellos y los encontrarán junto al arroyo, frente al desierto de Jeruel. 17Pero ustedes no tendrán que intervenir en esta batalla. Simplemente, quédense quietos en sus puestos, para que vean la *salvación que el SEÑOR les dará. ¡Habitantes de Judá y de Jerusalén, no tengan miedo ni se acobarden! Salgan mañana contra ellos, porque yo, el SEÑOR, estaré con ustedes."»

18Josafat y todos los habitantes de Judá y de Jerusalén se postraron rostro en tierra y adoraron al SEÑOR, 19y los levitas de los hijos de Coat y de Coré se pusieron de pie para alabar al SEÑOR a voz en cuello.

20Al día siguiente, madrugaron y fueron al desierto de Tecoa. Mientras avanzaban, Josafat se detuvo y dijo: «Habitantes de Judá y de Jerusalén, escúchenme: ¡Confíen en el SEÑOR, y serán librados! ¡Confíen en sus profetas, y tendrán éxito!»

21Después de consultar con el pueblo, Josafat designó a los que irían al frente del ejército para cantar al SEÑOR y alabar el esplendor de su santidadi con el cántico: «Den gracias al SEÑOR; su gran amor perdura para siempre.»

22Tan pronto como empezaron a entonar este cántico de alabanza, el SEÑOR puso emboscadas contra los amonitas, los moabitas y los del monte de Seír que habían venido contra Judá, y los derrotó. 23De hecho, los amonitas y los moabitas atacaron a los habitantes de los montes de Seír y los mataron hasta aniquilarlos. Luego de exterminar a los habitantes de Seír, ellos mismos se atacaron y se mataron unos a otros.

24Cuando los hombres de Judá llegaron a la torre del desierto para ver el gran ejército enemigo, no vieron sino los cadáveres que yacían en tierra. ¡Ninguno había escapado con vida! 25Entonces Josafat y su gente fueron para apoderarse del botín, y entre los cadáveres encontraron muchas riquezas, vestidos y joyas preciosas. Cada uno se apoderó de todo lo que quiso, hasta más no poder. Era tanto el botín, que tardaron tres días en recogerlo. 26El cuarto día se congregaron en el valle de Beracá, y alabaron al SEÑOR; por eso llamaron a ese lugar el valle de Beracá,k nombre con el que hasta hoy se lo conoce.

27Más tarde, todos los de Judá y Jerusalén, con Josafat a la cabeza, regresaron a Jerusalén llenos de gozo porque el SEÑOR los había librado de sus enemigos. 28Al llegar, entraron en el templo del SEÑOR al son de arpas, liras y trompetas.

29Al oír las naciones de la tierra cómo el SEÑOR había peleado contra los enemigos de Israel, el temor de Dios se apoderó de ellas. 30Por lo tanto, el reinado de Josafat disfrutó de tranquilidad, y Dios le dio *paz por todas partes.

Fin del reinado de Josafat
20:31—21:1 — 1R 22:41-50

31Josafat tenía treinta y cinco años cuando ascendió al trono de Judá, y reinó en Jerusalén veinticinco años. El nombre de su madre era Azuba hija de

---

g 19:11 de carácter religioso ... de carácter civil. Lit. del SEÑOR ... del rey.　h 20:1 meunitas (LXX); amonitas (TM).
i 20:2 Edom (un ms. hebreo y Vetus Latina); Aram (TM).　j 20:21 el esplendor de su santidad. Alt. vestidos de ropas sagradas.
k 20:26 En hebreo, Beracá significa bendición o alabanza.

Siljí. ³²Siguió el buen ejemplo de su padre Asá y nunca se desvió de él, sino que hizo lo que agrada al SEÑOR. ³³Sin embargo, no se quitaron los *santuarios paganos, pues el pueblo aún no se había consagrado al Dios de sus antepasados.

³⁴Los demás acontecimientos del reinado de Josafat, desde el primero hasta el último, están escritos en las crónicas de Jehú hijo de Jananí, que forman parte del libro de los reyes de Israel.

³⁵Después de esto, Josafat se alió con el perverso Ocozías, rey de Israel, ³⁶para construir una flota mercante que iría a Tarsis. Los barcos los hacían en Ezión Guéber. ³⁷Entonces Eliezer hijo de Dodías, de Maresá, profetizó contra Josafat: «Por haberte aliado con Ocozías, el SEÑOR destruirá lo que estás haciendo.» En efecto, los barcos naufragaron y no pudieron ir a Tarsis.

Jorán, rey de Judá
21:5-10,20 — 2R 8:16-24

21 Josafat murió y fue sepultado con sus antepasados en la Ciudad de David, y su hijo Jorán lo sucedió en el trono. ²Sus hermanos eran Azarías, Jehiel, Zacarías, Azarías, Micael y Sefatías. Todos éstos fueron hijos de Josafat, rey de Israel. ³Su padre le había regalado plata, oro y objetos de valor en abundancia, y les entregó también ciudades fortificadas en Judá, pero el reino se lo dio a Jorán, porque era el hijo mayor. ⁴Cuando Jorán se afirmó completamente en el trono de su padre, mató a espada a todos sus hermanos y también a algunos jefes de Israel.

⁵Jorán tenía treinta y dos años cuando ascendió al trono, y reinó en Jerusalén ocho años. ⁶Pero hizo lo que ofende al SEÑOR, pues siguió el mal ejemplo de los reyes de Israel, como lo había hecho la familia de Acab, y llegó incluso a casarse con la hija de Acab. ⁷Pero el SEÑOR no quiso destruir la dinastía de David por consideración al *pacto que había hecho con él, pues le había prometido mantener encendida para siempre una lámpara para él y sus descendientes.

⁸En tiempos de Jorán, los edomitas se sublevaron contra Judá y se nombraron su propio rey. ⁹Por lo tanto, Jorán marchó con sus capitanes y todos sus carros de combate. Los edomitas lo cercaron a él y a los capitanes de los carros, pero durante la noche Jorán logró abrirse paso. ¹⁰Desde entonces Edom ha estado en rebelión contra Judá, al igual que la ciudad de Libná, que en ese mismo tiempo se sublevó. Esto sucedió porque Jorán abandonó al SEÑOR, Dios de sus antepasados. ¹¹Además, Jorán construyó *santuarios paganos en las colinas de Judá, e indujo a los habitantes de Jerusalén y de Judá a la idolatría.

¹²El profeta Elías le envió una carta con este mensaje:

«Así dice el SEÑOR, Dios de tu antepasado David: "Por cuanto no seguiste el buen ejemplo de tu padre Josafat, ni el de Asá, rey de Judá, ¹³sino que seguiste el mal ejemplo de los reyes de Israel, haciendo que los habitantes de Judá y de Jerusalén fueran infieles a Dios,ˡ como lo hizo la familia de Acab; y por cuanto asesinaste a tus hermanos, la familia de tu padre, que eran mejores que tú, ¹⁴el SEÑOR herirá con una plaga terrible a tu pueblo, a tus hijos, a tus mujeres y todas tus posesiones. ¹⁵Y

a ti te enviará una enfermedad en las entrañas, tan grave que día tras día empeorará, hasta que se te salgan los intestinos."»

¹⁶El SEÑOR incitó a los filisteos y a los árabes vecinos de los *cusitas para que se rebelaran contra Jorán. ¹⁷Así que marcharon contra Judá y la invadieron, y se llevaron todos los objetos de valor que hallaron en el palacio real, junto con los hijos y las mujeres de Jorán. Ninguno de sus hijos escapó con vida, excepto Joacaz, que era el menor de todos.

¹⁸Después de esto, el SEÑOR hirió a Jorán con una enfermedad incurable en las entrañas. ¹⁹Pasaron los días y, al cabo de dos años, murió en medio de una terrible agonía, pues por causa de su enfermedad se le salieron los intestinos. Su pueblo no encendió ninguna hoguera en su honor, como se había hecho en honor de sus antepasados.

²⁰Jorán tenía treinta y dos años cuando ascendió al trono, y reinó en Jerusalén ocho años. Murió sin que nadie guardara luto por él, y fue sepultado en la Ciudad de David, pero no en el panteón de los reyes.

Ocozías, rey de Judá
22:1-6 — 2R 8:25-29
22:7-9 — 2R 9:21-29

22 A la muerte de Jorán, los habitantes de Jerusalén proclamaron rey a Ocozías, su hijo menor, pues a sus hijos mayores los habían asesinado las bandas de árabes que habían venido al campamento. Así fue como Ocozías hijo de Jorán ascendió al trono de Judá. ²Tenía cuarenta y dos años cuando ascendió al trono, y reinó en Jerusalén un año. Su madre era Atalía, nietaᵐ de Omrí.

³También Ocozías siguió el mal ejemplo de la familia de Acab, pues su madre le aconsejaba que hiciera lo malo. ⁴Hizo lo que ofende al SEÑOR, como lo había hecho la familia de Acab. En efecto, una vez muerto su padre, Ocozías tuvo como consejeros a miembros de esa familia, para su perdición. ⁵Por consejo de ellos, Ocozías se juntó con Jorán hijo de Acab, rey de Israel, y marchó hacia Ramot de Galaad para hacerle la guerra a Jazael, rey de *Siria, pero en la batalla los sirios hirieron a Jorán. ⁶Por eso tuvo que regresar a Jezrel, para reponerse de las heridas que había recibido en Ramotⁿ cuando luchó contra Jazael, rey de Siria. Como Jorán hijo de Acab convalecía en Jezrel, Ocozíasñ hijo de Jorán, rey de Judá, fue a visitarlo.

Jehú mata a Ocozías

⁷Dios había dispuesto que Ocozías muriera cuando fuera a visitar a Jorán. Tan pronto como Ocozías llegó, salió acompañado de Jorán para encontrarse con Jehú hijo de Nimsi, al que el SEÑOR había escogido para exterminar a la familia de Acab. ⁸Mientras Jehú ejecutaba el juicio contra la familia de Acab, se encontró con los jefes de Judá y con los parientes de Ocozías que estaban al servicio de éste, y los mató. ⁹Luego mandó a buscar a Ocozías, que se había escondido en Samaria; pero lo apresaron y lo llevaron ante Jehú, quien ordenó matarlo. Sin embargo, le dieron sepultura, porque decían: «Es el hijo de Josafat, que buscó al SEÑOR con todo su *corazón.» Y en la familia de Ocozías no quedó nadie capaz de retener el reino.

ˡ **21:13** *fueran infieles a Dios.* Lit. *se prostituyeran.* ᵐ **22:2** *nieta.* Lit. *Hija.* ⁿ **22:6** *Ramot.* Lit. *Ramá* (variante de este nombre). ñ **22:6** *Ocozías* (mss. hebreos, LXX, Siríaca; véase 2R 8:29); *Azarías* (TM).

Atalía y Joás
22:10—23:21 — 2R 11:1-21

¹⁰Cuando Atalía madre de Ocozías vio que su hijo había muerto, tomó medidas para eliminar a toda la familia real de Judá. ¹¹Pero Josaba,ᵒ que era hija del rey y esposa del sacerdote Joyadá, raptó a Joás hijo de Ocozías cuando los príncipes estaban a punto de ser asesinados. Metiéndolo en un dormitorio con su nodriza, logró esconderlo de Atalía, de modo que no lo mataron. Hizo esto porque era la hermana de Ocozías. ¹²Seis años estuvo Joás escondido con ellos en el templo de Dios, mientras Atalía reinaba en el país.

23 En el séptimo año, el sacerdote Joyadá se armó de valor y convocó a los siguientes capitanes: Azarías hijo de Jeroán, Ismael hijo de Johanán, Azarías hijo de Obed, Maseías hijo de Adaías, y Elisafat hijo de Zicrí. ²Éstos recorrieron todo el país convocando a los levitas de todos los pueblos de Judá y a los jefes de las familias de Israel, para que fueran a Jerusalén. ³Allí toda la asamblea reunida en el templo de Dios hizo un *pacto con el rey.

Joyadá les dijo: «Aquí tienen al hijo del rey. Él es quien debe reinar, tal como lo prometió el SEÑOR a los descendientes de David. ⁴Así que hagan lo siguiente: Una tercera parte de ustedes, los sacerdotes y levitas que están de servicio en el *sábado, hará la guardia en las puertas; ⁵otra tercera parte permanecerá en el palacio real, y la tercera parte restante ocupará la puerta de los Cimientos, mientras que todo el pueblo estará en los atrios del templo. ⁶Sólo los sacerdotes y levitas que estén de servicio entrarán en el templo, pues ellos están consagrados; nadie más podrá entrar. El pueblo deberá obedecer el precepto del SEÑOR. ⁷Arma en mano, los levitas rodearán por completo al rey; y si alguien se atreve a entrar en el templo, mátenlo. ¡No dejen solo al rey, vaya donde vaya!»

⁸Los levitas y todos los habitantes de Judá cumplieron con todo lo que el sacerdote Joyadá les había ordenado. Cada uno reunió a sus hombres, tanto a los que estaban de servicio el sábado como a los que estaban libres, pues el sacerdote Joyadá no eximió a ninguno de los turnos. ⁹Éste repartió entre los capitanes las lanzas y los escudos grandes y pequeños del rey David, que estaban guardados en el templo de Dios, ¹⁰y luego colocó en sus puestos a todos. Cada uno, arma en mano, protegía al rey cerca del altar y desde el lado sur hasta el lado norte del templo. ¹¹Luego sacaron al hijo del rey, le pusieron la corona, le entregaron una copia del pactoᴾ y lo proclamaron rey. Joyadá y sus hijos lo ungieron y gritaron: «¡Viva el rey!»

¹²Cuando Atalía oyó la gritería del pueblo que corría y aclamaba al rey, fue al templo del SEÑOR, donde estaba la gente. ¹³Allí vio al rey de pie, junto a la columna de la entrada, y a los capitanes y músicos a su lado. Toda la gente tocaba alegre las trompetas, y los cantores, acompañados de instrumentos musicales, dirigían la alabanza. Al ver esto, Atalía se rasgó las vestiduras y gritó: «¡Traición! ¡Traición!»

¹⁴Entonces el sacerdote Joyadá, como no quería que la mataran en el templo del SEÑOR, hizo que salieran los capitanes que estaban al mando de las fuerzas, y les ordenó: «¡Sáquenla de entre las filas! Y si alguien se pone a su lado, ¡mátenlo a filo de espada!» ¹⁵Así que la apresaron y la llevaron al palacio por la puerta de la caballería, y allí la mataron.

¹⁶Luego Joyadá hizo un pacto con toda la gente y con el rey, para que fueran el pueblo del SEÑOR. ¹⁷Entonces toda la gente fue al templo de *Baal y lo derribó. Destruyeron los altares y los ídolos, y en frente de los altares degollaron a Matán, sacerdote de Baal.

¹⁸Después Joyadá apostó guardias en el templo del SEÑOR, bajo las órdenes de los sacerdotes y levitas. A éstos David les había asignado sus turnos para que ofrecieran al SEÑOR los *holocaustos, como está escrito en la *ley de Moisés, y para que cantaran con gozo, como lo había ordenado David. ¹⁹También colocó porteros en la entrada del templo del SEÑOR, para que le impidieran el paso a todo el que estuviera *impuro.

²⁰Acto seguido, Joyadá, acompañado de los capitanes, los nobles, los gobernadores y todo el pueblo, llevó al rey desde el templo del SEÑOR hasta el palacio real, pasando por la puerta superior, y sentaron a Joás en el trono real. ²¹Todo el pueblo estaba alegre, y tranquila la ciudad, pues habían matado a Atalía a filo de espada.

Joás, rey de Judá
24:1-14 — 2R 12:1-16
24:23-27 — 2R 12:17-21

24 Joás tenía siete años cuando ascendió al trono, y reinó en Jerusalén cuarenta años. Su madre era Sibia, oriunda de Berseba. ²Mientras el sacerdote Joyadá vivió, Joás hizo lo que agradaba al SEÑOR. ³Joyadá eligió dos esposas para Joás, y con ellas Joás tuvo hijos e hijas.

⁴Algún tiempo después, Joás decidió reparar el templo del SEÑOR. ⁵Reunió a los sacerdotes y a los levitas, y les dijo: «Vayan por las ciudades de Judá y recojan dinero de todos los israelitas, para reparar cada año el templo de su Dios. Háganlo inmediatamente.» Sin embargo, los levitas fueron negligentes. ⁶Entonces el rey llamó al sumo sacerdote Joyadá y le dijo: «¿Por qué no has presionado a los levitas para que vayan y recojan en Judá y en Jerusalén la contribución que Moisés, siervo del SEÑOR, y la asamblea de Israel impusieron para la Tienda del *pacto?»

⁷Resulta que la malvada de Atalía y sus hijos habían destrozado el templo de Dios, y hasta habían ofrecido a los *baales los objetos sagrados del templo del SEÑOR. ⁸Por eso el rey ordenó que se hiciera un cofre y se colocara afuera, junto a la puerta del templo del SEÑOR. ⁹Luego mandó que se pregonara por Judá y Jerusalén que trajeran al SEÑOR la contribución que Moisés, siervo del SEÑOR, había ordenado a Israel en el desierto.

¹⁰Todos los jefes y todo el pueblo llevaron alegremente sus contribuciones, y las depositaron en el cofre hasta llenarlo. ¹¹Los levitas llevaban el cofre a los funcionarios del rey, para que lo examinaran. Cuando veían que había mucho dinero, se presentaban el secretario real y un oficial nombrado por el sumo sacerdote, y luego de vaciar el cofre, volvían a colocarlo en su lugar. Esto lo hacían todos los días, y así recogieron mucho dinero. ¹²El rey y Joyadá entregaban el dinero a los que supervisaban la restauración del templo del SEÑOR, y éstos contrataban canteros, carpinteros, y expertos en el manejo del hierro y del bronce, para repararlo.

¹³Los supervisores de la restauración trabajaron diligentemente hasta terminar la obra. Repararon el templo del SEÑOR y lo dejaron en buen estado y con-

---

ᵒ **22:11** *Josaba.* Lit. *Josabet* (variante de este nombre). ᴾ **23:11** *le pusieron ... pacto.* Alt. *le pusieron la corona y las insignias.*

forme al diseño original. ¹⁴Cuando terminaron, le llevaron al rey y a Joyadá el dinero que sobró, y éstos lo utilizaron para hacer utensilios para el templo del SEÑOR: utensilios para el culto y para los *holocaustos, y cucharones y vasos de oro y de plata.

Todos los días, mientras Joyadá vivió, se ofrecieron holocaustos en el templo del SEÑOR. ¹⁵Pero Joyadá envejeció, y murió muy anciano. Cuando murió, tenía ciento treinta años. ¹⁶Fue sepultado junto con los reyes en la Ciudad de David, porque había servido bien a Israel y a Dios y su templo.

Depravación de Joás

¹⁷Después de que Joyadá murió, los jefes de Judá se presentaron ante el rey para rendirle homenaje, y él escuchó sus consejos. ¹⁸Abandonaron el templo del SEÑOR, Dios de sus antepasados, y adoraron las imágenes de *Aserá y de los ídolos. Debido a este pecado, la ira de Dios cayó sobre Judá y Jerusalén. ¹⁹El SEÑOR les envió profetas para que los exhortaran a volver a él, pero no les hicieron caso.

²⁰El Espíritu de Dios vino sobre Zacarías, hijo del sacerdote Joyadá, y éste, presentándose ante el pueblo, declaró: «Así dice Dios el SEÑOR: ¿Por qué desobedecen mis mandamientos? De ese modo no prosperarán. Como me han abandonado, yo también los abandonaré.»

²¹⁻²²Pero ellos conspiraron contra Zacarías hijo de Joyadá y, por orden del rey, lo mataron a pedradas en el atrio del templo del SEÑOR. Así fue como el rey Joás, no tomando en cuenta la bondad de Joyadá, mató a su hijo Zacarías, quien al morir dijo: «¡Que el SEÑOR vea esto y te juzgue!»

²³Al cabo de un año, las tropas *sirias marcharon contra Joás, invadieron Judá y Jerusalén, y, después de matar a los jefes del pueblo, enviaron todo el botín al rey de Damasco. ²⁴Aunque el ejército sirio era pequeño, el SEÑOR permitió que derrotara a un ejército muy numeroso, porque los habitantes de Judá habían abandonado al SEÑOR, Dios de sus antepasados. De esta manera Joás recibió el castigo que merecía.

²⁵Cuando los sirios se retiraron, dejando a Joás gravemente herido, sus servidores conspiraron contra él y lo mataron en su propia cama, vengando así la muerte del hijo del sacerdote Joyadá. Luego lo sepultaron en la Ciudad de David, pero no en el panteón de los reyes. ²⁶Los que conspiraron contra Joás fueron Zabad hijo de Simat el amonita, y Jozabad hijo de Simrit el moabita.

²⁷Todo lo relacionado con los hijos de Joás, con las muchas profecías en su contra y con la restauración del templo de Dios, está escrito en el comentario sobre el libro de los reyes. Su hijo Amasías lo sucedió en el trono.

Amasías, rey de Judá
25:1-4 — 2R 14:1-6
25:11-12 — 2R 14:7
25:17-28 — 2R 14:8-20

25 Amasías tenía veinticinco años cuando ascendió al trono, y reinó en Jerusalén veintinueve años. Su madre era Joadán, oriunda de Jerusalén. ²Amasías hizo lo que agrada al SEÑOR, aunque no de todo *corazón. ³Después de afianzarse en el poder, Amasías mató a los ministros que habían asesinado a su padre el rey. ⁴Sin embargo, según lo que ordenó el SEÑOR, no mató a los hijos de los asesinos, pues está escrito en el libro de la *ley de

Moisés: «A los padres no se les dará muerte por la culpa de sus hijos, ni a los hijos se les dará muerte por la culpa de sus padres, sino que cada uno morirá por su propio pecado.»q

⁵Amasías reunió a los de Judá, y puso al frente de todo Judá y Benjamín jefes de mil y de cien soldados, agrupados según sus familias patriarcales. Censó a los hombres mayores de veinte años, y resultó que había trescientos mil hombres aptos para ir a la guerra y capaces de manejar la lanza y el escudo. ⁶Además, por la suma de tres mil trescientos kilosʳ de plata contrató a cien mil guerreros valientes de Israel.

⁷Pero un hombre de Dios fue a verlo y le dijo:
—Su Majestad, no permita que el ejército de Israel vaya con usted, porque el SEÑOR no está con esos efraimitas. ⁸Si usted va con ellos, Dios lo derribará en la cara misma de sus enemigos aunque luche valerosamente, porque Dios tiene poder para ayudar y poder para derribar.

⁹Amasías le preguntó al hombre de Dios:
—¿Qué va a pasar con los tres mil trescientos kilos de plata que pagué al ejército de Israel?
—El SEÑOR puede darle a usted mucho más que eso —respondió.

¹⁰Entonces Amasías dio de baja a las tropas israelitas que habían llegado de Efraín, y las hizo regresar a su país. A raíz de eso, las tropas se enojaron mucho con Judá y regresaron furiosas a sus casas.

¹¹Armándose de valor, Amasías guió al ejército hasta el valle de la Sal, donde mató a diez mil hombres de Seír. ¹²El ejército de Judá capturó vivos a otros diez mil. A éstos los hicieron subir a la cima de una roca, y desde allí los despeñaron. Todos murieron destrozados.

¹³Mientras esto sucedía, las tropas que Amasías había dado de baja se lanzaron contra las ciudades de Judá, y desde Samaria hasta Bet Jorón mataron a tres mil personas y se llevaron un enorme botín.

¹⁴Cuando Amasías regresó de derrotar a los edomitas, se llevó consigo los dioses de los habitantes de Seír y los adoptó como sus dioses, adorándolos y quemándoles incienso. ¹⁵Por eso el SEÑOR se encendió en ira contra Amasías y le envió un profeta con este mensaje:
—¿Por qué sigues a unos dioses que no pudieron librar de tus manos a su propio pueblo?

¹⁶El rey interrumpió al profeta y le replicó:
—¿Y quién te ha nombrado consejero del rey? Si no quieres que te maten, ¡no sigas fastidiándome!

El profeta se limitó a añadir:
—Sólo sé que, por haber hecho esto y por no seguir mi consejo, Dios ha resuelto destruirte.

¹⁷Sin embargo, Amasías, rey de Judá, siguiendo el consejo de otros, envió mensajeros a Joás, hijo de Joacaz y nieto de Jehú, rey de Israel, con este reto: «Ven acá, para que nos enfrentemos!»

¹⁸Pero Joás, rey de Israel, le respondió a Amasías, rey de Judá: «El cardo del Líbano le mandó este mensaje al cedro: "¡Entrega a tu hija como esposa a mi hijo!" Pero luego pasaron por allí las fieras del Líbano, y aplastaron al cardo. ¹⁹Tú te jactas de haber derrotado a los edomitas; el éxito se te ha subido a la cabeza! Está bien, jáctate si quieres, pero quédate en casa. ¿Para qué provocas una desgracia que significará tu perdición y la de Judá?»

²⁰Como estaba en los planes de Dios entregar a Amasías en poder del enemigo por haber seguido a los dioses de Edom, Amasías no le hizo caso a Joás.

---

q **25:4** Dt 24:16 r **25:6** *tres mil trescientos kilos.* Lit. *cien *talentos;* también en v. 9.

21Entonces Joás, rey de Israel, marchó a Bet Semes, que está en Judá, para enfrentarse con él. 22Los israelitas batieron a los de Judá, y éstos huyeron a sus hogares. 23En Bet Semes, Joás, rey de Israel, capturó a Amasías, rey de Judá, hijo de Joás y nieto de Joacaz.s Luego fue a Jerusalén y derribó ciento ochenta metrost de la muralla, desde la puerta de Efraín hasta la puerta de la Esquina. 24Además, se apoderó de todo el oro, la plata y los utensilios que estaban en el templo de Dios bajo el cuidado de Obed Edom. También se llevó los tesoros del palacio real, tomó rehenes y regresó a Samaria.

25Amasías hijo de Joás, rey de Judá, sobrevivió quince años a Joás hijo de Joacaz, rey de Israel. 26Los demás acontecimientos del reinado de Amasías, desde el primero hasta el último, están escritos en el libro de los reyes de Judá y de Israel. 27Desde el momento en que Amasías abandonó al SEÑOR, se tramó una conspiración contra él en Jerusalén. Entonces Amasías huyó a Laquis, pero lo persiguieron y allí lo mataron. 28Luego lo llevaron a caballo hasta la capital de Judá, donde fue sepultado con sus antepasados.

Uzías, rey de Judá
26:1-4 — 2R 14:21-22; 15:1-3
26:21-23 — 2R 15:5-7

26 Todo el pueblo de Judá tomó entonces a Uzías, que tenía dieciséis años, y lo proclamó rey en lugar de su padre Amasías. 2Y fue Uzías quien, después de la muerte del rey Amasías, reconstruyó la ciudad de Elat y la reintegró a Judá.

3Uzías tenía dieciséis años cuando ascendió al trono, y reinó en Jerusalén cincuenta y dos años. Su madre era Jecolías, oriunda de Jerusalén. 4Uzías hizo lo que agrada al SEÑOR, pues en todo siguió el buen ejemplo de su padre Amasías 5y, mientras vivió Zacarías, quien lo instruyó en el temor de Dios, se empeñó en buscar al SEÑOR. Mientras Uzías buscó a Dios, Dios le dio prosperidad.

6Uzías marchó contra los filisteos, y destruyó los muros de Gat, Jabnia y Asdod. Además, construyó ciudades en la región de Asdod, entre los filisteos. 7Dios lo ayudó en su guerra contra los filisteos, contra los árabes que vivían en Gur Baal, y contra los meunitas. 8Los amonitas fueron tributarios de Uzías, y éste llegó a tener tanto poder que su fama se difundió hasta la frontera de Egipto.

9Uzías también construyó y fortificó torres en Jerusalén, sobre las puertas de la Esquina y del Valle, y en el ángulo del muro. 10Así mismo, construyó torres en el desierto y cavó un gran número de pozos, pues tenía mucho ganado en la llanura y en la meseta. Tenía también labradores y viñadores que trabajaban en las montañas y en los valles, pues era un amante de la agricultura.

11Uzías contaba con un ejército que salía a la guerra por escuadrones, de acuerdo con el censo hecho por el cronista Jeyel y por el oficial Maseías, bajo la dirección de Jananías,

funcionario del rey. 12El total de los jefes de familia era de dos mil seiscientos, todos ellos guerreros valientes. 13Bajo el mando de éstos había un ejército bien entrenado, compuesto por trescientos siete mil quinientos soldados, que combatían con mucho valor para apoyar al rey en su lucha contra los enemi-

gos. 14A ese ejército Uzías lo dotó de escudos, lanzas, cascos, corazas, arcos y hondas. 15Construyó en Jerusalén unas máquinas diseñadas por hombres ingeniosos, y las colocó en las torres y en las esquinas de la ciudad para disparar flechas y piedras de gran tamaño. Con la poderosa ayuda de Dios, Uzías llegó a ser muy poderoso y su fama se extendió hasta muy lejos.

16Sin embargo, cuando aumentó su poder, Uzías se volvió arrogante, lo cual lo llevó a la desgracia. Se rebeló contra el SEÑOR, Dios de sus antepasados, y se atrevió a entrar en el templo del SEÑOR para quemar incienso en el altar. 17Detrás de él entró el sumo sacerdote Azarías, junto con ochenta sacerdotes del SEÑOR, todos ellos hombres valientes, 18quienes se le enfrentaron y le dijeron: «No corresponde a tu Majestad quemar el incienso al SEÑOR. Ésta es función de los sacerdotes descendientes de Aarón, pues son ellos los que están consagrados para quemar el incienso. Salga usted ahora mismo del santuario, pues ha pecado, y así Dios el SEÑOR no va a honrarlo.»

19Esto enfureció a Uzías, quien tenía en la mano un incensario listo para ofrecer el incienso. Pero en ese mismo instante, allí en el templo del SEÑOR, junto al altar del incienso y delante de los sacerdotes, la frente se le cubrió de *lepra. 20Al ver que Uzías estaba leproso, el sumo sacerdote Azarías y los demás sacerdotes lo expulsaron de allí a toda prisa. Es más, él mismo se apresuró a salir, pues el SEÑOR lo había castigado.

21El rey Uzías se quedó leproso hasta el día de su muerte. Tuvo que vivir aislado en su casa,u y le prohibieron entrar en el templo del SEÑOR. Su hijo Jotán quedó a cargo del palacio y del gobierno del país.

22Los demás acontecimientos del reinado de Uzías, desde el primero hasta el último, los escribió el profeta Isaías hijo de Amoz. 23Cuando Uzías murió, fue sepultado con sus antepasados en un campo cercano al panteón de los reyes, pues padecía de lepra. Y su hijo Jotán lo sucedió en el trono.

Jotán, rey de Judá
27:1-4,7-9 — 2R 15:33-38

27 Jotán tenía veinticinco años cuando ascendió al trono, y reinó en Jerusalén dieciséis años. Su madre era Jerusa hija de Sadoc. 2Jotán hizo lo que agrada al SEÑOR, pues en todo siguió el buen ejemplo de su padre Uzías, aunque no iba al templo del SEÑOR. El pueblo, por su parte, continuó con sus prácticas corruptas. 3Jotán fue quien reconstruyó la puerta superior del templo del SEÑOR. Hizo también muchas obras en el muro de Ofel, 4construyó ciudades en las montañas de Judá, y fortalezas y torres en los bosques.

5Jotán le declaró la guerra al rey de los amonitas y lo venció. Durante tres años consecutivos, los amonitas tuvieron que pagarle un tributo anual de cien barrasv de plata, diez mil cargas de trigo y diez mil cargasw de cebada.

6Jotán llegó a ser poderoso porque se propuso obedecer al SEÑOR su Dios.

7Los demás acontecimientos del reinado de Jotán, y sus guerras y su conducta, están escritos en el libro de los reyes de Israel y de Judá. 8Tenía Jotán veinticinco años cuando ascendió al trono, y reinó en Jerusalén dieciséis años. 9Cuando murió, fue sepul-

---

s **25:23** *Joacaz* es otra forma del nombre *Ocozías*. t **25:23** *ciento ochenta metros.* Lit. *cuatrocientos* *codos. u **26:21** *aislado en su casa.* Lit. *en casa de libertad*; es decir, libre de responsabilidades. v **27:5** *barras.* Lit. **talentos.* w **27:5** *cargas ... cargas.* Lit. **coros ... coros.*

tado en la Ciudad de David, y su hijo Acaz lo sucedió en el trono.

Acaz, rey de Judá
28:1-27 — 2R 16:1-20

28 Acaz tenía veinte años cuando ascendió al trono, y reinó en Jerusalén dieciséis años. Pero a diferencia de su antepasado David, Acaz no hizo lo que agrada al SEÑOR. ²Al contrario, siguió el mal ejemplo de los reyes de Israel, y también hizo imágenes fundidas de los *baales. ³Así mismo, quemó incienso en el valle de Ben Hinón y sacrificó en el fuego a sus hijos, según las repugnantes ceremonias de las naciones que el SEÑOR había expulsado al paso de los israelitas. ⁴También ofrecía sacrificios y quemaba incienso en los *santuarios paganos, en las colinas y bajo todo árbol frondoso.

⁵Por eso el SEÑOR su Dios lo entregó al poder del rey de *Siria. Los sirios lo derrotaron, y capturaron una gran cantidad de prisioneros que se llevaron a Damasco.

Acaz también cayó en poder del rey de Israel, quien le infligió una gran derrota. ⁶En un solo día, Pécaj hijo de Remalías mató en Judá a ciento veinte mil hombres, todos ellos soldados valientes, porque los habitantes de Judá habían abandonado al SEÑOR, Dios de sus antepasados. ⁷Zicrí, un guerrero de Efraín, mató a Maseías, hijo del rey, a Azricán, oficial encargado del palacio, y a Elcaná, que era el oficial más importante después del rey. ⁸De entre sus hermanos de Judá, los israelitas capturaron a doscientas mil personas, incluyendo a mujeres, niños y niñas. Además, se apoderaron de un enorme botín, que se llevaron a Samaria.

⁹Había allí un hombre llamado Oded, que era profeta del SEÑOR. Cuando el ejército regresaba a Samaria, este profeta salió a su encuentro y les dijo:

—El SEÑOR, Dios de sus antepasados, entregó a los de Judá en manos de ustedes, porque estaba enojado con ellos. Pero ustedes los mataron con tal furia, que repercutió en el cielo. ¹⁰Y como si fuera poco, ¡ahora pretenden convertir a los habitantes de Judá y de Jerusalén en sus esclavos! ¿Acaso no son también ustedes culpables de haber pecado contra el SEÑOR su Dios? ¹¹Por tanto, háganme caso: dejen libres a los prisioneros. ¿Acaso no son sus propios hermanos? ¡La ira del SEÑOR se ha encendido contra ustedes!

¹²Entonces Azarías hijo de Johanán, Berequías hijo de Mesilemot, Ezequías hijo de Salún, y Amasá hijo de Hadlay, que eran jefes de los efraimitas, se enfrentaron a los que regresaban de la guerra ¹³y les dijeron:

—No traigan aquí a los prisioneros, porque eso nos haría culpables ante el SEÑOR. ¿Acaso pretenden aumentar nuestros pecados y nuestras faltas? ¡Ya es muy grande nuestra culpa, y la ira del SEÑOR se ha encendido contra Israel!

¹⁴Así que los soldados dejaron libres a los prisioneros, y pusieron el botín a los pies de los jefes y de toda la asamblea. ¹⁵Algunos fueron nombrados para que se hicieran cargo de los prisioneros, y con la ropa y el calzado del botín vistieron a todos los que estaban desnudos. Luego les dieron de comer y de beber, y les untaron aceite. Finalmente, a los que estaban débiles los montaron en burros y los llevaron a Jericó, la ciudad de las palmeras, para reunirlos con sus hermanos. Después, aquellos hombres volvieron a Samaria.

¹⁶En aquel tiempo, el rey Acaz solicitó la ayuda de los reyes de Asiria, ¹⁷porque los edomitas habían atacado nuevamente a Judá y se habían llevado algunos prisioneros. ¹⁸Por su parte, los filisteos saquearon las ciudades de Judá que estaban en la llanura y en el Néguev, se apoderaron de Bet Semes, Ayalón, Guederot, Soco, Timná y Guimzó, junto con sus respectivas aldeas, y se establecieron en ellas. ¹⁹Así fue como el SEÑOR humilló a Judá, por culpa de Acaz su rey,ˣ quien permitió el desenfreno en Judá y se rebeló totalmente contra el SEÑOR.

²⁰Tiglat Piléser, rey de Asiria, en vez de apoyar a Acaz, marchó contra él y empeoró su situación. ²¹Entonces Acaz le entregó al rey de Asiria todo lo que había de valor en el templo del SEÑOR, en el palacio real y en las casas de sus oficiales; pero eso de nada le sirvió. ²²Y a pesar de encontrarse tan presionado, el rey Acaz se empecinó en su rebelión contra el SEÑOR. ²³Incluso ofreció sacrificios a los dioses de Damasco que lo habían derrotado, pues pensó: «Como los dioses de Siria ayudan a sus reyes, también me ayudarán a mí si les ofrezco sacrificios.» Pero esos dioses fueron su ruina y la de todo Israel. ²⁴Acaz también juntó y despedazó los utensilios del templo del SEÑOR, cerró sus puertas e hizo construir altares en cada esquina de Jerusalén. ²⁵Y en todas las ciudades de Judá hizo construir *santuarios paganos para quemar incienso a otros dioses, ofendiendo así al SEÑOR, Dios de sus antepasados.

²⁶Los demás acontecimientos de su reinado, desde el primero hasta el último, lo mismo que su conducta, están escritos en el libro de los reyes de Judá y de Israel. ²⁷Acaz murió y fue sepultado en la ciudad de Jerusalén, pero no en el panteón de los reyes de Israel. Su hijo Ezequías lo sucedió en el trono.

Ezequías, rey de Judá
29:1-2 — 2R 18:2-3

29 Ezequías tenía veinticinco años cuando ascendió al trono, y reinó en Jerusalén veintinueve años. Su madre era Abías hija de Zacarías. ²Ezequías hizo lo que agrada al SEÑOR, pues en todo siguió el buen ejemplo de su antepasado David.

³En el mes primero del primer año de su reinado, Ezequías mandó que se abrieran las puertas del templo del SEÑOR, y las reparó. ⁴En la plaza oriental convocó a los sacerdotes y a los levitas, ⁵y les dijo:

«¡Levitas, escúchenme! *Purifíquense ustedes, y purifiquen también el templo del SEÑOR, Dios de sus antepasados, y saquen las cosas profanas que hay en el santuario. ⁶Es un hecho que nuestros antepasados se rebelaron e hicieron lo que ofende al SEÑOR nuestro Dios, y que lo abandonaron. Es también un hecho que le dieron la espalda al SEÑOR, y que despreciaron el lugar donde él habita. ⁷Así mismo, cerraron las puertas del atrio, apagaron las lámparas, y dejaron de quemar incienso y de ofrecer *holocaustos en el santuario al Dios de Israel.

⁸»¡Por eso la ira del SEÑOR cayó sobre Judá y Jerusalén, y los convirtió en objeto de horror, de desolación y de burla, tal como ustedes pueden verlo ahora con sus propios ojos! ⁹¡Por eso nuestros antepasados murieron a filo de espada, y nuestros hijos, nuestras hijas y nuestras mujeres fueron llevados al cautiverio!

¹⁰»Yo me propongo ahora hacer un *pacto con el SEÑOR, Dios de Israel, para que retire de

---

ˣ **28:19** *su rey.* Lit. *rey de Israel.* En este libro se usa con frecuencia el nombre de Israel para referirse a Judá.

nosotros su ardiente ira. 11Así que, hijos míos, no sean negligentes, pues el SEÑOR los ha escogido a ustedes para que estén en su presencia, y le sirvan, y sean sus ministros y le quemen incienso.»

12Éstos son los levitas que se dispusieron a trabajar:

De los descendientes de Coat:
Mahat hijo de Amasay, y Joel hijo de Azarías.
De los descendientes de Merari:
Quis hijo de Abdí, y Azarías hijo de Yalelel.
De los descendientes de Guersón:
Joa hijo de Zimá, y Edén hijo de Joa.
13 De los descendientes de Elizafán:
Simri y Jeyel.
De los descendientes de Asaf:
Zacarías y Matanías.
14 De los descendientes de Hemán:
Jehiel y Simí.
De los descendientes de Jedutún:
Semaías y Uziel.

15Éstos reunieron a sus parientes, se purificaron y entraron en el templo del SEÑOR para purificarlo, cumpliendo así la orden del rey, según las palabras del SEÑOR. 16Después los sacerdotes entraron al interior del templo del SEÑOR para purificarlo. Sacaron al atrio del templo todos los objetos paganos y que encontraron allí, y los levitas los recogieron y los arrojaron al arroyo de Cedrón. 17Comenzaron a purificar el templo el primer día del mes primero, y al octavo día ya habían llegado al pórtico del templo. Para completar la purificación emplearon otros ocho días, de modo que terminaron el día dieciséis del mes primero.

18Más tarde, se presentaron ante el rey Ezequías y le dijeron: «Ya hemos purificado el templo del SEÑOR, el altar de los holocaustos con sus utensilios, y la mesa para el *pan de la Presencia con sus utensilios. 19Además, hemos reparado y purificado todos los utensilios que, en su rebeldía, el rey Acaz profanó durante su reinado, y los hemos puesto ante el altar del SEÑOR.»

20El rey Ezequías se levantó muy de mañana, reunió a los jefes de la ciudad y se fue con ellos al templo del SEÑOR. 21Llevaron siete bueyes, siete carneros y siete corderos; además, como ofrenda por el pecado del reino, del santuario y de Judá, llevaron siete machos cabríos. El rey ordenó a los sacerdotes descendientes de Aarón que los ofrecieran en holocausto sobre el altar del SEÑOR. 22Los sacerdotes mataron los toros, recogieron la sangre y la rociaron sobre el altar; luego mataron los carneros y rociaron la sangre sobre el altar; después mataron los corderos y rociaron la sangre sobre el altar. 23Finalmente, a los machos cabríos de la ofrenda por el pecado los llevaron y los colocaron delante del rey y de la asamblea para que pusieran las manos sobre ellos; 24luego los mataron y rociaron la sangre sobre el altar como una ofrenda por el pecado de todo Israel, pues el rey había ordenado que el holocausto y el sacrificio por el pecado se ofrecieran por todo Israel.

25Ezequías instaló también a los levitas en el templo del SEÑOR, con música de címbalos, arpas y liras, tal como lo habían ordenado David, Natán el profeta, y Gad, el vidente del rey. Este mandato lo dio el SEÑOR por medio de sus profetas.

26Los levitas estaban de pie con los instrumentos musicales de David, y los sacerdotes, con las trompetas. 27Entonces Ezequías ordenó que se ofreciera el holocausto sobre el altar. En cuanto comenzó el holocausto, comenzaron también los cantos al SEÑOR y el toque de trompetas, acompañados de los instrumentos musicales de David, rey de Israel. 28Toda la asamblea permaneció postrada hasta que terminó el holocausto, mientras los cantores entonaban los cantos y los trompetistas hacían resonar sus instrumentos.

29Cuando terminaron de ofrecer el holocausto, el rey y todos los que estaban con él se postraron para adorar al SEÑOR. 30El rey Ezequías y los jefes les ordenaron a los levitas que cantaran al SEÑOR las alabanzas que David y Asaf el vidente habían compuesto. Los levitas lo hicieron con alegría, y se postraron en adoración.

31Luego Ezequías dijo: «Ahora que ustedes se han consagrado al SEÑOR, acérquense y preséntenle en su templo los sacrificios y las ofrendas de acción de gracias.» 32Así que la asamblea llevó setenta bueyes, cien carneros y doscientos corderos, para ofrecerlos en holocausto al SEÑOR. 33También se consagraron seiscientos bueyes y tres mil ovejas. 34Pero como los sacerdotes eran pocos y no podían desollar tantos animales, sus parientes levitas tuvieron que ayudarlos para terminar el trabajo, a fin de que los otros sacerdotes pudieran purificarse, pues los levitas habían sido más diligentes en purificarse que los sacerdotes. 35Se ofrecieron muchos holocaustos, además de la grasa de los sacrificios de *comunión y de las libaciones para cada holocausto.

Así fue como se restableció el culto en el templo del SEÑOR. 36Y Ezequías y todo el pueblo se regocijaron de que Dios hubiera preparado al pueblo para hacerlo todo con rapidez.

Celebración de la Pascua

30 Ezequías escribió cartas a todo Israel y Judá, incluyendo a las tribus de Efraín y Manasés, y se las envió, para que acudieran al templo del SEÑOR en Jerusalén a celebrar la Pascua del SEÑOR, Dios de Israel. 2El rey, los jefes y toda la asamblea habían decidido celebrar la Pascua en el mes segundo. 3No pudieron hacerlo en la fecha correspondiente porque muchos de los sacerdotes aún no se habían *purificado, y el pueblo no se había reunido en Jerusalén. 4Como la propuesta les agradó al rey y a la asamblea, 5acordaron pregonar por todo Israel, desde Dan hasta Berseba, que todos debían acudir a Jerusalén para celebrar la Pascua del SEÑOR, Dios de Israel, pues muchos no la celebraban como está prescrito.

6Los mensajeros salieron por todo Israel y Judá con las cartas del rey y de sus oficiales, y de acuerdo con la orden del rey iban proclamando:

«Israelitas, vuélvanse al SEÑOR, Dios de Abraham, de Isaac y de Israel, para que él se vuelva al remanente de ustedes, que escapó del poder de los reyes de Asiria. 7No sean como sus antepasados, ni como sus hermanos, que se rebelaron contra el SEÑOR, Dios de sus antepasados. Por eso él los convirtió en objeto de burla, como ahora lo pueden ver. 8No sean tercos, como sus antepasados. Sométanse al SEÑOR, y entren en su santuario, que él consagró para siempre. Sirvan al SEÑOR su Dios, para que él retire su ardiente ira. 9Si se vuelven al SEÑOR, sus hermanos y sus hijos serán tratados con benevolencia por aquellos que los tienen cautivos, y podrán regresar a esta tierra. El SEÑOR su

---

y 29:16 todos los objetos paganos. Lit. toda la *impureza.

Dios es compasivo y misericordioso. Si ustedes se vuelven a él, jamás los abandonará.»

¹⁰Los mensajeros recorrieron toda la región de Efraín y Manasés de ciudad en ciudad, hasta llegar a la región de Zabulón, pero todos se reían y se burlaban de ellos. ¹¹No obstante, algunos de las tribus de Aser, Manasés y Zabulón se humillaron y fueron a Jerusalén. ¹²También los habitantes de Judá, movidos por Dios, cumplieron unánimes la orden del rey y de los jefes, conforme a la palabra del SEÑOR.

¹³En el mes segundo, una inmensa muchedumbre se reunió en Jerusalén para celebrar la fiesta de los Panes sin levadura. ¹⁴Quitaron los altares que había en Jerusalén y los altares donde se quemaba incienso, y los arrojaron al arroyo de Cedrón.

¹⁵El día catorce del mes segundo celebraronᶻ la Pascua. Los sacerdotes y los levitas, compungidos, se purificaron y llevaron *holocaustos al templo del SEÑOR, ¹⁶después de lo cual ocuparon sus respectivos puestos, conforme a la *ley de Moisés, hombre de Dios. Los levitas entregaban la sangre a los sacerdotes, y éstos la rociaban. ¹⁷Como muchos de la asamblea no se habían purificado, para consagrarlos al SEÑOR los levitas tuvieron que matar por ellos los corderos de la Pascua. ¹⁸En efecto, mucha gente de Efraín, de Manasés, de Isacar y de Zabulón participó de la comida pascual sin haberse purificado, con lo que transgredieron lo prescrito. Pero Ezequías oró así a favor de ellos: «Perdona, buen Dios, ¹⁹a todo el que se ha empeñado de todo *corazón en buscarte a ti, SEÑOR, Dios de sus antepasados, aunque no se haya purificado según las normas de *santidad.» ²⁰Y el SEÑOR escuchó a Ezequías y perdonóᵃ al pueblo.

²¹Los israelitas que se encontraban en Jerusalén celebraron con mucho gozo, y durante siete días, la fiesta de los Panes sin levadura. Los levitas y sacerdotes alababan al SEÑOR todos los días, y le entonaban cantos al son de sus instrumentos musicales.ᵇ ²²Y Ezequías felicitó a los levitas que habían tenido una buena disposición para servir al SEÑOR.

Durante siete días celebraron la fiesta y participaron de la comida pascual, ofreciendo sacrificios de *comunión y alabando al SEÑOR, Dios de sus antepasados. ²³Pero toda la asamblea acordó prolongar la fiesta siete días más, y llenos de gozo celebraron esos siete días. ²⁴Ezequías, rey de Judá, le obsequió a la asamblea mil bueyes y siete mil ovejas, y también los jefes regalaron mil bueyes y diez mil ovejas. Y muchos más sacerdotes se purificaron. ²⁵Toda la asamblea de Judá estaba alegre, lo mismo que todos los sacerdotes, levitas y extranjeros que habían llegado de Israel, así como los que vivían en Judá. ²⁶Desde la época de Salomón hijo de David, rey de Israel, no se había celebrado en Jerusalén una fiesta tan alegre. ²⁷Después los sacerdotes y los levitas se pusieron de pie y bendijeron al pueblo, y el SEÑOR los escuchó; su oración llegó hasta el cielo, el *santo lugar donde Dios habita.

31
Cuando terminó la fiesta, todos los israelitas que estaban allí recorrieron las ciudades de Judá para derribar las piedras sagradas y las imágenes de la diosa *Aserá. También derribaron por completo los altares y los *santuarios paganos que había en los territorios de Judá, Benjamín, Efraín y Manasés. Después de eso, todos ellos regresaron a sus ciudades, cada uno a su propiedad.

Reorganización del culto
31:20-21 — 2R 18:5-7

²Ezequías les asignó turnos a los sacerdotes y levitas, para que cada uno sirviera según su oficio, y así ofreciera los *holocaustos o los sacrificios de *comunión, oficiara en el culto, cantara las alabanzas al SEÑOR, o sirviera en las puertas del temploᶜ del SEÑOR. ³El rey destinó parte de sus bienes para los holocaustos matutinos y vespertinos, y para los holocaustos de los *sábados, de luna nueva y de las fiestas solemnes, como está escrito en la *ley del SEÑOR. ⁴También ordenó que los habitantes de Jerusalén entregaran a los sacerdotes y a los levitas la parte que les correspondía, para que pudieran dedicarse a la ley del SEÑOR. ⁵Tan pronto como se dio la orden, los israelitas entregaron en abundancia las *primicias del trigo, del vino, del aceite, de la miel y de todos los productos del campo. También dieron en abundancia el diezmo de todo. ⁶De igual manera, los habitantes de Israel y los que vivían en las ciudades de Judá entregaron el diezmo de bueyes y ovejas, y de todas aquellas cosas que eran consagradas al SEÑOR su Dios, y todo lo colocaron en montones. ⁷Comenzaron a formar los montones en el mes tercero, y terminaron en el séptimo. ⁸Cuando Ezequías y sus oficiales fueron y vieron los montones, bendijeron al SEÑOR y a su pueblo Israel.

⁹Entonces Ezequías pidió a los sacerdotes y a los levitas que le informaran acerca de esos montones, ¹⁰y el sumo sacerdote Azarías, descendiente de Sadoc, le contestó: «Desde que el pueblo comenzó a traer sus ofrendas al templo del SEÑOR, hemos tenido suficiente comida y nos ha sobrado mucho, porque el SEÑOR ha bendecido a su pueblo. En esos montones está lo que ha sobrado.»

¹¹Ezequías ordenó entonces que prepararan unos depósitos en el templo del SEÑOR, y así lo hicieron. ¹²Y todos llevaron fielmente las ofrendas, los diezmos y los dones consagrados. El encargado de administrar todo esto era el levita Conanías, y su hermano Simí le ayudaba. ¹³El rey Ezequías y Azarías, que administraba el templo de Dios, nombraron como inspectores a Jehiel, Azazías, Najat, Asael, Jerimot, Jozabad, Eliel, Ismaquías, Mahat y Benaías, y los pusieron bajo las órdenes de Conanías y su hermano Simí. ¹⁴El levita Coré hijo de Imná, guardián de la puerta oriental, estaba encargado de las ofrendas voluntarias que se hacían al SEÑOR, y de distribuir las ofrendas del SEÑOR y los dones consagrados. ¹⁵Bajo sus órdenes estaban Edén, Minjamín, Jesúa, Semaías, Amarías y Secanías. Éstos se hallaban en las ciudades de los sacerdotes y, según sus turnos, distribuían fielmente las ofrendas entre sus compañeros, grandes y pequeños. ¹⁶Se distribuían entre los varones de tres años para arriba que estuvieran inscritos en el registro genealógico y que prestaran diariamente sus servicios en el templo del SEÑOR, según sus respectivos turnos y oficios. ¹⁷A los sacerdotes se les registraba de acuerdo con sus familias patriarcales, y a los levitas mayores de veinte años, de acuerdo con sus oficios y turnos. ¹⁸En el registro se incluían los niños pequeños, las mujeres, los hijos y las hijas, es decir, todo el grupo, ya que se mantenían fielmente consagrados. ¹⁹Además, en todas las ciudades había personas encargadas de repartir las porciones entre los sacerdotes descendientes de Aarón, y entre

---

ᶻ **30:15** *celebraron.* Lit. *Sacrificaron.*   ᵃ **30:20** *perdonó.* Lit. *Sanó.*   ᵇ **30:21** *sus instrumentos musicales.* Lit. *los instrumentos poderosos del SEÑOR.*   ᶜ **31:2** *templo.* Lit. *campamento.*

los levitas que estaban inscritos en el registro y que vivían en las aldeas de sus ciudades.

²⁰Eso mismo hizo Ezequías en todo Judá, actuando con bondad, rectitud y fidelidad ante el SEÑOR su Dios. ²¹Todo lo que emprendió para el servicio del templo de Dios, lo hizo de todo *corazón, de acuerdo con la ley y el mandamiento de buscar a Dios, y tuvo éxito.

Senaquerib invade Judá
32:9-19 — 2R 18:17-35; Is 36:2-20
32:20-21 — 2R 19:35-37; Is 37:36-38

32 Después de semejante muestra de fidelidad por parte de Ezequías, Senaquerib, rey de Asiria, marchó contra Judá y sitió las ciudades fortificadas, dispuesto a conquistarlas. ²Cuando Ezequías se enteró de que Senaquerib se dirigía también hacia Jerusalén con el propósito de atacarla, ³se reunió con sus jefes civiles y militares y les propuso cegar los manantiales que había fuera de la ciudad, y ellos lo apoyaron. ⁴Entonces se juntó mucha gente, y entre todos cegaron los manantiales y el arroyo que atravesaba la región, pues no querían que al llegar los reyes de Asiria encontraran agua en abundancia.

⁵Armándose de valor, Ezequías reconstruyó toda la muralla que había sido derribada y levantó torres sobre ella; también construyó un muro exterior, fortificó los terraplenesᵈ de la Ciudad de David, y mandó fabricar muchas lanzas y escudos. ⁶Luego puso jefes militares al frente del ejército, y luego de reunirlos en la plaza frente a la *puerta de la ciudad, los arengó con estas palabras: ⁷«¡Cobren ánimo y ármense de valor! No se asusten ni se acobarden ante el rey de Asiria y su numeroso ejército, porque nosotros contamos con alguien que es más poderoso. ⁸Él se apoya en la fuerza *humana, mientras que nosotros contamos con el SEÑOR nuestro Dios, quien nos brinda su ayuda y pelea nuestras batallas.» Al oír las palabras de Ezequías, rey de Judá, el pueblo se tranquilizó.

⁹Senaquerib, que en ese momento se hallaba en Laquis con todo su ejército, envió a sus oficiales para que les dijeran a Ezequías, rey de Judá, y a todos los de Judá que estaban en Jerusalén:

¹⁰«Así dice Senaquerib, rey de Asiria: "¿En qué basan su confianza para permanecer dentro de Jerusalén, que ya es una ciudad sitiada? ¹¹¿No se dan cuenta de que Ezequías los va a hacer morir de hambre y de sed? Él los está engañando cuando les dice que el SEÑOR su Dios los librará de mis manos. ¹²¿No fue acaso Ezequías mismo quien eliminó los *santuarios y los altares paganos, y luego ordenó a Judá y Jerusalén adorar en un solo altar, y sólo en él quemar incienso? ¹³¿Es que no se han dado cuenta de lo que yo y mis antepasados les hemos hecho a todas las naciones de la tierra? ¿Acaso los dioses de esas naciones pudieron librarlas de mi mano? ¹⁴Pues así como ninguno de los dioses de esas naciones que mis antepasados *destruyeron por completo pudo librarlas de mi mano, tampoco este dios de ustedes podrá librarlos de mí. ¹⁵¡No se dejen engañar ni seducir por Ezequías! ¡No le crean! Si ningún dios de esas naciones y reinos pudo librarlos de mi poder y del poder de mis antepasados, ¡mucho menos el dios de ustedes podrá librarlos a ustedes de mi mano!"»

¹⁶Los oficiales de Senaquerib siguieron hablando contra Dios el SEÑOR y contra su siervo Ezequías. ¹⁷Además, Senaquerib escribió una carta en la que insultaba al SEÑOR, Dios de Israel, en estos términos: «Así como los dioses de otras naciones no han podido librarlas de mi mano, tampoco ese dios de Ezequías podrá librar de mi mano a su pueblo.»

¹⁸Los oficiales de Senaquerib les gritaban a voz en cuello a los habitantes de Jerusalén que estaban en la muralla. Lo hacían en lengua hebrea, para infundirles miedo y así poder conquistar la ciudad. ¹⁹Y se referían al Dios de Jerusalén como si fuera igual a los dioses de las otras naciones de la tierra, fabricados por manos humanas.

²⁰Por ese motivo, el rey Ezequías y el profeta Isaías hijo de Amoz clamaron al cielo en oración. ²¹Entonces el SEÑOR envió un ángel para que exterminara a todos los soldados y a los jefes y capitanes del campamento del rey de Asiria, y éste tuvo que volver avergonzado a su país. Al entrar en el templo de su dios, sus propios hijos lo asesinaron.

²²Así salvó el SEÑOR a Ezequías y a los habitantes de Jerusalén de la mano de Senaquerib, rey de Asiria, y de todos sus enemigos, y les dio *paz en todas sus fronteras. ²³Entonces muchos fueron a Jerusalén con ofrendas para el SEÑOR y regalos para Ezequías, rey de Judá. De este modo aumentó el prestigio de Ezequías entre todas las naciones.

Enfermedad y curación de Ezequías
32:24-33 — 2R 20:1-21; Is 37:21-38; 38:1-8

²⁴Por aquellos días Ezequías se enfermó gravemente y estuvo a punto de morir. Entonces oró al SEÑOR, quien le respondió y le dio una señal extraordinaria. ²⁵Pero Ezequías no correspondió al favor recibido, sino que se llenó de orgullo. Eso hizo que el SEÑOR se encendiera en ira contra él, y contra Judá y Jerusalén. ²⁶Luego Ezequías, junto con los habitantes de Jerusalén, se *arrepintió de su orgullo, y mientras él vivió, el SEÑOR no volvió a derramar su ira contra ellos.

Prosperidad y muerte de Ezequías

²⁷Ezequías llegó a tener muchas riquezas y a gozar de gran prestigio. Acumuló grandes cantidades de plata, oro, piedras preciosas, perfumes, escudos y toda clase de objetos valiosos. ²⁸Tenía depósitos para almacenar trigo, vino y aceite, establos para toda clase de ganado, y rediles para los rebaños. ²⁹También edificó ciudades, y era dueño de inmensos rebaños de ganado mayor y menor, pues Dios le concedió muchísimos bienes.

³⁰Ezequías fue también quien cegó la salida superior de las aguas de Guijón y las desvió por un canal subterráneo hacia la parte occidental de la Ciudad de David. En fin, Ezequías tuvo éxito en todas las obras que emprendió. ³¹Sin embargo, cuando los príncipes de Babilonia enviaron una embajada para investigar acerca de la señal extraordinaria que había tenido lugar en el país, Dios se retiró de Ezequías para probarlo y descubrir todo lo que había en su *corazón.

³²Los demás acontecimientos del reinado de Ezequías, incluyendo sus hazañas, están escritos en la visión del profeta Isaías hijo de Amoz y en el libro de los reyes de Judá e Israel. ³³Ezequías murió y fue sepultado con sus antepasados en la parte superior del panteón de los descendientes de David. Todos

---

ᵈ **32:5** *los terraplenes*. Alt. *el Milo*.

los habitantes de Judá y de Jerusalén le rindieron honores. Y su hijo Manasés lo sucedió en el trono.

Manasés, rey de Judá
33:1-10 — 2R 21:1-10
33:18-20 — 2R 21:17-18

33 Manasés tenía doce años cuando ascendió al trono, y reinó en Jerusalén cincuenta y cinco años. 2Pero hizo lo que ofende al SEÑOR, pues practicó las repugnantes ceremonias de las naciones que el SEÑOR había expulsado al paso de los israelitas. 3Reconstruyó los *santuarios paganos que su padre Ezequías había derribado; además, erigió altares en honor de los *baales e hizo imágenes de la diosa *Aserá. Se postró ante todos los astros del cielo y los adoró. 4Construyó altares en el templo del SEÑOR, lugar del cual el SEÑOR había dicho: «En Jerusalén habitaré para siempre.» 5En ambos atrios del templo del SEÑOR construyó altares en honor de los astros del cielo. 6Sacrificó en el fuego a sus hijos en el valle de Ben Hinón, practicó la magia, la hechicería y la adivinación, y consultó a nigromantes y a espiritistas. Hizo continuamente lo que ofende al SEÑOR, provocando así su ira.

7Tomó la imagen del ídolo que había hecho y lo puso en el templo de Dios, lugar del cual Dios había dicho a David y a su hijo Salomón: «En este templo en Jerusalén, la ciudad que he escogido de entre todas las tribus de Israel, habitaré para siempre. 8Nunca más arrojaré a los israelitas de la tierra en que establecí a sus antepasados, siempre y cuando tengan cuidado de cumplir todo lo que les he ordenado, es decir, toda la *ley, los estatutos y los mandamientos que les di por medio de Moisés.» 9Manasés descarrió a los habitantes de Judá y de Jerusalén, de modo que se condujeron peor que las naciones que el SEÑOR destruyó al paso de los israelitas.

10El SEÑOR les habló a Manasés y a su pueblo, pero no le hicieron caso. 11Por eso el SEÑOR envió contra ellos a los jefes del ejército del rey de Asiria, los cuales capturaron a Manasés y lo llevaron a Babilonia sujeto con garfios y cadenas de bronce. 12Estando en tal aflicción, imploró al SEÑOR, Dios de sus antepasados, y se humilló profundamente ante él. 13Oró al SEÑOR, y él escuchó sus súplicas y le permitió regresar a Jerusalén y volver a reinar. Así Manasés reconoció que sólo el SEÑOR es Dios.

14Después de esto, Manasés construyó una alta muralla exterior en la Ciudad de David, la cual iba desde el oeste de Guijón, en el valle, hasta la puerta del Pescado, y rodeaba Ofel. Además, colocó jefes militares en todas las ciudades fortificadas de Judá 15y sacó del templo del SEÑOR los dioses extranjeros y el ídolo, arrojando fuera de la ciudad todos los altares que había construido en el monte del templo del SEÑOR y en Jerusalén. 16Luego reconstruyó el altar del SEÑOR, y en él ofreció sacrificios de *comunión y de acción de gracias, y le ordenó a Judá que sirviera al SEÑOR, Dios de Israel. 17Sin embargo, el pueblo siguió ofreciendo sacrificios en los *santuarios paganos, aunque se los ofrecían sólo al SEÑOR su Dios.

18Los demás acontecimientos del reinado de Manasés, incluso su oración a Dios y las palabras de los profetas que le hablaban en *nombre del SEÑOR, Dios de Israel, están escritos en las crónicas de los reyes de Israel. 19Su oración y la respuesta que recibió, como también todos sus pecados y rebeldías, los sitios donde erigió santuarios paganos y colocó las imágenes de la diosa *Aserá o de otros ídolos, lo cual hizo antes de su humillación, todo esto está escrito en las crónicas de Jozay. 20Manasés murió y

fue sepultado en su palacio, y su hijo Amón lo sucedió en el trono.

Amón, rey de Judá
33:21-25 — 2R 21:19-24

21Amón tenía veintidós años cuando ascendió al trono, y reinó en Jerusalén dos años. 22Pero hizo lo que ofende al SEÑOR, como lo había hecho su padre Manasés, y ofreció sacrificios a todos los ídolos que había hecho su padre, y los adoró. 23Pero, a diferencia de su padre Manasés, no se humilló ante el SEÑOR, sino que multiplicó sus pecados.

24Los ministros de Amón conspiraron contra él y lo asesinaron en su palacio. 25A su vez, la gente mató a todos los que habían conspirado contra él, y en su lugar proclamaron rey a su hijo Josías.

Josías, rey de Judá
34:1-2 — 2R 22:1-2
34:8-13 — 2R 22:3-7

34 Josías tenía ocho años cuando ascendió al trono, y reinó en Jerusalén treinta y un años. 2Josías hizo lo que agrada al SEÑOR, pues siguió el buen ejemplo de su antepasado David; no se desvió de él en el más mínimo detalle.

3En el año octavo de su reinado, siendo aún muy joven, Josías comenzó a buscar al Dios de su antepasado David. En el año duodécimo empezó a *purificar a Judá y a Jerusalén, quitando los *santuarios paganos, las imágenes de la diosa *Aserá, y los ídolos y las imágenes de metal fundido. 4En su presencia fueron destruidos los altares de los *baales y los altares que sobre sí se quemaba incienso; también fueron despedazadas las imágenes para el culto a Aserá, y los ídolos y las imágenes de metal fundido fueron reducidos a polvo, el cual fue esparcido sobre las tumbas de los que les habían ofrecido sacrificios. 5Quemó sobre los altares los huesos de los sacerdotes, purificando así a Judá y a Jerusalén. 6Lo mismo hizo en las ciudades de Manasés, Efraín, Simeón y Neftalí, y en sus alrededores. 7En toda la región de Israel destruyó los altares, redujo a polvo los ídolos y las imágenes de la diosa Aserá, y derribó los altares para quemar incienso. Luego regresó a Jerusalén.

8En el año dieciocho de su reinado, después de haber purificado el país y el templo, Josías envió a Safán hijo de Asalías y a Maseías, gobernador de la ciudad, junto con el secretario Joa hijo de Joacaz, a que repararan el templo del SEÑOR su Dios. 9Éstos se presentaron ante el sumo sacerdote Jilquías y le entregaron el dinero que había sido recaudado en el templo del SEÑOR, y que los levitas porteros habían recibido de los habitantes de Manasés y Efraín, y de todo el resto de Israel, Judá y Benjamín, y de los habitantes de Jerusalén. 10Luego entregaron el dinero a los que supervisaban la restauración del templo, y éstos se lo dieron a los trabajadores que estaban reparando y restaurando el templo del SEÑOR. 11También les dieron dinero a los carpinteros y albañiles, a fin de que compraran piedras de cantera y madera para las vigas de los edificios que los reyes de Judá habían dejado deteriorar.

12Estos hombres realizaban su trabajo con honradez. Los que estaban al frente de ellos eran los levitas Yajat y Abdías, descendientes de Merari, y Zacarías y Mesulán, descendientes de Coat. Los levitas, que eran hábiles en tocar instrumentos de música, 13eran los jefes de los cargadores y de todos los que trabajaban en la obra, fuera cual fuera su tarea. Entre los levitas había cronistas, oficiales y porteros.

Hallazgo del libro de la ley
34:14-28 — 2R 22:8-20
34:29-32 — 2R 23:1-3

14Al sacar el dinero recaudado en el templo del SEÑOR, el sacerdote Jilquías encontró el libro de la *ley del SEÑOR, dada por medio de Moisés. **15**Jilquías le dijo al cronista Safán: «He encontrado el libro de la ley en el templo del SEÑOR.» Entonces se lo entregó, **16**y Safán se lo llevó al rey. Le dijo:

—Majestad, sus servidores están haciendo todo cuanto se les ha encargado. **17**Han recogido el dineroᵉ que estaba en el templo del SEÑOR, y se lo han entregado a los supervisores y a los trabajadores.

18En sus funciones de cronista, Safán también informó al rey que el sumo sacerdote Jilquías le había entregado un libro, el cual leyó en presencia del rey.

19Cuando el rey oyó las palabras de la ley, se rasgó las vestiduras en señal de duelo **20**y dio esta orden a Jilquías, a Ajicán hijo de Safán, a Abdón hijo de Micaías, al cronista Safán y a Asaías, su ministro personal:

21—Con respecto a lo que dice este libro que se ha encontrado, vayan a consultar al SEÑOR por mí y por el remanente de Israel y de Judá. Sin duda que la gran ira del SEÑOR se ha derramado contra nosotros porque nuestros antepasados no tuvieron en cuenta su palabra, ni actuaron según lo que está escrito en este libro.

22Jilquías y los demás comisionados del rey fueron a consultar a la profetisa Huldá, que vivía en el barrio nuevo de Jerusalén. Huldá era la esposa de Salún, el encargado del vestuario, quien era hijo de Ticváᶠ y nieto de Jarjás.

23Huldá les contestó: «Así dice el SEÑOR, Dios de Israel: "Díganle al que los ha enviado **24**que yo, el SEÑOR, les advierto: 'Voy a enviar una desgracia sobre este lugar y sus habitantes, y haré que se cumplan todas las maldiciones que están escritas en el libro que se ha leído ante el rey de Judá. **25**Ellos me han abandonado; han quemado incienso a otros dioses, y con todos sus ídolosᵍ han provocado mi furor. Por eso arde mi ira contra este lugar, y no se apagará.' **26**Pero al rey de Judá, que los envió para consultarme, díganle que yo, el SEÑOR, Dios de Israel, digo en cuanto a las palabras que él ha oído: **27**'Como te has conmovido y humillado ante mí al escuchar lo que he anunciado contra este lugar y sus habitantes, y te has rasgado las vestiduras y has llorado en mi presencia, yo te he escuchado. Yo, el SEÑOR, lo afirmo. **28**Por lo tanto, te reuniré con tus antepasados, y serás sepultado en *paz. Tus ojos no verán la desgracia que voy a enviar sobre este lugar y sobre sus habitantes.' "»

Así que ellos regresaron para informar al rey.

Renovación del pacto

29Entonces el rey mandó convocar a todos los *ancianos de Judá y Jerusalén. **30**Acompañado de todos los habitantes de Judá y de Jerusalén, de los sacerdotes, de los levitas y, en fin, de la nación entera, desde el más grande hasta el más pequeño, el rey subió al templo del SEÑOR y, en presencia de ellos, leyó todo lo que dice el libro del *pacto que fue hallado en el templo del SEÑOR. **31**Después se puso de pie, junto a la columna del rey, y ante el SEÑOR renovó el pacto. Se comprometió a seguir al SEÑOR y a poner en práctica, de todo *corazón y con toda el *alma, sus mandamientos, preceptos y decretos,

cumpliendo así las palabras del pacto escritas en este libro. **32**Después hizo que todos los que se encontraban en Jerusalén y en Benjamín confirmaran el pacto. Y así los habitantes de Jerusalén actuaron según el pacto del Dios de sus antepasados.

33Josías suprimió todas las costumbres detestables que había en todo el territorio de los israelitas, e hizo que todos los que se hallaban en Israel adoraran al SEÑOR su Dios. Mientras Josías vivió, no abandonaron al SEÑOR, Dios de sus antepasados.

Celebración de la Pascua
35:1,18-19 — 2R 23:21-23

35 Josías celebró en Jerusalén la Pascua del SEÑOR. El día catorce del mes primero celebraron la Pascua. **2**Josías asignó las funciones a los sacerdotes y los animó a dedicarse al servicio del templo del SEÑOR. **3**A los levitas, que eran los encargados de enseñar a los israelitas y que estaban consagrados al SEÑOR, les dijo: «Pongan el arca sagrada en el templo que construyó Salomón hijo de David, rey de Israel, para que ya no tengan que llevarla sobre los hombros. Sirvan al SEÑOR su Dios y a su pueblo Israel. **4**Organícense en turnos, según sus familias patriarcales, de acuerdo con las instrucciones que dejaron por escrito David, rey de Israel, y su hijo Salomón. **5**Ocupen sus puestos en el santuario, conforme a las familias patriarcales de sus hermanos israelitas, de manera que a cada grupo de familias del pueblo corresponda un grupo de levitas. **6**Celebren la Pascua, conságrense y preparen todo para sus hermanos, y cumplan con lo que el SEÑOR ordenó por medio de Moisés.»

7De sus propios bienes, Josías obsequió a todo el pueblo allí presente unos treinta mil corderos y cabritos y tres mil bueyes, para que celebraran la Pascua. **8**También los jefes hicieron sus donativos para el pueblo y para los sacerdotes y levitas. Por su parte, Jilquías, Zacarías y Jehiel, oficiales del templo de Dios, entregaron a los sacerdotes dos mil seiscientos animales de ganado menor y trescientos bueyes, para celebrar la Pascua. **9**Conanías y sus hermanos Semaías y Natanael, y Jasabías, Jeyel y Josabad, jefes de los levitas, entregaron a los levitas cinco mil animales de ganado menor y quinientos bueyes.

10Una vez preparada la ceremonia, los sacerdotes ocuparon sus puestos, y los levitas se organizaron según sus turnos, conforme a la orden del rey. **11**Al sacrificar los animales para la Pascua, los sacerdotes rociaban la sangre y los levitas desollaban los animales. **12**Luego entregaban a cada familia patriarcal del pueblo la porción que ésta debía ofrecerle al SEÑOR, como está escrito en el libro de Moisés. Lo mismo hicieron con los bueyes. **13**Después asaron los animales para la Pascua, conforme al mandamiento; además, cocieron las otras ofrendas en ollas, calderos y sartenes, y las repartieron rápidamente entre toda la gente. **14**Luego prepararon la Pascua para ellos mismos y para los sacerdotes descendientes de Aarón. Los levitas tuvieron que prepararla para ellos mismos y para los sacerdotes porque éstos estuvieron ocupados hasta la noche ofreciendo los *holocaustos y la grasa.

15Los cantores descendientes de Asaf ocuparon sus puestos, de acuerdo con lo que habían dispuesto David, Asaf, Hemán y Jedutún, vidente del rey. También los porteros permanecieron en sus respectivas puertas, y no tuvieron que abandonar sus pues-

---

ᵉ **34:17** *recogido el dinero.* Lit. *fundido la plata.*   ᶠ **34:22** Ticvá (mss. de LXX y Siríaca; véase 2R 22:14); *Tocat* (TM).
ᵍ **34:25** *todos sus ídolos.* Lit. *todas las obras de sus manos.*

tos de servicio, pues sus compañeros levitas les prepararon la Pascua.

16Así se organizó aquel día el servicio del SEÑOR para celebrar la Pascua y ofrecer los holocaustos en el altar del SEÑOR, tal como lo había ordenado el rey Josías. 17En aquella ocasión, los israelitas allí presentes celebraron durante siete días la fiesta de la Pascua y la de los Panes sin levadura. 18Desde la época del profeta Samuel no se había celebrado una Pascua semejante, y ninguno de los reyes había celebrado una Pascua así, como lo hizo Josías con los sacerdotes y levitas, con los habitantes de Judá y de Israel allí presentes, y con los de Jerusalén. 19Esta Pascua se celebró en el año dieciocho del reinado de Josías.

Muerte de Josías
35:20—36:1 — 2R 23:28-30

20Tiempo después de que Josías terminó la restauración del templo, Necao, rey de Egipto, salió a presentar batalla en Carquemis, ciudad que está junto al río Éufrates, pero Josías le salió al paso. 21Necao envió mensajeros a decirle: «No te entrometas, rey de Judá. Hoy no vengo a luchar contra ti, sino contra la nación que me hace la guerra. Dios, que está de mi parte, me ha ordenado que me apresure. Así que no interfieras con Dios, para que él no te destruya.»

22Josías no le hizo caso a la advertencia que Dios le dio por medio de Necao; al contrario, en vez de retirarse, se disfrazó y fue a la llanura de Meguido para pelear con Necao. 23Como los arqueros le dispararon, el rey Josías les dijo a sus servidores: «Sáquenme de aquí, porque estoy gravemente herido.» 24Sus servidores lo sacaron del carro en que estaba y lo trasladaron a otro carro, y lo llevaron a Jerusalén. Allí murió, y fue sepultado en el panteón de sus antepasados. Y todo Judá y todo Jerusalén hicieron duelo por él.

25Jeremías compuso un lamento por la muerte de Josías; además, hasta este día todos los cantores y las cantoras aluden a Josías en sus cantos fúnebres. Estos cantos, que se han hecho populares en Israel, forman parte de las Lamentaciones.

26Los demás acontecimientos del reinado de Josías, sus actos piadosos acordes con la *ley del SEÑOR, 27y sus hechos, desde el primero hasta el último, están escritos en el libro de los reyes de Israel y de Judá.

Joacaz, rey de Judá
36:2-4 — 2R 23:31-34

36 Entonces el pueblo tomó a Joacaz hijo de Josías y lo proclamó rey en Jerusalén, en lugar de su padre. 2Joacaz tenía veintitrés años cuando ascendió al trono, y reinó en Jerusalén tres meses. 3Sin embargo, el rey de Egipto le quitó del trono para que no reinara en Jerusalén, y le impuso al país un tributo de cien barras de plata y una barrah de oro. 4Luego hizo reinar sobre Judá y Jerusalén a Eliaquín, hermano de Joacaz, y le dio el nombre de Joacim. En cuanto a Joacaz, Necao se lo llevó a Egipto.

Joacim, rey de Judá
36:5-8 — 2R 23:36—24:6

5Joacim tenía veinticinco años cuando ascendió al trono, y reinó en Jerusalén once años, pero hizo lo que ofende al SEÑOR su Dios. 6Por eso Nabucodonosor, rey de Babilonia, marchó contra Joacim y lo

llevó a Babilonia sujeto con cadenas de bronce. 7Además, Nabucodonosor se llevó a Babilonia los utensilios del templo del SEÑOR y los puso en su templo en Babilonia.

8Los demás acontecimientos del reinado de Joacim, y sus pecados y todo cuanto le sucedió, están escritos en el libro de los reyes de Israel y de Judá. Y su hijo Joaquín lo sucedió en el trono.

Joaquín, rey de Judá
36:9-10 — 2R 24:8-17

9Joaquín tenía dieciochoi años cuando ascendió al trono, y reinó en Jerusalén tres meses y diez días, pero hizo lo que ofende al SEÑOR. 10Por eso, a comienzos del año el rey Nabucodonosor mandó que lo llevaran a Babilonia, junto con los utensilios más valiosos del templo del SEÑOR, e hizo reinar sobre Judá y Jerusalén a Sedequías, pariente de Joaquín.

Sedequías, rey de Judá
36:11-16 — 2R 24:18-20; Jer 52:1-3

11Sedequías tenía veintiún años cuando ascendió al trono, y reinó en Jerusalén once años, 12pero hizo lo que ofende al SEÑOR su Dios. No se humilló ante el profeta Jeremías, que hablaba en *nombre del SEÑOR, 13y además se rebeló contra el rey Nabucodonosor, a quien había jurado lealtad. Sedequías fue terco y, en su obstinación, no quiso volverse al SEÑOR, Dios de Israel.

14También los jefes de los sacerdotes y el pueblo aumentaron su maldad, pues siguieron las prácticas detestables de los países vecinos y *contaminaron el templo que el SEÑOR había consagrado para sí en Jerusalén. 15Por amor a su pueblo y al lugar donde habita, el SEÑOR, Dios de sus antepasados, con frecuencia les enviaba advertencias por medio de sus mensajeros. 16Pero ellos se burlaban de los mensajeros de Dios, tenían en poco sus palabras, y se mofaban de sus profetas. Por fin, el SEÑOR desató su ira contra el pueblo, y ya no hubo remedio.

La caída de Jerusalén
36:17-20 — 2R 25:1-21; Jer 52:4-27
36:22-23 — Esd 1:1-3

17Entonces el SEÑOR envió contra ellos al rey de los *babilonios, quien dentro del mismo templo mató a espada a los jóvenes, y no tuvo compasión de jóvenes ni de doncellas, ni de adultos ni de ancianos. A todos se los entregó Dios en sus manos. 18Todos los utensilios del templo de Dios, grandes y pequeños, más los tesoros del templo y los del rey y de sus oficiales, fueron llevados a Babilonia. 19Incendiaron el templo de Dios, derribaron la muralla de Jerusalén, prendieron fuego a sus palacios y destruyeron todos los objetos de valor que allí había.

20A los que se salvaron de la muerte, el rey se los llevó a Babilonia, y fueron esclavos suyos y de sus hijos hasta el establecimiento del reino persa. 21De este modo se cumplió la palabra que el SEÑOR había pronunciado por medio de Jeremías. La tierra disfrutó de su descanso sabático todo el tiempo que estuvo desolada, hasta que se cumplieron setenta años.

Decreto de Ciro

22En el primer año del reinado de Ciro, rey de Persia, el SEÑOR dispuso el *corazón del rey para que éste

---

h 36:3 barras ... una barra. Lit. *talentos ... un talento. i 36:9 dieciocho (un ms. hebreo, mss. de LXX y Siríaca; véase 2R 24:8); ocho (TM).

promulgara un decreto en todo su reino y así se cumpliera la palabra del SEÑOR por medio del profeta Jeremías. Tanto oralmente como por escrito, el rey decretó lo siguiente:

23 «Esto es lo que ordena Ciro, rey de Persia:

»"El SEÑOR, Dios del cielo, que me ha dado todos los reinos de la tierra, me ha encargado que le construya un templo en la ciudad de Jerusalén, que está en Judá. Por tanto, cualquiera que pertenezca a Judá, que se vaya, y que el SEÑOR su Dios lo acompañe."»

ESDRAS

Decreto de Ciro

1 En el primer año del reinado de Ciro, rey de Persia, el SEÑOR dispuso el corazón del rey para que éste promulgara un decreto en todo su reino y así se cumpliera la palabra del SEÑOR por medio del profeta Jeremías. Tanto oralmente como por escrito, el rey decretó lo siguiente:

2«Esto es lo que ordena Ciro, rey de Persia:

»El SEÑOR, Dios del cielo, que me ha dado todos los reinos de la tierra, me ha encargado que le construya un templo en la ciudad de Jerusalén, que está en Judá. 3Por tanto, cualquiera que pertenezca a Judá, vaya a Jerusalén a construir el templo del SEÑOR, Dios de Israel, el Dios que habita en Jerusalén; y que Dios lo acompañe. 4También ordeno que los habitantes de cada lugar donde haya judíos sobrevivientes los ayuden dándoles plata y oro, bienes y ganado, y ofrendas voluntarias para el templo de Dios en Jerusalén.»

El regreso de los judíos

5Entonces los jefes de familia de Benjamín y de Judá, junto con los sacerdotes y levitas, es decir, con todos aquellos en cuyo corazón Dios puso el deseo de construir el templo, se dispusieron a ir a Jerusalén. 6Todos sus vecinos los ayudaron con plata y oro, bienes y ganado, objetos valiosos y todo tipo de ofrendas voluntarias. 7Además, el rey Ciro hizo sacar los utensilios que Nabucodonosor se había llevado del templo del SEÑOR en Jerusalén y había depositado en el templo de su dios.ª 8Ciro los entregó a su tesorero Mitrídates, el cual los contó y se los pasó a Sesbasar, jefe de Judá.

9El inventario de dichos utensilios fue el siguiente:

tazones de oro	30
tazones de plata	1.000
cuchillos	29
10 tazas de oro	30
tazas de plata	410
objetos diversos	1.000

11En total fueron cinco mil cuatrocientos los utensilios de oro y de plata. Todos estos objetos los llevó Sesbasar a Jerusalén cuando a los deportados se les permitió regresar de Babilonia.

Lista de los que regresaron

2 La siguiente es la lista de la gente de la provincia que Nabucodonosor, rey de Babilonia, había llevado cautiva a Babilonia, y a la que se le permitió regresar a Jerusalén y a Judá. Cada uno volvió a su propia población 2en compañía de Zorobabel, Jesúa, Nehemías, Seraías, Relaías, Mardoqueo, Bilsán, Mispar, Bigvay, Rejún y Baná.

Ésta es la lista de los israelitas que regresaron:

3	de Parós	2.172
4	de Sefatías	372
5	de Araj	775
6	de Pajat Moab, es decir, de Jesúa y Joab	2.812
7	de Elam	1.254
8	de Zatú	945
9	de Zacay	760
10	de Baní	642

11	de Bebay	623
12	de Azgad	1.222
13	de Adonicán	666
14	de Bigvay	2.056
15	de Adín	454
16	de Ater, es decir, de Ezequías	98
17	de Bezay	323
18	de Jorá	112
19	de Jasún	223
20	de Guibar	95
21	de Belén	123
22	de Netofa	56
23	de Anatot	128
24	de Azmávet	42
25	de Quiriat Yearín, Cafira y Berot	743
26	de Ramá y Gueba	621
27	de Micmás	122
28	de Betel y de Hai	223
29	de Nebo	52
30	de Magbís	156
31	del otro Elam	1.254
32	de Jarín	320
33	de Lod, Jadid y Ono	725
34	de Jericó	345
35	de Sená	3.630

36	De los sacerdotes descendientes de Jedaías, de la familia de Jesúa	973
37	de Imer	1052
38	de Pasur	1247
39	de Jarín	1017

40	De los levitas descendientes de Jesúa y de Cadmiel, que pertenecían a la familia de Hodavías	74
41	De los cantores descendientes de Asaf	128
42	De los porteros descendientes de Salún, Ater, Talmón, Acub, Jatitá y Sobay	139

43 Los servidores del templo eran de las familias de Zijá, Jasufá, Tabaot, 44Querós, Sigajá, Padón, 45Lebaná, Jagabá, Acub, 46Jagab, Salmay, Janán, 47Guidel, Gajar, Reaías, 48Rezín, Necoda, Gazán, 49Uza, Paseaj, Besay, 50Asena, Meunín, Nefusín, 51Bacbuc, Jacufá, Jarjur, 52Baslut, Mejidá, Jarsa, 53Barcós, Sísara, Temá, 54Neziaj y Jatifá.

55 Los descendientes de los servidores de Salomón eran de las familias de Sotay, Soféret, Peruda, 56Jalá, Darcón, Guidel, 57Sefatías, Jatil, Poquéret Hasebayin y Amón.

58 Los servidores del templo y de los descendientes de los servidores de Salomón	392

59Los siguientes regresaron de Tel Melaj, Tel Jarsá, Querub, Adón e Imer, pero no pudieron demostrar ascendencia israelita:

60 De los descendientes de Delaías, Tobías y Necoda	652

61 De entre los sacerdotes, los siguientes tampoco pudieron demostrar su ascendencia israelita: los descendientes de Jabaías, Cos y Barzi-

a **1:7** *su dios.* Alt. *sus dioses.*

lay (este último se casó con una de las hijas de un galaadita llamado Barzilay, del cual tomó su nombre). 62Éstos buscaron sus registros genealógicos, pero como no los encontraron, fueron excluidos del sacerdocio. 63A ellos el gobernador les prohibió comer de los alimentos sagrados hasta que un sacerdote decidiera su suerte por medio del *urim y el tumim.

64 El número total de los miembros de la asamblea era de cuarenta y dos mil trescientas sesenta personas, 65sin contar a esclavos y esclavas, que sumaban siete mil trescientos treinta y siete; y tenían doscientos cantores y cantoras. 66Tenían además setecientos treinta y seis caballos, doscientas cuarenta y cinco mulas, 67cuatrocientos treinta y cinco camellos y seis mil setecientos veinte burros.

68Cuando llegaron al templo del SEÑOR en Jerusalén, algunos jefes de familia dieron donativos para que se reconstruyera el templo del SEÑOR en el mismo sitio. 69De acuerdo con sus capacidades económicas dieron, para la obra de reconstrucción, cuatrocientos ochenta y ocho kilosᵇ de oro, dos mil setecientos cincuenta kilosᶜde plata y cien túnicas sacerdotales.

70Los sacerdotes, los levitas y algunos del pueblo se establecieron en Jerusalén,ᵈ en tanto que los cantores, los porteros, los servidores del templo y los demás israelitas se fueron a vivir a sus propias poblaciones.

Restauración del altar

3 En el mes séptimo, cuando ya todos los israelitas se habían establecido en sus poblaciones, se reunió el pueblo en Jerusalén con un mismo propósito. 2Entonces Jesúa hijo de Josadac con sus parientes, que eran sacerdotes, y Zorobabel hijo de Salatiel con sus parientes empezaron a construir el altar del Dios de Israel para ofrecer *holocaustos, según lo estipulado en la *ley de Moisés, hombre de Dios. 3A pesar del miedo que tenían de los pueblos vecinos, colocaron el altar en su mismo sitio. Y todos los días, por la mañana y por la tarde, ofrecían holocaustos al SEÑOR. 4Luego, según lo estipulado en la ley, celebraron la fiesta de las *Enramadas, ofreciendo el número de holocaustos prescrito para cada día, 5como también los holocaustos diarios, los de luna nueva, los de las fiestas solemnes ordenadas por el SEÑOR, y los que el pueblo le ofrecía voluntariamente. 6A pesar de que aún no se habían echado los cimientos del templo, desde el primer día del mes séptimo el pueblo comenzó a ofrecer holocaustos al SEÑOR.

Se comienza la reconstrucción del templo

7Luego dieron dinero a los albañiles y carpinteros. A los de Sidón y Tiro les dieron comida, bebida y aceite para que por mar llevaran madera de cedro desde el Líbano hasta Jope, conforme a la autorización que había dado Ciro, rey de Persia. 8Zorobabel hijo de Salatiel, y Jesúa hijo de Josadac, junto con el resto de sus parientes, que eran sacerdotes, y con los levitas y con todos los que habían regresado del cautiverio, comenzaron la reconstrucción del templo en el mes segundo del segundo año de haber llegado a Jerusalén. A los levitas mayores de veinte años les encomendaron la tarea de supervisar las obras del

templo del SEÑOR. 9Entonces Jesúa, junto con sus hijos y hermanos, y Cadmiel y sus hijos, que eran descendientes de Hodavías,ᵉ y los descendientes de Henadad, y sus hijos y hermanos, que eran levitas, se unieron para supervisar a los obreros que trabajaban en el templo de Dios.

10Cuando los constructores echaron los cimientos del templo del SEÑOR, los sacerdotes llegaron con sus vestimentas sagradas y los levitas descendientes de Asaf, con sus platillos, ocuparon su lugar para alabar al SEÑOR, según lo establecido por David, rey de Israel. 11Todos daban gracias al SEÑOR, y a una le cantaban esta alabanza: «Dios es bueno; su gran amor por Israel perdura para siempre.» Y todo el pueblo alabó con grandes aclamaciones al SEÑOR, porque se habían echado los cimientos del templo. 12Muchos de los sacerdotes, levitas y jefes de familia, que eran ya ancianos y habían conocido el primer templo, prorrumpieron en llanto cuando vieron los cimientos del nuevo templo, mientras muchos otros gritaban de alegría. 13Y no se podía distinguir entre los gritos de alegría y las voces de llanto, pues la gente gritaba a voz en cuello, y el ruido se escuchaba desde muy lejos.

Oposición samaritana

4 Cuando los enemigos del pueblo de Judá y de Benjamín se enteraron de que los repatriados estaban reconstruyendo el templo del SEÑOR, Dios de Israel, 2se presentaron ante Zorobabel y ante los jefes de familia y les dijeron:

—Permítannos participar en la reconstrucción, pues nosotros, al igual que ustedes, hemos buscado a su Dios y le hemos ofrecido *holocaustos desde el día en que Esarjadón, rey de Asiria, nos trajo acá.

3Pero Zorobabel, Jesúa y los jefes de las familias de Israel les respondieron:

—No podemos permitir que ustedes se unan a nosotros en la reconstrucción del templo de nuestro Dios. Nosotros solos nos encargaremos de reedificar el templo para el SEÑOR, Dios de Israel, tal como lo decretó Ciro, rey de Persia.

4Entonces los habitantes de la región comenzaron a desanimar e intimidar a los de Judá para que abandonaran la reconstrucción. 5Y hasta llegaron a sobornar a algunos de los consejeros para impedirles llevar a cabo sus planes. Esto sucedió durante todo el reinado de Ciro, rey de Persia, y hasta el reinado de Darío, que también fue rey de Persia.

6También al comienzo del reinado de Jerjes,ᶠ aquellos enemigos enviaron una carta en la cual acusaban a los habitantes de Judá y de Jerusalén. 7Luego, cuando Artajerjes llegó a ser rey de Persia, también a él Bislán, Mitrídates, Tabel y sus demás compañeros le enviaron una carta, que fue traducida al arameo.

8Además, el comandante Rejún y el cronista Simsay enviaron a Artajerjes una carta en contra de los habitantes de Jerusalén. La carta decía:

9El comandante Rejún y el cronista Simsay escriben esta carta, junto con sus compañeros los jueces, gobernadores y funcionarios de Persia, Érec, Babilonia y Susa (es decir, Elam). 10Esta carta la suscriben también las demás naciones que el grande y noble Asnapar llevó cautivas y estable-

---

ᵇ **2:69** cuatrocientos ochenta y ocho kilos. Lit. sesenta y un mil *dracmas.   ᶜ **2:69** dos mil setecientos cincuenta y dos kilos. Lit. cinco mil *minas.   ᵈ **2:70** en Jerusalén (LXX, 3 Esdras 5:46); en sus ciudades (TM).   ᵉ **3:9** Hodavías (lectura probable; véase 2:40); Judá (TM).   ᶠ **4:6** Jerjes. Hebreo Asuero; véase nota en Est 1:1.

ció en la ciudad de Samaria y en las otras provincias al oeste del río Éufrates.

11Al rey Artajerjes, de parte de sus siervos que habitan al oeste del río Éufrates:

12Sepa Su Majestad que los judíos enviados por usted han llegado a Jerusalén y están reconstruyendo esa ciudad rebelde y mala. Ya están echados los cimientos.

13Sepa también Su Majestad que si esta gente reconstruye la ciudad y termina la muralla, sus habitantes se rebelarán y no pagarán tributos, ni impuestos ni contribución alguna, lo cual sería perjudicial para el tesoro real. 14Como nosotros somos vasallos de Su Majestad,g no podemos permitir que se le deshonre. Por eso le enviamos esta denuncia. 15Pida Su Majestad que se investigue en los archivos donde están las crónicas de los reyes que lo han precedido. Así comprobará que esta ciudad ha sido rebelde y nociva para los reyes y las provincias, y que fue destruida porque hace ya mucho tiempo allí se fraguaron sediciones. 16Por eso le advertimos que, si esa ciudad es reconstruida y la muralla levantada, Su Majestad perderá el dominio de la región al oeste del Éufrates.

17En respuesta, el rey les escribió:

Al comandante Rejún y al cronista Simsay, y al resto de sus compañeros que viven en Samaria y en las otras regiones al oeste del río Éufrates:

Saludos.

18La carta que ustedes enviaron ha sido traducida y leída en mi presencia. 19Di orden de investigar en los archivos y, en efecto, se encontró que anteriormente en dicha ciudad se fraguaron sediciones y se tramaron rebeliones contra los reyes; 20que en Jerusalén hubo reyes poderosos, gobernantes de toda la región al oeste del río Éufrates, a quienes se les pagaban impuestos, tributos y rentas. 21Por eso, ordénenles a esos hombres que cesen sus labores, que suspendan la reconstrucción de la ciudad, hasta que yo promulgue un nuevo edicto. 22Sean diligentes en hacer cumplir esta orden, para que no crezca la amenaza de perjuicio a los intereses reales.

23En cuanto la carta del rey Artajerjes se leyó en presencia de Rejún, del cronista Simsay y de sus compañeros, todos ellos fueron a Jerusalén y, por la fuerza de las armas, obligaron a los judíos a detener la obra. 24De este modo el trabajo de reconstrucción del templo de Dios en Jerusalén quedó suspendido hasta el año segundo del reinado de Darío, rey de Persia.

Se reinicia la reconstrucción del templo

5 Los profetas Hageo y Zacarías hijo de Idó profetizaron a los judíos que estaban en Judá y Jerusalén, en el *nombre del Dios de Israel, que velaba por ellos. 2Entonces Zorobabel hijo de Salatiel y Jesúa hijo de Josadac se dispusieron a continuar la reconstrucción del templo de Dios en Jerusalén. Y los profetas estaban con ellos ayudándolos.

3En ese mismo tiempo, Tatenay, gobernador de la provincia al oeste del río Éufrates, y Setar Bosnay y sus compañeros, se presentaron ante los judíos y les preguntaron: «¿Quién los autorizó a reconstruir ese templo y restaurar su estructura?» 4Y añadieron:h «¿Cómo se llaman los que están reconstruyendo ese edificio?» 5Pero como Dios velaba por los *dirigentes judíos, no los obligaron a interrumpir el trabajo hasta que se consultara a Darío y éste respondiera por escrito.

6Entonces Tatenay, gobernador de la provincia al oeste del río Éufrates, y Setar Bosnay y sus compañeros, que eran los funcionarios del gobierno de esa provincia, enviaron una carta al rey Darío, 7la cual decía:

Al rey Darío:

Un cordial saludo.

8Ponemos en conocimiento de Su Majestad que fuimos a la provincia de Judá, al templo del gran Dios, y vimos que se está reconstruyendo con grandes piedras, y que sus paredes se están recubriendo con madera. El trabajo se hace con esmero y avanza rápidamente.

9A los dirigentes les preguntamos quién los había autorizado a reconstruir ese templo y restaurar su estructura, 10y cómo se llaman los que dirigen la obra, para comunicárselo por escrito a Su Majestad.

11Ellos nos respondieron:

«Somos siervos del Dios del cielo y de la tierra, y estamos reconstruyendo el templo que fue edificado y terminado hace ya mucho tiempo por un gran rey de Israel. 12Pero como nuestros antepasados provocaron a ira al Dios del cielo, él los entregó en manos de Nabucodonosor, rey de Babilonia, el *caldeo que destruyó este templo y que llevó al pueblo cautivo a Babilonia.

13»Pero más tarde, en el primer año de su reinado, Ciro, rey de Babilonia, ordenó que este templo de Dios fuera reconstruido. 14También hizo sacar del templo de Babilonia los utensilios de oro y de plata que Nabucodonosor se había llevado del templo de Jerusalén y había puesto en el templo de Babilonia, y se los entregó a Sesbasar, a quien había nombrado gobernador. 15Ciro, pues, ordenó a Sesbasar que tomara esos utensilios y los devolviera al templo de Jerusalén, y que reedificara en el mismo sitio el templo de Dios. 16Entonces Sesbasar llegó a Jerusalén y echó los cimientos del templo de Dios. Desde entonces se ha estado trabajando en su reconstrucción, pero aún no se ha terminado.»

17Ahora bien, si Su Majestad lo considera conveniente, pedimos que se investiguen los archivos donde están las crónicas de los reyes de Babilonia, para saber si es verdad que el rey Ciro ordenó la reconstrucción del templo de Dios en Jerusalén. Además solicitamos que se nos dé a conocer la decisión de Su Majestad con respecto a este asunto.

Decreto de Darío

6 Entonces el rey Darío ordenó que se investigara en los archivos donde se guardaban los tesoros de Babilonia. 2Y en el palacio de Ecbatana, en la provincia de Media, se encontró un rollo que contenía la siguiente memoria:

---

g 4:14 *somos vasallos de Su Majestad.* Lit. *comemos la sal del palacio.* h 5:4 añadieron (lectura probable; véanse LXX y Siríaca); *les dijimos* (TM).

³En el primer año de su reinado, el rey Ciro promulgó el siguiente edicto respecto al templo de Dios en Jerusalén:

Que se echen los cimientos y se reconstruya el templo, para que en él se ofrezcan *holocaustos. Tendrá veintisiete metros[i] tanto de alto como de ancho, ⁴tres hileras de piedras grandes, y una de madera. Todos los gastos serán sufragados por el tesoro real. ⁵Con respecto a los utensilios de oro y de plata que Nabucodonosor sacó del templo de Jerusalén y llevó a Babilonia, que los devuelvan a Jerusalén, y que se pongan en el templo de Dios, donde deben estar.

⁶Entonces el rey Darío dio la siguiente orden[j] a Tatenay, gobernador de la provincia al oeste del río Éufrates, y a Setar Bosnay y a sus compañeros, los funcionarios de dicha provincia:

Aléjense de Jerusalén ⁷y no estorben la obra de reconstrucción del templo de Dios. Dejen que el gobernador de la provincia de Judá y los *dirigentes judíos reconstruyan el templo en su antiguo sitio.

⁸También he decidido que ustedes deben prestarles ayuda, sufragando los gastos de la reconstrucción del templo con los impuestos que la provincia al oeste del río Éufrates paga al tesoro real. No se tarden en pagar todos los gastos, para que no se interrumpan las obras. ⁹Además, todos los días, sin falta, deberán suministrarles becerros, carneros y corderos para ofrecerlos en holocausto al Dios del cielo, junto con trigo, sal, vino y aceite, y todo lo que necesiten, según las instrucciones de los sacerdotes que están en Jerusalén. ¹⁰Así podrán ellos ofrecer sacrificios gratos al Dios del cielo y rogar por la vida del rey y de sus hijos.

¹¹He determinado así mismo que, a quien desobedezca esta orden, lo empalen en una viga sacada de su propia casa, y que le derrumben la casa. ¹²¡Que el Dios que decidió habitar en Jerusalén derribe a cualquier rey o nación que intente modificar este decreto o destruir ese templo de Dios!

Yo, Darío, promulgo este decreto. Publíquese y cúmplase al pie de la letra.

Terminación y dedicación del templo

¹³Entonces Tatenay, gobernador de la provincia al oeste del río Éufrates, y Setar Bosnay y sus compañeros cumplieron al pie de la letra lo que el rey Darío les había ordenado. ¹⁴Así los *dirigentes judíos pudieron continuar y terminar la obra de reconstrucción, conforme a la palabra de los profetas Hageo y Zacarías hijo de Idó. Terminaron, pues, la obra de reconstrucción, según el mandato del Dios de Israel y por decreto de Ciro, Darío y Artajerjes, reyes de Persia. ¹⁵La reconstrucción del templo se terminó el día tres del mes de *adar, en el año sexto del reinado de Darío.

¹⁶Entonces los israelitas —es decir, los sacerdotes, los levitas y los demás que regresaron del cautiverio—, llenos de júbilo dedicaron el templo de Dios. ¹⁷Como ofrenda de dedicación, ofrecieron a Dios cien becerros, doscientos carneros, cuatrocientos corderos y doce chivos, conforme al número de las tribus de Israel, para *expiación por el pecado del pueblo. ¹⁸Luego, según lo que está escrito en el libro de Moisés, instalaron a los sacerdotes en sus turnos y a los levitas en sus funciones, para el culto que se ofrece a Dios en Jerusalén.

Celebración de la Pascua

¹⁹Los que regresaron del cautiverio celebraron la Pascua el día catorce del mes primero. ²⁰Los sacerdotes y levitas se habían unido para *purificarse y, ya estando ritualmente *limpios, mataron el cordero pascual por todos los que habían regresado del cautiverio, por sus compañeros los sacerdotes y por ellos mismos. ²¹Los israelitas que regresaron del cautiverio comieron la Pascua junto con los que se habían apartado de la impureza de sus vecinos para seguir al SEÑOR, Dios de Israel. ²²Durante siete días celebraron con mucho gozo la fiesta de los Panes sin levadura, porque el SEÑOR les había devuelto la alegría y había hecho que el rey de Persia[k] los ayudara y permitiera reconstruir el templo del Dios de Israel.

Esdras llega a Jerusalén

7 Durante el reinado de Artajerjes, rey de Persia, vivió un hombre llamado Esdras hijo de Seraías, que era descendiente en línea directa de Azarías, Jilquías, ²Salún, Sadoc, Ajitob, ³Amarías, Azarías, Merayot, ⁴Zeraías, Uzi, Buquí, ⁵Abisúa, Finés, Eleazar y Aarón, que fue el primer sacerdote. ⁶Este Esdras llegó de Babilonia. Era un maestro muy versado en la *ley que el SEÑOR, Dios de Israel, le había dado a Moisés. Gozaba de la simpatía del rey, y el SEÑOR su Dios estaba con él.

⁷Con Esdras regresaron a Jerusalén algunos israelitas, entre los cuales había sacerdotes, levitas, cantores, porteros y servidores del templo. Esto sucedió en el séptimo año del reinado de Artajerjes. ⁸Así que Esdras llegó a Jerusalén en el mes quinto del séptimo año del reinado de Artajerjes. ⁹Había salido de Babilonia el día primero del mes primero, y llegó a Jerusalén el día primero del mes quinto, porque la mano bondadosa de Dios estaba con él. ¹⁰Esdras se había dedicado por completo a estudiar la ley del SEÑOR, a ponerla en práctica y a enseñar sus preceptos y normas a los israelitas.

Carta de Artajerjes a Esdras

¹¹El rey Artajerjes le entregó la siguiente carta a Esdras, quien era sacerdote y maestro de los mandamientos y preceptos que el SEÑOR le dio a Israel:

¹²Artajerjes, rey de reyes,

a Esdras, sacerdote y maestro versado en la *ley del Dios del cielo:

Saludos.[l]

¹³He dispuesto que todos los israelitas que quieran ir contigo a Jerusalén puedan hacerlo, incluyendo a los sacerdotes y levitas. ¹⁴El rey y sus siete consejeros te mandan a investigar la situación de Jerusalén y de Judá, conforme a la ley de tu Dios que se te ha confiado. ¹⁵Lleva el oro y la plata que el rey y sus consejeros han ofrecido voluntariamente al Dios de Israel, que habita en Jerusalén. ¹⁶También lleva contigo toda la plata y el oro que obtengas de la provincia de Babilonia, junto con los donativos del pueblo y de los

i 6:3 *veintisiete metros*. Lit. *sesenta *codos*.   j 6:6 *Entonces el rey Darío dio la siguiente orden*. Se ha añadido esta frase para indicar el cambio de sujeto.   k 6:22 *rey de Persia*. Lit. *rey de Asiria* (uno de los títulos dado al rey persa).   l 7:12 *Saludos*. Texto de difícil traducción.

sacerdotes para el templo de su Dios en Jerusalén. 17Con ese dinero compra, sin falta, becerros, carneros y corderos, con sus respectivas ofrendas de cereales y de vino, para ofrecerlos en el altar del templo del Dios de ustedes en Jerusalén.

18Con el resto de la plata y del oro tú y tus compañeros podrán hacer lo que les parezca mejor, de acuerdo con la voluntad del Dios de ustedes. 19Pero deposita en el templo los utensilios sagrados que se te han entregado para rendir culto a tu Dios en Jerusalén. 20Cualquier otro gasto que sea necesario para el templo de tu Dios, se cubrirá del tesoro real.

21Ahora bien, yo, el rey Artajerjes, les ordeno a todos los tesoreros que están al oeste del río Éufrates, que entreguen de inmediato todo cuanto solicite Esdras, sacerdote y maestro versado en la ley del Dios del cielo. 22Pueden darle hasta tres mil trescientos kilos de plata, veintidós mil litros de trigo, dos mil doscientos litros de vino, dos mil doscientos litros de aceitem y toda la sal que se requiera.

23Todo lo que ha ordenado el Dios del cielo para su templo, háganlo de inmediato, de modo que no se descargue su ira contra el dominio del rey y su familia. 24También les ordeno que exoneren de impuestos a los sacerdotes, levitas, cantores, porteros y servidores del templo de Dios.

25Por cuanto tú, Esdras, posees la sabiduría de Dios, serás el encargado de nombrar funcionarios y jueces para que juzguen a los habitantes de la provincia al oeste del río Éufrates, es decir, a todos los que conocen la ley de Dios. Pero a quienes no la conozcan, enséñasela. 26Si alguien desobedece la ley de tu Dios y las órdenes del rey, haz que se le castigue de inmediato con la pena de muerte, el destierro, la confiscación de bienes o la cárcel.

Oración de Esdras

27«Bendito sea el SEÑOR, Dios de nuestros antepasados, que puso en el *corazón del rey el propósito de honrar el templo del SEÑOR en Jerusalén. 28Por su infinito amor, él me ha permitido recibir el favor del rey, de sus consejeros y de todos sus funcionarios más importantes. Y porque Dios estaba conmigo, cobré ánimo y reuní a los jefes de Israel para que me acompañaran a Jerusalén.»

Lista de los que regresaron con Esdras

8 Según los registros genealógicos, ésta es la lista de los jefes de familia que durante el reinado de Artajerjes regresaron conmigo de Babilonia:

2 de los descendientes de Finés: Guersón;
de Itamar: Daniel;
de David: Jatús, 3que era de la familia de Secanías;
de Parós: Zacarías y ciento cincuenta hombres que se registraron con él;
4 de Pajat Moab: Elihoenay hijo de Zeraías y doscientos hombres más;
5 de Secanías: el hijo de Jahaziel y trescientos hombres más;
6 de Adín: Ébed hijo de Jonatán y cincuenta hombres más;
7 de Elam: Isaías hijo de Atalías y setenta hombres más;

8 de Sefatías: Zebadías hijo de Micael y ochenta hombres más;
9 de Joab: Abdías hijo de Jehiel y doscientos dieciocho hombres más;
10 de Selomit: el hijo de Josifías y ciento sesenta hombres más;
11 de Bebay: Zacarías hijo de Bebay y veintiocho hombres más;
12 de Azgad: Johanán hijo de Hacatán y ciento diez hombres más;
13 de Adonicán: Elifelet, Jeyel y Semaías, los últimos de esta familia, con los cuales se registraron sesenta hombres más;
14 de Bigvay: Utay, Zabud y setenta hombres más.

El regreso a Jerusalén

15A estos jefes de familia los reuní junto al arroyo que corre hacia el río Ahava, y allí estuvimos acampados tres días. Cuando pasé revista a todo el pueblo y a los sacerdotes, no encontré a ningún descendiente de Leví. 16Entonces mandé llamar a Eliezer, Ariel, Semaías, Elnatán, Jarib, Elnatán, Natán, Zacarías y Mesulán, que eran jefes del pueblo, y también a Joyarib y Elnatán, que eran maestros, 17y los envié a Idó, que era el jefe de Casifia. Les encargué que les pidieran a Idó y a sus compañeros, quienes estaban al frente de Casifiá, que nos proveyeran servidores para el templo de nuestro Dios. 18Y como Dios estaba con nosotros, nos enviaron a un israelita muy capacitado llamado Serebías hijo de Majlí, descendiente de Leví. Con él vinieron sus hijos y sus hermanos, dieciocho personas en total. 19También nos enviaron a Jasabías y a Isaías, descendientes de Merari, junto con sus hijos y hermanos, veinte personas en total. 20Además, del grupo que David y sus oficiales habían asignado para que ayudaran a los levitas, nos enviaron doscientos veinte servidores, los cuales fueron registrados por su nombre.

21Luego, estando cerca del río Ahava, proclamé un ayuno para que nos humilláramos ante nuestro Dios y le pidiéramos que nos acompañara durante el camino, a nosotros, a nuestros hijos y nuestras posesiones. 22En realidad, sentí vergüenza de pedirle al rey que nos enviara un pelotón de caballería para que nos protegiera de los enemigos, ya que le habíamos dicho al rey que la mano de Dios protege a todos los que confían en él, pero que Dios descarga su poder y su ira contra quienes lo abandonan. 23Así que ayunamos y oramos a nuestro Dios pidiéndole su protección, y él nos escuchó.

24Después aparté a doce jefes de los sacerdotes: Serebías, Jasabías y diez de sus parientes. 25En presencia de ellos pesé el oro, los utensilios sagrados y las ofrendas que el rey, sus consejeros, sus funcionarios más importantes y todos los israelitas allí presentes habían entregado para el templo de Dios. 26Lo que pesé fue lo siguiente: veintiún mil cuatrocientos cincuenta kilos de plata, utensilios de plata que pesaban tres mil trescientos kilos, tres mil trescientos kilos de oro, 27veinte tazas de oro que pesaban ocho kilos,n y dos recipientes de bronce bruñido de la mejor calidad, tan preciosos como el oro.

28Luego les dije: «Ustedes y los utensilios han sido consagrados al SEÑOR. La plata y el oro son una ofrenda voluntaria para el SEÑOR, Dios de nuestros antepasados. 29Vigílenlos y guárdenlos hasta que los pesen en los aposentos del templo del SEÑOR en Jeru-

---

m 7:22 hasta ... aceite. Lit. hasta cien *talentos de plata y hasta cien *coros de trigo y hasta cien *batos de vino y hasta cien batos de aceite. n 8:26,27 veintiún mil ... ocho kilos. Lit. seiscientos cincuenta *talentos de plata, utensilios de plata que pesaban cien talentos, cien talentos de oro, 27 veinte tazas de oro que valían mil *dracmas.

salén, en presencia de los principales sacerdotes, de los levitas y de los jefes de familia del pueblo de Israel.» ³⁰Así que los sacerdotes y levitas recibieron la plata, el oro y los utensilios que fueron pesados para llevarlos al templo de nuestro Dios en Jerusalén.

³¹El día doce del mes primero partimos del río Ahava para ir a Jerusalén. Durante todo el trayecto Dios nos acompañó y nos libró de enemigos y asaltantes. ³²Al llegar a Jerusalén nos quedamos descansando tres días. ³³Al cuarto día pesamos la plata, el oro y los utensilios en el templo de nuestro Dios, y entregamos todo al sacerdote Meremot hijo de Urías. Eleazar hijo de Finés estaba allí con él, lo mismo que los levitas Jozabad hijo de Jesúa, y Noadías hijo de Binuy. ³⁴Ese día pesamos y contamos todo, y registramos el peso total.

³⁵Luego, en honor del SEÑOR, Dios de Israel, los que habían regresado del cautiverio ofrecieron, en *holocausto y como ofrenda de *expiación por todo el pueblo, doce novillos, noventa y seis carneros, setenta y siete corderos y doce chivos. ³⁶Y se les entregaron los decretos del rey a los *sátrapas del reino y a los gobernadores de la provincia al oeste del río Éufrates, los cuales prestaron todo su apoyo al pueblo y al templo de Dios.

Esdras confiesa el pecado del pueblo

9 Después de todo esto, se me acercaron los jefes y me dijeron: «El pueblo de Israel, incluso los sacerdotes y levitas, no se ha mantenido separado de los pueblos vecinos, sino que practica las costumbres abominables de todos ellos, es decir, de los cananeos, hititas, ferezeos, jebuseos, amonitas, moabitas, egipcios y amorreos. ²De entre las mujeres de esos pueblos han tomado esposas para sí mismos y para sus hijos, mezclando así la raza *santa con la de los pueblos vecinos. Y los primeros en cometer tal infidelidad han sido los jefes y los gobernantes.»

³Cuando escuché esto, me rasgué la túnica y el manto, me arranqué los pelos de la cabeza y de la barba, y me postré muy angustiado. ⁴Entonces, por causa del pecado cometido por los repatriados, se reunieron a mi alrededor todos los que obedecíanⁿ la palabra de Dios. Y yo seguí angustiado hasta la hora del sacrificio de la tarde.

⁵A la hora del sacrificio me recobré de mi abatimiento y, con la túnica y el manto rasgados, caí de rodillas, extendí mis manos hacia el SEÑOR mi Dios, ⁶y le dije en oración:

«Dios mío, estoy confundido y siento vergüenza de levantar el rostro hacia ti, porque nuestras maldades se han amontonado hasta cubrirnos por completo; nuestra culpa ha llegado hasta el cielo. ⁷Desde los días de nuestros antepasados hasta hoy, nuestra culpa ha sido grande. Debido a nuestras maldades, nosotros, nuestros reyes y nuestros sacerdotes fuimos entregados al poder de los reyes de los países vecinos. Hemos sufrido la espada, el cautiverio, el pillaje y la humillación, como nos sucede hasta hoy.

⁸»Pero ahora tú, SEÑOR y Dios nuestro, por un breve momento nos has mostrado tu bondad al permitir que un remanente quede en libertad y se establezca en tu lugar santo. Has permitido que nuestros ojos vean una nueva luz, y nos has concedido un pequeño alivio en medio de nuestra esclavitud. ⁹Aunque somos esclavos, no nos has abandonado, Dios nuestro, sino que nos has extendido tu misericordia a la vista de los reyes de Persia. Nos has dado nueva vida para reedificar tu templo y reparar sus ruinas, y nos has brindado tu protección en Judá y en Jerusalén.º

¹⁰»Y ahora, después de lo que hemos hecho, ¿qué podemos decirte? No hemos cumplido los mandamientos ¹¹que nos diste por medio de tus siervos los profetas, cuando nos advertiste: "La tierra que van a poseer está corrompida por la *impureza de los pueblos que la habitan, pues de un extremo a otro ellos la han llenado con sus abominaciones. ¹²Por eso, no permitan ustedes que sus hijas ni sus hijos se casen con los de esos pueblos. Nunca busquen el *bienestar ni la prosperidad que tienen ellos, para que ustedes se mantengan fuertes y coman de los frutos de la buena tierra y luego se la dejen por herencia a sus descendientes para siempre."

¹³»Después de todo lo que nos ha acontecido por causa de nuestras maldades y de nuestra grave culpa, reconocemos que tú, Dios nuestro, no nos has dado el castigo que merecemos, sino que nos has dejado un remanente. ¹⁴¿Cómo es posible que volvamos a quebrantar tus mandamientos contrayendo matrimonio con las mujeres de estos pueblos que tienen prácticas abominables? ¿Acaso no sería justo que te enojaras con nosotros y nos destruyeras hasta no dejar remanente ni que nadie escape? ¹⁵¡SEÑOR, Dios de Israel, tú eres justo! Tú has permitido que hasta hoy sobrevivamos como remanente. Culpables como somos, estamos en tu presencia, aunque no lo merecemos.»

El pueblo reconoce su pecado

10 Mientras Esdras oraba y hacía esta confesión llorando y postrándose delante del templo de Dios, a su alrededor se reunió una gran *asamblea de hombres, mujeres y niños del pueblo de Israel. Toda la multitud lloraba amargamente. ²Entonces uno de los descendientes de Elam, que se llamaba Secanías hijo de Jehiel, se dirigió a Esdras y le dijo:

«Nosotros hemos sido infieles a nuestro Dios, pues tomamos por esposas a mujeres de los pueblos vecinos; pero todavía hay esperanza para Israel. ³Hagamos un *pacto con nuestro Dios, comprometiéndonos a expulsar a todas estas mujeres y a sus hijos, conforme al consejo que nos has dado tú, y todos los que aman el mandamiento de Dios. ¡Que todo se haga de acuerdo con la ley! ⁴Levántate, pues ésta es tu responsabilidad; nosotros te apoyamos. ¡Cobra ánimo y pon manos a la obra!»

⁵Al oír esto, Esdras se levantó e hizo que los jefes de los sacerdotes, los levitas y todo el pueblo de Israel se comprometieran, bajo juramento, a cumplir con lo que habían dicho; y ellos lo juraron. ⁶Luego Esdras salió del templo de Dios y fue a la habitación de Johanán hijo de Eliasib. Allí se quedó sin comer pan ni beber agua, porque estaba muy deprimido por causa de la infidelidad de los repatriados.

⁷Posteriormente anunciaron en Judá y Jerusalén que todos los que habían regresado del cautiverio debían reunirse en Jerusalén. ⁸Y advirtieron que a todo el que no se presentara en el plazo de tres días, según la decisión de los jefes y *dirigentes, se le quitarían sus propiedades y se le expulsaría de la asamblea de los repatriados.

ⁿ **9:4** *obedecían.* Lit. *Temían.*   º **9:8,9** En el hebreo de estos versículos, Esdras se refiere a Dios en tercera persona.

9Por lo tanto, a los tres días, en el día veinte del mes noveno, se reunieron en Jerusalén todos los *hombres de Judá y de Benjamín. Todo el pueblo se sentó en la plaza del templo de Dios, temblando por causa de ese asunto e intimidados por el aguacero que caía. 10Entonces el sacerdote Esdras se puso en pie y les dijo:

—Ustedes han sido infieles y han aumentado la culpa de Israel, pues han contraído matrimonio con mujeres extranjeras. 11Ahora, pues, confiesen su pecadop al SEÑOR, Dios de nuestros antepasados, y hagan lo que a él le agrada. Sepárense de los *paganos y de las mujeres extranjeras.

12Toda la asamblea contestó en alta voz:

—Haremos todo lo que nos has dicho. 13Pero no podemos quedarnos a la intemperie; estamos en época de lluvias y esto no es asunto de uno o dos días, pues somos muchos los que hemos cometido este pecado. 14Proponemos que se queden sólo los jefes del pueblo, y que todos los que viven en nuestras ciudades y se han casado con mujeres extranjeras se presenten en fechas determinadas, junto con los dirigentes y jueces de cada ciudad, hasta que se aparte de nosotros la terrible ira de nuestro Dios por causa de esta infidelidad.

15Sólo se opusieron Jonatán hijo de Asael y Jahazías hijo de Ticvá, apoyados por los levitas Mesulán y Sabetay. 16Los que habían regresado del cautiverio actuaron según lo que se había convenido. Entonces el sacerdote Esdras seleccionó y llamó por nombre a ciertos jefes de familia, y a partir del primer día del mes décimo se reunió con ellos para tratar cada caso. 17Y el primer día del mes primero terminaron de resolver los casos de todos los que se habían casado con mujeres extranjeras.

Lista de los culpables

18 Los descendientes de los sacerdotes que se habían casado con mujeres extranjeras fueron los siguientes:

De Jesúa hijo de Josadac, y de sus hermanos: Maseías, Eliezer, Jarib y Guedalías, 19los cuales se comprometieron a despedir a sus mujeres extranjeras, y ofrecieron un carnero como ofrenda de *expiación por su pecado.

20 De Imer: Jananí y Zebadías.

21 De Jarín: Maseías, Elías, Semaías, Jehiel y Uzías.

22 De Pasur: Elihoenay, Maseías, Ismael, Natanael, Jozabad y Elasá.

23 De los levitas:

Jozabad, Simí, Quelaías o Quelitá, Petaías, Judá y Eliezer.

24 De los cantores: Eliasib.

De los porteros: Salún, Telén y Uri.

25 Y de los demás israelitas:

De Parós: Ramías, Jezías, Malquías, Mijamín, Eleazar, Malquías y Benaías.

26 De Elam: Matanías, Zacarías, Jehiel, Abdí, Jeremot y Elías.

27 De Zatú: Elihoenay, Eliasib, Matanías, Jeremot, Zabad y Azizá.

28 De Bebay: Johanán, Jananías, Zabay y Atlay.

29 De Baní: Mesulán, Maluc, Adaías, Yasub, Seal y Ramot.

30 De Pajat Moab: Adná, Quelal, Benaías, Maseías, Matanías, Bezalel, Binuy y Manasés.

31 De Jarín: Eliezer, Isías, Malquías, Semaías, Simeón, 32Benjamín, Maluc y Semarías.

33 De Jasún: Matenay, Matatá, Zabad, Elifelet, Jeremay, Manasés y Simí.

34 De Baní: Maday, Amirán, Uel, 35Benaías, Bedías, Queluhi, 36Vanías, Meremot, Eliasib, 37Matanías, Matenay, Jasay.

38 De Binuy:q Simí, 39Selemías, Natán, Adaías, 40Macnadebay, Sasay, Saray, 41Azarel, Selemías, Semarías, 42Salún, Amarías y José.

43 De Nebo: Jeyel, Matatías, Zabad, Zebiná, Jadau, Joel y Benaías.

44Todos éstos se habían casado con mujeres extranjeras, y algunos habían tenido hijos con ellas.

---

p **10:11** confiesen su pecado. Alt. den gracias. q **10:38** de Binuy. Alt. Bani, Binuy.

NEHEMÍAS

Nehemías ora por su pueblo

1 Éstas son las palabras de Nehemías hijo de Jacalías:

En el mes de *quisleu del año veinte, estando yo en la ciudadela de Susa, 2llegó Jananí, uno de mis hermanos, junto con algunos hombres de Judá. Entonces les pregunté por el resto de los judíos que se habían librado del destierro, y por Jerusalén.

3me respondieron: «Los que se libraron del destierro y se quedaron en la provincia están enfrentando una gran calamidad y humillación. La muralla de Jerusalén sigue derribada, con sus *puertas consumidas por el fuego.»

4Al escuchar esto, me senté a llorar; hice duelo por algunos días, ayuné y oré al Dios del cielo. 5Le dije:

«SEÑOR, Dios del cielo, grande y temible, que cumples el *pacto y eres fiel con los que te aman y obedecen tus mandamientos, 6te suplico que me prestes atención, que fijes tus ojos en este siervo tuyo que día y noche ora en favor de tu pueblo Israel. Confieso que los israelitas, entre los cuales estamos incluidos mi familia y yo, hemos pecado contra ti. 7Te hemos ofendido y nos hemos corrompido mucho; hemos desobedecido los mandamientos, preceptos y decretos que tú mismo diste a tu siervo Moisés.

8»Recuerda, te suplico, lo que le dijiste a tu siervo Moisés: "Si ustedes pecan, yo los dispersaré entre las naciones; 9pero si se vuelven a mí, y obedecen y ponen en práctica mis mandamientos, aunque hayan sido llevados al lugar más apartado del mundo los recogeré y los haré volver al lugar donde he decidido habitar."

10»Ellos son tus siervos y tu pueblo al cual redimiste con gran despliegue de fuerza y poder. 11SEÑOR, te suplico que escuches nuestra oración, pues somos tus siervos y nos complacemos en honrar tu *nombre. Y te pido que a este siervo tuyo le concedas tener éxito y ganarse el favor del rey.»

En aquel tiempo yo era copero del rey.

Nehemías vuelve a Jerusalén

2 Un día, en el mes de *nisán del año veinte del reinado de Artajerjes, al ofrecerle vino al rey, como él nunca antes me había visto triste, 2me preguntó:

—¿Por qué estás triste? No me parece que estés enfermo, así que debe haber algo que te está causando dolor.

Yo sentí mucho miedo 3y le respondí:

—¡Qué viva Su Majestad para siempre! ¿Cómo no he de estar triste, si la ciudad donde están los sepulcros de mis padres se halla en ruinas, con sus *puertas consumidas por el fuego?

4—¿Qué quieres que haga? —replicó el rey.

Encomendándome al Dios del cielo, 5le respondí:

—Si a Su Majestad le parece bien, y si este siervo suyo es digno de su favor, le ruego que me envíe a Judá para reedificar la ciudad donde están los sepulcros de mis padres. 6—¿Cuánto durará tu viaje? ¿Cuándo regresarás? —me preguntó el rey, que tenía a la reina sentada a su lado. En cuanto le propuse un plazo, el rey aceptó enviarme. 7Entonces añadí:

—Si a Su Majestad le parece bien, le ruego que envíe cartas a los gobernadores del oeste del río Éufrates para que me den vía libre y yo pueda llegar a Judá; 8y por favor ordene a su guardabosques Asaf que me dé madera para reparar las puertas de la ciudadela del templo, la muralla de la ciudad y la casa donde he de vivir.

El rey accedió a mi petición, porque Dios estaba actuando a mi favor. 9Cuando me presenté ante los gobernadores del oeste del río Éufrates, les entregué las cartas del rey. Además el rey había ordenado que me escoltaran su caballería y sus capitanes. 10Pero al oír que alguien había llegado a ayudar a los israelitas, Sambalat el horonita y Tobías el siervo amonita se disgustaron mucho.

Nehemías inspecciona la muralla

11Tres días después de haber llegado a Jerusalén, 12salí de noche acompañado de algunos hombres, pero a ninguno de ellos le conté lo que mi Dios me había motivado hacer por Jerusalén. La única bestia que llevábamos era la que yo montaba. 13Esa noche salí por la puerta del Valle hacia la fuente del Dragón y la puerta del Basurero. Inspeccioné las ruinas de la muralla de Jerusalén, y sus puertas consumidas por el fuego. 14Después me dirigí hacia la puerta de la Fuente y el estanque del Rey, pero no hallé por dónde pasar con mi cabalgadura. 15Así que, siendo aún de noche, subí por el arroyo mientras inspeccionaba la muralla. Finalmente regresé y entré por la puerta del Valle.

16Los gobernadores no supieron a dónde fui ni qué hice, porque hasta entonces no había dicho nada a ningún judío: ni a los sacerdotes, ni a los nobles, ni a los gobernadores ni a los que estaban trabajando en la obra. 17Por eso les dije:

—Ustedes son testigos de nuestra desgracia. Jerusalén está en ruinas, y sus *puertas han sido consumidas por el fuego. ¡Vamos, anímense! ¡Reconstruyamos la muralla de Jerusalén para que ya nadie se burle de nosotros!

18Entonces les conté cómo la bondadosa mano de Dios había estado conmigo y les relaté lo que el rey me había dicho. Al oír esto, exclamaron:

—¡Manos a la obra!

Y unieron la acción a la palabra.

19Cuando lo supieron, Sambalat el horonita, Tobías el oficial amonita y Guesén el árabe se burlaron de nosotros y nos preguntaron de manera despectiva:

—Pero, ¿qué están haciendo? ¿Acaso pretenden rebelarse contra el rey?

20Yo les contesté:

—El Dios del cielo nos concederá salir adelante. Nosotros, sus siervos, vamos a comenzar la reconstrucción. Ustedes no tienen arte ni parte en este asunto, ni raigambre en Jerusalén.

Se inicia la reconstrucción

3 Entonces el sumo sacerdote Eliasib y sus compañeros los sacerdotes trabajaron en la reconstrucción de la puerta de las Ovejas. La repararon y la colocaron en su lugar, y reconstruyerona también la muralla desde la torre de los Cien hasta la torre de Jananel. 2El tramo contiguo lo reconstruyeron los hombres de Jericó, y el tramo siguiente, Zacur hijo de Imrí.

---

a 3:1 repararon ... reconstruyeron (texto probable); consagraron ... consagraron (TM).

[3]La puerta de los Péscados la reconstruyeron los descendientes de Sená.[b] Colocaron las vigas y pusieron la puerta en su lugar, con sus cerrojos y barras. [4]El tramo contiguo lo reconstruyó Meremot, hijo de Urías y nieto de Cos, y el tramo siguiente Mesulán, hijo de Berequías y nieto de Mesezabel. El siguiente tramo lo reconstruyó Sadoc hijo de Baná. [5]Los de Tecoa reconstruyeron el siguiente tramo de la muralla, aunque sus notables no quisieron colaborar con sus dirigentes.

[6]La puerta de Jesaná[c] la reconstruyeron Joyadá hijo de Paseaj y Mesulán hijo de Besodías. Colocaron las vigas y pusieron en su lugar la puerta con sus cerrojos y barras. [7]El tramo contiguo lo reconstruyeron Melatías de Gabaón y Jadón de Meronot. A éstos se les unieron los de Gabaón y los de Mizpa, que estaban bajo el dominio del gobernador de la provincia al oeste del río Éufrates.

[8]Uziel hijo de Jaraías, que era uno de los plateros, reconstruyó el siguiente tramo de la muralla, y uno de los perfumistas, llamado Jananías, el siguiente. Entre los dos reconstruyeron la muralla de Jerusalén hasta la muralla Ancha. [9]El siguiente tramo lo reconstruyó Refaías hijo de Jur, que era gobernador de una mitad del distrito de Jerusalén; [10]el siguiente, Jedaías hijo de Jarumaf, cuya casa quedaba al frente, y el siguiente, Jatús hijo de Jasabnías.

[11]Malquías hijo de Jarín y Jasub hijo de Pajat Moab reconstruyeron el siguiente tramo de la muralla y la torre de los Hornos. [12]Salún hijo de Halojés, que era gobernador de la otra mitad del distrito de Jerusalén, reconstruyó el siguiente tramo con la ayuda de sus hijas.

[13]La puerta del Valle la reconstruyeron Janún y los habitantes de Zanoa, y la colocaron en su lugar con sus cerrojos y barras. Levantaron también quinientos metros[d] de muralla hasta la puerta del Basurero.

[14]Malquías hijo de Recab, gobernador del distrito de Bet Haqueren, reconstruyó la puerta del Basurero y la colocó en su lugar con sus cerrojos y barras.

[15]Salún hijo de Coljozé, gobernador del distrito de Mizpa, reconstruyó la puerta de la Fuente, la techó y la colocó en su lugar con sus cerrojos y barras. Reconstruyó también el muro del estanque de Siloé, que está junto al jardín del rey, hasta las gradas que llevan a la Ciudad de David. [16]Nehemías hijo de Azbuc, gobernador de una mitad del distrito de Betsur, reconstruyó el siguiente tramo hasta el lugar que está frente a los sepulcros de David, hasta el estanque artificial y hasta el cuartel de la guardia real.

[17]El sector que sigue lo reconstruyeron los levitas y Rejún hijo de Baní. En el tramo siguiente Jasabías, gobernador de una mitad del distrito de Queilá, hizo las obras de reconstrucción por cuenta de su distrito, [18]y las continuaron sus compañeros: Bavay hijo de Henadad, gobernador de la otra mitad del distrito de Queilá, [19]y Ezer hijo de Jesúa, gobernador de Mizpa, que reconstruyó el tramo que sube frente al arsenal de la esquina. [20]El tramo siguiente, es decir, el sector que va desde la esquina hasta la puerta de la casa del sumo sacerdote Eliasib, lo reconstruyó con entusiasmo Baruc hijo de Zabay. [21]El sector que va desde la puerta de la casa de Eliasib hasta el extremo de la misma lo reconstruyó Meremot, hijo de Urías y nieto de Cos.

[22]El siguiente tramo lo reconstruyeron los sacerdotes que vivían en los alrededores. [23]Benjamín y Jasub reconstruyeron el sector que está frente a sus propias casas. Azarías, hijo de Maseías y nieto de Ananías, reconstruyó el tramo que está junto a su propia casa. [24]Binuy hijo de Henadad reconstruyó el sector que va desde la casa de Azarías hasta el ángulo, es decir, hasta la esquina. [25]Palal hijo de Uzay reconstruyó el sector de la esquina que está frente a la torre alta que sobresale del palacio real, junto al patio de la guardia. El tramo contiguo lo reconstruyó Pedaías hijo de Parós. [26]Los servidores del templo que vivían en Ofel reconstruyeron el sector oriental que está frente a la puerta del Agua y la torre que allí sobresale. [27]Los hombres de Tecoa reconstruyeron el tramo que va desde el frente de la gran torre que allí sobresale, hasta la muralla de Ofel.

[28]Los sacerdotes, cada uno frente a su casa, reconstruyeron el sector de la muralla sobre la puerta de los Caballos, [29]El siguiente tramo lo reconstruyó Sadoc hijo de Imer, pues quedaba frente a su propia casa. El sector que sigue lo reparó Semaías hijo de Secanías, guardián de la puerta oriental. [30]Jananías hijo de Selemías, y Janún, el sexto hijo de Salaf, reconstruyeron otro tramo. Mesulán hijo de Berequías reconstruyó el siguiente tramo, pues quedaba frente a su casa. [31]Malquías, que era uno de los plateros, reconstruyó el tramo que llega hasta las casas de los servidores del templo y de los comerciantes, frente a la puerta de la Inspección y hasta el puesto de vigilancia. [32]Y el sector que va desde allí hasta la puerta de las Ovejas lo reconstruyeron los plateros y los comerciantes.

Se obstaculiza la reconstrucción

4 Cuando Sambalat se enteró de que estábamos reconstruyendo la muralla, se disgustó muchísimo y se burló de los judíos. [2]Ante sus compañeros y el ejército de Samaria dijo:

—¿Qué están haciendo estos miserables judíos? ¿Creen que se les va a dejar que reconstruyan y que vuelvan a ofrecer sacrificios? ¿Piensan acaso terminar en un solo día? ¿Cómo creen que de esas piedras quemadas, de esos escombros, van a hacer algo nuevo?

[3]Y Tobías el amonita, que estaba junto a él, añadió:

—¡Hasta una zorra, si se sube a ese montón de piedras, lo echa abajo!

[4]Por eso oramos:

«¡Escucha, Dios nuestro,
    cómo se burlan de nosotros!
Haz que sus ofensas recaigan sobre ellos
        mismos;
    entrégalos a sus enemigos;
    ¡que los lleven en cautiverio!
[5]No pases por alto su maldad
    ni olvides sus pecados,
    porque insultan a los que reconstruyen.»

[6]Continuamos con la reconstrucción y levantamos la muralla hasta media altura, pues el pueblo trabajó con entusiasmo. [7]Pero cuando Sambalat y Tobías, y los árabes, los amonitas y los asdodeos se enteraron de que avanzaba la reconstrucción de la muralla y de que ya estábamos cerrando las brechas, se enojaron muchísimo [8]y acordaron atacar a Jerusalén y provocar disturbios en ella. [9]Oramos entonces a nuestro Dios y decidimos montar guardia día y noche para defendernos de ellos.

---

b **3:3** *Sená.* Alt. *Hasená.* c **3:6** *La puerta de Jesaná.* Alt. *La puerta Vieja.* d **3:13** *quinientos metros.* Lit. *mil *codos.*

10Por su parte, la gente de Judá decía:

«Los cargadores desfallecen,
    pues son muchos los escombros;
¡no vamos a poder
    reconstruir esta muralla!»

11Y nuestros enemigos maquinaban: «Les caeremos por sorpresa y los mataremos; así haremos que la obra se suspenda.»

12Algunos de los judíos que vivían cerca de ellos venían constantemente y nos advertían: «Los van a atacar por todos lados.»

13Así que puse a la gente por familias, con sus espadas, arcos y lanzas, detrás de las murallas, en los lugares más vulnerables y desguarnecidos. 14Luego de examinar la situación, me levanté y dije a los nobles y gobernantes, y al resto del pueblo: «¡No les tengan miedo! Acuérdense del Señor, que es grande y temible, y peleen por sus hermanos, por sus hijos e hijas, y por sus esposas y sus hogares.»

15Una vez que nuestros enemigos se dieron cuenta de que conocíamos sus intenciones y de que Dios había frustrado sus planes, todos regresamos a la muralla, cada uno a su trabajo. 16A partir de aquel día la mitad de mi gente trabajaba en la obra, mientras la otra mitad permanecía armada con lanzas, escudos, arcos y corazas. Los jefes estaban pendientes de toda la gente de Judá. 17Tanto los que reconstruían la muralla como los que acarreaban los materiales, no descuidaban ni la obra ni la defensa.e 18Todos los que trabajaban en la reconstrucción lleaban la espada a la cintura. A mi lado estaba el en - cargado de dar el toque de alarma. 19Yo les había dicho a los nobles y gobernantes, y al resto del pueblo: «La tarea es grande y extensa, y nosotros estamos muy esparcidos en la muralla, distantes los unos de los otros. 20Por eso, al oír el toque de alarma, cerremos filas. ¡Nuestro Dios peleará por nosotros!»

21Así que, desde el amanecer hasta que aparecían las estrellas, mientras trabajábamos en la obra, la mitad de la gente montaba guardia lanza en mano. 22En aquella ocasión también le dije a la gente: «Todos ustedes, incluso los ayudantes, quédense en Jerusalén para que en la noche sirvan de centinelas y de día trabajen en la obra.» 23Ni yo ni mis parientes y ayudantes, ni los de mi guardia personal, nos desvestíamos para nada: cada uno de nosotros se mantenía listo para la defensa.f

Nehemías defiende a los pobres

5 Los hombres y las mujeres del pueblo protestaron enérgicamente contra sus hermanos judíos, 2pues había quienes decían: «Si contamos a nuestros hijos y a nuestras hijas, ya somos muchos. Necesitamos conseguir trigo para subsistir.» 3Otros se quejaban: «Por conseguir trigo para no morirnos de hambre, hemos hipotecado nuestros campos, viñedos y casas.» 4Había también quienes se quejaban: «Tuvimos que empeñar nuestros campos y viñedos para conseguir dinero prestado y así pagar el tributo al rey. 5Y aunque nosotros y nuestros hermanos somos de la misma sangre, y nuestros hijos y los suyos son iguales, a nosotros nos ha tocado vender a nuestros hijos e hijas como esclavos. De hecho, hay hijas nuestras sirviendo como esclavas, y no podemos rescatarlas, puesto que nuestros campos y viñedos están en poder de otros.»

6Cuando oí sus palabras de protesta, me enojé muchísimo. 7Y después de reflexionar, reprendí a los nobles y gobernantes:

—¡Es inconcebible que sus propios hermanos les exijan el pago de intereses!

Convoqué además una gran asamblea contra ellos, 8y allí les recriminé:

—Hasta donde nos ha sido posible, hemos rescatado a nuestros hermanos judíos que fueron vendidos a los *paganos. ¡Y ahora son ustedes quienes venden a sus hermanos, después de que nosotros los hemos rescatado!g

Todos se quedaron callados, pues no sabían qué responder.

9Yo añadí:

—Lo que están haciendo ustedes es incorrecto. ¿No deberían mostrar la debida reverencia a nuestro Dios y evitar así el reproche de los paganos, nuestros enemigos? 10Mis hermanos y mis criados, y hasta yo mismo, les hemos prestado dinero y trigo. Pero ahora, ¡quitémosles esa carga de encima! 11Yo les ruego que les devuelvan campos, viñedos, olivares y casas, y también el uno por ciento de la plata, del trigo, del vino y del aceite que ustedes les exigen.

12—Está bien —respondieron ellos—, haremos todo lo que nos has pedido. Se lo devolveremos todo, sin exigirles nada.

Entonces llamé a los sacerdotes, y ante éstos les hice jurar que cumplirían su promesa. 13Luego me sacudí el manto y afirmé:

—¡Así sacuda Dios y arroje de su casa y de sus propiedades a todo el que no cumpla esta promesa! ¡Así lo sacuda Dios y lo deje sin nada!

Toda la asamblea respondió:

—¡Amén!

Y alabaron al SEÑOR, y el pueblo cumplió lo prometido.

14Desde el año veinte del reinado de Artajerjes, cuando fui designado gobernador de la tierra de Judá, hasta el año treinta y dos, es decir, durante doce años, ni mis hermanos ni yo utilizamos el impuesto que me correspondía como gobernador. 15En cambio, los gobernadores que me precedieron habían impuesto cargas sobre el pueblo, y cada día les habían exigido comida y vino por un valor de cuarenta monedash de plata. También sus criados oprimían al pueblo. En cambio yo, por temor a Dios, no hice eso. 16Al contrario, tanto yo como mis criados trabajamos en la reconstrucción de la muralla y no compramos ningún terreno.

17A mi mesa se sentaban ciento cincuenta hombres, entre judíos y oficiales, sin contar a los que llegaban de países vecinos. 18Era tarea de todos los días preparar un buey, seis ovejas escogidas y algunas aves; y cada diez días se traía vino en abundancia. Pero nunca utilicé el impuesto que me correspondía como gobernador, porque ya el pueblo tenía una carga muy pesada.

19¡Recuerda, Dios mío, todo lo que he hecho por este pueblo, y favoréceme!

Nueva oposición de los enemigos

6 Sambalat, Tobías, Guesén el árabe y el resto de nuestros enemigos se enteraron de que yo había reconstruido la muralla, y de que se habían cerrado las brechas (aunque todavía no se habían puesto las *puertas en su sitio). 2Entonces Sambalat y Gue-

---

e 4:17 no descuidaban ... defensa. Lit. con una mano trabajaban en la obra y con la otra sostenían la lanza.   f 4:23 cada uno ... defensa. Lit. cada uno su arma el agua. Texto de difícil traducción.   g 5:8 después de que nosotros los hemos rescatado. Alt. para que nosotros tengamos que volver a rescatarlos.   h 5:15 monedas. Lit. *Siclos.

sén me enviaron este mensaje: «Tenemos que reunirnos contigo en alguna de las poblaciones del valle de Ono.» En realidad, lo que planeaban era hacerme daño. ³Así que envié unos mensajeros a decirles: «Estoy ocupado en una gran obra, y no puedo ir. Si bajara yo a reunirme con ustedes, la obra se vería interrumpida.» ⁴Cuatro veces me enviaron este mensaje, y otras tantas les respondí lo mismo. ⁵La quinta vez Sambalat me envió, por medio de uno de sus siervos, el mismo mensaje en una carta abierta, ⁶que a la letra decía:

«Corre el rumor entre la gente —y Guesénⁱ lo asegura— de que tú y los judíos están construyendo la muralla porque tienen planes de rebelarse. Según tal rumor, tú pretendes ser su rey, ⁷y has nombrado profetas para que te proclamen rey en Jerusalén, y se declare: "¡Tenemos rey en Judá!" Por eso, ven y hablemos de este asunto, antes de que todo esto llegue a oídos del rey.»

⁸Yo enseguida le decir: «Nada de lo que dices es cierto. Todo esto es pura invención tuya.»

⁹En realidad, lo que pretendían era asustarnos. Pensaban desanimarnos, para que no termináramos la obra.

«Y ahora, Señor, ¡fortalece mis manos!»

¹⁰Fui entonces a la casa de Semaías, hijo de Delaías y nieto de Mehitabel, que se había encerrado en su casa. Él me dijo:

«Reunámonos a puerta cerrada
en la casa de Dios,
en el interior del templo,
porque vendrán a matarte.
¡Sí, esta noche te quitarán la vida!»

¹¹Pero yo le respondí:
—¡Yo no soy de los que huyen! ¡Los hombres como yo no corren a esconderse en el templo para salvar la vida! ¡No me esconderé!

¹²Y es que me di cuenta de que Dios no lo había enviado, sino que se la daba de profeta porque Sambalat y Tobías lo habían sobornado. ¹³En efecto, le habían pagado para intimidarme y hacerme pecar siguiendo su consejo. De este modo podrían hablar mal de mí y desprestigiarme.

¹⁴¡Dios mío, recuerda las intrigas de Sambalat y Tobías! ¡Recuerda también a la profetisa Noadías y a los otros profetas que quisieron intimidarme!»

Termina la reconstrucción de la muralla

¹⁵La muralla se terminó el día veinticinco del mes de *elul. Su reconstrucción había durado cincuenta y dos días. ¹⁶Cuando todos nuestros enemigos se enteraron de esto, las naciones vecinas se sintieron humilladas, pues reconocieron que ese trabajo se había hecho con la ayuda de nuestro Dios.

¹⁷En aquellos días los nobles de Judá se mantuvieron en estrecho contacto con Tobías, ¹⁸pues muchos judíos estaban aliados con él en vista de que era yerno de Secanías hijo de Araj, y de que su hijo Johanán era yerno de Mesulán hijo de Berequías. ¹⁹En mi presencia hablaban bien de mí, pero luego le comunicaban todo lo que yo decía. Tobías, por su parte, trataba de intimidarme con sus cartas.

Plan para defender a Jerusalén

7 Una vez que se terminó la reconstrucción de la muralla y se colocaron sus *puertas, se nombraron porteros, cantores y levitas. ²A mi hermano Jananí, que era un hombre fiel y temeroso de Dios como pocos, lo puse a cargo de Jerusalén, junto con Jananías, comandante de la ciudadela. ³A los dos les dije: «Las puertas de Jerusalén se abrirán cuando ya haya salido el sol, y volverán a cerrarse y se asegurarán con sus barras cuando los porteros estén en sus puestos. Además, los habitantes de Jerusalén montarán guardia, unos en sus puestos y otros frente a su propia casa.»

⁴La ciudad ocupaba una gran extensión, pero tenía pocos habitantes porque no todas las casas se habían reconstruido.

Lista de los repatriados

⁵Mi Dios puso en mi *corazón el deseo de reunir a los nobles, a los oficiales y al pueblo, para registrarlos según su descendencia; y encontré el registro genealógico de los que habían regresado en la primera repatriación. Allí estaba escrito:

⁶La siguiente es la lista de la gente de la provincia, es decir, de aquellos que Nabucodonosor, rey de Babilonia, se había llevado cautivos, y a quienes se les permitió regresar a Jerusalén y a Judá. Cada uno volvió a su propia ciudad, ⁷bajo el mando de Zorobabel, Jesúa, Nehemías, Azarías, Raamías, Najamani, Mardoqueo, Bilsán, Mispéret, Bigvay, Nehúm y Baná.

Ésta es la lista de los israelitas que regresaron:

8	de Parós	2.172
9	de Sefatías	372
10	de Araj	652
11	de Pajat Moab, es decir, los de Jesúa y de Joab	2.818
12	de Elam	1.254
13	de Zatú	845
14	de Zacay	760
15	de Binuy	648
16	de Bebay	628
17	de Azgad	2.322
18	de Adonicán	667
19	de Bigvay	2.067
20	de Adín	655
21	de Ater, es decir, los de Ezequías	98
22	de Jasún	328
23	de Bezay	324
24	de Jarif	112
25	de Gabaón	95
26	de Belén y de Netofa	188
27	de Anatot	128
28	de Bet Azmávet	42
29	de Quiriat Yearín, Cafira y Berot	743
30	de Ramá y de Gueba	721
31	de Micmás	122
32	de Betel y de Hai	123
33	del otro Nebo	52
34	del otro Elam	1.254
35	de Jarín	320
36	de Jericó	345
37	de Lod, Jadid y Ono	721
38	de Sená	3.930
39	De los sacerdotes descendientes de Jedaías, de la familia de Jesúa	973
40	de Imer	1.052
41	de Pasur	1.247
42	de Jarín	1.017

ⁱ **6:6** *Guesén.* Lit. *Gasmu* (variante de este nombre).

43 De los levitas descendientes de
Jesúa y de Cadmiel, que pertenecían
a la familia de Hodavías   74

44 De los cantores descendientes de
Asaf   148

45 De los porteros descendientes de
Salún, Ater, Talmón, Acub, Jatitá
y Sobay   138

46 Los servidores del templo eran
descendientes de Zijá, Jasufá,
Tabaot, **47**Querós, Sigajá, Padón,
48Lebaná, Jagabá, Salmay, **49**Janán,
Guidel, Gajar, **50**Reaías, Rezín,
Necoda, **51**Gazán, Uza, Paseaj,
52Besay, Meunín, Nefisesín,
53Bacbuc, Jacufá, Jarjur, **54**Baslut,
Mejidá, Jarsa, **55**Barcós, Sísara,
Temá, **56**Neziaj y Jatifá.

57 Los descendientes de los servidores
de Salomón eran de las familias de
Sotay, Soféret, Peruda, **58**Jalá,
Darcón, Guidel, **59**Sefatías, Jatil,
Poquéret Hasebayin y Amón.

60 Los servidores del templo y de
los descendientes de los servidores
de Salomón   392

61Los siguientes regresaron de Tel Melaj, Tel Jarsá, Querub, Adón e Imer, pero no pudieron demostrar ascendencia israelita:

62 De los descendientes de Delaías,
Tobías y Necoda   642

63 De entre los sacerdotes, tampoco pudieron demostrar su ascendencia israelita los siguientes: los descendientes de Jabaías, Cos y
Barzilay (este último se casó con una de las
hijas de un galaadita llamado Barzilay, del
cual tomó su nombre). **64**Éstos buscaron sus
registros genealógicos, pero como no los encontraron, fueron excluidos del sacerdocio.
65A ellos el gobernador les prohibió comer
de los alimentos sagrados hasta que un sacerdote decidiera su suerte por medio del
*urim y el tumim.

66 El número total de los miembros de la asamblea
ascendía a cuarenta y dos mil trescientas sesenta personas, **67**sin contar a esclavos y esclavas, que sumaban siete mil trescientos
treinta y siete; y tenían doscientos cuarenta y
cinco cantores y cantoras. **68**Tenían además
setecientos treinta y seis caballos, doscientos
cuarenta y cinco mulas,ʲ **69**cuatrocientos
treinta y cinco camellos y seis mil setecientos
veinte burros.

70Algunos jefes de familia entregaron al tesoro
donativos para la obra: el gobernador entregó al tesoro ocho kilos de oro, cincuenta tazones y quinientas treinta túnicas sacerdotales; **71**los jefes de familia
entregaron ciento sesenta kilos de oro y mil doscientos diez kilos de plata, **72**y el resto del pueblo entregó
ciento sesenta kilos de oro, mil cien kilosᵏ de plata y
sesenta y siete túnicas sacerdotales.

73Los sacerdotes, los levitas, los porteros, los cantores, la gente del pueblo, los servidores del templo y
los demás israelitas se establecieron en sus propias
ciudades.

Esdras lee la ley

Al llegar el mes séptimo, los israelitas ya estaban
establecidos en sus ciudades.

8 Entonces todo el pueblo, como un solo *hombre, se reunió en la plaza que está frente a la
puerta del Agua y le pidió al *maestro Esdras traer el
libro de la *ley que el SEÑOR le había dado a Israel
por medio de Moisés. **2**Así que el día primero del mes
séptimo, el sacerdote Esdras llevó la ley ante la asamblea, que estaba compuesta de hombres y mujeres y
de todos los que podían comprender la lectura, **3**y la
leyó en presencia de ellos en la plaza que está frente
a la puerta del Agua. Todo el pueblo estaba muy
atento a la lectura del libro de la ley.

4El maestro Esdras se puso de pie sobre una plataforma de madera construida para la ocasión. A su
derecha estaban Matatías, Semá, Anías, Urías, Jilquías
y Maseías; a su izquierda, Pedaías, Misael, Malquías,
Jasún, Jasbadana, Zacarías y Mesulán. **5**Esdras, a
quien la gente podía ver porque él estaba en un lugar
más alto, abrió el libro y todo el pueblo se puso de pie.
6Entonces Esdras bendijo al SEÑOR, el gran Dios. Y
todo el pueblo, levantando las manos, respondió:
«¡Amén y amén!». Luego adoraron al SEÑOR, inclinándose hasta tocar el suelo con la frente.

7Los levitas Jesúa, Baní, Serebías, Jamín, Acub,
Sabetay, Hodías, Maseías, Quelitá, Azarías, Jozabed,
Janán y Pelaías le explicaban la ley al pueblo, que no
se movía de su sitio. **8**Ellos leían con claridad el libro
de la ley de Dios y lo interpretaban de modo que se
comprendiera su lectura.

9Al oír las palabras de la ley, la gente comenzó a
llorar. Por eso el gobernador Nehemías, el sacerdote
y maestro Esdras, y los levitas que enseñaban al pueblo, les dijeron: «No lloren ni se pongan tristes, porque este día ha sido consagrado al SEÑOR su Dios.»
10Luego Nehemías añadió: «Ya pueden irse. Coman bien, tomen bebidas dulces y compartan su comida con quienes no tengan nada, porque este día
ha sido consagrado a nuestro Señor. No estén tristes,
pues el gozo del Señor es nuestra fortaleza.»
11También los levitas tranquilizaban a todo el
pueblo. Les decían: «¡Tranquilos! ¡No estén tristes,
que éste es un día *santo!»

12Así que todo el pueblo se fue a comer y beber y
compartir su comida, felices de haber comprendido lo
que se les había enseñado.

La fiesta de las Enramadas

13Al día siguiente, los jefes de familia, junto con
los sacerdotes y los levitas, se reunieron con el maestro Esdras para estudiar los términos de la *ley. **14**Y
en ésta encontraron escrito que el SEÑOR le había
mandado a Moisés que durante la fiesta del mes séptimo los israelitas debían habitar en *enramadas **15**y
pregonar en todas sus ciudades y en Jerusalén esta
orden: «Vayan a la montaña y traigan ramas de olivo, de olivo silvestre, de arrayán, de palmera y de
todo árbol frondoso, para hacer enramadas, conforme a lo que está escrito.»

16De modo que la gente fue y trajo ramas, y con
ellas hizo enramadas en las azoteas, en los patios, en

ʲ **7:68** setecientos ... mulas (varios mss. hebreos; véase también Esd 2:66); TM no incluye estas frases. ᵏ **7:70-72** ocho kilos
... ciento sesenta kilos ... mil doscientos diez kilos ... ciento sesenta kilos ... miel cien kilos. Lit. mil *dracmas ... veinte mil dracmas ... dos mil doscientas *minas ... veinte mil dracmas ... dos mil minas.

el atrio del templo de Dios, en la plaza de la puerta del Agua y en la plaza de la puerta de Efraín. [17]Toda la asamblea de los que habían regresado del cautiverio hicieron enramadas y habitaron en ellas. Como los israelitas no habían hecho esto desde los días de Josué hijo de Nun, hicieron una gran fiesta.

[18]Todos los días, desde el primero hasta el último, se leyó el libro de la ley de Dios. Celebraron la fiesta durante siete días, y en el día octavo hubo una asamblea solemne, según lo ordenado.

Los israelitas confiesan sus pecados

9 El día veinticuatro de ese mes los israelitas se reunieron para ayunar, se vistieron de luto y se echaron ceniza sobre la cabeza. [2]Habiéndose separado de los extranjeros, confesaron públicamente sus propios pecados y la maldad de sus antepasados, [3]y asumieron así su responsabilidad. Durante tres horas leyeron el libro de la *ley del SEÑOR su Dios, y en las tres horas siguientes[l] le confesaron sus pecados y lo adoraron. [4]Luego los levitas Jesúa, Baní, Cadmiel, Sebanías, Buní, Serebías, Baní y Quenaní subieron a la plataforma y en alta voz invocaron al SEÑOR su Dios. [5]Y los levitas Jesúa, Cadmiel, Baní, Jasabnías, Serebías, Hodías, Sebanías y Petaías clamaron:

«¡Vamos, bendigan al SEÑOR su Dios
    desde ahora y para siempre!
¡Bendito seas, Señor!
    ¡Sea exaltado tu glorioso *nombre,
    que está por encima de toda bendición y
        alabanza!

[6]»¡Sólo tú eres el SEÑOR!
    Tú has hecho los cielos,
    y los cielos de los cielos
        con todas sus estrellas.[m]
    Tú le das vida a todo lo creado:
        la tierra y el mar
    con todo lo que hay en ellos.
        ¡Por eso te adoran los ejércitos del cielo!

[7]»Tú, SEÑOR y Dios,
    fuiste quien escogió a Abram.
    Tú lo sacaste de Ur de los *caldeos
    y le pusiste por nombre Abraham.
[8]Descubriste en él un *corazón fiel;
    por eso hiciste con él un *pacto.
    Le prometiste que a sus descendientes
        les darías la tierra de los cananeos,
        de los hititas, amorreos y ferezeos,
        de los jebuseos y gergeseos.
    Y cumpliste tu palabra
        porque eres justo.

[9]»En Egipto viste la aflicción de nuestros
        padres;
    junto al *Mar Rojo escuchaste sus
        lamentos.
[10]Lanzaste grandes señales y maravillas
    contra el faraón, sus siervos y toda su gente,
    porque viste la insolencia
    con que habían tratado a tu pueblo.
    Fue así como te ganaste
        la buena fama que hoy tienes.
[11]A la vista de ellos abriste el mar,
    y lo cruzaron sobre terreno seco.
    Pero a sus perseguidores
        en lo más profundo del mar,
        como piedra en aguas caudalosas.

[12]Con una columna de nube los guiaste de día,
    con una columna de fuego los guiaste de
        noche:
    les alumbraste el camino que debían seguir.

[13]»Descendiste al monte Sinaí;
    desde el cielo les hablaste.
    Les diste juicios rectos y leyes verdaderas,
    estatutos y mandamientos buenos.
[14]Les diste a conocer tu *sábado santo,
    y por medio de tu servidor Moisés
    les entregaste tus mandamientos,
    estatutos y leyes.

[15]»Saciaste su hambre con pan del cielo;
    calmaste su sed con agua de la roca.
    Les diste posesión de la tierra
    que bajo juramento les habías prometido.
[16]Pero ellos y nuestros padres fueron altivos;
    no quisieron obedecer tus mandamientos.
[17]Se negaron a escucharte;
    no se acordaron de las maravillas
    que hiciste por ellos.
    Fue tanta su terquedad y rebeldía
    que hasta se nombraron un jefe
    para que los hiciera volver
    a la esclavitud de Egipto.
    Pero tú no los abandonaste
    porque eres Dios perdonador,
    clemente y compasivo,
    lento para la ira y grande en amor.

[18]»Y a pesar de que se hicieron
    un becerro de metal fundido
    y dijeron: "Éste es tu dios
    que te hizo subir de Egipto",
    y aunque fueron terribles
    las ofensas que cometieron,
[19]tú no los abandonaste en el desierto
    porque eres muy compasivo.

»Jamás se apartó de ellos la columna de nube
    que los guiaba de día por el camino;
    ni dejó de alumbrarlos la columna de fuego
    que de noche les mostraba por dónde ir.

[20]»Con tu buen Espíritu les diste
        entendimiento.
    No les quitaste tu maná de la boca;
    les diste agua para calmar su sed.
[21]Cuarenta años los sustentaste en el desierto.
    ¡Nada les faltó!
    No se desgastaron sus vestidos
    ni se les hincharon los pies.

[22]»Les entregaste reinos y pueblos,
    y asignaste a cada cual su territorio.
    Conquistaron las tierras de Og y de Sijón,
    que eran reyes de Hesbón y de Basán.
[23]Multiplicaste sus hijos
    como las estrellas del cielo;
    los hiciste entrar en la tierra
    que bajo juramento les prometiste a sus
        padres.
[24]Y sus hijos entraron en la tierra
    y tomaron posesión de ella.
    Ante ellos sometiste a los cananeos que la
        habitaban;
    les entregaste reyes y pueblos de esa tierra,

---

[l] 9:3 tres horas ... tres horas siguientes. Lit. una cuarta parte del día ... una cuarta parte. [m] 9:6 todas sus estrellas. Lit. todo su ejército.

para que hicieran con ellos lo que
          quisieran.
²⁵Conquistaron ciudades fortificadas
     y una tierra fértil;
se adueñaron de casas repletas de bienes,
     de cisternas, viñedos y olivares,
     y de gran cantidad de árboles frutales.
Comieron y se hartaron y engordaron;
     ¡disfrutaron de tu gran bondad!

²⁶»Pero fueron desobedientes:
     se rebelaron contra ti,
     rechazaron tu ley,
mataron a tus profetas
     que los convocaban a volverse a ti;
     ¡te ofendieron mucho!
²⁷Por eso los entregaste a sus enemigos,
     y éstos los oprimieron.
En tiempo de angustia clamaron a ti,
     y desde el cielo los escuchaste;
por tu inmensa compasión les enviaste
          salvadores
     para que los liberaran de sus enemigos.
²⁸Pero en cuanto eran liberados,
     volvían a hacer lo que te ofende;
tú los entregabas a sus enemigos,
     y ellos los dominaban.
De nuevo clamaban a ti,
     y desde el cielo los escuchabas.
¡Por tu inmensa compasión
     muchas veces los libraste!
²⁹Les advertiste que volvieran a tu ley,
     pero ellos actuaron con soberbia
     y no obedecieron tus mandamientos.
Pecaron contra tus normas,
     que dan vida a quien las obedece.
En su rebeldía, te rechazaron;
     fueron tercos y no quisieron escuchar.

³⁰»Por años les tuviste paciencia;
     con tu Espíritu los amonestaste
     por medio de tus profetas,
     pero ellos no quisieron escuchar.
Por eso los dejaste caer en manos
     de los pueblos de esa tierra.
³¹Sin embargo, es tal tu compasión
     que no los destruiste ni abandonaste,
     porque eres Dios clemente y compasivo.

³²»Y ahora, Dios nuestro,
     Dios grande, temible y poderoso,
     que cumples el pacto y eres fiel,
no tengas en poco los sufrimientos
     que han padecido nuestros reyes,
     gobernantes, sacerdotes y profetas,
nuestros padres y todo tu pueblo,
     desde los reyes de Asiria hasta hoy.
³³Tú has sido justo en todo
     lo que nos ha sucedido,
     porque actúas con fidelidad.
     Nosotros, en cambio, actuamos con
          maldad.
³⁴Nuestros reyes y gobernantes,
     nuestros sacerdotes y antepasados
desobedecieron tu ley
     y no acataron tus mandamientos
     ni las advertencias con que los
          amonestabas.
³⁵Pero ellos, durante tu reinado,
     no quisieron servirte
     ni abandonar sus malas obras,
a pesar de que les diste muchos bienes
     y les regalaste una tierra extensa y fértil.

³⁶»Por eso ahora somos esclavos,
     esclavos en la tierra
que les diste a nuestros padres
     para que gozaran de sus frutos y sus
          bienes.
³⁷Sus abundantes cosechas son ahora de los
          reyes
     que nos has impuesto por nuestro pecado.
Como tienen el poder, hacen lo que quieren
     con nosotros y con nuestro ganado.
     ¡Grande es nuestra aflicción!

³⁸»Por todo esto, nosotros hacemos este pacto y
lo ponemos por escrito, firmado por nuestros gobernantes, levitas y sacerdotes.»

El pueblo se compromete a obedecer la ley

10 La siguiente es la lista de los que firmaron:

Nehemías hijo de Jacalías, que era el gobernador;
Sedequías, ²Seraías, Azarías, Jeremías,
³ Pasur, Amarías, Malquías,
⁴ Jatús, Sebanías, Maluc,
⁵ Jarín, Meremot, Abdías,
⁶ Daniel, Guinetón, Baruc,
⁷ Mesulán, Abías, Mijamín,
⁸ Maazías, Bilgay y Semaías.
Éstos eran los sacerdotes.

⁹ Los levitas:

Jesúa hijo de Azanías, Binuy, de los descendientes de Henadad, Cadmiel,
¹⁰y sus hermanos Sebanías, Hodías, Quelitá, Pelaías, Janán,
¹¹Micaías, Rejob, Jasabías,
¹²Zacur, Serebías, Sebanías,
¹³Hodías, Baní y Beninu.

¹⁴Los jefes del pueblo:

Parós, Pajat Moab, Elam, Zatú, Baní,
¹⁵Buní, Azgad, Bebay,
¹⁶Adonías, Bigvay, Adín,
¹⁷Ater, Ezequías, Azur,
¹⁸Hodías, Jasún, Bezay,
¹⁹Jarif, Anatot, Nebay,
²⁰Magpías, Mesulán, Hezir,
²¹Mesezabel, Sadoc, Jadúa,
²²Pelatías, Janán, Anaías,
²³Oseas, Jananías, Jasub,
²⁴Halojés, Piljá, Sobec,
²⁵Rejún, Jasabná, Maseías,
²⁶Ahías, Janán, Anán,
²⁷Maluc, Jarín y Baná.

²⁸El resto del pueblo —sacerdotes, levitas, porteros, cantores, servidores del templo, todos los que se
habían separado de los pueblos de aquella tierra
para cumplir con la *ley de Dios, más sus mujeres,
hijos e hijas, y todos los que tenían uso de razón—
²⁹se unió a sus parientes que ocupaban cargos importantes y se comprometió, bajo juramento, a vivir
de acuerdo con la ley que Dios les había dado por
medio de su servidor Moisés, y a obedecer todos los
mandamientos, normas y estatutos de nuestro
SEÑOR. ³⁰Además, todos nos comprometimos a no
casar a nuestras hijas con los habitantes del país ni
aceptar a sus hijas como esposas para nuestros hijos.
³¹También prometimos que si la gente del país venía
en *sábado, o en cualquier otro día de fiesta, a vender sus mercancías o alguna otra clase de víveres, nosotros no les compraríamos nada. Prometimos así

mismo que en el séptimo año no cultivaríamos la tierra, y que perdonaríamos toda deuda.

32Además, nos impusimos la obligación de contribuir cada año con cuatro gramos de plataⁿ para los gastos del templo de nuestro Dios: 33el *pan de la Presencia; las ofrendas y el *holocausto diarios; los sacrificios de los sábados, de la luna nueva y de las fiestas solemnes; las ofrendas sagradas; los sacrificios de *expiación por el pecado de Israel, y todo el servicio del templo de nuestro Dios.

34En cuanto a la ofrenda de la leña, echamos suertes entre nosotros los sacerdotes, los levitas y el pueblo en general, según nuestras familias, para determinar a quiénes les tocaría llevar, en los tiempos fijados cada año, la leña para el templo del SEÑOR nuestro Dios, para que ardiera en su altar, como está escrito en la ley. 35Además nos comprometimos a llevar cada año al templo del SEÑOR las *primicias del campo y de todo árbol frutal, 36como también a presentar nuestros primogénitos y las primeras crías de nuestro ganado, como lo manda la ley, y a llevar a los sacerdotes que sirven en el templo de nuestro Dios, como está escrito en la ley.

37Convinimos en llevar a los almacenes del templo de nuestro Dios las primicias de nuestra molienda, de nuestras ofrendas, del fruto de nuestros árboles, de nuestro vino nuevo y de nuestro aceite, para los sacerdotes que ministran en el templo de nuestro Dios. Convinimos también en dar la décima parte de nuestras cosechas a los levitas, pues son ellos quienes recolectan todo esto en los pueblos donde trabajamos. 38Un sacerdote de la familia de Aarón acompañará a los levitas cuando éstos vayan a recolectar los diezmos. Los levitas, por su parte, depositarán el diezmo de los diezmos en la tesorería del templo de nuestro Dios. 39Los israelitas y los levitas llevarán las ofrendas de trigo, de vino y de aceite a los almacenes donde se guardan los utensilios sagrados y donde permanecen los sacerdotes, los porteros y los cantores, cuando están de servicio.

De este modo nos comprometimos a no descuidar el templo de nuestro Dios.

Los que se establecieron en Jerusalén

11 Los jefes del pueblo se establecieron en Jerusalén. Entre el resto del pueblo se hizo un sorteo para que uno de cada diez se quedara a vivir en Jerusalén, la ciudad *santa, y los otros nueve se establecieran en las otras poblaciones. 2El pueblo bendijo a todos los que se ofrecieron voluntariamente a vivir en Jerusalén.

3Éstos son los jefes de la provincia que se establecieron en Jerusalén y en las otras poblaciones de Judá. Los israelitas, los sacerdotes, los levitas, los servidores del templo y los descendientes de los servidores de Salomón se establecieron, cada uno en su propia población y en su respectiva propiedad. 4Éstos fueron los judíos y benjaminitas que se establecieron en Jerusalén:

De los descendientes de Judá:

Ataías hijo de Uzías, hijo de Zacarías, hijo de Amarías, hijo de Sefatías, hijo de Malalel, de los descendientes de Fares; 5y Maseías hijo de Baruc, hijo de Coljozé, hijo de Jazaías, hijo de Adaías, hijo de Joyarib, hijo de Zacarías, hijo de Siloní. 6El total de los descendientes de Fares

que se establecieron en Jerusalén fue de cuatrocientos sesenta y ocho guerreros valientes.

7De los descendientes de Benjamín:

Salú hijo de Mesulán, hijo de Joed, hijo de Pedaías, hijo de Colaías, hijo de Maseías, hijo de Itiel, hijo de Isaías, 8y sus hermanosñ Gabay y Salay. En total eran novecientos veintiocho. 9Su jefe era Joel hijo de Zicrí, y el segundo jefe de la ciudad era Judá hijo de Senuá.º

10De los sacerdotes:

Jedaías hijo de Joyarib, Jaquín, 11Seraías hijo de Jilquías, hijo de Mesulán, hijo de Sadoc, hijo de Merayot, hijo de Ajitob, que era el jefe del templo de Dios, 12y sus parientes, que eran ochocientos veintidós y trabajaban en el templo; así mismo, Adaías hijo de Jeroán, hijo de Pelalías, hijo de Amsí, hijo de Zacarías, hijo de Pasur, hijo de Malquías, 13y sus parientes, los cuales eran jefes de familia y sumaban doscientos cuarenta y dos; también Amasay hijo de Azarel, hijo de Ajsay, hijo de Mesilemot, hijo de Imer, 14y sus parientes, los cuales eran ciento veintiocho valientes. Su jefe era Zabdiel hijo de Guedolín.

15De los levitas:

Semaías hijo de Jasub, hijo de Azricán, hijo de Jasabías, hijo de Buní; 16Sabetay y Jozabad, que eran jefes de los levitas y estaban encargados de la obra exterior del templo de Dios; 17Matanías hijo de Micaías, hijo de Zabdí, hijo de Asaf, que dirigía el coro de los que entonaban las acciones de gracias en el momento de la oración; Bacbuquías, segundo entre sus hermanos, y Abdá hijo de Samúa, hijo de Galal, hijo de Jedutún. 18Los levitas que se establecieron en la ciudad santa fueron doscientos ochenta y cuatro.

19De los porteros:

Acub, Talmón y sus parientes, que vigilaban las puertas. En total eran ciento setenta y dos.

20Los demás israelitas, de los sacerdotes y de los levitas, vivían en todas las poblaciones de Judá, cada uno en su propiedad.

21Los servidores del templo, que estaban bajo la dirección de Zijá y Guispa, se establecieron en Ofel.

22El jefe de los levitas que estaban en Jerusalén era Uzi hijo de Baní, hijo de Jasabías, hijo de Matanías, hijo de Micaías, uno de los descendientes de Asaf. Éstos tenían a su cargo el canto en el servicio del templo de Dios. 23Una orden real y un reglamento establecían los deberes diarios de los cantores.

24Para atender a todos los asuntos del pueblo, el rey había nombrado como su representante a Petaías hijo de Mesezabel, que era uno de los descendientes de Zera hijo de Judá.

Otras ciudades habitadas

25Algunos judíos se establecieron en las siguientes ciudades con sus poblaciones: Quiriat Arbá, Dibón, Yecabsel, 26Jesúa, Moladá, Bet Pelet, 27Jazar Súal, Berseba, 28Siclag, Mecona, 29Enrimón, Zora, Jarmut, 30Zanoa, Adulán, Laquis y Azeca, es decir, desde Berseba hasta el valle de Hinón.

31Los benjaminitas se establecieron en Gueba, Micmás, Aías, Betel y sus poblaciones, 32Anatot, Nob,

ⁿ **10:32** *cuatro gramos de plata.* Lit. *la tercera parte de un* *siclo.*   ñ **11:8** *y sus hermanos* (mss. de LXX); *y después de él* (TM).
º **11:9** *Senuá.* Alt. *Hasenuá.*

Ananías, 33Jazor, Ramá, Guitayin, 34Jadid, Seboyín, Nebalat, 35Lod y Ono, y en el valle de los Artesanos.

36Algunos levitas de Judá se unieron a los benjaminitas.

Sacerdotes y levitas repatriados

12 Éstos son los sacerdotes y los levitas que regresaron con Zorobabel hijo de Salatiel, y con Jesúa:

Seraías, Jeremías, Esdras,

2 Amarías, Maluc, Jatús,

3 Secanías, Rejún, Meremot,

4 Idó, Guinetón, Abías,

5 Mijamín, Madías, Bilgá,

6 Semaías, Joyarib, Jedaías,

7 Salú, Amoc, Jilquías y Jedaías.

Éstos eran los jefes de los sacerdotes y de sus parientes en los días de Jesúa.

8Los levitas eran Jesúa, Binuy, Cadmiel, Serebías, Judá y Matanías, quien dirigía las acciones de gracias junto con sus hermanos; 9Bacbuquías y Uni, sus hermanos, se colocaban frente a ellos en los servicios.

10Los descendientes de Jesúa eran Joaquim, Eliasib, Joyadá, 11Johanán y Jadúa.

12Los jefes de las familias sacerdotales, en la época de Joaquim, eran:

de Seraías: Meraías;

de Jeremías: Jananías;

13 de Esdras: Mesulán;

de Amarías: Johanán;

14 de Melicú: Jonatán;

de Sebanías: José;

15 de Jarín: Adná;

de Merayot: Jelcay;

16 de Idó: Zacarías;

de Guinetón: Mesulán;

17 de Abías: Zicrí;

de Minjamín;p

de Moadías: Piltay;

18 de Bilgá: Samúa;

de Semaías: Jonatán;

19 de Joyarib: Matenay;

de Jedaías: Uzi;

20 de Salay: Calay;

de Amoc: Éber;

21 de Jilquías: Jasabías;

de Jedaías: Natanael.

22Los jefes de familia de los levitas y de los sacerdotes en tiempos de Eliasib, Joyadá, Johanán y Jadúa fueron inscritos durante el reinado de Darío el persa. 23Los jefes de familia de los levitas hasta los días de Johanán hijo de Eliasib fueron inscritos en el libro de las crónicas. 24Los jefes de los levitas eran Jasabías, Serebías y Jesúa hijo de Cadmiel. Cuando les llegaba el turno de servicio, sus parientes se colocaban frente a ellos para la alabanza y la acción de gracias, según lo establecido por David, hombre de Dios.

25Matanías, Bacbuquías, Abdías, Mesulán, Talmón y Acub eran los porteros que montaban la guardia en los almacenes cercanos a las puertas. 26Todos éstos vivieron en tiempos de Joaquim, hijo de Jesúa y nieto de Josadac, y en tiempos del gobernador Nehemías y del sacerdote y maestro Esdras.

Dedicación de la muralla

27Cuando llegó el momento de dedicar la muralla, buscaron a los levitas en todos los lugares donde vivían, y los llevaron a Jerusalén para celebrar la dedicación con cánticos de acción de gracias, al son de címbalos, arpas y liras. 28Entonces se reunieron los cantores de los alrededores de Jerusalén y de las aldeas de Netofa 29y Bet Guilgal, así como de los campos de Gueba y de Azmávet, ya que los cantores se habían construido aldeas alrededor de Jerusalén. 30Después de *purificarse a sí mismos, los sacerdotes y los levitas purificaron también a la gente, las *puertas y la muralla.

31Luego hice que los jefes de Judá subieran a la muralla, y organicé dos grandes coros. Uno de ellos marchaba sobre la muralla hacia la derecha, rumbo a la puerta del Basurero, 32seguido de Osaías, la mitad de los jefes de Judá, 33Azarías, Esdras, Mesulán, 34Judá, Benjamín, Semaías y Jeremías. 35A éstos los acompañaban los siguientes sacerdotes, que llevaban trompetas: Zacarías hijo de Jonatán, hijo de Semaías, hijo de Matanías, hijo de Micaías, hijo de Zacur, hijo de Asaf, 36y sus parientes Semaías, Azarel, Milalay, Guilalay, May, Natanael, Judá y Janani, que llevaban los instrumentos musicales de David, hombre de Dios. Al frente de ellos iba Esdras. 37Al llegar a la puerta de la Fuente, subieron derecho por las gradas de la Ciudad de David, por la cuesta de la muralla, pasando junto al palacio de David, hasta la puerta del Agua, al este de la ciudad.

38El segundo coro marchaba en dirección opuesta, a lo largo de la torre de los Hornos hasta el muro Ancho. Yo iba detrás, sobre la muralla, junto con la otra mitad de la gente. 39Pasamos por encima de la puerta de Efraín, la de Jesanáq y la de los Pescados; por la torre de Jananel y la de los Cien, y por la puerta de las Ovejas, hasta llegar a la puerta de la Guardia. Allí nos detuvimos. 40Los dos coros ocuparon sus sitios en el templo de Dios. Lo mismo hicimos yo, la mitad de los oficiales del pueblo, 41y los sacerdotes Eliaquín, Maseías, Minjamín, Micaías, Elihoenay, Zacarías, Jananías, 42Maseías, Semaías, Eleazar, Uzi, Johanán, Malquías, Elam y Ezer. En seguida los cantores empezaron a cantar a toda voz, dirigidos por Izraías.

43Ese día se ofrecieron muchos sacrificios y hubo fiesta, porque Dios los llenó de alegría. Hasta las mujeres y los niños participaron. Era tal el regocijo de Jerusalén que se oía desde lejos.

Contribución para los sacerdotes y levitas

44Aquel día se nombró a los encargados de los depósitos donde se almacenaban los tesoros, las ofrendas, las *primicias y los diezmos, para que depositaran en ellos las contribuciones que provenían de los campos de cada población y que, según la *ley, les correspondían a los sacerdotes y a los levitas. La gente de Judá estaba contenta con el servicio que prestaban los sacerdotes y levitas, 45quienes según lo establecido por David y su hijo Salomón se ocupaban del servicio de su Dios y del servicio de *purificación, junto con los cantores y los porteros. 46Por mucho tiempo, desde los días de David y de Asaf, había directores de coro y cánticos de alabanza y de acción de gracias a Dios. 47En la época de Zorobabel y de Nehemías, todos los días los israelitas entregaban las porciones correspondientes a los cantores y a los porteros. Así mismo daban las ofrendas sagradas para los demás levitas, y los levitas a su vez les entregaban a los hijos de Aarón lo que a éstos les correspondía.

p 12:17 En TM no aparece el nombre del jefe de Minjamín. q 12:39 de Jesaná. Alt. Vieja.

Reforma final de Nehemías

13 Aquel día se leyó ante el pueblo el libro de Moisés, y allí se encontró escrito que los amonitas y moabitas no debían jamás formar parte del pueblo de Dios, 2porque no sólo no les habían dado de comer ni de beber a los israelitas sino que habían contratado a Balán para que los maldijera, aunque en realidad nuestro Dios cambió la maldición por bendición. 3Al escuchar lo que la *ley decía, apartaron de Israel a todos los que se habían mezclado con extranjeros.

4Antes de esto, el sacerdote Eliasib, encargado de los almacenes del templo de nuestro Dios, había emparentado con Tobías 5y le había acondicionado una habitación grande. Allí se almacenaban las ofrendas, el incienso, los utensilios, los diezmos del trigo, vino y aceite correspondientes a los levitas, cantores y porteros, y las contribuciones para los sacerdotes.

6Para ese entonces yo no estaba en Jerusalén, porque en el año treinta y dos de Artajerjes, rey de Babilonia, había ido a ver al rey. Después de algún tiempo, con permiso del rey regresé a Jerusalén y me enteré de la infracción cometida por Eliasib al proporcionarle a Tobías una habitación en los atrios del templo de Dios. 8Esto me disgustó tanto que hice sacar de la habitación todos los cachivaches de Tobías. 9Luego ordené que *purificaran las habitaciones y volvieran a colocar allí los utensilios sagrados del templo de Dios, las ofrendas y el incienso.

10También me enteré de que a los levitas no les habían entregado sus porciones, y de que los levitas y cantores encargados del servicio habían regresado a sus campos. 11Así que reprendí a los jefes y les dije: «¿Por qué está tan descuidado el templo de Dios?» Luego los reuní y los restablecí en sus puestos.

12Todo Judá trajo a los almacenes la décima parte del trigo, del vino y del aceite. 13Puse a cargo de los almacenes al sacerdote Selemías, al escriba Sadoc y al levita Pedaías; como ayudante de ellos nombré a Janán, hijo de Zacur y nieto de Matanías. Todos ellos eran dignos de confianza, y se encargarían de distribuir las porciones entre sus compañeros.

14«¡Recuerda esto, Dios mío, y favoréceme; no olvides todo el bien que hice por el templo de mi Dios y de su culto!»

15Durante aquellos días vi en Judá que en *sábado algunos exprimían uvas y otros acarreaban, a lomo de mula, manojos de trigo, vino, uvas, higos y toda clase de cargas que llevaban a Jerusalén. Los reprendí entonces por vender sus víveres en ese día.

16También los tirios que vivían en Jerusalén traían a la ciudad pescado y otras mercancías, y las vendían a los judíos en sábado. 17Así que censuré la actitud de los nobles de Judá, y les dije: «Ustedes están pecando al profanar el día sábado! 18Lo mismo hicieron sus antepasados, y por eso nuestro Dios envió toda esta desgracia sobre nosotros y sobre esta ciudad. ¿Acaso quieren que aumente la ira de Dios sobre Israel por profanar el sábado?»

19Entonces ordené que cerraran las *puertas de Jerusalén al caer la tarde, antes de que comenzara el sábado, y que no las abrieran hasta después de ese día. Así mismo, puse a algunos de mis servidores en las puertas para que no dejaran entrar ninguna carga en sábado. 20Una o dos veces, los comerciantes y los vendedores de toda clase de mercancías pasaron la noche fuera de Jerusalén. 21Así que les advertí: «¡No se queden junto a la muralla! Si vuelven a hacerlo, ¡los apresaré!» Desde entonces no volvieron a aparecerse más en sábado. 22Luego ordené a los levitas que se purificaran y que fueran a hacer guardia en las puertas, para que el sábado fuera respetado.

«Recuerda esto, Dios mío, y conforme a tu gran amor, ten compasión de mí!»

23En aquellos días también me di cuenta de que algunos judíos se habían casado con mujeres de Asdod, de Amón y de Moab. 24La mitad de sus hijos hablaban la lengua de Asdod o de otros pueblos, y no sabían hablar la lengua de los judíos. 25Entonces los reprendí y los maldije; a algunos de ellos los golpeé, y hasta les arranqué los pelos, y los obligué a jurar por Dios. Les dije: «No permitan que sus hijas se casen con los hijos de ellos, ni se casen ustedes ni sus hijos con las hijas de ellos. 26¿Acaso no fue ése el pecado de Salomón, rey de Israel? Entre todas las naciones no hubo un solo rey como él: Dios lo amó y lo hizo rey sobre todo Israel. Pero aun a él lo hicieron pecar las mujeres extranjeras. 27¿Será que también de ustedes se dirá que cometieron el gran pecado de ofender a nuestro Dios casándose con mujeres extranjeras?»

28A uno de los hijos de Joyadá, hijo del sumo sacerdote Eliasib, lo eché de mi lado porque era yerno de Sambalat el horonita.

29«¡Recuerda esto, Dios mío, en perjuicio de los que profanaron el sacerdocio y el pacto de los sacerdotes y de los levitas!»

30Yo los purifiqué de todo lo extranjero y asigné a los sacerdotes y levitas sus respectivas tareas. 31También organicé la ofrenda de la leña en las fechas establecidas, y la entrega de las *primicias.

«¡Acuérdate de mí, Dios mío, y favoréceme!»

ESTER

Destitución de la reina Vasti

1 El rey Asuero,[a] que reinó sobre ciento veintisiete provincias que se extendían desde la India hasta *Cus, 2estableció su trono real en la ciudadela de Susa.

3En el tercer año de su reinado ofreció un banquete para todos sus funcionarios y servidores, al que asistieron los jefes militares de Persia y Media, y los magistrados y los gobernadores de las provincias, 4y durante ciento ochenta días les mostró la enorme riqueza de su reino y la esplendorosa gloria de su majestad.

5Pasado este tiempo, el rey ofreció otro banquete, que duró siete días, para todos los que se encontraban en la ciudadela de Susa, tanto los más importantes como los de menor importancia. Este banquete tuvo lugar en el jardín interior de su palacio, 6el cual lucía cortinas blancas y azules, sostenidas por cordones de lino blanco y tela púrpura, las cuales pasaban por anillos de plata sujetos a columnas de mármol. También había sofás de oro y plata sobre un piso de mosaicos de pórfido, mármol, madreperla y otras piedras preciosas. 7En copas de oro de las más variadas formas se servía el vino real, el cual corría a raudales, como era de esperarse del rey. 8Todos los invitados podían beber cuanto quisieran, pues los camareros habían recibido instrucciones del rey de servir a cada uno lo que deseara.

9La reina Vasti, por su parte, ofreció también un banquete para las mujeres en el palacio del rey Asuero.

10Al séptimo día, como a causa del vino el rey Asuero estaba muy alegre, le ordenó a los siete *eunucos que le servían —Meumán, Biztá, Jarboná, Bigtá, Abagtá, Zetar y Carcás— 11que llevaran a su presencia a la reina, ceñida con la corona real, a fin de exhibir su belleza ante los pueblos y sus dignatarios, pues realmente era muy hermosa. 12Pero cuando los eunucos le comunicaron la orden del rey, la reina se negó a ir. Esto contrarió mucho al rey, y se enfureció.

13De inmediato el rey consultó a los sabios conocedores de leyes,[b] porque era costumbre que en cuestiones de ley y justicia el rey consultara a los expertos. 14Los más allegados a él eran: Carsena, Setar, Admata, Tarsis, Meres, Marsená y Memucán, los siete funcionarios de Persia y Media que tenían acceso especial a la presencia del rey y ocupaban los puestos más altos en el reino.

15—Según la ley, ¿qué se debe hacer con la reina Vasti por haber desobedecido la orden del rey transmitida por los eunucos? —preguntó el rey.

16En presencia del rey y de los funcionarios, Memucán respondió:

—La reina Vasti no sólo ha ofendido a Su Majestad, sino también a todos los funcionarios y a todos los pueblos de las provincias del reino. 17Porque todas las mujeres se enterarán de la conducta de la reina, y esto hará que desprecien a sus esposos, pues dirán: "El rey Asuero mandó que la reina Vasti se presentara ante él, pero ella no fue." 18El día en que las mujeres de la nobleza de Persia y de Media se enteren de la conducta de la reina, les responderán de la misma manera a todos los dignatarios de Su Majestad. ¡Entonces no habrá fin al desprecio y a la discordia!

19»Por lo tanto, si le parece bien a Su Majestad, emita un decreto real, el cual se inscribirá con carácter irrevocable en las leyes de Persia y Media: que Vasti nunca vuelva a presentarse ante Su Majestad, y que el título de reina se lo otorgue a otra mejor que ella. 20Así, cuando el edicto real se dé a conocer por todo su inmenso reino, todas las mujeres respetarán a sus esposos, desde los más importantes hasta los menos importantes.

21Al rey y a sus funcionarios les pareció bien ese consejo, de modo que el rey hizo lo que había propuesto Memucán: 22envió cartas por todo el reino, a cada provincia en su propia escritura y a cada pueblo en su propio idioma, proclamando en la lengua de cada pueblo que todo hombre debe ejercer autoridad sobre su familia.

Elección de Ester como reina

2 Algún tiempo después, ya aplacada su furia, el rey Asuero se acordó de Vasti y de lo que había hecho, y de lo que se había decretado contra ella. 2Entonces los ayudantes personales del rey hicieron esta propuesta: «Que se busquen jóvenes vírgenes y hermosas para el rey. 3Que nombre el rey para cada provincia de su reino delegados que reúnan a todas esas jóvenes hermosas en el harén de la ciudadela de Susa. Que sean puestas bajo el cuidado de Jegay, el *eunuco encargado de las mujeres del rey, y que se les dé un tratamiento de belleza. 4Y que reine en lugar de Vasti la joven que más le guste al rey.» Esta propuesta le agradó al rey, y ordenó que así se hiciera.

5En la ciudadela de Susa vivía un judío de la tribu de Benjamín, llamado Mardoqueo hijo de Yaír, hijo de Simí, hijo de Quis, 6uno de los capturados en Jerusalén y llevados al exilio cuando Nabucodonosor, rey de Babilonia, se llevó cautivo a Jeconías,[c] rey de Judá. 7Mardoqueo tenía una prima llamada Jadasá. Esta joven, conocida también como Ester, a quien había criado porque era huérfana de padre y madre, tenía una figura atractiva y era muy hermosa. Al morir sus padres, Mardoqueo la adoptó como su hija.

8Cuando se proclamaron el edicto y la orden del rey, muchas jóvenes fueron reunidas en la ciudadela de Susa y puestas al cuidado de Jegay. Ester también fue llevada al palacio del rey y confiada a Jegay, quien estaba a cargo del harén. 9La joven agradó a Jegay y se ganó su simpatía. Por eso él se apresuró a darle el tratamiento de belleza y los alimentos especiales. Le asignó las siete doncellas más distinguidas del palacio y la trasladó con sus doncellas al mejor lugar del harén.

10Ester no reveló su nacionalidad ni sus antecedentes familiares, porque Mardoqueo se lo había prohibido. 11Éste se paseaba diariamente frente al patio del harén para saber cómo le iba a Ester y cómo la trataban.

12Ahora bien, para poder presentarse ante el rey, una joven tenía que completar los doce meses de tratamiento de belleza prescritos: seis meses con aceite de mirra, y seis meses con perfumes y cosméticos. 13Terminado el tratamiento, la joven se presentaba ante el rey y podía llevarse del harén al palacio todo lo que quisiera. 14Iba al palacio por la noche, y a la mañana siguiente volvía a un segundo harén bajo el cuidado de Sasgaz, el eunuco encargado de las concubinas

---

a 1:1 *Asuero*. Variante hebrea de Jerjes, nombre persa; así en el resto de este libro. b 1:13 *leyes* (lectura probable); *los tiempos* (TM). c 2:6 *Jeconías*. Es decir, Joaquín (véase 2R 24:8-17).

del rey. Y no volvía a presentarse ante el rey, a no ser que él la deseara y la mandara a llamar.

15Cuando a Ester, la joven que Mardoqueo había adoptado y que era hija de su tío Abijaíl, le llegó el turno de presentarse ante el rey, ella no pidió nada fuera de lo sugerido por Jegay, el eunuco encargado del harén del rey. Para entonces, ella se había ganado la simpatía de todo el que la veía. 16Ester fue llevada al palacio real ante el rey Asuero en el mes décimo, el mes de *tébet, durante el séptimo año de su reinado.

17El rey se enamoró de Ester más que de todas las demás mujeres, y ella se ganó su aprobación y simpatía más que todas las otras vírgenes. Así que él le ciñó la corona real y la proclamó reina en lugar de Vasti. 18Luego el rey ofreció un gran banquete en honor de Ester para todos sus funcionarios y servidores. Declaró un día de fiesta en todas las provincias y distribuyó regalos con generosidad digna de un rey.

Conspiración contra Asuero

19Mientras se reunía a un segundo grupo de vírgenes, Mardoqueo permanecía sentado a la puerta del rey. 20Ester, por su parte, continuó guardando en secreto sus antecedentes familiares y su nacionalidad, tal como Mardoqueo le había ordenado, ya que seguía cumpliendo las instrucciones de Mardoqueo como cuando estaba bajo su cuidado.

21En aquellos días, mientras Mardoqueo seguía sentado a la puerta del rey, Bigtán y Teres, los dos *eunucos del rey, miembros de la guardia, se enojaron y tramaron el asesinato del rey Asuero. 22Al enterarse Mardoqueo de la conspiración, se lo contó a la reina Ester, quien a su vez se lo hizo saber al rey de parte de Mardoqueo. 23Cuando se investigó el informe y se descubrió que era cierto, los dos eunucos fueron empalados en una estaca. Todo esto fue debidamente anotado en los registros reales, en presencia del rey.

Conspiración de Amán contra los judíos

3 Después de estos acontecimientos, el rey Asuero honró a Amán hijo de Hamedata, el descendiente de Agag, ascendiéndolo a un puesto más alto que el de todos los demás funcionarios que estaban con él. 2Todos los servidores de palacio asignados a la puerta del rey se arrodillaban ante Amán, y le rendían homenaje, porque así lo había ordenado el rey. Pero Mardoqueo no se arrodillaba ante él ni le rendía homenaje.

3Entonces los servidores de palacio asignados a la puerta del rey le preguntaron a Mardoqueo: «¿Por qué desobedeces la orden del rey?» 4Día tras día se lo reclamaban; pero él no les hacía caso. No se denunciaron a Amán para ver si seguía tolerándose la conducta de Mardoqueo, ya que éste les había confiado que era judío.

5Cuando Amán se dio cuenta de que Mardoqueo no se arrodillaba ante él ni le rendía homenaje, se enfureció. 6Y cuando le informaron a qué pueblo pertenecía Mardoqueo, desechó la idea de matarlo sólo a él y buscó la manera de exterminar a todo el pueblo de Mardoqueo, es decir, a los judíos que vivían por todo el reino de Asuero.

7Para determinar el día y el mes, se echó el *pur, es decir, la suerte, en presencia de Amán, en el mes primero, que es el mes de *nisán, del año duodécimo del reinado de Asuero. Y la suerte cayó sobred el mes duodécimo, el mes de *adar.

8Entonces Amán le dijo al rey Asuero:

—Hay cierto pueblo disperso y diseminado entre los pueblos de todas las provincias del reino, cuyas leyes y costumbres son diferentes de las de todos los demás. ¡No obedecen las leyes del reino, y a Su Majestad no le conviene tolerarlos! 9Si le parece bien, emita Su Majestad un decreto para aniquilarlos, y yo depositaré en manos de los administradores trescientos treinta mil kilose de plata para el tesoro real.

10Entonces el rey se quitó el anillo que llevaba su sello y se lo dio a Amán hijo de Hamedata, descendiente de Agag y enemigo de los judíos.

11—Quédate con el dinero —le dijo el rey a Amán—, y haz con ese pueblo lo que mejor te parezca.

12El día trece del mes primero se convocó a los secretarios del rey. Redactaron en la escritura de cada provincia y en el idioma de cada pueblo todo lo que Amán ordenaba a los *sátrapas del rey, a los intendentes de las diversas provincias y a los funcionarios de los diversos pueblos. Todo se escribió en *nombre del rey Asuero y se selló con el anillo real. 13Luego se enviaron los documentos por medio de los mensajeros a todas las provincias del rey con la orden de exterminar, matar y aniquilar a todos los judíos —jóvenes y ancianos, mujeres y niños— y saquear sus bienes en un solo día: el día trece del mes duodécimo, es decir, el mes de *adar. 14En cada provincia se debía emitir como ley una copia del edicto, el cual se comunicaría a todos los pueblos a fin de que estuvieran preparados para ese día.

15Los mensajeros partieron de inmediato por orden del rey, y a la vez se publicó el edicto en la ciudadela de Susa. Luego el rey y Amán se sentaron a beber, mientras que en la ciudad de Susa reinaba la confusión.

Acuerdo entre Mardoqueo y Ester

4 Cuando Mardoqueo se enteró de todo lo que se había hecho, se rasgó las vestiduras, se vistió de luto, se cubrió de ceniza y salió por la ciudad dando gritos de amargura. 2Pero como a nadie se le permitía entrar a palacio vestido de luto, sólo pudo llegar hasta la puerta del rey. 3En cada provincia adonde llegaban el edicto y la orden del rey, había gran duelo entre los judíos, con ayuno, llanto y lamentos. Muchos de ellos, vestidos de luto, se tendían sobre la ceniza.

4Cuando las criadas y los *eunucos de la reina Ester llegaron y le contaron lo que pasaba, ella se angustió mucho y le envió ropa a Mardoqueo para que se la pusiera en lugar de la ropa de luto; pero él no la aceptó. 5Entonces Ester mandó llamar a Hatac, uno de los eunucos del rey puesto al servicio de ella, y le ordenó que averiguara qué preocupaba a Mardoqueo y por qué actuaba de esa manera.

6Así que Hatac salió a ver a Mardoqueo, que estaba en la plaza de la ciudad, frente a la puerta del rey. 7Mardoqueo le contó todo lo que había sucedido, mencionándole incluso la cantidad exacta de dinero que Amán había prometido pagar al tesoro real por la aniquilación de los judíos. 8También le dio una copia del texto del edicto promulgado en Susa, el cual ordenaba el exterminio, para que se lo mostrara a Ester, se lo explicara, y la exhortara a que se presentara ante el rey para implorar clemencia e interceder en favor de su pueblo.

9Hatac regresó y le informó a Ester lo que Mardoqueo había dicho. 10Entonces ella ordenó a Hatac que le dijera a Mardoqueo: 11«Todos los servidores

---

d 3:7 Y la suerte cayó sobre (LXX); TM no incluye esta frase.　e 3:9 trescientos treinta mil kilos. Lit. diez mil *talentos.

del rey y el pueblo de las provincias del reino saben que, para cualquier hombre o mujer que, sin ser invitado por el rey, se acerque a él en el patio interior, hay una sola ley: la pena de muerte. La única excepción es que el rey, extendiendo su cetro de oro, le perdone la vida. En cuanto a mí, hace ya treinta días que el rey no me ha pedido presentarme ante él.»

12Cuando Mardoqueo se enteró de lo que había dicho Ester, 13mandó a decirle: «No te imagines que por estar en la casa del rey serás la única que escape con vida de entre todos los judíos. 14Si ahora te quedas absolutamente callada, de otra parte vendrán el alivio y la liberación para los judíos, pero tú y la familia de tu padre perecerán. ¡Quién sabe si no has llegado al trono precisamente para un momento como éste!»

15Ester le envió a Mardoqueo esta respuesta: 16«Ve y reúne a todos los judíos que están en Susa, para que ayunen por mí. Durante tres días no coman ni beban, ni de día ni de noche. Yo, por mi parte, ayunaré con mis doncellas al igual que ustedes. Cuando cumpla con esto, me presentaré ante el rey, por más que vaya en contra de la ley. ¡Y si perezco, que perezca!»

17Entonces Mardoqueo fue y cumplió con todas las instrucciones de Ester.

Petición de Ester al rey Asuero

5 Al tercer día, Ester se puso sus vestiduras reales y fue a pararse en el patio interior del palacio, frente a la sala del rey. El rey estaba sentado allí en su trono real, frente a la puerta de entrada. 2Cuando vio a la reina Ester de pie en el patio, se mostró complacido con ella y le extendió el cetro de oro que tenía en la mano. Entonces Ester se acercó y tocó la punta del cetro.

3El rey le preguntó:

—¿Qué te pasa, reina Ester? ¿Cuál es tu petición? ¡Aun cuando fuera la mitad del reino, te lo concedería!

4—Si le parece bien a Su Majestad —respondió Ester—, venga hoy al banquete que ofrezco en su honor, y traiga también a Amán.

5—Vayan de inmediato por Amán, para que podamos cumplir con el deseo de Ester —ordenó el rey.

Así que el rey y Amán fueron al banquete que ofrecía Ester. 6Cuando estaban brindando, el rey volvió a preguntarle a Ester:

—Dime qué deseas, y te lo concederé. ¿Cuál es tu petición? ¡Aun cuando fuera la mitad del reino, te lo concedería!

7Ester respondió:

—Mi deseo y petición es que, 8si me he ganado el favor de Su Majestad, y si le agrada cumplir mi deseo y conceder mi petición, venga mañana con Amán al banquete que les voy a ofrecer, y entonces le daré la respuesta.

Odio de Amán contra Mardoqueo

9Amán salió aquel día muy contento y de buen humor; pero cuando vio a Mardoqueo en la puerta del rey y notó que no se levantaba ni temblaba ante su presencia, se llenó de ira contra él. 10No obstante, se contuvo y se fue a su casa.

Luego llamó Amán a sus amigos y a Zeres, su esposa, 11e hizo alarde de su enorme riqueza y de sus muchos hijos, y de cómo el rey lo había honrado en todo sentido ascendiéndolo sobre los funcionarios y demás servidores del rey.

12—Es más —añadió Amán—, yo soy el único a quien la reina Ester invitó al banquete que le ofreció al rey. Y también me ha invitado a acompañarlo mañana. 13Pero todo esto no significa nada para mí, mientras vea a ese judío Mardoqueo sentado a la puerta del rey.

14Su esposa Zeres y todos sus amigos le dijeron:

—Haz que se coloque una estaca a veinticinco metrosf de altura, y por la mañana pídele al rey que empale en ella a Mardoqueo. Así podrás ir contento al banquete con el rey.

La sugerencia le agradó a Amán, y mandó que se colocara la estaca.

Exaltación de Mardoqueo

6 Aquella noche el rey no podía dormir, así que mandó que le trajeran las crónicas reales —la historia de su reino— y que se las leyeran. 2Allí constaba que Mardoqueo había delatado a Bigtán y Teres, dos de los *eunucos del rey, miembros de la guardia, que habían tramado asesinar al rey Asuero.

3—¿Qué honor o reconocimiento ha recibido Mardoqueo por esto? —preguntó el rey.

—No se ha hecho nada por él —respondieron sus ayudantes personales.

4Amán acababa de entrar en el patio exterior del palacio para pedirle al rey que empalara a Mardoqueo en la estaca que había mandado levantar para él. Así que el rey preguntó:

—¿Quién anda en el patio?

5Sus ayudantes respondieron:

—El que anda en el patio es Amán.

—¡Que pase! —ordenó el rey.

6Cuando entró Amán, el rey le preguntó:

—¿Cómo se debe tratar al hombre a quien el rey desea honrar?

Entonces Amán dijo para sí: «¿A quién va a querer honrar el rey sino a mí?» 7Así que respondió:

—Para el hombre a quien el rey desea honrar, 8que se mande traer una vestidura real que el rey haya usado, y un caballo en el que haya montado y que lleve en la cabeza un adorno real. 9La vestidura y el caballo deberán entregarse a uno de los funcionarios más ilustres del rey, para que vista al hombre a quien el rey desea honrar, y que lo pasee a caballo por las calles de la ciudad, proclamando a su paso: "¡Así se trata al hombre a quien el rey desea honrar!"

10—Ve de inmediato —le dijo el rey a Amán—, toma la vestidura y el caballo, tal como lo has sugerido, y haz eso mismo con Mardoqueo, el judío que está sentado a la puerta del rey. No descuides ningún detalle de todo lo que has recomendado.

11Así que Amán tomó la vestidura y el caballo, vistió a Mardoqueo y lo llevó a caballo por las calles de la ciudad, proclamando a su paso: «¡Así se trata al hombre a quien el rey desea honrar!»

12Después Mardoqueo volvió a la puerta del rey. Pero Amán regresó apurado a su casa, triste y tapándose la cara. 13Y les contó a Zeres, su esposa, y a todos sus amigos todo lo que le había sucedido.

Entonces sus consejeros y su esposa Zeres le dijeron:

—Si Mardoqueo, ante quien has comenzado a caer, es de origen judío, no podrás contra él. ¡Sin duda acabarás siendo derrotado!

14Mientras todavía estaban hablando con Amán, llegaron los eunucos del rey y lo llevaron de prisa al banquete ofrecido por Ester.

---

f 5:14 veinticinco metros. Lit. cincuenta *codos.

Humillación y muerte de Amán

7 El rey y Amán fueron al banquete de la reina Ester, **2**y al segundo día, mientras brindaban, el rey le preguntó otra vez:

—Dime qué deseas, reina Ester, y te lo concederé. ¿Cuál es tu petición? ¡Aun cuando fuera la mitad del reino, te lo concedería!

3Ester respondió:

—Si me he ganado el favor de Su Majestad, y si le parece bien, mi deseo es que me conceda la *vida. Mi petición es que se compadezca de mi pueblo. **4**Porque a mí y a mi pueblo se nos ha vendido para exterminio, muerte y aniquilación. Si sólo se nos hubiera vendido como esclavos, yo me habría quedado callada, pues tal angustia no sería motivo suficiente para inquietar a Su Majestad.ᵍ

5El rey le preguntó:

—¿Y quién es ése que se ha atrevido a concebir semejante barbaridad? ¿Dónde está?

6—¡El adversario y enemigo es este miserable de Amán! —respondió Ester.

Amán quedó aterrorizado ante el rey y la reina. **7**El rey se levantó enfurecido, dejó de beber y salió al jardín del palacio. Pero Amán, dándose cuenta de que el rey ya había decidido su fin, se quedó para implorarle a la reina Ester que le perdonara la vida.

8Cuando el rey volvió del jardín del palacio a la sala del banquete, Amán estaba inclinado sobre el diván donde Ester estaba recostada. Al ver esto, el rey exclamó:

—¡Y todavía se atreve éste a violar a la reina en mi presencia y en mi casa!

Tan pronto como el rey pronunció estas palabras, cubrieron el rostro de Amán. **9**Y Jarboná, uno de los *eunucos que atendían al rey, dijo:

—Hay una estaca a veinticinco metrosʰ de altura, junto a la casa de Amán. Él mandó colocarla para Mardoqueo, el que intervino en favor del rey.

—¡Empálenlo en ella! —ordenó el rey.

10De modo que empalaron a Amán en la estaca que él había mandado levantar para Mardoqueo. Con eso se aplacó la furia del rey.

Edicto real en favor de los judíos

8 Ese mismo día el rey Asuero le dio a la reina Ester las propiedades de Amán, el enemigo de los judíos. Mardoqueo se presentó ante el rey, porque Ester le había dicho cuál era su parentesco con ella. **2**El rey se quitó el anillo con su sello, el cual había recuperado de Amán, y se lo obsequió a Mardoqueo. Ester, por su parte, lo designó administrador de las propiedades de Amán.

3Luego Ester volvió a interceder ante el rey. Se echó a sus pies y, con lágrimas en los ojos, le suplicó que pusiera fin al malvado plan que Amán el agagueo había maquinado contra los judíos. **4**El rey le extendió a Ester el cetro de oro. Entonces ella se levantó y, permaneciendo de pie ante él, **5**dijo:

—Si me he ganado el favor de Su Majestad, y si piensa que es correcto hacerlo y está contento conmigo, dígnese dar una contraorden que invalide los decretos para aniquilar a los judíos que están en todas las provincias del reino, los cuales fraguó y escribió Amán hijo de Hamedata, el agagueo. **6**¿cómo podría yo ver la calamidad que se cierne sobre mi pueblo? ¿Cómo podría ver impasible el exterminio de mi gente?

7El rey Asuero respondió entonces a la reina Ester y a Mardoqueo el judío:

—Debido a que Amán atentó contra los judíos, le he dado sus propiedades a Ester, y a él lo han empalado en la estaca. **8**Redacten ahora, en mi *nombre, otro decreto en favor de los judíos, como mejor les parezca, y séllenlo con mi anillo real. Un documento escrito en mi nombre, y sellado con mi anillo, es imposible revocarlo.

9De inmediato fueron convocados los secretarios del rey. Era el día veintitrés del mes tercero, el mes de *siván. Se escribió todo lo que Mardoqueo ordenó a los judíos y a los *sátrapas, intendentes y funcionarios de las ciento veintisiete provincias que se extendían desde la India hasta *Cus. Esas órdenes se promulgaron en la escritura de cada provincia y en el idioma de cada pueblo, y también en la escritura e idioma propios de los judíos. **10**Mardoqueo escribió los decretos en nombre del rey Asuero, los selló con el anillo real, y los envió por medio de mensajeros del rey, que montaban veloces corceles de las caballerizas reales.

11El edicto del rey facultaba a los judíos de cada ciudad a reunirse y defenderse, a exterminar, matar y aniquilar a cualquier fuerza armada de cualquier pueblo o provincia que los atacara a ellos o a sus mujeres y niños, y a apoderarse de los bienes de sus enemigos. **12**Para llevar esto a cabo en todas las provincias del rey Asuero, los judíos fijaron el día trece del mes doce, que es el mes de *adar. **13**En cada provincia se emitiría como ley una copia del edicto, y se daría a conocer a todos los pueblos. Así los judíos estarían preparados ese día para vengarse de sus enemigos.

14Los mensajeros, siguiendo las órdenes del rey, salieron de inmediato montando veloces corceles. El edicto se publicó también en la ciudadela de Susa. **15**Mardoqueo salió de la presencia del rey vistiendo ropas reales de azul y blanco, una gran corona de oro y un manto de lino fino color púrpura. La ciudad de Susa estalló en gritos de alegría. **16**Para los judíos, aquél fue un tiempo de luz y de alegría, júbilo y honor. **17**En cada provincia y ciudad adonde llegaban el edicto y la orden del rey, había alegría y regocijo entre los judíos, con banquetes y festejos. Y muchas personas de otros pueblos se hicieron judíos por miedo a ellos.

Triunfo de los judíos

9 El edicto y la orden del rey debían ejecutarse el día trece del mes doce, que es el mes de *adar. Los enemigos de los judíos esperaban dominarlos ese día; pero ahora se habían invertido los papeles, y los judíos dominaban a quienes los odiaban. **2**En todas las provincias del rey Asuero, los judíos se reunieron en sus respectivas ciudades para atacar a los que procuraban su ruina. Nadie podía combatirlos, porque el miedo a ellos se había apoderado de todos. **3**Los funcionarios de las provincias, los *sátrapas, los intendentes y los administradores del rey apoyaban a los judíos, porque el miedo a Mardoqueo se había apoderado de todos ellos. **4**Mardoqueo se había convertido en un personaje distinguido dentro del palacio real. Su fama se extendía por todas las provincias, y cada vez se hacía más poderoso.

---

g 7:4 *pues ... Majestad.* Alt. *pero la compensación que nuestro adversario ofrece no puede compararse con la pérdida que sufriría Su Majestad.* **h 7:9** *veinticinco metros.* Lit. *cincuenta *codos.*

⁵Los judíos mataron a filo de espada a todos sus enemigos. Los mataron y los aniquilaron, e hicieron lo que quisieron con quienes los odiaban. ⁶En la ciudadela de Susa mataron y aniquilaron a quinientos hombres. ⁷También mataron a Parsandata, Dalfón, Aspata, ⁸Porata, Adalías, Aridata, ⁹Parmasta, Arisay, Ariday y Vaizata, ¹⁰que eran los diez hijos de Amán hijo de Hamedata, el enemigo de los judíos. Pero no se apoderaron de sus bienes.

¹¹Ese mismo día, al enterarse el rey del número de muertos en la ciudadela de Susa, ¹²le dijo a la reina Ester:

—Si los judíos han matado y aniquilado a quinientos hombres y a los diez hijos de Amán en la ciudadela de Susa, ¡qué no habrán hecho en el resto de las provincias del reino! Dime cuál es tu deseo, y se te concederá. ¿Qué otra petición tienes? ¡Se cumplirá tu deseo!

¹³—Si a Su Majestad le parece bien —respondió Ester—, concédeles permiso a los judíos de Susa para prorrogar hasta mañana el edicto de este día, y permita que sean empalados en la estaca los diez hijos de Amán.

¹⁴El rey ordenó que se hiciera así. Se emitió un edicto en Susa, y los diez hijos de Amán fueron empalados. ¹⁵Los judíos de Susa se reunieron también el día catorce del mes de *adar*, y mataron allí a trescientos hombres, pero no se apoderaron de sus bienes.

¹⁶Mientras tanto, los judíos restantes que estaban en las provincias del rey también se reunieron para defenderse y librarse de sus enemigos. Mataron a setenta y cinco mil de quienes los odiaban, pero tampoco se apoderaron de sus bienes. ¹⁷Esto sucedió el día trece del mes de *adar*. El día catorce descansaron, y lo celebraron con un alegre banquete.

Celebración de *Purim*

¹⁸En cambio, los judíos de Susa que se habían reunido el trece y el catorce, descansaron el día quince, y lo celebraron con un alegre banquete.

¹⁹Por eso los judíos de las zonas rurales —los que viven en las aldeas— celebran el catorce del mes de *adar como día de alegría y de banquete, y se hacen regalos unos a otros.

²⁰Mardoqueo registró estos acontecimientos, y envió cartas a todos los judíos de todas las provincias lejanas y cercanas del rey Asuero, ²¹exigiéndoles que celebraran cada año los días catorce y quince del mes de *adar* ²²como el tiempo en que los judíos se libraron de sus enemigos, y como el mes en que su aflicción se convirtió en alegría, y su dolor en día de fiesta. Por eso debían celebrarlos como días de banquete y de alegría, compartiendo los alimentos los unos con los otros y dándoles regalos a los pobres.

²³Así los judíos acordaron convertir en costumbre lo que habían comenzado a festejar, cumpliendo lo que Mardoqueo les había ordenado por escrito. ²⁴Porque Amán hijo de Hamedata, el agagueo, el enemigo de todos los judíos, había maquinado aniquilar a los judíos y había echado el *pur* —es decir, la suerte— para confundirlos y aniquilarlos. ²⁵Pero cuando Ester se presentó ante el rey, éste ordenó por escrito que el malvado plan que Amán había maquinado contra los judíos debía recaer sobre su propia cabeza, y que él y sus hijos fueran empalados en la estaca. ²⁶Por tal razón, a estos días se los llamó *Purim*, de la palabra *pur*. Conforme a todo lo escrito en esta carta, y debido a lo que habían visto y a lo que les había sucedido, ²⁷los judíos establecieron para ellos y sus descendientes, y para todos los que se les unieran, la costumbre de celebrar sin falta estos dos días cada año, según la manera prescrita y en la fecha fijada. ²⁸Toda familia, y cada provincia y ciudad, debía recordar y celebrar estos días en cada generación. Y estos días de *Purim* no debían dejar de festejarse entre los judíos, ni debía morir su recuerdo entre sus descendientes.

²⁹La reina Ester, hija de Abijaíl, junto con Mardoqueo el judío, escribieron con plena autoridad para confirmar esta segunda carta con respecto a los días de *Purim*. ³⁰Él envió decretos a todos los judíos de las ciento veintisiete provincias del reino de Asuero —con palabras de buena voluntad y seguridad— ³¹para establecer los días de *Purim* en las fechas fijadas, como lo habían decretado para ellos Mardoqueo el judío y la reina Ester, y como lo habían establecido para sí mismos y para sus descendientes, con algunas cláusulas sobre ayunos y lamentos. ³²El decreto de Ester confirmó estas normas con respecto a *Purim*, y quedó registrado por escrito.

Grandeza de Mardoqueo

10 El rey Asuero impuso tributo por todo el imperio, incluyendo las islas del mar. ²Todos los hechos de poder y autoridad de Mardoqueo, junto con un relato completo de la grandeza a la cual lo elevó el rey, se hallan registrados en las crónicas de los reyes de Media y Persia. ³El judío Mardoqueo fue preeminente entre su pueblo y segundo en jerarquía después del rey Asuero. Alcanzó gran estima entre sus muchos compatriotas, porque procuraba el bien de su pueblo y promovía su *bienestar.

JOB

Prólogo

1 En la región de Uz había un hombre recto e intachable, que temía a Dios y vivía apartado del mal. Este hombre se llamaba Job. 2Tenía siete hijos y tres hijas; 3era dueño de siete mil ovejas, tres mil camellos, quinientas yuntas de bueyes y quinientas asnas, y su servidumbre era muy numerosa. Entre todos los habitantes del oriente era el personaje de mayor renombre.

4Sus hijos acostumbraban turnarse para celebrar banquetes en sus respectivas casas, e invitaban a sus tres hermanas a comer y beber con ellos. 5Una vez terminado el ciclo de los banquetes, Job se aseguraba de que sus hijos se *purificaran. Muy de mañana ofrecía un *holocausto por cada uno de ellos, pues pensaba: «Tal vez mis hijos hayan pecado y maldecidoᵃ en su *corazón a Dios.» Para Job ésta era una costumbre cotidiana.

Primera prueba de Job

6Llegó el día en que los ángelesᵇ debían hacer acto de presencia ante el SEÑOR, y con ellos se presentó también *Satanás. 7Y el SEÑOR le preguntó:

—¿De dónde vienes?

—Vengo de rondar la tierra, y de recorrerla de un extremo a otro —le respondió Satanás.

8—¿Te has puesto a pensar en mi siervo Job? —volvió a preguntarle el SEÑOR—. No hay en la tierra nadie como él; es un hombre recto e intachable, que me honra y vive apartado del mal.

9Satanás replicó:

—¿Y acaso Job te honra sin recibir nada a cambio? 10¿Acaso no están bajo tu protección él y su familia y todas sus posesiones? De tal modo has bendecido la obra de sus manos que sus rebaños y ganados llenan toda la tierra. 11Pero extiende la mano y quítale todo lo que posee, ¡a ver si no te maldice en tu propia cara!

12—Muy bien —le contestó el SEÑOR—. Todas sus posesiones están en tus manos, con la condición de que a él no le pongas la mano encima.

Dicho esto, Satanás se retiró de la presencia del SEÑOR.

13Llegó el día en que los hijos y las hijas de Job celebraban un banquete en casa de su hermano mayor. 14Entonces un mensajero llegó a decirle a Job: «Mientras los bueyes araban y los asnos pastaban por allí cerca, 15nos atacaron los sabeanos y se los llevaron. A los criados los mataron a filo de espada. ¡Sólo yo pude escapar, y ahora vengo a contárselo a usted!»

16No había terminado de hablar este mensajero cuando uno más llegó y dijo: «Del cielo cayó un rayo que calcinó a las ovejas y a los criados. ¡Sólo yo pude escapar para venir a contárselo!»

17No había terminado de hablar este mensajero cuando otro más llegó y dijo: «Unos salteadores caldeos vinieron y, dividiéndose en tres grupos, se apoderaron de los camellos y se los llevaron. A los criados los mataron a filo de espada. ¡Sólo yo pude escapar, y ahora vengo a contárselo!»

18No había terminado de hablar este mensajero cuando todavía otro llegó y dijo: «Los hijos y las hijas de usted estaban celebrando un banqueteᶜ en casa del mayor de todos ellos 19cuando, de pronto, un fuerte viento del desierto dio contra la casa y derribó sus cuatro esquinas. ¡Y la casa cayó sobre los jóvenes, y todos murieron! ¡Sólo yo pude escapar, y ahora vengo a contárselo!»

20Al llegar a este punto, Job se levantó, se rasgó las vestiduras, se rasuró la cabeza, y luego se dejó caer al suelo en actitud de adoración. 21Entonces dijo:

«Desnudo salí del vientre de mi madre,
   y desnudo he de partir.ᵈ
El SEÑOR ha dado; el SEÑOR ha quitado.
   ¡Bendito sea el *nombre del SEÑOR!»

22A pesar de todo esto, Job no pecó ni le echó la culpa a Dios.ᵉ

Segunda prueba de Job

2 Llegó el día en que los ángelesᶠ debían hacer acto de presencia ante el SEÑOR, y con ellos llegó también *Satanás para presentarse ante el SEÑOR.

2Y el SEÑOR le preguntó:

—¿De dónde vienes?

—Vengo de rondar la tierra, y de recorrerla de un extremo a otro —le respondió Satanás.

3—¿Te has puesto a pensar en mi siervo Job? —volvió a preguntarle el SEÑOR—. No hay en la tierra nadie como él; es un hombre recto e intachable, que me honra y vive apartado del mal. Y aunque tú me incitaste contra él para arruinarlo sin motivo, ¡todavía mantiene firme su integridad!

4—¡Una cosa por la otra! —replicó Satanás—. Con tal de salvar la vida, el *hombre da todo lo que tiene. 5Pero extiende la mano y hiérelo, ¡a ver si no te maldice en tu propia cara!

6—Muy bien —dijo el SEÑOR a Satanás—, Job está en tus manos. Eso sí, respeta su vida.

7Dicho esto, Satanás se retiró de la presencia del SEÑOR para afligir a Job con dolorosas llagas desde la planta del pie hasta la coronilla. 8Y Job, sentado en medio de las cenizas, tomó un pedazo de teja para rascarse constantemente.

9Su esposa le reprochó:

—¿Todavía mantienes firme tu integridad? ¡Maldice a Dios y muérete!

10Job le respondió:

—Mujer, hablas como una necia. Si de Dios sabemos recibir lo bueno, ¿no sabremos también recibir lo malo?

A pesar de todo esto, Job no pecó ni de palabra.

Los tres amigos de Job

11Tres amigos de Job se enteraron de todo el mal que le había sobrevenido, y de común acuerdo salieron de sus respectivos lugares para ir juntos a expresarle a Job sus condolencias y consuelo. Ellos eran Elifaz de Temán, Bildad de Súah, y Zofar de Namat. 12Desde cierta distancia alcanzaron a verlo, y casi no lo pudieron reconocer. Se echaron a llorar a voz en cuello, rasgándose las vestiduras y arrojándose polvo y ceniza sobre la cabeza, 13y durante siete días y siete noches se sentaron en el suelo para hacerle compañía. Ninguno de ellos se atrevía a decirle nada, pues veían cuán grande era su sufrimiento.

ᵃ **1:5** *maldecido.* Lit. *bendecido;* este eufemismo se usa también en 1:11; 2:5,9. ᵇ **1:6** *ángeles.* Lit. *hijos de Dios.* ᶜ **1:18** *celebrando un banquete.* Lit. *comiendo y bebiendo vino.* ᵈ **1:21** *he de partir.* Alt. *he de volver allá.* ᵉ **1:22** *ni le echó la culpa a Dios.* Lit. *ni dio oración a Dios;* véase nota en 1:5. ᶠ **2:1** *ángeles.* Lit. *hijos de Dios.*

Primer discurso de Job

3 Después de esto, Job rompió el silencio para maldecir el día en que había nacido. ²Dijo así:

³«Que perezca el día en que fui concebido
y la noche en que se anunció: "¡Ha nacido un niño!"

⁴Que ese día se vuelva oscuridad;
que Dios en lo alto no lo tome en cuenta;
que no brille en él ninguna luz.

⁵Que las tinieblas y las más pesadas sombras
vuelvan a reclamarlo;
Que una nube lo cubra con su sombra;
que la oscuridad domine su esplendor.

⁶Que densas tinieblas caigan sobre esa noche;
que no sea contada entre los días del año,
ni registrada en ninguno de los meses.

⁷Que permanezca estéril esa noche;
que no haya en ella gritos de alegría.

⁸Que maldigan ese día los que profieren maldiciones,
los expertos en provocar a *Leviatán.

⁹Que se oscurezcan sus estrellas matutinas;
que en vano esperen la luz del día,
y que no vean los primeros rayos de la aurora.

¹⁰Pues no cerró el vientre de mi madre
ni evitó que mis ojos vieran tanta miseria.

¹¹»¿Por qué no perecí al momento de nacer?
¿Por qué no morí cuando salí del vientre?

¹²¿Por qué hubo rodillas que me recibieran,
y pechos que me amamantaran?

¹³Ahora estaría yo descansando en paz;
estaría durmiendo tranquilo

¹⁴entre reyes y consejeros de este mundo,
que se construyeron monumentos hoy en ruinas;

¹⁵entre gobernantes que poseyeron mucho oro
y que llenaron de plata sus mansiones.

¹⁶¿Por qué no me enterraron como a un abortivo,
como a esos niños que jamás vieron la luz?

¹⁷¡Allí cesa el afán de los malvados!
¡Allí descansan las víctimas de la opresión!

¹⁸También los cautivos disfrutan del reposo,
pues ya no escuchan los gritos del capataz.

¹⁹Allí el pequeño se codea con el grande,
y el esclavo se libera de su amo.

²⁰»¿Por qué permite Dios que los sufridos vean la luz?
¿Por qué se les da vida a los amargados?

²¹Anhelan éstos una muerte que no llega,
aunque la buscan más que a tesoro escondido;

²²¡se llenarían de gran regocijo,
se alegrarían si llegaran al sepulcro!

²³¿Por qué arrincona Dios
al *hombre que desconoce su destino?

²⁴Antes que el pan, me llegan los suspiros;
mis gemidos se derraman como el agua.

²⁵Lo que más temía, me sobrevino;
lo que más me asustaba, me sucedió.

²⁶No encuentro paz ni sosiego;
no hallo reposo, sino sólo agitación.»

Primer discurso de Elifaz

4 A esto respondió así Elifaz de Temán:

²«Tal vez no puedas aguantar
que alguien se atreva a decirte algo,
pero ¿quién podría contener las palabras?

³Tú, que impartías instrucción a las multitudes
y fortalecías las manos decaídas;

⁴tú, que con tus palabras sostenías a los que tropezaban
y fortalecías las rodillas que flaqueaban;

⁵ahora que afrontas las calamidades, no las resistes!;
¡te ves golpeado y te desanimas!

⁶¿No debieras confiar en que temes a Dios
y en que tu conducta es intachable?

⁷»Ponte a pensar: ¿Quién que sea inocente ha perecido?
¿Cuándo se ha destruido a la gente íntegra?

⁸La experiencia me ha enseñado
que los que siembran maldad cosechan desventura.

⁹El soplo de Dios los destruye,
el aliento de su enojo los consume.

¹⁰Aunque ruja el león y gruña el cachorro,
acabarán con los colmillos destrozados;

¹¹el león perece por falta de presa,
y los cachorros de la leona se dispersan.

¹²»En lo secreto me llegó un mensaje;
mis oídos captaron sólo su murmullo.

¹³Entre inquietantes visiones nocturnas,
cuando cae sobre los *hombres un sueño profundo,

¹⁴me hallé presa del miedo y del temblor;
mi esqueleto entero se sacudía.

¹⁵Sentí sobre mi rostro el roce de un espíritu,
y se me erizaron los cabellos.

¹⁶Una silueta se plantó frente a mis ojos,
pero no pude ver quién era.
Detuvo su marcha,
y escuché una voz que susurraba:

¹⁷»"¿Puede un simple *mortal ser más justo que Dios?
¿Puede ser más puro el hombre que su Creador?

¹⁸Pues si Dios no confía en sus propios siervos,
y aun a sus ángeles acusa de cometer errores,

¹⁹¡cuánto más a los que habitan en casas de barro,
cimentadas sobre el polvo y aplastadas como polilla!

²⁰Entre la aurora y el ocaso pueden ser destruidos
y perecer para siempre, sin que a nadie le importe.

²¹¿No se arrancan acaso las estacas de su carpa?
¡Mueren sin haber adquirido sabiduría!"

5 »Llama, si quieres, pero ¿habrá quien te responda?
¿A cuál de los dioses⁸ te dirigirás?

²El resentimiento mata a los necios;
la envidia mata a los insensatos.

³Yo mismo he visto al necio echar raíces,
pero de pronto su casa fue maldecida.ʰ

4Sus hijos distan mucho de estar a salvo;
   en el tribunal se les oprime, y nadie los
   defiende.
5Los hambrientos se comen su cosecha,
   y la recogen de entre las espinas;
   los sedientos se beben sus riquezas.
6Y aunque las penas no brotan del suelo,
   ni los sufrimientos provienen de la tierra,
7con todo, el *hombre nace para sufrir,
   tan cierto como que las chispas vuelan.

8»Si se tratara de mí, yo apelaría a Dios;
   ante él expondría mi caso.
9Él realiza maravillas insondables,
   portentos que no pueden contarse.
10Él derrama lluvia sobre la tierra
   y envía agua sobre los campos.
11Él enaltece a los humildes
   y da seguridad a los enlutados.
12Él deshace las maquinaciones de los astutos,
   para que no prospere la obra de sus manos.
13Él atrapa a los astutos en su astucia,
   y desbarata los planes de los malvados.
14De día éstos se topan con las tinieblas;
   a plena luz andan a tientas, como si fuera
   de noche.
15Pero a los menesterosos los salva
   de la opresión de los poderosos
   y de su lengua viperina.
16Así es como los pobres recobran la esperanza,
   y a la injusticia se le tapa la boca.

17»¡Cuán *dichoso es el hombre a quien Dios
   corrige!
   No menosprecies la *disciplina del
   *Todopoderoso.
18Porque él hiere, pero venda la herida;
   golpea, pero trae alivio.
19De seis aflicciones te rescatará,
   y la séptima no te causará ningún daño.
20Cuando haya hambre, te salvará de la
   muerte;
   cuando haya guerra, te librará de la espada.
21Estarás a salvo del latigazo de la lengua,
   y no temerás cuando venga la destrucción.
22Te burlarás de la destrucción y del hambre,
   y no temerás a las bestias salvajes,
23pues harás un pacto con las piedras del
   campo
   y las bestias salvajes estarán en *paz
   contigo.
24Reconocerás tu casa como lugar seguro;
   contarás tu ganado, y ni un solo animal
   faltará.
25Llegarás a tener muchos hijos,
   y descendientes como la hierba del campo.
26Llegarás al sepulcro anciano pero vigoroso,
   como las gavillas que se recogen a tiempo.

27»Esto lo hemos examinado, y es verdad.
   Así que escúchalo y compruébalo tú
   mismo.»

Segundo discurso de Job

6 A esto Job respondió:

2«¡Cómo quisiera que mi angustia se pesara
   y se pusiera en la balanza, junto con mi
   desgracia!

3¡De seguro pesarían más que la arena de los
   mares!
   ¡Por algo mis palabras son tan impetuosas!
4Las saetas del *Todopoderoso me han herido,
   y mi espíritu absorbe su veneno.
   ¡Dios ha enviado sus terrores contra mí!
5¿Rebuzna el asno salvaje si tiene hierba?
   ¿Muge el buey si tiene forraje?
6¿Puede comerse sin sal la comida desabrida?
   ¿Tiene algún sabor la clara de huevo?i
7Mi paladar se niega a probarla;
   ¡esa comida me enferma!

8»¡Ah, si Dios me concediera lo que pido!
   ¡Si Dios me otorgara lo que anhelo!
9¡Ah, si Dios se decidiera a destrozarme por
   completo,
   a descargar su mano sobre mí, y
   aniquilarme!
10Aun así me quedaría este consuelo,
   esta alegría en medio de mi implacable
   dolor:
   ¡el no haber negado las palabras del Dios
   *Santo!

11»¿Qué fuerzas me quedan para seguir
   esperando?
   ¿Qué fin me espera para querer vivir?
12¿Tengo acaso la fuerza de la roca?
   ¿Acaso tengo piel de bronce?
13¿Cómo puedo valerme por mí mismo,
   si me han quitado todos mis recursos?

14»Aunque uno se aparte del temor al
   Todopoderoso,
   el amigo no le niega su lealtad.j
15Pero mis hermanos son arroyos inconstantes,
   son corrientes desbordadas:
16se enturbian cuando el hielo se derrite,
   se ensanchan al derretirse la nieve,
17pero dejan de fluir durante las sequías,
   ¡en pleno calor desaparecen de sus lechos!
18Las caravanas se apartan de sus rutas;
   se encaminan al desierto, y allí mueren.
19Las caravanas de Temá van en busca de agua,
   los mercaderes de Sabá abrigan esperanzas.
20Se desaniman, a pesar de su confianza;
   llegan allí y se quedan frustrados.
21Lo mismo pasa con ustedes:
   ¡ven algo espantoso, y se asustan!
22¿Quién les ha pedido que me den algo,
   o que paguen con su dinero mi rescate?
23¿Quién les ha pedido que me libren de mi
   enemigo,
   o que me rescaten de las garras de los
   tiranos?

24»Instrúyanme, y me quedaré callado;
   muéstrenme en qué estoy equivocado.
25Las palabras justas no ofenden,
   ¡pero los argumentos de ustedes no
   prueban nada!
26¿Me van a juzgar por mis palabras,
   sin ver que provienenk de un desesperado?
27¡Ustedes echarían suertes hasta por un
   huérfano,
   y venderían a su amigo por cualquier cosa!

28»Tengan la bondad de mirarme a los ojos;
   ¿Creen que les mentiría en su propia cara?

29Reflexionen, no sean injustos;
　reflexionen, que en esto radica mi
　　integridad.
30¿Acaso hay maldad en mi lengua?
　¿No puede mi paladar discernir la maldad?

7 »¿No tenemos todos una obligación en este
　　mundo?
　¿No son nuestros días como los de un
　　asalariado?
2Como el esclavo que espera con ansias la
　　noche,
　como el asalariado que ansioso espera su
　　paga,
3meses enteros he vivido en vano;
　¡me han tocado noches de miseria!
4Me acuesto y pienso:
　"¿Cuánto falta para que amanezca?"
　La noche se me hace interminable;
　me doy vueltas en la cama hasta el
　　amanecer.
5Tengo el cuerpo cubierto de gusanos y de
　　costras;
　¡la piel se me raja y me supura!

6»Mis días se van más veloces que una
　　lanzadera,
　y sin esperanza alguna llegan a su fin.
7Recuerda, oh Dios, que mi vida es un suspiro;
　que ya no verán mis ojos la felicidad.
8Los ojos que hoy me ven, no me verán
　　mañana;
　pondrás en mí tus ojos, pero ya no existiré.
9Como nubes que se diluyen y se pierden,
　los que bajan al *sepulcro ya no vuelven a
　　subir.
10Nunca más regresan a su casa;
　desaparecen de su lugar.

11»Por lo que a mí toca, no guardaré silencio;
　la angustia de mi alma me lleva a hablar,
　la amargura en que vivo me obliga a
　　protestar.
12¿Soy acaso el mar, el monstruo del abismo,
　para que me pongas bajo vigilancia?
13Cuando pienso que en mi lecho hallaré
　　consuelo
　o encontraré alivio a mi queja,
14aun allí me infundes miedo en mis sueños;
　¡me aterras con visiones!
15¡Preferiría que me estrangularan
　a seguir viviendo en este cuerpo!
16Tengo en poco mi vida; no quiero vivir para
　　siempre.
　¡Déjame en paz, que mi vida no tiene
　　sentido!

17»¿Qué es el *hombre, que le das tanta
　　importancia,
　que tanta atención le concedes,
18que cada mañana lo examinas
　y a toda hora lo pones a prueba?
19Aparta de mí la mirada;
　¡déjame al menos tragar saliva!
20Si he pecado, ¿en qué te afecta,
　vigilante de los *mortales?
　¿Por qué te ensañas conmigo?
　¿Acaso te soy una carga?l
21¿Por qué no me perdonas mis pecados?

¿Por qué no pasas por alto mi maldad?
Un poco más, y yaceré en el polvo;
　me buscarás, pero habré dejado de existir.»

Primer discurso de Bildad

8 A esto respondió Bildad de Súah:

2«¿Hasta cuándo seguirás hablando así?
　¡Tus palabras son un viento huracanado!
3¿Acaso Dios pervierte la justicia?
　¿Acaso tuerce el derecho el
　　*Todopoderoso?
4Si tus hijos pecaron contra Dios,
　él les dio lo que su pecado merecía.
5Pero si tú vuelves la mirada a Dios,
　si le pides perdón al Todopoderoso,
6y si eres puro y recto,
　él saldrá en tu defensam
　y te devolverá el lugar que te corresponde.
7Modestas parecerán tus primeras riquezas,
　comparadas con tu prosperidad futura.

8»Pregunta a las generaciones pasadas,
　averigua lo que descubrieron sus padres.
9Nosotros nacimos ayer, y nada sabemos;
　nuestros días en este mundo son como una
　　sombra.
10Pero ellos te instruirán, te lo harán saber;
　compartirán contigo su experiencia.
11¿Puede crecer el papiro donde no hay
　　pantano?
　¿Pueden crecer los juncos donde no hay
　　agua?
12Aunque estén floreciendo y nadie los haya
　　cortado,
　se marchitan antes que otra hierba.
13Tal es el destino de los que se olvidan de Dios;
　así termina la esperanza de los impíos.
14Muy débilesn son sus esperanzas;
　han puesto su confianza en una telaraña.
15No podrán sostenerse cuando se apoyen en
　　ella;
　no quedarán en pie cuando se prendan de
　　sus hilos.
16Son como plantas frondosas expuestas al sol,
　que extienden sus ramas por todo el jardín:
17hunden sus raíces en torno a un montón de
　　piedras
　y buscan arraigarse entre ellas.
18Pero si las arrancan de su sitio,
　ese lugar negará haberlas conocido.
19¡Así termina su alegría de vivir,
　y del suelo brotan otras plantas!

20»Dios no rechaza a quien es íntegro,
　ni brinda su apoyo a quien hace el mal.
21Pondrá de nuevo risas en tu boca,
　y gritos de alegría en tus labios.
22Tus enemigos se cubrirán de vergüenza,
　y desaparecerán las moradas de los
　　malvados.»

Tercer discurso de Job

9 Job entonces replicó:

2«Aunque sé muy bien que esto es cierto,
　¿cómo puede un *mortal justificarse ante
　　Dios?
3Si uno quisiera disputar con él,

---

l 7:20 ¿Acaso te soy una carga? (LXX, mss. hebreos y una tradición rabínica); Me he vuelto una carga para mí mismo (TM).
m 8:6 saldrá en tu defensa. Alt. velará por ti. n 8:14 débiles. Palabra de difícil traducción.

de mil cosas no podría responderle una
　　sola.
4Profunda es su sabiduría, vasto su poder.
　　¿Quién puede desafiarlo y salir bien
　　librado?
5Él mueve montañas sin que éstas lo sepan,
　　y en su enojo las trastorna.
6Él remueve los cimientos de la tierra
　　y hace que se estremezcan sus columnas.
7Reprende al sol, y su brillo se apaga;
　　eclipsa la luz de las estrellas.
8Él se basta para extender los cielos;
　　somete a su dominio las olas del mar.
9Él creó la Osa y el Orión,
　　las Pléyades y las constelaciones del sur.
10Él realiza maravillas insondables,
　　portentos que no pueden contarse.
11Si pasara junto a mí, no podría verlo;
　　si se alejara, no alcanzaría a percibirlo.
12Si de algo se adueñara, ¿quién lo haría
　　desistir?
　　¿Quién puede cuestionar sus actos?
13Dios no depone el enojo;
　　aun *Rahab y sus secuaces se postran a sus
　　pies.

14»¿Cómo entonces podré yo responderle?
　　¿Dónde hallar palabras para contradecirle?
15Aunque sea yo inocente, no puedo
　　defenderme;
　　de mi juez sólo puedo pedir misericordia.
16Y aunque lo llamara y me respondiera,
　　no creo que me concedería audiencia.
17Me despedazaría con una tormenta,
　　y por la menor cosa multiplicaría mis
　　heridas.
18No me dejaría recobrar el aliento;
　　más bien, me saturaría de amargura.
19Si de fuerza se trata, ¡él es más poderoso!
　　Si es cuestión de juicio, ¿quién loñ hará
　　comparecer?
20Aun siendo inocente, me condenará mi boca;
　　aun siendo íntegro, resultaré culpable.

21»Soy intachable, pero ya no me importa;
　　tengo en poco mi propia vida.
22Todo es lo mismo; por eso digo:
　　"A buenos y a malos destruye por igual."
23Si alguna plaga acarrea la muerte repentina,
　　él se burla de la angustia del inocente.
24Si algún malvado se apodera de un terreno,
　　él les tapa los ojos a los jueces.
　　Si no lo hace él, ¿entonces quién?

25»Transcurren mis días con más rapidez que
　　un corredor;
　　vuelan sin que hayan conocido la dicha.
26Se deslizan como barcas de papiro,
　　como veloces águilas al caer sobre su presa.
27Si acaso digo: "Olvidaré mi queja,
　　cambiaré de expresión, esbozaré una
　　sonrisa",
28me queda el miedo de tanto sufrimiento,
　　pues bien sé que no me consideran
　　inocente.
29Y ya que me tienen por culpable,
　　¿para qué voy a luchar en vano?
30Aunque me restriegue con jabónᵒ
　　y me limpie las manos con lejía,
31tú me lanzarás al muladar,

¡y hasta mis ropas me aborrecerán!

32»Dios no es *hombre como yo,
　　para que juntos comparezcamos ante un
　　tribunal.
33¡No hay un juez entre nosotros
　　que decida el caso por los dos!
34¡No hay quien aleje de mí el báculo divino
　　para que ya no me asuste su terror!
35Quisiera yo hablar sin temor,
　　pero no estoy en tales condiciones.

10 »¡Ya estoy harto de esta vida!
　　Por eso doy rienda suelta a mi queja;
　　desahogo la amargura de mi alma.
2Le he dicho a Dios: No me condenes.
　　Dime qué es lo que tienes contra mí.
3¿Te parece bien el oprimirme
　　y despreciar la obra de tus manos
mientras te muestras complaciente
　　ante los planes del malvado?
4¿Son tus ojos los de un simple *mortal?
　　¿Ves las cosas como las vemos nosotros?
5¿Son tus días como los nuestros,
　　tus años como los de un mortal,
6para que andes investigando mis faltas
　　y averiguándolo todo acerca de mi pecado?
7¡Tú bien sabes que no soy culpable
　　y que de tus manos no tengo escapatoria!

8»Tú me hiciste con tus propias manos;
　　tú me diste forma.
¿Vas ahora a cambiar de parecer
　　y a ponerle fin a mi vida?
9Recuerda que tú me modelaste, como al barro;
　　¿Vas ahora a devolverme al polvo?
10¿No fuiste tú quien me derramó como leche,
　　quien me hizo cuajar como queso?
11Fuiste tú quien me vistió de carne y piel,
　　quien me tejió con huesos y tendones.
12Me diste vida, me favoreciste con tu amor,
　　y tus cuidados me han infundido aliento.

13»Pero una cosa mantuviste en secreto,
　　y sé muy bien que la tuviste en mente:
14Que si yo peco, tú me vigilas
　　y no pasas por alto mi pecado.
15Si soy culpable, ¡ay de mí!
　　Si soy inocente, no puedo dar la cara.
　¡Lleno estoy de vergüenza,
　　y consciente de mi aflicción!
16Si me levanto, me acechas como un león
　　y despliegas contra mí tu gran poder.
17Contra mí presentas nuevos testigos,
　　contra mí acrecientas tu enojo.
　　¡Una tras otra, tus tropas me atacan!
18»¿Por qué me hiciste salir del vientre?
　　¡Quisiera haber muerto, sin que nadie me
　　viera!
19¡Preferiría no haber existido,
　　y haber pasado del vientre a la tumba!
20¿Acaso mis contados días no llegan ya a su fin?
　　¡Déjame disfrutar de un momento de
　　alegría
21antes de mi partida sin regreso
　　a la tierra de la penumbra y de las sombras,
22al país de la más profunda de las noches,
　　al país de las sombras y del caos,
　　donde aun la luz se asemeja a las tinieblas!»

ñ 9:19 *lo* (LXX); *me* (TM). ᵒ 9:30 *jabón*. Alt. *nieve*.

Primer discurso de Zofar

11 A esto respondió Zofar de Namat:

2«¿Quedará sin respuesta toda esta perorata?
¿Resultará inocente este hablador?
3¿Toda esa palabrería nos dejará callados?
¿Te burlarás sin que nadie te reprenda?
4Tú afirmas: "Mi postura es la correcta;
soy puro a los ojos de Dios."
5¡Cómo me gustaría que Dios interviniera
y abriera sus labios contra ti
6para mostrarte los secretos de la sabiduría,
pues ésta es muy compleja!p
Sabrías entonces que buena parte de tu
pecado
Dios no lo ha tomado en cuenta.

7»¿Puedes adentrarte en los misterios de Dios
o alcanzar la perfecciónq del
*Todopoderoso?
8Son más altos que los cielos;
¿qué puedes hacer?
Son más profundos que el *sepulcro;
¿qué puedes saber?
9Son más extensos que toda la tierra;
¡son más anchos que todo el mar!

10»Si viene y te pone en un calabozo,
y luego te llama a cuentas,
¿quién lo hará desistir?
11Bien conoce Dios a la gente sin escrúpulos;
cuando percibe el mal, no lo pasa por alto.
12¡El necio llegará a ser sabio
cuando de un asno salvaje nazca un
*hombre!r

13»Pero si le entregas tu *corazón
y hacia él extiendes las manos,
14si te apartas del pecado que has cometido
y en tu morada no das cabida al mal,
15entonces podrás llevar la frente en alto
y mantenerte firme y libre de temor.
16Ciertamente olvidarás tus pesares,
o los recordarás como el agua que pasó.
17Tu vida será más radiante que el sol de
mediodía,
y la oscuridad será como el amanecer.
18Vivirás tranquilo, porque hay esperanza;
estarás protegidos y dormirás confiado.
19Descansarás sin temer a nadie,
y muchos querrán ganarse tu favor.
20Pero los ojos de los malvados se apagarán;
no tendrán escapatoria.
¡Su esperanza es exhalar el último suspiro!»

Cuarto discurso de Job

12 A esto respondió Job:

2«¡No hay duda de que ustedes son el pueblo!
¡Muertos ustedes, morirá la sabiduría!
3Pero yo tengo tanto cerebro como ustedes;
en nada siento que me aventajen.
¿Quién no sabe todas esas cosas?

4»Yo, que llamaba a Dios y él me respondía,
me he vuelto el hazmerreír de mis amigos;
¡soy un hazmerreír, recto e intachable!
5Dice la gente que vive tranquila:

"¡Al daño se añade la injuria!",
"¡Al que está por caer, hay que empujarlo!"
6Los salteadores viven tranquilos en sus carpas;
confiados viven esos que irritan a Dios
y piensan que pueden controlarlo.

7»Pero interroga a los animales,
y ellos te darán una lección;
pregunta a las aves del cielo,
y ellas te lo contarán;
8habla con la tierra, y ella te enseñará;
con los peces del mar, y te lo harán saber.
9¿Quién de todos ellos no sabe
que la mano del SEÑOR ha hecho todo esto?
10En sus manos está la vida de todo *ser vivo,
y el hálito que anima a todo ser humano.
11¿Acaso no comprueba el oído las palabras
como la lengua prueba la comida?
12Entre los ancianos se halla la sabiduría;
en los muchos años, el entendimiento.

13»Con Dios están la sabiduría y el poder;
suyos son el consejo y el entendimiento.
14Lo que él derriba, nadie lo levanta;
a quien él apresa, nadie puede liberarlo.
15Si él retiene las lluvias, hay sequía;
si las deja caer, se inunda la tierra.
16Suyos son el poder y el buen juicio;
suyos son los engañados y los que
engañan.
17Él pone en ridículo a los consejeros
y hace que los jueces pierdan la cabeza.
18Despoja de su autoridad a los reyes,
y les ata a la cintura un simple taparrabo.t
19Él pone en ridículo a los sacerdotes,
y derroca a los que detentan el poder.
20Acalla los labios de los consejeros
y deja sin discernimiento a los ancianos.
21Derrama ignominia sobre los nobles
y deja en vergüenza au los poderosos.
22Pone al descubierto los más oscuros abismos
y saca a la luz las sombras más profundas.
23Engrandece o destruye a las naciones;
las hace prosperar o las dispersa.
24Priva de sensatez a los poderosos,
y los hace vagar por desiertos sin senderos.
25Andan a tientas en medio de la oscuridad,
y se tambalean como borrachos.

13 »Todo esto lo han visto mis ojos,
lo han captado y entendido mis oídos.
2Yo tengo tanto *conocimiento como ustedes;
en nada siento que me aventajen.
3Más bien quisiera hablar con el
*Todopoderoso;
me gustaría discutir mi caso con Dios.
4Porque ustedes son unos incriminadores;v
¡como médicos no valen nada!
5¡Si tan sólo se callaran la boca!
Eso, en ustedes, ¡ya sería sabiduría!
6Ahora les toca escuchar mi defensa;
presten atención a mi alegato.
7¿Se atreverán a mentir en *nombre de Dios?
¿Argumentarán en su favor con engaños?
8¿Le harán el favor de defenderlo?
¿Van a resultar sus abogados defensores?
9¿Qué pasaría si él los examinara?

p **11:6** *ésta es muy compleja.* Frase de difícil traducción. q **11:7** *alcanzar la perfección.* Alt. *llegar hasta los límites.*
r **11:12** *cuando de un asno salvaje nazca un hombre.* Alt. *cuando los asnos salvajes nazcan domesticados.* s **11:18** *estarás protegi-do.* Alt. *mirarás en torno tuyo* (TM). t **12:18** *un simple taparrabo.* Alt. *un cinturón.* u **12:21** *deja en vergüenza a.* Lit. *afloja el cinturón de.* v **13:4** *incriminadores.* Lit. *untadores de mentira.*

¿Podrían engañarlo como se engaña a la
gente?
10Lo más seguro es que él los reprendería
si en secreto se mostraran parciales.
11¿Acaso no les infundiría miedo su esplendor?
¿Y no caería sobre ustedes su terror?
12¡Han memorizado proverbios sin sentido!
¡Se defienden con apologías endebles!

13»¡Cállense la boca y déjenme hablar,
y que venga lo que venga!
14¿Por qué me pongo en peligro
y me juego el pellejo?
15¡Que me mate! ¡Ya no tengo esperanza!w
Pero en su propia cara defenderé mi
conducta.
16En esto radica mi liberación:
en que ningún impío comparecería ante él.

17»Presten atención a mis palabras;
presten oído a lo que digo:
18Vean que ya he preparado mi caso,
y sé muy bien que seré declarado inocente.
19¿Hay quien pueda presentar cargos contra mí?
Si lo hay, me quedaré callado hasta que
muera.

20»Concédeme, oh Dios, sólo dos cosas,
y no tendré que esconderme de ti:
21Quítame la mano de encima
y deja de infundirme temor.
22Llámame a comparecer, y te responderé;
o déjame hablar, y contéstame tú.
23Enumera mis iniquidades y pecados;
hazme ver mis transgresiones y ofensas.
24¿Por qué no me das la cara?
¿Por qué me tienes por enemigo?
25¿Acosarás a una hoja arrebatada por el viento?
¿Perseguirás a la paja seca?
26Has dictado contra mí penas amargas;
me estás cobrandox los pecados de mi
juventud.
27Me has puesto cadenas en los pies;
vigilas todos mis pasos;
¡examinas las huellas que dejo al caminar!

28»El *hombre es como un odrey desgastado;
como ropa carcomida por la polilla.

14 »Pocos son los días, y muchos los
problemas,
que vive el *hombre nacido de mujer.
2Es como las flores, que brotan y se marchitan;
es como efímera sombra que se esfuma.
3¿Y en alguien así has puesto los ojos?
¿Con alguien como yo entrarás en juicio?
4¿Quién de la inmundicia puede sacar pureza?
¡No hay nadie que pueda hacerlo!
5Los días del hombre ya están determinados;
tú has decretado los meses de su vida;
le has puesto límites que no puede rebasar.
6Aparta de él la mirada; déjalo en paz,
hasta que haya gozado de su día de
asalariado.

7»Si a un árbol se le derriba,
queda al menos la esperanza de que retoñe
y de que no se marchiten sus renuevos.
8Tal vez sus raíces envejezcan en la tierra
y su tronco muera en su terreno,

9pero al sentir el agua, florecerá;
echará ramas como árbol recién plantado.
10El hombre, en cambio, muere y pierde su
fuerza;
exhala el último suspiro, y deja de existir.
11Y así como del mar desaparece el agua,
y los ríos se agotan y se secan,
12así los *mortales, cuando se acuestan,
no se vuelven a levantar.
Mientras exista el cielo,
no se levantarán los mortales
ni se despertarán de su sueño.

13»¡Si al menos me ocultaras en el *sepulcro
y me escondieras hasta que pase tu enojo!
¡Si al menos me pusieras un plazo,
y luego me recordaras!
14Si el hombre muere, ya no vuelve a la vida.
Cada día de mi servicio obligatorio
esperaré a que llegue mi relevo.
15Tú me llamarás, y yo te responderé;
desearás ver la obra de tus manos.
16Desearás también contar mis pasos,
pero no tomarás en cuenta mi pecado.
17En saco sellado guardarás mis transgresiones,
y perdonarás del todo mi pecado.

18»Pero así como un monte se erosiona y se
derrumba,
y las piedras cambian de lugar;
19así como las aguas desgastan las rocas
y los torrentes deslavan el suelo,
así tú pones fin a la esperanza del hombre.
20Lo apabullas del todo, y él desaparece;
lo desfiguras, y entonces lo despides.
21Si sus hijos reciben honores, él no lo sabe;
si se les humilla, él no se da cuenta.
22Sólo siente el dolor de su propio cuerpo,
y sólo de sí mismo se conduele.»

Segundo discurso de Elifaz

15 Replicó entonces Elifaz de Temán:
2«El sabio no responde con vana sabiduría
ni explota en violenta verborrea.z
3Tampoco discute con argumentos vanos
ni con palabras huecas.
4Tú, en cambio, restas valor al temor a Dios
y tomas a la ligera la devoción que él
merece.
5Tu maldad pone en acción tu boca;
hablas igual que los pícaros.
6Tu propia boca te condena, no la mía;
tus propios labios atestiguan contra ti.

7»¿Eres acaso el primer *hombre que ha
nacido?
¿Naciste acaso antes que los montes?
8¿Tienes parte en el consejo de Dios?
¿Acaso eres tú el único sabio?
9¿Qué sabes tú que nosotros no sepamos?
¿Qué has percibido que nosotros
ignoremos?
10Las canas y la edad están de nuestra parte,
tenemos más experiencia que tu padre.
11¿No te basta que Dios mismo te consuele
y que se te hable con cariño?
12¿Por qué te dejas llevar por el enojo?
¿Por qué te relampaguean los ojos?

---

w **13:15** *¡Que me mate ... esperanza!* Alt. *Aunque él me mate, seguiré esperando en él.*   x **13:26** *cobrando.* Lit. *heredando.*
y **13:28** *como un odre.* Alt. *como algo podrido.*   z **15:2** *explota en violenta verborrea.* Lit. *llena su vientre con el viento del este.*

¹³¿Por qué desatas tu enojo contra Dios
　y das rienda suelta a tu lengua?

¹⁴»¿Qué es el hombre para creerse puro,
　y el nacido de mujer para alegar inocencia?
¹⁵Si Dios no confía ni en sus *santos siervos,
　y ni siquiera considera puros a los cielos,
¹⁶¡cuánto menos confiará en el hombre,
　que es vil y corrupto y tiene sed del mal!ᵃ

¹⁷»Escúchame, y te lo explicaré;
　déjame decirte lo que he visto.
¹⁸Es lo que han declarado los sabios,
　sin ocultar nada de lo aprendido de sus
　　padres,
¹⁹Sólo a ellos se les dio la tierra,
　y ningún extraño pasó entre ellos.
²⁰El impío se ve atormentado toda su vida,
　el desalmado tiene sus años contados.
²¹Sus oídos perciben sonidos espantosos;
　cuando está en *paz, los salteadores lo
　　atacan.
²²No espera escapar de las tinieblas;
　condenado está a morir a filo de espada.
²³Vaga sin rumbo; es comida de los buitres;ᵇ
　sabe que el día de las tinieblas le ha llegado.
²⁴La desgracia y la angustia lo llenan de terror;
　lo abruman como si un rey fuera a atacarlo,
²⁵y todo por levantar el puño contra Dios
　y atreverse a desafiar al *Todopoderoso.
²⁶Contra Dios se lanzó desafiante,
　blandiendo grueso y resistente escudo.

²⁷»Aunque su rostro esté hinchado de grasa,
　y le sobre carne en la cintura,
²⁸habitará en lugares desolados,
　en casas deshabitadas,
　en casas a punto de derrumbarse.
²⁹Dejará de ser rico; no durarán sus riquezas
　ni se extenderán sus posesiones en la tierra.
³⁰No podrá escapar de las tinieblas;
　una llama de fuego marchitará sus
　　renuevos,
　y el aliento de Dios lo arrebatará.
³¹Que no se engañe ni confíe en cosas vanas,
　porque nada obtendrá a cambio de ellas.
³²Antes de su término recibirá su merecido,
　y sus ramas no reverdecerán.
³³Quedará como vid que pierde sus uvas verdes,
　como olivo que no llega a florecer.
³⁴La compañía de los impíos no es de provecho;
　¡las moradas de los que aman el soborno
　　serán consumidas por el fuego!
³⁵Conciben iniquidad, y dan a luz maldad;
　en su vientre se genera el engaño.»

Quinto discurso de Job

16 A esto, Job contestó:

²«Cosas como éstas he escuchado muchas;
　¡valiente consuelo el deᶜ todos ustedes!
³¿No habrá fin a sus peroratas?
　¿Qué tanto les irrita que siguen
　　respondiendo?
⁴¡También yo podría hablar del mismo modo
　si estuvieran ustedes en mi lugar!
　¡También yo pronunciaría bellos discursos en
　　su contra,

　meneando con sarcasmo la cabeza!
⁵¡Les infundiría nuevos bríos con la boca;
　les daría consuelo con los labios!

⁶»Si hablo, mi dolor no disminuye;
　si me callo, tampoco se me calma.
⁷Ciertamente Dios me ha destruido;
　ha exterminadoᵈ a toda mi familia.
⁸Me tiene acorralado, y da testimonio contra mí;
　mi deplorable estado se levanta y me
　　condena.

⁹»En su enojo Dios me desgarra y me persigue;
　rechina los dientes contra mí;
　mi adversario me clava la mirada.
¹⁰La gente se mofa de mí abiertamente;
　burlones, me dan de bofetadas,
　y todos juntos se ponen en mi contra.
¹¹Dios me ha entregado en manos de gente
　　inicua;
　me ha arrojado en las garras de los
　　malvados.
¹²Yo vivía tranquilo, pero él me destrozó;
　me agarró por el cuello y me hizo pedazos;
　¡me hizo blanco de sus ataques!
¹³Sus arqueros me rodearon.
　Sin piedad me perforaron los riñones,
　y mi hígado se derramó por el suelo.
¹⁴Abriéndome herida tras herida,
　se lanzaron contra mí como un guerrero.

¹⁵»El luto es parte de mi cuerpo;
　en el polvo tengo enterrada la frente.ᵉ
¹⁶De tanto llorar tengo enrojecida la cara,
　profundas ojeras tengo en torno a los ojos;
¹⁷pero mis manos están libres de violencia,
　y es pura mi oración.

¹⁸»¡Ah, tierra, no cubras mi sangre!
　¡No dejes que se acalle mi clamor!
¹⁹Ahora mismo tengo en los cielos un testigo;
　en lo alto se encuentra mi abogado.
²⁰Mi intercesor es mi amigo,ᶠ
　y ante él me deshago en lágrimas
²¹para que interceda ante Dios en favor mío,
　como quien apela por su amigo.
²²Pasarán sólo unos cuantos años
　antes de que yo emprenda el viaje sin
　　regreso.

17 »Mi ánimo se agota,
　mis días se acortan,
　la tumba me espera.
²Estoy rodeado de burlones;
　¡sufren mis ojos su hostilidad!

³»Dame, oh Dios, la fianza que demandas.
　¿Quién más podría responder por mí?
⁴Tú has ofuscado su pensamiento,
　por eso no dejarás que triunfen.
⁵Quien por una recompensa denuncia a sus
　　amigos,
　verá a sus hijos desfallecer.

⁶»Dios me ha puesto en boca de todos;
　no falta quien me escupa en la cara.
⁷Los ojos se me apagan a causa del dolor;
　todo mi esqueleto no es más que una
　　sombra.

ᵃ 15:16 que tiene sed del mal. Lit. que bebe como agua el mal.　ᵇ 15:23 rumbo ... buitres. Alt. rumbo, en busca de alimento.
ᶜ 16:2 valiente consuelo el de. Lit. consoladores de calamidad son.　ᵈ 16:7 ha exterminado; Lit. tú has exterminado.　ᵉ 16:15 enterrada la frente. Lit. enterrado mi cuerno.　ᶠ 16:20 Mi intercesor es mi amigo. Alt. Mis amigos me tratan con burlas.

8Los justos ven esto, y se quedan asombrados;
los inocentes se indignan contra el impío,
9la gente recta se aferra a su camino
y los de manos limpias aumentan su
fuerza.

10»Vengan, pues, todos ustedes; ¡arremetan
contra mí!
No hallaré entre ustedes a un solo sabio.
11Mis días van pasando, mis planes se frustran
junto con los anhelos de mi *corazón.
12Esta gente convierte la noche en día;
todo está oscuro, pero insisten:
"La luz se acerca."
13Si el único hogar que espero es el *sepulcro,
he de tenderme a dormir en las tinieblas;
14he de llamar "Padre mío" a la corrupción,
y "Madre" y "Hermana" a los gusanos.
15¿Dónde queda entonces mi esperanza?
¿Quién ve alguna esperanza para mí?
16¿Bajará conmigo hasta las puertas de la
*muerte?
¿Descenderemos juntos hasta el polvo?»

Segundo discurso de Bildad

18 Respondió entonces Bildad de Súah:

2«¿Cuándo pondrás fin a tanta palabrería?
Entra en razón, y entonces hablaremos.
3¿Por qué nos tratas como si fuéramos bestias?
¿Por qué nos consideras unos tontos?
4Es tal tu enojo que te desgarras el alma;
¡mas no por ti quedará desierta la tierra,
ni se moverán de su lugar las rocas!

5»La lámpara del malvado se apagará;
la llama de su fuego dejará de arder.
6Languidece la luz de su morada,
la lámpara que lo alumbra se apagará.
7El vigor de sus pasos se irá debilitando;
sus propios planes lo derribarán.
8Sus pies lo harán caer en una trampa,
y entre sus redes quedará atrapado.
9Quedará sujeto por los tobillos,
quedará atrapado por completo.
10Un lazo le espera escondido en el suelo;
una trampa está tendida a su paso.
11El terror lo asalta por doquier,
y anda tras sus pasos.
12La calamidad lo acosa sin descanso;
el desastre no lo deja un solo instante.
13La enfermedad le carcome el cuerpo;
la muerte le devora las manos y los pies.g
14Lejos de la seguridad de su morada,
marcha ahora hacia el rey de los terrores.
15El fuego se ha apoderado de su carpa;h
hay azufre ardiente esparcido en su
morada.
16En el tronco, sus raíces se han secado;
en la copa, sus ramas se marchitan.
17Borrada de la tierra ha sido su memoria;
de su fama nada queda en el país.
18De la luz es lanzado a las tinieblas;
ha sido expulsado de este mundo.
19No tiene entre su pueblo hijos ni parientes;

nadie le sobrevive donde él habitó.
20Del oriente al occidente
los pueblos se asombran de su suerte
y se estremecen de terror.
21Así es la morada del malvado,
el lugar del que no conoce a Dios.»

Sexto discurso de Job

19 A esto, Job respondió:

2«¿Hasta cuándo van a estar atormentándome
y aplastándome con sus palabras?
3Una y otra vezi me hacen reproches;
descaradamente me atacan.
4Aun si fuera verdad que me he desviado,
mis errores son asunto mío.
5Si quieren darse importancia a costa mía,
y valerse de mi humillación para atacarme,
6sepan que es Dios quien me ha hecho daño,
quien me ha atrapado en su red.

7»Aunque grito: "¡Violencia!", no hallo
respuesta;
aunque pido ayuda, no se me hace justicia.
8Dios me ha cerrado el camino, y no puedo
pasar;
ha cubierto de oscuridad mis senderos.
9Me ha despojado de toda honra;
de la cabeza me ha quitado la corona.
10Por todos lados me destroza, como a un árbol;
me aniquila, y arranca de raíz mi
esperanza.
11Su enojo se ha encendido contra mí;
me cuenta entre sus enemigos.
12Sus tropas avanzan en tropel;
levantan una rampa para asediarme;
¡acampan alrededor de mi carpa!

13»Hizo que mis hermanos me abandonaran;
hasta mis amigos se han alejado de mí.
14Mis parientes y conocidos se distanciaron,
me echaron al olvido.
15Mis huéspedes y mis criadas me ven como a
un extraño,
me miran como a un desconocido.
16Llamo a mi criado, y no me responde,
aunque yo mismo se lo ruego.
17A mi esposa le da asco mi aliento;
a mis hermanosj les resulto repugnante.
18Hasta los niños se burlan de mí;
en cuanto me ven, me dan la espalda.k
19A todos mis amigos les resulto abominable;
mis seres queridos se han vuelto contra mí.
20La piel y la carne se me pegan a los huesos;
¡a duras penas he salvado el pellejo!l

21»¡Compadézcanse de mí, amigos míos;
compadézcanse, que la mano de Dios me
ha golpeado!
22¿Por qué me acosan como Dios?
¿No les basta con desollarme vivo?m

23»¡Ah, si fueran grabadas mis palabras,
si quedaran escritas en un libro!
24Si para siempre quedaran sobre la roca,
grabadas con cincel en una placa de plomo!

25Yo sé que mi redentorn vive,
　y que al final *triunfará sobre la muerte.ñ
26Y cuando mi piel haya sido destruida,
　todavía veré a Dios con mis propios ojos.o
27Yo mismo espero verlo;
　espero ser yo quien lo vea, y no otro.
　¡Este anhelo me consume las entrañas!

28»Ustedes dicen: "Vamos a acosarlo,
　porque en él está la raíz del mal."
29Pero cuídense de la espada,
　pues con ella viene la ira justiciera,
　para que sepan que hay un juez.»

Segundo discurso de Zofar

20 A esto respondió Zofar de Namat:

2«Mis turbados pensamientos me hacen
　　replicar,
　pues me hallo muy desconcertado.
3He escuchado una reprensión que me
　　deshonra,
　y mi inteligencia me obliga a responder.

4»Bien sabes tú que desde antaño,
　　desde que Dios puso al hombrep en la
　　tierra,
5muy breve ha sido la algarabía del malvado;
　la alegría del impío ha sido pasajera.
6Aunque su orgullo llegue hasta los cielos
　y alcance a tocar con la cabeza las nubes,
7él perecerá para siempre, como su excremento,
　y sus allegados dirán: "¿Qué se hizo?"
8Como un sueño, como una visión nocturna,
　se desvanecerá y no volverá a ser hallado.
9Los ojos que lo vieron no volverán a verlo;
　su lugar no volverá a contemplarlo.
10Sus hijos tendrán que resarcir a los pobres;
　ellos mismos restituirán las riquezas de su
　　padre.
11El vigor juvenil que hoy sostiene sus huesos
　un día reposará en el polvo con él.

12»Aunque en su boca el mal sabe dulce
　y lo disimula bajo la lengua,
13y aunque no lo suelta para nada,
　sino que tenazmente lo retiene,
14ese pan se le agriará en el estómago;
　dentro de él se volverá veneno de áspid.
15Vomitará las riquezas que se engulló;
　Dios hará que las arroje de su vientre.
16Chupará veneno de serpientes;
　la lengua de un áspid lo matará.
17No disfrutará de los arroyos,
　de los ríos de crema y miel;
18no se engullirá las ganancias de sus negocios;
　no disfrutará de sus riquezas,
19porque oprimió al pobre y lo dejó sin nada,
　y se adueñó de casas que nunca construyó.

20»Su ambición nunca quedó satisfecha;
　¡nada quedó a salvo de su codicia!
21Nada se libró de su voracidad;
　por eso no perdurará su bienestar.
22En medio de la abundancia, lo abrumará la
　　angustia;
　le sobrevendrá toda la fuerza de la
　　desgracia.

23Cuando el malvado se haya llenado el
　　vientre,
　Dios dará rienda suelta a su enojo contra él,
　y descargará sobre él sus golpes.
24Aunque huya de las armas de hierro,
　una flecha de bronce lo atravesará.
25Cuando del hígado y de la espalda
　intente sacarse la punta de la flecha,
　se verá sobrecogido de espanto,
26y la oscuridad total acechará sus tesoros.
Un fuego no atizado acabará con él
　y con todo lo que haya quedado de su casa.
27Los cielos harán pública su culpa;
　la tierra se levantará a denunciarlo.
28En el día de la ira de Dios,
　un aluvión arrasará con su casa.
29Tal es el fin que Dios reserva al malvado;
　tal es la herencia que le asignó.»

Séptimo discurso de Job

21 A esto, Job respondió:

2«Escuchen atentamente mis palabras;
　concédanme este consuelo.
3Tolérenme un poco mientras hablo,
　y búrlense si quieren cuando haya
　　terminado.

4»¿Acaso dirijo mi reclamo a los *mortales?
　¿Por qué creen que pierdo la paciencia?
5Mírenme, y queden asombrados;
　tápense la boca con la mano.
6Si pienso en esto, me lleno de espanto;
　un escalofrío me corre por el cuerpo.
7¿Por qué siguen con vida los malvados,
　cada vez más viejos y más ricos?
8Ven establecerse en torno suyo
　a sus hijos y a sus descendientes.
9Tienen *paz en su hogar, y están libres de
　　temores;
　la vara de Dios no los castiga.
10Sus toros son verdaderos sementales;
　sus vacas paren y no pierden las crías.
11Dejan correr a sus niños como si fueran
　　ovejas;
　sus pequeñuelos danzan alegres.
12Cantan al son del tamboril y del arpa;
　se divierten al son de la flauta.
13Pasan la vida con gran bienestar,
　y en pazq bajan al *sepulcro.
14A Dios increpan: "¡Déjanos tranquilos!
　No queremos conocer tu voluntad.
15¿Quién es el *Todopoderoso, para que le
　　sirvamos?
　¿Qué ganamos con dirigirle nuestras
　　oraciones?"
16Pero si bienestar no depende de ellos.
　¡Jamás me dejaré llevar por sus malos
　　consejos!

17»¿Cuándo se ha apagado la lámpara de los
　　malvados?
　¿Cuándo les ha sobrevenido el desastre?
　¿Cuándo Dios, en su enojo, los ha hecho sufrir
　18como paja que arrebata el viento,
　como tamo que se lleva la tormenta?
19Me dirán que Dios reserva el castigo
　para los hijos del pecador.

---

n **19:25** *redentor.* Alt. *defensor.*　ñ **19:25** *triunfará sobre la muerte.* Lit. *se levantará sobre el polvo.*　o **19:26** *con mis propios ojos.*
Lit. *desde mi carne.*　p **20:4** *al hombre.* Alt. *a Adán.*　q **21:13** *en paz.* Lit. *en un instante.*

¡Mejor que castigue al que peca,
para que escarmiente!
20¡Que sufra el pecador su propia destrucción!
¡Que beba de la ira del Todopoderoso!
21¿Qué le puede importar la familia que deja,
si le quedan pocos meses de vida?

22»¿Quién puede impartirle a Dios
*conocimientos,
si es él quien juzga a las grandes
eminencias?
23Hay quienes mueren en la flor de la vida,
rebosantes de salud y de paz;
24sus caderas,r llenas de grasa,
sus huesos, recios hasta la médula.
25Otros mueren con el ánimo amargado,
sin haber disfrutado de lo bueno.
26¡En el polvo yacen unos y otros,
todos ellos cubiertos de gusanos!

27»Sé muy bien lo que están pensando,
y los planes que tienen de hacerme daño.
28También sé que se preguntan:
"¿Dónde está la mansión del potentado?
¿Dónde están las moradas de los inicuos?"
29¿No han interrogado a los viajeros?
¿No han prestado atención a sus
argumentos?
30En el día del desastre, el malvado se salva;
¡en el día de la ira, es puesto a salvo!
31¿Y quién le echa en cara su conducta?
¿Quién le da su merecido por sus hechos?
32Cuando lo llevan al sepulcro,
sobre su tumba se pone vigilancia;
33mucha gente le abre paso,
y muchos más cierran el cortejo.
¡Descansa en paz bajo la tierra del valle!s

34»¿Cómo esperan consolarme con discursos
sin sentido?
¡Sus respuestas no son más que falacias!»

Tercer discurso de Elifaz

22 A esto respondió Elifaz de Temán:

2«¿Puede alguien, por muy sabio que sea,
serle a Dios de algún provecho?
3¿Sacará alguna ventaja el *Todopoderoso
con que seas un hombre justo?
¿Tendrá algún beneficio
si tu conducta es intachable?
4¿Acaso te reprende por temerlo,
y por eso te lleva a juicio?
5¿No es acaso demasiada tu maldad?
¿Y no son incontables tus pecados?
6Sin motivo demandabas fianza de tus
hermanos,
y en prenda los despojabas de sus mantos;
¡desnudos los dejabas!
7Al sediento no le dabas agua,
al hambriento le negabas la comida.
8Hombre de poder, te adueñaste de la tierra;
hombre prominente, en ella te asentaste.
9No les dabas nada a las viudas,
y para colmo les quitabas todot a los
huérfanos.
10Por eso ahora te ves rodeado de trampas,

y te asaltan temores repentinos;
11la oscuridad te impide ver,
y te ahogan las aguas torrenciales.

12»¿No está Dios en las alturas de los cielos?
¡Mira las estrellas, cuán altas y remotas!
13Sin embargo, cuestionas: "¿Y Dios qué sabe?
¿Puede acaso juzgar a través de las
tinieblas?
14Él recorre los cielos de uno a otro extremo,
y densas nubes lo envuelven,
¡así que no puede vernos!"

15»¿Vas a seguir por los trillados caminos
que han recorrido los malvados?
16Perdieron la vida antes de tiempo;
un diluvio arrasó sus cimientos.
17Increparon a Dios: "¡Déjanos tranquilos!
¿Qué puedes tú hacernos,u
Todopoderoso?"
18¡Y fue Dios quien llenó sus casas de bienes!
¡Yo no me dejaré llevar por sus malos
consejos!

19»Los justos se alegran al ver la ruina de los
malvados;
los inocentes dicen en son de burla:
20"Nuestros enemigos han sido destruidos,
¡el fuego ha consumido sus riquezas!"

21»Sométete a Dios; ponte en *paz con él,
y volverá a ti la prosperidad.
22Acepta la enseñanza que mana de su boca,
¡grábate sus palabras en el *corazón!
23Si te vuelves al Todopoderoso
y alejas de tu casa la maldad,
serás del todo restaurado;
24si tu oro refinadov lo arrojas por el suelo,
entre rocas y cañadas,
25tendrás por oro al Todopoderoso,
y será él para ti como plata refinada.
26En el Todopoderoso te deleitarás;
ante Dios levantarás tu rostro.
27Cuando ores, él te escuchará,
y tú le cumplirás tus votos.
28Tendrás éxito en todo lo que emprendas,
y en tus caminos brillará la luz.
29Porque Dios humilla a los altaneros,
y exalta a los humildes.
30Él salva al que es inocente,
y por tu honradez quedarás a salvo.»w

Octavo discurso de Job

23 A esto respondió Job:

2«Mi queja sigue siendo amarga;
gimo bajo el peso de su mano.x
3¡Ah, si supiera yo dónde encontrar a Dios!
¡Si pudiera llegar adonde él habita!
4Ante él expondría mi caso;
llenaría mi boca de argumentos.
5Podría conocer su respuesta,
y trataría de entenderla.
6¿Disputaría él conmigo, con todo su poder?
¡Claro que no! ¡Ni me acusaría!
7Ante él cualquier *hombre recto
podría presentar su caso,
y yo sería absuelto para siempre

---

r 21:24 *caderas.* Palabra de difícil traducción. s 21:33 *¡Descansa ... valle!* Lit. *Dulce le es el suelo del valle.* t 22:9 *les quitabas todo.* Alt. *les anulaste la fuerza.* Lit. *sus brazos fueron rotos.* u 22:17 *hacernos* (LXX y Siríaca); *hacerle* (TM). v 22:24 *oro refinado.* Lit. *oro de Ofir.* w 22:30 *Él salva ... salvo.* Alt. *Él salva al que es culpable, / y lo salva por la limpieza de tus manos.* x 23:2 *su mano* (LXX y Siríaca); *mi mano* (TM).

delante de mi juez.

8»Si me dirijo hacia el este, no está allí;
  si me encamino al oeste, no lo encuentro.
9Si está ocupado en el norte, no lo veo;
  si se vuelve al sur, no alcanzo a percibirlo.
10Él, en cambio, conoce mis caminos;
  si me pusiera a prueba, saldría yo puro
    como el oro.
11En sus sendas he afirmado mis pies;
  he seguido su camino sin desviarme.
12No me he apartado de los mandamientos de
    sus labios;
  en lo más profundo de mi ser*y*
  he atesorado las palabras de su boca.

13»Pero él es soberano;*z*
  ¿quién puede hacerlo desistir?
  Lo que él quiere hacer, lo hace.
14Hará conmigo lo que ha determinado;
  todo lo que tiene pensado lo realizará.
15Por eso me espanto en su presencia;
  si pienso en todo esto, me lleno de temor.
16Dios ha hecho que mi *corazón desmaye;
  me tiene aterrado el *Todopoderoso.
17Con todo, no logran acallarme las tinieblas
  ni la densa oscuridad que cubre mi rostro.

24 »Si los tiempos no se esconden del
      *Todopoderoso,
  ¿por qué no los perciben quienes dicen
    conocerlo?
2Hay quienes no respetan los linderos,
  y pastorean ganado robado;
3a los huérfanos los despojan de sus asnos;
  a las viudas les quitan en prenda sus
    bueyes;
4apartan del camino a los necesitados;
  a los pobres del país los obligan a
    esconderse.
5Como asnos salvajes del desierto,
  se afanan los pobres por encontrar su
    presa,
  y el páramo da de comer a sus hijos.
6En campos ajenos recogen forraje,
  y en las viñas de los malvados recogen uvas.
7Por no tener ropa, se pasan la noche
    desnudos;
  ¡no tienen con qué protegerse del frío!
8Las lluvias de las montañas los empapan;
  no teniendo más abrigo, se arriman a las
    peñas.
9Al huérfano se le aparta de los pechos de su
    madre;
  al pobre se le retiene a cambio de una
    deuda.
10Por no tener ropa, andan desnudos;
  aunque cargados de trigo, van muriéndose
    de hambre.
11Exprimen aceitunas en las terrazas;*a*
  pisan uvas en las cubas, pero desfallecen de
    sed.
12De la ciudad se eleva el clamor de los
    moribundos;
  la garganta de los heridos reclama ayuda,
  ¡pero Dios ni se da por enterado!

13»Hay quienes se oponen a la luz;
  no viven conforme a ella
  ni reconocen sus caminos.
14Apenas amanece, se levanta el asesino
  y mata al pobre y al necesitado;
  apenas cae la noche, actúa como ladrón.
15Los ojos del adúltero están pendientes de la
    noche;
  se dice a sí mismo: "No habrá quien me vea",
  y mantiene oculto el rostro.
16Por la noche, entra el ladrón a casa ajena,
  pero se encierra durante el día;
  ¡de la luz no quiere saber nada!
17Para todos ellos, la mañana es oscuridad;
  prefieren el horror de las tinieblas.»

Interrupción de Zofar*b*

18«Los malvados son como espuma sobre el
    agua;
  su parcela está bajo maldición;
  ya no van a trabajar a los viñedos.
19Y así como el calor y la sequía
  arrebatan con violencia la nieve derretida,
  así el *sepulcro arrebata a los pecadores.
20Su propia madre se olvida de ellos;
  los gusanos se los comen;
  nadie vuelve a recordarlos,
  ¡son desgajados como árboles!
21Maltratan a la estéril, a la mujer sin hijos;
  jamás buscan el bien de la viuda.
22Pero Dios, con su poder, arrastra a los
    poderosos;
  cuando él se levanta, nadie tiene segura la
    vida.
23Dios los deja sentirse seguros,
  pero no les quita la vista de encima.
24Por algún tiempo son exaltados,
  pero luego dejan de existir;
  son humillados y recogidos como hierba,*c*
  ¡son cortados como espigas!
25¿Quién puede probar que es falso lo que digo,
  y reducir mis palabras a la nada?»

Tercer discurso de Bildad

25 A esto respondió Bildad de Súah:

2«Dios es poderoso e infunde temor;
  él pone orden*d* en las alturas de los cielos.
3¿Pueden contarse acaso sus ejércitos?
  ¿Sobre quién no alumbra su luz?
4¿Cómo puede el *hombre
    declararse inocente ante Dios?
  ¿Cómo puede alegar pureza
    quien ha nacido de mujer?
5Si a sus ojos no tiene brillo la luna,
  ni son puras las estrellas,
6mucho menos el hombre, simple gusano;
  ¡mucho menos el hombre, miserable
    lombriz!»

Interrupción de Job

26 Pero Job intervino:

2«¡Tú sí que ayudas al débil!
  ¡Tú sí que salvas al que no tiene fuerza!
3¡Qué consejos sabes dar al ignorante!

---

y **23:12** *en lo más profundo de mi ser* (LXX y Vulgata); *más que mi porción* (TM).   *z* **23:13** *pero él es soberano.* Lit. *y él, en uno.*
a **24:11** *en las terrazas.* Alt. *entre las piedras de molino.*   *b* **24:18-25** Zofar no se menciona en el texto. Se considera que esta
porción, junto con 27:13-23, forma parte del tercer discurso de este personaje.   *c* **24:24** *como hierba* (LXX); *como todo*
(TM).   *d* **25:2** *pone orden.* Lit. *hace *paz.*

¡Qué gran discernimiento has demostrado!
⁴¿Quién te ayudó a pronunciar tal discurso?
¿Qué espíritu ha hablado por tu boca?»

Bildad reanuda su discurso

⁵«Un estremecimiento invade a los muertos,
a los que habitan debajo de las aguas.
⁶Ante Dios, queda el *sepulcro al descubierto;
nada hay que oculte a este *destructor.
⁷Dios extiende el cieloᵉ sobre el vacío;
sobre la nada tiene suspendida la tierra.
⁸En sus nubes envuelve las aguas,
pero no revientan las nubes con su peso.
⁹Cubre la faz de la luna llena
al extender sobre ella sus nubes.
¹⁰Dibuja el horizonte sobre la faz de las aguas
para dividir la luz de las tinieblas.
¹¹Aterrados por su represión,
tiemblan los pilares de los cielos.
¹²⁻¹³Con un soplo suyo se despejan los cielos;
con su poder Dios agita el mar.
Con su sabiduría descuartizó a *Rahab;
con su mano ensartó a la serpiente
escurridiza.
¹⁴¡Y esto es sólo una muestra de sus obras,ᶠ
un murmullo que logramos escuchar!
¿Quién podrá comprender su trueno
poderoso?»

Noveno discurso de Job

27 Job, retomando la palabra, dijo:

²«Juro por Dios,ᵍ el *Todopoderoso,
quien se niega a hacerme *justicia,
quien me ha amargado el ánimo,
³que mientras haya vida en mí
y aliento divino en mi nariz,
⁴mis labios no pronunciarán maldad alguna,
ni mi lengua proferirá mentiras.
⁵Jamás podré admitir que ustedes tengan la
razón;
mientras viva, insistiré en mi integridad.
⁶Insistiré en mi inocencia; no cederé.
Mientras viva, no me remorderá la
conciencia.

⁷»¡Que terminen mis enemigos como los
malvados
y mis adversarios como los injustos!
⁸¿Qué esperanza tienen los impíos
cuando son eliminados,
cuando Dios les quita la vida?
⁹¿Escucha Dios su clamor
cuando les sobreviene la angustia?
¹⁰¿Acaso se deleitan en el Todopoderoso,
o claman a Dios en todo tiempo?

¹¹»¡Yo les voy a mostrar algo del poder de Dios!
¡No les voy a ocultar los planes del
Todopoderoso!
¹²Si ustedes mismos han visto todo esto,
¿a qué viene tanta palabrería?»

Tercer discurso de Zofar

¹³«Ésta es la herencia que Dios
tiene reservada para los malvados;
ésta es la herencia que los desalmados
recibirán del *Todopoderoso:
¹⁴No importa cuántos hijos tengan,
la espada los aguarda;

jamás sus pequeños comerán hasta saciarse.
¹⁵La muerte sepultará a quienes les sobrevivan;
sus viudas no llorarán por ellos.
¹⁶Y aunque amontonen plata como polvo,
y apilen vestidos como arcilla,
¹⁷será el justo quien se ponga esos vestidos,
y el inocente quien reparta esa plata.
¹⁸Las casas que construyen parecen larvas de
polilla,
parecen cobertizo de vigilancia.
¹⁹Se acuestan siendo ricos, pero por última vez:
cuando despiertan, sus riquezas se han
esfumado.
²⁰Les sobreviene un diluvio de terrores;
la tempestad los arrebata por la noche.
²¹El viento del este se los lleva, y desaparecen;
los arranca del lugar donde viven.
²²Se lanza contra ellos sin clemencia,
mientras ellos tratan de huir de su poder.
²³Agita las manos y aplaude burlón;
entre silbidos, los arranca de su lugar.»

Elogio de la sabiduría

28 Hay minas de donde se saca la plata,
y crisoles donde se refina el oro.
²El hierro se extrae de la tierra;
el cobre se separa de la escoria.
³El minero ha puesto fin a las tinieblas:
hurga en los rincones más apartados,
busca piedras en la más densa oscuridad.
⁴Lejos de la gente
cava túneles en lugares nunca hollados;
lejos de la gente
se balancea en el aire.
⁵Extrae su sustento de la tierra,
cuyas entrañas se transforman como por
fuego.
⁶De sus rocas se obtienen zafiros,
y en el polvo se encuentra oro.
⁷No hay ave rapaz que conozca ese escondrijo
ni ojo de halcón que lo haya descubierto.
⁸Ninguna bestia salvaje ha puesto allí su pie;
tampoco merodean allí los leones.
⁹La mano del minero ataca el pedernal
y pone al descubierto la raíz de las
montañas.
¹⁰Abre túneles en la roca,
y sus ojos contemplan todos sus tesoros.
¹¹Anda en busca deʰ las fuentes de los ríos,
y trae a la luz cosas ocultas.

¹²Pero, ¿dónde se halla la sabiduría?
¿Dónde habita la inteligencia?
¹³Nadie sabe lo que ella vale,
pues no se encuentra en este mundo.
¹⁴«Aquí no está», dice el océano;
«Aquí tampoco», responde el mar.
¹⁵No se compra con el oro más fino,
ni su precio se calcula en plata.
¹⁶No se compra con oro refinado,ⁱ
ni con ónice ni zafiros.
¹⁷Ni el oro ni el cristal se comparan con ella,
ni se cambia por áureas joyas.
¹⁸¡Para qué mencionar el coral y el jaspe!
¡La sabiduría vale más que los rubíes!
¹⁹El topacio de Cus no se le iguala,
ni es posible comprarla con oro puro.

20¿De dónde, pues, viene la sabiduría?
    ¿Dónde habita la inteligencia?
21Se esconde de los ojos de toda criatura;
    ¡hasta de las aves del cielo se oculta!
22La *destrucción y la muerte afirman:
    «Algo acerca de su fama llegó a nuestros
      oídos.»
23Sólo Dios sabe llegar hasta ella;
    sólo él sabe dónde habita.
24Él puede ver los confines de la tierra;
    él ve todo lo que hay bajo los cielos.
25Cuando él establecía la fuerza del viento
    y determinaba el volumen de las aguas,
26cuando dictaba el decreto para las lluvias
    y la ruta de las tormentas,
27miró entonces a la sabiduría y ponderó su
      valor;
    la puso a prueba y la confirmó.
28Y dijo a los *mortales:
    «Temer al Señor: ¡eso es sabiduría!
    Apartarse del mal: ¡eso es discernimiento!»

Soliloquio de Job

29 Job, retomando la palabra, dijo:

2«¡Cómo añoro los meses que se han ido,
    los días en que Dios me cuidaba!
3Su lámpara alumbraba sobre mi cabeza,
    y por su luz podía andar entre tinieblas.
4¡Qué días aquellos, cuando yo estaba en mi
      apogeo
    y Dios bendecía mi casa con su íntima
      amistad!

5»Cuando aún estaba conmigo el
    *Todopoderoso,
    y mis hijos me rodeaban;
6cuando ante mí corrían ríos de crema,
    y de las rocas fluían arroyos de aceite;
7cuando ocupaba mi puesto en el consejo de la
      ciudad,j
    y en la plaza pública tomaba asiento,
8los jóvenes al verme se hacían a un lado,
    y los ancianos se ponían de pie;
9los jefes se abstenían de hablar
    y se tapaban la boca con las manos;
10los nobles bajaban la voz,
    y la lengua se les pegaba al paladar.
11Los que me oían, hablaban bien de mí;
    los que me veían, me alababan.
12Si el pobre recurría a mí, yo lo ponía a salvo,
    y también al huérfano, si no tenía quien lo
      ayudara.
13Me bendecían los desahuciados;
    ¡por mí gritaba de alegría
    el *corazón de las viudas!
14De justicia y rectitud me revestía;
    ellas eran mi manto y mi turbante.
15Para los ciegos fui sus ojos;
    para los tullidos, sus pies.
16Fui padre de los necesitados
    y defensor de los extranjeros.
17A los malvados les rompí la cara,
    ¡de sus fauces les arrebaté la presa!

18»Llegué a pensar: "Moriré en mi propia casa;

    mis días serán incontables como la arena
      del mar.
19Mis raíces llegarán hasta las aguas;
    el rocío de la noche se quedará en mis
      ramas.
20Mi gloria mantendrá en mí su lozanía,
    y el arco en mi mano se mantendrá firme."

21»La gente me escuchaba expectante,
    y en silencio aguardaba mi consejo.
22Hablaba yo, y nadie replicaba;
    mis palabras hallaban cabidak en sus oídos.
23Expectantes, absorbían mis palabras
    como quien espera las lluvias tardías.
24Si yo les sonreía, no podían creerlo;
    mi rostro sonriente los reanimaba.l
25Yo les indicaba el camino a seguir;
    me sentaba a la cabecera;
    habitaba entre ellos como un rey entre su
      tropa,
    como quien consuela a los que están de luto.

30 »¡Y ahora resulta que de mí se burlan
    jovencitos a cuyos padres no habría puesto
    ni con mis perros ovejeros!
2¿De qué me habría servido la fuerza de sus
      manos,
    si no tenían ya fuerza para nada?
3Retorciéndose de hambre y de necesidad,
    rondabanm en la noche por tierras
      desoladas,
    por páramos deshabitados.
4En las breñas recogían hierbas amargas
    y comíann raíces de *retama.
5Habían sido excluidos de la comunidad,
    acusados a gritos como ladrones.
6Se vieron obligados a vivir
    en el lecho de los arroyos secos,
    entre las grietas y en las cuevas.
7Bramaban entre los matorrales,
    se amontonaban entre la maleza.
8Gente vil, generación infame,
    fueron expulsados de la tierra.

9»¡Y ahora resulta que soy tema de sus
      parodias!
    ¡Me he vuelto su hazmerreír!
10Les doy asco, y se alejan de mí;
    no vacilan en escupirme en la cara.
11Ahora que Dios me ha humillado por
      completo,
    no se refrenan en mi presencia.
12A mi derecha, me ataca el populacho;ñ
    tienden trampas a mis pies
    y levantan rampas de asalto para atacarme.
13Han irrumpido en mi camino;
    sin ayuda de nadie han logrado
      destruirme.o
14Avanzan como a través de una brecha;
    irrumpen entre las ruinas.
15El terror me ha sobrecogido;
    mi dignidad se esfuma como el viento,
    ¡mi *salvación se desvanece como las
      nubes!

16»Y ahora la vida se me escapa;
    me oprimen los días de sufrimiento.

---

j **29:7** *cuando ocupaba ... ciudad.* Lit. *cuando salía yo a las *puertas de la ciudad.*   k **29:22** *hallaban cabida.* Lit. *caían como gotas.*
l **29:24** *mi rostro ... reanimaba.* Lit. *la luz de mi rostro no los hacía caer.*   m **30:3** *rondaban.* Alt. *roían.*   n **30:4** *comían.* Alt. *se ca-
lentaban con.*   ñ **30:12** *populacho.* Palabra de difícil traducción.   o **30:13** *sin ayuda ... destruirme.* Alt. *han logrado destruirme,
y dicen: "Nadie puede ayudarlo."*

17La noche me taladra los huesos;
el dolor que me corroe no tiene fin.
18Como con un manto, Dios me envuelve con
su poder;
me ahoga como el cuello de mi ropa.
19Me arroja con fuerza en el fango,
y me reduce a polvo y ceniza.

20»A ti clamo, oh Dios, pero no me respondes;
me hago presente, pero tú apenas me
miras.
21Implacable, te vuelves contra mí;
con el poder de tu brazo me atacas.
22Me arrebatas, me lanzas alp viento;
me arrojas al ojo de la tormenta.
23Sé muy bien que me harás bajar al sepulcro,
a la morada final de todos los vivientes.

24»Pero nadie golpea al que está derrotado,
al que en su angustia reclama auxilio.
25¿Acaso no he llorado por los que sufren?
¿No me he condolido por los pobres?
26Cuando esperaba lo bueno, vino lo malo;
cuando buscaba la luz, vinieron las
sombras.
27No cesa la agitación que me invade;
me enfrento a días de sufrimiento.
28Ando apesadumbrado, pero no a causa del
sol;
me presento en la asamblea, y pido ayuda.
29He llegado a ser hermano de los chacales,
compañero de las lechuzas.
30La piel se me ha requemado, y se me cae;
el cuerpo me arde por la fiebre.
31El tono de mi arpa es de lamento,
el son de mi flauta es de tristeza.

31 »Yo había convenido con mis ojos
no mirar con lujuria a ninguna mujer.q
2¿Qué se recibe del Dios altísimo?
¿Qué se hereda del *Todopoderoso en las
alturas?
3¿No es acaso la ruina para los malvados
y el desastre para los malhechores?
4¿Acaso no se fija Dios en mis caminos
y toma en cuenta todos mis pasos?

5»Si he andado en malos pasos,
o mis pies han corrido tras la mentira,
6¡que Dios me pese en una balanza justa,
y así sabrá que soy inocente!
7Si mis pies se han apartado del camino,
o mi *corazón se ha dejado llevar por mis
ojos,
o mis manos se han llenado de ignominia,
8¡que se coman otros lo que yo he sembrado,
y que sean destruidas mis cosechas!

9»Si por alguna mujer me he dejado seducir,
si a las puertas de mi prójimo he estado al
acecho,
10¡que mi esposa muela el grano de otro
hombre,
y que otros hombres se acuesten con ella!
11Eso habría sido una infamia,
¡un pecado que tendría que ser juzgado!
12¡Habría sido un incendio *destructor!
¡Habría arrancado mi cosecha de raíz!

13»Si me negué a hacerles justicia

a mis siervos y a mis siervas
cuando tuvieron queja contra mí,
14¿qué haré cuando Dios me llame a cuentas?
¿qué responderé cuando me haga
comparecer?
15El mismo Dios que me formó en el vientre
fue el que los formó también a ellos;
nos dio forma en el seno materno.

16»Jamás he desoído los ruegos de los pobres,
ni he dejado que las viudas desfallezcan;
17jamás el pan me lo he comido solo,
sin querer compartirlo con los huérfanos.
18Desde mi juventud he sido un padre para
ellos;
a las viudas las he guiado desde mi
nacimiento.
19Si he dejado que alguien muera por falta de
vestido,
o que un necesitado no tenga qué ponerse;
20si éste no me ha bendecido de corazón
por haberlo abrigado con lana de mis
rebaños;
21o si he levantado contra el huérfano mi mano
por contar con influencias en los
tribunales,r
22¡que los brazos se me caigan de los hombros!
¡que se me zafen de sus articulaciones!
23Siempre he sido temeroso del castigo de Dios;
¡ante su majestad no podría resistir!

24»¿Acaso he puesto en el oro mi confianza,
o le he dicho al oro puro: "En ti confío"?
25¿Me he ufanado de mi gran fortuna,
de las riquezas amasadas con mis manos?
26¿He admirado acaso el esplendor del sol
o el avance esplendoroso de la luna,
27como para rendirles culto en lo secreto
y enviarles un beso con la mano?
28¡También este pecado tendría que ser
juzgado,
pues habría yo traicionado al Dios de las
alturas!

29»¿Acaso me he alegrado de la ruina de mi
enemigo?
¿Acaso he celebrado su desgracia?
30¡Jamás he permitido que mi boca peque
pidiendo que le vaya mal!
31¿Quién bajo mi techo no sació su hambre
con los manjares de mi mesa?
32Jamás mis puertas se cerraron al viajero;
jamás un extraño pasó la noche en la calle.
33Jamás he ocultado mi pecado,s
como el común de la gente,
ni he mantenido mi culpa en secreto,
34por miedo al qué dirán.
Jamás me he quedado en silencio y encerrado
por miedo al desprecio de mis parientes.

35»¡Cómo quisiera que Dios me escuchara!
Estampo aquí mi firma;
que me responda el Todopoderoso.
Si él quiere contender conmigo,
que lo haga por escrito.
36Llevaré esa acusación sobre mis hombros;
me la pondré como diadema.
37Compareceré ante él con dignidad,
y le daré cuenta de cada uno de mis pasos.

38»Si mis tierras claman contra mí,
  y todos sus surcos se aniegan en llanto;
39si he tomado la cosecha de alguien sin
    pagarle,
  o quebrantado el ánimo de sus dueños,
40¡que nazcan en mi tierra zarzas en vez de
    trigo,
  y hierbas en vez de cebada!»

Con esto Job dio por terminado su discurso.

Intervención de Eliú

32 Al ver los tres amigos de Job que éste se consideraba un hombre recto, dejaron de responderle. 2Pero Eliú hijo de Baraquel de Buz, de la
familia de Ram, se enojó mucho con Job porque, en
vez de justificar a Dios, se había justificado a sí mismo. 3También se enojó con los tres amigos porque no
habían logrado refutar a Job, y sin embargo lo habían
condenado. 4Ahora bien, Eliú había estado esperando antes de dirigirse a Job, porque ellos eran mayores de edad; 5pero al ver que los tres amigos no
tenían ya nada que decir, se encendió su enojo. 6Y
habló Eliú hijo de Baraquel de Buz:

Primer discurso de Eliú

«Yo soy muy joven, y ustedes ancianos;
  por eso me sentía muy temeroso
  de expresarles mi opinión.
7Y me dije: "Que hable la voz de la experiencia;
  que demuestren los ancianos su sabiduría."
8Pero lo que da entendimiento al *hombre
  es el espíritut que en él habita;
  ies el hálito del *Todopoderoso!
9No son los ancianosu los únicos sabios,
  ni es la edad la que hace entender lo que es
    justo.

10»Les ruego, por tanto, que me escuchen;
  yo también tengo algo que decirles.
11Mientras hablaban, me propuse esperar
  y escuchar sus razonamientos;
  mientras buscaban las palabras,
    12les presté toda mi atención.
Pero no han podido probar que Job esté
    equivocado;
  ninguno ha respondido a sus argumentos.
13No vayan a decirme: "Hemos hallado la
    sabiduría;
  que lo refute Dios, y no los hombres."
14Ni Job se ha dirigido a mí,
  ni yo he de responderle como ustedes.

15»Job, tus amigos están desconcertados;
  no pueden responder, les faltan las
    palabras.
16¿Y voy a quedarme callado ante su silencio,
  ante su falta de respuesta?
17Yo también tengo algo que decir,
  y voy a demostrar mis *conocimientos.
18Palabras no me faltan;
  el espíritu que hay en mí me obliga a
    hablar.
19Estoy como vino embotellado,
  como vino en odre nuevo a punto de
    estallar.
20Tengo que hablar y desahogarme;
  tengo que abrir la boca y dar respuesta.

21No favoreceré a nadie
  ni halagaré a ninguno;
22Yo no sé adular a nadie;
  si lo hiciera,v mi Creador me castigaría.

33 »Te ruego, Job, que escuches mis palabras,
    que prestes atención a todo lo que digo.
2Estoy a punto de abrir la boca,
  y voy a hablar hasta por los codos.
3Mis palabras salen de un *corazón honrado;
  mis labios dan su opinión sincera.
4El Espíritu de Dios me ha creado;
  me infunde vida el hálito del
    *Todopoderoso.
5Contéstame, si puedes;
  prepárate y hazme frente.
6Ante Dios, tú y yo somos iguales;
  también yo fui tomado de la tierra.
7No debieras alarmarte ni temerme,
  ni debiera pesar mi mano sobre ti.

8»Pero me parece haber oído que decías
  (al menos, eso fue lo que escuché):
9"Soy inocente. No tengo pecado.
  Estoy limpio y libre de culpa.
10Sin embargo, Dios me ha encontrado faltas;
  me considera su enemigo.
11Me ha sujetado los pies con cadenas
  y vigila todos mis pasos."

12»Pero déjame decirte que estás equivocado,
  pues Dios es más grande que los *mortales.
13¿Por qué le echas en cara
  que no responda a todas tusw preguntas?x
14Dios nos habla una y otra vez,
  aunque no lo percibamos.
15Algunas veces en sueños,
  otras veces en visiones nocturnas,
  cuando caemos en un sopor profundo,
  o cuando dormitamos en el lecho,
16él nos habla al oído
  y nos aterra con sus advertencias,
17para apartarnos de hacer lo malo
  y alejarnos de la soberbia;
18para librarnos de caer en el sepulcro
  y de cruzar el umbral de la muerte.y
19A veces nos castiga con el lecho del dolor,
  con frecuentes dolencias en los huesos.
20Nuestro ser encuentra repugnante la comida,
  el mejor manjar nos parece aborrecible.
21Nuestra carne va perdiéndose en la nada,
  hasta se nos pueden contar los huesos.
22Nuestra vida va acercándose al sepulcro,
  se acerca a los heraldos de la muerte.

23»Mas si un ángel, uno entre mil,
  aboga por el *hombre y sale en su favor,
  y da constancia de su rectitud;
24si le tiene compasión y le ruega a Dios:
  "Sálvalo de caer en la tumba,
  que ya tengo su rescate",
25entonces el hombre rejuvenece;
  ¡vuelve a ser como cuando era niño!
26Orará a Dios, y él recibirá su favor;
  verá su rostro y gritará de alegría,
  y Dios lo hará volver a su estado de
    inocencia.
27El hombre reconocerá públicamente:z
  "He pecado, he pervertido la justicia,

---

t **32:8** *espíritu.* Alt. *Espíritu;* también en v. 18. u **32:9** *ancianos.* Alt. *muchos,* o *grandes.* v **32:22** *si lo hiciera.* Lit. *en poco
tiempo.* w **33:13** *tus.* Lit. *sus.* x **33:13** *que no ... preguntas.* Alt. *de que no responde por ninguno de sus actos.* y **33:18** *y de ...
muerte.* Lit. *y su vida del cruce del canal.* z **33:27** *El hombre reconocerá públicamente.* Lit. *Cantará ante los hombres y dirá.*

pero no recibí mi merecido.
28Dios me libró de caer en la tumba;
¡estoy vivo y disfruto de la luz!"

29»Todo esto Dios lo hace
una, dos y hasta tres veces,
30para salvarnos de la muerte,
para que la luz de la vida nos alumbre.

31»Préstame atención, Job, escúchame;
guarda silencio, que quiero hablar.
32Si tienes algo que decir, respóndeme;
habla, que quisiera darte la razón.
33De lo contrario, escúchame en silencio
y yo te impartiré sabiduría.»

Segundo discurso de Eliú

34 También dijo Eliú:

2«Ustedes los sabios, escuchen mis palabras;
ustedes los instruidos, préstenme atención.
3El oído saborea las palabras,
como saborea el paladar la comida.
4Examinemos juntos este caso;
decidamos entre nosotros lo mejor.
5»Job alega: "Soy inocente,
pero Dios se niega a hacerme *justicia.
6Tengo que resultar un mentiroso,
a pesar de que soy justo;
sus flechas me hieren de muerte,
a pesar de que no he pecado."
7¿Dónde hay alguien como Job,
que tiene el sarcasmo a flor de labios?a
8Le encanta hacer amistad con los malhechores
y andar en compañía de los malvados.
9Y nos alega que ningún provecho saca el
*hombre
tratando de agradar a Dios!

10»Escúchenme, hombres entendidos:
¡Es inconcebible que Dios haga lo malo,
que el *Todopoderoso cometa injusticias!
11Dios paga al hombre según sus obras;
lo trata como se merece.
12¡Ni pensar que Dios cometa injusticias!
¡El Todopoderoso no pervierte el derecho!
13¿Quién le dio poder sobre la tierra?
¿Quién lo puso a cargo de todo el mundo?
14Si pensara en retirarnos su espíritu,b
en quitarnos su hálito de vida,
15todo el *género humano perecería,
¡la humanidad entera volvería a ser polvo!

16»Escucha esto, si eres entendido;
presta atención a lo que digo.
17¿Puede acaso gobernar quien detesta la
justicia?
¿Condenarás entonces al Dios justo y
poderoso,
18al que niega el valor de los reyes
y denuncia la maldad de los nobles?
19Dios no se muestra parcial con los príncipes
ni favorece a los ricos más que a los pobres.
¡Unos y otros son obra de sus manos!
20Mueren de pronto, en medio de la noche;
la gente se estremece y muere;
los poderosos son derrocados
sin intervención *humana.

21»Los ojos de Dios ven los caminos del
hombre;

él vigila cada uno de sus pasos.
22No hay lugares oscuros ni sombras profundas
que puedan esconder a los malhechores.
23Dios no tiene que examinarlos
para someterlos a juicio.
24No tiene que indagar para derrocar a los
poderosos
y sustituirlos por otros.
25Dios toma nota de todo lo que hacen;
por la noche los derroca, y quedan
aplastados;
26los castiga por su maldad
para escarmiento de todos,c
27pues dejaron de seguirlo
y no tomaron en cuenta sus caminos.
28Hicieron llegar a su presencia
el clamor de los pobres y necesitados,
y Dios lo escuchó.
29¿Pero quién puede condenarlo
si él decide guardar silencio?
¿Quién puede verlo si oculta su rostro?
Él está por encima de pueblos y personas,
30para que no reinen los malvados
ni se le tiendan trampas a su pueblo.

31»Supongamos que le dijeras:
"Soy culpable; no volveré a ofenderte.
32Enséñame lo que no alcanzo a percibir;
si he cometido algo malo, no volveré a
hacerlo."
33¿Tendría Dios que recompensarte
como tú quieres que lo haga,
aunque lo hayas rechazado?
No seré yo quien lo decida, sino tú,
así que expresa lo que piensas.

34»Que me digan los sabios
y ustedes los entendidos que me escuchan:
35"Job no sabe lo que dice;
en sus palabras no hay inteligencia."
36¡Que sea Job examinado,
pues como un malvado ha respondido!
37A su pecado ha añadido rebeldía;
en nuestra propia cara se ha burlado de
nosotros,
y se ha excedido en sus palabras contra
Dios.»

Tercer discurso de Eliú

35 Además, Eliú dijo:

2«¿Crees tener la razón, Job, cuando afirmas:
"Mi justicia es mayor que la de Dios"?,d
3y cuando te atreves a preguntarle:
"¿En qué te beneficias si no peco?"
4Pues bien, voy a responderles
a ti y a tus amigos.
5Mira hacia el cielo, y fíjate bien;
contempla las nubes en lo alto.
6Si pecas, ¿en qué afectas a Dios?
Si multiplicas tus faltas, ¿en qué lo dañas?
7Si actúas con justicia, ¿qué puedes darle?
¿Qué puede recibir de parte tuya?
8Hagas el mal o hagas el bien,
los únicos afectados serán tus semejantes.

9»Todo el mundo clama bajo el peso de la
opresión,
y pide ser librado del brazo del poderoso.

---

a **34:7** tiene ... labios. Lit. bebe sarcasmo como agua.   b **34:14** espíritu. Alt. Espíritu.   c **34:26** para escarmiento de todos. Lit. en un lugar visible.   d **35:2** Mi justicia ... Dios. Alt. Dios habrá de justificarme.

10Pero nadie dice: "¿Dónde está Dios, mi
Hacedor,
que me infunde fuerzas^e por las noches,
11que nos enseña más que a las bestias del
campo,
que nos hace más sabios que las aves del
cielo?"
12Si Dios no responde al clamor de la gente,
es por la arrogancia de los malvados.
13Dios no escucha sus vanas peticiones;
el *Todopoderoso no les presta atención.
14Aun cuando digas que no puedes verlo,
tu caso está delante de él, y debes
aguardarlo.
15Tú dices que Dios no se enoja ni castiga,
y que no se da cuenta de tanta maldad;^f
16pero tú, Job, abres la boca y dices tonterías;
hablas mucho y no sabes lo que dices.»

Cuarto discurso de Eliú

36 Eliú continuó diciendo:

2«Ten paciencia conmigo y te mostraré
que aún quiero decir más en favor de Dios.
3Mi *conocimiento proviene de muy lejos;
voy a demostrar que mi Hacedor está en lo
justo.
4Te aseguro que no hay falsedad en mis
palabras,
¡tienes ante ti a la sabiduría en persona!

5»Dios es poderoso, pero no rechaza al
inocente;^g
Dios es poderoso, y todo lo entiende.^h
6Al malvado no lo mantiene con vida;
al afligido le hace valer sus derechos.
7Cuida siempre de los justos;
los hace reinar en compañía de reyes
y los exalta para siempre.
8Pero si son encadenados,
si la aflicción los domina,
9Dios denuncia sus acciones
y la arrogancia de su pecado.
10Les hace prestar oído a la *corrección
y les pide apartarse del mal.
11Si ellos le obedecen y le sirven,
pasan el resto de su vida en prosperidad,
pasan felices los años que les quedan.
12Pero si no le hacen caso,
sin darse cuenta cruzarán el umbral de la
muerte.^i

13»Los de *corazón impío abrigan
resentimiento;
no piden ayuda aun cuando Dios los
castigue.^j
14Mueren en la flor de la vida,
entre los que se prostituyen en los
santuarios.
15A los que sufren, Dios los libra mediante el
sufrimiento;
en su aflicción, los consuela.^k

16»Dios te libra de las fauces de la angustia,
te lleva a un lugar amplio y espacioso,
y llena tu mesa con la mejor comida.

17Pero tú te has ganado el juicio de los impíos;^l
el juicio y la justicia te tienen atrapado.
18Cuídate de no dejarte seducir por las
riquezas;
no te dejes desviar por el soborno.
19Tus grandes riquezas no podrán sostenerte,
ni tampoco todos tus esfuerzos.
20No ansíes que caiga la noche,
cuando la gente es arrancada de su sitio.^m
21Cuídate de no inclinarte a la maldad,
que por eso fuiste apartado de la aflicción.

22»Dios es exaltado por su poder.
¿Qué maestro hay que se le compare?
23¿Quién puede pedirle cuentas de sus actos?
¿Quién puede decirle que se ha
equivocado?
24No te olvides de exaltar sus obras,
que con cánticos han sido alabadas.
25Todo el *género humano puede
contemplarlas,
aunque sólo desde lejos.
26¡Tan grande es Dios que no lo conocemos!
¡Incontable es el número de sus años!

27»Él derrama las gotas de agua
que fluyen como lluvia hacia los ríos;^n
28las nubes derraman su lluvia,
que cae a raudales sobre el género
humano.
29¿Quién entiende la extensión de las nubes
y el estruendo que sale de su pabellón?
30Vean a Dios esparcir su luz en torno suyo,
y bañar con ella las profundidades del
océano.
31Dios gobierna a las naciones
y les da comida en abundancia.
32Toma entre sus manos el relámpago,
y le ordena dar en el blanco.
33Su trueno anuncia la inminente tormenta,
y hasta el ganado presagia su llegada.

37 »Al llegar a este punto,^ñ me palpita el
*corazón
como si fuera a salírseme del pecho.
2¡Escucha, escucha el estruendo de su voz,
el ruido estrepitoso que sale de su boca!
3Lanza sus rayos bajo el cielo entero;
su resplandor, hasta los confines de la
tierra.
4Sigue luego el rugido majestuoso de su voz;
¡resuena su voz, y no retiene sus rayos!
5Dios hace tronar su voz
y se producen maravillas:
¡Dios hace grandes cosas
que rebasan nuestra comprensión!
6A la nieve le ordena: "¡Cae sobre la tierra!",
y a la lluvia: "¡Muestra tu poder!"
7Hace que todo el mundo se encierre,
para que todos reconozcan sus obras.
8Los animales buscan abrigo
y se quedan en sus cuevas.
9De las cámaras del sur viene la tempestad;
de los vientos del norte, el frío.
10Por el aliento de Dios se forma el hielo

---

^e **35:10** *que me infunde fuerzas.* Alt. *que me inspira cánticos.* ^f **35:15** *maldad.* Palabra de difícil traducción. ^g **36:5** *no rechaza al inocente* (LXX); *no rechaza* (TM). ^h **36:5** *todo lo entiende.* Lit. *es fuerte de corazón.* ^i **36:12** *el umbral de la muerte.* Lit. *el canal.* ^j **36:13** *los castigue* (lectura probable); *los aprisione* (TM). ^k **36:15** *los consuela.* Alt. *los hace entender.* Lit. *abre sus oídos.* ^l **36:17** *te has ... impíos.* Texto de difícil traducción. ^m **36:20** Los vv. 18-20 son de difícil traducción. ^n **36:27** *que fluyen ... los ríos.* Alt. *que destila del rocío en forma de lluvia.* ^ñ **37:1** *Al llegar a este punto.* Alt. *Al ver esto.*

y se congelan las masas de agua.
11Con agua de lluvia carga las nubes,
   y lanza sus relámpagos desde ellas;
12y éstas van de un lado a otro,
   por toda la faz de la tierra,
   dispuestas a cumplir sus mandatos.
13Por su bondad, hace que vengan las nubes,
   ya sea para castigar o para bendecir.o

14»Espera un poco, Job, y escucha;
   ponte a pensar en las maravillas de Dios.
15¿Sabes cómo controla Dios las nubes,
   y cómo hace que su relámpago deslumbre?
16¿Sabes cómo las nubes,
   maravillas del conocimiento perfecto,p
   se mantienen suspendidas?
17Tú, que te sofocas de calor entre tus ropas
   cuando la tierra dormita bajo el viento del
   sur,
18¿puedes ayudarle a extender los cielos,
   sólidos como espejo de bronce bruñido?

19»Haznos saber qué debemos responderle,
   pues debido a nuestra ignoranciaq
   no tenemos argumentos.
20¿Le haré saber que estoy pidiendo la palabra?
   ¿Quién se atreve a hablar y ser destruido?
21No hay quien pueda mirar al sol brillante
   después de que el viento ha despejado los
   cielos.
22Un dorado resplandor viene del norte;
   ¡viene Dios, envuelto en terrible majestad!
23El *Todopoderoso no está a nuestro alcance;
   excelso es su poder.
Grandes son su justicia y rectitud;
   ¡a nadie oprime!
24Él no toma en cuenta a los que se creen
   sabios;
   por eso le temen los *mortales.»

Respuesta de Dios

38 El SEÑOR le respondió a Job desde la tempestad. Le dijo:

2«¿Quién es éste, que oscurece mi consejo
   con palabras carentes de sentido?
3Prepárate a hacerme frente;r
   yo te cuestionaré, y tú me responderás.

4¿Dónde estabas cuando puse las bases de la
   tierra?
   ¡Dímelo, si de veras sabes tanto!
5¡Seguramente sabes quién estableció sus
   dimensiones
   y quién tendió sobre ella la cinta de medir!
6¿Sobre qué están puestos sus cimientos,
   o quién puso su piedra angular
7mientras cantaban a coro las estrellas
   matutinas
   y todos los ángeless gritaban de alegría?

8¿Quién encerró el mar tras sus compuertas
   cuando éste brotó del vientre de la tierra?
9O cuando lo arropé con las nubes
   y lo envolví en densas tinieblas?
10O cuando establecí sus límites

y en sus compuertas coloqué cerrojos?
11¿O cuando le dije: "Sólo hasta aquí puedes
   llegar;
   de aquí no pasarán tus orgullosas olas"?

12»¿Alguna vez en tu vida le has dado órdenes
   a la mañana,
   o le has hecho saber a la aurora su lugar,
13para que tomen la tierra por sus extremos
   y sacudan de ella a los malvados?
14La tierra adquiere forma, como arcilla bajo un
   sello;
   resaltan sus rasgos como los de un vestido.
15Los malvados son privados de su luz,
   y es quebrantado su altanero brazo.

16¿Has viajado hasta las fuentes del océano,
   o recorrido los rincones del abismo?
17¿Te han mostrado los umbrales de la muerte?
   ¿Has visto las puertas de la región
   tenebrosa?t
18¿Tienes idea de cuán ancha es la tierra?
   Si de veras sabes todo esto, ¡dalo a conocer!

19»¿Qué camino lleva a la morada de la luz?
   ¿En qué lugar se encuentran las tinieblas?
20¿Puedes acaso llevarlas a sus linderos?
   ¿Conoces el camino a sus moradas?
21¡Con toda seguridad lo sabes,
   pues para entonces ya habrías nacido!
   ¡Son tantos los años que has vivido!

22»¿Has llegado a visitar
   los depósitos de nieve de granizo,
23que guardo para tiempos azarosos,
   cuando se libran guerras y batallas?
24¿Qué camino lleva a donde la luz se dispersa,
   o a donde los vientos del este
   se desatan sobre la tierra?
25¿Quién abre el canal para las lluvias
   torrenciales,
   y le da paso a la tormenta,
26para regar regiones despobladas,
   desiertos donde nadie vive,
27para saciar la sed del yermo desolado
   y hacer que en él brote la hierba?
28¿Acaso la lluvia tiene padre?
   ¿Ha engendrado alguien las gotas de rocío?
29¿De qué vientre nace el hielo?
   ¿Quién da a luz la escarcha de los cielos?
30¡Las aguas se endurecen como rocas,
   y la faz del mar profundo se congela!

31»¿Acaso puedes atar los lazos de las Pléyades,
   o desatar las cuerdas que sujetan al Orión?
32¿Puedes hacer que las constelaciones salganu
   a tiempo?
   ¿Puedes guiar a la Osa Mayor y a la
   Menor?v
33¿Conoces las leyes que rigen los cielos?
   ¿Puedes establecer miw dominio sobre la
   tierra?

34»¿Puedes elevar tu voz hasta las nubes
   para que te cubran aguas torrenciales?
35¿Eres tú quien señala el curso de los rayos?
   ¿Acaso te responden: "Estamos a tus
   órdenes"?

---

o 37:13 Versículo de difícil traducción. p 37:16 del conocimiento perfecto. Alt. del que todo lo sabe. q 37:19 nuestra ignorancia.
Lit. nuestra oscuridad. r 38:3 Prepárate a hacerme frente. Lit. Cíñe ahora, como hombre, tus lomos. s 38:7 ángeles. Lit. hijos de
Dios. t 38:17 la región tenebrosa. Lit. la profunda sombra. u 38:32 las constelaciones salgan. Alt. la estrella de la mañana salga.
v 38:32 a la Osa Mayor y a la Menor. Alt. a Leo y a sus cachorros. w 38:33 mí. Lit. su.

36¿Quién infundió sabiduría en el ibis,
o dio al gallox entendimiento?
37¿Quién tiene sabiduría para contar las nubes?
¿Quién puede vaciar los cántaros del cielo
38cuando el polvo se endurece
y los terrones se pegan entre sí?

39»¿Cazas tú la presa para las leonas
y sacias el hambre de sus cachorros
40cuando yacen escondidas en sus cuevas
o se tienden al acecho en sus guaridas?
41¿Eres tú quien alimenta a los cuervos
cuando sus crías claman a míy
y andan sin rumbo y sin comida?

39 »¿Sabes cuándo los íbices tienen sus crías?
¿Has visto el parto de las gacelas?
2¿Has contado los meses de su gestación?
¿Sabes cuándo dan a luz?
3Al tener sus crías se encorvan,
y allí terminan sus dolores de parto.
4Crecen sus crías, y en el bosque se hacen
fuertes;
luego se van y ya no vuelven.
5¿Quién deja sueltos a los asnos salvajes?
¿Quién les desata las cuerdas?
6Yo les di el páramo por morada,
el yermo por hábitat.
7Se burlan del ajetreo de la ciudad;
no prestan atención a los gritos del arriero.
8Recorren los cerros en busca de pastos,
en busca de verdes prados.

9»¿Crees tú que el toro salvaje se prestará a
servirte?
¿Pasará la noche en tus establos?
10¿Puedes mantenerlo en el surco con el arnés?
¿Irá en pos de ti labrando los valles?
11¿Pondrás tu confianza en su tremenda fuerza?
¿Echarás sobre sus lomos tu pesado
trabajo?
12¿Puedes confiar en él para que acarree tu
grano
y lo junte en el lugar donde lo trillas?

13»El avestruz bate alegremente sus alas,
pero su plumaje no es como el de la
cigüeña.z
14Pone sus huevos en la tierra,
los deja empollar en la arena,
15sin que le importe aplastarlos con sus patas,
o que las bestias salvajes los pisoteen.
16Maltrata a sus polluelos como si no fueran
suyos,
y no le importa haber trabajado en vano,
17pues Dios no le dio sabiduría
ni le impartió su porción de buen juicio.
18Pero cuando extiende sus alas y corre,
se ríe de jinetes y caballos.

19»¿Le has dado al caballo su fuerza?
¿Has cubierto su cuello con largas crines?
20¿Eres tú quien lo hace saltar como langosta,
con su orgulloso resoplido que infunde
terror?
21Patalea con furia, regocijándose en su fuerza,
y se lanza al galope hacia la llanura.
22Se burla del miedo; a nada le teme;
no rehuye hacerle frente a la espada.
23En torno suyo silban las flechas,

brillan las lanzas y las jabalinas.
24En frenética carrera devora las distancias;
al toque de trompeta no es posible
refrenarlo.
25En cuanto suena la trompeta, resopla
desafiante;
percibe desde lejos el fragora de la batalla,
los gritos de combate y las órdenes de
ataque.

26»¿Es tu sabiduría la que hace que el halcón
vuele
y que hacia el sur extienda sus alas?
27¿Acaso por tus órdenes remonta el vuelo el
águila
y construye su nido en las alturas?
28Habita en los riscos; allí pasa la noche;
en escarpadas grietas tiene su baluarte.
29Desde allí acecha la presa;
sus ojos la detectan desde lejos.
30Sus polluelos se regodean en la sangre;
donde hay un cadáver, allí está el halcón.»

40 El SEÑOR dijo también a Job:

2¿Corregirá al *Todopoderoso quien contra él
contiende?
¡Que le responda a Dios quien se atreve a
acusarlo!»

3Entonces Job le respondió:

4«¿Qué puedo responderte, si soy tan indigno?
¡Me tapo la boca con la mano!
5Hablé una vez, y no voy a responder;
hablé otra vez, y no voy a insistir.»

6El SEÑOR le respondió a Job desde la tempestad. Le dijo:

7«Prepárate a hacerme frente.
Yo te cuestionaré, y tú me responderás.

8»¿Vas acaso a invalidar mi *justicia?
¿Me harás quedar mal para que tú quedes
bien?
9¿Tienes acaso un brazo como el mío?
¿Puede tu voz tronar como la mía?
10Si es así, cúbrete de gloria y esplendor;
revístete de honra y majestad.
11Da rienda suelta a la furia de tu ira;
mira a los orgullosos, y humíllalos;
12mira a los soberbios, y somételos;
aplasta a los malvados donde se hallen.
13Entiérralos a todos en el polvo;
amortaja sus rostros en la fosa.
14Yo, por mi parte, reconoceré
que en tu mano *derecha está la
*salvación.

15»Mira a Behemot,b criatura mía igual que tú,
que se alimenta de hierba, como los
bueyes.
16¡Cuánta fuerza hay en sus lomos!
¡Su poder está en los músculos de su
vientre!
17Su rabo se mece como un cedro;
los tendones de sus muslos se entrelazan.
18Sus huesos son como barras de bronce;
sus piernas parecen barrotes de hierro.
19Entre mis obras ocupa el primer lugar,

sólo yo, su Hacedor, puedo acercármele
con la espada.
20Los montes le brindan sus frutos;
allí juguetean todos los animales salvajes.
21Debajo de los lotos se tiende a descansar;
se oculta entre los juncos del pantano.
22Los lotos le brindan su sombra;
los álamos junto al río lo envuelven.
23Vacía un río entero sin apresurarse;
con toda calma se traga el Jordán.c
24¿Quién ante sus ojos se atreve a capturarlo?
¿Quién puede atraparlo y perforarle la
nariz?

41 »¿Puedes pescar a *Leviatán con un
anzuelo,
o atarle la lengua con una cuerda?
2¿Puedes ponerle un cordel en la nariz,
o perforarle la quijada con un gancho?
3¿Acaso amablemente va a pedirte
o suplicarte que le tengas compasión?
4¿Acaso va a comprometerse
a ser tu esclavo de por vida?
5¿Podrás jugar con él como juegas con los
pájaros,
o atarlo para que tus niñas se entretengan?
6¿Podrán los mercaderes ofrecerlo como
mercancía,d
o cortarlo en pedazos para venderlo?
7¿Puedes atravesarle la piel con lanzas,
o la cabeza con arpones?
8Si llegas a ponerle la mano encima,
¡jamás te olvidarás de esa batalla,
y no querrás repetir la experiencia!
9Vana es la pretensión de llegar a someterlo;
basta con verlo para desmayarse.e
10No hay quien se atreva siquiera a provocarlo;
¿quién, pues, podría hacerle frente?
11¿Y quién tiene alguna cuenta que cobrarme?
¡Mío es todo cuanto hay bajo los cielos!

12»No puedo dejar de mencionar sus
extremidades,
su fuerza y su elegante apariencia.
13¿Quién puede despojarlo de su coraza?
¿Quién puede acercarse a él y ponerle un
freno?
14¿Quién se atreve a abrir el abismo de sus
fauces,
coronadas de terribles colmillos?
15Tiene el lomof recubierto de hileras de
escudos,
todos ellos unidos en cerrado tejido;
16tan juntos están uno al otro
que no dejan pasar ni el aire;
17tan prendidos están uno del otro,
tan unidos entre sí, que no pueden
separarse.
18Resopla y lanza deslumbrantes relámpagos;
sus ojos se parecen a los rayos de la aurora.
19Ascuas de fuego brotan de su hocico;
chispas de lumbre salen disparadas.
20Lanza humo por la nariz,
como olla hirviendo sobre un fuego de
juncos.
21Con su aliento enciende los carbones,

y lanza fuego por la boca.
22En su cuello radica su fuerza;
ante él, todo el mundo pierde el ánimo.
23Los pliegues de su piel son un tejido
apretado;
firmes son, e inconmovibles.
24Duro es su pecho, como una roca;
sólido, cual piedra de molino.
25Cuando se yergue, los poderosos tiemblan;
cuando se sacude, emprenden la huida.
26La espada, aunque lo alcance, no lo hiere,
ni lo hieren tampoco los dardos,
ni las lanzas y las jabalinas.
27Al hierro lo trata como a paja,
y al bronce como a madera podrida.
28No lo hacen huir las flechas;
ve como paja las piedras de las hondas.
29Los golpes del mazo apenas le hacen
cosquillas;
se burla del silbido de la lanza.
30Sus costados son dentados tiestos
que en el fango van dejando huellas de
rastrillos.
31Hace hervir las profundidades como un
caldero;
agita los mares como un frasco de
ungüento.
32Una estela brillante va dejando tras de sí,
cual si fuera la blanca cabellera del abismo.
33Es un monstruo que a nada teme;
nada hay en el mundo que se le parezca.
34Mira con desdén a todos los poderosos;
¡él es rey de todos los soberbios!»

Respuesta de Job

42 Job respondió entonces al SEÑOR. Le dijo:
2«Yo sé bien que tú lo puedes todo,
que no es posible frustrar ninguno de tus
planes.
3"¿Quién es éste —has preguntado—,
que sin *conocimiento oscurece mi
consejo?"
Reconozco que he hablado de cosas
que no alcanzo a comprender,
de cosas demasiado maravillosas
que me son desconocidas.

4»"Ahora escúchame, que voy a hablar
—dijiste—;g
yo te cuestionaré, y tú me responderás."
5De oídas había oído hablar de ti,
pero ahora te veo con mis propios ojos.
6Por tanto, me retracto de lo que he dicho,
y me arrepiento en polvo y ceniza.»

Epílogo

7Después de haberle dicho todo esto a Job, el
SEÑOR se dirigió a Elifaz de Temán y le dijo: «Estoy
muy irritado contigo y con tus dos amigos porque, a
diferencia de mi siervo Job, lo que ustedes han dicho
de mí no es verdad. 8Tomen ahora siete toros y siete
carneros, y vayan con mi siervo Job y ofrezcan un
*holocausto por ustedes mismos. Mi siervo Job orará
por ustedes, y yo atenderé a su oración y no los haré
quedar en vergüenza. Y conste que, a diferencia de

---

c **40:23** *Vacía un río ... el Jordán.* Alt. *No se alarma si brama el río; / vive tranquilo, aunque el Jordán le llegue al hocico.*
d **41:6** *como mercancía.* Alt. *en un banquete.*   e **41:9** *basta con ... para desmayarse.* Alt. *¡hasta un dios se desmayó al verlo!*
f **41:15** *lomo* (véanse LXX y Vulgata); *orgullo* (TM).   g **42:4** *dijiste.* Véase 38:3.

mi siervo Job, lo que ustedes han dicho de mí no es verdad.»

⁹Elifaz de Temán, Bildad de Súah y Zofar de Na-mat fueron y cumplieron con lo que el SEÑOR les ha-bía ordenado, y el SEÑOR atendió a la oración de Job.

¹⁰Después de haber orado Job por sus amigos, el SEÑOR lo hizo prosperar de nuevo y le dio dos veces más de lo que antes tenía. ¹¹Todos sus hermanos y hermanas, y todos los que antes lo habían conocido, fueron a su casa y celebraron con él un banquete. Lo animaron y lo consolaron por todas las calamidades que el SEÑOR le había enviado, y cada uno de ellos le dio una moneda de plata y un anillo de oro.

¹²El SEÑOR bendijo más los últimos años de Job que los primeros, pues llegó a tener catorce mil ove-jas, seis mil camellos, mil yuntas de bueyes y mil as-nas. ¹³Tuvo también catorceʰ hijos y tres hijas. ¹⁴A la primera de ellas le puso por nombre Paloma, a la se-gunda la llamó Canela, y a la tercera, Linda.ⁱ ¹⁵No ha-bía en todo el país mujeres tan bellas como las hijas de Job. Su padre les dejó una herencia, lo mismo que a sus hermanos.

¹⁶Después de estos sucesos Job vivió ciento cua-renta años. Llegó a ver a sus hijos, y a los hijos de sus hijos, hasta la cuarta generación. ¹⁷Disfrutó de una larga vida y murió en plena ancianidad.

ʰ **42:13** *catorce.* Alt. *siete.* ⁱ **42:14** *Linda.* Lit. *Frasquito de maquillaje.*

SALMOS

LIBRO I
Salmos 1-41

Salmo 1

¹*Dichoso el *hombre
que no sigue el consejo de los malvados,
ni se detiene en la senda de los pecadores
ni cultiva la amistad de los *blasfemos,
²sino que en la *ley del SEÑOR se deleita,
y día y noche medita en ella.
³Es como el árbol
plantado a la orilla de un río
que, cuando llega su tiempo, da fruto
y sus hojas jamás se marchitan.
¡Todo cuanto hace prospera!

⁴En cambio, los malvados
son como paja arrastrada por el viento.
⁵Por eso no se sostendrán los malvados en el
juicio,
ni los pecadores en la asamblea de los justos.

⁶Porque el SEÑOR cuida el *camino de los
justos,
mas la senda de los malos lleva a la
perdición.

Salmo 2

¹¿Por qué se sublevan las naciones,
y en vano conspiran los pueblos?
²Los reyes de la tierra se rebelan;
los gobernantes se confabulan contra el
SEÑOR
y contra su *ungido.
³Y dicen: «¡Hagamos pedazos sus cadenas!
¡Librémonos de su yugo!»

⁴El rey de los cielos se ríe;
el SEÑOR se burla de ellos.
⁵En su enojo los reprende,
en su furor los intimida y dice:
⁶«He establecido a mi rey
sobre *Sión, mi santo monte.»
⁷Yo proclamaré el decreto del SEÑOR:
«Tú eres mi hijo», me ha dicho;
«hoy mismo te he engendrado.
⁸Pídeme,
y como herencia te entregaré las naciones;
¡tuyos serán los confines de la tierra!
⁹Las gobernarás con puñoª de hierro;
las harás pedazos como a vasijas de barro.»

¹⁰Ustedes, los reyes, sean prudentes;
déjense enseñar, gobernantes de la tierra.
¹¹Sirvan al SEÑOR con temor;
con temblor ríndanle alabanza.
¹²Bésenle los pies,ᵇ no sea que se enoje
y sean ustedes destruidos en el camino,
pues su ira se inflama de repente.

*¡Dichosos los que en él buscan refugio!

Salmo 3

Salmo de David, cuando huía de su hijo Absalón.

¹Muchos son, SEÑOR, mis enemigos;
muchos son los que se me oponen,
²y muchos los que de mí aseguran:
«Dios no lo salvará.»
*Selah

³Pero tú, SEÑOR, me rodeas cual escudo;
tú eres mi gloria;
¡tú mantienes en alto mi cabeza!
⁴Clamo al SEÑOR a voz en cuello,
y desde su monte santo él me responde.
Selah

⁵Yo me acuesto, me duermo y vuelvo a
despertar,
porque el SEÑOR me sostiene.
⁶No me asustan los numerosos escuadrones
que me acosan por doquier.
⁷¡Levántate, SEÑOR!
¡Ponme a salvo, Dios mío!
¡Rómpeles la quijada a mis enemigos!
¡Rómpeles los dientes a los malvados!
⁸Tuya es, SEÑOR, la *salvación;
¡envía tu bendición sobre tu pueblo!
Selah

Salmo 4

Al director musical. Acompáñese con instrumentos
de cuerda. Salmo de David.

¹Responde a mi clamor,
Dios mío y defensor mío.
Dame alivio cuando esté angustiado,
apiádate de mí y escucha mi oración.

²Y ustedes, señores,
¿hasta cuándo cambiarán mi gloria en
vergüenza?
¿Hasta cuándo amarán ídolos vanos
e irán en pos de lo ilusorio?
*Selah

³Sepan que el SEÑOR honra al que le es fiel;
el SEÑOR me escucha cuando lo llamo.

⁴Si se enojan, no pequen;
en la quietud del descanso nocturno
examínense el *corazón.
Selah

⁵Ofrezcan sacrificios de *justicia
y confíen en el SEÑOR.

⁶Muchos son los que dicen:
«¿Quién puede mostrarnos algún bien?»
¡Haz, SEÑOR, que sobre nosotros
brille la luz de tu rostro!

⁷Tú has hecho que mi corazón rebose de
alegría,
alegría mayor que la que tienen los que
disfrutan de trigo y vino en
abundancia.

⁸En *paz me acuesto y me duermo,
porque sólo tú, SEÑOR, me haces vivir
confiado.

Salmo 5

Al director musical. Acompáñese con flautas.
Salmo de David.

¹Atiende, SEÑOR, a mis palabras;
toma en cuenta mis gemidos.

ª 2:9 *puño*. Lit. *cetro*.   ᵇ 2:12 *Bésenle los pies.* Texto de difícil traducción.

²Escucha mis súplicas, rey mío y Dios mío,
 porque a ti elevo mi plegaria.
³Por la mañana, SEÑOR, escuchas mi clamor;
 por la mañana te presento mis ruegos,
 y quedo a la espera de tu respuesta.

⁴Tú no eres un Dios que se complazca en lo malo;
 a tu lado no tienen cabida los malvados.
⁵No hay lugar en tu presencia para los altivos,
 pues aborreces a los malhechores.
⁶Tú destruyes a los mentirosos
 y aborreces a los tramposos y asesinos.

⁷Pero yo, por tu gran amor
 puedo entrar en tu casa;
 puedo postrarme reverente
 hacia tu santo templo.

⁸SEÑOR, por causa de mis enemigos,
 dirígeme en tu *justicia;
 empareja delante de mí tu senda.

⁹En sus palabras no hay sinceridad;
 en su interior sólo hay corrupción.
 Su garganta es un sepulcro abierto;
 con su lengua profieren engaños.

¹⁰¡Condénalos, oh Dios!
 ¡Que caigan por sus propias intrigas!
 ¡Recházalos por la multitud de sus crímenes,
 porque se han rebelado contra ti!

¹¹Pero que se alegren todos los que en ti buscan
 refugio;
 ¡que canten siempre jubilosos!
 Extiende tu protección, y que en ti se
 regocijen
 todos los que aman tu *nombre.
¹²Porque tú, SEÑOR, bendices a los justos;
 cual escudo los rodeas con tu buena
 voluntad.

Salmo 6

Al director musical. Acompáñese con instrumentos
de cuerda. Sobre la octava.c Salmo de David.

¹No me reprendas, SEÑOR, en tu ira;
 no me castigues en tu furor.
²Tenme compasión, SEÑOR, porque desfallezco;
 sáname, SEÑOR, que un frío de muerte
 recorre mis huesos.
³Angustiada está mi *alma;
 ¿hasta cuándo, SEÑOR, hasta cuándo?

⁴Vuélvete, SEÑOR, y sálvame la vida;
 por tu gran amor, ¡ponme a salvo!
⁵En la muerte nadie te recuerda;
 en el *sepulcro, ¿quién te alabará?

⁶Cansado estoy de sollozar;
 toda la noche inundo de lágrimas mi cama,
 ¡mi lecho empapo con mi llanto!
⁷Desfallecen mis ojos por causa del dolor;
 desfallecen por culpa de mis enemigos.

⁸¡Apártense de mí, todos los malhechores,
 que el SEÑOR ha escuchado mi llanto!
⁹El SEÑOR ha escuchado mis ruegos;
 el SEÑOR ha tomado en cuenta mi oración.
¹⁰Todos mis enemigos quedarán avergonzados
 y confundidos;
 ¡su repentina vergüenza los hará
 retroceder!

Salmo 7

*Sigaión de David, que elevó al SEÑOR acerca de
Cus el benjaminita.

¹¡Sálvame, SEÑOR mi Dios, porque en ti busco
 refugio!
 ¡Líbrame de todos mis perseguidores!
²De lo contrario, me devorarán como leones;
 me despedazarán, y no habrá quien me
 libre.

³SEÑOR mi Dios, ¿qué es lo que he hecho?
 ¿qué mal he cometido?
⁴Si le he hecho daño a mi amigo,
 si he despojado sin razón al que me
 oprime,
⁵entonces que mi enemigo me persiga y me
 alcance;
 que me haga morder el polvo
 y arrastre mi honra por los suelos.
      *Selah

⁶¡Levántate, SEÑOR, en tu ira;
 enfréntate al furor de mis enemigos!
 ¡Despierta, oh Dios, e imparte *justicia!
⁷Que en torno tuyo se reúnan los pueblos;
 reinad sobre ellos desde lo alto.
⁸¡El SEÑOR juzgará a los pueblos!

Júzgame, SEÑOR, conforme a mi justicia;
 págame conforme a mi inocencia.
⁹Dios justo, que examinas mente y corazón,
 acaba con la maldad de los malvados
 y mantén firme al que es justo.

¹⁰Mi escudo está en Dios,
 que salva a los de *corazón recto.
¹¹Dios es un juez justo,
 un Dios que en todo tiempo manifiesta su
 enojo.
¹²Si el malvado no se arrepiente,
 Dios afilará la espada y tensará el arco;
¹³ya ha preparado sus mortíferas armas;
 ya tiene listas sus llameantes saetas.

¹⁴Miren al preñado de maldad:
 Concibió iniquidad y parirá mentira.
¹⁵Cavó una fosa y la ahondó,
 y en esa misma fosa caerá.
¹⁶Su iniquidad se volverá contra él;
 su violencia recaerá sobre su cabeza.

¹⁷¡Alabaré al SEÑOR por su justicia!
 ¡Al *nombre del SEÑOR altísimo cantaré
 salmos!

Salmo 8

Al director musical. Sígase la tonada de «La canción
del lagar».e Salmo de David.

¹Oh SEÑOR, soberano nuestro,
 ¡qué imponente es tu *nombre en toda la
 tierra!
 ¡Has puesto tu gloria sobre los cielos!

²Por causa de tus adversarios
 has hecho que brote la alabanzaf
de labios de los pequeñitos y de los niños de
 pecho,
 para silenciar al enemigo y al rebelde.

³Cuando contemplo tus cielos,
 obra de tus dedos,

---

c **6 Tít.** *Sobre la octava*. Lit. *Sobre* *sheminit. d **7:7** *reina* (lectura probable); *vuélvete* (TM). e **8 Tít.** *Sígase ... lagar*. Lit. *Según
la* *gittith. f **8:2** *has hecho que brote la alabanza*. Lit. *fundaste la fortaleza.*

la luna y las estrellas que allí fijaste,
4me pregunto:
«¿Qué es el *hombre, para que en él
pienses?
¿Qué es el *ser humanog, para que lo
tomes en cuenta?»
5Pues lo hiciste poco menos que un dios,h
y lo coronaste de gloria y de honra;
6lo entronizaste sobre la obra de tus manos,
todo lo sometiste a su dominio:
7todas las ovejas, todos los bueyes,
todos los animales del campo,
8las aves del cielo, los peces del mar,
y todo lo que surca los senderos del mar.

9Oh SEÑOR, soberano nuestro,
¡qué imponente es tu nombre en toda la
tierra!

Salmo 9i

Al director musical. Sígase la tonada de «La muerte
del hijo». Salmo de David.

Álef 1Quiero alabarte, SEÑOR, con todo el
*corazón,
y contar todas tus maravillas.
2Quiero alegrarme y regocijarme en ti,
y cantar salmos a tu *nombre, oh
*Altísimo.

Bet 3Mis enemigos retroceden;
tropiezan y perecen ante ti.
4Porque tú me has hecho *justicia, me
has vindicado;
tú, juez justo, ocupas tu trono.

Guímel 5Reprendiste a los *paganos, destruiste
a los malvados;
¡para siempre borraste su
memoria!
6Desgracia sin fin cayó sobre el
enemigo;
arrancaste de raíz sus ciudades,
y hasta su recuerdo se ha
desvanecido.

He 7Pero el SEÑOR reina por siempre;
para emitir juicio ha establecido su
trono.
8Juzgará al mundo con justicia;
gobernará a los pueblos con
equidad.

Vav 9El SEÑOR es refugio de los oprimidos;
es su baluarte en momentos de
angustia.

10En ti confían los que conocen tu
nombre,
porque tú, SEÑOR, jamás
abandonas a los que te buscan.

Zayin 11Canten salmos al SEÑOR, el rey de
*Sión;
proclamen sus proezas entre las
naciones.
12El vengador de los inocentesj se
acuerda de ellos;
no pasa por alto el clamor de los
afligidos.

Jet 13Ten compasión de mí, SEÑOR;

mira cómo me afligen los que me
odian.
Sácame de las puertas de la muerte,
14para que en las *puertas de
Jerusalénk
proclame tus alabanzas y me
regocije en tu *salvación.

Tet 15Han caído los paganos
en la fosa que han cavado;
sus pies quedaron atrapados
en la red que ellos mismos
escondieron.

16Al SEÑOR se le conoce porque
imparte justicia;
el malvado cae en la trampa que él
mismo tendió.
*Higaión. *Selah

Yod 17Bajan al *sepulcro los malvados,
todos los paganos que de Dios se
olvidan.

Caf 18Pero no se olvidará para siempre al
necesitado,
ni para siempre se perderá la
esperanza del pobre.

19¡Levántate, SEÑOR!
No dejes que el *hombre
prevalezca;
¡haz que las naciones comparezcan
ante ti!
20Infúndeles terror, SEÑOR;
¡que los pueblos sepan que son
simples *mortales!
Selah

Salmo 10

Lámed 1¿Por qué, SEÑOR, te mantienes
distante?
¿Por qué te escondes en momentos
de angustia?
2Con arrogancia persigue el malvado al
indefenso,
pero se enredará en sus propias
artimañas.
3El malvado hace alarde de su propia
codicia;
alaba al ambicioso y menosprecia
al SEÑOR.
4El malvado levanta insolente la nariz,
y no da lugar a Dios en sus
pensamientos.
5Todas sus empresas son siempre
exitosas;
tan altos y alejados de él están tus
juicios
que se burla de todos sus
enemigos.
6Y se dice a sí mismo: «Nada me hará
caer.
Siempre seré feliz. Nunca tendré
problemas.»

Pe 7Llena está su boca de maldiciones,
de mentiras y amenazas;
bajo su lengua esconde maldad y
violencia.
8Se pone al acecho en las aldeas,

---

g 8:4 ser humano. Lit. hijo de hombre.　h 8:5 un dios. Alt. los ángeles o los seres celestiales.　i Sal 9 En el texto hebreo los salmos 9 y 10 son un solo poema (véase LXX), que forma un acróstico siguiendo el orden del alfabeto hebreo.
j 9:12 vengador de los inocentes. Lit. vengador de sangres.　k 9:14 Jerusalén. Lit. la hija de Sión.

se esconde en espera de sus
víctimas,
y asesina a mansalva al inocente.

Ayin 9Cual león en su guarida se agazapa,
listo para atrapar al indefenso;
le cae encima y lo arrastra en su
red.
10Bajo el peso de su poder,
sus víctimas caen por tierra.
11Se dice a sí mismo: «Dios se ha
olvidado.
Se cubre el rostro. Nunca ve nada.»

Qof 12¡Levántate, SEÑOR!
¡Levanta, oh Dios, tu brazo!
¡No te olvides de los indefensos!
13¿Por qué te ha de menospreciar el
malvado?
¿Por qué ha de pensar que no lo
llamarás a cuentas?

Resh 14Pero tú ves la opresión y la violencia,
las tomas en cuenta y te harás
cargo de ellas.
Las víctimas confían en ti;
tú eres la ayuda de los huérfanos.

Shin 15¡Rómpeles el brazo al malvado y al
impío!
¡Pídeles cuentas de su maldad,
y haz que desaparezcan por
completo!

16El SEÑOR es rey eterno;
los *paganos serán borrados de su
tierra.

Tav 17Tú, SEÑOR, escuchas la petición de
los indefensos,
les infundes aliento y atiendes a su
clamor.
18Tú defiendes al huérfano y al
oprimido,
para que el *hombre, hecho de
tierra,
no siga ya sembrando el terror.

Salmo 11

Al director musical. Salmo de David.
1En el SEÑOR hallo refugio.
¿Cómo, pues, se atreven a decirme:
«Huye al monte, como las aves»?
2Vean cómo tensan sus arcos los malvados:
preparan las flechas sobre la cuerda
para disparar desde las sombras
contra los rectos de *corazón.
3Cuando los fundamentos son destruidos,
¿qué le queda al justo?

4El SEÑOR está en su santo templo,
en los cielos tiene el SEÑOR su trono,
y atentamente observa al *ser humano;
con sus propios ojos lo examina.
5El SEÑOR examina a justos y a malvados,
y aborrece a los que aman la violencia.
6Hará llover sobre los malvados
ardientes brasas y candente azufre;
¡un viento abrasador será su suerte!

7Justo es el SEÑOR, y ama la *justicia;
por eso los íntegros contemplarán su
rostro.

Salmo 12

Al director musical. Sobre la octava.¹
Salmo de David.
1Sálvanos, SEÑOR, que ya no hay *gente fiel;
ya no queda gente sincera en este mundo.
2No hacen sino mentirse unos a otros;
sus labios lisonjeros hablan con doblez.

3El SEÑOR cortará todo labio lisonjero
y toda lengua jactanciosa
4que dice: «Venceremos con la lengua;
en nuestros labios confiamos.
¿Quién puede dominarnos a nosotros?»

5Dice el SEÑOR: «Voy ahora a levantarme,
y pondré a salvo a los oprimidos,
pues al pobre se le oprime,
y el necesitado se queja.»

6Las palabras del SEÑOR son puras,
son como la plata refinada,
siete veces purificada en el crisol.

7Tú, SEÑOR, nos protegerás;
tú siempre nos defenderás de esta gente,
8aun cuando los malvados sigan merodeando,
y la maldad sea exaltada en este mundo.

Salmo 13

Al director musical. Salmo de David.
1¿Hasta cuándo, SEÑOR, me seguirás
olvidando?
¿Hasta cuándo esconderás de mí tu rostro?
2¿Hasta cuándo he de estar angustiado
y he de sufrir cada día en mi *corazón?
¿Hasta cuándo el enemigo me seguirá
dominando?

3SEÑOR y Dios mío,
mírame y respóndeme;
ilumina mis ojos.
Así no caeré en el sueño de la muerte.
4así no dirá mi enemigo: «Lo he vencido»;
así mi adversario no se alegrará de mi caída.

5Pero yo confío en tu gran amor;
mi corazón se alegra en tu *salvación.
6Canto salmos al SEÑOR.
¡El SEÑOR ha sido bueno conmigo!

Salmo 14

14:1-7 — Sal 53:1-6
Al director musical. Salmo de David.
1Dice el *necio en su *corazón:
«No hay Dios.»
Están corrompidos, sus obras son detestables;
¡no hay uno solo que haga lo bueno!

2Desde el cielo el SEÑOR contempla a los
*mortales,
para ver si hay alguien
que sea sensato y busque a Dios.
3Pero todos se han descarriado,
a una se han corrompido.
No hay nadie que haga lo bueno;
¡no hay uno solo!

4¿Acaso no entienden todos los que hacen lo
malo,
los que devoran a mi pueblo como si fuera
pan?

¹ **12 Tít.** *Sobre la octava*. Lit. *Sobre* *sheminit.

¡Jamás invocan al SEÑOR!
5Allí los tienen, sobrecogidos de miedo,
  pero Dios está con los que son justos.

6Ustedes frustran los planes de los pobres,
  pero el SEÑOR los protege.

7¡Quiera Dios que de *Sión
  venga la *salvación de Israel!
Cuando el SEÑOR restaure a su pueblo,m
  ¡Jacob se regocijará, Israel se alegrará!

Salmo 15
Salmo de David.

1¿Quién, SEÑOR, puede habitar en tu
  santuario?
  ¿Quién puede vivir en tu santo monte?
2Sólo el de conducta intachable,
  que practica la *justicia
  y de *corazón dice la verdad;
3que no calumnia con la lengua,
  que no le hace mal a su prójimo
  ni le acarrea desgracias a su vecino;
4que desprecia al que Dios reprueba,
  pero honra al que teme al SEÑOR;
 que cumple lo prometido
  aunque salga perjudicado;
5que presta dinero sin ánimo de lucro,
  y no acepta sobornos que afecten al
  inocente.

El que así actúa no caerá jamás.

Salmo 16
*Mictam de David.

1Cuídame, oh Dios, porque en ti busco refugio.

2Yo le he dicho al SEÑOR: «Mi SEÑOR eres tú.
  Fuera de ti, no poseo bien alguno.»
3Poderosos son los sacerdotes *paganos del
  país,
  según todos sus seguidores.n
4Pero aumentarán los dolores
  de los que corren tras ellos.
 ¡Jamás derramaré sus sangrientas libaciones,
  ni con mis labios pronunciaré sus nombres!

5Tú, SEÑOR, eres mi porción y mi copa;
  eres tú quien ha afirmado mi suerte.
6Bellos lugares me han tocado en suerte;
  ¡preciosa herencia me ha correspondido!

7Bendeciré al SEÑOR, que me aconseja;
  aun de noche me reprende mi conciencia.
8Siempre tengo presente al SEÑOR;
  con él a mi derecha, nada me hará caer.

9Por eso mi *corazón se alegra,
  y se regocijan mis entrañas;ñ
  todo mi ser se llena de confianza.
10No dejarás que mi vida termine en el
  *sepulcro;
  no permitirás que sufra corrupción tu
  siervo fiel.
11Me has dado a conocer la senda de la vida;
  me llenarás de alegría en tu presencia,
  y de dicha eterna a tu derecha.

Salmo 17
Oración de David.

1SEÑOR, oye mi justo ruego;
  escucha mi clamor;
 presta oído a mi oración,
  pues no sale de labios engañosos.
2Sé tú mi defensor,
  pues tus ojos ven lo que es justo.

3Tú escudriñas mi *corazón,
  tú me examinas por las noches;
 ¡ponme, pues, a prueba,
  que no hallarás en mí maldad alguna!

¡No pasarán por mis labios
4palabras como las de otra *gente,
  pues yo cumplo con tu palabra!
Del *camino de la violencia
5he apartado mis pasos;
  mis pies están firmes en tus sendas.

6A ti clamo, oh Dios, porque tú me respondes;
  inclina a mí tu oído, y escucha mi oración.
7Tú, que salvas con tu diestra
  a los que buscan escapar de sus
  adversarios,
  dame una muestra de tu gran amor.
8Cuídame como a la niña de tus ojos;
  escóndeme, bajo la sombra de tus alas,
9de los malvados que me atacan,
  de los enemigos que me han cercado.
10Han cerrado su insensible corazón,
  y profieren insolencias con su boca.
11Vigilan de cerca mis pasos,
  prestos a derribarme.
12Parecen leones ávidos de presa,
  leones que yacen al acecho.

13¡Vamos, SEÑOR, enfréntate a ellos!
  ¡Derrótalos!
  ¡Con tu espada rescátame de los malvados!
14¡Con tu mano, SEÑOR, sálvame de estos
  *mortales
  que no tienen más herencia que esta vida!

Con tus tesoros les has llenado el vientre,
  sus hijos han tenido abundancia,
  y hasta ha sobrado para sus descendientes.
15Pero yo en *justicia contemplaré tu rostro;
  me bastará con verte cuando despierte.

Salmo 18
18 tít.-50 — 2S 22:1-51

Al director musical. De David, siervo del SEÑOR.
David dedicó al SEÑOR la letra de esta canción
cuando el SEÑOR lo libró de Saúl y de todos sus
enemigos. Dijo así:

1¡Cuánto te amo, SEÑOR, fuerza mía!

2El SEÑOR es mi *roca, mi amparo, mi
  libertador;
  es mi Dios, el peñasco en que me refugio.
Es mi escudo, el poder que me salva,o
  ¡mi más alto escondite!
3Invoco al SEÑOR, que es digno de alabanza,
  y quedo a salvo de mis enemigos.

4Los lazos de la muerte me envolvieron;
  los torrentes destructores me abrumaron.

---

m **14:7** restaure a su pueblo. Alt. haga que su pueblo vuelva del cautiverio.   n **16:3** Poderosos ... sus seguidores. Alt. En cuanto a los santos que están en la tierra, son los gloriosos en quienes está toda mi delicia.   ñ **16:9** mis entrañas. Lit. mi gloria.   o **18:2** el poder que me salva. Lit. el cuerno de mi salvación.

5Me enredaron los lazos del *sepulcro,
y me encontré ante las trampas de la muerte.
6En mi angustia invoqué al SEÑOR;
clamé a mi Dios,
y él me escuchó desde su templo;
¡mi clamor llegó a sus oídos!

7La tierra tembló, se estremeció;
se sacudieron los cimientos de los montes;
¡retemblaron a causa de su enojo!
8Por la nariz echaba humo,
por la boca, fuego consumidor;
¡lanzaba carbones encendidos!

9Rasgando el cielo, descendió,
pisando sobre oscuros nubarrones.
10Montando sobre un *querubín, surcó los cielos
y se remontó sobre las alas del viento.
11Hizo de las tinieblas su escondite,
de los oscuros y cargados nubarrones
un pabellón que lo rodeaba.
12De su radiante presencia brotaron nubes,
granizos y carbones encendidos.

13En el cielo, entre granizos y carbones encendidos,
se oyó el trueno del SEÑOR,
resonó la voz del *Altísimo.
14Lanzó sus flechas, sus grandes centellas;
dispersó a mis enemigos y los puso en fuga.
15A causa de tu reprensión, oh SEÑOR,
y por el resoplido de tu enojo,[p]
las cuencas del mar quedaron a la vista;
¡al descubierto quedaron los cimientos de la tierra!
16Extendiendo su mano desde lo alto,
tomó la mía y me sacó del mar profundo.
17Me libró de mi enemigo poderoso,
de aquellos que me odiaban
y eran más fuertes que yo.
18En el día de mi desgracia me salieron al encuentro,
pero mi apoyo fue el SEÑOR.
19Me sacó a un amplio espacio;
me libró porque se agradó de mí.

20El SEÑOR me ha pagado conforme a mi *justicia;
me ha premiado conforme a la limpieza de mis manos,
21pues he andado en los *caminos del SEÑOR;
no he cometido mal alguno
ni me he apartado de mi Dios.
22Presentes tengo todas sus sentencias;
no me he alejado de sus decretos.
23He sido íntegro con él
y me he abstenido de pecar.
24El SEÑOR me ha recompensado conforme a mi justicia,
conforme a la limpieza de mis manos.

25Tú eres fiel con quien es fiel,
e irreprochable con quien es irreprochable;
26sincero eres con quien es sincero,
pero sagaz con el que es tramposo.
27Tú das la *victoria a los humildes,
pero humillas a los altaneros.
28Tú, SEÑOR, mantienes mi lámpara encendida;
tú, Dios mío, iluminas mis tinieblas.
29Con tu apoyo me lanzaré contra un ejército;
contigo, Dios mío, podré asaltar murallas.

30El camino de Dios es perfecto;
la palabra del SEÑOR es intachable.
Escudo es Dios a los que en él se refugian.
31¿Quién es Dios, si no el SEÑOR?
¿Quién es la roca, si no nuestro Dios?
32Es él quien me arma de valor
y endereza mi camino;
33da a mis pies la ligereza del venado,
y me mantiene firme en las alturas;
34adiestra mis manos para la batalla,
y mis brazos para tensar arcos de bronce.
35Tú me cubres con el escudo de tu *salvación,
y con tu diestra me sostienes;
tu bondad me ha hecho prosperar.
36Me has despejado el camino,
así que mis tobillos no flaquean.

37Perseguí a mis enemigos, les di alcance,
y no retrocedí hasta verlos aniquilados.
38Los aplasté. Ya no pudieron levantarse.
¡Cayeron debajo de mis pies!
39Tú me armaste de valor para el combate;
bajo mi planta sometiste a los rebeldes.
40Hiciste retroceder a mis enemigos,
y así exterminé a los que me odiaban.
41Pedían ayuda; no hubo quien los salvara.
Al SEÑOR clamaron,[q] pero no les respondió.
42Los desmenucé. Parecían polvo disperso por el viento.
¡Los pisoteé[r] como al lodo de las calles!

43Me has librado de una turba amotinada;
me has puesto por encima de los *paganos;
me sirve *gente que yo no conocía.
44Apenas me oyen, me obedecen;
son extranjeros, y me rinden homenaje.
45¡Esos extraños se descorazonan,
y temblando salen de sus refugios!
46¡El SEÑOR vive! ¡Alabada sea mi roca!
¡Exaltado sea Dios mi Salvador!
47Él es el Dios que me vindica,
el que pone los pueblos a mis pies.

48Tú me libras del furor de mis enemigos,
me exaltas por encima de mis adversarios,
me salvas de los hombres violentos.
49Por eso, SEÑOR, te alabo entre las naciones
y canto salmos a tu *nombre.

50El SEÑOR da grandes victorias a su rey;
a su *ungido David y a sus descendientes
les muestra por siempre su gran amor.

Salmo 19

Al director musical. Salmo de David.

1Los cielos cuentan la gloria de Dios,
el firmamento proclama la obra de sus manos.
2Un día comparte al otro la noticia,
una noche a la otra se lo hace saber.
3Sin palabras, sin lenguaje,
sin una voz perceptible,
4por toda la tierra resuena su eco,

p **18:15** *por ... tu enojo.* Lit. *por el soplo del aliento de tu nariz.* q **18:41** *Al SEÑOR clamaron* (versiones antiguas); TM no incluye *clamaron.* r **18:42** *Los pisoteé* (LXX, Siríaca, Targum, mss. y 2S 22:43); *Los vacié* (TM).

¡sus palabras llegan hasta los confines del
    mundo!

Dios ha plantado en los cielos
    un pabellón para el sol.
5Y éste, como novio que sale de la cámara
    nupcial,
    se apresta, cual atleta, a recorrer el camino.
6Sale de un extremo de los cielos
    y, en su recorrido, llega al otro extremo,
    sin que nada se libre de su calor.

7La *ley del SEÑOR es perfecta:
    infunde nuevo *aliento.
El mandato del SEÑOR es digno de confianza:
    da sabiduría al *sencillo.
8Los preceptos del SEÑOR son rectos:
    traen alegría al *corazón.
El mandamiento del SEÑOR es claro:
    da luz a los ojos.
9El temor del SEÑOR es puro:
    permanece para siempre.
Las sentencias del SEÑOR son verdaderas:
    todas ellas son justas.
10Son más deseables que el oro,
    más que mucho oro refinado;
son más dulces que la miel,
    la miel que destila del panal.
11Por ellas queda advertido tu siervo;
    quien las obedece recibe una gran
    recompensa.
12¿Quién está consciente de sus propios
    errores?
    ¡Perdóname aquellos de los que no estoy
    consciente!
13Libra, además, a tu siervo de pecar a
    sabiendas;
    no permitas que tales pecados me
    dominen.
Así estaré libre de culpa
    y de multiplicar mis pecados.

14Sean, pues, aceptables ante ti
    mis palabras y mis pensamientos,
    oh SEÑOR, *roca mía y redentor mío.

Salmo 20

Al director musical. Salmo de David.
1Que el SEÑOR te responda cuando estés
    angustiado;
    que el *nombre del Dios de Jacob te
    proteja.
2Que te envíe ayuda desde el santuario;
    que desde *Sión te dé su apoyo.
3Que se acuerde de todas tus ofrendas;
    que acepte tus *holocaustos.
                      *Selah

4Que te conceda lo que tu *corazón desea;
    que haga que se cumplan todos tus planes.
5Nosotros celebraremos tu *victoria,
    y en el nombre de nuestro Dios
    desplegaremos las banderas.
¡Que el SEÑOR cumpla todas tus peticiones!

6Ahora sé que el SEÑOR salvará a su *ungido,
    que le responderá desde su santo cielo
    y con su poder le dará grandes victorias.
7Éstos confían en sus carros de guerra,
    aquéllos confían en sus corceles,
pero nosotros confiamos en el nombre
    del SEÑOR nuestro Dios.
8Ellos son vencidos y caen,

pero nosotros nos erguimos y de pie
    permanecemos.

9¡Concede, SEÑOR, la victoria al rey!
    ¡Respóndenos cuando te llamemos!

Salmo 21

Al director musical. Salmo de David.
1En tu fuerza, SEÑOR,
    se regocija el rey;
    ¡cuánto se alegra en tus *victorias!
2Le has concedido lo que su *corazón desea;
    no le has negado lo que sus labios piden.
                      *Selah

3Has salido a su encuentro con ricas
    bendiciones;
    lo has coronado con diadema de oro fino.
4Te pidió vida, se la concediste:
    una vida larga y duradera.
5Por tus victorias se acrecentó su gloria;
    lo revestiste de honor y majestad.
6Has hecho de él manantial de bendiciones;
    tu presencia lo ha llenado de alegría.

7El rey confía en el SEÑOR,
    en el gran amor del *Altísimo;
    por eso jamás caerá.

8Tu mano alcanzará a todos tus enemigos;
    tu diestra alcanzará a los que te aborrecen.
9Cuando tú, SEÑOR, te manifiestes,
    los convertirás en un horno encendido.

En su ira los devorará el SEÑOR;
    ¡un fuego los consumirá!
10Borrarás de la tierra a su simiente;
    de entre los *mortales, a su posteridad.
11Aunque tramen hacerte daño
    y maquinen perversidades,
    ¡no se saldrán con la suya!
12Porque tú los harás retroceder
    cuando tenses tu arco contra ellos.

13Enaltécete, SEÑOR, con tu poder,
    y con salmos celebraremos tus proezas.

Salmo 22

Al director musical. Sígase la tonada de «La cierva
de la aurora». Salmo de David.
1Dios mío, Dios mío,
    ¿por qué me has abandonado?
Lejos estás para salvarme,
    lejos de mis palabras de lamento.
2Dios mío, clamo de día y no me respondes;
    clamo de noche y no hallo reposo.

3Pero tú eres santo, tú eres rey,
    ¡tú eres la alabanza de Israel!
4En ti confiaron nuestros padres;
    confiaron, y tú los libraste;
5a ti clamaron, y tú los salvaste;
    se apoyaron en ti, y no los defraudaste.

6Pero yo, gusano soy y no *hombre;
    la *gente se burla de mí,
    el pueblo me desprecia.
7Cuantos me ven, se ríen de mí;
    lanzan insultos, meneando la cabeza:
8«Éste confía en el SEÑOR,
    ¡pues que el SEÑOR lo ponga a salvo!
Ya que en él se deleita,
    ¡que sea él quien lo libre!»

9Pero tú me sacaste del vientre materno;
    me hiciste reposar confiado

en el regazo de mi madre.
10Fui puesto a tu cuidado
    desde antes de nacer;
desde el vientre de mi madre
    mi Dios eres tú.
11No te alejes de mí,
    porque la angustia está cerca
    y no hay nadie que me ayude.

12Muchos toros me rodean;
    fuertes toros de Basán me cercan.
13Contra mí abren sus fauces
    leones que rugen y desgarran a su presa.
14Como agua he sido derramado;
    dislocados están todos mis huesos.
Mi *corazón se ha vuelto como cera,
    y se derrite en mis entrañas.
15Se ha secado mi vigor como una teja;
    la lengua se me pega al paladar.
    ¡Me has hundido en el polvo de la muerte!
16Como perros de presa, me han rodeado;
    me ha cercado una banda de malvados;
    me han traspasados las manos y los pies.
17Puedo contar todos mis huesos;
    con satisfacción perversa
    la gente se detiene a mirarme.
18Se reparten entre ellos mis vestidos
    y sobre mi ropa echan suertes.

19Pero tú, SEÑOR, no te alejes;
    fuerza mía, ven pronto en mi auxilio.
20Libra mi vida de la espada,
    mi preciosa vida del poder de esos perros.
21Rescátame de la boca de los leones;
    sálvame det los cuernos de los toros.

22Proclamaré tu *nombre a mis hermanos;
    en medio de la congregación te alabaré.
23¡Alaben al SEÑOR los que le temen!
    ¡Hónrenlo, descendientes de Jacob!
    ¡Venérenlo, descendientes de Israel!
24Porque él no desprecia ni tiene en poco
    el sufrimiento del pobre;
no esconde de él su rostro,
    sino que lo escucha cuando a él clama.

25Tú inspiras mi alabanza en la gran asamblea;
    ante los que te temen cumpliré mis
      promesas.
26Comerán los pobres y se saciarán;
    alabarán al SEÑOR quienes lo buscan;
    ¡que su corazón viva para siempre!
27Se acordarán del SEÑOR y se volverán a él
    todos los confines de la tierra;
    ante él se postrarán
    todas las familias de las naciones,
28porque del SEÑOR es el reino;
    él gobierna sobre las naciones.

29Festejarán y adorarán todos los ricos de la
      tierra;
    ante él se postrarán todos los que bajan al
      polvo,
    los que no pueden conservar su vida.
30La posteridad le servirá;
    del Señor se hablará a las generaciones
      futuras.
31A un pueblo que aún no ha nacido
    se le dirá que Dios hizo *justicia.

Salmo 23
Salmo de David.

1El SEÑOR es mi *pastor, nada me falta;
    2en verdes pastos me hace descansar.
Junto a tranquilas aguas me conduce;
    3me infunde nuevas *fuerzas.
Me guía por sendas de *justicia
    por amor a su *nombre.

4Aun si voy por valles tenebrosos,
    no temo peligro alguno
    porque tú estás a mi lado;
tu vara de pastor me reconforta.

5Dispones ante mí un banquete
    en presencia de mis enemigos.
Has ungido con perfume mi cabeza;
    has llenado mi copa a rebosar.

6La bondad y el amor me seguirán
    todos los días de mi vida;
y en la casa del SEÑOR
    habitaré para siempre.

Salmo 24
Salmo de David.

1Del SEÑOR es la tierra y todo cuanto hay en
      ella,
    el mundo y cuantos lo habitan;
2porque él la afirmó sobre los mares,
    la estableció sobre los ríos.

3¿Quién puede subir al monte del SEÑOR?
    ¿Quién puede estar en su lugar santo?
4Sólo el de manos limpias y *corazón puro,
    el que no adora ídolos vanos
    ni jura por dioses falsos.u

5Quien es así recibe bendiciones del SEÑOR;
    Dios su Salvador le hará *justicia.
6Tal es la generación de los que a ti acuden,
    de los que buscan tu rostro, oh Dios de
      Jacob.v
                          *Selah

7Eleven, *puertas, sus dinteles;
    levántense, puertas antiguas,
    que va a entrar el Rey de la gloria.

8¿Quién es este Rey de la gloria?
    El SEÑOR, el fuerte y valiente,
    el SEÑOR, el valiente guerrero.

9Eleven, puertas, sus dinteles;
    levántense, puertas antiguas,
    que va a entrar el Rey de la gloria.

10¿Quién es este Rey de la gloria?
    Es el SEÑOR *Todopoderoso;
    ¡él es el Rey de la gloria!
                          Selah

Salmo 25w
Salmo de David.

Álef   1A ti, SEÑOR, elevo mi *alma;
Bet   2mi Dios, en ti confío;
    no permitas que sea yo humillado,
    no dejes que mis enemigos se
      burlen de mí.
Guímel   3Quien en ti pone su esperanza

---

s **22:16** *me han traspasado* (LXX, Siríaca y algunos mss. hebreos); *como el león* (TM).   t **22:21** *sálvame de* (lectura probable); *me respondiste desde* (TM).   u **24:4** *por dioses falsos.* Alt. *con falsedad.*   v **24:6** *Dios de Jacob* (LXX, Siríaca, Targum y dos mss. hebreos); TM no incluye *Dios de.*   w **Sal 25** Este salmo es un poema acróstico, que sigue el orden del alfabeto hebreo.

jamás será avergonzado;
pero quedarán en vergüenza
los que traicionan sin razón.

Dálet ⁴SEÑOR, hazme conocer tus *caminos;
muéstrame tus sendas.

He ⁵Encamíname en tu verdad,
¡enséñame!
Tú eres mi Dios y Salvador;

Vav ¡en ti pongo mi esperanza todo el
día!

Zayin ⁶Acuérdate, SEÑOR, de tu ternura y
gran amor,
que siempre me has mostrado;

Jet ⁷olvida los pecados y transgresiones
que cometí en mi juventud.
Acuérdate de mí según tu gran amor,
porque tú, SEÑOR, eres bueno.

Tet ⁸Bueno y justo es el SEÑOR;
por eso les muestra a los pecadores
el camino.

Yod ⁹Él dirige en la *justicia a los humildes,
y les enseña su camino.

Caf ¹⁰Todas las sendas del SEÑOR son amor
y verdad
para quienes cumplen los
preceptos de su *pacto.

Lámed ¹¹Por amor a tu *nombre, SEÑOR,
perdona mi gran iniquidad.

Mem ¹²¿Quién es el *hombre que teme al
SEÑOR?
Será instruido en el mejor de los
caminos.

Nun ¹³Tendrá una vida placentera,
y sus descendientes heredarán la
tierra.

Sámej ¹⁴El SEÑOR brinda su amistad a
quienes le honran,
y les da a conocer su pacto.

Ayin ¹⁵Mis ojos están puestos siempre en el
SEÑOR,
pues sólo él puede sacarme de la
trampa.

Pe ¹⁶Vuelve a mí tu rostro y tenme
compasión,
pues me encuentro solo y afligido.

Tsade ¹⁷Crecen las angustias de mi *corazón;
líbrame de mis tribulaciones.
¹⁸Fíjate en mi aflicción y en mis
penurias,
y borra todos mis pecados.

Resh ¹⁹¡Mira cómo se han multiplicado mis
enemigos,
y cuán violento es el odio que me
tienen!

Shin ²⁰Protege mi vida, rescátame;
no permitas que sea avergonzado,
porque en ti busco refugio.

Tav ²¹Sean mi protección la integridad y la
rectitud,
porque en ti he puesto mi
esperanza.

²²¡Libra, oh Dios, a Israel
de todas sus angustias!

Salmo 26
Salmo de David.

¹Hazme *justicia, SEÑOR,

pues he llevado una vida intachable;
¡en el SEÑOR confío sin titubear!
²Examíname, SEÑOR; ¡ponme a prueba!
purifica mis entrañas y mi *corazón.

³Tu gran amor lo tengo presente,
y siempre ando en tu verdad.
⁴Yo no convivo con los mentirosos,
ni me junto con los hipócritas;
⁵aborrezco la compañía de los malvados;
no cultivo la amistad de los perversos.

⁶Con manos limpias e inocentes
camino, SEÑOR, en torno a tu altar,
⁷proclamando en voz alta tu alabanza
y contando todas tus maravillas.
⁸SEÑOR, yo amo la casa donde vives,
el lugar donde reside tu gloria.

⁹En la muerte, no me incluyas
entre pecadores y asesinos,
¹⁰entre *gente que tiene las manos
llenas de artimañas y sobornos.
¹¹Yo, en cambio, llevo una vida intachable;
líbrame y compadécete de mí.

¹²Tengo los pies en terreno firme,
y en la gran asamblea bendeciré al SEÑOR.

Salmo 27
Salmo de David.

¹El SEÑOR es mi luz y mi *salvación;
¿a quién temeré?
El SEÑOR es el baluarte de mi vida;
¿quién podrá amedrentarme?
²Cuando los malvados avanzan contra mí
para devorar mis carnes,
cuando mis enemigos y adversarios me
atacan,
son ellos los que tropiezan y caen.
³Aun cuando un ejército me asedie,
no temerá mi *corazón;
aun cuando una guerra estalle contra mí,
yo mantendré la confianza.

⁴Una sola cosa le pido al SEÑOR,
y es lo único que persigo:
habitar en la casa del SEÑOR
todos los días de mi vida,
para contemplar la hermosura del SEÑOR
y recrearme en su templo.
⁵Porque en el día de la aflicción
él me resguardará en su morada;
al amparo de su tabernáculo me protegerá,
y me pondrá en alto, sobre una roca.
⁶Me hará prevalecer
frente a los enemigos que me rodean;
en su templo ofreceré sacrificios de alabanza
y cantaré salmos al SEÑOR.

⁷Oye, SEÑOR, mi voz cuando a ti clamo;
compadécete de mí y respóndeme.
⁸El corazón me dice: «¡Busca su rostro!»ˣ
Y yo, SEÑOR, tu rostro busco.
⁹No te escondas de mí;
no rechaces, en tu enojo, a este siervo tuyo,
porque tú has sido mi ayuda.
No me desampares ni me abandones,
Dios de mi salvación.

¹⁰Aunque mi padre y mi madre me abandonen,
el SEÑOR me recibirá en sus brazos.

ˣ **27:8** *El corazón ... su rostro!»* (lectura probable); *A ti dice mi corazón: «Busquen mi rostro»* (TM).

11Guíame, SEÑOR, por tu *camino;
　dirígeme por la senda de rectitud,
　por causa de los que me acechan.
12No me entregues al capricho de mis
　　adversarios,
　pues contra mí se levantan falsos testigos
　que respiran violencia.

13Pero de una cosa estoy seguro:
　he de ver la bondad del SEÑOR
　en esta tierra de los vivientes.
14Pon tu esperanza en el SEÑOR;
　ten valor, cobra ánimo;
　¡pon tu esperanza en el SEÑOR!

Salmo 28
Salmo de David.

1A ti clamo, SEÑOR, *roca mía;
　no te desentiendas de mí,
　porque si guardas silencio,
　ya puedo contarme entre los muertos.
2Oye mi voz suplicante
　cuando a ti acudo en busca de ayuda,
　cuando tiendo los brazos hacia tu lugar
　　santísimo.
3No me arrastres con los malvados,
　con los que hacen iniquidad,
　con los que hablan de *paz con su prójimo
　pero en su *corazón albergan maldad.
4Págales conforme a sus obras,
　conforme a sus malas acciones.
　Págales conforme a las obras de sus manos;
　¡dales su merecido!
5Ya que no toman en cuenta las obras del SEÑOR
　y lo que él ha hecho con sus manos,
　él los derribará
　y nunca más volverá a levantarlos.

6Bendito sea el SEÑOR,
　que ha oído mi voz suplicante.
7El SEÑOR es mi fuerza y mi escudo;
　mi corazón en él confía;
　de él recibo ayuda.
　Mi corazón salta de alegría,
　y con cánticos le daré gracias.

8El SEÑOR es la fortaleza de su pueblo,
　y un baluarte de *salvación para su
　　*ungido.
9Salva a tu pueblo, bendice a tu heredad,
　y cual *pastor guíalos por siempre.

Salmo 29
Salmo de David.

1Tributen al SEÑOR, seres celestiales,y
　tributen al SEÑOR la gloria y el poder.
2Tributen al SEÑOR la gloria que merece su
　　*nombre;
　póstrense ante el SEÑOR en su santuario
　majestuoso.

3La voz del SEÑOR está sobre las aguas;
　resuena el trueno del Dios de la gloria;
　el SEÑOR está sobre las aguas impetuosas.
4La voz del SEÑOR resuena potente;
　la voz del SEÑOR resuena majestuosa.
5La voz del SEÑOR desgaja los cedros,
　desgaja el SEÑOR los cedros del Líbano;
6hace que el Líbano salte como becerro,
　y que el Hermónz salte cual toro salvaje.

7La voz del SEÑOR lanza ráfagas de fuego;
8la voz del SEÑOR sacude al desierto;
　el SEÑOR sacude al desierto de Cades.
9La voz del SEÑOR retuerce los roblesa
　y deja desnudos los bosques;
　en su templo todos gritan: «¡Gloria!»

10El SEÑOR tiene su trono sobre las lluvias;
　el SEÑOR reina por siempre.
11El SEÑOR fortalece a su pueblo;
　el SEÑOR bendice a su pueblo con la *paz.

Salmo 30
Cántico para la dedicación de la casa.b
Salmo de David.

1Te exaltaré, SEÑOR, porque me levantaste,
　porque no dejaste que mis enemigos se
　　burlaran de mí.
2SEÑOR mi Dios, te pedí ayuda
　y me sanaste.
3Tú, SEÑOR, me sacaste del *sepulcro;
　me hiciste revivir de entre los muertos.

4Canten al SEÑOR, ustedes sus fieles;
　alaben su santo *nombre.
5Porque sólo un instante dura su enojo,
　pero toda una vida su bondad.
　Si por la noche hay llanto,
　por la mañana habrá gritos de alegría.

6Cuando me sentí seguro, exclamé:
　«Jamás seré conmovido.»
7Tú, SEÑOR, en tu buena voluntad,
　me afirmaste en elevado baluarte;
　pero escondiste tu rostro,
　y yo quedé confundido.

8A ti clamo, SEÑOR soberano;
　a ti me vuelvo suplicante.
9¿Qué ganas tú con que yo muera,c
　con que descienda yo al sepulcro?
　¿Acaso el polvo te alabará
　o proclamará tu verdad?
10Oye, SEÑOR; compadécete de mí.
　¡Sé tú, SEÑOR, mi ayuda!

11Convertiste mi lamento en danza;
　me quitaste la ropa de luto
　y me vestiste de fiesta,
12para que te cante y te glorifique,
　y no me quede callado.

¡SEÑOR mi Dios, siempre te daré gracias!

Salmo 31
31:1-4 — Sal 71:1-3
Al director musical. Salmo de David.

1En ti, SEÑOR, busco refugio;
　jamás permitas que me avergüencen;
　en tu *justicia, líbrame.
2Inclina a mí tu oído,
　y acude pronto a socorrerme.
　Sé tú mi *roca protectora,
　la fortaleza de mi *salvación.
3Guíame, pues eres mi roca y mi fortaleza,
　dirígeme por amor a tu *nombre.
4Líbrame de la trampa que me han tendido,
　porque tú eres mi refugio.
5En tus manos encomiendo mi espíritu;
　líbrame, SEÑOR, Dios de la verdad.

---

y **29:1** *seres celestiales.* Lit. *hijos de los dioses.*　z **29:6** *Hermón* (lectura probable); *Sirión* (TM).　a **29:9** *retuerce los robles.* Alt. *hace parir a la cierva.*　b **30** Tít. *casa.* Alt. *palacio,* o *templo.*　c **30:9** *con que yo muera.* Lit. *con mi sangre.*

⁶Odio a los que veneran ídolos vanos;
   yo, por mi parte, confío en ti, SEÑOR.
⁷Me alegro y me regocijo en tu amor,
   porque tú has visto mi aflicción
   y conoces las angustias de mí *alma.
⁸No me entregaste al enemigo,
   sino que me pusiste en lugar espacioso.

⁹Tenme compasión, SEÑOR, que estoy
     angustiado;
   el dolor está acabando con mis ojos,
   con mi alma, icon mi cuerpo!
¹⁰La vida se me va en angustias,
   y los años en lamentos;
  la tristeza está acabando con mis fuerzas,
   y mis huesos se van debilitando.
¹¹Por causa de todos mis enemigos,
   soy el hazmerreír de mis vecinos;
  soy un espanto para mis amigos;
   de mí huyen los que me encuentran en la
     calle.
¹²Me han olvidado, como si hubiera muerto;
   soy como una vasija hecha pedazos.
¹³Son muchos a los que oigo cuchichear:
   «Hay terror por todas partes.»
  Se han confabulado contra mí,
   y traman quitarme la vida.

¹⁴Pero yo, SEÑOR, en ti confío,
   y digo: «Tú eres mi Dios.»
¹⁵Mi vida entera está en tus manos;
   líbrame de mis enemigos y perseguidores.
¹⁶Que irradie tu faz sobre tu siervo;
   por tu gran amor, sálvame.

¹⁷SEÑOR, no permitas que me avergüencen,
   porque a ti he clamado.
  Que sean avergonzados los malvados,
   y acallados en el *sepulcro.
¹⁸Que sean silenciados sus labios mentirosos,
   porque hablan contra los justos
   con orgullo, desdén e insolencia.

¹⁹Cuán grande es tu bondad,
   que atesoras para los que te temen,
  y que a la vista de la *gente derramas
   sobre los que en ti se refugian.
²⁰Al amparo de tu presencia los proteges
   de las intrigas *humanas;
  en tu morada los resguardas
   de las lenguas contenciosas.

²¹Bendito sea el SEÑOR,
   pues mostró su gran amor por mí
   cuando me hallaba en una ciudad sitiada.
²²En mi confusión llegué a decir:
   «¡He sido arrojado de tu presencia!»
  Pero tú oíste mi voz suplicante
   cuando te pedí que me ayudaras.

²³Amen al SEÑOR, todos sus fieles;
   él protege a los dignos de confianza,
  pero a los orgullosos les da su merecido.
²⁴Cobren ánimo y ármense de valor,
   todos los que en el SEÑOR esperan.

Salmo 32

Salmo de David. *Masquil.

¹*Dichoso aquel
   a quien se le perdonan sus transgresiones,
   a quien se le borran sus pecados.

²Dichoso aquel
   a quien el SEÑOR no toma en cuenta su
     maldad
   y en cuyo espíritu no hay engaño.
³Mientras guardé silencio,
   mis huesos se fueron consumiendo
   por mi gemir de todo el día.
⁴Mi fuerza se fue debilitando
   como al calor del verano,
  porque día y noche
   tu mano pesaba sobre mí.
                 *Selah

⁵Pero te confesé mi pecado,
   y no te oculté mi maldad.
  Me dije: «Voy a confesar mis transgresiones al
     SEÑOR»,
   y tú perdonaste mi maldad y mi pecado.
                 Selah

⁶Por eso los fieles te invocan
   en momentos de angustia;ᵈ
  caudalosas aguas podrán desbordarse,
   pero a ellos no los alcanzarán.
⁷Tú eres mi refugio;
   tú me protegerás del peligro
   y me rodearás con cánticos de liberación.
                 Selah

⁸El SEÑOR dice:
  «Yo te instruiré,
   yo te mostraré el *camino que debes
     seguir;
   yo te daré consejos y velaré por ti.
⁹No seas como el mulo o el caballo,
   que no tienen discernimiento,
  y cuyo brío hay que domar con brida y freno,
   para acercarlos a ti.»
¹⁰Muchas son las calamidades de los malvados,
   pero el gran amor del SEÑOR
   envuelve a los que en él confían.

¹¹¡Alégrense, ustedes los justos;
   regocíjense en el SEÑOR!
  icanten todos ustedes,
   los rectos de *corazón!

Salmo 33

¹Canten al SEÑOR con alegría, ustedes los
     justos;
   es propio de los íntegros alabar al SEÑOR.
²Alaben al SEÑOR al son del arpa;
   entonen alabanzas con el decacordio.
³Cántenle una canción nueva;
   toquen con destreza,
   y den voces de alegría.

⁴La palabra del SEÑOR es justa;
   fieles son todas sus obras.
⁵El SEÑOR ama la *justicia y el derecho;
   llena está la tierra de su amor.

⁶Por la palabra del SEÑOR fueron creados los
     cielos,
   y por el soplo de su boca, las estrellas.
⁷Él recoge en un cántaro el agua de los mares,
   y junta en vasijas los océanos.
⁸Tema toda la tierra al SEÑOR;
   hónrenlo todos los pueblos del mundo.
⁹porque él habló, y todo fue creado;
   dio una orden, y todo quedó firme.

ᵈ **32:6** *de angustia* (LXX y Siríaca); *de encontrar solamente* (TM).

¹⁰El SEÑOR frustra los planes de las naciones;
  desbarata los designios de los pueblos.
¹¹Pero los planes del SEÑOR quedan firmes para
    siempre;
  los designios de su *mente son eternos.
¹²Dichosa la nación cuyo Dios es el SEÑOR,
  el pueblo que escogió por su heredad.
¹³El SEÑOR observa desde el cielo
  y ve a toda la *humanidad;
¹⁴él contempla desde su trono
  a todos los habitantes de la tierra.
¹⁵Él es quien formó el *corazón de todos,
  y quien conoce a fondo todas sus acciones.
¹⁶No se salva el rey por sus muchos soldados,
  ni por su mucha fuerza se libra el valiente.
¹⁷Vana esperanza de *victoria es el caballo;
  a pesar de su mucha fuerza no puede salvar.
¹⁸Pero el SEÑOR cuida de los que le temen,
  de los que esperan en su gran amor;
¹⁹él los libra de la muerte,
  y en épocas de hambre los mantiene con
    vida.

²⁰Esperamos confiados en el SEÑOR;
  él es nuestro socorro y nuestro escudo.
²¹En él se regocija nuestro corazón,
  porque confiamos en su santo *nombre.
²²Que tu gran amor, SEÑOR, nos acompañe,
  tal como lo esperamos de ti.

Salmo 34 [e]

Salmo de David, cuando fingió estar demente ante
Abimélec, por lo cual éste lo arrojó de su presencia.

Álef   ¹Bendeciré al SEÑOR en todo tiempo;
              mis labios siempre lo alabarán.
Bet   ²Mi *alma se gloría en el SEÑOR;
              lo oirán los humildes y se
                alegrarán.
Guímel   ³Engrandezcan al SEÑOR conmigo;
              exaltemos a una su *nombre.
Dálet   ⁴Busqué al SEÑOR, y él me respondió;
              me libró de todos mis temores.
He   ⁵Radiantes están los que a él acuden;
              jamás su rostro se cubre de
                vergüenza.
Zayin   ⁶Este pobre clamó, y el SEÑOR le oyó
              y lo libró de todas sus angustias.
Jet   ⁷El ángel del SEÑOR acampa en torno a
                los que le temen;
              a su lado está para librarlos.
Tet   ⁸Prueben y vean que el SEÑOR es
                bueno;
              *dichosos los que en él se refugian.
Yod   ⁹Teman al SEÑOR, ustedes sus santos,
              pues nada les falta a los que le
                temen.
Caf   ¹⁰Los leoncillos se debilitan y tienen
                hambre,
              pero a los que buscan al SEÑOR
                nada les falta.
Lámed   ¹¹Vengan, hijos míos, y escúchenme,
              que voy a enseñarles el temor del
                SEÑOR.
Mem   ¹²El que quiera amar la vida
              y gozar de días felices,
Nun   ¹³que refrene su lengua de hablar el mal

Sámej   ¹⁴que se aparte del mal y haga el bien;
              que busque la *paz y la siga.
Ayin   ¹⁵Los ojos del SEÑOR están sobre los
                justos,
              y sus oídos, atentos a sus
                oraciones;
Pe   ¹⁶el rostro del SEÑOR está contra los
                que hacen el mal,
              para borrar de la tierra su
                memoria.
Tsade   ¹⁷Los justos claman, y el SEÑOR los oye;
              los libra de todas sus angustias.
Qof   ¹⁸El SEÑOR está cerca de los
                quebrantados de corazón,
              y salva a los de espíritu abatido.
Resh   ¹⁹Muchas son las angustias del justo,
              pero el SEÑOR lo librará de todas
                ellas;
Shin   ²⁰le protegerá todos los huesos,
              y ni uno solo le quebrarán.
Tav   ²¹La maldad destruye a los malvados;
              serán condenados los enemigos de
                los justos.
            ²²El SEÑOR libra a sus siervos;
              no serán condenados los que en él
                confían.

Salmo 35

Salmo de David.
¹Defiéndeme, SEÑOR, de los que me atacan;
  combate a los que me combaten.
²Toma tu adarga, tu escudo,
  y acude en mi ayuda.
³Empuña la lanza y el hacha,
  y haz frente a[f] los que me persiguen.
  Quiero oírte decir:
    «Yo soy tu *salvación.»

⁴Queden confundidos y avergonzados
  los que procuran matarme;
  retrocedan humillados
  los que traman mi ruina.
⁵Sean como la paja en el viento,
  acosados por el ángel del SEÑOR;
⁶sea su senda oscura y resbalosa,
  perseguidos por el ángel del SEÑOR.
⁷Ya que sin motivo me tendieron una trampa,
  y sin motivo cavaron una fosa para mí,
⁸que la ruina los tome por sorpresa;
  que caigan en su propia trampa,
  en la fosa que ellos mismos cavaron.

⁹Así mi *alma se alegrará en el SEÑOR
  y se deleitará en su salvación;
¹⁰así todo mi ser exclamará:
    «¿Quién como tú, SEÑOR?
  Tú libras de los poderosos a los pobres;
  a los pobres y necesitados libras
  de aquellos que los explotan.»

¹¹Se presentan testigos despiadados
  y me preguntan cosas que yo ignoro.
¹²Me devuelven mal por bien,
  y eso me hiere en el alma;
¹³pues cuando ellos enfermaban
  yo me vestía de luto,
  me afligía y ayunaba.

---

[e] **Sal 34** Este salmo es un poema acróstico, que sigue el orden del alfabeto hebreo. [f] **35:3** *el hacha, y haz frente a* (lectura probable); *cierra contra* (TM).

¡Ay, si pudiera retractarme de mis oraciones!
14Me vestía yo de luto,
   como por un amigo o un hermano.
Afligido, inclinaba la cabeza,
   como si llorara por mi madre.
15Pero yo tropecé, y ellos se alegraron,
   y a una se juntaron contra mí.
Gente extraña,g que yo no conocía,
   me calumniaba sin cesar.
16Me atormentaban, se burlaban de mí,h
   y contra mí rechinaban los dientes.

17¿Hasta cuándo, Señor, vas a tolerar esto?
   Libra mi vida, mi única vida,
   de los ataques de esos leones.
18Yo te daré gracias en la gran asamblea;
   ante una multitud te alabaré.

19No dejes que de mí se burlen
   mis enemigos traicioneros;
no dejes que se guiñen el ojo
   los que me odian sin motivo.
20Porque no vienen en son de *paz,
   sino que urden mentiras
   contra la gente apacible del país.
21De mí se ríen a carcajadas, y exclaman:
   «¡Miren en lo que vino a parar!»

22Señor, tú has visto todo esto;
   no te quedes callado.
¡Señor, no te alejes de mí!
23¡Despierta, Dios mío, levántate!
   ¡Hazme *justicia, Señor, defiéndeme!
24Júzgame según tu justicia, Señor mi Dios;
   no dejes que se burlen de mí.
25No permitas que piensen:
   «¡Así queríamos verlo!»
No permitas que digan:
   «Nos lo hemos tragado vivo.»

26Queden avergonzados y confundidos
   todos los que se alegran de mi desgracia;
sean cubiertos de oprobio y vergüenza
   todos los que se creen más que yo.
27Pero lancen voces de alegría y regocijo
   los que apoyan mi causa,
y digan siempre: «Exaltado sea el Señor,
   quien se deleita en el *bienestar de su
   siervo.»
28Con mi lengua proclamaré tu justicia,
   y todo el día te alabaré.

Salmo 36
Al director musical. De David, el siervo del Señor.

1Dice el pecador:
   «Ser impío lo llevo en el *corazón.»i
No hay temor de Dios
   delante de sus ojos.
2Cree que merece alabanzas
   y no halla aborrecible su pecado.
3Sus palabras son inicuas y engañosas;
   ha perdido el buen juicio
   y la capacidad de hacer el bien.
4Aun en su lecho trama hacer el mal;
   se aferra a su mal *camino
   y persiste en la maldad.

5Tu amor, Señor, llega hasta los cielos;
   tu fidelidad alcanza las nubes.
6Tu *justicia es como las altas montañas;j
   tus juicios, como el gran océano.

Tú, Señor, cuidas de *hombres y animales;
   7¡cuán precioso, oh Dios, es tu gran amor!
Todo *ser humano halla refugio
   a la sombra de tus alas.
8Se sacian de la abundancia de tu casa;
   les das a beber de tu río de deleites.
9Porque en ti está la fuente de la vida,
   y en tu luz podemos ver la luz.

10Extiende tu amor a los que te conocen,
   y tu justicia a los rectos de corazón.
11Que no me aplaste el pie del orgulloso,
   ni me desarraigue la mano del impío.
12Vean cómo fracasan los malvados:
   ¡caen a tierra, y ya no pueden levantarse!

Salmo 37 k
Salmo de David.

Álef
1No te irrites a causa de los impíos
   ni envidies a los que cometen
   injusticias;
2porque pronto se marchitan, como la
   hierba;
pronto se secan, como el verdor
   del pasto.

Bet
3Confía en el Señor y haz el bien;
   establécete en la tierra y manténte
   fiel.
4Deléitate en el Señor,
   y él te concederá los deseos de tu
   *corazón.

Guímel
5Encomienda al Señor tu *camino;
   confía en él, y él actuará.
6Hará que tu *justicia resplandezca
   como el alba;
tu justa causa, como el sol de
   mediodía.

Dálet
7Guarda silencio ante el Señor,
   y espera en él con paciencia;
no te irrites ante el éxito de otros,
   de los que maquinan planes
   malvados.

He
8Refrena tu enojo, abandona la ira;
   no te irrites, pues esto conduce al
   mal.
9Porque los impíos serán
   exterminados,
pero los que esperan en el Señor
   heredarán la tierra.

Vav
10Dentro de poco los malvados dejarán
   de existir;
por más que los busques, no los
   encontrarás.
11Pero los desposeídos heredarán la
   tierra
y disfrutarán de gran *bienestar.

Zayin
12Los malvados conspiran contra los
   justos
y crujen los dientes contra ellos;
13pero el Señor se ríe de los malvados,

---

g **35:15** *Gente extraña* (lectura probable); *Gente golpeada* (TM). h **35:16** *Me atormentaban, se burlaban de mí* (LXX); *Con inicuos burlones de una torta* (TM). i **36:1** *Dice el ... corazón*» (lectura probable); *Oráculo del pecado al malvado en medio de mi corazón* (TM). j **36:6** *las altas montañas.* Alt. *las montañas de Dios.* k **Sal 37** Este salmo es un poema acróstico, que sigue el orden del alfabeto hebreo.

pues sabe que les llegará su hora.

Jet ¹⁴Los malvados sacan la espada y
tensan el arco
para abatir al pobre y al
necesitado,
para matar a los que viven con
rectitud.
¹⁵Pero su propia espada les atravesará
el corazón,
y su arco quedará hecho pedazos.

Tet ¹⁶Más vale lo poco de un justo
que lo mucho de innumerables
malvados;
¹⁷porque el brazo de los impíos será
quebrado,
pero el SEÑOR sostendrá a los
justos.

Yod ¹⁸El SEÑOR protege la vida de los
íntegros,
y su herencia perdura por siempre.
¹⁹En tiempos difíciles serán
prosperados;
en épocas de hambre tendrán
abundancia.

Caf ²⁰Los malvados, los enemigos del
SEÑOR,
acabarán por ser destruidos;
desaparecerán como las flores
silvestres,
se desvanecerán como el humo.

Lámed ²¹Los malvados piden prestado y no
pagan,
pero los justos dan con
generosidad.
²²Los benditos del SEÑOR heredarán la
tierra,
pero los que él maldice serán
destruidos.

Mem ²³El SEÑOR afirma los pasos del
*hombre
cuando le agrada su modo de vivir;
²⁴podrá tropezar, pero no caerá,
porque el SEÑOR lo sostiene de la
mano.

Nun ²⁵He sido joven y ahora soy viejo,
pero nunca he visto justos en la
miseria,
ni que sus hijos mendiguen pan.
²⁶Prestan siempre con generosidad;
sus hijos son una bendición.

Sámej ²⁷Apártate del mal y haz el bien,
y siempre tendrás dónde vivir.
²⁸Porque el SEÑOR ama la justicia
y no abandona a quienes le son
fieles.

El SEÑOR los protegerá para siempre,
pero acabará con la descendencia
de los malvados.

Ayin ²⁹Los justos heredarán la tierra,
y por siempre vivirán en ella.

Pe ³⁰La boca del justo imparte sabiduría,
y su lengua emite justicia.
³¹La *ley de Dios está en su corazón,
y sus pies jamás resbalan.

Tsade ³²Los malvados acechan a los justos

con la intención de matarlos,
³³pero el SEÑOR no los dejará caer en
sus manos
ni permitirá que los condenen en
el juicio.

Qof ³⁴Pero tú, espera en el SEÑOR,
y vive según su voluntad,
que él te exaltará para que heredes
la tierra.
Cuando los malvados sean
destruidos,
tú lo verás con tus propios ojos.

Resh ³⁵He visto al déspota y malvado
extenderse como cedro frondoso.
³⁶Pero pasó al olvido y dejó de existir;
lo busqué, y ya no pude
encontrarlo.

Shin ³⁷Observa a los que son íntegros y
rectos:
hay porvenir para quien busca la
*paz.
³⁸Pero todos los pecadores serán
destruidos;
el porvenir de los malvados será el
exterminio.

Tav ³⁹La *salvación de los justos viene del
SEÑOR;
él es su fortaleza en tiempos de
angustia.
⁴⁰El SEÑOR los ayuda y los libra;
los libra de los malvados y los salva,
porque en él ponen su confianza.

Salmo 38

Salmo de David, para las ofrendas memoriales.

¹SEÑOR, no me reprendas en tu enojo
ni me castigues en tu ira.
²Porque tus flechas me han atravesado,
y sobre mí ha caído tu mano.
³Por causa de tu indignación
no hay nada sano en mi cuerpo;
por causa de mi pecado
mis huesos no hallan descanso.
⁴Mis maldades me abruman,
son una carga demasiado pesada.

⁵Por causa de mi insensatez
mis llagas hieden y supuran.
⁶Estoy agobiado, del todo abatido;
todo el día ando acongojado.
⁷Estoy ardiendo de fiebre;
no hay nada sano en mi cuerpo.
⁸Me siento débil, completamente deshecho;
mi *corazón gime angustiado.

⁹Ante ti, Señor, están todos mis deseos;
no te son un secreto mis anhelos.
¹⁰Late mi corazón con violencia,
las fuerzas me abandonan,
hasta la luz de mis ojos se apaga.
¹¹Mis amigos y vecinos se apartan de mis
llagas;
mis parientes se mantienen a distancia.
¹²Tienden sus trampas los que quieren
matarme;
maquinan mi ruina los que buscan mi mal
y todo el día urden engaños.

¹³Pero yo me hago el sordo, y no los escucho;
me hago el mudo, y no les respondo.
¹⁴Soy como los que no oyen

ni pueden defenderse.
15Yo, SEÑOR, espero en ti;
    tú, Señor y Dios mío, serás quien responda.
16Tan sólo pido que no se burlen de mí,
    que no se crean superiores si resbalo.

17Estoy por desfallecer;
    el dolor no me deja un solo instante.
18Voy a confesar mi iniquidad,
    pues mi pecado me angustia.
19Muchos son mis enemigos gratuitos;l
    abundan los que me odian sin motivo.
20Por hacer el bien, me pagan con el mal;
    por procurar lo bueno, se ponen en mi
        contra.

21SEÑOR, no me abandones;
    Dios mío, no te alejes de mí.
22Señor de mi *salvación,
    ¡ven pronto en mi ayuda!

Salmo 39

Al director musical. Para Jedutún. Salmo de David.
1Me dije a mí mismo:
«Mientras esté ante gente malvada
    vigilaré mi conducta,
    me abstendré de pecar con la lengua,
    me pondré una mordaza en la boca.»
2Así que guardé silencio, me mantuve callado.
    ¡Ni aun lo bueno salía de mi boca!
Pero mi angustia iba en aumento,
    3¡el corazón me ardía en el pecho!
Al meditar en esto, el fuego se inflamó
    y tuve que decir:

4«Hazme saber, SEÑOR, el límite de mis días,
    y el tiempo que me queda por vivir;
    hazme saber lo efímero que soy.
5Muy breve es la vida que me has dado;
    ante ti, mis años no son nada.
Un soplo nada más es el *mortal,

                                    *Selah

6un suspiro que se pierde entre las sombras.
Ilusorias son las riquezas que amontona,m
    pues no sabe quién se quedará con ellas.

7»Y ahora, Señor, ¿qué esperanza me queda?
    ¡Mi esperanza he puesto en ti!
8Líbrame de todas mis transgresiones.
    Que los *necios no se burlen de mí.

9»He guardado silencio; no he abierto la boca,
    pues tú eres quien actúa.
10Ya no me castigues,
    que los golpes de tu mano me aniquilan.
11Tú reprendes a los mortales,
    los castigas por su iniquidad;
como polilla, acabas con sus placeres.
    ¡Un soplo nada más es el mortal!

                                    Selah

12»SEÑOR, escucha mi oración,
    atiende a mi clamor;
    no cierres tus oídos a mi llanto.
Ante ti soy un extraño,
    un peregrino, como todos mis antepasados.
13No me mires con enojo, y volveré a alegrarme
    antes que me muera y deje de existir.»

Salmo 40

40:13-17 — Sal 70:1-5
Al director musical. Salmo de David.
1Puse en el SEÑOR toda mi esperanza;
    él se inclinó hacia mí y escuchó mi clamor.
2Me sacó de la fosa de la muerte,
    del lodo y del pantano;
puso mis pies sobre una roca,
    y me plantó en terreno firme.
3Puso en mis labios un cántico nuevo,
    un himno de alabanza a nuestro Dios.
Al ver esto, muchos tuvieron miedo
    y pusieron su confianza en el SEÑOR.

4*Dichoso el que pone su confianza en el
        SEÑOR
    y no recurre a los idólatras
    ni a los que adoran dioses falsos.
5Muchas son, SEÑOR mi Dios,
    las maravillas que tú has hecho.
No es posible enumerar
    tus bondades en favor nuestro.
Si quisiera anunciarlas y proclamarlas,
    serían más de lo que puedo contar.

6A ti no te complacen sacrificios ni ofrendas,
    pero me has hecho obediente;n
tú no has pedido *holocaustos
    ni sacrificios por el pecado.
7Por eso dije: «Aquí me tienes
    —como el libro dice de mí—.
8Me agrada, Dios mío, hacer tu voluntad;
    tu *ley la llevo dentro de mí.»

9En medio de la gran asamblea
    he dado a conocer tu *justicia.
Tú bien sabes, SEÑOR,
    que no he sellado mis labios.
10No escondo tu justicia en mi *corazón,
    sino que proclamo tu fidelidad y tu
        *salvación.
No oculto en la gran asamblea
    tu gran amor y tu verdad.
11No me niegues, SEÑOR, tu misericordia;
    que siempre me protejan tu amor y tu
        verdad.
12Muchos males me han rodeado;
    tantos son que no puedo contarlos.
Me han alcanzado mis iniquidades,
    y ya ni puedo ver.
Son más que los cabellos de mi cabeza,
    y mi corazón desfallece.

13Por favor, SEÑOR, ¡ven a librarme!
    ¡Ven pronto, SEÑOR, en mi auxilio!
14Sean confundidos y avergonzados
    todos los que tratan de matarme;
huyan derrotados
    todos los que procuran mi mal;
15que la vergüenza de su derrota
    humille a los que se burlan de mí.
16Pero que todos los que te buscan
    se alegren en ti y se regocijen;
que los que aman tu salvación digan siempre:
    «¡Cuán grande es el SEÑOR!»

17Y a mí, pobre y necesitado,
    quiera el Señor tomarme en cuenta.

Tú eres mi socorro y mi libertador;
    ¡no te tardes, Dios mío!

---

l 38:19 gratuitos (lectura probable); vivientes (TM). m 39:6 Ilusorias … que amontona (lectura probable); En vano hace ruido y amontona (TM).n 40:6 me has hecho obediente. Lit. me has perforado los oídos.

Salmo 41

Al director musical. Salmo de David.

[1]*Dichoso el que piensa en el débil;
 el SEÑOR lo librará en el día de la desgracia.
[2]El SEÑOR lo protegerá y lo mantendrá con vida;
 lo hará dichoso en la tierra
 y no lo entregará al capricho de sus
 adversarios.
[3]El SEÑOR lo confortará cuando esté enfermo;
 lo alentará en el lecho del dolor.

[4]Yo he dicho:
 «SEÑOR, compadécete de mí;
 sáname, pues contra ti he pecado.»
[5]Con saña dicen de mí mis enemigos:
 «¿Cuándo se morirá?
 ¿Cuándo pasará al olvido?»
[6]Si vienen a verme, no son sinceros;
 recogen calumnias y salen a contarlas.

[7]Mis enemigos se juntan y cuchichean contra
 mí;
 me hacen responsable de mi mal. Dicen:
[8]«Lo que le ha sobrevenido es cosa del
 demonio;
 de esa cama no volverá a levantarse.»
[9]Hasta mi mejor amigo, en quien yo confiaba
 y que compartía el pan conmigo,
 me ha puesto la zancadilla.

[10]Pero tú, SEÑOR, compadécete de mí;
 haz que vuelva a levantarme
 para darles su merecido.
[11]En esto sabré que te he agradado:
 en que mi enemigo no triunfe sobre mí.
[12]Por mi integridad habrás de sostenerme,
 y en tu presencia me mantendrás para
 siempre.

[13]Bendito sea el SEÑOR, el Dios de Israel,
 por los siglos de los siglos.
 Amén y amén.

LIBRO II
Salmos 42-72

Salmo 42 [ñ]

Al director musical. *Masquil* de los hijos de Coré.

[1]Cual ciervo jadeante en busca del agua,
 así te busca, oh Dios, todo mi ser.
[2]Tengo sed de Dios, del Dios de la vida.
 ¿Cuándo podré presentarme ante Dios?
[3]Mis lágrimas son mi pan de día y de noche,
 mientras me echan en cara a todas horas:
 «¿Dónde está tu Dios?»

[4]Recuerdo esto y me deshago en llanto:
 yo solía ir con la multitud,
 y la conducía a la casa de Dios.
 Entre voces de alegría y acciones de gracias
 hacíamos gran celebración.

[5]¿Por qué voy a inquietarme?
 ¿Por qué me voy a angustiar?
 En Dios pondré mi esperanza
 y todavía lo alabaré.
 ¡Él es mi Salvador y mi Dios!

[6]Me siento sumamente angustiado;
 por eso, mi Dios, pienso en ti

desde la tierra del Jordán,
 desde las alturas del Hermón,
 desde el monte Mizar.
[7]Un abismo llama a otro abismo
 en el rugir de tus cascadas;
 todas tus ondas y tus olas
 se han precipitado sobre mí.
[8]Ésta es la oración al Dios de mi vida:
 que de día el SEÑOR mande su amor,
 y de noche su canto me acompañe.
[9]Y le digo a Dios, a mi *Roca:
 «¿Por qué me has olvidado?
 ¿Por qué debo andar de luto
 y oprimido por el enemigo?»
[10]Mortal agonía me penetra hasta los huesos
 ante la burla de mis adversarios,
 mientras me echan en cara a todas horas:
 «¿Dónde está tu Dios?»

[11]¿Por qué voy a inquietarme?
 ¿Por qué me voy a angustiar?
 En Dios pondré mi esperanza,
 y todavía lo alabaré.
 ¡Él es mi Salvador y mi Dios!

Salmo 43

[1]¡Hazme *justicia, oh Dios!
 Defiende mi causa frente a esta nación
 impía;
 líbrame de *gente mentirosa y perversa.
[2]Tú eres mi Dios y mi fortaleza:
 ¿Por qué me has rechazado?
 ¿Por qué debo andar de luto
 y oprimido por el enemigo?
[3]Envía tu luz y tu verdad;
 que ellas me guíen a tu monte santo,
 que me lleven al lugar donde tú habitas.
[4]Llegaré entonces al altar de Dios,
 del Dios de mi alegría y mi deleite,
 y allí, oh Dios, mi Dios,
 te alabaré al son del arpa.

[5]¿Por qué voy a inquietarme?
 ¿Por qué me voy a angustiar?
 En Dios pondré mi esperanza,
 y todavía lo alabaré.
 ¡Él es mi Salvador y mi Dios!

Salmo 44

Al director musical. *Masquil* de los hijos de Coré.

[1]Oh Dios, nuestros oídos han oído
 y nuestros padres nos han contado
 las proezas que realizaste en sus días,
 en aquellos tiempos pasados:
[2]Con tu mano echaste fuera a las naciones
 y en su lugar estableciste a nuestros padres;
 aplastaste a aquellos pueblos,
 y a nuestros padres los hiciste prosperar.[o]
[3]Porque no fue su espada la que conquistó la
 tierra,
 ni fue su brazo el que les dio la victoria:
 fue tu brazo, tu mano derecha,
 fue la luz de tu rostro, porque tú los amabas.

[4]Sólo tú eres mi rey y mi Dios.
 ¡Decreta las *victorias de Jacob!
[5]Por ti derrotamos a nuestros enemigos;
 en tu *nombre aplastamos a nuestros
 agresores.

[ñ] **Sal 42** Por su contenido, los salmos 42 y 43 forman una sola unidad literaria. [o] **44:2** *los hiciste prosperar*. Lit. *los arrojaste*.

⁶Yo no confío en mi arco,
   ni puede mi espada darme la victoria;
⁷tú nos das la victoria sobre nuestros enemigos,
   y dejas en vergüenza a nuestros
      adversarios.
⁸¡Por siempre nos gloriaremos en Dios!
   ¡Por siempre alabaremos tu nombre!

                                              *Selah

⁹Pero ahora nos has rechazado y humillado;
   ya no sales con nuestros ejércitos.
¹⁰Nos hiciste retroceder ante el enemigo;
   nos han saqueado nuestros adversarios.
¹¹Cual si fuéramos ovejas
   nos has entregado para que nos devoren,
   nos has dispersado entre las naciones.
¹²Has vendido a tu pueblo muy barato,
   y nada has ganado con su venta.

¹³Nos has puesto en ridículo ante nuestros
      vecinos;
   somos la burla y el escarnio de los que nos
      rodean.
¹⁴Nos has hecho el hazmerreír de las naciones;
   todos los pueblos se burlan de nosotros.
¹⁵La ignominia no me deja un solo instante;
   se me cae la cara de vergüenza
¹⁶por las burlas de los que me injurian y me
      ultrajan,
   por culpa del enemigo que está presto a la
      venganza.

¹⁷Todo esto nos ha sucedido,
   a pesar de que nunca te olvidamos
   ni faltamos jamás a tu *pacto.
¹⁸No te hemos sido infieles,
   ni nos hemos apartado de tu senda.
¹⁹Pero tú nos arrojaste a una cueva de chacales;
   ¡nos envolviste en la más densa oscuridad!

²⁰Si hubiéramos olvidado el nombre de nuestro
      Dios,
   o tendido nuestras manos a un dios
      extraño,
²¹¿acaso Dios no lo habría descubierto,
   ya que él conoce los más íntimos secretos?
²²Por tu causa, siempre nos llevan a la muerte;
   ¡nos tratan como a ovejas para el matadero!

²³¡Despierta, Señor! ¿Por qué duermes?
   ¡Levántate! No nos rechaces para siempre.
²⁴¿Por qué escondes tu rostro
   y te olvidas de nuestro sufrimiento y
      opresión?
²⁵Estamos abatidos hasta el polvo;
   nuestro cuerpo se arrastra por el suelo.
²⁶Levántate, ven a ayudarnos,
   y por tu gran amor, ¡rescátanos!

Salmo 45

Al director musical. Sígase la tonada de «Los lirios».
*Masquil de los hijos de Coré. Canto nupcial.

¹En mi *corazón se agita un bello tema
   mientras recito mis versos ante el rey;
   mi lengua es como pluma de hábil escritor.

²Tú eres el más apuesto de los hombres;
   tus labios son fuente de elocuencia,
   ya que Dios te ha bendecido para siempre.
³¡Con esplendor y majestad,
   cíñete la espada, oh valiente!

⁴Con majestad, cabalga victorioso
   en nombre de la verdad, la humildad y la
      justicia;
   que tu diestra realice gloriosas hazañas.
⁵Que tus agudas flechas atraviesen
   el corazón de los enemigos del rey,
   y que caigan las naciones a tus pies.

⁶Tu trono, oh Dios, permanece para siempre;
   el cetro de tu reino es un cetro de justicia.
⁷Tú amas la justicia y odias la maldad;
   por eso Dios te escogió a ti y no a tus
      compañeros,
   ¡tu Dios te ungió con perfume de alegría!
⁸Aroma de mirra, áloe y canela
   exhalan todas tus vestiduras;
   desde los palacios adornados con marfil
   te alegra la música de cuerdas.
⁹Entre tus damas de honor se cuentan
      princesas;
   a tu derecha se halla la novia real
   luciendo el oro más fino.ᴾ

¹⁰Escucha, hija, fíjate bien y presta atención:
   Olvídate de tu pueblo y de tu familia.
¹¹El rey está cautivado por tu hermosura;
   él es tu señor: inclínate ante él.
¹²La gente de Tiro vendrá con presentes;
   los ricos del pueblo buscarán tu favor.

¹³La princesa es todo esplendor,
   luciendo en su alcoba brocados de oro.
¹⁴Vestida de finos bordados
   es conducida ante el rey,
   seguida por sus damas de compañía.
¹⁵Con alegría y regocijo son conducidas
   al interior del palacio real.

¹⁶Tus hijos ocuparán el trono de tus ancestros;
   los pondrás por príncipes en toda la tierra.
¹⁷Haré que tu *nombre se recuerde
   por todas las generaciones;
   por eso las naciones te alabarán
   eternamente y para siempre.

Salmo 46

Al director musical. De los hijos de Coré. Canción
según *alamot.

¹Dios es nuestro amparo y nuestra fortaleza,
   nuestra ayuda segura en momentos de
      angustia.
²Por eso, no temeremos
   aunque se desmorone la tierra
   y las montañas se hundan en el fondo del
      mar;
³aunque rujan y se encrespen sus aguas,
   y ante su furia retiemblen los montes.

                                              *Selah

⁴Hay un río cuyas corrientes alegran la ciudad
      de Dios,
   la santa habitación del *Altísimo.
⁵Dios está en ella, la ciudad no caerá;
   al rayar el alba Dios le brindará su ayuda.
⁶Se agitan las naciones, se tambalean los reinos;
   Dios deja oír su voz, y la tierra se
      derrumba.

⁷El SEÑOR *Todopoderoso está con nosotros;
   nuestro refugio es el Dios de Jacob.

                                              Selah

ᴾ **45:9** oro más fino. Lit. oro de Ofir.

8Vengan y vean los portentos del SEÑOR;
　él ha traído desolación sobre la tierra.
9Ha puesto fin a las guerras
　en todos los confines de la tierra;
　ha quebrado los arcos, ha destrozado las
　　　lanzas,
　ha arrojado los carros al fuego.
10«Quédense quietos, reconozcan que yo soy
　　　Dios.
　¡Yo seré exaltado entre las naciones!
　¡Yo seré enaltecido en la tierra!»

11El SEÑOR Todopoderoso está con nosotros;
　nuestro refugio es el Dios de Jacob.

Selah

Salmo 47

Al director musical. Salmo de los hijos de Coré.
1Aplaudan, pueblos todos;
　aclamen a Dios con gritos de alegría.
2¡Cuán imponente es el SEÑOR *Altísimo,
　el gran rey de toda la tierra!
3Sometió a nuestro dominio las naciones;
　puso a los pueblos bajo nuestros pies;
4escogió para nosotros una heredad
　que es el orgullo de Jacob, a quien amó.

Selah

5Dios el SEÑOR ha ascendido
　entre gritos de alegría y toques de
　　　trompeta.
6Canten salmos a Dios, cántenle salmos;
　canten, cántenle salmos a nuestro rey.

7Dios es el rey de toda la tierra;
　por eso, cántenle un salmo solemne.q
8Dios reina sobre las naciones;
　Dios está sentado en su santo trono.
9Los nobles de los pueblos se reúnen
　con el pueblo del Dios de Abraham,
10pues de Dios son los imperios de la tierra.
　¡Él es grandemente enaltecido!

Salmo 48

Canción. Salmo de los hijos de Coré.
1Grande es el SEÑOR, y digno de suprema
　　　alabanza
　en la ciudad de nuestro Dios.
　Su monte santo,
2bella colina,
　es la alegría de toda la tierra.
　El monte *Sión, en la parte norte,
　es la ciudad del gran Rey.
3En las fortificaciones de Sión
　Dios se ha dado a conocer como refugio
　　　seguro.

4Hubo reyes que unieron sus fuerzas
　y que juntos avanzaron contra la ciudad;
5pero al verla quedaron pasmados,
　y asustados emprendieron la retirada.
6Allí el miedo se apoderó de ellos,
　y un dolor de parturienta les sobrevino.
7¡Con un viento huracanado
　destruiste las naves de Tarsis!

8Tal como lo habíamos oído,
　ahora lo hemos visto
　en la ciudad del SEÑOR *Todopoderoso,
　en la ciudad de nuestro Dios:

¡Él la hará permanecer para siempre!

Selah

9Dentro de tu templo, oh Dios,
　meditamos en tu gran amor.
10Tu alabanza, oh Dios, como tu *nombre,
　llega a los confines de la tierra;
　tu derecha está llena de *justicia.
11Por causa de tus justas decisiones
　el monte Sión se alegra
　y las aldeas de Judá se regocijan.

12Caminen alrededor de Sión,
　caminen en torno suyo
　y cuenten sus torres.
13Observen bien sus murallas
　y examinen sus fortificaciones,
　para que se lo cuenten a las generaciones
　　　futuras.
14¡Este Dios es nuestro Dios eterno!
　¡Él nos guiará para siempre!r

Salmo 49

Al director musical. Salmo de los hijos de Coré.
1Oigan esto, pueblos todos;
　escuchen, habitantes todos del mundo,
2tanto débiles como poderosos,
　lo mismo los ricos que los pobres.
3Mi boca hablará con sabiduría;
　mi *corazón se expresará con inteligencia.
4Inclinaré mi oído a los *proverbios;
　propondré mi enigma al son del arpa.

5¿Por qué he de temer en tiempos de desgracia,
　cuando me rodeen inicuos detractores?
6¿Temeré a los que confían en sus riquezas
　y se jactan de sus muchas posesiones?
7Nadie puede salvar a nadie,
　ni pagarle a Dios rescate por la vida.
8Tal rescate es muy costoso;
　ningún pago es suficiente.
9Nadie vive para siempre
　sin llegar a ver la fosa.
10Nadie puede negar que todos mueren,
　que sabios e insensatos perecen por igual,
　y que sus riquezas se quedan para otros.
11Aunque tuvieron tierras a su nombre,
　sus tumbas seráns su hogar eterno,
　su morada por todas las generaciones.

12A pesar de sus riquezas, no perduran los
　　　*mortales;
　al igual que las bestias, perecen.

13Tal es el destino de los que confían en sí
　　　mismos,
　el final det los que se envanecen.

Selah

14Como ovejas, están destinados al *sepulcro;
　hacia allá los conduce la muerte.
　Sus cuerpos se pudrirán en el *sepulcro,
　lejos de sus mansiones suntuosas.
　Por la mañana los gobernarán los justos.
15Pero Dios me rescatará de las garras del
　　　sepulcro
　y con él me llevará.

Selah

16No te asombre ver que alguien se enriquezca
　y aumente el esplendor de su casa,

---

q **47:7** *un salmo solemne.* Lit. *un* *masquil. r **48:14** *para siempre* (LXX); *sobre muerte* (TM). s **49:11** *sus tumbas serán* (LXX y Siríaca); *su interior será* (TM). t **49:13** *el final de* (Targum); *tras ellos* (TM).

17porque al morir no se llevará nada,
ni con él descenderá su esplendor.
18Aunque en vida se considere dichoso,
y la gente lo elogie por sus logros,
19irá a reunirse con sus ancestros,
sin que vuelva jamás a ver la luz.
20A pesar de sus riquezas, no perduranu los
mortales;
al igual que las bestias, perecen.

Salmo 50

Salmo de Asaf.

1Habla el SEÑOR, el Dios de dioses:
convoca a la tierra de oriente a occidente.
2Dios resplandece desde *Sión,
la ciudad bella y perfecta.
3Nuestro Dios viene, pero no en silencio;
lo precede un fuego que todo lo destruye,
y en torno suyo ruge la tormenta.
4El SEÑOR convoca a los cielos y a la tierra,
para que presencien el juicio de su pueblo:
5«Reúnanme a los consagrados,
a los que pactaron conmigo mediante un
sacrificio.»
6El cielo proclama la *justicia divina:
¡Dios mismo es el juez!

Selah

7«Escucha, pueblo mío, que voy a hablar;
Israel, voy a testificar contra ti:
¡Yo soy tu Dios, el único Dios!
8No te reprendo por tus sacrificios
ni por tus *holocaustos, que siempre me
ofreces.
9No necesito becerros de tu establo
ni machos cabríos de tus apriscos,
10pues míos son los animales del bosque,
y mío también el ganado de los cerros.
11Conozco a las aves de las alturas;
todas las bestias del campo son mías.
12Si yo tuviera hambre, no te lo diría,
pues mío es el mundo, y todo lo que
contiene.
13¿Acaso me alimento con carne de toros,
o con sangre de machos cabríos?
14¡Ofrece a Dios tu gratitud,
cumple tus promesas al *Altísimo!
15Invócame en el día de la angustia;
yo te libraré y tú me honrarás.»
16Pero Dios le dice al malvado:
«¿Qué derecho tienes tú de recitar mis *leyes
o de mencionar mi *pacto con tus labios?
17Mi *instrucción, la aborreces;
mis palabras, las desechas.
18Ves a un ladrón, y lo acompañas;
con los adúlteros te identificas.
19Para lo malo, das rienda suelta a tu boca;
tu lengua está siempre dispuesta al
engaño.
20Tienes por costumbre hablar contra tu
prójimo,
y aun calumnias a tu propio hermano.
21Has hecho todo esto, y he guardado silencio;
¿acaso piensas que soy como tú?
Pero ahora voy a reprenderte;
cara a cara voy a denunciarte.

22»Ustedes que se olvidan de Dios,
consideren lo que he dicho;
de lo contrario, los haré pedazos,

y no habrá nadie que los salve.
23Quien me ofrece su gratitud, me honra;
al que enmiende su conducta le mostraré
mi *salvación.»

Salmo 51

Al director musical. Salmo de David, cuando el
profeta Natán fue a verlo por haber cometido David
adulterio con Betsabé.

1Ten compasión de mí, oh Dios,
conforme a tu gran amor;
conforme a tu inmensa bondad,
borra mis transgresiones.
2Lávame de toda mi maldad
y límpiame de mi pecado.

3Yo reconozco mis transgresiones;
siempre tengo presente mi pecado.
4Contra ti he pecado, sólo contra ti,
y he hecho lo que es malo ante tus ojos;
por eso, tu sentencia es justa,
y tu juicio, irreprochable.
5Yo sé que soy malo de nacimiento;
pecador me concibió mi madre.
6Yo sé que tú amas la verdad en lo íntimo;
en lo secreto me has enseñado sabiduría.

7Purifícame con *hisopo, y quedaré limpio;
lávame, y quedaré más blanco que la nieve.
8Anúnciame gozo y alegría;
infunde gozo en estos huesos que has
quebrantado.
9Aparta tu rostro de mis pecados
y borra toda mi maldad.

10Crea en mí, oh Dios, un *corazón limpio,
y renueva la firmeza de mi espíritu.
11No me alejes de tu presencia
ni me quites tu santo Espíritu.
12Devuélveme la alegría de tu *salvación;
que un espíritu obediente me sostenga.
13Así enseñaré a los transgresores tus *caminos,
y los pecadores se volverán a ti.

14Dios mío, Dios de mi salvación,
líbrame de derramar sangre,
y mi lengua alabará tu *justicia.
15Abre, *Señor, mis labios,
y mi boca proclamará tu alabanza.
16Tú no te deleitas en los sacrificios
ni te complacen los *holocaustos;
de lo contrario, te los ofrecería.
17El sacrificio que te agrada
es un espíritu quebrantado;
tú, oh Dios, no desprecias
al corazón quebrantado y arrepentido.

18En tu buena voluntad, haz que prospere
*Sión;
levanta los muros de Jerusalén.
19Entonces te agradarán los sacrificios de
justicia,
los holocaustos del todo quemados,
y sobre tu altar se ofrecerán becerros.

Salmo 52

Al director musical. *Masquil* de David, cuando
Doeg el edomita fue a informarle a Saúl:
«David ha ido a la casa de Ajimélec.»

1¿Por qué te jactas de tu maldad, varón
prepotente?

---

u 49:20 *no perduran* (algunos mss.; véase v. 12); *no entienden* (TM).

¡El amor de Dios es constante!
2Tu lengua, como navaja afilada,
    trama destrucción y practica el engaño.
3Más que el bien, amas la maldad;
    más que la verdad, amas la mentira.
                                    Selah

4Lengua embustera,
    te encanta ofender con tus palabras.
5Pero Dios te arruinará para siempre;
    te tomará y te arrojará de tu hogar;
    ¡te arrancará del mundo de los vivientes!
                                    Selah

6Los justos verán esto, y temerán;
    entre burlas dirán de él:
7«¡Aquí tienen al hombre
    que no buscó refugio en Dios,
sino que confió en su gran riqueza
    y se afirmó en su maldad!»

8Pero yo soy como un olivo verde
    que florece en la casa de Dios;
yo confío en el gran amor de Dios
    eternamente y para siempre.

9En todo tiempo te alabaré por tus obras;
    en ti pondré mi esperanza en presencia de
        tus fieles,
    porque tu *nombre es bueno.

Salmo 53

53:1-6 — Sal 14:1-7
Al director musical. Según *majalat. *Masquil* de
    David.

1Dice el *necio en su *corazón:
    «No hay Dios.»
Están corrompidos, sus obras son detestables;
    ¡no hay uno solo que haga lo bueno!

2Desde el cielo Dios contempla a los *mortales,
    para ver si hay alguien
    que sea sensato y busque a Dios.
3Pero todos se han descarriado,
    a una se han corrompido.
No hay nadie que haga lo bueno;
    ¡no hay uno solo!

4¿Acaso no entienden todos los que hacen lo
        malo,
    los que devoran a mi pueblo como si fuera
        pan?
    ¡Jamás invocan a Dios!
5Allí los tienen, sobrecogidos de miedo,
    cuando no hay nada que temer.
Dios dispersó los huesos de quienes te
        atacaban;
    tú los avergonzaste, porque Dios los
        rechazó.

6¡Quiera Dios que de *Sión
    venga la *salvación para Israel!
Cuando Dios restaure a su pueblo,v
    se regocijará Jacob; se alegrará todo Israel.

Salmo 54

Al director musical. Acompáñese con instrumentos
de cuerda. *Masquil* de David, cuando gente de Zif
fue a decirle a Saúl: «¿No estará David escondido
        entre nosotros?»

1Sálvame, oh Dios, por tu *nombre;
    defiéndeme con tu poder.

2Escucha, oh Dios, mi oración;
    presta oído a las palabras de mi boca.
3Pues *gente extraña me ataca;
    tratan de matarme los violentos,
    gente que no toma en cuenta a Dios.
                                    Selah

4Pero Dios es mi socorro;
    el Señor es quien me sostiene,
5y hará recaer el mal sobre mis adversarios.
    Por tu fidelidad, SEÑOR, ¡destrúyelos!

6Te presentaré una ofrenda voluntaria
    y alabaré, SEÑOR, tu buen nombre;
7pues me has librado de todas mis angustias,
    y mis ojos han visto la derrota de mis
        enemigos.

Salmo 55

Al director musical. Acompáñese con instrumentos
de cuerda. *Masquil* de David.

1Escucha, oh Dios, mi oración;
    no pases por alto mi súplica.
2¡Óyeme y respóndeme,
    porque mis angustias me perturban!
Me aterran 3las amenazas del enemigo
    y la opresión de los impíos,
pues me causan sufrimiento
    y en su enojo me insultan.

4Se me estremece el *corazón dentro del pecho,
    y me invade un pánico mortal.
5Temblando estoy de miedo,
    sobrecogido estoy de terror.
6¡Cómo quisiera tener las alas de una paloma
    y volar hasta encontrar reposo!
7Me iría muy lejos de aquí;
    me quedaría a vivir en el desierto.
                                    Selah

8Presuroso volaría a mi refugio,
    para librarme del viento borrascoso
    y de la tempestad.

9¡Destrúyelos, Señor! ¡Confunde su lenguaje!
    En la ciudad sólo veo contiendas y
        violencia;
10día y noche rondan por sus muros,
    y dentro de ella hay intrigas y maldad.
11En su seno hay fuerzas destructivas;
    de sus calles no se apartan la opresión y el
        engaño.

12Si un enemigo me insultara,
    yo lo podría soportar;
si un adversario me humillara,
    de él me podría yo esconder.
13Pero lo has hecho tú, un *hombre como yo,
    mi compañero, mi mejor amigo,
14a quien me unía una bella amistad,
    con quien convivía en la casa de Dios.

15¡Que sorprenda la muerte a mis enemigos!
    ¡Que caigan vivos al *sepulcro,
    pues en ellos habita la maldad!
16Pero yo clamaré a Dios,
    y el SEÑOR me salvará.
17Mañana, tarde y noche
    clamo angustiado, y él me escucha.
18Aunque son muchos los que me combaten,
    él me rescata, me salva la vida
    en la batalla que se libra contra mí.

---

v 53:6 *restaure a su pueblo.* Alt. *haga que su pueblo vuelva del cautiverio.*

19¡Dios, que reina para siempre,
    habrá de oírme y los afligirá!

Selah

Esa *gente no cambia de conducta,
    no tiene temor de Dios.
20Levantan la mano contra sus amigos
    y no cumplen sus compromisos.
21Su boca es blanda como la manteca,
    pero sus pensamientos son belicosos.
Sus palabras son más suaves que el aceite,
    pero no son sino espadas desenvainadas.

22Encomienda al SEÑOR tus afanes,
    y él te sostendrá;
no permitirá que el justo caiga
    y quede abatido para siempre.
23Tú, oh Dios, abatirás a los impíos
    y los arrojarás en la fosa de la muerte;
la gente sanguinaria y mentirosa
    no llegará ni a la mitad de su vida.
Yo, por mi parte, en ti confío.

Salmo 56

Al director musical. Sígase la tonada de «La tórtola
en los robles lejanos». *Mictam* de David, cuando
    los filisteos lo apresaron en Gat.

1Ten compasión de mí, oh Dios,
    pues hay *gente que me persigue.
Todo el día me atacan mis opresores,
    2todo el día me persiguen mis adversarios;
son muchos los arrogantes que me atacan.

3Cuando siento miedo,
    pongo en ti mi confianza.
4Confío en Dios y alabo su palabra;
    confío en Dios y no siento miedo.
    ¿Qué puede hacerme un simple *mortal?
5Todo el día tuercen mis palabras;
    siempre están pensando hacerme mal.
6Conspiran, se mantienen al acecho;
    ansiosos por quitarme la vida,
    vigilan todo lo que hago.
7¡En tu enojo, Dios mío, humilla a esos pueblos!
    ¡De ningún modo los dejes escapar!

8Toma en cuenta mis lamentos;
    registra mi llanto en tu libro.w
    ¿Acaso no lo tienes anotado?
9Cuando yo te pida ayuda,
    huirán mis enemigos.
    Una cosa sé: ¡Dios está de mi parte!
10Confío en Dios y alabo su palabra;
    confío en el SEÑOR y alabo su palabra;
11confío en Dios y no siento miedo.
    ¿Qué puede hacerme un simple mortal?

12He hecho votos delante de ti, oh Dios,
    y te presentaré mis ofrendas de gratitud.
13Tú, oh Dios, me has librado de tropiezos,
    me has librado de la muerte,
para que siempre, en tu presencia,
    camine en la luz de la vida.

Salmo 57

57:7-11 — Sal 108:1-5

Al director musical. Sígase la tonada de «No
destruyas». *Mictam* de David, cuando David había
    huido de Saúl y estaba en una cueva.

1Ten compasión de mí, oh Dios;
    ten compasión de mí, que en ti confío.

A la sombra de tus alas me refugiaré,
    hasta que haya pasado el peligro.

2Clamo al Dios *Altísimo,
    al Dios que me brinda su apoyo.
3Desde el cielo me tiende la mano y me salva;
    reprende a mis perseguidores.

Selah

    ¡Dios me envía su amor y su verdad!

4Me encuentro en medio de leones,
    rodeado de *gente rapaz.
Sus dientes son lanzas y flechas;
    su lengua, una espada afilada.

5Pero tú, oh Dios, estás sobre los cielos,
    ¡tu gloria cubre toda la tierra!

6Tendieron una red en mi camino,
    y mi ánimo quedó por los suelos.
En mi senda cavaron una fosa,
    pero ellos mismos cayeron en ella.

Selah

7Firme está, oh Dios, mi *corazón;
    firme está mi corazón.
Voy a cantarte salmos.
8¡Despierta, *alma mía!
    ¡Despierten, arpa y lira!
    ¡Haré despertar al nuevo día!

9Te alabaré, Señor, entre los pueblos,
    te cantaré salmos entre las naciones.
10Pues tu amor es tan grande que llega a los
    cielos;
    ¡tu verdad llega hasta el firmamento!

11¡Tú, oh Dios, estás sobre los cielos;
    tu gloria cubre toda la tierra!

Salmo 58

Al director musical. Sígase la tonada de «No
    destruyas». *Mictam* de David.

1¿Acaso ustedes, gobernantes, actúan con
    *justicia,
    y juzgan con rectitud a los *seres
    humanos?
2Al contrario, con la *mente traman injusticia,
    y la violencia de sus manos se desata en el
    país.
3Los malvados se pervierten desde que nacen;
    desde el vientre materno se desvían los
    mentirosos.
4Su veneno es como el de las serpientes,
    como el de una cobra que se hace la sorda
5para no escuchar la música del mago,
    del diestro en encantamientos.

6Rómpeles, oh Dios, los dientes;
    ¡arráncales, SEÑOR, los colmillos a esos
    leones!
7Que se escurran, como el agua entre los dedos;
    que se rompan sus flechas al tensar el arco.
8Que se disuelvan, como babosa rastrera;
    que no vean la luz, cual si fueran abortivos.
9Que sin darse cuenta, ardan como espinos;
    que el viento los arrastre, estén verdes o
    secos.

10Se alegrará el justo al ver la venganza,
    al empapar sus pies en la sangre del impío.
11Dirá entonces la *gente:

---

w **56:8** *registra mi llanto en tu libro.* Lit. *pon mis lágrimas en tu frasco.*

«Ciertamente los justos son
recompensados;
ciertamente hay un Dios que juzga en la
tierra.»

Salmo 59

Al director musical. Sígase la tonada de «No
destruyas». *Mictam de David, cuando Saúl había
ordenado que vigilaran la casa de David con el
propósito de matarlo.

¹Líbrame de mis enemigos, oh Dios;
protégeme de los que me atacan.
²Líbrame de los malhechores;
sálvame de los asesinos.

³¡Mira cómo me acechan!
*Hombres crueles conspiran contra mí
sin que yo, SEÑOR, haya delinquido ni
pecado.
⁴Presurosos se disponen a atacarme
sin que yo haya cometido mal alguno.

¡Levántate y ven en mi ayuda!
¡Mira mi condición!
⁵Tú, SEÑOR, eres el Dios *Todopoderoso,
¡eres el Dios de Israel!
¡Despiértate y castiga a todas las naciones;
no tengas compasión de esos viles
traidores!
*Selah

⁶Ellos vuelven por la noche,
gruñendo como perros
y acechando alrededor de la ciudad.
⁷Echan espuma por la boca,
lanzan espadas por sus fauces,
y dicen: «¿Quién va a oírnos?»
⁸Pero tú, SEÑOR, te burlas de ellos;
te ríes de todas las naciones.
⁹A ti, fortaleza mía, vuelvo los ojos,
pues tú, oh Dios, eres mi protector.
¹⁰Tú eres el Dios que me ama,
e irás delante de mí
para hacerme ver la derrota de mis
enemigos.
¹¹Pero no los mates,
para que mi pueblo no lo olvide.
Zarandéalos con tu poder; ¡humíllalos!
¡Tú, Señor, eres nuestro escudo!
¹²Por los pecados de su boca,
por las palabras de sus labios,
que caigan en la trampa de su orgullo.
Por las maldiciones y mentiras que profieren,
¹³consúmelos en tu enojo;
¡consúmelos hasta que dejen de existir!
Así todos sabrán que Dios gobierna en Jacob,
y hasta los confines de la tierra.
Selah

¹⁴Porque ellos vuelven por la noche,
gruñendo como perros
y acechando alrededor de la ciudad.
¹⁵Van de un lado a otro buscando comida,
y aúllan si no quedan satisfechos.
¹⁶Pero yo le cantaré a tu poder,
y por la mañana alabaré tu amor;
porque tú eres mi protector,
mi refugio en momentos de angustia.

¹⁷A ti, fortaleza mía, te cantaré salmos,
pues tú, oh Dios, eres mi protector.

¡Tú eres el Dios que me ama!

Salmo 60

60:5-12 — Sal 108:6-13

Al director musical. Sígase la tonada de «El lirio del
pacto». *Mictam didáctico de David, cuando luchó
contra los arameos del noroeste de Mesopotamia y
de Siria central, y cuando Joab volvió y abatió a
doce mil edomitas en el valle de la Sal.

¹Oh Dios, tú nos has rechazado
y has abierto brecha en nuestras filas;
te has enojado con nosotros:
¡restáuranos ahora!
²Has sacudido la tierra,
la has resquebrajado;
repara sus grietas,
porque se desmorona.
³Has sometido a tu pueblo a duras pruebas;
nos diste a beber un vino embriagador.
⁴Daˣ a tus fieles la señal de retirada,
para que puedan escapar de los arqueros.
*Selah

⁵Líbranos con tu diestra, respóndenos
para que tu pueblo amado quede a salvo.

⁶Dios ha dicho en su santuario:
«Triunfante repartiré a Siquén,
y dividiré el valle de Sucot.
⁷Mío es Galaad, mío es Manasés;
Efraín es mi yelmo y Judá mi cetro.
⁸En Moab me lavo las manos,
sobre Edom arrojo mi sandalia;
sobre Filistea lanzo gritos de triunfo.»

⁹¿Quién me llevará a la ciudad fortificada?
¿Quién me mostrará el camino a Edom?
¹⁰¿No eres tú, oh Dios, quien nos ha rechazado?
¡Ya no sales, oh Dios, con nuestros
ejércitos!
¹¹Bríndanos tu ayuda contra el enemigo,
pues de nada sirve la ayuda *humana.
¹²Con Dios obtendremos la victoria;
¡él pisoteará a nuestros enemigos!

Salmo 61

Al director musical. Acompáñese con instrumentos
de cuerda. De David.

¹Oh Dios, escucha mi clamor
y atiende a mi oración.

²Desde los confines de la tierra te invoco,
pues mi *corazón desfallece;
llévame a una roca donde esté yo a salvo.
³Porque tú eres mi refugio,
mi baluarte contra el enemigo.

⁴Anhelo habitar en tu casa para siempre
y refugiarme debajo de tus alas.
*Selah

⁵Tú, oh Dios, has aceptado mis votos
y me has dado la heredad de quienes te
honran.

⁶Concédele al rey más años de vida;
que sean sus días una eternidad.
⁷Que reine siempre en tu presencia,
y que tu amor y tu verdad lo protejan.
⁸Así cantaré siempre salmos a tu *nombre
y cumpliré mis votos día tras día.

ˣ **60:4** *Da* (lectura probable); *Diste* (TM).

Salmo 62

Al director musical. Para Jedutún. Salmo de David.
¹Sólo en Dios halla descanso mi *alma;
　de él viene mi *salvación.
²Sólo él es mi *roca y mi salvación;
　él es mi protector.
　¡Jamás habré de caer!

³¿Hasta cuándo atacarán todos ustedes
　a un *hombre para derribarlo?
Es como un muro inclinado,
　¡como una cerca a punto de derrumbarse!
⁴Sólo quieren derribarlo
　de su lugar de preeminencia.
Se complacen en la mentira:
　bendicen con la boca,
　pero maldicen con el *corazón.

　　　　　　　　　　　　　　*Selah

⁵Sólo en Dios halla descanso mi alma;
　de él viene mi esperanza.
⁶Sólo él es mi roca y mi salvación;
　él es mi protector
　y no habré de caer.
⁷Dios es mi salvación y mi gloria;
　es la roca que me fortalece;
　¡mi refugio está en Dios!
⁸Confía siempre en él, pueblo mío;
　ábrele tu corazón cuando estés ante él.
　¡Dios es nuestro refugio!

　　　　　　　　　　　　　　Selah

⁹Una quimera es la *gente de humilde cuna,
　y una mentira la gente de alta alcurnia;
si se les pone juntos en la balanza,
　todos ellos no pesan nada.

¹⁰No confíen en la extorsión
　ni se hagan ilusiones con sus rapiñas;
y aunque se multipliquen sus riquezas,
　no pongan el corazón en ellas.

¹¹Una cosa ha dicho Dios,
　y dos veces lo he escuchado:
Que tú, oh Dios, eres poderoso;
　¹²que tú, Señor, eres todo amor;
que tú pagarás a cada uno
　según lo que merezcan sus obras.

Salmo 63

Salmo de David, cuando estaba en el desierto
de Judá.
¹Oh Dios, tú eres mi Dios;
　yo te busco intensamente.
Mi *alma tiene sed de ti;
　todo mi ser te anhela,
　cual tierra seca, extenuada y sedienta.

²Te he visto en el santuario
　y he contemplado tu poder y tu gloria.
³Tu amor es mejor que la vida;
　por eso mis labios te alabarán.
⁴Te bendeciré mientras viva,
　y alzando mis manos te invocaré.

⁵Mi alma quedará satisfecha
　como de un suculento banquete,
y con labios jubilosos
　te alabará mi boca.

⁶En mi lecho me acuerdo de ti;
　pienso en ti toda la noche.
⁷A la sombra de tus alas cantaré,
　porque tú eres mi ayuda.
⁸Mi alma se aferra a ti;

tu mano derecha me sostiene.

⁹Los que buscan mi muerte serán destruidos;
　bajarán a las profundidades de la tierra.
¹⁰Serán entregados a la espada
　y acabarán devorados por los chacales.

¹¹El rey se regocijará en Dios;
　todos los que invocan a Dios lo alabarán,
　pero los mentirosos serán silenciados.

Salmo 64

Al director musical. Salmo de David.
¹Escucha, oh Dios, la voz de mi queja;
　protégeme del temor al enemigo.
²Escóndeme de esa pandilla de impíos,
　de esa caterva de malhechores.
³Afilan su lengua como espada
　y lanzan como flechas palabras
　　ponzoñosas.
⁴Emboscados, disparan contra el inocente;
　le tiran sin temor y sin aviso.

⁵Unos a otros se animan en sus planes impíos,
　calculan cómo tender sus trampas;
　y hasta dicen: «¿Quién las verá?»
⁶Maquinan injusticias, y dicen:
　　«¡Hemos tramado un plan perfecto!»
　¡Cuán incomprensibles son
　la *mente y los pensamientos *humanos!

⁷Pero Dios les disparará sus flechas,
　y sin aviso caerán heridos.
⁸Su propia lengua será su ruina,
　y quien los vea se burlará de ellos.

⁹La *humanidad entera sentirá temor:
　proclamará las proezas de Dios
　y meditará en sus obras.
¹⁰Que se regocijen en el SEÑOR los justos;
　que busquen refugio en él;
　¡que lo alaben todos los de recto *corazón!

Salmo 65

Al director musical. Salmo de David. Cántico.
¹A ti, oh Dios de *Sión,
　te pertenece la alabanza.
A ti se te deben cumplir los votos,
　²porque escuchas la oración.
A ti acude todo *mortal,
　³a causa de sus perversidades.
Nuestros delitos nos abruman,
　pero tú los perdonaste.
⁴*¡Dichoso aquel a quien tú escoges,
　al que atraes a ti para que viva en tus atrios!
Saciémonos de los bienes de tu casa,
　de los dones de tu santo templo.

⁵Tú, oh Dios y Salvador nuestro,
　nos respondes con imponentes obras de
　　*justicia;
tú eres la esperanza de los confines de la tierra
　y de los más lejanos mares.
⁶Tú, con tu poder, formaste las montañas,
　desplegando tu potencia.
⁷Tú calmaste el rugido de los mares,
　el estruendo de sus olas,
　y el tumulto de los pueblos.
⁸Los que viven en remotos lugares
　se asombran ante tus prodigios;
del oriente al occidente
　tú inspiras canciones de alegría.

⁹Con tus cuidados fecundas la tierra,
　y la colmas de abundancia.

Los arroyos de Dios se llenan de agua,
　para asegurarle trigo al pueblo.
　¡Así preparas el campo!
10Empapas los surcos, nivelas sus terrones,
　reblandeces la tierra con las lluvias
　y bendices sus renuevos.
11Tú coronas el año con tus bondades,
　y tus carretas se desbordan de abundancia.
12Rebosan los prados del desierto;
　las colinas se visten de alegría.
13Pobladas de rebaños las praderas,
　y cubiertos los valles de trigales,
　cantan y lanzan voces de alegría.

Salmo 66

Al director musical. Cántico. Salmo.
1¡Aclamen alegres a Dios,
　habitantes de toda la tierra!
2Canten salmos a su glorioso *nombre;
　¡ríndanle gloriosas alabanzas!
3Díganle a Dios:
　«¡Cuán imponentes son tus obras!
　Es tan grande tu poder
　que tus enemigos mismos se rinden ante ti.
4Toda la tierra se postra en tu presencia,
　y te cantan salmos;
　cantan salmos a tu nombre.»
　　　　　　　　　　　　　　　　*Selah

5¡Vengan y vean las proezas de Dios,
　sus obras portentosas en nuestro favor!
6Convirtió el mar en tierra seca,
　y el pueblo cruzó el río a pie.
　¡Regocijémonos en él!
7Con su poder gobierna eternamente;
　sus ojos vigilan a las naciones.
　¡Que no se levanten contra él los rebeldes!
　　　　　　　　　　　　　　　　Selah

8Pueblos todos, bendigan a nuestro Dios,
　hagan oír la voz de su alabanza.
9Él ha protegido nuestra vida,
　ha evitado que resbalen nuestros pies.

10Tú, oh Dios, nos has puesto a prueba;
　nos has purificado como a la plata.
11Nos has hecho caer en una red;
　¡pesada carga nos has echado a cuestas!
12Las caballerías nos han aplastado la cabeza;
　hemos pasado por el fuego y por el agua,
　pero al fin nos has dado un respiro.
13Me presentaré en tu templo con *holocaustos
　y cumpliré los votos que te hice,
14los votos de mis labios y mi boca
　que pronuncié en medio de mi angustia.
15Te ofreceré holocaustos de animales
　engordados,
　junto con el humo de ofrendas de carneros;
　te ofreceré toros y machos cabríos.
　　　　　　　　　　　　　　　　Selah

16Vengan ustedes, temerosos de Dios,
　escuchen, que voy a contarles
　todo lo que él ha hecho por mí.
17Clamé a él con mi boca;
　lo alabé con mi lengua.
18Si en mi *corazón hubiera yo abrigado
　maldad,
　el *Señor no me habría escuchado;
19pero Dios sí me ha escuchado,
　ha atendido a la voz de mi plegaria.
20¡Bendito sea Dios,
　que no rechazó mi plegaria

ni me negó su amor!

Salmo 67

Al director musical. Acompáñese con instrumentos
de cuerda. Salmo. Cántico.
1Dios nos tenga compasión y nos bendiga;
　Dios haga resplandecer su rostro sobre
　nosotros,
　　　　　　　　　　　　　　　　*Selah
2para que se conozcan en la tierra sus *caminos,
　y entre todas las naciones su *salvación.

3Que te alaben, oh Dios, los pueblos;
　que todos los pueblos te alaben.

4Alégrense y canten con júbilo las naciones,
　porque tú las gobiernas con rectitud;
　¡tú guías a las naciones de la tierra!
　　　　　　　　　　　　　　　　Selah

5Que te alaben, oh Dios, los pueblos;
　que todos los pueblos te alaben.

6La tierra dará entonces su fruto,
　y Dios, nuestro Dios, nos bendecirá.
7Dios nos bendecirá,
　y le temerán todos los confines de la tierra.

Salmo 68

Al director musical. Salmo de David. Cántico.
1Que se levante Dios,
　que sean dispersados sus enemigos,
　que huyan de su presencia los que le odian.
2Que desaparezcan del todo,
　como humo que se disipa con el viento;
　que perezcan ante Dios los impíos,
　como cera que se derrite en el fuego.
3Pero que los justos se alegren y se regocijen;
　que estén felices y alegres delante de Dios.

4Canten a Dios, canten salmos a su *nombre;
　aclamen a quien cabalga por las estepas,
　y regocíjense en su presencia.
　¡Su nombre es el SEÑOR!
5Padre de los huérfanos y defensor de las viudas
　es Dios en su morada santa.
6Dios da un hogar a los desamparados
　y libertad a los cautivos;
　los rebeldes habitarán en el desierto.

7Cuando saliste, oh Dios, al frente de tu pueblo,
　cuando a través de los páramos marchaste,
　　　　　　　　　　　　　　　　*Selah
8la tierra se estremeció,
　los cielos se vaciaron,
　delante de Dios, el Dios de Sinaí,
　delante de Dios, el Dios de Israel.
9Tú, oh Dios, diste abundantes lluvias;
　reanimaste a tu extenuada herencia.
10Tu familia se estableció en la tierra
　que en tu bondad, oh Dios, preparaste para
　el pobre.

11El Señor ha emitido la palabra,
　y millares de mensajeras la proclaman:
12«Van huyendo los reyes y sus tropas;
　en las casas, las mujeres se reparten el botín:
13alas de paloma cubiertas de plata,
　con plumas de oro resplandeciente.
　Tú te quedaste a dormir entre los rebaños.»
14Cuando el *Todopoderoso puso en fuga
　a los reyes de la tierra,
　parecían copos de nieve
　cayendo sobre la cumbre del Zalmón.

15Montañas de Basán, montañas imponentes;

montañas de Basán, montañas escarpadas:

16¿Por qué, montañas escarpadas, miran con
envidia
al monte donde a Dios le place residir,
donde el SEÑOR habitará por siempre?

17Los carros de guerra de Dios
se cuentan por millares;
del Sinaí vino en ellos el Señor
para entrar en su santuario.

18Cuando tú, Dios y SEÑOR,
ascendiste a las alturas,
te llevaste contigo a los cautivos;
tomaste tributo de los *hombres,
aun de los rebeldes,
para establecer tu morada.

19Bendito sea el Señor, nuestro Dios y Salvador,
que día tras día sobrelleva nuestras cargas.
Selah

20Nuestro Dios es un Dios que salva;
el SEÑOR Soberano nos libra de la muerte.

21Dios aplastará la cabeza de sus enemigos,
la testa enmarañada de los que viven
pecando.

22El Señor nos dice: «De Basán los regresaré;
de las profundidades del mar los haré
volver,

23para que se empapen los pies
en la sangre de sus enemigos;
para que, al lamerla, los perros
tengan también su parte.»

24En el santuario pueden verse
las procesiones de mi Dios,
las procesiones de mi Dios y rey.

25Los cantores van al frente,
seguidos de los músicos de cuerda,
entre doncellas que tocan panderetas.

26Bendigan a Dios en la gran congregación;
alaben al SEÑOR, descendientes de Israel.

27Los guía la joven tribu de Benjamín,
seguida de los múltiples príncipes de Judá
y de los príncipes de Zabulón y Neftalí.

28Despliega tu poder, oh Dios;
haz gala, oh Dios, de tu poder,
que has manifestado en favor nuestro.

29Por causa de tu templo en Jerusalén
los reyes te ofrecerán presentes.

30Reprende a esa bestia de los juncos,
a esa manada de toros bravos
entre naciones que parecen becerros.
Haz que, humillada, te lleve barras de plata;
dispersa a las naciones belicosas.

31Egipto enviará embajadores,
y *Cus se someterá a Dios.

32Cántenle a Dios, oh reinos de la tierra,
cántenle salmos al Señor,
Selah

33al que cabalga por los cielos,
los cielos antiguos,
al que hace oír su voz,
su voz de trueno.

34Reconozcan el poder de Dios;
su majestad está sobre Israel,
su poder está en las alturas.

35En tu santuario, oh Dios, eres imponente;
¡el Dios de Israel da poder y fuerza a su
pueblo!

¡Bendito sea Dios!

Salmo 69

Al director musical. Sígase la tonada de «Los lirios».
De David.

1Sálvame, Dios mío,
que las aguas ya me llegan al *cuello.

2Me estoy hundiendo en una ciénaga
profunda,
y no tengo dónde apoyar el pie.
Estoy en medio de profundas aguas,
y me arrastra la corriente.

3Cansado estoy de pedir ayuda;
tengo reseca la garganta.
Mis ojos languidecen,
esperando la ayuda de mi Dios.

4Más que los cabellos de mi cabeza
son los que me odian sin motivo;
muchos son los enemigos gratuitos
que se han propuesto destruirme.
¿Cómo voy a devolver lo que no he
robado?

5Oh Dios, tú sabes lo insensato que he sido;
no te puedo esconder mis transgresiones.

6SEÑOR Soberano, *Todopoderoso,
que no sean avergonzados por mi culpa
los que en ti esperan;
oh Dios de Israel,
que no sean humillados por mi culpa
los que te buscan.

7Por ti yo he sufrido insultos;
mi rostro se ha cubierto de ignominia.

8Soy como un extraño para mis hermanos;
soy un extranjero para los hijos de mi
madre.

9El celo por tu casa me consume;
sobre mí han recaído
los insultos de tus detractores.

10Cuando lloro y ayuno,
tengo que soportar sus ofensas;

11cuando me visto de luto,
soy objeto de burlas.

12Los que se sientan a la *puerta murmuran
contra mí;
los borrachos me dedican parodias.

13Pero yo, SEÑOR, te imploro
en el tiempo de tu buena voluntad.
Por tu gran amor, oh Dios, respóndeme;
por tu fidelidad, sálvame.

14Sácame del fango;
no permitas que me hunda.
Líbrame de los que me odian,
y de las aguas profundas.

15No dejes que me arrastre la corriente;
no permitas que me trague el abismo,
ni que el foso cierre sus fauces sobre mí.

16Respóndeme, SEÑOR, por tu bondad y tu
amor;
por tu gran compasión, vuélvete a mí.

17No escondas tu rostro de este siervo tuyo;
respóndeme pronto, que estoy angustiado.

18Ven a mi lado, y rescátame;
redímeme, por causa de mis enemigos.

19Tú bien sabes cómo me insultan,
me avergüenzan y denigran;
sabes quiénes son mis adversarios.

20Los insultos me han destrozado el corazón;
para mí ya no hay remedio.
Busqué compasión, y no la hubo;
busqué consuelo, y no lo hallé.

21En mi comida pusieron hiel;

para calmar mi sed me dieron vinagre.

22Que se conviertan en trampa sus banquetes,
　y su prosperidad en lazo.
23Que se les nublen los ojos, para que no vean;
　y que sus fuerzas flaqueen para siempre.
24Descarga tu furia sobre ellos;
　que tu ardiente ira los alcance.
25Quédense desiertos sus campamentos,
　y deshabitadas sus tiendas de campaña.
26Pues al que has afligido lo persiguen,
　y se burlan del dolor del que has herido.
27Añade a sus pecados más pecados;
　no los hagas partícipes de tu *salvación.
28Que sean borrados del libro de la vida;
　que no queden inscritos con los justos.

29Y a mí, que estoy pobre y adolorido,
　que me proteja, oh Dios, tu *salvación.
30Con cánticos alabaré el *nombre de Dios;
　con acción de gracias lo exaltaré.
31Esa ofrenda agradará más al SEÑOR
　que la de un toro o un novillo
　con sus cuernos y pezuñas.
32Los pobres verán esto y se alegrarán;
　¡reanímense ustedes, los que buscan a Dios!
33Porque el SEÑOR oye a los necesitados,
　y no desdeña a su pueblo cautivo.

34Que lo alaben los cielos y la tierra,
　los mares y todo lo que se mueve en ellos,
35porque Dios salvará a *Sión
　y reconstruirá las ciudades de Judá.
　Allí se establecerá el pueblo
　y tomará posesión de la tierra.
36La heredarán los hijos de sus siervos;
　la habitarán los que aman al Señor.

Salmo 70
70:1-5 — Sal 40:13-17
Al director musical. Petición de David.

1Apresúrate, oh Dios, a rescatarme;
　¡apresúrate, SEÑOR, a socorrerme!
2Que sean avergonzados y confundidos
　los que procuran matarme.
　Que retrocedan humillados
　todos los que desean mi ruina.
3Que vuelvan sobre sus pasos, avergonzados,
　todos los que se burlan de mí.
4Pero que todos los que te buscan
　se alegren en ti y se regocijen;
　que los que aman tu *salvación digan
　siempre:
　«¡Sea Dios exaltado!»

5Yo soy pobre y estoy necesitado;
　¡ven pronto a mí, oh Dios!
　Tú eres mi socorro y mi libertador;
　¡no te demores, SEÑOR!

Salmo 71
71:1-3 — Sal 31:1-4
1En ti, SEÑOR, me he refugiado;
　jamás me dejes quedar en vergüenza.
2Por tu justicia, rescátame y líbrame;
　dígnate escucharme, y sálvame.
3Sé tú mi *roca de refugio
　adonde pueda yo siempre acudir;
　da la orden de salvarme,
　porque tú eres mi roca, mi fortaleza.
4Líbrame, Dios mío, de manos de los impíos,
　del poder de los malvados y violentos.

5Tú, Soberano SEÑOR, has sido mi esperanza;

en ti he confiado desde mi juventud.
6De ti he dependido desde que nací;
　del vientre materno me hiciste nacer.
　¡Por siempre te alabaré!
7Para muchos, soy motivo de asombro,
　pero tú eres mi refugio inconmovible.
8Mi boca rebosa de alabanzas a tu *nombre,
　y todo el día proclama tu grandeza.

9No me rechaces cuando llegue a viejo;
　no me abandones cuando me falten las
　　fuerzas.
10Porque mis enemigos murmuran contra mí;
　los que me acechan se confabulan.
11Y dicen: «¡Dios lo ha abandonado!
　¡Persíganlo y agárrenlo, que nadie lo
　　rescatará!»
12Dios mío, no te alejes de mí;
　Dios mío, ven pronto a ayudarme.
13Que perezcan humillados mis acusadores;
　que se cubran de oprobio y de ignominia
　los que buscan mi ruina.

14Pero yo siempre tendré esperanza,
　y más y más te alabaré.
15Todo el día proclamará mi boca
　tu justicia y tu *salvación,
　aunque es algo que no alcanzo a descifrar.
16Soberano SEÑOR, relataré tus obras
　　poderosas,
　y haré memoria de tu justicia,
　de tu justicia solamente.
17Tú, oh Dios, me enseñaste desde mi
　　juventud,
　y aún hoy anuncio todos tus prodigios.
18Aun cuando sea yo anciano y peine canas,
　no me abandones, oh Dios,
　hasta que anuncie tu poder
　a la generación venidera,
　y dé a conocer tus proezas
　a los que aún no han nacido.

19Oh Dios, tú has hecho grandes cosas;
　tu justicia llega a las alturas.
　¿Quién como tú, oh Dios?
20Me has hecho pasar por muchos infortunios,
　pero volverás a darme vida;
　de las profundidades de la tierra
　volverás a levantarme.
21Acrecentarás mi honor
　y volverás a consolarme.

22Por tu fidelidad, Dios mío,
　te alabaré con instrumentos de cuerda;
　te cantaré, oh Santo de Israel,
　salmos con la lira.
23Gritarán de júbilo mis labios
　cuando yo te cante salmos,
　pues me has salvado la vida.
24Todo el día repetirá mi lengua
　la historia de tus justas acciones,
　pues quienes buscaban mi mal
　han quedado confundidos y avergonzados.

Salmo 72
De Salomón.

1Oh Dios, otorga tu justicia al rey,
　tu rectitud al príncipe heredero.
2Así juzgará con rectitud a tu pueblo
　y hará justicia a tus pobres.
3Brindarán los montes *bienestar al pueblo,
　y fruto de justicia las colinas.
4El rey hará justicia a los pobres del pueblo

y salvará a los necesitados;
  ¡él aplastará a los opresores!

⁵Que viva el rey¥ por mil generaciones,
  lo mismo que el sol y que la luna.
⁶Que sea como la lluvia sobre un campo
    sembrado,
  como las lluvias que empapan la tierra.
⁷Que en sus días florezca la justicia,
  y que haya gran prosperidad,
  hasta que la luna deje de existir.

⁸Que domine el rey de mar a mar,
  desde el río Éufrates hasta los confines de
    la tierra.
⁹Que se postren ante él las tribus del desierto;
  ¡que muerdan el polvo sus enemigos!
¹⁰Que le paguen tributo los reyes de Tarsis
  y de las costas remotas;
  que los reyes de Sabá y de Seba
  le traigan presentes.
¹¹Que ante él se inclinen todos los reyes;
  ¡que le sirvan todas las naciones!

¹²Él librará al indigente que pide auxilio,
  y al pobre que no tiene quien lo ayude.
¹³Se compadecerá del desvalido y del
    necesitado,
  y a los menesterosos les salvará la vida.
¹⁴Los librará de la opresión y la violencia,
  porque considera valiosa su vida.

¹⁵¡Que viva el rey!
  ¡Que se le entregue el oro de Sabá!
  Que se ore por él sin cesar;
  que todos los días se le bendiga.
¹⁶Que abunde el trigo en toda la tierra;
  que ondeen los trigales en la cumbre de los
    montes.
  Que el grano se dé como en el Líbano;
  que abunden las gavillas² como la hierba
    del campo.

¹⁷Que su *nombre perdure para siempre;
  que su fama permanezca como el sol.
  Que en su nombre las naciones
  se bendigan unas a otras;
  que todas ellas lo proclamen *dichoso.

¹⁸Bendito sea Dios el SEÑOR,
  el Dios de Israel,
  el único que hace obras portentosas.
¹⁹Bendito sea por siempre su glorioso nombre;
  ¡que toda la tierra se llene de su gloria!

      Amén y amén.

²⁰Aquí terminan las oraciones de David hijo de
    Isaí.

LIBRO III
Salmos 73-89

Salmo 73
Salmo de Asaf.

¹En verdad, ¡cuán bueno es Dios con Israel,
  con los puros de corazón!
²Yo estuve a punto de caer,
  y poco me faltó para que resbalara.
³Sentí envidia de los arrogantes,

al ver la prosperidad de esos malvados.

⁴Ellos no tienen ningún problema;
  su cuerpo está fuerte y saludable.ᵃ
⁵Libres están de los afanes de todos;
  no les afectan los infortunios humanos.
⁶Por eso lucen su orgullo como un collar,
  y hacen gala de su violencia.
⁷¡Están que revientan de malicia,
  y hasta se les ven sus malas intenciones!
⁸Son burlones, hablan con doblez,
  y arrogantes oprimen y amenazan.
⁹Con la boca increpan al cielo,
  con la lengua dominan la tierra.
¹⁰Por eso la gente acude a ellos
  y cree todo lo que afirman.
¹¹Hasta dicen: «¿Cómo puede Dios saberlo?
  ¿Acaso el *Altísimo tiene entendimiento?»

¹²Así son los impíos;
  sin afanarse, aumentan sus riquezas.
¹³En verdad, ¿de qué me sirve
  mantener mi corazón limpio
  y mis manos lavadas en la inocencia,
¹⁴si todo el día me golpean
  y de mañana me castigan?

¹⁵Si hubiera dicho: «Voy a hablar como ellos»,
  habría traicionado a tu linaje.
¹⁶Cuando traté de comprender todo esto,
  me resultó una carga insoportable.
¹⁷hasta que entré en el santuario de Dios;
  allí comprendí cuál será el destino de los
    malvados:
¹⁸En verdad, los has puesto en terreno
    resbaladizo,
  y los empujas a su propia destrucción.
¹⁹¡En un instante serán destruidos,
  totalmente consumidos por el terror!
²⁰Como quien despierta de un sueño,
  así, *Señor, cuando tú te levantes,
  desecharás su falsa apariencia.

²¹Se me afligía el corazón
  y se me amargaba el ánimo
²²por mi *necedad e ignorancia.
  ¡Me porté contigo como una bestia!
²³Pero yo siempre estoy contigo,
  pues tú me sostienes de la mano derecha.
²⁴Me guías con tu consejo,
  y más tarde me acogerás en gloria.
²⁵¿A quién tengo en el cielo sino a ti?
  Si estoy contigo, ya nada quiero en la tierra.
²⁶Podrán desfallecer mi cuerpo y mi espíritu,ᵇ
  pero Dios fortaleceᶜ mi corazón;
  él es mi herencia eterna.

²⁷Perecerán los que se alejen de ti;
  tú destruyes a los que te son infieles.
²⁸Para mí el bien es estar cerca de Dios.
  He hecho del SEÑOR Soberano mi refugio
  para contar todas sus obras.

Salmo 74
*Masquil de Asaf.

¹¿Por qué, oh Dios,
  nos has rechazado para siempre?
  ¿Por qué se ha encendido tu ira
  contra las ovejas de tu prado?

---

y **72:5** *Que viva el rey* (véase LXX); *Te temerán* (TM).   z **72:16** *que abunden las gavillas.* Alt. *que de la ciudad nazca gente.*
a **73:4** *no tienen ningún problema; / su cuerpo está fuerte y saludable.* Alt. *no tienen lucha alguna ante su muerte; / su cuerpo está saludable.*   b **73:26** *espíritu.* Lit. *corazón.*   c **73:26** *fortalece.* Lit. *es la roca de.*

²Acuérdate del pueblo que adquiriste
　　desde tiempos antiguos,
de la tribu que redimiste
　　para que fuera tu posesión.
Acuérdate de este monte *Sión,
　　que es donde tú habitas.
³Dirige tus pasos hacia estas ruinas eternas;
　　¡todo en el santuario lo ha destruido el
　　　enemigo!
⁴Tus adversarios rugen en el lugar de tus
　　asambleas
　　y plantan sus banderas en señal de victoria.
⁵Parecen leñadores en el bosque,
　　talando árboles con sus hachas.
⁶Con sus hachas y martillos
　　destrozaron todos los adornos de madera.
⁷Prendieron fuego a tu santuario;
　　profanaron el lugar donde habitas.
⁸En su corazón dijeron: «¡Los haremos polvo!»,
　　y quemaron en el país todos tus santuarios.
⁹Ya no vemos ondear nuestras banderas;
　　ya no hay ningún profeta,
　　y ni siquiera sabemos
　　　hasta cuándo durará todo esto.

¹⁰¿Hasta cuándo, oh Dios, se burlará el
　　adversario?
　　¿Por siempre insultará tu nombre el
　　　enemigo?
¹¹¿Por qué retraes tu mano, tu mano derecha?
　　¿Por qué te quedas cruzado de brazos?

¹²Tú, oh Dios, eres mi rey desde tiempos
　　antiguos;
　　tú traes *salvación sobre la tierra.
¹³Tú dividiste el mar con tu poder;
　　les rompiste la cabeza a los monstruos
　　　marinos.
¹⁴Tú aplastaste las cabezas de *Leviatán
　　y lo diste por comida a las jaurías del
　　　desierto.
¹⁵Tú hiciste que brotaran fuentes y arroyos;
　　secaste ríos de inagotables corrientes.
¹⁶Tuyo es el día, tuya también la noche;
　　tú estableciste la luna y el sol;
¹⁷trazaste los límites de la tierra,
　　y creaste el verano y el invierno.

¹⁸Recuerda, SEÑOR, que tu enemigo se burla,
　　y que un pueblo insensato ofende tu
　　　nombre.
¹⁹No entregues a las fieras
　　la vida de tu tórtola;
no te olvides, ni ahora ni nunca,
　　de la vida de tus pobres.
²⁰Toma en cuenta tu *pacto,
　　pues en todos los rincones del país
　　abunda la violencia.
²¹Que no vuelva humillado el oprimido;
　　que alaben tu nombre el pobre y el
　　　necesitado.

²²Levántate, oh Dios, y defiende tu causa;
　　recuerda que a todas horas te ofenden los
　　　*necios.
²³No pases por alto el griterío de tus
　　adversarios,
　　el creciente tumulto de tus enemigos.

Salmo 75

Al director musical. Sígase la tonada de «No
destruyas». Salmo de Asaf. Cántico.

¹ Te damos gracias, oh Dios,
　　te damos gracias e invocamosᵈ tu *nombre;
　　¡todos hablan de tus obras portentosas!

²Tú dices: «Cuando yo lo decida,
　　juzgaré con justicia.
³Cuando se estremece la tierra
　　con todos sus habitantes,
　　soy yo quien afirma sus columnas.»
　　　　　　　　　　　　　　　　*Selah

⁴«No sean altaneros», digo a los altivos;
　　«No sean soberbios», ordeno a los impíos;
⁵«No hagan gala de soberbia contra el cielo,
　　ni hablen con aires de suficiencia.»

⁶La exaltación no viene del oriente,
　　ni del occidente ni del sur,
⁷sino que es Dios el que juzga:
　　a unos humilla y a otros exalta.
⁸En la mano del SEÑOR hay una copa
　　de espumante vino mezclado con especias;
　　cuando él lo derrame, todos los impíos de la
　　　tierra
　　habrán de beberlo hasta las heces.
⁹Yo hablaré de esto siempre;
　　cantaré salmos al Dios de Jacob.
¹⁰Aniquilaré la altivez de todos los impíos,
　　y exaltaré el poder de los justos.

Salmo 76

Al director musical. Acompáñese con instrumentos
de cuerda. Salmo de Asaf. Cántico.

¹Dios es conocido en Judá;
　　su *nombre es exaltado en Israel.
²En *Salén se halla su santuario;
　　en *Sión está su morada.
³Allí hizo pedazos las centelleantes saetas,
　　los escudos, las espadas, las armas de
　　　guerra.
　　　　　　　　　　　　　　　　*Selah

⁴Estás rodeado de esplendor;
　　eres más imponente que las montañas
　　　eternas.ᵉ
⁵Los valientes yacen ahora despojados;
　　han caído en el sopor de la muerte.
Ninguno de esos hombres aguerridos
　　volverá a levantar sus manos.
⁶Cuando tú, Dios de Jacob, los reprendiste,
　　quedaron pasmados jinetes y corceles.
⁷Tú, y sólo tú, eres de temer.
　　¿Quién puede hacerte frente
　　cuando se enciende tu enojo?
⁸Desde el cielo diste a conocer tu veredicto;
　　la tierra, temerosa, guardó silencio
⁹cuando tú, oh Dios, te levantaste para juzgar,
　　para salvar a los pobres de la tierra.
　　　　　　　　　　　　　　　　Selah
¹⁰La furia de Edom se vuelve tu alabanza;
　　lo que aún queda de Jamat se vuelve tu
　　　corona.ᶠ
¹¹Hagan votos al SEÑOR su Dios, y cúmplanlos;
　　que todos los países vecinos
　　paguen tributo al Dios temible,

ᵈ **75:1** *e invocamos* (LXX y Siríaca); *y cercano está* (TM).　ᵉ **76:4** *montañas eternas* (LXX); *montañas donde hay presa* (TM).
ᶠ **76:10** *La furia ... tu corona* (lectura probable); *La furia del hombre te alabará, porque los sobrevivientes al castigo te harán fiesta* (TM).

12al que acaba con el valor de los gobernantes,
¡al que es temido por los reyes de la tierra!

Salmo 77

Al director musical. Para Jedutún. Salmo de Asaf.

1A Dios elevo mi voz suplicante;
a Dios elevo mi voz para que me escuche.
2Cuando estoy angustiado, recurro al *Señor;
sin cesar elevo mis manos por las noches,
pero me niego a recibir consuelo.
3Me acuerdo de Dios, y me lamento;
medito en él, y desfallezco.

Selah

4No me dejas conciliar el sueño;
tan turbado estoy que ni hablar puedo.
5Me pongo a pensar en los tiempos de antaño;
de los años ya idos 6me acuerdo.
Mi corazón reflexiona por las noches;g
mi espíritu medita e inquiere:
7¿Nos rechazará el Señor para siempre?
¿No volverá a mostrarnos su buena
voluntad?
8¿Se habrá agotado su gran amor eterno,
y sus promesas por todas las generaciones?
9¿Se habrá olvidado Dios de sus bondades,
y en su enojo ya no quiere tenernos
compasión?»

Selah

10Y me pongo a pensar: «Esto es lo que me
duele:
que haya cambiado la diestra del
*Altísimo.»
11Prefiero recordar las hazañas del SEÑOR,
traer a la memoria sus milagros de antaño.
12Meditaré en todas tus proezas;
evocaré tus obras poderosas.

13Santos, oh Dios, son tus *caminos;
¿qué dios hay tan excelso como nuestro
Dios?
14Tú eres el Dios que realiza maravillas;
el que despliega su poder entre los
pueblos.
15Con tu brazo poderoso redimiste a tu pueblo,
a los descendientes de Jacob y de José.

Selah

16Las aguas te vieron, oh Dios,
las aguas te vieron y se agitaron;
el propio abismo se estremeció con
violencia.
17Derramaron su lluvia las nubes;
retumbaron con estruendo los cielos;
rasgaron el espacio tus centellas.
18Tu estruendo retumbó en el torbellino
y tus relámpagos iluminaron el mundo;
la tierra se estremeció con temblores.
19Te abriste camino en el mar;
te hiciste paso entre las muchas aguas,
y no se hallaron tus huellas.
20Por medio de Moisés y de Aarón
guiaste como un rebaño a tu pueblo.

Salmo 78

*Masquil de Asaf.

1Pueblo mío, atiende a mi *enseñanza;
presta oído a las palabras de mi boca.
2Mis labios pronunciarán *parábolas
y evocarán misterios de antaño,

3cosas que hemos oído y conocido,
y que nuestros padres nos han contado.
4No las esconderemos de sus descendientes;
hablaremos a la generación venidera
del poder del SEÑOR, de sus proezas,
y de las maravillas que ha realizado.
5Él promulgó un decreto para Jacob,
dictó una *ley para Israel;
ordenó a nuestros antepasados
enseñarlos a sus descendientes,
6para que los conocieran las generaciones
venideras
y los hijos que habrían de nacer,
que a su vez los enseñarían a sus hijos.
7Así ellos pondrían su confianza en Dios
y no se olvidarían de sus proezas,
sino que cumplirían sus mandamientos.
8Así no serían como sus antepasados:
generación obstinada y rebelde,
gente de corazón fluctuante,
cuyo espíritu no se mantuvo fiel a Dios.
9La tribu de Efraín, con sus diestros arqueros,
se puso en fuga el día de la batalla.

10No cumplieron con el *pacto de Dios,
sino que se negaron a seguir sus
enseñanzas.
11Echaron al olvido sus proezas,
las maravillas que les había mostrado,
12los milagros que hizo a la vista de sus padres
en la tierra de Egipto, en la región de Zoán.
13Partió el mar en dos para que ellos lo
cruzaran,
mientras mantenía las aguas firmes como
un muro.
14De día los guió con una nube,
y toda la noche con luz de fuego.
15En el desierto partió en dos las rocas,
y les dio a beber torrentes de aguas;
16hizo que brotaran arroyos de la peña
y que las aguas fluyeran como ríos.

17Pero ellos volvieron a pecar contra él;
en el desierto se rebelaron contra el
*Altísimo.
18Con toda intención pusieron a Dios a prueba,
y le exigieron comida a su antojo.
19Murmuraron contra Dios, y aun dijeron:
«¿Podrá Dios tendernos una mesa en el
desierto?
20Cuando golpeó la roca,
el agua brotó en torrentes;
pero ¿podrá también darnos de comer?,
¿podrá proveerle carne a su pueblo?»
21Cuando el SEÑOR oyó esto, se puso muy
furioso;
su enojo se encendió contra Jacob,
su ira ardió contra Israel.
22Porque no confiaron en Dios,
ni creyeron que él los salvaría.
23Desde lo alto dio una orden a las nubes,
y se abrieron las puertas de los cielos.
24Hizo que les lloviera maná, para que
comieran;
pan del cielo les dio a comer.
25Todos ellos comieron pan de ángeles;
Dios les envió comida hasta saciarlos.
26Desató desde el cielo el viento solano,
y con su poder levantó el viento del sur.

---

g **77:6** *me acuerdo. / Mi ... las noches* (LXX); *Me acuerdo de mi cántico por las noches con mi corazón* (TM).

27Cual lluvia de polvo, hizo que les lloviera
carne;
¡nubes de pájaros, como la arena del mar!
28Los hizo caer en medio de su campamento
y en los alrededores de sus tiendas.
29Comieron y se hartaron,
pues Dios les cumplió su capricho.
30Pero el capricho no les duró mucho:
aún tenían la comida en la boca
31cuando el enojo de Dios vino sobre ellos:
dio muerte a sus hombres más robustos;
abatió a la flor y nata de Israel.

32A pesar de todo, siguieron pecando
y no creyeron en sus maravillas.
33Por tanto, Dios hizo que sus días
se esfumaran como un suspiro,
que sus años acabaran en medio del terror.
34Si Dios los castigaba, entonces lo buscaban,
y con ansias se volvían de nuevo a él.
35Se acordaban de que Dios era su *roca,
de que el Dios Altísimo era su redentor.
36Pero entonces lo halagaban con la boca,
y le mentían con la lengua.
37No fue su corazón sincero para con Dios;
no fueron fieles a su pacto.
38Sin embargo, él les tuvo compasión;
les perdonó su maldad y no los destruyó.
Una y otra vez contuvo su enojo,
y no se dejó llevar del todo por la ira.
39Se acordó de que eran simples *mortales,
un efímero suspiro que jamás regresa.

40¡Cuántas veces se rebelaron contra él en el
desierto,
y lo entristecieron en los páramos!
41Una y otra vez ponían a Dios a prueba,
provocaban al Santo de Israel.
42Jamás se acordaron de su poder,
de cuando los rescató del opresor,
43ni de sus señales milagrosas en Egipto,
ni de sus portentos en la región de Zoán,
44cuando convirtió en sangre los ríos egipcios
y no pudieron ellos beber de sus arroyos;
45cuando les envió tábanos que se los
devoraban,
y ranas que los destruían;
46cuando entregó sus cosechas a los
saltamontes,
y sus sembrados a la langosta;
47cuando con granizo destruyó sus viñas,
y con escarcha sus higueras;
48cuando entregó su ganado al granizo,
y sus rebaños a las centellas;
49cuando lanzó contra ellos el ardor de su ira,
de su furor, indignación y hostilidad:
¡todo un ejército de ángeles destructores!
50Dio rienda suelta a su enojo
y no los libró de la muerte,
sino que los entregó a la plaga.
51Dio muerte a todos los primogénitos de
Egipto,
a las primicias de su raza en los
campamentos de Cam.
52A su pueblo lo guió como a un rebaño;
los llevó por el desierto, como a ovejas,
53infundiéndoles confianza para que no
temieran.
Pero a sus enemigos se los tragó el mar.

54Trajo a su pueblo a esta su tierra santa,
a estas montañas que su diestra conquistó.
55Al paso de los israelitas expulsó naciones,
cuyas tierras dio a su pueblo en heredad;
¡así estableció en sus tiendas a las tribus de
Israel!

56Pero ellos pusieron a prueba a Dios:
se rebelaron contra el *Altísimo
y desobedecieron sus *estatutos.
57Fueron desleales y traidores, como sus
padres;
¡tan falsos como un arco defectuoso!
58Lo irritaron con sus santuarios paganos;
con sus ídolos despertaron sus celos.
59Dios lo supo y se puso muy furioso,
por lo que rechazó completamente a Israel.
60Abandonó el tabernáculo de Siló,
que era su santuario aquí en la tierra,
61y dejó que el símbolo de su poder y gloria
cayera cautivo en manos enemigas.
62Tan furioso estaba contra su pueblo
que dejó que los mataran a filo de espada.
63A sus jóvenes los consumió el fuego,
y no hubo cantos nupciales para sus
doncellas;
64a filo de espada cayeron sus sacerdotes,
y sus viudas no pudieron hacerles duelo.

65Despertó entonces el Señor,
como quien despierta de un sueño,
como un guerrero que, por causa del vino,
lanza gritos desaforados.
66Hizo retroceder a sus enemigos,
y los puso en vergüenza para siempre.
67Rechazó a los descendientesh de José,
y no escogió a la tribu de Efraín;
68más bien, escogió a la tribu de Judá
y al monte *Sión, al cual ama.
69Construyó su santuario, alto como los cielos,i
como la tierra, que él afirmó para siempre.
70Escogió a su siervo David,
al que sacó de los apriscos de las ovejas,
71y lo quitó de andar arreando los rebaños
para que fuera el *pastor de Jacob, su
pueblo;
el pastor de Israel, su herencia.
72Y David los pastoreó con corazón sincero;
con mano experta los dirigió.

Salmo 79

Salmo de Asaf.

1Oh Dios, los pueblos paganos han invadido tu
herencia;
han profanado tu santo templo,
han dejado en ruinas a Jerusalén.
2Han entregado los cadáveres de tus siervos
como alimento de las aves del cielo;
han destinado los cuerpos de tus fieles
para comida de los animales salvajes.
3Por toda Jerusalén han derramado su sangre,
como si derramaran agua,
y no hay quien entierre a los muertos.
4Nuestros vecinos hacen mofa de nosotros;
somos blanco de las burlas de quienes nos
rodean.

5¿Hasta cuándo, SEÑOR?
¿Vas a estar enojado para siempre?
¿Arderá tu celo como el fuego?

---

h 78:67 los descendientes. Lit. las tiendas (de campaña).   i 78:69 santuario, alto como los cielos. Lit. santuario como las alturas.

6¡Enójate con las naciones que no te reconocen,
con los reinos que no invocan tu *nombre!
7Porque a Jacob se lo han devorado,
y al país lo han dejado en ruinas.
8No nos tomes en cuenta los pecados de ayer;
¡venga pronto tu misericordia a nuestro
encuentro,
porque estamos totalmente abatidos!

9Oh Dios y salvador nuestro,
por la gloria de tu nombre, ayúdanos;
por tu nombre, líbranos y perdona
nuestros pecados.

10¿Por qué van a decir las naciones:
«¿Dónde está su Dios?»
Permítenos ver, y muéstrales a los pueblos
paganos
cómo tomas venganza de la sangre de tus
siervos.
11Que lleguen a tu presencia
los gemidos de los cautivos,
y por la fuerza de tu brazo
salva a los condenados a muerte.

12Señor, haz que sientan nuestros vecinos,
siete veces en carne propia,
el oprobio que han lanzado contra ti.
13Y nosotros, tu pueblo y ovejas de tu prado,
te alabaremos por siempre;
de generación en generación
cantaremos tus alabanzas.

Salmo 80

Al director musical. Sígase la tonada de «Los lirios
del *pacto». Salmo de Asaf.

1*Pastor de Israel,
tú que guías a José como a un rebaño,
tú que reinas entre los *querubines,
¡escúchanos!
¡Resplandece 2delante de Efraín, Benjamín y
Manasés!
¡Muestra tu poder, y ven a salvarnos!

3Restáuranos, oh Dios;
haz resplandecer tu rostro sobre nosotros,
y sálvanos.

4¿Hasta cuándo, SEÑOR, Dios *Todopoderoso,
arderá tu ira contra las oraciones de tu
pueblo?
5Por comida, le has dado pan de lágrimas;
por bebida, lágrimas en abundancia.
6Nos has hecho motivo de contienda
para nuestros vecinos;
nuestros enemigos se burlan de nosotros.

7Restáuranos, oh Dios Todopoderoso;
haz resplandecer tu rostro sobre nosotros,
y sálvanos.

8De Egipto trajiste una vid;
expulsaste a los pueblos paganos, y la
plantaste.
9Le limpiaste el terreno,
y ella echó raíces y llenó la tierra.
10Su sombra se extendía hasta las montañas,
su follaje cubría los más altos cedros.
11Sus ramas se extendieron hasta el
Mediterráneo
y sus renuevos hasta el Éufrates.

12¿Por qué has derribado sus muros?
¡Todos los que pasan le arrancan uvas!
13Los jabalíes del bosque la destruyen,
los animales salvajes la devoran.
14¡Vuélvete a nosotros, oh Dios Todopoderoso!
¡Asómate a vernos desde el cielo
y brinda tus cuidados a esta vid!
15¡Es la raíz que plantaste con tu diestra!
¡Es el vástago que has criado para ti!

16Tu vid está derribada, quemada por el fuego;
a tu reprensión perece tu pueblo.j
17Bríndale tu apoyo al *hombre de tu diestra,
al *ser humanok que para ti has criado.
18Nosotros no nos apartaremos de ti;
reavívanos, e invocaremos tu *nombre.

19Restáuranos, SEÑOR, Dios Todopoderoso;
haz resplandecer tu rostro sobre nosotros,
y sálvanos.

Salmo 81

Al director musical. Sígase la tonada de «La canción
del lagar». Salmo de Asaf.

1Canten alegres a Dios, nuestra fortaleza;
¡aclamen con regocijo al Dios de Jacob!
2¡Entonen salmos!
¡Toquen ya la pandereta,
la lira y el arpa melodiosa!

3Toquen el cuerno de carnero en la luna nueva,
y en la luna llena, día de nuestra fiesta.
4Éste es un decreto para Israel,
una ordenanza del Dios de Jacob.
5Lo estableció como un *pacto con José
cuando salió de la tierra de Egipto.

Escucho un idioma que no entiendo:
6«Te he quitado la carga de los hombros;
tus manos se han librado del pesado cesto.
7En tu angustia me llamaste, y te libré;
oculto en el nubarrón te respondí;
en las aguas de Meribá te puse a prueba.
Selah

8»Escucha, pueblo mío, mis advertencias;
¡ay Israel, si tan sólo me escucharas!
9No tendrás ningún dios extranjero,
ni te inclinarás ante ningún dios extraño.
10Yo soy el SEÑOR tu Dios,
que te sacó de la tierra de Egipto.
Abre bien la boca, y te la llenaré.

11»Pero mi pueblo no me escuchó;
Israel no quiso hacerme caso.
12Por eso los abandoné a su obstinada
voluntad,
para que actuaran como mejor les
pareciera.

13»Si mi pueblo tan sólo me escuchara,
si Israel quisiera andar por mis *caminos,
14¡cuán pronto sometería yo a sus enemigos,
y volvería mi mano contra sus adversarios!
15Los que aborrecen al SEÑOR se rendirían ante
él,
pero serían eternamente castigados.
16Y a ti te alimentaría con lo mejor del trigo;
con miel de la peña te saciaría.»

j **80:16** *Tu vid ... tu pueblo* (lectura probable); *Haz que perezcan, a tu reprensión, / los que la queman y destruyen* (TM).
k **80:17** *ser humano.* Lit. *hijo de hombre.*

Salmo 82

Salmo de Asaf.

1Dios preside el consejo celestial;
 entre los dioses dicta sentencia:

2«¿Hasta cuándo defenderán la injusticia
 y favorecerán a los impíos?

Selah

3Defiendan la causa del huérfano y del
 desvalido;
 al pobre y al oprimido háganles justicia.
4Salven al menesteroso y al necesitado;
 líbrenlos de la mano de los impíos.

5»Ellos no saben nada, no entienden nada.
 Deambulan en la oscuridad;
 se estremecen todos los cimientos de la
 tierra.

6»Yo les he dicho: "Ustedes son dioses;
 todos ustedes son hijos del *Altísimo."
7Pero morirán como cualquier *mortal;
 caerán como cualquier otro gobernante.»

8Levántate, oh Dios, y juzga a la tierra,
 pues tuyas son todas las naciones.

Salmo 83

Cántico. Salmo de Asaf.

1Oh Dios, no guardes silencio;
 no te quedes, oh Dios, callado e impasible.
2Mira cómo se alborotan tus enemigos,
 cómo te desafían los que te odian.
3Con astucia conspiran contra tu pueblo;
 conspiran contra aquellos a quienes tú
 estimas.
4Y dicen: «¡Vengan, destruyamos su nación!
 ¡Que el *nombre de Israel no vuelva a
 recordarse!»
5Como un solo hombre se confabulan;
 han hecho un *pacto contra ti:
6los campamentos de Edom y de Ismael,
 los de Moab y de Agar,
7Guebal,l Amón y Amalec,
 los de Filistea y los habitantes de Tiro.
8¡Hasta Asiria se les ha unido;
 ha apoyado a los descendientes de Lot!

Selah

9Haz con ellos como hiciste con Madián,
 como hiciste con Sísara y Jabín en el río
 Quisón,
10los cuales perecieron en Endor
 y quedaron en la tierra, como estiércol.
11Haz con sus nobles
 como hiciste con Oreb y con Zeb;
 haz con todos sus príncipes
 como hiciste con Zeba y con Zalmuna,
12que decían: «Vamos a adueñarnos
 de los pastizales de Dios.»

13Hazlos rodar como zarzas, Dios mío;
 ¡como paja que se lleva el viento!
14Y así como el fuego consume los bosques
 y las llamas incendian las montañas,
15así persíguelos con tus tormentas
 y aterrorízalos con tus tempestades.
16SEÑOR, cúbreles el rostro de ignominia,
 para que busquen tu nombre.

17Que sean siempre puestos en vergüenza;

que perezcan humillados.
18Que sepan que tú eres el SEÑOR,
 que ése es tu nombre;
 que sepan que sólo tú eres el *Altísimo
 sobre toda la tierra.

Salmo 84

Al director musical. Sígase la tonada de «La canción
del lagar». Salmo de los hijos de Coré.

1¡Cuán hermosas son tus moradas,
 SEÑOR *Todopoderoso!
2Anhelo con el *alma los atrios del SEÑOR;
 casi agonizo por estar en ellos.
 Con el corazón, con todo el cuerpo,
 canto alegre al Dios de la vida.

3SEÑOR Todopoderoso, rey mío y Dios mío,
 aun el gorrión halla casa cerca de tus
 altares;
 también la golondrina hace allí su nido,
 para poner sus polluelos.

4*Dichoso el que habita en tu templo,
 pues siempre te está alabando.

Selah

5Dichoso el que tiene en ti su fortaleza,
 que sólo piensa en recorrer tus sendas.
6Cuando pasa por el valle de las Lágrimas
 lo convierte en región de manantiales;
 también las lluvias tempranas
 cubren de bendiciones el valle.
7Según avanzan los peregrinos, cobran más
 fuerzas,
 y en *Sión se presentan ante el Dios de
 dioses.

8Oye mi oración, SEÑOR, Dios Todopoderoso;
 escúchame, Dios de Jacob.

Selah

9Oh Dios, escudo nuestro,
 pon sobre tu ungido tus ojos bondadosos.

10Vale más pasar un día en tus atrios
 que mil fuera de ellos;
 prefiero cuidar la entrada de la casa de mi Dios
 que habitar entre los impíos.

11El SEÑOR es sol y escudo;
 Dios nos concede honor y gloria.
 El SEÑOR brinda generosamente su bondad
 a los que se conducen sin tacha.

12SEÑOR Todopoderoso,
 ¡dichosos los que en ti confían!

Salmo 85

Al director musical. Salmo de los hijos de Coré.

1SEÑOR, tú has sido bondadoso con esta tierra
 tuya
 al restaurarm a Jacob;
2perdonaste la iniquidad de tu pueblo
 y cubriste todos sus pecados;

Selah

3depusiste por completo tu enojo,
 y contuviste el ardor de tu ira.

4Restáuranos una vez más, Dios y salvador
 nuestro;
 pon fin a tu disgusto con nosotros.
5¿Vas a estar enojado con nosotros para
 siempre?
 ¿Vas a seguir eternamente airado?

---

l **83:7** *Guebal.* Es decir, Biblos. m **85:1** *al restaurar.* Alt. *al hacer volver de la cautividad.*

6¿No volverás a darnos nueva vida,
para que tu pueblo se alegre en ti?
7Muéstranos, SEÑOR, tu amor inagotable,
y concédenos tu *salvación.

8Voy a escuchar lo que Dios el SEÑOR dice:
él promete *paz a su pueblo y a sus fieles,
siempre y cuando no se vuelvan a la
*necedad.n
9Muy cercano está para salvar a los que le
temen,
para establecer su gloria en nuestra tierra.

10El amor y la verdad se encontrarán;
se besarán la paz y la justicia.
11De la tierra brotará la verdad,
y desde el cielo se asomará la justicia.
12El SEÑOR mismo nos dará bienestar,
y nuestra tierra rendirá su fruto.
13La justicia será su heraldo
y le preparará el camino.

Salmo 86

Oración de David.

1Atiéndeme, SEÑOR; respóndeme,
pues pobre soy y estoy necesitado.
2Presérvame la vida, pues te soy fiel.
Tú eres mi Dios, y en ti confío;
¡salva a tu siervo!
3Compadécete, Señor, de mí,
porque a ti clamo todo el día.
4Reconforta el espíritu de tu siervo,
porque a ti, Señor, elevo mi *alma.

5Tú, Señor, eres bueno y perdonador;
grande es tu amor por todos los que te
invocan.
6Presta oído, SEÑOR, a mi oración;
atiende a la voz de mi clamor.
7En el día de mi angustia te invoco,
porque tú me respondes.

8No hay, SEÑOR, entre los dioses otro como tú,
ni hay obras semejantes a las tuyas.
9Todas las naciones que has creado
vendrán, Señor, y ante ti se postrarán
y glorificarán tu *nombre.
10Porque tú eres grande y haces maravillas;
¡sólo tú eres Dios!

11Instrúyeme, SEÑOR, en tu *camino
para conducirme con fidelidad.
Dame integridad de corazón
para temer tu nombre.
12Señor mi Dios, con todo el corazón te alabaré,
y por siempre glorificaré tu nombre.
13Porque grande es tu amor por mí:
me has librado de caer en el *sepulcro.

14Gente altanera me ataca, oh Dios;
una banda de asesinos procura matarme.
¡Son gente que no te toma en cuenta!
15Pero tú, Señor, eres Dios clemente y
compasivo,
lento para la ira, y grande en amor y
verdad.
16Vuélvete hacia mí, y tenme compasión;
concédele tu fuerza a este siervo tuyo.
¡Salva a tu hijo fiel!ñ
17Dame una muestra de tu amor,

para que mis enemigos la vean y se
avergüencen,
porque tú, SEÑOR, me has brindado ayuda
y consuelo.

Salmo 87

Salmo de los hijos de Coré. Cántico.

1Los cimientos de la ciudad de Dioso
están en el santo monte.
2El SEÑOR ama las *entradas de *Sión
más que a todas las moradas de Jacob.
3De ti, ciudad de Dios,
se dicen cosas gloriosas:
         *Selah
4«Entre los que me reconocen
puedo contar a *Rahab y a Babilonia,
a Filistea y a Tiro, lo mismo que a *Cus.
Se dice: "Éste nació en Sión."»
5De Sión se dirá, en efecto:
«Éste y aquél nacieron en ella.
El *Altísimo mismo la ha establecido.»
6El SEÑOR anotará en el registro de los pueblos:
«Éste nació en Sión.»
         Selah
7Y mientras cantan y bailan, dicen:
«En ti se hallan todos mis orígenes.»p

Salmo 88

Cántico. Salmo de los hijos de Coré. Al director musical. Según *majalat leannot. *Masquil de Hemán el ezraíta.

1SEÑOR, Dios de mi *salvación,
día y noche clamo en presencia tuya.
2Que llegue ante ti mi oración;
dígnate escuchar mi súplica.

3Tan colmado estoy de calamidades
que mi vida está al borde del *sepulcro.
4Ya me cuentan entre los que bajan a la fosa;
parezco un guerrero desvalido.
5Me han puesto aparte, entre los muertos;
parezco un cadáver que yace en el
sepulcro,
de esos que tú ya no recuerdas,
porque fueron arrebatados de tu mano.

6Me has echado en el foso más profundo,
en el más tenebroso de los abismos.
7El peso de tu enojo ha recaído sobre mí;
me has abrumado con tus olas.
         *Selah
8Me has quitado a todos mis amigos
y ante ellos me has hecho aborrecible.
Estoy aprisionado y no puedo librarme;
9los ojos se me nublan de tristeza.
Yo, SEÑOR, te invoco cada día,
y hacia ti extiendo las manos.
10¿Acaso entre los muertos realizas maravillas?
¿Pueden los muertos levantarse a darte
gracias?
         Selah
11¿Acaso en el sepulcro se habla de tu amor,
y de tu fidelidad en el abismo destructor?q
12¿Acaso en las tinieblas se conocen tus
maravillas,
o tu justicia en la tierra del olvido?
13Yo, SEÑOR, te ruego que me ayudes;

por la mañana busco tu presencia en
oración.
14¿Por qué me rechazas, SEÑOR?
¿Por qué escondes de mí tu rostro?

15Yo he sufrido desde mi juventud;
muy cerca he estado de la muerte.
Me has enviado terribles sufrimientos
y ya no puedo más.
16Tu ira se ha descargado sobre mí;
tus violentos ataques han acabado
conmigo.
17Todo el día me rodean como un océano;
me han cercado por completo.
18Me has quitado amigos y seres queridos;
ahora sólo tengo amistad con las tinieblas.

Salmo 89

*Masquil de Etán el ezraíta.

1Oh SEÑOR, por siempre cantaré
la grandeza de tu amor;
por todas las generaciones
proclamará mi boca tu fidelidad.
2Declararé que tu amor permanece firme para
siempre,
que has afirmado en el cielo tu fidelidad.

3Dijiste: «He hecho un *pacto con mi escogido;
le he jurado a David mi siervo:
4"Estableceré tu dinastía para siempre,
y afirmaré tu trono por todas las
generaciones."»
*Selah

5Los cielos, SEÑOR, celebran tus maravillas,
y tu fidelidad la asamblea de los santos.
6¿Quién en los cielos es comparable al SEÑOR?
¿Quién como él entre los seres celestiales?
7Dios es muy temido en la asamblea de los
santos;
grande y portentoso sobre cuantos lo
rodean.
8¿Quién como tú, SEÑOR, Dios *Todopoderoso,
rodeado de poder y de fidelidad?

9Tú gobiernas sobre el mar embravecido;
tú apaciguas sus encrespadas olas.
10Aplastaste a *Rahab como a un cadáver;
con tu brazo poderoso dispersaste a tus
enemigos.
11Tuyo es el cielo, y tuya la tierra;
tú fundaste el mundo y todo lo que
contiene.
12Por ti fueron creados el norte y el sur;
el Tabor y el Hermón cantan alegres a tu
*nombre.
13Tu brazo es capaz de grandes proezas;
fuerte es tu mano, exaltada tu diestra.

14La justicia y el derecho son el fundamento de
tu trono,
y tus heraldos, el amor y la verdad.
15*Dichosos los que saben aclamarte, SEÑOR,
y caminan a la luz de tu presencia;
16los que todo el día se alegran en tu nombre
y se regocijan en tu justicia.
17Porque tú eres su gloria y su poder;
por tu buena voluntad aumentas nuestra
fuerza.r
18Tú, SEÑOR, eres nuestro escudo;

tú, Santo de Israel, eres nuestro rey.

19Una vez hablaste en una visión,
y le dijiste a tu pueblo fiel:
«Le he brindado mi ayuda a un valiente;
al mejor hombre del pueblo lo he exaltado.
20He encontrado a David, mi siervo,
y lo he ungido con mi aceite santo.
21Mi mano siempre lo sostendrá;
mi brazo lo fortalecerá.
22Ningún enemigo lo someterá a tributo;
ningún inicuo lo oprimirá.
23Aplastaré a quienes se le enfrenten
y derribaré a quienes lo aborrezcan.
24La fidelidad de mi amor lo acompañará,
y por mi nombre será exaltada su fuerza.s
25Le daré poder sobre el mart
y dominio sobre los ríos.u
26Él me dirá: "Tú eres mi Padre,
mi Dios, la *roca de mi *salvación."
27Yo le daré los derechos de primogenitura,
la primacía sobre los reyes de la tierra.
28Mi amor por él será siempre constante,
y mi pacto con él se mantendrá fiel.
29Afirmaré su dinastía y su trono
para siempre, mientras el cielo exista.

30»Pero si sus hijos se apartan de mi *ley
y no viven según mis decretos,
31si violan mis *estatutos
y no observan mis mandamientos,
32con vara castigaré sus transgresiones
y con azotes su iniquidad.
33Con todo, jamás le negaré mi amor,
ni mi fidelidad le faltará.
34No violaré mi pacto
ni me retractaré de mis palabras.
35Una sola vez he jurado por mi santidad,
y no voy a mentirle a David:
36Su descendencia vivirá por siempre;
su trono durará como el sol en mi
presencia.
37Como la luna, fiel testigo en el cielo,
será establecido para siempre.»
Selah

38Pero tú has desechado, has rechazado a tu
ungido;
te has enfurecido contra él en gran manera.
39Has revocado el pacto con tu siervo;
has arrastrado por los suelos su corona.
40Has derribado todas sus murallas
y dejado en ruinas sus fortalezas.
41Todos los que pasan lo saquean;
ies motivo de burla para sus vecinos!
42Has exaltado el poder de sus adversarios
y llenado de gozo a sus enemigos.
43Le has quitado el filo a su espada,
y no lo has apoyado en la batalla.
44Has puesto fin a su esplendor
al derribar por tierra su trono.
45Has acortado los días de su juventud;
lo has cubierto con un manto de
vergüenza.
Selah

46¿Hasta cuándo, SEÑOR, te seguirás
escondiendo?

---

r 89:17 *aumentas nuestra fuerza.* Lit. *levantas nuestro cuerno.* s 89:24 *su fuerza.* Lit. *su cuerno.* t 89:25 *el mar.* Probable referencia al mar Mediterráneo. u 89:25 *los ríos.* Probable referencia a Mesopotamia.

¿Va a arder tu ira para siempre, como el
fuego?
47¡Recuerda cuán efímera es mi vida!v
Al fin y al cabo, ¿para qué creaste a los
*mortales?
48¿Quién hay que viva y no muera jamás,
o que pueda escapar del poder del
*sepulcro?

Selah

49¿Dónde está, Señor, tu amor de antaño,
que en tu fidelidad juraste a David?
50Recuerda, Señor, que se burlan de tus siervos;
que llevo en mi pecho los insultos de
muchos pueblos.
51Tus enemigos, SEÑOR, nos ultrajan;
a cada paso ofenden a tu ungido.
52¡Bendito sea el SEÑOR por siempre!
Amén y amén.

LIBRO IV
Salmos 90-106

Salmo 90
Oración de Moisés, hombre de Dios.
1*Señor, tú has sido nuestro refugio
generación tras generación.
2Desde antes que nacieran los montes
y que crearas la tierra y el mundo,
desde los tiempos antiguos
y hasta los tiempos postreros,
tú eres Dios.

3Tú haces que los *hombres vuelvan al polvo,
cuando dices: «¡Vuélvanse al polvo,
*mortales!»
4Mil años, para ti, son como el día de ayer, que
ya pasó;
son como unas cuantas horas de la noche.
5Arrasas a los mortales. Son como un sueño.
Nacen por la mañana, como la hierba
6que al amanecer brota lozana
y por la noche ya está marchita y seca.

7Tu ira en verdad nos consume,
tu indignación nos aterra.
8Ante ti has puesto nuestras iniquidades;
a la luz de tu presencia, nuestros pecados
secretos.
9Por causa de tu ira se nos va la vida entera;
se esfuman nuestros años como un suspiro.
10Algunos llegamos hasta los setenta años,
quizás alcancemos hasta los ochenta,
si las fuerzas nos acompañan.
Tantos años de vida,w sin embargo,
sólo traen pesadas cargas y calamidades:
pronto pasan, y con ellos pasamos
nosotros.

11¿Quién puede comprender el furor de tu
enojo?
¡Tu ira es tan grande como el temor que se
te debe!
12Enséñanos a contar bien nuestros días,
para que nuestro corazón adquiera
sabiduría.

13¿Cuándo, SEÑOR, te volverás hacia nosotros?
¡Compadécete ya de tus siervos!
14Sácianos de tu amor por la mañana,
y toda nuestra vida cantaremos de alegría.

15Días y años nos has afligido, nos has hecho
sufrir;
¡devuélvenos ahora ese tiempo en alegría!
16¡Sean manifiestas tus obras a tus siervos,
y tu esplendor a sus descendientes!

17Que el favorx del Señor nuestro Dios
esté sobre nosotros.
Confirma en nosotros la obra de nuestras
manos;
sí, confirma la obra de nuestras manos.

Salmo 91
1El que habita al abrigo del *Altísimo
se acoge a la sombra del *Todopoderoso.
2Yo le digo al SEÑOR: «Tú eres mi refugio,
mi fortaleza, el Dios en quien confío.»

3Sólo él puede librarte de las trampas del
cazador
y de mortíferas plagas,
4pues te cubrirá con sus plumas
y bajo sus alas hallarás refugio.
¡Su verdad será tu escudo y tu baluarte!
5No temerás el terror de la noche,
ni la flecha que vuela de día,
6ni la peste que acecha en las sombras
ni la plaga que destruye a mediodía.
7Podrán caer mil a tu izquierda,
y diez mil a tu derecha,
pero a ti no te afectará.
8No tendrás más que abrir bien los ojos,
para ver a los impíos recibir su merecido.

9Ya que has puesto al SEÑOR por tuy refugio,
al Altísimo por tu protección,
10ningún mal habrá de sobrevenirte,
ninguna calamidad llegará a tu hogar.
11Porque él ordenará que sus ángeles
te cuiden en todos tus *caminos.
12Con sus propias manos te levantarán
para que no tropieces con piedra alguna.
13Aplastarás al león y a la víbora;
¡hollarás fieras y serpientes!

14«Yo lo libraré, porque él se acoge a mí;
lo protegeré, porque reconoce mi *nombre.
15Él me invocará, y yo le responderé;
estaré con él en momentos de angustia;
lo libraré y lo llenaré de honores.
16Lo colmaré con muchos años de vida
y le haré gozar de mi *salvación.»

Salmo 92
Salmo para cantarse en *sábado.
1¡Cuán bueno, SEÑOR, es darte gracias
y entonar, oh *Altísimo, salmos a tu
*nombre;
2proclamar tu gran amor por la mañana,
y tu fidelidad por la noche,
3al son del decacordio y de la lira;
al son del arpa y del salterio!

4Tú, SEÑOR, me llenas de alegría con tus
maravillas;
por eso alabaré jubiloso las obras de tus
manos.
5Oh SEÑOR, ¡cuán imponentes son tus obras,
y cuán profundos tus pensamientos!
6Los insensatos no lo saben,
los *necios no lo entienden:

v 89:47 Véase 39:4. w 90:10 *Tantos años de vida*. Lit. *Su orgullo*. x 90:17 *Que el favor*. Alt. *Que la belleza*. y 91:9 *tu*. Lit. *mi*.

7aunque broten como hierba los impíos,
y florezcan todos los malhechores,
para siempre serán destruidos.
8Sólo tú, SEÑOR, serás exaltado para
siempre.

9Ciertamente tus enemigos, SEÑOR,
ciertamente tus enemigos perecerán;
idispersados por todas partes
serán todos los malhechores!

10Me has dado las fuerzas de un toro;
me has ungido con el mejor perfume.
11Me has hecho ver la caída de mis adversarios
y oír la derrota de mis malvados enemigos.

12Como palmeras florecen los justos;
como cedros del Líbano crecen.
13Plantados en la casa del SEÑOR,
florecen en los atrios de nuestro Dios.
14Aun en su vejez, darán fruto;
siempre estarán vigorosos y lozanos,
15para proclamar: «El SEÑOR es justo;
él es mi *Roca, y en él no hay injusticia.»

Salmo 93

1El SEÑOR reina, revestido de esplendor;
el SEÑOR se ha revestido de grandeza
y ha desplegado su poder.
Ha establecido el mundo con firmeza;
jamás será removido.
2Desde el principio se estableció tu trono,
y tú desde siempre has existido.

3Se levantan las aguas, SEÑOR;
se levantan las aguas con estruendo;
se levantan las aguas y sus batientes olas.
4Pero el SEÑOR, en las alturas, se muestra
poderoso:
más poderoso que el estruendo de las
muchas aguas,
más poderoso que los embates del mar.

5Dignos de confianza son, SEÑOR, tus
*estatutos;
ila santidad es para siempre el adorno de tu
casa!

Salmo 94

1SEÑOR, Dios de las venganzas;
Dios de las venganzas, imanifiéstate!z
2Levántate, Juez de la tierra,
y dales su merecido a los soberbios.
3¿Hasta cuándo, SEÑOR, hasta cuándo
habrán de ufanarse los impíos?

4Todos esos malhechores son unos fanfarrones;
a borbotones escupen su arrogancia.
5A tu pueblo, SEÑOR, lo pisotean;
ioprimen a tu herencia!
6Matan a las viudas y a los extranjeros;
a los huérfanos los asesinan.
7Y hasta dicen: «El SEÑOR no ve;
el Dios de Jacob no se da cuenta.»
8Entiendan esto, gente necia;
¿cuándo, insensatos, lo van a comprender?
9¿Acaso no oirá el que nos puso las orejas,
ni podrá ver el que nos formó los ojos?
10¿Y no habrá de castigar el que corrige a las
naciones

e instruye en el saber a todo el mundo?
11El SEÑOR conoce los pensamientos
*humanos,
y sabe que son absurdos.

12*Dichoso aquel a quien tú, SEÑOR, corriges;
aquel a quien instruyes en tu *ley,
13para que enfrente tranquilo los días de
aflicción
mientras al impío se le cava una fosa.
14El SEÑOR no rechazará a su pueblo;
no dejará a su herencia en el abandono.
15El juicio volverá a basarse en la justicia,
y todos los rectos de corazón lo seguirán.

16¿Quién se levantó a defenderme de los
impíos?
¿Quién se puso de mi parte contra los
malhechores?
17Si el SEÑOR no me hubiera brindado su
ayuda,
muy pronto me habría quedado en mortal
silencio.
18No bien decía: «Mis pies resbalan»,
cuando ya tu amor, SEÑOR, venía en mi
ayuda.
19Cuando en mí la angustia iba en aumento,
tu consuelo llenaba mi *alma de alegría.

20¿Podrías ser amigo de reyes corruptosa
que por decreto fraguan la maldad,
21que conspiran contra la gente honrada
y condenan a muerte al inocente?
22Pero el SEÑOR es mi protector,
es mi Dios y la *roca en que me refugio.
23Él les hará pagar por sus pecados
y los destruirá por su maldad;
iel SEÑOR nuestro Dios los destruirá!

Salmo 95

1Vengan, cantemos con júbilo al SEÑOR;
aclamemos a la *roca de nuestra
*salvación.
2Lleguemos ante él con acción de gracias,
aclamémoslo con cánticos.

3Porque el SEÑOR es el gran Dios,
el gran Rey sobre todos los dioses.
4En sus manos están los abismos de la tierra;
suyas son las cumbres de los montes.
5Suyo es el mar, porque él lo hizo;
con sus manos formó la tierra firme.

6Vengan, postrémonos reverentes,
doblemos la rodilla
ante el SEÑOR nuestro Hacedor.
7Porque él es nuestro Dios
y nosotros somos el pueblo de su prado;
isomos un rebaño bajo su cuidado!

Si ustedes oyen hoy su voz,
8no endurezcan el corazón, como en
Meribá,b
como aquel día en Masá,c en el desierto,
9cuando sus antepasados me tentaron,
cuando me pusieron a prueba,
a pesar de haber visto mis obras.
10Cuarenta años estuve enojado
con aquella generación,
y dije: «Son un pueblo mal encaminado

---

z **94:1** *imanifiéstate!* Lit. *resplandece.* a **94:20** *de reyes corruptos.* Lit. *del trono corrupto.* b **95:8** En hebreo, *Meribá* significa *altercado.* c **95:8** En hebreo, *Masá* significa *prueba* o *provocación.*

que no reconoce mis senderos.»
11Así que, en mi enojo, hice este juramento:
«Jamás entrarán en mi reposo.»

Salmo 96
96:1-13 — 1Cr 16:23-33

1Canten al SEÑOR un cántico nuevo;
   canten al SEÑOR, habitantes de toda la
     tierra.
2Canten al SEÑOR, alaben su *nombre;
   anuncien día tras día su *victoria.
3Proclamen su gloria entre las naciones,
   sus maravillas entre todos los pueblos.
4¡Grande es el SEÑOR y digno de alabanza,
   más temible que todos los dioses!
5Todos los dioses de las naciones no son nada,
   pero el SEÑOR ha creado los cielos.
6El esplendor y la majestad son sus heraldos;
   hay poder y belleza en su santuario.

7Tributen al SEÑOR, pueblos todos,
   tributen al SEÑOR la gloria y el poder.
8Tributen al SEÑOR la gloria que merece su
     nombre;
   traigan sus ofrendas y entren en sus atrios.
9Póstrense ante el SEÑOR en la majestad de su
     santuario;
   ¡tiemble delante de él toda la tierra!

10Que se diga entre las naciones:
   «¡El SEÑOR es rey!»
   Ha establecido el mundo con firmeza;
   jamás será removido.
   El juzga a los pueblos con equidad.
11¡Alégrense los cielos, regocíjese la tierra!
   ¡Brame el mar y todo lo que él contiene!
12¡Canten alegres los campos y todo lo que hay
     en ellos!
   ¡Canten jubilosos todos los árboles del
     bosque!
13¡Canten delante del SEÑOR, que ya viene!
   ¡Viene ya para juzgar la tierra!
   Y juzgará al mundo con justicia,
   y a los pueblos con fidelidad.

Salmo 97

1¡El SEÑOR es rey!
   ¡Regocíjese la tierra!
   ¡Alégrense las costas más remotas!

2Oscuros nubarrones lo rodean;
   la rectitud y la justicia son la base de su
     trono.
3El fuego va delante de él
   y consume a todos los adversarios que lo rodean.
4Sus relámpagos iluminan el mundo;
   al verlos, la tierra se estremece.
5Ante el SEÑOR, dueño de toda la tierra,
   las montañas se derriten como cera.
6Los cielos proclaman su justicia,
   y todos los pueblos contemplan su gloria.

7Sean avergonzados todos los idólatras,
   los que se jactan de sus ídolos inútiles.
   ¡Póstrense ante él todos los dioses!
8SEÑOR, por causa de tus juicios
   *Sión escucha esto y se alegra,
   y las ciudades de Judá se regocijan.
9Porque tú eres el SEÑOR *Altísimo,
   por encima de toda la tierra.

¡Tú estás muy por encima de todos los
   dioses!

10El SEÑOR ama[d] a los que odian[e] el mal;
   él protege la vida de sus fieles,
   y los libra de manos de los impíos.
11La luz se esparce sobre los justos,
   y la alegría sobre los rectos de corazón.
12Alégrense en el SEÑOR, ustedes los justos,
   y alaben su santo *nombre.

Salmo 98
Salmo.

1Canten al SEÑOR un cántico nuevo,
   porque ha hecho maravillas.
   Su diestra, su santo brazo,
   ha alcanzado la *victoria.
2El SEÑOR ha hecho gala de su *triunfo;
   ha mostrado su justicia a las naciones.
3Se ha acordado de su amor y de su fidelidad
   por el pueblo de Israel;
   ¡todos los confines de la tierra son testigos
   de la *salvación de nuestro Dios!

4¡Aclamen alegres al SEÑOR, habitantes de toda
     la tierra!
   ¡Prorrumpan en alegres cánticos y salmos!
5¡Canten salmos al SEÑOR al son del arpa,
   al son del arpa y de coros melodiosos!
6¡Aclamen alegres al SEÑOR, el Rey,
   al son de clarines y trompetas!
7¡Brame el mar y todo lo que él contiene;
   el mundo y todos sus habitantes!
8¡Batan palmas los ríos,
   y canten jubilosos todos los montes!
9Canten delante del SEÑOR,
   que ya viene a juzgar la tierra.
   Y juzgará al mundo con justicia,
   a los pueblos con equidad.

Salmo 99

1El SEÑOR es rey:
   que tiemblen las naciones.
   Él tiene su trono entre *querubines:
   que se estremezca la tierra.
2Grande es el SEÑOR en *Sión,
   ¡excelso sobre todos los pueblos!
3Sea alabado su *nombre grandioso e
     imponente:
   ¡él es santo!

4Rey poderoso, que amas la justicia:
   tú has establecido la equidad
   y has actuado en Jacob con justicia y
     rectitud.
5Exalten al SEÑOR nuestro Dios;
   adórenlo ante el estrado de sus pies:
   ¡él es santo!

6Moisés y Aarón se contaban entre sus
     sacerdotes,
   y Samuel, entre los que invocaron su
     nombre.
   Invocaron al SEÑOR, y él les respondió;
7les habló desde la columna de nube.
   Cumplieron con sus estatutos,
   con los decretos que él les entregó.

8SEÑOR y Dios nuestro, tú les respondiste;
   fuiste para ellos un Dios perdonador,

---

d 97:10 El SEÑOR ama (lectura probable); Los que aman al Señor (TM).   e 97:10 a los que odian (Siríaca y algunos mss. hebreos); ustedes odian (TM).

aun cuando castigaste sus rebeliones.

9Exalten al SEÑOR nuestro Dios;
adórenlo en su santo monte:
¡Santo es el SEÑOR nuestro Dios!

Salmo 100

Salmo de acción de gracias.

1Aclamen alegres al SEÑOR, habitantes de toda
la tierra;
2adoren al SEÑOR con regocijo.
Preséntense ante él
con cánticos de júbilo.
3Reconozcan que el SEÑOR es Dios;
él nos hizo, y somos suyos.f
Somos su pueblo, ovejas de su prado.

4Entren por sus *puertas con acción de gracias;
vengan a sus atrios con himnos de
alabanza;
denle gracias, alaben su *nombre.
5Porque el SEÑOR es bueno y su gran amor es
eterno;
su fidelidad permanece para siempre.

Salmo 101

Salmo de David.

1Quiero cantar al amor y a la justicia:
quiero, SEÑOR, cantarte salmos.
2Quiero triunfar en el *camino de perfección:
¿Cuándo me visitarás?
Quiero conducirme en mi propia casa
con integridad de corazón.
3No me pondré como meta
nada en que haya perversidad.

Las acciones de gente desleal las aborrezco;
no tendrán nada que ver conmigo.
4Alejaré de mí toda intención perversa;
no tendrá cabida en mí la maldad.

5Al que en secreto calumnie a su prójimo,
lo haré callar para siempre;
al de ojos altivos y corazón soberbio
no lo soportaré.

6Pondré mis ojos en los fieles de la tierra,
para que habiten conmigo;
sólo estarán a mi servicio
los de conducta intachable.

7Jamás habitará bajo mi techo
nadie que practique el engaño;
jamás prevalecerá en mi presencia
nadie que hable con falsedad.

8Cada mañana reduciré al silencio
a todos los impíos que hay en la tierra;
extirparé de la ciudad del SEÑOR
a todos los malhechores.

Salmo 102

Oración de un afligido que, a punto de desfallecer,
da rienda suelta a su lamento ante el SEÑOR.

1Escucha, SEÑOR, mi oración;
llegue a ti mi clamor.
2No escondas de mí tu rostro
cuando me encuentre angustiado.
Inclina a mí tu oído;
respóndeme pronto cuando te llame.

3Pues mis días se desvanecen como el humo,
los huesos me arden como brasas.
4Mi corazón decae y se marchita como la
hierba;
¡hasta he perdido el apetito!
5Por causa de mis fuertes gemidos
se me pueden contar los huesos.g
6Parezco una lechuza del desierto;
soy como un búho entre las ruinas.
7No logro conciliar el sueño;
parezco ave solitaria sobre el tejado.
8A todas horas me ofenden mis enemigos,
y hasta usan mi *nombre para maldecir.
9Las cenizas son todo mi alimento;
mis lágrimas se mezclan con mi bebida.
10¡Por tu enojo, por tu indignación,
me levantaste para luego arrojarme!
11Mis días son como sombras nocturnas;
me voy marchitando como la hierba.

12Pero tú, SEÑOR, reinas eternamente;
tu nombre perdura por todas las
generaciones.
13Te levantarás y tendrás piedad de *Sión,
pues ya es tiempo de que la compadezcas.
¡Ha llegado el momento señalado!
14Tus siervos sienten cariño por sus ruinas;
los mueven a compasión sus escombros.

15Las naciones temerán el nombre del SEÑOR;
todos los reyes de la tierra reconocerán su
majestad.
16Porque el SEÑOR reconstruirá a Sión,
y se manifestará en su esplendor.
17Atenderá a la oración de los desamparados,
y no desdeñará sus ruegos.
18Que se escriba esto para las generaciones
futuras,
y que el pueblo que será creado alabe al
SEÑOR.
19Miró el SEÑOR desde su altísimo santuario;
contempló la tierra desde el cielo,
20para oír los lamentos de los cautivos
y liberar a los condenados a muerte;
21para proclamar en Sión el nombre del SEÑOR
y anunciar en Jerusalén su alabanza,
22cuando todos los pueblos y los reinos
se reúnan para adorar al SEÑOR.

23En el curso de mi vida acabó Dios con mis
fuerzas;h
me redujo los días.
24Por eso dije:
«No me lleves, Dios mío, a la mitad de mi
vida;
tú permaneces por todas las generaciones.
25En el principio tú afirmaste la tierra,
y los cielos son la obra de tus manos.
26Ellos perecerán, pero tú permaneces.
Todos ellos se desgastarán como un
vestido.
Y como ropa los cambiarás,
y los dejarás de lado.
27Pero tú eres siempre el mismo,
y tus años no tienen fin.
28Los hijos de tus siervos se establecerán,
y sus descendientes habitarán en tu
presencia.»

---

f 100:3 y somos suyos (Targum, Qumrán y mss.); y no nosotros (TM). g 102:5 se me pueden contar los huesos. Lit. se me pegan los huesos a la carne. h 102:23 mis fuerzas. Lit. su fuerza.

Salmo 103

Salmo de David.

¹Alaba, *alma mía, al SEÑOR;
  alabe todo mi ser su santo *nombre.
²Alaba, alma mía, al SEÑOR,
  y no olvides ninguno de sus beneficios.
³Él perdona todos tus pecados
  y sana todas tus dolencias;
⁴él rescata tu vida del *sepulcro
  y te cubre de amor y compasión;
⁵él colma de bienes tu vidaⁱ
  y te rejuvenece como a las águilas.

⁶El SEÑOR hace *justicia
  y defiende a todos los oprimidos.
⁷Dio a conocer sus *caminos a Moisés;
  reveló sus obras al pueblo de Israel.

⁸El SEÑOR es clemente y compasivo,
  lento para la ira y grande en amor.
⁹No sostiene para siempre su querella
  ni guarda rencor eternamente.
¹⁰No nos trata conforme a nuestros pecados
  ni nos paga según nuestras maldades.
¹¹Tan grande es su amor por los que le temen
  como alto es el cielo sobre la tierra.
¹²Tan lejos de nosotros echó nuestras
    transgresiones
  como lejos del oriente está el occidente.
¹³Tan compasivo es el SEÑOR con los que le
    temen
  como lo es un padre con sus hijos,
¹⁴Él conoce nuestra condición;
  sabe que somos de barro.

¹⁵El *hombre es como la hierba,
  sus días florecen como la flor del campo:
¹⁶sacudida por el viento,
  desaparece sin dejar rastro alguno.
¹⁷Pero el amor del SEÑOR es eterno
  y siempre está con los que le temen;
  su justicia está con los hijos de sus hijos,
¹⁸con los que cumplen su *pacto
  y se acuerdan de sus preceptos
  para ponerlos por obra.

¹⁹El SEÑOR ha establecido su trono en el cielo;
  su reinado domina sobre todos.

²⁰Alaben al SEÑOR, ustedes sus ángeles,
  paladines que ejecutan su palabra
  y obedecen su mandato.
²¹Alaben al SEÑOR, todos sus ejércitos,
  siervos suyos que cumplen su voluntad.
²²Alaben al SEÑOR, todas sus obras
  en todos los ámbitos de su dominio.

¡Alaba, alma mía, al SEÑOR!

Salmo 104

¹¡Alaba, *alma mía, al SEÑOR!

SEÑOR mi Dios, tú eres grandioso;
  te has revestido de gloria y majestad.
²Te cubresʲ de luz como con un manto;
  extiendes los cielos como un velo.
³Afirmas sobre las aguas tus altos aposentos
  y haces de las nubes tus carros de guerra.
  ¡Tú cabalgas en las alas del viento!
⁴Haces de los vientos tus mensajeros,ᵏ

y de las llamas de fuego tus servidores.

⁵Tú pusiste la tierra sobre sus cimientos,
  y de allí jamás se moverá;
⁶la revestiste con el mar,
  y las aguas se detuvieron sobre los montes.
⁷Pero a tu reprensión huyeron las aguas;
  ante el estruendo de tu voz se dieron a la
    fuga.
⁸Ascendieron a los montes,
  descendieron a los valles,
  al lugar que tú les asignaste.
⁹Pusiste una frontera que ellas no pueden
    cruzar;
  ¡jamás volverán a cubrir la tierra!

¹⁰Tú haces que los manantiales
  viertan sus aguas en las cañadas,
  y que fluyan entre las montañas.
¹¹De ellas beben todas las bestias del campo;
  allí los asnos monteses calman su sed.
¹²Las aves del cielo anidan junto a las aguas
  y cantan entre el follaje.
¹³Desde tus altos aposentos riegas las
    montañas;
  la tierra se sacia con el fruto de tu trabajo.
¹⁴Haces que crezca la hierba para el ganado,
  y las plantas que la *gente cultiva
  para sacar de la tierra su alimento:
¹⁵el vino que alegra el corazón,
  el aceite que hace brillar el rostro,
  y el pan que sustenta la vida.
¹⁶Los árboles del SEÑOR están bien regados,
  los cedros del Líbano que él plantó.
¹⁷Allí las aves hacen sus nidos;
  en los cipreses tienen su hogar las cigüeñas.
¹⁸En las altas montañas están las cabras
    monteses,
  y en los escarpados peñascos tienen su
    madriguera los tejones.

¹⁹Tú hicisteˡ la luna, que marca las estaciones,
  y el sol, que sabe cuándo ocultarse.
²⁰Tú traes la oscuridad, y cae la noche,
  y en sus sombras se arrastran los animales
    del bosque.
²¹Los leones rugen, reclamando su presa,
  exigiendo que Dios les dé su alimento.
²²Pero al salir el sol se escabullen,
  y vuelven a echarse en sus guaridas.
²³Sale entonces la *gente a cumplir sus tareas,
  a hacer su trabajo hasta el anochecer.

²⁴¡Oh SEÑOR, cuán numerosas son tus obras!
  ¡Todas ellas las hiciste con sabiduría!
  ¡Rebosa la tierra con todas tus criaturas!
²⁵Allí está el mar, ancho e infinito,ᵐ
  que abunda en animales, grandes y
    pequeños,
  cuyo número es imposible conocer.
²⁶Allí navegan los barcos y se mece *Leviatán,
  que tú creaste para jugar con él.

²⁷Todos ellos esperan de ti
  que a su tiempo les des su alimento.
²⁸Tú les das, y ellos recogen;
  abres la mano, y se colman de bienes.
²⁹Si escondes tu rostro, se aterran;
  si les quitas el aliento, mueren y vuelven al
    polvo.

ⁱ 103:5 *vida.* Palabra de difícil traducción.   ʲ 104:2 *Te cubres.* Lit. *Él se cubre.*   ᵏ 104:4 *mensajeros.* Alt. *ángeles.*   ˡ 104:19 *Tú hiciste.* Lit. *Él hace.*   ᵐ 104:25 *infinito.* Lit. *amplio de manos.*

[30]Pero si envías tu Espíritu, son creados,
y así renuevas la faz de la tierra.

[31]Que la gloria del SEÑOR perdure
eternamente;
que el SEÑOR se regocije en sus obras.
[32]Él mira la tierra y la hace temblar;
toca los montes y los hace echar humo.

[33]Cantaré al SEÑOR toda mi vida;
cantaré salmos a mi Dios mientras tenga
aliento.
[34]Quiera él agradarse de mi meditación;
yo, por mi parte, me alegro en el SEÑOR.
[35]Que desaparezcan de la tierra los pecadores;
¡que no existan más los malvados!

¡Alaba, *alma mía, al SEÑOR!

*¡Aleluya! ¡Alabado sea el SEÑOR![n]

Salmo 105

105:1-15 — 1Cr 16:8-22

[1]Den gracias al SEÑOR, invoquen su *nombre;
den a conocer sus obras entre las naciones.
[2]Cántenle, entónenle salmos,
hablen de todas sus maravillas.
[3]Siéntanse orgullosos de su santo nombre;
alégrese el corazón de los que buscan al
SEÑOR.
[4]Recurran al SEÑOR y a su fuerza;
busquen siempre su rostro.
[5]Recuerden las maravillas que ha realizado,
sus señales, y los decretos que ha emitido.
[6]¡Ustedes, descendientes de Abraham su siervo!
¡Ustedes, hijos de Jacob, elegidos suyos!
[7]Él es el SEÑOR, nuestro Dios;
en toda la tierra están sus decretos.
[8]Él siempre tiene presente su *pacto,
la palabra que ordenó para mil
generaciones.
[9]Es el pacto que hizo con Abraham,
el juramento que le hizo a Isaac.
[10]Se lo confirmó a Jacob como un decreto,
a Israel como un pacto eterno,
[11]cuando dijo: «Te daré la tierra de Canaán
como la herencia que te toca.»

[12]Aun cuando eran pocos en número,
unos cuantos extranjeros en la tierra
[13]que andaban siempre de nación en nación
y de reino en reino,
[14]a nadie permitió que los oprimiera,
sino que por ellos reprendió a los reyes:
[15]«No toquen a mis ungidos;
no hagan daño a mis profetas.»

[16]Dios provocó hambre en la tierra
y destruyó todos sus trigales.[ñ]
[17]Pero envió delante de ellos a un hombre:
a José, vendido como esclavo.
[18]Le sujetaron los pies con grilletes,
entre hierros le aprisionaron el *cuello,
[19]hasta que se cumplió lo que él predijo
y la palabra del SEÑOR probó que él era
veraz.
[20]El rey ordenó ponerlo en libertad,

el gobernante de los pueblos lo dejó libre.
[21]Le dio autoridad sobre toda su casa
y lo puso a cargo de cuanto poseía,
[22]con pleno poder para instruir[o] a sus príncipes
e impartir sabiduría a sus ancianos.

[23]Entonces Israel vino a Egipto;
Jacob fue extranjero en el país de Cam.
[24]El SEÑOR hizo que su pueblo se multiplicara;
lo hizo más numeroso que sus adversarios,
[25]a quienes trastornó para que odiaran a su
pueblo
y se confabularan contra sus siervos.
[26]Envió a su siervo Moisés,
y a Aarón, a quien había escogido,
[27]y éstos hicieron señales milagrosas entre ellos,
¡maravillas en el país de Cam!
[28]Envió tinieblas, y la tierra se oscureció,
pero ellos no atendieron[p] a sus palabras.
[29]Convirtió en sangre sus aguas
y causó la muerte de sus peces.
[30]Todo Egipto[q] se infestó de ranas,
¡hasta las habitaciones de sus reyes!
[31]Habló Dios, e invadieron todo el país
enjambres de moscas y mosquitos.
[32]Convirtió la lluvia en granizo,
y lanzó relámpagos sobre su tierra;
[33]derribó sus vides y sus higueras,
y en todo el país hizo astillas los árboles.
[34]Dio una orden, y llegaron las langostas,
¡infinidad de saltamontes!
[35]Arrasaron con toda la vegetación del país,
devoraron los frutos de sus campos.
[36]Hirió de muerte a todos los primogénitos del
país,
a las primicias de sus descendientes.
[37]Sacó a los israelitas cargados de oro y plata,
y no hubo entre sus tribus nadie que
tropezara.

[38]Los egipcios se alegraron de su partida,
pues el miedo a los israelitas los dominaba.
[39]El SEÑOR les dio sombra con una nube,
y con fuego los alumbró de noche.
[40]Pidió el pueblo comida, y les envió
codornices;
los sació con pan del cielo.
[41]Abrió la roca, y brotó agua
que corrió por el desierto como un río.

[42]Ciertamente Dios se acordó de su santa
promesa,
la que hizo a su siervo Abraham.
[43]Sacó a su pueblo, a sus escogidos,
en medio de gran alegría y de gritos
jubilosos.
[44]Les entregó las tierras que poseían las
naciones;
heredaron el fruto del trabajo de otros
pueblos
[45]para que ellos observaran sus preceptos
y pusieran en práctica sus *leyes.

*¡Aleluya! ¡Alabado sea el SEÑOR!

---

n 104:35 En LXX este verso aparece al principio del Salmo 105.   ñ 105:16 *todos sus trigales*. Lit. *todo bastón de pan*.
o 105:22 *instruir* (LXX, Siríaca y Vulgata); *atar* (TM).   p 105:28 *no atendieron* (véanse LXX y Siríaca); *no se opusieron* (TM).
q 105:30 *Todo Egipto*. Lit. *La tierra de ellos*.

Salmo 106

106:1,47-48 — 1Cr 16:34-36

¹*¡Aleluya! ¡Alabado sea el SEÑOR!

Den gracias al SEÑOR, porque él es bueno;
    su gran amor perdura para siempre.
²¿Quién puede proclamar las proezas del
    SEÑOR,
    o expresar toda su alabanza?
³*Dichosos los que practican la justicia
    y hacen siempre lo que es justo.
⁴Recuérdame, SEÑOR, cuando te compadezcas
    de tu pueblo,
    ven en mi ayuda el día de tu *salvación.
⁵Hazme disfrutar del bienestar de tus
    escogidos,
    participar de la alegría de tu pueblo
    y expresar mis alabanzas con tu heredad.

⁶Hemos pecado, lo mismo que nuestros padres;
    hemos hecho lo malo y actuado con
    iniquidad.
⁷Cuando nuestros padres estaban en Egipto,
    no tomaron en cuenta tus maravillas;
    no tuvieron presente tu bondad infinita
    y se rebelaron junto al mar, el Mar Rojo.ʳ
⁸Pero Dios los salvó, haciendo honor a su
    *nombre,
    para mostrar su gran poder.
⁹Reprendió al Mar Rojo, y éste quedó seco;
    los condujo por las profundidades del mar
    como si cruzaran el desierto.
¹⁰Los salvó del poder de sus enemigos,
    del poder de quienes los odiaban.
¹¹Las aguas envolvieron a sus adversarios,
    y ninguno de éstos quedó con vida.
¹²Entonces ellos creyeron en sus promesas
    y le entonaron alabanzas.

¹³Pero muy pronto olvidaron sus acciones
    y no esperaron a conocer sus planes.
¹⁴En el desierto cedieron a sus propios deseos;
    en los páramos pusieron a prueba a Dios.
¹⁵Y él les dio lo que pidieron,
    pero les envió una enfermedad
    devastadora.

¹⁶En el campamento tuvieron envidia de
    Moisés
    y de Aarón, el que estaba consagrado al
    SEÑOR.
¹⁷Se abrió la tierra y se tragó a Datán;
    sepultó a los seguidores de Abirán.
¹⁸Un fuego devoró a esa pandilla;
    las llamas consumieron a los impíos.

¹⁹En Horeb hicieron un becerro;
    se postraron ante un ídolo de fundición.
²⁰Cambiaron al que era su motivo de orgulloˢ
    por la imagen de un toro que come hierba.
²¹Se olvidaron del Dios que los salvó
    y que había hecho grandes cosas en Egipto:
²²milagros en la tierra de Cam
    y portentos junto al Mar Rojo.
²³Dios amenazó con destruirlos,
    pero no lo hizo por Moisés, su escogido,
    que se puso ante él en la brecha
    e impidió que su ira los destruyera.

²⁴Menospreciaron esa bella tierra;

no creyeron en la promesa de Dios.
²⁵Refunfuñaron en sus tiendas de campaña
    y no obedecieron al SEÑOR.
²⁶Por tanto, él levantó su mano contra ellos
    para hacerlos caer en el desierto,
²⁷para hacer caer a sus descendientes entre las
    naciones
    y dispersarlos por todos los países.

²⁸Se sometieron al yugo de Baal Peor
    y comieron de las ofrendas a ídolos sin vida.ᵗ
²⁹Provocaron al SEÑOR con sus malvadas
    acciones,
    y les sobrevino una plaga.
³⁰Pero Finés se levantó e hizo justicia,
    y la plaga se detuvo.
³¹Esto se le acreditó como un acto de justicia
    para siempre, por todas las generaciones.

³²Junto a las aguas de Meribá hicieron enojar al
    SEÑOR,
    y a Moisés le fue mal por culpa de ellos,
³³pues lo sacaron de quicio
    y él habló sin pensar lo que decía.
³⁴No destruyeron a los pueblos
    que el SEÑOR les había señalado,
³⁵sino que se mezclaron con los paganos
    y adoptaron sus costumbres.
³⁶Rindieron culto a sus ídolos,
    y se les volvieron una trampa.
³⁷Ofrecieron a sus hijos y a sus hijas
    como sacrificio a esos demonios.
³⁸Derramaron sangre inocente,
    la sangre de sus hijos y sus hijas.
Al ofrecerlos en sacrificio a los ídolos de
    Canaán,
    su sangre derramada profanó la tierra.
³⁹Tales hechos los contaminaron;
    tales acciones los corrompieron.

⁴⁰La ira del SEÑOR se encendió contra su
    pueblo;
    su heredad le resultó aborrecible.
⁴¹Por eso los entregó a los paganos,
    y fueron dominados por quienes los
    odiaban.
⁴²Sus enemigos los oprimieron,
    los sometieron a su poder.
⁴³Muchas veces Dios los libró;
    pero ellos, empeñados en su rebeldía,
    se hundieron en la maldad.

⁴⁴Al verlos Dios angustiados,
    y al escuchar su clamor,
⁴⁵se acordó del pacto que había hecho con ellos
    y por su gran amor les tuvo compasión.
⁴⁶Hizo que todos sus opresores
    también se apiadaran de ellos.

⁴⁷Sálvanos, SEÑOR, Dios nuestro;
    vuelve a reunirnos de entre las naciones,
    para que demos gracias a tu santo nombre
    y orgullosos te alabemos.

⁴⁸¡Bendito sea el SEÑOR, el Dios de Israel,
    eternamente y para siempre!
    ¡Que todo el pueblo diga: «Amén»!

*¡Aleluya! ¡Alabado sea el SEÑOR!

ʳ **106:7** *Mar Rojo.* Lit. *mar de las Cañas* (heb. *Yam Suf*); también en vv. 9 y 22.   ˢ **106:20** *Cambiaron ... de orgullo.* Lit. *Cambiaron la gloria de ellos.*   ᵗ **106:28** *ofrendas a ídolos sin vida.* Lit. *ofrendas a los muertos.*

Libro V
Salmos 107-150
Salmo 107

¹Den gracias al SEÑOR, porque él es bueno;
su gran amor perdura para siempre.
²Que lo digan los redimidos del SEÑOR,
a quienes redimió del poder del adversario,
³a quienes reunió de todos los países,
de oriente y de occidente, del norte y del
sur.ᵘ

⁴Vagaban perdidos por parajes desiertos,
sin dar con el camino a una ciudad
habitable.
⁵Hambrientos y sedientos,
la vida se les iba consumiendo.
⁶En su angustia clamaron al SEÑOR,
y él los libró de su aflicción.
⁷Los llevó por el camino recto
hasta llegar a una ciudad habitable.

⁸¡Que den gracias al SEÑOR por su gran amor,
por sus maravillas en favor de los hombres!
⁹Él apaga la sed del sediento,
y sacia con lo mejor al hambriento!

¹⁰Afligidos y encadenados,
habitaban en las más densas tinieblas
¹¹por haberse rebelado contra las palabras de
Dios,
por menospreciar los designios del
*Altísimo.
¹²Los sometióᵛ a trabajos forzados;
tropezaban, y no había quien los ayudara.
¹³En su angustia clamaron al SEÑOR,
y él los salvó de su aflicción.
¹⁴Los sacó de las sombras tenebrosas
y rompió en pedazos sus cadenas.

¹⁵¡Que den gracias al SEÑOR por su gran amor,
por sus maravillas en favor de los hombres!
¹⁶¡Él hace añicos las puertas de bronce
y rompe en mil pedazos las barras de
hierro!

¹⁷Trastornados por su rebeldía,
afligidos por su iniquidad,
¹⁸todo alimento les causaba asco.
¡Llegaron a las puertas mismas de la
muerte!
¹⁹En su angustia clamaron al SEÑOR,
y él los salvó de su aflicción.
²⁰Envió su palabra para sanarlos,
y así los rescató del sepulcro.

²¹¡Que den gracias al SEÑOR por su gran amor,
por sus maravillas en favor de los hombres!
²²¡Que ofrezcan sacrificios de gratitud,
y jubilosos proclamen sus obras!

²³Se hicieron a la mar en sus barcos;
para comerciar surcaron las muchas aguas.
²⁴Allí, en las aguas profundas,
vieron las obras del SEÑOR y sus maravillas.
²⁵Habló Dios, y se desató un fuerte viento
que tanto encrespó las olas
²⁶que subían a los cielos y bajaban al abismo.
Ante el peligro, ellos perdieron el coraje.
²⁷Como ebrios tropezaban, se tambaleaban;
de nada les valía toda su pericia.
²⁸En su angustia clamaron al SEÑOR,

y él los sacó de su aflicción.
²⁹Cambió la tempestad en suave brisa:
se sosegaron las olas del mar.
³⁰Ante esa calma se alegraron,
y Dios los llevó al puerto anhelado.

³¹¡Que den gracias al SEÑOR por su gran amor,
por sus maravillas en favor de los hombres!
³²¡Que lo exalten en la asamblea del pueblo!
¡Que lo alaben en el consejo de los
ancianos!

³³Dios convirtió los ríos en desiertos,
los manantiales en tierra seca,
³⁴los fértiles terrenos en tierra salitrosa,
por la maldad de sus habitantes.
³⁵Convirtió el desierto en fuentes de agua,
la tierra seca en manantiales;
³⁶hizo habitar allí a los hambrientos,
y ellos fundaron una ciudad habitable.
³⁷Sembraron campos, plantaron viñedos,
obtuvieron abundantes cosechas.
³⁸Dios los bendijo y se multiplicaron,
y no dejó que menguaran sus rebaños.

³⁹Pero si merman y son humillados,
es por la opresión, la maldad y la aflicción.
⁴⁰Dios desdeña a los nobles
y los hace vagar por desiertos sin senderos.
⁴¹Pero a los necesitados los saca de su miseria,
y hace que sus familias crezcan como
rebaños.
⁴²Los rectos lo verán y se alegrarán,
pero todos los impíos serán acallados.

⁴³Quien sea sabio, que considere estas cosas
y entienda bien el gran amor del SEÑOR.

Salmo 108

108:1-5 — Sal 57:7-11
108:6-13 — Sal 60:5-12
Cántico. Salmo de David.

¹Firme está, oh Dios, mi corazón;
¡voy a cantarte salmos, gloria mía!
²¡Despierten, arpa y lira!
¡Haré despertar al nuevo día!
³Te alabaré, SEÑOR, entre los pueblos;
te cantaré salmos entre las naciones.
⁴Pues tu amor es tan grande que rebasa los
cielos;
¡tu verdad llega hasta el firmamento!
⁵Tú, oh Dios, estás sobre los cielos,
y tu gloria cubre toda la tierra.
⁶Líbranos con tu diestra, respóndeme
para que tu pueblo amado quede a salvo.

⁷Dios ha dicho en su santuario:
«Triunfante repartiré a Siquén,
y dividiré el valle de Sucot.
⁸Mío es Galaad, mío es Manasés;
Efraín es mi yelmo y Judá mi cetro.
⁹En Moab me lavo las manos,
sobre Edom arrojo mi sandalia;
sobre Filistea lanzo gritos de triunfo.»

¹⁰¿Quién me llevará a la ciudad fortificada?
¿Quién me mostrará el camino a Edom?
¹¹¿No es Dios quien nos ha rechazado?
¡Ya no sales, oh Dios, con nuestros
ejércitos!
¹²Bríndanos tu ayuda contra el enemigo,

ᵘ 107:3 *del sur.* Lit. *del mar.*   ᵛ 107:12 *Los sometió.* Lit. *Sometió sus corazones.*

pues de nada sirve la ayuda humana.
13Con Dios obtendremos la victoria;
¡él pisoteará a nuestros enemigos!

Salmo 109

Al director musical. Salmo de David.

1Oh Dios, alabanza mía,
no guardes silencio.
2Pues gente impía y mentirosa
ha declarado en mi contra,
y con lengua engañosa me difaman;
3con expresiones de odio me acosan,
y sin razón alguna me atacan.
4Mi amor me lo pagan con calumnias,
mientras yo me encomiendo a Dios.
5Mi bondad la pagan con maldad;
en vez de amarme, me aborrecen.

6Pon en su contra a un malvado;
que a su derecha esté su acusador.w
7Que resulte culpable al ser juzgado,
y que sus propias oraciones lo condenen.
8Que se acorten sus días,
y que otro se haga cargo de su oficio.
9Que se queden huérfanos sus hijos;
que se quede viuda su esposa.
10Que anden sus hijos vagando y mendigando;
que anden rebuscando entre las ruinas.
11Que sus acreedores se apoderen de sus
bienes;
que gente extraña saquee sus posesiones.
12Que nadie le extienda su bondad;
que nadie se compadezca de sus
huérfanos.
13Que sea exterminada su descendencia;
que desaparezca su *nombre en la próxima
generación.
14Que recuerde el SEÑOR la iniquidad de su
padre,
y no se olvide del pecado de su madre.
15Que no les quite el SEÑOR la vista de encima,
y que borre de la tierra su memoria.

16Por cuanto se olvidó de hacer el bien,
y persiguió hasta la muerte
a pobres, afligidos y menesterosos,
17y porque le encantaba maldecir,
¡que caiga sobre él la maldición!
Por cuanto no se complacía en bendecir,
¡que se aleje de él la bendición!
18Por cuanto se cubrió de maldición
como quien se pone un vestido,
¡que ésta se filtre en su cuerpo como el agua!,
¡que penetre en sus huesos como el aceite!
19¡Que lo envuelva como un manto!
¡Que lo apriete en todo tiempo como un
cinto!
20¡Que así les pague el SEÑOR a mis acusadores,
a los que me calumnian!

21Pero tú, SEÑOR Soberano,
trátame bien por causa de tu nombre;
líbrame por tu bondad y gran amor.
22Ciertamente soy pobre y estoy necesitado;
profundamente herido está mi corazón.
23Me voy desvaneciendo como sombra
vespertina;
se desprenden de mí como de una
langosta.

24De tanto ayunar me tiemblan las rodillas;
la piel se me pega a los huesos.
25Soy para ellos motivo de burla;
me ven, y menean la cabeza.

26SEÑOR, mi Dios, ¡ayúdame!;
por tu gran amor, ¡sálvame!
27Que sepan que ésta es tu mano;
que tú mismo, SEÑOR, lo has hecho.
28¿Qué importa que ellos me maldigan?
¡Bendíceme tú!
Pueden atacarme, pero quedarán
avergonzados;
en cambio, este siervo tuyo se alegrará.
29¡Queden mis acusadores cubiertos de
deshonra,
envueltos en un manto de vergüenza!

30Por mi parte, daré muchas gracias al SEÑOR;
lo alabaré entre una gran muchedumbre.
31Porque él defiende alx necesitado,
para salvarlo de quienes lo condenan.

Salmo 110

Salmo de David.

1Así dijo el SEÑOR a mi Señor:
«Siéntate a mi derecha
hasta que ponga a tus enemigos
por estrado de tus pies.»

2¡Que el SEÑOR extienda desde *Sión
el poder de tu cetro!
¡Domina tú en medio de tus enemigos!
3Tus tropas estarán dispuestas
el día de la batalla,
ordenadas en santa majestad.
De las entrañas de la aurora
recibirás el rocío de tu juventud.

4El SEÑOR ha jurado
y no cambiará de parecer:
«Tú eres sacerdote para siempre,
según el orden de Melquisedec.»

5El Señor está a tu mano derecha;
aplastará a los reyes en el día de su ira.
6Juzgará a las naciones y amontonará
cadáveres;
aplastará cabezas en toda la tierra.

7Beberá de un arroyo junto al camino,
y por lo tanto cobrará nuevas fuerzas.y

Salmo 111z

1*¡Aleluya! ¡Alabado sea el SEÑOR!

Álef	Alabaré al SEÑOR con todo el corazón
Bet	en la asamblea, en compañía de los rectos.
Guímel	2Grandes son las obras del SEÑOR;
Dálet	estudiadas por los que en ellas se deleitan.
He	3Gloriosas y majestuosas son sus obras;
Vav	su justicia permanece para siempre.
Zayin	4Ha hecho memorables sus maravillas.
Jet	¡El SEÑOR es clemente y compasivo!
Tet	5Da de comer a quienes le temen;
Yod	siempre recuerda su pacto.

---

w 109:6 esté su acusador. Lit. esté Satán.   x 109:31 defiende al. Lit. está de pie a la diestra del.   y 110:7 cobrará nuevas fuerzas.
Lit. levantará la cabeza.   z Sal 111 Este salmo es un poema acróstico, que sigue el orden del alfabeto hebreo.

Caf	6Ha mostrado a su pueblo el poder de sus obras
Lámed	al darle la heredad de otras naciones.
Mem	7Las obras de sus manos son fieles y justas;
Nun	todos sus preceptos son dignos de confianza,
Sámej	8inmutables por los siglos de los siglos,
Ayin	establecidos con fidelidad y rectitud.
Pe	9Pagó el precio del rescate de su pueblo
Tsade	y estableció su pacto para siempre.
Qof	¡Su *nombre es santo e imponente!
Resh	10El principio de la sabiduría es el temor del SEÑOR;
Shin	buen juicio demuestran quienes cumplen sus preceptos.ᵃ
Tav	¡Su alabanza permanece para siempre!

Salmo 112ᵇ

1*¡Aleluya! ¡Alabado sea el SEÑOR!

Álef	*Dichoso el que teme al SEÑOR,
Bet	el que halla gran deleite en sus mandamientos.
Guímel	2Sus hijos dominarán el país;
Dálet	la descendencia de los justos será bendecida.
He	3En su casa habrá abundantes riquezas,
Vav	y para siempre permanecerá su justicia.
Zayin	4Para los justos la luz brilla en las tinieblas.
Jet	¡Dios es clemente, compasivo y justo!
Tet	5Bien le va al que presta con generosidad,
Yod	y maneja sus negocios con justicia.
Lámed	6El justo será siempre recordado;
Caf	ciertamente nunca fracasará.
Mem	7No temerá recibir malas noticias;
Nun	su corazón estará firme, confiado en el SEÑOR.
Sámej	8Su corazón estará seguro, no tendrá temor,
Ayin	y al final verá derrotados a sus adversarios.
Pe	9Reparte sus bienes entre los pobres;
Tsade	su justicia permanece para siempre;
Qof	su poderᶜ será gloriosamente exaltado.
Resh	10El malvado verá esto, y se irritará;
Shin	rechinando los dientes se irá desvaneciendo.
Tav	¡La ambición de los impíos será destruida!

Salmo 113

1*¡Aleluya! ¡Alabado sea el SEÑOR!

Alaben, siervos del SEÑOR,
alaben el *nombre del SEÑOR.
2Bendito sea el nombre del SEÑOR,
desde ahora y para siempre.

3Desde la salida del sol hasta su ocaso,
sea alabado el nombre del SEÑOR.

4El SEÑOR domina sobre todas las naciones;
su gloria está sobre los cielos.
5¿Quién como el SEÑOR nuestro Dios,
que tiene su trono en las alturas
6y se digna contemplar los cielos y la tierra?

7Él levanta del polvo al pobre
y saca del muladar al necesitado;
8los hace sentarse con príncipes,
con los príncipes de su pueblo.
9A la mujer estéril le da un hogar
y le concede la dicha de ser madre.

*¡Aleluya! ¡Alabado sea el SEÑOR!

Salmo 114

1Cuando Israel, el pueblo de Jacob,
salió de Egipto, de un pueblo extraño,
2Judá se convirtió en el santuario de Dios,
Israel llegó a ser su dominio.

3Al ver esto, el mar huyó;
el Jordán se volvió atrás.
4Las montañas saltaron como carneros,
los cerros saltaron como ovejas.
5¿Qué te pasó, mar, que huiste,
y a ti, Jordán, que te volviste atrás?
6¿Y a ustedes montañas, que saltaron como carneros?
¿Y a ustedes cerros, que saltaron como ovejas?
7¡Tiembla, oh tierra, ante el *Señor,
tiembla ante el Dios de Jacob!
8¡Él convirtió la roca en un estanque,
el pedernal en manantiales de agua!

Salmo 115

115:4-11 – Sal 135:15-20

1La gloria, SEÑOR, no es para nosotros;
no es para nosotros sino para tu *nombre,
por causa de tu amor y tu verdad.

2¿Por qué tienen que decirnos las naciones:
«¿Dónde está su Dios?»
3Nuestro Dios está en los cielos
y puede hacer lo que le parezca.
4Pero sus ídolos son de oro y plata,
producto de manos humanas.
5Tienen boca, pero no pueden hablar;
ojos, pero no pueden ver;
6tienen oídos, pero no pueden oír;
nariz, pero no pueden oler;
7tienen manos, pero no pueden palpar;
pies, pero no pueden andar;
¡ni un solo sonido emite su garganta!
8Semejantes a ellos son sus hacedores,
y todos los que confían en ellos.

9Pueblo de Israel, confía en el SEÑOR;
él es tu ayuda y tu escudo.
10Descendientes de Aarón, confíen en el SEÑOR;
él es su ayuda y su escudo.
11Los que temen al SEÑOR, confíen en él;
él es su ayuda y su escudo.

12El SEÑOR nos recuerda y nos bendice:
bendice al pueblo de Israel,

ᵃ **111:10** *quienes cumplen sus preceptos.* Lit. *quienes hacen estas cosas.* ᵇ **Sal 112** Este salmo es un poema acróstico, que sigue el orden del alfabeto hebreo. ᶜ **112:9** *poder.* Lit. *cuerno.*

bendice a los descendientes de Aarón,
13bendice a los que temen al SEÑOR,
bendice a grandes y pequeños.

14Que el SEÑOR multiplique la descendencia
de ustedes y sus hijos.
15Que reciban bendiciones del SEÑOR,
creador del cielo y de la tierra.

16Los cielos le pertenecen al SEÑOR,
pero a la *humanidad le ha dado la tierra.
17Los muertos no alaban al SEÑOR,
ninguno de los que bajan al silencio.
18Somos nosotros los que alabamos al SEÑOR
desde ahora y para siempre.

*¡Aleluya! ¡Alabado sea el SEÑOR!

Salmo 116

1Yo amo al SEÑOR
porque él escuchad mi voz suplicante.
2Por cuanto él inclina a mí su oído,
lo invocaré toda mi vida.

3Los lazos de la muerte me enredaron;
me sorprendió la angustia del *sepulcro,
y caí en la ansiedad y la aflicción.
4Entonces clamé al SEÑOR:
«¡Te ruego, SEÑOR, que me salves la vida!»

5El SEÑOR es compasivo y justo;
nuestro Dios es todo ternura.
6El SEÑOR protege a la gente sencilla;
estaba yo muy débil, y él me salvó.

7¡Ya puedes, *alma mía, estar tranquila,
que el SEÑOR ha sido bueno contigo!

8Tú me has librado de la muerte,
has enjugado mis lágrimas,
no me has dejado tropezar.
9Por eso andaré siempre delante del SEÑOR
en esta tierra de los vivientes.
10Aunque digo: «Me encuentro muy afligido»,
sigo creyendo en Dios.
11En mi desesperación he exclamado:
«Todos son unos mentirosos.»

12¿Cómo puedo pagarle al SEÑOR
por tanta bondad que me ha mostrado?
13¡Tan sólo brindando con la copa de *salvación
e invocando el *nombre del SEÑOR!
14¡Tan sólo cumpliendo mis promesas al SEÑOR
en presencia de todo su pueblo!

15Mucho valor tiene a los ojos del SEÑOR
la muerte de sus fieles.
16Yo, SEÑOR, soy tu siervo;
soy siervo tuyo, tu hijo fiel;e
¡tú has roto mis cadenas!

17Te ofreceré un sacrificio de gratitud
e invocaré, SEÑOR, tu nombre.
18Cumpliré mis votos al SEÑOR
en presencia de todo su pueblo,
19en los atrios de la casa del SEÑOR,
en medio de ti, oh Jerusalén.

*¡Aleluya! ¡Alabado sea el SEÑOR!

Salmo 117

1¡Alaben al SEÑOR, naciones todas!
¡Pueblos todos, cántenle alabanzas!

2¡Grande es su amor por nosotros!
¡La fidelidad del SEÑOR es eterna!

*¡Aleluya! ¡Alabado sea el SEÑOR!

Salmo 118

1Den gracias al SEÑOR, porque él es bueno;
su gran amor perdura para siempre.

2Que proclame el pueblo de Israel:
«Su gran amor perdura para siempre.»
3Que proclamen los descendientes de Aarón:
«Su gran amor perdura para siempre.»
4Que proclamen los que temen al SEÑOR:
«Su gran amor perdura para siempre.»

5Desde mi angustia clamé al SEÑOR,
y él me respondió dándome libertad.
6El SEÑOR está conmigo, y no tengo miedo;
¿qué me puede hacer un simple *mortal?
7El SEÑOR está conmigo, él es mi ayuda;
¡ya veré por los suelos a los que me odian!

8Es mejor refugiarse en el SEÑOR
que confiar en el *hombre.
9Es mejor refugiarse en el SEÑOR
que fiarse de los poderosos.

10Todas las naciones me rodearon,
pero en el *nombre del SEÑOR las aniquilé.
11Me rodearon por completo,
pero en el nombre del SEÑOR las aniquilé.
12Me rodearon como avispas,
pero se consumieron como zarzas en el
fuego.
¡En el nombre del SEÑOR las aniquilé!

13Me empujaronf con violencia para que
cayera,
pero el SEÑOR me ayudó.
14El SEÑOR es mi fuerza y mi canto;
¡él es mi *salvación!

15Gritos de júbilo y *victoria
resuenan en las casas de los justos:
«¡La diestra del SEÑOR realiza proezas!
16¡La diestra del SEÑOR es exaltada!
¡La diestra del SEÑOR realiza proezas!»

17No he de morir; he de vivir
para proclamar las maravillas del SEÑOR.
18El SEÑOR me ha castigado con dureza,
pero no me ha entregado a la muerte.

19Ábranme las *puertas de la justicia
para que entre yo a dar gracias al SEÑOR.
20Son las puertas del SEÑOR,
por las que entran los justos.
21¡Te daré gracias porque me respondiste,
porque eres mi *salvación!

22La piedra que desecharon los constructores
ha llegado a ser la piedra angular.
23Esto ha sido obra del SEÑOR,
y nos deja maravillados.
24Éste es el día en que el SEÑOR actuó;
regocijémonos y alegrémonos en él.

25SEÑOR, ¡danos la *salvación!
SEÑOR, ¡concédenos la *victoria!
26Bendito el que viene en el nombre del SEÑOR.
Desde la casa del SEÑOR los bendecimos.
27El SEÑOR es Dios y nos ilumina.

Únanse a la procesión portando ramas en
la mano
hasta los cuernos del altar.g

28Tú eres mi Dios, por eso te doy gracias;
tú eres mi Dios, por eso te exalto.

29Den gracias al SEÑOR, porque él es bueno;
su gran amor perdura para siempre.

Salmo 119h

Álef

1*Dichosos los que van por *caminos
perfectos,
los que andan conforme a la *ley
del SEÑOR.
2Dichosos los que guardan sus
*estatutos
y de todo corazón lo buscan.
3Jamás hacen nada malo,
sino que siguen los *caminos de
Dios.
4Tú has establecido tus preceptos,
para que se cumplan fielmente.
5¡Cuánto deseo afirmar mis caminos
. para cumplir tus decretos!
6No tendré que pasar vergüenzas
cuando considere todos tus
mandamientos.
7Te alabaré con integridad de corazón,
cuando aprenda tus justos juicios.
8Tus decretos cumpliré;
no me abandones del todo.

Bet

9¿Cómo puede el joven llevar una vida
íntegra?
Viviendo conforme a tu palabra.
10Yo te busco con todo el corazón;
no dejes que me desvíe de tus
mandamientos.
11En mi corazón atesoro tus dichos
para no pecar contra ti.
12¡Bendito seas, SEÑOR!
¡Enséñame tus decretos!
13Con mis labios he proclamado
todos los juicios que has emitido.
14Me regocijo en el *camino de tus
estatutos
más que eni todas las riquezas.
15En tus preceptos medito,
y pongo mis ojos en tus sendas.
16En tus decretos hallo mi deleite,
y jamás olvidaré tu palabra.

Guímel

17Trata con bondad a este siervo tuyo;
así viviré y obedeceré tu palabra.
18Ábreme los ojos, para que contemple
las maravillas de tu ley.
19En esta tierra soy un extranjero;
no escondas de mí tus
mandamientos.
20A toda hora siento un nudo en la
garganta
por el deseo de conocer tus juicios.
21Tú reprendes a los insolentes;
¡malditos los que se apartan de tus
mandamientos!
22Aleja de mí el menosprecio y el
desdén,

pues yo cumplo tus estatutos.
23Aun los poderosos se confabulan
contra mí,
pero este siervo tuyo medita en tus
decretos.
24Tus estatutos son mi deleite;
son también mis consejeros.

Dálet

25Postrado estoy en el polvo;
dame vida conforme a tu palabra.
26Tú me respondiste cuando te hablé
de mis caminos.
¡Enséñame tus decretos!
27Hazme entender el *camino de tus
preceptos,
y meditaré en tus maravillas.
28De angustia se me derrite el *alma:
susténtame conforme a tu palabra.
29Mantenme alejado de caminos
torcidos;
concédeme las bondades de tu ley.
30He optado por el camino de la
fidelidad,
he escogido tus juicios.
31Yo, SEÑOR, me apego a tus estatutos;
no me hagas pasar vergüenza.
32Corro por el camino de tus
mandamientos,
porque has ampliado mi modo de
pensar.

He

33Enséñame, SEÑOR, a seguir tus
decretos,
y los cumpliré hasta el fin.
34Dame entendimiento para seguir tu
ley,
y la cumpliré de todo corazón.
35Dirígeme por la senda de tus
mandamientos,
porque en ella encuentro mi solaz.
36Inclina mi corazón hacia tus estatutos
y no hacia las ganancias
desmedidas.
37Aparta mi vista de cosas vanas,
dame vida conforme a tu palabra.j
38Confirma tu promesa a este siervo,
como lo has hecho con los que te
temen.
39Líbrame del oprobio que me aterra,
porque tus juicios son buenos.
40¡Yo amo tus preceptos!
¡Dame vida conforme a tu justicia!

Vav

41Envíame, SEÑOR, tu gran amor
y tu *salvación, conforme a tu
promesa.
42Así responderé a quien me desprecie,
porque yo confío en tu palabra.
43No me quites de la boca la palabra de
verdad,
pues en tus juicios he puesto mi
esperanza.
44Por toda la eternidad
obedeceré fielmente tu ley.
45Viviré con toda libertad,
porque he buscado tus preceptos.
46Hablaré de tus estatutos a los reyes

---

g **118:27** *Únanse ... del altar.* Alt. Aten el sacrificio festivo con sogas / y llévenlo hasta los cuernos del altar. h **Sal 119** Éste es un
salmo acróstico, dividido en 22 estrofas, conforme al número de las letras del alfabeto hebreo. En el texto hebreo
cada una de los ocho líneas principales de cada estrofa comienza con la letra que da nombre a la misma. i **119:14** *más
que en* (Siríaca); *como sobre* (TM). j **119:37** *conforme a tu palabra* (Targum y dos mss. hebreos); *en tu camino* (TM).

y no seré avergonzado,
47pues amo tus mandamientos,
y en ellos me regocijo.
48Yo amo tus mandamientos,
y hacia ellos elevo mis manos;
¡quiero meditar en tus decretos!

Zayin   49Acuérdate de la palabra que diste a
este siervo tuyo,
palabra con la que me infundiste
esperanza.
50Éste es mi consuelo en medio del
dolor:
que tu promesa me da vida.
51Los insolentes me ofenden hasta el
colmo,
pero yo no me aparto de tu ley.
52Me acuerdo, SEÑOR, de tus juicios de
antaño,
y encuentro consuelo en ellos.
53Me llenan de indignación los impíos,
que han abandonado tu ley.
54Tus decretos han sido mis cánticos
en el lugar de mi destierro.
55SEÑOR, por la noche evoco tu
*nombre;
¡quiero cumplir tu ley!
56Lo que a mí me corresponde
es obedecer tus preceptos.k

Jet   57¡Mi herencia eres tú, SEÑOR!
Prometo obedecer tus palabras.
58De todo corazón busco tu rostro;
compadécete de mí conforme a tu
promesa.
59Me he puesto a pensar en mis
caminos,
y he orientado mis pasos hacia tus
estatutos.
60Me doy prisa, no tardo nada
para cumplir tus mandamientos.
61Aunque los lazos de los impíos me
aprisionan,
yo no me olvido de tu ley.
62A medianoche me levanto a darte
gracias
por tus rectos juicios.
63Soy amigo de todos los que te
honran,
de todos los que observan tus
preceptos.
64Enséñame, SEÑOR, tus decretos,
¡la tierra está llena de tu gran
amor!

Tet   65Tú, SEÑOR, tratas bien a tu siervo,
conforme a tu palabra.
66Impárteme *conocimiento y buen
juicio,
pues yo creo en tus
mandamientos.
67Antes de sufrir anduve descarriado,
pero ahora obedezco tu palabra.
68Tú eres bueno, y haces el bien;
enséñame tus decretos.
69Aunque los insolentes me difaman,
yo cumplo tus preceptos con todo
el corazón.
70El corazón de ellos es torpe e
insensible,

pero yo me regocijo en tu ley.
71Me hizo bien haber sido afligido,
porque así llegué a conocer tus
decretos.
72Para mí es más valiosa tu *enseñanza
que millares de monedas de oro y
plata.

Yod   73Con tus manos me creaste, me diste
forma.
Dame entendimiento para
aprender tus mandamientos.
74Los que te honran se regocijan al
verme,
porque he puesto mi esperanza en
tu palabra.
75SEÑOR, yo sé que tus juicios son
justos,
y que con justa razón me afliges.
76Que sea tu gran amor mi consuelo,
conforme a la promesa que hiciste
a tu siervo.
77Que venga tu compasión a darme
vida,
porque en tu ley me regocijo.
78Sean avergonzados los insolentes
que sin motivo me maltratan;
yo, por mi parte, meditaré en tus
preceptos.
79Que se reconcilien conmigo los que
te temen,
los que conocen tus estatutos.
80Sea mi corazón íntegro hacia tus
decretos,
para que yo no sea avergonzado.

Caf   81Esperando tu salvación se me va la
vida.
En tu palabra he puesto mi
esperanza.
82Mis ojos se consumen esperando tu
promesa,
y digo: «¿Cuándo vendrás a
consolarme?»
83Parezco un odre ennegrecido por el
humo,
pero no me olvido de tus decretos.
84¿Cuánto más vivirá este siervo tuyo?
¿Cuándo juzgarás a mis
perseguidores?
85Me han cavado trampas los
insolentes,
los que no viven conforme a tu ley.
86Todos tus mandamientos son
fidedignos;
¡ayúdame!, pues falsos son mis
perseguidores.
87Por poco me borran de la tierra,
pero yo no abandono tus
preceptos.
88Por tu gran amor, dame vida
y cumpliré tus estatutos.

Lámed   89Tu palabra, SEÑOR, es eterna,
y está firme en los cielos.
90Tu fidelidad permanece para
siempre;
estableciste la tierra, y quedó
firme.

k 119:56 Lo que a mí ... tus preceptos. Alt. Esto es lo que me corresponde, porque obedezco tus preceptos.

91Todo subsiste hoy, conforme a tus
decretos,
porque todo está a tu servicio.
92Si tu ley no fuera mi regocijo,
la aflicción habría acabado
conmigo.
93Jamás me olvidaré de tus preceptos,
pues con ellos me has dado vida.
94¡Sálvame, pues te pertenezco
y escudriño tus preceptos!
95Los impíos me acechan para
destruirme,
pero yo me esfuerzo por entender
tus estatutos.
96He visto que aun la perfección tiene
sus límites;
¡sólo tus mandamientos son
infinitos!

Mem
97¡Cuánto amo yo tu ley!
Todo el día medito en ella.
98Tus mandamientos me hacen más
sabio que mis enemigos
porque me pertenecen para
siempre.
99Tengo más discernimiento que todos
mis maestros
porque medito en tus estatutos.
100Tengo más entendimiento que los
ancianos
porque obedezco tus preceptos.
101Aparto mis pies de toda mala senda
para cumplir con tu palabra.
102No me desvío de tus juicios
porque tú mismo me instruyes.
103¡Cuán dulces son a mi paladar tus
palabras!
¡Son más dulces que la miel a mi
boca!
104De tus preceptos adquiero
entendimiento;
por eso aborrezco toda senda de
mentira.

Nun
105Tu palabra es una lámpara a mis
pies;
es una luz en mi sendero.
106Hice un juramento, y lo he
confirmado:
que acataré tus rectos juicios.
107SEÑOR, es mucho lo que he sufrido;
dame vida conforme a tu palabra.
108SEÑOR, acepta la ofrenda que brota
de mis labios;
enséñame tus juicios.
109Mi vida pende de un hilo,l
pero no me olvido de tu ley.
110Los impíos me han tendido una
trampa,
pero no me aparto de tus
preceptos.
111Tus estatutos son mi herencia
permanente;
son el regocijo de mi corazón.
112Inclino mi corazón a cumplir tus
decretos
para siempre y hasta el fin.

Sámej
113Aborrezco a los hipócritas,

pero amo tu ley.
114Tú eres mi escondite y mi escudo;
en tu palabra he puesto mi
esperanza.
115¡Malhechores, apártense de mí,
que quiero cumplir los
mandamientos de mi Dios!
116Sosténme conforme a tu promesa, y
viviré;
no defraudes mis esperanzas.
117Defiéndeme, y estaré a salvo;
siempre optaré por tus decretos.
118Tú rechazas a los que se desvían de
tus decretos,
porque sólo maquinan falsedades.
119Tú desechas como escoria a los
impíos de la tierra;
por eso amo tus estatutos.
120Mi cuerpo se estremece por el temor
que me inspiras;
siento reverencia por tus leyes.

Ayin
121Yo practico la justicia y el derecho;
no me dejes en manos de mis
opresores.
122Garantiza el bienestar de tu siervo;
que no me opriman los arrogantes.
123Mis ojos se consumen esperando tu
salvación,
esperando que se cumpla tu
justicia.
124Trata a tu siervo conforme a tu gran
amor;
enséñame tus decretos.
125Tu siervo soy: dame entendimiento
y llegaré a conocer tus estatutos.
126SEÑOR, ya es tiempo de que actúes,
pues tu ley está siendo
quebrantada.
127Sobre todas las cosas amo tus
mandamientos,
más que el oro, más que el oro
refinado.
128Por eso tomo en cuenta todos tus
preceptosm
y aborrezco toda senda falsa.

Pe
129Tus estatutos son maravillosos;
por eso los obedezco.
130La exposición de tus palabras nos da
luz,
y da entendimiento al *sencillo.
131Jadeante abro la boca
porque ansío tus mandamientos.
132Vuélvete a mí, y tenme compasión
como haces siempre con los que
aman tu nombre.
133Guía mis pasos conforme a tu
promesa;
no dejes que me domine la
iniquidad.
134Líbrame de la opresión humana,
pues quiero obedecer tus
preceptos.
135Haz brillar tu rostro sobre tu siervo;
enséñame tus decretos.
136Ríos de lágrimas brotan de mis ojos,
porque tu ley no se obedece.

---

l **119:109** pende de un hilo. Lit. está siempre en mi puño.   m **119:128** Por eso ... tus preceptos (véanse LXX y Vulgata); Por eso
todos los estatutos de todo lo que hago recto (TM).

Tsade

137SEÑOR, tú eres justo,
y tus juicios son rectos.
138Justos son los estatutos que has
ordenado,
y muy dignos de confianza.
139Mi celo me consume,
porque mis adversarios pasan por
alto tus palabras.
140Tus promesas han superado muchas
pruebas,
por eso tu siervo las ama.
141Insignificante y menospreciable
como soy,
no me olvido de tus preceptos.
142Tu justicia es siempre justa;
tu ley es la verdad.
143He caído en la angustia y la
aflicción,
pero tus mandamientos son mi
regocijo.
144Tus estatutos son siempre justos;
dame entendimiento para poder
vivir.

Qof

145Con todo el corazón clamo a ti,
SEÑOR;
respóndeme, y obedeceré tus
decretos.
146A ti clamo: «¡Sálvame!»
Quiero cumplir tus estatutos.
147Muy de mañana me levanto a pedir
ayuda;
en tus palabras he puesto mi
esperanza.
148En toda la noche no pego los ojos,n
para meditar en tu promesa.
149Conforme a tu gran amor, escucha
mi voz;
conforme a tus juicios, SEÑOR,
dame vida.
150Ya se acercan mis crueles
perseguidores,
pero andan muy lejos de tu ley.
151Tú, SEÑOR, también estás cerca,
y todos tus mandamientos son
verdad.
152Desde hace mucho conozco tus
estatutos,
los cuales estableciste para
siempre.

Resh

153Considera mi aflicción, y líbrame,
pues no me he olvidado de tu ley.
154Defiende mi causa, rescátame;
dame vida conforme a tu promesa.
155La salvación está lejos de los impíos,
porque ellos no buscan tus
decretos.
156Grande es, SEÑOR, tu compasión;
dame vida conforme a tus juicios.
157Muchos son mis adversarios y mis
perseguidores,
pero yo no me aparto de tus
estatutos.
158Miro a esos renegados y me dan
náuseas,
porque no cumplen tus palabras.
159Mira, SEÑOR, cuánto amo tus
preceptos;

conforme a tu gran amor, dame
vida.
160La suma de tus palabras es la
verdad;
tus rectos juicios permanecen para
siempre.

Shin

161Gente poderosañ me persigue sin
motivo,
pero mi corazón se asombra ante
tu palabra.
162Yo me regocijo en tu promesa
como quien halla un gran botín.
163Aborrezco y repudio la falsedad,
pero amo tu ley.
164Siete veces al día te alabo
por tus rectos juicios.
165Los que aman tu ley disfrutan de
gran *bienestar,
y nada los hace tropezar.
166Yo, SEÑOR, espero tu salvación
y practico tus mandamientos.
167Con todo mi ser cumplo tus
estatutos.
¡Cuánto los amo!
168Obedezco tus preceptos y tus
estatutos,
porque conoces todos mis
caminos.

Tav

169Que llegue mi clamor a tu presencia;
dame entendimiento, SEÑOR,
conforme a tu palabra.
170Que llegue a tu presencia mi
súplica;
líbrame, conforme a tu promesa.
171Que rebosen mis labios de alabanza,
porque tú me enseñas tus
decretos.
172Que entone mi lengua un cántico a
tu palabra,
pues todos tus mandamientos son
justos.
173Que acuda tu mano en mi ayuda,
porque he escogido tus preceptos.
174Yo, SEÑOR, ansío tu salvación.
Tu ley es mi regocijo.
175Déjame vivir para alabarte;
que vengan tus juicios a
ayudarme.
176Cual oveja perdida me he
extraviado;
ven en busca de tu siervo,
porque no he olvidado tus
mandamientos.

Salmo 120

Cántico de los *peregrinos.

1En mi angustia invoqué al SEÑOR,
y él me respondió.
2SEÑOR, líbrame de los labios mentirosos
y de las lenguas embusteras.

3¡Ah, lengua embustera!
¿Qué se te habrá de dar?
¿Qué se te habrá de añadir?
4¡Puntiagudas flechas de guerrero,
con ardientes brasas de *retama!

5¡Ay de mí, que soy extranjero en Mésec,

---

n **119:148** *En toda ... los ojos.* Lit. *Se anticipan mis ojos a las vigilias.*   ñ **119:161** *Gente poderosa.* Lit. *Príncipes.*

que he acampado entre las tiendas de
Cedar!
6¡Ya es mucho el tiempo que he acampado
entre los que aborrecen la *paz!
7Yo amo la paz,
pero si hablo de paz,
ellos hablan de guerra.

Salmo 121

Cántico de los *peregrinos.

1A las montañas levanto mis ojos;
¿de dónde ha de venir mi ayuda?
2Mi ayuda proviene del SEÑOR,
creador del cielo y de la tierra.

3No permitirá que tu pie resbale;
jamás duerme el que te cuida.
4Jamás duerme ni se adormece
el que cuida de Israel.

5El SEÑOR es quien te cuida,
el SEÑOR es tu sombra protectora.o
6De día el sol no te hará daño,
ni la luna de noche.

7El SEÑOR te protegerá;
de todo mal protegerá tu vida.
8El SEÑOR te cuidará en el hogar y en el
camino,p
desde ahora y para siempre.

Salmo 122

Cántico de los *peregrinos. De David.

1Yo me alegro cuando me dicen:
«Vamos a la casa del SEÑOR.»
2*¡Jerusalén, ya nuestros pies
se han plantado ante tus *portones!

3¡Jerusalén, ciudad edificada
para que en ella todos se congreguen!q
4A ella suben las tribus,
las tribus del SEÑOR,
para alabar su *nombre
conforme a la ordenanza que recibió Israel.

5Allí están los tribunales de justicia,
los tribunales de la dinastía de David.

6Pidamos por la *paz de Jerusalén:
«Que vivan en paz los que te aman.
7Que haya paz dentro de tus murallas,
seguridad en tus fortalezas.»
8Y ahora, por mis hermanos y amigos te digo:
«¡Deseo que tengas paz!»
9Por la casa del SEÑOR nuestro Dios
procuraré tu bienestar.

Salmo 123

Cántico de los *peregrinos.

1Hacia ti dirijo la mirada,
hacia ti, cuyo trono está en el cielo.
2Como dirigen los esclavos la mirada
hacia la mano de su amo,
como dirige la esclava la mirada
hacia la mano de su ama,
así dirigimos la mirada al SEÑOR nuestro Dios,
hasta que nos muestre compasión.

3Compadécenos, SEÑOR, compadécenos,
¡ya estamos hartos de que nos desprecien!

4Ya son muchas las burlas que hemos sufrido;
muchos son los insultos de los altivos,
y mucho el menosprecio de los orgullosos.

Salmo 124

Cántico de los *peregrinos. De David.

1Si el SEÑOR no hubiera estado de nuestra parte
—que lo repita ahora Israel—,
2si el SEÑOR no hubiera estado de nuestra parte
cuando todo el mundo se levantó contra
nosotros,
3nos habrían tragado vivos
al encenderse su furor contra nosotros;
4nos habrían inundado las aguas,
el torrente nos habría arrastrado,
5inos habrían arrastrado las aguas
turbulentas!

6Bendito sea el SEÑOR, que no dejó
que nos despedazaran con sus dientes.
7Como las aves, hemos escapado
de la trampa del cazador;
¡la trampa se rompió,
y nosotros escapamos!
8Nuestra ayuda está en el *nombre del SEÑOR,
creador del cielo y de la tierra.

Salmo 125

Cántico de los *peregrinos.

1Los que confían en el SEÑOR
son como el monte *Sión,
que jamás será conmovido,
que permanecerá para siempre.
2Como rodean las colinas a Jerusalén,
así rodea el SEÑOR a su pueblo,
desde ahora y para siempre.

3No prevalecerá el cetro de los impíos
sobre la heredad asignada a los justos,
para que nunca los justos extiendan
sus manos hacia la maldad.

4Haz bien, SEÑOR, a los que son buenos,
a los de recto corazón.
5Pero a los que van por caminos torcidos
deséchalos, SEÑOR, junto con los
malhechores.

¡Que haya paz en Israel!

Salmo 126

Cántico de los *peregrinos.

1Cuando el SEÑOR hizo volver a *Sión a los
cautivos,
nos parecía estar soñando.
2Nuestra boca se llenó de risas;
nuestra lengua, de canciones jubilosas.
Hasta los otros pueblos decían:
«El SEÑOR ha hecho grandes cosas por
ellos.»
3Sí, el SEÑOR ha hecho grandes cosas por
nosotros,
y eso nos llena de alegría.

4Ahora, SEÑOR, haz volver a nuestros cautivos
como haces volver los arroyos del desierto.
5El que con lágrimas siembra,
con regocijo cosecha.
6El que llorando esparce la semilla,
cantando recoge sus gavillas.

---

o 121:5 tu sombra protectora. Lit. tu sombra a tu mano derecha. p 121:8 te cuidará en el hogar y en el camino. Lit. cuidará tu salida y tu entrada. q 122:3 ¡Jerusalén, ... se congreguen! Alt. Jerusalén, edificada como ciudad, en la que todo se mantiene bien unido.

Salmo 127

Cántico de los *peregrinos. De Salomón.

1Si el SEÑOR no edifica la casa,
en vano se esfuerzan los albañiles.
Si el SEÑOR no cuida la ciudad,
en vano hacen guardia los vigilantes.
2En vano madrugan ustedes,
y se acuestan muy tarde,
para comer un pan de fatigas,
porque Dios concede el sueño a sus
amados.

3Los hijos son una herencia del SEÑOR,
los frutos del vientre son una recompensa.
4Como flechas en las manos del guerrero
son los hijos de la juventud.
5*Dichosos los que llenan su aljaba
con esta clase de flechas.r
No serán avergonzados por sus enemigos
cuando litiguen con ellos en los tribunales.

Salmo 128

Cántico de los *peregrinos.

1*Dichosos todos los que temen al SEÑOR,
los que van por sus *caminos.
2Lo que ganes con tus manos, eso comerás;
gozarás de dicha y prosperidad.
3En el seno de tu hogar,
tu esposa será como vid llena de uvas;
alrededor de tu mesa,
tus hijos serán como vástagos de olivo.
4Tales son las bendiciones
de los que temen al SEÑOR.

5Que el SEÑOR te bendiga desde *Sión,
y veas la prosperidad de Jerusalén
todos los días de tu vida.
6Que vivas para ver a los hijos de tus hijos.

¡Que haya *paz en Israel!

Salmo 129

Cántico de los *peregrinos.

1Mucho me han angustiado desde mi juventud
—que lo repita ahora Israel—,
2mucho me han angustiado desde mi juventud,
pero no han logrado vencerme.
3Sobre la espalda me pasaron el arado,
abriéndome en ella profundoss surcos.
4Pero el SEÑOR, que es justo,
me libró de las ataduras de los impíos.

5Que retrocedan avergonzados
todos los que odian a *Sión.
6Que sean como la hierba en el techo,
que antes de crecer se marchita;
7por no llena las manos del segador
ni el regazo del que cosecha.
8Que al pasar nadie les diga:
«La bendición del SEÑOR sea con ustedes;
los bendecimos en el *nombre del SEÑOR.»

Salmo 130

Cántico de los *peregrinos.

1A ti, SEÑOR, elevo mi clamor
desde las profundidades del abismo.
2Escucha, Señor, mi voz.

Estén atentos tus oídos a mi voz suplicante.

3Si tú, SEÑOR, tomaras en cuenta los pecados,
¿quién, SEÑOR, sería declarado inocente?t
4Pero en ti se halla perdón,
y por eso debes ser temido.

5Espero al SEÑOR, lo espero con toda el *alma;
en su palabra he puesto mi esperanza.
6Espero al SEÑOR con toda el alma,
más que los centinelas la mañana.

Como esperan los centinelas la mañana,
7así tú, Israel, espera al SEÑOR.
Porque en él hay amor inagotable;
en él hay plena redención.
8Él mismo redimirá a Israel
de todos sus pecados.

Salmo 131

Cántico de los *peregrinos. De David.

1SEÑOR, mi corazón no es orgulloso,
ni son altivos mis ojos;
no busco grandezas desmedidas,
ni proezas que excedan a mis fuerzas.
2Todo lo contrario:
he calmado y aquietado mis ansias.
Soy como un niño recién amamantado en el
regazo de su madre.
¡Mi *alma es como un niño recién
amamantado!

3Israel, pon tu esperanza en el SEÑOR
desde ahora y para siempre.

Salmo 132

132:8-10 — 2Cr 6:41-42

Cántico de los *peregrinos.

1SEÑOR, acuérdate de David
y de todas sus penurias.
2Acuérdate de sus juramentos al SEÑOR,
de sus votos al Poderoso de Jacob:
3«No gozaré del calor del hogar,
ni me daré un momento de descanso;u
4no me permitiré cerrar los ojos,
y ni siquiera el menor pestañeo,
5antes de hallar un lugar para el SEÑOR,
una morada para el Poderoso de Jacob.»

6En Efrata oímos hablar del arca;v
dimos con ella en los campos de Yagar:w
7«Vayamos hasta su morada;
postrémonos ante el estrado de sus pies.»

8Levántate, SEÑOR; ven a tu lugar de reposo,
tú y tu arca poderosa.
9¡Que se revistan de justicia tus sacerdotes!
¡Que tus fieles canten jubilosos!
10Por amor a David, tu siervo,
no le des la espalda ax tu *ungido.

11El SEÑOR le ha hecho a David
un firme juramento que no revocará:
«A uno de tus propios descendientes
lo pondré en tu trono.
12Si tus hijos cumplen con mi pacto
y con los estatutos que les enseñaré,
también sus descendientes
te sucederán en el trono para siempre.»

---

r 127:5 con esta clase de flechas. Lit. con ellos.   s 129:3 profundos. Lit. largos.   t 130:3 ¿ ... sería declarado inocente? Lit. ¿ ... se mantendría en pie?   u 132:3 No gozaré ... de descanso. Lit. Si entrara yo en la tienda de mi casa, / si subiera yo al lecho de mi cama.   v 132:6 del arca. Lit. de ella; véase 1S 7:1.   w 132:6 Yagar. Es decir, Quiriat Yearín.   x 132:10 no le des la espalda a. Lit. no vuelvas el rostro de.

¹³El SEÑOR ha escogido a *Sión;
su deseo es hacer de este monte su morada:
¹⁴«Éste será para siempre mi lugar de reposo;
aquí pondré mi trono, porque así lo deseo.
¹⁵Bendeciré con creces sus provisiones,
y saciaré de pan a sus pobres.
¹⁶Revestiré de *salvación a sus sacerdotes,
y jubilosos cantarán sus fieles.

¹⁷»Aquí haré renacer el poderʸ de David,
y encenderé la lámpara de mi ungido.
¹⁸A sus enemigos los cubriré de vergüenza,
pero él lucirá su corona esplendorosa.»

Salmo 133

Cántico de los *peregrinos. De David.

¹¡Cuán bueno y cuán agradable es
que los hermanos convivan en armonía!
²Es como el buen aceite que, desde la cabeza,
va descendiendo por la barba,
por la barba de Aarón,
hasta el borde de sus vestiduras.
³Es como el rocío de Hermón
que va descendiendo sobre los montes de
*Sión.
Donde se da esta armonía,ᶻ
el SEÑOR concede bendición y vida eterna.

Salmo 134

Cántico de los *peregrinos.

¹Bendigan al SEÑOR todos ustedes sus siervos,
que de noche permanecen en la casa del
SEÑOR.
²Eleven sus manos hacia el santuario
y bendigan al SEÑOR.
³Que desde *Sión los bendiga el SEÑOR,
creador del cielo y de la tierra.

Salmo 135

135:15-20 — Sal 115:4-11

¹*¡Aleluya! ¡Alabado sea el SEÑOR!

¡Alaben el *nombre del SEÑOR!
¡Siervos del SEÑOR, alábenlo!
²Ustedes, que permanecen en la casa del
SEÑOR,
en los atrios de la casa del Dios nuestro.

³Alaben al SEÑOR, porque el SEÑOR es bueno;
canten salmos a su nombre, porque eso es
agradable.
⁴El SEÑOR escogió a Jacob como su propiedad,
a Israel como su posesión.

⁵Yo sé que el SEÑOR, nuestro Soberano,
es más grande que todos los dioses.
⁶El SEÑOR hace todo lo que quiere
en los cielos y en la tierra,
en los mares y en todos sus abismos.
⁷Levanta las nubes desde los confines de la
tierra;
envía relámpagos con la lluvia
y saca de sus depósitos a los vientos.

⁸A los primogénitos de Egipto hirió de muerte,
tanto a *hombres como a animales.
⁹En tu corazón mismo, oh Egipto,
Dios envió señales y maravillas
contra el faraón y todos sus siervos.
¹⁰A muchas naciones las hirió de muerte;

a reyes poderosos les quitó la vida:
¹¹a Sijón, el rey amorreo;
a Og, el rey de Basán,
y a todos los reyes de Canaán.
¹²Entregó sus tierras como herencia,
¡como herencia para su pueblo Israel!

¹³Tu nombre, SEÑOR, es eterno;
tu renombre, por todas las generaciones.
¹⁴Ciertamente el SEÑOR juzgará a su pueblo,
y de sus siervos tendrá compasión.

¹⁵Los ídolos de los paganos son de oro y plata,
producto de manos humanas.
¹⁶Tienen boca, pero no pueden hablar;
ojos, pero no pueden ver;
¹⁷tienen oídos, pero no pueden oír;
¡ni siquiera hay aliento en su boca!
¹⁸Semejantes a ellos son sus hacedores
y todos los que confían en ellos.

¹⁹Pueblo de Israel, bendice al SEÑOR;
descendientes de Aarón, bendigan al
SEÑOR;
²⁰descendientes de Leví, bendigan al SEÑOR;
los que temen al SEÑOR, bendíganlo.
²¹Desde *Sión sea bendito el SEÑOR,
el que habita en Jerusalén.

*¡Aleluya! ¡Alabado sea el SEÑOR!

Salmo 136

¹Den gracias al SEÑOR, porque él es bueno;
su gran amor perdura para siempre.
²Den gracias al Dios de dioses;
su gran amor perdura para siempre.
³Den gracias al SEÑOR omnipotente;
su gran amor perdura para siempre.
⁴Al único que hace grandes maravillas;
su gran amor perdura para siempre.
⁵Al que con inteligencia hizo los cielos;
su gran amor perdura para siempre.
⁶Al que expandió la tierra sobre las aguas;
su gran amor perdura para siempre.
⁷Al que hizo las grandes luminarias;
su gran amor perdura para siempre.
⁸El sol, para iluminarª el día;
su gran amor perdura para siempre.
⁹La luna y las estrellas, para iluminar la noche;
su gran amor perdura para siempre.
¹⁰Al que hirió a los primogénitos de Egipto;
su gran amor perdura para siempre.
¹¹Al que sacó de Egiptoᵇ a Israel;
su gran amor perdura para siempre.
¹²Con mano poderosa y con brazo extendido;
su gran amor perdura para siempre.
¹³Al que partió en dos el Mar Rojo;ᶜ
su gran amor perdura para siempre.
¹⁴Y por en medio hizo cruzar a Israel;
su gran amor perdura para siempre.
¹⁵Pero hundió en el Mar Rojo al faraón y a su
ejército;
su gran amor perdura para siempre.
¹⁶Al que guió a su pueblo por el desierto;
su gran amor perdura para siempre.
¹⁷Al que hirió de muerte a grandes reyes;
su gran amor perdura para siempre.
¹⁸Al que a reyes poderosos les quitó la vida;
su gran amor perdura para siempre.
¹⁹A Sijón, el rey amorreo;

ʸ **132:17** *poder.* Lit. *cuerno.* ᶻ **133:3** *Donde se da esta armonía.* Lit. *Ciertamente allí.* ª **136:8** *iluminar.* Lit. *dominar.*
ᵇ **136:11** *de Egipto.* Lit. *de entre ellos.* ᶜ **136:13** *Mar Rojo.* Lit. *mar de las Cañas* (heb. *Yam Suf*); también en v. 15.

su gran amor perdura para siempre.
²⁰A Og, el rey de Basán;
su gran amor perdura para siempre.
²¹Cuyas tierras entregó como herencia;
su gran amor perdura para siempre.
²²Como herencia para su siervo Israel;
su gran amor perdura para siempre.
²³Al que nunca nos olvida, aunque estemos humillados;
su gran amor perdura para siempre.
²⁴Al que nos libra de nuestros adversarios;
su gran amor perdura para siempre.
²⁵Al que alimenta a todo ser viviente;
su gran amor perdura para siempre.
²⁶¡Den gracias al Dios de los cielos!
¡Su gran amor perdura para siempre!

Salmo 137

¹Junto a los ríos de Babilonia nos sentábamos,
y llorábamos al acordarnos de *Sión.
²En los álamos que había en la ciudad
colgábamos nuestras arpas.
³Allí, los que nos tenían cautivos
nos pedían que entonáramos canciones;
nuestros opresores nos pedían estar alegres;
nos decían: «¡Cántennos un cántico de Sión!»

⁴¿Cómo cantar las canciones del SEÑOR
en una tierra extraña?
⁵Ah, Jerusalén, Jerusalén,
si llegara yo a olvidarte,
¡que la mano derecha se me seque!
⁶Si de ti no me acordara,
ni te pusiera por encima de mi propia alegría,
¡que la lengua se me pegue al paladar!

⁷SEÑOR, acuérdate de los edomitas
el día en que cayó Jerusalén.
«¡Arrásenla —gritaban—,
arrásenla hasta sus cimientos!»

⁸Hija de Babilonia, que has de ser destruida,
*¡dichoso el que te haga pagar
por todo lo que nos has hecho!
⁹¡Dichoso el que agarre a tus pequeños
y los estrelle contra las rocas!

Salmo 138
Salmo de David.

¹SEÑOR, quiero alabarte de todo corazón,
y cantarte salmos delante de los dioses.
²Quiero inclinarme hacia tu santo templo
y alabar tu *nombre por tu gran amor y fidelidad.
Porque has exaltado tu nombre y tu palabra
por sobre todas las cosas.
³Cuando te llamé, me respondiste;
me infundiste ánimo y renovaste mis *fuerzas.

⁴Oh SEÑOR, todos los reyes de la tierra
te alabarán al escuchar tus palabras.
⁵Celebrarán con cánticos tus *caminos,
porque tu gloria, SEÑOR, es grande.

⁶El SEÑOR es excelso,
pero toma en cuenta a los humildes

y mira^d de lejos a los orgullosos.
⁷Aunque pase yo por grandes angustias,
tú me darás vida;
contra el furor de mis enemigos extenderás la mano:
¡tu mano derecha me pondrá a salvo!
⁸El SEÑOR cumplirá en mí su propósito.^e
Tu gran amor, SEÑOR, perdura para siempre;
¡no abandones la obra de tus manos!

Salmo 139
Al director musical. Salmo de David.

¹SEÑOR, tú me examinas,
tú me conoces.
²Sabes cuándo me siento y cuándo me levanto;
aun a la distancia me lees el pensamiento.
³Mis trajines y descansos los conoces,
todos mis caminos te son familiares.
⁴No me llega aún la palabra a la lengua
cuando tú, SEÑOR, ya la sabes toda.
⁵Tu protección me envuelve por completo;
me cubres con la palma de tu mano.
⁶Conocimiento tan maravilloso rebasa mi comprensión;
tan sublime es que no puedo entenderlo.

⁷¿Adónde podría alejarme de tu Espíritu?
¿Adónde podría huir de tu presencia?
⁸Si subiera al cielo,
allí estás tú;
si tendiera mi lecho en el fondo del *abismo,
también estás allí.
⁹Si me elevara sobre las alas del alba,
o me estableciera en los extremos del mar,
¹⁰aun allí tu mano me guiaría,
¡me sostendría tu mano derecha!

¹¹Y si dijera: «Que me oculten las tinieblas;
que la luz se haga noche en torno mío»,
¹²ni las tinieblas serían oscuras para ti,
y aun la noche sería clara como el día.
¡Lo mismo son para ti las tinieblas que la luz!

¹³Tú creaste mis entrañas;
me formaste en el vientre de mi madre.
¹⁴¡Te alabo porque soy una creación admirable!
¡Tus obras son maravillosas,
y esto lo sé muy bien!
¹⁵Mis huesos no te fueron desconocidos
cuando en lo más recóndito era yo formado,
cuando en lo más profundo de la tierra
era yo entretejido.
¹⁶Tus ojos vieron mi cuerpo en gestación:
todo estaba ya escrito en tu libro;
todos mis días se estaban diseñando,
aunque no existía uno solo de ellos.

¹⁷¡Cuán preciosos, oh Dios, me son tus pensamientos!
¡Cuán inmensa es la suma de ellos!
¹⁸Si me propusiera contarlos,
sumarían más que los granos de arena.
Y si terminara de hacerlo,^f
aún estaría a tu lado.

¹⁹Oh Dios, ¡si les quitaras la vida a los impíos!
¡Si de mí se aparta la gente sanguinaria,

---

d **138:6** *mira.* Lit. *conoce.*   e **138:8** *El SEÑOR ... su propósito.* Lit. *El SEÑOR completará en mí.*   f **139:18** *Y si terminara de hacerlo* (algunos mss. hebreos); *Despierto y* (TM).

²⁰esos que con malicia te difaman
    y que en vano se rebelan contra ti!ᵍ
²¹¿Acaso no aborrezco, SEÑOR, a los que te
        odian,
    y abomino a los que te rechazan?
²²El odio que les tengo es un odio implacable;
    ¡los cuento entre mis enemigos!

²³Examíname, oh Dios, y sondea mi corazón;
    ponme a prueba y sondea mis
        pensamientos.
²⁴Fíjate si voy por mal camino,
    y guíame por el *camino eterno.

Salmo 140

Al director musical. Salmo de David.

¹Oh SEÑOR, líbrame de los impíos;
    protégeme de los violentos,
²de los que urden en su corazón planes
        malvados
    y todos los días fomentan la guerra.
³Afilan su lengua cual lengua de serpiente;
    ¡veneno de víbora hay en sus labios!
                                    *Selah
⁴SEÑOR, protégeme del poder de los impíos;
    protégeme de los violentos,
    de los que piensan hacerme caer.
⁵Esos engreídos me han tendido una trampa;
    han puesto los lazos de su red,
    han tendido trampas a mi paso.
                                    Selah

⁶Yo le digo al SEÑOR: «Tú eres mi Dios.
    Atiende, SEÑOR, a mi voz suplicante.»
⁷SEÑOR Soberano, mi salvador poderoso
    que me protege en el día de la batalla:
⁸No satisfagas, SEÑOR, los caprichos de los
        impíos;
    no permitas que sus planes prosperen,
    para que no se enorgullezcan.
                                    Selah

⁹Que sobre la cabeza de mis perseguidores
    recaiga el mal que sus labios proclaman.
¹⁰Que lluevan brasas sobre ellos;
    que sean echados en el fuego,
    en ciénagas profundas, de donde no
        vuelvan a salir.
¹¹Que no eche raíces en la tierra
    la *gente de lengua viperina;
    que la calamidad persiga y destruya
    a la gente que practica la violencia.

¹²Yo sé que el SEÑOR hace justicia a los pobres
    y defiende el derecho de los necesitados.
¹³Ciertamente los justos alabarán tu *nombre
    y los íntegros vivirán en tu presencia.

Salmo 141

Salmo de David.

¹A ti clamo, SEÑOR; ven pronto a mí.
    ¡Atiende a mi voz cuando a ti clamo!
²Que suba a tu presencia mi plegaria
    como una ofrenda de incienso;
    que hacia ti se eleven mis manos
    como un sacrificio vespertino.

³SEÑOR, ponme en la boca un centinela;
    un guardia a la puerta de mis labios.

⁴No permitas que mi corazón se incline a la
        maldad,
    ni que sea yo cómplice de iniquidades;
    no me dejes participar de banquetes
    en compañía de malhechores.

⁵Que la justicia me golpee,
    que el amor me reprenda;
    pero que el ungüento de los malvados
    no perfume mi cabeza,
    pues mi oración está siempre
    en contra de sus malas obras.
⁶Cuando sus gobernantes sean lanzados desde
        los despeñaderos,
    sabrán que mis palabras eran bien
        intencionadas.
⁷Y dirán: «Así como se dispersa la tierra
    cuando en ella se abren surcos con el
        arado,
    así se han dispersado nuestros huesos
    a la orilla del *sepulcro.»

⁸En ti, SEÑOR Soberano, tengo puestos los ojos;
    en ti busco refugio; no dejes que me maten.
⁹Protégeme de las trampas que me tienden,
    de las trampas que me tienden los
        malhechores.
¹⁰Que caigan los impíos en sus propias redes,
    mientras yo salgo bien librado.

Salmo 142

*Masquil de David. Cuando estaba en la cueva.
Oración.

¹A voz en cuello, al SEÑOR le pido ayuda;
    a voz en cuello, al SEÑOR le pido
        compasión.
²Ante él expongo mis quejas;
    ante él expreso mis angustias.

³Cuando ya no me queda aliento,
    tú me muestras el camino.ʰ
    Por la senda que transito
    algunos me han tendido una trampa.
⁴Mira a mi derecha, y ve:
    nadie me tiende la mano.
    No tengo dónde refugiarme;
    por mí nadie se preocupa.

⁵A ti, SEÑOR, te pido ayuda;
    a ti te digo: «Tú eres mi refugio,
    mi porción en la tierra de los vivientes.»
⁶Atiende a mi clamor,
    porque me siento muy débil;
    líbrame de mis perseguidores,
    porque son más fuertes que yo.
⁷Sácame de la prisión,
    para que alabe yo tu *nombre.
    Los justos se reunirán en torno mío
    por la bondad que me has mostrado.

Salmo 143

Salmo de David.

¹Escucha, SEÑOR, mi oración;
    atiende a mi súplica.
    Por tu fidelidad y tu justicia,
    respóndeme.
²No lleves a juicio a tu siervo,
    pues ante ti nadie puede alegar inocencia.
³El enemigo atenta contra mi vida:

ᵍ **139:20** *y que en vano ... contra ti* (tres versiones griegas y algunos mss. hebreos); *levantan en vano tus ciudades* (TM).
ʰ **142:3** *tú me muestras el camino.* Lit. *tú conoces mi encrucijada.*

quiere hacerme morder el polvo.
Me obliga a vivir en las tinieblas,
como los que murieron hace tiempo.
4Ya no me queda aliento;
dentro de mí siento paralizado el corazón.
5Traigo a la memoria los tiempos de antaño:
medito en todas tus proezas,
considero las obras de tus manos.
6Hacia ti extiendo las manos;
me haces falta, como el agua a la tierra seca.
Selah

7Respóndeme pronto, SEÑOR,
que el aliento se me escapa.
No escondas de mí tu rostro,
o seré como los que bajan a la fosa.
8Por la mañana hazme saber de tu gran amor,
porque en ti he puesto mi confianza.
Señálame el *camino que debo seguir,
porque a ti elevo mi *alma.
9SEÑOR, líbrame de mis enemigos,
porque en ti busco refugio.
10Enséñame a hacer tu voluntad,
porque tú eres mi Dios.
Que tu buen Espíritu me guíe
por un terreno sin obstáculos.

11Por tu *nombre, SEÑOR, dame vida;
por tu justicia, sácame de este aprieto.
12Por tu gran amor, destruye a mis enemigos;
acaba con todos mis adversarios.
¡Yo soy tu siervo!

Salmo 144

Salmo de David.

1Bendito sea el SEÑOR, mi *Roca,
que adiestra mis manos para la guerra,
mis dedos para la batalla.
2Él es mi Dios amoroso, mi amparo,
mi más alto escondite, mi libertador,
mi escudo, en quien me refugio.
Él es quien pone los pueblosⁱ a mis pies.

3SEÑOR, ¿qué es el *mortal para que lo cuides?
¿Qué es el *ser humano para que en él
pienses?
4Todo mortal es como un suspiro;
sus días son fugaces como una sombra.

5Abre tus cielos, SEÑOR, y desciende;
toca los montes y haz que echen humo.
6Lanza relámpagos y dispersa al enemigo;
dispara tus flechas y ponlo en retirada.
7Extiende tu mano desde las alturas
y sálvame de las aguas tumultuosas;
líbrame del poder de gente extraña.
8Cuando abren la boca, dicen mentiras;
cuando levantan su diestra, juran en falso.ʲ

9Te cantaré, oh Dios, un cántico nuevo;
con el arpa de diez cuerdas te cantaré
salmos.
10Tú das la *victoria a los reyes;
a tu siervo David lo libras de la cruenta
espada.
11Ponme a salvo,

líbrame del poder de gente extraña.
Cuando abren la boca, dicen mentiras;
cuando levantan su diestra, juran en falso.

12Que nuestros hijos, en su juventud,
crezcan como plantas frondosas;
que sean nuestras hijas como columnas
esculpidas para adornar un palacio.
13Que nuestros graneros se llenen
con provisiones de toda especie.
Que nuestros rebaños aumenten por millares,
por decenas de millares en nuestros
campos.
14Que nuestros bueyes arrastren cargas
pesadas;ᵏ
que no haya brechas ni salidas,
ni gritos de angustia en nuestras calles.

15*¡Dichoso el pueblo que recibe todo esto!
¡Dichoso el pueblo cuyo Dios es el SEÑOR!

Salmo 145ˡ

Salmo de alabanza. De David.

Álef	1Te exaltaré, mi Dios y rey; por siempre bendeciré tu *nombre.
Bet	2Todos los días te bendeciré; por siempre alabaré tu nombre.
Guímel	3Grande es el SEÑOR, y digno de toda alabanza; su grandeza es insondable.
Dálet	4Cada generación celebrará tus obras y proclamará tus proezas.
He	5Se hablará del esplendor de tu gloria y majestad, y yo meditaré en tus obras maravillosas.ᵐ
Vav	6Se hablará del poder de tus portentos, y yo anunciaré la grandeza de tus obras.
Zayin	7Se proclamará la memoria de tu inmensa bondad, y se cantará con júbilo tu *victoria.
Jet	8El SEÑOR es clemente y compasivo, lento para la ira y grande en amor.
Tet	9El SEÑOR es bueno con todos; él se compadece de toda su creación.
Yod	10Que te alaben, SEÑOR, todas tus obras; que te bendigan tus fieles.
Caf	11Que hablen de la gloria de tu reino; que proclamen tus proezas.
Lámed	12para que todo el mundo conozca tus proezas y la gloria y esplendor de tu reino.
Mem	13Tu reino es un reino eterno; tu dominio permanece por todas las edades.
Nun	Fiel es el SEÑOR a su palabra y bondadoso en todas sus obras.ⁿ
Sámej	14El SEÑOR levanta a los caídos

ⁱ **144:2** *los pueblos* (Targum, Vulgata, Siríaca, Aquila y varios mss. hebreos); *mi pueblo* (TM).   ʲ **144:8** *cuando ... en falso.* Lit. *su diestra es diestra de engaño;* también en v. 11.   ᵏ **144:14** *Que nuestros ... cargas pesadas.* Alt. *Que nuestros capitanes sean establecidos firmemente.*   ˡ **Sal 145** Este salmo es un poema acróstico, que sigue el orden del alfabeto hebreo. ᵐ **145:5** *Se hablará ... obras maravillosas.* (Qumrán y Siríaca; véase también LXX); *Meditaré en el esplendor glorioso de tu majestad / y en tus obras maravillosas* (TM).   ⁿ **145:13** *Fiel es el Señor a su palabra / y bondadoso en todas sus obras* (LXX, Siríaca, Vulgata y un ms. hebreo); TM no incluye estas dos líneas.

y sostiene a los agobiados.

Ayin
15Los ojos de todos se posan en ti,
y a su tiempo les das su alimento.

Pe
16Abres la mano y sacias con tus favores
a todo ser viviente.

Tsade
17El SEÑOR es justo en todos sus *caminos
y bondadoso en todas sus obras.

Qof
18El SEÑOR está cerca de quienes lo invocan,
de quienes lo invocan en verdad.

Resh
19Cumple los deseos de quienes le temen;
atiende a su clamor y los salva.

Shin
20El SEÑOR cuida a todos los que lo aman,
pero aniquilará a todos los impíos.

Tav
21¡Prorrumpa mi boca en alabanzas al SEÑOR!
¡Alabe todo el mundo su santo nombre,
por siempre y para siempre!

Salmo 146

1*¡Aleluya! ¡Alabado sea el SEÑOR!
Alaba, *alma mía, al SEÑOR.
2Alabaré al SEÑOR toda mi vida;
mientras haya aliento en mí, cantaré
salmos a mi Dios.

3No pongan su confianza en gente poderosa,
en simples *mortales, que no pueden salvar.
4Exhalan el espíritu y vuelven al polvo,
y ese mismo día se desbaratan sus planes.

5*Dichoso aquel cuya ayuda es el Dios de Jacob,
cuya esperanza está en el SEÑOR su Dios,
6creador del cielo y de la tierra,
del mar y de todo cuanto hay en ellos,
y que siempre mantiene la verdad.
7El SEÑOR hace justicia a los oprimidos,
da de comer a los hambrientos
y pone en libertad a los cautivos.
8El SEÑOR da vista a los ciegos,
el SEÑOR sostiene a los agobiados,
el SEÑOR ama a los justos.
9El SEÑOR protege al extranjero
y sostiene al huérfano y a la viuda,
pero frustra los planes de los impíos.

10¡Oh *Sión, que el SEÑOR reine para siempre!
¡Que tu Dios reine por todas las generaciones!

*¡Aleluya! ¡Alabado sea el SEÑOR!

Salmo 147

1*¡Aleluya! ¡Alabado sea el SEÑOR!

¡Cuán bueno es cantar salmos a nuestro Dios,
cuán agradable y justo es alabarlo!

2El SEÑOR reconstruye a Jerusalén
y reúne a los exiliados de Israel;
3restaura a los abatidosñ
y cubre con vendas sus heridas.
4Él determina el número de las estrellas

y a todas ellas les pone *nombre.
5Excelso es nuestro Señor, y grande su poder;
su entendimiento es infinito;
6El SEÑOR sostiene a los pobres,
pero hace morder el polvo a los impíos.

7Canten al SEÑOR con gratitud;
canten salmos a nuestro Dios al son del arpa.
8Él cubre de nubes el cielo,
envía la lluvia sobre la tierra
y hace crecer la hierba en los montes.
9Él alimenta a los ganados
y a las crías de los cuervos cuando graznan.

10El SEÑOR no se deleita en los bríos del caballo,
ni se complace en la agilidado del *hombre,
11sino que se complace en los que le temen,
en los que confían en su gran amor.

12Alaba al SEÑOR, Jerusalén;
alaba a tu Dios, oh *Sión.
13Él refuerza los cerrojos de tus *puertas
y bendice a los que en ti habitan.
14Él trae la *paz a tus fronteras
y te sacia con lo mejor del trigo.

15Envía su palabra a la tierra;
su palabra corre a toda prisa.
16Extiende la nieve cual blanco manto,p
esparce la escarcha cual ceniza.
17Deja caer el granizo como grava;
¿quién puede resistir sus ventiscas?
18Pero envía su palabra y lo derrite;
hace que el viento sople, y las aguas fluyen.
19A Jacob le ha revelado su palabra;
sus *leyes y decretos a Israel.
20Esto no lo ha hecho con ninguna otra nación;
jamás han conocido ellas sus decretos.

*¡Aleluya! ¡Alabado sea el SEÑOR!

Salmo 148

1*¡Aleluya! ¡Alabado sea el SEÑOR!

Alaben al SEÑOR desde los cielos,
alábenlo desde las alturas.
2Alábenlo, todos sus ángeles,
alábenlo, todos sus ejércitos.
3Alábenlo, sol y luna,
alábenlo, estrellas luminosas.
4Alábenlo ustedes, altísimos cielos,
y ustedes, las aguas que están sobre los cielos.
5Sea alabado el *nombre del SEÑOR,
porque él dio una orden y todo fue creado.
6Todo quedó afirmado para siempre;
emitió un decreto que no será abolido.

7Alaben al SEÑOR desde la tierra
los monstruos marinos y las profundidades del mar,
8el relámpago y el granizo, la nieve y la neblina,
el viento tempestuoso que cumple su mandato,
9los montes y las colinas,
los árboles frutales y todos los cedros,
10los animales salvajes y los domésticos,
los reptiles y las aves,
11los reyes de la tierra y todas las naciones,
los príncipes y los gobernantes de la tierra,

ñ **147:3** *a los abatidos.* Lit. *a los de corazón quebrantado.* o **147:10** *en la agilidad.* Lit. *en las piernas.* P **147:16** *cual blanco manto.* Lit. *como lana.*

12los jóvenes y las jóvenes,
los ancianos y los niños.

13Alaben el nombre del SEÑOR,
porque sólo su nombre es excelso;
su esplendor está por encima de la tierra y de
los cielos.
14¡Él ha dado poder a su pueblo!q

¡A él sea la alabanza de todos sus fieles,
de los hijos de Israel, su pueblo cercano!

*¡Aleluya! ¡Alabado sea el SEÑOR!

Salmo 149

1*¡Aleluya! ¡Alabado sea el SEÑOR!

Canten al SEÑOR un cántico nuevo,
alábenlo en la comunidad de los fieles.

2Que se alegre Israel por su creador;
que se regocijen los hijos de *Sión por su
rey.
3Que alaben su *nombre con danzas;
que le canten salmos al son de la lira y el
pandero.
4Porque el SEÑOR se complace en su pueblo;
a los humildes concede el honor de la
*victoria.
5Que se alegren los fieles por su triunfo;r
que aun en sus camas griten de júbilo.

6Que broten de su garganta alabanzas a Dios,

y haya en sus manos una espada de dos
filos
7para que tomen venganza de las naciones
y castiguen a los pueblos;
8para que sujeten a sus reyes con cadenas,
a sus nobles con grilletes de hierro;
9para que se cumpla en ellos la sentencia
escrita.
¡Ésta será la gloria de todos sus fieles!

*¡Aleluya! ¡Alabado sea el SEÑOR!

Salmo 150

1*¡Aleluya! ¡Alabado sea el SEÑOR!

Alaben a Dios en su santuario,
alábenlo en su poderoso firmamento.
2Alábenlo por sus proezas,
alábenlo por su inmensa grandeza.
3Alábenlo con sonido de trompeta,
alábenlo con el arpa y la lira.
4Alábenlo con panderos y danzas,
alábenlo con cuerdas y flautas.
5Alábenlo con címbalos sonoros,
alábenlo con címbalos resonantes.

6¡Que todo lo que respira alabe al SEÑOR!

*¡Aleluya! ¡Alabado sea el SEÑOR!

q **148:14** *¡Él ha dado ... su pueblo!* Lit. *¡Él levantó un cuerno para su pueblo!.* r **149:5** *por su triunfo.* Lit. *en gloria.*

PROVERBIOS

Prólogo: Propósito y tema

1 *Proverbios de Salomón hijo de David, rey de Israel:

²para adquirir sabiduría y *disciplina;
   para discernir palabras de inteligencia;
³para recibir la *corrección que dan la
      prudencia,
   la rectitud, la *justicia y la equidad;
⁴para infundir sagacidad en los *inexpertos,
   *conocimiento y discreción en los jóvenes.
⁵Escuche esto el sabio, y aumente su saber;
   reciba dirección el entendido,
⁶para discernir el proverbio y la *parábola,
   los dichos de los sabios y sus enigmas.

⁷El temor del SEÑOR es el principio del
      conocimiento;
   los *necios desprecian la sabiduría y la
      disciplina.

Exhortaciones a buscar la sabiduría

Advertencia contra el engaño

⁸Hijo mío, escucha las correcciones de tu padre
   y no abandones las *enseñanzas de tu
      madre.
⁹Adornarán tu cabeza como una diadema;
   adornarán tu cuello como un collar.

¹⁰Hijo mío, si los pecadores quieren engañarte,
   no vayas con ellos.
¹¹Éstos te dirán:
   «¡Ven con nosotros!
   Acechemos a algún inocente
   y démonos el gusto de matar a algún
      incauto;
¹²traguémonos a alguien vivo,
   como se traga el *sepulcro a la *gente;
   devorémoslo entero,
   como devora la fosa a los muertos.
¹³Obtendremos toda clase de riquezas;
   con el botín llenaremos nuestras casas.
¹⁴Comparte tu suerte con nosotros,
   y compartiremos contigo lo que
      obtengamos.»
¹⁵¡Pero no te dejes llevar por ellos,ᵃ hijo mío!
   ¡Apártate de sus senderos!
¹⁶Pues corren presurosos a hacer lo malo;
   ¡tienen prisa por derramar sangre!
¹⁷De nada sirve tender la red
   a la vista de todos los pájaros,
¹⁸pero aquéllos acechan su propia vidaᵇ
   y acabarán por destruirse a sí mismos.
¹⁹Así terminan los que van tras ganancias mal
      habidas;
   por éstas perderán la vida.

Advertencia contra el rechazo a la sabiduría

²⁰Clama la sabiduría en las calles;
   en los lugares públicos levanta su voz.
²¹Clama en las esquinas de calles transitadas;
   a la *entrada de la ciudad razona: ·

²²«¿Hasta cuándo, muchachos *inexpertos,
   seguirán aferrados a su inexperiencia?
   ¿Hasta cuándo, ustedes los *insolentes,

se complacerán en su insolencia?
   ¿Hasta cuándo, ustedes los necios,
      aborrecerán el conocimiento?
²³Respondan a mis reprensiones,
   y yo les abriré mi corazón;ᶜ
   les daré a conocer mis pensamientos.
²⁴Como ustedes no me atendieron cuando los
      llamé,
   ni me hicieron caso cuando les tendí la
      mano,
²⁵sino que rechazaron todos mis consejos
   y no acataron mis reprensiones,
²⁶ahora yo me burlaré de ustedes
   cuando caigan en desgracia.
   Yo seré el que se ría de ustedes
      cuando les sobrevenga el miedo,
²⁷cuando el miedo les sobrevenga como una
      tormenta
   y la desgracia los arrastre como un
      torbellino.

²⁸»Entonces me llamarán, pero no les
      responderé;
   me buscarán, pero no me encontrarán.
²⁹Por cuanto aborrecieron el conocimiento
   y no quisieron temer al SEÑOR;
³⁰por cuanto no siguieron mis consejos,
   sino que rechazaron mis reprensiones,
³¹cosecharán el fruto de su conducta,
   se hartarán con sus propias intrigas;
³²¡su descarrío e inexperiencia los destruirán,
   su complacencia y *necedad los
      aniquilarán!
³³Pero el que me obedezca vivirá tranquilo,
   sosegado y sin temor del mal.»

Ventajas de la sabiduría

2 Hijo mío, si haces tuyas mis palabras
   y atesoras mis mandamientos;
²si tu oído inclinas hacia la sabiduría
   y de corazón te entregas a la inteligencia;
³si llamas a la inteligencia
   y pides discernimiento;
⁴si la buscas como a la plata,
   como a un tesoro escondido,
⁵entonces comprenderás el temor del SEÑOR
   y hallarás el conocimiento de Dios.
⁶Porque el SEÑOR da la sabiduría;
   conocimiento y ciencia brotan de sus
      labios.
⁷Él reserva su ayuda para la gente íntegra
   y protege a los de conducta intachable.
⁸Él cuida el sendero de los justos
   y protege el camino de sus fieles.
⁹Entonces comprenderás la justicia y el
      derecho,
   la equidad y todo buen camino;
¹⁰la sabiduría vendrá a tu corazón,
   y el conocimiento te endulzará la vida.
¹¹La discreción te cuidará,
   la inteligencia te protegerá.

¹²La sabiduría te librará del camino de los
      malvados,
   de los que profieren palabras perversas,
¹³de los que se apartan del camino recto

ᵃ **1:15** *no ... por ellos.* Lit. *no vayas por sus caminos.* ᵇ **1:18** *vida.* Lit. *sangre.* ᶜ **1:23** *les abriré mi corazón.* Lit. *derramaré mi espíritu.*

para andar por sendas tenebrosas,
14de los que se complacen en hacer lo malo
y festejan la perversidad,
15de los que andan por caminos torcidos
y por sendas extraviadas;
16te librará de la mujer ajena,
de la extraña de palabras seductoras
17que, olvidándose de su pacto con Dios,
abandona al compañero de su juventud.
18Ciertamente su casa conduce a la muerte;
sus sendas llevan al reino de las sombras.
19El que se enreda con ella no vuelve jamás,
ni alcanza los senderos de la vida.

20Así andarás por el camino de los buenos
y seguirás la senda de los justos.
21Pues los íntegros, los perfectos,
habitarán la tierra y permanecerán en ella.
22Pero los malvados, los impíos,
serán desarraigados y expulsados de la
tierra.

Otras ventajas de la sabiduría

3 Hijo mío, no te olvides de mis *enseñanzas;
más bien, guarda en tu *corazón mis
mandamientos.
2Porque prolongarán tu vida muchos años
y te traerán prosperidad.
3Que nunca te abandonen el amor y la verdad:
llévalos siempre alrededor de tu cuello
y escríbelos en el libro de tu corazón.
4Contarás con el favor de Dios
y tendrás buena fama[d] entre la *gente.
5Confía en el SEÑOR de todo corazón,
y no en tu propia inteligencia.
6Reconócelo en todos tus *caminos,
y él allanará tus sendas.
7No seas sabio en tu propia opinión;
más bien, teme al SEÑOR y huye del mal.
8Esto infundirá salud a tu cuerpo
y fortalecerá tu ser.[e]
9Honra al SEÑOR con tus riquezas
y con los primeros frutos de tus cosechas.
10Así tus graneros se llenarán a reventar
y tus bodegas rebosarán de vino nuevo.
11Hijo mío, no desprecies la *disciplina del
SEÑOR,
ni te ofendas por sus represiones.
12Porque el SEÑOR disciplina a los que ama,
como corrige un padre a su hijo querido.

13*Dichoso el que halla sabiduría,
el que adquiere inteligencia.
14Porque ella es de más provecho que la plata
y rinde más ganancias que el oro.
15Es más valiosa que las piedras preciosas:
¡ni lo más deseable se le puede comparar!
16Con la mano derecha ofrece larga vida;
con la izquierda, honor y riquezas.
17Sus caminos son placenteros
y en sus senderos hay *paz.
18Ella es árbol de vida para quienes la abrazan;
¡dichosos los que la retienen!
19Con sabiduría afirmó el SEÑOR la tierra,
con inteligencia estableció los cielos.
20Por su *conocimiento se separaron las aguas,
y las nubes dejaron caer su rocío.

21Hijo mío, conserva el buen juicio;
no pierdas de vista la discreción.

22Te serán fuente de vida,
te adornarán como un collar.
23Podrás recorrer tranquilo tu camino,
y tus pies no tropezarán.
24Al acostarte, no tendrás temor alguno;
te acostarás y dormirás tranquilo.
25No temerás ningún desastre repentino,
ni la desgracia que sobreviene a los impíos.
26Porque el SEÑOR estará siempre a tu lado
y te librará de caer en la trampa.

27No niegues un favor a quien te lo pida,
si en tu mano está el otorgarlo.
28Nunca digas a tu prójimo:
«Vuelve más tarde; te ayudaré mañana»,
si hoy tienes con qué ayudarlo.
29No urdas el mal contra tu prójimo,
contra el que ha puesto en ti su confianza.
30No entres en pleito con nadie
que no te haya hecho ningún daño.
31No envidies a los violentos,
ni optes por andar en sus caminos.
32Porque el SEÑOR aborrece al perverso,
pero al íntegro le brinda su amistad.
33La maldición del SEÑOR cae sobre la casa del
malvado;
su bendición, sobre el hogar de los justos.
34El SEÑOR se burla de los *burlones,
pero muestra su favor a los humildes.
35Los sabios son dignos de honra,
pero los *necios sólo merecen deshonra.

La sabiduría es lo máximo

4 Escuchen, hijos, la corrección de un padre;
dispónganse a adquirir inteligencia.
2Yo les brindo buenas enseñanzas,
así que no abandonen mi instrucción.
3Cuando yo era pequeño y vivía con mi padre,
cuando era el niño consentido de mi
madre,
4mi padre me instruyó de esta manera:
«Aférrate de corazón a mis palabras;
obedece mis mandamientos, y vivirás.
5Adquiere sabiduría, adquiere inteligencia;
no olvides mis palabras ni te apartes de
ellas.
6No abandones nunca a la sabiduría,
y ella te protegerá;
ámala, y ella te cuidará.
7La sabiduría es lo primero. ¡Adquiere
sabiduría!
Por sobre todas las cosas, adquiere
discernimiento.
8Estima a la sabiduría, y ella te exaltará;
abrázala, y ella te honrará;
9te pondrá en la cabeza una hermosa diadema;
te obsequiará una bella corona.»

10Escucha, hijo mío; acoge mis palabras,
y los años de tu vida aumentarán.
11Yo te guío por el camino de la sabiduría,
te dirijo por sendas de rectitud.
12Cuando camines, no encontrarás obstáculos;
cuando corras, no tropezarás.
13Aférrate a la instrucción, no la dejes escapar;
cuídala bien, que ella es tu vida.
14No sigas la senda de los perversos
ni vayas por el camino de los malvados.
15¡Evita ese camino! ¡No pases por él!
¡Aléjate de allí, y sigue de largo!

---

d **3:4** *buena fama.* Lit. *prudencia.* e **3:8** *tu ser.* Lit. *tus huesos.*

16Los malvados no duermen si no hacen lo
  malo;
  pierden el sueño si no hacen que alguien
  caiga.
17Su pan es la maldad;
  su vino, la violencia.

18La senda de los justos se asemeja
  a los primeros albores de la aurora:
  su esplendor va en aumento
  hasta que el día alcanza su plenitud.
19Pero el camino de los malvados
  es como la más densa oscuridad;
  ¡ni siquiera saben con qué tropiezan!

20Hijo mío, atiende a mis consejos;
  escucha atentamente lo que digo.
21No pierdas de vista mis palabras;
  guárdalas muy dentro de tu corazón.
22Ellas dan vida a quienes las hallan;
  son la salud del cuerpo.
23Por sobre todas las cosas cuida tu corazón,
  porque de él mana la vida.
24Aleja de tu boca la perversidad;
  aparta de tus labios las palabras corruptas.
25Pon la mirada en lo que tienes delante;
  fija la vista en lo que está frente a ti.
26Endereza las sendas por donde andas;
  allana todos tus caminos.
27No te desvíes ni a diestra ni a siniestra;
  apártate de la maldad.

Advertencia contra el adulterio

5 Hijo mío, pon atención a mi sabiduría
  y presta oído a mi buen juicio,
2para que al hablar mantengas la discreción
  y retengas el conocimiento.
3De los labios de la adúltera fluye miel;
  su lengua es más suave que el aceite.
4Pero al fin resulta más amarga que la hiel
  y más cortante que una espada de dos filos.
5Sus pies descienden hasta la muerte;
  sus pasos van derecho al *sepulcro.
6No toma ella en cuenta el camino de la vida;f
  sus sendas son torcidas, y ella no lo
  reconoce.g

7Pues bien, hijo mío, préstame atención
  y no te apartes de mis palabras.
8Aléjate de la adúltera;
  no te acerques a la puerta de su casa,
9para que no entregues a otros tu vigor,
  ni tus años a gente cruel;
10para que no sacies con tu fuerza a gente
  extraña,
  ni vayan a dar en casa ajena tus esfuerzos.
11Porque al final acabarás por llorar,
  cuando todo tu serh se haya consumido.
12Y dirás: «¡Cómo pude aborrecer la corrección!
  ¡Cómo pudo mi corazón despreciar la
  disciplina!
13No atendí a la voz de mis maestros,
  ni presté oído a mis instructores.
14Ahora estoy al borde de la ruina,
  en medio de toda la comunidad.»

15Bebe el agua de tu propio pozo,
  el agua que fluye de tu propio manantial.

16¿Habrán de derramarse tus fuentes por las
  calles
  y tus corrientes de aguas por las plazas
  públicas?
17Son tuyas, solamente tuyas,
  y no para que las compartas con extraños.
18¡Bendita sea tu fuente!
  ¡Goza con la esposa de tu juventud!
19Es una gacela amorosa,
  es una cervatilla encantadora.
  ¡Que sus pechos te satisfagan siempre!
  ¡Que su amor te cautive todo el tiempo!
20¿Por qué, hijo mío, dejarte cautivar por una
  adúltera?
  ¿Por qué abrazarte al pecho de la mujer
  ajena?

21Nuestros caminos están a la vista del SEÑOR;
  él examina todas nuestras sendas.
22Al malvado lo atrapan sus malas obras;
  las cuerdas de su pecado lo aprisionan.
23Morirá por su falta de disciplina;
  perecerá por su gran insensatez.

Advertencia contra la insensatez

6 Hijo mío, si has salido fiador de tu vecino,
  si has hecho tratos para responder por otro,
2si verbalmente te has comprometido,
  enredándote con tus propias palabras,
3entonces has caído en manos de tu
  prójimo.
  Si quieres librarte, hijo mío, éste es el camino:
  Ve corriendo y humíllate ante él;
  procura deshacer tu compromiso.
4No permitas que se duerman tus ojos;
  no dejes que tus párpados se cierren.
5Líbrate, como se libra del cazadori la gacela,
  como se libra de la trampaj el ave.

6¡Anda, perezoso, fíjate en la hormiga!
  ¡Fíjate en lo que hace, y adquiere sabiduría!
7No tiene quien la mande,
  ni quien la vigile ni gobierne;
8con todo, en el verano almacena provisiones
  y durante la cosecha recoge alimentos.

9Perezoso, ¿cuánto tiempo más seguirás
  acostado?
  ¿Cuándo despertarás de tu sueño?
10Un corto sueño, una breve siesta,
  un pequeño descanso, cruzado de brazos...
11¡y te asaltará la pobreza como un bandido,
  y la escasez como un hombre armado!k

12El bribón y sinvergüenza,
  el vagabundo de boca corrupta,
13hace guiños con los ojos,
  y señas con los pies y con los dedos.
14El malvado trama el mal en su mente,
  y siempre anda provocando disensiones.
15Por eso le sobrevendrá la ruina;
  ¡de repente será destruido, y no podrá
  evitarlo!

16Hay seis cosas que el SEÑOR aborrece,
  y siete que le son detestables:
17 los ojos que se enaltecen,
    la lengua que miente,

---

f 5:6 No toma ... vida. Lit. El camino de la vida para que no lo prepare. g 5:6 y ella no lo reconoce. Alt. y tú no lo sabes.
h 5:11 todo tu ser. Lit. tu carne y tu cuerpo. i 6:5 del cazador (LXX y otras versiones antiguas); de la mano (TM). j 6:5 de la trampa (LXX y otras versiones antiguas); de la mano del trampero (TM). k 6:11 como un hombre armado. Alt. como un limosnero.

las manos que derraman sangre
   inocente,
18 el corazón que hace planes perversos,
   los pies que corren a hacer lo malo,
19 el falso testigo que esparce mentiras,
   y el que siembra discordia entre
      hermanos.

Advertencia contra el adulterio

20Hijo mío, obedece el mandamiento de tu
   padre
   y no abandones la enseñanza de tu madre.
21Grábatelos en el corazón;
   cuélgatelos al cuello.
22Cuando camines, te servirán de guía;
   cuando duermas, vigilarán tu sueño;
   cuando despiertes, hablarán contigo.
23El mandamiento es una lámpara,
   la enseñanza es una luz
   y la disciplina es el camino a la vida.
24Te protegerán de la mujer malvada,
   de la mujer ajena y de su lengua seductora.
25No abrigues en tu corazón deseos por su
   belleza,
   ni te dejes cautivar por sus ojos.
26pues la ramera va tras un pedazo de pan,
   pero la adúltera va tras el hombre que vale.l
27¿Puede alguien echarse brasas en el pecho
   sin quemarse la ropa?
28¿Puede alguien caminar sobre las brasas
   sin quemarse los pies?
29Pues tampoco quien se acuesta con la mujer
   ajena
   puede tocarla y quedar impune.

30No se desprecia al ladrón
   que roba para mitigar su hambre;
31pero si lo atrapan, deberá devolver
   siete tantos lo robado,
   aun cuando eso le cueste todas sus
      posesiones.
32Pero al que comete adulterio le faltan sesos;
   el que así actúa se destruye a sí mismo.
33No sacará más que golpes y vergüenzas,
   y no podrá borrar su oprobio.
34Porque los celos desatan la furia del esposo,
   y éste no perdonará en el día de la
      venganza.
35No aceptará nada en desagravio,
   ni se contentará con muchos regalos.

Advertencia contra la mujer adúltera

7 Hijo mío, pon en prácticam mis palabras
   y atesora mis mandamientos.
2Cumple con mis mandatos, y vivirás;
   cuida mis enseñanzas como a la niña de tus
      ojos.
3Llévalos atados en los dedos;
   anótalos en la tablilla de tu corazón.
4Di a la sabiduría: «Tú eres mi hermana»,
   y a la inteligencia: «Eres de mi sangre.»
5Ellas te librarán de la mujer ajena,
   de la adúltera y de sus palabras seductoras.

6Desde la ventana de mi casa
   miré a través de la celosía.
7Me puse a ver a los inexpertos,
   y entre los jóvenes observé

a uno de ellos falto de juicio.n
8Cruzó la calle, llegó a la esquina,
   y se encaminó hacia la casa de esa mujer.
9Caía la tarde. Llegaba el día a su fin.
   Avanzaban las sombras de la noche.

10De pronto la mujer salió a su encuentro,
   con toda la apariencia de una prostituta
   y con solapadas intenciones.
11(Como es escandalosa y descarada,
   nunca hallan sus pies reposo en su casa.
12Unas veces por las calles, otras veces por las
   plazas,
   siempre está al acecho en cada esquina.)
13Se prendió de su cuello, lo besó,
   y con todo descaro le dijo:

14«Tengo en mi casa sacrificios de *comunión,
   pues hoy he cumplido mis votos.
15Por eso he venido a tu encuentro;
   te buscaba, ¡y ya te he encontrado!
16Sobre la cama he tendido
   multicolores linos egipcios.
17He perfumado mi lecho
   con aroma de mirra, áloe y canela.
18Ven, bebamos hasta el fondo la copa del
   amor;
   ¡disfrutemos del amor hasta el amanecer!
19Mi esposo no está en casa,
   pues ha emprendido un largo viaje.
20Se ha llevado consigo la bolsa del dinero,
   y no regresará hasta el día de luna llena.»

21Con palabras persuasivas lo convenció;
   con lisonjas de sus labios lo sedujo.
22Y él en seguida fue tras ella,
   como el buey que va camino al matadero;
   como el ciervoñ que cae en la trampa,o
      23hasta que una flecha le abre las entrañas;
   como el ave que se lanza contra la red,
   sin saber que en ello le va la vida.

24Así que, hijo mío, escúchame;
   prestap atención a mis palabras.
25No desvíes tu corazón hacia sus sendas,
   ni te extravíes por sus caminos,
26pues muchos han muerto por su causa;
   sus víctimas han sido innumerables.
27Su casa lleva derecho al *sepulcro;
   ¡conduce al reino de la muerte!

Llamado de la sabiduría

8 ¿Acaso no está llamando la sabiduría?
   ¿No está elevando su voz la inteligencia?
2Toma su puesto en las alturas,
   a la vera del camino y en las encrucijadas.
3Junto a las *puertas que dan a la ciudad,
   a la *entrada misma, grita a voz en cuello:
4«A ustedes los *hombres, los estoy llamando;
   dirijo mi voz a toda la *humanidad.
5Ustedes los *inexpertos, ¡adquieran prudencia!
   Ustedes los *necios, ¡obtengan
      discernimiento!
6Escúchenme, que diré cosas importantes;
   mis labios hablarán con *justicia.
7Mi boca expresará la verdad,
   pues mis labios detestan la mentira.
8Las palabras de mi boca son todas justas;
   no hay en ellas maldad ni doblez.

---

l 6:26 el hombre que vale. Lit. un alma valiosa. m 7:1 pon en práctica. Lit. guarda. n 7:7 falto de juicio. Lit. falto de corazón.
ñ 7:22 ciervo (Siríaca; véase también LXX); necio (TM). o 7:22 Texto de difícil traducción. p 7:24 hijo mío, escúchame;
presta. Lit. hijos míos, escúchenme; presten.

9Son claras para los entendidos,
e irreprochables para los sabios.
10Opten por mi *instrucción, no por la plata;
por el *conocimiento, no por el oro
refinado.
11Vale más la sabiduría que las piedras
preciosas,
y ni lo más deseable se le compara.

12»Yo, la sabiduría, convivo con la prudencia
y poseo conocimiento y discreción.
13Quien teme al SEÑOR aborrece lo malo;
yo aborrezco el orgullo y la arrogancia,
la mala conducta y el lenguaje perverso.
14Míos son el consejo y el buen juicio;
míos son el entendimiento y el poder.
15Por mí reinan los reyes
y promulgan leyes justas los gobernantes.
16Por mí gobiernan los príncipes
y todos los nobles que rigen la tierra.q
17A los que me aman, les correspondo;
a los que me buscan, me doy a conocer.
18Conmigo están las riquezas y la honra,
la prosperidadr y los bienes duraderos.
19Mi fruto es mejor que el oro fino;
mi cosecha sobrepasa a la plata refinada.
20Voy por el *camino de la rectitud,
por los senderos de la justicia,
21enriqueciendo a los que me aman
y acrecentando sus tesoros.
22»El SEÑOR me dio la vidas como primicia de
sus obras,t
mucho antes de sus obras de antaño.
23Fui establecida desde la eternidad,
desde antes que existiera el mundo.
24No existían los grandes mares cuando yo
nací,
no había entonces manantiales de
abundantes aguas.
25Nací antes que fueran formadas las colinas,
antes que se cimentaran las montañas,
26antes que él creara la tierra y sus paisajes
y el polvo primordial con que hizo el
mundo.
27Cuando Dios cimentó la bóveda celeste
y trazó el horizonte sobre las aguas,
allí estaba yo presente.
28Cuando estableció las nubes en los cielos
y reforzó las fuentes del mar profundo;
29cuando señaló los límites del mar,
para que las aguas obedecieran su
mandato;
cuando plantó los fundamentos de la tierra,
30allí estaba yo, afirmando su obra.
Día tras día me llenaba yo de alegría,
siempre disfrutaba de estar en su
presencia;
31me regocijaba en el mundo que él creó;
¡en el *género humano me deleitaba!
32»Y ahora, hijos míos, escúchenme:
*dichosos los que van poru mis caminos.
33Atiendan a mi instrucción, y sean sabios;
no la descuiden.
34Dichosos los que me escuchan
y a mis puertas están atentos cada día,
esperando a la entrada de mi casa.
35En verdad, quien me encuentra, halla la vida

y recibe el favor del SEÑOR.
36Quien me rechaza, se perjudica a sí mismo;
quien me aborrece, ama la muerte.»

Invitación de la sabiduría y de la necedad

9 La sabiduría construyó su casa
y labró sus siete pilares.
2Preparó un banquete, mezcló su vino
y tendió la mesa.
3Envió a sus doncellas, y ahora clama
desde lo más alto de la ciudad.
4«¡Vengan conmigo los inexpertos!
—dice a los faltos de juicio—.
5Vengan, disfruten de mi pan
y beban del vino que he mezclado.
6Dejen su insensatez, y vivirán;
andarán por el camino del discernimiento.

7»El que corrige al burlón se gana que lo
insulten;
el que reprende al malvado se gana su
desprecio.
8No reprendas al insolente, no sea que acabe
por odiarte;
reprende al sabio, y te amará.
9Instruye al sabio, y se hará más sabio;
enseña al justo, y aumentará su saber.

10»El comienzo de la sabiduría es el temor del
SEÑOR;
conocer al Santov es tener discernimiento.
11Por mí aumentarán tus días;
muchos años de vida se serán añadidos.
12Si eres sabio, tu premio será tu sabiduría;
si eres insolente, sólo tú lo sufrirás.»

13La mujer necia es escandalosa,
frívola y desvergonzada.
14Se sienta a las puertas de su casa,
sienta sus reales en lo más alto de la
ciudad,
15y llama a los que van por el camino,
a los que no se apartan de su senda.
16«¡Vengan conmigo, inexpertos!
—dice a los faltos de juicio—.
17¡Las aguas robadas saben a gloria!
¡El pan sabe a miel si se come a
escondidas!»
18Pero éstos ignoran que allí está la muerte,
que sus invitados caen al fondo de la *fosa.

Proverbios de Salomón

10 Proverbios de Salomón:

El hijo sabio es la alegría de su padre;
el hijo necio es el pesar de su madre.

2Las riquezas mal habidas no sirven de nada,
pero la justicia libra de la muerte.

3El SEÑOR no deja sin comer al justo,
pero frustra la avidez de los malvados.

4Las manos ociosas conducen a la pobreza;
las manos hábiles atraen riquezas.

5El hijo prevenido se abastece en el verano,
pero el sinvergüenza duerme en tiempo de
cosecha.

6El justo se ve coronado de bendiciones,

---

q 8:16 y todos los nobles que rigen la tierra (varios mss. hebreos y LXX); y nobles, todos jueces justos (TM).   r 8:18 prosperidad. Lit. justicia.   s 8:22 me dio la vida. Alt. era mi dueño.   t 8:22 obras. Lit. caminos.   u 8:32 van por. Lit. guardan.   v 9:10 al
Santo. Alt. las cosas santas.

pero la boca del malvado encubre
violencia.

[7]La memoria de los justos es una bendición,
pero la fama de los malvados será pasto de
los gusanos.

[8]El de sabio corazón acata las órdenes,
pero el necio y rezongón va camino al
desastre.

[9]Quien se conduce con integridad, anda
seguro;
quien anda en malos pasos será
descubierto.

[10]Quien guiña el ojo con malicia provoca pesar;
el necio y rezongón va camino al desastre.

[11]Fuente de vida es la boca del justo,
pero la boca del malvado encubre
violencia.

[12]El odio es motivo de disensiones,
pero el amor cubre todas las faltas.

[13]En los labios del prudente hay sabiduría;
en la espalda del falto de juicio, sólo
garrotazos.

[14]El que es sabio atesora el conocimiento,
pero la boca del necio es un peligro
inminente.

[15]La riqueza del rico es su baluarte;
la pobreza del pobre es su ruina.

[16]El salario del justo es la vida;
la ganancia del malvado es el pecado.

[17]El que atiende a la corrección va camino a la
vida;
el que la rechaza se pierde.

[18]El de labios mentirosos disimula su odio,
y el que propaga calumnias es un necio.

[19]El que mucho habla, mucho yerra;
el que es sabio refrena su lengua.

[20]Plata refinada es la lengua del justo;
el corazón del malvado no vale nada.

[21]Los labios del justo orientan a muchos;
los necios mueren por falta de juicio.

[22]La bendición del SEÑOR trae riquezas,
y nada se gana con preocuparse.

[23]El necio se divierte con su mala conducta,
pero el sabio se recrea con la sabiduría.

[24]Lo que el malvado teme, eso le ocurre;
lo que el justo desea, eso recibe.

[25]Pasa la tormenta y desaparece el malvado,
pero el justo permanece firme para
siempre.

[26]Como vinagre a los dientes y humo a los ojos
es el perezoso para quienes lo emplean.

[27]El temor del SEÑOR prolonga la vida,
pero los años del malvado se acortan.

[28]El futuro de los justos es halagüeño;
la esperanza de los malvados se desvanece.

[29]El camino del SEÑOR es refugio de los justos

y ruina de los malhechores.

[30]Los justos no tropezarán jamás;
los malvados no habitarán la tierra.

[31]La boca del justo profiere sabiduría,
pero la lengua perversa será cercenada.

[32]Los labios del justo destilan[w] bondad;
de la boca del malvado brota perversidad.

11

El SEÑOR aborrece las balanzas adulteradas,
pero aprueba las pesas exactas.

[2]Con el orgullo viene el oprobio;
con la humildad, la sabiduría.

[3]A los justos los guía su integridad;
a los falsos los destruye su hipocresía.

[4]En el día de la ira de nada sirve ser rico,
pero la justicia libra de la muerte.

[5]La justicia endereza el camino de los íntegros,
pero la maldad hace caer a los impíos.

[6]La justicia libra a los justos,
pero la codicia atrapa a los falsos.

[7]Muere el malvado, y con él su esperanza;
muere también su ilusión de poder.

[8]El justo se salva de la calamidad,
pero la desgracia le sobreviene al malvado.

[9]Con la boca el impío destruye a su prójimo,
pero los justos se libran por el
conocimiento.

[10]Cuando el justo prospera, la ciudad se alegra;
cuando el malvado perece, hay gran
regocijo.

[11]La bendición de los justos enaltece a la
ciudad,
pero la boca de los malvados la destruye.

[12]El falto de juicio desprecia a su prójimo,
pero el entendido refrena su lengua.

[13]La gente chismosa revela los secretos;
la gente confiable es discreta.

[14]Sin dirección, la nación fracasa;
el éxito depende de los muchos consejeros.

[15]El fiador de un extraño saldrá perjudicado;
negarse a dar fianza[x] es vivir en paz.

[16]La mujer bondadosa se gana el respeto;
los hombres violentos sólo ganan riquezas.

[17]El que es bondadoso se beneficia a sí mismo;
el que es cruel, a sí mismo se perjudica.

[18]El malvado obtiene ganancias ilusorias;
el que siembra justicia asegura su ganancia.

[19]El que es justo obtiene la vida;
el que persigue el mal se encamina a la
muerte.

[20]El SEÑOR aborrece a los de corazón perverso,
pero se complace en los que viven con
rectitud.

[21]Una cosa es segura:[y] Los malvados no
quedarán impunes,

---

[w] **10:32** *destilan* (LXX); *saben* (TM).　[x] **11:15** *a dar fianza*. Lit. *a estrechar la mano.*　[y] **11:21** *Una cosa es segura.* Lit. *Mano a mano.*

pero los justos saldrán bien librados.

22Como argolla de oro en hocico de cerdo
es la mujer bella pero indiscreta.

23Los deseos de los justos terminan bien;
la esperanza de los malvados termina mal.z

24Unos dan a manos llenas, y reciben más de lo
que dan;
otros ni sus deudas pagan, y acaban en la
miseria.

25El que es generoso prospera;
el que reanima será reanimado.

26La gente maldice al que acapara el trigo,
pero colma de bendiciones al que gustoso
lo vende.

27El que madruga para el bien, halla buena
voluntad;
el que anda tras el mal, por el mal será
alcanzado.

28El que confía en sus riquezas se marchita,
pero el justo se renueva como el follaje.

29El que perturba su casa no hereda más que el
viento,
y el necio termina sirviendo al sabio.

30El fruto de la justiciaa es árbol de vida,
pero el que arrebata vidas es violento.b

31Si los justos reciben su pago aquí en la tierra,
¡cuánto más los impíos y los pecadores!

12 El que ama la disciplina ama el
conocimiento,
pero el que la aborrece es un necio.

2El hombre bueno recibe el favor del SEÑOR,
pero el intrigante recibe su condena.

3Nadie puede afirmarse por medio de la
maldad;
sólo queda firme la raíz de los justos.

4La mujer ejemplarc es corona de su esposo;
la desvergonzada es carcoma en los huesos.

5En los planes del justo hay justicia,
pero en los consejos del malvado hay
engaño.

6Las palabras del malvado son insidias de
muerte,
pero la boca de los justos los pone a salvo.

7Los malvados se derrumban y dejan de existir,
pero los hijos de los justos permanecen.

8Al hombre se le alaba según su sabiduría,
pero al de mal corazón se le desprecia.

9Vale más un Don Nadie con criado
que un Don Alguien sin pan.

10El justo atiende a las necesidades de su bestia,
pero el malvado es de mala entraña.

11El que labra su tierra tendrá abundante
comida,

pero el que sueña despiertod es un
imprudente.

12Los malos deseos son la trampae de los
malvados,
pero la raíz de los justos prospera.

13En el pecado de sus labios se enreda el
malvado,
pero el justo sale del aprieto.

14Cada uno se sacíaf del fruto de sus labios,
y de la obra de sus manos recibe su
recompensa.

15Al necio le parece bien lo que emprende,
pero el sabio atiende al consejo.

16El necio muestra en seguida su enojo,
pero el prudente pasa por alto el insulto.

17El testigo verdadero declara lo que es justo,
pero el testigo falso declara falsedades.

18El charlatán hiere con la lengua como con una
espada,
pero la lengua del sabio brinda alivio.

19Los labios sinceros permanecen para siempre,
pero la lengua mentirosa dura sólo un
instante.

20En los que fraguan el mal habita el engaño,
pero hay gozo para los que promueven la
paz.

21Al justo no le sobrevendrá ningún daño,
pero al malvado lo cubrirá la desgracia.

22El SEÑOR aborrece a los de labios mentirosos,
pero se complace en los que actúan con
lealtad.

23El hombre prudente no muestra lo que sabe,
pero el corazón de los necios proclama su
necedad.

24El de manos diligentes gobernará;
pero el perezoso será subyugado.

25La angustia abate el corazón del hombre,
pero una palabra amable lo alegra.

26El justo es guía de su prójimo,g
pero el camino del malvado lleva a la
perdición.

27El perezoso no atrapa presa,h
pero el diligente ya posee una gran
riqueza.

28En el camino de la justicia se halla la vida;
por ese camino se evita la muerte.

13 El hijo sabio atiende ai la *corrección de su
padre,
pero el *insolente no hace caso a la
represión.

2Quien habla el bien, del bien se nutre,
pero el infiel padece hambre de violencia.

3El que refrena su lengua protege su vida,

---

z **11:23** *termina mal* (LXX); *es ira* (TM). a **11:30** *de la justicia* (LXX); *del justo* (TM). b **11:30** *violento* (LXX); *sabio* (TM).
c **12:4** *ejemplar.* Alt. *fuerte;* véase 31:10-31. d **12:11** *el que sueña despierto.* Lit. *el que persigue lo vacío;* también en 28:19.
e **12:12** *la trampa* (texto probable); *el botín* (TM). f **12:14** *se sacia.* Lit. *se sacia de lo bueno.* g **12:26** Texto de difícil traducción. h **12:27** *no atrapa presa.* Alt. *no pone a asar lo que ha cazado.* Texto de difícil traducción. i **13:1** *atiende a* (LXX y Siríaca). TM no incluye verbo.

pero el ligero de labios provoca su ruina.

4El perezoso ambiciona, y nada consigue;
el diligente ve cumplidos sus deseos.

5El justo aborrece la mentira;
el malvado acarrea vergüenza y deshonra.

6La *justicia protege al que anda en integridad,
pero la maldad arruina al pecador.

7Hay quien pretende ser rico, y no tiene nada;
hay quien parece ser pobre, y todo lo tiene.

8Con su riqueza el rico pone a salvo su vida,
pero al pobre no hay ni quien lo amenace.

9La luz de los justos brilla radiante,j
pero los malvados son como lámpara
apagada.

10El orgullo sólo genera contiendas,
pero la sabiduría está con quienes oyen
consejos.

11El dinero mal habido pronto se acaba;
quien ahorra, poco a poco se enriquece.

12La esperanza frustrada aflige al *corazón;
el deseo cumplido es un árbol de vida.

13Quien se burla de la *instrucción tendrá su
merecido;
quien respeta el mandamiento tendrá su
recompensa.

14La enseñanza de los sabios es fuente de vida,
y libera de los lazos de la muerte.

15El buen juicio redunda en aprecio,
pero el *camino del infiel no cambia.

16El prudente actúa con cordura,
pero el *necio se jacta de su *necedad.

17El mensajero malvado se mete en problemas;
el enviado confiable aporta la solución.

18El que desprecia a la *disciplina sufre pobreza
y deshonra;
el que atiende a la corrección recibe
grandes honores.

19El deseo cumplido endulza el *alma,
pero el necio detesta alejarse del mal.

20El que con sabios anda, sabio se vuelve;
el que con necios se junta, saldrá mal
parado.

21Al pecador lo persigue el mal,
y al justo lo recompensa el bien.

22El *hombre de bien deja herencia a sus nietos;
las riquezas del pecador se quedan para los
justos.

23En el campo del pobre hay abundante
comida,
pero ésta se pierde donde hay injusticia.

24No corregir al hijo es no quererlo;
amarlo es disciplinarlo.

25El justo come hasta quedar saciado,
pero el malvado se queda con hambre.

14 La mujer sabia edifica su casa;
la necia, con sus manos la destruye.

2El que va por buen camino teme al SEÑOR;
el que va por mal camino lo desprecia.

3De la boca del necio brota arrogancia;
los labios del sabio son su propia
protección.

4Donde no hay bueyes el granero está vacío;
con la fuerza del buey aumenta la cosecha.

5El testigo verdadero jamás engaña;
el testigo falso propaga mentiras.

6El insolente busca sabiduría y no la halla;
para el entendido, el conocimiento es cosa
fácil.

7Manténte a distancia del necio,
pues en sus labios no hallarás
conocimiento.

8La sabiduría del prudente es discernir sus
caminos,
pero al necio lo engaña su propia necedad.

9Los necios hacen mofa de sus propias faltas,
pero los íntegros cuentan con el favor de
Dios.

10Cada corazón conoce sus propias amarguras,
y ningún extraño comparte su alegría.

11La casa del malvado será destruida,
pero la morada del justo prosperará.

12Hay caminos que al hombre le parecen rectos,
pero que acaban por ser caminos de
muerte.

13También de reírse duele el corazón,
y hay alegrías que acaban en tristeza.

14El inconstante recibirá todo el pago de su
inconstancia;
el hombre bueno, el premio de sus
acciones.

15El ingenuo cree todo lo que le dicen;
el prudente se fija por dónde va.

16El sabio teme al SEÑOR y se aparta del mal,
pero el necio es arrogante y se pasa de
confiado.

17El iracundo comete locuras,
pero el prudente sabe aguantar.k

18Herencia de los inexpertos es la necedad;
corona de los prudentes, el conocimiento.

19Los malvados se postrarán ante los buenos;
los impíos, ante el tribunall de los justos.

20Al pobre hasta sus amigos lo aborrecen,
pero son muchos los que aman al rico.

21Es un pecado despreciar al prójimo;
¡dichoso el que se compadece de los
pobres!

22Pierden el camino los que maquinan el mal,
pero hallan amor y verdad los que hacen el
bien.

23Todo esfuerzo tiene su recompensa,
pero quedarse sólo en palabras lleva a la
pobreza.

---

j **13:9** *brilla radiante.* Lit. *se alegra.*   k **14:17** *sabe aguantar* (LXX); *es odiado* (TM).   l **14:19** *ante el tribunal.* Lit. *ante la *puerta.*

24La corona del sabio es su sabiduría;m
   la de los necios, su necedad.

25El testigo veraz libra de la muerte,
   pero el testigo falso miente.

26El temor del SEÑOR es un baluarte seguro
   que sirve de refugio a los hijos.

27El temor del SEÑOR es fuente de vida,
   y aleja al hombre de las redes de la muerte.

28Gloria del rey es gobernar a muchos;
   un príncipe sin súbditos está arruinado.

29El que es paciente muestra gran
     discernimiento;
   el que es agresivo muestra mucha
     insensatez.

30El corazón tranquilo da vida al cuerpo,
   pero la envidia corroe los huesos.

31El que oprime al pobre ofende a su Creador,
   pero honra a Dios quien se apiada del
     necesitado.

32El malvado cae por su propia maldad;
   el justo halla refugio en su integridad.n

33En el corazón de los sabios mora la sabiduría,
   pero los necios ni siquiera la conocen.ñ

34La justicia enaltece a una nación,
   pero el pecado deshonra a todos los
     pueblos.

35El rey favorece al siervo inteligente,
   pero descarga su ira sobre el sinvergüenza.

15 La respuesta amable calma el enojo,
   pero la agresiva echa leña al fuego.

2La lengua de los sabios destila conocimiento;o
   la boca de los necios escupe necedades.

3Los ojos del SEÑOR están en todo lugar,
   vigilando a los buenos y a los malos.

4La lengua que brinda consuelop es árbol de
     vida;
   la lengua insidiosa deprime el espíritu.

5El necio desdeña la corrección de su padre;
   el que la acepta demuestra prudencia.

6En la casa del justo hay gran abundancia;
   en las ganancias del malvado, grandes
     problemas.

7Los labios de los sabios esparcen
     conocimiento;
   el corazón de los necios ni piensa en ello.

8El SEÑOR aborrece las ofrendas de los
     malvados,
   pero se complace en la oración de los
     justos.

9El SEÑOR aborrece el camino de los malvados,
   pero ama a quienes siguen la justicia.

10Para el descarriado, disciplina severa;
   para el que aborrece la corrección, la
     muerte.

11Si ante el SEÑOR están el *sepulcro y la
     *muerte,
   ¡cuánto más el corazón humano!

12Al insolente no le gusta que lo corrijan,
   ni busca la compañía de los sabios.

13El corazón alegre se refleja en el rostro,
   el corazón dolido deprime el espíritu.

14El corazón entendido va tras el conocimiento;
   la boca de los necios se nutre de tonterías.

15Para el afligido todos los días son malos;
   para el que es feliz siempre es día de fiesta.

16Más vale tener poco, con temor del SEÑOR,
   que muchas riquezas con grandes
     angustias.

17Más vale comer verduras sazonadas con amor
   que un festín de carneq sazonada con odio.

18El que es iracundo provoca contiendas;
   el que es paciente las apacigua.

19El camino del perezoso está plagado de
     espinas,
   pero la senda del justo es como una
     calzada.

20El hijo sabio alegra a su padre;
   el hijo necio menosprecia a su madre.

21Al necio le divierte su falta de juicio;
   el entendido endereza sus propios pasos.

22Cuando falta el consejo, fracasan los planes;
   cuando abunda el consejo, prosperan.

23Es muy grato dar la respuesta adecuada,
   y más grato aun cuando es oportuna.

24El sabio sube por el sendero de vida,
   para librarse de caer en el *sepulcro.

25El SEÑOR derriba la casa de los soberbios,
   pero mantiene intactos los linderos de las
     viudas.

26El SEÑOR aborrece los planes de los malvados,
   pero le agradan las palabras puras.

27El ambicioso acarrea mal sobre su familia;
   el que aborrece el soborno vivirá.

28El corazón del justo medita sus respuestas,
   pero la boca del malvado rebosa de
     maldad.

29El SEÑOR se mantiene lejos de los impíos,
   pero escucha las oraciones de los justos.

30Una mirada radiante alegra el corazón,
   y las buenas noticias renuevan las fuerzas.r

31El que atiende a la crítica edificante
   habitará entre los sabios.

32Rechazar la corrección es despreciarse a sí
     mismo;
   atender a la reprensión es ganar
     entendimiento.

33El temor del SEÑOR es corrección y sabiduría;s
   la humildad precede a la honra.

---

m **14:24** *su sabiduría* (LXX); *su riqueza* (TM).   n **14:32** *en su integridad* (LXX y Siríaca); *en su muerte* (TM).   ñ **14:33** *los necios ni siquiera la conocen* (LXX y Siríaca); *los necios la conocen* (TM).   o **15:2** *destila conocimiento* (LXX); *hace bien al conocimiento* (TM).   p **15:4** *que brinda consuelo.* Lit. *que sana.*   q **15:17** *que un festín de carne.* Lit. *que toro engordado.*   r **15:30** *las fuerzas.* Lit. *los huesos.*   s **15:33** *es corrección y sabiduría* (LXX); *es corrección de sabiduría* (TM).

16

El hombre propone
y Dios[t] dispone.

[2]A cada uno le parece correcto su proceder,[u]
pero el SEÑOR juzga los motivos.

[3]Pon en manos del SEÑOR todas tus obras,
y tus proyectos se cumplirán.

[4]Toda obra del SEÑOR tiene un propósito;
¡hasta el malvado fue hecho para el día del
desastre!

[5]El SEÑOR aborrece a los arrogantes.
Una cosa es segura: no quedarán impunes.

[6]Con amor y verdad se perdona el pecado,
y con temor del SEÑOR se evita el mal.

[7]Cuando el SEÑOR aprueba la conducta de un
hombre,
hasta con sus enemigos lo reconcilia.

[8]Más vale tener poco con justicia
que ganar mucho con injusticia.

[9]El corazón del hombre traza su rumbo,
pero sus pasos los dirige el SEÑOR.

[10]La sentencia[v] está en labios del rey;
en el veredicto que emite no hay error.

[11]Las pesas y las balanzas justas son del SEÑOR;
todas las medidas son hechura suya.

[12]El rey detesta las malas acciones,
porque el trono se afirma en la justicia.

[13]El rey se complace en los labios honestos;
aprecia a quien habla con la verdad.

[14]La ira del rey es presagio de muerte,
pero el sabio sabe apaciguarla.

[15]El rostro radiante del rey es signo de vida;
su favor es como lluvia en primavera.

[16]Más vale adquirir sabiduría que oro;
más vale adquirir inteligencia que plata.

[17]El camino del hombre recto evita el mal;
el que quiere salvar su vida, se fija por
dónde va.

[18]Al orgullo le sigue la destrucción;
a la altanería, el fracaso.

[19]Vale más humillarse con los oprimidos
que compartir el botín con los orgullosos.

[20]El que atiende a la palabra, prospera.
¡Dichoso el que confía en el SEÑOR!

[21]Al sabio de corazón se le llama inteligente;
los labios convincentes promueven el
saber.

[22]Fuente de vida es la prudencia para quien la
posee;
el castigo de los necios es su propia
necedad.

[23]El sabio de corazón controla su boca;
con sus labios promueve el saber.

[24]Panal de miel son las palabras amables:

endulzan la vida y dan salud al cuerpo.[w]

[25]Hay caminos que al hombre le parecen rectos,
pero que acaban por ser caminos de
muerte.

[26]Al que trabaja, el hambre lo obliga a trabajar,
pues su propio apetito lo estimula.

[27]El perverso hace[x] planes malvados;
en sus labios hay un fuego devorador.

[28]El perverso provoca contiendas,
y el chismoso divide a los buenos amigos.

[29]El violento engaña a su prójimo
y lo lleva por mal camino.

[30]El que guiña el ojo trama algo perverso;
el que aprieta los labios ya lo ha cometido.

[31]Las canas son una honrosa corona
que se obtiene en el camino de la justicia.

[32]Más vale ser paciente que valiente;
más vale dominarse a sí mismo que
conquistar ciudades.

[33]Las suertes se echan sobre la mesa,[y]
pero el veredicto proviene del SEÑOR.

17

Más vale comer pan duro donde hay
concordia
que hacer banquete[z] donde hay discordia.

[2]El siervo sabio gobernará al hijo sinvergüenza,
y compartirá la herencia con los otros
hermanos.

[3]En el crisol se prueba la plata
y en el horno se prueba el oro,
pero al corazón lo prueba el SEÑOR.

[4]El malvado hace caso a los labios impíos,
y el mentiroso presta oído a la lengua
maliciosa.

[5]El que se burla del pobre ofende a su Creador;
el que se alegra de verlo en la ruina no
quedará sin castigo.

[6]La corona del anciano son sus nietos;
el orgullo de los hijos son sus padres.

[7]No va bien con los necios el lenguaje refinado,
ni con los gobernantes, la mentira.

[8]Vara[a] mágica es el soborno para quien lo
ofrece,
pues todo lo que emprende lo consigue.

[9]El que perdona la ofensa cultiva el amor;
el que insiste en la ofensa divide a los
amigos.

[10]Cala más un regaño en el hombre prudente
que cien latigazos en el obstinado.

[11]El revoltoso siempre anda buscando camorra,
pero se las verá con un mensajero cruel.

[12]Más vale toparse con un oso enfurecido[b]
que con un necio empecinado en su
necedad.

[13]Al que devuelve mal por bien,

---

[t] 16:1 *Dios.* Lit. *el SEÑOR.* [u] 16:2 *A cada uno ... proceder.* Lit. *Todos los caminos del hombre son limpios a sus ojos.*
[v] 16:10 *La sentencia.* Alt. *El oráculo.* [w] 16:24 *al cuerpo.* Lit. *a los huesos.* [x] 16:27 *hace.* Lit. *cava.* [y] 16:33 *sobre la mesa.* Lit. *en
el regazo.* [z] 17:1 *banquete.* Lit. *sacrificios.* [a] 17:8 *Vara.* Lit. *Piedra.* [b] 17:12 *oso enfurecido.* Lit. *oso al que le robaron sus cachorros.*

nunca el mal se apartará de su familia.

14Iniciar una pelea es romper una represa;
vale más retirarse que comenzarla.

15Absolver al culpable y condenar al inocente
son dos cosas que el SEÑOR aborrece.

16¿De qué le sirve al necio poseer dinero?
¿Podrá adquirir sabiduría si le faltan
sesos?c

17En todo tiempo ama el amigo;
para ayudar en la adversidad nació el
hermano.

18El que es imprudente se compromete por
otros,
y sale fiador de su prójimo.

19Al que le gusta pecar, le gusta pelear;
el que abre mucho la boca, busca que se la
rompan.d

20El de corazón perverso jamás prospera;
el de lengua engañosa caerá en desgracia.

21Engendrar a un hijo necio es causa de pesar;
ser padre de un necio no es ninguna
alegría.

22Gran remedio es el corazón alegre,
pero el ánimo decaído seca los huesos.

23El malvado acepta soborno en secreto,
con lo que tuerce el curso de la justicia.

24La meta del prudente es la sabiduría;
el necio divaga contemplando vanos
horizontes.e

25El hijo necio irrita a su padre,
y causa amargura a su madre.

26No está bien castigar al inocente,
ni azotar por su rectitud a gente honorable.

27El que es entendido refrena sus palabras;
el que es prudente controla sus impulsos.

28Hasta un necio pasa por sabio si guarda
silencio;
se le considera prudente si cierra la boca.

18 El egoísta busca su propio bien;
contra todo sano juicio se rebela.

2Al necio no le complace el discernimiento;
tan sólo hace alarde de su propia opinión.

3Con la maldad, viene el desprecio,
y con la vergüenza llega el oprobio.

4Las palabras del hombre son aguas profundas,
arroyo de aguas vivas, fuente de sabiduría.

5No está bien declarar inocente alf malvado
y dejar de lado los derechos del justo.

6Los labios del necio son causa de contienda;
su boca incita a la riña.

7La boca del necio es su perdición;
sus labios son para él una trampa mortal.

8Los chismes son deliciosos manjares;

penetran hasta lo más íntimo del ser.

9El que es negligente en su trabajo
confraterniza con el que es destructivo.

10Torre inexpugnable es el nombre del SEÑOR;
a ella corren los justos y se ponen a salvo.

11Ciudad amurallada es la riqueza para el rico,
y éste cree que sus muros son
inexpugnables.

12Al fracaso lo precede la soberbia humana;
a los honores los precede la humildad.

13Es necio y vergonzoso
responder antes de escuchar.

14En la enfermedad, el ánimo levanta al
enfermo;
¿pero quién podrá levantar al abatido?

15El corazón prudente adquiere conocimiento;
los oídos de los sabios procuran hallarlo.

16Con regalos se abren todas las puertas
y se llega a la presencia de gente
importante.

17El primero en presentar su caso parece
inocente,
hasta que llega la otra parte y lo refuta.

18El echar suertes pone fin a los litigios
y decide entre las partes en pugna.

19Más resiste el hermano ofendido que una
ciudad amurallada;
los litigios son como cerrojos de ciudadela.

20Cada uno se llena con lo que dice
y se sacia con lo que habla.

21En la lengua hay poder de vida y muerte;
quienes la aman comerán de su fruto.

22Quien halla esposa halla la felicidad:
muestras de su favor le ha dado el SEÑOR.

23El pobre habla en tono suplicante;
el rico responde con aspereza.

24Hay amigosg que llevan a la ruina,
y hay amigos más fieles que un hermano.

19 Más vale pobre e intachable
que necio y embustero.

2El afán sin conocimiento no vale nada;
mucho yerra quien mucho corre.

3La necedad del hombre le hace perder el
rumbo,
y para colmo se irrita contra el SEÑOR.

4Con las riquezas aumentan los amigos,
pero al pobre hasta su amigo lo abandona.

5El testigo falso no quedará sin castigo;
el que esparce mentiras no saldrá bien
librado.

6Muchos buscan congraciarse con los
poderosos;
todos son amigos de quienes reparten
regalos.

---

c **17:16** sesos. Lit. corazón.　d **17:19** el que abre ... se la rompan. Lit. el que abre su puerta, busca destrucción.　e **17:24** el necio ...
horizontes. Lit. y los ojos del necio en los confines de la tierra.　f **18:5** declarar inocente al. Lit. levantar el rostro del.
g **18:24** Hay amigos (LXX, Siríaca y Targum); Hombre de amigos (TM).

7Si al pobre lo aborrecen sus parientes,
con más razón lo evitan sus amigos.
Aunque los busca suplicante,
por ninguna parte los encuentra.h

8El que adquiere cordurai a sí mismo se ama,
y el que retiene el discernimiento prospera.

9El testigo falso no quedará sin castigo;
el que difunde mentiras perecerá.

10No va a bien con el necio vivir entre lujos,
y menos con el esclavo gobernar a los
príncipes.

11El buen juicio hace al hombre paciente;
su gloria es pasar por alto la ofensa.

12Rugido de león es la ira del rey;
su favor es como rocío sobre el pasto.

13El hijo necio es la ruina del padre;
la mujer pendenciera es gotera constante.

14La casa y el dinero se heredan de los padres,
pero la esposa inteligente es un don del
SEÑOR.

15La pereza conduce al sueño profundo;
el holgazán pasará hambre.

16El que cumple el mandamiento cumple
consigo mismo;
el que descuida su conducta morirá.

17Servir al pobre es hacerle un préstamo al
SEÑOR;
Dios pagará esas buenas acciones.

18Corrige a tu hijo mientras aún hay esperanza;
no te hagas cómplice de su muerte.j

19El iracundo tendrá que afrontar el castigo;
el que intente disuadirlo aumentará su
enojo.k

20Atiende al consejo y acepta la corrección,
y llegarás a ser sabio.

21El corazón humano genera muchos
proyectos,
pero al final prevalecen los designios del
SEÑOR.

22De todo hombre se espera lealtad.l
Más vale ser pobre que mentiroso.

23El temor del SEÑOR conduce a la vida;
da un sueño tranquilo y evita los
problemas.

24El perezoso mete la mano en el plato,
pero es incapaz de llevarse el bocado a la
boca.

25Golpea al insolente, y se hará prudente el
inexperto;
reprende al entendido, y ganará en
conocimiento.

26El que roba a su padre y echa a la calle a su
madre
es un hijo infame y sinvergüenza.

27Hijo mío, si dejas de atender a la corrección,
te apartarás de las palabras del saber.

28El testigo corrupto se burla de la justicia,
y la boca del malvado engulle maldad.

29El castigo se dispuso para los insolentes,
y los azotes para la espalda de los necios.

20 El vino lleva a la insolencia,
y la bebida embriagante al escándalo;
¡nadie bajo sus efectos se comporta
sabiamente!

2Rugido de león es la furia del rey;
quien provoca su enojo se juega la vida.

3Honroso es al hombre evitar la contienda,
pero no hay necio que no inicie un pleito.

4El perezoso no labra la tierra en otoño;
en tiempo de cosecha buscará y no hallará.

5Los pensamientos humanos son aguas
profundas,
el que es inteligente los capta fácilmente.

6Son muchos los que proclaman su lealtad,
¿pero quién puede hallar a alguien digno
de confianza?

7Justo es quien lleva una vida sin tacha,
¡dichosos los hijos que sigan su ejemplo!m

8Cuando el rey se sienta en el tribunal,
con su sola mirada barre toda maldad.

9¿Quién puede afirmar: «Tengo puro el
corazón,
estoy limpio de pecado»?

10Pesas falsas y medidas engañosas:
¡vaya pareja que el SEÑOR detesta!

11Por sus hechos el niño deja entrever
si su conducta será pura y recta.

12Los oídos para oír y los ojos para ver:
¡hermosa pareja que el SEÑOR ha creado!

13No te des al sueño, o te quedarás pobre;
manténte despierto y tendrás pan de sobra.

14«¡No sirve, no sirve!», dice el comprador,
pero luego va y se jacta de su compra.

15Oro hay, y abundan las piedras preciosas,
pero aun más valiosos son los labios del
saber.

16Toma la prenda del que salga fiador de un
extraño;
reténla en garantía si la da en favor de
desconocidos.

17Tal vez sea agradable ganarse el pan con
engaños,
pero uno acaba con la boca llena de arena.

18Afirma tus planes con buenos consejos;
entabla el combate con buena estrategia.

19El chismoso traiciona la confianza;
no te juntes con la gente que habla de más.

20Al que maldiga a su padre y a su madre,
su lámpara se le apagará en la más densa
oscuridad.

21La herencia de fácil comienzo

h 19:7 Texto de difícil traducción. i 19:8 cordura. Lit. corazón. j 19:18 no te hagas ... muerte. Alt. pero no te excedas hasta matarlo. k 19:19 Texto de difícil traducción. l 19:22 De todo ... lealtad. Alt. El anhelo de todo hombre es su amor.
m 20:7 los hijos ... su ejemplo. Lit. sus hijos después de él.

no tendrá un final feliz.

22Nunca digas: «¡Me vengaré de ese daño!»
Confía en el SEÑOR, y él actuará por ti.

23El SEÑOR aborrece las pesas falsas
y reprueba el uso de medidas engañosas.

24Los pasos del hombre los dirige el SEÑOR.
¿Cómo puede el hombre entender su
propio camino?

25Trampa es consagrar algo sin pensarlo
y más tarde reconsiderar lo prometido.

26El rey sabio avienta como trigo a los
malvados,
y los desmenuza con rueda de molino.

27El espíritu humano es la lámpara del SEÑOR,
pues escudriña lo más recóndito del ser.

28La misericordia y la verdad sostienen al rey;
su trono se afirma en la misericordia.

29La gloria de los jóvenes radica en su fuerza;
la honra de los ancianos, en sus canas.

30Los golpes y las heridas curan la maldad;
los azotes purgan lo más íntimo del ser.

21 En las manos del SEÑOR el corazón del rey
es como un río:
sigue el curso que el SEÑOR le ha trazado.

2A cada uno le parece correcto su proceder,[n]
pero el SEÑOR juzga los corazones.

3Practicar la justicia y el derecho
lo prefiere el SEÑOR a los sacrificios.

4Los ojos altivos, el corazón orgulloso
y la lámpara de los malvados son pecado.

5Los planes bien pensados: ¡pura ganancia!
Los planes apresurados: ¡puro fracaso!

6La fortuna amasada por la lengua embustera
se esfuma como la niebla y es mortal como
una trampa.[ñ]

7La violencia de los malvados los destruirá,
porque se niegan a practicar la justicia.

8Torcido es el camino del culpable,
pero recta la conducta del hombre
honrado.

9Más vale habitar en un rincón de la azotea
que compartir el techo con mujer
pendenciera.

10El malvado sólo piensa en el mal;
jamás se compadece de su prójimo.

11Cuando se castiga al insolente,
aprende[o] el inexperto;
cuando se instruye al sabio,
el inexperto adquiere conocimiento.

12El justo se fija en la casa del malvado,
y ve cuando éste acaba en la ruina.

13Quien cierra sus oídos al clamor del pobre,
llorará también sin que nadie le responda.

14El regalo secreto apacigua el enojo;

el obsequio discreto calma la ira violenta.

15Cuando se hace justicia,
se alegra el justo y tiembla el malhechor.

16Quien se aparta de la senda del
discernimiento
irá a parar entre los muertos.

17El que ama el placer se quedará en la pobreza;
el que ama el vino y los perfumes jamás
será rico.

18El malvado pagará por el justo,
y el traidor por el hombre intachable.

19Más vale habitar en el desierto
que con mujer pendenciera y de mal genio.

20En casa del sabio abundan las riquezas y el
perfume,
pero el necio todo lo despilfarra.

21El que va tras la justicia y el amor
halla vida, prosperidad[p] y honra.

22El sabio conquista la ciudad de los valientes
y derriba el baluarte en que ellos confiaban.

23El que refrena su boca y su lengua
se libra de muchas angustias.

24Orgulloso y arrogante, y famoso por
insolente,
es quien se comporta con desmedida
soberbia.

25La codicia del perezoso lo lleva a la muerte,
porque sus manos se niegan a trabajar;
26todo el día se lo pasa codiciando,
pero el justo da con generosidad.

27El sacrificio de los malvados es detestable,
y más aun cuando se ofrece con mala
intención.

28El testigo falso perecerá,
y quien le haga caso será destruido[q] para
siempre.

29El malvado es inflexible en sus decisiones;
el justo examina[r] su propia conducta.

30De nada sirven ante el SEÑOR
la sabiduría, la inteligencia y el consejo.

31Se alista al caballo para el día de la batalla,
pero la victoria depende del SEÑOR.

22 Vale más la buena fama que las muchas
riquezas,
y más que oro y plata, la buena reputación.

2El rico y el pobre tienen esto en común:
a ambos los ha creado el SEÑOR.

3El prudente ve el peligro y lo evita;
el inexperto sigue adelante y sufre las
consecuencias.

4Recompensa de la humildad y del temor del
SEÑOR
son las riquezas, la honra y la vida.

5Espinas y trampas hay en la senda de los
impíos,

---

n **21:2** *A cada uno ... su proceder.* Lit. *Todo camino del hombre recto a sus ojos.* ñ **21:6** *se esfuma ... una trampa* (LXX, Vulgata
y algunos mss. hebreos); *es niebla llevada de los que buscan la muerte* (TM). o **21:11** *aprende.* Lit. *se hace sabio.*
p **21:21** *prosperidad.* Alt. *justicia.* q **21:28** *será destruido.* Alt. *hablará.* r **21:29** *examina* (LXX, Qumrán y varios mss. hebreos); *ordena* (TM).

pero el que cuida su vida se aleja de ellas.

6Instruye al niño en el camino correcto,
  y aun en su vejez no lo abandonará.

7Los ricos son los amos de los pobres;
  los deudores son esclavos de sus
    acreedores.

8El que siembra maldad cosecha desgracias;
  el SEÑOR lo destruirá con el cetro de su ira.s

9El que es generoso𝑡 será bendecido,
  pues comparte su comida con los pobres.

10Despide al insolente, y se irá la discordia
  y cesarán los pleitos y los insultos.

11El que ama la pureza de corazón y tiene
    gracia al hablar
  tendrá por amigo al rey.

12Los ojos del SEÑOR protegen el saber,
  pero desbaratan las palabras del traidor.

13«¡Hay un león allá afuera! —dice el
    holgazán—.
  ¡En plena calle me va a hacer pedazos!»
14La boca de la adúltera es una fosa profunda;
  en ella caerá quien esté bajo la ira del
    SEÑOR.

15La necedad es parte del corazón juvenil,
  pero la vara de la disciplina la corrige.

16Oprimir al pobre para enriquecerse,
  y hacerle regalos al rico,
  ¡buena manera de empobrecerse!

Los treinta dichos de los sabios
(22:17—24:22)

17Presta atención, escucha mis palabras;𝑢
  aplica tu corazón a mi conocimiento.
18Grato es retenerlas dentro de ti,
  y tenerlas todas a flor de labio.
19A ti te las enseño en este día,
  para que pongas tu confianza en el SEÑOR.
20¿Acaso no te he escrito treinta𝑣 dichos
  que contienen sabios consejos?
21Son para enseñarte palabras ciertas y
    confiables,
  para que sepas responder bien a quien te
    pregunte.𝑤

1

22No explotes al pobre porque es pobre,
  ni oprimas en los tribunales𝑥 a los
    necesitados;
23porque el SEÑOR defenderá su causa,
  y despojará a quienes los despojen.

2

24No te hagas amigo de gente violenta,
  ni te juntes con los iracundos,
25no sea que aprendas sus malas costumbres
  y tú mismo caigas en la trampa.

3

26No te comprometas por otros
  ni salgas fiador de deudas ajenas;
27porque si no tienes con qué pagar,
  te quitarán hasta la cama en que duermes.

4

28No cambies de lugar los linderos antiguos
  que establecieron tus antepasados.

5

29¿Has visto a alguien diligente en su trabajo?
  Se codeará con reyes, y nunca será un Don
    Nadie.

6

23

Cuando te sientes a comer con un
    gobernante,
  fíjate bien en lo que𝑦 tienes ante ti.
2Si eres dado a la glotonería,
  domina tu apetito.𝑧
3No codicies sus manjares,
  pues tal comida no es más que un engaño.

7

4No te afanes acumulando riquezas;
  no te obsesiones con ellas.
5¿Acaso has podido verlas? ¡No existen!
  Es como si les salieran alas,
  pues se van volando como las águilas.

8

6No te sientes a la mesa de un tacaño,𝑎
  ni codicies sus manjares,
7que son como un pelo en la garganta.𝑏
  «Come y bebe», te dirá,
  pero no te lo dirá de corazón.
8Acabarás vomitando lo que hayas comido,
  y tus cumplidos no habrán servido de
    nada.

9

9A oídos del necio jamás dirijas palabra,
  pues se burlará de tus sabios consejos.

10

10No cambies de lugar los linderos antiguos,
  ni invadas la propiedad de los huérfanos,
11porque su Defensor es muy poderoso
  y contra ti defenderá su causa.

11

12Aplica tu corazón a la disciplina
  y tus oídos al conocimiento.

12

13No dejes de disciplinar al joven,
  que de unos cuantos azotes no se morirá.
14Dale unos buenos azotes,
  y así lo librarás del *sepulcro.

13

15Hijo mío, si tu corazón es sabio,
  también mi corazón se regocijará;
16en lo íntimo de mi ser me alegraré
  cuando tus labios hablen con rectitud.

14

17No envidies en tu corazón a los pecadores;
  más bien, muéstrate siempre celoso en el
    temor del SEÑOR.
18Cuentas con una esperanza futura,
  la cual no será destruida.

15

19Hijo mío, presta atención y sé sabio;
  mantén tu corazón en el camino recto.
20No te juntes con los que beben mucho vino,

---

s **22:8** *el Señor ... su ira.* Lit. *el cetro de su ira perecerá.* t **22:9** *El que es generoso.* Lit. *El buen ojo.* u **22:17** *mis palabras* (LXX); *las palabras de los sabios* (TM). v **22:20** *escrito treinta.* Alt. *escrito antes* o *escrito excelentes.* w **22:21** *a quien te pregunte* (LXX); *al que te envíe* (TM). x **22:22** *en los tribunales.* Lit. *en la* **puerta.* y **23:1** *en lo que.* Alt. *en quién.* z **23:2** *domina tu apetito.* Lit. *ponle un cuchillo a tu garganta.* a **23:6** *un tacaño.* Alt. *un hombre mal intencionado.* b **23:7** *que son ... garganta* (LXX); *pues como él piensa en su interior, así es él* (TM).

ni con los que se hartan de carne,
²¹pues borrachos y glotones, por su indolencia,
acaban harapientos y en la pobreza.

16

²²Escucha a tu padre, que te engendró,
y no desprecies a tu madre cuando sea
anciana.
²³Adquiere la verdad y la sabiduría,
la disciplina y el discernimiento,
¡y no los vendas!
²⁴El padre del justo experimenta gran regocijo;
quien tiene un hijo sabio se solaza en él.
²⁵¡Que se alegren tu padre y tu madre!
¡Que se regocije la que te dio la vida!

17

²⁶Dame, hijo mío, tu corazón
y no pierdas de vista mis caminos.
²⁷Porque fosa profunda es la prostituta,
y estrecho pozo, la mujer ajena.
²⁸Se pone al acecho, como un bandido,
y multiplica la infidelidad de los hombres.

18

²⁹¿De quién son los lamentos? ¿De quién los
pesares?
¿De quién son los pleitos? ¿De quién las
quejas?
¿De quién son las heridas gratuitas?
¿De quién los ojos morados?
³⁰¡Del que no suelta la botella de vino
ni deja de probar licores!

³¹No te fijes en lo rojo que es el vino,
ni en cómo brilla en la copa,
ni en la suavidad con que se desliza;
³²porque acaba mordiendo como serpiente
y envenenando como víbora.
³³Tus ojos verán alucinaciones,
y tu mente imaginará estupideces.
³⁴Te parecerá estar durmiendo en alta mar,
acostado sobre el mástil mayor.
³⁵Y dirás: «Me han herido, pero no me duele.
Me han golpeado, pero no lo siento.
¿Cuándo despertaré de este sueño
para ir a buscar otro trago?»

19

24 No envidies a los malvados,
ni procures su compañía;
²porque en su corazón traman violencia,
y no hablan más que de cometer fechorías.

20

³Con sabiduría se construye la casa;
con inteligencia se echan los cimientos.
⁴Con buen juicio se llenan sus cuartos
de bellos y extraordinarios tesoros.

21

⁵El que es sabio tiene gran poder,
y el que es entendido aumenta su fuerza.
⁶La guerra se hace con buena estrategia;
la victoria se alcanza con muchos
consejeros.

22

⁷La sabiduría no está al alcance del necio,
que en la asamblea del puebloᶜ nada tiene
que decir.

23

⁸Al que hace planes malvados
lo llamarán intrigante.
⁹Las intrigas del necio son pecado,

y todos aborrecen a los insolentes.

24

¹⁰Si en el día de la aflicción te desanimas,
muy limitada es tu fortaleza.

25

¹¹Rescata a los que van rumbo a la muerte;
detén a los que a tumbos avanzan al
suplicio.
¹²Pues aunque digas, «Yo no lo sabía»,
¿no habrá de darse cuenta el que pesa los
corazones?
¿No habrá de saberlo el que vigila tu vida?
¡Él le paga a cada uno según sus acciones!

26

¹³Come la miel, hijo mío, que es deliciosa;
dulce al paladar es la miel del panal.
¹⁴Así de dulce sea la sabiduría a tu alma;
si das con ella, tendrás buen futuro;
tendrás una esperanza que no será
destruida.

27

¹⁵No aceches cual malvado la casa del justo,
ni arrases el lugar donde habita;
¹⁶porque siete veces podrá caer el justo,
pero otras tantas se levantará;
los malvados, en cambio,
se hundirán en la desgracia.

28

¹⁷No te alegres cuando caiga tu enemigo,
ni se regocije tu corazón ante su desgracia,
¹⁸no sea que el SEÑOR lo vea y no lo apruebe,
y aparte de él su enojo.

29

¹⁹No te alteres por causa de los malvados,
ni sientas envidia de los impíos,
²⁰porque el malvado no tiene porvenir;
¡la lámpara del impío se apagará!

30

²¹Hijo mío, teme al SEÑOR y honra al rey,
y no te juntes con los rebeldes,
²²porque de los dos recibirás un castigo
repentino
¡y quién sabe qué calamidades puedan
venir!

Otros dichos de los sabios

²³También éstos son dichos de los sabios:

No es correcto ser parcial en el juicio.

²⁴Maldecirán los pueblos, y despreciarán las
naciones,
a quien declare inocente al culpable.
²⁵Pero bien vistos serán, y bendecidos,
los que condenen al culpable.

²⁶Una respuesta sincera
es como un beso en los labios.

²⁷Prepara primero tus faenas de cultivo
y ten listos tus campos para la siembra;
después de eso, construye tu casa.

²⁸No testifiques sin razón contra tu prójimo,
ni mientas con tus labios.
²⁹No digas: «Le haré lo mismo que me hizo;
le pagaré con la misma moneda.»

³⁰Pasé por el campo del perezoso,
por la viña del falto de juicio.

ᶜ **24:7** *en la asamblea del pueblo.* Lit. *en la* **puerta.*

³¹Había espinas por todas partes;
la hierba cubría el terreno,
y el lindero de piedras estaba en ruinas.
³²Guardé en mi corazón lo observado,
y de lo visto saqué una lección:
³³Un corto sueño, una breve siesta,
un pequeño descanso, cruzado de brazos...
³⁴¡y te asaltará la pobreza como un bandido,
y la escasez, como un hombre armado!

Más proverbios de Salomón

25 Éstos son otros proverbios de Salomón,
copiados por los escribas de Ezequías,
rey de Judá.

²Gloria de Dios es ocultar un asunto,
y gloria de los reyes es el investigarlo.

³Tan impenetrable es el corazón de los reyes
como alto es el cielo y profunda la tierra.

⁴Quita la escoria de la plata,
y de allí saldrá material para ᵈ el orfebre;
⁵quita de la presencia del rey al malvado,
y el rey afirmará su trono en la justicia.

⁶No te des importancia en presencia del rey,
ni reclames un lugar entre los magnates;
⁷vale más que el rey te diga: «Sube acá»,
y no que te humille ante gente importante.

Lo que atestigües con tus ojos
⁸no lo lleves ᵉ de inmediato al tribunal,
pues ¿qué harás si a fin de cuentas
tu prójimo te pone en vergüenza?

⁹Defiende tu causa contra tu prójimo,
pero no traiciones la confianza de nadie,
¹⁰no sea que te avergüence el que te oiga
y ya no puedas quitarte la infamia.

¹¹Como naranjas de oro con incrustaciones de
plata
son las palabras dichas a tiempo.

¹²Como anillo o collar de oro fino
son los regaños del sabio en oídos atentos.

¹³Como frescura de nieve en día de verano
es el mensajero confiable para quien lo
envía,
pues infunde nuevo ánimo en sus amos.
¹⁴Nubes y viento, y nada de lluvia,
es quien presume de dar y nunca da nada.

¹⁵Con paciencia se convence al gobernante.
¡La lengua amable quebranta hasta los
huesos!

¹⁶Si encuentras miel, no te empalagues;
la mucha miel provoca náuseas.

¹⁷No frecuentes la casa de tu amigo;
no sea que lo fastidies y llegue a
aborrecerte.

¹⁸Un mazo, una espada, una aguda saeta,
¡eso es el falso testigo contra su amigo!

¹⁹Confiar en gente desleal en momentos de
angustia
es como tener un diente careado o una
pierna quebrada.

²⁰Dedicarle canciones al corazón afligido
es como echarle vinagre ᶠ a una herida
o como andar desabrigado en un día de
frío.

²¹Si tu enemigo tiene hambre, dale de comer;
si tiene sed, dale de beber.
²²Actuando así, harás que se avergüence de su
conducta,ᵍ
y el SEÑOR te lo recompensará.

²³Con el viento del norte vienen las lluvias;
con la lengua viperina, las malas caras.

²⁴Más vale habitar en un rincón de la azotea
que compartir el techo con mujer
pendenciera.

²⁵Como el agua fresca a la garganta reseca
son las buenas noticias desde lejanas
tierras.

²⁶Manantial turbio, contaminado pozo,
es el justo que flaquea ante el impío.

²⁷No hace bien comer mucha miel,
ni es honroso buscar la propia gloria.

²⁸Como ciudad sin defensa y sin murallas
es quien no sabe dominarse.

26 Ni la nieve es para el verano,
ni la lluvia para la cosecha,
ni los honores para el necio.

²Como el gorrión sin rumbo o la golondrina sin
nido,
la maldición sin motivo jamás llega a su
destino.

³El látigo es para los caballos,
el freno para los asnos,
y el garrote para la espalda del necio.

⁴No respondas al necio según su necedad,
o tú mismo pasarás por necio.

⁵Respóndele al necio como se merece,
para que no se tenga por sabio.

⁶Enviar un mensaje por medio de un necio
es como cortarse los pies o sufrir ʰ violencia.

⁷Inútil es el proverbio en la boca del necio
como inútiles son las piernas de un tullido.

⁸Rendirle honores al necio es tan absurdo
como atar una piedra a la honda.

⁹El proverbio en la boca del necio
es como espina en la mano del borracho.

¹⁰Como arquero que hiere a todo el que pasa
es quien contrata al necio en su casa.ⁱ

¹¹Como vuelve el perro a su vómito,
así el necio insiste en su necedad.

¹²¿Te has fijado en quien se cree muy sabio?
Más se puede esperar de un necio que de
gente así.

¹³Dice el perezoso: «Hay una fiera en el camino.
¡Por las calles un león anda suelto!»

¹⁴Sobre sus goznes gira la puerta;

ᵈ **25:4** *saldrá material para.* Alt. *sacará una copa para.* ᵉ **25:7,8** *gente importante. Lo que ... no lo lleves.* Alt. *gente importante /
sobre la que hayas posado tus ojos. /* ⁸ *No vayas* ᶠ **25:20** *vinagre* (LXX); *salitre* (TM). ᵍ **25:22** *harás ... conducta.* Lit. *ascuas
amontonarás sobre su cabeza.* ʰ **26:6** *sufrir.* Lit. *beber.* ⁱ **26:10** Texto de difícil traducción.

sobre la cama, el perezoso.

15 El perezoso mete la mano en el plato,
pero le pesa llevarse el bocado a la boca.

16 El perezoso se cree más sabio
que siete sabios que saben responder.

17 Meterse en pleitos ajenos
es como agarrar a un perro por las orejas.

18 Como loco que dispara
mortíferas flechas encendidas,
19 es quien engaña a su amigo y explica:
«¡Tan sólo estaba bromeando!»

20 Sin leña se apaga el fuego;
sin chismes se acaba el pleito.

21 Con el carbón se hacen brasas, con la leña se
prende fuego,
y con un pendenciero se inician los pleitos.

22 Los chismes son como ricos bocados:
se deslizan hasta las entrañas.

23 Como baño de plata ͥ sobre vasija de barro
son los labios zalameros de un corazón
malvado.

24 El que odia se esconde tras sus palabras,
pero en lo íntimo alberga perfidia.
25 No le creas, aunque te hable con dulzura,
porque su corazón rebosa de
abominaciones.ᵏ
26 Tal vez disimule con engaños su odio,
pero en la asamblea se descubrirá su
maldad.

27 Cava una fosa, y en ella caerás;
echa a rodar piedras, y te aplastarán.
28 La lengua mentirosa odia a sus víctimas;
la boca lisonjera lleva a la ruina.

27 No te jactes del día de mañana,
porque no sabes lo que el día traerá.

2 No te jactes de ti mismo;
que sean otros los que te alaben.

3 Pesada es la piedra, pesada es la arena,
pero más pesada es la ira del necio.

4 Cruel es la furia, y arrolladora la ira,
pero ¿quién puede enfrentarse a la
envidia?

5 Más vale ser reprendido con franqueza
que ser amado en secreto.

6 Más confiable es el amigo que hiere
que el enemigo que besa.

7 Al que no tiene hambre, hasta la miel lo
empalaga;
al hambriento, hasta lo amargo le es dulce.

8 Como ave que vaga lejos del nido
es el hombre que vaga lejos del hogar.

9 El perfume y el incienso alegran el corazón;
la dulzura de la amistad fortalece el ánimo.ˡ

10 No abandones a tu amigo ni al amigo de tu
padre.

No vayas a la casa de tu hermano cuando
tengas un problema.

Más vale vecino cercano que hermano
distante.

11 Hijo mío, sé sabio y alegra mi corazón;
así podré responder a los que me
desprecian.

12 El prudente ve el peligro y lo evita;
el inexperto sigue adelante y sufre las
consecuencias.

13 Toma la prenda del que salga fiador por un
extraño;
reténla en garantía si la entrega por la
mujer ajena.

14 El mejor saludo se juzga una impertinencia
cuando se da a gritos y de madrugada.

15 Gotera constante en un día lluvioso
es la mujer que siempre pelea.
16 Quien la domine, podrá dominar el viento
y retenerᵐ aceite en la mano.

17 El hierro se afila con el hierro,
y el hombre en el trato con el hombre.

18 El que cuida de la higuera comerá de sus
higos,
y el que vela por su amo recibirá honores.

19 En el agua se refleja el rostro,
y en el corazón se refleja la persona.

20 El *sepulcro, la *muerte y los ojos del hombre
jamás se dan por satisfechos.

21 En el crisol se prueba la plata;
en el horno se prueba el oro;
ante las alabanzas, el hombre.

22 Aunque al necio lo muelas y lo remuelas,
y lo machaques como al grano,
no le quitarás la necedad.

23 Asegúrate de saber cómo están tus rebaños;
cuida mucho de tus ovejas;
24 pues las riquezas no son eternas
ni la fortuna está siempre segura.
25 Cuando se limpien los campos y brote el
verdor,
y en los montes se recoja la hierba,
26 las ovejas te darán para el vestido,
y las cabras para comprar un campo;
27 tendrás leche de cabra en abundancia
para que se alimenten tú y tu familia,
y toda tu servidumbre.

28 El malvado huye aunque nadie lo persiga;
pero el justo vive confiado como un león.

2 Cuando hay rebelión en el país,
los caudillos se multiplican;
cuando el gobernante es entendido,
se mantiene el orden.

3 El gobernanteⁿ que oprime a los pobres
es como violenta lluvia que arrasa la
cosecha.

4 Los que abandonan la ley alaban a los
malvados;

ʲ **26:23** *como baño de plata.* Lit. *como plata de escoria.* ᵏ **26:25** *porque su corazón ... abominaciones.* Lit. *porque siete abominaciones hay en su corazón.* ˡ **27:9** Texto de difícil traducción. ᵐ **27:16** *y retener.* Lit. *y llamará.* ⁿ **28:3** *El gobernante* (texto probable); *El pobre* (TM).

los que la obedecen luchan contra ellos.

5 Los malvados nada entienden de la justicia;
los que buscan al SEÑOR lo entienden todo.

6 Más vale pobre pero honrado,
que rico pero perverso.

7 El hijo entendido se sujeta a la ley;
el derrochador deshonra a su padre.

8 El que amasa riquezas mediante la usura
las acumula para el que se compadece de
los pobres.

9 Dios aborrece hasta la oración
del que se niega a obedecer la ley.

10 El que lleva a los justos por el mal camino,
caerá en su propia trampa;
pero los íntegros heredarán el bien.

11 El rico se las da de sabio;
el pobre pero inteligente lo desenmascara.

12 Cuando los justos triunfan, se hace gran
fiesta;
cuando los impíos se imponen, todo el
mundo se esconde.

13 Quien encubre su pecado jamás prospera;
quien lo confiesa y lo deja, halla perdón.

14 ¡Dichoso el que siempre teme al SEÑOR!ñ
Pero el obstinado caerá en la desgracia.

15 Un león rugiente, un oso hambriento,
es el gobernante malvado que oprime a los
pobres.

16 El gobernante falto de juicio es terrible
opresor;
el que odia las riquezas prolonga su vida.

17 El que es perseguido poro homicidio
será un fugitivo hasta la muerte.
¡Que nadie le brinde su apoyo!

18 El que es honrado se mantendrá a salvo;
el de caminos perversos caerá en la fosa.p

19 El que trabaja la tierra tendrá abundante
comida;
el que sueña despiertoq sólo abundará en
pobreza.

20 El hombre fiel recibirá muchas bendiciones;
el que tiene prisa por enriquecerse no
quedará impune.

21 No es correcto mostrarse parcial con nadie.
Hay quienes pecan hasta por un mendrugo
de pan.

22 El tacaño ansía enriquecerse,
sin saber que la pobreza lo aguarda.

23 A fin de cuentas, más se aprecia
al que reprende que al que adula.

24 El que roba a su padre o a su madre,
e insiste en que no ha pecado,
amigo es de gente perversa.r

25 El que es ambicioso provoca peleas,
pero el que confía en el SEÑOR prospera.

26 Necio es el que confía en sí mismo;
el que actúa con sabiduría se pone a salvo.

27 El que ayuda al pobre no conocerá la pobreza;
el que le niega su ayuda será maldecido.

28 Cuando triunfan los impíos, la gente se
esconde;
cuando perecen, los justos prosperan.

29 El que es reacio a las represiones
será destruido de repente y sin remedio.

2 Cuando los justos prosperan, el pueblo se
alegra;
cuando los impíos gobiernan, el pueblo
gime.

3 El que ama la sabiduría alegra a su padre;
el que frecuenta rameras derrocha su
fortuna.

4 Con justicia el rey da estabilidad al país;
cuando lo abruma con tributos, lo destruye.

5 El que adula a su prójimo
le tiende una trampa.

6 Al malvado lo atrapa su propia maldad,
pero el justo puede cantar de alegría.

7 El justo se ocupa de la causa del desvalido;
el malvado ni sabe de qué se trata.

8 Los insolentes conmocionan a la ciudad,
pero los sabios apaciguan los ánimos.

9 Cuando el sabio entabla pleito contra un necio,
aunque se enoje o se ría, nada arreglará.

10 Los asesinos aborrecen a los íntegros,
y tratan de matar a los justos.

11 El necio da rienda suelta a su ira,
pero el sabio sabe dominarla.

12 Cuando un gobernante se deja llevar por
mentiras,
todos sus oficiales se corrompen.

13 Algo en común tienen el pobre y el opresor:
a los dos el SEÑOR les ha dado la vista.

14 El rey que juzga al pobre según la verdad
afirma su trono para siempre.

15 La vara de la disciplina imparte sabiduría,
pero el hijo malcriado avergüenza a su
madre.

16 Cuando prospera el impío, prospera el
pecado,
pero los justos presenciarán su caída.

17 Disciplina a tu hijo, y te traerá tranquilidad;
te dará muchas satisfacciones.

18 Donde no hay visión, el pueblo se extravía;
¡dichosos los que son obedientes a la ley!

19 No sólo con palabras se corrige al siervo;
aunque entienda, no obedecerá.

20 ¿Te has fijado en los que hablan sin pensar?
¡Más se puede esperar de un necio que de
gente así!

ñ **28:14** *teme al SEÑOR.* Lit. *teme.* o **28:17** *El que es perseguido por.* Alt. *El que carga con la culpa de.* p **28:18** *en la fosa* (Siríaca); *en uno* (TM). q **28:19** *el que sueña despierto.* Lit. *el que persigue lo vacío;* también en 12:11. r **28:24** *de gente perversa.* Lit.
del destructor.

21Quien consiente a su criado cuando éste es
   niño,
   al final habrá de lamentarlo.s

22El hombre iracundo provoca peleas;
   el hombre violento multiplica sus crímenes.

23El altivo será humillado,
   pero el humilde será enaltecido.

24El cómplice del ladrón atenta contra sí
   mismo;
   aunque esté bajo juramento,t no testificará.

25Temer a los hombres resulta una trampa,
   pero el que confía en el SEÑOR sale bien
   librado.

26Muchos buscan el favor del gobernante,
   pero la sentencia del hombre la dicta el
   SEÑOR.

27Los justos aborrecen a los malvados,
   y los malvados aborrecen a los justos.

Dichos de Agur

30 Dichos de Agur hijo de Jaqué. Oráculo.u
   Palabras de este varón:

«Cansado estoy, oh Dios;
   cansado estoy, oh Dios, y débil.v

2»Soy el más ignorante de todos los hombres;
   no hay en mí discernimiento humano.
3No he adquirido sabiduría,
   ni tengo conocimiento del Dios santo.

4»¿Quién ha subido a los cielos
   y descendido de ellos?
¿Quién puede atrapar el viento en su puño
   o envolver el mar en su manto?
¿Quién ha establecido los límites de la tierra?
   ¿Quién conoce su nombre o el de su hijo?

5»Toda palabra de Dios es digna de crédito;
   Dios protege a los que en él buscan refugio.
6No añadas nada a sus palabras,
   no sea que te reprenda
   y te exponga como a un mentiroso.

7»Sólo dos cosas te pido, SEÑOR;
   no me las niegues antes de que muera:
8Aleja de mí la falsedad y la mentira;
   no me des pobreza ni riquezas
   sino sólo el pan de cada día.
9Porque teniendo mucho, podría desconocerte
   y decir: "¿Y quién es el SEÑOR?"
   Y teniendo poco, podría llegar a robar
   y deshonrar así el nombre de mi Dios.

10»No ofendas al esclavo delante de su amo,
   pues podría maldecirte y sufrirías las
   consecuencias.
11»Hay quienes maldicen a su padre
   y no bendicen a su madre.
12Hay quienes se creen muy puros,
   pero no se han purificado de su impureza.
13Hay quienes se creen muy importantes,
   y a todos miran con desdén.
14Hay quienes tienen espadas por dientes
   y cuchillos por mandíbulas;

para devorar a los pobres de la tierra
   y a los menesterosos de este mundo.

15»La sanguijuela tiene dos hijas
   que sólo dicen: "Dame, dame."

»Tres cosas hay que nunca se sacian,
   y una cuarta que nunca dice "¡Basta!":
16el *sepulcro, el vientre estéril,
   la tierra, que nunca se sacia de agua,
   y el fuego, que no se cansa de consumir.

17»Al que mira con desdén a su padre,
   y rehúsa obedecer a su madre,
   que los cuervos del valle le saquen los ojos
   y que se lo coman vivo los buitres.

18»Tres cosas hay que me causan asombro,
   y una cuarta que no alcanzo a comprender:
19el rastro del águila en el cielo,
   el rastro de la serpiente en la roca,
   el rastro del barco en alta mar,
   y el rastro del hombre en la mujer.

20»Así procede la adúltera:
   come, se limpia la boca,
   y afirma: "Nada malo he cometido."

21»Tres cosas hacen temblar la tierra,
   y una cuarta la hace estremecer:
22el siervo que llega a ser rey,
   el necio al que le sobra comida,
23la mujer rechazada que llega a casarse,
   y la criada que suplanta a su señora.

24»Cuatro cosas hay pequeñas en el mundo,
   pero que son más sabias que los sabios:
25las hormigas, animalito de escasas fuerzas,
   pero que almacenan su comida en el
   verano;
26los tejones, animalitos de poca monta,
   pero que construyen su casa entre las
   rocas;
27las langostas, que no tienen rey,
   pero que avanzan en formación perfecta;
28las lagartijas, que se atrapan con la mano,
   pero que habitan hasta en los palacios.

29»Tres cosas hay que caminan con garbo,
   y una cuarta de paso imponente:
30el león, poderoso entre las bestias,
   que no retrocede ante nada;
31el gallo engreído,w el macho cabrío,
   y el rey al frente de su ejército.x

32»Si como un necio te has engreído,
   o si algo maquinas, ponte a pensary
33que batiendo la leche se obtiene mantequilla,
   que sonándose fuerte sangra la nariz,
   y que provocando la ira se acaba
   peleando.»

Dichos del rey Lemuel

31 Los dichos del rey Lemuel. Oráculo
   mediante el cualz su madre lo instruyó:

2«¿Qué pasa, hijo mío?
   ¿Qué pasa, hijo de mis entrañas?
   ¿Qué pasa, fruto de mis votosa al SEÑOR?
3No gastes tu vigor en las mujeres,

s **29:21** Texto de difícil traducción. t **29:24** bajo juramento. Alt. bajo maldición. u **30:1** hijo de Jaqué. Oráculo. Alt. hijo de Jaqué
de Masa. v **30:1** Cansado ... y débil. Alt. A Itiel, a Itiel y a Ucal. w **30:31** el gallo engreído. Lit. el apretado de hombros. x **30:31** el
rey ... ejército. Alt. el rey contra quien su pueblo no se subleva. y **30:32** ponte a pensar. Lit. mano a la boca. z **31:1** Lemuel. Oráculo
mediante el cual. Alt. Lemuel de Masa, mediante los cuales. a **31:2** fruto de mis votos. Alt. respuesta a mis oraciones.

ni tu fuerzab en las que arruinan a los
reyes.

4»No conviene que los reyes, oh Lemuel,
no conviene que los reyes se den al vino,
ni que los gobernantes se entreguen al
licor,
5no sea que al beber se olviden de lo que la *ley
ordena
y priven de sus derechos a todos los
oprimidos.
6Dales licor a los que están por morir,
y vino a los amargados;
7¡que beban y se olviden de su pobreza!
¡que no vuelvan a acordarse de sus penas!

8»¡Levanta la voz por los que no tienen voz!
¡Defiende los derechos de los desposeídos!
9¡Levanta la voz, y hazles *justicia!
¡Defiende a los pobres y necesitados!»

Epílogo: Acróstico a la mujer ejemplarc

Álef 10Mujer ejemplar,d ¿dónde se hallará?
¡Es más valiosa que las piedras
preciosas!

Bet 11Su esposo confía plenamente en ella
y no necesita de ganancias mal
habidas.

Guímel 12Ella le es fuente de bien, no de mal,
todos los días de su vida.

Dálet 13Anda en busca de lana y de lino,
y gustosa trabaja con sus manos.

He 14Es como los barcos mercantes,
que traen de muy lejos su
alimento.

Vav 15Se levanta de madrugada,
da de comere a su familia
y asigna tareas a sus criadas.

Zayin 16Calcula el valor de un campo y lo
compra;
con sus gananciasf planta un
viñedo.

Jet 17Decidida se ciñe la cinturag
y se apresta para el trabajo.

Tet 18Se complace en la prosperidad de sus
negocios,
y no se apaga su lámpara en la
noche.

Yod 19Con una mano sostiene el huso
y con la otra tuerce el hilo.

Caf 20Tiende la mano al pobre,
y con ella sostiene al necesitado.

Lámed 21Si nieva, no tiene que preocuparse de
su familia,
pues todos están bien abrigados.

Mem 22Las colchas las cose ella misma,
y se viste de púrpura y lino fino.

Nun 23Su esposo es respetado en la
comunidad;h
ocupa un puesto entre las
autoridades del lugar.

Sámej 24Confecciona ropa de lino y la vende;
provee cinturones a los
comerciantes.

Ayin 25Se reviste de fuerza y dignidad,
y afronta segura el porvenir.

Pe 26Cuando habla, lo hace con sabiduría;
cuando instruye, lo hace con amor.

Tsade 27Está atenta a la marcha de su hogar,
y el pan que come no es fruto del
ocio.

Qof 28Sus hijos se levantan y la felicitan;
también su esposo la alaba:

Resh 29«Muchas mujeres han realizado
proezas,
pero tú las superas a todas.»

Shin 30Engañoso es el encanto y pasajera la
belleza;
la mujer que teme al SEÑOR es
digna de alabanza.

Tav 31¡Sean reconocidosi sus logros,
y públicamentej alabadas sus
obras!

---

b **31:3** *tu fuerza*. Lit. *tus caminos*.   c **31:10** Los vv. 10-31 son un acróstico, en que cada verso comienza con una de las letras del alfabeto hebreo.   d **31:10** *ejemplar*. Alt. *fuerte*.   e **31:15** *da de comer*. Lit. *da presa*.   f **31:16** *sus ganancias*. Lit. *el fruto
de sus manos*.   g **31:17** *se ciñe la cintura*. Lit. *se ciñe con fuerza sus lomos*.   h **31:23** *en la comunidad*. Lit. *en las *puertas*.
i **31:31** *Sean reconocidos*. Alt. *Denle*.   j **31:31** *públicamente*. Lit. *en las puertas*.

ECLESIASTÉS

Discurso inicial

1 Éstas son las palabras del Maestro,[a] hijo de David, rey en Jerusalén.

[2] Lo más absurdo de lo absurdo,
—dice el Maestro—,
lo más absurdo de lo absurdo,
¡todo es un absurdo!

[3] ¿Qué provecho saca el hombre
de tanto afanarse en esta vida?

[4] Generación va, generación viene,
mas la tierra siempre es la misma.

[5] Sale el sol, se pone el sol,
y afanoso vuelve a su punto de origen
para de allí volver a salir.

[6] Dirigiéndose al sur,
o girando hacia el norte,
sin cesar va girando el viento
para de nuevo volver a girar.

[7] Todos los ríos van a dar al mar,
pero el mar jamás se sacia.
A su punto de origen vuelven los ríos,
para de allí volver a fluir.

[8] Todas las cosas hastían
más de lo que es posible expresar.
Ni se sacian los ojos de ver,
ni se hartan los oídos de oír.

[9] Lo que ya ha acontecido
volverá a acontecer;
lo que ya se ha hecho
se volverá a hacer
¡y no hay nada nuevo bajo el sol!

[10] Hay quien llega a decir:
«¡Mira que esto sí es una novedad!»
Pero eso ya existía desde siempre,
entre aquellos que nos precedieron.

[11] Nadie se acuerda de los hombres[b] primeros,
como nadie se acordará de los últimos.
¡No habrá memoria de ellos
entre los que habrán de sucedernos!

Primeras conclusiones

[12] Yo, el Maestro, reiné en Jerusalén sobre Israel. [13] Y me dediqué de lleno a explorar e investigar con sabiduría todo cuanto se hace bajo el cielo. ¡Penosa tarea ha impuesto Dios al *género humano para abrumarlo con ella! [14] Y he observado todo cuanto se hace en esta vida, y todo ello es absurdo, ¡es correr tras el viento!

[15] Ni se puede enderezar lo torcido,
ni se puede contar lo que falta.

[16] Me puse a reflexionar: «Aquí me tienen, engrandecido y con más sabiduría que todos mis antecesores en Jerusalén, y habiendo experimentado abundante sabiduría y conocimiento. [17] Me he dedicado de lleno a la comprensión de la sabiduría, y hasta conozco la *necedad y la insensatez. ¡Pero aun esto es querer alcanzar el viento! [18] Francamente,

»mientras más sabiduría, más problemas;
mientras más se sabe, más se sufre.»

2 Me dije entonces: «Vamos, pues, haré la prueba con los placeres y me daré la gran vida.» ¡Pero aun esto resultó un absurdo! [2] A la risa la considero una locura; en cuanto a los placeres, ¿para qué sirven? [3] Quise luego hacer la prueba de entregarme al vino —si bien mi *mente estaba bajo el control de la sabiduría—, y de aferrarme a la *necedad, hasta ver qué de bueno le encuentra el hombre a lo que hace bajo el cielo durante los contados días de su vida.

[4] Realicé grandes obras: me construí casas, me planté viñedos, [5] cultivé mis propios huertos y jardines, y en ellos planté toda clase de árboles frutales. [6] También me construí aljibes para irrigar los muchos árboles que allí crecían. [7] Me hice de esclavos y esclavas; y tuve criados, y mucho más ganado vacuno y lanar que todos los que me precedieron en Jerusalén. [8] Amontoné oro y plata, y tesoros que fueron de reyes y provincias. Me hice de cantores y cantoras, y disfruté de los deleites de los hombres: ¡formé mi propio harén![c]

[9] Me engrandecí en gran manera, más que todos los que me precedieron en Jerusalén; además, la sabiduría permanecía conmigo. [10] No le negué a mis ojos ningún deseo, ni a mi *corazón privé de placer alguno, sino que disfrutó de todos mis afanes. ¡Sólo eso saqué de tanto afanarme!

[11] Consideré luego todas mis obras y el trabajo que me había costado realizarlas, y vi que todo era absurdo, un correr tras el viento, y que ningún provecho se saca en esta vida.

Todos paran en lo mismo

[12] Consideré entonces la sabiduría, la *necedad y la insensatez —¿qué más puede hacer el sucesor del rey, aparte de lo ya hecho?—, [13] y pude observar que hay más provecho en la sabiduría que en la insensatez, así como hay más provecho en la luz que en las tinieblas.

[14] El sabio tiene los ojos bien puestos,
pero el necio anda a oscuras.

Pero también me di cuenta de que un mismo final les espera a todos. [15] Me dije entonces: «Si al fin voy a acabar igual que el necio, ¿de qué me sirve ser tan sabio?» Y concluí que también esto es absurdo, [16] pues nadie se acuerda jamás del sabio ni del necio; con el paso del tiempo todo cae en el olvido, y lo mismo mueren los sabios que los necios.

[17] Aborrecí entonces la vida, pues todo cuanto se hace en ella me resultaba repugnante. Realmente, todo es absurdo; ¡es correr tras el viento!

[18] Aborrecí también el haberme afanado tanto en esta vida, pues el fruto de tanto afán tendría que dejárselo a mi sucesor, [19] y ¿quién sabe si éste sería sabio o necio? Sin embargo, se adueñaría de lo que con tantos afanes y sabiduría logré hacer en esta vida. ¡Y también esto es absurdo!

[20] Volví a sentirme descorazonado de haberme afanado tanto en esta vida, [21] pues hay quienes ponen a trabajar su sabiduría y sus conocimientos y experiencia, para luego entregarle todos sus bienes a quien jamás movió un dedo. ¡Y también esto es absurdo, y un mal enorme! [22] Pues, ¿qué gana el *hombre con todos sus esfuerzos y con tanto preocuparse y afanarse bajo el sol? [23] Todos sus días están plagados de sufrimientos y tareas frustrantes, y ni siquiera de noche descansa su *mente. ¡Y también esto es absurdo!

---

a **1:1** *Maestro*. Alt. *Predicador*; así en el resto de este libro.   b **1:11** *hombres*. Alt. *tiempos*.   c **2:8** *¡formé mi propio harén!* Frase de difícil traducción.

²⁴Nada hay mejor para el hombre que comer y beber, y llegar a disfrutar de sus afanes. He visto que también esto proviene de Dios, ²⁵porque ¿quién puede comer y alegrarse, si no es por Dios?d ²⁶En realidad, Dios da sabiduría, conocimientos y alegría a quien es de su agrado; en cambio, al pecador le impone la tarea de acumular más y más, para luego dárselo todo a quien es de su agrado. Y también esto es absurdo; ¡es correr tras el viento!

Hay un tiempo para todo

3 Todo tiene su momento oportuno; hay un tiempo para todo lo que se hace bajo el cielo:

²un tiempo para nacer,
  y un tiempo para morir;
un tiempo para plantar,
  y un tiempo para cosechar;
³un tiempo para matar,
  y un tiempo para sanar;
un tiempo para destruir,
  y un tiempo para construir;
⁴un tiempo para llorar,
  y un tiempo para reír;
un tiempo para estar de luto,
  y un tiempo para saltar de gusto;
⁵un tiempo para esparcir piedras,
  y un tiempo para recogerlas;
un tiempo para abrazarse,
  y un tiempo para despedirse;
⁶un tiempo para intentar,
  y un tiempo para desistir;
un tiempo para guardar,
  y un tiempo para desechar;
⁷un tiempo para rasgar,
  y un tiempo para coser;
un tiempo para callar,
  y un tiempo para hablar;
⁸un tiempo para amar,
  y un tiempo para odiar;
un tiempo para la guerra,
  y un tiempo para la paz.

De nada sirve afanarse

⁹¿Qué provecho saca quien trabaja, de tanto afanarse? ¹⁰He visto la tarea que Dios ha impuesto al *género humano para abrumarlo con ella. ¹¹Dios hizo todo hermoso en su momento, y puso en la *mente humana el sentido del tiempo, aun cuando el *hombre no alcanza a comprender la obra que Dios realiza de principio a fin.

¹²Yo sé que nada hay mejor para el hombre que alegrarse y hacer el bien mientras viva; ¹³y sé también que es un don de Dios que el hombre coma o beba, y disfrute de todos sus afanes. ¹⁴Sé además que todo lo que Dios ha hecho permanece para siempre; que no hay nada que añadirle ni quitarle; y que Dios lo hizo así para que se le tema.

¹⁵Lo que ahora existe, ya existía,
  y lo que ha de existir, existe ya.
  Dios hace que la historia se repita.

Contradicciones de la vida

¹⁶He visto algo más en esta vida: maldad donde se dictan las sentencias, y maldad donde se imparte la justicia. ¹⁷Pensé entonces: «Al justo y al malvado los juzgará Dios, pues hay un tiempo para toda obra y un lugar para toda acción.»

¹⁸Pensé también con respecto a los *hombres: «Dios los está poniendo a prueba, para que ellos mismos se den cuenta de que son como los animales. ¹⁹Los hombres terminan igual que los animales; el destino de ambos es el mismo, pues unos y otros mueren por igual, y el aliento de vida es el mismo para todos, así que el hombre no es superior a los animales. Realmente, todo es absurdo, ²⁰y todo va hacia el mismo lugar.

»Todo surgió del polvo,
  y al polvo todo volverá.

²¹»¿Quién sabe si el espíritu del hombre se remonta a las alturas, y el de los animales desciendee a las profundidades de la tierra?» ²²He visto, pues, que nada hay mejor para el hombre que disfrutar de su trabajo, ya que eso le ha tocado. Pues, ¿quién lo traerá para que vea lo que sucederá después de él?

Opresores y oprimidos

4 Luego me fijé en tanta opresión que hay en esta vida. Vi llorar a los oprimidos, y no había quien los consolara; el poder estaba del lado de sus opresores, y no había quien los consolara. ²Y consideré más felices a los que ya han muerto que a los que aún viven, ³aunque en mejor situación están los que aún no han nacido, los que no han visto aún la maldad que se comete en esta vida.

⁴Vi además que tanto el afán como el éxito en la vida despiertan envidias. Y también esto es absurdo; ¡es correr tras el viento!

⁵El necio se cruza de brazos,
  y acaba muriéndose de hambre.
⁶Más vale poco con tranquilidad
  que muchof con fatiga …
  ¡corriendo tras el viento!

La unión hace la fuerza

⁷Me fijé entonces en otro absurdo en esta vida: ⁸vi a un hombre solitario, sin hijos ni hermanos, y que nunca dejaba de afanarse; ¡jamás le parecían demasiadas sus riquezas! «¿Para quién trabajo tanto, y me abstengo de las cosas buenas?», se preguntó. ¡También esto es absurdo, y una penosa tarea!

⁹Más valen dos que uno,
  porque obtienen más fruto de su esfuerzo.
¹⁰Si caen, el uno levanta al otro.
  ¡Ay del que cae
  y no tiene quien lo levante!
¹¹Si dos se acuestan juntos,
  entrarán en calor;
  uno solo ¿cómo va a calentarse?
¹²Uno solo puede ser vencido,
  pero dos pueden resistir.
  ¡La cuerda de tres hilos
  no se rompe fácilmente!

Juventud y sabiduría

¹³Más vale joven pobre pero sabio
  que rey viejo pero necio,
  que ya no sabe recibir consejos.

¹⁴Aunque de la cárcel haya ascendido al trono, o haya nacido pobre en ese reino, ¹⁵en esta vida he visto que la gente apoya al joven que sucede al rey. ¹⁶Y aunque es incontable la gente que sigue a los reyes,g muchos de los que vienen después tampoco quedan

---

d 2:25 por Dios (véanse mss. hebreos, LXX y Siríaca); por mí (TM).   e 3:21 sabe … desciende. Alt. conoce el espíritu del hombre, que se remonta a las alturas, o el de los animales, que desciende.   f 4:6 poco … mucho. Lit. un puñado … dos puñados.
g 4:16 los reyes. Lit. ellos.

contentos con el sucesor. Y también esto es absurdo; ¡es alcanzar el viento!

Hay que cumplir los votos

5 Cuando vayas a la casa de Dios, cuida tus pasos y acércate a escuchar en vez de ofrecer sacrificio de necios, que ni conciencia tienen de que hacen mal.

²No te apresures,
    ni con la boca ni con la *mente,
    a proferir ante Dios palabra alguna;
    él está en el cielo y tú estás en la tierra.
    Mide, pues, tus palabras.
³Quien mucho se preocupa tiene pesadillas,
    y quien mucho habla dice tonterías.

⁴Cuando hagas un voto a Dios, no tardes en cumplirlo, porque a Dios no le agradan los *necios. Cumple tus votos:

⁵Vale más no hacer votos
    que hacerlos y no cumplirlos.

⁶No permitas que tu boca te haga pecar, ni digas luego ante el mensajero de Diosʰ que lo hiciste sin querer. ¿Por qué ha de enojarse Dios por lo que dices, y destruir el fruto de tu trabajo? ⁷Más bien, entre tantos absurdos, pesadillas y palabrerías, muestra temor a Dios.

Futilidad de las riquezas

⁸Si en alguna provincia ves que se oprime al pobre, y que a la gente se le niega un juicio justo, no te asombres de tales cosas; porque a un alto oficial lo vigila otro más alto, y por encima de ellos hay otros altos oficiales. ⁹¿Qué provecho hay en todo esto para el país? ¿Está el rey al servicio del campo?ⁱ

¹⁰Quien ama el dinero, de dinero no se sacia. Quien ama las riquezas nunca tiene suficiente. ¡También esto es absurdo! ¹¹Donde abundan los bienes, sobra quien se los gaste; ¿y qué saca de esto su dueño, aparte de contemplarlos? ¹²El trabajador duerme tranquilo, coma mucho o coma poco. Al rico sus muchas riquezas no lo dejan dormir.

¹³He visto un mal terrible en esta vida: riquezas acumuladas que redundan en perjuicio de su dueño, ¹⁴y riquezas que se pierden en un mal negocio. Y si llega su dueño a tener un hijo, ya no tendrá nada que dejarle. ¹⁵Tal como salió del vientre de su madre, así se irá: desnudo como vino al mundo, y sin llevarse el fruto de tanto trabajo.

¹⁶Esto es un mal terrible: que tal como viene el hombre, así se va. ¿Y de qué le sirve afanarse tanto para nada? ¹⁷Además, toda su vida come en tinieblas, y en medio de muchas molestias, enfermedades y enojos.

¹⁸Esto es lo que he comprobado: que en esta vida lo mejor es comer y beber, y disfrutar del fruto de nuestros afanes. Es lo que Dios nos ha concedido; es lo que nos ha tocado. ¹⁹Además, a quien Dios le concede abundancia y riquezas, también le concede comer de ellas, y tomar su parte y disfrutar de sus afanes, pues esto es don de Dios. ²⁰Y como Dios le llena de alegría el *corazón, muy poco reflexiona el hombre en cuanto a su vida.

¿Qué sentido tiene la vida?

6 Hay un mal que he visto en esta vida y que abunda entre los *hombres: ²a algunos Dios les da abundancia, riquezas y honores, y no les falta

nada que pudieran desear, pero es a otros a quienes les concede disfrutar de todo ello. ¡Esto es absurdo, y un mal terrible!

³Si un hombre tiene cien hijos y vive muchos años, no importa cuánto viva, si no se ha saciado de las cosas buenas ni llega a recibir sepultura, yo digo que un abortivo vale más que él. ⁴Porque el abortivo vino de la nada, y a las tinieblas va, y en las tinieblas permanecerá anónimo. ⁵Nunca llegará a ver el sol, ni sabrá nada; sin embargo, habrá tenido más tranquilidad que el ⁶que pudo haber vivido dos mil años sin disfrutar jamás de lo bueno. ¿Y acaso no van todos a un mismo lugar? ⁷Mucho trabaja el hombre para comer, pero nunca se sacia. ⁸¿Qué ventaja tiene el sabio sobre el *necio? ¿Y qué gana el pobre con saber enfrentarse a la vida? ⁹Vale más lo visible que lo imaginario. Y también esto es absurdo; ¡es correr tras el viento!

¹⁰Lo que ahora existe ya ha recibido su
    *nombre,
    y se sabe lo que es: *humanidad.
Nadie puede luchar
    contra alguien más fuerte.
¹¹Aumentan las palabras,
    aumentan los absurdos.

¿Y qué se gana con eso? ¹²En realidad, ¿quién sabe qué le conviene al hombre en esta breve y absurda vida suya, por donde pasa como una sombra? ¿Y quién puede decirle lo que sucederá en esta vida después de su muerte?

Nueva escala de valores

7 Vale más el buen *nombre
    que el buen perfume.
Vale más el día en que se muere
    que el día en que se nace.
²Vale más ir a un funeral
    que a un festival.

Pues la muerte es el fin de todo *hombre, y los que viven debieran tenerlo presente.

³Vale más llorar que reír;
    pues entristece el rostro,
    pero le hace bien al *corazón.
⁴El sabio tiene presente la muerte;
    el *necio sólo piensa en la diversión.
⁵Vale más represión de sabios
    que lisonja de necios.

⁶Pues las carcajadas de los necios son como el crepitar de las espinas bajo la olla. ¡Y también esto es absurdo!

⁷La extorsión entorpece al sabio,
    y el soborno corrompe su corazón.
⁸Vale más el fin de algo
    que su principio.
Vale más la paciencia
    que la arrogancia.
⁹No te dejes llevar por el enojo
    que sólo abriga el corazón del necio.

¹⁰Nunca preguntes por qué todo tiempo pasado fue mejor. No es de sabios hacer tales preguntas.
¹¹Buena es la sabiduría sumada a la heredad, y provechosa para los que viven. ¹²Puedes ponerte a la sombra de la sabiduría o a la sombra del dinero, pero la sabiduría tiene la ventaja de dar vida a quien la posee.

ʰ **5:6** *mensajero de Dios.* Lit. *mensajero.*   ⁱ **5:9** Versículo de difícil traducción.

¹³Contempla las obras de Dios: ¿quién puede enderezar lo que él ha torcido? ¹⁴Cuando te vengan buenos tiempos, disfrútalos; pero cuando te lleguen los malos, piensa que unos y otros son obra de Dios, y que el hombre nunca sabe con qué habrá de encontrarse después.

¹⁵Todo esto he visto durante mi absurda vida: hombres justos a quienes su justicia los destruye, y hombres malvados a quienes su maldad les alarga la vida.

¹⁶No seas demasiado justo,
    ni tampoco demasiado sabio.
¿Para qué destruirte
    a ti mismo?

¹⁷No hay que pasarse de malo,
    ni portarse como un necio.
¿Para qué morir
    antes de tiempo?

¹⁸Conviene asirse bien de esto,
    sin soltar de la mano aquello.
Quien teme a Dios
    saldrá bien en todo.

¹⁹Más fortalece la sabiduría al sabio
    que diez gobernantes a una ciudad.
²⁰No hay en la tierra nadie tan justo
    que haga el bien y nunca peque.

²¹No prestes atención a lo que se dice, y así no oirás cuando tu siervo hable mal de ti, ²²aunque bien sabes que muchas veces también tú has hablado mal de otros.

Tras la razón de las cosas

²³Todo esto lo examiné muy bien y con sabiduría, pues me dispuse a ser sabio, pero la sabiduría estaba fuera de mi alcance. ²⁴Lejos y demasiado profundo está todo cuanto existe. ¿Quién puede dar con ello?

²⁵Volví entonces mi atención hacia el conocimiento, para investigar e indagar acerca de la sabiduría y la razón de las cosas, y me di cuenta de la insensatez de la maldad y la locura de la *necedad. ²⁶Y encontré algo más amargo que la muerte: a la mujer que es una trampa, que por *corazón tiene una red y por brazos tiene cadenas. Quien agrada a Dios se librará de ella, pero el pecador caerá en sus redes.

²⁷Y dijo el Maestro: «Miren lo que he hallado al buscar la razón de las cosas, una por una: ²⁸¡que todavía estoy buscando lo que no he encontrado! Ya he dado con un hombre entre mil, pero entre todas las mujeres aún no he encontrado ninguna. ²⁹Tan sólo he hallado lo siguiente: que Dios hizo perfecto al *género humano, pero éste se ha buscado demasiadas complicaciones.»

8 ¿Quién como el sabio? ¿Quién conoce las respuestas? La sabiduría del hombre hace que resplandezca su rostro y se ablanden sus facciones.

La obediencia al rey

²Yo digo: Obedece al rey, porque lo has jurado ante Dios. ³No te apresures a salir de su presencia. No defiendas una mala causa, porque lo que él quiere hacer, lo hace. ⁴Puesto que la palabra del rey tiene autoridad, ¿quién puede pedirle cuentas?

⁵El que acata sus órdenes no sufrirá daño alguno. El *corazón sabio sabe cuándo y cómo acatarlas.

⁶En realidad, para todo lo que se hace hay un cuándo y un cómo, aunque el *hombre tiene en su contra un gran problema: ⁷que no sabe lo que está por suceder, ni hay quien se lo pueda decir. ⁸No hay quien tenga poder sobre el aliento de vida, como para retenerlo, ni hay quien tenga poder sobre el día de su muerte. No hay licencias durante la batalla, ni la maldad deja libre al malvado.

Sinrazones de la vida

⁹Todo esto vi al dedicarme de lleno a conocer todo lo que se hace en esta vida: hay veces que el hombre domina sobre el hombre, para su mal. ¹⁰Vi también a los malvados ser sepultados —los que solían ir y venir del lugar santo—; a ellos se les echó al olvido en la ciudad donde así se condujeron.ʲ ¡Y también esto es absurdo! ¹¹Cuando no se ejecuta rápidamente la sentencia de un delito, el *corazón del pueblo se llena de razones para hacer lo malo.

¹²El pecador puede hacer lo malo cien veces, y vivir muchos años; pero sé también que le irá mejor a quien teme a Dios y le guarda reverencia. ¹³En cambio, a los malvados no les irá bien ni vivirán mucho tiempo. Serán como una sombra, porque no temen a Dios.

¹⁴En la tierra suceden cosas absurdas, pues hay hombres justos a quienes les va como si fueran malvados, y hay malvados a quienes les va como si fueran justos. ¡Y yo digo que también esto es absurdo!

¹⁵Por tanto, celebro la alegría, pues no hay para el hombre nada mejor en esta vida que comer, beber y divertirse, pues sólo eso le queda de tanto afanarse en esta vida que Dios le ha dado.

¹⁶Al dedicarme al *conocimiento de la sabiduría y a la observación de todo cuanto se hace en la tierra, sin que pudiera conciliar el sueño ni de día ni de noche, ¹⁷pude ver todo lo hecho por Dios. ¡El hombre no puede comprender todo lo que Dios ha hecho en esta vida! Por más que se esfuerce por hallarle sentido, no lo encontrará; aun cuando el sabio diga conocerlo, no lo puede comprender.

Un destino común

9 A todo esto me dediqué de lleno, y en todo esto comprobé que los justos y los sabios, y sus obras, están en las manos de Dios; que el hombre nada sabe del amor ni del odio, aunque los tenga ante sus ojos. ²Para todos hay un mismo final:

    para el justo y el injusto,
    para el bueno y el malo,
    para el puro y el impuro,
    para el que ofrece sacrificios
        y para el que no los ofrece;
    para el bueno y para el pecador,
    para el que hace juramentos
        y para el que no los hace.

³Hay un mal en todo lo que se hace en esta vida: que todos tienen un mismo final. Además, el *corazón del *hombre rebosa de maldad; la locura está en su corazón toda su vida, y su fin está entre los muertos. ⁴¿Por quién, pues, decidirse? Entre todos los vivos hay esperanza, pues

    vale más perro vivo
        que león muerto.

⁵Porque los vivos saben que han de morir, pero los muertos no saben nada ni esperan nada, pues su memoria cae en el olvido. ⁶Sus amores, odios y pasiones

---

ʲ **8:10** *a ellos … se condujeron.* Frase de difícil traducción.

llegan a su fin, y nunca más vuelven a tener parte en nada de lo que se hace en esta vida.

7¡Anda, come tu pan con alegría! ¡Bebe tu vino con buen ánimo, que Dios ya se ha agradado de tus obras! 8Que sean siempre blancos tus vestidos, y que no falte nunca el perfume en tus cabellos. 9Goza de la vida con la mujer amada cada día de la fugaz existencia que Dios te ha dado en este mundo. ¡Cada uno de tus absurdos días! Esto es lo que te ha tocado de todos tus afanes en este mundo. 10Y todo lo que te venga a la mano, hazlo con todo empeño; porque en el *sepulcro, adonde te diriges, no hay trabajo ni planes ni conocimiento ni sabiduría.

Más vale maña que fuerza

11Me fijé que en esta vida la carrera no la ganan los más veloces, ni ganan la batalla los más valientes; que tampoco los sabios tienen qué comer, ni los inteligentes abundan en dinero, ni los instruidos gozan de simpatía, sino que a todos les llegan buenos y malos tiempos.

12Vi además que nadie sabe cuándo le llegará su hora. Así como los peces caen en la red maligna y las aves caen en la trampa, también los *hombres se ven atrapados por una desgracia que de pronto les sobreviene.

13También vi en este mundo un notable caso de sabiduría: 14una ciudad pequeña, con pocos habitantes, contra la cual se dirigió un rey poderoso que la sitió, y construyó a su alrededor una impresionante maquinaria de asalto. 15En esa ciudad había un hombre, pobre pero sabio, que con su sabiduría podría haber salvado a la ciudad, ¡pero nadie se acordó de aquel hombre pobre!

16Yo digo que «más vale maña que fuerza», aun cuando se menosprecie la sabiduría del pobre y no se preste atención a sus palabras.

17Más se atiende a las palabras tranquilas de los sabios
que a los gritos del jefe de los necios.
18Vale más la sabiduría
que las armas de guerra.
Un solo error
acaba con muchos bienes.

Dichos de sabiduría

10 Las moscas muertas apestan
y echan a perder el perfume.
Pesa más una pequeña *necedad
que la sabiduría y la honra juntas.
2El *corazón del sabio busca el bien,
pero el del necio busca el mal.

3Y aun en el camino por el que va, el necio revela su falta de inteligencia y a todos va diciendo lo necio que es.

4Si el ánimo del gobernante se exalta contra ti, no abandones tu puesto. La paciencia es el remedio para los grandes errores.

5Hay un mal que he visto en esta vida, semejante al error que cometen los gobernantes: 6al necio se le dan muchos puestos elevados, pero a los capaces se les dan los puestos más bajos. 7He visto esclavos montar a caballo, y príncipes andar a pie como esclavos.

8El que cava la fosa,
en ella se cae.
Al que abre brecha en el muro,
la serpiente lo muerde.

9El que pica piedra,
con las piedras se hiere.

El que corta leña,
con los leños se lastima.

10Si el hacha pierde su filo,
y no se vuelve a afilar,
hay que golpear con más fuerza.
El éxito radica en la acción
sabia y bien ejecutada.

11Si la serpiente muerde antes de ser
encantada,
no hay ganancia para el encantador.

12Las palabras del sabio son placenteras,
pero los labios del necio son su ruina;
13sus primeras palabras son necedades,
y las últimas son terribles sandeces.
14¡Pero no le faltan las palabras!

Nadie sabe lo que ha de suceder,
y lo que será aun después,
¿quién podría decirlo?

15El trabajo del necio tanto lo fatiga
que ni el camino a la ciudad conoce.

16¡Ay del país cuyo rey es un inmaduro,
y cuyos príncipes banquetean desde
temprano!

17*¡Dichoso el país cuyo rey es un noble,
y cuyos príncipes comen cuando es debido,
para reponerse y no para embriagarse!

18Por causa del ocio se viene abajo el techo,
y por la pereza se desploma la casa.

19Para alegrarse, el pan;
para gozar, el vino;
para disfrutarlo, el dinero.

20No maldigas al rey ni con el pensamiento,
ni en privado maldigas al rico,
pues las aves del cielo pueden correr la voz.
Tienen alas y pueden divulgarlo.

11 Lanza tu pan sobre el agua;
después de algún tiempo volverás a
encontrarlo.

2Comparte lo que tienes entre siete,
y aun entre ocho,
pues no sabes qué calamidad
pueda venir sobre la tierra.

3Cuando las nubes están cargadas,
derraman su lluvia sobre la tierra.

Si el árbol cae hacia el sur,
o cae hacia el norte,
donde cae allí se queda.

4Quien vigila al viento, no siembra;
quien contempla las nubes, no cosecha.

5Así como no sabes por dónde va el viento ni cómo se forma el niño en el vientre de la madre, tampoco entiendes la obra de Dios, creador de todas las cosas.

6Siembra tu semilla en la mañana, y no te des reposo por la tarde, pues nunca sabes cuál siembra saldrá mejor, si ésta o aquélla, o si ambas serán igual de buenas.

7Grata es la luz, y qué bueno que los ojos disfruten del sol. 8Mas si el hombre vive muchos años, y todos ellos los disfruta, debe recordar que los días tenebrosos serán muchos y que lo venidero será un absurdo.

Acuérdate de tu Creador

9Alégrate, joven, en tu juventud; deja que tu *corazón disfrute de la adolescencia. Sigue los impulsos de tu corazón y responde al estímulo de tus ojos, pero toma en cuenta que Dios te juzgará por todo esto. **10**Aleja de tu corazón el enojo, y echa fuera de tu ser la maldad, porque confiar en la juventud y en la flor de la vida es un absurdo.

12 Acuérdate de tu Creador
en los días de tu juventud,
antes que lleguen los días malos
y vengan los años en que digas:
«No encuentro en ellos placer alguno»;
2antes que dejen de brillar
el sol y la luz,
la luna y las estrellas,
y vuelvan las nubes después de la lluvia.
3Un día temblarán los guardianes de la casa,
y se encorvarán los hombres de batalla;
se detendrán las molenderas por ser tan
pocas,
y se apagarán los que miran a través de las
ventanas.
4Se irán cerrando las puertas de la calle,
irá disminuyendo el ruido del molino,
las aves elevarán su canto,
pero apagados se oirán sus trinos.
5Sobrevendrá el temor por las alturas
y por los peligros del camino.
Florecerá el almendro,
la langosta resultará onerosa,
y no servirá de nada la alcaparra,
pues el hombre se encamina al hogar eterno

y rondan ya en la calle los que lloran su
muerte.

6Acuérdate de tu Creador
antes que se rompa el cordón de plata
y se quiebre la vasija de oro,
y se estrelle el cántaro contra la fuente
y se haga pedazos la polea del pozo.
7Volverá entonces el polvo a la tierra,
como antes fue,
y el espíritu volverá a Dios,
que es quien lo dio.

8Lo más absurdo de lo absurdo,
¡todo es un absurdo!
—ha dicho el Maestro.

Epílogo

9Además de ser sabio, el Maestro impartió conocimientos a la gente. Ponderó, investigó y ordenó muchísimos proverbios. **10**Procuró también hallar las palabras más adecuadas y escribirlas con honradez y veracidad.

11Las palabras de los sabios son como aguijones. Como clavos bien puestos son sus colecciones de dichos, dados por un solo pastor. **12**Además de ellas, hijo mío, ten presente que el hacer muchos libros es algo interminable y que el mucho leer causa fatiga. **13**El fin de este asunto es que ya se ha escuchado todo. Teme, pues, a Dios y cumple sus mandamientos, porque esto es todo para el hombre. **14**Pues Dios juzgará toda obra, buena o mala, aun la realizada en secreto.

CANTAR DE CANTARES

1 Cantar de los cantaresª de Salomón.

Primer Canto

La amada

²Ah, si me besaras con los besos de tu bocaᵇ...
¡grato en verdad es tu amor, más que el
vino!
³Grata es también, de tus perfumes, la
fragancia;
tú mismo eresᶜ bálsamo fragante.
¡Con razón te aman las doncellas!
⁴¡Hazme del todo tuya!ᵈ ¡Date prisa!
¡Llévame, oh rey, a tu alcoba!

Los amigos

Regocijémonos y deleitémonos juntos,
celebraremos tus caricias más que el vino.
¡Sobran las razones para amarte!

La amada

⁵Morena soy, pero hermosa,
hijas de Jerusalén;
morena como las carpas de Cedar,
hermosa como los pabellones de Salmá.ᵉ
⁶No se fijen en mi tez morena,
ni en que el sol me bronceó la piel.
Mis hermanos se enfadaron contra mí,
y me obligaron a cuidar las viñas;
¡y mi propia viña descuidé!
⁷Cuéntame, amor de mi *vida,
¿dónde apacientas tus rebaños?,
¿dónde a la hora de la siestaᶠ los haces
reposar?
¿Por qué he de andar vagandoᵍ
entre los rebaños de tus amigos?

Los amigos

⁸Si no lo sabes, bella entre las bellas,
ve tras la huella del rebaño
y apacienta a tus cabritos
junto a las moradas de los pastores.

El amado

⁹Tú y tus adornos, amada mía,
me recuerdan a las yeguas enjaezadas
de los carros del faraón.
¹⁰¡Qué hermosas lucen tus mejillas entre los
pendientes!
¡Qué hermoso luce tu cuello entre los
collares!
¹¹¡Haremos para ti pendientes de oro
con incrustaciones de plata!

La amada

¹²Mientras el rey se halla sentado a la mesa,
mi perfume esparce su fragancia.
¹³Mi amado es para mí como el saquito de
mirra
que duerme entre mis pechos.
¹⁴Mi amado es para mí como un ramito de
azaharʰ
de las viñas de Engadi.

El amado

¹⁵¡Cuán bella eres, amada mía!
¡Cuán bella eres!
¡Tus ojos son dos palomas!

La amada

¹⁶¡Cuán hermoso eres, amado mío!
¡Eres un encanto!

El amado

Una alfombra de verdor es nuestro lecho,
¹⁷los cedros son las vigas de la casa
y nos cubre un techo de cipreses.

La amada

2 Yo soy una rosa de Sarón,
una azucena de los valles.

El amado

²Como azucena entre las espinas
es mi amada entre las mujeres.

La amada

³Cual manzano entre los árboles del bosque
es mi amado entre los hombres.
Me encanta sentarme a su sombra;
dulce a mi paladar es su fruto.
⁴Me llevó a la sala del banquete,
y sobre mí enarboló su bandera de amor.
⁵¡Fortalézcanme con pasas,
susténtenme con manzanas,
porque desfallezco de amor!
⁶¡Ojalá pudiera mi cabeza
reposar sobre su izquierda!
¡Ojalá su derecha me abrazara!

El amado

⁷Yo les ruego, mujeres de Jerusalén,
por las gacelas y cervatillas del bosque,
que no desvelen ni molesten a mi amada
hasta que ella quiera despertar.

Segundo Canto

La amada

⁸¡La voz de mi amado!
¡Mírenlo, aquí viene!,
saltando por las colinas,
brincando por las montañas.
⁹Mi amado es como un venado;
se parece a un cervatillo.
¡Mírenlo, de pie tras nuestro muro,
espiando por las ventanas,
atisbando por las celosías!

¹⁰Mi amado me habló y me dijo:
«¡Levántate, amada mía;
ven conmigo, mujer hermosa!
¹¹¡Mira, el invierno se ha ido,
y con él han cesado y se han ido las lluvias!
¹²Ya brotan flores en los campos;
¡el tiempo de la canción ha llegado!
Ya se escucha por toda nuestra tierra
el arrullo de las tórtolas.
¹³La higuera ofrece ya sus primeros frutos,
y las viñas en ciernes esparcen su fragancia.
¡Levántate, amada mía;
ven conmigo, mujer hermosa!»

---

a **1:1** *Cantar de los cantares.* Alt. *El más bello cantar.* b **1:2** *si me besaras ... tu boca.* Lit. *béseme él con los besos de su boca.*
c **1:3** *tú mismo eres.* Lit. *tu *nombre es.* d **1:4** *Hazme del todo tuya.* Lit. *Arrástrame tras de ti.* e **1:5** *Salmá.* Alt. *Salomón.*
f **1:7** *a la hora de la siesta.* Lit. *al mediodía.* g **1:7** *vagando* (véanse Siríaca, Targum y Vulgata); *como una mujer cubierta con un velo* (TM). h **1:14** *azahar.* Lit. *alheña.*

El amado

14Paloma mía, que te escondes
en las grietas de las rocas,
en las hendiduras de las montañas,
muéstrame tu rostro,
déjame oír tu voz;
pues tu voz es placentera
y hermoso tu semblante.

El amado y la amada

15Atrapen a las zorras,
a esas zorras pequeñas
que arruinan nuestros viñedos,
nuestros viñedos en flor.

La amada

16Mi amado es mío, y yo soy suya;
él apacienta su rebaño entre azucenas.
17Antes de que el día despunte
y se desvanezcan las sombras,
regresa a mí, amado mío.
Corre como un venado,
como un cervatillo
por colinas escarpadas.i

3 Por las noches, sobre mi lecho,
busco al amor de mi *vida;
lo busco y no lo hallo.
2Me levanto, y voy por la ciudad,
por sus calles y mercados,
buscando al amor de mi vida.
¡Lo busco y no lo hallo!

3Me encuentran los centinelas
mientras rondan la ciudad.
Les pregunto:
«¿Han visto ustedes al amor de mi vida?»
4No bien los he dejado,
cuando encuentro al amor de mi vida.
Lo abrazo y, sin soltarlo,
lo llevo a la casa de mi madre,
a la alcoba donde ella me concibió.

El amado

5Yo les ruego, mujeres de Jerusalén,
por las gacelas y cervatillas del bosque,
que no desvelen ni molesten a mi amada
hasta que ella quiera despertar.

Tercer Canto

El coro

6¿Qué es eso que sube por el desierto
semejante a una columna de humo,
entre aromas de mirra e incienso,
entre exóticos perfumes?j
7¡Miren!
¡Es el carruaje de Salomón!
Viene escoltado por sesenta guerreros,
escogidos entre los más valientes de Israel.
8Todos ellos portan espadas,
y han sido adiestrados para el combate;
cada uno lleva la espada al cinto
por causa de los peligros de la noche.
9Salomón mismo se hizo el carruaje
con finas maderas del Líbano.
10Hizo de plata las columnas,
y de oro los soportes.
El asiento lo tapizó de púrpura,
y su interior fue decorado con esmero

por las hijas de Jerusalén.

11¡Salgan, mujeres de *Sión!
¡Contemplen al rey Salomón!
¡Lleva puesta la corona que le ciñó su madre
el día en que contrajo nupcias,
el día en que se alegró su *corazón!

El amado

4 ¡Cuán bella eres, amada mía!
¡Cuán bella eres!
Tus ojos, tras el velo, son dos palomas.
Tus cabellos son como los rebaños de cabras
que retozan en los montes de Galaad.
2Tus dientes son como ovejas recién
trasquiladas,
que ascienden luego de haber sido
bañadas.
Cada una de ellas tiene su pareja;
ninguna de ellas está sola.
3Tus labios son cual cinta escarlata;
tus palabras me tienen hechizado.
Tus mejillas, tras el velo,
parecen dos mitades de granadas.
4Tu cuello se asemeja a la torre de David,
construida con piedras labradas;
de ella penden mil escudos,
escudos de guerreros todos ellos.
5Tus pechos parecen dos cervatillos,
dos crías mellizas de gacela
que pastan entre azucenas.
6Antes de que el día despunte
y se desvanezcan las sombras,
subiré a la montaña de la mirra,
a la colina del incienso.

7Toda tú eres bella, amada mía;
no hay en ti defecto alguno.
8Desciende del Líbano conmigo, novia mía;
desciende del Líbano conmigo.
Baja de la cumbre del Amaná,
de la cima del Senir y del Hermón.
Baja de las guaridas de los leones,
de los montes donde habitan los leopardos.

9Cautivaste mi *corazón,
hermana y novia mía,
con una mirada de tus ojos;
con una vuelta de tu collar
cautivaste mi corazón.
10¡Cuán delicioso es tu amor,
hermana y novia mía!
¡Más agradable que el vino es tu amor,
y más que toda especia
la fragancia de tu perfume!
11Tus labios, novia mía, destilan miel;
leche y miel escondes bajo la lengua.
Cual fragancia del Líbano
es la fragancia de tus vestidos.

12Jardín cerrado eres tú,
hermana y novia mía;
¡jardín cerrado, sellado manantial!
13Tus pechosk son un huerto de granadas
con frutos exquisitos,
con flores de nardo y azahar;
14con toda clase de árbol resinoso,l
con nardo y azafrán,
con cálamo y canela,

---

i 2:17 *por colinas escarpadas.* Alt. *por las colinas de Beter.* j 3:6 *exóticos perfumes.* Lit. *perfumes de mercaderes.* k 4:13 *Tus pechos.* Lit. *Tus brotes.* l 4:14 *resinoso.* Lit. *de incienso.*

con mirra y áloe,
y con las más finas especias.
15Eres fuente de los jardines,
manantial de aguas vivas,
¡arroyo que del Líbano desciende!

La amada

16¡Viento del norte, despierta!
¡Viento del sur, ven acá!
Soplen en mi jardín;
¡esparzan su fragancia!
Que venga mi amado a su jardín
y pruebe sus frutos exquisitos.

El amado

5 He entrado ya en mi jardín,
hermana y novia mía,
y en él recojo mirra y bálsamo;
allí me sacio del panal y de su miel.
Allí me embriago de vino y leche;
¡todo esto me pertenece!

Los amigos

¡Coman y beban, amigos,
y embriáguense de amor!

Cuarto Canto

La amada

2Yo dormía, pero mi *corazón velaba.
¡Y oí una voz!
¡Mi amado estaba a la puerta!

«Hermana, amada mía;
preciosa paloma mía,
¡déjame entrar!
Mi cabeza está empapada de rocío;
la humedad de la noche corre por mi pelo.»

3Ya me he quitado la ropa;
¡cómo volver a vestirme!
Ya me he lavado los pies;
¡cómo ensuciarlos de nuevo!

4Mi amado pasó la mano
por la abertura del cerrojo;
¡se estremecieron mis entrañas al sentirlo!
5Me levanté y le abrí a mi amado;
¡gotas de mirra corrían por mis manos!
¡Se deslizaban entre mis dedos
y caían sobre la aldaba!

6Le abrí a mi amado,
pero ya no estaba allí.
Se había marchado,
y tras su voz se fue mi *alma.
Lo busqué, y no lo hallé.
Lo llamé, y no me respondió.
7Me encontraron los centinelas
mientras rondaban la ciudad;
los que vigilan las murallas
me hirieron, me golpearon;
¡me despojaron de mi manto!

8Yo les ruego, mujeres de Jerusalén,
que si encuentran a mi amado,
¡le digan que estoy enferma de amor!

El coro

9Dinos, bella entre las bellas,
¿en qué aventaja tu amado a otros
hombres?
¿En qué aventaja tu amado a otros hombres,
que nos haces tales ruegos?

La amada

10Mi amado es apuesto y trigueño,
y entre diez mil hombres se le distingue.
11Su cabeza es oro puro;
su cabellera es ondulada
y negra como un cuervo.
12Sus ojos parecen palomas
posadas junto a los arroyos,
bañadas en leche,
montadas como joyas.
13Sus mejillas son como lechos de bálsamo,
como cultivos de aromáticas hierbas.
Sus labios son azucenas
por las que fluye mirra.
14Sus brazos son barras de oro
montadas sobre topacios.
Su cuerpo es pulido marfil
incrustado de zafiros.
15Sus piernas son pilares de mármol
que descansan sobre bases de oro puro.
Su porte es como el del Líbano,
esbelto como sus cedros.
16Su paladar es la dulzura misma;
¡él es todo un encanto!

¡Tal es mi amado, tal es mi amigo,
mujeres de Jerusalén!

El coro

6 ¿A dónde se ha ido tu amado,
tú, bella entre las bellas?
¿Hacia dónde se ha encaminado?
¡Iremos contigo a buscarlo!

La amada

2Mi amado ha bajado a su jardín,
a los lechos de bálsamo,
para retozar en los jardines
y recoger azucenas.
3Yo soy de mi amado, y mi amado es mío;
él apacienta su rebaño entre azucenas.

Quinto Canto

El amado

4Tú, amada mía, eres bella como Tirsá,
encantadora como Jerusalén,
majestuosa como las estrellas del cielo.
5Aparta de mí la mirada,
que tus ojos me tienen fascinado.
Tus cabellos son como los rebaños de cabras
que retozan en Galaad.
6Tus dientes son como rebaños de cabritas
recién salidas del baño.
Cada una de ellas tiene su pareja,
ninguna de ellas marcha sola.
7Tus mejillas, tras el velo,
parecen dos mitades de granadas.
8Pueden ser sesenta las reinas,
ochenta las concubinas
e innumerables las vírgenes,
9pero una sola es mi palomita preciosa,
la hija consentida de su madre,
la favorita de quien le dio la vida.
Las mujeres la ven y la bendicen;
las reinas y las concubinas la alaban.

El coro

10¿Quién es ésta, admirable como la aurora?
¡Es bella como la luna,
radiante como el sol,
majestuosa como las estrellas del cielo!

El amado

11Descendí al huerto de los nogales
  para admirar los nuevos brotes en el valle,
para admirar los retoños de las vides
  y los granados en flor.
12Sin darme cuenta, mi pasión me puso
  entre las carrozas reales de mi pueblo.m

Los amigos

13Vuelve, Sulamita, vuelve;
  vuélvete a nosotros,
  ¡queremos contemplarte!

El amado

¿Y por qué han de contemplar a la Sulamita,
  como en las danzas de los campamentos?

7 ¡Ah, princesa mía,
  cuán bellos son tus pies en las sandalias!
Las curvas de tus caderas son como alhajas
  labradas por hábil artesano.
2Tu ombligo es una copa redonda,
  rebosante de buen vino.
Tu vientre es un monte de trigo
  rodeado de azucenas.
3Tus pechos parecen dos cervatillos,
  dos crías mellizas de gacela.
4Tu cuello parece torre de marfil.
Tus ojos son los manantiales de Hesbón,
  junto a la entrada de Bat Rabín.
Tu nariz se asemeja a la torre del Líbano,
  que mira hacia Damasco.
5Tu cabeza se yergue como la cumbre del
  Carmelo.
Hilos de púrpura son tus cabellos;
  ¡con tus rizos has cautivado al rey!

6¡Cuán bella eres, amor mío,
  ¡cuán encantadora en tus delicias!
7Tu talle se asemeja al talle de la palmera,
  y tus pechos a sus racimos.
8Me dije: «Me treparé a la palmera;
  de sus racimos me adueñaré.»
¡Sean tus pechos como racimos de uvas,
  tu aliento cual fragancia de manzanas,
9y como el buen vino tu boca!

La amada

¡Corra el vino hacia mi amado,
  y le resbale por labios y dientes!n

10Yo soy de mi amado,
  y él me busca con pasión.
11Ven, amado mío,
  vayamos a los campos,
  pasemos la noche entre los azahares.
12Vayamos temprano a los viñedos,
  para ver si han retoñado las vides,
si sus pimpollos se han abierto,
  y si ya florecen los granados.
¡Allí te brindaré mis caricias!

13Las mandrágoras esparcen su fragancia,
  y hay a nuestras puertas
toda clase de exquisitos frutos,
lo mismo nuevos que añejos,
  que he guardado para ti, amor mío.

8 ¡Ah, si fueras mi propio hermano,
  criado a los pechos de mi madre!

Al encontrarte en la calle podría besarte,
  y nadie me juzgaría mal.
2Tomándote de la mano,
  te llevaría a la casa de mi madre,
  y me enseñarías el arte del amor.
Te daría a beber vino con especias,
  y el néctar de mis granadas.

3¡Ojalá pudiera mi cabeza
  reposar sobre su izquierda!
¡Ojalá su derecha me abrazara!

El amado

4Yo les ruego, mujeres de Jerusalén,
  que no desvelen ni molesten a mi amada,
  hasta que ella quiera despertar.

Sexto Canto

El coro

5¿Quién es ésta que sube por el desierto
  apoyada sobre el hombro de su amado?

El amado

Bajo el manzano te desperté;
  allí te concibió tu madre,
  allí mismo te dio a luz.

La amada

6Grábame como un sello sobre tu *corazón;
  llévame como una marca sobre tu brazo.
Fuerte es el amor, como la muerte,
  y tenaz la pasión, como el *sepulcro.
Como llama divina
  es el fuego ardiente del amor.
7Ni las muchas aguas pueden apagarlo,
  ni los ríos pueden extinguirlo.
Si alguien ofreciera todas sus riquezas
  a cambio del amor,
  sólo conseguiría el desprecio.

El coro

8Tan pequeña es nuestra hermana
  que no le han crecido los pechos.
¿Qué haremos por nuestra hermana
  cuando vengan a pedirla?
9Si fuera una muralla,
  construiríamos sobre ella almenas de plata.
Si acaso fuera una puerta,
  la recubriríamos con paneles de cedro.

La amada

10Una muralla soy yo,
  y mis pechos, sus dos torres.
Por eso a los ojos de mi amado
  soy como quien ha hallado la paz.

11Salomón tenía una viña en Baal Jamón,
  que dejó al cuidado de aparceros.
Cada uno entregaba, por sus frutos,
  mil monedasñ de plata.
12¡Quédate, Salomón, con las mil monedas,
  y ustedes, aparceros, con doscientas,
  pero mi viña sólo a mí me pertenece!

El amado

13Tú, que reinas en los jardines,
  pendientes de tu voz están nuestros
    amigos;
  ¡déjanos escucharla!

---

m 6:12 *entre ... mi pueblo.* Alt. *entre los carros de Aminadab.* n 7:9 *labios y dientes* (LXX y Aquila; véanse Siríaca y Vulgata);
labios de dormilones (TM). ñ 8:11 *mil monedas de plata.* Lit. *mil* {*siclos*} *de plata.*

La amada

14¡Apresúrate, amado mío!

¡Corre como venado, como cervato,
sobre los montes de bálsamo cubiertos!

ISAÍAS

1 Visión que recibió Isaías hijo de Amoz acerca de Judá y Jerusalén, durante los reinados de Uzías, Jotán, Acaz y Ezequías, reyes de Judá.

Judá, nación rebelde

2¡Oigan, cielos! ¡Escucha, tierra!
    Así dice el SEÑOR:
    «Yo crié hijos hasta hacerlos *hombres,
    pero ellos se rebelaron contra mí.
3El buey conoce a su dueño
    y el asno el pesebre de su amo;
    ¡pero Israel no conoce,
    mi pueblo no entiende!»

4¡Ay, nación pecadora,
    pueblo cargado de culpa,
    generación de malhechores,
    hijos corruptos!
    ¡Han abandonado al SEÑOR!
    ¡Han despreciado al *Santo de Israel!
    ¡Se han vuelto atrás!

5¿Para qué recibir más golpes?
    ¿Para qué insistir en la rebelión?
    Toda su cabeza está herida,
    todo su corazón está enfermo.
6Desde la planta del pie hasta la coronilla
    no les queda nada sano:
    todo en ellos es heridas, moretones,
    y llagas abiertas,
    que no les han sido curadas ni vendadas,
    ni aliviadas con aceite.

7Su país está desolado,
    sus ciudades son presa del fuego;
    ante sus propios ojos
    los extraños devoran sus campos;
    su país está desolado,
    como si hubiera sido destruido por
        extranjeros.
8La bella *Sión ha quedado
    como cobertizo en un viñedo,
    como choza en un melonar,
    como ciudad sitiada.
9Si el SEÑOR *Todopoderoso
    no nos hubiera dejado algunos
        sobrevivientes,
    seríamos ya como Sodoma,
    nos pareceríamos a Gomorra.

10¡Oigan la palabra del SEÑOR,
    gobernantes de Sodoma!
    ¡Escuchen la *enseñanza de nuestro Dios,
    pueblo de Gomorra!
11«¿De qué me sirven sus muchos sacrificios?
    —dice el SEÑOR—.
    Harto estoy de *holocaustos de carneros
    y de la grasa de animales engordados;
    la sangre de toros, corderos y cabras
    no me complace.
12¿Por qué vienen a presentarse ante mí?
    ¿Quién les mandó traer animales
    para que pisotearan mis atrios?
13No me sigan trayendo vanas ofrendas;
    el incienso es para mí una abominación.
    Luna nueva, día de reposo, asambleas
        convocadas,
    ¡no soporto que con su adoración me
        ofendan!
14Yo aborrezco sus lunas nuevas y festividades;
    se me han vuelto una carga

que estoy cansado de soportar.
15Cuando levantan sus manos,
    yo aparto de ustedes mis ojos;
    aunque multipliquen sus oraciones,
    no las escucharé,
    pues tienen las manos llenas de sangre.
16¡Lávense, límpiense!
    ¡Aparten de mi vista sus obras malvadas!
    ¡Dejen de hacer el mal!
    17¡Aprendan a hacer el bien!
    ¡Busquen la justicia y reprendan al opresor!
    ¡Aboguen por el huérfano y defiendan a la
        viuda!

18»Vengan, pongamos las cosas en claro
    —dice el SEÑOR—.
    ¿Son sus pecados como escarlata?
    ¡Quedarán blancos como la nieve!
    ¿Son rojos como la púrpura?
    ¡Quedarán como la lana!
19¿Están ustedes dispuestos a obedecer?
    ¡Comerán lo mejor de la tierra!
20¿Se niegan y se rebelan?
    ¡Serán devorados por la espada!»
        El SEÑOR mismo lo ha dicho.

21¡Cómo se ha prostituido la ciudad fiel!
    Antes estaba llena de justicia.
    La rectitud moraba en ella,
    pero ahora sólo quedan asesinos.
22Tu plata se ha convertido en escoria;
    tu buen vino, en agua.
23Tus gobernantes son rebeldes,
    cómplices de ladrones;
    todos aman el soborno
    y van detrás de las prebendas.
    No abogan por el huérfano,
    ni se ocupan de la causa de la viuda.

24Por eso afirma el Señor,
    el SEÑOR Todopoderoso,
        el Fuerte de Israel:
    «Me desquitaré de mis adversarios,
    me vengaré de mis enemigos.
25Volveré mi mano contra ti,
    limpiaré tus escorias con lejía
    y quitaré todas tus *impurezas.
26Restauraré a tus jueces como al principio,
    y a tus consejeros como al comienzo.
    Entonces serás llamada "Ciudad de justicia",
    "Ciudad fiel".»

27Sión será redimida con justicia,
    y con rectitud, los que se *arrepientan.
28Pero los rebeldes y pecadores a una serán
        quebrantados,
    y perecerán los que abandonan al SEÑOR.
29Se avergonzarán de las encinas que ustedes
        tanto aman;
    los jardines que eligieron serán para ellos
        una afrenta.
30Serán como una encina con hojas marchitas,
    como un jardín sin agua.
31El hombre fuerte se convertirá en estopa,
    y su trabajo en chispa;
    arderán los dos juntos,
    y no habrá quien los apague.

El monte del SEÑOR
2:1-4 — Mi 4:1-3

2 Palabra que Isaías hijo de Amoz recibió en visión acerca de Judá y Jerusalén:

²En los últimos días,
el monte de la casa del SEÑOR será
establecido
como el más alto de los montes;
se alzará por encima de las colinas,
y hacia él confluirán todas las naciones.
³Muchos pueblos vendrán y dirán:
«¡Vengan, subamos al monte del SEÑOR,
a la casa del Dios de Jacob!,
para que nos enseñe sus *caminos
y andemos por sus sendas.»
Porque de *Sión saldrá la enseñanza,
de Jerusalén la palabra del SEÑOR.
⁴Él juzgará entre las naciones
y será árbitro de muchos pueblos.
Convertirán sus espadas en arados
y sus lanzas en hoces.
No levantará espada nación contra nación,
y nunca más se adiestrarán para la guerra.
⁵¡Ven, pueblo de Jacob,
y caminemos a la luz del SEÑOR!

El día del SEÑOR

⁶Has abandonado a tu pueblo,
a los descendientes de Jacob,
porque están llenos de astrólogos de Oriente,
de adivinos como entre los filisteos,
y hacen tratos con extranjeros.
⁷Su tierra está llena de oro y plata,
y sus tesoros son incalculables.
En su tierra abundan los caballos,
y sus carros de guerra son incontables.
⁸Su país está lleno de ídolos;
el pueblo adora la obra de sus manos,
lo que han hecho con sus propios dedos.
⁹Al *hombre se le humilla,
a la humanidad se le degrada.
¡Imposible que los perdones!

¹⁰¡Métete en la roca,
y escóndete en el polvo
ante el terror del SEÑOR
y el esplendor de su majestad!
¹¹Los ojos del altivo serán humillados
y la arrogancia humana será doblegada.
¡En aquel día sólo el SEÑOR será exaltado!
¹²Un día vendrá el SEÑOR *Todopoderoso
contra todos los orgullosos y arrogantes,
contra todos los altaneros, para
humillarlos;
¹³contra todos los cedros del Líbano,
arrogantes y erguidos,
contra todas las encinas de Basán,
¹⁴contra todas las montañas altivas,
contra todas las colinas erguidas,
¹⁵contra todas las torres altas,
contra todo muro fortificado,
¹⁶contra todas las naves de Tarsis,
contra todos los barcos lujosos.
¹⁷La altivez del hombre será abatida,
y la arrogancia humana será humillada.
En aquel día sólo el SEÑOR será exaltado,
¹⁸y los ídolos desaparecerán por completo.

¹⁹Los hombres se meterán en las cuevas de las
rocas,
y en las grietas del suelo,

ante el terror del SEÑOR
y el esplendor de su majestad,
cuando él se levante
para hacer temblar la tierra.
²⁰En aquel día arrojará el hombre
a los topos y murciélagos,
a sus ídolos de oro y plata
que él fabricó para adorarlos.
²¹Se meterá en las grutas de las rocas
y en las hendiduras de los peñascos,
ante el terror del SEÑOR
y el esplendor de su majestad,
cuando él se levante
para hacer temblar la tierra.
²²¡Dejen de confiar en el hombre,
que es muy poco lo que vale!
¡Su vida es un soplo nada más!

Juicio sobre Jerusalén y Judá

3 ¡Presten atención!
El Señor, el SEÑOR *Todopoderoso,
retira de Jerusalén y de Judá
todo apoyo y sustento:
toda provisión de pan,
toda provisión de agua.
²Él retira al valiente y al guerrero,
al juez y al profeta,
al adivino y al anciano,
³al capitán y al dignatario,
al consejero, al artesano experto
y al hábil encantador.

⁴Les pondré como jefes a muchachos,
y los gobernarán niños caprichosos.
⁵Unos a otros se maltratarán:
hombre contra hombre,
vecino contra vecino,
joven contra anciano,
plebeyo contra noble.

⁶Entonces un hombre agarrará a su hermano
en la casa de su padre, y le dirá:
«Sé nuestro líder, que tienes un manto;
¡hazte cargo de este montón de ruinas!»
⁷Pero entonces el otro protestará:
«Yo no soy médico,
y en mi casa no hay pan ni manto;
¡no me hagas líder del pueblo!»

⁸Jerusalén se tambalea,
Judá se derrumba,
porque su hablar y su actuar
son contrarios al SEÑOR:
¡desafían su gloriosa presencia!
⁹Su propio descaro los acusa
y, como Sodoma, se jactan de su pecado;
¡ni siquiera lo disimulan!
¡Ay de ellos,
porque causan su propia desgracia!
¹⁰Díganle al justo que le irá bien,
pues gozará del fruto de sus acciones.
¹¹¡Ay del malvado, pues le irá mal!
¡Según la obra de sus manos se le pagará!

¹²¡Pobre pueblo mío, oprimido por niños
y gobernado por mujeres!
¡Pobre pueblo mío, extraviado por tus guías,
que tuercen el curso de tu senda!
¹³El SEÑOR se dispone a denunciar;
se levanta para enjuiciar al pueblo.
¹⁴El SEÑOR entra en juicio
contra los *ancianos y jefes de su pueblo:
«¡Ustedes han devorado la viña,

y el despojo del pobre está en sus casas!
15¿Con qué derecho aplastan a mi pueblo
y pasan por encima de los pobres?»,
afirma el Señor,
el SEÑOR Todopoderoso.

16El SEÑOR dice:
«Las hijas de *Sión son tan orgullosas
que caminan con el cuello estirado,
con ojos seductores y pasitos cortos,
haciendo sonar los adornos de sus pies.
17Por eso el Señor cubrirá de sarna
la cabeza de las hijas de Sión;
el SEÑOR las dejará completamente calvas.»

18En aquel día, el Señor arrancará todo adorno:
hebillas, diademas, broches, 19pendientes, pulseras,
velos, 20pañuelos, cadenillas de los pies, cinturones,
frasquitos de perfume, amuletos, 21anillos, argollas
para la nariz, 22ropas de gala, mantos, chales, bol-
sos, 23espejos, telas finas, turbantes y mantillas.

24Habrá pestilencia en vez de perfume,
soga en vez de cinturón,
calvicie en vez de peinado elegante,
ropa de luto en vez de trajes lujosos,
vergüenzaa en vez de belleza.
25Tus hombres caerán a filo de espada,
y tus valientes, en el campo de batalla.*
26Las *puertas de la ciudad gemirán y se
vestirán de luto;
desolada, la ciudad se sentará en el suelo.

4 En aquel día, siete mujeres agarrarán
a un solo hombre y le dirán:
«De alimentarnos y de vestirnos
nosotras nos ocuparemos;
tan sólo déjanos llevar tu *nombre:
¡Líbranos de nuestra afrenta!»

2En aquel día, el retoño del SEÑOR será bello y
glorioso, y el fruto de la tierra será el orgullo y el honor de los sobrevivientes de Israel. 3Entonces tanto el
que quede en *Sión como el que sobreviva en Jerusalén serán llamados *santos, e inscritos para vida en Jerusalén. 4Con espíritu de juicio y espíritub abrasador,
el Señor lavará la inmundicia de las hijas de Sión y
limpiará la sangre que haya en Jerusalén. 5Entonces el
SEÑOR creará una nube de humo durante el día y un
resplandor de fuego llameante durante la noche, sobre el monte Sión y sobre los que allí se reúnan. Por
sobre toda la gloria habrá un toldo 6que servirá de cobertizo, para dar sombra contra el calor del día, y de
refugio y protección contra la lluvia y la tormenta.

El canto a la viña

5 Cantaré en nombre de mi amigo querido
una canción dedicada a su viña.
Mi amigo querido tenía una viña
en una ladera fértil.
2La cavó, la limpió de piedras
y la plantó con las mejores cepas.
Edificó una torre en medio de ella
y además preparó un lagar.
Él esperaba que diera buenas uvas,
pero acabó dando uvas agrias.
3Y ahora, *hombres de Judá,
habitantes de Jerusalén,
juzguen entre mi viña y yo.
4¿Qué más se podría hacer por mi viña

que yo no lo haya hecho?
Yo esperaba que diera buenas uvas;
¿por qué dio uvas agrias?
5Voy a decirles
lo que haré con mi viña:
Le quitaré su cerco, y será destruida;
derribaré su muro, y será pisoteada.
6La dejaré desolada,
y no será podada ni cultivada;
le crecerán espinos y cardos.
Mandaré que las nubes
no lluevan sobre ella.
7La viña del SEÑOR *Todopoderoso es el
pueblo de Israel;
los hombres de Judá son su huerto preferido.
Él esperaba justicia,
pero encontró ríos de sangre;
esperaba rectitud,
pero encontró gritos de angustia.

Maldiciones contra los explotadores

8¡Ay de aquellos que acaparan casa tras casa
y se apropian de campo tras campo
hasta que no dejan lugar para nadie más,
y terminan viviendo solos en el país!
9El SEÑOR *Todopoderoso me ha dicho al oído:
«Muchas casas quedarán desoladas,
y no habrá quien habite las grandes
mansiones.
10Tres hectáreas de viña sólo producirán un
tonel,
y diez medidas de semilla
darán tan sólo una.»c

11¡Ay de los que madrugan
para ir tras bebidas embriagantes,
que quedan hasta muy tarde
embriagándose con vino!
12En sus banquetes hay vino y arpas,
liras, tambores y flautas;
pero no se fijan en los hechos del SEÑOR
ni tienen en cuenta las obras de sus manos.
13Por eso mi pueblo será exiliado
porque no me conoce;
sus nobles perecerán de hambre
y la multitud se morirá de sed.
14Por eso el *sepulcro ensancha su garganta,
y desmesuradamente abre sus fauces.
Allí bajan nobles y plebeyos,
con sus juergas y diversiones.
15El *hombre será humillado,
la humanidad, doblegada,
y abatidos los ojos altivos.
16Pero el SEÑOR Todopoderoso será exaltado en
*justicia,
el Dios *santo se mostrará santo en
rectitud.
17Los corderos pastarán como en praderas
propias,
y las cabrasd comerán entre las ruinas de
los ricos.
18¡Ay de los que arrastran iniquidad con
cuerdas de mentira,
y el pecado con sogas de carreta!
19Dicen: «¡Que Dios se apure,
que apresure su obra
para que la veamos;

---

a **3:24** vergüenza (Qumrán); TM no incluye esta palabra. b **4:4** espíritu ... espíritu. Alt. el Espíritu de juicio y el Espíritu.
c **5:10** tres hectáreas ... un tonel ... diez medidas ... tan sólo una. Lit. diez yugadas ... un *bato ... un *jómer ... un *efa. d **5:17** las
cabras (LXX); los forasteros (TM).

que se acerque y se cumpla
el plan del Santo de Israel,
para que lo conozcamos!»
20¡Ay de los que llaman a lo malo bueno
y a lo bueno malo,
que tienen las tinieblas por luz
y la luz por tinieblas,
que tienen lo amargo por dulce
y lo dulce por amargo!

21¡Ay de los que se consideran sabios,
de los que se creen inteligentes!

22¡Ay de los valientes para beber vino,
de los valentones que mezclan bebidas
embriagantes,
23de los que por soborno absuelven al culpable,
y le niegan sus derechos al indefenso!

24Por eso, así como las lenguas de fuego
devoran la paja
y el pasto seco se consume en las llamas,
su raíz se pudrirá
y, como el polvo, se disipará su flor.
Porque han rechazado la *ley del SEÑOR
Todopoderoso
y han desdeñado la palabra del Santo de
Israel.

25Por eso se enciende la ira del SEÑOR contra su
pueblo,
levanta la mano contra él y lo golpea;
las montañas se estremecen,
los cadáveres quedan como basura
en medio de las calles.

Con todo, no se aplacó su ira,
y su brazo aún sigue extendido.

26Con una bandera le hará señas a una nación
lejana,
con un silbido la llamará desde el extremo
de la tierra,
y esta nación llegará presta y veloz.
27Ninguno de ellos se cansa ni tropieza,
ni dormita ni se duerme;
a ninguno se le afloja el cinturón
ni se le rompe la correa de las sandalias.
28Sus flechas son puntiagudas,
tensos todos sus arcos;
parecen pedernal los cascos de sus caballos,
y torbellino las ruedas de sus carros.
29Su rugido es el de una leona,
como el de los leoncillos:
gruñe y atrapa la presa,
y se la lleva sin que nadie se la arrebate.
30En aquel día bramará contra ella
como brama el mar.
Si alguien contempla la tierra,
la verá sombría y angustiada,
y la luz se ocultará tras negros nubarrones.

La misión de Isaías

6 El año de la muerte del rey Uzías, vi al Señor excelso y sublime, sentado en un trono; las orlas de su manto llenaban el templo. **2**Por encima de él había serafines, cada uno de los cuales tenía seis alas: con dos de ellas se cubrían el rostro, con dos se cubrían los pies, y con dos volaban. **3**Y se decían el uno al otro:

«*Santo, santo, santo es el SEÑOR
*Todopoderoso;

toda la tierra está llena de su gloria.»

4Al sonido de sus voces, se estremecieron los umbrales de las puertas y el templo se llenó de humo. **5**Entonces grité: «¡Ay de mí, que estoy perdido! Soy un hombre de labios *impuros y vivo en medio de un pueblo de labios blasfemos, ¡y no obstante mis ojos han visto al Rey, al SEÑOR Todopoderoso!»

6En ese momento voló hacia mí uno de los serafines. Traía en la mano una brasa que, con unas tenazas, había tomado del altar. **7**Con ella me tocó los labios y me dijo:

«Mira, esto ha tocado tus labios;
tu maldad ha sido borrada,
y tu pecado, perdonado.»

8Entonces oí la voz del Señor que decía:
—¿A quién enviaré? ¿Quién irá por nosotros?
Y respondí:
—Aquí estoy. ¡Envíame a mí!
9Él dijo:
—Ve y dile a este pueblo:

»"Oigan bien, pero no entiendan;
miren bien, pero no perciban."

10Haz insensible el *corazón de este pueblo;
embota sus oídos
y cierra sus ojos,
no sea que vea con sus ojos,
oiga con sus oídos,
y entienda con su corazón,
y se convierta
y sea sanado.

11Entonces exclamé:
—¿Hasta cuándo, Señor?
Y él respondió:

«Hasta que las ciudades queden destruidas
y sin habitante alguno;
hasta que las casas queden deshabitadas,
y los campos, asolados y en ruinas;
12hasta que el SEÑOR haya enviado lejos a todo
el pueblo,
y el país quede en total abandono.
13Si aún queda en la tierra una décima parte,
ésta volverá a ser devastada.
Pero así como al talar la encina y el roble
queda parte del tronco,
esa parte es la simiente santa.»

La señal de Emanuel

7 Acaz, hijo de Jotán y nieto de Uzías, reinaba en Judá. En ese tiempo Rezín, rey de *Siria, y Pécaj hijo de Remalías, rey de Israel, subieron contra Jerusalén para atacarla, pero no pudieron conquistarla.

2En el palacio de David se recibió la noticia de que Siria se había aliado con Efraín, y se estremeció el *corazón de Acaz y el de su pueblo, como se estremecen por el viento los árboles del bosque.

3El SEÑOR le dijo a Isaías: «Ve con tu hijo Sear Yasub[e] a encontrarte con Acaz donde termina el canal del estanque superior, en el camino que conduce al Campo del Lavandero. **4**Dile que tenga cuidado y no pierda la calma; que no tema ante el enojo ardiente de Rezín el sirio, ni ante el hijo de Remalías; que no se descorazone a causa de esos dos tizones humeantes. **5**Dile también que Efraín, junto con el hijo de Remalías y el sirio, han tramado hacerle mal, pues piensan **6**subir contra Judá, provocar el pánico, conquistarla y

---

e **7:3** En hebreo, *Sear Yasub* significa *un remanente volverá*.

poner allí como rey al hijo de Tabel. **7**Pero dile además que yo, el SEÑOR omnipotente, digo:

»"Eso no se cumplirá ni sucederá.
8La cabeza de Siria es Damasco,
  y la cabeza de Damasco es Rezín;
pero dentro de sesenta y cinco años
  Efraín será destrozado hasta dejar de ser
    pueblo.
9La cabeza de Efraín es Samaria,
  y la cabeza de Samaria es el hijo de
    Remalías,
si ustedes no creen en mí,
  no permanecerán‍f firmes."»

10El SEÑOR se dirigió a Acaz de nuevo: **11**—Pide que el SEÑOR tu Dios te dé una señal, ya sea en lo más profundo de la tierra o en lo más alto del cielo.

12Pero Acaz respondió:
—No pondré a prueba al SEÑOR, ni le pediré nada.

13Entonces Isaías dijo: «¡Escuchen ahora ustedes, los de la dinastía de David! ¿No les basta con agotar la paciencia de los *hombres, que hacen lo mismo con mi Dios? **14**Por eso, el Señor mismo les dará una señal: La joven concebirá y dará a luz un hijo, y lo llamará Emanuel.g **15**Cuando sepa elegir lo bueno y rechazar lo malo, comerá cuajada con miel. **16**Porque antes de que el niño sepa elegir lo bueno y rechazar lo malo, la tierra de los dos reyes que tú temes quedará abandonada.

17»El SEÑOR hará venir sobre ti, sobre tu pueblo y sobre la dinastía de tu padre, días como no se conocieron desde que Efraín se separó de Judá, pues hará venir al rey de Asiria.»

18En aquel día el SEÑOR llamará con un silbido a la mosca que está en los lejanos ríos de Egipto, y a la abeja que está en la tierra de Asiria. **19**Todas ellas vendrán y anidarán en las quebradas profundas, en las hendiduras de las rocas, en todos los matorrales espinosos y sobre todos los abrevaderos.

20En aquel día, con el rey de Asiria como navaja prestada del otro lado del río Éufrates, el Señor le afeitará a Israel la cabeza y el vello púbico,h y también la barba.

21En aquel día, un hombre criará un ternero y dos cabras; **22**y le darán tanta leche que tendrá leche cuajada para comer. Además, todos los que permanezcan en la tierra comerán cuajada con miel.

23En aquel día, allí donde hubo mil viñedos que costaban mil monedas de platai cada uno, no quedarán más que zarzas y espinos. **24**los cuales cubrirán toda la tierra. Sólo se podrá entrar allí con arco y flecha. **25**Y por temor a estos espinos y a estas zarzas, ya no irás a los cerros que antes se cultivaban con el azadón, pues se convertirán en lugares donde suelta el ganado y corretean las ovejas.

Asiria, el instrumento del SEÑOR

8 El SEÑOR me dijo: «Toma una tablilla grande y, con un estilete común, escribe sobre ella: "Tocante a Maher Salal Jasbaz".j **2**Yo convocaré como testigos confiables al sacerdote Urías y a Zacarías hijo de Jeberequías.»

3Luego tuve relaciones con la profetisa, y ella concibió y dio a luz un hijo. Entonces el SEÑOR me

dijo: «Ponle por nombre Maher Salal Jasbaz. **4**Antes de que el niño aprenda a decir "papá" y "mamá", la riqueza de Damasco y el botín de Samaria serán llevados ante el rey de Asiria.»

5El SEÑOR volvió a decirme:

6«Por cuanto este pueblo ha rechazado
  las mansas corrientes de Siloé
y se regocija con Rezín
  y con el hijo de Remalías,
7el Señor está a punto de traer contra ellos
  las impetuosas crecientes del río Éufrates:
    al rey de Asiria con toda su gloria.
Rebasará todos sus canales,
  desbordará todas sus orillas;
8pasará hasta Judá, la inundará,
  y crecerá hasta llegarle al cuello.
Sus alas extendidas, ¡oh Emanuel!,k
  cubrirán la anchura de tu tierra.»

9Escuchen esto, naciones,
  todas las naciones lejanas:
¡Alcen el grito de guerra,
  y serán destrozadas!
¡Prepárense para la batalla,
  y serán despedazadas!
¡Prepárense para la batalla,
  y serán desmenuzadas!
10Tracen su estrategia,
  pero será desbaratada;
propongan su plan,
  pero no se realizará,
porque Dios está con nosotros.l

Hay que temer a Dios

11El SEÑOR me habló fuertemente y me advirtió que no siguiera el *camino de este pueblo. Me dijo:

12«No digan ustedes que es conspiración
  todo lo que llama conspiración esta gente;
no teman lo que ellos temen,
  ni se dejen asustar.
13Sólo al SEÑOR *Todopoderoso
  tendrán ustedes por *santo,
sólo a él se deben honrarlo,
  sólo a él han de temerlo.
14El SEÑOR será un santuario.
Pero será una piedra de tropiezo
  para las dos casas de Israel;
¡una *roca que los hará caer!
¡Será para los habitantes de Jerusalén
  un lazo y una trampa!
15Muchos de ellos tropezarán;
  caerán y serán quebrantados.
Se les tenderán trampas,
  y en ellas quedarán atrapados.»

16Guarda bien el testimonio;
  sella la ley entre mis discípulos.
17El SEÑOR ha escondido su rostro
  del pueblo de Jacob,
pero yo esperaré en él,
  pues en él tengo puesta mi esperanza.

18Aquí me tienen, con los hijos que el SEÑOR me ha dado. Somos en Israel señales y presagios del SEÑOR Todopoderoso, que habita en el monte *Sión.

---

f **7:9** *no creen en mí, / no permanecerán* (lectura probable); *no creen, / ciertamente no permanecerán* (TM). g **7:14** En hebreo, *Emanuel* significa *Dios con nosotros.* h **7:20** *vello público.* Lit. *vello de los pies.* i **7:23** *mil monedas de plata.* Lit. *mil [*siclos] de plata.* j **8:1** En hebreo, *Maher Salal Jasbaz* significa *Pronto al saqueo, presto al botín;* también en v. 3. k **8:8** En hebreo, *Emanuel* significa *Dios con nosotros;* véase también v. 10. l **8:10** *Dios está con nosotros.* Lit. *Emanuel;* véase v. 8.

19Si alguien les dice: «Consulten a las pitonisas y a los agoreros que susurran y musitan; ¿acaso no es deber de un pueblo consultar a sus dioses y a los muertos, en favor de los vivos?», 20yo les digo: «¡Aténganse a la ley y al testimonio!» Para quienes no se atengan a esto, no habrá un amanecer.

21Ustedes habrán de enfurecerse cuando, angustiados y hambrientos, vaguen por la tierra. Levantando los ojos al cielo, maldecirán a su rey y a su Dios, 22y clavando la mirada en la tierra, sólo verán aflicción, tinieblas y espantosa penumbra; ¡serán arrojados a una oscuridad total!

Nos ha nacido un niño

9 A pesar de todo, no habrá más penumbra para la que estuvo angustiada. En el pasado Dios humilló a la tierra de Zabulón y a la tierra de Neftalí; pero en el futuro honrará a Galilea, tierra de *paganos, en el camino del mar, al otro lado del Jordán.

2El pueblo que andaba en la oscuridad
  ha visto una gran luz;
sobre los que vivían en densas tinieblas
  la luz ha resplandecido.
3Tú has hecho que la nación crezca;
  has aumentado su alegría.
Y se alegran ellos en tu presencia
  como cuando recogen la cosecha,
  como cuando reparten el botín.
4Ciertamente tú has quebrado,
  como en la derrota de Madián,
el yugo que los oprimía,
  la barra que pesaba sobre sus hombros,
  el bastón de mando que los subyugaba.
5Todas las botas guerreras
  que resonaron en la batalla,
y toda la ropa teñida en sangre
  serán arrojadas al fuego,
  serán consumidas por las llamas.
6Porque nos ha nacido un niño,
  se nos ha concedido un hijo;
la soberanía reposará sobre sus hombros,
  y se le darán estos *nombres:
Consejero admirable, Dios fuerte,
  Padre eterno, Príncipe de *paz.
7Se extenderán su soberanía y su paz,
  y no tendrán fin.
Gobernará sobre el trono de David
  y sobre su reino,
para establecerlo y sostenerlo
  con justicia y rectitud
  desde ahora y para siempre.
Esto lo llevará a cabo
  el celo del SEÑOR *Todopoderoso.

El enojo del SEÑOR contra Israel

8El Señor ha enviado su palabra;
  la ha enviado contra Jacob,
  ¡ya cae sobre Israel!
9De esto se entera todo el pueblo
  —Efraín y los habitantes de Samaria—,
todos los que dicen con orgullo
  y con altivez de *corazón:
10«Si se caen los ladrillos,
  reconstruiremos con piedra tallada;
si se caen las vigas de higuera,
  las repondremos con vigas de cedro.»

11Pero el SEÑOR ha fortalecido
  a los adversarios de Rezín;

ha incitado a sus enemigos.
12Los *sirios en el este y los filisteos en el oeste
  se comieron a Israel de un solo bocado.

A pesar de todo esto,
  la ira de Dios no se ha aplacado;
  ¡su mano aún sigue extendida!

13Pero el pueblo no ha querido reconocer
  al que lo ha castigado;
no ha buscado al SEÑOR *Todopoderoso.
14Por eso en un mismo día
  el SEÑOR le cortará a Israel
la cabeza y la cola,
  la palmera y el junco.
15La cabeza son los *ancianos
  y la gente de alto rango;
la cola son los profetas,
  maestros de mentiras.
16Los guías de este pueblo lo han extraviado;
  los que se dejan guiar son confundidos.
17Por eso no se complacerá el Señor en los
    jóvenes,
  ni se apiadará de huérfanos y viudas,
porque todos ellos son impíos y malvados;
  sus labios profieren *necedades.

A pesar de todo esto,
  la ira de Dios no se ha aplacado;
  ¡su mano aún sigue extendida!

18La maldad arde como un fuego
  que consume zarzas y espinos,
que incendia la espesura del bosque
  y sube luego, como torbellino,
  en una columna de humo.
19Por la ira del SEÑOR Todopoderoso
  arderá en fuego la tierra.
Y el pueblo será el combustible:
  ¡Nadie se compadecerá de su hermano!
20Unos comerán lo que esté a su mano derecha,
  pero se quedarán con hambre;
otros comerán lo que esté a su izquierda,
  pero no quedarán satisfechos.
  ¡Se comerán a sus propios hijos!m
21Manasés se comerá a Efraín,
  y Efraín a Manasés,
  y los dos juntos atacarán a Judá.

A pesar de todo esto,
  la ira de Dios no se ha aplacado;
  ¡su mano aún sigue extendida!

10 ¡Ay de los que emiten decretos inicuos
   y publican edictos opresivos!
2Privan de sus derechos a los pobres,
  y no les hacen justicia a los oprimidos de
    mi pueblo;
hacen de las viudas su presa
  y saquean a los huérfanos.
3¿Qué van a hacer cuando deban rendir
    cuentas,
  cuando llegue desde lejos la tormenta?
¿A quién acudirán en busca de ayuda?
  ¿En dónde dejarán sus riquezas?
4No les quedará más remedio
  que humillarse entre los cautivos
  o morir entre los masacrados.

A pesar de todo esto,
  la ira de Dios no se ha aplacado;

---

m 9:20 a sus propios hijos. Lit. la carne de su brazo.

¡su mano aún sigue extendida!

Juicio de Dios sobre Asiria

5«¡Ay de Asiria, vara de mi ira!
    ¡El garrote de mi enojo está en su mano!
6Lo envío contra una nación impía,
    lo mando contra un pueblo que me
        enfurece,
para saquearlo y despojarlo,
    para pisotearlo como al barro de las calles.
7Pero esto Asiria no se lo propuso;
    ¡ni siquiera lo pensó!
Sólo busca destruir
    y aniquilar a muchas naciones.
8Pues dice: "¿Acaso no son reyes todos mis
        jefes?
    9¿No es Calnó como Carquemis?
¿No es Jamat como Arfad,
    y Samaria como Damasco?
10Así como alcanzó mi mano
    a los reinos de los ídolos,
reinos cuyas imágenes superaban
    a las de Jerusalén y de Samaria,
11y así como hice con Samaria y sus dioses,
    también haré con Jerusalén y sus ídolos."»

12Cuando el Señor termine lo que va a hacer contra el monte *Sión y contra Jerusalén, él dirá: «Castigaré el fruto del orgulloso *corazón del rey de Asiria y la arrogancia de sus ojos.» 13Porque afirma:

«Esto lo hizo el poder de mi mano;
    lo hizo mi sabiduría,
    porque soy inteligente.
He cambiado las fronteras de los pueblos,
    he saqueado sus tesoros;
como un guerrero poderoso
    he derribado a sus reyes.
14Como quien mete la mano en un nido,
    me he adueñado de la riqueza de los
        pueblos;
como quien recoge huevos abandonados,
    me he apoderado de toda la tierra;
y no hubo nadie que aleteara
    ni abriera el pico y chillara.»

15¿Puede acaso gloriarse el hacha
    más que el que la maneja,
o jactarse la sierra contra quien la usa?
¡Como si pudiera el bastón manejar
    a quien lo tiene en la mano,
o la frágil vara pudiera levantar
    a quien pesa más que la madera!
16Por eso enviará el Señor,
    el SEÑOR *Todopoderoso,
una enfermedad devastadora
    sobre sus robustos guerreros.
En vez de honrarlos, les prenderá fuego,
    un fuego como de llama ardiente.
17La luz de Israel se convertirá en fuego;
    su *Santo se volverá una llama.
En un solo día quemará sus espinos
    y consumirá sus zarzas.
18Destruirá de extremo a extremo
    el esplendor de sus bosques y de sus
        huertos,
como enfermo carcomido por la plaga.
19Tan pocos árboles quedarán en su bosque
    que hasta un niño podrá contarlos.

El remanente de Israel

20En aquel día ni el remanente de Israel
    ni los sobrevivientes del pueblo de Jacob
volverán a apoyarse
    en quien los hirió de muerte,
sino que su apoyo verdadero
    será el SEÑOR, el *Santo de Israel.
21Y un remanente volverá;[n]
    un remanente de Jacob volverá al Dios
        Poderoso.
22Israel,
    aunque tu pueblo sea como la arena del
        mar,
sólo un remanente volverá.
Se ha decretado destrucción,
    abrumadora justicia.
23Porque el Señor, el SEÑOR *Todopoderoso,
    ejecutará la destrucción decretada
    en medio de todo el país.
24Por eso, así dice el Señor, el SEÑOR Todopoderoso:

«Pueblo mío, que vives en *Sión,
    no tengas temor de Asiria.
Aunque te golpee con el bastón
    y contra ti levante una vara,
    como lo hizo Egipto.
25Dentro de muy poco tiempo
    mi indignación contra ti llegará a su fin,
    y mi ira destruirá a tus enemigos.»

26Con un látigo los azotará
    el SEÑOR Todopoderoso,
como cuando abatió a Madián
    en la *roca de Oreb;
levantará sobre el mar su vara,
    como lo hizo en Egipto.
27En aquel día
    esa carga se te quitará de los hombros,
y a causa de la gordura
    se romperá el yugo que llevas en el cuello.

28Llega el enemigo hasta Ayat,
    pasa por Migrón,
    y deja en Micmás su equipaje.
29Cruza el vado, y dice:
    «Acamparemos en Gueba.»
Ramá se pone a temblar,
    y huye Guibeá, ciudad de Saúl.
30¡Clama a gritos, hija de Galín!
    ¡Escucha, Lais!
    ¡Pobre Anatot!
31Se ha puesto en fuga Madmena;
    los habitantes de Guebín buscan refugio.
32Hoy mismo se detendrá en Nob;
    agitará su puño contra el monte
    de la ciudad de Sión,
    el monte de Jerusalén.

33¡Miren! El Señor, el SEÑOR Todopoderoso,
    desgaja las ramas con fuerza increíble.
Los árboles más altos son talados;
    los más elevados son abatidos.
34Derriba con un hacha la espesura del bosque,
    y el esplendor del Líbano se viene abajo.

El retoño de Isaí

11 Del tronco de Isaí brotará un retoño;
    un vástago nacerá de sus raíces.
2El Espíritu del SEÑOR reposará sobre él:

---

n 10:21 *un remanente volverá.* Véase nota en 7:3.

espíritu de sabiduría y de entendimiento,
espíritu de consejo y de poder,
espíritu de conocimiento y de temor del
    SEÑOR.

3Él se deleitará en el temor del SEÑOR;
no juzgará según las apariencias,
ni decidirá por lo que oiga decir,
4sino que juzgará con justicia a los desvalidos,
y dará un fallo justo
en favor de los pobres de la tierra.
Destruirá la tierra con la vara de su boca;
matará al malvado con el aliento de sus
    labios.
5La *justicia será el cinto de sus lomos
y la fidelidad el ceñidor de su cintura.

6El lobo vivirá con el cordero,
el leopardo se echará con el cabrito,
y juntos andarán el ternero y el cachorro de
    león,
y un niño pequeño los guiará.
7La vaca pastará con la osa,
sus crías se echarán juntas,
y el león comerá paja como el buey.
8Jugará el niño de pecho
junto a la cueva de la cobra,
y el recién destetado meterá la mano
en el nido de la víbora.
9No harán ningún daño ni estrago
en todo mi monte *santo,
porque rebosará la tierra
con el conocimiento del SEÑOR
como rebosa el mar con las aguas.

10En aquel día se alzará la raíz de Isaí
como estandarte de los pueblos;
hacia él correrán las naciones,
y glorioso será el lugar donde repose.
11En aquel día el Señor volverá a extender su
    mano
para recuperar al remanente de su pueblo,
a los que hayan quedado en Asiria,
en Egipto, Patros y *Cus;
en Elam, Sinar y Jamat,
y en las regiones más remotas.
12Izará una bandera para las naciones,
reunirá a los desterrados de Israel,
y de los cuatro puntos cardinales
juntará al pueblo esparcido de Judá.
13Desaparecerán los celos de Efraín;
los opresores de Judá serán aniquilados.
Efraín no tendrá más celos de Judá,
ni oprimirá Judá a Efraín.
14Juntos se lanzarán hacia el oeste,
contra las laderas de los filisteos;
juntos saquearán a los pueblos del este,
dejarán sentir su poder sobre Edom y
    Moab,
y se les someterán los amonitas.
15Secará el SEÑOR el golfo del mar de Egipto;
pasará su mano sobre el río Éufrates
y lanzará un viento ardiente;
lo dividirá en siete arroyos
para que lo puedan cruzar en sandalias.
16Para el remanente de su pueblo,
para los que hayan quedado de Asiria,
habrá un camino, como lo hubo para Israel
cuando salió de Egipto.

Canciones de alabanza

12 En aquel día tú dirás:

«SEÑOR, yo te alabaré
aunque te hayas enojado conmigo.
Tu ira se ha calmado,
y me has dado consuelo.
2¡Dios es mi *salvación!
Confiaré en él y no temeré.
El SEÑOR es mi fuerza,
el SEÑOR es mi canción;
¡él es mi salvación!»
3Con alegría sacarán ustedes agua
de las fuentes de la salvación.

4En aquel día se dirá:

«Alaben al SEÑOR, invoquen su *nombre;
den a conocer entre los pueblos sus obras;
proclamen la grandeza de su nombre.
5Canten salmos al SEÑOR,
porque ha hecho maravillas;
que esto se dé a conocer
en toda la tierra.
6¡Canta y grita de alegría,
habitante de *Sión;
realmente es grande, en medio de ti,
el *Santo de Israel!»

Profecía contra Babilonia

13 Profecía contra Babilonia que recibió Isaías
hijo de Amoz:

2Sobre un monte pelado agiten la bandera;
llamen a gritos a los soldados,
háganles señas con la mano
para que entren por las puertas de los
    nobles.
3Ya he dado orden a mis consagrados;
he reclutado a mis valientes,
a los que se alegran de mi *triunfo,
para que ejecuten mi castigo.
4¡Escuchen! Se oye tumulto en las montañas,
como el de una gran multitud.
¡Escuchen! Se oye un estruendo de reinos,
de naciones que se han reunido.
El SEÑOR *Todopoderoso pasa revista
a un ejército para la batalla.
5Vienen de tierras lejanas,
de los confines del horizonte.
Viene el SEÑOR con las armas de su ira
para destruir toda la tierra.
6¡Giman, que el día del SEÑOR está cerca!
Llega de parte del *Todopoderoso como
una devastación.
7Por eso todas las manos desfallecen,
todo el mundo pierde el ánimo.
8Quedan todos aterrados;
dolores y angustias los atrapan,
¡se retuercen de dolor,
como si estuvieran de parto!
Espantados, se miran unos a otros,
¡tienen el rostro encendido!
9¡Miren! ¡Ya viene el día del SEÑOR
—día cruel, de furor y ardiente ira—;
convertirá en desolación la tierra
y exterminará de ella a los pecadores!
10Las estrellas y las constelaciones del cielo
dejarán de irradiar su luz;
se oscurecerá el sol al salir

ñ 11:15 *Secará* (LXX); *Destruirá (TM).

y no brillará más la luna.
11Castigaré por su maldad al mundo,
y por su iniquidad a los malvados.
Pondré fin a la soberbia de los arrogantes
y humillaré el orgullo de los violentos.
12Voy a hacer que haya menos gente que oro
fino,
menos *mortales que oro de Ofir.
13Por eso haré que tiemble el cielo
y que la tierra se mueva de su sitio,
por el furor del SEÑOR *Todopoderoso
en el día de su ardiente ira.
14Como gacela acosada,
como rebaño sin *pastor,
cada uno se volverá a su propio pueblo,
cada cual huirá a su propia tierra.
15Al que atrapen lo traspasarán;
el que caiga preso morirá a filo de espada.
16Ante sus propios ojos
estrellarán a sus pequeños,
saquearán sus casas
y violarán a sus mujeres.
17¡Miren! Yo incito contra ellos a los medos,
pueblo al que no le importa la plata
ni se deleita en el oro.
18Con sus arcos traspasarán a los jóvenes;
no se apiadarán del fruto del vientre
ni tendrán compasión de los niños.
19Babilonia, la perla de los reinos,
la gloria y el orgullo de los *caldeos,
quedará como Sodoma y Gomorra
cuando Dios las destruyó.
20Nunca más volverá a ser habitada,
ni poblada en los tiempos venideros.
No volverá a acampar allí el beduino,
ni hará el pastor descansar a su rebaño.
21Allí descansarán las fieras del desierto;
sus casas se llenarán de búhos.
Allí habitarán los avestruces
y brincarán las cabras salvajes.
22En sus fortalezas aullarán las hienas,
y en sus lujosos palacios, los chacales.
Su hora está por llegar,
y no se prolongarán sus días.

14 En verdad, el SEÑOR tendrá compasión de
Jacob y elegirá de nuevo a Israel. Los asenta-
rá en su propia tierra. Los extranjeros se juntarán con
ellos, y se unirán a los descendientes de Jacob. 2Los
pueblos los acogerán y los llevarán hasta su patria.
Los israelitas los tomarán como siervos y siervas en el
suelo del SEÑOR; apresarán a sus captores y dominarán a sus opresores.

3Cuando el SEÑOR los haga descansar de su sufrimiento, de su tormento y de la cruel esclavitud a
la que fueron sometidos, 4pronunciarán esta sátira
contra el rey de Babilonia:

¡Hay que ver cómo terminó el opresor,
y cómo acabó su furia insolente!o
5Quebró el SEÑOR la vara de los malvados;
rompió el bastón de los tiranos
6que con furia y continuos golpes
castigaba a los pueblos,
que con implacable enojo
dominaba y perseguía a las naciones.
7Toda la tierra descansa tranquila
y prorrumpe en gritos de alegría.
8Hasta los pinos y cedros del Líbano

se burlan de ti y te dicen:
«Desde que yaces tendido,
nadie viene a derribarnos.»
9Allá en lo profundo, por tu causa,
el *sepulcro se estremece
al salir a tu encuentro;
por causa tuya despierta a los muertos,
a los que fueron jefes de la tierra.
Hace que los reyes de todas las naciones
se levanten de sus tronos.
10Todos ellos responden y te dicen:
«¡También tú te has debilitado!
¡Ya eres uno más de los nuestros!»
11Tu majestad ha sido arrojada al *sepulcro,
junto con el sonido de tus arpas.
¡Duermes entre gusanos,
y te cubren las lombrices!
12¡Cómo has caído del cielo,
lucero de la mañana!
Tú, que sometías a las naciones,
has caído por tierra.
13Decías en tu *corazón:
«Subiré hasta los cielos.
¡Levantaré mi trono
por encima de las estrellas de Dios!
Gobernaré desde el extremo norte,
en el monte de los dioses.p
14Subiré a la cresta de las más altas nubes,
seré semejante al *Altísimo.»
15¡Pero has sido arrojado al sepulcro,
a lo más profundo de la fosa!
16Los que te ven, te clavan la mirada
y reflexionan en cuanto a tu destino:
«¿Y éste es el que sacudía a la tierra
y hacía temblar a los reinos,
17el que dejaba el mundo hecho un desierto,
el que arrasaba sus ciudades
y nunca dejaba libres a los presos?»
18Todos los reyes de las naciones
reposan con honor,
cada uno en su tumba.
19Pero a ti, el sepulcro te ha vomitado
como a un vástago repugnante.
Los que murieron a filo de espada,
los que bajaron al fondo de la fosa,
te han cubierto por completo.
¡Pareces un cadáver pisoteado!
20No tendrás sepultura con los reyes,
porque destruiste a tu tierra
y asesinaste a tu pueblo.

¡Jamás volverá a mencionarse
la descendencia de los malhechores!
21Por causa de la maldad de los padres,
preparen un matadero para los hijos.
¡Que no se levanten para heredar la tierra
ni cubran con ciudades la faz del mundo!

22«Yo me levantaré contra ellos
—afirma el SEÑOR—.

Yo extirparé de Babilonia
*nombre y descendencia,
vástago y posteridad
—afirma el SEÑOR—.
23La convertiré en lugar de erizos,
en charco de agua estancada;
la barreré con la escoba de la destrucción»,
afirma el SEÑOR Todopoderoso.

---

o 14:4 insolente (LXX, Qumrán y Siríaca); en TM, palabra de difícil traducción. p 14:13 monte de los dioses. Lit. monte de
la asamblea.

Profecía contra Asiria

24El SEÑOR Todopoderoso ha jurado:
«Tal como lo he planeado, se cumplirá;
tal como lo he decidido, se realizará.
25Destrozaré a Asiria en mi tierra;
la pisotearé sobre mis montes.
Mi pueblo dejará de llevar su yugo;
ya no pesará esa carga sobre sus hombros.»
26Esto es lo que he determinado
para toda la tierra;
ésta es la mano que he extendido
sobre todas las naciones.
27Si lo ha determinado el SEÑOR
*Todopoderoso,
¿quién podrá impedirlo?
Si él ha extendido su mano,
¿quién podrá detenerla?

Profecía contra los filisteos

28Esta profecía vino a Isaías el año en que murió
el rey Acaz:

29Todos ustedes filisteos,
no se alegren de que se haya roto
el bastón que los golpeaba;
porque una víbora saldrá
de la raíz de la serpiente;
su fruto será una serpiente voladora.
30Los más desvalidos pacerán como ovejas,
los necesitados descansarán seguros.
Pero mataré de hambre a su raíz;
destruiré a sus sobrevivientes.
31¡Gime y grita, *puerta de la ciudad!
¡Ponte a temblar de miedo, Filistea entera!
Porque viene del norte una nube de humo,
y nadie rompe la formación.
32¿Qué respuesta se dará a los mensajeros de
esa nación?
Pues que el SEÑOR ha afirmado a *Sión,
y que allí se refugiarán
los afligidos de su pueblo.

Profecía contra Moab
16:6-12 — Jer 48:29-36

15 Profecía contra Moab:

La ciudad moabita de Ar está arruinada,
¡destruida en una noche!
La ciudad moabita de Quir está arruinada,
¡destruida en una noche!
2Acuden los de Dibón al templo,
a sus *altares paganos, para llorar.
Moab está gimiendo
por Nebo y por Medeba.
Rapadas están todas las cabezas,
y afeitadas todas las barbas.
3Todos, deshechos en llanto,
van por las calles, vestidos de luto;
¡gimen en los techos y en las plazas!
4Hesbón y Elalé claman a gritos,
hasta Yahaza se escuchan sus clamores.
Por eso gritan los valientes de Moab,
y flaquea su entereza.
5Mi *corazón grita por Moab;
sus fugitivos huyen hasta Zoar,
hasta Eglat Selisiyá.
Suben llorando por la cuesta de Luhit;
ante el desastre, gritan desesperados
por el camino de Joronayin.
6Se han secado las aguas de Nimrín;
se ha marchitado la hierba.
Ya no hay vegetación,

no ha quedado nada verde.
7Por eso se llevaron,
más allá del arroyo de los Sauces,
las muchas riquezas que amasaron.
8Su grito desesperado
va recorriendo la frontera de Moab.
Llega su gemido hasta Eglayin,
y aun llega hasta Ber Elín.
9Llenas están de sangre las aguas de Dimón,
y aun más plagas le añadiré:
enviaré un león contra los moabitas fugitivos
y contra los que permanezcan en la tierra.

16 Envíen corderos al gobernante del país,
desde Selá, por el desierto,
y hasta el monte de la hija de *Sión.
2Las mujeres de Moab,
en los vados del Arnón,
parecen aves que, espantadas,
abandonan el nido.

3«Danos un consejo;
toma una decisión.
A plena luz del día,
extiende tu sombra como la noche.
Esconde a los fugitivos;
no traiciones a los refugiados.
4Deja que los fugitivos de Moab
encuentren en ti un refugio;
¡protégelos del destructor!»

Cuando la opresión llegue a su fin
y la destrucción se acabe,
el agresor desaparecerá de la tierra.
5El trono se fundará en la lealtad,
y un descendiente de David
reinará sobre él con fidelidad:
será un juez celoso del derecho
y ansioso de hacer justicia.

6Hemos sabido que Moab
es extremadamente orgulloso;
hemos sabido de su soberbia,
de su orgullo y arrogancia,
de su charlatanería sin sentido.
7Por eso gimen los moabitas;
todos ellos gimen por Moab.
Laméntense, aflíjanse,
por las tortas de pasas de Quir Jaréset.
8Se han marchitado los campos de Hesbón,
lo mismo que las vides de Sibma.
Los gobernantes de las naciones
han pisoteado los viñedos más selectos,
los que llegaban hasta Jazer
y se extendían hacia el desierto.
Sus sarmientos se extendían
y llegaban hasta el mar.
9Por eso lloro, como llora Jazer,
por los viñedos de Sibma.
¡Y a ustedes, ciudades de Hesbón y de Elalé,
las empapo con mis lágrimas!
Se han acallado los gritos de alegría
por tu fruto maduro y tus cosechas.
10Ya no hay en los huertos alegría ni regocijo.
Nadie canta ni grita en los viñedos,
nadie pisa la uva en los lagares;
yo le puse fin al clamor en la vendimia.
11Por eso vibran mis entrañas por Moab
como las cuerdas de un arpa;
vibra todo mi ser por Quir Jaréset.
12Por más que acuda Moab a sus *altares
paganos
no logrará sino fatigarse;

cuando vaya a orar a su santuario,
todo lo que haga será en vano.

¹³Ésta es la palabra que el SEÑOR pronunció en el pasado contra Moab. ¹⁴Pero ahora el SEÑOR dice: «Dentro de tres años, contados como los cuenta un jornalero, el esplendor de Moab y de toda su inmensa multitud será despreciado, y muy pocos y débiles serán sus sobrevivientes.»

Profecía contra Damasco

17 Profecía contra Damasco:

«¡Miren a Damasco!
¡Ya no será una ciudad!
¡Será convertida en un montón de
escombros!
²Abandonadas quedarán
las ciudades de Aroer;
serán pastizales donde los rebaños
comerán sin que nadie los asuste.
³Efraín perderá la ciudad fortificada;
Damasco se quedará sin realeza.
Los sobrevivientes de Aram y sus riquezas
serán para los hijos de Israel
—afirma el SEÑOR *Todopoderoso—.

⁴»En aquel día
se debilitará la gloria de Jacob
y se consumirá la gordura de su cuerpo.
⁵Será como el segador que recoge la mies
y cosecha el grano con su brazo;
será como cuando se recoge el grano
en el valle de Refayin.
⁶Pero quedarán algunos rebuscos,
como cuando se sacude el olivo
y dos o tres aceitunas se quedan
en las ramas más altas,
y tal vez cuatro o cinco
en todas las ramas del árbol.»
Lo afirma el SEÑOR, el Dios de Israel.

⁷En aquel día
buscará el *hombre a su Hacedor;
fijará la mirada en el *Santo de Israel.
⁸Ya no se fijará en los altares,
que son obra de sus manos;
ni volverá la mirada a las imágenes de *Aserá,
ni a los altares de incienso
que sus dedos fabricaron.

⁹En aquel día las ciudades fortificadas, que fueron abandonadas por causa de los israelitas, serán como lugares abandonados que se convierten en bosques y matorrales. Todo será desolación.

¹⁰Porque te olvidaste del Dios de tu *salvación;
no te acordaste de la *Roca de tu fortaleza.
Por eso, aunque siembres las plantas más
selectas
y plantes vides importadas,
¹¹aunque las hagas crecer el día que las plantes,
y las hagas florecer al día siguiente,
en el día del dolor y de la enfermedad
incurable
la cosecha se malogrará.

¹²¡Ay del rugido de muchas naciones!
¡Braman como brama el mar!
¡Ay del clamor de los pueblos!
¡Su estruendo es como el de aguas
caudalosas!

¹³Aunque esos pueblos braman como aguas
encrespadas,
huyen cuando él los reprende,
arrastrados por el viento
como la paja de los cerros,
como el polvo con el vendaval.
¹⁴Al atardecer, ¡terror repentino!
Antes del amanecer, ¡ya no existen!
Tal es el destino de quienes nos despojan;
eso les espera a quienes nos saquean.

Profecía contra Etiopía

18 ¡Ay de la tierra de zumbantes langostasq
más allá de los ríos de *Cus,
²que por las aguas del río Nilo
envía emisarios en barcas de papiro!

Vayan, veloces mensajeros,
a una nación de gente alta y lampiña;
a un pueblo temido por doquier,
a una nación agresiva y dominante,
cuya tierra está surcada por ríos.

³Cuando sobre las montañas
se alce el estandarte y suene la trompeta,
¡fíjense, habitantes del mundo!;
¡escuchen, pobladores de la tierra!

⁴Así me dijo el SEÑOR:
«Desde mi morada miraré impasible,
como los candentes rayos del sol,
como las nubes de rocío en el calor de la
vendimia.»
⁵Porque antes de la vendimia,
cuando la flor se cae y madura la uva,
se podarán los retoños
y se arrancarán de raíz los sarmientos.
⁶Todos ellos quedarán abandonados
a los buitres de las montañas
y a los animales salvajes;
durante el verano
serán el alimento de las aves de rapiña;
durante el invierno,
de todos los animales salvajes.

⁷En aquel tiempo ese pueblo de alta estatura y de lampiña piel, ese pueblo temido en todas partes, esa nación agresiva y dominante, cuya tierra está surcada por ríos, le llevará ofrendas al SEÑOR *Todopoderoso. Se las llevará al monte *Sión, al lugar donde habita el *nombre del SEÑOR Todopoderoso.

Profecía contra Egipto

19 Profecía contra Egipto:

¡Miren al SEÑOR!
Llega a Egipto montado sobre una nube
ligera.
Los ídolos de Egipto
tiemblan en su presencia;
el *corazón de los egipcios
desfallece en su interior.

²«Incitaré a egipcio contra egipcio;
luchará hermano contra hermano,
amigo contra amigo,
ciudad contra ciudad,
reino contra reino.
³Los egipcios quedarán desanimados
y consultarán a los ídolos:
a los espíritus de los muertos,
a las pitonisas y a los agoreros,

q **18:1** *langostas.* Lit. *alas.*

¡pero yo frustraré sus planes!
4Dejaré que crueles amos los dominen;
    un rey de mano dura los gobernará»,
afirma el Señor,
    el SEÑOR *Todopoderoso.

5Se agotarán las aguas del Nilo;
    árido y reseco quedará el lecho del río.
6Apestarán los canales,
    y bajará el nivel de los arroyos de Egipto
hasta dejarlos completamente secos.
    ¡Las cañas y los juncos quedarán
        marchitos!
7A orillas del Nilo,
    en la desembocadura del río,
    la vegetación perderá su verdor.
Todos los sembrados junto al Nilo
    quedarán asolados, dejarán de existir.
8Gemirán y harán lamentos todos los
        pescadores,
    los que lanzan anzuelos en el Nilo;
desfallecerán los que echan redes en el agua.
9Quedarán frustrados los que trabajan el lino
        peinado;
    perderán la esperanza los tejedores de lino
        fino.
10Quedarán desalentados los fabricantes de
        telas;
    todos los asalariados se llenarán de
        angustia.
11Los jefes de Zoán no son más que unos necios;
    los consejeros más sabios
    le dan a Faraón consejos insensatos.
¿Cómo se les ocurre decirle:
    «Yo soy uno de los sabios,
discípulo de los antiguos reyes»?

12¿Dónde quedaron tus sabios?
    Que te muestren y te hagan saber
lo que el SEÑOR Todopoderoso
    ha planeado contra Egipto.
13Los jefes de Zoán se han vuelto necios;
    los jefes de Menfis se dejaron engañar.
Las piedras angulares de sus pueblos
    han hecho que Egipto pierda el rumbo.
14El SEÑOR ha infundido en ellos
    un espíritu de desconcierto.
En todo lo que hace Egipto
    le han hecho perder el rumbo.
Como un borracho en su vómito,
    Egipto se tambalea.
15Nada puede hacerse por Egipto,
    sea cabeza o cola, palmera o caña.

16En aquel día los egipcios parecerán mujeres. Se estremecerán de terror ante la mano amenazante que el SEÑOR Todopoderoso agita contra ellos. 17La tierra de Judá será un espanto para los egipcios. Por causa de lo que el SEÑOR Todopoderoso está planeando contra ellos, la sola mención de Judá llenará de espanto a los que oigan este *nombre.r 18En aquel día habrá en Egipto cinco ciudades que hablarán el idioma de Canaán, y que jurarán lealtad al SEÑOR Todopoderoso. Una de ellas se llamará Ciudad del Sol.r 19En aquel día habrá un altar para el SEÑOR en el corazón mismo de Egipto, y en su frontera un monumento al SEÑOR. 20Esto servirá en Egipto de señal y testimonio del SEÑOR Todopoderoso. Cuando ellos

clamen al SEÑOR por causa de sus opresores, él les enviará un salvador y defensor que los librará. 21De modo que el SEÑOR se dará a conocer a los egipcios, y en aquel día ellos reconocerán al SEÑOR: lo servirán con sacrificios y ofrendas de grano; harán votos al SEÑOR y se los cumplirán. 22El SEÑOR herirá a los egipcios con una plaga, y aun hiriéndolos, los sanará. Ellos se volverán al SEÑOR, y él responderá a sus ruegos y los sanará.

23En aquel día habrá una carretera desde Egipto hasta Asiria. Los asirios irán a Egipto y los egipcios a Asiria, y unos y otros adorarán juntos. 24En aquel día Israel será, junto con Egipto y Asiria, una bendición en medio de la tierra. 25El SEÑOR Todopoderoso los bendecirá, diciendo: «Bendito sea Egipto mi pueblo, y Asiria obra de mis manos, e Israel mi heredad.»

Profecía contra Egipto y Cus

20 El año en que el comandante en jefe enviado por Sargón, rey de Asiria, fue a Asdod, atacó esa ciudad y la conquistó. 2En aquel tiempo el SEÑOR habló por medio de Isaías hijo de Amoz. Le dijo: «Anda, quítate la ropa de luto y las sandalias.» Así lo hizo Isaías, y anduvo desnudo y descalzo.

3Entonces el SEÑOR dijo: «Así como durante tres años mi siervo Isaías ha andado desnudo y descalzo, como señal y presagio contra Egipto y *Cus, 4así también, para vergüenza de Egipto, el rey de Asiria llevará desnudos y descalzos, y con las nalgas al aire, a los cautivos de Egipto y a los desterrados de Cus, lo mismo jóvenes que viejos. 5Y los que confían en Etiopía y se enorgullecen de Egipto quedarán aterrados y avergonzados. 6En aquel día los habitantes de esta costa dirán: "Fíjense, ahí tienen a los que eran nuestra esperanza, ¡aquellos a quienes acudíamos en busca de ayuda, para que nos libraran del rey de Asiria! ¿Y ahora, ¿cómo podremos escapar?"»

Profecía contra Babilonia

21 Profecía contra el desierto junto al mar:s
Como torbellinos que pasan por el Néguev,
    se acercan invasores de una temible tierra
        del desierto.
2Una visión terrible
    me ha sido revelada:
    el traidor traiciona,
        el destructor destruye.
¡Al ataque, Elam! ¡Al asedio, Media!
    Pondré fin a todo gemido.

3Por eso mi cuerpo se estremece de dolor,
    sufro de agudos dolores,
    como los de una parturienta;
lo que oigo, me aturde;
    lo que veo, me desconcierta.
4Se me turba la *mente,
    me hace temblar el terror;
    el crepúsculo tan anhelado
se me ha vuelto un espanto.

5¡Ellos tienden las mesas,
    extienden los tapices,
    y comen y beben!
¡Jefes, pónganse de pie!
    ¡Levántense y engrasen los escudos!

6Porque así me ha dicho el SEÑOR:

    «Ve y pon un centinela,

---

r 19:18 del Sol (mss. hebreos, Qumrán y Vulgata); de la destrucción (TM).   s 21:1 el desierto junto al mar. Probable referencia al golfo Pérsico o a la llanura al sur de Babilonia.

que informe de todo lo que vea.
7Cuando vea carros de combate tirados por
   caballos,
o gente montada en asnos o en camellos,
que preste atención,
   mucha atención.»

8Y el centinela[t] gritó:

«¡Día tras día, Señor,
   estoy de pie en la torre;
cada noche permanezco
   en mi puesto de guardia!
9¡Ahí viene un hombre
   en un carro de combate tirado por caballos!
Y éste es su mensaje:
   "¡Ha caído, ha caído Babilonia!
¡Todas las imágenes de sus dioses
   han rodado por el suelo!"»

10Pueblo mío, trillado como el trigo,
   yo te he anunciado lo que he oído
de parte del SEÑOR *Todopoderoso,
   del Dios de Israel.

Profecía contra Edom

11Profecía contra Dumá:[u]

Alguien me grita desde Seír:
   «Centinela, ¿cuánto queda de la noche?
Centinela, ¿cuánto falta para que
   amanezca?»
12El centinela responde:
   «Ya viene la mañana, pero también la
     noche.
Si quieren preguntar, pregunten;
   si quieren volver, vuelvan.»

Profecía contra Arabia

13Profecía contra Arabia:

Caravanas de Dedán,
   acampadas en los matorrales del desierto:
14salgan al encuentro del sediento
   y ofrézcanle agua.
Habitantes de la tierra de Temá,
   ofrezcan alimento a los fugitivos,
15porque huyen de la espada,
   de la espada desnuda,
del arco tenso
   y del fragor de la batalla.

16Porque así me dijo el Señor: «Dentro de un
año, contado como lo cuenta un jornalero, toda la
magnificencia de Cedar llegará a su fin. 17Pocos serán los arqueros, los guerreros de Cedar, que sobrevivan.» Lo ha dicho el SEÑOR, el Dios de Israel.

Profecía contra Jerusalén

22 Profecía contra el valle de la Visión:

¿Qué te pasa ahora,
   que has subido a las azoteas,
2ciudad llena de disturbios,
   de tumultos y parrandas?
Tus víctimas no cayeron a filo de espada
   ni murieron en batalla.
3Todos tus jefes huyeron juntos,
   pero fueron capturados
sin haber disparado el arco.
Todos tus prisioneros fueron capturados

mientras trataban de huir.

4Por eso dije: «Apártense de mí;
   déjenme llorar amargamente.
No insistan en consolarme:
   ¡la hija de mi pueblo ha sido destruida!»

5El Señor, el SEÑOR *Todopoderoso,
   ha decretado un día de pánico,
un día de humillación y desconcierto
   en el valle de la Visión,
un día para derribar muros
   y para clamar a las montañas.
6Montado en sus carros de combate,
   Elam toma la aljaba;
Quir saca el escudo a relucir.
7Llenos de carros de combate
   están tus valles preferidos;
apostados a la puerta están los jinetes.
8¡Judá se ha quedado indefensa!

Aquel día ustedes se fijaron
   en el arsenal del Palacio del bosque.
9Vieron que en la ciudad de David
   había muchas brechas,
en el estanque inferior
   guardaron agua,
10contaron las casas de Jerusalén
   y derribaron algunas para reforzar el muro,
11entre los dos muros construyeron un
     depósito
para las aguas del estanque antiguo,
pero no se fijaron en quien lo hizo,
   ni consideraron al que hace tiempo lo
     planeó.

12En aquel día el Señor,
   el SEÑOR Todopoderoso,
los llamó a llorar y a lamentarse,
   a raparse la cabeza y a hacer duelo.
13¡Pero miren, hay gozo y alegría!
   ¡Se sacrifican vacas, se matan ovejas,
se come carne y se bebe vino!

«¡Comamos y bebamos,
   que mañana moriremos!»

14El SEÑOR Todopoderoso me reveló al oído:
«No se te perdonará este pecado hasta el día de tu
muerte. Lo digo yo, el Señor, el SEÑOR Todopoderoso.»

15Así dice el Señor, el SEÑOR Todopoderoso: «Ve
a encontrarte con Sebna, el mayordomo, que está a
cargo del palacio, y dile:

16»¿Qué haces aquí?
   ¿Quién te dio permiso
para cavarte aquí un sepulcro?
¿Por qué tallas en las alturas tu lugar de
     reposo,
y lo esculpes en la roca?

17» "Mira, hombre poderoso,
   el SEÑOR está a punto de agarrarte
y arrojarte con violencia.
18Te hará rodar como pelota,
   y te lanzará a una tierra inmensa.
Allí morirás; allí quedarán
   tus gloriosos carros de combate.
¡Serás la vergüenza de la casa de tu señor!
19Te destituiré de tu cargo,

---

t **21:8** *el centinela* (Qumrán y Siríaca); *un león* (TM).   u **21:11** En hebreo, *Dumá* significa *silencio* o *quietud;* juego de palabras con *Edom.*

y serás expulsado de tu puesto."

20»En aquel día llamaré a mi siervo Eliaquín hijo de Jilquías. **21**Le pondré tu túnica, le colocaré tu cinto, y le daré tu autoridad. Será como un padre para los habitantes de Jerusalén y para la tribu de Judá. **22**Sobre sus hombros pondré la llave de la casa de David; lo que él abra, nadie podrá cerrarlo; lo que él cierre, nadie podrá abrirlo. **23**Como a una estaca, lo clavaré en un lugar firme, y será como un trono de honor para la dinastía de su padre. **24**De él penderá toda la gloria de su familia: sus descendientes y sus vástagos, y toda la vajilla pequeña, desde los cántaros hasta las tazas.

25»En aquel día —afirma el SEÑOR Todopoderoso—, cederá la estaca clavada en el lugar firme; será arrancada de raíz y se vendrá abajo, con la carga que colgaba de ella.» El SEÑOR mismo lo ha dicho.

Profecía contra Tiro

23 Profecía contra Tiro:

¡Giman, barcos de Tarsis!,
     porque destruidas están su casa y su
          puerto.
Desde la tierra de Chipre
     les ha llegado la noticia.

2¡Callen, habitantes de la costa,
     comerciantes de Sidón,
     ciudad que han enriquecido los marinos!
3Sobre las grandes aguas
     llegó el grano de Sijor;
Tiro se volvió el centro comercial de las
          naciones;
     la cosecha del Nilo le aportaba ganancias.
4Avergüénzate, Sidón, fortaleza del mar,
     porque el mar ha dicho:
«No he estado con dolores de parto ni he dado
          a luz;
     no he criado hijos ni educado hijas.»
5Cuando la noticia llegue a Egipto,
     lo que se diga de Tiro los angustiará.

6Pasen a Tarsis;
     giman, habitantes de la costa.
7¿Es ésta su ciudad alegre,
     la ciudad tan antigua,
cuyos pies la han llevado
     a establecerse en tierras lejanas?
8¿Quién planeó esto contra Tiro,
     la ciudad que confiere coronas,
cuyos comerciantes son príncipes,
     y sus negociantes reconocidos en la tierra?
9Lo planeó el SEÑOR *Todopoderoso
     para abatir la altivez de toda gloria
     y humillar a toda la gente importante de la
          tierra.

10Hija de Tarsis,
     cultiva^v tu tierra como en el Nilo,
     porque tu puerto ya no existe.
11El SEÑOR ha extendido su mano sobre el mar
     y ha puesto a temblar a los reinos,
     ha ordenado destruir las fortalezas de
          Canaán.
12Él dijo:
«¡Virgen violentada, hija de Sidón:
     no volverás a alegrarte!

»Levántate y cruza hasta Chipre;

¡ni siquiera allí encontrarás descanso!»
13¡Mira la tierra de los *caldeos!
     ¡Ese pueblo ya no existe!
Asiria la ha convertido
     en refugio de las fieras del desierto;
levantaron torres de asalto,
     demolieron sus fortalezas
     y las convirtieron en ruinas.

14¡Giman, barcos de Tarsis,
     porque destruida está su fortaleza!

15En aquel tiempo Tiro será olvidada durante setenta años, que es lo que vive un rey. Pero al cabo de esos setenta años le sucederá a Tiro lo que dice la canción de la prostituta:

16«Tú, prostituta olvidada,
     toma un arpa y recorre la ciudad;
toca lo mejor que puedas,
     y canta muchas canciones,
     para que te recuerden.»

17Al cabo de setenta años, el SEÑOR se ocupará de Tiro, la cual volverá a venderse y prostituirse con todos los reinos de la tierra. **18**Pero sus ingresos y ganancias se consagrarán al SEÑOR; no serán almacenados ni atesorados. Sus ganancias serán para los que habitan en presencia del SEÑOR, para que se alimenten en abundancia y se vistan con ropas finas.

Juicio universal

24 Miren, el SEÑOR arrasa la tierra y la devasta, trastorna su faz y dispersa a sus habitantes. **2**Lo mismo les pasará
     al sacerdote y al pueblo,
     al amo y al esclavo,
     a la señora y a la esclava,
     al comprador y al vendedor,
     al prestamista y al prestatario,
     al acreedor y al deudor.
3La tierra queda totalmente arrasada,
     saqueada por completo,
     porque el SEÑOR lo ha dicho.
4La tierra languidece y se marchita;
     el mundo se marchita y desfallece;
     desfallecen los notables de la tierra.
5La tierra yace profanada,
     pisoteada por sus habitantes,
porque han desobedecido las leyes,
     han violado los estatutos,
     han quebrantado el *pacto eterno.
6Por eso una maldición consume a la tierra,
     y los culpables son sus habitantes.
Por eso el fuego los consume,
     y sólo quedan unos cuantos.
7Languidece el vino nuevo, desfallece la vid;
     gimen todos los corazones alegres.
8Cesó el ritmo de los tambores,
     se aplacó el bullicio de los que se divierten,
     se apagó el júbilo del arpa.
9Ya no beben vino mientras cantan;
     a los borrachos el licor les sabe amargo.
10La ciudad del caos yace desolada;
     cerrado está el acceso a toda casa.
11Clamor hay en las calles porque falta el vino;
     toda alegría se ha extinguido;
     el júbilo ha sido desterrado.
12La ciudad está en ruinas;
     su *puerta está hecha pedazos.
13Así sucederá en medio de la tierra

---

v 23:10 *cultiva* (Qumrán y LXX); *atraviesa* (TM).

y entre las naciones,
como cuando a golpes se cosechan aceitunas,
como cuando se recogen rebuscos
después de la vendimia.
14El remanente eleva su voz y grita de alegría;
desde el occidente aclama la majestad del
SEÑOR.
15Por eso, glorifiquen al SEÑOR en el oriente;
el *nombre del SEÑOR, Dios de Israel,
en las costas del mar.
16Desde los confines de la tierra oímos cantar:
«¡Gloria al justo!»
Pero yo digo: «¡Ay de mí!
¡Qué dolor, que me consumo!»
Los traidores traicionan,
los traidores maquinan traiciones.
17¡Terror, fosa y trampa
están contra ti, habitante de la tierra!
18Quien huya del grito de terror
caerá en la fosa,
y quien suba del fondo de la fosa
caerá en la trampa,
porque abiertas están las ventanas de lo alto,
y tiemblan los cimientos de la tierra.
19La tierra se quiebra, se desintegra;
la tierra se agrieta, se resquebraja;
la tierra tiembla y retiembla.
20La tierra se tambalea como un borracho,
se sacude como una choza.
Tanto pesa sobre ella su rebelión
que caerá para no volver a levantarse.
21En aquel día el SEÑOR castigará
a los poderes celestiales en el cielo
y a los reyes terrenales en la tierra.
22Serán amontonados en un pozo,
como prisioneros entre rejas,
y después de muchos días se les castigará.
23La luna se sonrojará
y el sol se avergonzará,
porque sobre el monte *Sión,
sobre Jerusalén,
reinará el SEÑOR *Todopoderoso,
glorioso entre sus *ancianos.

Canto de alabanza al SEÑOR

25 SEÑOR, tú eres mi Dios;
te exaltaré y alabaré tu *nombre
porque has hecho maravillas.
Desde tiempos antiguos
tus planes son fieles y seguros.
2Has convertido la ciudad en un montón de
escombros,
la ciudad fortificada en una ruina.
Ya no es ciudad la ciudadela de extranjeros;
nunca más volverá a ser reconstruida.
3Por eso te glorifica un pueblo poderoso;
te teme la ciudad de las naciones crueles.
4Porque tú has sido,
en su angustia,
un baluarte para el desvalido,
un refugio para el necesitado,
un resguardo contra la tormenta,
una sombra contra el calor.
En cambio, el aliento de los crueles
es como una tormenta contra un muro,
5como el calor en el desierto.
Tú aplacas el tumulto de los extranjeros,
como se aplaca el calor bajo la sombra de
una nube,

y ahogas la alharaca de los tiranos.
6Sobre este monte, el SEÑOR *Todopoderoso
preparará para todos los pueblos
un banquete de manjares especiales,
un banquete de vinos añejos,
de manjares especiales y de selectos vinos
añejos.
7Sobre este monte rasgará
el velo que cubre a todos los pueblos,
el manto que envuelve a todas las naciones.
8Devorará a la muerte para siempre;
el SEÑOR omnipotente enjugará las
lágrimas de todo rostro,
y quitará de toda la tierra
el oprobio de su pueblo.
El SEÑOR mismo lo ha dicho.

9En aquel día se dirá:

«¡Sí, éste es nuestro Dios;
en él confiamos, y él nos salvó!
¡Éste es el SEÑOR, en él hemos confiado;
regocijémonos y alegrémonos en su
*salvación!»

10La mano del SEÑOR se posará sobre este
monte,
pero Moab será pisoteada en su sitio,
como se pisotea la paja en el muladar.
11Allí extenderán sus manos,
como al nadar las extiende un nadador.
Pero el SEÑOR abatirá su orgullo,
junto con la destrezaw de sus manos.
12Derribará, hará caer y abatirá
tus muros altos y fortificados,
hasta dejarlos hechos polvo sobre la tierra.

Canto de victoria

26 En aquel día se entonará esta canción en la
tierra de Judá:

«Tenemos una ciudad fuerte.
Como un muro, como un baluarte,
Dios ha interpuesto su *salvación.
2Abran las *puertas, para que entre
la nación justa que se mantiene fiel.
3Al de carácter firme
lo guardarás en perfecta *paz,
porque en ti confía.
4Confíen en el SEÑOR para siempre,
porque el SEÑOR es una *Roca eterna.
5Él hace caer a los que habitan en lo alto
y abate a la ciudad enaltecida:
la abate hasta dejarla por el suelo,
la derriba hasta hacerla morder el polvo.
6¡Los débiles y los desvalidos
la pisotean con sus propios pies!»

7La senda del justo es llana;
tú, que eres recto, allanas su *camino.
8Sí, en ti esperamos, SEÑOR,
y en la senda de tus juicios;
tu *nombre y tu memoria
son el deseo de nuestra *vida.
9Todo mi ser te desea por las noches;
por la mañana mi espíritu te busca.
Pues cuando tus juicios llegan a la tierra,
los habitantes del mundo aprenden lo que
es justicia.
10Aunque al malvado se le tenga compasión,
no aprende lo que es justicia;

---

w 25:11 *la destreza.* Palabra de difícil traducción.

en tierra de rectitud actúa con iniquidad,
y no reconoce la majestad del SEÑOR.

11Levantada está, SEÑOR, tu mano,
pero ellos no la ven.
¡Que vean tu celo por el pueblo, y sean
avergonzados;
que sean consumidos por el fuego
destinado a tus enemigos!

12SEÑOR, tú estableces la paz en favor nuestro,
porque tú eres quien realiza todas nuestras
obras.
13SEÑOR y Dios nuestro,
otros señores nos han gobernado,
pero sólo a tu nombre damos honra.
14Ya están muertos, y no revivirán;
ya son sombras, y no se levantarán.
Tú los has castigado y destruido;
has hecho que perezca su memoria.
15Tú, SEÑOR, has engrandecido a la nación;
la has engrandecido y te has glorificado;
has extendido las fronteras de todo el país.
16SEÑOR, en la angustia te buscaron;
apenas si lograban susurrar una oración[x]
cuando tú ya los corregías.
17SEÑOR, nosotros estuvimos ante ti
como cuando una mujer embarazada
se retuerce y grita de dolor
al momento de dar a luz.
18Concebimos, nos retorcimos,
pero dimos a luz tan sólo viento.
No trajimos salvación a la tierra,
ni nacieron los habitantes del mundo.

19Pero tus muertos vivirán,
sus cadáveres volverán a la vida.
¡Despierten y griten de alegría,
moradores del polvo!
Porque tu rocío es como el rocío de la mañana,
y la tierra devolverá sus muertos.

20¡Anda, pueblo mío, entra en tus habitaciones
y cierra tus puertas tras de ti;
escóndete por un momento,
hasta que pase la ira!
21¡Estén alerta!,
que el SEÑOR va a salir de su morada
para castigar la maldad
de los habitantes del país.
La tierra pondrá al descubierto la sangre
derramada;
¡ya no ocultará a los masacrados en ella!

Liberación de Israel

27 En aquel día el SEÑOR castigará
a *Leviatán, la serpiente huidiza,
a Leviatán, la serpiente tortuosa.
Con su espada violenta, grande y poderosa,
matará al Dragón que está en el mar.
2«Canten en aquel día
a la viña escogida:
3Yo, el SEÑOR, soy su guardián;
todo el tiempo riego mi viña.
Día y noche cuido de ella
para que nadie le haga daño.
4No estoy enojado.
Si tuviera zarzas y espinos,
pelearía contra ella
y la quemaría totalmente,
5a menos que ella acudiera a mi refugio

e hiciera las paces conmigo,
sí, que hiciera las paces conmigo.»

6Días vendrán en que Jacob echará raíces,
en que Israel retoñará y florecerá,
y llenará el mundo con sus frutos.
7¿Acaso el SEÑOR lo ha golpeado
como hizo con quien lo golpeaba?
¿Acaso le dio muerte
como hizo con quienes lo mataron?
8Contendió con él con guerra[y] y destierro;
lo expulsó con su soplo violento
al soplar el viento del este.
9Así quedará *expiada la iniquidad de Jacob;
ésta será la única condición
para que se le perdone su pecado:
que reduzca a polvo todas las piedras del altar,
como si moliera piedra caliza,
y no deje en pie ninguna imagen de *Aserá
ni altar de incienso alguno.

10En ruinas está la ciudad fortificada;
es un sitio sin habitantes,
abandonado como el desierto.
Allí se echa el ternero,
allí pace y deshoja las ramas.
11Una vez secas, las ramas se quiebran;
vienen luego las mujeres y con ellas hacen
fuego.
Porque éste es un pueblo sin entendimiento;
por eso su Creador no le tiene compasión,
ni de él se apiada quien lo formó.

12En aquel día el SEÑOR trillará desde las corrientes del Éufrates hasta el torrente de Egipto, y ustedes, israelitas, serán recogidos uno por uno. **13**En
aquel día sonará una gran trompeta. Los que fueron
llevados a Asiria y los que fueron desterrados a Egipto vendrán y adorarán al SEÑOR sobre el monte *santo en Jerusalén.

Ay de Efraín

28 ¡Ay de la altiva corona de los borrachos de
Efraín,
de la flor marchita de su gloriosa
hermosura,
que está sobre la cumbre de un valle fértil!
¡Ay de los abatidos por el vino!
2Miren, el Señor cuenta con alguien
que es fuerte y poderoso:
Éste echará todo por tierra con violencia,
como tormenta de granizo,
como tempestad destructora,
como tormenta de aguas torrenciales,
como torrente desbordado.
3La altiva corona de los borrachos de Efraín,
será pisoteada.
4Esa flor marchita de su gloriosa hermosura,
sobre la cumbre de un valle fértil,
será como higo maduro antes de la cosecha:
apenas alguien lo ve y lo tiene en la mano,
se lo traga.

5En aquel día el SEÑOR *Todopoderoso
será una hermosa corona,
una diadema gloriosa
para el remanente de su pueblo.
6Él infundirá espíritu de justicia
al que se sienta en el tribunal,
y valor a los que rechazan

---

x 26:16 *apenas … oración.* Frase de difícil traducción. **y 27:8** *guerra.* Palabra de difícil traducción.

los asaltos a la puerta.

7También sacerdotes y profetas
se tambalean por causa del vino,
trastabillan por causa del licor;
quedan aturdidos con el vino,
tropiezan a causa del licor.
Cuando tienen visiones, titubean;
cuando toman decisiones, vacilan.
8¡Sí, regadas de vómito están todas las mesas,
y no queda limpio ni un solo lugar!

9«¿A quién creen que están enseñando?
¿A quién le están explicando su mensaje?
¿Creen que somos niños recién destetados,
que acaban de dejar el pecho?
10¿Niños que repiten:
"a-b-c-ch-d, a-e-i-o-u,
un poquito aquí, un poquito allá"?»z

11Pues bien, Dios hablará a este pueblo
con labios burlones y lenguas extrañas,
12pueblo al que dijo:
«Éste es el lugar de descanso;
que descanse el fatigado»;
y también:
«Éste es el lugar de reposo.»
¡Pero no quisieron escuchar!
13Pues la palabra del SEÑOR
para ellos será también:
«a-b-c-ch-d, a-e-i-o-u,
un poquito aquí, un poquito allá.»
Para que se vayan de espaldas cuando
caminen,
y queden heridos, enredados y atrapados.

14Por tanto, gobernantes insolentes
de este pueblo de Jerusalén,
escuchen la palabra del SEÑOR:

15Ustedes dicen: «Hemos hecho un pacto con la
muerte,
hemos hecho una alianza con el *sepulcro.
Cuando venga una calamidad abrumadora,
no nos podrá alcanzar,
porque hemos hecho de la mentira nuestro
refugio
y del engaño nuestro escondite.»

16Por eso dice el SEÑOR omnipotente:

«¡Yo pongo en *Sión una piedra probada!,
piedra angular y preciosa para un cimiento
firme;
el que confíe no andará desorientado.
17Pondré como nivel la justicia,
y la rectitud como plomada.
El granizo arrasará con el refugio de la
mentira,
y las aguas inundarán el escondite.
18Se anulará el pacto que hicieron con la
muerte,
quedará sin efecto su alianza con el
sepulcro.
Cuando venga la calamidad abrumadora,
a ustedes los aplastará.
19Cada vez que pase, los arrebatará;
pasará mañana tras mañana, de día y de
noche.»

La comprensión de este mensaje
causará terror absoluto.
20La cama es demasiado estrecha para estirarse
en ella,
la manta es demasiado corta para
envolverse en ella.
21Sí, el SEÑOR se levantará como en el monte
Perasín,
se moverá como en el valle de Gabaón;
para llevar a cabo su extraña obra,
para realizar su insólita tarea.
22Ahora bien, dejen de burlarse,
no sea que se aprieten más sus cadenas;
porque me ha hecho saber el Señor,
el SEÑOR Todopoderoso,
acerca de la destrucción decretada
contra todo el país.

23Escuchen, oigan mi voz;
presten atención, oigan mi palabra:
24Cuando un agricultor ara para sembrar,
¿lo hace sin descanso?
¿Se pasa todos los días rompiendo y
rastrillando su terreno?
25Después de que ha emparejado la superficie,
¿no siembra eneldo y esparce comino?
¿No siembra trigo en hileras,a
cebada en el lugar debido,
y centeno en las orillas?
26Es Dios quien lo instruye
y le enseña cómo hacerlo.

27Porque no se trilla el eneldo con rastrillo,
ni sobre el comino se pasa una rueda de
carreta,
sino que el eneldo se golpea con una vara,
y el comino con un palo.
28El grano se tritura, pero no demasiado,
ni tampoco se trilla sin descanso.
Se le pasan las ruedas de la carreta,
pero los caballos no lo trituran.
29También esto viene del SEÑOR
Todopoderoso,
admirable por su consejo
y magnífico por su sabiduría.

Ay de la Ciudad de David

29 ¡Ay, Ariel, Ariel,
ciudad donde acampó David!
Añadan a un año otro año más,
y que prosiga el ciclo de las fiestas.
2Pero a Ariel la sitiaré;
habrá llanto y lamento,
y será para mí como un brasero del altar.b
3Acamparé contra ti, y te rodearé;
te cercaré con empalizadas,
y levantaré contra ti torres de asalto.
4Humillada, desde el suelo elevarás tu voz;
tu palabra apenas se levantará del polvo.
Saldrá tu voz de la tierra
como si fuera la de un fantasma;
tu palabra, desde el polvo,
apenas será un susurro.

5Pero la multitud de tus enemigos
quedará hecha polvo fino,
y la multitud de despiadados
será como la paja que se lleva el viento.

z 28:10 Versículo de difícil traducción (posiblemente remedo burlón de una lección de abecedario); también en v. 13.
a 28:25 hileras. Palabra de difícil traducción. b 29:2 un brasero del altar. Esta frase traduce una palabra hebrea que es
idéntica al nombre Ariel.

De repente, en un instante,
6vendrá contra ti el SEÑOR *Todopoderoso;
vendrá con truenos, terremotos
y gran estruendo,
vendrá con una violenta tormenta
y con devoradoras llamas de fuego.
7La multitud de todas las naciones
que batallan contra Ariel,
todos los que luchan contra ella
y contra su fortaleza,
aquellos que la asedian,
serán como un sueño,
como una visión nocturna.
8Como el hambriento que sueña que está
comiendo,
pero despierta y aún tiene hambre;
como el sediento que sueña que está
bebiendo,
pero despierta y la sed le reseca la
garganta.
Así sucederá con la multitud de todas las
naciones
que luchan contra el monte *Sión.

9Pierdan el juicio, quédense pasmados,
pierdan la vista, quédense ciegos;
embriáguense, pero no con vino;
tambaléense, pero no por el licor.
10El SEÑOR ha derramado sobre ustedes
un espíritu de profundo sueño;
a los profetas les cubrió los ojos,
a los videntes les tapó la cara.

11Para ustedes, toda esta visión no es otra cosa
que palabras en un rollo de pergamino sellado. Si le
dan el rollo a alguien que sepa leer, y le dicen: «Lea
esto, por favor», éste responderá: «No puedo hacerlo; está sellado.» 12Y si le dan el rollo a alguien que no
sepa leer, y le dicen: «Lea esto, por favor», éste responderá: «No sé leer.»

13El Señor dice:

«Este pueblo me alaba con la boca
y me honra con los labios,
pero su *corazón está lejos de mí.
Su adoración no es más que un mandato
enseñado por *hombres.
14Por eso, una vez más asombraré a este pueblo
con prodigios maravillosos;
perecerá la sabiduría de sus sabios,
y se esfumará la inteligencia de sus
inteligentes.»

15¡Ay de los que, para esconder sus planes,
se ocultan del SEÑOR en las profundidades;
cometen sus fechorías en la oscuridad, y
piensan:
«¿Quién nos ve? ¿Quién nos conoce?»!
16¡Qué manera de falsear las cosas!
¿Acaso el alfarero es igual al barro?
¿Acaso le dirá el objeto al que lo modeló:
«Él no me hizo»?
¿Puede la vasija decir del alfarero:
«Él no entiende nada»?

17Muy pronto el Líbano
se convertirá en campo fértil,
y el campo fértil se convertirá en bosque.
18En aquel día podrán los sordos
oír la lectura del rollo,
y los ojos de los ciegos podrán ver
desde la oscuridad y la penumbra.
19Los pobres volverán a alegrarse en el SEÑOR,

los más necesitados se regocijarán en el
*Santo de Israel.
20Se desvanecerán los despiadados,
desaparecerán los insolentes,
y todos los que no duermen para hacer el mal
serán exterminados;
21los que con una palabra hacen culpable a una
persona,
los que en el tribunal ponen trampas al
defensor
y con engaños perjudican al indefenso.

22Por eso, el SEÑOR, el redentor de Abraham, dice
así a los descendientes de Jacob:

«Jacob ya no será avergonzado,
ni palidecerá su rostro.
23Cuando él vea a sus hijos,
y la obra de mis manos en medio de él,
todos ellos santificarán mi *nombre;
santificarán al Santo de Jacob,
y temerán al Dios de Israel.
24Los de espíritu extraviado recibirán
entendimiento;
y los murmuradores aceptarán ser
instruidos.»

Ay de la nación obstinada

30 El SEÑOR ha dictado esta sentencia:

«Ay de los hijos rebeldes
que ejecutan planes que no son míos,
que hacen alianzas contrarias a mi Espíritu,
que amontonan pecado sobre pecado,
2que bajan a Egipto sin consultarme,
que se acogen a la protección de Faraón,
y se refugian bajo la sombra de Egipto.
3¡La protección de Faraón será su vergüenza!
¡El refugiarse bajo la sombra de Egipto, su
humillación!
4Aunque en Zoán tengan funcionarios,
y a Janés hayan llegado sus mensajeros,
5todos quedarán avergonzados
por culpa de un pueblo que les resulta
inútil,
que no les brinda ninguna ayuda ni provecho,
sino sólo vergüenza y frustración.»

6Ésta es la sentencia que se ha dictado contra los
animales del Néguev:

Por tierra de dificultades y angustias,
de leones y leonas,
de víboras y serpientes voladoras,
llevan ellos a lomo de burro
las riquezas de esa nación inútil,
y sus tesoros, a lomo de camello.
7La ayuda de Egipto no sirve para nada;
por eso la llamo: «*Rahab, la inmóvil».

8Anda, pues, delante de ellos,
y grábalo en una tablilla.
Escríbelo en un rollo de cuero,
para que en los días venideros
quede como un testimonio eterno.
9Porque éste es un pueblo rebelde;
son hijos engañosos,
hijos que no quieren escuchar
la enseñanza del SEÑOR.
10A los videntes les dicen:
«¡No tengan más visiones!»,
y a los profetas:
«¡No nos sigan profetizando la verdad!
Dígannos cosas agradables,

profeticen ilusiones.
11 ¡Apártense del camino,
    retírense de esta senda,
y dejen de enfrentarnos
    con el *Santo de Israel!»

12 Así dice el Santo de Israel:

«Ustedes han rechazado esta palabra;
    han confiado en la opresión y en la
        perversidad,
    y se han apoyado en ellas.
13 Por eso su iniquidad se alzará frente a ustedes
    como un muro alto y agrietado,
    a punto de derrumbarse:
        ¡de repente, en un instante, se desplomará!
14 Su iniquidad quedará hecha pedazos,
    hecha añicos sin piedad, como vasija de
        barro:
    ni uno solo de sus pedazos servirá
    para sacar brasas del fuego
    ni agua de una cisterna.»

15 Porque así dice el SEÑOR omnipotente, el Santo de Israel:

«En el *arrepentimiento y la calma está su
        *salvación,
    en la serenidad y la confianza está su
        fuerza,
    ¡pero ustedes no lo quieren reconocer!
16 Se resisten y dicen: "Huiremos a caballo."
    ¡Por eso, así tendrán que huir!
Dicen: "Cabalgaremos sobre caballos veloces."
    ¡Por eso, veloces serán sus perseguidores!
17 Ante la amenaza de uno solo;
    mil de ustedes saldrán huyendo;
ante la amenaza de cinco,
    huirán todos ustedes;
hasta quedar abandonados
    como un mástil en la cima de una montaña,
    como una señal sobre una colina.»

18 Por eso el SEÑOR los espera, para tenerles
        piedad;
    por eso se levanta para mostrarles
        compasión.
Porque el SEÑOR es un Dios de *justicia.
    *¡Dichosos todos los que en él esperan!

19 Pueblo de *Sión, que habitas en Jerusalén, ya no llorarás más. ¡El Dios de piedad se apiadará de ti cuando clames pidiendo ayuda! Tan pronto como te oiga, te responderá. 20 Aunque el Señor te dé pan de adversidad y agua de aflicción, tu maestro no se esconderá más; con tus propios ojos lo verás. 21 Ya sea que te desvíes a la derecha o a la izquierda, tus oídos percibirán a tus espaldas una voz que te dirá: «Éste es el *camino; síguelo.» 22 Entonces profanarás tus ídolos enchapados en plata y tus imágenes revestidas de oro; los arrojarás como cosa *impura, y les dirás: «¡Fuera de aquí!»
    23 El SEÑOR te enviará lluvia para la semilla que siembren en la tierra, y el alimento que produzca la tierra será suculento y abundante. En aquel día tu ganado pacerá en extensas praderas. 24 Los bueyes y los burros que trabajan la tierra comerán el mejor forraje, aventado con bieldo y horquilla. 25 En el día de la gran masacre, cuando caigan las torres, habrá arroyos y corrientes de agua en toda montaña alta y en toda colina elevada. 26 Cuando el SEÑOR ponga

una venda en la fractura de su pueblo y sane las heridas que le causó, brillará la luna como el sol, y será la luz del sol siete veces más intensa, como la luz de siete días enteros.

27 ¡Miren! El *nombre del SEÑOR viene de lejos,
    con ardiente ira y densa humareda.
Sus labios están llenos de furor;
    su lengua es como un fuego consumidor.
28 Su aliento es cual torrente desbordado
    que llega hasta el cuello,
para zarandear a las naciones
    en la zaranda destructora.
Pone en las quijadas de los pueblos
    un freno que los desvía.
29 Ustedes cantarán como en noche de fiesta
        solemne;
    su *corazón se alegrará,
como cuando uno sube con flautas
    a la montaña del SEÑOR,
    a la *Roca de Israel.
30 El SEÑOR hará oír su majestuosa voz,
    y descargará su brazo:
con rugiente ira y llama de fuego consumidor,
    con aguacero, tormenta y granizo.
31 La voz del SEÑOR quebrantará a Asiria;
    la golpeará con su bastón.
32 Cada golpe que el SEÑOR descargue sobre ella
    con su vara de castigo
será al son de panderos y de arpas;
    agitando su brazo, peleará contra ellos.
33 Porque Tofet[c] está preparada desde hace
        tiempo;
    está dispuesta incluso para el rey.
Se ha hecho una pira de fuego profunda y
        ancha,
    con abundancia de fuego y leña;
el soplo del SEÑOR la encenderá
    como un torrente de azufre ardiente.

Ay de los que confían en Egipto

31 ¡Ay de los que descienden a Egipto en busca
        de ayuda,
de los que se apoyan en la caballería,
de los que confían en la multitud de sus carros
        de guerra
    y en la gran fuerza de sus jinetes,
pero no toman en cuenta al *Santo de Israel,
    ni buscan al SEÑOR!
2 Sin embargo, el SEÑOR es también sabio,
    y traerá calamidad,
    y no se retractará de sus palabras.
Se levantará contra la dinastía de los
        malvados,
    contra los que ayudan a los malhechores.
3 Los egipcios, en cambio, son *hombres y no
        dioses;
    sus caballos son carne y no espíritu.
Cuando el SEÑOR extienda su mano,
    tropezará el que presta ayuda
y caerá el que la recibe.
    ¡Todos juntos perecerán!

4 Porque así me dice el SEÑOR:

«Como león que gruñe sobre la presa
    cuando contra él se reúne
        toda una cuadrilla de pastores;
como cachorro de león
    que no se asusta por sus gritos

---

c **30:33** *Tofet.* Lugar de incineración, cercano a Jerusalén.

ni se inquieta por su tumulto,
así también el SEÑOR *Todopoderoso
descenderá para combatir
sobre el monte *Sión, sobre su cumbre.
⁵Como aves que revolotean sobre el nido,
así también el SEÑOR Todopoderoso
protegerá a Jerusalén;
la protegerá y la librará,
la defenderá y la rescatará.»

⁶Israelitas, ¡vuélvanse a aquel contra quien ustedes se han rebelado tan abiertamente! ⁷Porque en aquel día cada uno de ustedes rechazará a los ídolos de plata y oro que sus propias manos pecadoras fabricaron.

⁸«Asiria caerá a espada, pero no de hombre;
una espada, pero no de hombre, la
consumirá.
Huirá para escapar de la espada,
y sus jóvenes serán sometidos a trabajos
forzados.
⁹A causa del terror caerá su fortaleza;
¡sus jefes dejarán abandonada su bandera!»
Lo afirma el SEÑOR,
cuyo fuego está en Sión,
y cuyo horno está en Jerusalén.

El reino de justicia

32 Miren, un rey reinará con rectitud
y los gobernantes gobernarán con
justicia.
²Cada uno será como un refugio contra el
viento,
como un resguardo contra la tormenta;
como arroyos de agua en tierra seca,
como la sombra de un peñasco en el
desierto.

³No se nublarán los ojos de los que ven;
prestarán atención los oídos de los que
oyen.
⁴La *mente impulsiva comprenderá y
entenderá,
la lengua tartamuda hablará con fluidez y
claridad.
⁵Ya no se llamará noble al necio
ni será respetado el canalla.
⁶Porque el necio profiere *necedades,
y su mente maquina iniquidad;
practica la impiedad,
y habla falsedades contra el SEÑOR;
deja con hambre al hambriento,
y le niega el agua al sediento.
⁷El canalla recurre a artimañas malignas,
y trama designios infames;
destruye a los pobres con mentiras,
aunque el necesitado reclama justicia.
⁸El noble, por el contrario,
concibe nobles planes,
y en sus nobles acciones se afirma.

Las mujeres de Jerusalén

⁹Mujeres despreocupadas,
¡levántense y escúchenme!
Hijas que se sienten tan confiadas,
¡presten atención a lo que voy a decirles!
¹⁰Ustedes, que se sienten tan confiadas,
en poco más de un año temblarán;
porque fallará la vendimia,

y no llegará la cosecha.
¹¹Mujeres despreocupadas, ¡estremézcanse!
Ustedes, que se sienten tan confiadas,
¡pónganse a temblar!
Desvístanse, desnúdense;
pónganse ropa de luto.
¹²Golpéense el pecho,
por los campos agradables,
por los viñedos fértiles,
¹³por el suelo de mi pueblo
cubierto de espinos y de zarzas,
por todas las casas donde hay alegría
y por esta ciudad donde hay diversión.
¹⁴La fortaleza será abandonada,
y desamparada la ciudad populosa;
para siempre convertidas en cuevas
quedarán la ciudadela y la atalaya;
convertidas en deleite de asnos,
en pastizal de rebaños,
¹⁵hasta que desde lo alto
el Espíritu sea derramado sobre nosotros.
Entonces el desierto se volverá un campo
fértil,
y el campo fértil se convertirá en bosque.
¹⁶La justicia morará en el desierto,
y en el campo fértil habitará la rectitud.
¹⁷El producto de la justicia será la *paz;
tranquilidad y seguridad perpetuas serán
su fruto.
¹⁸Mi pueblo habitará en un lugar de paz,
en moradas seguras,
en serenos lugares de reposo.
¹⁹Aunque el granizo arrase con el bosque
y la ciudad sea completamente allanada,
²⁰*¡dichosos ustedes,
los que siembran junto al agua,
y dejan sueltos al buey y al asno!

Angustia y auxilio

33 ¡Ay de ti, destructor, que no has sido
destruido!
¡Ay de ti, traidor, que no has sido
traicionado!
Cuando dejes de destruir, te destruirán;
cuando dejes de traicionar, te traicionarán.

²SEÑOR, ten compasión de nosotros;
pues en ti esperamos.
Sé nuestra fortaleza^d cada mañana,
nuestra *salvación en tiempo de angustia.
³Al estruendo de tu voz, huyen los pueblos;
cuando te levantas, se dispersan las
naciones.
⁴Los despojos de ustedes se recogen
como si fueran devorados por orugas;
sobre ellos se lanza el enemigo
como una bandada de langostas.

⁵Exaltado es el SEÑOR porque mora en las
alturas,
y llena a *Sión de justicia y rectitud.
⁶Él será la seguridad de tus tiempos,
te dará en abundancia salvación, sabiduría
y conocimiento;
el temor del SEÑOR será tu tesoro.

⁷¡Miren cómo gritan sus valientes en las calles!
¡amargamente lloran los mensajeros de
*paz!
⁸Los caminos están desolados,

---

^d **33:2** *nuestra fortaleza* (Siríaca, Targum y Vulgata); *la fortaleza de ellos* (TM).

nadie transita por los senderos.
El *pacto se ha quebrantado,
se desprecia a los testigos,[e]
ia nadie se le respeta!
9La tierra está de luto y languidece;
el Líbano se avergüenza y se marchita;
Sarón es como un desierto;
Basán y el Carmelo pierden su follaje.

10«Ahora me levantaré —dice el SEÑOR—.
Ahora seré exaltado,
ahora seré ensalzado.
11Ustedes conciben cizaña
y dan a luz paja;
ipero el fuego de mi aliento los consumirá!
12Los pueblos serán calcinados,
como espinos cortados arderán en el
fuego.»

13Ustedes, que están lejos,
oigan lo que he hecho;
y ustedes, que están cerca,
reconozcan mi poder.
14Los pecadores están aterrados en Sión;
el temblor atrapa a los impíos:
«¿Quién de nosotros puede habitar
en el fuego consumidor?
¿Quién de nosotros puede habitar
en la hoguera eterna?»
15Sólo el que procede con justicia
y habla con rectitud,
el que rechaza la ganancia de la extorsión
y se sacude las manos para no aceptar
soborno,
el que no presta oído a las conjuras de
asesinato
y cierra los ojos para no contemplar el mal.
16Ese tal morará en las alturas;
tendrá como refugio una fortaleza de rocas,
se le proveerá de pan,
y no le faltará el agua.

17Tus ojos verán al rey en su esplendor
y contemplarán una tierra que se extiende
hasta muy lejos.
18Dentro de ti meditarás acerca del terror, y
dirás:
«¿Dónde está el contador?
¿Dónde el recaudador de impuestos?
¿Dónde el que lleva el registro de las
torres?»
19No verás más a ese pueblo insolente,
a ese pueblo de idioma confuso,
de lengua extraña e incomprensible.

20Mira a Sión, la ciudad de nuestras fiestas;
tus ojos verán a Jerusalén,
morada apacible, campamento bien plantado;
sus estacas jamás se arrancarán,
ni se romperá ninguna de sus sogas.
21Allí el SEÑOR nos mostrará su poder.
Será como un lugar de anchos ríos y
canales.
Ningún barco de remos surcará sus aguas,
ni barcos poderosos navegarán por ellas.
22Porque el SEÑOR es nuestro guía;
el SEÑOR es nuestro gobernante.
El SEÑOR es nuestro rey:
iÉl nos salvará!

23Tus cuerdas se han aflojado:

No sostienen el mástil con firmeza
ni se despliegan las velas.
Abundante botín habrá de repartirse,
y aun los cojos se dedicarán al saqueo.
24Ningún habitante dirá: «Estoy enfermo»;
y se perdonará la iniquidad del pueblo que
allí habita.

Juicio contra las naciones

34 Naciones, iacérquense a escuchar!
Pueblos, ipresten atención!
iQue lo oiga la tierra, y todo lo que hay en ella;
el mundo, y todo lo que él produce!
2El SEÑOR está enojado con todas las naciones,
airado con todos sus ejércitos.
Él los ha *destruido por completo,
los ha entregado a la matanza.
3Serán arrojados sus muertos,
hedor despedirán sus cadáveres,
su sangre derretirá las montañas.
4Se desintegrarán todos los astros del cielo
y se enrollará el cielo como un pergamino;
toda la multitud de astros perderá su brillo,
como lo pierde la hoja marchita de la vid,
o los higos secos de la higuera.

5Mi espada se ha embriagado en el cielo;
miren cómo desciende en juicio sobre
Edom,
pueblo que he condenado a la destrucción
total.
6La espada del SEÑOR está bañada en sangre,
en la sangre de cabras y corderos;
cubierta está de grasa,
de la grasa de los riñones de carneros.
Porque el SEÑOR celebra un sacrificio en Bosra
y una gran matanza en tierra de Edom.
7Y con ellos caerán los búfalos,
los terneros y los toros.
Su tierra quedará empapada en sangre,
y su polvo se llenará de grasa.

8Porque el SEÑOR celebra un día de venganza,
un año de desagravio
para defender la causa de *Sión.
9Los arroyos de Edom se volverán ríos de brea,
su polvo se convertirá en azufre
y ardiente brea se volverá su tierra.
10Ni de día ni de noche se extinguirá,
y su humo subirá por siempre.
Quedará desolada por todas las generaciones;
nunca más transitará nadie por ella.
11Se adueñarán de ella el pelícano y el erizo;
anidarán allí el búho y el cuervo.
Dios extenderá sobre Edom
el cordel del caos
y la plomada de la desolación.
12Sus nobles no tendrán allí
nada que pueda llamarse reino;
todos sus príncipes desaparecerán.
13Los espinos invadirán sus palacios;
las ortigas y las zarzas, sus fortalezas.
Se volverá guarida de chacales
y nido de avestruces.
14Las fieras del desierto se juntarán con las
hienas,
y las cabras monteses se llamarán unas a
otras;
allí también reposarán las aves nocturnas
y encontrarán un lugar de descanso.

---

e **33:8** *los testigos* (Qumrán); *las ciudades* (TM).

¹⁵Allí el búho anidará y pondrá sus huevos;
    bajo sus alas incubará y cuidará a sus crías.
También allí se reunirán los buitres,
    cada cual con su pareja.

¹⁶Consulten el libro del SEÑOR y lean:

Ninguno de estos animales faltará;
    cada cual tendrá su pareja.
El SEÑOR mismo ha dado la orden,
    y su Espíritu los ha de reunir.
¹⁷Él les ha asignado sus lugares;
    su mano les señaló su territorio.
Ellos los poseerán para siempre,
    y morarán allí por todas las generaciones.

La alegría de los redimidos

35 Se alegrarán el desierto y el sequedal;
    se regocijará el desierto
    y florecerá como el azafrán.
²Florecerá y se regocijará:
    ¡gritará de alegría!
Se le dará la gloria del Líbano,
    y el esplendor del Carmelo y de Sarón.
Ellos verán la gloria del SEÑOR,
    el esplendor de nuestro Dios.

³Fortalezcan las manos débiles,
    afirmen las rodillas temblorosas;
⁴digan a los de *corazón temeroso:
    «Sean fuertes, no tengan miedo.
Su Dios vendrá,
    vendrá con venganza;
con retribución divina
    vendrá a salvarlos.»

⁵Se abrirán entonces los ojos de los ciegos
    y se destaparán los oídos de los sordos;
⁶saltará el cojo como un ciervo,
    y gritará de alegría la lengua del mudo.
Porque aguas brotarán en el desierto,
    y torrentes en el sequedal.
⁷La arena ardiente se convertirá en estanque,
    la tierra sedienta en manantiales
    burbujeantes.
Las guaridas donde se tendían los chacales,
    serán morada de juncos y papiros.

⁸Habrá allí una calzada
    que será llamada *Camino de *santidad.
No viajarán por ella los *impuros,
    ni transitarán por ella los necios;
    será sólo para los que siguen el camino.
⁹No habrá allí ningún león,
    ni bestia feroz que por él pase;
    ¡allí no se les encontrará!
    ¡Por allí pasarán solamente los redimidos!
¹⁰Y volverán los rescatados por el SEÑOR,
    y entrarán en *Sión con cantos de alegría,
    coronados de una alegría eterna.
Los alcanzarán la alegría y el regocijo,
    y se alejarán la tristeza y el gemido.

Senaquerib amenaza a Jerusalén
36:1-22 — 2R 18:13,17-37; 2Cr 32:9-19

36 En el año catorce del reinado de Ezequías, Senaquerib, rey de Asiria, atacó y tomó todas las ciudades fortificadas de Judá. ²Desde Laquis el rey de Asiria envió a su comandante en jefe,ᶠ al frente de un gran ejército, para hablar con el rey Ezequías en Jerusalén. Cuando el comandante se detuvo en el acueducto del estanque superior, en el camino que lleva al Campo del Lavandero, ³salió a recibirlo Eliaquín hijo de Jilquías, que era el administrador del palacio, junto con el cronista Sebna y el secretario Joa hijo de Asaf.

⁴El comandante en jefe les dijo:

—Díganle a Ezequías que así dice el gran rey, el rey de Asiria: "¿En qué se basa tu confianza? ⁵Túᵍ dices que tienes estrategia y fuerza militar, pero éstas no son más que palabras sin fundamento. ¿En quién confías, que te rebelas contra mí? ⁶Mira, tú confías en Egipto, ¡ese bastón de caña astillada, que traspasa la mano y hiere al que se apoya en él! Porque eso es el faraón, el rey de Egipto, para todos los que en él confían. ⁷Y si tú me dices: 'Nosotros confiamos en el SEÑOR, nuestro Dios', ¿no se trata acaso, Ezequías, del Dios cuyos altares y *santuarios paganos tú mismo quitaste, diciéndoles a Judá y a Jerusalén: 'Deben adorar solamente ante este altar'?"

⁸»Ahora bien, Ezequías, haz este trato con mi señor, el rey de Asiria: Yo te doy dos mil caballos, si tú consigues otros tantos jinetes para montarlos. ⁹¿Cómo podrás rechazar el ataque de uno solo de los funcionarios más insignificantes de mi señor, si confías en obtener de Egipto carros de combate y jinetes? ¹⁰¿Acaso he venido a atacar y a destruir esta tierra sin el apoyo del SEÑOR? ¡Si fue él mismo quien me ordenó: "Marcha contra este país y destrúyelo"!

¹¹Eliaquín, Sebna y Joa le dijeron al comandante en jefe:

—Por favor, hábleles usted a sus siervos en arameo, ya que lo entendemos. No nos hable en hebreo, que el pueblo que está sobre el muro nos escucha.

¹²Pero el comandante en jefe respondió:

—¿Acaso mi señor me envió a decirles estas cosas sólo a ti y a tu señor, y no a los que están sentados en el muro? ¡Si tanto ellos como ustedes tendrán que comerse su excremento y beberse su orina!

¹³Dicho esto, el comandante en jefe se puso de pie y a voz en cuello gritó en hebreo:

—¡Oigan las palabras del gran rey, el rey de Asiria! ¹⁴Así dice el rey: "No se dejen engañar por Ezequías. ¡Él no puede librarlos! ¹⁵No dejen que Ezequías los persuada a confiar en el SEÑOR, diciendo: 'Sin duda el SEÑOR nos librará; ¡esta ciudad no caerá en manos del rey de Asiria!' "

¹⁶»No le hagan caso a Ezequías. Así dice el rey de Asiria: "Hagan las paces conmigo, y ríndanse. De este modo cada uno podrá comer de su vid y de su higuera, y beber agua de su propio pozo, ¹⁷hasta que yo venga y los lleve a un país como el de ustedes, país de grano y de mosto, de pan y de viñedos."

¹⁸»No se dejen seducir por Ezequías cuando dice: "El SEÑOR nos librará." ¿Acaso alguno de los dioses de las naciones pudo librar a su país de las manos del rey de Asiria? ¹⁹¿Dónde están los dioses de Jamat y de Arfad? ¿Dónde están los dioses de Sefarvayin? ¿Acaso libraron a Samaria de mis manos? ²⁰¿Cuál de todos los dioses de estos países ha podido salvar de mis manos a su país? ¿Cómo entonces podrá el SEÑOR librar de mis manos a Jerusalén?"

²¹Pero el pueblo permaneció en silencio y no respondió ni una sola palabra, porque el rey había ordenado: «No le respondan.»

²²Entonces Eliaquín hijo de Jilquías, administrador del palacio, el cronista Sebna y el secretario Joa hijo de Asaf, con las vestiduras rasgadas en señal de duelo, fueron a ver a Ezequías y le contaron lo que había dicho el comandante en jefe.

ᶠ **36:2** *comandante en jefe.* Alt. *copero mayor.*   ᵍ **36:5** *Tú dices* (mss. hebreos y Qumrán; véase 2R 18:20); *Yo digo* (TM).

Se profetiza la liberación de Jerusalén
37:1-13 — 2R 19:1-13

37 Cuando el rey Ezequías escuchó esto, se rasgó las vestiduras, se vistió de luto y fue al templo del SEÑOR. 2Además, envió a Eliaquín, administrador del palacio, al cronista Sebna y a los sacerdotes más ancianos, todos vestidos de luto, para hablar con el profeta Isaías hijo de Amoz. 3Y le dijeron: «Así dice Ezequías: "Hoy es un día de angustia, castigo y deshonra, como cuando los hijos están a punto de nacer y no se tienen fuerzas para darlos a luz. 4Tal vez el SEÑOR tu Dios oiga las palabras del comandante en jefe, a quien su señor, el rey de Asiria, envió para insultar al Dios viviente. ¡Que el SEÑOR tu Dios le castigue por las palabras que ha oído! Eleva, pues, una oración por el remanente del pueblo que aún sobrevive."»

5Cuando los funcionarios del rey Ezequías fueron a ver a Isaías, 6éste les dijo: «Díganle a su señor que así dice el SEÑOR: "No temas por las blasfemias que has oído, y que han pronunciado contra mí los subalternos del rey de Asiria. 7¡Mira! Voy a poner un espíritu en él, de manera que cuando oiga cierto rumor se regrese a su propio país. ¡Allí haré que lo maten a filo de espada!"»

8Cuando el comandante en jefe se enteró de que el rey de Asiria había salido de Laquis, se retiró y encontró al rey luchando contra Libná.

9Luego Senaquerib recibió el informe de que Tiracá, rey de *Cus, había salido para luchar contra él. Al enterarse de esto, envió mensajeros a Ezequías 10para que le dijeran: «Tú, Ezequías, rey de Judá: No dejes que tu Dios, en quien confías, te engañe cuando dice: "No caerá Jerusalén en manos del rey de Asiria." 11Sin duda te habrás enterado de lo que han hecho los reyes de Asiria en todos los países, *destruyéndolos por completo. ¿Y acaso vas tú a librarte? 12¿Libraron sus dioses a las naciones que mis antepasados han destruido: Gozán, Jarán, Résef y la gente de Edén que vivía en Telasar? 13¿Dónde están el rey de Jamat, el rey de Arfad, el rey de la ciudad de Sefarvayin, o de Hená o Ivá?»

Oración de Ezequías
37:14-20 — 2R 19:14-19

14Ezequías tomó la carta de mano de los mensajeros, y la leyó. Luego subió al templo del SEÑOR, la desplegó delante del SEÑOR, 15y oró así: 16«SEÑOR *Todopoderoso, Dios de Israel, entronizado sobre los *querubines: sólo tú eres el Dios de todos los reinos de la tierra. Tú has hecho los cielos y la tierra. 17Presta atención, SEÑOR, y escucha; abre tus ojos, SEÑOR, y mira; escucha todas las palabras que Senaquerib ha mandado a decir para insultar al Dios viviente.

18»Es verdad, SEÑOR, que los reyes asirios han asolado todas estas naciones y sus tierras. 19Han arrojado al fuego sus dioses, y los han destruido, porque no eran dioses sino sólo madera y piedra, obra de manos *humanas. 20Ahora, pues, SEÑOR y Dios nuestro, sálvanos de su mano, para que todos los reinos de la tierra sepan que sólo tú, SEÑOR, eres Dios.»h

Muerte de Senaquerib
37:21-38 — 2R 19:20-37; 2Cr 32:20-21

21Entonces Isaías hijo de Amoz le envió este mensaje a Ezequías: «Así dice el SEÑOR, Dios de Israel: "Por cuanto me has rogado respecto a Senaquerib, rey de Asiria, 22ésta es la palabra que yo, el SEÑOR, he pronunciado contra él:

» "La virginal hija de *Sión
    te desprecia y se burla de ti.
La hija de Jerusalén
    menea la cabeza al verte huir.
23¿A quién has insultado?
    ¿Contra quién has blasfemado?
¿Contra quién has alzado la voz
    y levantado los ojos con orgullo?
¡Contra el *Santo de Israel!
24Has enviado a tus siervos
    a insultar al Señor, diciendo:
'Con mis numerosos carros de combate
    escalé las cumbres de las montañas,
    ¡las laderas del Líbano!
Talé sus cedros más altos,
    sus cipreses más selectos.
Alcancé sus cumbres más lejanas,
    y sus bosques más frondosos.
25Cavé pozos en tierras extranjeras,i
    y en esas aguas apagué mi sed.
Con las plantas de mis pies
    sequé todos los ríos de Egipto.'

26» "¿No te has dado cuenta?
    ¡Hace mucho tiempo que lo he preparado!
Desde tiempo atrás lo vengo planeando,
    y ahora lo he llevado a cabo;
por eso tú has dejado en ruinas
    a las ciudades fortificadas.
27Sus habitantes, impotentes,
    están desalentados y avergonzados.
Son como plantas en el campo,
    como tiernos pastos verdes,
como hierba que brota sobre el techo
    y que se quemaj antes de crecer.

28» "Yo sé bien cuándo te sientas,
    cuándo sales, cuándo entras,
    y cuánto ruges contra mí.
29Porque has rugido contra mí
    y tu insolencia ha llegado a mis oídos,
te pondré una argolla en la nariz
    y un freno en la boca,
y por el mismo camino por donde viniste
    te haré regresar.

30» "Ésta será la señal para ti, Ezequías:

» "Este año comerán lo que crezca por sí solo,
    y el segundo año lo que de allí brote.
Pero al tercer año sembrarán y cosecharán,
    plantarán viñas y comerán su fruto.
31Una vez más los sobrevivientes de la tribu de Judá
    echarán raíces abajo, y arriba darán fruto.
32Porque de Jerusalén saldrá un remanente,
    del monte Sión un grupo de
    sobrevivientes.
Esto lo hará mi celo,
    celo del SEÑOR *Todopoderoso.

33»"Yo, el SEÑOR, declaro esto acerca del rey de Asiria:

»"No entrará en esta ciudad,
    ni lanzará contra ella una sola flecha.

---

h **37:20** *sólo tú, SEÑOR, eres Dios* (Qumrán y LXX; véase también 2R 19:19); *sólo tú eres el SEÑOR* (TM). i **37:25** *en tierras extranjeras* (Qumrán; véase también 2R 19:24); TM no incluye esta frase. j **37:27** *y que se quema* (mss. hebreos; véanse Qumrán y 2R 19:26); *y como un campo* (TM).

No se enfrentará a ella con escudos,
ni cónstruirá contra ella una rampa de
asalto.
34Volverá por el mismo camino que vino;
¡en esta ciudad no entrará!
Yo, el SEÑOR, lo afirmo.
35Por mi causa, y por consideración a David mi
siervo,
defenderé esta ciudad y la salvaré."»

36Entonces el ángel del SEÑOR salió y mató a
ciento ochenta y cinco mil hombres del campamento
asirio. A la mañana siguiente, cuando los demás se
levantaron, ¡allí estaban tendidos todos los cadáveres! 37Así que Senaquerib, rey de Asiria, levantó el
campamento y se retiró. Volvió a Nínive y permaneció allí. 38Pero un día, mientras adoraba en el templo
de su dios Nisroc, sus hijos Adramélec y Saréezer lo
mataron a espada y escaparon a la tierra de Ararat. Y
su hijo Esarjadón lo sucedió en el trono.

Enfermedad de Ezequías
38:1-8 — 2R 20:1-11; 2Cr 32:24-26

38 Por aquellos días Ezequías se enfermó gravemente y estuvo a punto de morir. El profeta
Isaías hijo de Amoz fue a verlo y le dijo: «Así dice el
SEÑOR: "Pon tu casa en orden, porque vas a morir; no
te recuperarás."»

2Ezequías volvió el rostro hacia la pared y le rogó
al SEÑOR: 3«Recuerda, SEÑOR, que yo me he conducido delante de ti con lealtad y con un *corazón íntegro,
y que he hecho lo que te agrada.» Y Ezequías lloró
amargamente.

4Entonces la palabra del SEÑOR vino a Isaías:
5«Ve y dile a Ezequías que así dice el SEÑOR, Dios de
su antepasado David: "He escuchado tu oración y
he visto tus lágrimas; voy a darte quince años más
de vida. 6Y a ti y a esta ciudad los libraré de caer en
manos del rey de Asiria. Yo defenderé esta ciudad.
7Y ésta es la señal que te daré para confirmar lo que
te he prometido: 8Haré que en la escala de Acaz la
sombra del sol retroceda las diez gradas que ya ha
bajado."» ¡Y la luz del sol retrocedió las diez gradas
que ya había bajado!

Escrito de Ezequías

9Después de su enfermedad y recuperación Ezequías, rey de Judá, escribió:

10«Yo decía: "¿Debo, en la plenitud de mi vida,
pasar por las puertas del *sepulcro
y ser privado del resto de mis días?"
11Yo decía: "Ya no veré más al SEÑOR
en esta tierra de los vivientes;
ya no contemplaré más a los *seres humanos,
a los que habitan este mundo."k
12Me quitaron mi casa, me la arrebataron,
como si fuera la carpa de un pastor.
Como un tejedor, enrollé mi vida,
y él me la arrancó del telar.
¡De la noche a la mañana acabó conmigo!
13Pacientemente esperé hasta la aurora,
pero él, como león, me quebró todos los
huesos.
¡De la noche a la mañana acabó conmigo!
14Chillé como golondrina, como grulla;
¡me quejé como paloma!
Mis ojos se cansaron de mirar al cielo.
¡Angustiado estoy, Señor!
¡Acude en mi ayuda!

15»Pero ¿qué puedo decir?
Él mismo me lo anunció, y así lo ha hecho.
La amargura de mi *alma
me ha quitado el sueño.
16Señor, por tales cosas viven los *hombres,
y también mi espíritu encuentra vida en
ellas.
Tú me devolviste la salud
y me diste vida.
17Sin duda, fue para mi bien
pasar por tal angustia.
Con tu amor me guardaste
de la fosa destructora,
y le diste la espalda a mis pecados.
18El sepulcro nada te agradece;
la muerte no te alaba.
Los que descienden a la fosa
nada esperan de tu fidelidad.
19Los que viven, y sólo los que viven,
son los que te alaban,
como hoy te alabo yo.
Todo padre hablará a sus hijos
acerca de tu fidelidad.

20»El SEÑOR me salvará,
y en el templo del SEÑOR
todos los días de nuestra vida
cantaremos con instrumentos de cuerda.»

21Isaías había dicho: «Preparen una pasta de higos, aplíquensela en la llaga, y él se recuperará.»
22Y Ezequías había preguntado: «¿Qué señal recibiré de que se me permitirá subir al templo del
SEÑOR?»

Mensajeros de Babilonia
39:1-8 — 2R 20:12-19

39 En aquel tiempo Merodac Baladán hijo de
Baladán, rey de Babilonia, le envió cartas y
un regalo a Ezequías, porque supo que había estado
enfermo y que se había recuperado. 2Ezequías se alegró al recibir esto, y les mostró a los mensajeros todos
sus tesoros: la plata, el oro, las especias, el aceite fino,
todo su arsenal y todo lo que había en ellos. No hubo
nada en su palacio ni en todo su reino que Ezequías
no les mostrara.

3Entonces el profeta Isaías fue a ver al rey Ezequías y le preguntó:

—¿Qué querían esos hombres? ¿De dónde vinieron?

—De un país lejano —respondió Ezequías—. Vinieron a verme desde Babilonia.

4—¿Y qué vieron en tu palacio? —preguntó el
profeta.

—Vieron todo lo que hay en él —contestó Ezequías—. No hay nada en mis tesoros que yo no les
haya mostrado.

5Entonces Isaías le dijo:

—Oye la palabra del SEÑOR *Todopoderoso:
6"Sin duda vendrán días en que todo lo que hay en tu
palacio, y todo lo que tus antepasados atesoraron hasta
el día de hoy, será llevado a Babilonia. No quedará
nada —dice el SEÑOR—. 7Y algunos de tus hijos y de
tus descendientes serán llevados para servir como *eunucos en el palacio del rey de Babilonia."

8—El mensaje del SEÑOR que tú me has traído es
bueno —respondió Ezequías.

Y es que pensaba: «Al menos mientras yo viva,
habrá *paz y seguridad.»

k 38:11 *este mundo* (mss. hebreos); *el lugar de cesación* (TM).

Consuelo para el pueblo de Dios

40 ¡Consuelen, consuelen a mi pueblo!
—dice su Dios—.
2Hablen con cariño a Jerusalén,
y anúncienle
que ya ha cumplido su tiempo de servicio,
que ya ha pagado por su iniquidad,
que ya ha recibido de la mano del SEÑOR
el doble por todos sus pecados.

3Una voz proclama:
«Preparen en el desierto
un camino para el SEÑOR;
enderecen en la estepa
un sendero para nuestro Dios.
4Que se levanten todos los valles,
y se allanen todos los montes y colinas;
que el terreno escabroso se nivele
y se alisen las quebradas.
5Entonces se revelará la gloria del SEÑOR,
y la verá toda la humanidad.
El SEÑOR mismo lo ha dicho.»

6Una voz dice: «Proclama.»
«¿Y qué voy a proclamar?», respondo yo.[1]

«Que todo *mortal es como la hierba,
y toda su gloria como la flor del campo.
7La hierba se seca y la flor se marchita,
porque el aliento del SEÑOR sopla sobre
ellas.
Sin duda, el pueblo es hierba.
8La hierba se seca y la flor se marchita,
pero la palabra de nuestro Dios
permanece para siempre.»

9Sión, portadora de buenas noticias,
¡súbete a una alta montaña!
Jerusalén, portadora de buenas noticias,
¡alza con fuerza tu voz!
Álzala, no temas;
di a las ciudades de Judá:
«¡Aquí está su Dios!»

10Miren, el SEÑOR omnipotente llega con poder,
y con su brazo gobierna.
Su galardón lo acompaña;
su recompensa lo precede.
11Como un *pastor que cuida su rebaño,
recoge los corderos en sus brazos;
los lleva junto a su pecho,
y guía con cuidado a las recién paridas.

12¿Quién ha medido las aguas con la palma de
su mano,
y abarcado entre sus dedos la extensión de
los cielos?
¿Quién metió en una medida el polvo de la
tierra?
¿Quién pesó en una balanza las montañas
y los cerros?
13¿Quién puede medir el alcance del espíritu
del SEÑOR,
o quién puede servirle de consejero?
14¿A quién consultó el SEÑOR para ilustrarse,
y quién le enseñó el *camino de la justicia?
¿Quién le impartió *conocimiento
o le hizo conocer la senda de la
inteligencia?

15A los ojos de Dios, las naciones son
como una gota de agua en un balde,

como una brizna de polvo en una balanza.
El SEÑOR pesa las islas
como si fueran polvo fino.
16El Líbano no alcanza para el fuego de su altar,
ni todos sus animales para los
*holocaustos.
17Todas las naciones no son nada en su
presencia;
no tienen para él valor alguno.

18¿Con quién compararán a Dios?
¿Con qué imagen lo representarán?
19Al ídolo un escultor lo funde;
un joyero lo enchapa en oro
y le labra cadenas de plata.
20El que es muy pobre para ofrendar
escoge madera que no se pudra,
y busca un hábil artesano
para erigir un ídolo que no se caiga.

21¿Acaso no lo sabían ustedes?
¿No se habían enterado?
¿No se les dijo desde el principio?
¿No lo entendieron desde la fundación del
mundo?
22Él reina sobre la bóveda de la tierra,
cuyos habitantes son como langostas.
Él extiende los cielos como un toldo,
y los despliega como carpa para ser
habitada.
23Él anula a los poderosos,
y a nada reduce a los gobernantes de este
mundo.
24Escasamente han sido plantados,
apenas han sido sembrados,
apenas echan raíces en la tierra,
cuando él sopla sobre ellos y se marchitan;
¡y el huracán los arrasa como paja!

25«¿Con quién, entonces, me compararán
ustedes?
¿Quién es igual a mí?», dice el *Santo.
26Alcen los ojos y miren a los cielos:
¿Quién ha creado todo esto?
El que ordena la multitud de estrellas una por
una,
y llama a cada una por su *nombre.
¡Es tan grande su poder, y tan poderosa su
fuerza,
que no falta ninguna de ellas!

27¿Por qué murmuras, Jacob?
¿Por qué refunfuñas, Israel:
«Mi camino está escondido del SEÑOR;
mi Dios ignora mi derecho»?
28¿Acaso no lo sabes?
¿Acaso no te has enterado?
El SEÑOR es el Dios eterno,
creador de los confines de la tierra.
No se cansa ni se fatiga,
y su inteligencia es insondable.
29Él fortalece al cansado
y acrecienta las fuerzas del débil.
30Aun los jóvenes se cansan, se fatigan,
y los muchachos tropiezan y caen;
31pero los que confían en el SEÑOR
renovarán sus fuerzas;
volarán como las águilas:
correrán y no se fatigarán,
caminarán y no se cansarán.

[1] **40:6** *respondo yo* (LXX, Qumrán y Vulgata); *responde él* (TM).

El amparo de Israel

41 «¡Callen en mi presencia, costas lejanas!
      ¡Naciones, renueven sus fuerzas!
   Acérquense y hablen;
      reunámonos para juicio.

2»¿Quién ha hecho venir desde el oriente
   a aquel que siempre sale *victorioso?
 Pone a las naciones en sus manos;
   ante él los reyes se rinden.
 Con su espada los vuelve polvo,
   con su arco los dispersa como paja.
3Con paso firme los persigue
   por una senda que nunca antes pisó.
4¿Quién realizó esto? ¿Quién lo hizo posible?
   ¿Quién llamó a las generaciones desde el
      principio?
 Yo, el SEÑOR, soy el primero,
   y seré el mismo hasta el fin.»

5Lo han visto las costas lejanas, y temen;
   tiemblan los confines de la tierra.
 ¡Ya se acercan, ya vienen!
6Cada uno ayuda a su compañero,
   y le infunde aliento a su hermano.
7El artesano anima al joyero;
   y el que aplana con el martillo
 le dice al que golpea el yunque:
   «¡Es buena la soldadura!»;
 luego asegura el ídolo con clavos
   para que no se tambalee.

8«Pero tú, Israel, mi siervo,
   tú Jacob, a quien he escogido,
   simiente de Abraham, mi amigo;
9Te tomé de los confines de la tierra,
   te llamé de los rincones más remotos,
 y te dije: "Tú eres mi siervo."
   Yo te escogí; no te rechacé.
10Así que no temas, porque yo estoy contigo;
   no te angusties, porque yo soy tu Dios.
 Te fortaleceré y te ayudaré;
   te sostendré con mi diestra victoriosa.

11»Todos los que se enardecen contra ti
   sin duda serán avergonzados y humillados;
 los que se te oponen serán como nada,
   como si no existieran.
12Aunque busques a tus enemigos,
   no los encontrarás.
 Los que te hacen la guerra serán como nada,
   como si no existieran.
13Porque yo soy el SEÑOR, tu Dios,
   que sostiene tu mano *derecha;
 yo soy quien te dice:
   "No temas, yo te ayudaré."
14No temas, gusano Jacob, pequeño Israel
   —afirma el SEÑOR—,
 porque yo mismo te ayudaré;
   ¡el *Santo de Israel es tu redentor!

15»Te convertiré en una trilladora
   nueva y afilada, de doble filo.
 Trillarás las montañas y las harás polvo;
   convertirás en paja las colinas.
16Las aventarás y se las llevará el viento;
   ¡un vendaval las dispersará!
 Pero tú te alegrarás en el SEÑOR,
   te gloriarás en el Santo de Israel.

17»Los pobres y los necesitados buscan agua,
   pero no la encuentran;
 la sed les ha resecado la lengua.
 Pero yo, el SEÑOR, les responderé;
   yo, el Dios de Israel, no los abandonaré.
18Haré brotar ríos en las áridas cumbres,
   y manantiales entre los valles.
 Transformaré el desierto en estanques de agua,
   y el sequedal en manantiales.
19Plantaré en el desierto
   cedros, acacias, mirtos y olivos;
 en áridas tierras plantaré cipreses,
   junto con pinos y abetos,
20para que la gente vea y sepa,
   y considere y entienda,
 que la mano del SEÑOR ha hecho esto,
   que el Santo de Israel lo ha creado.

21»Expongan su caso —dice el SEÑOR—;
   presenten sus pruebas —demanda el rey
      de Jacob—.
22Acérquensem y anuncien
   lo que ha de suceder,
 y cómo fueron las cosas del pasado,
   para que las consideremos
 y conozcamos su desenlace.
   ¡Cuéntennos lo que está por venir!
23Digan qué nos depara el futuro;
   así sabremos que ustedes son dioses.
 Hagan algo, bueno o malo,
   para verlo y llenarnos de terror.
24¡La verdad es que ustedes no son nada,
   y aun menos que nada son sus obras!
 ¡Abominable es quien los escoge!

25»Del norte hice venir a uno,
   y acudió a mi llamado;
 desde el oriente invoca mi *nombre.
 Como alfarero que amasa arcilla con los pies,
   aplasta gobernantes como si fueran barro.
26¿Quién lo anunció desde el principio,
   para que lo supiéramos?
 ¿Quién lo anunció de antemano,
   para que dijéramos: "Tenía razón"?
 Nadie lo anunció ni lo proclamó;
   nadie les oyó proclamar mensaje alguno.
27Yo fui el primero en decirle a *Sión:
   "¡Mira, ya están aquí!"
 Yo fui quien envió a Jerusalén
   un mensajero de buenas noticias.
28Miro entre ellos, y no hay nadie;
   no hay entre ellos quien aconseje,
 no hay quien me responda cuando les
      pregunto.
29¡Todos ellos son falsos!
   Sus obras no son nada;
 sus ídolos no son más que viento y
   confusión.

El siervo del SEÑOR

42 »Éste es mi siervo, a quien sostengo,
      mi escogido, en quien me deleito;
 sobre él he puesto mi Espíritu,
   y llevará *justicia a las naciones.
2No clamará, ni gritará,
   ni alzará su voz por las calles.
3No acabará de romper la caña quebrada,
   ni apagará la mecha que apenas arde.
 Con fidelidad hará justicia;
   4no vacilará ni se desanimará
 hasta implantar la justicia en la tierra.

---

m **41:22** *Acérquense* (LXX, Qumrán, Targum y Vulgata); *Traigan* (TM).

Las costas lejanas esperan su enseñanza.»

5Así dice Dios, el SEÑOR,
  el que creó y desplegó los cielos;
el que expandió la tierra
  y todo lo que ella produce;
el que da aliento al pueblo que la habita,
  y vida a los que en ella se mueven:
6«Yo, el SEÑOR, te he llamado en justicia;
  te he tomado de la mano.
Yo te formé, yo te constituí
  como *pacto para el pueblo,
  como luz para las naciones,
7para abrir los ojos de los ciegos,
  para librar de la cárcel a los presos,
  y del calabozo a los que habitan en
    tinieblas.

8»Yo soy el SEÑOR; íese es mi *nombre!
  No entrego a otros mi gloria,
  ni mi alabanza a los ídolos.
9Las cosas pasadas se han cumplido,
  y ahora anuncio cosas nuevas;
  ílas anuncio antes que sucedan!»

Canción de alabanza al SEÑOR

10Canten al SEÑOR un cántico nuevo,
  ustedes, que descienden al mar,
  y todo lo que hay en él;
canten su alabanza desde los confines de la
    tierra,
  ustedes, costas lejanas y sus habitantes.
11Que alcen la voz el desierto y sus ciudades,
  y los poblados donde Cedar habita.
Que canten de alegría los habitantes de Selá,
  y griten desde las cimas de las montañas.
12Den gloria al SEÑOR
  y proclamen su alabanza en las costas
    lejanas.
13El SEÑOR marchará como guerrero;
  como hombre de guerra despertará su celo.
Con gritos y alaridos se lanzará al combate,
  y *triunfará sobre sus enemigos.

14«Por mucho tiempo he guardado silencio,
  he estado callado y me he contenido.
Pero ahora voy a gritar como parturienta,
  voy a resollar y jadear al mismo tiempo.
15Devastaré montañas y cerros,
  y secaré toda su vegetación;
convertiré los ríos en tierra seca,
  y secaré los estanques.
16conduciré a los ciegos por caminos
    desconocidos,
  los guiaré por senderos inexplorados;
ante ellos convertiré en luz las tinieblas,
  y allanaré los lugares escabrosos.
Esto haré,
  y no los abandonaré.
17Pero retrocederán llenos de vergüenza
  los que confían en los ídolos,
los que dicen a las imágenes:
  "Ustedes son nuestros dioses."

Israel ciego y sordo

18»Sordos, íescuchen!
  Ciegos, ífíjense bien!
19¿Quién es más ciego que mi siervo,
  y más sordo que mi mensajero?
¿Quién es más ciego que mi enviado,
  y más ciego que el siervo del SEÑOR?
20Tú has visto muchas cosas,
  pero no las has captado;
tienes abiertos los oídos,

  pero no oyes nada.»
21Le agradó al SEÑOR,
  por amor a su justicia,
hacer su *ley grande y gloriosa.
22Pero éste es un pueblo saqueado y despojado,
  todos atrapados en cuevas
  o encerrados en cárceles.
Son saqueados,
  y nadie los libra;
son despojados,
  y nadie reclama.

23¿Quién de ustedes escuchará esto
  y prestará atención en el futuro?
24¿Quién entregó a Jacob para el despojo,
  a Israel para el saqueo?
¿No es acaso el SEÑOR
  a quien su pueblo ha ofendido?
No siguió sus *caminos
  ni obedeció su ley.
25Por eso el SEÑOR derramó sobre él
  su ardiente ira y el furor de la guerra.
Lo envolvió en llamas, pero no comprendió;
  lo consumió, pero no lo tomó en serio.

El único Salvador de Israel

43 Pero ahora, así dice el SEÑOR,
  el que te creó, Jacob,
  el que te formó, Israel:
«No temas, que yo te he redimido;
  te he llamado por tu *nombre; tú eres mío.
2Cuando cruces las aguas,
  yo estaré contigo;
cuando cruces los ríos,
  no te cubrirán sus aguas;
cuando camines por el fuego,
  no te quemarás ni te abrasarán las llamas.
3Yo soy el SEÑOR, tu Dios,
  el *Santo de Israel, tu salvador;
yo he entregado a Egipto como precio por tu
    rescate,
  a *Cus y a Seba en tu lugar.
4A cambio de ti entregaré *hombres;
  ia cambio de tu *vida entregaré pueblos!
Porque te amo y eres ante mis ojos
  precioso y digno de honra.
5No temas, porque yo estoy contigo;
  desde el oriente traeré a tu descendencia,
  desde el occidente te reuniré.
6Al norte le diré: "íEntrégalos!"
  y al sur: "íNo los retengas!
Trae a mis hijos desde lejos
  y a mis hijas desde los confines de la tierra.
7Trae a todo el que sea llamado por mi nombre,
  al que yo he creado para mi gloria,
  al que yo hice y formé."»

8Saquen al pueblo ciego, aunque tiene ojos,
  al pueblo sordo, aunque tiene oídos.
9Que se reúnan todas las naciones
  y se congreguen los pueblos.
¿Quién de entre ellos profetizó estas cosas
  y nos anunció lo ocurrido en el pasado?
Que presenten a sus testigos
  y demuestren tener razón,
para que otros oigan y digan:
  «Es verdad.»
10«Ustedes son mis testigos —afirma el
    SEÑOR—,
  son mis siervos escogidos,
para que me conozcan y crean en mí,
  y entiendan que yo soy.
Antes de mí no hubo ningún otro dios,

ni habrá ninguno después de mí.
¹¹Yo, yo soy el SEÑOR,
     fuera de mí no hay ningún otro salvador.
¹²Yo he anunciado, salvado y proclamado;
     yo entre ustedes, y no un dios extraño.
Ustedes son mis testigos —afirma el SEÑOR—,
     y yo soy Dios.
¹³Desde los tiempos antiguos, yo soy.
     No hay quien pueda librar de mi mano.
     Lo que yo hago, nadie puede
          desbaratarlo.»

La misericordia de Dios y la infidelidad de Israel

¹⁴Así dice el SEÑOR,
     su Redentor, el *Santo de Israel:
«Por ustedes enviaré gente a Babilonia;
     abatiré a todos como fugitivos.
En los barcos que eran su orgullo,
     abatiré también a los *caldeos.
¹⁵Yo soy el SEÑOR, su santo;
     soy su rey, el creador de Israel.»

¹⁶Así dice el SEÑOR,
     el que abrió un camino en el mar,
     una senda a través de las aguas
          impetuosas,
¹⁷el que hizo salir carros de combate y caballos,
     ejército y guerrero al mismo tiempo,
los cuales quedaron tendidos para nunca más
          levantarse,
     extinguidos como mecha que se apaga:
¹⁸«Olviden las cosas de antaño;
     ya no vivan en el pasado.
¹⁹¡Voy a hacer algo nuevo!
     Ya está sucediendo, ¿no se dan cuenta?
Estoy abriendo un camino en el desierto,
     y ríos en lugares desolados.
²⁰Me honran los animales salvajes,
     los chacales y los avestruces;
yo hago brotar agua en el desierto,
     ríos en lugares desolados,
para dar de beber a mi pueblo escogido,
²¹al pueblo que formé para mí mismo,
     para que proclame mi alabanza.

²²»Pero tú, Jacob, no me has invocado;
     tú, Israel, te has cansado de mí.
²³No me has traído el cordero de tus
          *holocaustos,
     ni me has honrado con tus sacrificios.
No te he abrumado exigiendo ofrendas de
          grano,
     ni te he agobiado reclamando incienso.
²⁴No me has comprado caña aromática,
     ni me has saciado con el sebo de tus
          sacrificios.
¡En cambio, tú me has abrumado con tus
          pecados
     y me has agobiado con tus iniquidades!

²⁵»Yo soy el que por amor a mí mismo
     borra tus transgresiones
     y no se acuerda más de tus pecados.
²⁶¡Hazme recordar! Presentémonos a juicio;
     plantea el argumento de tu inocencia.
²⁷Tu primer antepasado pecó;
     tus voceros se rebelaron contra mí.
²⁸Por eso humillé a las autoridades del templo;
     entregué a Jacob a la *destrucción total,
     entregué a Israel al menosprecio.

Israel, el escogido

44 »Pero ahora, Jacob, mi siervo,
     Israel, a quien he escogido, ¡escucha!
²Así dice el SEÑOR, el que te hizo,
     el que te formó en el seno materno
     y te brinda su ayuda:
"No temas, Jacob, mi siervo,
     Jesurún, a quien he escogido,
³que regaré con agua la tierra sedienta,
     y con arroyos el suelo seco;
derramaré mi Espíritu sobre tu descendencia,
     y mi bendición sobre tus vástagos,
⁴y brotarán como hierba en un prado,
     como sauces junto a arroyos.
⁵Uno dirá: 'Pertenezco al SEÑOR';
     otro llevará el *nombre de Jacob,
y otro escribirá en su mano: 'Yo soy del
          SEÑOR',
     y tomará para sí el nombre de Israel."

El SEÑOR y los ídolos

⁶»Así dice el SEÑOR, el SEÑOR *Todopoderoso,
     rey y redentor de Israel:
"Yo soy el primero y el último;
     fuera de mí no hay otro dios.
⁷¿Quién es como yo?
     Que lo diga.
Que declare lo que ha ocurrido
     desde que establecí a mi antiguo pueblo;
que exponga ante mí lo que está por venir,
     ¡que anuncie lo que va a suceder!
⁸No tiemblen ni se asusten.
     ¿Acaso no lo anuncié y profeticé hace
          tiempo?
Ustedes son mis testigos.
     ¿Hay algún Dios fuera de mí?
No, no hay otra *Roca,
     no conozco ninguna."»

⁹Los que fabrican ídolos no valen nada;
     inútiles son sus obras más preciadas.
Para su propia vergüenza,
     sus propios testigos no ven ni conocen.
¹⁰¿Quién modela un dios o funde un ídolo,
     que no le sirve para nada?
¹¹Todos sus devotos quedarán avergonzados;
     ¡simples *mortales son los artesanos!
Que todos se reúnan y comparezcan;
     ¡aterrados y avergonzados quedarán todos
          ellos!

¹²El herrero toma una herramienta,
     y con ella trabaja sobre las brasas;
con martillo modela un ídolo,
     con la fuerza de su brazo lo forja.
Siente hambre, y pierde las fuerzas;
     no bebe agua, y desfallece.
¹³El carpintero mide con un cordel,
     hace un boceto con un estilete,
lo trabaja con el escoplo
     y lo traza con el compás.
Le da forma *humana;
     le imprime la belleza de un ser humano,
     para que habite en un santuario.
¹⁴Derriba los cedros,
     y escoge un ciprés o un roble,
y lo deja crecer entre los árboles del bosque;
     o planta un pino, que la lluvia hace crecer.
¹⁵Al *hombre le sirve de combustible,
     y toma una parte para calentarse;
     enciende un fuego y hornea pan.
Pero también labra un dios y lo adora;

hace un ídolo y se postra ante él.
16La mitad de la madera la quema en el fuego,
　sobre esa mitad prepara su comida;
　asa la carne y se sacia.
También se calienta y dice:
　«¡Ah! Ya voy entrando en calor,
　mientras contemplo las llamas.»
17Con el resto hace un dios, su ídolo;
　se postra ante él y lo adora.
Y suplicante le dice:
　«Sálvame, pues tú eres mi dios.»

18No saben nada, no entienden nada;
　sus ojos están velados, y no ven;
　su *mente está cerrada, y no entienden.
19Les falta *conocimiento y entendimiento;
　no se ponen a pensar ni a decir:
«Usé la mitad para combustible;
　incluso horneé pan sobre las brasas,
　asé carne y la comí.
¿Y haré algo abominable con lo que queda?
　¿Me postraré ante un pedazo de madera?»
20Se alimentan de cenizas,
　se dejan engañar por su iluso *corazón,
no pueden salvarse a sí mismos, ni decir:
　«¡Lo que tengo en mi diestra es una
　mentira!»

21«Recuerda estas cosas, Jacob,
　porque tú eres mi siervo, Israel.
Yo te formé, tú eres mi siervo;
　Israel, yo no te olvidaré.
22He disipado tus transgresiones como el rocío,
　y tus pecados como la bruma de la mañana.
Vuelve a mí, que te he redimido.»

23¡Canten de alegría, cielos,
　que esto lo ha hecho el SEÑOR!
¡Griten con fuerte voz,
　profundidades de la tierra!
¡Prorrumpan en canciones, montañas;
　y bosques, con todos sus árboles!
Porque el SEÑOR ha redimido a Jacob,
　Dios ha manifestado su gloria en Israel.

Jerusalén vuelve a ser habitada

24«Así dice el SEÑOR, tu Redentor,
　quien te formó en el seno materno:
"Yo soy el SEÑOR,
　que ha hecho todas las cosas,
yo solo desplegué los cielos
　y expandí la tierra.
　¿Quién estaba conmigo?

25» "Yo frustro las señales de los falsos profetas
　y ridiculizo a los adivinos;
yo hago retroceder a los sabios
　y convierto su sabiduría en necedad.
26Yo confirmo la palabra de mis siervos
　y cumplo el consejo de mis mensajeros.
Yo digo que Jerusalén será habitada,
　que los pueblos de Judá serán
　reconstruidos;
　y sus ruinas las restauraré.
27Yo mando que se seque lo profundo del mar,
　y ordeno que se sequen sus corrientes.
28Yo afirmo que Ciro es mi pastor,
　y dará cumplimiento a mis deseos;
dispondrá que Jerusalén sea reconstruida,
　y que se repongan los cimientos del
　templo."»

45 Así dice el SEÑOR a Ciro, su ungido,
　a quien tomó de la mano *derecha
para someter a su dominio las naciones
　y despojar de su armadura a los reyes,
para abrir a su paso las *puertas
　y dejar abiertas las entradas:

2«Marcharé al frente de ti,
　y allanaré las montañas;n
haré pedazos las puertas de bronce
　y cortaré los cerrojos de hierro.
3Te daré los tesoros de las tinieblas,
　y las riquezas guardadas en lugares
　secretos,
para que sepas que yo soy el SEÑOR,
　el Dios de Israel, que te llama por tu
　*nombre.
4Por causa de Jacob mi siervo,
　de Israel mi escogido,
te llamo por tu nombre
　y te confiero un título de honor,
　aunque tú no me conoces.
5Yo soy el SEÑOR, y no hay otro;
　fuera de mí no hay ningún Dios.
Aunque tú no me conoces,
　te fortaleceré,
6para que sepan de oriente a occidente
　que no hay ningún otro fuera de mí.
Yo soy el SEÑOR, y no hay ningún otro.
7Yo formo la luz y creo las tinieblas,
　traigo *bienestar y creo calamidad;
Yo, el SEÑOR, hago todas estas cosas.

8»¡Destilen, cielos, desde lo alto!
　¡Nubes, hagan llover *justicia!
¡Que se abra la tierra de par en par!
　¡Que brote la *salvación!
¡Que crezca con ella la justicia!
　Yo, el SEÑOR, lo he creado.»

9¡Ay del que contiende con su Hacedor!
　¡Ay del que no es más que un tiesto
　entre los tiestos de la tierra!
¿Acaso el barro le reclama al alfarero:
　«¡Fíjate en lo que haces!
　¡Tu vasija no tiene agarraderas!»?

10¡Ay del que le reprocha a su padre:
　«¡Mira lo que has engendrado!»!
¡Ay del que le reclama a su madre:
　«¡Mira lo que has dado a luz!»!

11Así dice el SEÑOR,
　el *Santo de Israel, su artífice:
«¿Van acaso a pedirme cuentas del futuro de
　mis hijos,
o a darme órdenes sobre la obra de mis
　manos?
12Yo hice la tierra,
　y sobre ella formé a la *humanidad.
Mis propias manos extendieron los cielos,
　y di órdenes a sus constelaciones.
13Levantaré a Ciro en justicia;
　allanaré todos sus caminos.
Él reconstruirá mi ciudad
　y pondrá en libertad a mis cautivos,
pero no por precio ni soborno.
　Lo digo yo, el SEÑOR *Todopoderoso.»

14Así dice el SEÑOR:

---

n 45:2 las montañas (Qumrán y LXX); en TM, palabra de difícil traducción.

«Los productos de Egipto y la mercancía de
　　*Cus,
　　pasarán a ser de tu propiedad;
los sabeos, hombres de elevada estatura,
　　marcharán detrás de ti en cadenas.
Se inclinarán en tu presencia,
　　y suplicantes te dirán:
"Hay un solo Dios, no hay ningún otro,
　　y ese Dios está contigo."»

15Tú, Dios y salvador de Israel,
　　eres un Dios que se oculta.
16Todos los que hacen ídolos
　　serán avergonzados y humillados,
　　y juntos marcharán con su humillación.
17Pero Israel será salvada por el SEÑOR
　　con salvación eterna;
y nunca más volverá a ser
　　avergonzada ni humillada.

18Porque así dice el SEÑOR,
　　el que creó los cielos;
el Dios que formó la tierra,
　　que la hizo y la estableció;
que no la creó para dejarla vacía,
　　sino que la formó para ser habitada:
«Yo soy el SEÑOR,
　　y no hay ningún otro.
19Desde ningún lugar de esta tierra tenebrosa
　　les he hablado en secreto.
Ni he dicho a los descendientes de Jacob:
　　"Búsquenme en el vacío."
Yo, el SEÑOR, digo lo que es justo,
　　y declaro lo que es recto.

20»Reúnanse, fugitivos de las naciones;
　　congréguense y vengan.
Ignorantes son los que cargan ídolos de
　　madera
y oran a dioses que no pueden salvar.
21Declaren y presenten sus pruebas,
　　deliberen juntos.
¿Quién predijo esto hace tiempo,
　　quién lo declaró desde tiempos antiguos?
¿Acaso no lo hice yo, el SEÑOR?
Fuera de mí no hay otro Dios;
Dios justo y Salvador,
　　no hay ningún otro fuera de mí.
22»Vuelvan a mí y sean salvos,
　　todos los confines de la tierra,
porque yo soy Dios, y no hay ningún otro.
23He jurado por mí mismo,
　　con integridad he pronunciado
　　una palabra irrevocable:
Ante mí se doblará toda rodilla,
　　y por mí jurará toda lengua.
24Ellos dirán de mí: "Sólo en el SEÑOR
　　están la justicia y el poder."»
Todos los que contra él se enfurecieron
　　ante él comparecerán
　　y quedarán avergonzados.
25Pero toda la descendencia de Israel
　　será vindicada y exaltada en el SEÑOR.

Los dioses de Babilonia

46 Bel se inclina, Nebo se somete;
　　sus ídolos son llevados por bestias de
　　carga.ñ
Pesadas son las imágenes que por todas partes
　　llevan;

son una carga para el agotado.
2Todos a la vez se someten y se inclinan;
　　no pudieron rescatar la carga,
　　y ellos mismos van al cautiverio.

3«Escúchame, familia de Jacob,
　　todo el resto de la familia de Israel,
a quienes he cargado desde el vientre,
　　y he llevado desde la cuna.
4Aun en la vejez, cuando ya peinen canas,
　　yo seré el mismo, yo los sostendré.
Yo los hice, y cuidaré de ustedes;
　　los sostendré y los libraré.

5»¿Con quién vas a compararme,
　　o a quién me vas a igualar?
¿A quién vas a asemejarme,
　　para que seamos parecidos?
6Algunos derrochan oro de sus bolsas
　　y pesan plata en la balanza;
contratan a un joyero para que les haga un
　　dios,
　　y ante ese dios se inclinan para adorarlo.
7Lo levantan en hombros y lo cargan;
　　lo ponen en su lugar, y allí se queda.
No se puede mover de su sitio.
Por más que clamen a él, no habrá de
　　responderles,
　　ni podrá salvarlos de sus aflicciones.

8»Recuerden esto, rebeldes;
　　piénsenlo bien, ¡fíjenlo en su *mente!
9Recuerden las cosas pasadas, aquellas de
　　antaño;
yo soy Dios, y no hay ningún otro,
　　yo soy Dios, y no hay nadie igual a mí.
10Yo anuncio el fin desde el principio,
　　desde los tiempos antiguos, lo que está por
　　venir.
Yo digo: Mi propósito se cumplirá,
　　y haré todo lo que deseo.
11Del oriente llamo
　　al ave de rapiña;
de tierra distante,
　　al hombre que cumplirá mi propósito.
Lo que he dicho, haré que se cumpla;
　　lo que he planeado, lo realizaré.
12Escúchenme ustedes, obstinados de *corazón,
　　que están lejos de la *justicia.
13Mi justicia no está lejana;
　　mi *salvación ya no tarda.
¡Estoy por traerlas!
Concederé salvación a *Sión,
　　y mi esplendor a Israel.

La caída de Babilonia

47 »Desciende, siéntate en el polvo,
　　hija virginal de Babilonia;
siéntate en el suelo, hija de los *caldeos,
　　pues ya no hay trono.
Nunca más se te llamará
　　tierna y delicada.
2Toma piedras de molino, y muele la harina;
　　quítate el velo.
Levántate las faldas, desnúdate las piernas,
　　y cruza los ríos.
3Tu desnudez quedará al descubierto;
　　quedará expuesta tu vergüenza.
Voy a tomar venganza,
　　y a nadie perdonaré.»

ñ **46:1** son llevados por bestias de carga. Alt. no son más que bestias y ganados.

4Nuestro Redentor es el *Santo de Israel;
su *nombre es el SEÑOR *Todopoderoso.

5«Siéntate en silencio, hija de los caldeos;
entra en las tinieblas.
Porque nunca más se te llamará
"soberana de los reinos".
6Yo estaba enojado con mi pueblo;
por eso profané mi heredad.
Los entregué en tu mano,
y no les tuviste compasión.
Pusiste sobre los ancianos
un yugo muy pesado.
7Dijiste: "¡Por siempre seré la soberana!"
Pero no consideraste esto,
ni reflexionaste sobre su final.

8»Ahora escucha esto, voluptuosa;
tú, que moras confiada y te dices a ti
misma:
"Yo soy, y no hay otra fuera de mí.
Nunca enviudaré ni me quedaré sin hijos."
9De repente, en un solo día,
ambas cosas te sorprenderán:
la pérdida de tus hijos y la viudez
te abrumarán por completo,
a pesar de tus muchas hechicerías
y de tus poderosos encantamientos.
10Tú has confiado en tu maldad,
y has dicho: "Nadie me ve."
Tu sabiduría y tu conocimiento te engañan
cuando a ti misma te dices:
"Yo soy, y no hay otra fuera de mí."
11Pero vendrá sobre ti una desgracia
que no sabrás conjurar;
caerá sobre ti una calamidad
que no podrás evitar.
¡Una catástrofe que ni te imaginas
vendrá de repente sobre ti!

12»Persiste, entonces, con tus encantamientos
y con tus muchas hechicerías,
en las que te has ejercitado desde la niñez.
Tal vez tengas éxito,
tal vez puedas provocar terror.
13¡Los muchos consejos te han fatigado!
Que se presenten tus astrólogos,
los que observan las estrellas,
los que hacen predicciones mes a mes,
¡que te salven de lo que viene sobre ti!
14¡Míralos! Son como la paja,
y el fuego los consumirá.
Ni a sí mismos pueden salvarse
del poder de las llamas.
Aquí no hay brasas para calentarse,
ni fuego para sentarse ante él.
15Eso son para ti los hechiceros
con quienes te has ejercitado,
y con los que has negociado desde tu
juventud.
Cada uno sigue en su error;
no habrá quien pueda salvarte.

El Israel obstinado

48 »Escuchen esto ustedes,
los de la familia de Jacob,
descendientes de Judá,
que llevan el *nombre de Israel;
que juran en el nombre del SEÑOR,
e invocan al Dios de Israel,
pero no con sinceridad ni justicia.
2Ustedes que se llaman ciudadanos de la
ciudad *santa

y confían en el Dios de Israel,
cuyo nombre es el SEÑOR *Todopoderoso:
3Desde hace mucho tiempo
anuncié las cosas pasadas.
Yo las profeticé;
yo mismo las di a conocer.
Actué de repente,
y se hicieron realidad.
4Porque yo sabía que eres muy obstinado,
que tu cuello es un tendón de hierro,
y que tu frente es de bronce.
5Por eso te declaré esas cosas desde hace
tiempo;
te las di a conocer antes que sucedieran,
para que no dijeras:
"¡Fue mi ídolo quien las hizo!
¡Mi imagen tallada o fundida las dispuso!"
6De todo esto has tenido noticia,
¿y no vas a proclamarlo?

»Desde ahora te haré conocer cosas nuevas;
cosas que te son ocultas y desconocidas.
7Son cosas creadas ahora, y no hace tiempo;
hasta hoy no habías oído hablar de ellas,
para que no dijeras:
"¡Sí, ya las sabía!"
8Nunca habías oído ni entendido;
nunca antes se te había abierto el oído.
Yo sé bien que eres muy traicionero,
y que desde tu nacimiento te llaman
rebelde.
9Por amor a mi nombre contengo mi ira;
por causa de mi alabanza me refreno,
para no aniquilarte.
10¡Mira! Te he refinado pero no como a la plata;
te he probado en el horno de la aflicción.
11Y lo he hecho por mí, por mí mismo.
¿Cómo puedo permitir que se me profane?
¡No cederé mi gloria a ningún otro!

Liberación de Israel

12»Escúchame, Jacob,
Israel, a quien he llamado:
Yo soy Dios;
yo soy el primero, y yo soy el último.
13Con la mano izquierda afirmé la tierra,
y con la derecha desplegué los cielos.
Yo pronuncié su *nombre,
y todos ellos aparecieron.

14»Reúnanse, todos ustedes, y escuchen:
¿Quién de ellos ha profetizado estas cosas?
El amado del SEÑOR
ejecutará su propósito contra Babilonia;
su brazo estará contra los *caldeos.
15Sólo yo he hablado;
sólo yo lo he llamado.
Lo haré venir,
y triunfará en su misión.

16»Acérquense a mí, escuchen esto:

»Desde el principio, jamás hablé en secreto;
cuando las cosas suceden, allí estoy yo.»

Y ahora el SEÑOR omnipotente
me ha enviado con su Espíritu.

17Así dice el SEÑOR,
tu Redentor, el *Santo de Israel:
«Yo soy el SEÑOR tu Dios,
que te enseña lo que te conviene,
que te guía por el *camino en que debes
andar.

18Si hubieras prestado atención a mis
    mandamientos,
  tu *paz habría sido como un río;
  tu justicia, como las olas del mar.
19Como la arena serían tus descendientes;
  como los granos de arena, tus hijos;
  su nombre nunca habría sido eliminado
  ni borrado de mi presencia.»

20¡Salgan de Babilonia!
  ¡Huyan de los caldeos!
  Anuncien esto con gritos de alegría
  y háganlo saber.
  Publíquenlo hasta en los confines de la tierra;
  digan: «El SEÑOR ha redimido a su siervo
    Jacob.»
21Cuando los guió a través de los desiertos,
  no tuvieron sed;
  hizo que de la *roca brotara agua para ellos;
  partió la roca, y manaron las aguas.

22«No hay paz para el malvado»,
  dice el SEÑOR.

El Siervo del SEÑOR

49 Escúchenme, costas lejanas,
    oigan esto, naciones distantes:
  El SEÑOR me llamó antes de que yo naciera,
  en el vientre de mi madre pronunció mi
    *nombre.
2Hizo de mi boca una espada afilada,
  y me escondió en la sombra de su mano;
  me convirtió en una flecha pulida,
  y me escondió en su aljaba.
3Me dijo: «Israel, tú eres mi siervo;
  en ti seré glorificado.»
4Y respondí: «En vano he trabajado;
  he gastado mis fuerzas sin provecho
    alguno.
  Pero mi justicia está en manos del SEÑOR;
  mi recompensa está con mi Dios.»

5Y ahora dice el SEÑOR,
  que desde el seno materno me formó
  para que fuera yo su siervo,
  para hacer que Jacob se vuelva a él,
  que Israel se reúna a su alrededor;
  porque a los ojos del SEÑOR soy digno de
    honra,
  y mi Dios ha sido mi fortaleza:
6«No es gran cosa que seas mi siervo,
  ni que restaures a las tribus de Jacob,
  ni que hagas volver a los de Israel,
  a quienes he preservado.
  Yo te pongo ahora como luz para las naciones,
  a fin de que lleves mi *salvación
  hasta los confines de la tierra.»

7Así dice el SEÑOR,
  el Redentor y *Santo de Israel,
  al despreciado y aborrecido por las naciones,
  al siervo de los gobernantes:
  «Los reyes te verán y se pondrán de pie,
  los príncipes te verán y se inclinarán,
  por causa del SEÑOR, el Santo de Israel,
  que es fiel y te ha escogido.»

Restauración de Israel

8Así dice el SEÑOR:

  «En el momento propicio te respondí,

  y en el día de *salvación te ayudé.
  Ahora te guardaré, y haré de ti
  un *pacto para el pueblo,
  para que restaures el país
  y repartas las propiedades asoladas;
9para que digas a los cautivos:
  "¡Salgan!",
  y a los que viven en tinieblas:
  "¡Están en libertad!"

  »Junto a los caminos pastarán
  y en todo cerro árido hallarán pastos.
10No tendrán hambre ni sed,
  no los abatirá el sol ni el calor,
  porque los guiará quien les tiene compasión,
  y los conducirá junto a manantiales de agua.
11Convertiré en caminos todas mis montañas,
  y construiré mis calzadas.
12¡Miren! Ellos vendrán de muy lejos;
  unos desde el norte, otros desde el oeste,
  y aun otros desde la región de Asuán.»o

13Ustedes los cielos, ¡griten de alegría!
  Tierra, ¡regocíjate!
  Montañas, ¡prorrumpan en canciones!
  Porque el SEÑOR consuela a su pueblo
  y tiene compasión de sus pobres.

14Pero *Sión dijo: «El SEÑOR me ha
    abandonado;
  el Señor se ha olvidado de mí.»

15¿Puede una madre olvidar a su niño de
    pecho,
  y dejar de amar al hijo que ha dado a luz?
  Aun cuando ella lo olvidara,
  ¡yo no te olvidaré!
16Grabada te llevo en las palmas de mis manos;
  tus muros siempre los tengo presentes.
17Tus constructoresp se apresuran;
  de ti se apartan tus destructores
  y los que te asolaron.
18Alza tus ojos, y mira a tu alrededor;
  todos se reúnen y vienen hacia ti.
  Tan cierto como que yo vivo,
    —afirma el SEÑOR—,
  a todos ellos los usarás como adorno,
  los lucirás en tu vestido de novia.

19»Aunque te arrasaron y te dejaron en ruinas,
  y tu tierra quedó asolada,
  ahora serás demasiado pequeña para tus
    habitantes,
  y lejos quedarán los que te devoraban.
20Los hijos que dabas por perdidos
  todavía te dirán al oído:
  "Este lugar es demasiado pequeño para mí;
  hazme lugar para poder vivir."
21Y te pondrás a pensar:
  "¿Quién me engendró estos hijos?
  Yo no tenía hijos, era estéril,
  desterrada y rechazada;
  pero a éstos, ¿quién los ha criado?
  Me había quedado sola,
  pero éstos, ¿de dónde han salido?"»

22Así dice el SEÑOR omnipotente:
  «Hacia las naciones alzaré mi mano,
  hacia los pueblos levantaré mi estandarte.
  Ellos traerán a tus hijos en sus brazos,
  y cargarán a tus hijas en sus hombros.

o **49:12** *Asuán* (Qumrán); *Sinín* (TM). p **49:17** *constructores.* Alt. *hijos.*

²³Los reyes te adoptarán como hijo,
   y sus reinas serán tus nodrizas.
Se postrarán ante ti rostro en tierra,
   y lamerán el polvo que tú pises.
Sabrás entonces que yo soy el SEÑOR,
   y que no quedarán avergonzados
   los que en mí confían.»

²⁴¿Se le puede quitar el botín a los guerreros?
   ¿Puede el cautivo ser rescatado del tirano?q

²⁵Pero así dice el SEÑOR:

   «Sí, al guerrero se le arrebatará el cautivo,
   y del tirano se rescatará el botín;
contenderé con los que contiendan contigo,
   y yo mismo salvaré a tus hijos.
²⁶Haré que tus opresores se coman su propia
    carne
   y se embriaguen con su propia sangre,
   como si fuera vino.
Toda la *humanidad sabrá entonces
   que yo, el SEÑOR, soy tu Salvador;
   que yo, el Poderoso de Jacob, soy tu
    Redentor.»

El pecado de Israel y la obediencia del Siervo

50 Así dice el SEÑOR:

   «A la madre de ustedes, yo la repudié;
   ¿dónde está el acta de divorcio?
   ¿A cuál de mis acreedores los he vendido?
Por causa de sus iniquidades,
   fueron ustedes vendidos;
por las transgresiones de ustedes
   fue despedida su madre.
²¿Por qué no había nadie cuando vine?
   ¿Por qué nadie respondió cuando llamé?
¿Tan corta es mi mano que no puede rescatar?
   ¿Me falta acaso fuerza para liberarlos?
Yo seco el mar con una simple represión,
   y convierto los ríos en desierto;
por falta de agua sus peces se pudren
   y se mueren de sed.
³A los cielos los revisto de tinieblas
   y los cubro de ceniza.»

⁴El SEÑOR omnipotente me ha concedido
   tener una lengua instruida,
para sostener con mi palabra al fatigado.
Todas las mañanas me despierta,
   y también me despierta el oído,
para que escuche como los discípulos.
⁵El SEÑOR omnipotente me ha abierto los oídos,
   y no he sido rebelde ni me he vuelto atrás.
⁶Ofrecí mi espalda a los que me golpeaban,
   mis mejillas a los que me arrancaban la
    barba;
ante las burlas y los escupitajos
   no escondí mi rostro.
⁷Por cuanto el SEÑOR omnipotente me ayuda,
   no seré humillado.
Por eso endurecí mi rostro como el pedernal,
   y sé que no seré avergonzado.
⁸Cercano está el que me justifica;
   ¿quién entonces contenderá conmigo?
   ¡Comparezcamos juntos!
¿Quién es mi acusador?
   ¡Que se me enfrente!
⁹¡El SEÑOR omnipotente es quien me ayuda!
   ¿Quién me condenará?

Todos ellos se gastarán;
   como a la ropa, la polilla se los comerá.

¹⁰¿Quién entre ustedes teme al SEÑOR
   y obedece la voz de su siervo?
Aunque camine en la oscuridad,
   y sin un rayo de luz,
que confíe en el *nombre del SEÑOR
   y dependa de su Dios.
¹¹Pero ustedes que encienden fuegos
   y preparan antorchas encendidas,
caminen a la luz de su propio fuego
   y de las antorchas que han encendido.
Esto es lo que ustedes recibirán de mi mano:
   en medio de tormentos quedarán tendidos.

Salvación eterna para Sión

51 «Ustedes, los que van tras la *justicia
   y buscan al SEÑOR, ¡escúchenme!
Miren la roca de la que fueron tallados,
   la cantera de la que fueron extraídos.
²Miren a Abraham, su padre,
   y a Sara, que los dio a luz.
Cuando yo lo llamé, él era solo uno,
   pero lo bendije y lo multipliqué.
³Sin duda, el SEÑOR consolará a *Sión;
   consolará todas sus ruinas.
Convertirá en un Edén su desierto;
   en huerto del SEÑOR sus tierras secas.
En ella encontrarán alegría y regocijo,
   acción de gracias y música de salmos.

⁴»Préstame atención, pueblo mío;
   óyeme, nación mía:
porque de mí saldrá la enseñanza,
   y mi justicia será luz para las naciones.
⁵Ya se acerca mi justicia,
   mi *salvación está en camino;
   ¡mi brazo juzgará a las naciones!
Las costas lejanas confían en mí,
   y ponen su esperanza en mi brazo.
⁶Levanten los ojos al cielo;
   miren la tierra aquí abajo:
como humo se esfumarán los cielos,
   como ropa se gastará la tierra,
   y como moscas morirán sus habitantes.
Pero mi salvación permanecerá para siempre,
   mi justicia nunca fallará.

⁷»Escúchenme, ustedes que conocen lo que es
    recto;
   pueblo que lleva mi *ley en su *corazón:
No teman el reproche de los *hombres,
   ni se desalienten por sus insultos.
⁸porque la polilla se los comerá como ropa
   y el gusano los devorará como lana.
Pero mi justicia permanecerá para siempre;
   mi salvación, por todas las generaciones.»

⁹¡Despierta, brazo del SEÑOR!
   ¡Despierta y vístete de fuerza!
Despierta, como en los días pasados,
   como en las generaciones de antaño.
¿No fuiste tú el que despedazó a *Rahab,
   el que traspasó a ese monstruo marino?
¹⁰¿No fuiste tú el que secó el mar,
   esas aguas del gran abismo?
¿El que en las profundidades del mar hizo un
    camino
   para que por él pasaran los redimidos?
¹¹Volverán los rescatados del SEÑOR,

---

q **49:24** *tirano* (Qumrán, Vulgata y Siríaca; véanse también LXX y v. 25); *justo* (TM).

y entrarán en Sión con cánticos de júbilo;
su corona será el gozo eterno.
Se llenarán de regocijo y alegría,
y se apartarán de ellos el dolor y los
gemidos.

12«Soy yo mismo el que los consuela.
¿Quién eres tú, que temes a los hombres,
a simples *mortales, que no son más que
hierba?
13¿Has olvidado al SEÑOR, que te hizo;
al que extendió los cielos y afirmó la tierra?
¿Vivirás cada día en terror constante
por causa de la furia del opresor
que está dispuesto a destruir?
Pero ¿dónde está esa furia?
14Pronto serán liberados los prisioneros;
no morirán en el calabozo,
ni les faltará el pan.
15Porque yo soy el SEÑOR tu Dios,
yo agito el mar, y rugen sus olas;
el SEÑOR *Todopoderoso es mi *nombre.
16He puesto mis palabras en tu boca
y te he cubierto con la sombra de mi mano;
he establecido los cielos y afirmado la tierra,
y he dicho a Sión: "Tú eres mi pueblo."»

La copa de la ira de Dios

17¡Despierta, Jerusalén, despierta!
Levántate, tú, que de la mano del SEÑOR
has bebido la copa de su furia;
tú, que has bebido hasta el fondo
la copa que entorpece a los *hombres.
18De todos los hijos que diste a luz,
no hubo ninguno que te guiara;
de todos los hijos que criaste,
ninguno te tomó de la mano.
19Estos dos males han venido sobre ti:
Ruina y destrucción, hambre y espada.
¿Quién se apiadará de ti?
¿Quién te consolará?ʳ
20Tus hijos han desfallecido;
como antílopes atrapados en la red,
han caído en las esquinas de las calles.
Sobre ellos recae toda la furia del SEÑOR,
todo el reproche de su Dios.

21Por eso escucha esto, tú que estás afligida;
que estás ebria, pero no de vino.
22Así dice tu SEÑOR y Dios,
tu Dios, que aboga por su pueblo:
«Te he quitado de la mano
la copa que te hacía tambalear.
De esa copa, que es el cáliz de mi furia,
jamás volverás a beber.
23La pondré en manos de los que te
atormentan,
de los que te dijeron:
"¡Tiéndete en el suelo,
para que pasemos sobre ti!"
¡Y te echaste boca abajo, sobre el suelo,
para que te pisoteara todo mundo!»

52 ¡Despierta, *Sión, despierta!
¡Revístete de poder!
Jerusalén, ciudad *santa,
ponte tus vestidos de gala,
que los incircuncisos e *impuros

no volverán a entrar en ti.
2¡Sacúdete el polvo, Jerusalén!
¡Levántate, vuelve al trono!
¡Libérate de las cadenas de tu cuello,
cautiva hija de Sión!

3Porque así dice el SEÑOR:

«Ustedes fueron vendidos por nada,
y sin dinero serán redimidos.»

4Porque así dice el SEÑOR omnipotente:

«En tiempos pasados,
mi pueblo descendió a Egipto y vivió allí;
en estos últimos tiempos,
Asiria los ha oprimido sin razón.

5»Y ahora —afirma el SEÑOR—,
¿qué estoy haciendo aquí?
Sin motivo se han llevado a mi pueblo;
sus gobernantes se mofan de él.ˢ
No hay un solo momento
en que mi *nombre no lo blasfemen.
6Por eso mi pueblo conocerá mi nombre,
y en aquel día sabrán
que yo soy quien dice: "¡Aquí estoy!"»

7¡Qué hermosos son, sobre los montes,
los pies del que trae buenas nuevas;
del que proclama la *paz,
del que anuncia buenas noticias,
del que proclama la *salvación,
del que dice a Sión: «Tu Dios reina»!
8¡Escucha! Tus centinelas alzan la voz,
y juntos gritan de alegría,
porque ven con sus propios ojos
que el SEÑOR vuelve a Sión.
9Ruinas de Jerusalén,
¡prorrumpan juntas en canciones de
alegría!
Porque el SEÑOR ha consolado a su pueblo,
¡ha redimido a Jerusalén!
10El SEÑOR desnudará su santo brazo
a la vista de todas las naciones,
y todos los confines de la tierra
verán la salvación de nuestro Dios.
11Ustedes, que transportan los utensilios del
SEÑOR,
¡pónganse en marcha, salgan de allí!
¡Salgan de en medio de ella, purifíquense!
¡No toquen nada impuro!
12Pero no tendrán que apresurarse ni salir
huyendo,
porque el SEÑOR marchará a la cabeza;
¡el Dios de Israel les cubrirá la espalda!

El sufrimiento y la gloria del Siervo

13Miren, mi siervo triunfará;
será exaltado, levantado y muy enaltecido.
14Muchos se asombraron de él,ᵗ
pues tenía desfigurado el semblante;
¡nada de *humano tenía su aspecto!
15Del mismo modo, muchas naciones se
asombrarán,ᵘ
y en su presencia enmudecerán los reyes,
porque verán lo que no se les había
anunciado,
y entenderán lo que no habían oído.

ʳ **51:19** *¿Quién te consolará?* (Qumrán, LXX, Vulgata y Siríaca); *¿Cómo te consolaré?* (TM). ˢ **52:5** *se mofan de él* (Qumrán, Aquila, Targum y Vulgata); *lanzan alaridos* (TM). ᵗ **52:14** *de él* (dos mss. hebreos, Siríaca y Targum); *de ti* (TM).
ᵘ **52:15** *muchas naciones se asombrarán* (LXX); *rociará a muchas naciones* (TM).

53 ¿Quién ha creído a nuestro mensaje
y a quién se le ha revelado el poder del
SEÑOR?
2Creció en su presencia como vástago tierno,
como raíz de tierra seca.
No había en él belleza ni majestad alguna;
su aspecto no era atractivo
y nada en su apariencia lo hacía deseable.
3Despreciado y rechazado por los *hombres,
varón de dolores, hecho para el
sufrimiento.
Todos evitaban mirarlo;
fue despreciado, y no lo estimamos.

4Ciertamente él cargó con nuestras
enfermedades
y soportó nuestros dolores,
pero nosotros lo consideramos herido,
golpeado por Dios, y humillado.
5Él fue traspasado por nuestras rebeliones,
y molido por nuestras iniquidades;
sobre él recayó el castigo, precio de nuestra
*paz,
y gracias a sus heridas fuimos sanados.
6Todos andábamos perdidos, como ovejas;
cada uno seguía su propio *camino,
pero el SEÑOR hizo recaer sobre él
la iniquidad de todos nosotros.
7Maltratado y humillado,
ni siquiera abrió su boca;
como cordero, fue llevado al matadero;
como oveja, enmudeció ante su
trasquilador;
y ni siquiera abrió su boca.
8Después de aprehenderlo y juzgarlo, le dieron
muerte;
nadie se preocupó de su descendencia.
Fue arrancado de la tierra de los vivientes,
y golpeado por la transgresión de mi
pueblo.
9Se le asignó un sepulcro con los malvados,
y murió entre los malhechores,[v]
aunque nunca cometió violencia alguna,
ni hubo engaño en su boca.

10Pero el SEÑOR quiso quebrantarlo y hacerlo
sufrir,
y como él ofreció[w] su *vida en *expiación,
verá su descendencia y prolongará sus días,
y llevará a cabo la voluntad del SEÑOR.
11Después de su sufrimiento,
verá la luz[x] y quedará satisfecho;
por su *conocimiento
mi siervo justo justificará a muchos,
y cargará con las iniquidades de ellos.
12Por lo tanto, le daré un puesto entre los
grandes,
y repartirá el botín con los fuertes,
porque derramó su vida hasta la muerte,
y fue contado entre los transgresores.
Cargó con el pecado de muchos,
e intercedió por los pecadores.

La futura gloria de Sión

54 «Tú, mujer estéril que nunca has dado a luz,
¡grita de alegría!
Tú, que nunca tuviste dolores de parto,
¡prorrumpe en canciones y grita con júbilo!
Porque más hijos que la casada
tendrá la desamparada
—dice el SEÑOR—.
2Ensancha el espacio de tu carpa,
y despliega las cortinas de tu morada.
¡No te limites!
Alarga tus cuerdas y refuerza tus estacas.
3Porque a derecha y a izquierda te extenderás;
tu descendencia desalojará naciones,
y poblará ciudades desoladas.

4»No temas,
porque no serás avergonzada.
No te turbes,
porque no serás humillada.
Olvidarás la vergüenza de tu juventud,
y no recordarás más el oprobio de tu
viudez.
5Porque el que te hizo es tu esposo;
su *nombre es el SEÑOR *Todopoderoso.
Tu Redentor es el *Santo de Israel;
¡Dios de toda la tierra es su nombre!
6El SEÑOR te llamará
como a esposa abandonada;
como a mujer angustiada de espíritu,
como a esposa que se casó joven
tan sólo para ser rechazada
—dice tu Dios—.
7Te abandoné por un instante,
pero con profunda compasión
volveré a unirme contigo.
8Por un momento, en un arrebato de enojo,
escondí mi rostro de ti;
pero con amor eterno
te tendré compasión
—dice el SEÑOR, tu Redentor—.
9»Para mí es como en los días de Noé,
cuando juré que las aguas del diluvio[y]
no volverían a cubrir la tierra.
Así he jurado no enojarme más contigo,
ni volver a reprenderte.
10Aunque cambien de lugar las montañas
y se tambaleen las colinas,
no cambiará mi fiel amor por ti
ni vacilará mi *pacto de *paz,
—dice el SEÑOR, que de ti se compadece—.

11»¡Mira tú, ciudad afligida,
atormentada y sin consuelo!
¡Te afirmaré con turquesas,[z]
y te cimentaré con zafiros![a]
12Con rubíes construiré tus almenas,
con joyas brillantes tus *puertas,
y con piedras preciosas todos tus muros.
13El SEÑOR mismo instruirá a todos tus hijos,
y grande será su *bienestar.
14Serás establecida en justicia;
lejos de ti estará la opresión,
y nada tendrás que temer;
el terror se apartará de ti,
y no se te acercará.
15Si alguien te ataca,
no será de mi parte;
cualquiera que te ataque
caerá ante ti.

16»Mira, yo he creado al herrero
que aviva las brasas del fuego

[v] **53:9** *malhechores* (lectura probable); *un rico* (TM). [w] **53:10** *él ofreció* (lectura probable); *tú ofreciste* (TM). [x] **53:11** *la luz* (Qumrán y LXX); TM no incluye esta palabra. [y] **54:9** *del diluvio*. Lit. *de Noé*. [z] **54:11** *turquesas*. Alt. *jaspe*, o *antimonio*, o *argamasa*. [a] **54:11** *zafiros*. Alt. *azul ultramarino*.

y forja armas para sus propios fines.
Yo también he creado al destructor
para que haga estragos.
17No prevalecerá ninguna arma que se forje
contra ti;
toda lengua que te acuse será refutada.
Ésta es la herencia de los siervos del SEÑOR,
la *justicia que de mí procede
—afirma el SEÑOR—.

Invitación a los sedientos

55 »¡Vengan a las aguas
todos los que tengan sed!
¡Vengan a comprar y a comer
los que no tengan dinero!
Vengan, compren vino y leche
sin pago alguno.
2¿Por qué gastan dinero en lo que no es pan,
y su salario en lo que no satisface?
Escúchenme bien, y comerán lo que es bueno,
y se deleitarán con manjares deliciosos.
3Presten atención y vengan a mí,
escúchenme y vivirán.
Haré con ustedes un *pacto eterno,
conforme a mi constante amor por David.
4Lo he puesto como testigo para los pueblos,
como su jefe supremo.
5Sin duda convocarás a naciones
que no conocías,
y naciones que no te conocían
correrán hacia ti,
gracias al SEÑOR tu Dios,
el *Santo de Israel,
que te ha colmado de honor.»

6Busquen al SEÑOR mientras se deje encontrar,
llámenlo mientras esté cercano.
7Que abandone el malvado su *camino,
y el perverso sus pensamientos.
Que se vuelva al SEÑOR, a nuestro Dios,
que es generoso para perdonar,
y de él recibirá misericordia.
8«Porque mis pensamientos no son los de
ustedes,
ni sus caminos son los míos
—afirma el SEÑOR—.
9Mis caminos y mis pensamientos
son más altos que los de ustedes;
¡más altos que los cielos sobre la tierra!
10Así como la lluvia y la nieve
descienden del cielo,
y no vuelven allá sin regar antes la tierra
y hacerla fecundar y germinar
para que dé semilla al que siembra
y pan al que come,
11así es también la palabra que sale de mi boca:
No volverá a mí vacía,
sino que hará lo que yo deseo
y cumplirá con mis propósitos.
12Ustedes saldrán con alegría
y serán guiados en *paz.
A su paso, las montañas y las colinas
prorrumpirán en gritos de júbilo
y aplaudirán todos los árboles del bosque.
13En vez de zarzas, crecerán cipreses;
mirtos, en lugar de ortigas.
Esto le dará renombre al SEÑOR;
será una señal que durará para siempre.»

Salvación para los demás

56 Así dice el SEÑOR:
«Observen el derecho

y practiquen la justicia,
porque mi *salvación está por llegar;
mi justicia va a manifestarse.
2*Dichoso el que así actúa,
y se mantiene firme en sus convicciones;
el que observa el *sábado sin profanarlo,
y se cuida de hacer lo malo.»

3El extranjero que por su propia voluntad
se ha unido al Señor, no debe decir:
«El SEÑOR me excluirá de su pueblo.»
Tampoco debe decir el *eunuco:
«No soy más que un árbol seco.»

4Porque así dice el SEÑOR:

«A los *eunucos que observen mis sábados,
que elijan lo que me agrada,
y sean fieles a mi *pacto,
5les concederé ver grabado su *nombre
dentro de mi templo y de mi ciudad;
¡eso les será mejor que tener hijos e hijas!
También les daré un nombre eterno
que jamás será borrado.
6Y a los extranjeros que se han unido al SEÑOR
para servirle,
para amar el nombre del SEÑOR,
y adorarlo,
a todos los que observan el sábado sin
profanarlo
y se mantienen firmes en mi pacto,
7los llevaré a mi monte *santo;
¡los llenaré de alegría en mi casa de
oración!
Aceptaré los *holocaustos y sacrificios
que ofrezcan sobre mi altar,
porque mi casa será llamada
casa de oración para todos los pueblos.»

8Así dice el SEÑOR omnipotente,
el que reúne a los desterrados de Israel:
«Reuniré a mi pueblo con otros pueblos,
además de los que ya he reunido.»

La acusación de Dios contra los malvados

9Animales del campo y fieras del bosque,
¡vengan todos y devoren!
10Ciegos están todos los guardianes de Israel;
ninguno de ellos sabe nada.
Todos ellos son perros mudos,
que no pueden ladrar.
Se acuestan y desvarían;
les encanta dormitar.
11Son perros de voraz apetito;
nunca parecen saciarse.
Son *pastores sin discernimiento;
cada uno anda por su propio *camino.
Todos, sin excepción,
procuran su propia ganancia.
12«¡Vengan, busquemos vino!
¡emborrachémonos con licor!
—gritan a una voz—.
¡Y mañana haremos lo mismo que hoy,
pero mucho mejor!»

57 El justo perece, y a nadie le importa;
mueren tus siervos fieles, y nadie
comprende
que mueren los justos a causa del mal.
2Los que van por el *camino recto mueren en
*paz;
hallan reposo en su lecho de muerte.

3«Ustedes, hijos de hechicera,

descendientes de adúltero con prostituta,
¡acérquense!

4¿De quién quieren burlarse?
¿A quién le hacen muecas despectivas
y le sacan la lengua?
¿Acaso no son ustedes una camada de
rebeldes,
y una descendencia de mentirosos?
5Entre los robles, y debajo de todo árbol
frondoso,
dan rienda suelta a su lujuria;
junto a los arroyos, y en las grietas de las rocas,
sacrifican a niños pequeños.
6Las piedras lisas de los arroyos,
serán tu herencia;
sí, ellas serán tu destino.
Ante ellas has derramado libaciones
y has presentado ofrendas de grano.
Ante estas cosas, ¿me quedaré callado?
7Sobre un monte alto y encumbrado,
pusiste tu lecho,
y hasta allí subiste
para ofrecer sacrificios.
8Detrás de tu puerta y de sus postes
has puesto tus símbolos paganos.
Te alejaste de mí, te desnudaste,
subiste al lecho que habías preparado;
entraste en arreglos con la gente
con quienes deseabas acostarte,
y contemplaste su desnudez.
9Acudiste a Moloc y le llevaste aceite de oliva,
y multiplicaste tus perfumes.
Enviaste muy lejos a tus embajadores;
¡hasta el *sepulcro mismo los hiciste bajar!
10De tanto andar te cansaste,
pero no dijiste: "Hasta aquí llego."
Lograste renovar tus fuerzas;
por eso no desmayaste.

11»¿Quién te asustó, quién te metió miedo,
que me has engañado?
No te acordaste de mí,
ni me tomaste en cuenta.
¿Será que no me temes
porque guardé silencio tanto tiempo?
12Yo denunciaré tu justicia y tus obras,
y de nada te servirán.
13Cuando grites pidiendo ayuda,
¡que te salve tu colección de ídolos!
A todos ellos se los llevará el viento;
con un simple soplo desaparecerán.
Pero el que se refugia en mí
recibirá la tierra por herencia
y tomará posesión de mi monte *santo.»

Consuelo para los contritos

14Y se dirá:

«¡Construyan, construyan, preparen el
camino!
¡Quiten los obstáculos del camino de mi
pueblo!»
15Porque lo dice el excelso y sublime,
el que vive para siempre, cuyo *nombre es
*santo:
«Yo habito en un lugar santo y sublime,
pero también con el contrito y humilde de
espíritu,
para reanimar el espíritu de los humildes
y alentar el *corazón de los quebrantados.
16Mi litigio no será eterno,
ni estaré siempre enojado,
porque ante mí desfallecerían

todos los seres vivientes que he creado.
17La codicia de mi pueblo es irritable,
por perversa,
en mi enojo, lo he castigado;
le he dado la espalda,
pero él prefirió seguir
sus obstinados *caminos.
18He visto sus caminos, pero lo sanaré;
lo guiaré y lo colmaré de consuelo.
Y a los que lloran por él
19les haré proclamar esta alabanza:
*¡Paz a los que están lejos,
y paz a los que están cerca!
Yo los sanaré —dice el SEÑOR—,
20pero los malvados son como el mar agitado,
que no puede calmarse,
cuyas olas arrojan fango y lodo.
21No hay paz para los malvados
—dice mi Dios—.

El verdadero ayuno

58 »¡Grita con toda tu fuerza, no te reprimas!
Alza tu voz como trompeta.
Denúnciale a mi pueblo sus rebeldías;
sus pecados, a los descendientes de Jacob.
2Porque día tras día me buscan,
y desean conocer mis *caminos,
como si fueran una nación
que practicara la justicia,
como si no hubieran abandonado
mis mandamientos.
Me piden decisiones justas,
y desean acercarse a mí,
3y hasta me reclaman:
"¿Para qué ayunamos, si no lo tomas en
cuenta?
¿Para qué nos afligimos, si tú no lo notas?"

»Pero el día en que ustedes ayunan,
hacen negocios y explotan a sus obreros.
4Ustedes sólo ayunan para pelear y reñir,
y darse puñetazos a mansalva.
Si quieren que el cielo atienda sus ruegos,
¡ayunen, pero no como ahora lo hacen!
5¿Acaso el ayuno que he escogido
es sólo un día para que el *hombre se
mortifique?
¿Y sólo para que incline la cabeza como un
junco,
haga duelo y se cubra de ceniza?
¿A eso llaman ustedes día de ayuno
y el día aceptable al SEÑOR?

6»El ayuno que he escogido,
¿no es más bien romper las cadenas de
injusticia
y desatar las correas del yugo,
poner en libertad a los oprimidos
y romper toda atadura?
7¿No es acaso el ayuno compartir tu pan con el
hambriento
y dar refugio a los pobres sin techo,
vestir al desnudo
y no dejar de lado a tus semejantes?
8Si así procedes,
tu luz despuntará como la aurora,
y al instante llegará tu sanidad;
tu justicia te abrirá el camino,
y la gloria del SEÑOR te seguirá.
9Llamarás, y el SEÑOR responderá;
pedirás ayuda, y él dirá: "¡Aquí estoy!"
»Si desechas el yugo de opresión,

el dedo acusador y la lengua maliciosa,
10si te dedicas a ayudar a los hambrientos
y a saciar la necesidad del desvalido,
entonces brillará tu luz en las tinieblas,
y como el mediodía será tu noche.
11El Señor te guiará siempre;
te saciará en tierras resecas,
y fortalecerá tus huesos.
Serás como jardín bien regado,
como manantial cuyas aguas no se agotan.
12Tu pueblo reconstruirá las ruinas antiguas
y levantará los cimientos de antaño;
serás llamado "reparador de muros
derruidos",
"restaurador de calles transitables".

13»Si dejas de profanar el *sábado,
y no haces negocios en mi día *santo;
si llamas al sábado "delicia",
y al día santo del Señor, "honorable";
si te abstienes de profanarlo,
y lo honras no haciendo negocios
ni profiriendo palabras inútiles,
14entonces hallarás tu gozo en el Señor;
sobre las cumbres de la tierra te haré
cabalgar,
y haré que te deleites
en la herencia de tu padre Jacob.»
                El Señor mismo lo ha dicho.

Pecado, confesión y redención

59 La mano del Señor
no es corta para salvar,
ni es sordo su oído para oír.
2Son las iniquidades de ustedes
las que los separan de su Dios.
Son estos pecados los que lo llevan
a ocultar su rostro para no escuchar.
3Ustedes tienen las manos manchadas de sangre
y los dedos manchados de iniquidad.
Sus labios dicen mentiras;
su lengua murmura maldades.
4Nadie clama por la justicia,
nadie va a juicio con integridad.
Se confía en argumentos sin sentido,
y se mienten unos a otros.
Conciben malicia
y dan a luz perversidad.
5Incuban huevos de víboras
y tejen telarañas.
El que coma de estos huevos morirá;
si uno de ellos se rompe, saldrá una culebra.
6Sus tejidos no sirven para vestido;
no podrán cubrirse con lo que fabrican.
Sus obras son obras de iniquidad,
y sus manos generan violencia.
7Sus pies corren hacia el mal;
se apresuran a derramar sangre inocente.
Sus pensamientos son perversos;
dejan ruina y destrucción en sus caminos.
8No conocen la senda de la *paz;
no hay justicia alguna en su *camino.
Abren senderos tortuosos,
y el que anda por ellos no conoce la paz.

9Por eso el derecho está lejos de nosotros,
y la justicia queda fuera de nuestro alcance.
Esperábamos luz, pero todo es tinieblas;
claridad, pero andamos en densa
oscuridad.
10Vamos palpando la pared como los ciegos,

andamos a tientas como los que no tienen
ojos.
En pleno mediodía tropezamos como si fuera
de noche;
teniendo fuerzas, estamos como muertos.
11Todos nosotros gruñimos como osos,
gemimos como palomas.
Esperábamos la *justicia, y no llegó;
¡la liberación sigue lejos de nosotros!

12Tú sabes que son muchas nuestras rebeliones;
nuestros pecados nos acusan.
Nuestras rebeliones no nos dejan;
conocemos nuestras iniquidades.
13Hemos sido rebeldes; hemos negado al Señor.
¡Le hemos vuelto la espalda a nuestro Dios!
Fomentamos la opresión y la traición;
proferimos las mentiras concebidas en
nuestro *corazón.
14Así se le vuelve la espalda al derecho,
y se mantiene alejada la justicia;
a la verdad se le hace tropezar en la plaza,
y no le damos lugar a la honradez.
15No se ve la verdad por ninguna parte;
al que se aparta del mal lo despojan de todo.

El Señor lo ha visto, y le ha disgustado
ver que no hay justicia alguna.
16Lo ha visto, y le ha asombrado
ver que no hay nadie que intervenga.
Por eso su propio brazo vendrá a salvarlos;
su propia justicia los sostendrá.
17Se pondrá la justicia como coraza,
y se cubrirá la cabeza con el casco de la
*salvación;
se vestirá con ropas de venganza,
y se envolverá en el manto de sus celos.
18Les pagará según sus obras;
a las costas lejanas les dará su merecido:
furor para sus adversarios,
y retribución para sus enemigos.

19Desde el occidente temerán el *nombre del
Señor,
y desde el oriente respetarán su gloria.
Porque vendrá como un torrente caudaloso,
impulsado por el soplo del Señor.

20«El Redentor vendrá a *Sión;
¡vendrá a todos los de Jacob
que se *arrepientan de su rebeldía!
                —afirma el Señor—.

21»En cuanto a mí —dice el Señor—,
éste es mi *pacto con ellos:
Mi Espíritu que está sobre ti,
y mis palabras que he puesto en tus labios,
no se apartarán más de ti,
ni de tus hijos ni de sus descendientes,
desde ahora y para siempre
                —dice el Señor—.

La gloria de Sión

60 »¡Levántate y resplandece, que tu luz ha
llegado!
¡La gloria del Señor brilla sobre ti!
2Mira, las tinieblas cubren la tierra,
y una densa oscuridad se cierne sobre los
pueblos.
Pero la aurora del Señor brillará sobre ti;
¡sobre ti se manifestará su gloria!
3Las naciones serán guiadas por tu luz,
y los reyes, por tu amanecer esplendoroso.
4»Alza los ojos, mira a tu alrededor:

todos se reúnen y acuden a ti.
Tus hijos llegan desde lejos;
   a tus hijas las traen en brazos.
5Verás esto y te pondrás radiante de alegría;
   vibrará tu *corazón y se henchirá de gozo;
porque te traerán los tesoros del mar,
   y te llegarán las riquezas de las naciones.
6Te llenarás con caravanas de camellos,
   con dromedarios de Madián y de Efa.
Vendrán todos los de Sabá,
   cargando oro e incienso
   y proclamando las alabanzas del SEÑOR.
7En ti se reunirán todos los rebaños de Cedar,
   te servirán los carneros de Nebayot;
subirán como ofrendas agradables sobre mi
     altar,
   y yo embelleceré mi templo glorioso.

8»¿Quiénes son los que pasan como nubes,
   y como palomas rumbo a su palomar?
9En mí esperarán las costas lejanas,
   a la cabeza vendrán los barcos de Tarsis
trayendo de lejos a tus hijos,
   y con ellos su oro y su plata,
para la honra del SEÑOR tu Dios,
   el *Santo de Israel,
   porque él te ha llenado de gloria.

10»Los extranjeros reconstruirán tus muros,
   y sus reyes te servirán.
Aunque en mi furor te castigué,
   por mi bondad tendré compasión de ti.
11Tus *puertas estarán siempre abiertas,
   ni de día ni de noche se cerrarán;
a ti serán traídas las riquezas de las naciones;
   ante ti desfilarán sus derrotados reyes.
12La nación o el reino que no te sirva, perecerá;
   quedarán arruinados por completo.

13»Te llegará la gloria del Líbano,
   con el ciprés, el olmo y el abeto,
   para embellecer el lugar de mi santuario.
Glorificaré el lugar donde reposan mis pies.
14Ante ti vendrán a inclinarse
   los hijos de tus opresores;
todos los que te desprecian
   se postrarán a tus pies,
y te llamarán "Ciudad del SEÑOR",
   "Sión del Santo de Israel".

15»Aunque fuiste abandonada y aborrecida,
   y nadie transitaba por tus calles,
haré de ti el orgullo eterno
   y la alegría de todas las generaciones.
16Te alimentarás con la leche de las naciones,
   con la riqueza de los reyes serás
     amamantada.
Sabrás entonces que yo, el SEÑOR, soy tu
     Salvador;
que yo, el Poderoso de Jacob, soy tu
     Redentor.
17En vez de bronce te traeré oro;
   en lugar de hierro, plata.
En vez de madera te traeré bronce,
   y en lugar de piedras, hierro.
Haré que la *paz te gobierne,
   y que la justicia te rija.
18Ya no se sabrá de violencia en tu tierra,
   ni de ruina y destrucción en tus fronteras,
sino que llamarás a tus muros *"Salvación",
   y a tus puertas, "Alabanza".
19Ya no será el sol tu luz durante el día,
   ni con su resplandor te alumbrará la luna,

porque el SEÑOR será tu luz eterna;
   tu Dios será tu gloria.
20Tu sol no volverá a ponerse,
   ni menguará tu luna;
será el SEÑOR tu luz eterna,
   y llegarán a su fin tus días de duelo.
21Entonces todo tu pueblo será justo
   y poseerá la tierra para siempre.
Serán el retoño plantado por mí mismo,
   la obra maestra que me glorificará.
22El más débil se multiplicará por miles,
   y el menor llegará a ser una nación
     poderosa.
Yo soy el SEÑOR;
   cuando llegue el momento, actuaré sin
     demora.»

El año del favor del SEÑOR

61 El Espíritu del SEÑOR omnipotente está
     sobre mí,
   por cuanto me ha ungido
para anunciar buenas nuevas a los pobres.
Me ha enviado a sanar los corazones heridos,
   a proclamar liberación a los cautivos
   y libertad a los prisioneros,
2a pregonar el año del favor del SEÑOR
   y el día de la venganza de nuestro Dios,
a consolar a todos los que están de duelo,
3y a confortar a los dolientes de *Sión.
Me ha enviado a darles una corona
   en vez de cenizas,
aceite de alegría
   en vez de luto,
traje de fiesta
   en vez de espíritu de desaliento.
Serán llamados robles de justicia,
   plantío del SEÑOR, para mostrar su gloria.
4Reconstruirán las ruinas antiguas,
   y restaurarán los escombros de antaño;
repararán las ciudades en ruinas,
   y los escombros de muchas generaciones.
5Gente extraña pastoreará
   los rebaños de ustedes,
y sus campos y viñedos serán labrados
   por un pueblo extranjero.
6Pero a ustedes los llamarán «sacerdotes del
     SEÑOR»;
les dirán «ministros de nuestro Dios».
Se alimentarán de las riquezas de las naciones,
   y se jactarán de los tesoros de ellas.
7En vez de su vergüenza,
   mi pueblo recibirá doble porción;
en vez de deshonra,
   se regocijará en su herencia;
y así en su tierra recibirá doble herencia,
   y su alegría será eterna.

8«Yo, el SEÑOR, amo la justicia,
   pero odio el robo y la iniquidad.
En mi fidelidad los recompensaré
   y haré con ellos un *pacto eterno.
9Sus descendientes serán conocidos entre las
     naciones,
   y sus vástagos, entre los pueblos.
Quienes los vean, reconocerán
   que ellos son descendencia bendecida del
     SEÑOR.»

10Me deleito mucho en el SEÑOR;
   me regocijo en mi Dios.
Porque él me vistió con ropas de *salvación
   y me cubrió con el manto de la justicia.

Soy semejante a un novio que luce su
diadema,
o una novia adornada con sus joyas.
¹¹Porque así como la tierra hace que broten los
retoños,
y el huerto hace que germinen las semillas,
así el SEÑOR omnipotente hará que broten
la justicia y la alabanza ante todas las
naciones.

El nuevo nombre de Sión

62 Por amor a *Sión no guardaré silencio,
por amor a Jerusalén no desmayaré,
hasta que su justicia resplandezca como la
aurora,
y como antorcha encendida su *salvación.
²Las naciones verán tu justicia,
y todos los reyes tu gloria;
recibirás un *nombre nuevo,
que el Señor mismo te dará.
³Serás en la mano del SEÑOR como una corona
esplendorosa,
¡como una diadema real en la palma de tu
Dios!
⁴Ya no te llamarán «Abandonada»,
ni a tu tierra la llamarán «Desolada»,
sino que serás llamada «Mi deleite»;
tu tierra se llamará «Mi esposa»;
porque el SEÑOR se deleitará en ti,
y tu tierra tendrá esposo.
⁵Como un joven que se casa con una doncella,
así el que te edifica se casará contigo;
como un novio que se regocija por su novia,
así tu Dios se regocijará por ti.

⁶Jerusalén, sobre tus muros he puesto
centinelas
que nunca callarán, ni de día ni de noche.
Ustedes, los que invocan al SEÑOR,
no se den descanso,
⁷ni tampoco lo dejen descansar,
hasta que establezca a Jerusalén
y la convierta en la alabanza de la tierra.

⁸Por su mano *derecha, por su brazo poderoso,
ha jurado el SEÑOR:
«Nunca más daré a tus enemigos
tu grano como alimento,
ni se beberá gente extranjera
el vino nuevo por el que trabajaste.
⁹Alabando al Señor comerán el grano
quienes lo hayan cosechado;
en los atrios de mi santuario beberán el vino
quienes hayan trabajado en la vendimia.»

¹⁰¡Pasen, pasen por las *puertas!
Preparen el camino para el pueblo.
¡Construyan la carretera!
¡Quítenle todas las piedras!
¡Desplieguen sobre los pueblos la bandera!

¹¹He aquí lo que el SEÑOR ha proclamado
hasta los confines de la tierra:
«Digan a la hija de Sión:
"¡Ahí viene tu Salvador!
Trae su premio consigo;
su recompensa lo acompaña."»
¹²Serán llamados «Pueblo *santo»,
«Redimidos del SEÑOR»;
y tú serás llamada «Ciudad anhelada»,

«Ciudad nunca abandonada».

El día de la venganza y la redención de Dios

63 ¿Quién es este que viene de Edom,
desde Bosra, vestido de púrpura?
¿Quién es este de espléndido ropaje,
que avanza^b con fuerza arrolladora?

«Soy yo, el que habla con justicia,
el que tiene poder para salvar.»

²¿Por qué están rojos tus vestidos,
como los del que pisa las uvas en el lagar?

³«He pisado el lagar yo solo;
ninguno de los pueblos estuvo conmigo.
Los he pisoteado en mi enojo;
los he aplastado en mi ira.
Su sangre salpicó mis vestidos,
y me manché toda la ropa.
⁴¡Ya tengo planeado el día de la venganza!
¡El año de mi redención ha llegado!
⁵Miré, pero no hubo quien me ayudara,
me asombró que nadie me diera apoyo.
Mi propio brazo me dio la victoria;
¡mi propia ira me sostuvo!
⁶En mi enojo pisoteé a los pueblos,
y los embriagué con la copa de mi ira;
¡hice correr su sangre sobre la tierra!»

Alabanza y oración

⁷Recordaré el gran amor del SEÑOR,
y sus hechos dignos de alabanza,
por todo lo que hizo por nosotros,
por su compasión y gran amor.
¡Sí, por la multitud de cosas buenas
que ha hecho por los descendientes de
Israel!
⁸Declaró: «Verdaderamente son mi pueblo,
hijos que no me engañarán.»
Así se convirtió en el Salvador
⁹de todas sus angustias.
Él mismo los salvó;
no envió un emisario ni un ángel.^c
En su amor y misericordia los rescató;
los levantó y los llevó en sus brazos
como en los tiempos de antaño.
¹⁰Pero ellos se rebelaron
y afligieron a su *santo Espíritu.
Por eso se convirtió en su enemigo,
y luchó él mismo contra ellos.

¹¹Su pueblo recordó los tiempos pasados,
los tiempos de Moisés:
¿Dónde está el que los guió a través del mar,
como guía el *pastor a su rebaño?^d
¿Dónde está el que puso
su santo Espíritu entre ellos,
¹²el que hizo que su glorioso brazo
marchara a la *derecha de Moisés,
el que separó las aguas a su paso,
para ganarse renombre eterno?
¹³¿Dónde está el que los guió a través del mar,^e
como a caballo en el desierto,
sin que ellos tropezaran?
¹⁴El Espíritu del SEÑOR les dio descanso,
como a ganado que pasta en la llanura.
Fue así como guiaste a tu pueblo,
para hacerte un *nombre glorioso.

¹⁵Mira bien desde el cielo;

^b **63:1** *avanza* (Vulgata); *se inclina* (TM). ^c **63:9** *de todas ... un ángel.* Frases de difícil traducción. ^d **63:11** *¿Dónde está ... su rebaño?* Alt. *¿Dónde está el que sacó de las aguas al pastor de su rebaño?* ^e **63:13** *mar.* Lit. *abismo.*

observa desde tu morada santa y gloriosa.
¿Dónde están tu celo y tu poder?
  ¡Se nos niega tu abundante compasión y
    ternura!
16Pero tú eres nuestro Padre,
  aunque Abraham no nos conozca
  ni nos reconozca Israel;
  tú, SEÑOR, eres nuestro Padre;
  ¡tu nombre ha sido siempre «nuestro
    Redentor»!
17¿Por qué, SEÑOR, nos desvías de tus *caminos,
  y endureces nuestro *corazón
    para que no te temamos?
  Vuelve por amor a tus siervos,
  por las tribus que son tu herencia.
18Tu pueblo poseyó por un tiempo tu
    santuario,
  pero ahora lo han pisoteado nuestros
    enemigos.
19Estamos como si nunca nos hubieras
    gobernado,
  como si nunca hubiéramos llevado tu
    nombre.

64 ¡Ojalá rasgaras los cielos, y descendieras!
  ¡Las montañas temblarían ante ti,
2como cuando el fuego enciende la leña
  y hace que hierva el agua!
  Así darías a conocer tu *nombre entre tus
    enemigos,
  y ante ti temblarían las naciones.
3Hiciste portentos inesperados cuando
    descendiste;
  ante tu presencia temblaron las montañas.
4Fuera de ti, desde tiempos antiguos
  nadie ha escuchado ni percibido,
  ni ojo alguno ha visto,
  a un Dios que, como tú,
  actúe en favor de quienes en él confían.
5Sales al encuentro de los que, alegres,
  practican la justicia y recuerdan tus
    *caminos.
  Pero te enojas si persistimos
  en desviarnos de ellos.f
  ¿Cómo podremos ser salvos?
6Todos somos como gente *impura;
  todos nuestros actos de justicia
  son como trapos de inmundicia.
  Todos nos marchitamos como hojas:
  nuestras iniquidades nos arrastran como el
    viento.
7Nadie invoca tu nombre,
  ni se esfuerza por aferrarse a ti.
  Pues nos has dado la espalda
  y nos has entregadog en poder de nuestras
    iniquidades.

8A pesar de todo, SEÑOR, tú eres nuestro Padre;
  nosotros somos el barro, y tú el alfarero.
  Todos somos obra de tu mano.
9No te enojes demasiado, SEÑOR;
  no te acuerdes siempre de nuestras
    iniquidades.
  ¡Considera, por favor,
  que todos somos tu pueblo!
10Tus ciudades *santas han quedado
    devastadas,
  y hasta *Sión se ha vuelto un desierto;
  Jerusalén es una desolación.

11Nuestro santo y glorioso templo,
  donde te alababan nuestros padres,
  ha sido devorado por el fuego.
  Ha quedado en ruinas
  todo lo que más queríamos.
12Ante todo esto, SEÑOR, ¿no vas a hacer nada?
  ¿Vas a guardar silencio y afligirnos sin
    medida?

Juicio y salvación

65 «Me di a conocer a los que no preguntaban
  por mí;
  dejé que me hallaran los que no me
    buscaban.
  A una nación que no invocaba mi *nombre,
  le dije: "¡Aquí estoy!"
2Todo el día extendí mis manos
  hacia un pueblo rebelde,
  que va por mal *camino,
  siguiendo sus propias ideas.
3Es un pueblo que en mi propia cara
  constantemente me provoca;
  que ofrece sacrificios en los jardines
  y quema incienso en los altares;
4que se sienta entre los sepulcros
  y pasa la noche en vigilias secretas;
  que come carne de cerdo,
  y en sus ollas cocina caldo *impuro;
5que dice: "¡Manténganse alejados!
  ¡No se me acerquen!
  ¡Soy demasiado sagrado para ustedes!"
  Todo esto me fastidia como humo en la nariz;
  ¡es un fuego que arde todo el día!

6»Ante mí ha quedado escrito;
  no guardaré silencio.
  Les daré su merecido;
  lo sufrirán en carne propia.
7tanto por las iniquidades de ustedes
  como por las de sus padres
                —dice el SEÑOR—.
  Por cuanto ellos quemaron incienso en las
    montañas
  y me desafiaron en las colinas,
  les haré sufrir en carne propia
  las consecuencias de sus acciones pasadas.»

8Así dice el SEÑOR:

«Cuando alguien encuentra un buen racimo
  de uvas,
  dice: "No voy a dañarlo,
  porque todavía tiene jugo".
  Del mismo modo actuaré yo por amor a mis
    siervos:
  No los destruiré a todos.
9De Jacob sacaré descendientes,
  y de Judá, a los que poseerán mis
    montañas.
  Las heredarán mis elegidos,
  y allí morarán mis siervos.
10Para mi pueblo que me busca,
  Sarón será redil de ovejas;
  el valle de Acor, corral de vacas.

11»Pero a ustedes que abandonan al SEÑOR
  y se olvidan de mi monte *santo,
  que para los dioses de la Fortuna y del Destino
  preparan mesas y sirven vino mezclado,
12los destinaré a la espada;

---

f **64:5** te enojas … de ellos. Frase de difícil traducción. g **64:7** entregado (LXX, Targum y Siríaca); derretido (TM).

¡todos ustedes se inclinarán para el
   degüello!
Porque llamé y no me respondieron,
   hablé y no me escucharon.
Más bien, hicieron lo malo ante mis ojos
   y optaron por lo que no me agrada.»

13Por eso, así dice el SEÑOR omnipotente:

«Mis siervos comerán,
   pero ustedes pasarán hambre;
mis siervos beberán,
   pero ustedes sufrirán de sed;
mis siervos se alegrarán,
   pero ustedes serán avergonzados.
14Mis siervos cantarán
   con alegría de *corazón,
pero ustedes clamarán
   con corazón angustiado;
   ¡gemirán con espíritu quebrantado!
15Mis escogidos heredarán el nombre de
      ustedes
   como una maldición.
El SEÑOR omnipotente les dará muerte,
   pero a sus siervos les dará un nombre
      diferente.
16Cualquiera que en el país invoque una
      bendición,
   lo hará por el Dios de la verdad;
y cualquiera que jure en esta tierra,
   lo hará por el Dios de la verdad.
Las angustias del pasado han quedado en el
      olvido,
   las he borrado de mi vista.

Nuevos cielos y nueva tierra

17»Presten atención, que estoy por crear
   un cielo nuevo y una tierra nueva.
No volverán a mencionarse las cosas pasadas,
   ni se traerán a la memoria.
18Alégrense más bien, y regocíjense por
      siempre,
   por lo que estoy a punto de crear:
Estoy por crear una Jerusalén feliz,
   un pueblo lleno de alegría.
19Me regocijaré por Jerusalén
   y me alegraré en mi pueblo;
no volverán a oírse en ella
   voces de llanto ni gritos de clamor.

20»Nunca más habrá en ella
   niños que vivan pocos días,
   ni ancianos que no completen sus años.
El que muera a los cien años
   será considerado joven;
pero el que no llegueh a esa edad
   será considerado maldito.
21Construirán casas y las habitarán;
   plantarán viñas y comerán de su fruto.
22Ya no construirán casas para que otros las
      habiten,
   ni plantarán viñas para que otros coman.
Porque los días de mi pueblo
   serán como los de un árbol;
mis escogidos disfrutarán
   de las obras de sus manos.
23No trabajarán en vano,
   ni tendrán hijos para la desgracia;
tanto ellos como su descendencia
   serán simiente bendecida del SEÑOR.

24Antes que me llamen,
   yo les responderé;
todavía estarán hablando
   cuando ya los habré escuchado.
25El lobo y el cordero pacerán juntos;
   el león comerá paja como el buey,
   y la serpiente se alimentará de polvo.
En todo mi monte *santo
   no habrá quien haga daño ni destruya»,
                          dice el SEÑOR.

Juicio y esperanza

66 Así dice el SEÑOR:

«El cielo es mi trono,
   y la tierra, el estrado de mis pies.
¿Qué casa me pueden construir?
   ¿Qué morada me pueden ofrecer?
2Fue mi mano la que hizo todas estas cosas;
   fue así como llegaron a existir
                     —afirma el SEÑOR—.

»Yo estimo a los pobres y contritos de espíritu,
   a los que tiemblan ante mi palabra.
3Pero los que sacrifican toros
   son como los que matan *hombres;
los que ofrecen corderos
   son como los que desnucan perros;
los que presentan ofrendas de grano
   son como los que ofrecen sangre de cerdo,
y los que queman ofrendas de incienso
   son como los que adoran ídolos.
Ellos han escogido sus propios *caminos,
   y se deleitan en sus abominaciones.
4Pues yo también escogeré aflicciones para ellos
   y enviaré sobre ellos lo que tanto temen.
Porque nadie respondió cuando llamé;
   cuando hablé, nadie escuchó.
Más bien, hicieron lo malo ante mis ojos
   y optaron por lo que no me agrada.»
5¡Escuchen la palabra del SEÑOR,
   ustedes que tiemblan ante su palabra!:
«Así dicen sus hermanos que los odian
   y los excluyen por causa de mi *nombre:
"¡Que el SEÑOR sea glorificado,
   para que veamos la alegría de ustedes!"
Pero ellos serán los avergonzados.
6Una voz resuena desde la ciudad,
   una voz surge del templo:
Es la voz del SEÑOR
   que da a sus enemigos su merecido.

7»Antes de estar con dolores de parto,
   Jerusalén tuvo un hijo;
antes que le llegaran los dolores,
   dio a luz un varón.
8¿Quién ha oído cosa semejante?
   ¿Quién ha visto jamás cosa igual?
¿Puede una nación nacer en un solo día?
   ¿Se da a luz un pueblo en un momento?
Sin embargo, *Sión dio a luz sus hijos
   cuando apenas comenzaban sus dolores.
9¿Podría yo abrir la matriz,
   y no provocar el parto?
                     —dice el SEÑOR—.
¿O cerraría yo el seno materno,
   siendo que yo hago dar a luz?
                     —dice tu Dios—.
10Mas alégrense con Jerusalén, y regocíjense
   por ella,

---

h **65:20** *el que no llegue.* Alt. *el pecador que llegue.*

todos los que la aman;
salten con ella de alegría,
todos los que por ella se conduelen.
11Porque ustedes serán amamantados y
    saciados,
y hallarán consuelo en sus pechos;
beberán hasta saciarse,
y se deleitarán en sus henchidos senos.»

12Porque así dice el SEÑOR:
«Hacia ella extenderé la *paz como un
    torrente,
y la riqueza de las naciones como río
    desbordado.
Ustedes serán amamantados, llevados en sus
    brazos,
mecidos en sus rodillas.
13Como madre que consuela a su hijo,
así yo los consolaré a ustedes;
en Jerusalén serán consolados.»

14Cuando ustedes vean esto,
se regocijará su *corazón,
y su cuerpo florecerá como la hierba;
el SEÑOR dará a conocer
    su poder entre sus siervos,
    y su furor entre sus enemigos.
15¡Ya viene el SEÑOR con fuego!
    ¡Sus carros de combate son como un
    torbellino!
Descargará su enojo con furor,
y su represión con llamas de fuego.
16Con fuego y con espada
juzgará el SEÑOR a todo *mortal.
¡Muchos morirán a manos del SEÑOR!

ⁱ 66:17 *al frente.* Lit. *en medio.*

17«Juntos perecerán los que se *santifican y se
*purifican para entrar en los jardines, siguiendo a
uno que va al frente,ⁱ y los que comen carne de cerdo, ratas y otras cosas abominables —afirma el
SEÑOR—.

18»Yo, por causa de sus acciones y sus ideas, estoy a punto de reunir a gente de toda nación y lengua; vendrán y verán mi gloria.

19»Les daré una señal, y a algunos de sus sobrevivientes los enviaré a las naciones: a Tarsis, Pul, Lidia (famosa por sus arqueros), Tubal y Grecia, y a las
costas lejanas que no han oído hablar de mi fama ni
han visto mi gloria. Ellos anunciarán mi gloria entre
las naciones. 20Y a todos los hermanos que ustedes
tienen entre las naciones los traerán a mi monte santo en Jerusalén, como una ofrenda al SEÑOR; los traerán en caballos, en carros de combate y en literas, y
en mulas y camellos —dice el SEÑOR—. Los traerán
como traen los israelitas, en recipientes limpios, sus
ofrendas de grano al templo del SEÑOR. 21Y de ellos
escogeré también a algunos, para que sean sacerdotes y levitas —dice el SEÑOR—.

22»Porque así como perdurarán en mi presencia
el cielo nuevo y la tierra nueva que yo haré, así también perdurarán el nombre y los descendientes de
ustedes —afirma el SEÑOR—. 23Sucederá que de una
luna nueva a otra, y de un *sábado a otro, toda la humanidad vendrá a postrarse ante mí —dice el
SEÑOR—. 24Entonces saldrán y contemplarán los cadáveres de los que se rebelaron contra mí.

»Porque no morirá el gusano que los devora,
ni se apagará el fuego que los consume:
¡repulsivos serán a toda la humanidad!»

JEREMÍAS

1 Éstas son las palabras de Jeremías hijo de Jilquías. Jeremías provenía de una familia sacerdotal de Anatot, ciudad del territorio de Benjamín. [2]La palabra del SEÑOR vino a Jeremías en el año trece del reinado de Josías hijo de Amón, rey de Judá. [3]También vino a él durante el reinado de Joacim hijo de Josías, rey de Judá, y hasta el fin del reinado de Sedequías hijo de Josías, rey de Judá; es decir, hasta el quinto mes del año undécimo de su reinado, cuando la población de Jerusalén fue deportada.

Llamamiento de Jeremías

[4]La palabra del SEÑOR vino a mí:

[5]«Antes de formarte en el vientre,
    ya te había elegido;
antes de que nacieras,
    ya te había apartado;
te había nombrado profeta para las
    naciones.»

[6]Yo le respondí:

«¡Ah, SEÑOR mi Dios! ¡Soy muy joven, y no sé hablar!»

[7]Pero el SEÑOR me dijo:

«No digas: "Soy muy joven", porque vas a ir adondequiera que yo te envíe, y vas a decir todo lo que yo te ordene. [8]No le temas a nadie, que yo estoy contigo para librarte.» Lo afirma el SEÑOR.

[9]Luego extendió el SEÑOR la mano y, tocándome la boca, me dijo:

«He puesto en tu boca mis palabras. [10]Mira, hoy te doy autoridad sobre naciones y reinos,

»para arrancar y derribar,
    para destruir y demoler,
    para construir y plantar.»

[11]La palabra del SEÑOR vino a mí, y me dijo:
«¿Qué es lo que ves, Jeremías?»
«Veo una rama de almendro», respondí.
[12]«Has visto bien —dijo el SEÑOR—, porque yo estoy alerta[a] para que se cumpla mi palabra.»
[13]La palabra del SEÑOR vino a mí por segunda vez, y me dijo:
«¿Qué es lo que ves?»
«Veo una olla que hierve y se derrama desde el norte», respondí.
[14]Entonces el SEÑOR me dijo:
«Desde el norte se derramará la calamidad sobre todos los habitantes del país. [15]Yo estoy por convocar a todas las tribus de los reinos del norte —afirma el SEÑOR—.

»Vendrán, y cada uno pondrá su trono
    a la *entrada misma de Jerusalén;
vendrán contra todos los muros que la rodean,
    y contra todas las ciudades de Judá.
[16]Yo dictaré sentencia contra mi pueblo,
    por toda su maldad,
porque me han abandonado;
han quemado incienso a otros dioses,
    y han adorado las obras de sus manos.

[17]»Pero tú, ¡prepárate! Ve y diles todo lo que yo te ordene. No temas ante ellos, pues de lo contrario yo haré que sí les temas. [18]Hoy te he puesto como ciudad fortificada, como columna de hierro y muro de bronce, contra todo el país, contra los reyes de Judá, contra sus autoridades y sus sacerdotes, contra la gente del país. [19]Pelearán contra ti, pero no te podrán vencer, porque yo estoy contigo para librarte», afirma el SEÑOR.

Israel abandona a Dios

2 La palabra del SEÑOR vino a mí: [2]«Ve y proclama a oídos de Jerusalén que así dice el SEÑOR:

»"Recuerdo el amor de tu juventud,
    tu cariño de novia,
cuando me seguías por el desierto,
    por tierras no cultivadas.
[3]Israel estaba consagrada al SEÑOR,
    era las *primicias de su cosecha;
todo el que comía de ella sufría las
        consecuencias,
    les sobrevenía la calamidad"»,
                                afirma el SEÑOR.
[4]¡Escuchen la palabra del SEÑOR, descendientes
        de Jacob,
    tribus todas del pueblo de Israel!

[5]Así dice el SEÑOR:

«¿Qué injusticia vieron en mí sus antepasados,
    que se alejaron tanto de mí?
Se fueron tras lo que nada vale,
    y en nada se convirtieron.
[6]Nunca preguntaron:
    "¿Dónde está el SEÑOR
    que nos hizo subir de Egipto,
que nos guió por el desierto,
    por tierra árida y accidentada,
por tierra reseca y tenebrosa,
    por tierra que nadie transita
    y en la que nadie vive?"
[7]Yo los traje a una tierra fértil,
    para que comieran de sus frutos
    y de su abundancia.
Pero ustedes vinieron y *contaminaron mi
        tierra;
    hicieron de mi heredad algo abominable.
[8]Nunca preguntaron los sacerdotes:
    "¿Dónde está el SEÑOR?"
Los expertos en la ley jamás me conocieron;
    los *pastores se rebelaron contra mí,
los profetas hablaron en nombre de *Baal
    y se fueron tras dioses que para nada
        sirven.
[9]Por eso, aún voy a entablar un litigio contra
        ustedes,
    y también litigaré contra los hijos de sus
        hijos
                            —afirma el SEÑOR—.

[10]»Crucen a las costas de Chipre, y miren;
    envíen mensajeros a Cedar,[b] e infórmense
        bien;
    fíjense si ha sucedido algo semejante:
[11]¿Hay alguna nación que haya cambiado de
        dioses,
    a pesar de que no son dioses?
¡Pues mi pueblo ha cambiado al que es su
        gloria,
    por lo que no sirve para nada!

---

[a] **1:11,12** En hebreo, las palabras que corresponden a *almendro* y *yo estoy alerta* tienen un sonido parecido.
[b] **2:10** *Cedar*. Asentamiento de tribus beduinas en el desierto siro-arábigo.

12¡Espántense, cielos, ante esto!
    ¡Tiemblen y queden horrorizados!
              —afirma el SEÑOR—.

13»Dos son los pecados
    que ha cometido mi pueblo:
Me han abandonado a mí,
    fuente de agua viva,
y han cavado sus propias cisternas,
    cisternas rotas que no retienen agua.
14¿Acaso es Israel un esclavo?
    ¿Nació en la esclavitud?
    ¿Por qué entonces lo saquean?
15Los leones rugieron contra él,
    lanzaron fuertes gruñidos.
Dejaron desolado su país,
    sus ciudades fueron incendiadas,
    y ya nadie las habita.

16»Para colmo de males,
    los de Menfis c y los de Tafnes
    te raparon la cabeza.
17¿No te ha pasado todo esto
    por haber abandonado al SEÑOR tu Dios,
    mientras él te guiaba por el camino?
18Y ahora, ¿qué sacas con ir a Egipto
    a beber agua del Nilo?
¿Qué sacas con ir a Asiria
    a beber agua del Éufrates?
19Tu maldad te castigará,
    tu infidelidad te recriminará.
Ponte a pensar cuán malo y amargo
    es abandonar al SEÑOR tu Dios
    y no sentir temor de mí
—afirma el Señor, el SEÑOR *Todopoderoso—.

20»Desde hace mucho quebraste el yugo;
    te quitaste las ataduras
    y dijiste: "¡No quiero servirte!"
Sobre toda colina alta,
    y bajo todo árbol frondoso,
    te entregaste a la prostitución.
21Yo te planté, como vid selecta,
    con semilla genuina.
¿Cómo es que te has convertido
    en una vid degenerada y extraña?
22Aunque te laves con lejía,
    y te frotes con mucho jabón,
ante mí seguirá presente
    la mancha de tu iniquidad
              —afirma el SEÑOR omnipotente—.
23»¿Cómo puedes decir:
    "No me he contaminado,
    ni me he ido tras los baales"?
¡Considera tu conducta en el valle!
    ¡Reconoce lo que has hecho!
¡Camella ligera de cascos,
    que no puedes quedarte quieta!
24¡Asna salvaje que tiras al monte!
Cuando ardes en deseos, olfateas el viento;
    cuando estás en celo, no hay quien te
        detenga.
Ningún macho que te busque tiene que
        fatigarse:
    cuando estás en celo, fácilmente te
        encuentra.

25»No andes con pies descalzos, que te lastimas,
    ni dejes que la garganta se te reseque.
Pero tú insistes: "¡No tengo remedio!

Amo a dioses extraños, y tras ellos me iré."

26»El pueblo de Israel se avergonzará,
    junto con sus reyes y autoridades,
sacerdotes y profetas,
    como se avergüenza el ladrón cuando lo
        descubren.
27A un trozo de madera le dicen:
    "Tú eres mi padre",
y a una piedra le repiten:
    "Tú me has dado a luz."
Me han vuelto la espalda;
    no me quieren dar la cara.
Pero les llega la desgracia y me dicen:
    "¡Levántate y sálvanos!"
28¿Dónde están, Judá, los dioses que te
        fabricaste?
    ¡Tienes tantos dioses como ciudades!
¡Diles que se levanten!
    ¡A ver si te salvan cuando caigas en
        desgracia!

29»¿Por qué litigan conmigo?
    Todos ustedes se han rebelado contra mí
              —afirma el SEÑOR—.

30»En vano castigo a mi pueblo,
    pues rechaza mi *corrección.
Cual si fuera un león feroz,
    la espada de ustedes devoró a sus profetas.

31»Pero ustedes, los de esta generación,
    presten atención a la palabra del SEÑOR:
¿Acaso he sido para Israel
    un desierto o una tierra tenebrosa?
¿Por qué dice mi pueblo:
    "Somos libres, nunca más volveremos a ti"?
32¿Acaso una joven se olvida de sus joyas,
    o una novia se su atavío?
¡Pues hace muchísimo tiempo
    que mi pueblo se olvidó de mí!
33¡Qué mañosa eres
    para conseguir amantes!
¡Hasta las malas mujeres
    han aprendido de ti!
34Tienes la ropa manchada de sangre,
    de sangre de gente pobre e inocente,
    a los que nunca sorprendiste robando.
Por todo esto
35te voy a juzgar:
    por alegar que no has pecado,
por insistir en tu inocencia,
    por afirmar: "Dios ya no está enojado
        conmigo!"
36Con qué ligereza cambias de parecer d
    Pues también Egipto te defraudará,
    como te defraudó Asiria.
37Saldrás de allí con las manos en la nuca,
    porque el SEÑOR ha rechazado
a aquellos en quienes confías,
    y no prosperarás con ellos.

3 »Supongamos que un hombre se divorcia de su mujer, y que ella lo deja para casarse con otro. ¿Volvería el primero a casarse con ella? ¡Claro que no! Semejante acción *contaminaría por completo la tierra. Pues bien, tú te has prostituido con muchos amantes, y ya no podrás volver a mí —afirma el SEÑOR—.

2»Fíjate bien en esas lomas estériles:

---

c **2:16** *Menfis.* Lit. *Nof.* d **2:36** *de parecer.* Alt. *de aliados.*

¡Dónde no se han acostado contigo!
Como un beduino en el desierto,
te sentabas junto al camino,
a la espera de tus amantes.
Has contaminado la tierra
con tus infames prostituciones.
³Por eso se demoraron las lluvias,
y no llegaron los aguaceros de primavera.
Tienes el descaro de una prostituta;
¡no conoces la vergüenza!
⁴No hace mucho me llamabas:
"Padre mío, amigo de mi juventud,
⁵¿vas a estar siempre enojado?
¿Guardarás rencor eternamente?"
Y mientras hablabas,
hacías todo el mal posible.»

La infidelidad de Israel

⁶Durante el reinado del rey Josías el SEÑOR me dijo: «¿Has visto lo que ha hecho Israel, la infiel? Se fue a todo monte alto, y allí, bajo todo árbol frondoso, se prostituyó. ⁷Yo pensaba que después de hacer todo esto ella volvería a mí. Pero no lo hizo. Esto lo vio su hermana, la infiel Judá, ⁸y vioᵉ también que yo había repudiado a la apóstata Israel, y que le había dado carta de divorcio por todos los adulterios que había cometido. No obstante, su hermana, la infiel Judá, no tuvo ningún temor, sino que también ella se prostituyó.

⁹»Como Israel no tuvo ningún reparo en prostituirse, *contaminó la tierra y cometió adulterio al adorar ídolos de piedra y de madera. ¹⁰A pesar de todo esto, su hermana, la infiel Judá, no se volvió a mí de todo *corazón, sino que sólo fingió volverse», afirma el SEÑOR.

¹¹El SEÑOR me dijo: «La apóstata Israel ha resultado ser más justa que la infiel Judá. ¹²Ve al norte y proclama este mensaje:

»¡Vuelve, apóstata Israel!
No te miraré con ira
—afirma el SEÑOR—.
No te guardaré rencor para siempre,
porque soy misericordioso
—afirma el SEÑOR—.
¹³Tan solo reconoce tu culpa,
y que te rebelaste contra el SEÑOR tu Dios.
Bajo todo árbol frondoso
has brindado a dioses extraños tus favores,
y no has querido obedecerme»
—afirma el SEÑOR—.

¹⁴»¡Vuélvanse a mí, apóstatas —afirma el SEÑOR—, porque yo soy su esposo! De ustedes tomaré uno de cada ciudad y dos de cada familia, y los traeré a *Sión. ¹⁵Les daré *pastores que cumplan mi voluntad, para que los guíen con sabiduría y entendimiento.

¹⁶»En aquellos días, cuando ustedes se hayan multiplicado y sean numerosos en el país, ya no se dirá más: "Arca del *pacto del SEÑOR". Nadie pensará más en ella ni la recordará; nadie la echará de menos ni volverá a fabricarla —afirma el SEÑOR—.

¹⁷»En aquel tiempo llamarán a Jerusalén: "Trono del SEÑOR". Todas las naciones se reunirán en Jerusalén para honrar el *nombre del SEÑOR, y ya no volverán a obedecer ciegamente a su malvado corazón.

¹⁸»En aquellos días la tribu de Judá se unirá al pueblo de Israel, y juntos vendrán del país del norte, a la tierra que di como herencia a sus antepasados.

¹⁹»Yo mismo dije:

»"¡Cómo quisiera tratarte como a un hijo,
y darte una tierra codiciable,
la heredad más hermosa de las naciones!"
Yo creía que me llamarías "Padre mío",
y que nunca dejarías de seguirme.
²⁰Pero tú, pueblo de Israel,
me has sido infiel
como una mujer infiel a su esposo»,
afirma el SEÑOR.

²¹Se escucha un grito en las lomas estériles,
la súplica angustiosa del pueblo de Israel,
porque han pervertido su conducta,
se han olvidado del SEÑOR su Dios.

²²«¡Vuélvanse, apóstatas,
y los curaré de su infidelidad!»

«Aquí estamos, a ti venimos,
porque tú eres el SEÑOR nuestro Dios.
²³Ciertamente son un engaño las colinas,
y una mentira el estruendo sobre las montañas.
Ciertamente en el SEÑOR nuestro Dios
está la *salvación de Israel.
²⁴Desde nuestra juventud, la vergonzosa idolatría
se ha engullido el esfuerzo de nuestros antepasados:
sus rebaños y su ganado,
sus hijos y sus hijas.
²⁵¡Acostémonos en nuestra vergüenza,
y que nos cubra nuestra desgracia!
¡Nosotros y nuestros antepasados
hemos pecado contra el SEÑOR nuestro Dios!
Desde nuestra juventud y hasta el día de hoy,
no hemos obedecido al SEÑOR nuestro Dios.»

4 «Israel, si piensas volver,
vuélvete a mí
—afirma el SEÑOR—.
Si quitas de mi vista tus ídolos abominables
y no te alejas de mí,
²si con fidelidad, justicia y rectitud
juras: "Por la vida del SEÑOR",
entonces "en él serán benditas las naciones,
y en él se gloriarán".»

³Así dice el SEÑOR
a los habitantes de Judá y de Jerusalén:
«Abran surcos en terrenos no labrados,
y no siembren entre espinos.
⁴Habitantes de Judá y de Jerusalén,
marquen su *corazón con la señal del *pacto:
circuncídense para honrar al SEÑOR,
no sea que por la maldad de sus obras
mi furor se encienda como el fuego
y arda sin que nadie pueda apagarlo.

La amenaza del norte

⁵»¡Anúncienlo en Judá,
proclámenlo en Jerusalén!
¡Toquen la trompeta por todo el país!
Griten a voz en cuello:
"¡Reúnanse y entremos
en las ciudades fortificadas!"
⁶Señalen a *Sión con la bandera;

ᵉ **3:8** *vio* (un ms. hebreo, mss. de LXX y Siríaca); *yo vi* (TM).

¡busquen refugio, no se detengan!
Porque yo traigo del norte
    calamidad y gran destrucción.
7Un león ha salido del matorral,
    un destructor de naciones se ha puesto en
        marcha;
ha salido de su lugar de origen
    para desolar tu tierra;
tus ciudades quedarán en ruinas
    y totalmente despobladas.
8Por esto, vístanse de luto,
    laméntense y giman,
porque la ardiente ira del SEÑOR
    no se ha apartado de nosotros.

9»En aquel día desfallecerá
    el *corazón del rey y de los jefes;
los sacerdotes se llenarán de pánico
    y los profetas quedarán atónitos»,
                    afirma el SEÑOR.

10Yo dije: «¡Ah, SEÑOR mi Dios,
    cómo has engañado a este pueblo y a
        Jerusalén!
Dijiste: "Tendrán *paz",
    pero tienen la espada en el cuello.»

11En aquel tiempo se les dirá
    a este pueblo y a Jerusalén:
«Desde las estériles lomas del desierto
    sopla un viento abrasador
    en dirección a la capital de mi pueblo.
No es el viento que sirve para aventar
    ni para limpiar el trigo;
12el viento que haré venir
    es demasiado fuerte para eso,
porque yo mismo
    dictaré sentencia contra ellos.»

13¡Mírenlo avanzar como las nubes!
    ¡Sus carros de guerra parecen un huracán!
¡Sus caballos son más veloces que las águilas!
    ¡Ay de nosotros! ¡Estamos perdidos!
14Jerusalén, limpia de maldad tu corazón
    para que seas salvada.
¿Hasta cuándo hallarán lugar en ti
    los pensamientos perversos?
15Una voz anuncia desgracia
    desde Dan y desde las colinas de Efraín.
16«Adviertan a las naciones,
    proclámenlo contra Jerusalén:
"De lejanas tierras vienen sitiadores
    lanzando gritos de guerra
    contra las ciudades de Judá."
17La rodean como quien cuida un campo,
    porque ella se rebeló contra mí
                    —afirma el SEÑOR—.
18Tu conducta y tus acciones
    te han causado todo esto.
Ésta es tu desgracia. ¡Qué amarga es!
    ¡Cómo te ha calado en el propio corazón!»

19¡Qué angustia, qué angustia!
    ¡Me retuerzo de dolor!
Mi corazón se agita. ¡Ay, corazón mío!
    ¡No puedo callarme!
Puedo escuchar el toque de trompeta
    y el grito de guerra.
20Un desastre llama a otro desastre;
    todo el país está devastado.
De repente fueron destruidos
    las carpas y los pabellones donde habito.
21¿Hasta cuándo tendré que ver la bandera
    y escuchar el toque de la trompeta?

22«Mi pueblo es *necio,
    no me conoce;
son hijos insensatos
    que no tienen entendimiento.
Son hábiles para hacer el mal;
    no saben hacer el bien.»

23Miré a la tierra, y era un caos total;
    miré a los cielos, y todo era tinieblas.
24Miré a las montañas, y estaban temblando;
    ¡se sacudían todas las colinas!
25Miré, y no quedaba nadie;
    habían huido todas las aves del cielo.
26Miré, y la tierra fértil era un desierto;
    yacían en ruinas todas las ciudades,
por la acción del SEÑOR,
    por causa de su ardiente ira.

27Así dice el SEÑOR:

«Todo el país quedará desolado,
    pero no lo destruiré por completo.
28Por eso el país estará de luto,
    y los altos cielos se oscurecerán,
pues ya lo dije, y no me retractaré;
    lo he decidido, y no me volveré atrás.»

29Ante el ruido de arqueros y jinetes
    huye toda la ciudad.
Algunos se meten en los matorrales,
    otros trepan por los peñascos.
Toda la ciudad queda abandonada;
    ¡no queda un solo habitante!

30¿Qué piensas hacer, ciudad devastada?
    ¿Para qué te vistes de púrpura?
¿Para qué te pones joyas de oro?
    ¿Para qué te maquillas los ojos?
En vano te embelleces,
    pues tus amantes te desprecian;
    sólo buscan tu muerte.

31Oigo gritos como de parturienta,
    gemidos como de primeriza.
Son los gemidos de la bella Sión,
    que respira con dificultad;
que extiende los brazos y dice:
    «¡Ay de mí, que desfallezco!
    ¡Estoy en manos de asesinos!»

La corrupción de Jerusalén y de Judá

5 «Recorran las calles de Jerusalén,
    observen con cuidado,
    busquen por las plazas.
Si encuentran una sola persona
    que practique la justicia y busque la
        verdad,
    yo perdonaré a esta ciudad.
2Aunque juran: "Por la vida del SEÑOR",
    de hecho juran en falso.»

3SEÑOR, ¿acaso no buscan tus ojos la verdad?
    Golpeaste a esa gente, y no les dolió;
acabaste con ellos, y no quisieron ser
        corregidos.
Endurecieron su rostro más que una roca,
    y no quisieron *arrepentirse.
4Entonces pensé: «Así es la plebe;
    siempre actúan como *necios,
porque no conocen el *camino del SEÑOR
    ni las demandas de su Dios.
5Me dirigiré a los líderes
    y les hablaré;
porque ellos sí conocen el camino del SEÑOR

y las demandas de su Dios.»
Pero ellos también quebrantaron el yugo
y rompieron las ataduras.
⁶Por eso los herirá el león de la selva
y los despedazará el lobo del desierto;
frente a sus ciudades está el leopardo al acecho,
y todo el que salga de ellas será
despedazado,
pues son muchas sus rebeliones
y numerosas sus infidelidades.

⁷«¿Por qué habré de perdonarte?
Tus hijos me han abandonado,
han jurado por los que no son dioses.
Cuando suplí sus necesidades,
ellos cometieron adulterio
y en tropel se volcaron a los prostíbulos.
⁸Son como caballos bien cebados y fogosos;
todos relinchan por la mujer ajena.
⁹¿Y no los he de castigar por esto?
—afirma el SEÑOR—.
¿Acaso no he de vengarme de semejante
nación?

¹⁰»Suban por los surcos de esta viña
y arrásenla, pero no acaben con ella.
Arránquenle sus sarmientos,
porque no son del SEÑOR.
¹¹Pues las casas de Israel y de Judá
me han sido más que infieles»,
afirma el SEÑOR.

¹²Ellas han negado al SEÑOR,
y hasta dicen: «¡Dios no existe!
Ningún mal vendrá sobre nosotros,
no sufriremos guerras ni hambre.»
¹³Los profetas son como el viento:
la palabra del SEÑORᶠ no está en ellos.
¡Que así les suceda!

¹⁴Por eso, así dice el SEÑOR,
el Dios *Todopoderoso:
«Por cuanto el pueblo ha hablado así,
mis palabras serán como fuego en tu boca,
y este pueblo, como un montón de leña.
Ese fuego los consumirá.

¹⁵»Pueblo de Israel,
voy a traer contra ustedes una nación
lejana,
una nación fuerte y antigua,
una nación cuyo idioma no conocen,
cuyo lenguaje no entienden
—afirma el SEÑOR—.
¹⁶Todos ellos son guerreros valientes;
sus flechas presagian la muerte.
¹⁷Acabarán con tu cosecha y tu alimento,
devorarán a tus hijos e hijas,
matarán a tus rebaños y ganados,
y destruirán tus viñas y tus higueras.
Tus ciudades fortificadas,
en las que pusiste tu confianza,
serán pasadas a filo de espada.

¹⁸»Sin embargo, aun en aquellos días no los destruiré por completo —afirma el SEÑOR—. ¹⁹Y cuando te pregunten: "¿Por qué el SEÑOR, nuestro Dios,
nos ha hecho todo esto?", tú les responderás: "Así
como ustedes me han abandonado y en su propia
tierra han servido a dioses extranjeros, así también
en tierra extraña servirán a gente extranjera."

²⁰»Anuncien esto entre los descendientes de
Jacob
y proclámenlo en Judá:
²¹Escucha esto, pueblo necio e insensato,
que tiene ojos pero no ve,
que tiene oídos pero no oye.
²²¿Acaso has dejado de temerme?
—afirma el SEÑOR—.
¿No debieras temblar ante mí?
Yo puse la arena como límite del mar,
como frontera perpetua e infranqueable.
Aunque se agiten sus olas,
no podrán prevalecer;
aunque bramen,
no franquearán esa frontera.
²³Pero este pueblo tiene un *corazón terco y
rebelde;
se ha descarriado, ha sido infiel.
²⁴No reflexionan ni dicen:
"Temamos al SEÑOR, nuestro Dios,
quien a su debido tiempo nos da lluvia,
las lluvias de otoño y primavera,
y nos asegura las semanas señaladas
para la cosecha."
²⁵Las iniquidades de ustedes
les han quitado estos beneficios;
sus pecados los han privado
de estas bendiciones.
²⁶Sin duda en mi pueblo hay malvados,
que están al acecho como cazadores de aves,
que ponen trampas para atrapar a la gente.
²⁷Como jaulas llenas de pájaros,
llenas de engaño están sus casas;
por eso se han vuelto poderosos y ricos,
²⁸gordos y pedantes.
Sus obras de maldad no tienen límite:
no le hacen justicia al huérfano,
para que su causa prospere;
ni defienden tampoco
el derecho de los menesterosos.
²⁹¿Y no los he de castigar por esto?
¿No he de vengarme de semejante nación?
—afirma el SEÑOR—.

³⁰»Algo espantoso y terrible
ha ocurrido en este país.
³¹Los profetas profieren mentiras,
los sacerdotes gobiernan a su antojo,
¡y mi pueblo tan campante!
Pero, ¿qué van a hacer ustedes
cuando todo haya terminado?

Jerusalén es sitiada

6 »¡Huyan de Jerusalén, benjaminitas!
¡Toquen la trompeta en Tecoa!
¡Levanten señal en Bet Haqueren!
Una desgracia, una gran destrucción,
nos amenaza desde el norte.
²Estoy por destruir a *Sión,
tan hermosa y delicada.
³Los pastores y sus rebaños vienen contra ella:
acampan a su alrededor,
y cada uno escoge su pastizal.»

⁴«¡Prepárense para pelear contra ella!
¡Ataquémosla a plena luz del día!
Pero, ¡ay de nosotros, que el día se acaba
y se alargan las sombras de la noche!
⁵¡Vamos, ataquémosla de noche,
y destruyamos sus fortalezas!»

ᶠ **5:13** *del SEÑOR* (LXX); TM no incluye esta frase.

6Así dice el SEÑOR *Todopoderoso:

«¡Talen árboles
   y levanten una rampa contra Jerusalén!
Esta ciudad debe ser castigada,
   pues en ella no hay más que opresión.
7Como agua que brota de un pozo,
   así brota de Jerusalén la maldad.
En ella se oye de violencia y destrucción;
   no veo otra cosa que enfermedades y
     heridas.
8¡Escarmienta, Jerusalén,
   para que no me aparte de ti!
De lo contrario, te convertiré en desolación,
   en una tierra inhabitable.»

9Así dice el SEÑOR Todopoderoso:

«Busquen al remanente de Israel.
Rebusquen, como en una viña;
repasen los sarmientos,
   como lo hace el vendimiador.»

10¿A quién le hablaré?
   ¿A quién le advertiré?
   ¿Quién podrá escucharme?
Tienen tapadosᵍ los oídos
   y no pueden comprender.
La palabra del SEÑOR los ofende;
   detestan escucharla.
11Pero yo estoy lleno de la ira del SEÑOR,
   y ya no puedo contenerme.

«Derrama tu ira sobre los niños de la calle,
   sobre los grupos de jóvenes,
porque serán apresados el marido y la mujer,
   la gente madura y la entrada en años.
12Sus casas, sus campos y sus mujeres
   caerán en manos extrañas,
porque yo voy a extender mi mano
   contra los habitantes del país
          —afirma el SEÑOR—.

13»Desde el más pequeño hasta el más grande,
   todos codician ganancias injustas;
desde el profeta hasta el sacerdote,
   todos practican el engaño.
14Curan por encima la herida de mi pueblo,
   y les desean: *"¡Paz, paz!",
   cuando en realidad no hay paz.
15¿Acaso se han avergonzado
   de la abominación que han cometido?
¡No, no se han avergonzado de nada,
   ni saben siquiera lo que es la vergüenza!
Por eso, caerán con los que caigan;
   cuando los castigue, serán derribados»,
          dice el SEÑOR.

16Así dice el SEÑOR:

«Deténganse en los caminos y miren;
   pregunten por los senderos antiguos.
Pregunten por el buen *camino,
   y no se aparten de él.
Así hallarán el descanso anhelado.
Pero ellos dijeron:
   "No lo seguiremos."
17Yo aposté centinelas para ustedes, y dije:
   "Presten atención al toque de trompeta."
Pero ellos dijeron:
   "No prestaremos atención."
18Por eso, ¡escuchen, naciones!

¡Sepa la congregación lo que le espera!
19Escucha, tierra:
Traigo sobre este pueblo una desgracia,
   fruto de sus maquinaciones,
porque no prestaron atención a mis palabras,
   sino que rechazaron mi enseñanza.
20¿De qué me sirve este incienso que llega de
     Sabá,
o la caña dulce de un país lejano?
Sus *holocaustos no me gustan;
   sus sacrificios no me agradan.»

21Por eso, así dice el SEÑOR:

«Voy a ponerle obstáculos a este pueblo.
Padres e hijos tropezarán contra ellos,
   vecinos y amigos perecerán.»

22Así dice el SEÑOR:

«¡Miren! Del norte viene un ejército;
   una gran nación se moviliza
   desde los confines de la tierra.
23Empuñan el arco y la lanza;
   son crueles y no tienen compasión.
Lanzan gritos como bramidos del mar,
   y cabalgan sobre sus corceles.
¡Vienen contra ti, hija de Sión,
   listos para la batalla!»

24Nos ha llegado la noticia,
   y nuestras manos flaquean;
la angustia nos domina,
   como si tuviéramos dolores de parto.
25¡Viene el enemigo armado con espada!
No salgan al campo,
   ni transiten por los caminos.
¡Hay terror por todas partes!
26Vístete de luto, pueblo mío;
   revuélcate en las cenizas.
Llora amargamente,
   como lo harías por tu primogénito,
porque nos cae por sorpresa
   el que viene a destruirnos.

27«Te he puesto entre mi pueblo
   como vigía y atalaya,
para que escudriñes
   y examines su conducta.
28Todos ellos son muy rebeldes,
   y andan sembrando calumnias;
sean de bronce o de hierro,
   todos son unos corruptos.
29Los fuelles soplan con furor,
   y el plomo se derrite en el fuego,
pero los malvados no se *purifican;
   ¡de nada sirve que se les refine!
30Por eso se les llama "Escoria de la plata":
   ¡para el SEÑOR son un desecho!»

La religión falsa e inútil

7 Ésta es la palabra que vino a Jeremías de parte del SEÑOR. 2«Párate a la entrada de la casa del SEÑOR, y desde allí proclama este mensaje: ¡Escuchen la palabra del SEÑOR, todos ustedes, habitantes de Judá que entran por estas puertas para adorar al SEÑOR! 3Así dice el SEÑOR *Todopoderoso, el Dios de Israel: "Enmienden su conducta y sus acciones, y yo los dejaré seguir viviendo en este país. 4No confíen en esas palabras engañosas que repiten: '¡Éste es el templo del SEÑOR,

ᵍ **6:10** *tapados.* Lit. *incircuncisos.*

el templo del SEÑOR, el templo del SEÑOR!' ⁵Si en verdad enmienden su conducta y sus acciones, si en verdad practican la justicia los unos con los otros, ⁶si no oprimen al extranjero ni al huérfano ni a la viuda, si no derraman sangre inocente en este lugar, ni siguen a otros dioses para su propio mal, ⁷entonces los dejaré seguir viviendo en este país, en la tierra que di a sus antepasados para siempre.

⁸»¡Pero ustedes confían en palabras engañosas, que no tienen validez alguna! ⁹Roban, matan, cometen adulterio, juran en falso, queman incienso a *Baal, siguen a otros dioses que jamás conocieron, ¹⁰¡y vienen y se presentan ante mí en esta casa que lleva mi *nombre, y dicen: 'Estamos a salvo', para luego seguir cometiendo todas estas abominaciones! ¹¹¿Creen acaso que esta casa que lleva mi nombre es una cueva de ladrones? ¡Pero si yo mismo lo he visto! —afirma el SEÑOR—.

¹²»Vayan ahora a mi santuario en Siló, donde al principio hice habitar mi nombre, y vean lo que hice con él por culpa de la maldad de mi pueblo Israel. ¹³Y ahora, puesto que ustedes han hecho todas estas cosas —afirma el SEÑOR—, y puesto que una y otra vez les he hablado y no me han querido escuchar, y puesto que los he llamado y no me han respondido, ¹⁴lo mismo que hice con Siló haré con esta casa, que lleva mi nombre y en la que ustedes confían, y con el lugar que les di a ustedes y a sus antepasados. ¹⁵Los echaré de mi presencia, así como eché a todos sus hermanos, a toda la descendencia de Efraín."

¹⁶»Pero en cuanto a ti, Jeremías, no intercedas por este pueblo. No me ruegues ni me supliques por ellos. No me insistas, porque no te escucharé. ¹⁷¿Acaso no ves lo que hacen en las ciudades de Judá y en las calles de Jerusalén? ¹⁸Los niños juntan la leña, los padres encienden el fuego, y las mujeres hacen la masa para cocer tortas y ofrecérselas a la "reina del cielo". Además, para ofenderme derraman libaciones a otros dioses. ¹⁹Pero no es a mí al que ofenden —afirma el SEÑOR—. Más bien se ofenden a sí mismos, para su propia vergüenza.

²⁰»Por eso, así dice el SEÑOR omnipotente: "Descargaré mi enojo y mi furor sobre este lugar: sobre los *hombres y los animales, sobre los árboles del campo y los frutos de la tierra, ¡y arderá mi enojo y no se apagará!"

²¹»Así dice el SEÑOR Todopoderoso, el Dios de Israel: "¡Junten sus *holocaustos con sus sacrificios, y cómanse la carne! ²²En verdad, cuando yo saqué de Egipto a sus antepasados, no les dije nada ni les ordené nada acerca de holocaustos y sacrificios. ²³Lo que sí les ordené fue lo siguiente: 'Obedézcanme. Así yo seré su Dios, y ustedes serán mi pueblo. Condúzcanse conforme a todo lo que yo les ordene, a fin de que les vaya bien.' ²⁴Pero ellos no me obedecieron ni me prestaron atención, sino que siguieron los consejos de su terco y malvado *corazón. Fue así como, en vez de avanzar, retrocedieron. ²⁵Desde el día en que sus antepasados salieron de Egipto hasta ahora, no he dejado de enviarles, día tras día, a mis servidores los profetas. ²⁶Con todo, no me obedecieron ni me prestaron atención, sino que se obstinaron y fueron peores que sus antepasados."

²⁷»Tú les dirás todas estas cosas, pero no te escucharán. Los llamarás, pero no te responderán. ²⁸Entonces les dirás: "Ésta es la nación que no ha obedecido la voz del SEÑOR su Dios, ni ha aceptado su *corrección. La verdad ha muerto, ha sido arrancada de su boca.

²⁹»"Córtate la cabellera, y tírala;
　　eleva tu lamento en las lomas desoladas,

porque el SEÑOR ha rechazado y abandonado
　　a la generación que provocó su ira.

El valle de la Matanza

³⁰» "La gente de Judá ha hecho el mal que yo detesto —afirma el SEÑOR—. Han profanado la casa que lleva mi *nombre al instalar allí sus ídolos abominables. ³¹Además, construyeron el *santuario pagano de Tofet, en el valle de Ben Hinón, para quemar a sus hijos y a sus hijas en el fuego, cosa que jamás ordené ni me pasó siquiera por la *mente. ³²Por eso llegarán días —afirma el SEÑOR—, cuando ya no lo llamarán más Tofet ni Valle de Ben Hinón, ino Valle de la Matanza; y a falta de otro lugar, en Tofet enterrarán a sus muertos. ³³Los cadáveres de este pueblo servirán de comida a las aves del cielo y a los animales de la tierra, y no habrá quien los espante. ³⁴Haré que en las ciudades de Judá y en las calles de Jerusalén se apaguen los gritos de alegría, las voces de júbilo, y los cánticos del novio y de la novia, porque el país se convertirá en desolación.

8 »"En aquel tiempo —afirma el SEÑOR—, se exhumarán los huesos de los reyes y de los jefes de Judá, de los sacerdotes y de los profetas, y de los habitantes de Jerusalén. ²Quedarán expuestos al sol y a la luna, y a todas las estrellas del cielo, cuerpos celestes a los que ellos amaron, sirvieron, consultaron y adoraron. No se les recogerá ni se les enterrará; ¡como estiércol quedarán sobre la faz de la tierra! ³En todos los lugares por donde yo disperse a los sobrevivientes de esta nación malvada, los que hayan quedado preferirán la muerte a la vida. Lo afirma el SEÑOR *Todopoderoso."

Pecado y castigo

⁴»Pero tú les advertirás que así dice el SEÑOR:

»"Cuando los *hombres caen,
　　¿acaso no se levantan?
Cuando uno se desvía,
　　¿acaso no vuelve al camino?
⁵¿Por qué entonces este pueblo se ha desviado?
　　¿Por qué persiste Jerusalén en su apostasía?
Se aferran al engaño,
　　y no quieren volver a mí.
⁶He escuchado con suma atención,
　　para ver si alguien habla con rectitud,
pero nadie se *arrepiente de su maldad;
　　nadie reconoce el mal que ha hecho.
Todos siguen su loca carrera,
　　como caballos desbocados en combate.
⁷Aun la cigüeña en el cielo
　　conoce sus estaciones;
la tórtola, la golondrina y la grulla
　　saben cuándo deben emigrar.
Pero mi pueblo no conoce
　　las *leyes del SEÑOR.

⁸»"¿Cómo se atreven a decir:
　　'Somos sabios; la ley del SEÑOR nos apoya',
si la pluma engañosa de los escribas
　　la ha falsificado?
⁹Los sabios serán avergonzados,
　　serán atrapados y abatidos.
Si han rechazado la palabra del SEÑOR,
　　¿qué sabiduría pueden tener?
¹⁰Por eso entregaré sus mujeres a otros
　　hombres,
　　y sus campos a otros dueños.
Porque desde el más pequeño hasta el más
　　grande,
　　todos codician ganancias injustas;
desde el profeta hasta el sacerdote,

todos practican el engaño.
11Curan por encima la herida de mi pueblo,
y les desean: '*¡Paz, paz!',
cuando en realidad no hay paz.
12¿Acaso se han avergonzado
de la abominación que han cometido?
¡No, no se han avergonzado de nada,
y ni siquiera saben lo que es la vergüenza!
Por eso, caerán con los que caigan;
cuando los castigue, serán derribados
—dice el SEÑOR—.

13»"Cuando quiero cosechar
—afirma el SEÑOR—,
no encuentro uvas en la viña,
ni hay higos en la higuera;
sus hojas están marchitas.
¡Voy, pues, a quitarles
lo que les he dado!"ʰ

14«¿Qué hacemos aquí sentados?
¡Vengan, y vámonos juntos a las ciudades
fortificadas
para morir allí!
El SEÑOR nuestro Dios nos está destruyendo.
Nos ha dado a beber agua envenenada,
porque hemos pecado contra él.
15Esperábamos paz,
pero no llegó nada bueno.
Esperábamos un tiempo de salud,
pero sólo nos llegó el terror.
16Desde Dan se escucha
el resoplar de sus caballos;
cuando relinchan sus corceles,
tiembla toda la tierra.
Vienen a devorarse el país,
y todo lo que hay en él,
la ciudad y todos sus habitantes.»

17«¡Miren! Estoy lanzando contra ustedes
serpientes venenosas que los morderán,
y contra ellas no hay encantamiento»,
afirma el SEÑOR.

18La aflicción me abruma;ⁱ
mi *corazón desfallece.
19El clamor de mi pueblo se levanta
desde todos los rincones del país:
«¿Acaso no está el SEÑOR en *Sión?
¿No está allí su rey?»

«¿Por qué me provocan con sus ídolos,
con sus dioses inútiles y extraños?»

20«Pasó la cosecha, se acabó el verano,
y nosotros no hemos sido salvados.»

21Por la herida de mi pueblo estoy herido;
estoy de luto, el terror se apoderó de mí.
22¿No queda bálsamo en Galaad?
¿No queda allí médico alguno?
¿Por qué no se ha restaurado
la salud de mi pueblo?

9 ¡Ojalá mi cabeza fuera un manantial,
y mis ojos una fuente de lágrimas,
para llorar de día y de noche
por los muertos de mi pueblo!
2¡Ojalá tuviera yo en el desierto
una posada junto al camino!
Abandonaría a mi pueblo,
y me alejaría de ellos.

Porque todos ellos son adúlteros,
son una banda de traidores.
3«Tensan su lengua como un arco;
en el país prevalece la mentira, no la
verdad,
porque van de mal en peor,
y a mí no me conocen
—afirma el SEÑOR—.
4Cuídese cada uno de su amigo,
no confíe ni siquiera en el hermano,
porque todo hermano engaña,
y todo amigo difama.
5Se engañan unos a otros;
no se hablan con la verdad.
Han enseñado sus lenguas a mentir,
y pecan hasta el cansancio.

6»Tú, Jeremías, vives en medio de engañadores,
que por su engaño no quieren
reconocerme»,
afirma el SEÑOR.

7Por eso, así dice el SEÑOR *Todopoderoso:

«Voy a refinarlos, a ponerlos a prueba.
¿Qué más puedo hacer con mi pueblo?
8Su lengua es una flecha mortífera,
su boca sólo sabe engañar;
hablan cordialmente con su amigo,
mientras en su interior le tienden una
trampa.
9¿Y no los he de castigar por esto?
—afirma el SEÑOR—.
¿Acaso no he de vengarme de semejante
nación?»

10Lloraré y gemiré por las montañas,
haré lamentos por las praderas del
desierto,
porque están desoladas:
ya nadie las transita
ni se escuchan los mugidos del ganado.
Desde las aves del cielo hasta los animales del
campo,
todos han huido.

11«Convertiré a Jerusalén en un montón de
ruinas,
en una guarida de chacales.
Convertiré en desolación las ciudades de Judá;
¡las dejaré sin habitantes!»

12¿Quién es tan sabio como para entender esto?
¿A quién le habló el SEÑOR, para que lo anuncie?
¿Por qué está arruinado el país, desolado como un
desierto por el que nadie pasa?
13El SEÑOR dice: «Ellos abandonaron la *ley que
yo les entregué; no me obedecieron ni vivieron conforme a ella. 14Siguieron la terquedad de su *corazón; se fueron tras los *baales, como les habían
enseñado sus antepasados.» 15Por eso, así dice el
SEÑOR Todopoderoso, el Dios de Israel: «A este pueblo le daré a comer ajenjo y a beber agua envena-
da. 16Los dispersaré entre naciones que ni ellos ni sus
antepasados conocieron; los perseguiré con espada
hasta aniquilarlos.»

17Así dice el SEÑOR Todopoderoso:

«¡Atención! Llamen a las plañideras.
Que vengan las más expertas.
18Que se den prisa,
que hagan lamentación por nosotros.

Nuestros ojos se inundarán de lágrimas,
  y brotará de nuestros párpados el llanto.
19Desde *Sión se escuchan gemidos y
    lamentos:
  "Hemos sido devastados;
  nos han avergonzado por completo.
Tenemos que abandonar el país,
  porque han derribado nuestros hogares."»

20Escuchen, mujeres, la palabra del SEÑOR;
  reciban sus oídos la palabra de su boca.
Enseñen a sus hijas a entonar endechas;
  que unas a otras se enseñen este lamento:
21«La muerte se ha metido por nuestras
    ventanas,
  ha entrado en nuestros palacios;
ha eliminado en las calles a los niños,
  y en las plazas a los jóvenes.
22Yacen tendidos los cadáveres
  como estiércol sobre los campos,
como gavillas que caen tras el segador,
  sin que nadie las recoja»,

                afirma el SEÑOR.

23Así dice el SEÑOR:

  «Que no se gloríe el sabio de su sabiduría,
    ni el poderoso de su poder,
    ni el rico de su riqueza.
24Si alguien ha de gloriarse,
  que se gloríe de conocerme
y de comprender que yo soy el SEÑOR,
  que actúo en la tierra con amor,
con derecho y justicia,
  pues es lo que a mí me agrada
             —afirma el SEÑOR—.

25»Vienen días —afirma el SEÑOR— en que castigaré al que sólo haya sido circuncidado del prepucio: 26castigaré a Egipto, Judá, Edom, Amón, Moab, y a todos los que viven en el desierto y se rapan las sienes. Todas las naciones son incircuncisas, pero el pueblo de Israel es incircunciso de corazón.»

Dios y los ídolos
10:12-16 — Jer 51:15-19

10 Escucha, pueblo de Israel, la palabra del SEÑOR. 2Dice así:

  «No aprendan ustedes la conducta de las
    naciones,
  ni se aterroricen ante las señales del cielo,
  aunque las naciones les tengan miedo.
3Las costumbres de los pueblos
  no tienen valor alguno.
Cortan un tronco en el bosque,
  y un artífice lo labra con un cincel.
4Lo adornan con oro y plata,
  y lo afirman con clavos y martillo
  para que no se tambalee.

5»Sus ídolos no pueden hablar;
  ¡parecen espantapájaros
en un campo sembrado de melones!
Tienen que ser transportados,
  porque no pueden caminar.
No les tengan miedo,
  que ningún mal pueden hacerles,
  pero tampoco ningún bien.»

6¡No hay nadie como tú, SEÑOR!
  ¡Grande eres tú,

  y grande y poderoso es tu *nombre!
7¿Quién no te temerá, Rey de las naciones?
  ¡Es lo que te corresponde!
Entre todos los sabios de las naciones,
  y entre todos los reinos,
  no hay nadie como tú.
8Todos son *necios e insensatos,
  educados por inútiles ídolos de palo.
9De Tarsis se trae plata laminada,
  y de Ufaz se importa oro.
Los ídolos, vestidos de púrpura y carmesí,
  son obra de artífices y orfebres;
  ¡todos ellos son obra de artesanos!
10Pero el SEÑOR es el Dios verdadero,
  el Dios viviente, el Rey eterno.
Cuando se enoja, tiembla la tierra;
  las naciones no pueden soportar su ira.

11«Así les dirás: "Los dioses que no hicieron los cielos ni la tierra, desaparecerán de la tierra y de debajo del cielo."»j
12Dios hizo la tierra con su poder,
  afirmó el mundo con su sabiduría,
  ¡extendió los cielos con su inteligencia!
13Cuando él deja oír su voz,
  rugen las aguas en los cielos;
hace que vengan las nubes
  desde los confines de la tierra.
Entre relámpagos hace llover,
  y saca de sus depósitos al viento.
14La *humanidad es necia e ignorante;
  todo orfebre se avergüenza de sus ídolos.
Sus imágenes son un engaño,
  y no hay en ellas aliento de vida.
15No valen nada, son obras ridículas;
  cuando llegue el día de su castigo, serán
    destruidas.
16La heredad de Jacob no es como ellos,
  porque él es quien hace todas las cosas;
su nombre es el SEÑOR *Todopoderoso,
  e Israel es la tribu de su herencia.

Destrucción inminente

17Recoge del suelo tus cosas,
  tú que te encuentras sitiado.
18Porque así dice el SEÑOR:
  «Esta vez arrojaré a los habitantes del país
  como si los lanzara con una honda.
Los pondré en aprietos
  y dejaré que los capturen.»

19¡Ay de mí, que estoy quebrantado!
  ¡Mi herida es incurable!
Pero es mi enfermedad,
  y me toca soportarla.
20Devastada está mi carpa,
  y rotas todas mis cuerdas.
Mis hijos me han abandonado;
  han dejado de existir.
Ya no hay nadie que arme mi carpa,
  y que levante mis toldos.
21Los *pastores se han vuelto *necios,
  no buscan al SEÑOR;
por eso no han prosperado,
  y su rebaño anda disperso.

22¡Escuchen! ¡Llega un mensaje!
  Un gran estruendo viene de un país del
    norte,
que convertirá las ciudades de Judá

---

j **10:11** Este versículo está escrito en arameo.

en guarida de chacales, en un montón de
ruinas.

Oración de Jeremías

23SEÑOR, yo sé que el *hombre
no es dueño de su destino,
que no le es dado al caminante
dirigir sus propios pasos.
24Corrígeme, SEÑOR, pero con *justicia,
y no según tu ira, pues me destruirías.
25Derrama tu furor
sobre las naciones que no te reconocen,
y sobre las familias que no invocan tu
*nombre.
Porque se han devorado a Jacob;
se lo han tragado por completo,
y han asolado su morada.

Violación del pacto

11 Ésta es la palabra que vino a Jeremías de parte del SEÑOR: 2«Atiende a los términos de
este *pacto, y comunícaselos a la gente de Judá y a
los habitantes de Jerusalén. 3Diles que así ha dicho el
SEÑOR, Dios de Israel: "Maldito sea el *hombre que
no obedezca los términos de este pacto, 4que yo mismo prescribí a los antepasados de ustedes el día que
los hice salir de Egipto, de esa caldera para fundir
hierro." Les dije: "Obedézcanme y cumplan con
todo lo que les prescribo, y ustedes serán mi pueblo y
yo seré su Dios. 5Así cumpliré el juramento que les
hice a sus antepasados, de darles una tierra donde
abundan la leche y la miel, como la que hoy tienen
ustedes."»

Yo respondí: «Amén, SEÑOR.»

6El SEÑOR me dijo: «Proclama todo esto en las
ciudades de Judá y en las calles de Jerusalén, diciendo: "Escuchen los términos de este pacto, y cúmplanlos. 7Desde el día en que hice salir a sus
antepasados de la tierra de Egipto hasta el día de
hoy, una y otra vez les he advertido: 'Obedézcanme.' 8Pero no obedecieron ni prestaron atención,
sino que siguieron la terquedad de su malvado *corazón. Por eso hice caer sobre ellos todo el peso de
las palabras de este pacto, que yo les había ordenado cumplir, pero que no cumplieron."»

9El SEÑOR también me dijo: «Se está fraguando
una conspiración entre los hombres de Judá y los habitantes de Jerusalén. 10Han vuelto a los mismos pecados de sus antepasados, quienes se negaron a
obedecerme. Se han ido tras otros dioses para servirles. Tanto el pueblo de Israel como la tribu de Judá
han quebrantado el pacto que hice con sus antepasados. 11Por eso, así dice el SEÑOR: "Les enviaré una calamidad de la cual no podrán escapar. Aunque
clamen a mí, no los escucharé. 12Entonces las ciudades de Judá y los habitantes de Jerusalén irán a clamar a los dioses a los que quemaron incienso, pero
ellos no podrán salvarlos cuando llegue el tiempo de
su calamidad. 13Tú, Judá, tienes tantos dioses como
ciudades. Erigiste tantos altares como calles hay en
Jerusalén; altares para quemar incienso a *Baal, para
vergüenza tuya."

14»Pero en cuanto a ti, Jeremías, no intercedas
por este pueblo. No me ruegues ni me supliques
por ellos, porque yo no escucharé cuando clamen a
mí por causa de su calamidad.

15»¿Qué hace mi amada en mi casa,
después de haber cometido tantas vilezas?
¿Acaso la carne consagrada
alejará de ti la calamidad?
¿Podrás así regocijarte?»

16El SEÑOR te puso por *nombre:
«Olivo frondoso, lleno de hermosos
frutos».
Pero en medio de grandes estruendos,
te ha prendido fuego,
y tus ramas se consumen.

17El SEÑOR *Todopoderoso, el que te plantó, ha
decretado una calamidad contra ti, por causa de la
maldad que cometieron el pueblo de Israel y la tribu
de Judá. Dice el SEÑOR: «Me han agraviado al quemar incienso a Baal.»

18El SEÑOR me lo hizo saber y lo comprendí. Me
mostró las maldades que habían cometido. 19Pero yo
era como un manso cordero que es llevado al matadero; no sabía lo que estaban maquinando contra mí,
y que decían:

«Destruyamos el árbol con su fruto,
arranquémoslo de la tierra de los vivientes,
para que nadie recuerde más su nombre.»
20Pero tú, SEÑOR Todopoderoso,
que juzgas con *justicia,
que pruebas los sentimientos y la *mente,
¡Déjame ver cómo te vengas de ellos,
porque en tus manos he puesto mi causa!

21«Por eso, así dice el SEÑOR en contra de los
hombres de Anatot, que buscan quitarte la vida y
afirman: "¡No profetices en nombre del SEÑOR, si no
quieres morir a manos nuestras!" 22Por eso, así dice
el SEÑOR Todopoderoso: "Voy a castigarlos. Los jóvenes morirán a filo de espada, y sus hijos y sus hijas
se morirán de hambre. 23No quedará ni uno solo de
ellos. En el año de su castigo haré venir una calamidad sobre los hombres de Anatot."»

Queja de Jeremías

12 Tú, SEÑOR, eres justo
cuando argumento contigo.
Sin embargo, quisiera exponerte
algunas cuestiones de justicia.
¿Por qué prosperan los malvados?
¿Por qué viven tranquilos los traidores?
2Tú los plantas, y ellos echan raíces;
crecen y dan fruto.
Te tienen a flor de labio,
pero estás lejos de su *corazón.
3A mí, SEÑOR, tú me conoces;
tú me ves y sabes lo que siento por ti.
Arrástralos, como ovejas, al matadero;
apártalos para el día de la matanza.
4¿Hasta cuándo estará seca la tierra,
y marchita la hierba de todos los campos?
Los animales y las aves se mueren
por la maldad de los que habitan el país,
quienes se atreven a decir:
«Dios no verá nuestro fin.»

Respuesta de Dios

5«Si los que corren a pie han hecho que te
canses,
¿cómo competirás con los caballos?
Si te sientes confiado en una tierra tranquila,
¿qué harás en la espesura del Jordán?
6Aun tus hermanos, los de tu propia familia,
te han traicionado y gritan contra ti.
Por más que te digan cosas agradables,
no confíes en ellos.

7»He abandonado mi casa,
he rechazado mi herencia,
he entregado a mi pueblo amado
en poder de sus enemigos.

8Mis herederos se han comportado conmigo
    como leones en la selva.
Lanzan rugidos contra mí;
    por eso los aborrezco.
9Mi heredad es para mí
    como un ave de muchos colores
acosada por las aves de rapiña.
¡Vayan y reúnan a todos los animales salvajes!
    ¡Tráiganlos para que la devoren!
10Muchos *pastores han destruido mi viña,
    han pisoteado mi terreno;
han hecho de mi hermosa parcela
    un desierto desolado.
11La han dejado en ruinas,
    seca y desolada ante mis ojos;
todo el país ha sido arrasado
    porque a nadie le importa.
12Sobre todas las lomas del desierto
    vinieron depredadores.
La espada del SEÑOR destruirá al país
    de un extremo al otro,
y para nadie habrá *paz.
13Sembraron trigo y cosecharon espinos;
    ¡de nada les valió su esfuerzo!
Por causa de la ardiente ira del SEÑOR
    se avergonzarán de sus cosechas.»

14Así dice el SEÑOR: «En cuanto a todos los vecinos malvados que tocaron la heredad que le di a mi
pueblo Israel, los arrancaré de sus tierras, y a la tribu
de Judá la quitaré de en medio de ellos. 15Después
que los haya desarraigado, volveré a tener compasión de ellos, y los haré regresar, cada uno a su heredad y a su propio país. 16Y si aprenden bien los
*caminos de mi pueblo y, si así como enseñaron a mi
pueblo a jurar por *Baal, aprenden a jurar por mi
*nombre y dicen: "Por la vida del SEÑOR", entonces
serán establecidos en medio de mi pueblo. 17Pero a la
nación que no obedezca, la desarraigaré por completo y la destruiré», afirma el SEÑOR.

El cinturón de lino

13 Así me dijo el SEÑOR: «Ve y cómprate un cinturón de lino, y póntelo en la cintura, pero
no lo metas en agua.» 2Conforme a las instrucciones
del SEÑOR, compré el cinturón y me lo puse en la cintura. 3Entonces el SEÑOR me dijo por segunda vez:
4«Toma el cinturón que has comprado y que tienes
puesto en la cintura, y ve a Perat,k y escóndelo allí, en
la grieta de una roca.» 5Fui entonces y lo escondí en
Perat, tal como el SEÑOR me lo había ordenado.

6Al cabo de muchos días, el SEÑOR me dijo: «Ve a
Perat y busca el cinturón que te mandé a esconder
allí.» 7Fui a Perat, cavé y saqué el cinturón del lugar
donde lo había escondido, pero ya estaba podrido y
no servía para nada.

8Entonces el SEÑOR volvió a decirme: 9«Así dice
el SEÑOR: "De esta misma manera destruiré el orgullo de Judá y el gran orgullo de Jerusalén. 10Este pueblo malvado, que se niega a obedecerme, que sigue
la terquedad de su *corazón y va tras otros dioses
para servirlos y adorarlos, será como este cinturón,
que no sirve para nada. 11Porque así como el cinturón se ajusta a la cintura del hombre, así procuré que
todo el pueblo de Israel y toda la tribu de Judá se
ajustaran a mí —afirma el SEÑOR— para que fueran
mi pueblo y mi renombre, mi honor y mi gloria.
¡Pero no obedecieron!"

Los cántaros rotos

12»Diles también lo siguiente: "Así dice el
SEÑOR, el Dios de Israel: 'Todo cántaro se llenará de
vino.' Y si ellos te dicen: '¿Acaso no sabemos bien
que todo cántaro se debe llenar de vino?', 13entonces
les responderás que así dice el SEÑOR: 'Voy a llenar
de vino a todos los habitantes de este país: a los reyes
que se sientan en el trono de David, a los sacerdotes
y a todos los habitantes de Jerusalén. 14Haré que se
despedacen unos a otros, padres e hijos por igual.
No les tendré piedad ni lástima, sino que los destruiré sin compasión.' Lo afirma el SEÑOR."»

Advertencia oportuna

15¡Escúchenme, préstenme atención!
    ¡No sean soberbios, que el SEÑOR mismo lo
        ha dicho!
16Glorifiquen al SEÑOR su Dios,
    antes de que haga venir la oscuridad
y ustedes tropiecen contra los montes
        sombríos.
Ustedes esperan la luz,
    pero Él la cambiará en densas tinieblas,
¡la convertirá en profunda oscuridad!
17Pero si ustedes no obedecen,
    lloraré en secreto
por causa de su orgullo;
mis ojos llorarán amargamente
    y se desharán en lágrimas,
porque el rebaño del SEÑOR
    será llevado al cautiverio.
18Di al rey y a la reina madre:
    «¡Humíllense, siéntense en el suelo,
que ya no ostentan sobre su cabeza
    la corona de gloria!»
19Las ciudades del Néguev están cerradas,
    y no hay quien abra sus *puertas.
Todo Judá se ha ido al destierro,
    exiliado en su totalidad.
20Alcen los ojos y miren
    a los que vienen del norte.
¿Dónde está el rebaño que te fue confiado,
    el rebaño que era tu orgullo?
21¿Qué dirás cuando el SEÑOR te imponga
        como jefes
a los que tú mismo enseñaste
    a ser tus aliados predilectos?
¿No tendrás dolores
    como de mujer de parto?
22Y si preguntas:
    «¿Por qué me pasa esto?»,
¡por tus muchos pecados
    te han arrancado las faldas
    y te han violado!l
23¿Puede el etíope cambiar de piel,
    o el leopardo quitarse sus manchas?
¡Pues tampoco ustedes pueden hacer el bien,
    acostumbrados como están a hacer el mal!
24«Los dispersaré como a la paja
    que arrastra el viento del desierto.
25Esto es lo que te ha tocado en suerte,
    ¡la porción que he medido para ti!
        —afirma el SEÑOR—.
Ya que me has olvidado,
    y has confiado en la mentira,
26¡yo también te alzaré las faldas
    hasta cubrirte el rostro
y descubrir tus vergüenzas!
27He visto tus adulterios,

---

k 13:4 *Perat.* Posiblemente *el río Éufrates*; también en vv. 5-7. l 13:22 *te han violado.* Lit. *tus talones han sufrido violencia.*

tus relinchos,
tu vergonzosa prostitución
y tus abominaciones,
en los campos y sobre las colinas.
¡Ay de ti, Jerusalén!
¿Hasta cuándo seguirás en tu *impureza?»

Sequía, hambre y espada

14 Ésta es la palabra del SEÑOR, que vino a Jeremías con motivo de la sequía:

2«Judá está de luto
y sus ciudades desfallecen;
hay lamentos en el país,
y sube el clamor de Jerusalén.
3Los nobles mandan por agua a sus siervos,
y éstos van a las cisternas,
pero no la encuentran.
Avergonzados y confundidos,
vuelven con sus cántaros vacíos
y agarrándosem la cabeza.
4El suelo está agrietado,
porque no llueve en el país.
Avergonzados están los campesinos,
agarrándose la cabeza.
5Aun las ciervas, en el campo,
abandonan a sus crías por falta de pastos.
6Parados sobre las lomas desiertas,
y con los ojos desfallecientes,
los asnos salvajes jadean como chacales
porque ya no tienen hierba.»

7Aunque nuestras iniquidades nos acusan,
tú, SEÑOR, actúas en razón de tu *nombre;
muchas nuestras infidelidades;
¡contra ti hemos pecado!
8Tú, esperanza y *salvación de Israel
en momentos de angustia,
¿por qué actúas en el país como un peregrino,
como un viajero que sólo pasa la noche?
9¿Por qué te encuentras confundido,
como un guerrero impotente para salvar?
SEÑOR, tú estás en medio de nosotros,
y se nos llama por tu nombre;
¡no nos abandones!

10Así dice el SEÑOR acerca de este pueblo:

«Les encanta vagabundear;
no refrenan sus pies.
Por eso yo no los acepto,
sino que voy a recordar sus iniquidades
y a castigar sus pecados.»

11Entonces el SEÑOR me dijo: «No ruegues por el bienestar de este pueblo. 12Aunque ayunen, no escucharé sus clamores; aunque me ofrezcan *holocaustos y ofrendas de cereal, no los aceptaré. En verdad, voy a exterminarlos con la espada, el hambre y la peste.»

13Pero yo respondí: «¡Ah, SEÑOR mi Dios! Los profetas les dicen que no se enfrentarán con la espada ni pasarán hambre, sino que tú les concederás una *paz duradera en este lugar.»

14El SEÑOR me contestó: «Mentira es lo que están profetizando en mi nombre esos profetas. Yo no los he enviado, ni les he dado ninguna orden, y ni siquiera les he hablado. Lo que les están profetizando son visiones engañosas, adivinaciones vanas y delirios de su propia imaginación. 15Por eso, así dice el

SEÑOR: "En cuanto a los profetas que profetizan en mi nombre sin que yo los haya enviado, y que además dicen que no habrá espada ni hambre en este país, ellos mismos morirán de hambre y a filo de espada. 16Y el pueblo al que profetizan será arrojado a las calles de Jerusalén a causa del hambre y de la espada, y no habrá quien los entierre, ni a ellos ni a sus esposas, ni a sus hijos, ni a sus hijas; también les echaré encima su propia maldad."

17»Tú les dirás lo siguiente:

»"Que corran lágrimas de mis ojos
día y noche, sin cesar,
porque la virginal hija de mi pueblo
ha sufrido una herida terrible,
¡un golpe muy duro!
18Si salgo al campo, veo los cuerpos
de los muertos a filo de espada;
si entro en la ciudad, veo los estragos
que el hambre ha producido.
Tanto el profeta como el sacerdote
ejercen en el país, sin *conocimiento."»n

19¿Has rechazado por completo a Judá?
¿Detestas a *Sión?
¿Por qué nos has herido de tal modo
que ya no tenemos remedio?
Esperábamos tiempos de paz,
pero nada bueno recibimos.
Esperábamos tiempos de salud,
pero sólo nos llegó el terror.
20Reconocemos, Señor, nuestra maldad,
y la iniquidad de nuestros padres;
¡hemos pecado contra ti!
21En razón de tu nombre, no nos desprecies;
no deshonres tu trono glorioso.
¡Acuérdate de tu *pacto con nosotros!
¡No lo quebrantes!
22¿Acaso hay entre los ídolos falsos
alguno que pueda hacer llover?
SEÑOR y Dios nuestro,
¿acaso no eres tú, y no el cielo mismo,
el que manda los aguaceros?
Tú has hecho todas estas cosas;
por eso esperamos en ti.

15 El SEÑOR me dijo: «Aunque Moisés y Samuel se presentaran ante mí, no tendría compasión de este pueblo. ¡Échalos de mi presencia! ¡Que se vayan! 2Y si te preguntan: "¿Adónde iremos?", adviérteles que así dice el SEÑOR:

»"Los destinados a la muerte, a la muerte;
los destinados a la espada, a la espada;
los destinados al hambre, al hambre;
los destinados al cautiverio, al cautiverio."

3»Enviaré contra ellos cuatro clases de calamidades —afirma el SEÑOR—: la espada para matar, los perros para arrastrar, las aves del cielo para devorar, y las bestias de la tierra para destruir. 4Los haré motivo de espanto para todos los reinos de la tierra, por causa de lo que Manasés hijo de Ezequías, rey de Judá, hizo en Jerusalén.

5»¿Quién tendrá compasión de ti, Jerusalén?
¿Quién llorará por ti?
¿Quién se detendrá a preguntar por tu salud?
6Tú me has rechazado,
te has vuelto atrás

—afirma el SEÑOR—.

---

m **14:3** *agarrándose*. Lit. *cubriéndose*; también en v. 4.   n **14:18** *ejercen ... sin conocimiento*. Alt. *andan errantes en una tierra que no conocen.*

Extenderé mi mano contra ti,
y te destruiré;
estoy cansado de tenerte compasión.
[7]Te aventaré con la horquilla
por las *puertas de la ciudad.
A ti te dejaré sin hijos,
y a mi pueblo lo destruiré,
porque no cambió su conducta.
[8]Haré que sus viudas sean más numerosas
que la arena de los mares;
en pleno día enviaré destrucción
contra las madres de los jóvenes.
De repente haré que caigan sobre ellas
la angustia y el pavor.
[9]Se desmaya la que tuvo siete hijos;
se queda sin *aliento.
Su sol se pone en pleno día;
¡se queda avergonzada y humillada!
A sus sobrevivientes los entregaré a la espada
delante de sus enemigos»,
afirma el SEÑOR.

[10]¡Ay de mí, madre mía,
que me diste a luz
como hombre de contiendas y disputas
contra toda la nación!
No he prestado ni me han prestado,
pero todos me maldicen.

[11]El SEÑOR dijo:

«De veras te libraré para bien;
haré que el enemigo te suplique
en tiempos de calamidad y de angustia.

[12]»¿Puede el *hombre romper el hierro,
el hierro del norte, y el bronce?
[13]Por causa de todos tus pecados
entregaré como botín, sin costo alguno,
tu riqueza y tus tesoros,
por todo tu territorio.
[14]Haré que sirvasñ a tus enemigos
en una tierra que no conoces,
porque en mi ira un fuego se ha encendido,
y arde contra ustedes.»

[15]Tú comprendes, SEÑOR;
¡acuérdate de mí, y cuídame!
¡Toma venganza de los que me persiguen!
Por causa de tu paciencia,
no permitas que sea yo arrebatado;
mira que por ti sufro injurias.
[16]Al encontrarme con tus palabras,
yo las devoraba;
ellas eran mi gozo
y la alegría de mi *corazón,
porque yo llevo tu *nombre,
SEÑOR, Dios *Todopoderoso.
[17]No he formado parte de grupos libertinos,
ni me he divertido con ellos;
he vivido solo, porque tú estás conmigo
y me has llenado de indignación.
[18]¿Por qué no cesa mi dolor?
¿Por qué es incurable mi herida?
¿Por qué se resiste a sanar?
¿Serás para mí un torrente engañoso
de aguas no confiables?

[19]Por eso, así dice el SEÑOR:

«Si te *arrepientes,
yo te restauraré y podrás servirme.

Si evitas hablar en vano,
y hablas lo que en verdad vale,
tú serás mi portavoz.
Que ellos se vuelvan hacia ti,
pero tú no te vuelvas hacia ellos.
[20]Haré que seas para este pueblo
como invencible muro de bronce;
pelearán contra ti,
pero no te podrán vencer,
porque yo estoy contigo
para salvarte y librarte
—afirma el SEÑOR—.
[21]Te libraré del poder de los malvados;
¡te rescataré de las garras de los violentos!»

Mensaje de juicio

16 La palabra del SEÑOR vino a mí, y me dijo: [2]«No te cases, ni tengas hijos ni hijas en este lugar.» [3]Porque así dice el SEÑOR en cuanto a los hijos y las hijas que han nacido en este lugar, y en cuanto a las madres que los dieron a luz y los padres que los engendraron en este país: [4]«Morirán de enfermedades horribles. Nadie llorará por ellos, ni los sepultará; se quedarán sobre la faz de la tierra, como el estiércol. La espada y el hambre acabarán con ellos, y sus cadáveres servirán de alimento para las aves del cielo y para las bestias de la tierra.»

[5]Así dice el SEÑOR: «No entres en una casa donde estén de luto, ni vayas a llorar, ni los consueles, porque a este pueblo le he retirado mi *paz, mi amor y mi compasión —afirma el SEÑOR—. [6]En este país morirán grandes y pequeños; nadie llorará por ellos, ni los sepultará; nadie se hará heridas en el cuerpo ni se rapará la cabeza por ellos. [7]Nadie ofrecerá un banquete fúnebre a los que estén de duelo, para consolarlos por el muerto, ni a nadie se le dará a beber la copa del consuelo, aun cuando quien haya muerto sea su padre o su madre.

[8]»No entres en una casa donde haya una celebración, ni te sientes con ellos a comer y beber. [9]Porque así dice el SEÑOR *Todopoderoso, el Dios de Israel: Voy a poner fin en este lugar a toda expresión de alegría y de regocijo, y al cántico del novio y de la novia. Esto sucederá en sus propios días, y ustedes lo verán.

[10]»Cuando anuncies a este pueblo todas estas cosas, ellos te preguntarán: "¿Por qué ha decretado el SEÑOR contra nosotros esta calamidad tan grande? ¿Cuál es nuestra iniquidad? ¿Qué pecado hemos cometido contra el SEÑOR nuestro Dios?" [11]Entonces les responderás: "Esto es porque sus antepasados me abandonaron y se fueron tras otros dioses, y los sirvieron y los adoraron. Pero a mí me abandonaron, y no cumplieron mi *ley —afirma el SEÑOR—. [12]Pero ustedes se han comportado peor que sus antepasados. Cada uno sigue la terquedad de su *corazón malvado, y no me ha obedecido. [13]Por eso los voy a arrojar de esta tierra, a un país que ni ustedes ni sus antepasados conocieron, y allí servirán a otros dioses día y noche. No les tendré clemencia."

[14]»Por eso —afirma el SEÑOR—, vienen días en que ya no se dirá: "Por la vida del SEÑOR, que hizo salir a los israelitas de la tierra de Egipto", [15]sino: "Por la vida del SEÑOR, que hizo salir a los israelitas de la tierra del norte, y de todos los países adonde los había expulsado." Yo los haré volver a su tierra, la que antes di a sus antepasados.

[16]»Voy a enviar a muchos pescadores —afirma el SEÑOR—, y ellos los pescarán a ustedes. Después,

---

ñ **15:14** *Haré que sirvas* (mss. hebreos, LXX y Siríaca); *Haré pasar* (TM).

enviaré a muchos cazadores, y ellos los cazarán a ustedes por todas las montañas y colinas, y por las grietas de las rocas. 17Ciertamente mis ojos ven todas sus acciones; ninguna de ellas me es oculta. Su iniquidad no puede esconderse de mi vista. 18Primero les pagaré el doble por su iniquidad y su pecado, porque con los cadáveres de sus ídolos detestables han profanado mi tierra, y han llenado mi herencia con sus abominaciones.»

19SEÑOR, fuerza y fortaleza mía,
     mi refugio en el día de la angustia:
desde los confines de la tierra
     vendrán a ti las naciones, y dirán:
«Sólo mentira heredaron nuestros
          antepasados;
     heredaron lo absurdo,
     lo que no sirve para nada.
20¿Acaso puede el *hombre hacer sus propios
          dioses?
     ¡Pero si no son dioses!»

21Por eso, esta vez les daré una lección;
     les daré a conocer mi mano poderosa.
¡Así sabrán que mi *nombre es el SEÑOR!

17 «El pecado de Judá está escrito
     con cincel de hierro;
grabado está con punta de diamante
     sobre la tabla de su *corazón
     y sobre los cuernos de sus altares.
2Bien que se acuerdan sus hijos
     de sus altares junto a árboles frondosos;
de sus imágenes de *Aserá sobre altas colinas
3y sobre mi montaña a campo abierto.

»Entregaré como botín tu riqueza,
     tus tesoros y tus *santuarios paganos,
por todos tus pecados
     en todo tu territorio.
4Por tu culpa perderás la herencia
     que yo te había dado.
Te haré esclava de tus enemigos,
     en un país para ti desconocido,
porque has encendido mi ira,
     la cual se mantendrá ardiendo para
          siempre.»

5Así dice el SEÑOR:

«¡Maldito el *hombre que confía en el hombre!
     ¡Maldito el que se apoya en su propia
          fuerza
     y aparta su corazón del SEÑOR!
6Será como una zarza en el desierto:
     no se dará cuenta cuando llegue el bien.
Morará en la sequedad del desierto,
     en tierras de sal, donde nadie habita.

7»Bendito el hombre que confía en el SEÑOR,
     y pone su confianza en él.
8Será como un árbol plantado junto al agua,
     que extiende sus raíces hacia la corriente;
no teme que llegue el calor,
     y sus hojas están siempre verdes.
En época de sequía no se angustia,
     y nunca deja de dar fruto.»

9Nada hay tan engañoso como el corazón.
     No tiene remedio.
     ¿Quién puede comprenderlo?

10«Yo, el SEÑOR, sondeo el corazón
     y examino los pensamientos,
para darle a cada uno según sus acciones

y según el fruto de sus obras.»

11El que acapara riquezas injustas
     es perdiz que empolla huevos ajenos.
En la mitad de la vida las perderá,
     y al final no será más que un insensato.

12Trono de gloria,
     exaltado desde el principio,
     es el lugar de nuestro santuario.
13SEÑOR, tú eres la esperanza de Israel,
     todo el que te abandona quedará
          avergonzado.
El que se aparta de ti
     quedará como algo escrito en el polvo,
porque abandonó al SEÑOR,
     al manantial de aguas vivas.

14Sáname, SEÑOR, y seré sanado;
     sálvame, y seré salvado,
     porque tú eres mi alabanza.
15No falta quien me pregunte:
     «¿Dónde está la palabra del SEÑOR?
     ¡Que se haga realidad!»
16Pero yo no me he apresurado
     a abandonarte y dejar de ser tu *pastor,
     ni he deseado que venga el día de la
          calamidad.
Tú bien sabes lo que he dicho,
     pues lo dije en tu presencia.
17No seas para mí un motivo de terror;
     tú eres mi refugio en tiempos de
          calamidad.
18¡No me pongas a mí en vergüenza;
     avergüénzalos a ellos!
¡No me llenes de terror a mí;
     aterrorízalos a ellos!
Envíales tiempos difíciles;
     ¡destrózalos, y vuelve a destrozarlos!

La observancia del sábado

19Así me dijo el SEÑOR: «Ve y párate en la puerta del Pueblo, por donde entran y salen los reyes de Judá, y luego en todas las *puertas de Jerusalén, 20y diles: "¡Escuchen la palabra del SEÑOR, reyes de Judá, y toda la gente de Judá y todos los habitantes de Jerusalén que entran por estas puertas! 21Así dice el SEÑOR: 'Cuídense bien de no llevar ninguna carga en día *sábado, y de no meterla por las puertas de Jerusalén. 22Tampoco saquen ninguna carga de sus casas en día sábado, ni hagan ningún tipo de trabajo. Observen el reposo del sábado, tal como se lo ordené a sus antepasados. 23Pero ellos no me prestaron atención ni me obedecieron, sino que se obstinaron y no quisieron escuchar ni recibir *corrección.

24»" 'Si de veras me obedecen —afirma el SEÑOR— y no meten ninguna carga por las puertas de esta ciudad en día sábado, sino que observan este día no haciendo ningún trabajo, 25entonces entrarán por las puertas de esta ciudad reyes y príncipes que se sentarán en el trono de David. Ellos y los príncipes entrarán montados en carros y caballos, acompañados por la gente de Judá y por los habitantes de Jerusalén, y esta ciudad será habitada para siempre. 26Vendrá gente de las ciudades de Judá y de los alrededores de Jerusalén, del territorio de Benjamín y de la Sefelá, de la región montañosa y del Néguev. Traerán a la casa del SEÑOR *holocaustos y sacrificios, ofrendas de cereal y de incienso, y ofrendas de acción de gracias. 27Pero si no obedecen ustedes mi mandato de observar el reposo del sábado, y de no llevar carga al entrar en sábado por las puertas de Jerusalén, entonces les prenderé fuego a sus puertas, que no podrá ser apagado y que consumirá los palacios de Jerusalén.' "»

Parábola del alfarero

18 Ésta es la palabra del SEÑOR, que vino a Jeremías: 2«Baja ahora mismo a la casa del alfarero, y allí te comunicaré mi mensaje.»

3Entonces bajé a la casa del alfarero, y lo encontré trabajando en el torno. 4Pero la vasija que estaba modelando se le deshizo en las manos; así que volvió a hacer otra vasija, hasta que le pareció que le había quedado bien.

5En ese momento la palabra del SEÑOR vino a mí, y me dijo: 6«Pueblo de Israel, ¿acaso no puedo hacer con ustedes lo mismo que hace este alfarero con el barro? —afirma el SEÑOR—. Ustedes, pueblo de Israel, son en mis manos como el barro en las manos del alfarero. 7En un momento puedo hablar de arrancar, derribar y destruir a una nación o a un reino; 8pero si la nación de la cual hablé se *arrepiente de su maldad, también yo me arrepentiré del castigo que había pensado infligirles. 9En otro momento puedo hablar de construir y plantar a una nación o a un reino. 10Pero si esa nación hace lo malo ante mis ojos y no me obedece, me arrepentiré del bien que había pensado hacerles. 11Y ahora habla con los habitantes de Judá y de Jerusalén, y adviérteles que así dice el SEÑOR: "Estoy preparando una calamidad contra ustedes, y elaborando un plan en su contra. ¡Vuélvanse ya de su mal *camino; enmienden su conducta y sus acciones!" 12Ellos objetarán: "Es inútil. Vamos a seguir nuestros propios planes", y cada uno cometerá la maldad que le dicte su obstinado *corazón.»

13Por eso, así dice el SEÑOR:

«Pregunten entre las naciones:
    ¿Quién ha oído algo semejante?
La virginal Israel
    ha cometido algo terrible.
14¿Acaso la nieve del Líbano
    desaparece de las colinas escarpadas?
¿Se agotan las aguas frías
    que fluyen de las montañas?º
15Sin embargo, mi pueblo me ha olvidado;
    quema incienso a ídolos inútiles.
Ha tropezado en sus caminos,
    en los senderos antiguos,
para andar por sendas
    y caminos escabrosos.
16Así ha dejado desolado su país;
    lo ha hecho objeto de burla constante.
Todo el que pase por él
    meneará atónito la cabeza.
17Como un viento del este,
    los esparciré delante del enemigo.
En el día de su calamidad
    les daré la espalda y no la cara.»

18Ellos dijeron: «Vengan, tramemos un plan contra Jeremías. Porque no le faltará ni la ley al sacerdote, ni el consejo al sabio, ni la palabra al profeta. Ataquémoslo de palabra, y no hagamos caso de nada de lo que diga.»

19¡SEÑOR, préstame atención!
    ¡Escucha a los que me acusan!
20¿Acaso el bien se paga con el mal?
    ¡Pues ellos me han cavado una fosa!

Recuerda que me presenté ante ti
    para interceder por ellos,
    para apartar de ellos tu ira.
21Por eso, entrega ahora sus hijos al hambre;
    abandónalos a merced de la espada.
Que sus esposas se queden viudas y sin hijos;
    que sus maridos mueran asesinados,
y que sus jóvenes caigan en combate
    a filo de espada.
22¡Que se oigan los gritos desde sus casas,
    cuando de repente mandes contra ellos
    una banda de asaltantes!
Han cavado una fosa para atraparme,
    y han puesto trampas a mi paso.
23Pero tú, SEÑOR, conoces
    todos sus planes para matarme.
¡No perdones su iniquidad,
    ni borres de tu presencia sus pecados!
¡Que caigan derribados ante ti!
    ¡Enfréntate a ellos en el momento de tu ira!

19 Así dice el SEÑOR: «Ve a un alfarero, y cómprale un cántaro de barro. Pide luego que te acompañen algunos de los *ancianos del pueblo y de los ancianos de los sacerdotes, 2y ve al valle de Ben Hinón, que está a la entrada de la puerta de los Alfareros, y proclama allí las palabras que yo te comunicaré. 3Diles: "Reyes de Judá y habitantes de Jerusalén, escuchen la palabra del SEÑOR. Así dice el SEÑOR *Todopoderoso, el Dios de Israel: 'Haré venir tal calamidad sobre este lugar, que a todo el que se entere le zumbarán los oídos. 4Porque ellos me han abandonado. Han profanado este lugar, quemando en él incienso a otros dioses que no conocían ni ellos ni sus antepasados ni los reyes de Judá. Además, han llenado de sangre inocente este lugar. 5Han construido *santuarios paganos en honor de *Baal, para quemar a sus hijos en el fuego como *holocaustos a Baal, cosa que yo jamás les ordené ni mencioné, ni jamás me pasó por la *mente. 6Por eso vendrán días en que este lugar ya no se llamará Tofet, ni Valle de Ben Hinón, sino Valle de la Matanza —afirma el SEÑOR—. 7En este lugar anularé los planes de Judá y de Jerusalén, y los haré caer a filo de espada delante de sus enemigos, es decir, a manos de los que atentan contra su vida, y dejaré sus cadáveres a las aves del cielo y a las bestias de la tierra, para que les sirvan de comida. 8Convertiré a esta ciudad en un lugar desolado y en objeto de burla. Todo el que pase por ella quedará atónito y se burlará de todas sus heridas. 9Ante el angustioso asedio que les impondrán los enemigos que atentan contra ustedes, haré que se coman la carne de sus propios hijos e hijas, y que se devoren entre sí.' "

10»Rompe después el cántaro en mil pedazos, a la vista de los hombres que te acompañaron, 11y adviérteles que así dice el SEÑOR Todopoderoso: "Voy a hacer pedazos esta nación y esta ciudad, como quien hace pedazos un cántaro de alfarero, que ya no se puede reparar; y a falta de otro lugar, enterrarán a sus muertos en Tofet. 12Así haré con este lugar y con sus habitantes —afirma el SEÑOR—; esta ciudad quedará tal y como quedó Tofet. 13Todas las casas de Jerusalén y todos los palacios de los reyes de Judá, es decir, todas esas casas en cuyas azoteas se quemó incienso a los astros de los cielos y donde se derramaron libaciones a otros dioses, quedarán tan *impuras como quedó Tofet."»

14Cuando Jeremías regresó de Tofet, adonde el SEÑOR lo había enviado a profetizar, se paró en el

---

º **18:14** *¿Se agotan ... montañas?* Texto de difícil traducción.

atrio de la casa del Señor y dijo a todo el pueblo: 15«Así dice el SEÑOR Todopoderoso, el Dios de Israel: "Como esta ciudad y todos sus pueblos vecinos se han obstinado en desobedecer mis palabras, voy a mandarles toda la calamidad que les había prometido."»

Jeremías y Pasur

20 Cuando el sacerdote Pasur hijo de Imer, que era el oficial principal de la casa del SEÑOR, oyó lo que Jeremías profetizaba, 2mandó que golpearan al profeta Jeremías y que lo colocaran en el cepo ubicado en la puerta alta de Benjamín, junto a la casa del SEÑOR. 3A la mañana siguiente, cuando Pasur liberó a Jeremías del cepo, Jeremías le dijo: «El SEÑOR ya no te llama Pasur, sino "Terror por todas partes". 4Porque así dice el SEÑOR: "Te voy a convertir en terror para ti mismo y para tus amigos, los cuales caerán bajo la espada de sus enemigos, y tú mismo lo verás. Entregaré a todo Judá en manos del rey de Babilonia, el cual los deportará a Babilonia o los matará a filo de espada. 5Además, pondré en manos de sus enemigos toda la riqueza de esta ciudad, todos sus productos y objetos de valor, y todos los tesoros de los reyes de Judá, para que los saqueen y se los lleven a Babilonia. 6Y tú, Pasur, irás al cautiverio de Babilonia junto con toda tu familia. Allí morirás, y allí serás enterrado, con todos tus amigos, a quienes les profetizabas mentiras."»

Quejas de Jeremías

7Me sedujiste, SEÑOR,
y yo me dejé seducir!
Fuiste más fuerte que yo,
y me venciste.
Todo el mundo se burla de mí;
se ríen de mí todo el tiempo.
8Cada vez que hablo, es para gritar:
«¡Violencia! ¡Violencia!»
Por eso la palabra del SEÑOR
no deja de ser para mí
un oprobio y una burla.
9Si digo: «No me acordaré más de él,
ni hablaré más en su *nombre»,
entonces su palabra en mi interior
se vuelve un fuego ardiente
que me cala hasta los huesos.
He hecho todo lo posible por contenerla,
pero ya no puedo más.
10Escucho a muchos decir con sorna:
«¡Hay terror por todas partes!»
y hasta agregan: «¡Denúncienlo!
¡Vamos a denunciarlo!»
Aun mis mejores amigos
esperan que tropiece.
También dicen: «Quizá lo podamos seducir.
Entonces lo venceremos
y nos vengaremos de él.»
11Pero el SEÑOR está conmigo
como un guerrero poderoso;
por eso los que me persiguen
caerán y no podrán prevalecer,
fracasarán y quedarán avergonzados.
Eterna será su deshonra;
jamás será olvidada.
12Tú, SEÑOR *Todopoderoso,
que examinas al justo,
que sondeas el *corazón y la *mente,
hazme ver tu venganza sobre ellos,
pues a ti he encomendado mi causa.
13¡Canten al SEÑOR, alábenlo!

Él salva a los pobres
del poder de los malvados.
14¡Maldito el día en que nací!
¡Maldito el día en que mi madre me dio a
luz!
15¡Maldito el hombre que alegró a mi padre
cuando le dijo: «¡Te ha nacido un hijo
varón!»!
16¡Que sea tal hombre como las ciudades
que el SEÑOR destruyó sin compasión.
Que oiga gritos en la mañana
y alaridos de guerra al mediodía!
17¿Por qué Dios no me dejó morir
en el seno de mi madre?
Así ella habría sido mi tumba,
y yo jamás habría salido de su vientre.
18¿Por qué tuve que salir del vientre
sólo para ver problemas y aflicción,
y para terminar mis días en vergüenza?

Dios rechaza la petición de Sedequías

21 Ésta es la palabra del SEÑOR, que vino a Jeremías cuando el rey Sedequías envió a Pasur hijo de Malquías, y al sacerdote Sofonías hijo de Maseías, a que le dijeran:
2«Consulta ahora al SEÑOR por nosotros, porque Nabucodonosor, rey de Babilonia, nos está atacando. Tal vez el SEÑOR haga uno de sus milagros, y lo obligue a retirarse.»
3Jeremías les respondió:
«Adviértanle a Sedequías 4que así dice el SEÑOR, el Dios de Israel: "Yo haré retroceder tus tropas, las que pelean contra el rey de Babilonia y contra los *caldeos, que desde fuera de los muros los tienen sitiados. Haré que tus tropas se repliegen dentro de la ciudad. 5Yo mismo pelearé contra ustedes. Con gran despliegue de poder, y con ira, furor y gran indignación, 6heriré a *hombres y animales, y los habitantes de esta ciudad morirán por causa de una peste terrible. 7Después de eso entregaré a Sedequías, rey de Judá, y a sus oficiales y a la gente que haya quedado con vida después de la peste, la espada y el hambre —afirma el SEÑOR—. Los entregaré en manos de Nabucodonosor, rey de Babilonia, y de los enemigos que buscan matarlos. Sin ninguna piedad, clemencia ni compasión, Nabucodonosor los herirá a filo de espada."
8»Y a este pueblo adviértele que así dice el SEÑOR: "Pongo delante de ustedes el *camino de la vida y el camino de la muerte. 9El que se quede en esta ciudad morirá por la espada y la peste, o de hambre. Pero el que salga y se rinda a los caldeos que los están sitiando, vivirá. Así salvará su vida. 10Porque he decidido hacerle a esta ciudad el mal y no el bien —afirma el SEÑOR—. Será entregada en manos del rey de Babilonia, quien le prenderá fuego."
11»Di también a la casa real de Judá que escuchen la palabra del SEÑOR. 12Adviértele a la dinastía de David que así dice el SEÑOR:

»"Hagan justicia cada mañana,
y libren al explotado del poder del opresor,
no sea que mi ira se encienda como un fuego
y arda sin que nadie pueda extinguirla,
a causa de la maldad de sus acciones.
13¡Yo estoy contra ti, Jerusalén,
reina del valle, roca de la llanura!
—afirma el SEÑOR—.
Ustedes dicen: '¿Quién podrá venir contra
nosotros?
¿Quién podrá entrar en nuestros refugios?'
14Yo los castigaré conforme al fruto de sus
acciones

—afirma el SEÑOR—;
a su bosque le prenderé fuego,
y ese fuego consumirá todos sus
    alrededores."»

Juicio contra reyes malvados

22 Así dice el SEÑOR: «Ve a la casa del rey de Judá, y proclama allí este mensaje:
2"Tú, rey de Judá, que estás sentado sobre el trono de David, y tus oficiales y tu pueblo, que entran por estas puertas, escuchen la palabra del SEÑOR. 3Así dice el SEÑOR: 'Practiquen el derecho y la justicia. Libren al oprimido del poder del opresor. No maltraten ni hagan violencia al extranjero, ni al huérfano ni a la viuda, ni·derramen sangre inocente en este lugar. 4Si de veras cumplen con esta palabra, entonces por las puertas de este palacio entrarán reyes que ocuparán el trono de David; entrarán en carros y a caballo, acompañados por sus oficiales y su pueblo. 5Pero si no obedecen estas palabras, juro por mí mismo que este palacio se convertirá en un montón de ruinas. Yo, el SEÑOR, lo afirmo.' "»

6Porque así dice el SEÑOR acerca de la casa real de Judá:

«Para mí, tú eres como Galaad
    y como la cima del Líbano,
pero juro que te convertiré en un desierto,
    en ciudades deshabitadas.
7Enviaré contra ti destructores,
    cada uno con sus armas,
que talarán tus cedros más hermosos
    y los echarán en el fuego.

8»Gente de muchas naciones pasará por esta ciudad, y se preguntará: "¿Por qué habrá tratado así el SEÑOR a esta gran ciudad?" 9Y se le responderá: "Porque abandonaron el *pacto del SEÑOR su Dios, adorando y sirviendo a otros dioses."»

10No lloren por el que está muerto,
    ni hagan lamentaciones por él.
Lloren más bien por el exiliado,
    por el que nunca volverá
    ni verá más la tierra en que nació.

11Así dice el SEÑOR acerca de Salún hijo de Josías, rey de Judá, que ascendió al trono después de su padre Josías y que salió de este lugar: «Nunca más volverá, 12sino que morirá en el lugar donde ha sido desterrado. No volverá a ver más este país.»

13»¡Ay del que edifica su casa
    y sus habitaciones superiores
    violentando la justicia y el derecho!
¡Ay del que obliga a su prójimo
    a trabajar de balde,
    y no le paga por su trabajo!
14¡Ay del que dice: "Me edificaré una casa
    señorial,
    con habitaciones amplias en el piso
      superior"!
Y le abre grandes ventanas,
    y la recubre de cedro y la pinta de rojo.

15»¿Acaso eres rey
    sólo por acaparar mucho cedro?
Tu padre no sólo comía y bebía,
    sino que practicaba el derecho y la justicia,

y por eso le fue bien.
16Defendía la causa del pobre y del necesitado,
    y por eso le fue bien.
¿Acaso no es esto conocerme?
    —afirma el SEÑOR—.

17»Pero tus ojos y tu *corazón
    sólo buscan ganancias deshonestas,
sólo buscan derramar sangre inocente
    y practicar la opresión y la violencia.»

18Por eso, así dice el SEÑOR acerca de Joacim hijo de Josías, rey de Judá:

«Nadie lamentará su muerte ni gritará:
    "¡Ay, mi hermano! ¡Ay, mi hermana!"
Nadie lamentará su muerte ni gritará:
    "¡Ay, señor! ¡Ay, Su Majestad!"
19Será enterrado como un asno,
    y lo arrastrarán y lo arrojarán
    fuera de las *puertas de Jerusalén.»

20«¡Sube al Líbano y grita;
    levanta tu voz en Basán!
¡Grita desde Abarín,
    pues todos tus amantes han sido
      destruidos!
21Yo te hablé cuando te iba bien,
    pero tú dijiste: "¡No escucharé!"
Así te has comportado desde tu juventud:
    ¡nunca me has obedecido!
22El viento arrastrará a todos tus *pastores,
    y tus amantes irán al cautiverio.
Por culpa de toda tu maldad
    quedarás avergonzada y humillada.
23Tú, que habitas en el Líbano,p
    que has puesto tu nido entre los cedros,
¡cómo gemirás cuando te vengan los dolores,
    dolores como de parturienta!

24»¡Tan cierto como que yo vivo —afirma el SEÑOR—, que aunque Jeconíasq hijo de Joacim, rey de Judá, sea un anillo en mi mano *derecha, aun de allí lo arrancaré! 25Yo te entregaré en manos de los que buscan matarte, y en manos de los que tú más temes, es decir, en poder de Nabucodonosor, rey de Babilonia, y de los *babilonios. 26A ti y a la madre que te dio a luz los arrojaré a un país que no vio nacer, y allí morirán. 27Jamás volverán al país al que tanto anhelan volver.»

28¿Es Jeconías una vasija despreciable y rota,
    un objeto que nadie desea?
¿Por qué son arrojados él y su descendencia,
    y echados a un país que no conocen?
29¡Tierra, tierra, tierra!
    ¡Escucha la palabra del SEÑOR!
30Así dice el SEÑOR: «Anoten a este hombre
    como si fuera un hombre sin hijos;
    como alguien que fracasó en su vida.
Porque ninguno de sus descendientes
    logrará ocupar el trono de David,
    ni reinar de nuevo en Judá.»

El Rey justo

23 «¡Ay de los *pastores que destruyen y dispersan el rebaño de mis praderas!», afirma el SEÑOR. 2Por eso, así dice el SEÑOR, el Dios de Israel, a los pastores que apacientan a mi pueblo: «Ustedes han dispersado a mis ovejas; las han expulsado y no

---

p **22:23** *el Líbano.* Es decir, en el palacio en Jerusalén (véase 1R 7:2). q **22:24** *Jeconías.* Lit. *Conías* (variante de este nombre); también en v. 28.

se han encargado de ellas. Pues bien, yo me encargaré de castigarlos a ustedes por sus malas acciones —afirma el SEÑOR—. **3**Al resto de mis ovejas yo mismo las reuniré de todos los países adonde las expulsé; y las haré volver a sus pastos, donde crecerán y se multiplicarán. **4**Pondré sobre ellas pastores que las pastorearán, y ya no temerán ni se espantarán, ni faltará ninguna de ellas —afirma el SEÑOR—.

5»Vienen días —afirma el SEÑOR—,
  en que de la simiente de David
  haré surgir un vástago justo;
  él reinará con sabiduría en el país,
  y practicará el derecho y la justicia.
6En esos días Judá será salvada,
  Israel morará seguro.
Y éste es el *nombre que se le dará:
  "El SEÑOR es nuestra *salvación."

7»Por eso —afirma el SEÑOR— vienen días en que ya no se dirá: "Por la vida del SEÑOR, que hizo salir a los israelitas de la tierra de Egipto", **8**sino: "Por la vida del SEÑOR, que hizo salir a los descendientes de la familia de Israel, y los hizo llegar del país del norte, y de todos los países adonde los había expulsado." Y habitarán en su propia tierra.»

Profetas mentirosos

9En cuanto a los profetas:

Se me parte el *corazón en el pecho
  y se me estremecen los huesos.
Por causa del SEÑOR
  y de sus santas palabras,
hasta parezco un borracho,
  alguien dominado por el vino.
10A causa de la maldición,
  el país está lleno de adúlteros,
la tierra está de luto
  y los pastos del desierto se han secado.
Los profetas corren tras la maldad,
  y usan su poder para la injusticia.

11«Impíos son los profetas y los sacerdotes;
  aun en mi propia casa encuentro su
    maldad

          —afirma el SEÑOR—.

12»Por eso su *camino será resbaladizo;
  serán empujados a las tinieblas,
  y en ellas se hundirán.
Yo traeré sobre ellos una calamidad
  en el año de su castigo

          —afirma el SEÑOR—.

13»Algo insólito he observado
  entre los profetas de Samaria:
profetizaron en nombre de *Baal,
  y descarriaron a mi pueblo Israel.
14Y entre los profetas de Jerusalén
  he observado cosas terribles:
cometen adulterio, y viven en la mentira;
  fortalecen las manos de los malhechores,
  ninguno se convierte de su maldad.
Todos ellos son para mí como Sodoma,
  los habitantes de Jerusalén son como
    Gomorra.»

15Por tanto, así dice el SEÑOR *Todopoderoso contra los profetas:

«Haré que coman alimentos amargos
  y que beban agua envenenada,
porque los profetas de Jerusalén
  han llenado de corrupción todo el país.»

16Así dice el SEÑOR Todopoderoso:

«No hagan caso de lo que dicen los profetas,
  pues alientan en ustedes falsas esperanzas;
cuentan visiones que se han imaginado
  y que no proceden de la boca del SEÑOR.
17A los que me desprecian les aseguran
  que yo digo que gozarán de *bienestar;
a los que obedecen los dictados de su terco
    corazón
  les dicen que no les sobrevendrá ningún
    mal.
18¿Quién de ellos ha estado en el consejo del
    SEÑOR?
  ¿Quién ha recibido o escuchado su
    palabra?
  ¿Quién ha atendido y escuchado su
    palabra?
19El huracán del SEÑOR se ha desatado con
    furor;
  un torbellino se cierne amenazante
  sobre la cabeza de los malvados.
20La ira del SEÑOR no cesará
  hasta que haya realizado por completo
  los propósitos de su corazón.
Al final de los tiempos
  lo comprenderán con claridad.
21Yo no envié a esos profetas,
  pero ellos corrieron;
ni siquiera les hablé,
  pero ellos profetizaron.
22Si hubieran estado en mi consejo,
  habrían proclamado mis palabras a mi
    pueblo;
lo habrían hecho volver de su mal camino
  y de sus malas acciones.

23»¿Soy acaso Dios sólo de cerca?
  ¿No soy Dios también de lejos?
          —afirma el SEÑOR—.
24¿Podrá el *hombre hallar un escondite
  donde yo no pueda encontrarlo?
          —afirma el SEÑOR—.
  ¿Acaso no soy yo el que llena los cielos y la
    tierra?
          —afirma el SEÑOR—.

25»He escuchado lo que dicen los profetas que profieren mentiras en mi nombre, los cuales dicen: "¡He tenido un sueño, he tenido un sueño!" **26**¿Hasta cuándo seguirán dándole valor de profecía a las mentiras y delirios de su *mente? **27**Con los sueños que se cuentan unos a otros pretenden hacer que mi pueblo se olvide de mi nombre, como sus antepasados se olvidaron de mi nombre por el de Baal. **28**El profeta que tenga un sueño, que lo cuente; pero el que reciba mi palabra, que la proclame con fidelidad. ¿Qué tiene que ver la paja con el grano? —afirma el SEÑOR—. **29**¿No es acaso mi palabra como fuego, y como martillo que pulveriza la roca? —afirma el SEÑOR—.

30»Por eso yo estoy contra los profetas que se roban mis palabras entre sí —afirma el SEÑOR—. **31**Yo estoy contra los profetas que sueltan la lengua y hablan por hablar —afirma el SEÑOR—. **32**Yo estoy contra los profetas que cuentan sueños mentirosos, y que al contarlos hacen que mi pueblo se extravíe con sus mentiras y sus presunciones —afirma el SEÑOR—. Yo no los he enviado ni les he dado ninguna orden. Son del todo inútiles para este pueblo —afirma el SEÑOR—.

Profecías falsas

33»Y si este pueblo, o algún profeta o sacerdote, te pregunta: "¿Qué mensaje tenemos del SEÑOR?", tú les responderás: "¿De qué mensaje hablan?" Yo los abandonaré —afirma el SEÑOR—. 34Y si un profeta o un sacerdote, o alguien del pueblo, dice: "Éste es el mensaje del SEÑOR", yo castigaré a ese hombre y a su casa. 35Así deberán hablarse entre amigos y hermanos: "¿Qué ha respondido el SEÑOR?", o "¿Qué ha dicho el SEÑOR?" 36Pero no deberán mencionar más la frase "Mensaje del SEÑOR", porque el mensaje de cada uno será su propia palabra, ya que ustedes han distorsionado las palabras del Dios viviente, del SEÑOR *Todopoderoso, nuestro Dios. 37Así les dirás a los profetas: "¿Qué les ha respondido el SEÑOR? ¿Qué les ha dicho?" 38Pero si ustedes responden: "¡Mensaje del SEÑOR!", el SEÑOR dice: "Por cuanto ustedes han dicho: '¡Mensaje del SEÑOR!', siendo que yo les había prohibido que pronunciaran esta frase, 39entonces me olvidaré de ustedes y los echaré de mi presencia, junto con la ciudad que les di a ustedes y a sus antepasados. 40Y los afligiré con un oprobio eterno, con una humillación eterna que jamás será olvidada."»

Dos canastas de higos

24 Después de que Nabucodonosor, rey de Babilonia, deportó de Jerusalén a Jeconías hijo de Joacim, rey de Judá, junto con los jefes de Judá y con los artesanos y herreros, el SEÑOR me mostró dos canastas de higos colocadas frente al templo del SEÑOR. 2Una de ellas tenía higos muy buenos, como los que maduran primero; la otra tenía higos muy malos, tan malos que no se podían comer.

3Entonces el SEÑOR me preguntó: «¿Qué ves, Jeremías?» Yo respondí: «Veo higos. Unos están muy buenos, pero otros están tan malos que no se pueden comer.»

4Y la palabra del SEÑOR vino a mí: 5»Así dice el SEÑOR, el Dios de Israel: "A los deportados de Judá, que envié de este lugar al país de los *babilonios, los consideraré como a estos higos buenos. 6Los miraré favorablemente, y los haré volver a este país. Los edificaré y no los derribaré, los plantaré y no los arrancaré. 7Les daré un *corazón que me conozca, porque yo soy el SEÑOR. Ellos serán mi pueblo, y yo seré su Dios, porque volverán a mí de todo corazón.

8»"Pero a Sedequías, rey de Judá, y a sus jefes y a los sobrevivientes de Jerusalén —lo mismo a los que se quedaron en este país como a los que viven en Egipto— los trataré como a los higos malos, que de tan malos no se pueden comer —afirma el SEÑOR—. 9Los convertiré en motivo de espanto y de calamidad, para todos los reinos de la tierra. En todos los lugares por donde los disperse, serán objeto de escarnio, desprecio, burla y maldición. 10Enviaré contra ellos espada, hambre y pestilencia, hasta que sean exterminados de la tierra que les di a ellos y a sus antepasados."»

Setenta años de cautiverio

25 Ésta es la palabra que vino a Jeremías con relación a todo el pueblo de Judá. La recibió en el año cuarto del reinado de Joacim hijo de Josías, rey de Judá, es decir, durante el año primero del reinado de Nabucodonosor, rey de Babilonia. 2El profeta Jeremías les dijo lo siguiente a todo el pueblo de Judá y a todos los habitantes de Jerusalén: 3«Desde el año

trece de Josías hijo de Amón, rey de Judá, hasta el día de hoy —¡y conste que ya han pasado veintitrés años!—, el SEÑOR me ha dirigido su palabra, y yo les he hablado en repetidas ocasiones, pero ustedes no me han hecho caso.

4»Además, una y otra vez el SEÑOR les ha enviado a sus siervos los profetas, pero ustedes no los han escuchado ni les han prestado atención. 5Ellos los exhortaban: "Dejen ya su mal *camino y sus malas acciones. Así podrán habitar en la tierra que, desde siempre y para siempre, el SEÑOR les ha dado a ustedes y a sus antepasados. 6No vayan tras otros dioses para servirles y adorarlos; no me irriten con la obra de sus manos, y no les haré ningún mal."

7»Pero ustedes no me obedecieron —afirma el SEÑOR—, sino que me irritaron con la obra de sus manos, para su propia desgracia.

8»Por eso, así dice el SEÑOR *Todopoderoso: "Por cuanto no han obedecido mis palabras, 9yo haré que vengan todos los pueblos del norte, y también mi siervo Nabucodonosor, rey de Babilonia. Los traeré contra este país, contra sus habitantes y contra todas las naciones vecinas, y los *destruiré por completo: ¡los convertiré en objeto de horror, de burla y de eterna desolación! —afirma el SEÑOR—. 10Haré que desaparezcan entre ellos los gritos de gozo y alegría, los cantos de bodas, el ruido del molino y la luz de la lámpara. 11Todo este país quedará reducido a horror y desolación, y estas naciones servirán al rey de Babilonia durante setenta años."

12»Pero cuando se hayan cumplido los setenta años, yo castigaré por su iniquidad al rey de Babilonia y a aquella nación, país de los *caldeos, y los convertiré en desolación perpetua —afirma el SEÑOR—. 13Haré que vengan sobre ese país todas las amenazas que le anuncié, y todo lo que está registrado en este libro y que Jeremías ha profetizado contra las naciones. 14Los caldeos, a su vez, caerán bajo el yugo de muchas naciones y reyes poderosos. Así les daré lo que merecen su conducta y sus hechos.»

15El SEÑOR, el Dios de Israel, me dijo: «Toma de mi mano esta copa del vino de mi ira, y dásela a beber a todas las naciones a las que yo te envíe. 16Cuando ellas la beban, se tambalearán y perderán el juicio, a causa de la espada que voy a enviar contra ellos.»

17Tomé de la mano del SEÑOR la copa, y se la di a beber a todas las naciones a las cuales el SEÑOR me envió: 18a Jerusalén y a las ciudades de Judá, a sus reyes y a sus jefes, para convertirlos en ruinas, en motivo de horror, burla y maldición, como hoy se puede ver. 19También se la di a beber al faraón, rey de Egipto, y a sus siervos y jefes y a todo su pueblo; 20a todos los forasteros, a todos los reyes del país de Uz, y a todos los reyes del país de los filisteos: a los de Ascalón, Gaza y Ecrón, y a los sobrevivientes de Asdod; 21a Edom y Moab, y a los hijos de Amón; 22a todos los reyes de Tiro y de Sidón; a todos los reyes de las costas al otro lado del mar; 23a Dedán, Temá y Buz; a todos los pueblos que se rapan las sienes; 24a todos los reyes de Arabia; a todos los reyes de las diferentes tribus del desierto; 25a todos los reyes de Zimri, Elam y Media; 26a todos los reyes del norte, cercanos o lejanos entre sí, y a todos los reinos que están sobre la faz de la tierra. Y después de ellos beberá el rey de Sesac.s

27«Tú les dirás: "Así dice el SEÑOR Todopoderoso, el Dios de Israel: 'Beban, emborráchense, vomiten y caigan para no levantarse más, por causa de la

---

r 23:33 *mensaje.* Juego de palabras aquí y en los vv. siguientes; el vocablo hebreo también significa *carga.*
s 25:26 *Sesac* es un criptograma que alude a Babilonia.

espada que estoy por mandar contra ustedes.' " 28Pero si se niegan a tomar de tu mano la copa y beberla, tú les dirás: "Así dice el SEÑOR Todopoderoso: '¡Tendrán que beberla!' 29Desataré calamidades contra la ciudad que lleva mi *nombre. ¿Y creen ustedes que no los voy a castigar? Al contrario, serán castigados —afirma el SEÑOR Todopoderoso—, porque yo desenvaino la espada contra todos los habitantes de la tierra."

30»Tú, Jeremías, profetiza contra ellos todas estas palabras:

»"Ruge el SEÑOR desde lo alto;
   desde su *santa morada hace tronar su voz.
Ruge violento contra su rebaño,
   grita como los que pisan la uva,
   contra todos los habitantes del mundo.
31El estruendo llega hasta los confines de la
     tierra,
   porque el SEÑOR litiga contra las naciones;
enjuicia a todos los *mortales,
   y pasa por la espada a los malvados"»,
                    afirma el SEÑOR.

32Así dice el SEÑOR Todopoderoso:

«La calamidad se extiende de nación en
     nación;
una terrible tempestad se desata
   desde los confines de la tierra.»

33En aquel día, las víctimas del SEÑOR quedarán tendidas de un extremo a otro de la tierra. Nadie las llorará ni las recogerá ni las enterrará; se quedarán sobre la faz de la tierra, como el estiércol.

34Giman, *pastores, y clamen;
   revuélquense en el polvo, jefes del rebaño,
porque les ha llegado el día de la matanza;
     serán dispersados, y caerán como carneros
     escogidos.t
35Los pastores no tendrán escapatoria;
   no podrán huir los jefes del rebaño.
36Escuchen el clamor de los pastores
   y el gemido de los jefes del rebaño,
porque el SEÑOR destruye sus pastizales.
37Las hermosas praderas son asoladas,
   a causa de la ardiente ira del SEÑOR.
38Como león que deja abandonada su guarida,
   el SEÑOR ha dejado desolado su país,
a causa de la espadau devastadora,
   a causa de la ardiente ira del SEÑOR.

Jeremías bajo amenaza de muerte

26 Al comienzo del reinado de Joacim hijo de Josías, rey de Judá, vino a Jeremías esta palabra del SEÑOR: 2«Así dice el SEÑOR: "Párate en el atrio de la casa del SEÑOR, y di todas las palabras que yo te ordene a todas las ciudades de Judá que vienen a adorar en la casa del SEÑOR. No omitas ni una sola palabra. 3Tal vez te hagan caso y se conviertan de su mal *camino. Si lo hacen, me arrepentiré del mal que pensaba hacerles por causa de sus malas acciones. 4Tú les advertirás que así dice el SEÑOR: 'Si no me obedecen ni se ciñen a la *ley que yo les he entregado, 5y si no escuchan las palabras de mis siervos los profetas, a quienes una y otra vez he enviado y ustedes han desobedecido, 6entonces haré con esta casa

lo mismo que hice con Siló: ¡Haré de esta ciudad una maldición para todas las naciones de la tierra!' "»

7Los sacerdotes, los profetas y el pueblo entero oyeron estas palabras que el profeta Jeremías pronunció en la casa del SEÑOR. 8Pero en cuanto Jeremías terminó de decirle al pueblo todo lo que el SEÑOR le había ordenado, los sacerdotes y los profetas y todo el pueblo lo apresaron y le dijeron: «¡Vas a morir! ¿Por qué has profetizado en el *nombre del SEÑOR que esta casa se quedará como Siló, y que esta ciudad quedará desolada y deshabitada?» Y todo el pueblo que estaba en la casa del SEÑOR se abalanzó sobre Jeremías.

10Cuando los jefes de Judá escucharon estas cosas, fueron del palacio del rey a la casa del SEÑOR, y se apostaron a la entrada de la Puerta Nueva del templo. 11Allí los sacerdotes y los profetas dijeron a los jefes y a todo el pueblo: «Este hombre debe ser condenado a muerte, porque ha profetizado contra esta ciudad, tal como ustedes lo han escuchado con sus propios oídos.»

12Pero Jeremías les dijo a todos los jefes y a todo el pueblo: «El SEÑOR me envió para profetizar contra esta casa y contra esta ciudad todas las cosas que ustedes han escuchado. 13Así que enmienden ya su conducta y sus acciones, y obedezcan al SEÑOR su Dios, y el SEÑOR se arrepentirá del mal que les ha anunciado. 14En cuanto a mí, estoy en manos de ustedes; hagan conmigo lo que mejor les parezca. 15Pero sepan que si ustedes me matan, estarán derramando sangre inocente sobre ustedes mismos y sobre los habitantes de esta ciudad. Lo cierto es que el SEÑOR me ha enviado a que les anuncie claramente todas estas cosas.»

16Los jefes y todo el pueblo dijeron a los sacerdotes y a los profetas: «Este hombre no debe ser condenado a muerte, porque nos ha hablado en el nombre del SEÑOR nuestro Dios.»

17Entonces algunos de los *ancianos del país se levantaron y le recordaron a toda la asamblea del pueblo 18que, durante el reinado de Ezequías, Miqueas de Moréset había profetizado a todo el pueblo de Judá:

«Así dice el SEÑOR *Todopoderoso:
"Sión será arada como un campo,
Jerusalén quedará en ruinas,
   y la montaña del templo se volverá un
     bosque."

19»¿Acaso Ezequías, rey de Judá, y todo su pueblo mataron a Miqueas? ¿No es verdad que Ezequías temió al SEÑOR y le pidió su ayuda, y que el SEÑOR se arrepintió del mal que les había anunciado? Sin embargo, nosotros estamos por provocar nuestro propio mal.»

20Hubo también otro profeta, de nombre Urías hijo de Semaías, de Quiriat Yearín, que profetizaba en el nombre del SEÑOR. Éste profetizó contra la ciudad y contra el país, tal y como lo hizo Jeremías. 21Cuando el rey Joacim y sus funcionarios y jefes oyeron sus palabras, el rey intentó matarlo; pero al enterarse Urías, tuvo miedo y escapó a Egipto. 22Después el rey Joacim envió a Egipto a Elnatán hijo de Acbor, junto con otros hombres, 23y ellos sacaron de Egipto a Urías y lo llevaron ante el rey Joacim, quien mandó que mataran a Urías a filo de espada, y que arrojaran su cadáver a la fosa común.

---

t 25:34 *carneros escogidos* (LXX); *vasijas escogidas* (TM).   u 25:38 *la espada* (mss. hebreos, LXX y Targum; véanse también Jer 46:16 y 50:16); *la ira* (TM).

24Sin embargo, Ajicán hijo de Safán protegió a Jeremías y no permitió que cayera en manos del pueblo ni que lo mataran.

Parábola del yugo

27 Al comienzo del reinado de Sedequías hijo de Josías, rey de Judá, vino a Jeremías esta palabra del SEÑOR:

2Así me dijo el SEÑOR: «Hazte un yugo y unas correas, y póntelos sobre el cuello. 3Envía luego a los reyes de Edom, Moab, Amón, Tiro y Sidón, un mensaje por medio de los mensajeros que vienen a Jerusalén para ver a Sedequías, rey de Judá. 4Entrégales este mensaje para sus señores: "Así dice el SEÑOR *Todopoderoso, el Dios de Israel: 'Digan a sus señores: 5Yo, con mi gran poder y mi brazo poderoso, hice la tierra, y los *hombres y los animales que están sobre ella, y puedo dárselos a quien me plazca. 6Ahora mismo entrego todos estos países en manos de mi siervo Nabucodonosor, rey de Babilonia, y hasta las bestias del campo las he puesto bajo su poder. 7Todas las naciones le servirán a él, y a su hijo y a su nieto, hasta que también a su país le llegue la hora y sea sometido por numerosas naciones y grandes reyes. 8Y si alguna nación o reino rehúsa someterse a Nabucodonosor, rey de Babilonia, y no dobla el cuello bajo el yugo del rey de Babilonia, yo castigaré a esa nación con espada, hambre y pestilencia, hasta que Nabucodonosor la destruya por completo —afirma el SEÑOR—.

9»" 'Por tanto, no les hagan caso a sus profetas ni a sus adivinos, intérpretes de sueños, astrólogos y hechiceros, que les dicen que no se sometan al rey de Babilonia. 10Las mentiras que ellos les profetizan sólo sirven para que ustedes se alejen de su propia tierra, y para que yo los expulse y mueran. 11En cambio, a la nación que doble el cuello bajo el yugo del rey de Babilonia y se someta a él —afirma el SEÑOR—, yo la dejaré en su propia tierra para que la trabaje y viva en ella.' "»

12A Sedequías, rey de Judá, le dije lo mismo: «Doblen el cuello bajo el yugo del rey de Babilonia; sométanse a él y a su pueblo, y seguirán con vida. 13¿Para qué van a morir tú y tu pueblo por la espada, el hambre y la pestilencia, tal como lo ha prometido el SEÑOR a toda nación que no se someta al rey de Babilonia? 14No le hagan caso a las palabras de los profetas que les dicen que no se sometan al rey de Babilonia, porque lo que les profetizan son mentiras. 15"¡Yo no los envié! —afirma el SEÑOR—. Ellos profetizan mentiras en mi *nombre, que sólo servirán para que yo los expulse a ustedes, y mueran tanto ustedes como sus profetas." »

16También les comuniqué a los sacerdotes y a todo el pueblo que así dice el SEÑOR:

«No les hagan caso a los profetas que les aseguran que muy pronto les serán devueltos de Babilonia los utensilios de la casa del SEÑOR. ¡Tales profecías son puras mentiras! 17No les hagan caso. Sométanse al rey de Babilonia, y seguirán con vida. ¿Por qué ha de convertirse en ruinas esta ciudad? 18Si de veras son profetas y tienen palabra del SEÑOR, que le supliquen al SEÑOR Todopoderoso que no sean llevados a Babilonia los utensilios que aún quedan en la casa del SEÑOR, y en el palacio del rey de Judá y en Jerusalén.

19»En cuanto a las columnas, la fuente de agua, las bases y los demás utensilios que quedaron en esta ciudad, 20los cuales no se llevó Nabucodonosor, rey de Babilonia, cuando deportó de Jerusalén a Babilonia a Jeconías hijo de Joacim, rey de Judá, junto con todos los nobles de Judá y Jerusalén, 21es decir, en cuanto a los utensilios que quedaron en la casa del SEÑOR y en el palacio del rey de Judá y en Jerusalén, así dice el SEÑOR Todopoderoso, el Dios de Israel: 22"Todo esto será llevado a Babilonia —afirma el SEÑOR—, y allí permanecerá hasta el día en que yo lo vaya a buscar y lo devuelva a este lugar." »

Jananías, el falso profeta

28 En el quinto mes de ese mismo año cuarto, es decir, al comienzo del reinado de Sedequías, rey de Judá, el profeta Jananías hijo de Azur, que era de Gabaón, me dijo en la casa del SEÑOR, en presencia de los sacerdotes y de todo el pueblo:

2—Así dice el SEÑOR *Todopoderoso, el Dios de Israel: "Voy a quebrar el yugo del rey de Babilonia. 3Dentro de dos años devolveré a este lugar todos los utensilios que Nabucodonosor, rey de Babilonia, se llevó de la casa del SEÑOR a Babilonia. 4También haré que vuelvan a este lugar Jeconías hijo de Joacim, rey de Judá, y todos los que fueron deportados de Judá a Babilonia. ¡Voy a quebrar el yugo del rey de Babilonia! Yo, el SEÑOR, lo afirmo."

5En presencia de los sacerdotes y de todo el pueblo que estaba en la casa del SEÑOR, el profeta Jeremías le respondió al profeta Jananías:

6—¡Amén! Que así lo haga el SEÑOR. Que cumpla el SEÑOR las palabras que has profetizado. Que devuelva a este lugar los utensilios de la casa del SEÑOR y a todos los que fueron deportados a Babilonia. 7Pero presta atención a lo que voy a decirles a ti y a todo el pueblo: 8Los profetas que nos han precedido profetizaron guerra, hambre y pestilencia contra numerosas naciones y grandes reinos. 9Pero a un profeta que anuncia *paz se le reconoce como profeta verdaderamente enviado por el SEÑOR, sólo si se cumplen sus palabras.

10Entonces el profeta Jananías tomó el yugo que estaba sobre el cuello del profeta Jeremías, y lo quebró. 11Y dijo en presencia de todo el pueblo:

—Así dice el SEÑOR: "De esta manera voy a quebrar, dentro de dos años, el yugo de Nabucodonosor, rey de Babilonia, que pesa sobre el cuello de todas las naciones."

El profeta Jeremías, por su parte, optó por seguir su camino.

12Algún tiempo después de que el profeta Jananías quebrara el yugo que pesaba sobre el cuello de Jeremías, la palabra del SEÑOR vino a este profeta:

13«Ve y adviértele a Jananías que así dice el SEÑOR: "Tú has quebrado un yugo de madera, pero yo haré w en su lugar un yugo de hierro. 14Porque así dice el SEÑOR Todopoderoso, el Dios de Israel: 'Voy a poner un yugo de hierro sobre el cuello de todas estas naciones, para someterlas a Nabucodonosor, rey de Babilonia, y ellas se sujetarán a él. También a las bestias del campo las someteré a su poder.' "»

Entonces el profeta Jeremías le dijo al profeta Jananías:

—Presta mucha atención. A pesar de que el SEÑOR no te ha enviado, tú has hecho que este pueblo confíe en una mentira. 16Por eso, así dice el SEÑOR: "Voy a hacer que desaparezcas de la faz de la tierra. Puesto que has incitado a la rebelión contra el SEÑOR, este mismo año morirás."

17En efecto, el profeta Jananías murió en el mes séptimo de ese mismo año.

---

v 27:20 Jeconías. Es decir, Joaquín; también en 28:4. w 28:13 yo haré (LXX); tú harás (TM).

Carta a los exiliados

29 Ésta es la carta que el profeta Jeremías envió desde Jerusalén al resto de los *ancianos que estaban en el exilio, a los sacerdotes y los profetas, y a todo el pueblo que Nabucodonosor había desterrado de Jerusalén a Babilonia. ²Esto sucedió después de que el rey Jeconías había salido de Jerusalén, junto con la reina madre, los *eunucos, los jefes de Judá y de Jerusalén, los artesanos y los herreros. ³La carta fue enviada por medio de Elasá hijo de Safán, y de Guemarías hijo de Jilquías, a quienes Sedequías, rey de Judá, había enviado al rey Nabucodonosor, rey de Babilonia. La carta decía:

⁴Así dice el SEÑOR *Todopoderoso, el Dios de Israel, a todos los que he deportado de Jerusalén a Babilonia: ⁵«Construyan casas y habítenlas; planten huertos y coman de su fruto. ⁶Cásense, y tengan hijos e hijas; y casen a sus hijos e hijas, para que a su vez ellos les den nietos. Multiplíquense allá, y no disminuyan. ⁷Además, busquen el *bienestar de la ciudad adonde los he deportado, y pidan al SEÑOR por ella, porque el bienestar de ustedes depende del bienestar de la ciudad.» ⁸Así dice el SEÑOR Todopoderoso, el Dios de Israel: «No se dejen engañar por los profetas ni por los adivinos que están entre ustedes. No hagan caso de los sueños que ellos tienen.ˣ ⁹Lo que ellos les profetizan en mi *nombre es una mentira. Yo no los he enviado», afirma el SEÑOR.

¹⁰Así dice el SEÑOR: «Cuando a Babilonia se le hayan cumplido los setenta años, yo los visitaré; y haré honor a mi promesa en favor de ustedes, y los haré volver a este lugar. ¹¹Porque yo sé muy bien los planes que tengo para ustedes —afirma el SEÑOR—, planes de bienestar y no de calamidad, a fin de darles un futuro y una esperanza. ¹²Entonces ustedes me invocarán, y vendrán a suplicarme, y yo los escucharé. ¹³Me buscarán y me encontrarán, cuando me busquen de todo *corazón. ¹⁴Me dejaré encontrar —afirma el SEÑOR—, y los haré volver del cautiverio.ʸ Yo los reuniré de todas las naciones y de todos los lugares adonde los haya dispersado, y los haré volver al lugar del cual los deporté», afirma el SEÑOR.

¹⁵Ustedes podrán decir: «El SEÑOR nos ha dado profetas en Babilonia», ¹⁶pero esto es lo que dice el SEÑOR acerca del rey que ocupa el trono de David, y acerca de todo el pueblo que aún queda en esta ciudad, es decir, de sus hermanos que no fueron con ustedes al exilio. ¹⁷Así dice el SEÑOR Todopoderoso: «Voy a mandar contra ellos la espada, el hambre y la pestilencia. Haré que sean como higos podridos, que de tan malos no se pueden comer. ¹⁸Los perseguiré con espada, hambre y pestilencia, y haré que sean motivo de espanto para todos los reinos de la tierra, y una maldición y objeto de horror, de burla y de escarnio en todas las naciones por donde yo los disperse. ¹⁹Porque ustedes no han escuchado ni han hecho caso de las palabras que, una y otra vez, les envié por medio de mis siervos los profetas —afirma el SEÑOR—.

²⁰»Pero ahora todos ustedes los exiliados que hice deportar de Jerusalén a Babilonia, ¡obedezcan mi palabra!» ²¹Así dice el SEÑOR Todo-poderoso, el Dios de Israel, acerca de Acab hijo de Colaías, y de Sedequías hijo de Maseías, que les profetizan una mentira en mi nombre: «Voy a entregarlos en manos de Nabucodonosor, rey de Babilonia, y él los matará ante sus propios ojos. ²²Por culpa de ellos, todos los deportados de Judá que están en Babilonia pronunciarán esta maldición: "Que haga el SEÑOR contigo lo mismo que hizo con Sedequías y Acab, a quienes el rey de Babilonia asó en el fuego." ²³Porque cometieron una infamia en Israel: adulteraron con la mujer de su prójimo y dijeron mentiras en mi nombre, cosas que jamás les ordené. Yo lo sé, y de eso soy testigo», afirma el SEÑOR.

Mensaje de Semaías

²⁴También a Semaías hijo de Nejelán le comunicarás ²⁵que así dice el SEÑOR *Todopoderoso, el Dios de Israel: «Tú, en tu propio nombre, enviaste cartas a todo el pueblo que está en Jerusalén, al sacerdote Sofonías hijo de Maseías, y a todos los sacerdotes. En esas cartas decías: ²⁶"El SEÑOR te ha puesto como sacerdote en lugar del sacerdote Joyadá, para que vigiles en la casa del SEÑOR. A todo loco que se haga pasar por profeta, lo pondrás en el cepo y en el calabozo. ²⁷¿Por qué, pues, no has reprendido a Jeremías de Anatot, que entre ustedes se hace pasar por profeta? ²⁸Resulta que él nos envió un mensaje a Babilonia, en el cual decía: 'La deportación va a durar mucho tiempo; así que construyan casas, y habítenlas; planten huertos y coman de su fruto.' "»

²⁹El sacerdote Sofonías leyó esta carta al profeta Jeremías. ³⁰Entonces vino a Jeremías la palabra del SEÑOR: ³¹«Comunícales a todos los deportados que así dice el SEÑOR acerca de Semaías de Nejelán: "Puesto que Semaías les ha profetizado sin que yo lo haya enviado, y les ha hecho confiar en una mentira, ³²yo, el SEÑOR, castigaré a Semaías de Nejelán y a su descendencia, porque ha incitado al pueblo a rebelarse contra mí. Ninguno de su familia vivirá para contar el bien que le haré a mi pueblo"», afirma el SEÑOR.

Restauración de Israel

30 La palabra del SEÑOR vino a Jeremías: ²«Así dice el SEÑOR, el Dios de Israel: "Escribe en un libro todas las palabras que te he dicho. ³Porque vienen días —afirma el SEÑOR— cuando yo haré volver del cautiverio a mi pueblo Israel y Judá, ᶻ y los traeré a la tierra que di a sus antepasados, y la poseerán"», afirma el SEÑOR.

⁴Esto fue lo que el SEÑOR le dijo a Jeremías acerca de Israel y Judá:

⁵«Así dice el SEÑOR:

»"Hemos escuchado un grito de espanto;
    no hay *paz, sino terror.
⁶Pregunten y vean
    si acaso los varones dan a luz.
¿Por qué, pues, veo a todos los *hombres
    con las manos sobre las caderas,
    como mujeres con dolores de parto?
¿Por qué han palidecido
    todos los rostros?
⁷¡Ay! Será un día terrible,
    un día que no tiene parangón.
Será un tiempo de angustia para Jacob,
    pero será librado de ella.

ˣ **29:8** *que ellos tienen.* Lit. *que ustedes hacen soñar.* ʸ **29:14** *los haré volver del cautiverio.* Alt. *cambiaré la suerte de ustedes.*
ᶻ **30:3** *haré volver del cautiverio a.* Alt. *cambiaré la suerte de.*

8»"En aquel día —afirma el SEÑOR
      *Todopoderoso—,
    quebraré el yugo que mi pueblo lleva sobre
      el cuello,
romperé sus ataduras,
    y ya no serán esclavos de extranjeros.
9Servirán al SEÑOR, su Dios,
    y a David, a quien pondré como su rey.

10»"No temas, Jacob, siervo mío;
    no te asustes, Israel
             —afirma el SEÑOR—.
A ti, Jacob, te libraré de ese país lejano;
    a tus descendientes los libraré del exilio.
Volverás a vivir en paz y tranquilidad,
    y ya nadie te infundirá temor.
11Porque yo estoy contigo para salvarte
             —afirma el SEÑOR—.
Destruiré por completo a todas las naciones
    entre las que te había dispersado.
Pero a ti no te destruiré del todo,
    sino que te castigaré con *justicia;
    ¡de ninguna manera quedarás impune!"

12»Así dice el SEÑOR:

»"Tu herida es incurable,
    tu llaga no tiene remedio.
13No hay quien defienda tu causa;
    no hay remedio para tu mal
    ni sanidad para tu enfermedad.
14Todos tus amantes te han olvidado;
    ya no se ocupan de ti.
Por causa de tu enorme iniquidad,
    y por tus muchos pecados,
te he golpeado, te he corregido,
    como lo haría un adversario cruel.
15¿Por qué te quejas de tus heridas,
    si tu dolor es incurable?
Por causa de tu enorme iniquidad
    y por tus muchos pecados,
yo te he tratado así.

16»"Todos los que te devoren serán devorados;
    todos tus enemigos serán deportados.
Todos los que te saqueen serán saqueados;
    todos los que te despojen serán
      despojados.
17Pero yo te restauraré
    y sanaré tus heridas
             —afirma el SEÑOR—
porque te han llamado la Desechada,
    la pobre *Sión, la que a nadie le importa."

18»Así dice el SEÑOR:

»"Restauraré las fortunas de las carpas de
    Jacob,
    y tendré compasión de sus moradas;
la ciudad resurgirá sobre sus ruinas,
    y el palacio se asentará en el lugar debido.
19Surgirán de ellos cánticos de gratitud,
    y gritos de alegría.
Multiplicaré su descendencia, y no
    disminuirá;
    los honraré, y no serán menospreciados.
20Sus hijos volverán a ser como antes;
    ante mí será restablecida su comunidad,
    pero castigaré a todos sus opresores.
21De entre ellos surgirá su líder;
    uno de ellos será su gobernante.

Lo acercaré hacia mí, y él estará a mi lado,
    pues ¿quién arriesgaría su vida por
      acercarse a mí?
                  —afirma el SEÑOR—.
22Ustedes serán mi pueblo,
    y yo seré su Dios."»

23La tempestad del SEÑOR
    ha estallado con furor;
una tempestad huracanada
    se ha desatado sobre los malvados.
24La ardiente ira del SEÑOR no pasará
    hasta que haya realizado del todo
    los propósitos de su *corazón.
Todo esto lo comprenderán ustedes
    al final de los tiempos.

31 «En aquel tiempo —afirma el SEÑOR— seré el Dios de todas las familias de Israel, y ellos serán mi pueblo.»

2Así dice el SEÑOR:

«El pueblo que escapó de la espada
    ha hallado gracia en el desierto;
Israel va en busca de su reposo.»

3Hace mucho tiempoa se me apareció el SEÑOR y me dijo:

«Con amor eterno te he amado;
    por eso te sigo con fidelidad,
4oh virginal Israel.
Te edificaré de nuevo;
    ¡sí, serás reedificada!
De nuevo tomarás panderetas
    y saldrás a bailar con alegría.
5Volverás a plantar viñedos
    en las colinas de Samaria,
y quienes los planten
    gozarán de sus frutos
6Vendrá un día en que los centinelas
    gritarán por las colinas de Efraín:
"¡Vengan, subamos a *Sión,
    al monte del SEÑOR, nuestro Dios!"»

7Así dice el SEÑOR:

«Canten jubilosos en honor de Jacob;
    griten de alegría por la mejor de las
      naciones.
Hagan oír sus alabanzas y clamen:
    "¡Salva, SEÑOR, a tu pueblo;
salva al remanente de Israel!"
8Yo los traeré del país del norte;
    los reuniré de los confines de la tierra.
    ¡Volverá una gran multitud!
Entre ellos vendrán ciegos y cojos,
    embarazadas y parturientas.
9Entre llantos vendrán,
    y entre consuelos los conduciré.
Los guiaré a corrientes de agua
    por un camino llano
    en el que no tropezarán.
Yo soy el padre de Israel;
    mi primogénito es Efraín.

10»Naciones, escuchen la palabra del SEÑOR,
    y anuncien en las costas más lejanas:
"El que dispersó a Israel, lo reunirá;
    lo cuidará como un *pastor a su rebaño."
11Porque el SEÑOR rescató a Jacob;
    lo redimió de una mano más poderosa.

---

a **31:3** *Hace mucho tiempo.* Alt. *Desde lejos.*

¹²Vendrán y cantarán jubilosos en las alturas de
      Sión;
   disfrutarán de las bondades del SEÑOR:
el trigo, el vino nuevo y el aceite,
   las crías de las ovejas y las vacas.
Serán como un jardín bien regado,
   y no volverán a desmayar.
¹³Entonces las jóvenes danzarán con alegría,
   y los jóvenes junto con los ancianos.
Convertiré su duelo en gozo, y los consolaré;
   transformaré su dolor en alegría.
¹⁴Colmaré de abundancia a los sacerdotes,
   y saciaré con mis bienes a mi pueblo»,
                     afirma el SEÑOR.

¹⁵Así dice el SEÑOR:

«Se oye un grito en Ramá,
   lamentos y amargo llanto.
Es Raquel, que llora por sus hijos
   y no quiere ser consolada;
   ¡sus hijos ya no existen!»

¹⁶Así dice el SEÑOR:

«Reprime tu llanto,
   las lágrimas de tus ojos,
pues tus obras tendrán su recompensa:
   tus hijos volverán del país enemigo
                —afirma el SEÑOR—.
¹⁷Se vislumbra esperanza en tu futuro:
   tus hijos volverán a su patria
                —afirma el SEÑOR—.

¹⁸»Por cierto, he escuchado el lamento de
      Efraín:
   "Me has escarmentado como a un ternero
      sin domar,
   y he aceptado tu *corrección.
Hazme volver, y seré restaurado;
   porque tú, mi Dios, eres el SEÑOR.
¹⁹Yo me aparté, pero me *arrepentí;
   al comprenderlo me di golpes de pecho.ᵇ
Me siento avergonzado y humillado
   porque cargo con el oprobio de mi
      juventud."

²⁰¿Acaso no es Efraín mi hijo amado?
   ¿Acaso no es mi niño preferido?
Cada vez que lo reprendo,
   vuelvo a acordarme de él.
Por él mi *corazón se conmueve;
   por él siento mucha compasión
                —afirma el SEÑOR—.

²¹»Ponte señales en el camino,
   coloca marcas por donde pasaste,
fíjate bien en el sendero.
¡Vuelve, virginal Israel;
   vuelve a tus ciudades!
²²¿Hasta cuándo andarás errante,
   hija infiel?
El SEÑOR creará algo nuevo en la tierra,
   la mujer regresará a su esposo.»ᶜ

²³Así dice el SEÑOR *Todopoderoso, el Dios de
Israel: «Cuando yo cambie su suerte, en la tierra de
Judá y en sus ciudades volverá a decirse:

»"Monte *santo, morada de justicia:
   ¡que el SEÑOR te bendiga!"

²⁴Allí habitarán juntos Judá y todas sus ciudades, los
agricultores y los pastores de rebaños. ²⁵Daré de beber a los sedientos y saciaré a los que estén agotados.»
   ²⁶En ese momento me desperté, y abrí los ojos.
Había tenido un sueño agradable.
   ²⁷»Vienen días —afirma el SEÑOR— en que con
la simiente de *hombres y de animales sembraré el
pueblo de Israel y la tribu de Judá. ²⁸Y así como he estado vigilándolos para arrancar y derribar, para destruir y demoler, y para traer calamidad, así también
habré de vigilarlos para construir y plantar —afirma
el SEÑOR—. ²⁹En aquellos días no volverá a decirse:

»"Los padres comieron uvas agrias,
   y a los hijos se les destemplaron los
      dientes."

³⁰Al contrario, al que coma uvas agrias se le destem-
plarán los dientes, es decir, que cada uno morirá por
su propia iniquidad.
   ³¹»Vienen días —afirma el SEÑOR— en que haré
un nuevo *pacto con el pueblo de Israel y con la tribu
de Judá. ³²No será un pacto como el que hice con sus
antepasados el día en que los tomé de la mano y los
saqué de Egipto, ya que ellos lo quebrantaron a pesar
de que yo era su esposo —afirma el SEÑOR—.
   ³³»Este es el pacto que después de aquel tiempo
haré con el pueblo de Israel —afirma el SEÑOR—:
Pondré mi *ley en su *mente, y la escribiré en su *corazón. Yo seré su Dios, y ellos serán mi pueblo. ³⁴Ya
no tendrá nadie que enseñar a su prójimo, ni dirá nadie a su hermano: "¡Conoce al SEÑOR!", porque todos,
desde el más pequeño hasta el más grande, me conocerán —afirma el SEÑOR—. Yo les perdonaré su iniquidad, y nunca más me acordaré de sus pecados.»

³⁵Así dice el SEÑOR,
   cuyo *nombre es el SEÑOR Todopoderoso,
quien estableció el sol para alumbrar el día,
   y la luna y las estrellas para alumbrar la
      noche,
   y agita el mar para que rujan sus olas:

³⁶«Si alguna vez fallaran estas leyes
            —afirma el SEÑOR—,
entonces la descendencia de Israel
   ya nunca más sería mi nación especial.»

³⁷Así dice el SEÑOR:

«Si se pudieran medir los cielos en lo alto,
   y en lo bajo explorar los cimientos de la
      tierra,
entonces yo rechazaría a la descendencia de
      Israel
   por todo lo que ha hecho
            —afirma el SEÑOR—.

³⁸»Vienen días —afirma el SEÑOR—, en que la
ciudad del SEÑOR será reconstruida, desde la torre
de Jananel hasta la puerta de la Esquina. ³⁹El cordel
para medir se extenderá en línea recta, desde allí
hasta la colina de Gareb, y luego girará hacia Goa.
⁴⁰Y todo el valle donde se arrojan los cadáveres y las
cenizas, y todos los campos, hasta el arroyo de Cedrón y hasta la puerta de los Caballos, en la esquina
oriental, estarán consagrados al SEÑOR. ¡Nunca más
la ciudad será arrancada ni derribada!»

Parábola del terreno

32 Esta es la palabra del SEÑOR, que vino a Jere-
      mías en el año décimo del reinado de Sede-

ᵇ **31:19** *de pecho.* Lit. *en el muslo.*   ᶜ **31:22** *regresará a su esposo.* Frase de difícil traducción.

quías en Judá, es decir, en el año dieciocho de Nabucodonosor. ²En aquel tiempo el ejército del rey de Babilonia mantuvo sitiada a Jerusalén, y el profeta Jeremías estuvo preso en el patio de la guardia del palacio real.

³Sedequías, el rey de Judá, lo tenía preso y le reprochaba: «¿Por qué andas profetizando: "Así dice el SEÑOR"? Andas proclamando que el SEÑOR dice: "Voy a entregar esta ciudad en manos del rey de Babilonia, y él la tomará; ⁴y Sedequías, rey de Judá, no escapará de la mano de los *babilonios, sino que será entregado en manos del rey de Babilonia y tendrá que enfrentarse con él cara a cara." ⁵Además, dices que el SEÑOR afirma: "Nabucodonosor se llevará a Sedequías a Babilonia, y allí se quedará hasta que yo vuelva a ocuparme de él", y también: "Si ustedes combaten contra los babilonios, no vencerán."»

⁶Jeremías respondió: «La palabra del SEÑOR vino a mí, ⁷y me dijo: "Janamel, hijo de tu tío Salún, vendrá a pedirte que le compres el campo que está en Anatot, pues tienes el derecho y la responsabilidad de comprarlo por ser el pariente más cercano."ᵈ

⁸»En efecto, conforme a la palabra del SEÑOR, mi primo Janamel vino a verme en el patio de la guardia y me dijo: "Compra ahora mi campo que está en Anatot, en el territorio de Benjamín, ya que tú tienes el derecho y la responsabilidad de comprarlo por ser el pariente más cercano." Entonces comprendí que esto era palabra del SEÑOR, ⁹y le compré a mi primo Janamel el campo de Anatot por diecisiete monedas de plata. ¹⁰Reuní a los testigos, firmé la escritura, la sellé, y pagué el precio convenido. ¹¹Luego tomé la copia sellada y la copia abierta de la escritura con las condiciones de compra, ¹²y se las entregué a Baruc, hijo de Nerías y nieto de Maseías, en presencia de Janamel, de los testigos que habían firmado la escritura, y de todos los judíos que estaban sentados en el patio de la guardia. ¹³Con ellos como testigos, le ordené a Baruc: ¹⁴"Así dice el SEÑOR *Todopoderoso, el Dios de Israel: 'Toma la copia sellada y la copia abierta de esta escritura, y guárdalas en una vasija de barro, para que se conserven mucho tiempo.' ¹⁵Porque así dice el SEÑOR Todopoderoso, el Dios de Israel: 'De nuevo volverán a comprarse casas, campos y viñedos en esta tierra.' "

¹⁶»Después de entregarle la escritura a Baruc hijo de Nerías, oré al SEÑOR:

¹⁷»¡Ah, SEÑOR mi Dios! Tú, con tu gran fuerza y tu brazo poderoso, has hecho los cielos y la tierra. Para ti no hay nada imposible. ¹⁸Muestras tu fiel amor a multitud de generaciones, pero también castigas a los hijos por la iniquidad de sus antepasados. ¡Oh Dios grande y fuerte, tu *nombre es el SEÑOR Todopoderoso! ¹⁹Tus proyectos son grandiosos, y magníficas tus obras. Tus ojos observan todo lo que hace la *humanidad, para dar a cada uno lo que merece, según su conducta y los frutos de sus acciones. ²⁰Tú hiciste milagros y prodigios en la tierra de Egipto, y hasta el día de hoy los sigues haciendo, tanto en Israel como en todo el mundo; así te has conquistado la fama que hoy tienes. ²¹Tú, con gran despliegue de poder, y con milagros, prodigios y gran terror, sacaste de Egipto a tu pueblo. ²²Le diste a Israel esta tierra, donde abundan la leche y la miel, tal como se lo habías jurado a sus antepasados. ²³Pero cuando entraron y tomaron po-

sesión de ella, no te obedecieron ni acataron tu *ley, ni tampoco hicieron lo que les habías ordenado. Por eso les enviaste toda esta desgracia. ²⁴Ahora las rampas de ataque han llegado hasta la ciudad para conquistarla. A causa de la espada, el hambre y la pestilencia, la ciudad caerá en manos de los babilonios que la atacan. SEÑOR, todo lo que habías anunciado se está cumpliendo, y tú mismo lo estás viendo. ²⁵SEÑOR mi Dios, a pesar de que la ciudad caerá en manos de los babilonios, tú me has dicho: "Cómprate el campo al contado en presencia de testigos."»

²⁶Entonces vino la palabra del SEÑOR a Jeremías: ²⁷«Yo soy el SEÑOR, Dios de toda la humanidad. ¿Hay algo imposible para mí? ²⁸Por eso, así dice el SEÑOR: Voy a entregar esta ciudad en manos de los babilonios y de Nabucodonosor, su rey, y él la capturará. ²⁹Y los babilonios que ataquen esta ciudad, entrarán en ella y le prenderán fuego, así como a las casas en cuyas azoteas se quemaba incienso a *Baal y, para provocarme a ira, se derramaban libaciones a otros dioses. ³⁰Porque desde su juventud el pueblo de Israel y el de Judá no han hecho sino lo malo delante de mí. El pueblo de Israel no ha dejado de provocarme a ira con la obra de sus manos —afirma el SEÑOR—. ³¹Desde el día en que construyeron esta ciudad hasta hoy, ella ha sido para mí motivo de ira y de furor. Por eso la quitaré de mi presencia, ³²por todo el mal que han cometido los pueblos de Israel y de Judá: ellos, sus reyes, sus jefes, sus sacerdotes y sus profetas, todos los habitantes de Judá y de Jerusalén. ³³Ellos no me miraron de frente, sino que me dieron la espalda. Y aunque una y otra vez les enseñaba, no escuchaban ni aceptaban *corrección. ³⁴Colocaban sus ídolos abominables en la casa que lleva mi nombre, y así la profanaban. ³⁵También construían altares a Baal en el valle de Ben Hinón, para pasar por el fuego a sus hijos e hijas en sacrificio a Moloc, cosa detestable que yo no les había ordenado, y que ni siquiera se me había ocurrido. De ese modo hacían pecar a Judá.

³⁶»Por tanto, así dice el SEÑOR, Dios de Israel, acerca de esta ciudad que, según ustedes, caerá en manos del rey de Babilonia por la espada, el hambre y la pestilencia: ³⁷Voy a reunirlos de todos los países adonde en mi ira, furor y terrible enojo los dispersé, y los haré volver a este lugar para que vivan seguros. ³⁸Ellos serán mi pueblo, y yo seré su Dios. ³⁹Haré que haya coherencia entre su pensamiento y su conducta, a fin de que siempre me teman, para su propio bien y el de sus hijos. ⁴⁰Haré con ellos un *pacto eterno: Nunca dejaré de estar con ellos para mostrarles mi favor; pondré mi temor en sus corazones, y así no se apartarán de mí. ⁴¹Me regocijaré en favorecerlos, y con todo mi *corazón y con toda mi *alma los plantaré firmemente en esta tierra.

⁴²»Así dice el SEÑOR: Tal como traje esta gran calamidad sobre este pueblo, yo mismo voy a traer sobre ellos todo el bien que les he prometido. ⁴³Se comprarán campos en esta tierra, de la cual ustedes dicen: "Es una tierra desolada, sin gente ni animales, porque fue entregada en manos de los babilonios." ⁴⁴En la tierra de Benjamín y en los alrededores de Jerusalén, en las ciudades de Judá, de la región montañosa, de la llanura, y del Néguev, se comprarán campos por dinero, se firmarán escrituras, y se sella-

---

ᵈ **32:7** *el derecho ... más cercano.* Lit. *el derecho de rescate para comprarlo;* también en v. 8 (véase Lv 25:25-28).   ᵉ **32:9** *monedas.* Lit. **siclos.*

rán ante testigos —afirma el SEÑOR—, porque yo cambiaré su suerte.»

Promesas de restauración

33 La palabra del SEÑOR vino a Jeremías por segunda vez, cuando éste aún se hallaba preso en el patio de la guardia: 2«Así dice aquel cuyo *nombre es el SEÑOR, el que hizo la tierra, y la formó y la estableció con firmeza: 3"Clama a mí y te responderé, y te daré a conocer cosas grandes y ocultas que tú no sabes." 4Porque así dice el SEÑOR, Dios de Israel, acerca de las casas de esta ciudad y de los palacios de los reyes de Judá, que van a ser derribados para levantar defensas contra la espada y contra las rampas de asalto: 5"Los *babilonios vienen para atacar la ciudad y llenarla de cadáveres. En mi ira y furor he ocultado mi rostro de esta ciudad; la heriré de muerte a causa de todas sus maldades.

6" "Sin embargo, les daré salud y los curaré; los sanaré y haré que disfruten de abundante *paz y seguridad. 7Cambiaré la suerte de Judá y de Israel, y los reconstruiré como al principio. 8Los *purificaré de todas las iniquidades que cometieron contra mí; les perdonaré todos los pecados con que se rebelaron contra mí. 9Jerusalén será para mí motivo de gozo, de alabanza y de gloria a la vista de todas las naciones de la tierra. Se enterarán de todo el bien que yo le hago, y temerán y temblarán por todo el bienestar y toda la paz que yo le ofrezco.

10»Así dice el SEÑOR: "Ustedes dicen que este lugar está en ruinas, sin gente ni animales. Sin embargo, en las ciudades de Judá y en las calles de Jerusalén, que están desoladas y sin gente ni animales, se oirá de nuevo 11el grito de gozo y alegría, el canto del novio y de la novia, y la voz de los que traen a la casa del SEÑOR ofrendas de acción de gracias y cantan:

»" 'Den gracias al SEÑOR *Todopoderoso,
    porque el SEÑOR es bueno,
    porque su amor es eterno.'

Yo cambiaré la suerte de este país —afirma el SEÑOR—, y volverá a ser como al principio."

12»Así dice el SEÑOR Todopoderoso: "En este lugar que está en ruinas, sin gente ni animales, y en todas sus ciudades, de nuevo habrá pastos en donde los *pastores harán descansar a sus rebaños. 13En las ciudades de la región montañosa, de la llanura, y del Néguev, en el territorio de Benjamín, en los alrededores de Jerusalén y en las ciudades de Judá, las ovejas volverán a ser contadas por los pastores —dice el SEÑOR—.

14»"Llegarán días —afirma el SEÑOR—, en que cumpliré la promesa de bendición que hice al pueblo de Israel y a la tribu de Judá.

15» "En aquellos días, y en aquel tiempo,
    haré que brote de David un renuevo justo,
    y él practicará la justicia y el derecho en el
    país.
16En aquellos días Judá estará a salvo,
    y Jerusalén morará segura.
    Y será llamada así:
    'El SEÑOR es nuestra *justicia.' "

17Porque así dice el SEÑOR: "Nunca le faltará a David un descendiente que ocupe el trono del pueblo de Israel. 18Tampoco a los sacerdotes levitas les faltará un descendiente que en mi presencia ofrezca *holocausto, queme ofrendas de grano, y presente sacrificios todos los días."»

19La palabra del SEÑOR vino a Jeremías: 20«Así dice el SEÑOR: "Si ustedes pudieran romper mi *pacto con el día y mi pacto con la noche, de modo que el día y la noche no llegaran a su debido tiempo, 21también podrían romper mi pacto con mi siervo David, que no tendría un sucesor que ocupara su trono, y con los sacerdotes levitas, que son mis ministros. 22Yo multiplicaré la descendencia de mi siervo David, y la de los levitas, mis ministros, como las incontables estrellas del cielo y los granos de arena del mar."»

23La palabra del SEÑOR vino a Jeremías: 24«¿No te has dado cuenta de que esta gente afirma que yo, el SEÑOR, he rechazado a los dos reinos que había escogido? Con esto desprecian a mi pueblo, y ya no lo consideran una nación. 25Así dice el SEÑOR: "Si yo no hubiera establecido mi pacto con el día ni con la noche, ni hubiera fijado las leyes que rigen el cielo y la tierra, 26entonces habría rechazado a los descendientes de Jacob y de mi siervo David, y no habría escogido a uno de su estirpe para gobernar sobre la descendencia de Abraham, Isaac y Jacob. ¡Pero yo cambiaré su suerte y les tendré compasión!"»

Advertencia al rey Sedequías

34 La palabra del SEÑOR vino a Jeremías cuando Nabucodonosor, rey de Babilonia, estaba atacando a Jerusalén y a sus ciudades vecinas con todo su ejército y con todos los reinos y pueblos de la tierra regidos por él: 2«Así dice el SEÑOR, el Dios de Israel: "Ve y adviértele a Sedequías, rey de Judá, que así dice el SEÑOR: 'Voy a entregar esta ciudad en manos del rey de Babilonia, quien la incendiará. 3Y tú no te escaparás de su poder, porque ciertamente serás capturado y entregado en sus manos. Tus ojos verán los ojos del rey de Babilonia, y él te hablará cara a cara, y serás llevado a Babilonia.'

4» "No obstante, Sedequías, rey de Judá, escucha la promesa del SEÑOR para ti. Así dice el SEÑOR: 'Tú no morirás a filo de espada 5sino en *paz.' También afirma el SEÑOR: 'Yo te prometo que, así como los reyes de antaño que te precedieron quemaron especias por tus antepasados, así también lo harán en tu funeral, lamentándose por ti y clamando: ¡Ay, señor!'."»

6El profeta Jeremías dijo todo esto a Sedequías, rey de Judá, en Jerusalén. 7Mientras tanto, el ejército del rey de Babilonia estaba combatiendo contra Jerusalén y contra las ciudades de Judá que aún quedaban, es decir, Laquis y Azeca, que eran las únicas ciudades fortificadas.

Liberación para los esclavos

8La palabra del SEÑOR vino a Jeremías después de que el rey Sedequías hizo un pacto con todo el pueblo de Jerusalén para dejar libres a los esclavos. 9El acuerdo estipulaba que cada israelita debía dejar libre a sus esclavas y esclavos hebreos, y que nadie debía esclavizar a un compatriota judío. 10Todo el pueblo y los jefes que habían hecho el acuerdo liberaron a sus esclavos, de manera que nadie quedaba obligado a servirlos. 11Pero después se retractaron y volvieron a someter a esclavitud a los que habían liberado.

12Una vez más la palabra del SEÑOR vino a Jeremías: 13«Así dice el SEÑOR, el Dios de Israel: "Yo hice un *pacto con sus antepasados cuando los saqué de Egipto, lugar de esclavitud. Les ordené 14que cada siete años liberaran a todo esclavo hebreo que se hubiera vendido a sí mismo con ellos. Después de haber servido como esclavo durante seis años, debía ser liberado.f Pero sus antepasados no me obedecieron

f **34:14** Véanse Éx 21:2; Dt 15:12.

ni me hicieron caso. 15Ustedes, en cambio, al proclamar la libertad de su prójimo, se habían convertido y habían hecho lo que yo apruebo. Además, se habían comprometido con un pacto en mi presencia, en la casa que lleva mi *nombre. 16Pero ahora se han vuelto atrás y han profanado mi nombre. Cada uno ha obligado a sus esclavas y esclavos que había liberado a someterse de nuevo a la esclavitud."

17»Por tanto, así dice el SEÑOR: "No me han obedecido, pues no han dejado en libertad a sus hermanos. Por tanto, yo proclamo contra ustedes una liberación —afirma el SEÑOR—: dejaré en libertad a la guerra, la pestilencia y el hambre, para que lo que les pase a ustedes sirva de escarmiento para todos los reinos de la tierra. 18Puesto que han violado mi pacto, y no han cumplido las estipulaciones del pacto que acordaron en mi presencia, los trataré como al novillo que cortaron en dos, y entre cuyos pedazos pasaron para rubricar el pacto.g 19A los jefes de Judá y de Jerusalén, y a los oficiales de la corte y a los sacerdotes, y a todo el pueblo que pasaron entre los pedazos del novillo, 20los entregaré en manos de sus enemigos, que atentan contra su vida, y sus cadáveres servirán de alimento a las aves de rapiña y a las fieras del campo.

21»"A Sedequías, rey de Judá, y a sus jefes, los entregaré en manos de sus enemigos, que atentan contra sus vidas, es decir, en poder del ejército del rey de Babilonia, que por el momento se ha replegado. 22Voy a dar una orden —afirma el SEÑOR—, y los haré volver a esta ciudad. La atacarán, y luego de tomarla, la incendiarán. Dejaré las ciudades de Judá en total desolación, sin habitantes."»

El ejemplo de los recabitas

35 La palabra del SEÑOR vino a mí, Jeremías, en los días de Joacim hijo de Josías, rey de Judá: 2«Ve a la familia de los recabitas, e invítalos para que vengan a una de las salas de la casa del SEÑOR, y ofréceles vino.»

3Entonces fui a buscar a Jazanías, hijo de mi tocayo Jeremías y nieto de Jabasinías, y a sus hermanos y a todos sus hijos, y a toda la familia de los recabitas. 4Entonces los llevé a la casa del SEÑOR, a la sala de los hijos de Janán hijo de Igdalías, hombre de Dios. Esta sala se encontraba junto a la de los jefes, que a su vez estaba encima de la de Maseías hijo de Salún, guardián del umbral. 5Les serví a los recabitas jarras y copas llenas de vino, y les dije: «¡Beban!»

6Ellos me respondieron: «Nosotros no bebemos vino, porque Jonadab hijo de Recab, nuestro antepasado, nos ordenó lo siguiente: "Nunca beban vino, ni ustedes ni sus descendientes. 7Tampoco edifiquen casas, ni siembren semillas, ni planten viñedos, ni posean ninguna de estas cosas. Habiten siempre en tiendas de campaña, para que vivan mucho tiempo en esta tierra donde son extranjeros." 8Nosotros obedecemos todo lo que nos ordenó Jonadab hijo de Recab, nuestro antepasado. Nunca bebemos vino, ni tampoco lo hacen nuestras mujeres ni nuestros hijos. 9No edificamos casas para habitarlas; no poseemos viñedos ni campos sembrados. 10Vivimos en tiendas de campaña y obedecemos todo lo que nos ordenó Jonadab, nuestro antepasado. 11Pero cuando Nabucodonosor, rey de Babilonia, invadió esta tierra, dijimos: "Vámonos a Jerusalén, para escapar del ejército *babilonio y del ejército *sirio." Por eso ahora vivimos en Jerusalén.»

12Entonces la palabra del SEÑOR vino a Jeremías: 13«Así dice el SEÑOR *Todopoderoso, el Dios de Israel: "Ve y dile a toda la gente de Judá y Jerusalén: ¿No pueden aprender esta lección, y obedecer mis palabras? —afirma el SEÑOR—. 14Los descendientes de Jonadab hijo de Recab han cumplido con la orden de no beber vino, y hasta el día de hoy no lo beben porque obedecen lo que su antepasado les ordenó. En cambio ustedes, aunque yo les he hablado en repetidas ocasiones, no me han hecho caso. 15Además, no he dejado de enviarles a mis siervos, los profetas, para decirles: 'Conviértanse ya de su mal *camino, enmienden sus acciones y no sigan a otros dioses para servirlos; entonces habitarán en la tierra que yo les he dado a ustedes y a sus antepasados.' Pero ustedes no me han prestado atención; no me han hecho caso. 16Los descendientes de Jonadab hijo de Recab cumplieron la orden dada por su antepasado; en cambio, este pueblo no me obedece."

17»Por eso, así dice el SEÑOR, Dios Todopoderoso, el Dios de Israel: "Voy a enviar contra Judá y contra todos los habitantes de Jerusalén todas las calamidades que ya les he anunciado, porque les hablé y no me obedecieron; los llamé y no me respondieron."»

18Jeremías también les dijo a los recabitas: «Así dice el SEÑOR Todopoderoso, el Dios de Israel: "Por cuanto ustedes han obedecido las órdenes de Jonadab, su antepasado, y han cumplido con todos sus mandamientos y han hecho todo lo que él les ordenó, 19así dice el SEÑOR Todopoderoso, el Dios de Israel: 'Nunca le faltará a Jonadab hijo de Recab un descendiente que esté a mi servicio todos los días.' "»

El rey Joacim quema el rollo de Jeremías

36 Esta palabra del SEÑOR vino a Jeremías en el año cuarto del rey Joacim hijo de Josías: 2«Toma un rollo y escribe en él todas las palabras que desde los tiempos de Josías, desde que comencé a hablarte hasta ahora, te he dicho acerca de Israel, de Judá y de las otras naciones. 3Cuando los de Judá se enteren de todas las calamidades que pienso enviar contra ellos, tal vez abandonen su mal *camino y pueda yo perdonarles su iniquidad y su pecado.»

4Jeremías llamó a Baruc hijo de Nerías, y mientras la dictaba, Baruc escribía en el rollo todo lo que el SEÑOR le había dicho al profeta. 5Luego Jeremías le dio esta orden a Baruc: «Estoy detenido y no puedo ir a la casa del SEÑOR. 6Por tanto, ve a la casa del SEÑOR en el día de ayuno, y lee en voz alta ante el pueblo de Jerusalén las palabras del SEÑOR que he dictado y que escribiste en el rollo. Léeselas también a toda la gente de Judá que haya venido de sus ciudades. 7A lo mejor su oración llega a la presencia del SEÑOR y cada uno se convierte de su mal camino! ¡Ciertamente son terribles la ira y el furor con que el SEÑOR ha amenazado a este pueblo!»

8Baruc hijo de Nerías hizo tal y como se lo había ordenado el profeta Jeremías: Leyó en la casa del SEÑOR las palabras contenidas en el rollo.

9En el mes noveno del año quinto de Joacim hijo de Josías, rey de Judá, todo el pueblo de Jerusalén y todos los que habían venido de las otras ciudades de Judá fueron convocados a ayunar en honor del SEÑOR. 10Baruc se dirigió al atrio superior de la casa del SEÑOR, a la entrada de la Puerta Nueva, y desde la sala de Guemarías hijo de Safán, el cronista, leyó ante todo el pueblo el rollo que contenía las palabras de Jeremías.

g **34:18** Véase Gn 15:9-10,17-18.

11Micaías hijo de Guemarías, nieto de Safán, escuchó todas las palabras del SEÑOR que estaban escritas en el rollo. 12Entonces bajó al palacio del rey, a la sala del cronista, donde estaban reunidos todos los jefes, es decir, el cronista Elisama, Delaías hijo de Semaías, Elnatán hijo de Acbor, Guemarías hijo de Safán, Sedequías hijo de Ananías, y todos los demás jefes. 13Micaías les contó todo lo que había escuchado de lo que Baruc había leído ante el pueblo. 14Entonces todos los jefes enviaron a Yehudi hijo de Netanías, nieto de Selemías y bisnieto de Cusí, para que le dijera a Baruc: «Toma el rollo que has leído ante el pueblo, y ven.» Baruc hijo de Nerías lo tomó y se presentó ante ellos. 15Los jefes le dijeron:

—Siéntate y léenos lo que está en el rollo.

Baruc lo leyó ante ellos. 16Terminada la lectura, se miraron temerosos unos a otros y le dijeron:

—Tenemos que informar de todo esto al rey.

17Luego le preguntaron a Baruc:

—Dinos, ¿cómo fue que escribiste todo esto? ¿Te lo dictó Jeremías?

18—Sí —les respondió Baruc—, él me lo dictó, y yo lo escribí con tinta, en el rollo.

19Entonces los jefes le dijeron a Baruc:

—Tú y Jeremías, vayan a esconderse. ¡Que nadie sepa dónde están!

20Después de dejar el rollo en la sala del cronista Elisama, los jefes se presentaron en el atrio, delante del rey, y lo pusieron al tanto de todo lo ocurrido. 21El rey envió a Yehudi a buscar el rollo, y Yehudi lo tomó de la sala de Elisama y lo leyó en presencia del rey y de todos los jefes que estaban con él. 22Era el mes noveno, y por eso el rey estaba en su casa de invierno, sentado junto a un brasero encendido. 23A medida que Yehudi terminaba de leer tres o cuatro columnas, el rey las cortaba con un estilete de escriba y las echaba al fuego del brasero. Así lo hizo con todo el rollo, hasta que éste se consumió en el fuego. 24Ni el rey ni los jefes que escucharon todas estas palabras tuvieron temor ni se rasgaron las vestiduras. 25Esto sucedió a pesar de que Elnatán, Delaías y Guemarías le habían suplicado al rey que no quemara el rollo; pero el rey no les hizo caso. 26Por el contrario, mandó a Jeramel, su hijo, a Seraías hijo de Azriel, y a Selemías hijo de Abdel que arrestaran al escriba Baruc y al profeta Jeremías. Pero el SEÑOR los había escondido.

27Luego que el rey quemó el rollo con las palabras que Jeremías le había dictado a Baruc, la palabra del SEÑOR vino a Jeremías: 28«Toma otro rollo, y escribe exactamente lo mismo que estaba escrito en el primer rollo quemado por Joacim, rey de Judá. 29Y adviértele a Joacim que así dice el SEÑOR: "Tú quemaste aquel rollo, diciendo: '¿Por qué has escrito en él que con toda seguridad el rey de Babilonia vendrá a destruir esta tierra, y a borrar de ella a toda persona y animal?' " 30Por eso, así dice el SEÑOR acerca de Joacim, rey de Judá: "Ninguno de sus descendientes ocupará el trono de David; su cadáver será arrojado, y quedará expuesto al calor del día y a las heladas de la noche. 31Castigaré la iniquidad de él, la de su descendencia y la de sus siervos. Enviaré contra ellos, y contra los habitantes de Jerusalén y de Judá, todas las calamidades con que los amenacé, porque no me hicieron caso."»

32Entonces Jeremías tomó otro rollo y se lo dio al escriba Baruc hijo de Nerías. Baruc escribió en el rollo todo lo que Jeremías le dictó, lo cual era idéntico a lo escrito en el rollo quemado por el rey Joacim. Se agregaron, además, muchas otras cosas semejantes.

Encarcelamiento de Jeremías

37 Nabucodonosor, rey de Babilonia, puso como rey de Judá a Sedequías hijo de Josías, en lugar de Jeconíash hijo de Joacim. 2Pero ni Sedequías ni sus siervos ni la gente de Judá hicieron caso a las palabras que el SEÑOR había hablado a través del profeta Jeremías. 3No obstante, el rey Sedequías envió a Jucal hijo de Selemías y al sacerdote Sofonías hijo de Maseías a decirle al profeta Jeremías: «Ora por nosotros al SEÑOR nuestro Dios.»

4Mientras tanto, Jeremías se movía con total libertad entre la gente, pues todavía no lo habían encarcelado. 5Por otra parte, el ejército del faraón había salido de Egipto. Y cuando los *babilonios, que estaban sitiando a Jerusalén, se enteraron de la noticia, emprendieron la retirada.

6La palabra del SEÑOR vino al profeta Jeremías: 7«Así dice el SEÑOR, el Dios de Israel: "Díganle al rey de Judá que los mandó a consultarme: 'El ejército del faraón, que salió para apoyarlos, se volverá a Egipto. 8Los babilonios regresarán para atacar esta ciudad, y la capturarán y la incendiarán.' "

9»Así dice el SEÑOR: "No se hagan ilusiones creyendo que los babilonios se van a retirar. ¡Se equivocan! No se van a retirar. 10Y aunque ustedes derrotaran a todo el ejército babilonio, y sólo quedaran en sus campamentos algunos hombres heridos, éstos se levantarían e incendiarían esta ciudad."»

11Cuando por causa de la incursión del ejército del faraón el ejército de Babilonia se retiró de Jerusalén, 12Jeremías quiso trasladarse de Jerusalén al territorio de Benjamín para tomar posesión de una herencia. 13Pero al llegar a la puerta de Benjamín, un capitán de la guardia llamado Irías, hijo de Selemías y nieto de Jananías, detuvo al profeta Jeremías y lo acusó:

—¡Estás por pasarte a los babilonios!

14Jeremías respondió:

—¡Mentira, no voy a pasarme a los babilonios!

Pero Irías no le hizo caso, sino que lo detuvo y lo llevó ante los jefes. 15Éstos estaban enfurecidos contra Jeremías, así que luego de golpearlo lo encarcelaron en la casa del cronista Jonatán, ya que la habían convertido en prisión. 16Así Jeremías fue encerrado en un calabozo subterráneo, donde permaneció mucho tiempo.

17El rey Sedequías mandó que trajeran a Jeremías al palacio, y allí le preguntó en secreto:

—¿Has recibido alguna palabra del SEÑOR?

—Sí —respondió Jeremías—, Su Majestad será entregado en manos del rey de Babilonia.

18A su vez, Jeremías le preguntó al rey Sedequías:

—¿Qué crimen he cometido contra Su Majestad, o contra sus ministros o este pueblo, para que me hayan encarcelado? 19¿Dónde están sus profetas, los que profetizaban que el rey de Babilonia no los atacaría ni a ustedes ni a este país? 20Pero ahora, ruego a Su Majestad me preste atención. Le pido que no me mande de vuelta a la casa del cronista Jonatán, no sea que yo muera allí.

21Entonces el rey Sedequías ordenó que pusieran a Jeremías en el patio de la guardia y que, mientras hubiera pan en la ciudad, todos los días le dieran una porción del pan horneado en la calle de los Panaderos. Así fue como Jeremías permaneció en el patio de la guardia.

---

h 37:1 *Jeconías.* Lit. *Conías* (variante de este nombre).

Jeremías en la cisterna

38 Sefatías hijo de Matán, Guedalías hijo de Pasur, Jucal hijo de Selemías, y Pasur hijo de Malquías, oyeron que Jeremías le decía a todo el pueblo: 2«Así dice el SEÑOR: "El que se quede en esta ciudad morirá de hambre, por la espada o por la peste. Pero el que se pase a los *babilonios vivirá. ¡Se entregará como botín de guerra, pero salvará su vida!" 3Así dice el SEÑOR: "Ésta ciudad caerá en poder del ejército del rey de Babilonia, y será capturada."»

4Los jefes le dijeron al rey:

—Hay que matar a este hombre. Con semejantes discursos está desmoralizando a los soldados y a todo el pueblo que aún quedan en esta ciudad. Este hombre no busca el bien del pueblo, sino su desgracia.

5El rey Sedequías respondió:

—Lo dejo en sus manos. Ni yo, que soy el rey, puedo oponerme a ustedes.

6Ellos tomaron a Jeremías y, bajándolo con cuerdas, lo echaron en la cisterna del patio de la guardia, la cual era de Malquías, el hijo del rey. Pero como en la cisterna no había agua, sino lodo, Jeremías se hundió en él.

7El etíope Ebedmélec, funcionario[i] de la casa real, se enteró de que habían echado a Jeremías en la cisterna. En cierta ocasión cuando el rey estaba participando en una sesión frente al portón de Benjamín, 8Ebedmélec salió del palacio real y le dijo:

9—Mi rey y señor, estos hombres han actuado con saña. Han arrojado a Jeremías a la cisterna, y allí se morirá de hambre, porque ya no hay pan en la ciudad.

10Entonces el rey ordenó al etíope Ebedmélec:

—Toma contigo tres[j] hombres, y rescata de la cisterna al profeta Jeremías antes de que se muera.

11Ebedmélec lo hizo así, y fue al depósito de ropa[k] del palacio real, sacó de allí ropas y trapos viejos, y con unas sogas se los bajó a la cisterna a Jeremías. 12Ebedmélec le dijo a Jeremías:

—Ponte en los sobacos estas ropas y trapos viejos, para protegerte de las sogas.

Así lo hizo Jeremías. 13Los hombres tiraron de las sogas y lo sacaron de la cisterna. Y Jeremías permaneció en el patio de la guardia.

Sedequías interroga a Jeremías

14El rey Sedequías mandó que llevaran a Jeremías a la tercera entrada de la casa del SEÑOR, y allí le dijo:

—Te voy a preguntar algo, y por favor no me ocultes nada.

15Jeremías le respondió al rey:

—Si respondo a la pregunta de Su Majestad, lo más seguro es que me mate. Y si le doy un consejo, no me va a hacer caso.

16Pero en secreto el rey Sedequías le hizo este juramento a Jeremías:

—¡Te juro por el SEÑOR, que nos ha dado esta vida, que no te mataré ni te entregaré en manos de estos hombres que atentan contra tu vida!

17Jeremías le dijo a Sedequías:

—Así dice el SEÑOR *Todopoderoso, el Dios de Israel: "Si Su Majestad se rinde ante los jefes del rey de Babilonia, salvará su vida, y esta ciudad no será incendiada; Su Majestad y su familia vivirán. 18Pero si no se rinde ante los jefes del rey de Babilonia, la

ciudad caerá bajo el poder de los *caldeos, y será incendiada, y usted no tendrá escapatoria."

19El rey Sedequías respondió:

—Yo le tengo terror a los judíos que se pasaron al bando de los *babilonios, pues me pueden entregar en sus manos para que me torturen.

20Jeremías le contestó:

—Obedezca Su Majestad la voz del SEÑOR que yo le estoy comunicando, y no caerá en manos de los babilonios. Así le irá bien a usted, y salvará su vida. 21Pero si Su Majestad se empecina en no rendirse, ésta es la palabra que el SEÑOR me ha revelado: 22Todas las mujeres que aún quedan en el palacio del rey de Judá serán entregadas a los jefes del rey de Babilonia, y ellas mismas le echarán en cara:

»"Tus amigos más confiables
    te han engañado y te han vencido.
Tienes los pies hundidos en el fango,
    pues tus amigos te dieron la espalda."

23»Todas las mujeres y los hijos de Su Majestad serán entregados a los babilonios, y ni Su Majestad podrá escapar, sino que caerá bajo el poder del rey de Babilonia, y la ciudad será incendiada.

24Sedequías le contestó a Jeremías:

—Que nadie se entere de estas palabras, pues de lo contrario morirás. 25Si los jefes se enteran de que yo hablé contigo, y vienen y te dicen: "Dinos ya lo que le has informado al rey, y lo que él te dijo; no nos ocultes nada, pues de lo contrario te mataremos", 26tú les dirás: "Vine a suplicarle al rey que no me mandara de vuelta a casa de Jonatán, a morir allí."

27Y así fue. Todos los jefes vinieron a interrogar a Jeremías, pero él les contestó de acuerdo con lo que el rey le había ordenado. Entonces lo dejaron tranquilo, porque nadie había escuchado la conversación. 28Y Jeremías se quedó en el patio de la guardia hasta el día en que Jerusalén fue capturada.

La caída de Jerusalén

39:1-10 — 2R 25:1-12; Jer 52:4-16

39 Jerusalén fue tomada de la siguiente manera: 1En el mes décimo del año noveno del reinado de Sedequías en Judá, el rey Nabucodonosor de Babilonia y todo su ejército marcharon contra Jerusalén y la sitiaron. 2El día nueve del mes cuarto del año undécimo del reinado de Sedequías, abrieron una brecha en el muro de la ciudad, 3por la que entraron todos los jefes del rey de Babilonia, hasta instalarse en la puerta central: Nergal Sarézer de Samgar, Nebo Sarsequín,[l] un oficial principal, Nergal Sarézer, también un alto funcionario, y todos los otros jefes del rey de Babilonia. 4Al verlos, el rey Sedequías de Judá y todos los soldados huyeron de la ciudad. Salieron de noche por el camino del jardín del rey, por la *puerta que está entre los dos muros, tomando el camino del Arabá.[m]

5Pero el ejército babilónico los persiguió hasta alcanzarlos en las llanuras de Jericó. Capturaron a Sedequías y lo llevaron ante Nabucodonosor, rey de Babilonia, que estaba en Riblá, en el territorio de Jamat. Allí dictó sentencia contra Sedequías, 6y ante sus propios ojos hizo degollar a sus hijos, lo mismo que a todos los nobles de Judá. 7Luego mandó que a Sedequías le sacaran los ojos y le pusieran cadenas de bronce, para llevarlo a Babilonia.

---

i 38:7 *funcionario*. Lit. *eunuco*. j 38:10 *tres* (un mss. hebreo); *treinta* (TM). k 38:11 *al depósito de ropa*. Lit. *debajo de la tesorería*; véase 2R 10:22. l 39:3 *Nergal Sarézer de Samgar, Nebo Sarsequín*. Alt. *Nergal Sarézer, Samgar Nebo, Sarsequín*. m 39:4 *del Arabá*. Alt. *del valle del Jordán*.

⁸Los *babilonios prendieron fuego al palacio real y a las casas del pueblo, y derribaron los muros de Jerusalén. ⁹Finalmente Nabuzaradán, el comandante de la guardia, llevó cautivos a Babilonia tanto al resto de la población como a los desertores, es decir, a todos los que quedaban. ¹⁰Nabuzaradán, comandante de la guardia, sólo dejó en el territorio de Judá a algunos de los más pobres, que no poseían nada. En aquel día les asignó campos y viñedos.

¹¹En cuanto a Jeremías, el rey Nabucodonosor de Babilonia había dado la siguiente orden a Nabuzaradán, el comandante de la guardia: ¹²«Vigílalo bien, sin hacerle ningún daño, y atiende a todas sus necesidades.» ¹³Nabuzaradán, comandante de la guardia, Nebusazbán, un oficial principal, Nergal Sarézer, un alto funcionario, y todos los demás oficiales del rey de Babilonia, ¹⁴mandaron sacar a Jeremías del patio de la guardia y se lo confiaron a Guedalías hijo de Ajicán, nieto de Safán, para que lo llevaran de vuelta a su casa. Así Jeremías se quedó a vivir en medio del pueblo.

¹⁵Aún estaba Jeremías preso en el patio de la guardia cuando la palabra del SEÑOR vino a él: ¹⁶«Ve y dile a Ebedmélec, el etíope, que así dice el SEÑOR *Todopoderoso, el Dios de Israel: "Voy a cumplir las palabras que anuncié contra esta ciudad, para mal y no para bien. En aquel día, tú serás testigo de todo esto. ¹⁷Pero en ese mismo día yo te rescataré —afirma el SEÑOR—, y no caerás en las manos de los hombres que temes. ¹⁸Porque ciertamente yo te libraré —afirma el SEÑOR—, y no caerás a filo de espada; antes bien, tu vida será tu botín, porque has confiado en mí."»

Liberación de Jeremías

40 La palabra del SEÑOR vino a Jeremías después de que Nabuzaradán, el comandante de la guardia, lo había dejado libre en Ramá. Allí lo había encontrado Nabuzaradán preso y encadenado, entre todos los cautivos de Judá y Jerusalén que eran deportados a Babilonia. ²El comandante de la guardia tomó aparte a Jeremías, y le dijo: «El SEÑOR tu Dios decretó esta calamidad para este lugar, ³y ahora el SEÑOR ha cumplido sus amenazas. Todo esto les ha pasado porque pecaron contra el SEÑOR y desobedecieron su voz. ⁴No obstante, hoy te libero de las cadenas que te sujetan las manos. Si quieres venir conmigo a Babilonia, ven, que yo te cuidaré. Pero si no quieres, no lo hagas. Mira, tienes ante tus ojos toda la tierra: ve a donde más te convenga.»

⁵Como Jeremías no se decidía, Nabuzaradán añadió: «Vuelve junto a Guedalías hijo de Ajicán, nieto de Safán, a quien el rey de Babilonia ha nombrado gobernador de las ciudades de Judá, y vive con él y con tu pueblo, o ve a donde más te convenga.»

Luego el comandante de la guardia le dio provisiones y un regalo, y lo dejó en libertad. ⁶Jeremías se fue entonces junto a Guedalías hijo de Ajicán, en Mizpa, y se quedó con él, en medio del pueblo que había permanecido en el país.

Asesinato de Guedalías
40:7-9; 41:1-3 — 2R 25:22-26

⁷Cuando todos los jefes y soldados del ejército que estaban en el campo se enteraron de que el rey de Babilonia había puesto a Guedalías hijo de Ajicán como gobernador del país, y de que le había confiado el cuidado de hombres, mujeres y niños, así como de los más pobres del país que no habían sido deportados a Babilonia, ⁸fueron a Mizpa para presentarse ante Guedalías. Entre ellos estaban: Ismael hijo de Netanías, Johanán y Jonatán hijos de Carea, Seraías

hijo de Tanjumet, los hijos de Efay de Netofa, y Jezanías, hijo de un hombre de Macá, y sus hombres. ⁹Guedalías hijo de Ajicán, nieto de Safán, les hizo este juramento a ellos y a sus tropas: «No teman al rey de Babilonia. Si ustedes se quedan en el país y sirven al rey de Babilonia, les aseguro que les irá bien. ¹⁰Yo me quedaré en Mizpa, para representarlos ante los babilonios que vengan hasta acá. Pero ustedes, comiencen a almacenar en recipientes vino, frutos de verano y aceite, y vivan en las ciudades que han ocupado.»

¹¹Todos los judíos que estaban en Moab, Amón y Edom, y en todos los otros países, se enteraron también de que el rey de Babilonia había dejado un remanente en Judá, y nombrado como gobernador a Guedalías hijo de Ajicán, nieto de Safán. ¹²Entonces todos estos judíos regresaron a la tierra de Judá, de todos los países donde estaban dispersos. Al llegar, se presentaron en Mizpa ante Guedalías, y también almacenaron vino y frutos de verano en abundancia.

¹³Johanán hijo de Carea, y todos los demás jefes militares que estaban en el campo, se presentaron ante Guedalías en Mizpa, ¹⁴y le dijeron:

—¿No sabes que Balís, rey de Amón, ha mandado a Ismael hijo de Netanías, para matarte?

Pero Guedalías hijo de Ajicán no les creyó. ¹⁵Y allí en Mizpa, Johanán hijo de Carea le propuso en secreto a Guedalías:

—Déjame ir a matar a Ismael hijo de Netanías. ¡Nadie tiene que enterarse! ¿Por qué vamos a permitir que te asesine? Eso causaría la dispersión de todos los judíos que se han reunido a tu alrededor, y acabaría con lo que queda de Judá.

¹⁶Pero Guedalías hijo de Ajicán le respondió a Johanán hijo de Carea:

—¡Ni lo pienses! ¡Lo que dices acerca de Ismael es mentira!

41 En el mes séptimo Ismael, hijo de Netanías y nieto de Elisama, que era de estirpe real y había sido uno de los oficiales del rey, vino a Mizpa con diez hombres y se presentó ante Guedalías hijo de Ajicán. Y ahí en Mizpa, mientras comían juntos, ²Ismael hijo de Netanías se levantó y, junto con los diez hombres que lo acompañaban, hirió a filo de espada a Guedalías hijo de Ajicán, nieto de Safán, quitándole la vida. Así hicieron con quien había sido nombrado gobernador del país por el rey de Babilonia. ³Ismael mató también a todos los judíos y soldados que se encontraban en Mizpa con Guedalías.

⁴Al día siguiente del asesinato de Guedalías, cuando todavía nadie se había enterado, ⁵llegaron de Siquén, Siló y Samaria ochenta hombres con la barba afeitada, la ropa rasgada, y el cuerpo lleno de cortaduras que ellos mismos se habían hecho. Traían ofrendas de cereales, e incienso, para presentarlas en la casa del SEÑOR. ⁶Desde Mizpa salió a su encuentro Ismael hijo de Netanías; iba llorando y, cuando los encontró, les dijo:

—Vengan a ver a Guedalías hijo de Ajicán.

⁷Pero no habían llegado al centro de la ciudad cuando Ismael hijo de Netanías y sus secuaces los mataron y los arrojaron en una cisterna. ⁸Había entre ellos diez hombres, que le rogaron a Ismael:

—¡No nos mates; tenemos escondidos en el campo trigo, cebada, aceite y miel!

Ismael accedió, y no los mató como a sus compañeros. ⁹El rey Asá había hecho una fosa para defenderse de Basá, rey de Israel, y en esa fosa fue donde Ismael arrojó los cadáveres de los hombres que había matado, junto con Guedalías, llenándola de cadáveres.

¹⁰Después Ismael se llevó en cautiverio a las hijas del rey y a todo el resto del pueblo que había quedado en Mizpa, a quienes Nabuzaradán, comandante de la guardia, había puesto bajo el mando de Guedalías hijo de Ajicán. Ismael hijo de Netanías salió con sus cautivos hacia el territorio de los amonitas.

¹¹Cuando Johanán hijo de Carea, y todos los jefes militares que estaban con él, se enteraron del crimen que había cometido Ismael hijo de Netanías, ¹²reunieron a todos sus hombres y fueron a pelear contra él. Lo encontraron cerca del gran estanque que está en Gabaón. ¹³Y sucedió que toda la gente que estaba con Ismael se alegró al ver a Johanán hijo de Carea, acompañado de todos los jefes militares. ¹⁴Todo el pueblo que Ismael llevaba cautivo desde Mizpa se dio la vuelta y se fue con Johanán hijo de Carea. ¹⁵Pero Ismael hijo de Netanías y ocho de sus hombres se escaparon de Johanán y huyeron hacia Amón.

Huida a Egipto

¹⁶Entonces Johanán hijo de Carea, junto con todos los jefes militares que lo acompañaban, tomaron y rescataron al resto del pueblo que desde Mizpa se había llevado Ismael hijo de Netanías, luego de haber asesinado a Guedalías hijo de Ajicán: eran soldados, mujeres, niños y altos funcionarios. ¹⁷Se pusieron en marcha hasta llegar a Guerut Quimán, que está junto a Belén, desde donde pensaban continuar a Egipto ¹⁸para huir de los *babilonios. Estaban con temor, ya que Ismael hijo de Netanías había matado a Guedalías hijo de Ajicán, a quien el rey de Babilonia había nombrado gobernador del país.

42 Entonces se acercaron Johanán hijo de Carea y Azaríasⁿ hijo de Osaías, junto con los jefes militares y todo el pueblo, desde el más chico hasta el más grande, ²y le dijeron al profeta Jeremías:

—Por favor, atiende a nuestra súplica y ruega al SEÑOR tu Dios por todos nosotros los que quedamos. Como podrás darte cuenta, antes éramos muchos, pero ahora quedamos sólo unos cuantos. ³Ruega para que el SEÑOR tu Dios nos indique el *camino que debemos seguir, y lo que debemos hacer.

⁴Jeremías les respondió:

—Ya los he oído. Voy a rogar al SEÑOR, al Dios de ustedes, tal como me lo han pedido. Les comunicaré todo lo que el SEÑOR me diga, y no les ocultaré absolutamente nada.

⁵Ellos le dijeron a Jeremías:

—Que el SEÑOR tu Dios sea un testigo fiel y verdadero contra nosotros, si no actuamos conforme a todo lo que él nos ordene por medio de ti. ⁶Sea o no de nuestro agrado, obedeceremos la voz del SEÑOR nuestro Dios, a quien te enviamos a consultar. Así, al obedecer la voz del SEÑOR nuestro Dios, nos irá bien.

⁷Diez días después, la palabra del SEÑOR vino a Jeremías. ⁸Éste llamó a Johanán hijo de Carea, a todos los jefes militares que lo acompañaban, y a todo el pueblo, desde el más chico hasta el más grande, ⁹y les dijo: «Así dice el SEÑOR, Dios de Israel, a quien ustedes me enviaron para interceder por ustedes: ¹⁰"Si se quedan en este país, yo los edificaré y no los derribaré, los plantaré y no los arrancaré, porque me duele haberles causado esta calamidad. ¹¹No teman al rey de Babilonia, al que ahora temen —afirma el SEÑOR—; no le teman, porque yo estoy con ustedes para salvarlos y librarlos de su poder. ¹²Tendré compasión de ustedes, y de esa manera él también tendrá compasión y les permitirá volver a su tierra."

¹³»Pero si desobedecen la voz del SEÑOR, Dios de ustedes, y dicen: "No nos quedaremos en esta tierra, ¹⁴sino que nos iremos a Egipto, donde no veremos guerra, ni escucharemos el sonido de la trompeta, ni pasaremos hambre, y allí nos quedaremos a vivir", ¹⁵entonces presten atención a la palabra del SEÑOR, ustedes los que quedan en Judá: Así dice el SEÑOR *Todopoderoso, el Dios de Israel: "Si ustedes insisten en trasladarse a Egipto para vivir allá, ¹⁶la guerra que tanto temen los alcanzará, y el hambre que los aterra los seguirá de cerca hasta Egipto, y en ese lugar morirán. ¹⁷Todos los que están empecinados en trasladarse a Egipto para vivir allá, morirán por la guerra, el hambre y la peste. Ninguno sobrevivirá ni escapará a la calamidad que haré caer sobre ellos." ¹⁸Porque así dice el SEÑOR Todopoderoso, el Dios de Israel: "Así como se ha derramado mi ira y mi furor sobre los habitantes de Jerusalén, así se derramará mi furor sobre ustedes, si se van a Egipto. Se convertirán en objeto de maldición, de horror, de imprecación y de oprobio, y nunca más volverán a ver este lugar."

¹⁹¡Remanente de Judá! El SEÑOR les ha dicho que no vayan a Egipto. Sepan bien que hoy les hago una advertencia seria. ²⁰Ustedes cometieron un error fatal cuando me enviaron al SEÑOR, Dios de ustedes, y me dijeron: "Ruega al SEÑOR nuestro Dios por nosotros, y comunícanos todo lo que él te diga, para que lo cumplamos." ²¹Hoy se lo he hecho saber a ustedes, pero no han querido obedecer la voz del SEÑOR su Dios en nada de lo que él me encargó comunicarles. ²²Por lo tanto, sepan bien que en el lugar donde quieren residir morirán por la guerra, el hambre y la peste.»

43 Cuando Jeremías terminó de comunicarle al pueblo todo lo que el SEÑOR su Dios le había encomendado decirles, ²Azarías hijo de Osaías, Johanán hijo de Carea, y todos los arrogantes le respondieron a Jeremías: «¡Lo que dices es una mentira! El SEÑOR nuestro Dios no te mandó a decirnos que no vayamos a vivir a Egipto. ³Es Baruc hijo de Nerías el que te incita contra nosotros, para entregarnos en poder de los *babilonios, para que nos maten o nos lleven cautivos a Babilonia.»

⁴Así que ni Johanán hijo de Carea, ni los jefes militares, ni nadie del pueblo, obedecieron el mandato del SEÑOR, de quedarse a vivir en el país de Judá. ⁵Por el contrario, Johanán hijo de Carea y todos los jefes militares se llevaron a la gente que aún quedaba en Judá, es decir, a los que habían vuelto para vivir en Judá luego de haber sido dispersados por todas las naciones: ⁶los hombres, las mujeres y los niños, las hijas del rey, y toda la gente que Nabuzaradán, comandante de la guardia, había confiado a Guedalías hijo de Ajicán, nieto de Safán, y también a Jeremías el profeta y a Baruc hijo de Nerías; ⁷y contrariando el mandato del SEÑOR se dirigieron al país de Egipto, llegando hasta la ciudad de Tafnes.

⁸En Tafnes, la palabra del SEÑOR vino a Jeremías: ⁹«Toma en tus manos unas piedras grandes y, a la vista de los judíos, entiérralas con argamasa en el pavimento, frente a la entrada del palacio del faraón en Tafnes. ¹⁰Luego comunícales que así dice el SEÑOR *Todopoderoso, el Dios de Israel: "Voy a mandar a buscar a mi siervo Nabucodonosor, rey de Babilonia; voy a colocar su trono sobre estas piedras que he enterrado, y él armará sobre ellas su toldo real. ¹¹Vendrá al país de Egipto y lo atacará: el que esté destinado a la

---

ⁿ **42:1** *Azarías* (LXX; véase 43:2); *Jezanías* (TM).

muerte, morirá; el que esté destinado al exilio, será exiliado; el que esté destinado a la guerra, a la guerra irá. 12Prenderán fuego a los templos de los dioses de Egipto; los quemará y los llevará cautivos. Sacudirá a Egipto, como un pastor que se sacude sus piojos de la ropa, y luego se irá de allí sin inmutarse. 13Destruirá los obeliscos de Bet Semes,o y prenderá fuego a los templos de los dioses de Egipto."»

Desastre causado por la idolatría

44 La palabra del SEÑOR vino a Jeremías para todos los judíos que habitaban en Egipto, es decir, para los que vivían en las ciudades de Migdol, Tafnes y Menfis,p y en la región del sur: 2«Así dice el SEÑOR *Todopoderoso, el Dios de Israel: "Ustedes han visto todas las calamidades que yo provoqué sobre Jerusalén y sobre todas las ciudades de Judá. Hoy yacen en ruinas, sin morador alguno, 3a causa de las maldades que cometieron. Ellos provocaron mi enojo al adorar y ofrecer incienso a otros dioses, que ni ellos ni sus antepasados conocieron. 4Una y otra vez les envié a mis siervos los profetas, para que los advirtieran que no incurrieran en estas cosas tan abominables que yo detesto. 5Pero ellos no escucharon ni prestaron atención; no se *arrepintieron de sus maldades, sino que siguieron ofreciendo incienso a otros dioses. 6Por eso se derramó mi ira contra las ciudades de Judá; por eso se encendió mi furor contra las calles de Jerusalén, las cuales se convirtieron en desolación hasta el día de hoy."

7»Y ahora, así dice el SEÑOR, el Dios Todopoderoso, el Dios de Israel: "¿Por qué se provocan ustedes mismos un mal tan grande? ¿Por qué provocan la muerte de la gente de Judá, de hombres, mujeres, niños y recién nacidos, hasta acabar con todos? 8Me agravian con las obras de sus manos, al ofrecer incienso a otros dioses en el país de Egipto, donde han ido a vivir. Lo único que están logrando es ganarse su propia destrucción, y convertirse en maldición y oprobio entre todas las naciones de la tierra. 9¿Acaso ya se han olvidado de todas las maldades que cometieron sus antepasados, de las que cometieron los reyes de Judá y sus esposas, y de las que ustedes y sus esposas cometieron en Judá y en las calles de Jerusalén? 10Sin embargo, hasta el día de hoy no se han humillado ni han sentido temor; no se han comportado según mi *ley y mis preceptos, que les di a ustedes y a sus antepasados."

11»Por eso, así dice el SEÑOR Todopoderoso, el Dios de Israel: "He decidido ponerme en contra de ustedes, para su mal, y destruir a todo Judá. 12Tomaré al resto de Judá, que se empecinó en ir a vivir a Egipto, y todos perecerán allí; caerán a filo de espada, o el hambre los exterminará. Desde el más pequeño hasta el más grande, morirán de hambre o a filo de espada. Se convertirán en objeto de maldición, de horror, de imprecación y de oprobio. 13Con hambre, peste y espada castigaré a los que habitan en Egipto, como castigué a Jerusalén. 14No escapará ninguno del resto de Judá que se fue a vivir a Egipto, ni sobrevivirá para volver a Judá. Aunque deseen y añoren volver a vivir en Judá, no podrán regresar, salvo algunos fugitivos."»

15Entonces los hombres que sabían que sus esposas ofrecían incienso a otros dioses, así como las mujeres que estaban presentes, es decir, un grupo numeroso, y todo el pueblo que vivía en la región sur de Egipto, respondieron a Jeremías:

16—No le haremos caso al mensaje que nos diste en el *nombre del SEÑOR. 17Al contrario, seguiremos haciendo lo que ya hemos dicho: Ofreceremos incienso y libaciones a la Reina del Cielo,q como lo hemos hecho nosotros, y como antes lo hicieron nuestros antepasados, nuestros reyes y nuestros funcionarios, en las ciudades de Judá y en las calles de Jerusalén. En aquel tiempo teníamos comida en abundancia, nos iba muy bien y no sufríamos ninguna calamidad. 18Pero desde que dejamos de ofrecer incienso y libaciones a la Reina del Cielo nos ha faltado todo, y el hambre y la espada están acabando con nosotros.

19Y las mujeres añadieron:

—Cuando nosotras ofrecíamos incienso y libaciones a la Reina del Cielo, ¿acaso no sabían nuestros maridos que hacíamos tortas con su imagen, y que les ofrecíamos libaciones?

20Entonces Jeremías le respondió a todo el pueblo, es decir, a los hombres y mujeres que le habían contestado:

21—¿Piensan ustedes que el SEÑOR no se acuerda, o no se daba cuenta de que ustedes y sus antepasados, sus reyes y sus funcionarios, y todo el pueblo, ofrecían incienso en las ciudades de Judá y en las calles de Jerusalén? 22Cuando el SEÑOR ya no pudo soportar más las malas acciones y las cosas abominables que ustedes hacían, su país se convirtió en objeto de maldición, en un lugar desértico, desolado y sin habitantes, tal como está hoy. 23Ustedes ofrecieron incienso y pecaron contra el SEÑOR, y no obedecieron su voz ni cumplieron con su ley, sus preceptos y estipulaciones. Por eso en este día les ha sobrevenido esta desgracia.

24Jeremías le dijo a todo el pueblo, incluyendo a las mujeres:

—Escuchen la palabra del SEÑOR todos ustedes, gente de Judá que vive en Egipto: 25Así dice el SEÑOR Todopoderoso, el Dios de Israel: "Cuando ustedes y sus mujeres dicen: 'Ciertamente cumpliremos nuestros votos de ofrecer incienso y libaciones a la Reina del Cielo', demuestran con sus acciones que cumplen lo que prometen. ¡Está bien, vayan y cumplan sus promesas, lleven a cabo sus votos! 26Pero escuchen la palabra del SEÑOR todos ustedes, gente de Judá que vive en Egipto: 'Juro por mi nombre soberano —dice el SEÑOR— que ninguno de los de Judá que vive en Egipto volverá a invocar mi nombre, ni a jurar diciendo: ¡Por la vida del SEÑOR omnipotente! 27Porque yo los estoy vigilando, para mal y no para bien. El hambre y la espada acabarán con todos los judíos que viven en Egipto. 28Tan sólo unos pocos lograrán escapar de la espada y regresar a Judá. Entonces todo el resto de Judá que se fue a vivir a Egipto sabrá si se cumple mi palabra o la de ellos.'

29» "Ésta será la señal de que voy a castigarlos en este lugar, para que sepan que mis amenazas contra ustedes se habrán de cumplir —afirma el SEÑOR—. 30Así dice el SEÑOR: 'Voy a entregar al faraón Hofra, rey de Egipto, en poder de los enemigos que atentan contra su vida, tal como entregué a Sedequías, rey de Judá, en poder de su enemigo Nabucodonosor, rey de Babilonia, que atentaba contra su vida.' "»

Mensaje para Baruc

45 Ésta es la palabra que el profeta Jeremías le comunicó a Baruc hijo de Nerías, en el año cuarto del gobierno de Joacim hijo de Josías, cuando

---

ñ 43:12 Prenderá (LXX, Siríaca y Vulgata); Prenderé (TM). o 43:13 En hebreo, Bet Semes significa casa del sol; posible alusión al templo del sol o a la ciudad de Heliópolis. p 44:1 Menfis. Lit. Nof. q 44:17 Reina del Cielo. Nombre de una diosa.

Baruc escribía en un rollo estas palabras que Jeremías le dictaba: ²«Así dice el SEÑOR, Dios de Israel, acerca de ti, Baruc: ³"Tú dijiste: 'iAy de mí! iEl SEÑOR añade angustia a mi dolor! Estoy agotado de tanto gemir, y no encuentro descanso.'

⁴»"Pues le dirás que así dice el SEÑOR: 'Voy a destruir lo que he construido, y a arrancar lo que he plantado; es decir, arrasaré con toda esta tierra. ⁵¿Buscas grandes cosas para ti? No las pidas, porque voy a provocar una desgracia sobre toda la gente, pero a ti te concederé la posibilidad de conservar la vida dondequiera que vayas —afirma el SEÑOR—. Ése será tu botín.' "»

Mensaje para Egipto

46 La palabra del SEÑOR acerca de las naciones vino a Jeremías el profeta.

²En cuanto a Egipto, éste es el mensaje contra el ejército del faraón Necao, rey de Egipto, que en el año cuarto del gobierno de Joacim hijo de Josías, rey de Judá, fue derrotado en Carquemis, junto al río Éufrates, por Nabucodonosor, rey de Babilonia:

³«iPreparen el escudo y el broquel,
    y avancen al combate!
⁴iEnsillen los caballos,
    monten los corceles!
  iAlístense, pónganse los cascos!
    iAfilen las lanzas, vístanse las corazas!
⁵iPero ¿qué es lo que veo?
    Sus guerreros están derrotados;
    aterrados retroceden.
Sin mirar atrás, huyen despavoridos.
    iCunde el terror por todas partes!
        —afirma el SEÑOR—.
⁶El más veloz no puede huir
    ni el más fuerte, escapar.
  En el norte, a orillas del río Éufrates
    trastabillan y caen.

⁷¿Quién es ése que sube como el Nilo,
    como ríos de aguas agitadas?
⁸Es Egipto, que trepa como el Nilo,
    como ríos de aguas agitadas.
  Dice Egipto: "Subiré y cubriré toda la tierra;
    destruiré las ciudades y sus habitantes."
⁹iAtaquen, corceles!
    iCarros, avancen con furia!
  iQue marchen los guerreros!
  iQue tomen sus escudos
    los soldados de *Cus y de Fut!
  iQue tensen el arco
    los soldados de Lidia!

¹⁰»Aquel día pertenece
    al Señor, al SEÑOR *Todopoderoso.
  Será un día de venganza;
    se vengará de sus enemigos.
  La espada devorará hasta saciarse;
    con sangre apagará su sed.
  En la tierra del norte,
    a orillas del río Éufrates,
  el Señor, el SEÑOR Todopoderoso,
    realizará una matanza.ʳ

¹¹»iVirginal hija de Egipto,
    ve a Galaad y consigue bálsamo!
  En vano multiplicas los remedios;
    ya no sanarás.
¹²Las naciones ya saben de tu humillación;

    tus gritos llenan la tierra.
  Un guerrero tropieza contra otro,
    y juntos caen por tierra.»

¹³Ésta es la palabra del SEÑOR, que vino a Jeremías el profeta cuando Nabucodonosor, rey de Babilonia, vino para atacar el país de Egipto:

¹⁴«Anuncien esto en Egipto,
    proclámenlo en Migdol, Menfisˢ y Tafnes:
  "iA sus puestos! iManténganse alerta!
    iLa espada devora a su alrededor!"
¹⁵¿Por qué yacen postrados tus guerreros?
    iNo pueden mantenerse en pie,
    porque el SEÑOR los ha derribado!
¹⁶Tropiezan una y otra vez,
    se caen uno sobre otro.
  Se dicen: "iLevántate,
    volvamos a nuestra gente,
  a la tierra donde nacimos,
    lejos de la espada del opresor!"
¹⁷Allí gritan: "iEl faraón es puro ruido!
    iel rey de Egipto ya perdió su
        oportunidad!"

¹⁸»iVivo yo! —declara el Rey,
    cuyo *nombre es el SEÑOR
        Todopoderoso—:
  Como el Tabor, que sobresale de entre los
        montes,
    y como el Carmelo, que se erige sobre el
        mar,
    así será el enemigo que viene.
¹⁹Tú, que habitas en Egipto,
    prepara tu equipaje para el exilio,
  porque Menfis se convertirá en desolación,
    en una ruina deshabitada.

²⁰»Novilla hermosa es Egipto,
    pero viene contra ella un tábano del norte.
²¹Los mercenarios en sus filas
    son como novillos cebados;
  también ellos se vuelven atrás,
    todos juntos huyen sin detenerse,
  porque ha llegado el día de su ruina,
    el momento de su castigo.
²²Egipto huye silbando como serpiente,
    pues el enemigo avanza con fuerza.
  Se acercan contra ella con hachas,
    como si fueran leñadores.
²³por impenetrables que sean sus bosques,
    los talan por completo
        —afirma el SEÑOR—.
  Más numerosos que langostas,
    son los leñadores;
    nadie los puede contar.
²⁴Egipto la hermosa será avergonzada
    y entregada a la gente del norte.»

²⁵El SEÑOR Todopoderoso, el Dios de Israel, dice: «Voy a castigar a Amón, dios de Tebas,ᵗ a Egipto, a sus dioses y reyes, al faraón y a los que en él confían.

²⁶Los entregaré al poder de quienes atentan contra su vida, al poder de Nabucodonosor, rey de Babilonia, y de sus siervos. Luego Egipto será habitada como en los días de antaño —afirma el SEÑOR—.

²⁷»Pero tú, Jacob siervo mío, no temas;
    no te asustes, Israel.

ʳ **46:10** *realizará una matanza.* Lit. *tiene un sacrificio.* ˢ **46:14** *Menfis.* Lit. *Nof;* también en v. 19. ᵗ **46:25** *Amón, dios de Tebas.* Lit. *Amón de No*

Porque te salvaré de un lugar remoto;
y a tu descendencia, del destierro.
Jacob volverá a vivir en *paz;
estará seguro y tranquilo.
[28]Tú, Jacob, siervo mío, no temas,
porque yo estoy contigo —afirma el
SEÑOR—.

»Aunque aniquile a todas las naciones
por las que te he dispersado,
a ti no te aniquilaré.
Te corregiré con *justicia,
pero no te dejaré sin castigo.»

Mensaje para los filisteos

47 Antes de que el faraón atacara Gaza, la palabra del SEÑOR acerca de los filisteos vino al profeta Jeremías:

[2]«Así dice el SEÑOR:

»"¡Miren! Las aguas del norte
suben cual torrente desbordado.
Inundan la tierra y todo lo que contiene,
sus ciudades y sus habitantes.
¡Grita toda la gente!
¡Gimen los habitantes de la tierra!
[3]Al oír el galope de sus corceles,
el estruendo de sus carros
y el estrépito de sus ruedas,
los padres abandonan a sus hijos
porque sus fuerzas desfallecen.
[4]Ha llegado el día
de exterminar a los filisteos,
y de quitarles a Tiro y Sidón
todos los aliados con que aún cuenten.
El SEÑOR exterminará a los filisteos
y al resto de las costas de Caftor.[u]
[5]Se rapan la cabeza los de Gaza;
se quedan mudos los de Ascalón.
Tú, resto de las llanuras,
¿hasta cuándo te harás incisiones?

[6]»"¡Ay, espada del SEÑOR!
¿Cuándo vas a descansar?
¡Vuélvete a la vaina!
¡Detente, quédate quieta!

[7]»"¿Cómo va a descansar,
si el SEÑOR le ha dado órdenes
de atacar a Ascalón
y a la costa del mar?"»

Mensaje para Moab
48:29-36 — Is 16:6-12

48 Así dice el SEÑOR *Todopoderoso, el Dios de Israel, acerca de Moab:

«¡Ay de Nebo, porque será devastada!
¡Quiriatayin será capturada y puesta en
vergüenza!
¡Su fortaleza[v] será humillada y destruida!
[2]La gloria de Moab ha desaparecido;
en Hesbón[w] maquinan el mal contra ella:
"¡Vengan, hagamos desaparecer a esta
nación!"
También tú, Madmén,[x] serás silenciada,
y la espada te perseguirá.
[3]Se oye el clamor desde Joronayin:

¡devastación y gran destrucción!
[4]Moab será quebrantada;
ya se oyen los gritos de sus pequeños.
[5]Por la cuesta de Luhit
suben llorando sin cesar;
por la bajada de Joronayin
se oyen gritos de dolor,
por causa de la destrucción.
[6]¡Huyan! ¡Sálvese quien pueda!
¡Sean como las zarzas[y] del desierto!
[7]Por cuanto confías en tus obras y en tus
riquezas,
también tú serás capturada.
Quemós, tu dios, irá al exilio,
junto con sus sacerdotes y oficiales.
[8]El destructor vendrá contra toda ciudad,
y ni una sola de ellas escapará.
El valle quedará en ruinas,
y la meseta quedará destruida,
tal como lo ha dicho el SEÑOR.
[9]Coloquen una lápida[z] para Moab,
porque yace destruida;
sus ciudades están desoladas,
y sin habitante alguno.

[10]»¡Maldito el que sea negligente
para realizar el trabajo del SEÑOR!
¡Maldito el que de la sangre
retraiga su espada!

[11]»Moab ha vivido en paz desde su juventud;
ha reposado sobre sus heces.
No ha pasado de vasija en vasija,
ni ha ido jamás al exilio.
Por eso conserva su sabor
y no pierde su aroma.
[12]Pero vienen días
—afirma el SEÑOR—
en que enviaré gente que transvasará a
Moab;
y vaciará sus vasijas
y romperá sus cántaros.
[13]Entonces Moab se avergonzará de Quemós,
como el pueblo de Israel se avergonzó de
Betel,
santuario en el que había depositado su
confianza.

[14]»¿Cómo se atreven a decir:
"Somos guerreros,
hombres valientes para la guerra"?
[15]Moab será devastada
y sus ciudades, invadidas
—afirma el Rey,
cuyo *nombre es el SEÑOR
Todopoderoso—:
Lo mejor de su juventud
descenderá al matadero.
[16]La ruina de Moab se acerca;
su calamidad es inminente.
[17]Lloren por él todos sus vecinos,
los que saben de su fama.
Digan: "¡Cómo se ha quebrado el cetro
tan poderoso e imponente!"
[18]»Tú, que habitas en Dibón:
desciende de tu lugar de honor
y siéntate en el sequedal,

---

u 47:4 *Caftor*. Es decir, *Creta*.   **v** 48:1 *Su fortaleza*. Alt. *Misgab*.   **w** 48:2 En hebreo, *Hesbón* suena como el verbo que significa *maquinan*.   **x** 48:2 En hebreo, *Madmén* suena como el verbo que significa *serás silenciada*.   **y** 48:6 *las zarzas* (véanse Aquila y Vulgata). Alt. *Aroer*.   **z** 48:9 *lápida* (LXX); en TM, palabra de difícil traducción.

porque el destructor de Moab te ataca
   y destruye tus fortificaciones.
¹⁹Tú, que habitas en Aroer,
   párate a la vera del camino, y observa;
pregunta a los que huyen, hombres y mujeres:
   "¿Qué es lo que ha sucedido?"
²⁰Moab está humillado;
   ha sido destrozado.
¡Giman y clamen!
   ¡Anuncien por el río Arnón
   que Moab ha sido devastado!
²¹El juicio ha llegado hasta la meseta
   contra Holón, Yahaza y Mefat;
²²contra Dibón, Nebo y Bet Diblatayin;
²³contra Quiriatayin, Bet Gamul y Bet Megón,
²⁴contra Queriot y Bosra,
   y contra todas las ciudades de Moab,
   cercanas y lejanas.
²⁵El poderᵃ de Moab ha desaparecido;
   ¡su fuerza está abatida!
                    —afirma el SEÑOR—.

²⁶»¡Emborrachen a Moab,
   porque ha desafiado al SEÑOR!
¡Que se regodee en su vómito,
   y se convierta en objeto de burla!
²⁷¿Acaso no te burlabas de Israel,
   y con tus palabras lo despreciabas,
   como si hubiera sido sorprendido entre
      ladrones?
²⁸Habitantes de Moab,
   ¡abandonen las ciudades
   y vivan entre las rocas!
Sean como las palomas
   que anidan al borde de los precipicios.

²⁹»Conocemos bien el orgullo de Moab,
   ese orgullo exagerado.
¡Tanta soberbia y tanto orgullo!
   ¡Tanta arrogancia y altivez!
³⁰Yo conozco su insolencia,
   pero sus jactancias no logran nada
                    —afirma el SEÑOR—.
³¹Por eso lloro por Moab;
   gimo por toda su gente,
   sollozo por el pueblo de Quir Jeres.
³²Lloro por ti, viña de Sibma,
   más que por Jazer;
tus sarmientos sobrepasan el mar
   y llegan hasta Jazer,
pero caerá el destructor
   sobre tu cosecha y sobre tu vendimia.
³³De los fértiles campos de Moab
   han desaparecido el gozo y alegría.
Acabé con el vino de tus lagares;
   ya nadie pisa las uvas entre gritos de
      alborozo;
   los gritos ya no son de regocijo.

³⁴»El clamor de Hesbón llega hasta Elalé y
      Yahaza,
   su voz se alza desde Zoar
   hasta Joronayin y Eglat Selisiyá.
Porque hasta las aguas de Nimrín
   se han secado.
³⁵Acabaré con la gente de Moab
   que ofrece sacrificios en *altares paganos
   y quema incienso a sus dioses
                    —afirma el SEÑOR—.

³⁶»Por eso, con sonido de flautas
   gime por Moab mi *corazón;
con sonido de flautas
   gime mi corazón por Quir Jeres,
porque han desaparecido
   las riquezas que acumularon.
³⁷Toda cabeza está rapada
   y toda barba rasurada;
en todas las manos hay incisiones,
   y todos están vestidos de luto.
³⁸Sobre todos los techos de Moab,
   y por todas sus plazas,
   sólo se escuchan lamentos;
porque rompí en pedazos a Moab
   como a una vasija desechada
                    —afirma el SEÑOR—.
³⁹¡Cómo quedó hecha pedazos!
   ¡Cómo gimen!
Moab ha vuelto la espalda
   del todo avergonzada.
Es para todos sus vecinos
   objeto de burla y de terror.»

⁴⁰Así dice el SEÑOR:

«¡Miren! Vuela el enemigo como águila;
   sobre Moab despliega sus alas.
⁴¹Sus ciudades serán capturadas,
   y conquistadas sus fortalezas.
En aquel día, el corazón de los guerreros de
      Moab
   será como el de una parturienta.
⁴²Moab será destruida como nación,
   porque ha desafiado al SEÑOR.
⁴³El terror, la fosa y la trampa,
   aguardan al habitante de Moab
                    —afirma el SEÑOR—.
⁴⁴El que huya del terror caerá en la fosa;
   el que salga de la fosa caerá en la trampa;
porque yo hago venir sobre Moab
   el tiempo de su castigo
                    —afirma el SEÑOR—.

⁴⁵»A la sombra de Hesbón
   se detienen exhaustos los fugitivos.
De Hesbón sale un fuego;
   de la ciudad de Sijón, una llama
que consume las sienes de Moab
   y el cráneo de los arrogantes y revoltosos.
⁴⁶¡Ay de ti, Moab!
   El pueblo de Quemós está destruido;
tus hijos son llevados al exilio;
   tus hijas, al cautiverio.
⁴⁷Pero en los días venideros
   yo cambiaré la suerte de Moab»,
                    afirma el SEÑOR.

Aquí concluye el juicio contra Moab.

Mensaje para Amón

49 Así dice el SEÑOR acerca de los amonitas:

«¿Acaso Israel no tiene hijos?
   ¿Acaso no tiene herederos?
¿Por qué el dios Molocᵇ ha heredado Gad,
   y su pueblo vive en sus ciudades?
²Vienen días —afirma el SEÑOR—
   en que yo haré resonar el grito de guerra
   contra Rabá de los amonitas;
y se convertirá en un montón de ruinas,
   y sus ciudades serán incendiadas.

ᵃ **48:25** *poder.* Lit. *cuerno.*   ᵇ **49:1** *Moloc.* Lit. *Malcán;* es decir, Milcón. Alt. *su rey.* También en v. 3.

Entonces Israel despojará de todo
a los que de todo la despojaron
　　　　—afirma el SEÑOR—.

3»¡Gime, Hesbón, porque Hai ha sido
destruida!
¡Griten, hijas de Rabá!
¡Vístanse de luto, y hagan lamentación;
corran de un lado a otro, dentro de los
muros!,
porque Moloc marcha al destierro,
junto con sus sacerdotes y oficiales.
4¿Por qué te jactas de tus valles,
de tus fértiles valles,
hija rebelde, que confías en tus tesoros
y dices: "¿Quién me atacará?"?
5Voy a hacer que te acose
el terror por todas partes
　　　—afirma el SEÑOR *Todopoderoso—.
Todos serán expulsados, cada uno por su lado,
y nadie reunirá a los fugitivos.

6»Pero después de esto,
cambiaré la suerte de los amonitas»,
afirma el SEÑOR.

Mensaje para Edom
49:9-10 — Abd 5-6
49:14-16 — Abd 1-4

7Así dice el SEÑOR Todopoderoso acerca de
Edom:

«¿Ya no hay sabiduría en Temán?
¿Se acabó el consejo de los inteligentes?
¿Acaso se ha echado a perder su sabiduría?
8Habitantes de Dedán:
¡Huyan, vuélvanse atrás!
¡Escóndanse en lo más profundo de la
tierra!
Yo provocaré un desastre sobre Esaú,
pues le llegó la hora del castigo.
9Si los vendimiadores llegaran a ti,
¿no te dejarían algunos racimos?
Si de noche te llegaran ladrones,
¿no se llevarían sólo lo que pudieran?
10Pero yo despojaré por completo a Esaú;
descubriré sus escondites, y no podrá
ocultarse.
Sus hijos, parientes y vecinos,
serán destruidos y dejarán de existir.
11¡Abandona a tus huérfanos,
que yo les protegeré la vida!
¡Tus viudas pueden confiar en mí!»

12Así dice el SEÑOR: «Los que no estaban condenados a beber la copa de castigo, la bebieron. ¿Y acaso tú vas a quedarte sin castigo? ¡De ninguna manera
quedarás impune, sino que también beberás de esa
copa! 13Juro por mí mismo —afirma el SEÑOR—, que
Bosra se convertirá en objeto de maldición, y en horror, oprobio y desolación. Para siempre quedarán
en ruinas todas sus ciudades.»

14He oído un mensaje del SEÑOR.
Un heraldo lo anuncia entre las naciones:
«¡Reúnanse, ataquen a la ciudad!
¡Prepárense para la guerra!»

15«Te haré pequeño entre las naciones,
menospreciado entre los *hombres.
16Tú, que habitas en las hendiduras de las
rocas;
tú, que ocupas las alturas de los montes:
fuiste engañado por el terror que infundías

y por el orgullo de tu *corazón.
Aunque pongas tu nido tan alto como el del
águila,
desde allí te haré caer
　　　　—afirma el SEÑOR—.
17Tan espantosa será la caída de Edom,
que todo el que pase junto a la ciudad
quedará pasmado al ver todas sus heridas.
18Será como en la destrucción de Sodoma y
Gomorra
y de sus ciudades vecinas;
nadie volverá a vivir allí,
ni la habitará ningún *ser humano
　　　　—afirma el SEÑOR—.
19»Como león que sale de los matorrales del
Jordán
hacia praderas de verdes pastos,
en un instante espantaré de su tierra a los de
Edom,
y sobre ellos nombraré a mi elegido.
Porque, ¿quién como yo?
¿Quién me puede desafiar?
¿Qué *pastor se me puede oponer?»
20Por eso, escuchen el plan que el SEÑOR
ha diseñado contra Edom;
escuchen lo que tiene proyectado
contra los habitantes de Temán:
Serán arrastrados
los más pequeños del rebaño;
por causa de ellos
sus praderas quedarán asoladas.
21Tiembla la tierra
por el estruendo de su caída;
hasta en el *Mar Rojo
resuenan sus gritos.
22Remonta vuelo el enemigo,
se desliza como un águila,
extiende sus alas sobre Bosra.
En aquel día se angustiarán los valientes de
Edom,
como se angustia una mujer de parto.

Mensaje para Damasco

23Mensaje acerca de Damasco:

«Jamat y Arfad están desconcertadas,
pues ya saben de la mala noticia.
Naufragan en el mar de la angustia,
y no pueden calmarse.
24Damasco desfallece;
trató de huir, pero la dominó el pánico.
Se halla presa de la angustia y el dolor,
como si estuviera de parto.
25¿Por qué no ha sido abandonada
la ciudad famosa, la que era mi delicia?
26En aquel día sus jóvenes
quedarán tendidos en las calles;
¡perecerán todos sus soldados!
　　　—afirma el SEÑOR *Todopoderoso—.
27Prenderé fuego al muro de Damasco,
y los palacios de Ben Adad serán
consumidos.»

Mensaje para Cedar y Jazor

28Así dice el SEÑOR acerca de Cedar y de los reinos de Jazor que fueron atacados por Nabucodonosor, rey de Babilonia:

«¡Vamos, ataquen a Cedar!
¡Destruyan a esa gente del oriente!
29Sus carpas y rebaños les serán arrebatados,
se llevarán sus toldos, bienes y camellos.
La gente les gritará:

"¡Cunde el terror por todas partes!"

30»¡Huyan, habitantes de Jazor!
Escapen ya, escóndanse
en lo más profundo de la tierra
—afirma el SEÑOR—.
Nabucodonosor, rey de Babilonia,
maquina planes contra ustedes;
contra ustedes ha diseñado un plan.

31»¡Vamos, ataquen a esta nación indolente
que vive del todo confiada,
nación que no tiene puertas ni cerrojos,
y que vive muy aislada!
—afirma el SEÑOR—.
32Sus camellos serán el botín,
y su numeroso ganado, el despojo.
Dispersaré a los cuatro vientos
a los que se rapan las sienes;
de todas partes les traeré su ruina
—afirma el SEÑOR—.
33Jazor se convertirá en una guarida de
chacales,
en un lugar desolado para siempre.
Ningún *ser humano vivirá allí,
nadie habitará en ese lugar.»

Mensaje para Elam

34La palabra del SEÑOR acerca de Elam vino al
profeta Jeremías al comienzo del reinado de Sedequías, rey de Judá.

35Así dice el SEÑOR *Todopoderoso:

«Voy a quebrar el arco de Elam;
voy a acabar con lo mejor de su poderío.
36Voy a desatar contra Elam los cuatro vientos
desde los cuatro confines de la tierra.
Los voy a esparcir por los cuatro vientos,
y no quedará nación alguna
adonde no lleguen sus desterrados.
37Aterraré a Elam frente a sus enemigos,
frente a los que atentan contra su vida;
desataré mi ardiente ira,
y traeré sobre ellos calamidad
—afirma el SEÑOR—.
Haré que la espada los persiga
hasta que los haya exterminado.
38Estableceré mi trono en Elam,
y destruiré a su rey y a sus oficiales
—afirma el SEÑOR—.

39»Pero en los días venideros
cambiaré la suerte de Elam»,
afirma el SEÑOR.

Mensaje para Babilonia
51:15-19 — Jer 10:12-16

50 La palabra del SEÑOR acerca de los *babilonios y de su país vino al profeta Jeremías:

2«¡Anuncien y proclamen entre las naciones!
¡Proclámenlo, levanten un estandarte!
No oculten nada, sino digan:
"¡Babilonia será conquistada!
¡Bel quedará en vergüenza!
¡Marduc quedará aterrado!
¡Sus imágenes quedan humilladas,
y aterrados sus ídolos!"
3Porque la ataca una nación del norte,
que dejará desolada a su tierra.
*Hombres y animales saldrán huyendo,
y no habrá nadie que la habite.

4En aquellos días, en aquel tiempo,

la gente de Israel y de Judá
irá llorando en busca del SEÑOR su Dios
—afirma el SEÑOR—.
5Preguntarán por el camino de *Sión,
y hacia allá se encaminarán.
Vendrán y se aferrarán al SEÑOR
en un *pacto eterno, que ya no olvidarán.

6»Mi pueblo ha sido como un rebaño perdido;
sus *pastores lo han descarriado,
lo han hecho vagar por las montañas.
Ha ido de colina en colina,
y se ha olvidado de su redil.
7Todos los que lo encuentran, lo devoran;
"No somos culpables —decían sus
enemigos—,
porque ellos pecaron contra el SEÑOR;
iél es morada de *justicia,
esperanza de sus antepasados!"

8»¡Huyan de Babilonia;
abandonen ese país!
Sean como los machos cabríos
que guían a las ovejas.
9Porque yo movilizo contra Babilonia,
una alianza de grandes naciones del norte.
Se alistarán contra ella,
y desde el norte será conquistada.
Sus flechas son como expertos guerreros
que no vuelven con las manos vacías.
10Babilonia será saqueada,
y todos sus saqueadores se saciarán
—afirma el SEÑOR—.

11»Ustedes, que saquean mi heredad,
alégrense y regocíjense!
¡Salten como terneros en la pradera,
relinchen como sementales!
12Pero la patria de ustedes
quedará humillada;
la que les dio la vida quedará en
vergüenza.
Será la última de las naciones;
se convertirá en sequedal, desierto y estepa.
13Por el enojo del SEÑOR
no será habitada,
sino que quedará en desolación.
Todo el que pase por Babilonia
quedará pasmado al ver todas sus heridas.

14»¡Tomen posiciones alrededor de Babilonia,
todos los que tensan el arco!
¡Dispárenle, no escatimen flechas,
porque ha pecado contra el SEÑOR!
15Griten en torno de ella:
¡Babilonia se rinde!
¡Cayeron sus torres,
se derrumbaron sus muros!
¡Ésta es la venganza del SEÑOR!
¡Vénguense de ella!
¡Páguenle con la misma moneda!
16Exterminen al que siembra en Babilonia,
y al que maneja la hoz en la cosecha.
Ante la espada del opresor,
cada uno retorna a su pueblo,
cada cual huye a su país.

17»Israel es como un rebaño descarriado,
acosado por los leones.
Primero lo devoró el rey de Asiria,
y luego Nabucodonosor, rey de Babilonia,
le quebró todos los huesos.»

[18]Por eso, así dice el SEÑOR *Todopoderoso, el Dios de Israel:

> «Castigaré al rey de Babilonia y a su país
> como castigué al rey de Asiria.
> [19]Haré que Israel vuelva a su prado
> y que se alimente en el Carmelo y en Basán.
> Su apetito quedará saciado
> en las montañas de Efraín y Galaad.
> [20]En aquellos días se buscará la iniquidad de
> Israel,
> pero ya no se encontrará.
> En aquel tiempo se buscarán los pecados de
> Judá,
> pero ya no se hallarán,
> porque yo perdonaré a los que deje con vida
> —afirma el SEÑOR—.

> [21]»¡Ataca el país de Meratayin!
> y a los que viven en Pecod!
> ¡Mátalos, *destrúyelos por completo!
> ¡Cumple con todas mis órdenes!
> —afirma el SEÑOR—.
> [22]¡En el país hay estruendo de guerra
> y de impresionante destrucción!
> [23]¡Cómo ha sido quebrado y derribado
> el martillo de toda la tierra!
> ¡Babilonia ha quedado desolada
> en medio de las naciones!
> [24]Te tendí una trampa, y en ella caíste
> antes de que te dieras cuenta.
> Fuiste sorprendida y apresada,
> porque te opusiste al SEÑOR.
> [25]El SEÑOR ha abierto su arsenal,
> y ha sacado las armas de su ira;
> el SEÑOR omnipotente, el Todopoderoso,
> tiene una tarea que cumplir
> en el país de los babilonios.
> [26]¡Atáquenla desde los confines de la tierra!
> ¡Abran sus graneros!
> ¡Amontónenla como a las gavillas!
> ¡Destrúyanla por completo!
> ¡Que no quede nada de ella!
> [27]¡Maten a todos sus novillos!
> ¡Llévenlos al matadero!
> ¡Ay de ellos, pues les ha llegado el día,
> el día de su castigo!
> [28]Se oye la voz de los fugitivos,
> de los que escaparon de Babilonia;
> vienen a anunciar en Sión
> la venganza del SEÑOR nuestro Dios,
> la venganza por su templo.

> [29]»Recluten contra Babilonia a los arqueros,
> a todos los que tensan el arco;
> acampen a su alrededor,
> y que no escape ninguno.
> Retribúyanle según sus obras,
> páguenle con la misma moneda.
> Porque ella ha desafiado al SEÑOR,
> al *Santo de Israel.
> [30]Por eso en aquel día
> caerán sus jóvenes en las calles
> y perecerán todos sus soldados
> —afirma el SEÑOR—.

> [31]»Estoy contra ti, nación arrogante
> —afirma el Señor, el SEÑOR
> Todopoderoso—;
> al fin ha llegado el día,

el día de tu castigo.
> [32]El arrogante tropezará y caerá,
> y no habrá quien lo ayude a levantarse.
> Prenderé fuego a todas sus ciudades,
> fuego que consumirá cuanto le rodea.»

[33]Así dice el SEÑOR Todopoderoso:

> «Israel y Judá son pueblos oprimidos;
> sus enemigos los tienen apresados,
> no los dejan en libertad.
> [34]Pero su redentor es fuerte,
> su *nombre es el SEÑOR Todopoderoso.
> Con vigor defenderá su causa;
> traerá la *paz a la tierra,
> pero a Babilonia, el terror.

> [35]»¡Muerte a[c] los babilonios!
> ¡Muerte a sus jefes y sabios!
>   —afirma el SEÑOR—.
> [36]¡Muerte a sus falsos profetas!
> ¡Que pierdan la razón!
> ¡Muerte a sus guerreros!
> ¡Que queden aterrorizados!
> [37]¡Muerte a sus caballos y carros!
> ¡Muerte a todos sus mercenarios!
> ¡Que se vuelvan como mujeres!
> ¡Muerte a sus tesoros!
> ¡Que sean saqueados!
> [38]¡Muerte a sus aguas!
> ¡Que queden secas!
> Porque Babilonia es un país de ídolos,
> de ídolos terribles que provocan la locura.

> [39]»Por eso las fieras del desierto
> vivirán allí con las hienas;
> también los avestruces harán allí su
> morada.
> Nunca más volverá a ser habitada;
> quedará despoblada para siempre.
> [40]Será como cuando Dios destruyó a Sodoma y
> Gomorra,
> y a sus ciudades vecinas;
> allí nadie volverá a vivir,
> ni la habitará ningún *ser humano
> —afirma el SEÑOR—.

> [41]»Del norte viene un ejército;
> desde los confines de la tierra
> se preparan una gran nación y muchos
> reyes.
> [42]Vienen armados con arcos y lanzas;
> son crueles y desalmados.
> Vienen montados a caballo;
> su estruendo es como el bramido del mar.
> Contra ti, bella Babilonia, contra ti
> marchan en formación de combate,
> alineados como un solo hombre.
> [43]El rey de Babilonia ha escuchado la noticia,
> y sus brazos flaquean;
> de él se apodera la angustia
> y le vienen dolores de parto.
> [44]Como león que sale de los matorrales del
> Jordán
> hacia praderas de verdes pastos,
> en un instante espantaré de su tierra a los de
> Babilonia,
> y sobre ellos nombraré a mi elegido.
> Porque, ¿quién como yo?
> ¿Quién me puede desafiar?
> ¿Qué pastor se me puede oponer?»

---

c **50:35** *Muerte a.* Lit. *Espada contra;* también en vv. 36 y 37.

45Por eso, escuchen el plan que el SEÑOR
    ha diseñado contra Babilonia,
escuchen lo que tiene proyectado
    en contra del país de los babilonios:
Serán arrastrados
    los más pequeños del rebaño;
por causa de ellos,
    sus praderas quedarán asoladas.
46Tiembla la tierra
    por la estruendosa caída de Babilonia;
resuenan sus gritos
    en medio de las naciones.

51

Así dice el SEÑOR:

«Voy a levantar un viento destructor
    contra Babilonia y la gente de Leb Camay.d
2Enviaré contra Babilonia
    gente que la lance por los aires,
que la aviente como se avienta el trigo,
    hasta dejarla vacía.
En el día de su calamidad
    la atacarán por todas partes.
3Que no tense el arquero su arco,e
    ni se vista la coraza.
No perdonen a sus jóvenes;
    *destruyan a su ejército por completo.
4Caerán muertos en el país de los *babilonios;
    serán traspasados en las calles.
5Aunque Israel y Judá están llenos de culpa
    delante del *Santo de Israel,
no han sido abandonados por su Dios,
    el SEÑOR *Todopoderoso.

6»¡Huyan de Babilonia!
    ¡Sálvese quien pueda!
    No perezcan por causa de su iniquidad.
Porque ha llegado la hora
    de que el SEÑOR tome venganza;
    ¡él le dará su merecido!
7En la mano del SEÑOR
    Babilonia era una copa de oro
    que embriagaba a toda la tierra.
Las naciones bebieron de su vino
    y se enloquecieron.
8Pero de pronto Babilonia cayó hecha pedazos.
    ¡Giman por ella!
Traigan bálsamo para su dolor;
    tal vez pueda ser curada.

9»"Quisimos curar a Babilonia,
    pero no pudo ser sanada;
abandonémosla, y regrese cada uno a su país,
    porque llega su condena hasta los cielos;
    ¡se eleva hasta las nubes!"

10»"¡El SEÑOR nos ha vindicado!
    Vengan, que en *Sión daremos a conocer
    lo que ha hecho el SEÑOR nuestro Dios."

11»¡Afilen las flechas!
    ¡Ármense con escudos!
El SEÑOR ha despertado el espíritu
    de los reyes de Media
    para destruir a Babilonia.
Ésta es la venganza del SEÑOR,
    la venganza por su templo.
12¡Levanten el estandarte
    contra los muros de Babilonia!
¡Refuercen la guardia!

¡Pongan centinelas!
    ¡Preparen la emboscada!
El SEÑOR cumplirá su propósito;
    cumplirá su decreto contra los babilonios.
13Tú, que habitas junto a muchas aguas
    y eres rica en tesoros,
has llegado a tu fin,
    al final de tu existencia.
14El SEÑOR Todopoderoso ha jurado por sí
    mismo:
"Te llenaré de enemigos, como de
    langostas,
    y sobre ti lanzarán gritos de victoria."
15»Con su poder hizo el SEÑOR la tierra;
    con su sabiduría afirmó el mundo;
    con su inteligencia extendió los cielos.
16Ante su trueno, braman las lluvias en el cielo,
    y desde los confines de la tierra
    hace que suban las nubes;
entre relámpagos desata la lluvia,
    y saca de sus depósitos el viento.

17»Todo *hombre es *necio e ignorante;
    todo orfebre se avergüenza de sus ídolos.
Sus ídolos son una mentira,
    no tienen aliento de vida.
18Son absurdos, objetos de burla;
    en el tiempo del juicio serán destruidos.
19La porción de Jacob no es como aquéllos;
    su Dios es el creador de todas las cosas.
Su *nombre es el SEÑOR Todopoderoso;
    Israel es la tribu de su heredad.

20»Tú eres mi mazo, mi arma de guerra;
    contigo destrozo naciones y reinos.
21Contigo destrozo jinetes y caballos;
    contigo destrozo aurigas y carros de
    guerra.
22Contigo destrozo hombres y mujeres;
    contigo destrozo jóvenes y ancianos,
    contigo destrozo jóvenes y doncellas.
23Contigo destrozo pastores y rebaños;
    contigo destrozo labradores y yuntas,
    contigo destrozo jefes y gobernantes.

24»Pero en presencia de ustedes les daré su merecido a Babilonia y a todos sus habitantes por todo
el mal que han hecho en Sión —afirma el SEÑOR—.

25»Estoy en contra tuya,
    monte del exterminio,
    que destruyes toda la tierra
           —afirma el SEÑOR—.
Extenderé mi mano contra ti;
    te haré rodar desde los peñascos
    y te convertiré en monte quemado.
26No volverán a tomar de ti piedra angular,
    ni piedra de cimiento,
porque para siempre quedarás desolada
           —afirma el SEÑOR—.
27»¡Levanten la bandera en el país!
    ¡Toquen la trompeta entre las naciones!
¡Convoquen contra ella
    a los reinos de Ararat, Mini y Asquenaz!
¡Pongan al frente un general!
    ¡Que avancen los caballos cual plaga de
    langostas!
28¡Convoquen contra ella a las naciones,
    a los reyes de Media,

---

d 51:1 *Leb Camay* es un criptograma que alude a *Caldea, es decir, Babilonia.   e 51:3 *Que no tense el arquero su arco.* Frase de difícil traducción.

y a sus gobernadores y oficiales!
¡Convoquen a todo su imperio!
²⁹La tierra tiembla y se sacude;
se cumplen los planes de Dios contra
Babilonia,
al convertirla en un desierto desolado
donde nadie ha de habitar.
³⁰Dejaron de combatir los guerreros de
Babilonia;
se escondieron en las fortalezas.
Sus fuerzas se agotaron;
se volvieron como mujeres.
Sus moradas fueron incendiadas
y destrozados sus cerrojos.
³¹Corre un emisario tras el otro;
un mensajero sigue a otro mensajero,
para anunciarle al rey de Babilonia
que toda la ciudad ha sido conquistada.
³²Los vados han sido ocupados,
e incendiados los esteros;
llenos de pánico quedaron los guerreros.»

³³Porque así dice el SEÑOR Todopoderoso, el
Dios de Israel:

«La bella Babilonia es como una era
en el momento de la trilla;
¡ya le llega el tiempo de la cosecha!»

³⁴«Nabucodonosor, el rey de Babilonia,
me devoró, me confundió;
me dejó como un plato vacío.
Me tragó como un monstruo marino,
con mis delicias se ha llenado el estómago
para luego vomitarme.
³⁵Dice Jerusalén:
"¡Que recaiga sobre Babilonia
la violencia que me hizo!"
Dice la moradora de Sión:
"¡Que mi sangre se derrame
sobre los babilonios!"»

³⁶Por eso, así dice el SEÑOR:

«Voy a defender tu causa,
y llevaré a cabo tu venganza;
voy a secar el agua de su mar,
y dejaré secos sus manantiales.
³⁷Babilonia se convertirá en un montón de
ruinas,
en guarida de chacales,
en objeto de horror y de burla,
en un lugar sin habitantes.
³⁸Juntos rugen como leones;
gruñen como cachorros de león.
³⁹Cuando entren en calor, les serviré bebida;
los embriagaré para que se diviertan.
Así dormirán un sueño eterno
del que ya no despertarán
—afirma el SEÑOR—.
⁴⁰Voy a llevarlos al matadero,
como si fueran corderos;
como carneros y chivos.

⁴¹»¡Cómo ha sido capturada Sesac!ᶠ
¡Cómo ha sido conquistado
el orgullo de toda la tierra!
Babilonia se ha convertido
en un horror para las naciones.
⁴²El mar ha subido contra Babilonia;
agitadas olas la han cubierto.

⁴³Desoladas han quedado sus ciudades:
como un sequedal, como un desierto.
Nadie habita allí;
nadie pasa por ese lugar.
⁴⁴Voy a castigar al dios Bel en Babilonia;
haré que vomite lo que se ha tragado.
Ya no acudirán a él las naciones,
ni quedará en pie el muro de Babilonia.

⁴⁵»¡Huye de ella, pueblo mío!
¡Sálvese quien pueda de mi ardiente ira!
⁴⁶No desfallezcan, no se acobarden
por los rumores que corren por el país.
Año tras año surgen nuevos rumores;
cunde la violencia en el país,
y un gobernante se levanta contra otro.
⁴⁷Se acercan ya los días
en que castigaré a los ídolos de Babilonia.
Toda su tierra será avergonzada;
caerán sus víctimas en medio de ella.
⁴⁸Entonces el cielo y la tierra,
y todo lo que hay en ellos,
lanzarán gritos de júbilo contra Babilonia,
porque del norte vendrán sus destructores
—afirma el SEÑOR—.

⁴⁹»Babilonia tiene que caer
por las víctimas de Israel,
así como en toda la tierra
cayeron las víctimas de Babilonia.
⁵⁰Ustedes, los que escaparon de la espada,
huyan sin demora.
Invoquen al SEÑOR en tierras lejanas,
y no dejen de pensar en Jerusalén.»

⁵¹«Sentimos vergüenza por los insultos;
estamos cubiertos de deshonra,
porque han penetrado extranjeros
en el santuario del SEÑOR.»

⁵²«Por eso, vienen días
en que castigaré a sus ídolos;
a lo largo de todo el país
gemirán sus heridos
—afirma el SEÑOR—.
⁵³Aunque Babilonia suba hasta los cielos,
y en lo alto fortifique sus baluartes,
yo enviaré destructores contra ella
—afirma el SEÑOR—.

⁵⁴»Se oyen clamores por la gran destrucción
del país de Babilonia.
⁵⁵El SEÑOR la destruye por completo;
pone fin a su bullicio.
Rugen sus enemigos como olas agitadas;
resuena el estruendo de su voz.
⁵⁶Llega contra Babilonia el destructor;
sus guerreros serán capturados,
y sus arcos serán hechos pedazos.
Porque el SEÑOR es un Dios
que a cada cual le da su merecido.
⁵⁷Voy a embriagar a sus jefes y a sus sabios;
a sus gobernadores, oficiales y guerreros;
y dormirán un sueño eterno,
del que no despertarán»,
afirma el Rey,
cuyo nombre es el SEÑOR Todopoderoso.

⁵⁸Así dice el SEÑOR Todopoderoso:

«Los anchos muros de Babilonia
serán derribados por completo;

ᶠ **51:41** *Sesac* es un criptograma que alude a Babilonia.

sus imponentes *puertas serán
incendiadas.
Los pueblos se agotan en vano,
y las naciones se fatigan
por lo que se desvanece como el humo.»

59Éste es el mandato que el profeta Jeremías dio
a Seraías, hijo de Nerías y nieto de Maseías, cuando
fue a Babilonia con Sedequías, rey de Judá, durante
el año cuarto de su reinado. Seraías era el jefe de este
viaje. 60Jeremías había descrito en un rollo todas las
calamidades que le sobrevendrían a Babilonia, es decir, todo lo concerniente a ella. 61Jeremías le dijo a Seraías: «En cuanto llegues a Babilonia, asegúrate de
leerles todas estas palabras. 62Luego diles: "SEÑOR,
tú has dicho que vas a destruir este lugar, y que lo
convertirás en una desolación perpetua, hasta que
no quede en él un solo habitante, ni hombre ni animal." 63Cuando termines de leer el rollo, átale una
piedra y arrójalo al Éufrates. 64Luego diles: "Así se
hundirá Babilonia, y nunca más se levantará del desastre que voy a traer sobre ella."»

Aquí concluyen las palabras de Jeremías.

La caída de Jerusalén
52:1-3 — 2R 24:18-20; 2Cr 36:11-16
52:4-16 — Jer 39:1-10
52:4-21 — 2R 25:1-21; 2Cr 36:17-20

52 Sedequías tenía veintiún años cuando ascendió al trono, y reinó en Jerusalén once años.
Su madre se llamaba Jamutal hija de Jeremías, oriunda de Libná. 2Al igual que Joacim, Sedequías hizo lo
que ofende al SEÑOR, 3a tal grado que el SEÑOR, en su
ira, los echó de su presencia. Todo esto sucedió en Jerusalén y en Judá.

Sedequías se rebeló contra el rey de Babilonia.
4En el año noveno del reinado de Sedequías, a los diez
días del mes décimo, Nabucodonosor, rey de Babilonia, marchó con todo su ejército y atacó a Jerusalén.
Acampó frente a la ciudad y construyó una rampa de
asalto a su alrededor. 5La ciudad estuvo sitiada hasta
el año undécimo del reinado de Sedequías.

6A los nueve días del mes cuarto, cuando el
hambre se agravó en la ciudad y no había más alimento para el pueblo, 7se abrió una brecha en el
muro de la ciudad, de modo que, aunque los *babilonios la tenían cercada, todo el ejército se escapó.
Salieron de noche, por la *puerta que estaba entre
los dos muros, junto al jardín real. Huyeron camino
al Arabá,g 8pero el ejército babilonio persiguió al rey
Sedequías hasta alcanzarlo en la llanura de Jericó.
Sus soldados se dispersaron, abandonándolo, 9y los
babilonios lo capturaron. Entonces lo llevaron ante
el rey de Babilonia, que estaba en Riblá, en el territorio de Jamat. Allí Nabucodonosor dictó sentencia
contra Sedequías, 10y ante sus propios ojos hizo degollar a sus hijos, lo mismo que a todos los nobles de
Judá. 11Luego mandó que a Sedequías le sacaran los
ojos y que le pusieran cadenas de bronce para llevarlo a Babilonia, donde permaneció preso hasta el
día en que murió.

12A los diez días del mes quinto del año diecinueve del reinado de Nabucodonosor, rey de Babilonia, su servidor Nabuzaradán, que era comandante

de la guardia, fue a Jerusalén 13y le prendió fuego al
templo del SEÑOR, al palacio real y a todas las casas
de Jerusalén, incluso a todos los edificios importantes. 14Entonces el ejército de los babilonios bajo su
mando derribó todas las murallas que rodeaban la
ciudad. 15Nabuzaradán además deportóh a la gente
que quedaba en la ciudad, es decir, al resto de los artesanos y a los que se habían aliado con el rey de Babilonia. 16Sin embargo, dejó a algunos de los más
pobres para que se encargaran de los viñedos y de
los campos.

17Los babilonios quebraron las columnas de
bronce, las bases y la fuentei de bronce que estaban
en el templo del SEÑOR, y se llevaron todo el bronce
a Babilonia. 18También se llevaron las ollas, las tenazas, las despabiladeras, los tazones, la vajilla y todos
los utensilios de bronce que se usaban para el culto.
19Además, el comandante de la guardia se apoderó
de las palanganas, los incensarios, los aspersorios, las
ollas, los candelabros, los platos y fuentes para las libaciones, todo lo cual era de oro y de plata.

20El bronce de las dos columnas, de la fuente,
de los doce toros que estaban debajo de la fuente,j y
de las bases, que el rey Salomón había hecho para el
templo del SEÑOR, era tanto que no se podía pesar.
21Cada columna medía ocho metros de altura y cinco y medio de circunferencia; su espesor era de
ocho centímetros,k y era hueca por dentro. 22El capitel de bronce que estaba encima de cada columna
medía dos metrosl de altura y estaba decorado alrededor con una red y con granadas de bronce. Las
dos columnas tenían el mismo adorno. 23De cada
columna pendían noventa y seis granadas, y las
granadas que estaban alrededor de la red eran cien
en total.

24El comandante de la guardia tomó presos a Seraías, sacerdote principal, a Sofonías, sacerdote de
segundo rango, y a los tres porteros. 25De los que
quedaban en la ciudad, apresó al oficial encargado
de las tropas, a siete de los servidores personales del
rey, al cronista principal del ejército, encargado de
reclutar soldados de entre el pueblo, y a sesenta ciudadanos que todavía estaban dentro de la ciudad.
26Después de apresarlos, Nabuzaradán, comandante de la guardia, se los llevó al rey de Babilonia, que
estaba en Riblá. 27Allí, en el territorio de Jamat, el rey
los hizo ejecutar.

Así Judá fue desterrado y llevado cautivo.
28Éste es el número de personas desterradas por
Nabucodonosor:

en el año séptimo de su reinado, tres mil veintitrés judíos;
29 en el año dieciocho de su reinado, ochocientas
treinta y dos personas de Jerusalén;
30 en el año veintitrés de su reinado, Nabuzaradán,
el capitán de la guardia real, desterró a setecientos cuarenta y cinco judíos.
En total fueron desterradas cuatro mil seiscientas personas.

Liberación del rey Joaquín
52:31-34 — 2R 25:27-30

31En el día veintisiete del mes duodécimo del
año treinta y siete del exilio de Joaquín, rey de Judá,
Evil Merodac, rey de Babilonia, en el año primero

---

g **52:7** Arabá. Alt. valle del Jordán.   h **52:15** deportó (lectura probable; véase 2R 25:11); deportó a algunos de los más pobres del
pueblo y (TM).   i **52:17** la fuente. Lit. el mar; también en v. 20.   j **52:20** debajo de la fuente (LXX y Siríaca); debajo (TM).
k **52:21** ocho metros ... cinco y medio ... ocho centímetros. Lit. dieciocho *codos ... doce codos ... cuatro codos.   l **52:22** dos metros.
Lit. cinco codos.

de su reinado, indultó a Joaquín y lo sacó de la cárcel. ³²Lo trató amablemente y le dio una posición más alta que la de los otros reyes que estaban con él en Babilonia. ³³Joaquín dejó su ropa de prisionero, y por el resto de su vida comió a la mesa del rey. ³⁴Además, durante toda su vida y hasta el día de su muerte, Joaquín gozó de una pensión diaria que le proveía el rey de Babilonia.

LAMENTACIONES

Álef

1 a ¡Ay, cuán desolada se encuentra
la que fue ciudad populosa!
¡Tiene apariencia de viuda
la que fue grande entre las naciones!
¡Hoy es esclava de las provincias
la que fue gran señora entre ellas!

Bet

2Amargas lágrimas derrama por las noches;
corre el llanto por sus mejillas.
No hay entre sus amantes
uno solo que la consuele.
Todos sus amigos la traicionaron;
se volvieron sus enemigos.

Guímel

3Humillada, cargada de cadenas,
Judá marchó al exilio.
Una más entre las naciones,
no encuentra reposo.
Todos sus perseguidores la acosan,
la ponen en aprietos.

Dálet

4Los caminos a *Sión están de duelo;
ya nadie asiste a sus fiestas solemnes.
Las *puertas de la ciudad se ven desoladas:
sollozan sus sacerdotes,
se turban sus doncellas,
¡toda ella es amargura!

He

5Sus enemigos se volvieron sus amos;
¡tranquilos ven sus adversarios!
El SEÑOR la ha acongojado
por causa de sus muchos pecados.
Sus hijos marcharon al cautiverio,
arrastrados por sus enemigos.

Vav

6La bella Sión ha perdido
todo su antiguo esplendor.
Sus príncipes parecen venados
que vagan en busca de pastos.
Exhaustos, se dan a la fuga
frente a sus perseguidores.

Zayin

7Jerusalén trae a la memoria
los tristes días de su peregrinaje;
se acuerda de todos los tesoros
que en el pasado fueron suyos.
Cuando su pueblo cayó en manos enemigas
nadie acudió en su ayuda.
Sus adversarios vieron su caída
y se burlaron de ella.

Jet

8Grave es el pecado de Jerusalén;
¡por eso se ha vuelto *impura!
Los que antes la honraban ahora la
desprecian,
pues han visto su desnudez;
ella misma se deshace en llanto,
y no se atreve a dar la cara.

Tet

9Sus vestidos están llenos de inmundicia;
no tomó en cuenta lo que le esperaba.
Su caída fue sorprendente;
no hubo nadie que la consolara.
«¡Mira, SEÑOR, mi aflicción!
¡El enemigo ha triunfado!»

Yod

10El enemigo se adueñó
de todos los tesoros de Jerusalén;
vio ella penetrar en su santuario
a las naciones *paganas,
a las que tú prohibiste
entrar en tu asamblea.

Caf

11Todo su pueblo solloza
y anda en busca de pan;
para mantenerse con *vida
cambian por comida sus tesoros.
«¡Mira, SEÑOR, date cuenta
de cómo me están humillando!»

Lámed

12«Fíjense ustedes, los que pasan por el camino:
¿Acaso no les importa?
¿Dónde hay un sufrimiento como el mío,
como el que el SEÑOR me ha hecho
padecer,
como el que el SEÑOR lanzó sobre mí
en el día de su furor?

Mem

13»Desde lo alto envió el Señor un fuego
que me caló hasta los huesos.
A mi paso tendió una trampa
y me hizo retroceder.
Me abandonó por completo;
a todas horas me sentía morir.

Nun

14»Pesan mis pecados como un yugo sobre mí;
Dios mismo me los ató con sus manos.b
Me los ha colgado al cuello,
y ha debilitado mis fuerzas.
Me ha entregado en manos de gente
a la que no puedo ofrecer resistencia.

Sámej

15»En mi ciudad el SEÑOR ha rechazado
a todos los guerreros;
ha reunido un ejército para atacarme,
para despedazarc a mis jóvenes.
El SEÑOR ha aplastado a la virginal hija de
Judá
como quien pisa uvas para hacer vino.

Ayin

16»Todo esto me hace llorar;
los ojos se me nublan de llanto.
No tengo cerca a nadie que me consuele;
no tengo a nadie que me reanime.
Mis hijos quedaron abandonados
porque el enemigo salió victorioso.»

Pe

17Sión clama pidiendo ayuda,d
pero no hay quien la consuele.
Por decreto del SEÑOR

---

a **Cap. 1** Este capítulo es un poema acróstico, que sigue el orden del alfabeto hebreo. b **1:14** *como un yugo ... sus manos.*
Texto de difícil traducción. c **1:15** *ha reunido ... despedazar.* Alt. *ha establecido mi tiempo, / cuando él despedazará.* d **1:17** *clama pidiendo ayuda.* Lit. *extiende los brazos.*

los vecinos de Jacob son ahora sus
  enemigos;
Jerusalén ha llegado a ser
  basura e inmundicia.

Tsade
18«El SEÑOR es justo,
  pero yo me rebelé contra sus *leyes.
Escuchen, ustedes los pueblos;
  fíjense en mi sufrimiento.
Mis jóvenes y mis doncellas
  han marchado al destierro.

Qof
19»Llamé a mis amantes,
  pero ellos me traicionaron.
Mis sacerdotes y mis *ancianos
  perecieron en la ciudad,
mientras buscaban alimentos
  para mantenerse con vida.

Resh
20»¡Mírame, SEÑOR, que me encuentro
  angustiada!
  ¡Siento una profunda agonía!e
Mi corazón está desconcertado,
  pues he sido muy rebelde.
Allá afuera, la espada me deja sin hijos;
  aquí adentro, hay un ambiente de muerte.

Shin
21»La gente ha escuchado mi gemir,
  pero no hay quien me consuele.
Todos mis enemigos conocen mi pesar
  y se alegran de lo que has hecho conmigo.
¡Manda ya tu castigo anunciado,
  para que sufran lo que he sufrido!

Tav
22»¡Que llegue a tu presencia
  toda su maldad!
¡Trátalos como me has tratado a mí
  por causa de todos mis pecados!
Son muchos mis gemidos,
  y mi *corazón desfallece.»

Álef
2 f ¡Ay, el SEÑOR ha eclipsado a la bella *Sión
  con la nube de su furor!g
Desde el cielo echó por tierra
  el esplendor de Israel;
en el día de su ira se olvidó
  del estrado de sus pies.

Bet
2Sin compasión el Señor ha destruido
  todas las moradas de Jacob;
en su furor ha derribado
  los baluartes de la bella Judá
y ha puesto su honra por los suelos
  al derrocar a su rey y a sus príncipes.

Guímel
3Dio rienda suelta a su furor
  y deshizo todo el poderh de Israel.
Nos vimos frente al enemigo,
  y el Señor nos negó su ayuda.i
Ardió en Jacob como un fuego encendido
  que consumía cuanto le rodeaba.

Dálet
4Como enemigo, tensó el arco;
  lista estaba su mano derecha.
Como enemigo, eliminó
  a nuestros seres queridos.
Como fuego, derramó su ira
  sobre las tiendas de la bella Sión.

He
5El Señor se porta como enemigo:
  ha destruido a Israel.
Ha destruido todos sus palacios
  y derribado sus baluartes.
Ha multiplicado el luto y los lamentos
  por la bella Judá.

Vav
6Ha desolado su morada como a un jardín;
  ha derribado su lugar de reunión.
El SEÑOR ha hecho que Sión olvide
  sus fiestas solemnes y sus *sábados;
se desató su furia contra el rey
  y dejó de lado al sacerdote.

Zayin
7El Señor ha rechazado su altar;
  ha abandonado su santuario.
Ha puesto en manos del enemigo
  las murallas de sus palacios.
¡Lanzan gritos en la casa del SEÑOR
  como en día de fiesta!

Jet
8El SEÑOR decidió derribar
  la muralla que rodea a la bella Sión.
Tomó la vara y midió;
  destruyó sin compasión.
Hubo lamentos en rampas y muros;
  todos ellos se derrumbaron.

Tet
9Las *puertas se han desplomado;
  él rompió por completo sus cerrojos.
Su rey y sus príncipes
  andan entre las naciones;
ya no hay ley ni profetas,
  ni visiones de parte del SEÑOR.

Yod
10En la bella Sión los ancianos
  se sientan silenciosos en el suelo;
se echan ceniza sobre la cabeza
  y se visten de luto.
Postradas yacen en el suelo
  las jóvenes de Jerusalén.

Caf
11El llanto me consume los ojos;
  siento una profunda agonía.j
Estoy con el ánimok por los suelos
  porque mi pueblo ha sido destruido.
Niños e infantes desfallecen
  por las calles de la ciudad.

Lámed
12«¿Dónde hay pan y vino?»,
  preguntan a sus madres
mientras caen por las calles
  como heridos de muerte,

---

e **1:20** *¡Siento ... agonía!* Lit. *Mis entrañas se agitan.* f **Cap. 2** Este capítulo es un poema acróstico, que sigue el orden del alfabeto hebreo. g **2:1** *¡Ay ... furor!* Alt. *¡Cómo el Señor, en su enojo, / ha tratado con reproches a la hija de Sión!* h **2:3** *todo el poder.* Lit. *todo cuerno.* i **2:3** *nos negó su ayuda.* Lit. *retiró su mano derecha.* j **2:11** *siento ... agonía.* Lit. *mis entrañas se agitan.* k **2:11** *Estoy con el ánimo.* Lit. *Mi hígado está derramado.*

mientras en los brazos maternos
exhalan el último suspiro.

Mem
13¿Qué puedo decir de ti, bella Jerusalén?
¿A qué te puedo comparar?
¿Qué ejemplo darte como consuelo,
virginal ciudad de Sión?
Profundas como el mar son tus heridas.
¿Quién podría devolverte la salud?

Nun
14Tus profetas te anunciaron
visiones falsas y engañosas.
No denunciaron tu maldad;
no evitaron tu cautiverio.
Los mensajes que te anunciaban
eran falsas patrañas.

Sámej
15Cuantos pasan por el camino
aplauden burlones al verte.
Ante ti, bella Jerusalén, hacen muecas,
y entre silbidos preguntan:
«¿Es ésta la ciudad de belleza perfecta?
¿Es ésta la alegría de toda la tierra?»

Pe
16Todos tus enemigos abren la boca
para hablar mal de ti;
rechinando los dientes, declaran burlones:
«Nos la hemos comido viva.
Llegó el día tan esperado;
¡hemos vivido para verlo!»

Ayin
17Él SEÑOR ha llevado a cabo sus planes;
ha cumplido su palabra,
que decretó hace mucho tiempo.
Sin piedad, te echó por tierra;
dejó que el enemigo se burlara de ti,
y enalteció el poderl de tus oponentes.

Tsade
18El *corazón de la gente
clama al Señor con angustia.
Bella Sión amurallada,
¡deja que día y noche
corran tus lágrimas como un río!
¡No te des un momento de descanso!
¡No retengas el llanto de tus ojos!m

Qof
19Levántate y clama por las noches,
cuando empiece la vigilancia nocturna.
Deja correr el llanto de tu corazón
como ofrenda derramada ante el Señor.
Eleva tus manos a Dios en oración
por la *vida de tus hijos,
que desfallecen de hambre
y quedan tendidos por las calles.

Resh
20«Mira, SEÑOR, y ponte a pensar:
¿A quién trataste alguna vez así?
¿Habrán de comerse las mujeres
a sus hijos, fruto de sus entrañas?
¿Habrán de matar a sacerdotes y profetas
en el santuario del Señor?

Shin
21»Jóvenes y ancianos por igual
yacen en el polvo de las calles;
mis jóvenes y mis doncellas
cayeron a filo de espada.
En tu enojo les quitaste la vida;
¡los masacraste sin piedad!

Tav
22»Como si invitaras a una fiesta solemne,
enviaste contra mí terror de todas partes.
En el día de la ira del SEÑOR
nadie pudo escapar, nadie quedó con vida.
A mis seres queridos, a los que eduqué,
los aniquiló el enemigo.»

Álef
3 n Yo soy aquel que ha sufrido la aflicción
bajo la vara de su ira.
2Me ha hecho andar en las tinieblas;
me ha apartado de la luz.
3Una y otra vez, y a todas horas,
su mano se ha vuelto contra mí.

Bet
4Me ha marchitado la carne y la piel;
me ha quebrantado los huesos.
5Me ha tendido un cerco
de amargura y tribulaciones.
6Me obliga a vivir en las tinieblas,
como a los que hace tiempo murieron.

Guímel
7Me tiene encerrado, no puedo escapar;
me ha puesto pesadas cadenas.
8Por más que grito y pido ayuda,
él se niega a escuchar mi oración.
9Ha sembrado de piedras mi camino;
ha torcido mis senderos.

Dálet
10Me vigila como oso agazapado;
me acecha como león.
11Me aparta del camino para despedazarme;
¡me deja del todo desvalido!
12Con el arco tenso,
me ha hecho el blanco de sus flechas.

He
13Me ha partido el *corazón
con las flechas de su aljaba.
14Soy el hazmerreír de todo mi pueblo;
todo el día me cantan parodias.
15Me ha llenado de amargura,
me ha saturado de hiel.

Vav
16Me ha estrellado contra el suelo;
me ha hecho morder el polvo.
17Me ha quitado la *paz;
ya no recuerdo lo que es la dicha.
18Y digo: «La vida se me acaba,
junto con mi esperanza en el SEÑOR.»

Zayin
19Recuerda que ando errante y afligido,
que me embargan la hiel y la amargura.
20Siempre tengo esto presente,
y por eso me deprimo.
21Pero algo más me viene a la memoria,

---

l **2:17** *poder.* Lit. *Cuerno.* m **2:18** *no retengas ... ojos.* Lit. *no acalles a la niña de tus ojos.* n **Cap. 3** Este capítulo es un poema
acróstico, que sigue el orden del alfabeto hebreo.

lo cual me llena de esperanza:

Jet

22El gran amor del SEÑOR nunca se acaba,ñ
　　y su compasión jamás se agota.
23Cada mañana se renuevan sus bondades;
　　¡muy grande es su fidelidad!
24Por tanto, digo:
　　«El SEÑOR es todo lo que tengo.
　　¡En él esperaré!»

Tet

25Bueno es el SEÑOR con quienes en él confían,
　　con todos los que lo buscan.
26Bueno es esperar calladamente
　　a que el SEÑOR venga a *salvarnos.
27Bueno es que el hombre aprenda
　　a llevar el yugo desde su juventud.

Yod

28¡Déjenlo estar solo y en silencio,
　　porque así el SEÑOR se lo impuso!
29¡Que hunda el rostro en el polvo!
　　¡Tal vez haya esperanza todavía!
30¡Que dé la otra mejilla a quien lo hiera,
　　y quede así cubierto de oprobio!

Caf

31El Señor nos ha rechazado,
　　pero no será para siempre.
32Nos hace sufrir, pero también nos
　　　　compadece,
　　porque es muy grande su amor.
33El SEÑOR nos hiere y nos aflige,
　　pero no porque sea de su agrado.

Lámed

34Cuando se aplasta bajo el pie
　　a todos los prisioneros de la tierra,
35cuando en presencia del *Altísimo
　　se le niegan al *hombre sus derechos
36y no se le hace justicia,
　　¿el Señor no se da cuenta?

Mem

37¿Quién puede anunciar algo y hacerlo
　　　　realidad
　　sin que el Señor dé la orden?
38¿No es acaso por mandato del Altísimo
　　que acontece lo bueno y lo malo?
39¿Por qué habría de quejarse en vida
　　quien es castigado por sus pecados?

Nun

40Hagamos un examen de conciencia
　　y volvamos al *camino del SEÑOR.
41Elevemos al Dios de los cielos
　　nuestro corazón y nuestras manos.
42Hemos pecado, hemos sido rebeldes,
　　y tú no has querido perdonarnos.

Sámej

43Ardiendo en ira nos persigues;
　　nos masacras sin piedad.
44Te envuelves en una nube
　　para no escuchar nuestra oración.
45Como a escoria despreciable,
　　nos has arrojado entre las naciones.

Pe

46Todos nuestros enemigos abren la boca

para hablar mal de nosotros.
47Hemos sufrido terrores, caídas,
　　ruina y destrucción.
48Ríos de lágrimas corren por mis mejillas
　　porque ha sido destruida la capital de mi
　　　　pueblo.

Ayin

49Se inundarán en llanto mis ojos,
　　sin cesar y sin consuelo,
50hasta que desde el cielo
　　el SEÑOR se digne mirarnos.
51Me duele en lo más profundo del *alma
　　ver sufrir a las mujeres de mi ciudad.

Tsade

52Mis enemigos me persiguen sin razón,
　　y quieren atraparme como a un ave.
53Me quieren enterrar vivo
　　y taparme con piedras la salida.
54Las aguas me han cubierto la cabeza;
　　tal parece que me ha llegado el fin.

Qof

55Desde lo más profundo de la fosa
　　invoqué, SEÑOR, tu nombre,
56y tú escuchaste mi plegaria;
　　no cerraste tus oídos a mi clamor.
57Te invoqué, y viniste a mí;
　　«No temas», me dijiste.

Resh

58Tú, Señor, te pusiste de mi parte
　　y me salvaste la vida.
59Tú, SEÑOR, viste el mal que me causaron;
　　¡hazme justicia!
60Tú notaste su sed de venganza
　　y todas sus maquinaciones en mi contra.

Shin

61SEÑOR, tú has escuchado sus insultos
　　y todas sus maquinaciones en mi contra;
62tú sabes que todo el día mis enemigos
　　cuchichean y se confabulan contra mí.
63¡Míralos! Hagan lo que hagan,o
　　se burlan de mí en sus canciones.

Tav

64¡Dales, SEÑOR, su merecido
　　por todo lo que han hecho!
65Oscurece su entendimiento,
　　¡y caiga sobre ellos tu maldición!
66Persíguelos, SEÑOR, en tu enojo,
　　y bórralos de este mundo.

Álef

4 p ¡El oro ha perdido su lustre!
　　¡Se ha empañado el oro fino!
　　¡Regadas por las esquinas de las calles
　　se han quedado las joyas sagradas!

Bet

2A los apuestos habitantes de *Sión,
　　que antaño valían su peso en oro,
hoy se les ve como vasijas de barro,
　　¡como la obra de un alfarero!

Guímel

3Hasta los chacales ofrecen el pecho
　　y dan leche a sus cachorros,
pero Jerusalénq ya no tiene sentimientos;

ñ **3:22** *El gran ... acaba* (Siríaca y Targum); *Por el gran amor del SEÑOR no somos consumidos* (TM).　o **3:63** *¡Míralos! Hagan
lo que hagan.* Lit. *Su sentarse y su levantarse mira.*　p **Cap. 4** Este capítulo es un poema acróstico, que sigue el orden del
alfabeto hebreo.　q **4:3** *Jerusalén.* Lit. *la hija de mi pueblo;* también en vv. 6 y 10.

ies como los avestruces del desierto!

Dálet

4Tanta es la sed que tienen los niños,
que la lengua se les pega al paladar.
Piden pan los pequeñuelos,
pero nadie se lo da.

He

5Quienes antes comían los más ricos manjares
hoy desfallecen de hambre por las calles.
Quienes antes se vestían de fina púrpura
hoy se revuelcan en la inmundicia.

Vav

6Más grande que los pecados de Sodoma
es la iniquidad de Jerusalén;
¡fue derribada en un instante,
y nadie le tendió la mano!

Zayin

7Más radiantes que la nieve eran sus príncipes,
y más blancos que la leche;
más rosado que el coral era su cuerpo;
su apariencia era la del zafiro.

Jet

8Pero ahora se ven más sucios que el hollín;
en la calle nadie los reconoce.
Su piel, reseca como la leña,
se les pega a los huesos.

Tet

9*¡Dichosos los que mueren por la espada,
más que los que mueren de hambre!
Torturados por el hambre desfallecen,
pues no cuentan con los frutos del campo.

Yod

10Con sus manos, mujeres compasivas
cocinaron a sus propios hijos,
y esos niños fueron su alimento
cuando Jerusalén fue destruida.

Caf

11El SEÑOR dio rienda suelta a su enojo;
dejó correr el ardor de su ira.
Le prendió fuego a Sión
y la consumió hasta sus cimientos.

Lámed

12No creían los reyes de la tierra,
ni tampoco los habitantes del mundo,
que los enemigos y adversarios de Jerusalén
cruzarían alguna vez sus *puertas.

Mem

13Pero sucedió.
Por los pecados de sus profetas.
Por las iniquidades de sus sacerdotes.
¡Por derramar sangre inocente
en las calles de la ciudad!

Nun

14Con las manos manchadas de sangre,
andan por las calles como ciegos.
No hay nadie que se atreva
a tocar siquiera sus vestidos.

Sámej

15«¡Largo de aquí, *impuros!», les grita la gente.
«¡Fuera! ¡Fuera! ¡No nos toquen!»
Entre las naciones *paganas les dicen:

«Son unos vagabundos, que andan
huyendo.
No pueden quedarse aquí más tiempo.»

Pe

16El SEÑOR mismo los ha dispersado;
ya no se preocupa por ellos.
Ya no hay respeto para los sacerdotes
ni compasión para los ancianos.

Ayin

17Para colmo, desfallecen nuestros ojos
esperando en vano que alguien nos ayude.
Desde nuestras torres estamos en espera
de una nación que no puede salvarnos.

Tsade

18A cada paso nos acechan;
no podemos ya andar por las calles.
Nuestro fin se acerca, nos ha llegado la hora;
¡nuestros días están contados!

Qof

19Nuestros perseguidores resultaron
más veloces que las águilas del cielo;
nos persiguieron por las montañas,
nos acecharon en el desierto.

Resh

20También cayó en sus redes el *ungido del
SEÑOR,
que era nuestra razón de vivir.
Era él de quien decíamos:
¡Viviremos bajo su sombra entre las
naciones!

Shin

21¡Regocíjate y alégrate, capital de Edom,
que vives como reina en la tierra de Uz!
¡Pero ya tendrás que beber de esta copa,
y quedarás embriagada y desnuda!

Tav

22Tu castigo se ha cumplido, bella Sión;
Dios no volverá a desterrarte.
Pero a ti, capital de Edom, te castigará por tu
maldad
y pondrá al descubierto tus pecados.

5 Recuerda, SEÑOR, lo que nos ha sucedido;
toma en cuenta nuestro oprobio.
2Nuestra heredad ha caído en manos extrañas;
nuestro hogar, en manos de extranjeros.
3No tenemos padre, hemos quedado
huérfanos;
viudas han quedado nuestras madres.
4El agua que bebemos, tenemos que pagarla;
la leña, tenemos que comprarla.
5Los que nos persiguen nos pisan los talones;r
estamos fatigados y no hallamos descanso.
6Entramos en tratoss con Egipto y con Asiria
para conseguir alimentos.
7Nuestros padres pecaron y murieron,
pero a nosotros nos tocó el castigo.
8Ahora nos gobiernan los esclavos,
y no hay quien nos libre de sus manos.
9Exponiéndonos a los peligrost del desierto,
nos jugamos la *vida para obtener
alimentos.
10La piel nos arde como un horno;
¡de hambre nos da fiebre!

---

r 5:5 *Los que ... los talones.* Lit. *Sobre nuestro cuello nos persiguen.*   s 5:6 *Entramos en tratos.* Lit. *Dimos la mano.*   t 5:9 *Exponiéndonos a los peligros.* Lit. *Por causa de la espada.*

11En *Sión y en los pueblos de Judá
   fueron violadas casadas y solteras.
12A nuestros jefes los colgaron de las manos,
   y ni siquiera respetaron a nuestros
      ancianos.
13A nuestros mejores jóvenes los pusieron a
      moler;
   los niños tropezaban bajo el peso de la
      leña.
14Ya no se sientan los *ancianos
   a las *puertas de la ciudad;
   no se escucha ya la música de los jóvenes.
15En nuestro corazón ya no hay gozo;
   la alegría de nuestras danzas se convirtió
      en tristeza.
16Nuestra cabeza se ha quedado sin corona.

¡Ay de nosotros; hemos pecado!
17Desfallece nuestro *corazón;
   se apagan nuestros ojos,
18porque el monte Sión se halla desolado,
   y sobre él rondan los chacales.

19Pero tú, SEÑOR, reinas por siempre;
   tu trono permanece eternamente.
20¿Por qué siempre nos olvidas?
   ¿Por qué nos abandonas tanto tiempo?
21Permítenos volver a ti, SEÑOR, y volveremos;
   devuélvenos la gloria de antaño.u
22La verdad es que nos has rechazado
   y te has excedido en tu enojo contra
      nosotros.

u **5:21** *devuélvenos ... antaño.* Lit. *renueva nuestros días como antes.*

EZEQUIEL

1 En el día quinto del mes cuarto del año treinta, mientras me encontraba entre los deportados a orillas del río Quebar, los cielos se abrieron y recibí visiones de Dios. ²Habían pasado cinco años y cinco meses desde que el rey Joaquín fue deportado.

³(En este tiempo, mientras Ezequiel hijo de Buzí estaba a orillas del río Quebar, en la tierra de los *caldeos, el SEÑOR le dirigió la palabra, y su mano se posó sobre él.)

⁴De pronto me fijé y vi que del norte venían un viento huracanado y una nube inmensa rodeada de un fuego fulgurante y de un gran resplandor. En medio del fuego se veía algo semejante a un metal refulgente. ⁵También en medio del fuego vi algo parecido a cuatro seres vivientes, ⁶cada uno de los cuales tenía cuatro caras y cuatro alas. ⁷Sus piernas eran rectas, y sus pies parecían pezuñas de ternero y brillaban como el bronce bruñido. ⁸En sus cuatro costados, debajo de las alas, tenían manos humanas. Estos cuatro seres tenían caras y alas, ⁹y las alas se tocaban entre sí. Cuando avanzaban no se volvían, sino que cada uno caminaba de frente. ¹⁰Sus rostros tenían el siguiente aspecto: de frente, los cuatro tenían rostro humano; a la derecha tenían cara de león; a la izquierda, de toro; y por detrás, de águila. ¹¹Tales eran sus caras. Sus alas se desplegaban hacia arriba. Con dos alas se tocaban entre sí, mientras que con las otras dos se cubrían el cuerpo. ¹²Los cuatro seres avanzaban de frente. Iban a donde el espíritu los impulsaba, y no se volvían al andar. ¹³Estos seres vivientes parecían carbones encendidos, o antorchas, que se movían de un lado a otro. El fuego resplandecía, y de él se desprendían relámpagos. ¹⁴Los seres vivientes se desplazaban de un lado a otro con la rapidez de un rayo.

¹⁵Miré a los seres vivientes de cuatro caras, y vi que en el suelo, junto a cada uno de ellos, había una rueda. ¹⁶Las cuatro ruedas tenían el mismo aspecto, es decir, brillaban como el topacio y tenían la misma forma. Su estructura era tal que cada rueda parecía estar encajada dentro de la otra. ¹⁷Las ruedas podían avanzar en las cuatro direcciones sin tener que volverse. ¹⁸Las cuatro ruedas tenían grandes aros y estaban llenas de ojos por todas partes. ¹⁹Cuando los seres vivientes avanzaban, las ruedas a su lado hacían lo mismo, y cuando se levantaban del suelo, también se levantaban las ruedas. ²⁰Los seres iban a donde el espíritu los impulsaba, y las ruedas se elevaban juntamente con ellos, porque el espíritu de los seres vivientes estaba en las ruedas. ²¹Cuando los seres se movían, las ruedas también se movían; cuando se detenían, las ruedas también se detenían; cuando se elevaban del suelo, las ruedas también se elevaban. Las ruedas hacían lo mismo que ellos, porque el espíritu de los seres vivientes estaba en las ruedas.

²²Sobre las cabezas de los seres vivientes había una especie de bóveda, muy hermosa y reluciente como el cristal. ²³Debajo de la bóveda las alas de estos seres se extendían y se tocaban entre sí, y cada uno de ellos tenía otras dos alas con las que se cubría el cuerpo. ²⁴Cuando los seres avanzaban, yo podía oír el ruido de sus alas: era como el estruendo de muchas aguas, como la voz del *Todopoderoso, como el tumultuoso ruido de un campamento militar. Cuando se detenían, replegaban sus alas. ²⁵Luego, mientras estaban parados con sus alas replegadas, se

produjo un estruendo por encima de la bóveda que estaba sobre sus cabezas. ²⁶Por encima de esa bóveda había algo semejante a un trono de zafiro, y sobre lo que parecía un trono había una figura de aspecto humano. ²⁷De lo que parecía ser su cintura para arriba, vi algo que brillaba como el metal bruñido, rodeado de fuego. De su cintura para abajo, vi algo semejante al fuego, y un resplandor a su alrededor. ²⁸El resplandor era semejante al del arco iris cuando aparece en las nubes un día de lluvia. Tal era el aspecto de la gloria del SEÑOR. Ante esa visión, caí rostro en tierra y oí que una voz me hablaba.

Llamamiento de Ezequiel

2 Esa voz me dijo: «Hijo de hombre, ponte en pie, que voy a hablarte.»

²Mientras me hablaba, el Espíritu entró en mí, hizo que me pusiera de pie, y pude oír al que me hablaba. ³Me dijo: «Hijo de hombre, te voy a enviar a los israelitas. Es una nación rebelde que se ha sublevado contra mí. Ellos y sus antepasados se han rebelado contra mí hasta el día de hoy. ⁴Te estoy enviando a un pueblo obstinado y terco, al que deberás advertirle: "Así dice el SEÑOR omnipotente." ⁵Tal vez te escuchen, tal vez no, pues son un pueblo rebelde; pero al menos sabrán que entre ellos hay un profeta. ⁶Tú, hijo de hombre, no tengas miedo de ellos ni de sus palabras, por más que estés en medio de cardos y espinas, y vivas rodeado de escorpiones. No temas por lo que digan, ni te sientas atemorizado, porque son un pueblo obstinado. ⁷Tal vez te escuchen, tal vez no, pues son un pueblo rebelde; pero tú les proclamarás mis palabras. ⁸Tú, hijo de hombre, atiende bien a lo que te voy a decir, y no seas rebelde como ellos. Abre tu boca y come lo que te voy a dar.»

⁹Entonces miré, y vi que una mano con un rollo escrito se extendía hacia mí. ¹⁰La mano abrió ante mis ojos el rollo, el cual estaba escrito por ambos lados, y contenía lamentos, gemidos y amenazas.

3 Y me dijo: «Hijo de hombre, cómete este rollo escrito, y luego ve a hablarles a los israelitas.»

²Yo abrí la boca y él hizo que me comiera el rollo. ³Luego me dijo: «Hijo de hombre, cómete el rollo que te estoy dando hasta que te sacies.» Y yo me lo comí, y era tan dulce como la miel.

⁴Otra vez me dijo: «Hijo de hombre, ve a la nación de Israel y proclámale mis palabras. ⁵No te envío a un pueblo de lenguaje complicado y difícil de entender, sino a la nación de Israel. ⁶No te mando a naciones numerosas de lenguaje complicado y difícil de entender, aunque si te hubiera mandado a ellas seguramente te escucharían. ⁷Pero el pueblo de Israel no va a escucharte porque no quiere obedecerme. Todo el pueblo de Israel es terco y obstinado. ⁸No obstante, yo te haré tan terco y obstinado como ellos. ⁹¡Te haré inquebrantable como el diamante, inconmovible como la roca! No les tengas miedo ni te asustes, por más que sean un pueblo rebelde.»

¹⁰Luego me dijo: «Hijo de hombre, escucha bien todo lo que voy a decirte, y atesóralo en tu *corazón. ¹¹Ahora ve a donde están exiliados tus compatriotas. Tal vez te escuchen, tal vez no; pero tú adviérteles: "Así dice el SEÑOR omnipotente."»

¹²Entonces el Espíritu de Diosª me levantó, y detrás de mí oí decir con el estruendo de un terremoto: «¡Bendita sea la gloria del SEÑOR, donde él habita!»

ª **3:12** *Espíritu de Dios.* Lit. *espíritu o viento;* también en v. 24.

13Oí el ruido de las alas de los seres vivientes al rozarse unas con otras, y el de las ruedas que estaban junto a ellas, y el ruido era estruendoso. 14El Espíritu me levantó y se apoderó de mí, y me fui amargado y enardecido, mientras la mano del SEÑOR me sujetaba con fuerza. 15Así llegué a Tel Aviv, a orillas del río Quebar, adonde estaban los israelitas exiliados, y totalmente abatido me quedé con ellos durante siete días.

Advertencia a Israel

16Al cabo de los siete días, el SEÑOR me dijo lo siguiente: 17«Hijo de hombre, a ti te he puesto como centinela del pueblo de Israel. Por tanto, cuando oigas mi palabra, adviérteles de mi parte 18al malvado: "Estás condenado a muerte." Si tú no le hablas al malvado ni le haces ver su mala conducta, para que siga viviendo, ese malvado morirá por causa de su pecado, pero yo te pediré cuentas de su muerte. 19En cambio, si tú se lo adviertes, y él no se *arrepiente de su maldad ni de su mala conducta, morirá por causa de su pecado, pero tú habrás salvado tu vida. 20Por otra parte, si un justo se desvía de su buena conducta y hace lo malo, y yo lo hago caer y tú no se lo adviertes, él morirá sin que se le tome en cuenta todo el bien que haya hecho. Por no haberle hecho ver su maldad, él morirá por causa de su pecado, pero yo te pediré cuentas de su muerte. 21Pero si tú le adviertes al justo que no peque, y en efecto él no peca, él seguirá viviendo porque hizo caso de tu advertencia, y tú habrás salvado tu vida.»

22Luego el SEÑOR puso su mano sobre mí, y me dijo: «Levántate y dirígete al campo, que allí voy a hablarte.» 23Yo me levanté y salí al campo. Allí vi la gloria del SEÑOR, tal como la había visto a orillas del río Quebar, y caí rostro en tierra. 24Entonces el Espíritu de Dios entró en mí, hizo que me pusiera de pie, y me dijo: «Ve y enciérrate en tu casa. 25A ti, hijo de hombre, te atarán con sogas para que no puedas salir ni andar entre el pueblo. 26Yo haré que se te pegue la lengua al paladar, y así te quedarás mudo y no podrás reprenderlos, por más que sean un pueblo rebelde. 27Pero cuando yo te hable, te soltaré la lengua y les advertirás: "Así dice el SEÑOR omnipotente." El que quiera oír, que oiga; y el que no quiera, que no oiga, porque son un pueblo rebelde.

Anuncio del sitio a Jerusalén

4 »Hijo de hombre, toma ahora un ladrillo, ponlo delante de ti y dibuja en él la ciudad de Jerusalén. 2Acampa a su alrededor y ponle sitio; levanta torres de asalto contra ella y construye una rampa que llegue hasta la ciudad; instala máquinas para derribar sus murallas. 3Toma una plancha de hierro y colócala como un muro entre ti y la ciudad, y fija tu mirada contra ella. De esa manera quedará sitiada: tú mismo la sitiarás. Eso les servirá de señal a los israelitas.

4»Acuéstate sobre tu lado izquierdo, y echa sobre ti la culpa de los israelitas. Todo el tiempo que estés acostado sobre ese lado, cargarás con sus culpas. 5Yo te he puesto un plazo de trescientos noventa días, es decir, un lapso de tiempo equivalente a los años de la culpa de Israel. 6Cuando cumplas ese plazo, volverás a acostarte, pero esta vez sobre tu lado derecho, y cuarenta días cargarás con la culpa del pueblo de Judá, o sea, un día por cada año. 7Luego mirarás el asedio de Jerusalén, y con brazo amenazante profetizarás contra ella. 8Yo te ataré con sogas

para que no puedas darte vuelta de un lado a otro mientras no se cumplan los días del asedio.

9»Toma trigo, cebada, habas, lentejas, mijo y avena; viértelos en un recipiente y amásalos para hacer pan, pues ése será tu alimento durante los trescientos noventa días que estarás acostado sobre tu lado izquierdo. 10Cada día comerás, a una hora fija, una ración de un cuarto de kilo.b 11También a una hora fija beberás medio litroc de agua. 12Cocerás ese pan con excremento humano, y a la vista de todos lo comerás, como si fuera una torta de cebada.»

13Luego el SEÑOR añadió: «De igual manera, los israelitas comerán alimentos *impuros en medio de las naciones por donde los voy a dispersar.»

14Entonces exclamé: «¡No, SEÑOR mi Dios! ¡Yo jamás me he *contaminado con nada! Desde mi niñez y hasta el día de hoy, jamás he comido carne de ningún animal que se haya encontrado muerto, o que haya sido despedazado por las fieras. ¡Por mi boca no ha entrado ningún tipo de carne impura!»

15«Está bien —me respondió—, te doy permiso para que hornees tu pan con excremento de vaca en vez de excremento humano.»

16Luego me dijo: «Hijo de hombre, voy a hacer que escasee el trigo en Jerusalén. La gente comerá el pan racionado y con mucha angustia; también el agua será racionada, la beberán con mucha ansiedad. 17Escasearán el pan y el agua, y cuando cada uno vea la condición del otro, todos irán perdiendo las fuerzas y acabarán muriéndose a causa de sus pecados.

5 »Hijo de hombre, toma ahora una espada afilada, y úsala como navaja de afeitar para raparte la cabeza y afeitarte la barba. Toma luego una balanza y divide tu cabello cortado. 2Cuando se cumplan los días del sitio, quemarás en medio de la ciudad una tercera parte del cabello; otra tercera parte la cortarás con la espada alrededor de la ciudad, y la parte restante la esparcirás al viento. Yo, por mi parte, desenvainaré la espada y perseguiré a sus habitantes. 3Toma algunos de los cabellos y átalos al borde de tu manto. 4Luego toma otros pocos y arrójalos en el fuego para que se quemen. Desde allí se extenderá el fuego sobre todo el pueblo de Israel.

5»Así dice el SEÑOR omnipotente: Ésta es la ciudad de Jerusalén. Yo la coloqué en medio de las naciones y de los territorios a su alrededor. 6Pero ella se rebeló contra mis *leyes y decretos, con una perversidad mayor a la de las naciones y territorios vecinos. En otras palabras, rechazó por completo mis leyes y decretos.

7»Por eso yo, el SEÑOR omnipotente, declaro: Ustedes han sido más rebeldes que las naciones a su alrededor; no han seguido mis decretos ni obedecido mis leyes, y ni siquiera se han sujetado a las costumbres de esas naciones. 8Por lo tanto yo, el SEÑOR omnipotente, declaro: Estoy contra ti, Jerusalén, y te voy a castigar a la vista de todas las naciones. 9Por causa de tus ídolos repugnantes, haré contigo lo que jamás he hecho ni volveré a hacer. 10Entre ustedes habrá padres que se comerán a sus hijos, y también hijos que se comerán a sus padres. Yo los castigaré, y a quien sobreviva lo dispersaré por los cuatro vientos.

11»Por esta razón yo, el SEÑOR omnipotente, juro por mí mismo: Como ustedes han profanado mi santuario con sus ídolos repugnantes y con prácticas detestables, yo los destruiré sin misericordia y sin piedad. 12Una tercera parte de tu pueblo morirá en tus calles por la peste y por el hambre; otra tercera

---

b 4:10 un cuarto de kilo. Lit. veinte *siclos.   c 4:11 medio litro. Lit. la sexta parte de un *hin.

parte caerá a filo de espada en tus alrededores, y a la tercera parte restante la dispersaré por los cuatro vientos. Yo desenvainaré la espada y perseguiré a la gente. 13Entonces se apaciguará mi ira, mi enojo contra ellos será saciado, y me daré por satisfecho. Y cuando en mi celo haya desahogado mi enojo contra ellos, sabrán que yo, el SEÑOR, lo he dicho.

14»Yo te convertiré en un montón de ruinas; te haré objeto de burla de todas las naciones que te rodean. Todos los que pasen junto a ti, lo verán. 15Cuando yo te castigue con indignación, enojo y durísimos reproches, serás objeto de burla y de oprobio, y motivo de advertencia y escarmiento para las naciones que te rodean. Yo, el SEÑOR, lo he dicho.

16»Yo te haré blanco del hambre, esa mortífera flecha que todo lo destruye. Dispararé a matar, pues traeré sobre ti hambre y escasez de provisiones. 17Por si fuera poco, lanzaré contra ti animales salvajes que te dejarán sin hijos. Te verás abrumado por las plagas y por el derramamiento de sangre, pues haré que caigas a filo de espada. Yo, el SEÑOR, lo he dicho.»

Profecía contra los montes de Israel

6 El SEÑOR me dirigió la palabra: 2«Hijo de hombre, alza tu mirada hacia los cerros de Israel, y profetiza contra ellos. 3Diles: "Escuchen, cerros de Israel, la palabra del SEÑOR. Esto dice el SEÑOR omnipotente a cerros y colinas, a ríos y valles: 'Haré que venga contra ustedes la espada, y destruiré sus lugares de culto idolátrico. 4Despedazaré sus altares, haré añicos sus quemadores de incienso, y haré también que sus muertos caigan frente a sus ídolos malolientes. 5¡Sí! Delante de sus ídolos malolientes arrojaré los cadáveres de los israelitas, y esparciré sus huesos en torno a sus altares. 6No importa dónde vivan ustedes, sus ciudades serán destruidas y sus lugares de culto idolátrico serán devastados. Sus altares quedarán completamente destrozados; sus ídolos malolientes, hechos un montón de ruinas; sus quemadores de incienso, hechos añicos. ¡Todas sus obras desaparecerán! 7Su propia gente caerá muerta, y así sabrán ustedes que yo soy el SEÑOR.

8»" 'Pero yo dejaré que algunos de ustedes se escapen de la muerte y queden esparcidos entre las naciones y los pueblos. 9Los sobrevivientes se acordarán de mí en las naciones donde hayan sido llevados cautivos. Se acordarán de cómo sufrí por culpa de su *corazón adúltero, y de cómo se apartaron de mí y se fueron tras sus ídolos malolientes. ¡Sentirán asco de ellos mismos por todas las maldades que hicieron y por sus obras repugnantes! 10Entonces sabrán que no en vano yo, el SEÑOR, los amenacé con estas calamidades.' '

11»Así dice el SEÑOR omnipotente: "Aplaude, patalea y grita: ¡Felicitaciones por todas las terribles abominaciones del pueblo de Israel!' Morirán por la espada, el hambre y la peste. 12Quien esté lejos perecerá por la peste, y quien esté cerca morirá a filo de espada, y el que quede con vida se morirá de hambre. Así descargaré sobre ellos toda mi ira, 13y sus cadáveres quedarán tendidos entre sus ídolos malolientes y alrededor de sus altares, en las colinas altas y en las cumbres de los cerros, o debajo de todo árbol frondoso y de toda encina tupida, es decir, en los lugares donde ofrecieron incienso de olor agradable a sus ídolos malolientes. ¡Entonces sabrán que yo soy el

SEÑOR! 14Extenderé mi mano contra ellos, y convertiré en tierra desolada su país y todo lugar donde habiten, desde el desierto hasta Riblá. ¡Entonces sabrán que yo soy el SEÑOR!"»

El fin ha llegado

7 El SEÑOR me dirigió la palabra: 2«Hijo de hombre, así dice el SEÑOR omnipotente al pueblo de Israel: ¡He llegado la hora! Ha llegado el fin para todo el país. 3¡Te ha llegado el fin! Descargaré mi ira sobre ti; te juzgaré según tu conducta y te pediré cuentas de todas tus acciones detestables. 4No voy a tratarte con piedad ni a tenerte compasión, sino que te haré pagar cara tu conducta y tus prácticas repugnantes. Así sabrás que yo soy el SEÑOR.

5»Así dice el SEÑOR omnipotente: ¡Las desgracias se siguen unas a otras! 6¡Ya viene la hecatombe; tu fin es inminente! 7Te ha llegado la hora, habitante del país. Ya viene la hora, ya se acerca el día. En las montañas hay pánico y no alegría. 8Ya estoy por descargar sobre ti mi furor; desahogaré mi enojo contra ti. Te juzgaré según tu conducta; te pediré cuentas por todas tus acciones detestables. 9No voy a tratarte con piedad ni a tenerte compasión, sino que te haré pagar cara tu conducta y tus prácticas repugnantes. Así sabrás que yo, el SEÑOR, también puedo herir.

10»¡Ya llegó el día! ¡Ya está aquí! ¡Tu suerte está echada! Florece la injusticia,d germina el orgullo, 11y la violencia produce frutos de maldad. Nada quedará de ustedese ni de su multitud; nada de su riqueza ni de su opulencia.f 12Llegó la hora; éste es el día. Que no se alegre el que compra ni llore el que vende, porque mi enojo caerá sobre toda la multitud. 13Y aunque el vendedor siga con vida, no recuperará lo vendido. Porque no se revocará la visión referente a toda su multitud, y por su culpa nadie podrá conservar la vida. 14Aunque toquen la trompeta y preparen todo, nadie saldrá a la batalla, porque mi enojo caerá sobre toda la multitud.

15»Allá afuera hay guerra; y aquí adentro, peste y hambre. El que esté en el campo morirá a filo de espada, y el que esté en la ciudad se morirá de hambre y de peste. 16Los que logren escapar se quedarán en las montañas como palomas del valle, cada uno llorando por su maldad. 17Desfallecerá todo brazo y temblará toda rodilla. 18Se vestirán de luto, y el terror los dominará. Se llenarán de vergüenza y se convertirán en objeto de burla.g 19La plata la arrojarán a las calles, y el oro lo verán como basura. En el día de la ira del SEÑOR, ni su oro ni su plata podrán salvarlos, ni les servirán para saciar su hambre y llenarse el estómago, porque el oro fue el causante de su caída. 20Se enorgullecían de sus joyas hermosas, y las usaron para fabricar sus imágenes detestables y sus ídolos despreciables. Por esta razón convertiré esas joyas en algo repugnante. 21Haré que vengan los extranjeros y se las roben, y los malvados de la tierra se las lleven y las profanen. 22Alejaré de ellos mi presencia, y mi templo será profanado; entrarán los invasores y lo profanarán.

23»Prepara las cadenash porque el país se ha llenado de sangre, y la ciudad está llena de violencia. 24Haré que las naciones más violentas vengan y se apoderen de sus casas. Pondré fin a la soberbia de los poderosos, y sus santuarios serán profanados. 25Cuando la desesperación los atrape, en vano bus-

---

d 7:10 injusticia. Lit. vara.   e 7:11 ustedes. Lit. ellos; es decir, el pueblo de Israel.   f 7:11 nada quedará ... opulencia. Frases de difícil traducción.   g 7:18 se convertirán en objeto de burla. Lit. todas sus cabezas serán rapadas.   h 7:23 cadenas. Palabra de difícil traducción.

carán la *paz. 26Una tras otra vendrán las desgracias, al igual que las malas noticias. Del profeta demandarán visiones; la instrucción se alejará del sacerdote, y a los *jefes del pueblo no les quedarán consejos. 27El rey hará duelo, el príncipe se cubrirá de tristeza, y temblarán las manos del pueblo. Yo los trataré según su conducta, y los juzgaré según sus acciones. Así sabrán que yo soy el SEÑOR.»

Idolatría en el templo

8 En el día quinto del mes sexto del año sexto, yo estaba sentado en mi casa, junto con los *jefes de Judá. De pronto, el SEÑOR puso su mano sobre mí.

2Miré entonces, y vi una figura de aspecto humano: de la cintura para abajo, ardía como fuego; de la cintura para arriba, brillaba como el metal bruñido. 3Aquella figura extendió lo que parecía ser una mano, y me tomó del cabello. Un viento me sostuvo entre la tierra y el cielo, y en visiones divinas me llevó a la parte norte de Jerusalén, hasta la entrada de la puerta interior, que es donde está el ídolo que provoca los celos de Dios. 4Allí estaba la gloria del Dios de Israel, como la visión que yo había visto en el campo. 5Y Dios me dijo: «Hijo de hombre, levanta la vista hacia el norte.» Yo miré en esa dirección, y en la entrada misma, al norte de la puerta del altar, vi el ídolo que provoca los celos de Dios. 6También me dijo: «Hijo de hombre, ¿ves las grandes abominaciones que cometen los israelitas en este lugar, y que me hacen alejarme de mi santuario? Realmente no has visto nada todavía; peores abominaciones verás.»

7Después me llevó a la entrada del atrio. En el muro había un agujero. 8Entonces me dijo: «Hijo de hombre, agranda el agujero del muro.» Yo agrandé el agujero en el muro y me encontré con una puerta. 9Dios me dijo: «Entra y observa las abominaciones que allí cometen.» 10Yo entré y a lo largo del muro vi pinturas de todo tipo: figuras de reptiles y de otros animales repugnantes, y de todos los malolientes ídolos de Israel. 11Setenta jefes israelitas estaban de pie frente a los ídolos, rindiéndoles culto. Entre ellos se encontraba Jazanías hijo de Safán. Cada uno tenía en la mano un incensario, del cual subía una fragante nube de incienso.

12Y él me dijo: «Hijo de hombre, ¿ves lo que hacen los jefes israelitas en los oscuros nichos de sus ídolos? Andan diciendo: "No hay ningún SEÑOR que nos vea. El SEÑOR ha abandonado el país."» 13Y añadió: «Ya los verás cometer mayores atrocidades.»

14Luego me llevó a la entrada del templo del SEÑOR, a la puerta que da hacia el norte. Allí estaban unas mujeres sentadas, que lloraban por el dios Tamuz. 15Entonces Dios me dijo: «Hijo de hombre, ¿ves esto? Pues aún las verás cometer mayores atrocidades.»

16Y me llevó al atrio interior del templo. A la entrada del templo, entre el vestíbulo y el altar, había unos veinticinco hombres que estaban mirando hacia el oriente y adoraban al sol, de espaldas al templo del SEÑOR. 17Me dijo: «Hijo de hombre, ¿ves esto? ¿Tan poca cosa le parece a Judá cometer tales abominaciones, que también ha llenado la tierra de violencia y no deja de provocarme? ¡Mira cómo me enardecen, pasándome[i] por la nariz sus pestilentes ramos! 18Por eso, voy a actuar con furor. No les tendré piedad ni compasión. Por más que me imploren a gritos, ¡no los escucharé!»

El castigo de los culpables

9 Después oí que Dios clamaba con fuerte voz: «¡Acérquense, verdugos de la ciudad, cada uno con su arma destructora en la mano!» 2Entonces vi que por el camino de la puerta superior que da hacia el norte venían seis hombres, cada uno con un arma mortal en la mano. Con ellos venía un hombre vestido de lino, que llevaba en la cintura un estuche de escriba. Todos ellos entraron y se pararon junto al altar de bronce. 3La gloria del Dios de Israel, que estaba sobre los *querubines, se elevó y se dirigió hacia el umbral del templo. Al hombre vestido de lino que llevaba en la cintura un estuche de escriba, el SEÑOR lo llamó 4y le dijo: «Recorre la ciudad de Jerusalén, y coloca una señal en la frente de quienes giman y hagan lamentación por todos los actos detestables que se cometen en la ciudad.» 5Pero oí que a los otros les dijo: «Síganlo. Recorran la ciudad y maten sin piedad ni compasión. 6Maten a viejos y a jóvenes, a muchachas, niños y mujeres; comiencen en el templo, y no dejen a nadie con vida. Pero no toquen a los que tengan la señal.» Y aquellos hombres comenzaron por matar a los viejos que estaban frente al templo.

7Después les dijo: «Salgan y profanen el templo; llenen de cadáveres los atrios.»

Ellos salieron y comenzaron a matar gente en toda la ciudad. 8Y mientras mataban, yo me quedé solo, caí rostro en tierra y grité: «¡Ay, SEÑOR y Dios! ¿Descargarás tu furor sobre Jerusalén y destruirás a todo el resto de Israel?»

9El SEÑOR me respondió: «La iniquidad del pueblo de Israel y de Judá es extremadamente grande. El país está lleno de violencia; la ciudad, llena de injusticia. Ellos piensan: "El SEÑOR ha abandonado el país. No hay ningún SEÑOR que vea." 10Por eso no les tendré piedad ni compasión, sino que les pediré cuentas de su conducta.»

11Entonces el hombre vestido de lino que llevaba en la cintura un estuche de escriba me informó: «Ya hice lo que me mandaste hacer.»

La gloria del SEÑOR abandona el templo

10 Después miré, y sobre la bóveda que estaba encima de la cabeza de los *querubines vi una especie de piedra de zafiro que tenía la forma de un trono. 2Y el SEÑOR le dijo al hombre vestido de lino: «Métete entre las ruedas que están debajo de los querubines, toma un puñado de las brasas que están entre los querubines, y espárcelas por toda la ciudad.» Y el hombre se metió allí, mientras yo miraba.

3En el momento en que el hombre entró, los querubines estaban en la parte sur del templo y una nube llenaba el atrio interior. 4Entonces la gloria del SEÑOR, que estaba sobre los querubines, se elevó y se dirigió hacia el umbral del templo. La nube llenó el templo, y el atrio se llenó del resplandor de la gloria del SEÑOR. 5El ruido de las alas de los querubines llegaba hasta el atrio exterior, y era semejante a la voz del Dios *Todopoderoso.

6El SEÑOR le ordenó al hombre vestido de lino: «Toma fuego de en medio de las ruedas que están entre los querubines.» Así que el hombre fue y se paró entre las ruedas. 7Uno de los querubines extendió la mano, tomó el fuego que estaba entre ellos, y lo puso en las manos del hombre vestido de lino. Aquél lo recibió y se fue. 8(Debajo de las alas de los querubines se veía algo semejante a la mano de un hombre.)

---

i 8:17 *pasándome.* Lit. *pasándose.*

9Me fijé, y al lado de los querubines vi cuatro ruedas, una junto a cada uno de ellos. Las ruedas tenían un aspecto brillante como el crisólito. 10Las cuatro ruedas se asemejaban, y parecía como si una rueda estuviera encajada en la otra. 11Al avanzar, podían hacerlo en las cuatro direcciones sin necesidad de volverse. Avanzaban en la dirección a que apuntaba la cabeza del querubín, y no tenían que volverse. 12Todo el cuerpo, la espalda, las manos y las alas de los querubines, al igual que las cuatro ruedas, estaban llenos de ojos. 13Alcancé a oír que a las ruedas se les llamaba «círculos». 14Cada uno de los querubines tenía cuatro caras: la primera, de querubín; la segunda, de hombre; la tercera, de león; y la cuarta, de águila.

15Los querubines, que eran los mismos seres que yo había visto junto al río Quebar, se elevaron. 16Cuando avanzaban, las ruedas a su costado hacían lo mismo; cuando desplegaban sus alas para levantarse del suelo, las ruedas no se apartaban de ellos; 17cuando se detenían, las ruedas hacían lo mismo; cuando se levantaban, las ruedas se levantaban también, porque el espíritu de esos seres vivientes estaba en las ruedas.

18La gloria del SEÑOR se elevó por encima del umbral del templo y se detuvo sobre los querubines. 19Y mientras yo miraba, los querubines desplegaron sus alas y se elevaron del suelo, y junto con las ruedas salieron y se detuvieron en la puerta oriental del templo del SEÑOR. La gloria del Dios de Israel estaba por encima de ellos. 20Eran los mismos seres vivientes que, estando yo junto al río Quebar, había visto debajo del Dios de Israel. Entonces me di cuenta de que eran querubines. 21Cada uno tenía cuatro caras y cuatro alas, y bajo las alas tenían algo que se parecía a las manos de un hombre. 22Sus caras eran iguales a las que yo había visto junto al río Quebar. Cada uno de ellos caminaba de frente.

Juicio contra los líderes de Israel

11 Un viento me levantó y me llevó hasta la entrada oriental del templo del SEÑOR. A la entrada vi a veinticinco hombres, entre los cuales estaban Jazanías hijo de Azur y Pelatías hijo de Benaías, que eran jefes del pueblo. 2Dios me dijo: «Hijo de hombre, éstos son los que están tramando maldades y dando malos consejos en esta ciudad. 3Dicen: "Todavía no es el momento de reconstruir las casas. La ciudad es la olla y nosotros somos la carne." 4Por eso, hijo de hombre, profetiza contra ellos; ¡sí, profetiza!»

5El Espíritu del SEÑOR vino sobre mí y me ordenó proclamar: «Así dice el SEÑOR: "Ustedes, pueblo de Israel, han dicho esto, y yo conozco sus pensamientos. 6Han matado a mucha gente en esta ciudad y han llenado las calles de cadáveres. 7Por eso yo, el SEÑOR omnipotente, les aseguro que los cadáveres que ustedes han arrojado en medio de la ciudad son la carne, y la ciudad es la olla de la que yo los arrojaré. 8¿Temen la guerra? Pues bien, yo, el SEÑOR omnipotente, declaro que enviaré guerra contra ustedes. 9Los echaré de la ciudad, los entregaré en manos de extranjeros y los castigaré con justicia. 10Morirán a filo de espada; yo los juzgaré en las mismas fronteras de Israel, y así sabrán que yo soy el SEÑOR. 11La ciudad no les servirá de olla, ni serán ustedes la carne dentro de ella. Yo los juzgaré en la frontera misma de Israel. 12Entonces sabrán que yo soy el SEÑOR. No han seguido mis decretos ni han cumplido con mis *leyes, sino que han adoptado las costumbres de las naciones que los rodean."»

13Mientras yo profetizaba, Pelatías hijo de Benaías cayó muerto. Entonces caí rostro en tierra y clamé a gritos: «¡Ay, SEÑOR mi Dios! ¿Vas a exterminar al resto de Israel?»

14El SEÑOR me dirigió la palabra: 15«Hijo de hombre, esto es lo que dicen los habitantes de Jerusalén en cuanto a tus hermanos, tus parientes y todo el pueblo de Israel: "Ellos se han alejado del SEÑOR, y por eso se nos ha dado esta tierra en posesión." 16Por tanto, adviérteles que así dice el SEÑOR omnipotente: "Aunque los desterré a naciones lejanas y los dispersé por países extraños, por un tiempo les he servido de santuario en las tierras adonde han ido."

17»Adviérteles también que así dice el SEÑOR omnipotente: "Yo los reuniré de entre las naciones; los juntaré de los países donde han estado dispersos, y les daré la tierra de Israel. 18Ellos volverán a su tierra y echarán de allí a los ídolos detestables y pondrán fin a las prácticas repugnantes. 19Yo les daré un *corazón íntegro, y pondré en ellos un espíritu renovado. Les arrancaré el corazón de piedra que ahora tienen, y pondré en ellos un corazón de carne, 20para que cumplan mis decretos y pongan en práctica mis leyes. Entonces ellos serán mi pueblo, y yo seré su Dios. 21Pero a los que van tras esos ídolos detestables y siguen prácticas repugnantes, yo les pediré cuentas de su conducta. Lo afirma el SEÑOR omnipotente."»

La gloria del Señor abandona Jerusalén

22Los *querubines desplegaron sus alas. Las ruedas estaban junto a ellos, y la gloria del Dios de Israel estaba por encima de ellos. 23La gloria del SEÑOR se elevó de en medio de la ciudad y se detuvo sobre el cerro que está al oriente de Jerusalén. 24En una visión, un viento me levantó y me trasladó hasta donde estaban los exiliados en Babilonia; y la visión desapareció. 25Entonces les comuniqué a los exiliados lo que el SEÑOR me había revelado.

Símbolo del exilio

12 El SEÑOR me dirigió la palabra: 2«Hijo de hombre, vives en medio de un pueblo rebelde. Tienen ojos para ver, pero no ven; tienen oídos para oír, pero no oyen. ¡Son un pueblo rebelde!

3»Por tanto, hijo de hombre, prepara tu equipaje; prepáralo para el exilio, y a plena luz del día, a la vista de todos, saldrás como quien va exiliado sin destino fijo. Tal vez así entiendan, aunque son un pueblo rebelde. 4Saca tu equipaje a plena luz del día, a la vista de todos, y al caer la tarde ponte en marcha, a la vista de todos, como quien va al exilio. 5También en presencia de todos, abre un agujero en el muro y sal por ahí con tu equipaje. 6Al llegar la noche, mientras todos te estén viendo, ponte en marcha con el equipaje al hombro. Cúbrete la cara para que no puedas ver la tierra, porque de ti he hecho un presagio para el pueblo de Israel.»

7Hice lo que se me había mandado, y a plena luz del día saqué mi bagaje, como quien va al exilio. Al caer la tarde abrí el agujero con mis propias manos, y al llegar la noche, en presencia de todos, salí con mi equipaje al hombro.

8Por la mañana el SEÑOR me dirigió la palabra: 9«Hijo de hombre, con toda seguridad el pueblo rebelde de Israel te preguntará: "¿Qué estás haciendo?" 10Pero tú explícales: "Así dice el SEÑOR omnipotente: Este mensaje se refiere al pueblo de Israel que vive en Jerusalén, y también a su gobernante." 11Diles: "Yo soy un presagio para ustedes. Lo que hice yo, les va a pasar a ustedes, pues serán llevados cautivos al exilio." 12Y su gobernante se echará el equipaje al hombro, y saldrá de noche por un agujero que abrirán en el muro. Se cubrirá la cara para que no pueda ver la tierra. 13Yo tenderé mi red sobre él, y quedará atrapado en mi trampa. Así lo llevaré a Babilonia, la tierra de los *caldeos, pero no podrá verla porque allá morirá. 14Dispersaré a los cuatro vientos a todos los que lo rodean, tanto a sus ayudantes como a todas sus tropas, y los perseguiré espada en mano. 15Entonces sabrán que yo soy el SEÑOR.

»Cuando los haya dispersado y esparcido por las naciones, 16dejaré que unos pocos de ellos se escapen de la guerra, del hambre y de la peste, para que en las naciones por donde vayan den cuenta de sus prácticas repugnantes. Entonces sabrán que yo soy el SEÑOR.»

17El SEÑOR me dirigió la palabra: 18«Hijo de hombre, tiembla al comer tu pan, y llénate de espanto y miedo al beber tu agua. 19Adviértele a la gente del país que así dice el SEÑOR omnipotente acerca de los que habitan en Jerusalén y en la tierra de Israel: "Con mucho miedo comerán su pan, y con gran angustia beberán su agua. Por la violencia de sus habitantes la tierra será despojada de todo lo que hay en ella. 20Las ciudades habitadas serán arrasadas, y su país quedará en ruinas. Entonces sabrán ustedes que yo soy el SEÑOR."»

21El SEÑOR me dirigió la palabra: 22«Hijo de hombre, ¿qué quiere decir este refrán que se repite en la tierra de Israel: "Se cumple el tiempo, pero no la visión"? 23Por lo tanto, adviérteles que así dice el SEÑOR omnipotente: "Pondré fin a ese refrán, y ya no volverán a repetirlo en Israel." Y adviérteles también: "Ya vienen los días en que se cumplirán las visiones. 24Pues ya no habrá visiones engañosas ni predicciones que susciten falsas expectativas en el pueblo de Israel. 25Porque yo, el SEÑOR, hablaré, y lo que diga se cumplirá sin retraso. Pueblo rebelde, mientras ustedes aún tengan vida, yo cumpliré mi palabra. Lo afirma el SEÑOR omnipotente."»

26El SEÑOR me dirigió la palabra: 27«Hijo de hombre, el pueblo de Israel anda diciendo que tus visiones son para un futuro distante, y que tus profecías son a largo plazo. 28Por lo tanto, adviérteles que así dice el SEÑOR omnipotente: "Mis palabras se cumplirán sin retraso: yo cumpliré con lo que digo. Lo afirma el SEÑOR omnipotente."»

Condena a los falsos profetas

13 El SEÑOR me dirigió la palabra: 2«Hijo de hombre, denuncia a los profetas de Israel que hacen vaticinios según sus propios delirios, y diles que escuchen la palabra del SEÑOR. 3Así dice el SEÑOR omnipotente: "¡Ay de los profetas insensatos que, sin haber recibido ninguna visión, siguen su propia inspiración! 4¡Ay, Israel! Tus profetas son como chacales entre las ruinas. 5No han ocupado su lugar en las brechas, ni han reparado los muros del pueblo de Israel, para que en el día del SEÑOR se mantenga firme en la batalla. 6Sus visiones son falsas, y mentirosas sus adivinaciones. Dicen: 'Lo afirma el SEÑOR', pero el SEÑOR no los ha enviado; sin embargo, ellos esperan que se cumpla lo que profetizan. 7¿Acaso no son falsas sus visiones, y mentirosas sus adivinaciones, cuando dicen: 'Lo afirma el SEÑOR', sin que yo haya hablado?

8»"Por tanto, así dice el SEÑOR omnipotente: A causa de sus palabras falsas y visiones mentirosas,

aquí estoy contra ustedes. Lo afirma el SEÑOR omnipotente. 9Levantaré mi mano contra los profetas; contra aquellos que tienen visiones falsas y ofrecen adivinaciones mentirosas. No participarán en la asamblea de mi pueblo, ni aparecerán sus nombres en los registros de los israelitas, ni entrarán en el país de Israel. Así sabrán ustedes que yo soy el SEÑOR omnipotente.

10»"Así es, en efecto. Estos profetas han engañado a mi pueblo diciendo: ¡Todo anda bien!', pero las cosas no andan bien; construyen paredes endebles de hermosa fachada. 11Pues diles a esos constructores que sus fachadas se vendrán abajo con una lluvia torrencial, abundante granizo y viento huracanado. 12Y cuando la pared se haya caído, les preguntarán: '¿Qué pasó con la hermosa fachada?'

13»"Por tanto, así dice el SEÑOR omnipotente: En mi furia desataré un viento huracanado; en mi ira, una lluvia torrencial; en mi furia, granizo destructor. 14Echaré por los suelos la pared con su hermosa fachada; sus endebles cimientos quedarán al descubierto. Y cuando caiga, ustedes perecerán. Así sabrán que yo soy el SEÑOR. 15Descargaré mi furia sobre esa pared y sobre los que hicieron su hermosa fachada. A ustedes les diré que ya no queda la pared ni los que hicieron su hermosa fachada: 16esos profetas de Israel que profetizaban acerca de Jerusalén, y tenían visiones falsas, y anunciaban que todo andaba bien, cuando en realidad era todo lo contrario. Lo afirma el SEÑOR omnipotente."

Condena a las profetisas

17»Y ahora tú, hijo de hombre, enfréntate a esas mujeres de tu pueblo que profetizan según sus propios delirios. ¡Denúncialas! 18Adviérteles que así dice el SEÑOR omnipotente: "¡Ay de las que hacen objetos de hechicería y sortilegios para atrapar a la gente!j ¿Acaso creen que pueden atrapar la vida de mi pueblo y salvar su propio pellejo? 19Ustedes me han profanado delante de mi pueblo por un puñado de cebada y unas migajas de pan. Por las mentiras que dicen, y que mi pueblo cree, se mata a los que no deberían morir y se deja con vida a los que no merecen vivir.

20»"Por tanto, así dice el SEÑOR omnipotente: Estoy contra sus hechicerías, con las que ustedes atrapan a la gente como a pájaros. Pero yo los liberaré de sus poderes mágicos, y los dejaré volar. 21Rescataré a mi pueblo de esos sortilegios, para que dejen de ser presa en sus manos. Así sabrán que yo soy el SEÑOR. 22Porque ustedes han descorazonado al justo con sus mentiras, sin que yo lo haya afligido. Han alentado al malvado para que no se convierta de su mala conducta y se salve. 23Por eso ya no volverán a tener visiones falsas ni a practicar la adivinación. Yo rescataré a mi pueblo del poder de ustedes, y así sabrán que yo soy el SEÑOR."»

Contra la idolatría

14 Unos *jefes de Israel vinieron a visitarme, y se sentaron frente a mí. 2Entonces el SEÑOR me dirigió la palabra: 3«Hijo de hombre, estas personas han hecho de su *corazón un altar de ídolos malolientes, y a su paso han colocado trampas que los hacen pecar. ¿Cómo voy a permitir que me consulten? 4Por tanto, habla con ellos y adviérteles que así dice el SEÑOR omnipotente: "A todo israelita que haya hecho de su corazón un altar de ídolos malolientes, y que después de haber colocado a su paso

---

j **13:18** *las que hacen ... la gente.* Texto de difícil traducción.

trampas que lo hagan pecar consulte al profeta, yo el SEÑOR le responderé según la multitud de sus ídolos malolientes. 5Así cautivaré el corazón de los israelitas que por causa de todos esos ídolos malolientes se hayan alejado de mí."

6»Por tanto, adviértele al pueblo de Israel que así dice el SEÑOR omnipotente: "*¡Arrepiéntanse! Apártense de una vez por todas de su idolatría y de toda práctica repugnante." 7Yo seré quien le responda a todo israelita o inmigrante que resida en Israel y que se haya alejado de mí: al que haya hecho de su corazón un altar de ídolos malolientes, o haya colocado ante sí trampas que lo hayan hecho pecar, y luego haya acudido al profeta para consultarme. 8Me enfrentaré a él, y de él haré una señal de escarmiento, y lo extirparé de mi pueblo. Así sabrán que yo soy el SEÑOR.

9»Si un profeta es seducido y pronuncia un mensaje, será porque yo, el SEÑOR, lo he seducido. Así que levantaré mi mano contra él, y lo haré pedazos en presencia de mi pueblo. 10Tanto el profeta como quien lo haya consultado cargarán con la misma culpa, 11para que el pueblo de Israel ya no se aparte de mí ni vuelva a mancharse con sus pecados. Entonces ellos serán mi pueblo y yo seré su Dios. Lo afirma el SEÑOR omnipotente.»

Contra falsas esperanzas

12El SEÑOR me dirigió la palabra: 13«Hijo de hombre, si un país peca contra mí y persiste en su infidelidad, yo levantaré mi mano contra él; le quitaré las provisiones, lo sumiré en el hambre, y arrasaré a sus habitantes y a sus animales. 14Y aun si Noé, Danielᵏ y Job vivieran en ese país, sólo ellos se salvarían por su justicia. Lo afirmo yo, el SEÑOR omnipotente.

15»Y si por todo el país yo mandara bestias feroces que lo arrasaran y lo convirtieran en desierto desolado, de modo que por temor a las fieras nadie se atreviera a pasar, 16aun si aquellos tres hombres vivieran allí, ni sus hijos ni sus hijas sobrevivirían. Sólo ellos se salvarían, pero el país quedaría desolado. ¡Yo, el SEÑOR omnipotente, lo juro por mí mismo!

17»Y si yo enviara guerra sobre ese país y dejara que la espada arrasara la tierra y eliminara a sus habitantes y a sus animales, 18aun si aquellos tres hombres vivieran allí, ni sus hijos ni sus hijas sobrevivirían. Sólo ellos se salvarían. ¡Yo, el SEÑOR omnipotente, lo juro por mí mismo!

19»Y si yo enviara peste a ese país y derramara sobre él mi ira mortal para eliminar a sus habitantes y a sus animales, 20aun si Noé, Daniel y Job vivieran allí, ni sus hijos ni sus hijas sobrevivirían. Sólo ellos se salvarían por su justicia. ¡Yo, el SEÑOR omnipotente, lo juro por mí mismo!

21»Así dice el SEÑOR omnipotente: ¡Peor será cuando mande contra Jerusalén mis cuatro castigos fatales: la guerra, el hambre, las bestias feroces y la peste! Con ellas arrasaré a sus habitantes y a sus animales. 22Sin embargo, quedarán algunos sobrevivientes que serán liberados y harán salir del exilio a sus hijos y a sus hijas. Cuando lleguen a donde están ustedes, y ustedes vean su conducta y sus obras, se consolarán del desastre que envié contra Jerusalén, y de todo lo que hice contra ella. 23Ustedes se consolarán cuando vean la conducta y las obras de esa gente, y sabrán que lo que hice contra Jerusalén no fue sin razón. Lo afirma el SEÑOR omnipotente.»

Jerusalén, una vid inútil

15 El SEÑOR me dirigió la palabra: 2«Hijo de hombre, ¿en qué supera la leña de la vid a la madera de los árboles del bosque? 3Esa leña no sirve para hacer muebles, ¡y ni siquiera para hacer una percha! 4¡Escasamente sirve para alimentar el fuego! Pero ¿de qué sirve cuando sus extremos se consumen y ya se ha quemado por dentro? 5Si cuando estaba entera no servía para nada, ¡mucho menos cuando ya ha sido consumida por el fuego!

6»Por tanto, así dice el SEÑOR omnipotente: Como la leña de la vid, que sólo sirve para echarla al fuego, así haré con los habitantes de Jerusalén. 7Voy a enfrentarme a ellos; ise han librado de un fuego, pero serán consumidos por otro! Cuando me enfrente a ellos, ustedes sabrán que yo soy el SEÑOR. 8Convertiré a este país en desolación, porque ha sido infiel. Lo afirma el SEÑOR omnipotente.»

Infidelidad de Jerusalén

16 El SEÑOR me dirigió la palabra: 2«Hijo de hombre, échale en cara a Jerusalén sus prácticas repugnantes. 3Adviértele que así dice el SEÑOR omnipotente: "Jerusalén, tú eres cananea de origen y de nacimiento; tu padre era amorreo y tu madre, hitita. 4El día en que naciste no te cortaron el cordón umbilical; no te bañaron, no te frotaron con sal, ni te envolvieron en pañales. 5Nadie se apiadó de ti ni te mostró compasión brindándote estos cuidados. Al contrario, el día en que naciste te arrojaron al campo como a un objeto despreciable.

6»"Pasé junto a ti, y te vi revolcándote en tu propia sangre y te dije: ¡Sigue viviendo; 7crece como planta silvestre!

»"Tú te desarrollaste, y creciste y te hiciste mujer. Y se formaron tus senos, y te brotó el vello, pero tú seguías completamente desnuda.

8»"Tiempo después pasé de nuevo junto a ti, y te miré. Estabas en la edad del amor. Extendí entonces mi manto sobre ti, y cubrí tu desnudez. Me comprometí e hice alianza contigo, y fuiste mía. Lo afirma el SEÑOR omnipotente.

9»"Te bañé, te limpié la sangre y te perfumé. 10Te puse un vestido bordado y te calcé con finas sandalias de cuero. Te vestí con ropa de lino y de seda. 11Te adorné con joyas: te puse pulseras, collares, 12aretes, un anillo en la nariz y una hermosa corona en la cabeza. 13Quedaste adornada de oro y plata, vestida de lino fino, de seda y de telas bordadas. Te alimentabas con el mejor trigo, y con miel y aceite de oliva. Llegaste a ser muy hermosa; ite sobraban cualidades para ser reina! 14Tan perfecta era tu belleza que tu fama se extendió por todas las naciones, pues yo te adorné con mi esplendor. Lo afirma el SEÑOR omnipotente.

15»"Sin embargo, confiaste en tu belleza y, valiéndote de tu fama, te prostituiste. ¡Sin ningún pudor te entregaste a cualquiera que pasaba! 16Con tus mismos vestidos te hiciste aposentos idolátricos de vistosos colores, y allí te prostituiste. ¡Algo nunca visto! 17Con las joyas de oro y plata que yo te había obsequiado, hiciste imágenes masculinas, y con ellas te prostituiste ofreciéndoles culto. 18Les pusiste tus vestidos bordados, y les ofreciste mi aceite y mi perfume. 19Como ofrenda de olor fragante les presentaste el alimento que yo

---

ᵏ **14:14** *Daniel.* Alt. *Danel.*

te había dado: el mejor trigo, el aceite de oliva y la miel. Lo afirma el SEÑOR omnipotente.

20»"Tomaste también a los hijos y a las hijas que tuviste conmigo y los sacrificaste como alimento a esas imágenes. ¡No te bastaron tus prostituciones! 21Inmolaste a mis hijos y los pasaste por fuego como ofrenda en honor de esos ídolos. 22En todas tus repugnantes prácticas y prostituciones no te acordaste de los días de tu infancia, cuando estabas completamente desnuda y te revolcabas en tu propia sangre.

23»¡Ay de ti, ay de ti! —afirma el SEÑOR omnipotente—. Para colmo de tus perversidades, 24construiste prostíbulos en cada plaza. 25¡No hubo esquina donde no te exhibieras para prostituirte! Te abriste de piernas a cualquiera que pasaba, y fornicaste sin cesar. 26Te acostaste con los egipcios, tus vecinos de grandes genitales, y para enfurecerme multiplicaste tus fornicaciones. 27Yo levanté mi mano para castigarte y reduje tu territorio; te entregué a las ciudadesˡ filisteas, que se avergonzaban de tu conducta depravada. 28Una y otra vez fornicaste con los asirios, porque eras insaciable. 29Lo mismo hiciste con los comerciantes de Babilonia, y ni así quedaste satisfecha.

30»¡Qué *mente tan depravada la tuya! —afirma el SEÑOR omnipotente—. ¡Te comportabas como una vil prostituta! 31Pero cuando en cada plaza armabas un prostíbulo y te exhibías en cada esquina, no te comportabas como una prostituta, ¡pues no cobrabas nada!

32»¡Adúltera! Prefieres a los extraños, en vez de a tu marido. 33A todas las prostitutas se les paga; tú, en cambio, les pagas a tus amantes. Los sobornas para que vengan de todas partes a acostarse contigo. 34En tu prostitución has sido diferente de otras mujeres: como nadie se te ofrecía, tú pagabas en vez de que te pagaran a ti. ¡En eso sí eras diferente de las demás!

35»"Por tanto, prostituta, escucha la palabra del SEÑOR. 36Así dice el SEÑOR omnipotente: Has expuesto tus vergüenzas y exhibido tu desnudez al fornicar con tus amantes y con tus malolientes ídolos; a éstos les has ofrecido la sangre de tus hijos. 37Por tanto, reuniré a todos tus amantes, a quienes brindaste placer; tanto a los que amaste como a los que odiaste. Los reuniré contra ti de todas partes, y expondré tu desnudez ante ellos, y ellos te verán completamente desnuda. 38Te juzgaré como a una adúltera y homicida, y derramaré sobre ti mi ira y mi celo. 39Te entregaré en sus manos, y ellos derribarán tus prostíbulos y demolerán tus puestos. Te arrancarán la ropa y te despojarán de tus joyas, dejándote completamente desnuda. 40Convocarán a la asamblea contra ti, y te apedrearán y te descuartizarán a filo de espada. 41Incendiarán tus casas, y en presencia de muchas mujeres ejecutarán la sentencia contra ti. Yo pondré fin a tu prostitución, y ya no volverás a pagarles a tus amantes. 42Así calmaré mi ira contra ti y se apaciguarán mis celos; me quedaré tranquilo y sin enojo. 43Yo te hago responsable de tu conducta por haberte olvidado de los días de tu infancia, por haberme irritado con todas estas cosas, y por haber agregado infamia a tus prácticas repugnantes. Lo afirma el SEÑOR.

44»"Los que acostumbran citar refranes, dirán esto de ti: 'De tal palo, tal astilla.' 45Tú eres igual a tu madre, que despreció a su marido y a sus hijos; eres igual a tus hermanas, que despreciaron a sus maridos y a sus hijos. La madre de ustedes era hitita, y su padre, amorreo. 46Tu hermana mayor es Samaria,

ubicada al norte de ti con sus aldeas.ᵐ Tu hermana menor es Sodoma, ubicada al sur de ti con sus aldeas. 47No sólo has seguido su conducta, sino que has actuado según sus prácticas repugnantes. En poco tiempo llegaste a ser peor que ellas. 48Yo, el SEÑOR, lo juro por mí mismo: ni tu hermana Sodoma ni sus aldeas hicieron jamás lo que tú y tus aldeas han hecho. 49Tu hermana Sodoma y sus aldeas pecaron de soberbia, gula, apatía, e indiferencia hacia el pobre y el indigente. 50Se creían superiores a otras, y en mi presencia se entregaron a prácticas repugnantes. Por eso, tal como lo has visto, las he destruido. 51¡Pero ni Samaria ni sus aldeas cometieron la mitad de tus pecados! Tú te entregaste a más prácticas repugnantes que ellas, haciendo que ellas parecieran justas en comparación contigo. 52Ahora tú, carga con tu desgracia; porque son tantos tus pecados que has favorecido a tus hermanas al hacerlas parecer más justas que tú. ¡Avergüénzate y carga con tu desgracia! Has hecho que tus hermanas parezcan más justas que tú.

53»"Pero yo cambiaré su suerte, la suerte de Sodoma y de Samaria, con sus respectivas aldeas, y haré lo mismo contigo. 54Así cargarás con tu desgracia y te avergonzarás de todo lo que hiciste, y les servirás de consuelo. 55Tú y tus dos hermanas, con sus respectivas aldeas, volverán a ser como antes. 56¿Acaso no te burlabas de tu hermana Sodoma en tu época de orgullo, 57antes de que se hiciera pública tu maldad? Ahora te has vuelto el hazmerreír de las aldeas edomitas y filisteas, ¡y por todas partes te desprecian! 58Sobre tus hombros llevas el peso de tu infamia y de tus prácticas repugnantes. Lo afirma el SEÑOR.

59»"Así dice el SEÑOR omnipotente: Te daré tu merecido, porque has menospreciado el juramento y quebrantado la alianza. 60Sin embargo, yo sí me acordaré de la alianza que hice contigo en los días de tu infancia, y estableceré contigo una alianza eterna. 61Tú te acordarás de tu conducta pasada, y te avergonzarás cuando yo acojaⁿ a tus hermanas, la mayor y la menor, para dártelas como hijas, aunque no participan de mi alianza contigo. 62Yo estableceré mi alianza contigo, y sabrás que yo soy el SEÑOR. 63Cuando yo te perdone por todo lo que has hecho, tú te acordarás de tu maldad y te avergonzarás, y en tu humillación no volverás a jactarte. Lo afirma el SEÑOR omnipotente."»

La vid y el águila

17 El SEÑOR me dirigió la palabra: 2«Hijo de hombre: Plantéale al pueblo de Israel este enigma, y nárrale esta parábola. 3Adviértele que así dice el SEÑOR:

»Llegó al Líbano un águila enorme,
    de grandes alas, tupido plumaje y vivos
    colores.
Se posó sobre la copa de un cedro,
    4y arrancó el retoño más alto.
Lo llevó a un país de mercaderes,
    y lo plantó en una ciudad de comerciantes.
5Tomó luego semilla de aquel país
    y la plantó en terreno fértil.
La sembró como un sauce,
    junto a aguas abundantes.
6La semilla germinó
    y se hizo una vid frondosa, de poca altura;
    volvió sus ramas hacia el águila,

ˡ **16:27** ciudades. Lit. hijas. ᵐ **16:46** aldeas. Lit. hijas; así en el resto de este capítulo. ⁿ **16:61** yo acoja (mss. de LXX y Siríaca); tú acojas (TM).

y hundió sus raíces bajo sí misma.
Así se convirtió en una vid
　　con retoños y exuberante follaje.
⁷Pero había otra águila grande,
　　de gigantescas alas y abundante plumaje.
Y la vid volvió sus raíces
　　y orientó sus ramas hacia ella,
　　para recibir más agua
　　de la que ya tenía.
⁸¡Había estado plantada en tierra fértil
　　junto a aguas abundantes,
　　para echar retoños y dar frutos,
　　y convertirse en una hermosa vid!

⁹»Adviértele que así dice el SEÑOR:

»¿Prosperará esa vid?
　　¿El águila no la arrancará de raíz?
¿No le quitará su fruto,
　　y así la vid se marchitará?
Sí, los tiernos retoños se secarán.
　　No hará falta un brazo fuerte ni mucha
　　　gente
　　para arrancarla de cuajo.
¹⁰¿Prosperará aunque sea trasplantada?
　　¿Acaso el viento del este
　　no la marchitará cuando la azote?
¡claro que sí se marchitará
　　en el lugar donde había nacido!»

¹¹El SEÑOR me dirigió la palabra: ¹²«Pregúntale a este pueblo rebelde si tiene idea de lo que significa todo esto. Recuérdale que el rey de Babilonia vino a Jerusalén y se llevó a su país al rey de Judá y a sus funcionarios. ¹³Luego tomó a uno de la familia real y lo obligó a firmar con él un tratado bajo juramento, y se llevó a la flor y nata del país. ¹⁴Esto lo hizo para humillar a Judá. Así le impidió sublevarse y lo obligó a cumplir el tratado para poder subsistir. ¹⁵Sin embargo, este príncipe se rebeló contra el rey de Babilonia, y envió mensajeros a Egipto para conseguir caballos y un numeroso ejército. ¿Y tendrá éxito y podrá escapar el que se atreva a hacer esto? ¿Acaso podrá violar el tratado y salir con vida? ¹⁶¡No, sino que morirá en Babilonia, el país del rey que lo nombró y con quien hizo un juramento que no cumplió, y firmó un tratado que violó! Yo, el SEÑOR omnipotente, lo juro por mí mismo. ¹⁷Ni el faraón con su gran ejército y numerosas tropas podrá auxiliarlo en la guerra, cuando se levanten rampas y se construyan torres de asalto para matar a mucha gente. ¹⁸El príncipe de Judá quebrantó el juramento y violó el tratado. Así que por haber hecho todo esto a pesar de su compromiso, ¡no escapará!

¹⁹»Por tanto, así dice el SEÑOR omnipotente: "Juro por mí mismo que lo castigaré por haber faltado al juramento y violado el tratado. ²⁰Le tenderé mis redes, y caerá en mi trampa. Lo llevaré a Babilonia, y allí lo someteré a juicio por haberme sido infiel. ²¹Lo mejorⁿ de sus tropas caerá a filo de espada, y los que aún queden con vida serán esparcidos a los cuatro vientos. Así sabrán que yo, el SEÑOR, lo he dicho.

²²»"Así dice el SEÑOR omnipotente:

»"De la copa de un cedro tomaré un retoño,
　　de las ramas más altas arrancaré un brote,
　　y lo plantaré sobre un cerro muy elevado.
²³Lo plantaré sobre el cerro
　　más alto de Israel,
　　para que eche ramas y produzca fruto

y se convierta en un magnífico cedro.
Toda clase de aves anidará en él,
　　y vivirá a la sombra de sus ramas.
²⁴Y todos los árboles del campo
　　sabrán que yo soy el SEÑOR.
Al árbol grande lo corto,
　　y al pequeño lo hago crecer.
Al árbol verde lo seco,
　　y al seco, lo hago florecer.
Yo, el SEÑOR, lo he dicho,
　　y lo cumpliré."»

La responsabilidad personal

18 El SEÑOR me dirigió la palabra: ²«¿A qué viene tanta repetición de este *proverbio tan conocido en Israel: "Los padres comieron uvas agrias, y a los hijos se les destemplaron los dientes?" ³Yo, el SEÑOR omnipotente, juro por mí mismo que jamás se volverá a repetir este proverbio en Israel. ⁴La persona que peque morirá. Sepan que todas las vidas me pertenecen, tanto la del padre como la del hijo.

⁵Quien es justo practica el derecho y la justicia; ⁶no participa de los banquetes idolátricos en los cerros, ni eleva plegarias a los ídolos malolientes de Israel. No deshonra a la mujer de su prójimo, ni se une a la mujer en los días de su menstruación. ⁷No oprime a nadie, ni roba, sino que devuelve la prenda al deudor, da de comer al hambriento y viste al desnudo. ⁸No presta dinero con usura ni exige intereses. Se abstiene de hacer el mal y juzga imparcialmente entre los rivales. ⁹Obedece mis decretos y cumple fielmente mis *leyes. Tal persona es justa, y ciertamente vivirá. Lo afirma el SEÑOR omnipotente.

¹⁰»Pero bien puede suceder que esa persona tenga un hijo violento y homicida, que no siga su ejemplo ¹¹y participe de los banquetes idolátricos en los cerros; que deshonre a la mujer de su prójimo, ¹²oprima al pobre y al indigente, robe y no devuelva la prenda al deudor, y eleve plegarias a los ídolos e incurra en actos repugnantes; ¹³que, además, preste dinero con usura y exija intereses. ¿Tal hijo merece vivir? ¡Claro que no! Por haber incurrido en estos actos asquerosos, será condenado a muerte, y de su muerte sólo él será responsable.

¹⁴»Ahora bien, ese hijo podría a su vez tener un hijo que observa todos los pecados de su padre, pero no los imita, ¹⁵pues no participa de los banquetes idolátricos en los cerros, ni eleva plegarias a los ídolos malolientes de Israel, ni deshonra a la mujer de su prójimo; ¹⁶no oprime a nadie, no roba, devuelve la prenda al deudor, da de comer al hambriento y viste al desnudo; ¹⁷se abstiene de hacer el mal, no presta dinero con usura ni exige intereses; cumple mis leyes y obedece mis decretos. Un hijo así no merece morir por la maldad de su padre; ¡merece vivir! ¹⁸En cuanto a su padre, que fue un opresor, que robó a su prójimo y que hizo lo malo en medio de su pueblo, ¡morirá por su propio pecado!

¹⁹»Pero ustedes preguntan: "¿Por qué no carga el hijo con las culpas de su padre?" ¡Porque el hijo era justo y recto, pues obedeció mis decretos y los puso en práctica! ¡Tal hijo merece vivir! ²⁰Todo el que peque, merece la muerte, pero ningún hijo cargará con la culpa de su padre, ni ningún padre con la del hijo: al justo se le pagará con justicia y al malvado se le pagará con maldad.

²¹»Si el malvado se *arrepiente de todos los pecados que ha cometido, y obedece todos mis decre-

---

ⁿ 17:21 *Lo mejor* (mss. hebreos, mss. de LXX, Siríaca y Targum); *Los fugitivos* (TM).

tos y practica el derecho y la justicia, no morirá; 22vivirá por practicar la justicia, y Dios se olvidará de todos los pecados que ese malvado haya cometido. 23¿Acaso creen que me complace la muerte del malvado? ¿No quiero más bien que abandone su mala conducta y que viva? Yo, el SEÑOR, lo afirmo.

24»Si el justo se aparta de la justicia y hace lo malo y practica los mismos actos repugnantes del malvado, ¿merece vivir? No, sino que morirá por causa de su infidelidad y de sus pecados, y no se recordará ninguna de sus obras justas.

25»Ustedes dicen: "El SEÑOR es injusto." Pero escucha, pueblo de Israel: ¿En qué soy injusto? ¿No son más bien ustedes los injustos? 26Cuando el justo se aparta de la justicia, cae en la maldad y muere, ¡pero muere por su maldad! 27Por otra parte, si el malvado se aleja de su maldad y practica el derecho y la justicia, salvará su vida. 28Si recapacita y se aparta de todas sus maldades, no morirá sino que vivirá.

29»Sin embargo, el pueblo de Israel anda diciendo: "El SEÑOR es injusto." Pueblo de Israel, ¿en qué soy injusto? ¿No son más bien ustedes los injustos? 30Por tanto, a cada uno de ustedes, los israelitas, los juzgaré según su conducta. Lo afirma el SEÑOR omnipotente. Arrepiéntanse y apártense de todas sus maldades, para que el pecado no les acarree la ruina. 31Arrojen de una vez por todas las maldades que cometieron contra mí, y háganse de un *corazón y de un espíritu nuevos. ¿Por qué habrás de morir, pueblo de Israel? 32Yo no quiero la muerte de nadie. ¡Conviértanse, y vivirán! Lo afirma el SEÑOR omnipotente.

Lamento por los príncipes de Israel

19 »Dedícale este lamento a la nobleza de Israel: 2»"En medio de los leones,
tu madre era toda una leona.
Recostada entre leoncillos,
amamantaba a sus cachorros.
3A uno de ellos lo crió,
y éste llegó a ser un león bravo
que aprendió a desgarrar su presa
y a devorar a la gente.
4Las naciones supieron de sus excesos,
y lo atraparon en una fosa;
¡se lo llevaron encadenado a Egipto!
5Cuando la leona madre perdió toda esperanza
de que volviera su cachorro,
tomó a otra de sus crías
y la convirtió en una fiera.
6Cuando este león se hizo fuerte,
se paseaba muy orondo entre los leones.
Aprendió a desgarrar su presa
y a devorar a la gente.
7Demolía palacios,o
asolaba ciudades,
y amedrentaba con sus rugidos
a todo el país y a sus habitantes.
8Las naciones y provincias vecinas
se dispusieron a atacarlo.
Le tendieron trampas,
y quedó atrapado en la fosa.
9Encadenado y enjaulado
lo llevaron ante el rey de Babilonia.
Enjaulado lo llevaron
para que no se oyeran sus rugidos
en los cerros de Israel.

10»"En medio del viñedop

tu madre era una vid
plantada junto al agua:
¡fructífera y frondosa,
gracias al agua abundante!
11Sus ramas crecieron vigorosas,
¡aptas para ser cetros de reyes!
Tanto creció que se destacaba
por encima del follaje.
Se le reconocía por su altura
y por sus ramas frondosas.
12Pero fue desarraigada con furia
y arrojada por el suelo.
El viento del este la dejó marchita,
y la gente le arrancó sus frutos.
Secas quedaron sus vigorosas ramas,
y fueron consumidas por el fuego.
13Ahora se halla en el desierto,
plantada en tierra árida y reseca.
14De una de sus ramas brotó un fuego,
y ese fuego devoró sus frutos.
¡Nada queda de esas vigorosas ramas,
aptas para ser cetros de reyes!"

Éste es un lamento, y debe entonarse como tal.»

Historia de una rebelión

20 El día diez del mes quinto del año séptimo, unos *jefes de Israel vinieron a consultar al SEÑOR, y se sentaron frente a mí. 2Allí el SEÑOR me dirigió la palabra: 3«Hijo de hombre, habla con los jefes de Israel y adviérteles que yo, el SEÑOR omnipotente, digo: "¿Así que ustedes vienen a consultarme? ¡Pues juro por mí mismo que no dejaré que me consulten! Lo afirmo yo, el SEÑOR omnipotente."

4»¡Júzgalos tú, hijo de hombre; júzgalos tú! Hazles ver las repugnantes prácticas de sus antepasados. 5Adviérteles que así dice el SEÑOR omnipotente: "El día en que elegí a Israel, con la mano en alto le hice un juramento a la descendencia de Jacob. El día en que me di a conocer a ellos en Egipto, volví a hacerles este juramento: 'Yo soy el SEÑOR su Dios.' 6En aquel día, con la mano en alto les juré que los sacaría de Egipto y los llevaría a una tierra que yo mismo había explorado. Es una tierra donde abundan la leche y la miel, ¡la más hermosa de todas! 7A cada uno de ellos le ordené que arrojara sus ídolos detestables, con los que estaba obsesionado, y que no se *contaminara con los malolientes ídolos de Egipto; porque yo soy el SEÑOR su Dios.

8»"Sin embargo, ellos se rebelaron contra mí, y me desobedecieron. No arrojaron los ídolos con que estaban obsesionados, ni abandonaron los ídolos de Egipto. Por eso, cuando estaban en Egipto, pensé agotar mi furor y descargar mi ira sobre ellos. 9Pero decidí actuar en honor a mi *nombre, para que no fuera profanado ante las naciones entre las cuales vivían los israelitas. Porque al sacar a los israelitas de Egipto yo me di a conocer a ellos en presencia de las naciones.

10»"Yo los saqué de Egipto y los llevé al desierto. 11Les di mis decretos, y les hice conocer mis *leyes, que son vida para quienes los obedecen. 12También les di mis *sábados como una señal entre ellos y yo, para que reconocieran que yo, el SEÑOR, he consagrado los sábados para mí. 13Pero el pueblo de Israel se rebeló contra mí en el desierto; desobedeció mis decretos y rechazó mis leyes, que son vida para quienes los obedecen. ¡Hasta el colmo profanaron mis sá-

---

o **19:7** Demolía palacios (lectura probable; véanse LXX y Targum); Conocía viudas (TM). p **19:10** del viñedo (dos mss. hebreos); de tu sangre (TM).

bados! Por eso, cuando estaban en el desierto, pensé descargar mi ira sobre ellos y exterminarlos. 14Pero decidí actuar en honor a mi nombre, para que no fuera profanado ante las naciones, las cuales me vieron sacarlos de Egipto.

15»"También con la mano en alto, en el desierto les juré que no los llevaría a la tierra que les había dado, ¡la tierra más hermosa de todas, donde abundan la leche y la miel! 16Rechazaron mis leyes, desobedecieron mis decretos y profanaron mis sábados, ¡y todo esto lo hicieron por haber andado tras esos ídolos malolientes! 17Sin embargo, les tuve compasión, y en el desierto no los destruí ni los exterminé.

18»"Allí en el desierto les dije a sus descendientes: 'No sigan los preceptos de sus padres; no obedezcan sus leyes ni se contaminen con sus ídolos malolientes. 19Yo soy el SEÑOR su Dios. Sigan mis decretos, obedezcan mis leyes 20y observen mis sábados como días consagrados a mí, como señal entre ustedes y yo, para que reconozcan que yo soy el SEÑOR su Dios.'

21»"Sin embargo, los israelitas se rebelaron contra mí. No siguieron mis decretos y no obedecieron mis leyes, que son vida para quienes los obedecen. Además, profanaron mis sábados. Por eso, cuando estaban en el desierto, pensé agotar mi furor y descargar mi ira sobre ellos. 22Pero me contuve en honor a mi nombre, para que no fuera profanado ante las naciones, las cuales me vieron sacarlos de Egipto. 23También con la mano en alto les juré en el desierto que los dispersaría entre las naciones. Los esparciría entre los países 24porque, obsesionados como estaban con los ídolos malolientes de sus antepasados, desobedecieron mis leyes, rechazaron mis decretos y profanaron mis sábados. 25¡Hasta les di decretos que no eran buenos y leyes que no podían dar vida! 26Los contaminé con sus propias ofrendas, dejándolos ofrecer en sacrificio a sus primogénitos, para horrorizarlos y hacerles reconocer que yo soy el SEÑOR."

27»Por tanto, hijo de hombre, habla con el pueblo de Israel y adviértele que yo, el SEÑOR omnipotente, digo: "En esto también me ofendieron tus antepasados y me trataron con absoluta infidelidad: 28Cuando los hice entrar en la tierra que con la mano en alto había jurado darles, cualquier cerro o árbol frondoso que veían les venía bien para hacer sacrificios y presentarme esas ofrendas que tanto me ofenden. Allí quemaban incienso y derramaban sus libaciones. 29Y les pregunté: ¿Qué significa ese *santuario pagano que tanto frecuentan?' Y hasta el día de hoy ese lugar de culto idolátrico se conoce como 'santuario pagano'."

Juicio y restauración

30»Por tanto, adviértele al pueblo de Israel que así dice el SEÑOR omnipotente: "¿Se *contaminarán ustedes a la manera de sus antepasados, y se prostituirán con sus ídolos detestables? 31Hasta el día de hoy, ustedes se contaminan al hacer sus ofrendas y al sacrificar a sus hijos, pasándolos por fuego en honor a los ídolos malolientes. ¿Y ahora ustedes, israelitas, vienen a consultarme? Juro por mí mismo que no dejaré que me consulten. Yo, el SEÑOR omnipotente, lo afirmo. 32Jamás sucederá lo que ustedes tienen en mente: 'Queremos ser como las otras naciones, como los pueblos del mundo, que adoran al culto a la piedra.' 33Yo, el SEÑOR omnipotente, juro por mí mismo que reinaré sobre ustedes con gran despliegue de fuerza y de poder,q y con furia incontenible. 34Los

sacaré de las naciones y de los pueblos por donde estaban esparcidos, y los reuniré con gran despliegue de fuerza y de poder, y con furia incontenible. 35Los llevaré al desierto que está entre las naciones, y allí los juzgaré cara a cara. 36Así como juzgué a sus antepasados en el desierto de Egipto, también los juzgaré a ustedes. Yo, el SEÑOR omnipotente, lo afirmo. 37Así como al *pastor selecciona sus ovejas, también yo los haré pasar a ustedes bajo mi vara y los seleccionaré para que formen parte de la alianza. 38Apartaré a los rebeldes, a los que se rebelan contra mí, y los sacaré del país donde ahora viven como extranjeros, pero no entrarán en la tierra de Israel. Entonces ustedes reconocerán que yo soy el SEÑOR.

39»"En cuanto a ustedes, pueblo de Israel, así dice el SEÑOR omnipotente: Si no quieren obedecerme, ¡vayan y adoren a sus ídolos malolientes! Pero no sigan profanando mi *santo *nombre con sus ofrendas y sus ídolos apestosos. 40Porque en mi monte santo, el monte elevado de Israel, me adorará todo el pueblo de Israel; todos los que habitan en el país. Yo, el SEÑOR, lo afirmo. Allí los recibiré, y exigiré sus ofrendas y sus *primicias, junto con todo lo que quieran dedicarme. 41Cuando yo los saque a ustedes y los reúna de todas las naciones y pueblos donde estarán esparcidos, en presencia de las naciones los recibiré como incienso agradable y les manifestaré mi santidad. 42Y cuando yo los lleve a la tierra de Israel, al país que con la mano en alto había jurado a sus antepasados que les daría, entonces reconocerán que yo soy el SEÑOR. 43Allí se acordarán de su conducta y de todas sus acciones con las que se contaminaron, y sentirán asco de sí mismos por todas las maldades que cometieron. 44Pueblo de Israel, cuando yo actúe en favor de ustedes, en honor a mi nombre y no según su mala conducta y sus obras corruptas, entonces ustedes reconocerán que yo soy el SEÑOR. Yo, el SEÑOR omnipotente, lo afirmo."»

Profecía contra el sur

45El SEÑOR me dirigió la palabra: 46«Hijo de hombre, mira hacia el sur y en esa dirección profetiza contra el bosque del Néguev. 47Dile: "Escucha, bosque del Néguev, la palabra del SEÑOR. Así dice el SEÑOR omnipotente: 'En medio de ti voy a prender un fuego que devorará todos los árboles, tanto los secos como los verdes. Este incendio no se podrá apagar, y quemará toda la superficie, de norte a sur. 48Todos los *mortales verán que yo, el SEÑOR, lo he encendido, y no podrá apagarse.' "»

49Entonces yo exclamé: «¡Ay, SEÑOR omnipotente, todo el mundo anda diciendo que soy un charlatán!»

La espada justiciera

21 El SEÑOR me dirigió la palabra: 2«Hijo de hombre, vuélvele la espalda a Jerusalén; clama contra sus santuarios, profetiza contra la tierra de Israel, 3anúnciale que así dice el SEÑOR: "Me declaro contra ti. Desenvainaré mi espada y mataré a justos y a malvados por igual. 4Puesto que he de extirpar de ti tanto al justo como al malvado, mi espada saldrá contra todo el mundo, desde el norte hasta el sur. 5Así todos sabrán que yo, el SEÑOR, la desenvainado la espada y no volveré a envainarla."

6»Y tú, hijo de hombre, con el *corazón quebrantado y en presencia de todo el mundo, llora con amargura. 7Y cuando te pregunten por qué lloras así, diles que es por la noticia de lo que va a suceder. Esta noti-

---

q 20:33 *gran despliegue ... poder.* Lit. *mano fuerte y brazo extendido;* también en v. 34.

cia hará que todos los corazones desfallezcan, que se dejen caer todos los brazos, y que tiemblen todas las rodillas. ¡Ya está por llegar! ¡Ya es una realidad! Yo, el SEÑOR, lo afirmo.»

8El SEÑOR me dirigió la palabra: 9«Hijo de hombre, profetiza y proclama que así dice el SEÑOR:

»"¡La espada, la espada,
    afilada y bruñida!,
10bruñida para fulgurar
    y afilada para masacrar.r
11La bruñeron y la afilaron
    para ponerla en manos del asesino.

12»"¡Grita y gime, hijo de hombre,
    que la espada se perfila contra mi pueblo
    y contra todos los jefes de Israel.
Han sido arrojados contra ella,
    lo mismo que mi pueblo.
Por eso, ¡date golpes de pecho!

13»"El SEÑOR omnipotente afirma:s

14»"Hijo de hombre, profetiza y bate palmas;
    que hiera la espada, y vuelva a herir.
Es la espada de la muerte
    que a todos mantiene amenazados,
15para que el corazón desfallezca
    y aumente el número de víctimas.
Ya he colocado en las puertas
    la espada asesina.t
Es la espada bruñida para centellear
    y afilada para matar.
16Muévete a diestra y a siniestra,
    y hiere por todas partes.
¡Exhibe tu filo, espada asesina!
17También yo batiré palmas
    y aplacaré mi furor.
Yo, el SEÑOR, lo he dicho."»

18El SEÑOR me dirigió la palabra: 19«Tú, hijo de hombre, traza dos caminos para que llegue por ellos la espada del rey de Babilonia. Estos dos caminos partirán del mismo país, y a la entrada de cada uno de ellos colocarás una señal que indique a qué ciudad conduce. 20Traza un camino para que la espada llegue contra Rabá de los amonitas y contra Jerusalén, la ciudad fortificada de Judá. 21El rey de Babilonia se ha colocado en la bifurcación del camino y consulta los augurios: sacude las saetas, consulta los ídolos domésticos y examina el hígado de un animal. 22Con su mano *derecha ha marcado el destino de Jerusalén: prepara arietes para derribar las *puertas, levanta terraplenes y edifica torres de asedio; alza la voz en grito de batalla y da la orden para la matanza. 23Por las alianzas ya hechas, los habitantes de Jerusalén creerán que se trata de una falsa profecía; pero aquel rey les recordará la iniquidad por la que serán capturados.

24»Por eso dice el SEÑOR omnipotente:

»Se les ha recordado su iniquidad,
    y han quedado al descubierto sus
        rebeliones;
expuestas están sus acciones pecaminosas,
    ¡y por tanto serán capturados!

25»Y en cuanto a ti, príncipe de Israel, infame y malvado, tu día ha llegado; ¡la hora de tu castigo es inminente! 26Así dice el SEÑOR omnipotente: Quítate el turbante, renuncia a la corona, que todo cambiará. Lo humilde será exaltado, y lo excelso será humillado. 27¡Ruinas, ruinas, todo lo convertiré en ruinas! Esto no sucederá hasta que venga aquel a quien le asiste el derecho, y a quien le pediré que establezca la justicia.

28»Y tú, hijo de hombre, profetiza y declara que esto afirma el SEÑOR omnipotente acerca de los amonitas y de sus insultos: "La espada, la espada está desenvainada para la masacre; pulida está para devorar y centellear como relámpago. 29La espada degollará a esos infames malvados, pues sus visiones son falsas y sus adivinanzas, mentiras. Pero su día ha llegado; ¡la hora de su castigo es inminente! 30»"¡Espada, vuelve a tu vaina! Allí, en tu tierra de origen, donde fuiste forjada, ¡allí te juzgaré! 31Sobre ti derramaré mi ira, sobre ti soplaré el fuego de mi furor; te entregaré en manos de gente sanguinaria y destructora. 32Serás pasto para el fuego; salpicaré con tu sangre todo el país, y borraré tu memoria de la faz de la tierra. Yo, el SEÑOR, lo he dicho."»

Los pecados de Jerusalén

22 El SEÑOR me dirigió la palabra: 2«Tú, hijo de hombre, juzga a la ciudad sanguinaria; denúnciala por todas sus prácticas detestables. 3Adviértele que así dice el SEÑOR omnipotente: "¡Ay de ti, ciudad que derramas sangre en tus calles, y te *contaminas fabricando ídolos malolientes! ¡Cómo provocas tu ruina! 4Te has hecho culpable por la sangre que has derramado, te has contaminado con los ídolos malolientes que has fabricado; has hecho que se avecine tu hora, ¡has llegado al final de tus años! Por eso te haré objeto de oprobio y de burla entre las naciones y los pueblos. 5Ciudad caótica y de mala fama, ¡gente de cerca y de lejos se burlará de ti! 6Mira, ahí tienes a los gobernadores de Israel, que en tus calles abusan del poder sólo para derramar sangre. 7Tus habitantes tratan con desprecio a su padre y a su madre, oprimen al extranjero, explotan al huérfano y a la viuda. 8Menosprecian mis objetos sagrados, profanan mis *sábados. 9En ti habita gente que con sus calumnias incita a derramar sangre; gente que come en los santuarios de los montes y que hace cosas detestables. 10Hay quienes deshonran la cama de su padre y obligan a la mujer a tener relaciones en su período de menstruación. 11Algunos cometen adulterio con la mujer de su prójimo, otros tienen relaciones vergonzosas con sus nueras, y hasta hay quienes violan a su hermana, ¡a la hija de su propio padre! 12También hay entre tus tuyos quienes aceptan soborno para derramar sangre. Tú practicas la usura y cobras altísimos intereses; extorsionas a tu prójimo y te olvidas de mí. Lo afirma el SEÑOR.

13»"Pero yo voy a batir palmas en contra de las ganancias injustas que has acumulado, y en contra de la sangre que se ha derramado en tus calles. 14Y cuando yo te haga frente, ¿podrá resistir tu *corazón, y tendrán fuerza tus manos? Yo, el SEÑOR, lo he dicho, y lo cumpliré. 15Te dispersaré entre las naciones, te esparciré entre los pueblos, y pondré fin a tu inmundicia. 16Serás una deshonra frente a las naciones, pero sabrás que yo soy el SEÑOR."»

17El SEÑOR me dirigió la palabra: 18«Hijo de hombre, todo el pueblo de Israel se ha vuelto para mí

---

r 21:10 *bruñida para ... masacrar* (véanse LXX, Vetus Latina, y Siríaca); TM incluye una frase de difícil traducción. s 21:13 *El SEÑOR* | d *omnipotente afirma* (lectura probable); TM incluye frases de difícil traducción. t 21:15 *asesina*. Palabra de difícil traducción.

como la escoria del cobre y del estaño, del hierro y del plomo, que se queda en el horno. ¡Son como la escoria de la plata! [19]Por eso, así dice el SEÑOR omnipotente: "Como todos ustedes se han convertido en escoria, los voy a reunir en medio de Jerusalén. [20]Así como la plata, el cobre, el hierro, el plomo y el estaño se juntan y se echan en el horno, y se atiza el fuego para fundirlos, así también yo, en mi ira, los juntaré a ustedes y los fundiré. [21]Los amontonaré y atizaré contra ustedes el fuego de mi ira, y los fundiré en medio de la ciudad. [22]Así como se funde la plata en medio del horno, así serán fundidos ustedes en medio de la ciudad, y sabrán que yo, el SEÑOR, he derramado mi ira contra ustedes."»

[23]El SEÑOR me dirigió la palabra: [24]«Hijo de hombre, dile a Israel: "Tú eres una tierra que no ha sido *purificada ni mojada por la lluvia en el día de la ira." [25]Como leones rugientes que despedazan a la presa, hay una conspiración de profetas que devoran a la gente, que se apoderan de las riquezas y los objetos de valor, y que aumentan el número de viudas. [26]Sus sacerdotes violan mi *ley y profanan mis objetos sagrados. Ellos no hacen distinción entre lo sagrado y lo profano, ni enseñan a otros la diferencia entre lo puro y lo impuro. Tampoco le prestan atención a mis sábados, y he sido profanado entre ellos. [27]Los jefes de la ciudad son como lobos que desgarran a su presa; siempre están listos a derramar sangre y a destruir vidas, con tal de lograr ganancias injustas. [28]Los profetas todo lo blanquean[u] mediante visiones falsas y predicciones mentirosas. Alegan que lo ha dicho el SEÑOR omnipotente, cuando en realidad el SEÑOR no les ha dicho nada. [29]Los terratenientes roban y extorsionan a la gente, explotan al indigente y al pobre, y maltratan injustamente al extranjero. [30]Yo he buscado entre ellos a alguien que se interponga entre mi pueblo y yo, y saque la cara por él[v] para que yo no lo destruya. ¡Y no lo he hallado! [31]Por eso derramaré mi ira sobre ellos; los consumiré con el fuego de mi ira, y haré recaer sobre ellos todo el mal que han hecho. Lo afirma el SEÑOR omnipotente.»

Las dos hermanas adúlteras

23 El SEÑOR me dirigió la palabra: [2]«Hijo de hombre, te cuento que había dos mujeres, hijas de una misma madre. [3]Desde jóvenes se dejaron manosear los senos; en Egipto se prostituyeron y dejaron que les acariciaran sus pechos virginales. [4]La mayor se llamaba Aholá, y la menor, Aholibá. Me uní a ellas, y me dieron hijos e hijas. (Aholá representa a Samaria, y su hermana Aholibá, a Jerusalén.) [5]Mientras Aholá me pertenecía, me fue infiel y se enamoró perdidamente de sus amantes los asirios, [6]todos ellos guerreros vestidos de púrpura, gobernadores y oficiales, jóvenes apuestos y hábiles jinetes. [7]Como una prostituta, se entregó a lo mejor de los asirios; se *contaminó con todos los ídolos malolientes que pertenecían a sus amantes. [8]Jamás abandonó la prostitución que había comenzado a practicar en Egipto. Desde su juventud, fueron muchos los que se acostaron con ella; fueron muchos los que acariciaron sus pechos virginales y se apasionaron con ella. [9]Por eso la entregué en manos de sus amantes, los asirios, con quienes ella se apasionó. [10]Y ellos la desnudaron, le quitaron sus hijos y sus hijas, y a ella la mataron a filo de espada. Fue tal el castigo que ella recibió, que su caso se volvió una advertencia para las mujeres.

[11]»Aunque su hermana Aholibá vio esto, dio rienda suelta a sus pasiones y se prostituyó aun más que su hermana. [12]Ella también se enamoró perdidamente de los asirios, todos ellos gobernadores y oficiales, guerreros vestidos con mucho lujo, hábiles jinetes, y jóvenes muy apuestos. [13]Yo pude darme cuenta de que ella se había contaminado y seguido el ejemplo de su hermana. [14]Pero Aholibá llevó más allá sus prostituciones. Vio en la pared figuras de *caldeos pintadas de rojo, [15]con cinturones y amplios turbantes en la cabeza. Todos ellos tenían aspecto de oficiales, y se parecían a los *babilonios originarios de Caldea. [16]Al verlos, se enamoró de ellos perdidamente y envió mensajeros a Caldea. [17]Los babilonios vinieron y se acostaron con ella en el lecho de sus pasiones. A tal punto la contaminaron con sus prostituciones que se hastió de ellos. [18]Pero exhibiendo su desnudez, practicó con descaro la prostitución. Entonces me hastié de ella, como antes me había hastiado de su hermana. [19]Pero ella multiplicó sus prostituciones, recordando los días de su juventud cuando en Egipto había sido una prostituta. [20]Allí se había enamorado perdidamente de sus amantes, cuyos genitales eran como los de un asno y su semen como el de un caballo. [21]Así echó de menos la lujuria de su juventud, cuando los egipcios la manoseaban los senos y le acariciaban sus pechos virginales.

[22]»Por eso, Aholibá, así dice el SEÑOR omnipotente: "Voy a incitar contra ti a tus amantes, de los que ahora estás hastiada. De todas partes traeré contra ti [23]a los babilonios y a todos los caldeos, a los de Pecod, Soa y Coa, y con ellos a los asirios, todos ellos jóvenes apuestos, gobernantes y oficiales, guerreros y hombres distinguidos, montados a caballo. [24]Vendrán contra ti con muchos carros y carretas, y con una multitud de ejércitos, cascos y escudos. Les encargaré que te juzguen, y te juzgarán según sus costumbres. [25]Descargaré sobre ti el furor de mi ira, y ellos te maltratarán con saña. Te cortarán la nariz y las orejas, y a tus sobrevivientes los matarán a filo de espada. Te arrebatarán a tus hijos y a tus hijas, y los que aún queden con vida serán consumidos por el fuego. [26]Te arrancarán tus vestidos y te quitarán tus joyas. [27]Así pondré fin a tu lujuria y a tu prostitución, que comenzaste en Egipto. Ya no desearás esas cosas ni te acordarás más de Egipto.

[28]»"Así dice el SEÑOR omnipotente: Voy a entregarte en manos de los que odias, en manos de quienes te hartaron. [29]Ellos te tratarán con odio y te despojarán de todas tus posesiones. Te dejarán completamente desnuda, y tus prostituciones quedarán al descubierto. Tu lujuria y tu promiscuidad [30]son la causa de todo esto, porque te prostituiste con las naciones y te contaminaste con sus ídolos malolientes. [31]Por cuanto has seguido los pasos de tu hermana, en castigo beberás la misma copa.

[32]»"Así dice el SEÑOR omnipotente:

»"Beberás la copa de tu hermana,
        una copa grande y profunda.
Llena está de burla y escarnio,
[33]llena de embriaguez y dolor.
Es la copa de ruina y desolación;
        ¡es la copa de tu hermana Samaria!
[34]La beberás hasta las heces,
        la romperás en mil pedazos,
y te desgarrarás los pechos
        porque yo lo he dicho.

        Lo afirma el SEÑOR omnipotente.

---

u 22:28 Los profetas todo lo blanquean. Lit. Sus profetas los recubren con cal. v 22:30 se interponga ... por él. Lit. construya un muro y se ponga en la brecha delante de mí por la tierra.

35»"Por eso, así dice el SEÑOR omnipotente: Por cuanto me has olvidado y me has dado la espalda, sufrirás las consecuencias de tu lujuria y de tus prostituciones."»

36El SEÑOR me dijo: «Hijo de hombre, ¿acaso no juzgarás a Aholá y a Aholibá? ¡Échales en cara sus actos detestables! 37Ellas han cometido adulterio, y tienen las manos manchadas de sangre. Han cometido adulterio con sus ídolos malolientes, han sacrificado a los hijos que me dieron, y los han ofrecido como alimento a esos ídolos. 38Además, me han ofendido contaminando mi santuario y, a la vez, profanando mis *sábados. 39El mismo día que sacrificaron a sus hijos para adorar a sus ídolos malolientes, entraron a mi santuario y lo profanaron. ¡Y lo hicieron en mi propia casa!

40»Y por si fuera poco, mandaron traer gente de muy lejos. Cuando esa gente llegó, ellas se bañaron, se pintaron los ojos y se adornaron con joyas; 41luego se sentaron en un diván lujoso, frente a una mesa donde previamente habían colocado el incienso y el aceite que me pertenecen. 42Podía escucharse el bullicio de una multitud: eran los sabeos, que venían del desierto. Adornaron a las mujeres poniéndoles brazaletes en los brazos y hermosas coronas sobre la cabeza. 43Pensé entonces en esa mujer desgastada por sus adulterios: "Ahora van a seguir aprovechándose de esa mujer prostituida." 44Y se acostaron con ella como quien se acuesta con una prostituta. Fue así como se acostaron con esas mujeres lascivas llamadas Aholá y Aholibá. 45Pero los hombres justos les darán el castigo que merecen las mujeres asesinas y adúlteras, ¡porque son unas adúlteras, y tienen las manos manchadas de sangre!

46»En efecto, así dice el SEÑOR: ¡Que se convoque a una multitud contra ellas, y que sean entregadas al terror y al saqueo! 47¡Que la multitud las apedree y las despedace con la espada! ¡Que maten a sus hijos y a sus hijas, y les prendan fuego a sus casas! 48Yo pondré fin en el país a esta conducta llena de lascivia. Todas las mujeres quedarán advertidas y no seguirán su ejemplo. 49Sobre estas dos hermanas recaerá su propia lascivia, y pagarán las consecuencias de sus pecados de idolatría. Entonces sabrán que yo soy el SEÑOR omnipotente.»

La olla hirviente

24 El día diez del mes décimo del año noveno, el SEÑOR me dirigió la palabra: 2«Hijo de hombre, anota la fecha de hoy, de este mismo día, porque el rey de Babilonia se ha puesto en marcha contra Jerusalén. 3Cuéntale una parábola a este pueblo rebelde, y adviértele que así dice el SEÑOR omnipotente:

»"Coloca la olla sobre el fuego
   y échale agua.
4Agrégale pedazos de carne,
   los mejores trozos de pata y de lomo,
   y lo mejor de los huesos.
5Toma luego la oveja más gorda
   y amontona leña debajo de ella,
para que hierva bien el agua
   y se cuezan bien los huesos.

6»"Porque el SEÑOR omnipotente dice:

»"¡Ay de la ciudad sanguinaria!
   ¡Ay de esa olla herrumbrada,

cuya herrumbre no se puede quitar!
Saca uno a uno los trozos de carne,
   tal como vayan saliendo.w
7La ciudad está empapada en su sangre,
   pues ella la derramó sobre la roca desnuda;
   no la derramó por el suelo,
   para impedir que el polvo la cubriera.
8Sobre la roca desnuda he vertido su sangre,
   para que no quede cubierta.
Así haré que se encienda mi ira,
   y daré lugar a mi venganza.

9»"Porque así dice el SEÑOR omnipotente:

»"¡Ay de la ciudad sanguinaria!
   Yo también amontonaré la leña.
10¡Vamos, apilen la leña y enciendan el fuego!
   ¡Cocinen la carne y preparen las especias,
   y que se quemen bien los huesos!
11¡Pongan la olla vacía sobre las brasas,
   hasta que el bronce esté al rojo vivo!
¡Que se fundan en ella sus *impurezas,
   y se consuma su herrumbre!
12¡Aunque esa olla está tan oxidada
   que ya ni con fuego se purifica!x

13»"Jerusalén, yo he querido purificarte de tu infame lujuria, pero no has dejado que te purifique. Por eso, no quedarás *limpia hasta que se apacigüe mi ira contra ti. 14Yo, el SEÑOR, lo he dicho, y lo cumpliré. Yo mismo actuaré, y no me voy a retractar. No tendré compasión ni me arrepentiré. Te juzgaré conforme a tu conducta y a tus acciones. Lo afirma el SEÑOR omnipotente."»

Muerte de la esposa de Ezequiel

15El SEÑOR me dirigió la palabra: 16«Hijo de hombre, voy a quitarte de golpe la mujer que te deleita la vista. Pero no llores ni hagas lamentos, ni dejes tampoco que te corran las lágrimas. 17Gime en silencio y no hagas duelo por los muertos. Átate el turbante, cálzate los pies, y no te cubras la barba ni comas el pan de duelo.»

18Por la mañana le hablé al pueblo, y por la tarde murió mi esposa. A la mañana siguiente hice lo que se me había ordenado. 19La gente del pueblo me preguntó: «¿No nos vas a explicar qué significado tiene para nosotros lo que estás haciendo?» 20Yo les contesté: «El SEÑOR me dirigió la palabra y me ordenó 21advertirle al pueblo de Israel que así dice el SEÑOR omnipotente: "Voy a profanar mi santuario, orgullo de su fortaleza, el templo que les deleita la vista y en el que depositan su afecto. Los hijos y las hijas que ustedes dejaron morirán a filo de espada, 22y ustedes harán lo mismo que yo: no se cubrirán la barba ni comerán el pan de duelo. 23Llevarán el turbante sobre la cabeza y se calzarán los pies. No llorarán ni harán lamentos, sino que se pudrirán a causa de sus pecados y gemirán unos con otros. 24Ezequiel les servirá de señal, y ustedes harán lo mismo que él hizo. Cuando esto suceda, sabrán que yo soy el SEÑOR omnipotente."

25»Y tú, hijo de hombre, el día en que yo les quite su fortaleza, su alegría y su gozo, el templo que les deleita la vista, el deseo de su *corazón, y a sus hijos e hijas, 26vendrá un fugitivo a comunicarte la noticia. 27Ese mismo día se te soltará la lengua y dejarás de estar mudo. Entonces podrás hablar con el fugitivo; servirás de señal para ellos, y sabrán que yo soy el SEÑOR.»

---

w 24:6 tal como vayan saliendo. Lit. sin echar suertes sobre ella.   x 24:12 Aunque ... purifica. Texto de difícil traducción.

Profecía contra Amón

25 El SEÑOR me dirigió la palabra: 2«Hijo de hombre, encara a los amonitas y profetiza contra ellos. 3Diles que presten atención a la palabra del SEÑOR omnipotente: "Por cuanto ustedes se burlaron cuando vieron que mi santuario era profanado, y que el país de Israel era devastado y que a los habitantes de Judá se los llevaban al exilio, 4yo los entregaré a ustedes al poder de los pueblos del oriente. Ellos armarán sus campamentos y establecerán entre ustedes sus moradas; comerán los frutos y beberán la leche de ustedes. 5Convertiré a Rabá en un pastizal de camellos, y a Amón en un corral de ovejas. Entonces sabrán ustedes que yo soy el SEÑOR.

6»"Así dice el SEÑOR omnipotente: Por cuanto ustedes los amonitas aplaudieron y saltaron de alegría, y maliciosamente se rieron de Israel, 7yo voy a extender mi mano contra ustedes y los entregaré a las naciones como despojo. Los arrancaré de entre los pueblos, y los destruiré por completo. Entonces sabrán que yo soy el SEÑOR."»

Profecía contra Moab

8«Así dice el SEÑOR omnipotente: Por cuanto Moab y Seír dicen: "Judá es igual a todas las naciones," 9voy a abrir el flanco de Moab. De un extremo a otro la dejaré sin Bet Yesimot, Baal Megón y Quiriatayin, ciudades que son su orgullo. 10Entregaré a Moab y a los amonitas en manos de los pueblos del oriente, y de los amonitas no quedará ni el recuerdo. 11Además, castigaré a Moab. Entonces sabrán que yo soy el SEÑOR.»

Profecía contra Edom

12«Así dice el SEÑOR omnipotente: Edom se ha vengado completamente de Judá, y de esta manera resulta más grave su culpa. 13Por eso, así dice el SEÑOR omnipotente: Extenderé mi mano contra Edom, y exterminaré a *hombres y animales. Lo dejaré en ruinas. Desde Temán hasta Dedán, todos morirán a filo de espada. 14Por medio de mi pueblo Israel me vengaré de Edom. Mi pueblo hará con Edom lo que le dicten mi ira y mi furor. Así conocerán lo que es mi venganza. Lo afirma el SEÑOR omnipotente.»

Profecía contra los filisteos

15«Así dice el SEÑOR omnipotente: Los filisteos se vengaron con alevosía; con profundo desprecio intentaron destruir a Judá por causa de una antigua enemistad. 16Por eso, así dice el SEÑOR omnipotente: Extenderé mi mano contra los filisteos. Exterminaré a los quereteos, y destruiré a los que aún quedan en la costa del mar. 17Mi venganza contra ellos será terrible. Los castigaré con mi ira. Y cuando ejecute mi venganza, sabrán que yo soy el SEÑOR.»

Profecía contra Tiro

26 El día primero del mes primeroy del año undécimo, el SEÑOR me dirigió la palabra: 2«Tiro ha dicho de Jerusalén: "Las *puertas de las naciones se han derrumbado. Sus puertas se me han abierto de par en par, y yo me estoy enriqueciendo mientras ellas yacen en ruinas." 3Por eso, así dice el SEÑOR omnipotente: Tiro, yo me declaro contra ti, y así como el mar levanta sus olas, voy a hacer que contra ti se levanten muchas naciones. 4Destruirán los muros de Tiro, y derribarán sus torres. Hasta los escombros barreré de su lugar; ¡la dejaré como roca desnuda! 5¡Quedará en medio del mar como un tendedero de redes! Yo, el SEÑOR omnipotente, lo afir-

mo. Tiro será despojo de las naciones, 6y sus poblados tierra adentro serán devastados a filo de espada. Entonces sabrán que yo soy el SEÑOR.

7»Así dice el SEÑOR omnipotente: Desde el norte voy a traer contra Tiro a Nabucodonosor, rey de Babilonia, rey de reyes. Vendrá con un gran ejército de caballos, y con carros de guerra y jinetes. 8Tus poblados tierra adentro serán devastados a filo de espada. Y Nabucodonosor construirá contra ti muros de asedio, levantará rampas para atacarte y alzará sus escudos. 9Atacará tus muros con arietes, y con sus armas destruirá tus torres. 10Cuando el rey de Babilonia entre por tus puertas, como se entra en una ciudad conquistada, sus caballos serán tan numerosos que te cubrirán de polvo, y tus muros temblarán por el estruendo de su caballería y sus carros. 11Con los cascos de sus caballos pisoteará todas tus calles; matará a tu pueblo a filo de espada, y tus sólidas columnas caerán por tierra. 12Además, saquearán tus riquezas y robarán tus mercancías. Derribarán tus muros, demolerán tus suntuosos palacios, y arrojarán al mar tus piedras, vigas y escombros. 13Así pondré fin al ruido de tus canciones, y no se volverá a escuchar la melodía de tus arpas. 14Te convertiré en una roca desnuda, en un tendedero de redes, y no volverás a ser edificada. Yo, el SEÑOR, lo he dicho. Yo, el SEÑOR omnipotente, lo afirmo.

15»Así le dice el SEÑOR omnipotente a Tiro: Las naciones costeras temblarán ante el estruendo de tu caída, el gemido de tus heridos y la masacre de tus habitantes. 16Todos los príncipes del mar descenderán de sus tronos, se quitarán los mantos y se despojarán de las vestiduras bordadas. Llenos de pánico se sentarán en el suelo; espantados por tu condición temblarán sin cesar,

17y sobre ti entonarán este lamento:

»¡Cómo has sido destruida, ciudad famosa,
    habitada por gente del mar!
¡Tú en el mar eras poderosa!
¡Con tus habitantes infundías
    terror a todo el continente!
18Ahora, en el día de tu caída,
    tiemblan los pueblos costeros,
y las islas que están en el mar
    se aterrorizan ante tu debacle."

19»Así dice el SEÑOR omnipotente: Te convertiré en lugar de ruinas, como toda ciudad deshabitada. Haré que te cubran las aguas caudalosas del océano. 20Te haré descender con los que descienden a la fosa; te haré habitar en lo más profundo de la tierra, en el país de eternas ruinas, con los que descienden a la fosa. No volverás a ser habitada ni reconstruidaz en la tierra de los vivientes. 21Te convertiré en objeto de espanto, y ya no volverás a existir. Te buscarán, pero jamás podrán encontrarte. Lo afirma el SEÑOR omnipotente.»

Lamento por la caída de Tiro

27 El SEÑOR me dirigió la palabra: 2«Hijo de hombre, dedícale este canto fúnebre a Tiro, 3ciudad asentada junto al mar y que trafica con pueblos de muchas costas lejanas:

»Así dice el SEÑOR omnipotente:

»"Tú, ciudad de Tiro,
    pretendes ser hermosa y perfecta.
4Tu dominio está en alta mar,
    tus constructores resaltaron tu hermosura.

---

y 26:1 *primero* (mss. de LXX); TM no incluye esta palabra.   z 26:20 *ni reconstruida* (LXX); *y daré gloria* (TM).

5Con pinos del monte Senir
  hicieron todos tus entablados.
Con cedros del Líbano
  armaron tu mástil.
6Con encinas de Basán
  construyeron tus remos,
y con cipreses de Chipre
  ensamblaron tu cubierta,
la cual fue decorada
  con incrustaciones de marfil.
7Con lino bordado de Egipto
  hicieron tus velas,
  y éstas te sirvieron de bandera.
De las costas de Elisá trajeron
  telas moradas y rojas para tu toldo.
8Oh, Tiro, tus remeros vinieron de Sidón y de
  Arvad.
  A bordo iban tus propios timoneles,
  los más expertos hombres de mar.
9Los hábiles veteranos de Guebala
  repararon los daños en la nave.
Los marineros de todas las naves del mar
  negociaron con tus mercancías.
10Hombres de Persia, Lidia y Fut
  militaron en tu ejército.
Te adornaron con escudos y cascos;
  ¡sacaron a relucir tu esplendor!

11»"Los de Arvad, junto con tu ejército, defendían los muros que te rodean, y los de Gamad estaban apostados en tus torres. A lo largo de tus muros colgaban sus escudos, haciendo resaltar tu hermosura. 12Era tal tu riqueza que Tarsis comerciaba contigo. A cambio de tu mercadería, ella te ofrecía plata, hierro, estaño y plomo. 13También Grecia, Tubal y Mésec negociaban contigo, y a cambio de tus mercancías te ofrecían esclavos y objetos de bronce. 14La gente de Bet Togarma te pagaba con caballos de trabajo, caballos de montar y mulos. 15Los habitantes de Rodasb también comerciaban contigo. Concretabas negocios con muchas islas del mar, las cuales te pagaban con ébano y colmillos de marfil. 16Por los muchos productos que tenías, Siria comerciaba contigo y a cambio te entregaba topacio, telas teñidas de púrpura, telas bordadas, lino fino, corales y rubíes. 17Judá e Israel también comerciaban contigo. Te ofrecían trigo de Minit, pasteles,c miel, aceite y bálsamo. 18Por la gran cantidad de tus productos, y por la abundancia de tu riqueza, también Damasco comerciaba contigo. Te pagaba con vino de Jelbón y lana de Sajar. 19A cambio de tus mercancías, los danitas y los griegos te traían de Uzal hierro forjado, canela y caña aromática. 20Dedán te vendía aparejos para montar. 21Tus clientes eran Arabia y todos los príncipes de Cedar, quienes te pagaban con corderos, carneros y chivos. 22También eran tus clientes los comerciantes de Sabá y Ragama. A cambio de mercancías, te entregaban oro, piedras preciosas y los mejores perfumes. 23Jarán, Cané, Edén y los comerciantes de Sabá, Asiria y Quilmad negociaban contigo. 24Para abastecer tus mercados te vendían hermosas telas, mantos de color púrpura, bordados, tapices de muchos colores y cuerdas muy bien trenzadas. 25Las naves de Tarsis transportaban tus mercancías.

»"Cargada de riquezas,
  navegabas en alta mar.
26Tus remeros te llevaron por los mares
  inmensos,

en alta mar el viento del este te hizo
  pedazos.
27El día de tu naufragio
  se hundirán en el fondo del mar
tu riqueza, tu mercancía y tus productos,
  tus marineros y tus timoneles,
los que reparan tus naves y tus comerciantes,
  tus soldados y toda tu tripulación.
28Al grito de tus timoneles
  temblarán las costas.
29Todos los remeros abandonarán las naves;
  marineros y timoneles bajarán a tierra.
30Por ti levantarán la voz
  y llorarán con amargura;
se echarán ceniza sobre la cabeza,
  y se revolcarán en ella.
31Por tu culpa se raparán la cabeza,
  y se vestirán de luto.
Llorarán por ti con gran amargura,
  y con angustiosos gemidos.
32Entonarán sentidos lamentos,
  y en tono de amarga queja dirán:
  '¿Quién en medio de los mares
  podía compararse a Tiro?'
33Cuando desembarcaban tus productos
  muchas naciones quedaban satisfechas.
Con tus muchas riquezas y mercancías,
  enriquecías a los reyes de la tierra.
34Pero ahora el mar te ha hecho pedazos,
  ¡yaces en lo profundo de las aguas!
Tus mercancías y toda tu tripulación
  se hundieron contigo.
35Por ti están horrorizados
  todos los habitantes de las costas;
sus reyes tiemblan de miedo,
  y en su rostro dibujan el terror.
36Atónitos se han quedado
  los comerciantes de otros países;
¡tu fin ha llegado!,
  ¡nunca más volverás a existir!"»

Profecía contra el rey de Tiro

28 El Señor me dirigió la palabra: 2«Hijo de
hombre, adviértele al rey de Tiro que así dice
el Señor omnipotente:

»"En la intimidad de tu arrogancia dijiste:
  'Yo soy un dios.
Me encuentro en alta mar
  sentado en un trono de dioses.'
¡Pero tú no eres un dios,
  aunque te creas que lo eres!
¡Tú eres un simple *mortal!
3¿Acaso eres más sabio que Daniel?
  ¿Acaso conoces todos los secretos?
4Con tu sabiduría y tu inteligencia
  has acumulado muchas riquezas,
y en tus cofres has amontonado
  mucho oro y mucha plata.
5Eres muy hábil para el comercio;
  por eso te has hecho muy rico.
Con tus grandes riquezas
  te has vuelto muy arrogante.

6Por eso, así dice el Señor omnipotente:

»"Ya que pretendes ser
  tan sabio como un dios,
7haré que vengan extranjeros contra ti,
  los más feroces de las naciones:

---

a 27:9 *Guebal.* Es decir, Byblos.   b 27:15 *Rodas* (LXX); *Dedán* (TM).   c 27:17 *pasteles.* Palabra de difícil traducción.

desenvainarán la espada
  contra tu hermosura y sabiduría,
  y profanarán tu esplendor.
8Te hundirán en la fosa,
  y en alta mar sufrirás una muerte violenta.
9Y aun así, en presencia de tus verdugos,
  ¿te atreverás a decir: ¡Soy un dios!?
¡Pues en manos de tus asesinos
  no serás un dios sino un simple mortal!
10Sufrirás a manos de extranjeros
  la muerte de los incircuncisos,
  porque yo lo he dicho.

Lo afirma el SEÑOR omnipotente."»

11El SEÑOR me dirigió la palabra: 12«Hijo de hombre, entona una elegía al rey de Tiro y adviértele que así dice el SEÑOR omnipotente:

»"Eras un modelo de perfección,
  lleno de sabiduría y de hermosura perfecta.
13Estabas en Edén, en el jardín de Dios,
  adornado con toda clase de piedras
     preciosas:
rubí, crisólito, jade,
  topacio, cornalina, jaspe,
  zafiro, granate y esmeralda.
Tus joyas y encajes estaban cubiertos de oro,
  y especialmente preparados para ti
  desde el día en que fuiste creado.
14Fuiste elegido *querubín protector,
  porque yo así lo dispuse.d
Estabas en el *santo monte de Dios,
  y caminabas sobre piedras de fuego.
15Desde el día en que fuiste creado
  tu conducta fue irreprochable,
  hasta que la maldad halló cabida en ti.
16Por la abundancia de tu comercio,
  te llenaste de violencia, y pecaste.
Por eso te expulsé del monte de Dios,
  como a un objeto profano.
A ti, querubín protector,
  te borré de entre las piedras de fuego.
17A causa de tu hermosura
  te llenaste de orgullo.
A causa de tu esplendor,
  corrompiste tu sabiduría.
Por eso te arrojé por tierra,
  y delante de los reyes
  te expuse al ridículo.
18Has profanado tus santuarios,
  por la gran cantidad de tus pecados,
  ¡por tu comercio corrupto!
Por eso hice salir de ti
  un fuego que te devorara.
A la vista de todos los que te admiran
  te eché por tierra y te reduje a cenizas.
19Al verte, han quedado espantadas
  todas las naciones que te conocen.
Has llegado a un final terrible,
  y ya no volverás a existir."»

Profecía contra Sidón

20El SEÑOR me dirigió la palabra: 21«Hijo de hombre, encara a Sidón y profetiza contra ella. 22Adviértele que así dice el SEÑOR omnipotente:

»"Aquí estoy, Sidón, para acusarte
  y para ser glorificado en ti.
Cuando traiga sobre ti un justo castigo,

y manifieste sobre ti mi *santidad,
  se sabrá que yo soy el SEÑOR.
23Mandaré contra ti una peste,
  y por tus calles correrá la sangre;
por la espada que ataca por todos lados
  los heridos caerán en tus calles,
  y se sabrá que yo soy el SEÑOR.
24Los israelitas no volverán a sufrir
  el desprecio de sus vecinos,
que duele como aguijones
  y punza como espinas,
  ¡y se sabrá que yo soy el SEÑOR!"

25»Así dice el SEÑOR omnipotente: "Cuando yo reúna al pueblo de Israel de entre las naciones donde se encuentra disperso, le mostraré mi santidad en presencia de todas las naciones. Entonces Israel vivirá en su propio país, el mismo que le di a mi siervo Jacob. 26Allí vivirán seguros, y se construirán casas y plantarán viñedos, porque yo ejecutaré un justo castigo sobre los vecinos que desprecian al pueblo de Israel. ¡y se sabrá que yo soy el SEÑOR su Dios!"»

Profecía contra Egipto

29 A los doce días del mes décimo del año décimo, el SEÑOR me dirigió la palabra: 2«Hijo de hombre, encara al faraón, rey de Egipto, y profetiza contra él y contra todo Egipto. 3Adviértele que así dice el SEÑOR omnipotente:

»"A ti, Faraón, rey de Egipto,
  gran monstruo que yaces
  en el cauce de tus ríos,
que dices: 'El Nilo es mío,
  el Nilo es mi creación,'
  ¡te declaro que estoy en tu contra!
4Te pondré garfios en las mandíbulas,
  y haré que los peces del río
  se te peguen a las escamas.
Y con todos los peces pegados a tus escamas
  te sacaré de la corriente.
5Te abandonaré a tu suerte en el desierto,
  junto con todos los peces de tu río.
Caerás en campo abierto,
  y no serás recogido ni enterrado.e
Las bestias de la tierra y las aves del cielo
  te las daré como alimento.
6Entonces todos los habitantes de Egipto
  sabrán que yo soy el SEÑOR.
No fuiste para el pueblo de Israel
  más que un bastón de caña.
7Cuando se agarraron de tu mano,
  te quebraste, y les desgarraste las manos;f
cuando en ti se apoyaron te rompiste,
  y sus espaldas se estremecieron.g

8»"Por eso, así dice el SEÑOR omnipotente: Contra ti traeré la espada, y haré que mate a *hombres y animales. 9La tierra de Egipto se convertirá en desolación. Entonces sabrán que yo soy el SEÑOR. Tú dijiste: 'El Nilo es mío, el Nilo es mi creación.' 10Por eso me declaro en contra tuya y en contra de tus ríos. Desde Migdol hasta Asuán, y hasta la frontera con Etiopía, convertiré a la tierra de Egipto en ruina y desolación total. 11Durante cuarenta años quedará completamente deshabitada, y ni hombres ni animales pasarán por allí. 12Haré de Egipto la más desolada de todas las tierras, y durante cuarenta años sus ciudades quedarán en ruinas y

---

d 28:14 Fuiste ... dispuse. Texto de difícil traducción.   e 29:5 enterrado (mss. hebreos y Targum); juntado (TM).   f 29:7 manos (LXX y Siríaca); hombros (TM).   g 29:7 se estremecieron (Siríaca; véanse LXX y Vulgata); hiciste que se pararan (TM).

en medio de gran desolación. Yo dispersaré a los egipcios entre las naciones, y los esparciré por los países.

13»"Así dice el SEÑOR omnipotente: Al cabo de los cuarenta años reuniré a los egipcios de entre los pueblos donde fueron dispersados. 14Cambiaré la suerte de Egipto y los haré volver a Patros, tierra de sus antepasados. Allí formarán un reino humilde. 15Será el reino de menor importancia, y nunca podrá levantarse por encima de las demás naciones. Yo mismo los haré tan pequeños que no podrán dominar a las otras naciones. 16El pueblo de Israel no confiará más en Egipto. Al contrario, será Egipto quien les sirva para recordar el pecado que cometieron los israelitas al seguirlo. Así sabrán que yo soy el SEÑOR."»

17El día primero del mes primero del año veintisiete, el SEÑOR me dirigió la palabra: 18«Toma en cuenta, hijo de hombre, que el rey de Babilonia, Nabucodonosor, y su ejército llevaron a cabo una gran campaña contra Tiro. Todos ellos quedaron con la cabeza rapada y con llagas en la espalda. Pero, a pesar del tremendo esfuerzo, ni él ni su ejército sacaron provecho alguno de la campaña emprendida contra Tiro. 19Por eso, así dice el SEÑOR omnipotente: Pondré a Egipto en manos de Nabucodonosor, rey de Babilonia, quien se apoderará de sus riquezas, saqueará sus despojos, y se llevará el botín que servirá de recompensa para su ejército. 20Al rey de Babilonia le entregaré Egipto como recompensa por lo que hizo contra Tiro, porque ellos lo hicieron por mí. Lo afirma el SEÑOR omnipotente.

21»En aquel día acrecentaré la fuerza del pueblo de Israel, y entonces tú, Ezequiel, les hablarás con libertad. Entonces sabrán que yo soy el SEÑOR.»

Lamento por Egipto

30 El SEÑOR me dirigió la palabra: 2«Hijo de hombre, profetiza y adviérteles:

»Así dice el SEÑOR:
　"Giman: '¡Ay de aquel día!'
3El día del SEÑOR se acerca,
　sí, ya se acerca el día.
Día cargado de nubarrones,
　día nefasto para los pueblos.
4Vendrá una espada contra Egipto
　y Etiopía será presa de la angustia.
Cuando caigan heridos los egipcios,
　serán saqueadas sus riquezas
　y destruidos sus cimientos.
5Etiopía, Fut, toda Arabia y Lidia
　caerán a filo de espada,
　lo mismo que los hijos del país del *pacto.

6»"Así dice el SEÑOR;
　esto afirma el SEÑOR omnipotente:
Caerán los aliados de Egipto,
　se derrumbará el orgullo de su poder.
Desde Migdol hasta Asuán
　caerán a filo de espada.
7Sus ciudades quedarán en ruinas,
　entre las más desoladas de las tierras.
8Cuando yo le prenda fuego a Egipto
　y sean destrozados todos sus aliados,
　sabrán que yo soy el SEÑOR.

9»"En aquel día saldrán en barcos mis mensajeros para aterrorizar a la confiada Etiopía; en el día de Egipto, que ya está a la puerta, les sobrevendrá la angustia.

10»"Así dice el SEÑOR omnipotente:

»"Por medio de Nabucodonosor, rey de Babilonia,
　acabaré con la opulencia de Egipto.
11Nabucodonosor y su ejército,
　el más poderoso de las naciones,
　vendrán a destruir el país.
Desenvainarán la espada contra Egipto
　y llenarán de cadáveres el país.
12Secaré los canales del Nilo,
　y entregaré el país en manos de gente
　malvada.
Por medio de manos extranjeras
　desolaré el país y cuanto haya en él.
　Yo, el SEÑOR, lo he dicho.

13»"Así dice el SEÑOR omnipotente:

»"Voy a destruir a todos los ídolos de Menfis;
　pondré fin a sus dioses falsos.
Haré que cunda el pánico por todo el país,
　y no habrá más príncipes en Egipto.
14Devastaré a Patros,
　le prenderé fuego a Zoán,
　y dictaré sentencia contra Tebas.

15»"Desataré mi ira sobre Sin, la fortaleza de Egipto, y extirparé la riqueza de Tebas. 16Le prenderé fuego a Egipto, y Sin se retorcerá de dolor. Se abrirán brechas en Tebas, y Menfis vivirá en constante angustia. 17Los jóvenes de On y de Bubastis caerán a filo de espada, y las mujeres irán al cautiverio. 18Cuando yo haga pedazos el yugo de Egipto, el día se oscurecerá en Tafnes. Así llegará a su fin el orgullo de su fuerza. Egipto quedará cubierto de nubes, y sus hijas irán al cautiverio. 19Éste será su castigo, y así Egipto sabrá que yo soy el SEÑOR."»

20El día siete del mes primero del año undécimo, el SEÑOR me dirigió la palabra: 21«Hijo de hombre, yo le he quebrado el brazo al faraón, rey de Egipto. Nadie se lo ha vendado ni curado para que recobre su fuerza y pueda empuñar la espada. 22Por eso, así dice el SEÑOR: "Estoy contra el faraón, rey de Egipto. Le quebraré los dos brazos, el sano y el fracturado, y haré que la espada se le caiga de la mano. 23Voy a dispersar a los egipcios entre las naciones; voy a esparcirlos entre los países. 24Fortaleceré a su vez los brazos del rey de Babilonia: pondré mi espada en sus manos y quebraré los brazos del faraón. Entonces él gemirá ante su enemigo como herido de muerte. 25Fortaleceré los brazos del rey de Babilonia, y haré que desfallezcan los brazos del faraón. Y cuando ponga yo mi espada en manos del rey de Babilonia, y él la extienda contra Egipto, se sabrá que yo soy el SEÑOR. 26Dispersaré por las naciones a los egipcios; los esparciré entre los países. Entonces sabrán que yo soy el SEÑOR."»

El cedro del Líbano

31 El día primero del mes tercero del año undécimo, el SEÑOR me dirigió la palabra: 2«Hijo de hombre, dile al faraón y a toda su gente:

»¿Quién se puede comparar con tu
　grandeza?
3Fíjate en Asiria,
　que alguna vez fue cedro del Líbano,
con bello y frondoso ramaje;
　su copa llegaba hasta las nubes.
4Las aguas lo hicieron crecer;
　las corrientes profundas lo nutrieron.
Sus ríos corrían en torno a sus raíces;
　sus acequias regaban todos los árboles del
　campo.

5Así el cedro creció
　　más alto que todos los árboles.
Gracias a las abundantes aguas,
　　se extendió su frondoso ramaje.
6Todas las aves del cielo
　　anidaban en sus ramas.
Todas las bestias del campo
　　parían bajo su follaje.
Todas las naciones
　　vivían bajo su sombra.
7Era un árbol imponente y majestuoso,
　　de ramas extendidas;
sus raíces se hundían
　　hasta las aguas caudalosas.
8Ningún cedro en el jardín de Dios
　　se le podía comparar;
ningún pino ostentaba un follaje parecido,
　　ni tenían su fronda los castaños.
Ningún árbol del jardín de Dios
　　se le comparaba en hermosura.
9Yo lo hice bello
　　y con un ramaje majestuoso.
En el Edén, jardín de Dios,
　　era la envidia de todos los árboles.

10»"Por eso, así dice el SEÑOR omnipotente: 'Por cuanto el árbol creció tan alto, y ufano de su altura irguió su copa hasta las nubes, 11yo lo he desechado; lo he dejado en manos de un déspota invasor, para que lo trate según su maldad. 12Los extranjeros más crueles lo han talado, abandonándolo a su suerte. Sus ramas han caído en los montes y en los valles; yacen rotas por todas las cañadas del país. Huyeron y lo abandonaron todas las naciones que buscaban protección bajo su sombra. 13Ahora las aves del cielo se posan sobre su tronco caído, y los animales salvajes se meten entre sus ramas. 14Y esto es para que ningún árbol que esté junto a las aguas vuelva a crecer tanto; para que ningún árbol, por bien regado que esté, vuelva a elevar su copa hasta las nubes. Todos están destinados a la muerte, a bajar a las regiones profundas de la tierra y quedarse entre los *mortales que descienden a la fosa.

15»'Así dice el SEÑOR omnipotente: El día en que el cedro bajó al *abismo, hice que el mar subterráneo se secara en señal de duelo. Detuve sus corrientes, y contuve sus ríos; por él cubrí de luto al Líbano, y todos los árboles del campo se marchitaron. 16Cuando lo hice bajar al abismo, junto con los que descienden a la fosa, con el estruendo de su caída hice temblar a las naciones. Todos los árboles del Edén, los más selectos y hermosos del Líbano, los que estaban mejor regados, se consolaron en las regiones subterráneas. 17Sus aliados entre las naciones que buscaban protección bajo su sombra también descendieron con él al abismo, junto con los que habían muerto a filo de espada. 18Ningún árbol del Edén se le podía comparar en grandeza y majestad. No obstante, también él descendió con los árboles del Edén a las regiones subterráneas. Allí quedó tendido en medio de los *paganos, junto con los que murieron a filo de espada. ¡Y así será la muerte del faraón y de todos sus súbditos! Lo afirma el SEÑOR omnipotente.' "»

Lamento por el faraón

32 El día primero del mes duodécimo del año duodécimo, el SEÑOR me dirigió la palabra: 2«Hijo de hombre, entona este lamento dedicado al faraón, rey de Egipto:

»"Pareces un león entre las naciones;
　　pareces un monstruo marino
　　chapoteando en el río;

con tus patas enturbias el agua
　　y revuelves sus corrientes.

3»"Así dice el SEÑOR omnipotente:

»"Aunque estés entre numerosos pueblos,
　　tenderé sobre ti mi red
　　y te atraparé con ella.
4Te arrastraré por tierra,
　　y en pleno campo te dejaré tendido.
Dejaré que sobre ti se posen
　　todas las aves del cielo.
Dejaré que con tu carne
　　se sacien todas las bestias salvajes.
5Desparramaré tu carne por los montes,
　　y con tu carroña llenaré los valles.
6Con tu sangre empaparé la tierra
　　hasta la cima de las montañas;
con tu sangre llenaré
　　los cauces de los ríos.
7Cuando te hayas consumido,
　　haré que el cielo se oscurezca
　　y se apaguen las estrellas;
cubriré el sol con una nube,
　　y no brillará más la luna.
8Por ti haré que se oscurezcan
　　todos los astros luminosos de los cielos,
　　y que tu país quede envuelto en las
　　　tinieblas.
　　　　　Lo afirma el SEÑOR omnipotente.

9»"'Cuando yo haga que la noticia de tu destrucción llegue hasta tierras que tú no conocías, haré temblar a muchas naciones. 10También haré que por tu causa muchos pueblos queden consternados. Cuando yo esgrima mi espada delante de ellos, sus reyes se estremecerán. En el día de tu debacle, en todo momento temblarán de miedo por temor a perder la vida.

11»"'Así dice el SEÑOR omnipotente: La espada del rey de Babilonia vendrá contra ti. 12Haré que tu pueblo numeroso caiga a filo de espada, empuñada por los guerreros más crueles entre las naciones. Ellos arrasarán la soberbia de Egipto, y toda su multitud será derrotada. 13Voy a destruir a todo el ganado que pasta junto a las aguas abundantes, y éstas nunca más serán enturbiadas por *hombres ni animales. 14Entonces dejaré que las aguas se asienten y que corran tranquilas, como el aceite. Lo afirma el SEÑOR omnipotente. 15Cuando convierta en desolación la tierra de Egipto, y la despoje de todo lo que hay en ella, y hiera a todos los que la habitan, entonces sabrán que yo soy el SEÑOR.' "

16»Éste es el lamento que las ciudades de las naciones entonarán sobre Egipto y toda su multitud. Lo afirma el SEÑOR omnipotente.»

17En el día quince del mes duodécimo del año duodécimo, el SEÑOR me dirigió la palabra: 18«Hijo de hombre, entona un lamento sobre las multitudes de Egipto, y junto con las ciudades de las naciones más poderosas hazlas descender con los que bajan a la fosa, a las regiones más profundas. 19Pregúntales: "¿Se creen acaso más privilegiados que otros? ¡Pues bajen y tiéndanse entre los *paganos!" 20Y caerán entre los que murieron a filo de espada. Ya tienen la espada en la mano: ¡que se arrastre a Egipto y a sus multitudes! 21En medio del *abismo, los guerreros más fuertes y valientes hablarán de Egipto y de sus aliados. Y dirán: "¡Ya han descendido a la fosa! ¡Yacen tendidos entre los paganos que murieron a filo de espada!"

²²»Allí está Asiria, con toda su multitud en torno a su sepulcro. Todos ellos murieron a filo de espada. ²³Todos los que sembraban el terror en la tierra de los vivientes yacen muertos, víctimas de la espada. Ahora están sepultados en lo más profundo de la fosa, ¡tendidos alrededor de su tumba!

²⁴»Allí está Elam, con toda su multitud en torno a su sepulcro. Todos ellos murieron a filo de espada. Todos los que sembraban el terror en la tierra de los vivientes bajaron como paganos a lo más profundo de la fosa. Yacen tendidos sin honor entre los que descendieron a la fosa. ²⁵A Elam le han preparado una cama en medio de los muertos, entre los paganos que murieron a filo de espada y que ahora rodean su tumba. Ellos sembraron el terror en la tierra de los vivientes, pero ahora yacen tendidos sin honor entre los que descendieron a la fosa. Allí quedaron, entre gente que murió asesinada.

²⁶»Allí están Mésec y Tubal, con toda su multitud en torno a su sepulcro. Todos ellos son paganos, muertos a filo de espada porque sembraron el terror en la tierra de los vivientes. ²⁷No yacen con los héroes caídos de entre los paganos, que bajaron al abismo con sus armas de guerra y que tienen sus espadas bajo la cabeza. El castigo de sus pecados cayó sobre sus huesos, porque estos héroes sembraron el terror en la tierra de los vivientes.

²⁸»Ahí estarás tú, Egipto, en medio de los paganos, quebrado y sepultado junto con los que murieron a filo de espada.

²⁹»Allí está Edom, con sus reyes y príncipes. A pesar de todo su poder, también ellos yacen tendidos junto a los que murieron a filo de espada. Yacen entre los paganos, con los que descendieron a la fosa.

³⁰»Allí están todos los príncipes del norte, y todos los de Sidón. A pesar del terror que sembraron con su poderío, también ellos bajaron, envueltos en deshonra, con los que murieron a filo de espada. Son paganos, y ahora yacen tendidos entre los que murieron a filo de espada, en medio de los que descendieron a la fosa.

³¹»El faraón los verá y se consolará de la muerte de toda su gente, pues él y todo su ejército morirán a filo de espada. Lo afirma el SEÑOR omnipotente.

³²»Aunque yo hice que el faraón sembrara el terror en la tierra de los vivientes, él y todo su ejército serán sepultados entre los paganos, con los que murieron a filo de espada. Lo afirma el SEÑOR omnipotente.»

El profeta centinela de su pueblo

33 El SEÑOR me dirigió la palabra: ²«Hijo de hombre, habla con tu pueblo y dile: "Cuando yo envío la guerra a algún país, y la gente de ese país escoge a un hombre y lo pone por centinela, ³si éste ve acercarse al ejército enemigo, toca la trompeta para advertir al pueblo. ⁴Entonces, si alguien escucha la trompeta pero no se da por advertido, y llega la espada y lo mata, él mismo será el culpable de su propia muerte. ⁵Como escuchó el sonido de la trompeta pero no le hizo caso, será responsable de su propia muerte, pues si hubiera estado atento se habría salvado.

⁶»"Ahora bien, si el centinela ve que se acerca el enemigo y no toca la trompeta para prevenir al pueblo, y viene la espada y mata a alguien, esa persona perecerá por su maldad, pero al centinela yo le pediré cuentas de esa muerte."

⁷»A ti, hijo de hombre, te he puesto por centinela del pueblo de Israel. Por lo tanto, oirás la palabra de mi boca, y advertirás de mi parte al pueblo. ⁸Cuando yo le diga al malvado: "¡Vas a morir!", si tú no lo adviertes que cambie su mala conducta, el malvado morirá por su pecado, pero a ti te pediré cuentas de su sangre. ⁹En cambio, si le adviertes al malvado que cambie su mala conducta, y no lo hace, él morirá por su pecado pero tú habrás salvado tu vida.

¹⁰»Hijo de hombre, diles a los israelitas: "Ustedes dicen: 'Nuestras rebeliones y nuestros pecados pesan sobre nosotros, y nos estamos consumiendo en vida. ¿Cómo podremos vivir?' " ¹¹Diles: "Tan cierto como que yo vivo —afirma el SEÑOR omnipotente—, que no me alegro con la muerte del malvado, sino con que se convierta de su mala conducta y viva. ¡Conviértete, pueblo de Israel; conviértete de tu conducta perversa! ¿Por qué habrás de morir?"

¹²»Tú, hijo de hombre, diles a los hijos de tu pueblo: "Al justo no lo salvará su propia justicia si comete algún pecado; y la maldad del impío no le será motivo de tropiezo si se convierte. Si el justo peca, no se podrá salvar por su justicia anterior. ¹³Si yo le digo al justo: '¡Vivirás!', pero él se atiene a su propia justicia y hace lo malo, no se le tomará en cuenta su justicia, sino que morirá por la maldad que cometió. ¹⁴En cambio, si le digo al malvado: '¡Morirás!', pero luego él se convierte de su pecado y actúa con justicia y rectitud, ¹⁵y devuelve lo que tomó en prenda y restituye lo que robó, y obedece los preceptos de vida, sin cometer ninguna iniquidad, ciertamente vivirá y no morirá. ¹⁶No se le tomará en cuenta ninguno de los pecados que antes cometió, sino que vivirá por haber actuado con justicia y rectitud."

¹⁷»Los hijos de tu pueblo dicen: "El SEÑOR no actúa con justicia." En realidad, los que no actúan con justicia son ellos. ¹⁸Si el justo se aparta de su justicia y hace lo malo, morirá a causa de ello. ¹⁹Y si el malvado deja de hacer lo malo y actúa con justicia y rectitud, vivirá. ²⁰A pesar de esto, ustedes siguen repitiendo: "El SEÑOR no actúa con justicia." Pero yo, israelitas, los juzgaré a cada uno de ustedes según su conducta.»

La caída de Jerusalén

²¹El día quinto del mes décimo del año duodécimo de nuestro exilio, un fugitivo que había huido de Jerusalén vino y me dio esta noticia: «La ciudad ha sido conquistada.» ²²La noche antes de que llegara el fugitivo, la mano del SEÑOR vino sobre mí y me dejó mudo. A la mañana siguiente, cuando vino el hombre, el SEÑOR me devolvió el habla.

²³Luego el SEÑOR me dirigió la palabra: ²⁴«Hijo de hombre, la gente que vive en esas ruinas en la tierra de Israel, anda diciendo: "Si Abraham, que era uno solo, llegó a poseer todo el país, con mayor razón nosotros, que somos muchos, habremos de recibir la tierra en posesión." ²⁵Por tanto, adviérteles que así dice el SEÑOR omnipotente: "Ustedes comen carne con sangre, adoran a sus ídolos, y derraman sangre, ¿y aun así pretenden poseer el país? ²⁶Además, confían en sus espadas, cometen abominaciones, viven en adulterio con la mujer de su prójimo, ¿y aun así pretenden poseer el país?"

²⁷»Por tanto, adviérteles que así dice el SEÑOR omnipotente: "Tan cierto como que yo vivo, que los que habitan en las ruinas morirán a filo de espada; a los que andan por el campo abierto se los daré como pasto a las fieras, y los que están en las fortalezas y en las cuevas morirán de peste. ²⁸Convertiré al país en un desierto desolado, y se acabará el orgullo de su poder. Los montes de Israel quedarán devastados, y nadie más pasará por ellos. ²⁹Y cuando yo deje a este país como un desierto desolado por culpa de los actos detestables que ellos cometieron, sabrán que yo soy el SEÑOR."

³⁰»En cuanto a ti, hijo de hombre, los de tu pueblo hablan de ti junto a los muros y en las puertas de

las casas, y se dicen unos a otros: "Vamos a escuchar el mensaje que nos envía el SEÑOR." ³¹Y se te acercan en masa, y se sientan delante de ti y escuchan tus palabras, pero luego no las practican. Me halagan de labios para afuera, pero después sólo buscan las ganancias injustas. ³²En realidad, tú eres para ellos tan sólo alguien que entona canciones de amor con una voz hermosa, y que toca bien un instrumento; oyen tus palabras, pero no las ponen en práctica. ³³No obstante, cuando todo esto suceda —y en verdad está a punto de cumplirse—, sabrán que hubo un profeta entre ellos.»

Pastores y ovejas

34 El SEÑOR me dirigió la palabra: ²«Hijo de hombre, profetiza contra los pastores de Israel; profetiza y adviérteles que así dice el SEÑOR omnipotente: "¡Ay de ustedes, *pastores de Israel, que tan sólo se cuidan a sí mismos! ¿Acaso los pastores no deben cuidar al rebaño? ³Ustedes se beben la leche, se visten con la lana, y matan las ovejas más gordas, pero no cuidan del rebaño. ⁴No fortalecen a la oveja débil, no cuidan de la enferma, ni curan a la herida; no van por la descarriada ni buscan a la perdida. Al contrario, tratan al rebaño con crueldad y violencia. ⁵Por eso las ovejas se han dispersado: ¡por falta de pastor! Por eso están a la merced de las fieras salvajes. ⁶Mis ovejas andan descarriadas por montes y colinas, dispersas por toda la tierra, sin que nadie se preocupe por buscarlas.

⁷»"Por tanto, pastores, escuchen bien la palabra del SEÑOR; ⁸Tan cierto como que yo vivo —afirma el SEÑOR omnipotente—, que por falta de pastor mis ovejas han sido objeto del pillaje y han estado a merced de las fieras salvajes. Mis pastores no se ocupan de mis ovejas; cuidan de sí mismos pero no de mis ovejas. ⁹Por tanto, pastores, escuchen la palabra del SEÑOR. ¹⁰Así dice el SEÑOR omnipotente: Yo estoy en contra de mis pastores. Les pediré cuentas de mi rebaño; les quitaré la responsabilidad de apacentar a mis ovejas, y no se apacentarán más a sí mismos. Arrebataré de sus fauces a mis ovejas, para que no les sirvan de alimento.

¹¹»"Así dice el SEÑOR omnipotente: Yo mismo me encargaré de buscar y de cuidar a mi rebaño. ¹²Como un pastor que cuida de sus ovejas cuando están dispersas, así me ocuparé de mis ovejas y las rescataré de todos los lugares donde, en un día oscuro y de nubarrones, se hayan dispersado. ¹³Yo las sacaré de entre las naciones; las reuniré de los países, y las llevaré a su tierra. Las apacentaré en los montes de Israel, en los vados y en todos los poblados del país. ¹⁴Las haré pastar en los mejores pastos, y su aprisco estará en los montes altos de Israel. Allí descansarán en un buen lugar de pastoreo y se alimentarán de los mejores pastos de los montes de Israel. ¹⁵Yo mismo apacentaré a mi rebaño, y lo llevaré a descansar. Lo afirma el SEÑOR omnipotente. ¹⁶Buscaré a las ovejas perdidas, recogeré a las extraviadas, vendaré a las que estén heridas y fortaleceré a las débiles, pero exterminaré a las ovejas gordas y robustas. Yo las pastorearé con *justicia.

¹⁷»"En cuanto a ti, rebaño mío, esto es lo que dice el SEÑOR omnipotente: Juzgaré entre ovejas y ovejas, y entre carneros y chivos. ¹⁸¿No les basta con comerse los mejores pastos, sino que tienen también que pisotear lo que queda? ¿No les basta con beber agua limpia, sino que tienen que enturbiar el resto con las patas? ¹⁹Por eso mis ovejas tienen ahora que comerse el pasto que ustedes han pisoteado, y beberse el agua que ustedes han enturbiado.

²⁰»"Por eso, así dice el SEÑOR omnipotente: Yo mismo voy a juzgar entre las ovejas gordas y las flacas. ²¹Por cuanto ustedes han empujado con el costado y con la espalda, y han atacado a cornadas a las más débiles, hasta dispersarlas, ²²voy a salvar a mis ovejas, y ya no les servirán de presa. Yo juzgaré entre ovejas y ovejas. ²³Entonces les daré un pastor, mi siervo David, que las apacentará y será su único pastor. ²⁴Yo, el SEÑOR, seré su Dios, y mi siervo David será su príncipe. Yo, el SEÑOR, lo he dicho.

²⁵»"Estableceré con ellas un *pacto de *paz: haré desaparecer del país a las bestias feroces, para que mis ovejas puedan habitar seguras en el desierto y dormir tranquilas en los bosques. ²⁶Haré que ellas y los alrededores de mi colina sean una fuente de bendición. Haré caer lluvias de bendición en el tiempo oportuno. ²⁷Los árboles del campo darán su fruto, la tierra entregará sus cosechas, y ellas vivirán seguras en su propia tierra. Y cuando yo haga pedazos su yugo y las libere de sus tiranos, entonces sabrán que yo soy el SEÑOR. ²⁸Ya no volverán a ser presa de las naciones, ni serán devoradas por las fieras. Vivirán seguras y nadie les infundirá temor. ²⁹Les daré una tierra famosa por sus cosechas. No sufrirán hambre en la tierra, ni tendrán que soportar los insultos de las naciones. ³⁰Entonces sabrán que yo, el SEÑOR su Dios, estoy con ellos, y que ellos, el pueblo de Israel, son mi pueblo. Yo, el SEÑOR omnipotente, lo afirmo. ³¹y afirmo también que yo soy su Dios y que ustedes son mis ovejas, las ovejas de mi prado."»

Profecía contra Edom

35 El SEÑOR me dirigió la palabra: ²«Hijo de hombre, vuélvete hacia la montaña de Seír y profetiza contra ella. ³Adviértele que así dice el SEÑOR omnipotente:

»"Aquí estoy contra ti, montaña de Seír.
Contra ti extenderé mi mano,
   y te convertiré en un desierto desolado.
⁴Tus ciudades quedarán en ruinas,
   y tú serás una desolación.
Entonces sabrán que yo soy el SEÑOR.

⁵»"En el día del castigo final de los israelitas, en el tiempo de su calamidad, tú les hiciste la guerra, y has mantenido contra ellos una enemistad proverbial. Por lo tanto, ⁶tan cierto como que yo vivo, que te anegaré en sangre, y la sangre te perseguirá. Lo afirma el SEÑOR omnipotente: eres culpable de muerte, y la muerte no te dará tregua. ⁷Haré de la montaña de Seír un desierto desolado, y exterminaré a todo el que pase o venga por allí. ⁸Llenaré de víctimas tus montes; los que han muerto a filo de espada cubrirán tus colinas, tus valles, y los cauces de tus ríos. ⁹Para siempre te convertiré en una desolación; tus ciudades quedarán deshabitadas. Entonces sabrás que yo soy el SEÑOR.

¹⁰»"Porque tú has dicho: 'A pesar de que el Señor viva allí, las dos naciones y los dos territorios serán míos, y yo seré su dueño.' ¹¹Por eso, tan cierto como que yo vivo, que haré contigo conforme al furor y celo con que tú actuaste en tu odio contra ellos. Lo afirma el SEÑOR. Y cuando yo te castigue me haré conocer entre ellos. ¹²Entonces sabrás que yo, el SEÑOR, he oído todas las injurias que has proferido contra las montañas de Israel. Tú dijiste desafiante: ¡Están devastados! ¡Ahora sí me los puedo devorar!' ¹³Me has desafiado con arrogancia e insolencia, y te he escuchado.

¹⁴»"Así dice el SEÑOR omnipotente: Para alegría de toda la tierra, yo los voy a destruir. ¹⁵Así como se alegraron cuando quedó devastada la herencia del

pueblo de Israel, también yo me alegraré de ti. Tú, montaña de Seír, y todo el territorio de Edom, quedarán desolados. Así sabrán que yo soy el SEÑOR."

Profecía sobre las montañas de Israel

36 »Tú, hijo de hombre, profetiza contra los montes de Israel y diles: "Montes de Israel, escuchen la palabra del SEÑOR. 2Así dice el SEÑOR omnipotente: El enemigo se ha burlado de ustedes diciendo: 'Las antiguas colinas ya son nuestras.' 3Por eso, profetiza y adviérteles que así dice el SEÑOR omnipotente: "A ustedes los han asolado y arrasado por todas partes; se han convertido en posesión del resto de las naciones, y además han sido objeto de burla y de insultos por parte de la gente. 4Por eso, montes de Israel, escuchen la palabra del SEÑOR omnipotente. Así habla el SEÑOR omnipotente a los montes y a las colinas, a los torrentes y a los valles, a las ruinas desoladas y a los pueblos deshabitados, saqueados y escarnecidos por los pueblos vecinos. 5Esto dice el SEÑOR omnipotente: En el ardor de mi celo me he pronunciado contra el resto de las naciones y contra todo Edom, porque con mucha alegría y profundo desprecio se han apoderado de mi tierra para destruirla y saquearla."

6»Por eso, profetiza contra Israel, y adviérteles a los montes y a las colinas, a los torrentes y a los valles, que así dice el SEÑOR omnipotente: "En mi celo y en mi furor he hablado, porque ustedes han sufrido el oprobio de las naciones. 7Por eso, así dice el SEÑOR omnipotente: Juro con la mano en alto que las naciones vecinas también sufrirán su propia deshonra.

8» "Ustedes, en cambio, montes de Israel, echarán ramas y producirán frutos para mi pueblo Israel, porque ya está por regresar. 9Yo estoy preocupado por ustedes, y los voy a proteger. Ustedes, los montes, volverán a ser sembrados y cultivados, 10y multiplicaré a mi pueblo de Israel. Las ciudades serán repobladas, y reconstruidas las ruinas. 11Sobre ustedes multiplicaré a los *hombres y animales, y ellos serán fecundos y numerosos. Los poblaré como en tiempos pasados, y los haré prosperar más que antes. Entonces sabrán que yo soy el SEÑOR. 12Haré que mi pueblo Israel transite por el territorio de ustedes. Él te poseerá, y tú serás parte de su herencia, y ya nunca más los privarás de sus hijos.

13»"Así dice el SEÑOR omnipotente: Por cuanto te han dicho que tú devoras a los hombres y dejas sin hijos a tu propio pueblo, 14el SEÑOR omnipotente afirma: Ya no devorarás más hombres, ni dejarás sin hijos a tu pueblo. 15Nunca más te haré oír el ultraje de las naciones; no tendrás que volver a soportar los insultos de los pueblos, ni serás causa de tropiezo para tu nación. Lo afirma el SEÑOR omnipotente."»

16El SEÑOR me dirigió otra vez la palabra: 17«Hijo de hombre, cuando los israelitas habitaban en su propia tierra, ellos mismos la *contaminaron con su conducta y sus acciones. Su conducta ante mí era semejante a la *impureza de una mujer en sus días de menstruación. 18Por eso, por haber derramado tanta sangre sobre la tierra y por haberla contaminado con sus ídolos, desaté mi furor contra ellos. 19Los dispersé entre las naciones, y quedaron esparcidos entre diversos pueblos. Los juzgué según su conducta y sus acciones. 20Pero al llegar a las distintas naciones, ellos profanaban mi *santo *nombre, pues se decía de ellos: "Son el pueblo del SEÑOR, pero han tenido que abandonar su tierra." 21Así que tuve que defender mi santo nombre, el cual los israelitas profanaban entre las naciones por donde iban.

22»Por eso, adviértele al pueblo de Israel que así dice el SEÑOR omnipotente: "Voy a actuar, pero no por ustedes sino por causa de mi santo nombre, que ustedes han profanado entre las naciones por donde han ido. 23Daré a conocer la grandeza de mi santo nombre, el cual ha sido profanado entre las naciones, el mismo que ustedes han profanado entre ellas. Cuando dé a conocer mi santidad entre ustedes, las naciones sabrán que yo soy el SEÑOR. Lo afirma el SEÑOR omnipotente. 24Los sacaré de entre las naciones, los reuniré de entre todos los pueblos, y los haré regresar a su propia tierra. 25Los rociaré con agua pura, y quedarán purificados. Los *limpiaré de todas sus impurezas e idolatrías. 26Les daré un nuevo *corazón, y les infundiré un espíritu nuevo; les quitaré ese corazón de piedra que ahora tienen, y les pondré un corazón de carne. 27Infundiré mi Espíritu en ustedes, y haré que sigan mis preceptos y obedezcan mis *leyes. 28Vivirán en la tierra que les di a sus antepasados, y ustedes serán mi pueblo y yo seré su Dios. 29Los libraré de todas sus impurezas. Haré que tengan trigo en abundancia, y no permitiré que sufran hambre. 30Multiplicaré el fruto de los árboles y las cosechas del campo, para que no sufran más entre las naciones el oprobio de pasar hambre. 31Así se acordarán ustedes de su mala conducta y de sus acciones perversas, y sentirán vergüenza por sus propias iniquidades y prácticas detestables. 32Y quiero que sepan que esto no lo hago por consideración a ustedes. Lo afirma el SEÑOR omnipotente. iOh, pueblo de Israel, sientan vergüenza y confusión por su conducta!

33»"Así dice el SEÑOR omnipotente: El día que yo los purifique de todas sus iniquidades, poblaré las ciudades y reconstruiré las ruinas. 34Se cultivará la tierra desolada, y ya no estará desierta a la vista de cuantos pasan por ella. 35Entonces se dirá: 'Esta tierra, que antes yacía desolada, es ahora un jardín de Edén; las ciudades que antes estaban en ruinas, desoladas y destruidas, están ahora habitadas y fortalecidas.' 36Entonces las naciones que quedaron a su alrededor sabrán que yo, el SEÑOR, reconstruí lo que estaba derribado y replanté lo que había quedado como desierto. Yo, el SEÑOR, lo he dicho, y lo cumpliré."

37»Así dice el SEÑOR omnipotente: Todavía he de concederle al pueblo de Israel que me suplique aumentar el número de sus hombres, hasta que sean como un rebaño. 38Entonces las ciudades desoladas se llenarán de mucha gente. Serán como las ovejas que, durante las fiestas solemnes, se llevan a Jerusalén para los sacrificios. Entonces sabrán que yo soy el SEÑOR.»

El valle de los huesos secos

37 La mano del SEÑOR vino sobre mí, y su Espíritu me llevó y me colocó en medio de un valle que estaba lleno de huesos. 2Me hizo pasearme entre ellos, y pude observar que había muchísimos huesos en el valle, huesos que estaban completamente secos. 3Y me dijo: «Hijo de hombre, ¿podrán revivir estos huesos?» Y yo le contesté: «SEÑOR omnipotente, tú lo sabes.»

4Entonces me dijo: «Profetiza sobre estos huesos, y diles: "¡Huesos secos, escuchen la palabra del SEÑOR! 5Así dice el SEÑOR omnipotente a estos huesos: 'Yo les daré aliento de vida, y ustedes volverán a vivir. 6Les pondré tendones, haré que les salga carne, y los cubriré de piel; les daré aliento de vida, y así revivirán. Entonces sabrán que yo soy el SEÑOR.' "»

7Tal y como el SEÑOR me lo había mandado, profeticé. Y mientras profetizaba, se escuchó un ruido que sacudió la tierra, y los huesos comenzaron a unirse entre sí. 8Yo me fijé, y vi que en ellos aparecían tendones, y les salía carne y se recubrían de piel, ¡pero no tenían vida!

9Entonces el SEÑOR me dijo: «Profetiza, hijo de hombre; conjura al aliento de vida y dile: "Esto ordena el SEÑOR omnipotente: 'Ven de los cuatro vientos, y dales vida a estos huesos muertos para que revivan.'"» 10Yo profeticé, tal como el SEÑOR me lo había ordenado, y el aliento de vida entró en ellos; entonces los huesos revivieron y se pusieron de pie. ¡Era un ejército numeroso!

11Luego me dijo: «Hijo de hombre, estos huesos son el pueblo de Israel. Ellos andan diciendo: "Nuestros huesos se han secado. Ya no tenemos esperanza. ¡Estamos perdidos!" 12Por eso, profetiza y adviérteles que así dice el SEÑOR omnipotente: "Pueblo mío, abriré tus tumbas y te sacaré de ellas, y te haré regresar a la tierra de Israel. 13Y cuando haya abierto tus tumbas y te haya sacado de allí, entonces, pueblo mío, sabrás que yo soy el SEÑOR. 14Pondré en ti mi aliento de vida, y volverás a vivir. Y te estableceré en tu propia tierra. Entonces sabrás que yo, el SEÑOR, lo he dicho, y lo cumpliré. Lo afirma el SEÑOR."»

Unificación de Judá e Israel

15El SEÑOR me dirigió la palabra: 16«Hijo de hombre, toma una vara y escribe sobre ella: "Para Judá y sus aliados los israelitas." Luego toma otra vara y escribe: "Para José, vara de Efraín, y todos sus aliados los israelitas." 17Júntalas, la una con la otra, de modo que formen una sola vara en tu mano.

18»Cuando la gente de tu pueblo te pregunte: "¿Qué significa todo esto?", 19tú les responderás que así dice el SEÑOR omnipotente: "Voy a tomar la vara de José que está en la mano de Efraín, y a las tribus de Israel que están unidas a él, y la uniré a la vara de Judá. Así haré con ellos una sola vara, y en mi mano serán una sola." 20Sostén en tu mano las varas sobre las cuales has escrito, de modo que ellos las vean, 21y adviérteles que así dice el SEÑOR omnipotente: "Tomaré a los israelitas de entre las naciones por donde han andado, y de todas partes los reuniré y los haré regresar a su propia tierra. 22Y en esta tierra, en los montes de Israel, haré de ellos una sola nación. Todos estarán bajo un solo rey, y nunca más serán dos naciones ni estarán divididos en dos reinos. 23Ya no se *contaminarán más con sus ídolos, ni con sus iniquidades ni actos abominables. Yo los libraré de todas sus infidelidades.h Ellos serán mi pueblo y yo seré su Dios. 24Mi siervo David será su rey, y todos tendrán un solo *pastor. Caminarán según mis *leyes, y cumplirán mis preceptos y los pondrán en práctica. 25Habitarán en la tierra que le di a mi siervo Jacob, donde vivieron sus antepasados. Ellos, sus hijos y sus nietos vivirán allí para siempre, y mi siervo David será su príncipe eterno. 26Y haré con ellos un *pacto de *paz. Será un pacto eterno. Haré que se multipliquen, y para siempre colocaré mi santuario en medio de ellos. 27Habitaré entre ellos, y yo seré su Dios y ellos serán mi pueblo. 28Y cuando mi santuario esté para siempre en medio de ellos, las naciones sabrán que yo, el SEÑOR, he hecho de Israel un pueblo *santo."»

Profecía contra Gog

38 El SEÑOR me dirigió la palabra: 2«Hijo de hombre, encara a Gog, de la tierra de Magog, príncipe soberano de Mésec y Tubal. Profetiza contra él 3y adviértele que así dice el SEÑOR omnipotente: "Yo estoy contra ti, Gog, príncipe supremo de Mésec

y Tubal. 4Te haré volver, te pondré garfios en la boca y te sacaré con todo tu ejército, caballos y jinetes. Todos ellos están bien armados; son una multitud enorme, con escudos y broqueles; todos ellos empuñan la espada. 5Con ellos están Persia, Etiopía y Fut, todos ellos armados con escudos y yelmos. 6Gómer también está allí, con todas sus tropas, y también Bet Togarma, desde el lejano norte, con todas sus tropas y muchos ejércitos que son tus aliados.

7»"Prepárate, mantente alerta, tú y toda la multitud que está reunida a tu alrededor; ponlos bajo tu mando. 8Al cabo de muchos días se te encomendará una misión. Después de muchos años invadirás un país que se ha recuperado de la guerra, una nación que durante mucho tiempo estuvo en ruinas, pero que ha sido reunido de entre los muchos pueblos en los montes de Israel. Ha sido sacado de entre las naciones, y ahora vive confiado. 9Pero tú lo invadirás como un huracán. Tú, con todas tus tropas y todos tus aliados, serás como un nubarrón que cubrirá la tierra.

10»"Así dice el SEÑOR omnipotente: En aquel día harás proyectos, y maquinarás un plan perverso. 11Y dirás: 'Invadiré a un país indefenso; atacaré a un pueblo pacífico que habita confiado en ciudades sin muros, *puertas y cerrojos. 12Lo saquearé y me llevaré el botín; atacaré las ciudades reconstruidas de entre las ruinas, al pueblo reunido allí de entre las naciones; es un pueblo rico en ganado y posesiones, que se cree el centro del mundo.' 13La gente de Sabá y Dedán, y los comerciantes de Tarsis y todos sus potentados, te preguntarán: '¿A qué vienes? ¿A despojarnos de todo lo nuestro? ¿Para eso reúnes a tus tropas? ¿Para quitarnos la plata y el oro, y llevarte nuestros ganados y posesiones? ¿Para alzarte con un enorme botín?'"

14»Por eso, hijo de hombre, profetiza contra Gog y adviértele que así dice el SEÑOR omnipotente: "En aquel día, ¿acaso no te enterarás de que mi pueblo Israel vive confiado? 15Vendrás desde el lejano norte, desde el lugar donde habitas, junto con otros pueblos numerosos. Todos ellos vendrán montados a caballo, y serán una gran multitud, un ejército poderoso. 16En los últimos días atacarás a mi pueblo Israel, y como un nubarrón cubrirás el país. Yo haré que tú, Gog, vengas contra mi tierra, para que las naciones me conozcan y para que, por medio de ti, mi *santidad se manifieste ante todos ellos.

17»Así dice el SEÑOR omnipotente: A ti me refería yo cuando en tiempos pasados hablé por medio de mis siervos, los profetas de Israel. En aquel tiempo, y durante años, ellos profetizaron que yo te haría venir contra los israelitas. 18Pero el día en que Gog invada a Israel, mi ira se encenderá con furor. Lo afirma el SEÑOR omnipotente. 19En el ardor de mi ira, declaro que en aquel momento habrá un gran terremoto en la tierra de Israel. 20Ante mí temblarán los peces del mar, las aves del cielo, las bestias del campo, los reptiles que se arrastran, y toda la gente que hay sobre la faz de la tierra. Se derrumbarán los montes, se desplomarán las pendientes escarpadas, y todos los muros se vendrán abajo. 21En todos los montes convocaré a la guerra contra Gog, y la espada de cada cual se volverá contra su prójimo —afirma el SEÑOR—. 22Yo juzgaré a Gog con peste y con sangre; sobre él y sobre sus tropas, lo mismo que sobre todas sus naciones aliadas, haré caer lluvias torrenciales, granizo, fuego y azufre. 23De esta manera mostraré mi grandeza y mi santidad, y me daré a co-

---

h 37:23 infidelidades (mss. hebreos y LXX); moradas (TM).

nocer ante muchas naciones. Entonces sabrán que yo soy el SEÑOR."

Derrota de Gog

39 »Hijo de hombre, profetiza contra Gog y adviértele que así dice el SEÑOR omnipotente: "Yo estoy contra ti, Gog, príncipe soberano de Mésec y Tubal. 2Te haré volver y te arrastraré; te haré salir del lejano norte, y te haré venir contra los montes de Israel. 3Quebraré el arco que llevas en la mano izquierda, y arrojaré a la basura las flechas que llevas en la mano derecha. 4Caerás sobre los montes de Israel, junto con tus tropas y las naciones que te acompañan. Te arrojaré a las aves de rapiña y a las fieras salvajes para que te devoren. 5-6Y caerás en campo abierto, porque yo lo he dicho. Y enviaré fuego sobre Magog y sobre los que confiados habitan en las costas. Entonces sabrán que yo soy el SEÑOR. Yo, el SEÑOR omnipotente, lo afirmo.

7»"Y me daré a conocer en medio de mi pueblo Israel. Ya no permitiré que mi *santo *nombre sea profanado; las naciones sabrán que yo soy el SEÑOR, el santo de Israel. 8Todo esto se acerca, y está a punto de suceder. Éste es el día del que he hablado. Yo, el SEÑOR, lo afirmo.

9»"Entonces los habitantes de las ciudades de Israel saldrán y prenderán una hoguera, y allí quemarán sus armas: escudos y broqueles, arcos y flechas, mazas y lanzas. ¡Tendrán suficiente leña para hacer fuego durante siete años! 10No tendrán que ir a buscar leña al monte, ni tendrán que cortarla de los bosques, porque la leña que usarán serán sus propias armas. Además, saquearán a sus saqueadores y despojarán a sus despojadores. Lo afirma el SEÑOR.

11»"En aquel día abriré en Israel, en el valle de los Viajeros, frente al mar, una tumba para Gog. Ese lugar le cortará el paso a los viajeros. Allí enterrarán a Gog y a todo su ejército, y lo llamarán Valle del ejército de Gog. 12Para enterrarlos, y *purificar así el país, los israelitas necesitarán siete meses. 13Toda la gente del país los enterrará. Y el día en que yo me glorifique será para ellos un día memorable. Yo, el SEÑOR omnipotente, lo afirmo.

14»"Al cabo de esos siete meses, elegirán hombres que se encarguen de recorrer el país, y junto con otros enterrarán a los que aún queden sobre la tierra, y así purificarán al país. 15Cuando al recorrer el país uno de estos hombres encuentre algún hueso humano, colocará a su lado una señal, hasta que los enterradores lo sepulten en el Valle del ejército de Gog. 16De esa manera purificarán al país. También allí habrá una ciudad llamada 'El ejército'."

17»Hijo de hombre, así dice el SEÑOR omnipotente: Diles a todas las aves del cielo, y a todas las fieras, que se reúnan de todos los alrededores y vengan al sacrificio que les ofrezco, un gran sacrificio sobre los montes de Israel. Allí comerán carne y beberán sangre: 18carne de poderosos guerreros, sangre de los príncipes de la tierra, como si fuera de carneros o corderos, de chivos o becerros, todos ellos engordados en Basán. 19Del sacrificio que voy a preparar, comerán grasa hasta hastiarse y beberán sangre hasta emborracharse. 20En mi mesa se hartarán de caballos y de jinetes, de guerreros valientes y de toda clase de soldados. Yo, el SEÑOR, lo afirmo.

21»Yo manifestaré mi gloria entre las naciones. Todas ellas verán cómo los he juzgado y castigado. 22Y a partir de ese día, los israelitas sabrán que yo soy

el SEÑOR su Dios. 23Y sabrán las naciones que el pueblo de Israel fue al exilio por causa de sus iniquidades, y porque me fueron infieles. Por eso les di la espalda y los entregué en manos de sus enemigos, y todos ellos cayeron a filo de espada. 24Los traté conforme a sus impurezas y rebeliones, y les volví la espalda.

25»Por eso, así dice el SEÑOR omnipotente: Ahora voy a cambiar la suerte de Jacob. Tendré compasión de todo el pueblo de Israel, y celaré el prestigio de mi santo nombre. 26Cuando habiten tranquilos en su tierra, sin que nadie los perturbe, olvidarán su vergüenza y todas las infidelidades que cometieron contra mí. 27Cuando yo los haga volver de entre las naciones, y los reúna de entre los pueblos enemigos, en presencia de muchas naciones y por medio de ellos manifestaré mi *santidad. 28Entonces sabrán que yo soy el SEÑOR su Dios, quien los envió al exilio entre las naciones, pero que después volví a reunirlos en su propia tierra, sin dejar a nadie atrás. 29Ya no volveré a darles la espalda, pues derramaré mi Espíritu sobre Israel. Yo, el SEÑOR, lo afirmo.»

Visión del templo futuro

40 Transcurría el año veinticinco del exilio cuando el SEÑOR puso su mano sobre mí, y me llevó a Jerusalén. Esto sucedió al comenzar el año, el día diez del mes primero, es decir, catorce años después de la toma de Jerusalén. 2En una visión divina, Dios me trasladó a la tierra de Israel y me colocó sobre un monte muy alto. Desde allí, mirando al sur, había unos edificios que parecían una ciudad. 3Dios me llevó allí, y vi un hombre que parecía hecho de bronce. Estaba de pie junto a la puerta, y en su mano tenía una cuerda de lino y una vara de medir. 4Aquel hombre me dijo: «Hijo de hombre, abre los ojos y presta atención a todo lo que estoy por mostrarte, pues para eso se te ha traído aquí. Anda luego y comunícale a Israel todo lo que veas.»

La puerta oriental

5Entonces vi un muro que rodeaba el templo por fuera. El hombre tenía en la mano una vara de tres metros,ⁱ que le servía para medir, y midió el muro, el cual tenía tres metros de ancho por tres metros de alto.

6Luego se dirigió a la puerta que mira hacia el oriente. Subió sus gradas y midió el umbral de la puerta, el cual medía tres metros de ancho.^j 7Cada celda lateral medía tres metros de largo por tres metros de ancho. Entre las celdas había un espacio de dos metros y medio. El umbral junto al vestíbulo de la puerta que daba al templo medía tres metros. 8Luego midió el vestíbulo de la puerta, hacia el interior, y medía tres metros. 9Midió el vestíbulo de la puerta que daba al templo, y éste medía cuatro metros; sus pilares eran de un metro de ancho. 10A cada lado de la puerta que daba al oriente había tres celdas del mismo tamaño. A su vez, los pilares que estaban a los lados tenían la misma medida.

11Aquel hombre midió también la entrada de la puerta, y tenía cinco metros de ancho por seis metros y medio de largo. 12Delante de cada celda había un pequeño muro que medía medio metro de ancho por lado. Cada celda medía tres metros de ancho por tres metros de largo. 13Luego midió la puerta, desde el techo de una celda hasta el techo de la celda de enfrente, y entre una y otra abertura había una distancia de doce metros y medio. 14Luego midió el vestíbulo, que

i **40:5** *tres metros.* Lit. *seis *codos, a razón de codo y *palmo*. En el resto de este libro, las medidas se han convertido al sistema métrico, sin explicación en las notas.   j **40:6** *ancho* (LXX); *ancho, y un umbral, una vara de ancho* (TM).

era de diez metros. El vestíbulo daba al atrio, que lo rodeaba por completo. 15Desde el frente de la puerta de entrada hasta la parte interior del vestíbulo, el corredor tenía una extensión de veinticinco metros. 16En torno de las celdas y de los pilares había ventanas con rejas que daban al interior. También en torno al vestíbulo había ventanas que daban a su interior. Sobre los pilares había grabados de palmeras.

El atrio exterior

17Luego el hombre me llevó al atrio exterior. Allí vi unas habitaciones y un enlosado construido alrededor del atrio; las habitaciones que daban al enlosado eran treinta. 18Este enlosado, que estaba en el piso inferior, bordeaba las puertas y correspondía a la longitud de las mismas. 19Luego midió la distancia desde el frente de la puerta de abajo hasta el frente del atrio interior, y al este y al norte la distancia era de cincuenta metros.

La puerta norte

20El hombre midió el largo y el ancho de la puerta que daba hacia el norte, es decir, hacia el atrio exterior. 21Sus celdas, que también eran tres de cada lado, más sus pilares y su vestíbulo, tenían las mismas medidas que la primera puerta: veinticinco metros de largo por doce metros y medio de ancho. 22Sus ventanas, su vestíbulo y sus palmeras tenían las mismas medidas que las de la puerta oriental. A esta puerta se subía por medio de siete gradas, y su vestíbulo estaba frente a ellas. 23En el atrio interior había una puerta que daba a la puerta del norte, igual que en la puerta del este. El hombre midió la distancia entre las dos puertas, y era de cincuenta metros.

La puerta sur

24Luego me condujo hacia el sur, y allí había una puerta que daba al sur. Midió las celdas, los pilares y el vestíbulo, y todos éstos tenían las mismas medidas que las anteriores. 25La puerta y el vestíbulo también tenían ventanas a su alrededor, al igual que los otros, y medían veinticinco metros de largo por doce metros y medio de ancho. 26También se subía a la puerta por medio de siete gradas, y frente a ella estaba su vestíbulo. Los pilares a ambos lados tenían grabados de palmeras. 27El atrio interior tenía una puerta que daba al sur. El hombre midió la distancia entre una puerta y otra en dirección sur, y era de cincuenta metros.

Las puertas del atrio interior: la puerta sur

28Luego me llevó por la puerta del sur hacia el atrio interior. Midió la puerta del sur, la cual tenía las mismas medidas que las anteriores. 29Sus celdas, sus pilares y su vestíbulo también tenían las mismas medidas que los anteriores. La puerta y el vestíbulo tenían ventanas a su alrededor, y medían veinticinco metros de largo por doce metros y medio de ancho. 30En su derredor había unos vestíbulos de doce metros y medio de largo por dos metros y medio de ancho. 31Su vestíbulo daba hacia el atrio exterior; sus pilares también tenían grabados de palmeras. A esta puerta se llegaba subiendo ocho gradas.

El atrio interior: la puerta oriental

32También me llevó al atrio interior que daba al oriente, y midió la entrada, y medía igual que las anteriores. 33Sus celdas, sus pilares y su vestíbulo también tenían las mismas medidas que los anteriores. La puerta y el vestíbulo tenían ventanas a su alrede-

dor, y medían veinticinco metros de largo por doce metros y medio de ancho. 34Su vestíbulo daba al atrio exterior. Los pilares tenían a cada lado grabados de palmeras, y a esta puerta se llegaba subiendo ocho gradas.

El atrio interior: la puerta norte

35Luego el mismo hombre me llevó a la puerta del norte y la midió: ésta tenía las mismas medidas que las otras. 36También tenía celdas, pilares, vestíbulo y ventanas a su alrededor, y medían veinticinco metros de largo por doce metros y medio de ancho. 37Su vestíbulo miraba hacia el atrio exterior. Los pilares tenían grabados de palmera a cada lado. A esta puerta se llegaba subiendo ocho gradas.

Los anexos de las puertas

38Había una sala que se comunicaba con el vestíbulo de cada puerta. Allí se lavaba el *holocausto. 39En el vestíbulo de la puerta había cuatro mesas, dos de cada lado, donde se mataba a los animales para el holocausto, para la ofrenda por el pecado y para la ofrenda por la culpa. 40Fuera del vestíbulo, por donde se subía hacia la entrada de la puerta norte, había otras dos mesas; y al otro lado del vestíbulo de la puerta había otras dos mesas. 41De manera que había cuatro mesas de un lado de la puerta y cuatro del otro, es decir, ocho mesas en total, donde se mataba a los animales. 42Para el holocausto había cuatro mesas talladas en piedra, que medían setenta y cinco centímetros de largo por setenta y cinco centímetros de ancho, y cincuenta centímetros de alto. Sobre ellas se colocaban los instrumentos con que se mataba a los animales para el holocausto y otros sacrificios. 43Colocados en el interior, sobre las paredes en derredor, estaban los ganchos dobles, que medían unos veinticinco centímetros de largo. Sobre las mesas se ponía la carne de las ofrendas.

Las habitaciones para los sacerdotes

44En el atrio interior, fuera de las puertas interiores, había dos salas.k Una de ellas estaba junto a la puerta del norte que daba al sur, y la otra estaba junto a la puerta del surl que daba al norte. 45Aquel hombre me dijo: «La sala que da al sur es para los sacerdotes que están encargados del servicio en el templo, 46mientras que la sala que da al norte es para los sacerdotes encargados del servicio en el altar. Éstos son los hijos de Sadoc, y son los únicos levitas que pueden acercarse al SEÑOR para servirle.»

El atrio interior y el templo

47El hombre midió el atrio, que era un cuadrado de cincuenta metros de largo por cincuenta metros de ancho. El altar estaba frente al templo. 48Entonces me llevó al vestíbulo del templo y midió sus pilares, y cada uno medía dos metros y medio de grueso. El ancho de la puerta era de siete metros, mientras que las paredes laterales de la puerta medían un metro y medio de ancho. 49El vestíbulo medía seis metros de largo por diez metros de ancho, y se llegaba a él por una escalera de diez gradas.m Junto a cada pilar había una columna.

41 Luego el hombre me llevó al templo y midió los pilares, los cuales tenían tres metros de un lado y tres metros del otro. 2El ancho de la entrada era de cinco metros, y cada una de las paredes laterales medía dos metros y medio de ancho. También midió

---

k **40:44** dos salas (LXX); salas para cantores (TM). l **40:44** sur (LXX); este (TM). m **40:49** diez gradas (LXX); gradas (TM)

la nave central, la cual medía veinte metros de largo por diez de ancho.

[3]Después entró en el recinto interior y midió los pilares de la entrada, los cuales eran de un metro cada uno. La entrada medía tres metros de ancho, y las paredes laterales de la entrada medían tres metros y medio. [4]Después midió la longitud del recinto interior, que era de diez metros de largo; su anchura era de la misma medida. Entonces me dijo: «Éste es el Lugar Santísimo.»

[5]Luego midió el muro del templo, que era de tres metros de espesor. Las salas alrededor del templo medían dos metros de fondo. [6]Estas salas laterales estaban puestas una sobre otra, formando tres pisos. En cada piso había treinta salas. Alrededor de todo el muro del templo había soportes que sobresalían para sostener a las salas laterales, de modo que no estuvieran empotradas en el muro del templo. [7]Las salas laterales alrededor del templo se ensanchaban en cada piso sucesivo. La estructura alrededor del templo estaba construida en niveles ascendentes, de modo que, a medida que se subía, las salas de arriba adquirían mayor amplitud. Una rampa subía desde el piso inferior hasta el superior, pasando por el piso intermedio.

[8]También vi que alrededor de todo el templo había una plataforma elevada que servía de base para las salas laterales. Esta base medía tres metros de altura. [9]La pared exterior de las salas tenía un espesor de dos metros y medio, y entre las salas laterales del templo [10]y las habitaciones de los sacerdotes que rodeaban el templo quedaba un espacio libre de diez metros de ancho. [11]Las salas laterales se comunicaban con el espacio libre por medio de dos entradas, una al norte y otra al sur. El ancho del espacio libre alrededor de las salas laterales era de dos metros y medio.

[12]El edificio que por el lado oeste quedaba frente al patio medía treinta y cinco metros de ancho, con un muro de dos metros y medio de ancho por cuarenta y cinco metros de largo.

[13]El hombre midió el templo, el cual tenía un total de cincuenta metros de largo. También el patio con el edificio adyacente y el muro medían cincuenta metros de largo. [14]El ancho de la fachada del templo, más la parte del patio que da hacia el este, medía cincuenta metros. [15]Luego midió la longitud del edificio posterior del templo que daba al patio, junto con las galerías de ambos lados, y medía cincuenta metros.

La nave interior del templo, los vestíbulos del atrio, [16]los umbrales, las ventanas con rejas y las galerías alrededor de los tres pisos, comenzando desde la entrada, estaban recubiertos de madera por todas partes. De arriba a abajo, todo estaba recubierto, incluso las ventanas. [17]Desde la entrada hasta el recinto interior, y alrededor de todo el muro, por dentro y por fuera, en el interior y el exterior, [18]se alternaban los grabados de *querubines y palmeras. Cada querubín tenía dos rostros, [19]uno de hombre y otro de león. Cada rostro miraba hacia la palmera que tenía a su costado. Alrededor de todo el templo podían verse los grabados de estos querubines. [20]Desde el suelo hasta la parte superior de las puertas había grabados de querubines y palmeras sobre todas las paredes del templo.

[21]Los postes de la entrada al templo eran cuadrados, y frente al Lugar Santísimo había algo que parecía [22]un altar de madera, el cual medía un metro

y medio de alto por uno de largo y uno de ancho. Sus esquinas, la base[n] y sus costados eran de madera. El hombre me dijo: «Ésta es la mesa que está delante del SEÑOR.» [23]Tanto el templo como el Lugar Santísimo tenían puertas dobles. [24]Cada puerta tenía dos hojas; dos hojas giratorias para cada puerta. [25]Sobre la puerta del templo había grabados de querubines y palmeras, como los que había en las paredes. En la fachada del vestíbulo, por la parte exterior, había un alero de madera. [26]Sobre ambos lados del vestíbulo había ventanas con rejas y con grabados de palmeras. Las salas laterales también tenían aleros.

Las habitaciones para los sacerdotes

42 El hombre me sacó al atrio exterior, en dirección al norte, y me hizo entrar a las habitaciones que estaban hacia el norte, frente al patio cerrado y frente al edificio detrás del templo. [2]Todo esto medía cincuenta metros de largo por el lado norte, y veinticinco metros de ancho. [3]Frente a los diez metros del atrio interior, y frente al enlosado del atrio exterior, había en los tres pisos unas galerías, las cuales quedaban unas frente a las otras. [4]Frente a las habitaciones había un pasillo interior de cinco metros de ancho y cincuenta[ñ] de largo. Las puertas de las habitaciones daban al norte. [5]Las habitaciones del piso superior eran más estrechas que las del piso inferior y las del piso intermedio, porque las galerías les quitaban más espacio a las de arriba. [6]Las habitaciones en el tercer piso no tenían columnas como las habitaciones del atrio, y por eso eran más estrechas que las del piso intermedio y las del piso inferior. [7]Había un muro exterior que corría paralelo y de frente a las habitaciones del atrio exterior, el cual medía veinticinco metros de largo. [8]Las habitaciones que daban al atrio exterior medían veinticinco metros, mientras que las que daban al frente del templo medían cincuenta metros. [9]A las habitaciones del piso inferior se entraba por el atrio exterior, es decir, por el este.

[10]Por el lado sur,[o] a lo largo del muro del atrio, frente al patio y frente al edificio detrás del templo, había unas habitaciones. [11]Tenían un pasillo frente a ellas, como el de las habitaciones de la parte norte. A su vez, tenían la misma longitud, el mismo ancho, las mismas salidas, las mismas disposiciones y las mismas entradas. [12]Bajo las habitaciones que daban al sur, frente al muro que daba al este, que era por donde se podía entrar a ellas, había una entrada al comienzo de cada pasillo.

[13]El hombre me dijo: «Las habitaciones del norte y del sur, que están frente al patio, son las habitaciones sagradas. Allí es donde los sacerdotes que se acercan al SEÑOR comerán las ofrendas más sagradas. Allí colocarán la ofrenda de cereal, la ofrenda por el pecado y la ofrenda por la culpa, porque el lugar es *santo. [14]Cuando los sacerdotes entren allí, no saldrán al atrio exterior sin dejar antes las vestiduras con que ministran, porque esas vestiduras son santas. Antes de acercarse a los lugares destinados para el pueblo deberán vestirse con otra ropa.»

[15]Cuando el hombre terminó de medir el interior del templo, me hizo salir por la puerta que da al oriente, y midió todo el contorno. [16]Tomó la vara para medir el lado oriental, y éste midió doscientos cincuenta metros.[p] [17]Después midió el lado norte, y también medía doscientos cincuenta metros; [18]luego el lado sur: doscientos cincuenta metros; [19]luego se volvió hacia el lado oeste y lo midió: doscientos cincuenta metros. [20]El

---

[n] **41:22** *la base* (LXX); *la longitud* (TM). [ñ] **42:4** *cincuenta* (LXX; lit. *cien* *codos*); *medio metro* (TM; lit. *un codo*). [o] **42:10** *sur* (LXX); *este* (TM). [p] **42:16** *doscientos cincuenta metros.* Texto de difícil traducción.

hombre tomó las medidas de los cuatro lados. La zona estaba rodeada por un muro que medía doscientos cincuenta metros de largo por doscientos cincuenta metros de ancho. Este muro separaba lo sagrado de lo profano.

La gloria del SEÑOR vuelve al templo

43 Entonces el hombre me llevó a la puerta que da al oriente, ²y vi que la gloria del Dios de Israel venía del oriente, en medio de un ruido ensordecedor, semejante al de un río caudaloso; y la tierra se llenó de su gloria. ³Esta visión era semejante a la que tuve cuando el SEÑOR vino a destruir la ciudad de Jerusalén, y a la que tuve junto al río Quebar. Me incliné rostro en tierra, ⁴y la gloria del SEÑOR entró al templo por la puerta que daba al oriente. ⁵Entonces el Espíritu me levantó y me introdujo en el atrio interior, y vi que la gloria del SEÑOR había llenado el templo.

⁶Mientras el hombre estaba de pie a mi lado, oí que alguien me hablaba desde el templo. ⁷Me decía: «Hijo de hombre, éste es el lugar de mi trono, el lugar donde pongo la planta de mis pies; aquí habitaré entre los israelitas para siempre. El pueblo de Israel y sus reyes no volverán a profanar mi *santo *nombre con sus infidelidades, ni con sus tumbas reales y sus cultos idolátricos. ⁸Los israelitas profanaron mi santo nombre con sus acciones detestables, pues colocaron su umbral y sus postes junto a los míos, con tan sólo un muro de por medio. Por eso, en mi ira los exterminé. ⁹Que alejen ahora de mí sus infidelidades y sus tumbas reales, y yo habitaré en medio de ellos para siempre.

¹⁰»Hijo de hombre, cuéntale al pueblo de Israel acerca del templo, con sus planos y medidas, para que se avergüencen de sus iniquidades. ¹¹Y si se avergüenzan de todo lo que han hecho, hazles conocer el diseño del templo y su estructura, con sus salidas y entradas, es decir, todo su diseño, al igual que sus preceptos y sus *leyes. Pon todo esto por escrito ante sus ojos, para que sean fieles a todo su diseño y cumplan todos sus preceptos.

¹²»Ésta es la ley del templo: todo el terreno que lo rodea sobre la cumbre del monte será un Lugar Santísimo. Tal es la ley del templo.»

El altar

¹³Éstas son las medidas del altar:q Alrededor del altar había una fosa de medio metro de hondo por medio metro de ancho, con un reborde de veinticinco centímetros alrededor de toda la orilla. La altura del altar era la siguiente: ¹⁴Desde la fosa en el suelo hasta el zócalo inferior tenía un metro de alto y medio metro de ancho; y desde el zócalo inferior hasta el zócalo superior, dos metros de alto y medio metro de ancho. ¹⁵El fogón del altar medía dos metros, y desde allí se erguían cuatro cuernos. ¹⁶El fogón del altar era un cuadrado perfecto de seis metros de largo por seis de ancho. ¹⁷El zócalo superior también era un cuadrado de siete metros de largo por siete de ancho, con un reborde de veinticinco centímetros. La fosa alrededor del altar tenía medio metro de ancho. Las gradas del altar daban al oriente.

¹⁸Luego el hombre me dijo: «Hijo de hombre, así dice el SEÑOR omnipotente: El día que se construya el altar para ofrecer un *holocausto y para derramar la sangre, se deberán seguir estas normas: ¹⁹A los sacerdotes levitas descendientes de Sadoc que se acercan

para servirme les darás un ternero para que lo ofrezcan como sacrificio por el pecado. Lo afirma el SEÑOR omnipotente. ²⁰Luego tomarás un poco de la sangre, y con ella rociarás los cuatro cuernos, las cuatro esquinas del zócalo superior y todo el reborde que lo rodea. Así lo *purificarás y harás *expiación por él. ²¹Después tomarás el ternero del sacrificio por el pecado, y éste será quemado en el lugar señalado en el templo, fuera del santuario.

²²»Al segundo día, ofrecerás como sacrificio por el pecado un macho cabrío sin defecto, y el altar quedará purificado de la misma manera que se purificó con el ternero. ²³Cuando hayas terminado de purificarlo, ofrecerás un ternero y un carnero sin defecto ²⁴en presencia del SEÑOR, y los sacerdotes los rociarán con sal y los ofrecerán como holocausto al SEÑOR. ²⁵Durante siete días ofrecerás diariamente un macho cabrío para el sacrificio por el pecado, y también un ternero y un carnero del rebaño, ambos sin defecto. ²⁶Durante siete días los sacerdotes harán la expiación por el altar y lo purificarán; de este modo quedará consagrado. ²⁷Al cabo de estos siete días, y a partir del día octavo, comenzarán a ofrecer sobre el altar los holocaustos y sacrificios de *comunión que ustedes ofrezcan. Entonces yo los aceptaré. Lo afirma el SEÑOR.»

Deberes de levitas y sacerdotes

44 El hombre me hizo regresar por la puerta exterior del templo, la que daba al oriente, pero estaba cerrada. ²Allí el SEÑOR me dijo: «Esta puerta quedará cerrada. No se abrirá, y nadie deberá entrar por ella. Deberá quedar cerrada porque por ella ha entrado el SEÑOR, Dios de Israel. ³Tan sólo el príncipe podrá sentarse junto a la puerta para comer en presencia del SEÑOR. Deberá entrar por el vestíbulo de la puerta, y salir por el mismo lugar.»

Los levitas

⁴Después el hombre me llevó por el camino de la puerta del norte, que está frente al templo. Al ver que la gloria del SEÑOR llenaba el templo, me postré rostro en tierra. ⁵Entonces el SEÑOR me dijo: «Hijo de hombre, presta mucha atención. Abre bien los ojos y escucha atentamente todo lo que voy a decirte sobre las normas y las leyes concernientes al templo. Fíjate bien en quiénes pueden entrar al santuario, y quiénes no.

⁶»Adviértele a este pueblo rebelde de Israel que así dice el SEÑOR omnipotente: "Pueblo de Israel, ¡basta ya de tus prácticas detestables! ⁷Ustedes dejaron entrar en mi santuario a extranjeros, incircuncisos de *corazón y de cuerpo, para que profanaran mi templo. Mientras tanto, ustedes me ofrecían alimentos, grasa y sangre, violando así mi *pacto con sus acciones detestables. ⁸No se ocuparon de cumplir con mi culto sagrado, sino que pusieron a extranjeros a cargo de mi santuario. ⁹Así dice el SEÑOR omnipotente: ¡No entrará en mi templo ningún extranjero incircunciso de corazón y de cuerpo; ni siquiera los extranjeros que habitan entre los israelitas!

¹⁰»"Tendrán que pagar por su iniquidad los levitas que se alejaron de mí cuando Israel se descarriaba para ir tras sus ídolos malolientes. ¹¹Podrán servir en mi santuario como custodios de las puertas, y en algunos otros menesteres del templo. Ellos serán los que maten los animales para el *holocausto y para el sacrificio que presenta el pueblo, y deberán estar dispuestos a servir al pueblo. ¹²Pero yo he levantado mi mano

q 43:13 del altar. Lit. del altar en codos, a razón de *codo y *palmo.

contra ellos, y por haber servido al pueblo de Israel delante de sus ídolos malolientes, y por hacerlo caer, tendrán que pagar por su iniquidad. Yo, el SEÑOR, lo afirmo. 13No podrán acercarse a mí para servir como sacerdotes, ni se acercarán a mis objetos sagrados, y menos aún a los objetos santísimos. Tendrán que cargar con la vergüenza de las acciones detestables que han cometido. 14Sin embargo, los pondré a cargo de la custodia del templo, y de todo el servicio que se deba cumplir en él.

15»"En cambio, se acercarán para servirme los sacerdotes levitas descendientes de Sadoc, que estuvieron al servicio de mi santuario cuando los israelitas se descarriaban de mí; y se presentarán ante mí para ofrecerme la grasa y la sangre. Yo, el SEÑOR omnipotente, lo afirmo. 16Sólo ellos entrarán en mi santuario y podrán acercarse a mi mesa para servirme y encargarse de mi servicio. 17Y cuando entren por la puerta del atrio interior, se pondrán vestiduras de lino. Cuando estén sirviendo a las puertas del atrio interior, o en el templo, no llevarán ropa de lana. 18Llevarán turbantes de lino sobre la cabeza, y alrededor de la cintura usarán ropa interior de lino. No se pondrán nada en la cintura que los haga transpirar. 19Y cuando salgan al atrio exterior, donde está el pueblo, deberán quitarse la ropa con que hayan servido y dejarla en las salas sagradas. Luego se cambiarán de ropa, a fin de no *santificar al pueblo por medio de sus vestiduras.

20»"No se raparán la cabeza, pero tampoco se dejarán largo el cabello, sino que se lo recortarán prolijamente.

21»"Ningún sacerdote deberá beber vino cuando entre en el atrio interior.

22»"No deberá casarse con una viuda o una divorciada, sino sólo con una israelita que aún sea virgen o con la viuda de un sacerdote.

·23»"Deberán enseñarle a mi pueblo a distinguir entre lo sagrado y lo profano, y mostrarle cómo diferenciar entre lo *puro y lo impuro.

24»"En cualquier pleito, los sacerdotes fungirán como jueces y juzgarán según mis ordenanzas. En todas mis fiestas observarán mis *leyes y mis preceptos, y observarán mis *sábados, pues son días *santos.

25»"El sacerdote no deberá acercarse a un cadáver, para no *contaminarse. Sólo podrá contaminarse si el cadáver es de su propio padre, o de su madre, hijo, hija, hermano, o hermana soltera. 26Si queda contaminado, deberá purificarse, y luego esperar siete días. 27El día que vuelva a entrar en el atrio interior del santuario para cumplir su servicio, deberá ofrecer su sacrificio por el pecado. Lo afirma el SEÑOR omnipotente.

28»"Los sacerdotes no tendrán ninguna heredad, porque su heredad soy yo. Ustedes no les darán ninguna propiedad en Israel. Su propiedad soy yo. 29Ellos se alimentarán de la ofrenda de cereal y de las víctimas ofrecidas por el pecado y por la culpa. Además, todo lo que los israelitas consagren al SEÑOR será para ellos. 30También recibirán lo mejor de todas las *primicias y de todas las ofrendas que ustedes presenten. Les darán a los sacerdotes, para su pan, lo mejor de sus masas. Así mi bendición reposará sobre los hogares de ustedes. 31Los sacerdotes no comerán ningún animal, sea ave o bestia, que sea encontrado muerto o despedazado por una fiera.

División de la tierra

45 »"Cuando por sorteo se repartan la tierra como herencia, deberán reservar una porción de terreno, la cual será consagrada al SEÑOR. Esta porción santa será de doce mil quinientos metros de largo por diez milʳ de ancho. Todo este territorio será *santo. 2De allí se adjudicará para el santuario un terreno cuadrado de doscientos cincuenta metros por lado. Además, alrededor de ese terreno se reservará un espacio libre de veinticinco metros de ancho. 3En esa sección reservada apartarás una parcela de doce mil quinientos metros de largo por cinco mil de ancho, donde estará el santuario, el Lugar Santísimo. 4Ésta será la porción santa de tierra para los sacerdotes que sirven en el santuario y que se acercan para servir al SEÑOR. Allí construirán sus casas, y también el santuario del SEÑOR. 5Además, a los levitas que sirven en el templo se les adjudicará un espacio de doce mil quinientos metros de largo por cinco mil de ancho, para que tengan ciudades donde vivir.ˢ 6Y como territorio para la ciudad se asignará, junto a la sección reservada para el santuario, un espacio de dos mil quinientos metros de ancho por doce mil quinientos de largo. Este terreno pertenecerá a todo el pueblo de Israel.

7»"Al príncipe se le asignará una porción de tierra a ambos lados de la sección reservada para el santuario y de la sección reservada para la ciudad. Por el lado oeste se extenderá hacia el oeste, y hacia el este por el lado oriental. Su longitud de este a oeste será igual a la de los terrenos asignados a una de las tribus. 8Esta tierra será su posesión en Israel; así mis príncipes no volverán a oprimir a mi pueblo, sino que dejarán que las tribus de Israel ocupen la tierra.

9»"Así dice el SEÑOR omnipotente: ¡Basta ya, príncipes de Israel! ¡Abandonen la violencia y la explotación! ¡Practiquen el derecho y la justicia! ¡Dejen de extorsionar a mi pueblo! Lo afirma el SEÑOR. 10¡Usen balanzas justas, y pesas y medidas exactas! 11Para sólidos y líquidos usarán la misma unidad de medida. El *jómer de doscientos veinte litros servirá de patrón. Un *bato de líquido será igual a una décima de jómer, y un *efa de granos será igual a una décima de jómer. 12En cuanto a las medidas de peso: una mina será igual a veinte siclos, y un siclo será igual a veinte guerás.

13»""Ésta es la ofrenda especial que presentarán: por cada jómer de trigo, la sexta parte de un efa; por cada jómer de cebada, la sexta parte de un efa. 14La medida para el aceite es la siguiente: por cada coro, la décima parte de un bato; esto equivale a diez batos, y también a un jómer, ya que diez batos equivalen a un jómer.

15»"En cuanto a las ovejas, se tomará una de cada doscientas de los rebaños que pastan en las mejores praderas de Israel. Éstas se usarán para las ofrendas de cereales, el *holocausto y el sacrificio de *comunión, a fin de hacer *expiación por ellos —afirma el SEÑOR—. 16Todo el pueblo estará obligado a contribuir para esta ofrenda especial del príncipe de Israel. 17Pero en las fiestas, lunas nuevas y *sábados, y en todas las fiestas señaladas en el pueblo de Israel, al príncipe le corresponderá proveer los holocaustos, las ofrendas de cereales y las libaciones. Deberá también proveer la ofrenda por el pecado, las ofrendas de cereales, el holocausto y los sacrificios de

---

ʳ 45:1 diez mil (LXX; lit. veinte mil *codos); cinco mil (TM; lit. diez mil codos). ˢ 45:5 ciudades donde vivir (LXX); veinte habitaciones (TM).

comunión, para hacer expiación por los pecados de Israel.

18»"Así dice el SEÑOR omnipotente: El día primero del mes primero tomarás un ternero sin defecto y lo ofrecerás como sacrificio para *purificar de pecado al templo. 19De la ofrenda por el pecado el sacerdote tomará un poco de sangre y la pondrá sobre los postes de la puerta del templo, en las cuatro esquinas del zócalo superior del altar, y en los postes de la puerta del atrio interior. 20Lo mismo harás el día siete del mes con todo el que haya pecado sin intención o por ignorancia. Así el templo quedará purificado.

21»"El día catorce del mes primero deberás celebrar la fiesta de la Pascua. Durante siete días comerás pan sin levadura. 22Ese día el príncipe deberá ofrecer un ternero como sacrificio por su pecado y el del todo el pueblo. 23Y cada día, durante los siete días de la fiesta, el príncipe deberá ofrecer en holocausto al Señor siete terneros y siete carneros sin defecto. Además, cada día ofrecerá un macho cabrío como sacrificio por el pecado. 24También ofrecerá, como ofrenda de cereal, un *efa* por cada ternero, un *efa* por cada carnero, y un *hin* de aceite por cada *efa*.

25»"Durante los siete días de la fiesta, que comienza el día quince del mes séptimo, el príncipe deberá proveer lo mismo para el sacrificio por el pecado, el holocausto y las ofrendas de cereales y de aceite.

46

»"Así dice el SEÑOR omnipotente: La puerta oriental del atrio interior permanecerá cerrada durante los días laborables, pero se abrirá los *sábados y los días de luna nueva. 2El príncipe entrará por el vestíbulo de la puerta, y se detendrá junto a uno de los postes de la puerta; entonces los sacerdotes ofrecerán sus *holocaustos y sus sacrificios de *comunión. El príncipe adorará junto al umbral de la puerta, y luego saldrá; la puerta, sin embargo, no se cerrará hasta el atardecer.

3»"Los sábados y los días de luna nueva el pueblo de esta tierra adorará en presencia del SEÑOR, frente a la misma puerta. 4El holocausto que el príncipe ofrecerá al SEÑOR el día sábado será de seis corderos y un carnero, todos ellos sin defecto alguno. 5La ofrenda de cereales será de un *efa* por carnero, y por los corderos, lo que pueda darse; por cada *efa* deberá ofrecer un *hin* de aceite. 6En el día de luna nueva deberá ofrecer un ternero, seis corderos y un carnero, todos ellos sin defecto alguno. 7Por el ternero ofrecerá una ofrenda de cereales de un *efa*, y lo mismo por el carnero. Por los corderos, la ofrenda de cereales será según lo que pueda darse, y por cada *efa* deberá ofrecer un *hin* de aceite.

8»"Cuando el príncipe entre, lo hará por el vestíbulo de la puerta, y saldrá por el mismo lugar. 9Pero cuando el pueblo se presente delante del SEÑOR durante las fiestas señaladas, el que entre para adorar por la puerta del norte saldrá por la puerta del sur; así mismo, el que entre por la puerta del sur saldrá por la puerta del norte. Nadie saldrá por la misma puerta por la que entró, sino que siempre saldrá por la de enfrente. 10Y cuando entren y cuando salgan, el príncipe deberá estar entre ellos. 11En los festivales y en las fiestas señaladas, la ofrenda de cereales será de un *efa* por cada ternero y lo mismo por cada carnero. Por los corderos será según lo que pueda darse, y por cada *efa* deberá ofrecerse un *hin* de aceite.

12»"Y cuando el príncipe presente una ofrenda voluntaria al SEÑOR, ya sea un holocausto o un sacrificio de comunión, se le abrirá la puerta oriental, y

ofrecerá su holocausto o su sacrificio de comunión de la misma manera que lo hace el día sábado. Luego saldrá, y tras él cerrarán la puerta.

13»"Todas las mañanas ofrecerás, en holocausto al SEÑOR, un cordero de un año sin defecto. 14De la misma manera, ofrecerás cada mañana una ofrenda de cereales. Será de una sexta parte de un *efa*, con una tercera parte de un *hin* de aceite para humedecer la harina. Ésta será una ofrenda al SEÑOR, que se presentará siempre, por ordenanza perpetua. 15Por lo tanto, cada mañana se ofrecerán, como holocausto perpetuo, el cordero, la ofrenda de cereales y la ofrenda de aceite.

16»"Así dice el SEÑOR omnipotente: Si el príncipe le regala a alguno de sus hijos parte de su herencia, ese regalo le pertenecerá a sus descendientes, pues es su herencia. 17Pero si le regala parte de su herencia a alguno de sus siervos, ésta sólo le pertenecerá al siervo hasta el año del jubileo, después de lo cual el siervo se la devolverá al príncipe. La herencia del príncipe es patrimonio de sus descendientes. 18El príncipe no se apoderará de la herencia del pueblo, ni lo privará de lo que le pertenece. A sus hijos les dará solamente lo que sea parte de su propiedad personal; así en mi pueblo nadie quedará despojado de su propiedad."»

19Luego el hombre me llevó a la entrada que estaba al lado de la puerta, a las habitaciones que dan al norte y que estaban consagradas para los sacerdotes. Desde allí me mostró un espacio en el fondo, al lado oeste. 20Y me dijo: «Éste es el lugar donde los sacerdotes hervirán la carne de los animales ofrecidos en sacrificio por la culpa o por el pecado. También aquí se cocerán las ofrendas de cereales. Esto es para que no tengan que sacarlas al atrio exterior, pues el pueblo podría entrar en contacto con los objetos sagrados.»

21Entonces me llevó al atrio exterior y me hizo pasar por los cuatro ángulos del atrio. Vi que en cada ángulo había un pequeño atrio. 22En los cuatro ángulos del atrio había atrios cercados,t todos del mismo tamaño, de veinte metros de largo por quince de ancho. 23Alrededor de los cuatro atrios había un muro, y en todo el derredor de la parte baja del muro había unos fogones. 24Entonces me dijo: «Éstas son las cocinas donde los servidores del templo hervirán los animales para los sacrificios del pueblo.»

El río del templo

47

El hombre me trajo de vuelta a la entrada del templo, y vi que brotaba agua por debajo del umbral, en dirección al oriente, que es hacia donde da la fachada del templo. El agua corría por la parte baja del lado derecho del templo, al sur del altar. 2Luego el hombre me sacó por la puerta del norte, y me hizo dar la vuelta por fuera, hasta la puerta exterior que mira hacia el oriente; y vi que las aguas fluían del lado sur. 3El hombre salió hacia el oriente con una cuerda en la mano, midió quinientos metros y me hizo cruzar el agua, la cual me llegaba a los tobillos. 4Luego midió otros quinientos metros y me hizo cruzar el agua, que ahora me llegaba a las rodillas. Midió otros quinientos metros, y me hizo cruzar el agua, que esta vez me llegaba a la cintura. 5Midió otros quinientos metros, pero la corriente se había convertido ya en un río que yo no podía cruzar. Había crecido tanto que sólo se podía cruzar a nado. 6Entonces me preguntó: «¿Lo has visto, hijo de hombre?»

En seguida me hizo volver a la orilla del río, 7y al llegar vi que en sus márgenes había muchos árboles.

---

t **46:22** *cercados*. Palabra de difícil traducción.

8Allí me dijo: «Estas aguas fluyen hacia la región oriental, descienden hasta el Arabá, y van a dar al Mar Muerto. Cuando desembocan en ese mar, las aguas se vuelven dulces. 9Por donde corra este río, todo ser viviente que en él se mueva vivirá. Habrá peces en abundancia porque el agua de este río transformará el agua salada en agua dulce, y todo lo que se mueva en sus aguas vivirá. 10Junto al río se detendrán los pescadores, desde Engadi hasta Eneglayin, porque allí habrá lugar para secar sus redes. Los peces allí serán tan variados y numerosos como en el mar Mediterráneo.u 11Pero sus pantanos y marismas no tendrán agua dulce, sino que quedarán como salinas. 12Junto a las orillas del río crecerá toda clase de árboles frutales; sus hojas no se marchitarán, y siempre tendrán frutos. Cada mes darán frutos nuevos, porque el agua que los riega sale del templo. Sus frutos servirán de alimento y sus hojas serán medicinales.

Los límites del país

13»Así dice el SEÑOR omnipotente: Éstos son los límites del país que se repartirá como herencia a las doce tribus de Israel, tomando en cuenta que a José le tocará una doble porción. 14A los antepasados de ustedes les juré darles este país como herencia. Ahora cada uno de ustedes recibirá una parte igual, porque este país es su herencia.

15»Por el lado norte, comenzando desde el mar Mediterráneo y pasando por la ciudad de Hetlón hasta la entrada de Zedad, los límites del país serán: 16Jamat, Berotá, Sibrayin —que está entre el territorio de Damasco y el de Jamat— y Jazar Haticón, que limita con Jaurán. 17Así el límite norte se extenderá desde el mar Mediterráneo hasta Jazar Enán. Al norte quedarán los territorios de Jamat y Jaurán.

18»Por el oriente, la frontera entre la tierra de Israel y Jaurán, Damasco y Galaad, será el río Jordán, hasta la ciudad de Tamar, que está junto al Mar Muerto; éste será el límite oriental.

19»Por el sur, la frontera irá desde Tamar hasta el oasis de Meribá Cades, en dirección del torrente de Egipto, hasta el mar Mediterráneo. Éste será el límite sur.

20»Por el occidente, la frontera será el mar Mediterráneo, desde el límite sur hasta la costa que está a la altura de Lebó Jamat.v Éste será el límite occidental.

21»Ustedes deberán repartirse esta tierra entre las doce tribus de Israel. 22La sortearán como herencia entre ustedes, y entre los extranjeros que habiten entre ustedes y que entre ustedes hayan tenido, a los cuales deberán considerar israelitas por nacimiento. Por tanto, estos extranjeros recibirán una herencia con ustedes entre las tribus de Israel. 23Y en la tribu donde esté residiendo el extranjero, allí le darán su herencia. Lo afirma el SEÑOR omnipotente.

Reparto de la tierra

48 »Éstos son los nombres de las tribus, partiendo desde la frontera norte y comenzando con la tribu de Dan, de este a oeste, y desde el Mediterráneo, pasando por Hetlón, hasta Lebó Jamat y Jazar Enán, que es la parte al sur de Damasco y Jamat:

2»Debajo de Dan, de este a oeste, está la porción de territorio de Aser.

3»Debajo de Aser, de este a oeste, está la porción de territorio de Neftalí.

4»Debajo de Neftalí, de este a oeste, está la porción de territorio de Manasés.

5»Debajo de Manasés, de este a oeste, está la porción de territorio de Efraín.

6»Debajo de Efraín, de este a oeste, está la porción de territorio de Rubén.

7»Debajo de Rubén, de este a oeste, está la porción de territorio de Judá.

8»Debajo de Judá, de este a oeste, está la porción de territorio que reservarás. Será de doce mil quinientos metros de ancho, y de este a oeste su longitud será la misma que la de los otros territorios. En medio de esta porción estará el santuario.

9»La parcela que ustedes deben reservar para el SEÑOR tendrá doce mil quinientos metros de largo por diez mil metrosw de ancho. 10Dentro de esta parcela sagrada, a los sacerdotes les corresponderá una sección exclusiva que medirá doce mil quinientos metros por el norte, y cinco mil metros por el sur. En medio de ella se levantará el santuario del SEÑOR. 11Esta sección estará destinada a los sacerdotes consagrados, descendientes de Sadoc, que cuando se descarrió el pueblo de Israel se encargaron de mi servicio y no se descarriaron, como los levitas. 12Por eso, a los sacerdotes les corresponderá una sección santísima de la parcela consagrada al SEÑOR, junto al territorio de los levitas. 13También los levitas tendrán una parcela de doce mil quinientos metros de largo por cinco mil de ancho, a lo largo del territorio de los sacerdotes. En total, la parcela reservada tendrá doce mil quinientos metros de largo por diez mil metros de ancho. 14Como parcela escogida del país, no se podrá vender, permutar ni expropiar ninguna parte de ella, pues está consagrada al SEÑOR.

15»La sección restante de doce mil quinientos metros de largo por dos mil quinientos metros de ancho es terreno profano. Se dedicará al uso común de la ciudad, para la construcción de viviendas y para pastizales. La ciudad quedará en el centro, 16y medirá dos mil doscientos cincuenta metros de largo por el lado norte, y lo mismo por sus lados sur, este y oeste. 17Los pastizales de la ciudad medirán ciento veinticinco metros de ancho alrededor de toda la ciudad. 18A los costados de la ciudad quedará una sección, junto a la parcela consagrada al SEÑOR, que tendrá cinco mil metros de largo por la parte este, y otros tantos por el oeste. Todo lo que allí se produzca servirá de alimento para los trabajadores de la ciudad. 19La cultivarán los trabajadores de la ciudad, sin importar a qué tribu pertenezcan. 20Toda la parcela consagrada, incluso lo que pertenece a la ciudad, formará un cuadrado de doce mil quinientos metros por lado.

21»El terreno que quede a ambos lados de la parcela consagrada y de la que pertenece a la ciudad, será para el príncipe. A él le tocará una parcela de doce mil quinientos metros por el lado este, hasta la frontera oriental, y doce mil quinientos metros por el oeste, hasta la frontera occidental. Todo esto quedará paralelo a las otras secciones. En el centro estarán la parcela consagrada y el santuario del templo. 22Así mismo, la propiedad de los levitas y la de la ciudad se ubicarán entre las fronteras de Judá y Benjamín, en medio de la parcela que le corresponde al príncipe.

23»En cuanto a las demás tribus, a Benjamín le tocará una sección de este a oeste.

---

u 47:10 mar Mediterráneo. Lit. mar grande; también en vv. 15,19,20. v 47:20 Lebó Jamat. Alt. la entrada de Jamat; también en 48:1. w 48:9 diez mil metros (lectura probable; lit. veinte mil [*codos]); cinco mil metros (TM; lit. diez mil [codos]); también en v. 13.

24»Debajo de Benjamín, a Simeón le tocará una sección de este a oeste.

25»Debajo de Simeón, a Isacar le tocará una sección de este a oeste.

26»Debajo de Isacar, a Zabulón le tocará una sección de este a oeste.

27»Debajo de Zabulón, a Gad le tocará una sección de este a oeste.

28»Debajo de Gad, partiendo de este a oeste, la frontera irá desde Tamar hasta el oasis de Meribá Cades y el arroyo de Egipto, y hasta el mar Mediterráneo.

29»Éste es el territorio que ustedes repartirán por sorteo entre las tribus de Israel, y que será su herencia. Así quedará distribuido el territorio. Lo afirma el SEÑOR omnipotente.

Las puertas de Jerusalén

30»Éstas son las salidas de la ciudad:

»Por el norte, la ciudad medirá dos mil doscientos cincuenta metros. 31Las *puertas de la ciudad tendrán los nombres de las tribus de Israel. Al norte habrá tres puertas: la de Rubén, la de Judá y la de Leví.

32»Por el este, la ciudad medirá dos mil doscientos cincuenta metros, y tendrá tres puertas: la de José, la de Benjamín y la de Dan.

33»Por el sur, la ciudad medirá dos mil doscientos cincuenta metros, y tendrá tres puertas: la de Simeón, la de Isacar y la de Zabulón.

34»Por el oeste, la ciudad medirá dos mil doscientos cincuenta metros, y tendrá tres puertas: la de Gad, la de Aser y la de Neftalí.

35»El perímetro urbano será de nueve mil metros.

»Y desde aquel día el *nombre de la ciudad será:

AQUÍ HABITA EL SEÑOR.»

DANIEL

Daniel en Babilonia

1 En el año tercero del reinado del rey Joacim de Judá, el rey Nabucodonosor de Babilonia vino a Jerusalén y la sitió. 2El SEÑOR permitió que Joacim cayera en manos de Nabucodonosor. Junto con él, cayeron en sus manos algunos de los utensilios del templo de Dios, los cuales Nabucodonosor se llevó a Babilonia y puso en el tesoro del templo de sus dioses. 3Además, el rey le ordenó a Aspenaz, jefe de los oficiales de su corte, que llevara a su presencia a algunos de los israelitas pertenecientes a la familia real y a la nobleza. 4Debían ser jóvenes apuestos y sin ningún defecto físico, que tuvieran aptitudes para aprender de todo y que actuaran con sensatez; jóvenes sabios y aptos para el servicio en el palacio real, a los cuales Aspenaz debía enseñarles la lengua y la literatura de los *babilonios. 5El rey les asignó raciones diarias de la comida y del vino que se servía en la mesa real. Su preparación habría de durar tres años, después de lo cual entrarían al servicio del rey.

6Entre estos jóvenes se encontraban Daniel, Ananías, Misael y Azarías, que eran de Judá, 7y a los cuales el jefe de oficiales les cambió el nombre: a Daniel lo llamó Beltsasar; a Ananías, Sadrac; a Misael, Mesac; y a Azarías, Abednego.

8Pero Daniel se propuso no *contaminarse con la comida y el vino del rey, así que le pidió al jefe de oficiales que no lo obligara a contaminarse. 9Y aunque Dios había hecho que Daniel se ganara el afecto y la simpatía del jefe de oficiales, 10éste se vio obligado a responderle a Daniel: «Tengo miedo de mi señor el rey, pues fue él quien te asignó la comida y el vino. Si el rey llega a verte más flaco y demacrado que los otros jóvenes de tu edad, por culpa tuya me cortará la cabeza.»

11El jefe de oficiales le ordenó a un guardia atender a Daniel, Ananías, Misael y Azarías. Por su parte, Daniel habló con ese guardia y le dijo: 12«Por favor, haz con tus siervos una prueba de diez días. Danos de comer sólo verduras, y de beber sólo agua. 13Pasado ese tiempo, compara nuestro semblante con el de los jóvenes que se alimentan con la comida real, y procede de acuerdo con lo que veas en nosotros.»

14El guardia aceptó la propuesta, y los sometió a una prueba de diez días. 15Al cumplirse el plazo, estos jóvenes se veían más sanos y mejor alimentados que cualquiera de los que participaban de la comida real. 16Así que el guardia les retiró la comida y el vino del rey, y en su lugar siguió alimentándolos con verduras.

17A estos cuatro jóvenes Dios los dotó de sabiduría e inteligencia para entender toda clase de literatura y ciencia. Además, Daniel podía entender toda visión y todo sueño.

18Cumplido el plazo fijado por el rey Nabucodonosor, y conforme a sus instrucciones, el jefe de oficiales los llevó ante su presencia. 19Luego de hablar el rey con Daniel, Ananías, Misael y Azarías, no encontró a nadie que los igualara, de modo que los cuatro entraron a su servicio. 20El rey los interrogó, y en todos los temas que requerían de sabiduría y discernimiento los halló diez veces más inteligentes que todos los magos y hechiceros de su reino. 21Fue así como Daniel se quedó en Babilonia hasta el primer año del rey Ciro.

El sueño del rey Nabucodonosor

2 En el segundo año de su reinado, Nabucodonosor tuvo varios sueños que lo perturbaron y no lo dejaban dormir. 2Mandó entonces que se reunieran los magos, hechiceros, adivinos y astrólogos[a] de su reino, para que le dijeran lo que había soñado. Una vez reunidos, y ya en presencia del rey, 3éste les dijo:

—Tuve un sueño que me tiene preocupado, y quiero saber lo que significa.

4Los astrólogos le respondieron:[b]

—¡Que viva Su Majestad por siempre! Estamos a su servicio. Cuéntenos el sueño, y nosotros le diremos lo que significa.

5Pero el rey les advirtió:

—Mi decisión ya está tomada: Si no me dicen lo que soñé, ni me dan su interpretación, ordenaré que los corten en pedazos y que sus casas sean reducidas a cenizas. 6Pero si me dicen lo que soñé y me explican su significado, yo les daré regalos, recompensas y grandes honores. Así que comiencen por decirme lo que soñé, y luego explíquenme su significado.

7Los astrólogos insistieron:

—Si Su Majestad les cuenta a estos siervos suyos lo que soñó, nosotros le diremos lo que significa.

8Pero el rey les contestó:

—Mi decisión ya está tomada. Eso ustedes bien lo saben, y por eso quieren ganar tiempo. 9Si no me dicen lo que soñé, ya saben lo que les espera. Ustedes se han puesto de acuerdo para salirme con cuestiones engañosas y mal intencionadas, esperando que cambie yo de parecer. Díganme lo que soñé, y así sabré que son capaces de darme su interpretación.

10Entonces los astrólogos le respondieron:

—¡No hay nadie en la tierra capaz de hacer lo que Su Majestad nos pide! ¡Jamás a ningún rey se le ha ocurrido pedirle tal cosa a ningún mago, hechicero o astrólogo! 11Lo que Su Majestad nos pide raya en lo imposible, y nadie podrá revelárselo, a no ser los dioses. ¡Pero ellos no viven entre nosotros!

12Tanto enfureció al rey la respuesta de los astrólogos, que mandó ejecutar a todos los sabios de Babilonia. 13Se publicó entonces un edicto que decretaba la muerte de todos los sabios, de modo que se ordenó la búsqueda de Daniel y de sus compañeros para que fueran ejecutados.

14Cuando el comandante de la guardia real, que se llamaba Arioc, salió para ejecutar a los sabios *babilonios, Daniel habló con mucho tacto e inteligencia. 15Le dijo: «¿Por qué ha emitido el rey un edicto tan violento?» Y una vez que Arioc le explicó cuál era el problema, 16Daniel fue a ver al rey y le pidió tiempo para poder interpretarle su sueño. 17Después volvió a su casa y les contó a sus amigos Ananías, Misael y Azarías cómo se presentaba la situación. 18Al mismo tiempo, les pidió que imploraran la misericordia del Dios del cielo en cuanto a ese sueño misterioso, para que ni él ni sus amigos fueran ejecutados con el resto de los sabios babilonios.

19Durante la noche, Daniel recibió en una visión la respuesta al misterio. Entonces alabó al Dios del cielo 20y dijo:

«¡Alabado sea por siempre el *nombre de Dios!

---

a 2:2 astrólogos. Lit. *caldeos; así en el resto de este libro. b 2:4 le respondieron. Lit. le respondieron en arameo. En efecto, de aquí al final del cap. 7 el texto bíblico está escrito en la lengua aramea.

Suyos son la sabiduría y el poder.
²¹Él cambia los tiempos y las épocas,
    pone y depone reyes.
 A los sabios da sabiduría,
    y a los inteligentes, discernimiento.
²²Él revela lo profundo y lo escondido,
    y sabe lo que se oculta en las sombras.
 ¡En él habita la luz!
²³A ti, Dios de mis padres,
    te alabo y te doy gracias.
 Me has dado sabiduría y poder,
    me has dado a conocer lo que te pedimos,
    ¡me has dado a conocer el sueño del rey!»

Daniel interpreta el sueño del rey

²⁴Entonces Daniel fue a ver a Arioc, a quien el rey le había dado la orden de ejecutar a los sabios de Babilonia, y le dijo:

—No mates a los sabios *babilonios. Llévame ante el rey, y le interpretaré el sueño que tuvo.

²⁵Inmediatamente Arioc condujo a Daniel a la presencia del rey, y le dijo:

—Entre los exiliados de Judá he hallado a alguien que puede interpretar el sueño de Su Majestad.

²⁶El rey le preguntó a Daniel, a quien los babilonios le habían puesto por nombre Beltsasar:

—¿Puedes decirme lo que vi en mi sueño, y darme su interpretación?

²⁷A esto Daniel respondió:

—No hay ningún sabio ni hechicero, ni mago o adivino, que pueda explicarle a Su Majestad el misterio que lo preocupa. ²⁸Pero hay un Dios en el cielo que revela los misterios. Ese Dios le ha mostrado a usted lo que tendrá lugar en los días venideros. Éstos son el sueño y las visiones que pasaron por la mente de Su Majestad mientras dormía: ²⁹Allí, en su cama, Su Majestad dirigió sus pensamientos a las cosas por venir, y el que revela los misterios le mostró lo que está por suceder. ³⁰Por lo que a mí toca, este misterio me ha sido revelado, no porque yo sea más sabio que el resto de la humanidad, sino para que Su Majestad llegue a conocer su interpretación y entienda lo que pasaba por su *mente.

³¹»En su sueño Su Majestad veía una estatua enorme, de tamaño impresionante y de aspecto horrible. ³²La cabeza de la estatua era de oro puro, el pecho y los brazos eran de plata, el vientre y los muslos eran de bronce, ³³y las piernas eran de hierro, lo mismo que la mitad de los pies, en tanto que la otra mitad era de barro cocido. ³⁴De pronto, y mientras Su Majestad contemplaba la estatua, una roca que nadie desprendió vino y golpeó los pies de hierro y barro de la estatua, y los hizo pedazos. ³⁵Con ellos se hicieron añicos el hierro y el barro, junto con el bronce, la plata y el oro. La estatua se hizo polvo, como el que vuela en el verano cuando se trilla el trigo. El viento barrió con la estatua, y no quedó ni rastro de ella. En cambio, la roca que dio contra la estatua se convirtió en una montaña enorme que llenó toda la tierra.

³⁶»Éste fue el sueño que tuvo Su Majestad, y éste es su significado: ³⁷Su Majestad es rey entre los reyes; el Dios del cielo le ha dado el reino, el poder, la majestad y la gloria. ³⁸Además, ha puesto en manos de Su Majestad a la *humanidad entera, a las bestias del campo y a las aves del cielo. No importa dónde vivan, Dios ha hecho de Su Majestad el gobernante de todos ellos. ¡Su Majestad es la cabeza de oro!

³⁹»Después de Su Majestad surgirá otro reino de menor importancia. Luego vendrá un tercer reino, que será de bronce, y dominará sobre toda la tierra. ⁴⁰Finalmente, vendrá un cuarto reino, sólido como el hierro. Y así como el hierro todo lo rompe, destroza y pulveriza, este cuarto reino hará polvo a los otros reinos.

⁴¹»Su Majestad veía que los pies y los dedos de la estatua eran mitad hierro y mitad barro cocido. El hierro y el barro, que Su Majestad vio mezclados, significan que éste será un reino dividido, aunque tendrá la fuerza del hierro. ⁴²Y como los dedos eran también mitad hierro y mitad barro, este reino será medianamente fuerte y medianamente débil. ⁴³Su Majestad vio mezclados el hierro y el barro, dos elementos que no pueden fundirse entre sí. De igual manera, el pueblo será una mezcla que no podrá mantenerse unida.

⁴⁴»En los días de estos reyes el Dios del cielo establecerá un reino que jamás será destruido ni entregado a otro pueblo, sino que permanecerá para siempre y hará pedazos a todos estos reinos. ⁴⁵Tal es el sentido del sueño donde la roca se desprendía de una montaña; roca que, sin la intervención de nadie, hizo añicos al hierro, al bronce, al barro, a la plata y al oro. El gran Dios le ha mostrado a Su Majestad lo que tendrá lugar en el futuro. El sueño es verdadero, y esta interpretación, digna de confianza.

⁴⁶Al oír esto, el rey Nabucodonosor se postró ante Daniel y le rindió pleitesía, ordenó que se le presentara una ofrenda e incienso, ⁴⁷y le dijo:

—¡Tu Dios es el Dios de dioses y el soberano de los reyes! ¡Tu Dios revela todos los misterios, pues fuiste capaz de revelarme este sueño misterioso!

⁴⁸Luego el rey puso a Daniel en un puesto prominente y lo colmó de regalos, lo nombró gobernador de toda la provincia de Babilonia y jefe de todos sus sabios. ⁴⁹Además, a solicitud de Daniel, el rey nombró a Sadrac, Mesac y Abednego administradores de la provincia de Babilonia. Daniel, por su parte, permaneció en la corte real.

El horno en llamas

3 El rey Nabucodonosor mandó hacer una estatua de oro, de veintisiete metros de alto por dos metros y medioᶜ de ancho, y mandó que la colocaran en los llanos de Dura, en la provincia de Babilonia. ²Luego les ordenó a los *sátrapas, prefectos, gobernadores, consejeros, tesoreros, jueces, magistrados y demás oficiales de las provincias, que asistieran a la dedicación de la estatua que había mandado erigir. ³Para celebrar tal dedicación, los sátrapas, prefectos, gobernadores, consejeros, tesoreros, jueces, magistrados y demás oficiales de las provincias se reunieron ante la estatua. ⁴Entonces los heraldos proclamaron a voz en cuello: «A ustedes, pueblos, naciones y gente de toda lengua, se les ordena lo siguiente: ⁵Tan pronto como escuchen la música de trompetas, flautas, cítaras, liras, arpas, zampoñas y otros instrumentos musicales, deberán inclinarse y adorar la estatua de oro que el rey Nabucodonosor ha mandado erigir. ⁶Todo el que no se incline ante ella ni la adore será arrojado de inmediato a un horno en llamas.»

⁷Ante tal amenaza, tan pronto como se escuchó la música de todos esos instrumentos musicales, todos los pueblos y naciones, y gente de toda lengua, se inclinaron y adoraron la estatua de oro que el rey Nabucodonosor había mandado erigir. ⁸Pero algu-

---

ᶜ **3:1** *veintisiete metros ... dos metros y medio.* Lit. *sesenta* *codos ... seis codos.*

nos astrólogos se presentaron ante el rey y acusaron a los judíos:

9—¡Que viva Su Majestad por siempre! —exclamaron—. 10Usted ha emitido un decreto ordenando que todo el que oiga la música de trompetas, flautas, cítaras, liras, arpas, zampoñas y otros instrumentos musicales, se incline ante la estatua de oro y la adore. 11También ha ordenado que todo el que no se incline ante la estatua de oro será arrojado a un horno en llamas. 12Pero hay algunos judíos, a quienes Su Majestad ha puesto al frente de la provincia de Babilonia, que no acatan sus órdenes. No adoran a los dioses de Su Majestad ni a la estatua de oro que mandó erigir. Se trata de Sadrac, Mesac y Abednego.

13Lleno de ira, Nabucodonosor los mandó llamar. Cuando los jóvenes se presentaron ante el rey, 14Nabucodonosor les dijo:

—Ustedes tres, ¿es verdad que no honran a mis dioses ni adoran a la estatua de oro que he mandado erigir? 15Ahora que escuchen la música de los instrumentos musicales, más les vale que se inclinen ante la estatua que he mandado hacer, y que la adoren. De lo contrario, serán lanzados de inmediato a un horno en llamas, ¡y no habrá dios capaz de librarlos de mis manos!

16Sadrac, Mesac y Abednego le respondieron a Nabucodonosor:

—¡No hace falta que nos defendamos ante Su Majestad! 17Si se nos arroja al horno en llamas, el Dios al que servimos puede librarnos del horno y de las manos de Su Majestad. 18Pero aun si nuestro Dios no lo hace así, sepa usted que no honraremos a sus dioses ni adoraremos a su estatua.

19Ante la respuesta de Sadrac, Mesac y Abednego, Nabucodonosor se puso muy furioso y cambió su actitud hacia ellos. Mandó entonces que se calentara el horno siete veces más de lo normal, 20y que algunos de los soldados más fuertes de su ejército ataran a los tres jóvenes y los arrojaran al horno en llamas. 21Fue así como los arrojaron al horno con sus mantos, sandalias, turbantes y todo, es decir, tal y como estaban vestidos. 22Tan inmediata fue la orden del rey, y tan caliente estaba el horno, que las llamas alcanzaron y mataron a los soldados que arrojaron a Sadrac, Mesac y Abednego, 23los cuales, atados de pies y manos, cayeron dentro del horno en llamas.

24En ese momento Nabucodonosor se puso de pie, y sorprendido les preguntó a sus consejeros:

—¿Acaso no eran tres los hombres que atamos y arrojamos al fuego?

—Así es, Su Majestad —le respondieron.

25—¡Pues miren! —exclamó—. Allí en el fuego veo a cuatro hombres, sin ataduras y sin daño alguno, ¡y el cuarto tiene la apariencia de un dios!d

26Dicho esto, Nabucodonosor se acercó a la puerta del horno en llamas y gritó:

—Sadrac, Mesac y Abednego, siervos del Dios *Altísimo, ¡salgan de allí, y vengan acá!

Cuando los tres jóvenes salieron del horno, 27los sátrapas, prefectos, gobernadores y consejeros reales se arremolinaron en torno a ellos y vieron que el fuego no les había causado ningún daño, y que ni uno solo de sus cabellos se había chamuscado; es más, su ropa no estaba quemada ¡y ni siquiera olía a humo!

28Entonces exclamó Nabucodonosor: «¡Alabado sea el Dios de estos jóvenes, que envió a su ángel y los salvó! Ellos confiaron en él y, desafiando la orden real, optaron por la muerte antes que honrar o adorar a otro dios que no fuera el suyo. 29Por tanto, yo

decreto que se descuartice a cualquiera que hable en contra del Dios de Sadrac, Mesac y Abednego, y que su casa sea reducida a cenizas, sin importar la nación a que pertenezca o la lengua que hable. ¡No hay otro dios que pueda salvar de esta manera!»

30Después de eso el rey promovió a Sadrac, Mesac y Abednego a un alto puesto en la provincia de Babilonia.

Nabucodonosor, árbol caído

4 El rey Nabucodonosor,

a todos los pueblos y naciones que habitan en este mundo, y a toda lengua:

¡Paz y prosperidad para todos!

2Me es grato darles a conocer las señales y maravillas que el Dios *Altísimo ha realizado en mi favor. 3¡Cuán grandes son sus señales! ¡Cuán portentosas son sus maravillas! ¡Su reino es un reino eterno! ¡Su soberanía permanece de generación en generación!

4Yo, Nabucodonosor, estaba en mi palacio, feliz y lleno de prosperidad, 5cuando tuve un sueño que me infundió miedo. Recostado en mi lecho, las imágenes y visiones que pasaron por mi mente me llenaron de terror. 6Ordené entonces que vinieran a mi presencia todos los sabios de Babilonia para que me interpretaran el sueño. 7Cuando llegaron los magos, hechiceros, astrólogos y adivinos, les conté mi sueño pero no me lo pudieron interpretar. 8Finalmente Daniel, que en honor a mi Dios también se llama Beltsasar, se presentó ante mí y le conté mi sueño, pues en él reposa el espíritu de los *santos dioses.

9Yo le dije: «Beltsasar, jefe de los magos, yo sé que en ti reposa el espíritu de los santos dioses, y que no hay para ti ningún misterio demasiado difícil de resolver. Te voy a contar mi sueño, y quiero que me digas lo que significa. 10Y ésta es la tremenda visión que tuve mientras reposaba en mi lecho: Veía ante mí un árbol de altura impresionante, plantado en medio de la tierra. 11El árbol creció y se hizo fuerte, y su copa tocaba el cielo, ¡hasta podía verse desde cualquier punto de la tierra! 12Tenía un hermoso follaje y abundantes frutos; ¡todo el mundo hallaba en él su alimento! Hasta las bestias salvajes venían a refugiarse bajo su sombra, y en sus ramas anidaban las aves del cielo. ¡Ese árbol alimentaba a todos los animales!

13»En la visión que tuve mientras reposaba en mi lecho, vi ante mí a un mensajero santo que descendía del cielo 14y que a voz en cuello me gritaba: "¡Derriba el árbol y córtale las ramas; arráncale las hojas y esparce sus frutos! ¡Haz que las bestias huyan de su sombra, y que las aves abandonen sus nidos! 15Pero deja enterrados el tocón y las raíces; sujétalos con hierro y bronce entre la hierba del campo. Deja que se empape con el rocío del cielo, y que habite con los animales y entre las plantas de la tierra. 16Deja que su *mente *humana se trastorne y se vuelva como la de un animal, hasta que hayan transcurrido siete años."e

17»Los santos mensajeros han anunciado la decisión, es decir, el veredicto, para que todos los vivientes reconozcan que el Dios Altísimo es el soberano de todos los reinos humanos, y que se los entrega a quien él quiere, y hasta pone sobre ellos al más humilde de los hombres.

18»Yo, Nabucodonosor, tuve este sueño. Ahora tú, Beltsasar, dime qué es lo que significa, ya que ninguno de los sabios de mi reino me lo pudo interpretar. ¡Pero tú sí puedes hacerlo, porque en ti reposa el espíritu de los santos dioses!»

Daniel interpreta el sueño del rey

19Daniel, conocido también como Beltsasar, se quedó desconcertado por algún tiempo y aterrorizado por sus propios pensamientos; por eso el rey le dijo:

—Beltsasar, no te dejes alarmar por este sueño y su significado.

A esto Daniel respondió:

—¡Ojalá que el sueño y su significado tengan que ver con los acérrimos enemigos de Su Majestad! 20La copa del árbol que Su Majestad veía crecer y fortalecerse, tocaba el cielo; ¡hasta podía verse desde cualquier punto de la tierra! 21Ese árbol tenía un hermoso follaje y daba abundantes frutos, y alimentaba a todo el mundo; bajo su sombra se refugiaban las bestias salvajes, y en sus ramas anidaban las aves del cielo. 22Ese árbol es Su Majestad, que se ha hecho fuerte y poderoso, y con su grandeza ha alcanzado el cielo. ¡Su dominio se extiende a los lugares más remotos de la tierra!

23»Su Majestad veía que del cielo bajaba un mensajero *santo, el cual le ordenaba derribar el árbol y destruirlo, y dejarlo enterrado para que se empapara con el rocío del cielo, aunque tenía que sujetar con hierro y bronce el tocón y las raíces. De este modo viviría como los animales salvajes hasta que transcurrieran siete años.

24»La interpretación del sueño, y el decreto que el *Altísimo ha emitido contra Su Majestad, es como sigue: 25Usted será apartado de la gente y habitará con los animales salvajes; comerá pasto como el ganado, y se empapará con el rocío del cielo. Siete años pasarán hasta que Su Majestad reconozca que el Altísimo es el soberano de los reinos del mundo, y que se los entrega a quien él quiere. 26La orden de dejar el tocón y las raíces del árbol quiere decir que Su Majestad recibirá nuevamente el reino, cuando haya reconocido que el verdadero reino es el del cielo. 27Por lo tanto, yo le ruego a Su Majestad aceptar el consejo que le voy a dar: Renuncie usted a sus pecados y actúe con justicia; renuncie a su maldad y sea bondadoso con los oprimidos. Tal vez entonces su prosperidad vuelva a ser la de antes.»

28En efecto, todo esto le sucedió al rey Nabucodonosor. 29Doce meses después, mientras daba un paseo por la terraza del palacio real de Babilonia, 30exclamó: «¡Miren la gran Babilonia que he construido como capital del reino! ¡La he construido con mi gran poder, para mi propia honra!»

31No había terminado de hablar cuando, desde el cielo, se escuchó una voz que decía:

«Éste es el decreto en cuanto a ti, rey Nabucodonosor. Tu autoridad real se te ha quitado. 32Serás apartado de la gente y vivirás entre los animales salvajes; comerás pasto como el ganado, y siete años transcurrirán hasta que reconozcas que el Altísimo es el soberano de todos los reinos del mundo, y que se los entrega a quien él quiere.»

33Y al instante se cumplió lo anunciado a Nabucodonosor. Lo separaron de la gente, y comió pasto como el ganado. Su cuerpo se empapó con el rocío del cielo, y hasta el pelo y las uñas le crecieron como plumas y garras de águila.

34Pasado ese tiempo yo, Nabucodonosor, elevé los ojos al cielo, y recobré el juicio. Entonces alabé al Altísimo; honré y glorifiqué al que vive para siempre:

Su dominio es eterno;
su reino permanece para siempre.
35Ninguno de los pueblos de la tierra
merece ser tomado en cuenta.
Dios hace lo que quiere
con los poderes celestiales
y con los pueblos de la tierra.
No hay quien se oponga a su poder
ni quien le pida cuentas de sus actos.

36Recobré el juicio, y al momento me fueron devueltos la honra, el esplendor y la gloria de mi reino. Mis consejeros y cortesanos vinieron a buscarme, y me fue devuelto el trono. ¡Llegué a ser más poderoso que antes! 37Por eso yo, Nabucodonosor, alabo, exalto y glorifico al Rey del cielo, porque siempre procede con rectitud y justicia, y es capaz de humillar a los soberbios.

La escritura en la pared

5 El rey Belsasar ofreció un gran banquete a mil miembros de la nobleza, y bebió vino con ellos hasta emborracharse. 2-3Mientras brindaban, Belsasar mandó que le trajeran las copas de oro y de plata que Nabucodonosor, su padre, había tomado del templo de Jerusalén. Y así se hizo. Le llevaron las copas, y en ellas bebieron el rey y sus nobles, junto con sus esposas y concubinas. 4Ya borrachos, se deshacían en alabanzas a los dioses de oro, plata, bronce, hierro, madera y piedra.

5En ese momento, en la sala del palacio apareció una mano que, a la luz de las lámparas, escribía con el dedo sobre la parte blanca de la pared. Mientras el rey observaba la mano que escribía, 6el rostro le palideció del susto, las rodillas comenzaron a temblarle, y apenas podía sostenerse. 7Mandó entonces que vinieran los hechiceros, astrólogos y adivinos, y a estos sabios *babilonios les dijo:

—Al que lea lo que allí está escrito, y me diga lo que significa, lo vestiré de púrpura, le pondré una cadena de oro en el cuello, y lo nombraré tercer gobernante del reino.

8Todos los sabios del reino se presentaron, pero no pudieron descifrar lo escrito ni decirle al rey lo que significaba. 9Esto hizo que el rey Belsasar se asustara y palideciera más todavía. Los nobles, por su parte, se hallaban confundidos.

10Al oír el alboroto que hacían el rey y sus nobles, la reina misma entró en la sala del banquete y exclamó:

—¡Que viva Su Majestad por siempre! ¡Y no se alarme ni se ponga pálido! 11En el reino de Su Majestad hay un hombre en quien reposa el espíritu de los *santos dioses. Cuando vivía el rey Nabucodonosor, padre de Su Majestad, se halló que ese hombre poseía sabiduría, inteligencia y gran percepción, semejantes a las de los dioses. El padre de Su Majestad llegó a nombrar a ese hombre jefe de los magos, hechiceros, astrólogos y adivinos. 12Y es que ese hombre tiene una mente aguda, amplios *conocimientos, e inteligencia y capacidad para interpretar sueños, explicar misterios y resolver problemas difíciles. Llame usted a ese hombre, y él le dirá lo que significa ese escrito. Se llama Daniel, aunque el padre de Su Majestad le puso por nombre Beltsasar.

13Daniel fue llevado a la presencia del rey, y éste le preguntó:

—¿Así que tú eres Daniel, uno de los exiliados que mi padre trajo de Judá?

14Me han contado que en ti reposa el espíritu de los dioses, y que posees gran agudeza e inteligencia, y una sabiduría sorprendente. 15Los sabios y hechiceros se presentaron ante mí para leer esta escritura y decirme lo que significa, pero no pudieron descifrarla. 16Según me han dicho, tú puedes dar interpretaciones y resolver problemas difíciles. Si logras descifrar e interpretar lo que allí está escrito, te vestiré de púrpura, te pondré una cadena de oro en el cuello, y te nombraré tercer gobernante del reino.

17—Su Majestad puede quedarse con sus regalos, o dárselos a otro —le respondió Daniel—. Yo voy a leerle a Su Majestad lo que dice en la pared, y le explicaré lo que significa.

18»El Dios *Altísimo dio al rey Nabucodonosor, padre de usted, grandeza, gloria, majestad y esplendor. 19Gracias a la autoridad que Dios le dio, ante él temblaban de miedo todos los pueblos, naciones y gente de toda lengua. A quien él quería matar, lo mandaba matar; a quien quería perdonar, lo perdonaba; si quería promover a alguien, lo promovía; y si quería humillarlo, lo humillaba. 20Pero, cuando su *corazón se volvió arrogante y orgulloso, se le arrebató el trono real y se le despojó de su gloria; 21fue apartado de la gente y recibió la *mente de un animal; vivió entre los asnos salvajes y se alimentó con pasto como el ganado; ¡el rocío de la noche empapaba su cuerpo! Todo esto le sucedió hasta que reconoció que el Dios Altísimo es el soberano de todos los reinos del mundo, y que se los entrega a quien él quiere.

22»Sin embargo, y a pesar de saber todo esto, usted, hijo de Nabucodonosor, no se ha humillado. 23Por el contrario, se ha opuesto al Dios del cielo mandando traer de su templo las copas, para que beban en ellas usted y sus nobles, y sus esposas y concubinas. Usted se ha deshecho en alabanzas a los dioses de oro, plata, hierro, madera y piedra, dioses que no pueden ver ni oír ni entender; en cambio, no ha honrado al Dios en cuyas manos se hallan la vida y las acciones de Su Majestad. 24Por eso Dios ha enviado esa mano a escribir 25lo que allí aparece: *Mene, Mene, Téquel, Parsin.*

26»Pues bien, esto es lo que significan esas palabras:

»*Mene*: Dios ha contado los días del reino de Su Majestad, y les ha puesto un límite.
27»*Téquel*: Su Majestad ha sido puesto en la balanza, y no pesa lo que debería pesar.
28»*Parsin*: El reino de Su Majestad se ha dividido, y ha sido entregado a medos y persas.

29Entonces Belsasar ordenó que se vistiera a Daniel de púrpura, que se le pusiera una cadena de oro en el cuello, y que se le nombrara tercer gobernante del reino. 30Esa misma noche fue asesinado Belsasar, rey de los babilonios, y Darío el Persa se apoderó del reino. 31Para entonces, Darío tenía sesenta y dos años.

Daniel en el foso de los leones

6 Para el control eficaz de su reino, Darío consideró prudente nombrar a ciento veinte *sátrapas 2y tres administradores, uno de los cuales era Daniel. Estos sátrapas eran responsables ante los administradores, a fin de que los intereses del rey no se vieran afectados. 3Y tanto se distinguió Daniel por sus extraordinarias cualidades administrativas, que el rey pensó en ponerlo al frente de todo el reino. 4Entonces los administradores y los sátrapas empezaron a buscar algún motivo para acusar a Daniel de malos manejos en los negocios del reino. Sin embargo, no encontraron de qué acusarlo porque, lejos de ser corrupto o negligente, Daniel era un hombre digno de confianza. 5Por eso concluyeron: «Nunca encontraremos nada de qué acusar a Daniel, a no ser algo relacionado con la *ley de su Dios.»

6Formaron entonces una comisión para ir a hablar con el rey, y estando en su presencia le dijeron:

—¡Que viva para siempre Su Majestad, el rey Darío! 7Nosotros los administradores reales, junto con los prefectos, sátrapas, consejeros y gobernadores, convenimos en que Su Majestad debiera emitir y confirmar un decreto que exija que, durante los próximos treinta días, sea arrojado al foso de los leones todo el que adore a cualquier dios u *hombre que no sea Su Majestad. 8Expida usted ahora ese decreto, y póngalo por escrito. Así, conforme a la ley de los medos y los persas, no podrá ser revocado.

9El rey Darío expidió el decreto y lo puso por escrito. 10Cuando Daniel se enteró de la publicación del decreto, se fue a su casa y subió a su dormitorio, cuyas ventanas se abrían en dirección a Jerusalén. Allí se arrodilló y se puso a orar y alabar a Dios, pues tenía por costumbre orar tres veces al día. 11Cuando aquellos hombres llegaron y encontraron a Daniel orando e implorando la ayuda de Dios, 12fueron a hablar con el rey respecto al decreto real:

—¿No es verdad que Su Majestad publicó un decreto? Según entendemos, todo el que en los próximos treinta días adore a otro dios u hombre que no sea Su Majestad, será arrojado al foso de los leones.

—El decreto sigue en pie —contestó el rey—. Según la ley de los medos y los persas, no puede ser derogado.

13—¡Pues Daniel —respondieron ellos—, que es uno de los exiliados de Judá, no toma en cuenta a Su Majestad ni al decreto que ha promulgado! ¡Todavía sigue orando a su Dios tres veces al día!

14Cuando el rey escuchó esto, se deprimió mucho y se propuso salvar a Daniel, así que durante todo el día buscó la forma de salvarlo. 15Pero aquellos hombres fueron a ver al rey y lo presionaron:

—No olvide Su Majestad que, según la ley de los medos y los persas, ningún decreto ni edicto emitido por el rey puede ser derogado.

16El rey dio entonces la orden, y Daniel fue arrojado al foso de los leones. Allí el rey animaba a Daniel:

—¡Que tu Dios, a quien siempre sirves, se digne salvarte!

17Trajeron entonces una piedra, y con ella taparon la boca del foso. El rey lo selló con su propio anillo y con el de sus nobles, para que la sentencia contra Daniel no pudiera ser cambiada. 18Luego volvió a su palacio y pasó la noche sin comer y sin divertirse, y hasta el sueño se le fue. 19Tan pronto como amaneció, se levantó y fue al foso de los leones. 20Ya cerca, lleno de ansiedad gritó:

—Daniel, siervo del Dios viviente, ¿pudo tu Dios, a quien siempre sirves, salvarte de los leones?

21—¡Que viva Su Majestad por siempre! —contestó Daniel desde el foso—. 22Mi Dios envió a su ángel y les cerró la boca a los leones. No me han hecho ningún daño, porque Dios bien sabe que soy inocente. ¡Tampoco he cometido nada malo contra Su Majestad!

23Sin ocultar su alegría, el rey ordenó que sacaran del foso a Daniel. Cuando lo sacaron, no se le halló un solo rasguño, pues Daniel confiaba en su Dios. 24Entonces el rey mandó traer a los que falsamente lo habían acusado, y ordenó que los arrojaran al foso de los leones, junto con sus esposas y sus hijos. ¡No habían tocado el suelo cuando ya los leones habían caído sobre ellos y les habían triturado los huesos!

25Más tarde el rey Darío firmó este decreto:

«A todos los pueblos, naciones y lenguas de este mundo:

»¡Paz y prosperidad para todos!

26»He decretado que en todo lugar de mi reino mi gente adore y honre al Dios de Daniel.

»Porque él es el Dios vivo,
    y permanece para siempre.
Su reino jamás será destruido,
    y su dominio jamás tendrá fin.
27Él rescata y salva;
    hace prodigios en el cielo
    y maravillas en la tierra.
¡Ha salvado a Daniel
    de las garras de los leones!»

28Fue así como Daniel prosperó durante los reinados de Darío y de Ciro el Persa.

Las cuatro bestias

7 En el primer año del reinado de Belsasar en Babilonia, Daniel tuvo un sueño y visiones mientras yacía en su lecho. Entonces puso por escrito lo más importante de su sueño, 2y esto es lo que escribió:

«Durante la noche tuve una visión, y en ella veía al gran mar, agitado por los cuatro vientos del cielo. 3Del mar salían cuatro bestias enormes, cada una diferente de la otra.

4»La primera de ellas se parecía a un león, pero sus alas eran las de un águila. Mientras yo la observaba, le arrancaron las alas, la levantaron del suelo, y la obligaron a pararse sobre sus patas traseras, como si fuera un hombre. Y se le dio un corazón *humano.

5»La segunda bestia que vi se parecía a un oso. Se levantaba sobre uno de sus costados, y entre sus fauces tenía tres costillas. A esta bestia se le dijo: "¡Levántate y come carne hasta que te hartes!"

6»Ante mis propios ojos vi aparecer otra bestia, la cual se parecía a un leopardo, aunque en el lomo tenía cuatro alas, como las de un ave. Esta bestia tenía cuatro cabezas, y recibió autoridad para gobernar.

7»Después de esto, en mis visiones nocturnas vi ante mí una cuarta bestia, la cual era extremadamente horrible y poseía una fuerza descomunal. Con sus grandes colmillos de hierro aplastaba y devoraba a sus víctimas, para luego pisotear los restos. Tenía diez cuernos, y no se parecía en nada a las otras bestias.

8»Mientras me fijaba en los cuernos, vi surgir entre ellos otro cuerno más pequeño. Por causa de éste fueron arrancados tres de los primeros. El cuerno pequeño parecía tener ojos humanos, y una boca que profería insolencias.

Canto al Anciano

9»Mientras yo observaba esto,
    se colocaron unos tronos,
    y tomó asiento un venerable Anciano.
Su ropa era blanca como la nieve,
    y su cabello, blanco como la lana.
Su trono con sus ruedas
    centelleaban como el fuego.
10De su presencia brotaba
    un torrente de fuego.

Miles y millares le servían,
    centenares de miles lo atendían.
Al iniciarse el juicio,
    los libros fueron abiertos.

11»Yo me quedé mirando por causa de las grandes insolencias que profería el cuerno. Seguí mirando hasta que a esta bestia la mataron, la descuartizaron y echaron los pedazos al fuego ardiente. 12A las otras bestias les quitaron el poder, aunque las dejaron vivir por algún tiempo.

13»En esa visión nocturna, vi que alguien con aspecto humanof venía entre las nubes del cielo. Se acercó al venerable Anciano y fue llevado a su presencia, 14y se le dio autoridad, poder y majestad. ¡Todos los pueblos, naciones y lenguas lo adoraron! ¡Su dominio es un dominio eterno, que no pasará, y su reino jamás será destruido!

La interpretación del sueño

15»Yo, Daniel, me quedé aterrorizado, y muy preocupado por las visiones que pasaban por mi mente. 16Me acerqué entonces a uno de los que estaban allí, y le pregunté el verdadero significado de todo esto. Y ésta fue su interpretación: 17"Las cuatro grandes bestias son cuatro reinos que se levantarán en la tierra, 18pero los *santos del *Altísimo recibirán el reino, y será suyo para siempre, ¡para siempre jamás!"

19»Quise entonces saber el verdadero significado de la cuarta bestia, la cual desmenuzaba a sus víctimas y las devoraba, pisoteando luego sus restos. Era muy distinta a las otras tres, pues tenía colmillos de hierro y garras de bronce. ¡Tenía un aspecto espantoso! 20Quise saber también acerca de los diez cuernos que tenía en la cabeza, y del otro cuerno que le había salido y ante el cual habían caído tres de ellos. Este cuerno se veía más impresionante que los otros, pues tenía ojos y hablaba con insolencia.

21»Mientras observaba yo, este cuerno libró una guerra contra los santos y los venció. 22Entonces vino el Anciano y emitió juicio en favor de los santos del Altísimo. En ese momento los santos recibieron el reino.

23»Ésta fue la explicación que me dio el venerable Anciano:

"La cuarta bestia es un cuarto reino
    que surgirá en este mundo.
Será diferente a los otros reinos;
    devorará a toda la tierra;
    ¡la aplastará y la pisoteará!
24Los diez cuernos son diez reyes
    que saldrán de este reino.
Otro rey les sucederá,
    distinto a los anteriores,
    el cual derrocará a tres reyes.
25Hablará en contra del Altísimo
    y oprimirá a sus santos;
tratará de cambiar las festividades
    y también las leyes,
y los santos quedarán bajo su poder
    durante tres años y medio.g
26Los jueces tomarán asiento,
    y al cuerno se le quitará el poder
    y se le destruirá para siempre.
27Entonces se dará a los santos,
    que son el pueblo del Altísimo,
la majestad y el poder
    y la grandeza de los reinos.

---

f 7:13 alguien con aspecto humano. Lit. como un hijo de hombre.   g 7:25 tres años y medio. Lit. un tiempo y tiempos y medio tiempo.

Su reino será un reino eterno,
　　y lo adorarán y obedecerán
　　todos los gobernantes de la tierra."

28»Aquí termina la visión. Yo, Daniel, me quedé desconcertado por tantas ideas que me pasaban por la *mente, a tal grado que palideció mi rostro. Pero preferí mantener todo esto en secreto.»h

Visión del carnero y del macho cabrío

8 «En el tercer año del reinado de Belsasar, yo, Daniel, tuve otra visión. 2En ella, me veía en la ciudadela de Susa, en la provincia de Elam, junto al río Ulay. 3Me fijé, y vi ante mí un carnero con sus dos cuernos. Estaba junto al río, y tenía cuernos largos. Uno de ellos era más largo, y le había salido después.

4»Me quedé observando cómo el carnero atacaba hacia el norte y hacia el sur. Ningún animal podía hacerle frente, ni había tampoco quien pudiera librarse de su poder. El carnero hacía lo que quería, y cada vez cobraba más fuerza.

5»Mientras reflexionaba yo al respecto, de pronto surgió del oeste un macho cabrío, con un cuerno enorme entre los ojos, y cruzó toda la tierra sin tocar siquiera el suelo. 6Se lanzó contra el carnero que yo había visto junto al río, y lo atacó furiosamente. 7Yo vi cómo lo golpeó y le rompió los dos cuernos. El carnero no pudo hacerle frente, pues el macho cabrío lo derribó y lo pisoteó. Nadie pudo librar al carnero del poder del macho cabrío.

8»El macho cabrío cobró gran fuerza, pero en el momento de su mayor grandeza se le rompió el cuerno más largo, y en su lugar brotaron cuatro grandes cuernos que se alzaron contra los cuatro vientos del cielo. 9De uno de ellos salió otro cuerno, pequeño al principio, que extendió su poder hacia el sur y hacia el este, y también hacia nuestra hermosa tierra. 10Creció hasta alcanzar al ejército de los cielos, derribó algunas estrellas y las pisoteó, 11y aun llegó a sentirse más importante que el jefe del ejército de los cielos. Por causa de él se eliminó el sacrificio diario y se profanó el santuario. 12Por la rebeldía de nuestro pueblo, su ejército echó por tierra la verdad y quitó el sacrificio diario. En fin, ese cuerno hizo y deshizo.

13»Escuché entonces que uno de los *santos hablaba, y que otro le preguntaba: "¿Cuánto más va a durar esta visión del sacrificio diario, de la rebeldía desoladora, de la entrega del santuario y de la humillación del ejército?" 14Y aquel santo me dijo: "Va a tardar dos mil trescientos días con sus noches. Después de eso, se *purificará el santuario."

Significado de la visión

15»Mientras yo, Daniel, contemplaba la visión y trataba de entenderla, de repente apareció ante mí alguien de apariencia *humana. 16Escuché entonces una voz que desde el río Ulay gritaba: "¡Gabriel, dile a este hombre lo que significa la visión!"

17»Cuando Gabriel se acercó al lugar donde yo estaba, me sentí aterrorizado y caí de rodillas. Pero él me dijo: "Toma en cuenta, criatura humana,i que la visión tiene que ver con la hora final."

18»Mientras Gabriel me hablaba, yo caí en un sueño profundo, de cara al suelo. Pero él me despertó y me obligó a levantarme, 19mientras me decía: "Voy a darte a conocer lo que sucederá cuando llegue a su fin el tiempo de la ira de Dios, porque el fin llegará en el momento señalado. 20El carnero de dos cuernos que has visto simboliza a los reyes de Media y de Persia. 21El macho cabrío es el rey de Grecia, y el cuerno grande que tiene entre los ojos es el primer rey. 22Los cuatro cuernos que salieron en lugar del que fue hecho pedazos simbolizan los cuatro reinos que surgirán de esa nación, pero que no tendrán el mismo poder.

23»Hacia el final de esos reinos, cuando los rebeldes lleguen al colmo de su maldad, surgirá un rey de rostro adusto, maestro de la intriga, 24que llegará a tener mucho poder, pero no por sí mismo. Ese rey causará impresionantes destrozos y saldrá airoso en todo lo que emprenda. Destruirá a los poderosos y al pueblo *santo. 25Con su astucia propagará el engaño, creyéndose un ser superior. Destruirá a mucha gente que creía estar segura, y se enfrentará al Príncipe de los príncipes, pero será destruido sin la intervención humana. 26Esta visión de los días con sus noches, que se te ha dado a conocer, es verdadera. Pero no la hagas pública, pues para eso falta mucho tiempo."

27»Yo, Daniel, quedé exhausto, y durante varios días guardé cama. Luego me levanté para seguir atendiendo los asuntos del reino. Pero la visión me dejó pasmado, pues no lograba comprenderla.

Oración de Daniel

9 1-2»Corría el primer año del reinado de Darío hijo de Jerjes, un medo que llegó a ser rey de los *babilonios, cuando yo, Daniel, logré entender ese pasaje de las Escrituras¡ donde el SEÑOR le comunicó al profeta Jeremías que la desolación de Jerusalén duraría setenta años. 3Entonces me puse a orar y a dirigir mis súplicas al Señor mi Dios. Además de orar, ayuné y me vestí de luto y me senté sobre cenizas. 4Ésta fue la oración y confesión que le hice:

»"Señor, Dios grande y terrible, que cumples tu *pacto de fidelidad con los que te aman y obedecen tus mandamientos: 5Hemos pecado y hecho lo malo; hemos sido malvados y rebeldes; nos hemos apartado de tus mandamientos y de tus *leyes. 6No hemos prestado atención a tus siervos los profetas, que en tu *nombre hablaron a nuestros reyes y príncipes, a nuestros antepasados y a todos los habitantes de la tierra.

7»"Tú, Señor, eres justo. Nosotros, en cambio, somos motivo de vergüenza en este día; nosotros, pueblo de Judá, habitantes de Jerusalén y de todo Israel, tanto los que vivimos cerca como los que se hallan lejos, en todos los países por los que nos has dispersado por haberte sido infieles.

8»"Señor, tanto nosotros como nuestros reyes y príncipes, y nuestros antepasados, somos motivo de vergüenza por haber pecado contra ti. 9Pero aun cuando nos hemos rebelado contra ti, tú, Señor nuestro, eres un Dios compasivo y perdonador.

10»"SEÑOR y Dios nuestro, no hemos obedecido ni seguido tus leyes, las cuales nos diste por medio de tus siervos los profetas. 11Todo Israel se ha apartado de tu ley y se ha negado a obedecerte. Por eso, porque pecamos contra ti, nos han sobrevenido las maldiciones que nos anunciaste, las cuales están escritas en la ley de tu siervo Moisés.

12»"Tú has cumplido las advertencias que nos hiciste, a nosotros y a nuestros gobernantes,

---

h 7:28 Aquí termina la porción aramea. Véase nota en 2:4. i 8:17 criatura humana. Lit. hijo de hombre. j 9:2 Alusión a Jer 25:11-12.

y has traído sobre nosotros esta gran calamidad. ¡Jamás ha ocurrido bajo el cielo nada semejante a lo que sucedió con Jerusalén!

13»"SEÑOR y Dios, todo este desastre ha venido sobre nosotros, tal y como está escrito en la ley de Moisés, y ni aun así hemos buscado tu favor. No nos hemos apartado de nuestros pecados ni hemos procurado entender tu verdad.

14»"Tú, SEÑOR y Dios nuestro, dispusiste esta calamidad y la has dejado caer sobre nosotros, porque eres justo en todos tus actos. ¡A pesar de todo, no te hemos obedecido!

15»"Señor y Dios nuestro, que con mano poderosa sacaste de Egipto a tu pueblo y te has hecho famoso, como hoy podemos ver: ¡Hemos pecado; hemos hecho lo malo! 16Aparta tu ira y tu furor de Jerusalén, como corresponde a tus actos de *justicia. Ella es tu ciudad y tu monte *santo. Por nuestros pecados, y por la iniquidad de nuestros antepasados, Jerusalén y tu pueblo son objeto de burla de cuantos nos rodean.

17»"Y ahora, Dios y Señor nuestro, escucha las oraciones y súplicas de este siervo tuyo. Haz honor a tu nombre y mira con amor a tu santuario, que ha quedado desolado. 18Préstanos oído, Dios nuestro; abre los ojos y mira nuestra desolación y la ciudad sobre la cual se invoca tu nombre. Al hacerte estas peticiones, no apelamos a nuestra rectitud sino a tu gran misericordia. 19¡Señor, escúchanos! ¡Señor, perdónanos! ¡Señor, atiéndenos y actúa! Dios mío, haz honor a tu nombre y no tardes más; itu nombre se invoca sobre tu ciudad y sobre tu pueblo!"

Las setenta semanas

20»Yo seguí hablando y orando al SEÑOR mi Dios. Le confesé mi pecado y el de mi pueblo Israel, y le supliqué en favor de su *santo monte. 21Se acercaba la hora del sacrificio vespertino. Y mientras yo seguía orando, el ángel Gabriel, a quien había visto en mi visión anterior, vino en raudo vuelo a verme 22y me hizo la siguiente aclaración:

»"Daniel, he venido en este momento para que entiendas todo con claridad. 23Tan pronto como empezaste a orar, Dios contestó tu oración. He venido a decírtelo porque tú eres muy apreciado. Presta, pues, atención a mis palabras, para que entiendas la visión.

24»"Setenta semanask han sido decretadas para que tu pueblo y tu santa ciudad pongan fin a sus transgresiones y pecados, pidan perdón por su maldad, establezcan para siempre la justicia, sellen la visión y la profecía, y consagren el lugar santísimo.

25»"Entiende bien lo siguiente: Habrá siete semanas desde la promulgación del decreto que ordena la reconstrucción de Jerusalén hasta la llegada del príncipe elegido.l Después de eso, habrá sesenta y dos semanas más. Entonces será reconstruida Jerusalén, con sus calles y murallas.m Pero cuando los tiempos apremien, 26después de las sesenta y dos semanas, se le quitará la vida al príncipe elegido. Éste se quedará sin ciudad y sin santuario, porque un futuro gobernante los destruirá. El fin vendrá como una inundación, y la destrucción no cesaráⁿ hasta que termine la guerra. 27Durante una semana ese gobernante hará un pacto con muchos, pero a media semana pon-

drá fin a los sacrificios y ofrendas. Sobre una de las alas del templo cometerá horribles sacrilegios, hasta que le sobrevenga el desastroso fin que le ha sido decretado." »

Daniel junto al río Tigris

10 En el tercer año del reinado de Ciro de Persia, Daniel tuvo una visión acerca de un gran ejército. El mensaje era verdadero, y Daniel, que también se llamaba Beltsasar, pudo comprender su significado en la visión.

2«En aquella ocasión yo, Daniel, pasé tres semanas como si estuviera de luto. 3En todo ese tiempo no comí nada especial, ni probé carne ni vino, ni usé ningún perfume. 4El día veinticuatro del mes primero, mientras me encontraba yo a la orilla del gran río Tigris, 5levanté los ojos y vi ante mí a un hombre vestido de lino, con un cinturón del oro más refinado. 6Su cuerpo brillaba como el topacio, y su rostro resplandecía como el relámpago; sus ojos eran dos antorchas encendidas, y sus brazos y piernas parecían de bronce bruñido; su voz resonaba como el eco de una multitud.

7»Yo, Daniel, fui el único que tuvo esta visión. Los que estaban conmigo, aunque no vieron nada, se asustaron y corrieron a esconderse. 8Nadie se quedó conmigo cuando tuve esta gran visión. Las fuerzas me abandonaron, palideció mi rostro, y me sentí totalmente desvalido. 9Fue entonces cuando oí que aquel hombre me hablaba. Mientras lo oía, caí en un profundo sueño, de cara al suelo. 10En ese momento una mano me agarró, me puso sobre mis manos y rodillas, 11y me dijo: "Levántate, Daniel, pues has sido enviado a verte. Tú eres muy apreciado, así que presta atención a lo que voy a decirte."

»En cuanto aquel hombre me habló, tembloroso me puse de pie. 12Entonces me dijo: "No tengas miedo, Daniel. Tu petición fue escuchada desde el primer día en que te propusiste ganar entendimiento y humillarte ante tu Dios. En respuesta a ella estoy aquí. 13Durante veintiún días el príncipe de Persia se me opuso, así que acudió en mi ayuda Miguel, uno de los príncipes de primer rango. Y me quedé allí, con los reyes de Persia. 14Pero ahora he venido a explicarte lo que va a suceder con tu pueblo en el futuro, pues la visión tiene que ver con el porvenir."

15»Mientras aquel hombre me decía esto, yo me incliné de cara al suelo y guardé silencio. 16Entonces alguien con aspecto *humano me tocó los labios, y yo los abrí y comencé a hablar. Y le dije a quien había estado hablando conmigo: "Señor, por causa de esta visión me siento muy angustiado y sin fuerzas. 17¿Cómo es posible que yo, que soy tu siervo, hable contigo? ¡Las fuerzas me han abandonado, y apenas puedo respirar!"

18»Una vez más, el de aspecto humano me tocó y me infundió fuerzas, 19al tiempo que me decía: "¡La *paz sea contigo, hombre altamente estimado! ¡Cobra ánimo, no tengas miedo!"

»Mientras él me hablaba, yo fui recobrando el ánimo y le dije: "Ya que me has reanimado, ¡háblame, Señor!" 20Y me dijo: "¿Sabes por qué he venido a verte? Pues porque debo volver a pelear contra el príncipe de Persia. Y cuando termine de luchar con él, hará su aparición el príncipe de Grecia. 21Pero antes de eso, te diré lo que está escrito en el libro de la verdad. En mi lucha contra ellos, sólo cuento con el apoyo de Miguel, el capitán de ustedes.

---

k **9:24** semanas. Lit. sietes; también en vv. 25-27. l **9:25** príncipe elegido. Lit. *Mesías príncipe. m **9:25** murallas. Alt. trincheras, o diques. n **9:26** no cesará. Lit. ha sido decretada.

11 »"Cuando Darío el Medo estaba en el primer año de su reinado, también le brindé mi apoyo y mi ayuda.

Los reyes del norte y del sur

2»"Pero ahora voy a darte a conocer la verdad. Van a levantarse en Persia tres reyes más, y hasta un cuarto, el cual será más rico que los otros tres. En cuanto haya cobrado fuerza con sus riquezas, incitará a todos contra el reino griego. 3Surgirá entonces un rey muy aguerrido, el cual gobernará con lujo de fuerza y hará lo que mejor le parezca. 4Pero tan pronto como surja su imperio, se resquebrajará y se esparcirá hacia los cuatro vientos del cielo. Este imperio no será para sus descendientes, ni tendrá el poder que tuvo bajo su gobierno, porque Dios lo dividirá y se lo entregará a otros.

5»"El rey del sur cobrará fuerza, pero uno de sus comandantes se hará más fuerte que él, y con alarde de poder gobernará sobre su propio imperio. 6Pasados algunos años harán una alianza: la hija del rey del sur se casará con el rey del norte, y harán las paces, aunque ella no retendrá su poder, y el poder del rey tampoco durará. Ella será traicionada, junto con su escolta, su hijo y su esposo.

»"En esos días, 7uno de la familia real usurpará el trono de la hija del rey del sur, y con su ejército atacará al rey del norte y a la fortaleza real, saliendo victorioso de la lucha. 8Se apoderará de las estatuas de metal de sus dioses, y de sus objetos de oro y plata, y se los llevará a Egipto, dejando tranquilo al rey del norte durante algunos años. 9Luego el rey del norte invadirá los dominios del rey del sur, pero se verá forzado a volver a su país. 10Tocará a sus hijos alistarse para la guerra, y reunirán a un gran ejército que, como una inundación, avanzará arrasándolo todo hasta llegar a la fortaleza.

11»"Enfurecido, el rey del sur marchará en contra del rey del norte, que será derrotado a pesar de contar con un gran ejército. 12Ante el triunfo obtenido, el rey del sur se llenará de orgullo y matará a miles, pero su victoria no durará 13porque el rey del norte reunirá a otro ejército, más numeroso y mejor armado que el anterior, y después de algunos años volverá a atacar al rey del sur.

14»"Mira, Daniel, por ese tiempo habrá muchos que se rebelarán contra el rey del sur, incluso gente violenta de tu pueblo, pero no saldrán victoriosos. Así se cumplirá la visión. 15Entonces el rey del norte vendrá y levantará rampas de asalto y conquistará la ciudad fortificada, pues las fuerzas del sur no podrán resistir, ¡ni siquiera las mejores tropas podrán ofrecer resistencia! 16El ejército invasor hará de las suyas, pues nadie podrá hacerle frente, y se establecerá en nuestra hermosa tierra, la cual quedará bajo su dominio. 17El rey del norte se dispondrá a atacar con todo el poder de su reino, pero hará una alianza con el rey del sur: éste le dará su hija en matrimonio, con miras a derrocar su reino, pero sus planes no tendrán el éxito esperado. 18Dirigirá entonces sus ataques contra las ciudades costeras, y conquistará muchas de ellas, pero un general responderá a su insolencia y lo hará quedar en ridículo. 19Después de eso, el rey del norte regresará a la fortaleza de su país, pero sufrirá un tropiezo y no volverá a saberse nada de él.

20»"Después del rey del norte, ocupará el trono un rey que, para mantener el esplendor del reino, enviará a un recaudador de impuestos. Pero poco tiempo después ese rey perderá la vida, aunque no en el fragor de la batalla.

21»"En su lugar reinará un hombre despreciable, indigno de ser rey, que invadirá el reino cuando la gente se sienta más segura y, recurriendo a artimañas, usurpará el trono. 22Arrasará como una inundación a las fuerzas que se le opongan; las derrotará por completo, lo mismo que al príncipe del pacto. 23Engañará a los que pacten con él, y con un grupo reducido usurpará el trono. 24Cuando las provincias más ricas se sientan más seguras, las invadirá, logrando así lo que jamás lograron sus padres y abuelos. Repartirá entre sus seguidores el botín y las riquezas que haya ganado en la guerra, y hará planes para atacar las ciudades fortificadas.

»"Pero esto no durará mucho tiempo. 25Envalentonado por su fuerza, ese hombre atacará al rey del sur con un gran ejército. Al frente de un ejército muy grande y poderoso, el rey del sur responderá al ataque; pero no podrá vencerlo, porque será traicionado. 26Los mismos que compartían su mesa buscarán su ruina; su ejército será derrotado por completo, y muchos caerán en batalla. 27Sentados a la misma mesa, estos dos reyes pensarán sólo en hacerse daño, y se mentirán el uno al otro; pero esto de nada servirá, porque el momento del fin todavía no habrá llegado. 28El rey del norte regresará a su país con grandes riquezas, pero antes profanará el *santo templo,ñ así que llevará a cabo sus planes y luego volverá a su país.

29»"En el momento preciso, el rey del norte volverá a invadir el sur, aunque esta vez el resultado será diferente, 30porque los barcos de guerra de las costas occidentales se opondrán a él y le harán perder el valor. Entonces retrocederá y descargará su enojo contra el santo templo. En su retirada, se mostrará bondadoso con los que renegaron de él. 31Sus fuerzas armadas se dedicarán a profanar la fortaleza del templo, y suspenderán el sacrificio diario, estableciendo el horrible sacrilegio. 32Corromperá con halagos a los que hayan renegado del pacto, pero los que conozcan a su Dios se le opondrán con firmeza.

33»"Los sabios instruirán a muchos, aunque durante algún tiempo morirán a filo de espada, o serán quemados, o se les tomará cautivos y se les despojará de todo. 34Cuando caigan, recibirán muy poca ayuda, aunque mucha gente hipócrita se les unirá. 35Algunos de los sabios caerán, pero esa prueba los *purificará y *perfeccionará, para que cuando llegue la hora final no tengan mancha alguna. Todavía falta mucho para que llegue el momento preciso.

El rey se exalta a sí mismo

36»"El rey hará lo que mejor le parezca. Se exaltará a sí mismo, se creerá superior a todos los dioses, y dirá cosas del Dios de dioses que nadie antes se atrevió a decir. Su éxito durará mientras la ira de Dios no llegue a su colmo, aunque lo que ha de suceder, sucederá. 37Ese rey no tomará en cuenta a los dioses de sus antepasados, ni al dios que adoran las mujeres, ni a ningún otro dios, sino que se exaltará a sí mismo por encima de todos ellos. 38En su lugar, adorará al dios de las fortalezas; honrará a un dios que sus antepasados no conocieron, y les presentará costosas ofrendas de oro, plata y piedras preciosas. 39Con la ayuda de un dios extraño atacará las fortalezas más poderosas, y rendirá grandes honores a aquellos que lo reconozcan, pues en recompensa

---

ñ **11:28** *templo.* Lit. *pacto;* también en v. 30.

los pondrá como gobernadores de grandes multitudes y les dará tierras.

40»"Cuando llegue la hora final, el rey del sur trabará combate contra el rey del norte, pero éste responderá a su ataque con carros y caballos y con toda una flota de barcos de guerra. Invadirá muchos países, y los arrasará como una inundación. 41También invadirá nuestro hermoso país, y muchos países caerán bajo su poder, aunque Edom y Moab y los jefes de Amón escaparán de sus manos. 42Extenderá su poder sobre muchos países, y ni Egipto podrá salvarse. 43Se adueñará de los tesoros de oro y plata de Egipto, y de todas sus riquezas, y también someterá a los libios y a los etíopes. 44Sin embargo, le llegarán noticias alarmantes del este y del norte, y en su furor se pondrá en marcha dispuesto a destruir y matar a mucha gente. 45Plantará su campamento real entre el mar y el bello monte *santo; pero allí le llegará su fin, y nadie acudirá en su ayuda.

La hora final

12 »"Entonces se levantará Miguel,
el gran príncipe protector de tu pueblo.
Habrá un período de angustia,
como no lo ha habido jamás
desde que las naciones existen.
Serán salvados los de tu pueblo,
cuyo *nombre se halla anotado en el libro,
2y del polvo de la tierra se levantarán
las multitudes de los que duermen,
algunos de ellos para vivir por siempre,
pero otros para quedar en la vergüenza
y en la confusión perpetuas.
3Los sabios resplandecerán
con el brillo de la bóveda celeste;

los que instruyen a las multitudes
en el *camino de la justicia
brillarán como las estrellas
por toda la eternidad.

4»"Tú, Daniel, guarda estas cosas en secreto y sella el libro hasta la hora final, pues muchos andarán de un lado a otro en busca de cualquier conocimiento."

5»Yo, Daniel, vi ante mí a otros dos hombres; uno de ellos estaba en una orilla del río, y el otro en la orilla opuesta. 6Uno de ellos le dijo al hombre vestido de lino, que estaba sobre las aguas del río: "¿Cuánto falta para que se cumplan estas cosas tan increíbles?"

7»Yo pude ver y oír cuando el hombre vestido de lino, que estaba sobre las aguas del río, levantó las manos al cielo y juró por el que vive para siempre: "Faltan tres años y medio.º Todo esto se cumplirá cuando el poder del pueblo *santo no vuelva a ser destruido."

8»Aunque escuché lo que dijo ese hombre, no pude entenderlo, así que le pregunté: "Señor, ¿en qué va a parar todo esto?" 9Y él me respondió: "Sigue adelante, Daniel, que estas cosas se mantendrán selladas y en secreto hasta que llegue la hora final. 10Muchos serán *purificados y *perfeccionados, y quedarán limpios, pero los malvados seguirán en su maldad. Ninguno de ellos entenderá nada, pero los sabios lo entenderán todo. 11A partir del momento en que se suspenda el sacrificio diario y se imponga el horrible sacrilegio, transcurrirán mil doscientos noventa días. 12¡*Dichoso el que espere a que hayan transcurrido mil trescientos treinta y cinco días! 13Pero tú, persevera hasta el fin y descansa, que al final de los tiempos te levantarás para recibir tu recompensa."»

º 12:7 *tres años y medio.* Lit. *un tiempo, tiempos y medio tiempo.*

OSEAS

1 Ésta es la palabra del SEÑOR que vino a Oseas hijo de Beerí durante los reinados de Uzías, Jotán, Acaz y Ezequías, reyes de Judá, y durante el reinado de Jeroboán hijo de Joás, rey de Israel.

La esposa y los hijos de Oseas

2La primera vez que el SEÑOR habló por medio de Oseas, le dijo: «Ve y toma por esposa una prostituta, y ten con ella hijos de prostitución, porque el país se ha prostituido por completo. ¡Se ha apartado del SEÑOR!»

3Oseas fue y tomó por esposa a Gómer, hija de Diblayin, la cual concibió y le dio a luz un hijo.

4Entonces el SEÑOR le dijo: «Ponle por *nombre Jezrel, porque dentro de poco haré que la casa real de Jehú pague por la masacre en Jezrel. Así pondré fin al dominio del reino de Israel. 5Ese día quebraré el arco de Israel en el valle de Jezrel.»

6Gómer volvió a concebir y dio a luz una niña. Entonces el SEÑOR le dijo a Oseas: «Ponle por nombre: "Indigna de compasión",a porque no volveré a compadecerme del reino de Israel, sino que le negaré el perdón. 7En cambio, tendré compasión de la tribu de Judá, y la salvaré; pero no por medio de arco, ni de espada ni de batallas, ni tampoco por medio de caballos y jinetes, sino por medio del SEÑOR su Dios.»

8Cuando Gómer destetó a la llamada «Indigna de compasión», volvió a concebir y tuvo otro hijo. 9Entonces el SEÑOR le dijo a Oseas: «Ponle por nombre: "Pueblo ajeno",b porque ni ustedes son mi pueblo, ni yo soy su Dios.

10»Con todo, los israelitas serán tan numerosos como la arena del mar, que no se puede medir ni contar. Y en el mismo lugar donde se les llamó: "Pueblo ajeno", se les llamará: "Hijos del Dios viviente". 11El pueblo de Judá se reunirá con el pueblo de Israel, y nombrarán un solo jefe y resurgirán en su país, porque grande será el día de Jezrel.

2 »Llamen a sus hermanos: "Pueblo mío",c y a sus hermanas: "Compadecidas".d

Castigo y restauración de Israel

2»¡Échenle en cara a su madre
que ni ella es mi esposa ni yo su esposo!
¡Que se quite del rostro el maquillaje de
prostituta,
y de entre los pechos los adornos de
ramera!
3De lo contrario, la desnudaré por completo;
la dejaré como el día en que nació.
La pondré como un desierto:
¡la convertiré en tierra seca y la mataré de
sed!
4No tendré compasión de sus hijos,
porque son hijos de prostitución.
5Su madre es una prostituta;
¡la que lo concibió es una sinvergüenza!
Pues dijo: "Quiero ir tras mis amantes,
que me dan mi pan y mi agua,
mi lana y mi lino, mi aceite y mis bebidas."
6Por eso le cerraré el paso con espinos;
la encerraré para que no encuentre el
camino.
7Con ardor perseguirá a sus amantes,

y al no encontrarlos dirá:
"Prefiero volver con mi primer esposo,
porque antes me iba mejor que ahora."
8Ella no ha querido reconocer que soy yo
quien le da el grano, el vino nuevo y el
aceite.
Yo le he multiplicado la plata y el oro,
¿y que hizo con ellos? ¡Falsos dioses!e

9»Por eso, llegado el momento
le quitaré mi trigo y mi vino nuevo.
La dejaré sin la lana y el lino
que le di para cubrir su desnudez.
10Voy a exhibir su desvergüenza
a la vista de sus amantes,
y nadie la librará de mi mano.
11Pondré fin a todo su jolgorio:
sus peregrinaciones, sus lunas nuevas,
sus días de reposo, y sus fiestas solemnes.
12Devastaré sus vides y sus higueras,
que consideraba la paga de sus amantes.
Las convertiré en maleza,
y los animales del campo acabarán con ellas.
13La llamaré a cuentas por los días
en que quemaba ofrendas a sus falsos
dioses,
cuando se adornaba con zarcillos y joyas,
y olvidándose de mí, se iba tras sus
amantes
—afirma el SEÑOR—.

14»Por eso, ahora voy a seducirla:
me la llevaré al desierto
y le hablaré con ternura.
15Allí le devolveré sus viñedos,
y convertiré el valle de la Desgraciaf
en el paso de la Esperanza.
Allí me corresponderá, como en los días de su
juventud,
como en el día en que salió de Egipto.

16»En aquel día —afirma el SEÑOR—,
ya no me llamarás: "mi señor",g
sino que me dirás: "esposo mío".
17Te quitaré de los labios el nombre de tus
falsos dioses,
y nunca más volverás a invocarlos.
18Aquel día haré en tu favor un pacto
con los animales del campo,
con las aves de los cielos
y con los reptiles de la tierra.
Eliminaré del país arcos, espadas y guerra,
para que todos duerman seguros.
19Yo te haré mi esposa para siempre,
y te daré como dote el derecho y la justicia,
el amor y la compasión.
20Te daré como dote mi fidelidad,
y entonces conocerás al SEÑOR.

21»En aquel día yo responderé
—afirma el SEÑOR—;
yo le responderé al cielo,
y el cielo le responderá a la tierra;
22la tierra les responderá al cereal,
al vino nuevo y al aceite,
y éstos le responderán a Jezrel.h

---

a **1:6** *Indigna de compasión.* Lit. *Lorrujama;* también en v. 8, y véase 2:23. b **1:9** *Pueblo ajeno.* Lit. *Loamí.* c **2:1** *Pueblo mío.* Lit. *Amí.* d **2:1** *Compadecidas.* Lit. *Rujama.* e **2:8** *Falsos dioses.* Lit. **Baales;* también en vv. 13 y 17. f **2:15** *la Desgracia.* Lit. *Acor;* véase Jos 7:24-26. g **2:16** *señor.* Lit. *baal.* h **2:22** En hebreo, *Jezrel* significa *Dios siembra.*

²³Yo la sembraré para mí en la tierra;
  me compadeceré de la "Indigna de
    compasión",
a "Pueblo ajeno" lo llamaré: "Pueblo mío";ⁱ
y él me dirá: "Mi Dios".»

Oseas se reconcilia con su esposa

3 Me habló una vez más el SEÑOR, y me dijo: «Ve y ama a esa mujer adúltera, que es amante de otro. Ámala como ama el SEÑOR a los israelitas, aunque se hayan vuelto a dioses ajenos y se deleiten con las tortas de pasas que les ofrecen.»

²Compré entonces a esa mujer por quince monedas de plataⁱ y una carga y media de cebada,ᵏ ³y le dije: «Vas a vivir conmigo mucho tiempo, pero sin prostituirte. No tendrás relaciones sexuales con ningún otro hombre. ¡Ni yo te voy a tocar!»

⁴Ciertamente los israelitas vivirán mucho tiempo sin rey ni gobernante, sin sacrificio ni altares, ni *efod ni ídolos. ⁵Pero después los israelitas buscarán nuevamente al SEÑOR su Dios, y a David su rey. En los últimos días acudirán con temor reverente al Señor y a sus bondades.

Pleito contra Israel

4 Escuchen, israelitas,
    la palabra del SEÑOR,
  porque el SEÑOR va a entrar en juicio
    contra los habitantes del país:

«Ya no hay entre mi pueblo fidelidad ni amor,
  ni *conocimiento de Dios.
²Cunden, más bien, el perjurio y la mentira.
  Abundan el robo, el adulterio y el
    asesinato.
  ¡Un homicidio sigue a otro!
³Por tanto, se resecará la tierra,
  y desfallecerán todos sus habitantes.
  ¡Morirán las bestias del campo,
  las aves del cielo y los peces del mar!
⁴»¡Que nadie acuse ni reprenda a nadie!
  ¡Tu pueblo parece acusar al sacerdote!
⁵Tropiezas de día y de noche,
  y los profetas tropiezan contigo;
tu madre dejará de existir,
  ⁶pues por falta de conocimiento
mi pueblo ha sido destruido.

»Puesto que rechazaste el conocimiento,
yo también te rechazo como mi sacerdote.
Ya que te olvidaste de la *ley de tu Dios,
  yo también me olvidaré de tus hijos.
⁷Mientras más aumentaban los sacerdotes,
  más pecaban contra mí;
cambiaron a quien es su gloria
  en algo deshonroso.
⁸El pecado de mi pueblo es su comida;
  se regodean en su perversidad.
⁹¡De tal pueblo, tal sacerdote!ˡ
  ¡Por eso les pediré cuentas de su conducta
  y les daré la paga de sus acciones!

¹⁰»Comerán, pero no quedarán satisfechos;
  se prostituirán, pero no se saciarán;ᵐ
porque han abandonado al SEÑOR
  para entregarse

¹¹a la prostitución y al vino,
  ¡al mosto que hace perder la razón!
¹²Mi pueblo consulta a su ídolo de madera,
  y ese pedazo de palo le responde;
su tendencia a prostituirse los descarría;
  se prostituyen en abierto desafío a su Dios.
¹³En la cumbre de montes y colinas
  queman ofrendas y ofrecen sacrificios,
bajo la agradable sombra
  de robles, álamos y encinas.
Por eso se prostituyen sus hijas
  y cometen adulterio sus nueras.
¹⁴Pero no las castigaré
  por sus prostituciones y adulterios,
porque sus propios maridos
  se juntan con prostitutas
y celebran banquetes paganos
  con las sacerdotisas del templo.
¡Es así como acaba por hundirse
  un pueblo falto de entendimiento!

¹⁵»Si tú, Israel, te prostituyes,
  ¡que no resulte culpable Judá!

»No vayan a Guilgal ni suban a Bet Avén,ⁿ
  ni juren: "¡Por la vida del SEÑOR!"
¹⁶Israel es tan indómito como una novilla.
  ¿Cómo podrá el SEÑOR pastorearlos
  en campo abierto, como a corderos?
¹⁷Efraín se ha aliado con las imágenes;
  ¡pues que se quede con ellas!
¹⁸Cuando ya no tienen licor,
  se entregan de lleno a la prostitución,
  ¡y hasta sus gobernantes aman la deshonra!
¹⁹¡Por eso un torbellino los arrastrará,
  y quedarán avergonzados por sus
    sacrificios!

Juicio contra Israel

5 »¡Oigan esto, sacerdotes!
    ¡Pon atención, reino de Israel!
  ¡Escucha, casa real!
    ¡Contra ustedes es la sentencia!
  En Mizpa han sido ustedes una trampa;
    en el monte Tabor, una red tendida;
²en Sitín, una fosa abierta.ñ
  Por eso, yo los disciplinaré.
³Yo conozco bien a Efraín;
  Israel no me es desconocido.
Pero ahora Efraín se ha prostituido;
  e Israel se ha mancillado.

⁴»No les permiten sus malas obras
  volverse a su Dios;
su tendencia a prostituirse
  les impide conocer al SEÑOR.
⁵La arrogancia de Israel testificará en su contra,
  Israel y Efraín tropezarán con su maldad,
  y hasta Judá caerá con ellos.
⁶Con sus ovejas y sus vacas
  irán en busca del SEÑOR,
pero no lo encontrarán
  porque él se ha apartado de ellos.
⁷Han traicionado al SEÑOR;
  han dado a luz hijos de otros padres.
  ¡Ahora la destruccióno devorará sus fincas!

ⁱ **2:23** *Indigna de compasión ... Pueblo ajeno ... Pueblo mío.* Véanse 1:6,8; 2:1 y notas. ʲ **3:2** *quince monedas de plata.* Lit. *quince {*siclos} de plata.* ᵏ **3:2** *una carga y media de cebada.* Lit. *un *jómer de cebada y un *létec de cebada.* ˡ **4:9** *¡De tal ... sacerdote!* Alt. *Al pueblo le irá como al sacerdote.* ᵐ **4:10** *no se saciarán.* Alt. *no tendrán hijos.* ⁿ **4:15** *Bet Avén,* nombre que significa *casa de iniquidad,* se aplica aquí a la ciudad de Betel, que significa *casa de Dios* (véase también 5:8). ñ **5:2** *en Sitín ... abierta* (lectura probable); en TM, texto de difícil traducción. o **5:7** *la destrucción* (lectura probable); *la fiesta de luna nueva* (TM).

8»Toquen la corneta en Guibeá,
　　hagan sonar la trompeta en Ramá,
　lancen el grito de guerra en Bet Avén:p
　　"¡Cuídate las espaldas, Benjamín!"
9En el día de la represión,
　　Efraín quedará desolado.
　Entre las tribus de Israel
　　doy a conocer lo que les va a pasar.
10Las autoridades de Judá se parecen
　a los que alteran los linderos.
　¡Pues derramaré mi enojo sobre ellos
　　como si derramara un torrente de agua!
11Efraín está deprimido,
　　aplastado por el juicio,
　empeñado en seguir a los ídolos.q
12¡Pues seré para Efraín como polilla,
　　como carcoma para el pueblo de Judá!

13»Cuando Efraín vio su enfermedad
　　y Judá reparó en sus llagas,
　Efraín recurrió a Asiria
　　y pidió la ayuda del gran rey.
　Pero el rey no podrá sanarlo,
　　ni tampoco curar sus llagas.
14Yo seré como un león para Efraín,
　　como un cachorro para Judá.
　Yo mismo los haré pedazos,
　　y luego me alejaré;
　yo mismo me llevaré la presa,
　　y no habrá quien me la arrebate.
15Volveré luego a mi morada,
　　hasta que reconozcan su culpa.
　Buscarán ganarse mi favor;
　　angustiados, me buscarán con ansias.»

Impenitencia de Israel

6 ¡Vengan, volvámonos al SEÑOR!
　　Él nos ha despedazado, pero nos sanará;
　nos ha herido, pero nos vendará.
2Después de dos días nos dará vida;
　al tercer día nos levantará,
　y así viviremos en su presencia.
3Conozcamos al SEÑOR;
　vayamos tras su conocimiento.
　Tan cierto como que sale el sol,
　　él habrá de manifestarse;
　vendrá a nosotros como la lluvia de invierno,
　como la lluvia de primavera que riega la
　　　tierra.

4«¿Qué voy a hacer contigo, Efraín?
　　¿Qué voy a hacer contigo, Judá?
　El amor de ustedes es como nube matutina,
　　como rocío que temprano se evapora.
5Por eso los hice pedazos por medio de los
　　　profetas;
　los herí con las palabras de mi boca.
　¡Mi sentencia los fulminará como un
　　　relámpago!
6Lo que pido de ustedes es amor y no
　　　sacrificios,
　conocimiento de Dios y no *holocaustos
7Son como Adán:
　　han quebrantado el *pacto,
　¡me han traicionado!
8Galaad es una ciudad de malhechores;
　　sus pisadas dejan huellas de sangre.
9Una pandilla de sacerdotes
　　está al acecho en el camino a Siquén,

　y como banda de salteadores,
　　comete toda clase de infamias.
10En el reino de Israel
　　he visto algo horrible:
　Allí se prostituye Efraín
　　y se mancilla Israel.

11»¡A ti también, Judá,
　　te espera la cosecha de tu maldad!

　»Cuando cambie yo la suerte de mi pueblo,

7 cuando sane yo a Israel,
　　la perversidad de Efraín y la maldad de
　　　Samaria
　quedarán al descubierto.
　Porque ellos cometen fraudes;
　　mientras el ladrón se mete en las casas,
　una banda de salteadores roba en las calles.
2No se ponen a pensar
　　que yo tomo en cuenta todas sus maldades.
　Sus malas acciones los tienen cercados,
　　y las tengo muy presentes.

3»Con su maldad deleitan al rey;
　　con sus mentiras, a las autoridades.
4Parecen un horno encendido
　　cuyo fuego no hace falta atizar
　desde que el panadero prepara la harina
　　hasta que la masa fermenta.
　¡Todos ellos son adúlteros!
5En la fiesta del rey las autoridades se
　　　encienden
　　bajo los efectos del vino,
　y el rey pierde su dignidad
　　codeándose con la plebe.
6Como el horno, se les prende el corazón,
　　dispuesto para la intriga.
　Su ira se adormece por la noche,
　　pero se reaviva por la mañana.
7Todos ellos arden como un horno;
　　devoran a sus gobernantes.
　Caen todos sus reyes,
　　pero ninguno de ellos me invoca.

8»Efraín se mezcla con las naciones;
　　parece una torta cocida de un solo lado.
9Los extranjeros le minan las fuerzas,
　　pero él ni cuenta se da.
　Su pelo se ha encanecido,
　　pero él ni cuenta se da.
10La arrogancia de Israel testifica en su contra,
　　pero él no se vuelve al SEÑOR su Dios;
　a pesar de todo esto, no lo busca.

11»Efraín es como una paloma
　　torpe y sin entendimiento,
　que unas veces pide ayuda a Egipto
　　y otras, recurre a Asiria.
12Pero tan pronto como lo hagan,
　　lanzaré mi red sobre ellos;
　los derribaré como a las aves del cielo,
　　¡siete veces los castigaré por sus pecados!r
13¡Ay de ellos, que de mí se alejaron!
　　¡Que sean destruidos por rebelarse contra
　　　mí!
　Yo bien podría redimirlos,
　　pero ellos no me hablan con la verdad.
14No me invocan de *corazón,
　　sino que se lamentan echados en sus
　　　camas.

Para obtener grano y vino nuevo se laceran[s]
y se ponen en mi contra.
[15]Yo adiestré y fortalecí sus brazos,
pero ellos maquinan maldades contra mí.
[16]No se vuelven al *Altísimo;
son como un arco engañoso.
Sus autoridades caerán a filo de espada
por sus palabras insolentes,
y en la tierra de Egipto
se burlarán de ellos.

Siembran vientos y cosechan torbellinos

8 »¡Da el toque de trompeta!
¡Un águila se cierne sobre la casa del SEÑOR!
Han quebrantado mi *pacto
y se han rebelado contra mi *ley,
[2]y ahora vienen a suplicarme:
"¡Dios de Israel, te conocemos!"
[3]Pero Israel ha rechazado el bien,
así que un enemigo lo perseguirá.
[4]Establecen reyes que yo no apruebo,
y escogen autoridades que no conozco.
Con su plata y con su oro se hacen imágenes
para su propia destrucción.
[5]Samaria, ¡arroja el becerro
que tienes por ídolo!
Contra ustedes se ha encendido mi ira.
¿Hasta cuándo estarán sin *purificarse?
[6]Oye, Israel: Ese becerro no es Dios;
es obra de un escultor.
Ese becerro de Samaria
será hecho pedazos.

[7]»Sembraron vientos
y cosecharán tempestades.
El tallo no tiene espiga
y no producirá harina;
si acaso llegara a producirla,
se la tragarían los extranjeros.
[8]Pues a Israel se lo han tragado,
y hoy es de poca estima entre las naciones.
[9]Los israelitas subieron a Asiria;
se apartaron como terco asno salvaje,
y Efraín se ha comprado amantes.
[10]Pero aunque se los compre entre las naciones,
de allí volveré a reunirlos;
y comenzarán a retorcerse
bajo la opresión de un rey poderoso.

[11]»Efraín edificó muchos altares
para *expiar sus pecados,
pero éstos se han convertido
en altares para pecar.
[12]Yo podría escribirles mi ley muchas veces,
pero ellos la verían como algo extraño.
[13]Me han ofrecido sacrificios y ofrendas,
y se han comido la carne,
pero eso a mí no me agrada.
Voy ahora a tomar en cuenta sus
perversidades,
y castigaré sus pecados;
¡y tendrán que regresar a Egipto!
[14]Israel se olvidó de su Hacedor y se edificó
palacios;
Judá multiplicó las ciudades amuralladas;
pero yo lanzaré sobre sus ciudades y
fortalezas
un fuego que las consuma.»

El castigo a Israel

9 No te alegres, Israel;
no hagas fiesta como las naciones.
Porque te has prostituido:
¡le has sido infiel a tu Dios!
Prefieres la paga de prostituta
que recibes en todos los trigales.[t]
[2]Ni el trigo ni las uvas podrán alimentarlos;
el vino nuevo no tendrá el gusto que
esperaban.
[3]No habitarán en la tierra del SEÑOR;
Efraín regresará a Egipto
y comerá inmundicias en Asiria.
[4]No le ofrecerán al SEÑOR más libaciones de
vino,
ni le serán gratos sus sacrificios.
Se les volverá pan de lágrimas;
quienes lo coman quedarán *impuros.
Tal vez les sirva para matar el hambre,
pero no tendrá cabida en la casa del SEÑOR.

[5]¿Qué harán ustedes en los días de fiesta,
o en las peregrinaciones en honor del
SEÑOR?
[6]Aunque escapen de la destrucción,
los recogerá Egipto y los enterrará Menfis.
Sus tesoros de plata se llenarán de ortigas,
y los espinos invadirán sus carpas.
[7]Han llegado los días del castigo;
han llegado los días de la retribución.
¡Que lo sepa Israel!
Es tan grande tu maldad,
y tan intensa tu hostilidad,
que al profeta se le tiene por necio,
y al hombre inspirado por loco.
[8]El profeta, junto con Dios,
es el centinela de Efraín,[u]
pero enfrenta trampas en todos sus caminos,
y hostilidad en la casa de su Dios.
[9]Han llegado al colmo de la corrupción,
como en los días de Guibeá;
¡pero Dios se acordará de sus perversidades
y los castigará por sus pecados!

[10]«Cuando encontré a Israel,
fue como hallar uvas en el desierto;
cuando vi a sus antepasados,
fue como ver higos tiernos en la higuera.
Pero ellos se fueron a Baal Peor
y se entregaron a la vergüenza;
¡se volvieron tan detestables
como el objeto de su amor!
[11]El esplendor de Efraín saldrá volando, como
un ave;
no habrá más concepción ni embarazo ni
nacimiento.
[12]Y aun cuando vean crecer a sus hijos,
yo los arrebataré de este mundo.
¡Ay de ellos cuando los abandone!
[13]He visto a Efraín y a Tiro plantados en una
pradera.[v]
¡Pero Efraín entregará sus hijos al
verdugo!»
[14]Dales, SEÑOR ... ¿qué les darás?
¡Dales vientres que aborten y pechos
resecos!

[15]«Toda su maldad comenzó en Guilgal;

---

[s] **7:14** *se laceran* (mss. hebreos y LXX); *residen como extranjeros* (TM).   [t] **9:1** *trigales.* Lit. *eras.*   [u] **9:8** *El profeta ... de Efraín.*
Alt. *El profeta es el centinela de Efraín,* / *el pueblo de mi Dios.*   [v] **9:13** *He visto ... pradera.* Texto de difícil traducción.

allí comencé a aborrecerlos.
Por causa de sus maldades,
los expulsaré de mi casa.
No volveré a amarlos,
pues todas sus autoridades son rebeldes.
16Efraín se ha marchitado:
su raíz se secó y no produce fruto.
Aunque llegue a tener hijos,
mataré el precioso fruto de su vientre.»

17Como no lo obedecieron, mi Dios los
rechazará;
¡andarán errantes entre las naciones!

10 Israel era una vid frondosa
que daba fruto a su antojo.
Pero cuanto más aumentaba su fruto,
más altares se construía;
cuanto más prosperaba su país,
más hermosas hacía sus *piedras sagradas.
2Su *corazón es escurridizo,
pero tendrá que cargar con su culpa.
El SEÑOR destrozará sus altares
y devastará sus piedras sagradas.
3Tal vez dirán: «No hemos temido al SEÑOR,
y por eso no tenemos rey.
Pero aun si lo tuviéramos,
¿qué podría hacer por nosotros?»
4Hablan sólo por hablar;
juran en falso y hacen tratos;
¡por eso florecen los pleitos
como la mala yerba en el campo!
5Temen los moradores de Samaria
por el becerro que adoran en Bet Avén.w
El pueblo del becerro hará duelo por él,
lo mismo que sus sacerdotes idólatras.
Harán lamentos por su esplendor,
porque se lo llevarán al destierro.
6El becerro será llevado a Asiria
como tributo para el gran rey.
Efraín quedará avergonzado;
Israel se avergonzará de sus ídolos.x
7Samaria y su rey desaparecerán
como rama arrastrada por el agua.
8Serán destruidos sus *santuarios paganos,
lugares de pecado de Israel.
¡Cardos y espinos crecerán sobre sus
altares!
Entonces dirán a las montañas: «¡Cúbrannos!»,
y a las colinas: «¡Caigan sobre nosotros!»

9«Tú, Israel, has venido pecando
desde los días de Guibeá,
y allí te has mantenido.
¡En Guibeá la guerra
tomará por sorpresa a los malvados!
10Cuando yo quiera, los castigaré;
entonces las naciones se juntarán contra
ellos
para aprisionarlos por su doble perversión.
11Efraín es una novilla adiestrada
a la que le gusta trillar,
pero yo no quise ponerle el yugo.
Pero ahora voy a uncir a Efraín,
y Judá tendrá que arar,
y Jacob emparejará la tierra.»

12¡Siembren para ustedes *justicia!
¡Cosechen el fruto del amor,

y pónganse a labrar el barbecho!
¡Ya es tiempo de buscar al SEÑOR!,
hasta que él venga y les envíe lluvias de
justicia.
13Pero ustedes sembraron maldad, cosecharon
crímenes
y comieron el fruto de la mentira,
porque confiaron en sus carros
y en la multitud de sus guerreros.
14Un estruendo de guerra se levantará contra
su pueblo,
y todas sus fortalezas serán devastadas,
como devastó Salmán a Bet Arbel en el día de
la batalla,
cuando las madres fueron destrozadas
junto con sus hijos.
15Esto es lo que Betel les hizo a ustedes,
a causa de su extrema maldad.
¡Pues el rey de Israel será destruido por
completo
en cuanto amanezca!

El amor de Dios por Israel

11 «Desde que Israel era niño, yo lo amé;
de Egipto llamé a mi hijo.
2Pero cuanto más lo llamaba,
más se alejaba de mí.y
Ofrecía sacrificios a sus falsos diosesz
y quemaba incienso a las imágenes.
3Yo fui quien enseñó a caminar a Efraín;
yo fui quien lo tomó de la mano.
Pero él no quiso reconocer
que era yo quien lo sanaba.
4Lo atraje con cuerdas de ternura,a
lo atraje con lazos de amor.
Le quité de la cerviz el yugo,
y con ternura me acerqué para alimentarlo.

5»No volverán a Egipto,
sino que Asiria reinará sobre ellos,
porque no quisieron volverse a mí.
6En sus ciudades se blandirán espadas,
que destrozarán los barrotes de sus
*puertas
y acabarán con sus planes.
7Mi pueblo está resuelto a renegar de mi
*nombre;
por eso, aunque me invoquen, no los
exaltaré.

8»¿Cómo podría yo entregarte, Efraín?
¿Cómo podría abandonarte, Israel?
¡Yo no podría entregarte como entregué a
Admá!
¡Yo no podría abandonarte como a
Zeboyín!
Dentro de mí, el *corazón me da vuelcos,
y se me conmueven las entrañas.
9Pero no daré rienda suelta a mi ira,
ni volveré a destruir a Efraín.
Porque en medio de ti no está un *hombre,
sino estoy yo, el Dios *santo,
y no atacaré la ciudad.»

10El SEÑOR rugirá como león,
y ellos lo seguirán.
Cuando el SEÑOR lance su rugido,
sus hijos vendrán temblando de occidente.

w 10:5 Véase nota en 4:15. x 10:6 sus ídolos (lectura probable); sus planes (TM). y 11:2 llamaba ... de mí (LXX); llamaban ...
de ellos (TM). z 11:2 falsos dioses. Lit. *baales. a 11:4 de ternura. Lit. humanas.

11«Vendrán desde Egipto, temblando como
        aves;
    vendrán desde Asiria, temblando como
        palomas,
    y yo los estableceré en sus casas
        —afirma el SEÑOR—.

El pecado de Israel

12»Efraín me ha rodeado de mentiras,
    y el reino de Israel con fraude;
Judá anda errante, lejos de Dios;
    ¡lejos del Dios santísimo y fiel!

12 Efraín se alimenta de viento:
    todo el día va tras el viento solano,
    y multiplica la mentira y la violencia.
Hace pactos con Asiria,
    y a Egipto le da aceite como tributo.»

2El SEÑOR tiene un pleito contra Judá:
    le hará pagar a Jacobᵇ todo lo que ha hecho,
    le dará lo que merecen sus obras.
3Ya en el seno materno suplantó a su hermano,
    y cuando se hizo hombre luchó con Dios.
4Luchó con el ángel, y lo venció;
    lloró y le rogó que lo favoreciera.
Se lo encontró en Betel,
    y allí habló con él;
5¡habló con el SEÑOR, Dios *Todopoderoso,
    cuyo *nombre es el SEÑOR!
6Pero tú debes volverte a tu Dios,
    practicar el amor y la justicia,
    y confiar siempre en él.

7Canaánᶜ usa balanzas fraudulentas,
    pues le gusta explotar a los demás.
8Efraín dice con jactancia:
    «¡Cómo me he enriquecido!
    ¡He amasado una gran fortuna!
    En todas mis ganancias no encontrarán
    que haya pecado en algo.»

9«Yo soy el SEÑOR tu Dios
    desde que estabas en Egipto,
    y haré que vuelvas a vivir en carpas,
    como en los días de nuestro encuentro en
        el desierto.ᵈ
10Yo les hablé a los profetas;
    les hice tener muchas visiones,
    y por medio de ellos les hablé en
        parábolas.»

11¿Es Galaad malvado?
    ¡No hay duda de que no vale nada!
    En Guilgal sacrifica toros;
    por eso sus altares quedarán reducidos a
        montones de piedra
    entre los surcos del campo.
12Jacob huyó a un campo de Aram;ᵉ
    Israel trabajó cuidando ovejas
    en pago por su esposa.
13Para sacar a Israel de Egipto, y después
        cuidarlo,
    el SEÑOR usó a un profeta.
14Pero Efraín ha irritado a su SEÑOR;
    le ha causado un amargo disgusto.
    Por eso el SEÑOR le hará pagar sus crímenes
    y le devolverá sus injurias.

La ira del SEÑOR contra Israel

13 Efraín tenía la preeminencia en Israel.
    Cuando él hablaba, la gente temblaba.
Pero le rindió culto a *Baal,
    y por ese pecado murió.
2Sin embargo, siguen pecando,
    pues se fabrican, según su ingenio,
    imágenes de fundición e ídolos de plata
    que no son más que obra de artesanos.
De ellos se dice:
    «Ofrecen sacrificios humanos
    y besan ídolos en forma de becerros.»ᶠ
3Por eso serán como nube matutina,
    como rocío que temprano se evapora,
    como paja que se lleva el viento,
    como humo que se escapa por la chimenea.

4«Pero yo soy el SEÑOR tu Dios
    desde que estabas en Egipto.
No conocerás a otro Dios fuera de mí,
    ni a otro Salvador que no sea yo.
5Porque yo fui el que te conoció en el desierto,
    en esa tierra de terrible aridez.
6Les di de comer, y quedaron saciados,
    y una vez satisfechos, se volvieron
        arrogantes
    y se olvidaron de mí.
7Por eso, yo seré para ellos como un león;
    los acecharé junto al camino, como un
        leopardo.
8Los atacaré y les desgarraré el pecho
    como una osa a quien le quitan sus
        cachorros.
    ¡Los devoraré como un león!
    ¡Los despedazaré como fiera del campo!

9»Voy a destruirte, Israel,
    porque estás contra quien te ayuda.
10¿Dónde está tu rey,
    para que te salve en todas tus ciudades?
¿Dónde están los gobernantes, de los que
        decías:
    "Dame rey y autoridades"?
11En mi ira te di rey,
    y en mi enojo te lo quité.
12La perversidad de Efraín está bien guardada;
    se ha tomado nota de su pecado.
13Llegan los dolores de parto,
    pero él es una criatura necia:
    ¡cuando llega la hora del parto,
    no se acomoda para salir!

14»¿Habré de rescatarlos del poder del
        *sepulcro?
    ¿Los redimiré de la muerte?
¿Dónde está, oh muerte, tus plagas?
    ¿Dónde está, oh sepulcro, tu destrucción?
    ¡Vengan, que no les tendré misericordia!»

15Aunque Efraín prospere entre sus hermanos,
    vendrá el viento del SEÑOR,
    el viento solano que se levanta del desierto,
    y se agotarán sus fuentes y manantiales.
    ¡Y arrebatará sus tesoros,
    todos sus objetos preciosos!
16El pueblo de Samaria cargará con su culpa
    por haberse rebelado contra su Dios.

ᵇ **12:2** En hebreo, *Jacob* significa *él agarra el talón* (en sentido figurado: *él suplanta* o *engaña*).   ᶜ **12:7** *Canaán.* Alt. *El merca-der.*   ᵈ **12:9** *de nuestro encuentro en el desierto.* Alt. *de fiestas solemnes.*   ᵉ **12:12** *Aram.* Es decir, al noroeste de Mesopota-mia.   ᶠ **13:2** *De ellos ... becerros.* Alt. *Dicen a la gente: «Quien ofrezca sacrificios, que bese a los becerros.»*   ᵍ **13:4** *No conocerás.* Alt. *No deberías haber conocido.*

Caerán a filo de espada;
ia los niños los lanzarán contra el suelo,
y a las embarazadas les abrirán el vientre!

Arrepentimiento para traer bendición

14 Vuélvete, Israel, al SEÑOR tu Dios.
iTu perversidad te ha hecho caer!
2Piensa bien lo que le dirás,
y vuélvete al SEÑOR con este ruego:
«Perdónanos nuestra perversidad,
y recíbenos con benevolencia,
pues queremos ofrecerte
el fruto de nuestros labios.
3Asiria no podrá salvarnos;
no montaremos caballos de guerra.
Nunca más llamaremos "dios nuestro"
a cosas hechas por nuestras manos,
pues en ti el huérfano halla compasión.»

Respuesta de Dios

4«Yo corregiré su rebeldía
y los amaré de pura gracia,
porque mi ira contra ellos se ha calmado.

5Yo seré para Israel como el rocío,
y lo haré florecer como lirio.
iHundirá sus raíces como cedro del Líbano!
6Sus vástagos crecerán,
y tendrán el esplendor del olivo
y la fragancia del cedro del Líbano.
7Volverán a habitar bajo mi sombra,
y crecerán como el trigo.
Echarán renuevos, como la vid,
y serán tan famosos como el vino del
Líbano.
8Efraín, ¿yo qué tengo que ver con las
imágenes?
iSoy yo quien te responde y cuida de ti!
Soy como un pino siempre verde;
tu fruto procede de mí.»

9El que es sabio entiende estas cosas;
el que es inteligente las comprende.
Ciertamente son rectos los *caminos del
SEÑOR:
en ellos caminan los justos,
mientras que allí tropiezan los rebeldes.

JOEL

1 Ésta es la palabra del SEÑOR, que vino a Joel hijo de Petuel.

La invasión de langostas

²¡Oigan esto, *ancianos del pueblo!
¡Presten atención, habitantes todos del país!
¿Alguna vez sucedió cosa semejante
en sus tiempos o en los de sus
antepasados?
³Cuéntenselo a sus hijos,
y que ellos se lo cuenten a los suyos,
y éstos a la siguiente generación.
⁴Lo que dejaron las langostas grandes
lo devoraron las langostas pequeñas;
lo que dejaron las langostas pequeñas
se lo comieron las larvas;
y lo que dejaron las larvas
se lo comieron las orugas.ᵃ

⁵¡Despierten, borrachos, y lloren!
Giman, todos los entregados al vino,
porque el vino dulce les fue arrebatado de
los labios.
⁶Una nación poderosa e innumerable
ha invadido mi país:
tiene dientes de león,
colmillos de leona.
⁷Asoló mis vides,
desgajó mis higueras.
Las peló hasta dejar blancas sus ramas;
¡las derribó por completo!

⁸Mi pueblo gime como virgen vestida de luto
por la muerte de su prometido.
⁹Las ofrendas de cereales y las libaciones
no se ofrecen ya en la casa del SEÑOR.
Hacen duelo los sacerdotes,
los ministros del SEÑOR.
¹⁰Los campos yacen devastados,
reseca está la tierra;
han sido arrasados los cereales,
se ha secado el vino nuevo
y agotado el aceite.
¹¹Séquense también ustedes, labradores;
giman, viñadores,
por el trigo y la cebada,
porque se ha perdido la cosecha de los
campos.
¹²La vid se marchitó;
languideció la higuera;
se marchitaron los granados,
las palmeras, los manzanos,
¡todos los árboles del campo!
¡Y hasta la alegría de la gente acabó por
marchitarse!

Llamado al arrepentimiento

¹³Vístanse de duelo y giman, sacerdotes;
laméntense, ministros del altar.
Vengan, ministros de mi Dios,
y pasen la noche vestidos de luto,
porque las ofrendas de cereales y las
libaciones
han sido suspendidas en la casa de su Dios.
¹⁴Entréguense al ayuno,
convoquen a una asamblea solemne.
Reúnan a los *ancianos del pueblo

en la casa del SEÑOR su Dios;
reúnan a todos los habitantes del país,
y clamen al SEÑOR.

¹⁵¡Ay de aquel día, el día del SEÑOR, que ya se
aproxima!
Vendrá como devastación de parte del
*Todopoderoso.

¹⁶¿No se nos arrebató el alimento
ante nuestros propios ojos,
y la alegría y el regocijo
de la casa de nuestro Dios?
¹⁷La semilla se pudrió
a pesar de haber sido cultivada.ᵇ
Los silos están en ruinas
y los graneros derribados
porque la cosecha se perdió.
¹⁸¡Cómo brama el ganado!
Vagan sin rumbo las vacas
porque no tienen donde pastar,
·y sufren también las ovejas.

¹⁹A ti clamo, SEÑOR,
porque el fuego ha devorado los pastizales
de la estepa;
las llamas han consumido todos los árboles
silvestres.
²⁰Aun los animales del campo te buscan con
ansias,
porque se han secado los arroyos
y el fuego ha devorado los pastizales de la
estepa.

Un ejército de langostas

2 Toquen la trompeta en *Sión;
den la voz de alarma en mi *santo monte.
Tiemblen todos los habitantes del país,
pues ya viene el día del SEÑOR;
en realidad ya está cerca.
²Día de tinieblas y oscuridad,
día de nubes y densos nubarrones.
Como la aurora que se extiende sobre los
montes,
así avanza un pueblo fuerte y numeroso,
pueblo como nunca lo hubo en la antigüedad
ni lo habrá en las generaciones futuras.
³Antes de que llegue, devora el fuego;
cuando ya ha pasado, las llamas lo
inflaman todo.
Antes de que llegue, el país se parece al jardín
del Edén;
cuando ya ha pasado, queda un desolado
desierto;
¡nada escapa su poder!
⁴Tienen aspecto de caballos;
galopan como corceles.
⁵Y al saltar sobre las cumbres de los montes,
producen un estruendo como el de carros
de guerra,
como el crepitar del fuego al consumir la
hojarasca.
¡Son como un ejército poderoso en
formación de batalla!

⁶Ante él se estremecen las naciones;
todo rostro palidece.

ᵃ **1:4** El texto hebreo en este versículo usa cuatro términos que se refieren a langostas y que son de difícil traducción; también en 2:25. ᵇ **1:17** *La semilla ... cultivada.* Texto de difícil traducción.

7Atacan como guerreros,
    escalan muros como soldados.
Cada uno mantiene la marcha
    sin romper la formación.
8No se atropellan entre sí;
    cada uno marcha en línea.
Se lanzan entre las flechas
    sin romper filas.
9Se abalanzan contra la ciudad,
    arremeten contra los muros,
trepan por las casas,
    se meten por las ventanas como ladrones.

10Ante este ejército tiembla la tierra
    y se estremece el cielo,
el sol y la luna se oscurecen
    y las estrellas dejan de brillar.
11Truena la voz del SEÑOR
    al frente de su ejército;
son innumerables sus tropas
    y poderosos los que ejecutan su palabra.
El día del SEÑOR es grande y terrible.
    ¿Quién lo podrá resistir?

Exhortación al arrepentimiento

12«Ahora bien —afirma el SEÑOR—,
    vuélvanse a mí de todo *corazón,
    con ayuno, llantos y lamentos.»

13Rásguense el corazón
    y no las vestiduras.
Vuélvanse al SEÑOR su Dios,
    porque él es bondadoso y compasivo,
lento para la ira y lleno de amor,
    cambia de parecer y no castiga.
14Tal vez Dios reconsidere y cambie de parecer,
    y deje tras de sí una bendición.
Las ofrendas de cereales y las libaciones
    son del SEÑOR su Dios.

15Toquen la trompeta en *Sión,
    proclamen el ayuno,
convoquen a una asamblea solemne.
16Congreguen al pueblo,
    *purifiquen la asamblea;
junten a los *ancianos del pueblo,
    reúnan a los pequeños
    y a los niños de pecho.
Que salga de su alcoba el recién casado,
    y la recién casada de su cámara nupcial.
17Lloren, sacerdotes, ministros del SEÑOR,
    entre el pórtico y el altar;
y digan: «Compadécete, SEÑOR, de tu pueblo.
    No entregues tu propiedad al oprobio,
    para que las naciones no se burlen de ella.c
¿Por qué habrán de decir entre los pueblos:
    "Dónde está su Dios?"»

La respuesta del SEÑOR

18Entonces el SEÑOR mostró amor por su tierra
    y perdonó a su pueblo.

19Y les respondió el SEÑOR:

«Miren, les enviaré cereales, vino nuevo y
    aceite,
    hasta dejarlos plenamente satisfechos;
y no volveré a entregarlos
    al oprobio entre las naciones.

20»Alejaré de ustedes al que viene del norte,
    arrojándolo hacia una tierra seca y
    desolada:
lanzaré su vanguardia hacia el mar oriental,
    y su retaguardia hacia el mar occidental.d
Subirá su hedor
    y se elevará su fetidez.»
¡El Señor hará grandes cosas!
21No temas, tierra,
    sino alégrate y regocíjate,
porque el SEÑOR hará grandes cosas.
22No teman, animales del campo,
    porque los pastizales de la estepa
    reverdecerán;
los árboles producirán su fruto,
    y la higuera y la vid darán su riqueza.
23Alégrense, hijos de Sión,
    regocíjense en el SEÑOR su Dios,
    que a su tiempo les dará las lluvias de otoño.
Les enviará la lluvia,
    la de otoño y la de primavera,
    como en tiempos pasados.
24Las eras se llenarán de grano;
    los lagares rebosarán de vino nuevo y de
    aceite.
25«Yo les compensaré a ustedes
    por los años en que todo lo devoró
    ese gran ejército de langostas
    que envié contra ustedes:
las grandes, las pequeñas,
    las larvas y las orugas.e
26Ustedes comerán en abundancia, hasta
    saciarse,
    y alabarán el *nombre del SEÑOR su Dios,
que hará maravillas por ustedes.
    ¡Nunca más será avergonzado mi
    pueblo!
27Entonces sabrán que yo estoy en medio de
    Israel,
    que yo soy el SEÑOR su Dios,
    y no hay otro fuera de mí.
¡Nunca más será avergonzado mi pueblo!

El día del SEÑOR

28»Después de esto,
    derramaré mi Espíritu sobre todo el
    *género humano.
Los hijos y las hijas de ustedes profetizarán,
    tendrán sueños los ancianos
    y visiones los jóvenes.
29En esos días derramaré mi Espíritu
    aun sobre los siervos y las siervas.
30En el cielo y en la tierra mostraré prodigios:
    sangre, fuego y columnas de humo.
31El sol se convertirá en tinieblas
    y la luna en sangre
antes que llegue el día del SEÑOR,
    día grande y terrible.
32Y todo el que invoque el *nombre del SEÑOR
    escapará con vida,
porque en el monte *Sión y en Jerusalén
    habrá escapatoria,
    como lo ha dicho el SEÑOR.
Y entre los sobrevivientes
    estarán los llamados del SEÑOR.

---

c 2:17 no se burlen de ella. Alt. no la sometan. d 2:20 el mar oriental ... el mar occidental. Es decir, el Mar Muerto y el Mediterráneo. e 2:25 Véase nota en 1:4.

El juicio de las naciones

3 »En aquellos días, en el tiempo señalado,
cuando restaure yo la suerte de Judá y de
    Jerusalén,
²reuniré a todas las naciones
    y las haré bajar al valle de Josafat.ᶠ
Allí entraré en juicio contra los pueblos
    en cuanto a mi propiedad, mi pueblo Israel,
pues lo dispersaron entre las naciones
    y se repartieron mi tierra.
³Se repartieron a mi pueblo echando suertes,
    cambiaron a niños por prostitutas
y, para emborracharse,
    vendieron niñas por vino.

⁴»Ahora bien, Tiro y Sidón, y regiones todas de
Filistea, ¿qué tienen en contra mía? ¿Quieren acaso
vengarse de mí? Si es así, yo haré que muy pronto recaiga sobre ustedes su propia venganza, ⁵pues se robaron mi oro y mi plata, y se llevaron a sus templos
mis valiosos tesoros. ⁶A los griegos les vendieron el
pueblo de Jerusalén y de Judá, para alejarlos de su
tierra.

⁷»Sepan, pues, que voy a sacarlos de los lugares
donde fueron vendidos, y haré que recaiga sobre ustedes su propia venganza. ⁸Venderé sus hijos y sus hijas
al pueblo de Judá, y ellos a su vez los venderán a los sabeos, una nación lejana.» El SEÑOR lo ha dicho.

⁹Proclamen esto entre las naciones:
    ¡Prepárenseᵍ para la batalla!
¡Movilicen a los soldados!
    ¡Alístense para el combate todos los
        hombres de guerra!
¹⁰Forjen espadas con los azadones
    y hagan lanzas con las hoces.
Que diga el cobarde:
    «¡Soy un valiente!»
¹¹Dense prisa, naciones vecinas,
    reúnanse en ese lugar.

¡Haz bajar, SEÑOR, a tus valientes!

¹²«Movilícense las naciones;
    suban hasta el valle de Josafat,
que allí me sentaré
    para juzgar a los pueblos vecinos.
¹³Mano a la hoz,
    que la mies está madura.
Vengan a pisar las uvas,
    que está lleno el lagar.
Sus cubas se desbordan:
    ¡tan grande es su maldad!»

¹⁴¡Multitud tras multitud
    en el valle de la Decisión!
¡Cercano está el día del SEÑOR
    en el valle de la Decisión!
¹⁵Se oscurecerán el sol y la luna;
    dejarán de brillar las estrellas.
¹⁶Rugirá el SEÑOR desde *Sión,
    tronará su voz desde Jerusalén,
    y la tierra y el cielo temblarán.
Pero el SEÑOR será un refugio para su pueblo,
    una fortaleza para los israelitas.

Bendiciones para el pueblo de Dios

¹⁷«Entonces ustedes sabrán que yo, el SEÑOR su
    Dios,
habito en Sión, mi monte *santo.
Santa será Jerusalén,
    y nunca más la invadirán los extranjeros.

¹⁸»En aquel día las montañas destilarán vino
    dulce,
    y de las colinas fluirá leche;
corerrá el agua por los arroyos de Judá.
De la casa del SEÑOR brotará una fuente
    que irrigará el valle de las Acacias.
¹⁹Pero Egipto quedará desolado,
    y Edom convertido en desierto,
por la violencia cometida contra el pueblo de
    Judá,
en cuya tierra derramaron sangre inocente.
²⁰Judá y Jerusalén serán habitadas
    para siempre, por todas las generaciones.
²¹¿Perdonaré la sangre que derramaron?
    ¡Claro que no la perdonaré!»

¡El SEÑOR hará su morada en Sión!

ᶠ **3:2** En hebreo, *Josafat* significa *el SEÑOR juzga*; también en v. 12.   ᵍ **3:9** *Prepárense.* Lit. *Santifíquense.*

AMÓS

1 Éstas son las palabras de Amós, pastor de Tecoa. Es la visión que recibió acerca de Israel dos años antes del terremoto, cuando Uzías era rey de Judá, y Jeroboán hijo de Joás era rey de Israel. ²Amós dijo:

«Ruge el SEÑOR desde *Sión;
 truena su voz desde Jerusalén.
Los pastizales de los pastores quedan
  asolados,
 y se seca la cumbre del Carmelo.»

Juicio contra las naciones vecinas

³Así dice el SEÑOR:

«Los delitos de Damasco han llegado a su
  colmo;ᵃ
 por tanto, no revocaré su castigo:
Porque trillaron a Galaad
 con trillos de hierro,
⁴yo enviaré fuego contra el palacio de Jazael,
 que consumirá las fortalezas de Ben Adad.
⁵Romperé el cerrojo de la *puerta de Damasco,
 destruiré al que reina en el valle de Avénᵇ
 y al que empuña el cetro en Bet Edén.
Y el pueblo de Siria
 será desterrado a Quir»,
                    dice el SEÑOR.

⁶Así dice el SEÑOR:

«Los delitos de Gaza han llegado a su colmo;
 por tanto, no revocaré su castigo:
Porque desterraron a poblaciones enteras
 para venderlas a Edom,
⁷yo enviaré fuego contra los muros de Gaza,
 que consumirá sus fortalezas.
⁸Destruiré al que reina en Asdod
 y al que empuña el cetro en Ascalón.
Volveré mi mano contra Ecrón,
 y perecerá hasta el último de los filisteos»,
                dice el SEÑOR omnipotente.

⁹Así dice el SEÑOR:

«Los delitos de Tiro han llegado a su colmo;
 por tanto, no revocaré su castigo:
Porque le vendieron a Edom poblaciones
  enteras de cautivos,
 olvidando así una alianza entre hermanos,
¹⁰yo enviaré fuego contra los muros de Tiro,
 que consumirá sus fortalezas.»

¹¹Así dice el SEÑOR:

«Los delitos de Edom han llegado a su colmo;
 por tanto, no revocaré su castigo:
Porque sin mostrar ninguna compasión
 persiguieron con espada a su hermano;
porque dieron rienda suelta a su ira
 y no dejaron de alimentar su enojo,
¹²yo enviaré fuego contra Temán,
 que consumirá las fortalezas de Bosra.»

¹³Así dice el SEÑOR:

«Los delitos de Amón han llegado a su colmo;
 por tanto, no revocaré su castigo:
Porque, a fin de extender sus fronteras,

 a las mujeres encintas de la región de
  Galaad
 les abrieron el vientre,
¹⁴yo prenderé fuego a los muros de Rabá,
 que consumirá sus fortalezas
entre gritos de guerra en el día de la batalla,
 y en el rugir de la tormenta en un día de
  tempestad.
¹⁵Su reyᶜ marchará al destierro,
 junto con sus oficiales»,
                    dice el SEÑOR.

2 Así dice el SEÑOR:

«Los delitos de Moab han llegado a su colmo;
 por tanto, no revocaré su castigo:
Porque quemaron los huesos del rey de Edom
 hasta reducirlos a ceniza,
²yo enviaré fuego sobre Moab
 que consumirá las fortalezas de Queriot,
y morirá Moab en medio del estrépito
 de gritos de guerra y toques de trompeta.
³Destruiré al gobernante en medio de su
  pueblo,
 y junto con él mataré a todos sus oficiales»,
                    dice el SEÑOR.

⁴Así dice el SEÑOR:

«Los delitos de Judá han llegado a su colmo;
 por tanto, no revocaré su castigo:
Porque, dejándose descarriar por sus
  mentiras,
 tras las cuales anduvieron sus antepasados,
rechazaron la *ley del SEÑOR
 y no obedecieron sus preceptos.
⁵Por eso yo enviaré fuego contra Judá,
 que consumirá las fortalezas de Jerusalén.»

Juicio contra Israel

⁶Así dice el SEÑOR:

«Los delitos de Israel han llegado a su colmo;
 por tanto, no revocaré su castigo:
Venden al justo por monedas,
 y al necesitado, por un par de sandalias.
⁷Pisotean la cabeza de los desvalidos
 como si fuera el polvo de la tierra,
 y pervierten el camino de los pobres.
Padre e hijo se acuestan con la misma mujer,
 profanando así mi *santo *nombre.
⁸Junto a cualquier altar
 se acuestan sobre ropa que tomaron en
  prenda,
 y el vino que han cobrado como multa
 lo beben en la casa de su Dios.ᵈ

⁹»Todo esto, a pesar de que por ellos
 yo destruí a los amorreos;
destruí su fruto arriba
 y sus raíces abajo,
aunque eran altos como el cedro
 y fuertes como la encina.

¹⁰»Yo mismo los hice subir desde Egipto,
 y los conduje cuarenta años por el desierto,
 a fin de conquistar para ustedes
 la tierra de los amorreos.
¹¹También levanté profetas de entre sus hijos

---

a **1:3** Los delitos ... su colmo. Lit. Por tres delitos de ..., y por cuatro (hebraísmo que indica plenitud); también en
1:6,9,11,13; 2:1,4,6. b **1:5** Avén. Alt. maldad. c **1:15** Su rey. Alt. Milcón. d **2:8** su Dios. Alt. sus dioses.

y nazareos de entre sus jóvenes.
¿Acaso no fue así, israelitas?
—afirma el SEÑOR—.
12Pero ustedes les hicieron beber vino a los
nazareos
y les ordenaron a los profetas que no
profetizaran.

13»Pues bien, estoy por aplastarlos a ustedes
como aplasta una carreta cargada de trigo.
14Entonces no habrá escapatoria para el ágil,
ni el fuerte podrá valerse de su fuerza,
ni el valiente librará su vida.
15El arquero no resistirá,
ni escapará con vida el ágil de piernas,
ni se salvará el que monta a caballo.
16En aquel día huirá desnudo
aun el más valiente de los guerreros»,
afirma el SEÑOR.

Vocación del profeta Amós

3 Oigan, israelitas, esta palabra que el SEÑOR pronuncia contra ustedes, contra toda la familia
que saqué de Egipto:

2«Sólo a ustedes los he escogido
entre todas las familias de la tierra.
Por tanto, les haré pagar
todas sus perversidades.»

3¿Pueden dos caminar juntos
sin antes ponerse de acuerdo?
4¿Ruge el león en la espesura
sin tener presa alguna?
¿Gruñe el leoncillo en su guarida
sin haber atrapado nada?
5¿Cae el pájaro en la trampa
sin que haya carnada?
¿Salta del suelo la trampa
sin haber atrapado nada?
6¿Se toca la trompeta en la ciudad
sin que el pueblo se alarme?
¿Ocurrirá en la ciudad alguna desgracia
que el SEÑOR no haya provocado?

7En verdad, nada hace el SEÑOR omnipotente
sin antes revelar sus designios
a sus siervos los profetas.

8Ruge el león;
¿quién no temblará de miedo?
Habla el SEÑOR omnipotente;
¿quién no profetizará?

El castigo a Israel

9Proclamen en las fortalezas de Asdod
y en los baluartes de Egipto:
«Reúnanse sobre los montes de Samaria
y vean cuánto pánico hay en ella,
¡cuánta opresión hay en su medio!»

10«Los que acumulan en sus fortalezas
el fruto de la violencia y el saqueo
no saben actuar con rectitud»,
afirma el SEÑOR.

11Por lo tanto, así dice el SEÑOR omnipotente:

«Un enemigo invadirá tu tierra;
echará abajo tu poderío
y saqueará tus fortalezas.»

12Así dice el SEÑOR:

«Como el pastor arrebata de las fauces del león
si acaso dos patas o un pedazo de oreja,
así serán rescatados los israelitas,
los que en Samaria se reclinan
en el borde de la cama y en divanes de
Damasco.e

13»Oigan esto y testifiquen contra el pueblo de
Jacob —afirma el SEÑOR omnipotente, el Dios *Todopoderoso—:

14El día en que haga pagar a Israel sus delitos,
destruiré los altares de Betel;
los cuernos del altar serán arrancados,
y caerán por tierra.
15Derribaré tanto la casa de invierno
como la de verano;
serán destruidas las casas adornadas de marfil
y serán demolidas muchas mansiones»,
afirma el SEÑOR.

4 Oigan esta palabra ustedes, vacas de Basán,
que viven en el monte de Samaria,
que oprimen a los desvalidos
y maltratan a los necesitados,
que dicen a sus esposos:
«¡Tráigannos de beber!»
2El SEÑOR omnipotente ha jurado por su
*santidad:
«Vendrán días en que hasta la última de
ustedes
será arreada con garfios y arpones.
3Una tras otra saldrán por las brechas del muro,
y hacia Hermón serán expulsadas
—afirma el SEÑOR—.

4»Vayan a Betel y pequen;
vayan a Guilgal y sigan pecando.
Ofrezcan sus sacrificios por la mañana,
y al tercer día sus diezmos.
5Quemen pan leudado como ofrenda de
gratitud
y proclamen ofrendas voluntarias.
Háganlo saber a todos, israelitas;
¡eso es lo que a ustedes les encanta!
—afirma el SEÑOR omnipotente—.

Dureza de Israel

6»Yo les hice pasar hambre en todas sus
ciudades,
y los privé de pan en todos sus poblados.
Con todo, ustedes no se volvieron a mí
—afirma el SEÑOR—.

7»Yo les retuve la lluvia
cuando aún faltaban tres meses para la
cosecha.
En una ciudad hacía llover,
pero en otra no;
una parcela recibía lluvia,
mientras que otra no, y se secó.
8Vagando de ciudad en ciudad, iba la gente en
busca de agua,
pero no calmaba su sed.
Con todo, ustedes no se volvieron a mí
—afirma el SEÑOR—.

9»Castigué sus campos con plagas y sequía;
la langosta devoró sus huertos y viñedos,
sus higueras y olivares.
Con todo, ustedes no se volvieron a mí
—afirma el SEÑOR—.

---

e **3:12** en el borde ... Damasco. Texto de difícil traducción.

10»Les mandé plagas
　　como las de Egipto.
Pasé por la espada a sus mejores jóvenes,
　　junto con los caballos capturados.
Hice que llegara hasta sus propias narices
　　el hedor de los cadáveres.
Con todo, ustedes no se volvieron a mí
　　　　—afirma el SEÑOR—.

11»Yo les envié destrucción
　　como la de Sodoma y Gomorra;
¡quedaron como tizones arrebatados del
　　fuego!
Con todo, ustedes no se volvieron a mí
　　　　—afirma el SEÑOR—.

12»Por eso, Israel, voy a actuar contra ti;
　　y como voy a hacerlo,
¡prepárate, Israel, para encontrarte con tu
　　Dios!»

13He aquí el que forma las montañas,
　　el que crea el viento,
　　el que revela al hombre sus designios,
el que convierte la aurora en tinieblas,
　　el que marcha sobre las alturas de la tierra:
　　su nombre es el SEÑOR Dios
　　*Todopoderoso.

Advertencias y lamentos

5 Oye esta palabra, reino de Israel,
　este canto fúnebre que por ti entono:
2«Ha caído la joven Israel,
　　y no volverá a levantarse;
postrada en su propia tierra,
　　no hay quien la levante.»

3Así dice el SEÑOR omnipotente al reino de Israel:

«La ciudad que salía a la guerra con mil
　　hombres
se quedará sólo con cien,
y la que salía con cien
　　se quedará sólo con diez.»

4Así dice el SEÑOR al reino de Israel:

«Búsquenme y vivirán.
　5Pero no acudan a Betel,
ni vayan a Guilgal,
　　ni pasen a Berseba,
porque Guilgal será llevada cautiva,
　　y Betel, reducida a la nada.»

6Busquen al SEÑOR y vivirán,
　　no sea que él caiga como fuego
　　sobre los descendientes de José,
fuego que devore a Betel
　　sin que haya quien lo apague.
7Ustedes convierten el derecho en amargura
　　y echan por tierra la justicia.

8El SEÑOR hizo las Pléyades y el Orión,
　　convierte en aurora las densas tinieblas
　　y oscurece el día hasta convertirlo en noche.
Él convoca las aguas del mar
　　y las derrama sobre la tierra.
　　¡Su nombre es el SEÑOR!
9Él reduce a la nada la fortaleza
　　y trae la ruina sobre la plaza fuerte.

10Ustedes odian al que defiende la justicia en el
　　tribunal
　　y detestan al que dice la verdad.
11Por eso, como pisotean al desvalido
　　y le imponen tributo de grano,

no vivirán en las casas de piedra labrada que
　　han construido,
ni beberán del vino de los selectos viñedos
　　que han plantado.
12¡Yo sé cuán numerosos son sus delitos,
　　cuán grandes sus pecados!

Ustedes oprimen al justo, exigen soborno
　　y en los tribunales atropellan al necesitado.
13Por eso en circunstancias como éstas guarda
　　silencio el prudente,
　　porque estos tiempos son malos.

14Busquen el bien y no el mal, y vivirán;
　　y así estará con ustedes el SEÑOR Dios
　　*Todopoderoso,
　　tal como ustedes lo afirman.

15¡Odien el mal y amen el bien!
　　Hagan que impere la justicia en los
　　tribunales;
　　tal vez así el SEÑOR, el Dios Todopoderoso,
　　tenga compasión del remanente de José.

16Por eso, así dice el SEÑOR omnipotente, el Dios
Todopoderoso:

«En todas las plazas se escucharán lamentos,
　　y gritos de angustia en todas las calles.
Llamarán a duelo a los campesinos,
　　y a los llorones profesionales, a hacer
　　lamentación.
17Se escucharán lamentos en todos los viñedos
　　cuando yo pase en medio de ti»,
　　　　　　　　dice el SEÑOR.

18¡Ay de los que suspiran
　　por el día del SEÑOR!
¿De qué les servirá ese día
　　si va a ser de oscuridad y no de luz?
19Será como cuando alguien huye de un león
　　y se le viene encima un oso,
o como cuando al llegar a su casa,
　　apoya la mano en la pared
　　y lo muerde una serpiente.
20¿No será el día del SEÑOR de oscuridad y no
　　de luz?
　　¡Será por cierto sombrío y sin resplandor!

21«Yo aborrezco sus fiestas religiosas;
　　no me agradan sus cultos solemnes.
22Aunque me traigan holocaustos y ofrendas de
　　cereal,
　　no los aceptaré,
ni prestaré atención
　　a los sacrificios de *comunión de novillos
　　cebados.
23Aleja de mí el bullicio de tus canciones;
　　no quiero oír la música de tus cítaras.
24¡Pero que fluya el derecho como las aguas,
　　y la justicia como arroyo inagotable!

25»Pueblo de Israel, ¿acaso me ofrecieron
　　sacrificios y ofrendas
　　durante los cuarenta años en el desierto?
26Ustedes tendrán que cargar con la imagen de
　　Sicut, su rey,
　　y también con la de Quiyún,
imágenes de esos dioses astrales
　　que ustedes mismos se han fabricado.
27Entonces los mandaré al exilio más allá de
　　Damasco»,
　　dice el SEÑOR, cuyo nombre es Dios
　　Todopoderoso.

6

¡Ay de los que viven tranquilos en *Sión
    y de los que viven confiados en el monte
      de Samaria!
¡Ay de los notables de la nación más
    importante,
    a quienes acude el pueblo de Israel!
²Pasen a Calné y obsérvenla;
    vayan de allí a Jamat la grande,
    bajen luego a Gat de los filisteos.
¿Acaso son ustedes superiores a estos reinos,
    o es más grande su territorio que el de
      ustedes?
³Ustedes creen alejar el día de la desgracia,
    pero están acercando el imperio de la
      violencia.
⁴Ustedes que se acuestan en camas incrustadas
    de marfil
    y se arrellanan en divanes;
que comen corderos selectos
    y terneros engordados;
⁵que, a la manera de David,
    improvisan canciones al son de la cítara
    e inventan instrumentos musicales;
⁶que beben vino en tazones
    y se perfuman con las esencias más finas
sin afligirse por la ruina de José,
⁷marcharán a la cabeza de los desterrados,
    y así terminará el banquete de los
      holgazanes.

⁸El SEÑOR omnipotente jura por sí mismo;
    esto afirma el SEÑOR Dios *Todopoderoso:

«Yo detesto la arrogancia de Jacob;
    yo aborrezco sus fortalezas;
por eso entregaré la ciudad al enemigo,
    con todo lo que hay en ella.»

⁹Sucederá que si en una casa quedan diez hombres con vida, todos morirán. ¹⁰Y cuando vengan a la casa para levantar los cadáveres y quemarlos, algún pariente le preguntará a otro que ande en la casa: «¿Queda alguien más contigo?» Y aquél le responderá: «No.» Entonces le dirá: «¡Cállate! No vayamos a mencionar el *nombre del SEÑOR.»

¹¹Mira, el SEÑOR da la orden
    de golpear la casa grande hasta hacerla
      añicos
    y de hacer trizas la casa pequeña.

¹²¿Acaso galopan los caballos por las rocas
    o se ara en éstas con bueyes?
Pero ustedes han convertido el derecho en
    veneno,
    y en amargura el fruto de la justicia.
¹³Ustedes se regocijan por la conquista de Lo
    Debarᶠ
    y agregan: «¿No fue con nuestras propias
      fuerzas
como nos apoderamos de Carnayin?»ᵍ

¹⁴«Por tanto, pueblo de Israel,
    voy a levantar contra ti a una nación
que te oprimirá desde Lebó Jamatʰ
    hasta el torrente del Arabá»,
    afirma el SEÑOR, el Dios Todopoderoso.

Tres visiones

7

El SEÑOR omnipotente me mostró esta visión: Empezaba a crecer la hierba después de la siega que corresponde al rey, y vi al Señor preparando enjambres de langostas. ²Cuando las langostas acababan con la hierba de la tierra, exclamé:

—¡SEÑOR mi Dios, te ruego que perdones a Jacob! ¿Cómo va a sobrevivir, si es tan pequeño?

³Entonces el SEÑOR se compadeció y dijo:

—Esto no va a suceder.

⁴El SEÑOR omnipotente me mostró entonces otra visión: Vi al SEÑOR llamar a juicio con un fuego que devoraba el gran abismo y consumía los campos. ⁵Y exclamé:

—¡Deténte, SEÑOR mi Dios, te lo ruego! ¿Cómo sobrevivirá Jacob, si es tan pequeño?

⁶Entonces el SEÑOR se compadeció y dijo:

—Esto tampoco va a suceder.

⁷El SEÑOR me mostró otra visión: Estaba él de pie junto a un muro construido a plomo, y tenía una cuerda de plomada en la mano. ⁸Y el SEÑOR me preguntó:

—¿Qué ves, Amós?

—Una cuerda de plomada —respondí.

Entonces el Señor dijo:

—Mira, voy a tirar la plomada en medio de mi pueblo Israel; no volveré a perdonarlo.

⁹»Los *altares paganos de Isaac serán
    destruidos,
    y arruinados los santuarios de Israel;
me levantaré con espada
    contra el palacio de Jeroboán.

Amasías contra Amós

¹⁰Entonces Amasías, sacerdote de Betel, envió un mensaje a Jeroboán rey de Israel: «Amós está conspirando contra ti en medio de Israel. El país ya no aguanta tanta palabrería de Amós, ¹¹porque anda diciendo:

»"Jeroboán morirá a espada,
    e Israel será llevado cautivo
      lejos de su tierra."»

¹²Entonces Amasías le dijo a Amós:

—¡Largo de aquí, vidente! ¡Si quieres ganarte el pan profetizando, vete a la tierra de Judá! ¹³No vuelvas a profetizar en Betel, porque éste es el santuario del rey; es el templo del reino.

¹⁴Amós le respondió a Amasías:

—Yo no soy profeta ni hijo de profeta, sino que cuido ovejas y cultivo higueras. ¹⁵Pero el SEÑOR me sacó de detrás del rebaño y me dijo: "Ve y profetiza a mi pueblo Israel." ¹⁶Así que oye la palabra del SEÑOR. Tú dices:

»"No profetices contra Israel;
    deja de predicar contra los descendientes
      de Isaac."

¹⁷»Por eso, así dice el SEÑOR:

»"Tu esposa se prostituirá en la ciudad,
    y tus hijos y tus hijas caerán a espada.
Tu tierra será medida y repartida,
    y tú mismo morirás en un país *pagano.
E Israel será llevado cautivo
    lejos de su tierra."

ᶠ **6:13** En hebreo, *Lo Debar* significa *nada*. ᵍ **6:13** En hebreo, *Carnayin* significa *dos cuernos*; el cuerno es símbolo del poder. ʰ **6:14** *Lebó Jamat*. Alt. *la entrada de Jamat*.

Cuarta visión y advertencias

8 El SEÑOR omnipotente me mostró en una visión una canasta de fruta madura, 2y me preguntó:

—¿Qué ves, Amós?

—Una canasta de fruta madura —respondí.

Entonces el SEÑOR me dijo:

—Ha llegado el tiempo de que Israel caiga como fruta madura; no volveré a perdonarlo.

3»En aquel día —afirma el SEÑOR omnipotente—, las canciones del palacio se volverán lamentos. ¡Muchos serán los cadáveres tirados por todas partes! ¡Silencio!

4Oigan esto, los que pisotean a los necesitados
    y exterminan a los pobres de la tierra.
5Ustedes dicen:

«¿Cuándo pasará la fiesta de luna nueva
    para que podamos vender grano,
o el día de reposo
    para que pongamos a la venta el trigo?»

Ustedes buscan

achicar la medida
    y aumentar el precio,
falsear las balanzas
    6y vender los deshechos del trigo,
comprar al desvalido por dinero,
    y al necesitado, por un par de sandalias.

7Jura el SEÑOR por el orgullo de Jacob: «Jamás olvidaré nada de lo que han hecho.

8»¿Y con todo esto no temblará la tierra?
    ¿No se enlutarán sus habitantes?
Subirá la tierra entera como el Nilo;
    se agitará y bajará,
    como el río de Egipto.

9»En aquel día —afirma el SEÑOR omnipotente—,

»haré que el sol se ponga al mediodía,
    y que en pleno día la tierra se oscurezca.
10Convertiré en luto sus fiestas religiosas,
    y en cantos fúnebres todas sus canciones.
Los vestiré de luto
    y les afeitaré la cabeza.
Será como si lloraran la muerte de un hijo
        único,
    y terminarán el día en amargura.

11»Vienen días —afirma el SEÑOR
        omnipotente—,
    en que enviaré hambre al país;
no será hambre de pan ni sed de agua,
    sino hambre de oír las palabras del SEÑOR.
12La gente vagará sin rumbo de mar a mar;
    andarán errantes del norte al este,
buscando la palabra del SEÑOR,
    pero no la encontrarán.

13»En aquel día se desmayarán de sed
    las jóvenes hermosas y los jóvenes fuertes.
14Y caerán para no levantarse jamás
    los que juran por la culpa*i* de Samaria,
los que dicen: "¡Por la vida de tu dios, oh Dan!
    ¡Por la vida de tu dios, Berseba!"»*j*

Quinta visión

9 Vi al Señor de pie junto al altar, y él dijo:

«Golpea los capiteles de las columnas
    para que se estremezcan los umbrales,
y que caigan en pedazos sobre sus cabezas.
    A los que queden los mataré a espada.
Ni uno solo escapará,
    ninguno saldrá con vida.
2Aunque se escondan en lo profundo del
        *sepulcro,
    de allí los sacará mi mano.
Aunque suban hasta el cielo,
    de allí los derribaré.
3Aunque se oculten en la cumbre del Carmelo,
    allí los buscaré y los atraparé.
Aunque de mí se escondan en el fondo del mar,
    allí ordenaré a la serpiente que los muerda.
4Aunque vayan al destierro arriados por sus
        enemigos,
    allí ordenaré que los mate la espada.
Para mal, y no para bien,
    fijaré en ellos mis ojos.»

5El SEÑOR omnipotente, el Todopoderoso,
    toca la tierra, y ella se desmorona.
Sube y baja la tierra
    como las aguas del Nilo, el río de Egipto,
    y se enlutan todos los que en ella viven.
6Dios construye su excelso palacio en el cielo
    y pone su cimiento*k* en la tierra,
llama a las aguas del mar
    y las derrama sobre la superficie de la
        tierra:
    su *nombre es el SEÑOR.
7«Israelitas, ¿acaso ustedes
    no son para mí como *cusitas?
¿Acaso no saqué de Egipto a Israel,
    de Creta*l* a los filisteos
    y de Quir a los *sirios?
                    —afirma el SEÑOR—.
8Por eso los ojos del SEÑOR omnipotente
    están sobre este reino pecaminoso.
Borraré de la faz de la tierra a los
        descendientes de Jacob,
    aunque no del todo
                    —afirma el SEÑOR—.
9Daré la orden de zarandear al pueblo de Israel
    entre todas las naciones,
como se zarandea la arena en una criba,
    sin que caiga a tierra ni una sola piedra.
10Morirán a filo de espada
    todos los pecadores de mi pueblo,
todos los que dicen:
    "No nos alcanzará la calamidad;
    ¡jamás se nos acercará!"

Restauración de Israel

11»En aquel día levantaré
    la choza caída de David.
Repararé sus grietas,
    restauraré sus ruinas
    y la reconstruiré tal como era en días
        pasados.
12para que ellos posean el remanente de Edom
    y todas las naciones que llevan mi *nombre
                    —afirma el SEÑOR,

---

i **8:14** *por la culpa.* Alt. *por Asima;* es decir, el ídolo samaritano. j **8:14** *de tu dios, Berseba.* Lit. *del camino de Berseba.*
k **9:6** *excelso palacio ... cimiento.* Palabras de difícil traducción. l **9:7** *Creta.* Lit. *Caftor.*

que hará estas cosas—.

13»Vienen días —afirma el SEÑOR—,

»en los cuales el que ara alcanzará al segador
y el que pisa las uvas, al sembrador.
Los montes destilarán vino dulce,
el cual correrá por todas las colinas.
14Restauraré am mi pueblo Israel;

ellos reconstruirán las ciudades arruinadas
y vivirán en ellas.
Plantarán viñedos y beberán su vino;
cultivarán huertos y comerán sus frutos.
15Plantaré a Israel en su propia tierra,
para que nunca más sea arrancado
de la tierra que yo le di»,

dice el SEÑOR tu Dios.

m 9:14 *Restauraré a.* Alt. *Haré volver a los cautivos de.*

ABDÍAS

¹Visión de Abdías.

Orgullo y caída de Edom
1-4 — Jer 49:14-16
5-6 — Jer 49:9-10

Hemos oído una noticia de parte del SEÑOR y un mensajero ha sido enviado a las naciones, diciendo: «¡Vamos, marchemos a la guerra contra ella!»

Así dice el SEÑOR omnipotente acerca de Edom:

²«¡Te haré insignificante entre las naciones,
    serás tremendamente despreciado!
³Tu carácter soberbio te ha engañado.
  Como habitas en las hendiduras de los
    desfiladeros,
    en la altura de tu morada,
  te dices a ti mismo:
    ¿Quién podrá arrojarme a tierra?
⁴Pero aunque vueles a lo alto como águila,
  y tu nido esté puesto en las estrellas,
  de allí te arrojaré
            —afirma el SEÑOR—.

⁵Si vinieran a ti ladrones
  o saqueadores nocturnos,
  ¿no robarían sólo lo que les bastara?
  ¡Pero tú, cómo serás destruido!
  Si vinieran a ti vendimiadores,
  ¿no dejarían algunos racimos?
⁶¡Pero cómo registrarán a Esaú!
  ¡Cómo rebuscarán sus escondrijos!
⁷Hasta la frontera te expulsarán
  tus propios aliados,
  te engañarán y dominarán
  tus propios amigos.
  Los que se sientan a tu mesa
  te pondrán una trampa.
  ¡Es que Edom ya no tiene inteligencia!
⁸¿Acaso no destruiré yo en aquel día
  a los sabios de Edom,
  a la inteligencia del monte de Esaú?
            —afirma el SEÑOR—.
⁹Ciudad de Temán, tus guerreros se caerán de
    miedo,
  a fin de que todo hombre sea exterminado
  del monte de Esaú por la masacre.
¹⁰»Por la violencia hecha contra tu hermano
    Jacob,
  te cubrirá la vergüenza
  y serás exterminado para siempre.
¹¹En el día que te mantuviste aparte,
  en el día que extranjeros llevaron su
    ejército cautivo,
  cuando extraños entraron por su puerta
  y sobre Jerusalén echaron suerte,

tú eras como uno de ellos.
¹²No debiste reírte de tu hermano en su mal día,
  en el día de su desgracia.
  No debiste alegrarte a costa del pueblo de Judá
  en el día de su ruina.
  No debiste proferir arrogancia
  en el día de su angustia.
¹³No debiste entrar por la *puerta de mi pueblo
  en el día de su calamidad.
  No debiste recrear la vista con su desgracia
  en el día de su calamidad.
  No debiste echar mano a sus riquezas
  en el día de su calamidad.
¹⁴No debiste aguardar en los angostos caminos
  para matar a los que huían.
  No debiste entregar a los sobrevivientes
  en el día de su angustia.

¹⁵»Porque cercano está el día del SEÑOR
  contra todas las naciones.
  ¡Edom, como hiciste, se te hará!
  ¡sobre tu cabeza recaerá tu merecido!
¹⁶Pues sin duda que así como ustedes,
    israelitas,
  bebieron de mi copa en mi santo monte,
  así también la beberán sin cesar todas las
    naciones;
  beberán y engullirán,
  y entonces serán como si nunca hubieran
    existido.
¹⁷Pero en el monte *Sión habrá liberación, y
  será sagrado.
  El pueblo de Jacob recuperará sus
    posesiones.
¹⁸Los descendientes de Jacob serán fuego,
  y los de José, llama;
  pero la casa real de Esaú será estopa:
  le pondrán fuego y la consumirán,
  de tal forma que no quedará sobreviviente
  entre los descendientes de Esaú.»
            El SEÑOR lo ha dicho.

Restauración del pueblo de Dios

¹⁹Los del Néguev poseerán el monte de Esaú, y los de la Sefelá poseerán Filistea. Los israelitas poseerán los campos de Efraín y de Samaria, y los de Benjamín poseerán Galaad.

²⁰Los exiliados, este ejército de israelitas que viven entre los cananeos, poseerán la tierra hasta Sarepta. Los desterrados de Jerusalén, que viven en Sefarad, poseerán las ciudades del Néguev, ²¹y los libertadores subirán al monte Sión para gobernar la región montañosa de Esaú. Y el reino será del SEÑOR.

JONÁS

Jonás desobedece al SEÑOR

1 La palabra del SEÑOR vino a Jonás hijo de Amitay: 2«Anda, ve a la gran ciudad de Nínive y proclama contra ella que su maldad ha llegado hasta mi presencia.»

3Jonás se fue, pero en dirección a Tarsis, para huir del SEÑOR. Bajó a Jope, donde encontró un barco que zarpaba rumbo a Tarsis. Pagó su pasaje y se embarcó con los que iban a esa ciudad, huyendo así del SEÑOR. 4Pero el SEÑOR lanzó sobre el mar un fuerte viento, y se desencadenó una tormenta tan violenta que el barco amenazaba con hacerse pedazos.

5Los marineros, aterrados y a fin de aliviar la situación, comenzaron a clamar cada uno a su dios y a lanzar al mar lo que había en el barco. Jonás, en cambio, que había bajado al fondo de la nave para acostarse, ahora dormía profundamente. 6El capitán del barco se le acercó y le dijo:

—¿Cómo puedes estar durmiendo? ¡Levántate! ¡Clama a tu dios! Quizá se fije en nosotros, y no perezcamos.

7Los marineros, por su parte, se dijeron unos a otros:

—¡Vamos, echemos suertes para averiguar quién tiene la culpa de que nos haya venido este desastre!

Así lo hicieron, y la suerte recayó en Jonás. 8Entonces le preguntaron:

—Dinos ahora, ¿quién tiene la culpa de que nos haya venido este desastre? ¿A qué te dedicas? ¿De dónde vienes? ¿Cuál es tu país? ¿A qué pueblo perteneces?

9—Soy hebreo y temo al SEÑOR, Dios del cielo, que hizo el mar y la tierra firme —les respondió.

10Al oír esto, los marineros se aterraron aun más, y como sabían que Jonás huía del SEÑOR, pues él mismo se lo había contado, le dijeron:

—¡Qué es lo que has hecho!

11Pero el mar se iba enfureciendo más y más, así que le preguntaron:

—¿Qué vamos a hacer contigo para que el mar deje de azotarnos?

12—Tómenme y láncenme al mar, y el mar dejará de azotarlos —les respondió—. Yo sé bien que por mi culpa se ha desatado sobre ustedes esta terrible tormenta.

13Sin embargo, en un intento por regresar a tierra firme, los marineros se pusieron a remar con todas sus fuerzas; pero como el mar se enfurecía más y más contra ellos, no lo consiguieron. 14Entonces clamaron al SEÑOR: «Oh SEÑOR, tú haces lo que quieres. No nos hagas perecer por quitarle la *vida a este hombre, ni nos hagas responsables de la muerte de un inocente.» 15Así que tomaron a Jonás y lo lanzaron al agua, y la furia del mar se aplacó. 16Al ver esto, se apoderó de ellos un profundo temor al SEÑOR, a quien le ofrecieron un sacrificio y le hicieron votos.

17El SEÑOR, por su parte, dispuso un enorme pez para que se tragara a Jonás, quien pasó tres días y tres noches en su vientre.

Oración de Jonás

2 Entonces Jonás oró al SEÑOR su Dios desde el vientre del pez.

2Dijo:

«En mi angustia clamé al SEÑOR,
   y él me respondió.
Desde las entrañas del *sepulcro pedí auxilio,
   y tú escuchaste mi clamor.
3A lo profundo me arrojaste,
   al corazón mismo de los mares;
las corrientes me envolvían,
   todas tus ondas y tus olas pasaban sobre mí.
4Y pensé: "He sido expulsado
   de tu presencia.
¿Cómo volveré a contemplar
   tu santo templo?"a
5Las aguas me llegaban hasta el *cuello,
   lo profundo del océano me envolvía;
las algas se me enredaban en la cabeza,
   6arrastrándome a los cimientos de las montañas.
Me tragó la tierra, y para siempre
   sus cerrojos se cerraron tras de mí.
Pero tú, SEÑOR, Dios mío,
   me rescataste de la fosa.

7»Al sentir que se me iba la *vida,
   me acordé del SEÑOR,
y mi oración llegó hasta ti,
   hasta tu *santo templo.

8»Los que siguen a ídolos vanos
   abandonan el amor de Dios.b
9Yo, en cambio, te ofreceré sacrificios
   y cánticos de gratitud.
Cumpliré las promesas que te hice.
   ¡La *salvación viene del SEÑOR!»

10Entonces el SEÑOR dio una orden y el pez vomitó a Jonás en tierra firme.

Jonás obedece al SEÑOR

3 La palabra del SEÑOR vino por segunda vez a Jonás: 2«Anda, ve a la gran ciudad de Nínive y proclámale el mensaje que te voy a dar.»

3Jonás se fue hacia Nínive, conforme al mandato del SEÑOR. Ahora bien, Nínive era una ciudad grande y de mucha importancia.c 4Jonás se fue internando en la ciudad, y la recorrió todo un día, mientras proclamaba: «¡Dentro de cuarenta días Nínive será destruida!» 5Y los ninivitas le creyeron a Dios, proclamaron ayuno y, desde el mayor hasta el menor, se vistieron de luto en señal de *arrepentimiento.

6Cuando el rey de Nínive se enteró del mensaje, se levantó de su trono, se quitó su manto real, hizo duelo y se cubrió de ceniza. 7Luego mandó que se pregonara en Nínive:

«Por decreto del rey y de su corte:

»Ninguna persona o animal, ni ganado lanar o vacuno, probará alimento alguno, ni tampoco pastará ni beberá agua. 8Al contrario, el rey ordena que toda persona, junto con sus animales, haga duelo y clame a Dios con todas sus fuerzas. Ordena así mismo que cada uno se convierta de su mal camino y de sus hechos violentos. 9¡Quién sabe! Tal vez Dios cambie de

---

a 2:4 ¿Cómo ... templo? Alt. Sin embargo, volveré a contemplar / tu santo templo.   b 2:8 abandonan el amor de Dios. Alt. desprecian la misericordia suya.   c 3:3 grande y de mucha importancia. Lit. grande para Dios, viaje de tres días.

parecer, y aplaque el ardor de su ira, y no perezcamos.»

10Al ver Dios lo que hicieron, es decir, que se habían convertido de su mal camino, cambió de parecer y no llevó a cabo la destrucción que les había anunciado.

Enojo de Jonás

4 Pero esto disgustó mucho a Jonás, y lo hizo enfurecerse. 2Así que oró al SEÑOR de esta manera:

—¡Oh SEÑOR! ¿No era esto lo que yo decía cuando todavía estaba en mi tierra? Por eso me anticipé a huir a Tarsis, pues bien sabía que tú eres un Dios bondadoso y compasivo, lento para la ira y lleno de amor, que cambias de parecer y no destruyes. 3Así que ahora, SEÑOR, te suplico que me quites la *vida. ¡Prefiero morir que seguir viviendo!

4—¿Tienes razón de enfurecerte tanto? —le respondió el SEÑOR.

5Jonás salió y acampó al este de la ciudad. Allí hizo una enramada y se sentó bajo su sombra para

ver qué iba a suceder con la ciudad. 6Para aliviarlo de su malestar, Dios el SEÑOR dispuso una planta,d la cual creció hasta cubrirle a Jonás la cabeza con su sombra. Jonás se alegró muchísimo por la planta. 7Pero al amanecer del día siguiente Dios dispuso que un gusano la hiriera, y la planta se marchitó. 8Al salir el sol, Dios dispuso un viento oriental abrasador. Además, el sol hería a Jonás en la cabeza, de modo que éste desfallecía. Con deseos de morirse, exclamó: «¡Prefiero morir que seguir viviendo!»

9Pero Dios le dijo a Jonás:

—¿Tienes razón de enfurecerte tanto por la planta?

—¡Claro que la tengo! —le respondió—. ¡Me muero de rabia!

10El SEÑOR le dijo:

—Tú te compadeces de una planta que, sin ningún esfuerzo de tu parte, creció en una noche y en la otra pereció. 11Y de Nínive, una gran ciudad donde hay más de ciento veinte mil personas que no distinguen su derecha de su izquierda, y tanto ganado, ¿no habría yo de compadecerme?

---

d 4:6 *planta*. Palabra de difícil traducción.

MIQUEAS

1 Ésta es la palabra que el SEÑOR dirigió a Miqueas de Moréset, durante los reinados de Jotán, Acaz y Ezequías, reyes de Judá. Ésta es la visión que tuvo acerca de Samaria y de Jerusalén.

La venida del Señor

2Escuchen, pueblos todos;
 preste atención la tierra
 y todo lo que hay en ella.
Desde su *santo templo
 el Señor, el SEÑOR omnipotente,
 será testigo en contra de ustedes.
3¡Miren! Ya sale el SEÑOR de su morada;
 ya baja y se encamina
 hacia las cumbres de la tierra.
4A su paso se derriten las montañas
 como la cera junto al fuego;
se parten en los valles
 como partidos por el agua de un torrente.
5Y todo esto por la transgresión de Jacob,
 por los pecados del pueblo de Israel.
¿Acaso no representa Samaria
 la transgresión de Jacob?
¿Y no es acaso en Jerusalén
 donde están los *santuarios paganos de
 Judá?
6Dejaré a Samaria hecha un montón de ruinas:
 ¡convertida en campo arado para viñedos!
Arrojaré sus piedras al valle,
 y pondré al descubierto sus cimientos.
7Todos sus ídolos serán hechos pedazos;
 toda su paga de prostituta será arrojada al
 fuego.
Yo destrozaré todas sus imágenes.
Todo cuanto ganó como prostituta,
 en paga de prostituta se convertirá.

Lamento de Miqueas

8Por eso lloraré y gritaré de dolor,
 y andaré descalzo y desnudo.
Aullaré como chacal
 y gemiré como avestruz.
9Porque la herida de Samaria es incurable:
 ha llegado hasta Judá.
Se ha extendido hasta mi pueblo,
 ¡hasta la *entrada misma de Jerusalén!
10No lo anuncien en Gat,a
 no se entreguen al llanto;
¡revuélquense de dolor
 en el polvo de Bet Leafrá!b
11Habitantes de Safir,c
 emigren desnudos y humillados.
Los habitantes de Zanánd
 no se atrevieron a salir.
Bet Ésel está gimiendo,
 y va a retirarles su apoyo.
12Se retuercen esperando el bien,
 los habitantes de Marot;e
el SEÑOR ha enviado el mal
 hasta la entrada misma de Jerusalén.
13Habitantes de Laquis,f
 ¡enganchen al carro los corceles!

Con ustedes comenzó el pecado de la hija de
 *Sión;
en ustedes se hallaron los delitos de Israel.
14Por tanto, despídanse de Moréset Gat.
Los edificios de la ciudad de Aczibg
 son una trampa para los reyes de Israel.

15Habitantes de Maresá,h
 yo enviaré contra ustedes un conquistador,
y hasta Adulán irá a parar
 la flor y nata de Israel.
16Así que rasúrate la barba y rápate la cabeza;
 haz duelo por tus amados hijos;
agranda tu calva como la del buitre,
 pues tus hijos te serán arrebatados.

El castigo a los ricos opresores

2 ¡Ay de los que sólo piensan en el mal,
 y aun acostados hacen planes malvados!
En cuanto amanece, los llevan a cabo
 porque tienen el poder en sus manos.
2Codician campos, y se apropian de ellos;
 casas, y de ellas se adueñan.
Oprimen al varón y a su familia,
 al hombre y a su propiedad.

3Por tanto, así dice el SEÑOR:

«Ahora soy yo el que piensa
 traer sobre ellos una desgracia,
 de la que no podrán escapar.
Ya no andarán erguidos,
 porque ha llegado la hora de su desgracia.
4En aquel día se les hará burla,
 y se les cantará este lamento:
"¡Estamos perdidos!
 Se están repartiendo los campos de mi
 pueblo.
¡Cómo me los arrebatan!
 Nuestra tierra se la reparten los traidores."»

5Por eso no tendrán en la asamblea del SEÑOR
 a nadie que reparta la tierra.

Falsos profetas

6Estos profetas me dicen:
 «¡Deja ya de profetizarnos!
¡No nos vengas con que el oprobio nos
 alcanzará!»
7Los descendientes de Jacob declaran:
 «¿Acaso ha perdido el SEÑOR la paciencia?
¿Es ésta su manera de actuar?
¿Acaso no hacen bien sus palabras?
 ¿Acaso no caminamos con el Justo?»
8Ayer ustedes eran mi pueblo,
 pero hoy se han vuelto mis enemigos.
A los que pasan confiados,
 a los que vuelven de la guerra,
 los despojan de su manto.
9A las mujeres de mi pueblo
 las echan de sus preciadas casas,
y a sus niños los despojan para siempre
 del honor que les di.

10¡Levántense! ¡Pónganse en marcha,

---

a 1:10 En hebreo, *Gat* suena como el verbo que significa *anuncien*. b 1:10 En hebreo, *Bet Leafrá* significa *casa de polvo*. c 1:11 En hebreo, *Safir* significa *placentero*. d 1:11 En hebreo, *Zanán* suena como el verbo que significa *salir*. e 1:12 En hebreo, *Marot* suena como la palabra que significa *amargura*. f 1:13 En hebreo, *Laquis* suena como la palabra que significa *corceles*. g 1:14 En hebreo, *Aczib* significa *destrucción*. h 1:15 En hebreo, *Maresá* suena como la palabra que significa *conquistador*.

que éste no es un lugar de reposo!
¡Está *contaminado,
destruido sin remedio!
11Si con la intención de mentirles,
llega algún embustero y les dice:
«Yo les anuncio vino y cerveza»,
este pueblo lo verá como un profeta.

Promesa de liberación

12Te aseguro, Jacob,
que yo reuniré a todo tu pueblo.
Te aseguro, Israel,
que yo juntaré a tu remanente.
Los congregaré como a rebaño en el aprisco,
como a ovejas que, en medio del pastizal,
balan huyendo de la gente.
13El que abre brecha marchará al frente,
y también ellos se abrirán camino;
atravesarán la puerta y se irán,
mientras su rey avanza al frente,
mientras el SEÑOR va a la cabeza.

El castigo a los gobernantes corruptos

3 Entonces dije:

«Escuchen, gobernantes de Jacob,
autoridades del pueblo de Israel:
¿Acaso no les corresponde a ustedes
conocer el derecho?
2Ustedes odian el bien y aman el mal;
a mi pueblo le arrancan la piel del cuerpo
y la carne de los huesos;
3ustedes se devoran a mi pueblo,
le arrancan la piel, le rompen los huesos;
lo descuartizan como carne para la olla,
como carne para el horno.»

4Ya le pedirán auxilio al SEÑOR,
pero él no les responderá;
esconderá de ellos su rostro
porque hicieron lo malo.

Contraste entre el profeta falso y el verdadero

5Esto es lo que dice el SEÑOR contra ustedes,
profetas que descarrían a mi pueblo:

«Con el estómago lleno, invitan a la paz;
con el vientre vacío, declaran la guerra.
6Por tanto, tendrán noches sin visiones,
oscuridad sin presagios.»

El sol se ocultará de estos profetas;
¡el día se les volverá tinieblas!
7Los videntes quedarán en vergüenza;
los adivinos serán humillados.
Dios les tapará la boca,
pues no les dará respuesta.
8Yo, en cambio, estoy lleno de poder,
lleno del Espíritu del SEÑOR,
y lleno de justicia y de fuerza,
para echarle en cara a Jacob su delito;
para reprocharle a Israel su pecado.

El gobierno corrupto, causa de la caída de Sión

9Escuchen esto ustedes,
gobernantes del pueblo de Jacob,
y autoridades del reino de Israel,
que abominan la justicia y tuercen el
derecho,
10que edifican a *Sión con sangre
y a Jerusalén con injusticia.
11Sus gobernantes juzgan por soborno,
sus sacerdotes instruyen por paga,
y sus profetas predicen por dinero;
para colmo, se apoyan en el SEÑOR, diciendo:

«¿No está el SEÑOR entre nosotros?
¡No vendrá sobre nosotros ningún mal!»
12Por lo tanto, por culpa de ustedes
Sión será como un campo arado;
Jerusalén quedará en ruinas,
y el monte del templo se volverá un
matorral.

Futura exaltación de Sión
4:1-3 — Is 2:1-4

4 En los últimos días,
el monte del templo del SEÑOR
será puesto sobre la cumbre de las montañas
y elevado por encima de las colinas.
Entonces los pueblos marcharán hacia ella,
2y muchas naciones se acercarán, diciendo:
«Vengan, subamos al monte del SEÑOR,
a la casa del Dios de Jacob.
Dios mismo nos instruirá en sus *caminos,
y así andaremos en sus sendas.»
Porque de *Sión viene la instrucción;
de Jerusalén, la palabra del SEÑOR.
3Dios mismo juzgará entre muchos pueblos,
y administrará *justicia
a naciones poderosas y lejanas.
Convertirán en azadones sus espadas,
y en hoces sus lanzas.
Ya no alzará su espada nación contra nación,
ni se adiestrarán más para la guerra.
4Cada uno se sentará
bajo su parra y su higuera;
y nadie perturbará su solaz
—el SEÑOR *Todopoderoso lo ha dicho—.
5Todos los pueblos marchan
en *nombre de sus dioses,
pero nosotros marchamos en el nombre del
SEÑOR,
en el nombre de nuestro Dios,
desde ahora y para siempre.

Futura restauración de Sión

6«En aquel día —afirma el SEÑOR—
reuniré a las ovejas lastimadas,
dispersas y maltratadas.
7Con las ovejas heridas formaré un remanente,
y con las desterradas, una nación poderosa.
El SEÑOR reinará sobre ellas en el monte Sión
desde ahora y para siempre.
8Y tú, Torre del Rebaño,
colina fortificada de la ciudad de Sión:
a ti volverá tu antiguo poderío,
la soberanía de la ciudad de Jerusalén.»

Castigo y triunfo de Sión

9Ahora, ¿por qué gritas tanto?
¿Acaso no tienes rey?
¿Por qué te han venido dolores de parto?
¿Murió acaso tu consejero?
10Retuércete y puja, hija de Sión,
como mujer a punto de dar a luz,
porque ahora vas a salir de tu ciudad,
y tendrás que vivir a campo abierto.
Irás a Babilonia, pero de allí serás rescatada;
el SEÑOR te librará del poder de tus
enemigos.
11Ahora muchas naciones se han reunido
contra ti.
Y dicen: «¡Que sea profanada Sión!
¡Disfrutemos del espectáculo!»
12Pero ellas no saben lo que piensa el SEÑOR,
ni comprenden sus designios;

no saben que él las junta
como a gavillas en la era.
13¡Levántate, hija de Sión!
¡Ponte a trillar!
Yo haré de hierro tus cuernos
y de bronce tus pezuñas,
para que conviertas en polvo a muchos
pueblos,
y consagres al SEÑOR sus ganancias injustas;
sus riquezas, al Señor de toda la tierra.

Humillación y exaltación de la dinastía davídica

5 Reagrupa tus tropas, ciudad guerrera,
porque nos asedian.
Con vara golpearán en la mejilla
al gobernante de Israel.
2Pero de ti, Belén Efrata,
pequeña entre los clanes de Judá,
saldrá el que gobernará a Israel;
sus orígenes se remontan hasta la antigüedad,
hasta tiempos inmemoriales.
3Por eso Dios los entregará al enemigo
hasta que tenga su hijo la que va a ser
madre,
y vuelva junto al pueblo de Israel
el resto de sus hermanos.
4Pero surgirá uno para *pastorearlos
con el poder del SEÑOR,
con la majestad del nombre del SEÑOR su
Dios.
Vivirán seguros, porque él dominará
hasta los confines de la tierra.
5¡Él traerá la *paz!
Si Asiria llegara a invadir nuestro país
para pisotear nuestras fortalezas,
le haremos frente con siete pastores,
y aun con ocho líderes del pueblo;
6ellos pastorearán a Asiria con la espada;
con la daga, a la tierra de Nimrod.
Si Asiria llegara a invadir nuestro país,
si llegara a profanar nuestras fronteras,
¡él nos rescatará!

El remanente

7Será el remanente de Jacob,
en medio de muchos pueblos,
como rocío que viene del SEÑOR,
como abundante lluvia sobre la hierba,
que no depende de los hombres,
ni espera nada de ellos.
8Será el remanente de Jacob entre las naciones,
en medio de muchos pueblos,
como un león entre los animales del bosque,
como un cachorro entre las ovejas del
rebaño,
que al pasar las pisotea y las desgarra,
sin que nadie pueda rescatarlas.
9Levantarás la mano contra tus enemigos,
y acabarás con todos tus agresores.

Purificación de un pueblo idólatra y belicoso

10Esto afirma el SEÑOR:

«En aquel día exterminaré tu caballería,
y destruiré tus carros de guerra.
11Exterminaré las ciudades de tu país
y derribaré todas tus fortalezas.
12Pondré fin a tus hechicerías
y no tendrás más adivinos.
13Acabaré con tus ídolos

y con tus monumentos sagrados;
nunca más volverás a postrarte
ante las obras de tus manos.
14Arrancaré tus imágenes de *Aserá,
y reduciré a escombros tus ciudades;
15con ira y con furor me vengaré
de las naciones que no me obedecieron.»

Querella de Dios contra su pueblo

6 Escuchen lo que dice el SEÑOR:

«Levántate, presenta tu caso ante las
montañas;
deja que las colinas oigan tu voz.»

2Escuchen, montañas, la querella del SEÑOR;
presten atención, firmes cimientos de la
tierra;
el SEÑOR entra en juicio contra su pueblo,
entabla un pleito contra Israel:
3«Pueblo mío, ¿qué te he hecho?
¡Dime en qué te he ofendido!
4Yo fui quien te sacó de Egipto,
quien te libró de esa tierra de esclavitud.
Yo envié a Moisés, Aarón y Miriam,
para que te dirigieran.
5Recuerda, pueblo mío,
lo que tramaba Balac, rey de Moab,
y lo que le respondió Balán hijo de Beor.
Recuerda tu paso desde Sitín hasta Guilgal,
y reconoce las hazañas redentoras del
SEÑOR.»

6¿Cómo podré acercarme al SEÑOR
y postrarme ante el Dios Altísimo?
¿Podré presentarme con *holocaustos
o con becerros de un año?
7¿Se complacerá el SEÑOR con miles de
carneros,
o con diez mil arroyos de aceite?
¿Ofreceré a mi primogénito por mi delito,
al fruto de mis entrañas por mi pecado?

8¡Ya se te ha declarado lo que es bueno!
Ya se te ha dicho lo que de ti espera el
SEÑOR:
Practicar la justicia,
amar la misericordia,
y humillarte ante tu Dios.

Castigo por delitos económicos y sociales

9Tribu y asamblea de la ciudad,
escuchen la voz del SEÑOR, que los
convoca,
pues es de sabios temer su *nombre.i
10¡Malvados!
¿Debo tolerar sus tesoros mal habidos,
y sus odiosas medidas adulteradas?
11¿Debo tener por justas la balanza falsa
y la bolsa de pesas alteradas?
12Los ricos de la ciudad son gente violenta;
sus habitantes son gente mentirosa;
¡engañan con la boca y con la lengua!
13Por lo que a mí toca, te demoleré a golpes,
te destruiré por tus pecados.
14Comerás, pero no te saciarás,
sino que seguirás padeciendo hambre.j
Lo que recojas no lo podrás retener,
y lo que retengas lo entregaré a la espada.
15Lo que siembres no lo cosecharás,

---

i 6:9 Versículo de difícil traducción. j 6:14 *seguirás padeciendo hambre.* Texto de difícil traducción.

ni usarás el aceite de las aceitunas que
exprimas,
ni beberás el vino de las uvas que pises.
16Tú sigues fielmente los decretos de Omrí
y todas las prácticas de la dinastía de Acab;
te conduces según sus consejos.
Por eso voy a entregarte a la destrucción,
y a poner en ridículo a tus habitantes.
¡Tendrás que soportar el insulto de los
pueblos!»k

Lamento ante una sociedad corrupta

7 ¡Pobre de mí!
　No llegué a tiempo para la cosecha de verano
ni para los rebuscos de la vendimia;
no tengo un solo racimo que comer,
ni un higo tierno, por el que me muero.
2La gente piadosa ha sido eliminada del país,
¡ya no hay gente honrada en este mundo!
Todos tratan de matar a alguien,
y unos a otros se tienden redes.
3Nadie les gana en cuanto a hacer lo malo;
funcionarios y jueces exigen soborno.
Los magnates no hacen más que pedir,
y todos complacen su codicia.
4El mejor de ellos es más enmarañado que una
zarza;
el más recto, más torcido que un espino.
Pero ya viene el día de su confusión;
¡ya se acerca el día de tu castigo
anunciado por tus centinelas!
5No creas en tu prójimo,
ni confíes en tus amigos;
cuídate de lo que hablas
con la que duerme en tus brazos.
6El hijo ultraja al padre,
la hija se rebela contra la madre,
la nuera contra la suegra,
y los enemigos de cada cual
están en su propia casa.
7Pero yo he puesto mi esperanza en el SEÑOR;
yo espero en el Dios de mi *salvación.
¡Mi Dios me escuchará!

Esperanza de redención

8Enemiga mía, no te alegres de mi mal.
Caí, pero he de levantarme;
vivo en tinieblas, pero el SEÑOR es mi luz.
9He pecado contra el SEÑOR,
así que soportaré su furia
hasta que él juzgue mi causa
y me haga justicia.

Entonces me sacará a la luz
y gozaré de su salvación.
10Cuando lo vea mi enemiga,
la que me decía: «¿Dónde está tu Dios?»,
se llenará de vergüenza.
Mis ojos contemplarán su desgracia,
pues será pisoteada como el lodo de las
calles.

11El día que tus muros sean reconstruidos
será el momento de extender tus fronteras.
12Ese día acudirán a ti los pueblos,
desde Asiria hasta las ciudades de Egipto,
desde el río Nilo hasta el río Éufrates,
de mar a mar y de montaña a montaña.
13La tierra quedará desolada
por culpa de sus habitantes,
como resultado de su maldad.

14Pastorea con tu cayado a tu pueblo,
al rebaño de tu propiedad,
que habita solitario en el bosque,
en medio de la espesura.
Hazlo pastar en Basán y en Galaad
como en los tiempos pasados.
15Muéstrale tus prodigios,
como cuando lo sacaste de Egipto.l
16Las naciones verán tus maravillas
y se avergonzarán de toda su prepotencia;
se llevarán la mano a la boca
y sus oídos se ensordecerán.
17Lamerán el polvo como serpientes,
como los reptiles de la tierra.
Saldrán temblando de sus escondrijos
y, temerosos ante tu presencia,
se volverán a ti, SEÑOR y Dios nuestro.

18¿Qué Dios hay como tú,
que perdone la maldad
y pase por alto el delito
del remanente de su pueblo?
No siempre estarás airado,
porque tu mayor placer es amar.
19Vuelve a compadecerte de nosotros.
Pon tu pie sobre nuestras maldades
y arroja al fondo del mar todos nuestros
pecados.
20Muestra tu fidelidad a Jacob,
y tu lealtad a Abraham,
como desde tiempos antiguos
se lo juraste a nuestros antepasados.

---

k 6:16 los pueblos (LXX); mi pueblo (TM). l 7:15 Muéstrale ... Egipto (lectura probable); Le mostraré maravillas / como cuando
saliste de la tierra de Egipto (TM).

NAHÚM

1 Profecía acerca de Nínive. Libro de la visión que tuvo Nahúm de Elcós.

Manifestación del SEÑOR

2El SEÑOR es un Dios celoso y vengador.
¡SEÑOR de la venganza, Señor de la ira!
El SEÑOR se venga de sus adversarios;
es implacable con sus enemigos.
3El SEÑOR es lento para la ira,
imponente en su fuerza.
El SEÑOR no deja a nadie sin castigo.
Camina en el huracán y en la tormenta;
las nubes son el polvo de sus pies.
4Increpa al mar y lo seca;
hace que todos los ríos se evaporen.
Los montes Basán y Carmelo pierden su
lozanía;
el verdor del Líbano se marchita.
5Ante él tiemblan las montañas
y se desmoronan las colinas.
Ante él se agita la tierra,
el mundo y cuanto en él habita.
6¿Quién podrá enfrentarse a su indignación?
¿Quién resistirá el ardor de su ira?
Su furor se derrama como fuego;
ante él se resquebrajan las rocas.

Destrucción de Nínive

7Bueno es el SEÑOR;
es refugio en el día de la angustia,
y protector de los que en él confían.
8Pero destruirá a Nínivea
con una inundación arrasadora;
¡aun en las tinieblas perseguirá a sus
enemigos!
9¿Qué traman contra el SEÑOR?
¡Él desbaratará sus planes!
¡La calamidad no se repetirá!
10Serán consumidos como paja seca,
como espinos enmarañados,
como borrachos ahogados en vino.
11Tú, Nínive, engendraste
al que trama el mal contra el SEÑOR,
al infame consejero.

Liberación del opresor

12Así dice el SEÑOR:
«Aunque los asirios sean fuertes y numerosos,
serán arrancados y morirán.
Y a ti, Judá, aunque te he afligido,
no volveré a afligirte.
13Voy a quebrar el yugo que te oprime,
voy a romper tus ataduras.»
14Pero acerca de ti, Nínive,
el SEÑOR ha decretado:
«No tendrás más hijos que perpetúen tu
*nombre;
extirparé de la casa de tus dioses
las imágenes talladas y los ídolos fundidos.
Te voy a preparar una tumba,
porque eres una infame.»

Anuncio de la victoria sobre Nínive

15¡Miren! Ya se acerca por los montes
el que anuncia las buenas nuevas de
*victoria,
el que proclama la *paz.

¡Celebra tus peregrinaciones, Judá!
¡Paga tus votos!
Porque no volverán a invadirte los malvados,
pues han sido destruidos por completo.

La destrucción de Nínive

2 Nínive, un destructor avanza contra ti,
así que monta guardia en el terraplén,
vigila el camino, renueva tus fuerzas,
acrecienta tu poder.
2Porque el SEÑOR restaura la majestad de Jacob,
como la majestad de Israel,
pues los destructores lo han arrasado;
han arruinado sus sarmientos.

3Rojo es el escudo de sus valientes;
de púrpura se visten los guerreros.
El metal de sus carros brilla como fuego
mientras se alistan para la batalla
y los guerreros agitan sus lanzas.
4Desaforados corren los carros por las calles,
irrumpen con violencia por las plazas.
Son como antorchas de fuego,
como relámpagos zigzagueantes.

Caída y saqueo de Nínive

5Convoca el rey de Nínive a sus tropas
escogidas,
que en su carrera se atropellan.
Se lanzan contra la muralla
para levantar la barricada,
6pero se abren las compuertas de los ríos
y el palacio se derrumba.
7Ya está decidido:
la ciudadb será llevada al exilio.
Gimen sus criadas como palomas,
y se golpean el pecho.

8Nínive es como un estanque roto
cuyas aguas se derraman.
«¡Deténganse!» «¡Deténganse!», les gritan,
pero nadie vuelve atrás.
9¡Saqueen la plata!
¡Saqueen el oro!
El tesoro es inagotable,
y abundan las riquezas y los objetos
preciosos.
10¡Destrucción, desolación, devastación!
Desfallecen los *corazones,
tiemblan las rodillas,
se estremecen los cuerpos,
palidecen los rostros.

La bestia salvaje morirá

11¿Qué fue de la guarida de los leones
y de la cueva de los leoncillos,
donde el león, la leona y sus cachorros
se guarecían sin que nadie los perturbara?
12¿Qué fue del león,
que despedazaba para sus crías
y estrangulaba para sus leonas,
que llenaba de presas su caverna
y de carne su guarida?
13Pero ahora yo vengo contra ti
—afirma el SEÑOR omnipotente—.
Reduciré a cenizas tus carros de guerra
y mataré a filo de espada a tus leoncillos.
Pondré fin en el país a tus rapiñas,

y no volverá a oírse la voz de tus
mensajeros.

Descripción del fin de Nínive

3 ¡Ay de la ciudad sedienta de sangre,
   repleta de mentira,
insaciable en su rapiña,
   aferrada a la presa!
2Se oye el chasquido de los látigos,
   el estrépito de las ruedas,
el galopar de los caballos,
   el chirrido de los carros,
3la carga de la caballería,
   el fulgor de las espadas,
el centellear de las lanzas,
   la multitud de muertos,
los cuerpos amontonados,
   los cadáveres por doquier,
en los que todos tropiezan.
4¡Y todo por las muchas prostituciones
   de esa ramera de encantos zalameros,
   de esa maestra de la seducción!
Engañó a los pueblos con sus fornicaciones,
   y a los clanes con sus embrujos.

5«¡Aquí estoy contra ti!
   —afirma el SEÑOR *Todopoderoso—.
Te levantaré la falda hasta la cara,
   para que las naciones vean tu desnudez,
   y los reinos descubran tus vergüenzas.
6Te cubriré de inmundicias,
   te ultrajaré y te exhibiré en público.
7Todos los que te vean huirán de ti,
   y dirán: "¡Nínive ha sido devastada!
¿Quién hará duelo por ella?"
   ¿Dónde hallaré quien la consuele?»

Destrucción total de Nínive

8¿Acaso eres mejor que Tebas,c
   ciudad rodeada de aguas,
asentada junto a las corrientes del Nilo,
que tiene al mar por terraplén
   y a las aguas por muralla?
9*Cus y Egipto eran su fuerza ilimitada,
   Fut y Libia eran sus aliados.
10Con todo, Tebas marchó al exilio;
   fue llevada al cautiverio.
A sus hijos los estrellaron

contra las esquinas de las calles.
Sobre sus nobles echaron suertes,
   y encadenaron a su gente ilustre.

11También tú, Nínive, te embriagarás,
   y se embotarán tus sentidos.
También tú, por causa del enemigo,
   tendrás que buscar refugio.
12Todas tus fortalezas son higueras
   cargadas de brevas maduras:
si las sacuden,
   caen en la boca del que se las come.
13Mira, al enfrentarse al enemigo
   tus tropas se portan como mujeres.
Las *puertas de tu país quedarán abiertas de
      par en par,
   porque el fuego consumirá tus cerrojos.

Defensa inútil

14Abastécete de agua para el asedio,
   refuerza tus fortificaciones.
Métete al barro, pisa la mezcla
   y moldea los ladrillos.
15Porque allí mismo te consumirá el fuego
   y te exterminará la espada;
¡como larva de langosta te devorará!
Multiplícate como larva,
   reprodúcete como langosta.
16Aumentaste tus mercaderes
   más que las estrellas del cielo.d
17Tus dignatarios son como langostas
   y tus oficiales, como insectos
que en días fríos se posan sobre los muros,
   pero que al salir el sol desaparecen,
   y nadie sabe dónde hallarlos.

18Rey de Asiria,
   tus pastores están amodorrados,
¡tus tropas escogidas se echaron a dormir!
Tu pueblo anda disperso por los montes,
   y no hay quien lo reúna.
19Tu herida no tiene remedio;
   tu llaga es incurable.

Todos los que sepan lo que te ha pasado,
   celebrarán tu desgracia.
Pues ¿quién no fue víctima
   de tu constante maldad?

---

c **3:8** *Tebas.* Lit. *No Amón.*   d **3:16** *cielo* (lectura probable); *cielo. La larva se desprende del capullo y vuela* (TM).

HABACUC

1 Ésta es la profecía que el profeta Habacuc recibió en visión.

La primera queja de Habacuc

2¿Hasta cuándo, SEÑOR, he de pedirte ayuda
 sin que tú me escuches?
¿Hasta cuándo he de quejarme de la violencia
 sin que tú nos salves?
3¿Por qué me haces presenciar calamidades?
 ¿Por qué debo contemplar el sufrimiento?
Veo ante mis ojos destrucción y violencia;
 surgen riñas y abundan las contiendas.
4Por lo tanto, se entorpece la ley
 y no se da curso a la justicia.
El impío acosa al justo,
 y las sentencias que se dictan son injustas.

La respuesta del SEÑOR

5«¡Miren a las naciones!
 ¡Contémplenlas y quédense asombrados!
Estoy por hacer en estos días cosas tan
 sorprendentes
 que no las creerán aunque alguien se las
 explique.
6Estoy incitando a los *caldeos,
 ese pueblo despiadado e impetuoso,
que recorre toda la tierra
 para apoderarse de territorios ajenos.
7Son un pueblo temible y espantoso,
 que impone su propia justicia y grandeza.
8Sus caballos son más veloces que leopardos,
 más feroces que lobos nocturnos.
Su caballería se lanza a todo galope;
 sus jinetes vienen de muy lejos.
¡Caen como buitres sobre su presa!
9Vienen en son de violencia;
 avanzan sus hordasa como el viento del
 desierto,
 hacen prisioneros como quien recoge arena.
10Ridiculizan a los reyes,
 se burlan de los gobernantes;
se ríen de toda ciudad amurallada,
 pues construyen terraplenes y la toman.
11Son un viento que a su paso arrasa todo;
 su pecado es hacer de su fuerza un dios.»

La segunda queja de Habacuc

12¡Tú, SEÑOR, existes desde la eternidad!
 ¡Tú, mi *santo Dios, eres inmortal!b
Tú, SEÑOR, los has puesto para hacer justicia;
 tú, mi *Roca, los has puesto para ejecutar
 tu castigo.
13Son tan puros tus ojos que no puedes ver el
 mal;
 no te es posible contemplar el sufrimiento.
¿Por qué entonces toleras a los traidores?
 ¿Por qué guardas silencio
mientras los impíos se tragan a los justos?
14Has hecho que a los *hombres como peces del mar,
 como reptiles que no tienen jefe.
15Babilonia los saca a todos con anzuelo,
 los arrastra con sus redes,
los recoge entre sus mallas,
 y así se alegra y regocija.
16Por lo tanto, ofrece sacrificios a sus redes
 y quema incienso a sus mallas,

pues gracias a sus redes su porción es sabrosa
 y su comida es suculenta.
17¿Continuará vaciando sus redes
 y matando sin piedad a las naciones?

2 Me mantendré alerta,
 me apostaré en los terraplenes;
estaré pendiente de lo que me diga,
 de su respuesta a mi reclamo.

La respuesta del SEÑOR

2Y el SEÑOR me respondió:

«Escribe la visión,
 y haz que resalte claramente en las tablillas,
 para que pueda leerse de corrido.
3Pues la visión se realizará en el tiempo
 señalado;
 marcha hacia su cumplimiento, y no dejará
 de cumplirse.
Aunque parezca tardar, espérala;
 porque sin falta vendrá.

4»El insolente no tiene el *alma recta,
 pero el justo vivirá por su fe.
5Además, la riqueza es traicionera;c
 por eso el soberbio no permanecerá.
Pues ensancha su garganta, como el
 *sepulcro,
 y es insaciable como la muerte.
Reúne en torno suyo a todas las naciones
 y toma cautivos a todos los pueblos.
6Y éstos lo harán objeto de burla
 en sus sátiras y adivinanzas.

»¡Ay del que se hace rico con lo ajeno
 y acumula prendas empeñadas!
 ¿Hasta cuándo seguirá con esta práctica?
7¿No se levantarán de repente tus acreedores?
 ¿No se despertarán para sacudirte
 y despojarte con violencia?
8Son tantas las naciones que has saqueado,
 que los pueblos que se salven te saquearán
 a ti;
porque es mucha la sangre que has
 derramado,
 y mucha tu violencia contra este país,
 contra esta ciudad y sus habitantes.

9»¡Ay del que llena su casa de ganancias
 injustas
 en un intento por salvar su nido
 y escapar de las garras del infortunio!
10»Son tus maquinaciones la vergüenza de tu
 casa:
 exterminaste a muchas naciones,
 pero causaste tu propia desgracia.
11Por eso hasta las piedras del muro claman,
 y resuenan las vigas del enmaderado.

12»¡Ay del que construye una ciudad con
 asesinatos
 y establece un poblado mediante el crimen!
13¿No ha determinado el SEÑOR
 *Todopoderoso
 que los pueblos trabajen para el fuego
 y las naciones se fatiguen por nada?

---

a 1:9 hordas. Palabra de difícil traducción. b 1:12 eres inmortal (lit. no morirás; según una tradición rabínica); no moriremos (TM). c 2:5 la riqueza es traicionera (Qumrán); el vino es traicionero (TM).

14Porque así como las aguas cubren los mares,
　　así también se llenará la tierra
　　del conocimiento de la gloria del SEÑOR.

15»¡Ay de ti, que emborrachas a tu prójimo!
　　¡Ay de ti, que lo embriagas con vinod
　　para contemplar su cuerpo desnudo!
16Con esto te has cubierto de ignominia y no de
　　　gloria.
　　¡Pues bebe también tú, y muestra lo pagano
　　　que eres!e
　　¡Que se vuelque sobre ti la copa de la diestra
　　　del SEÑOR,
　　y sobre tu gloria, la ignominia!
17¡Que te aplaste la violencia que cometiste
　　　contra el Líbano!
　　¡Que te abata la destrucción que hiciste de
　　　los animales!
　　¡Porque es mucha la sangre que has
　　　derramado,
　　y mucha tu violencia contra este país,
　　contra esta ciudad y sus habitantes!

18»¿De qué sirve una imagen,
　　si quien la esculpe es un artesano?
　　¿De qué sirve un ídolo fundido,
　　si tan sólo enseña mentiras?
　　El artesano que hace ídolos que no pueden
　　　hablar
　　sólo está confiando en su propio artificio.
19¡Ay del que le dice al madero: "Despierta",
　　y a la piedra muda: "Levántate"!
　　Aunque están recubiertos de oro y plata,
　　nada pueden enseñarle,
　　pues carecen de aliento de vida.
20En cambio, el SEÑOR está en su *santo templo;
　　¡guarde toda la tierra silencio en su
　　　presencia!»

La oración de Habacuc

3 Oración del profeta Habacuc. Según sigionot.f

2SEÑOR, he sabido de tu fama;
　　tus obras, SEÑOR, me dejan pasmado.
　　Realízalas de nuevo en nuestros días,
　　dalas a conocer en nuestro tiempo;
　　en tu ira, ten presente tu misericordia.

3De Temán viene Dios,
　　del monte de Parán viene el *Santo.
　　　　　　　　　　　　　　　　*Selah
　Su gloria cubre el cielo
　　y su alabanza llena la tierra.
4Su brillantez es la del relámpago;
　　rayos brotan de sus manos;
　　¡tras ellos se esconde su poder!
5Una plaga mortal lo precede,
　　un fuego abrasador le sigue los pasos.
6Se detiene, y la tierra se estremece;
　　lanza una mirada, y las naciones tiemblan.
　Se desmoronan las antiguas montañas
　　y se desploman las viejas colinas,
　　pero los caminos de Dios son eternos.

7He visto afligidos los campamentos de Cusán,
　　y angustiadas las moradas de Madián.

8¿Te enojaste, oh SEÑOR, con los ríos?
　　¿Estuviste airado contra las corrientes?
　¿Tan enfurecido estabas contra el mar
　　que cabalgaste en tus caballos
　　y montaste en tus carros victoriosos?
9Descubriste tu arco,
　　llenaste de flechas tu aljaba.g
　　　　　　　　　　　　　　　　Selah
　Tus ríos surcan la tierra;
10　las montañas te ven y se retuercen.
　Pasan los torrentes de agua,
　　y ruge el abismo, levantando sus manos.
11El sol y la luna se detienen en el cielo
　　por el fulgor de tus veloces flechas,
　　por el deslumbrante brillo de tu lanza.
12Indignado, marchas sobre la tierra;
　　lleno de ira, trillas a las naciones.

13Saliste a liberar a tu pueblo,
　　saliste a salvar a tu *ungido.
　Aplastaste al rey de la perversa dinastía,
　　¡lo desnudaste de pies a cabeza!
　　　　　　　　　　　　　　　　Selah
14Con tu lanza les partiste la cabeza a sus
　　　guerreros,
　　que enfurecidos querían dispersarme,
　que con placer arrogante se lanzaron contra mí,
　　como quien se lanza contra un pobre
　　　indefenso.h
15Pisoteaste el mar con tus corceles,
　　agitando las inmensas aguas.

16Al oírlo, se estremecieron mis entrañas;
　　a su voz, me temblaron los labios;
　la carcoma me caló en los huesos,
　　y se me aflojaron las piernas.
　Pero yo espero con paciencia
　　el día en que la calamidad
　　vendrá sobre la nación que nos invade.
17Aunque la higuera no dé renuevos,
　　ni haya frutos en las vides;
　aunque falle la cosecha del olivo,
　　y los campos no produzcan alimentos;
　aunque en el aprisco no haya ovejas,
　　ni ganado alguno en los establos;
18aun así, yo me regocijaré en el SEÑOR,
　　¡me alegraré en Dios, mi libertador!

19El SEÑOR omnipotente es mi fuerza;
　　da a mis pies la ligereza de una gacela
　　y me hace caminar por las alturas.

　　　　　　Al director musical.
　　　　　Sobre instrumentos de cuerda.

---

d 2:15 que lo embriagas con vino. Texto de difícil traducción. e 2:16 lo pagano que eres. Lit. tu prepucio. f 3:1 Sigionot. Probablemente un término literario o musical. g 3:9 llenaste de flechas tu aljaba (mss. de LXX); en TM, texto de difícil traducción. h 3:14 Versículo de difícil traducción.

SOFONÍAS

1 Ésta es la palabra del SEÑOR, que vino a Sofonías hijo de Cusí, hijo de Guedalías, hijo de Amarías, hijo de Ezequías, durante el reinado de Josías hijo de Amón, rey de Judá:

Advertencia sobre la destrucción venidera

2«Arrasaré por completo
cuanto hay sobre la faz de la tierra
—afirma el SEÑOR—.
3Arrasaré con *hombres y animales,
con las aves del cielo,
con los peces del mar,
con ídolos e impíos por igual.a

»Exterminaré al hombre
de sobre la faz de la tierra
—afirma el SEÑOR—.

Juicio contra Judá

4»Extenderé mi mano contra Judá
y contra todos los habitantes de Jerusalén.
Exterminaré de este lugar todo rastro de *Baal,
y hasta el nombre de sus sacerdotes;b
5a los que en las azoteas se postran en
adoración
ante las estrellas del cielo,
a los que, postrados en adoración,
juran lealtad al SEÑOR,
y al mismo tiempo a Moloc,c
6a los que se apartan del SEÑOR,
y no lo buscan ni lo consultan.
7¡Silencio ante el SEÑOR omnipotente,
porque cercano está el día del SEÑOR;
ha preparado el SEÑOR un sacrificio
y ha *purificado a sus invitados!
8En el día del sacrificio del SEÑOR
castigaré a los funcionarios y oficiales del
rey,
y a cuantos se visten según modas
extrañas.
9En aquel día castigaré
a cuantos evitan pisar el umbral,d
a los que llenan de violencia y engaño
la casa de sus dioses.e
10»Aquel día se oirán gritos de auxilio,
desde la puerta del Pescado,
gemidos desde el Barrio Nuevo,
y gran quebranto desde las colinas
—afirma el SEÑOR—.

11»¡Giman, habitantes del Barrio del Mercado!f
Aniquilados serán todos sus mercaderes,
exterminados cuantos comercian con plata.
12En aquel tiempo registraré Jerusalén con
lámparas
para castigar a los que reposan tranquilos
como vino en su sedimento,
a los que piensan: "El SEÑOR no va a hacer
nada,
ni para bien ni para mal."
13En botín se convertirán sus riquezas,
sus casas en desolación:
"Edificarán casas,
pero no las habitarán;

plantarán viñas,
pero del vino no beberán."

El gran día del SEÑOR

14»Ya se acerca el gran día del SEÑOR;
a toda prisa se acerca.
El estruendo del día del SEÑOR será amargo,
y aun el más valiente gritará.
15Día de ira será aquel día,
día de acoso y angustia,
día de devastación y ruina,
día de tinieblas y penumbra,
día de niebla y densos nubarrones,
16día de trompeta y grito de batalla
contra las ciudades fortificadas,
contra los altos bastiones.
17De tal manera acosaré a los *hombres,
que andarán como ciegos,
porque pecaron contra el SEÑOR.
Su sangre será derramada como polvo
y sus entrañas como estiércol.
18No los podrán librar
ni su plata ni su oro
en el día de la ira del SEÑOR.
En el fuego de su celo
será toda la tierra consumida;
en un instante reducirá a la nada
a todos los habitantes de la tierra.»

2 Humíllate hasta el polvo,g
nación no quebrantada;
2hazlo antes que se cumpla lo que he
determinado
y ese día se desvanezca como la brizna,
antes que caiga sobre ti la ira ardiente del
SEÑOR,
antes que venga sobre ti el día de la ira del
SEÑOR.
3Busquen al SEÑOR, todos los humildes de la
tierra,
los que han puesto en práctica sus normas.
Busquen la justicia, busquen la humildad;
tal vez encontrarán refugio
en el día de la ira del SEÑOR.

Juicio contra los filisteos

4Gaza quedará abandonada
y Ascalón acabará en desolación.
Asdod será expulsada a plena luz del día
y Ecrón será desarraigada.
5¡Ay de la nación quereta
que habita a la orilla del mar!
La palabra del SEÑOR es contra ti,
Canaán, tierra de los filisteos:

«Te aniquilaré
hasta no dejar en ti habitante.»

6El litoral se convertirá en praderas,
en camposh de pastoreo y corrales de
ovejas.
7Y allí pastarán las ovejas
del remanente de la tribu de Judá.
Al atardecer se echarán a descansar
en las casas de Ascalón;

---

a 1:3 con ídolos e impíos por igual. Texto de difícil traducción. b 1:4 de sus sacerdotes (LXX); de los sacerdotes paganos con los sacerdotes (TM). c 1:5 Moloc. Lit. Malcán; es decir, Milcón. d 1:9 evitan pisar el umbral. Alusión a una práctica supersticiosa; véase 1S 5:5. e 1:9 la casa de sus dioses. Alt. el palacio de su señor. f 1:11 Mercado. Alt. Mortero. g 2:1 Humíllate hasta el polvo. Texto de difícil traducción. h 2:6 campos. Palabra de difícil traducción.

el SEÑOR su Dios vendrá en su ayuda
para restaurarlos.i

Juicio contra Moab y Amón

8«He oído los insultos de Moab
y las burlas de los amonitas,
que injuriaron a mi pueblo
y se mostraron arrogantes contra su
territorio.
9Tan cierto como que yo vivo
—afirma el SEÑOR *Todopoderoso, el Dios
de Israel—,
que Moab vendrá a ser como Sodoma
y los amonitas como Gomorra:
se volverán campos de espinos y minas de sal,
desolación perpetua.
El remanente de mi pueblo los saqueará;
los sobrevivientes de mi nación heredarán
su tierra.»

10Éste será el pago por su soberbia
y por injuriar y despreciar al pueblo del
SEÑOR Todopoderoso.
11El SEÑOR los aterrará
cuando destruya a todos los dioses de la
tierra;
y así hasta las naciones más remotas
se postrarán en adoración ante él,
cada cual en su propia tierra.

Juicio contra Cus

12«También ustedes, *cusitas,
serán atravesados por mi espada.»

Juicio contra Asiria

13Él extenderá su mano contra el norte;
aniquilará a Asiria
y convertirá a Nínive en desolación,
árida como un desierto.
14Se tenderán en medio de ella los rebaños,
todos los animales del campo.
Pasarán la noche sobre sus columnas
tanto el pelícano como la garza.
Resonarán por las ventanas sus graznidos,
habrá asolamiento en los umbrales,
las vigas de cedro quedarán al descubierto.
15Ésta es la ciudad alegre
que habitaba segura,
la que se decía a sí misma:
«Yo y nadie más.»
¡Cómo ha quedado convertida en espanto,
en guarida de fieras!
Todo el que pasa junto a ella
se mofa y amenaza con los puños.

El futuro de Jerusalén

3 ¡Ay de la ciudad opresora,
rebelde y contaminada!
2No atiende a consejos,
ni acepta *corrección.
No confía en el SEÑOR,
ni se acerca a su Dios.
3Las autoridades que están en ella
son leones rugientes,
sus gobernantes son lobos nocturnos
que no dejan nada para la mañana.
4Sus profetas son impertinentes,
hombres traicioneros.
Sus sacerdotes profanan las cosas *santas
y violentan la ley.

5Pero el SEÑOR que está en ella es justo;
no comete iniquidad.
Cada mañana imparte su justicia,
y no deja de hacerlo cada nuevo día,
pero el inicuo no conoce la vergüenza.

6«Exterminé naciones;
quedaron desolados sus bastiones.
Dejé sus calles desiertas,
y nadie pasa por ellas.
Quedaron arrasadas sus ciudades,
sin ningún habitante.
7Dije a la ciudad:
"¡Ciertamente me temerás;
aceptarás corrección!"
Entonces no sería destruida su morada,
según todo lo que decreté contra ella.
A pesar de todo, se empeñaron
en corromper todas sus obras.
8Espérenme, por tanto,
hasta el día que me levante a buscar el botín
—afirma el SEÑOR—,
porque he decidido reunir a las naciones
y juntar a los reinos
para derramar sobre ellos mi indignación,
toda mi ardiente ira.
En el fuego de mi celo
será toda la tierra consumida.

9»*Purificaré los labios de los pueblos
para que todos invoquen el *nombre del
SEÑOR
y le sirvan de común acuerdo.
10Desde más allá de los ríos de *Cus
me traerán ofrendas
mis adoradores, mi pueblo disperso.
11Aquel día no tendrás que avergonzarte más
de todas tus rebeliones contra mí.
Quitaré de en medio de ti
a esa gente altanera y jactanciosa,
y así nunca más volverás a ser arrogante
en mi santo monte.
12Dejaré un remanente en medio de ti,
un pueblo pobre y humilde.
En el nombre del SEÑOR,
se cobijará
13el remanente de Israel;
no cometerá iniquidad,
no dirá mentiras,
ni se hablará engaño en su boca.
Pastarán y se echarán a descansar
sin que nadie los espante.»

14¡Lanza gritos de alegría, hija de *Sión!
¡da gritos de victoria, Israel!
¡Regocíjate y alégrate de todo corazón,
hija de Jerusalén!
15El SEÑOR te ha levantado el castigo,
ha puesto en retirada a tus enemigos.
El SEÑOR, rey de Israel, está en medio de ti:
nunca más temerás mal alguno.
16Aquel día le dirán a Jerusalén:
«No temas, Sión, ni te desanimes,
17porque el SEÑOR tu Dios está en medio de ti
como guerrero victorioso.
Se deleitará en ti con gozo,
te renovará con su amor,
se alegrará por ti con cantos
18como en los días de fiesta.

»Yo te libraré de las tristezas,

---

i **2:7** *para restaurarlos.* Alt. *y hará volver a sus cautivos.*

que son para ti una carga deshonrosa.j
19En aquel tiempo yo mismo me ocuparé
de todos los que te oprimen;
salvaré a la oveja que cojea
y juntaré a la descarriada.
Les daré a ustedes fama y renombre
en los países donde fueron avergonzados.

20En aquel tiempo yo los traeré,
en aquel tiempo los reuniré.
Daré a ustedes fama y renombre
entre todos los pueblos de la tierra
cuando yo los restaurek
ante sus mismos ojos.»

Así lo ha dicho el Señor.

---

j **3:18** Versículo de difícil traducción. k **3:20** *los restaure.* Alt. *haga volver a sus cautivos.*

HAGEO

Primer oráculo: Exhortación a reedificar el templo

1 El día primero del mes sexto del segundo año del rey Darío, vino palabra del SEÑOR por medio del profeta Hageo a Zorobabel hijo de Salatiel, gobernador de Judá, y al sumo sacerdote Josué hijo de Josadac: 2«Así dice el SEÑOR *Todopoderoso: "Este pueblo alega que todavía no es el momento apropiado para ir a reconstruir la casa del SEÑOR."»

3También vino esta palabra del SEÑOR por medio del profeta Hageo:

4«¿Acaso es el momento apropiado
    para que ustedes residan en casas techadas
    mientras que esta casa está en ruinas?»

5Así dice ahora el SEÑOR Todopoderoso:

«¡Reflexionen sobre su proceder!

6»Ustedes siembran mucho, pero cosechan poco;
    comen, pero no quedan satisfechos;
    beben, pero no llegan a saciarse;
        se visten, pero no logran abrigarse;
    y al jornalero se le va su salario
        como por saco roto.»

7Así dice el SEÑOR Todopoderoso:

«¡Reflexionen sobre su proceder!

8»Vayan ustedes a los montes;
    traigan madera y reconstruyan mi casa.
Yo veré su reconstrucción con gusto,
    y manifestaré mi gloria

—dice el SEÑOR—.

9»Ustedes esperan mucho,
    pero cosechan poco;
lo que almacenan en su casa,
    yo lo disipo de un soplo.
¿Por qué? ¡Porque mi casa está en ruinas,
    mientras ustedes sólo se ocupan de la suya!

—afirma el SEÑOR Todopoderoso—.

10»Por eso, por culpa de ustedes, los cielos retuvieron el rocío y la tierra se negó a dar sus productos. 11Yo hice venir una sequía sobre los campos y las montañas, sobre el trigo y el vino nuevo, sobre el aceite fresco y el fruto de la tierra, sobre los animales y los hombres, y sobre toda la obra de sus manos.»

12Zorobabel hijo de Salatiel, el sumo sacerdote Josué hijo de Josadac, y todo el resto del pueblo, obedecieron al SEÑOR su Dios, es decir, obedecieron las palabras del profeta Hageo, a quien el SEÑOR su Dios había enviado. Y el pueblo sintió temor en la presencia del SEÑOR. 13Entonces Hageo su mensajero comunicó al pueblo del mensaje del SEÑOR: «Yo estoy con ustedes. Yo, el SEÑOR, lo afirmo.» 14Y el SEÑOR inquietó de tal manera a Zorobabel hijo de Salatiel, gobernador de Judá, y al sumo sacerdote Josué hijo de Josadac, y a todo el resto del pueblo, que vinieron y empezaron a trabajar en la casa de su Dios, el SEÑOR Todopoderoso. 15Era el día veinticuatro del mes sexto del segundo año del rey Darío.

Segundo oráculo: La presencia del Señor

2 El día veintiuno del mes séptimo, vino palabra del SEÑOR por medio del profeta Hageo: 2«Pregunta a Zorobabel hijo de Salatiel, gobernador de Judá, al sumo sacerdote Josué hijo de Josadac, y al resto del pueblo: 3"¿Queda alguien entre ustedes que haya visto esta casa en su antiguo esplendor? ¿Qué les parece ahora? ¿No la ven como muy poca cosa? 4Pues ahora, ¡ánimo, Zorobabel! —afirma el SEÑOR—. ¡Ánimo, Josué hijo de Josadac! ¡Tú eres el sumo sacerdote! ¡Ánimo, pueblo de esta tierra! —afirma el SEÑOR—. ¡Manos a la obra, que yo estoy con ustedes! —afirma el SEÑOR *Todopoderoso—. 5Y mi Espíritu permanece en medio de ustedes, conforme al *pacto que hice con ustedes cuando salieron de Egipto.

»No teman, 6porque así dice el SEÑOR Todopoderoso: "Dentro de muy poco haré que se estremezcan los cielos y la tierra, el mar y la tierra firme; 7¡haré temblar a todas las naciones! Sus riquezas llegarán aquí, y así llenaré de esplendor esta casa —dice el SEÑOR Todopoderoso—. 8¡Mía es la plata, y mío es el oro —afirma el SEÑOR Todopoderoso—. 9El esplendor de esta segunda casa será mayor que el de la primera —dice el SEÑOR Todopoderoso—. Y en este lugar concederé la *paz", afirma el SEÑOR Todopoderoso.»

Tercer oráculo: Consulta a los sacerdotes

10El día veinticuatro del mes noveno del segundo año de Darío, vino palabra del SEÑOR al profeta Hageo: 11«Así dice el SEÑOR Todopoderoso: "Consulta a los sacerdotes sobre las cosas sagradas."» Entonces Hageo les planteó lo siguiente:

12—Supongamos que alguien lleva carne consagrada en la falda de su vestido, y sucede que la falda toca pan, o guiso, o vino, o aceite, o cualquier otro alimento; ¿quedarán también consagrados?

—¡No! —contestaron los sacerdotes.

13—Supongamos ahora —prosiguió Hageo— que una persona inmunda por el contacto de un cadáver toca cualquiera de estas cosas; ¿también ellas quedarán inmundas?

—¡Sí! —contestaron los sacerdotes.

14Entonces Hageo respondió:

«¡Así es este pueblo!
    ¡Así es para mí esta nación!

—afirma el SEÑOR—.

¡Así es cualquier obra de sus manos!
    ¡y aun lo que allí ofrecen es inmundo!

15»Ahora bien, desde hoy en adelante, reflexionen. Antes que ustedes pusieran piedra sobre piedra en la casa del SEÑOR, 16¿cómo les iba? Cuando alguien se acercaba a un montón de grano esperando encontrar veinte medidas, sólo hallaba diez; y si se iba al lagar esperando sacar cincuenta medidas de la artesa del mosto, sólo sacaba veinte. 17Herí sus campos con quemazón y con plaga, y con granizo toda obra de sus manos. Pero ustedes no se volvieron[a] a mí —afirma el SEÑOR—. 18Reflexionen desde hoy en adelante, desde el día veinticuatro del mes noveno, día en que se colocaron los cimientos de la casa del SEÑOR. Reflexionen: 19¿Queda todavía alguna semilla en el granero? ¿Todavía no producen nada la vid ni la higuera, ni el granado ni el olivo? ¡Pues a partir de hoy yo los bendeciré!»

---

a 2:17 no se volvieron (LXX y Siríaca); en TM, texto de difícil traducción.

Cuarto oráculo: Promesas a Zorobabel

²⁰El día veinticuatro del mismo mes vino por segunda vez palabra del SEÑOR a Hageo: ²¹«Di a Zorobabel, gobernante de Judá: "Yo estoy por estremecer los cielos y la tierra. ²²Volcaré los tronos reales y haré pedazos el poderío de los reinos del mundo. Volcaré los carros con sus conductores, y caerán caballos y jinetes, y éstos se matarán a espada unos a otros. ²³En aquel día —afirma el SEÑOR *Todopoderoso— te tomaré a ti, mi siervo Zorobabel hijo de Salatiel —afirma el SEÑOR—, y te haré semejante a un anillo de sellar, porque yo te he elegido", afirma el SEÑOR Todopoderoso.»

ZACARÍAS

Un llamado a volver al SEÑOR

1 En el mes octavo del segundo año del reinado de Darío, la palabra del SEÑOR vino al profeta Zacarías, hijo de Berequías y nieto de Idó:
²«El SEÑOR está ardiendo en ira contra los antepasados de ustedes. ³Por lo tanto, adviértele al pueblo que así dice el SEÑOR *Todopoderoso:

»"Vuélvanse a mí,
    y yo me volveré a ustedes
        —afirma el SEÑOR Todopoderoso—.

⁴»"No sean como sus antepasados,
    a quienes les proclamaron
    los profetas de antaño
que así dice el SEÑOR Todopoderoso:
    'Vuélvanse de su mala conducta
    y de sus malas prácticas.'
Porque ellos no me obedecieron
    ni me prestaron atención
        —afirma el SEÑOR—.

⁵» "¿Dónde están los antepasados de ustedes?
    ¿Acaso los profetas siguen con vida?
⁶¿No se cumplieron en sus antepasados
    las palabras y los decretos
    que a mis siervos los profetas
    ordené comunicarles?

»"Entonces ellos se volvieron al SEÑOR, y dijeron: 'El SEÑOR Todopoderoso nos ha tratado tal y como había resuelto hacerlo: conforme a lo que merecen nuestra conducta y nuestras acciones.' "»

El hombre entre los arrayanes

⁷En el segundo año del reinado de Darío, en el día veinticuatro del mes de *sebat, que es el mes undécimo, la palabra del SEÑOR vino al profeta Zacarías, hijo de Berequías y de Idó: ⁸Una noche tuve una visión, en la que vi a un hombre montado en un caballo alazán. Ese hombre se detuvo entre los arrayanes que había en una hondonada. Detrás de él había jinetes en caballos alazanes, bayos y blancos. ⁹Yo le pregunté: «¿Qué significan estos jinetes, mi señor?» El ángel que hablaba conmigo me respondió: «Voy a explicarte lo que significan.» ¹⁰Y el hombre que estaba entre los arrayanes me dijo: «El SEÑOR ha enviado estos jinetes a recorrer toda la tierra.»

¹¹Los jinetes informaron al ángel del SEÑOR, que estaba entre los arrayanes: «Hemos recorrido toda la tierra. Por cierto, la encontramos tranquila y en paz.» ¹²Ante esto, el ángel del SEÑOR replicó: «SEÑOR Todopoderoso, ¿hasta cuándo te negarás a compadecerte de Jerusalén y de las ciudades de Judá, con las que has estado enojado estos setenta años?» ¹³El SEÑOR le respondió con palabras buenas y consoladoras al ángel que hablaba conmigo, ¹⁴y luego el ángel me dijo: «Proclama este mensaje de parte del SEÑOR Todopoderoso:

»"Mi amor por *Sión y por Jerusalén
    me hace sentir celos por ellas.
¹⁵En cambio, estoy lleno de ira
    con las naciones engreídas.
Mi enojo no era tan grave,
    pero ellas lo agravaron más."

¹⁶»Por lo tanto, así dice el SEÑOR:
    "Volveré a compadecerme de Jerusalén.
Allí se reconstruirá mi templo,
    y se extenderá el cordel de medir,

afirma el Señor Todopoderoso."

¹⁷»Proclama además lo siguiente de parte del SEÑOR Todopoderoso:

»"Otra vez mis ciudades rebosarán de bienes,
    otra vez el SEÑOR consolará a Sión,
    otra vez escogerá a Jerusalén."»

¹⁸Alcé la vista, ¡y vi ante mí cuatro cuernos! ¹⁹Le pregunté entonces al ángel que hablaba conmigo: «¿Qué significan estos cuernos?» Y el ángel me respondió: «Estos cuernos son los poderes que dispersaron a Judá, a Israel y a Jerusalén.»

²⁰Luego el SEÑOR me mostró cuatro herreros. ²¹Le pregunté: «¿Y éstos qué han venido a hacer?» Y el SEÑOR me respondió: «Los cuernos son los poderes que dispersaron a Judá, a tal punto que nadie pudo volver a levantar la cabeza. Los herreros han venido para aterrorizarlos, y para deshacer el poder de las naciones que levantaron su cuerno contra la tierra de Judá y dispersaron a sus habitantes.»

El hombre con el cordel de medir

2 Alcé la vista, ¡y vi ante mí a un hombre que tenía en la mano un cordel de medir! ²Le pregunté: «¿A dónde vas?» Y él me respondió: «Voy a medir a Jerusalén. Quiero ver cuánto mide de ancho y cuánto de largo.»

³Ya salía el ángel que hablaba conmigo cuando otro ángel vino a su encuentro ⁴y le dijo: «Corre a decirle a ese joven:

»"Tanta gente habrá en Jerusalén,
    y tanto ganado,
    que Jerusalén llegará a ser
    una ciudad sin muros.
⁵En torno suyo —afirma el SEÑOR—
    seré un muro de fuego,
    y dentro de ella
    seré su gloria."

⁶»¡Salgan, salgan!
    ¡Huyan del país del norte!
        —afirma el SEÑOR—.

»¡Fui yo quien los dispersó a ustedes
    por los cuatro vientos del cielo!
        —afirma el SEÑOR—.

⁷»Sión, tú que habitas en Babilonia, ¡sal de allí; escápate! ⁸Porque así dice el SEÑOR *Todopoderoso, cuya gloria me envió contra las naciones que los saquearon a ustedes:

«La nación que toca a mi pueblo,
    me toca la niña de los ojos.
⁹Yo agitaré mi mano contra esa nación,
    y sus propios esclavos la saquearán.

»Así sabrán que me ha enviado el SEÑOR Todopoderoso.

¹⁰»¡Grita de alegría, hija de *Sión!
    ¡Yo vengo a habitar en medio de ti!
        —afirma el SEÑOR—.

¹¹»En aquel día,
    muchas naciones se unirán al SEÑOR.
Ellas serán mi pueblo,
    y yo habitaré entre ellas.

»Así sabrán que el SEÑOR Todopoderoso es quien me ha enviado a ustedes. ¹²El SEÑOR tomará posesión de Judá, su porción en tierra *santa, y de nuevo escogerá a Jerusalén. 13¡Que todo el mundo guarde silencio ante el SEÑOR, que ya avanza desde su santa morada!»

Ropas limpias para el sumo sacerdote

3 Entonces me mostró a Josué, el sumo sacerdote, que estaba de pie ante el ángel del SEÑOR, y a *Satanás, que estaba a su mano derecha como parte acusadora. 2El ángel del SEÑOR le dijo a Satanás:

«¡Que te reprenda el SEÑOR,
    que ha escogido a Jerusalén!
¡Que el SEÑOR te reprenda, Satanás!
¿Acaso no es este hombre
    un tizón rescatado del fuego?»

3Josué estaba vestido con ropas sucias en presencia del ángel. 4Así que el ángel les dijo a los que estaban allí, dispuestos a servirle: «¡Quítenle las ropas sucias!» Y a Josué le dijo: «Como puedes ver, ya te he liberado de tu culpa, y ahora voy a vestirte con ropas espléndidas.»

5Entonces dije yo: «¡Pónganle también un turbante limpio en la cabeza!» Y le pusieron en la cabeza un turbante limpio, y lo vistieron, mientras el ángel del SEÑOR permanecía de pie. 6Luego el ángel del SEÑOR le hizo esta advertencia a Josué: 7«Así dice el SEÑOR *Todopoderoso:

»"Si andas en mis *caminos
    y me cumples como sacerdote,
entonces gobernarás mi templo
    y te harás cargo de mis atrios.
¡Yo te concederé un lugar
    entre estos que están aquí!

8»"Escucha, Josué, sumo sacerdote,
    y que lo oigan tus compañeros,
que se sientan en tu presencia
    y que son un buen presagio:
Estoy por traer a mi siervo,
    estoy por traer al Renuevo.
9¡Mira, Josué, la piedra
    que ante ti he puesto!
Hay en ella siete ojos,ᵃ
    y en ella pondré una inscripción.
¡En un solo día borraré
    el pecado de esta tierra!
    —afirma el SEÑOR Todopoderoso—.

10»"En aquel día, cada uno de ustedes invitará a su vecino a sentarse debajo de su vid y de su higuera, afirma el SEÑOR Todopoderoso."»

El candelabro de oro y los dos olivos

4 Entonces el ángel que hablaba conmigo volvió y me despertó, como a quien se despierta de su sueño. 2Y me preguntó: «¿Qué es lo que ves?» Yo le respondí: «Veo un candelabro de oro macizo, con un recipiente en la parte superior. Encima del candelabro hay siete lámparas, con siete tubos para las mismas. 3Hay también junto a él dos olivos, uno a la derecha del recipiente, y el otro a la izquierda.

4Le pregunté entonces al ángel que hablaba conmigo: «¿Qué significa todo esto, mi señor?» 5Y el ángel me respondió: «¿Acaso no sabes lo que significa?»

Tuve que admitir que no lo sabía. 6Así que el ángel me dijo: «Ésta es la palabra del SEÑOR para Zorobabel:

» "No será por la fuerza
    ni por ningún poder,
sino por mi Espíritu
    —dice el SEÑOR *Todopoderoso—.
7¿Quién te crees tú, gigantesca montaña?
    ¡Ante Zorobabel sólo eres una llanura!
Y él sacará la piedra principal
    entre gritos de alabanza a su belleza."»

8Entonces vino a mí la palabra del SEÑOR:

9«Zorobabel ha puesto los cimientos de este
        templo,
    y él mismo terminará de construirlo.
¡Así sabrán que me ha enviado a ustedes
    el SEÑOR Todopoderoso!
10Cuando vean la plomada
    en las manos de Zorobabel,
se alegrarán que menospreciaron
    los días de los modestos comienzos.
¡Éstos son los siete ojos del SEÑOR,
    que recorren toda la tierra!»

11Entonces le pregunté al ángel: «¿Qué significan estos dos olivos a la derecha y a la izquierda del candelabro?» 12Y también le pregunté: «¿Qué significan estas dos ramas de olivo junto a los dos tubos de oro, por los que fluye el aceite dorado?»

13El ángel me respondió: «¿Acaso no sabes lo que significan?» Y yo tuve que admitir que no lo sabía. 14Así que el ángel me explicó: «Éstos son los dos *ungidos que están al servicio del Señor de toda la tierra.»

El rollo que volaba

5 Alcé otra vez la vista, ¡y vi ante mí un rollo que volaba! 2El ángel me preguntó: «¿Qué es lo que ves?» Y yo respondí: «Veo un rollo que vuela, de diez metros de largo por cinco de ancho.»ᵇ

3Entonces el ángel me dijo: Ésta es la maldición que caerá sobre todo el país. Según lo escrito en el rollo, alcanzará tanto al ladrón como al perjuro. 4Así que he desencadenado esta maldición para que entre en la casa del ladrón y en la casa del que jura en falso por mi nombre. Se alojará dentro de su casa y la destruirá, junto con sus vigas y sus piedras, afirma el SEÑOR *Todopoderoso.»

La mujer en un recipiente

5Entonces el ángel que hablaba conmigo salió y me dijo: «Alza la vista y fíjate en esto que ha aparecido.»

6«¿Y qué es?», le pregunté. Y él me contestó: «Es una medida de veintidós litros.ᶜ Es la maldad de la gente de todo el país.»

7Se levantó entonces la tapa de plomo, ¡y dentro de esa medida había una mujer sentada! 8El ángel dijo: «Ésta es la maldad», e inmediatamente arrojó a la mujer dentro de la medida, la cual cubrió luego con la tapa de plomo.

9Alcé la vista, ¡y vi ante mí dos mujeres que salían batiendo sus alas al viento! Tenían alas como de cigüeña, y elevaban la medida por los aires.

10Yo le pregunté al ángel que hablaba conmigo: «¿Adónde se llevan la medida?» 11Y él me respondió: «Se la llevan al país de Babilonia, para construirle un templo. Cuando el templo esté listo, colocarán la medida allí, sobre un pedestal.»

ᵃ 3:9 ojos. Alt. caras.   ᵇ 5:2 diez metros de largo por cinco de ancho. Lit. veinte *codos de largo y diez codos de ancho.   ᶜ 5:6 una medida de veintidós litros. Lit. un *efa; también en vv. 7,9,10.

Los cuatro carros

6 Alcé de nuevo la vista, ¡y vi ante mí cuatro carros de guerra que salían de entre dos montañas, las cuales eran de bronce! **2**El primer carro era tirado por caballos alazanes, el segundo por caballos negros, **3**el tercero por caballos blancos, y el cuarto por caballos pintos. Todos ellos eran caballos briosos. **4**Le pregunté al ángel que hablaba conmigo: «¿Qué significan estos carros, mi señor?»

5El ángel me respondió: «Éstos son los cuatro espíritus[d] del cielo, que salen después de haberse presentado ante el Señor de toda la tierra. **6**El carro de los caballos negros va hacia el país del norte; el de los caballos blancos, hacia el occidente;[e] y el de los caballos pintos, hacia el país del sur.»

7Esos briosos caballos estaban impacientes por recorrer toda la tierra. Y el ángel les dijo: «¡Vayan, recorran la tierra de uno a otro extremo!» Y así lo hicieron.

8Entonces el ángel me llamó y me dijo: «Mira, los que van hacia el país del norte van a calmar mi enojo en ese país.»

La corona para Josué

9La palabra del SEÑOR vino a mí, y me dijo: **10**«Ve hoy mismo a la casa de Josías hijo de Sofonías, que es adonde han llegado de Babilonia los exiliados Jelday, Tobías y Jedaías. Recíbeles **11**la plata y el oro que traen consigo, y con ese oro y esa plata haz una corona, la cual pondrás en la cabeza del sumo sacerdote Josué hijo de Josadac. **12**Y le dirás a Josué de parte del SEÑOR *Todopoderoso:

»"Éste es aquel cuyo *nombre es Renuevo,
    pues echará renuevos de sus raíces
    y reconstruirá el templo del SEÑOR.
13Él reconstruirá el templo del SEÑOR,
    se revestirá de majestad
    y se sentará a gobernar en su trono.
También un sacerdote se sentará en su propio
    trono,
y entre ambos habrá armonía."

14»La corona permanecerá en el templo del SEÑOR como un recordatorio para Jelday,[f] Tobías, Jedaías y Hen[g] hijo de Sofonías. **15**Si ustedes se esmeran en obedecer al SEÑOR su Dios, los que están lejos vendrán para ayudar en la reconstrucción del templo del SEÑOR. Así sabrán que el SEÑOR Todopoderoso me ha enviado a ustedes.»

Justicia y misericordia en lugar de ayuno

7 En el cuarto año del reinado del rey Darío, en el día cuatro del mes noveno, que es el mes de *quisleu, la palabra del SEÑOR vino a Zacarías. **2**El pueblo de Betel había enviado a Sarézer y a Reguen Mélec, y a sus hombres, a buscar el favor del SEÑOR **3**y a preguntarles a los sacerdotes de la casa del SEÑOR *Todopoderoso y a los profetas: «¿Debemos observar en el quinto mes un día de duelo y abstinencia, tal como lo hemos hecho todos estos años?»

4Vino entonces a mí esta palabra de parte del SEÑOR Todopoderoso:

5«Dile a todo el pueblo de la tierra,
    y también a los sacerdotes:
"Cuando ustedes ayunaban y se lamentaban
    en los meses quinto y séptimo
de los últimos setenta años,
    ¿realmente ayunaban por mí?
6Y cuando ustedes comen y beben,

¿acaso no lo hacen para sí mismos?"»

7¿No son éstas las palabras
    que por medio de los antiguos profetas
    el SEÑOR mismo proclamó
cuando Jerusalén y las ciudades cercanas
    estaban habitadas y tenían paz,
cuando el Néguev y las llanuras del oeste
    también estaban habitadas?

8La palabra del SEÑOR vino de nuevo a Zacarías. Le advirtió:

9«Así dice el SEÑOR Todopoderoso:

»"Juzguen con verdadera justicia;
    muestren amor y compasión
    los unos por los otros.
10No opriman a las viudas ni a los huérfanos,
    ni a los extranjeros ni a los pobres.
No maquinen el mal en su *corazón
    los unos contra los otros."

11»Pero ellos se negaron a hacer caso. Desafiantes volvieron la espalda, y se taparon los oídos. **12**Para no oír las instrucciones ni las palabras que por medio de los antiguos profetas el SEÑOR Todopoderoso había enviado con su Espíritu, endurecieron su corazón como el diamante. Por lo tanto, el SEÑOR Todopoderoso se llenó de ira. **13**"Como no me escucharon cuando los llamé, tampoco yo los escucharé cuando ellos me llamen —dice el SEÑOR Todopoderoso—. **14**Como con un torbellino, los dispersé entre todas las naciones que no conocían. La tierra que dejaron quedó tan desolada que nadie siquiera pasaba por ella. Fue así como convirtieron en desolación la tierra que antes era una delicia."»

El SEÑOR promete bendecir a Jerusalén

8 Otra vez vino a mí la palabra del SEÑOR *Todopoderoso. Me hizo saber lo siguiente:

2«Así dice el SEÑOR Todopoderoso:

»"Siento grandes celos por *Sión.
Son tantos mis celos por ella
    que me llenan de furia."

3»Así dice el SEÑOR:

»"Regresaré a Sión,
    y habitaré en Jerusalén.
Y Jerusalén será conocida
    como la Ciudad de la Verdad,
y el monte del SEÑOR Todopoderoso
    como el Monte de la *Santidad."

4»Así dice el SEÑOR Todopoderoso:

»"Los ancianos y las ancianas volverán a
    sentarse
    en las calles de Jerusalén,
cada uno con su bastón en la mano
    debido a su avanzada edad.
5Los niños y las niñas volverán a jugar
    en las calles de la ciudad."
6»Así dice el SEÑOR Todopoderoso:

»"Al remanente de este pueblo
    podrá parecerle imposible en aquellos días,
¿pero también a mí me parecerá imposible?,
    afirma el SEÑOR Todopoderoso."

---

d 6:5 *espíritus.* Alt. *vientos.*   **e 6:6** *hacia el occidente* (lectura probable); *tras ellos* (TM).   **f 6:14** *Jelday* (Siríaca; véase v. 10); *Hélem* (TM).   **g 6:14** *Hen.* Alt. *el piadoso, el.*

7»Así dice el SEÑOR Todopoderoso:

»"Salvaré a mi pueblo
de los países de oriente y de occidente.
8Los haré volver
para que vivan en Jerusalén;
ellos serán mi pueblo
y yo seré su Dios,
en la verdad y en la justicia."

9»Así dice el SEÑOR Todopoderoso:

»"¡Cobren ánimo, ustedes,
los que en estos días han escuchado
las palabras de los profetas,
mientras se echan los cimientos
para la reconstrucción del templo
del SEÑOR Todopoderoso!
10Porque antes de estos días
ni los hombres recibían su jornal
ni los animales su alimento.
Por culpa del enemigo
tampoco los viajeros tenían seguridad,
pues yo puse a la *humanidad entera
en contra de sus semejantes.
11Pero ya no trataré al remanente de este pueblo
como lo hice en el pasado
—afirma el SEÑOR Todopoderoso—.
12Habrá *paz cuando se siembre,
y las vides darán su fruto;
la tierra producirá sus cosechas
y el cielo enviará su rocío.
Todo esto se lo daré como herencia
al remanente de este pueblo.
13Judá e Israel,
¡no teman, sino cobren ánimo!
Ustedes han sido entre las naciones
objeto de maldición,
pero yo los salvaré,
y serán una bendición."

14»Así dice el SEÑOR Todopoderoso:
»"Cuando sus antepasados me hicieron enojar,
yo decidí destruirlos sin ninguna
compasión
—afirma el SEÑOR Todopoderoso—.
15Pero ahora he decidido
hacerles bien a Jerusalén y a Judá.
¡Así que no tengan miedo!

16»"Lo que ustedes deben hacer
es decirse la verdad,
y juzgar en sus tribunales
con la verdad y la justicia.
¡Eso trae la paz!
17No maquinen el mal contra su prójimo,
ni sean dados al falso testimonio,
porque yo aborrezco todo eso,
afirma el SEÑOR."»

18Vino a mí la palabra del SEÑOR Todopoderoso,
y me declaró:

19«Así dice el SEÑOR Todopoderoso:

»"Para Judá, los ayunos de los meses
cuarto, quinto, séptimo y décimo,
serán motivo de gozo y de alegría,
y de animadas festividades.
Amen, pues, la verdad y la paz."

20»Así dice el SEÑOR Todopoderoso:

»"Todavía vendrán pueblos
y habitantes de muchas ciudades,
21que irán de una ciudad a otra
diciendo a los que allí vivan:
'¡Vayamos al SEÑOR para buscar su bendición!
¡Busquemos al SEÑOR Todopoderoso!
¡Yo también voy a buscarlo!'
22Y muchos pueblos y potentes naciones
vendrán a Jerusalén
en busca del SEÑOR Todopoderoso
y de su bendición."

23»Así dice el SEÑOR Todopoderoso: "En aquellos días habrá mucha gente, de todo idioma y de toda nación, que tomará a un judío por el borde de su capa y le dirá: ¡Déjanos acompañarte! ¡Hemos sabido que Dios está con ustedes!"»

Juicio contra los enemigos de Israel

9 Esta profecía es la palabra del SEÑOR, la cual caerá sobre la tierra de Jadrac y sobre Damasco. Ciertamente el SEÑOR tiene puestos los ojos sobre la humanidad y sobre todas las tribus de Israel,h 2como también sobre Jamat, su vecina, y sobre Tiro y Sidón, aunque sean muy sabias.

3Tiro se ha edificado una fortaleza;
ha amontonado plata como polvo,
y oro como lodo de las calles.
4Pero el Señor le quitará sus posesiones;
arrojará al mar sus riquezas,
y el fuego la devorará.
5Lo verá Ascalón, y se llenará de miedo;
Gaza se retorcerá en agonía,
y lo mismo hará Ecrón
al ver marchita su esperanza.
Gaza se quedará sin rey,
y Ascalón sin habitantes.
6Bastardos habitarán en Asdod,
y yo aniquilaré el orgullo de los filisteos.
7De la boca les quitaré la sangre,
y de entre los dientes el alimento
prohibido.
También los filisteos serán
un remanente de nuestro Dios;
se convertirán en jefes de Judá,
y Ecrón será como los jebuseos.
8Montaré guardia junto a mi casa
para que nadie entre ni salga.
¡Nunca más un opresor invadirá a mi pueblo,
porque ahora me mantengo vigilante!

El rey de Sión

9¡Alégrate mucho, hija de *Sión!
¡Grita de alegría, hija de Jerusalén!
Mira, tu rey viene hacia ti,
justo, salvador y humilde.
Viene montado en un asno,
en un pollino, cría de asna.
10Destruiré los carros de Efraín
y los caballos de Jerusalén.
Quebrará el arco de combate
y proclamará *paz a las naciones.
Su dominio se extenderá de mar a mar,
¡desde el río Éufrates
hasta los confines de la tierra!

Restauración de Israel

11En cuanto a ti,
por la sangre de mi *pacto contigo
libraré de la cisterna seca a tus cautivos.

---

h 9:1 *Damasco ... Israel*. Alt. *Damasco. Porque la humanidad y todas las tribus de Israel tienen los ojos puestos en el SEÑOR.*

12Vuelvan a su fortaleza,
   cautivos de la esperanza,
pues hoy mismo les hago saber
   que les devolveré el doble.
13Tensaré a Judá como mi arco,
   y pondré a Efraín como mi flecha.
Incitaré a tus hijos, a los hijos de Sión,
   contra tus hijos, los hijos de Grecia,
   y te usaré como espada de guerrero.

14El SEÑOR se aparecerá sobre ellos,
   y como un relámpago saldrá su flecha.
¡El SEÑOR omnipotente tocará la trompeta
   y marchará sobre las tempestades del sur!
15El SEÑOR Todopoderoso los protegerá,
   y ellos destruirán por completo
   los proyectiles de la honda.
Beberán y reirán como embriagados de vino;
   se llenarán como un tazón de libaciones,
   como los cuernos del altar.
16En aquel día el SEÑOR su Dios
   salvará a su pueblo como a un rebaño,
y en la tierra del SEÑOR
   brillarán como las joyas de una corona.
17¡Qué bueno y hermoso será todo ello!
   El trigo dará nuevos bríos a los jóvenes,
   y el mosto alegrará a las muchachas.

El SEÑOR cuidará de Judá

10 ¡Pídanle al SEÑOR que llueva en primavera!
   ¡Él es quien hace los nubarrones
   y envía los aguaceros!
¡Él es quien da a todo *hombre
   la hierba del campo!
2Los ídolos hablan con engaño,
   los adivinos tienen sueños falsos;
hablan de visiones engañosas
   y consuelan con fantasías.
¡Y el pueblo vaga como rebaño agobiado
   porque carece de *pastor!

3Se enciende mi ira contra los pastores;
   castigaré a esos machos cabríos.
Ciertamente el SEÑOR *Todopoderoso
   cuida de Judá, que es su rebaño,
¡y lo convertirá en su corcel de honor
   el día de la batalla!
4De Judá saldrán
   la piedra angular y la estaca de la carpa,
   el arco de guerra y todo gobernante.
5Juntos serán como héroes
   que combaten sobre el lodo de las calles,
que luchan contra jinetes y los derriban
   porque el SEÑOR está con ellos.

6«Yo fortaleceré a la tribu de Judá
   y salvaré a los descendientes de José.
Me he compadecido de ellos
   y los haré volver.
Será como si nunca los hubiera rechazado,
   porque yo soy el SEÑOR su Dios,
   y les responderé.
7Efraín se volverá como un guerrero,
   y su *corazón se alegrará
   como si tomara vino.
Sus hijos lo verán y se pondrán felices;
   su corazón se alegrará en el SEÑOR.
8Yo los llamaré y los recogeré.
   Cuando los haya redimido,

   serán tan numerosos como antes.
9Aunque los dispersé entre los pueblos,
   en tierras remotas se acordarán de mí.
Aunque vivieron allí con sus hijos,
   regresarán a su tierra.
10Los traeré de Egipto,
   los recogeré de Asiria,
   los llevaré a Galaad y al Líbano,
   y hasta espacio les faltará.
11Cruzarán el mar de la angustia,
   pero yo heriré sus olas,
   y las profundidades del Nilo se secarán.
Abatiré el orgullo de Asiria,
   y pondré fin al dominio de Egipto.
12Yo mismo los fortaleceré,
   y ellos caminarán en mi nombre»,
                 afirma el SEÑOR.

11 ¡Abre tus puertas, monte Líbano,
   para que el fuego devore tus cedros!
2¡Gime tú, ciprés, porque los cedros se han
   caído
   y los majestuosos árboles se han
   derrumbado!
¡Giman, robles de Basán!
   ¡Los tupidos bosques han sido derribados!
3Escuchen el gemido de los pastores;
   ¡sus ricos pastizales han sido destruidos!
Escuchen el rugido de los leones;
   ¡la espesura del Jordán ha quedado
   devastada!

Los dos pastores

4Así dice el SEÑOR mi Dios: «Cuida de las ovejas destinadas al matadero. 5Quienes las compran las matan impunemente, y quienes las venden dicen: "¡Bendito sea el SEÑOR, porque me he enriquecido!" Ni sus propios pastores se compadecen de ellas. 6Pero yo no tendré piedad de los que habitan este país —afirma el SEÑOR—, sino que los entregaré en manos de su prójimo y de su rey. Aunque devasten el país, no los rescataré de sus manos.»

7Así que me dediqué a cuidar las ovejas que los mercaderes habían destinado al matadero. Tomé dos varas de *pastor: a una le puse por nombre Gracia, y a la otra Unión, y me dediqué a cuidar del rebaño. 8En un solo mes me deshice de tres pastores.

Pero me cansé de las ovejas, y ellas se cansaron de mí. 9Así que les dije:[i] «Ya no voy a ser su pastor. Las que se vayan a morir, que se mueran; las que deban perecer, que perezcan; y las que queden con vida, que se devoren unas a otras.»

10Tomé entonces la vara a la que había llamado Gracia, y la quebré. De ese modo anulé el pacto que había hecho con todas las naciones. 11Ese mismo día quedó anulado, y los mercaderes de ovejas que me observaban supieron que se trataba de la palabra del SEÑOR.

12Les dije: «Si les parece bien, páguenme mi jornal; de lo contrario, quédense con él.» Y me pagaron sólo treinta monedas de plata.[j] 13¡Valiente precio el que me pusieron!

Entonces el SEÑOR me dijo: «Entrégaselas al fundidor.» Así que tomé las treinta monedas de plata y se las di al fundidor del templo del SEÑOR.

14Quebré luego la segunda vara, a la que había llamado Unión, y anulé el vínculo fraternal entre Judá e Israel. 15El SEÑOR me dijo entonces: «Vístete

---

ahora como uno de esos pastores insensatos, ¹⁶porque voy a poner sobre el país a un pastor que no se preocupará por las ovejas moribundas, ni buscará a las ovejas pequeñas, ni curará a las ovejas heridas ni dará de comer a las ovejas sanas, sino que devorará a las más gordas y les arrancará las pezuñas.»

¹⁷¡Ay del pastor inútil
que abandona su rebaño!
¡Que la espada le hiera el brazo,
y el puñal le saque el ojo derecho!
¡Que del brazo quede tullido,
y del ojo derecho, ciego!

Destrucción de los enemigos de Jerusalén

12 Esta profecía es la palabra del SEÑOR con respecto a Israel.

Afirma el SEÑOR, que extendió los cielos,
que echó los cimientos de la tierra,
y que puso en el *hombre aliento de vida:

²«Convertiré a Jerusalén en una copa que embriagará a todos los pueblos vecinos. Judá será sitiada, lo mismo que Jerusalén, ³y todas las naciones de la tierra se juntarán contra ella.

»En aquel día convertiré a Jerusalén en una roca inconmovible para todos los pueblos. Los que intenten moverla quedarán despedazados.

⁴»En aquel día espantaré a todos los caballos y enloqueceré a sus jinetes —afirma el SEÑOR—. Me mantendré vigilante sobre Judá, pero dejaré ciegos a los caballos de todas las naciones. ⁵Entonces los jefes de Judá proclamarán: "La fortaleza de los habitantes de Jerusalén es su Dios, el SEÑOR *Todopoderoso."

⁶»En aquel día convertiré a los jefes de Judá en un brasero ardiente dentro de un bosque, en una antorcha encendida entre las gavillas. A diestra y a siniestra devorarán a todos los pueblos vecinos, pero Jerusalén misma volverá a ser habitada. ⁷El SEÑOR salvará primero las viviendas de Judá, para que no sea mayor la gloria de la casa real de David, y la de los habitantes de Jerusalén, que la de Judá.

⁸»En aquel día yo, el SEÑOR, protegeré a los habitantes de Jerusalén. El más débil entre ellos será como David, y la casa real de David será como Dios mismo, como el ángel del SEÑOR que marcha al frente de ellos.

Lamento por el que fue traspasado

⁹»En aquel día me dispondré a destruir a todas las naciones que ataquen a Jerusalén. ¹⁰Sobre la casa real de David y los habitantes de Jerusalén derramaré un espíritu[k] de gracia y de súplica, y entonces pondrán sus ojos en mí. Harán lamentación por el que traspasaron, como quien hace lamentación por su hijo único; llorarán amargamente, como quien llora por su primogénito.

¹¹»En aquel día habrá una gran lamentación en Jerusalén, como la de Hadad Rimón en la llanura de Meguido. ¹²Todo el país hará duelo, familia por familia:

»la parentela de David
y sus esposas,
la parentela de Natán
y sus esposas,
¹³la parentela de Leví
y sus esposas,
la parentela de Simí
y sus esposas,

¹⁴y todas las demás familias
y sus esposas.

Limpieza del pecado

13 »En aquel día se abrirá una fuente para lavar del pecado y de la *impureza a la casa real de David y a los habitantes de *Jerusalén.

²»En aquel día arrancaré del país los *nombres de los ídolos, y nunca más volverán a ser invocados —afirma el SEÑOR *Todopoderoso—. También eliminaré del país a los profetas y la impureza que los inspira. ³Y si hubiera todavía alguno que quisiera profetizar, sus propios padres le dirán: "Has mentido en el nombre del SEÑOR. Por tanto, debes morir." Y por meterse a profeta, sus propios padres lo apuñalarán.

⁴»En aquel día los profetas se avergonzarán de sus visiones proféticas. Ya no engañarán a nadie vistiéndose con mantos de piel, ⁵sino que cada cual dirá: "Yo no soy profeta sino agricultor. Desde mi juventud, la tierra ha sido mi ocupación."[l] ⁶Y si alguien le pregunta: "¿Por qué tienes esas heridas en las manos?", él responderá: "Son las heridas que me hicieron en casa de mis amigos."

El pastor herido, las ovejas dispersas

⁷»¡Despierta, espada, contra mi *pastor,
contra el hombre en quien confío!
—afirma el SEÑOR Todopoderoso—.
Hiere al pastor
para que se dispersen las ovejas
y vuelva yo mi mano contra los corderitos.
⁸Las dos terceras partes del país
serán abatidas y perecerán;
sólo una tercera parte quedará con vida
—afirma el SEÑOR—.
⁹Pero a esa parte restante la pasaré por el fuego;
la refinaré como se refina la plata,
la probaré como se prueba el oro.
Entonces ellos me invocarán
y yo les responderé.
Yo diré: "Ellos son mi pueblo",
y ellos dirán: "El SEÑOR es nuestro Dios."

El reinado venidero del SEÑOR

14 »¡Jerusalén! Viene un día para el SEÑOR cuando tus despojos serán repartidos en tus propias calles. ²Movilizaré a todas las naciones para que peleen contra ti. Te conquistarán, saquearán tus casas y violarán a tus mujeres. La mitad de los habitantes irá al exilio, pero el resto del pueblo se quedará contigo. ³Entonces saldrá el SEÑOR y peleará contra aquellas naciones, como cuando pelea en el día de la batalla.

⁴»En aquel día pondrá el SEÑOR sus pies en el monte de los Olivos, que se encuentra al este de Jerusalén, y el monte de los Olivos se partirá en dos de este a oeste, y formará un gran valle, con una mitad del monte desplazándose al norte y la otra mitad al sur. ⁵Ustedes huirán por el valle de mi monte, porque se extenderá hasta Asal. Huirán como huyeron del terremoto en los días de Uzías, rey de Judá. Entonces vendrá el SEÑOR mi Dios, acompañado de todos sus fieles.

⁶»En aquel día no habrá luz, ni hará frío. ⁷Será un día excepcional, que sólo el SEÑOR conoce: no tendrá día ni noche, pues cuando llegue la noche, seguirá alumbrando la luz.

---

k **12:10** *un espíritu.* Alt. *el Espíritu.*   l **13:5** *Desde ... ocupación.* Alt. *Un hombre me vendió en mi juventud.*

8»En aquel día fluirá agua viva desde Jerusalén, tanto en verano como en invierno. Y una mitad correrá hacia el Mar Muerto, y la otra hacia el mar Mediterráneo. 9El SEÑOR reinará sobre toda la tierra. En aquel día el SEÑOR será el único Dios, y su *nombre será el único nombre.

10»Desde Gueba hasta Rimón, al sur de Jerusalén, todo el país se volverá un desierto.m Pero Jerusalén se levantará y permanecerá en su lugar, desde la puerta de Benjamín hasta el sitio de la puerta Primera, hasta la puerta del Ángulo, y desde la torre de Jananel hasta los lagares del rey. 11Jerusalén volverá a ser habitada, tendrá tranquilidad, y nunca más será *destruida.

12»Ésta es la plaga con la que el SEÑOR herirá a todos los pueblos que pelearon contra Jerusalén: Se les pudrirá la carne en vida, se les pudrirán los ojos en las cuencas, y se les pudrirá la lengua en la boca. 13En aquel día el SEÑOR los llenará de pánico. Cada uno levantará la mano contra el otro, y se atacarán entre sí. 14También Judá peleará en Jerusalén, y se recogerán las riquezas de todas las naciones vecinas, y grandes cantidades de oro y plata y de ropa. 15Una plaga semejante herirá también a caballos y mulos,

camellos y asnos, y a todo animal que esté en aquellos campamentos.

16»Entonces los sobrevivientes de todas las naciones que atacaron a Jerusalén subirán año tras año para adorar al Rey, al SEÑOR *Todopoderoso, y para celebrar la fiesta de las *Enramadas. 17Si alguno de los pueblos de la tierra no sube a Jerusalén para adorar al Rey, al SEÑOR Todopoderoso, tampoco recibirá lluvia. 18Y si el pueblo egipcio no sube ni participa, tampoco recibirá lluvia. El SEÑOR enviará una plaga para castigar a las naciones que no suban a celebrar la fiesta de las Enramadas. 19¡Así será castigado Egipto, y todas las naciones que no suban a celebrar la fiesta de las Enramadas!

20»En aquel día los cascabeles de los caballos llevarán esta inscripción: CONSAGRADO AL SEÑOR. Las ollas de cocina del templo del SEÑOR serán como los tazones sagrados que están frente al altar del sacrificio. 21Toda olla de Jerusalén y de Judá será consagrada al SEÑOR Todopoderoso, y todo el que vaya a sacrificar tomará algunas de esas ollas y cocinará en ellas. En aquel día no habrá más mercaderes[n] en el templo del SEÑOR Todopoderoso.»

---

m 14:10 un desierto. Lit. como el Arabá. n 14:21 mercaderes. Alt. cananeos.

MALAQUÍAS

1 Esta profecía es la palabra del SEÑOR dirigida a Israel por medio de Malaquías.[a]

El amor de Dios por su pueblo

2«Yo los he amado», dice el SEÑOR.

«"¿Y cómo nos has amado?", replican ustedes.

»¿No era Esaú hermano de Jacob? Sin embargo, amé a Jacob 3pero aborrecí a Esaú, y convertí sus montañas en desolación y entregué su heredad a los chacales del desierto.»

4Edom dice: «Aunque nos han hecho pedazos, reconstruiremos sobre las ruinas.» Pero el SEÑOR Todopoderoso dice: «Ustedes podrán reconstruir, pero yo derribaré. Serán llamados territorio malvado, pueblo contra el cual siempre estará indignado el SEÑOR. 5Ustedes lo verán con sus propios ojos y dirán: "¡Se ha engrandecido el SEÑOR aun más allá de las fronteras[b] de Israel!"

El culto al SEÑOR

6»El hijo honra a su padre y el siervo a su señor. Ahora bien, si soy padre, ¿dónde está el honor que merezco? Y si soy señor, ¿dónde está el respeto que se me debe? Yo, el SEÑOR *Todopoderoso, les pregunto a ustedes, sacerdotes que desprecian mi *nombre.

»Y encima preguntan: "¿En qué hemos despreciado tu nombre?"

7»Pues en que ustedes traen a mi altar alimento mancillado.

»Y todavía preguntan: "¿En qué te hemos mancillado?"

»Pues en que tienen la mesa del SEÑOR como algo despreciable. 8Ustedes traen animales ciegos para el sacrificio, y piensan que no tiene nada de malo; sacrifican animales cojos o enfermos, y piensan que no tiene nada de malo. ¿Por qué no tratan de ofrecérselos a su gobernante? ¿Creen que estaría él contento con ustedes? ¿Se ganarían su favor? —dice el SEÑOR Todopoderoso—.

9»Ahora pues, traten de apaciguar a Dios para que se apiade de nosotros. ¿Creen que con esta clase de ofrendas se van a ganar su favor? —dice el SEÑOR Todopoderoso—. 10¡Cómo quisiera que alguno de ustedes clausurara el templo, para que no encendieran en vano el fuego de mi altar! No estoy nada contento con ustedes —dice el SEÑOR Todopoderoso—, y no voy a aceptar ni una sola ofrenda de sus manos. 11Porque desde donde nace el sol hasta donde se pone, grande es mi nombre entre las naciones. En todo lugar se ofrece incienso y ofrendas puras a mi nombre, porque grande es mi nombre entre las naciones —dice el SEÑOR Todopoderoso—. 12Pero ustedes lo profanan cuando dicen que la mesa del Señor está mancillada y que su alimento es despreciable. 13Y exclaman: "¡Qué hastío!" Y me tratan con desdén —dice el SEÑOR Todopoderoso—. ¿Y creen que voy a aceptar de sus manos los animales lesionados, cojos o enfermos que ustedes me traen como sacrificio? —dice el SEÑOR—.

14»¡Maldito sea el tramposo que, teniendo un macho aceptable en su rebaño, se lo dedica al Señor y luego le ofrece un animal mutilado! Porque yo soy el gran rey —dice el SEÑOR Todopoderoso—, y temido es mi nombre entre las naciones.

Juicio contra los sacerdotes

2 »Ahora, pues, este mandato es para ustedes, los sacerdotes. 2Si no me hacen caso ni se deciden a honrar mi *nombre —dice el SEÑOR *Todopoderoso—, les enviaré una maldición, y maldeciré sus bendiciones. Ya las he maldecido, porque ustedes no se han decidido a honrarme.

3»Por esto, voy a reprender a sus descendientes. Les arrojaré a la cara los desperdicios de los sacrificios de sus fiestas, y los barreré junto con ellos. 4Entonces sabrán que les he dado este mandato, a fin de que continúe mi *pacto con Leví —dice el SEÑOR Todopoderoso—. 5Mi pacto con él era de vida y *paz, y se las di; era también de temor, y él me temió, y mostró ante mí profunda reverencia. 6En su boca había instrucción fidedigna; en sus labios no se encontraba perversidad. En paz y rectitud caminó conmigo, y apartó del pecado a muchos.

7»Los labios de un sacerdote atesoran sabiduría, y de su boca los hombres buscan instrucción, porque es mensajero del SEÑOR Todopoderoso. 8Pero ustedes se han desviado del *camino y mediante su instrucción han hecho tropezar a muchos; ustedes han arruinado el pacto con Leví —dice el SEÑOR Todopoderoso—. 9Por mi parte, yo he hecho que ustedes sean despreciables y viles ante todo el pueblo, porque no han guardado mis caminos sino que han mostrado parcialidad en cuestiones de la *ley.»

Deslealtad de Judá

10»¿No tenemos todos un solo Padre? ¿No nos creó un solo Dios? ¿Por qué, pues, profanamos el *pacto de nuestros antepasados al traicionarnos unos a otros?

11Judá ha sido traicionero. En Israel y en Jerusalén se ha cometido algo detestable: al casarse Judá con la hija de un dios extraño, ha profanado el santuario[c] que el SEÑOR ama. 12En cuanto al hombre que haga eso, quienquiera que sea, que el SEÑOR *Todopoderoso lo excluya de los campamentos de Jacob, aun cuando le lleve ofrendas.

13Otra cosa que ustedes hacen es inundar de lágrimas el altar del SEÑOR; lloran y se lamentan porque él ya no presta atención a sus ofrendas ni las acepta de sus manos con agrado.

14Y todavía preguntan por qué.

Pues porque el SEÑOR actúa como testigo entre ti y la esposa de tu juventud, a la que traicionaste aunque es tu compañera, la esposa de tu pacto.[d] 15¿Acaso no hizo el SEÑOR un solo ser, que es cuerpo y espíritu? Y ¿por qué es uno solo? Porque busca descendencia dada por Dios.[e] Así pues cuídense ustedes en su propio espíritu, y no traicionen a la esposa de su juventud. 16»Yo aborrezco el divorcio —dice el SEÑOR, Dios de Israel—, y al que cubre[f] de violencia sus vestiduras», dice el SEÑOR Todopoderoso.

Así que cuídense en su espíritu, y no sean traicioneros.

Acusaciones contra Judá

17Ustedes han cansado al SEÑOR con sus palabras.

Y encima preguntan: «¿En qué lo hemos cansado?»

---

a 1:1 En hebreo, *Malaquías* significa *mi mensajero*. b 1:5 *aun más allá de las fronteras*. Alt. *sobre el territorio*. c 2:11 *el santuario*. Alt. *las cosas santas*. d 2:14 *pacto*. Alt. *vínculo matrimonial*, o *misma nacionalidad*. e 2:15 *¿Acaso ... Dios*. Texto de difícil traducción. f 2:16 *Yo aborrezco el divorcio ... y al que cubre*. Alt. *El que odia y se divorcia ... cubre*.

En que dicen: «Todo el que hace lo malo agrada al SEÑOR, y él se complace con ellos»; y murmuran: «¿Dónde está el Dios de *justicia?»

3 El SEÑOR *Todopoderoso responde: «Yo estoy por enviar a mi mensajero para que prepare el camino delante de mí. De pronto vendrá a su templo el Señor a quien ustedes buscan; vendrá el mensajero del *pacto, en quien ustedes se complacen.»

²Pero ¿quién podrá soportar el día de su venida? ¿Quién podrá mantenerse en pie cuando él aparezca? Porque será como fuego de fundidor o lejía de lavandero. ³Se sentará como fundidor y purificador de plata; *purificará a los levitas y los refinará como se refinan el oro y la plata. Entonces traerán al SEÑOR ofrendas conforme a la justicia, ⁴y las ofrendas de Judá y Jerusalén serán aceptables al SEÑOR, como en tiempos antiguos, en años pasados.

⁵«De modo que me acercaré a ustedes para juicio. Estaré presto a testificar contra los hechiceros, los adúlteros y los perjuros, contra los que explotan a sus asalariados; contra los que oprimen a las viudas y a los huérfanos, y niegan el derecho del extranjero, sin mostrarme ningún temor —dice el SEÑOR Todopoderoso—.

Fidelidad en las ofrendas

⁶»Yo, el SEÑOR, no cambio. Por eso ustedes, descendientes de Jacob, no han sido exterminados. ⁷Desde la época de sus antepasados se han apartado de mis preceptos y no los han guardado. Vuélvanse a mí, y yo me volveré a ustedes —dice el SEÑOR Todopoderoso—.

»Pero ustedes replican: "¿En qué sentido tenemos que volvernos?"

⁸»¿Acaso roba el hombre a Dios? ¡Ustedes me están robando!

»Y todavía preguntan: "¿En qué te robamos?"

»En los diezmos y en las ofrendas. ⁹Ustedes —la nación entera— están bajo gran maldición, pues es a mí a quien están robando.

¹⁰»Traigan íntegro el diezmo para los fondos del templo, y así habrá alimento en mi casa. Pruébenme en esto —dice el SEÑOR Todopoderoso—, y vean si no abro las compuertas del cielo y derramo sobre ustedes bendición hasta que sobreabunde. ¹¹Exterminaré a la langosta, para que no arruine sus cultivos y las vides en los campos no pierdan su fruto —dice el

SEÑOR Todopoderoso—. ¹²Entonces todas las naciones los llamarán a ustedes *dichosos, porque ustedes tendrán una nación encantadora —dice el SEÑOR Todopoderoso—.

Insolencia de Judá

¹³»Ustedes profieren insolencias contra mí —dice el SEÑOR—.

»Y encima preguntan: "¿Qué insolencias hemos dicho contra ti?"

¹⁴»Ustedes han dicho: "Servir a Dios no vale la pena. ¿Qué ganamos con cumplir sus mandatos y vestirnos de luto delante del SEÑOR Todopoderoso ¹⁵si nos toca llamar dichosos a los soberbios, y los que hacen lo malo no sólo prosperan sino que incluso desafían a Dios y se salen con la suya?"»

¹⁶Los que temían al SEÑOR hablaron entre sí, y él los escuchó y les prestó atención. Entonces se escribió en su presencia un libro de memorias de aquellos que temen al SEÑOR y honran su nombre. ¹⁷«El día que yo actúe ellos serán mi propiedad exclusiva —dice el SEÑOR Todopoderoso—. Tendré compasión de ellos, como se compadece un hombre del hijo que le sirve. ¹⁸Y ustedes volverán a distinguir entre los buenos y los malos, entre los que sirven a Dios y los que no le sirven.

El día del SEÑOR

4 »Miren, ya viene el día, ardiente como un horno. Todos los soberbios y todos los malvados serán como paja, y aquel día les prenderá fuego hasta dejarlos sin raíz ni rama —dice el SEÑOR *Todopoderoso—. ²Pero para ustedes que temen mi *nombre, se levantará el sol de justicia trayendo en sus rayosg salud. Y ustedes saldrán saltando como becerros recién alimentados. ³El día que yo actúe ustedes pisotearán a los malvados, y bajo sus pies quedarán hechos polvo —dice el SEÑOR Todopoderoso—.

⁴»Acuérdense de la *ley de mi siervo Moisés. Recuerden los preceptos y las leyes que le di en Horeb para todo Israel.

⁵»Estoy por enviarles al profeta Elías antes que llegue el día del SEÑOR, día grande y terrible. ⁶Él hará que los padres se reconcilien con sus hijos y los hijos con sus padres, y así no vendré a herir la tierra con *destrucción total.»

g **4:2** *rayos.* Lit. *alas.*

NUEVO TESTAMENTO

MATEO

Genealogía de Jesucristo
1:1-17 — Lc 3:23-38
1:3-6 — Rt 4:18-22
1:7-11 — 1Cr 3:10-17

1 Tabla genealógica de *Jesucristo, hijo de David, hijo de Abraham:

2 Abraham fue el padre dea Isaac;
Isaac, padre de Jacob;
Jacob, padre de Judá y de sus hermanos;

3 Judá, padre de Fares y de Zera, cuya madre fue Tamar;
Fares, padre de Jezrón;
Jezrón, padre de Aram;

4 Aram, padre de Aminadab;
Aminadab, padre de Naasón;
Naasón, padre de Salmón;

5 Salmón, padre de Booz, cuya madre fue Rajab;
Booz, padre de Obed, cuya madre fue Rut;
Obed, padre de Isaí;

6 e Isaí, padre del rey David.

David fue el padre de Salomón, cuya madre había sido la esposa de Urías;

7 Salomón, padre de Roboán;
Roboán, padre de Abías;
Abías, padre de Asá;

8 Asá, padre de Josafat;
Josafat, padre de Jorán;
Jorán, padre de Uzías;

9 Uzías, padre de Jotán;
Jotán, padre de Acaz;
Acaz, padre de Ezequías;

10 Ezequías, padre de Manasés;
Manasés, padre de Amón;
Amón, padre de Josías;

11 y Josías, padre de Jeconíasb y de sus hermanos en tiempos de la deportación a Babilonia.

12 Después de la deportación a Babilonia,
Jeconías fue el padre de Salatiel;
Salatiel, padre de Zorobabel;

13 Zorobabel, padre de Abiud;
Abiud, padre de Eliaquín;
Eliaquín, padre de Azor;

14 Azor, padre de Sadoc;
Sadoc, padre de Aquín;
Aquín, padre de Eliud;

15 Eliud, padre de Eleazar;
Eleazar, padre de Matán;
Matán, padre de Jacob;

16 y Jacob fue padre de José, que fue el esposo de María, de la cual nació Jesús, llamado el *Cristo.

17Así que hubo en total catorce generaciones desde Abraham hasta David, catorce desde David hasta la deportación a Babilonia, y catorce desde la deportación hasta el Cristo.

Nacimiento de Jesucristo

18El nacimiento de Jesús, el *Cristo, fue así: Su madre, María, estaba comprometida para casarse con José, pero antes de unirse a él, resultó que estaba encinta por obra del Espíritu Santo. 19Como José, su esposo, era un hombre justo y no quería exponerla a vergüenza pública, resolvió divorciarse de ella en secreto.

20Pero cuando él estaba considerando hacerlo, se le apareció en sueños un ángel del Señor y le dijo: «José, hijo de David, no temas recibir a María por esposa, porque ella ha concebido por obra del Espíritu Santo. 21Dará a luz un hijo, y le pondrás por nombre Jesús,c porque él salvará a su pueblo de sus pecados.»

22Todo esto sucedió para que se cumpliera lo que el Señor había dicho por medio del profeta: 23«La virgen concebirá y dará a luz un hijo, y lo llamarán Emanuel»d (que significa «Dios con nosotros»).

24Cuando José se despertó, hizo lo que el ángel del Señor le había mandado y recibió a María por esposa. 25Pero no tuvo relaciones conyugales con ella hasta que dio a luz un hijo,e a quien le puso por nombre Jesús.

Visita de los sabios

2 Después de que Jesús nació en Belén de Judea en tiempos del rey Herodes, llegaron a Jerusalén unos sabiosf procedentes del Oriente.

2—¿Dónde está el que ha nacido rey de los judíos? —preguntaron—. Vimos levantarseg su estrella y hemos venido a adorarlo.

3Cuando lo oyó el rey Herodes, se turbó, y toda Jerusalén con él. 4Así que convocó de entre el pueblo a todos los jefes de los sacerdotes y *maestros de la ley, y les preguntó dónde había de nacer el *Cristo.

5—En Belén de Judea —le respondieron—, porque esto es lo que ha escrito el profeta:

6»"Pero tú, Belén, en la tierra de Judá,
de ninguna manera eres la menor entre los principales de Judá;
porque de ti saldrá un príncipe
que será el pastor de mi pueblo Israel."h

7Luego Herodes llamó en secreto a los sabios y se enteró por ellos del tiempo exacto en que había aparecido la estrella. 8Los envió a Belén y les dijo:

—Vayan e infórmense bien de ese niño y, tan pronto como lo encuentren, avísenme para que yo también vaya y lo adore.

9Después de oír al rey, siguieron su camino, y sucedió que la estrella que habían visto levantarse iba delante de ellos hasta que se detuvo sobre el lugar donde estaba el niño. 10Al ver la estrella, se llenaron de alegría. 11Cuando llegaron a la casa, vieron al niño con María, su madre; y postrándose lo adoraron. Abrieron sus cofres y le presentaron como regalos oro, incienso y mirra. 12Entonces, advertidos en sueños de que no volvieran a Herodes, regresaron a su tierra por otro camino.

La huida a Egipto

13Cuando ya se habían ido, un ángel del Señor se le apareció en sueños a José y le dijo: «Levántate,

---

a 1:2 *fue el padre de.* Lit. *engendró a;* y así sucesivamente en el resto de esta genealogía. b 1:11 *Jeconías.* Es decir, Joaquín; también en v. 12. c 1:21 *Jesús* es la forma griega del nombre hebreo *Josué,* que significa *el SEÑOR salva.* d 1:23 Is 7:14
e 1:25 *un hijo.* Var. *su hijo primogénito.* f 2:1 *sabios.* Lit. *magos;* también en vv. 7, 16. g 2:2 *levantarse.* Alt. *en el oriente;*
también en v. 9. h 2:6 Mi 5:2

toma al niño y a su madre, y huye a Egipto. Quédate allí hasta que yo te avise, porque Herodes va a buscar al niño para matarlo.»

14Así que se levantó cuando todavía era de noche, tomó al niño y a su madre, y partió para Egipto, 15donde permaneció hasta la muerte de Herodes. De este modo se cumplió lo que el Señor había dicho por medio del profeta: «De Egipto llamé a mi hijo.»i

16Cuando Herodes se dio cuenta de que los sabios se habían burlado de él, se enfureció y mandó matar a todos los niños menores de dos años en Belén y en sus alrededores, de acuerdo con el tiempo que había averiguado de los sabios. 17Entonces se cumplió lo dicho por el profeta Jeremías:

18«Se oye un grito en Ramá,
　　　　llanto y gran lamentación;
　　es Raquel, que llora por sus hijos
　　　　y no quiere ser consolada;
　　　　¡sus hijos ya no existen!»j

El regreso a Nazaret

19Después de que murió Herodes, un ángel del Señor se le apareció en sueños a José en Egipto 20y le dijo: «Levántate, toma al niño y a su madre, y vete a la tierra de Israel, que ya murieron los que amenazaban con quitarle la *vida al niño.»

21Así que se levantó José, tomó al niño y a su madre, y regresó a la tierra de Israel. 22Pero al oír que Arquelao reinaba en Judea en lugar de su padre Herodes, tuvo miedo de ir allá. Advertido por Dios en sueños, se retiró al distrito de Galilea, 23y fue a vivir en un pueblo llamado Nazaret. Con esto se cumplió lo dicho por los profetas: «Lo llamarán nazareno.»

Juan el Bautista prepara el camino
3:1-12 — Mr 1:3-8; Lc 3:2-17

3 En aquellos días se presentó Juan el Bautista predicando en el desierto de Judea.

2Decía: «*Arrepiéntanse, porque el reino de los cielos está cerca.» 3Juan era aquel de quien había escrito el profeta Isaías:

«Voz de uno que grita en el desierto:
"Preparen el camino para el Señor,
　　háganle sendas derechas." »k

4La ropa de Juan estaba hecha de pelo de camello. Llevaba puesto un cinturón de cuero y se alimentaba de langostas y miel silvestre. 5Acudía a él la gente de Jerusalén, de toda Judea y de toda la región del Jordán. 6Cuando confesaban sus pecados, él los bautizaba en el río Jordán.

7Pero al ver que muchos fariseos y saduceos llegaban adonde él estaba bautizando, les advirtió: «¡Camada de víboras! ¿Quién les dijo que podrán escapar del castigo que se acerca?

8Produzcan frutos que demuestren arrepentimiento. 9No piensen que podrán alegar: "Tenemos a Abraham por padre." Porque les digo que aun de estas piedras Dios es capaz de darle hijos a Abraham. 10El hacha ya está puesta a la raíz de los árboles, y todo árbol que no produzca buen fruto será cortado y arrojado al fuego.

11»Yo los bautizo a ustedes conl agua para que se arrepientan. Pero el que viene después de mí es más poderoso que yo, y ni siquiera merezco llevarle las sandalias. Él los bautizará con el Espíritu Santo y con fuego. 12Tiene el rastrillo en la mano y limpiará su era,

recogiendo el trigo en su granero; la paja, en cambio, la quemará con fuego que nunca se apagará.»

Bautismo de Jesús
3:13-17 — Mr 1:9-11; Lc 3:21-22; Jn 1:31-34

13Un día Jesús fue de Galilea al Jordán para que Juan lo bautizara. 14Pero Juan trató de disuadirlo.

—Yo soy el que necesita ser bautizado por ti, ¿y tú vienes a mí? —objetó.

15—Dejémoslo así por ahora, pues nos conviene cumplir con lo que es justo —le contestó Jesús.

Entonces Juan consintió.

16Tan pronto como Jesús fue bautizado, subió del agua. En ese momento se abrió el cielo, y él vio al Espíritu de Dios bajar como una paloma y posarse sobre él. 17Y una voz del cielo decía: «Éste es mi Hijo amado; estoy muy complacido con él.»

Tentación de Jesús
4:1-11 — Mr 1:12-13; Lc 4:1-13

4 Luego el Espíritu llevó a Jesús al desierto para que el diablo lo sometiera a *tentación. 2Después de ayunar cuarenta días y cuarenta noches, tuvo hambre.3El tentador se le acercó y le propuso:

—Si eres el Hijo de Dios, ordena a estas piedras que se conviertan en pan.

4Jesús le respondió:

—Escrito está: "No sólo de pan vive el hombre, sino de toda palabra que sale de la boca de Dios."m

5Luego el diablo lo llevó a la ciudad santa e hizo que se pusiera de pie sobre la parte más alta del *templo, y le dijo:

6—Si eres el Hijo de Dios, tírate abajo. Porque escrito está:

"Ordenará que sus ángeles
　　te sostengan en sus manos,
　　para que no tropieces con piedra alguna."n

7—También está escrito: "No pongas a prueba al Señor tu Dios"ñ —le contestó Jesús.

8De nuevo lo tentó el diablo, llevándolo a una montaña muy alta, y le mostró todos los reinos del mundo y su esplendor.

9—Todo esto te daré si te postras y me adoras.

10—¡Vete, Satanás! —le dijo Jesús—. Porque escrito está: "Adora al Señor tu Dios y sírvele solamente a él."o

11Entonces el diablo lo dejó, y unos ángeles acudieron a servirle.

Jesús comienza a predicar

12Cuando Jesús oyó que habían encarcelado a Juan, regresó a Galilea. 13Partió de Nazaret y se fue a vivir a Capernaúm, que está junto al lago en la región de Zabulón y de Neftalí, 14para cumplir lo dicho por el profeta Isaías:

15«Tierra de Zabulón y tierra de Neftalí,
　　camino del mar, al otro lado del Jordán,
　　Galilea de los *gentiles;
16el pueblo que habitaba en la oscuridad
　　ha visto una gran luz;
　　sobre los que vivían en densas tinieblasp
　　la luz ha resplandecido.»q

17Desde entonces comenzó Jesús a predicar: «*Arrepiéntanse, porque el reino de los cielos está cerca.»

i 2:15 Os 11:1　j 2:18 Jer 31:15　k 3:3 Is 40:3　l 3:11 con. Alt. En.　m 4:4 Dt 8:3　n 4:6 Sal 91:11,12　ñ 4:7 Dt 6:16　o 4:10 Dt 6:13　p 4:16 vivían en densas tinieblas. Lit. habitaban en tierra y sombra de muerte.　q 4:16 Is 9:1,2

Llamamiento de los primeros discípulos
4:18-22 — Mr 1:16-20; Lc 5:2-11; Jn 1:35-42

18Mientras caminaba junto al mar de Galilea, Jesús vio a dos hermanos: uno era Simón, llamado Pedro, y el otro Andrés. Estaban echando la red al lago, pues eran pescadores. 19«Vengan, síganme —les dijo Jesús—, y los haré pescadores de hombres.» 20Al instante dejaron las redes y lo siguieron.

21Más adelante vio a otros dos hermanos: *Jacobo y Juan, hijos de Zebedeo, que estaban con su padre en una barca remendando las redes. Jesús los llamó, 22y dejaron en seguida la barca y a su padre, y lo siguieron.

Jesús sana a los enfermos

23Jesús recorría toda Galilea, enseñando en las sinagogas, anunciando las buenas *nuevas del reino, y sanando toda enfermedad y dolencia entre la gente. 24Su fama se extendió por toda Siria, y le llevaban todos los que padecían de diversas enfermedades, los que sufrían de dolores graves, los endemoniados, los epilépticos y los paralíticos, y él los sanaba. 25Lo seguían grandes multitudes de Galilea, *Decápolis, Jerusalén, Judea y de la región al otro lado del Jordán.

Las bienaventuranzas
5:3-12 — Lc 6:20-23

5 Cuando vio a las multitudes, subió a la ladera de una montaña y se sentó. Sus discípulos se le acercaron, 2y tomando él la palabra, comenzó a enseñarles diciendo:

3«*Dichosos los pobres en espíritu,
　　porque de ellos es el reino de los cielos les pertenece.
4Dichosos los que lloran,
　　porque serán consolados.
5Dichosos los humildes,
　　porque recibirán la tierra como herencia.
6Dichosos los que tienen hambre y sed de
　　　　justicia,
　　porque serán saciados.
7Dichosos los compasivos,
　　porque serán tratados con compasión.
8Dichosos los de corazón limpio,
　　porque ellos verán a Dios.
9Dichosos los que trabajan por la paz,
　　porque serán llamados hijos de Dios.
10Dichosos los perseguidos por causa de la
　　　　justicia,
　　porque el reino de los cielos les pertenece.

11»Dichosos serán ustedes cuando por mi causa la gente los insulte, los persiga y levante contra ustedes toda clase de calumnias. 12Alégrense y llénense de júbilo, porque les espera una gran recompensa en el cielo. Así también persiguieron a los profetas que los precedieron a ustedes.

La sal y la luz

13»Ustedes son la sal de la tierra. Pero si la sal se vuelve insípida, ¿cómo recobrará su sabor? Ya no sirve para nada, sino para que la gente la deseche y la pisotee.

14»Ustedes son la luz del mundo. Una ciudad en lo alto de una colina no puede esconderse. 15Ni se enciende una lámpara para cubrirla con un cajón. Por el contrario, se pone en la repisa para que alumbre a todos los que están en la casa. 16Hagan brillar su luz delante de todos, para que ellos puedan ver las buenas obras de ustedes y alaben al Padre que está en el cielo.

El cumplimiento de la ley

17»No piensen que he venido a anular la ley o los profetas; no he venido a anularlos sino a darles cumplimiento. 18Les aseguro que mientras existan el cielo y la tierra, ni una letra ni una tilde de la ley desaparecerán hasta que todo se haya cumplido. 19Todo el que infrinja uno solo de estos mandamientos, por pequeño que sea, y enseñe a otros a hacer lo mismo, será considerado el más pequeño en el reino de los cielos; pero el que los practique y enseñe será considerado grande en el reino de los cielos. 20Porque les digo a ustedes, que no van a entrar en el reino de los cielos a menos que su justicia supere a la de los fariseos y de los *maestros de la ley.

El homicidio
5:25-26 — Lc 12:58-59

21»Ustedes han oído que se dijo a sus antepasados: "No mates,r y todo el que mate quedará sujeto al juicio del tribunal." 22Pero yo les digo que todo el que se enojes con su hermano quedará sujeto al juicio del tribunal. Es más,cualquiera que insultet a su hermano quedará sujeto al juicio del *Consejo. Pero cualquiera que lo maldigau quedará sujeto al juicio del infiernov.

23»Por lo tanto, si estás presentando tu ofrenda en el altar y allí recuerdas que tu hermano tiene algo contra ti, 24deja tu ofrenda allí delante del altar. Ve primero y reconcíliate con tu hermano; luego vuelve y presenta tu ofrenda.

25»Si tu adversario te va a denunciar, llega a un acuerdo con él lo más pronto posible. Hazlo mientras vayan de camino al juzgado, no sea que te entregue al juez, y el juez al guardia, y te echen en la cárcel. 26Te aseguro que no saldrás de allí hasta que pagues el último centavo.w

El adulterio

27»Ustedes han oído que se dijo: "No cometas adulterio."x 28Pero yo les digo que cualquiera que mira a una mujer y la codicia ya ha cometido adulterio con ella en el corazón. 29Por tanto, si tu ojo derecho te hace *pecar, sácatelo y tíralo. Más te vale perder una sola parte de tu cuerpo, y no que todo él sea arrojado al infierno.y 30Y si tu mano derecha te hace pecar, córtatela y arrójala. Más te vale perder una sola parte de tu cuerpo, y no que todo él vaya al infierno.

El divorcio

31»Se ha dicho: "El que repudia a su esposa debe darle un certificado de divorcio."z 32Pero yo les digo que, excepto en caso de infidelidad conyugal, todo el que se divorcia de su esposa, la induce a cometer adulterio, y el que se casa con la divorciada comete adulterio también.

Los juramentos

33»También han oído que se dijo a sus antepasados: "No faltes a tu juramento, sino cumple con tus promesas al Señor." 34Pero yo les digo: No juren de ningún modo: ni por el cielo, porque es el trono de

---

r 5:21 Éx 20:13　s 5:22 se enoje. Var. se enoje sin causa.　t 5:22 insulte. Lit. le diga: "Raca" (estúpido en arameo).　u 5:22 lo maldiga. Lit. le diga: "Necio."　v 5:22 del infierno. Lit. de la *Gehenna del fuego.　w 5:26 centavo. Lit. Cuadrante.　x 5:27 Éx 20:14　y 5:29 al infierno. Lit. a la *Gehenna; también en v. 30.　z 5:31 Dt 24:1

Dios; 35ni por la tierra, porque es el estrado de sus pies; ni por Jerusalén, porque es la ciudad del gran Rey. 36Tampoco jures por tu cabeza, porque no puedes hacer que ni uno solo de tus cabellos se vuelva blanco o negro. 37Cuando ustedes digan "sí", que sea realmente sí; y cuando digan "no", que sea no. Cualquier cosa de más, proviene del maligno.

Ojo por ojo

38»Ustedes han oído que se dijo: "Ojo por ojo y diente por diente."a 39Pero yo les digo: No resistan al que les haga mal. Si alguien te da una bofetada en la mejilla derecha, vuélvele también la otra. 40Si alguien te pone pleito para quitarte la capa, déjale también la *camisa. 41Si alguien te obliga a llevarte la carga un kilómetro, llévasela dos. 42Al que te pida, dale; y al que quiera tomar de ti prestado, no le vuelvas la espalda.

El amor a los enemigos

43»Ustedes han oído que se dijo: "Ama a tu prójimob y odia a tu enemigo." 44Pero yo les digo: Amen a sus enemigos y oren por quienes los persiguen,c 45para que sean hijos de su Padre que está en el cielo. Él hace que salga el sol sobre malos y buenos, y que llueva sobre justos e injustos. 46Si ustedes aman solamente a quienes los aman, ¿qué recompensa recibirán? ¿Acaso no hacen eso hasta los *recaudadores de impuestos? 47Y si saludan a sus hermanos solamente, ¿qué de más hacen ustedes? ¿Acaso no hacen esto hasta los *gentiles? 48Por tanto, sean *perfectos, así como su Padre celestial es perfecto.

El dar a los necesitados

6 »Cuídense de no hacer sus obras de justicia delante de la gente para llamar la atención. Si actúan así, su Padre que está en el cielo no les dará ninguna recompensa.

2»Por eso, cuando des a los necesitados, no lo anuncies al son de trompeta, como lo hacen los *hipócritas en las sinagogas y en las calles para que la gente los rinda homenaje. Les aseguro que ellos ya han recibido toda su recompensa. 3Más bien, cuando des a los necesitados, que no se entere tu mano izquierda de lo que hace la derecha, 4para que tu limosna sea en secreto. Así tu Padre, que ve lo que se hace en secreto, te recompensará.

La oración
6:9-13 — Lc 11:2-4

5»Cuando oren, no sean como los *hipócritas, porque a ellos les encanta orar de pie en las sinagogas y en las esquinas de las plazas para que la gente los vea. Les aseguro que ya han obtenido toda su recompensa. 6Pero tú, cuando te pongas a orar, entra en tu cuarto, cierra la puerta y ora a tu Padre, que está en lo secreto. Así tu Padre, que ve lo que se hace en secreto, te recompensará. 7Y al orar, no hablen sólo por hablar como hacen los *gentiles, porque ellos se imaginan que serán escuchados por sus muchas palabras. 8No sean como ellos, porque su Padre sabe lo que ustedes necesitan antes de que se lo pidan.

9»Ustedes deben orar así:

»"Padre nuestro que estás en el cielo,

*santificado sea tu nombre,
10venga tu reino,
　hágase tu voluntad
　　en la tierra como en el cielo.
11Danos hoy nuestro pan cotidiano.d
12Perdónanos nuestras deudas,
　como también nosotros hemos perdonado
　　a nuestros deudores.
13Y no nos dejes caer en *tentación,
　sino líbranos del maligno."e

14»Porque si perdonan a otros sus ofensas, también los perdonará a ustedes su Padre celestial. 15Pero si no perdonan a otros sus ofensas, tampoco su Padre les perdonará a ustedes las suyas.

El ayuno

16»Cuando ayunen, no pongan cara triste como hacen los *hipócritas, que demudan sus rostros para mostrar que están ayunando. Les aseguro que éstos ya han obtenido toda su recompensa. 17Pero tú, cuando ayunes, perfúmate la cabeza y lávate la cara 18para que no sea evidente ante los demás que estás ayunando, sino sólo ante tu Padre, que está en lo secreto; y tu Padre, que ve lo que se hace en secreto, te recompensará.

Tesoros en el cielo
6:22-23 — Lc 11:34-36

19»No acumulen para sí tesoros en la tierra, donde la polilla y el óxido destruyen, y donde los ladrones se meten a robar. 20Más bien, acumulen para sí tesoros en el cielo, donde ni la polilla ni el óxido carcomen, ni los ladrones se meten a robar. 21Porque donde esté tu tesoro, allí estará también tu corazón.

22»El ojo es la *lámpara del cuerpo. Por tanto, si tu visión es clara, todo tu ser disfrutará de la luz. 23Pero si tu visión está nublada, todo tu ser estará en oscuridad. Si la luz que hay en ti es oscuridad, ¡qué densa será esa oscuridad!

24»Nadie puede servir a dos señores, pues menospreciará a uno y amará al otro, o querrá mucho a uno y despreciará al otro. No se puede servir a la vez a Dios y a las riquezas.

De nada sirve preocuparse
6:25-33 — Lc 12:22-31

25»Por eso les digo: No se preocupen por su *vida, qué comerán o beberán; ni por su cuerpo, cómo se vestirán. ¿No tiene la vida más valor que la comida, y el cuerpo más que la ropa? 26Fíjense en las aves del cielo: no siembran ni cosechan ni almacenan en graneros; sin embargo, el Padre celestial las alimenta. ¿No valen ustedes mucho más que ellas? 27¿Quién de ustedes, por mucho que se preocupe, puede añadir una sola hora al curso de su vida?f

28»¿Y por qué se preocupan por la ropa? Observen cómo crecen los lirios del campo. No trabajan ni hilan; 29sin embargo, les digo que ni siquiera Salomón, con todo su esplendor, se vestía como uno de ellos. 30Si así viste Dios a la hierba que hoy está en el campo y mañana es arrojada al horno, ¿no hará mucho más por ustedes, gente de poca fe? 31Así que no se preocupen diciendo: "¿Qué comeremos?" o "¿Qué beberemos?" o "¿Con qué nos vestiremos?" 32Porque los *paganos andan tras todas estas cosas, y el Padre

---

a 5:38 Éx 21:24; Lv 24:20; Dt 19:21　b 5:43 Lv 19:18　c 5:44 Amen . . . persiguen. Var. Amen a sus enemigos, bendigan a quienes los maldicen, hagan bien a quienes los odian, y oren por quienes los ultrajan y los persiguen (véase Lc 6:27,28).　d 6:11 nuestro pan cotidiano. Alt. el pan que necesitamos.　e 6:13 del maligno. Alt. del mal. Var. del maligno, porque tuyos son el reino y el poder y la gloria para siempre. Amén.　f 6:27 puede añadir . . . su vida. Alt. puede aumentar su estatura siquiera medio metro? (lit. un *codo).

celestial sabe que ustedes las necesitan. ³³Más bien, busquen primeramente el reino de Dios y su justicia, y todas estas cosas les serán añadidas. ³⁴Por lo tanto, no se angustien por el mañana, el cual tendrá sus propios afanes. Cada día tiene ya sus problemas.

El juzgar a los demás
7:3-5 — Lc 6:41-42

7 »No juzguen a nadie, para que nadie los juzgue a ustedes. ²Porque tal como juzguen se les juzgará, y con la medida que midan a otros, se les medirá a ustedes.

³¿Por qué te fijas en la astilla que tiene tu hermano en el ojo, y no le das importancia a la viga que está en el tuyo? ⁴¿Cómo puedes decirle a tu hermano: "Déjame sacarte la astilla del ojo", cuando ahí tienes una viga en el tuyo? ⁵¡*Hipócrita!, saca primero la viga de tu propio ojo, y entonces verás con claridad para sacar la astilla del ojo de tu hermano.

⁶»No den lo sagrado a los *perros, no sea que se vuelvan contra ustedes y los despedacen; ni echen sus perlas a los cerdos, no sea que las pisoteen.

Pidan, busquen, llamen
7:7-11 — Lc 11:9-13

⁷»Pidan, y se les dará; busquen, y encontrarán; llamen, y se les abrirá. ⁸Porque todo el que pide, recibe; el que busca, encuentra; y al que llama, se le abre.

⁹¿Quién de ustedes, si su hijo le pide pan, le da una piedra? ¹⁰¿O si le pide un pescado, le da una serpiente? ¹¹Pues si ustedes, aun siendo malos, saben dar cosas buenas a sus hijos, ¡cuánto más su Padre que está en el cielo dará cosas buenas a los que le pidan! ¹²Así que en todo traten ustedes a los demás tal y como quieren que ellos los traten a ustedes. De hecho, esto es la ley y los profetas.

La puerta estrecha y la puerta ancha

¹³»Entren por la puerta estrecha. Porque es ancha la puerta y espacioso el camino que conduce a la destrucción, y muchos entran por ella. ¹⁴Pero estrecha es la puerta y angosto el camino que conduce a la vida, y son pocos los que la encuentran.

El árbol y sus frutos

¹⁵»Cuídense de los falsos profetas. Vienen a ustedes disfrazados de ovejas, pero por dentro son lobos feroces. ¹⁶Por sus frutos los conocerán. ¿Acaso se recogen uvas de los espinos, o higos de los cardos? ¹⁷Del mismo modo, todo árbol bueno da fruto bueno, pero el árbol malo da fruto malo. ¹⁸Un árbol bueno no puede dar fruto malo, y un árbol malo no puede dar fruto bueno. ¹⁹Todo árbol que no da buen fruto se corta y se arroja al fuego. ²⁰Así que por sus frutos los conocerán.

²¹»No todo el que me dice: "Señor, Señor", entrará en el reino de los cielos, sino sólo el que hace la voluntad de mi Padre que está en el cielo. ²²Muchos me dirán en aquel día: "Señor, Señor, ¿no profetizamos en tu nombre, y en tu nombre expulsamos demonios e hicimos muchos milagros?" ²³Entonces les diré claramente: "Jamás los conocí. ¡Aléjense de mí, hacedores de maldad!"

El prudente y el insensato
7:24-27 — Lc 6:47-49

²⁴»Por tanto, todo el que me oye estas palabras y las pone en práctica es como un hombre prudente que construyó su casa sobre la roca. ²⁵Cayeron las lluvias, crecieron los ríos, y soplaron los vientos y azotaron aquella casa; con todo, la casa no se derrumbó

porque estaba cimentada sobre la roca. ²⁶Pero todo el que me oye estas palabras y no las pone en práctica es como un hombre insensato que construyó su casa sobre la arena. ²⁷Cayeron las lluvias, crecieron los ríos, y soplaron los vientos y azotaron aquella casa, y ésta se derrumbó, y grande fue su ruina.»

²⁸Cuando Jesús terminó de decir estas cosas, las multitudes se asombraron de su enseñanza, ²⁹porque les enseñaba como quien tenía autoridad, y no como los *maestros de la ley.

Jesús sana a un leproso
8:2-4 — Mr 1:40-44; Lc 5:12-14

8 Cuando Jesús bajó de la ladera de la montaña, lo siguieron grandes multitudes. ²Un hombre que tenía *lepra se le acercó y se arrodilló delante de él.

—Señor, si quieres, puedes *limpiarme —le dijo.

³Jesús extendió la mano y tocó al hombre.

—Sí quiero —le dijo—. ¡Queda limpio!

Y al instante quedó sano[g] de la lepra.

⁴—Mira, no se lo digas a nadie —le dijo Jesús—; sólo ve, preséntate al sacerdote, y lleva la ofrenda que ordenó Moisés, para que sirva de testimonio.

La fe del centurión
8:5-13 — Lc 7:1-10

⁵Al entrar Jesús en Capernaúm, se le acercó un centurión pidiendo ayuda.

⁶—Señor, mi siervo está postrado en casa con parálisis, y sufre terriblemente.

⁷—Iré a sanarlo —respondió Jesús.

⁸—Señor, no merezco que entres bajo mi techo. Pero basta con que digas una sola palabra, y mi siervo quedará sano. ⁹Porque yo mismo soy un hombre sujeto a órdenes superiores, y además tengo soldados bajo mi autoridad. Le digo a uno: "Ve", y va, y al otro: "Ven", y viene. Le digo a mi siervo: "Haz esto", y lo hace.

¹⁰Al oír esto, Jesús se asombró y dijo a quienes lo seguían:

—Les aseguro que no he encontrado en Israel a nadie que tenga tanta fe. ¹¹Les digo que muchos vendrán del oriente y del occidente, y participarán en el banquete con Abraham, Isaac y Jacob en el reino de los cielos. ¹²Pero a los súbditos del reino se les echará afuera, a la oscuridad, donde habrá llanto y rechinar de dientes.

¹³Luego Jesús le dijo al centurión:

—¡Ve! Todo se hará tal como creíste.

Y en esa misma hora aquel siervo quedó sano.

Jesús sana a muchos enfermos
8:14-16 — Mr 1:29-34; Lc 4:38-41

¹⁴Cuando Jesús entró en casa de Pedro, vio a la suegra de éste en cama, con fiebre. ¹⁵Le tocó la mano y la fiebre se le quitó; luego ella se levantó y comenzó a servirle.

¹⁶Al atardecer, le llevaron muchos endemoniados, y con una sola palabra expulsó a los espíritus, y sanó a todos los enfermos. ¹⁷Esto sucedió para que se cumpliera lo dicho por el profeta Isaías:

«Él cargó con nuestras enfermedades
y soportó nuestros dolores.»[h]

---

g 8:3 *sano*. Lit. *Limpio.*   h 8:17 Is 53:4

Lo que cuesta seguir a Jesús
8:19-22 — Lc 9:57-60

18Cuando Jesús vio a la multitud que lo rodeaba, dio orden de pasar al otro lado del lago. 19Se le acercó un *maestro de la ley y le dijo:

—Maestro, te seguiré a dondequiera que vayas.

20—Las zorras tienen madrigueras y las aves tienen nidos —le respondió Jesús—, pero el Hijo del hombre no tiene dónde recostar la cabeza.

21Otro discípulo le pidió:

—Señor, primero déjame ir a enterrar a mi padre.

22—Sígueme —le replicó Jesús—, y deja que los muertos entierren a sus muertos.

Jesús calma la tormenta
8:23-27 — Mr 4:36-41; Lc 8:22-25

23Luego subió a la barca y sus discípulos lo siguieron. 24De repente, se levantó en el lago una tormenta tan fuerte que las olas inundaban la barca. Pero Jesús estaba dormido. 25Los discípulos fueron a despertarlo.

—¡Señor —gritaron—, sálvanos, que nos vamos a ahogar!

26—Hombres de poca fe —les contestó—, ¿por qué tienen tanto miedo?

Entonces se levantó y reprendió a los vientos y a las olas, y todo quedó completamente tranquilo.

27Los discípulos no salían de su asombro, y decían: «¿Qué clase de hombre es éste, que hasta los vientos y las olas le obedecen?»

Liberación de dos endemoniados
8:28-34 — Mr 5:1-17; Lc 8:26-37

28Cuando Jesús llegó al otro lado, a la región de los gadarenos,[i] dos endemoniados le salieron al encuentro de entre los sepulcros. Eran tan violentos que nadie se atrevía a pasar por aquel camino. 29De pronto le gritaron:

—¿Por qué te entrometes, Hijo de Dios? ¿Has venido aquí a atormentarnos antes del tiempo señalado?

30A cierta distancia de ellos estaba paciendo una gran manada de cerdos. 31Los demonios le rogaron a Jesús:

—Si nos expulsas, mándanos a la manada de cerdos.

32—Vayan —les dijo.

Así que salieron de los hombres y entraron en los cerdos, y toda la manada se precipitó al lago por el despeñadero y murió en el agua. 33Los que cuidaban los cerdos salieron corriendo al pueblo y dieron aviso de todo, incluso de lo que les había sucedido a los endemoniados. 34Entonces todos del pueblo fueron al encuentro de Jesús. Y cuando lo vieron, le suplicaron que se aleja de esa región.

Jesús sana a un paralítico
9:2-8 — Mr 2:3-12; Lc 5:18-26

9 Subió Jesús a una barca, cruzó al otro lado y llegó a su propio pueblo. 2Unos hombres le llevaron un paralítico, acostado en una camilla. Al ver Jesús la fe de ellos, le dijo al paralítico:

—¡Ánimo, hijo; tus pecados quedan perdonados!

3Algunos de los *maestros de la ley murmuraron entre ellos: «¡Este hombre *blasfema!»

4Como Jesús conocía sus pensamientos, les dijo:

—¿Por qué dan lugar a tan malos pensamientos? 5¿Qué es más fácil, decir: "Tus pecados quedan perdonados", o decir: "Levántate y anda"? 6Pues para

que sepan que el Hijo del hombre tiene autoridad en la tierra para perdonar pecados —se dirigió entonces al paralítico—: Levántate, toma tu camilla y vete a tu casa.

7Y el hombre se levantó y se fue a su casa. 8Al ver esto, la multitud se llenó de temor, y glorificó a Dios por haber dado tal autoridad a los *mortales.

Llamamiento de Mateo
9:9-13 — Mr 2:14-17; Lc 5:27-32

9Al irse de allí, Jesús vio a un hombre llamado Mateo, sentado a la mesa de recaudación de impuestos. «Sígueme», le dijo. Mateo se levantó y lo siguió.

10Mientras Jesús estaba comiendo en casa de Mateo, muchos *recaudadores de impuestos y *pecadores llegaron y comieron con él y sus discípulos. 11Cuando los fariseos vieron esto, les preguntaron a sus discípulos:

—¿Por qué come su maestro con recaudadores de impuestos y con pecadores?

12Al oír esto, Jesús les contestó:

—No son los sanos los que necesitan médico sino los enfermos. 13Pero vayan y aprendan lo que significa: "Lo que pido de ustedes es misericordia y no sacrificios."[j] Porque no he venido a llamar a justos sino a pecadores.

Le preguntan a Jesús sobre el ayuno
9:14-17 — Mr 2:18-22; Lc 5:33-39

14Un día se le acercaron los discípulos de Juan y le preguntaron:

—¿Cómo es que nosotros y los fariseos ayunamos, pero no así tus discípulos?

Jesús les contestó:

15—¿Acaso pueden estar de luto los invitados del novio mientras él está con ellos? Llegará el día en que se les quitará el novio; entonces sí ayunarán. 16Nadie remienda un vestido viejo con un retazo de tela nueva, porque el remiendo fruncirá el vestido y la rotura se hará peor. 17Ni tampoco se echa vino nuevo en odres viejos. De hacerlo así, se reventarán los odres, se derramará el vino y los odres se arruinarán. Más bien, el vino nuevo se echa en odres nuevos, y así ambos se conservan.

Una niña muerta y una mujer enferma
9:18-26 — Mr 5:22-43; Lc 8:41-56

18Mientras él les decía esto, un dirigente judío llegó, se arrodilló delante de él y le dijo:

—Mi hija acaba de morir. Pero ven y pon tu mano sobre ella, y vivirá.

19Jesús se levantó y fue con él, acompañado de sus discípulos. 20En esto, una mujer que hacía doce años padecía de hemorragias se le acercó por detrás y le tocó el borde del manto. 21Pensaba: «Si al menos logro tocar su manto, quedaré *sana.» 22Jesús se dio vuelta, la vio y le dijo:

—¡Ánimo, hija! Tu fe te ha sanado.

Y la mujer quedó sana en aquel momento.

23Cuando Jesús entró en la casa del dirigente y vio a los flautistas y el alboroto de la gente, 24les dijo:

—Váyanse. La niña no está muerta sino dormida.

Entonces empezaron a burlarse de él. 25Pero cuando se les hizo salir, entró él, tomó de la mano a la niña, y ésta se levantó. 26La noticia se divulgó por toda aquella región.

---

i **8:28** *gadarenos.* Var. *gergesenos;* otra var. *gerasenos.*   j **9:13** Os 6:6

Jesús sana a los ciegos y a los mudos

27Al irse Jesús de allí, dos ciegos lo siguieron, gritándole:

—¡Ten compasión de nosotros, Hijo de David!

28Cuando entró en la casa, se le acercaron los ciegos, y él les preguntó:

—¿Creen que puedo sanarlos?

—Sí, Señor —le respondieron.

29Entonces les tocó los ojos y les dijo:

—Se hará con ustedes conforme a su fe.

30Y recobraron la vista. Jesús les advirtió con firmeza:

—Asegúrense de que nadie se entere de esto.

31Pero ellos salieron para divulgar por toda aquella región la noticia acerca de Jesús.

32Mientras ellos salían, le llevaron un mudo endemoniado. 33Así que Jesús expulsó al demonio, y el que había estado mudo habló. La multitud se maravillaba y decía: «Jamás se ha visto nada igual en Israel.»

34Pero los fariseos afirmaban: «Éste expulsa a los demonios por medio del príncipe de los demonios.»

Son pocos los obreros

35Jesús recorría todos los pueblos y aldeas enseñando en las sinagogas, anunciando las buenas *nuevas del reino, y sanando toda enfermedad y toda dolencia. 36Al ver a las multitudes, tuvo compasión de ellas, porque estaban agobiadas y desamparadas, como ovejas sin pastor. 37«La cosecha es abundante, pero son pocos los obreros —les dijo a sus discípulos— 38Pídanle, por tanto, al Señor de la cosecha que envíe obreros a su campo.»

Jesús envía a los doce

10:2-4 — Mr 3:16-19; Lc 6:14-16; Hch 1:13
10:9-15 — Mr 6:8-11; Lc 9:3-5; 10:4-12
10:19-22 — Mr 13:11-13; Lc 21:12-17
10:26-33 — Lc 12:2-9
10:34-35 — Lc 12:51-53

10 Reunió a sus doce discípulos y les dio autoridad para expulsar a los *espíritus malignos y sanar toda enfermedad y toda dolencia.

2Éstos son los nombres de los doce apóstoles: primero Simón, llamado Pedro, y su hermano Andrés; *Jacobo y su hermano Juan, hijos de Zebedeo; 3Felipe y Bartolomé; Tomás y Mateo, el *recaudador de impuestos; Jacobo, hijo de Alfeo, y Tadeo; 4Simón el Zelote y Judas Iscariote, el que lo traicionó.

5Jesús envió a estos doce con las siguientes instrucciones: «No vayan entre los *gentiles ni entren en ningún pueblo de los samaritanos. 6Vayan más bien a las ovejas descarriadas del pueblo de Israel. 7Dondequiera que vayan, prediquen este mensaje: "El reino de los cielos está cerca." 8Sanen a los enfermos, resuciten a los muertos, *limpien de su enfermedad a los que tienen *lepra, expulsen a los demonios. Lo que ustedes recibieron gratis, denlo gratuitamente. 9No lleven oro ni plata ni cobre en el cinturón, 10ni bolsa para el camino, ni dos mudas de ropa, ni sandalias, ni bastón; porque el trabajador merece que se le dé su sustento.

11»En cualquier pueblo o aldea donde entren, busquen a alguien que merezca recibirlos, y quédense en su casa hasta que se vayan de ese lugar. 12Al entrar, digan: "Paz a esta casa."k 13Si el hogar se lo merece,

que la paz de ustedes reine en él; y si no, que la paz se vaya con ustedes. 14Si alguno no los recibe bien ni escucha sus palabras, al salir de esa casa o de ese pueblo, sacúdanse el polvo de los pies. 15Les aseguro que en el día del juicio el castigo para Sodoma y Gomorra será más tolerable que para ese pueblo. 16Los envío como ovejas en medio de lobos. Por tanto, sean astutos como serpientes y sencillos como palomas.

17»Tengan cuidado con la gente; los entregarán a los tribunales y los azotarán en las sinagogas. 18Por mi causa los llevarán ante gobernadores y reyes para dar testimonio a ellos y a los gentiles. 19Pero cuando los arresten, no se preocupen por lo que van a decir o cómo van a decirlo. En ese momento se les dará lo que han de decir, 20porque no serán ustedes los que hablen, sino que el Espíritu de su Padre hablará por medio de ustedes.

21»El hermano entregará a la muerte al hermano, y el padre al hijo. Los hijos se rebelarán contra sus padres y harán que los maten. 22Por causa de mi nombre todo el mundo los odiará, pero el que se mantenga firme hasta el fin será salvo. 23Cuando los persigan en una ciudad, huyan a otra. Les aseguro que no terminarán de recorrer las ciudades de Israel antes de que venga el Hijo del hombre.

24»El discípulo no es superior a su maestro, ni el *siervo superior a su amo. 25Basta con que el discípulo sea como su maestro, y el siervo como su amo. Si al jefe de la casa lo han llamado *Beelzebú, ¡cuánto más a los de su familia!

26»Así que no les tengan miedo; porque no hay nada encubierto que no llegue a revelarse, ni nada escondido que no llegue a conocerse. 27Lo que les digo en la oscuridad, díganlo ustedes a plena luz; lo que se les susurra al oído, proclámenlo desde las azoteas. 28No teman a los que matan el cuerpo pero no pueden matar el alma.l Teman más bien al que puede destruir alma y cuerpo en el infierno.m 29¿No se venden dos gorriones por una monedita?n Sin embargo, ni uno de ellos caerá a tierra sin que lo permita el Padre; 30y él les tiene contados a ustedes aun los cabellos de la cabeza. 31Así que no tengan miedo; ustedes valen más que muchos gorriones.

32»A cualquiera que me reconozca delante de los demás, yo también lo reconoceré delante de mi Padre que está en el cielo. 33Pero a cualquiera que me desconozca delante de los demás, yo también lo desconoceré delante de mi Padre que está en el cielo.

34»No crean que he venido a traer paz a la tierra. No vine a traer paz sino espada. 35Porque he venido a poner en conflicto

> "al hombre contra su padre,
>   a la hija contra su madre,
>   a la nuera contra su suegra;
> 36los enemigos de cada cual
>   serán los de su propia familia".ñ

37»El que quiere a su padre o a su madre más que a mí no es digno de mí; el que quiere a su hijo o a su hija más que a mí no es digno de mí; 38y el que no toma su cruz y me sigue no es digno de mí. 39El que encuentre su *vida, la perderá, y el que la pierda por mi causa, la encontrará.

40»Quien los recibe a ustedes, me recibe a mí; y quien me recibe a mí, recibe al que me envió. 41Cualquiera que reciba a un profeta por tratarse de un profeta, recibirá recompensa de profeta; y el que

---

k **10:12** El entrar . . . casa". Lit. Al entrar en la casa, salúdenla. l **10:28** alma. Este vocablo griego también puede significar *vida. m **10:28** infierno. Lit. *Gehenna. n **10:29** una monedita. Lit. un *asarion. ñ **10:36** Mi 7:6

recibe a un justo por tratarse de un justo, recibirá recompensa de justo. ⁴²Y quien dé siquiera un vaso de agua fresca a uno de estos pequeños por tratarse de uno de mis discípulos, les aseguro que no perderá su recompensa.»

Jesús y Juan el Bautista
11:2-19 — Lc 7:18-35

11 Cuando Jesús terminó de dar instrucciones a sus doce discípulos, se fue de allí a enseñar y a predicar en otros pueblos.

²Juan estaba en la cárcel, y al enterarse de lo que *Cristo estaba haciendo, envió a sus discípulos a que le preguntaran:

³—¿Eres tú el que ha de venir, o debemos esperar a otro?

⁴Les respondió Jesús:

—Vayan y cuéntenle a Juan lo que están viendo y oyendo: ⁵Los ciegos ven, los cojos andan, los que tienen *lepra son sanados, los sordos oyen, los muertos resucitan y a los pobres se les anuncian las buenas *nuevas. ⁶*Dichoso el que no *tropieza por causa mía.

⁷Mientras se iban los discípulos de Juan, Jesús comenzó a hablarle a la multitud acerca de Juan: «¿Qué salieron a ver al desierto? ¿Una caña sacudida por el viento? ⁸Si no, ¿qué salieron a ver? ¿A un hombre vestido con ropa fina? Claro que no, pues los que usan ropa de lujo están en los palacios de los reyes. ⁹Entonces, ¿qué salieron a ver? ¿A un profeta? Sí, les digo, y más que profeta. ¹⁰Éste es de quien está escrito:

»"Yo estoy por enviar a mi mensajero delante
    de ti,
el cual preparará tu camino."o

¹¹Les aseguro que entre los mortales no se ha levantado nadie más grande que Juan el Bautista; sin embargo, el más pequeño en el reino de los cielos es más grande que él. ¹²Desde los días de Juan el Bautista hasta ahora, el reino de los cielos ha venido avanzando contra viento y marea, y los que se esfuerzan logran aferrarse a él.p ¹³Porque todos los profetas y la ley profetizaron hasta Juan. ¹⁴Y si quieren aceptar mi palabra, Juan es el Elías que había de venir. ¹⁵El que tenga oídos, que oiga.

¹⁶¿Con qué puedo comparar a esta generación? Se parece a los niños sentados en la plaza que gritan a los demás:

¹⁷»"Tocamos la flauta,
    y ustedes no bailaron;
Cantamos por los muertos,
    y ustedes no lloraron."

¹⁸»Porque vino Juan, que no comía ni bebía, y ellos dicen: "Tiene un demonio." ¹⁹Vino el Hijo del hombre, que come y bebe, y dicen: "Éste es un glotón y un borracho, amigo de *recaudadores de impuestos y de *pecadores." Pero la sabiduría queda demostrada por sus hechos.»

Ayes sobre ciudades no arrepentidas
11:21-23 — Lc 10:13-15

²⁰Entonces comenzó Jesús a denunciar a las ciudades en que había hecho la mayor parte de sus milagros, porque no se habían *arrepentido. ²¹«¡Ay de ti, Corazín! ¡Ay de ti, Betsaida! Si se hubieran hecho en Tiro y en Sidón los milagros que se hicieron en medio de ustedes, ya hace tiempo que se habrían

arrepentido con muchos lamentos.q ²²Pero les digo que en el día del juicio será más tolerable el castigo para Tiro y Sidón que para ustedes. ²³Y tú, Capernaúm, ¿acaso serás levantada hasta el cielo? No, sino que descenderás hasta el *abismo. Si los milagros que se hicieron en ti se hubieran hecho en Sodoma, ésta habría permanecido hasta el día de hoy. ²⁴Pero ter digo que en el día del juicio será más tolerable el castigo para Sodoma que para ti.»

Descanso para los cansados
11:25-27 — Lc 10:21-22

²⁵En aquel tiempo Jesús dijo: «Te alabo, Padre, Señor del cielo y de la tierra, porque habiendo escondido estas cosas de los sabios e instruidos, se las has revelado a los que son como niños. ²⁶Sí, Padre, porque esa fue tu buena voluntad.

²⁷»Mi Padre me ha entregado todas las cosas. Nadie conoce al Hijo sino el Padre, y nadie conoce al Padre sino el Hijo y aquel a quien el Hijo quiera revelarlo.

²⁸»Vengan a mí todos ustedes que están cansados y agobiados, y yo les daré descanso. ²⁹Carguen con mi yugo y aprendan de mí, pues yo soy apacible y humilde de corazón, y encontrarán descanso para su alma. ³⁰Porque mi yugo es suave y mi carga es liviana.»

Señor del sábado
12:1-8 — Mr 2:23-28; Lc 6:1-5
12:9-14 — Mr 3:1-6; Lc 6:6-11

12 Por aquel tiempo pasaba Jesús por los sembrados en *sábado. Sus discípulos tenían hambre, así que comenzaron a arrancar algunas espigas de trigo y comérselas. ²Al ver esto, los fariseos le dijeron:

—¡Mira! Tus discípulos están haciendo lo que está prohibido en sábado.

³Él les contestó:

—¿No han leído lo que hizo David en aquella ocasión en que él y sus compañeros tuvieron hambre? ⁴Entró en la casa de Dios, y él y sus compañeros comieron los panes consagrados a Dios, lo que no se permitía a ellos sino sólo a los sacerdotes. ⁵¿O no han leído en la ley que los sacerdotes en el *templo profanan el sábado sin incurrir en culpa? ⁶Pues yo les digo que aquí está uno más grande que el templo. ⁷Si ustedes supieran lo que significa: "Lo que pido de ustedes es misericordia y no sacrificios",ˢ no condenarían a los que no son culpables. ⁸Sepan que el Hijo del hombre es Señor del sábado.

⁹Pasando de allí, entró en la sinagoga, ¹⁰donde había un hombre que tenía una mano paralizada. Como buscaban un motivo para acusar a Jesús, le preguntaron:

—¿Está permitido sanar en sábado?

¹¹Él les contestó:

—Si alguno de ustedes tiene una oveja y en sábado se le cae en un hoyo, ¿no la agarra y la saca? ¹²¡Cuánto más vale un hombre que una oveja! Por lo tanto, está permitido hacer el bien en sábado.

¹³Entonces le dijo al hombre:

—Extiende la mano.

Así que la extendió y le quedó restablecida, tan sana como la otra. ¹⁴Pero los fariseos salieron y tramaban cómo matar a Jesús.

o 11:10 Mal 3:1 p 11:12 ha venido . . . aferrarse a él. Alt. sufre violencia y los violentos quieren arrebatarlo. q 11:21 con muchos lamentos. Lit. en saco y ceniza. r 11:24 te. Lit. les. s 12:7 Os 6:6

El siervo escogido por Dios

15Consciente de esto, Jesús se retiró de aquel lugar. Muchos lo siguieron, y él sanó a todos los enfermos, 16pero les ordenó que no dijeran quién era él. 17Esto fue para que se cumpliera lo dicho por el profeta Isaías:

18«Éste es mi siervo, a quien he escogido,
mi amado, en quien estoy muy
complacido;
sobre él pondré mi Espíritu,
y proclamará justicia a las *naciones.
19No disputará ni gritará;
nadie oirá su voz en las calles.
20No acabará de romper la caña quebrada
ni apagará la mecha que apenas arde,
hasta que haga triunfar la justicia.
21Y en su nombre pondrán las naciones su
esperanza.»t

Jesús y Beelzebú

12:25-29 — Mr 3:23-27; Lc 11:17-22

22Un día le llevaron un endemoniado que estaba ciego y mudo, y Jesús lo sanó, de modo que pudo ver y hablar. 23Toda la gente se quedó asombrada y decía: «¿No será éste el Hijo de David?»

24Pero al oírlo los fariseos, dijeron: «Éste no expulsa a los demonios sino por medio de *Beelzebú, príncipe de los demonios.»

25Jesús conocía sus pensamientos, y les dijo: «Todo reino dividido contra sí mismo quedará asolado, y toda ciudad o familia dividida contra sí misma no se mantendrá en pie. 26Si Satanás expulsa a Satanás, está dividido contra sí mismo. ¿Cómo puede, entonces, mantenerse en pie su reino? 27Ahora bien, si yo expulso a los demonios por medio de Beelzebú, ¿los seguidores de ustedes por medio de quién los expulsan? Por eso ellos mismos los juzgarán a ustedes. 28En cambio, si expulso a los demonios por medio del Espíritu de Dios, eso significa que el reino de Dios ha llegado a ustedes.

29»¿O cómo puede entrar alguien en la casa de un hombre fuerte y arrebatarle sus bienes, a menos que primero lo ate? Sólo entonces podrá robar su casa.

30»El que no está de mi parte, está contra mí; y el que conmigo no recoge, esparce. 31Por eso les digo que a todos se les podrá perdonar todo pecado y toda *blasfemia, pero la blasfemia contra el Espíritu no se le perdonará a nadie. 32A cualquiera que pronuncie alguna palabra contra el Hijo del hombre se le perdonará, pero el que hable contra el Espíritu Santo no tendrá perdón ni en este mundo ni en el venidero.

33»Si tienen un buen árbol, su fruto es bueno; si tienen un mal árbol, su fruto es malo. Al árbol se le reconoce por su fruto. 34Camada de víboras, ¿cómo pueden ustedes que son malos decir algo bueno? De la abundancia del corazón habla la boca. 35El que es bueno, de la bondad que atesora en el corazón saca el bien, pero el que es malo, de su maldad saca el mal. 36Pero yo les digo que en el día del juicio todos tendrán que dar cuenta de toda palabra ociosa que hayan pronunciado. 37Porque por tus palabras se te absolverá, y por tus palabras se te condenará.»

La señal de Jonás

12:39-42 — Lc 11:29-32
12:43-45 — Lc 11:24-26

38Algunos de los fariseos y de los *maestros de la ley le dijeron:

—Maestro, queremos ver alguna señal milagrosa de parte tuya.

39Jesús les contestó:

—¡Esta generación malvada y adúltera pide una señal milagrosa! Pero no se le dará más señal que la del profeta Jonás. 40Porque así como tres días y tres noches estuvo Jonás en el vientre de un gran pez, también tres días y tres noches estará el Hijo del hombre en las entrañas de la tierra. 41Los habitantes de Nínive se levantarán en el juicio contra esta generación y la condenarán; porque ellos se *arrepintieron al escuchar la predicación de Jonás, y aquí tienen ustedes a uno más grande que Jonás. 42La reina del Sur se levantará en el día del juicio y condenará a esta generación; porque ella vino desde los confines de la tierra para escuchar la sabiduría de Salomón, y aquí tienen ustedes a uno más grande que Salomón.

43»Cuando un *espíritu maligno sale de una persona, va por lugares áridos, buscando descanso sin encontrarlo. 44Entonces dice: "Volveré a la casa de donde salí." Cuando llega, la encuentra desocupada, barrida y arreglada. 45Luego va y trae a otros siete espíritus más malvados que él, y entran a vivir allí. Así que el estado postrero de aquella persona resulta peor que el primero. Así le pasará también a esta generación malvada.

La madre y los hermanos de Jesús

12:46-50 — Mr 3:31-35; Lc 8:19-21

46Mientras Jesús le hablaba a la multitud, se presentaron su madre y sus hermanos. Se quedaron afuera, y deseaban hablar con él. 47Alguien le dijo:

—Tu madre y tus hermanos están afuera y quieren hablar contigo.u

48—¿Quién es mi madre, y quiénes son mis hermanos? —replicó Jesús.

49Señalando a sus discípulos, añadió:

—Aquí tienen a mi madre y a mis hermanos. 50Pues mi hermano, mi hermana y mi madre son los que hacen la voluntad de mi Padre que está en el cielo.

Parábola del sembrador

13:1-15 — Mr 4:1-12; Lc 8:4-10
13:16-17 — Lc 10:23-24
13:18-23 — Mr 4:13-20; Lc 8:11-15

13 Ese mismo día salió Jesús de la casa y se sentó junto al lago. 2Era tal la multitud que se reunió para verlo que él tuvo que subir a una barca donde se sentó mientras toda la gente estaba de pie en la orilla. 3Y les dijo en parábolas muchas cosas como éstas: «Un sembrador salió a sembrar. 4Mientras iba esparciendo la semilla, una parte cayó junto al camino, y llegaron los pájaros y se la comieron. 5Otra parte cayó en terreno pedregoso, sin mucha tierra. Esa semilla brotó pronto porque la tierra no era profunda. 6pero cuando salió el sol, las plantas se marchitaron y, por no tener raíz, se secaron. 7Otra parte de la semilla cayó entre espinos que, al crecer, la ahogaron. 8Pero las otras semillas cayeron en buen terreno, en el que se dio una cosecha que rindió treinta, sesenta

---

t 12:21 Is 42:1-4   u 12:47 Var. no incluye v. 47.

y hasta cien veces más de lo que se había sembrado. ⁹El que tenga oídos, que oiga.»

¹⁰Los discípulos se acercaron y le preguntaron:

—¿Por qué le hablas a la gente en parábolas?

¹¹—A ustedes se les ha concedido conocer los *secretos del reino de los cielos; pero a ellos no. ¹²Al que tiene, se le dará más, y tendrá en abundancia. Al que no tiene, hasta lo poco que tiene se le quitará. ¹³Por eso les hablo a ellos en parábolas:

»Aunque miran, no ven;
    aunque oyen, no escuchan ni entienden.

¹⁴En ellos se cumple la profecía de Isaías:

»"Por mucho que oigan, no entenderán;
    por mucho que vean, no percibirán.
¹⁵Porque el corazón de este pueblo se ha vuelto
    insensible;
se les han embotado los oídos,
    y se les han cerrado los ojos.
De lo contrario, verían con los ojos,
    oirían con los oídos,
    entenderían con el corazón
y se convertirían, y yo los sanaría."ᵛ

¹⁶Pero *dichosos los ojos de ustedes porque ven, y sus oídos porque oyen. ¹⁷Porque les aseguro que muchos profetas y otros justos anhelaron ver lo que ustedes ven, pero no lo vieron; y oír lo que ustedes oyen, pero no lo oyeron.

¹⁸»Escuchen lo que significa la parábola del sembrador: ¹⁹Cuando alguien oye la palabra acerca del reino y no la entiende, viene el maligno y arrebata lo que se sembró en su corazón. Ésta es la semilla sembrada junto al camino. ²⁰El que recibió la semilla que cayó en terreno pedregoso es el que oye la palabra e inmediatamente la recibe con alegría; ²¹pero como no tiene raíz, dura poco tiempo. Cuando surgen problemas o persecución a causa de la palabra, en seguida se aparta de ella. ²²El que recibió la semilla que cayó entre espinos es el que oye la palabra, pero las preocupaciones de esta vida y el engaño de las riquezas la ahogan, de modo que ésta no llega a dar fruto. ²³Pero el que recibió la semilla que cayó en buen terreno es el que oye la palabra y la entiende. Éste sí produce una cosecha al treinta, al sesenta y hasta al ciento por uno.

Parábola de la mala hierba

²⁴Jesús les contó otra parábola: «El reino de los cielos es como un hombre que sembró buena semilla en su campo. ²⁵Pero mientras todos dormían, llegó su enemigo y sembró mala hierba entre el trigo, y se fue. ²⁶Cuando brotó el trigo y se formó la espiga, apareció también la mala hierba. ²⁷Los siervos fueron al dueño y le dijeron: "Señor, ¿no sembró usted semilla buena en su campo? Entonces, ¿de dónde salió la mala hierba?" ²⁸"Esto es obra de un enemigo", les respondió. Le preguntaron los siervos: "¿Quiere usted que vayamos a arrancarla?" ²⁹"¡No! —les contestó—, no sea que, al arrancar la mala hierba, arranquen con ella el trigo. ³⁰Dejen que crezcan juntos hasta la cosecha. Entonces les diré a los segadores: Recojan primero la mala hierba, y átenla en manojos para quemarla; después recojan el trigo y guárdenlo en mi granero."»

Parábolas del grano de mostaza y de la levadura

13:31-32 — Mr 4:30-32
13:31-33 — Lc 13:18-21

³¹Les contó otra parábola: «El reino de los cielos es como un grano de mostaza que un hombre sembró en su campo. ³²Aunque es la más pequeña de todas las semillas, cuando crece es la más grande de las hortalizas y se convierte en árbol, de modo que vienen las aves y anidan en sus ramas.»

³³Les contó otra parábola más: «El reino de los cielos es como la levadura que una mujer tomó y mezcló en una gran cantidadʷ de harina, hasta que fermentó toda la masa.»

³⁴Jesús le dijo a la multitud todas estas cosas en parábolas. Sin emplear parábolas no les decía nada. ³⁵Así se cumplió lo dicho por el profeta:

«Hablaré por medio de parábolas;
    revelaré cosas que han estado ocultas
    desde la creación del mundo.»ˣ

Explicación de la parábola de la mala hierba

³⁶Una vez que se despidió de la multitud, entró en la casa. Se le acercaron sus discípulos y le pidieron:

—Explícanos la parábola de la mala hierba del campo.

³⁷—El que sembró la buena semilla es el Hijo del hombre —les respondió Jesús—. ³⁸El campo es el mundo, y la buena semilla representa a los hijos del reino. La mala hierba son los hijos del maligno, ³⁹y el enemigo que la siembra es el diablo. La cosecha es el fin del mundo, y los segadores son los ángeles.

⁴⁰»Así como se recoge la mala hierba y se quema en el fuego, ocurrirá también al fin del mundo. ⁴¹El Hijo del hombre enviará a sus ángeles, y arrancarán de su reino a todos los que *pecan y hacen pecar. ⁴²Los arrojarán al horno encendido, donde habrá llanto y rechinar de dientes. ⁴³Entonces los justos brillarán en el reino de su Padre como el sol. El que tenga oídos, que oiga.

Parábolas del tesoro escondido y de la perla

⁴⁴»El reino de los cielos es como un tesoro escondido en un campo. Cuando un hombre lo descubrió, lo volvió a esconder, y lleno de alegría fue y vendió todo lo que tenía y compró ese campo.

⁴⁵»También se parece el reino de los cielos a un comerciante que andaba buscando perlas finas. ⁴⁶Cuando encontró una de gran valor, fue y vendió todo lo que tenía y la compró.

Parábola de la red

⁴⁷»También se parece el reino de los cielos a una red echada al lago, que recoge peces de toda clase. ⁴⁸Cuando se llena, los pescadores la sacan a la orilla, se sientan y recogen en canastas los peces buenos, y desechan los malos. ⁴⁹Así será al fin del mundo. Vendrán los ángeles y apartarán de los justos a los malvados, ⁵⁰y los arrojarán al horno encendido, donde habrá llanto y rechinar de dientes.

⁵¹—¿Han entendido todo esto? —les preguntó Jesús.

—Sí —respondieron ellos.

Entonces concluyó Jesús:

⁵²—Todo *maestro de la ley que ha sido instruido acerca del reino de los cielos es como el dueño de

---

ᵛ **13:15** Is 6:9,10   ʷ **13:33** *una gran cantidad.* Lit. *tres satas* (probablemente unos 22 litros).   ˣ **13:35** Sal 78:2

una casa, que de lo que tiene guardado saca tesoros nuevos y viejos.

Un profeta sin honra
13:54-58 — Mr 6:1-6

53Cuando Jesús terminó de contar estas parábolas, se fue de allí. 54Al llegar a su tierra, comenzó a enseñar a la gente en la sinagoga.

—¿De dónde sacó éste tal sabiduría y tales poderes milagrosos? —decían maravillados—. 55¿No es acaso el hijo del carpintero? ¿No se llama su madre María; y no son sus hermanos *Jacobo, José, Simón y Judas? 56¿No están con nosotros todas sus hermanas? ¿Así que de dónde sacó todas estas cosas?

57Y se *escandalizaban a causa de él. Pero Jesús les dijo:

—En todas partes se honra a un profeta, menos en su tierra y en su propia casa.

58Y por la incredulidad de ellos, no hizo allí muchos milagros.

Decapitación de Juan el Bautista
14:1-12 — Mr 6:14-29

14 En aquel tiempo Herodes el tetrarca se enteró de lo que decían de Jesús, 2y comentó a sus sirvientes: «Ése es Juan el Bautista; ha *resucitado! Por eso tiene poder para realizar milagros.»

3En efecto, Herodes había arrestado a Juan. Lo había encadenado y metido en la cárcel por causa de Herodías, esposa de su hermano Felipe. 4Es que Juan había estado diciéndole: «La ley te prohíbe tenerla por esposa.» 5Herodes quería matarlo, pero le tenía miedo a la gente, porque consideraban a Juan como un profeta.

6En el cumpleaños de Herodes, la hija de Herodías bailó delante de todos; y tanto le agradó a Herodes 7que le prometió bajo juramento darle cualquier cosa que pidiera. 8Instigada por su madre, le pidió: «Dame en una bandeja la cabeza de Juan el Bautista.»

9El rey se entristeció, pero a causa de sus juramentos y en atención a los invitados, ordenó que se le concediera la petición, 10y mandó decapitar a Juan en la cárcel. 11Llevaron la cabeza en una bandeja y se la dieron a la muchacha, quien se la entregó a su madre. 12Luego llegaron los discípulos de Juan, recogieron el cuerpo y le dieron sepultura. Después fueron y avisaron a Jesús.

Jesús alimenta a los cinco mil
14:13-21 — Mr 6:32-44; Lc 9:10-17; Jn 6:1-13

13Cuando Jesús recibió la noticia, se retiró él solo en una barca a un lugar solitario. Las multitudes se enteraron y lo siguieron a pie desde los poblados. 14Cuando Jesús desembarcó y vio a tanta gente, tuvo compasión de ellos y sanó a los que estaban enfermos. 15Al atardecer se le acercaron sus discípulos y le dijeron:

—Éste es un lugar apartado y ya se hace tarde. Despide a la gente, para que vayan a los pueblos y se compren algo de comer.

16—No tienen que irse —contestó Jesús—. Denles ustedes mismos de comer.

17Ellos objetaron:

—No tenemos aquí más que cinco panes y dos pescados.

18—Tráiganmelos acá —les dijo Jesús.

19Y mandó a la gente que se sentara sobre la hierba. Tomó los cinco panes y los dos pescados y, miran-

do al cielo, los bendijo. Luego partió los panes y se los dio a los discípulos, quienes los repartieron a la gente. 20Todos comieron hasta quedar satisfechos, y los discípulos recogieron doce canastas llenas de pedazos que sobraron. 21Los que comieron fueron unos cinco mil hombres, sin contar a las mujeres y a los niños.

Jesús camina sobre el agua
14:22-33 — Mr 6:45-51; Jn 6:15-21
14:34-36 — Mr 6:53-56

22En seguida Jesús hizo que los discípulos subieran a la barca y se le adelantaran al otro lado mientras tras él despedía a la multitud. 23Después de despedir a la gente, subió a la montaña para orar a solas. Al anochecer, estaba allí él solo, 24y la barca ya estaba bastante lejosy de la tierra, zarandeada por las olas, porque el viento le era contrario.

25En la madrugada,z Jesús se acercó a ellos caminando sobre el lago. 26Cuando los discípulos lo vieron caminando sobre el agua, quedaron aterrados.

—¡Es un fantasma! —gritaron de miedo.

27Pero Jesús les dijo en seguida:

—¡Cálmense! Soy yo. No tengan miedo.

28—Señor, si eres tú —respondió Pedro—, mándame que vaya a ti sobre el agua.

29—Ven —dijo Jesús.

Pedro bajó de la barca y caminó sobre el agua en dirección a Jesús. 30Pero al sentir el viento fuerte, tuvo miedo y comenzó a hundirse. Entonces gritó:

—¡Señor, sálvame!

31En seguida Jesús le tendió la mano y, sujetándolo, lo reprendió:

—¡Hombre de poca fe! ¿Por qué dudaste?

32Cuando subieron a la barca, se calmó el viento. 33Y los que estaban en la barca lo adoraron diciendo:

—Verdaderamente tú eres el Hijo de Dios.

34Después de cruzar el lago, desembarcaron en Genesaret. 35Los habitantes de aquel lugar reconocieron a Jesús y divulgaron la noticia por todos los alrededores. Le llevaban todos los enfermos, 36suplicándole que les permitiera tocar siquiera el borde de su manto, y quienes lo tocaban quedaban sanos.

Lo limpio y lo impuro
15:1-20 — Mr 7:1-23

15 Se acercaron a Jesús algunos fariseos y *maestros de la ley que habían llegado de Jerusalén, y le preguntaron:

2—¿Por qué quebrantan tus discípulos la tradición de los *ancianos? ¡Comen sin cumplir primero el rito de lavarse las manos!

3Jesús les contestó:

—¿Y por qué ustedes quebrantan el mandamiento de Dios a causa de la tradición? 4Dios dijo: "Honra a tu padre y a tu madre",a y también: "El que maldiga a su padre o a su madre será condenado a muerte."b 5Ustedes, en cambio, enseñan que un hijo puede decir a su padre o a su madre: "Cualquier ayuda que pudiera darte ya la he dedicado como ofrenda a Dios." 6En ese caso, el tal hijo no tiene que honrar a su padre.c Así por causa de la tradición anulan ustedes la palabra de Dios. 7¡*Hipócritas! Tenía razón Isaías cuando profetizó de ustedes:

8»"Este pueblo me honra con los labios,
    pero su corazón está lejos de mí.
9En vano me adoran;

y **14:24** bastante lejos. Lit. a muchos *estadios. z **14:25** la madrugada. Lit. la cuarta vigilia de la noche. a **15:4** Éx 20:12; Dt 5:16 b **15:4** Éx 21:17; Lv 20:9 c **15:6** padre. Var. padre ni a su madre.

sus enseñanzas no son más que reglas *humanas."d

10Jesús llamó a la multitud y dijo:

—Escuchen y entiendan. 11Lo que *contamina a una persona no es lo que entra en la boca sino lo que sale de ella.

12Entonces se le acercaron los discípulos y le dijeron:

—¿Sabes que los fariseos se *escandalizaron al oír eso?

13—Toda planta que mi Padre celestial no haya plantado será arrancada de raíz —les respondió—. 14Déjenlos; son guías ciegos.e Y si un ciego guía a otro ciego, ambos caerán en un hoyo.

15—Explícanos la comparación —le pidió Pedro.

16—¿También ustedes son todavía tan torpes? —les dijo Jesús—. 17¿No se dan cuenta de que todo lo que entra en la boca va al estómago y después se echa en la letrina? 18Pero lo que sale de la boca viene del corazón y contamina a la persona. 19Porque del corazón salen los malos pensamientos, los homicidios, los adulterios, la inmoralidad sexual, los robos, los falsos testimonios y las calumnias. 20Éstas son las cosas que contaminan a la persona, y no el comer sin lavarse las manos.

La fe de la mujer cananea
15:21-28 — Mr 7:24-30

21Partiendo de allí, Jesús se retiró a la región de Tiro y Sidón. 22Una mujer cananea de las inmediaciones salió a su encuentro, gritando:

—¡Señor, Hijo de David, ten compasión de mí! Mi hija sufre terriblemente por estar endemoniada.

23Jesús no le respondió palabra. Así que sus discípulos se acercaron a él y le rogaron:

—Despídela, porque viene detrás de nosotros gritando.

24—No fui enviado sino a las ovejas perdidas del pueblo de Israel —contestó Jesús.

25La mujer se acercó y, arrodillándose delante de él, le suplicó:

—¡Señor, ayúdame!

26Él le respondió:

—No está bien quitarles el pan a los hijos y echárselo a los *perros.

27—Sí, Señor; pero hasta los perros comen las migajas que caen de la mesa de sus amos.

28—¡Mujer, qué grande es tu fe! —contestó Jesús—. Que se cumpla lo que quieres.

Y desde ese mismo momento quedó sana su hija.

Jesús alimenta a los cuatro mil
15:29-31 — Mr 7:31-37
15:32-39 — Mr 8:1-10

29Salió Jesús de allí y llegó a orillas del mar de Galilea. Luego subió a la montaña y se sentó. 30Se le acercaron grandes multitudes que llevaban cojos, ciegos, lisiados, mudos y muchos enfermos más, y los pusieron a sus pies; y él los sanó. 31La gente se asombraba al ver a los mudos hablar, a los lisiados recobrar la salud, a los cojos andar y a los ciegos ver. Y alababan al Dios de Israel.

32Jesús llamó a sus discípulos y les dijo:

—Siento compasión de esta gente porque ya llevan tres días conmigo y no tienen nada que comer.

No quiero despedirlos sin comer, no sea que se desmayen por el camino.

33Los discípulos objetaron:

—¿Dónde podríamos conseguir en este lugar despoblado suficiente pan para dar de comer a toda esta multitud?

34—¿Cuántos panes tienen? —les preguntó Jesús.

—Siete, y unos pocos pescaditos.

35Luego mandó que la gente se sentara en el suelo. 36Tomando los siete panes y los pescados, dio gracias, los partió y se los fue dando a los discípulos. Éstos, a su vez, los distribuyeron a la gente. 37Todos comieron hasta quedar satisfechos. Después los discípulos recogieron siete cestas llenas de pedazos que sobraron. 38Los que comieron eran cuatro mil hombres, sin contar a las mujeres y a los niños. 39Después de despedir a la gente, subió Jesús a la barca y se fue a la región de Magadán.f

Le piden a Jesús una señal
16:1-12 — Mr 8:11-21

16 Los fariseos y los saduceos se acercaron a Jesús y, para ponerlo a prueba, le pidieron que les mostrara una señal del cielo.

2Él les contestó:g «Al atardecer, ustedes dicen que hará buen tiempo porque el cielo está rojizo, 3y por la mañana, que habrá tempestad porque el cielo está nublado y amenazante.h Ustedes saben discernir el aspecto del cielo, pero no las señales de los tiempos. 4Esta generación malvada y adúltera busca una señal milagrosa, pero no se le dará más señal que la de Jonás.» Entonces Jesús los dejó y se fue.

La levadura de los fariseos y de los saduceos

5Cruzaron el lago, pero a los discípulos se les había olvidado llevar pan.

6—Tengan cuidado —les advirtió Jesús—; eviten la levadura de los fariseos y de los saduceos.

7Ellos comentaban entre sí: «Lo dice porque no trajimos pan.» 8Al darse cuenta de esto, Jesús les recriminó:

—Hombres de poca fe, ¿por qué están hablando de que no tienen pan? 9¿Todavía no entienden? ¿No recuerdan los cinco panes para los cinco mil, y el número de canastas que recogieron? 10¿Ni los siete panes para los cuatro mil, y el número de cestas que recogieron? 11¿Cómo es que no entienden que no hablaba yo del pan sino de tener cuidado de la levadura de fariseos y saduceos?

12Entonces comprendieron que no les decía que se cuidaran de la levadura del pan sino de la enseñanza de los fariseos y de los saduceos.

La confesión de Pedro
16:13-16 — Mr 8:27-29; Lc 9:18-20

13Cuando llegó a la región de Cesarea de Filipo, Jesús preguntó a sus discípulos:

—¿Quién dice la gente que es el Hijo del hombre?

Le respondieron:

14—Unos dicen que es Juan el Bautista, otros que Elías, y otros que Jeremías o uno de los profetas.

15—Y ustedes, ¿quién dicen que soy yo?

16—Tú eres el *Cristo, el Hijo del Dios viviente —afirmó Simón Pedro.

17—*Dichoso tú, Simón, hijo de Jonás —le dijo Jesús—, porque eso no te lo reveló ningún mortal,i

---

d **15:9** Is 29:13 e **15:14** *guías ciegos.* Var. *ciegos guías de ciegos.* f **15:39** *Magadán.* Var. *Magdala.* g **16:2** Var. no incluye el resto del v. 2 y todo el v. 3. h **16:3** *amenazante.* Lit. *Rojizo.* i **16:17** *ningún mortal.* Lit. *carne y sangre.*

sino mi Padre que está en el cielo. 18Yo te digo que tú eres Pedro,j y sobre esta piedra edificaré mi iglesia, y las puertas del reino de los muertek no prevalecerán contra ella. 19Te daré las llaves del reino de los cielos; todo lo que ates en la tierra quedará atado en el cielo, y todo lo que desates en la tierra quedará desatado en el cielo.

20Luego les ordenó a sus discípulos que no dijeran a nadie que él era el Cristo.

Jesús predice su muerte
16:21-28 — Mr 8:31—9:1; Lc 9:22-27

21Desde entonces comenzó Jesús a advertir a sus discípulos que tenía que ir a Jerusalén y sufrir muchas cosas a manos de los *ancianos, de los jefes de los sacerdotes y de los *maestros de la ley, y que era necesario que lo mataran y que al tercer día resucitara. 22Pedro lo llevó aparte y comenzó a reprenderlo:

—iDe ninguna manera, Señor! iEsto no te sucederá jamás!

23Jesús se volvió y le dijo a Pedro:

—iAléjate de mí, Satanás! Quieres hacerme *tropezar; no piensas en las cosas de Dios sino en las de los hombres.

24Luego dijo Jesús a sus discípulos:

—Si alguien quiere ser mi discípulo, tiene que negarse a sí mismo, tomar su cruz y seguirme. 25Porque el que quiera salvar su *vida, la perderá; pero el que pierda su vida por mi causa, la encontrará. 26¿De qué sirve ganar el mundo entero si se pierde la vida? ¿O qué se puede dar a cambio de la vida? 27Porque el Hijo del hombre ha de venir en la gloria de su Padre con sus ángeles, y entonces recompensará a cada persona según lo que haya hecho. 28Les aseguro que algunos de los aquí presentes no sufrirán la muerte sin antes haber visto al Hijo del hombre llegar en su reino.

La transfiguración
17:1-8 — Lc 9:28-36
17:1-13 — Mr 9:2-13

17 Seis días después, Jesús tomó consigo a Pedro, a *Jacobo y a Juan, el hermano de Jacobo, y los llevó aparte, a una montaña alta. 2Allí se transfiguró en presencia de ellos; su rostro resplandeció como el sol, y su ropa se volvió blanca como la luz. 3En esto, se les aparecieron Moisés y Elías conversando con Jesús. 4Pedro le dijo a Jesús:

—Señor, iqué bien que estemos aquí! Si quieres, levantaré tres albergues: uno para ti, otro para Moisés y otro para Elías.

5Mientras estaba aún hablando, apareció una nube luminosa que los envolvió, de la cual salió una voz que dijo: «Éste es mi Hijo amado; estoy muy complacido con él. iEscúchenlo!»

6Al oír esto, los discípulos se postraron sobre sus rostros, aterrorizados. 7Pero Jesús se acercó a ellos y los tocó.

—Levántense —les dijo—. No tengan miedo.

8Cuando alzaron la vista, no vieron a nadie más que a Jesús.

9Mientras bajaban de la montaña, Jesús les encargó:

—No le cuenten a nadie lo que han visto hasta que el Hijo del hombre *resucite.

10Entonces los discípulos le preguntaron a Jesús:

—¿Por qué dicen los *maestros de la ley que Elías tiene que venir primero?

11—Sin duda Elías viene, y restaurará todas las cosas —respondió Jesús—. 12Pero les digo que Elías ya vino, y no lo reconocieron sino que hicieron con él todo lo que quisieron. De la misma manera va a sufrir el Hijo del hombre a manos de ellos.

13Entonces entendieron los discípulos que les estaba hablando de Juan el Bautista.

Jesús sana a un muchacho endemoniado
17:14-19 — Mr 9:14-28; Lc 9:37-42

14Cuando llegaron a la multitud, un hombre se acercó a Jesús y se arrodilló delante de él.

15—Señor, ten compasión de mi hijo. Le dan ataques y sufre terriblemente. Muchas veces cae en el fuego o en el agua. 16Se lo traje a tus discípulos, pero no pudieron sanarlo.

17—iAh, generación incrédula y perversa! —respondió Jesús—. ¿Hasta cuándo tendré que estar con ustedes? ¿Hasta cuándo tendré que soportarlos? Tráiganme acá al muchacho.

18Jesús reprendió al demonio, el cual salió del muchacho, y éste quedó sano desde aquel momento.

19Después los discípulos se acercaron a Jesús y, en privado, le preguntaron:

—¿Por qué nosotros no pudimos expulsarlo?

20—Porque ustedes tienen tan poca fe —les respondió—. Les aseguro que si tienen fe tan pequeña como un grano de mostaza, podrán decirle a esta montaña: "Trasládate de aquí para allá", y se trasladará. Para ustedes nada será imposible.l

22Estando reunidos en Galilea, Jesús les dijo: «El Hijo del hombre va a ser entregado en manos de los hombres. 23Lo matarán, pero al tercer día resucitará.» Y los discípulos se entristecieron mucho.

El impuesto del templo

24Cuando Jesús y sus discípulos llegaron a Capernaúm, los que cobraban el impuesto del *templom se acercaron a Pedro y le preguntaron:

—¿Su maestro no paga el impuesto del templo?

25—Sí, lo paga —respondió Pedro.

Al entrar Pedro en la casa, se adelantó Jesús a preguntarle:

—¿Tú qué opinas, Simón? Los reyes de la tierra, ¿a quiénes cobran tributos e impuestos: a los suyos o a los demás?

26—A los demás —contestó Pedro.

—Entonces los suyos están exentos —le dijo Jesús—. 27Pero, para no *escandalizar a esta gente, vete al lago y echa el anzuelo. Saca el primer pez que pique; ábrele la boca y encontrarás una moneda.n Tómala y dásela a ellos por mi impuesto y por el tuyo.

El más importante en el reino de los cielos
18:1-5 — Mr 9:33-37; Lc 9:46-48

18 En ese momento los discípulos se acercaron a Jesús y le preguntaron:

—¿Quién es el más importante en el reino de los cielos?

2Él llamó a un niño y lo puso en medio de ellos. 3Entonces dijo:

—Les aseguro que a menos que ustedes cambien y se vuelvan como niños, no entrarán en el rei-

---

j **16:18** *Pedro* significa *piedra.* k **16:18** *del reino de la muerte.* Lit. *del *Hades.* l **17:20** *imposible.* Var. *imposible. v. 21 Pero esta clase no sale sino con oración y ayuno.* m **17:24** *el impuesto del templo.* Lit. *las dos *dracmas.* n **17:27** *una moneda.* Lit. *un estatero* (moneda que equivale a cuatro *dracmas).

no de los cielos. 4Por tanto, el que se humilla como este niño será el más grande en el reino de los cielos.

5»Y el que recibe en mi nombre a un niño como éste, me recibe a mí. 6Pero si alguien hace *pecar a uno de estos pequeños que creen en mí, más le valdría que le colgaran al cuello una gran piedra de molino y lo hundieran en lo profundo del mar.

7»¡Ay del mundo por las cosas que hacen pecar a la gente! Inevitable es que sucedan, pero ¡ay del que hace pecar a los demás! 8Si tu mano o tu pie te hace pecar, córtatelo y arrójalo. Más te vale entrar en la vida manco o cojo que ser arrojado al fuego eterno con tus dos manos y tus dos pies. 9Y si tu ojo te hace pecar, sácatelo y arrójalo. Más te vale entrar tuerto en la vida que con dos ojos ser arrojado al fuego del infierno.ñ

Parábola de la oveja perdida
18:12-14 — Lc 15:4-7

10»Miren que no menosprecien a uno de estos pequeños. Porque les digo que en el cielo los ángeles de ellos contemplan siempre el rostro de mi Padre celestial.o

12»¿Qué les parece? Si un hombre tiene cien ovejas y se le extravía una de ellas, ¿no dejará las noventa y nueve en las colinas para ir en busca de la extraviada? 13Y si llega a encontrarla, les aseguro que se pondrá más feliz por esa sola oveja que por las noventa y nueve que no se extraviaron. 14Así también, el Padre de ustedes que está en el cielo no quiere que se pierda ninguno de estos pequeños.

El hermano que peca contra ti

15»Si tu hermano peca contra ti,p ve a solas con él y hazle ver su falta. Si te hace caso, has ganado a tu hermano. 16Pero si no, lleva contigo a uno o dos más, para que "todo asunto se resuelva mediante el testimonio de dos o tres testigos".q 17Si se niega a hacerles caso a ellos, díselo a la iglesia; y si incluso a la iglesia no le hace caso, trátalo como si fuera un incrédulo o un renegado.r

18»Les aseguro que todo lo que ustedes aten en la tierra quedará atado en el cielo, y todo lo que desaten en la tierra quedará desatado en el cielo.

19»Además les digo que si dos de ustedes en la tierra se ponen de acuerdo sobre cualquier cosa que pidan, les será concedida por mi Padre que está en el cielo. 20Porque donde dos o tres se reúnen en mi nombre, allí estoy yo en medio de ellos.

Parábola del siervo despiadado

21Pedro se acercó a Jesús y le preguntó:
—Señor, ¿cuántas veces tengo que perdonar a mi hermano que peca contra mí? ¿Hasta siete veces?

22—No te digo que hasta siete veces, sino hasta setenta y siete vecess —le contestó Jesús—.

23»Por eso el reino de los cielos se parece a un rey que quiso ajustar cuentas con sus *siervos. 24Al comenzar a hacerlo, se le presentó uno que le debía miles y miles de monedas de oro.t 25Como él no tenía con qué pagar, el señor mandó que lo vendieran a él, a su esposa y a sus hijos, y todo lo que tenía, para así saldar la deuda. 26El siervo se postró delante de él. "Tenga paciencia conmigo —le rogó—, y se lo pagaré todo." 27El señor se compadeció de su siervo, le perdonó la deuda y lo dejó en libertad.

28»Al salir, aquel siervo se encontró con uno de sus compañeros que le debía cien monedas de plata.u Lo agarró por el cuello y comenzó a estrangularlo. "¡Págame lo que me debes!", le exigió. 29Su compañero se postró delante de él. "Ten paciencia conmigo —le rogó—, y te lo pagaré." 30Pero él se negó. Más bien fue y lo hizo meter en la cárcel hasta que pagara la deuda. 31Cuando los demás siervos vieron lo ocurrido, se entristecieron mucho y fueron a contarle a su señor todo lo que había sucedido. 32Entonces el señor mandó llamar al siervo. "¡Siervo malvado! —le increpó—. Te perdoné toda aquella deuda porque me lo suplicaste. 33¿No debías tú también haberte compadecido de tu compañero, así como yo me compadecí de ti?" 34Y enojado, su señor lo entregó a los carceleros para que lo torturaran hasta que pagara todo lo que debía.

35»Así también mi Padre celestial los tratará a ustedes, a menos que cada uno perdone de corazón a su hermano.

El divorcio
19:1-9 — Mr 10:1-12

19 Cuando Jesús acabó de decir estas cosas, salió de Galilea y se fue a la región de Judea, al otro lado del Jordán. 2Lo siguieron grandes multitudes, y sanó allí a los enfermos.

3Algunos fariseos se le acercaron y, para ponerlo a *prueba, le preguntaron:
—¿Está permitido que un hombre se divorcie de su esposa por cualquier motivo?

4—¿No han leído —replicó Jesús— que en el principio el Creador "los hizo hombre y mujer",v 5y dijo: "Por eso dejará el hombre a su padre y a su madre, y se unirá a su esposa, y los dos llegarán a ser un solo cuerpo"?w 6Así que ya no son dos, sino uno solo. Por tanto, lo que Dios ha unido, que no lo separe el hombre.

7Le replicaron:
—¿Por qué, entonces, mandó Moisés que un hombre le diera a su esposa un certificado de divorcio y la despidiera?

8—Moisés les permitió divorciarse de su esposa por los obstinados que sonx —respondió Jesús—. Pero no fue así desde el principio. 9Les digo que, excepto en caso de infidelidad conyugal, el que se divorcia de su esposa, y se casa con otra, comete adulterio.

10—Si tal es la situación entre esposo y esposa —comentaron los discípulos—, es mejor no casarse.

11—No todos pueden comprender este asunto —respondió Jesús—, sino sólo aquellos a quienes se les ha concedido entenderlo. 12Pues algunos son *eunucos porque nacieron así; a otros los hicieron así los hombres; y otros se han hecho así por causa del reino de los cielos. El que pueda aceptar esto, que lo acepte.

Jesús y los niños
19:13-15 — Mr 10:13-16; Lc 18:15-17

13Llevaron unos niños a Jesús para que les impusiera las manos y orara por ellos, pero los discípulos reprendían a quienes los llevaban.

14Jesús dijo: «Dejen que los niños vengan a mí, y no se lo impidan, porque el reino de los cielos es de

---

ñ **18:9** al fuego del infierno. Lit. a la *Gehenna del fuego. o **18:10** celestial. Var. celestial. v. 11 El Hijo del hombre vino a salvar lo que se había perdido. p **18:15** peca contra ti. Var. peca. q**18:16** Dt 19:15 r **18:17** incrédulo o un renegado. Lit. un *gentil o un *recaudador de impuestos. s **18:22** setenta y siete veces. Alt. setenta veces siete. t **18:24** miles y miles de monedas de oro. Lit. una miríada de *talentos. u **18:28** monedas de plata. Lit. *denarios. v **19:4** Gn 1:27 w **19:5** Gn 2:24 x **19:8** por lo obstinados que son. Lit. por su dureza de corazón.

quienes son como ellos.» ¹⁵Después de poner las manos sobre ellos, se fue de allí.

El joven rico
19:16-29 — Mr 10:17-30; Lc 18:18-30

¹⁶Sucedió que un hombre se acercó a Jesús y le preguntó:

—Maestro, ¿qué de bueno tengo que hacer para obtener la vida eterna?

¹⁷—¿Por qué me preguntas sobre lo que es bueno? —respondió Jesús—. Solamente hay uno que es bueno. Si quieres entrar en la vida, obedece los mandamientos.

¹⁸—¿Cuáles? —preguntó el hombre.

Contestó Jesús:

—"No mates, no cometas adulterio, no robes, no presentes falso testimonio, ¹⁹honra a tu padre y a tu madre",ʸ y "ama a tu prójimo como a ti mismo"ᶻ.

²⁰—Todos ésos los he cumplido —dijo el joven—. ¿Qué más me falta?

²¹—Si quieres ser *perfecto, anda, vende lo que tienes y dáselo a los pobres, y tendrás tesoro en el cielo. Luego ven y sígueme.

²²Cuando el joven oyó esto, se fue triste porque tenía muchas riquezas.

²³—Les aseguro —comentó Jesús a sus discípulos— que es difícil para un rico entrar en el reino de los cielos. ²⁴De hecho, le resulta más fácil a un camello pasar por el ojo de una aguja, que a un rico entrar en el reino de Dios.

²⁵Al oír esto, los discípulos quedaron desconcertados y decían:

—En ese caso, ¿quién podrá salvarse?

²⁶—Para los hombres es imposible —aclaró Jesús, mirándolos fijamente—, mas para Dios todo es posible.

²⁷—¡Mira, nosotros lo hemos dejado todo por seguirte! —le reclamó Pedro—. ¿Y qué ganamos con eso?

²⁸—Les aseguro —respondió Jesús— que en la renovación de todas las cosas, cuando el Hijo del hombre se siente en su trono glorioso, ustedes que me han seguido se sentarán también en doce tronos para gobernar a las doce tribus de Israel. ²⁹Y todo el que por mi causa haya dejado casas, hermanos, hermanas, padre, madre,ᵃ hijos o terrenos, recibirá cien veces más y heredará la vida eterna. ³⁰Pero muchos de los primeros serán últimos, y muchos de los últimos serán primeros.

Parábola de los viñadores

20 »Así mismo el reino de los cielos se parece a un propietario que salió de madrugada a contratar obreros para su viñedo. ²Acordó darles la paga de un día de trabajoᵇ y los envió a su viñedo. ³Cerca de las nueve de la mañana,ᶜ salió y vio a otros que estaban desocupados en la plaza. ⁴Les dijo: "Vayan también ustedes a trabajar en mi viñedo, y les pagaré lo que sea justo. ⁵Así que fueron. Salió de nuevo a eso del mediodía y a la media tarde, e hizo lo mismo. ⁶Alrededor de las cinco de la tarde, salió y encontró a otros más que estaban sin trabajo. Les preguntó: "¿Por qué han estado aquí desocupados todo el día?" ⁷"Porque nadie nos ha contratado", contestaron. Él les dijo: "Vayan también ustedes a trabajar en mi viñedo."

⁸»Al atardecer, el dueño del viñedo le ordenó a su capataz: "Llama a los obreros y págales su jornal, comenzando por los últimos contratados hasta llegar a los primeros." ⁹Se presentaron los obreros que habían sido contratados cerca de las cinco de la tarde, y cada uno recibió la paga de un día. ¹⁰Por eso cuando llegaron los que fueron contratados primero, esperaban que recibirían más. Pero cada uno de ellos recibió también la paga de un día. ¹¹Al recibirla, comenzaron a murmurar contra el propietario. ¹²Estos que fueron los últimos en ser contratados trabajaron una sola hora —dijeron—, y usted los ha tratado como a nosotros que hemos soportado el peso del trabajo y el calor del día." ¹³Pero él les contestó a uno de ellos: "Amigo, no estoy cometiendo ninguna injusticia contigo. ¿Acaso no aceptaste trabajar por esa paga? ¹⁴Tómala y vete. Quiero darle al último obrero contratado lo mismo que te di a ti. ¹⁵¿Es que no tengo derecho a hacer lo que quiera con mi dinero? ¿O te da envidia de que yo sea generoso?"ᵈ

¹⁶»Así que los últimos serán primeros, y los primeros, últimos.

Jesús predice de nuevo su muerte
20:17-19 — Mr 10:32-34; Lc 18:31-33

¹⁷Mientras subía Jesús rumbo a Jerusalén, tomó aparte a los doce discípulos y les dijo: ¹⁸«Ahora vamos rumbo a Jerusalén, y el Hijo del hombre será entregado a los jefes de los sacerdotes y a los *maestros de la ley. Ellos lo condenarán a muerte ¹⁹y lo entregarán a los *gentiles para que se burlen de él, lo azoten y lo crucifiquen. Pero al tercer día resucitará.»

La petición de una madre
20:20-28 — Mr 10:35-45

²⁰Entonces la madre de *Jacobo y de Juan,ᵉ junto con ellos, se acercó a Jesús y, arrodillándose, le pidió un favor.

²¹—¿Qué quieres? —le preguntó Jesús.

—Ordena que en tu reino uno de estos dos hijos míos se siente a tu *derecha y el otro a tu izquierda.

²²—No saben lo que están pidiendo —les replicó Jesús—. ¿Pueden acaso beber el trago amargo de la copa que yo voy a beber?

—Sí, podemos.

²³—Ciertamente beberán de mi copa —les dijo Jesús—, pero el sentarse a mi derecha o a mi izquierda no me corresponde concederlo. Eso ya lo ha decididoᶠ mi Padre.

²⁴Cuando lo oyeron los otros diez, se indignaron contra los dos hermanos.

²⁵Jesús los llamó y les dijo:

—Como ustedes saben, los gobernantes de las *naciones oprimen a los súbditos, y los altos oficiales abusan de su autoridad. ²⁶Pero entre ustedes no debe ser así. Al contrario, el que quiera hacerse grande entre ustedes deberá ser su servidor, ²⁷y el que quiera ser el primero deberá ser *esclavo de los demás; ²⁸así como el Hijo del hombre no vino para que le sirvan, sino para servir y para dar su *vida en rescate por muchos.

ʸ **19:19** Éx 20:12-16; Dt 5:16-20　ᶻ **19:19** Lv 19:18　ᵃ **19:29** *madre.* Var. *madre, esposa.*　ᵇ **20:2** *la paga de un día de trabajo.* Lit. *un *denario por el día;* también en vv. 9,10,13.　ᶜ **20:3** *las nueve de la mañana.* Lit. *la hora tercera;* en v. 5 *la hora sexta y novena;* en vv. 6 y 9 *la hora undécima.*　ᵈ **20:15** *¿O . . . generoso?* Lit. *¿O es tu ojo malo porque yo soy bueno?*　ᵉ **20:20** *de Jacobo y de Juan.* Lit. *de los hijos de Zebedeo.*　ᶠ **20:23** *concederlo. Eso ya lo ha decidido.* Lit. *concederlo, sino para quienes lo ha preparado.*

Dos ciegos reciben la vista
20:29-34 — Mr 10:46-52; Lc 18:35-43

²⁹Una gran multitud seguía a Jesús cuando él salía de Jericó con sus discípulos. ³⁰Dos ciegos que estaban sentados junto al camino, al oír que pasaba Jesús, gritaron:

—¡Señor, Hijo de David, ten compasión de nosotros!

³¹La multitud los reprendía para que se callaran, pero ellos gritaban con más fuerza:

—¡Señor, Hijo de David, ten compasión de nosotros!

³²Jesús se detuvo y los llamó.

—¿Qué quieren que haga por ustedes?

³³—Señor, queremos recibir la vista.

³⁴Jesús se compadeció de ellos y les tocó los ojos. Al instante recobraron la vista y lo siguieron.

La entrada triunfal
21:1-9 — Mr 11:1-10; Lc 19:29-38
21:4-9 — Jn 12:12-15

21 Cuando se acercaban a Jerusalén y llegaron a Betfagué, al monte de los Olivos, Jesús envió a dos discípulos ²con este encargo: «Vayan a la aldea que tienen enfrente, y ahí mismo encontrarán una burra atada, y un burrito con ella. Desátenlos y tráiganmelos. ³Si alguien les dice algo, díganle que el Señor los necesita, pero que ya los devolverá.»

⁴Esto sucedió para que se cumpliera lo dicho por el profeta:

⁵«Digan a la hija de Sión:
　　"Mira, tu rey viene hacia ti,
　humilde y montado en un burro,
　　en un burrito, cría de una bestia de carga."»g

⁶Los discípulos fueron e hicieron como les había mandado Jesús. ⁷Llevaron la burra y el burrito, y pusieron encima sus mantos, sobre los cuales se sentó Jesús. ⁸Había mucha gente que tendía sus mantos sobre el camino; otros cortaban ramas de los árboles y las esparcían en el camino. ⁹Tanto la gente que iba delante de él como la que iba detrás, gritaba:

—¡Hosannah al Hijo de David!

—¡Bendito el que viene en el nombre del Señor!i

—¡Hosanna en las alturas!

¹⁰Cuando Jesús entró en Jerusalén, toda la ciudad se conmovió.

—¿Quién es éste? —preguntaban.

¹¹—Éste es el profeta Jesús, de Nazaret de Galilea —contestaba la gente.

Jesús en el templo
21:12-16 — Mr 11:15-18; Lc 19:45-47

¹²Jesús entró en el *temploj y echó de allí a todos los que compraban y vendían. Volcó las mesas de los que cambiaban dinero y los puestos de los que vendían palomas. ¹³«Escrito está —les dijo—: "Mi casa será llamada casa de oración";k pero ustedes la están convirtiendo en "cueva de ladrones".l»

¹⁴Se le acercaron en el templo ciegos y cojos, y los sanó. ¹⁵Pero cuando los jefes de los sacerdotes y los *maestros de la ley vieron que hacía cosas mara-

villosas, y que los niños gritaban en el templo: «¡Hosanna al Hijo de David!», se indignaron.

¹⁶—¿Oyes lo que ésos están diciendo? —protestaron.

—Claro que sí —respondió Jesús—; ¿no han leído nunca:

»"En los labios de los pequeños
　y de los niños de pecho
　has puesto la perfecta alabanza"?m

¹⁷Entonces los dejó y, saliendo de la ciudad, se fue a pasar la noche en Betania.

Se seca la higuera
21:18-22 — Mr 11:12-14,20-24

¹⁸Muy de mañana, cuando volvía a la ciudad, tuvo hambre. ¹⁹Al ver una higuera junto al camino, se acercó a ella, pero no encontró nada más que hojas.

—¡Nunca más vuelvas a dar fruto! —le dijo.

Y al instante se secó la higuera.

²⁰Los discípulos se asombraron al ver esto.

—¿Cómo es que se secó la higuera tan pronto? —preguntaron ellos.

²¹—Les aseguro que si tienen fe y no dudan —les respondió Jesús—, no sólo harán lo que he hecho con la higuera, sino que podrán decirle a este monte: "¡Quítate de ahí y tírate al mar!", y así se hará. ²²Si ustedes creen, recibirán todo lo que pidan en oración.

La autoridad de Jesús puesta en duda
21:23-27 — Mr 11:27-33; Lc 20:1-8

²³Jesús entró en el *templo y, mientras enseñaba, se le acercaron los jefes de los sacerdotes y los *ancianos del pueblo.

—¿Con qué autoridad haces esto? —lo interrogaron—. ¿Quién te dio esa autoridad?

²⁴—Yo también voy a hacerles una pregunta. Si me la contestan, les diré con qué autoridad hago esto. ²⁵El bautismo de Juan, ¿de dónde procedía? ¿Del cielo o de la tierra?n

Ellos se pusieron a discutir entre sí: «Si respondemos: "Del cielo", nos dirá: "Entonces, ¿por qué no le creyeron?" ²⁶Pero si decimos: "De la tierra"... tememos al pueblo, porque todos consideran que Juan era un profeta.» Así que le respondieron a Jesús:

²⁷—No lo sabemos.

—Pues yo tampoco les voy a decir con qué autoridad hago esto.

Parábola de los dos hijos

²⁸»¿Qué les parece? —continuó Jesús—. Había un hombre que tenía dos hijos. Se dirigió al primero y le pidió: "Hijo, ve a trabajar hoy en el viñedo." ²⁹"No quiero", contestó, pero después se *arrepintió y fue. ³⁰Luego el padre se dirigió al otro hijo y le pidió lo mismo. Éste contestó: "Sí, señor"; pero no fue. ³¹¿Cuál de los dos hizo lo que su padre quería?

—El primero —contestaron ellos.

Jesús les dijo:

—Les aseguro que los *recaudadores de impuestos y las prostitutas van delante de ustedes hacia el reino de Dios. ³²Porque Juan ha venido a ustedes a señalarles el camino de la justicia, y no le creyeron, pero los recaudadores de impuestos y las prostitutas sí le creyeron. E incluso después de ver esto, ustedes no se arrepintieron para creerle.

---

g **21:5** Zac 9:9　h **21:9** Expresión hebrea que significa «¡Salva!», y que llegó a ser una exclamación de alabanza; también en v. 15.　i **21:9** Sal 118:26　j **21:12** Es decir, en el área general del templo; también en vv. 14,15,23.　k **21:13** Is 56:7　l **21:13** Jer 7:11　m **21:16** Sal 8:2　n **21:25** *la tierra.* Lit. *los hombres;* también en v. 26.

Parábola de los labradores malvados
21:33-46 — Mr 12:1-12; Lc 20:9-19

33»Escuchen otra parábola: Había un propietario que plantó un viñedo. Lo cercó, cavó un lagar y construyó una torre de vigilancia. Luego arrendó el viñedo a unos labradores y se fue de viaje. 34Cuando se acercó el tiempo de la cosecha, mandó sus *siervos a los labradores para recibir de éstos lo que le correspondía. 35Los labradores agarraron a esos siervos; golpearon a uno, mataron a otro y apedrearon a un tercero. 36Después les mandó otros siervos, en mayor número que la primera vez, y también los maltrataron.

37»Por último, les mandó a su propio hijo, pensando: "¡A mi hijo sí lo respetarán!" 38Pero cuando los labradores vieron al hijo, se dijeron unos a otros: "Éste es el heredero. Matémoslo, para quedarnos con su herencia." 39Así que le echaron mano, lo arrojaron fuera del viñedo y lo mataron.

40»Ahora bien, cuando vuelva el dueño, ¿qué hará con esos labradores?

41—Hará que esos malvados tengan un fin miserable —respondieron—, y arrendará el viñedo a otros labradores que le den lo que le corresponde cuando llegue el tiempo de la cosecha.

42Les dijo Jesús:

—¿No han leído nunca en las Escrituras:

»"La piedra que desecharon los constructores
    ha llegado a ser la piedra angular;
esto es obra del Señor,
    y nos deja maravillados"?ñ

43»Por eso les digo que el reino de Dios se les quitará a ustedes y se le entregará a un pueblo que produzca los frutos del reino. 44El que caiga sobre esta piedra quedará despedazado, y si ella cae sobre alguien, lo hará polvo.o

45Cuando los jefes de los sacerdotes y los fariseos oyeron las parábolas de Jesús, se dieron cuenta de que hablaba de ellos. 46Buscaban la manera de arrestarlo, pero temían a la gente porque ésta lo consideraba un profeta.

Parábola del banquete de bodas

22 Jesús volvió a hablarles en parábolas, y les dijo: 2«El reino de los cielos es como un rey que preparó un banquete de bodas para su hijo. 3Mandó a sus *siervos que llamaran a los invitados, pero éstos se negaron a asistir al banquete. 4Luego mandó a otros siervos y les ordenó: "Digan a los invitados que ya he preparado mi comida: Ya han matado mis bueyes y mis reses cebadas, y todo está listo. Vengan al banquete de bodas." 5Pero ellos no hicieron caso y se fueron: uno a su campo, otro a su negocio. 6Los demás agarraron a los siervos, los maltrataron y los mataron. 7El rey se enfureció. Mandó su ejército a destruir a los asesinos y a incendiar su ciudad. 8Luego dijo a sus siervos: "El banquete de bodas está preparado, pero los que invité no merecían venir. 9Vayan al cruce de los caminos e inviten al banquete a todos los que encuentren." 10Así que los siervos salieron a los caminos y reunieron a todos los que pudieron encontrar, buenos y malos, y se llenó de invitados el salón de bodas.

11»Cuando el rey entró a ver a los invitados, notó que allí había un hombre que no estaba vestido con el traje de boda. 12"Amigo, ¿cómo entraste aquí sin el traje de boda?", le dijo. El hombre se quedó callado. 13Entonces el rey dijo a los sirvientes: "Átenlo de pies y manos, y échenlo afuera, a la oscuridad, donde habrá llanto y rechinar de dientes." 14Porque muchos son los invitados, pero pocos los escogidos.»

El pago de impuestos al césar
22:15-22 — Mr 12:13-17; Lc 20:20-26

15Entonces salieron los fariseos y tramaron cómo tenderle a Jesús una trampa con sus mismas palabras. 16Enviaron algunos de sus discípulos junto con los herodianos, los cuales le dijeron:

—Maestro, sabemos que eres un hombre íntegro y que enseñas el camino de Dios de acuerdo con la verdad. No te dejas influir por nadie porque no te fijas en las apariencias. 17Danos tu opinión: ¿Está permitido pagar impuestos al *césar o no?

18Conociendo sus malas intenciones, Jesús replicó:

—¡Hipócritas! ¿Por qué me tienden *trampas? 19Muéstrenme la moneda para el impuesto.

Y se la enseñaron.p

20—¿De quién son esta imagen y esta inscripción? —les preguntó.

21—Del césar —respondieron.

—Entonces denle al césar lo que es del césar y a Dios lo que es de Dios.

22Al oír esto, se quedaron asombrados. Así que lo dejaron y se fueron.

El matrimonio en la resurrección
22:23-33 — Mr 12:18-27; Lc 20:27-40

23Ese mismo día los saduceos, que decían que no hay resurrección, se le acercaron y le plantearon un problema:

24—Maestro, Moisés nos enseñó que si un hombre sin tener hijos, el hermano de ése se debe casar con la viuda para que su hermano tenga descendencia. 25Pues bien, había entre nosotros siete hermanos. El primero se casó y murió y, como no tuvo hijos, dejó la esposa a su hermano. 26Lo mismo les pasó al segundo y al tercer hermano, y así hasta llegar al séptimo. 27Por último, murió la mujer. 28Ahora bien, en la resurrección, ¿de cuál de los siete será esposa esta mujer, ya que todos estuvieron casados con ella?

29Jesús les contestó:

—Ustedes andan equivocados porque desconocen las Escrituras y el poder de Dios. 30En la resurrección, las personas no se casarán ni serán dadas en casamiento, sino que serán como los ángeles que están en el cielo. 31Pero en cuanto a la resurrección de los muertos, ¿no han leído lo que Dios les dijo a ustedes: 32"Yo soy el Dios de Abraham, de Isaac y de Jacob"?q Él no es Dios de muertos, sino de vivos.

33Al oír esto, la gente quedó admirada de su enseñanza.

El mandamiento más importante
22:34-40 — Mr 12:28-31

34Los fariseos se reunieron al oír que Jesús había hecho callar a los saduceos. 35Uno de ellos, *experto en la ley, le tendió una *trampa con esta pregunta:

36—Maestro, ¿cuál es el mandamiento más importante de la ley?

37—"Ama al Señor tu Dios con todo tu corazón, con todo tu ser y con toda tu mente"r —le respondió

ñ **21:42** Sal 118:22,23   o **21:44** Var. no incluye v. 44.   p **22:19** *se la enseñaron*. Lit. *le trajeron un *denario*.   q **22:32** Éx 3:6
r **22:37** Dt 6:5

Jesús—. ³⁸Éste es el primero y el más importante de los mandamientos. ³⁹El segundo se parece a éste: "Ama a tu prójimo como a ti mismo."ˢ ⁴⁰De estos dos mandamientos dependen toda la ley y los profetas.

¿De quién es hijo el Cristo?
22:41-46 — Mr 12:35-37; Lc 20:41-44

⁴¹Mientras estaban reunidos los fariseos, Jesús les preguntó:

⁴²—¿Qué piensan ustedes acerca del *Cristo? ¿De quién es hijo?

—De David —le respondieron ellos.

⁴³—Entonces, ¿cómo es que David, hablando por el Espíritu, lo llama "Señor"? Él afirma:

⁴⁴»"Dijo el Señor a mi Señor:
  'Siéntate a mi *derecha,
  hasta que ponga a tus enemigos
    debajo de tus pies.' "ᵗ

⁴⁵Si David lo llama "Señor", ¿cómo puede entonces ser su hijo?

⁴⁶Nadie pudo responderle ni una sola palabra, y desde ese día ninguno se atrevía a hacerle más preguntas.

Jesús denuncia a los fariseos y a los maestros de la ley
23:1-7 — Mr 12:38-39; Lc 20:45-46
23:37-39 — Lc 13:34-35

23 Después de esto, Jesús dijo a la gente y a sus discípulos: ²«Los *maestros de la ley y los fariseos tienen la responsabilidad de interpretar a Moisés.ᵘ ³Así que ustedes deben obedecerlos y hacer todo lo que les digan. Pero no hagan lo que hacen ellos, porque no practican lo que predican. ⁴Atan cargas pesadas y las ponen sobre la espalda de los demás, pero ellos mismos no están dispuestos a mover ni un dedo para levantarlas.

⁵»Todo lo hacen para que la gente los vea: Usan filacterias grandes y adornan sus ropas con borlas vistosas;ᵛ ⁶se mueren por el lugar de honor en los banquetes y los primeros asientos en las sinagogas, ⁷y por que la gente los salude en las plazas y los llame "Rabí".

⁸»Pero no permitan que a ustedes se les llame "Rabí", porque tienen un solo Maestro y todos ustedes son hermanos. ⁹Y no llamen "padre" a nadie en la tierra, porque ustedes tienen un solo Padre, y él está en el cielo. ¹⁰Ni permitan que los llamen "maestro", porque tienen un solo Maestro, el *Cristo. ¹¹El más importante entre ustedes será siervo de los demás. ¹²Porque el que a sí mismo se enaltece será humillado, y el que se humilla será enaltecido.

¹³»¡Ay de ustedes, maestros de la ley y fariseos, *hipócritas! Les cierran a los demás el reino de los cielos, y ni entran ustedes ni dejan entrar a los que intentan hacerlo.ʷ

¹⁵»¡Ay de ustedes, maestros de la ley y fariseos, hipócritas! Recorren tierra y mar para ganar un solo adepto, y cuando lo han logrado lo hacen dos veces más merecedor del infiernoˣ que ustedes.

¹⁶»¡Ay de ustedes, guías ciegos!, que dicen: "Si alguien jura por el templo, no significa nada; pero si jura por el oro del templo, queda obligado por su juramento." ¹⁷¡Ciegos insensatos! ¿Qué es más importante: el oro, o el templo que hace sagrado al oro? ¹⁸También dicen ustedes: "Si alguien jura por el altar, no significa nada; pero si jura por la ofrenda que está sobre él, queda obligado por su juramento." ¹⁹¡Ciegos! ¿Qué es más importante: la ofrenda, o el altar que hace sagrada la ofrenda? ²⁰Por tanto, el que jura por el altar, jura no sólo por el altar sino por todo lo que está sobre él. ²¹El que jura por el templo, jura no sólo por el templo sino por quien habita en él. ²²Y el que jura por el cielo, jura por el trono de Dios y por aquel que lo ocupa.

²³»¡Ay de ustedes, maestros de la ley y fariseos, hipócritas! Dan la décima parte de sus especias: la menta, el anís y el comino. Pero han descuidado los asuntos más importantes de la ley, tales como la justicia, la misericordia y la *fidelidad. Debían haber practicado esto sin descuidar aquello. ²⁴¡Guías ciegos! Cuelan el mosquito pero se tragan el camello.

²⁵»¡Ay de ustedes, maestros de la ley y fariseos, hipócritas! *Limpian el exterior del vaso y del plato, pero por dentro están llenos de robo y de desenfreno. ²⁶¡Fariseo ciego! Limpia primero por dentro el vaso y el plato, y así quedará limpio también por fuera.

²⁷»¡Ay de ustedes, maestros de la ley y fariseos, hipócritas!, que son como sepulcros blanqueados. Por fuera lucen hermosos pero por dentro están llenos de huesos de muertos y de podredumbre. ²⁸Así también ustedes, por fuera dan la impresión de ser justos pero por dentro están llenos de hipocresía y de maldad.

²⁹»¡Ay de ustedes, maestros de la ley y fariseos, hipócritas! Construyen sepulcros para los profetas y adornan los monumentos de los justos. ³⁰Y dicen: "Si hubiéramos vivido nosotros en los días de nuestros antepasados, no habríamos sido cómplices de ellos para derramar la sangre de los profetas." ³¹Pero así quedan implicados ustedes al declararse descendientes de los que asesinaron a los profetas. ³²¡Completen de una vez por todas lo que sus antepasados comenzaron!

³³»¡Serpientes! ¡Camada de víboras! ¿Cómo escaparán ustedes de la condenación del infierno?ʸ ³⁴Por eso yo les voy a enviar profetas, sabios y maestros. A algunos de ellos ustedes los matarán y crucificarán; a otros los azotarán en sus sinagogas y los perseguirán de pueblo en pueblo. ³⁵Así recaerá sobre ustedes la culpa de toda la sangre justa que ha sido derramada sobre la tierra, desde la sangre del justo Abel hasta la de Zacarías, hijo de Berequías, a quien ustedes asesinaron entre el *santuario y el altar de los sacrificios. ³⁶Les aseguro que todo esto vendrá sobre esta generación.

³⁷»¡Jerusalén, Jerusalén, que matas a los profetas y apedreas a los que se te envían! ¡Cuántas veces quise reunir a tus hijos, como reúne la gallina a sus pollitos debajo de sus alas, pero no quisiste! ³⁸Pues bien, la casa de ustedes va a quedar abandonada. ³⁹Y les advierto que ya no volverán a verme hasta que digan: "¡Bendito el que viene en el nombre del Señor!"ᶻ»

ˢ **22:39** Lv 19:18. ᵗ **22:44** Sal 110:1. ᵘ **23:2** *tienen . . . Moisés.* Lit. *se sientan en la cátedra de Moisés.* ᵛ **23:5** *Usan . . . vistosas.* Lit. *Ensanchan sus filacterias y engrandecen las borlas.* Las filacterias eran pequeñas cajas en las que llevaban textos de las Escrituras en la frente y en los brazos; las borlas simbolizaban obediencia a los mandamientos (véanse Nm 15:38-39; Dt 68; 11:18). ʷ **23:13** *hacerlo.* Var. *hacerlo. v. 14 ¡Ay de ustedes, maestros de la ley y fariseos, hipócritas! Ustedes devoran las casas de las viudas y por las apariencias hacen largas plegarias. Por esto se les castigará con más severidad.* ˣ **23:15** *merecedor del infierno.* Lit. *hijo de la *Gehenna.* ʸ **23:33** *del infierno.* Lit. *de la *Gehenna.* ᶻ **23:39** Sal 118:26

Señales del fin del mundo
24:1-51 — Mr 13:1-37; Lc 21:5-36

24 Jesús salió del *templo y, mientras caminaba, se le acercaron sus discípulos y le mostraron los edificios del templo.

²Pero él les dijo:

—¿Ven todo esto? Les aseguro que no quedará piedra sobre piedra, pues todo será derribado.

³Más tarde estaba Jesús sentado en el monte de los Olivos, cuando llegaron los discípulos y le preguntaron en privado:

—¿Cuándo sucederá eso, y cuál será la señal de tu venida y del fin del mundo?

⁴—Tengan cuidado de que nadie los engañe —les advirtió Jesús—. ⁵Vendrán muchos que, usando mi nombre, dirán: "Yo soy el *Cristo", y engañarán a muchos. ⁶Ustedes oirán de guerras y de rumores de guerras, pero procuren no alarmarse. Es necesario que eso suceda, pero no será todavía el fin. ⁷Se levantará nación contra nación, y reino contra reino. Habrá hambres y terremotos por todas partes. ⁸Todo esto será apenas el comienzo de los dolores.

⁹»Entonces los entregarán a ustedes para que los persigan y los maten, y los odiarán todas las *naciones por causa de mi nombre. ¹⁰En aquel tiempo muchos se apartarán de la fe; unos a otros se traicionarán y se odiarán; ¹¹y surgirá un gran número de falsos profetas que engañarán a muchos. ¹²Habrá tanta maldad que el amor de muchos se enfriará, ¹³pero el que se mantenga firme hasta el fin será salvo. ¹⁴Y este *evangelio del reino se predicará en todo el mundo como testimonio a todas las naciones, y entonces vendrá el fin.

¹⁵»Así que cuando vean en el lugar santo "el horrible sacrilegio",ᵃ el que habló el profeta Daniel (el que lee, que lo entienda), ¹⁶los que estén en Judea huyan a las montañas. ¹⁷El que esté en la azotea no baje a llevarse nada de su casa. ¹⁸El que esté en el campo no regrese para buscar su capa. ¹⁹¡Qué terrible será en aquellos días para las que estén embarazadas o amamantando! ²⁰Oren para que su huida no suceda en invierno ni en *sábado. ²¹Porque habrá una gran tribulación, como no la ha habido desde el principio del mundo hasta ahora, ni la habrá jamás. ²²Si no se acortaran esos días, nadie sobreviviría, pero por causa de los elegidos se acortarán. ²³Entonces, si alguien les dice a ustedes: "¡Miren, aquí está el Cristo!" o "¡Allí está!", no lo crean. ²⁴Porque surgirán falsos Cristos y falsos profetas que harán grandes señales y milagros para engañar, de ser posible, aun a los elegidos. ²⁵Fíjense que se lo he dicho a ustedes de antemano.

²⁶»Por eso, si les dicen: "¡Miren que está en el desierto!", no salgan; o: "¡Miren que está en la casa!", no lo crean. ²⁷Porque así como el relámpago que sale del oriente se ve hasta en el occidente, así será la venida del Hijo del hombre. ²⁸Donde esté el cadáver, allí se reunirán los buitres.

²⁹»Inmediatamente después de la tribulación de aquellos días,

»"se oscurecerá el sol
   y no brillará más la luna;
las estrellas caerán del cielo
   y los cuerpos celestes serán sacudidos".ᵇ

³⁰»La señal del Hijo del hombre aparecerá en el cielo, y se angustiarán todas las razas de la tierra. Ve-

rán al Hijo del hombre venir sobre las nubes del cielo con poder y gran gloria. ³¹Y al sonido de la gran trompeta mandará a sus ángeles, y reunirán de los cuatro vientos a los elegidos, de un extremo al otro del cielo.

³²»Aprendan de la higuera esta lección: Tan pronto como se ponen tiernas sus ramas y brotan sus hojas, ustedes saben que el verano está cerca. ³³Igualmente, cuando vean todas estas cosas, sepan que el tiempo está cerca, a las puertas. ³⁴Les aseguro que no pasará esta generación hasta que todas estas cosas sucedan. ³⁵El cielo y la tierra pasarán, pero mis palabras jamás pasarán.

Se desconocen el día y la hora
24:37-39 — Lc 17:26-27
24:45-51 — Lc 12:42-46

³⁶»Pero en cuanto al día y la hora, nadie lo sabe, ni siquiera los ángeles en el cielo, ni el Hijo,ᶜ sino sólo el Padre. ³⁷La venida del Hijo del hombre será como en tiempos de Noé. ³⁸Porque en los días antes del diluvio comían, bebían y se casaban y daban en casamiento, hasta el día en que Noé entró en el arca; ³⁹y no supieron nada de lo que sucedería hasta que llegó el diluvio y se los llevó a todos. Así será la venida del Hijo del hombre. ⁴⁰Estarán dos hombres en el campo: uno será llevado y el otro será dejado. ⁴¹Dos mujeres estarán moliendo: una será llevada y la otra será dejada.

⁴²»Por lo tanto, manténganse despiertos, porque no saben qué día vendrá su Señor. ⁴³Pero entiendan esto: Si un dueño de casa supiera a qué hora de la noche va a llegar el ladrón, se mantendría despierto para no dejarlo forzar la entrada. ⁴⁴Por eso también ustedes deben estar preparados, porque el Hijo del hombre vendrá cuando menos lo esperen.

⁴⁵»¿Quién es el *siervo fiel y prudente a quien su señor ha dejado encargado de los sirvientes para darles la comida a su debido tiempo? ⁴⁶*Dichoso el siervo cuando su señor, al regresar, lo encuentra cumpliendo con su deber. ⁴⁷Les aseguro que lo pondrá a cargo de todos sus bienes. ⁴⁸Pero ¿qué tal si ese siervo malo se pone a pensar: "Mi señor se está demorando", ⁴⁹y luego comienza a golpear a sus compañeros, y a comer y beber con los borrachos? ⁵⁰El día en que el siervo menos lo espere y a la hora menos pensada el señor volverá. ⁵¹Lo castigará severamente y le impondrá la condena que reciben los *hipócritas. Y habrá llanto y rechinar de dientes.

Parábola de las diez jóvenes

25 »El reino de los cielos será entonces como diez jóvenes solteras que tomaron sus lámparas y salieron a recibir al novio. ²Cinco de ellas eran insensatas y cinco prudentes. ³Las insensatas llevaron sus lámparas, pero no se abastecieron de aceite. ⁴En cambio, las prudentes llevaron vasijas de aceite junto con sus lámparas. ⁵Y como el novio tardaba en llegar, a todas les dio sueño y se durmieron.

⁶A medianoche se oyó un grito: "¡Ahí viene el novio! ¡Salgan a recibirlo!" ⁷Entonces todas las jóvenes se despertaron y se pusieron a preparar sus lámparas. ⁸Las insensatas dijeron a las prudentes: "Dennos un poco de su aceite porque nuestras lámparas se están apagando." ⁹"No —respondieron éstas—, porque así no va a alcanzar ni para nosotras ni para ustedes. Es mejor que vayan a los que venden aceite, y compren para ustedes mismas." ¹⁰Pero mientras iban a

---

a **24:15** *el horrible sacrilegio.* Lit. *la abominación de la desolación;* Dn 9:27; 11:31; 12:11.   b **24:29** Is 13:10; 34:4   c **24:36** Var. no incluye: *ni el Hijo.*

comprar el aceite llegó el novio, y las jóvenes que estaban preparadas entraron con él al banquete de bodas. Y se cerró la puerta. [11]Después llegaron también las otras. "¡Señor! ¡Señor! —suplicaban—. ¡Ábrenos la puerta!" [12]"¡No, no las conozco!", respondió él.

[13]»Por tanto —agregó Jesús—, manténganse despiertos porque no saben ni el día ni la hora.

Parábola de las monedas de oro

[14]»El reino de los cielos será también como un hombre que, al emprender un viaje, llamó a sus *siervos y les encargó sus bienes. [15]A uno le dio cinco mil monedas de oro,[d] a otro dos mil y a otro sólo mil, a cada uno según su capacidad. Luego se fue de viaje. [16]El que había recibido las cinco mil fue en seguida y negoció con ellas y ganó otras cinco mil. [17]Así mismo, el que recibió dos mil ganó otras dos mil. [18]Pero el que había recibido mil fue, cavó un hoyo en la tierra y escondió el dinero de su señor.

[19]»Después de mucho tiempo volvió el señor de aquellos siervos y arregló cuentas con ellos. [20]El que había recibido las cinco mil monedas llegó con las otras cinco mil. "Señor —dijo—, usted me encargó cinco mil monedas. Mire, he ganado otras cinco mil." [21]Su señor le respondió: "¡Hiciste bien, siervo bueno y fiel! En lo poco has sido fiel; te pondré a cargo de mucho más. ¡Ven a compartir la felicidad de tu señor!" [22]Llegó también el que recibió dos mil monedas. "Señor —informó—, usted me encargó dos mil monedas. Mire, he ganado otras dos mil." [23]Su señor le respondió: "¡Hiciste bien, siervo bueno y fiel! Has sido fiel en lo poco; te pondré a cargo de mucho más. ¡Ven a compartir la felicidad de tu señor!"

[24]»Después llegó el que había recibido sólo mil monedas. "Señor —explicó—, yo sabía que usted es un hombre duro, que cosecha donde no ha sembrado y recoge donde no ha esparcido. [25]Así que tuve miedo, y fui y escondí su dinero en la tierra. Mire, aquí tiene lo que es suyo." [26]Pero su señor le contestó: "¡Siervo malo y perezoso! ¿Así que sabías que cosecho donde no he sembrado y recojo donde no he esparcido? [27]Pues debías haber depositado mi dinero en el banco, para que a mi regreso lo hubiera recibido con intereses.

[28]» "Quítenle las mil monedas y dénselas al que tiene las diez mil. [29]Porque a todo el que tiene, se le dará más, y tendrá en abundancia. Al que no tiene se le quitará hasta lo que tiene. [30]Y a ese siervo inútil échenlo afuera, a la oscuridad, donde habrá llanto y rechinar de dientes."

Las ovejas y las cabras

[31]»Cuando el Hijo del hombre venga en su gloria, con todos sus ángeles, se sentará en su trono glorioso. [32]Todas las naciones se reunirán delante de él, y él separará a unos de otros, como separa el pastor las ovejas de las cabras. [33]Pondrá las ovejas a su *derecha, y las cabras a su izquierda.

[34]»Entonces dirá el Rey a los que estén a su derecha: "Vengan ustedes, a quienes mi Padre ha bendecido; reciban su herencia, el reino preparado para ustedes desde la creación del mundo. [35]Porque tuve hambre, y ustedes me dieron de comer; tuve sed, y me dieron de beber; fui forastero, y me dieron alojamiento; [36]necesité ropa, y me vistieron; estuve enfermo, y me atendieron; estuve en la cárcel, y me visitaron." [37]Y le contestarán los justos: "Señor, ¿cuándo te vimos hambriento y te alimentamos, o sediento y te dimos de beber? [38]¿Cuándo te vimos como forastero y te dimos alojamiento, o necesitado de ropa y te vestimos? [39]¿Cuándo te vimos enfermo o en la cárcel y te visitamos?" [40]El Rey les responderá: "Les aseguro que todo lo que hicieron por uno de mis hermanos, aun por el más pequeño, lo hicieron por mí."

[41]»Luego dirá a los que estén a su izquierda: "Apártense de mí, malditos, al fuego eterno preparado para el diablo y sus ángeles. [42]Porque tuve hambre, y ustedes no me dieron nada de comer; tuve sed, y no me dieron nada de beber; [43]fui forastero, y no me dieron alojamiento; necesité ropa, y no me vistieron; estuve enfermo y en la cárcel, y no me atendieron." [44]Ellos también le contestarán: "Señor, ¿cuándo te vimos hambriento o sediento, o como forastero, o necesitado de ropa, o enfermo, o en la cárcel, y no te ayudamos?" [45]Él les responderá: "Les aseguro que todo lo que no hicieron por el más pequeño de mis hermanos, tampoco lo hicieron por mí."

[46]»Aquéllos irán al castigo eterno, y los justos a la vida eterna.

La conspiración contra Jesús
26:2-5 — Mr 14:1-2; Lc 22:1-2

26 Después de exponer todas estas cosas, Jesús les dijo a sus discípulos: [2]«Como ya saben, faltan dos días para la Pascua, y el Hijo del hombre será entregado para que lo crucifiquen.»

[3]Se reunieron entonces los jefes de los sacerdotes y los *ancianos del pueblo en el palacio de Caifás, el sumo sacerdote, [4]y con artimañas buscaban cómo arrestar a Jesús para matarlo. [5]«Pero no durante la fiesta —decían—, no sea que se amotine el pueblo.»

Una mujer unge a Jesús en Betania
26:6-13 — Mr 14:3-9

[6]Estando Jesús en Betania, en casa de Simón llamado el Leproso, [7]se acercó una mujer con un frasco de alabastro lleno de un perfume muy caro, y lo derramó sobre la cabeza de Jesús mientras él estaba *sentado a la mesa.

[8]Al ver esto, los discípulos se indignaron.

—¿Para qué este desperdicio? —dijeron—. [9]Podía haberse vendido este perfume por mucho dinero para darlo a los pobres.

[10]Consciente de ello, Jesús les dijo:

—¿Por qué molestan a esta mujer? Ella ha hecho una obra hermosa conmigo. [11]A los pobres siempre los tendrán con ustedes, pero a mí no me van a tener siempre. [12]Al derramar ella este perfume sobre mi cuerpo, lo hizo a fin de prepararme para la sepultura. [13]Les aseguro que en cualquier parte del mundo donde se predique este *evangelio, se contará también, en memoria de esta mujer, lo que ella hizo.

Judas acuerda traicionar a Jesús
26:14-16 — Mr 14:10-11; Lc 22:3-6

[14]Uno de los doce, el que se llamaba Judas Iscariote, fue a ver a los jefes de los sacerdotes.

[15]—¿Cuánto me dan, y yo les entrego a Jesús? —les propuso.

Decidieron pagarle treinta monedas de plata. [16]Y desde entonces Judas buscaba una oportunidad para entregarlo.

---

[d] **25:15** *cinco mil monedas de oro*. Lit. *cinco* *talentos* (y así sucesivamente en el resto de este pasaje).

La Cena del Señor

26:17-19 — Mr 14:12-16; Lc 22:7-13
26:20-24 — Mr 14:17-21
26:26-29 — Mr 14:22-25; Lc 22:17-20;
   1Co 11:23-25

17El primer día de la fiesta de los Panes sin levadura, se acercaron los discípulos a Jesús y le preguntaron:

—¿Dónde quieres que hagamos los preparativos para que comas la Pascua?

18Él les respondió que fueran a la ciudad, a la casa de cierto hombre, y le dijeran: «El Maestro dice: "Mi tiempo está cerca. Voy a celebrar la Pascua en tu casa con mis discípulos."» **19**Los discípulos hicieron entonces como Jesús les había mandado, y prepararon la Pascua.

20Al anochecer, Jesús estaba *sentado a la mesa con los doce. **21**Mientras comían, les dijo:

—Les aseguro que uno de ustedes me va a traicionar.

22Ellos se entristecieron mucho, y uno por uno comenzaron a preguntarle:

—¿Acaso seré yo, Señor?

23—El que mete la mano conmigo en el plato es el que me va a traicionar —respondió Jesús. **24**A la verdad el Hijo del hombre se irá, tal como está escrito de él, pero ¡ay de aquel que lo traiciona! Más le valdría a ese hombre no haber nacido.

25—¿Acaso seré yo, Rabí? —le dijo Judas, el que lo iba a traicionar.

—Tú lo has dicho —le contestó Jesús.

26Mientras comían, Jesús tomó pan y lo bendijo. Luego lo partió y se lo dio a sus discípulos, diciéndoles:

—Tomen y coman; esto es mi cuerpo.

27Después tomó la copa, dio gracias, y se la ofreció diciéndoles:

—Beban de ella todos ustedes. **28**Esto es mi sangre del pacto,ᵉ que es derramada por muchos para el perdón de pecados. **29**Les digo que no beberé de este fruto de la vid desde ahora en adelante, hasta el día en que beba con ustedes el vino nuevo en el reino de mi Padre.

30Después de cantar los salmos, salieron al monte de los Olivos.

Jesús predice la negación de Pedro

26:31-35 — Mr 14:27-31; Lc 22:31-34

31—Esta misma noche —les dijo Jesús— todos ustedes me abandonarán, porque está escrito:

»"Heriré al pastor,
   y se dispersarán las ovejas del rebaño."ᶠ

32Pero después de que yo resucite, iré delante de ustedes a Galilea.

33—Aunque todos te abandonen —declaró Pedro—, yo jamás lo haré.

34—Te aseguro —le contestó Jesús— que esta misma noche, antes de que cante el gallo, me negarás tres veces.

35—Aunque tenga que morir contigo —insistió Pedro—, jamás te negaré. Y los demás discípulos dijeron lo mismo.

Jesús en Getsemaní

26:36-46 — Mr 14:32-42; Lc 22:40-46

36Luego fue Jesús con sus discípulos a un lugar llamado Getsemaní, y les dijo: «Siéntense aquí mientras voy más allá a orar.» **37**Se llevó a Pedro y a los dos hijos de Zebedeo, y comenzó a sentirse triste y angustiado. **38**«Es tal la angustia que me invade, que me siento morir —les dijo—. Quédense aquí y manténganse despiertos conmigo.»

39Yendo un poco más allá, se postró sobre su rostro y oró: «Padre mío, si es posible, no me hagas beber este trago amargo.ᵍ Pero no sea lo que yo quiero, sino lo que quieres tú.»

40Luego volvió adonde estaban sus discípulos y los encontró dormidos. «¿No pudieron mantenerse despiertos conmigo ni una hora? —le dijo a Pedro—. **41**Estén alerta y oren para que no caigan en *tentación. El espíritu está dispuesto, pero el cuerpoʰ es débil.»

42Por segunda vez se retiró y oró: «Padre mío, si no es posible evitar que yo beba este trago amargo,ⁱ hágase tu voluntad.»

43Cuando volvió, otra vez los encontró dormidos, porque se les cerraban los ojos de sueño. **44**Así que los dejó y se retiró a orar por tercera vez, diciendo lo mismo.

45Volvió de nuevo a los discípulos y les dijo: «¿Siguen durmiendo y descansando? Miren, se acerca la hora, y el Hijo del hombre va a ser entregado en manos de *pecadores. **46**¡Levántense! ¡Vámonos! ¡Ahí viene el que me traiciona!»

Arresto de Jesús

26:47-56 — Mr 14:43-50; Lc 22:47-53

47Todavía estaba hablando Jesús cuando llegó Judas, uno de los doce. Lo acompañaba una gran turba armada con espadas y palos, enviada por los jefes de los sacerdotes y los *ancianos del pueblo. **48**El traidor les había dado esta contraseña: «Al que le dé un beso, ése es; arréstenlo.» **49**En seguida Judas se acercó a Jesús y lo saludó.

—¡Rabí! —le dijo, y lo besó.

50—Amigo —le replicó Jesús—, ¿a qué vienes?ʲ

Entonces los hombres se acercaron y prendieron a Jesús. **51**En eso, uno de los que estaban con él extendió la mano, sacó la espada e hirió al siervo del sumo sacerdote, cortándole una oreja.

52—Guarda tu espada —le dijo Jesús—, porque los que a hierro matan, a hierro mueren.ᵏ **53**¿Crees que no puedo acudir a mi Padre, y al instante pondría a mi disposición más de doce batallonesˡ de ángeles? **54**Pero entonces, ¿cómo se cumplirían las Escrituras que dicen que así tiene que suceder?

55Y de inmediato dijo a la turba:

—¿Acaso soy un bandido,ᵐ para que vengan con espadas y palos a arrestarme? Todos los días me sentaba a enseñar en el *templo, y no me prendieron. **56**Pero todo esto ha sucedido para que se cumpla lo que escribieron los profetas.

Entonces todos los discípulos lo abandonaron y huyeron.

Jesús ante el Consejo

26:57-68 — Mr 14:53-65; Jn 18:12-13,19-24

57Los que habían arrestado a Jesús lo llevaron ante Caifás, el sumo sacerdote, donde se habían reu-

---

ᵉ **26:28** *del pacto.* Var. *del nuevo pacto* (véase Lc 22:20). ᶠ **26:31** Zac 13:7 ᵍ **26:39** *no ... amargo.* Lit. *que pase de mí esta copa.* ʰ **26:41** *el cuerpo.* Lit. *la *carne.* ⁱ **26:42** *evitar ... amargo.* Lit. *que esto pase de mí.* ʲ **26:50** *¿a qué vienes?* Alt. *haz lo que viniste a hacer.* ᵏ **26:52** *porque ... mueren.* Lit. *porque todos los que toman espada, por espada perecerán.* ˡ **26:53** *batallones.* Lit. *legiones.* ᵐ **26:55** *bandido.* Alt. *insurgente.*

nido los *maestros de la ley y los *ancianos. 58Pero Pedro lo siguió de lejos hasta el patio del sumo sacerdote. Entró y se sentó con los guardias para ver en qué terminaba aquello.

59Los jefes de los sacerdotes y el *Consejo en pleno buscaban alguna prueba falsa contra Jesús para poder condenarlo a muerte. 60Pero no la encontraron, a pesar de que se presentaron muchos falsos testigos.

Por fin se presentaron dos, 61que declararon:

—Este hombre dijo: "Puedo destruir el *templo de Dios y reconstruirlo en tres días."

62Poniéndose en pie, el sumo sacerdote le dijo a Jesús:

—¿No vas a responder? ¿Qué significan estas denuncias en tu contra?

63Pero Jesús se quedó callado. Así que el sumo sacerdote insistió:

—Te ordeno en el nombre del Dios viviente que nos digas si eres el *Cristo, el Hijo de Dios.

64—Tú lo has dicho —respondió Jesús—. Pero yo les digo a todos: De ahora en adelante verán ustedes al Hijo del hombre sentado a la *derecha del Todopoderoso, y viniendo en las nubes del cielo.

65—¡Ha *blasfemado! —exclamó el sumo sacerdote, rasgándose las vestiduras—. ¿Para qué necesitamos más testigos? ¡Miren, ustedes mismos han oído la blasfemia! 66¿Qué piensan de esto?

—Merece la muerte —le contestaron.

67Entonces algunos le escupieron en el rostro y le dieron puñetazos. Otros lo abofeteaban 68y decían:

—A ver, Cristo, ¡adivina quién te pegó!

Pedro niega a Jesús
26:69-75 — Mr 14:66-72; Lc 22:55-62; Jn 18:16-18,25-27

69Mientras tanto, Pedro estaba sentado afuera, en el patio, y una criada se le acercó.

—Tú también estabas con Jesús de Galilea —le dijo.

70Pero él lo negó delante de todos, diciendo:

—No sé de qué estás hablando.

71Luego salió a la puerta, donde otra criada lo vio y dijo a los que estaban allí:

—Éste estaba con Jesús de Nazaret.

72Él lo volvió a negar, jurándoles:

—¡A ese hombre ni lo conozco!

73Poco después se acercaron a Pedro los que estaban allí y le dijeron:

—Seguro que eres uno de ellos; se te nota por tu acento.

74Y comenzó a echarse maldiciones, y les juró:

—¡A ese hombre ni lo conozco!

En ese instante cantó un gallo. 75Entonces Pedro se acordó de lo que Jesús había dicho: «Antes de que cante el gallo, me negarás tres veces.» Y saliendo de allí, lloró amargamente.

Judas se ahorca

27 Muy de mañana, todos los jefes de los sacerdotes y los *ancianos del pueblo tomaron la decisión de condenar a muerte a Jesús. 2Lo ataron, se lo llevaron y se lo entregaron a Pilato, el gobernador.

3Cuando Judas, el que lo había traicionado, vio que habían condenado a Jesús, sintió remordimiento y devolvió las treinta monedas de plata a los jefes de los sacerdotes y a los ancianos.

4—He pecado —les dijo— porque he entregado sangre inocente.

—¿Y eso a nosotros qué nos importa? —respondieron—. ¡Allá tú!

5Entonces Judas arrojó el dinero en el *santuario y salió de allí. Luego fue y se ahorcó.

6Los jefes de los sacerdotes recogieron las monedas y dijeron: «La ley no permite echar esto al tesoro, porque es precio de sangre.» 7Así que resolvieron comprar con ese dinero un terreno conocido como Campo del Alfarero, para sepultar allí a los extranjeros. 8Por eso se le ha llamado Campo de Sangre hasta el día de hoy. 9Así se cumplió lo dicho por el profeta Jeremías: «Tomaron las treinta monedas de plata, el precio que puso el pueblo de Israel le había fijado, 10y con ellas compraron el campo del alfarero, como me ordenó el Señor.»n

Jesús ante Pilato
27:11-26 — Mr 15:12-15; Lc 23:2-3,18-25; Jn 18:29—19:16

11Mientras tanto, Jesús compareció ante el gobernador, y éste le preguntó:

—¿Eres tú el rey de los judíos?

—Tú lo dices —respondió Jesús.

12Al ser acusado por los jefes de los sacerdotes y por los *ancianos, Jesús no contestó nada.

13—¿No oyes lo que declaran contra ti? —le dijo Pilato.

14Pero Jesús no respondió ni a una sola acusación, por lo que el gobernador se llenó de asombro.

15Ahora bien, durante la fiesta el gobernador acostumbraba soltar un preso que la gente escogiera. 16Tenían un preso famoso llamado Barrabás. 17-18Así que cuando se reunió la multitud, Pilato, que sabía que le habían entregado a Jesús por envidia, les preguntó:

—¿A quién quieren que les suelte: a Barrabás o a Jesús, al que llaman *Cristo?

19Mientras Pilato estaba sentado en el tribunal, su esposa le envió el siguiente recado: «No te metas con ese justo, pues por causa de él, hoy he sufrido mucho en un sueño.»

20Pero los jefes de los sacerdotes y los ancianos persuadieron a la multitud a que le pidiera a Pilato soltar a Barrabás y ejecutar a Jesús.

21—¿A cuál de los dos quieren que les suelte? —preguntó el gobernador.

—A Barrabás.

22—¿Y qué voy a hacer con Jesús, al que llaman Cristo?

—¡Crucifícalo! —respondieron todos.

23—¿Por qué? ¿Qué crimen ha cometido?

Pero ellos gritaban aún más fuerte:

—¡Crucifícalo!

24Cuando Pilato vio que no conseguía nada, sino que más bien se estaba formando un tumulto, pidió agua y se lavó las manos delante de la gente.

—Soy inocente de la sangre de este hombre —dijo—. ¡Allá ustedes!

25—¡Que su sangre caiga sobre nosotros y sobre nuestros hijos! —contestó todo el pueblo.

26Entonces les soltó a Barrabás; pero a Jesús lo mandó azotar, y lo entregó para que lo crucificaran.

Los soldados se burlan de Jesús
27:27-31 — Mr 15:16-20

27Los soldados del gobernador llevaron a Jesús al palacioñ y reunieron a toda la tropa alrededor de

n 27:10 Véanse Zac 11:12,13; Jer 19:1-13; 32:6-9.   ñ 27:27 palacio. Lit. pretorio.

él. **28**Le quitaron la ropa y le pusieron un manto de color escarlata. **29**Luego trenzaron una corona de espinas y se la colocaron en la cabeza, y en la mano derecha le pusieron una caña. Arrodillándose delante de él, se burlaban diciendo:

—¡Salve, rey de los judíos!

30Y le escupían, y con la caña le golpeaban la cabeza. **31**Después de burlarse de él, le quitaron el manto, le pusieron su propia ropa y se lo llevaron para crucificarlo.

La crucifixión
27:33-44 — Mr 15:22-32; Lc 23:33-43; Jn 19:17-24

32Al salir encontraron a un hombre de Cirene que se llamaba Simón, y lo obligaron a llevar la cruz. **33**Llegaron a un lugar llamado Gólgota (que significa «Lugar de la Calavera»). **34**Allí le dieron a Jesús vino mezclado con hiel; pero después de probarlo, se negó a beberlo. **35**Lo crucificaron y repartieron sus ropa echando suertes.o **36**Y se sentaron a vigilarlo. **37**Encima de su cabeza pusieron por escrito la causa de su condena: «ÉSTE ES JESÚS, EL REY DE LOS JUDÍOS.» **38**Con él crucificaron a dos bandidos,p uno a su derecha y otro a su izquierda. **39**Los que pasaban meneaban la cabeza y *blasfemaban contra él:

40—Tú, que destruyes el *templo y en tres días lo reconstruyes, ¡sálvate a ti mismo! ¡Si eres el Hijo de Dios, baja de la cruz!

41De la misma manera se burlaban de él los jefes de los sacerdotes, junto con los *maestros de la ley y los *ancianos.

42—Salvó a otros —decían—, ¡pero no puede salvarse a sí mismo! ¡Y es el Rey de Israel! Que baje ahora de la cruz, y así creeremos en él. **43**Él confía en Dios; pues que lo libre Dios ahora, si de veras lo quiere. ¿Acaso no dijo: "Yo soy el Hijo de Dios"?

44Así también lo insultaban los bandidos que estaban crucificados con él.

Muerte de Jesús
27:45-56 — Mr 15:31-41; Lc 23:44-49

45Desde el mediodía y hasta la media tardeq toda la tierra quedó en oscuridad. **46**Como a las tres de la tarde,r Jesús gritó con fuerza:

—Elí, Elí,s ¿lama sabactani? (que significa: "Dios mío, Dios mío, ¿por qué me has desamparado?").t

47Cuando lo oyeron, algunos de los que estaban allí dijeron:

—Está llamando a Elías.

48Al instante uno de ellos corrió en busca de una esponja. La empapó en vinagre, la puso en una caña y se la ofreció a Jesús para que bebiera. **49**Los demás decían:

—Déjalo, a ver si viene Elías a salvarlo.

50Entonces Jesús volvió a gritar con fuerza, y entregó su espíritu.

51En ese momento la cortina del *santuario del templo se rasgó en dos, de arriba abajo. La tierra tembló y se partieron las rocas. **52**Se abrieron los sepulcros, y muchos *santos que habían muerto resucitaron. **53**Salieron de los sepulcros y, después de la resurrección de Jesús, entraron en la ciudad santa y se aparecieron a muchos.

54Cuando el centurión y los que con él estaban custodiando a Jesús vieron el terremoto y todo lo que había sucedido, quedaron aterrados y exclamaron:

—¡Verdaderamente éste era el Hijou de Dios!

55Estaban allí, mirando de lejos, muchas mujeres que habían seguido a Jesús desde Galilea para servirle. **56**Entre ellas se encontraban María Magdalena, María la madre de *Jacobo y de José, y la madre de los hijos de Zebedeo.

Sepultura de Jesús
27:57-61 — Mr 15:42-47; Lc 23:50-56; Jn 19:38-42

57Al atardecer, llegó un hombre rico de Arimatea, llamado José, que también se había convertido en discípulo de Jesús. **58**Se presentó ante Pilato para pedirle el cuerpo de Jesús, y Pilato ordenó que se lo dieran. **59**José tomó el cuerpo, lo envolvió en una sábana limpia **60**y lo puso en un sepulcro nuevo de su propiedad que había cavado en la roca. Luego hizo rodar una piedra grande a la entrada del sepulcro, y se fue. **61**Allí estaban, sentadas frente al sepulcro, María Magdalena y la otra María.

La guardia ante el sepulcro

62Al día siguiente, después del día de la preparación, los jefes de los sacerdotes y los fariseos se presentaron ante Pilato.

63—Señor —le dijeron—, nosotros recordamos que mientras ese engañador aún vivía, dijo: "A los tres días resucitaré." **64**Por eso, ordene usted que se selle el sepulcro hasta el tercer día, no sea que vengan sus discípulos, se roben el cuerpo y le digan al pueblo que ha *resucitado. Ese último engaño sería peor que el primero.

65—Llévense una guardia de soldados —les ordenó Pilato—, y vayan a asegurar el sepulcro lo mejor que puedan.

66Así que ellos fueron, cerraron el sepulcro con una piedra, y lo sellaron; y dejaron puesta la guardia.

La resurrección
28:1-8 — Mr 16:1-8; Lc 24:1-10

28 Después del *sábado, al amanecer del primer día de la semana, María Magdalena y la otra María fueron a ver el sepulcro.

2Sucedió que hubo un terremoto violento, porque un ángel del Señor bajó del cielo y, acercándose al sepulcro, quitó la piedra y se sentó sobre ella. **3**Su aspecto era como el de un relámpago, y su ropa era blanca como la nieve. **4**Los guardias tuvieron tanto miedo de él que se pusieron a temblar y quedaron como muertos.

5El ángel dijo a las mujeres:

—No tengan miedo; sé que ustedes buscan a Jesús, el que fue crucificado. **6**No está aquí, pues ha resucitado, tal como dijo. Vengan a ver el lugar donde lo pusieron. **7**Luego vayan pronto a decirles a sus discípulos: "Él se ha *levantado de entre los muertos y va delante de ustedes a Galilea. Allí lo verán." Ahora ya lo saben.

8Así que las mujeres se alejaron a toda prisa del sepulcro, asustadas pero muy alegres, y corrieron a dar la noticia a los discípulos. **9**En eso Jesús les salió al

---

o **27:35** suertes. Var. suertes, para que se cumpliera lo dicho por medio del profeta: «Se repartieron entre ellos mi manto y sobre mi ropa echaron suertes» (Sal 22:18; véase Jn 19:24).   p **27:38** bandidos. Alt. insurgentes; también en v. 44.   q **27:45** Desde . . . tarde. Lit. Desde la hora sexta hasta la hora novena.   r **27:46** Como . . . tarde. Lit. Como a la hora novena.   s **27:46** Elí, Elí. Var. Eloi, Eloi.   t **27:46** Sal 22:1   u **27:54** era el Hijo. Alt. era hijo.

encuentro y las saludó. Ellas se le acercaron, le abrazaron los pies y lo adoraron.

10—No tengan miedo —les dijo Jesús—. Vayan a decirles a mis hermanos que se dirijan a Galilea, y allí me verán.

El informe de los guardias

11Mientras las mujeres iban de camino, algunos de los guardias entraron en la ciudad e informaron a los jefes de los sacerdotes de todo lo que había sucedido. 12Después de reunirse estos jefes con los *ancianos y de trazar un plan, les dieron a los soldados una fuerte suma de dinero 13y les encargaron: «Digan que los discípulos de Jesús vinieron por la noche y que, mientras ustedes dormían, se robaron el cuerpo. 14Y si el gobernador llega a enterarse de esto, nosotros responderemos por ustedes y les evitaremos cualquier problema.»

v **28:20** *el fin del mundo.* Lit. *la consumación del siglo.*

15Así que los soldados tomaron el dinero e hicieron como se les había instruido. Esta es la versión de los sucesos que hasta el día de hoy ha circulado entre los judíos.

La gran comisión

16Los once discípulos fueron a Galilea, a la montaña que Jesús les había indicado. 17Cuando lo vieron, lo adoraron; pero algunos dudaban. 18Jesús se acercó entonces a ellos y les dijo:

—Se me ha dado toda autoridad en el cielo y en la tierra. 19Por tanto, vayan y hagan discípulos de todas las *naciones, bautizándolos en el nombre del Padre y del Hijo y del Espíritu Santo, 20enseñándoles a obedecer todo lo que les he mandado a ustedes. Y les aseguro que estaré con ustedes siempre, hasta el fin del mundo.v

MARCOS

Juan el Bautista prepara el camino
1:2-8 — Mt 3:1-11; Lc 3:2-16

1 Comienzo del *evangelio de *Jesucristo, el Hijo de Dios.a

2Sucedió como está escrito en el profeta Isaías:

«Yo estoy por enviar a mi mensajero delante de ti,
el cual preparará tu camino.»b
3«Voz de uno que grita en el desierto:
"Preparen el camino del Señor,
háganle sendas derechas." »c

4Así se presentó Juan, bautizando en el desierto y predicando el bautismo de *arrepentimiento para el perdón de pecados. 5Toda la gente de la región de Judea y de la ciudad de Jerusalén acudía a él. Cuando confesaban sus pecados, él los bautizaba en el río Jordán. 6La ropa de Juan estaba hecha de pelo de camello. Llevaba puesto un cinturón de cuero, y comía langostas y miel silvestre. 7Predicaba de esta manera: «Después de mí viene uno más poderoso que yo; ni siquiera merezco agacharme para desatar la correa de sus sandalias. 8Yo los he bautizado a ustedes cond agua, pero él los bautizará con el Espíritu Santo.»

Bautismo y tentación de Jesús
1:9-11 — Mt 3:13-17; Lc 3:21-22
1:12-13 — Mt 4:1-11; Lc 4:1-13

9En esos días llegó Jesús desde Nazaret de Galilea y fue bautizado por Juan en el Jordán. 10En seguida, al subir del agua, Jesús vio que el cielo se abría y que el Espíritu bajaba sobre él como una paloma. 11También se oyó una voz del cielo que decía: «Tú eres mi Hijo amado; estoy muy complacido contigo.»

12En seguida el Espíritu lo impulsó a ir al desierto, 13y allí fue *tentado por Satanás durante cuarenta días. Estaba entre las fieras, y los ángeles le servían.

Llamamiento de los primeros discípulos
1:16-20 — Mt 4:18-22; Lc 5:2-11; Jn 1:35-42

14Después de que encarcelaron a Juan, Jesús se fue a Galilea a anunciar las buenas *nuevas de Dios. 15«Se ha cumplido el tiempo —decía—. El reino de Dios está cerca. ¡*Arrepiéntanse y crean las buenas *nuevas!»

16Pasando por la orilla del mar de Galilea, Jesús vio a Simón y a su hermano Andrés que echaban la red al lago, pues eran pescadores. 17«Vengan, síganme —les dijo Jesús—, y los haré pescadores de hombres.» 18Al momento dejaron las redes y lo siguieron.

19Un poco más adelante vio a *Jacobo y a su hermano Juan, hijos de Zebedeo, que estaban en la barca remendando las redes. 20En seguida los llamó, y ellos, dejando a su padre Zebedeo en la barca con los jornaleros, se fueron con Jesús.

Jesús expulsa a un espíritu maligno
1:21-28 — Lc 4:31-37

21Entraron en Capernaúm, y tan pronto como llegó el *sábado, Jesús fue a la sinagoga y se puso a enseñar. 22La gente se asombraba de su enseñanza, porque la impartía como quien tiene autoridad y no como los *maestros de la ley. 23De repente, en la sinagoga, un hombre que estaba poseído por un *espíritu maligno gritó:

24—¿Por qué te entrometes, Jesús de Nazaret? ¿Has venido a destruirnos? Yo sé quién eres tú: ¡el Santo de Dios!

25—¡Cállate! —lo reprendió Jesús—. ¡Sal de ese hombre!

26Entonces el espíritu maligno sacudió al hombre violentamente y salió de él dando un alarido. 27Todos se quedaron tan asustados que se preguntaban unos a otros: «¿Qué es esto? ¡Una enseñanza nueva, pues lo hace con autoridad! Les da órdenes incluso a los espíritus malignos, y le obedecen.» 28Como resultado, su fama se extendió rápidamente por toda la región de Galilea.

Jesús sana a muchos enfermos
1:29-31 — Mt 8:14-15; Lc 4:38-39
1:32-34 — Mt 8:16-17; Lc 4:40-41

29Tan pronto como salieron de la sinagoga, Jesús fue con *Jacobo y Juan a casa de Simón y Andrés. 30La suegra de Simón estaba en cama con fiebre, y en seguida se lo dijeron a Jesús. 31Él se le acercó, la tomó de la mano y la ayudó a levantarse. Entonces se le quitó la fiebre y se puso a servirles.

32Al atardecer, cuando ya se ponía el sol, la gente le llevó a Jesús todos los enfermos y endemoniados, 33de manera que la población entera se estaba congregando a la puerta. 34Jesús sanó a muchos que padecían de diversas enfermedades. También expulsó a muchos demonios, pero no los dejaba hablar porque sabían quién era él.

Jesús ora en un lugar solitario
1:35-38 — Lc 4:42-43

35Muy de madrugada, cuando todavía estaba oscuro, Jesús se levantó, salió de la casa y se fue a un lugar solitario, donde se puso a orar. 36Simón y sus compañeros salieron a buscarlo.

37Por fin lo encontraron y le dijeron:

—Todo el mundo te busca.

38Jesús respondió:

—Vámonos de aquí a otras aldeas cercanas donde también pueda predicar; para esto he venido.

39Así que recorrió toda Galilea, predicando en las sinagogas y expulsando demonios.

Jesús sana a un leproso
1:40-44 — Mt 8:2-4; Lc 5:12-14

40Un hombre que tenía *lepra se le acercó, y de rodillas le suplicó:

—Si quieres, puedes *limpiarme.

41Movido a compasión, Jesús extendió la mano y tocó al hombre, diciéndole:

—Sí quiero. ¡Queda limpio!

42Al instante se le quitó la lepra y quedó sano.e 43Jesús lo despidió en seguida con una fuerte advertencia:

44—Mira, no se lo digas a nadie; sólo ve, preséntate al sacerdote y lleva por tu *purificación lo que ordenó Moisés, para que sirva de testimonio.

45Pero él salió y comenzó a hablar sin reserva, divulgando lo sucedido. Como resultado, Jesús ya no podía entrar en ningún pueblo abiertamente, sino que se quedaba afuera, en lugares solitarios. Aun así, gente de todas partes seguía acudiendo a él.

---

a 1:1 Var. no incluye: *el Hijo de Dios.* b 1:2 Mal 3:1 c 1:3 Is 40:3 d 1:8 *con.* Alt. *en.* e 1:42 *sano.* Lit. *limpio.*

Jesús sana a un paralítico
2:3-12 — Mt 9:2-8; Lc 5:18-26

2 Unos días después, cuando Jesús entró de nuevo en Capernaúm, corrió la voz de que estaba en casa. ²Se aglomeraron tantos que ya no quedaba sitio ni siquiera frente a la puerta mientras él les predicaba la palabra. ³Entonces llegaron cuatro hombres que le llevaban un paralítico. ⁴Como no podían acercarlo a Jesús por causa de la multitud, quitaron parte del techo encima de donde estaba Jesús y, luego de hacer una abertura, bajaron la camilla en la que estaba acostado el paralítico. ⁵Al ver Jesús la fe de ellos, le dijo al paralítico:

—Hijo, tus pecados quedan perdonados.

⁶Estaban sentados allí algunos *maestros de la ley, que pensaban: ⁷«¿Por qué habla éste así? ¡Está *blasfemando! ¿Quién puede perdonar pecados sino sólo Dios?»

⁸En ese mismo instante supo Jesús en su espíritu que esto era lo que estaban pensando.

—¿Por qué razonan así? —les dijo—. ⁹¿Qué es más fácil, decirle al paralítico: "Tus pecados son perdonados", o decirle: "Levántate, toma tu camilla y anda"? ¹⁰Pues para que sepan que el Hijo del hombre tiene autoridad en la tierra para perdonar pecados —se dirigió entonces al paralítico—: ¹¹A ti te digo, levántate, toma tu camilla y vete a tu casa.

¹²Él se levantó, tomó su camilla en seguida y salió caminando a la vista de todos. Ellos se quedaron asombrados y comenzaron a alabar a Dios.

—Jamás habíamos visto cosa igual —decían.

Llamamiento de Leví
2:14-17 — Mt 9:9-13; Lc 5:27-32

¹³De nuevo salió Jesús a la orilla del lago. Toda la gente acudía a él, y él les enseñaba. ¹⁴Al pasar vio a Leví hijo de Alfeo, donde éste cobraba impuestos.

—Sígueme —le dijo Jesús.

Y Leví se levantó y lo siguió.

¹⁵Sucedió que, estando Jesús a la mesa en casa de Leví, muchos *recaudadores de impuestos y *pecadores se *sentaron con él y sus discípulos, pues ya eran muchos los que lo seguían. ¹⁶Cuando los *maestros de la ley, que eran *fariseos, vieron con quién comía, les preguntaron a sus discípulos:

—¿Y éste come con recaudadores de impuestos y con pecadores?

¹⁷Al oírlos, Jesús les contestó:

—No son los sanos los que necesitan médico sino los enfermos. Y yo no he venido a llamar a justos sino a pecadores.

Le preguntan a Jesús sobre el ayuno
2:18-22 — Mt 9:14-17; Lc 5:33-38

¹⁸Al ver que los discípulos de Juan y los *fariseos ayunaban, algunos se acercaron a Jesús y le preguntaron:

—¿Cómo es que los discípulos de Juan y de los fariseos ayunan, pero los tuyos no?

¹⁹Jesús les contestó:

—¿Acaso pueden ayunar los invitados del novio mientras él está con ellos? No pueden hacerlo mientras lo tienen con ellos. ²⁰Pero llegará el día en que se les quitará el novio, y ese día sí ayunarán. ²¹Nadie remienda un vestido viejo con un retazo de tela nueva. De hacerlo así, el remiendo fruncirá el vestido y la rotura se hará peor. ²²Ni echa nadie vino nuevo en odres viejos. De hacerlo así, el vino hará reventar los

odres y se arruinarán tanto el vino como los odres. Más bien, el vino nuevo se echa en odres nuevos.

Señor del sábado
2:23-28 — Mt 12:1-8; Lc 6:1-5
3:1-6 — Mt 12:9-14; Lc 6:6-11

²³Un *sábado, al cruzar Jesús los sembrados, sus discípulos comenzaron a arrancar a su paso unas espigas de trigo.

²⁴—Mira —le preguntaron los *fariseos—, ¿por qué hacen ellos lo que está prohibido hacer en sábado?

²⁵Él les contestó:

—¿Nunca han leído lo que hizo David en aquella ocasión, cuando él y sus compañeros tuvieron hambre y pasaron necesidad? ²⁶Entró en la casa de Dios cuando Abiatar era el sumo sacerdote, y comió los panes consagrados a Dios, que sólo a los sacerdotes les es permitido comer. Y dio también a sus compañeros.

²⁷»El sábado se hizo para el hombre, y no el hombre para el sábado —añadió—. ²⁸Así que el Hijo del hombre es Señor incluso del sábado.

3 En otra ocasión entró en la sinagoga, y había allí un hombre que tenía la mano paralizada. ²Algunos que buscaban un motivo para acusar a Jesús no le quitaban la vista de encima para ver si sanaba al enfermo en *sábado. ³Entonces Jesús le dijo al hombre de la mano paralizada:

—Ponte de pie frente a todos.

⁴Luego dijo a los otros:

—¿Qué está permitido en sábado: hacer el bien o hacer el mal, salvar una *vida o matar?

Pero ellos permanecieron callados. ⁵Jesús se les quedó mirando, enojado y entristecido por la dureza de su corazón, y le dijo al hombre:

—Extiende la mano.

La extendió, y la mano le quedó restablecida. ⁶Tan pronto como salieron los fariseos, comenzaron a tramar con los herodianos cómo matar a Jesús.

La multitud sigue a Jesús
3:7-12 — Mt 12:15-16; Lc 6:17-19

⁷Jesús se retiró al lago con sus discípulos, y mucha gente de Galilea lo siguió. ⁸Cuando se enteraron de todo lo que hacía, acudieron también a él muchos de Judea y Jerusalén, de Idumea, del otro lado del Jordán y de las regiones de Tiro y Sidón. ⁹Entonces, para evitar que la gente lo atropellara, encargó a sus discípulos que le tuvieran preparada una pequeña barca; ¹⁰pues como había sanado a muchos, todos los que sufrían dolencias se abalanzaban sobre él para tocarlo. ¹¹Además, los *espíritus malignos, al verlo, se postraban ante él, gritando: «¡Tú eres el Hijo de Dios!» ¹²Pero él les ordenó terminantemente que no dijeran quién era él.

Nombramiento de los doce apóstoles
3:16-19 — Mt 10:2-4; Lc 6:14-16; Hch 1:13

¹³Subió Jesús a una montaña y llamó a los que quiso, los cuales se reunieron con él. ¹⁴Designó a doce, a quienes nombró apóstoles,ᶠ para que lo acompañaran y para enviarlos a predicar ¹⁵y ejercer autoridad para expulsar demonios. ¹⁶Éstos son los doce que él nombró: Simón (a quien llamó Pedro); ¹⁷*Jacobo y su hermano Juan, hijos de Zebedeo (a quienes llamó Boanerges, que significa: Hijos del

---

ᶠ **3:14** Var. no incluye: *a quienes nombró apóstoles*.

trueno); 18Andrés, Felipe, Bartolomé, Mateo, Tomás, Jacobo, hijo de Alfeo; Tadeo, Simón el Zelote 19y Judas Iscariote, el que lo traicionó.

Jesús y Beelzebú
3:23-27 — Mt 12:25-29; Lc 11:14-22

20Luego entró en una casa, y de nuevo se aglomeró tanta gente que ni siquiera podían comer él y sus discípulos. 21Cuando se enteraron sus parientes, salieron a hacerse cargo de él, porque decían: «Está fuera de sí.»

22Los *maestros de la ley que habían llegado de Jerusalén decían: «¡Está poseído por *Beelzebú! Expulsa a los demonios por medio del príncipe de los demonios.»

23Entonces Jesús los llamó y les habló en parábolas: «¿Cómo puede Satanás expulsar a Satanás? 24Si un reino está dividido contra sí mismo, ese reino no puede mantenerse en pie. 25Y si una familia está dividida contra sí misma, esa familia no puede mantenerse en pie. 26Igualmente, si Satanás se levanta contra sí mismo y se divide, no puede mantenerse en pie, sino que ha llegado su fin. 27Ahora bien, nadie puede entrar en la casa de alguien fuerte y arrebatarle sus bienes a menos que primero lo ate. Sólo entonces podrá robar su casa. 28Les aseguro que todos los pecados y *blasfemias se les perdonarán a todos por igual, 29excepto a quien blasfeme contra el Espíritu Santo. Éste no tendrá perdón jamás; es culpable de un pecado eterno.»

30Es que ellos habían dicho: «Tiene un *espíritu maligno.»

La madre y los hermanos de Jesús
3:31-33 — Mt 12:46-50; Lc 8:19-21

31En eso llegaron la madre y los hermanos de Jesús. Se quedaron afuera y enviaron a alguien a llamarlo, 32pues había mucha gente sentada alrededor de él.

—Mira, tu madre y tus hermanosg están afuera y te buscan —le dijeron.

33—¿Quiénes son mi madre y mis hermanos? —replicó Jesús.

34Luego echó una mirada a los que estaban sentados alrededor de él y añadió:

—Aquí tienen a mi madre y a mis hermanos. 35Cualquiera que hace la voluntad de Dios es mi hermano, mi hermana y mi madre.

Parábola del sembrador
4:1-12 — Mt 13:1-15; Lc 8:4-10
4:13-20 — Mt 13:18-23; Lc 8:11-15

4 De nuevo comenzó Jesús a enseñar a la orilla del lago. La multitud que se reunió para verlo era tan grande que él subió y se sentó en una barca que estaba en el lago, mientras toda la gente se quedaba en la playa. 2Entonces se puso a enseñarles muchas cosas por medio de parábolas y, como parte de su instrucción, les dijo: 3«¡Pongan atención! Un sembrador salió a sembrar. 4Sucedió que al esparcir él la semilla, una parte cayó junto al camino, y llegaron los pájaros y se la comieron. 5Otra parte cayó en terreno pedregoso, sin mucha tierra. Esa semilla brotó pronto porque la tierra no era profunda; 6pero cuando salió el sol, las plantas se marchitaron y, por no tener raíz, se secaron. 7Otra parte de la semilla cayó entre espinos que, al crecer, la ahogaron, de modo que no dio fruto. 8Pero las otras semillas cayeron en buen terreno. Brotaron, crecieron y produjeron una cosecha

que rindió el treinta, el sesenta y hasta el ciento por uno.

9»El que tenga oídos para oír, que oiga», añadió Jesús.

10Cuando se quedó solo, los doce y los que estaban alrededor de él le hicieron preguntas sobre las parábolas. 11«A ustedes se les ha revelado el *secreto del reino de Dios —les contestó—; pero a los de afuera todo les llega por medio de parábolas, 12para que

»"por mucho que vean, no perciban;
    y por mucho que oigan, no entiendan;
no sea que se conviertan y sean perdonados."h

13»¿No entienden esta parábola? —continuó Jesús—. ¿Cómo podrán, entonces, entender las demás? 14El sembrador siembra la palabra. 15Algunos son como lo sembrado junto al camino, donde se siembra la palabra. Tan pronto como la oyen, viene Satanás y les quita la palabra sembrada en ellos. 16Otros son como lo sembrado en terreno pedregoso: cuando oyen la palabra, en seguida la reciben con alegría, 17pero como no tienen raíz, duran poco tiempo. Cuando surgen problemas o persecución a causa de la palabra, en seguida se apartan de ella. 18Otros son como lo sembrado entre espinos: oyen la palabra, 19pero las preocupaciones de esta vida, el engaño de las riquezas y muchos otros malos deseos entran hasta ahogar la palabra, de modo que ésta no llega a dar fruto. 20Pero otros son como lo sembrado en buen terreno: oyen la palabra, la aceptan y producen una cosecha que rinde el treinta, el sesenta y hasta el ciento por uno.»

Una lámpara en una repisa

21También les dijo: «¿Acaso se trae una lámpara para ponerla debajo de un cajón o debajo de la cama? ¿No es, por el contrario, para ponerla en una repisa? 22No hay nada escondido que no esté destinado a descubrirse; tampoco hay nada oculto que no esté destinado a ser revelado. 23El que tenga oídos para oír, que oiga.

24»Pongan mucha atención —añadió—. Con la medida que midan a otros, se les medirá a ustedes, y aún más se les añadirá. 25Al que tiene, se le dará más; al que no tiene, hasta lo poco que tiene se le quitará.»

Parábola de la semilla que crece

26Jesús continuó: «El reino de Dios se parece a quien esparce semilla en la tierra. 27Sin que éste sepa cómo, y ya sea que duerma o esté despierto, día y noche brota y crece la semilla. 28La tierra da fruto por sí sola; primero el tallo, luego la espiga, y después el grano lleno en la espiga. 29Tan pronto como el grano está maduro, se le mete la hoz, pues ha llegado el tiempo de la cosecha.»

Parábola del grano de mostaza
4:30-32 — Mt 13:31-32; Lc 13:18-19

30También dijo: «¿Con qué vamos a comparar el reino de Dios? ¿Qué parábola podemos usar para describirlo? 31Es como un grano de mostaza: cuando se siembra en la tierra, es la semilla más pequeña que hay, 32pero una vez sembrada crece hasta convertirse en la más grande de las hortalizas, y echa ramas tan grandes que las aves pueden anidar bajo su sombra.»

33Y con muchas parábolas semejantes les enseñaba Jesús la palabra hasta donde podían entender. 34No les decía nada sin emplear parábolas. Pero cuando estaba a solas con sus discípulos, les explicaba todo.

---

g 3:32 tus hermanos. Var. tus hermanos y tus hermanas.   h 4:12 Is 6:9,10

Jesús calma la tormenta
4:35-41 — Mt 8:18,23-27; Lc 8:22-25

³⁵Ese día al anochecer, les dijo a sus discípulos:

—Crucemos al otro lado.

³⁶Dejaron a la multitud y se fueron con él en la barca donde estaba. También lo acompañaban otras barcas. ³⁷Se desató entonces una fuerte tormenta, y las olas azotaban la barca, tanto que ya comenzaba a inundarse. ³⁸Jesús, mientras tanto, estaba en la popa, durmiendo sobre un cabezal, así que los discípulos lo despertaron.

—¡Maestro! —gritaron—, ¿no te importa que nos ahoguemos?

³⁹Él se levantó, reprendió al viento y ordenó al mar:

—¡Silencio! ¡Cálmate!

El viento se calmó y todo quedó completamente tranquilo.

⁴⁰—¿Por qué tienen tanto miedo? —dijo a sus discípulos—. ¿Todavíaⁱ no tienen fe?

⁴¹Ellos estaban espantados y se decían unos a otros:

—¿Quién es éste, que hasta el viento y el mar le obedecen?

Liberación de un endemoniado
5:1-17 — Mt 8:28-34; Lc 8:26-37
5:18-20 — Lc 8:38-39

5 Cruzaron el lago hasta llegar a la región de los gerasenos.ʲ ²Tan pronto como desembarcó Jesús, un hombre poseído por un *espíritu maligno le salió al encuentro de entre los sepulcros. ³Este hombre vivía en los sepulcros, y ya nadie podía sujetarlo, ni siquiera con cadenas. ⁴Muchas veces lo habían atado con cadenas y grilletes, pero él las destrozaba, y nadie tenía fuerza para dominarlo. ⁵Noche y día andaba por los sepulcros y por las colinas, gritando y golpeándose con piedras.

⁶Cuando vio a Jesús desde lejos, corrió y se postró delante de él.

⁷—¿Por qué te entrometes, Jesús, Hijo del Dios Altísimo? —gritó con fuerza—. ¡Te ruego por Dios que no me atormentes!

⁸Es que Jesús le había dicho: «¡Sal de este hombre, espíritu maligno!»

⁹—¿Cómo te llamas? —le preguntó Jesús.

—Me llamo Legión —respondió—, porque somos muchos.

¹⁰Y con insistencia le suplicaba a Jesús que no los expulsara de aquella región.

¹¹Como en una colina estaba paciendo una manada de muchos cerdos, los demonios le rogaron a Jesús:

¹²—Mándanos a los cerdos; déjanos entrar en ellos.

¹³Así que él les dio permiso. Cuando los espíritus malignos salieron del hombre, entraron en los cerdos, que eran unos dos mil, y la manada se precipitó al lago por el despeñadero y allí se ahogó.

¹⁴Los que cuidaban los cerdos salieron huyendo y dieron la noticia en el pueblo y por los campos, y la gente fue a ver lo que había pasado. ¹⁵Llegaron adonde estaba Jesús, y cuando vieron al que había estado poseído por la legión de demonios, sentado, vestido y en su sano juicio, tuvieron miedo. ¹⁶Los que habían presenciado estos hechos le contaron a la gente lo que había sucedido con el endemoniado y con los cerdos. ¹⁷Entonces la gente comenzó a suplicarle a Jesús que se fuera de la región.

¹⁸Mientras subía Jesús a la barca, el que había estado endemoniado le rogaba que le permitiera acompañarlo. ¹⁹Jesús no se lo permitió, sino que le dijo:

—Vete a tu casa, a los de tu familia, y diles todo lo que el Señor ha hecho por ti y cómo te ha tenido compasión.

²⁰Así que el hombre se fue y se puso a proclamar en *Decápolis lo mucho que Jesús había hecho por él. Y toda la gente se quedó asombrada.

Una niña muerta y una mujer enferma
5:22-43 — Mt 9:18-26; Lc 8:41-56

²¹Después de que Jesús regresó en la barca al otro lado del lago, se reunió alrededor de él una gran multitud, por lo que él se quedó en la orilla. ²²Llegó entonces uno de los jefes de la sinagoga, llamado Jairo. Al ver a Jesús, se arrojó a sus pies, ²³suplicándole con insistencia:

—Mi hijita se está muriendo. Ven y pon tus manos sobre ella para que se *sane y viva.

²⁴Jesús se fue con él, y lo seguía una gran multitud, la cual lo apretujaba. ²⁵Había entre la gente una mujer que hacía doce años padecía de hemorragias. ²⁶Había sufrido mucho a manos de varios médicos, y se había gastado todo lo que tenía sin que le hubiera servido de nada, pues en vez de mejorar, iba de mal en peor. ²⁷Cuando oyó hablar de Jesús, se le acercó por detrás entre la gente y le tocó el manto. ²⁸Pensaba: «Si logro tocar siquiera su ropa, quedaré sana.» ²⁹Al instante cesó su hemorragia, y se dio cuenta de que su cuerpo había quedado libre de esa aflicción.

³⁰Al momento también Jesús se dio cuenta de que de él había salido poder, así que se volvió hacia la gente y preguntó:

—¿Quién me ha tocado la ropa?

³¹—Ves que te apretuja la gente —le contestaron sus discípulos—, y aun así preguntas: "¿Quién me ha tocado?"

³²Pero Jesús seguía mirando a su alrededor para ver quién lo había hecho. ³³La mujer, sabiendo lo que le había sucedido, se acercó temblando de miedo y, arrojándose a sus pies, le confesó toda la verdad.

³⁴—¡Hija, tu fe te ha sanado! —le dijo Jesús—. Vete en paz y queda sana de tu aflicción.

³⁵Todavía estaba hablando Jesús, cuando llegaron unos hombres de la casa de Jairo, jefe de la sinagoga, para decirle:

—Tu hija ha muerto. ¿Para qué sigues molestando al Maestro?

³⁶Sin hacer caso de la noticia, Jesús le dijo al jefe de la sinagoga:

—No tengas miedo; cree nada más.

³⁷No dejó que nadie lo acompañara, excepto Pedro, *Jacobo y Juan, el hermano de Jacobo. ³⁸Cuando llegaron a la casa del jefe de la sinagoga, Jesús notó el alboroto, y que la gente lloraba y daba grandes alaridos. ³⁹Entró y les dijo:

—¿Por qué tanto alboroto y llanto? La niña no está muerta sino dormida.

⁴⁰Entonces empezaron a burlarse de él, pero él los sacó a todos, tomó consigo al padre y a la madre de la niña y a los discípulos que estaban con él, y entró adonde estaba la niña. ⁴¹La tomó de la mano y le dijo:

ⁱ **4:40** *Todavía.* Var. *Cómo es que.* ʲ **5:1** *gerasenos.* Var. *gadarenos;* otra var. *gergesenos.*

—*Talita cum*k (que significa: Niña, a ti te digo, ilevántate!).

42La niña, que tenía doce años, se levantó en seguida y comenzó a andar. Ante este hecho todos se llenaron de asombro. 43Él dio órdenes estrictas de que nadie se enterara de lo ocurrido, y les mandó que le dieran de comer a la niña.

Un profeta sin honra
6:1-6 — Mt 13:54-58

6 Salió Jesús de allí y fue a su tierra, en compañía de sus discípulos. 2Cuando llegó el *sábado, comenzó a enseñar en la sinagoga.

—¿De dónde sacó éste tales cosas? —decían maravillados muchos de los que le oían—. ¿Qué sabiduría es ésta que se le ha dado? ¿Cómo se explican estos milagros que vienen de sus manos? 3¿No es acaso el carpintero, el hijo de María y hermano de *Jacobo, de José, de Judas y de Simón? ¿No están sus hermanas aquí con nosotros?

Y se *escandalizaban a causa de él. Por tanto, Jesús les dijo:

4—En todas partes se honra a un profeta, menos en su tierra, entre sus familiares y en su propia casa.

5En efecto, no pudo hacer allí ningún milagro, excepto sanar a unos pocos enfermos al imponerles las manos. 6Y él se quedó asombrado por la incredulidad de ellos.

Jesús envía a los doce
6:7-11 — Mt 10:1,9-14; Lc 9:1,3-5

Jesús recorría los alrededores, enseñando de pueblo en pueblo. 7Reunió a los doce, y comenzó a enviarlos de dos en dos, dándoles autoridad sobre los *espíritus malignos.

8Les ordenó que no llevaran nada para el camino, ni pan, ni bolsa, ni dinero en el cinturón, sino sólo un bastón. 9«Lleven sandalias —dijo—, pero no dos mudas de ropa.» 10Y añadió: «Cuando entren en una casa, quédense allí hasta que salgan del pueblo. 11Y si en algún lugar no los reciben bien o no los escuchan, al salir de allí sacúdanse el polvo de los pies, como un testimonio contra ellos.»

12Los doce salieron y exhortaban a la gente a que se *arrepintiera. 13También expulsaban a muchos demonios y sanaban a muchos enfermos, ungiéndolos con aceite.

Decapitación de Juan el Bautista
6:14-29 — Mt 14:1-12
6:14-16 — Lc 9:7-9

14El rey Herodes se enteró de esto, pues el nombre de Jesús se había hecho famoso. Algunos decían:l «Juan el Bautista ha *resucitado, y por eso tiene poder para realizar milagros.» 15Otros decían: «Es Elías.» Otros, en fin, afirmaban: «Es un profeta, como los de antes.» 16Pero cuando Herodes oyó esto, exclamó: «¡Juan, al que yo mandé que le cortaran la cabeza, ha resucitado!»

17En efecto, Herodes mismo había mandado que arrestaran a Juan y que lo encadenaran en la cárcel. Herodes se había casado con Herodías, esposa de Felipe su hermano, 18y Juan le había estado diciendo a Herodes: «La ley te prohíbe tener a la esposa de tu hermano.» 19Por eso Herodías le guardaba rencor a Juan y deseaba matarlo. Pero no había logrado hacerlo, 20ya que Herodes temía a Juan y lo protegía, pues sabía que era un hombre justo y *santo. Cuando He-

rodes oía a Juan, se quedaba muy desconcertado, pero lo escuchaba con gusto.

21Por fin se presentó la oportunidad. En su cumpleaños Herodes dio un banquete a sus altos oficiales, a los comandantes militares y a los notables de Galilea. 22La hija de Herodías entró en el banquete y bailó, y esto agradó a Herodes y a los invitados.

—Pídeme lo que quieras y te lo daré —le dijo el rey a la muchacha.

23Y le prometió bajo juramento:

—Te daré cualquier cosa que me pidas, aun cuando sea la mitad de mi reino.

24Ella salió a preguntarle a su madre:

—¿Qué debo pedir?

—La cabeza de Juan el Bautista —contestó.

25En seguida se fue corriendo la muchacha a presentarle al rey su petición:

—Quiero que ahora mismo me des en una bandeja la cabeza de Juan el Bautista.

26El rey se quedó angustiado, pero a causa de sus juramentos y en atención a los invitados, no quiso desairarla. 27Así que en seguida envió a un verdugo con la orden de llevarle la cabeza de Juan. El hombre fue, decapitó a Juan en la cárcel 28y volvió con la cabeza en una bandeja. Se la entregó a la muchacha, y ella se la dio a su madre. 29Al enterarse de esto, los discípulos de Juan fueron a recoger el cuerpo y le dieron sepultura.

Jesús alimenta a los cinco mil
6:32-44 — Mt 14:13-21; Lc 9:10-17; Jn 6:5-13

30Los apóstoles se reunieron con Jesús y le contaron lo que habían hecho y enseñado.

31Y como no tenían tiempo ni para comer, pues era tanta la gente que iba y venía, Jesús les dijo:

—Vengan conmigo ustedes solos a un lugar tranquilo y descansen un poco.

32Así que se fueron solos en la barca a un lugar solitario. 33Pero muchos que los vieron salir los reconocieron y, desde todos los poblados, corrieron por tierra hasta allá y llegaron antes que ellos. 34Cuando Jesús desembarcó y vio tanta gente, tuvo compasión de ellos, porque eran como ovejas sin pastor. Así que comenzó a enseñarles muchas cosas.

35Cuando ya se hizo tarde, se le acercaron sus discípulos y le dijeron:

—Éste es un lugar apartado y ya es muy tarde. 36Despide a la gente, para que vayan a los campos y pueblos cercanos y se compren algo de comer.

37—Denles ustedes mismos de comer —contestó Jesús.

—¡Eso costaría casi un año de trabajo!m —objetaron—. ¿Quieres que vayamos y gastemos todo ese dinero en pan para darles de comer?

38—¿Cuántos panes tienen ustedes? —preguntó—. Vayan a ver.

Después de averiguarlo, le dijeron:

—Cinco, y dos pescados.

39Entonces les mandó que hicieran que la gente se sentara por grupos sobre la hierba verde. 40Así que ellos se acomodaron en grupos de cien y de cincuenta. 41Jesús tomó los cinco panes y los dos pescados y, mirando al cielo, los bendijo. Luego partió los panes y se los dio a los discípulos para que se los repartieran a la gente. También repartió los dos pescados entre todos. 42Comieron todos hasta quedar satisfechos, 43y los discípulos recogieron doce canastas llenas de pedazos de pan y de pescado. 44Los que comieron fueron cinco mil.

---

k 5:41 *cum.* Var. *cumi.* l 6:14 *Algunos decían.* Var. *Él decía.* m 6:37 *casi un año de trabajo.* Lit. *doscientos *denarios.*

Jesús camina sobre el agua
6:45-51 — Mt 14:22-32; Jn 6:15-21
6:53-56 — Mt 14:34-36

45En seguida Jesús hizo que sus discípulos subieran a la barca y se le adelantaran al otro lado, a Betsaida, mientras él despedía a la multitud. 46Cuando se despidió, fue a la montaña para orar.

47Al anochecer, la barca se hallaba en medio del lago, y Jesús estaba en tierra solo. 48En la madrugada,[n] vio que los discípulos hacían grandes esfuerzos para remar, pues tenían el viento en contra. Se acercó a ellos caminando sobre el lago, e iba a pasarlos de largo. 49Los discípulos, al verlo caminar sobre el agua, creyeron que era un fantasma y se pusieron a gritar, 50llenos de miedo por lo que veían. Pero él habló en seguida con ellos y les dijo: «¡Cálmense! Soy yo. No tengan miedo.»

51Subió entonces a la barca con ellos, y el viento se calmó. Estaban sumamente asombrados, 52porque tenían la mente embotada y no habían comprendido lo de los panes.

53Después de cruzar el lago, llegaron a tierra en Genesaret y atracaron allí. 54Al bajar ellos de la barca, la gente en seguida reconoció a Jesús. 55Lo siguieron por toda aquella región y, a donde oían que él estaba, le llevaban en camillas a los que tenían enfermedades. 56Y dondequiera que iba, en pueblos, ciudades o caseríos, colocaban a los enfermos en las plazas. Le suplicaban que les permitiera tocar siquiera el borde de su manto, y quienes lo tocaban quedaban *sanos.

Lo puro y lo impuro
7:1-23 — Mt 15:1-20

7 Los *fariseos y algunos de los *maestros de la ley que habían llegado de Jerusalén se reunieron alrededor de Jesús, 2y vieron a algunos de sus discípulos que comían con manos *impuras, es decir, sin habérselas lavado. 3(En efecto, los fariseos y los demás judíos no comen nada sin primero cumplir con el rito de lavarse las manos, ya que están aferrados a la tradición de los *ancianos. 4Al regresar del mercado, no comen nada antes de lavarse. Y siguen otras muchas tradiciones, tales como el rito de lavar copas, jarras y bandejas de cobre.)[ñ] 5Así que los fariseos y los maestros de la ley le preguntaron a Jesús:

—¿Por qué no siguen tus discípulos la tradición de los ancianos, en vez de comer con manos impuras?

6Él les contestó:

—Tenía razón Isaías cuando profetizó acerca de ustedes, *hipócritas, según está escrito:

»"Este pueblo me honra con los labios,
pero su corazón está lejos de mí.
7En vano me adoran;
sus enseñanzas no son más que reglas
*humanas."[o]

8Ustedes han desechado los mandamientos divinos y se aferran a las tradiciones humanas.

9Y añadió:

—¡Qué buena manera tienen ustedes de dejar a un lado los mandamientos de Dios para mantener[p] sus propias tradiciones! 10Por ejemplo, Moisés dijo: "Honra a tu padre y a tu madre",[q] y: "El que maldiga a su padre o a su madre será condenado a muerte".[r] 11Ustedes, en cambio, enseñan que un hijo puede decirle a su padre o a su madre: "Cualquier ayuda que pudiera haberte dado es corbán" (es decir, ofrenda dedicada a Dios). 12En ese caso, el tal hijo ya no está obligado a hacer nada por su padre ni por su madre. 13Así, por la tradición que se transmiten entre ustedes, anulan la palabra de Dios. Y hacen muchas cosas parecidas.

14De nuevo Jesús llamó a la multitud.

—Escúchenme todos —dijo— y entiendan esto: 15Nada de lo que viene de afuera puede *contaminar a una persona. Más bien, lo que sale de la persona es lo que la contamina.[s]

17Después de que dejó a la gente y entró en la casa, sus discípulos le preguntaron sobre la comparación que había hecho.

18—¿Tampoco ustedes pueden entenderlo? —les dijo—. ¿No se dan cuenta de que nada de lo que entra en una persona puede contaminarla? 19Porque no entra en su corazón sino en su estómago, y después va a dar a la letrina.

Con esto Jesús declaraba *limpios todos los alimentos. 20Luego añadió:

—Lo que sale de la persona es lo que la contamina. 21Porque de adentro, del corazón humano, salen los malos pensamientos, la inmoralidad sexual, los robos, los homicidios, los adulterios, 22la avaricia, la maldad, el engaño, el libertinaje, la envidia, la calumnia, la arrogancia y la necedad. 23Todos estos males vienen de adentro y contaminan a la persona.

La fe de una mujer sirofenicia
7:24-30 — Mt 15:21-28

24Jesús partió de allí y fue a la región de Tiro.[t] Entró en una casa y no quería que nadie lo supiera, pero no pudo pasar inadvertido. 25De hecho, muy pronto se enteró de su llegada una mujer que tenía una niña poseída por un *espíritu maligno, así que fue y se arrojó a sus pies. 26Esta mujer era extranjera,[u] sirofenicia de nacimiento, y le rogaba que expulsara al demonio que tenía su hija.

27—Deja que primero se sacien los hijos —replicó Jesús—, porque no está bien quitarles el pan a los hijos y echárselo a los *perros.

28—Sí, Señor —respondió la mujer—, pero hasta los perros comen debajo de la mesa las migajas que dejan los hijos.

29Jesús le dijo:

—Por haberme respondido así, puedes irte tranquila; el demonio ha salido de tu hija.

30Cuando ella llegó a su casa, encontró a la niña acostada en la cama. El demonio ya había salido de ella.

Jesús sana a un sordomudo
7:31-37 — Mt 15:29-31

31Luego regresó Jesús de la región de Tiro y se dirigió por Sidón al mar de Galilea, internándose en la región de *Decápolis. 32Allí le llevaron un sordo tartamudo, y le suplicaban que pusiera la mano sobre él.

33Jesús lo apartó de la multitud para estar a solas con él, le puso los dedos en los oídos y le tocó la lengua con saliva.[v] 34Luego, mirando al cielo, suspiró profundamente y le dijo: «*¡Efatá!*» (que significa: ¡Ábrete!). 35Con esto, se le abrieron los oídos al hombre, se le destrabó la lengua y comenzó a hablar normalmente.

[n] **6:48** *En la madrugada.* Lit. *Alrededor de la cuarta vigilia de la noche.* [ñ] **7:4** *bandejas de cobre.* Var. *bandejas de cobre y divanes.* [o] **7:6,7** Is 29:13 [p] **7:9** *mantener.* Var. *establecer.* [q] **7:10** Éx 20:12; Dt 5:16 [r] **7:10** Éx 21:17; Lv 20:9 [s] **7:15** *contamina.* Var. *contamina. v. 16 El que tenga oídos para oír, que oiga.* [t] **7:24** *de Tiro.* Var. *de Tiro y Sidón.* [u] **7:26** *extranjera.* Lit. *helénica* (es decir, de cultura griega). [v] **7:33** *con saliva.* Lit. *escupiendo.*

36Jesús les mandó que no se lo dijeran a nadie, pero cuanto más se lo prohibía, tanto más lo seguían propagando. 37La gente estaba sumamente asombrada, y decía: «Todo lo hace bien. Hasta hace oír a los sordos y hablar a los mudos.»

Jesús alimenta a los cuatro mil

8:1-9 — Mt 15:32-39
8:11-21 — Mt 16:1-12

8 En aquellos días se reunió de nuevo mucha gente. Como no tenían nada que comer, Jesús llamó a sus discípulos y les dijo:

2—Siento compasión de esta gente porque ya llevan tres días conmigo y no tienen nada que comer. 3Si los despido a sus casas sin haber comido, se van a desmayar por el camino, porque algunos de ellos han venido de lejos.

4Los discípulos objetaron:

—¿Dónde se va a conseguir suficiente pan en este lugar despoblado para darles de comer?

5—¿Cuántos panes tienen? —les preguntó Jesús.

—Siete —respondieron.

6Entonces mandó que la gente se sentara en el suelo. Tomando los siete panes, dio gracias, los partió y se los fue dando a sus discípulos para que los repartieran a la gente, y así lo hicieron. 7Tenían además unos cuantos pescaditos. Dio gracias por ellos también y les dijo a los discípulos que los repartieran. 8La gente comió hasta quedar satisfecha. Después los discípulos recogieron siete cestas llenas de pedazos que sobraron. 9Los que comieron eran unos cuatro mil. Tan pronto como los despidió, 10Jesús se embarcó con sus discípulos y se fue a la región de Dalmanuta.

11Llegaron los *fariseos y comenzaron a discutir con Jesús. Para ponerlo a *prueba, le pidieron una señal del cielo. 12Él lanzó un profundo suspiro y dijo:w «¿Por qué pide esta generación una señal milagrosa? Les aseguro que no se le dará ninguna señal.» 13Entonces los dejó, volvió a embarcarse y cruzó al otro lado.

La levadura de los fariseos y la de Herodes

14A los discípulos se les había olvidado llevar comida, y sólo tenían un pan en la barca.

15—Tengan cuidado —les advirtió Jesús—; ¡ojo con la levadura de los *fariseos y con la de Herodes!

16Ellos comentaban entre sí: «Lo dice porque no tenemos pan.» 17Al darse cuenta de esto, Jesús les dijo:

—¿Por qué están hablando de que no tienen pan? ¿Todavía no ven ni entienden? ¿Tienen la mente embotada? 18¿Es que tienen ojos, pero no ven, y oídos, pero no oyen? ¿Acaso no recuerdan? 19Cuando partí los cinco panes para los cinco mil, ¿cuántas canastas llenas de pedazos recogieron?

—Doce —respondieron.

20—Y cuando partí los siete panes para los cuatro mil, ¿cuántas cestas llenas de pedazos recogieron?

—Siete.

21Entonces concluyó:

—¿Y todavía no entienden?

Jesús sana a un ciego en Betsaida

22Cuando llegaron a Betsaida, algunas personas le llevaron un ciego a Jesús y le rogaron que lo tocara. 23Él tomó de la mano al ciego y lo sacó fuera del pueblo. Después de escupirle en los ojos y de poner las manos sobre él, le preguntó:

—¿Puedes ver ahora?

24El hombre alzó los ojos y dijo:

—Veo gente; parecen árboles que caminan.

25Entonces le puso de nuevo las manos sobre los ojos, y el ciego fue curado: recobró la vista y comenzó a ver todo con claridad. 26Jesús lo mandó a su casa con esta advertencia:

—No vayas a entrar en el pueblo.x

La confesión de Pedro

8:27-29 — Mt 16:13-16; Lc 9:18-20

27Jesús y sus discípulos salieron hacia las aldeas de Cesarea de Filipo. En el camino les preguntó:

—¿Quién dice la gente que soy yo?

28—Unos dicen que Juan el Bautista, otros que Elías, y otros que uno de los profetas —contestaron.

29—Y ustedes, ¿quién dicen que soy yo?

—Tú eres el *Cristo —afirmó Pedro.

30Jesús les ordenó que no hablaran a nadie acerca de él.

Jesús predice su muerte

8:31—9:1 — Mt 16:21-28; Lc 9:22-27

31Luego comenzó a enseñarles:

—El Hijo del hombre tiene que sufrir muchas cosas y ser rechazado por los *ancianos, por los jefes de los sacerdotes y por los *maestros de la ley. Es necesario que lo maten y que a los tres días resucite.

32Habló de esto con toda claridad. Pedro lo llevó aparte y comenzó a reprenderlo. 33Pero Jesús se dio la vuelta, miró a sus discípulos, y reprendió a Pedro.

—¡Aléjate de mí, Satanás! —le dijo—. Tú no piensas en las cosas de Dios sino en las de los hombres.

34Entonces llamó a la multitud y a sus discípulos.

—Si alguien quiere ser mi discípulo —les dijo—, que se niegue a sí mismo, lleve su cruz y me siga. 35Porque el que quiera salvar su *vida, la perderá; pero el que pierda su vida por mi causa y por el *evangelio, la salvará. 36¿De qué sirve ganar el mundo entero si se pierde la vida? 37¿O qué se puede dar a cambio de la vida? 38Si alguien se avergüenza de mí y de mis palabras en medio de esta generación adúltera y pecadora, también el Hijo del hombre se avergonzará de él cuando venga en la gloria de su Padre con los santos ángeles.

9 Y añadió:

—Les aseguro que algunos de los aquí presentes no sufrirán la muerte sin antes haber visto el reino de Dios llegar con poder.

La transfiguración

9:2-8 — Lc 9:28-36
9:2-13 — Mt 17:1-13

2Seis días después Jesús tomó consigo a Pedro, a *Jacobo y a Juan, y los llevó a una montaña alta, donde estaban solos. Allí se transfiguró en presencia de ellos. 3Su ropa se volvió de un blanco resplandeciente como nadie en el mundo podría blanquearla. 4Y se les aparecieron Elías y Moisés, los cuales conversaban con Jesús. Tomando la palabra, 5Pedro le dijo a Jesús:

—Rabí, ¡qué bien que estemos aquí! Podemos levantar tres albergues: uno para ti, otro para Moisés y otro para Elías.

6No sabía qué decir, porque todos estaban asustados. 7Entonces apareció una nube que los envol-

---

w 8:12 *lanzó . . . dijo*. Lit. *suspirando en su espíritu dijo.*   x 8:26 *pueblo.* Var. *pueblo, ni a decírselo a nadie en el pueblo.*

vió, de la cual salió una voz que dijo: «Éste es mi Hijo amado. ¡Escúchenlo!»

⁸De repente, cuando miraron a su alrededor, ya no vieron a nadie más que a Jesús.

⁹Mientras bajaban de la montaña, Jesús les ordenó que no contaran a nadie lo que habían visto hasta que el Hijo del hombre se *levantara de entre los muertos. ¹⁰Guardaron el secreto, pero discutían entre ellos qué significaría eso de «levantarse de entre los muertos».

¹¹—¿Por qué dicen los *maestros de la ley que Elías tiene que venir primero? —le preguntaron.

¹²—Sin duda Elías ha de venir primero para restaurar todas las cosas —respondió Jesús—. Pero entonces, ¿cómo es que está escrito que el Hijo del hombre tiene que sufrir mucho y ser rechazado? ¹³Pues bien, les digo que Elías ya ha venido, y le hicieron todo lo que quisieron, tal como está escrito de él.

Jesús sana a un muchacho endemoniado
9:14-28,30-32 — Mt 17:14-19,22-23; Lc 9:37-45

¹⁴Cuando llegaron a donde estaban los otros discípulos, vieron que a su alrededor había mucha gente y que los *maestros de la ley discutían con ellos. ¹⁵Tan pronto como la gente vio a Jesús, todos se sorprendieron y corrieron a saludarlo.

¹⁶—¿Qué están discutiendo con ellos? —les preguntó.

¹⁷—Maestro —respondió un hombre de entre la multitud—, te he traído a mi hijo, pues está poseído por un espíritu que le ha quitado el habla. ¹⁸Cada vez que se apodera de él, lo derriba. Echa espumarajos, cruje los dientes y se queda rígido. Les pedí a tus discípulos que expulsaran al espíritu, pero no lo lograron.

¹⁹—¡Ah, generación incrédula! —respondió Jesús—. ¿Hasta cuándo tendré que estar con ustedes? ¿Hasta cuándo tendré que soportarlos? Tráiganme al muchacho.

²⁰Así que se lo llevaron. Tan pronto como vio a Jesús, el espíritu sacudió de tal modo al muchacho que éste cayó al suelo y comenzó a revolcarse echando espumarajos.

²¹—¿Cuánto tiempo hace que le pasa esto? —le preguntó Jesús al padre.

—Desde que era niño —contestó—. ²²Muchas veces lo ha echado al fuego y al agua para matarlo. Si puedes hacer algo, ten compasión de nosotros y ayúdanos.

²³—¿Cómo que si puedo? Para el que cree, todo es posible.

²⁴—¡Sí creo! —exclamó de inmediato el padre del muchacho—. ¡Ayúdame en mi poca fe!

²⁵Al ver Jesús que se agolpaba mucha gente, reprendió al *espíritu maligno.

—Espíritu sordo y mudo —dijo—, te mando que salgas y que jamás vuelvas a entrar en él.

²⁶El espíritu, dando un alarido y sacudiendo violentamente al muchacho, salió de él. Éste quedó como muerto, tanto que muchos decían: «Ya se murió.» ²⁷Pero Jesús lo tomó de la mano y lo levantó, y el muchacho se puso de pie.

²⁸Cuando Jesús entró en casa, sus discípulos le preguntaron en privado:

—¿Por qué nosotros no pudimos expulsarlo?

²⁹—Esta clase de demonios sólo puede ser expulsada a fuerza de oraciónᶻ —respondió Jesús.

³⁰Dejaron aquel lugar y pasaron por Galilea. Pero Jesús no quería que nadie lo supiera, ³¹porque estaba instruyendo a sus discípulos. Les decía: «El Hijo del hombre va a ser entregado en manos de los hombres. Lo matarán, y a los tres días de muerto resucitará.» ³²Pero ellos no entendían lo que quería decir con esto, y no se atrevían a preguntárselo.

¿Quién es el más importante?
9:33-37 — Mt 18:1-5; Lc 9:46-48

³³Llegaron a Capernaúm. Cuando ya estaba en casa, Jesús les preguntó:

—¿Qué venían discutiendo por el camino?

³⁴Pero ellos se quedaron callados, porque en el camino habían discutido entre sí quién era el más importante.

³⁵Entonces Jesús se sentó, llamó a los doce y les dijo:

—Si alguno quiere ser el primero, que sea el último de todos y el servidor de todos.

³⁶Luego tomó a un niño y lo puso en medio de ellos. Abrazándolo, les dijo:

³⁷—El que recibe en mi nombre a uno de estos niños, me recibe a mí; y el que me recibe a mí, no me recibe a mí sino al que me envió.

El que no está contra nosotros está a favor de nosotros
9:38-40 — Lc 9:49-50

³⁸—Maestro —dijo Juan—, vimos a uno que expulsaba demonios en tu nombre y se lo impedimos porque no es de los nuestros.ᵃ

³⁹—No se lo impidan —replicó Jesús—. Nadie que haga un milagro en mi nombre puede a la vez hablar mal de mí. ⁴⁰El que no está contra nosotros está a favor de nosotros. ⁴¹Les aseguro que cualquiera que les dé un vaso de agua en mi nombre por ser ustedes de *Cristo no perderá su recompensa.

El hacer pecar

⁴²»Pero si alguien hace *pecar a uno de estos pequeños que creen en mí, más le valdría que le ataran al cuello una piedra de molino y lo arrojaran al mar. ⁴³Si tu mano te hace pecar, córtatela. Más te vale entrar en la vida manco, que ir con las dos manos al infierno,ᵇ donde el fuego nunca se apaga.ᶜ ⁴⁵Y si tu pie te hace pecar, córtatelo. Más te vale entrar en la vida cojo, que ser arrojado con los dos pies al infierno.ᵈ ⁴⁷Y si tu ojo te hace pecar, sácatelo. Más te vale entrar tuerto en el reino de Dios, que ser arrojado con los dos ojos al infierno, ⁴⁸donde

> »"su gusano no muere,
>   y el fuego no se apaga".ᵉ

⁴⁹La sal con que todos serán sazonados es el fuego.

⁵⁰»La sal es buena, pero si deja de ser salada, ¿cómo le pueden volver a dar sabor? Que no falte la sal entre ustedes, para que puedan vivir en paz unos con otros.

El divorcio
10:1-12 — Mt 19:1-9

10 Jesús partió de aquel lugar y se fue a la región de Judea y al otro lado del Jordán. Otra vez se le reunieron las multitudes, y como era su costumbre, les enseñaba.

ʸ **9:14** *Cuando llegaron . . . vieron.* Var. *Cuando llegó . . . vio.*   ᶻ **9:29** *oración.* Var. *oración y ayuno.*   ᵃ **9:38** *no es de los nuestros.* Lit. *no nos sigue.*   ᵇ **9:43** *al infierno.* Lit. *a la *Gehenna;* también en vv. 45 y 47.   ᶜ **9:43** *apaga.* Var. *apaga, v. 44 donde "su gusano no muere, y el fuego no se apaga".*   ᵈ **9:45** *infierno.* Var. *infierno, v. 46 donde "su gusano no muere, y el fuego no se apaga".*   ᵉ **9:48** Is 66:24

2En eso, unos *fariseos se le acercaron y, para ponerlo a *prueba, le preguntaron:

—¿Está permitido que un hombre se divorcie de su esposa?

3—¿Qué les mandó Moisés? —replicó Jesús.

4—Moisés permitió que un hombre le escribiera un certificado de divorcio y la despidiera —contestaron ellos.

5—Esa ley la escribió Moisés para ustedes por lo obstinados que sonf —aclaró Jesús—. 6Pero al principio de la creación Dios "los hizo hombre y mujer".g 7"Por eso dejará el hombre a su padre y a su madre, y se unirá a su esposa,h 8y los dos llegarán a ser un solo cuerpo."i Así que ya no son dos, sino uno solo. 9Por tanto, lo que Dios ha unido, que no lo separe el hombre.

10Vueltos a casa, los discípulos le preguntaron a Jesús sobre este asunto.

11—El que se divorcia de su esposa y se casa con otra, comete adulterio contra la primera —respondió—. 12Y si la mujer se divorcia de su esposo y se casa con otro, comete adulterio.

Jesús y los niños
10:13-16 — Mt 19:13-15; Lc 18:15-17

13Empezaron a llevarle niños a Jesús para que los tocara, pero los discípulos reprendían a quienes los llevaban. 14Cuando Jesús se dio cuenta, se indignó y les dijo: «Dejen que los niños vengan a mí, y no se lo impidan, porque el reino de Dios es de quienes son como ellos. 15Les aseguro que el que no reciba el reino de Dios como un niño, de ninguna manera entrará en él.» 16Y después de abrazarlos, los bendecía poniendo las manos sobre ellos.

El joven rico
10:17-31 — Mt 19:16-30; Lc 18:18-30

17Cuando Jesús ya para irse, un hombre llegó corriendo y se postró delante de él.

—Maestro bueno —le preguntó—, ¿qué debo hacer para heredar la vida eterna?

18—¿Por qué me llamas bueno? —respondió Jesús—. Nadie es bueno sino sólo Dios. 19Ya sabes los mandamientos: "No mates, no cometas adulterio, no robes, no presentes falso testimonio, no defraudes, honra a tu padre y a tu madre."j

20—Maestro —dijo el hombre—, todo eso lo he cumplido desde que era joven.

21Jesús lo miró con amor y añadió:

—Una sola cosa te falta: anda, vende todo lo que tienes y dáselo a los pobres, y tendrás tesoro en el cielo. Luego ven y sígueme.

22Al oír esto, el hombre se desanimó y se fue triste porque tenía muchas riquezas.

23Jesús miró alrededor y les comentó a sus discípulos:

—¡Qué difícil es para los ricos entrar en el reino de Dios!

24Los discípulos se asombraron de sus palabras.

—Hijos, ¡qué difícil es entrark en el reino de Dios! —repitió Jesús—. 25Le resulta más fácil a un camello pasar por el ojo de una aguja, que a un rico entrar en el reino de Dios.

26Los discípulos se asombraron aun más, y decían entre sí: «Entonces, ¿quién podrá salvarse?»

27—Para los hombres es imposible —aclaró Jesús, mirándolos fijamente—, pero no para Dios; de hecho, para Dios todo es posible.

28—¿Qué de nosotros, que lo hemos dejado todo y te hemos seguido? —comenzó a reclamarle Pedro.

29—Les aseguro —respondió Jesús— que todo el que por mí causa y a la del *evangelio haya dejado casa, hermanos, hermanas, madre, padre, hijos o terrenos, 30recibirá cien veces más ahora en este tiempo (casas, hermanos, hermanas, madres, hijos y terrenos, aunque con persecuciones); y en la edad venidera, la vida eterna. 31Pero muchos de los primeros serán últimos, y los últimos, primeros.

Jesús predice de nuevo su muerte
10:32-34 — Mt 20:17-19; Lc 18:31-33

32Iban de camino subiendo a Jerusalén, y Jesús se les adelantó. Los discípulos estaban asombrados, y los otros que venían detrás tenían miedo. De nuevo tomó aparte a los doce y comenzó a decirles lo que le iba a suceder. 33«Ahora vamos rumbo a Jerusalén, y el Hijo del hombre será entregado a los jefes de los sacerdotes y a los *maestros de la ley. Ellos lo condenarán a muerte y lo entregarán a los *gentiles. 34Se burlarán de él, le escupirán, lo azotarán y lo matarán. Pero a los tres días resucitará.»

La petición de Jacobo y Juan
10:35-45 — Mt 20:20-28

35Se le acercaron *Jacobo y Juan, hijos de Zebedeo.

—Maestro —le dijeron—, queremos que nos concedas lo que te vamos a pedir.

36—¿Qué quieren que haga por ustedes?

37—Concédenos que en tu glorioso reino uno de nosotros se siente a tu *derecha y el otro a tu izquierda.

38—No saben lo que están pidiendo —les replicó Jesús—. ¿Pueden acaso beber el trago amargo de la copa que yo bebo, o pasar por la prueba del bautismo con el que voy a ser probado?l

39—Sí, podemos.

—Ustedes beberán de la copa que yo bebo —les respondió Jesús— y pasarán por la prueba del bautismo con el que voy a ser probado, 40pero el sentarse a mi derecha o a mi izquierda no me corresponde a mí concederlo. Eso ya está decidido.m

41Los otros diez, al oír la conversación, se indignaron contra Jacobo y Juan.

42Así que Jesús los llamó y les dijo:

—Como ustedes saben, los que se consideran jefes de las *naciones oprimen a los súbditos, y los altos oficiales abusan de su autoridad. 43Pero entre ustedes no debe ser así. Al contrario, el que quiera hacerse grande entre ustedes deberá ser su servidor, 44y el que quiera ser el primero deberá ser *esclavo de todos. 45Porque ni aun el Hijo del hombre vino para que le sirvan, sino para servir y para dar su *vida en rescate por muchos.

El ciego Bartimeo recibe la vista
10:46-52 — Mt 20:29-34; Lc 18:35-43

46Después llegaron a Jericó. Más tarde, salió Jesús de la ciudad acompañado de sus discípulos y de una gran multitud. Un mendigo ciego llamado Bartimeo (el hijo de Timeo) estaba sentado junto al camino. 47Al oír que el que venía era Jesús de Nazaret, se puso a gritar:

---

f 10:5 por lo obstinados que son. Lit. por su dureza de corazón. g 10:6 Gn 1:27 h 10:7 Var. no incluye: y se unirá a su esposa. i 10:8 Gn 2:24 j 10:19 Éx 20:12-16; Dt 5:16-20 k 10:24 es entrar. Var. es para los que confían en las riquezas entrar. l 10:38 beber . . . probado? Lit. beber la copa que yo bebo, o ser bautizados con el bautismo con que yo soy bautizado? m 10:40 concederlo. Eso ya está decidido. Lit. concederlo, sino para quienes está preparado.

—¡Jesús, Hijo de David, ten compasión de mí!

48Muchos lo reprendían para que se callara, pero él se puso a gritar aun más:

—¡Hijo de David, ten compasión de mí!

49Jesús se detuvo y dijo:

—Llámenlo.

Así que llamaron al ciego.

—¡Ánimo! —le dijeron—. ¡Levántate! Te llama.

50Él, arrojando la capa, dio un salto y se acercó a Jesús.

51—¿Qué quieres que haga por ti? —le preguntó.

—Rabí, quiero ver —respondió el ciego.

52—Puedes irte —le dijo Jesús—; tu fe te ha *sanado.

Al momento recobró la vista y empezó a seguir a Jesús por el camino.

La entrada triunfal
11:1-10 — Mt 21:1-9; Lc 19:29-38
11:7-10 — Jn 12:12-15

11 Cuando se acercaban a Jerusalén y llegaron a Betfagué y a Betania, junto al monte de los Olivos, Jesús envió a dos de sus discípulos 2con este encargo: «Vayan a la aldea que tienen enfrente. Tan pronto como entren en ella, encontrarán atado un burrito, en el que nunca se ha montado nadie. Desátenlo y tráiganlo acá. 3Y si alguien les dice: "¿Por qué hacen eso?", díganle: "El Señor lo necesita, y en seguida lo devolverá."»

4Fueron, encontraron un burrito afuera en la calle, atado a un portón, y lo desataron. 5Entonces algunos de los que estaban allí les preguntaron: «¿Qué hacen desatando el burrito?» 6Ellos contestaron como Jesús les había dicho, y les dejaron desatarlo. 7Le llevaron, pues, el burrito a Jesús. Luego pusieron encima sus mantos, y él se montó. 8Muchos tendieron sus mantos sobre el camino; otros usaron ramas que habían cortado en los campos. 9Tanto los que iban delante como los que iban detrás, gritaban:

—¡Hosanna!n

—¡Bendito el que viene en el nombre del Señor!ñ

10—¡Bendito el reino venidero de nuestro padre David!

—¡Hosanna en las alturas!

11Jesús entró en Jerusalén y fue al *templo. Después de observarlo todo, como ya era tarde, salió para Betania con los doce.

Jesús purifica el templo
11:12-14 — Mt 21:18-22
11:15-18 — Mt 21:12-16; Lc 19:45-47;
Jn 2:13-16

12Al día siguiente, cuando salían de Betania, Jesús tuvo hambre. 13Viendo a lo lejos una higuera que tenía hojas, fue a ver si hallaba algún fruto. Cuando llegó a ella sólo encontró hojas, porque no era tiempo de higos. 14«¡Nadie vuelva jamás a comer fruto de ti!», le dijo a la higuera. Y lo oyeron sus discípulos.

15Llegaron, pues, a Jerusalén. Jesús entró en el *temploo y comenzó a echar de allí a los que compraban y vendían. Volcó las mesas de los que cambiaban dinero y los puestos de los que vendían palomas, 16y no permitía que nadie atravesara el templo llevando mercancías. 17También les enseñaba con estas palabras: «¿No está escrito:

»"Mi casa será llamada
casa de oración para todas las *naciones"?p

Pero ustedes la han convertido en "cueva de ladrones".»q

18Los jefes de los sacerdotes y los *maestros de la ley lo oyeron y comenzaron a buscar la manera de matarlo, pues le temían, ya que toda la gente se maravillaba de sus enseñanzas.

19Cuando cayó la tarde, salieronr de la ciudad.

La higuera seca
11:20-24 — Mt 21:19-22

20Por la mañana, al pasar junto a la higuera, vieron que se había secado de raíz. 21Pedro, acordándose, le dijo a Jesús:

—¡Rabí, mira, se ha secado la higuera que maldijiste!

22—Tengan fe en Dios —respondió Jesús—. 23Les aseguros que si alguno le dice a este monte: "Quítate de ahí y tírate al mar", creyendo, sin abrigar la menor duda de que lo que dice sucederá, lo obtendrá. 24Por eso les digo: Crean que ya han recibido todo lo que estén pidiendo en oración, y lo obtendrán. 25Y cuando estén orando, si tienen algo contra alguien, perdónenlo, para que también su Padre que está en el cielo les perdone a ustedes sus pecados.t

La autoridad de Jesús puesta en duda
11:27-33 — Mt 21:23-27; Lc 20:1-8

27Llegaron de nuevo a Jerusalén, y mientras Jesús andaba por el *templo, se le acercaron los jefes de los sacerdotes, los *maestros de la ley y los *ancianos.

28—¿Con qué autoridad haces esto? —lo interrogaron—. ¿Quién te dio autoridad para actuar así?

29—Yo voy a hacerles una pregunta a ustedes —replicó él—. Contéstenmela, y les diré con qué autoridad hago esto: 30El bautismo de Juan, ¿procedía del cielo o de la tierra?u Respóndanme.

31Ellos se pusieron a discutir entre sí: «Si respondemos: "Del cielo", nos dirá: "Entonces, ¿por qué no le creyeron?" 32Pero si decimos: "De la tierra"...» Es que temían al pueblo, porque todos consideraban que Juan era realmente un profeta. 33Así que le respondieron a Jesús:

—No lo sabemos.

—Pues yo tampoco les voy a decir con qué autoridad hago esto.

Parábola de los labradores malvados
12:1-12 — Mt 21:33-46; Lc 20:9-19

12 Entonces comenzó Jesús a hablarles en parábolas: «Un hombre plantó un viñedo. Lo cercó, cavó un lagar y construyó una torre de vigilancia. Luego arrendó el viñedo a unos labradores y se fue de viaje. 2Llegada la cosecha, mandó un *siervo a los labradores para recibir de ellos una parte del fruto.

---

n 11:9 Expresión hebrea que significa «¡Salva!», y que llegó a ser una exclamación de alabanza; también en v. 10.
ñ 11:9 Sal 118:25,26 o 11:15 Es decir, en el área general del templo; también en v. 16. p 11:17 Is 56:7 q 11:17 Jer 7:11
r 11:19 salieron. Var. salió. s 11:22,23 Tengan fe . . . Les aseguro. Var. Si tienen fe . . . les aseguro. t 11:25 pecados. Var. pecados. 26Pero si ustedes no perdonan, tampoco su Padre que está en el cielo les perdonará a ustedes sus pecados. u 11:30 la tierra.
Lit. los hombres; también en v. 32.

3Pero ellos lo agarraron, lo golpearon y lo despidieron con las manos vacías. 4Entonces les mandó otro siervo; a éste le rompieron la cabeza y lo humillaron. 5Mandó a otro, y a éste lo mataron. Mandó a otros muchos, a unos los golpearon, a otros los mataron.

6»Le quedaba todavía uno, su hijo amado. Por último, lo mandó a él, pensando: "¡A mi hijo sí lo respetarán!" 7Pero aquellos labradores se dijeron unos a otros: "Éste es el heredero. Matémoslo, y la herencia será nuestra." 8Así que le echaron mano y lo mataron, y lo arrojaron fuera del viñedo.

9»¿Qué hará el dueño? Volverá, acabará con los labradores, y dará el viñedo a otros.

10¿No han leído ustedes esta Escritura:

»"La piedra que desecharon los constructores
ha llegado a ser la piedra angular;
11esto es obra del Señor,
y nos deja maravillados"?»v

12Cayendo en la cuenta de que la parábola iba dirigida contra ellos, buscaban la manera de arrestarlo. Pero temían a la multitud; así que lo dejaron y se fueron.

El pago de impuestos al césar
12:13-17 — Mt 22:15-22; Lc 20:20-26

13Luego enviaron a Jesús algunos de los *fariseos y de los herodianos para tenderle una trampa con sus mismas palabras. 14Al llegar le dijeron:

—Maestro, sabemos que eres un hombre íntegro. No te dejas influir por nadie porque no te fijas en las apariencias, sino que de verdad enseñas el camino de Dios. ¿Está permitido pagar impuestos al *césar o no? 15¿Debemos pagar o no?

Pero Jesús, sabiendo que fingían, les replicó:

—¿Por qué me tienden *trampas? Tráiganme una moneda romanaw para verla.

16Le llevaron la moneda, y él les preguntó:

—¿De quién son esta imagen y esta inscripción?

—Del césar —contestaron.

17—Denle, pues, al césar lo que es del césar, y a Dios lo que es de Dios.

Y se quedaron admirados de él.

El matrimonio en la resurrección
12:18-27 — Mt 22:23-33; Lc 20:27-38

18Entonces los saduceos, que dicen que no hay resurrección, fueron a verlo y le plantearon un problema:

19—Maestro, Moisés nos enseñó en sus escritos que si un hombre muere y deja a la viuda sin hijos, el hermano de ese hombre tiene que casarse con la viuda para que su hermano tenga descendencia. 20Ahora bien, había siete hermanos. El primero se casó y murió sin dejar descendencia. 21El segundo se casó con la viuda, pero también murió sin dejar descendencia. Lo mismo le pasó al tercero. 22En fin, ninguno de los siete dejó descendencia. Por último, murió también la mujer. 23Cuando resuciten, ¿de cuál será esposa esta mujer, ya que los siete estuvieron casados con ella?

24—¿Acaso no andan ustedes equivocados? —les replicó Jesús—. ¡Es que desconocen las Escrituras y el poder de Dios! 25Cuando resuciten los muertos, no se casarán ni serán dados en casamiento, sino que serán como los ángeles que están en el cielo. 26Pero en cuanto a que los muertos resucitan, ¿no han leído en el libro de Moisés, en el pasaje sobre la zarza, cómo Dios le dijo: "Yo soy el Dios de Abraham, de Isaac y de Jacob"?x 27Él no es Dios de muertos, sino de vivos. ¡Ustedes andan muy equivocados!

El mandamiento más importante
12:28-34 — Mt 22:34-40

28Uno de los *maestros de la ley se acercó y los oyó discutiendo. Al ver lo bien que Jesús les había contestado, le preguntó:

—De todos los mandamientos, ¿cuál es el más importante?

29—El más importante es: "Oye, Israel. El Señor nuestro Dios es el único Señory —contestó Jesús—. 30Ama al Señor tu Dios con todo tu corazón, con toda tu alma, con toda tu mente y con todas tus fuerzas."z 31El segundo es: "Ama a tu prójimo como a ti mismo."a No hay otro mandamiento más importante que éstos.

32—Bien dicho, Maestro —respondió el hombre—. Tienes razón al decir que Dios es uno solo y que no hay otro fuera de él. 33Amarlo con todo el corazón, con todo el entendimiento y con todas las fuerzas, y amar al prójimo como a uno mismo, es más importante que todos los holocaustos y sacrificios.

34Al ver Jesús que había respondido con inteligencia, le dijo:

—No estás lejos del reino de Dios.

Y desde entonces nadie se atrevió a hacerle más preguntas.

¿De quién es hijo el Cristo?
12:35-37 — Mt 22:41-46; Lc 20:41-44
12:38-40 — Mt 23:1-7; Lc 20:45-47

35Mientras enseñaba en el *templo, Jesús les propuso:

—¿Cómo es que los *maestros de la ley dicen que el *Cristo es hijo de David? 36David mismo, hablando por el Espíritu Santo, declaró:

»"Dijo el Señor a mi Señor:
'Siéntate a mi *derecha,
hasta que ponga a tus enemigos
debajo de tus pies.' "b

37Si David mismo lo llama "Señor", ¿cómo puede ser su hijo?

La muchedumbre lo escuchaba con agrado. 38Como parte de su enseñanza Jesús decía:

—Tengan cuidado de los *maestros de la ley. Les gusta pasearse con ropas ostentosas y que los saluden en las plazas, 39ocupar los primeros asientos en las sinagogas y los lugares de honor en los banquetes. 40Se apoderan de los bienes de las viudas y a la vez hacen largas plegarias para impresionar a los demás. Éstos recibirán peor castigo.

La ofrenda de la viuda
12:41-44 — Lc 21:1-4

41Jesús se sentó frente al lugar donde se depositaban las ofrendas, y estuvo observando cómo la gente echaba sus monedas en las alcancías del *templo. Muchos ricos echaban grandes cantidades. 42Pero una viuda pobre llegó y echó dos moneditas de muy poco valor.c

43Jesús llamó a sus discípulos y les dijo: «Les aseguro que esta viuda pobre ha echado en el tesoro más que todos los demás. 44Éstos dieron de lo que les

v 12:11 Sal 118:22,23 w 12:15 una moneda romana. Lit. un *denario. x 12:26 Éx 3:6 y 12:29 Dios es el único Señor. Alt. Dios, el Señor es uno. z 12:30 Dt 6:4,5 a 12:31 Lv 19:18 b 12:36 Sal 110:1 c 12:42 dos moneditas de muy poco valor. Lit. dos *lepta, que es un cuadrante.

sobraba; pero ella, de su pobreza, echó todo lo que tenía, todo su sustento.»

Señales del fin del mundo
13:1-37 — Mt 24:1-51; Lc 21:5-36

13 Cuando salía Jesús del *templo, le dijo uno de sus discípulos:

—¡Mira, Maestro! ¡Qué piedras! ¡Qué edificios!

2—¿Ves todos estos grandiosos edificios? —contestó Jesús—. No quedará piedra sobre piedra; todo será derribado.

3Más tarde estaba Jesús sentado en el monte de los Olivos, frente al templo. Y Pedro, *Jacobo, Juan y Andrés le preguntaron en privado:

4—Dinos, ¿cuándo sucederá eso? ¿Y cuál será la señal de que todo está a punto de cumplirse?

5—Tengan cuidado de que nadie los engañe —comenzó Jesús a advertirles—. 6Vendrán muchos que, usando mi nombre, dirán: "Yo soy", y engañarán a muchos. 7Cuando sepan de guerras y de rumores de guerras, no se alarmen. Es necesario que eso suceda, pero no será todavía el fin. 8Se levantará nación contra nación, y reino contra reino. Habrá terremotos por todas partes; también habrá hambre. Esto será apenas el comienzo de los dolores.

9»Pero ustedes cuídense. Los entregarán a los tribunales y los azotarán en las sinagogas. Por mi causa comparecerán ante gobernadores y reyes para dar testimonio ante ellos. 10Pero primero tendrá que predicarse el *evangelio a todas las *naciones. 11Y cuando los arresten y los sometan a juicio, no se preocupen de antemano por lo que van a decir. Sólo declaren lo que se les dé a decir en ese momento, porque no serán ustedes los que hablen, sino el Espíritu Santo.

12»El hermano entregará a la muerte al hermano, y el padre al hijo. Los hijos se rebelarán contra sus padres y les darán muerte. 13Todo el mundo los odiará a ustedes por causa de mi nombre, pero el que se mantenga firme hasta el fin será salvo.

14»Ahora bien, cuando vean "el horrible sacrilegio"d donde no debe estar (el que lee, que lo entienda), entonces los que estén en Judea huyan a las montañas. 15El que esté en la azotea no baje ni entre en casa para llevarse nada. 16Y el que esté en el campo no regrese para buscar su capa. 17¡Ay de las que estén embarazadas o amamantando en aquellos días! 18Oren para que no suceda en invierno, 19porque serán días de tribulación como no la ha habido desde el principio, cuando Dios creó el mundo,e ni la habrá jamás. 20Si el Señor no hubiera acortado esos días, nadie sobreviviría. Pero por causa de los que él ha elegido, los ha acortado. 21Entonces, si alguien les dice a ustedes: "¡Miren, aquí está el *Cristo!" o "¡Miren, allí está!", no lo crean. 22Porque surgirán falsos Cristos y falsos profetas que harán señales y milagros para engañar, de ser posible, aun a los elegidos. 23Así que tengan cuidado; los he prevenido de todo.

24»Pero en aquellos días, después de esa tribulación,

»"se oscurecerá el sol
    y no brillará más la luna;
25las estrellas caerán del cielo
    y los cuerpos celestes serán sacudidos".f

26»Verán entonces al Hijo del hombre venir en las nubes con gran poder y gloria. 27Y él enviará a sus ángeles para reunir de los cuatro vientos a los elegidos, desde los confines de la tierra hasta los confines del cielo.

28»Aprendan de la higuera esta lección: Tan pronto como se ponen tiernas sus ramas y brotan sus hojas, ustedes saben que el verano está cerca. 29Igualmente, cuando vean que suceden estas cosas, sepan que el tiempo está cerca, a las puertas. 30Les aseguro que no pasará esta generación hasta que todas estas cosas sucedan. 31El cielo y la tierra pasarán, pero mis palabras jamás pasarán.

Se desconocen el día y la hora

32»Pero en cuanto al día y la hora, nadie lo sabe, ni siquiera los ángeles en el cielo, ni el Hijo, sino sólo el Padre. 33¡Estén alerta! ¡Vigilen!g Porque ustedes no saben cuándo llegará ese momento. 34Es como cuando un hombre sale de viaje y deja su casa al cuidado de sus siervos, cada uno con su tarea, y le manda al portero que vigile.

35»Por lo tanto, manténganse despiertos, porque no saben cuándo volverá el dueño de la casa, si al atardecer, o a la medianoche, o al canto del gallo, o al amanecer; 36no sea que venga de repente y los encuentre dormidos. 37Lo que les digo a ustedes, se lo digo a todos: ¡Manténganse despiertos!

Una mujer unge a Jesús en Betania
14:1-11 — Mt 26:2-16
14:1-2,10-11 — Lc 22:1-6

14 Faltaban sólo dos días para la Pascua y para la fiesta de los Panes sin levadura. Los jefes de los sacerdotes y los *maestros de la ley buscaban con artimañas cómo arrestar a Jesús para matarlo. 2Por eso decían: «No durante la fiesta, no sea que se amotine el pueblo.»

3En Betania, mientras estaba él *sentado a la mesa en casa de Simón llamado el leproso, llegó una mujer con un frasco de alabastro lleno de un perfume muy costoso, hecho de nardo puro. Rompió el frasco y derramó el perfume sobre la cabeza de Jesús.

4Algunos de los presentes comentaban indignados:

—¿Para qué este desperdicio de perfume? 5Podía haberse vendido por muchísimo dineroh para darlo a los pobres.

Y la reprendían con severidad.

6—Déjenla en paz —dijo Jesús—. ¿Por qué la molestan? Ella ha hecho una obra hermosa conmigo. 7A los pobres siempre los tendrán con ustedes, y podrán ayudarlos cuando quieran; pero a mí no me van a tener siempre. 8Ella hizo lo que pudo. Ungió mi cuerpo de antemano, preparándolo para la sepultura. 9Les aseguro que en cualquier parte del mundo donde se predique el *evangelio, se contará también, en memoria de esta mujer, lo que ella hizo.

10Judas Iscariote, uno de los doce, fue a los jefes de los sacerdotes para entregarles a Jesús. 11Ellos se alegraron al oírlo, y prometieron darle dinero. Así que él buscaba la ocasión propicia para entregarlo.

La Cena del Señor
14:12-26 — Mt 26:17-30; Lc 22:7-23
14:22-25 — 1Co 11:23-25

12El primer día de la fiesta de los Panes sin levadura, cuando se acostumbraba sacrificar el cordero de la Pascua, los discípulos le preguntaron a Jesús:

---

d **13:14** *el horrible sacrilegio*. Lit. *la abominación de desolación*; Dn 9:27; 11:31; 12:11. e **13:19** *desde . . . mundo*. Lit. *desde el principio de la creación que creó Dios hasta ahora*. f **13:25** Is 13:10; 34:4 g **13:33** *¡Vigilen!* Var. *¡Vigilen y oren!* h **14:5** *muchísimo dinero*. Lit. *más de trescientos *denarios*.

—¿Dónde quieres que vayamos a hacer los preparativos para que comas la Pascua?

¹³Él envió a dos de sus discípulos con este encargo:

—Vayan a la ciudad y les saldrá al encuentro un hombre que lleva un cántaro de agua. Síganlo, ¹⁴y allí donde entre díganle al dueño: "El Maestro pregunta: ¿Dónde está la sala en la que pueda comer la Pascua con mis discípulos?" ¹⁵Él les mostrará en la planta alta una sala amplia, amueblada y arreglada. Preparen allí nuestra cena.

¹⁶Los discípulos salieron, entraron en la ciudad y encontraron todo tal y como se los había dicho Jesús. Así que prepararon la Pascua.

¹⁷Al anochecer llegó Jesús con los doce. ¹⁸Mientras estaban *sentados a la mesa comiendo, dijo:

—Les aseguro que uno de ustedes, que está comiendo conmigo, me va a traicionar.

¹⁹Ellos se pusieron tristes, y uno tras otro empezaron a preguntarle:

—¿Acaso seré yo?

²⁰—Es uno de los doce —contestó—, uno que moja el pan conmigo en el plato. ²¹A la verdad, el Hijo del hombre se irá tal como está escrito de él, pero ¡ay de aquel que lo traiciona! Más le valdría a ese hombre no haber nacido.

²²Mientras comían, Jesús tomó pan y lo bendijo. Luego lo partió y se lo dio a ellos, diciéndoles:

—Tomen; esto es mi cuerpo.

²³Después tomó una copa, dio gracias y se la dio a ellos, y todos bebieron de ella.

²⁴—Esto es mi sangre del pacto,ⁱ que es derramada por muchos —les dijo—. ²⁵Les aseguro que no volveré a beber del fruto de la vid hasta aquel día en que beba el vino nuevo en el reino de Dios.

²⁶Después de cantar los salmos, salieron al monte de los Olivos.

Jesús predice la negación de Pedro
14:27-31 — Mt 26:31-35

²⁷—Todos ustedes me abandonarán —les dijo Jesús—, porque está escrito:

»"Heriré al pastor,
    y se dispersarán las ovejas."ʲ

²⁸Pero después de que yo resucite, iré delante de ustedes a Galilea.

²⁹—Aunque todos te abandonen, yo no —declaró Pedro.

³⁰—Te aseguro —le contestó Jesús— que hoy, esta misma noche, antes de que el gallo cante por segunda vez,ᵏ me negarás tres veces.

³¹—Aunque tenga que morir contigo —insistió Pedro con vehemencia—, jamás te negaré.

Y los demás dijeron lo mismo.

Getsemaní
14:32-42 — Mt 26:36-46; Lc 22:40-46

³²Fueron a un lugar llamado Getsemaní, y Jesús les dijo a sus discípulos: «Siéntense aquí mientras yo oro.» ³³Se llevó a Pedro, a *Jacobo y a Juan, y comenzó a sentir temor y tristeza. ³⁴«Es tal la angustia que me invade que me siento morir —les dijo—. Quédense aquí y vigilen.»

³⁵Yendo un poco más allá, se postró en tierra y empezó a orar que, de ser posible, no tuviera él que pasar por aquella hora. ³⁶Decía: «*Abba, Padre, todo es posible para ti. No me hagas beber este trago amargo,ˡ pero no sea lo que yo quiero, sino lo que quieres tú.»

³⁷Luego volvió a sus discípulos y los encontró dormidos. «Simón —le dijo a Pedro—, ¿estás dormido? ¿No pudiste mantenerte despierto ni una hora? ³⁸Vigilen y oren para que no caigan en *tentación. El espíritu está dispuesto, pero el cuerpoᵐ es débil.»

³⁹Una vez más se retiró e hizo la misma oración. ⁴⁰Cuando volvió, los encontró dormidos otra vez, porque se les cerraban los ojos de sueño. No sabían qué decirle. ⁴¹Al volver por tercera vez, les dijo: «¿Siguen durmiendo y descansando? ¡Se acabó! Ha llegado la hora. Miren, el Hijo del hombre va a ser entregado en manos de *pecadores. ⁴²¡Levántense! ¡Vámonos! ¡Ahí viene el que me traiciona!»

Arresto de Jesús
14:43-50 — Mt 26:14-56; Lc 22:47-50;
Jn 18:3-11

⁴³Todavía estaba hablando Jesús cuando de repente llegó Judas, uno de los doce. Lo acompañaba una turba armada con espadas y palos, enviada por los jefes de los sacerdotes, los *maestros de la ley y los *ancianos.

⁴⁴El traidor les había dado esta contraseña: «Al que yo le dé un beso, ése es; arréstenlo y llévenselo bien asegurado.»

⁴⁵Tan pronto como llegó, Judas se acercó a Jesús.

—¡Rabí! —le dijo, y lo besó.

⁴⁶Entonces los hombres prendieron a Jesús. ⁴⁷Pero uno de los que estaban ahí desenfundó la espada e hirió al siervo del sumo sacerdote, cortándole una oreja.

⁴⁸—¿Acaso soy un bandidoⁿ —dijo Jesús—, para que vengan con espadas y palos a arrestarme? ⁴⁹Día tras día estaba con ustedes, enseñando en el *templo, y no me prendieron. Pero es preciso que se cumplan las Escrituras.

⁵⁰Entonces todos lo abandonaron y huyeron. ⁵¹Cierto joven que se cubría con sólo una sábana iba siguiendo a Jesús. Lo detuvieron, ⁵²pero él soltó la sábana y escapó desnudo.

Jesús ante el Consejo
14:53-65 — Mt 26:57-68; Jn 18:12-13,19-24
14:61-63 — Lc 22:67-71

⁵³Llevaron a Jesús ante el sumo sacerdote y se reunieron allí todos los jefes de los sacerdotes, los *ancianos y los *maestros de la ley. ⁵⁴Pedro lo siguió de lejos hasta dentro del patio del sumo sacerdote. Allí se sentó con los guardias, y se calentaba junto al fuego.

⁵⁵Los jefes de los sacerdotes y el *Consejo en pleno buscaban alguna prueba contra Jesús para poder condenarlo a muerte, pero no la encontraban. ⁵⁶Muchos testificaban falsamente contra él, pero sus declaraciones no coincidían. ⁵⁷Entonces unos decidieron dar este falso testimonio contra él:

⁵⁸—Nosotros le oímos decir: "Destruiré este *templo hecho por hombres y en tres días construiré otro, no hecho por hombres."

⁵⁹Pero ni aun así concordaban sus declaraciones.

⁶⁰Poniéndose de pie en el medio, el sumo sacerdote interrogó a Jesús:

—¿No tienes nada que contestar? ¿Qué significan estas denuncias en tu contra?

ⁱ 14:24 del pacto. Var. del nuevo pacto (véase Lc 22:20). ʲ 14:27 Zac 13:7 ᵏ 14:30 Var. no incluye: por segunda vez.
ˡ 14:36 No . . . amargo. Lit. Quita de mí esta copa. ᵐ 14:38 el cuerpo. Lit. la *carne. ⁿ 14:48 bandido. Alt. Insurgente.

61Pero Jesús se quedó callado y no contestó nada.

—¿Eres el *Cristo, el Hijo del Bendito? —le preguntó de nuevo el sumo sacerdote.

62—Sí, yo soy —dijo Jesús—. Y ustedes verán al Hijo del hombre sentado a la *derecha del Todopoderoso, y viniendo en las nubes del cielo.

63—¿Para qué necesitamos más testigos? —dijo el sumo sacerdote, rasgándose las vestiduras—. 64¡Ustedes han oído la *blasfemia! ¿Qué les parece?

Todos ellos lo condenaron como digno de muerte. 65Algunos comenzaron a escupirle; le vendaron los ojos y le daban puñetazos.

—¡Profetiza! —le gritaban.

Los guardias también le daban bofetadas.

Pedro niega a Jesús
14:66-72 — Mt 26:69-75; Lc 22:56-62; Jn 18:16-18,25-27

66Mientras Pedro estaba abajo en el patio, pasó una de las criadas del sumo sacerdote. 67Cuando vio a Pedro calentándose, se fijó en él.

—Tú también estabas con ese nazareno, con Jesús —le dijo ella.

68Pero él lo negó:

—No lo conozco. Ni siquiera sé de qué estás hablando.

Y salió afuera, a la entrada.ñ

69Cuando la criada lo vio allí, les dijo de nuevo a los presentes:

—Éste es uno de ellos.

70Él lo volvió a negar.

Poco después, los que estaban allí le dijeron a Pedro:

—Seguro que tú eres uno de ellos, pues eres galileo.

71Él comenzó a echarse maldiciones.

—¡No conozco a ese hombre del que hablan! —les juró.

72Al instante un gallo cantó por segunda vez.o Pedro se acordó de lo que Jesús le había dicho: «Antes de que el gallo cante por segunda vez,p me negarás tres veces.» Y se echó a llorar.

Jesús ante Pilato
15:2-15 — Mt 27:11-26; Lc 23:2-3,18-25; Jn 18:29—19:16

15 Tan pronto como amaneció, los jefes de los sacerdotes, con los *ancianos, los *maestros de la ley y el *Consejo en pleno, llegaron a una decisión. Ataron a Jesús, se lo llevaron y se lo entregaron a Pilato.

2—¿Eres tú el rey de los judíos? —le preguntó Pilato.

—Tú mismo lo dices —respondió.

3Los jefes de los sacerdotes se pusieron a acusarlo de muchas cosas.

4—¿No vas a contestar? —le preguntó de nuevo Pilato—. Mira de cuántas cosas te están acusando.

5Pero Jesús ni aun con eso contestó nada, de modo que Pilato se quedó asombrado.

6Ahora bien, durante la fiesta él acostumbraba soltarles un preso, el que la gente pidiera. 7Y resulta que un hombre llamado Barrabás estaba encarcelado con los rebeldes condenados por haber cometido homici-

dio en una insurrección. 8Subió la multitud y le pidió a Pilato que le concediera lo que acostumbraba.

9—¿Quieren que les suelte al rey de los judíos? —replicó Pilato, 10porque se daba cuenta de que los jefes de los sacerdotes habían entregado a Jesús por envidia.

11Pero los jefes de los sacerdotes incitaron a la multitud para que Pilato les soltara más bien a Barrabás.

12—¿Y qué voy a hacer con el que ustedes llaman el rey de los judíos? —les preguntó Pilato.

13—¡Crucifícalo! —gritaron.

14—¿Por qué? ¿Qué crimen ha cometido?

Pero ellos gritaron aun más fuerte:

—¡Crucifícalo!

15Como quería satisfacer a la multitud, Pilato les soltó a Barrabás; a Jesús lo mandó azotar, y lo entregó para que lo crucificaran.

Los soldados se burlan de Jesús
15:16-20 — Mt 27:27-31

16Los soldados llevaron a Jesús al interior del palacio (es decir, al pretorio) y reunieron a toda la tropa. 17Le pusieron un manto de color púrpura; luego trenzaron una corona de espinas, y se la colocaron.

18—¡Salve, rey de los judíos! —lo aclamaban.

19Lo golpeaban en la cabeza con una caña y le escupían. Doblando la rodilla, le rendían homenaje. 20Después de burlarse de él, le quitaron el manto y le pusieron su propia ropa. Por fin, lo sacaron para crucificarlo.

La crucifixión
15:22-32 — Mt 27:33-44; Lc 23:33-43; Jn 19:17-24

21A uno que pasaba por allí de vuelta del campo, un tal Simón de Cirene, padre de Alejandro y de Rufo, lo obligaron a llevar la cruz. 22Condujeron a Jesús al lugar llamado Gólgota (que significa: Lugar de la Calavera). 23Le ofrecieron vino mezclado con mirra, pero no lo tomó. 24Y lo crucificaron. Repartieron su ropa, echando suertes para ver qué le tocaría a cada uno.

25Eran las nueve de la mañanaq cuando lo crucificaron. 26Un letrero tenía escrita la causa de su condena: «EL REY DE LOS JUDÍOS.» 27Con él crucificaron a dos bandidos,r uno a su derecha y otro a su izquierda.s 29Los que pasaban meneaban la cabeza y *blasfemaban contra él.

—¡Eh! Tú que destruyes el *templo y en tres días lo reconstruyes —decían—, 30¡baja de la cruz y sálvate a ti mismo!

31De la misma manera se burlaban de él los jefes de los sacerdotes junto con los maestros de la ley.

—Salvó a otros —decían—, ¡pero no puede salvarse a sí mismo! 32Que baje ahora de la cruz ese *Cristo, el rey de Israel, para que veamos y creamos. También lo insultaban los que estaban crucificados con él.

Muerte de Jesús
15:33-41 — Mt 27:45-56; Lc 23:44-49

33Desde el mediodía y hasta la media tarde quedó toda la tierra en oscuridad. 34A las tres de la tardet Jesús gritó a voz en cuello:

ñ **14:68** entrada. Var. entrada; y cantó el gallo. o **14:72** Var. no incluye: por segunda vez. p **14:72** Var. no incluye: por segunda vez. q **15:25** Eran . . . mañana. Lit. Era la hora tercera. r **15:27** bandidos. Alt. insurgentes. s **15:27** izquierda. Var. izquierda. v. 28 Así se cumplió la Escritura que dice: «Fue contado con los malhechores.» (Is 53:12) t **15:33,34** Desde . . . tarde. Lit. Y llegando la hora sexta vino oscuridad sobre toda la tierra hasta la hora novena. v. 34 Y en la hora novena.

—*Eloi, Eloi, ¿lama sabactani?* (que significa: "Dios mío, Dios mío, ¿por qué me has desamparado?").u

35Cuando lo oyeron, algunos de los que estaban cerca dijeron:

—Escuchen, está llamando a Elías.

36Un hombre corrió, empapó una esponja en vinagre, la puso en una caña y se la ofreció a Jesús para que bebiera.

—Déjenlo, a ver si viene Elías a bajarlo —dijo.

37Entonces Jesús, lanzando un fuerte grito, expiró.

38La cortina del *santuario del templo se rasgó en dos, de arriba abajo. 39Y el centurión, que estaba frente a Jesús, al oír el grito yv ver cómo murió, dijo:

—¡Verdaderamente este hombre era el Hijow de Dios!

40Algunas mujeres miraban desde lejos. Entre ellas estaban María Magdalena, María la madre de *Jacobo el menor y de José, y Salomé. 41Estas mujeres lo habían seguido y atendido cuando estaba en Galilea. Además había allí muchas otras que habían subido con él a Jerusalén.

Sepultura de Jesús
15:42-47 — Mt 27:57-61; Lc 23:50-56; Jn 19:38-42

42Era el día de preparación (es decir, la víspera del *sábado). Así que al atardecer, 43José de Arimatea, miembro distinguido del *Consejo, y que también esperaba el reino de Dios, se atrevió a presentarse ante Pilato para pedirle el cuerpo de Jesús. 44Pilato, sorprendido de que ya hubiera muerto, llamó al centurión y le preguntó si hacía mucho quex había muerto. 45Una vez informado por el centurión, le entregó el cuerpo a José. 46Entonces José bajó el cuerpo, lo envolvió en una sábana que había comprado, y lo puso en un sepulcro cavado en la roca. Luego hizo rodar una piedra a la entrada del sepulcro. 47María Magdalena y María la madre de José vieron dónde lo pusieron.

La resurrección
16:1-8 — Mt 28:1-8; Lc 24:1-10

16 Cuando pasó el *sábado, María Magdalena, María la madre de *Jacobo, y Salomé compraron especias aromáticas para ir a ungir el cuerpo de Jesús. 2Muy de mañana el primer día de la semana, apenas salido el sol, se dirigieron al sepulcro.

3Iban diciéndose unas a otras: «¿Quién nos quitará la piedra de la entrada del sepulcro?» 4Pues la piedra era muy grande.

Pero al fijarse bien, se dieron cuenta de que estaba corrida. 5Al entrar en el sepulcro vieron a un joven vestido con un manto blanco, sentado a la derecha, y se asustaron.

6—No se asusten —les dijo—. Ustedes buscan a Jesús el nazareno, el que fue crucificado. ¡Ha resucitado! No está aquí. Miren el lugar donde lo pusieron. 7Pero vayan a decirles a los discípulos y a Pedro: "Él va delante de ustedes a Galilea. Allí lo verán, tal como les dijo."

8Temblorosas y desconcertadas, las mujeres salieron huyendo del sepulcro. No dijeron nada a nadie, porque tenían miedo.y

Apariciones y ascensión de Jesús

9Cuando Jesús resucitó en la madrugada del primer día de la semana, se apareció primero a María Magdalena, de la que había expulsado siete demonios. 10Ella fue y avisó a los que habían estado con él, que estaban lamentándose y llorando. 11Pero ellos, al oír que Jesús estaba vivo y que ella lo había visto, no lo creyeron.

12Después se apareció Jesús en otra forma a dos de ellos que iban de camino al campo. 13Éstos volvieron y avisaron a los demás, pero no les creyeron a ellos tampoco.

14Por último se apareció Jesús a los once mientras comían; los reprendió por su falta de fe y por su obstinación en no creerles a los que lo habían visto *resucitado.

15Les dijo: «Vayan por todo el mundo y anuncien las buenas *nuevas a toda criatura.z 16El que crea y sea bautizado será salvo, pero el que no crea será condenado. 17Estas señales acompañarán a los que crean: en mi nombre expulsarán demonios; hablarán en nuevas lenguas; 18tomarán en sus manos serpientes; y cuando beban algo venenoso, no les hará daño alguno; pondrán las manos sobre los enfermos, y éstos recobrarán la salud.»

19Después de hablar con ellos, el Señor Jesús fue llevado al cielo y se sentó a la *derecha de Dios. 20Los discípulos salieron y predicaron por todas partes, y el Señor los ayudaba en la obra y confirmaba su palabra con las señales que la acompañaban.

---

u 15:34 Sal 22:1   v 15:39 Var. no incluye: *oír el grito y.*   w 15:39 *era el Hijo.* Alt. *era hijo.*   x 15:44 *hacía mucho que.* Var. *ya.*   y 16:8 Los mss. más antiguos y otros testimonios de la antigüedad no incluyen Mr 16:9-20. En lugar de este pasaje, algunos mss. incluyen una conclusión más breve.   z 16:15 *criatura.* Lit. *creación.*

LUCAS

Prólogo

1 Muchos han intentado hacer un relato de las cosas que se han cumplidoa entre nosotros, 2tal y como nos las transmitieron los que desde el principio fueron testigos presenciales y servidores de la palabra. 3Por lo tanto, yo también, excelentísimo Teófilo, habiendo investigado todo esto con esmero desde su origen, he decidido escribírtelo ordenadamente, 4para que llegues a tener plena seguridad de lo que te enseñaron.

Anuncio del nacimiento de Juan el Bautista

5En tiempos de Herodes, rey de Judea, hubo un sacerdote llamado Zacarías, miembro del grupo de Abías. Su esposa Elisabet también era descendiente de Aarón. 6Ambos eran rectos e intachables delante de Dios; obedecían todos los mandamientos y preceptos del Señor. 7Pero no tenían hijos, porque Elisabet era estéril; y los dos eran de edad avanzada.

8Un día en que Zacarías, por haber llegado el turno de su grupo, oficiaba como sacerdote delante de Dios, 9le tocó en suerte, según la costumbre del sacerdocio, entrar en el *santuario del Señor para quemar incienso. 10Cuando llegó la hora de ofrecer el incienso, la multitud reunida afuera estaba orando. 11En esto un ángel del Señor se le apareció a Zacarías a la derecha del altar del incienso. 12Al verlo, Zacarías se asustó, y el temor se apoderó de él. 13El ángel le dijo:

—No tengas miedo, Zacarías, pues ha sido escuchada tu oración. Tu esposa Elisabet te dará un hijo, y le pondrás por nombre Juan. 14Tendrás gozo y alegría, y muchos se regocijarán por su nacimiento, 15porque él será un gran hombre delante del Señor. Jamás tomará vino ni licor, y será lleno del Espíritu Santo aun desde su nacimiento.b 16Hará que muchos israelitas se vuelvan al Señor su Dios. 17Él irá primero, delante del Señor, con el espíritu y el poder de Elías, para reconciliar ac los padres con los hijos y guiar a los desobedientes a la sabiduría de los justos. De este modo preparará un pueblo bien dispuesto para recibir al Señor.

18—¿Cómo podré estar seguro de esto? —preguntó Zacarías al ángel—. Ya soy anciano y mi esposa también es de edad avanzada.

19—Yo soy Gabriel y estoy a las órdenes de Dios —le contestó el ángel—. He sido enviado para hablar contigo y darte estas buenas *noticias. 20Pero como no creíste en mis palabras, las cuales se cumplirán a su debido tiempo, te vas a quedar mudo. No podrás hablar hasta el día en que todo esto suceda.

21Mientras tanto, el pueblo estaba esperando a Zacarías y les extrañaba que se demorara tanto en el santuario. 22Cuando por fin salió, no podía hablarles, así que se dieron cuenta de que allí había tenido una visión. Se podía comunicar sólo por señas, pues seguía mudo.

23Cuando terminaron los días de su servicio, regresó a su casa. 24Poco después, su esposa Elisabet quedó encinta y se mantuvo recluida por cinco meses. 25«Esto —decía ella— es obra del Señor, que ahora ha mostrado su bondad al quitarme la vergüenza que yo tenía ante los demás.»

Anuncio del nacimiento de Jesús

26A los seis meses, Dios envió al ángel Gabriel a Nazaret, pueblo de Galilea, 27a visitar a una joven virgen comprometida para casarse con un hombre que se llamaba José, descendiente de David. La virgen se llamaba María. 28El ángel se acercó a ella y le dijo:

—¡Te saludo,d tú que has recibido el favor de Dios! El Señor está contigo.

29Ante estas palabras, María se perturbó, y se preguntaba qué podría significar este saludo.

30—No tengas miedo, María; Dios te ha concedido su favor —le dijo el ángel—. 31Quedarás encinta y darás a luz un hijo, y le pondrás por nombre Jesús. 32Él será un gran hombre, y lo llamarán Hijo del Altísimo. Dios el Señor le dará el trono de su padre David, 33y reinará sobre el pueblo de Jacob para siempre. Su reinado no tendrá fin.

34—¿Cómo podrá suceder esto —le preguntó María al ángel—, puesto que soy virgen?e

35—El Espíritu Santo vendrá sobre ti, y el poder del Altísimo te cubrirá con su sombra. Así que al santo niño que va a nacer lo llamarán Hijo de Dios. 36También tu parienta Elisabet va a tener un hijo en su vejez; de hecho, la que decían que era estéril ya está en el sexto mes de embarazo. 37Porque para Dios no hay nada imposible.

38—Aquí tienes a la sierva del Señor —contestó María—. Que él haga conmigo como me has dicho.

Con esto, el ángel la dejó.

María visita a Elisabet

39A los pocos días María emprendió el viaje y se fue de prisa a un pueblo en la región montañosa de Judea. 40Al llegar, entró en casa de Zacarías y saludó a Elisabet. 41Tan pronto como Elisabet oyó el saludo de María, la criatura saltó en su vientre. Entonces Elisabet, llena del Espíritu Santo, 42exclamó:

—¡Bendita tú entre las mujeres, y bendito el hijo que darás a luz!f 43Pero, ¿cómo es esto, que la madre de mi Señor venga a verme? 44Te digo que tan pronto como llegó a mis oídos la voz de tu saludo, saltó de alegría la criatura que llevo en el vientre. 45¡*Dichosa tú que has creído, porque lo que el Señor te ha dicho se cumplirá!

El cántico de María
1:46-53 — 1S 2:1-10

46Entonces dijo María:

—Mi alma glorifica al Señor,
47 y mi espíritu se regocija en Dios mi
     Salvador,
48porque se ha dignado fijarse en su humilde
     sierva.
Desde ahora me llamarán *dichosa todas las
     generaciones,
49 porque el Poderoso ha hecho grandes cosas
     por mí.
¡Santo es su nombre!
50De generación en generación
     se extiende su misericordia a los que le
     temen.
51Hizo proezas con su brazo;

---

a 1:1 se han cumplido. Alt. se han recibido con convicción. b 1:15 desde su nacimiento. Alt. antes de nacer. Lit. desde el vientre de su madre. c 1:17 reconciliar a. Lit. hacer volver los corazones de; véase Mal 4:6. d 1:28 ¡Te saludo. Alt. ¡Alégrate. e 1:34 soy virgen? Lit. no conozco a hombre? f 1:42 el hijo que darás a luz! Lit. el fruto de tu vientre!

desbarató las intrigas de los soberbios.g
52De sus tronos derrocó a los poderosos,
    mientras que ha exaltado a los humildes.
53A los hambrientos los colmó de bienes,
    y a los ricos los despidió con las manos
        vacías.
54-55Acudió en ayuda de su siervo Israel
    y, cumpliendo su promesa a nuestros
        padres,
    mostróh su misericordia a Abraham
    y a su descendencia para siempre.

56María se quedó con Elisabet unos tres meses y luego regresó a su casa.

Nacimiento de Juan el Bautista

57Cuando se le cumplió el tiempo, Elisabet dio a luz un hijo. 58Sus vecinos y parientes se enteraron de que el Señor le había mostrado gran misericordia, y compartieron su alegría.

59A los ocho días llevaron a circuncidar al niño. Como querían ponerle el nombre de su padre, Zacarías, 60su madre se opuso.

—¡No! —dijo ella—. Tiene que llamarse Juan.

61—Pero si nadie en tu familia tiene ese nombre —le dijeron.

62Entonces le hicieron señas a su padre, para saber qué nombre quería ponerle al niño. 63Él pidió una tablilla, en la que escribió: «Su nombre es Juan.» Y todos quedaron asombrados. 64Al instante se le desató la lengua, recuperó el habla y comenzó a alabar a Dios. 65Todos los vecinos se llenaron de temor, y por toda la región montañosa de Judea se comentaba lo sucedido. 66Quienes lo oían se preguntaban: «¿Qué llegará a ser este niño?» Porque la mano del Señor lo protegía.

El cántico de Zacarías

67Entonces su padre Zacarías, lleno del Espíritu Santo, profetizó:
68«Bendito sea el Señor, Dios de Israel,
    porque ha venido a redimiri a su pueblo.
69Nos envió un poderoso salvadorj
    en la casa de David su siervo
70(como lo prometió en el pasado por medio de
    sus *santos profetas),
71para librarnos de nuestros enemigos
    y del poder de todos los que nos aborrecen;
72para mostrar misericordia a nuestros padres
    al acordarse de su santo pacto.
73   Así lo juró a Abraham nuestro padre:
74nos concedió que fuéramos libres del temor,
    al rescatarnos del poder de nuestros
        enemigos,
    para que le sirviéramos 75con *santidad y
        justicia,
    viviendo en su presencia todos nuestros
        días.
76Y tú, hijito mío, serás llamado profeta del
        Altísimo,
    porque irás delante del Señor para
        prepararle el camino,
77Darás a conocer a su pueblo la salvación
    mediante el perdón de sus pecados,
78gracias a la entrañable misericordia de
    nuestro Dios.

Así nos visitará desde el cielo el sol
        naciente,
79para dar luz a los que viven en tinieblas,
    en la más terrible oscuridad,k
    para guiar nuestros pasos por la senda de la
        paz.»

80El niño crecía y se fortalecía en espíritu; y vivió en el desierto hasta el día en que se presentó públicamente al pueblo de Israel.

Nacimiento de Jesús

2 Por aquellos días Augusto *César decretó que se levantara un censo en todo el imperio romano.l 2(Este primer censo se efectuó cuando Cirenio gobernaba en Siria.) 3Así que iban todos a inscribirse, cada cual a su propio pueblo.

4También José, que era descendiente del rey David, subió de Nazaret, ciudad de Galilea, a Judea. Fue a Belén, la ciudad de David, 5para inscribirse junto con María su esposa.m Ella se encontraba encinta 6y, mientras estaban allí, se le cumplió el tiempo. 7Así que dio a luz a su hijo primogénito. Lo envolvió en pañales y lo acostó en un pesebre, porque no había lugar para ellos en la posada.

Los pastores y los ángeles

8En esa misma región había unos pastores que pasaban la noche en el campo, turnándose para cuidar sus rebaños. 9Sucedió que un ángel del Señor se les apareció. La gloria del Señor los envolvió en su luz, y se llenaron de temor. 10Pero el ángel les dijo: «No tengan miedo. Miren que les traigo buenas *noticias que serán motivo de mucha alegría para todo el pueblo. 11Hoy les ha nacido en la ciudad de David un Salvador, que es *Cristo el Señor. 12Esto les servirá de señal: Encontrarán a un niño envuelto en pañales y acostado en un pesebre.»

13De repente apareció una multitud de ángeles del cielo, que alababan a Dios y decían:

14«Gloria a Dios en las alturas,
    y en la tierra paz a los que gozan de su
        buena voluntad.»n

15Cuando los ángeles se fueron al cielo, los pastores se dijeron unos a otros: «Vamos a Belén, a ver esto que ha pasado y que el Señor nos ha dado a conocer.»

16Así que fueron de prisa y encontraron a María y a José, y al niño que estaba acostado en el pesebre. 17Cuando vieron al niño, contaron lo que les habían dicho acerca de él, 18y cuantos lo oyeron se asombraron de lo que los pastores decían. 19María, por su parte, guardaba todas estas cosas en su corazón y meditaba acerca de ellas. 20Los pastores regresaron glorificando y alabando a Dios por lo que habían visto y oído, pues todo sucedió tal como se les había dicho.

Presentación de Jesús en el templo

21Cuando se cumplieron los ocho días y fueron a circuncidarlo, le llamaron Jesús, nombre que el ángel le había puesto antes de que fuera concebido.

22Así mismo, cuando se cumplió el tiempo en que, según la ley de Moisés, ellos debían *purificarse, José y María llevaron al niño a Jerusalén para presentarlo al Señor. 23Así cumplieron con lo que en la ley del Señor está escrito: «Todo varón primogénito

---

g 1:51 desbarató . . . soberbios. Lit. dispersó a los orgullosos en el pensamiento del corazón de ellos. h 1:54,55 mostró. Lit. recordó. i 1:68 ha venido a redimir. Lit. ha visitado y ha redimido. j 1:69 envió un poderoso salvador. Lit. levantó un cuerno de salvación. k 1:79 en la más terrible oscuridad. Lit. y en sombra de muerte. l 2:1 el imperio romano. Lit. el mundo. m 2:5 María su esposa. Lit. María, que estaba comprometida para casarse con él. n 2:14 paz . . . voluntad. Lit. paz a los hombres de buena voluntad. Var. paz, buena voluntad a los hombres.

será consagradoñ al Señor».º 24También ofrecieron un sacrificio conforme a lo que la ley del Señor dice: «un par de tórtolas o dos pichones de paloma».P

25Ahora bien, en Jerusalén había un hombre llamado Simeón, que era justo y devoto, y aguardaba con esperanza la redención q de Israel. El Espíritu Santo estaba con él 26y le había revelado que no moriría sin antes ver al *Cristo del Señor. 27Movido por el Espíritu, fue al *templo. Cuando al niño Jesús lo llevaron sus padres para cumplir con la costumbre establecida por la ley, 28Simeón lo tomó en sus brazos y bendijo a Dios:

29«Según tu palabra, Soberano Señor,
 ya puedes despedir a tu *siervo en paz.
30Porque han visto mis ojos tu salvación,
 31que has preparado a la vista de todos los
 pueblos:
32luz que ilumina a las *naciones
 y gloria de tu pueblo Israel.»

33El padre y la madre del niño se quedaron maravillados por lo que se decía de él. 34Simeón les dio su bendición y le dijo a María, la madre de Jesús: «Este niño está destinado a causar la caída y el levantamiento de muchos en Israel, y a crear mucha oposición,r 35a fin de que se manifiesten las intenciones de muchos corazones. En cuanto a ti, una espada te atravesará el alma.»

36Había también una profetisa, Ana, hija de Penuel, de la tribu de Aser. Era muy anciana; casada de joven, había vivido con su esposo siete años, 37y luego permaneció viuda hasta la edad de ochenta y cuatro.s Nunca salía del *templo, sino que día y noche adoraba a Dios con ayunos y oraciones. 38Llegando en ese mismo momento, Ana dio gracias a Dios y comenzó a hablar del niño a todos los que esperaban la redención de Jerusalén.

39Después de haber cumplido con todo lo que exigía la ley del Señor, José y María regresaron a Galilea, a su propio pueblo de Nazaret. 40El niño crecía y se fortalecía; progresaba en sabiduría, y la gracia de Dios lo acompañaba.

El niño Jesús en el templo

41Los padres de Jesús subían todos los años a Jerusalén para la fiesta de la Pascua. 42Cuando cumplió doce años, fueron allá según era la costumbre. 43Terminada la fiesta, emprendieron el viaje de regreso, pero el niño Jesús se había quedado en Jerusalén, sin que sus padres se dieran cuenta. 44Ellos, pensando que él estaba entre el grupo de viajeros, hicieron un día de camino mientras lo buscaban entre los parientes y conocidos. 45Al no encontrarlo, volvieron a Jerusalén en busca de él. 46Al cabo de tres días lo encontraron en el *templo, sentado entre los maestros, escuchándolos y haciéndoles preguntas. 47Todos los que le oían se asombraban de su inteligencia y de sus respuestas. 48Cuando lo vieron sus padres, se quedaron admirados.

—Hijo, ¿por qué te has portado así con nosotros? —le dijo su madre—. ¡Mira que tu padre y yo te hemos estado buscando angustiados!

49—¿Por qué me buscaban? ¿No sabían que tengo que estar en la casa de mi Padre?

50Pero ellos no entendieron lo que les decía.

51Así que Jesús bajó con sus padres a Nazaret y vivió sujeto a ellos. Pero su madre conservaba todas estas cosas en el corazón. 52Jesús siguió creciendo en sabiduría y estatura, y cada vez más gozaba del favor de Dios y de toda la gente.

Juan el Bautista prepara el camino
3:2-10 — Mt 3:1-10; Mr 1:3-5
3:16-17 — Mt 3:11-12; Mr 1:7-8

3 En el año quince del reinado de Tiberio *César, Poncio Pilato gobernaba la provincia de Judea, Herodest era tetrarca en Galilea, su hermano Felipe en Iturea y Traconite, y Lisanias en Abilene; 2el sumo sacerdocio lo ejercían Anás y Caifás. En aquel entonces, la palabra de Dios llegó a Juan hijo de Zacarías, en el desierto. 3Juan recorría toda la región del Jordán predicando el bautismo de *arrepentimiento para el perdón de pecados. 4Así está escrito en el libro del profeta Isaías:

«Voz de uno que grita en el desierto:
"Preparen el camino del Señor,
 háganle sendas derechas.
5Todo valle será rellenado,
 toda montaña y colina será allanada.
Los caminos torcidos se enderezarán,
 las sendas escabrosas quedarán llanas.
6Y todo *mortal verá la salvación de Dios." »u

7Muchos acudían a Juan para que los bautizara.

—¡Camada de víboras! —les advirtió—. ¿Quién les dijo que podrán escapar del castigo que se acerca? 8Produzcan frutos que demuestren arrepentimiento. Y no se pongan a pensar: "Tenemos a Abraham por padre." Porque les digo que aun de estas piedras Dios es capaz de darle hijos a Abraham. 9Es más, el hacha ya está puesta a la raíz de los árboles, y todo árbol que no produzca buen fruto será cortado y arrojado al fuego.

10—¿Entonces qué debemos hacer? —le preguntaba la gente.

11—El que tiene dos *camisas debe compartir con el que no tiene ninguna —les contestó Juan—, y el que tiene comida debe hacer lo mismo.

12Llegaron a bautizarse unos *recaudadores de impuestos para que los bautizara.

—Maestro, ¿qué debemos hacer nosotros? —le preguntaron.

13—No cobren más de lo debido —les respondió.

14—Y nosotros, ¿qué debemos hacer? —le preguntaron unos soldados.

—No extorsionen a nadie ni hagan denuncias falsas; más bien confórmense con lo que les pagan.

15La gente estaba a la expectativa, y todos se preguntaban si acaso Juan sería el *Cristo.

16—Yo los bautizo a ustedes conv agua —les respondió Juan a todos—. Pero está por llegar uno más poderoso que yo, a quien ni siquiera merezco desatarle la correa de sus sandalias. Él los bautizará con el Espíritu Santo y con fuego. 17Tiene el rastrillo en la mano para limpiar su *era y recoger el trigo en su granero; la paja, en cambio, la quemará con fuego que nunca se apagará.

18Y con muchas otras palabras exhortaba Juan a la gente y le anunciaba las buenas *nuevas. 19Pero

---

ñ2:23 Todo . . . consagrado. Lit. Todo varón que abre la matriz será llamado santo. º 2:23 Éx 13:2,12 P 2:24 Lv 12:8 q 2:25 redención. Lit. consolación. r 2:34 a crear mucha oposición. Lit. a ser una señal contra la cual se hablará. s 2:37 hasta la edad de ochenta y cuatro. Alt. durante ochenta y cuatro años. t 3:1 Es decir, Herodes Antipas, hijo del rey Herodes (1:5). u 3:6 Is 40:3-5 v 3:16 con. Alt. en.

cuando reprendió al tetrarca Herodes por el asunto de su cuñada Herodías,w y por todas las otras maldades que había cometido, 20Herodes llegó hasta el colmo de encerrar a Juan en la cárcel.

Bautismo y genealogía de Jesús
3:21-22 — Mt 3:13-17; Mr 1:9-11
3:23-38 — Mt 1:1-17

21Un día en que todos acudían a Juan para que los bautizara, Jesús fue bautizado también. Y mientras oraba, se abrió el cielo, 22y el Espíritu Santo bajó sobre él en forma de paloma. Entonces se oyó una voz del cielo que decía: «Tú eres mi Hijo amado; estoy muy complacido contigo.»

23Jesús tenía unos treinta años cuando comenzó su ministerio. Era hijo, según se creía, de José,

hijo de Elí, 24hijo de Matat,
hijo de Leví, hijo de Melquí,
hijo de Janay, hijo de José,
25 hijo de Matatías, hijo de Amós,
hijo de Nahúm, hijo de Eslí,
hijo de Nagay, 26hijo de Máat,
hijo de Matatías, hijo de Semeí,
hijo de Josec, hijo de Judá,
27 hijo de Yojanán, hijo de Resa,
hijo de Zorobabel, hijo de Salatiel,
hijo de Neri, 28hijo de Melquí,
hijo de Adí, hijo de Cosán,
hijo de Elmadán, hijo de Er,
29 hijo de Josué, hijo de Eliezer,
hijo de Jorín, hijo de Matat,
hijo de Leví, 30hijo de Simeón,
hijo de Judá, hijo de José,
hijo de Jonán, hijo de Eliaquín,
31 hijo de Melea, hijo de Mainán,
hijo de Matata, hijo de Natán,
hijo de David, 32hijo de Isaí,
hijo de Obed, hijo de Booz,
hijo de Salmón,x hijo de Naasón,
33 hijo de Aminadab, hijo de Aram,y
hijo de Jezrón, hijo de Fares,
hijo de Judá, 34hijo de Jacob,
hijo de Isaac, hijo de Abraham,
hijo de Téraj, hijo de Najor,
35 hijo de Serug, hijo de Ragau,
hijo de Péleg, hijo de Éber,
hijo de Selaj, 36hijo de Cainán,
hijo de Arfaxad, hijo de Sem,
hijo de Noé, hijo de Lamec,
37 hijo de Matusalén, hijo de Enoc,
hijo de Jared, hijo de Malalel,
hijo de Cainán, 38hijo de Enós,
hijo de Set, hijo de Adán,
hijo de Dios.

Tentación de Jesús
4:1-13 — Mt 4:1-11; Mr 1:12-13

4 Jesús, lleno del Espíritu Santo, volvió del Jordán y fue llevado por el Espíritu al desierto. 2Allí estuvo cuarenta días y fue *tentado por el diablo. No comió nada durante esos días, pasados los cuales tuvo hambre.

3—Si eres el Hijo de Dios —le propuso el diablo—, dile a esta piedra que se convierta en pan.

4Jesús le respondió:
—Escrito está: "No sólo de pan vive el hombre."z

5Entonces el diablo lo llevó a un lugar alto y le mostró en un instante todos los reinos del mundo.

6—Sobre estos reinos y todo su esplendor —le dijo—, te daré la autoridad, porque a mí me ha sido entregada, y puedo dársela a quien yo quiera. 7Así que, si me adoras, todo será tuyo.

Jesús le contestó:
8—Escrito está: "Adora al Señor tu Dios y sírvele solamente a él."a

9El diablo lo llevó luego a Jerusalén e hizo que se pusiera de pie en la parte más alta del *templo, y le dijo:
—Si eres el Hijo de Dios, ¡tírate de aquí! 10Pues escrito está:

»"Ordenará que sus ángeles te cuiden.
  Te sostendrán en sus manos
11para que no tropieces con piedra alguna."b

12—También está escrito: "No pongas a prueba al Señor tu Dios"c —le replicó Jesús.

13Así que el diablo, habiendo agotado todo recurso de tentación, lo dejó hasta otra oportunidad.

Rechazan a Jesús en Nazaret

14Jesús regresó a Galilea en el poder del Espíritu, y se extendió su fama por toda aquella región. 15Enseñaba en las sinagogas, y todos lo admiraban.

16Fue a Nazaret, donde se había criado, y un *sábado entró en la sinagoga, como era su costumbre. Se levantó para hacer la lectura, 17y le entregaron el libro del profeta Isaías. Al desenrollarlo, encontró el lugar donde está escrito:

18«El Espíritu del Señor está sobre mí,
  por cuanto me ha ungido
  para anunciar buenas *nuevas a los pobres.
Me ha enviado a proclamar libertad a los
      cautivos
  y dar vista a los ciegos,
a poner en libertad a los oprimidos,
  19a pregonar el año del favor del Señor.»d

20Luego enrolló el libro, se lo devolvió al ayudante y se sentó. Todos los que estaban en la sinagoga lo miraban detenidamente, 21y él comenzó a hablarles: «Hoy se cumple esta Escritura en presencia de ustedes.»

22Todos dieron su aprobación, impresionados por las hermosas palabrase que salían de su boca. «¿No es éste el hijo de José?», se preguntaban.

23Jesús continuó: «Seguramente ustedes me van a citar el proverbio: "¡Médico, cúrate a ti mismo! Haz aquí en tu tierra lo que hemos oído que hiciste en Capernaúm." 24Pues bien, les aseguro que a ningún profeta lo aceptan en su propia tierra. 25No cabe duda de que en tiempos de Elías, cuando el cielo se cerró por tres años y medio, de manera que hubo una gran hambre en toda la tierra, muchas viudas vivían en Israel. 26Sin embargo, Elías no fue enviado a ninguna de ellas, sino a una viuda de Sarepta, en los alrededores de Sidón. 27Así mismo, había en Israel muchos enfermos de *lepra en tiempos del profeta Eliseo, pero ninguno de ellos fue sanado, sino Naamán el sirio.»

w 3:19 Esposa de Felipe, hermano de Herodes Antipas. x 3:32 Salmón. Var. Sala. y 3:33 Aminadab, hijo de Aram. Var. Aminadab, el hijo de Admín, el hijo de Arní; los mss. varían mucho en este versículo. z 4:4 Dt 8:3 a 4:8 Dt 6:13 b 4:10,11 Sal 91:11,12 c 4:12 Dt 6:16 d 4:19 Is 61:1,2 e 4:22 Todos . . . palabras. Lit. Todos daban testimonio de él y estaban asombrados de las palabras de gracia.

28Al oír esto, todos los que estaban en la sinagoga se enfurecieron. 29Se levantaron, lo expulsaron del pueblo y lo llevaron hasta la cumbre de la colina sobre la que estaba construido el pueblo, para tirarlo por el precipicio. 30Pero él pasó por en medio de ellos y se fue.

Jesús expulsa a un espíritu maligno
4:31-37 — Mr 1:21-28

31Jesús pasó a Capernaúm, un pueblo de Galilea, y el día *sábado enseñaba a la gente. 32Estaban asombrados de su enseñanza, porque les hablaba con autoridad.

33Había en la sinagoga un hombre que estaba poseído por un *espíritu maligno, quien gritó con todas sus fuerzas:

34—¡Ah! ¿Por qué te entrometes, Jesús de Nazaret? ¿Has venido a destruirnos? Yo sé quién eres tú: ¡el Santo de Dios!

35—¡Cállate! —lo reprendió Jesús—. ¡Sal de ese hombre!

Entonces el demonio derribó al hombre en medio de la gente y salió de él sin hacerle ningún daño.

36Todos se asustaron y se decían unos a otros: «¿Qué clase de palabra es ésta? ¡Con autoridad y poder les da órdenes a los espíritus malignos, y salen!» 37Y se extendió su fama por todo aquel lugar.

Jesús sana a muchos enfermos
4:38-41 — Mt 8:14-17
4:38-43 — Mr 1:29-38

38Cuando Jesús salió de la sinagoga, se fue a casa de Simón, cuya suegra estaba enferma con una fiebre muy alta. Le pidieron a Jesús que la ayudara, 39así que se inclinó sobre ella y reprendió a la fiebre, la cual se le quitó. Ella se levantó en seguida y se puso a servirles.

40Al ponerse el sol, la gente le llevó a Jesús todos los que padecían de diversas enfermedades; él puso las manos sobre cada uno de ellos y los sanó. 41Además, de muchas personas salían demonios que gritaban: «¡Tú eres el Hijo de Dios!» Pero él los reprendía y no los dejaba hablar porque sabían que él era el *Cristo.

42Cuando amaneció, Jesús salió y se fue a un lugar solitario. La gente andaba buscándolo, y cuando llegaron adonde él estaba, procuraban detenerlo para que no se fuera. 43Pero él les dijo: «Es preciso que anuncie también a los demás pueblos las buenas *nuevas del reino de Dios, porque para esto fui enviado.»

44Y siguió predicando en las sinagogas de los judíos.f

Llamamiento de los primeros discípulos
5:1-11 — Mt 4:18-22; Mr 1:16-20; Jn 1:40-42

5 Un día estaba Jesús a orillas del lago de Genesaret,g y la gente lo apretujaba para escuchar el mensaje de Dios. 2Entonces vio dos barcas que los pescadores habían dejado en la playa mientras lavaban las redes. 3Subió a una de las barcas, que pertenecía a Simón, y le pidió que la alejara un poco de la orilla. Luego se sentó, y enseñaba a la gente desde la barca.

4Cuando acabó de hablar, le dijo a Simón:

—Lleva la barca hacia aguas más profundas, y echen allí las redes para pescar.

5—Maestro, hemos estado trabajando duro toda la noche y no hemos pescado nada —le contestó Simón—. Pero como tú me lo mandas, echaré las redes.

6Así lo hicieron, y recogieron una cantidad tan grande de peces que las redes se les rompían. 7Entonces llamaron por señas a sus compañeros de la otra barca para que los ayudaran. Ellos se acercaron y llenaron tanto las dos barcas que comenzaron a hundirse.

8Al ver esto, Simón Pedro cayó de rodillas delante de Jesús y le dijo:

—¡Apártate de mí, Señor; soy un pecador!

9Es que él y todos sus compañeros estaban asombrados ante la pesca que habían hecho, 10como también lo estaban *Jacobo y Juan, hijos de Zebedeo, que eran socios de Simón.

—No temas; desde ahora serás pescador de hombres —le dijo Jesús a Simón.

11Así que llevaron las barcas a tierra y, dejándolo todo, siguieron a Jesús.

Jesús sana a un leproso
5:12-14 — Mt 8:2-4; Mr 1:40-44

12En otra ocasión, cuando Jesús estaba en un pueblo, se presentó un hombre cubierto de *lepra. Al ver a Jesús, cayó rostro en tierra y le suplicó:

—Señor, si quieres, puedes *limpiarme.

13Jesús extendió la mano y tocó al hombre.

—Sí quiero —le dijo—. ¡Queda limpio!

Y al instante se le quitó la lepra.

14—No se lo digas a nadie —le ordenó Jesús—; sólo ve, preséntate al sacerdote y lleva por tu *purificación lo que ordenó Moisés, para que sirva de testimonio.

15Sin embargo, la fama de Jesús se extendía cada vez más, de modo que acudían a él multitudes para oírlo y para que los sanara de sus enfermedades. 16Él, por su parte, solía retirarse a lugares solitarios para orar.

Jesús sana a un paralítico
5:18-26 — Mt 9:2-8; Mr 2:3-12

17Un día, mientras enseñaba, estaban sentados allí algunos *fariseos y *maestros de la ley que habían venido de todas las aldeas de Galilea y Judea, y también de Jerusalén. Y el poder del Señor estaba con él para sanar a los enfermos. 18Entonces llegaron unos hombres que llevaban en una camilla a un paralítico. Procuraron entrar para ponerlo delante de Jesús, 19pero no pudieron a causa de la multitud. Así que subieron a la azotea y, separando las tejas, lo bajaron en la camilla hasta ponerlo en medio de la gente, frente a Jesús.

20Al ver la fe de ellos, Jesús dijo:

—Amigo, tus pecados quedan perdonados.

21Los fariseos y los maestros de la ley comenzaron a pensar: «¿Quién es éste que dice *blasfemias? ¿Quién puede perdonar pecados sino sólo Dios?»

22Pero Jesús supo lo que estaban pensando y les dijo:

—¿Por qué razonan así? 23¿Qué es más fácil decir: "Tus pecados quedan perdonados", o "Levántate y anda"? 24Pues para que sepan que el Hijo del hombre tiene autoridad en la tierra para perdonar pecados —se dirigió entonces al paralítico—: A ti te digo, levántate, toma tu camilla y vete a tu casa.

25Al instante se levantó a la vista de todos, tomó la camilla en que había estado acostado, y se fue a su casa alabando a Dios. 26Todos quedaron asombrados

---

f **4:44** los judíos. Lit. Judea. Var. Galilea. g **5:1** Es decir, el mar de Galilea.

y ellos también alababan a Dios. Estaban llenos de temor y decían: «Hoy hemos visto maravillas.»

Llamamiento de Leví
5:27-32 — Mt 9:9-13; Mr 2:14-17

27Después de esto salió Jesús y se fijó en un *recaudador de impuestos llamado Leví, sentado a la mesa donde cobraba.

—Sígueme —le dijo Jesús.

28Y Leví se levantó, lo dejó todo y lo siguió.

29Luego Leví le ofreció a Jesús un gran banquete en su casa, y había allí un grupo numeroso de recaudadores de impuestos y otras personas que estaban comiendo con ellos. 30Pero los *fariseos y los *maestros de la ley que eran de la misma secta les reclamaban a los discípulos de Jesús:

—¿Por qué comen y beben ustedes con recaudadores de impuestos y *pecadores?

31—No son los sanos los que necesitan médico sino los enfermos —les contestó Jesús—. 32No he venido a llamar a justos sino a pecadores para que se *arrepientan.

Le preguntan a Jesús sobre el ayuno
5:33-39 — Mt 9:14-17; Mr 2:18-22

33Algunos dijeron a Jesús:

—Los discípulos de Juan ayunan y oran con frecuencia, lo mismo que los discípulos de los *fariseos, pero los tuyos se la pasan comiendo y bebiendo.

34Jesús les replicó:

—¿Acaso pueden obligar a los invitados del novio a que ayunen mientras él está con ellos? 35Llegará el día en que se les quitará el novio; en aquellos días sí ayunarán.

36Les contó esta parábola:

—Nadie quita un retazo de un vestido nuevo para remendar un vestido viejo. De hacerlo así, habrá rasgado el vestido nuevo, y el retazo nuevo no hará juego con el vestido viejo. 37Ni echa nadie vino nuevo en odres viejos. De hacerlo así, el vino nuevo hará reventar los odres, se derramará y el vino y los odres se arruinarán. 38Más bien, el vino nuevo debe echarse en odres nuevos. 39Y nadie que haya bebido vino añejo quiere el nuevo, porque dice: "El añejo es mejor."

Señor del sábado
6:1-11 — Mt 12:1-14; Mr 2:23—3:6

6 Un *sábado, al pasar Jesús por los sembrados, sus discípulos se pusieron a arrancar unas espigas de trigo, y las desgranaban para comérselas. 2Por eso algunos de los *fariseos les dijeron:

—¿Por qué hacen ustedes lo que está prohibido hacer en sábado?

3Jesús les contestó:

—¿Nunca han leído lo que hizo David en aquella ocasión en que él y sus compañeros tuvieron hambre? 4Entró en la casa de Dios y, tomando los panes consagrados a Dios, comió lo que sólo a los sacerdotes les es permitido comer. Y les dio también a sus compañeros.

5Entonces añadió:

—El Hijo del hombre es Señor del sábado.

6Otro sábado entró en la sinagoga y comenzó a enseñar. Había allí un hombre que tenía la mano derecha paralizada; 7así que los *maestros de la ley y los fariseos, buscando un motivo para acusar a Jesús, no le quitaban la vista de encima para ver si sanaría

en sábado. 8Pero Jesús, que sabía lo que estaban pensando, le dijo al hombre de la mano paralizada:

—Levántate y ponte frente a todos.

Así que el hombre se puso de pie. Entonces Jesús dijo a los otros:

9—Voy a hacerles una pregunta: ¿Qué está permitido hacer en sábado: hacer el bien o el mal, salvar una *vida o destruirla?

10Jesús se quedó mirando a todos los que lo rodeaban, y le dijo al hombre:

—Extiende la mano.

Así lo hizo, y la mano le quedó restablecida. 11Pero ellos se enfurecieron y comenzaron a discutir qué podrían hacer contra Jesús.

Los doce apóstoles
6:13-16 — Mt 10:2-4; Mr 3:16-19; Hch 1:13

12Por aquel tiempo se fue Jesús a la montaña a orar, y pasó toda la noche en oración a Dios. 13Al llegar la mañana, llamó a sus discípulos y escogió a doce de ellos, a los que nombró apóstoles: 14Simón (a quien llamó Pedro), su hermano Andrés, *Jacobo, Juan, Felipe, Bartolomé, 15Mateo, Tomás, Jacobo hijo de Alfeo, Simón, al que llamaban el Zelote, 16Judas hijo de Jacobo, y Judas Iscariote, que llegó a ser el traidor.

Bendiciones y ayes
6:20-23 — Mt 5:3-12

17Luego bajó con ellos y se detuvo en un llano. Había allí una gran multitud de sus discípulos y mucha gente de toda Judea, de Jerusalén y de la costa de Tiro y Sidón, 18que habían llegado para oírlo y para que los sanara de sus enfermedades. Los que eran atormentados por *espíritus malignos quedaban liberados; 19así que toda la gente procuraba tocarlo, porque de él salía poder que sanaba a todos.

20Él entonces dirigió la mirada a sus discípulos y dijo:

«*Dichosos ustedes los pobres,
    porque el reino de Dios les pertenece.
21Dichosos ustedes que ahora pasan hambre,
    porque serán saciados.
Dichosos ustedes que ahora lloran,
    porque luego habrán de reír.
22Dichosos ustedes cuando los odien,
    cuando los discriminen, los insulten y los
        desprestigienh
    por causa del Hijo del hombre.

23»Alégrense en aquel día y salten de gozo, pues miren que les espera una gran recompensa en el cielo. Dense cuenta de que los antepasados de esta gente trataron así a los profetas.

24»Pero iay de ustedes los ricos,
    porque ya han recibido su consuelo!
25¡Ay de ustedes los que ahora están saciados,
    porque sabrán lo que es pasar hambre!
¡Ay de ustedes los que ahora ríen,
    porque sabrán lo que es derramar lágrimas!
26¡Ay de ustedes cuando todos los elogien!
    Dense cuenta de que los antepasados de
    esta gente trataron así a los falsos
        profetas.

---

h 6:22 los desprestigien. Lit. echen su nombre como malo.

El amor a los enemigos
6:29-30 — Mt 5:39-42

27»Pero a ustedes que me escuchan les digo: Amen a sus enemigos, hagan bien a quienes los odian, 28bendigan a quienes los maldicen, oren por quienes los maltratan. 29Si alguien te pega en una mejilla, vuélvele también la otra. Si alguien te quita tu *camisa, no le impidas que se lleve también la capa. 30Dale a todo el que te pida, y si alguien se lleva lo que es tuyo, no se lo reclames. 31Traten a los demás tal y como quieren que ellos los traten a ustedes.

32»¿Qué mérito tienen ustedes al amar a quienes los aman? Aun los *pecadores lo hacen así. 33¿Y qué mérito tienen ustedes al hacer bien a quienes les hacen bien? Aun los pecadores actúan así. 34¿Y qué mérito tienen ustedes al dar prestado a quienes pueden corresponderles? Aun los pecadores se prestan entre sí, esperando recibir el mismo trato. 35Ustedes, por el contrario, amen a sus enemigos, háganles bien y denles prestado sin esperar nada a cambio. Así tendrán una gran recompensa y serán hijos del Altísimo, porque él es bondadoso con los ingratos y malvados. 36Sean compasivos, así como su Padre es compasivo.

El juzgar a los demás
6:37-42 — Mt 7:1-5

37»No juzguen, y no se les juzgará. No condenen, y no se les condenará. Perdonen, y se les perdonará. 38Den, y se les dará: se les echará en el regazo una medida llena, apretada, sacudida y desbordante. Porque con la medida que midan a otros, se les medirá a ustedes.»

39También les contó esta parábola: «¿Acaso puede un ciego guiar a otro ciego? ¿No caerán ambos en el hoyo? 40El discípulo no está por encima de su maestro, pero todo el que haya completado su aprendizaje, a lo sumo llega al nivel de su maestro.

41»¿Por qué te fijas en la astilla que tiene tu hermano en el ojo y no ha das importancia a la viga que tienes en el tuyo? 42¿Cómo puedes decirle a tu hermano: "Hermano, déjame sacarte la astilla del ojo", cuando tú mismo no te das cuenta de la viga en el tuyo? *¡Hipócrita! Saca primero la viga de tu propio ojo, y entonces verás con claridad para sacar la astilla del ojo de tu hermano.

El árbol y su fruto
6:43-44 — Mt 7:16,18,20

43»Ningún árbol bueno da fruto malo; tampoco da buen fruto el árbol malo. 44A cada árbol se le reconoce por su propio fruto. No se recogen higos de los espinos ni se cosechan uvas de las zarzas. 45El que es bueno, de la bondad que atesora en el corazón produce el bien; pero el que es malo, de su maldad produce el mal, porque de lo que abunda en el corazón habla la boca.

El prudente y el insensato
6:47-49 — Mt 7:24-27

46»¿Por qué me llaman ustedes "Señor, Señor", y no hacen lo que les digo? 47Voy a decirles a quién se parece todo el que viene a mí, y oye mis palabras y las pone en práctica. 48Se parece a un hombre que, al construir una casa, cavó bien hondo y puso el cimiento sobre la roca. De manera que cuando vino una inundación, el torrente azotó aquella casa, pero no pudo ni siquiera hacerla tambalear porque estaba bien construida. 49Pero el que oye mis palabras y no las pone en práctica se parece a un hombre que construyó una casa sobre tierra y sin cimientos. Tan pronto como la azotó el torrente, la casa se derrumbó, y el desastre fue terrible.»

La fe del centurión
7:1-10 — Mt 8:5-13

7 Cuando terminó de hablar al pueblo, Jesús entró en Capernaúm. 2Había allí un centurión, cuyo *siervo, a quien él estimaba mucho, estaba enfermo, a punto de morir. 3Como oyó hablar de Jesús, el centurión mandó a unos dirigentesi de los judíos a pedirle que fuera a sanar a su siervo. 4Cuando llegaron ante Jesús, le rogaron con insistencia:

—Este hombre merece que le concedas lo que te pide: 5aprecia tanto a nuestra nación, que nos ha construido una sinagoga.

6Así que Jesús fue con ellos. No estaba lejos de la casa cuando el centurión mandó unos amigos a decirle:

—Señor, no te tomes tanta molestia, pues no merezco que entres bajo mi techo. 7Por eso ni siquiera me atreví a presentarme ante ti. Pero con una sola palabra que digas, quedará sano mi siervo. 8Yo mismo obedezco órdenes superiores y, además, tengo soldados bajo mi autoridad. Le digo a uno: "Ve", y va, y al otro: "Ven", y viene. Le digo a mi siervo: "Haz esto", y lo hace.

9Al oírlo, Jesús se asombró de él y, volviéndose a la multitud que lo seguía, comentó:

—Les digo que ni siquiera en Israel he encontrado una fe tan grande.

10Al regresar a casa, los enviados encontraron sano al siervo.

Jesús resucita al hijo de una viuda

11Poco después Jesús, en compañía de sus discípulos y de una gran multitud, se dirigió a un pueblo llamado Naín. 12Cuando ya se acercaba a las puertas del pueblo, vio que sacaban de allí a un muerto, hijo único de madre viuda. La acompañaba un grupo grande de la población. 13Al verla, el Señor se compadeció de ella y le dijo:

—No llores.

14Entonces se acercó y tocó el féretro. Los que lo llevaban se detuvieron, y Jesús dijo:

—Joven, ¡te ordeno que te levantes!

15El muerto se incorporó y comenzó a hablar, y Jesús se lo entregó a su madre. 16Todos se llenaron de temor y alababan a Dios.

—Ha surgido entre nosotros un gran profeta —decían—. Dios ha venido en ayuda dej su pueblo.

17Así que esta noticia acerca de Jesús se divulgó por toda Judeak y por todas las regiones vecinas.

Jesús y Juan el Bautista
7:18-35 — Mt 11:2-19

18Los discípulos de Juan le contaron todo esto. Él llamó a dos de ellos 19y los envió al Señor a preguntarle:

—¿Eres tú el que ha de venir, o debemos esperar a otro?

20Cuando se acercaron a Jesús, ellos le dijeron:

—Juan el Bautista nos ha enviado a preguntarte: "¿Eres tú el que ha de venir, o debemos esperar a otro?"

21En ese mismo momento Jesús sanó a muchos que tenían enfermedades, dolencias y *espíritus ma-

---

i 7:3 dirigentes. Lit. *ancianos. j 7:16 ha venido en ayuda de. Lit. ha visitado a. k 7:17 Judea. Alt. la tierra de los judíos.

lignos, y les dio la vista a muchos ciegos. [22]Entonces les respondió a los enviados:

—Vayan y cuéntenle a Juan lo que han visto y oído: Los ciegos ven, los cojos andan, los que tienen *lepra son sanados, los sordos oyen, los muertos resucitan y a los pobres se les anuncian las buenas *nuevas. [23]*Dichoso el que no *tropieza por causa mía.

[24]Cuando se fueron los enviados, Jesús comenzó a hablarle a la multitud acerca de Juan: «¿Qué salieron a ver al desierto? ¿Una caña sacudida por el viento? [25]Si no, ¿qué salieron a ver? ¿A un hombre vestido con ropa fina? Claro que no, pues los que se visten ostentosamente y llevan una vida de lujo están en los palacios reales. [26]Entonces, ¿qué salieron a ver? ¿A un profeta? Sí, les digo, y más que profeta. [27]Éste es de quien está escrito:

»"Yo estoy por enviar a mi mensajero delante
        de ti,
   el cual preparará el camino."[l]

[28]Les digo que entre los mortales no ha habido nadie más grande que Juan; sin embargo, el más pequeño en el reino de Dios es más grande que él.»

[29]Al oír esto, todo el pueblo, y hasta los *recaudadores de impuestos, reconocieron que el camino de Dios era justo, y fueron bautizados por Juan. [30]Pero los *fariseos y los *expertos en la ley no se hicieron bautizar por Juan, rechazando así el propósito de Dios respecto a ellos.[m]

[31]«Entonces, ¿con qué puedo comparar a la gente de esta generación? ¿A quién se parecen ellos? [32]Se parecen a niños sentados en la plaza que se gritan unos a otros:

»"Tocamos la flauta,
   y ustedes no bailaron;
entonamos un canto fúnebre,
   y ustedes no lloraron."

[33]Porque vino Juan el Bautista, que no comía pan ni bebía vino, y ustedes dicen: "Tiene un demonio." [34]Vino el Hijo del hombre, que come y bebe, y ustedes dicen: "Éste es un glotón y un borracho, amigo de recaudadores de impuestos y de *pecadores." [35]Pero la sabiduría queda demostrada por los que la siguen.»[n]

Una mujer pecadora unge a Jesús

[36]Uno de los *fariseos invitó a Jesús a comer, así que fue a la casa del fariseo y se *sentó a la mesa.[ñ] [37]Ahora bien, vivía en aquel pueblo una mujer que tenía fama de *pecadora. Cuando ella se enteró de que Jesús estaba comiendo en casa del fariseo, se presentó con un frasco de alabastro lleno de perfume. [38]Llorando, se arrojó a los pies de Jesús,[o] de manera que se los bañaba en lágrimas. Luego se los secó con los cabellos; también se los besaba y se los ungía con el perfume. [39]Al ver esto, el fariseo que lo había invitado dijo para sí: «Si este hombre fuera profeta, sabría quién es la que le está tocando, y qué clase de mujer es: una pecadora.»

[40]Entonces Jesús le dijo a manera de respuesta:

—Simón, tengo algo que decirte.

—Dime, Maestro —respondió.

[41]—Dos hombres le debían dinero a cierto prestamista. Uno le debía quinientas monedas de plata,[p]

y el otro cincuenta. [42]Como no tenían con qué pagarle, les perdonó la deuda a los dos. Ahora bien, ¿cuál de los dos lo amará más?

[43]—Supongo que aquel a quien más le perdonó —contestó Simón.

—Has juzgado bien —le dijo Jesús.

[44]Luego se volvió hacia la mujer y le dijo a Simón:

—¿Ves a esta mujer? Cuando entré en tu casa, no me diste agua para los pies, pero ella me ha bañado los pies en lágrimas y me los ha secado con sus cabellos. [45]Tú no me besaste, pero ella, desde que entré, no ha dejado de besarme los pies. [46]Tú no me ungiste la cabeza con aceite, pero ella me ungió los pies con perfume. [47]Por esto te digo: si ella ha amado mucho, es que sus muchos pecados le han sido perdonados.[q] Pero a quien poco se le perdona, poco ama.

[48]Entonces le dijo Jesús a ella:

—Tus pecados quedan perdonados.

[49]Los otros invitados comenzaron a decir entre sí: «¿Quién es éste, que hasta perdona pecados?»

[50]—Tu fe te ha salvado —le dijo Jesús a la mujer—; vete en paz.

Parábola del sembrador
8:4-15 — Mt 13:2-23; Mr 4:1-20

8 Después de esto, Jesús estuvo recorriendo los pueblos y las aldeas, proclamando las buenas *nuevas del reino de Dios. Lo acompañaban los doce, [2]y también algunas mujeres que habían sido sanadas de *espíritus malignos y de enfermedades: María, a la que llamaban Magdalena, y la que habían salido siete demonios; [3]Juana, esposa de Cuza, el administrador de Herodes; Susana y muchas más que los ayudaban con sus propios recursos.

[4]De cada pueblo salía gente para ver a Jesús, y cuando se reunió una gran multitud, él les contó esta parábola: [5]«Un sembrador salió a sembrar. Al esparcir la semilla, una parte cayó junto al camino; fue pisoteada, y los pájaros se la comieron. [6]Otra parte cayó sobre las piedras y, cuando brotó, las plantas se secaron por falta de humedad. [7]Otra parte cayó entre espinos que, al crecer junto con la semilla, la ahogaron. [8]Pero otra parte cayó en buen terreno; así que brotó y produjo una cosecha del ciento por uno.»

Dicho esto, exclamó: «El que tenga ðídos para oír, que oiga.»

[9]Sus discípulos le preguntaron cuál era el significado de esta parábola. [10]«A ustedes se les ha concedido que conozcan los *secretos del reino de Dios —les contestó—; pero a los demás se les habla por medio de parábolas para que

»"aunque miren, no vean;
   aunque oigan, no entiendan".[r]

[11]»Éste es el significado de la parábola: La semilla es la palabra de Dios. [12]Los que están junto al camino son los que oyen, pero luego viene el diablo y les quita la palabra del corazón, no sea que crean y se salven. [13]Los que están sobre las piedras son los que reciben la palabra con alegría cuando la oyen, pero no tienen raíz. Éstos creen por algún tiempo, pero se apartan cuando llega la *prueba. [14]La parte que cayó entre espinos son los que oyen, pero, con el correr

---

l 7:27 Mal 3:1   m 7:29,30 Algunos intérpretes piensan que estos versículos forman parte del discurso de Jesús.
n 7:35 queda . . . siguen. Lit. ha sido justificada por todos sus hijos.   ñ 7:36 se sentó a la mesa. Lit. se recostó.   o 7:38 se arrojó a los pies de Jesús. Lit. se puso detrás junto a sus pies; es decir, detrás del recostadero.   p 7:41 quinientas monedas de plata. Lit. quinientos *denarios.   q 7:47 te digo ... perdonados. Lit. te digo que sus muchos pecados han sido perdonados porque amó mucho.
r 8:10 Is 6:9

del tiempo, los ahogan las preocupaciones, las riquezas y los placeres de esta vida, y no maduran. 15Pero la parte que cayó en buen terreno son los que oyen la palabra con corazón noble y bueno, y la retienen; y como perseveran, producen una buena cosecha.

Una lámpara en una repisa

16»Nadie enciende una lámpara para después cubrirla con una vasija o ponerla debajo de la cama, sino para ponerla en una repisa, a fin de que los que entren tengan luz. 17No hay nada escondido que no llegue a descubrirse, ni nada oculto que no llegue a conocerse públicamente. 18Por lo tanto, pongan mucha atención. Al que tiene, se le dará más; al que no tiene, hasta lo que cree tener se le quitará.»

La madre y los hermanos de Jesús
8:19-21 — Mt 12:46-50; Mr 3:31-35

19La madre y los hermanos de Jesús fueron a verlo, pero como había mucha gente, no lograban acercársele.

20—Tu madre y tus hermanos están afuera y quieren verte —le avisaron.

21Pero él les contestó:

—Mi madre y mis hermanos son los que oyen la palabra de Dios y la ponen en práctica.

Jesús calma la tormenta
8:22-25 — Mt 8:23-27; Mr 4:36-41

22Un día subió Jesús con sus discípulos a una barca.

—Crucemos al otro lado del lago —les dijo.

Así que partieron, 23y mientras navegaban, él se durmió. Entonces se desató una tormenta sobre el lago, de modo que la barca comenzó a inundarse y corrían gran peligro.

24Los discípulos fueron a despertarlo.

—¡Maestro, Maestro, nos vamos a ahogar! —gritaron.

Él se levantó y reprendió al viento y a las olas; la tormenta se apaciguó y todo quedó tranquilo.

25—¿Dónde está la fe de ustedes? —les dijo a sus discípulos.

Con temor y asombro ellos se decían unos a otros: «¿Quién es éste, que manda aun a los vientos y al agua, y le obedecen?»

Liberación de un endemoniado
8:26-37 — Mt 8:28-34
8:26-39 — Mr 5:1-20

26Navegaron hasta la región de los gerasenos,s que está al otro lado del lago, frente a Galilea. 27Al desembarcar Jesús, un endemoniado que venía del pueblo le salió al encuentro. Hacía mucho tiempo que este hombre no se vestía; tampoco vivía en una casa sino en los sepulcros. 28Cuando vio a Jesús, dio un grito y se arrojó a sus pies. Entonces exclamó con fuerza:

—¿Por qué te entrometes, Jesús, Hijo del Dios Altísimo? ¡Te ruego que no me atormentes!

29Es que Jesús le había ordenado al *espíritu maligno que saliera del hombre. Se había apoderado de él muchas veces y, aunque le sujetaban los pies y las manos con cadenas y lo mantenían bajo custodia, rompía las cadenas y el demonio lo arrastraba a lugares solitarios.

30—¿Cómo te llamas? —le preguntó Jesús.

—Legión —respondió, ya que habían entrado en él muchos demonios.

31Y éstos le suplicaban a Jesús que no los mandara al *abismo. 32Como había una manada grande de cerdos paciendo en la colina, le rogaron a Jesús que los dejara entrar en ellos. Así que él les dio permiso. 33Y cuando los demonios salieron del hombre, entraron en los cerdos, y la manada se precipitó al lago por el despeñadero y se ahogó.

34Al ver lo sucedido, los que cuidaban los cerdos huyeron y dieron la noticia en el pueblo y por los campos, 35y la gente salió a ver lo que había pasado. Llegaron a donde estaba Jesús y encontraron, sentado a sus pies, al hombre de quien habían salido los demonios. Cuando lo vieron vestido y en su sano juicio, tuvieron miedo. 36Los que habían presenciado estas cosas le contaron a la gente cómo el endemoniado había sido *sanado. 37Entonces toda la gente de la región de los gerasenos le pidió a Jesús que se fuera de allí, porque les había entrado mucho miedo. Así que él subió a la barca para irse.

38Ahora bien, el hombre de quien habían salido los demonios le rogaba que le permitiera acompañarlo, pero Jesús lo despidió y le dijo:

39—Vuelve a tu casa y cuenta todo lo que Dios ha hecho por ti.

Así que el hombre se fue y proclamó por todo el pueblo lo mucho que Jesús había hecho por él.

Una niña muerta y una mujer enferma
8:40-56 — Mt 9:18-26; Mr 5:22-43

40Cuando Jesús regresó, la multitud se alegró de verlo, pues todos estaban esperándolo. 41En esto llegó un hombre llamado Jairo, que era un jefe de la sinagoga. Arrojándose a los pies de Jesús, le suplicaba que fuera a su casa, 42porque su única hija, de unos doce años, se estaba muriendo.

Jesús se puso en camino y las multitudes lo apretujaban. 43Había entre la gente una mujer que hacía doce años padecía de hemorragias,t sin que nadie pudiera sanarla. 44Ella se le acercó por detrás y le tocó el borde del manto, y al instante cesó su hemorragia.

45—¿Quién me ha tocado? —preguntó Jesús.

Como todos negaban haberlo tocado, Pedro le dijo:

—Maestro, son multitudes las que te aprietan y te oprimen.

46—No, alguien me ha tocado —replicó Jesús—; yo sé que de mí ha salido poder.

47La mujer, al ver que no podía pasar inadvertida, se acercó temblando y se arrojó a sus pies. En presencia de toda la gente, contó por qué lo había tocado y cómo había sido sanada al instante.

48—Hija, tu fe te ha *sanado —le dijo Jesús—. Vete en paz.

49Todavía estaba hablando Jesús, cuando alguien llegó de la casa de Jairo, jefe de la sinagoga, para decirle:

—Tu hija ha muerto. No molestes más al Maestro.

50Al oír esto, Jesús le dijo a Jairo:

—No tengas miedo; cree nada más, y ella será sanada.

51Cuando llegó a la casa de Jairo, no dejó que nadie entrara con él, excepto Pedro, Juan y *Jacobo, y el padre y la madre de la niña. 52Todos estaban llorando, muy afligidos por ella.

—Dejen de llorar —les dijo Jesús—. No está muerta sino dormida.

---

s 8:26 gerasenos. Var. gadarenos; otra var. gergesenos; también en v. 37.   t 8:43 hemorragias. Var. hemorragias y que había gastado en médicos todo lo que tenía.

⁵³Entonces ellos empezaron a burlarse de él porque sabían que estaba muerta. ⁵⁴Pero él la tomó de la mano y le dijo:

—¡Niña, levántate!

⁵⁵Recobró la vida^u y al instante se levantó. Jesús mandó darle de comer. ⁵⁶Los padres se quedaron atónitos, pero él les advirtió que no contaran a nadie lo que había sucedido.

Jesús envía a los doce
9:3-5 — Mt 10:9-15; Mr 6:8-11
9:7-9 — Mt 14:1-2; Mr 6:14-16

9 Habiendo reunido a los doce, Jesús les dio poder y autoridad para expulsar a todos los demonios y para sanar enfermedades. ²Entonces los envió a predicar el reino de Dios y a sanar a los enfermos. ³«No lleven nada para el camino: ni bastón, ni bolsa, ni pan, ni dinero, ni dos mudas de ropa —les dijo—. ⁴En cualquier casa que entren, quédense allí hasta que salgan del pueblo. ⁵Si no los reciben bien, al salir de ese pueblo, sacúdanse el polvo de los pies como un testimonio contra sus habitantes.» ⁶Así que partieron y fueron por todas partes de pueblo en pueblo, predicando el evangelio y sanando a la gente.

⁷Herodes el tetrarca se enteró de todo lo que estaba sucediendo. Estaba perplejo porque algunos decían que Juan había *resucitado; ⁸otros, que se había aparecido Elías; y otros, en fin, que había resucitado alguno de los antiguos profetas. ⁹Pero Herodes dijo: «A Juan mandé que le cortaran la cabeza; ¿quién es, entonces, éste de quien oigo tales cosas?» Y procuraba verlo.

Jesús alimenta a los cinco mil
9:10-17 — Mt 14:13-21; Mr 6:32-44; Jn 6:5-13

¹⁰Cuando regresaron los apóstoles, le relataron a Jesús lo que habían hecho. Él se los llevó consigo y se retiraron solos a un pueblo llamado Betsaida, ¹¹pero la gente se enteró y lo siguió. Él los recibió y les habló del reino de Dios. También sanó a los que lo necesitaban.

¹²Al atardecer se le acercaron los doce y le dijeron:

—Despide a la gente, para que vaya a buscar alojamiento y comida en los campos y pueblos cercanos, pues donde estamos no hay nada.^v

¹³—Denles ustedes mismos de comer —les dijo Jesús.

—No tenemos más que cinco panes y dos pescados, a menos que vayamos a comprar comida para toda esta gente —objetaron ellos, ¹⁴porque había allí unos cinco mil hombres.

Pero Jesús dijo a sus discípulos:

—Hagan que se sienten en grupos de cincuenta cada uno.

¹⁵Así lo hicieron los discípulos, y se sentaron todos. ¹⁶Entonces Jesús tomó los cinco panes y los dos pescados, y mirando al cielo, los bendijo. Luego los partió y se los dio a los discípulos para que se los repartieran a la gente. ¹⁷Todos comieron hasta quedar satisfechos, y de los pedazos que sobraron se recogieron doce canastas.

La confesión de Pedro
9:18-20 — Mt 16:13-16; Mr 8:27-29
9:22-27 — Mt 16:21-28; Mr 8:31—9:1

¹⁸Un día cuando Jesús estaba orando para sí, estando allí sus discípulos, les preguntó:

—¿Quién dice la gente que soy yo?

¹⁹—Unos dicen que Juan el Bautista, otros que Elías, y otros que uno de los antiguos profetas ha resucitado —respondieron.

²⁰—Y ustedes, ¿quién dicen que soy yo?

—El *Cristo de Dios —afirmó Pedro.

²¹Jesús les ordenó terminantemente que no dijeran esto a nadie. Y les dijo:

²²—El Hijo del hombre tiene que sufrir muchas cosas y ser rechazado por los *ancianos, los jefes de los sacerdotes y los *maestros de la ley. Es necesario que lo maten y que resucite al tercer día.

²³Dirigiéndose a todos, declaró:

—Si alguien quiere ser mi discípulo, que se niegue a sí mismo, lleve su cruz cada día y me siga. ²⁴Porque el que quiera salvar su *vida, la perderá; pero el que pierda su vida por mi causa, la salvará. ²⁵¿De qué le sirve a uno ganar el mundo entero si se pierde o se destruye a sí mismo? ²⁶Si alguien se avergüenza de mí y de mis palabras, el Hijo del hombre se avergonzará de él cuando venga en su gloria y en la gloria del Padre y de los santos ángeles. ²⁷Además, les aseguro que algunos de los aquí presentes no sufrirán la muerte sin antes haber visto el reino de Dios.

La transfiguración
9:28-36 — Mt 17:1-8; Mr 9:2-8

²⁸Unos ocho días después de decir esto, Jesús, acompañado de Pedro, Juan y *Jacobo, subió a una montaña a orar. ²⁹Mientras oraba, su rostro se transformó, y su ropa se tornó blanca y radiante. ³⁰Y aparecieron dos personajes —Moisés y Elías— que conversaban con Jesús. ³¹Tenían un aspecto glorioso, y hablaban de la partida^w de Jesús, que él estaba por llevar a cabo en Jerusalén. ³²Pedro y sus compañeros estaban rendidos de sueño, pero cuando se despabilaron, vieron su gloria y a los dos personajes que estaban con él. ³³Mientras éstos se apartaban de Jesús, Pedro, sin saber lo que estaba diciendo, propuso:

—Maestro, ¡qué bien que estemos aquí! Podemos levantar tres albergues: uno para ti, otro para Moisés y otro para Elías.

³⁴Estaba hablando todavía cuando apareció una nube que los envolvió, de modo que se asustaron. ³⁵Entonces salió de la nube una voz que dijo: «Éste es mi Hijo, mi escogido; escúchenlo.» ³⁶Después de oírse la voz, Jesús quedó solo. Los discípulos guardaron esto en secreto, y por algún tiempo a nadie contaron nada de lo que habían visto.

Jesús sana a un muchacho endemoniado
9:37-42,43-45 — Mt 17:14-18,22-23;
Mr 9:14-27,30-32

³⁷Al día siguiente, cuando bajaron de la montaña, le salió al encuentro mucha gente. ³⁸Y un hombre de entre la multitud exclamó:

—Maestro, te ruego que atiendas a mi hijo, pues es el único que tengo. ³⁹Resulta que un espíritu se posesiona de él, y de repente el muchacho se pone a gritar; también lo sacude con violencia y hace que eche espumarajos. Cuando lo atormenta, a duras penas lo suelta. ⁴⁰Ya le rogué a tus discípulos que lo expulsaran, pero no pudieron.

⁴¹—¡Ah, generación incrédula y perversa! —respondió Jesús—. ¿Hasta cuándo tendré que estar con ustedes y soportarlos? Trae acá a tu hijo.

⁴²Estaba acercándose el muchacho cuando el demonio lo derribó con una convulsión. Pero Jesús re-

---

^u **8:55** *Recobró la vida.* Lit. *Y volvió el espíritu de ella.* ^v **9:12** *donde estamos no hay nada.* Lit. *aquí estamos en un lugar desierto.*
^w **9:31** *de la partida.* Lit. *del éxodo.*

prendió al *espíritu maligno, sanó al muchacho y se lo devolvió al padre. ⁴³Y todos se quedaron asombrados de la grandeza de Dios.

En medio de tanta admiración por todo lo que hacía, Jesús dijo a sus discípulos:

⁴⁴—Presten mucha atención a lo que les voy a decir: El Hijo del hombre va a ser entregado en manos de los hombres.

⁴⁵Pero ellos no entendían lo que quería decir con esto. Les estaba encubierto para que no lo comprendieran, y no se atrevían a preguntárselo.

¿Quién va a ser el más importante?
9:46-48 — Mt 18:1-5
9:46-50 — Mr 9:33-40

⁴⁶Surgió entre los discípulos una discusión sobre quién de ellos sería el más importante. ⁴⁷Como Jesús sabía bien lo que pensaban, tomó a un niño y lo puso a su lado.

⁴⁸—El que recibe en mi nombre a este niño —les dijo—, me recibe a mí; y el que me recibe a mí, recibe al que me envió. El que es más insignificante entre todos ustedes, ése es el más importante.

⁴⁹—Maestro —intervino Juan—, vimos a un hombre que expulsaba demonios en tu nombre; pero como no anda con nosotros, tratamos de impedírselo.

⁵⁰—No se lo impidan —les replicó Jesús—, porque el que no está contra ustedes está a favor de ustedes.

La oposición de los samaritanos

⁵¹Como se acercaba el tiempo de que fuera llevado al cielo, Jesús se hizo el firme propósito de ir a Jerusalén. ⁵²Envió por delante mensajeros, que entraron en un pueblo samaritano para prepararle alojamiento; ⁵³pero allí la gente no quiso recibirlo porque se dirigía a Jerusalén. ⁵⁴Cuando los discípulos *Jacobo y Juan vieron esto, le preguntaron:

—Señor, ¿quieres que hagamos caer fuego del cielo paraˣ que los destruya?

⁵⁵Pero Jesús se volvió a ellos y los reprendió. ⁵⁶Luegoy siguieron la jornada a otra aldea.

Lo que cuesta seguir a Jesús
9:57-60 — Mt 8:19-22

⁵⁷Iban por el camino cuando alguien le dijo:

—Te seguiré a dondequiera que vayas.

⁵⁸—Las zorras tienen madrigueras y las aves tienen nidos —le respondió Jesús—, pero el Hijo del hombre no tiene dónde recostar la cabeza.

⁵⁹A otro le dijo:

—Sígueme.

—Señor —le contestó—, primero déjame ir a enterrar a mi padre.

⁶⁰—Deja que los muertos entierren a sus propios muertos, pero tú ve y proclama el reino de Dios —le replicó Jesús.

⁶¹Otro afirmó:

—Te seguiré, Señor; pero primero déjame despedirme de mi familia.

⁶²Jesús le respondió:

—Nadie que mire atrás después de poner la mano en el arado es apto para el reino de Dios.

Jesús envía a los setenta y dos
10:4-12 — Lc 9:3-5
10:13-15,21-22 — Mt 11:21-23,25-27
10:23-24 — Mt 13:16-17

10 Después de esto, el Señor escogió a otros setenta y dosᶻ para enviarlos de dos en dos delante de él a todo pueblo y lugar a donde él pensaba ir. ²«Es abundante la cosecha —les dijo—, pero son pocos los obreros. Pídanle, por tanto, al Señor de la cosecha que mande obreros a su campo. ³¡Vayan ustedes! Miren que los envío como corderos en medio de lobos. ⁴No lleven monedero ni bolsa ni sandalias; ni se detengan a saludar a nadie por el camino.

⁵»Cuando entren en una casa, digan primero: "Paz a esta casa." ⁶Si hay allí alguien digno de paz, gozará de ella; y si no, la bendición no se cumplirá.ᵃ ⁷Quédense en esa casa, y coman y beban de lo que ellos tengan, porque el trabajador tiene derecho a su sueldo. No anden de casa en casa.

⁸»Cuando entren en un pueblo y los reciban, coman lo que les sirvan. ⁹Sanen a los enfermos que encuentren allí y díganles: "El reino de Dios ya está cerca de ustedes." ¹⁰Pero cuando entren en un pueblo donde no los reciban, salgan a las plazas y digan: ¹¹"Aun el polvo de este pueblo, que se nos ha pegado a los pies, nos lo sacudimos en protesta contra ustedes. Pero tengan por seguro que ya está cerca el reino de Dios." ¹²Les digo que en aquel día será más tolerable el castigo para Sodoma que para ese pueblo.

¹³»¡Ay de ti, Corazín! ¡Ay de ti, Betsaida! Si se hubieran hecho en Tiro y en Sidón los milagros que se hicieron en medio de ustedes, ya hace tiempo que se habrían *arrepentido con grandes lamentos.ᵇ ¹⁴Pero en el juicio será más tolerable el castigo para Tiro y Sidón que para ustedes. ¹⁵Y tú, Capernaúm, ¿acaso serás levantada hasta el cielo? No, sino que descenderás hasta el *abismo.

¹⁶»El que los escucha a ustedes, me escucha a mí; el que los rechaza a ustedes, me rechaza a mí; y el que me rechaza a mí, rechaza al que me envió.»

¹⁷Cuando los setenta y dos regresaron, dijeron contentos:

—Señor, hasta los demonios se nos someten en tu nombre.

¹⁸—Yo veía a Satanás caer del cielo como un rayo —respondió él—. ¹⁹Sí, les he dado autoridad a ustedes para pisotear serpientes y escorpiones y vencer todo el poder del enemigo; nada les podrá hacer daño. ²⁰Sin embargo, no se alegren de que puedan someter a los espíritus, sino alégrense de que sus nombres están escritos en el cielo.

²¹En aquel momento Jesús, lleno de alegría por el Espíritu Santo, dijo: «Te alabo, Padre, Señor del cielo y de la tierra, porque habiendo escondido estas cosas de los sabios e instruidos, se las has revelado a los que son como niños. Sí, Padre, porque así fue tu buena voluntad.

²²»Mi Padre me ha entregado todas las cosas. Nadie sabe quién es el Hijo, sino el Padre, y nadie sabe quién es el Padre, sino el Hijo y aquel a quien el Hijo quiera revelárselo.»

²³Volviéndose a sus discípulos, les dijo aparte: «*Dichosos los ojos que ven lo que ustedes ven. ²⁴Les digo que muchos profetas y reyes quisieron ver lo

---

ˣ **9:54** *cielo para.* Var. *cielo, como hizo Elías, para.* ʸ **9:55,56** *reprendió. v. 56 Luego.* Var. *reprendió. /—Ustedes no saben de qué espíritu son —les dijo—, v. 56 porque el Hijo del Hombre no vino para destruir la vida de las personas sino para salvarla. / Luego.* ᶻ **10:1** *setenta y dos.* Var. *setenta;* también en v. 17. ᵃ **10:6** *Si hay . . . se cumplirá.* Lit. *Si hay allí un hijo de paz, la paz de ustedes reposará sobre él; y si no, volverá a ustedes.* ᵇ **10:13** *con grandes lamentos.* Lit. *sentados en saco y ceniza.*

que ustedes ven, pero no lo vieron; y oír lo que ustedes oyen, pero no lo oyeron.»

Parábola del buen samaritano
10:25-28 — Mt 22:34-40; Mr 12:28-31

25En esto se presentó un *experto en la ley y, para poner a prueba a Jesús, le hizo esta pregunta:

—Maestro, ¿qué tengo que hacer para heredar la vida eterna?

26Jesús replicó:

—¿Qué está escrito en la ley? ¿Cómo la interpretas tú?

27Como respuesta el hombre citó:

—"Ama al Señor tu Dios con todo tu corazón, con todo tu ser, con todas tus fuerzas y con toda tu mente",c y: "Ama a tu prójimo como a ti mismo."d

28—Bien contestado —le dijo Jesús—. Haz eso y vivirás.

29Pero él quería justificarse, así que le preguntó a Jesús:

—¿Y quién es mi prójimo?

30Jesús respondió:

—Bajaba un hombre de Jerusalén a Jericó, y cayó en manos de unos ladrones. Le quitaron la ropa, lo golpearon y se fueron, dejándolo medio muerto. 31Resulta que viajaba por el mismo camino un sacerdote quien, al verlo, se desvió y siguió de largo. 32Así también llegó a aquel lugar un levita, y al verlo, se desvió y siguió de largo. 33Pero un samaritano que iba de viaje llegó a donde estaba el hombre y, viéndolo, se compadeció de él. 34Se acercó, le curó las heridas con vino y aceite, y se las vendó. Luego lo montó sobre su propia cabalgadura, lo llevó a un alojamiento y lo cuidó. 35Al día siguiente, sacó dos monedas de platae y se las dio al dueño del alojamiento. "Cuídemelo —le dijo—, y lo que gaste usted de más, se lo pagaré cuando yo vuelva." 36¿Cuál de estos tres piensas que demostró ser el prójimo del que cayó en manos de los ladrones?

37—El que se compadeció de él —contestó el experto en la ley.

—Anda entonces y haz tú lo mismo —concluyó Jesús.

En casa de Marta y María

38Mientras iba de camino con sus discípulos, Jesús entró en una aldea, y una mujer llamada Marta lo recibió en su casa. 39Tenía ella una hermana llamada María que, sentada a los pies del Señor, escuchaba lo que él decía. 40Marta, por su parte, se sentía abrumada porque tenía mucho que hacer. Así que se acercó a él y le dijo:

—Señor, ¿no te importa que mi hermana me haya dejado sirviendo sola? ¡Dile que me ayude!

41—Marta, Marta —le contestó Jesús—, estás inquieta y preocupada por muchas cosas, 42pero sólo una es necesaria.f María ha escogido la mejor, y nadie se la quitará.

Jesús enseña sobre la oración
11:2-4 — Mt 6:9-13
11:9-13 — Mt 7:7-11

11 Un día estaba Jesús orando en cierto lugar. Cuando terminó, le dijo uno de sus discípulos:

—Señor, enséñanos a orar, así como Juan enseñó a sus discípulos.

2Él les dijo:

—Cuando oren, digan:

»"Padre,g
*santificado sea tu nombre.
Venga tu reino.h
3Danos cada día nuestro pan cotidiano.i
4Perdónanos nuestros pecados,
    porque también nosotros perdonamos a
    todos los que nos ofenden.j
Y no nos metas en *tentación."k

5»Supongamos —continuó— que uno de ustedes tiene un amigo, y a medianoche va y le dice: "Amigo, préstame tres panes, 6pues se me ha presentado un amigo recién llegado de viaje, y no tengo nada que ofrecerle." 7Y el que está adentro le contesta: "No me molestes. Ya está cerrada la puerta, y mis hijos y yo estamos acostados. No puedo levantarme a darte nada." 8Les digo que, aunque no se levante a darle pan por ser amigo suyo, sí se levantará por su impertinencia y le dará cuanto necesite.

9»Así que yo les digo: Pidan, y se les dará; busquen, y encontrarán; llamen, y se les abrirá la puerta. 10Porque todo el que pide, recibe; el que busca, encuentra; y al que llama, se le abre.

11»¿Quién de ustedes que sea padre, si su hijo le pidel un pescado, le dará en cambio una serpiente? 12O si le pide un huevo, le dará un escorpión? 13Pues si ustedes, aun siendo malos, saben dar cosas buenas a sus hijos, ¡cuánto más el Padre celestial dará el Espíritu Santo a quienes se lo pidan!

Jesús y Beelzebú
11:14-15,17-22,24-26 — Mt 12:22,24-29,43-45
11:17-22 — Mr 3:23-27

14En otra ocasión Jesús expulsaba de un hombre a un demonio que lo había dejado mudo. Cuando salió el demonio, el mudo habló, y la gente se quedó asombrada. 15Pero algunos dijeron: «Éste expulsa a los demonios por medio de *Beelzebú, príncipe de los demonios.» 16Otros, para ponerlo a *prueba, le pedían una señal del cielo.

17Como él conocía sus pensamientos, les dijo: «Todo reino dividido contra sí mismo quedará asolado, y una casa dividida contra sí misma se derrumbará.m 18Por tanto, si Satanás está dividido contra sí mismo, ¿cómo puede mantenerse en pie su reino? Lo pregunto porque ustedes dicen que yo expulso a los demonios por medio de Beelzebú. 19Ahora bien, si yo expulso a los demonios por medio de Beelzebú, ¿los seguidores de ustedes por medio de quién los expulsan? Por eso ellos mismos los juzgarán a ustedes. 20Pero si expulso a los demonios con el podern de Dios, eso significa que ha llegado a ustedes el reino de Dios.

21»Cuando un hombre fuerte y bien armado cuida su hacienda, sus bienes están seguros. 22Pero si lo ataca otro más fuerte que él y lo vence, le quita las armas en que confiaba y reparte el botín.

23»El que no está de mi parte, está contra mí; y el que conmigo no recoge, esparce.

---

c **10:27** Dt 6:5 d **10:27** Lv 19:18 e **10:35** *monedas de plata*. Lit. *denarios*. f **10:42** *sólo una es necesaria*. Var. *se necesitan pocas cosas, o una sola*. g **11:2** *Padre*. Var. *Padre nuestro que estás en el cielo* (véase Mt 6:9). h **11:2** *reino*. Var. *reino. Hágase tu voluntad en la tierra como en el cielo* (véase Mt 6:10). i **11:3** *nuestro pan cotidiano*. Alt. *el pan que necesitamos*. j **11:4** *nos ofenden*. Lit. *nos deben*. k **11:4** *tentación*. Var. *tentación, sino líbranos del maligno* (véase Mt 6:13). l **11:11** *le pide pan, le dará una piedra; o si le pide*. m **11:17** *y una casa . . . derrumbará*. Alt. *y sus casas se derrumbarán unas sobre otras*. n **11:20** *poder*. Lit. *dedo*.

24»Cuando un *espíritu maligno sale de una persona, va por lugares áridos buscando un descanso. Y al no encontrarlo, dice: "Volveré a mi casa, de donde salí." 25Cuando llega, la encuentra barrida y arreglada. 26Luego va y trae otros siete espíritus más malvados que él, y entran a vivir allí. Así que el estado final de aquella persona resulta peor que el inicial.»

27Mientras Jesús decía estas cosas, una mujer de entre la multitud exclamó:

—*¡Dichosa la mujer que te dio a luz y te amamantó!ñ

28—Dichosos más bien —contestó Jesús— los que oyen la palabra de Dios y la obedecen.

La señal de Jonás
11:29-32 — Mt 12:39-42

29Como crecía la multitud, Jesús se puso a decirles: «Ésta es una generación malvada. Pide una señal milagrosa, pero no se le dará más señal que la de Jonás. 30Así como Jonás fue una señal para los habitantes de Nínive, también lo será el Hijo del hombre para esta generación. 31La reina del Sur se levantará en el día del juicio y condenará a esta gente; porque ella vino desde los confines de la tierra para escuchar la sabiduría de Salomón, y aquí tienen ustedes a uno más grande que Salomón. 32Los ninivitas se levantarán en el día del juicio y condenarán a esta generación; porque ellos se *arrepintieron al escuchar la predicación de Jonás, y aquí tienen ustedes a uno más grande que Jonás.

La lámpara del cuerpo
11:34-35 — Mt 6:22-23

33»Nadie enciende una lámpara para luego ponerla en un lugar escondido o cubrirla con un cajón, sino para ponerla en una repisa, a fin de que los que entren tengan luz. 34Tus ojos son la lámpara de tu cuerpo. Si tu visión es clara, todo tu ser disfrutará de la luz; pero si está nublada, todo tu ser estará en la oscuridad.o 35Asegúrate de que la luz que crees tener no sea oscuridad. 36Por tanto, si todo tu ser disfruta de la luz, sin que ninguna parte quede en la oscuridad, estarás completamente iluminado, como cuando una lámpara te alumbra con su luz.»

Jesús denuncia a los fariseos y a los expertos en la ley

37Cuando Jesús terminó de hablar, un *fariseo lo invitó a comer con él; así que entró en la casa y se *sentó a la mesa. 38Pero el fariseo se sorprendió al ver que Jesús no había cumplido con el rito de lavarse antes de comer.

39—Resulta que ustedes los fariseos —les dijo el Señor—, *limpian el vaso y el plato por fuera, pero por dentro están ustedes llenos de codicia y de maldad. 40¡Necios! ¿Acaso el que hizo lo de afuera no hizo también lo de adentro? 41Den más bien a los pobres de lo que está dentro,p y así todo quedará limpio para ustedes.

42»¡Ay de ustedes, fariseos!, que dan la décima parte de la menta, de la ruda y de toda clase de legumbres, pero descuidan la justicia y el amor de Dios. Debían haber practicado esto, sin dejar de hacer aquello.

43»¡Ay de ustedes, fariseos!, que se mueren por los primeros puestos en las sinagogas y los saludos en las plazas.

44»¡Ay de ustedes!, que son como tumbas sin lápida, sobre las que anda la gente sin darse cuenta.

45Uno de los *expertos en la ley le respondió:

—Maestro, al hablar así nos insultas también a nosotros.

46Contestó Jesús:

—¡Ay de ustedes también, expertos en la ley! Abruman a los demás con cargas que apenas se pueden soportar, pero ustedes mismos no levantan ni un dedo para ayudarlos.

47»¡Ay de ustedes!, que construyen monumentos para los profetas, a quienes los antepasados de ustedes mataron. 48En realidadq aprueban lo que hicieron sus antepasados; ellos mataron a los profetas, y ustedes les construyen los sepulcros. 49Por eso dijo Dios en su sabiduría: "Les enviaré profetas y apóstoles, de los cuales matarán a unos y perseguirán a otros." 50Por lo tanto, a esta generación se le pedirán cuentas de la sangre de todos los profetas derramada desde el principio del mundo, 51desde la sangre de Abel hasta la sangre de Zacarías, el que murió entre el altar y el *santuario. Sí, les aseguro que de todo esto se le pedirán cuentas a esta generación.

52»¡Ay de ustedes, expertos en la ley!, porque se han adueñado de la llave del conocimiento. Ustedes mismos no han entrado, y a los que querían entrar les han cerrado el paso.

53Cuando Jesús salió de allí, los *maestros de la ley y los fariseos, resentidos, se pusieron a acosarlo a preguntas. 54Estaban tendiéndole trampas para ver si fallaba en algo.

Advertencias y estímulos
12:2-9 — Mt 10:26-33

12 Mientras tanto, se habían reunido millares de personas, tantas que se atropellaban unas a otras. Jesús comenzó a hablar, dirigiéndose primero a sus discípulos: «Cuídense de la levadura de los *fariseos, o sea, de la *hipocresía. 2No hay nada encubierto que no llegue a revelarse, ni nada escondido que no llegue a conocerse. 3Así que todo lo que ustedes han dicho en la oscuridad se dará a conocer a plena luz, y lo que han susurrado a puerta cerrada se proclamará desde las azoteas.

4»A ustedes, mis amigos, les digo que no teman a los que matan el cuerpo pero después no pueden hacer más. 5Les voy a enseñar más bien a quién deben temer: teman al que, después de dar muerte, tiene poder para echarlos al infierno.r Sí, les aseguro que a él deben temerle. 6¿No se venden cinco gorriones por dos monedas?s Sin embargo, Dios no se olvida de ninguno de ellos. 7Así mismo sucede con ustedes: aun los cabellos de su cabeza están contados. No tengan miedo; ustedes valen más que muchos gorriones.

8»Les aseguro que a cualquiera que me reconozca delante de la gente, también el Hijo del hombre lo reconocerá delante de los ángeles de Dios. 9Pero al que me desconozca delante de la gente se le desconocerá delante de los ángeles de Dios. 10Y todo el que pronuncie alguna palabra contra el Hijo del hombre será perdonado, pero el que *blasfeme contra el Espíritu Santo no tendrá perdón.

ñ 11:27 ¡Dichosa . . . amamantó! Lit. ¡Dichoso el vientre que te llevó y los pechos que te criaron! o 11:34 Si tu visión . . . oscuridad. Lit. Cuando tu ojo es bueno, todo tu cuerpo está iluminado; pero cuando es malo, también tu cuerpo está oscuro P 11:41 lo que está dentro. Alt. lo que tienen. q 11:48 En realidad. Lit. Así que ustedes son testigos y. r 12:5 al infierno. Lit. a la *Gehenna. s 12:6 monedas. Lit. asaria.

11»Cuando los hagan comparecer ante las sinagogas, los gobernantes y las autoridades, no se preocupen de cómo van a defenderse o de qué van a decir, 12porque en ese momento el Espíritu Santo les enseñará lo que deben responder.»

Parábola del rico insensato

13Uno de entre la multitud le pidió:

—Maestro, dile a mi hermano que comparta la herencia conmigo.

14—Hombre —replicó Jesús—, ¿quién me nombró a mí juez o árbitro entre ustedes?

15»¡Tengan cuidado! —advirtió a la gente—. Absténganse de toda avaricia; la vida de una persona no depende de la abundancia de sus bienes.

16Entonces les contó esta parábola:

—El terreno de un hombre rico le produjo una buena cosecha. 17Así que se puso a pensar: "¿Qué voy a hacer? No tengo dónde almacenar mi cosecha." 18Por fin dijo: "Ya sé lo que voy a hacer: derribaré mis graneros y construiré otros más grandes, donde pueda almacenar todo mi grano y mis bienes. 19Y diré: Alma mía, ya tienes bastantes cosas buenas guardadas para muchos años. Descansa, come, bebe y goza de la vida." 20Pero Dios le dijo: "¡Necio! Esta misma noche te van a reclamar la *vida. ¿Y quién se quedará con lo que has acumulado?"

21»Así le sucede al que acumula riquezas para sí mismo, en vez de ser rico delante de Dios.

No se preocupe
12:22-31 — Mt 6:25-33

22Luego dijo Jesús a sus discípulos:

—Por eso les digo: No se preocupen por su *vida, qué comerán; ni por su cuerpo, con qué se vestirán. 23La vida tiene más valor que la comida, y el cuerpo más que la ropa. 24Fíjense en los cuervos: no siembran ni cosechan, ni tienen almacén ni granero; sin embargo, Dios los alimenta. ¡Cuánto más valen ustedes que las aves! 25¿Quién de ustedes, por mucho que se preocupe, puede añadir una sola hora al curso de su vida?t 26Ya que no pueden hacer algo tan insignificante, ¿por qué se preocupan por lo demás?

27»Fíjense cómo crecen los lirios. No trabajan ni hilan; sin embargo, les digo que ni siquiera Salomón, con todo su esplendor, se vestía como uno de ellos. 28Si así viste Dios a la hierba que hoy está en el campo y mañana es arrojada al horno, ¡cuánto más hará por ustedes, gente de poca fe! 29Así que no se afanen por lo que han de comer o beber; dejen de atormentarse. 30El mundo *pagano anda tras todas estas cosas, pero el Padre sabe que ustedes las necesitan. 31Ustedes, por el contrario, busquen el reino de Dios, y estas cosas les serán añadidas.

32»No tengan miedo, mi rebaño pequeño, porque es la buena voluntad del Padre darles el reino. 33Vendan sus bienes y den a los pobres. Proveánse de bolsas que no se desgasten; acumulen un tesoro inagotable en el cielo, donde no hay ladrón que aceche ni polilla que destruya. 34Pues donde tengan ustedes su tesoro, allí estará también su corazón.

La vigilancia
12:35-36 — Mt 25:1-13; Mr 13:33-37
12:39-40,42-46 — Mt 24:43-51

35»Manténganse listos, con la ropa bien ajustadau y la luz encendida. 36Pórtense como siervos que esperan a que regrese su señor de un banquete de bodas, para abrirle la puerta tan pronto como él llegue y toque. 37*Dichosos los *siervos a quienes su señor encuentre pendientes de su llegada. Créanme que se ajustará la ropa, hará que los siervos se sienten a la mesa, y él mismo se pondrá a servirles. 38Sí, dichosos aquellos siervos a quienes su señor encuentre preparados, aunque llegue a la medianoche o de madrugada. 39Pero entiendan esto: Si un dueño de casa supiera a qué hora va a llegar el ladrón, estaría pendiente para no dejarlo forzar la entrada. 40Así mismo deben ustedes estar preparados, porque el Hijo del hombre vendrá cuando menos lo esperen.

41—Señor —le preguntó Pedro—, ¿cuentas esta parábola para nosotros, o para todos?

42Respondió el Señor:

—¿Dónde se halla un mayordomo fiel y prudente a quien su señor deja encargado de los siervos para repartirles la comida a su debido tiempo? 43Dichoso el siervo cuyo señor, al regresar, lo encuentra cumpliendo con su deber. 44Les aseguro que lo pondrá a cargo de todos sus bienes. 45Pero iqué tal si ese siervo se pone a pensar: "Mi señor tarda en volver", y luego comienza a golpear a los criados y a las criadas, a comer y beber y emborracharse! 46El señor de ese siervo volverá el día en que el siervo menos lo espere y a la hora menos pensada. Entonces lo castigará severamente y le impondrá la condena que reciben los incrédulos.v

47»El siervo que conoce la voluntad de su señor, y no se prepara para cumplirla, recibirá muchos golpes. 48En cambio, el que no la conoce y hace algo que merezca castigo, recibirá pocos golpes. A todo el que se le ha dado mucho, se le exigirá mucho; y al que se le ha confiado mucho, se le pedirá aun más.

División en vez de paz
12:51-53 — Mt 10:34-36

49»He venido a traer fuego a la tierra, y ¡cómo quisiera que ya estuviera ardiendo! 50Pero tengo que pasar por la prueba de un bautismo, y ¡cuánta angustia siento hasta que se cumpla! 51¿Creen ustedes que vine a traer paz a la tierra? ¡Les digo que no, sino división! 52De ahora en adelante estarán divididos cinco en una familia, tres contra dos, y dos contra tres. 53Se enfrentarán el padre contra su hijo y el hijo contra su padre, la madre contra su hija y la hija contra su madre, la suegra contra su nuera y la nuera contra su suegra.

Señales de los tiempos

54Luego añadió Jesús, dirigiéndose a la multitud:

—Cuando ustedes ven que se levanta una nube en el occidente, en seguida dicen: "Va a llover", y así sucede. 55Y cuando sopla el viento del sur, dicen: "Va a hacer calor", y así sucede. 56*¡Hipócritas! Ustedes saben interpretar la apariencia de la tierra y del cielo. ¿Cómo es que no saben interpretar el tiempo actual?

57¿Por qué no juzgan por ustedes mismos lo que es justo? 58Si tienes que ir con un adversario al magistrado, procura reconciliarte con él en el camino, no sea que te lleve por la fuerza ante el juez, y el juez te entregue al alguacil, y el alguacil te meta en la cárcel. 59Te digo que no saldrás de allí hasta que pagues el último centavo.w

---

t 12:25 puede añadir . . . su vida. Alt. puede aumentar su estatura siquiera medio metro (lit. un *codo). u 12:35 Manténganse . . . ajustada. Lit. Tengan sus lomos ceñidos. v 12:46 lo castigará . . . incrédulos. Lit. lo cortará en dos y fijará su porción con los incrédulos. w 12:59 centavo. Lit. *lepton.

El que no se arrepiente perecerá

13 En aquella ocasión algunos que habían llegado le contaron a Jesús cómo Pilato había dado muerte a unos galileos cuando ellos ofrecían sus sacrificios.ˣ 2Jesús les respondió: «¿Piensan ustedes que esos galileos, por haber sufrido así, eran más pecadores que todos los demás? 3¡Les digo que no! De la misma manera, todos ustedes perecerán, a menos que se *arrepientan. 4¿O piensan que aquellos dieciocho que fueron aplastados por la torre de Siloé eran más culpables que todos los demás habitantes de Jerusalén? 5¡Les digo que no! De la misma manera, todos ustedes perecerán, a menos que se arrepientan.»

6Entonces les contó esta parábola: «Un hombre tenía una higuera plantada en su viñedo, pero cuando fue a buscar fruto en ella, no encontró nada. 7Así que le dijo al viñador: "Mira, ya hace tres años que vengo a buscar fruto en esta higuera, y no he encontrado nada. ¡Córtala! ¿Para qué ha de ocupar terreno?" 8"Señor —le contestó el viñador—, déjala todavía por un año más, para que yo pueda cavar a su alrededor y echarle abono. 9Así tal vez en adelante dé fruto; si no, córtela."»

Jesús sana en sábado a una mujer encorvada

10Un *sábado Jesús estaba enseñando en una de las sinagogas, 11y estaba allí una mujer que por causa de un demonio llevaba dieciocho años enferma. Andaba encorvada y de ningún modo podía enderezarse. 12Cuando Jesús la vio, la llamó y le dijo:

—Mujer, quedas libre de tu enfermedad.

13Al mismo tiempo, puso las manos sobre ella, y al instante la mujer se enderezó y empezó a alabar a Dios. 14Indignado porque Jesús había sanado en sábado, el jefe de la sinagoga intervino, dirigiéndose a la gente:

—Hay seis días en que se puede trabajar, así que vengan esos días para ser sanados, y no el sábado.

15—*¡Hipócritas! —le contestó el Señor—. ¿Acaso no desata cada uno de ustedes su buey o su burro en sábado, y lo saca del establo para llevarlo a tomar agua? 16Sin embargo, a esta mujer, que es hija de Abraham, y a quien Satanás tenía atada durante dieciocho largos años, ¿no se le debía quitar esta cadena en sábado?

17Cuando razonó así, quedaron humillados todos sus adversarios, pero la gente estaba encantada de tantas maravillas que él hacía.

Parábolas del grano de mostaza y de la levadura

13:18-19 — Mr 4:30-32
13:18-21 — Mt 13:31-33

18—¿A qué se parece el reino de Dios? —continuó Jesús—. ¿Con qué voy a compararlo? 19Se parece a un grano de mostaza que un hombre sembró en su huerto. Creció hasta convertirse en un árbol, y las aves anidaron en sus ramas.

20Volvió a decir:

—¿Con qué voy a comparar el reino de Dios? 21Es como la levadura que una mujer tomó y mezcló con una gran cantidad de harina, hasta que fermentó toda la masa.

La puerta estrecha

22Continuando su viaje a Jerusalén, Jesús enseñaba en los pueblos y aldeas por donde pasaba. 23—Señor, ¿son pocos los que van a salvarse? —le preguntó uno.

24—Esfuércense por entrar por la puerta estrecha —contestó—, porque les digo que muchos tratarán de entrar y no podrán. 25Tan pronto como el dueño de la casa se haya levantado a cerrar la puerta, ustedes desde afuera se pondrán a golpear la puerta, diciendo: "Señor, ábrenos." Pero él les contestará: "No sé quiénes son ustedes." 26Entonces dirán: "Comimos y bebimos contigo, y tú enseñaste en nuestras plazas." 27Pero él les contestará: "Les repito que no sé quiénes son ustedes. ¡Apártense de mí, todos ustedes hacedores de injusticia!"

28»Allí habrá llanto y rechinar de dientes cuando vean en el reino de Dios a Abraham, Isaac, Jacob y a todos los profetas, mientras a ustedes los echan fuera. 29Habrá quienes lleguen del oriente y del occidente, del norte y del sur, para *sentarse al banquete en el reino de Dios. 30En efecto, hay últimos que serán primeros, y primeros que serán últimos.

Lamento de Jesús sobre Jerusalén

13:34-35 — Mt 23:37-39

31En ese momento se acercaron a Jesús unos *fariseos y le dijeron:

—Sal de aquí y vete a otro lugar, porque Herodes quiere matarte.

32Él les contestó:

—Vayan y díganle a ese zorro: "Mira, hoy y mañana seguiré expulsando demonios y sanando a la gente, y al tercer día terminaré lo que debo hacer." 33Tengo que seguir adelante hoy, mañana y pasado mañana, porque no puede ser que muera un profeta fuera de Jerusalén.

34»¡Jerusalén, Jerusalén, que matas a los profetas y apedreas a los que se te envían! ¡Cuántas veces quise reunir a tus hijos, como reúne la gallina a sus pollitos debajo de sus alas, pero no quisiste! 35Pues bien, la casa de ustedes va a quedar abandonada. Y les advierto que ya no volverán a verme hasta el día que digan: "¡Bendito el que viene en el nombre del Señor!"ᶻ

Jesús en casa de un fariseo

14 Un día Jesús fue a comer a casa de un notable de los *fariseos. Era *sábado, así que éstos estaban acechando a Jesús. 2Allí, delante de él, estaba un hombre enfermo de hidropesía. 3Jesús les preguntó a los *expertos en la ley y a los fariseos:

—¿Está permitido o no sanar en sábado?

4Pero ellos se quedaron callados. Entonces tomó al hombre, lo sanó y lo despidió.

5También les dijo:

—Si uno de ustedes tiene un hijoᵃ o un buey que se le cae en un pozo, ¿no lo saca en seguida aunque sea sábado?

6Y no pudieron contestarle nada.

7Al notar cómo los invitados escogían los lugares de honor en la mesa, les contó esta parábola:

8—Cuando alguien te invite a una fiesta de bodas, no te sientes en el lugar de honor, no sea que haya algún invitado más distinguido que tú. 9Si es así, el que los invitó a los dos vendrá y te dirá: "Cédele tu asiento a este hombre." Entonces, avergonzado, tendrás que ocupar el último asiento. 10Más bien, cuando te inviten, siéntate en el último lugar, para que cuando venga el que te invitó, te diga: "Amigo, pasa más adelante a un lugar mejor." Así recibirás honor en presencia de todos los demás invitados.

ˣ **13:1** *le contaron . . . sacrificios.* Lit. *le contaron acerca de los galileos cuya sangre Pilato mezcló con sus sacrificios.* ʸ **13:21** *una gran cantidad.* Lit. *tres satas* (probablemente unos 22 litros). ᶻ **13:35** Sal 118:26 ᵃ **14:5** *hijo.* Var. *burro.*

11Todo el que a sí mismo se enaltece será humillado, y el que se humilla será enaltecido.

12También dijo Jesús al que lo había invitado:

—Cuando des una comida o una cena, no invites a tus amigos, ni a tus hermanos, ni a tus parientes, ni a tus vecinos ricos; no sea que ellos, a su vez, te inviten y así seas recompensado. 13Más bien, cuando des un banquete, invita a los pobres, a los inválidos, a los cojos y a los ciegos. 14Entonces serás *dichoso, pues aunque ellos no tienen con qué recompensarte, serás recompensado en la resurrección de los justos.

Parábola del gran banquete

15Al oír esto, uno de los que estaban *sentados a la mesa con Jesús le dijo:

—*¡Dichoso el que coma en el banquete del reino de Dios!

16Jesús le contestó:

—Cierto hombre preparó un gran banquete e invitó a muchas personas. 17A la hora del banquete mandó a su siervo a decirles a los invitados: "Vengan, porque ya todo está listo." 18Pero todos, sin excepción, comenzaron a disculparse. El primero le dijo: "Acabo de comprar un terreno y tengo que ir a verlo. Te ruego que me disculpes." 19Otro adujo: "Acabo de comprar cinco yuntas de bueyes, y voy a probarlas. Te ruego que me disculpes." 20Otro alegó: "Acabo de casarme y por eso no puedo ir." 21El siervo regresó y le informó de esto a su señor. Entonces el dueño de la casa se enojó y le mandó a su siervo: "Sal de prisa por las plazas y los callejones del pueblo, y trae acá a los pobres, a los inválidos, a los cojos y a los ciegos." 22"Señor —le dijo luego el siervo—, ya hice lo que usted me mandó, pero todavía hay lugar." 23Entonces el señor le respondió: "Ve por los caminos y las veredas, y oblígalos a entrar para que se llene mi casa. 24Les digo que ninguno de aquellos invitados disfrutará de mi banquete."

El precio del discipulado

25Grandes multitudes seguían a Jesús, y se volvió y les dijo: 26«Si alguno viene a mí y no sacrifica el amorb a su padre y a su madre, a su esposa y a sus hijos, a sus hermanos y a sus hermanas, y aun a su propia *vida, no puede ser mi discípulo. 27Y el que no carga su cruz y me sigue, no puede ser mi discípulo.

28»Supongamos que alguno de ustedes quiere construir una torre. ¿Acaso no se sienta primero a calcular el costo, para ver si tiene suficiente dinero para terminarla? 29Si echa los cimientos y no puede terminarla, todos los que la vean comenzarán a burlarse de él, 30y dirán: "Este hombre ya no pudo terminar lo que comenzó a construir."

31»O supongamos que un rey está a punto de ir a la guerra contra otro rey. ¿Acaso no se sienta primero a calcular si con diez mil hombres puede enfrentarse al que viene contra él con veinte mil? 32Si no puede, enviará una delegación mientras el otro está todavía lejos, para pedir condiciones de paz. 33De la misma manera, cualquiera de ustedes que no renuncie a todos sus bienes, no puede ser mi discípulo.

34»La sal es buena, pero si se vuelve insípida, ¿cómo recuperará el sabor? 35No sirve ni para la tierra ni para el abono; hay que tirarla fuera.

»El que tenga oídos para oír, que oiga.»

Parábola de la oveja perdida
15:4-7 – Mt 18:12-14

15 Muchos *recaudadores de impuestos y *pecadores se acercaban a Jesús para oírlo, 2de modo que los *fariseos y los *maestros de la ley se pusieron a murmurar: «Este hombre recibe a los pecadores y come con ellos.»

3Él entonces les contó esta parábola: 4«Supongamos que uno de ustedes tiene cien ovejas y pierde una de ellas. ¿No deja las noventa y nueve en el campo, y va en busca de la oveja perdida hasta encontrarla? 5Y cuando la encuentra, lleno de alegría la carga en los hombros 6y vuelve a la casa. Al llegar, reúne a sus amigos y vecinos, y les dice: "Alégrense conmigo; ya encontré la oveja que se me había perdido." 7Les digo que así es también en el cielo: habrá más alegría por un solo pecador que se *arrepienta, que por noventa y nueve justos que no necesitan arrepentirse.

Parábola de la moneda perdida

8»O supongamos que una mujer tiene diez monedas de platac y pierde una. ¿No enciende una lámpara, barre la casa y busca con cuidado hasta encontrarla? 9Y cuando la encuentra, reúne a sus amigas y vecinas, y les dice: "Alégrense conmigo; ya encontré la moneda que se me había perdido." 10Les digo que así mismo se alegra Dios con sus ángelesd por un pecador que se arrepiente.

Parábola del hijo perdido

11»Un hombre tenía dos hijos —continuó Jesús—. 12El menor de ellos le dijo a su padre: "Papá, dame lo que me toca de la herencia." Así que el padre repartió sus bienes entre los dos. 13Poco después el hijo menor juntó todo lo que tenía y se fue a un país lejano; allí vivió desenfrenadamente y derrochó su herencia.

14»Cuando ya lo había gastado todo, sobrevino una gran escasez en la región, y él comenzó a pasar necesidad. 15Así que fue y consiguió empleo con un ciudadano de aquel país, quien lo mandó a sus campos a cuidar cerdos. 16Tanta hambre tenía que hubiera querido llenarse el estómago con la comida que daban a los cerdos, pero aun así nadie le daba nada. 17Por fin recapacitó y dijo: "¡Cuántos jornaleros de mi padre tienen comida de sobra, y yo aquí me muero de hambre! 18Tengo que volver a mi padre y decirle: Papá, he pecado contra el cielo y contra ti. 19Ya no merezco que se me llame tu hijo; trátame como si fuera uno de tus jornaleros." 20Así que emprendió el viaje y se fue a su padre.

»Todavía estaba lejos cuando su padre lo vio y se compadeció de él; salió corriendo a su encuentro, lo abrazó y lo besó. 21El joven le dijo: "Papá, he pecado contra el cielo y contra ti. Ya no merezco que se me llame tu hijo."e 22Pero el padre ordenó a sus *siervos: "¡Pronto! Traigan la mejor ropa para vestirlo. Pónganle también un anillo en el dedo y sandalias en los pies. 23Traigan el ternero más gordo y mátenlo para celebrar un banquete. 24Porque este hijo mío estaba muerto, pero ahora ha vuelto a la vida; se había perdido, pero ya lo hemos encontrado." Así que empezaron a hacer fiesta.

25»Mientras tanto, el hijo mayor estaba en el campo. Al volver, cuando se acercó a la casa, oyó la música del baile. 26Entonces llamó a uno de los siervos y le preguntó qué pasaba. 27"Ha llegado tu her-

---

b **14:26** no sacrifica el amor. Lit. no odia.   c **15:8** monedas de plata. Lit. *dracmas.   d **15:10** se alegra … ángeles. Lit. hay alegría en la presencia de los ángeles de Dios.   e **15:21** hijo. Var. hijo; trátame como si fuera uno de tus jornaleros.

mano —le respondió—, y tu papá ha matado el ternero más gordo porque ha recobrado a su hijo sano y salvo." 28Indignado, el hermano mayor se negó a entrar. Así que su padre salió a suplicarle que lo hiciera. 29Pero él le contestó: "¡Fíjate cuántos años te he servido sin desobedecer jamás tus órdenes, y ni un cabrito me has dado para celebrar una fiesta con mis amigos! 30¡Pero ahora llega ese hijo tuyo, que ha despilfarrado tu fortuna con prostitutas, y tú mandas matar en su honor el ternero más gordo!"

31»"Hijo mío —le dijo su padre—, tú siempre estás conmigo, y todo lo que tengo es tuyo. 32Pero teníamos que hacer fiesta y alegrarnos, porque este hermano tuyo estaba muerto, pero ahora ha vuelto a la vida; se había perdido, pero ya lo hemos encontrado."»

Parábola del administrador astuto

16 Jesús contó otra parábola a sus discípulos: «Un hombre rico tenía un administrador a quien acusaron de derrochar sus bienes. 2Así que lo mandó a llamar y le dijo: "¿Qué es esto que me dicen de ti? Rinde cuentas de tu administración, porque ya no puedes seguir en tu puesto." 3El administrador reflexionó: "¿Qué voy a hacer ahora que mi patrón está por quitarme el puesto? No tengo fuerzas para cavar, y me da vergüenza pedir limosna. 4Tengo que asegurarme de que, cuando me echen de la administración, haya gente que me reciba en su casa. ¡Ya sé lo que voy a hacer!"

5»Llamó entonces a cada uno de los que le debían algo a su patrón. Al primero le preguntó: "¿Cuánto le debes a mi patrón?" 6"Cien barrilesf de aceite", le contestó él. El administrador le dijo: "Toma tu factura, siéntate en seguida y escribe cincuenta." 7Luego preguntó al segundo: "Y tú, ¿cuánto debes?" "Cien bultosg de trigo", contestó. El administrador le dijo: "Toma tu factura y escribe ochenta."

8»Pues bien, el patrón elogió al administrador de riquezas mundanash por haber actuado con astucia. Es que lo de este mundo, en su trato con los que son como ellos, son más astutos que los que han recibido la luz. 9Por eso les digo que se valgan de las riquezas mundanas para ganar amigos,i a fin de que cuando éstas se acaben haya quienes los reciban a ustedes en las viviendas eternas.

10»El que es honradoj en lo poco, también lo será en lo mucho; y el que no es íntegrok en lo poco, tampoco lo será en lo mucho. 11Por eso, si ustedes no han sido honrados en el uso de las riquezas mundanas,l ¿quién les confiará las verdaderas? 12Y si con lo ajeno no han sido honrados, ¿quién les dará a ustedes lo que les pertenece?

13»Ningún sirviente puede servir a dos patrones. Menospreciará a uno y amará al otro, o querrá mucho a uno y despreciará al otro. Ustedes no pueden servir a la vez a Dios y a las riquezas.»

14Oían todo esto los *fariseos, a quienes les encantaba el dinero, y se burlaban de Jesús. 15Él les dijo: «Ustedes se hacen los buenos ante la gente, pero Dios conoce sus corazones. Dense cuenta de que aquello que la gente tiene en gran estima es detestable delante de Dios.

Otras enseñanzas

16»La ley y los profetas se proclamaron hasta Juan. Desde entonces se anuncian las buenas *nuevas del reino de Dios, y todos se esfuerzan por entrar en él.m 17Es más fácil que desaparezcan el cielo y la tierra, que caiga una sola tilde de la ley.

18»Todo el que se divorcia de su esposa y se casa con otra, comete adulterio; y el que se casa con la divorciada, comete adulterio.

El rico y Lázaro

19»Había un hombre rico que se vestía lujosamenten y daba espléndidos banquetes todos los días. 20A la puerta de su casa se tendía un mendigo llamado Lázaro, que estaba cubierto de llagas 21y que hubiera querido llenarse el estómago con lo que caía de la mesa del rico. Hasta los perros se acercaban y le lamían las llagas.

22»Resulta que murió el mendigo, y los ángeles se lo llevaron para que estuviera al lado de Abraham. También murió el rico, y lo sepultaron. 23En el infierno,ñ en medio de sus tormentos, el rico levantó los ojos y vio de lejos a Abraham, y a Lázaro junto a él. 24Así que alzó la voz y lo llamó: "Padre Abraham, ten compasión de mí y manda a Lázaro que moje la punta del dedo en agua y me refresque la lengua, porque estoy sufriendo mucho en este fuego." 25Pero Abraham le contestó: "Hijo, recuerda que durante tu vida te fue muy bien, mientras que a Lázaro le fue muy mal; pero ahora a él le toca recibir consuelo aquí, y a ti, sufrir terriblemente. 26Además de eso, hay un gran abismo entre nosotros y ustedes, de modo que los que quieren pasar de aquí para allá no pueden, ni tampoco pueden los de allá para acá."

27»Él respondió: "Entonces te ruego, padre, que mandes a Lázaro a la casa de mi padre, 28para que advierta a mis cinco hermanos y no vengan ellos también a este lugar de tormento." 29Pero Abraham le contestó: "Ya tienen a Moisés y a los profetas; ¡que les hagan caso a ellos!" 30"No les harán caso, padre Abraham —replicó el rico—; en cambio, sí se les presentara uno de entre los muertos, entonces sí se *arrepentirían." 31Abraham le dijo: "Si no les hacen caso a Moisés y a los profetas, tampoco se convencerán aunque alguien se *levante de entre los muertos."»

El pecado, la fe y el deber

17 Luego dijo Jesús a sus discípulos:
—Los *tropiezos son inevitables, pero ¡ay de aquel que los ocasiona! 2Más le valdría ser arrojado al mar con una piedra de molino atada al cuello, que servir de tropiezo a uno solo de estos pequeños. 3Así que, ¡cuídense!

»Si tu hermano peca, repréndelo; y si se *arrepiente, perdónalo. 4Aun si peca contra ti siete veces en un día, y siete veces regresa a decirte "Me arrepiento", perdónalo.

5Entonces los apóstoles le dijeron al Señor:
—¡Aumenta nuestra fe!

6—Si ustedes tuvieran una fe tan pequeña como un grano de mostaza —les respondió el Señor—, po-

---

f **16:6** *cien barriles.* Lit. *cien* *batos* (unos 3.700 litros). g **16:7** *cien bultos.* Lit. *cien* *coros* (unos 37.000 litros). h **16:8** *administrador de riquezas mundanas.* Alt. *administrador deshonesto.* Lit. *administrador de injusticia.* i **16:9** *se valgan . . . amigos.* Lit. *se hagan amigos por medio del dinero de injusticia.* j **16:10** *honrado.* Alt. *digno de confianza.* Lit. *fiel*; también en vv. 11,12. k **16:10** *el que no es íntegro.* Lit. *el que es injusto.* l **16:11** *las riquezas mundanas.* Lit. *el dinero injusto.* m **16:16** *se esfuerzan por entrar en él.* Alt. *hacen violencia por entrar en él,* o *hacen violencia contra él.* n **16:19** *lujosamente.* Lit. *con púrpura y tela fina.* ñ **16:23** *infierno.* Lit. **Hades.*

drían decirle a este árbol: "Desarráigate y plántate en el mar", y les obedecería.

7»Supongamos que uno de ustedes tiene un *siervo que ha estado arando el campo o cuidando las ovejas. Cuando el siervo regresa del campo, ¿acaso se le dice: "Ven en seguida a sentarte a la mesa"? 8¿No se le diría más bien: "Prepárame la comida y cámbiate de ropa para atenderme mientras yo ceno; después tú podrás cenar"? 9¿Acaso se le darían las gracias al siervo por haber hecho lo que se le mandó? 10Así también ustedes, cuando hayan hecho todo lo que se les ha mandado, deben decir: "Somos siervos inútiles; no hemos hecho más que cumplir con nuestro deber."

Jesús sana a diez leprosos

11Un día, siguiendo su viaje a Jerusalén, Jesús pasaba por Samaria y Galilea. 12Cuando estaba por entrar en un pueblo, salieron a su encuentro diez hombres enfermos de *lepra. Como se habían quedado a cierta distancia, 13gritaron:

—¡Jesús, Maestro, ten compasión de nosotros!

14Al verlos, les dijo:

—Vayan a presentarse a los sacerdotes.

Resultó que, mientras iban de camino, quedaron *limpios.

15Uno de ellos, al verse ya sano, regresó alabando a Dios a grandes voces. 16Cayó rostro en tierra a los pies de Jesús y le dio las gracias, no obstante que era samaritano.

17—¿Acaso no quedaron limpios los diez? —preguntó Jesús—. ¿Dónde están los otros nueve? 18¿No hubo ninguno que regresara a dar gloria a Dios, excepto este extranjero? 19Levántate y vete —le dijo al hombre—; tu fe te ha *sanado.

La venida del reino de Dios
17:26-27 — Mt 24:37-39

20Los *fariseos le preguntaron a Jesús cuándo iba a venir el reino de Dios, y él les respondió:

—La venida del reino de Dios no se puede someter a cálculos.º 21No van a decir: "¡Mírenlo acá! ¡Mírenlo allá!" Dense cuenta de que el reino de Dios está entrep ustedes.

22A sus discípulos les dijo:

—Llegará el tiempo en que ustedes anhelarán vivir siquiera uno de los días del Hijo del hombre, pero no podrán. 23Les dirán: "¡Mírenlo allá! ¡Mírenlo acá!" No vayan; no los sigan. 24Porque en su díaq el Hijo del hombre será como el relámpago que fulgura e ilumina el cielo de uno a otro extremo. 25Pero antes él tiene que sufrir muchas cosas y ser rechazado por esta generación.

26»Tal como sucedió en tiempos de Noé, así también será cuando venga el Hijo del hombre. 27Comían, bebían, y se casaban y daban en casamiento, hasta el día en que Noé entró en el arca; entonces llegó el diluvio y los destruyó a todos.

28»Lo mismo sucedió en tiempos de Lot: comían y bebían, compraban y vendían, sembraban y edificaban. 29Pero el día en que Lot salió de Sodoma, llovió del cielo fuego y azufre y acabó con todos.

30»Así será el día en que se manifieste el Hijo del hombre. 31En aquel día, el que esté en la azotea y tenga sus cosas dentro de la casa, que no baje a buscarlas. Así mismo el que esté en el campo, que no regrese por lo que haya dejado atrás. 32¡Acuérdense de la esposa de Lot! 33El que procure conservar su

*vida, la perderá; y el que la pierda, la conservará. 34Les digo que en aquella noche estarán dos personas en una misma cama: una será llevada y la otra será dejada. 35Dos mujeres estarán moliendo juntas: una será llevada y la otra será dejada.r

37—¿Dónde, Señor? —preguntaron.

—Donde esté el cadáver, allí se reunirán los buitres —respondió él.

Parábola de la viuda insistente

18 Jesús les contó a sus discípulos una parábola para mostrarles que debían orar siempre, sin desanimarse. 2Les dijo: «Había en cierto pueblo un juez que no tenía temor de Dios ni consideración de nadie. 3En el mismo pueblo había una viuda que insistía en pedirle: "Hágame usted justicia contra mi adversario." 4Durante algún tiempo él se negó, pero por fin concluyó: "Aunque no temo a Dios ni tengo consideración de nadie, 5como esta viuda no deja de molestarme, voy a tener que hacerle justicia, no sea que con sus visitas me haga la vida imposible."»

6Continuó el Señor: «Tengan en cuenta lo que dijo el juez injusto. 7¿Acaso Dios no hará justicia a sus escogidos, que claman a él día y noche? ¿Se tardará mucho en responderles? 8Les digo que sí les hará justicia, y sin demora. No obstante, cuando venga el Hijo del hombre, ¿encontrará fe en la tierra?»

Parábola del fariseo y del recaudador de impuestos

9A algunos que, confiando en sí mismos, se creían justos y que despreciaban a los demás, Jesús les contó esta parábola: 10«Dos hombres subieron al *templo a orar; uno era *fariseo y el otro, *recaudador de impuestos. 11El fariseo se puso a orar consigo mismo: "Oh Dios, te doy gracias porque no soy como otros hombres —ladrones, malhechores, adúlteros— ni mucho menos como ese recaudador de impuestos. 12Ayuno dos veces a la semana y doy la décima parte de todo lo que recibo." 13En cambio, el recaudador de impuestos, que se había quedado a cierta distancia, ni siquiera se atrevía a alzar la vista al cielo, sino que se golpeaba el pecho y decía: "¡Oh Dios, ten compasión de mí, que soy pecador!"

14»Les digo que éste, y no aquél, volvió a su casa *justificado ante Dios. Pues todo el que a sí mismo se enaltece será humillado, y el que se humilla será enaltecido.»

Jesús y los niños
18:15-17 — Mt 19:13-15; Mr 10:13-16

15También le llevaban niños pequeños a Jesús para que los tocara. Al ver esto, los discípulos reprendían a quienes los llevaban. 16Pero Jesús llamó a los niños y dijo: «Dejen que los niños vengan a mí, y no se lo impidan, porque el reino de Dios es de quienes son como ellos. 17Les aseguro que el que no reciba el reino de Dios como un niño, de ninguna manera entrará en él.»

El dirigente rico
18:18-30 — Mt 19:16-29; Mr 10:17-30

18Cierto dirigente le preguntó:

—Maestro bueno, ¿qué tengo que hacer para heredar la vida eterna?

19—¿Por qué me llamas bueno? —respondió Jesús—. Nadie es bueno sino sólo Dios. 20Ya sabes

---

º **17:20** *La venida . . . cálculos.* Lit. *El reino de Dios no viene con observación.* p **17:21** *entre.* Alt. *dentro de.* q **17:24** Var. no incluye: *en su día.* r **17:35** *dejada.* Var. *dejada.* 36Estarán *dos hombres en el campo: uno será llevado y el otro será dejado* (véase Mt 24:40).

los mandamientos: "No cometas adulterio, no mates, no robes, no presentes falso testimonio, honra a
tu padre y a tu madre."s

²¹—Todo eso lo he cumplido desde que era joven —dijo el hombre.

²²Al oír esto, Jesús añadió:

—Todavía te falta una cosa: vende todo lo que
tienes y repártelo entre los pobres, y tendrás tesoro
en el cielo. Luego ven y sígueme.

²³Cuando el hombre oyó esto, se entristeció mucho, pues era muy rico. ²⁴Al verlo tan afligido, Jesús
comentó:

—¡Qué difícil es para los ricos entrar en el reino
de Dios! ²⁵En realidad, le resulta más fácil a un camello pasar por el ojo de una aguja, que a un rico entrar
en el reino de Dios.

²⁶Los que lo oyeron preguntaron:

—Entonces, ¿quién podrá salvarse?

²⁷—Lo que es imposible para los hombres es posible para Dios —aclaró Jesús.

²⁸—Mira —le dijo Pedro—, nosotros hemos dejado todo lo que teníamos para seguirte.

²⁹—Les aseguro —respondió Jesús— que todo el
que por causa del reino de Dios haya dejado casa, esposa, hermanos, padres o hijos, ³⁰recibirá mucho
más en este tiempo; y en la edad venidera, la vida
eterna.

Jesús predice de nuevo su muerte
18:31-33 — Mt 20:17-19; Mr 10:32-34

³¹Entonces Jesús tomó aparte a los doce y les
dijo: «Ahora vamos rumbo a Jerusalén, donde se
cumplirá todo lo que escribieron los profetas acerca
del Hijo del hombre. ³²En efecto, será entregado a los
*gentiles. Se burlarán de él, lo insultarán, le escupi-
rán; ³³y después de azotarlo, lo matarán. Pero al tercer día resucitará.»

³⁴Los discípulos no entendieron nada de esto.
Les era incomprensible, pues no captaban el sentido
de lo que les hablaba.

Un mendigo ciego recibe la vista
18:35-43 — Mt 20:29-34; Mr 10:46-52

³⁵Sucedió que al acercarse Jesús a Jericó, estaba
un ciego sentado junto al camino pidiendo limosna.
³⁶Cuando oyó a la multitud que pasaba, preguntó
qué acontecía.

³⁷—Jesús de Nazaret está pasando por aquí —le
respondieron.

³⁸—¡Jesús, Hijo de David, ten compasión de mí!
—gritó el ciego.

³⁹Los que iban delante lo reprendían para que se
callara, pero él se puso a gritar aun más fuerte:

—¡Hijo de David, ten compasión de mí!

⁴⁰Jesús se detuvo y mandó que se lo trajeran.
Cuando el ciego se acercó, le preguntó Jesús:

⁴¹—¿Qué quieres que haga por ti?

—Señor, quiero ver.

⁴²—¡Recibe la vista! —le dijo Jesús—. Tu fe te ha
*sanado.

⁴³Al instante recobró la vista. Entonces, glorificando a Dios, comenzó a seguir a Jesús, y todos los
que lo vieron daban alabanza a Dios.

Zaqueo, el recaudador de impuestos

19 Jesús llegó a Jericó y comenzó a cruzar la ciudad. ²Resulta que había allí un hombre llamado Zaqueo, jefe de los *recaudadores de
impuestos, que era muy rico. ³Estaba tratando de ver
quién era Jesús, pero la multitud se lo impedía, pues
era de baja estatura. ⁴Por eso se adelantó corriendo y
se subió a un árbol para poder verlo, ya que Jesús iba
a pasar por allí.

⁵Llegando al lugar, Jesús miró hacia arriba y le
dijo:

—Zaqueo, baja enseguida. Tengo que quedarme hoy en tu casa.

⁶Así que se apresuró a bajar y, muy contento, recibió a Jesús en su casa.

⁷Al ver esto, todos empezaron a murmurar: «Ha
ido a hospedarse con un *pecador.»

⁸Pero Zaqueo dijo resueltamente:

—Mira, Señor: Ahora mismo voy a dar a los pobres la mitad de mis bienes, y si en algo he defraudado a alguien, le devolveré cuatro veces la cantidad
que sea.

⁹—Hoy ha llegado la salvación a esta casa —le
dijo Jesús—, ya que éste también es hijo de Abraham. ¹⁰Porque el Hijo del hombre vino a buscar y a
salvar lo que se había perdido.

Parábola del dinero

¹¹Como la gente lo escuchaba, pasó a contarles
una parábola, porque estaba cerca de Jerusalén y la
gente pensaba que el reino de Dios iba a manifestarse en cualquier momento. ¹²Así que les dijo: «Un
hombre de la nobleza se fue a un país lejano para ser
coronado rey y luego regresar. ¹³Llamó a diez de sus
*siervos y entregó a cada cual una buena cantidad de
dinero.t Les instruyó: "Hagan negocio con este dinero hasta que yo vuelva." ¹⁴Pero sus súbditos lo odiaban y mandaron tras él una delegación a decir: "No
queremos a éste por rey."

¹⁵»A pesar de todo, fue nombrado rey. Cuando
regresó a su país, mandó llamar a los siervos a quienes había entregado el dinero, para enterarse de lo
que habían ganado. ¹⁶Se presentó el primero y dijo:
"Señor, su dinerou ha producido diez veces más."
¹⁷"¡Hiciste bien, siervo bueno! —le respondió el
rey—. Puesto que has sido fiel en tan poca cosa, te
doy el gobierno de diez ciudades." ¹⁸Se presentó el
segundo y dijo: "Señor, su dinero ha producido cinco veces más." ¹⁹El rey le respondió: "A ti te pongo
sobre cinco ciudades."

²⁰»Llegó otro siervo y dijo: "Señor, aquí tiene su
dinero; lo he tenido guardado, envuelto en un pañue-
lo. ²¹Es que le tenía miedo a usted, que es un hombre
muy exigente: toma lo que no depositó y cosecha lo
que no sembró." ²²El rey le contestó: "Siervo malo,
con tus propias palabras te voy a juzgar. ¿Así que sabías que soy muy exigente, que tomo lo que no depo-
sité y cosecho lo que no sembré? ²³Entonces, ¿por qué
no pusiste mi dinero en el banco, para que al regresar
pudiera reclamar los intereses?" ²⁴Luego dijo a los
presentes: "Quítenle el dinero y dénselo al que recibió
diez veces más." ²⁵"Señor —protestaron—, ¡él ya tiene diez veces más!" ²⁶El rey contestó: "Les aseguro
que a todo el que tiene, se le dará más, pero al que no
tiene, se le quitará hasta lo que tiene. ²⁷Pero en cuanto

---

s **18:20** Éx 20:12-16; Dt 5:16-20   t **19:13** y entregó . . . de dinero. Lit. y les entregó diez *minas (una mina equivalía al salario
de unos tres meses).   u **19:16** dinero. Lit. mina; también en vv. 18,20,24.

a esos enemigos míos que no me querían por rey, tráiganlos acá y mátenlos delante de mí."»

La entrada triunfal
19:29-38 — Mt 21:1-9; Mr 11:1-10
19:35-38 — Jn 12:12-15

28Dicho esto, Jesús siguió adelante, subiendo hacia Jerusalén. 29Cuando se acercó a Betfagué y a Betania, junto al monte llamado de los Olivos, envió a dos de sus discípulos con este encargo: 30«Vayan a la aldea que está enfrente y, al entrar en ella, encontrarán atado a un burrito en el que nadie se ha montado. Desátenlo y tráiganlo acá. 31Y si alguien les pregunta: "¿Por qué lo desatan?", díganle: "El Señor lo necesita."»

32Fueron y lo encontraron tal como él les había dicho. 33Cuando estaban desatando el burrito, los dueños les preguntaron:

—¿Por qué desatan el burrito?

34—El Señor lo necesita —contestaron.

35Se lo llevaron, pues, a Jesús. Luego pusieron sus mantos encima del burrito y ayudaron a Jesús a montarse. 36A medida que avanzaba, la gente tendía sus mantos sobre el camino.

37Al acercarse él a la bajada del monte de los Olivos, todos los discípulos se entusiasmaron y comenzaron a alabar a Dios por tantos milagros que habían visto. Gritaban:

38—¡Bendito el Rey que viene en el nombre del Señor!v

—¡Paz en el cielo y gloria en las alturas!

39Algunos de los *fariseos que estaban entre la gente le reclamaron a Jesús:

—¡Maestro, reprende a tus discípulos!

40Pero él respondió:

—Les aseguro que si ellos se callan, gritarán las piedras.

Jesús en el templo
19:45-46 — Mt 21:12-16; Mr 11:15-18;
Jn 2:13-16

41Cuando se acercaba a Jerusalén, Jesús vio la ciudad y lloró por ella. 42Dijo:

—¡Cómo quisiera que hoy supieras lo que te puede traer paz! Pero eso ahora está oculto a tus ojos. 43Te sobrevendrán días en que tus enemigos levantarán un muro y te rodearán, y te encerrarán por todos lados. 44Te derribarán a ti y a tus hijos dentro de tus murallas. No dejarán ni una piedra sobre otra, porque no reconociste el tiempo en que Dios vino a salvarte.w

45Luego entró en el *templox y comenzó a echar de allí a los que estaban vendiendo. 46«Escrito está —les dijo—: "Mi casa será casa de oración";y pero ustedes la han convertido en "cueva de ladrones".z»

47Todos los días enseñaba en el templo, y los jefes de los sacerdotes, los *maestros de la ley y los dirigentes del pueblo procuraban matarlo. 48Sin embargo, no encontraban la manera de hacerlo, porque todo el pueblo lo escuchaba con gran interés.

La autoridad de Jesús puesta en duda
20:1-8 — Mt 21:23-27; Mr 11:27-33

20 Un día, mientras Jesús enseñaba al pueblo en el *templo y les predicaba el *evangelio, se le acercaron los jefes de los sacerdotes y los *maestros de la ley, junto con los *ancianos. 2—Dinos con qué autoridad haces esto —lo interrogaron—. ¿Quién te dio esa autoridad?

3—Yo también voy a hacerles una pregunta a ustedes —replicó él—. Díganme: 4El bautismo de Juan, ¿procedía del cielo o de la tierra?a

5Ellos, pues, lo discutieron entre sí: «Si respondemos: "Del cielo", nos dirá: "¿Por qué no le creyeron?" 6Pero si decimos: "De la tierra", todo el pueblo nos apedreará, porque están convencidos de que Juan era un profeta.»

Así que le respondieron:

7—No sabemos de dónde era.

8—Pues yo tampoco les voy a decir con qué autoridad hago esto.

Parábola de los labradores malvados
20:9-19 — Mt 21:33-46; Mr 12:1-12

9Pasó luego a contarle a la gente esta parábola:

—Un hombre plantó un viñedo, se lo arrendó a unos labradores y se fue de viaje por largo tiempo. 10Llegada la cosecha, mandó un *siervo a los labradores para que le dieran parte de la cosecha. Pero los labradores lo golpearon y lo despidieron con las manos vacías. 11Les envió otro siervo, pero también a éste lo golpearon, lo humillaron y lo despidieron con las manos vacías. 12Entonces envió un tercero, pero aun a éste lo hirieron y lo expulsaron.

13»Entonces pensó el dueño del viñedo: "¿Qué voy a hacer? Enviaré a mi hijo amado; seguro que a él sí lo respetarán." 14Pero cuando lo vieron los labradores, trataron el asunto. "Éste es el heredero —dijeron—. Matémoslo, y la herencia será nuestra." 15Así que lo arrojaron fuera del viñedo y lo mataron.

»¿Qué les hará el dueño? 16Volverá, acabará con esos labradores y dará el viñedo a otros.

Al oír esto, la gente exclamó:

—¡Dios no lo quiera!

17Mirándolos fijamente, Jesús les dijo:

—Entonces, ¿qué significa esto que está escrito:

»"La piedra que desecharon los constructores ha llegado a ser la piedra angular"?b

18Todo el que caiga sobre esa piedra quedará despedazado, y si ella cae sobre alguien, lo hará polvo.

19Los maestros de la ley y los jefes de los sacerdotes, cayendo en cuenta que la parábola iba dirigida contra ellos, buscaron la manera de echarle mano en aquel mismo momento. Pero temían al pueblo.

El pago de impuestos al césar
20:20-26 — Mt 22:15-22; Mr 12:13-17

20Entonces, para acecharlo, enviaron espías que fingían ser gente honorable. Pensaban atrapar a Jesús en algo que él dijera, y así poder entregarlo a la jurisdicción del gobernador.

21—Maestro —dijeron los espías—, sabemos que lo que dices y enseñas es correcto. No juzgas por las apariencias, sino que de verdad enseñas el camino de Dios. 22¿Nos está permitido pagar impuestos al *césar o no?

23Pero Jesús, dándose cuenta de sus malas intenciones, replicó:

24—Muéstrenme una moneda romana.c ¿De quién son esta imagen y esta inscripción?

v 19:38 Sal 118:26   w 19:44 el tiempo . . . salvarte. Lit. el tiempo de tu visitación.   x 19:45 Es decir, en el área general del templo.   y 19:46 Is 56:7   z 19:46 Jer 7:11   a 20:4 la tierra. Lit. los hombres; también en v. 6.   b 20:17 Sal 118:22   c 20:24 una moneda romana. Lit. un *denario.

—Del césar —contestaron.

²⁵—Entonces denle al césar lo que es del césar, y a Dios lo que es de Dios.

²⁶No pudieron atraparlo en lo que decía en público. Así que, admirados de su respuesta, se callaron.

La resurrección y el matrimonio
20:27-40 — Mt 22:23-33; Mr 12:18-27

²⁷Luego, algunos de los saduceos, que decían que no hay resurrección, se acercaron a Jesús y le plantearon un problema:

²⁸—Maestro, Moisés nos enseñó en sus escritos que si un hombre muere y deja a la viuda sin hijos, el hermano de ese hombre tiene que casarse con la viuda para que su hermano tenga descendencia. ²⁹Pues bien, había siete hermanos. El primero se casó y murió sin dejar hijos. ³⁰Entonces el segundo ³¹y el tercero se casaron con ella, y así sucesivamente murieron los siete sin dejar hijos. ³²Por último, murió también la mujer. ³³Ahora bien, en la resurrección, ¿de cuál será esposa esta mujer, ya que los siete estuvieron casados con ella?

³⁴—La gente de este mundo se casa y se da en casamiento —les contestó Jesús—. ³⁵Pero en cuanto a los que sean dignos de tomar parte en el mundo venidero por la resurrección: ésos no se casarán ni serán dados en casamiento, ³⁶ni tampoco podrán morir, pues serán como los ángeles. Son hijos de Dios porque toman parte en la resurrección. ³⁷Pero que los muertos resucitan lo dio a entender Moisés mismo en el pasaje sobre la zarza, pues llama al Señor "el Dios de Abraham, de Isaac y de Jacob".ᵈ ³⁸Él no es Dios de muertos, sino de vivos; en efecto, para él todos ellos viven.

³⁹Algunos de los *maestros de la ley le respondieron:

—¡Bien dicho, Maestro!

⁴⁰Y ya no se atrevieron a hacerle más preguntas.

¿De quién es hijo el Cristo?
20:41-47 — Mt 22:41—23:7; Mr 12:35-40

⁴¹Pero Jesús les preguntó:

—¿Cómo es que dicen que el *Cristo es hijo de David? ⁴²David mismo declara en el libro de los Salmos:

»"Dijo el Señor a mi Señor:
　'Siéntate a mi *derecha,
⁴³hasta que ponga a tus enemigos
　por estrado de tus pies.' "ᵉ

⁴⁴David lo llama "Señor". ¿Cómo puede entonces ser su hijo?

⁴⁵Mientras todo el pueblo lo escuchaba, Jesús les dijo a sus discípulos:

⁴⁶—Cuídense de los *maestros de la ley. Les gusta pasearse con ropas ostentosas y les encanta que los saluden en las plazas, y ocupar el primer puesto en las sinagogas y los lugares de honor en los banquetes. ⁴⁷Devoran los bienes de las viudas y a la vez hacen largas plegarias para impresionar a los demás. Éstos recibirán peor castigo.

La ofrenda de la viuda
21:1-4 — Mr 12:41-44

21 Jesús se detuvo a observar y vio a los ricos que echaban sus ofrendas en las alcancías del *templo. ²También vio a una viuda pobre que echaba dos monteditas de cobre.ᶠ

³—Les aseguro —dijo— que esta viuda pobre ha echado más que todos los demás. ⁴Todos ellos dieron sus ofrendas de lo que les sobraba; pero ella, de su pobreza, echó todo lo que tenía para su sustento.

Señales del fin del mundo
21:5-36 — Mt 24; Mr 13
21:12-17 — Mt 10:17-22

⁵Algunos de sus discípulos comentaban acerca del *templo, de cómo estaba adornado con hermosas piedras y con ofrendas dedicadas a Dios. Pero Jesús dijo:

⁶—En cuanto a todo esto que ven ustedes, llegará el día en que no quedará piedra sobre piedra; todo será derribado.

⁷—Maestro —le preguntaron—, ¿cuándo sucederá eso, y cuál será la señal de que está a punto de suceder?

⁸—Tengan cuidado; no se dejen engañar —les advirtió Jesús—. Vendrán muchos que usando mi nombre dirán: "Yo soy", y: "El tiempo está cerca." No los sigan ustedes. ⁹Cuando sepan de guerras y de revoluciones, no se asusten. Es necesario que eso suceda primero, pero el fin no vendrá en seguida.

¹⁰Se levantará nación contra nación, y reino contra reino —continuó—. ¹¹Habrá grandes terremotos, hambre y epidemias por todas partes, cosas espantosas y grandes señales del cielo.

¹²Pero antes de todo esto, echarán mano de ustedes y los perseguirán. Los entregarán a las sinagogas y a las cárceles, y por causa de mi nombre los llevarán ante reyes y gobernadores. ¹³Así tendrán ustedes la oportunidad de dar testimonio ante ellos. ¹⁴Pero tengan en cuenta que no hay por qué preparar una defensa de antemano, ¹⁵pues yo mismo les daré tal elocuencia y sabiduría para responder, que ningún adversario podrá resistirles ni contradecirles. ¹⁶Ustedes serán traicionados aun por sus padres, hermanos, parientes y amigos, y a algunos de ustedes se les dará muerte. ¹⁷Todo el mundo los odiará por causa de mi nombre. ¹⁸Pero no se perderá ni un solo cabello de su cabeza. ¹⁹Si se mantienen firmes, se salvarán.ᵍ

²⁰»Ahora bien, cuando vean a Jerusalén rodeada de ejércitos, sepan que su desolación ya está cerca. ²¹Entonces los que estén en Judea huyan a las montañas, los que estén en la ciudad salgan de ella, y los que estén en el campo no entren en la ciudad. ²²Ése será el tiempo del juicio cuando se cumplirá todo lo que está escrito. ²³¡Ay de las que estén embarazadas o amamantando en aquellos días! Porque habrá gran aflicción en la tierra, y castigo contra este pueblo. ²⁴Caerán a filo de espada y los llevarán cautivos a todas las naciones. Los *gentiles pisotearán a Jerusalén, hasta que se cumplan los tiempos señalados para ellos.

²⁵»Habrá señales en el sol, la luna y las estrellas. En la tierra, las naciones estarán angustiadas y perplejas por el bramido y la agitación del mar. ²⁶Se desmayarán de terror los hombres, temerosos por lo que va a sucederle al mundo, porque los cuerpos celestes serán sacudidos. ²⁷Entonces verán al Hijo del hombre venir en una nube con poder y gran gloria. ²⁸Cuando comiencen a suceder estas cosas, cobren ánimo y levanten la cabeza, porque se acerca su redención.

²⁹Jesús también les propuso esta comparación:

ᵈ **20:37** Éx 3:6　ᵉ **20:43** Sal 110:1　ᶠ **21:2** *dos monteditas de cobre.* Lit. *dos *lepta.*　ᵍ **21:19** *Si . . . salvarán.* Lit. *Por su perseverancia obtendrán sus almas.*

—Fíjense en la higuera y en los demás árboles. ³⁰Cuando brotan las hojas, ustedes pueden ver por sí mismos y saber que el verano está cerca. ³¹Igualmente, cuando vean que suceden estas cosas, sepan que el reino de Dios está cerca.

³²»Les aseguro que no pasará esta generación hasta que todas estas cosas sucedan. ³³El cielo y la tierra pasarán, pero mis palabras jamás pasarán.

³⁴»Tengan cuidado, no sea que se les endurezca el corazón por el vicio, la embriaguez y las preocupaciones de esta vida. De otra manera, aquel día caerá de improviso sobre ustedes, ³⁵pues vendrá como una trampa sobre todos los habitantes de la tierra. ³⁶Estén siempre vigilantes, y oren para que puedan escapar de todo lo que está por suceder, y presentarse delante del Hijo del hombre.

³⁷De día Jesús enseñaba en el templo, pero salía a pasar la noche en el monte llamado de los Olivos, ³⁸y toda la gente madrugaba para ir al templo a oírlo.

Judas acuerda traicionar a Jesús
22:1-2 — Mt 26:2-5; Mr 14:1-2,10-11

22 Se aproximaba la fiesta de los Panes sin levadura, llamada la Pascua. ²Los jefes de los sacerdotes y los *maestros de la ley buscaban algún modo de acabar con Jesús, porque temían al pueblo. ³Entonces entró Satanás en Judas, uno de los doce, al que llamaban Iscariote. ⁴Éste fue a los jefes de los sacerdotes y a los capitanes del *templo para tratar con ellos cómo les entregaría a Jesús. ⁵Ellos se alegraron y acordaron darle dinero. ⁶Él aceptó, y comenzó a buscar una oportunidad para entregarles a Jesús cuando no hubiera gente.

La última cena
22:7-13 — Mt 26:17-19; Mr 14:12-16
22:17-20 — Mt 26:26-29; Mr 14:22-25; 1Co 11:23-25
22:21-23 — Mt 26:21-24; Mr 14:18-21; Jn 13:21-30
22:25-27 — Mt 20:25-28; Mr 10:42-45
22:33-34 — Mt 26:33-35; Mr 14:29-31; Jn 13:37-38

⁷Cuando llegó el día de la fiesta de los Panes sin levadura, en que debía sacrificarse el cordero de la Pascua, ⁸Jesús envió a Pedro y a Juan, diciéndoles:

—Vayan a hacer los preparativos para que comamos la Pascua.

⁹—¿Dónde quieres que la preparemos? —le preguntaron.

¹⁰—Miren —contestó él—: al entrar ustedes en la ciudad les saldrá al encuentro un hombre que lleva un cántaro de agua. Síganlo hasta la casa en que entre, ¹¹y díganle al dueño de la casa: "El Maestro pregunta: ¿Dónde está la sala en la que voy a comer la Pascua con mis discípulos?" ¹²Él les mostrará en la planta alta una sala amplia y amueblada. Preparen allí la cena.

¹³Ellos fueron y encontraron todo tal como les había dicho Jesús. Así que prepararon la Pascua.

¹⁴Cuando llegó la hora, Jesús y sus apóstoles se *sentaron a la mesa. ¹⁵Entonces les dijo:

—He tenido muchísimos deseos de comer esta Pascua con ustedes antes de padecer, ¹⁶pues les digo que no volveré a comerla hasta que tenga su pleno cumplimiento en el reino de Dios.

¹⁷Luego tomó la copa, dio gracias y dijo:

—Tomen esto y repártanlo entre ustedes. ¹⁸Les digo que no volveré a beber del fruto de la vid hasta que venga el reino de Dios.

¹⁹También tomó pan y, después de dar gracias, lo partió, se lo dio a ellos y dijo:

—Este pan es mi cuerpo, entregado por ustedes; hagan esto en memoria de mí.

²⁰De la misma manera tomó la copa después de la cena, y dijo:

—Esta copa es el nuevo pacto en mi sangre, que es derramada por ustedes. ²¹Pero sepan que la mano del que va a traicionarme está con la mía, sobre la mesa. ²²A la verdad el Hijo del hombre se irá según está decretado, pero ¡ay de aquel que lo traiciona!

²³Entonces comenzaron a preguntarse unos a otros quién de ellos haría esto.

²⁴Tuvieron además un altercado sobre cuál de ellos sería el más importante.

²⁵Jesús les dijo:

—Los reyes de las *naciones oprimen a sus súbditos, y los que ejercen autoridad sobre ellos se llaman a sí mismos benefactores. ²⁶No sea así entre ustedes. Al contrario, el mayor debe comportarse como el menor, y el que manda como el que sirve. ²⁷Porque, ¿quién es más importante, el que está a la mesa o el que sirve? ¿No lo es el que está sentado a la mesa? Sin embargo, yo estoy entre ustedes como uno que sirve. ²⁸Ahora bien, ustedes son los que han estado siempre a mi lado en mis *pruebas. ²⁹Por eso, yo mismo les concedo un reino, así como mi Padre me lo concedió a mí, ³⁰para que coman y beban a mi mesa en mi reino, y se sienten en tronos para juzgar a las doce tribus de Israel.

³¹»Simón, Simón, mira que Satanás ha pedido zarandearlos a ustedes como si fueran trigo. ³²Pero yo he orado por ti, para que no falle tu fe. Y tú, cuando te hayas vuelto a mí, fortalece a tus hermanos.

³³—Señor —respondió Pedro—, estoy dispuesto a ir contigo tanto a la cárcel como a la muerte.

³⁴—Pedro, te digo que hoy mismo, antes de que cante el gallo, tres veces negarás que me conoces.

³⁵Luego Jesús dijo a todos:

—Cuando los envié a ustedes sin monedero ni bolsa ni sandalias, ¿acaso les faltó algo?

—Nada —respondieron.

³⁶—Ahora, en cambio, el que tenga un monedero, que lo lleve; así mismo, el que tenga una bolsa. Y el que nada tenga, que venda su manto y compre una espada. ³⁷Porque les digo que tiene que cumplirse en mí aquello que está escrito: "Y fue contado entre los transgresores."ʰ En efecto, lo que se ha escrito de mí se está cumpliendo.ⁱ

³⁸—Mira, Señor —le señalaron los discípulos—, aquí hay dos espadas.

—¡Basta! —les contestó.

Jesús ora en el monte de los Olivos
22:40-46 — Mt 26:36-46; Mr 14:32-42

³⁹Jesús salió de la ciudad y, como de costumbre, se dirigió al monte de los Olivos, y sus discípulos lo siguieron. ⁴⁰Cuando llegaron al lugar, les dijo: «Oren para que no caigan en *tentación.» ⁴¹Entonces se separó de ellos a una buena distancia,ʲ se arrodilló y empezó a orar: ⁴²«Padre, si quieres, no me hagas beber este trago amargo;ᵏ pero no se cumpla mi voluntad, sino la tuya.» ⁴³Entonces se le apareció un ángel del cielo para fortalecerlo. ⁴⁴Pero, como estaba an-

---

ʰ **22:37** Is 53:12   ⁱ **22:37** *En efecto . . . cumpliendo.* Lit. *Porque lo que es acerca de mí tiene fin.*   ʲ **22:41** *a una buena distancia.* Lit. *como a un tiro de piedra.*   ᵏ **22:42** *no . . . amargo.* Lit. *quita de mí esta copa.*

gustiado, se puso a orar con más fervor, y su sudor era como gotas de sangre que caían a tierra.[l]

45Cuando terminó de orar y volvió a los discípulos, los encontró dormidos, agotados por la tristeza. 46«¿Por qué están durmiendo? —les exhortó—. Levántense y oren para que no caigan en tentación.»

Arresto de Jesús
22:47-53 — Mt 26:47-56; Mr 14:43-50; Jn 18:3-11

47Todavía estaba hablando Jesús cuando se apareció una turba, y al frente iba uno de los doce, el que se llamaba Judas. Éste se acercó a Jesús para besarlo, 48pero Jesús le preguntó:

—Judas, ¿con un beso traicionas al Hijo del hombre?

49Los discípulos que lo rodeaban, al darse cuenta de lo que pasaba, dijeron:

—Señor, ¿atacamos con la espada?

50Y uno de ellos hirió al siervo del sumo sacerdote, cortándole la oreja derecha.

51—¡Déjenlos! —ordenó Jesús.

Entonces le tocó la oreja al hombre, y lo sanó. 52Luego dijo a los jefes de los sacerdotes, a los capitanes del *templo y a los *ancianos, que habían venido a prenderlo:

—¿Acaso soy un bandido,[m] para que vengan contra mí con espadas y palos? 53Todos los días estaba con ustedes en el templo, y no se atrevieron a ponerme las manos encima. Pero ya ha llegado la hora de ustedes, cuando reinan las tinieblas.

Pedro niega a Jesús
22:55-62 — Mt 26:69-75; Mr 14:66-72; Jn 18:16-18,25-27

54Prendieron entonces a Jesús y lo llevaron a la casa del sumo sacerdote. Pedro los seguía de lejos. 55Pero luego, cuando encendieron una fogata en medio del patio y se sentaron alrededor, Pedro se les unió. 56Una criada lo vio allí sentado a la lumbre, lo miró detenidamente y dijo:

—Éste estaba con él.

57Pero él lo negó.

—Muchacha, yo no lo conozco.

58Poco después lo vio otro y afirmó:

—Tú también eres uno de ellos.

—¡No, hombre, no lo soy! —contestó Pedro.

59Como una hora más tarde, otro lo acusó:

—Seguro que éste estaba con él; miren que es galileo.

60—¡Hombre, no sé de qué estás hablando! —replicó Pedro.

En el mismo momento en que dijo eso, cantó el gallo. 61El Señor se volvió y miró directamente a Pedro. Entonces Pedro se acordó de que el Señor le había dicho: «Hoy mismo, antes de que el gallo cante, me negarás tres veces.» 62Y saliendo de allí, lloró amargamente.

Los soldados se burlan de Jesús
22:63-65 — Mt 26:67-68; Mr 14:65; Jn 18:22-23

63Los hombres que vigilaban a Jesús comenzaron a burlarse de él y a golpearlo. 64Le vendaron los ojos, y le increpaban:

—¡Adivina quién te pegó!

65Y le lanzaban muchos otros insultos.

Jesús ante Pilato y Herodes
22:67-71 — Mt 26:63-66; Mr 14:61-63; Jn 18:19-21
23:2-3 — Mt 27:11-14; Mr 15:2-5; Jn 18:29-37
23:18-25 — Mt 27:15-26; Mr 15:6-15; Jn 18:39—19:16

66Al amanecer, se reunieron los *ancianos del pueblo, tanto los jefes de los sacerdotes como los *maestros de la ley, e hicieron comparecer a Jesús ante el *Consejo.

67—Si eres el *Cristo, dínoslo —le exigieron.

Jesús les contestó:

—Si se lo dijera a ustedes, no me lo creerían, 68y si les hiciera preguntas, no me contestarían. 69Pero de ahora en adelante el Hijo del hombre estará sentado a la *derecha del Dios Todopoderoso.

70—¿Eres tú, entonces, el Hijo de Dios? —le preguntaron a una voz.

—Ustedes mismos lo dicen.

71—¿Para qué necesitamos más testimonios? —resolvieron—. Acabamos de oírlo de sus propios labios.

23 Así que la asamblea en pleno se levantó, y lo llevaron a Pilato. 2Y comenzaron la acusación con estas palabras:

—Hemos descubierto a este hombre agitando a nuestra nación. Se opone al pago de impuestos al *emperador y afirma que él es el *Cristo, un rey.

3Así que Pilato le preguntó a Jesús:

—¿Eres tú el rey de los judíos?

—Tú mismo lo dices —respondió.

4Entonces Pilato declaró a los jefes de los sacerdotes y a la multitud:

—No encuentro que este hombre sea culpable de nada.

5Pero ellos insistían:

—Con sus enseñanzas agita al pueblo por toda Judea.[n] Comenzó en Galilea y ha llegado hasta aquí.

6Al oír esto, Pilato preguntó si el hombre era galileo. 7Cuando se enteró de que pertenecía a la jurisdicción de Herodes, se lo mandó a él, ya que en aquellos días también Herodes estaba en Jerusalén.

8Al ver a Jesús, Herodes se puso muy contento; hacía tiempo que quería verlo por lo que oía acerca de él, y esperaba presenciar algún milagro que hiciera Jesús. 9Lo acosó con muchas preguntas, pero Jesús no le contestaba nada. 10Allí estaban también los jefes de los sacerdotes y los *maestros de la ley, acusándolo con vehemencia. 11Entonces Herodes y sus soldados, con desprecio y burlas, le pusieron un manto lujoso y lo mandaron de vuelta a Pilato. 12Anteriormente, Herodes y Pilato no se llevaban bien, pero ese mismo día se hicieron amigos.

13Pilato entonces reunió a los jefes de los sacerdotes, a los gobernantes y al pueblo, 14y les dijo:

—Ustedes me trajeron a este hombre acusado de fomentar la rebelión entre el pueblo, pero resulta que lo he interrogado delante de ustedes sin encontrar que sea culpable de lo que ustedes lo acusan. 15Y es claro que tampoco Herodes lo ha juzgado culpable, puesto que nos lo devolvió. Como pueden ver, no ha cometido ningún delito que merezca la muerte, 16así que le daré una paliza y después lo soltaré.[ñ]

18Pero todos gritaron a una voz:

—¡Llévate a ése! ¡Suéltanos a Barrabás!

---

[l] **22:44** Var. no incluye vv. 43 y 44. [m] **22:52** bandido. Alt. Insurgente. [n] **23:5** toda Judea. Alt. toda la tierra de los judíos. [ñ] **23:16** soltaré. Var. soltaré. v. 17 Ahora bien, durante la fiesta tenía la obligación de soltarles un preso (véanse Mt 27:15 y Mr 15:6).

[19]A Barrabás lo habían metido en la cárcel por
una insurrección en la ciudad, y por homicidio. [20]Pi-
lato, como quería soltar a Jesús, apeló al pueblo otra
vez, [21]pero ellos se pusieron a gritar:
—¡Crucifícalo! ¡Crucifícalo!
[22]Por tercera vez les habló:
—Pero, ¿qué crimen ha cometido este hombre?
No encuentro que él sea culpable de nada que merezca la pena de muerte, así que le daré una paliza y
después lo soltaré.
[23]Pero a voz en cuello ellos siguieron insistiendo
en que lo crucificara, y con sus gritos se impusieron.
[24]Por fin Pilato decidió concederles su demanda:
[25]soltó al hombre que le pedían, el que por insurrección y homicidio había sido echado en la cárcel, y
dejó que hicieran con Jesús lo que quisieran.

La crucifixión

23:33-43 — Mt 27:33-44; Mr 15:22-32; Jn 19:17-24

[26]Cuando se lo llevaban, echaron mano de un tal
Simón de Cirene, que volvía del campo, y le cargaron
la cruz para que la llevara detrás de Jesús. [27]Lo seguía
mucha gente del pueblo, incluso mujeres que se golpeaban el pecho, lamentándose por él. [28]Jesús se volvió hacia ellas y les dijo:
—Hijas de Jerusalén, no lloren por mí; lloren
más bien por ustedes y por sus hijos. [29]Miren, va a
llegar el tiempo en que se dirá: "*¡Dichosas las estériles, que nunca dieron a luz ni amamantaron!"
[30]Entonces

»"dirán a las montañas: '¡Caigan sobre
nosotros!',
y a las colinas: '¡Cúbrannos!' "[o]

[31]Porque si esto se hace cuando el árbol está verde,
¿qué no sucederá cuando esté seco?
[32]También llevaban con él a otros dos, ambos criminales, para ser ejecutados. [33]Cuando llegaron al lugar llamado la Calavera, lo crucificaron allí, junto con
los criminales, uno a su derecha y otro a su izquierda.
[34]—Padre —dijo Jesús—, perdónalos, porque no
saben lo que hacen.[p]
Mientras tanto, echaban suertes para repartirse
entre sí la ropa de Jesús.
[35]La gente, por su parte, se quedó allí observando, y aun los gobernantes estaban burlándose de él.
—Salvó a otros —decían—; que se salve a sí mismo, si es el *Cristo de Dios, el Escogido.
[36]También los soldados se acercaron para burlarse de él. Le ofrecieron vinagre [37]y le dijeron:
—Si eres el rey de los judíos, sálvate a ti mismo.
[38]Resulta que había sobre él un letrero, que decía: «ÉSTE ES EL REY DE LOS JUDÍOS.»
[39]Uno de los criminales allí colgados empezó a
insultarlo:
—¿No eres tú el Cristo? ¡Sálvate a ti mismo y a
nosotros!
[40]Pero el otro criminal lo reprendió:
—¿Ni siquiera temor de Dios tienes, aunque su-
fres la misma condena? [41]En nuestro caso, el castigo
es justo, pues sufrimos lo que merecen nuestros delitos; éste, en cambio, no ha hecho nada malo.
[42]Luego dijo:
—Jesús, acuérdate de mí cuando vengas en tu
reino.
[43]—Te aseguro que hoy estarás conmigo en el
paraíso —le contestó Jesús.

Muerte de Jesús

23:44-49 — Mt 27:45-56; Mr 15:33-41

[44]Desde el mediodía y hasta la media tarde[q] toda
la tierra quedó sumida en la oscuridad, [45]pues el sol
se ocultó. Y la cortina del *santuario del templo se
rasgó en dos. [46]Entonces Jesús exclamó con fuerza:
—¡Padre, en tus manos encomiendo mi espíritu!
Y al decir esto, expiró.
[47]El centurión, al ver lo que había sucedido, alabó a Dios y dijo:
—Verdaderamente este hombre era justo.
[48]Entonces los que se habían reunido para presenciar aquel espectáculo, al ver lo ocurrido, se fueron de allí golpeándose el pecho. [49]Pero todos los
conocidos de Jesús, incluso las mujeres que lo habían
seguido desde Galilea, se quedaron mirando desde
lejos.

Sepultura de Jesús

23:50-56 — Mt 27:57-61; Mr 15:42-47; Jn 19:38-42

[50]Había un hombre bueno y justo llamado José,
miembro del *Consejo, [51]que no había estado de
acuerdo con la decisión ni con la conducta de ellos.
Era natural de un pueblo de Judea llamado Arimatea, y esperaba el reino de Dios. [52]Éste se presentó
ante Pilato y le pidió el cuerpo de Jesús. [53]Después
de bajarlo, lo envolvió en una sábana de lino y lo
puso en un sepulcro cavado en la roca, en el que todavía no se había sepultado a nadie. [54]Era el día de
preparación para el *sábado, que estaba a punto de
comenzar.
[55]Las mujeres que habían acompañado a Jesús
desde Galilea siguieron a José para ver el sepulcro y
cómo colocaban el cuerpo. [56]Luego volvieron a casa y
prepararon especias aromáticas y perfumes. Entonces
descansaron el sábado, conforme al mandamiento.

La resurrección

24:1-10 — Mt 28:1-8; Mr 16:1-8; Jn 20:1-8

24 El primer día de la semana, muy de mañana,
las mujeres fueron al sepulcro, llevando las
especias aromáticas que habían preparado. [2]Encon-
traron que había sido quitada la piedra que cubría el
sepulcro [3]y, al entrar, no hallaron el cuerpo del Señor
Jesús. [4]Mientras se preguntaban qué habría pasado,
se les presentaron dos hombres con ropas resplande-
cientes. [5]Asustadas, se postraron sobre su rostro,
pero ellos les dijeron:
—¿Por qué buscan ustedes entre los muertos al
que vive? [6]No está aquí; ¡ha resucitado! Recuerden
lo que les dijo cuando todavía estaba con ustedes en
Galilea: [7]"El Hijo del hombre tiene que ser entregado
en manos de hombres *pecadores, y ser crucificado,
pero al tercer día resucitará."
[8]Entonces ellas se acordaron de las palabras de
Jesús. [9]Al regresar del sepulcro, les contaron todas
estas cosas a los once y a todos los demás. [10]Las mujeres eran María Magdalena, Juana, María la madre
de *Jacobo, y las demás que las acompañaban. [11]Pero
a los discípulos el relato les pareció una tontería, así
que no les creyeron. [12]Pedro, sin embargo, salió corriendo al sepulcro. Se asomó y vio sólo las vendas
de lino. Luego volvió a su casa, extrañado de lo que
había sucedido.

[o] **23:30** Os 10:8 [p] **23:34** Var. no incluye esta oración. [q] **23:44** *el mediodía . . . la media tarde.* Lit. *la hora sexta ... la hora novena.*

De camino a Emaús

¹³Aquel mismo día dos de ellos se dirigían a un pueblo llamado Emaús, a unos once kilómetrosʳ de Jerusalén. ¹⁴Iban conversando sobre todo lo que había acontecido. ¹⁵Sucedió que, mientras hablaban y discutían, Jesús mismo se acercó y comenzó a caminar con ellos; ¹⁶pero no lo reconocieron, pues sus ojos estaban velados.

¹⁷—¿Qué vienen discutiendo por el camino? —les preguntó.

Se detuvieron, cabizbajos; ¹⁸y uno de ellos, llamado Cleofas, le dijo:

—¿Eres tú el único peregrino en Jerusalén que no se ha enterado de todo lo que ha pasado recientemente?

¹⁹—¿Qué es lo que ha pasado? —les preguntó.

—Lo de Jesús de Nazaret. Era un profeta, poderoso en obras y en palabras delante de Dios y de todo el pueblo. ²⁰Los jefes de los sacerdotes y nuestros gobernantes lo entregaron para ser condenado a muerte, y lo crucificaron; ²¹pero nosotros abrigábamos la esperanza de que era él quien redimiría a Israel. Es más, ya hace tres días que sucedió todo esto. ²²También algunas mujeres de nuestro grupo nos dejaron asombrados. Esta mañana, muy temprano, fueron al sepulcro ²³pero no hallaron su cuerpo. Cuando volvieron, nos contaron que se les habían aparecido unos ángeles quienes les dijeron que él está vivo. ²⁴Algunos de nuestros compañeros fueron después al sepulcro y lo encontraron tal como habían dicho las mujeres, pero a él no lo vieron.

²⁵—¡Qué torpes son ustedes —les dijo—, y qué tardos de corazón para creer todo lo que han dicho los profetas! ²⁶¿Acaso no tenía que sufrir el *Cristo estas cosas antes de entrar en su gloria?

²⁷Entonces, comenzando por Moisés y por todos los profetas, les explicó lo que se refería a él en todas las Escrituras.

²⁸Al acercarse al pueblo adonde se dirigían, Jesús hizo como que iba más lejos. ²⁹Pero ellos insistieron:

—Quédate con nosotros, que está atardeciendo; ya es casi de noche.

Así que entró para quedarse con ellos. ³⁰Luego, estando con ellos a la mesa, tomó el pan, lo bendijo, lo partió y se lo dio. ³¹Entonces se les abrieron los ojos y lo reconocieron, pero él desapareció. ³²Se decían el uno al otro:

—¿No ardía nuestro corazón mientras conversaba con nosotros en el camino y nos explicaba las Escrituras?

³³Al instante se pusieron en camino y regresaron a Jerusalén. Allí encontraron a los once y a los que estaban reunidos con ellos. ³⁴«¡Es cierto! —decían—. El Señor ha resucitado y se le ha aparecido a Simón.»

³⁵Los dos, por su parte, contaron lo que les había sucedido en el camino, y cómo habían reconocido a Jesús cuando partió el pan.

Jesús se aparece a los discípulos

³⁶Todavía estaban ellos hablando acerca de esto, cuando Jesús mismo se puso en medio de ellos y les dijo:

—Paz a ustedes.

³⁷Aterrorizados, creyeron que veían a un espíritu. ³⁸—¿Por qué se asustan tanto? —les preguntó—. ¿Por qué les vienen dudas? ³⁹Miren mis manos y mis pies. ¡Soy yo mismo! Tóquenme y vean; un espíritu no tiene carne ni huesos, como ven que los tengo yo.

⁴⁰Dicho esto, les mostró las manos y los pies. ⁴¹Como ellos no acababan de creerlo a causa de la alegría y del asombro, les preguntó:

—¿Tienen aquí algo de comer?

⁴²Le dieron un pedazo de pescado asado, ⁴³así que lo tomó y se lo comió delante de ellos. Luego les dijo:

⁴⁴—Cuando todavía estaba yo con ustedes, les decía que tenía que cumplirse todo lo que está escrito acerca de mí en la ley de Moisés, en los profetas y en los salmos.

⁴⁵Entonces les abrió el entendimiento para que comprendieran las Escrituras.

⁴⁶—Esto es lo que está escrito —les explicó—: que el *Cristo padecerá y *resucitará al tercer día, ⁴⁷y en su nombre se predicarán el *arrepentimiento y el perdón de pecados a todas las *naciones, comenzando por Jerusalén. ⁴⁸Ustedes son testigos de estas cosas. ⁴⁹Ahora voy a enviarles lo que ha prometido mi Padre; pero ustedes quédense en la ciudad hasta que sean revestidos del poder de lo alto.

La ascensión

⁵⁰Después los llevó Jesús hasta Betania; allí alzó las manos y los bendijo. ⁵¹Sucedió que, mientras los bendecía, se alejó de ellos y fue llevado al cielo. ⁵²Ellos, entonces, lo adoraron y luego regresaron a Jerusalén con gran alegría. ⁵³Y estaban continuamente en el *templo, alabando a Dios.

ʳ **24:13** *unos once kilómetros.* Lit. *sesenta* *estadios.*

JUAN

El Verbo se hizo hombre

1 En el principio ya existía el *Verbo,
y el Verbo estaba con Dios,
y el Verbo era Dios.
²Él estaba con Dios en el principio.
³Por medio de él todas las cosas fueron creadas;
sin él, nada de lo creado llegó a existir.
⁴En él estaba la vida,
y la vida era la luz de la *humanidad.
⁵Esta luz resplandece en las tinieblas,
y las tinieblas no han podido extinguirla.ᵃ

⁶Vino un hombre llamado Juan. Dios lo envió ⁷como testigo para dar testimonio de la luz, a fin de que por medio de él todos creyeran. ⁸Juan no era la luz, sino que vino para dar testimonio de la luz. ⁹Esa luz verdadera, la que alumbra a todo *ser humano, venía a este mundo.ᵇ

¹⁰El que era la luz ya estaba en el mundo, y el mundo fue creado por medio de él, pero el mundo no lo reconoció. ¹¹Vino a lo que era suyo, pero los suyos no lo recibieron. ¹²Mas a cuantos lo recibieron, a los que creen en su nombre, les dio el derecho de ser hijos de Dios. ¹³Éstos no nacen de la sangre, ni por deseos *naturales, ni por voluntad humana, sino que nacen de Dios.

¹⁴Y el Verbo se hizo hombre y habitóᶜ entre nosotros. Y hemos contemplado su gloria, la gloria que corresponde al Hijo *unigénito del Padre, lleno de gracia y de verdad.

¹⁵Juan dio testimonio de él, y a voz en cuello proclamó: «Éste es aquel de quien yo decía: "El que viene después de mí es superior a mí, porque existía antes que yo."» ¹⁶De su plenitud todos hemos recibido gracia sobre gracia, ¹⁷pues la ley fue dada por medio de Moisés, mientras que la gracia y la verdad nos han llegado por medio de *Jesucristo. ¹⁸A Dios nadie lo ha visto nunca; el Hijo unigénito, que es Diosᵈ y que vive en unión íntima con el Padre, nos lo ha dado a conocer.

Juan el Bautista niega ser el Cristo

¹⁹Éste es el testimonio de Juan cuando los judíos de Jerusalén enviaron sacerdotes y levitas a preguntarle quién era. ²⁰No se negó a declararlo, sino que confesó con franqueza:

—Yo no soy el *Cristo.

²¹—¿Quién eres entonces? —le preguntaron—. ¿Acaso eres Elías?

—No lo soy.

—¿Eres el profeta?

—No lo soy.

²²—¿Entonces quién eres? ¡Tenemos que llevar una respuesta a los que nos enviaron! ¿Cómo te ves a ti mismo?

²³—Yo soy la voz del que grita en el desierto: "Enderecen el camino del Señor"ᵉ —respondió Juan, con las palabras del profeta Isaías.

²⁴Algunos que habían sido enviados por los *fariseos ²⁵lo interrogaron:

—Pues si no eres el Cristo, ni Elías ni el profeta, ¿por qué bautizas?

²⁶—Yo bautizo conᶠ agua, pero entre ustedes hay alguien a quien no conocen, ²⁷y que viene después de mí, al cual yo no soy digno ni siquiera de desatarle la correa de las sandalias.

²⁸Todo esto sucedió en Betania, al otro lado del río Jordán, donde Juan estaba bautizando.

Jesús, el Cordero de Dios

²⁹Al día siguiente Juan vio a Jesús que se acercaba a él, y dijo: «¡Aquí tienen al Cordero de Dios, que quita el pecado del mundo! ³⁰De éste hablaba yo cuando dije: "Después de mí viene un hombre que es superior a mí, porque existía antes que yo." ³¹Yo ni siquiera lo conocía, pero, para que él se revelara al pueblo de Israel, vine bautizando con agua.»

³²Juan declaró: «Vi al Espíritu descender del cielo como una paloma y permanecer sobre él. ³³Yo mismo no lo conocía, pero el que me envió a bautizar con agua me dijo: "Aquel sobre quien veas que el Espíritu desciende y permanece, es el que bautiza con el Espíritu Santo." ³⁴Yo lo he visto y por eso testifico que éste es el Hijo de Dios.»

Los primeros discípulos de Jesús
1:40-42 — Mt 4:18-22; Mr 1:16-20; Lc 5:2-11

³⁵Al día siguiente Juan estaba de nuevo allí, con dos de sus discípulos. ³⁶Al ver a Jesús que pasaba por ahí, dijo:

—¡Aquí tienen al Cordero de Dios!

³⁷Cuando los dos discípulos le oyeron decir esto, siguieron a Jesús. ³⁸Jesús se volvió y, al ver que lo seguían, les preguntó:

—¿Qué buscan?

—Rabí, ¿dónde te hospedas? (Rabí significa: Maestro.)

³⁹—Vengan a ver —les contestó Jesús.

Ellos fueron, pues, y vieron dónde se hospedaba, y aquel mismo día se quedaron con él. Eran como las cuatro de la tarde.ᵍ

⁴⁰Andrés, hermano de Simón Pedro, era uno de los dos que, al oír a Juan, habían seguido a Jesús. ⁴¹Andrés encontró primero a su hermano Simón, y le dijo:

—Hemos encontrado al Mesías (es decir, el *Cristo).

⁴²Luego lo llevó a Jesús, quien mirándolo fijamente, le dijo:

—Tú eres Simón, hijo de Juan. Serás llamado *Cefas (es decir, Pedro).

Jesús llama a Felipe y a Natanael

⁴³Al día siguiente, Jesús decidió salir hacia Galilea. Se encontró con Felipe, y lo llamó:

—Sígueme.

⁴⁴Felipe era del pueblo de Betsaida, lo mismo que Andrés y Pedro. ⁴⁵Felipe buscó a Natanael y le dijo:

—Hemos encontrado a Jesús de Nazaret, el hijo de José, aquel de quien escribió Moisés en la ley, y de quien escribieron los profetas.

⁴⁶—¡De Nazaret! —replicó Natanael—. ¿Acaso de allí puede salir algo bueno?

—Ven a ver —le contestó Felipe.

ᵃ **1:5** *extinguirla.* Alt. *comprenderla.* ᵇ **1:9** *Esa . . . mundo.* Alt. *Esa era la luz verdadera que alumbra a todo *ser humano que viene al mundo.* ᶜ **1:14** *habitó.* Lit. *puso su carpa.* ᵈ **1:18** *el Hijo unigénito, que es Dios.* Var. *el Hijo unigénito.* ᵉ **1:23** Is 40:3 ᶠ **1:26** *con.* Alt. *en;* también en vv. 31 y 33. ᵍ **1:39** *Eran . . . tarde* (si se cuentan las horas a partir de las seis de la mañana, según la hora judía). Lit. *Era como la hora décima;* véase nota en 19:14.

47Cuando Jesús vio que Natanael se le acercaba, comentó:

—Aquí tienen a un verdadero israelita, en quien no hay falsedad.

48—¿De dónde me conoces? —le preguntó Natanael.

—Antes de que Felipe te llamara, cuando aún estabas bajo la higuera, ya te había visto.

49—Rabí, ¡tú eres el Hijo de Dios! ¡Tú eres el Rey de Israel! —declaró Natanael.

50—¿Lo crees porque te dije que te vi cuando estabas debajo de la higuera? ¡Vas a ver aun cosas más grandes que éstas!

Y añadió:

51—Ciertamente les aseguro que ustedes verán abrirse el cielo, y a los ángeles de Dios subir y bajar sobre el Hijo del hombre.

Jesús cambia el agua en vino

2 Al tercer día se celebró una boda en Caná de Galilea, y la madre de Jesús se encontraba allí. 2También habían sido invitados a la boda Jesús y sus discípulos. 3Cuando el vino se acabó, la madre de Jesús le dijo:

—Ya no tienen vino.

4—Mujer, ¿eso qué tiene que ver conmigo? —respondió Jesús—. Todavía no ha llegado mi hora.

5Su madre dijo a los sirvientes:

—Hagan lo que él les ordene.

6Había allí seis tinajas de piedra, de las que usan los judíos en sus ceremonias de *purificación. En cada una cabían unos cien litros.h

7Jesús dijo a los sirvientes:

—Llenen de agua las tinajas.

Y los sirvientes las llenaron hasta el borde.

8—Ahora saquen un poco y llévenlo al encargado del banquete —les dijo Jesús.

Así lo hicieron. 9El encargado del banquete probó el agua convertida en vino sin saber de dónde había salido, aunque sí lo sabían los sirvientes que habían sacado el agua. Entonces llamó aparte al novio 10y le dijo:

—Todos sirven primero el mejor vino, y cuando los invitados ya han bebido mucho, entonces sirven el más barato; pero tú has guardado el mejor vino hasta ahora.

11Ésta, la primera de sus señales, la hizo Jesús en Caná de Galilea. Así reveló su gloria, y sus discípulos creyeron en él.

12Después de esto Jesús bajó a Capernaúm con su madre, sus hermanos y sus discípulos, y se quedaron allí unos días.

Jesús purifica el templo
2:14-16 — Mt 21:12-13; Mr 11:15-17; Lc 19:45-46

13Cuando se aproximaba la Pascua de los judíos, subió Jesús a Jerusalén. 14Y en el *temploi halló a los que vendían bueyes, ovejas y palomas, e instalados en sus mesas a los que cambiaban dinero. 15Entonces, haciendo un látigo de cuerdas, echó a todos del templo, juntamente con sus ovejas y sus bueyes; regó por el suelo las monedas de los que cambiaban dinero y derribó sus mesas. 16A los que vendían las palomas les dijo:

—¡Saquen esto de aquí! ¿Cómo se atreven a convertir la casa de mi Padre en un mercado?

17Sus discípulos se acordaron de que está escrito: «El celo por tu casa me consumirá.»j 18Entonces los judíos reaccionaron, preguntándole:

—¿Qué señal puedes mostrarnos para actuar de esta manera?

19—Destruyan este templo —respondió Jesús—, y lo levantaré de nuevo en tres días.

20—Tardaron cuarenta y seis años en construir este templo, ¿y tú vas a levantarlo en tres días?

21Pero el templo al que se refería era su propio cuerpo. 22Así, pues, cuando se *levantó de entre los muertos, sus discípulos se acordaron de lo que había dicho, y creyeron en la Escritura y en las palabras de Jesús.

23Mientras estaba en Jerusalén, durante la fiesta de la Pascua, muchos creyeron en su nombre al ver las señales que hacía. 24En cambio Jesús no les creía porque los conocía a todos; 25no necesitaba que nadie le informara nadak acerca de los demás, pues él conocía el interior del *ser humano.

Jesús enseña a Nicodemo

3 Había entre los *fariseos un dirigente de los judíos llamado Nicodemo. 2Éste fue de noche a visitar a Jesús.

—Rabí —le dijo—, sabemos que eres un maestro que ha venido de parte de Dios, porque nadie podría hacer las señales que tú haces si Dios no estuviera con él.

3—De veras te aseguro que quien no nazca de nuevol no puede ver el reino de Dios —dijo Jesús.

4—¿Cómo puede uno nacer de nuevo siendo ya viejo? —preguntó Nicodemo—. ¿Acaso puede entrar por segunda vez en el vientre de su madre y volver a nacer?

5—Yo te aseguro que quien no nazca de agua y del Espíritu, no puede entrar en el reino de Dios —respondió Jesús—. 6Lo que nace del cuerpo es cuerpo; lo que nace del Espíritu es espíritu. 7No te sorprendas de que te haya dicho: "Tienen que nacer de nuevo." 8El viento sopla por donde quiere, y lo oyes silbar, aunque ignoras de dónde viene y a dónde va. Lo mismo pasa con todo el que nace del Espíritu.

9Nicodemo replicó:

—¿Cómo es posible que esto suceda?

10—Tú eres maestro de Israel, ¿y no entiendes estas cosas? —respondió Jesús—. 11Te digo con seguridad y verdad que hablamos de lo que sabemos y damos testimonio de lo que hemos visto personalmente, pero ustedes no aceptan nuestro testimonio. 12Si les he hablado de las cosas terrenales, y no creen, ¿entonces cómo van a creer si les hablo de las celestiales? 13Nadie ha subido jamás al cielo sino el que descendió del cielo, el Hijo del hombre.m

Jesús y el amor del Padre

14»Como levantó Moisés la serpiente en el desierto, así también tiene que ser levantado el Hijo del hombre, 15para que todo el que crea en él tenga vida eterna.n

16»Porque tanto amó Dios al mundo, que dio a su Hijo *unigénito, para que todo el que cree en él no se pierda, sino que tenga vida eterna. 17Dios no envió a su Hijo al mundo para condenar al mundo, sino para salvarlo por medio de él. 18El que cree en él no es condenado, pero el que no cree ya está condenado por no haber creído en el nombre del Hijo unigénito

h 2:6 unos cien litros. Lit. entre dos y tres *metretas. i 2:14 Es decir, en el área general del templo; en vv. 19-21 el término griego significa *santuario. j 2:17 Sal 69:9 k 2:25 le informara nada. Lit. le diera testimonio. l 3:3 de nuevo. Alt. de arriba; también en v. 7. m 3:13 hombre. Var. hombre que está en el cielo. n 3:15 todo . . . eterna. Alt. todo el que cree tenga vida eterna en él.

de Dios. [19]Ésta es la causa de la condenación: que la luz vino al mundo, pero la *humanidad prefirió las tinieblas a la luz, porque sus hechos eran perversos. [20]Pues todo el que hace lo malo aborrece la luz, y no se acerca a ella por temor a que sus obras queden al descubierto. [21]En cambio, el que practica la verdad se acerca a la luz, para que se vea claramente que ha hecho sus obras en obediencia a Dios.ñ

Testimonio de Juan el Bautista acerca de Jesús

[22]Después de esto Jesús fue con sus discípulos a la región de Judea. Allí pasó algún tiempo con ellos, y bautizaba. [23]También Juan estaba bautizando en Enón, cerca de Salín, porque allí había mucha agua. Así que la gente iba para ser bautizada. [24](Esto sucedió antes de que encarcelaran a Juan.) [25]Se entabló entonces una discusión entre los discípulos de Juan y un judíoº en torno a los ritos de *purificación. [26]Aquéllos fueron a ver a Juan y le dijeron:

—Rabí, fíjate, el que estaba contigo al otro lado del Jordán, y de quien tú diste testimonio, ahora está bautizando, y todos acuden a él.

[27]—Nadie puede recibir nada a menos que Dios se lo conceda —les respondió Juan—. [28]Ustedes me son testigos de que dije: "Yo no soy el *Cristo, sino que he sido enviado delante de él." [29]El que tiene a la novia es el novio. Pero el amigo del novio, que está a su lado y lo escucha, se llena de alegría cuando oye la voz del novio. Ésa es la alegría que me inunda. [30]A él le toca crecer, y a mí menguar.

El que viene del cielo

[31]»El que viene de arriba está por encima de todos; el que es de la tierra, es terrenal y de lo terrenal habla. El que viene del cielo está por encima de todos [32]y da testimonio de lo que ha visto y oído, pero nadie recibe su testimonio. [33]El que lo recibe certifica que Dios es veraz. [34]El enviado de Dios comunica el mensaje divino, pues Dios mismo le da su Espíritu sin restricción. [35]El Padre ama al Hijo, y ha puesto todo en sus manos. [36]El que cree en el Hijo tiene vida eterna; pero el que rechaza al Hijo no sabrá lo que es esa vida, sino que permanecerá bajo el castigo de Dios.p

Jesús y la samaritana

4 Jesúsq se enteró de que los *fariseos sabían que él estaba haciendo y bautizando más discípulos que Juan [2](aunque en realidad no era Jesús quien bautizaba sino sus discípulos). [3]Por eso se fue de Judea y volvió otra vez a Galilea. [4]Como tenía que pasar por Samaria, [5]llegó a un pueblo samaritano llamado Sicar, cerca del terreno que Jacob le había dado a su hijo José. [6]Allí estaba el pozo de Jacob. Jesús, fatigado del camino, se sentó junto al pozo. Era cerca del mediodía.r [7-8]Sus discípulos habían ido al pueblo a comprar comida.

En eso llegó a sacar agua una mujer de Samaria, y Jesús le dijo:

—Dame un poco de agua.

[9]Pero como los judíos no usan nada en comúns con los samaritanos, la mujer le respondió:

—¿Cómo se te ocurre pedirme agua, si tú eres judío y yo soy samaritana?

[10]—Si supieras lo que Dios puede dar, y conocieras al que te está pidiendo agua —contestó Jesús—, tú le habrías pedido a él, y él te habría dado agua que da vida.

[11]—Señor, ni siquiera tienes con qué sacar agua, y el pozo es muy hondo; ¿de dónde, pues, vas a sacar esa agua que da vida? [12]¿Acaso eres tú superior a nuestro padre Jacob, que nos dejó este pozo, del cual bebieron él, sus hijos y su ganado?

[13]—Todo el que beba de esta agua volverá a tener sed —respondió Jesús—, [14]pero el que beba del agua que yo le daré, no volverá a tener sed jamás, sino que dentro de él esa agua se convertirá en un manantial del que brotará vida eterna.

[15]—Señor, dame de esa agua para que no vuelva a tener sed ni siga viniendo aquí a sacarla.

[16]—Ve a llamar a tu esposo, y vuelve acá —le dijo Jesús.

[17]—No tengo esposo —respondió la mujer.

—Bien has dicho que no tienes esposo. [18]Es cierto que has tenido cinco, y el que ahora tienes no es tu esposo. En esto has dicho la verdad.

[19]—Señor, me doy cuenta de que tú eres profeta. [20]Nuestros antepasados adoraron en este monte, pero ustedes los judíos dicen que el lugar donde debemos adorar está en Jerusalén.

[21]—Créeme, mujer, que se acerca la hora en que ni en este monte ni en Jerusalén adorarán ustedes al Padre. [22]Ahora ustedes adoran lo que no conocen; nosotros adoramos lo que conocemos, porque la salvación proviene de los judíos. [23]Pero se acerca la hora, y ha llegado ya, en que los verdaderos adoradores rendirán culto al Padre en espíritu y en verdad,t porque así quiere el Padre que sean los que le adoren. [24]Dios es espíritu, y quienes lo adoran deben hacerlo en espíritu y en verdad.

[25]—Sé que viene el Mesías, al que llaman el *Cristo —respondió la mujer—. Cuando él venga nos explicará todas las cosas.

[26]—Ése soy yo, el que habla contigo —le dijo Jesús.

Los discípulos vuelven a reunirse con Jesús

[27]En esto llegaron sus discípulos y se sorprendieron de verlo hablando con una mujer, aunque ninguno le preguntó: «¿Qué pretendes?» o «¿De qué hablas con ella?»

[28]La mujer dejó su cántaro, volvió al pueblo y le decía a la gente:

[29]—Vengan a ver a un hombre que me ha dicho todo lo que he hecho. ¿No será éste el *Cristo?

[30]Salieron del pueblo y fueron a ver a Jesús. [31]Mientras tanto, sus discípulos le insistían:

—Rabí, come algo.

[32]—Yo tengo un alimento que ustedes no conocen —replicó él.

[33]¿Le habrán traído algo de comer?», comentaban entre sí los discípulos.

[34]—Mi alimento es hacer la voluntad del que me envió y terminar su obra —les dijo Jesús—. [35]¿No dicen ustedes: "Todavía faltan cuatro meses para la cosecha"? Yo les digo: ¡Abran los ojos y miren los campos sembrados! Ya la cosecha está madura; [36]ya el segador recibe su salario y recoge el fruto para vida eterna. Ahora tanto el sembrador como el segador se alegran juntos. [37]Porque como dice el refrán: "Uno

---

ñ **3:21** Algunos intérpretes consideran que el discurso de Jesús termina en el v. 15. o **3:25** *un judío.* Var. *unos judíos.* p **3:36** Algunos intérpretes consideran que los vv. 31-36 son comentario del autor del evangelio. q **4:1** *Jesús.* Var. *El Señor.* r **4:6** *del mediodía.* Lit. *de la hora sexta;* véase nota en 1:39. s **4:9** *no usan nada en común.* Alt. *no se llevan bien.* t **4:23** *en espíritu y en verdad.* Alt. *por el Espíritu y la verdad;* también en v. 24.

es el que siembra y otro el que cosecha." 38Yo los he enviado a ustedes a cosechar lo que no les costó ningún trabajo. Otros se han fatigado trabajando, y ustedes han cosechado el fruto de ese trabajo.

Muchos samaritanos creen en Jesús

39Muchos de los samaritanos que vivían en aquel pueblo creyeron en él por el testimonio que daba la mujer: «Me dijo todo lo que he hecho.» 40Así que cuando los samaritanos fueron a su encuentro le insistieron en que se quedara con ellos. Jesús permaneció allí dos días, 41y muchos más llegaron a creer por lo que él mismo decía.

42—Ya no creemos sólo por lo que tú dijiste —le decían a la mujer—; ahora lo hemos oído nosotros mismos, y sabemos que verdaderamente éste es el Salvador del mundo.

Jesús sana al hijo de un funcionario

43Después de esos dos días Jesús salió de allí rumbo a Galilea 44(pues, como él mismo había dicho, a ningún profeta se le honra en su propia tierra). 45Cuando llegó a Galilea, fue bien recibido por los galileos, pues éstos habían visto personalmente todo lo que había hecho en Jerusalén durante la fiesta de la Pascua, ya que ellos habían estado también allí.

46Y volvió otra vez Jesús a Caná de Galilea, donde había convertido el agua en vino. Había allí un funcionario real, cuyo hijo estaba enfermo en Capernaúm. 47Cuando este hombre se enteró de que Jesús había llegado de Judea a Galilea, fue a su encuentro y le suplicó que bajara a sanar a su hijo, pues estaba a punto de morir.

48—Ustedes nunca van a creer si no ven señales y prodigios —le dijo Jesús.

49—Señor —rogó el funcionario—, baja antes de que se muera mi hijo.

50—Vuelve a casa, que tu hijo vive —le dijo Jesús.

El hombre creyó lo que Jesús le dijo, y se fue. 51Cuando se dirigía a su casa, sus siervos salieron a su encuentro y le dieron la noticia de que su hijo estaba vivo. 52Cuando les preguntó a qué hora había comenzado su hijo a sentirse mejor, le contestaron:

—Ayer a la una de la tarde[u] se le quitó la fiebre.

53Entonces el padre se dio cuenta de que precisamente a esa hora Jesús le había dicho: «Tu hijo vive.» Así que creyó él con toda su familia.

54Ésta fue la segunda señal que hizo Jesús después de que volvió de Judea a Galilea.

Jesús sana a un inválido

5 Algún tiempo después, se celebraba una fiesta de los judíos, y subió Jesús a Jerusalén. 2Había allí, junto a la puerta de las Ovejas, un estanque rodeado de cinco pórticos, cuyo nombre en arameo es Betzatá.[v] 3En esos pórticos se hallaban tendidos muchos enfermos, ciegos, cojos y paralíticos.[w] 5Entre ellos se encontraba un hombre inválido que llevaba enfermo treinta y ocho años. 6Cuando Jesús lo vio allí, tirado en el suelo, y se enteró de que ya tenía mucho tiempo de estar así, le preguntó:

—¿Quieres quedar sano?

7—Señor —respondió—, no tengo a nadie que me meta en el estanque mientras se agita el agua, y cuando trato de hacerlo, otro se mete antes.

8—Levántate, recoge tu camilla y anda —le contestó Jesús.

9Al instante aquel hombre quedó sano, así que tomó su camilla y echó a andar. Pero ese día era *sábado. 10Por eso los judíos le dijeron al que había sido sanado:

—Hoy es sábado; no te está permitido cargar tu camilla.

11—El que me sanó me dijo: "Recoge tu camilla y anda" —les respondió.

12—¿Quién es ese hombre que te dijo: "Recógela y anda"? —le interpelaron.

13El que había sido sanado no tenía idea de quién era, porque Jesús se había escabullido entre la mucha gente que había en el lugar.

14Después de esto Jesús lo encontró en el *templo y le dijo:

—Mira, ya has quedado sano. No vuelvas a pecar, no sea que te ocurra algo peor.

15El hombre se fue e informó a los judíos que Jesús era quien lo había sanado.

Vida mediante el Hijo

16Precisamente por esto los judíos perseguían a Jesús, pues hacía tales cosas en *sábado. 17Pero Jesús les respondía:

—Mi Padre aun hoy está trabajando, y yo también trabajo.

18Así que los judíos redoblaban sus esfuerzos para matarlo, pues no sólo quebrantaba el sábado sino que incluso llamaba a Dios su propio Padre, con lo que él mismo se hacía igual a Dios.

19Entonces Jesús afirmó:

—Ciertamente les aseguro que el hijo no puede hacer nada por su propia cuenta, sino solamente lo que ve que su padre hace, porque cualquier cosa que hace el padre, la hace también el hijo. 20Pues el padre ama al hijo y le muestra todo lo que hace. Sí, y aun cosas más grandes que éstas le mostrará, que los dejará a ustedes asombrados. 21Porque así como el Padre resucita a los muertos y les da vida, así también el Hijo da vida a quienes a él le place. 22Además, el Padre no juzga a nadie, sino que todo juicio lo ha delegado en el Hijo, 23para que todos honren al Hijo como lo honran a él. El que se niega a honrar al Hijo no honra al Padre que lo envió.

24»Ciertamente les aseguro que el que oye mi palabra y cree al que me envió, tiene vida eterna y no será juzgado, sino que ha pasado de la muerte a la vida. 25Ciertamente les aseguro que ya viene la hora, y ha llegado ya, en que los muertos oirán la voz del Hijo de Dios, y los que la oigan vivirán. 26Porque así como el Padre tiene vida en sí mismo, así también ha concedido al Hijo el tener vida en sí mismo, 27y le ha dado autoridad para juzgar, puesto que es el Hijo del hombre.

28»No se asombren de esto, porque viene la hora en que todos los que están en los sepulcros oirán su voz, 29y saldrán de allí. Los que han hecho el bien resucitarán para tener vida, pero los que han practicado el mal resucitarán para ser juzgados. 30Yo no puedo hacer nada por mi propia cuenta; juzgo sólo según lo que oigo, y mi juicio es justo, pues no busco hacer mi propia voluntad sino cumplir la voluntad del que me envió.

Los testimonios a favor del Hijo

31»Si yo testifico en mi favor, ese testimonio no es válido. 32Otro es el que testifica en mi favor, y me consta que es válido el testimonio que él da de mí.

33»Ustedes enviaron a preguntarle a Juan, y él dio un testimonio válido. 34Y no es que acepte yo el testimonio de un hombre; más bien lo menciono para que ustedes sean salvos. 35Juan era una lámpara encendida y brillante, y ustedes decidieron disfrutar de su luz por algún tiempo.

36»El testimonio con que yo cuento tiene más peso que el de Juan. Porque esa misma tarea que el Padre me ha encomendado que lleve a cabo, y que estoy haciendo, es la que testifica que el Padre me ha enviado. 37Y el Padre mismo que me envió ha testificado en mi favor. Ustedes nunca han oído su voz, ni visto su figura, 38ni vive su palabra en ustedes, porque no creen en aquel a quien él envió. 39Ustedes estudianˣ con diligencia las Escrituras porque piensan que en ellas hallan la vida eterna. ¡Y son ellas las que dan testimonio en mi favor! 40Sin embargo, ustedes no quieren venir a mí para tener esa vida.

41»La gloria *humana no la acepto, 42pero a ustedes los conozco, y sé que no aman realmente a Dios.ʸ 43Yo he venido en nombre de mi Padre, y ustedes no me aceptan; pero si otro viniera por su propia cuenta, a ése sí lo aceptarían. 44¿Cómo va a ser posible que ustedes crean, si unos a otros se rinden gloria pero no buscan la gloria que viene del Dios único?ᶻ

45»Pero no piensen que yo voy a acusarlos delante del Padre. Quien los va a acusar es Moisés, en quien tienen puesta su esperanza. 46Si le creyeran a Moisés, me creerían a mí, porque de mí escribió él. 47Pero si no creen lo que él escribió, ¿cómo van a creer mis palabras?

Jesús alimenta a los cinco mil
6:1-13 — Mt 14:13-21; Mr 6:32-44; Lc 9:10-17

6 Algún tiempo después, Jesús se fue a la otra orilla del mar de Galilea (o de Tiberíades). 2Y mucha gente lo seguía, porque veían las señales milagrosas que hacía en los enfermos. 3Entonces subió Jesús a una colina y se sentó con sus discípulos.

4Faltaba muy poco tiempo para la fiesta judía de la Pascua.

5Cuando Jesús alzó la vista y vio una gran multitud que venía hacia él, le dijo a Felipe:

—¿Dónde vamos a comprar pan para que coma esta gente?

6Esto lo dijo sólo para ponerlo a *prueba, porque él ya sabía lo que iba a hacer.

7—Ni con el salario de ocho mesesª podríamos comprar suficiente pan para darle un pedazo a cada uno —respondió Felipe.

8Otro de sus discípulos, Andrés, que era hermano de Simón Pedro, le dijo:

9—Aquí hay un muchacho que tiene cinco panes de cebada y dos pescados, pero ¿qué es esto para tanta gente?

10—Hagan que se sienten todos —ordenó Jesús.

En ese lugar había mucha hierba. Así que se sentaron, y los varones adultos eran como cinco mil. 11Jesús tomó entonces los panes, dio gracias y distribuyó a los que estaban sentados todo lo que quisieron. Lo mismo hizo con los pescados.

12Una vez que quedaron satisfechos, dijo a sus discípulos:

—Recojan los pedazos que sobraron, para que no se desperdicie nada.

13Así lo hicieron, y con los pedazos de los cinco panes de cebada que les sobraron a los que habían comido, llenaron doce canastas.

14Al ver la señal que Jesús había realizado, la gente comenzó a decir: «En verdad éste es el profeta, el que ha de venir al mundo.» 15Pero Jesús, dándose cuenta de que querían llevárselo a la fuerza y declararlo rey, se retiró de nuevo a la montaña él solo.

Jesús camina sobre el agua
6:16-21 — Mt 14:22-33; Mr 6:47-51

16Cuando ya anochecía, sus discípulos bajaron al lago 17y subieron a una barca, y comenzaron a cruzar el lago en dirección a Capernaúm. Para entonces ya había oscurecido, y Jesús todavía no se había unido. 18Por causa del fuerte viento que soplaba, el lago estaba picado. 19Habrían remado unos cinco o seis kilómetrosᵇ cuando vieron que Jesús se acercaba a la barca, caminando sobre el agua, y se asustaron. 20Pero él les dijo: «No tengan miedo, que soy yo.» 21Así que se dispusieron a recibirlo a bordo, y en seguida la barca llegó a la orilla adonde se dirigían.

22Al día siguiente, la multitud que se había quedado en el otro lado del lago se dio cuenta de que los discípulos se habían embarcado solos. Allí había estado una sola barca, y Jesús no había entrado en ella con sus discípulos. 23Sin embargo, algunas barcas de Tiberíades se aproximaron al lugar donde la gente había comido el pan después de haber dado gracias el Señor. 24En cuanto la multitud se dio cuenta de que ni Jesús ni sus discípulos estaban allí, subieron a las barcas y se fueron a Capernaúm a buscar a Jesús.

Jesús, el pan de vida

25Cuando lo encontraron al otro lado del lago, le preguntaron:

—Rabí, ¿cuándo llegaste acá?

26—Ciertamente les aseguro que ustedes me buscan, no porque han visto señales sino porque comieron pan hasta llenarse. 27Trabajen, pero no por la comida que es perecedera, sino por la que permanece para vida eterna, la cual les dará el Hijo del hombre. Sobre éste ha puesto Dios el Padre su sello de aprobación.

28—¿Qué tenemos que hacer para realizar las obras que Dios exige? —le preguntaron.

29—Ésta es la obra de Dios: que crean en aquel a quien él envió —les respondió Jesús.

30—¿Y qué señal harás para que la veamos y te creamos? ¿Qué puedes hacer? —insistieron ellos—. 31Nuestros antepasados comieron el maná en el desierto, como está escrito: "Pan del cielo les dio a comer."ᶜ

32—Ciertamente les aseguro que no fue Moisés el que les dio a ustedes el pan del cielo —afirmó Jesús—. El que da el verdadero pan del cielo es mi Padre. 33El pan de Dios es el que baja del cielo y da vida al mundo.

34—Señor —le pidieron—, danos siempre ese pan.

35—Yo soy el pan de vida —declaró Jesús—. El que a mí viene nunca pasará hambre, y el que en mí cree nunca más volverá a tener sed. 36Pero como ya

---

ˣ **5:39** Ustedes estudian. Alt. Estudien. ʸ **5:42** no aman . . . Dios. Lit. no tienen el amor de Dios en sí mismos. ᶻ **5:44** del Dios único. Var. del Único. ª **6:7** el salario de ocho meses. Lit. doscientos *denarios. ᵇ **6:19** cinco o seis kilómetros. Lit. veinticinco o treinta *estadios. ᶜ **6:31** Éx 16:4; Neh 9:15; Sal 78:24,25

les dije, a pesar de que ustedes me han visto, no creen. 37Todos los que el Padre me da vendrán a mí; y al que a mí viene, no lo rechazo. 38Porque he bajado del cielo no para hacer mi voluntad sino la del que me envió. 39Y ésta es la voluntad del que me envió: que yo no pierda nada de lo que él me ha dado, sino que lo resucite en el día final. 40Porque la voluntad de mi Padre es que todo el que reconozca al Hijo y crea en él, tenga vida eterna, y yo lo resucitaré en el día final.

41Entonces los judíos comenzaron a murmurar contra él, porque dijo: «Yo soy el pan que bajó del cielo.» 42Y se decían: «¿Acaso no es éste Jesús, el hijo de José? ¿No conocemos a su padre y a su madre? ¿Cómo es que sale diciendo: "Yo bajé del cielo"?»

43—Dejen de murmurar —replicó Jesús—. 44Nadie puede venir a mí si no lo atrae el Padre que me envió, y yo lo resucitaré en el día final. 45En los profetas está escrito: "A todos los instruirá Dios."d En efecto, todo el que escucha al Padre y aprende de él, viene a mí. 46Al Padre nadie lo ha visto, excepto el que viene de Dios; sólo él ha visto al Padre. 47Ciertamente les aseguro que el que cree tiene vida eterna. 48Yo soy el pan de vida. 49Los antepasados de ustedes comieron el maná en el desierto, y sin embargo murieron. 50Pero éste es el pan que baja del cielo; el que come de él, no muere. 51Yo soy el pan vivo que bajó del cielo. Si alguno come de este pan, vivirá para siempre. Este pan es mi carne, que daré para que el mundo viva.

52Los judíos comenzaron a disputar acaloradamente entre sí: «¿Cómo puede éste darnos a comer su carne?»

53—Ciertamente les aseguro —afirmó Jesús— que si no comen la carne del Hijo del hombre ni beben su sangre, no tienen realmente vida. 54El que comee mi carne y bebe mi sangre tiene vida eterna, y yo lo resucitaré en el día final. 55Porque mi carne es verdadera comida y mi sangre es verdadera bebida. 56El que come mi carne y bebe mi sangre, permanece en mí y yo en él. 57Así como me envió el Padre viviente, y yo vivo por el Padre, también el que come de mí, vivirá por mí. 58Éste es el pan que bajó del cielo. Los antepasados de ustedes comieron maná y murieron, pero el que come de este pan vivirá para siempre.

59Todo esto lo dijo Jesús mientras enseñaba en la sinagoga de Capernaúm.

Muchos discípulos abandonan a Jesús

60Al escucharlo, muchos de sus discípulos exclamaron: «Esta enseñanza es muy difícil; ¿quién puede aceptarla?»

61Jesús, muy consciente de que sus discípulos murmuraban por lo que había dicho, les reprochó:

—¿Esto les causa *tropiezo? 62¿Qué tal si vieran al Hijo del hombre subir a donde antes estaba? 63El Espíritu da vida; la *carne no vale para nada. Las palabras que les he hablado son espíritu y son vida. 64Sin embargo, hay algunos de ustedes que no creen.

Es que Jesús conocía desde el principio quiénes eran los que no creían y quién era el que iba a traicionarlo. Así que añadió:

65—Por esto les dije que nadie puede venir a mí, a menos que se lo haya concedido el Padre.

66Desde entonces muchos de sus discípulos le volvieron la espalda y ya no andaban con él. Así que Jesús les preguntó a los doce:

67—¿También ustedes quieren marcharse?

68—Señor —contestó Simón Pedro—, ¿a quién iremos? Tú tienes palabras de vida eterna. 69Y nosotros hemos creído, y sabemos que tú eres el Santo de Dios.f

70—¿No los he escogido yo a ustedes doce? —repuso Jesús—. No obstante, uno de ustedes es un diablo.

71Se refería a Judas, hijo de Simón Iscariote, uno de los doce, que iba a traicionarlo.

Jesús va a la fiesta de los Tabernáculos

7 Algún tiempo después, Jesús andaba por Galilea. No tenía ningún interés en ir a Judea, porque allí los judíos buscaban la oportunidad para matarlo. 2Faltaba poco tiempo para la fiesta judía de los Tabernáculos,g 3así que los hermanos de Jesús le dijeron:

—Deberías salir de aquí e ir a Judea, para que tus discípulos vean las obras que realizas, 4porque nadie que quiera darse a conocer actúa en secreto. Ya que haces estas cosas, deja que el mundo te conozca.

5Lo cierto es que ni siquiera sus hermanos creían en él. 6Por eso Jesús les dijo:

—Para ustedes cualquier tiempo es bueno, pero el tiempo mío aún no ha llegado. 7El mundo no tiene motivos para aborrecerlos; a mí, sin embargo, me aborrece porque yo testifico que sus obras son malas. 8Suban ustedes a la fiesta. Yo no voy todavíah a esta fiesta porque mi tiempo aún no ha llegado.

9Dicho esto, se quedó en Galilea. 10Sin embargo, después de que sus hermanos se fueron a la fiesta, fue también él, no públicamente sino en secreto. 11Por eso las autoridades judías lo buscaban durante la fiesta, y decían: «¿Dónde se habrá metido?»

12Entre la multitud corrían muchos rumores acerca de él. Unos decían: «Es una buena persona.» Otros alegaban: «No, lo que pasa es que engaña a la gente.» 13Sin embargo, por temor a los judíos nadie hablaba de él abiertamente.

Jesús enseña en la fiesta

14Jesús esperó hasta la mitad de la fiesta para subir al *templo y comenzar a enseñar. 15Los judíos se admiraban y decían: «¿De dónde sacó éste tantos conocimientos sin haber estudiado?»

16—Mi enseñanza no es mía —replicó Jesús— sino del que me envió. 17El que esté dispuesto a hacer la voluntad de Dios reconocerá si mi enseñanza proviene de Dios o si yo hablo por mi propia cuenta. 18El que habla por cuenta propia busca su vanagloria; en cambio, el que busca glorificar al que lo envió es una persona íntegra y sin doblez. 19¿No les ha dado Moisés la ley a ustedes? Sin embargo, ninguno de ustedes la cumple. ¿Por qué tratan entonces de matarme?

20—Estás endemoniado —contestó la multitud—. ¿Quién quiere matarte?

21—Hice un milagro y todos ustedes han quedado asombrados. 22Por eso Moisés les dio la circuncisión, que en realidad no proviene de Moisés sino de los patriarcas, y aun en *sábado la practican. 23Ahora bien, si para cumplir la ley de Moisés circuncidan a un varón incluso en sábado, ¿por qué se enfurecen conmigo si en sábado lo sano por completo? 24No juzguen por las apariencias; juzguen con justicia.

¿Es éste el Cristo?

25Algunos de los que vivían en Jerusalén comentaban: «¿No es éste al que quieren matar? 26Ahí está,

d 6:45 Is 54:13 e 6:54 come. Lit. masca, o casca. f 6:69 el Santo de Dios. Var. el *Cristo, el hijo del Dios viviente. g 7:2 los Tabernáculos. Alt. las *Enramadas. h 7:8 Var. no incluye: todavía.

hablando abiertamente, y nadie le dice nada. ¿Será que las autoridades se han convencido de que es el *Cristo? 27Nosotros sabemos de dónde viene este hombre, pero cuando venga el Cristo nadie sabrá su procedencia.»

28Por eso Jesús, que seguía enseñando en el *templo, exclamó:

—¡Conque ustedes me conocen y saben de dónde vengo! No he venido por mi propia cuenta, sino que me envió uno que es digno de confianza. Ustedes no lo conocen, 29pero yo sí lo conozco porque vengo de parte suya, y él mismo me ha enviado.

30Entonces quisieron arrestarlo, pero nadie le echó mano porque aún no había llegado su hora. 31Con todo, muchos de entre la multitud creyeron en él y decían: «Cuando venga el Cristo, ¿acaso va a hacer más señales que este hombre?»

32Los *fariseos oyeron a la multitud que murmuraba estas cosas acerca de él, y junto con los jefes de los sacerdotes mandaron unos guardias del templo para arrestarlo. 33—Voy a estar con ustedes un poco más de tiempo —afirmó Jesús—, y luego volveré al que me envió. 34Me buscarán, pero no me encontrarán, porque a dónde yo esté no podrán ustedes llegar.

35«¿Y éste adónde piensa irse que no podamos encontrarlo? —comentaban entre sí los judíos—. ¿Será que piensa ir a nuestra gente dispersa entre las naciones,i para enseñar a los *griegos? 36¿Qué quiso decir con eso de que "me buscarán, pero no me encontrarán", y "a donde yo esté no podrán ustedes llegar"?»

Jesús en el último día de la fiesta

37En el último día, el más solemne de la fiesta, Jesús se puso de pie y exclamó:

—¡Si alguno tiene sed, que venga a mí y beba! 38De aquel que cree en mí, como dicej la Escritura, brotarán ríos de agua viva.

39Con esto se refería al Espíritu que habrían de recibir, más tarde los que creyeran en él. Hasta ese momento el Espíritu no había sido dado, porque Jesús no había sido glorificado todavía.

40Al oír sus palabras, algunos de entre la multitud decían: «Verdaderamente éste es el profeta.» 41Otros afirmaban: «¡Es el *Cristo!» Pero otros objetaban: «¿Cómo puede el Cristo venir de Galilea? 42¿Acaso no dice la Escritura que el Cristo vendrá de la descendencia de David, y de Belén, el pueblo de donde era David?» 43Por causa de Jesús la gente estaba dividida. 44Algunos querían arrestarlo, pero nadie le puso las manos encima.

Incredulidad de los dirigentes judíos

45Los guardias del *templo volvieron a los jefes de los sacerdotes y a los *fariseos, quienes los interrogaron:

—¿Se puede saber por qué no lo han traído?

46—¡Nunca nadie ha hablado como ese hombre! —declararon los guardias.

47—¿Así que también ustedes se han dejado engañar? —replicaron los fariseos—. 48¿Acaso ha creído en él alguno de los gobernantes o de los fariseos? 49¡No! Pero esta gente, que no sabe nada de la ley, está bajo maldición.

50Nicodemo, que era uno de ellos y que antes había ido a ver a Jesús, les interpeló:

51—¿Acaso nuestra ley condena a un hombre sin antes escucharlo y averiguar lo que hace?

52—¿No eres tú también de Galilea? —protestaron—. Investiga y verás que de Galilea no ha salido ningún profeta.k

---

53Entonces todos se fueron a casa.

La mujer sorprendida en adulterio

8 Pero Jesús se fue al monte de los Olivos. 2Al amanecer se presentó de nuevo en el *templo. Toda la gente se le acercó, y él se sentó a enseñarles. 3Los *maestros de la ley y los *fariseos llevaron entonces a una mujer sorprendida en adulterio, y poniéndola en medio del grupo 4le dijeron a Jesús:

—Maestro, a esta mujer se le ha sorprendido en el acto mismo de adulterio. 5En la ley Moisés nos ordenó apedrear a tales mujeres. ¿Tú qué dices?

6Con esta pregunta le estaban tendiendo una *trampa, para tener de qué acusarlo. Pero Jesús se inclinó y con el dedo comenzó a escribir en el suelo. 7Y como ellos lo acosaban a preguntas, Jesús se incorporó y les dijo:

—Aquel de ustedes que esté libre de pecado, que tire la primera piedra.

8E inclinándose de nuevo, siguió escribiendo en el suelo. 9Al oír esto, se fueron retirando uno tras otro, comenzando por los más viejos, hasta dejar a Jesús solo con la mujer, que aún seguía allí. 10Entonces él se incorporó y le preguntó:

—Mujer, ¿dónde están?l ¿Ya nadie te condena?

11—Nadie, Señor.

—Tampoco yo te condeno. Ahora vete, y no vuelvas a pecar.

Validez del testimonio de Jesús

12Una vez más Jesús se dirigió a la gente, y les dijo:

—Yo soy la luz del mundo. El que me sigue no andará en tinieblas, sino que tendrá la luz de la vida.

13—Tú te presentas como tu propio testigo —alegaron los *fariseos—, así que tu testimonio no es válido.

14—Aunque yo sea mi propio testigo —repuso Jesús—, mi testimonio es válido, porque sé de dónde he venido y a dónde voy. Pero ustedes no saben de dónde vengo ni a dónde voy. 15Ustedes juzgan según criterios *humanos; yo, en cambio, no juzgo a nadie. 16Y si lo hago, mis juicios son válidos porque no los emito por mi cuenta sino en unión con el Padre que me envió. 17En la ley de ustedes está escrito que el testimonio de dos personas es válido. 18Uno de mis testigos soy yo mismo, y el Padre que me envió también da testimonio de mí.

19—¿Dónde está tu padre?

—Si supieran quién soy yo, sabrían también quién es mi Padre.

20Estas palabras las dijo Jesús en el lugar donde se depositaban las ofrendas, mientras enseñaba en

---

i **7:35** nuestra . . . naciones. Lit. la diáspora de los griegos. j **7:37,38** que venga . . . como dice. Alt. que venga a mí! ¡Y que beba 38el que cree en mí! De él, como dice. k **7:52** Los mss. más antiguos y otros testimonios de la antigüedad no incluyen Jn 7:53—8:11. En algunos códices y versiones que contienen el relato de la adúltera, esta sección aparece en diferentes lugares; por ejemplo, después de 7:44, o al final de este evangelio, o después de Lc 21:38. l **8:10** ¿dónde están? Var. ¿dónde están los que te acusaban?

el *templo. Pero nadie le echó mano porque aún no había llegado su tiempo.

Yo no soy de este mundo

21De nuevo Jesús les dijo:

—Yo me voy, y ustedes me buscarán, pero en su pecado morirán. A donde yo voy, ustedes no pueden ir.

22Comentaban, por tanto, los judíos: «¿Acaso piensa suicidarse? ¿Será por eso que dice: "A donde yo voy, ustedes no pueden ir"?»

23—Ustedes son de aquí abajo —continuó Jesús—; yo soy de allá arriba. Ustedes son de este mundo; yo no soy de este mundo. 24Por eso les he dicho que morirán en sus pecados, pues si no creen que yo soy el que afirmo ser,m en sus pecados morirán.

25—¿Quién eres tú? —le preguntaron.

—En primer lugar, ¿qué tengo que explicarles?n —contestó Jesús—. 26Son muchas las cosas que tengo que decir y juzgar de ustedes. Pero el que me envió es veraz, y lo que le he oído decir es lo mismo que le repito al mundo.

27Ellos no entendieron que les hablaba de su Padre. 28Por eso Jesús añadió:

—Cuando hayan levantado al Hijo del hombre, sabrán ustedes que yo soy, y que no hago nada por mi propia cuenta, sino que hablo conforme a lo que el Padre me ha enseñado. 29El que me envió está conmigo; no me ha dejado solo, porque siempre hago lo que le agrada.

30Mientras aún hablaba, muchos creyeron en él.

Los hijos de Abraham

31Jesús se dirigió entonces a los judíos que habían creído en él, y les dijo:

—Si se mantienen fieles a mis enseñanzas, serán realmente mis discípulos; 32y conocerán la verdad, y la verdad los hará libres.

33—Nosotros somos descendientes de Abraham —le contestaron—, y nunca hemos sido esclavos de nadie. ¿Cómo puedes decir que seremos liberados?

34—Ciertamente les aseguro que todo el que peca es esclavo del pecado —respondió Jesús—. 35Ahora bien, el esclavo no se queda para siempre en la familia; pero el hijo sí se queda en ella para siempre. 36Así que si el Hijo los libera, serán ustedes verdaderamente libres. 37Yo sé que ustedes son descendientes de Abraham. Sin embargo, procuran matarme porque no está en sus planes aceptar mi palabra. 38Yo hablo de lo que he visto en presencia del Padre; así también ustedes, hagan lo que del Padre han escuchado.

39—Nuestro padre es Abraham —replicaron.

—Si fueran hijos de Abraham, harían lo mismo que él hizo. 40Ustedes, en cambio, quieren matarme, ¡a mí, que les he expuesto la verdad que he recibido de parte de Dios! Abraham jamás haría tal cosa. 41Las obras de ustedes son como las de su padre.

—Nosotros no somos hijos nacidos de prostitución —le reclamaron—. Un solo Padre tenemos, y es Dios mismo.

Los hijos del diablo

42—Si Dios fuera su Padre —les contestó Jesús—, ustedes me amarían, porque yo he venido de Dios y aquí me tienen. No he venido por mi propia cuenta, sino que él me envió. 43¿Por qué no entienden mi modo de hablar? Porque no pueden aceptar mi palabra. 44Ustedes son de su padre, el dia-

blo, cuyos deseos quieren cumplir. Desde el principio éste ha sido un asesino, y no se mantiene en la verdad, porque no hay verdad en él. Cuando miente, expresa su propia naturaleza, porque es un mentiroso. ¡Es el padre de la mentira! 45Y sin embargo a mí, que les digo la verdad, no me creen. 46¿Quién de ustedes me puede probar que soy culpable de pecado? Si digo la verdad, ¿por qué no me creen? 47El que es de Dios escucha lo que Dios dice. Pero ustedes no escuchan, porque no son de Dios.

Declaración de Jesús acerca de sí mismo

48—¿No tenemos razón al decir que eres un samaritano, y que estás endemoniado? —replicaron los judíos.

49—No estoy poseído por ningún demonio —contestó Jesús—. Tan sólo honro a mi Padre; pero ustedes me deshonran a mí. 50Yo no busco mi propia gloria; pero hay uno que la busca, y él es el juez. 51Ciertamente les aseguro que el que cumple mi palabra, nunca morirá.

52—¡Ahora estamos convencidos de que estás endemoniado! —exclamaron los judíos—. Abraham murió, y también los profetas, pero tú sales diciendo que si alguno guarda tu palabra, nunca morirá. 53¿Acaso eres tú mayor que nuestro padre Abraham? Él murió, y también murieron los profetas. ¿Quién te crees tú?

54—Si yo me glorifico a mí mismo —les respondió Jesús—, mi gloria no significa nada. Pero quien me glorifica es mi Padre, el que ustedes dicen que es su Dios, 55aunque no lo conocen. Yo, en cambio, sí lo conozco. Si dijera que no lo conozco, sería tan mentiroso como ustedes; pero lo conozco y cumplo su palabra. 56Abraham, el padre de ustedes, se regocijó al pensar que vería mi día; y lo vio y se alegró.

57—Ni a los cincuenta años llegas —le dijeron los judíos—, ¿y has visto a Abraham?

58—Ciertamente les aseguro que, antes de que Abraham naciera, ¡yo soy!

59Entonces los judíos tomaron piedras para arrojárselas, pero Jesús se escondió y salió inadvertido del templo.ñ

Jesús sana a un ciego de nacimiento

9 A su paso, Jesús vio a un hombre que era ciego de nacimiento. 2Y sus discípulos le preguntaron:

—Rabí, para que este hombre haya nacido ciego, ¿quién pecó, él o sus padres?

3—Ni él pecó, ni sus padres —respondió Jesús—, sino que esto sucedió para que la obra de Dios se hiciera evidente en su vida. 4Mientras sea de día, tenemos que llevar a cabo la obra del que me envió. Viene la noche cuando nadie puede trabajar. 5Mientras esté yo en el mundo, luz soy del mundo.

6Dicho esto, escupió en el suelo, hizo barro con la saliva y se lo untó en los ojos al ciego, diciéndole:

7—Ve y lávate en el estanque de Siloé (que significa: Enviado).

El ciego fue y se lavó, y al volver ya veía.

8Sus vecinos y los que lo habían visto pedir limosna decían: «¿No es éste el que se sienta a mendigar?» 9Unos aseguraban: «Sí, es él.» Otros decían: «No es él, sino que se le parece.» Pero él insistía: «Soy yo.»

10—¿Cómo entonces se te han abierto los ojos? —le preguntaron.

---

m **8:24** el que afirmo ser. Alt. aquél; también en v. 28. ñ **8:25** En primer . . . explicarles? Alt. Lo que desde el principio he venido diciéndoles. ñ **8:59** templo. Var. templo atravesando por en medio de ellos, y así se fue.

11—Ese hombre que se llama Jesús hizo un poco de barro, me lo untó en los ojos y me dijo: "Ve y lávate en Siloé." Así que fui, me lavé, y entonces pude ver.

12—¿Y dónde está ese hombre? —le preguntaron.

—No lo sé —respondió.

Las autoridades investigan la sanidad del ciego

13Llevaron ante los *fariseos al que había sido ciego. **14**Era *sábado cuando Jesús hizo el barro y le abrió los ojos al ciego. **15**Por eso los fariseos, a su vez, le preguntaron cómo había recibido la vista.

—Me untó barro en los ojos, me lavé, y ahora veo —respondió.

16Algunos de los fariseos comentaban: «Ese hombre no viene de parte de Dios, porque no respeta el sábado.» Otros objetaban: «¿Cómo puede un pecador hacer semejantes señales?» Y había desacuerdo entre ellos.

17Por eso interrogaron de nuevo al ciego:

—¿Y qué opinas tú de él? Fue a ti a quien te abrió los ojos.

—Yo digo que es profeta —contestó.

18Pero los judíos no creían que el hombre hubiera sido ciego y que ahora viera, y hasta llamaron a sus padres **19**y les preguntaron:

—¿Es éste su hijo, el que dicen ustedes que nació ciego? ¿Cómo es que ahora puede ver?

20—Sabemos que éste es nuestro hijo —contestaron los padres—, y sabemos también que nació ciego. **21**Lo que no sabemos es cómo ahora puede ver, ni quién le abrió los ojos. Pregúntenselo a él, que ya es mayor de edad y puede responder por sí mismo.

22Sus padres contestaron así por miedo a los judíos, pues ya éstos habían convenido que se expulsara de la sinagoga a todo el que reconociera que Jesús era el *Cristo. **23**Por eso dijeron sus padres: «Pregúntenselo a él, que es mayor de edad.»

24Por segunda vez llamaron los judíos al que había sido ciego, y le dijeron:

—Júralo por Dios.º A nosotros nos consta que ese hombre es *pecador.

25—Si es pecador, no lo sé —respondió el hombre—. Lo único que sé es que yo era ciego y ahora veo.

26Pero ellos le insistieron:

—¿Qué te hizo? ¿Cómo te abrió los ojos?

27—Ya les dije yo no me hicieron caso. ¿Por qué quieren oírlo de nuevo? ¿Es que también ustedes quieren hacerse sus discípulos?

28Entonces lo insultaron y le dijeron:

—¡Discípulo de ése lo serás tú! ¡Nosotros somos discípulos de Moisés! **29**Y sabemos que a Moisés le habló Dios; pero de éste no sabemos ni de dónde salió.

30—¡Allí está lo sorprendente! —respondió el hombre—: que ustedes no sepan de dónde salió, y que a mí me haya abierto los ojos. **31**Sabemos que Dios no escucha a los pecadores, pero sí a los piadosos y a quienes hacen su voluntad. **32**Jamás se ha sabido que alguien le haya abierto los ojos a uno que nació ciego. **33**Si este hombre no viniera de parte de Dios, no podría hacer nada.

34Ellos replicaron:

—Tú, que naciste sumido en pecado, ¿vas a darnos lecciones?

Y lo expulsaron.

La ceguera espiritual

35Jesús se enteró de que habían expulsado a aquel hombre, y al encontrarlo le preguntó:

—¿Crees en el Hijo del hombre?

36—¿Quién es, Señor? Dímelo, para que crea en él.

37—Pues ya lo has visto —le contestó Jesús—; es el que está hablando contigo.

38—Creo, Señor —declaró el hombre.

Y, postrándose, lo adoró.

39Entonces Jesús dijo:

—Yo he venido a este mundo para juzgarlo, para que los ciegos vean, y los que ven se queden ciegos.

40Algunos fariseos que estaban con él, al oírlo hablar así, le preguntaron:

—¿Qué? ¿Acaso también nosotros somos ciegos?

41Jesús les contestó:

—Si fueran ciegos, no serían culpables de pecado, pero como afirman que ven, su pecado permanece.

Jesús, el buen pastor

10 »Ciertamente les aseguro que el que no entra por la puerta al redil de las ovejas, sino que trepa y se mete por otro lado, es un ladrón y un bandido. **2**El que entra por la puerta es el pastor de las ovejas. **3**El portero le abre la puerta, y las ovejas oyen su voz. Llama por nombre a las ovejas y las saca del redil. **4**Cuando ya ha sacado a todas las que son suyas, va delante de ellas, y las ovejas lo siguen porque reconocen su voz. **5**Pero a un desconocido jamás lo siguen; más bien, huyen de él porque no reconocen voces extrañas.

6Jesús les puso este ejemplo, pero ellos no captaron el sentido de sus palabras. **7**Por eso volvió a decirles: «Ciertamente les aseguro que yo soy la puerta de las ovejas. **8**Todos los que vinieron antes de mí eran unos ladrones y unos bandidos, pero las ovejas no les hicieron caso. **9**Yo soy la puerta; el que entre por esta puerta, que soy yo, será salvo.P Se moverá con entera libertad,q y hallará pastos. **10**El ladrón no viene más que a robar, matar y destruir; yo he venido para que tengan vida, y la tengan en abundancia.

11Yo soy el buen pastor. El buen pastor da su *vida por las ovejas. **12**El asalariado no es el pastor, y a él no le pertenecen las ovejas. Cuando ve que el lobo se acerca, abandona las ovejas y huye; entonces el lobo ataca al rebaño y lo dispersa. **13**Y ese hombre huye porque, siendo asalariado, no le importan las ovejas.

14»Yo soy el buen pastor; conozco a mis ovejas, y ellas me conocen a mí, **15**así como el Padre me conoce a mí y yo lo conozco a él, y doy mi vida por las ovejas. **16**Tengo otras ovejas que no son de este redil, y también a ellas debo traerlas. Así ellas escucharán mi voz, y habrá un solo rebaño y un solo pastor. **17**Por eso me ama el Padre: porque entrego mi vida para volver a recibirla. **18**Nadie me la arrebata, sino que yo la entrego por mi propia voluntad. Tengo autoridad para entregarla, y tengo también autoridad para volver a recibirla. Éste es el mandamiento que recibí de mi Padre.»

19De nuevo las palabras de Jesús fueron motivo de disensión entre los judíos. **20**Muchos de ellos decían: «Está endemoniado y loco de remate. ¿Para qué hacerle caso?» **21**Pero otros opinaban: «Estas palabras no son de un endemoniado. ¿Puede acaso un demonio abrirles los ojos a los ciegos?»

º **9:24** *Júralo por Dios.* Lit. *Da gloria a Dios;* véase Jos 7:19. P **10:9** *será salvo.* Alt. *se mantendrá seguro.* q **10:9** *Se moverá . . . libertad.* Lit. *Entrará y saldrá.*

Jesús y la fiesta de la Dedicación

²²Por esos días se celebraba en Jerusalén la fiesta de la Dedicación.ʳ Era invierno, ²³y Jesús andaba en el *templo, por el pórtico de Salomón. ²⁴Entonces lo rodearon los judíos y le preguntaron:

—¿Hasta cuándo vas a tenernos en suspenso? Si tú eres el *Cristo, dínoslo con franqueza.

²⁵—Ya se lo he dicho a ustedes, y no lo creen. Las obras que hago en nombre de mi Padre son las que me acreditan, ²⁶pero ustedes no creen porque no son de mi rebaño. ²⁷Mis ovejas oyen mi voz; yo las conozco y ellas me siguen. ²⁸Yo les doy vida eterna, y nunca perecerán, ni nadie podrá arrebatármelas de la mano. ²⁹Mi Padre, que me las ha dado, es más grande que todos;ˢ y de la mano del Padre nadie las puede arrebatar. ³⁰El Padre y yo somos uno.

³¹Una vez más los judíos tomaron piedras para arrojárselas, ³²pero Jesús les dijo:

—Yo les he mostrado muchas obras irreprochables que proceden del Padre. ¿Por cuál de ellas me quieren apedrear?

³³—No te apedreamos por ninguna de ellas sino por *blasfemia; porque tú, siendo hombre, te haces pasar por Dios.

³⁴—¿Y acaso —respondió Jesús— no está escrito en su ley: "Yo he dicho que ustedes son dioses"?ᵗ ³⁵Si Dios llamó "dioses" a aquellos para quienes vino la palabra (y la Escritura no puede ser quebrantada), ³⁶¿por qué acusan de blasfemia a quien el Padre apartó para sí y envió al mundo? ¿Tan sólo porque dijo: "Yo soy el Hijo de Dios"? ³⁷Si no hago las obras de mi Padre, no me crean. ³⁸Pero si las hago, aunque no me crean a mí, crean a mis obras, para que sepan y entiendan que el Padre está en mí, y que yo estoy en el Padre.

³⁹Nuevamente intentaron arrestarlo, pero él se les escapó de las manos.

⁴⁰Volvió Jesús al otro lado del Jordán, al lugar donde Juan había estado bautizando antes; y allí se quedó. ⁴¹Mucha gente acudía a él, y decía: «Aunque Juan nunca hizo ninguna señal milagrosa, todo lo que dijo acerca de este hombre era verdad.» ⁴²Y muchos en aquel lugar creyeron en Jesús.

Muerte de Lázaro

11 Había un hombre enfermo llamado Lázaro, que era de Betania, el pueblo de María y Marta, sus hermanas. ²María era la misma que ungió con perfume al Señor, y le secó los pies con sus cabellos. ³Las dos hermanas mandaron a decirle a Jesús: «Señor, tu amigo querido está enfermo.»

⁴Cuando Jesús oyó esto, dijo: «Esta enfermedad no terminará en muerte, sino que es para la gloria de Dios, para que por ella el Hijo de Dios sea glorificado.»

⁵Jesús amaba a Marta, a su hermana y a Lázaro. ⁶A pesar de eso, cuando oyó que Lázaro estaba enfermo, se quedó dos días más donde se encontraba. ⁷Después dijo a sus discípulos:

—Volvamos a Judea.

⁸—Rabí —objetaron ellos—, hace muy poco los judíos intentaron apedrearte, ¿y todavía quieres volver allá?

⁹—¿Acaso el día no tiene doce horas? —respondió Jesús—. El que anda de día no tropieza, porque tiene la luz de este mundo. ¹⁰Pero el que anda de noche sí tropieza, porque no tiene luz.

¹¹Dicho esto, añadió:

—Nuestro amigo Lázaro duerme, pero voy a despertarlo.

¹²—Señor —respondieron sus discípulos—, si duerme, es que va a recuperarse. ¹³Jesús les hablaba de la muerte de Lázaro, pero sus discípulos pensaron que se refería al sueño natural. ¹⁴Por eso les dijo claramente:

—Lázaro ha muerto, ¹⁵y por causa de ustedes me alegro de no haber estado allí, para que crean. Pero vamos a verlo.

¹⁶Entonces Tomás, apodado el Gemelo,ᵘ dijo a los otros discípulos:

—Vayamos también nosotros, para morir con él.

Jesús consuela a las hermanas de Lázaro

¹⁷A su llegada, Jesús se encontró con que Lázaro llevaba ya cuatro días en el sepulcro. ¹⁸Betania estaba cerca de Jerusalén, como a tres kilómetrosᵛ de distancia, ¹⁹y muchos judíos habían ido a casa de Marta y de María, a darles el pésame por la muerte de su hermano. ²⁰Cuando Marta supo que Jesús llegaba, fue a su encuentro; pero María se quedó en la casa.

²¹—Señor —le dijo Marta a Jesús—, si hubieras estado aquí, mi hermano no habría muerto. ²²Pero yo sé que aun ahora Dios te dará todo lo que le pidas.

²³—Tu hermano resucitará —le dijo Jesús.

²⁴—Yo sé que resucitará en la resurrección, en el día final —respondió Marta.

²⁵Entonces Jesús le dijo:

—Yo soy la resurrección y la vida. El que cree en mí vivirá, aunque muera; ²⁶y todo el que vive y cree en mí no morirá jamás. ¿Crees esto?

²⁷—Sí, Señor; yo creo que tú eres el *Cristo, el Hijo de Dios, el que había de venir al mundo.

²⁸Dicho esto, Marta regresó a la casa y, llamando a su hermana María, le dijo en privado:

—El Maestro está aquí y te llama.

²⁹Cuando María oyó esto, se levantó rápidamente y fue a su encuentro. ³⁰Jesús aún no había entrado en el pueblo, sino que todavía estaba en el lugar donde Marta se había encontrado con él. ³¹Los judíos que habían estado con María en la casa, dándole el pésame, al ver que se había levantado y había salido de prisa, la siguieron, pensando que iba al sepulcro a llorar.

³²Cuando María llegó a donde estaba Jesús y lo vio, se arrojó a sus pies y le dijo:

—Señor, si hubieras estado aquí, mi hermano no habría muerto.

³³Al ver llorar a María y a los judíos que la habían acompañado, Jesús se turbó y se conmovió profundamente.

³⁴—¿Dónde lo han puesto? —preguntó.

—Ven a verlo, Señor —le respondieron.

³⁵Jesús lloró.

³⁶—¡Miren cuánto lo quería! —dijeron los judíos.

³⁷Pero algunos de ellos comentaban:

—Éste, que le abrió los ojos al ciego, ¿no podría haber impedido que Lázaro muriera?

Jesús resucita a Lázaro

³⁸Conmovido una vez más, Jesús se acercó al sepulcro. Era una cueva cuya entrada estaba tapada con una piedra.

³⁹—Quiten la piedra —ordenó Jesús.

Marta, la hermana del difunto, objetó:

—Señor, ya debe oler mal, pues lleva cuatro días allí.

ʳ **10:22** *la fiesta de la Dedicación*..Es decir, Hanukkah. ˢ **10:29** *Mi Padre . . . todos.* Var. *Lo que mi Padre me ha dado es más grande que todo.* ᵗ **10:34** Sal 82:6 ᵘ **11:16** *apodado el Gemelo.* Lit. *llamado Dídimos.* ᵛ **11:18** *tres kilómetros.* Lit. *quince* *estadios.*

40—¿No te dije que si crees verás la gloria de Dios? —le contestó Jesús.
41Entonces quitaron la piedra. Jesús, alzando la vista, dijo:

—Padre, te doy gracias porque me has escuchado. 42Ya sabía yo que siempre me escuchas, pero lo dije por la gente que está aquí presente, para que crean que tú me enviaste.

43Dicho esto, gritó con todas sus fuerzas:

—¡Lázaro, sal fuera!

44El muerto salió, con vendas en las manos y en los pies, y el rostro cubierto con un sudario.

—Quítenle las vendas y dejen que se vaya —les dijo Jesús.

La conspiración para matar a Jesús

45Muchos de los judíos que habían ido a ver a María y que habían presenciado lo hecho por Jesús, creyeron en él. 46Pero algunos de ellos fueron a ver a los *fariseos y les contaron lo que Jesús había hecho. 47Entonces los jefes de los sacerdotes y los fariseos convocaron a una reunión del *Consejo.

—¿Qué vamos a hacer? —dijeron—. Este hombre está haciendo muchas señales milagrosas. 48Si lo dejamos seguir así, todos van a creer en él, y vendrán los romanos y acabarán con nuestro lugar sagrado, e incluso con nuestra nación.

49Uno de ellos, llamado Caifás, que ese año era el sumo sacerdote, les dijo:

—¡Ustedes no saben nada en absoluto! 50No entienden que les conviene más que muera un solo hombre por el pueblo, y no que perezca toda la nación.

51Pero esto no lo dijo por su propia cuenta sino que, como era sumo sacerdote ese año, profetizó que Jesús moriría por la nación judía, 52y no sólo por esa nación sino también por los hijos de Dios que estaban dispersos, para congregarlos y unificarlos. 53Así que desde ese día convinieron en quitarle la vida.

54Por eso Jesús ya no andaba en público entre los judíos. Se retiró más bien a una región cercana al desierto, a un pueblo llamado Efraín, donde se quedó con sus discípulos.

55Faltaba poco para la Pascua judía, así que muchos subieron del campo a Jerusalén para su *purificación ceremonial antes de la Pascua. 56Andaban buscando a Jesús, y mientras estaban en el *templo comentaban entre sí: «¿Qué les parece? ¿Acaso no vendrá a la fiesta?» 57Por su parte, los jefes de los sacerdotes y los fariseos habían dado la orden de que si alguien llegaba a saber dónde estaba Jesús, debía denunciarlo para que lo arrestaran.

María unge a Jesús en Betania

12 Seis días antes de la Pascua llegó Jesús a Betania, donde vivía Lázaro, a quien Jesús había *resucitado. 2Allí se dio una cena en honor de Jesús. Marta servía, y Lázaro era uno de los que estaban a la mesa con él. 3María tomó entonces como medio litro de nardo puro, que era un perfume muy caro, y lo derramó sobre los pies de Jesús, secándoselos luego con su cabellos. Y la casa se llenó de la fragancia del perfume.

4Judas Iscariote, que era uno de sus discípulos y que más tarde lo traicionaría, objetó:

5—¿Por qué no se vendió este perfume, que vale muchísimo dinero,w para dárselo a los pobres?

6Dijo esto, no porque se interesara por los pobres sino porque era un ladrón y, como tenía a su cargo la bolsa del dinero, acostumbraba robarse lo que echaban en ella.

7—Déjala en paz —respondió Jesús—. Ella ha estado guardando este perfume para el día de mi sepultura.x 8A los pobres siempre los tendrán con ustedes, pero a mí no siempre me tendrán.

9Mientras tanto, muchos de los judíos se enteraron de que Jesús estaba allí, y fueron a ver no sólo a Jesús sino también a Lázaro, a quien Jesús había resucitado. 10Entonces los jefes de los sacerdotes resolvieron matar también a Lázaro, 11pues por su causa muchos se apartaban de los judíos y creían en Jesús.

La entrada triunfal
12:12-15 — Mt 21:4-9; Mr 11:7-10; Lc 19:35-38

12Al día siguiente muchos de los que habían ido a la fiesta se enteraron de que Jesús se dirigía a Jerusalén; 13tomaron ramas de palma y salieron a recibirlo, gritando a voz en cuello:

—¡Hosanna!

—¡Bendito el que viene en el nombre del Señor!y

—¡Bendito el Rey de Israel!

14Jesús encontró un burrito y se montó en él, como dice la Escritura:

15«No temas, oh hija de Sión;
    mira, que aquí viene tu rey,
    montado sobre un burrito.»z

16Al principio, sus discípulos no entendieron lo que sucedía. Sólo después de que Jesús fue glorificado se dieron cuenta de que se había cumplido en él lo que de él ya estaba escrito.

17La gente que había estado con Jesús cuando él llamó a Lázaro del sepulcro y lo resucitó de entre los muertos, seguía difundiendo la noticia. 18Muchos que se habían enterado de la señal realizada por Jesús salían a su encuentro. 19Por eso los *fariseos comentaban entre sí: «Como pueden ver, así no vamos a lograr nada. ¡Miren cómo lo sigue todo el mundo!»

Jesús predice su muerte

20Entre los que habían subido a adorar en la fiesta había algunos *griegos. 21Éstos se acercaron a Felipe, que era de Betsaida de Galilea, y le pidieron:

—Señor, queremos ver a Jesús.

22Felipe fue a decírselo a Andrés, y ambos fueron a decírselo a Jesús.

23—Ha llegado la hora de que el Hijo del hombre sea glorificado —les contestó Jesús—. 24Ciertamente les aseguro que si el grano de trigo no cae en tierra y muere, se queda solo. Pero si muere, produce mucho fruto. 25El que se apega a su *vida la pierde; en cambio, el que aborrece su vida en este mundo, la conserva para la vida eterna. 26Quien quiera servirme, debe seguirme; y donde yo esté, allí también estará mi siervo. A quien me sirva, mi Padre lo honrará.

27»Ahora todo mi ser está angustiado, ¿y acaso voy a decir: "Padre, sálvame de esta hora difícil"? ¡Si precisamente para afrontarla he venido! 28¡Padre, glorifica tu nombre!

Se oyó entonces, desde el cielo, una voz que decía: «Ya lo he glorificado, y volveré a glorificarlo.» 29La multitud que estaba allí, y que oyó la voz, decía que había sido un trueno; otros decían que un ángel le había hablado.

---

w **12:5** perfume . . . dinero. Lit. perfume por trescientos *denarios. x **12:7** Jesús—. Ella … sepultura. Var. Jesús— para que guarde [es decir, se acuerde de] esto el día de mi sepultura. y **12:13** Sal 118:25,26 z **12:15** Zac 9:9

674

³⁰—Esa voz no vino por mí sino por ustedes —dijo Jesús—. ³¹El juicio de este mundo ha llegado ya, y el príncipe de este mundo va a ser expulsado. ³²Pero yo, cuando sea levantado de la tierra, atraeré a todos a mí mismo.

³³Con esto daba Jesús a entender de qué manera iba a morir.

³⁴—De la ley hemos sabido —le respondió la gente— que el *Cristo permanecerá para siempre; ¿cómo, pues, dices que el Hijo del hombre tiene que ser levantado? ¿Quién es ese Hijo del hombre?

³⁵—Ustedes van a tener la luz sólo un poco más de tiempo —les dijo Jesús—. Caminen mientras tienen la luz, antes de que los envuelvan las tinieblas. El que camina en las tinieblas no sabe a dónde va. ³⁶Mientras tienen la luz, crean en ella, para que sean hijos de la luz.

Cuando terminó de hablar, Jesús se fue y se escondió de ellos.

Los judíos siguen en su incredulidad

³⁷A pesar de haber hecho Jesús todas estas señales en presencia de ellos, todavía no creían en él. ³⁸Así se cumplió lo dicho por el profeta Isaías:

«Señor, ¿quién ha creído a nuestro mensaje,
y a quién se le ha revelado el poder del
Señor?»ᵃ

³⁹Por eso no podían creer, pues también había dicho Isaías:

⁴⁰«Les ha cegado los ojos
y endurecido el corazón,
para que no vean con los ojos,
ni entiendan con el corazón
ni se conviertan; y yo los sane.»ᵇ

⁴¹Esto lo dijo Isaías porque vio la gloria de Jesús y habló de él.

⁴²Sin embargo, muchos de ellos, incluso de entre los jefes, creyeron en él, pero no lo confesaban porque temían que los *fariseos los expulsaran de la sinagoga. ⁴³Preferían recibir honores de los hombres más que de parte de Dios.

⁴⁴«El que cree en mí —clamó Jesús con voz fuerte—, cree no sólo en mí sino en el que me envió. ⁴⁵Y el que me ve a mí, ve al que me envió. ⁴⁶Yo soy la luz que ha venido al mundo, para que todo el que crea en mí no viva en tinieblas.

⁴⁷»Si alguno escucha mis palabras, pero no las obedece, no seré yo quien lo juzgue; pues no vine a juzgar al mundo sino a salvarlo. ⁴⁸El que me rechaza y no acepta mis palabras tiene quien lo juzgue. La palabra que yo he proclamado lo condenará en el día final. ⁴⁹Yo no he hablado por mi propia cuenta; el Padre que me envió me ordenó qué decir y cómo decirlo. ⁵⁰Y sé muy bien que su mandato es vida eterna. Así que todo lo que digo es lo que el Padre me ha ordenado decir.»

Jesús les lava los pies a sus discípulos

13 Se acercaba la fiesta de la Pascua. Jesús sabía que le había llegado la hora de abandonar este mundo para volver al Padre. Y habiendo amado a los suyos que estaban en el mundo, los amó hasta el fin.ᶜ

²Llegó la hora de la cena. El diablo ya había incitado a Judas Iscariote, hijo de Simón, para que traicionara a Jesús. ³Sabía Jesús que el Padre había puesto todas las cosas bajo su dominio, y que había salido de Dios y a él volvía; ⁴así que se levantó de la mesa, se quitó el manto y se ató una toalla a la cintura. ⁵Luego echó agua en un recipiente y comenzó a lavarles los pies a sus discípulos y a secárselos con la toalla que llevaba a la cintura.

⁶Cuando llegó a Simón Pedro, éste le dijo:

—¿Y tú, Señor, me vas a lavar los pies a mí?

⁷—Ahora no entiendes lo que estoy haciendo —le respondió Jesús—, pero lo entenderás más tarde.

⁸—¡No! —protestó Pedro—. ¡Jamás me lavarás los pies!

—Si no te los lavo,ᵈ no tendrás parte conmigo.

⁹—Entonces, Señor, ¡no sólo los pies sino también las manos y la cabeza!

¹⁰—El que ya se ha bañado no necesita lavarse más que los pies —le contestó Jesús—; pues ya todo su cuerpo está limpio. Y ustedes ya están limpios, aunque no todos.

¹¹Jesús sabía quién lo iba a traicionar, y por eso dijo que no todos estaban limpios.

¹²Cuando terminó de lavarles los pies, se puso el manto y volvió a su lugar. Entonces les dijo:

—¿Entienden lo que he hecho con ustedes? ¹³Ustedes me llaman Maestro y Señor, y dicen bien, porque lo soy. ¹⁴Pues si yo, el Señor y el Maestro, les he lavado los pies, también ustedes deben lavarse los pies los unos a los otros. ¹⁵Les he puesto el ejemplo, para que hagan lo mismo que yo he hecho con ustedes. ¹⁶Ciertamente les aseguro que ningún *siervo es más que su amo, y ningún mensajero es más que el que lo envió. ¹⁷¿Entienden esto? *Dichosos serán si lo ponen en práctica.

Jesús predice la traición de Judas

¹⁸»No me refiero a todos ustedes; yo sé a quiénes he escogido. Pero esto es para que se cumpla la Escritura: "El que comparte el pan conmigo me ha puesto la zancadilla."ᵉ

¹⁹»Les digo esto ahora, antes de que suceda, para que cuando suceda crean que yo soy. ²⁰Ciertamente les aseguro que el que recibe al que yo envío me recibe a mí, y el que me recibe a mí recibe al que me envió.

²¹Dicho esto, Jesús se angustió profundamente y declaró:

—Ciertamente les aseguro que uno de ustedes me va a traicionar.

²²Los discípulos se miraban unos a otros sin saber a cuál de ellos se refería. ²³Uno de ellos, el discípulo a quien Jesús amaba, estaba a su lado. ²⁴Simón Pedro le hizo señas a ese discípulo y le dijo:

—Pregúntale a quién se refiere.

²⁵—Señor, ¿quién es? —preguntó él, reclinándose sobre Jesús.

²⁶—Aquel a quien yo le dé este pedazo de pan que voy a mojar en el plato —le contestó Jesús.

Acto seguido, mojó el pedazo de pan y se lo dio a Judas Iscariote, hijo de Simón. ²⁷Tan pronto como Judas tomó el pan, Satanás entró en él.

—Lo que vas a hacer, hazlo pronto —le dijo Jesús.

²⁸Ninguno de los que estaban a la mesa entendió por qué le dijo eso Jesús. ²⁹Como Judas era el encargado del dinero, algunos pensaron que Jesús le estaba diciendo que comprara lo necesario para la fiesta, o que diera algo a los pobres. ³⁰En cuanto Judas tomó el pan, salió de allí. Ya era de noche.

Jesús predice la negación de Pedro

³¹Cuando Judas hubo salido, Jesús dijo:

ᵃ **12:38** Is 53:1   ᵇ **12:40** Is 6:10   ᶜ **13:1** *hasta el fin.* Alt. *hasta lo sumo.*   ᵈ **13:8** *te los lavo.* Lit. *te lavo.*   ᵉ **13:18** Sal 41:9

—Ahora es glorificado el Hijo del hombre, y Dios es glorificado en él. 32Si Dios es glorificado en él,f Dios glorificará al Hijo en sí mismo, y lo hará muy pronto.

33»Mis queridos hijos, poco tiempo me queda para estar con ustedes. Me buscarán, y lo que antes les dije a los judíos, ahora se lo digo a ustedes: Adonde yo voy, ustedes no pueden ir.

34»Este mandamiento nuevo les doy: que se amen los unos a los otros. Así como yo los he amado, también ustedes deben amarse los unos a los otros. 35De este modo todos sabrán que son mis discípulos, si se aman los unos a los otros.

36—¿Y adónde vas, Señor? —preguntó Simón Pedro.

—Adonde yo voy, no puedes seguirme ahora, pero me seguirás más tarde.

37—Señor —insistió Pedro—, ¿por qué no puedo seguirte ahora? Por ti daré hasta la *vida.

38—¿Tú darás la vida por mí? ¡De veras te aseguro que antes de que cante el gallo, me negarás tres veces!

Jesús consuela a sus discípulos

14 »No se angustien. Confíen en Dios, y confíen también en mí.g 2En el hogar de mi Padre hay muchas viviendas. Voy a prepararles un lugar. 3Y si me voy y se lo preparo, vendré para llevármelos conmigo. Así ustedes estarán donde yo esté. 4Ustedes ya conocen el camino para ir a donde yo voy.

Jesús, el camino al Padre

5Dijo entonces Tomás:

—Señor, no sabemos a dónde vas, así que ¿cómo podemos conocer el camino?

6—Yo soy el camino, la verdad y la vida —le contestó Jesús—. Nadie llega al Padre sino por mí. 7Si ustedes realmente me conocieran, conoceríanh también a mi Padre. Y ya desde este momento lo conocen y lo han visto.

8—Señor —dijo Felipe—, muéstranos al Padre y con eso nos basta.

9—¡Pero, Felipe! ¿Tanto tiempo llevo ya entre ustedes, y todavía no me conoces? El que me ha visto a mí, ha visto al Padre. ¿Cómo puedes decirme: "Muéstranos al Padre"? 10¿Acaso no crees que yo estoy en el Padre, y que el Padre está en mí? Las palabras que yo les comunico, no las hablo como cosa mía, sino que es el Padre, que está en mí, el que realiza sus obras. 11Créanme cuando les digo que yo estoy en el Padre y que el Padre está en mí; o al menos créanme por las obras mismas. 12Ciertamente les aseguro que el que cree en mí las obras que yo hago también él las hará, y aun las hará mayores, porque yo vuelvo al Padre. 13Cualquier cosa que ustedes pidan en mi nombre, yo la haré; así será glorificado el Padre en el Hijo. 14Lo que pidan en mi nombre, yo lo haré.

Jesús promete el Espíritu Santo

15»Si ustedes me aman, obedecerán mis mandamientos. 16Y yo le pediré al Padre, y él les dará otro *Consolador para que los acompañe siempre: 17el Espíritu de verdad, a quien el mundo no puede aceptar porque no lo ve ni lo conoce. Pero ustedes sí lo conocen, porque vive con ustedes y estarái en ustedes. 18No los voy a dejar huérfanos; volveré a ustedes. 19Dentro de poco el mundo ya no me verá más, pero ustedes sí me verán. Y porque yo vivo, también ustedes vivirán. 20En aquel día ustedes se darán cuenta de que yo estoy en mi Padre, y ustedes en mí, y yo en ustedes. 21¿Quién es el que me ama? El que hace suyos mis mandamientos y los obedece. Y al que me ama, mi Padre lo amará, y yo también lo amaré y me manifestaré a él.

22Judas (no el Iscariote) le dijo:

—¿Por qué, Señor, estás dispuesto a manifestarte a nosotros, y no al mundo?

23Le contestó Jesús:

—El que me ama, obedecerá mi palabra, y mi Padre lo amará, y haremos nuestra vivienda en él. 24El que no me ama, no obedece mis palabras. Pero estas palabras que ustedes oyen no son mías sino del Padre, que me envió.

25»Todo esto lo digo ahora que estoy con ustedes. 26Pero el Consolador, el Espíritu Santo, a quien el Padre enviará en mi nombre, les enseñará todas las cosas y les hará recordar todo lo que les he dicho. 27La paz les dejo; mi paz les doy. Yo no se la doy a ustedes como la da el mundo. No se angustien ni se acobarden.

28»Ya me han oído decirles: "Me voy, pero vuelvo a ustedes." Si me amaran, se alegrarían de que voy al Padre, porque el Padre es más grande que yo. 29Y les he dicho esto ahora, antes de que suceda, para que cuando suceda, crean. 30Ya no hablaré más con ustedes, porque viene el príncipe de este mundo. Él no tiene ningún dominio sobre mí, 31pero el mundo tiene que saber que amo al Padre, y hago exactamente lo que él me ha ordenado que haga.

»¡Levántense, vámonos de aquí!

Jesús, la vid verdadera

15 »Yo soy la vid verdadera, y mi Padre es el labrador. 2Toda rama que en mí no da fruto, la corta; pero toda rama que da fruto la podai para que dé más fruto todavía. 3Ustedes ya están limpios por la palabra que les he comunicado. 4Permanezcan en mí, y yo permaneceré en ustedes. Así como ninguna rama puede dar fruto por sí misma, sino que tiene que permanecer en la vid, así tampoco ustedes pueden dar fruto si no permanecen en mí.

5»Yo soy la vid y ustedes son las ramas. El que permanece en mí, como yo en él, dará mucho fruto; separados de mí no pueden ustedes hacer nada. 6El que no permanece en mí es desechado y se seca, como las ramas que se recogen, se arrojan al fuego y se queman. 7Si permanecen en mí y mis palabras permanecen en ustedes, pidan lo que quieran, y se les concederá. 8Mi Padre es glorificado cuando ustedes dan mucho fruto y muestran así que son mis discípulos.

9»Así como el Padre me ha amado a mí, también yo los he amado a ustedes. Permanezcan en mi amor. 10Si obedecen mis mandamientos, permanecerán en mi amor, así como yo he obedecido los mandamientos de mi Padre y permanezco en su amor. 11Les he dicho esto para que tengan mi alegría y así su alegría sea completa. 12Y éste es mi mandamiento: que se amen los unos a los otros, como yo los he amado. 13Nadie tiene amor más grande que el dar la *vida por sus amigos. 14Ustedes son mis amigos si hacen lo que yo les mando. 15Ya no los llamo *siervos, porque el siervo no está al tanto de lo que hace su amo; los he llamado amigos, porque todo lo que a mi Padre le oí decir se lo he dado a conocer a ustedes.

---

f **13:32** Var. no incluye: *Si Dios es glorificado en él.*   g **14:1** *Confíen . . . en mí.* Alt. *Ustedes confían en Dios; confíen también en mí.*   h **14:7** *me conocieran, conocerían.* Var. *me han conocido, conocerán.*   i **14:17** estará. Var. *está.*   j **15:2** *poda.* Alt. *limpia.*

16No me escogieron ustedes a mí, sino que yo los escogí a ustedes y los comisioné para que vayan y den fruto, un fruto que perdure. Así el Padre les dará todo lo que le pidan en mi nombre. 17Éste es mi mandamiento: que se amen los unos a los otros.

Jesús y sus discípulos aborrecidos por el mundo

18»Si el mundo los aborrece, tengan presente que antes que a ustedes, me aborreció a mí. 19Si fueran del mundo, el mundo los querría como a los suyos. Pero ustedes no son del mundo, sino que yo los he escogido de entre el mundo. Por eso el mundo los aborrece. 20Recuerden lo que les dije: "Ningún *siervo es más que su amo."k Si a mí me han perseguido, también a ustedes los perseguirán. Si han obedecido mis enseñanzas, también obedecerán las de ustedes. 21Los tratarán así por causa de mi nombre, porque no conocen al que me envió. 22Si yo no hubiera venido ni les hubiera hablado, no serían culpables de pecado. Pero ahora no tienen excusa por su pecado. 23El que me aborrece a mí, también aborrece a mi Padre. 24Si yo no hubiera hecho entre ellos las obras que ningún otro antes ha realizado, no serían culpables de pecado. Pero ahora las han visto, y sin embargo a mí y a mi Padre nos han aborrecido. 25Pero esto sucede para que se cumpla lo que está escrito en la ley de ellos: "Me odiaron sin motivo."l

26»Cuando venga el *Consolador, que yo les enviaré de parte del Padre, el Espíritu de verdad que procede del Padre, él testificará acerca de mí. 27Y también ustedes darán testimonio porque han estado conmigo desde el principio.

16 »Todo esto les he dicho para que no flaquee su fe. 2Los expulsarán de las sinagogas; y hasta viene el día en que cualquiera que los mate pensará que le está prestando un servicio a Dios. 3Actuarán de este modo porque no nos han conocido ni al Padre ni a mí. 4Y les digo esto para que cuando llegue ese día se acuerden de que ya se lo había advertido. Sin embargo, no les dije esto al principio porque yo estaba con ustedes.

La obra del Espíritu Santo

5»Ahora vuelvo al que me envió, pero ninguno de ustedes me pregunta: "¿Adónde vas?" 6Al contrario, como les he dicho estas cosas, se han entristecido mucho. 7Pero les digo la verdad: Les conviene que me vaya porque, si no lo hago, el *Consolador no vendrá a ustedes; en cambio, si me voy, se lo enviaré a ustedes. 8Y cuando él venga, convencerá al mundo de su errorm en cuanto al pecado, a la justicia y al juicio; 9en cuanto al pecado, porque no creen en mí; 10en cuanto a la justicia, porque voy al Padre y ustedes ya no podrán verme; 11y en cuanto al juicio, porque el príncipe de este mundo ya ha sido juzgado.

12»Muchas cosas me quedan aún por decirles, que por ahora no podrían soportar. 13Pero cuando venga el Espíritu de la verdad, él los guiará a toda la verdad, porque no hablará por su propia cuenta sino que dirá sólo lo que oiga y les anunciará las cosas por venir. 14Él me glorificará porque tomará de lo mío y se lo dará a conocer a ustedes. 15Todo cuanto tiene el Padre es mío. Por eso les dije que el Espíritu tomará de lo mío y se lo dará a conocer a ustedes.

16»Dentro de poco ya no me verán; pero un poco después volverán a verme.

La despedida de Jesús

17Algunos de sus discípulos comentaban entre sí: «¿Qué quiere decir con eso de que "dentro de poco ya no me verán", y "un poco después volverán a verme", y "porque voy al Padre"?» 18E insistían: «¿Qué quiere decir con eso de "dentro de poco"? No sabemos de qué habla.»

19Jesús se dio cuenta de que querían hacerle preguntas acerca de esto, así que les dijo:

—¿Se están preguntando qué quise decir cuando dije: "Dentro de poco ya no me verán", y "un poco después volverán a verme"? 20Ciertamente les aseguro que ustedes llorarán y se pondrán tristes, mientras que el mundo se alegrará. Se pondrán tristes, pero su tristeza se convertirá en alegría. 21La mujer que está por dar a luz siente dolores porque ha llegado su momento, pero en cuanto nace la criatura se olvida de su angustia por la alegría de haber traído al mundo un nuevo ser. 22Lo mismo les pasa a ustedes: Ahora están tristes, pero cuando vuelva a verlos se alegrarán, y nadie les va a quitar esa alegría. 23En aquel día ya no me preguntarán nada. Ciertamente les aseguro que mi Padre les dará todo lo que le pidan en mi nombre. 24Hasta ahora no han pedido nada en mi nombre. Pidan y recibirán, para que su alegría sea completa.

25»Les he dicho todo esto por medio de comparaciones, pero viene la hora en que ya no les hablaré así, sino que les hablaré claramente acerca de mi Padre. 26En aquel día pedirán en mi nombre. Y no digo que voy a rogar por ustedes al Padre, 27ya que el Padre mismo los ama porque me han amado y han creído que yo he venido de parte de Dios. 28Salí del Padre y vine al mundo; ahora dejo de nuevo el mundo y vuelvo al Padre.

29—Ahora sí estás hablando directamente, sin vueltas ni rodeos —le dijeron sus discípulos—. 30Ya podemos ver que sabes todas las cosas, y que ni siquiera necesitas que nadie te haga preguntas. Por esto creemos que saliste de Dios.

31—¿Hasta ahora me creen?n —contestó Jesús—. 32Miren que la hora viene, y ya está aquí, en que ustedes serán dispersados, y cada uno se irá a su propia casa y a mí me dejarán solo. Sin embargo, solo no estoy, porque el Padre está conmigo. 33Yo les he dicho estas cosas para que en mí hallen paz. En este mundo afrontarán aflicciones, pero ¡anímense! Yo he vencido al mundo.

Jesús ora por sí mismo

17 Después de que Jesús dijo esto, dirigió la mirada al cielo y oró así:

«Padre, ha llegado la hora. Glorifica a tu Hijo, para que tu Hijo te glorifique a ti, 2ya que le has conferido autoridad sobre todo *mortal para que él le conceda vida eterna a todos los que le has dado. 3Y ésta es la vida eterna: que te conozcan a ti, el único Dios verdadero, y a *Jesucristo, a quien tú has enviado. 4Yo te he glorificado en la tierra, y he llevado a cabo la obra que me encomendaste. 5Y ahora, Padre, glorifícame en tu presencia con la gloria que tuve contigo antes de que el mundo existiera.

Jesús ora por sus discípulos

6»A los que me diste del mundo les has revelado quién eres.ñ Eran tuyos; tú me los diste y ellos han obedecido tu palabra. 7Ahora saben

---

k 15:20 Jn 13:16 l 15:25 Sal 35:19; 69:4 m 16:8 convencerá . . . error. Alt. pondrá en evidencia la culpa del mundo.
n 16:31 ¿Hasta . . . creen? Alt. ¿Ahora creen? ñ 17:6 quién eres. Lit. tu nombre; también en v. 26.

que todo lo que me has dado viene de ti, **8**porque les he entregado las palabras que me diste, y ellos las aceptaron; saben con certeza que salí de ti, y han creído que tú me enviaste. **9**Ruego por ellos. No ruego por el mundo, sino por los que me has dado, porque son tuyos. **10**Todo lo que yo tengo es tuyo, y todo lo que tú tienes es mío; y por medio de ellos he sido glorificado. **11**Ya no voy a estar por más tiempo en el mundo, pero ellos están todavía en el mundo, y yo vuelvo a ti.

»Padre santo, protégelos con el poder de tu nombre, el nombre que me diste, para que sean uno, lo mismo que nosotros. **12**Mientras estaba con ellos, los protegía y los preservaba mediante el nombre que me diste, y ninguno se perdió sino aquel que nació para perderse, a fin de que se cumpliera la Escritura.

13»Ahora vuelvo a ti, pero digo estas cosas mientras todavía estoy en el mundo, para que tengan mi alegría en plenitud. **14**Yo les he entregado tu palabra, y el mundo los ha odiado porque no son del mundo, como tampoco yo soy del mundo. **15**No te pido que los quites del mundo, sino que los protejas del maligno. **16**Ellos no son del mundo, como tampoco lo soy yo. **17***Santifícalos en la verdad; tu palabra es la verdad. **18**Como tú me enviaste al mundo, así los envío también al mundo. **19**Y por ellos me santifico a mí mismo, para que también ellos sean santificados en la verdad.

Jesús ora por todos los creyentes

20»No ruego sólo por éstos. Ruego también por los que han de creer en mí por el mensaje de ellos, **21**para que todos sean uno. Padre, así como tú estás en mí y yo en ti, permite que ellos también estén en nosotros, para que el mundo crea que tú me has enviado. **22**Yo les he dado la gloria que me diste, para que sean uno, así como nosotros somos uno: **23**yo en ellos y tú en mí. Permite que alcancen la *perfección en la unidad, y así el mundo reconozca que tú me enviaste y que los has amado a ellos tal como me has amado a mí.

24»Padre, quiero que los que me has dado estén conmigo donde yo estoy. Que vean mi gloria, la gloria que me has dado porque me amaste desde antes de la creación del mundo. **25**»Padre justo, aunque el mundo no te conoce, yo sí te conozco, y éstos reconocen que tú me enviaste. **26**Yo les he dado a conocer quién eres, y seguiré haciéndolo, para que el amor con que me has amado esté en ellos, y yo mismo esté en ellos.»

Arresto de Jesús
18:3-11 — Mt 26:47-56; Mr 14:43-50;
Lc 22:47-53

18 Cuando Jesús terminó de orar, salió con sus discípulos y cruzó el arroyo de Cedrón. Al otro lado había un huerto en el que entró con sus discípulos.

2También Judas, el que lo traicionaba, conocía aquel lugar, porque muchas veces Jesús se había reunido allí con sus discípulos. **3**Así que Judas llegó al huerto, a la cabeza de un destacamento*o* de soldados y guardias de los jefes de los sacerdotes y de los *fariseos. Llevaban antorchas, lámparas y armas.

4Jesús, que sabía todo lo que le iba a suceder, les salió al encuentro.

—¿A quién buscan? —les preguntó.

5—A Jesús de Nazaret —contestaron.

—Yo soy.

Judas, el traidor, estaba con ellos. **6**Cuando Jesús les dijo: «Yo soy», dieron un paso atrás y se desplomaron.

7—¿A quién buscan? —volvió a preguntarles Jesús.

—A Jesús de Nazaret —repitieron.

8—Ya les dije que yo soy. Si es a mí a quien buscan, dejen que éstos se vayan.

9Esto sucedió para que se cumpliera lo que había dicho: «De los que me diste ninguno se perdió.»*p*

10Simón Pedro, que tenía una espada, la desenfundó e hirió al siervo del sumo sacerdote, cortándole la oreja derecha. (El siervo se llamaba Malco.)

11—¡Vuelve esa espada a su funda! —le ordenó Jesús a Pedro—. ¿Acaso no he de beber el trago amargo que el Padre me da a beber?

Jesús ante Anás
18:12-13 — Mt 26:57

12Entonces los soldados, con su comandante, y los guardias de los judíos, arrestaron a Jesús. Lo ataron **13**y lo llevaron primeramente a Anás, que era suegro de Caifás, el sumo sacerdote de aquel año. **14**Caifás era el que había aconsejado a los judíos que era preferible que muriera un solo hombre por el pueblo.

Pedro niega a Jesús
18:16-18 — Mt 26:69-70; Mr 14:66-68;
Lc 22:55-57

15Simón Pedro y otro discípulo seguían a Jesús. Y como el otro discípulo era conocido del sumo sacerdote, entró en el patio del sumo sacerdote con Jesús; **16**Pedro, en cambio, tuvo que quedarse afuera, junto a la puerta. El discípulo conocido del sumo sacerdote volvió entonces a salir, habló con la portera de turno y consiguió que Pedro entrara.

17—¿No eres tú también uno de los discípulos de ese hombre? —le preguntó la portera.

—No lo soy —respondió Pedro.

18Los criados y los guardias estaban de pie alrededor de una fogata que habían hecho para calentarse, pues hacía frío. Pedro también estaba de pie con ellos, calentándose.

Jesús ante el sumo sacerdote
18:19-24 — Mt 26:59-68; Mr 14:55-65;
Lc 22:63-71

19Mientras tanto, el sumo sacerdote interrogaba a Jesús acerca de sus discípulos y de sus enseñanzas.

20—Yo he hablado abiertamente al mundo —respondió Jesús—. Siempre he enseñado en las sinagogas o en el *templo, donde se congregan todos los judíos. En secreto no he dicho nada. **21**¿Por qué me interrogas a mí? ¡Interroga a los que me han oído hablar! Ellos deben saber lo que dije.

22Apenas dijo esto, uno de los guardias que estaba allí cerca le dio una bofetada y le dijo:

—¿Así contestas al sumo sacerdote?

23—Si he dicho algo malo —replicó Jesús—, demuéstramelo. Pero si lo que dije es correcto, ¿por qué me pegas?

---

24 Entonces Anás lo envió,[q] todavía atado, a Caifás, el sumo sacerdote.

Pedro niega de nuevo a Jesús

18:25-27 — Mt 26:71-75; Mr 14:69-72; Lc 22:58-62

25 Mientras tanto, Simón Pedro seguía de pie, calentándose.

—¿No eres tú también uno de sus discípulos? —le preguntaron.

—No lo soy —dijo Pedro, negándolo.

26 —¿Acaso no te vi en el huerto con él? —insistió uno de los siervos del sumo sacerdote, pariente de aquel a quien Pedro le había cortado la oreja.

27 Pedro volvió a negarlo, y en ese instante cantó el gallo.

Jesús ante Pilato

18:29-40 — Mt 27:11-18,20-23; Mr 15:2-15; Lc 23:2-3,18-25

28 Luego los judíos llevaron a Jesús de la casa de Caifás al palacio del gobernador romano.[r] Como ya amanecía, los judíos no entraron en el palacio, pues de hacerlo se *contaminarían ritualmente y no podrían comer la Pascua. 29 Así que Pilato salió a interrogarlos:

—¿De qué delito acusan a este hombre?

30 —Si no fuera un malhechor —respondieron—, no te lo habríamos entregado.

31 —Pues llévenselo ustedes y júzguenlo según su propia ley —les dijo Pilato.

—Nosotros no tenemos ninguna autoridad para ejecutar a nadie —objetaron los judíos.

32 Esto sucedió para que se cumpliera lo que Jesús había dicho, al indicar la clase de muerte que iba a sufrir.

33 Pilato volvió a entrar en el palacio y llamó a Jesús.

—¿Eres tú el rey de los judíos? —le preguntó.

34 —¿Eso lo dices tú —le respondió Jesús—, o es que otros te han hablado de mí?

35 —¿Acaso soy judío? —replicó Pilato—. Han sido tu propio pueblo y los jefes de los sacerdotes los que te entregaron a mí. ¿Qué has hecho?

36 —Mi reino no es de este mundo —contestó Jesús—. Si lo fuera, mis propios guardias pelearían para impedir que los judíos me arrestaran. Pero mi reino no es de este mundo.

37 —¡Así que eres rey! —le dijo Pilato.

—Eres tú quien dice que soy rey. Yo para esto nací, y para esto vine al mundo: para dar testimonio de la verdad. Todo el que está de parte de la verdad escucha mi voz.

38 —¿Y qué es la verdad? —preguntó Pilato.

Dicho esto, salió otra vez a ver a los judíos.

—Yo no encuentro que éste sea culpable de nada —declaró—. 39 Pero como ustedes tienen la costumbre de que les suelte a un preso durante la Pascua, ¿quieren que les suelte al "rey de los judíos"?

40 —¡No, no sueltes a ése; suelta a Barrabás! —volvieron a gritar desaforadamente.

Y Barrabás era un bandido.[s]

La sentencia

19:1-16 — Mt 27:27-31; Mr 15:16-20

19 Pilato tomó entonces a Jesús y mandó que lo azotaran. 2 Los soldados, que habían tejido una corona de espinas, se la pusieron a Jesús en la cabeza y lo vistieron con un manto de color púrpura.

3 —¡Viva el rey de los judíos! —le gritaban, mientras se le acercaban para abofetearlo.

4 Pilato volvió a salir.

—Aquí lo tienen —dijo a los judíos—. Lo he sacado para que sepan que no lo encuentro culpable de nada.

5 Cuando salió Jesús, llevaba puestos la corona de espinas y el manto de color púrpura.

—¡Aquí tienen al hombre! —les dijo Pilato.

6 Tan pronto como lo vieron, los jefes de los sacerdotes y los guardias gritaron a voz en cuello:

—¡Crucifícalo! ¡Crucifícalo!

—Pues llévenselo y crucifíquenlo ustedes —replicó Pilato—. Por mi parte, no lo encuentro culpable de nada.

7 —Nosotros tenemos una ley, y según esa ley debe morir, porque se ha hecho pasar por Hijo de Dios —insistieron los judíos.

8 Al oír esto, Pilato se atemorizó aun más, 9 así que entró de nuevo en el palacio y le preguntó a Jesús:

—¿De dónde eres tú?

Pero Jesús no le contestó nada.

10 —¿Te niegas a hablarme? —le dijo Pilato—. ¿No te das cuenta de que tengo poder para ponerte en libertad o para mandar que te crucifiquen?

11 —No tendrías ningún poder sobre mí si no se te hubiera dado de arriba —le contestó Jesús—. Por eso el que me puso en tus manos es culpable de un pecado más grande.

12 Desde entonces Pilato procuraba poner en libertad a Jesús, pero los judíos gritaban desaforadamente:

—Si dejas en libertad a este hombre, no eres amigo del *emperador. Cualquiera que pretende ser rey se hace su enemigo.

13 Al oír esto, Pilato llevó a Jesús hacia fuera y se sentó en el tribunal, en un lugar al que llamaban el Empedrado (que en arameo se dice Gabatá). 14 Era el día de la preparación para la Pascua, cerca del mediodía.[t]

—Aquí tienen a su rey —dijo Pilato a los judíos.

15 —¡Fuera! ¡Fuera! ¡Crucifícalo! —vociferaron.

—¿Acaso voy a crucificar a su rey? —replicó Pilato.

—No tenemos más rey que el emperador romano —contestaron los jefes de los sacerdotes.

16 Entonces Pilato se lo entregó para que lo crucificaran, y los soldados se lo llevaron.

La crucifixión

19:17-24 — Mt 27:33-44; Mr 15:22-32; Lc 23:33-43

17 Jesús salió cargando su propia cruz hacia el lugar de la Calavera (que en arameo se llama Gólgota). 18 Allí lo crucificaron, y con él a otros dos, uno a cada lado y Jesús en medio.

19 Pilato mandó que se pusiera sobre la cruz un letrero en el que estuviera escrito: «JESÚS DE NAZARET, REY DE LOS JUDÍOS.» 20 Muchos de los judíos lo leyeron, porque el sitio en que crucificaron a Jesús estaba cerca de la ciudad. El letrero estaba escrito en arameo, latín y griego.

21 —No escribas "Rey de los judíos" —protestaron ante Pilato los jefes de los sacerdotes judíos—. Era él quien decía ser rey de los judíos.

[q] **18:24** *Entonces . . . envió.* Alt. *Ahora bien, Anás lo había enviado.* [r] **18:28** *al . . . romano.* Lit. *al pretorio.* [s] **18:40** *bandido.* Alt. *insurgente.* [t] **19:14** *del mediodía.* Alt. *de las seis de la mañana* (si se cuentan las horas a partir de la medianoche, según la hora romana). Lit. *de la hora sexta*; véase nota en 1:39.

²²—Lo que he escrito, escrito queda —les contestó Pilato.

²³Cuando los soldados crucificaron a Jesús, tomaron su manto y lo partieron en cuatro partes, una para cada uno de ellos. Tomaron también la túnica, la cual no tenía costura, sino que era de una sola pieza, tejida de arriba abajo.

²⁴—No la dividamos —se dijeron unos a otros—. Echemos suertes para ver a quién le toca.

Y así lo hicieron los soldados. Esto sucedió para que se cumpliera la Escritura que dice:

«Se repartieron entre ellos mi manto,
    y sobre mi ropa echaron suertes.»ᵘ

²⁵Junto a la cruz de Jesús estaban su madre, la hermana de su madre, María la esposa de Cleofas, y María Magdalena. ²⁶Cuando Jesús vio a su madre, y a su lado al discípulo a quien él amaba, dijo a su madre:

—Mujer, ahí tienes a tu hijo.

²⁷Luego dijo al discípulo:

—Ahí tienes a tu madre.

Y desde aquel momento ese discípulo la recibió en su casa.

Muerte de Jesús
19:29-30 — Mt 27:48,50; Mr 15:36-37; Lc 23:36

²⁸Después de esto, como Jesús sabía que ya todo había terminado, y para que se cumpliera la Escritura, dijo:

—Tengo sed.

²⁹Había allí una vasija llena de vinagre; así que empaparon una esponja en el vinagre, la pusieron en una cañaᵛ y se la acercaron a la boca. ³⁰Al probar Jesús el vinagre, dijo:

—Todo se ha cumplido.

Luego inclinó la cabeza y entregó el espíritu.

³¹Era el día de la preparación para la Pascua. Los judíos no querían que los cuerpos permanecieran en la cruz en *sábado, por ser éste un día muy solemne. Así que le pidieron a Pilato ordenar que les quebraran las piernas a los crucificados y bajaran sus cuerpos. ³²Fueron entonces los soldados y le quebraron las piernas al primer hombre que había sido crucificado con Jesús, y luego al otro. ³³Pero cuando se acercaron a Jesús y vieron que ya estaba muerto, no le quebraron las piernas, ³⁴sino que uno de los soldados le abrió el costado con una lanza, y al instante le brotó sangre y agua. ³⁵El que lo vio ha dado testimonio de ello, y su testimonio es verídico. Él sabe que dice la verdad, para que también ustedes crean. ³⁶Estas cosas sucedieron para que se cumpliera la Escritura: «No le quebrarán ningún hueso»ᵂ ³⁷y, como dice otra Escritura: «Mirarán al que han traspasado.»ˣ

Sepultura de Jesús
19:38-42 — Mt 27:57-61; Mr 15:42-47; Lc 23:50-56

³⁸Después de esto, José de Arimatea le pidió a Pilato el cuerpo de Jesús. José era discípulo de Jesús, aunque en secreto por miedo a los judíos. Con el permiso de Pilato, fue y retiró el cuerpo. ³⁹También Nicodemo, el que antes había visitado a Jesús de noche, llegó con unos treinta y cuatro kilosʸ de una mezcla de mirra y áloe. ⁴⁰Ambos tomaron el cuerpo de Jesús y, conforme a la costumbre judía de dar sepultura, lo envolvieron en vendas con las especias aromáticas. ⁴¹En el lugar donde crucificaron a Jesús había un huerto, y en el huerto un sepulcro nuevo en el que todavía no se había sepultado a nadie. ⁴²Como era el día judío de la preparación, y el sepulcro estaba cerca, pusieron allí a Jesús.

El sepulcro vacío
20:1-8 — Mt 28:1-8; Mr 16:1-8; Lc 24:1-10

20 El primer día de la semana, muy de mañana, cuando todavía estaba oscuro, María Magdalena fue al sepulcro y vio que habían quitado la piedra que cubría la entrada. ²Así que fue corriendo a ver a Simón Pedro y al otro discípulo, a quien Jesús amaba, y les dijo:

—¡Se han llevado del sepulcro al Señor, y no sabemos dónde lo han puesto!

³Pedro y el otro discípulo se dirigieron entonces al sepulcro. ⁴Ambos fueron corriendo, pero como el otro discípulo corría más aprisa que Pedro, llegó primero al sepulcro. ⁵Inclinándose, se asomó y vio allí las vendas, pero no entró. ⁶Tras él llegó Simón Pedro, y entró en el sepulcro. Vio allí las vendas ⁷y el sudario que había cubierto la cabeza de Jesús, aunque el sudario no estaba con las vendas sino enrollado en un lugar aparte. ⁸En ese momento entró también el otro discípulo, el que había llegado primero al sepulcro; y vio y creyó. ⁹Hasta entonces no habían entendido la Escritura, que dice que Jesús tenía que resucitar.

Jesús se aparece a María Magdalena

¹⁰Los discípulos regresaron a su casa, ¹¹pero María se quedó afuera, llorando junto al sepulcro. Mientras lloraba, se inclinó para mirar dentro del sepulcro, ¹²y vio a dos ángeles vestidos de blanco, sentados donde había estado el cuerpo de Jesús, uno a la cabecera y otro a los pies.

¹³—¿Por qué lloras, mujer? —le preguntaron los ángeles.

—Es que se han llevado a mi Señor, y no sé dónde lo han puesto —les respondió.

¹⁴Apenas dijo esto, volvió la mirada y allí vio a Jesús de pie, aunque no sabía que era él. ¹⁵Jesús le dijo:

—¿Por qué lloras, mujer? ¿A quién buscas?

Ella, pensando que se trataba del que cuidaba el huerto, le dijo:

—Señor, si usted se lo ha llevado, dígame dónde lo ha puesto, y yo iré por él.

¹⁶—María —le dijo Jesús.

Ella se volvió y exclamó:

—¡Raboni! (que en arameo significa: Maestro).

¹⁷—Suéltame,ᶻ porque todavía no he vuelto al Padre. Ve más bien a mis hermanos y diles: "Vuelvo a mi Padre, que es Padre de ustedes; a mi Dios, que es Dios de ustedes."

¹⁸María Magdalena fue a darles la noticia a los discípulos. «¡He visto al Señor!», exclamaba, y les contaba lo que él le había dicho.

Jesús se aparece a sus discípulos

¹⁹Al atardecer de aquel primer día de la semana, estando reunidos los discípulos a puerta cerrada por temor a los judíos, entró Jesús y, poniéndose en medio de ellos, los saludó:

—¡La paz sea con ustedes!

²⁰Dicho esto, les mostró las manos y el costado. Al ver al Señor, los discípulos se alegraron.

ᵘ **19:24** Sal 22:18. ᵛ **19:29** *una caña.* Lit. *una rama de hisopo.* ᵂ **19:36** Éx 12:46; Nm 9:12; Sal 34:20. ˣ **19:37** Zac 12:10. ʸ **19:39** *unos . . . kilos.* Lit. *como cien litrai.* ᶻ **20:17** *Suéltame.* Lit. *No me toques.*

²¹—¡La paz sea con ustedes! —repitió Jesús—. Como el Padre me envió a mí, así yo los envío a ustedes.

²²Acto seguido, sopló sobre ellos y les dijo:

—Reciban el Espíritu Santo. ²³A quienes les perdonen sus pecados, les serán perdonados; a quienes no se los perdonen, no les serán perdonados.

Jesús se aparece a Tomás

²⁴Tomás, al que apodaban el Gemelo,ᵃ y que era uno de los doce, no estaba con los discípulos cuando llegó Jesús. ²⁵Así que los otros discípulos le dijeron:

—¡Hemos visto al Señor!

—Mientras no vea yo la marca de los clavos en sus manos, y meta mi dedo en las marcas y mi mano en su costado, no lo creeré —repuso Tomás.

²⁶Una semana más tarde estaban los discípulos de nuevo en la casa, y Tomás estaba con ellos. Aunque las puertas estaban cerradas, Jesús entró y, poniéndose en medio de ellos, los saludó.

—¡La paz sea con ustedes!

²⁷Luego le dijo a Tomás:

—Pon tu dedo aquí y mira mis manos. Acerca tu mano y métela en mi costado. Y no seas incrédulo, sino hombre de fe.

²⁸—¡Señor mío y Dios mío! —exclamó Tomás.

²⁹—Porque me has visto, has creído —le dijo Jesús—; *dichosos los que no han visto y sin embargo creen.

³⁰Jesús hizo muchas otras señales milagrosas en presencia de sus discípulos, las cuales no están registradas en este libro. ³¹Pero éstas se han escrito para que ustedes crean que Jesús es el *Cristo, el Hijo de Dios, y para que al creer en su nombre tengan vida.

Jesús y la pesca milagrosa

21 Después de esto Jesús se apareció de nuevo a sus discípulos, junto al lago de Tiberíades.ᵇ Sucedió de esta manera: ²Estaban juntos Simón Pedro, Tomás (al que apodaban el Geméloᶜ), Natanael, el de Caná de Galilea, los hijos de Zebedeo, y otros dos discípulos.

³—Me voy a pescar —dijo Simón Pedro.

—Nos vamos contigo —contestaron ellos.

Salieron, pues, de allí y se embarcaron, pero esa noche no pescaron nada. ⁴Al despuntar el alba Jesús se hizo presente en la orilla, pero los discípulos no se dieron cuenta de que era él.

⁵—Muchachos, ¿no tienen algo de comer? —les preguntó Jesús.

—No —respondieron ellos.

⁶—Tiren la red a la derecha de la barca, y pescarán algo.

Así lo hicieron, y era tal la cantidad de pescados que ya no podían sacar la red.

⁷—¡Es el Señor! —dijo a Pedro el discípulo a quien Jesús amaba.

Tan pronto como Simón Pedro le oyó decir: «Es el Señor», se puso la ropa, pues estaba semidesnudo, y se tiró al agua. ⁸Los otros discípulos lo siguieron en la barca, arrastrando la red llena de pescados, pues estaban a escasos cien metrosᵈ de la orilla. ⁹Al de-

sembarcar, vieron unas brasas con un pescado encima, y un pan.

¹⁰—Traigan algunos de los pescados que acaban de sacar —les dijo Jesús.

¹¹Simón Pedro subió a bordo y arrastró hasta la orilla la red, la cual estaba llena de pescados de buen tamaño. Eran ciento cincuenta y tres, pero a pesar de ser tantos la red no se rompió.

¹²—Vengan a desayunar —les dijo Jesús.

Ninguno de los discípulos se atrevía a preguntarle: «¿Quién eres tú?», porque sabían que era el Señor. ¹³Jesús se acercó, tomó el pan y se lo dio a ellos, e hizo lo mismo con el pescado. ¹⁴Ésta fue la tercera vez que Jesús se apareció a sus discípulos después de haber *resucitado.

Jesús restituye a Pedro

¹⁵Cuando terminaron de desayunar, Jesús le preguntó a Simón Pedro:

—Simón, hijo de Juan, ¿me amas más que éstos?

—Sí, Señor, tú sabes que te quiero —contestó Pedro.

—Apacienta mis corderos —le dijo Jesús.

¹⁶Y volvió a preguntarle:

—Simón, hijo de Juan, ¿me amas?

—Sí, Señor, tú sabes que te quiero.

—Cuida de mis ovejas.

¹⁷Por tercera vez Jesús le preguntó:

—Simón, hijo de Juan, ¿me quieres?

A Pedro le dolió que por tercera vez Jesús le hubiera preguntado: «¿Me quieres?» Así que le dijo:

—Señor, tú lo sabes todo; tú sabes que te quiero.

—Apacienta mis ovejas —le dijo Jesús—. ¹⁸De veras te aseguro que cuando eras más joven te vestías tú mismo e ibas a donde querías; pero cuando seas viejo, extenderás las manos y otro te vestirá y te llevará a donde no quieras ir.

¹⁹Esto dijo Jesús para dar a entender la clase de muerte con que Pedro glorificaría a Dios. Después de eso añadió:

—¡Sígueme!

²⁰Al volverse, Pedro vio que los seguía el discípulo a quien Jesús amaba, el mismo que en la cena se había reclinado sobre Jesús y le había dicho: «Señor, ¿quién es el que va a traicionarte?» ²¹Al verlo, Pedro preguntó:

—Señor, ¿y éste, qué?

²²—Si quiero que él permanezca vivo hasta que yo vuelva, ¿a ti qué? Tú sígueme no más.

²³Por este motivo corrió entre los hermanos el rumor de que aquel discípulo no moriría. Pero Jesús no dijo que no moriría, sino solamente: «Si quiero que él permanezca vivo hasta que yo vuelva, ¿a ti qué?»

²⁴Éste es el discípulo que da testimonio de estas cosas, y las escribió. Y estamos convencidos de que su testimonio es verídico.

²⁵Jesús hizo también muchas otras cosas, tantas que, si se escribiera cada una de ellas, pienso que los libros escritos no cabrían en el mundo entero.

ᵃ **20:24** *apodaban el Gemelo.* Lit. *llamaban Dídimos.*   ᵇ **21:1** Es decir, el mar de Galilea.   ᶜ **21:2** *apodaban el Gemelo.* Lit. *llamaban Dídimos.*   ᵈ **21:8** *a escasos cien metros.* Lit. *a unos doscientos *codos.*

HECHOS DE LOS APÓSTOLES

Jesús llevado al cielo

1 Estimado Teófilo, en mi primer libro me referí a todo lo que Jesús comenzó a hacer y enseñar [2]hasta el día en que fue llevado al cielo, luego de darles instrucciones por medio del Espíritu Santo a los apóstoles que había escogido. [3]Después de padecer la muerte, se les presentó dándoles muchas pruebas convincentes de que estaba vivo. Durante cuarenta días se les apareció y les habló acerca del reino de Dios. [4]Una vez, mientras comía con ellos, les ordenó:

—No se alejen de Jerusalén, sino esperen la promesa del Padre, de la cual les he hablado. [5]Juan bautizó con[a] agua, pero dentro de pocos días ustedes serán bautizados con el Espíritu Santo.

[6]Entonces los que estaban reunidos con él le preguntaron:

—Señor, ¿es ahora cuando vas a restablecer el reino a Israel?

[7]—No les toca a ustedes conocer la hora ni el momento determinados por la autoridad misma del Padre —les contestó Jesús—. [8]Pero cuando venga el Espíritu Santo sobre ustedes, recibirán poder y serán mis testigos tanto en Jerusalén como en toda Judea y Samaria, y hasta los confines de la tierra.

[9]Habiendo dicho esto, mientras ellos lo miraban, fue llevado a las alturas hasta que una nube lo ocultó de su vista. [10]Ellos se quedaron mirando fijamente al cielo mientras se alejaba. De repente, se les acercaron dos hombres vestidos de blanco, que les dijeron:

[11]—Galileos, ¿qué hacen aquí mirando al cielo? Este mismo Jesús, que ha sido llevado de entre ustedes al cielo, vendrá otra vez de la misma manera que lo han visto irse.

Elección de Matías para reemplazar a Judas

[12]Entonces regresaron a Jerusalén desde el monte llamado de los Olivos, situado aproximadamente a un kilómetro de la ciudad.[b] [13]Cuando llegaron, subieron al lugar donde se alojaban. Estaban allí Pedro, Juan, *Jacobo, Andrés, Felipe, Tomás, Bartolomé, Mateo, Jacobo hijo de Alfeo, Simón el Zelote y Judas hijo de Jacobo. [14]Todos, en un mismo espíritu, se dedicaban a la oración, junto con las mujeres y con los hermanos de Jesús y su madre María.

[15]Por aquellos días Pedro se puso de pie en medio de los creyentes,[c] que eran un grupo como de ciento veinte personas, [16]y les dijo: «Hermanos, tenía que cumplirse la Escritura que, por boca de David, había predicho el Espíritu Santo en cuanto a Judas, el que sirvió de guía a los que arrestaron a Jesús. [17]Judas se contaba entre los nuestros y participaba en nuestro ministerio. [18](Con el dinero que obtuvo por su crimen, Judas compró un terreno; allí cayó de cabeza, se reventó, y se le salieron las vísceras. [19]Todos en Jerusalén se enteraron de ello, así que aquel terreno fue llamado Acéldama, que en su propio idioma quiere decir "Campo de Sangre".)

[20]»Porque en el libro de los Salmos —continuó Pedro— está escrito:

»"Que su lugar quede desierto,
y que nadie lo habite."[d]

También está escrito:

»"Que otro se haga cargo de su oficio".[e]

[21-22]Por tanto, es preciso que se una a nosotros un testigo de la resurrección, uno de los que nos acompañaban todo el tiempo que el Señor Jesús vivió entre nosotros, desde que Juan bautizaba hasta el día en que Jesús fue llevado de entre nosotros.»

[23]Así que propusieron a dos: a José, llamado Barsabás, apodado el Justo, y a Matías. [24]Y oraron así: «Señor, tú que conoces el corazón de todos, muéstranos a cuál de estos dos has elegido [25]para que se haga cargo del servicio apostólico que Judas dejó para irse al lugar que le correspondía.» [26]Luego echaron suertes y la elección recayó en Matías; así que él fue reconocido junto con los once apóstoles.

El Espíritu Santo desciende en Pentecostés

2 Cuando llegó el día de Pentecostés, estaban todos juntos en el mismo lugar. [2]De repente, vino del cielo un ruido como el de una violenta ráfaga de viento y llenó toda la casa donde estaban reunidos. [3]Se les aparecieron entonces unas lenguas como de fuego que se repartieron y se posaron sobre cada uno de ellos. [4]Todos fueron llenos del Espíritu Santo y comenzaron a hablar en diferentes *lenguas, según el Espíritu les concedía expresarse.

[5]Estaban de visita en Jerusalén judíos piadosos, procedentes de todas las naciones de la tierra. [6]Al oír aquel bullicio, se agolparon y quedaron todos pasmados porque cada uno los escuchaba hablar en su propio idioma. [7]Desconcertados y maravillados, decían: «¿No son galileos todos estos que están hablando? [8]¿Cómo es que cada uno de nosotros los oye hablar en su lengua materna? [9]Partos, medos y elamitas; habitantes de Mesopotamia, de Judea y de Capadocia, del Ponto y de *Asia, [10]de Frigia y de Panfilia, de Egipto y de las regiones de Libia cercanas a Cirene; visitantes llegados de Roma; [11]judíos y *prosélitos; cretenses y árabes: ¡todos por igual los oímos proclamar en nuestra propia lengua las maravillas de Dios!»

[12]Desconcertados y perplejos, se preguntaban: «¿Qué quiere decir esto?» [13]Otros se burlaban y decían: «Lo que pasa es que están borrachos.»

Pedro se dirige a la multitud

[14]Entonces Pedro, con los once, se puso de pie y dijo a voz en cuello: «Compatriotas judíos y todos ustedes que están en Jerusalén, déjenme explicarles lo que sucede; presten atención a lo que les voy a decir. [15]Éstos no están borrachos, como suponen ustedes. ¡Apenas son las nueve de la mañana![f] [16]En realidad lo que pasa es lo que anunció el profeta Joel:

[17]»Sucederá que en los últimos días —dice Dios—,
derramaré mi Espíritu sobre todo el género *humano.
Los hijos y las hijas de ustedes profetizarán,
tendrán visiones los jóvenes
y sueños los ancianos.
[18]En esos días derramaré mi Espíritu
aun sobre mis *siervos y mis siervas,
y profetizarán.
[19]Arriba en el cielo y abajo en la tierra mostraré prodigios:

---

a [1:5] con. Alt. en. b [1:12] situado . . . ciudad. Lit. que está cerca de Jerusalén, camino de un *sábado (es decir, lo que la ley permitía caminar en el día de reposo). c [1:15] creyentes. Lit. hermanos. d [1:20] Sal 69:25 e [1:20] Sal 109:8 f [2:15] son las nueve de la mañana. Lit. es la hora tercera del día.

sangre, fuego y nubes de humo.
²⁰El sol se convertirá en tinieblas
y la luna en sangre
antes que llegue el día del Señor,
día grande y esplendoroso.
²¹Y todo el que invoque el nombre del Señor
será salvo."g

²²»Pueblo de Israel, escuchen esto: Jesús de Nazaret fue un hombre acreditado por Dios ante ustedes con milagros, señales y prodigios, los cuales realizó Dios entre ustedes por medio de él, como bien lo saben. ²³Éste fue entregado según el determinado propósito y el previo conocimiento de Dios; y por medio de gente malvada,h ustedes lo mataron, clavándolo en la cruz. ²⁴Sin embargo, Dios lo resucitó, librándolo de las angustias de la muerte, porque era imposible que la muerte lo mantuviera bajo su dominio. ²⁵En efecto, David dijo de él:

»"Veía yo al Señor siempre delante de mí,
porque él está a mi *derecha
para que no caiga.
²⁶Por eso mi corazón se alegra, y canta con gozo
mi lengua;
mi cuerpo también vivirá en esperanza.
²⁷No dejarás que mi *vida termine en el
sepulcro;i
no permitirás que tu santo sufra
corrupción.
²⁸Me has dado a conocer los caminos de la vida;
me llenarás de alegría en tu presencia."j

²⁹»Hermanos, permítanme hablarles con franqueza acerca del patriarca David, que murió y fue sepultado, y cuyo sepulcro está entre nosotros hasta el día de hoy. ³⁰Era profeta y sabía que Dios le había prometido bajo juramento poner en el trono a uno de sus descendientes.k ³¹Fue así como previó lo que iba a suceder. Refiriéndose a la resurrección del *Mesías, afirmó que Dios no dejaría que su vida terminara en el sepulcro, ni que su fin fuera la corrupción. ³²A este Jesús, Dios lo resucitó, y de ello todos nosotros somos testigos. ³³Exaltado por el poderl de Dios, y habiendo recibido del Padre el Espíritu Santo prometido, ha derramado esto que ustedes ahora ven y oyen. ³⁴David no subió al cielo, y sin embargo declaró:

»"Dijo el Señor a mi Señor:
Siéntate a mi derecha,
³⁵hasta que ponga a tus enemigos
por estrado de tus pies."m

³⁶»Por tanto, sépalo bien todo Israel que a este Jesús, a quien ustedes crucificaron, Dios lo ha hecho Señor y Mesías.»

³⁷Cuando oyeron esto, todos se sintieron profundamente conmovidos y les dijeron a Pedro y a los otros apóstoles:

—Hermanos, ¿qué debemos hacer?

³⁸—*Arrepiéntase y bautícese cada uno de ustedes en el nombre de *Jesucristo para perdón de sus pecados —les contestó Pedro—, y recibirán el don del Espíritu Santo. ³⁹En efecto, la promesa es para ustedes, para sus hijos y para todos los extranjeros,n es decir, para todos aquellos a quienes el Señor nuestro Dios quiera llamar.

⁴⁰Y con muchas otras razones les exhortaba insistentemente:

—¡Sálvense de esta generación perversa!

La comunidad de los creyentes

⁴¹Así, pues, los que recibieron su mensaje fueron bautizados, y aquel día se unieron a la iglesia unas tres mil personas. ⁴²Se mantenían firmes en la enseñanza de los apóstoles, en la comunión, en el partimiento del pan y en la oración. ⁴³Todos estaban asombrados por los muchos prodigios y señales que realizaban los apóstoles. ⁴⁴Todos los creyentes estaban juntos y tenían todo en común: ⁴⁵vendían sus propiedades y posesiones, y compartían sus bienes entre sí según la necesidad de cada uno. ⁴⁶No dejaban de reunirse en el *templo ni un solo día. De casa en casa partían el pan y compartían la comida con alegría y generosidad, ⁴⁷alabando a Dios y disfrutando de la estimación general del pueblo. Y cada día el Señor añadía al grupo los que iban siendo salvos.

Pedro sana a un mendigo lisiado

3 Un día subían Pedro y Juan al *templo a las tres de la tarde,ñ que es la hora de la oración. ²Junto a la puerta llamada Hermosa había un hombre lisiado de nacimiento, al que todos los días dejaban allí para que pidiera limosna a los que entraban en el templo. ³Cuando éste vio que Pedro y Juan estaban por entrar, les pidió limosna. ⁴Pedro, con Juan, mirándolo fijamente, le dijo:

—¡Míranos!

⁵El hombre fijó en ellos la mirada, esperando recibir algo.

⁶—No tengo plata ni oro —declaró Pedro—, pero lo que tengo te doy. En el nombre de *Jesucristo de Nazaret, ¡levántate y anda!

⁷Y tomándolo por la mano derecha, lo levantó. Al instante los pies y los tobillos del hombre cobraron fuerza. ⁸De un salto se puso en pie y comenzó a caminar. Luego entró con ellos en el templo con sus propios pies, saltando y alabando a Dios. ⁹Cuando todo el pueblo lo vio caminar y alabar a Dios, ¹⁰lo reconocieron como el mismo hombre que acostumbraba pedir limosna sentado junto a la puerta llamada Hermosa, y se llenaron de admiración y asombro por lo que le había ocurrido.

Pedro se dirige a los espectadores

¹¹Mientras el hombre seguía aferrado a Pedro y a Juan, toda la gente, que no salía de su asombro, corrió hacia ellos al lugar conocido como Pórtico de Salomón. ¹²Al ver esto, Pedro les dijo: «Pueblo de Israel, ¿por qué les sorprende lo que ha pasado? ¿Por qué nos miran como si, por nuestro propio poder o virtud, hubiéramos hecho caminar a este hombre? ¹³El Dios de Abraham, de Isaac y de Jacob, el Dios de nuestros antepasados, ha glorificado a su siervo Jesús. Ustedes lo entregaron y lo rechazaron ante Pilato, aunque éste había decidido soltarlo. ¹⁴Rechazaron al Santo y Justo, y pidieron que se indultara a un asesino. ¹⁵Mataron al autor de la vida, pero Dios lo *levantó de entre los muertos, y de eso nosotros somos testigos. ¹⁶Por la fe en el nombre de Jesús, él ha restablecido a este hombre a quien ustedes ven y conocen. Esta fe que viene por medio de Jesús lo ha sanado por completo, como les consta a ustedes.

¹⁷»Ahora bien, hermanos, yo sé que ustedes y sus dirigentes actuaron así por ignorancia. ¹⁸Pero de este modo Dios cumplió lo que de antemano había anunciado por medio de todos los profetas: que su

---

g **2:21** Jl 2:28-32 h **2:23** gente malvada. Lit. quienes carecían de la ley. i **2:27** sepulcro. Lit. *Hades; también en v. 31. j **2:28** Sal 16:8-11 k **2:30** Sal 132:11 l **2:33** por el poder. Alt. a la derecha. m **2:35** Sal 110:1 n **2:39** los extranjeros. Lit. los que están lejos. ñ **3:1** las tres de la tarde. Lit. la hora novena.

*Mesías tenía que padecer. 19Por tanto, para que sean borrados sus pecados, *arrepiéntanse y vuélvanse a Dios, a fin de que vengan tiempos de descanso de parte del Señor, 20enviándoles el Mesías que ya había sido preparado para ustedes, el cual es Jesús. 21Es necesario que él permanezca en el cielo hasta que llegue el tiempo de la restauración de todas las cosas, como Dios lo ha anunciado desde hace siglos por medio de sus *santos profetas. 22Moisés dijo: "El Señor su Dios hará surgir para ustedes, de entre sus propios hermanos, a un profeta como yo; presten atención a todo lo que les diga. 23Porque quien no le haga caso será eliminado del pueblo."o

24»En efecto, a partir de Samuel todos los profetas han anunciado estos días. 25Ustedes, pues, son herederos de los profetas y del pacto que Dios estableció con nuestros antepasados al decirle a Abraham: "Todos los pueblos del mundo serán bendecidos por medio de tu descendencia."p 26Cuando Dios resucitó a su siervo, lo envió primero a ustedes para darles la bendición de que cada uno se convierta de sus maldades.»

Pedro y Juan ante el Consejo

4 Mientras Pedro y Juan le hablaban a la gente, se les presentaron los sacerdotes, el capitán de la guardia del *templo y los saduceos. 2Estaban muy disgustados porque los apóstoles enseñaban a la gente y proclamaban la resurrección, que se había hecho evidente en el caso de Jesús. 3Prendieron a Pedro y a Juan y, como ya anochecía, los metieron en la cárcel hasta el día siguiente. 4Pero muchos de los que oyeron el mensaje creyeron, y el número de éstos llegaba a unos cinco mil.

5Al día siguiente se reunieron en Jerusalén los gobernantes, los *ancianos y los *maestros de la ley. 6Allí estaban el sumo sacerdote Anás, Caifás, Juan, Alejandro y los otros miembros de la familia del sumo sacerdote. 7Hicieron que Pedro y Juan comparecieran ante ellos y comenzaron a interrogarlos:

—¿Con qué poder, o en nombre de quién, hicieron ustedes esto?

8Pedro, lleno del Espíritu Santo, les respondió:

—Gobernantes del pueblo y ancianos: 9Hoy se nos procesa por haber favorecido a un inválido, ¡y se nos pregunta cómo fue sanado! 10Sepan, pues, todos ustedes y todo el pueblo de Israel que este hombre está aquí delante de ustedes, sano gracias al nombre de *Jesucristo de Nazaret, crucificado por ustedes pero *resucitado por Dios. 11Jesucristo es "la piedra que desecharon ustedes los constructores, y que ha llegado a ser la piedra angular".q 12De hecho, en ningún otro hay salvación, porque no hay bajo el cielo otro nombre dado a los hombres mediante el cual podamos ser salvos.

13Los gobernantes, al ver la osadía con que hablaban Pedro y Juan, y al darse cuenta de que eran gente sin estudios ni preparación, quedaron asombrados y reconocieron que habían estado con Jesús. 14Además, como vieron que los acompañaba el hombre que había sido sanado, no tenían nada que alegar. 15Así que les mandaron que se retiraran del *Consejo, y se pusieron a deliberar entre sí: 16«¿Qué vamos a hacer con estos sujetos? Es un hecho que por medio de ellos ha ocurrido un milagro evidente; todos los que viven en Jerusalén lo saben, y no podemos negarlo. 17Pero para evitar que este asunto siga divulgándose entre la gente, vamos a amenazarlos para que no vuelvan a hablar de ese nombre a nadie.»

18Los llamaron y les ordenaron terminantemente que dejaran de hablar y enseñar acerca del nombre de Jesús. 19Pero Pedro y Juan replicaron:

—¿Es justo delante de Dios obedecerlos a ustedes en vez de obedecerlo a él? ¡Júzguenlo ustedes mismos! 20Nosotros no podemos dejar de hablar de lo que hemos visto y oído.

21Después de nuevas amenazas, los dejaron irse. Por causa de la gente, no hallaban manera de castigarlos: todos alababan a Dios por lo que había sucedido, 22pues el hombre que había sido milagrosamente sanado tenía más de cuarenta años.

La oración de los creyentes

23Al quedar libres, Pedro y Juan volvieron a los suyos y les relataron todo lo que les habían dicho los jefes de los sacerdotes y los *ancianos. 24Cuando lo oyeron, alzaron unánimes la voz en oración a Dios: «Soberano Señor, creador del cielo y de la tierra, del mar y de todo lo que hay en ellos, 25tú, por medio del Espíritu Santo, dijiste en labios de nuestro padre David, tu siervo:

»"¿Por qué se sublevan las *naciones
    y en vano conspiran los pueblos?
26Los reyes de la tierra se rebelan
    y los gobernantes se confabulan
        contra el Señor
    y contra su ungido."r

27En efecto, en esta ciudad se reunieron Herodes y Poncio Pilato, con los *gentiles y con el pueblos de Israel, contra tu santo siervo Jesús, a quien ungiste 28para hacer lo que de antemano tu poder y tu voluntad habían determinado que sucediera. 29Ahora, Señor, toma en cuenta sus amenazas y concede a tus *siervos el proclamar tu palabra sin temor alguno. 30Por eso, extiende tu mano para sanar y hacer señales y prodigios mediante el nombre de tu santo siervo Jesús.»

31Después de haber orado, tembló el lugar en que estaban reunidos; todos fueron llenos del Espíritu Santo, y proclamaban la palabra de Dios sin temor alguno.

Los creyentes comparten sus bienes

32Todos los creyentes eran de un solo sentir y pensar. Nadie consideraba suya ninguna de sus posesiones, sino que las compartían. 33Los apóstoles, a su vez, con gran poder seguían dando testimonio de la resurrección del Señor Jesús. La gracia de Dios se derramaba abundantemente sobre todos ellos, 34pues no había ningún necesitado en la comunidad. Quienes poseían casas o terrenos los vendían, llevaban el dinero de las ventas 35y lo entregaban a los apóstoles para que se distribuyera a cada uno según su necesidad.

36José, un levita natural de Chipre, a quien los apóstoles llamaban Bernabé (que significa: Consolador[t]), 37vendió un terreno que poseía, llevó el dinero y lo puso a disposición de los apóstoles.

Ananías y Safira

5 1-2Un hombre llamado Ananías también vendió una propiedad y, en complicidad con su esposa Safira, se quedó con parte del dinero y puso el resto a disposición de los apóstoles.

---

o 3:23 Lv 23:29; Dt 18:15,18,19   p 3:25 Gn 22:18; 26:4   q 4:11 Sal 118:22   r 4:26 *ungido*. Lit. *Cristo*; Sal 2:1,2.   s 4:27 *el pueblo*. Lit. *los pueblos*.   t 4:36 *Consolador*. Lit. *Hijo de consolación*.

3—Ananías —le reclamó Pedro—, ¿cómo es posible que Satanás haya llenado tu corazón para que le mintieras al Espíritu Santo y te quedaras con parte del dinero que recibiste por el terreno? 4¿Acaso no era tuyo antes de venderlo? Y una vez vendido, ¿no estaba el dinero en tu poder? ¿Cómo se te ocurrió hacer esto? ¡No has mentido a los hombres sino a Dios!

5Al oír estas palabras, Ananías cayó muerto. Y un gran temor se apoderó de todos los que se enteraron de lo sucedido. 6Entonces se acercaron los más jóvenes, envolvieron el cuerpo, se lo llevaron y le dieron sepultura.

7Unas tres horas más tarde entró la esposa, sin saber lo que había ocurrido.

8—Dime —le preguntó Pedro—, ¿vendieron ustedes el terreno por tal precio?

—Sí —dijo ella—, por tal precio.

9—¿Por qué se pusieron de acuerdo para poner a *prueba al Espíritu del Señor? —le recriminó Pedro—. ¡Mira! Los que sepultaron a tu esposo acaban de regresar y ahora te llevarán a ti.

10En ese mismo instante ella cayó muerta a los pies de Pedro. Entonces entraron los jóvenes y, al verla muerta, se la llevaron y le dieron sepultura al lado de su esposo. 11Y un gran temor se apoderó de toda la iglesia y de todos los que se enteraron de estos sucesos.

Los apóstoles sanan a muchas personas

12Por medio de los apóstoles ocurrían muchas señales y prodigios entre el pueblo; y todos los creyentes se reunían de común acuerdo en el Pórtico de Salomón. 13Nadie entre el pueblo se atrevía a juntarse con ellos, aunque los elogiaban. 14Y seguía aumentando el número de los que creían y aceptaban al Señor. 15Era tal la multitud de hombres y mujeres, que hasta sacaban a los enfermos a las plazas y los ponían en colchonetas y camillas para que, al pasar Pedro, por lo menos su sombra cayera sobre alguno de ellos. 16También de los pueblos vecinos a Jerusalén acudían multitudes que llevaban personas enfermas y atormentadas por *espíritus malignos, y todas eran sanadas.

Persiguen a los apóstoles

17El sumo sacerdote y todos sus partidarios, que pertenecían a la secta de los saduceos, se llenaron de envidia. 18Entonces arrestaron a los apóstoles y los metieron en la cárcel común. 19Pero en la noche un ángel del Señor abrió las puertas de la cárcel y los sacó. 20«Vayan —les dijo—, preséntense en el *templo y comuniquen al pueblo todo este mensaje de vida.»

21Conforme a lo que habían oído, al amanecer entraron en el templo y se pusieron a enseñar. Cuando llegaron el sumo sacerdote y sus partidarios, convocaron al *Consejo, es decir, a la asamblea general de los *ancianos de Israel, y mandaron traer de la cárcel a los apóstoles. 22Pero al llegar los guardias a la cárcel, no los encontraron. Así que volvieron con el siguiente informe: 23«Encontramos la cárcel cerrada, con todas las medidas de seguridad, y a los guardias firmes a las puertas; pero cuando abrimos, no encontramos a nadie adentro.»

24Al oírlo, el capitán de la guardia del templo y los jefes de los sacerdotes se quedaron perplejos, preguntándose en qué terminaría todo aquello. 25En esto, se presentó alguien que les informó: «¡Miren! Los hombres que ustedes metieron en la cárcel están en el templo y siguen enseñando al pueblo.» 26Fue entonces el capitán con sus guardias y trajo a los apóstoles sin recurrir a la fuerza, porque temían ser apedreados por la gente. 27Los condujeron ante el Consejo, y el sumo sacerdote les reclamó:

28—Terminantemente les hemos prohibido enseñar en ese nombre. Sin embargo, ustedes han llenado a Jerusalén con sus enseñanzas, y se han propuesto echarnos la culpa a nosotros de la muerteu de ese hombre.

29—¡Es necesario obedecer a Dios antes que a los hombres! —respondieron Pedro y los demás apóstoles—. 30El Dios de nuestros antepasados resucitó a Jesús, a quien ustedes mataron colgándolo de un madero. 31Por su poder,v Dios lo exaltó como Príncipe y Salvador, para que diera a Israel *arrepentimiento y perdón de pecados. 32Nosotros somos testigos de estos acontecimientos, y también lo es el Espíritu Santo que Dios ha dado a quienes le obedecen.

33A los que oyeron esto se les subió la sangre a la cabeza y querían matarlos.

34Pero un *fariseo llamado Gamaliel, *maestro de la ley muy respetado por todo el pueblo, se puso de pie en el Consejo y mandó que hicieran salir por un momento a los apóstoles. 35Luego dijo: «Hombres de Israel, piensen dos veces en lo que están a punto de hacer con estos hombres. 36Hace algún tiempo surgió Teudas, jactándose de ser alguien, y se le unieron unos cuatrocientos hombres. Pero lo mataron y todos sus seguidores se dispersaron y allí se acabó todo. 37Después de él surgió Judas el galileo, en los días del censo, y logró que la gente lo siguiera. A él también lo mataron, y todos sus secuaces se dispersaron. 38En este caso les aconsejo que dejen a estos hombres en paz. ¡Suéltenlos! Si lo que se proponen y hacen es de origen humano, fracasará; 39pero si es de Dios, no podrán destruirlos, y ustedes se encontrarán luchando contra Dios.»

Se dejaron persuadir por Gamaliel. 40Entonces llamaron a los apóstoles y, luego de azotarlos, les ordenaron que no hablaran más en el nombre de Jesús. Después de eso los soltaron.

41Así, pues, los apóstoles salieron del Consejo, llenos de gozo por haber sido considerados dignos de sufrir afrentas por causa del Nombre. 42Y día tras día, en el templo y de casa en casa, no dejaban de enseñar y anunciar las buenas *nuevas de que Jesús es el *Mesías.

Elección de los siete

6 En aquellos días, al aumentar el número de los discípulos, se quejaron los judíos de habla griega contra los de habla arameaw de que sus viudas eran desatendidas en la distribución diaria de los alimentos. 2Así que los doce reunieron a toda la comunidad de discípulos y les dijeron: «No está bien que nosotros los apóstoles descuidemos el ministerio de la palabra de Dios para servir las mesas. 3Hermanos, escojan de entre ustedes a siete hombres de buena reputación, llenos del Espíritu y de sabiduría, para encargarles esta responsabilidad. 4Así nosotros nos dedicaremos de lleno a la oración y al ministerio de la palabra.»

5Esta propuesta agradó a toda la asamblea. Escogieron a Esteban, hombre lleno de fe y del Espíritu Santo, y a Felipe, a Prócoro, a Nicanor, a Timón, a Parmenas y a Nicolás, un prosélito de Antioquía.

---

u 5:28 muerte. Lit. Sangre. v 5:31 Par su poder. Alt. A su derecha. w 6:1 los judíos . . . aramea. Lit. los helenistas contra los hebreos.

⁶Los presentaron a los apóstoles, quienes oraron y les impusieron las manos.

⁷Y la palabra de Dios se difundía: el número de los discípulos aumentaba considerablemente en Jerusalén, e incluso muchos de los sacerdotes obedecían a la fe.

Arresto de Esteban

⁸Esteban, hombre lleno de la gracia y del poder de Dios, hacía grandes prodigios y señales milagrosas entre el pueblo. ⁹Con él se pusieron a discutir ciertos individuos de la sinagoga llamada de los Libertos, donde había judíos de Cirene y de Alejandría, de Cilicia y de la provincia de *Asia. ¹⁰Como no podían hacer frente a la sabiduría ni al Espíritu con que hablaba Esteban, ¹¹instigaron a unos hombres a decir: «Hemos oído a Esteban *blasfemar contra Moisés y contra Dios.»

¹²Agitaron al pueblo, a los *ancianos y a los *maestros de la ley. Se apoderaron de Esteban y lo llevaron ante el *Consejo. ¹³Presentaron testigos falsos, que declararon: «Este hombre no deja de hablar contra este lugar santo y contra la ley. ¹⁴Le hemos oído decir que ese Jesús de Nazaret destruirá este lugar y cambiará las tradiciones que nos dejó Moisés.»

¹⁵Todos los que estaban sentados en el Consejo fijaron la mirada en Esteban y vieron que su rostro se parecía al de un ángel.

Discurso de Esteban ante el Consejo

7 —¿Son ciertas estas acusaciones? —le preguntó el sumo sacerdote.

²Él contestó:

—Hermanos y padres, ¡escúchenme! El Dios de la gloria se apareció a nuestro padre Abraham cuando éste aún vivía en Mesopotamia, antes de radicarse en Jarán. ³"Deja tu tierra y a tus parientes —le dijo Dios—, y ve a la tierra que yo te mostraré."ˣ

⁴»Entonces salió de la tierra de los caldeos y se estableció en Jarán. Desde allí, después de la muerte de su padre, Dios lo trasladó a esta tierra donde ustedes viven ahora. ⁵No le dio herencia alguna en ella, ni siquiera dónde plantar el pie, pero le prometió dársela en posesión a él y a su descendencia, aunque Abraham no tenía ni un solo hijo todavía. ⁶Dios le dijo así: "Tus descendientes vivirán como extranjeros en tierra extraña, donde serán esclavizados y maltratados durante cuatrocientos años. ⁷Pero sea cual sea la nación que los esclavice, yo la castigaré, y luego tus descendientes saldrán de esa tierra y me adorarán en este lugar."ʸ ⁸Hizo con Abraham el pacto que tenía por señal la circuncisión. Así, cuando Abraham tuvo a su hijo Isaac, lo circuncidó a los ocho días de nacido, e Isaac a Jacob, y Jacob a los doce patriarcas.

⁹»Por envidia los patriarcas vendieron a José como esclavo, quien fue llevado a Egipto; pero Dios estaba con él ¹⁰y lo libró de todas sus desgracias. Le dio sabiduría para ganarse el favor del faraón, rey de Egipto, que lo nombró gobernador del país y del palacio real.

¹¹»Hubo entonces un hambre que azotó a todo Egipto y a Canaán, causando mucho sufrimiento, y nuestros antepasados no encontraban alimentos. ¹²Al enterarse Jacob de que había comida en Egipto, mandó allá a nuestros antepasados en una primera visita. ¹³En la segunda, José se dio a conocer a sus hermanos, y el faraón supo del origen de José. ¹⁴Después de esto, José mandó llamar a su padre Jacob y a toda su familia, setenta y cinco personas en total. ¹⁵Bajó entonces Jacob a Egipto, y allí murieron él y nuestros antepasados. ¹⁶Sus restos fueron llevados a Siquén y puestos en el sepulcro que a buen precio Abraham había comprado a los hijos de Jamor en Siquén.

¹⁷»Cuando ya se acercaba el tiempo de que se cumpliera la promesa que Dios le había hecho a Abraham, el pueblo crecía y se multiplicaba en Egipto. ¹⁸Por aquel entonces subió al trono de Egipto un nuevo rey que no sabía nada de José. ¹⁹Este rey usó de artimañas con nuestro pueblo y oprimió a nuestros antepasados, obligándolos a dejar abandonados a sus hijos recién nacidos para que murieran.

²⁰»En aquel tiempo nació Moisés, y fue agradable a los ojos de Dios.ᶻ Por tres meses se crió en la casa de su padre ²¹y, al quedar abandonado, la hija del faraón lo adoptó y lo crió como a su propio hijo. ²²Así Moisés fue instruido en toda la sabiduría de los egipcios, y era poderoso en palabra y en obra.

²³»Cuando cumplió cuarenta años, Moisés tuvo el deseo de allegarse a sus hermanos israelitas. ²⁴Al ver que un egipcio maltrataba a uno de ellos, acudió en su defensa y lo vengó matando al egipcio. ²⁵Moisés suponía que sus hermanos reconocerían que Dios iba a liberarlos por medio de él, pero ellos no lo comprendieron así. ²⁶Al día siguiente, Moisés sorprendió a dos israelitas que estaban peleando. Trató de reconciliarlos, diciéndoles: "Señores, ustedes son hermanos; ¿por qué quieren hacerse daño?"

²⁷»Pero el que estaba maltratando al otro empujó a Moisés y le dijo: "¿Y quién te nombró a ti gobernante y juez sobre nosotros? ²⁸¿Acaso quieres matarme a mí, como mataste ayer al egipcio?"ᵃ ²⁹Al oír esto, Moisés huyó a Madián; allí vivió como extranjero y tuvo dos hijos.

³⁰»Pasados cuarenta años, se le apareció un ángel en el desierto cercano al monte Sinaí, en las llamas de una zarza que ardía. ³¹Moisés se asombró de lo que veía. Al acercarse para observar, oyó la voz del Señor: ³²"Yo soy el Dios de tus antepasados, el Dios de Abraham, de Isaac y de Jacob."ᵇ Moisés se puso a temblar de miedo, y no se atrevía a mirar.

³³»Le dijo el Señor: "Quítate las sandalias, porque estás pisando tierra santa. ³⁴Ciertamente he visto la opresión que sufre mi pueblo en Egipto. Los he escuchado quejarse, así que he descendido para librarlos. Ahora ven y te enviaré de vuelta a Egipto."ᶜ

³⁵»A este mismo Moisés, a quien habían rechazado diciéndole: "¿Y quién te nombró gobernante y juez?", Dios lo envió para ser gobernante y libertador, mediante el poder del ángel que se le apareció en la zarza. ³⁶Él los sacó de Egipto haciendo prodigios y señales milagrosas tanto en la tierra de Egipto como en el Mar Rojo, y en el desierto durante cuarenta años.

³⁷Este Moisés les dijo a los israelitas: "Dios hará surgir para ustedes, de entre sus propios hermanos, un profeta como yo."ᵈ ³⁸Este mismo Moisés estuvo en la asamblea en el desierto, con el ángel que le habló en el monte Sinaí, y con nuestros antepasados. Fue también él quien recibió palabras de vida para comunicárnoslas a nosotros.

³⁹»Nuestros antepasados no quisieron obedecerlo a él, sino que lo rechazaron. Lo que realmente deseaban era volver a Egipto, ⁴⁰por lo cual le dijeron a Aarón: "Tienes que hacernos dioses que va-

---

ˣ 7:3 Gn 12:1 ʸ 7:7 Gn 15:13,14; Éx 3:12 ᶻ 7:20 *fue . . . Dios.* Alt. *era sumamente hermoso.* ᵃ 7:28 Éx 2:14 ᵇ 7:32 Éx 3:6
ᶜ 7:34 Éx 3:5,7,8,10 ᵈ 7:37 Dt 18:15

yan delante de nosotros, porque a ese Moisés que nos sacó de Egipto, ino sabemos qué pudo haberle pasado!"e

41»Entonces se hicieron un ídolo en forma de becerro. Le ofrecieron sacrificios y tuvieron fiesta en honor de la obra de sus manos. **42**Pero Dios les volvió la espalda y los entregó a que rindieran culto a los astros. Así está escrito en el libro de los profetas:

»"Casa de Israel, ¿acaso me ofrecieron ustedes
    sacrificios y ofrendas
durante los cuarenta años en el desierto?
43Por el contrario, ustedes se hicieron cargo del
    tabernáculo de Moloc,
de la estrella del dios Refán,
y de las imágenes que hicieron para
    adorarlas.
Por lo tanto, los mandaré al exilio"f más allá de
    Babilonia.

44»Nuestros antepasados tenían en el desierto el tabernáculo del testimonio, hecho como Dios le había ordenado a Moisés, según el modelo que éste había visto. **45**Después de haber recibido el tabernáculo, lo trajeron consigo bajo el mando de Josué, cuando conquistaron la tierra de las naciones que Dios expulsó de la presencia de ellos. Allí permaneció hasta el tiempo de David, **46**quien disfrutó del favor de Dios y pidió que le permitiera proveer una morada para el Diosg de Jacob. **47**Pero fue Salomón quien construyó la casa.

48»Sin embargo, el Altísimo no habita en casas construidas por manos humanas. Como dice el profeta:

49»"El cielo es mi trono,
y la tierra, el estrado de mis pies.
¿Qué clase de casa me construirán?
    —dice el Señor—.
¿O qué lugar de descanso?
50¿No es mi mano la que ha hecho todas estas
    cosas?"h

51»¡Tercos, duros de corazón y torpes de oídos!i Ustedes son iguales que sus antepasados: ¡Siempre resisten al Espíritu Santo! **52**¿A cuál de los profetas no persiguieron sus antepasados? Ellos mataron a los que de antemano anunciaron la venida del Justo, y ahora a éste lo han traicionado y asesinado **53**ustedes, que recibieron la ley promulgada por medio de ángeles y no la han obedecido.

Muerte de Esteban

54Al oír esto, rechinando los dientes montaron en cólera contra él. **55**Pero Esteban, lleno del Espíritu Santo, fijó la mirada en el cielo y vio la gloria de Dios, y a Jesús de pie a la *derecha de Dios.

56—¡Veo el cielo abierto —exclamó—, y al Hijo del hombre de pie a la derecha de Dios!

57Entonces ellos, gritando a voz en cuello, se taparon los oídos y todos a una se abalanzaron sobre él, **58**lo sacaron a empellones fuera de la ciudad y comenzaron a apedrearlo. Los acusadores le encargaron sus mantos a un joven llamado Saulo.

59Mientras lo apedreaban, Esteban oraba.

—Señor Jesús —decía—, recibe mi espíritu.

60Luego cayó de rodillas y gritó:

—¡Señor, no les tomes en cuenta este pecado! Cuando hubo dicho esto, murió.

8 Y Saulo estaba allí, aprobando la muerte de Esteban.

La iglesia perseguida y dispersa

Aquel día se desató una gran persecución contra la iglesia en Jerusalén, y todos, excepto los apóstoles, se dispersaron por las regiones de Judea y Samaria. **2**Unos hombres piadosos sepultaron a Esteban e hicieron gran duelo por él. **3**Saulo, por su parte, causaba estragos en la iglesia: entrando de casa en casa, arrastraba a hombres y mujeres y los metía en la cárcel.

Felipe en Samaria

4Los que se habían dispersado predicaban la palabra por dondequiera que iban. **5**Felipe bajó a una ciudad de Samaria y les anunciaba al *Mesías. **6**Al oír a Felipe y ver las señales milagrosas que realizaba, mucha gente se reunía y todos prestaban atención a su mensaje. **7**De muchos endemoniados los *espíritus malignos salían dando alaridos, y un gran número de paralíticos y cojos quedaban sanos. **8**Y aquella ciudad se llenó de alegría.

Simón el hechicero

9Ya desde antes había en esa ciudad un hombre llamado Simón que, jactándose de ser un gran personaje, practicaba la hechicería y asombraba a la gente de Samaria. **10**Todos, desde el más pequeño hasta el más grande, le prestaban atención y exclamaban: «¡Este hombre es al que llaman el Gran Poder de Dios!»

11Lo seguían porque por mucho tiempo los había tenido deslumbrados con sus artes mágicas. **12**Pero cuando creyeron a Felipe, que les anunciaba las buenas *nuevas del reino de Dios y el nombre de *Jesucristo, tanto hombres como mujeres se bautizaron. **13**Simón mismo creyó y, después de bautizarse, seguía a Felipe por todas partes, asombrado de los grandes milagros y señales que veía.

14Cuando los apóstoles que estaban en Jerusalén se enteraron de que los samaritanos habían aceptado la palabra de Dios, les enviaron a Pedro y a Juan. **15**Estos, al llegar, oraron por ellos para que recibieran el Espíritu Santo, **16**porque el Espíritu aún no había descendido sobre ninguno de ellos; solamente habían sido bautizados en el nombre del Señor Jesús. **17**Entonces Pedro y Juan les impusieron las manos, y ellos recibieron el Espíritu Santo.

18Al ver Simón que mediante la imposición de las manos de los apóstoles se daba el Espíritu Santo, les ofreció dinero **19**y les pidió:

—Denme también a mí ese poder, para que todos a quienes yo les imponga las manos reciban el Espíritu Santo.

20—¡Que tu dinero perezca contigo —le contestó Pedro—, porque intentaste comprar el don de Dios con dinero! **21**No tienes arte ni parte en este asunto, porque no eres íntegro delante de Dios. **22**Por eso, *arrepiéntete de tu maldad y ruega al Señor. Tal vez te perdone el haber tenido esa mala intención. **23**Veo que vas camino a la amargura y a la esclavitud del pecado.

24—Rueguen al Señor por mí —respondió Simón—, para que no me suceda nada de lo que han dicho.

25Después de testificar y proclamar la palabra del Señor, Pedro y Juan se pusieron en camino de vuelta a Jerusalén, y de paso predicaron el *evangelio en muchas poblaciones de los samaritanos.

---

e **7:40** Éx 32:1   f **7:43** Am 5:25-27   g **7:46** *para el Dios.* Var. *para la casa* (es decir, la familia). h **7:50** Is 66:1,2   i **7:51** *iTercos . . . oídos!* Lit. *¡Duros de cuello e incircuncisos en los corazones y los oídos!*

Felipe y el etíope

26Un ángel del Señor le dijo a Felipe: «Ponte en marcha hacia el sur, por el camino del desierto que baja de Jerusalén a Gaza.» 27Felipe emprendió el viaje, y resulta que se encontró con un etíope *eunuco, alto funcionario encargado de todo el tesoro de la Candace, reina de los etíopes. Éste había ido a Jerusalén para adorar 28y, en el viaje de regreso a su país, iba sentado en su carro, leyendo el libro del profeta Isaías. 29El Espíritu le dijo a Felipe: «Acércate y júntate a ese carro.»

30Felipe se acercó deprisa al carro y, al oír que el hombre leía al profeta Isaías, le preguntó:

—¿Acaso entiende usted lo que está leyendo?

31—¿Y cómo voy a entenderlo —contestó— si nadie me lo explica?

Así que invitó a Felipe a subir y sentarse con él. 32El pasaje de la Escritura que estaba leyendo era el siguiente:

«Como oveja, fue llevado al matadero;
    y como cordero que enmudece ante su
        trasquilador,
    ni siquiera abrió su boca.
33Lo humillaron y no le hicieron justicia.
    ¿Quién describirá su descendencia?
    Porque su vida fue arrancada de la tierra.»ʲ

34—Dígame usted, por favor, ¿de quién habla aquí el profeta, de sí mismo o de algún otro? —le preguntó el eunuco a Felipe.

35Entonces Felipe, comenzando con ese mismo pasaje de la Escritura, le anunció las buenas *nuevas acerca de Jesús. 36Mientras iban por el camino, llegaron a un lugar donde había agua, y dijo el eunuco:

—Mire usted, aquí hay agua. ¿Qué impide que yo sea bautizado?ᵏ

38Entonces mandó parar el carro, y ambos bajaron al agua, y Felipe lo bautizó. 39Cuando subieron del agua, el Espíritu del Señor se llevó de repente a Felipe. El eunuco no volvió a verlo, pero siguió alegre su camino. 40En cuanto a Felipe, apareció en Azoto, y se fue predicando el *evangelio en todos los pueblos hasta que llegó a Cesarea.

Conversión de Saulo
9:1-19 — Hch 23:3-16; 26:9-18

9 Mientras tanto, Saulo, respirando aún amenazas de muerte contra los discípulos del Señor, se presentó al sumo sacerdote 2y le pidió cartas de extradición para las sinagogas de Damasco. Tenía la intención de encontrar y llevarse presos a Jerusalén a todos los que pertenecieran al Camino, fueran hombres o mujeres. 3En el viaje sucedió que, al acercarse a Damasco, una luz del cielo relampagueó de repente a su alrededor. 4Él cayó al suelo y oyó una voz que le decía:

—Saulo, Saulo, ¿por qué me persigues?

5—¿Quién eres, Señor? —preguntó.

—Yo soy Jesús, a quien tú persigues —contestó la voz—. 6Levántate y entra en la ciudad, que allí se te dirá lo que tienes que hacer.

7Los hombres que viajaban con Saulo se detuvieron atónitos, porque oían la voz pero no veían a nadie. 8Saulo se levantó del suelo, pero cuando abrió los ojos no podía ver, así que lo tomaron de la mano y lo llevaron a Damasco. 9Estuvo ciego tres días, sin comer ni beber nada.

10Había en Damasco un discípulo llamado Ananías, a quien el Señor llamó en una visión.

—¡Ananías!

—Aquí estoy, Señor.

11—Anda, ve a la casa de Judas, en la calle llamada Derecha, y pregunta por un tal Saulo de Tarso. Está orando, 12y ha visto en una visión a un hombre llamado Ananías, que entra y pone las manos sobre él para que recobre la vista.

13Entonces Ananías respondió:

—Señor, he oído hablar mucho de ese hombre y de todo el mal que ha causado a tus *santos en Jerusalén. 14Y ahora lo tenemos aquí, autorizado por los jefes de los sacerdotes, para llevarse presos a todos los que invocan tu nombre.

15—¡Ve! —insistió el Señor—, porque ese hombre es mi instrumento escogido para dar a conocer mi nombre tanto a las *naciones y a sus reyes como al pueblo de Israel. 16Yo le mostraré cuánto tendrá que padecer por mi nombre.

17Ananías se fue y, cuando llegó a la casa, le impuso las manos a Saulo y le dijo: «Hermano Saulo, el Señor Jesús, que se te apareció en el camino, me ha enviado para que recobres la vista y seas lleno del Espíritu Santo.» 18Al instante cayó de los ojos de Saulo algo como escamas, y recobró la vista. Se levantó y fue bautizado; 19y habiendo comido, recobró las fuerzas.

Saulo en Damasco y en Jerusalén

Saulo pasó varios días con los discípulos que estaban en Damasco, 20y en seguida se dedicó a predicar en las sinagogas, afirmando que Jesús es el Hijo de Dios.

21Todos los que le oían se quedaban asombrados, y preguntaban: «¿No es éste el que en Jerusalén perseguía a muerte a los que invocan ese nombre? ¿Y no ha venido aquí para llevárselos presos y entregarlos a los jefes de los sacerdotes?» 22Pero Saulo cobraba cada vez más fuerza y confundía a los judíos que vivían en Damasco, demostrándoles que Jesús es el *Mesías.

23Después de muchos días, los judíos se pusieron de acuerdo para hacerlo desaparecer, 24pero Saulo se enteró de sus maquinaciones. Día y noche vigilaban de cerca las puertas de la ciudad con el fin de eliminarlo. 25Pero sus discípulos se lo llevaron de noche y lo bajaron en un canasto por una abertura en la muralla.

26Cuando llegó a Jerusalén, trataba de juntarse con los discípulos, pero todos tenían miedo de él, porque no creían que de veras fuera discípulo. 27Entonces Bernabé lo tomó a su cargo y lo llevó a los apóstoles. Saulo les describió en detalle cómo en el camino había visto al Señor, el cual le había hablado, y cómo en Damasco había predicado con libertad en el nombre de Jesús. 28Así que se quedó con ellos, y andaba por todas partes en Jerusalén, hablando abiertamente en el nombre del Señor. 29Conversaba y discutía con los judíos de habla griega,ˡ pero ellos se proponían eliminarlo. 30Cuando se enteraron de ello los hermanos, se lo llevaron a Cesarea y de allí lo mandaron a Tarso.

31Mientras tanto, la iglesia disfrutaba de paz a la vez que se consolidaba en toda Judea, Galilea y Samaria, pues vivía en el temor del Señor. E iba creciendo en número, fortalecida por el Espíritu Santo.

ʲ 8:33 Is 53:7,8 ᵏ 8:36 bautizado? Var. bautizado? / 37—Si cree usted de todo corazón, bien puede —le dijo Felipe. / —Creo que Jesucristo es el Hijo de Dios —contestó el hombre. ˡ 9:29 los judíos de habla griega. Lit. los helenistas.

Eneas y Dorcas

³²Pedro, que estaba recorriendo toda la región, fue también a visitar a los *santos que vivían en Lida. ³³Allí encontró a un paralítico llamado Eneas, que llevaba ocho años en cama. ³⁴«Eneas —le dijo Pedro—, *Jesucristo te sana. Levántate y tiende tu cama.» Y al instante se levantó. ³⁵Todos los que vivían en Lida y en Sarón lo vieron, y se convirtieron al Señor.

³⁶Había en Jope una discípula llamada Tabita (que traducido es Dorcasᵐ). Ésta se esmeraba en hacer buenas obras y en ayudar a los pobres. ³⁷Sucedió que en esos días cayó enferma y murió. Pusieron el cadáver, después de lavarlo, en un cuarto de la planta alta. ³⁸Y como Lida estaba cerca de Jope, los discípulos, al enterarse de que Pedro se encontraba en Lida, enviaron a dos hombres a rogarle: «¡Por favor, venga usted a Jope en seguida!»

³⁹Sin demora, Pedro se fue con ellos, y cuando llegó lo llevaron al cuarto de arriba. Todas las viudas se presentaron, llorando y mostrándole las túnicas y otros vestidos que Dorcas había hecho cuando aún estaba con ellas.

⁴⁰Pedro hizo que todos salieran del cuarto; luego se puso de rodillas y oró. Volviéndose hacia la muerta, dijo: «Tabita, levántate.» Ella abrió los ojos y, al ver a Pedro, se incorporó. ⁴¹Él, tomándola de la mano, la levantó. Luego llamó a los *creyentes y a las viudas, a quienes la presentó viva. ⁴²La noticia se difundió por todo Jope, y muchos creyeron en el Señor. ⁴³Pedro se quedó en Jope un buen tiempo, en casa de un tal Simón, que era curtidor.

Cornelio manda llamar a Pedro

10 Vivía en Cesarea un centurión llamado Cornelio, del regimiento conocido como el Italiano. ²Él y toda su familia eran devotos y temerosos de Dios. Realizaba muchas obras de beneficencia para el pueblo judío y oraba a Dios constantemente. ³Un día, como a las tres de la tarde,ⁿ tuvo una visión. Vio claramente a un ángel de Dios que se acercaba y le decía:

—¡Cornelio!

⁴—¿Qué quieres, Señor? —le preguntó Cornelio, mirándolo fijamente y con mucho miedo.

—Dios ha recibido tus oraciones y tus obras de beneficencia como una ofrenda —le contestó el ángel—. ⁵Envía de inmediato a algunos hombres a Jope para que hagan venir a un tal Simón, apodado Pedro. ⁶Él se hospeda con Simón el curtidor, que tiene su casa junto al mar.

⁷Después de que se fue el ángel que le había hablado, Cornelio llamó a dos de sus siervos y a un soldado devoto de los que le servían regularmente. ⁸Les explicó todo lo que había sucedido y los envió a Jope.

La visión de Pedro

⁹Al día siguiente, mientras ellos iban de camino y se acercaban a la ciudad, Pedro subió a la azotea a orar. Era casi el mediodía.ñ ¹⁰Tuvo hambre y quiso algo de comer. Mientras se lo preparaban, le sobrevino un éxtasis. ¹¹Vio el cielo abierto y algo parecido a una gran sábana que, suspendida por las cuatro puntas, descendía hacia la tierra. ¹²En ella había toda clase de cuadrúpedos, como también reptiles y aves.

¹³—Levántate, Pedro; mata y come —le dijo una voz.

¹⁴—¡De ninguna manera, Señor! —replicó Pedro—. Jamás he comido nada *impuro o inmundo.

¹⁵Por segunda vez le insistió la voz:

—Lo que Dios ha purificado, tú no lo llames impuro.

¹⁶Esto sucedió tres veces, y en seguida la sábana fue recogida al cielo.

¹⁷Pedro no atinaba a explicarse cuál podría ser el significado de la visión. Mientras tanto, los hombres enviados por Cornelio, que estaban preguntando por la casa de Simón, se presentaron a la puerta. ¹⁸Llamando, averiguaron si allí se hospedaba Simón, apodado Pedro.

¹⁹Mientras Pedro seguía reflexionando sobre el significado de la visión, el Espíritu le dijo: «Mira, Simón, tres⁰ hombres te buscan. ²⁰Date prisa, baja y no dudes en ir con ellos, porque yo los he enviado.»

²¹Pedro bajó y les dijo a los hombres:

—Aquí estoy; yo soy el que ustedes buscan. ¿Qué asunto los ha traído por acá?

²²Ellos le contestaron:

—Venimos de parte del centurión Cornelio, un hombre justo y temeroso de Dios, respetado por todo el pueblo judío. Un ángel de Dios le dio instrucciones de invitarlo a usted a su casa para escuchar lo que usted tiene que decirle.

²³Entonces Pedro los invitó a pasar y los hospedó.

Pedro en casa de Cornelio

Al día siguiente, Pedro se fue con ellos acompañado de algunos creyentes de Jope.

²⁴Un día después llegó a Cesarea. Cornelio estaba esperándolo con los parientes y amigos íntimos que había reunido. ²⁵Al llegar Pedro a la casa, Cornelio salió a recibirlo y, postrándose delante de él, le rindió homenaje. ²⁶Pero Pedro hizo que se levantara, y le dijo:

—Ponte de pie, que sólo soy un hombre como tú.

²⁷Pedro entró en la casa conversando con él, y encontró a muchos reunidos.

²⁸Entonces les habló así:

—Ustedes saben muy bien que nuestra ley prohíbe que un judío se junte con un extranjero o lo visite. Pero Dios me ha hecho ver que a nadie debe llamar *impuro o inmundo. ²⁹Por eso, cuando mandaron por mí, vine sin poner ninguna objeción. Ahora permítanme preguntarles: ¿para qué me hicieron venir?

³⁰Cornelio contestó:

—Hace cuatro días a esta misma hora, las tres de la tarde, estaba yo en casa orando.ᵖ De repente apareció delante de mí un hombre vestido con ropa brillante, ³¹y me dijo: "Cornelio, Dios ha oído tu oración y se ha acordado de tus obras de beneficencia. ³²Por lo tanto, envía a alguien a Jope para hacer venir a Simón, apodado Pedro, que se hospeda en casa de Simón el curtidor, junto al mar." ³³Así que inmediatamente mandé a llamarte, y tú has tenido la bondad de venir. Ahora estamos todos aquí, en la presencia de Dios, para escuchar todo lo que el Señor te ha encomendado que nos digas.

³⁴Pedro tomó la palabra y dijo:

—Ahora comprendo que en realidad para Dios no hay favoritismos, ³⁵sino que en toda nación él ve con agrado a los que le temen y actúan con justicia. ³⁶Dios envió su mensaje al pueblo de Israel, anunciando las buenas *nuevas de la paz por medio de *Je-

---

ᵐ **9:36** Tanto *Tabita* (arameo) como *Dorcas* (griego) significan *gacela.* ⁿ **10:3** *las tres de la tarde.* Lit. *la hora novena;* también en v. 30. ñ **10:9** *casi el mediodía.* Lit. *alrededor de la hora sexta.* ⁰ **10:19** Var. no incluye *tres* (un ms. antiguo dice: *dos*). ᵖ **10:30** *en casa orando.* Var. *en casa ayunando y orando.*

sucristo, que es el Señor de todos. ³⁷Ustedes conocen este mensaje que se difundió por toda Judea, comenzando desde Galilea, después del bautismo que predicó Juan. ³⁸Me refiero a Jesús de Nazaret: cómo lo ungió Dios con el Espíritu Santo y con poder, y cómo anduvo haciendo el bien y sanando a todos los que estaban oprimidos por el diablo, porque Dios estaba con él. ³⁹Nosotros somos testigos de todo lo que hizo en la tierra de los judíos y en Jerusalén. Lo mataron, colgándolo de un madero, ⁴⁰pero Dios lo resucitó al tercer día y dispuso que se apareciera, ⁴¹no a todo el pueblo, sino a nosotros, testigos previamente escogidos por Dios, que comimos y bebimos con él después de su *resurrección. ⁴²Él nos mandó a predicar al pueblo y a dar solemne testimonio de que ha sido nombrado por Dios como juez de vivos y muertos. ⁴³De él dan testimonio todos los profetas, que todo el que cree en él recibe, por medio de su nombre, el perdón de los pecados.

⁴⁴Mientras Pedro estaba todavía hablando, el Espíritu Santo descendió sobre todos los que escuchaban el mensaje. ⁴⁵Los defensores de la circuncisión que habían llegado con Pedro se quedaron asombrados de que el don del Espíritu Santo se hubiera derramado también sobre los *gentiles, ⁴⁶pues los oían hablar en *lenguas y alabar a Dios. Entonces Pedro respondió:

⁴⁷—¿Acaso puede alguien negar el agua para que sean bautizados estos que han recibido el Espíritu Santo lo mismo que nosotros?

⁴⁸Y mandó que fueran bautizados en el nombre de Jesucristo. Entonces le pidieron que se quedara con ellos algunos días.

Pedro explica su comportamiento

11 Los apóstoles y los hermanos de toda Judea se enteraron de que también los *gentiles habían recibido la palabra de Dios. ²Así que cuando Pedro subió a Jerusalén, los defensores de la circuncisión lo criticaron ³diciendo:

—Entraste en casa de hombres incircuncisos y comiste con ellos.

⁴Entonces Pedro comenzó a explicarles paso a paso lo que había sucedido:

⁵—Yo estaba orando en la ciudad de Jope y tuve en éxtasis una visión. Vi que del cielo descendía algo parecido a una gran sábana, que, suspendida por las cuatro puntas, bajaba hasta donde yo estaba. ⁶Me fijé en lo que había en ella, y vi cuadrúpedos, fieras, reptiles y aves. ⁷Luego oí una voz que me decía: "Levántate, Pedro; mata y come." ⁸Repliqué: "¡De ninguna manera, Señor! Jamás ha entrado en mi boca nada *impuro o inmundo." ⁹Por segunda vez insistió la voz del cielo: "Lo que Dios ha purificado, tú no lo llames impuro." ¹⁰Esto sucedió tres veces, y luego todo volvió a ser llevado al cielo.

¹¹»En aquel momento se presentaron en la casa donde yo estaba tres hombres que desde Cesarea habían sido enviados a verme. ¹²El Espíritu me dijo que fuera con ellos sin dudar. También fueron conmigo estos seis hermanos, y entramos en la casa de aquel hombre. ¹³Él nos contó cómo en su casa se le había aparecido un ángel que le dijo: "Manda a alguien a Jope para hacer venir a Simón, apodado Pedro. ¹⁴Él te traerá un mensaje mediante el cual serán salvos tú y toda tu familia."

¹⁵»Cuando comencé a hablarles, el Espíritu Santo descendió sobre ellos tal como al principio descendió sobre nosotros. ¹⁶Entonces recordé lo que había dicho el Señor: "Juan bautizó con⁹ agua, pero ustedes serán bautizados con el Espíritu Santo." ¹⁷Por tanto, si Dios les ha dado a ellos el mismo don que a nosotros al creer en el Señor *Jesucristo, ¿quién soy yo para pretender estorbar a Dios?

¹⁸Al oír esto, se apaciguaron y alabaron a Dios diciendo:

—¡Así que también a los gentiles les ha concedido Dios el *arrepentimiento para vida!

La iglesia en Antioquía

¹⁹Los que se habían dispersado a causa de la persecución que se desató por el caso de Esteban llegaron hasta Fenicia, Chipre y Antioquía, sin anunciar a nadie el mensaje excepto a los judíos. ²⁰Sin embargo, había entre ellos algunas personas de Chipre y de Cirene que, al llegar a Antioquía, comenzaron a hablarles también a los de habla griega, anunciándoles las buenas *nuevas acerca del Señor Jesús. ²¹El poder del Señor estaba con ellos, y un gran número creyó y se convirtió al Señor.

²²La noticia de estos sucesos llegó a oídos de la iglesia de Jerusalén, y mandaron a Bernabé a Antioquía. ²³Cuando él llegó y vio las evidencias de la gracia de Dios, se alegró y animó a todos a hacerse el firme propósito de permanecer fieles al Señor, ²⁴pues era un hombre bueno, lleno del Espíritu Santo y de fe. Un gran número de personas aceptó al Señor.

²⁵Después partió Bernabé para Tarso en busca de Saulo, ²⁶y cuando lo encontró, lo llevó a Antioquía. Durante todo un año se reunieron los dos con la iglesia y enseñaron a mucha gente. Fue en Antioquía donde a los discípulos se les llamó «cristianos» por primera vez.

²⁷Por aquel tiempo unos profetas bajaron de Jerusalén a Antioquía. ²⁸Uno de ellos, llamado Ágabo, se puso de pie y predijo por medio del Espíritu que iba a haber una gran hambre en todo el mundo, lo cual sucedió durante el reinado de Claudio. ²⁹Entonces decidieron que cada uno de los discípulos, según los recursos de cada cual, enviaría ayuda a los hermanos que vivían en Judea. ³⁰Así lo hicieron, mandando su ofrenda a los *ancianos por medio de Bernabé y de Saulo.

Pedro escapa milagrosamente de la cárcel

12 En ese tiempo el rey Herodes hizo arrestar a algunos de la iglesia con el fin de maltratarlos. ²A *Jacobo, hermano de Juan, lo mandó matar a espada. ³Al ver que esto agradaba a los judíos, procedió a prender también a Pedro. Esto sucedió durante la fiesta de los Panes sin levadura. ⁴Después de arrestarlo, lo metió en la cárcel y lo puso bajo la vigilancia de cuatro grupos de cuatro soldados cada uno. Tenía la intención de hacerlo comparecer en juicio público después de la Pascua. ⁵Pero mientras mantenían a Pedro en la cárcel, la iglesia oraba constante y fervientemente a Dios por él.

⁶La misma noche en que Herodes estaba a punto de sacar a Pedro para someterlo a juicio, éste dormía entre dos soldados, sujeto con dos cadenas. Unos guardias vigilaban la entrada de la cárcel. ⁷De repente apareció un ángel del Señor y una luz resplandeció en la celda. Despertó a Pedro con unas palmadas en el costado y le dijo: «¡Date prisa, levántate!» Las cadenas cayeron de las manos de Pedro. ⁸Le dijo además el ángel: «Vístete y cálzate las sandalias.» Así

---

q **11:16** con. Alt. *en.*

lo hizo, y el ángel añadió: «Échate la capa encima y sígueme.»

[9]Pedro salió tras él, pero no sabía si realmente estaba sucediendo lo que el ángel hacía. Le parecía que se trataba de una visión. [10]Pasaron por la primera y la segunda guardia, y llegaron al portón de hierro que daba a la ciudad. El portón se les abrió por sí solo, y salieron. Caminaron unas cuadras, y de repente el ángel lo dejó solo.

[11]Entonces Pedro volvió en sí y se dijo: «Ahora estoy completamente seguro de que el Señor ha enviado a su ángel para librarme del poder de Herodes y de todo lo que el pueblo judío esperaba.»

[12]Cuando cayó en cuenta de esto, fue a casa de María, la madre de Juan, apodado Marcos, donde muchas personas estaban reunidas orando. [13]Llamó a la puerta de la calle, y salió a responder una sierva llamada Rode. [14]Al reconocer la voz de Pedro, se puso tan contenta que volvió corriendo sin abrir.

—¡Pedro está a la puerta! —exclamó.

[15]—¡Estás loca! —le dijeron.

Ella insistía en que así era, pero los otros decían:

—Debe de ser su ángel.

[16]Entre tanto, Pedro seguía llamando. Cuando abrieron la puerta y lo vieron, quedaron pasmados. [17]Con la mano Pedro les hizo señas de que se callaran, y les contó cómo el Señor lo había sacado de la cárcel.

—Cuéntenles esto a Jacobo y a los hermanos —les dijo.

Luego salió y se fue a otro lugar.

[18]Al amanecer se produjo un gran alboroto entre los soldados respecto al paradero de Pedro. [19]Herodes hizo averiguaciones, pero al no encontrarlo, les tomó declaración a las guardias y mandó matarlos. Después viajó de Judea a Cesarea y se quedó allí.

Muerte de Herodes

[20]Herodes estaba furioso con los de Tiro y de Sidón, pero ellos se pusieron de acuerdo y se presentaron ante él. Habiéndose ganado el favor de Blasto, camarero del rey, pidieron paz, porque su región dependía del país del rey para obtener sus provisiones. [21]El día señalado, Herodes, ataviado con su ropaje real y sentado en su trono, le dirigió un discurso al pueblo. [22]La gente gritaba: «¡Voz de un dios, no de hombre!» [23]Al instante un ángel del Señor lo hirió, porque no le había dado la gloria a Dios; y Herodes murió comido de gusanos.

[24]Pero la palabra de Dios seguía extendiéndose y difundiéndose.

[25]Cuando Bernabé y Saulo cumplieron su servicio, regresaron de[r] Jerusalén llevando con ellos a Juan, llamado también Marcos.

Despedida de Bernabé y Saulo

13 En la iglesia de Antioquía eran profetas y maestros Bernabé; Simeón, apodado el Negro; Lucio de Cirene; Manaén, que se había criado con Herodes el tetrarca; y Saulo. [2]Mientras ayunaban y participaban en el culto al Señor, el Espíritu Santo dijo: «Apártenme ahora a Bernabé y a Saulo para el trabajo al que los he llamado.»

[3]Así que después de ayunar, orar e imponerles las manos, los despidieron.

En Chipre

[4]Bernabé y Saulo, enviados por el Espíritu Santo, bajaron a Seleucia, y de allí navegaron a Chipre. [5]Al llegar a Salamina, predicaron la palabra de Dios en las sinagogas de los judíos. Tenían también a Juan como ayudante.

[6]Recorrieron toda la isla hasta Pafos. Allí se encontraron con un hechicero, un falso profeta judío llamado Barjesús, [7]que estaba con el gobernador[s] Sergio Paulo. El gobernador, hombre inteligente, mandó llamar a Bernabé y a Saulo, en un esfuerzo por escuchar la palabra de Dios. [8]Pero Elimas el hechicero (que es lo que significa su nombre) se les oponía y procuraba apartar de la fe al gobernador. [9]Entonces Saulo, o sea Pablo, lleno del Espíritu Santo, clavó los ojos en Elimas y le dijo: [10]«¡Hijo del diablo y enemigo de toda justicia, lleno de todo tipo de engaño y de fraude! ¿Nunca dejarás de torcer los caminos rectos del Señor? [11]Ahora la mano del Señor está contra ti; vas a quedarte ciego y por algún tiempo no podrás ver la luz del sol.»

Al instante cayeron sobre él sombra y oscuridad, y comenzó a buscar a tientas quien lo llevara de la mano. [12]Al ver lo sucedido, el gobernador creyó, maravillado de la enseñanza acerca del Señor.

En Antioquía de Pisidia

[13]Pablo y sus compañeros se hicieron a la mar desde Pafos, y llegaron a Perge de Panfilia. Juan se separó de ellos y regresó a Jerusalén; [14]ellos, por su parte, siguieron su viaje desde Perge hasta Antioquía de Pisidia. El *sábado entraron en la sinagoga y se sentaron. [15]Al terminar la lectura de la ley y los profetas, los jefes de la sinagoga mandaron a decirles: «Hermanos, si tienen algún mensaje de aliento para el pueblo, hablen.»

[16]Pablo se puso en pie, hizo una señal con la mano y dijo: «Escúchenme, israelitas, y ustedes, los *gentiles temerosos de Dios: [17]El Dios de este pueblo de Israel escogió a nuestros antepasados y engrandeció al pueblo mientras vivían como extranjeros en Egipto. Con gran poder los sacó de aquella tierra [18]y soportó su mal proceder[t] en el desierto unos cuarenta años. [19]Luego de destruir siete naciones en Canaán, dio a su pueblo la tierra de ellas en herencia. [20]Todo esto duró unos cuatrocientos cincuenta años.

»Después de esto, Dios les asignó jueces hasta los días del profeta Samuel. [21]Entonces pidieron un rey, y Dios les dio a Saúl, hijo de Quis, de la tribu de Benjamín, que gobernó por cuarenta años. [22]Tras destituir a Saúl, les puso por rey a David, de quien dio este testimonio: "He encontrado en David, hijo de Isaí, un hombre conforme a mi corazón; él realizará todo lo que yo quiero."

[23]»De los descendientes de éste, conforme a la promesa, Dios ha provisto a Israel un salvador, que es Jesús. [24]Antes de la venida de Jesús, Juan predicó un bautismo de *arrepentimiento a todo el pueblo de Israel. [25]Cuando estaba completando su carrera, Juan decía: "¿Quién suponen ustedes que soy? No soy aquél. Miren, después de mí viene uno a quien no soy digno ni siquiera de desatarle las sandalias."

[26]»Hermanos, descendientes de Abraham, y ustedes, los gentiles temerosos de Dios: a nosotros se nos ha enviado este mensaje de salvación. [27]Los habitantes de Jerusalén y sus gobernantes no reconocieron a Jesús. Por tanto, al condenarlo, cumplieron las palabras de los profetas que se leen todos los sábados. [28]Aunque no encontraron ninguna causa digna de muerte, le pidieron a Pilato que lo mandara a ejecutar. [29]Después de llevar a cabo todas las cosas que

---

[r] **12:25** *regresaron de.* Var. *regresaron a.* [s] **13:7** *gobernador.* Lit. *procónsul;* también en vv. 8 y 12. [t] **13:18** *soportó su mal proceder.* Var. *los cuidó.*

estaban escritas acerca de él, lo bajaron del madero y lo sepultaron. ³⁰Pero Dios lo *levantó de entre los muertos. ³¹Durante muchos días lo vieron los que habían subido con él de Galilea a Jerusalén, y ellos son ahora sus testigos ante el pueblo.

³²»Nosotros les anunciamos a ustedes las buenas *nuevas respecto a la promesa hecha a nuestros antepasados. ³³Dios nos la ha cumplido plenamente a nosotros, los descendientes de ellos, al resucitar a Jesús. Como está escrito en el segundo salmo:

»"Tú eres mi hijo;
    hoy mismo te he engendrado."^u

³⁴Dios lo *resucitó para que no volviera jamás a la corrupción. Así se cumplieron estas palabras:

»"Yo les daré las bendiciones santas y seguras
    prometidas a David."^v

³⁵Por eso dice en otro pasaje:

»"No permitirás que el fin de tu santo sea la
    corrupción."^w

³⁶»Ciertamente David, después de servir a su propia generación conforme al propósito de Dios, murió, fue sepultado con sus antepasados, y su cuerpo sufrió la corrupción. ³⁷Pero aquel a quien Dios resucitó no sufrió la corrupción de su cuerpo. ³⁸Por tanto, hermanos, sepan que por medio de Jesús se les anuncia a ustedes el perdón de los pecados. ³⁹Ustedes no pudieron ser *justificados de esos pecados por la ley de Moisés, pero todo el que cree es justificado por medio de Jesús. ⁴⁰Tengan cuidado, no sea que les suceda lo que han dicho los profetas:

⁴¹»"¡Miren, burlones!
    ¡Asómbrense y desaparezcan!
Estoy por hacer en estos días una obra
    que ustedes nunca creerán,
    aunque alguien se la explique."^x»

⁴²Al salir ellos de la sinagoga, los invitaron a que el siguiente sábado les hablaran más de estas cosas. ⁴³Cuando se disolvió la asamblea, muchos judíos y prosélitos fieles acompañaron a Pablo y a Bernabé, los cuales en su conversación con ellos les instaron a perseverar en la gracia de Dios.

⁴⁴El siguiente sábado casi toda la ciudad se congregó para oír la palabra del Señor. ⁴⁵Pero cuando los judíos vieron a las multitudes, se llenaron de celos y contradecían con maldiciones lo que Pablo decía. ⁴⁶Pablo y Bernabé les contestaron valientemente: «Era necesario que les anunciáramos la palabra de Dios primero a ustedes. Como la rechazan y no se consideran dignos de la vida eterna, ahora vamos a dirigirnos a los gentiles. ⁴⁷Así nos lo ha mandado el Señor:

»"Te he puesto por luz para las *naciones,
    a fin de que lleves mi salvación hasta los
    confines de la tierra."^y»

⁴⁸Al oír esto, los gentiles se alegraron y celebraron la palabra del Señor; y creyeron todos los que estaban destinados a la vida eterna.

⁴⁹La palabra del Señor se difundía por toda la región. ⁵⁰Pero los judíos incitaron a mujeres muy distinguidas y favorables al judaísmo, y a los hombres más prominentes de la ciudad, y provocaron una persecución contra Pablo y Bernabé. Por tanto, los expulsaron de la región. ⁵¹Ellos, por su parte, se sa-

cudieron el polvo de los pies en señal de protesta contra la ciudad, y se fueron a Iconio. ⁵²Y los discípulos quedaron llenos de alegría y del Espíritu Santo.

En Iconio

¹⁴ En Iconio, Pablo y Bernabé entraron, como de costumbre, en la sinagoga judía y hablaron de tal manera que creyó una multitud de judíos y de *griegos. ²Pero los judíos incrédulos incitaron a los *gentiles y les amargaron el ánimo contra los hermanos. ³En todo caso, Pablo y Bernabé pasaron allí bastante tiempo, hablando valientemente en el nombre del Señor, quien confirmaba el mensaje de su gracia, haciendo señales y prodigios por medio de ellos. ⁴La gente de la ciudad estaba dividida: unos estaban de parte de los judíos, y otros de parte de los apóstoles. ⁵Hubo un complot tanto de los gentiles como de los judíos, apoyados por sus dirigentes, para maltratarlos y apedrearlos. ⁶Al darse cuenta de esto, los apóstoles huyeron a Listra y a Derbe, ciudades de Licaonia, y a sus alrededores, ⁷donde siguieron anunciando las buenas *nuevas.

En Listra y Derbe

⁸En Listra vivía un hombre lisiado de nacimiento, que no podía mover las piernas y nunca había caminado. Estaba sentado, ⁹escuchando a Pablo, quien al reparar en él y ver que tenía fe para ser sanado, ¹⁰le ordenó con voz fuerte:

—¡Ponte en pie y enderézate!

El hombre dio un salto y empezó a caminar. ¹¹Al ver lo que Pablo había hecho, la gente comenzó a gritar en el idioma de Licaonia:

—¡Los dioses han tomado forma humana y han venido a visitarnos!

¹²A Bernabé lo llamaban Zeus, y a Pablo, Hermes, porque era el que dirigía la palabra. ¹³El sacerdote de Zeus, cuyo templo estaba a las afueras de la ciudad, llevó toros y guirnaldas a las puertas y, con toda la multitud, quería ofrecerles sacrificios.

¹⁴Al enterarse de esto los apóstoles Bernabé y Pablo, se rasgaron las vestiduras y se lanzaron por entre la multitud, gritando:

¹⁵—Señores, ¿por qué hacen esto? Nosotros también somos hombres mortales como ustedes. Las buenas *nuevas que les anunciamos es que dejen estas cosas sin valor y se vuelvan al Dios viviente, que hizo el cielo, la tierra, el mar y todo lo que hay en ellos. ¹⁶En épocas pasadas él permitió que todas las *naciones siguieran su propio camino. ¹⁷Sin embargo, no ha dejado de dar testimonio de sí mismo haciendo el bien, dándoles lluvias del cielo y estaciones fructíferas, proporcionándoles comida y alegría de corazón.

¹⁸A pesar de todo lo que dijeron, a duras penas evitaron que la multitud les ofreciera sacrificios.

¹⁹En eso llegaron de Antioquía y de Iconio unos judíos que hicieron cambiar de parecer a la multitud. Apedrearon a Pablo y lo arrastraron fuera de la ciudad, creyendo que estaba muerto. ²⁰Pero cuando lo rodearon los discípulos, él se levantó y volvió a entrar en la ciudad. Al día siguiente, partió para Derbe en compañía de Bernabé.

El regreso a Antioquía de Siria

²¹Después de anunciar las buenas *nuevas en aquella ciudad y de hacer muchos discípulos, Pablo y Bernabé regresaron a Listra, a Iconio y a Antioquía, ²²fortaleciendo a los discípulos y animándolos a perseverar en la fe. «Es necesario pasar por mu-

u 13:33 Sal 2:7   v 13:34 Is 55:3   w 13:35 Sal 16:10   x 13:41 Hab 1:5   y 13:47 Is 49:6

chas dificultades para entrar en el reino de Dios», les decían.

²³En cada iglesia nombraron *ancianos y, con oración y ayuno, los encomendaron al Señor, en quien habían creído. ²⁴Atravesando Pisidia, llegaron a Panfilia,

²⁵y cuando terminaron de predicar la palabra en Perge, bajaron a Atalia.

²⁶De Atalia navegaron a Antioquía, donde se los había encomendado a la gracia de Dios para la obra que ya habían realizado.

²⁷Cuando llegaron, reunieron a la iglesia e informaron de todo lo que Dios había hecho por medio de ellos, y de cómo había abierto la puerta de la fe a los *gentiles.

²⁸Y se quedaron allí mucho tiempo con los discípulos.

El concilio de Jerusalén

15 Algunos que habían llegado de Judea a Antioquía se pusieron a enseñar a los hermanos: «A menos que ustedes se circunciden, conforme a la tradición de Moisés, no pueden ser salvos.» ²Esto provocó un altercado y un serio debate de Pablo y Bernabé con ellos. Entonces se decidió que Pablo y Bernabé, y algunos otros creyentes, subieran a Jerusalén para tratar este asunto con los apóstoles y los *ancianos. ³Enviados por la iglesia, al pasar por Fenicia y Samaria contaron cómo se habían convertido los *gentiles. Estas noticias llenaron de alegría a todos los creyentes. ⁴Al llegar a Jerusalén, fueron muy bien recibidos tanto por la iglesia como por los apóstoles y los ancianos, a quienes informaron de todo lo que Dios había hecho por medio de ellos.

⁵Entonces intervinieron algunos creyentes que pertenecían a la secta de los *fariseos y afirmaron:

—Es necesario circuncidar a los gentiles y exigirles que obedezcan la ley de Moisés.

⁶Los apóstoles y los ancianos se reunieron para examinar este asunto. ⁷Después de una larga discusión, Pedro tomó la palabra:

—Hermanos, ustedes saben que desde un principio Dios me escogió de entre ustedes para que por mi boca los gentiles oyeran el mensaje del *evangelio y creyeran. ⁸Dios, que conoce el corazón humano, mostró que los aceptaba dándoles el Espíritu Santo, lo mismo que a nosotros. ⁹Sin hacer distinción alguna entre nosotros y ellos, purificó sus corazones por la fe. ¹⁰Entonces, ¿por qué tratan ahora de provocar a Dios poniendo sobre el cuello de esos discípulos un yugo que ni nosotros ni nuestros antepasados hemos podido soportar? ¹¹¡No puede ser! Más bien, como ellos, creemos que somos salvos^z por la gracia de nuestro Señor Jesús.

¹²Toda la asamblea guardó silencio para escuchar a Bernabé y a Pablo, que les contaron las señales y prodigios que Dios había hecho por medio de ellos entre los gentiles. ¹³Cuando terminaron, *Jacobo tomó la palabra y dijo:

—Hermanos, escúchenme. ¹⁴*Simón^a nos ha expuesto cómo Dios desde el principio tuvo a bien escoger de entre los gentiles un pueblo para honra de su nombre. ¹⁵Con esto concuerdan las palabras de los profetas, tal como está escrito:

¹⁶»"Después de esto volveré

y reedificaré la choza caída de David.
Reedificaré sus ruinas,
y la restauraré,
¹⁷para que busque al Señor el resto de la
*humanidad,
todas las *naciones que llevan mi nombre.
¹⁸Así dice el Señor, que hace estas cosas"^b
conocidas desde tiempos antiguos.^c

¹⁹»Por lo tanto, yo considero que debemos dejar de ponerles trabas a los gentiles que se convierten a Dios. ²⁰Más bien debemos escribirles que se abstengan de lo *contaminado por los ídolos, de la inmoralidad sexual, de la carne de animales estrangulados y de sangre. ²¹En efecto, desde tiempos antiguos Moisés siempre ha tenido en cada ciudad quien lo predique y lo lea en las sinagogas todos los *sábados.

Carta del concilio a los creyentes gentiles

²²Entonces los apóstoles y los *ancianos, de común acuerdo con toda la iglesia, decidieron escoger a algunos de ellos y enviarlos a Antioquía con Pablo y Bernabé. Escogieron a Judas, llamado Barsabás, y a Silas, que tenían buena reputación entre los hermanos. ²³Con ellos mandaron la siguiente carta:

Los apóstoles y los ancianos,

a nuestros hermanos *gentiles en Antioquía, Siria y Cilicia:

Saludos.

²⁴Nos hemos enterado de que algunos de los nuestros, sin nuestra autorización, los han inquietado a ustedes, alarmándolos con lo que les han dicho. ²⁵Así que de común acuerdo hemos decidido escoger a algunos hombres y enviarlos a ustedes con nuestros queridos hermanos Pablo y Bernabé, ²⁶quienes han arriesgado su *vida por el nombre de nuestro Señor *Jesucristo. ²⁷Por tanto, les enviamos a Judas y a Silas para que les confirmen personalmente lo que les escribimos. ²⁸Nos pareció bien al Espíritu Santo y a nosotros no imponerles a ustedes ninguna carga aparte de los siguientes requisitos: ²⁹abstenerse de lo sacrificado a los ídolos, de sangre, de la carne de animales estrangulados y de la inmoralidad sexual. Bien harán ustedes si evitan estas cosas.

Con nuestros mejores deseos.

³⁰Una vez despedidos, ellos bajaron a Antioquía, donde reunieron a la congregación y entregaron la carta. ³¹Los creyentes la leyeron y se alegraron por su mensaje alentador. ³²Judas y Silas, que también eran profetas, hablaron extensamente para animarlos y fortalecerlos. ³³Después de pasar algún tiempo allí, los hermanos los despidieron en paz, para que regresaran a quienes los habían enviado.^d ³⁵Pablo y Bernabé permanecieron en Antioquía, enseñando y anunciando la palabra del Señor en compañía de muchos otros.

Desacuerdo entre Pablo y Bernabé

³⁶Algún tiempo después, Pablo le dijo a Bernabé: «Volvamos a visitar a los creyentes en todas las ciudades en donde hemos anunciado la palabra del Señor, y veamos cómo están.» ³⁷Resulta que Bernabé

---

^z **15:11** *que somos salvos.* Alt. *a fin de ser salvos.* ^a **15:14** *Simón.* Lit. *Simeón.* ^b **15:18** Am 9:11,12 ^c **15:18** "*... que hace ... antiguos.* Var. "*... que hace todas estas cosas*"; *conocidas del Señor son todas sus obras desde tiempos antiguos.* ^d **15:33** *enviado.* Var. *enviado,* 34*pero Silas decidió quedarse.*

quería llevar con ellos a Juan Marcos, 38pero a Pablo no le pareció prudente llevarlo, porque los había abandonado en Panfilia y no había seguido con ellos en el trabajo. 39Se produjo entre ellos un conflicto tan serio que acabaron por separarse. Bernabé se llevó a Marcos y se embarcó rumbo a Chipre, 40mientras que Pablo escogió a Silas. Después de que los hermanos lo encomendaron a la gracia del Señor, Pablo partió 41y viajó por Siria y Cilicia, consolidando a las iglesias.

Timoteo se une a Pablo y a Silas

16 Llegó Pablo a Derbe y después a Listra, donde se encontró con un discípulo llamado Timoteo, hijo de una mujer judía creyente, pero de padre *griego. 2Los hermanos en Listra y en Iconio hablaban bien de Timoteo, 3así que Pablo decidió llevárselo. Por causa de los judíos que vivían en aquella región, lo circuncidó, pues todos sabían que su padre era griego. 4Al pasar por las ciudades, entregaban los acuerdos tomados por los apóstoles y los *ancianos de Jerusalén, para que los pusieran en práctica. 5Y así las iglesias se fortalecían en la fe y crecían en número día tras día.

La visión de Pablo del hombre macedonio

6Atravesaron la región de Frigia y Galacia, ya que el Espíritu Santo les había impedido que predicaran la palabra en la provincia de *Asia. 7Cuando llegaron cerca de Misia, intentaron pasar a Bitinia, pero el Espíritu de Jesús no se lo permitió. 8Entonces, pasando de largo por Misia, bajaron a Troas. 9Durante la noche Pablo tuvo una visión en la que un hombre de Macedonia, puesto de pie, le rogaba: «Pasa a Macedonia y ayúdanos.» 10Después de que Pablo tuvo la visión, en seguida nos preparamos para partir hacia Macedonia, convencidos de que Dios nos había llamado a anunciar el *evangelio a los macedonios.

Conversión de Lidia en Filipos

11Zarpando de Troas, navegamos directamente a Samotracia, y al día siguiente a Neápolis. 12De allí fuimos a Filipos, que es una colonia romana y la ciudad principal de ese distrito de Macedonia. En esa ciudad nos quedamos varios días.

13El *sábado salimos a las afueras de la ciudad, y fuimos por la orilla del río, donde esperábamos encontrar un lugar de oración. Nos sentamos y nos pusimos a conversar con las mujeres que se habían reunido. 14Una de ellas, que se llamaba Lidia, adoraba a Dios. Era de la ciudad de Tiatira y vendía telas de púrpura. Mientras escuchaba, el Señor le abrió el corazón para que respondiera al mensaje de Pablo. 15Cuando fue bautizada con su familia, nos hizo la siguiente invitación: «Si ustedes me consideran creyente en el Señor, vengan a hospedarse en mi casa.» Y nos persuadió.

Pablo y Silas en la cárcel

16Una vez, cuando íbamos al lugar de oración, nos salió al encuentro una joven esclava que tenía un espíritu de adivinación. Con sus poderes ganaba mucho dinero para sus amos. 17Nos seguía a Pablo y a nosotros, gritando:

—Estos hombres son *siervos del Dios Altísimo, y les anuncian a ustedes el camino de salvación.

18Así continuó durante muchos días. Por fin Pablo se molestó tanto que se volvió y reprendió al espíritu:

—¡En el nombre de *Jesucristo, te ordeno que salgas de ella!

Y en aquel mismo momento el espíritu la dejó.

19Cuando los amos de la joven se dieron cuenta de que se les había esfumado la esperanza de ganar dinero, echaron mano a Pablo y a Silas y los arrastraron a la plaza, ante las autoridades. 20Los presentaron ante los magistrados y dijeron:

—Estos hombres son judíos, y están alborotando a nuestra ciudad, 21enseñando costumbres que a los romanos se nos prohíbe admitir o practicar.

22Entonces la multitud se amotinó contra Pablo y Silas, y los magistrados mandaron que les arrancaran la ropa y los azotaran. 23Después de darles muchos golpes, los echaron en la cárcel, y ordenaron al carcelero que los custodiara con la mayor seguridad. 24Al recibir tal orden, éste los metió en el calabozo interior y les sujetó los pies en el cepo.

25A eso de la medianoche, Pablo y Silas se pusieron a orar y a cantar himnos a Dios, y los otros presos los escuchaban. 26De repente se produjo un terremoto tan fuerte que la cárcel se estremeció hasta sus cimientos. Al instante se abrieron todas las puertas y a los presos se les soltaron las cadenas. 27El carcelero despertó y, al ver las puertas de la cárcel de par en par, sacó la espada y estuvo a punto de matarse, porque pensaba que los presos se habían escapado. Pero Pablo le gritó:

28—¡No te hagas ningún daño! ¡Todos estamos aquí!

29El carcelero pidió luz, entró precipitadamente y se echó temblando a los pies de Pablo y de Silas. 30Luego los sacó y les preguntó:

—Señores, ¿qué tengo que hacer para ser salvo?

31—Cree en el Señor Jesús; así tú y tu familia serán salvos —le contestaron.

32Luego les expusieron la palabra de Dios a él y a todos los demás que estaban en su casa. 33A esas horas de la noche, el carcelero se los llevó y les lavó las heridas; en seguida fueron bautizados él y toda su familia. 34El carcelero los llevó a su casa, les sirvió comida y se alegró mucho junto con toda su familia por haber creído en Dios.

35Al amanecer, los magistrados mandaron a unos guardias al carcelero con esta orden: «Suelta a esos hombres.» 36El carcelero, entonces, le informó a Pablo:

—Los magistrados han ordenado que los suelte. Así que pueden irse. Vayan en paz.

37Pero Pablo respondió a los guardias:

—¿Cómo? A nosotros, que somos ciudadanos romanos, que nos han azotado públicamente y sin proceso alguno, y nos han echado en la cárcel, ¿ahora quieren expulsarnos a escondidas? ¡Nada de eso! Que vengan ellos personalmente a escoltarnos hasta la salida.

38Los guardias comunicaron la respuesta a los magistrados. Éstos se asustaron cuando oyeron que Pablo y Silas eran ciudadanos romanos, 39así que fueron a presentarles sus disculpas. Los escoltaron desde la cárcel, pidiéndoles que se fueran de la ciudad. 40Al salir de la cárcel, Pablo y Silas se dirigieron a la casa de Lidia, donde se vieron con los hermanos y los animaron. Después se fueron.

En Tesalónica

17 Atravesando Anfípolis y Apolonia, Pablo y Silas llegaron a Tesalónica, donde había una sinagoga de los judíos. 2Como era su costumbre, Pablo entró en la sinagoga y tres *sábados seguidos discutió con ellos. Basándose en las Escrituras, 3les explicaba y demostraba que era necesario que el *Mesías padeciera y *resucitara. Les decía: «Este Jesús que les anuncio es el Mesías.» 4Algunos de los judíos se convencieron y se unieron a Pablo y a Silas, como también lo hicieron un buen número de mujeres prominentes y muchos *griegos que adoraban a Dios.

5Pero los judíos, llenos de envidia, reclutaron a unos maleantes callejeros, con los que armaron una turba y empezaron a alborotar la ciudad. Asaltaron la casa de Jasón en busca de Pablo y Silas, con el fin de procesarlos públicamente. 6Pero como no los encontraron, arrastraron a Jasón y a algunos otros hermanos ante las autoridades de la ciudad, gritando: «¡Estos que han trastornado el mundo entero han venido también acá, 7y Jasón los ha recibido en su casa! Todos ellos actúan en contra de los decretos del *emperador, afirmando que hay otro rey, uno que se llama Jesús.» 8Al oír esto, la multitud y las autoridades de la ciudad se alborotaron; 9entonces éstas exigieron fianza a Jasón y a los demás para dejarlos en libertad.

En Berea

10Tan pronto como se hizo de noche, los hermanos enviaron a Pablo y a Silas a Berea, quienes al llegar se dirigieron a la sinagoga de los judíos. 11Éstos eran de sentimientos más nobles que los de Tesalónica, de modo que recibieron el mensaje con toda avidez y todos los días examinaban las Escrituras para ver si era verdad lo que se les anunciaba. 12Muchos de los judíos creyeron, y también un buen número de *griegos, incluso mujeres distinguidas y no pocos hombres.

13Cuando los judíos de Tesalónica se enteraron de que también en Berea estaba Pablo predicando la palabra de Dios, fueron allá para agitar y alborotar a las multitudes. 14En seguida los hermanos enviaron a Pablo hasta la costa, pero Silas y Timoteo se quedaron en Berea. 15Los que acompañaban a Pablo lo llevaron hasta Atenas. Luego regresaron con instrucciones de que Silas y Timoteo se reunieran con él tan pronto como les fuera posible.

En Atenas

16Mientras Pablo los esperaba en Atenas, le dolió en el alma ver que la ciudad estaba llena de ídolos. 17Así que discutía en la sinagoga con los judíos y con los *griegos que adoraban a Dios, y a diario hablaba en la plaza con los que se encontraban por allí. 18Algunos filósofos epicúreos y estoicos entablaron conversación con él. Unos decían: «¿Qué querrá decir este charlatán?» Otros comentaban: «Parece que es predicador de dioses extranjeros.» Decían esto porque Pablo les anunciaba las buenas *nuevas de Jesús y de la resurrección. 19Entonces se lo llevaron a una reunión del Areópago.

—¿Se puede saber qué nueva enseñanza es esta que usted presenta? —le preguntaron—. 20Porque nos viene usted con ideas que nos suenan extrañas, y queremos saber qué significan.

21Es que todos los atenienses y los extranjeros que vivían allí se pasaban el tiempo sin hacer otra cosa más que escuchar y comentar las últimas novedades.

22Pablo se puso en medio del Areópago y tomó la palabra:

—¡Ciudadanos atenienses! Observo que ustedes son sumamente religiosos en todo lo que hacen. 23Al pasar y fijarme en sus lugares sagrados, encontré incluso un altar con esta inscripción: A UN DIOS DESCONOCIDO. Pues bien, eso que ustedes adoran como algo desconocido es lo que yo les anuncio.

24»El Dios que hizo el mundo y todo lo que hay en él es Señor del cielo y de la tierra. No vive en templos construidos por hombres, 25ni se deja servir por manos *humanas, como si necesitara de algo. Por el contrario, él es quien da a todos la vida, el aliento y todas las cosas. 26De un solo hombre hizo todas las nacionese para que habitaran toda la tierra; y determinó los períodos de su historia y las fronteras de sus territorios. 27Esto lo hizo Dios para que todos lo busquen y, aunque sea a tientas, lo encuentren. En verdad, él no está lejos de ninguno de nosotros, 28»puesto que en él vivimos, nos movemos y existimos». Como algunos de sus propios poetas griegos han dicho: "De él somos descendientes."

29»Por tanto, siendo descendientes de Dios, no debemos pensar que la divinidad sea como el oro, la plata o la piedra: escultura hecha como resultado del ingenio y de la destreza del *ser humano. 30Pues bien, Dios pasó por alto aquellos tiempos de tal ignorancia, pero ahora manda a todos, en todas partes, que se *arrepientan. 31Él ha fijado un día en que juzgará al mundo con justicia, por medio del hombre que ha designado. De ello ha dado pruebas a todos al *levantarlo de entre los muertos.

32Cuando oyeron de la resurrección, unos se burlaron; pero otros le dijeron:

—Queremos que usted nos hable en otra ocasión sobre este tema.

33En ese momento Pablo salió de la reunión. 34Algunas personas se unieron a Pablo y creyeron. Entre ellos estaba Dionisio, miembro del Areópago, también una mujer llamada Dámaris, y otros más.

En Corinto

18 Después de esto, Pablo se marchó de Atenas y se fue a Corinto. 2Allí se encontró con un judío llamado Aquila, natural del Ponto, y con su esposa Priscila. Hacía poco habían llegado de Italia, porque Claudio había mandado que todos los judíos fueran expulsados de Roma. Pablo fue a verlos 3y, como hacía tiendas de campaña al igual que ellos, se quedó para que trabajaran juntos. 4Todos los *sábados discutía en la sinagoga, tratando de persuadir a judíos y a *griegos.

5Cuando Silas y Timoteo llegaron de Macedonia, Pablo se dedicó exclusivamente a la predicación, testificándoles a los judíos que Jesús era el *Mesías. 6Pero cuando los judíos se opusieron a Pablo y lo insultaron, éste se sacudió la ropa en señal de protesta y les dijo: «¡Caiga la sangre de ustedes sobre su propia cabeza! Estoy libre de responsabilidad. De ahora en adelante me dirigiré a los *gentiles.»

7Entonces Pablo salió de la sinagoga y se fue a la casa de un tal Ticio Justo, que adoraba a Dios y que vivía al lado de la sinagoga. 8Crispo, el jefe de la sinagoga, creyó en el Señor con toda su familia. También creyeron y fueron bautizados muchos de los corintios que oyeron a Pablo.

9Una noche el Señor le dijo a Pablo en una visión: «No tengas miedo; sigue hablando y no te calles, 10pues estoy contigo. Aunque te ataquen, no voy a dejar que nadie te haga daño, porque tengo mucha gente en esta ciudad.» 11Así que Pablo se quedó allí un año y medio, enseñando entre el pueblo la palabra de Dios.

12Mientras Galión era gobernadorf de Acaya, los judíos a una atacaron a Pablo y lo condujeron al tribunal.

13—Este hombre —denunciaron ellos— anda persuadiendo a la gente a adorar a Dios de una manera que va en contra de nuestra ley.

---

e 17:26 todas las naciones. Alt. todo el género humano.   f 18:12 gobernador. Lit. procónsul.

14Pablo ya iba a hablar cuando Galión les dijo:

—Si ustedes los judíos estuvieran entablando una demanda sobre algún delito o algún crimen grave, sería razonable que los escuchara. 15Pero como se trata de cuestiones de palabras, de nombres y de su propia ley, arréglense entre ustedes. No quiero ser juez de tales cosas.

16Así que mandó que los expulsaran del tribunal. 17Entonces se abalanzaron todos sobre Sóstenes, el jefe de la sinagoga, y lo golpearon delante del tribunal. Pero Galión no le dio ninguna importancia al asunto.

Priscila, Aquila y Apolos

18Pablo permaneció en Corinto algún tiempo más.

Después se despidió de los hermanos y emprendió el viaje rumbo a Siria, acompañado de Priscila y Aquila. En Cencreas, antes de embarcarse, se hizo rapar la cabeza a causa de un voto que había hecho. 19Al llegar a Éfeso, Pablo se separó de sus acompañantes y entró en la sinagoga, donde se puso a discutir con los judíos. 20Éstos le pidieron que se quedara más tiempo con ellos. Él no accedió, 21pero al despedirse les prometió: «Ya volveré, si Dios quiere.» Y zarpó de Éfeso. 22Cuando desembarcó en Cesarea, subió a Jerusalén a saludar a la iglesia y luego bajó a Antioquía.

23Después de pasar algún tiempo allí, Pablo se fue a visitar una por una las congregaciones*g* de Galacia y Frigia, animando a todos los discípulos.

24Por aquel entonces llegó a Éfeso un judío llamado Apolos, natural de Alejandría. Era un hombre ilustrado y convincente en el uso de las Escrituras. 25Había sido instruido en el camino del Señor, y con gran fervor*h* hablaba y enseñaba con la mayor exactitud acerca de Jesús, aunque conocía sólo el bautismo de Juan. 26Comenzó a hablar valientemente en la sinagoga. Al oírlo Priscila y Aquila, lo tomaron a su cargo y le explicaron con mayor precisión el camino de Dios.

27Como Apolos quería pasar a Acaya, los hermanos lo animaron y les escribieron a los discípulos de allá para que lo recibieran. Cuando llegó, ayudó mucho a quienes por la gracia habían creído, 28pues refutaba vigorosamente en público a los judíos, demostrando por las Escrituras que Jesús es el *Mesías.

Pablo en Éfeso

19 Mientras Apolos estaba en Corinto, Pablo recorrió las regiones del interior y llegó a Éfeso. Allí encontró a algunos discípulos.

2—¿Recibieron ustedes el Espíritu Santo cuando creyeron? —les preguntó.

—No, ni siquiera hemos oído hablar del Espíritu Santo —respondieron.

3—Entonces, ¿qué bautismo recibieron?

—El bautismo de Juan.

4Pablo les explicó:

—El bautismo de Juan no era más que un bautismo de *arrepentimiento. Él le decía al pueblo que creyera en el que venía después de él, es decir, en Jesús.

5Al oír esto, fueron bautizados en el nombre del Señor Jesús. 6Cuando Pablo les impuso las manos, el Espíritu Santo vino sobre ellos, y empezaron a ha-

blar en *lenguas y a profetizar. 7Eran en total unos doce hombres.

8Pablo entró en la sinagoga y habló allí con toda valentía durante tres meses. Discutía acerca del reino de Dios, tratando de convencerlos, 9pero algunos se negaron obstinadamente a creer, y ante la congregación hablaban mal del Camino. Así que Pablo se alejó de ellos y formó un grupo aparte con los discípulos; y a diario debatía en la escuela de Tirano. 10Esto continuó por espacio de dos años, de modo que todos los judíos y los *griegos que vivían en la provincia de *Asia llegaron a escuchar la palabra del Señor.

11Dios hacía milagros extraordinarios por medio de Pablo, 12a tal grado que a los enfermos les llevaban pañuelos y delantales que habían tocado el cuerpo de Pablo, y quedaban sanos de sus enfermedades, y los espíritus malignos salían de ellos.

13Algunos judíos que andaban expulsando espíritus malignos intentaron invocar sobre los endemoniados el nombre del Señor Jesús. Decían: «En el nombre de Jesús, a quien Pablo predica, les ordeno que salgan!» 14Esto lo hacían siete hijos de un tal Esceva, que era uno de los jefes de los sacerdotes judíos.

15Un día el *espíritu maligno les replicó: «Conozco a Jesús, y sé quién es Pablo, pero ustedes ¿quiénes son?» 16Y abalanzándose sobre ellos, el hombre que tenía el espíritu maligno los dominó a todos. Los maltrató con tanta violencia que huyeron de la casa desnudos y heridos.

17Cuando se enteraron los judíos y los griegos que vivían en Éfeso, el temor se apoderó de todos ellos, y el nombre del Señor Jesús era glorificado. 18Muchos de los que habían creído llegaban ahora y confesaban públicamente sus prácticas malvadas. 19Un buen número de los que practicaban la hechicería juntaron sus libros en un montón y los quemaron delante de todos. Cuando calcularon el precio de aquellos libros, resultó un total de cincuenta mil monedas de plata.*i* 20Así la palabra del Señor crecía y se difundía con poder arrollador.

21Después de todos estos sucesos, Pablo tomó la determinación de ir a Jerusalén, pasando por Macedonia y Acaya. Decía: «Después de estar allí, tengo que visitar Roma.» 22Entonces envió a Macedonia a dos de sus ayudantes, Timoteo y Erasto, mientras él se quedaba por algún tiempo en la provincia de Asia.

El disturbio en Éfeso

23Por aquellos días se produjo un gran disturbio a propósito del Camino. 24Un platero llamado Demetrio, que hacía figuras en plata del templo de Artemisa,*j* proporcionaba a los artesanos no poca ganancia. 25Los reunió con otros obreros del ramo, y les dijo:

—Compañeros, ustedes saben que obtenemos buenos ingresos de este oficio. 26Les consta además que el tal Pablo ha logrado persuadir a mucha gente, no sólo en Éfeso sino en casi toda la provincia de *Asia. Él sostiene que no son dioses los que se hacen con las manos. 27Ahora bien, no sólo hay el peligro de que se desprestigie nuestro oficio, sino también el de que el templo de la gran diosa Artemisa sea menospreciado, y que la diosa misma, a quien adoran toda la provincia de Asia y el mundo entero, sea despojada de su divina majestad.

---

g **18:23** *una por una las congregaciones.* Lit. *por orden de la región.* h **18:25** *con gran fervor.* Lit. *con fervor en el Espíritu.*
i **19:19** *monedas de plata.* Es decir, *dracmas.* j **19:24** Nombre griego de la Diana de los romanos; también en vv. 27,28,34 y 35.

28Al oír esto, se enfurecieron y comenzaron a gritar:

—¡Grande es Artemisa de los efesios!

29En seguida toda la ciudad se alborotó. La turba en masa se precipitó en el teatro, arrastrando a Gayo y a Aristarco, compañeros de viaje de Pablo, que eran de Macedonia. 30Pablo quiso presentarse ante la multitud, pero los discípulos no se lo permitieron. 31Incluso algunas autoridades de la provincia, que eran amigos de Pablo, le enviaron un recado, rogándole que no se arriesgara a entrar en el teatro.

32Había confusión en la asamblea. Cada uno gritaba una cosa distinta, y la mayoría ni siquiera sabía para qué se habían reunido. 33Los judíos empujaron a un tal Alejandro hacia adelante, y algunos de entre la multitud lo sacaron para que tomara la palabra. Él agitó la mano para pedir silencio y presentar su defensa ante el pueblo. 34Pero cuando se dieron cuenta de que era judío, todos se pusieron a gritar al unísono como por dos horas:

—¡Grande es Artemisa de los efesios!

35El secretario del concejo municipal logró calmar a la multitud y dijo:

—Ciudadanos de Éfeso, ¿acaso no sabe todo el mundo que la ciudad de Éfeso es guardiana del templo de la gran Artemisa y de su estatua bajada del cielo? 36Ya que estos hechos son innegables, es preciso que ustedes se calmen y no hagan nada precipitadamente. 37Ustedes han traído a estos hombres, aunque ellos no han cometido ningún sacrilegio ni han *blasfemado contra nuestra diosa. 38Así que si Demetrio y sus compañeros de oficio tienen alguna queja contra alguien, para eso hay tribunales y gobernadores.k Vayan y presenten allí sus acusaciones unos contra otros. 39Si tienen alguna otra demanda, que se resuelva en legítima asamblea. 40Tal y como están las cosas, con los sucesos de hoy corremos el riesgo de que nos acusen de causar disturbios. ¿Qué razón podríamos dar de este alboroto, si no hay ninguna? 41Dicho esto, despidió la asamblea.

Recorrido por Macedonia y Grecia

20 Cuando cesó el alboroto, Pablo mandó llamar a los discípulos y, después de animarlos, se despidió y salió rumbo a Macedonia. 2Recorrió aquellas regiones, alentando a los creyentes en muchas ocasiones, y por fin llegó a Grecia, 3donde se quedó tres meses. Como los judíos tramaban un atentado contra él cuando estaba a punto de embarcarse para Siria, decidió regresar por Macedonia. 4Lo acompañaron Sópater hijo de Pirro, de Berea; Aristarco y Segundo, de Tesalónica; Gayo, de Derbe; Timoteo; y por último, Tíquico y Trófimo, de la provincia de *Asia. 5Éstos se adelantaron y nos esperaron en Troas. 6Pero nosotros zarpamos de Filipos después de la fiesta de los Panes sin levadura, y a los cinco días nos reunimos con los otros en Troas, donde pasamos siete días.

Visita de Pablo a Troas

7El primer día de la semana nos reunimos para partir el pan. Como iba a salir al día siguiente, Pablo estuvo hablando a los creyentes, y prolongó su discurso hasta la medianoche. 8En el cuarto del piso superior donde estábamos reunidos había muchas lámparas. 9Un joven llamado Eutico, que estaba sentado en una ventana, comenzó a dormirse mientras Pablo alargaba su discurso. Cuando se quedó profundamente dormido, se cayó desde el tercer piso y lo recogieron muerto. 10Pablo bajó, se echó sobre el joven y lo abrazó. «No se alarmen! —les dijo—. ¡Está vivo!» 11Luego volvió a subir, partió el pan y comió. Siguió hablando hasta el amanecer, y entonces se fue. 12Al joven se lo llevaron vivo a su casa, para gran consuelo de todos.

Pablo se despide de los ancianos de Éfeso

13Nosotros, por nuestra parte, nos embarcamos anticipadamente y zarpamos para Asón, donde íbamos a recoger a Pablo. Así se había planeado, ya que él iba a hacer esa parte del viaje por tierra. 14Cuando se encontró con nosotros en Asón, lo tomamos a bordo y fuimos a Mitilene. 15Desde allí zarpamos al día siguiente y llegamos frente a Quío. Al otro día cruzamos en dirección a Samos, y un día después llegamos a Mileto. 16Pablo había decidido pasar de largo a Éfeso para no demorarse en la provincia de *Asia, porque tenía prisa por llegar a Jerusalén para el día de Pentecostés, si fuera posible.

17Desde Mileto, Pablo mandó llamar a los *ancianos de la iglesia de Éfeso. 18Cuando llegaron, les dijo: «Ustedes saben cómo me porté todo el tiempo que estuve con ustedes, desde el primer día que vine a la provincia de Asia. 19He servido al Señor con toda humildad y con lágrimas, a pesar de haber sido sometido a duras *pruebas por las maquinaciones de los judíos. 20Ustedes saben que no he vacilado en predicarles nada que les fuera de provecho, sino que les he enseñado públicamente y en las casas. 21A judíos y a *griegos les he instado a convertirse a Dios y a creer en nuestro Señor Jesús.

22»Y ahora tengan en cuenta que voy a Jerusalén obligadol por el Espíritu, sin saber lo que allí me espera. 23Lo único que sé es que en todas las ciudades el Espíritu Santo me asegura que me esperan prisiones y sufrimientos. 24Sin embargo, considero que mi *vida carece de valor para mí mismo, con tal de que termine mi carrera y lleve a cabo el servicio que me ha encomendado el Señor Jesús, que es el de dar testimonio del *evangelio de la gracia de Dios.

25»Escuchen, yo sé que ninguno de ustedes, entre quienes he andado predicando el reino de Dios, volverá a verme. 26Por tanto, hoy les declaro que soy inocente de la sangre de todos, 27porque sin vacilar les he proclamado todo el propósito de Dios. 28Tengan cuidado de sí mismos y de todo el rebaño sobre el cual el Espíritu Santo los ha puesto como *obispos para pastorear la iglesia de Dios,m que él adquirió con su propia sangre.n 29Sé que después de mi partida entrarán en medio de ustedes lobos feroces que procurarán acabar con el rebaño. 30Aun de entre ustedes mismos se levantarán algunos que enseñarán falsedades para arrastrar a los discípulos que los sigan. 31Así que estén alerta. Recuerden que día y noche, durante tres años, no he dejado de amonestar con lágrimas a cada uno en particular.

32»Ahora los encomiendo a Dios y al mensaje de su gracia, mensaje que tiene poder para edificarlos y darles herencia entre todos los *santificados. 33No he codiciado ni la plata ni el oro ni la ropa de nadie. 34Ustedes mismos saben bien que estas manos se han ocupado de mis propias necesidades y las de mis compañeros. 35Con mi ejemplo les he mostrado que es preciso trabajar duro para ayudar a los necesi-

k 19:38 gobernadores. Lit. procónsules. l 20:22 obligado. Lit. Atado. m 20:28 de Dios. Var. del Señor. n 20:28 su propia sangre. Var. la sangre de su propio hijo.

tados, recordando las palabras del Señor Jesús: "Hay más *dicha en dar que en recibir."»

36Después de decir esto, Pablo se puso de rodillas con todos ellos y oró. 37Todos lloraban inconsolablemente mientras lo abrazaban y lo besaban. 38Lo que más los entristecía era su declaración de que ellos no volverían a verlo. Luego lo acompañaron hasta el barco.

Rumbo a Jerusalén

21 Después de separarnos de ellos, zarpamos y navegamos directamente a Cos. Al día siguiente fuimos a Rodas, y de allí a Pátara. 2Como encontramos un barco que iba para Fenicia, subimos a bordo y zarpamos. 3Después de avistar Chipre y de pasar al sur de la isla, navegamos hacia Siria y llegamos a Tiro, donde el barco tenía que descargar. 4Allí encontramos a los discípulos y nos quedamos con ellos siete días. Ellos, por medio del Espíritu, exhortaron a Pablo a que no subiera a Jerusalén. 5Pero al cabo de algunos días, partimos y continuamos nuestro viaje. Todos los discípulos, incluso las mujeres y los niños, nos acompañaron hasta las afueras de la ciudad, y allí en la playa nos arrodillamos y oramos. 6Luego de despedirnos, subimos a bordo y ellos regresaron a sus hogares.

7Nosotros continuamos nuestro viaje en barco desde Tiro y arribamos a Tolemaida, donde saludamos a los hermanos y nos quedamos con ellos un día. 8Al día siguiente salimos y llegamos a Cesarea, y nos hospedamos en casa de Felipe el evangelista, que era uno de los siete; 9éste tenía cuatro hijas solteras que profetizaban.

10Llevábamos allí varios días, cuando bajó de Judea un profeta llamado Ágabo. 11Éste vino a vernos y, tomando el cinturón de Pablo, se ató con él de pies y manos, y dijo:

—Así dice el Espíritu Santo: "De esta manera atarán los judíos de Jerusalén al dueño de este cinturón, y lo entregarán en manos de los *gentiles."

12Al oír esto, nosotros y los de aquel lugar le rogamos a Pablo que no subiera a Jerusalén.

13—¿Por qué lloran? ¡Me parten el alma! —respondió Pablo—. Por el nombre del Señor Jesús estoy dispuesto no sólo a ser atado sino también a morir en Jerusalén.

14Como no se dejaba convencer, desistimos exclamando:

—¡Que se haga la voluntad del Señor!

15Después de esto, acabamos los preparativos y subimos a Jerusalén. 16Algunos de los discípulos de Cesarea nos acompañaron y nos llevaron a la casa de Mnasón, donde íbamos a alojarnos. Éste era de Chipre, y uno de los primeros discípulos.

Llegada de Pablo a Jerusalén

17Cuando llegamos a Jerusalén, los creyentes nos recibieron calurosamente. 18Al día siguiente Pablo fue con nosotros a ver a *Jacobo, y todos los *ancianos estaban presentes. 19Después de saludarlos, Pablo les relató detalladamente lo que Dios había hecho entre los *gentiles por medio de su ministerio.

20Al oírlo, alabaron a Dios. Luego le dijeron a Pablo: «Ya ves, hermano, cuántos miles de judíos han creído, y todos ellos siguen aferrados a la ley. 21Ahora bien, han oído decir que tú enseñas a todos los judíos que viven entre los gentiles. Les recomiendas que no circunciden a sus hijos ni vivan según nuestras costumbres. 22¿Qué vamos a hacer? Sin duda se van a enterar de que has llegado.

23Por eso, será mejor que sigas nuestro consejo. Hay aquí entre nosotros cuatro hombres que tienen que cumplir un voto. 24Llévatelos, toma parte en sus ritos de *purificación y paga los gastos que corresponden al voto de rasurarse la cabeza. Así todos sabrán que no son ciertos esos informes acerca de ti, sino que tú también vives en obediencia a la ley. 25En cuanto a los creyentes gentiles, ya les hemos comunicado por escrito nuestra decisión de que se abstengan de lo sacrificado a los ídolos, de sangre, de la carne de animales estrangulados y de la inmoralidad sexual.»

26Al día siguiente Pablo se llevó a los hombres y se purificó con ellos. Luego entró en el *templo para dar aviso de la fecha en que vencería el plazo de la purificación y se haría la ofrenda por cada uno de ellos.

Arresto de Pablo

27Cuando estaban a punto de cumplirse los siete días, unos judíos de la provincia de *Asia vieron a Pablo en el *templo. Alborotaron a toda la multitud y le echaron mano, 28gritando: «¡Israelitas! ¡Ayúdennos! Éste es el individuo que anda por todas partes enseñando a toda la gente contra nuestro pueblo, nuestra ley y este lugar. Además, hasta ha metido a unos *griegos en el templo, y ha profanado este lugar santo.»

29Ya antes habían visto en la ciudad a Trófimo el efesio en compañía de Pablo, y suponían que Pablo lo había metido en el templo.

30Toda la ciudad se alborotó. La gente se precipitó en masa, agarró a Pablo y lo sacó del templo a rastras, e inmediatamente se cerraron las puertas. 31Estaban por matarlo, cuando se le informó al comandante del batallón romano que toda la ciudad de Jerusalén estaba amotinada. 32En seguida tomó algunos centuriones con sus tropas, y bajó corriendo hacia la multitud. Al ver al comandante y a sus soldados, los amotinados dejaron de golpear a Pablo.

33El comandante se abrió paso, lo arrestó y ordenó que lo sujetaran con dos cadenas. Luego preguntó quién era y qué había hecho. 34Entre la multitud unos gritaban una cosa distinta. Como el comandante no pudo averiguar la verdad a causa del alboroto, mandó que condujeran a Pablo al cuartel. 35Cuando Pablo llegó a las gradas, los soldados tuvieron que llevárselo en vilo debido a la violencia de la turba. 36El pueblo en masa iba detrás gritando: «¡Que lo maten!»

Pablo se dirige a la multitud
22:3-16 – Hch 9:1-22; 26:9-18

37Cuando los soldados estaban a punto de meterlo en el cuartel, Pablo le preguntó al comandante:

—¿Me permite decirle algo?

—¿Hablas griego? —replicó el comandante—. 38¿No eres el egipcio que hace algún tiempo provocó una rebelión y llevó al desierto a cuatro mil guerrilleros?

39—No, yo soy judío, natural de Tarso, una ciudad muy importante de Cilicia —le respondió Pablo—. Por favor, permítame hablarle al pueblo.

40Con el permiso del comandante, Pablo se puso de pie en las gradas e hizo una señal con la mano a la multitud. Cuando todos guardaron silencio, les dijo en arameo:[ñ]

22 «Padres y hermanos, escuchen ahora mi defensa.»

2Al oír que les hablaba en arameo, guardaron más silencio.

ñ **21:40** arameo. Lit. el dialecto hebreo; también en 22:2.

Pablo continuó: ³«Yo soy judío, nacido en Tarso de Cilicia, pero criado en esta ciudad. Bajo la tutela de Gamaliel recibí instrucción cabal en la ley de nuestros antepasados, y fui tan celoso de Dios como cualquiera de ustedes lo es hoy día. ⁴Perseguí a muerte a los seguidores de este Camino, arrestando y echando en la cárcel a hombres y mujeres por igual, ⁵y así lo pueden atestiguar el sumo sacerdote y todo el *Consejo de *ancianos. Incluso obtuve de parte de ellos cartas de extradición para nuestros hermanos judíos en Damasco, y fui allá con el fin de traer presos a Jerusalén a los que encontrara, para que fueran castigados.

⁶»Sucedió que a eso del mediodía, cuando me acercaba a Damasco, una intensa luz del cielo relampagueó de repente a mi alrededor. ⁷Caí al suelo y oí una voz que me decía: "Saulo, Saulo, ¿por qué me persigues?" ⁸¿Quién eres, Señor?", pregunté. "Yo soy Jesús de Nazaret, a quien tú persigues", me contestó él. ⁹Los que me acompañaban vieron la luz, pero no percibieron la voz del que me hablaba. ¹⁰¿Qué debo hacer, Señor?", le pregunté. "Levántate —dijo el Señor—, y entra en Damasco. Allí se te dirá todo lo que se ha dispuesto que hagas." ¹¹Mis compañeros me llevaron de la mano hasta Damasco porque el resplandor de aquella luz me había dejado ciego.

¹²»Vino a verme un tal Ananías, hombre devoto que observaba la ley y a quien respetaban mucho los judíos que allí vivían. ¹³Se puso a mi lado y me dijo: "Hermano Saulo, ¡recibe la vista!" Y en aquel mismo instante recobré la vista y pude verlo. ¹⁴Luego dijo: "El Dios de nuestros antepasados te ha escogido para que conozcas su voluntad, y para que veas al Justo y oigas las palabras de su boca. ¹⁵Tú le serás testigo ante toda persona de lo que has visto y oído. ¹⁶Y ahora, ¿qué esperas? Levántate, bautízate y lávate de tus pecados, invocando su nombre."

¹⁷»Cuando volví a Jerusalén, mientras oraba en el *templo tuve una visión ¹⁸y vi al Señor que me hablaba: "¡Date prisa! Sal inmediatamente de Jerusalén, porque no aceptarán tu testimonio acerca de mí." ¹⁹"Señor —le respondí—, ellos saben que yo andaba de sinagoga en sinagoga encarcelando y azotando a los que creen en ti; ²⁰y cuando se derramaba la sangre de tu testigoᵒ Esteban, ahí estaba yo, dando mi aprobación y cuidando la ropa de quienes lo mataban." ²¹Pero el Señor me replicó: "Vete; yo te enviaré lejos, a los *gentiles."»

Pablo el ciudadano romano

²²La multitud estuvo escuchando a Pablo hasta que pronunció esas palabras. Entonces levantaron la voz y gritaron: «¡Bórralo de la tierra! ¡Ese tipo no merece vivir!»

²³Como seguían gritando, tirando sus mantos y arrojando polvo al aire, ²⁴el comandante ordenó que metieran a Pablo en el cuartel. Mandó que lo interrogaran a latigazos con el fin de averiguar por qué gritaban así contra él. ²⁵Cuando lo estaban sujetando con cadenas para azotarlo, Pablo le dijo al centurión que estaba allí:

—¿Permite la ley que ustedes azoten a un ciudadano romano antes de ser juzgado?

²⁶Al oír esto, el centurión fue y avisó al comandante.

—¿Qué va a hacer usted? Resulta que ese hombre es ciudadano romano.

²⁷El comandante se acercó a Pablo y le dijo:

—Dime, ¿eres ciudadano romano?

—Sí, lo soy.

²⁸—A mí me costó una fortuna adquirir mi ciudadanía —le dijo el comandante.

—Pues yo la tengo de nacimiento —replicó Pablo.

²⁹Los que iban a interrogarlo se retiraron en seguida. Al darse cuenta de que Pablo era ciudadano romano, el comandante mismo se asustó de haberlo encadenado.

Pablo ante el Consejo

³⁰Al día siguiente, como el comandante quería saber con certeza de qué acusaban los judíos a Pablo, lo desató y mandó que se reunieran los jefes de los sacerdotes y el *Consejo en pleno. Luego llevó a Pablo para que compareciera ante ellos.

23 Pablo se quedó mirando fijamente al Consejo y dijo:

—Hermanos, hasta hoy yo he actuado delante de Dios con toda buena conciencia.

²Ante esto, el sumo sacerdote Ananías ordenó a los que estaban cerca de Pablo que lo golpearan en la boca.

³—¡Hipócrita,ᴾ a usted también lo va a golpear Dios! —reaccionó Pablo—. ¡Ahí está sentado para juzgarme según la ley!, ¿y usted mismo viola la ley al mandar que me golpeen?

⁴Los que estaban junto a Pablo le interpelaron:

—¿Cómo te atreves a insultar al sumo sacerdote de Dios?

⁵—Hermanos, no me había dado cuenta de que es el sumo sacerdote —respondió Pablo—; de hecho está escrito: "No hables mal del jefe de tu pueblo."ᑫ

⁶Pablo, sabiendo que unos de ellos eran saduceos y los demás *fariseos, exclamó en el Consejo:

—Hermanos, yo soy fariseo de pura cepa. Me están juzgando porque he puesto mi esperanza en la resurrección de los muertos.

⁷Apenas dijo esto, surgió un altercado entre los fariseos y los saduceos, y la asamblea quedó dividida. ⁸(Los saduceos sostienen que no hay resurrección, ni ángeles ni espíritus; los fariseos, en cambio, reconocen todo esto.)

⁹Se produjo un gran alboroto, y algunos de los *maestros de la ley que eran fariseos se pusieron de pie y protestaron. «No encontramos ningún delito en este hombre —decían—. ¿Acaso no podría haberle hablado un espíritu o un ángel?» ¹⁰Se tornó tan violento el altercado que el comandante tuvo miedo de que hicieran pedazos a Pablo. Así que ordenó a los soldados que bajaran para sacarlo de allí por la fuerza y llevárselo al cuartel.

¹¹A la noche siguiente el Señor se apareció a Pablo, y le dijo: «¡Ánimo! Así como has dado testimonio de mí en Jerusalén, es necesario que lo des también en Roma.»

Conspiración para matar a Pablo

¹²Muy de mañana los judíos tramaron una conspiración y juraron bajo maldición no comer ni beber hasta que lograran matar a Pablo. ¹³Más de cuarenta hombres estaban implicados en esta conspiración. ¹⁴Se presentaron ante los jefes de los sacerdotes y los *ancianos, y les dijeron:

—Nosotros hemos jurado bajo maldición no comer nada hasta que logremos matar a Pablo. ¹⁵Ahora, con el respaldo del *Consejo, pídanle al comandante que haga comparecer al reo ante ustedes, con el pretexto de obtener información más

---

ᵒ **22:20** testigo. Alt. Mártir. ᴾ **23:3** Hipócrita. Lit. Pared blanqueada. ᑫ **23:5** Éx 22:28

precisa sobre su caso. Nosotros estaremos listos para matarlo en el camino.

16Pero cuando el hijo de la hermana de Pablo se enteró de esta emboscada, entró en el cuartel y avisó a Pablo. 17Éste llamó entonces a uno de los centuriones y le pidió:

—Lleve a este joven al comandante, porque tiene algo que decirle.

18Así que el centurión lo llevó al comandante, y le dijo:

—El preso Pablo me llamó y me pidió que le trajera este joven, porque tiene algo que decirle.

19El comandante tomó de la mano al joven, lo llevó aparte y le preguntó:

—¿Qué quieres decirme?

20—Los judíos se han puesto de acuerdo para pedirle a usted que mañana lleve a Pablo ante el Consejo con el pretexto de obtener información más precisa acerca de él. 21No se deje convencer, porque más de cuarenta de ellos lo esperan emboscados. Han jurado bajo maldición no comer ni beber hasta que hayan logrado matarlo. Ya están listos; sólo aguardan a que usted les conceda su petición.

22El comandante despidió al joven con esta advertencia:

—No le digas a nadie que me has informado de esto.

Trasladan a Pablo a Cesarea

23Entonces el comandante llamó a dos de sus centuriones y les ordenó:

—Alisten un destacamento de doscientos soldados de infantería, setenta de caballería y doscientos lanceros para que vayan a Cesarea esta noche a las nueve.r 24Y preparen cabalgaduras para llevar a Pablo sano y salvo al gobernador Félix.

25Además, escribió una carta en estos términos:

26Claudio Lisias,

a su excelencia el gobernador Félix:

Saludos.

27Los judíos prendieron a este hombre y estaban a punto de matarlo, pero yo llegué con mis soldados y lo rescaté, porque me había enterado de que es ciudadano romano. 28Yo quería saber de qué lo acusaban, así que lo llevé al *Consejo judío. 29Descubrí que lo acusaban de algunas cuestiones de su ley, pero no había contra él cargo alguno que mereciera la muerte o la cárcel. 30Cuando me informaron que se tramaba una conspiración contra este hombre, decidí enviarlo a usted en seguida. También les ordené a sus acusadores que expongan delante de usted los cargos que tengan contra él.

31Así que los soldados, según se les había ordenado, tomaron a Pablo y lo llevaron de noche hasta Antípatris. 32Al día siguiente dejaron que la caballería siguiera con él mientras ellos volvían al cuartel. 33Cuando la caballería llegó a Cesarea, le entregaron la carta al gobernador y le presentaron también a Pablo. 34Félix leyó la carta y le preguntó de qué provincia era. Al enterarse de que Pablo era de Cilicia, 35le dijo: «Te daré audiencia cuando lleguen tus acusadores.» Y ordenó que lo dejaran bajo custodia en el palacio de Herodes.

El proceso ante Félix

24 Cinco días después, el sumo sacerdote Ananías bajó a Cesarea con algunos de los *ancianos y un abogado llamado Tértulo, para presentar ante el gobernador las acusaciones contra Pablo. 2Cuando se hizo comparecer al acusado, Tértulo expuso su caso ante Félix:

—Excelentísimo Félix, bajo su mandato hemos disfrutado de un largo período de paz, y gracias a la previsión suya se han llevado a cabo reformas en pro de esta nación. 3En todas partes y en toda ocasión reconocemos esto con profunda gratitud. 4Pero a fin de no importunarlo más, le ruego que, con la bondad que lo caracteriza, nos escuche brevemente. 5Hemos descubierto que este hombre es una plaga que por todas partes anda provocando disturbios entre los judíos. Es cabecilla de la secta de los nazarenos. 6Incluso trató de profanar el *templo; por eso lo prendimos. 8Usteds mismo, al interrogarlo, podrá cerciorarse de la verdad de todas las acusaciones que presentamos contra él.

9Los judíos corroboraron la acusación, afirmando que todo esto era cierto. 10Cuando el gobernador, con un gesto, le concedió la palabra, Pablo respondió:

—Sé que desde hace muchos años usted ha sido juez de esta nación; así que de buena gana presento mi defensa. 11Usted puede comprobar fácilmente que no hace más de doce días que subí a Jerusalén para adorar. 12Mis acusadores no me encontraron discutiendo con nadie en el templo, ni promoviendo motines entre la gente en las sinagogas ni en ninguna otra parte de la ciudad. 13Tampoco pueden probarle a usted las cosas de que ahora me acusan. 14Sin embargo, esto sí confieso: que adoro al Dios de nuestros antepasados siguiendo este Camino que mis acusadores llaman secta, pues estoy de acuerdo con todo lo que enseña la ley y creo lo que está escrito en los profetas. 15Tengo en Dios la misma esperanza que estos hombres profesan, de que habrá una resurrección de los justos y de los injustos. 16En todo esto procuro conservar siempre limpia mi conciencia delante de Dios y de los hombres.

17»Después de una ausencia de varios años, volví a Jerusalén para traerle donativos a mi pueblo y presentar ofrendas. 18En esto estaba, habiéndome ya *purificado, cuando me encontraron en el templo. No me acompañaba ninguna multitud, ni estaba implicado en ningún disturbio. 19Los que me vieron eran algunos judíos de la provincia de *Asia, y son ellos los que deberían estar delante de usted para formular sus acusaciones, si es que tienen algo contra mí. 20De otro modo, estos que están aquí deberían declarar qué delito hallaron en mí cuando comparecí ante el *Consejo, 21a no ser lo que exclamé en presencia de ellos: "Es por la resurrección de los muertos por lo que hoy me encuentro procesado delante de ustedes."

22Entonces Félix, que estaba bien informado del Camino, suspendió la sesión.

—Cuando venga el comandante Lisias, decidiré su caso —les dijo.

23Luego le ordenó al centurión que mantuviera custodiado a Pablo, pero que le diera cierta libertad y permitiera que sus amigos lo atendieran.

24Algunos días después llegó Félix con su esposa Drusila, que era judía. Mandó llamar a Pablo y lo es-

---

r 23:23 esta . . . nueve. Lit. a la tercera hora de la noche.   s 24:6-8 prendimos. 8Usted. Var. prendimos y quisimos juzgarlo según nuestra ley. 7Pero el comandante Lisias intervino, y con mucha fuerza lo arrebató de nuestras manos 8y mandó que sus acusadores se presentaran ante usted. Usted

cuchó hablar acerca de la fe en *Cristo Jesús. 25Al disertar Pablo sobre la justicia, el dominio propio y el juicio venidero, Félix tuvo miedo y le dijo: «¡Basta por ahora! Puedes retirarte. Cuando sea oportuno te mandaré llamar otra vez.» 26Félix también esperaba que Pablo le ofreciera dinero; por eso mandaba llamarlo con frecuencia y conversaba con él.

27Transcurridos dos años, Félix tuvo como sucesor a Porcio Festo, pero como Félix quería congraciarse con los judíos, dejó preso a Pablo.

El proceso ante Festo

25 Tres días después de llegar a la provincia, Festo subió de Cesarea a Jerusalén. 2Entonces los jefes de los sacerdotes y los dirigentes de los judíos presentaron sus acusaciones contra Pablo. 3Insistentemente le pidieron a Festo que les hiciera el favor de trasladar a Pablo a Jerusalén. Lo cierto es que ellos estaban preparando una emboscada para matarlo en el camino. 4Festo respondió: «Pablo está preso en Cesarea, y yo mismo partiré en breve para allá. 5Que vayan conmigo algunos de los dirigentes de ustedes y formulen allí sus acusaciones contra él, si es que ha hecho algo malo.»

6Después de pasar entre los judíos unos ocho o diez días, Festo bajó a Cesarea, y al día siguiente convocó al tribunal y mandó que le trajeran a Pablo. 7Cuando éste se presentó, los judíos que habían bajado de Jerusalén lo rodearon, formulando contra él muchas acusaciones graves que no podían probar.

8Pablo se defendía:

—No he cometido ninguna falta, ni contra la ley de los judíos ni contra el templo ni contra el *emperador.

9Pero Festo, queriendo congraciarse con los judíos, le preguntó:

—¿Estás dispuesto a subir a Jerusalén para ser juzgado allí ante mí?

10Pablo contestó:

—Ya estoy ante el tribunal del emperador, que es donde se me debe juzgar. No les he hecho ningún agravio a los judíos, como usted sabe muy bien. 11Si soy culpable de haber hecho algo que merezca la muerte, no me niego a morir. Pero si no son ciertas las acusaciones que estos judíos formulan contra mí, nadie tiene el derecho de entregarme a ellos para complacerlos. ¡Apelo al emperador!

12Después de consultar con sus asesores, Festo declaró:

—Has apelado al emperador. ¡Al emperador irás!

Festo consulta al rey Agripa

13Pasados algunos días, el rey Agripa y Berenice llegaron a Cesarea para saludar a Festo. 14Como se entretuvieron allí varios días, Festo le presentó al rey el caso de Pablo.

—Hay aquí un hombre —le dijo— que Félix dejó preso. 15Cuando fui a Jerusalén, los jefes de los sacerdotes y los *ancianos de los judíos presentaron acusaciones contra él y exigieron que se le condenara. 16Les respondí que no es costumbre de los romanos entregar a ninguna persona sin antes concederle al acusado un careo con sus acusadores, y darle la oportunidad de defenderse de los cargos. 17Cuando acudieron a mí, no dilaté el caso, sino que convoqué al tribunal el día siguiente y mandé traer a este hombre. 18Al levantarse para hablar, sus acusadores no alegaron en su contra ninguno de los delitos que yo había supuesto. 19Más bien, tenían contra él algunas cuestiones tocantes a su propia religión y sobre un tal Jesús, ya muerto, que Pablo sostiene que está vivo. 20Yo no sabía cómo investigar tales cuestiones, así que le pregunté si estaba dispuesto a ir a Jerusalén para ser juzgado allí con respecto a esos cargos. 21Pero como Pablo apeló para que se le reservara el fallo al emperador,[t] ordené que quedara detenido hasta ser remitido a Roma.[u]

22—A mí también me gustaría oír a ese hombre —le dijo Agripa a Festo.

—Pues mañana mismo lo oirá usted —le contestó Festo.

Pablo ante Agripa
26:12-18 — Hch 9:3-8; 22:6-11

23Al día siguiente Agripa y Berenice se presentaron con gran pompa, y entraron en la sala de la audiencia acompañados por oficiales de alto rango y por las personalidades más distinguidas de la ciudad. 24Festo mandó que le trajeran a Pablo, 24y dijo:

—Rey Agripa y todos los presentes: Aquí tienen a este hombre. Todo el pueblo judío me ha presentado una demanda contra él, tanto en Jerusalén como aquí en Cesarea, pidiendo a gritos su muerte. 25He llegado a la conclusión de que él no ha hecho nada que merezca la muerte, pero como apeló al emperador, he decidido enviarlo a Roma. 26El problema es que no tengo definido nada que escribir al soberano acerca de él. Por eso lo he hecho comparecer ante ustedes, y especialmente delante de usted, rey Agripa, para que como resultado de esta investigación tenga yo algunos datos para mi carta; 27me parece absurdo enviar a un preso sin especificar los cargos contra él.

26 Entonces Agripa le dijo a Pablo: —Tienes permiso para defenderte.

Pablo hizo un además con la mano y comenzó así su defensa:

2—Rey Agripa, para mí es un privilegio presentarme hoy ante usted para defenderme de las acusaciones de los judíos, 3sobre todo porque usted está bien informado de todas las tradiciones y controversias de los judíos. Por eso le ruego que me escuche con paciencia.

4»Todos los judíos saben cómo he vivido desde que era niño, desde mi edad temprana entre mi gente y también en Jerusalén. 5Ellos me conocen desde hace mucho tiempo y pueden atestiguar, si quieren, que viví como *fariseo, de acuerdo con la secta más estricta de nuestra religión. 6Y ahora me juzgan por la esperanza que tengo en la promesa que Dios hizo a nuestros antepasados. 7Ésta es la promesa que nuestras doce tribus esperan alcanzar rindiendo culto a Dios con diligencia día y noche. Es por esta esperanza, oh rey, por lo que me acusan los judíos. 8¿Por qué les parece a ustedes increíble que Dios resucite a los muertos?

9»Pues bien, yo mismo estaba convencido de que debía hacer todo lo posible por combatir el nombre de Jesús de Nazaret. 10Eso es precisamente lo que hice en Jerusalén. Con la autoridad de los jefes de los sacerdotes metí en la cárcel a muchos de los *santos, y cuando los mataban, yo manifestaba mi aprobación. 11Muchas veces anduve de sinagoga en sinagoga castigándolos para obligarlos a *blasfemar. Mi obsesión contra ellos me llevaba al extremo de perseguirlos incluso en ciudades del extranjero.

---

t **25:21** al emperador. Lit. al augusto; también en v. 25. u **25:21** a Roma. Lit. al *césar.

12»En uno de esos viajes iba yo hacia Damasco con la autoridad y la comisión de los jefes de los sacerdotes. 13A eso del mediodía, oh rey, mientras iba por el camino, vi una luz del cielo, más refulgente que el sol, que con su resplandor nos envolvió a mí y a mis acompañantes. 14Todos caímos al suelo, y yo oí una voz que me decía en arameo:v "Saulo, Saulo, ¿por qué me persigues? ¿Qué sacas con darte cabezazos contra la pared?"w 15Entonces pregunté: "¿Quién eres, Señor?" "Yo soy Jesús, a quien tú persigues —me contestó el Señor—. 16Ahora, ponte en pie y escúchame. Me he aparecido a ti con el fin de designarte siervo y testigo de lo que has visto de mí y de lo que te voy a revelar. 17Te libraré de tu propio pueblo y de los *gentiles. Te envío a éstos 18para que les abras los ojos y se conviertan de las tinieblas a la luz, y del poder de Satanás a Dios, a fin de que, por la fe en mí, reciban el perdón de los pecados y la herencia entre los *santificados."

19»Así que, rey Agripa, no fui desobediente a esa visión celestial. 20Al contrario, comenzando con los que estaban en Damasco, siguiendo con los que estaban en Jerusalén y en toda Judea, y luego con los gentiles, a todos les prediqué que se *arrepintieran y se convirtieran a Dios, y que demostraran su arrepentimiento con sus buenas obras. 21Sólo por eso los judíos me prendieron en el *templo y trataron de matarme. 22Pero Dios me ha ayudado hasta hoy, y así me mantengo firme, testificando a grandes y pequeños. No he dicho sino lo que los profetas y Moisés ya dijeron que sucedería: 23que el *Cristo padecería y que, siendo el primero en resucitar, proclamaría la luz a su propio pueblo y a los gentiles.

24Al llegar Pablo a este punto de su defensa, Festo interrumpió.

—¡Estás loco, Pablo! —le gritó—. El mucho estudio te ha hecho perder la cabeza.

25—No estoy loco, excelentísimo Festo —contestó Pablo—. Lo que digo es cierto y sensato. 26El rey está familiarizado con estas cosas, y por eso hablo ante él con tanto atrevimiento. Estoy convencido de que nada de esto ignora, porque no sucedió en un rincón. 27Rey Agripa, ¿cree usted en los profetas? ¡A mí me consta que sí!

28—Un poco más y me convences a hacerme cristianox —le dijo Agripa.

29—Sea por poco o por mucho —le replicó Pablo—, le pido a Dios que no sólo usted, sino también todos los que me están escuchando hoy, lleguen a ser como yo, aunque sin estas cadenas.

30Se levantó el rey, y también el gobernador, Berenice y los que estaban sentados con ellos. 31Al retirarse, decían entre sí:

—Este hombre no ha hecho nada que merezca la muerte ni la cárcel.

32Y Agripa le dijo a Festo:

—Se podría poner en libertad a este hombre si no hubiera apelado al *emperador.

Pablo viaja a Roma

27 Cuando se decidió que navegáramos rumbo a Italia, entregaron a Pablo y a algunos otros presos a un centurión llamado Julio, que pertenecía al batallón imperial. 2Subimos a bordo de un barco, con matrícula de Adramitio, que estaba a punto de zarpar hacia los puertos de la provincia de *Asia, y nos hicimos a la mar. Nos acompañaba Aristarco, un macedonio de Tesalónica.

3Al día siguiente hicimos escala en Sidón; y Julio, con mucha amabilidad, le permitió a Pablo visitar a sus amigos para que lo atendieran. 4Desde Sidón zarpamos y navegamos al abrigo de Chipre, porque los vientos nos eran contrarios. 5Después de atravesar el mar frente a las costas de Cilicia y Panfilia, arribamos a Mira de Licia. 6Allí el centurión encontró un barco de Alejandría que iba para Italia, y nos hizo subir a bordo. 7Durante muchos días la navegación fue lenta, y a duras penas llegamos frente a Gnido. Como el viento nos era desfavorable para seguir el rumbo trazado, navegamos al abrigo de Creta, frente a Salmona. 8Seguimos con dificultad a lo largo de la costa y llegamos a un lugar llamado Buenos Puertos, cerca de la ciudad de Lasea.

9Se había perdido mucho tiempo, y era peligrosa la navegación por haber pasado ya la fiesta del ayuno.y Así que Pablo les advirtió: 10«Señores, veo que nuestro viaje va a ser desastroso y que va a causar mucho perjuicio tanto para el barco y su carga como para nuestras propias *vidas». 11Pero el centurión, en vez de hacerle caso, siguió el consejo del timonel y del dueño del barco. 12Como el puerto no era adecuado para invernar, la mayoría decidió que debíamos seguir adelante, con la esperanza de llegar a Fenice, puerto de Creta que da al suroeste y al noroeste, y pasar allí el invierno.

La tempestad

13Cuando comenzó a soplar un viento suave del sur, creyeron que podían conseguir lo que querían, así que levaron anclas y navegaron junto a la costa de Creta. 14Poco después se nos vino encima un viento huracanado, llamado Nordeste, que venía desde la isla. 15El barco quedó atrapado por la tempestad y no podía hacerle frente al viento, así que nos dejamos llevar a la deriva. 16Mientras pasábamos al abrigo de un islote llamado Cauda, a duras penas pudimos sujetar el bote salvavidas. 17Después de subirlo a bordo, amarraron con sogas todo el casco del barco para reforzarlo. Temiendo que fueran a encallar en los bancos de arena de la Sirte, echaron el ancla flotante y dejaron el barco a la deriva. 18Al día siguiente, dado que la tempestad seguía arremetiendo con mucha fuerza contra nosotros, comenzaron a arrojar la carga por la borda. 19Al tercer día, con sus propias manos arrojaron al mar los aparejos del barco. 20Como pasaron muchos días sin que apareciera ni el sol ni las estrellas, y la tempestad seguía arreciando, perdimos al fin toda esperanza de salvarnos.

21Llevábamos ya mucho tiempo sin comer, así que Pablo se puso en medio de todos y dijo: «Señores, debían haber seguido mi consejo y no haber zarpado de Creta; así se habrían ahorrado este perjuicio y esta pérdida. 22Pero ahora los exhorto a cobrar ánimo, porque ninguno de ustedes perderá la *vida; sólo se perderá el barco. 23Anoche se me apareció un ángel del Dios a quien pertenezco y a quien sirvo, 24y me dijo: "No tengas miedo, Pablo. Tienes que comparecer ante el *emperador; y Dios te ha concedido la vida de todos los que navegan contigo." 25Así que ¡ánimo, señores! Confío en Dios que sucederá tal y

---

v 26:14 arameo. Lit. el dialecto hebreo. w 26:14 ¿Qué sacas . . . pared? Lit. Te es difícil dar coces contra el aguijón. x 26:28 Un poco . . . cristiano. Alt. ¿Con tan poco pretendes hacerme cristiano? y 27:9 Es decir, el día de la *Expiación (Yom Kippur) en septiembre, de manera que se acercaba el invierno.

como se me dijo. ²⁶Sin embargo, tenemos que encallar en alguna isla.»

El naufragio

²⁷Ya habíamos pasado catorce noches a la deriva por el mar Adriático,ᶻ cuando a eso de la medianoche los marineros presintieron que se aproximaban a tierra. ²⁸Echaron la sonda y encontraron que el agua tenía unos treinta y siete metros de profundidad. Más adelante volvieron a echar la sonda y encontraron que tenía cerca de veintisiete metrosᵃ de profundidad. ²⁹Temiendo que fuéramos a estrellarnos contra las rocas, echaron cuatro anclas por la popa y se pusieron a rogar que amaneciera. ³⁰En un intento por escapar del barco, los marineros comenzaron a bajar el bote salvavidas al mar, con el pretexto de que iban a echar algunas anclas desde la proa. ³¹Pero Pablo les advirtió al centurión y a los soldados: «Si ésos no se quedan en el barco, no podrán salvarse ustedes.» ³²Así que los soldados cortaron las amarras del bote salvavidas y lo dejaron caer al agua.

³³Estaba a punto de amanecer cuando Pablo animó a todos a tomar alimento: «Hoy hace ya catorce días que ustedes están con la vida en un hilo, y siguen sin probar bocado. ³⁴Les ruego que coman algo, pues lo necesitan para sobrevivir. Ninguno de ustedes perderá ni un solo cabello de la cabeza.» ³⁵Dicho esto, tomó pan y dio gracias a Dios delante de todos. Luego lo partió y comenzó a comer. ³⁶Todos se animaron y también comieron. ³⁷Éramos en total doscientas setenta y seis personas en el barco. ³⁸Una vez satisfechos, aligeraron el barco echando el trigo al mar.

³⁹Cuando amaneció, no reconocieron la tierra, pero vieron una bahía que tenía playa, donde decidieron encallar el barco a como diera lugar. ⁴⁰Cortaron las anclas y las dejaron caer en el mar, desatando a la vez las amarras de los timones. Luego izaron a favor del viento la vela de proa y se dirigieron a la playa. ⁴¹Pero el barco fue a dar en un banco de arena y encalló. La proa se encajó en el fondo y quedó varada, mientras la popa se hacía pedazos al embate de las olas.

⁴²Los soldados pensaron matar a los presos para que ninguno escapara a nado. ⁴³Pero el centurión quería salvarle la vida a Pablo, y les impidió llevar a cabo el plan. Dio orden de que los que pudieran nadar saltaran primero por la borda para llegar a tierra, ⁴⁴y de que los demás salieran valiéndose de tablas o de restos del barco. De esta manera todos llegamos sanos y salvos a tierra.

En la isla de Malta

28 Una vez a salvo, nos enteramos de que la isla se llamaba Malta. ²Los isleños nos trataron con toda clase de atenciones. Encendieron una fogata y nos invitaron a acercarnos, porque estaba lloviendo y hacía frío. ³Sucedió que Pablo recogió un montón de leña y la estaba echando al fuego, cuando una víbora que huía del calor se le prendió en la mano. ⁴Al ver la serpiente colgada de la mano de Pablo, los isleños se pusieron a comentar entre sí: «Sin duda este hombre es un asesino, pues aunque se salvó del mar, la justicia divina no va a consentir que siga con vida.» ⁵Pero Pablo sacudió la mano y la serpiente cayó en el fuego, y él no sufrió ningún daño.

⁶La gente esperaba que se hinchara o cayera muerto de repente, pero después de esperar un buen rato y de ver que nada extraño le sucedía, cambiaron de parecer y decían que era un dios.

⁷Cerca de allí había una finca que pertenecía a Publio, el funcionario principal de la isla. Éste nos recibió en su casa con amabilidad y nos hospedó durante tres días. ⁸El padre de Publio estaba en cama, enfermo con fiebre y disentería. Pablo entró a verlo y, después de orar, le impuso las manos y lo sanó. ⁹Como consecuencia de esto, los demás enfermos de la isla también acudían y eran sanados. ¹⁰Nos colmaron de muchas atenciones y nos proveyeron de todo lo necesario para el viaje.

Llegada a Roma

¹¹Al cabo de tres meses en la isla, zarpamos en un barco que había invernado allí. Era una nave de Alejandría que tenía por insignia a los dioses Dióscuros.ᵇ ¹²Hicimos escala en Siracusa, donde nos quedamos tres días. ¹³Desde allí navegamos bordeando la costa y llegamos a Regio. Al día siguiente se levantó el viento del sur, y al segundo día llegamos a Poteoli. ¹⁴Allí encontramos a algunos creyentes que nos invitaron a pasar una semana con ellos. Y por fin llegamos a Roma. ¹⁵Los hermanos de Roma, habiéndose enterado de nuestra situación, salieron hasta el Foro de Apio y Tres Tabernas a recibirnos. Al verlos, Pablo dio gracias a Dios y cobró ánimo. ¹⁶Cuando llegamos a Roma, a Pablo se le permitió tener su domicilio particular, con un soldado que lo custodiara.

Pablo predica bajo custodia en Roma

¹⁷Tres días más tarde, Pablo convocó a los dirigentes de los judíos. Cuando estuvieron reunidos, les dijo:

—A mí, hermanos, a pesar de no haber hecho nada contra mi pueblo ni contra las costumbres de nuestros antepasados, me arrestaron en Jerusalén y me entregaron a los romanos. ¹⁸Éstos me interrogaron y quisieron soltarme por no ser yo culpable de ningún delito que mereciera la muerte. ¹⁹Cuando los judíos se opusieron, me vi obligado a apelar al *emperador, pero no porque tuviera alguna acusación que presentar contra mi nación. ²⁰Por este motivo he pedido verlos y hablar con ustedes. Precisamente por la esperanza de Israel estoy encadenado.

²¹—Nosotros no hemos recibido ninguna carta de Judea que tenga que ver contigo —le contestaron ellos—, ni ha llegado ninguno de los hermanos de allá con malos informes o que haya hablado mal de ti. ²²Pero queremos oír tu punto de vista, porque lo único que sabemos es que en todas partes se habla en contra de esa secta.

²³Señalaron un día para reunirse con Pablo, y acudieron en mayor número a la casa donde estaba alojado. Desde la mañana hasta la tarde estuvo explicándoles y testificándoles acerca del reino de Dios y tratando de convencerlos respecto a Jesús, partiendo de la ley de Moisés y de los profetas. ²⁴Unos se convencieron por lo que él decía, pero otros se negaron a creer. ²⁵No pudieron ponerse de acuerdo entre sí, y comenzaron a irse cuando Pablo añadió esta última declaración: «Con razón el Espíritu Santo les habló a sus antepasados por medio del profeta Isaías diciendo:

ᶻ **27:27** En la antigüedad el nombre *Adriático* se refería a una zona que se extendía muy al sur de Italia. ᵃ **27:28** *treinta y siete metros ... veintisiete metros.* Lit. *veinte *brazas ... quince brazas.* ᵇ **28:11** Dioses gemelos de la mitología griega, probablemente Cástor y Pólux

26»"Ve a este pueblo y dile:
  'Por mucho que oigan, no entenderán;
    por mucho que vean, no percibirán.'
27Porque el corazón de este pueblo se ha vuelto
    insensible;
  se les han embotado los oídos,
  y se les han cerrado los ojos.
De lo contrario, verían con los ojos,
  oirían con los oídos,
  entenderían con el corazón

y se convertirían, y yo los sanaría."c

28»Por tanto, quiero que sepan que esta salvación de Dios se ha enviado a los *gentiles, y ellos sí escucharán.»d

30Durante dos años completos permaneció Pablo en la casa que tenía alquilada, y recibía a todos los que iban a verlo. 31Y predicaba el reino de Dios y enseñaba acerca del Señor *Jesucristo sin impedimento y sin temor alguno.

---

c **28:27** Is 6:9,10   d **28:28** *escucharán.»* Var. *escucharán.»* 29*Después que él dijo esto, los judíos se fueron, discutiendo acaloradamente entre ellos.*

Carta a los ROMANOS

1 Pablo, *siervo de *Cristo Jesús, llamado a ser apóstol, apartado para anunciar el *evangelio de Dios, 2que por medio de sus profetas ya había prometido en las sagradas Escrituras. 3Este evangelio habla de su Hijo, que según la *naturaleza humana era descendiente de David, 4pero que según el Espíritu de *santidad fue designadoa con poder Hijo de Dios por la resurrección. Él es Jesucristo nuestro Señor. 5Por medio de él, y en honor a su nombre, recibimos el don apostólico para persuadir a todas las *naciones que obedezcan a la fe.b 6Entre ellas están incluidos también ustedes, a quienes Jesucristo ha llamado.

7Les escribo a todos ustedes, los amados de Dios que están en Roma, que han sido llamados a ser *santos.

Que Dios nuestro Padre y el Señor Jesucristo les concedan gracia y paz.

Pablo anhela visitar Roma

8En primer lugar, por medio de Jesucristo doy gracias a mi Dios por todos ustedes, pues en el mundo entero se habla bien de su fe. 9Dios, a quien sirvo de corazón predicando el *evangelio de su Hijo, me es testigo de que los recuerdo a ustedes sin cesar. 10Siempre pido en mis oraciones que, si es la voluntad de Dios, por fin se me abra ahora el camino para ir a visitarlos.

11Tengo muchos deseos de verlos para impartirles algún don espiritual que los fortalezca; 12mejor dicho, para que unos a otros nos animemos con la fe que compartimos. 13Quiero que sepan, hermanos, que aunque hasta ahora no he podido visitarlos, muchas veces me he propuesto hacerlo, para recoger algún fruto entre ustedes, tal como lo he recogido entre las otras naciones.

14Estoy en deuda con todos, sean cultos o incultos,c instruidos o ignorantes. 15De allí mi gran anhelo de predicarles el evangelio también a ustedes que están en Roma.

16A la verdad, no me avergüenzo del evangelio, pues es poder de Dios para la salvación de todos los que creen: de los judíos primeramente, pero también de los *gentiles. 17De hecho, en el evangelio se revela la justicia que proviene de Dios, la cual es por fe de principio a fin,d tal como está escrito: «El justo vivirá por la fe.»e

La ira de Dios contra la humanidad

18Ciertamente, la ira de Dios viene revelándose desde el cielo contra toda impiedad e injusticia de los *seres humanos, que con su maldad obstruyen la verdad. 19Me explico: lo que se puede conocer acerca de Dios es evidente para ellos, pues él mismo se lo ha revelado. 20Porque desde la creación del mundo las cualidades invisibles de Dios, es decir, su eterno poder y su naturaleza divina, se perciben claramente a través de lo que él creó, de modo que nadie tiene excusa. 21A pesar de haber conocido a Dios, no lo glorificaron como a Dios ni le dieron gracias, sino que se extraviaron en sus inútiles razonamientos, y se les oscureció su insensato corazón. 22Aunque afirmaban ser sabios, se volvieron necios 23y cambiaron la gloria del Dios inmortal por imágenes que eran réplicas del hombre mortal, de las aves, de los cuadrúpedos y de los reptiles.

24Por eso Dios los entregó a los malos deseos de sus corazones, que conducen a la impureza sexual, de modo que degradaron sus cuerpos los unos con los otros. 25Cambiaron la verdad de Dios por la mentira, adorando y sirviendo a los seres creados antes que al Creador, quien es bendito por siempre. Amén.

26Por tanto, Dios los entregó a pasiones vergonzosas. En efecto, las mujeres cambiaron las relaciones naturales por las que van contra la naturaleza. 27Así mismo los hombres dejaron las relaciones naturales con la mujer y se encendieron en pasiones lujuriosas los unos con los otros. Hombres con hombres cometieron actos indecentes, y en sí mismos recibieron el castigo que merecía su perversión.

28Además, como estimaron que no valía la pena tomar en cuenta el conocimiento de Dios, él a su vez los entregó a la depravación mental, para que hicieran lo que no debían hacer. 29Se han llenado de toda clase de maldad, perversidad, avaricia y depravación. Están repletos de envidia, homicidios, disensiones, engaño y malicia. Son chismosos, 30calumniadores, enemigos de Dios, insolentes, soberbios y arrogantes; se ingenian maldades; se rebelan contra sus padres; 31son insensatos, desleales, insensibles, despiadados. 32Saben bien que, según el justo decreto de Dios, quienes practican tales cosas merecen la muerte; sin embargo, no sólo siguen practicándolas sino que incluso aprueban a quienes las practican.

El justo juicio de Dios

2 Por tanto, no tienes excusa tú, quienquiera que seas, cuando juzgas a los demás, pues al juzgar a otros te condenas a ti mismo, ya que practicas las mismas cosas. 2Ahora bien, sabemos que el juicio de Dios contra los que practican tales cosas se basa en la verdad. 3¿Piensas entonces que vas a escapar del juicio de Dios, tú que juzgas a otros y sin embargo haces lo mismo que ellos? 4¿O no ves que desprecias las riquezas de la bondad de Dios, de su tolerancia y de su paciencia, al no reconocer que su bondad quiere llevarte al *arrepentimiento?

5Pero por tu obstinación y por tu corazón empedernido sigues acumulando castigo contra ti mismo para el día de la ira, cuando Dios revelará su justo juicio. 6Porque Dios «pagará a cada uno según lo que merezcan sus obras».f 7Él dará vida eterna a los que, perseverando en las buenas obras, buscan gloria, honor e inmortalidad. 8Pero los que por egoísmo rechazan la verdad para aferrarse a la maldad, recibirán el gran castigo de Dios. 9Habrá sufrimiento y angustia para todos los que hacen el mal, los judíos primeramente, y también los *gentiles; 10pero gloria, honor y paz para todos los que hacen el bien, los judíos primeramente, y también los gentiles. 11Porque con Dios no hay favoritismos.

12Todos los que han pecado sin conocer la ley, también perecerán sin la ley; y todos los que han pecado conociendo la ley, por la ley serán juzgados. 13Porque Dios no considera justos a los que oyen la ley sino a los que la cumplen. 14De hecho, cuando los gentiles, que no tienen la ley, cumplen por naturaleza lo que la ley exige,g ellos son ley para sí mismos,

a 1:4 según el Espíritu *santidad fue designado. Alt. según su espíritu de santidad fue declarado. b 1:5 para . . . la fe. Lit. para la obediencia de la fe entre todas las naciones. c 1:14 sean cultos o incultos. Lit. **griegos y bárbaros. d 1:17 por fe . . . fin. Lit. de fe a fe. e 1.17 Hab 2:4 f 2:6 Sal 62:12; Pr 24:12 g 2:14 que no tienen . . . exige. Alt. que por naturaleza no tienen la ley, cumplen lo que la ley exige.

705

aunque no tengan la ley. 15Éstos muestran que llevan escrito en el corazón lo que la ley exige, como lo atestigua su conciencia, pues sus propios pensamientos algunas veces los acusan y otras veces los excusan. 16Así sucederá el día en que, por medio de Jesucristo, Dios juzgará los secretos de toda persona, como lo declara mi *evangelio.

Los judíos y la ley

17Ahora bien, tú que llevas el nombre de judío; que dependes de la ley y te *jactas de tu relación con Dios; 18que conoces su voluntad y sabes discernir lo que es mejor porque eres instruido por la ley; 19que estás convencido de ser guía de los ciegos y luz de los que están en la oscuridad, 20instructor de los ignorantes, maestro de los sencillos, pues tienes en la ley la esencia misma del conocimiento y de la verdad; 21en fin, tú que enseñas a otros, ¿no te enseñas a ti mismo? Tú que predicas contra el robo, ¿robas? 22Tú que dices que no se debe cometer adulterio, ¿adulteras? Tú que aborreces a los ídolos, ¿robas de sus templos? 23Tú que te jactas de la ley, ¿deshonras a Dios quebrantando la ley? 24Así está escrito: "Por causa de ustedes se *blasfema el nombre de Dios entre los *gentiles."h

25La circuncisión tiene valor si observas la ley; pero si la quebrantas, vienes a ser como un *incircunciso. 26Por lo tanto, si los gentiles cumpleni los requisitos de la ley, ¿no se les considerará como si estuvieran circuncidados? 27El que no está físicamente circuncidado, pero obedece la ley, te condenará a ti que, a pesar de tener el mandamiento escritoj y la circuncisión, quebrantas la ley.

28Lo exterior no hace a nadie judío, ni consiste la circuncisión en una señal en el cuerpo. 29El verdadero judío lo es interiormente; y la circuncisión es la del corazón, la que realiza el Espíritu, no el mandamiento escrito. Al que es judío así, lo alaba Dios y no la gente.

Fidelidad de Dios

3 Entonces, ¿qué se gana con ser judío, o qué valor tiene la circuncisión? 2Mucho, desde cualquier punto de vista. En primer lugar, a los judíos se les confiaron las palabras mismas de Dios.

3Pero entonces, si a algunos les faltó la fe, ¿acaso su falta de fe anula la *fidelidad de Dios? 4¡De ninguna manera! Dios es siempre veraz, aunque el hombre sea mentiroso. Así está escrito:

«Por eso, eres justo en tu sentencia,
y triunfarás cuando te juzguen.»k

5Pero si nuestra injusticia pone de relieve la justicia de Dios, ¿qué diremos? ¿Que Dios es injusto al descargar sobre nosotros su ira? (Hablo en términos humanos.) 6¡De ninguna manera! Si así fuera, ¿cómo podría Dios juzgar al mundo? 7Alguien podría objetar: «Si mi mentira destaca la verdad de Dios y así aumenta su gloria, ¿por qué todavía se me juzga como pecador? 8¿Por qué no decir: Hagamos lo malo para que venga lo bueno?» Así nos calumnian algunos, asegurando que eso es lo que enseñamos. ¡Pero bien merecida se tienen la condenación!

No hay un solo justo

9¿A qué conclusión llegamos? ¿Acaso los judíos somos mejores? ¡De ninguna manera! Ya hemos demostrado que tanto los judíos como los *gentiles están bajo el pecado. 10Así está escrito:

«No hay un solo justo, ni siquiera uno;
11   no hay nadie que entienda,
    nadie que busque a Dios.
12Todos se han descarriado,
    a una se han corrompido.
No hay nadie que haga lo bueno;
    ino hay uno solo!»l
13«Su garganta es un sepulcro abierto;
    con su lengua profieren engaños.»m
«¡Veneno de víbora hay en sus labios!»n
14   «Llena está su boca de maldiciones y de
    amargura.»ñ
15«Veloces son sus pies para ir a derramar
    sangre;
16   dejan ruina y miseria en sus caminos,
17y no conocen la senda de la paz.»o
18   «No hay temor de Dios delante de sus
    ojos.»p

19Ahora bien, sabemos que todo lo que dice la ley, lo dice a quienes están sujetos a ella, para que todo el mundo se calle la boca y quede convicto delante de Dios. 20Por tanto, nadie será *justificado en presencia de Dios por hacer las obras que exige la ley; más bien, mediante la ley cobramos conciencia del pecado.

La justicia mediante la fe

21Pero ahora, sin la mediación de la ley, se ha manifestado la justicia de Dios, de la que dan testimonio la ley y los profetas. 22Esta justicia de Dios llega, mediante la *fe en Jesucristo, a todos los que creen. De hecho, no hay distinción, 23pues todos han pecado y están privados de la gloria de Dios, 24pero por su gracia son *justificados gratuitamente mediante la redención que Cristo Jesús efectuó.q 25Dios lo ofreció como un sacrificio de *expiación que se recibe por la fe en su sangre, para así demostrar su justicia. Anteriormente, en su paciencia, Dios había pasado por alto los pecados; 26pero en el tiempo presente ha ofrecido a Jesucristo para manifestar su justicia. De este modo Dios es justo y, a la vez, el que justifica a los que tienen fe en Jesús.

27¿Dónde, pues, está la *jactancia? Queda excluida. ¿Por cuál principio? ¿Por el de la observancia de la ley? No, sino por el de la fe. 28Porque sostenemos que todos somos justificados por la fe, y no por las obras que la ley exige. 29¿Es acaso Dios sólo Dios de los judíos? ¿No lo es también de los *gentiles? Sí, también es Dios de los gentiles, 30pues no hay más que un solo Dios. Él justificará por la fe a los que están circuncidados y, mediante esa misma fe, a los que no lo están. 31¿Quiere decir que anulamos la ley con la fe? ¡De ninguna manera! Más bien, confirmamos la ley.

Abraham, justificado por la fe

4 Entonces, ¿qué diremos en el caso de nuestro antepasado Abraham?s 2En realidad, si Abraham hubiera sido *justificado por las obras, habría

---

h 2:24 Is 52:5; Ez 36:22   i 2:26 si . . . cumplen. Lit. si la incircuncisión guarda.   j 2:27 el mandamiento escrito. Lit. la letra; también en v. 29.   k 3:4 Sal 51:4   l 3:12 Sal 14:1-3; 53:1-3; Ec 7:20   m 3:13 Sal 5:9   n 3:13 Sal 140:3   ñ 3:14 Sal 10:7   o 3:17 Is 59:7,8   p 3:18 Sal 36:1   q 3:24 redención . . . efectuó. Lit. redención en Cristo Jesús.   r 3:25 un sacrificio de *expiación. Lit. propiciación.   s 4:1 ¿qué . . . Abraham? Lit. ¿qué diremos que descubrió Abraham, nuestro antepasado según la *carne?

tenido de qué *jactarse, pero no delante de Dios. ³Pues ¿qué dice la Escritura? «Le creyó Abraham a Dios, y esto se le tomó en cuenta como justicia.»ᵗ

⁴Ahora bien, cuando alguien trabaja, no se le toma en cuenta el salario como un favor sino como una deuda. ⁵Sin embargo, al que no trabaja, sino que cree en el que justifica al malvado, se le toma en cuenta la fe como justicia. ⁶David dice lo mismo cuando habla de la dicha de aquel a quien Dios le atribuye justicia sin la mediación de las obras:

⁷«*¡Dichosos aquellos
a quienes se les perdonan las
transgresiones
y se les cubren los pecados!
⁸¡Dichoso aquel
cuyo pecado el Señor no tomará en
cuenta!»ᵘ

⁹¿Acaso se ha reservado esta dicha sólo para los que están circuncidados? ¿Acaso no es también para los *gentiles?ᵛ Hemos dicho que a Abraham se le tomó en cuenta la fe como justicia. ¹⁰¿Bajo qué circunstancias sucedió esto? ¿Fue antes o después de ser circuncidado? ¡Antes, y no después! ¹¹Es más, cuando todavía no estaba circuncidado, recibió la señal de la circuncisión como sello de la justicia que se le había tomado en cuenta por la fe. Por tanto, Abraham es padre de todos los que creen, aunque no hayan sido circuncidados, y a éstos se les toma en cuenta su fe como justicia. ¹²Y también es padre de aquellos que, además de haber sido circuncidados, siguen las huellas de nuestro padre Abraham, quien creyó cuando todavía era incircunciso.

¹³En efecto, no fue mediante la ley como Abraham y su descendencia recibieron la promesa de que él sería heredero del mundo, sino mediante la fe, la cual se le tomó en cuenta como justicia. ¹⁴Porque si los que viven por la ley fueran los herederos, entonces la fe no tendría ya ningún valor y la promesa no serviría de nada. ¹⁵La ley, en efecto, acarrea castigo. Pero donde no hay ley, tampoco hay transgresión.

¹⁶Por eso la promesa viene por la fe, a fin de que por la gracia quede garantizada para toda la descendencia de Abraham; esta promesa no es sólo para los que son de la ley sino para los que son también de la fe de Abraham, quien es el padre que tenemos en común ¹⁷delante de Dios, tal como está escrito: «Te he confirmado como padre de muchas naciones.»ʷ Así que Abraham creyó en el Dios que da vida a los muertos y que llama las cosas que no son como si ya existieran.

¹⁸Contra toda esperanza, Abraham creyó y esperó, y de este modo llegó a ser padre de muchas naciones, tal como se le había dicho: «¡Así de numerosa será tu descendencia!»ˣ ¹⁹Su fe no flaqueó, aunque reconocía que su cuerpo estaba como muerto, pues ya tenía unos cien años, y que también estaba muerta la matriz de Sara. ²⁰Ante la promesa de Dios no vaciló como un incrédulo, sino que se reafirmó en su fe y dio gloria a Dios, ²¹plenamente convencido de que Dios tenía poder para cumplir lo que había prometido. ²²Por eso se le tomó en cuenta su fe como justicia. ²³Y esto de que «se le tomó en cuenta» no se escribió sólo para Abraham, ²⁴sino también para nosotros. Dios tomará en cuenta

nuestra fe como justicia, pues creemos en aquel que *levantó de entre los muertos a Jesús nuestro Señor. ²⁵Él fue entregado a la muerte por nuestros pecados, y resucitó para nuestra justificación.

Paz y alegría

5 En consecuencia, ya que hemos sido *justificados mediante la fe, tenemos y paz con Dios por medio de nuestro Señor Jesucristo. ²También por medio de él, y mediante la fe, tenemos acceso a esta gracia en la cual nos mantenemos firmes. Así que nos *regocijamos en la esperanza de alcanzar la gloria de Dios. ³Y no sólo en esto, sino también en nuestros sufrimientos, porque sabemos que el sufrimiento produce perseverancia; ⁴la perseverancia, entereza de carácter; la entereza de carácter, esperanza. ⁵Y esta esperanza no nos defrauda, porque Dios ha derramado su amor en nuestro corazón por el Espíritu Santo que nos ha dado.

⁶A la verdad, como éramos incapaces de salvarnos,ᶻ en el tiempo señalado Cristo murió por los malvados. ⁷Difícilmente habrá quien muera por un justo, aunque tal vez haya quien se atreva a morir por una persona buena. ⁸Pero Dios demuestra su amor por nosotros en esto: en que cuando todavía éramos pecadores, Cristo murió por nosotros.

⁹Y ahora que hemos sido justificados por su sangre, ¡con cuánta más razón, por medio de él, seremos salvados del castigo de Dios! ¹⁰Porque si, cuando éramos enemigos de Dios, fuimos reconciliados con él mediante la muerte de su Hijo, ¡con cuánta más razón, habiendo sido reconciliados, seremos salvados por su vida! ¹¹Y no sólo esto, sino que también nos regocijamos en Dios por nuestro Señor Jesucristo, pues gracias a él ya hemos recibido la reconciliación.

De Adán, la muerte; de Cristo, la vida

¹²Por medio de un solo hombre el pecado entró en el mundo, y por medio del pecado entró la muerte; fue así como la muerte pasó a toda la *humanidad, porque todos pecaron.ᵃ ¹³Antes de promulgarse la ley, ya existía el pecado en el mundo. Es cierto que el pecado no se toma en cuenta cuando no hay ley; ¹⁴sin embargo, desde Adán hasta Moisés la muerte reinó, incluso sobre los que no pecaron quebrantando un mandato, como lo hizo Adán, quien es figura de aquel que había de venir.

¹⁵Pero la transgresión de Adán no puede compararse con la gracia de Dios. Pues si por la transgresión de un solo hombre murieron todos, ¡cuánto más el don que vino por la gracia de un solo hombre, Jesucristo, abundó para todos! ¹⁶Tampoco se puede comparar la dádiva de Dios con las consecuencias del pecado de Adán. El juicio que lleva a la condenación fue resultado de un solo pecado, pero la dádiva que lleva a la *justificación tiene que ver conᵇ una multitud de transgresiones. ¹⁷Pues si por la transgresión de un solo hombre reinó la muerte, con mayor razón los que reciben en abundancia la gracia y el don de la justicia reinarán en vida por medio de un solo hombre, Jesucristo.

¹⁸Por tanto, así como una sola transgresión causó la condenación de todos, también un solo acto de justicia produjo la justificación que da vida a todos. ¹⁹Porque así como por la desobediencia de uno solo muchos fueron constituidos pecadores, también por

---

ᵗ 4:3 Gn 15:6; también en v. 22 ᵘ 4:8 Sal 32:1,2 ᵛ 4:9 los *gentiles. Lit. la *incircuncisión. ʷ 4:17 Gn 17:5 ˣ 4:18 Gn 15:5 y 5:1 tenemos. Var. tengamos. ᶻ 5:6 como . . . salvarnos. Lit. cuando todavía éramos débiles. ᵃ 5:12 En el griego este versículo es la primera parte de una oración comparativa que se reinicia y concluye en el v. 18. ᵇ 5:16 resultado . . . con. Alt. resultado del pecado de uno solo, pero la dádiva que lleva a la justificación fue resultado de.

la obediencia de uno solo muchos serán constituidos justos.

20En lo que atañe a la ley, ésta intervino para que aumentara la transgresión. Pero allí donde abundó el pecado, sobreabundó la gracia, 21a fin de que, así como reinó el pecado en la muerte, reine también la gracia que nos trae justificación y vida eterna por medio de Jesucristo nuestro Señor.

Muertos al pecado, vivos en Cristo

6 ¿Qué concluiremos? ¿Vamos a persistir en el pecado, para que la gracia abunde? 2¡De ninguna manera! Nosotros, que hemos muerto al pecado, ¿cómo podemos seguir viviendo en él? 3¿Acaso no saben ustedes que todos los que fuimos bautizados para unirnos con Cristo Jesús, en realidad fuimos bautizados para participar en su muerte? 4Por tanto, mediante el bautismo fuimos sepultados con él en su muerte, a fin de que, así como Cristo *resucitó por el poderc del Padre, también nosotros llevemos una vida nueva.

5En efecto, si hemos estado unidos con él en su muerte, sin duda también estaremos unidos con él en su resurrección. 6Sabemos que nuestra vieja naturaleza fue crucificada con él para que nuestro cuerpo pecaminoso perdiera su poder, de modo que ya no siguiéramos siendo esclavos del pecado; 7porque el que muere queda liberado del pecado.

8Ahora bien, si hemos muerto con Cristo, confiamos que también viviremos con él. 9Pues sabemos que Cristo, por haber sido *levantado de entre los muertos, ya no puede volver a morir; la muerte ya no tiene dominio sobre él. 10En cuanto a su muerte, murió al pecado una vez y para siempre; en cuanto a su vida, vive para Dios.

11De la misma manera, también ustedes considérense muertos al pecado, pero vivos para Dios en Cristo Jesús. 12Por lo tanto, no permitan ustedes que el pecado reine en su cuerpo mortal, ni obedezcan a sus malos deseos. 13No ofrezcan los miembros de su cuerpo al pecado como instrumentos de injusticia; al contrario, ofrézcanse más bien a Dios como quienes han vuelto de la muerte a la vida, presentando los miembros de su cuerpo como instrumentos de justicia. 14Así el pecado no tendrá dominio sobre ustedes, porque ya no están bajo la ley sino bajo la gracia.

Esclavos de la justicia

15Entonces, ¿qué? ¿Vamos a pecar porque no estamos ya bajo la ley sino bajo la gracia? ¡De ninguna manera! 16¿Acaso no saben ustedes que, cuando se entregan a alguien para obedecerlo, son *esclavos de aquel a quien obedecen? Claro que lo son, ya sea del pecado que lleva a la muerte, o de la obediencia que lleva a la justicia. 17Pero gracias a Dios que, aunque antes eran esclavos del pecado, ya se han sometido de corazón a la enseñanzad que les fue transmitida. 18En efecto, habiendo sido liberados del pecado, ahora son ustedes esclavos de la justicia.

19Hablo en términos humanos, por las limitaciones de su *naturaleza humana. Antes ofrecían ustedes los miembros de su cuerpo para servir a la impureza, que lleva más y más a la maldad; ofrézcanlos ahora para servir a la justicia que lleva a la *santidad. 20Cuando ustedes eran esclavos del pecado, estaban libres del dominio de la justicia. 21¿Qué fruto cosechaban entonces? ¡Cosas que ahora los avergüenzan y que conducen a la muerte! 22Pero

ahora que han sido liberados del pecado y se han puesto al servicio de Dios, cosechan la santidad que conduce a la vida eterna. 23Porque la paga del pecado es muerte, mientras que la dádiva de Dios es vida eterna en Cristo Jesús, nuestro Señor.

Analogía tomada del matrimonio

7 Hermanos, les hablo como a quienes conocen la ley. ¿Acaso no saben que uno está sujeto a la ley solamente en vida? 2Por ejemplo, la casada está ligada por ley a su esposo sólo mientras éste vive; pero si su esposo muere, ella queda libre de la ley que la unía a su esposo. 3Por eso, si se casa con otro hombre mientras su esposo vive, se le considera adúltera. Pero si muere su esposo, ella queda libre de esa ley, y no es adúltera aunque se case con otro hombre.

4Así mismo, hermanos míos, ustedes murieron a la ley mediante el cuerpo crucificado de Cristo, a fin de pertenecer al que fue *levantado de entre los muertos. De este modo daremos fruto para Dios. 5Porque cuando nuestra *naturaleza pecaminosa aún nos dominaba,e las malas pasiones que la ley nos despertaba actuaban en los miembros de nuestro cuerpo, y dábamos fruto para muerte. 6Pero ahora, al morir a lo que nos tenía subyugados, hemos quedado libres de la ley, a fin de servir a Dios con el nuevo poder que nos da el Espíritu, y no por medio del antiguo mandamiento escrito.

Conflicto con el pecado

7¿Qué concluiremos? ¿Que la ley es pecado? ¡De ninguna manera! Sin embargo, si no fuera por la ley, no me habría dado cuenta de lo que es el pecado. Por ejemplo, nunca habría sabido yo lo que es codiciar si la ley no hubiera dicho: «No codicies.»f 8Pero el pecado, aprovechando la oportunidad que le proporcionó el mandamiento, despertó en mí toda clase de codicia. Porque aparte de la ley el pecado está muerto. 9En otro tiempo yo tenía vida aparte de la ley; pero cuando vino el mandamiento, cobró vida el pecado y yo morí. 10Se me hizo evidente que el mismo mandamiento que debía haberme dado vida me llevó a la muerte; 11porque el pecado se aprovechó del mandamiento, me engañó, y por medio de él me mató.

12Concluimos, pues, que la ley es santa, y que el mandamiento es santo, justo y bueno. 13Pero entonces, ¿lo que es bueno se convirtió en muerte para mí? ¡De ninguna manera! Más bien fue el pecado lo que, valiéndose de lo bueno, me produjo la muerte; ocurrió así para que el pecado se manifestara claramente, o sea, para que mediante el mandamiento se demostrara lo extremadamente malo que es el pecado.

14Sabemos, en efecto, que la ley es espiritual. Pero yo soy meramente *humano, y estoy vendido como esclavo al pecado. 15No entiendo lo que me pasa, pues no hago lo que quiero, sino lo que aborrezco. 16Ahora bien, si hago lo que no quiero, estoy de acuerdo en que la ley es buena; 17pero, en ese caso, ya no soy yo quien lo lleva a cabo sino el pecado que habita en mí. 18Yo sé que en mí, es decir, en mi *naturaleza pecaminosa, nada bueno habita. Aunque deseo hacer lo bueno, no soy capaz de hacerlo. 19De hecho, no hago el bien que quiero, sino el mal que no quiero. 20Y si hago lo que no quiero, ya no soy yo quien lo hace sino el pecado que habita en mí.

21Así que descubro esta ley: que cuando quiero hacer el bien, me acompaña el mal. 22Porque en lo íntimo de mi ser me deleito en la ley de Dios; 23pero me

---

c **6:4** *el poder.* Lit. *la gloria.*   d **6:17** *a la enseñanza.* Lit. *al modelo de enseñanza.*   e **7:5** *cuando . . . dominaba.* Lit. *cuando estábamos en la *carne.*   f **7:7** Éx 20:17; Dt 5:21

doy cuenta de que en los miembros de mi cuerpo hay otra ley, que es la ley del pecado. Esta ley lucha contra la ley de mi mente, y me tiene cautivo. 24¡Soy un pobre miserable! ¿Quién me librará de este cuerpo mortal? 25¡Gracias a Dios por medio de Jesucristo nuestro Señor!

En conclusión, con la mente yo mismo me someto a la ley de Dios, pero mi *naturaleza pecaminosa está sujeta a la ley del pecado.

Vida mediante el Espíritu

8 Por lo tanto, ya no hay ninguna condenación para los que están unidos a Cristo Jesús,g 2pues por medio de él la ley del Espíritu de vida meh ha liberado de la ley del pecado y de la muerte. 3En efecto, la ley no pudo liberarnos porque la *naturaleza pecaminosa anuló su poder; por eso Dios envió a su propio Hijo en condición semejante a nuestra condición de pecadores,i para que se ofreciera en sacrificio por el pecado. Así condenó Dios al pecado en la naturaleza humana, 4a fin de que las justas demandas de la ley se cumplieran en nosotros, que no vivimos según la naturaleza pecaminosa sino según el Espíritu.

5Los que viven conforme a la naturaleza pecaminosa fijan la mente en los deseos de tal naturaleza; en cambio, los que viven conforme al Espíritu fijan la mente en los deseos del Espíritu. 6La mentalidad pecaminosa es muerte, mientras que la mentalidad que proviene del Espíritu es vida y paz. 7La mentalidad pecaminosa es enemiga de Dios, pues no se somete a la ley de Dios, ni es capaz de hacerlo. 8Los que viven según la naturaleza pecaminosa no pueden agradar a Dios.

9Sin embargo, ustedes no viven según la naturaleza pecaminosa sino según el Espíritu, si es que el Espíritu de Dios vive en ustedes. Y si alguno no tiene el Espíritu de Cristo, no es de Cristo. 10Pero si Cristo está en ustedes, el cuerpo está muerto a causa del pecado, pero el Espíritu que está en ustedes es vidaj a causa de la justicia. 11Y si el Espíritu de aquel que *levantó a Jesús de entre los muertos vive en ustedes, el mismo que levantó a Cristo de entre los muertos también dará vida a sus cuerpos mortales por medio de su Espíritu, que vive en ustedes.

12Por tanto, hermanos, tenemos una obligación, pero no es la de vivir conforme a la naturaleza pecaminosa. 13Porque si ustedes viven conforme a ella, morirán; pero si por medio del Espíritu dan muerte a los malos hábitos del cuerpo, vivirán. 14Porque todos los que son guiados por el Espíritu de Dios son hijos de Dios. 15Y ustedes no recibieron un espíritu que de nuevo los esclavice al miedo, sino el Espíritu que los adopta como hijos y les permite clamar: «¡*Abba! ¡Padre!» 16El Espíritu mismo le asegura a nuestro espíritu que somos hijos de Dios. 17Y si somos hijos, somos herederos; herederos de Dios y coherederos de Cristo, pues si ahora sufrimos con él, también tendremos parte con él en su gloria.

La gloria futura

18De hecho, considero que en nada se comparan los sufrimientos actuales con la gloria que habrá de revelarse en nosotros. 19La creación aguarda con ansiedad la revelación de los hijos de Dios, 20porque fue sometida a la frustración. Esto no sucedió por su propia voluntad, sino por la del que así lo dispuso.

Pero queda la firme esperanza 21de que la creación misma ha de ser liberada de la corrupción que la esclaviza, para así alcanzar la gloriosa libertad de los hijos de Dios.

22Sabemos que toda la creación todavía gime a una, como si tuviera dolores de parto. 23Y no sólo ella, sino también nosotros mismos, que tenemos las *primicias del Espíritu, gemimos interiormente, mientras aguardamos nuestra adopción como hijos, es decir, la redención de nuestro cuerpo. 24Porque en esa esperanza fuimos salvados. Pero la esperanza que se ve, ya no es esperanza. ¿Quién espera lo que ya tiene? 25Pero si esperamos lo que todavía no tenemos, en la espera mostramos nuestra constancia.

26Así mismo, en nuestra debilidad el Espíritu acude a ayudarnos. No sabemos qué pedir, pero el Espíritu mismo intercede por nosotros con gemidos que no pueden expresarse con palabras. 27Y Dios, que examina los corazones, sabe cuál es la intención del Espíritu, porque el Espíritu intercede por los *creyentes conforme a la voluntad de Dios.

Más que vencedores

28Ahora bien, sabemos que Dios dispone todas las cosas para el bien de quienes lo aman,k los que han sido llamados de acuerdo con su propósito. 29Porque a los que Dios conoció de antemano, también los predestinó a ser transformados según la imagen de su Hijo, para que él sea el primogénito entre muchos hermanos. 30A los que predestinó, también los llamó; a los que llamó, también los *justificó; y a los que justificó, también los glorificó.

31¿Qué diremos frente a esto? Si Dios está de nuestra parte, ¿quién puede estar en contra nuestra? 32El que no escatimó ni a su propio Hijo, sino que lo entregó por todos nosotros, ¿cómo no habrá de darnos generosamente, junto con él, todas las cosas? 33¿Quién acusará a los que Dios ha escogido? Dios es el que justifica. 34¿Quién condenará? Cristo Jesús es el que murió, e incluso *resucitó, y está a la *derecha de Dios e intercede por nosotros. 35¿Quién nos apartará del amor de Cristo? ¿La tribulación, o la angustia, la persecución, el hambre, la indigencia, el peligro, o la violencia? 36Así está escrito:

«Por tu causa siempre nos llevan a la muerte;
¡nos tratan como a ovejas para el
matadero!»l

37Sin embargo, en todo esto somos más que vencedores por medio de aquel que nos amó. 38Pues estoy convencido de que ni la muerte ni la vida, ni los ángeles ni los demonios,m ni lo presente ni lo por venir, ni los poderes, 39ni lo alto ni lo profundo, ni cosa alguna en toda la creación, podrá apartarnos del amor que Dios nos ha manifestado en Cristo Jesús nuestro Señor.

La elección soberana de Dios

9 Digo la verdad en Cristo; no miento. Mi conciencia me lo confirma en el Espíritu Santo. 2Me invade una gran tristeza y me embarga un continuo dolor. 3Desearía yo mismo ser maldecido y separado de Cristo por el bien de mis hermanos, los de mi propia raza, 4el pueblo de Israel. De ellos son la adopción como hijos, la gloria divina, los pactos, la ley, y el privilegio de adorar a Dios y contar con sus pro-

---

g 8:1 Jesús. Var. Jesús, los que no viven según la naturaleza pecaminosa sino según el Espíritu (véase v. 4).   h 8:2 me. Var. te.   i 8:3 en condición semejante . . . pecadores. Lit. en semejanza de *carne de pecado.   j 8:10 el Espíritu . . . vida. Alt. el espíritu de ustedes vive.   k 8:28 Dios . . . aman. Var. todo actúa para el bien de quienes aman a Dios.   l 8:36 Sal 44:22   m 8:38 demonios. Alt. gobernantes celestiales.

mesas. [5]De ellos son los patriarcas, y de ellos, según la *naturaleza humana, nació Cristo, quien es Dios sobre todas las cosas. ¡Alabado sea por siempre![n] Amén.

[6]Ahora bien, no digamos que la Palabra de Dios ha fracasado. Lo que sucede es que no todos los que descienden de Israel son Israel. [7]Tampoco por ser descendientes de Abraham son todos hijos suyos. Al contrario: «Tu descendencia se establecerá por medio de Isaac.»[ñ] [8]En otras palabras, los hijos de Dios no son los descendientes *naturales; más bien, se considera descendencia de Abraham a los hijos de la promesa. [9]Y ésta fue la promesa: «Dentro de un año vendré, y para entonces Sara tendrá un hijo.»[o]

[10]No sólo eso. También sucedió que los hijos de Rebeca tuvieron un mismo padre, que fue nuestro antepasado Isaac. [11]Sin embargo, antes de que los mellizos nacieran, o hicieran algo bueno o malo, y para confirmar el propósito de la elección divina, [12]no en base a las obras sino al llamado de Dios, se le dijo a ella: «El mayor servirá al menor.»[p] [13]Y así está escrito: «Amé a Jacob, pero aborrecí a Esaú.»[q]

[14]¿Qué concluiremos? ¿Acaso es Dios injusto? ¡De ninguna manera! [15]Es un hecho que a Moisés le dice:

«Tendré clemencia de quien yo quiera tenerla, y seré compasivo con quien yo quiera serlo.»[r]

[16]Por lo tanto, la elección no depende del deseo ni del esfuerzo humano sino de la misericordia de Dios. [17]Porque la Escritura le dice al faraón: «Te he levantado precisamente para mostrar en ti mi poder, y para que mi nombre sea proclamado por toda la tierra.»[s] [18]Así que Dios tiene misericordia de quien él quiere tenerla, y endurece a quien él quiere endurecer.

[19]Pero tú me dirás: «Entonces, ¿por qué todavía nos echa la culpa Dios? ¿Quién puede oponerse a su voluntad?» [20]Respondo: ¿Quién eres tú para pedirle cuentas a Dios? ¿Acaso le dirá la olla de barro al que la modeló: "¿Por qué me hiciste así?"»[t] [21]¿No tiene derecho el alfarero de hacer del mismo barro unas vasijas para usos especiales y otras para fines ordinarios?

[22]¿Y qué si Dios, queriendo mostrar su ira y dar a conocer su poder, soportó con mucha paciencia a los que eran objeto de su castigo[u] y estaban destinados a la destrucción? [23]¿Qué si lo hizo para dar a conocer sus gloriosas riquezas a los que eran objeto de su misericordia, a quienes de antemano preparó para esa gloria? [24]Ésos somos nosotros, a quienes Dios llamó no sólo de entre los judíos sino también de entre los *gentiles. [25]Así lo dice Dios en el libro de Oseas:

«Llamaré "mi pueblo" a los que no son mi pueblo;
y llamaré "mi amada" a la que no es mi amada».[v]

[26]«Y sucederá que en el mismo lugar donde se les dijo:
"Ustedes no son mi pueblo",
serán llamados "hijos del Dios viviente".»[w]

[27]Isaías, por su parte, proclama respecto de Israel:

«Aunque los israelitas sean tan numerosos

como la arena del mar,
sólo el remanente será salvo;
[28]porque plenamente y sin demora
el Señor cumplirá su sentencia en la tierra.»[x]

[29]Así había dicho Isaías:

«Si el Señor Todopoderoso
no nos hubiera dejado descendientes,
seríamos ya como Sodoma,
nos pareceríamos a Gomorra.»[y]

Incredulidad de Israel

[30]¿Qué concluiremos? Pues que los *gentiles, que no buscaban la justicia, la han alcanzado. Me refiero a la justicia que es por la fe. [31]En cambio Israel, que iba en busca de una ley que le diera justicia, no ha alcanzado esa justicia. [32]¿Por qué no? Porque no la buscaron mediante la fe sino mediante las obras, como si fuera posible alcanzarla así. Por eso tropezaron con la «piedra de tropiezo», [33]como está escrito:

«Miren que pongo en Sión una piedra de tropiezo
y una roca que hace *caer;
pero el que confíe en él no será defraudado.»[z]

10 Hermanos, el deseo de mi corazón, y mi oración a Dios por los israelitas, es que lleguen a ser salvos. [2]Puedo declarar en favor de ellos que muestran celo por Dios, pero su celo no se basa en el conocimiento. [3]No conociendo la justicia que proviene de Dios, y procurando establecer la suya propia, no se sometieron a la justicia de Dios. [4]De hecho, Cristo es el fin de la ley, para que todo el que cree reciba la justicia.

[5]Así describe Moisés la justicia que se basa en la ley: «Quien practique estas cosas vivirá por ellas.»[a] [6]Pero la justicia que se basa en la fe afirma: «No digas en tu corazón: "¿Quién subirá al cielo?"[b] (es decir, para hacer bajar a Cristo), [7]o "¿Quién bajará al *abismo?" » (es decir, para hacer subir a Cristo de entre los muertos). [8]¿Qué afirma entonces? «La palabra está cerca de ti; la tienes en la boca y en el corazón.»[c] Ésta es la palabra de fe que predicamos: [9]que si confiesas con tu boca que Jesús es el Señor, y crees en tu corazón que Dios lo *levantó de entre los muertos, serás salvo. [10]Porque con el corazón se cree para ser *justificado, pero con la boca se confiesa para ser salvo. [11]Así dice la Escritura: «Todo el que confíe en él no será jamás defraudado.»[d] [12]No hay diferencia entre judíos y *gentiles, pues el mismo Señor es Señor de todos y bendice abundantemente a cuantos lo invocan, [13]porque «todo el que invoque el nombre del Señor será salvo».[e]

[14]Ahora bien, ¿cómo invocarán a aquel en quien no han creído? ¿Y cómo creerán en aquel de quien no han oído? ¿Y cómo oirán si no hay quien les predique? [15]¿Y quién predicará sin ser enviado? Así está escrito: «¡Qué hermoso es recibir al mensajero que trae[f] buenas *nuevas!»

[16]Sin embargo, no todos los israelitas aceptaron las buenas nuevas. Isaías dice: «Señor, ¿quién ha creído a nuestro mensaje?»[g] [17]Así que la fe viene como resultado de oír el mensaje, y el mensaje que se

---

[n] 9:5 *Cristo . . . siempre!* Alt. *Cristo. ¡Dios, que está sobre todas las cosas, sea alabado por siempre!* [ñ] 9:7 Gn 21:12 [o] 9:9 Gn 18:10,14 [p] 9:12 Gn 25:23 [q] 9:13 Mal 1:2,3 [r] 9:15 Éx 33:19 [s] 9:17 Éx 9:16 [t] 9:20 Is 29:16; 45:9 [u] 9:22 *objeto de su castigo.* Lit. *vasijas de ira.* [v] 9:25 Os 2:23 [w] 9:26 Os 1:10 [x] 9:28 Is 10:22,23 [y] 9:29 Is 1:9 [z] 9:33 Is 8:14; 28:16 [a] 10:5 Lv 18:5 [b] 10:6 Dt 30:12 [c] 10:8 Dt 30:14 [d] 10:11 Is 28:16 [e] 10:13 Jl 2:32 [f] 10:15 *¡Qué hermoso . . . trae.* Lit. *¡Qué hermosos son los pies de los que anuncian;* Is 52:7. [g] 10:16 Is 53:1

oye es la palabra de Cristo.ʰ ¹⁸Pero pregunto: ¿Acaso no oyeron? ¡Claro que sí!

> «Por toda la tierra se difundió su voz,
> ¡sus palabras llegan hasta los confines del
>   mundo!»ⁱ

¹⁹Pero insisto: ¿Acaso no entendió Israel? En primer lugar, Moisés dice:

> «Yo haré que ustedes sientan envidia de los
>   que no son nación;
> voy a irritarlos con una nación insensata.»ʲ

²⁰Luego Isaías se atreve a decir:

> «Dejé que me hallaran los que no me
>   buscaban;
> me di a conocer a los que no preguntaban
>   por mí.»ᵏ

²¹En cambio, respecto de Israel, dice:

> «Todo el día extendí mis manos
> hacia un pueblo desobediente y rebelde.»ˡ

El remanente de Israel

11 Por lo tanto, pregunto: ¿Acaso rechazó Dios a su pueblo? ¡De ninguna manera! Yo mismo soy israelita, descendiente de Abraham, de la tribu de Benjamín. ²Dios no rechazó a su pueblo, al que de antemano conoció. ¿No saben lo que relata la Escritura en cuanto a Elías? Acusó a Israel delante de Dios: ³«Señor, han matado a tus profetas y han derribado tus altares. Yo soy el único que ha quedado con vida, ¡y ahora quieren matarme a mí también!»ᵐ ⁴¿Y qué le contestó la voz divina? «He apartado para mí siete mil hombres, los que no se han arrodillado ante Baal.»ⁿ ⁵Así también hay en la actualidad un remanente escogido por gracia. ⁶Y si es por gracia, ya no es por obras; porque en tal caso la gracia ya no sería gracia.ñ

⁷¿Qué concluiremos? Pues que Israel no consiguió lo que tanto deseaba, pero sí lo consiguieron los elegidos. Los demás fueron endurecidos, ⁸como está escrito:

> «Dios les dio un espíritu insensible,
> ojos con los que no pueden ver
> y oídos con los que no pueden oír,
> hasta el día de hoy.»ᵒ

⁹Y David dice:

> «Que sus banquetes se les conviertan en red y
>   en trampa,
> en *tropezadero y en castigo.
> ¹⁰Que se les nublen los ojos para que no vean,
> y se encorven sus espaldas para siempre.»ᵖ

Ramas injertadas

¹¹Ahora pregunto: ¿Acaso tropezaron para no volver a levantarse? ¡De ninguna manera! Más bien, gracias a su transgresión ha venido la salvación a los *gentiles, para que Israel sienta celos. ¹²Pero si su transgresión ha enriquecido al mundo, es decir, si su fracaso ha enriquecido a los gentiles, ¡cuánto mayor será la riqueza que su plena restauración producirá!

¹³Me dirijo ahora a ustedes, los gentiles. Como apóstol que soy de ustedes, le hago honor a mi ministerio, ¹⁴pues quisiera ver si de algún modo despierto los celos de mi propio pueblo, para así salvar a algunos de ellos. ¹⁵Pues si el haberlos rechazado dio como resultado la reconciliación entre Dios y el mundo, ¿no será su restitución una vuelta a la vida? ¹⁶Si se consagra la parte de la masa que se ofrece como *primicias, también se consagra toda la masa; si la raíz es santa, también lo son las ramas.

¹⁷Ahora bien, es verdad que algunas de las ramas han sido desgajadas, y que tú, siendo de olivo silvestre, has sido injertado entre las otras ramas. Ahora participas de la savia nutritiva de la raíz del olivo. ¹⁸Sin embargo, no te vayas a creer mejor que las ramas originales. Y si te jactas de ello, ten en cuenta que no eres tú quien nutre a la raíz, sino que es la raíz la que te nutre a ti. ¹⁹Tal vez dirás: «Desgajaron unas ramas para que yo fuera injertado.» ²⁰De acuerdo. Pero ellas fueron desgajadas por su falta de fe, y tú por la fe te mantienes firme. Así que no seas arrogante sino temeroso; ²¹porque si Dios no tuvo miramientos con las ramas originales, tampoco los tendrá contigo.

²²Por tanto, considera la bondad y la severidad de Dios: severidad hacia los que cayeron y bondad hacia ti. Pero si no te mantienes en su bondad, tú también serás desgajado. ²³Y si ellos dejan de ser incrédulos, serán injertados, porque Dios tiene poder para injertarlos de nuevo. ²⁴Después de todo, si tú fuiste cortado de un olivo silvestre, al que por naturaleza pertenecías, y contra tu condición natural fuiste injertado en un olivo cultivado, ¡con cuánta mayor facilidad las ramas naturales de ese olivo serán injertadas de nuevo en él!

Todo Israel será salvo

²⁵Hermanos, quiero que entiendan este *misterio para que no se vuelvan presuntuosos. Parte de Israel se ha endurecido, y así permanecerá hasta que haya entrado la totalidad de los *gentiles. ²⁶De esta manera todo Israel será salvo, como está escrito:

> «El redentor vendrá de Sión
> y apartará de Jacob la impiedad.
> ²⁷Y éste será mi pacto con ellos
> cuando perdone sus pecados.»q

²⁸Con respecto al *evangelio, los israelitas son enemigos de Dios para bien de ustedes; pero si tomamos en cuenta la elección, son amados de Dios por causa de los patriarcas, ²⁹porque las dádivas de Dios son irrevocables, como lo es también su llamamiento. ³⁰De hecho, en otro tiempo ustedes fueron desobedientes a Dios; pero ahora, por la desobediencia de los israelitas, han sido objeto de su misericordia. ³¹Así mismo, estos que han desobedecido recibirán misericordia ahora, como resultado de la misericordia de Dios hacia ustedes. ³²En fin, Dios ha sujetado a todos a la desobediencia, con el fin de tener misericordia de todos.

Doxología

³³¡Qué profundas son las riquezas de la sabiduría y del conocimiento de Dios!

> ¡Qué indescifrables sus juicios
> e impenetrables sus caminos!
> ³⁴«¿Quién ha conocido la mente del Señor,
> o quién ha sido su consejero?»ʳ
> ³⁵«¿Quién le ha dado primero a Dios,
> para que luego Dios le pague?»ˢ

ʰ **10:17** *Cristo.* Var. *Dios.* ⁱ **10:18** Sal 19:4 ʲ **10:19** Dt 32:21 ᵏ **10:20** Is 65:1 ˡ **10:21** Is 65:2 ᵐ **11:3** 1R 19:10,14 ⁿ **11:4** 1R 19:18 ñ **11:6** *no sería gracia.* Var. *no sería gracia. Pero si es por obras, ya no es gracia; porque en tal caso la obra ya no sería obra.* ᵒ **11:8** Dt 29:4; Is 29:10 ᵖ **11:10** Sal 69:22,23 q **11:27** Is 59:20,21; 27:9; Jer 31:33,34 ʳ **11:34** Is 40:13 ˢ **11:35** Job 41:11

36Porque todas las cosas proceden de él,
y existen por él y para él.
¡A él sea la gloria por siempre! Amén.

Sacrificios vivos

12 Por lo tanto, hermanos, tomando en cuenta la misericordia de Dios, les ruego que cada uno de ustedes, en adoración espiritual,t ofrezca su cuerpo como sacrificio vivo, *santo y agradable a Dios. 2No se amolden al mundo actual, sino sean transformados mediante la renovación de su mente. Así podrán comprobar cuál es la voluntad de Dios, buena, agradable y perfecta.

3Por la gracia que se me ha dado, les digo a todos ustedes: Nadie tenga un concepto de sí más alto que el que debe tener, sino más bien piense de sí mismo con moderación, según la medida de fe que Dios le haya dado. 4Pues así como cada uno de nosotros tiene un solo cuerpo con muchos miembros, y no todos estos miembros desempeñan la misma función, 5también nosotros, siendo muchos, formamos un solo cuerpo en Cristo, y cada miembro está unido a todos los demás. 6Tenemos dones diferentes, según la gracia que se nos ha dado. Si el don de alguien es el de profecía, que lo use en proporción con su fe;u 7si es el de prestar un servicio, que lo preste; si es el de enseñar, que enseñe; 8si es el de animar a otros, que los anime; si es el de socorrer a los necesitados, que dé con generosidad; si es el de dirigir, que dirija con esmero; si es el de mostrar compasión, que lo haga con alegría.

El amor

9El amor debe ser sincero. Aborrezcan el mal; aférrense al bien. 10Ámense los unos a los otros con amor fraternal, respetándose y honrándose mutuamente. 11Nunca dejen de ser diligentes; antes bien, sirvan al Señor con el fervor que da el Espíritu. 12Alégrense en la esperanza, muestren paciencia en el sufrimiento, perseveren en la oración. 13Ayuden a sus hermanos necesitados. Practiquen la hospitalidad. 14Bendigan a quienes los persigan; bendigan y no maldigan. 15Alégrense con los que están alegres; lloren con los que lloran. 16Vivan en armonía los unos con los otros. No sean arrogantes, sino háganse solidarios con los humildes.v No se crean los únicos que saben.

17No paguen a nadie mal por mal. Procuren hacer lo bueno delante de todos. 18Si es posible, y en cuanto dependa de ustedes, vivan en paz con todos. 19No tomen venganza, hermanos míos, sino dejen el castigo en las manos de Dios, porque está escrito: «Mía es la venganza; yo pagaré»,w dice el Señor. 20Antes bien,

«Si tu enemigo tiene hambre, dale de comer;
si tiene sed, dale de beber.
Actuando así, harás que se avergüence de su
conducta.»x

21No te dejes vencer por el mal; al contrario, vence el mal con el bien.

El respeto a las autoridades

13 Todos deben someterse a las autoridades públicas, pues no hay autoridad que Dios no haya dispuesto, así que las que existen fueron establecidas por él. 2Por lo tanto, todo el que se opone a la autoridad se rebela contra lo que Dios ha instituido. Los que así proceden recibirán castigo. 3Porque los gobernantes no están para infundir terror a los que hacen lo bueno sino a los que hacen lo malo. ¿Quieres librarte del miedo a la autoridad? Haz lo bueno, y tendrás su aprobación, 4pues está al servicio de Dios para tu bien. Pero si haces lo malo, entonces debes tener miedo. No en vano lleva la espada, pues está al servicio de Dios para impartir justicia y castigar al malhechor. 5Así que es necesario someterse a las autoridades, no sólo para evitar el castigo sino también por razones de conciencia.

6Por eso mismo pagan ustedes impuestos, pues las autoridades están al servicio de Dios, dedicadas precisamente a gobernar. 7Paguen a cada uno lo que le corresponda: si deben impuestos, paguen los impuestos; si deben contribuciones, paguen las contribuciones; al que deban respeto, muéstrenle respeto; al que deban honor, ríndanle honor.

La responsabilidad hacia los demás

8No tengan deudas pendientes con nadie, a no ser la de amarse unos a otros. De hecho, quien ama al prójimo ha cumplido la ley. 9Porque los mandamientos que dicen: «No cometas adulterio», «No mates», «No robes», «No codicies»,y y todos los demás mandamientos, se resumen en este precepto: «Ama a tu prójimo como a ti mismo.»z 10El amor no perjudica al prójimo. Así que el amor es el cumplimiento de la ley.

11Hagan todo esto estando conscientes del tiempo en que vivimos. Ya es hora de que despierten del sueño, pues nuestra salvación está ahora más cerca que cuando inicialmente creímos. 12La noche está muy avanzada y ya se acerca el día. Por eso, dejemos a un lado las obras de la oscuridad y pongámonos la armadura de la luz. 13Vivamos decentemente, como a la luz del día, no en orgías y borracheras, ni en inmoralidad sexual y libertinaje, ni en disensiones y envidias. 14Más bien, revístanse ustedes del Señor Jesucristo, y no se preocupen por satisfacer los deseos de la *naturaleza pecaminosa.

Los débiles y los fuertes

14 Reciban al que es débil en la fe, pero no para entrar en discusiones. 2A algunos su fe les permite comer de todo, pero hay quienes son débiles en la fe, y sólo comen verduras. 3El que come de todo no debe menospreciar al que no come ciertas cosas, y el que no come de todo no debe condenar al que lo hace, pues Dios lo ha aceptado. 4¿Quién eres tú para juzgar al siervo de otro? Que se mantenga en pie, o que caiga, es asunto de su propio señor. Y se mantendrá en pie, porque el Señor tiene poder para sostenerlo.

5Hay quien considera que un día tiene más importancia que otro, pero hay quien considera iguales todos los días. Cada uno debe estar firme en sus propias opiniones. 6El que le da importancia especial a cierto día, lo hace para el Señor. El que come de todo, come para el Señor, y lo demuestra dándole gracias a Dios; y el que no come, para el Señor se abstiene, y también da gracias a Dios. 7Porque ninguno de nosotros vive para sí mismo, ni tampoco muere para sí mismo. 8Si vivimos, para el Señor vivimos; y si morimos, para el Señor morimos. Así pues, sea que vivamos o

---

t **12:1** espiritual. Alt. racional. u **12:6** en proporción con su fe. Alt. de acuerdo con la fe. v **12:16** háganse . . . humildes. Alt. estén dispuestos a ocuparse en oficios humildes. w **12:19** Dt 32:35 x **12:20** harás . . . conducta. Lit. ascuas de fuego amontonarás sobre su cabeza (Pr 25:21,22). y **13:9** Éx 20:13-15,17; Dt 5:17-19,21 z **13:9** Lv 19:18

que muramos, del Señor somos. **9**Para esto mismo murió Cristo, y volvió a vivir, para ser Señor tanto de los que han muerto como de los que aún viven. **10**Tú, entonces, ¿por qué juzgas a tu hermano? O tú, ¿por qué lo menosprecias? ¡Todos tendremos que comparecer ante el tribunal de Dios! **11**Está escrito:

«Tan cierto como que yo vivo —dice el Señor—,
    ante mí se doblará toda rodilla
    y toda lengua confesará a Dios.»a

12Así que cada uno de nosotros tendrá que dar cuentas de sí a Dios.

13Por tanto, dejemos de juzgarnos unos a otros. Más bien, propónganse no poner *tropiezos ni obstáculos al hermano. **14**Yo, de mi parte, estoy plenamente convencido en el Señor Jesús de que no hay nada *impuro en sí mismo. Si algo es impuro, lo es solamente para quien así lo considera. **15**Ahora bien, si tu hermano se angustia por causa de lo que comes, ya no te comportas con amor. No destruyas, por causa de la comida, al hermano por quien Cristo murió. **16**En una palabra, no den lugar a que se hable mal del bien que ustedes practican, **17**porque el reino de Dios no es cuestión de comidas o bebidas sino de justicia, paz y alegría en el Espíritu Santo. **18**El que de esta manera sirve a Cristo, agrada a Dios y es aprobado por sus semejantes.

19Por lo tanto, esforcémonos por promover todo lo que conduzca a la paz y a la mutua edificación. **20**No destruyas la obra de Dios por causa de la comida. Todo alimento es puro; lo malo es hacer tropezar a otros por lo que uno come. **21**Más vale no comer carne ni beber vino, ni hacer nada que haga *caer a tu hermano.

22Así que la convicciónb que tengas tú al respecto, manténla como algo entre Dios y tú. *Dichoso aquel a quien su conciencia no lo acusa por lo que hace. **23**Pero el que tiene dudas en cuanto a lo que come, se condena; porque no lo hace por convicción. Y todo lo que no se hace por convicción es pecado.

15 Los fuertes en la fe debemos apoyar a los débiles, en vez de hacer lo que nos agrada. **2**Cada uno debe agradar al prójimo para su bien, con el fin de edificarlo. **3**Porque ni siquiera Cristo se agradó a sí mismo sino que, como está escrito: «Sobre mí han recaído los insultos de tus detractores.»c **4**De hecho, todo lo que se escribió en el pasado se escribió para enseñarnos, a fin de que, alentados por las Escrituras, perseveremos en mantener nuestra esperanza.

5Que el Dios que infunde aliento y perseverancia les conceda vivir juntos en armonía, conforme al ejemplo de Cristo Jesús, **6**para que con un solo corazón y una sola voz glorifiquen al Dios y Padre de nuestro Señor Jesucristo.

7Por tanto, acéptense mutuamente, así como Cristo los aceptó a ustedes para gloria de Dios. **8**Les digo que Cristo se hizo servidor de los judíosd para demostrar la fidelidad de Dios, a fin de confirmar las promesas hechas a los patriarcas, **9**y para que los *gentiles glorifiquen a Dios por su compasión, como está escrito:

«Por eso te alabaré entre las *naciones;
    cantaré salmos a tu nombre.»e

10En otro pasaje dice:

«Alégrense, naciones, con el pueblo de Dios.»f

11Y en otra parte:

«¡Alaben al Señor, naciones todas!
    ¡Pueblos todos, cántenle alabanzas!»g

12A su vez, Isaías afirma:

«Brotará la raíz de Isaí,
    el que se levantará para gobernar a las
        naciones;
en él los pueblos pondrán su esperanza.»h

13Que el Dios de la esperanza los llene de toda alegría y paz a ustedes que creen en él, para que rebosen de esperanza por el poder del Espíritu Santo.

Pablo, ministro de los gentiles

14Por mi parte, hermanos míos, estoy seguro de que ustedes mismos rebosan de bondad, abundan en conocimiento y están capacitados para instruirse unos a otros. **15**Sin embargo, les he escrito con mucha franqueza sobre algunos asuntos, como para refrescarles la memoria. Me he atrevido a hacerlo por causa de la gracia que Dios me dio **16**para ser ministro de Cristo Jesús a los *gentiles. Yo tengo el deber sacerdotal de proclamar el *evangelio de Dios, a fin de que los gentiles lleguen a ser una ofrenda aceptable a Dios, *santificada por el Espíritu Santo.

17Por tanto, mi servicio a Dios es para mí motivo de *orgullo en Cristo Jesús. **18**No me atreveré a hablar de nada sino de lo que Cristo ha hecho por medio de mí para que los gentiles lleguen a obedecer a Dios. Lo ha hecho con palabras y obras, **19**mediante poderosas señales y milagros, por el poder del Espíritu de Dios. Así que, habiendo comenzado en Jerusalén, he completado la proclamación del evangelio de Cristo por todas partes, hasta la región de Iliria. **20**En efecto, mi propósito ha sido predicar el evangelio donde Cristo no sea conocido, para no edificar sobre fundamento ajeno. **21**Más bien, como está escrito:

«Los que nunca habían recibido noticia de él,
    lo verán;
    y entenderán los que no habían oído hablar
        de él.»i

22Este trabajo es lo que muchas veces me ha impedido ir a visitarlos.

Pablo piensa visitar Roma

23Pero ahora que ya no me queda un lugar dónde trabajar en estas regiones, y como desde hace muchos años anhelo verlos, **24**tengo planes de visitarlos cuando vaya rumbo a España. Espero que, después de que haya disfrutado de la compañía de ustedes por algún tiempo, me ayuden a continuar el viaje. **25**Por ahora, voy a Jerusalén para llevar ayuda a los *hermanos, **26**ya que Macedonia y Acaya tuvieron a bien hacer una colecta para los hermanos pobres de Jerusalén. **27**Lo hicieron de buena voluntad, aunque en realidad están en obligación de hacerlo. Porque si los *gentiles han participado de las bendiciones espirituales de los judíos, están en deuda con ellos para servirles con las bendiciones materiales. **28**Así que, una vez que yo haya cumplido esta tarea y entregado en sus manos este fruto, saldré para España y de paso los visitaré a ustedes. **29**Sé que, cuando los visite, iré con la abundante bendición de Cristo.

30Les ruego, hermanos, por nuestro Señor Jesucristo y por el amor del Espíritu, que se unan conmigo en esta lucha y que oren a Dios por mí. **31**Pídanle

---

a **14:11** Is 45:23 b **14:22** *convicción.* Lit. *fe;* también en v. 23. c **15:3** Sal 69:9 d **15:8** *de los judíos.* Lit. *de la *circuncisión.* e **15:9** 2S 22:50; Sal 18:49 f **15:10** Dt 32:43 g **15:11** Sal 117:1 h **15:12** Is 11:10 i **15:21** Is 52:15

que me libre de caer en manos de los incrédulos que están en Judea, y que los hermanos de Jerusalén reciban bien la ayuda que les llevo. **32**De este modo, por la voluntad de Dios, llegaré a ustedes con alegría y podré descansar entre ustedes por algún tiempo. **33**El Dios de paz sea con todos ustedes. Amén.

Saludos personales

16 Les recomiendo a nuestra hermana Febe, diaconisa de la iglesia de Cencreas. **2**Les pido que la reciban dignamente en el Señor, como conviene hacerlo entre hermanos en la fe; préstenle toda la ayuda que necesite, porque ella ha ayudado a muchas personas, entre las que me cuento yo.

3 Saluden a *Priscila y a Aquila, mis compañeros de trabajo en Cristo Jesús. **4**Por salvarme la *vida, ellos arriesgaron la suya. Tanto yo como todas las iglesias de los *gentiles les estamos agradecidos.

5 Saluden igualmente a la iglesia que se reúne en la casa de ellos.

Saluden a mi querido hermano Epeneto, el primer convertido a Cristo en la provincia de *Asia.j

6 Saluden a María, que tanto ha trabajado por ustedes.

7 Saluden a Andrónico y a Junías,k mis parientes y compañeros de cárcel, destacados entre los apóstoles y convertidos a Cristo antes que yo.

8 Saluden a Amplias, mi querido hermano en el Señor.

9 Saluden a Urbano, nuestro compañero de trabajo en Cristo, y a mi querido hermano Estaquis.

10 Saluden a Apeles, que ha dado tantas pruebas de su fe en Cristo.

Saluden a los de la familia de Aristóbulo.

11 Saluden a Herodión, mi pariente.

Saluden a los de la familia de Narciso, fieles en el Señor.

12 Saluden a Trifena y a Trifosa, las cuales se esfuerzan trabajando por el Señor.

Saluden a mi querida hermana Pérsida, que ha trabajado muchísimo en el Señor.

13 Saluden a Rufo, distinguido creyente,l y a su madre, que ha sido también como una madre para mí.

14 Saluden a Asíncrito, a Flegonte, a Hermes, a Patrobas, a Hermas y a los hermanos que están con ellos.

15 Saluden a Filólogo, a Julia, a Nereo y a su hermana, a Olimpas y a todos los hermanos que están con ellos.

16 Salúdense unos a otros con un beso santo.

Todas las iglesias de Cristo les mandan saludos.

17Les ruego, hermanos, que se cuiden de los que causan divisiones y dificultades, y van en contra de lo que a ustedes se les ha enseñado. Apártense de ellos. **18**Tales individuos no sirven a Cristo nuestro Señor, sino a sus propios deseos.m Con palabras suaves y lisonjeras engañan a los ingenuos. **19**Es cierto que ustedes viven en obediencia, lo que es bien conocido de todos y me alegra mucho; pero quiero que sean sagaces para el bien e inocentes para el mal.

20Muy pronto el Dios de paz aplastará a Satanás bajo los pies de ustedes.

Que la gracia de nuestro Señor Jesús sea con ustedes.

21Saludos de parte de Timoteo, mi compañero de trabajo, como también de Lucio, Jasón y Sosípater, mis parientes.

22Yo, Tercio, que escribo esta carta, los saludo en el Señor.

23Saludos de parte de Gayo, de cuya hospitalidad disfrutamos yo y toda la iglesia de este lugar.

También les mandan saludos Erasto, que es el tesorero de la ciudad, y nuestro hermano Cuarto.n

25-26 El Dios eterno ocultó su *misterio durante largos siglos, pero ahora lo ha revelado por medio de los escritos proféticos, según su propio mandato, para que todas las *naciones obedezcan a la fe.ñ ¡Al que puede fortalecerlos a ustedes conforme a mi *evangelio y a la predicación acerca de Jesucristo, **27**al único sabio Dios, sea la gloria para siempre por medio de Jesucristo! Amén.

---

j **16:5** *el primer . . . *Asia.* Lit. *las *primicias de Asia.* k **16:7** *Junías.* Alt. *Junia.* l **16:13** *distinguido creyente.* Lit. *escogido en el Señor.* m **16:18** *sus propios deseos.* Lit. *su propio estómago.* n **16:23** *Cuarto.* Var. *Cuarto.* v. 24 *La gracia de nuestro Señor Jesucristo sea con todos ustedes. Amén.* ñ **16:25,26** *para . . . la fe.* Lit. *para la obediencia de la fe a todas las naciones.*

Primera Carta a los CORINTIOS

1 Pablo, llamado por la voluntad de Dios a ser apóstol de *Cristo Jesús, y nuestro hermano Sóstenes,

2a la iglesia de Dios que está en Corinto, a los que han sido *santificados en Cristo Jesús y llamados a ser su santo pueblo, junto con todos los que en todas partes invocan el nombre de nuestro Señor Jesucristo, Señor de ellos y de nosotros:

3Que Dios nuestro Padre y el Señor Jesucristo les concedan gracia y paz.

Acción de gracias

4Siempre doy gracias a Dios por ustedes, pues él, en Cristo Jesús, les ha dado su gracia. 5Unidos a Cristo ustedes se han llenado de toda riqueza, tanto en palabra como en conocimiento. 6Así se ha confirmado en ustedes nuestro testimonio acerca de Cristo, 7de modo que no les falta ningún don espiritual mientras esperan con ansias que se manifieste nuestro Señor Jesucristo. 8Él los mantendrá firmes hasta el fin, para que sean irreprochables en el día de nuestro Señor Jesucristo. 9Fiel es Dios, quien los ha llamado a tener comunión con su Hijo Jesucristo, nuestro Señor.

Divisiones en la iglesia

10Les suplico, hermanos, en el nombre de nuestro Señor Jesucristo, que todos vivan en armonía y que no haya divisiones entre ustedes, sino que se mantengan unidos en un mismo pensar y en un mismo propósito. 11Digo esto, hermanos míos, porque algunos de la familia de Cloé me han informado que hay rivalidades entre ustedes. 12Me refiero a que unos dicen: «Yo sigo a Pablo»; otros afirman: «Yo, a Apolos»; otros: «Yo, a *Cefas»; y otros: «Yo, a Cristo.» 13¡Cómo! ¿Está dividido Cristo? ¿Acaso Pablo fue crucificado por ustedes? ¿O es que fueron bautizados en el nombre de Pablo? 14Gracias a Dios que no bauticé a ninguno de ustedes, excepto a Crispo y a Gayo, 15de modo que nadie puede decir que fue bautizado en mi nombre. 16Bueno, también bauticé a la familia de Estéfanas; fuera de éstos, no recuerdo haber bautizado a ningún otro. 17Pues Cristo no me envió a bautizar sino a predicar el *evangelio, y eso sin discursos de sabiduría humana, para que la cruz de Cristo no perdiera su eficacia.

Cristo, sabiduría y poder de Dios

18Me explico: El mensaje de la cruz es una locura para los que se pierden; en cambio, para los que se salvan, es decir, para nosotros, este mensaje es el poder de Dios. 19Pues está escrito:

«Destruiré la sabiduría de los sabios;
frustraré la inteligencia de los
inteligentes.»a

20¿Dónde está el sabio? ¿Dónde el erudito? ¿Dónde el filósofo de esta época? ¿No ha convertido Dios en locura la sabiduría de este mundo? 21Ya que Dios, en su sabio designio, dispuso que el mundo no lo conociera mediante la sabiduría humana, tuvo a bien salvar, mediante la locura de la predicación, a los que creen. 22Los judíos piden señales milagrosas y los *gentiles buscan sabiduría, 23mientras que nosotros predicamos a Cristo crucificado. Este mensaje es motivo de *tropiezo para los judíos, y es locura para los gentiles, 24pero para los que Dios ha llamado, lo mismo judíos que gentiles, Cristo es el poder de Dios y la sabiduría de Dios. 25Pues la locura de Dios es más sabia que la sabiduría humana, y la debilidad de Dios es más fuerte que la fuerza humana.

26Hermanos, consideren su propio llamamiento: No muchos de ustedes son sabios, según criterios meramente *humanos; ni son muchos los poderosos ni muchos los de noble cuna. 27Pero Dios escogió lo insensato del mundo para avergonzar a los sabios, y escogió lo débil del mundo para avergonzar a los poderosos. 28También escogió Dios lo más bajo y despreciado, y lo que no es nada, para anular lo que es, 29a fin de que en su presencia nadie pueda *jactarse. 30Pero gracias a él ustedes están unidos a Cristo Jesús, a quien Dios ha hecho nuestra sabiduría —es decir, nuestra *justificación, *santificación y redención— 31para que, como está escrito: «Si alguien ha de gloriarse, que se gloríe en el Señor.»b

2 Yo mismo, hermanos, cuando fui a anunciarles el testimonioc de Dios, no lo hice con gran elocuencia y sabiduría. 2Me propuse más bien, estando entre ustedes, no saber de cosa alguna, excepto de Jesucristo, y de éste crucificado. 3Es más, me presenté ante ustedes con tanta debilidad que temblaba de miedo. 4No les hablé ni les prediqué con palabras sabias y elocuentes sino con demostración del poder del Espíritu, 5para que la fe de ustedes no dependiera de la sabiduría humana sino del poder de Dios.

Sabiduría procedente del Espíritu

6En cambio, hablamos con sabiduría entre los que han alcanzado madurez,d pero no con la sabiduría de este mundo ni con la de sus gobernantes, los cuales terminarán en nada. 7Más bien, exponemos el *misterio de la sabiduría de Dios, una sabiduría que ha estado escondida y que Dios había predestinado para nuestra gloria desde la eternidad. 8Ninguno de los gobernantes de este mundo la entendió, porque de haberla entendido no habrían crucificado al Señor de la gloria. 9Sin embargo, como está escrito:

«Ningún ojo ha visto,
ningún oído ha escuchado,
ninguna mente humana ha concebido
lo que Dios ha preparado para quienes lo
aman.»e

10Ahora bien, Dios nos ha revelado esto por medio de su Espíritu, pues el Espíritu lo examina todo, hasta las profundidades de Dios. 11En efecto, ¿quién conoce los pensamientos del *ser humano sino su propio espíritu que está en él? Así mismo, nadie conoce los pensamientos de Dios sino el Espíritu de Dios. 12Nosotros no hemos recibido el espíritu del mundo sino el Espíritu que procede de Dios, para que entendamos lo que por su gracia él nos ha concedido. 13Esto es precisamente de lo que hablamos, no con las palabras que enseña la sabiduría humana sino con las que enseña el Espíritu, de modo que expresamos verdades espirituales en términos espirituales.f 14El que no tiene el Espíritug no acepta lo que procede del Espíritu de Dios, pues para él es locura.

---

a 1:19 Is 29:14 b 1:31 Jer 9:24 c 2:1 testimonio. Var. *Misterio. d 2:6 los que . . . madurez. Lit. los *perfectos. e 2:9 Is 64:4
f 2:13 expresamos . . . espirituales. Alt. interpretamos verdades espirituales a personas espirituales. g 2:14 El que no tiene el
Espíritu. Lit. El hombre *síquico (o natural).

No puede entenderlo, porque hay que discernirlo espiritualmente. 15En cambio, el que es espiritual lo juzga todo, aunque él mismo no está sujeto al juicio de nadie, porque

16«¿quién ha conocido la mente del Señor
para que pueda instruirlo?»h

Nosotros, por nuestra parte, tenemos la mente de Cristo.

Sobre las divisiones en la iglesia

3 Yo, hermanos, no pude dirigirme a ustedes como a espirituales sino como a inmaduros,i apenas niños en Cristo. 2Les di leche porque no podían asimilar alimento sólido, ni pueden todavía, 3pues aún son inmaduros. Mientras haya entre ustedes celos y contiendas, ¿no serán inmaduros? ¿Acaso no se están comportando según criterios meramente *humanos? 4Cuando uno afirma: «Yo sigo a Pablo», y otro: «Yo sigo a Apolos», ¿no es porque están actuando con criterios humanos?j

5Después de todo, ¿qué es Apolos? ¿Y qué es Pablo? Nada más que servidores por medio de los cuales ustedes llegaron a creer, según lo que el Señor le asignó a cada uno. 6Yo sembré, Apolos regó, pero Dios ha dado el crecimiento. 7Así que no cuenta ni el que siembra ni el que riega, sino sólo Dios, quien es el que hace crecer. 8El que siembra y el que riega están al mismo nivel, aunque cada uno será recompensado según su propio trabajo. 9En efecto, nosotros somos colaboradores al servicio de Dios; y ustedes son el campo de cultivo de Dios, son el edificio de Dios.

10Según la gracia que Dios me ha dado, yo, como maestro constructor, eché los cimientos, y otro construye sobre ellos. Pero cada uno tenga cuidado de cómo construye, 11porque nadie puede poner un fundamento diferente del que ya está puesto, que es Jesucristo. 12Si alguien construye sobre este fundamento, ya sea con oro, plata y piedras preciosas, o con madera, heno y paja, 13su obra se mostrará tal cual es, pues el día del juicio la dejará al descubierto. El fuego la dará a conocer, y pondrá a prueba la calidad del trabajo de cada uno. 14Si lo que alguien ha construido permanece, recibirá su recompensa, 15pero si su obra es consumida por las llamas, él sufrirá pérdida. Será salvo, pero como quien pasa por el fuego.

16¿No saben que ustedes son templo de Dios y que el Espíritu de Dios habita en ustedes? 17Si alguno destruye el templo de Dios, él mismo será destruido por Dios; porque el templo de Dios es sagrado, y ustedes son ese templo.

18Que nadie se engañe. Si alguno de ustedes se cree sabio según las normas de esta época, hágase ignorante para así llegar a ser sabio. 19Porque a los ojos de Dios la sabiduría de este mundo es locura. Como está escrito: «Él atrapa a los sabios en su propia astucia»;k 20y también dice: «El Señor conoce los pensamientos de los sabios y sabe que son absurdos.»l 21Por lo tanto, ¡que nadie base su *orgullo en el hombre! Al fin y al cabo, todo es de ustedes, 22ya sea Pablo, o Apolos, o *Cefas, o el universo, o la vida, o la muerte, o lo presente o lo por venir; todo es de ustedes, 23y ustedes son de Cristo, y Cristo es de Dios.

Apóstoles de Cristo

4 Que todos nos consideren servidores de Cristo, encargados de administrar los *misterios de Dios. 2Ahora bien, a los que reciben un encargo se les exige que demuestren ser dignos de confianza. 3Por mi parte, muy poco me preocupa que me juzguen ustedes o cualquier tribunal humano; es más, ni siquiera me juzgo a mí mismo. 4Porque aunque la conciencia no me remuerde, no por eso quedo absuelto; el que me juzga es el Señor. 5Por lo tanto, no juzguen nada antes de tiempo; esperen hasta que venga el Señor. Él sacará a la luz lo que está oculto en la oscuridad y pondrá al descubierto las intenciones de cada corazón. Entonces cada uno recibirá de Dios la alabanza que le corresponda.

6Hermanos, todo esto lo he aplicado a Apolos y a mí mismo para beneficio de ustedes, con el fin de que aprendan de nosotros aquello de «no ir más allá de lo que está escrito». Así ninguno de ustedes podrá engreírse de haber favorecido al uno en perjuicio del otro. 7¿Quién te distingue de los demás? ¿Qué tienes que no hayas recibido? Y si lo recibiste, ¿por qué presumes como si no te lo hubieran dado?

8¡Ya tienen todo lo que desean! ¡Ya se han enriquecido! ¡Han llegado a ser reyes, y eso sin nosotros! ¡Ojalá fueran de veras reyes para que también nosotros reináramos con ustedes! 9Por lo que veo, a nosotros los apóstoles Dios nos ha hecho desfilar en el último lugar, como a los sentenciados a muerte. Hemos llegado a ser un espectáculo para todo el universo, tanto para los ángeles como para los hombres. 10¡Por causa de Cristo, nosotros somos los ignorantes; ustedes, en Cristo, son los inteligentes! ¡Los débiles somos nosotros; los fuertes son ustedes! ¡A ustedes se les estima; a nosotros se nos desprecia! 11Hasta el momento pasamos hambre, tenemos sed, nos falta ropa, se nos maltrata, no tenemos dónde vivir. 12Con estas manos nos matamos trabajando. Si nos maldicen, bendecimos; si nos persiguen, lo soportamos; 13si nos calumnian, los tratamos con gentileza. Se nos considera la escoria de la tierra, la basura del mundo, y así hasta el día de hoy.

14No les escribo esto para avergonzarlos sino para amonestarlos, como a hijos míos amados. 15De hecho, aunque tuvieran ustedes miles de tutores en Cristo, padres sí que no tienen muchos, porque mediante el *evangelio yo fui el padre que los engendró en Cristo Jesús. 16Por tanto, les ruego que sigan mi ejemplo. 17Con este propósito les envié a Timoteo, mi amado y fiel hijo en el Señor. Él les recordará mi manera de comportarme en Cristo Jesús, como enseño por todas partes y en todas las iglesias.

18Ahora bien, algunos de ustedes se han vuelto presuntuosos, pensando que no iré a verlos. 19Lo cierto es que, si Dios quiere, iré a visitarlos muy pronto, y ya veremos no sólo cómo hablan sino cuánto poder tienen esos presumidos. 20Porque el reino de Dios no es cuestión de palabras sino de poder. 21¿Qué prefieren? ¿Que vaya a verlos con un látigo, o con amor y espíritu apacible?

¡Expulsen al hermano inmoral!

5 Es ya del dominio público que hay entre ustedes un caso de inmoralidad sexual que ni siquiera entre los *paganos se tolera, a saber, que uno de ustedes tiene por mujer a la esposa de su padre. 2¡Y de esto se sienten orgullosos! ¿No debieran, más bien, haber lamentado lo sucedido y expulsado de entre ustedes al que hizo tal cosa? 3Yo, por mi parte, aunque no estoy físicamente entre ustedes, sí estoy presente en espíritu, y ya he juzgado, como si estu-

h 2:16 Is 40:13. i 3:1 inmaduros. Lit. *carnales; también en v. 3. j 3:4 ¿no es . . . humanos? Lit. ¿no son ustedes hombres?
k 3:19 Job 5:13 l 3:20 Sal 94:11

viera presente, al que cometió este pecado. ⁴Cuando se reúnan en el nombre de nuestro Señor Jesús, y con su poder yo los acompañe en espíritu, ⁵entreguen a este hombre a Satanás para destrucción de su *naturaleza pecaminosaᵐ a fin de que su espíritu sea salvo en el día del Señor.

⁶Hacen mal en *jactarse. ¿No se dan cuenta de que un poco de levadura hace fermentar toda la masa? ⁷Deshágansе de la vieja levadura para que sean masa nueva, panes sin levadura, como lo son en realidad. Porque Cristo, nuestro Cordero pascual, ya ha sido sacrificado. ⁸Así que celebremos nuestra Pascua no con la vieja levadura, que es la malicia y la perversidad, sino con pan sin levadura, que es la sinceridad y la verdad.

⁹Por carta ya les he dicho que no se relacionen con personas inmorales. ¹⁰Por supuesto, no me refería a la gente inmoral de este mundo, ni a los avaros, estafadores o idólatras. En tal caso, tendrían ustedes que salirse de este mundo. ¹¹Pero en esta carta quiero aclararles que no deben relacionarse con nadie que, llamándose hermano, sea inmoral o avaro, idólatra, calumniador, borracho o estafador. Con tal persona ni siquiera deben juntarse para comer.

¹²¿Acaso me toca a mí juzgar a los de afuera? ¿No son ustedes los que deben juzgar a los de adentro? ¹³Dios juzgará a los de afuera. «Expulsen al malvado de entre ustedes.»ⁿ

Pleitos entre creyentes

6 Si alguno de ustedes tiene un pleito con otro, ¿cómo se atreve a presentar demanda ante los inconversos, en vez de acudir a los *creyentes? ²¿Acaso no saben que los creyentes juzgarán al mundo? Y si ustedes han de juzgar al mundo, ¿cómo no van a ser capaces de juzgar casos insignificantes? ³¿No saben que aun a los ángeles los juzgaremos? ¡Cuánto más los asuntos de esta vida! ⁴Por tanto, si tienen pleitos sobre tales asuntos, ¿cómo es que nombran como jueces a los que no cuentan para nada ante la iglesia?ñ ⁵Digo esto para que les dé vergüenza. ¿Acaso no hay entre ustedes nadie lo bastante sabio como para juzgar un pleito entre creyentes? ⁶Al contrario, un hermano demanda a otro, ¡y esto ante los incrédulos!

⁷En realidad, ya es una grave falla el solo hecho de que haya pleitos entre ustedes. ¿No sería mejor soportar la injusticia? ¿No sería mejor dejar que los defrauden? ⁸Lejos de eso, son ustedes los que defraudan y cometen injusticias, ¡y conste que se trata de sus hermanos!

⁹¿No saben que los malvados no heredarán el reino de Dios? ¡No se dejen engañar! Ni los fornicarios, ni los idólatras, ni los adúlteros, ni los sodomitas, ni los pervertidos sexuales, ¹⁰ni los ladrones, ni los avaros, ni los borrachos, ni los calumniadores, ni los estafadores heredarán el reino de Dios. ¹¹Y eso eran algunos de ustedes. Pero ya han sido lavados, ya han sido *santificados, ya han sido *justificados en el nombre del Señor Jesucristo y por el Espíritu de nuestro Dios.

La inmoralidad sexual

¹²«Todo me está permitido», pero no todo es para mi bien. «Todo me está permitido», pero no dejaré que nada me domine. ¹³«Los alimentos son para el estómago y el estómago para los alimentos»;

así es, y Dios los destruirá a ambos. Pero el cuerpo no es para la inmoralidad sexual sino para el Señor, y el Señor para el cuerpo. ¹⁴Con su poder Dios resucitó al Señor, y nos resucitará también a nosotros. ¹⁵¿No saben que sus cuerpos son miembros de Cristo mismo? ¿Tomaré acaso los miembros de Cristo para unirlos con una prostituta? ¡Jamás! ¹⁶¿No saben que el que se une a una prostituta se hace un solo cuerpo con ella? Pues la Escritura dice: «Los dos llegarán a ser un solo cuerpo.»ᵒ ¹⁷Pero el que se une al Señor se hace uno con él en espíritu.

¹⁸Huyan de la inmoralidad sexual. Todos los demás pecados que una persona comete quedan fuera de su cuerpo; pero el que comete inmoralidades sexuales peca contra su propio cuerpo. ¹⁹¿Acaso no saben que su cuerpo es templo del Espíritu Santo, quien está en ustedes y al que han recibido de parte de Dios? Ustedes no son sus propios dueños; ²⁰fueron comprados por un precio. Por tanto, honren con su cuerpo a Dios.

Consejos matrimoniales

7 Paso ahora a los asuntos que me plantearon por escrito: «Es mejor no tener relaciones sexuales.»ᵖ ²Pero en vista de tanta inmoralidad, cada hombre debe tener su propia esposa, y cada mujer su propio esposo. ³El hombre debe cumplir su deber conyugal con su esposa, e igualmente la mujer con su esposo. ⁴La mujer ya no tiene derecho sobre su propio cuerpo, sino su esposo. Tampoco el hombre tiene derecho sobre su propio cuerpo, sino su esposa. ⁵No se nieguen el uno al otro, a no ser de común acuerdo, y sólo por un tiempo, para dedicarse a la oración. No tarden en volver a unirse nuevamente; de lo contrario, pueden caer en *tentación de Satanás, por falta de dominio propio. ⁶Ahora bien, esto lo digo como una concesión y no como una orden. ⁷En realidad, preferiría que todos fueran como yo. No obstante, cada uno tiene de Dios su propio don: éste posee uno; aquél, otro.

⁸A los solteros y a las viudas les digo que sería mejor que se quedaran como yo. ⁹Pero si no pueden dominarse, que se casen, porque es preferible casarse que quemarse de pasión.

¹⁰A los casados les doy la siguiente orden (no yo sino el Señor): que la mujer no se separe de su esposo. ¹¹Sin embargo, si se separa, que no se vuelva a casar; de lo contrario, que se reconcilie con su esposo. Así mismo, que el hombre no se divorcie de su esposa.

¹²A los demás les digo yo (no es mandamiento del Señor): Si algún hermano tiene una esposa que no es creyente, y ella consiente en vivir con él, que no se divorcie de ella. ¹³Y si una mujer tiene un esposo que no es creyente, y él consiente en vivir con ella, que no se divorcie de él. ¹⁴Porque el esposo no creyente ha sido *santificado por la unión con su esposa, y la esposa no creyente ha sido santificada por la unión con su esposo creyente. Si así no fuera, sus hijos serían impuros, mientras que, de hecho, son santos.

¹⁵Sin embargo, si el cónyuge no creyente decide separarse, no se lo impidan. En tales circunstancias, el cónyuge creyente queda sin obligación; Dios nos ha llamado a vivir en paz. ¹⁶¿Cómo sabes tú, mujer, si acaso salvarás a tu esposo? ¿O cómo sabes tú, hombre, si acaso salvarás a tu esposa?

ᵐ **5:5** su *naturaleza pecaminosa. Alt. su cuerpo. Lit. la *carne. ⁿ **5:13** Dt 17:7; 19:19; 21:21; 22:21,24; 24:7 ñ **6:4** ¿cómo . . . iglesia? Alt. ¡nombren como jueces aun a los que no cuentan para nada ante la iglesia! ᵒ **6:16** un solo cuerpo. Lit. una sola *carne; Gn 2:24. ᵖ **7:1** «Es . . . sexuales.» Alt. «Es mejor no casarse.» Lit. Es bueno para el hombre no tocar mujer.

17En cualquier caso, cada uno debe vivir conforme a la condición que el Señor le asignó y a la cual Dios lo ha llamado. Ésta es la norma que establezco en todas las iglesias. 18¿Fue llamado alguno estando ya *circuncidado? Que no disimule su condición. ¿Fue llamado alguno sin estar circuncidado? Que no se circuncide. 19Para nada cuenta estar o no estar circuncidado; lo que importa es cumplir los mandatos de Dios. 20Que cada uno permanezca en la condición en que estaba cuando Dios lo llamó. 21¿Eras *esclavo cuando fuiste llamado? No te preocupes, aunque si tienes la oportunidad de conseguir tu libertad, aprovéchala. 22Porque el que era esclavo cuando el Señor lo llamó es un liberto del Señor; del mismo modo, el que era libre cuando fue llamado es un esclavo de Cristo. 23Ustedes fueron comprados por un precio; no se vuelvan esclavos de nadie. 24Hermanos, cada uno permanezca ante Dios en la condición en que estaba cuando Dios lo llamó.

25En cuanto a las personas solteras,q no tengo ningún mandato del Señor, pero doy mi opinión como quien por la misericordia del Señor es digno de confianza. 26Pienso que, a causa de la crisis actual, es bueno que cada persona se quede como está. 27¿Estás casado? No procures divorciarte. ¿Estás soltero? No busques esposa. 28Pero si te casas, no pecas; y si una jovenr se casa, tampoco comete pecado. Sin embargo, los que se casan tendrán que pasar por muchos aprietos,s y yo quiero evitárselos.

29Lo que quiero decir, hermanos, es que nos queda poco tiempo. De aquí en adelante los que tienen esposa deben vivir como si no la tuvieran; 30los que lloran, como si no lloraran; los que se alegran, como si no se alegraran; los que compran algo, como si no lo poseyeran; 31los que disfrutan de las cosas de este mundo, como si no disfrutaran de ellas; porque este mundo, en su forma actual, está por desaparecer.

32Yo preferiría que estuvieran libres de preocupaciones. El soltero se preocupa de las cosas del Señor y de cómo agradarlo. 33Pero el casado se preocupa de las cosas de este mundo y de cómo agradar a su esposa; 34sus intereses están divididos. La mujer no casada, lo mismo que la joven soltera,t se preocupau de las cosas del Señor; se afana por consagrarse al Señor tanto en cuerpo como en espíritu. Pero la casada se preocupa de las cosas de este mundo y de cómo agradar a su esposo. 35Les digo esto por su propio bien, no para ponerles restricciones sino para que vivan con decoro y plenamente dedicados al Señor.

36Si alguno piensa que no está tratando a su prometidav como es debido, y ella ha llegado ya a su madurez, por lo cual él se siente obligado a casarse, que lo haga. Con eso no peca; que se casen. 37Pero el que se mantiene firme en su propósito, y no está dominado por sus impulsos sino que domina su propia voluntad, y ha resuelto no casarse con su prometida, también hace bien. 38De modo que el que se casa con su prometida hace bien, pero el que no se casa hace mejor.w

39La mujer está ligada a su esposo mientras él vive; pero si el esposo muere, ella queda libre para casarse con quien quiera, con tal de que sea en el Señor. 40En mi opinión, ella será más feliz si no se casa, y creo que yo también tengo el Espíritu de Dios.

Lo sacrificado a los ídolos

8 En cuanto a lo sacrificado a los ídolos, es cierto que todos tenemos conocimiento. El conocimiento envanece, mientras que el amor edifica. 2El que cree que sabe algo, todavía no sabe como debiera saber. 3Pero el que ama a Dios es conocido por él.

4De modo que, en cuanto a comer lo sacrificado a los ídolos, sabemos que un ídolo no es absolutamente nada, y que hay un solo Dios. 5Pues aunque haya los así llamados dioses, ya sea en el cielo o en la tierra (y por cierto que hay muchos «dioses» y muchos «señores»), 6para nosotros no hay más que un solo Dios, el Padre, de quien todo procede y para el cual vivimos; y no hay más que un solo Señor, es decir, Jesucristo, por quien todo existe y por medio del cual vivimos.

7Pero no todos tienen conocimiento de esto. Algunos siguen tan acostumbrados a los ídolos, que comen carne a sabiendas de que ha sido sacrificada a un ídolo, y su conciencia se contamina por ser débil. 8Pero lo que comemos no nos acerca a Dios; no somos mejores por comer ni peores por no comer.

9Sin embargo, tengan cuidado de que su libertad no se convierta en motivo de tropiezo para los débiles. 10Porque si alguien de conciencia débil te ve a ti, que tienes este conocimiento, comer en el templo de un ídolo, ¿no se sentirá animado a comer lo que ha sido sacrificado a los ídolos? 11Entonces ese hermano débil, por quien Cristo murió, se perderá a causa de tu conocimiento. 12Al pecar así contra los hermanos, hiriendo su débil conciencia, pecan ustedes contra Cristo. 13Por lo tanto, si mi comida ocasiona la caída de mi hermano, no comeré carne jamás, para no hacerlo *caer en pecado.

Los derechos de un apóstol

9 ¿No soy libre? ¿No soy apóstol? ¿No he visto a Jesús nuestro Señor? ¿No son ustedes el fruto de mi trabajo en el Señor? 2Aunque otros no me reconozcan como apóstol, ¡para ustedes sí lo soy! Porque ustedes mismos son el sello de mi apostolado en el Señor.

3Ésta es mi defensa contra los que me critican: 4¿Acaso no tenemos derecho a comer y a beber? 5¿No tenemos derecho a viajar acompañados por una esposa creyente, como hacen los demás apóstoles y *Cefas y los hermanos del Señor? 6¿O es que sólo Bernabé y yo estamos obligados a ganarnos la vida con otros trabajos?

7¿Qué soldado presta servicio militar pagándose sus propios gastos? ¿Qué agricultor planta una viñedo y no come de sus uvas? ¿Qué pastor cuida un rebaño y no toma de la leche que ordeña? 8No piensen que digo esto solamente desde un punto de vista humano. ¿No lo dice también la ley? 9Porque en la ley de Moisés está escrito: «No le pongas bozal al buey mientras esté trillando.»x ¿Acaso se preocupa Dios por los bueyes, 10o lo dice más bien por noso-

---

q **7:25** *personas solteras.* Lit. *vírgenes.*   r **7:28** *joven.* Lit. *Virgen.*   s **7:28** *tendrán . . . aprietos.* Lit. *tendrán aflicción en la* *carne.   t **7:34** *La mujer . . . soltera.* Lit. *La mujer no casada y la virgen.*   u **7:33,34** *su esposa; . . . se preocupa.* Var. *se esposa.* v. 34 También hay diferencia entre la esposa y la joven soltera. La que no es casada se preocupa.   v **7:36** *prometida.* Lit. *virgen;* también en vv. 37 y 38.   w **7:36,38** Alt. v. 36 *Si alguno piensa que no está tratando a su hija como es debido, y ella ha llegado a su madurez, por lo cual él se siente obligado a darla en matrimonio, que lo haga. Con eso no peca; que la dé en matrimonio.* v. 37 *Pero el que se mantiene firme en su propósito, y no está dominado por sus impulsos sino que domina su propia voluntad, y ha resuelto mantener soltera a su hija, también hace bien.* v. 38 *De modo que el que da a su hija en matrimonio hace bien, pero el que no la da en matrimonio hace mejor.*   x **9:9** Dt 25:4

tros? Por supuesto que lo dice por nosotros, porque cuando el labrador ara y el segador trilla, deben hacerlo con la esperanza de participar de la cosecha. [11]Si hemos sembrado semilla espiritual entre ustedes, ¿será mucho pedir que cosechemos de ustedes lo material?[y] [12]Si otros tienen derecho a este sustento de parte de ustedes, ¿no lo tendremos aun más nosotros?

Sin embargo, no ejercimos este derecho, sino que lo soportamos todo con tal de no crear obstáculo al *evangelio de Cristo. [13]¿No saben que los que sirven en el templo reciben su alimento del templo, y que los que atienden el altar participan de lo que se ofrece en el altar? [14]Así también el Señor ha ordenado que quienes predican el evangelio vivan de este ministerio.

[15]Pero no me he aprovechado de ninguno de estos derechos, ni escribo de esta manera porque quiera reclamarlos. Prefiero morir a que alguien me prive de este motivo de *orgullo. [16]Sin embargo, cuando predico el evangelio, no tengo de qué enorgullecerme, ya que estoy bajo la obligación de hacerlo. ¡Ay de mí si no predico el evangelio! [17]En efecto, si lo hiciera por mi propia voluntad, tendría recompensa; pero si lo hago por obligación, no hago más que cumplir la tarea que se me ha encomendado. [18]¿Cuál es, entonces, mi recompensa? Pues que al predicar el evangelio pueda presentarlo gratuitamente, sin hacer valer mi derecho.

[19]Aunque soy libre respecto a todos, de todos me he hecho *esclavo para ganar a tantos como sea posible. [20]Entre los judíos me volví judío, a fin de ganarlos a ellos. Entre los que viven bajo la ley me volví como los que están sometidos a ella (aunque yo mismo no vivo bajo la ley), a fin de ganar a éstos. [21]Entre los que no tienen la ley me volví como los que están sin ley (aunque no estoy libre de la ley de Dios sino comprometido con la ley de Cristo), a fin de ganar a los que están sin ley. [22]Entre los débiles me hice débil, a fin de ganar a los débiles. Me hice todo para todos, a fin de salvar a algunos por todos los medios posibles. [23]Todo esto lo hago por causa del evangelio, para participar de sus frutos.

[24]¿No saben que en una carrera todos los corredores compiten, pero sólo uno obtiene el premio? Corran, pues, de tal modo que lo obtengan. [25]Todos los deportistas se entrenan con mucha disciplina. Ellos lo hacen para obtener un premio que se echa a perder; nosotros, en cambio, por uno que dura para siempre. [26]Así que yo no corro como quien no tiene meta; no lucho como quien da golpes al aire. [27]Más bien, golpeo mi cuerpo y lo domino, no sea que, después de haber predicado a otros, yo mismo quede descalificado.

Advertencias basadas en la historia de Israel

10 No quiero que desconozcan, hermanos, que nuestros antepasados estuvieron todos bajo la nube y que todos atravesaron el mar. [2]Todos ellos fueron bautizados en la nube y en el mar para unirse a Moisés. [3]Todos también comieron el mismo alimento espiritual [4]y tomaron la misma bebida espiritual, pues bebían de la roca espiritual que los acompañaba, y la roca era Cristo. [5]Sin embargo, la mayoría de ellos no agradaron a Dios, y sus cuerpos quedaron tendidos en el desierto.

[6]Todo eso sucedió para servirnos de ejemplo,[z] a fin de que no nos apasionemos por lo malo, como lo hicieron ellos. [7]No sean idólatras, como lo fueron algunos de ellos, según está escrito: «Se sentó el pueblo a comer y a beber, y se entregó al desenfreno.»[a] [8]No cometamos inmoralidad sexual, como algunos lo hicieron, por lo que en un solo día perecieron veintitrés mil. [9]Tampoco pongamos a *prueba al Señor, como lo hicieron algunos y murieron víctimas de las serpientes. [10]Ni murmuren contra Dios, como lo hicieron algunos y sucumbieron a manos del ángel destructor.

[11]Todo eso les sucedió para servir de ejemplo, y quedó escrito para advertencia nuestra, pues a nosotros nos ha llegado el fin de los tiempos. [12]Por lo tanto, si alguien piensa que está firme, tenga cuidado de no caer. [13]Ustedes no han sufrido ninguna *tentación que no sea común al género *humano. Pero Dios es fiel, y no permitirá que ustedes sean tentados más allá de lo que puedan aguantar. Más bien, cuando llegue la tentación, él les dará también una salida a fin de que puedan resistir.

Las fiestas idólatras y la Cena del Señor

[14]Por tanto, mis queridos hermanos, huyan de la idolatría. [15]Me dirijo a personas sensatas; juzguen ustedes mismos lo que digo. [16]Esa copa de bendición por la cual damos gracias,[b] ¿no significa que entramos en comunión con la sangre de Cristo? Ese pan que partimos, ¿no significa que entramos en comunión con el cuerpo de Cristo? [17]Hay un solo pan del cual todos participamos; por eso, aunque somos muchos, formamos un solo cuerpo.

[18]Consideren al pueblo de Israel como tal:[c] ¿No entran en comunión con el altar los que comen de lo sacrificado? [19]¿Qué quiero decir con esta comparación? ¿Que el sacrificio que los *gentiles ofrecen a los ídolos sea algo, o que el ídolo mismo sea algo? [20]No, sino que cuando ellos ofrecen sacrificios, lo hacen para los demonios, no para Dios, y no quiero que ustedes entren en comunión con los demonios. [21]No pueden beber de la copa del Señor y también de la copa de los demonios; no pueden participar de la mesa del Señor y también de la mesa de los demonios. [22]¿O vamos a provocar a celos al Señor? ¿Somos acaso más fuertes que él?

La libertad del creyente

[23]«Todo está permitido», pero no todo es provechoso. «Todo está permitido», pero no todo es constructivo. [24]Que nadie busque sus propios intereses sino los del prójimo.

[25]Coman de todo lo que se vende en la carnicería, sin preguntar nada por motivos de conciencia, [26]porque «del Señor es la tierra y todo cuanto hay en ella».[d]

[27]Si algún incrédulo los invita a comer, y ustedes aceptan la invitación, coman de todo lo que les sirvan sin preguntar nada por motivos de conciencia. [28]Ahora bien, si alguien les dice: «Esto ha sido ofrecido en sacrificio a los ídolos», entonces no lo coman, por consideración al que se lo mencionó, y por motivos de conciencia.[e] [29](Me refiero a la conciencia del otro, no a la de ustedes.) ¿Por qué se ha de juzgar mi libertad de acuerdo con la conciencia ajena? [30]Si con gratitud participo de la comida, ¿me van a condenar por comer algo por lo cual doy gracias a Dios?

---

y **9:11** *lo material*. Lit. *las cosas* *carnales*. z **10:6** *ejemplo*. Lit. *tipo*; también en v. 11. a **10:7** Éx 32:6 b **10:16** *por la cual damos gracias*. Lit. *que bendecimos*. c **10:18** *como tal*. Lit. *según la* *carne*. d **10:26** Sal 24:1 e **10:28** *conciencia*. Var. *conciencia, porque «del Señor es la tierra y todo cuanto hay en ella».*

31En conclusión, ya sea que coman o beban o hagan cualquier otra cosa, háganlo todo para la gloria de Dios. 32No hagan *tropezar a nadie, ni a judíos, ni a *gentiles ni a la iglesia de Dios. 33Hagan como yo, que procuro agradar a todos en todo. No busco mis propios intereses sino los de los demás, para que sean salvos.

11
Imítenme a mí, como yo imito a Cristo.

Decoro en el culto

2Los elogio porque se acuerdan de mí en todo y retienen las enseñanzas,f tal como se las transmití.

3Ahora bien, quiero que entiendan que Cristo es cabeza de todo hombre, mientras que el hombre es cabeza de la mujer y Dios es cabeza de Cristo. 4Todo hombre que ora o profetiza con la cabeza cubierta deshonra al que es su cabeza. 5En cambio, toda mujer que ora o profetiza con la cabeza descubierta deshonra al que es su cabeza; es como si estuviera rasurada. 6Si la mujer no se cubre la cabeza, que se corte también el cabello; pero si es vergonzoso para la mujer tener el pelo corto o la cabeza rasurada, que se la cubra. 7El hombre no debe cubrirse la cabeza, ya que él es imagen y gloria de Dios, mientras que la mujer es gloria del hombre. 8De hecho, el hombre no procede de la mujer sino la mujer del hombre; 9ni tampoco fue creado el hombre a causa de la mujer, sino la mujer a causa del hombre. 10Por esta razón, y a causa de los ángeles, la mujer debe llevar sobre la cabeza señal de autoridad.h

11Sin embargo, en el Señor, ni la mujer existe aparte del hombre ni el hombre aparte de la mujer. 12Porque así como la mujer procede del hombre, también el hombre nace de la mujer; pero todo proviene de Dios. 13Juzguen ustedes mismos: ¿Es apropiado que la mujer ore a Dios sin cubrirse la cabeza? 14¿No les enseña el mismo orden natural de las cosas que es una vergüenza para el hombre dejarse crecer el cabello, 15mientras que es una gloria para la mujer llevar cabello largo? Es que a ella se le ha dado su cabellera como velo. 16Si alguien insiste en discutir este asunto, tenga en cuenta que nosotros no tenemos otra costumbre, ni tampoco las iglesias de Dios.

La Cena del Señor
11:23-25 — Mt 26:26-28; Mr 14:22-24; Lc 22:17-20

17Al darles las siguientes instrucciones, no puedo elogiarlos, ya que sus reuniones traen más perjuicio que beneficio. 18En primer lugar, oigo decir que cuando se reúnen como iglesia hay divisiones entre ustedes, y hasta cierto punto lo creo. 19Sin duda, tiene que haber grupos sectarios entre ustedes, para que se demuestre quiénes cuentan con la aprobación de Dios. 20De hecho, cuando se reúnen, ya no es para comer la Cena del Señor, 21porque cada uno se adelanta a comer su propia cena, de manera que unos se quedan con hambre mientras otros se emborrachan. 22¿Acaso no tienen casas donde comer y beber? ¿O es que menosprecian a la iglesia de Dios y quieren avergonzar a los que no tienen nada? ¿Qué les diré? ¿Voy a elogiarlos por esto? ¡Claro que no!

23Yo recibí del Señor lo mismo que les transmití a ustedes: Que el Señor Jesús, la noche en que fue traicionado, tomó pan, 24y después de dar gracias, lo partió y dijo: «Este pan es mi cuerpo, que por ustedes entrego; hagan esto en memoria de mí.» 25De la misma manera, después de cenar, tomó la copa y dijo: «Esta copa es el nuevo pacto en mi sangre; hagan esto, cada vez que beban de ella, en memoria de mí.» 26Porque cada vez que comen este pan y beben de esta copa, proclaman la muerte del Señor hasta que él venga.

27Por lo tanto, cualquiera que coma el pan o beba de la copa del Señor de manera indigna, será culpable de pecar contra el cuerpo y la sangre del Señor. 28Así que cada uno debe examinarse a sí mismo antes de comer el pan y beber de la copa. 29Porque el que come y bebe sin discernir el cuerpo,i come y bebe su propia condena. 30Por eso hay entre ustedes muchos débiles y enfermos, e incluso varios han muerto. 31Si nos examináramos a nosotros mismos, no se nos juzgaría; 32pero si nos juzga el Señor, nos disciplina para que no seamos condenados con el mundo.

33Así que, hermanos míos, cuando se reúnan para comer, espérense unos a otros. 34Si alguno tiene hambre, que coma en su casa, para que las reuniones de ustedes no resulten dignas de condenación.

Los demás asuntos los arreglaré cuando los visite.

Los dones espirituales

12
En cuanto a los dones espirituales, hermanos, quiero que entiendan bien este asunto. 2Ustedes saben que cuando eran *paganos se dejaban arrastrar hacia los ídolos mudos. 3Por eso les advierto que nadie que esté hablando por el Espíritu de Dios puede maldecir a Jesús; ni nadie puede decir: «Jesús es el Señor» sino por el Espíritu Santo.

4Ahora bien, hay diversos dones, pero un mismo Espíritu. 5Hay diversas maneras de servir, pero un mismo Señor. 6Hay diversas funciones, pero es un mismo Dios el que hace todas las cosas en todos.

7A cada uno se le da una manifestación especial del Espíritu para el bien de los demás. 8A unos Dios les da por el Espíritu palabra de sabiduría; a otros, por el mismo Espíritu, palabra de conocimiento; 9a otros, fe por medio del mismo Espíritu; a otros, y por ese mismo Espíritu, dones para sanar enfermos; 10a otros, poderes milagrosos; a otros, profecía; a otros, el discernir espíritus; a otros, el hablar en diversas *lenguas; y a otros, el interpretar lenguas. 11Todo esto lo hace un mismo y único Espíritu, quien reparte a cada uno según él lo determina.

Un cuerpo con muchos miembros

12De hecho, aunque el cuerpo es uno solo, tiene muchos miembros, y todos los miembros, no obstante ser muchos, forman un solo cuerpo. Así sucede con Cristo. 13Todos fuimos bautizados porj un solo Espíritu para constituir un solo cuerpo —ya seamos judíos o *gentiles, esclavos o libres—, y a todos se nos dio a beber de un mismo Espíritu.

14Ahora bien, el cuerpo no consta de un solo miembro sino de muchos. 15Si el pie dijera: «Como no soy mano, no soy del cuerpo», no por eso dejaría de ser parte del cuerpo. 16Y si la oreja dijera: «Como no soy ojo, no soy del cuerpo», no por eso dejaría de ser parte del cuerpo. 17Si todo el cuerpo fuera ojo, ¿qué sería del olfato? 18En realidad, Dios colocó cada miembro del cuerpo como mejor le pareció. 19Si todos ellos fueran un solo miembro, ¿qué sería del

---

f 11:2 enseñanzas. Alt. Tradiciones . g 11:4 la cabeza cubierta. Alt. el cabello largo; también en el resto del pasaje.
h 11:10 debe . . . autoridad. Lit. debe tener autoridad sobre la cabeza. i 11:29 cuerpo. Var. cuerpo del Señor. j 12:13 por. Alt. con, o en.

cuerpo? 20Lo cierto es que hay muchos miembros, pero el cuerpo es uno solo.

21El ojo no puede decirle a la mano: «No te necesito.» Ni puede la cabeza decirles a los pies: «No los necesito.» 22Al contrario, los miembros del cuerpo que parecen más débiles son indispensables, 23y a los que nos parecen menos honrosos los tratamos con honra especial. Y se les trata con especial modestia a los miembros que nos parecen menos presentables, 24mientras que los más presentables no requieren trato especial. Así Dios ha dispuesto los miembros de nuestro cuerpo, dando mayor honra a los que menos tenían, 25a fin de que no haya división en el cuerpo, sino que sus miembros se preocupen por igual unos por otros. 26Si uno de los miembros sufre, los demás comparten su sufrimiento; y si uno de ellos recibe honor, los demás se alegran con él.

27Ahora bien, ustedes son el cuerpo de Cristo, y cada uno es miembro de ese cuerpo. 28En la iglesia Dios ha puesto, en primer lugar, apóstoles; en segundo lugar, profetas; en tercer lugar, maestros; luego los que hacen milagros; después los que tienen dones para sanar enfermos, los que ayudan a otros, los que administran y los que hablan en diversas *lenguas. 29¿Son todos apóstoles? ¿Son todos profetas? ¿Son todos maestros? ¿Hacen todos milagros? 30¿Tienen todos dones para sanar enfermos? ¿Hablan todos en lenguas? ¿Acaso interpretan todos? 31Ustedes, por su parte, ambicionenk los mejores dones.

El amor

Ahora les voy a mostrar un camino más excelente.

13 Si hablo en *lenguas *humanas y angelicales, pero no tengo amor, no soy más que un metal que resuena o un platillo que hace ruido. 2Si tengo el don de profecía y entiendo todos los *misterios y poseo todo conocimiento, y si tengo una fe que logra trasladar montañas, pero me falta el amor, no soy nada. 3Si reparto entre los pobres todo lo que poseo, y si entrego mi cuerpo para que lo consuman las llamas,l pero no tengo amor, nada gano con eso.

4El amor es paciente, es bondadoso. El amor no es envidioso ni jactancioso ni orgulloso. 5El amor no se comporta con rudeza, no es egoísta, no se enoja fácilmente, no guarda rencor. 6El amor no se deleita en la maldad sino que se regocija con la verdad. 7Todo lo disculpa, todo lo cree, todo lo espera, todo lo soporta.

8El amor jamás se extingue, mientras que el don de profecía cesará, el de lenguas será silenciado y el de conocimiento desaparecerá. 9Porque conocemos y profetizamos de manera imperfecta; 10pero cuando llegue lo perfecto, lo imperfecto desaparecerá. 11Cuando yo era niño, hablaba como niño, pensaba como niño, razonaba como niño; cuando llegué a ser adulto, dejé atrás las cosas de niño. 12Ahora vemos de manera indirecta y velada, como en un espejo; pero entonces veremos cara a cara. Ahora conozco de manera imperfecta, pero entonces conoceré tal y como soy conocido.

13Ahora, pues, permanecen estas tres virtudes: la fe, la esperanza y el amor. Pero la más excelente de ellas es el amor.

El don de lenguas y el de profecía

14 Empéñense en seguir el amor y ambicionen los dones espirituales, sobre todo el de profecía. 2Porque el que habla en *lenguas no habla a los demás sino a Dios. En realidad, nadie le entien-

de lo que dice, pues habla *misterios por el Espíritu.m 3En cambio, el que profetiza habla a los demás para edificarlos, animarlos y consolarlos. 4El que habla en lenguas se edifica a sí mismo; en cambio, el que profetiza edifica a la iglesia. 5Yo quisiera que todos ustedes hablaran en lenguas, pero mucho más que profetizaran. El que profetiza aventaja al que habla en lenguas, a menos que éste también interprete, para que la iglesia reciba edificación.

6Hermanos, si ahora fuera a visitarlos y les hablara en lenguas, ¿de qué les serviría, a menos que les presentara alguna revelación, conocimiento, profecía o enseñanza? 7Aun en el caso de los instrumentos musicales, tales como la flauta o el arpa, ¿cómo se reconocerá lo que tocan si no dan distintamente sus sonidos? 8Y si la trompeta no da un toque claro, ¿quién se va a preparar para la batalla? 9Así sucede con ustedes. A menos que su lengua pronuncie palabras comprensibles, ¿cómo se sabrá lo que dicen? Será como si hablaran al aire. 10¡Quién sabe cuántos idiomas hay en el mundo, y ninguno carece de sentido! 11Pero si no capto el sentido de lo que alguien dice, seré como un extranjero para el que me habla, y él lo será para mí. 12Por eso ustedes, ya que tanto ambicionan dones espirituales, procuren que éstos abunden para la edificación de la iglesia.

13Por esta razón, el que habla en lenguas pida en oración el don de interpretar lo que diga. 14Porque si yo oro en lenguas, mi espíritu ora, pero mi entendimiento no se beneficia en nada. 15¿Qué debo hacer entonces? Pues orar con el espíritu, pero también con el entendimiento; cantar con el espíritu, pero también con el entendimiento. 16De otra manera, si alabas a Dios con el espíritu, ¿cómo podrá quien no es instruidon decir «amén» a tu acción de gracias, puesto que no entiende lo que dices? 17En ese caso tu acción de gracias es admirable, pero no edifica al otro.

18Doy gracias a Dios porque hablo en lenguas más que todos ustedes. 19Sin embargo, en la iglesia prefiero emplear cinco palabras comprensibles y que me sirvan para instruir a los demás, que diez mil palabras en lenguas.

20Hermanos, no sean niños en su modo de pensar. Sean niños en cuanto a la malicia, pero adultos en su modo de pensar. 21En la ley está escrito:

«Por medio de gente de lengua extraña
   y por boca de extranjeros
hablaré a este pueblo,
   pero ni aun así me escucharán»,ñ dice el
     Señor.

22De modo que el hablar en lenguas es una señal, no para los creyentes sino para los incrédulos; en cambio, la profecía no es señal para los incrédulos sino para los creyentes. 23Así que, si toda la iglesia se reúne y todos hablan en lenguas, y entran algunos que no entienden o no creen, ¿no dirán que ustedes están locos? 24Pero si uno que no cree o uno que no entiende entra cuando todos están profetizando, se sentirá reprendido y juzgado por todos, 25y los secretos de su corazón quedarán al descubierto. Así que se postrará ante Dios y lo adorará, exclamando: «¡Realmente Dios está entre ustedes!»

Orden en los cultos

26¿Qué concluimos, hermanos? Que cuando se reúnan, cada uno puede tener un himno, una ense-

k 12:31 ambicionen. Alt. Ambicionan . l 13:3 para . . . llamas. Var. para tener de qué *jactarme. m 14:2 por el Espíritu. Alt. en su espíritu. n 14:16 quien no es instruido. Lit. el que ocupa el lugar del indocto. ñ 14:21 Is 28:11,12

ñanza, una revelación, un mensaje en *lenguas, o una interpretación. Todo esto debe hacerse para la edificación de la iglesia. 27Si se habla en lenguas, que hablen dos —o cuando mucho tres—, cada uno por turno; y que alguien interprete. 28Si no hay intérprete, que guarden silencio en la iglesia y cada uno hable para sí mismo y para Dios.

29En cuanto a los profetas, que hablen dos o tres, y que los demás examinen con cuidado lo dicho. 30Si alguien que está sentado recibe una revelación, el que esté hablando ceda la palabra. 31Así todos pueden profetizar por turno, para que todos reciban instrucción y aliento. 32El don de profecía está bajo el control de los profetas, 33porque Dios no es un Dios de desorden sino de paz.

Como es costumbre en las congregaciones de los *creyentes, 34guarden las mujeres silencio en la iglesia, pues no les está permitido hablar. Que estén sumisas, como lo establece la ley. 35Si quieren saber algo, que se lo pregunten en casa a sus esposos; porque no está bien visto que una mujer hable en la iglesia.

36¿Acaso la palabra de Dios procedió de ustedes? ¿O son ustedes los únicos que la han recibido? 37Si alguno se cree profeta o espiritual, reconozca que esto que les escribo es mandato del Señor. 38Si no lo reconoce, tampoco él será reconocido.P

39Así que, hermanos míos, ambicionen el don de profetizar, y no prohíban que se hable en lenguas. 40Pero todo debe hacerse de una manera apropiada y con orden.

La resurrección de Cristo

15 Ahora, hermanos, quiero recordarles el *evangelio que les prediqué, el mismo que recibieron y en el cual se mantienen firmes. 2Mediante este evangelio son salvos, si se aferran a la palabra que les prediqué. De otro modo, habrán creído en vano.

3Porque ante todoq les transmití a ustedes lo que yo mismo recibí: que Cristo murió por nuestros pecados según las Escrituras, 4que fue sepultado, que resucitó al tercer día según las Escrituras, 5y que se apareció a *Cefas, y luego a los doce. 6Después se apareció a más de quinientos hermanos a la vez, la mayoría de los cuales vive todavía, aunque algunos han muerto. 7Luego se apareció a *Jacobo, más tarde a todos los apóstoles, 8y por último, como a uno nacido fuera de tiempo, se me apareció también a mí.

9Admito que yo soy el más insignificante de los apóstoles y que ni siquiera merezco ser llamado apóstol, porque perseguí a la iglesia de Dios. 10Pero por la gracia de Dios soy lo que soy, y la gracia que él me concedió no fue infructuosa. Al contrario, he trabajado con más tesón que todos ellos, aunque no yo sino la gracia de Dios que está conmigo. 11En fin, ya sea que se trate de mí o de ellos, esto es lo que predicamos, y esto es lo que ustedes han creído.

La resurrección de los muertos

12Ahora bien, si se predica que Cristo ha sido levantado de entre los muertos, ¿cómo dicen algunos de ustedes que no hay resurrección? 13Si no hay resurrección, entonces ni siquiera Cristo ha resucitado. 14Y si Cristo no ha resucitado, nuestra predicación no sirve para nada, como tampoco la fe de ustedes. 15Aun más, resultaríamos falsos testigos de Dios por haber testificado que Dios resucitó a Cristo, lo cual no habría sucedido, si en verdad los muertos

no resucitan. 16Porque si los muertos no resucitan, tampoco Cristo ha resucitado. 17Y si Cristo no ha resucitado, la fe de ustedes es ilusoria y todavía están en sus pecados. 18En este caso, también están perdidos los que murieron en Cristo. 19Si la esperanza que tenemos en Cristo fuera sólo para esta vida, seríamos los más desdichados de todos los *mortales.

20Lo cierto es que Cristo ha sido *levantado de entre los muertos, como *primicias de los que murieron. 21De hecho, ya que la muerte vino por medio de un hombre, también por medio de un hombre viene la resurrección de los muertos. 22Pues así como en Adán todos mueren, también en Cristo todos volverán a vivir, 23pero cada uno en su debido orden: Cristo, las primicias; después, cuando él venga, los que le pertenecen. 24Entonces vendrá el fin, cuando él entregue el reino a Dios el Padre, luego de destruir todo dominio, autoridad y poder. 25Porque es necesario que Cristo reine hasta poner a todos sus enemigos debajo de sus pies. 26El último enemigo que será destruido es la muerte, 27pues Dios «ha sometido todo a su dominio».r Al decir que «todo» ha quedado sometido a su dominio, es claro que no se incluye a Dios mismo, quien todo lo sometió a Cristo. 28Y cuando todo le sea sometido, entonces el Hijo se someterá a aquel que le sometió todo, para que Dios sea todo en todos.

29Si no hay resurrección, ¿qué sacan los que se bautizan por los muertos? Si en definitiva los muertos no resucitan, ¿por qué se bautizan por ellos? 30Y nosotros, ¿por qué nos exponemos al peligro a todas horas? 31Que cada día muero, hermanos, es tan cierto como el *orgullo que siento por ustedes en Cristo Jesús nuestro Señor. 32¿Qué he ganado si, sólo por motivos humanos, en Éfeso luché contra las fieras? Si los muertos no resucitan,

«comamos y bebamos,
    que mañana moriremos».s

33No se dejen engañar: «Las malas compañías corrompen las buenas costumbres.» 34Vuelvan a su sano juicio, como conviene, y dejen de pecar. En efecto, hay algunos de ustedes que no tienen conocimiento de Dios; para vergüenza de ustedes lo digo.

El cuerpo resucitado

35Tal vez alguien pregunte: «¿Cómo resucitarán los muertos? ¿Con qué clase de cuerpo vendrán?» 36¡Qué tontería! Lo que tú siembras no cobra vida a menos que muera. 37No plantas el cuerpo que luego ha de nacer sino que siembras una simple semilla de trigo o de otro grano. 38Pero Dios le da el cuerpo que quiso darle, y a cada clase de semilla le da un cuerpo propio. 39No todos los cuerpos son iguales: hay cuerpos *humanos; también los hay de animales terrestres, de aves y de peces. 40Así mismo hay cuerpos celestes y cuerpos terrestres; pero el esplendor de los cuerpos celestes es uno, y el de los cuerpos terrestres es otro. 41Uno es el esplendor del sol, otro el de la luna y otro el de las estrellas. Cada estrella tiene su propio brillo.

42Así sucederá también con la resurrección de los muertos. Lo que se siembra en corrupción, resucita en incorrupción; 43lo que se siembra en oprobio, resucita en gloria; lo que se siembra en debilidad, resucita en poder; 44se siembra un cuerpo natural,t resucita un cuerpo espiritual.

---

o **14:32** El don . . . está. Lit. Los espíritus de los profetas están. p **14:38** tampoco . . . reconocido. Var. que no lo reconozca. q **15:3** ante todo. Alt. al principio. r **15:27** Sal 8:6 s **15:32** Is 22:13 t **15:44** natural. Lit. *síquico; también en v. 46.

Si hay un cuerpo natural, también hay un cuerpo espiritual. [45]Así está escrito: «El primer hombre, Adán, se convirtió en un ser viviente»;[u] el último Adán, en el Espíritu que da vida. [46]No vino primero lo espiritual sino lo natural, y después lo espiritual. [47]El primer hombre era del polvo de la tierra; el segundo hombre, del cielo. [48]Como es aquel hombre terrenal, así son también los de la tierra; y como es el celestial, así son también los del cielo. [49]Y así como hemos llevado la imagen de aquel hombre terrenal, llevaremos[v] también la imagen del celestial.

[50]Les declaro, hermanos, que el cuerpo mortal[w] no puede heredar el reino de Dios, ni lo corruptible puede heredar lo incorruptible. [51]Fíjense bien en el *misterio que les voy a revelar: No todos moriremos, pero todos seremos transformados, [52]en un instante, en un abrir y cerrar de ojos, al toque final de la trompeta. Pues sonará la trompeta y los muertos resucitarán con un cuerpo incorruptible, y nosotros seremos transformados. [53]Porque lo corruptible tiene que revestirse de lo incorruptible, y lo mortal, de inmortalidad. [54]Cuando lo corruptible se revista de lo incorruptible, y lo mortal, de inmortalidad, entonces se cumplirá lo que está escrito: «La muerte ha sido devorada por la victoria.»[x]

[55]«¿Dónde está, oh muerte, tu victoria?
¿Dónde está, oh muerte, tu aguijón?»[y]

[56]El aguijón de la muerte es el pecado, y el poder del pecado es la ley. [57]¡Pero gracias a Dios, que nos da la victoria por medio de nuestro Señor Jesucristo!

[58]Por lo tanto, mis queridos hermanos, manténganse firmes e inconmovibles, progresando siempre en la obra del Señor, conscientes de que su trabajo en el Señor no es en vano.

La colecta para el pueblo de Dios

16 En cuanto a la colecta para los *creyentes, sigan las instrucciones que di a las iglesias de Galacia. [2]El primer día de la semana, cada uno de ustedes aparte y guarde algún dinero conforme a sus ingresos, para que no se tengan que hacer colectas cuando yo vaya. [3]Luego, cuando llegue, daré cartas de presentación a los que ustedes hayan aprobado y los enviaré a Jerusalén con los donativos que hayan recogido. [4]Si conviene que yo también vaya, iremos juntos.

Encargos personales

[5]Después de pasar por Macedonia, pues tengo que atravesar esa región, iré a verlos. [6]Es posible que me quede con ustedes algún tiempo, y tal vez pase allí el invierno, para que me ayuden a seguir el viaje a dondequiera que vaya. [7]Esta vez no quiero verlos sólo de paso; más bien, espero permanecer algún tiempo con ustedes, si el Señor así lo permite. [8]Pero me quedaré en Éfeso hasta Pentecostés, [9]porque se me ha presentado una gran oportunidad para un trabajo eficaz, a pesar de que hay muchos en mi contra.

[10]Si llega Timoteo, procuren que se sienta cómodo entre ustedes, porque él trabaja como yo en la obra del Señor. [11]Por tanto, que nadie lo menosprecie. Ayúdenlo a seguir su viaje en paz para que pueda volver a reunirse conmigo, pues estoy esperándolo junto con los hermanos.

[12]En cuanto a nuestro hermano Apolos, le rogué encarecidamente que en compañía de otros hermanos les hiciera una visita. No quiso de ninguna manera ir ahora, pero lo hará cuando se le presente la oportunidad.

[13]Manténganse alerta; permanezcan firmes en la fe; sean valientes y fuertes. [14]Hagan todo con amor.

[15]Bien saben que los de la familia de Estéfanas fueron los primeros convertidos de Acaya,[z] y que se han dedicado a servir a los *creyentes. Les recomiendo, hermanos, [16]que se pongan a disposición de aquéllos y de todo el que colabore en este arduo trabajo. [17]Me alegré cuando llegaron Estéfanas, Fortunato y Acaico, porque ellos han suplido lo que ustedes no podían darme, [18]ya que han tranquilizado mi espíritu y también el de ustedes. Tales personas merecen que se les exprese reconocimiento.

Saludos finales

[19]Las iglesias de la provincia de *Asia les mandan saludos. Aquila y *Priscila los saludan cordialmente en el Señor, como también la iglesia que se reúne en la casa de ellos. [20]Todos los hermanos les mandan saludos. Salúdense unos a otros con un beso santo.

[21]Yo, Pablo, escribo este saludo de mi puño y letra.

[22]Si alguno no ama al Señor, quede bajo maldición. ¡Marana ta![a]

[23]Que la gracia del Señor Jesús sea con ustedes.

[24]Los amo a todos ustedes en Cristo Jesús. Amén.[b]

---

u **15:45** Gn 2:7　v **15:49** llevaremos. Var. Llevemos .　w **15:50** el cuerpo mortal. Lit. *carne y sangre.　x **15:54** Is 25:8　y **15:55** Os 13:14　z **16:15** los primeros convertidos de Acaya. Lit. las *primicias de Acaya.　a **16:22** ¡Marana ta! Expresión aramea que significa: «Ven, Señor»; otra posible lectura es Maran ata, que significa: «El Señor viene.»　b **16:24** Var. no incluye: Amén.

Segunda Carta a los CORINTIOS

1 Pablo, apóstol de *Cristo Jesús por la voluntad de Dios, y Timoteo nuestro hermano,

a la iglesia de Dios que está en Corinto y a todos los *santos en toda la región de Acaya:

2Que Dios nuestro padre y el Señor Jesucristo les concedan gracia y paz.

El Dios de toda consolación

3Alabado sea el Dios y Padre de nuestro Señor Jesucristo, Padre misericordioso y Dios de toda consolación, 4quien nos consuela en todas nuestras tribulaciones para que con el mismo consuelo que de Dios hemos recibido, también nosotros podamos consolar a todos los que sufren. 5Pues así como participamos abundantemente en los sufrimientos de Cristo, así también por medio de él tenemos abundante consuelo. 6Si sufrimos, es para que ustedes tengan consuelo y salvación; y si somos consolados, es para que ustedes tengan el consuelo que los ayude a soportar con paciencia los mismos sufrimientos que nosotros padecemos. 7Firme es la esperanza que tenemos en cuanto a ustedes, porque sabemos que así como participan de nuestros sufrimientos, así también participan de nuestro consuelo.

8Hermanos, no queremos que desconozcan las aflicciones que sufrimos en la provincia de *Asia. Estábamos tan agobiados bajo tanta presión, que hasta perdimos la esperanza de salir con vida: 9nos sentíamos como sentenciados a muerte. Pero eso sucedió para que no confiáramos en nosotros mismos sino en Dios, que resucita a los muertos. 10Él nos libró y nos librará de tal peligro de muerte. En él tenemos puesta nuestra esperanza, y él seguirá librándonos. 11Mientras tanto, ustedes nos ayudan orando por nosotros. Así muchos darán gracias a Dios por nosotrosa a causa del don que se nos ha concedido en respuesta a tantas oraciones.

Pablo cambia de planes

12Para nosotros, el motivo de *satisfacción es el testimonio de nuestra conciencia: Nos hemos comportado en el mundo, y especialmente entre ustedes, con la *santidad y sinceridad que vienen de Dios. Nuestra conducta no se ha ajustado a la sabiduría *humana sino a la gracia de Dios. 13No estamos escribiéndoles nada que no puedan leer ni entender. Espero que comprenderán del todo, 14así como ya nos han comprendido en parte, que pueden sentirse *orgullosos de nosotros como también nosotros nos sentiremos orgullosos de ustedes en el día del Señor Jesús.

15Confiando en esto, quise visitarlos primero a ustedes para que recibieran una doble bendición; 16es decir, visitarlos de paso a Macedonia, y verlos otra vez a mi regreso de allá. Así podrían ayudarme a seguir el viaje a Judea. 17Al proponerme esto, ¿acaso lo hice a la ligera? ¿O es que hago mis planes según criterios meramente *humanos, de manera que diga «sí, sí» y «no, no» al mismo tiempo?

18Pero tan cierto como que Dios es fiel, el mensaje que les hemos dirigido no es «sí» y «no». 19Porque el Hijo de Dios, Jesucristo, a quien *Silvano, Timoteo y yo predicamos entre ustedes, no fue «sí» y «no»; en él siempre ha sido «sí». 20Todas las promesas que ha hecho Dios son «sí» en Cristo. Así que por medio de Cristo respondemos «amén» para la gloria de Dios.

21Dios es el que nos mantiene firmes en Cristo, tanto a nosotros como a ustedes. Él nos ungió, 22nos selló como propiedad suya y puso su Espíritu en nuestro corazón, como garantía de sus promesas.

23¡Por mi *vida! Pongo a Dios por testigo de que es sólo por consideración a ustedes por lo que todavía no he ido a Corinto. 24No es que intentemos imponerles la fe, sino que deseamos contribuir a la alegría de ustedes, pues por la fe se mantienen firmes.

2 En efecto, decidí no hacerles otra visita que les causara tristeza. 2Porque si yo los entristezco, ¿quién me brindará alegría sino aquel a quien yo haya entristecido? 3Les escribí como lo hice para no, al llegar yo, los que debían alegrarme no me causaran tristeza. Estaba confiado de que todos ustedes harían suya mi alegría. 4Les escribí con gran tristeza y angustia de corazón, y con muchas lágrimas, no para entristecerlos sino para darles a conocer la profundidad del amor que les tengo.

Perdón para el pecador

5Si alguno ha causado tristeza, no me la ha causado sólo a mí; hasta cierto punto —y lo digo para no exagerar— se la ha causado a todos ustedes. 6Para él es suficiente el castigo que le impuso la mayoría. 7Más bien debieran perdonarlo y consolarlo para que no sea consumido por la excesiva tristeza. 8Por eso les ruego que reafirmen su amor hacia él. 9Con este propósito les escribí: para ver si pasan la prueba de la completa obediencia. 10A quien ustedes perdonen, yo también lo perdono. De hecho, si había algo que perdonar, lo he perdonado por consideración a ustedes en presencia de Cristo, 11para que Satanás no se aproveche de nosotros, pues no ignoramos sus artimañas.

Ministros del nuevo pacto

12Ahora bien, cuando llegué a Troas para predicar el *evangelio de Cristo, descubrí que el Señor me había abierto las puertas. 13Aun así, me sentí intranquilo por no haber encontrado allí a mi hermano Tito, por lo cual me despedí de ellos y me fui a Macedonia.

14Sin embargo, gracias a Dios que en Cristo siempre nos lleva triunfantesb y, por medio de nosotros, esparce por todas partes la fragancia de su conocimiento. 15Porque para Dios nosotros somos el aroma de Cristo entre los que se salvan y entre los que se pierden. 16Para éstos somos olor de muerte que los lleva a la muerte; para aquéllos, olor de vida que los lleva a la vida. ¿Y quién es competente para semejante tarea? 17A diferencia de muchos, nosotros no somos de los que trafican con la palabra de Dios. Más bien, hablamos con sinceridad delante de él en Cristo, como enviados de Dios que somos.

3 ¿Acaso comenzamos otra vez a recomendarnos a nosotros mismos? ¿O acaso tenemos que presentarles o pedirles a ustedes cartas de recomendación, como hacen algunos? 2Ustedes mismos son nuestra carta, escrita en nuestro corazón, conocida y leída por todos. 3Es evidente que ustedes son una carta de Cristo, expedidac por medio de nosotros, escrita no con tinta sino con el Espíritu del Dios viviente; no en tablas de piedra sino en tablas de carne, en los corazones.

4Ésta es la confianza que delante de Dios tenemos por medio de Cristo. 5No es que nos consideremos competentes en nosotros mismos. Nuestra

---

a 1:11 *nosotros.* Var. *ustedes.*   b 2:14 *nos lleva triunfantes.* Alt. *nos conduce en desfile victorioso.*   c 3:3 *expedida.* Lit. *Ministrada.*

capacidad viene de Dios. [6]Él nos ha capacitado para ser servidores de un nuevo pacto, no el de la letra sino el del Espíritu; porque la letra mata, pero el Espíritu da vida.

La gloria del nuevo pacto

[7]El ministerio que causaba muerte, el que estaba grabado con letras en piedra, fue tan glorioso que los israelitas no podían mirar la cara de Moisés debido a la gloria que se reflejaba en su rostro, la cual ya se estaba extinguiendo. [8]Pues bien, si aquel ministerio fue así, ¿no será todavía más glorioso el ministerio del Espíritu? [9]Si es glorioso el ministerio que trae condenación, ¡cuánto más glorioso será el ministerio que trae la justicia! [10]En efecto, lo que fue glorioso ya no lo es, si se le compara con esta excelsa gloria. [11]Y si vino con gloria lo que ya se estaba extinguiendo, ¡cuánto mayor será la gloria de lo que permanece!

[12]Así que, como tenemos tal esperanza, actuamos con plena confianza. [13]No hacemos como Moisés, quien se ponía un velo sobre el rostro para que los israelitas no vieran el fin del resplandor que se iba extinguiendo. [14]Sin embargo, la mente de ellos se embotó, de modo que hasta el día de hoy tienen puesto el mismo velo al leer el antiguo pacto. El velo no les ha sido quitado, porque sólo se quita en Cristo. [15]Hasta el día de hoy, siempre que leen a Moisés, un velo les cubre el corazón. [16]Pero cada vez que alguien se vuelve al Señor, el velo es quitado. [17]Ahora bien, el Señor es el Espíritu; y donde está el Espíritu del Señor, allí hay libertad. [18]Así, todos nosotros, que con el rostro descubierto reflejamos[d] como en un espejo la gloria del Señor, somos transformados a su semejanza con más y más gloria por la acción del Señor, que es el Espíritu.

Tesoros en vasijas de barro

4 Por esto, ya que por la misericordia de Dios tenemos este ministerio, no nos desanimamos. [2]Más bien, hemos renunciado a todo lo vergonzoso que se hace a escondidas; no actuamos con engaño ni torcemos la palabra de Dios. Al contrario, mediante la clara exposición de la verdad, nos recomendamos a toda conciencia *humana en la presencia de Dios. [3]Pero si nuestro *evangelio está encubierto, lo está para los que se pierden. [4]El dios de este mundo ha cegado la mente de estos incrédulos, para que no vean la luz del glorioso evangelio de Cristo, el cual es la imagen de Dios. [5]No nos predicamos a nosotros mismos sino a Jesucristo como Señor; nosotros no somos más que servidores de ustedes por causa de Jesús. [6]Porque Dios, que ordenó que la luz resplandeciera en las tinieblas,[e] hizo brillar su luz en nuestro corazón para que conociéramos la gloria de Dios que resplandece en el rostro de Cristo.

[7]Pero tenemos este tesoro en vasijas de barro para que se vea que tan sublime poder viene de Dios y no de nosotros. [8]Nos vemos atribulados en todo, pero no abatidos; perplejos, pero no desesperados; [9]perseguidos, pero no abandonados; derribados, pero no destruidos. [10]Dondequiera que vamos, siempre llevamos en nuestro cuerpo la muerte de Jesús, para que también su vida se manifieste en nuestro cuerpo. [11]Pues a nosotros, los que vivimos, siempre se nos entrega a la muerte por causa de Jesús, para que también su vida se manifieste en nuestro cuerpo[f] mortal. [12]Así que la muerte actúa en nosotros, y en ustedes la vida.

[13]Escrito está: «Creí, y por eso hablé.»[g] Con ese mismo espíritu de fe también nosotros creemos, y por eso hablamos. [14]Pues sabemos que aquel que resucitó al Señor Jesús nos resucitará también a nosotros con él y nos llevará junto con ustedes a su presencia. [15]Todo esto es por el bien de ustedes, para que la gracia que está alcanzando a más y más personas haga abundar la acción de gracias para la gloria de Dios.

[16]Por tanto, no nos desanimamos. Al contrario, aunque por fuera nos vamos desgastando, por dentro nos vamos renovando día tras día. [17]Pues los sufrimientos ligeros y efímeros que ahora padecemos producen una gloria eterna que vale muchísimo más que todo sufrimiento. [18]Así que no nos fijamos en lo visible sino en lo invisible, ya que lo que se ve es pasajero, mientras que lo que no se ve es eterno.

Nuestra morada celestial

5 De hecho, sabemos que si esta tienda de campaña en que vivimos se deshace, tenemos de Dios un edificio, una casa eterna en el cielo, no construida por manos humanas. [2]Mientras tanto suspiramos, anhelando ser revestidos de nuestra morada celestial, [3]porque cuando seamos revestidos, no se nos hallará desnudos. [4]Realmente, vivimos en esta tienda de campaña, suspirando y agobiados, pues no deseamos ser desvestidos sino revestidos, para que lo mortal sea absorbido por la vida. [5]Es Dios quien nos ha hecho para este fin y nos ha dado su Espíritu como garantía de sus promesas.

[6]Por eso mantenemos siempre la confianza, aunque sabemos que mientras vivamos en este cuerpo estaremos alejados del Señor. [7]Vivimos por fe, no por vista. [8]Así que nos mantenemos confiados, y preferiríamos ausentarnos de este cuerpo y vivir junto al Señor. [9]Por eso nos empeñamos en agradarle, ya sea que vivamos en nuestro cuerpo o que lo hayamos dejado. [10]Porque es necesario que todos comparezcamos ante el tribunal de Cristo, para que cada uno reciba lo que le corresponda, según lo bueno o malo que haya hecho mientras vivió en el cuerpo.

El ministerio de la reconciliación

[11]Por tanto, como sabemos lo que es temer al Señor, tratamos de persuadir a todos, aunque para Dios es evidente lo que somos, y espero que también lo sea para la conciencia de ustedes. [12]No buscamos el recomendarnos otra vez a ustedes, sino que les damos una oportunidad de sentirse *orgullosos de nosotros, para que tengan con qué responder a los que se dejan llevar por las apariencias y no por lo que hay dentro del corazón. [13]Si estamos locos, es por Dios; y si estamos cuerdos, es por ustedes. [14]El amor de Cristo nos obliga, porque estamos convencidos de que uno murió por todos, y por consiguiente todos murieron. [15]Y él murió por todos, para que los que viven ya no vivan para sí, sino para el que murió por ellos y fue resucitado.

[16]Así que de ahora en adelante no consideramos a nadie según criterios meramente *humanos.[h] Aunque antes conocimos a Cristo de esta manera, ya no lo conocemos así. [17]Por lo tanto, si alguno está en Cristo, es una nueva creación. ¡Lo viejo ha pasado, ha llegado ya lo nuevo! [18]Todo esto proviene de Dios, quien por medio de Cristo nos reconcilió consigo mismo y nos dio el ministerio de la reconciliación: [19]esto es, que en Cristo, Dios estaba reconciliando al

---

[d] **3:18** *reflejamos.* Alt. *contemplamos.*　[e] **4:6** Gn 1:3　[f] **4:11** *nuestro cuerpo.* Lit. *nuestra *carne.*　[g] **4:13** Sal 116:10　[h] **5:16** *criterios . . . humanos.* Lit. *la carne.*

mundo consigo mismo, no tomándole en cuenta sus pecados y encargándonos a nosotros el mensaje de la reconciliación. 20Así que somos embajadores de Cristo, como si Dios los exhortara a ustedes por medio de nosotros: «En nombre de Cristo les rogamos que se reconcilien con Dios.» 21Al que no cometió pecado alguno, por nosotros Dios lo trató como pecador,i para que en él recibiéramosi la justicia de Dios.

6 Nosotros, colaboradores de Dios, les rogamos que no reciban su gracia en vano. 2Porque él dice:

«En el momento propicio te escuché,
    y en el día de salvación te ayudé.»k

Les digo que éste es el momento propicio de Dios; ¡hoy es el día de salvación!

Privaciones de Pablo

3Por nuestra parte, a nadie damos motivo alguno de tropiezo, para que no se desacredite nuestro servicio. 4Más bien, en todo y con mucha paciencia nos acreditamos como servidores de Dios: en sufrimientos, privaciones y angustias; 5en azotes, cárceles y tumultos; en trabajos pesados, desvelos y hambre. 6Servimos con pureza, conocimiento, constancia y bondad; en el Espíritu Santo y en amor sincero; 7con palabras de verdad y con el poder de Dios; con armas de justicia, tanto ofensivas como defensivas;l 8por honra y por deshonra, por mala y por buena fama; veraces, pero tenidos por engañadores; 9conocidos, pero tenidos por desconocidos; como moribundos, pero aún con vida; golpeados, pero no muertos; 10aparentemente tristes, pero siempre alegres; pobres en apariencia, pero enriqueciendo a muchos; como si no tuviéramos nada, pero poseyéndolo todo.

11Hermanos corintios, les hemos hablado con toda franqueza; les hemos abierto de par en par nuestro corazón. 12Nunca les hemos negado nuestro afecto, pero ustedes sí nos niegan el suyo. 13Para corresponder del mismo modo —les hablo como si fueran mis hijos—, ¡abran también su corazón de par en par!

No formen yunta con los incrédulos

14No formen yunta con los incrédulos. ¿Qué tienen en común la justicia y la maldad? ¿O qué comunión puede tener la luz con la oscuridad? 15¿Qué armonía tiene Cristo con el diablo?m ¿Qué tiene en común un creyente con un incrédulo? 16¿En qué concuerdan el templo de Dios y los ídolos? Porque nosotros somos templo del Dios viviente. Como él ha dicho: «Viviré con ellos y caminaré entre ellos. Yo seré su Dios, y ellos serán mi pueblo.»n Por tanto, el Señor añade:

17«Salgan de en medio de ellos
    y apártense.
No toquen nada *impuro,
    y yo los recibiré.»ñ
18«Yo seré un padre para ustedes,
    y ustedes serán mis hijos y mis hijas,
        dice el Señor Todopoderoso.»o

7 Como tenemos estas promesas, queridos hermanos, purifiquémonos de todo lo que contamina el cuerpo y el espíritu, para completar en el temor de Dios la obra de nuestra *santificación.

La alegría de Pablo

2Hagan lugar para nosotros en su corazón. A nadie hemos agraviado, a nadie hemos corrompido, a nadie hemos explotado. 3No digo esto para condenarlos; ya les he dicho que tienen un lugar tan amplio en nuestro corazón que con ustedes viviríamos o moriríamos. 4Les tengo mucha confianza y me siento muy *orgulloso de ustedes. Estoy muy animado; en medio de todas nuestras aflicciones se desborda mi alegría.

5Cuando llegamos a Macedonia, nuestro cuerpo no tuvo ningún descanso, sino que nos vimos acosados por todas partes; conflictos por fuera, temores por dentro. 6Pero Dios, que consuela a los abatidos, nos consoló con la llegada de Tito, 7y no sólo con su llegada sino también con el consuelo que él había recibido de ustedes. Él nos habló del anhelo, de la profunda tristeza y de la honda preocupación que ustedes tienen por mí, lo cual me llenó de alegría.

8Si bien los entristecí con mi carta, no me pesa. Es verdad que antes me pesó, porque me di cuenta de que por un tiempo mi carta los había entristecido. 9Sin embargo, ahora me alegro, no porque se hayan entristecido sino porque su tristeza los llevó al *arrepentimiento. Ustedes se entristecieron tal como Dios lo quiere, de modo que nosotros de ninguna manera los hemos perjudicado. 10La tristeza que proviene de Dios produce el arrepentimiento que lleva a la salvación, de la cual no hay que arrepentirse, mientras que la tristeza del mundo produce la muerte. 11¡Fíjense lo que ha producido en ustedes esta tristeza que proviene de Dios: ¡qué empeño, qué afán por disculparse, qué indignación, qué temor, qué anhelo, qué preocupación, qué disposición para ver que se haga justicia! En todo han demostrado su inocencia en este asunto. 12Así que, a pesar de que les escribí, no fue por causa del ofensor ni del ofendido, sino más bien para que delante de Dios se dieran cuenta por ustedes mismos de cuánto interés tienen en nosotros. 13Todo esto nos reanima.

Además del consuelo que hemos recibido, nos alegró muchísimo el ver lo feliz que estaba Tito debido a que todos ustedes fortalecieron su espíritu. 14Ya le había dicho que me sentía orgulloso de ustedes, y no me han hecho quedar mal. Al contrario, así como todo lo que les dijimos es verdad, también resultaron ciertos los elogios que hice de ustedes delante de Tito. 15Y él les tiene aun más cariño al recordar que todos ustedes fueron obedientes y lo recibieron con temor y temblor. 16Me alegro de que puedo confiar plenamente en ustedes.

Estímulo a la generosidad

8 Ahora, hermanos, queremos que se enteren de la gracia que Dios ha dado a las iglesias de Macedonia. 2En medio de las pruebas más difíciles, su desbordante alegría y su extrema pobreza abundaron en rica generosidad. 3Soy testigo de que dieron espontáneamente tanto como podían, y aun más de lo que podían, 4rogándonos con insistencia que les concediéramos el privilegio de tomar parte en esta ayuda para los *santos. 5Incluso hicieron más de lo que esperábamos, ya que se entregaron a sí mismos, primeramente al Señor y después a nosotros, conforme a la voluntad de Dios. 6De modo que rogamos a Tito que llevara a feliz término esta obra de gracia entre ustedes, puesto que ya la había comenzado. 7Pero

i 5:21 lo trató como pecador. Alt. lo hizo sacrificio por el pecado. Lit. lo hizo pecado.   j 5:21 recibiéramos. Lit. llegáramos a ser.   k 6:2 Is 49:8   l 6:7 ofensivas como defensivas. Lit. en la mano derecha como en la izquierda.   m 6:15 el diablo. Lit. Beliar, otra forma de Belial.   n 6:16 Lv 26:12; Jer 32:38; Ez 37:27   ñ 6:17 Is 52:11; Ez 20:34,41   o 6:18 2S 7:8,14; 1Cr 17:13

ustedes, así como sobresalen en todo —en fe, en palabras, en conocimiento, en dedicación y en su amor hacia nosotrosᵖ—, procuren también sobresalir en esta gracia de dar.

8No es que esté dándoles órdenes, sino que quiero probar la sinceridad de su amor en comparación con la dedicación de los demás. 9Ya conocen la gracia de nuestro Señor Jesucristo, que aunque era rico, por causa de ustedes se hizo pobre, para que mediante su pobreza ustedes llegaran a ser ricos.

10Aquí va mi consejo sobre lo que les conviene en este asunto: El año pasado ustedes fueron los primeros no sólo en dar sino también en querer hacerlo. 11Lleven ahora a feliz término la obra, para que, según sus posibilidades, cumplan con lo que de buena gana propusieron. 12Porque si uno lo hace de buena voluntad, lo que da es bien recibido según lo que tiene, y no según lo que no tiene.

13No se trata de que otros encuentren alivio mientras que ustedes sufren escasez; es más bien cuestión de igualdad. 14En las circunstancias actuales la abundancia de ustedes suplirá lo que ellos necesitan, para que a su vez la abundancia de ellos supla lo que ustedes necesitan. Así habrá igualdad, 15como está escrito: «Ni al que recogió mucho le sobraba, ni al que recogió poco le faltaba.»q

Tito enviado a Corinto

16Gracias a Dios que puso en el corazón de Tito la misma preocupación que yo tengo por ustedes. 17De hecho, cuando accedió a nuestra petición de ir a verlos, lo hizo con mucho entusiasmo y por su propia voluntad. 18Junto con él les enviamos al hermano que se ha ganado el reconocimiento de todas las iglesias por los servicios prestados al *evangelio. 19Además, las iglesias lo escogieron para que nos acompañe cuando llevemos la ofrenda, la cual administramos para honrar al Señor y demostrar nuestro ardiente deseo de servir. 20Queremos evitar cualquier crítica sobre la forma en que administramos este generoso donativo; 21porque procuramos hacer lo correcto, no sólo delante del Señor sino también delante de los demás.

22Con ellos les enviamos a nuestro hermano que nos ha demostrado con frecuencia y de muchas maneras que es diligente, y ahora lo es aun más por la gran confianza que tiene en ustedes. 23En cuanto a Tito, es mi compañero y colaborador entre ustedes; y en cuanto a los otros hermanos, son enviados de las iglesias, son una honra para Cristo. 24Por tanto, den a estos hombres una prueba de su amor y muéstrenles por qué nos sentimos *orgullosos de ustedes, para testimonio ante las iglesias.

9 No hace falta que les escriba acerca de esta ayuda para los *santos, 2porque conozco la buena disposición que ustedes tienen. Esto lo he comentado con orgullo entre los macedonios, diciéndoles que desde el año pasado ustedes los de Acaya estaban preparados para dar. El entusiasmo de ustedes ha servido de estímulo a la mayoría de ellos. 3Con todo, les envío a estos hermanos para que en este asunto no resulte vano nuestro *orgullo por ustedes, sino que estén preparados, como ya he dicho que lo estarían, 4no sea que algunos macedonios vayan conmigo y los encuentren desprevenidos. En ese caso nosotros —por no decir nada de ustedes— nos avergonzaríamos por haber estado tan seguros. 5Así que me pareció necesario rogar a estos hermanos

que se adelantaran a visitarlos y completaran los preparativos para esa generosa colecta que ustedes habían prometido. Entonces estará lista como una ofrenda generosa,r y no como una tacañería.

Sembrar con generosidad

6Recuerden esto: El que siembra escasamente, escasamente cosechará, y el que siembra en abundancia, en abundancia cosechará.s 7Cada uno debe dar según lo que haya decidido en su corazón, no de mala gana ni por obligación, porque Dios ama al que da con alegría. 8Y Dios puede hacer que toda gracia abunde para ustedes, de manera que siempre, en toda circunstancia, tengan todo lo necesario, y toda buena obra abunde en ustedes. 9Como está escrito:

«Repartió sus bienes entre los pobres;
    su justicia permanece para siempre.»t

10El que le suple semilla al que siembra también le suplirá pan para que coma, aumentará los cultivos y hará que ustedes produzcan una abundante cosecha de justicia. 11Ustedes serán enriquecidos en todo sentido para que en toda ocasión puedan ser generosos, y para que por medio de nosotros la generosidad de ustedes resulte en acciones de gracias a Dios.

12Esta ayuda que es un servicio sagrado no sólo suple las necesidades de los *santos sino que también redunda en abundantes acciones de gracias a Dios. 13En efecto, al recibir esta demostración de servicio, ellos alabarán a Dios por la obediencia con que ustedes acompañan la confesión del *evangelio de Cristo, y por su generosa solidaridad con ellos y con todos. 14Además, en las oraciones de ellos por ustedes, expresarán el afecto que les tienen por la sobreabundante gracia que ustedes han recibido de Dios. 15¡Gracias a Dios por su don inefable!

Pablo defiende su ministerio

10 Por la ternura y la bondad de Cristo, yo, Pablo, apelo a ustedes personalmente; yo mismo que, según dicen, soy tímido cuando me encuentro cara a cara con ustedes pero atrevido cuando estoy lejos. 2Les ruego que cuando vaya no tenga que ser tan atrevido como me he propuesto ser con algunos que opinan que vivimos según criterios meramente *humanos, 3pues aunque vivimos en el *mundo, no libramos batallas como lo hace el mundo. 4Las armas con que luchamos no son del mundo, sino que tienen el poder divino para derribar fortalezas. 5Destruimos argumentos y toda altivez que se levanta contra el conocimiento de Dios, y llevamos cautivo todo pensamiento para que se someta a Cristo. 6Y estamos dispuestos a castigar cualquier acto de desobediencia una vez que yo pueda contar con la completa obediencia de ustedes.

7Fíjense en lo que está a la vista.u Si alguno está convencido de ser de Cristo, considere esto de nuevo: nosotros somos tan de Cristo como él. 8No me avergonzaré de *jactarme de nuestra autoridad más de la cuenta, autoridad que el Señor nos ha dado para la edificación y no para la destrucción de ustedes. 9No quiero dar la impresión de que trato de asustarlos con mis cartas, 10pues algunos dicen: «Sus cartas son duras y fuertes, pero él en persona no impresiona a nadie, y como orador es un fracaso.» 11Tales personas deben darse cuenta de que lo que somos

---

p 8:7 su amor hacia nosotros. Var. nuestro amor hacia ustedes.   q 8:15 Éx 16:18   r 9:5 una ofrenda generosa. Lit. una bendición.   s 9:6 siembra . . . cosechará. Lit. siembra en bendición, en bendición cosechará.   t 9:9 Sal 112:9   u 10:7 Fíjense . . . vista. Alt. Ustedes se fijan en las apariencias.

por escrito estando ausentes, lo seremos con hechos estando presentes.

12No nos atrevemos a igualarnos ni a compararnos con algunos que tanto se recomiendan a sí mismos. Al medirse con su propia medida y compararse unos con otros, no saben lo que hacen. 13Nosotros, por nuestra parte, no vamos a jactarnos más de lo debido. Nos limitaremos al campo que Dios nos ha asignado según su medida, en la cual también ustedes están incluidos. 14Si no hubiéramos estado antes entre ustedes, se podría alegar que estamos rebasando estos límites, cuando lo cierto es que fuimos los primeros en llevarles el *evangelio de Cristo. 15No nos jactamos desmedidamente a costa del trabajo que otros han hecho. Al contrario, esperamos que, según vaya creciendo la fe de ustedes, también nuestro campo de acción entre ustedes se amplíe grandemente, 16para poder predicar el evangelio más allá de sus regiones, sin tener que jactarnos del trabajo ya hecho por otros. 17Más bien, «Si alguien ha de gloriarse, que se gloríe en el Señor».v 18Porque no es aprobado el que se recomienda a sí mismo sino aquel a quien recomienda el Señor.

Pablo y los falsos apóstoles

11 ¡Ojalá me aguanten unas cuantas tonterías! ¡Sí, aguántenmelas!w 2El celo que siento por ustedes proviene de Dios, pues los tengo prometidos a un solo esposo, que es Cristo, para presentarles como una virgen pura. 3Pero me temo que, así como la serpiente con su astucia engañó a Eva, los pensamientos de ustedes sean desviados de un compromiso puro yx sincero con Cristo. 4Si alguien llega a ustedes predicando a un Jesús diferente del que les hemos predicado nosotros, o si reciben un espíritu o un *evangelio diferentes de los que ya recibieron, a ése lo aguantan con facilidad. 5Pero considero que en nada soy inferior a esos «superapóstoles». 6Quizás yo sea un mal orador, pero tengo conocimiento. Esto se lo hemos demostrado a ustedes de una y mil maneras.

7¿Es que cometí un pecado al humillarme yo para enaltecerlos a ustedes, predicándoles el *evangelio de Dios gratuitamente? 8De hecho, despojé a otras iglesias al recibir de ellas ayuda para servirles a ustedes. 9Cuando estuve entre ustedes y necesité algo, no fui una carga para nadie, ya que los hermanos que llegaron de Macedonia suplieron mis necesidades. He evitado serles una carga en cualquier sentido, y seguiré evitándolo. 10Es tan cierto que la verdad de Cristo está en mí, como lo es que nadie en las regiones de Acaya podrá privarme de este motivo de *orgullo. 11¿Por qué? ¿Porque no los amo? Dios sabe que sí! 12Pero seguiré haciendo lo que hago, a fin de quitar todo pretexto a aquellos que, buscando una oportunidad para hacerse iguales a nosotros, se *jactan de lo que hacen.

13Tales individuos son falsos apóstoles, obreros estafadores, que se disfrazan de apóstoles de Cristo. 14Y no es de extrañar, ya que Satanás mismo se disfraza de ángel de luz. 15Por eso no es de sorprenderse que sus servidores se disfracen de servidores de la justicia. Su fin corresponderá con lo que merecen sus acciones.

Los sufrimientos de Pablo

16Lo repito: Que nadie me tenga por insensato. Pero aun cuando así me consideren, de todos modos

recíbanme, para poder *jactarme un poco. 17Al jactarme tan confiadamente, no hablo como quisiera el Señor sino con insensatez. 18Ya que muchos se ufanan como lo hace el mundo,y yo también lo haré. 19Por ser tan sensatos, ustedes de buena gana aguantan a los insensatos. 20Aguantan incluso a cualquiera que los esclaviza, o los explota, o se aprovecha de ustedes, o se comporta con altanería, o les da de bofetadas. 21¡Para vergüenza mía, confieso que hemos sido demasiado débiles!

Si alguien se atreve a dárselas de algo, también yo me atrevo a hacerlo; lo digo como un insensato. 22¿Son ellos hebreos? Pues yo también. ¿Son israelitas? También yo lo soy. ¿Son descendientes de Abraham? Yo también. 23¿Son servidores de Cristo? ¡Qué locura! Yo lo soy más que ellos. He trabajado más arduamente, he sido encarcelado más veces, he recibido los azotes más severos, he estado en peligro de muerte repetidas veces. 24Cinco veces recibí de los judíos los treinta y nueve azotes. 25Tres veces me golpearon con varas, una vez me apedrearon, tres veces naufragué, y pasé un día y una noche como náufrago en alta mar. 26Mi vida ha sido un continuo ir y venir de un sitio a otro; en peligros de ríos, peligros de bandidos, peligros de parte de mis compatriotas, peligros a manos de los *gentiles, peligros en la ciudad, peligros en el campo, peligros en el mar y peligros de parte de falsos hermanos. 27He pasado muchos trabajos y fatigas, y muchas veces me he quedado sin dormir; he sufrido hambre y sed, y muchas veces me he quedado en ayunas; he sufrido frío y desnudez. 28Y como si fuera poco, cada día pesa sobre mí la preocupación por todas las iglesias. 29¿Cuando alguien se siente débil, no comparto yo su debilidad? ¿Y cuando a alguien se le hace *tropezar, no ardo yo de indignación?

30Si me veo obligado a jactarme, me jactaré de mi debilidad. 31El Dios y Padre del Señor Jesús (sea por siempre alabado!) sabe que no miento. 32En Damasco, el gobernador bajo el rey Aretas mandó que se vigilara la ciudad de los damascenos con el fin de arrestarme; 33pero me bajaron en un canasto por una ventana de la muralla, y así escapé de las manos del gobernador.

Visión y debilidad de Pablo

12 Me veo obligado a *jactarme, aunque nada se gane con ello. Paso a referirme a las visiones y revelaciones del Señor. 2Conozco a un seguidor de Cristo que hace catorce años fue llevado al tercer cielo (no sé si en el cuerpo o fuera del cuerpo; Dios lo sabe). 3Y sé que este hombre (no sé si en el cuerpo o aparte del cuerpo; Dios lo sabe) 4fue llevado al paraíso y escuchó cosas indecibles que a los *humanos no se nos permite expresar. 5De tal hombre podría hacer alarde; pero de mí no haré alarde sino de mis debilidades. 6Sin embargo, no sería insensato si decidiera jactarme, porque estaría diciendo la verdad. Pero no lo hago, para que nadie suponga que soy más de lo que aparento o de lo que digo.

7Para evitar que me volviera presumido por estas sublimes revelaciones, una espina me fue clavada en el cuerpo, es decir, un mensajero de Satanás, para que me atormentara. 8Tres veces le rogué al Señor que me la quitara; 9pero él me dijo: «Te basta con mi gracia, pues mi poder se perfecciona en la debilidad.» Por lo tanto, gustosamente haré más bien alarde de mis debilidades, para que permanezca sobre mí el poder de Cristo. 10Por eso me regocijo en debilidades, insultos, privaciones, persecuciones y dificultades que sufro por Cristo; porque cuando soy débil, entonces soy fuerte.

Preocupación de Pablo por los corintios

11Me he portado como un insensato, pero ustedes me han obligado a ello. Ustedes debían haberme elogiado, pues de ningún modo soy inferior a los «superapóstoles», aunque yo no soy nada. 12Las marcas distintivas de un apóstol, tales como señales, prodigios y milagros, se dieron constantemente entre ustedes. 13¿En qué fueron ustedes inferiores a las demás iglesias? Pues sólo en que yo mismo nunca les fui una carga. ¡Perdónenme si los ofendo!

14Miren que por tercera vez estoy listo para visitarlos, y no les seré una carga, pues no me interesa lo que ustedes tienen sino lo que ustedes son. Después de todo, no son los hijos los que deben ahorrar para los padres, sino los padres para los hijos. 15Así que de buena gana gastaré todo lo que tengo, y hasta yo mismo me desgastaré del todo por ustedes. Si los amo hasta el extremo, ¿me amarán menos? 16En todo caso, no les he sido una carga. ¿Es que, como soy tan astuto, les tendí una trampa para estafarlos? 17¿Acaso los exploté por medio de alguno de mis enviados? 18Le rogué a Tito que fuera a verlos y con él envié al hermano. ¿Acaso se aprovechó Tito de ustedes? ¿No procedimos los dos con el mismo espíritu y seguimos el mismo camino?

19¿Todo este tiempo han venido pensando que nos estábamos justificando ante ustedes? ¡Más bien, hemos estado hablando delante de Dios en Cristo! Todo lo que hacemos, queridos hermanos, es para su edificación. 20En realidad, me temo que cuando vaya a verlos no los encuentre como quisiera, ni ustedes me encuentren a mí como quisieran. Temo que haya peleas, celos, arrebatos de ira, rivalidades, calumnias, chismes, insultos y alborotos. 21Temo que, al volver a visitarlos, mi Dios me humille delante de ustedes, y que yo tenga que llorar por muchos que han pecado desde hace algún tiempo pero no se han *arrepentido

de la impureza, de la inmoralidad sexual y de los vicios a que se han entregado.

Advertencias finales

13 Ésta será la tercera vez que los visito. «Todo asunto se resolverá mediante el testimonio de dos o tres testigos.»z 2Cuando estuve con ustedes por segunda vez les advertí, y ahora que estoy ausente se lo repito: Cuando vuelva a verlos, no seré indulgente con los que antes pecaron ni con ningún otro, 3ya que están exigiendo una prueba de que Cristo habla por medio de mí. Él no se muestra débil en su trato con ustedes, sino que ejerce su poder entre ustedes. 4Es cierto que fue crucificado en debilidad, pero ahora vive por el poder de Dios. De igual manera, nosotros participamos de su debilidad, pero por el poder de Dios viviremos con Cristo para ustedes.

5Examínense para ver si están en la fe; pruébense a sí mismos. ¿No se dan cuenta de que Cristo Jesús está en ustedes? ¡A menos que fracasen en la *prueba! 6Espero que reconozcan que nosotros no hemos fracasado. 7Pedimos a Dios que no hagan nada malo, no para demostrar mi éxito, sino para que hagan lo bueno, aunque parezca que nosotros hemos fracasado. 8Pues nada podemos hacer contra la verdad, sino a favor de la verdad. 9De hecho, nos alegramos cuando nosotros somos débiles y ustedes fuertes; y oramos a Dios para que los restaure plenamente. 10Por eso les escribo todo esto en mi ausencia, para que cuando vaya no tenga que ser severo en el uso de mi autoridad, la cual el Señor me ha dado para edificación y no para destrucción.

Saludos finales

11En fin, hermanos, alégrense, busquena su restauración, hagan caso de mi exhortación, sean de un mismo sentir, vivan en paz. Y el Dios de amor y de paz estará con ustedes.

12Salúdense unos a otros con un beso santo. 13Todos los *santos les mandan saludos.

14Que la gracia del Señor Jesucristo, el amor de Dios y la comunión del Espíritu Santo sean con todos ustedes.

---

z **13:1** Dt 19:15   a **13:11** *alégrense, busquen*. Alt. *los saludo. Busquen*.

Carta a los GÁLATAS

1 Pablo, apóstol, no por investidura ni mediación *humanas, sino por *Jesucristo y por Dios Padre, que lo *levantó de entre los muertos; 2y todos los hermanos que están conmigo,

a las iglesias de Galacia:

3Que Dios nuestro Padre y el Señor Jesucristo les concedan gracia y paz. 4Jesucristo dio su vida por nuestros pecados para rescatarnos de este mundo malvado, según la voluntad de nuestro Dios y Padre, 5a quien sea la gloria por los siglos de los siglos. Amén.

No hay otro evangelio

6Me asombra que tan pronto estén dejando ustedes a quien los llamó por la gracia de Cristo, para pasarse a otro *evangelio. 7No es que haya otro evangelio, sino que ciertos individuos están sembrando confusión entre ustedes y quieren tergiversar el evangelio de Cristo. 8Pero aun si alguno de nosotros o un ángel del cielo les predicara un evangelio distinto del que les hemos predicado, ¡que caiga bajo maldición! 9Como ya lo hemos dicho, ahora lo repito: si alguien les anda predicando un evangelio distinto del que recibieron, ¡que caiga bajo maldición!

10¿Qué busco con esto: ganarme la aprobación *humana o la de Dios? ¿Piensan que procuro agradar a los demás? Si yo buscara agradar a otros, no sería *siervo de Cristo.

Pablo, llamado por Dios

11Quiero que sepan, hermanos, que el *evangelio que yo predico no es invención *humana. 12No lo recibí ni lo aprendí de ningún *ser humano, sino que me llegó por revelación de Jesucristo.

13Ustedes ya están enterados de mi conducta cuando pertenecía al judaísmo, de la furia con que perseguía a la iglesia de Dios, tratando de destruirla. 14En la práctica del judaísmo, yo aventajaba a muchos de mis contemporáneos en mi celo exagerado por las tradiciones de mis antepasados. 15Sin embargo, Dios me había apartado desde el vientre de mi madre y me llamó por su gracia. Cuando él tuvo a bien 16revelarme a su Hijo para que yo lo predicara entre los *gentiles, no consulté con nadie. 17Tampoco subí a Jerusalén para ver a los que eran apóstoles antes que yo, sino que fui de inmediato a Arabia, de donde luego regresé a Damasco.

18Después de tres años, subí a Jerusalén para visitar a Pedro,ᵃ y me quedé con él quince días. 19No vi a ningún otro de los apóstoles; sólo vi a *Jacobo, el hermano del Señor. 20Dios me es testigo que en esto que les escribo no miento. 21Más tarde fui a las regiones de Siria y Cilicia. 22Pero en Judea las iglesias deᵇ Cristo no me conocían personalmente. 23Sólo habían oído decir: «El que antes nos perseguía ahora predica la fe que procuraba destruir.» 24Y por causa mía glorificaban a Dios.

Los apóstoles aceptan a Pablo

2 Catorce años después subí de nuevo a Jerusalén, esta vez con Bernabé, llevando también a Tito. 2Fui en obediencia a una revelación, y me reuní en privado con los que eran reconocidos como dirigentes, y les expliqué el *evangelio que predico entre los *gentiles, para que todo mi esfuerzo no fuera en vano.ᶜ 3Ahora bien, ni siquiera Tito, que me acompañaba, fue obligado a circuncidarse, aunque era *griego. 4El problema era que algunos falsos hermanos se habían infiltrado entre nosotros para coartar la libertad que tenemos en Cristo Jesús a fin de esclavizarnos. 5Ni por un momento accedimos a someternos a ellos, pues queríamos que se preservara entre ustedes la integridad del evangelio.

6En cuanto a los que eran reconocidos como personas importantes —aunque no me interesa lo que fueran, porque Dios no juzga por las apariencias—, me impusieron nada nuevo. 7Al contrario, reconocieron que a mí se me había encomendado predicar el evangelio a los gentiles, de la misma manera que se le había encomendado a Pedro predicarlo a los judíos.ᵈ 8El mismo Dios que facultó a Pedro como apóstol de los judíosᵉ me facultó también a mí como apóstol de los gentiles. 9En efecto, *Jacobo, Pedro y Juan, que eran considerados columnas, al reconocer la gracia que yo había recibido, nos dieron la mano a Bernabé y a mí en señal de compañerismo, de modo que nosotros fuéramos a los gentiles y ellos a los judíos. 10Sólo nos pidieron que nos acordáramos de los pobres, y eso es precisamente lo que he venido haciendo con esmero.

Pablo se opone a Pedro

11Pues bien, cuando Pedro fue a Antioquía, le eché en cara su comportamiento condenable. 12Antes que llegaran algunos de parte de *Jacobo, Pedro solía comer con los *gentiles. Pero cuando aquéllos llegaron, comenzó a retraerse y a separarse de los gentiles por temor a los partidarios de la *circuncisión.ᶠ 13Entonces los demás judíos se unieron a Pedro en su *hipocresía, y hasta el mismo Bernabé se dejó arrastrar por esa conducta hipócrita.

14Cuando vi que no actuaban rectamente, como corresponde a la integridad del *evangelio, le dije a Pedro delante de todos: «Si tú, que eres judío, vives como si no lo fueras, ¿por qué obligas a los gentiles a practicar el judaísmo?

15»Nosotros somos judíos de nacimiento y no *"pecadores paganos". 16Sin embargo, al reconocer que nadie es *justificado por las obras que demanda la ley sino por la *fe en Jesucristo, también nosotros hemos puesto nuestra fe en Cristo Jesús, para ser justificados por la fe en él y no por las obras de la ley; porque por éstas nadie será justificado.

17»Ahora bien, cuando buscamos ser justificados porᵍ Cristo, se hace evidente que nosotros mismos somos pecadores. ¿Quiere esto decir que Cristo está al servicio del pecado? ¡De ninguna manera! 18Si uno vuelve a edificar lo que antes había destruido, se haceʰ transgresor. 19Yo, por mi parte, mediante la ley he muerto a la ley, a fin de vivir para Dios. 20He sido crucificado con Cristo, y ya no vivo yo sino que Cristo vive en mí. Lo que ahora vivo en el cuerpo, lo vivo por la fe en el Hijo de Dios, quien me amó y dio su vida por mí. 21No desecho la gracia de Dios. Si la justicia se obtuviera mediante la ley, Cristo habría muerto en vano.»ⁱ

ᵃ **1:18** Aquí el autor usa *Cefas, nombre arameo de Pedro; también en 2:9,11,14. ᵇ **1:22** *de.* Lit. *en.* ᶜ **2:2** *para … vano* Lit. *Para que yo no estuviera corriendo o hubiera corrido en vano.* ᵈ **2:7** *el evangelio … judíos.* Lit. *el evangelio de la incircuncisión, como a Pedro el de la *circuncisión.* ᵉ **2:8** *los judíos.* Lit. *la circuncisión; también en v. 9.* ᶠ **2:12** *los partidarios de la circuncisión.* Alt. *los judíos.* ᵍ **2:17** *por.* Lit. *En.* ʰ **2:18** *Si uno vuelve … se hace.* Lit. *Si vuelvo … me hago.* ⁱ **2:21** Algunos intérpretes consideran que la cita termina al final del v. 14.

La fe o la observancia de la ley

3 ¡Gálatas torpes! ¿Quién los ha hechizado a ustedes, ante quienes Jesucristo crucificado ha sido presentado tan claramente? 2Sólo quiero que me respondan a esto: ¿Recibieron el Espíritu por las obras que demanda la ley, o por la fe con que aceptaron el mensaje? 3¿Tan torpes son? Después de haber comenzado con el Espíritu, ¿pretenden ahora perfeccionarse con esfuerzos *humanos?j 4¿Tanto sufrir, para nada?k ¡Si es que de veras fue para nada! 5Al darles Dios su Espíritu y hacer milagros entre ustedes, ¿lo hace por las obras que demanda la ley o por la fe con que han aceptado el mensaje? 6Así fue con Abraham: «Le creyó a Dios, y esto se le tomó en cuenta como justicia.»l

7Por lo tanto, sepan que los descendientes de Abraham son aquellos que viven por la fe. 8En efecto, la Escritura, habiendo previsto que Dios *justificaría por la fe a las *naciones, anunció de antemano el *evangelio a Abraham: «Por medio de ti serán bendecidas todas las naciones.»m 9Así que los que viven por la fe son bendecidos junto con Abraham, el hombre de fe.

10Todos los que viven por las obras que demanda la ley están bajo maldición, porque está escrito: «Maldito sea quien no practique fielmente todo lo que está escrito en el libro de la ley.»n 11Ahora bien, es evidente que por la ley nadie es justificado delante de Dios, porque «el justo vivirá por la fe».ñ 12La ley no se basa en la fe; por el contrario, «quien practique estas cosas vivirá por ellas».o 13Cristo nos rescató de la maldición de la ley al hacerse maldición por nosotros, pues está escrito: «Maldito todo el que es colgado de un madero.»p 14Así sucedió, para que, por medio de Cristo Jesús, la bendición prometida a Abraham llegara a las naciones, y para que por la fe recibiéramos el Espíritu según la promesa.

La ley y la promesa

15Hermanos, voy a ponerles un ejemplo: aun en el caso de un pactoq *humano, nadie puede anularlo ni añadirle nada una vez que ha sido ratificado. 16Ahora bien, las promesas se le hicieron a Abraham y a su descendencia. La Escritura no dice: «y a los descendientes», como refiriéndose a muchos, sino: «y a tu descendencia»,r dando a entender uno solo, que es Cristo. 17Lo que quiero decir es esto: La ley, que vino cuatrocientos treinta años después, no anula el pacto que Dios había ratificado previamente; de haber sido así, quedaría sin efecto la promesa. 18Si la herencia se basa en la ley, ya no se basa en la promesa; pero Dios se la concedió gratuitamente a Abraham mediante una promesa.

19Entonces, ¿cuál era el propósito de la ley? Fue añadida por causa des las transgresiones hasta que viniera la descendencia a la cual se hizo la promesa. La ley se promulgó por medio de ángeles, por conducto de un mediador. 20Ahora bien, no hace falta mediador si hay una sola parte, y sin embargo Dios es uno solo.

21Si esto es así, ¿estará la ley en contra de las promesas de Dios? ¡De ninguna manera! Si se hubiera promulgado una ley capaz de dar vida, entonces sí que la justicia se basaría en la ley. 22Pero la Escritura declara que todo el mundo es prisionero del pecado,t para que mediante la *fe en Jesucristo lo prometido se les conceda a los que creen.

23Antes de venir esta fe, la ley nos tenía presos, encerrados hasta que la fe se revelara. 24Así que la ley vino a ser nuestro guía encargado de conducirnos a Cristo,u para que fuéramos *justificados por la fe. 25Pero ahora que ha llegado la fe, ya no estamos sujetos al guía.

Hijos de Dios

26Todos ustedes son hijos de Dios mediante la *fe en Cristo Jesús, 27porque todos los que han sido bautizados en Cristo se han revestido de Cristo. 28Ya no hay judío ni *griego, esclavo ni libre, hombre ni mujer, sino que todos ustedes son uno solo en Cristo Jesús. 29Y si ustedes pertenecen a Cristo, son la descendencia de Abraham y herederos según la promesa.

4 En otras palabras, mientras el heredero es menor de edad, en nada se diferencia de un *esclavo, a pesar de ser dueño de todo. 2Al contrario, está bajo el cuidado de tutores y administradores hasta la fecha fijada por su padre. 3Así también nosotros, cuando éramos menores, estábamos esclavizados por los *principiosv de este mundo. 4Pero cuando se cumplió el plazo,w Dios envió a su Hijo, nacido de una mujer, nacido bajo la ley, 5para rescatar a los que estaban bajo la ley, a fin de que fuéramos adoptados como hijos. 6Ustedes ya son hijos. Dios ha enviado a nuestros corazones el Espíritu de su Hijo, que clama: «¡*Abba! ¡Padre!» 7Así que ya no eres esclavo sino hijo; y como eres hijo, Dios te ha hecho también heredero.

Preocupación de Pablo por los gálatas

8Antes, cuando ustedes no conocían a Dios, eran esclavos de los que en realidad no son dioses. 9Pero ahora que conocen a Dios —o más bien que Dios los conoce a ustedes—, ¿cómo es que quieren regresar a esos *principios ineficaces y sin valor? ¿Quieren volver a ser esclavos de ellos? 10¡Ustedes siguen guardando unos días de fiesta, meses, estaciones y años! 11Temo por ustedes, que tal vez me haya estado esforzando en vano.

12Hermanos, yo me he identificado con ustedes. Les suplico que ahora se identifiquen conmigo. No es que me hayan ofendido en algo. 13Como bien saben, la primera vez que les prediqué el *evangelio fue debido a una enfermedad, 14y aunque ésta fue una *prueba para ustedes, no me trataron con desprecio ni desdén. Al contrario, me recibieron como a un ángel de Dios, como si se tratara de Cristo Jesús. 15Pues bien, ¿qué pasó con todo ese entusiasmo? Me consta que, de haberles sido posible, se habrían sacado los ojos para dármelos. 16¡Y ahora resulta que por decirles la verdad me he vuelto su enemigo!

17Esos que muestran mucho interés por ganárselos a ustedes no abrigan buenas intenciones. Lo que quieren es alejarlos de nosotros para que ustedes se entreguen a ellos. 18Está bien mostrar interés, con tal de que ese interés sea bien intencionado y constante, y que no se manifieste sólo cuando yo es-

---

j 3:3 ¿pretenden … humanos? Lit. ¿se perfeccionan ahora con la *carne? k 3:4 ¿Tanto sufrir, para nada? Alt. ¿Han tenido tan grandes experiencias en vano? l 3:6 Gn 15:6 m 3:8 Gn 12:3; 18:18; 22:18 n 3:10 Dt 27:26 ñ 3:11 Hab 2:4 o 3:12 Lv 18:5 p 3:13 Dt 21:23 q 3:15 pacto. Alt. Testamento. r 3:16 Gn 12:7; 13:15; 24:7 s 3:19 por causa de. Alt. para manifestar, o para aumentar. t 3:22 declara … pecado. Lit. lo ha encerrado todo bajo pecado. u 3:24 la ley … Cristo. Alt. la ley fue nuestro guía hasta que vino Cristo. v 4:3 los principios. Alt. los poderes espirituales, o las normas; también en v. 9. w 4:4 se cumplió el plazo. Lit. vino la plenitud del tiempo.

toy con ustedes. 19Queridos hijos, por quienes vuelvo a sufrir dolores de parto hasta que Cristo sea formado en ustedes, 20¡cómo quisiera estar ahora con ustedes y hablarles de otra manera, porque lo que están haciendo me tiene perplejo!

Agar y Sara

21Díganme ustedes, los que quieren estar bajo la ley: ¿por qué no le prestan atención a lo que la ley misma dice? 22¿Acaso no está escrito que Abraham tuvo dos hijos, uno de la esclava y otro de la libre? 23El de la esclava nació por decisión *humana, pero el de la libre nació en cumplimiento de una promesa.

24Ese relato puede interpretarse en sentido figurado: estas mujeres representan dos pactos. Uno, que es Agar, procede del monte Sinaí y tiene hijos que nacen para ser esclavos. 25Agar representa el monte Sinaí en Arabia, y corresponde a la actual ciudad de Jerusalén, porque junto con sus hijos vive en esclavitud. 26Pero la Jerusalén celestial es libre, y ésa es nuestra madre. 27Porque está escrito:

«Tú, mujer estéril que nunca has dado a luz,
¡grita de alegría!
Tú, que nunca tuviste dolores de parto,
¡prorrumpe en gritos de júbilo!
Porque más hijos que la casada
tendrá la desamparada.»x

28Ustedes, hermanos, al igual que Isaac, son hijos por la promesa. 29Y así como en aquel tiempo el hijo nacido por decisión humana persiguió al hijo nacido por el Espíritu, así también sucede ahora. 30Pero, ¿qué dice la Escritura? «¡Echa de aquí a la esclava y a su hijo! El hijo de la esclava jamás tendrá parte en la herencia con el hijo de la libre.»y 31Así que, hermanos, no somos hijos de la esclava sino de la libre.

Libertad en Cristo

5 Cristo nos libertó para que vivamos en libertad. Por lo tanto, manténganse firmesz y no se sometan nuevamente al yugo de esclavitud.

2Escuchen bien: yo, Pablo, les digo que si se hacen circuncidar, Cristo no les servirá de nada. 3De nuevo declaro que todo el que se hace circuncidar está obligado a practicar toda la ley. 4Aquellos de entre ustedes que tratan de ser *justificados por la ley, han roto con Cristo; han caído de la gracia. 5Nosotros, en cambio, por obra del Espíritu y mediante la fe, aguardamos con ansias la justicia que es nuestra esperanza. 6En Cristo Jesús de nada vale estar o no estar circuncidados; lo que vale es la fe que actúa mediante el amor.

7Ustedes estaban corriendo bien. ¿Quién los estorbó para que dejaran de obedecer a la verdad? 8Tal instigación no puede venir de Dios, que es quien los ha llamado.

9«Un poco de levadura fermenta toda la masa.» 10Yo por mi parte confío en el Señor que ustedes no pensarán de otra manera. El que los está perturbando será castigado, sea quien sea. 11Hermanos, si es verdad que yo todavía predico la circuncisión, ¿por qué se me sigue persiguiendo? Si tal fuera mi predicación, la cruz no *ofendería tanto. 12¡Ojalá que esos instigadores acabaran por mutilarse del todo!

13Les hablo así, hermanos, porque ustedes han sido llamados a ser libres; pero no se valgan de esa libertad para dar rienda suelta a sus *pasiones. Más bien sírvanse unos a otros con amor. 14En efecto, toda la ley se resume en un solo mandamiento: «Ama a tu prójimo como a ti mismo.»a 15Pero si siguen mordiéndose y devorándose, tengan cuidado, no sea que acaben por destruirse unos a otros.

La vida por el Espíritu

16Así que les digo: Vivan por el Espíritu, y no seguirán los deseos de la *naturaleza pecaminosa. 17Porque ésta desea lo que es contrario al Espíritu, y el Espíritu desea lo que es contrario a ella. Los dos se oponen entre sí, de modo que ustedes no pueden hacer lo que quieren. 18Pero si los guía el Espíritu, no están bajo la ley.

19Las obras de la naturaleza pecaminosa se conocen bien: inmoralidad sexual, impureza y libertinaje; 20idolatría y brujería; odio, discordia, celos, arrebatos de ira, rivalidades, disensiones, sectarismos 21y envidia; borracheras, orgías, y otras cosas parecidas. Les advierto ahora, como antes lo hice, que los que practican tales cosas no heredarán el reino de Dios.

22En cambio, el fruto del Espíritu es amor, alegría, paz, paciencia, amabilidad, bondad, *fidelidad, 23humildad y dominio propio. No hay ley que condene estas cosas. 24Los que son de Cristo Jesús han crucificado la naturaleza pecaminosa, con sus pasiones y deseos. 25Si el Espíritu nos da vida, andemos guiados por el Espíritu. 26No dejemos que la vanidad nos lleve a irritarnos y a envidiarnos unos a otros.

La ayuda mutua

6 Hermanos, si alguien es sorprendido en pecado, ustedes que son espirituales deben restaurarlo con una actitud humilde. Pero cuídese cada uno, porque también puede ser *tentado. 2Ayúdense unos a otros a llevar sus cargas, y así cumplirán la ley de Cristo. 3Si alguien cree ser algo, cuando en realidad no es nada, se engaña a sí mismo. 4Cada cual examine su propia conducta; y si tiene algo de qué presumir, que no se compare con nadie. 5Que cada uno cargue con su propia responsabilidad.

6El que recibe instrucción en la palabra de Dios, comparta todo lo bueno con quien le enseña.

7No se engañen: de Dios nadie se burla. Cada uno cosecha lo que siembra. 8El que siembra para agradar a su *naturaleza pecaminosa, de esa misma naturaleza cosechará destrucción; el que siembra para agradar al Espíritu, del Espíritu cosechará vida eterna. 9No nos cansemos de hacer el bien, porque a su debido tiempo cosecharemos si no nos damos por vencidos. 10Por lo tanto, siempre que tengamos la oportunidad, hagamos bien a todos, y en especial a los de la familia de la fe.

No la circuncisión, sino una nueva creación

11Miren que les escribo de mi puño y letra, ¡y con letras bien grandes!

12Los que tratan de obligarlos a ustedes a circuncidarse lo hacen únicamente para dar una buena impresión y evitar ser perseguidos por causa de la cruz de Cristo. 13Ni siquiera esos que están circuncidados obedecen la ley; lo que desea es que ustedes quieren obligarlos a circuncidarse para luego *jactarse de la señal que ustedes llevarían en el cuerpo.b 14En cuanto a mí, jamás se me ocurra jactarme de otra cosa sino de la cruz

---

x **4:27** Is 54:1 y **4:30** Gn 21:10 z **5:1** Cristo … firmes. Var. Por lo tanto, manténganse firmes en la libertad con que Cristo nos libertó. a **5:14** Lv 19:18 b **6:13** jactarse … cuerpo. Lit. jactarse en la *carne.

de nuestro Señor Jesucristo, por quien^c el mundo ha sido crucificado para mí, y yo para el mundo. ¹⁵Para nada cuenta estar o no estar circuncidados; lo que importa es ser parte de una nueva creación. ¹⁶Paz y misericordia desciendan sobre todos los que siguen esta norma, y sobre el Israel de Dios.

^c **6:14** *por quien.* Alt. *por la cual.*

¹⁷Por lo demás, que nadie me cause más problemas, porque yo llevo en el cuerpo las cicatrices de Jesús.

¹⁸Hermanos, que la gracia de nuestro Señor Jesucristo sea con el espíritu de cada uno de ustedes. Amén.

Carta a los EFESIOS

1 Pablo, apóstol de *Cristo Jesús por la voluntad de Dios,

a los *santos y fieles[a] en Cristo Jesús que están en Éfeso:[b]

2Que Dios nuestro Padre y el Señor Jesucristo les concedan gracia y paz.

Bendiciones espirituales en Cristo

3Alabado sea Dios, Padre de nuestro Señor Jesucristo, que nos ha bendecido en las regiones celestiales con toda bendición espiritual en Cristo. 4Dios nos escogió en él antes de la creación del mundo, para que seamos santos y sin mancha delante de él. En amor 5nos predestinó para ser adoptados como hijos suyos por medio de Jesucristo, según el buen propósito de su voluntad, 6para alabanza de su gloriosa gracia, que nos concedió en su Amado. 7En él tenemos la redención mediante su sangre, el perdón de nuestros pecados, conforme a las riquezas de la gracia 8que Dios dio en abundancia con toda sabiduría y entendimiento. 9Él nos hizo conocer el *misterio de su voluntad conforme al buen propósito de su antemano estableció en Cristo, 10para llevarlo a cabo cuando se cumpliera el tiempo: reunir en él todas las cosas, tanto las del cielo como las de la tierra.

11En Cristo también fuimos hechos herederos,[c] pues fuimos predestinados según el plan de aquel que hace todas las cosas conforme al designio de su voluntad, 12a fin de que nosotros, que ya hemos puesto nuestra esperanza en Cristo, seamos para alabanza de su gloria. 13En él también ustedes, cuando oyeron el mensaje de la verdad, el *evangelio que les trajo la salvación, y lo creyeron, fueron marcados con el sello que es el Espíritu Santo prometido. 14Éste garantiza nuestra herencia hasta que llegue la redención final del pueblo adquirido por Dios,[d] para alabanza de su gloria.

Acción de gracias e intercesión

15Por eso yo, por mi parte, desde que me enteré de la fe que tienen en el Señor Jesús y del amor que demuestran por todos los *santos, 16no he dejado de dar gracias por ustedes al recordarlos en mis oraciones. 17Pido que el Dios de nuestro Señor Jesucristo, el Padre glorioso, les dé el Espíritu de sabiduría y de revelación, para que lo conozcan mejor. 18Pido también que les sean iluminados los ojos del corazón para que sepan a qué esperanza él los ha llamado, cuál es la riqueza de su gloriosa herencia entre los santos, 19y cuán incomparable es la grandeza de su poder a favor de los que creemos. Ese poder es la fuerza grandiosa y eficaz 20que Dios ejerció en Cristo cuando lo resucitó de entre los muertos y lo sentó a su *derecha en las regiones celestiales, 21muy por encima de todo gobierno y autoridad, poder y dominio, y de cualquier otro nombre que se invoque, no sólo en este mundo sino también en el venidero. 22Dios sometió todas las cosas al dominio de Cristo,[e] y lo dio como cabeza de todo a la iglesia. 23Ésta, que es su cuerpo, es la plenitud de aquel que lo llena todo por completo.

La vida en Cristo

2 En otro tiempo ustedes estaban muertos en sus transgresiones y pecados, 2en los cuales andaban conforme a los poderes de este mundo. Se conducían según el que gobierna las tinieblas, según el espíritu que ahora ejerce su poder en los que viven en la desobediencia. 3En ese tiempo también todos nosotros vivíamos como ellos, impulsados por nuestros deseos pecaminosos, siguiendo nuestra propia voluntad y nuestros propósitos.[f] Como los demás, éramos por naturaleza objeto de la ira de Dios. 4Pero Dios, que es rico en misericordia, por su gran amor por nosotros, 5nos dio vida con Cristo, aun cuando estábamos muertos en pecados. ¡Por gracia ustedes han sido salvados! 6Y en unión con Cristo Jesús, Dios nos resucitó y nos hizo sentar con él en las regiones celestiales, 7para mostrar en los tiempos venideros la incomparable riqueza de su gracia, que por su bondad derramó sobre nosotros en Cristo Jesús. 8Porque por gracia ustedes han sido salvados mediante la fe; esto no procede de ustedes, sino que es el regalo de Dios, 9no por obras, para que nadie se *jacte. 10Porque somos hechura de Dios, creados en Cristo Jesús para buenas obras, las cuales Dios dispuso de antemano a fin de que las pongamos en práctica.

Unidad en Cristo

11Por lo tanto, recuerden ustedes los *gentiles de nacimiento —los que son llamados «incircuncisos» por aquellos que se llaman «de la *circuncisión», la cual se hace en el cuerpo por mano humana—, 12recuerden que en ese entonces estaban separados de Cristo, excluidos de la ciudadanía de Israel y ajenos a los pactos de la promesa, sin esperanza y sin Dios en el mundo. 13Pero ahora en Cristo Jesús, a ustedes que antes estaban lejos, Dios los ha acercado mediante la sangre de Cristo.

14Porque Cristo es nuestra paz: de los dos pueblos ha hecho uno solo, derribando mediante su sacrificio[g] el muro de enemistad que nos separaba, 15pues anuló la ley con sus mandamientos y requisitos. Esto lo hizo para crear en sí mismo de los dos pueblos una nueva *humanidad al hacer la paz, 16para reconciliar con Dios a ambos en un solo cuerpo mediante la cruz, por la que dio muerte a la enemistad. 17Él vino y proclamó paz a ustedes que estaban lejos y paz a los que estaban cerca. 18Pues por medio de él tenemos acceso al Padre por un mismo Espíritu.

19Por lo tanto, ustedes ya no son extraños ni extranjeros, sino conciudadanos de los *santos y miembros de la familia de Dios, 20edificados sobre el fundamento de los apóstoles y los profetas, siendo Cristo Jesús mismo la piedra angular. 21En él todo el edificio, bien armado, se va levantando para llegar a ser un templo santo en el Señor. 22En él también ustedes son edificados juntamente para ser morada de Dios por su Espíritu.

Pablo y el misterio de Cristo

3 Por esta razón yo, Pablo, prisionero de Cristo Jesús por el bien de ustedes los *gentiles, me arrodillo en oración.[h] 2Sin duda se han enterado del

---

a **1:1** fieles. Alt. Creyentes. b **1:1** los santos . . . Éfeso. Var. los santos que también son fieles en Cristo Jesús (es decir, sin indicación de lugar). c **1:11** fuimos hechos herederos. Alt. fuimos escogidos. d **1:14** hasta . . . Dios. Alt. hasta que lleguemos a adquirirla. e **1:22** Dios . . . Cristo. Lit. Dios sujetó todas las cosas debajo de sus pies. f **2:3** impulsados . . . propósitos. Lit. en los deseos de nuestra *carne, haciendo la voluntad de la carne y los pensamientos. g **2:14** mediante su sacrificio. Lit. en su carne. h **3:1** En el griego este versículo termina con la palabra gentiles, y el tema se reinicia en el v. 14.

plan de la gracia de Dios que él me encomendó para ustedes, **3**es decir, el *misterio que me dio a conocer por revelación, como ya les escribí brevemente. **4**Al leer esto, podrán darse cuenta de que comprendo el misterio de Cristo. **5**Ese misterio, que en otras generaciones no se les dio a conocer a los *seres humanos, ahora se les ha revelado por el Espíritu a los santos apóstoles y profetas de Dios; **6**es decir, que los gentiles son, junto con Israel, beneficiarios de la misma herencia, miembros de un mismo cuerpo y participantes igualmente de la promesa en Cristo Jesús mediante el *evangelio.

7De este evangelio llegué a ser servidor como regalo que Dios, en su gracia, me dio conforme a su poder eficaz. **8**Aunque soy el más insignificante de todos los *santos, recibí esta gracia de predicar a las *naciones las incalculables riquezas de Cristo, **9**y de hacer entender a todos la realización del plan de Dios, el misterio que desde los tiempos eternos se mantuvo oculto en Dios, creador de todas las cosas. **10**El fin de todo esto es que la sabiduría de Dios, en toda su diversidad, se dé a conocer ahora, por medio de la iglesia, a los poderes y autoridades en las regiones celestiales, **11**conforme a su eterno propósito realizado en Cristo Jesús nuestro Señor. **12**En él, mediante la fe, disfrutamos de libertad y confianza para acercarnos a Dios. **13**Así que les pido que no se desanimen a causa de lo que sufro por ustedes, ya que estos sufrimientos míos son para ustedes un honor.

Oración por los efesios

14Por esta razón me arrodillo delante del Padre, **15**de quien recibe nombre toda familia[i] en el cielo y en la tierra. **16**Le pido que, por medio del Espíritu y con el poder que procede de sus gloriosas riquezas, los fortalezca a ustedes en lo íntimo de su ser, **17**para que por fe Cristo habite en sus corazones. Y pido que, arraigados y cimentados en amor, **18**puedan comprender, junto con todos los *santos, cuán ancho y largo, alto y profundo es el amor de Cristo; **19**en fin, que conozcan ese amor que sobrepasa nuestro conocimiento, para que sean llenos de la plenitud de Dios.

20Al que puede hacer muchísimo más que todo lo que podamos imaginarnos o pedir, por el poder que obra eficazmente en nosotros, **21**¡a él sea la gloria en la iglesia y en Cristo Jesús por todas las generaciones, por los siglos de los siglos! Amén.

Unidad en el cuerpo de Cristo

4 Por eso yo, que estoy preso por la causa del Señor, les ruego que vivan de una manera digna del llamamiento que han recibido, **2**siempre humildes y amables, pacientes, tolerantes unos con otros en amor. **3**Esfuércense por mantener la unidad del Espíritu mediante el vínculo de la paz. **4**Hay un solo cuerpo y un solo Espíritu, así como también fueron llamados a una sola esperanza; **5**un solo Señor, una sola fe, un solo bautismo; **6**un solo Dios y Padre de todos, que está sobre todos y por medio de todos y en todos.

7Pero a cada uno de nosotros se nos ha dado gracia en la medida en que Cristo ha repartido los dones. **8**Por esto dice:

«Cuando ascendió a lo alto,
se llevó consigo a los cautivos
y dio dones a los hombres.»[j]

9(¿Qué quiere decir eso de que «ascendió», sino que también descendió a las partes bajas, o sea, a la tierra?[k] **10**El que descendió es el mismo que ascendió por encima de todos los cielos, para llenarlo todo.) **11**Él mismo constituyó a unos, apóstoles; a otros, profetas; a otros, evangelistas; y a otros, pastores y maestros, **12**a fin de capacitar al *pueblo de Dios para la obra de servicio, para edificar el cuerpo de Cristo. **13**De este modo, todos llegaremos a la unidad de la fe y del conocimiento del Hijo de Dios, a una *humanidad *perfecta que se conforme a la plena estatura de Cristo.

14Así ya no seremos niños, zarandeados por las olas y llevados de aquí para allá por todo viento de enseñanza y por la astucia y los artificios de quienes emplean artimañas engañosas. **15**Más bien, al vivir la verdad con amor, creceremos hasta ser en todo como aquel que es la cabeza, es decir, Cristo. **16**Por su acción todo el cuerpo crece y se edifica en amor, sostenido y ajustado por todos los ligamentos, según la actividad propia de cada miembro.

Vivan como hijos de luz

17Así que les digo esto y les insisto en el Señor: no vivan más con pensamientos frívolos como los *paganos. **18**A causa de la ignorancia que los domina y por la dureza de su corazón, éstos tienen oscurecido el entendimiento y están alejados de la vida que proviene de Dios. **19**Han perdido toda vergüenza, se han entregado a la inmoralidad, y no se sacian de cometer toda clase de actos indecentes.

20No fue ésta la enseñanza que ustedes recibieron acerca de Cristo, **21**si de veras se les habló y enseñó de Jesús según la verdad que está en él. **22**Con respecto a la vida que antes llevaban, se les enseñó que debían quitarse el ropaje de la vieja naturaleza, la cual está corrompida por los deseos engañosos; **23**ser renovados en la actitud de su mente; **24**y ponerse el ropaje de la nueva naturaleza, creada a imagen de Dios, en verdadera justicia y *santidad.

25Por lo tanto, dejando la mentira, hable cada uno a su prójimo con la verdad, porque todos somos miembros de un mismo cuerpo. **26**«Si se enojan, no pequen.»[l] No dejen que el sol se ponga estando aún enojados, **27**ni den cabida al diablo. **28**El que robaba, que no robe más, sino que trabaje honradamente con las manos para tener qué compartir con los necesitados.

29Eviten toda conversación obscena. Por el contrario, que sus palabras contribuyan a la necesaria edificación y sean de bendición para quienes escuchan. **30**No agravien al Espíritu Santo de Dios, con el cual fueron sellados para el día de la redención. **31**Abandonen toda amargura, ira y enojo, gritos y calumnias, y toda forma de malicia. **32**Más bien, sean bondadosos y compasivos unos con otros, y perdónense mutuamente, así como Dios los perdonó a ustedes en Cristo.

5 Por tanto, imiten a Dios, como hijos muy amados, **2**y lleven una vida de amor, así como Cristo nos amó y se entregó por nosotros como ofrenda y sacrificio fragante para Dios.

3Entre ustedes ni siquiera debe mencionarse la inmoralidad sexual, ni ninguna clase de impureza o de avaricia, porque eso no es propio del *pueblo santo de Dios. **4**Tampoco debe haber palabras indecentes, conversaciones necias ni chistes groseros, todo lo cual está fuera de lugar; haya más bien acción de gra-

---

i **3:15** *familia*. Alt. *paternidad*.   j **4:8** Sal 68:18   k **4:9** *las partes bajas, o sea, a la tierra?* Alt. *las partes bajas de la tierra?*
l **4:26** Sal 4:4

cias. [5]Porque pueden estar seguros de que nadie que sea avaro (es decir, idólatra), inmoral o impuro tendrá herencia en el reino de Cristo y de Dios.[m] [6]Que nadie los engañe con argumentaciones vanas, porque por esto viene el castigo de Dios sobre los que viven en la desobediencia. [7]Así que no se hagan cómplices de ellos.

[8]Porque ustedes antes eran oscuridad, pero ahora son luz en el Señor. Vivan como hijos de luz [9](el fruto de la luz consiste en toda bondad, justicia y verdad) [10]y comprueben lo que agrada al Señor. [11]No tengan nada que ver con las obras infructuosas de la oscuridad, sino más bien denúncienlas, [12]porque da vergüenza aun mencionar lo que los desobedientes hacen en secreto. [13]Pero todo lo que la luz pone al descubierto se hace visible, [14]porque la luz es lo que hace que todo sea visible. Por eso se dice:

«Despiértate, tú que duermes,
    *levántate de entre los muertos,
  y te alumbrará Cristo.»

[15]Así que tengan cuidado de su manera de vivir. No vivan como necios sino como sabios, [16]aprovechando al máximo cada momento oportuno, porque los días son malos. [17]Por tanto, no sean insensatos, sino entiendan cuál es la voluntad del Señor. [18]No se emborrachen con vino, que lleva al desenfreno. Al contrario, sean llenos del Espíritu. [19]Anímense unos a otros con salmos, himnos y canciones espirituales. Canten y alaben al Señor con el corazón, [20]dando siempre gracias a Dios el Padre por todo, en el nombre de nuestro Señor Jesucristo.

Deberes conyugales

[21]Sométanse unos a otros, por reverencia a Cristo. [22]Esposas, sométanse a sus propios esposos como al Señor. [23]Porque el esposo es cabeza de su esposa, así como Cristo es cabeza y salvador de la iglesia, la cual es su cuerpo. [24]Así como la iglesia se somete a Cristo, también las esposas deben someterse a sus esposos en todo.

[25]Esposos, amen a sus esposas, así como Cristo amó a la iglesia y se entregó por ella [26]para hacerla santa. Él la purificó, lavándola con agua mediante la palabra, [27]para presentársela a sí mismo como una iglesia radiante, sin mancha ni arruga ni ninguna otra imperfección, sino santa e intachable. [28]Así mismo el esposo debe amar a su esposa como a su propio cuerpo. El que ama a su esposa se ama a sí mismo, [29]pues nadie ha odiado jamás a su propio cuerpo; al contrario, lo alimenta y lo cuida, así como Cristo hace con la iglesia, [30]porque somos miembros de su cuerpo. [31]«Por eso dejará el hombre a su padre y a su madre, y se unirá a su esposa, y los dos llegarán a ser un solo cuerpo.»[n] [32]Esto es un *misterio profundo; yo me refiero a Cristo y a la iglesia. [33]En todo caso, cada uno de ustedes ame también a su esposa como a sí mismo, y que la esposa respete a su esposo.

Deberes filiales

6 Hijos, obedezcan en el Señor a sus padres, porque esto es justo. [2]«Honra a tu padre y a tu madre —que es el primer mandamiento con promesa— [3]para que te vaya bien y disfrutes de una larga vida en la tierra.»[ñ]

[4]Y ustedes, padres, no hagan enojar a sus hijos, sino críenlos según la disciplina e instrucción del Señor.

Deberes de los esclavos y de sus amos

[5]*Esclavos, obedezcan a sus amos terrenales con respeto y temor, y con integridad de corazón, como a Cristo. [6]No lo hagan sólo cuando los estén mirando, como los que quieren ganarse el favor *humano, sino como esclavos de Cristo, haciendo de todo corazón la voluntad de Dios. [7]Sirvan de buena gana, como quien sirve al Señor y no a los hombres, [8]sabiendo que el Señor recompensará a cada uno por el bien que haya hecho, sea esclavo o sea libre.

[9]Y ustedes, amos, correspondan a esta actitud de sus esclavos, dejando de amenazarlos. Recuerden que tanto ellos como ustedes tienen un mismo Amo[o] en el cielo, y que con él no hay favoritismos.

La armadura de Dios

[10]Por último, fortalézcanse con el gran poder del Señor. [11]Pónganse toda la armadura de Dios para que puedan hacer frente a las artimañas del diablo. [12]Porque nuestra lucha no es contra *seres humanos, sino contra poderes, contra autoridades, contra potestades que dominan este mundo de tinieblas, contra fuerzas espirituales malignas en las regiones celestiales. [13]Por lo tanto, pónganse toda la armadura de Dios, para que cuando llegue el día malo puedan resistir hasta el fin con firmeza. [14]Manténganse firmes, ceñidos con el cinturón de la verdad, protegidos por la coraza de justicia, [15]y calzados con la disposición de proclamar el *evangelio de la paz. [16]Además de todo esto, tomen el escudo de la fe, con el cual pueden apagar todas las flechas encendidas del maligno. [17]Tomen el casco de la salvación y la espada del Espíritu, que es la palabra de Dios.

[18]Oren en el Espíritu en todo momento, con peticiones y ruegos. Manténganse alerta y perseveren en oración por todos los *santos.

[19]Oren también por mí para que, cuando hable, Dios me dé las palabras para dar a conocer con valor el *misterio del evangelio, [20]por el cual soy embajador en cadenas. Oren para que lo proclame valerosamente, como debo hacerlo.

Saludos finales

[21]Nuestro querido hermano Tíquico, fiel servidor en el Señor, les contará todo, para que también ustedes sepan cómo me va y qué estoy haciendo. [22]Lo envío a ustedes precisamente para que sepan cómo estamos y para que cobren ánimo.

[23]Que Dios el Padre y el Señor Jesucristo les concedan paz, amor y fe a los hermanos. [24]La gracia sea con todos los que aman a nuestro Señor Jesucristo con amor imperecedero.

---

[m] **5:5** *de Cristo y de Dios.* Alt. *de Cristo, que es Dios.*   [n] **5:31** Gn 2:24   [ñ] **6:3** Éx 20:12; Dt 5:16   [o] **6:9** *Amo.* Lit. *Señor.*

Carta a los FILIPENSES

1 Pablo y Timoteo, *siervos de *Cristo Jesús,

a todos los *santos en Cristo Jesús que están en Filipos, junto con los *obispos y diáconos:

2Que Dios nuestro Padre y el Señor Jesucristo les concedan gracia y paz.

Acción de gracias e intercesión

3Doy gracias a mi Dios cada vez que me acuerdo de ustedes. 4En todas mis oraciones por todos ustedes, siempre oro con alegría, 5porque han participado en el *evangelio desde el primer día hasta ahora. 6Estoy convencido de esto: el que comenzó tan buena obra en ustedes la irá *perfeccionando hasta el día de Cristo Jesús. 7Es justo que yo piense así de todos ustedes porque los llevo[a] en el corazón; pues, ya sea que me encuentre preso o defendiendo y confirmando el evangelio, todos ustedes participan conmigo de la gracia que Dios me ha dado. 8Dios es testigo de cuánto los quiero a todos con el entrañable amor de Cristo Jesús.

9Esto es lo que pido en oración: que el amor de ustedes abunde cada vez más en conocimiento y en buen juicio, 10para que disciernan lo que es mejor, y sean puros e irreprochables para el día de Cristo, 11llenos del fruto de justicia que se produce por medio de Jesucristo, para gloria y alabanza de Dios.

El vivir es Cristo

12Hermanos, quiero que sepan que, en realidad, lo que me ha pasado ha contribuido al avance del *evangelio. 13Es más, se ha hecho evidente a toda la guardia del palacio[b] y a todos los demás que estoy encadenado por causa de Cristo. 14Gracias a mis cadenas, ahora más que nunca la mayoría de los hermanos, confiados en el Señor, se han atrevido a anunciar sin temor la palabra de Dios.

15Es cierto que algunos predican a Cristo por envidia y rivalidad, pero otros lo hacen con buenas intenciones. 16Estos últimos lo hacen por amor, pues saben que he sido puesto para la defensa del evangelio. 17Aquéllos predican a Cristo por ambición personal y no por motivos puros, creyendo que así van a aumentar las angustias que sufro en mi prisión.[c]

18¿Qué importa? Al fin y al cabo, y sea como sea, con motivos falsos o con sinceridad, se predica a Cristo. Por eso me alegro; es más, seguiré alegrándome 19porque sé que, gracias a las oraciones de ustedes y a la ayuda que me da el Espíritu de Jesucristo, todo esto resultará en mi liberación.[d] 20Mi ardiente anhelo y esperanza es que en nada seré avergonzado, sino que con toda libertad, ya sea que yo viva o muera, ahora como siempre, Cristo será exaltado en mi cuerpo. 21Porque para mí el vivir es Cristo y el morir es ganancia. 22Ahora bien, si seguir viviendo en este mundo[e] representa para mí un trabajo fructífero, ¿qué escogeré? ¡No lo sé! 23Me siento presionado por dos posibilidades: deseo partir y estar con Cristo, que es muchísimo mejor, 24pero por el bien de ustedes es preferible que yo permanezca en este mundo. 25Convencido de esto, sé que permaneceré y continuaré con todos ustedes para contribuir a su jubiloso avance en la fe. 26Así,

cuando yo vuelva, su *satisfacción en Cristo Jesús abundará por causa mía.

27Pase lo que pase, compórtense de una manera digna del evangelio de Cristo. De este modo, ya sea que vaya a verlos o que, estando ausente, sólo tenga noticias de ustedes, sabré que siguen firmes en un mismo propósito, luchando unánimes por la fe del evangelio 28y sin temor alguno a sus adversarios, lo cual es para ellos señal de destrucción. Para ustedes, en cambio, es señal de salvación, y esto proviene de Dios. 29Porque a ustedes se les ha concedido no sólo creer en Cristo, sino también sufrir por él, 30pues sostienen la misma lucha que antes me vieron sostener, y que ahora saben que sigo sosteniendo.

Humillación y exaltación de Cristo

2 Por tanto, si sienten algún estímulo en su unión con Cristo, algún consuelo en su amor, algún compañerismo en el Espíritu, algún afecto entrañable, 2llénenme de alegría teniendo un mismo parecer, un mismo amor, unidos en alma y pensamiento. 3No hagan nada por egoísmo o vanidad; más bien, con humildad consideren a los demás como superiores a ustedes mismos. 4Cada uno debe velar no sólo por sus propios intereses sino también por los intereses de los demás.

5La actitud de ustedes debe ser como la de Cristo Jesús,

6quien, siendo por naturaleza[f] Dios,
no consideró el ser igual a Dios como algo a qué aferrarse,
7por el contrario, se rebajó voluntariamente,
tomando la naturaleza[g] de *siervo
y haciéndose semejante a los seres *humanos.
8Y al manifestarse como hombre,
se humilló a sí mismo
y se hizo obediente hasta la muerte,
¡y muerte de cruz!
9Por eso Dios lo exaltó hasta lo sumo
y le otorgó el nombre
que está sobre todo nombre,
10para que ante el nombre de Jesús
se doble toda rodilla
en el cielo y en la tierra
y debajo de la tierra,
11y toda lengua confiese que Jesucristo es el Señor,
para gloria de Dios Padre.

Testimonio de luz

12Así que, mis queridos hermanos, como han obedecido siempre —no sólo en mi presencia sino mucho más ahora en mi ausencia— lleven a cabo su salvación con temor y temblor, 13pues Dios es quien produce en ustedes tanto el querer como el hacer para que se cumpla su buena voluntad.

14Háganlo todo sin quejas ni contiendas, 15para que sean intachables y puros, hijos de Dios sin culpa en medio de una generación torcida y depravada. En ella ustedes brillan como estrellas en el firmamento, 16manteniendo en alto[h] la palabra de vida. Así en el día de Cristo me sentiré *satisfecho de no haber corrido ni trabajado en vano. 17Y aunque mi vida fuera

---

a **1:7** los llevo. Alt. me llevan.   b **1:13** a toda la guardia del palacio. Alt. en todo el palacio.   c **1:16,17** Var. invierte el orden de vv. 16 y 17.   d **1:19** liberación. Alt. Salvación.   e **1:22** este mundo. Lit. la *carne; también en v. 24.   f **2:6** por naturaleza. Lit. en forma de.   g **2:7** la naturaleza. Lit. la forma.   h **2:16** manteniendo en alto. Alt. ya que se aferran a.

derramada[i] sobre el sacrificio y servicio que proceden de su fe, me alegro y comparto con todos ustedes mi alegría. [18]Así también ustedes, alégrense y compartan su alegría conmigo.

Dos colaboradores ejemplares

[19]Espero en el Señor Jesús enviarles pronto a Timoteo, para que también yo cobre ánimo al recibir noticias de ustedes. [20]No tengo a nadie más que, como él, se preocupe de veras por el bienestar de ustedes, [21]pues todos los demás buscan sus propios intereses y no los de Jesucristo. [22]Pero ustedes conocen bien la entereza de carácter de Timoteo, que ha servido conmigo en la obra del *evangelio, como un hijo junto a su padre. [23]Así que espero enviárselo tan pronto como se aclaren mis asuntos. [24]Y confío en el Señor que yo mismo iré pronto.

[25]Ahora bien, creo que es necesario enviarles de vuelta a Epafrodito, mi hermano, colaborador y compañero de lucha, a quien ustedes han enviado para atenderme en mis necesidades. [26]Él los extraña mucho a todos y está afligido porque ustedes se enteraron de que estaba enfermo. [27]En efecto, estuvo enfermo y al borde de la muerte; pero Dios se compadeció de él, y no sólo de él sino también de mí, para no añadir tristeza a mi tristeza. [28]Así que lo envío urgentemente para que, al verlo de nuevo, ustedes se alegren y yo esté menos preocupado. [29]Recíbanlo en el Señor con toda alegría y honren a los que son como él, [30]porque estuvo a punto de morir por la obra de Cristo, arriesgando la *vida para suplir el servicio que ustedes no podían prestarme.

Plena confianza en Cristo

3 Por lo demás, hermanos míos, alégrense en el Señor. Para mí no es molestia volver a escribirles lo mismo, y a ustedes les da seguridad.

[2]Cuídense de esos *perros, cuídense de esos que hacen el mal, cuídense de esos que mutilan el cuerpo. [3]Porque la *circuncisión somos nosotros, los que por medio del Espíritu de Dios adoramos, nos *enorgullecemos en Cristo Jesús y no ponemos nuestra confianza en esfuerzos *humanos. [4]Yo mismo tengo motivos para tal confianza. Si cualquier otro cree tener motivos para confiar en esfuerzos humanos, yo más: [5]circuncidado al octavo día, del pueblo de Israel, de la tribu de Benjamín, hebreo de pura cepa; en cuanto a la interpretación de la ley, *fariseo; [6]en cuanto al celo, perseguidor de la iglesia; en cuanto a la justicia que la ley exige, intachable.

[7]Sin embargo, todo aquello que para mí era ganancia, ahora lo considero pérdida por causa de Cristo. [8]Es más, todo lo considero pérdida por razón del incomparable valor de conocer a Cristo Jesús, mi Señor. Por él lo he perdido todo, y lo tengo por estiércol, a fin de ganar a Cristo [9]y encontrarme unido a él. No quiero mi propia justicia que procede de la ley, sino la que se obtiene mediante la *fe en Cristo, la justicia que procede de Dios, basada en la fe. [10]Lo he perdido todo a fin de conocer a Cristo, experimentar el poder que se manifestó en su resurrección, participar en sus sufrimientos y llegar a ser semejante a él en su muerte. [11]Así espero alcanzar la resurrección de entre los muertos.

Ciudadanos del cielo

[12]No es que ya lo haya conseguido todo, o que ya sea *perfecto. Sin embargo, sigo adelante esperando alcanzar aquello para lo cual Cristo Jesús me alcanzó a mí. [13]Hermanos, no pienso que yo mismo lo haya logrado ya. Más bien, una cosa hago: olvidando lo que queda atrás y esforzándome por alcanzar lo que está delante, [14]sigo avanzando hacia la meta para ganar el premio que Dios ofrece mediante su llamamiento celestial en Cristo Jesús.

[15]Así que, ¡escuchen los perfectos! Todos debemos[j] tener este modo de pensar. Y si en algo piensan de forma diferente, Dios les hará ver esto también. [16]En todo caso, vivamos de acuerdo con lo que ya hemos alcanzado.[k]

[17]Hermanos, sigan todos mi ejemplo, y fíjense en los que se comportan conforme al modelo que les hemos dado. [18]Como les he dicho a menudo, y ahora lo repito hasta con lágrimas, muchos se comportan como enemigos de la cruz de Cristo. [19]Su destino es la destrucción, adoran al dios de sus propios deseos[l] y se enorgullecen de lo que es su vergüenza. Sólo piensan en lo terrenal. [20]En cambio, nosotros somos ciudadanos del cielo, de donde anhelamos recibir al Salvador, el Señor Jesucristo. [21]Él transformará nuestro cuerpo miserable para que sea como su cuerpo glorioso, mediante el poder con que somete a sí mismo todas las cosas.

4 Por lo tanto, queridos hermanos míos, a quienes amo y extraño mucho, ustedes que son mi alegría y mi corona, manténganse así firmes en el Señor.

Exhortaciones

[2]Ruego a Evodia y también a Síntique que se pongan de acuerdo en el Señor. [3]Y a ti, mi fiel compañero,[m] te pido que ayudes a estas mujeres que han luchado a mi lado en la obra del *evangelio, junto con Clemente y los demás colaboradores míos, cuyos nombres están en el libro de la vida.

[4]Alégrense siempre en el Señor. Insisto: ¡Alégrense! [5]Que su amabilidad sea evidente a todos. El Señor está cerca. [6]No se inquieten por nada; más bien, en toda ocasión, con oración y ruego, presenten sus peticiones a Dios y denle gracias. [7]Y la paz de Dios, que sobrepasa todo entendimiento, cuidará sus corazones y sus pensamientos en Cristo Jesús.

[8]Por último, hermanos, consideren bien todo lo verdadero, todo lo respetable, todo lo justo, todo lo puro, todo lo amable, todo lo digno de admiración, en fin, todo lo que sea excelente o merezca elogio. [9]Pongan en práctica lo que de mí han aprendido, recibido y oído, y lo que han visto en mí, y el Dios de paz estará con ustedes.

Gratitud por la ayuda recibida

[10]Me alegro muchísimo en el Señor de que al fin hayan vuelto a interesarse en mí. Claro está que tenían interés, sólo que no habían tenido la oportunidad de demostrarlo. [11]No digo esto porque esté necesitado, pues he aprendido a estar satisfecho en cualquier situación en que me encuentre. [12]Sé lo que es vivir en la pobreza, y lo que es vivir en la abundancia. He aprendido a vivir en todas y cada una de las circunstancias, tanto a quedar saciado como a pasar hambre, a tener de sobra como a sufrir escasez. [13]Todo lo puedo en Cristo que me fortalece.

---

i **2:17** *derramada.* Es decir, como libación. j **3:15** *Así . . . debemos.* Alt. *Así que los que somos perfectos debemos.* k **3:16** *alcanzado.* Var. *alcanzado, una misma regla, un mismo modo de pensar.* l **3:19** *adoran . . . deseos.* Lit. *su dios es el estómago.* m **4:3** *mi fiel compañero.* Alt. *fiel Sícigo.*

[14]Sin embargo, han hecho bien en participar conmigo en mi angustia. [15]Y ustedes mismos, filipenses, saben que en el principio de la obra del *evangelio, cuando salí de Macedonia, ninguna iglesia participó conmigo en mis ingresos y gastos, excepto ustedes. [16]Incluso a Tesalónica me enviaron ayuda una y otra vez para suplir mis necesidades. [17]No digo esto porque esté tratando de conseguir más ofrendas, sino que trato de aumentar el crédito a su cuenta. [18]Ya he recibido todo lo que necesito y aun más; tengo hasta de sobra ahora que he recibido de Epafrodito lo que me enviaron. Es una ofrenda fragante, un sacrificio que Dios acepta con agrado. [19]Así que mi Dios les proveerá de todo lo que necesiten, conforme a las gloriosas riquezas que tiene en Cristo Jesús.

[20]A nuestro Dios y Padre sea la gloria por los siglos de los siglos. Amén.

Saludos finales

[21]Saluden a todos los *santos en Cristo Jesús. Los hermanos que están conmigo les mandan saludos. [22]Saludos de parte de todos los santos, especialmente los de la casa del *emperador.

[23]Que la gracia del Señor Jesucristo sea con su espíritu. Amén.[n]

n **4:23** Var. no incluye: *Amén.*

Carta a los COLOSENSES

1 Pablo, apóstol de *Cristo Jesús por la voluntad de Dios, y el hermano Timoteo,

[2]a los *santos y fieles hermanos[a] en Cristo que están en Colosas:

Que Dios nuestro Padre les conceda[b] gracia y paz.

Acción de gracias e intercesión

[3]Siempre que oramos por ustedes, damos gracias a Dios, el Padre de nuestro Señor Jesucristo, [4]pues hemos recibido noticias de su fe en Cristo Jesús y del amor que tienen por todos los *santos [5]a causa de la esperanza reservada para ustedes en el cielo. De esta esperanza ya han sabido por la palabra de verdad, que es el *evangelio [6]que ha llegado hasta ustedes. Este evangelio está dando fruto y creciendo en todo el mundo, como también ha sucedido entre ustedes desde el día en que supieron de la gracia de Dios y la comprendieron plenamente. [7]Así lo aprendieron de Epafras, nuestro querido colaborador[c] y fiel servidor de Cristo para el bien de ustedes.[d] [8]Fue él quien nos contó del amor que tienen en el Espíritu.

[9]Por eso, desde el día en que lo supimos no hemos dejado de orar por ustedes. Pedimos que Dios les haga conocer plenamente su voluntad con toda sabiduría y comprensión espiritual, [10]para que vivan de manera digna del Señor, agradándole en todo. Esto implica dar fruto en toda buena obra, crecer en el conocimiento de Dios [11]y ser fortalecidos en todo sentido con su glorioso poder. Así perseverarán con paciencia en toda situación, [12]dando gracias con alegría al Padre. Él los[e] ha facultado para participar de la herencia de los santos en el reino de la luz. [13]Él nos libró del dominio de la oscuridad y nos trasladó al reino de su amado Hijo, [14]en quien tenemos redención,[f] el perdón de pecados.

La supremacía de Cristo

[15]Él es la imagen del Dios invisible,
    el primogénito[g] de toda creación,
[16]porque por medio de él fueron creadas todas
        las cosas
    en el cielo y en la tierra, visibles e invisibles,
    sean tronos, poderes, principados o
        autoridades:
    todo ha sido creado
        por medio de él y para él.
[17]Él es anterior a todas las cosas,
    que por medio de él forman un todo
        coherente.[h]
[18]Él es la cabeza del cuerpo,
    que es la iglesia.
    Él es el principio,
    el primogénito de la resurrección,
    para ser en todo el primero.
[19]Porque a Dios le agradó habitar en él con toda
        su plenitud,
[20]   y, por medio de él, reconciliar consigo
        todas las cosas,

tanto las que están en la tierra como las que
        están en el cielo,
    haciendo la paz mediante la sangre que
        derramó en la cruz.

[21]En otro tiempo ustedes, por su actitud y sus malas acciones, estaban alejados de Dios y eran sus enemigos. [22]Pero ahora Dios, a fin de presentarlos *santos, intachables e irreprochables delante de él, los ha reconciliado en el cuerpo mortal de Cristo mediante su muerte, [23]con tal de que se mantengan firmes en la fe, bien cimentados y estables, sin abandonar la esperanza que ofrece el *evangelio. Éste es el evangelio que ustedes oyeron y que ha sido proclamado en toda la creación debajo del cielo, y del que yo, Pablo, he llegado a ser servidor.

Trabajo de Pablo por la iglesia

[24]Ahora me alegro en medio de mis sufrimientos por ustedes, y voy completando en mí mismo[i] lo que falta de las aflicciones de Cristo, en favor de su cuerpo, que es la iglesia. [25]De ésta llegué a ser servidor según el plan que Dios me encomendó para ustedes: el dar cumplimiento a la palabra de Dios, [26]anunciando el *misterio que se ha mantenido oculto por siglos y generaciones, pero que ahora se ha manifestado a sus *santos. [27]A éstos Dios se propuso dar a conocer cuál es la gloriosa riqueza de este misterio entre las *naciones, que es Cristo en ustedes, la esperanza de gloria.

[28]A este Cristo proclamamos, aconsejando y enseñando a todos los *seres humanos, para presentarlos a todos *perfectos en él. [29]Con este fin trabajo y lucho fortalecido por el poder de Cristo que obra en mí.

2 Quiero que sepan qué gran lucha sostengo por el bien de ustedes y de los que están en Laodicea, y de tantos que no me conocen personalmente. [2]Quiero que lo sepan para que cobren ánimo, permanezcan unidos por amor, y tengan toda la riqueza que proviene de la convicción y del entendimiento. Así conocerán el *misterio de Dios, es decir, a Cristo, [3]en quien están escondidos todos los tesoros de la sabiduría y del conocimiento. [4]Les digo esto para que nadie los engañe con argumentos capciosos. [5]Aunque estoy físicamente ausente, los acompaño en espíritu, y me alegro al ver su buen orden y la firmeza de su fe en Cristo.

Libertad en Cristo

[6]Por eso, de la manera que recibieron a Cristo Jesús como Señor, vivan ahora en él, [7]arraigados y edificados en él, confirmados en la fe como se les enseñó, y llenos de gratitud.

[8]Cuídense de que nadie los cautive con la vana y engañosa filosofía que sigue tradiciones *humanas, la que va de acuerdo con los *principios[j] de este mundo y no conforme a Cristo.

[9]Toda la plenitud de la divinidad habita en forma corporal en Cristo; [10]y en él, que es la cabeza de todo poder y autoridad, ustedes han recibido esa plenitud. [11]Además, en él fueron *circuncidados, no

---

a **1:2** santos y fieles hermanos. Alt. santos hermanos creyentes. b **1:2** Padre les conceda. Var. Padre y el Señor Jesucristo les concedan. c **1:7** colaborador. Lit. Coesclavo. d[1:7] de ustedes. Var. de nosotros. e **1:12** los. Var. Nos. f **1:14** redención. Var. redención mediante su sangre (véase Ef 1:7). g **1:15** el primogénito. Es decir, el que tiene anterioridad y preeminencia; también en v. 18. h **1:17** por medio . . . coherente. Alt. por medio de él continúan existiendo. i **1:24** en mí mismo. Lit. en mi *carne. j **2:8** los principios. Alt. los poderes espirituales, o las normas; también en v. 20.

por mano humana sino con la circuncisión que consiste en despojarse del cuerpo pecaminoso.k Esta circuncisión la efectuó Cristo. 12Ustedes la recibieron al ser sepultados con él en el bautismo. En él también fueron resucitados mediante la fe en el poder de Dios, quien lo resucitó de entre los muertos.

13Antes de recibir esa circuncisión, ustedes estaban muertos en sus pecados. Sin embargo, Dios nosl dio vida en unión con Cristo, al perdonarnos todos los pecados 14y anular la deudam que teníamos pendiente por los requisitos de la ley. Él anuló esa deuda que nos era adversa, clavándola en la cruz. 15Desarmó a los poderes y a las potestades, y por medio de Criston los humilló en público al exhibirlos en su desfile triunfal.

16Así que nadie los juzgue a ustedes por lo que comen o beben, o con respecto a días de fiesta religiosa, de luna nueva o de reposo. 17Todo esto es una sombra de las cosas que están por venir; la realidad se halla en Cristo. 18No dejen que les prive de esta realidad ninguno de esos que se ufanan en fingir humildad y adoración de ángeles. Los tales hacen alarde de lo que no han visto; y, envanecidos por su razonamiento *humano, 19no se mantienen firmemente unidos a la Cabeza. Por la acción de ésta, todo el cuerpo, sostenido y ajustado mediante las articulaciones y ligamentos, va creciendo como Dios quiere.

20Si con Cristo ustedes ya han muerto a los principios de este mundo, ¿por qué, como si todavía pertenecieran al mundo, se someten a preceptos tales como: 21«No tomes en tus manos, no pruebes, no toques»? 22Estos preceptos, basados en reglas y enseñanzas humanas, se refieren a cosas que van a desaparecer con el uso. 23Tienen sin duda apariencia de sabiduría, con su afectada piedad, falsa humildad y severo trato del cuerpo, pero de nada sirven frente a los apetitos de la naturaleza pecaminosa.ñ

Normas para una vida santa

3 Ya que han resucitado con Cristo, busquen las cosas de arriba, donde está Cristo sentado a la *derecha de Dios. 2Concentren su atención en las cosas de arriba, no en las de la tierra, 3pues ustedes han muerto y su vida está escondida con Cristo en Dios. 4Cuando Cristo, que es la vida de ustedes,o se manifieste, entonces también ustedes serán manifestados con él en gloria.

5Por tanto, hagan morir todo lo que es propio de la naturaleza terrenal: inmoralidad sexual, impureza, bajas pasiones, malos deseos y avaricia, la cual es idolatría. 6Por estas cosas viene el castigo de Dios.p 7Ustedes las practicaron en otro tiempo, cuando vivían en ellas. 8Pero ahora abandonen también todo esto: enojo, ira, malicia, calumnia y lenguaje obsceno. 9Dejen de mentirse unos a otros, ahora que se han quitado el ropaje de la vieja naturaleza con sus vicios, 10y se han puesto el de la nueva naturaleza, que se va renovando en conocimiento a imagen de su Creador. 11En esta nueva naturaleza no hay *griego ni judío, *circunciso ni incircunciso, culto ni inculto,q esclavo ni libre, sino que Cristo es todo y está en todos.

12Por lo tanto, como escogidos de Dios, *santos y amados, revístanse de afecto entrañable y de bondad, humildad, amabilidad y paciencia, 13de modo que se toleren unos a otros y se perdonen si alguno tiene queja contra otro. Así como el Señor los perdonó, perdonen también ustedes. 14Por encima de todo, vístanse de amor, que es el vínculo perfecto.

15Que gobierne en sus corazones la paz de Cristo, a la cual fueron llamados en un solo cuerpo. Y sean agradecidos. 16Que habite en ustedes la palabra de Cristo con toda su riqueza: instrúyanse y aconséjense unos a otros con toda sabiduría; canten salmos, himnos y canciones espirituales a Dios, con gratitud de corazón. 17Y todo lo que hagan, de palabra o de obra, háganlo en el nombre del Señor Jesús, dando gracias a Dios el Padre por medio de él.

Normas para la familia cristiana

18Esposas, sométanse a sus esposos, como conviene en el Señor.

19Esposos, amen a sus esposas y no sean duros con ellas.

20Hijos, obedezcan a sus padres en todo, porque esto agrada al Señor.

21Padres, no exasperen a sus hijos, no sea que se desanimen.

22*Esclavos, obedezcan en todo a sus amos terrenales, no sólo cuando ellos los estén mirando, como si ustedes quisieran ganarse el favor *humano, sino con integridad de corazón y por respeto al Señor. 23Hagan lo que hagan, trabajen de buena gana, como para el Señor y no como para nadie en este mundo, 24conscientes de que el Señor los recompensará con la herencia. Ustedes sirven a Cristo el Señor. 25El que hace el mal pagará por su propia maldad, y en esto no hay favoritismos.

4 Amos, proporcionen a sus esclavos lo que es justo y equitativo, conscientes de que ustedes también tienen un Amo en el cielo.

Instrucciones adicionales

2Dedíquense a la oración: perseveren en ella con agradecimiento 3y, al mismo tiempo, intercedan por nosotros a fin de que Dios nos abra las puertas para proclamar la palabra, el *misterio de Cristo por el cual estoy preso. 4Oren para que yo lo anuncie con claridad, como debo hacerlo. 5Compórtense sabiamente con los que no creen en Cristo,r aprovechando al máximo cada momento oportuno. 6Que su conversación sea siempre amena y de buen gusto. Así sabrán cómo responder a cada uno.

Saludos finales

7Nuestro querido hermano Tíquico, fiel servidor y colaboradors en el Señor, les contará en detalle cómo me va. 8Lo envío a ustedes precisamente para que tengan noticias de nosotros, y así cobren ánimo.t 9Va con Onésimo, querido y fiel hermano, que es uno de ustedes. Ellos les pondrán al tanto de todo lo que sucede aquí.

10Aristarco, mi compañero de cárcel, les manda saludos, como también Marcos, el primo de Bernabé. En cuanto a Marcos, ustedes ya han recibido instrucciones; si va a visitarlos, recíbanlo bien. 11También los saluda Jesús, llamado el Justo. Éstos son los úni-

---

k **2:11** *cuerpo pecaminoso.* Lit. *cuerpo de la* *carne. l **2:13** *nos.* Var. *Les.* m **2:14** *la deuda.* Lit. *el pagaré.* n **2:15** *por medio de Cristo.* Alt. *mediante la cruz.* ñ **2:23** *los apetitos de la naturaleza pecaminosa.* Lit. *la satisfacción de la* *carne. o **3:4** *de ustedes.* Var. *de nosotros.* p **3:6** *de Dios.* Var. *de Dios sobre los que son desobedientes.* q **3:11** *culto ni inculto.* Lit. *bárbaro, escita.* r **4:5** *los que no creen en Cristo.* Lit. *los de afuera.* s **4:7** *colaborador.* Lit. *Coesclavo.* t **4:8** *para que … ánimo.* Var. *Para que él tenga noticias de ustedes, y los anime.*

cos judíos que colaboran conmigo en pro del reino de Dios, y me han sido de mucho consuelo. [12]Les manda saludos Epafras, que es uno de ustedes. Este *siervo de Cristo Jesús está siempre luchando en oración por ustedes, para que, plenamente convencidos,[u] se mantengan firmes, cumpliendo en todo la voluntad de Dios. [13]A mí me consta que él se preocupa mucho por ustedes y por los que están en Laodicea y en Hierápolis. [14]Los saludan Lucas, el querido médico, y Demas. [15]Saluden a los hermanos que es-

tán en Laodicea, como también a Ninfas y a la iglesia que se reúne en su casa.

[16]Una vez que se les haya leído a ustedes esta carta, que se lea también en la iglesia de Laodicea, y ustedes lean la carta dirigida a esa iglesia.

[17]Díganle a Arquipo que se ocupe de la tarea que recibió en el Señor, y que la lleve a cabo.

[18]Yo, Pablo, escribo este saludo de mi puño y letra. Recuerden que estoy preso. Que la gracia sea con ustedes.

---

u **4:12** *plenamente convencidos*. Alt. *perfectos y convencidos*.

Primera Carta a los TESALONICENSES

1 Pablo, *Silvano y Timoteo,

a la iglesia de los tesalonicenses que está en Dios el Padre y en el Señor *Jesucristo:

Gracia y paz a ustedes.a

Acción de gracias por los tesalonicenses

[2]Siempre damos gracias a Dios por todos ustedes cuando los mencionamos en nuestras oraciones. [3]Los recordamos constantemente delante de nuestro Dios y Padre a causa de la obra realizada por su fe, el trabajo motivado por su amor, y la constancia sostenida por su esperanza en nuestro Señor Jesucristo.

[4]Hermanos amados de Dios, sabemos que él los ha escogido, [5]porque nuestro *evangelio les llegó no sólo con palabras sino también con poder, es decir, con el Espíritu Santo y con profunda convicción. Como bien saben, estuvimos entre ustedes buscando su bien. [6]Ustedes se hicieron imitadores nuestros y del Señor cuando, a pesar de mucho sufrimiento, recibieron el mensaje con la alegría que infunde el Espíritu Santo. [7]De esta manera se constituyeron en ejemplo para todos los creyentes de Macedonia y de Acaya. [8]Partiendo de ustedes, el mensaje del Señor se ha proclamado no sólo en Macedonia y en Acaya sino en todo lugar; a tal punto se ha divulgado su fe en Dios que ya no es necesario que nosotros digamos nada. [9]Ellos mismos cuentan de lo bien que ustedes nos recibieron, y de cómo se convirtieron a Dios dejando los ídolos para servir al Dios vivo y verdadero, [10]y esperar del cielo a Jesús, su Hijo a quien *resucitó, que nos libra del castigo venidero.

Ministerio de Pablo en Tesalónica

2 Hermanos, saben que nuestra visita a ustedes no fue un fracaso. [2]Y saben también que, a pesar de las aflicciones e insultos que antes sufrimos en Filipos, cobramos confianza en nuestro Dios y nos atrevimos a comunicarles el *evangelio en medio de una gran lucha. [3]Nuestra predicación no se origina en el error ni en malas intenciones, ni procura engañar a nadie. [4]Al contrario, hablamos como hombres a quienes Dios aprobó y les confió el evangelio: no tratamos de agradar a la gente sino a Dios, que examina nuestro corazón. [5]Como saben, nunca hemos recurrido a las adulaciones ni a las excusas para obtener dinero; Dios es testigo. [6]Tampoco hemos buscado honores de nadie; ni de ustedes ni de otros. [7]Aunque como apóstoles de Cristo hubiéramos podido ser exigentes con ustedes, los tratamos con delicadeza.b Como una madrec que amamanta y cuida a sus hijos, [8]así nosotros, por el cariño que les tenemos, nos deleitamos en compartir con ustedes no sólo el evangelio de Dios sino también nuestra *vida. ¡Tanto llegamos a quererlos! [9]Recordarán, hermanos, nuestros esfuerzos y fatigas para proclamarles el evangelio de Dios, y cómo trabajamos día y noche para no serles una carga.

[10]Dios y ustedes me son testigos de que nos comportamos con ustedes los creyentes en una forma santa, justa e irreprochable. [11]Saben también que a cada uno de ustedes lo hemos tratado como trata un padre a sus propios hijos. [12]Los hemos animado,

consolado y exhortado a llevar una vida digna de Dios, que los llama a su reino y a su gloria.

[13]Así que no dejamos de dar gracias a Dios, porque al oír ustedes la palabra de Dios que les predicamos, la aceptaron no como palabra *humana sino como lo que realmente es, palabra de Dios, la cual actúa en ustedes los creyentes. [14]Ustedes, hermanos, siguieron el ejemplo de las iglesias de Dios en Cristo Jesús que están en Judea, ya que sufrieron a manos de sus compatriotas lo mismo que sufrieron aquellas iglesias a manos de los judíos. [15]Éstos mataron al Señor Jesús y a los profetas, y a nosotros nos expulsaron. No agradan a Dios y son hostiles a todos, [16]pues procuran impedir que prediquemos a los *gentiles para que sean salvos. Así en todo lo que hacen llegan al colmo de su pecado. Pero el castigo de Dios vendrá sobre ellos con toda severidad.d

Pablo anhela ver a los tesalonicenses

[17]Nosotros, hermanos, luego de estar separados de ustedes por algún tiempo, en lo físico pero no en lo espiritual, con ferviente anhelo hicimos todo lo humanamente posible por ir a verlos. [18]Sí, deseábamos visitarlos —yo mismo, Pablo, más de una vez intenté ir—, pero Satanás nos lo impidió. [19]En resumidas cuentas, ¿cuál es nuestra esperanza, alegría o motivoe de *orgullo delante de nuestro Señor Jesús para cuando él venga? ¿Quién más sino ustedes? [20]Sí, ustedes son nuestro orgullo y alegría.

3 Por tanto, cuando ya no pudimos soportarlo más, pensamos que era mejor quedarnos solos en Atenas. [2]Así que les enviamos a Timoteo, hermano nuestro y colaborador de Diosf en el *evangelio de Cristo, con el fin de afianzarlos y animarlos en la fe [3]para que nadie fuera perturbado por estos sufrimientos. Ustedes mismos saben que se nos destinó para esto, [4]pues cuando estábamos con ustedes les advertimos que íbamos a padecer sufrimientos. Y así sucedió. [5]Por eso, cuando ya no pude soportarlo más, mandé a Timoteo a indagar acerca de su fe, no fuera que el *tentador los hubiera inducido a hacer lo malo y que nuestro trabajo hubiera sido en vano.

El informe alentador de Timoteo

[6]Ahora Timoteo acaba de volver de Tesalónica con buenas noticias de la fe y del amor de ustedes. Nos dice que conservan gratos recuerdos de nosotros y que tienen muchas ganas de vernos, tanto como nosotros a ustedes. [7]Por eso, hermanos, en medio de todas nuestras angustias y sufrimientos ustedes nos han dado ánimo por su fe. [8]¡Ahora sí que vivimos al saber que están firmes en el Señor! [9]¿Cómo podemos agradecer bastante a nuestro Dios por ustedes y por toda la alegría que nos han proporcionado delante de él? [10]Día y noche le suplicamos que nos permita verlos de nuevo para suplir lo que le falta a su fe.

[11]Que el Dios y Padre nuestro, y nuestro Señor Jesús, nos preparen el camino para ir a verlos. [12]Que el Señor los haga crecer para que se amen más y más unos a otros, y a todos, como nosotros los amamos a ustedes. [13]Que los fortalezca interiormente para que, cuando nuestro Señor Jesús venga con todos sus *santos, la santidad de ustedes sea intachable delante de nuestro Dios y Padre.

a 1:1 *a ustedes.* Var. *a ustedes de nuestro Padre y del Señor Jesucristo.* b 2:7 *exigentes ... delicadeza.* Var. *exigentes, fuimos niños entre ustedes.* c 2:7 *madre.* Alt. *Nodriza.* d 2:16 *Pero ... severidad.* Lit. *Pero la ira vino sobre ellos hasta el fin.* e 2:19 *motivo.* Lit. *Corona.* f 3:2 *colaborador de Dios.* Var. *servidor de Dios;* otra var. *servidor de Dios y colaborador nuestro.*

La vida que agrada a Dios

4 Por lo demás, hermanos, les pedimos encarecidamente en el nombre del Señor Jesús que sigan progresando en el modo de vivir que agrada a Dios, tal como lo aprendieron de nosotros. De hecho, ya lo están practicando. 2Ustedes saben cuáles son las instrucciones que les dimos de parte del Señor Jesús.

3La voluntad de Dios es que sean *santificados; que se aparten de la inmoralidad sexual; 4que cada uno aprenda a controlar su propio cuerpoᵍ de una manera santa y honrosa, 5sin dejarse llevar por los malos deseos como hacen los *paganos, que no conocen a Dios; 6y que nadie perjudique a su hermano ni se aproveche de él en este asunto. El Señor castiga todo esto, como ya les hemos dicho y advertido. 7Dios no nos llamó a la impureza sino a la santidad; 8por tanto, el que rechaza estas instrucciones no rechaza a un hombre sino a Dios, quien les da a ustedes su Espíritu Santo.

9En cuanto al amor fraternal, no necesitan que les escribamos, porque Dios mismo les ha enseñado a amarse unos a otros. 10En efecto, ustedes aman a todos los hermanos que viven en Macedonia. No obstante, hermanos, les animamos a amarse aun más, 11a procurar vivir en paz con todos, a ocuparse de sus propias responsabilidades y a trabajar con sus propias manos. Así les he mandado, 12para que por su modo de vivir se ganen el respeto de los que no son creyentes, y no tengan que depender de nadie.

La venida del Señor

13Hermanos, no queremos que ignoren lo que va a pasar con los que ya han muerto,ʰ para que no se entristezcan como esos otros que no tienen esperanza. 14¿Acaso no creemos que Jesús murió y resucitó? Así también Dios resucitará con Jesús a los que han muerto en unión con él. 15Conforme a lo dicho por el Señor, afirmamos que nosotros, los que estemos vivos y hayamos quedado hasta la venida del Señor, de ninguna manera nos adelantaremos a los que hayan muerto. 16El Señor mismo descenderá del cielo con voz de mando, con voz de arcángel y con trompeta de Dios, y los muertos en Cristo resucitarán primero. 17Luego los que estemos vivos, los que hayamos quedado, seremos arrebatados junto con ellos en las nubes para encontrarnos con el Señor en el aire. Y así estaremos con el Señor para siempre. 18Por lo tanto, anímense unos a otros con estas palabras.

5 Ahora bien, hermanos, ustedes no necesitan que se les escriba acerca de tiempos y fechas, 2porque ya saben que el día del Señor llegará como ladrón en la noche. 3Cuando estén diciendo: «Paz y seguridad», vendrá de improviso sobre ellos la destrucción, como le llega a la mujer encinta los dolores de parto. De ninguna manera podrán escapar.

4Ustedes, en cambio, hermanos, no están en la oscuridad para que ese día los sorprenda como un ladrón. 5Todos ustedes son hijos de la luz y del día. No somos de la noche ni de la oscuridad. 6No debemos, pues, dormirnos como los demás, sino mantenernos alerta y en nuestro sano juicio. 7Los que duermen, de noche duermen, y los que se emborrachan, de noche se emborrachan. 8Nosotros que somos del día, por el contrario, estemos siempre en nuestro sano juicio, protegidos por la coraza de la fe y del amor, y por el casco de la esperanza de salvación; 9pues Dios no nos destinó a sufrir el castigo sino a recibir la salvación por medio de nuestro Señor Jesucristo. 10Él murió por nosotros para que, en la vida o en la muerte,ⁱ vivamos junto con él. 11Por eso, anímense y edifíquense unos a otros, tal como lo vienen haciendo.

Instrucciones finales

12Hermanos, les pedimos que sean considerados con los que trabajan arduamente entre ustedes, y los guían y amonestan en el Señor. 13Ténganlos en alta estima, y ámenlos por el trabajo que hacen. Vivan en paz unos con otros. 14Hermanos, también les rogamos que amonesten a los holgazanes, estimulen a los desanimados, ayuden a los débiles y sean pacientes con todos. 15Asegúrense de que nadie pague mal por mal; más bien, esfuércense siempre por hacer el bien, no sólo entre ustedes sino a todos.

16Estén siempre alegres, 17oren sin cesar, 18den gracias a Dios en toda situación, porque esta es su voluntad para ustedes en Cristo Jesús.

19No apaguen el Espíritu, 20no desprecien las profecías, 21sométanlo todo a prueba, aférrense a lo bueno, 22eviten toda clase de mal.

23Que Dios mismo, el Dios de paz, los *santifique por completo, y conserve todo su ser —espíritu, alma y cuerpo— irreprochable para la venida de nuestro Señor Jesucristo. 24El que los llama es fiel, y así lo hará.

25Hermanos, oren también por nosotros. 26Saluden a todos los hermanos con un beso santo. 27Les encargo delante del Señor que lean esta carta a todos los hermanos.

28Que la gracia de nuestro Señor Jesucristo sea con ustedes.

---

g **4:4** *aprenda . . . cuerpo.* Alt. *trate a su esposa,* o *consiga esposa.* h **4:13** *han muerto.* Lit. *duermen;* el mismo verbo en vv. 14 y 15. i **5:10** *en la vida o en la muerte.* Lit. *despiertos o dormidos.*

Segunda Carta a los TESALONICENSES

1 Pablo, *Silvano y Timoteo,

a la iglesia de los tesalonicenses, unida a Dios nuestro Padre y al Señor *Jesucristo:

²Que Dios el Padre y el Señor Jesucristo les concedan gracia y paz.

Acción de gracias y oración

³Hermanos, siempre debemos dar gracias a Dios por ustedes, como es justo, porque su fe se acrecienta cada vez más, y en cada uno de ustedes sigue abundando el amor hacia los otros. ⁴Así que nos sentimos orgullosos de ustedes ante las iglesias de Dios por la perseverancia y la fe que muestran al soportar toda clase de persecuciones y sufrimientos. ⁵Todo esto prueba que el juicio de Dios es justo, y por tanto él los considera dignos de su reino, por el cual están sufriendo.

⁶Dios, que es justo, pagará con sufrimiento a quienes los hacen sufrir a ustedes. ⁷Y a ustedes que sufren, les dará descanso, lo mismo que a nosotros. Esto sucederá cuando el Señor Jesús se manifieste desde el cielo entre llamas de fuego, con sus poderosos ángeles, ⁸para castigar a los que no conocen a Dios ni obedecen el *evangelio de nuestro Señor Jesús. ⁹Ellos sufrirán el castigo de la destrucción eterna, lejos de la presencia del Señor y de la majestad de su poder, ¹⁰el día en que venga para ser glorificado por medio de sus *santos y admirado por todos los que hayan creído, entre los cuales están ustedes porque creyeron el testimonio que les dimos.

¹¹Por eso oramos constantemente por ustedes, para que nuestro Dios los considere dignos del llamamiento que les ha hecho, y por su poder *perfeccione toda disposición al bien y toda obra que realicen por la fe. ¹²Oramos así, de modo que el nombre de nuestro Señor Jesús sea glorificado por medio de ustedes, y ustedes por él, conforme a la gracia de nuestro Dios y del Señor Jesucristo.ᵃ

Manifestación y juicio del malvado

2 Ahora bien, hermanos, en cuanto a la venida de nuestro Señor Jesucristo y a nuestra reunión con él, les pedimos que ²no pierdan la cabeza ni se alarmen por ciertas profecías,ᵇ ni por mensajes orales o escritos supuestamente nuestros, que digan: «¡Ya llegó el día del Señor!» ³No se dejen engañar de ninguna manera, porque primero tiene que llegar la rebelión contra Diosᶜ y manifestarse el hombre de maldad,ᵈ el destructor por naturaleza.ᵉ ⁴Éste se opone y se levanta contra todo lo que lleva el nombre de Dios o es objeto de adoración, hasta el punto de adueñarse del templo de Dios y pretender ser Dios.

⁵¿No recuerdan que ya les hablaba de esto cuando estaba con ustedes? ⁶Bien saben que hay algo que detiene a este hombre, a fin de que él se manifieste a su debido tiempo. ⁷Es cierto que el *misterio de la maldad ya está ejerciendo su poder; pero falta que sea quitado de en medio el que ahora lo detiene. ⁸Entonces se manifestará aquel malvado, a quien el Señor Jesús derrocará con el soplo de su boca, y destruirá con el esplendor de su venida. ⁹El malvado vendrá, por obra de Satanás, con toda clase de mila-

gros, señales y prodigios falsos. ¹⁰Con toda perversidad engañará a los que se pierden por haberse negado a amar la verdad y así ser salvos. ¹¹Por eso Dios permite que, por el poder del engaño, crean en la mentira. ¹²Así serán condenados todos los que no creyeron en la verdad sino que se deleitaron en el mal.

Exhortación a la perseverancia

¹³Nosotros, en cambio, siempre debemos dar gracias a Dios por ustedes, hermanos amados por el Señor, porque desde el principio Dios los escogióᶠ para ser salvos, mediante la obra *santificadora del Espíritu y la fe que tienen en la verdad. ¹⁴Para esto Dios los llamó por nuestro *evangelio, a fin de que tengan parte en la gloria de nuestro Señor Jesucristo. ¹⁵Así que, hermanos, sigan firmes y manténganse fieles a las enseñanzasᵍ que, oralmente o por carta, les hemos transmitido.

¹⁶Que nuestro Señor Jesucristo mismo y Dios nuestro Padre, que nos amó y por su gracia nos dio consuelo eterno y una buena esperanza, ¹⁷los anime y les fortalezca el corazón, para que tanto en palabra como en obra hagan todo lo que sea bueno.

Oración por la difusión del evangelio

3 Por último, hermanos, oren por nosotros para que el mensaje del Señor se difunda rápidamente y se reciba con honor, tal como sucedió entre ustedes. ²Oren además para que seamos librados de personas perversas y malvadas, porque no todos tienen fe. ³Pero el Señor es fiel, y él los fortalecerá y los protegerá del maligno. ⁴Confiamos en el Señor de que ustedes cumplen y seguirán cumpliendo lo que les hemos enseñado. ⁵Que el Señor los lleve a amar como Dios ama, y a perseverar como Cristo perseveró.

Exhortación al trabajo

⁶Hermanos, en el nombre del Señor Jesucristo les ordenamos que se aparten de todo hermano que esté viviendo como un vago y no según las enseñanzas recibidasʰ de nosotros. ⁷Ustedes mismos saben cómo deben seguir nuestro ejemplo. Nosotros no vivimos como ociosos entre ustedes, ⁸ni comimos el pan de nadie sin pagarlo. Al contrario, día y noche trabajamos arduamente y sin descanso para no ser una carga a ninguno de ustedes. ⁹Y lo hicimos así, no porque no tuviéramos derecho a tal ayuda, sino para darles buen ejemplo. ¹⁰Porque incluso cuando estábamos con ustedes, les ordenamos: «El que no quiera trabajar, que tampoco coma.»

¹¹Nos hemos enterado de que entre ustedes hay algunos que andan de vagos, sin trabajar en nada, y que sólo se ocupan de lo que no les importa. ¹²A tales personas les ordenamos y exhortamos en el Señor Jesucristo que tranquilamente se pongan a trabajar para ganarse la vida. ¹³Ustedes, hermanos, no se cansen de hacer el bien.

¹⁴Si alguno no obedece las instrucciones que les damos en esta carta, denúncienlo públicamente y no se relacionen con él, para que se avergüence. ¹⁵Sin embargo, no lo tengan por enemigo, sino amonéstenlo como a hermano.

---

a **1:12** *Dios y del Señor Jesucristo.* Alt. *Dios y Señor, Jesucristo.* b **2:2** *por ciertas profecías.* Lit. *por espíritu.* c **2:3** *la rebelión contra Dios.* Lit. *la apostasía.* d **2:3** *maldad.* Var. *Pecado.* e **2:3** *el destructor por naturaleza.* Alt. *el que está destinado a la destrucción.* Lit. *el hijo de la destrucción.* f **2:13** *desde . . . escogió.* Var. *Dios los escogió como sus *primicias.* g **2:15** *enseñanzas.* Alt. *tradiciones.* h **3:6** *las enseñanzas recibidas.* Alt. *la tradición recibida.*

Saludos finales

16Que el Señor de paz les conceda su paz siempre y en todas las circunstancias. El Señor sea con todos ustedes.

17Yo, Pablo, escribo este saludo de mi puño y letra. Ésta es la señal distintiva de todas mis cartas; así escribo yo.

18Que la gracia de nuestro Señor Jesucristo sea con todos ustedes.

Primera Carta a TIMOTEO

1 Pablo, apóstol de *Cristo Jesús por mandato de Dios nuestro Salvador y de Cristo Jesús nuestra esperanza,

2a Timoteo, mi verdadero hijo en la fe:

Que Dios el Padre y Cristo Jesús nuestro Señor te concedan gracia, misericordia y paz.

Advertencia contra los falsos maestros de la ley

3Al partir para Macedonia, te encargué que permanecieras en Éfeso y les ordenaras a algunos supuestos maestros que dejen de enseñar doctrinas falsas 4y de prestar atención a leyendas y genealogías interminables. Esas cosas provocan controversias en vez de llevar adelante la obra de Dios que es por la fe. 5Debes hacerlo así para que el amor brote de un corazón limpio, de una buena conciencia y de una fe sincera. 6Algunos se han desviado de esa línea de conducta y se han enredado en discusiones inútiles. 7Pretenden ser maestros de la ley, pero en realidad no saben de qué hablan ni entienden lo que con tanta seguridad afirman.

8Ahora bien, sabemos que la ley es buena, si se aplica como es debido. 9Tengamos en cuenta que la ley no se ha instituido para los justos sino para los desobedientes y rebeldes, para los impíos y pecadores, para los irreverentes y profanos. La ley es para los que maltratan a sus propios padres,a para los asesinos, 10para los adúlteros y los homosexuales, para los traficantes de esclavos, los embusteros y los que juran en falso. En fin, la ley es para todo lo que está en contra de la sana doctrina 11enseñada por el glorioso *evangelio que el Dios bendito me ha confiado.

La gracia que el Señor dio a Pablo

12Doy gracias al que me fortalece, Cristo Jesús nuestro Señor, pues me consideró digno de confianza al ponerme a su servicio. 13Anteriormente, yo era un *blasfemo, un perseguidor y un insolente; pero Dios tuvo misericordia de mí porque yo era un incrédulo y actuaba con ignorancia. 14Pero la gracia de nuestro Señor se derramó sobre mí con abundancia, junto con la fe y el amor que hay en Cristo Jesús.

15Este mensaje es digno de crédito y merece ser aceptado por todos: que Cristo Jesús vino al mundo a salvar a los pecadores, de los cuales yo soy el primero. 16Pero precisamente por eso Dios fue misericordioso conmigo, a fin de que en mí, el peor de los pecadores, pudiera Cristo Jesús mostrar su infinita bondad. Así vengo a ser ejemplo para los que, creyendo en él, recibirán la vida eterna. 17Por tanto, al Rey eterno, inmortal, invisible, al único Dios, sea honor y gloria por los siglos de los siglos. Amén.

18Timoteo, hijo mío, te doy este encargo porque tengo en cuenta las profecías que antes se hicieron acerca de ti. Deseo que, apoyado en ellas, pelees la buena batalla 19y mantengas la fe y una buena conciencia. Por no hacerle caso a su conciencia, algunos han naufragado en la fe. 20Entre ellos están Himeneo y Alejandro, a quienes he entregado a Satanás para que aprendan a no blasfemar.

Instrucciones sobre la adoración

2 Así que recomiendo, ante todo, que se hagan plegarias, oraciones, súplicas y acciones de gracias por todos, 2especialmente por los gobernantesb y por todas las autoridades, para que tengamos paz y tranquilidad, y llevemos una vida piadosa y digna. 3Esto es bueno y agradable a Dios nuestro Salvador, 4pues él quiere que todos sean salvos y lleguen a conocer la verdad. 5Porque hay un solo Dios y un solo mediador entre Dios y los hombres, Jesucristo hombre, 6quien dio su vida como rescate por todos. Este testimonio Dios lo ha dado a su debido tiempo, 7y para proclamarlo me nombró heraldo y apóstol. Digo la verdad y no miento: Dios me hizo maestro de los *gentiles para enseñarles la verdadera fe.

8Quiero, pues, que en todas partes los hombres levanten las manos al cielo con pureza de corazón, sin enojos ni contiendas.

9En cuanto a las mujeres, quiero que ellas se vistan decorosamente, con modestia y recato, sin peinados ostentosos, ni oro, ni perlas ni vestidos costosos. 10Que se adornen más bien con buenas obras, como corresponde a mujeres que profesan servir a Dios.

11La mujer debe aprender con serenidad,c con toda sumisión. 12No permito que la mujer enseñe al hombre y ejerza autoridad sobre él; debe mantenerse ecuánime.d 13Porque primero fue formado Adán, y Eva después. 14Además, no fue Adán el engañado, sino la mujer; y ella, una vez engañada, incurrió en pecado. 15Pero la mujer se salvaráe siendo madre y permaneciendo con sensatez en la fe, el amor y la *santidad.

Obispos y diáconos

3 Se dice, y es verdad, que si alguno desea ser *obispo, a noble función aspira. 2Así que el obispo debe ser intachable, esposo de una sola mujer, moderado, sensato, respetable, hospitalario, capaz de enseñar; 3no debe ser borracho ni pendenciero, ni amigo del dinero, sino amable y apacible. 4Debe gobernar bien su casa y hacer que sus hijos le obedezcan con el debido respeto; 5porque el que no sabe gobernar su propia familia, ¿cómo podrá cuidar de la iglesia de Dios? 6No debe ser un recién convertido, no sea que se vuelva presuntuoso y caiga en la misma condenación en que cayó el diablo. 7Se requiere además que hablen bien de él los que no pertenecen a la iglesia,f para que no caiga en descrédito y en la trampa del diablo.

8Los diáconos, igualmente, deben ser honorables, sinceros, no amigos del mucho vino ni codiciosos de las ganancias mal habidas. 9Deben guardar, con una conciencia limpia, las grandes verdadesg de la fe. 10Que primero sean puestos a prueba, y después, si no hay nada que reprocharles, que sirvan como diáconos.

11Así mismo, las esposas de los diáconosh deben ser honorables, no calumniadoras sino moderadas y dignas de toda confianza.

12El diácono debe ser esposo de una sola mujer y gobernar bien a sus hijos y su propia casa. 13Los que ejercen bien el diaconado se ganan un lugar de

---

a 1:9 *los que maltratan a sus propios padres.* Lit. *los parricidas y matricidas.* b 2:2 *gobernantes.* Lit. *reyes.* c 2:11 *con serenidad.* Alt. *en silencio.* d 2:12 *debe mantenerse ecuánime.* Alt. *debe guardar silencio.* e 2:15 *se salvará.* Alt. *será restaurada.* f 3:7 *hablen . . . iglesia.* Lit. *tenga buen testimonio de los de afuera.* g 3:9 *las grandes verdades.* Lit. *el *misterio.* h 3:11 *las esposas de los diáconos.* Alt. *las diaconisas.*

honor y adquieren mayor confianza para hablar de su fe en Cristo Jesús.

14Aunque espero ir pronto a verte, escribo estas instrucciones para que, 15si me retraso, sepas cómo hay que portarse en la casa de Dios, que es la iglesia del Dios viviente, columna y fundamento de la verdad. 16No hay duda de que es grande el *misterio de nuestra fe:i

Éli se manifestó como hombre;k
fue vindicado porl el Espíritu,
visto por los ángeles,
proclamado entre las *naciones,
creído en el mundo,
recibido en la gloria.

Instrucciones a Timoteo

4 El Espíritu dice claramente que, en los últimos tiempos, algunos abandonarán la fe para seguir a inspiraciones engañosas y doctrinas diabólicas. 2Tales enseñanzas provienen de embusteros hipócritas, que tienen la conciencia encallecida.m 3Prohíben el matrimonio y no permiten comer ciertos alimentos que Dios ha creado para que los creyentes,n conocedores de la verdad, los coman con acción de gracias. 4Todo lo que Dios ha creado es bueno, y nada es despreciable si se recibe con acción de gracias, 5porque la palabra de Dios y la oración lo *santifican.

6Si enseñas estas cosas a los hermanos, serás un buen servidor de Cristo Jesús, nutrido con las verdades de la fe y de la buena enseñanza que paso a paso has seguido. 7Rechaza las leyendas profanas y otros mitos semejantes.ñ Más bien, ejercítate en la piedad, 8pues aunque el ejercicio físico trae algún provecho, la piedad es útil para todo, ya que incluye una promesa no sólo para la vida presente sino también para la venidera. 9Este mensaje es digno de crédito y merece ser aceptado por todos. 10En efecto, si trabajamos y nos esforzamos es porque hemos puesto nuestra esperanza en el Dios viviente, que es el Salvador de todos, especialmente de los que creen.

11Encarga y enseña estas cosas. 12Que nadie te menosprecie por ser joven. Al contrario, que los creyentes vean en ti un ejemplo a seguir en la manera de hablar, en la conducta, y en amor, fe y pureza. 13En tanto que llego, dedícate a la lectura pública de las Escrituras, y a enseñar y animar a los hermanos. 14Ejercita el don que recibiste mediante profecía, cuando los *ancianos te impusieron las manos.

15Sé diligente en estos asuntos; entrégate de lleno a ellos, de modo que todos puedan ver que estás progresando. 16Ten cuidado de tu conducta y de tu enseñanza. Persevera en todo ello, porque así te salvarás a ti mismo y a los que te escuchen.

Cómo tratar a viudas, ancianos y esclavos

5 No reprendas con dureza al anciano, sino aconséjalo como si fuera tu padre. Trata a los jóvenes como a hermanos; 2a las ancianas, como a madres; a las jóvenes, como a hermanas, con toda pureza.

3Reconoce debidamente a las viudas que de veras están desamparadas. 4Pero si una viuda tiene hijos o nietos, que éstos aprendan primero a cumplir sus obligaciones con su propia familia y correspondan así a sus padres y abuelos, porque eso agrada a

Dios. 5La viuda desamparada, como ha quedado sola, pone su esperanza en Dios y persevera noche y día en sus oraciones y súplicas. 6En cambio, la viuda que se entrega al placer ya está muerta en vida. 7Encárgales estas cosas para que sean intachables. 8El que no provee para los suyos, y sobre todo para los de su propia casa, ha negado la fe y es peor que un incrédulo.

9En la lista de las viudas debe figurar únicamente la que tenga más de sesenta años, que haya sido fiel a su esposo,o 10y que sea reconocida por sus buenas obras, tales como criar hijos, practicar la hospitalidad, lavar los pies de los *creyentes, ayudar a los que sufren y aprovechar toda oportunidad para hacer el bien.

11No incluyas en esa lista a las viudas más jóvenes, porque cuando sus pasiones las alejan de Cristo, les da por casarse. 12Así resultan culpables de faltar a su primer compromiso. 13Además se acostumbran a estar ociosas y andar de casa en casa. Y no sólo se vuelven holgazanas sino también chismosas y entrometidas, hablando de lo que no deben. 14Por eso exhorto a las viudas jóvenes a que se casen y tengan hijos, y a que lleven bien su hogar y no den lugar a las críticas del enemigo. 15Y es que algunas ya se han descarriado para seguir a Satanás.

16Si alguna creyente tiene viudas en su familia, debe ayudarlas para que no sean una carga a la iglesia; así la iglesia podrá atender a las viudas desamparadas.

17Los *ancianos que dirigen bien los asuntos de la iglesia son dignos de doble honor,p especialmente los que dedican sus esfuerzos a la predicación y a la enseñanza. 18Pues la Escritura dice: «No le pongas bozal al buey mientras esté trillando»,q y «El trabajador merece que se le pague su salario».r 19No admitas ninguna acusación contra un anciano, a no ser que esté respaldada por dos o tres testigos. 20A los que pecan, repréndelos en público para que sirva de escarmiento.

21Te insto delante de Dios, de Cristo Jesús y de los santos ángeles, a que sigas estas instrucciones sin dejarte llevar de prejuicios ni favoritismos.

22No te apresures a imponerle las manos a nadie, no sea que te hagas cómplice de pecados ajenos. Consérvate puro.

23No sigas bebiendo sólo agua; toma también un poco de vino a causa de tu mal de estómago y tus frecuentes enfermedades.

24Los pecados de algunos son evidentes aun antes de ser investigados, mientras que los pecados de otros se descubren después. 25De igual manera son evidentes las buenas obras, y aunque estén ocultas, tarde o temprano se manifestarán.s

6 Todos los que aún son esclavos deben reconocer que sus amos merecen todo respeto; así evitarán que se hable mal del nombre de Dios y de nuestra enseñanza. 2Los que tienen amos creyentes no deben faltarles al respeto por ser hermanos. Al contrario, deben servirles todavía mejor, porque los que se benefician de sus servicios son creyentes y hermanos queridos. Esto es lo que debes enseñar y recomendar.

El amor al dinero

3Si alguien enseña falsas doctrinas, apartándose de la sana enseñanza de nuestro Señor Jesucristo y de la doctrina que se ciñe a la verdadera religión,t

---

i **3:16** de nuestra fe. Lit. de la piedad. j **3:16** Él. Lit. Quien. Var. Dios. k **3:16** como hombre. Lit. en la *carne. l **3:16** vindicado por. Lit. justificado en. m **4:2** encallecida. Lit. Cauterizada. n **4:3** creyentes. Alt. Fieles. ñ **4:7** Rechaza . . . semejantes. Lit. Rechaza los mitos profanos y de viejas. o **5:9** que haya sido fiel a su esposo. Alt. que no haya tenido más de un esposo. p **5:17** honor. Alt. Honorario. q **5:18** Dt 25:4 r **5:18** Lc 10:7 s **5:25** y aunque . . . se manifestarán. Alt. y si son malas, no podrán quedar ocultas. t **6:3** la verdadera religión. Lit. la piedad; también en vv. 5 y 6.

⁴es un obstinado que nada entiende. Ese tal padece del afán enfermizo de provocar discusiones inútiles que generan envidias, discordias, insultos, suspicacias ⁵y altercados entre personas de mente depravada, carentes de la verdad. Éste es de los que piensan que la religión es un medio de obtener ganancias. ⁶Es cierto que con la verdadera religión se obtienen grandes ganancias, pero sólo si uno está satisfecho con lo que tiene. ⁷Porque nada trajimos a este mundo, y nada podemos llevarnos. ⁸Así que, si tenemos ropa y comida, contentémonos con eso. ⁹Los que quieren enriquecerse caen en la *tentación y se vuelven esclavos de sus muchos deseos. Estos afanes insensatos y dañinos hunden a la gente en la ruina y en la destrucción. ¹⁰Porque el amor al dinero es la raíz de toda clase de males. Por codiciarlo, algunos se han desviado de la fe y se han causado muchísimos sinsabores.

Encargo de Pablo a Timoteo

¹¹Tú, en cambio, hombre de Dios, huye de todo eso, y esmérate en seguir la justicia, la piedad, la fe, el amor, la constancia y la humildad. ¹²Pelea la buena batalla de la fe; haz tuya la vida eterna, a la que fuiste llamado y por la cual hiciste aquella admirable declaración de fe delante de muchos testigos. ¹³Teniendo a Dios por testigo, el cual da vida a todas las cosas, y a Cristo Jesús, que dio su admirable testimonio delante de Poncio Pilato, te encargo ¹⁴que guardes este mandato sin mancha ni reproche hasta la venida de nuestro Señor Jesucristo, ¹⁵la cual Dios a su debido tiempo hará que se cumpla.

Al único y bendito Soberano,
    Rey de reyes y Señor de señores,
¹⁶al único inmortal,
    que vive en luz inaccesible,
    a quien nadie ha visto ni puede ver,
a él sea el honor y el poder eternamente.
    Amén.

¹⁷A los ricos de este mundo, mándales que no sean arrogantes ni pongan su esperanza en las riquezas, que son tan inseguras, sino en Dios, que nos provee de todo en abundancia para que lo disfrutemos. ¹⁸Mándales que hagan el bien, que sean ricos en buenas obras, y generosos, dispuestos a compartir lo que tienen. ¹⁹De este modo atesorarán para sí un seguro caudal para el futuro y obtendrán la vida verdadera.

²⁰Timoteo, ¡cuida bien lo que se te ha confiado! Evita las discusiones profanas e inútiles, y los argumentos de la falsa ciencia. ²¹Algunos, por abrazarla, se han desviado de la fe.

Que la gracia sea con ustedes.

Segunda Carta a TIMOTEO

1 Pablo, apóstol de *Cristo Jesús por la voluntad de Dios, según la promesa de vida que tenemos en Cristo Jesús,

2a mi querido hijo Timoteo:

Que Dios el Padre y Cristo Jesús nuestro Señor te concedan gracia, misericordia y paz.

Exhortación a la fidelidad

3Al recordarte de día y de noche en mis oraciones, siempre doy gracias a Dios, a quien sirvo con una conciencia limpia como lo hicieron mis antepasados. 4Y al acordarme de tus lágrimas, anhelo verte para llenarme de alegría. 5Traigo a la memoria tu fe sincera, la cual animó primero a tu abuela Loida y a tu madre Eunice, y ahora te anima a ti. De eso estoy convencido. 6Por eso te recomiendo que avives la llama del don de Dios que recibiste cuando te impuse las manos. 7Pues Dios no nos ha dado un espíritu de timidez, sino de poder, de amor y de dominio propio.

8Así que no te avergüences de dar testimonio de nuestro Señor, ni tampoco de mí, que por su causa soy prisionero. Al contrario, tú también, con el poder de Dios, debes soportar sufrimientos por el *evangelio. 9Pues Dios nos salvó y nos llamó a una vida *santa, no por nuestras propias obras, sino por su propia determinación y gracia. Nos concedió este favor en Cristo Jesús antes del comienzo del tiempo; 10y ahora lo ha revelado con la venida de nuestro Salvador Cristo Jesús, quien destruyó la muerte y sacó a la luz la vida incorruptible mediante el evangelio. 11De este evangelio he sido yo designado heraldo, apóstol y maestro. 12Por ese motivo padezco estos sufrimientos. Pero no me avergüenzo, porque sé en quién he creído, y estoy seguro de que tiene poder para guardar hasta aquel día lo que le he confiado.a

13Con fe y amor en Cristo Jesús, sigue el ejemplo de la sana doctrina que de mí aprendiste. 14Con el poder del Espíritu Santo que vive en nosotros, cuida la preciosa enseñanzab que se te ha confiado.

15Ya sabes que todos los de la provincia de *Asia me han abandonado, incluso Figelo y Hermógenes.

16Que el Señor le conceda misericordia a la familia de Onesíforo, porque muchas veces me dio ánimo y no se avergonzó de mis cadenas. 17Al contrario, cuando estuvo en Roma me buscó sin descanso hasta encontrarme. 18Que el Señor le conceda hallar misericordia divina en aquel día. Tú conoces muy bien los muchos servicios que me prestó en Éfeso.

2 Así que tú, hijo mío, fortalécete por la gracia que tenemos en Cristo Jesús. 2Lo que me has oído decir en presencia de muchos testigos, encomiéndalo a creyentes dignos de confianza, que a su vez estén capacitados para enseñar a otros. 3Comparte nuestros sufrimientos, como buen soldado de Cristo Jesús. 4Ningún soldado que quiera agradar a su superior se enreda en cuestiones civiles. 5Así mismo, el atleta no recibe la corona de vencedor si no compite según el reglamento. 6El labrador que trabaja duro tiene derecho a recibir primero parte de la cosecha. 7Reflexiona en lo que te digo, y el Señor te dará una mayor comprensión de todo esto.

8No dejes de recordar a Jesucristo, descendiente de David, *levantado de entre los muertos. Este es mi *evangelio, 9por el que sufro al extremo de llevar

cadenas como un criminal. Pero la palabra de Dios no está encadenada. 10Así que todo lo soporto por el bien de los elegidos, para que también ellos alcancen la gloriosa y eterna salvación que tenemos en Cristo Jesús.

11Este mensaje es digno de crédito:

Si morimos con él,
    también viviremos con él;
12si resistimos,
    también reinaremos con él.
Si lo negamos,
    también él nos negará;
13si somos infieles,
    él sigue siendo fiel,
    ya que no puede negarse a sí mismo.

Un obrero aprobado por Dios

14No dejes de recordarles esto. Adviérteles delante de Dios que eviten las discusiones inútiles, pues no sirven nada más que para destruir a los oyentes. 15Esfuérzate por presentarte a Dios aprobado, como obrero que no tiene de qué avergonzarse y que interpreta rectamente la palabra de verdad. 16Evita las palabrerías profanas, porque los que se dan a ellas se alejan cada vez más de la vida piadosa, 17y sus enseñanzas se extienden como gangrena. Entre ellos están Himeneo y Fileto, 18que se han desviado de la verdad. Andan diciendo que la resurrección ya tuvo lugar, y así trastornan la fe de algunos. 19A pesar de todo, el fundamento de Dios es sólido y se mantiene firme, pues está sellado con esta inscripción: «El Señor conoce a los suyos»,c y esta otra: «Que se aparte de la maldad todo el que invoca el nombre del Señor».d

20En una casa grande no sólo hay vasos de oro y de plata sino también de madera y de barro, unos para los usos más nobles y otros para los usos más bajos. 21Si alguien se mantiene limpio, llegará a ser un vaso noble, *santificado, útil para el Señor y preparado para toda obra buena.

22Huye de las malas pasiones de la juventud, y esmérate en seguir la justicia, la fe, el amor y la paz, junto con los que invocan al Señor con un corazón limpio. 23No tengas nada que ver con discusiones necias y sin sentido, pues ya sabes que terminan en pleitos. 24Y un *siervo del Señor no debe andar peleando; más bien, debe ser amable con todos, capaz de enseñar y no propenso a irritarse. 25Así, humildemente, debe corregir a los adversarios, con la esperanza de que Dios les conceda el *arrepentimiento para conocer la verdad, 26de modo que se despierten y escapen de la trampa en que el diablo los tiene cautivos, sumisos a su voluntad.

La impiedad en los últimos días

3 Ahora bien, ten en cuenta que en los últimos días vendrán tiempos difíciles. 2La gente estará llena de egoísmo y avaricia; serán jactanciosos, arrogantes, *blasfemos, desobedientes a los padres, ingratos, impíos, 3insensibles, implacables, calumniadores, libertinos, despiadados, enemigos de todo lo bueno, 4traicioneros, impetuosos, vanidosos y más amigos del placer que de Dios. 5Aparentarán ser piadosos, pero su conducta desmentirá el poder de la piedad. ¡Con esa gente ni te metas!

a **1:12** *lo que le he confiado.* Alt. *lo que me ha confiado.* b **1:14** *la preciosa enseñanza.* Lit. *el buen depósito.* c **2:19** Nm 16:5, según LXX d **2:19** Véanse Nm 16:26 y Jl 3:5

⁶Así son los que van de casa en casa cautivando a mujeres débiles cargadas de pecados, que se dejan llevar de toda clase de pasiones. ⁷Ellas siempre están aprendiendo, pero nunca logran conocer la verdad. ⁸Del mismo modo que Janes y Jambres se opusieron a Moisés, también esa gente se opone a la verdad. Son personas de mente depravada, reprobadas en la fe. ⁹Pero no llegarán muy lejos, porque todo el mundo se dará cuenta de su insensatez, como pasó con aquellos dos.

Encargo de Pablo a Timoteo

¹⁰Tú, en cambio, has seguido paso a paso mis enseñanzas, mi manera de vivir, mi propósito, mi fe, mi paciencia, mi amor, mi constancia, ¹¹mis persecuciones y mis sufrimientos. Estás enterado de lo que sufrí en Antioquía, Iconio y Listra, y de las persecuciones que soporté. Y de todas ellas me libró el Señor. ¹²Así mismo serán perseguidos todos los que quieran llevar una vida piadosa en Cristo Jesús, ¹³mientras que esos malvados embaucadores irán de mal en peor, engañando y siendo engañados. ¹⁴Pero tú, permanece firme en lo que has aprendido y de lo cual estás convencido, pues sabes de quiénes lo aprendiste. ¹⁵Desde tu niñez conoces las Sagradas Escrituras, que pueden darte la sabiduría necesaria para la salvación mediante la fe en Cristo Jesús. ¹⁶Toda la Escritura es inspirada por Dios y útil para enseñar, para reprender, para corregir y para instruir en la justicia, ¹⁷a fin de que el siervo de Dios esté enteramente capacitado para toda buena obra.

4 En presencia de Dios y de Cristo Jesús, que ha de venir en su reino y que juzgará a los vivos y a los muertos, te doy este solemne encargo: ²Predica la Palabra; persiste en hacerlo, sea o no sea oportuno; corrige, reprende y anima con mucha paciencia, sin dejar de enseñar. ³Porque llegará el tiempo en que no van a tolerar la sana doctrina, sino que, llevados de sus propios deseos, se rodearán de maestros que les digan las novelerías que quieren oír. ⁴Dejarán de escuchar la verdad y se volverán a los mitos. ⁵Tú, por el contrario, sé prudente en todas las circunstancias,

soporta los sufrimientos, dedícate a la evangelización; cumple con los deberes de tu ministerio.

⁶Yo, por mi parte, ya estoy a punto de ser ofrecido como un sacrificio, y el tiempo de mi partida ha llegado. ⁷He peleado la buena batalla, he terminado la carrera, me he mantenido en la fe. ⁸Por lo demás me espera la corona de justicia que el Señor, el juez justo, me otorgará en aquel día; y no sólo a mí, sino también a todos los que con amor hayan esperado su venida.

Instrucciones personales

⁹Haz todo lo posible por venir a verme cuanto antes, ¹⁰pues Demas, por amor a este mundo, me ha abandonado y se ha ido a Tesalónica. Crescente se ha ido a Galacia y Tito a Dalmacia. ¹¹Sólo Lucas está conmigo. Recoge a Marcos y tráelo contigo, porque me es de ayuda en mi ministerio. ¹²A Tíquico lo mandé a Éfeso. ¹³Cuando vengas, trae la capa que dejé en Troas, en casa de Carpo; trae también los libros, especialmente los pergaminos.

¹⁴Alejandro el herrero me ha hecho mucho daño. El Señor le dará su merecido. ¹⁵Tú también cuídate de él, porque se opuso tenazmente a nuestro mensaje.

¹⁶En mi primera defensa, nadie me respaldó, sino que todos me abandonaron. Que no les sea tomado en cuenta. ¹⁷Pero el Señor estuvo a mi lado y me dio fuerzas para que por medio de mí se llevara a cabo la predicación del mensaje y lo oyeran todos los *paganos. Y fui librado de la boca del león. ¹⁸El Señor me librará de todo mal y me preservará para su reino celestial. A él sea la gloria por los siglos de los siglos. Amén.

Saludos finales

¹⁹Saludos a *Priscila y a Aquila, y a la familia de Onesíforo. ²⁰Erasto se quedó en Corinto; a Trófimo lo dejé enfermo en Mileto. ²¹Haz todo lo posible por venir antes del invierno. Te mandan saludos Eubulo, Pudente, Lino, Claudia y todos los hermanos. ²²El Señor esté con tu espíritu. Que la gracia sea con ustedes.

Carta a TITO

1 Pablo, *siervo de Dios y apóstol de Jesucristo, llamado para que, mediante la fe, los elegidos de Dios lleguen a conocer la verdadera religión.a 2Nuestra esperanza es la vida eterna, la cual Dios, que no miente, ya había prometido antes de la creación. 3Ahora, a su debido tiempo, él ha cumplido esta promesa mediante la predicación que se me ha confiado por orden de Dios nuestro Salvador.

4A Tito, mi verdadero hijo en esta fe que compartimos:

Que Dios el Padre y Cristo Jesús nuestro Salvador te concedan gracia y paz.

Tarea de Tito en Creta

5Te dejé en Creta para que pusieras en orden lo que quedaba por hacer y en cada pueblo nombrarasb *ancianos de la iglesia, de acuerdo con las instrucciones que te di. 6El anciano debe ser intachable, esposo de una sola mujer; sus hijos deben ser creyentes,c libres de sospecha de libertinaje o de desobediencia. 7El *obispo tiene a su cargo la obra de Dios, y por lo tanto debe ser intachable: no arrogante, ni iracundo, ni borracho, ni violento, ni codicioso de ganancias mal habidas. 8Al contrario, debe ser hospitalario, amigo del bien, sensato, justo, santo y disciplinado. 9Debe apegarse a la palabra fiel, según la enseñanza que recibió, de modo que también pueda exhortar a otros con la sana doctrina y refutar a los que se opongan.

10Y es que hay muchos rebeldes, charlatanes y engañadores, especialmente los partidarios de la *circuncisión. 11A ésos hay que taparles la boca, ya que están arruinando familias enteras al enseñar lo que no se debe; y lo hacen para obtener ganancias mal habidas. 12Fue precisamente uno de sus propios profetas el que dijo: «Los cretenses son siempre mentirosos, malas bestias, glotones perezosos.» 13¡Y es la verdad! Por eso, repréndelos con severidad a fin de que sean sanos en la fe 14y no hagan caso de leyendas judías ni de lo que exigen esos que rechazan la verdad. 15Para los puros todo es puro, pero para los corruptos e incrédulos no hay nada puro. Al contrario, tienen corrompidas la mente y la conciencia. 16Profesan conocer a Dios, pero con sus acciones lo niegan; son abominables, desobedientes e incapaces de hacer nada bueno.

Lo que se debe enseñar

2 Tú, en cambio, predica lo que va de acuerdo con la sana doctrina. 2A los *ancianos, enséñales que sean moderados, respetables, sensatos, e íntegros en la fe, en el amor y en la constancia.

3A las ancianas, enséñales que sean reverentes en su conducta, y no calumniadoras ni adictas al mucho vino. Deben enseñar lo bueno 4y aconsejar a las jóvenes a amar a sus esposos y a sus hijos, 5a ser sensatas y puras, cuidadosas del hogar, bondadosas y sumisas a sus esposos, para que no se hable mal de la palabra de Dios.

6A los jóvenes, exhórtalos a ser sensatos. 7Con tus buenas obras, dales tú mismo ejemplo en todo. Cuando enseñes, hazlo con integridad y seriedad, 8y con un mensaje sano e intachable. Así se avergonzará cualquiera que se oponga, pues no podrá decir nada malo de nosotros.

9Enseña a los *esclavos a someterse en todo a sus amos, a procurar agradarles y a no ser respondones. 10No deben robarles sino demostrar que son dignos de toda confianza, para que en todo hagan honor a la enseñanza de Dios nuestro Salvador.

11En verdad, Dios ha manifestado a toda la *humanidad su gracia, la cual trae salvación 12y nos enseña a rechazar la impiedad y las pasiones mundanas. Así podremos vivir en este mundo con justicia, piedad y dominio propio, 13mientras aguardamos la bendita esperanza, es decir, la gloriosa venida de nuestro gran Dios y Salvador Jesucristo. 14Él se entregó por nosotros para rescatarnos de toda maldad y purificar para sí un pueblo elegido, dedicado a hacer el bien.

15Esto es lo que debes enseñar. Exhorta y reprende con toda autoridad. Que nadie te menosprecie.

La conducta del creyente

3 Recuérdales a todos que deben mostrarse obedientes y sumisos ante los gobernantes y las autoridades. Siempre deben estar dispuestos a hacer lo bueno: 2a no hablar mal de nadie, sino a buscar la paz y ser respetuosos, demostrando plena humildad en su trato con todo el mundo.

3En otro tiempo también nosotros éramos necios y desobedientes. Estábamos descarriados y éramos esclavos de todo género de pasiones y placeres. Vivíamos en la malicia y en la envidia. Éramos detestables y nos odiábamos unos a otros. 4Pero cuando se manifestaron la bondad y el amor de Dios nuestro Salvador, 5él nos salvó, no por nuestras propias obras de justicia sino por su misericordia. Nos salvó mediante el lavamiento de la regeneración y de la renovación por el Espíritu Santo, 6el cual fue derramado abundantemente sobre nosotros por medio de Jesucristo nuestro Salvador. 7Así lo hizo para que, *justificados por su gracia, llegáramos a ser herederos que abrigan la esperanza de recibir la vida eterna. 8Este mensaje es digno de confianza, y quiero que lo recalques, para que los que han creído en Dios se empeñen en hacer buenas obras. Esto es excelente y provechoso para todos.

9Evita las necias controversias y genealogías, las discusiones y peleas sobre la ley, porque carecen de provecho y de sentido. 10Al que cause divisiones, amonéstalo dos veces, y después evítalo. 11Puedes estar seguro de que tal individuo se condena a sí mismo por ser un perverso pecador.

Instrucciones personales y saludos finales

12Tan pronto como te haya enviado a Artemas o a Tíquico, haz todo lo posible por ir a Nicópolis a verme, pues he decidido pasar allí el invierno. 13Ayuda en todo lo que puedas al abogado Zenas y a Apolos, de modo que no les falte nada para su viaje. 14Que aprendan los nuestros a empeñarse en hacer buenas obras, a fin de que atiendan a lo que es realmente necesario y no lleven una vida inútil.

15Saludos de parte de todos los que me acompañan. Saludos a los que nos aman en la fe.

Que la gracia sea con todos ustedes.

---

a 1:1 *la verdadera religión.* Lit. *la verdad que es según la piedad.*   b 1:5 *nombraras.* Alt. *Ordenaras.*   c 1:6 *creyentes.* Alt. *fieles.*

Carta a FILEMÓN

1Pablo, prisionero de *Cristo Jesús, y el hermano Timoteo,

a ti, querido Filemón, compañero de trabajo, 2a la hermana Apia, a Arquipo nuestro compañero de lucha, y a la iglesia que se reúne en tu casa:

3Que Dios nuestro Padre y el Señor Jesucristo les concedan gracia y paz.

Acción de gracias y petición

4Siempre doy gracias a mi Dios al recordarte en mis oraciones, 5porque tengo noticias de tu amor y tu *fidelidad hacia el Señor Jesús y hacia todos los creyentes. 6Pido a Dios que el compañerismo que brota de tu fe sea eficaz para la causa de Cristo mediante el reconocimiento de todo lo bueno que compartimos. 7Hermano, tu amor me ha alegrado y animado mucho porque has reconfortado el corazón de los *santos.

Intercesión de Pablo por Onésimo

8Por eso, aunque en Cristo tengo la franqueza suficiente para ordenarte lo que debes hacer, 9prefiero rogártelo en nombre del amor. Yo, Pablo, ya anciano y ahora, además, prisionero de Cristo Jesús, 10te suplico por mi hijo Onésimo,a quien llegó a ser hijo mío mientras yo estaba preso. 11En otro tiempo te era inútil, pero ahora nos es útil tanto a ti como a mí.

12Te lo envío de vuelta, y con él va mi propio corazón. 13Yo hubiera querido retenerlo para que me sirviera en tu lugar mientras estoy preso por causa del *evangelio. 14Sin embargo, no he querido hacer nada sin tu consentimiento, para que tu favor no sea por obligación sino espontáneo. 15Tal vez por eso Onésimo se alejó de ti por algún tiempo, para que ahora lo recibas para siempre, 16ya no como a esclavo, sino como algo mejor: como a un hermano querido, muy especial para mí, pero mucho más para ti, como persona y como hermano en el Señor.

17De modo que, si me tienes por compañero, recíbelo como a mí mismo. 18Si te ha perjudicado o te debe algo, cárgalo a mi cuenta. 19Yo, Pablo, lo escribo de mi puño y letra: te lo pagaré; por no decirte que tú mismo me debes lo que eres. 20Sí, hermano, ¡que reciba yo de ti algún beneficio en el Señor! Reconforta mi corazón en Cristo. 21Te escribo confiado en tu obediencia, seguro de que harás aun más de lo que te pido.

22Además de eso, prepárame alojamiento, porque espero que Dios les conceda el tenerme otra vez con ustedes en respuesta a sus oraciones.

23Te mandan saludos Epafras, mi compañero de cárcel en Cristo Jesús, 24y también Marcos, Aristarco, Demas y Lucas, mis compañeros de trabajo.

25Que la gracia del Señor Jesucristo sea con su espíritu.

---

a 10 *Onésimo* significa *útil*.

Carta a los HEBREOS

El Hijo, superior a los ángeles

1 Dios, que muchas veces y de varias maneras habló a nuestros antepasados en otras épocas por medio de los profetas, [2]en estos días finales nos ha hablado por medio de su Hijo. A éste lo designó heredero de todo, y por medio de él hizo el universo. [3]El Hijo es el resplandor de la gloria de Dios, la fiel imagen de lo que él es, y el que sostiene todas las cosas con su palabra poderosa. Después de llevar a cabo la purificación de los pecados, se sentó a la *derecha de la Majestad en las alturas. [4]Así llegó a ser superior a los ángeles en la misma medida en que el nombre que ha heredado supera en excelencia al de ellos.

[5]Porque, ¿a cuál de los ángeles dijo Dios jamás:

«Tú eres mi hijo;
hoy mismo te he engendrado»;[a]

y en otro pasaje:

«Yo seré su padre,
y él será mi hijo»?[b]

[6]Además, al introducir a su Primogénito en el mundo, Dios dice:

«Que lo adoren todos los ángeles de Dios.»[c]

[7]En cuanto a los ángeles dice:

«Él hace de los vientos sus ángeles,
y de las llamas de fuego sus servidores.»[d]

[8]Pero con respecto al Hijo dice:

«Tu trono, oh Dios, permanece por los siglos
de los siglos,
y el cetro de tu reino es un cetro de justicia.
[9]Has amado la justicia y odiado la maldad;
por eso Dios, tu Dios, te ha ungido con
aceite de alegría,
exaltándote por encima de tus
compañeros.»[e]

[10]También dice:

«En el principio, oh Señor, tú afirmaste la tierra,
y los cielos son la obra de tus manos.
[11]Ellos perecerán, pero tú permaneces para
siempre.
Todos ellos se desgastarán como un vestido.
[12]Los doblarás como un manto,
y cambiarán como ropa que se muda;
pero tú eres siempre el mismo,
y tus años no tienen fin.»[f]

[13]¿A cuál de los ángeles dijo Dios jamás:

«Siéntate a mi derecha,
hasta que ponga a tus enemigos
por estrado de tus pies»?[g]

[14]¿No son todos los ángeles espíritus dedicados al servicio divino, enviados para ayudar a los que han de heredar la salvación?

Advertencia a prestar atención

2 Por eso es necesario que prestemos más atención a lo que hemos oído, no sea que perdamos el rumbo. [2]Porque si el mensaje anunciado por los ángeles tuvo validez, y toda transgresión y desobediencia recibió su justo castigo, [3]¿cómo escaparemos nosotros si descuidamos una salvación tan grande? Esta salvación fue anunciada primeramente por el Señor, y los que la oyeron nos la confirmaron. [4]A la vez, Dios ratificó su testimonio acerca de ella con señales, prodigios, diversos milagros y dones distribuidos por el Espíritu Santo según su voluntad.

Jesús, hecho igual a sus hermanos

[5]Dios no puso bajo el dominio de los ángeles el mundo venidero del que estamos hablando. [6]Como alguien ha atestiguado en algún lugar:

«¿Qué es el hombre, para que en él pienses?
¿Qué es el *ser humano,[h] para que lo
tomes en cuenta?
[7]Lo hiciste un poco[i] menor que los ángeles,
y lo coronaste de gloria y de honra;
[8]¡todo lo sometiste a su dominio!»[j]

Si Dios puso bajo él todas las cosas, entonces no hay nada que no le esté sujeto. Ahora bien, es cierto que todavía no vemos que todo le esté sujeto. [9]Sin embargo, vemos a Jesús, que fue hecho un poco inferior a los ángeles, coronado de gloria y honra por haber padecido la muerte. Así, por la gracia de Dios, la muerte que él sufrió resulta en beneficio de todos.

[10]En efecto, a fin de llevar a muchos hijos a la gloria, convenía que Dios, para quien y por medio de quien todo existe, *perfeccionara mediante el sufrimiento al autor de la salvación de ellos. [11]Tanto el que *santifica como los que son santificados tienen un mismo origen, por lo cual Jesús no se avergüenza de llamarlos hermanos, [12]cuando dice:

«Proclamaré tu nombre a mis hermanos;
en medio de la congregación te alabaré.»[k]

[13]En otra parte dice:

«Yo confiaré en él.»[l]

Y añade:

«Aquí me tienen, con los hijos que Dios me ha
dado.»[m]

[14]Por tanto, ya que ellos son de carne y hueso,[n] él también compartió esa naturaleza humana para anular, mediante la muerte, al que tiene el dominio de la muerte —es decir, al diablo—, [15]y librar a todos los que por temor a la muerte estaban sometidos a esclavitud durante toda la vida. [16]Pues, ciertamente, no vino en auxilio de los ángeles sino de los descendientes de Abraham. [17]Por eso era preciso que en todo se asemejara a sus hermanos, para ser un sumo sacerdote fiel y misericordioso al servicio de Dios, a fin de *expiar[ñ] los pecados del pueblo. [18]Por haber sufrido él mismo la *tentación, puede socorrer a los que son tentados.

a **1:5** Sal 2:7 b **1:5** 2 S 7:14; 1 Cr 17:13 c **1:6** Dt 32:43 (según Qumrán y LXX). d **1:7** Sal 104:4 e **1:9** Sal 45:6,7 f **1:12** Sal 102:25-27 g **1:13** Sal 110:1 h **2:6** el *ser humano. Lit. o hijo de hombre. i **2:7** un poco. Alt. por un poco de tiempo; también en v. 9. j **2:8** Sal 8:4-6 k **2:12** Sal 22:22 l **2:13** Is 8:17 m **2:13** Is 8:18 n **2:14** carne y hueso. Lit. sangre y carne. ñ **2:17** expiar. Lit. hacer propiciación por.

Jesús, superior a Moisés

3 Por lo tanto, hermanos, ustedes que han sido *santificados y que tienen parte en el mismo llamamiento celestial, consideren a Jesús, apóstol y sumo sacerdote de la fe que profesamos. ²Él fue fiel al que lo nombró, como lo fue también Moisés en toda la casa de Dios. ³De hecho, Jesús ha sido estimado digno de mayor honor que Moisés, así como el constructor de una casa recibe mayor honor que la casa misma. ⁴Porque toda casa tiene su constructor, pero el constructor de todo es Dios. ⁵Moisés fue fiel como siervo en toda la casa de Dios, para dar testimonio de lo que Dios diría en el futuro. ⁶*Cristo, en cambio, es fiel como Hijo al frente de la casa de Dios. Y esa casa somos nosotros, con tal que mantengamos° nuestra confianza y la esperanza que nos *enorgullece.

Advertencia contra la incredulidad

⁷Por eso, como dice el Espíritu Santo:

«Si ustedes oyen hoy su voz,
8   no endurezcan el corazón
como sucedió en la rebelión,
    en aquel día de *prueba en el desierto.
⁹Allí sus antepasados me *tentaron y me
    pusieron a prueba,
    a pesar de haber visto mis obras cuarenta
    años.
¹⁰Por eso me enojé con aquella generación,
    y dije: "Siempre se descarría su corazón,
    y no han reconocido mis caminos."
¹¹Así que, en mi enojo, hice este juramento:
    "Jamás entrarán en mi reposo." »ᵖ

¹²Cuídense, hermanos, de que ninguno de ustedes tenga un corazón pecaminoso e incrédulo que los haga apartarse del Dios vivo. ¹³Más bien, mientras dure ese «hoy», anímense unos a otros cada día, para que ninguno de ustedes se endurezca por el engaño del pecado. ¹⁴Hemos llegado a tener parte con *Cristo, con tal que retengamos firme hasta el fin la confianza que tuvimos al principio. ¹⁵Como se acaba de decir:

«Si ustedes oyen hoy su voz,
    no endurezcan el corazón
    como sucedió en la rebelión.»q

¹⁶Ahora bien, ¿quiénes fueron los que oyeron y se rebelaron? ¿No fueron acaso todos los que salieron de Egipto guiados por Moisés? ¹⁷¿Y con quiénes se enojó Dios durante cuarenta años? ¿No fue acaso con los que pecaron, los cuales cayeron muertos en el desierto? ¹⁸¿Y a quiénes juró Dios que jamás entrarían en su reposo, sino a los que desobedecieron?ʳ ¹⁹Como podemos ver, no pudieron entrar por causa de su incredulidad.

Reposo del pueblo de Dios

4 Cuidémonos, por tanto, no sea que, aunque la promesa de entrar en su reposo sigue vigente, alguno de ustedes parezca quedarse atrás. ²Porque a nosotros, lo mismo que a ellos, se nos ha anunciado la buena *noticia; pero el mensaje que escucharon no les sirvió de nada, porque no se unieron en la feᵃˢ los que habían prestado atención a ese mensaje. ³En

tal reposo entramos los que somos creyentes, conforme Dios ha dicho:

«Así que, en mi enojo, hice este juramento:
    "Jamás entrarán en mi reposo." »ᵗ

Es cierto que su trabajo quedó terminado con la creación del mundo, ⁴pues en algún lugar se ha dicho así del séptimo día: «Y en el séptimo día reposó Dios de todas sus obras.»ᵘ ⁵Y en el pasaje citado también dice: «Jamás entrarán en mi reposo.»

⁶Sin embargo, todavía falta que algunos entren en ese reposo, y los primeros a quienes se les anunció la buena noticia no entraron por causa de su desobediencia. ⁷Por eso, Dios volvió a fijar un día, que es «hoy», cuando mucho después declaró por medio de David lo que ya se ha mencionado:

«Si ustedes oyen hoy su voz,
    no endurezcan el corazón.»v

⁸Si Josué les hubiera dado el reposo, Dios no habría hablado posteriormente de otro día. ⁹Por consiguiente, queda todavía un reposo especialʷ para el pueblo de Dios; ¹⁰porque el que entra en el reposo de Dios descansa también de sus obras, así como Dios descansó de las suyas. ¹¹Esforcémonos, pues, por entrar en ese reposo, para que nadie caiga al seguir aquel ejemplo de desobediencia.

¹²Ciertamente, la palabra de Dios es viva y poderosa, y más cortante que cualquier espada de dos filos. Penetra hasta lo más profundo del alma y del espíritu, hasta la médula de los huesos,ˣ y juzga los pensamientos y las intenciones del corazón. ¹³Ninguna cosa creada escapa a la vista de Dios. Todo está al descubierto, expuesto a los ojos de aquel a quien hemos de rendir cuentas.

Jesús, el gran sumo sacerdote

¹⁴Por lo tanto, ya que en Jesús, el Hijo de Dios, tenemos un gran sumo sacerdote que ha atravesado los cielos, aferrémonos a la fe que profesamos. ¹⁵Porque no tenemos un sumo sacerdote incapaz de compadecerse de nuestras debilidades, sino uno que ha sido *tentado en todo de la misma manera que nosotros, aunque sin pecado. ¹⁶Así que acerquémonos confiadamente al trono de la gracia para recibir misericordia y hallar la gracia que nos ayude en el momento que más la necesitemos.

5 Todo sumo sacerdote es escogido de entre los hombres. Él mismo es nombrado para representar a su pueblo ante Dios, y ofrecer dones y sacrificios por los pecados. ²Puede tratar con paciencia a los ignorantes y extraviados, ya que él mismo está sujeto a las debilidades humanas. ³Por tal razón se ve obligado a ofrecer sacrificios por sus propios pecados, como también por los del pueblo.

⁴Nadie ocupa ese cargo por iniciativa propia; más bien, lo ocupa el que es llamado por Dios, como sucedió con Aarón. ⁵Tampoco *Cristo se glorificó a sí mismo haciéndose sumo sacerdote, sino que Dios le dijo:

«Tú eres mi hijo,
    hoy mismo te he engendrado.»y
⁶Y en otro pasaje dice:

«Tú eres sacerdote para siempre,
    según el orden de Melquisedec.»z

ᵒ **3:6** *mantengamos.* Var. *mantengamos firme hasta el fin.* ᵖ **3:11** Sal 95:7-11 q **3:15** Sal 95:7,8 ʳ **3:18** *los que desobedecieron.* Alt. *los que no creyeron.* ˢ **4:2** *no se unieron en la fe a.* Var. *no se combinó con fe para.* ᵗ **4:3** Sal 95:11; también en v. 5. ᵘ **4:4** Gn 2:2 ᵛ **4:7** Sal 95:7,8 ʷ **4:9** *un reposo especial.* Lit. *un sabático.* ˣ **4:12** *Penetra . . . huesos.* Lit. *Penetra hasta la división de alma y espíritu, y de articulaciones y médulas.* ʸ **5:5** Sal 2:7 ᶻ **5:6** Sal 110:4

7En los días de su vida *mortal, Jesús ofreció oraciones y súplicas con fuerte clamor y lágrimas al que podía salvarlo de la muerte, y fue escuchado por su reverente sumisión. 8Aunque era Hijo, mediante el sufrimiento aprendió a obedecer; 9y consumada su *perfección, llegó a ser autor de salvación eterna para todos los que le obedecen, 10y Dios lo nombró sumo sacerdote según el orden de Melquisedec.

Advertencia contra la apostasía

11Sobre este tema tenemos mucho que decir aunque es difícil explicarlo, porque a ustedes lo que les entra por un oído les sale por el otro.a 12En realidad, a estas alturas ya deberían ser maestros, y sin embargo necesitan que alguien vuelva a enseñarles las verdades más elementales de la palabra de Dios. Dicho de otro modo, necesitan leche en vez de alimento sólido. 13El que sólo se alimenta de leche es inexperto en el mensaje de justicia; es como un niño de pecho. 14En cambio, el alimento sólido es para los adultos, para los que tienen la capacidad de distinguir entre lo bueno y lo malo, pues han ejercitado su facultad de percepción espiritual.

6 Por eso, dejando a un lado las enseñanzas elementales acerca de *Cristo, avancemos hacia la madurez. No volvamos a poner los fundamentos, tales como el *arrepentimiento de las obras que conducen a la muerte, la fe en Dios, 2la instrucción sobre bautismos, la imposición de manos, la resurrección de los muertos y el juicio eterno. 3Así procederemos, si Dios lo permite.

4-6Es imposible que renueven su arrepentimiento aquellos que han sido una vez iluminados, que han saboreado el don celestial, que han tenido parte en el Espíritu Santo y que han experimentado la buena palabra de Dios y los poderes del mundo venidero, y después de todo esto se han apartado. Es imposible, porque así vuelven a crucificar, para su propio mal, al Hijo de Dios, y lo exponen a la vergüenza pública.

7Cuando la tierra bebe la lluvia que con frecuencia cae sobre ella, y produce una buena cosecha para los que la cultivan, recibe una bendición de Dios. 8En cambio, cuando produce espinos y cardos, no vale nada; está a punto de ser maldecida, y acabará por ser quemada.

9En cuanto a ustedes, queridos hermanos, aunque nos expresamos así, estamos seguros de que les espera lo mejor, es decir, lo que atañe a la salvación. 10Porque Dios no es injusto como para olvidarse de las obras y del amor que, para su gloria,b ustedes han mostrado sirviendo a los *santos, como lo siguen haciendo. 11Deseamos, sin embargo, que cada uno de ustedes siga mostrando ese mismo empeño hasta la realización final y completa de su esperanza. 12No sean perezosos; más bien, imiten a quienes por su fe y paciencia heredan las promesas.

La certeza de la promesa de Dios

13Cuando Dios hizo su promesa a Abraham, como no tenía a nadie superior por quien jurar, juró por sí mismo, 14y dijo: «Te bendeciré en gran manera y multiplicaré tu descendencia.»c 15Y así, después de esperar con paciencia, Abraham recibió lo que se le había prometido.

16Los *seres humanos juran por alguien superior a ellos mismos, y el juramento, al confirmar lo que se ha dicho, pone punto final a toda discusión.

17Por eso Dios, queriendo demostrar claramente a los herederos de la promesa que su propósito es inmutable, la confirmó con un juramento. 18Lo hizo así para que, mediante la promesa y el juramento, que son dos realidades inmutables en las cuales es imposible que Dios mienta, tengamos un estímulo poderoso los que, buscando refugio, nos aferramos a la esperanza que está delante de nosotros. 19Tenemos como firme y segura ancla del alma una esperanza que penetra hasta detrás de la cortina del *santuario, 20hasta donde Jesús, el precursor, entró por nosotros, llegando a ser sumo sacerdote para siempre, según el orden de Melquisedec.

El sacerdocio de Melquisedec

7 Este Melquisedec, rey de Salén y sacerdote del Dios Altísimo, salió al encuentro de Abraham, que regresaba de derrotar a los reyes, y lo bendijo. 2Abraham, a su vez, le dio la décima parte de todo. El nombre Melquisedec significa, en primer lugar, «rey de justicia» y, además, «rey de Salén» es, «rey de paz». 3No tiene padre ni madre ni genealogía; no tiene comienzo ni fin, pero a semejanza del Hijo de Dios, permanece como sacerdote para siempre.

4Consideren la grandeza de ese hombre, a quien nada menos que el patriarca Abraham dio la décima parte del botín. 5Ahora bien, los descendientes de Leví que reciben el sacerdocio tienen, por ley, el mandato de cobrar los diezmos del pueblo, es decir, de sus hermanos, aunque éstos también son descendientes de Abraham. 6En cambio, Melquisedec, que no era descendiente de Leví, recibió los diezmos de Abraham y bendijo al que tenía las promesas. 7Es indiscutible que la persona que bendice es superior a la que recibe la bendición. 8En el caso de los levitas, los diezmos los reciben hombres mortales; en el otro caso, los recibe Melquisedec, de quien se da testimonio de que vive. 9Hasta podría decirse que Leví, quien ahora recibe los diezmos, los pagó por medio de Abraham, 10ya que Leví estaba presente en su antepasado Abraham cuando Melquisedec le salió al encuentro.

Jesús, semejante a Melquisedec

11Si hubiera sido posible alcanzar la *perfección mediante el sacerdocio levítico (pues bajo éste se le dio la ley al pueblo), ¿qué necesidad había de que más adelante surgiera otro sacerdote, según el orden de Melquisedec y no según el de Aarón? 12Porque cuando cambia el sacerdocio, también tiene que cambiarse la ley. 13En efecto, Jesús, de quien se dicen estas cosas, era de otra tribu, de la cual nadie se ha dedicado al servicio del altar. 14Es evidente que nuestro Señor procedía de la tribu de Judá, respecto a la cual nada dijo Moisés con relación al sacerdocio. 15Y lo que hemos dicho resulta aún más evidente si, a semejanza de Melquisedec, surge otro sacerdote 16que ha llegado a serlo, no conforme a un requisito legal respecto a linaje *humano, sino conforme al poder de una vida indestructible. 17Pues de él se da testimonio:

«Tú eres sacerdote para siempre,
    según el orden de Melquisedec.»d

18Por una parte, la ley anterior queda anulada por ser inútil e ineficaz, 19ya que no *perfeccionó nada. Y por la otra, se introduce una esperanza mejor, mediante la cual nos acercamos a Dios.

---

a **5:11** a ustedes . . . por el otro. Lit. se han vuelto torpes en los oídos. b **6:10** gloria. Lit. nombre. c **6:14** Gn 22:17 d **7:17** Sal 110:4; también en v. 21

20¡Y no fue sin juramento! Los otros sacerdotes llegaron a serlo sin juramento, 21mientras que éste llegó a serlo con el juramento de aquel que le dijo:

«El Señor ha jurado,
y no cambiará de parecer:
"Tú eres sacerdote para siempre." »

22Por tanto, Jesús ha llegado a ser el que garantiza un pacto superior.

23Ahora bien, como a aquellos sacerdotes la muerte les impedía seguir ejerciendo sus funciones, ha habido muchos de ellos; 24pero como Jesús permanece para siempre, su sacerdocio es imperecedero. 25Por eso también puede salvar por completo[e] a los que por medio de él se acercan a Dios, ya que vive siempre para interceder por ellos.

26Nos convenía tener un sumo sacerdote así: santo, irreprochable, puro, apartado de los pecadores y exaltado sobre los cielos. 27A diferencia de los otros sumos sacerdotes, él no tiene que ofrecer sacrificios día tras día, primero por sus propios pecados y luego por los del pueblo; porque él ofreció el sacrificio una sola vez y para siempre cuando se ofreció a sí mismo. 28De hecho, la ley designa como sumos sacerdotes a hombres débiles; pero el juramento, posterior a la ley, designa al Hijo, quien ha sido hecho *perfecto para siempre.

El sumo sacerdote de un nuevo pacto

8 Ahora bien, el punto principal de lo que venimos diciendo es que tenemos tal sumo sacerdote, aquel que se sentó a la *derecha del trono de la Majestad en el cielo, 2el que sirve en el *santuario, es decir, en el verdadero tabernáculo levantado por el Señor y no por ningún *ser humano.

3A todo sumo sacerdote se le nombra para presentar ofrendas y sacrificios, por lo cual es necesario que también tenga algo que ofrecer. 4Si Jesús estuviera en la tierra, no sería sacerdote, pues aquí ya hay sacerdotes que presentan las ofrendas en conformidad con la ley. 5Estos sacerdotes sirven en un santuario que es copia y sombra del que está en el cielo, tal como se le advirtió a Moisés cuando estaba a punto de construir el tabernáculo: «Asegúrate de hacerlo todo según el modelo que se te ha mostrado en la montaña.»[f] 6Pero el servicio sacerdotal que Jesús ha recibido es superior al de ellos, así como el pacto del cual es mediador es superior al antiguo, puesto que se basa en mejores promesas.

7Efectivamente, si ese primer pacto hubiera sido *perfecto, no habría lugar para un segundo pacto. 8Pero Dios, reprochándoles sus defectos, dijo:

«Vienen días —dice el Señor—,
en que haré un nuevo pacto
con la casa de Israel
y con la casa de Judá.
9No será un pacto
como el que hice con sus antepasados
el día en que los tomé de la mano
y los saqué de Egipto,
ya que ellos no permanecieron fieles a mi
pacto,
y yo los abandoné
—dice el Señor—.
10Éste es el pacto que después de aquel tiempo
haré con la casa de Israel —dice el Señor—:
Pondré mis leyes en su mente

y las escribiré en su corazón.
Yo seré su Dios,
y ellos serán mi pueblo.
11Ya no tendrá nadie que enseñar a su prójimo,
ni dirá nadie a su hermano: "¡Conoce al
Señor!",
porque todos, desde el más pequeño hasta el
más grande,
me conocerán.
12Yo les perdonaré sus iniquidades,
y nunca más me acordaré de sus
pecados.»[g]

13Al llamar «nuevo» a ese pacto, ha declarado obsoleto al anterior; y lo que se vuelve obsoleto y envejece ya está por desaparecer.

El culto en el tabernáculo terrenal

9 Ahora bien, el primer pacto tenía sus normas para el culto, y un *santuario terrenal. 2En efecto, se habilitó un tabernáculo de tal modo que en su primera parte, llamada el Lugar Santo, estaban el candelabro, la mesa y los panes consagrados. 3Tras la segunda cortina estaba la parte llamada el Lugar Santísimo, 4el cual tenía el altar de oro para el incienso y el arca del pacto, toda recubierta de oro. Dentro del arca había una urna de oro que contenía el maná, la vara de Aarón que había retoñado, y las tablas del pacto. 5Encima del arca estaban los *querubines de la gloria, que cubrían con su sombra el lugar de la *expiación.[h] Pero ahora no se puede hablar de eso en detalle.

6Así dispuestas todas estas cosas, los sacerdotes entran continuamente en la primera parte del tabernáculo para celebrar el culto. 7Pero en la segunda parte entra únicamente el sumo sacerdote, y sólo una vez al año, provisto siempre de sangre que ofrece por sí mismo y por los pecados de ignorancia cometidos por el pueblo. 8Con esto el Espíritu Santo da a entender que, mientras siga en pie el primer tabernáculo, aún no se habrá revelado el camino que conduce al Lugar Santísimo. 9Esto nos ilustra hoy día que las ofrendas y los sacrificios que allí se ofrecen no tienen poder alguno para *perfeccionar la conciencia de los que celebran ese culto. 10No se trata más que de reglas externas relacionadas con alimentos, bebidas y diversas ceremonias de *purificación, válidas sólo hasta el tiempo señalado para reformarlo todo.

La sangre de Cristo

11*Cristo, por el contrario, al presentarse como sumo sacerdote de los bienes definitivos[i] en el tabernáculo más excelente y *perfecto, no hecho por manos humanas (es decir, que no es de esta creación), 12entró una sola vez y para siempre en el Lugar Santísimo. No lo hizo con sangre de machos cabríos y becerros, sino con su propia sangre, logrando así un rescate eterno. 13La sangre de machos cabríos y de toros, y las cenizas de una novilla rociadas sobre personas *impuras, las *santifican de modo que quedan *limpias por fuera. 14Si esto es así, ¡cuánto más la sangre de Cristo, quien por medio del Espíritu eterno se ofreció sin mancha a Dios, purificará nuestra conciencia de las obras que conducen a la muerte, a fin de que sirvamos al Dios viviente!

15Por eso Cristo es mediador de un nuevo pacto, para que los llamados reciban la herencia eterna pro-

---

e 7:25 por completo. Alt. para siempre. f 8:5 Éx 25:40 g 8:12 Jer 31:31-34 h 9:5 el lugar de la expiación. Lit. el *propiciatorio. i 9:11 definitivos. Var. venideros.

metida, ahora que él ha muerto para liberarlos de los pecados cometidos bajo el primer pacto.

16En el caso de un testamento,ʲ es necesario constatar la muerte del testador, 17pues un testamento sólo adquiere validez cuando el testador muere, y no entra en vigor mientras vive. 18De ahí que ni siquiera el primer pacto se haya establecido sin sangre. 19Después de promulgar todos los mandamientos de la ley a todo el pueblo, Moisés tomó la sangre de los becerros junto con agua, lana escarlata y ramas de hisopo, y roció el libro de la ley y a todo el pueblo, 20diciendo: «Ésta es la sangre del pacto que Dios ha mandado que ustedes cumplan.»ᵏ 21De la misma manera roció con la sangre el tabernáculo y todos los objetos que se usaban en el culto. 22De hecho, la ley exige que casi todo sea purificado con sangre, pues sin derramamiento de sangre no hay perdón.

23Así que era necesario que las copias de las realidades celestiales fueran purificadas con esos sacrificios, pero que las realidades mismas lo fueran con sacrificios superiores a aquéllos. 24En efecto, Cristo no entró en un santuario hecho por manos humanas, simple copia del verdadero santuario, sino en el cielo mismo, para presentarse ahora ante Dios en favor nuestro. 25Ni entró en el cielo para ofrecerse vez tras vez, como entra el sumo sacerdote en el Lugar Santísimo cada año con sangre ajena. 26Si así fuera, Cristo habría tenido que sufrir muchas veces desde la creación del mundo. Al contrario, ahora, al final de los tiempos, se ha presentado una sola vez y para siempre a fin de acabar con el pecado mediante el sacrificio de sí mismo. 27Y así como está establecido que los seres *humanos mueran una sola vez, y después venga el juicio, 28también Cristo fue ofrecido en sacrificio una sola vez para quitar los pecados de muchos; y aparecerá por segunda vez, ya no para cargar con pecado alguno, sino para traer salvación a quienes lo esperan.

El sacrificio de Cristo, ofrecido una vez y para siempre

10 La ley es sólo una sombra de los bienes venideros, y no la presencia misma de estas realidades. Por eso nunca puede, mediante los mismos sacrificios que se ofrecen sin cesar año tras año, hacer *perfectos a los que adoran. 2De otra manera, ¿no habrían dejado ya de hacerse sacrificios? Pues los que rinden culto, *purificados de una vez por todas, no se habrían sentido culpables de pecado. 3Pero esos sacrificios son un recordatorio anual de los pecados, 4ya que es imposible que la sangre de los toros y de los machos cabríos quite los pecados.

5Por eso, al entrar en el mundo, *Cristo dijo:

«A ti no te complacen sacrificios ni ofrendas;
en su lugar, me preparaste un cuerpo;
6no te agradaron ni holocaustos
ni sacrificios por el pecado.
7Por eso dije: "Aquí me tienes
—como el libro dice de mí—.
He venido, oh Dios, a hacer tu voluntad."»ᵐ

8Primero dijo: «Sacrificios y ofrendas, holocaustos y expiaciones no te complacen ni fueron de tu agrado» (a pesar de que la ley exigía que se ofrecieran). 9Luego añadió: «Aquí me tienes: He venido a hacer tu vo-

luntad.» Así quitó lo primero para establecer lo segundo. 10Y en virtud de esa voluntad somos *santificados mediante el sacrificio del cuerpo de *Jesucristo, ofrecido una vez y para siempre.

11Todo sacerdote celebra el culto día tras día ofreciendo repetidas veces los mismos sacrificios, que nunca pueden quitar los pecados. 12Pero este sacerdote, después de ofrecer por los pecados un solo sacrificio para siempre, se sentó a la *derecha de Dios, 13en espera de que sus enemigos sean puestos por estrado de sus pies. 14Porque con un solo sacrificio ha hecho perfectos para siempre a los que está santificando.

15También el Espíritu Santo nos da testimonio de ello. Primero dice:

16«Éste es el pacto que haré con ellos
después de aquel tiempo —dice el Señor—:
Pondré mis leyes en su corazón,
y las escribiré en su mente.»ⁿ

17Después añade:

«Y nunca más me acordaré de sus pecados y
maldades.»ñ

18Y cuando éstos han sido perdonados, ya no hace falta otro sacrificio por el pecado.

Llamada a la perseverancia

19Así pues, hermanos, mediante la sangre de Jesús, tenemos plena libertad para entrar en el Lugar Santísimo, 20por el camino nuevo y vivo que él nos ha abierto a través de la cortina, es decir, a través de su cuerpo; 21y tenemos además un gran sacerdote al frente de la familia de Dios. 22Acerquémonos, pues, a Dios con corazón sincero y con la plena seguridad que da la fe, interiormente purificados de una conciencia culpable y exteriormente lavados con agua pura. 23Mantengamos firme la esperanza que profesamos, porque fiel es el que hizo la promesa. 24Preocupémonos los unos por los otros, a fin de estimularnos al amor y a las buenas obras. 25No dejemos de congregarnos, como acostumbran hacerlo algunos, sino animémonos unos a otros, y con mayor razón ahora que vemos que aquel día se acerca.

26Si después de recibir el conocimiento de la verdad pecamos obstinadamente, ya no hay sacrificio por los pecados. 27Sólo queda una terrible expectativa de juicio, el fuego ardiente que ha de devorar a los enemigos de Dios. 28Cualquiera que rechazaba la ley de Moisés moría irremediablemente por el testimonio de dos o tres testigos. 29¿Cuánto mayor castigo piensan ustedes que merece·el que ha pisoteado al Hijo de Dios, que ha profanado la sangre del pacto por la cual había sido *santificado, y que ha insultado al Espíritu de la gracia? 30Pues conocemos al que dijo: «Mía es la venganza; yo pagaré»;ᵒ y también: «El Señor juzgará a su pueblo.»ᵖ 31¡Terrible cosa es caer en las manos del Dios vivo!

32Recuerden aquellos días pasados cuando ustedes, después de haber sido iluminados, sostuvieron una dura lucha y soportaron mucho sufrimiento. 33Unas veces se vieron expuestos públicamente al insulto y a la persecución; otras veces se solidarizaron con los que eran tratados de igual manera. 34También se compadecieron de los encarcelados, y cuando a ustedes les confiscaron sus bienes, lo aceptaron con alegría, conscientes de que tenían un patrimonio mejor y más permanente.

³⁵Así que no pierdan la confianza, porque ésta será grandemente recompensada. ³⁶Ustedes necesitan perseverar para que, después de haber cumplido la voluntad de Dios, reciban lo que él ha prometido. ³⁷Pues dentro de muy poco tiempo,

«el que ha de venir vendrá, y no tardará.
³⁸ Pero mi justo⁹ vivirá por la fe.
Y si se vuelve atrás,
no será de mi agrado.»ʳ

³⁹Pero nosotros no somos de los que se vuelven atrás y acaban por perderse, sino de los que tienen fe y preservan su *vida.

Por la fe

11 Ahora bien, la fe es la garantía de lo que se espera, la certeza de lo que no se ve. ²Gracias a ella fueron aprobados los antiguos.

³Por la fe entendemos que el universo fue formado por la palabra de Dios, de modo que lo visible no provino de lo que se ve.

⁴Por la fe Abel ofreció a Dios un sacrificio más aceptable que el de Caín, por lo cual recibió testimonio de ser justo, pues Dios aceptó su ofrenda. Y por la fe Abel, a pesar de estar muerto, habla todavía.

⁵Por la fe Enoc fue sacado de este mundo sin experimentar la muerte; no fue hallado porque Dios se lo llevó, pero antes de ser llevado recibió testimonio de haber agradado a Dios. ⁶En realidad, sin fe es imposible agradar a Dios, ya que cualquiera que se acerca a Dios tiene que creer que él existe y que recompensa a quienes lo buscan.

⁷Por la fe Noé, advertido sobre cosas que aún no se veían, con temor reverente construyó un arca para salvar a su familia. Por esa fe condenó al mundo y llegó a ser heredero de la justicia que viene por la fe.

⁸Por la fe Abraham, cuando fue llamado para ir a un lugar que más tarde recibiría como herencia, obedeció y salió sin saber a dónde iba. ⁹Por la fe se radicó como extranjero en la tierra prometida, y habitó en tiendas de campaña con Isaac y Jacob, herederos también de la misma promesa, ¹⁰porque esperaba la ciudad de cimientos sólidos, de la cual Dios es arquitecto y constructor.

¹¹Por la fe Abraham, a pesar de su avanzada edad y de que Sara misma era estéril,ˢ recibió fuerza para tener hijos, porque consideró fiel al que le había hecho la promesa. ¹²Así que de este solo hombre, ya en decadencia, nacieron descendientes numerosos como las estrellas del cielo e incontables como la arena a la orilla del mar.

¹³Todos ellos vivieron por la fe, y murieron sin haber recibido las cosas prometidas; más bien, las reconocieron a lo lejos, y confesaron que eran extranjeros y peregrinos en la tierra. ¹⁴Al expresarse así, claramente dieron a entender que andaban en busca de una patria. ¹⁵Si hubieran estado pensando en aquella patria de donde habían emigrado, habrían tenido oportunidad de regresar a ella. ¹⁶Antes bien, anhelaban una patria mejor, es decir, la celestial. Por lo tanto, Dios no se avergonzó de ser llamado su Dios, y les preparó una ciudad.

¹⁷Por la fe Abraham, que había recibido las promesas, fue puesto a *prueba y ofreció a Isaac, su hijo único, ¹⁸a pesar de que Dios le había dicho: «Tu *descendencia se establecerá por medio de Isaac.»ᵗ ¹⁹Consideraba Abraham que Dios tiene poder hasta para resucitar a los muertos, y así, en sentido figurado, recobró a Isaac de entre los muertos.

²⁰Por la fe Isaac bendijo a Jacob y a Esaú, previendo lo que les esperaba en el futuro.

²¹Por la fe Jacob, cuando estaba a punto de morir, bendijo a cada uno de los hijos de José, y adoró apoyándose en la punta de su bastón.

²²Por la fe José, al fin de su vida, se refirió a la salida de los israelitas de Egipto y dio instrucciones acerca de sus restos mortales.

²³Por la fe Moisés, recién nacido, fue escondido por sus padres durante tres meses, porque vieron que era un niño precioso, y no tuvieron miedo del edicto del rey.

²⁴Por la fe Moisés, ya adulto, renunció a ser llamado hijo de la hija del faraón. ²⁵Prefirió ser maltratado con el pueblo de Dios a disfrutar de los efímeros placeres del pecado. ²⁶Consideró que el oprobio por causa del *Mesías era una mayor riqueza que los tesoros de Egipto, porque tenía la mirada puesta en la recompensa. ²⁷Por la fe salió de Egipto sin tenerle miedo a la ira del rey, pues se mantuvo firme como si estuviera viendo al Invisible. ²⁸Por la fe celebró la Pascua y el rociamiento de la sangre, para que el exterminador de los primogénitos no tocara a los de Israel.

²⁹Por la fe el pueblo cruzó el Mar Rojo como por tierra seca; pero cuando los egipcios intentaron cruzarlo, se ahogaron.

³⁰Por la fe cayeron las murallas de Jericó, después de haber marchado el pueblo siete días a su alrededor.

³¹Por la fe la prostituta Rajab no murió junto con los desobedientes,ᵘ pues había recibido en paz a los espías.

³²¿Qué más voy a decir? Me faltaría tiempo para hablar de Gedeón, Barac, Sansón, Jefté, David, Samuel y los profetas, ³³los cuales por la fe conquistaron reinos, hicieron justicia y alcanzaron lo prometido; cerraron bocas de leones, ³⁴apagaron la furia de las llamas y escaparon del filo de la espada; sacaron fuerzas de flaqueza; se mostraron valientes en la guerra y pusieron en fuga a ejércitos extranjeros. ³⁵Hubo mujeres que por la resurrección recobraron a sus muertos. Otros, en cambio, fueron muertos a golpes, pues para alcanzar una mejor resurrección no aceptaron que los pusieran en libertad. ³⁶Otros sufrieron la prueba de burlas y azotes, e incluso de cadenas y cárceles. ³⁷Fueron apedreados,ᵛ aserrados por la mitad, asesinados a filo de espada. Anduvieron fugitivos de aquí para allá, cubiertos de pieles de oveja y de cabra, pasando necesidades, afligidos y maltratados. ³⁸¡El mundo no merecía gente así! Anduvieron sin rumbo por desiertos y montañas, por cuevas y cavernas.

³⁹Aunque todos obtuvieron un testimonio favorable mediante la fe, ninguno de ellos vio el cumplimiento de la promesa. ⁴⁰Esto sucedió para que ellos no llegaran a la metaʷ sin nosotros, pues Dios nos había preparado algo mejor.

Dios disciplina a sus hijos

12 Por tanto, también nosotros, que estamos rodeados de una multitud tan grande de testigos, despojémonos del lastre que nos estorba, en

---

especial del pecado que nos asedia, y corramos con perseverancia la carrera que tenemos por delante. ²Fijemos la mirada en Jesús, el iniciador y *perfeccionador de nuestra fe, quien por el gozo que le esperaba, soportó la cruz, menospreciando la vergüenza que ella significaba, y ahora está sentado a la *derecha del trono de Dios. ³Así, pues, consideren a aquel que perseveró frente a tanta oposición por parte de los pecadores, para que no se cansen ni pierdan el ánimo.

⁴En la lucha que ustedes libran contra el pecado, todavía no han tenido que resistir hasta derramar su sangre. ⁵Y ya han olvidado por completo las palabras de aliento que como a hijos se les dirige:

«Hijo mío, no tomes a la ligera la disciplina del Señor
ni te desanimes cuando te reprenda,
⁶porque el Señor disciplina a los que ama,
y azota a todo el que recibe como hijo.»ˣ

⁷Lo que soportan es para su disciplina, pues Dios los está tratando como a hijos. ¿Qué hijo hay a quien el padre no disciplina? ⁸Si a ustedes se les deja sin la disciplina que todos reciben, entonces son bastardos y no hijos legítimos. ⁹Después de todo, aunque nuestros padres *humanos nos disciplinaban, los respetábamos. ¿No hemos de someternos, con mayor razón, al Padre de los espíritus, para que vivamos? ¹⁰En efecto, nuestros padres nos disciplinaban por un breve tiempo, como mejor les parecía; pero Dios lo hace para nuestro bien, a fin de que participemos de su *santidad. ¹¹Ciertamente, ninguna disciplina, en el momento de recibirla, parece agradable, sino más bien penosa; después, sin embargo, después produce una cosecha de justicia y paz para quienes han sido entrenados por ella.

¹²Por tanto, renueven las fuerzas de sus manos cansadas y de sus rodillas debilitadas. ¹³«Hagan sendas derechas para sus pies»,ʸ para que la pierna coja no se disloque sino que sane.

Advertencia a los que rechazan a Dios

¹⁴Busquen la paz con todos, y la *santidad, sin la cual nadie verá al Señor. ¹⁵Asegúrense de que nadie deje de alcanzar la gracia de Dios; de que ninguna raíz amarga brote y cause dificultades y corrompa a muchos; ¹⁶y de que nadie sea inmoral ni profano como Esaú, quien por un solo plato de comida vendió sus derechos de hijo mayor.ᶻ ¹⁷Después, como ya saben, cuando quiso heredar esa bendición, fue rechazado: No se le dio lugar para el *arrepentimiento, aunque con lágrimas buscó la bendición.

¹⁸Ustedes no se han acercado a una montaña que se pueda tocar o que esté ardiendo en fuego; ni a oscuridad, tinieblas y tormenta; ¹⁹ni a sonido de trompeta, ni a tal clamor de palabras que quienes lo oyeron suplicaron que no se les hablara más, ²⁰porque no podían soportar esta orden: «¡Será apedreado todo el que toque la montaña, aunque sea un animal!»ᵃ ²¹Tan terrible era este espectáculo que Moisés dijo: «Estoy temblando de miedo.»ᵇ

²²Por el contrario, ustedes se han acercado al monte Sión, a la Jerusalén celestial, la ciudad del Dios viviente. Se han acercado a millares y millares de ángeles, a una asamblea gozosa, ²³a la iglesia de los primogénitos inscritos en el cielo. Se han acercado a Dios, el juez de todos; a los espíritus de los justos que han llegado a la *perfección; ²⁴a Jesús, el mediador de

un nuevo pacto; y a la sangre rociada, que habla con más fuerza que la de Abel.

²⁵Tengan cuidado de no rechazar al que habla, pues si no escaparon aquellos que rechazaron al que los amonestaba en la tierra, mucho menos escaparemos nosotros si le volvemos las espaldas al que nos amonesta desde el cielo. ²⁶En aquella ocasión, su voz conmovió la tierra, pero ahora ha prometido: «Una vez más haré que se estremezca no sólo la tierra sino también el cielo.»ᶜ ²⁷La frase «una vez más» indica la transformaciónᵈ de las cosas movibles, es decir, las creadas, para que permanezca lo inconmovible.

²⁸Así que nosotros, que estamos recibiendo un reino inconmovible, seamos agradecidos. Inspirados por esta gratitud, adoremos a Dios como a él le agrada, con temor reverente, ²⁹porque nuestro «Dios es fuego consumidor».ᵉ

Exhortaciones finales

13 Sigan amándose unos a otros fraternalmente. ²No se olviden de practicar la hospitalidad, pues gracias a ella algunos, sin saberlo, hospedaron ángeles. ³Acuérdense de los presos, como si ustedes fueran sus compañeros de cárcel, y también de los que son maltratados, como si fueran ustedes mismos los que sufren.

⁴Tengan todos en alta estima el matrimonio y la fidelidad conyugal, porque Dios juzgará a los adúlteros y a todos los que cometen inmoralidades sexuales. ⁵Manténganse libres del amor al dinero, y conténtense con lo que tienen, porque Dios ha dicho:

«Nunca te dejaré;
jamás te abandonaré.»ᶠ

⁶Así que podemos decir con toda confianza:

«El Señor es quien me ayuda; no temeré.
¿Qué me puede hacer un simple mortal?»ᵍ

⁷Acuérdense de sus dirigentes, que les comunicaron la palabra de Dios. Consideren cuál fue el resultado de su estilo de vida, e imiten su fe. ⁸*Jesucristo es el mismo ayer y hoy y por los siglos.

⁹No se dejen llevar por ninguna clase de enseñanzas extrañas. Conviene que el corazón sea fortalecido por la gracia, y no por alimentos rituales que de nada aprovechan a quienes los comen. ¹⁰Nosotros tenemos un altar del cual no tienen derecho a comer los que oficianen en el tabernáculo. ¹¹Porque el sumo sacerdote introduce la sangre de los animales en el Lugar Santísimo como sacrificio por el pecado, pero los cuerpos de esos animales se queman fuera del campamento. ¹²Por eso también Jesús, para *santificar al pueblo mediante su propia sangre, sufrió fuera de la puerta de la ciudad. ¹³Por lo tanto, salgamos a su encuentro fuera del campamento, llevando la deshonra que él llevó, ¹⁴pues aquí no tenemos una ciudad permanente, sino que buscamos la ciudad venidera.

¹⁵Así que ofrezcamos continuamente a Dios, por medio de Jesucristo, un sacrificio de alabanza, es decir, el fruto de los labios que confiesan su nombre. ¹⁶No se olviden de hacer el bien y de compartir con otros lo que tienen, porque ésos son los sacrificios que agradan a Dios.

¹⁷Obedezcan a sus dirigentes y sométanse a ellos, pues cuidan de ustedes como quienes tienen que rendir cuentas. Obedézcanlos a fin de que ellos

---

ˣ **12:6** Pr 3:11,12   y **12:13** Pr 4:26   ᶻ **12:16** *sus derechos de hijo mayor.* Lit. *su primogenitura.*   ᵃ **12:20** Éx 19:12,13
ᵇ **12:21** Dt 9:19   ᶜ **12:26** Hag 2:6   ᵈ **12:27** *transformación.* Alt. *Remoción.*   ᵉ **12:29** Dt 4:24   ᶠ **13:5** Dt 31:6   ᵍ **13:6** Sal 118:6,7

cumplan su tarea con alegría y sin quejarse, pues el quejarse no les trae ningún provecho.

18Oren por nosotros, porque estamos seguros de tener la conciencia tranquila y queremos portarnos honradamente en todo. 19Les ruego encarecidamente que oren para que cuanto antes se me permita estar de nuevo con ustedes.

20El Dios que da la paz levantó de entre los muertos al gran Pastor de las ovejas, a nuestro Señor Jesús, por la sangre del pacto eterno. 21Que él los capacite en todo lo bueno para hacer su voluntad. Y que, por medio de Jesucristo, Dios cumpla en noso-tros lo que le agrada. A él sea la gloria por los siglos de los siglos. Amén.

22Hermanos, les ruego que reciban bien estas palabras de exhortación, ya que les he escrito brevemente.

23Quiero que sepan que nuestro hermano Timoteo ha sido puesto en libertad. Si llega pronto, iré con él a verlos.

24Saluden a todos sus dirigentes y a todos los *santos. Los de Italia les mandan saludos.

25Que la gracia sea con todos ustedes.

Carta de SANTIAGO

1 *Santiago, *siervo de Dios y del Señor *Jesucristo, a las doce tribus que se hallan dispersas por el mundo:

Saludos.

Pruebas y tentaciones

2Hermanos míos, considérense muy dichosos cuando tengan que enfrentarse con diversas *pruebas, 3pues ya saben que la prueba de su fe produce constancia. 4Y la constancia debe llevar a feliz término la obra, para que sean *perfectos e íntegros, sin que les falte nada. 5Si a alguno de ustedes le falta sabiduría, pídasela a Dios, y él se la dará, pues Dios da a todos generosamente sin menospreciar a nadie. 6Pero que pida con fe, sin dudar, porque quien duda es como las olas del mar, agitadas y llevadas de un lado a otro por el viento. 7Quien es así no piense que va a recibir cosa alguna del Señor; 8es indeciso e inconstante en todo lo que hace.

9El hermano de condición humilde debe sentirse *orgulloso de su alta dignidad, 10y el rico, de su humilde condición. El rico pasará como la flor del campo. 11El sol, cuando sale, seca la planta con su calor abrasador. A ésta se le cae la flor y pierde su belleza. Así se marchitará también el rico en todas sus empresas.

12*Dichoso el que resiste la *tentación porque, al salir aprobado, recibirá la corona de la vida que Dios ha prometido a quienes lo aman.

13Que nadie, al ser tentado, diga: «Es Dios quien me tienta.» Porque Dios no puede ser tentado por el mal, ni tampoco tienta él a nadie. 14Todo lo contrario, cada uno es tentado cuando sus propios malos deseos lo arrastran y seducen. 15Luego, cuando el deseo ha concebido, engendra el pecado; y el pecado, una vez que ha sido consumado, da a luz la muerte.

16Mis queridos hermanos, no se engañen. 17Toda buena dádiva y todo don perfecto descienden de lo alto, donde está el Padre que creó las lumbreras celestes, y que no cambia como los astros ni se mueve como las sombras. 18Por su propia voluntad nos hizo nacer mediante la palabra de verdad, para que fuéramos como los primeros y mejores frutos de su creación.

Hay que poner en práctica la palabra

19Mis queridos hermanos, tengan presente esto: Todos deben estar listos para escuchar, y ser lentos para hablar y para enojarse; 20pues la ira *humana no produce la vida justa que Dios quiere. 21Por esto, despójense de toda inmundicia y de la maldad que tanto abunda, para que puedan recibir con humildad la palabra sembrada en ustedes, la cual tiene poder para salvarles la *vida.

22No se contenten sólo con escuchar la palabra, pues así se engañan ustedes mismos. Llévenla a la práctica. 23El que escucha la palabra pero no la pone en práctica es como el que se mira el rostro en un espejo 24y, después de mirarse, se va y se olvida en seguida de cómo es. 25Pero quien se fija atentamente en la ley perfecta de la libertad, y persevera en ella, no olvidando lo que ha oído sino haciéndolo, recibirá bendición al practicarla.

26Si alguien se cree religioso pero no le pone freno a su lengua, se engaña a sí mismo, y su religión no sirve para nada. 27La religión pura y sin mancha delante de Dios nuestro Padre es ésta: atender a los huérfanos y a las viudas en sus aflicciones, y conservarse limpio de la corrupción del mundo.

Prohibición del favoritismo

2 Hermanos míos, la fe que tienen en nuestro glorioso Señor *Jesucristo no debe dar lugar a favoritismos. 2Supongamos que en el lugar donde se reúnen entra un hombre con anillo de oro y ropa elegante, y entra también un pobre desarrapado. 3Si atienden bien al que lleva ropa elegante y le dicen: «Siéntese usted aquí, en este lugar cómodo», pero al pobre le dicen: «Quédate ahí de pie» o «Siéntate en el suelo, a mis pies», 4¿acaso no hacen discriminación entre ustedes, juzgando con malas intenciones?

5Escuchen, mis queridos hermanos: ¿No ha escogido Dios a los que son pobres según el mundo para que sean ricos en la fe y hereden el reino que prometió a quienes lo aman? 6¡Pero ustedes han menospreciado al pobre! ¿No son los ricos quienes los explotan a ustedes y los arrastran ante los tribunales? 7¿No son ellos los que *blasfeman el buen nombre de aquel a quien ustedes pertenecen?

8Hacen muy bien si de veras cumplen la ley suprema de la Escritura: «Ama a tu prójimo como a ti mismo»;a 9pero si muestran algún favoritismo, pecan y son culpables, pues la misma ley los acusa de ser transgresores. 10Porque el que cumple con toda la ley pero falla en un solo punto ya es culpable de haberla quebrantado toda. 11Pues el que dijo: «No cometas adulterio»,b también dijo: «No mates.»c Si no cometes adulterio, pero matas, ya has violado la ley.

12Hablen y pórtense como quienes han de ser juzgados por la ley que nos da libertad, 13porque habrá un juicio sin compasión para el que actúe sin compasión. ¡La compasión triunfa en el juicio!

La fe y las obras

14Hermanos míos, ¿de qué le sirve a uno alegar que tiene fe, si no tiene obras? ¿Acaso podrá salvarlo esa fe? 15Supongamos que un hermano o una hermana no tienen con qué vestirse y carecen del alimento diario, 16y uno de ustedes les dice: «Que les vaya bien; abríguense y coman hasta saciarse», pero no les da lo necesario para el cuerpo. ¿De qué servirá eso? 17Así también la fe por sí sola, si no tiene obras, está muerta.

18Sin embargo, alguien dirá: «Tú tienes fe, y yo tengo obras.»

Pues bien, muéstrame tu fe sin las obras, y yo te mostraré la fe por mis obras. 19¿Tú crees que hay un solo Dios? ¡Magnífico! También los demonios lo creen, y tiemblan.

20¡Qué tonto eres! ¿Quieres convencerte de que la fe sin obras es estéril?d 21¿No fue declarado justo nuestro padre Abraham por lo que hizo cuando ofreció sobre el altar a su hijo Isaac? 22Ya lo ves: Su fe y sus obras actuaban conjuntamente, y su fe llegó a la *perfección por las obras que hizo. 23Así se cumplió la Escritura que dice: «Le creyó Abraham a Dios, y esto se le tomó en cuenta como justicia»,e y fue llamado amigo de Dios. 24Como pueden ver, a una persona se le declara justa por las obras, y no sólo por la fe.

25De igual manera, ¿no fue declarada justa por las obras aun la prostituta Rajab, cuando hospedó a los espías y les ayudó a huir por otro camino? 26Pues

a 2:8 Lv 19:18 b 2:11 Éx 20:14; Dt 5:18 c 2:11 Éx 20:13; Dt 5:17 d 2:20 es estéril. Var. está muerta. e 2:23 Gn 15:6

como el cuerpo sin el espíritu está muerto, así también la fe sin obras está muerta.

Hay que domar la lengua

3 Hermanos míos, no pretendan muchos de ustedes ser maestros, pues, como saben, seremos juzgados con más severidad. 2Todos fallamos mucho. Si alguien nunca falla en lo que dice, es una persona *perfecta, capaz también de controlar todo su cuerpo.

3Cuando ponemos freno en la boca de los caballos para que nos obedezcan, podemos controlar todo el animal. 4Fíjense también en los barcos. A pesar de ser tan grandes y de ser impulsados por fuertes vientos, se gobiernan por un pequeño timón a voluntad del piloto. 5Así también la lengua es un miembro muy pequeño del cuerpo, pero hace alarde de grandes hazañas. ¡Imagínense qué gran bosque se incendia con tan pequeña chispa! 6También la lengua es un fuego, un mundo de maldad. Siendo uno de nuestros órganos, contamina todo el cuerpo y, encendida por el infierno,f prende a su vez fuego a todo el curso de la vida.

7El *ser humano sabe domar y, en efecto, ha domado toda clase de fieras, de aves, de reptiles y de bestias marinas; 8pero nadie puede domar la lengua. Es un mal irrefrenable, lleno de veneno mortal.

9Con la lengua bendecimos a nuestro Señor y Padre, y con ella maldecimos a las personas, creadas a imagen de Dios. 10De una misma boca salen bendición y maldición. Hermanos míos, esto no debe ser así. 11¿Puede acaso brotar de una misma fuente agua dulce y agua salada?g 12Hermanos míos, ¿acaso puede dar aceitunas una higuera o higos una vid? Pues tampoco una fuente de agua salada puede dar agua dulce.

Dos clases de sabiduría

13¿Quién es sabio y entendido entre ustedes? Que lo demuestre con su buena conducta, mediante obras hechas con la humildad que le da su sabiduría. 14Pero si ustedes tienen envidias amargas y rivalidades en el corazón, dejen de presumir y de faltar a la verdad. 15Ésa no es la sabiduría que desciende del cielo, sino que es terrenal, puramente *humana y diabólica. 16Porque donde hay envidias y rivalidades, también hay confusión y toda clase de acciones malvadas.

17En cambio, la sabiduría que desciende del cielo es ante todo pura, y además pacífica, bondadosa, dócil, llena de compasión y de buenos frutos, imparcial y sincera. 18En fin, el fruto de la justicia se siembra en paz parah los que hacen la paz.

Sométanse a Dios

4 ¿De dónde surgen las guerras y los conflictos entre ustedes? ¿No es precisamente de las pasiones que luchan dentro de ustedes mismos?i 2Desean algo y no lo consiguen. Matan y sienten envidia, y no pueden obtener lo que quieren. Riñen y se hacen la guerra. No tienen, porque no piden. 3Y cuando piden, no reciben porque piden con malas intenciones, para satisfacer sus propias pasiones.

4¡Oh gente adúltera! ¿No saben que la amistad con el mundo es enemistad con Dios? Si alguien quiere ser amigo del mundo se vuelve enemigo de Dios. 5¿O creen que la Escritura dice en vano que Dios ama celosamente al espíritu que hizo morar en nosotros?j 6Pero él nos da mayor ayuda con su gracia. Por eso dice la Escritura:

«Dios se opone a los orgullosos,
pero da gracia a los humildes.»k

7Así que sométanse a Dios. Resistan al diablo, y él huirá de ustedes. 8Acérquense a Dios, y él se acercará a ustedes. ¡Pecadores, límpiense las manos! ¡Ustedes los inconstantes, purifiquen su corazón! 9Reconozcan sus miserias, lloren y laméntense. Que su risa se convierta en llanto, y su alegría en tristeza. 10Humíllense delante del Señor, y él los exaltará.

11Hermanos, no hablen mal unos de otros. Si alguien habla mal de su hermano, o lo juzga, habla mal de la ley y la juzga. Y si juzgas la ley, ya no eres cumplidor de la ley, sino su juez. 12No hay más que un solo legislador y juez, aquel que puede salvar y destruir. Tú, en cambio, ¿quién eres para juzgar a tu prójimo?

Alarde sobre el mañana

13Ahora escuchen esto, ustedes que dicen: «Hoy o mañana iremos a tal o cual ciudad, pasaremos allí un año, haremos negocios y ganaremos dinero.» 14¡Y eso que ni siquiera saben qué sucederá mañana! ¿Qué es su vida? Ustedes son como la niebla, que aparece por un momento y luego se desvanece. 15Más bien, debieran decir: «Si el Señor quiere, viviremos y haremos esto o aquello.» 16Pero ahora se *jactan en sus fanfarronerías. Toda esta jactancia es mala. 17Así que comete pecado todo el que sabe hacer el bien y no lo hace.

Advertencia a los ricos opresores

5 Ahora escuchen, ustedes los ricos: lloren a gritos por las calamidades que se les vienen encima. 2Se ha podrido su riqueza, y sus ropas están comidas por la polilla. 3Se han oxidado su oro y su plata. Ese óxido dará testimonio contra ustedes y consumirá como fuego sus cuerpos. Han amontonado riquezas, ¡y eso que estamos en los últimos tiempos! 4Oigan cómo clama contra ustedes el salario no pagado a los obreros que les trabajaron sus campos. El clamor de esos trabajadores ha llegado a oídos del Señor Todopoderoso. 5Ustedes han llevado en este mundo una vida de lujo y de placer desenfrenado. Lo que han hecho es engordar para el día de la matanza.l 6Han condenado y matado al justo sin que él les ofreciera resistencia.

Paciencia en los sufrimientos

7Por tanto, hermanos, tengan paciencia hasta la venida del Señor. Miren cómo espera el agricultor a que la tierra dé su precioso fruto y con qué paciencia aguarda las temporadas de lluvia. 8Así también ustedes, manténganse firmes y aguarden con paciencia la venida del Señor, que ya se acerca. 9No se quejen unos de otros, hermanos, para que no sean juzgados. ¡El juez ya está a la puerta!

10Hermanos, tomen como ejemplo de sufrimiento y de paciencia a los profetas que hablaron en el nombre del Señor. 11En verdad, consideramos *dichosos a los que perseveraron. Ustedes han oído hablar de la perseverancia de Job, y han visto lo que al final le dio el Señor. Es que el Señor es muy compasivo y misericordioso.

¹²Sobre todo, hermanos míos, no juren ni por el cielo ni por la tierra ni por ninguna otra cosa. Que su «sí» sea «sí», y su «no», «no», para que no sean condenados.

La oración de fe

¹³¿Está afligido alguno entre ustedes? Que ore. ¿Está alguno de buen ánimo? Que cante alabanzas. ¹⁴¿Está enfermo alguno de ustedes? Haga llamar a los *ancianos de la iglesia para que oren por él y lo unjan con aceite en el nombre del Señor. ¹⁵La oración de fe sanará al enfermo y el Señor lo levantará. Y si ha pecado, su pecado se le perdonará. ¹⁶Por eso, confiésense unos a otros sus pecados, y oren unos por otros, para que sean sanados. La oración del justo es poderosa y eficaz.

¹⁷Elías era un hombre con debilidades como las nuestras. Con fervor oró que no lloviera, y no llovió sobre la tierra durante tres años y medio. ¹⁸Volvió a orar, y el cielo dio su lluvia y la tierra produjo sus frutos.

¹⁹Hermanos míos, si alguno de ustedes se extravía de la verdad, y otro lo hace volver a ella, ²⁰recuerden que quien hace volver a un pecador de su extravío, lo salvará de la muerte y cubrirá muchísimos pecados.

Primera Carta de PEDRO

1 Pedro, apóstol de *Jesucristo,

a los elegidos, extranjeros dispersos por el Ponto, Galacia, Capadocia, *Asia y Bitinia, 2según la previsióna de Dios el Padre, mediante la obra *santificadora del Espíritu, para obedecer a Jesucristo y ser redimidosb por su sangre:

Que abunden en ustedes la gracia y la paz.

Alabanza a Dios por una esperanza viva

3¡Alabado sea Dios, Padre de nuestro Señor Jesucristo! Por su gran misericordia, nos ha hecho nacer de nuevo mediante la resurrección de Jesucristo, para que tengamos una esperanza viva 4y recibamos una herencia indestructible, incontaminada e inmarchitable. Tal herencia está reservada en el cielo para ustedes, 5a quienes el poder de Dios protege mediante la fe hasta que llegue la salvación que se ha de revelar en los últimos tiempos. 6Esto es para ustedes motivo de gran alegría, a pesar de que hasta ahora han tenido que sufrir diversas *pruebas por un tiempo. 7El oro, aunque perecedero, se acrisola al fuego. Así también la fe de ustedes, que vale mucho más que el oro, al ser acrisolada por las pruebas demostrará que es digna de aprobación, gloria y honor cuando Jesucristo se revele. 8Ustedes lo aman a pesar de no haberlo visto; y aunque no lo ven ahora, creen en él y se alegran con un gozo indescriptible y glorioso, 9pues están obteniendo la meta de su fe, que es su salvación.

10Los profetas, que anunciaron la gracia reservada para ustedes, estudiaron y observaron esta salvación. 11Querían descubrir a qué tiempo y a cuáles circunstancias se refería el Espíritu de *Cristo, que estaba en ellos, cuando testificó de antemano acerca de los sufrimientos de Cristo y de la gloria que vendría después de éstos. 12A ellos se les reveló que no se estaban sirviendo a sí mismos, sino que les servían a ustedes. Hablaban de las cosas que ahora les han anunciado los que les predicaron el *evangelio por medio del Espíritu Santo enviado del cielo. Aun los mismos ángeles anhelan contemplar esas cosas.

Sean santos

13Por eso, dispónganse para actuar con inteligencia;c tengan dominio propio; pongan su esperanza completamente en la gracia que se les dará cuando se revele *Jesucristo. 14Como hijos obedientes, no se amolden a los malos deseos que tenían antes, cuando vivían en la ignorancia. 15Más bien, sean ustedes *santos en todo lo que hagan, como también es santo quien los llamó; 16pues está escrito: «Sean santos, porque yo soy santo.»d 17Ya que invocan como Padre al que juzga con imparcialidad las obras de cada uno, vivan con temor reverente mientras sean peregrinos en este mundo. 18Como bien saben, ustedes fueron rescatados de la vida absurda que heredaron de sus antepasados. El precio de su rescate no se pagó con cosas perecederas, como el oro o la plata, 19sino con la preciosa sangre de Cristo, como de un cordero sin mancha y sin defecto. 20Cristo, a quien Dios escogió antes de la creación del mundo, se ha manifestado en estos últimos tiempos en beneficio de ustedes. 21Por medio de él ustedes creen en Dios, que lo *resucitó y glorificó, de modo que su fe y su esperanza están puestas en Dios.

22Ahora que se han purificado obedeciendo a la verdad y tienen un amor sincero por sus hermanos, ámense de todo corazóne los unos a los otros. 23Pues ustedes han nacido de nuevo, no de simiente perecedera, sino de simiente imperecedera, mediante la palabra de Dios que vive y permanece. 24Porque

«todo *mortal es como la hierba,
    y toda su gloria como la flor del campo;
la hierba se seca y la flor se cae,
25   pero la palabra del Señor permanece para
        siempre.»f

Y ésta es la palabra del evangelio que se les ha anunciado a ustedes.

2 Por lo tanto, abandonando toda maldad y todo engaño, hipocresía, envidias y toda calumnia, 2deseen con ansias la leche pura de la palabra,g como niños recién nacidos. Así, por medio de ella, crecerán en su salvación, 3ahora que han probado lo bueno que es el Señor.

La piedra viva y su pueblo escogido

4*Cristo es la piedra viva, rechazada por los *seres humanos pero escogida y preciosa ante Dios. Al acercarse a él, 5también ustedes son como piedras vivas, con las cuales se está edificando una casa espiritual. De este modo llegan a ser un sacerdocio *santo, para ofrecer sacrificios espirituales que Dios acepta por medio de Jesucristo. 6Así dice la Escritura:

«Miren que pongo en Sión
    una piedra principal escogida y preciosa,
y el que confíe en ella
    no será jamás defraudado.»h

7Para ustedes los creyentes, esta piedra es preciosa; pero para los incrédulos,

«la piedra que desecharon los constructores
    ha llegado a ser la piedra angular»,i

8y también:

«una piedra de *tropiezo
    y una roca que hace *caer.»j

Tropiezan al desobedecer la palabra, para lo cual estaban destinados.

9Pero ustedes son linaje escogido, real sacerdocio, nación santa, pueblo que pertenece a Dios, para que proclamen las obras maravillosas de aquel que los llamó de las tinieblas a su luz admirable. 10Ustedes antes ni siquiera eran pueblo, pero ahora son pueblo de Dios; antes no habían recibido misericordia, pero ahora ya la han recibido.

11Queridos hermanos, les ruego como a extranjeros y peregrinos en este mundo, que se aparten de los deseos pecaminososk que combaten contra la *vida. 12Mantengan entre los incrédulosl una conducta tan ejemplar que, aunque los acusen de hacer el mal, ellos observen las buenas obras de ustedes y glorifiquen a Dios en el día de la salvación.m

---

a 1:2 la previsión. Lit. el conocimiento previo. b 1:2 redimidos. Lit. Rociados. c 1:13 dispónganse . . . inteligencia. Lit. ceñidos los lomos de su mente. d 1:16 Lv 11:44,45; 19:2; 20:7; Is 40:6-8 e 1:22 de todo corazón. Var. con corazón puro. f 1:25 Is 40:6-8 g 2:2 leche pura de la palabra. Alt. leche espiritual pura. h 2:6 Is 28:16 i 2:7 Sal 118:22 j 2:8 Is 8:14 k 2:11 pecaminosos. Lit. *carnales. l 2:12 incrédulos. Lit. *Gentiles. m 2:12 de la salvación. Alt. del juicio. Lit. de la visitación.

Sumisión a los gobernantes y a los superiores

13Sométanse por causa del Señor a toda autoridad humana, ya sea al rey como suprema autoridad,
14o a los gobernadores que él envía para castigar a los
que hacen el mal y reconocer a los que hacen el bien.
15Porque ésta es la voluntad de Dios: que, practicando el bien, hagan callar la ignorancia de los insensatos. 16Eso es actuar como personas libres que no se
valen de su libertad para disimular la maldad, sino
que viven como *siervos de Dios. 17Den a todos el
debido respeto: amen a los hermanos, teman a Dios,
respeten al rey.

18Criados, sométanse con todo respeto a sus
amos, no sólo a los buenos y comprensivos sino también a los insoportables. 19Porque es digno de elogio
que, por sentido de responsabilidad delante de Dios,
se soporten las penalidades, aun sufriendo injustamente. 20Pero ¿cómo pueden ustedes atribuirse mérito alguno si soportan que los maltraten por hacer el
mal? En cambio, si sufren por hacer el bien, eso merece elogio delante de Dios. 21Para esto fueron llamados, porque *Cristo sufrió por ustedes, dándoles
ejemplo para que sigan sus pasos.

22«Él no cometió ningún pecado,
ni hubo engaño en su boca.»[n]

23Cuando proferían insultos contra él, no replicaba
con insultos; cuando padecía, no amenazaba, sino
que se entregaba a aquel que juzga con justicia. 24Él
mismo, en su cuerpo, llevó al madero nuestros pecados, para que muramos al pecado y vivamos para la
justicia. Por sus heridas ustedes han sido sanados.
25Antes eran ustedes como ovejas descarriadas, pero
ahora han vuelto al Pastor que cuida[ñ] de sus vidas.

Deberes conyugales

3 Así mismo, esposas, sométanse a sus esposos, de
modo que si algunos de ellos no creen en la palabra, puedan ser ganados más por el comportamiento de ustedes que por sus palabras, 2al observar
su conducta íntegra y respetuosa. 3Que la belleza de
ustedes no sea la externa, que consiste en adornos tales como peinados ostentosos, joyas de oro y vestidos lujosos. 4Que su belleza sea más bien la
incorruptible, la que procede de lo íntimo del corazón y consiste en un espíritu suave y apacible. Ésta sí
que tiene mucho valor delante de Dios. 5Así se ador-
naban en tiempos antiguos las *santas mujeres que
esperaban en Dios, cada una sumisa a su esposo. 6Tal
es el caso de Sara, que obedecía a Abraham y lo llamaba su señor. Ustedes son hijas de ella si hacen el
bien y viven sin ningún temor.

7De igual manera, ustedes esposos, sean comprensivos en su vida conyugal, tratando cada uno a
su esposa con respeto, ya que como mujer es más delicada,[o] y ambos son herederos del grato don de la
vida. Así nada estorbará las oraciones de ustedes.

Sufrir por hacer el bien

8En fin, vivan en armonía los unos con los otros;
compartan penas y alegrías, practiquen el amor fraternal, sean compasivos y humildes. 9No devuelvan
mal por mal ni insulto por insulto; más bien, bendigan, porque para esto fueron llamados, para heredar
una bendición. 10En efecto,

«el que quiera amar la vida
y gozar de días felices,
que refrene su lengua de hablar el mal
y sus labios de proferir engaños;
11que se aparte del mal y haga el bien;
que busque la paz y la siga.
12Porque los ojos del Señor están sobre los
justos,
y sus oídos, atentos a sus oraciones;
pero el rostro del Señor está contra los que
hacen el mal».[p]

13Y a ustedes, ¿quién les va a hacer daño si se esfuerzan por hacer el bien? 14*¡Dichosos si sufren por
causa de la justicia! «No teman lo que ellos temen,[q]
ni se dejen asustar.»[r] 15Más bien, honren en su corazón a *Cristo como Señor. Estén siempre preparados
para responder a todo el que les pida razón de la esperanza que hay en ustedes. 16Pero háganlo con
gentileza y respeto, manteniendo la conciencia limpia, para que los que hablan mal de la buena conducta de ustedes en Cristo, se avergüencen de sus
calumnias. 17Si es la voluntad de Dios, es preferible
sufrir por hacer el bien que por hacer el mal.

18Porque Cristo murió por los pecados una vez
por todas, el justo por los injustos, a fin de llevarlos a
ustedes a Dios. Él sufrió la muerte en su *cuerpo,
pero el Espíritu hizo que volviera a la vida.[s] 19Por
medio del Espíritu fue y predicó a los espíritus encarcelados, 20que en los tiempos antiguos, en los días de
Noé, desobedecieron, cuando Dios esperaba con paciencia mientras se construía el arca. En ella sólo pocas personas, ocho en total, se salvaron mediante el
agua, 21la cual simboliza el bautismo que ahora los
salva también a ustedes. El bautismo no consiste en
la limpieza del cuerpo, sino en el compromiso de tener una buena conciencia delante de Dios. Esta salvación es posible por la resurrección de Jesucristo,
22quien subió al cielo y tomó su lugar a la *derecha
de Dios, y a quien están sometidos los ángeles, las
autoridades y los poderes.

Vivir el ejemplo de Cristo

4 Por tanto, ya que *Cristo sufrió en el cuerpo,
asuman también ustedes la misma actitud; porque el que ha sufrido en el *cuerpo ha roto con el pecado, 2para vivir el resto de su vida terrenal no
satisfaciendo sus pasiones *humanas sino cumpliendo la voluntad de Dios. 3Pues ya basta con el tiempo
que han desperdiciado haciendo lo que agrada a los
incrédulos,[t] entregados al desenfreno, a las pasiones,
a las borracheras, a las orgías, a las parrandas y a las
idolatrías abominables. 4A ellos les parece extraño
que ustedes ya no corran con ellos en ese mismo des-
bordamiento de inmoralidad, y por eso los insultan.
5Pero ellos tendrán que rendirle cuentas a aquel que
está preparado para juzgar a los vivos y a los muertos. 6Por esto también se les predicó el *evangelio
aun a los muertos, para que, a pesar de haber sido
juzgados según criterios *humanos en lo que atañe
al cuerpo, vivan conforme a Dios en lo que atañe al
espíritu.[u]

7Ya se acerca el fin de todas las cosas. Así que,
para orar bien, manténganse sobrios y con la mente
despejada. 8Sobre todo, ámense los unos a los otros
profundamente, porque el amor cubre multitud de
pecados. 9Practiquen la hospitalidad entre ustedes
sin quejarse. 10Cada uno ponga al servicio de los demás el don que haya recibido, administrando fiel-

[n] **2:22** Is 53:9 [ñ] **2:25** *Pastor que cuida.* Lit. *Pastor y *Obispo.* [o] **3:7** *ya que . . . delicada.* Lit. *como a vaso más frágil.* [p] **3:12** Sal 34:12-16 [q] **3:14** *lo que ellos temen.* Alt. *sus amenazas.* [r] **3:14** Is 8:12 [s] **3:18** *pero . . . vida.* Alt. *pero volvió a la vida en su espíritu.* [t] **4:3** *incrédulos.* Lit. **gentiles.* [u] **4:6** *en lo que atañe al espíritu.* Alt. *en el Espíritu.*

mente la gracia de Dios en sus diversas formas. [11]El que habla, hágalo como quien expresa las palabras mismas de Dios; el que presta algún servicio, hágalo como quien tiene el poder de Dios. Así Dios será en todo alabado por medio de Jesucristo, a quien sea la gloria y el poder por los siglos de los siglos. Amén.

Sufrir por seguir a Cristo

[12]Queridos hermanos, no se extrañen del fuego de la *prueba que están soportando, como si fuera algo insólito. [13]Al contrario, alégrense de tener parte en los sufrimientos de *Cristo, para que también sea inmensa su alegría cuando se revele la gloria de Cristo. [14]*Dichosos ustedes si los insultan por causa del nombre de Cristo, porque el glorioso Espíritu de Dios reposa sobre ustedes. [15]Que ninguno tenga que sufrir por asesino, ladrón o delincuente, ni siquiera por entrometido. [16]Pero si alguien sufre por ser cristiano, que no se avergüence, sino que alabe a Dios por llevar el nombre de Cristo. [17]Porque es tiempo de que el juicio comience por la familia de Dios; y si comienza por nosotros, ¡cuál no será el fin de los que se rebelan contra el *evangelio de Dios!

[18]«Si el justo a duras penas se salva,
¿qué será del impío y del pecador?»v

[19]Así pues, los que sufren según la voluntad de Dios, entréguense a su fiel Creador y sigan practicando el bien.

Exhortación a los ancianos y a los jóvenes

5 A los *ancianos que están entre ustedes, yo, que soy anciano como ellos, testigo de los sufrimientos de *Cristo y partícipe con ellos de la gloria que se ha de revelar, les ruego esto: [2]cuiden como pastores el rebaño de Dios que está a su cargo, no por obligación ni por ambición de dinero, sino con afán de ser-

vir, como Dios quiere. [3]No sean tiranos con los que están a su cuidado, sino sean ejemplos para el rebaño. [4]Así, cuando aparezca el Pastor supremo, ustedes recibirán la inmarcesible corona de gloria.

[5]Así mismo, jóvenes, sométanse a los ancianos. Revístanse todos de humildad en su trato mutuo, porque

«Dios se opone a los orgullosos,
pero da gracia a los humildes».w

[6]Humíllense, pues, bajo la poderosa mano de Dios, para que él los exalte a su debido tiempo. [7]Depositen en él toda ansiedad, porque él cuida de ustedes. [8]Practiquen el dominio propio y manténganse alerta. Su enemigo el diablo ronda como león rugiente, buscando a quién devorar. [9]Resístanlo, manteniéndose firmes en la fe, sabiendo que sus hermanos en todo el mundo están soportando la misma clase de sufrimientos.

[10]Y después de que ustedes hayan sufrido un poco de tiempo, Dios mismo, el Dios de toda gracia que los llamó a su gloria eterna en Cristo, los restaurará y los hará fuertes, firmes y estables. [11]A él sea el poder por los siglos de los siglos. Amén.

Saludos finales

[12]Con la ayuda de *Silvano, a quien considero un hermano fiel, les he escrito brevemente, para animarlos y confirmarles que ésta es la verdadera gracia de Dios. Manténganse firmes en ella.

[13]Saludos de parte de la que está en Babilonia, escogida como ustedes, y también de mi hijo Marcos. [14]Salúdense los unos a los otros con un beso de amor fraternal.

Paz a todos ustedes que están en *Cristo.

v 4:18 Pr 11:31   w 5:5 Pr 3:34

Segunda Carta de PEDRO

1 Simón Pedro, *siervo y apóstol de *Jesucristo,

a los que por la justicia de nuestro Dios y Salvador Jesucristo han recibido una fe tan preciosa como la nuestra.

2Que abunden en ustedes la gracia y la paz por medio del conocimiento que tienen de Dios y de Jesús nuestro Señor.

Firmeza en el llamamiento y en la elección

3Su divino poder, al darnos el conocimiento de aquel que nos llamó por su propia gloria y potencia, nos ha concedido todas las cosas que necesitamos para vivir como Dios manda.a 4Así Dios nos ha entregado sus preciosas y magníficas promesas para que ustedes, luego de escapar de la corrupción que hay en el mundo debido a los malos deseos, lleguen a tener parte en la naturaleza divina.b

5Precisamente por eso, esfuércense por añadir a su fe, virtud; a su virtud, entendimiento; 6al entendimiento, dominio propio; al dominio propio, constancia; a la constancia, devoción a Dios; 7a la devoción a Dios, afecto fraternal; y al afecto fraternal, amor. 8Porque estas cualidades, si abundan en ustedes, les harán crecer en el conocimiento de nuestro Señor Jesucristo, y evitarán que sean inútiles e improductivos. 9En cambio, el que no las tiene es tan corto de vista que ya ni ve, y se olvida de que ha sido limpiado de sus antiguos pecados. 10Por lo tanto, hermanos, esfuércense más todavía por asegurarse del llamado de Dios, que fue quien los eligió. Si hacen estas cosas, no caerán jamás, 11y se les abrirán de par en par las puertas del reino eterno de nuestro Señor y Salvador Jesucristo.

La veracidad de la Escritura

12Por eso siempre les recordaré estas cosas, por más que las sepan y estén afianzados en la verdad que ahora tienen. 13Además, considero que tengo la obligación de refrescarles la memoria mientras viva en esta habitación pasajera que es mi cuerpo; 14porque sé que dentro de poco tendré que abandonarlo, según me lo ha manifestado nuestro Señor *Jesucristo. 15También me esforzaré con empeño para que aun después de mi partidac ustedes puedan recordar estas cosas en todo tiempo.

16Cuando les dimos a conocer la venida de nuestro Señor Jesucristo en todo su poder, no estábamos siguiendo sutiles cuentos supersticiosos sino dando testimonio de su grandeza, ya que vimos con nuestros propios ojos. 17Él recibió honor y gloria de parte de Dios el Padre, cuando desde la majestuosa gloria se le dirigió aquella voz que dijo: «Éste es mi Hijo amado; estoy muy complacido con él.»d 18Nosotros mismos oímos esa voz que vino del cielo cuando estábamos con él en el monte santo. 19Esto ha venido a confirmarnos la palabrae de los profetas, a la cual ustedes hacen bien en prestar atención, como a una lámpara que brilla en un lugar oscuro, hasta que despunte el día y salga el lucero de la mañana en sus corazones. 20Ante todo, tengan muy presente que ninguna profecía de la Escritura surge de la interpretación particular de nadie. 21Porque la profecía no ha tenido su origen en la voluntad *humana, sino que

los profetas hablaron de parte de Dios, impulsados por el Espíritu Santo.

Los falsos maestros y su destrucción

2 En el pueblo judío hubo falsos profetas, y también entre ustedes habrá falsos maestros que encubiertamente introducirán herejías destructivas, al extremo de negar al mismo Señor que los rescató. Esto les traerá una pronta destrucción. 2Muchos los seguirán en sus prácticas vergonzosas, y por causa de ellos se difamará el camino de la verdad. 3Llevados por la avaricia, estos maestros los explotarán a ustedes con palabras engañosas. Desde hace mucho tiempo su condenación está preparada y su destrucción los acecha.

4Dios no perdonó a los ángeles cuando pecaron, sino que los arrojó al *abismo, metiéndolos en tenebrosas cavernasf y reservándolos para el juicio. 5Tampoco perdonó al mundo antiguo cuando mandó un diluvio sobre los impíos, aunque protegió a ocho personas, incluyendo a Noé, predicador de la justicia. 6Además, condenó a las ciudades de Sodoma y Gomorra, y las redujo a cenizas, poniéndolas como escarmiento para los impíos. 7Por otra parte, libró al justo Lot, que se hallaba abrumado por la vida desenfrenada de esos perversos, 8pues este justo, que convivía con ellos y amaba el bien, día tras día sentía que se le despedazaba el alma por las obras inicuas que veía y oía. 9Todo esto demuestra que el Señor sabe librar de la *prueba a los que viven como Dios quiere, y mantener castigados a los impíos para el día del juicio. 10Esto les espera sobre todo a los que siguen los corrompidos deseos de la *naturaleza humana y desprecian la autoridad del Señor.

¡Atrevidos y arrogantes que son! No tienen reparo en insultar a los seres celestiales, 11mientras que los ángeles, a pesar de superarlos en fuerza y en poder, no pronuncian contra tales seres ninguna acusación insultante en la presencia del Señor. 12Pero aquéllos blasfeman en asuntos que no entienden. Como animales irracionales, se guían únicamente por el instinto, y nacieron para ser atrapados y degollados. Lo mismo que esos animales, perecerán también en su corrupción 13y recibirán el justo pago por sus injusticias. Su concepto de placer es entregarse a las pasiones desenfrenadas en pleno día. Son manchas y suciedad, que gozan de sus placeres mientras los acompañan a ustedes en sus comidas. 14Tienen los ojos llenos de adulterio y son insaciables en el pecar; seducen a las personas inconstantes; son expertos en la avaricia, ¡hijos de maldición! 15Han abandonado el camino recto, y se han extraviado para seguir la senda de Balán, hijo de Bosor,g a quien le encantaba el salario de la injusticia. 16Pero fue reprendido por su maldad: su burra —una muda bestia de carga— habló con voz humana y refrenó la locura del profeta.

17Estos individuos son fuentes sin agua, niebla empujada por la tormenta, para quienes está reservada la más densa oscuridad. 18Pronunciando discursos arrogantes y sin sentido, seducen con los instintos *naturales desenfrenados a quienes apenas comienzan a apartarse de los que viven en el error. 19Les prometen libertad, cuando ellos mismos son *esclavos de la corrupción, ya que cada uno es escla-

a 1:3 para vivir como Dios manda. Lit. para la vida y la piedad.   b 1:4 lleguen . . . divina. Alt. lleguen a ser colaboradores con Dios.   c 1:15 partida. Lit. Éxodo.   d 1:17 Mt 17:5; Mr 9:7; Lc 9:35   e 1:19 Esto . . . palabra. Lit. También tenemos la muy segura palabra.   f 2:4 cavernas. Var. Cadenas.   g 2:15 Bosor. Var. Beor.

vo de aquello que lo ha dominado. ²⁰Si habiendo escapado de la contaminación del mundo por haber conocido a nuestro Señor y Salvador *Jesucristo, vuelven a enredarse en ella y son vencidos, terminan en peores condiciones que al principio. ²¹Más les hubiera valido no conocer el camino de la justicia, que abandonarlo después de haber conocido el santo mandamiento que se les dio. ²²En su caso ha sucedido lo que acertadamente afirman estos proverbios: «El *perro vuelve a su vómito»,ʰ y «la puerca lavada, a revolcarse en el lodo».

El día del Señor

3 Queridos hermanos, ésta es ya la segunda carta que les escribo. En las dos he procurado refrescarles la memoria para que, con una mente íntegra, ²recuerden las palabras que los *santos profetas pronunciaron en el pasado, y el mandamiento que dio nuestro Señor y Salvador por medio de los apóstoles.

³Ante todo, deben saber que en los últimos días vendrá gente burlona que, siguiendo sus malos deseos, se mofará: ⁴«¿Qué hubo de esa promesa de su venida? Nuestros padres murieron, y nada ha cambiado desde el principio de la creación.» ⁵Pero intencionalmente olvidan que desde tiempos antiguos, por la palabra de Dios, existía el cielo y también la tierra, que surgió del agua y mediante el agua. ⁶Por la palabra y el agua, el mundo de aquel entonces pereció inundado. ⁷Y ahora, por esa misma palabra, el cielo y la tierra están guardados para el fuego, reservados para el día del juicio y de la destrucción de los impíos.

⁸Pero no olviden, queridos hermanos, que para el Señor un día es como mil años, y mil años como un día. ⁹El Señor no tarda en cumplir su promesa, según entienden algunos la tardanza. Más bien, él tiene paciencia con ustedes, porque no quiere que nadie perezca sino que todos se *arrepientan.

¹⁰Pero el día del Señor vendrá como un ladrón. En aquel día los cielos desaparecerán con un estruendo espantoso, los elementos serán destruidos por el fuego, y la tierra, con todo lo que hay en ella, será quemada.ⁱ

¹¹Ya que todo será destruido de esa manera, ¿no deberían vivir ustedes como Dios manda, siguiendo una conducta intachable ¹²y esperando ansiosamente la venida del día de Dios? Ese día los cielos serán destruidos por el fuego, y los elementos se derretirán con el calor de las llamas. ¹³Pero, según su promesa, esperamos un cielo nuevo y una tierra nueva, en los que habite la justicia.

¹⁴Por eso, queridos hermanos, mientras esperan estos acontecimientos, esfuércense para que Dios los halle sin mancha y sin defecto, y en paz con él. ¹⁵Tengan presente que la paciencia de nuestro Señor significa salvación, tal como les escribió también nuestro querido hermano Pablo, con la sabiduría que Dios le dio. ¹⁶En todas sus cartas se refiere a estos mismos temas. Hay en ellas algunos puntos difíciles de entender, que los ignorantes e inconstantes tergiversan, como lo hacen también con las demás Escrituras, para su propia perdición.

¹⁷Así que ustedes, queridos hermanos, puesto que ya saben esto de antemano, manténganse alerta, no sea que, arrastrados por el error de esos libertinos, pierdan la estabilidad y caigan. ¹⁸Más bien, crezcan en la gracia y en el conocimiento de nuestro Señor y Salvador *Jesucristo. ¡A él sea la gloria ahora y para siempre! Amén.ᵏ

ʰ **2:22** Pr 26:11   ⁱ **3:10** *será quemada.* Var. *quedará al descubierto.*   ʲ **3:12** *esperando ansiosamente.* Alt. *esperando y apresurando.* ᵏ **3:18** Var. no incluye: *Amén.*

Primera Carta de JUAN

El Verbo de vida

1 Lo que ha sido desde el principio, lo que hemos oído, lo que hemos visto con nuestros propios ojos, lo que hemos contemplado, lo que hemos tocado con las manos, esto es lo que les anunciamos respecto al *Verbo que es vida. ²Esta vida se manifestó. Nosotros la hemos visto y damos testimonio de ella, y les anunciamos a ustedes la vida eterna que estaba con el Padre y que se nos ha manifestado. ³Les anunciamos lo que hemos visto y oído, para que también ustedes tengan comunión con nosotros. Y nuestra comunión es con el Padre y con su Hijo *Jesucristo. ⁴Les escribimos estas cosas para que nuestra alegríaᵃ sea completa.

Caminemos en la luz

⁵Éste es el mensaje que hemos oído de él y que les anunciamos: Dios es luz y en él no hay ninguna oscuridad. ⁶Si afirmamos que tenemos comunión con él, pero vivimos en la oscuridad, mentimos y no ponemos en práctica la verdad. ⁷Pero si vivimos en la luz, así como él está en la luz, tenemos comunión unos con otros, y la sangre de su Hijo Jesucristo nos limpia de todo pecado.

⁸Si afirmamos que no tenemos pecado, nos engañamos a nosotros mismos y no tenemos la verdad. ⁹Si confesamos nuestros pecados, Dios, que es fiel y justo, nos los perdonará y nos limpiará de toda maldad. ¹⁰Si afirmamos que no hemos pecado, lo hacemos pasar por mentiroso y su palabra no habita en nosotros.

2 Mis queridos hijos, les escribo estas cosas para que no pequen. Pero si alguno peca, tenemos ante el Padre a un *intercesor, a *Jesucristo, el Justo. ²Él es el sacrificio por el perdón de nuestros pecados,ᵇ y no sólo por los nuestros sino por los de todo el mundo.

³¿Cómo sabemos si hemos llegado a conocer a Dios? Si obedecemos sus mandamientos. ⁴El que afirma: «Lo conozco», pero no obedece sus mandamientos, es un mentiroso y no tiene la verdad. ⁵En cambio, el amor de Dios se manifiesta plenamenteᶜ en la vida del que obedece su palabra. De este modo sabemos que estamos unidos a él: ⁶el que afirma que permanece en él, debe vivir como él vivió.

⁷Queridos hermanos, lo que les escribo no es un mandamiento nuevo, sino uno antiguo que han tenido desde el principio. Este mandamiento antiguo es el mensaje que ya oyeron. ⁸Por otra parte, lo que les escribo es un mandamiento nuevo, cuya verdad se manifiesta tanto en la vida de *Cristo como en la de ustedes, porque la oscuridad se va desvaneciendo y ya brilla la luz verdadera.

⁹El que afirma que está en la luz, pero odia a su hermano, todavía está en la oscuridad. ¹⁰El que ama a su hermano permanece en la luz, y no hay nada en su vidaᵈ que lo haga *tropezar. ¹¹Pero el que odia a su hermano está en la oscuridad y en ella vive, y no sabe a dónde va porque la oscuridad no lo deja ver.

¹²Les escribo a ustedes, queridos hijos,
porque sus pecados han sido perdonados
por el nombre de Cristo.

¹³Les escribo a ustedes, padres,
porque han conocido al que es desde el
principio.
Les escribo a ustedes, jóvenes,
porque han vencido al maligno.
Les he escrito a ustedes, queridos hijos,
porque han conocido al Padre.
¹⁴Les he escrito a ustedes, padres,
porque han conocido al que es desde el
principio.
Les he escrito a ustedes, jóvenes,
porque son fuertes,
y la palabra de Dios permanece en ustedes,
y han vencido al maligno.

No amemos al mundo

¹⁵No amen al mundo ni nada de lo que hay en él. Si alguien ama al mundo, no tiene el amor del Padre. ¹⁶Porque nada de lo que hay en el mundo —los malos deseos del *cuerpo, la codicia de los ojos y la arrogancia de la vida— proviene del Padre sino del mundo. ¹⁷El mundo se acaba con sus malos deseos, pero el que hace la voluntad de Dios permanece para siempre.

Cuidémonos de los anticristos

¹⁸Queridos hijos, ésta es la hora final, y así como ustedes oyeron que el anticristo vendría, muchos son los anticristos que han surgido ya. Por eso nos damos cuenta de que ésta es la hora final. ¹⁹Aunque salieron de entre nosotros, en realidad no eran de los nuestros; si lo hubieran sido, se habrían quedado con nosotros. Su salida sirvió para comprobar que ninguno de ellos era de los nuestros.

²⁰Todos ustedes, en cambio, han recibido unción del Santo, de manera que conocen la verdad.ᵉ ²¹No les escribo porque ignoren la verdad, sino porque la conocen y porque ninguna mentira procede de la verdad. ²²¿Quién es el mentiroso sino el que niega que Jesús es el *Cristo? Es el anticristo, el que niega al Padre y al Hijo. ²³Todo el que niega al Hijo no tiene al Padre; el que reconoce al Hijo tiene también al Padre.

²⁴Permanezca en ustedes lo que han oído desde el principio, y así ustedesᶠ permanecerán también en el Hijo y en el Padre. ²⁵Ésta es la promesa que él nos dio: la vida eterna. ²⁶Estas cosas les escribo acerca de los que procuran engañarlos. ²⁷En cuanto a ustedes, la unción que de él recibieron permanece en ustedes, y no necesitan que nadie les enseñe. Esa unción es auténtica —no es falsa— y les enseña todas las cosas. Permanezcan en él, tal y como él les enseñó.

Permanezcamos en Dios

²⁸Y ahora, queridos hijos, permanezcamosᵍ en él para que, cuando se manifieste, podamos presentarnos ante él confiadamente, seguros de no ser avergonzados en su venida.

²⁹Si reconocen que *Jesucristo es justo, reconozcan también que todo el que practica la justicia ha nacido de él.

3 ¡Fíjense qué gran amor nos ha dado el Padre, que se nos llame hijos de Dios! ¡Y lo somos! El mundo no nos conoce, precisamente porque no lo conoció a

---

ᵃ **1:4** *nuestra alegría.* Var. *la alegría de ustedes.* ᵇ **2:2** *el sacrificio por el perdón de.* Lit. *la *propiciación por.* ᶜ **2:5** *se manifiesta plenamente.* Lit. *se ha *perfeccionado.* ᵈ **2:10** *en su vida.* Alt. *en la luz.* ᵉ **2:20** *la verdad.* Var. *todas las cosas.* ᶠ **2:24** *principio . . . ustedes.* Lit. *principio. Si permanece en ustedes lo que han oído desde el principio, ustedes.* ᵍ **2:28** *permanezcamos.* Lit. *Permanezcan.*

él. 2Queridos hermanos, ahora somos hijos de Dios, pero todavía no se ha manifestado lo que habremos de ser. Sabemos, sin embargo, que cuando Cristo venga seremos semejantes a él, porque lo veremos tal como él es. 3Todo el que tiene esta esperanza en Cristo, se purifica a sí mismo, así como él es puro.

4Todo el que comete pecado quebranta la ley; de hecho, el pecado es transgresión de la ley. 5Pero ustedes saben que Jesucristo se manifestó para quitar nuestros pecados. Y él no tiene pecado. 6Todo el que permanece en él, no practica el pecado.h Todo el que practica el pecado, no lo ha visto ni lo ha conocido.

7Queridos hijos, que nadie los engañe. El que practica la justicia es justo, así como él es justo. 8El que practica el pecado es del diablo, porque el diablo ha estado pecando desde el principio. El Hijo de Dios fue enviado precisamente para destruir las obras del diablo. 9Ninguno que haya nacido de Dios practica el pecado, porque la semilla de Dios permanece en él; no puede practicar el pecado,i porque ha nacido de Dios. 10Así distinguimos entre los hijos de Dios y los hijos del diablo: el que no practica la justicia no es hijo de Dios; ni tampoco lo es el que no ama a su hermano.

Amémonos los unos a los otros

11Éste es el mensaje que han oído desde el principio: que nos amemos los unos a los otros. 12No seamos como Caín que, por ser del maligno, asesinó a su hermano. ¿Y por qué lo hizo? Porque sus propias obras eran malas, y las de su hermano justas. 13Hermanos, no se extrañen si el mundo los odia. 14Nosotros sabemos que hemos pasado de la muerte a la vida porque amamos a nuestros hermanos. El que no ama permanece en la muerte. 15Todo el que odia a su hermano es un asesino, y ustedes saben que en ningún asesino permanece la vida eterna.

16En esto conocemos lo que es el amor: en que Jesucristo entregó su *vida por nosotros. Así también nosotros debemos entregar la vida por nuestros hermanos. 17Si alguien que posee bienes materiales ve que su hermano está pasando necesidad, y no tiene compasión de él, ¿cómo se puede decir que el amor de Dios habita en él? 18Queridos hijos, no amemos de palabra ni de labios para afuera, sino con hechos y de verdad.

19En esto sabremos que somos de la verdad, y nos sentiremos seguros delante de él: 20que aunque nuestro corazón nos condene, Dios es más grande que nuestro corazón y lo sabe todo. 21Queridos hermanos, si el corazón no nos condena, tenemos confianza delante de Dios, 22y recibimos todo lo que le pedimos porque obedecemos sus mandamientos y hacemos lo que le agrada. 23Y éste es su mandamiento: que creamos en el nombre de su Hijo Jesucristo, y que nos amemos los unos a los otros, pues así lo ha dispuesto. 24El que obedece sus mandamientos permanece en Dios, y Dios en él. ¿Cómo sabemos que él permanece en nosotros? Por el Espíritu que nos dio.

Vivamos en el Espíritu

4 Queridos hermanos, no crean a cualquiera que pretenda estar inspirado por el Espíritu,j sino sométanlo a prueba para ver si es de Dios, porque han salido por el mundo muchos falsos profetas. 2En esto pueden discernir quién tiene el Espíritu de Dios: todo profetak que reconoce que *Jesucristo ha venido en cuerpo humano, es de Dios; 3todo profeta que no reconoce a Jesús, no es de Dios sino del anticristo. Ustedes han oído que éste viene; en efecto, ya está en el mundo.

4Ustedes, queridos hijos, son de Dios y han vencido a esos falsos profetas, porque el que está en ustedes es más poderoso que el que está en el mundo. 5Ellos son del mundo; por eso hablan desde el punto de vista del mundo, y el mundo los escucha. 6Nosotros somos de Dios, y todo el que conoce a Dios nos escucha; pero el que no es de Dios no nos escucha. Así distinguimos entre el Espíritu de la verdad y el espíritu del engaño.

Permanezcamos en el amor

7Queridos hermanos, amémonos los unos a los otros, porque el amor viene de Dios, y todo el que ama ha nacido de él y lo conoce. 8El que no ama no conoce a Dios, porque Dios es amor. 9Así manifestó Dios su amor entre nosotros: en que envió a su Hijo unigénito al mundo para que vivamos por medio de él. 10En esto consiste el amor: no en que nosotros hayamos amado a Dios, sino en que él nos amó y envió a su Hijo para que fuera ofrecido como sacrificio por el perdón del nuestros pecados. 11Queridos hermanos, ya que Dios nos ha amado así, también nosotros debemos amarnos los unos a los otros. 12Nadie ha visto jamás a Dios, pero si nos amamos los unos a los otros, Dios permanece entre nosotros, y entrem nosotros su amor se ha manifestado plenamente.n

13¿Cómo sabemos que permanecemos en él, y que él permanece en nosotros? Porque nos ha dado de su Espíritu. 14Y nosotros hemos visto y declaramos que el Padre envió a su Hijo para ser el Salvador del mundo. 15Si alguien reconoce que Jesús es el Hijo de Dios, Dios permanece en él, y él en Dios. 16Y nosotros hemos llegado a saber y creer que Dios nos ama.

Dios es amor. El que permanece en amor, permanece en Dios, y Dios en él. 17Ese amor se manifiesta plenamenteñ entre nosotros para que en el día del juicio comparezcamos con toda confianza, porque en este mundo hemos vivido como vivió Jesús. En el amor no hay temor, 18sino que el amor *perfecto echa fuera el temor. El que teme espera el castigo, así que no ha sido perfeccionado en el amor.

19Nosotros amamos a Dios porque él nos amó primero. 20Si alguien afirma: «Yo amo a Dios», pero odia a su hermano, es un mentiroso; pues el que no ama a su hermano, a quien ha visto, no puede amar a Dios, a quien no ha visto. 21Y él nos ha dado este mandamiento: el que ama a Dios, ame también a su hermano.

Vivamos en la fe

5 Todo el que cree que Jesús es el *Cristo, ha nacido de Dios, y todo el que ama al padre, ama también a sus hijos. 2Así, cuando amamos a Dios y cumplimos sus mandamientos, sabemos que amamos a los hijos de Dios. 3En esto consiste el amor a Dios: en que obedezcamos sus mandamientos. Y éstos no son difíciles de cumplir, 4porque todo el que ha nacido de Dios vence al mundo. Ésta es la victoria que vence al mundo: nuestra fe. 5¿Quién es el que vence al mundo sino el que cree que Jesús es el Hijo de Dios?

---

h 3:6 no practica el pecado. Alt. no peca. i 3:9 no puede practicar el pecado. Alt. no puede pecar. j 4:1 no crean . . . por el Espíritu. Lit. no crean a todo espíritu. k 4:2 profeta. Lit. espíritu; también en v. 3. l 4:10 sacrificio por el perdón de. Lit. *propiciación por. m 4:12 entre . . . entre. Alt. en . . . En. n 4:12 se ha manifestado plenamente. Lit. se ha *perfeccionado. ñ 4:17 se manifiesta plenamente. Lit. se ha perfeccionado.

⁶Éste es el que vino mediante agua y sangre, Jesucristo; no sólo mediante agua, sino mediante agua y sangre. El Espíritu es quien da testimonio de esto, porque el Espíritu es la verdad. ⁷Tres son los que dan testimonio, ⁸y los tres están de acuerdo: el Espíritu,º el agua y la sangre. ⁹Aceptamos el testimonio *humano, pero el testimonio de Dios vale mucho más, precisamente porque es el testimonio de Dios, que él ha dado acerca de su Hijo. ¹⁰El que cree en el Hijo de Dios acepta este testimonio. El que no cree a Dios lo hace pasar por mentiroso, por no haber creído el testimonio que Dios ha dado acerca de su Hijo. ¹¹Y el testimonio es éste: que Dios nos ha dado vida eterna, y esa vida está en su Hijo. ¹²El que tiene al Hijo, tiene la vida; el que no tiene al Hijo de Dios, no tiene la vida.

Observaciones finales

¹³Les escribo estas cosas a ustedes que creen en el nombre del Hijo de Dios, para que sepan que tienen vida eterna. ¹⁴Ésta es la confianza que tenemos al acercarnos a Dios: que si pedimos conforme a su voluntad, él nos oye. ¹⁵Y si sabemos que Dios oye todas nuestras oraciones, podemos estar seguros de que ya tenemos lo que le hemos pedido.

¹⁶Si alguno ve a su hermano cometer un pecado que no lleva a la muerte, ore por él y Dios le dará vida. Me refiero a quien comete un pecado que no lleva a la muerte. Hay un pecado que sí lleva a la muerte, y en ese caso no digo que se ore por él. ¹⁷Toda maldad es pecado, pero hay pecado que no lleva a la muerte.

¹⁸Sabemos que el que ha nacido de Dios no está en pecado: *Jesucristo, que nació de Dios, lo protege, y el maligno no llega a tocarlo. ¹⁹Sabemos que somos hijos de Dios, y que el mundo entero está bajo el control del maligno. ²⁰También sabemos que el Hijo de Dios ha venido y nos ha dado entendimiento para que conozcamos al Dios verdadero. Y estamos con el Verdadero, conᴾ su Hijo Jesucristo. Éste es el Dios verdadero y la vida eterna.

²¹Queridos hijos, apártense de los ídolos.

º **5:7,8** *testimonio . . . Espíritu.* Var. *testimonio en el cielo: el Padre, el Verbo y el Espíritu Santo, y estos tres son uno.* v. 8 *Y hay tres que dan testimonio en la tierra: el Espíritu* (este pasaje se encuentra en mss. posteriores de la Vulgata, pero no está en ningún ms. griego anterior al siglo XVI). ᴾ **5:20** *con.* Alt. *por medio de.*

Segunda Carta de JUAN

[1]El *anciano,

a la iglesia elegida y a sus miembros,[a] a quienes amo en la verdad —y no sólo yo sino todos los que han conocido la verdad—, [2]a causa de esa verdad que permanece en nosotros y que estará con nosotros para siempre:

[3]La gracia, la misericordia y la paz de Dios el Padre y de *Jesucristo, el Hijo del Padre, estarán con nosotros en verdad y en amor.

[4]Me alegré muchísimo al encontrarme con algunos de ustedes[b] que están practicando la verdad, según el mandamiento que nos dio el Padre. [5]Y ahora, hermanos, les ruego que nos amemos los unos a los otros. Y no es que les[c] esté escribiendo un mandamiento nuevo sino el que hemos tenido desde el principio. [6]En esto consiste el amor: en que pongamos en práctica sus mandamientos. Y éste es el mandamiento: que vivan en este amor, tal como ustedes lo han escuchado desde el principio.

[7]Es que han salido por el mundo muchos engañadores que no reconocen que Jesucristo ha venido en cuerpo humano. El que así actúa es el engañador y el anticristo. [8]Cuídense de no echar a perder el fruto de nuestro trabajo;[d] procuren más bien recibir la recompensa completa. [9]Todo el que se descarría y no permanece en la enseñanza de Cristo, no tiene a Dios; el que permanece en la enseñanza[e] sí tiene al Padre y al Hijo. [10]Si alguien los visita y no lleva esta enseñanza, no lo reciban en casa ni le den la bienvenida, [11]pues quien le da la bienvenida se hace cómplice de sus malas obras.

[12]Aunque tengo muchas cosas que decirles, no he querido hacerlo por escrito, pues espero visitarlos y hablar personalmente con ustedes para que nuestra alegría sea completa.

[13]Los miembros de la iglesia hermana, la elegida, les[f] mandan saludos.

---

[a] 1 *la iglesia . . . miembros.* Lit. *la señora elegida y a sus hijos.* [b] 4 *ustedes.* Lit. *tus hijos.* [c] 5 *hermanos, les ruego . . . Y no es que les.* Lit. *señora, te ruego . . . Y no es que te.* [d] 8 *el fruto de nuestro trabajo.* Lit. *lo que hemos trabajado.* Var. *lo que ustedes han trabajado.* [e] 9 *enseñanza.* Var. *enseñanza de Cristo.* [f] 13 *Los miembros . . . les.* Lit. *Los hijos de tu hermana, la elegida, te.*

Tercera Carta de JUAN

¹El *anciano,

al querido hermano Gayo, a quien amo en la verdad.

²Querido hermano, oro para que te vaya bien en todos tus asuntos y goces de buena salud, así como prosperas espiritualmente. ³Me alegré mucho cuando vinieron unos hermanos y dieron testimonio de tu fidelidad,ᵃ y de cómo estás poniendo en práctica la verdad. ⁴Nada me produce más alegría que oír que mis hijos practican la verdad.

⁵Querido hermano, te comportas fielmente en todo lo que haces por los hermanos, aunque no los conozcas.ᵇ ⁶Delante de la iglesia ellos han dado testimonio de tu amor. Harás bien en ayudarlos a seguir su viaje, como es digno de Dios. ⁷Ellos salieron por causa del Nombre, sin nunca recibir nada de los *paganos; ⁸nosotros, por lo tanto, debemos brindarles hospitalidad, y así colaborar con ellos en la verdad.

⁹Le escribí algunas líneas a la iglesia, pero Diótrefes, a quien le encanta ser el primero entre ellos, no nos recibe. ¹⁰Por eso, si voy no dejaré de reprocharle su comportamiento, ya que, con palabras malintencionadas, habla contra nosotros sólo por hablar. Como si fuera poco, ni siquiera recibe a los hermanos, y a quienes quieren hacerlo, no los deja y los expulsa de la iglesia.

¹¹Querido hermano, no imites lo malo sino lo bueno. El que hace lo bueno es de Dios; el que hace lo malo no ha visto a Dios. ¹²En cuanto a Demetrio, todos dan buen testimonio de él, incluso la verdad misma. También nosotros lo recomendamos, y bien sabes que nuestro testimonio es verdadero.

¹³Tengo muchas cosas que decirte, pero prefiero no hacerlo por escrito; ¹⁴espero verte muy pronto, y entonces hablaremos personalmente.

¹⁵La paz sea contigo. Tus amigos aquí te mandan saludos. Saluda a los amigos allá, a cada uno en particular.

ᵃ **3** *fidelidad.* Lit. *Verdad.* ᵇ **5** *aunque no los conozcas.* Alt. *aunque para ti sean extraños.*

Carta de JUDAS

[1]Judas, *siervo de *Jesucristo y hermano de *Jacobo,

a los que son amados por Dios el Padre, guardados por[a] Jesucristo y llamados a la salvación:

[2]Que reciban misericordia, paz y amor en abundancia.

Pecado y condenación de los impíos

[3]Queridos hermanos, he deseado intensamente escribirles acerca de la salvación que tenemos en común, y ahora siento la necesidad de hacerlo para rogarles que sigan luchando vigorosamente por la fe encomendada una vez por todas a los *santos. [4]El problema es que se han infiltrado entre ustedes ciertos individuos que desde hace mucho tiempo han estado señalados[b] para condenación. Son impíos que cambian en libertinaje la gracia de nuestro Dios y niegan a Jesucristo, nuestro único Soberano y Señor.

[5]Aunque ustedes ya saben muy bien todo esto, quiero recordarles que el Señor,[c] después de liberar de la tierra de Egipto a su pueblo, destruyó a los que no creían. [6]Y a los ángeles que no mantuvieron su posición de autoridad, sino que abandonaron su propia morada, los tiene perpetuamente encarcelados en oscuridad para el juicio del gran Día. [7]Así también Sodoma y Gomorra y las ciudades vecinas son puestas como escarmiento, al sufrir el castigo de un fuego eterno, por haber practicado, como aquéllos, inmoralidad sexual y vicios contra la naturaleza.

[8]De la misma manera estos individuos, llevados por sus delirios, contaminan su *cuerpo, desprecian la autoridad y maldicen a los seres celestiales. [9]Ni siquiera el arcángel Miguel, cuando argumentaba con el diablo disputándole el cuerpo de Moisés, se atrevió a pronunciar contra él un juicio de maldición, sino que dijo: «¡Que el Señor te reprenda!» [10]Éstos, en cambio, maldicen todo lo que no entienden; y como animales irracionales, lo que entienden por instinto es precisamente lo que los corrompe.

[11]¡Ay de los que siguieron el camino de Caín! Por ganar dinero se entregaron al error de Balán y perecieron en la rebelión de Coré.

[12]Estos individuos son un peligro oculto:[d] sin ningún respeto convierten en parrandas las fiestas de amor fraternal que ustedes celebran. Buscan sólo su propio provecho.[e] Son nubes sin agua, llevadas por el viento. Son árboles que no dan fruto cuando debieran darlo; están doblemente muertos, arrancados de raíz. [13]Son violentas olas del mar, que arrojan la espuma de sus actos vergonzosos. Son estrellas fugaces, para quienes está reservada eternamente la más densa oscuridad.

[14]También Enoc, el séptimo patriarca a partir de Adán, profetizó acerca de ellos: «Miren, el Señor viene con millares y millares de sus ángeles[f] [15]para someter a juicio a todos y para reprender a todos los pecadores impíos por todas las malas obras que han cometido, y por todas las injurias que han proferido contra él.» [16]Estos individuos son refunfuñadores y criticones; se dejan llevar por sus propias pasiones; hablan con arrogancia y adulan a los demás para sacar ventaja.

Exhortación a la perseverancia

[17]Ustedes, queridos hermanos, recuerden el mensaje anunciado anteriormente por los apóstoles de nuestro Señor Jesucristo. [18]Ellos les decían: «En los últimos tiempos habrá burladores que vivirán según sus propias pasiones impías.» [19]Éstos son los que causan divisiones y se dejan llevar por sus propios instintos, pues no tienen el Espíritu.

[20-21]Ustedes, en cambio, queridos hermanos, manténganse en el amor de Dios, edificándose sobre la base de su santísima fe y orando en el Espíritu Santo, mientras esperan que nuestro Señor Jesucristo, en su misericordia, les conceda vida eterna.

[22]Tengan compasión de los que dudan; [23]a otros, sálvenlos arrebatándolos del fuego. Compadézcanse de los demás, pero tengan cuidado; aborrezcan hasta la ropa que haya sido contaminada por su *cuerpo.

Doxología

[24]¡Al único Dios, nuestro Salvador, que puede guardarlos para que no *caigan, y establecerlos sin tacha y con gran alegría ante su gloriosa presencia, [25]sea la gloria, la majestad, el dominio y la autoridad, por medio de Jesucristo nuestro Señor, antes de todos los siglos, ahora y para siempre! Amén.

---

a **1** por. Alt. Para. b **4** señalados. Lit. inscritos de antemano. c **5** el Señor. Var. Jesús. d **12** un peligro oculto. Lit. escollos, o manchas. e **12** Buscan . . . provecho. Lit. Se pastorean a sí mismos. f **14** ángeles. Lit. *santos.

APOCALIPSIS

Prólogo

1 Ésta es la revelación de *Jesucristo, que Dios le dio para mostrar a sus *siervos lo que sin demora tiene que suceder. Jesucristo envió a su ángel para dar a conocer la revelación a su siervo Juan, 2quien por su parte da fe de la verdad, escribiendo todo lo que vio, a saber, la palabra de Dios y el testimonio de Jesucristo. 3*Dichoso el que lee y dichosos los que escuchan las palabras de este mensaje profético y hacen caso de lo que aquí está escrito, porque el tiempo de su cumplimiento está cerca.

Saludos y doxología

4Yo, Juan, escribo a las siete iglesias que están en la provincia de *Asia:

Gracia y paz a ustedes de parte de aquel que es y que era y que ha de venir; de parte de los siete espíritus que están delante de su trono; 5y de parte de *Jesucristo, el testigo fiel, el primogénito de la resurrección, el soberano de los reyes de la tierra.

Al que nos ama
y que por su sangre
nos ha librado de nuestros pecados,
6al que ha hecho de nosotros un reino,
sacerdotes al servicio de Dios su Padre,
¡a él sea la gloria y el poder
por los siglos de los siglos! Amén.

7¡Miren que viene en las nubes!
Y todos lo verán con sus propios ojos,
incluso quienes lo traspasaron;
y por él harán lamentación
todos los pueblos de la tierra.
¡Así será! Amén.

8«Yo soy el Alfa y la Omega —dice el Señor Dios—, el que es y que era y que ha de venir, el Todopoderoso.»

Alguien semejante al Hijo del hombre

9Yo, Juan, hermano de ustedes y compañero en el sufrimiento, en el reino y en la perseverancia que tenemos en unión con Jesús, estaba en la isla de Patmos por causa de la palabra de Dios y del testimonio de Jesús. 10En el día del Señor vino sobre mí el Espíritu, y oí detrás de mí una voz fuerte, como de trompeta, 11que decía: «Escribe en un libro lo que veas y envíalo a las siete iglesias: a Éfeso, a Esmirna, a Pérgamo, a Tiatira, a Sardis, a Filadelfia y a Laodicea.»

12Me volví para ver de quién era la voz que me hablaba y, al volverme, vi siete candelabros de oro. 13En medio de los candelabros estaba alguien «semejante al Hijo del hombre»,[a] vestido con una túnica que le llegaba hasta los pies y ceñido con una banda de oro a la altura del pecho. 14Su cabellera lucía blanca como la lana, como la nieve; y sus ojos resplandecían como llama de fuego. 15Sus pies parecían bronce al rojo vivo en un horno, y su voz era tan fuerte como el estruendo de una catarata. 16En su mano derecha tenía siete estrellas, y de su boca salía una aguda espada de dos filos. Su rostro era como el sol cuando brilla en todo su esplendor.

17Al verlo, caí a sus pies como muerto; pero él, poniendo su mano derecha sobre mí, me dijo: «No tengas miedo. Yo soy el Primero y el Último, 18y el que vive. Estuve muerto, pero ahora vivo por los siglos de los siglos, y tengo las llaves de la muerte y del infierno.[b]

19»Escribe, pues, lo que has visto, lo que sucede ahora y lo que sucederá después. 20Ésta es la explicación del *misterio de las siete estrellas que viste en mi mano derecha, y de los siete candelabros de oro: las siete estrellas son los ángeles[c] de las siete iglesias, y los siete candelabros son las siete iglesias.

A la iglesia de Éfeso

2 »Escribe al ángel[d] de la iglesia de Éfeso:

Esto dice el que tiene las siete estrellas en su mano derecha y se pasea en medio de los siete candelabros de oro: 2Conozco tus obras, tu duro trabajo y tu perseverancia. Sé que no puedes soportar a los malvados, y que has puesto a *prueba a los que dicen ser apóstoles pero no lo son; y has descubierto que son falsos. 3Has perseverado y sufrido por mi nombre, sin desanimarte.

4Sin embargo, tengo en tu contra que has abandonado tu primer amor. 5¡Recuerda de dónde has caído! *Arrepiéntete y vuelve a practicar las obras que hacías al principio. Si no te arrepientes, iré y quitaré de su lugar tu candelabro. 6Pero tienes a tu favor que aborreces las prácticas de los nicolaítas, las cuales yo también aborrezco.

7El que tenga oídos, que oiga lo que el Espíritu dice a las iglesias. Al que salga vencedor le daré derecho a comer del árbol de la vida, que está en el paraíso de Dios.

A la iglesia de Esmirna

8»Escribe al ángel de la iglesia de Esmirna:

Esto dice el Primero y el Último, el que murió y volvió a vivir: 9Conozco tus sufrimientos y tu pobreza. ¡Sin embargo, eres rico! Sé cómo te calumnian los que dicen ser judíos pero que, en realidad, no son más que una sinagoga de Satanás. 10No tengas miedo de lo que estás por sufrir. Te advierto que a algunos de ustedes el diablo los meterá en la cárcel para ponerlos a *prueba, y sufrirán persecución durante diez días. Sé fiel hasta la muerte, y yo te daré la corona de la vida.

11El que tenga oídos, que oiga lo que el Espíritu dice a las iglesias. El que salga vencedor no sufrirá daño alguno de la segunda muerte.

A la iglesia de Pérgamo

12»Escribe al ángel de la iglesia de Pérgamo:

Esto dice el que tiene la aguda espada de dos filos: 13Sé dónde vives: allí donde Satanás tiene su trono. Sin embargo, sigues fiel a mi nombre. No renegaste de tu fe en mí, ni siquiera en los días en que Antipas, mi testigo fiel, sufrió la muerte en esa ciudad donde vive Satanás.

14No obstante, tengo unas cuantas cosas en tu contra: que toleras ahí a los que se aferran a la doctrina de Balán, el que enseñó a Balac a poner *tropiezos a los israelitas, incitándolos a co-

a 1:13 Dn 7:13 b 1:18 infierno. Lit. *Hades. c 1:20 ángeles. Alt. Mensajeros. d 2:1 ángel. Alt. mensajero; también en vv. 8, 12 y 18.

mer alimentos sacrificados a los ídolos y a cometer inmoralidades sexuales. 15Toleras así mismo a los que sostienen la doctrina de los nicolaítas. 16Por lo tanto, ¡*arrepiéntete! De otra manera, iré pronto a ti para pelear contra ellos con la espada que sale de mi boca.

17El que tenga oídos, que oiga lo que el Espíritu dice a las iglesias. Al que salga vencedor le daré del maná escondido, y le daré también una piedrecita blanca en la que está escrito un nombre nuevo que sólo conoce el que lo recibe.

A la iglesia de Tiatira

18»Escribe al ángel de la iglesia de Tiatira:

Esto dice el Hijo de Dios, el que tiene ojos que resplandecen como llamas de fuego y pies que parecen bronce al rojo vivo: 19Conozco tus obras, tu amor y tu fe, tu servicio y tu perseverancia, y sé que tus últimas obras son más abundantes que las primeras.

20Sin embargo, tengo en tu contra que toleras a Jezabel, esa mujer que dice ser profetisa. Con su enseñanza engaña a mis *siervos, pues los induce a cometer inmoralidades sexuales y a comer alimentos sacrificados a los ídolos. 21Le he dado tiempo para que se *arrepienta de su inmoralidad, pero no quiere hacerlo. 22Por eso la voy a postrar en un lecho de dolor, y a los que cometen adulterio con ella los haré sufrir terriblemente, a menos que se arrepientan de lo que aprendieron de ella. 23A los hijos de esa mujer los heriré de muerte. Así sabrán todas las iglesias que yo soy el que escudriña la mente y el corazón; y a cada uno de ustedes lo trataré de acuerdo con sus obras. 24Ahora, al resto de los que están en Tiatira, es decir, a ustedes que no siguen esa enseñanza ni han aprendido los mal llamados "profundos secretos de Satanás", les digo que ya no les impondré ninguna otra carga. 25Eso sí, retengan con firmeza lo que ya tienen, hasta que yo venga.

26Al que salga vencedor y cumpla mi voluntadᵉ hasta el fin, le daré autoridad sobre las *naciones 27—así como yo la he recibido de mi Padre— y

"él las gobernará con puño de hierro;ᶠ
las hará pedazos como a vasijas de barro".ᵍ

28También le daré la estrella de la mañana. 29El que tenga oídos, que oiga lo que el Espíritu dice a las iglesias.

A la iglesia de Sardis

3 »Escribe al ángelʰ de la iglesia de Sardis:

Esto dice el que tiene los siete espíritus de Dios y las siete estrellas: Conozco tus obras; tienes fama de estar vivo, pero en realidad estás muerto. 2¡Despierta! Reaviva lo que aún es rescatable,ⁱ pues no he encontrado que tus obras sean perfectas delante de mi Dios. 3Así que recuerda lo que has recibido y oído; obedécelo y *arrepiéntete. Si no te mantienes despierto, cuando menos lo esperes caeré sobre ti como un ladrón.

4Sin embargo, tienes en Sardis a unos cuantos que no se han manchado la ropa. Ellos, por

ser dignos, andarán conmigo vestidos de blanco. 5El que salga vencedor se vestirá de blanco. Jamás borraré su nombre del libro de la vida, sino que reconoceré su nombre delante de mi Padre y delante de sus ángeles. 6El que tenga oídos, que oiga lo que el Espíritu dice a las iglesias.

A la iglesia de Filadelfia

7»Escribe al ángel de la iglesia de Filadelfia:

Esto dice el Santo, el Verdadero, el que tiene la llave de David, el que abre y nadie puede cerrar, el que cierra y nadie puede abrir: 8Conozco tus obras. Mira que delante de ti he dejado abierta una puerta que nadie puede cerrar. Ya sé que tus fuerzas son pocas, pero has obedecido mi palabra y no has renegado de mi nombre. 9Voy a hacer que los de la sinagoga de Satanás, que dicen ser judíos pero que en realidad mienten, vayan y se postren a tus pies, y reconozcan que yo te he amado. 10Ya que has guardado mi mandato de ser constante, yo por mi parte te guardaré de la hora de *tentación, que vendrá sobre el mundo entero para poner a prueba a los que viven en la tierra.

11Vengo pronto. Aférrate a lo que tienes, para que nadie te quite la corona. 12Al que salga vencedor lo haré columna del templo de mi Dios, y ya no saldrá jamás de allí. Sobre él grabaré el nombre de mi Dios y el nombre de la nueva Jerusalén, ciudad de mi Dios, la que baja del cielo de parte de mi Dios; y también grabaré sobre él mi nombre nuevo. 13El que tenga oídos, que oiga lo que el Espíritu dice a las iglesias.

A la iglesia de Laodicea

14»Escribe al ángel de la iglesia de Laodicea:

Esto dice el Amén, el testigo fiel y veraz, el soberanoj de la creación de Dios: 15Conozco tus obras; sé que no eres ni frío ni caliente. ¡Ojalá fueras lo uno o lo otro! 16Por tanto, como no eres ni frío ni caliente, sino tibio, estoy por vomitarte de mi boca. 17Dices: "Soy rico; me he enriquecido y no me hace falta nada"; pero no te das cuenta de que el infeliz y miserable, el pobre, ciego y desnudo eres tú. 18Por eso te aconsejo que de mí compres oro refinado por el fuego, para que te hagas rico; ropas blancas para que te vistas y cubras tu vergonzosa desnudez; y colirio para que te lo pongas en los ojos y recobres la vista.

19Yo reprendo y disciplino a todos los que amo. Por lo tanto, sé fervoroso y *arrepiéntete. 20Mira que estoy a la puerta y llamo. Si alguno oye mi voz y abre la puerta, entraré, y cenaré con él, y él conmigo.

21Al que salga vencedor le daré el derecho de sentarse conmigo en mi trono, como también yo vencí y me senté con mi Padre en su trono. 22El que tenga oídos, que oiga lo que el Espíritu dice a las iglesias.»

El trono en el cielo

4 Después de esto miré, y allí en el cielo había una puerta abierta. Y la voz que me había hablado antes con sonido como de trompeta me dijo: «Sube acá: voy a mostrarte lo que tiene que suceder después de esto.» 2Al instante vino sobre mí el Espí-

---

ᵉ 2:26 cumpla mi voluntad. Lit. guarde mis obras. ᶠ 2:27 gobernará . . . hierro. Lit. pastoreará con cetro de hierro. ᵍ 2:27 Sal 2:9 ʰ 3:1 ángel. Alt. mensajero; también en vv. 7 y 14. ⁱ 3:2 Reaviva . . . rescatable. Lit. Fortalece las otras cosas que están por morir. ʲ 3:14 soberano. Lit. comienzo u origen.

ritu y vi un trono en el cielo, y a alguien sentado en el trono. ³El que estaba sentado tenía un aspecto semejante a una piedra de jaspe y de cornalina. Alrededor del trono había un arco iris que se asemejaba a una esmeralda. ⁴Rodeaban al trono otros veinticuatro tronos, en los que estaban sentados veinticuatro *ancianos vestidos de blanco y con una corona de oro en la cabeza. ⁵Del trono salían relámpagos, estruendos^k y truenos. Delante del trono ardían siete antorchas de fuego, que son los siete espíritus de Dios, ⁶y había algo parecido a un mar de vidrio, como de cristal transparente.

En el centro, alrededor del trono, había cuatro seres vivientes cubiertos de ojos por delante y por detrás. ⁷El primero de los seres vivientes era semejante a un león; el segundo, a un toro; el tercero tenía rostro como de hombre; el cuarto era semejante a un águila en vuelo. ⁸Cada uno de ellos tenía seis alas y estaba cubierto de ojos, por encima y por debajo de las alas. Y día y noche repetían sin cesar:

> «Santo, santo, santo
> es el Señor Dios Todopoderoso,
> el que era y que es y que ha de venir.»

⁹Cada vez que estos seres vivientes daban gloria, honra y acción de gracias al que estaba sentado en el trono, al que vive por los siglos de los siglos, ¹⁰los veinticuatro ancianos se postraban ante él y adoraban al que vive por los siglos de los siglos. Y rendían sus coronas delante del trono exclamando:

> ¹¹«Digno eres, Señor y Dios nuestro,
> de recibir la gloria, la honra y el poder,
> porque tú creaste todas las cosas;
> por tu voluntad existen
> y fueron creadas.»

El rollo escrito y el Cordero

5 En la mano derecha del que estaba sentado en el trono vi un rollo escrito por ambos lados y sellado con siete sellos. ²También vi a un ángel poderoso que proclamaba a gran voz: «¿Quién es digno de romper los sellos y de abrir el rollo?» ³Pero ni en el cielo ni en la tierra, ni debajo de la tierra, hubo nadie capaz de abrirlo ni de examinar su contenido. ⁴Y lloraba yo mucho porque no se había encontrado a nadie que fuera digno de abrir el rollo ni de examinar su contenido. ⁵Uno de los *ancianos me dijo: «Deja de llorar, que ya el León de la tribu de Judá, la Raíz de David, ha vencido! Él sí puede abrir el rollo y sus siete sellos.»

⁶Entonces vi, en medio de los cuatro seres vivientes y del trono y los ancianos, a un Cordero que estaba de pie y parecía haber sido sacrificado. Tenía siete cuernos y siete ojos, que son los siete espíritus de Dios enviados por toda la tierra. ⁷Se acercó y recibió el rollo de la mano derecha del que estaba sentado en el trono. ⁸Cuando lo tomó, los cuatro seres vivientes y los veinticuatro ancianos se postraron delante del Cordero. Cada uno tenía un arpa y copas de oro llenas de incienso, que son las oraciones del *pueblo de Dios. ⁹Y entonaban este nuevo cántico:

> «Digno eres de recibir el rollo escrito
> y de romper sus sellos,
> porque fuiste sacrificado,
> y con tu sangre compraste para Dios

> gente de toda raza, lengua, pueblo y
> nación.
> ¹⁰De ellos hiciste un reino;
> los hiciste sacerdotes al servicio de nuestro
> Dios,
> y reinarán sobre la tierra.»

¹¹Luego miré, y oí la voz de muchos ángeles que estaban alrededor del trono, de los seres vivientes y de los ancianos. El número de ellos era millares de millares y millones de millones. ¹²Cantaban con todas sus fuerzas:

> «¡Digno es el Cordero, que ha sido sacrificado,
> de recibir el poder,
> la riqueza y la sabiduría,
> la fortaleza y la honra,
> la gloria y la alabanza!»

¹³Y oí a cuanta criatura hay en el cielo, y en la tierra, y debajo de la tierra y en el mar, a todos en la creación, que cantaban:

> «¡Al que está sentado en el trono y al Cordero,
> sean la alabanza y la honra, la gloria y el
> poder,
> por los siglos de los siglos!»

¹⁴Los cuatro seres vivientes exclamaron: «¡Amén!», y los ancianos se postraron y adoraron.

Los sellos

6 Vi cuando el Cordero rompió el primero de los siete sellos, y oí a uno de los cuatro seres vivientes, que gritaba con voz de trueno: «¡Ven!» ²Miré, ¡y apareció un caballo blanco! El jinete llevaba un arco; se le dio una corona, y salió como vencedor, para seguir venciendo.

³Cuando el Cordero rompió el segundo sello, oí al segundo ser viviente, que gritaba: «¡Ven!» ⁴En eso salió otro caballo, de color rojo encendido. Al jinete se le entregó una gran espada; se le permitió quitar la paz de la tierra y hacer que sus habitantes se mataran unos a otros.

⁵Cuando el Cordero rompió el tercer sello, oí al tercero de los seres vivientes, que gritaba: «¡Ven!» Miré, ¡y apareció un caballo negro! El jinete tenía una balanza en la mano. ⁶Y oí como una voz en medio de los cuatro seres vivientes, que decía: «Un kilo de trigo, o tres kilos de cebada, por el salario de un día; pero no afectes el precio del aceite y del vino.»^l

⁷Cuando el Cordero rompió el cuarto sello, oí la voz del cuarto ser viviente, que gritaba: «¡Ven!» ⁸Miré, ¡y apareció un caballo amarillento! El jinete se llamaba Muerte, y el Infierno^m no seguía de cerca. Y se le otorgó poder sobre la cuarta parte de la tierra, para matar por medio de la espada, el hambre, las epidemias y las fieras de la tierra.

⁹Cuando el Cordero rompió el quinto sello, vi debajo del altar las almas de los que habían sufrido el martirio por causa de la palabra de Dios y por mantenerse fieles en su testimonio. ¹⁰Gritaban a gran voz: «¿Hasta cuándo, Soberano Señor, santo y veraz, seguirás sin juzgar a los habitantes de la tierra y sin vengar nuestra muerte?» ¹¹Entonces cada uno de ellos recibió ropas blancas, y se les dijo que esperaran un poco más, hasta que se completara el número de sus consiervos y hermanos que iban a sufrir el martirio como ellos.

---

^k **4:5** *estruendos.* Lit. *voces;* y así en otros pasajes semejantes. ^l **6:6** *por el salario . . . vino.* Lit. *por un *denario, y no dañes el aceite ni el vino.* ^m **6:8** *Infierno.* Lit. **Hades.*

[12]Vi que el Cordero rompió el sexto sello, y se produjo un gran terremoto. El sol se oscureció como si se hubiera vestido de luto,[n] la luna entera se tornó roja como la sangre, [13]y las estrellas del firmamento cayeron sobre la tierra, como caen los higos verdes de la higuera sacudida por el vendaval. [14]El firmamento desapareció como cuando se enrolla un pergamino, y todas las montañas y las islas fueron removidas de su lugar.

[15]Los reyes de la tierra, los magnates, los jefes militares, los ricos, los poderosos, y todos los demás, esclavos y libres, se escondieron en las cuevas y entre las peñas de las montañas. [16]Todos gritaban a las montañas y a las peñas: «¡Caigan sobre nosotros y escóndannos de la mirada del que está sentado en el trono y de la ira del Cordero, [17]porque ha llegado el gran día del castigo! ¿Quién podrá mantenerse en pie?»

Los 144.000 sellados

7 Después de esto vi a cuatro ángeles en los cuatro ángulos de la tierra. Estaban allí de pie, deteniendo los cuatro vientos para que éstos no se desataran sobre la tierra, el mar y los árboles. [2]Vi también a otro ángel que venía del oriente con el sello del Dios vivo. Gritó con voz potente a los cuatro ángeles a quienes se les había permitido hacer daño a la tierra y al mar: [3]«¡No hagan daño ni a la tierra, ni al mar ni a los árboles, hasta que hayamos puesto un sello en la frente de los *siervos de nuestro Dios!» [4]Y oí el número de los que fueron sellados: ciento cuarenta y cuatro mil de todas las tribus de Israel.

[5] De la tribu de Judá fueron sellados doce mil;
de la tribu de Rubén, doce mil;
de la tribu de Gad, doce mil;
[6] de la tribu de Aser, doce mil;
de la tribu de Neftalí, doce mil;
de la tribu de Manasés, doce mil;
[7] de la tribu de Simeón, doce mil;
de la tribu de Leví, doce mil;
de la tribu de Isacar, doce mil;
[8] de la tribu de Zabulón, doce mil;
de la tribu de José, doce mil;
de la tribu de Benjamín, doce mil.

La gran multitud con túnicas blancas

[9]Después de esto miré, y apareció una multitud tomada de todas las naciones, tribus, pueblos y lenguas; era tan grande que nadie podía contarla. Estaban de pie delante del trono y del Cordero, vestidos de túnicas blancas y con ramas de palma en la mano. [10]Gritaban a gran voz:

«¡La salvación viene de nuestro Dios,
que está sentado en el trono,
y del Cordero!»

[11]Todos los ángeles estaban de pie alrededor del trono, de los *ancianos y de los cuatro seres vivientes. Se postraron rostro en tierra delante del trono, y adoraron a Dios [12]diciendo:

«¡Amén!
La alabanza, la gloria,
la sabiduría, la acción de gracias,
la honra, el poder y la fortaleza
son de nuestro Dios por los siglos de los siglos.
¡Amén!»

[13]Entonces uno de los ancianos me preguntó:

—Esos que están vestidos de blanco, ¿quiénes son, y de dónde vienen?

[14]—Eso usted lo sabe, mi señor —respondí.

Él me dijo:

—Aquéllos son los que están saliendo de la
gran tribulación;
han lavado y blanqueado sus túnicas en la
sangre del Cordero.

[15]Por eso, están delante del trono de Dios,
y día y noche le sirven en su templo;
y el que está sentado en el trono
les dará refugio en su santuario.[ñ]
[16]Ya no sufrirán hambre ni sed.
No los abatirá el sol ni ningún calor
abrasador.
[17]Porque el Cordero que está en el trono los
pastoreará
y los guiará a fuentes de agua viva;
y Dios les enjugará toda lágrima de sus ojos.

El séptimo sello y el incensario de oro

8 Cuando el Cordero rompió el séptimo sello, hubo silencio en el cielo como por media hora.

[2]Vi a los siete ángeles que están de pie delante de Dios, a los cuales se les dieron siete trompetas.

[3]Se acercó otro ángel y se puso de pie frente al altar. Tenía un incensario de oro, y se le entregó mucho incienso para ofrecerlo, junto con las oraciones de todo el *pueblo de Dios, sobre el altar de oro que está delante del trono. [4]Y junto con esas oraciones, subió el humo del incienso desde la mano del ángel hasta la presencia de Dios. [5]Luego el ángel tomó el incensario y lo llenó con brasas del altar, las cuales arrojó sobre la tierra; y se produjeron truenos, estruendos,[o] relámpagos y un terremoto.

Las trompetas

[6]Los siete ángeles que tenían las siete trompetas se dispusieron a tocarlas.

[7]Tocó el primero su trompeta, y fueron arrojados sobre la tierra granizo y fuego mezclados con sangre. Y se quemó la tercera parte de la tierra, la tercera parte de los árboles y toda la hierba verde.

[8]Tocó el segundo ángel su trompeta, y fue arrojado al mar algo que parecía una enorme montaña envuelta en llamas. La tercera parte del mar se convirtió en sangre, [9]y murió la tercera parte de las criaturas que viven en el mar; también fue destruida la tercera parte de los barcos.

[10]Tocó el tercer ángel su trompeta, y una enorme estrella, que ardía como una antorcha, cayó desde el cielo sobre la tercera parte de los ríos y sobre los manantiales. [11]La estrella se llama Amargura.[p] Y la tercera parte de las aguas se volvió amarga, y por causa de esas aguas murió mucha gente.

[12]Tocó el cuarto ángel su trompeta, y fue asolada la tercera parte del sol, de la luna y de las estrellas, de modo que se oscureció la tercera parte de ellos. Así quedó sin luz la tercera parte del día y la tercera parte de la noche.

[13]Seguí observando, y oí un águila que volaba en medio del cielo y gritaba fuertemente: «¡Ay! ¡Ay! ¡Ay de los habitantes de la tierra cuando suenen las tres trompetas que los últimos tres ángeles están a punto de tocar!»

---

[n] **6:12** *se oscureció . . . luto.* Lit. *se puso negro como un saco hecho de pelo* (es decir, pelo de cabra).   [ñ] **7:15** *les dará . . . santuario.* Lit. *extenderá su tienda sobre ellos.*   [o] **8:5** *estruendos.* Lit. *Voces.*   [p] **8:11** *Amargura.* Lit. *Ajenjo.*

9 Tocó el quinto ángel su trompeta, y vi que había caído del cielo a la tierra una estrella, a la cual se le entregó la llave del pozo del *abismo. 2Lo abrió, y del pozo subió una humareda, como la de un horno gigantesco; y la humareda oscureció el sol y el aire. 3De la humareda descendieron langostas sobre la tierra, y se les dio poder como el que tienen los escorpiones de la tierra. 4Se les ordenó que no dañaran la hierba de la tierra, ni ninguna planta ni ningún árbol, sino sólo a las personas que no llevaran en la frente el sello de Dios. 5No se les dio permiso para matarlas sino sólo para torturarlas durante cinco meses. Su tormento es como el producido por la picadura de un escorpión. 6En aquellos días la gente buscará la muerte, pero no la encontrará; desearán morir, pero la muerte huirá de ellos.

7El aspecto de las langostas era como de caballos equipados para la guerra. Llevaban en la cabeza algo que parecía una corona de oro, y su cara se asemejaba a un rostro humano. 8Su crin parecía cabello de mujer, y sus dientes eran como de león. 9Llevaban coraza como de hierro, y el ruido de sus alas se escuchaba como el estruendo de carros de muchos caballos que se lanzan a la batalla. 10Tenían cola y aguijón como de escorpión; y en la cola tenían poder para torturar a la gente durante cinco meses. 11El rey que los dirigía era el ángel del abismo, que en hebreo se llama Abadón y en griego Apolión.q

12El primer ¡ay! ya pasó, pero vienen todavía otros dos.

13Tocó el sexto ángel su trompeta, y oí una voz que salía de entre los cuernos del altar de oro que está delante de Dios. 14A este ángel que tenía la trompeta, la voz le dijo: «Suelta a los cuatro ángeles que están atados a la orilla del gran río Éufrates.» 15Así que los cuatro ángeles que habían sido preparados precisamente para esa hora, y ese día, mes y año, quedaron sueltos para matar a la tercera parte de la *humanidad. 16Oí que el número de las tropas de caballería llegaba a doscientos millones.

17Así vi en la visión a los caballos y a sus jinetes: Tenían coraza de color rojo encendido, azul violeta y amarillo como azufre. La cabeza de los caballos era como de león, y por la boca echaban fuego, humo y azufre. 18La tercera parte de la humanidad murió a causa de las tres plagas de fuego, humo y azufre que salían de la boca de los caballos. 19Es que el poder de los caballos radicaba en su boca y en su cola; pues sus colas, semejantes a serpientes, tenían cabezas con las que hacían daño.

20El resto de la humanidad, los que no murieron a causa de estas plagas, tampoco se *arrepintieron de sus malas acciones ni dejaron de adorar a los demonios y a los ídolos de oro, plata, bronce, piedra y madera, los cuales no pueden ver ni oír ni caminar. 21Tampoco se arrepintieron de sus asesinatos ni de sus artes mágicas, inmoralidad sexual y robos.

El ángel y el rollo pequeño

10 Después vi a otro ángel poderoso que bajaba del cielo envuelto en una nube. Un arco iris rodeaba su cabeza; su rostro era como el sol, y sus piernas parecían columnas de fuego. 2Llevaba en la mano un pequeño rollo escrito que estaba abierto. Puso el pie derecho sobre el mar y el izquierdo sobre la tierra, 3y dio un grito tan fuerte que parecía el rugido de un león. Entonces los siete truenos levantaron también sus voces. 4Una vez que hablaron los siete truenos, estaba yo por escribir, pero oí una voz del cielo que me decía: «Guarda en secreto lo que han dicho los siete truenos, y no lo escribas.»

5El ángel que yo había visto de pie sobre el mar y sobre la tierra levantó al cielo su mano derecha 6y juró por el que vive por los siglos de los siglos, el que creó el cielo, la tierra, el mar y todo lo que hay en ellos, y dijo: «¡El tiempo ha terminado! 7En los días en que hable el séptimo ángel, cuando comience a tocar su trompeta, se cumplirá el designio *secreto de Dios, tal y como lo anunció a sus *siervos los profetas.»

8La voz del cielo que yo había escuchado se dirigió a mí de nuevo: «Acércate al ángel que está de pie sobre el mar y sobre la tierra, y toma el rollo que tiene abierto en la mano.»

9Me acerqué al ángel y le pedí que me diera el rollo. Él me dijo: «Tómalo y cómetelo. Te amargará las entrañas, pero en la boca te sabrá dulce como la miel.» 10Lo tomé de la mano del ángel y me lo comí. Me supo dulce como la miel, pero al comérmelo se me amargaron las entrañas. 11Entonces se me ordenó: «Tienes que volver a profetizar acerca de muchos pueblos, naciones, lenguas y reyes.»

Los dos testigos

11 Se me dio una caña que servía para medir, y se me ordenó: «Levántate y mide el templo de Dios y el altar, y calcula cuántos pueden adorar allí. 2Pero no incluyas el atrio exterior del templo; no lo midas, porque ha sido entregado a las naciones paganas, las cuales pisotearán la ciudad santa durante cuarenta y dos meses. 3Por mi parte, yo encargaré a mis dos testigos que, vestidos de luto,r profeticen durante mil doscientos sesenta días.» 4Estos dos testigos son los dos olivos y los dos candelabros que permanecen delante del Señor de la tierra. 5Si alguien quiere hacerles daño, ellos lanzan fuego por la boca y consumen a sus enemigos. Así habrá de morir cualquiera que intente hacerles daño. 6Estos testigos tienen poder para cerrar el cielo a fin de que no llueva mientras estén profetizando; y tienen poder para convertir las aguas en sangre y para azotar la tierra, cuantas veces quieran, con toda clase de plagas.

7Ahora bien, cuando hayan terminado de dar su testimonio, la bestia que sube del *abismo les hará la guerra, los vencerá y los matará. 8Sus cadáveres quedarán tendidos en la plaza de la gran ciudad, llamada en sentido figurados Sodoma y Egipto, donde también fue crucificado su Señor. 9Y gente de todo pueblo, tribu, lengua y nación contemplará sus cadáveres por tres días y medio, y no permitirá que se les dé sepultura. 10Los habitantes de la tierra se alegrarán de su muerte y harán fiesta e intercambiarán regalos, porque estos dos profetas les estaban haciendo la vida imposible.

11Pasados los tres días y medio, entró en ellos un aliento de vida enviado por Dios, y se pusieron de pie, y quienes los observaban quedaron sobrecogidos de terror. 12Entonces los dos testigos oyeron una potente voz del cielo que les decía: «Suban acá.» Y subieron al cielo en una nube, a la vista de sus enemigos.

13En ese mismo instante se produjo un violento terremoto y se derrumbó la décima parte de la ciudad. Perecieron siete mil personas, pero los sobrevivientes, llenos de temor, dieron gloria al Dios del cielo.

14El segundo ¡ay! ya pasó, pero se acerca el tercero.

---

q 9:11 *Abadón* y *Apolión* significan *Destructor.* r 11:3 *luto.* Lit. *Cilicio.* s 11:8 *en sentido figurado.* Lit. *Espiritualmente.*

La séptima trompeta

15Tocó el séptimo ángel su trompeta, y en el cielo resonaron fuertes voces que decían:

«El reino del mundo ha pasado a ser de
    nuestro Señor y de su *Cristo,
    y él reinará por los siglos de los siglos.»

16Los veinticuatro *ancianos que estaban sentados en sus tronos delante de Dios se postraron rostro en tierra y adoraron a Dios 17diciendo:

«Señor, Dios Todopoderoso,
    que eres y que eras,t
te damos gracias porque has asumido tu gran
    poder
    y has comenzado a reinar.
18Las *naciones se han enfurecido;
    pero ha llegado tu castigo,
el momento de juzgar a los muertos,
    y de recompensar a tus *siervos los profetas,
a tus *santos y a los que temen tu nombre,
    sean grandes o pequeños,
y de destruir a los que destruyen la tierra.»

19Entonces se abrió en el cielo el templo de Dios; allí se vio el arca de su pacto, y hubo relámpagos, estruendos, truenos, un terremoto y una fuerte granizada.

La mujer y el dragón

12 Apareció en el cielo una señal maravillosa: una mujer revestida del sol, con la luna debajo de sus pies y con una corona de doce estrellas en la cabeza. 2Estaba encinta y gritaba por los dolores y angustias del parto. 3Y apareció en el cielo otra señal: un enorme dragón de color rojo encendido que tenía siete cabezas y diez cuernos, y una diadema en cada cabeza. 4Con la cola arrastró la tercera parte de las estrellas del cielo y las arrojó sobre la tierra. Cuando la mujer estaba a punto de dar a luz, el dragón se plantó delante de ella para devorar a su hijo tan pronto como naciera. 5Ella dio a luz un hijo varón que gobernará a todas las *naciones con puño de hierro.u Pero su hijo fue arrebatado y llevado hasta Dios, que está en su trono. 6Y la mujer huyó al desierto, a un lugar que Dios le había preparado para que allí la sustentaran durante mil doscientos sesenta días.

7Se desató entonces una guerra en el cielo: Miguel y sus ángeles combatieron al dragón; éste y sus ángeles, a su vez, les hicieron frente, 8pero no pudieron vencer, y ya no hubo lugar para ellos en el cielo. 9Así fue expulsado el gran dragón, aquella serpiente antigua que se llama Diablo y Satanás, y que engaña al mundo entero. Junto con sus ángeles, fue arrojado a la tierra.

10Luego oí en el cielo un gran clamor:

«Han llegado ya la salvación y el poder y el
    reino de nuestro Dios;
    ha llegado ya la autoridad de su *Cristo.
Porque ha sido expulsado
    el acusador de nuestros hermanos,
    el que los acusaba día y noche delante de
        nuestro Dios.
11Ellos lo han vencido
    por medio de la sangre del Cordero

y por el mensaje del cual dieron
    testimonio;
no valoraron tanto su *vida
    como para evitar la muerte.
12Por eso, ¡alégrense, cielos,
    y ustedes que los habitan!
Pero ¡ay de la tierra y del mar!
    El diablo, lleno de furor, ha descendido a
        ustedes,
porque sabe que le queda poco tiempo.»

13Cuando el dragón se vio arrojado a la tierra, persiguió a la mujer que había dado a luz al varón. 14Pero a la mujer se le dieron las dos alas de la gran águila, para que volara al desierto, al lugar donde sería sustentada durante un tiempo y tiempos y medio tiempo, lejos de la vista de la serpiente. 15La serpiente, persiguiendo a la mujer, arrojó por sus fauces agua como un río, para que la corriente la arrastrara. 16Pero la tierra ayudó a la mujer: abrió la boca y se tragó el río que el dragón había arrojado por sus fauces. 17Entonces el dragón se enfureció contra la mujer, y se fue a hacer guerra contra el resto de sus descendientes, los cuales obedecen los mandamientos de Dios y se mantienen fieles al testimonio de Jesús.

13 Y el dragón se plantóv a la orilla del mar.

La bestia que surge del mar

Entonces vi que del mar subía una bestia, la cual tenía diez cuernos y siete cabezas. En cada cuerno tenía una diadema, y en cada cabeza un nombre *blasfemo contra Dios. 2La bestia parecía un leopardo, pero tenía patas como de oso y fauces como de león. El dragón le confirió a la bestia su poder, su trono y gran autoridad. 3Una de las cabezas de la bestia parecía haber sufrido una herida mortal, pero esa herida ya había sido sanada. El mundo entero, fascinado, iba tras la bestia 4y adoraba al dragón porque había dado su autoridad a la bestia. También adoraban a la bestia y decían: «¿Quién como la bestia? ¿Quién puede combatirla?»

5A la bestia se le permitió hablar con arrogancia y proferir blasfemias contra Dios, y se le confirió autoridad para actuar durante cuarenta y dos meses. 6Abrió la boca para blasfemar contra Dios, para maldecir su nombre y su morada y a los que viven en el cielo. 7También se le permitió hacer la guerra a los *santos y vencerlos, y se le dio autoridad sobre toda raza, pueblo, lengua y nación. 8A la bestia la adorarán todos los habitantes de la tierra, aquellos cuyos nombres no han sido escritos en el libro de la vida, el libro del Cordero que fue sacrificado desde la creación del mundo.w

9El que tenga oídos, que oiga.

10El que deba ser llevado cautivo,
    a la cautividad irá.
El que deba morirx a espada,
    a filo de espada morirá.

¡En esto consisteny la perseverancia y la *fidelidad de los santos!

La bestia que sube de la tierra

11Después vi que de la tierra subía otra bestia. Tenía dos cuernos como de cordero, pero hablaba

---

como dragón. 12Ejercía toda la autoridad de la primera bestia en presencia de ella, y hacía que la tierra y sus habitantes adoraran a la primera bestia, cuya herida mortal había sido sanada. 13También hacía grandes señales milagrosas, incluso la de hacer caer fuego del cielo a la tierra, a la vista de todos. 14Con estas señales que se le permitió hacer en presencia de la primera bestia, engañó a los habitantes de la tierra. Les ordenó que hicieran una imagen en honor de la bestia que, después de ser herida a espada, revivió. 15Se le permitió infundir vida a la imagen de la primera bestia, para que hablara y mandara matar a quienes no adoraran la imagen. 16Además logró que a todos, grandes y pequeños, ricos o pobres, libres y esclavos, se les pusiera una marca en la mano derecha o en la frente, 17de modo que nadie pudiera comprar ni vender, a menos que llevara la marca, que es el nombre de la bestia o el número de ese nombre.

18En esto consiste^z la sabiduría: el que tenga entendimiento, calcule el número de la bestia, pues es número de un ser *humano: seiscientos sesenta y seis.

El Cordero y los 144.000

14 Luego miré, y apareció el Cordero. Estaba de pie sobre el monte Sión, en compañía de ciento cuarenta y cuatro mil personas que llevaban escrito en la frente el nombre del Cordero y de su Padre. 2Oí un sonido que venía del cielo, como el estruendo de una catarata y el retumbar de un gran trueno. El sonido se parecía al de músicos que tañen sus arpas. 3Y cantaban un himno nuevo delante del trono y delante de los cuatro seres vivientes y de los *ancianos. Nadie podía aprender aquel himno, aparte de los ciento cuarenta y cuatro mil que habían sido rescatados de la tierra. 4Éstos se mantuvieron puros, sin contaminarse con ritos sexuales.^a Son los que siguen al Cordero por dondequiera que va. Fueron rescatados como los primeros frutos de la *humanidad para Dios y el Cordero. 5No se encontró mentira alguna en su boca, pues son intachables.

Los tres ángeles

6Luego vi a otro ángel que volaba en medio del cielo, y que llevaba el *evangelio eterno para anunciarlo a los que viven en la tierra, a toda nación, raza, lengua y pueblo. 7Gritaba a gran voz: «Teman a Dios y denle gloria, porque ha llegado la hora de su juicio. Adoren al que hizo el cielo, la tierra, el mar y los manantiales.»

8Lo seguía un segundo ángel que gritaba: «¡Ya cayó! Ya cayó la gran Babilonia, la que hizo que todas las *naciones bebieran el excitante vino^b de su adulterio.»

9Lo seguía un tercer ángel que clamaba a grandes voces: «Si alguien adora a la bestia y a su imagen, y se deja poner en la frente o en la mano la marca de la bestia, 10beberá también el vino del furor de Dios, que en la copa de su ira está puro, ni diluido. Será atormentado con fuego y azufre, en presencia de los santos ángeles y del Cordero. 11El humo de ese tormento sube por los siglos de los siglos. No habrá descanso ni de día ni de noche para el que adore a la bestia y su imagen, ni para quien se deje poner la marca de su nombre.» 12¡En esto consiste^c la perseverancia de los *santos, los cuales obedecen los mandamientos de Dios y se mantienen fieles a Jesús!

13Entonces oí una voz del cielo, que decía: «Escribe: *Dichosos los que de ahora en adelante mueren en el Señor.»

«Sí —dice el Espíritu—, ellos descansarán de sus fatigosas tareas, pues sus obras los acompañan.»

La cosecha de la tierra

14Miré, y apareció una nube blanca, sobre la cual estaba sentado alguien «semejante al Hijo del hombre».^d En la cabeza tenía una corona de oro, y en la mano, una hoz afilada. 15Entonces salió del templo otro ángel y le gritó al que estaba sentado en la nube: «Mete la hoz y recoge la cosecha; ya es tiempo de segar, pues la cosecha de la tierra está madura.» 16Así que el que estaba sentado sobre la nube pasó la hoz, y la tierra fue segada.

17Del templo que está en el cielo salió otro ángel, que también llevaba una hoz afilada. 18Del altar salió otro ángel, que tenía autoridad sobre el fuego, y le gritó al que llevaba la hoz afilada: «Mete tu hoz y corta los racimos del viñedo de la tierra, porque sus uvas ya están maduras.» 19El ángel pasó la hoz sobre la tierra, recogió las uvas y las echó en el gran lagar de la ira de Dios. 20Las uvas fueron exprimidas fuera de la ciudad, y del lagar salió sangre, la cual llegó hasta los frenos de los caballos en una extensión de trescientos kilómetros.^e

Siete ángeles con siete plagas

15 Vi en el cielo otra señal grande y maravillosa: siete ángeles con las siete plagas, que son las últimas, pues con ellas se consumará la ira de Dios. 2Vi también un mar como de vidrio mezclado con fuego. De pie, a la orilla del mar, estaban los que habían vencido a la bestia, a su imagen y al número de su nombre. Tenían las arpas que Dios les había dado, 3y cantaban el himno de Moisés, *siervo de Dios, y el himno del Cordero:

«Grandes y maravillosas son tus obras,
    Señor, Dios Todopoderoso.
Justos y verdaderos son tus caminos,
    Rey de las *naciones.^f
4¿Quién no te temerá, oh Señor?
    ¿Quién no glorificará tu nombre?
Sólo tú eres santo.
Todas las naciones vendrán
    y te adorarán,
porque han salido a la luz
    las obras de tu justicia.»

5Después de esto miré, y en el cielo se abrió el templo, el tabernáculo del testimonio. 6Del templo salieron los siete ángeles que llevaban las siete plagas. Estaban vestidos de lino limpio y resplandeciente, y ceñidos con bandas de oro a la altura del pecho. 7Uno de los cuatro seres vivientes dio a cada uno de los siete ángeles una copa de oro llena del furor de Dios, quien vive por los siglos de los siglos. 8El templo se llenó del humo que procedía de la gloria y del poder de Dios, y nadie podía entrar allí hasta que se terminaran las siete plagas de los siete ángeles.

Las siete copas de la ira de Dios

16 Oí una voz que desde el templo decía a gritos a los siete ángeles: «¡Vayan y derramen sobre la tierra las siete copas del furor de Dios!»

---

z **13:18** *En esto consiste.* Alt. *Aquí se verá.* a **14:4** *Éstos . . . sexuales.* Lit. *Éstos no se contaminaron con mujeres, pues son vírgenes.* b **14:8** *el excitante vino.* Lit. *el vino del furor.* c **14:12** *En esto consiste.* Alt. *Aquí se verá.* d **14:14** Dn 7:13 e **14:20** *trescientos kilómetros.* Lit. *mil seiscientos *estadios.* f **15:3** *de las naciones.* Var. *de los siglos.*

²El primer ángel fue y derramó su copa sobre la tierra, y a toda la gente que tenía la marca de la bestia y que adoraba su imagen le salió una llaga maligna y repugnante.

³El segundo ángel derramó su copa sobre el mar, y el mar se convirtió en sangre como de gente masacrada, y murió todo ser viviente que había en el mar.

⁴El tercer ángel derramó su copa sobre los ríos y los manantiales, y éstos se convirtieron en sangre. ⁵Oí que el ángel de las aguas decía:

«Justo eres tú, el Santo,
    que eres y que eras,
    porque juzgas así:
⁶ellos derramaron la sangre de *santos y de
    profetas,
    y tú les has dado a beber sangre, como se lo
    merecen.»

⁷Oí también que el altar respondía:

«Así es, Señor, Dios Todopoderoso,
    verdaderos y justos son tus juicios.»

⁸El cuarto ángel derramó su copa sobre el sol, al cual se le permitió quemar con fuego a la gente. ⁹Todos sufrieron terribles quemaduras, pero ni así se *arrepintieron; en vez de darle gloria a Dios, que tiene poder sobre esas plagas, maldijeron su nombre.

¹⁰El quinto ángel derramó su copa sobre el trono de la bestia, y el reino de la bestia quedó sumido en la oscuridad. La gente se mordía la lengua de dolor ¹¹y, por causa de sus padecimientos y de sus llagas, maldecían al Dios del cielo, pero no se arrepintieron de sus malas obras.

¹²El sexto ángel derramó su copa sobre el gran río Éufrates, y se secaron sus aguas para abrir paso a los reyes del oriente. ¹³Y vi salir de la boca del dragón, de la boca de la bestia y de la boca del falso profeta tres espíritus malignos que parecían ranas. ¹⁴Son espíritus de demonios que hacen señales milagrosas y que salen a reunir a los reyes del mundo entero para la batalla del gran día del Dios Todopoderoso.

¹⁵«¡Cuidado! ¡Vengo como un ladrón! *Dichoso el que se mantenga despierto, con su ropa a la mano, no sea que ande desnudo y sufra vergüenza por su desnudez.»

¹⁶Entonces los espíritus de los demonios reunieron a los reyes en el lugar que en hebreo se llama Armagedón.

¹⁷El séptimo ángel derramó su copa en el aire, y desde el trono del templo salió un vozarrón que decía: «¡Se acabó!» ¹⁸Y hubo relámpagos, estruendos, truenos y un violento terremoto. Nunca, desde que el género *humano existe en la tierra, se había sentido un terremoto tan grande y violento. ¹⁹La gran ciudad se partió en tres, y las ciudades de las *naciones se desplomaron. Dios se acordó de la gran Babilonia y le dio a beber de la copa llena del vino del furor de su castigo. ²⁰Entonces huyeron todas las islas y desaparecieron las montañas. ²¹Del cielo cayeron sobre la gente enormes granizos, de casi cuarenta kilos cada uno.ᵍ Y maldecían a Dios por esa terrible plaga.

La mujer montada en la bestia

17 Uno de los siete ángeles que tenían las siete copas se me acercó y me dijo: «Ven, te mostraré el castigo de la gran prostituta que está sentada sobre muchas aguas. ²Con ella cometieron adulterio

los reyes de la tierra, y los habitantes de la tierra se embriagaron con el vino de su inmoralidad.»

³Luego el ángel me llevó en el Espíritu a un desierto. Allí vi a una mujer montada en una bestia escarlata. La bestia estaba cubierta de nombres *blasfemos contra Dios, y tenía siete cabezas y diez cuernos. ⁴La mujer estaba vestida de púrpura y escarlata, y adornada con oro, piedras preciosas y perlas. Tenía en la mano una copa de oro llena de abominaciones y de la inmundicia de sus adulterios. ⁵En la frente llevaba escrito un nombre misterioso:

LA GRAN BABILONIA
MADRE DE LAS PROSTITUTAS
Y DE LAS ABOMINABLES IDOLATRÍAS
DE LA TIERRA.

⁶Vi que la mujer se había emborrachado con la sangre de los *santos y de los mártires de Jesús.

Al verla, quedé sumamente asombrado. ⁷Entonces el ángel me dijo: «¿Por qué te asombras? Yo te explicaré el misterio de esa mujer y de la bestia de siete cabezas y diez cuernos en la que va montada. ⁸La bestia que has visto es la que antes era pero ya no es, y está a punto de subir del *abismo, pero va rumbo a la destrucción. Los habitantes de la tierra, cuyos nombres, desde la creación del mundo, no han sido escritos en el libro de la vida, se asombrarán al ver a la bestia, porque antes era pero ya no es, y sin embargo reaparecerá.

⁹»¡En esto consisteʰ el entendimiento y la sabiduría! Las siete cabezas son siete colinas sobre las que está sentada esa mujer. ¹⁰También son siete reyes: cinco han caído, uno está gobernando, el otro no ha llegado todavía; pero cuando llegue, es preciso que dure poco tiempo. ¹¹La bestia, que antes era pero ya no es, es el octavo rey. Está incluido entre los siete, y va rumbo a la destrucción.

¹²»Los diez cuernos que has visto son diez reyes que todavía no han comenzado a reinar, pero que por una hora recibirán autoridad como reyes, junto con la bestia. ¹³Éstos tienen un mismo propósito, que es poner su poder y autoridad a disposición de la bestia. ¹⁴Le harán la guerra al Cordero, pero el Cordero los vencerá, porque es Señor de señores y Rey de reyes, y los que están con él son sus llamados, sus escogidos y sus fieles.»

¹⁵Además el ángel me dijo: «Las aguas que has visto, donde está sentada la prostituta, son pueblos, multitudes, naciones y lenguas. ¹⁶Los diez cuernos y la bestia que has visto le cobrarán odio a la prostituta. Causarán su ruina y la dejarán desnuda; devorarán su cuerpo y la destruirán con fuego, ¹⁷porque Dios les ha puesto en el corazón que lleven a cabo su divino propósito. Por eso, y de común acuerdo, ellos entregarán a la bestia el poder que tienen de gobernar, hasta que se cumplan las palabras de Dios. ¹⁸La mujer que has visto es aquella gran ciudad que tiene poder de gobernar sobre los reyes de la tierra.»

La caída de Babilonia

18 Después de esto vi a otro ángel que bajaba del cielo. Tenía mucho poder, y la tierra se iluminó con su resplandor. ²Gritó a gran voz:

«¡Ha caído! ¡Ha caído la gran Babilonia!
    Se ha convertido en morada de demonios
    y en guarida de todo espíritu *maligno,
    en nido de toda ave *impura y detestable.
³Porque todas las *naciones han bebido

ᵍ **16:21** *granizos . . . cada uno.* Lit. *granizos como *talentos.* ʰ **17:9** *En esto consisten.* Alt. *Aquí se verán.*

el excitante vino de su adulterio;
los reyes de la tierra cometieron adulterio con
ella,
y los comerciantes de la tierra se
enriquecieron
a costa de lo que ella despilfarraba en sus
lujos.»

⁴Luego oí otra voz del cielo que decía:

«Salgan de ella, pueblo mío,
para que no sean cómplices de sus pecados,
ni los alcance ninguna de sus plagas;
⁵pues sus pecados se han amontonado hasta el
cielo,
y de sus injusticias se ha acordado Dios.
⁶Páguenle con la misma moneda;
denle el doble de lo que ha cometido,
y en la misma copa en que ella preparó bebida
mézclenle una doble porción.
⁷En la medida en que ella se entregó a la
vanagloria y al arrogante lujo
denle tormento y aflicción;
porque en su corazón se jacta:
"Estoy sentada como reina;
no soy viuda ni sufriré jamás."
⁸Por eso, en un solo día le sobrevendrán sus
plagas:
pestilencia, aflicción y hambre.
Será consumida por el fuego,
porque poderoso es el Señor Dios que la
juzga.»

⁹Cuando los reyes de la tierra que cometieron
adulterio con ella y compartieron su lujo vean el
humo del fuego que la consume, llorarán de dolor
por ella. ¹⁰Aterrorizados al ver semejante castigo, se
mantendrán a distancia y gritarán:

«¡Ay! ¡Ay de ti, la gran ciudad,
Babilonia, ciudad poderosa,
porque en una sola hora ha llegado tu juicio!»

¹¹Los comerciantes de la tierra llorarán y harán
duelo por ella, porque ya no habrá quien les compre
sus mercaderías: ¹²artículos de oro, plata, piedras
preciosas y perlas; lino fino, púrpura, telas de seda y
escarlata; toda clase de maderas de cedro; los más
variados objetos, hechos de marfil, de madera preciosa, de bronce, de hierro y de mármol; ¹³cargamen-
tos de canela y especias aromáticas; de incienso, mirra y perfumes; de vino y aceite; de harina refinada y
trigo; de ganado vacuno y de corderos; de caballos y
carruajes; y hasta de seres *humanos, vendidos
como esclavos.
¹⁴Y dirán: «Se ha apartado de ti el fruto que con
toda el alma codiciabas. Has perdido todas tus cosas
suntuosas y espléndidas, y nunca las recuperarás.»
¹⁵Los comerciantes que vendían estas mercaderías y
se habían enriquecido a costa de ella se mantendrán
a distancia, aterrorizados al ver semejante castigo.
Llorarán y harán lamentación:

¹⁶«¡Ay! ¡Ay de la gran ciudad,
vestida de lino fino, de púrpura y escarlata,
y adornada con oro, piedras preciosas y
perlas,
¹⁷porque en una sola hora ha quedado
destruida toda tu riqueza!»

Todos los capitanes de barco, los pasajeros, los
marineros y todos los que viven del mar se deten-

drán a lo lejos. ¹⁸Al ver el humo del fuego que la consume, exclamarán: «¿Hubo jamás alguna ciudad
como esta gran ciudad?» ¹⁹Harán duelo,ⁱ llorando y
lamentándose a gritos:

«¡Ay! ¡Ay de la gran ciudad,
con cuya opulencia se enriquecieron
todos los dueños de flotas navieras!
¡En una sola hora ha quedado destruida!
²⁰¡Alégrate, oh cielo, por lo que le ha sucedido!
¡Alégrense también ustedes, *santos,
apóstoles y profetas!,
porque Dios, al juzgarla,
les ha hecho justicia a ustedes.»

²¹Entonces un ángel poderoso levantó una piedra del tamaño de una gran rueda de molino, y la
arrojó al mar diciendo:

«Así también tú, Babilonia, gran ciudad,
serás derribada con la misma violencia,
y desaparecerás de la faz de la tierra.
²²Jamás volverá a oírse en ti
la música de los cantantes
y de arpas, flautas y trompetas.
Jamás volverá a hallarse en ti
ningún tipo de artesano.
Jamás volverá a oírse en ti
el ruido de la rueda de molino.
²³Jamás volverá a brillar en ti
la luz de ninguna lámpara.
Jamás volverá a sentirse en ti
el regocijo de las nupcias.ʲ
Porque tus comerciantes
eran los magnates del mundo,
porque con tus hechicerías
engañaste a todas las naciones.
²⁴porque en ti se halló sangre de profetas y de
santos,
y de todos los que han sido asesinados en
la tierra.»

¡Aleluya!

19 Después de esto oí en el cielo un tremendo
bullicio, como el de una inmensa multitud
que exclamaba:

«¡Aleluya!
La salvación, la gloria y el poder son de
nuestro Dios,
2 pues sus juicios son verdaderos y justos,
ha condenado a la famosa prostituta
que con sus adulterios corrompía la tierra;
ha vindicado la sangre de los *siervos de Dios
derramada por ella.»

³Y volvieron a exclamar:

«¡Aleluya!
El humo de ella sube por los siglos de los
siglos.»

⁴Entonces los veinticuatro *ancianos y los cuatro
seres vivientes se postraron y adoraron a Dios, que
estaba sentado en el trono, y dijeron:

«¡Amén, Aleluya!»

⁵Y del trono salió una voz que decía:

«¡Alaben ustedes a nuestro Dios,
todos sus siervos, grandes y pequeños,
que con reverente temor le sirven!»

---

i **18:19** *Harán duelo.* Lit. *Se echaron polvo en la cabeza.* j **18:23** *el regocijo de las nupcias.* Lit. *la voz del novio y de la novia.*

6Después oí voces como el rumor de una inmensa multitud, como el estruendo de una catarata y como el retumbar de potentes truenos, que exclamaban:

«¡Aleluya!
Ya ha comenzado a reinar el Señor,
nuestro Dios Todopoderoso.
7¡Alegrémonos y regocijémonos
y démosle gloria!
Ya ha llegado el día de las bodas del Cordero.
Su novia se ha preparado,
8y se le ha concedido vestirse
de lino fino, limpio y resplandeciente.»

(El lino fino representa las acciones justas de los *santos.)

9El ángel me dijo: «Escribe: "¡*Dichosos los que han sido convidados a la cena de las bodas del Cordero!"» Y añadió: «Estas son las palabras verdaderas de Dios.»

10Me postré a sus pies para adorarlo. Pero él me dijo: «¡No, cuidado! Soy un siervo como tú y como tus hermanos que se mantienen fieles al testimonio de Jesús. ¡Adora sólo a Dios! El testimonio de Jesús es el espíritu que inspira la profecía.»

El jinete del caballo blanco

11Luego vi el cielo abierto, y apareció un caballo blanco. Su jinete se llama Fiel y Verdadero. Con justicia dicta sentencia y hace la guerra. 12Sus ojos resplandecen como llamas de fuego, y muchas diademas ciñen su cabeza. Lleva escrito un nombre que nadie conoce sino sólo él. 13Está vestido de un manto teñido en sangre, y su nombre es «el *Verbo de Dios». 14Lo siguen los ejércitos del cielo, montados en caballos blancos y vestidos de lino fino, blanco y limpio. 15De su boca sale una espada afilada, con la que herirá a las *naciones. «Las gobernará con puño de hierro.»k Él mismo exprime uvas en el lagar del furor del castigo que viene de Dios Todopoderoso. 16En su manto y sobre el muslo lleva escrito este nombre:

REY DE REYES Y SEÑOR DE SEÑORES.

17Vi a un ángel que, parado sobre el sol, gritaba a todas las aves que vuelan en medio del cielo: «Vengan, reúnanse para la gran cena de Dios, 18para que coman carne de reyes, de jefes militares y de magnates; carne de caballos y de sus jinetes; carne de toda clase de gente, libres y esclavos, grandes y pequeños.»

19Entonces vi a la bestia y a los reyes de la tierra con sus ejércitos, reunidos para hacer guerra contra el jinete de aquel caballo y contra su ejército. 20Pero la bestia fue capturada junto con el falso profeta. Éste es el que hacía señales milagrosas en presencia de ella, con las cuales engañaba a los que habían recibido la marca de la bestia y adoraban su imagen. Los dos fueron arrojados vivos al lago de fuego y azufre. 21Los demás fueron exterminados por la espada que salía de la boca del que montaba a caballo, y todas las aves se hartaron de la carne de ellos.

Los mil años

20 Vi además a un ángel que bajaba del cielo con la llave del *abismo y una gran cadena en la mano. 2Sujetó al dragón, a aquella serpiente antigua que es el diablo y Satanás, y lo encadenó por mil años. 3Lo arrojó al abismo, lo encerró y tapó la salida para que no engañara más a las *naciones, hasta

que se cumplieran los mil años. Después habrá de ser soltado por algún tiempo.

4Entonces vi tronos donde se sentaron los que recibieron autoridad para juzgar. Vi también las almas de los que habían sido decapitados por causa del testimonio de Jesús y por la palabra de Dios. No habían adorado a la bestia ni a su imagen, ni se habían dejado poner su marca en la frente ni en la mano. Volvieron a vivir y reinaron con *Cristo mil años. 5Ésta es la primera resurrección; los demás muertos no volvieron a vivir hasta que se cumplieron los mil años. 6*Dichosos y santos los que tienen parte en la primera resurrección. La segunda muerte no tiene poder sobre ellos, sino que serán sacerdotes de Dios y de Cristo, y reinarán con él mil años.

Juicio final de Satanás

7Cuando se cumplan los mil años, Satanás será liberado de su prisión, 8y saldrá para engañar a las *naciones que están en los cuatro ángulos de la tierra —a Gog y a Magog—, a fin de reunirlas para la batalla. Su número será como el de las arenas del mar. 9Marcharán a lo largo y a lo ancho de la tierra, y rodearán el campamento del *pueblo de Dios, la ciudad que él ama. Pero caerá fuego del cielo y los consumirá por completo. 10El diablo, que los había engañado, será arrojado al lago de fuego y azufre, donde también habrán sido arrojados la bestia y el falso profeta. Allí serán atormentados día y noche por los siglos de los siglos.

Juicio de los muertos

11Luego vi un gran trono blanco y a alguien que estaba sentado en él. De su presencia huyeron la tierra y el cielo, sin dejar rastro alguno. 12Vi también a los muertos, grandes y pequeños, de pie delante del trono. Se abrieron unos libros, y luego otro, que es el libro de la vida. Los muertos fueron juzgados según lo que habían hecho, conforme a lo que estaba escrito en los libros. 13El mar devolvió sus muertos; la muerte y el infiernol devolvieron los suyos; y cada uno fue juzgado según lo que había hecho. 14La muerte y el infierno fueron arrojados al lago de fuego. Este lago de fuego es la muerte segunda. 15Aquel cuyo nombre no estaba escrito en el libro de la vida era arrojado al lago de fuego.

La nueva Jerusalén

21 Después vi un cielo nuevo y una tierra nueva, porque el primer cielo y la primera tierra habían dejado de existir, lo mismo que el mar. 2Vi además la ciudad santa, la nueva Jerusalén, que bajaba del cielo, procedente de Dios, preparada como una novia hermosamente vestida para su prometido. 3Oí una potente voz que provenía del trono y decía: «¡Aquí, entre los seres *humanos, está la morada de Dios! Él acampará en medio de ellos, y ellos serán su pueblo; Dios mismo estará con ellos y será su Dios. 4Él les enjugará toda lágrima de los ojos. Ya no habrá muerte, ni llanto, ni lamento ni dolor, porque las primeras cosas han dejado de existir.»

5El que estaba sentado en el trono dijo: «¡Yo hago nuevas todas las cosas!» Y añadió: «Escribe, porque estas palabras son verdaderas y dignas de confianza.»

6También me dijo: «Ya todo está hecho. Yo soy el Alfa y la Omega, el Principio y el Fin. Al que tenga sed le daré a beber gratuitamente de la fuente del agua de la vida. 7El que salga vencedor heredará todo esto, y yo seré su Dios y él será mi hijo. 8Pero los

---

k 19:15 gobernará . . . hierro. Lit. pastoreará con cetro de hierro; Sal 2:9. l 20:13 infierno. Lit. *Hades; también en v. 14.

cobardes, los incrédulos, los abominables, los asesinos, los que cometen inmoralidades sexuales, los que practican artes mágicas, los idólatras y todos los mentirosos recibirán como herencia el lago de fuego y azufre. Ésta es la segunda muerte.»

9Se acercó uno de los siete ángeles que tenían las siete copas llenas con las últimas siete plagas. Me habló así: «Ven, que te voy a presentar a la novia, la esposa del Cordero.» 10Me llevó en el Espíritu a una montaña grande y elevada, y me mostró la ciudad santa, Jerusalén, que bajaba del cielo, procedente de Dios. 11Resplandecía con la gloria de Dios, y su brillo era como el de una piedra preciosa, semejante a una piedra de jaspe transparente. 12Tenía una muralla grande y alta, y doce puertas custodiadas por doce ángeles, en las que estaban escritos los nombres de las doce tribus de Israel. 13Tres puertas daban al este, tres al norte, tres al sur y tres al oeste. 14La muralla de la ciudad tenía doce cimientos, en los que estaban los nombres de los doce apóstoles del Cordero.

15El ángel que hablaba conmigo llevaba una caña de oro para medir la ciudad, sus puertas y su muralla. 16La ciudad era cuadrada; medía lo mismo de largo que de ancho. El ángel midió la ciudad con la caña, y tenía dos mil doscientos kilómetros:m su longitud, su anchura y su altura eran iguales. 17Midió también la muralla, y tenía sesenta y cinco metros,n según las medidas humanas que el ángel emplea. 18La muralla estaba hecha de jaspe, y la ciudad era de oro puro, semejante a cristal pulido. 19Los cimientos de la muralla de la ciudad estaban decorados con toda clase de piedras preciosas: el primero con jaspe, el segundo con zafiro, el tercero con ágata, el cuarto con esmeralda, 20el quinto con ónice, el sexto con cornalina, el séptimo con crisólito, el octavo con berilo, el noveno con topacio, el décimo con crisoprasa, el undécimo con jacinto y el duodécimo con amatista.ñ 21Las doce puertas eran doce perlas, y cada puerta estaba hecha de una sola perla. La calleo principal de la ciudad era de oro puro, como cristal transparente.

22No vi ningún templo en la ciudad, porque el Señor Dios Todopoderoso y el Cordero son su templo. 23La ciudad no necesita ni sol ni luna que la alumbren, porque la gloria de Dios la ilumina, y el Cordero es su lumbrera. 24Las *naciones caminarán a la luz de la ciudad, y los reyes de la tierra le entregarán sus espléndidas riquezas.p 25Sus puertas estarán abiertas todo el día, pues allí no habrá noche. 26Y llevarán a ella las todas las riquezasq y el honor de las *naciones. 27Nunca entrará en ella nada impuro, ni los idólatras ni los farsantes, sino sólo aquellos que tienen su nombre escrito en el libro de la vida, el libro del Cordero.

El río de vida

22 Luego el ángel me mostró un río de agua de vida, claro como el cristal, que salía del trono de Dios y del Cordero, 2y corría por el centro de la caller principal de la ciudad. A cada lado del río estaba el árbol de la vida, que produce doce cosechas al año,

una por mes; y las hojas del árbol son para la salud de las *naciones. 3Ya no habrá maldición. El trono de Dios y del Cordero estará en la ciudad. Sus *siervos lo adorarán; 4lo verán cara a cara, y llevarán su nombre en la frente. 5Ya no habrá noche; no necesitarán luz de lámpara ni de sol, porque el Señor Dios los alumbrará. Y reinarán por los siglos de los siglos.

6El ángel me dijo: «Estas palabras son verdaderas y dignas de confianza. El Señor, el Dios que inspira a los profetas,s ha enviado a su ángel para mostrar a sus siervos lo que tiene que suceder sin demora.»

Cristo viene pronto

7«¡Miren que vengo pronto! *Dichoso el que cumple las palabras del mensaje profético de este libro.»

8Yo, Juan, soy el que vio y oyó todas estas cosas. Y cuando lo vi y oí, me postré para adorar al ángel que me había estado mostrando todo esto. 9Pero él me dijo: «¡No, cuidado! Soy un siervo como tú, como tus hermanos los profetas y como todos los que cumplen las palabras de este libro. ¡Adora sólo a Dios!»

10También me dijo: «No guardes en secreto las palabras del mensaje profético de este libro, porque el tiempo de su cumplimiento está cerca. 11Deja que el malo siga haciendo el mal y que el vil siga envileciéndose; deja que el justo siga practicando la justicia y que el *santo siga santificándose.»

12«¡Miren que vengo pronto! Traigo conmigo mi recompensa, y le pagaré a cada uno según lo que haya hecho. 13Yo soy el Alfa y la Omega, el Primero y el Último, el Principio y el Fin.

14»Dichosos los que lavan sus ropas para tener derecho al árbol de la vida y para poder entrar por las puertas de la ciudad. 15Pero afuera se quedarán los *perros, los que practican las artes mágicas, los que cometen inmoralidades sexuales, los asesinos, los idólatras y todo el que ama y practica la mentira.

16»Yo, Jesús, he enviado a mi ángel para darles a ustedes testimonio de estas cosas que conciernen a las iglesias. Yo soy la raíz y la descendencia de David, la brillante estrella de la mañana.»

17El Espíritu y la novia dicen: «¡Ven!»; y el que escuche diga: «¡Ven!» El que tenga sed, venga; y el que quiera, tome gratuitamente del agua de la vida.

18A todo el que escuche las palabras del mensaje profético de este libro le advierto esto: Si alguno le añade algo, Dios le añadirá a él las plagas descritas en este libro. 19Y si alguno quita palabras de este libro de profecía, Dios le quitará su parte del árbol de la vida y de la ciudad santa, descritos en este libro.

20El que da testimonio de estas cosas, dice: «Sí, vengo pronto.»

Amén. ¡Ven, Señor Jesús!

21Que la gracia del Señor Jesús sea con todos. Amén.

---

m 21:16 dos mil doscientos kilómetros. Lit. doce mil *estadios. n 21:17 sesenta y cinco metros. Lit. ciento cuarenta y cuatro *codos. ñ 21:20 No se sabe con certeza la identificación precisa de algunas de estas piedras. o 21:21 calle. Alt. Plaza. p 21:24 entregarán . . . riquezas. Lit. llevarán su gloria. q 21:26 todas las riquezas. Lit. la gloria. r 22:2 calle. Alt. Plaza. s 22:6 el Dios . . . profetas. Lit. El Dios de los espíritus de los profetas.

GLOSARIO

Este glosario no pretende ser un diccionario bíblico en miniatura, sino sólo una ayuda relacionada con los principios y métodos de la traducción. Muchos términos culturales y teológicos no están incluidos, pero la lista abarca todas las palabras marcadas con un asterisco en el texto bíblico. (Nótese que si la palabra se usa más de una vez en el mismo pasaje bíblico, el asterisco no se repite.) Se trata principalmente de palabras difíciles de traducir, debido a las diferencias entre los idiomas bíblicos y el español.

abba. Palabra aramea que significa «padre» o «papá». Como fue usada por Jesús de modo característico para referirse a Dios, su Padre celestial (véase Mr 14:36), la iglesia cristiana también la adoptó, aun cuando el idioma de los creyentes era el griego (Ro 8:15; Gá 4:6).

abadón. Literalmente significa «destructor». En el Antiguo Testamento, término hebreo para referirse al reino de la muerte. Aparece como sinónimo de «muerte» y «sepulcro». En el Nuevo Testamento aparece como personificación del ángel de la muerte (Ap 9:11).

abismo. Ya en la tradición judía se usaba este término en oposición a «cielo» (véase Ro 10:6-8); más específicamente, puede designar la morada de los demonios (p.ej. Lc 8:31; Ap 9:1). En un pasaje (Mt 11:23 = Lc 10:15) se ha usado para traducir *Hades*. En otro pasaje la expresión «arrojar al abismo» (2P 2:4) traduce el verbo *tartaróō*, literalmente «meter en el Tártaro», nombre que entre los griegos se refería a un lugar subterráneo (más profundo que el Hades), donde se imponía el castigo divino. Véase también **sepulcro.**

adar. Duodécimo mes en el calendario hebreo (mediados de febrero a mediados de marzo).

alamot. Probable anotación musical en cuanto al instrumento que debía tocarse o en tono en que debía cantarse un salmo. Por su etimología, posible indicación de que la melodía era para voces femeninas.

aleluya. (heb. *hallelu Yah*) Exclamación de alabanza a Dios que significa «¡Alaben al SEÑOR!» En esta versión aparece la expresión junto con su traducción literal.

aliento. Véase **vida.**

alma. Véase **vida.**

altares paganos (también santuarios paganos). Es traducción de la palabra hebrea *bamoth*, que literalmente significa «lugares altos». En 1 y 2 Reyes y en 2 Crónicas se usa para designar santuarios donde se practicaban cultos idolátricos cananeos.

Altísimo. (heb. *'elyón*, arameo *'illa'á*) Uno de los nombres de Dios, que también puede entenderse como «el Excelso».

anaquitas. Habitantes de Palestina, identificados como descendientes de cierto Anac; eran de gran estatura e infundían terror en las poblaciones de la región. En otras versiones castellanas se traduce «anaceos».

anciano. Además de su significado literal, esta palabra se usa con sentido especializado para designar a los jefes y dirigentes del pueblo hebreo, los cuales tenían responsabilidades tanto religiosas como civiles. En el Nuevo Testamento (griego *presbúteros*) se usa también para designar a los encargados de gobernar las iglesias (p.ej. Hch 14:23; 1Ti 5:17). En Apocalipsis se usa en un sentido más exaltado con referencia a veinticuatro seres en el cielo (p.ej. Ap 4:4). Véase también **obispo.**

Aram/arameos. Véase **Siria/sirios.**

arrasar. Véase **destrucción.**

arrepentimiento/arrepentirse. Significa no sólo el sentimiento de tristeza o remordimiento por haber pecado, sino también la acción de cambiar el modo de pensar y de actuar; implica un profundo cambio espiritual.

asarion. Moneda romana (latín *as*) de poco valor. Véase **Tabla de pesas, medidas y monedas.**

Aserá. Nombre de una diosa cananea. En el plural (heb. *'aserim*) se refiere a objetos hechos para adorarla, y generalmente se ha traducido con alguna frase, tal como «imágenes para el culto a Aserá».

Asia. En el Nuevo Testamento este nombre no se refiere al Lejano Oriente sino a una provincia romana al suroeste de Asia Menor (lo que hoy es Turquía), cuya capital era Éfeso.

aviv. Primer mes en el calendario hebreo (mediados de marzo a mediados de abril); después del exilio se usó el nombre *nisán*.

Astarté. (En otras traducciones, «Astoret».) Nombre de una diosa, común entre los pueblos semíticos de la antigüedad. En el plural puede referirse a la variedad de diosas que tenían este nombre, o a imágenes hechas en su honor.

Baal. La palabra hebrea significa «amo» o «esposo», pero como nombre propio se refiere a una deidad cananea, el dios de la tormenta, consorte de **Aserá** y **Astarté.** El uso del plural, «baales», parece indicar que el nombre podía referirse a distintas deidades locales.

babilonios. Generalmente es traducción de la palabra hebrea *kasdim*, que puede significar «Caldea» (un país antiguo al sur de Babilonia) o «caldeos». El nombre llegó a designar todo el territorio babilónico o a sus habitantes.

bato. Medida de capacidad equivalente aproximadamente a 22 litros; en el Nuevo Testamento, alrededor de 37 litros. Véase **Tabla de pesas, medidas y monedas.**

becá. Medida de peso equivalente aproximadamente a 6 gramos. Véase **Tabla de pesas, medidas y monedas.**

Beelzebú. Nombre que se usa en los evangelios con referencia a Satanás.

bienestar. Véase **paz.**

blasfemar. Acción de proferir blasfemias, o sea, pronunciar maldiciones o palabras injuriosas contra Dios o contra alguien que lo representa. La «blasfemia contra el Espíritu» (Mt 12:31 y paralelos) consiste en atribuir a Satanás las obras de Jesús, lo cual parece indicar un rechazo total del mensaje de Dios. El término griego también se puede usar en el sentido menos fuerte de «calumniar» o «insultar» (p.ej. Mr 7:22; Ef 4:31).

blasfemo. (heb. *letz*) Término tradicionalmente traducido «escarnecedor» (Sal 1:1), que alude a quienes no tienen respeto por nada ni nadie, ni siquiera por Dios.

braza. Medida de longitud equivalente aproximadamente a 1,80 metros. Véase **Tabla de pesas, medidas y monedas.**

bul. Octavo mes en el calendario hebreo (mediados de octubre a mediados de noviembre).

burlón. Véase **blasfemo.**

cab. Medida de capacidad equivalente aproximadamente a 1,2 litros. Véase **Tabla de pesas, medidas y monedas.**

caer, hacer caer. Véase **tropiezo.**

Caldea/caldeos. Véase **babilonios.**

camino. Además de su sentido primario, en el lenguaje bíblico este término alude simbólicamente a la conducta y voluntad divinas y humanas, así como a sus métodos, hábitos, actitudes y propósitos.

camisa. Se ha usado esta palabra unas cuantas veces (Mt 5:40 = Lc 6:29; Lc 3:11) para representar el vocablo griego *jitōn*, que también puede traducirse con un término general, «ropa» (p.ej. Mt 10:10; Mr 14:63; Jud 23). Con más precisión, se trata de la túnica (y así se tradujo en Jn 19:23; Hch 9:39), que en español puede implicar una vestidura formal o religiosa, y que daría un sentido incorrecto a los pasajes anteriores.

caña. Medida de longitud equivalente aproximadamente a 3 metros. También se ha traducido «vara». Véase **Tabla de pesas, medidas y monedas.**

carne/carnal. El término griego *sarx* tiene un uso muy variado, y frecuentemente contrasta con **Espíritu** (o **espíritu**). En su sentido literal y físico, puede traducirse «carne» o «cuerpo». En un sentido más amplio, se usa para designar lo que es meramente humano y por lo tanto débil. (Nótese también la frase «carne y sangre», que se ha traducido con varias expresiones; p.ej. Mt 16:17; 1Co 15:50; Ef 6:12.) En un sentido moral, indica lo que caracteriza a este mundo pecaminoso (véanse 2Co 10:3-4; Fil 1:22,24). Es difícil representar el concepto en español, por lo que también se han usado frases tales como «naturaleza humana», «naturaleza pecaminosa», «esfuerzos (o criterios, o razonamiento) humanos», «pasiones», y otras más (p.ej. Ro 8:3-9; 1Co 1:26; Gá 3:3; 4:23,29; 5:13-19; Fil 3:3-4; Col 2:18). La dificultad de distinguir entre el sentido literal y el figurado se nota especialmente en Ro 7:18,25; 1P 3:18; 4:1,2 («terrenal»),6.

Cefas. Nombre arameo que significa «roca» y que corresponde al nombre griego Pedro (véase Jn 1:42).

César/césar. Nombre que los emperadores romanos usaban como título (véanse Lc 2:1; 3:1) y que llegó a usarse en el sentido general de «emperador» (así se ha traducido en la mayoría de los pasajes, p.ej. Jn 19:12; Hch 17:7).

cielo(s). En la cosmogonía bíblica, bóveda sólida y firme (de allí que también se le llame «firmamento») que separa las aguas de arriba de las aguas de abajo (Gn 1), en la que Dios tiene su habitación. También se le concibe como una tienda de campaña, como una cortina y como un manto.

cilicio. Tela áspera, generalmente de pelo de cabra. Como se usaba entre los hebreos para expresar la pena y el dolor, la expresión «cubrirse de cilicio» (y otras parecidas) generalmente se ha traducido «vestirse de luto» o «hacer duelo».

circuncisión. Como esta operación era la señal física de que un hombre pertenecía al pueblo de Dios, la palabra se podía usar para designar a los judíos (p.ej. Ro 15:8; Gá 2:8-9; en Fil 3:3 con referencia a los cristianos). Por consiguiente, los términos «incircunciso» e «incircuncisión» (Ro 2:20) se refieren a los no judíos. Véase también **gentiles.**

codo. Medida antigua, basada en el largo del brazo desde el codo hasta la punta de los dedos, equivalente a 45-50 centímetros. Véase **Tabla de pesas, medidas y monedas.**

comunión, sacrificios de. (heb. *shelamim*) Tradicionalmente traducido como «sacrificios de paz», el vocablo hebreo parece referirse a varios tipos de ofrenda relacionados con la acción de gracias.

condenar a muerte. Véase **destrucción.**

conocimiento. Término sinónimo de **sabiduría**, que implica una relación estrecha e íntima entre dos personas, más que una simple acumulación de información y datos.

Consejo. Se ha usado este término como traducción del griego *sunédrion* (tradicionalmente «sanedrín»; en Hch 22:5 el griego es *presbutérion*). Se trata del más importante consejo de gobierno entre los judíos. Incluía a los **ancianos**, los **maestros de la ley** y los jefes de los sacerdotes.

Consolador. Traducción tradicional del término griego *paráklētos* en Jn 14:16,26; 15:26; 16:7. La palabra puede significar «abogado», pero más probable es el sentido general de «mediador» o «ayudador». En 1Jn 2:1 se tradujo «intercesor».

contaminar. Véase **puro.**

corazón. Además de su sentido primario, el lenguaje bíblico alude con este término al órgano cardíaco como la sede principal de las emociones y los sentimientos humanos, así como de sus esperanzas y temores. El corazón es también la sede de la actividad intelectual; de allí que en algunos casos se traduzca como «mente».

coro. Medida de capacidad equivalente aproximadamente a 220 litros. Véase **Tabla de pesas, medidas y monedas.**

corrección. Véase **disciplina.**

creyentes. Véase **santos.**

Cristo. Vocablo griego que significa «ungido» (véase Hch 4:26). Es primeramente un título descriptivo, pero también se usa como nombre propio de Jesús. En ciertos pasajes se ha traducido «Mesías» (término hebreo que corresponde a Cristo) para aclarar el uso titular, pero hay muchos otros pasajes en que puede entenderse como nombre o como título. La combinación «Jesús Cristo» (traducido como nombre, «Jesucristo») o «Cristo Jesús» también puede tener un sentido titular, es decir, «Jesús el Mesías». Nótese que en las cartas de Pablo, el uso de este vocablo es muy frecuente y se ha marcado con asterisco sólo la primera vez que aparece en cada carta.

cuello. Véase **vida.**

Cus/cusita. Se refiere a Nubia, una región al sur de Egipto, en la parte norte de lo que hoy es el Sudán. Los escritores clásicos llamaban a esta región «Etiopía», pero no debe confundirse con el país moderno que lleva ese nombre y que queda más al sur.

cuerpo. Véase **carne.**

Decápolis. Significa «las diez ciudades». Era una región de la Palestina habitada por gentiles.

denario. Moneda romana de plata, cuyo valor correspondía al salario de un obrero por un día de trabajo.

derecha. Se usa en sentido figurado para señalar la posición de honor. También es un símbolo del poder (véanse Hch 2:33; 5:31).

destrucción, destruir. Cuando estas palabras llevan asterisco, son traducción de vocablos hebreos (*jé-rem*, verbo *hejerim*) que se refieren a lo que Dios ha declarado anatema, es decir, algo prohibido y consagrado a Dios para ser destruido totalmente. En esta traducción también se han usado las expresiones «arrasar», «condenar a muerte», «destruir por completo» y «exterminar».

dichoso. En el Antiguo Testamento representa la palabra hebrea *'ashrey*, término tradicionalmente traducido «bienaventurado». En el Nuevo Testamento, con frecuencia representa la palabra griega *makários*, que significa «feliz» y que tradicionalmente se ha traducido «bienaventurado». En ambos casos se refiere a la persona que recibe la bendición de Dios y así experimenta la verdadera felicidad.

dirigente. Cuando esta palabra lleva asterisco, es traducción del vocablo hebreo que literalmente significa **anciano**.

disciplina. (heb. *musar*) Término típico de la literatura sapiencial que implica la **enseñanza** o **instrucción** correctiva de la ley, más la educación de los padres, incluido el castigo físico.

discreción. Véase **sabiduría**.

dracma. En el Antiguo Testamento se refiere al *dárico*, moneda persa de oro que pesaba alrededor de 125 gramos. En el Nuevo Testamento se refiere a una moneda griega de plata equivalente al **denario**.

efa. Medida de capacidad equivalente aproximadamente a 22 litros. Véase **Tabla de pesas, medidas y monedas**.

efod. Parte de la vestimenta sacerdotal, que se describe en Éx 28:6-14.

elul. Sexto mes en el calendario hebreo (mediados de agosto a mediados de septiembre).

emperador. Véase **César**.

enorgullecerse. Véase **jactancia**.

Enramadas, fiesta de las. Tradicionalmente traducida «Tabernáculos», esta fiesta se celebraba en el mes de *tisrí*. Durante los siete días de celebración, los israelitas vivían en cabañas hechas de ramas de árboles.

entrada(s). Véase **puerta(s)**.

escándalo/escandalizar. Véase **tropiezo**.

esclavo. Véase **siervo**.

Espíritu/espíritu. En ciertos pasajes donde la palabra griega *pneuma* aparece sin el calificativo «Santo», no es seguro si la referencia es al Espíritu Santo o al espíritu humano (p.ej. Jn 4:23-24; Ro 1:4; 8:10). Véase también **síquico**.

espíritu maligno. Una traducción más literal es «espíritu impuro». Se refiere a los demonios que se posesionan de algunas personas.

estela. Véase **piedra sagrada**.

estadio. Medida de longitud equivalente aproximadamente a 180 metros. Véase **Tabla de pesas, medidas y monedas**.

etanim. Séptimo mes en el calendario hebreo (mediados de septiembre a mediados de octubre).

eunuco. Hombre castrado que servía en la corte como guardián de las mujeres. A veces los eunucos llegaban a ser funcionarios de alto rango (véase Hch 8:27). En sentido figurado, se aplica a los que se mantienen solteros (Mt 19:11-12).

evangelio. Término de origen griego que significa «buena noticia». Principalmente en las cartas, el término se usa con sentido especializado, es decir, el mensaje acerca de Jesucristo. En otros pasajes se ha traducido como «buenas nuevas» o «buenas noticias» (p.ej. Lc 1:19; Hch 5:42). Más tarde, el término llegó a usarse para referirse a los libros que relatan la historia de Jesús.

experto en la ley. Véase **maestro de la ley**.

expiar/expiación. Se refiere a la acción divina de cubrir o quitar el pecado por medio del sacrificio. El término **propiciación** describe la misma acción desde otro punto de vista: el sacrificio aplaca la ira de Dios (véanse Ro 3:25; Heb 2:17; 1Jn 2:2; 4:10).

exterminar. Véase **destrucción**.

fariseo. Hoy día este término se usa en sentido despectivo y equivale a «hipócrita» (porque así calificó Jesús a los fariseos; p.ej. Mt 23:13-29), pero es necesario recordar que los fariseos constituían un grupo religioso que la mayoría de los judíos admiraba. Estudiaban la ley minuciosamente (muchos **maestros de la ley** estaban relacionados con este grupo) y deseaban obedecerla, aunque su modo de interpretación a veces los llevaba a ignorar los mandatos de Dios (véase especialmente Mr 7:1-13).

fidelidad. El término griego *pístis* generalmente tiene el sentido activo de «fe», indicando la acción de «confiar en alguien», pero en algunas ocasiones puede tener sentido pasivo, «ser confiable». En este segundo caso, se puede traducir «fidelidad» (p.ej. Ro 3:3; Gá 5:22). Algunos eruditos piensan que la frase «la fe en Jesucristo» (p.ej. Gá 2:16; 3:22) debe traducirse «la fidelidad de Cristo». Nótese también que el adjetivo *pistós* puede significar «creyente» o «fiel».

fosa. Véase **sepulcro**.

fuerza(s). Véase **vida**.

Gehenna. Nombre de un barranco en Jerusalén donde se quemaban los desperdicios. Entre los judíos llegó a ser un símbolo del fuego eterno, por lo cual se puede traducir «infierno».

género humano. Véase **hombre**.

gente. Véase **hombre**.

gentiles. Designa a los que no son judíos. Por lo general traduce el término que literalmente significa «naciones»; en otros pasajes traduce el término que significa «griegos» (en Ro 2:26 y 4:9 corresponde a «incircuncisión»; véase **circuncisión**). Cuando hay énfasis en el sentido religioso o moral, se traduce «paganos».

gittith. Término hebreo que aparece como título de algunos salmos (8, 81, 84), probablemente en relación con una melodía popular que se cantaba en los lagares.

gómer. Medida de capacidad equivalente aproximadamente a 2,2 litros. Véase **Tabla de pesas, medidas y monedas**.

griegos. Se usa no solamente en un sentido étnico estricto sino también para designar a cualquier persona que haya adoptado la cultura griega. Véase también **gentiles**.

guerá. Medida de peso equivalente aproximadamente a 0,6 gramos. Véase **Tabla de pesas, medidas y monedas**.

Hades. En la mitología griega era el nombre del dios del inframundo, y también se usaba para designar el lugar de los muertos. En el Nuevo Testamento equivale a «infierno»; también se ha traducido como **abismo** (Mt 11:23 = Lc 10:15), «muerte» (Mt 16:18), y «sepulcro» (Hch 2:27).

higaión. Término hebreo que aparece en algunos salmos (19 tít., 9, 92) y en otros libros del Antiguo Testamento (Is y Lm), probablemente para indicar un murmullo (Sal 19:14; Lm 3:62) o una queja (Is 16:7), o bien la vibración de algún instrumento de cuerdas (Sal 92:3).

hijo de hombre. Véase **hombre**.

hin. Medida de capacidad equivalente aproximadamente a 4 litros. Véase **Tabla de pesas, medidas y monedas**.

hipócrita/hipocresía. El término griego *hupokritēs* se refería a los actores de teatro. Posteriormente, incluso en el Nuevo Testamento, se usaba en sentido más general de cualquier persona que fingía ser lo que no era (p.ej. Mt 6:2), o que actuaba de manera incongruente con sus convicciones (Gá 2:13, donde se usan el verbo y el sustantivo). El término no implica necesariamente que la persona fuera mal intencionada.

hisopo. Planta pequeña y frondosa, no del todo identificada, que se usaba en ritos de purificación (Lv 14; Nm 19), y para aplicar la sangre a los dinteles de las puertas (Éx 12).

holocausto. Uno de los sacrificios en que el animal ofrecido se quemaba del todo.

hombre. Tanto en el Antiguo Testamento (heb. *'adam, 'enosh, o 'ish*) como en el Nuevo (griego *ánzrōpos*), el término castellano **hombre** puede usarse en sentido genérico, que contrasta al ser humano con Dios y abarca a toda la humanidad, o en sentido más restrictivo, que contrasta al *hombre* con la *mujer*. En la actualidad, el segundo sentido ha adquirido más prominencia, lo cual crea nuevos problemas de traducción. Cuando el texto original y el estilo castellano lo permiten, se han usado expresiones tales como «género humano», «gente», «humanidad», «mortal», «persona» y «ser humano».

humanidad/humano. Véanse **carne**, **hombre** y **síquico**.

impuro. Véase **puro**.

incircunciso. Véase **circuncisión**.

inexperto. (heb. *pety*) En la literatura sapiencial, referencia al joven simple e ingenuo, ignorante de la **ley** e incapaz de discernir por sí mismo entre el bien y el mal.

insolente. Véase **blasfemo**.

instrucción. Véase **ley (del S**eñor**)** y **disciplina**.

inteligencia. Véase **sabiduría**.

intercesor. Véase **Consolador**.

Jacobo. En la evolución de la lengua española, el nombre «San Jacobo» llegó a pronunciarse «Santiago». Tradicionalmente, se ha usado «Santiago» en la carta que se conoce por ese nombre, pero se ha mantenido «Jacobo» en los demás pasajes. En esta versión se sigue la misma costumbre.

jactancia/jactarse. Uno de los términos más característicos de las cartas de Pablo es el verbo griego *kaujáomai* (sustantivo *kaújēma*), que puede usarse tanto en sentido positivo como negativo. En castellano, el vocablo «jactarse» siempre tiene una acepción peyorativa («alabarse presuntuosamente»), de manera que se han usado varios términos para traducir el griego según el contexto (p.ej. «presumir», «orgullo/enorgullecerse», «satisfacción/estar satisfecho», «regocijarse»).

Jerusalén. Ciudad importante de Palestina. Conocida como Ciudad de David, fue la capital del reino davídico y, más tarde, del reino de Judá. Reconstruida después del exilio babilónico, era para los judíos la ciudad escogida por Dios para habitar entre su pueblo. Fue destruida nuevamente en el año 70 d.C.

Jesucristo. Véase **Cristo**.

jómer. Medida de capacidad equivalente aproximadamente a 220 litros. Véase **Tabla de pesas, medidas y monedas**.

juicio. (heb. *mishpat*) Véase **ley (del S**eñor**)**.

justicia. (heb. *tsedeq, tsedeqah*) Véase **salvación**.

justificar/justificación. El sustantivo generalmente traduce la palabra griega *dikaiosúnē*, que también significa «justicia». El verbo lo usa especialmente Pablo para designar la acción de Dios de «declarar justos» a los que ponen su fe en Jesucristo.

lenguas. En el libro de los Hechos y en 1 Corintios, la expresión «hablar en lenguas» es traducción literal del griego; otra posible traducción es «hablar en otros idiomas».

lepra. Varios tipos de enfermedades de la piel se agrupaban bajo esta categoría en la antigüedad. No se trata necesariamente de la aflicción que la medicina moderna llama «lepra».

lepton. Moneda judía de muy poco valor. Véase **Tabla de pesas, medidas y monedas**.

létec. Medida de capacidad equivalente aproximadamente a 110 litros. Véase **Tabla de pesas, medidas y monedas**.

levantar de entre los muertos. Esta expresión se ha traducido literalmente en algunos casos, según el contexto, pero por lo general se ha usado sencillamente el verbo «resucitar» o el sustantivo «resurrección».

Leviatán. Nombre del monstruo marino vencido por Dios al principio de la creación (Sal 74:14; Is 27:1), y que por lo general aparece como sinónimo de «mar». En Job este nombre alude a algún animal acuático de enormes proporciones, probablemente el hipopótamo.

ley (del Señor**/de Moisés)**. (heb. *torah*) Término que significa «enseñanza» o «instrucción», más que un código legislativo. Bajo este término genérico se incluían «mandamientos», «mandatos», «decretos», «sentencias», «preceptos», «ordenanzas» y «juicios», que debían ser enseñados de padres a hijos (Dt 6:1-9).

limpio. Véase **puro**.

log. Medida de capacidad equivalente aproximadamente a 0,3 litros. Véase **Tabla de pesas, medidas y monedas**.

maestro de la ley. Esta frase representa un vocablo griego (*grammateús*) que tradicionalmente se ha traducido «escriba». Entre el pueblo judío, los escribas estaban encargados no solamente de copiar y preservar los libros del Antiguo Testamento, sino principalmente de interpretar y enseñar su contenido. La expresión **experto en la ley** corresponde a otro vocablo griego (*nomikós*) pero se refiere a la misma profesión.

majalat (leannot). Término hebreo que aparece en el título de algunos salmos (53, 88), y que posiblemente se refiera a la manera triste y melancólica en que estos salmos debían cantarse.

Mar Rojo. Es traducción del nombre hebreo *yam suf*, que literalmente significa «mar de las cañas». En el Antiguo Testamento este nombre se usa principalmente para designar los golfos de Suez y Acaba, y también la región de los «lagos Amargos» al norte de Suez.

masquil. Término hebreo que aparece en el título de varios salmos (32, 42, 44, 45, 47:7, 52, 53, 54, 55, 74, 78, 88, 89, 142), y que parece referirse al carácter didáctico del salmo, o bien a su alta calidad literaria (Sal 45, p.ej.).

mente. Véase **corazón**.

Mesías. Véase **Cristo**.

metreta. Medida de capacidad equivalente aproximadamente a 39 litros. Véase **Tabla de pesas, medidas y monedas**.

mictam. Término hebreo que aparece en el título de algunos salmos (16, 56, 57, 58, 59, 60), y que posiblemente aluda a su carácter enigmático o esotérico.

milla. Medida de longitud equivalente aproximadamente a 1.500 metros. Véase **Tabla de pesas, medidas y monedas.**

mina. Medida de peso equivalente aproximadamente a 0,6 kilogramos. En el Nuevo Testamento se refiere a una moneda valiosa. Véase **Tabla de pesas, medidas y monedas.**

misterio. Este término (griego *mustērion*) lo usa Pablo con referencia a los planes eternos de Dios para las naciones, planes que sólo fueron revelados con la venida de Cristo (p.ej. Ro 16:25-26; Ef 3:2-6). Se ha traducido literalmente cuando el contexto evita que haya confusión. Como el vocablo en español puede implicar un sentido esotérico, en varios pasajes se ha empleado la palabra «secreto».

mortal. Véase **hombre.**

muerte. Véase **abadón.**

mundo. Véase **carne.**

naciones. Véase **gentiles.**

naturaleza humana/pecaminosa. Véase **carne.**

necedad. En la literatura sapiencial, actitud contraria a la **sabiduría,** característica de los jóvenes **inexpertos.** La necedad llega a ser personificada, y su discurso es del todo contrario al de la **sabiduría** (Pr 9:1-12; 13-18).

necio. Se dice de todo el que se resiste a cumplir los mandamientos de Dios y a seguir los sabios consejos de sus padres y maestros. Por extensión, el necio es también **insolente** y **blasfemo.**

nisán. Véase *aviv.*

nombre. En el lenguaje bíblico, el nombre está íntimamente ligado al ser mismo de la persona. El nombre *es* la persona. Sin nombre nada puede existir (Gn 2:18-23; Ec 6:10). La conducta de la persona está condicionada por su nombre (1S 25:25) Un cambio de nombre implica un cambio total de la persona, que deja de ser la misma (Gn 32:28; Mt 16:18). Hablar en nombre de alguien es actuar con la misma personalidad y autoridad de la persona nombrada. Conocer el nombre de alguien equivale a tener poder sobre esa persona.

nuevas/noticias, buenas. Véase **evangelio.**

obispo. Traducción tradicional del término griego *epískopos,* que significa «supervisor, superintendente». Parece ser equivalente a **anciano** (véase Hch 20:17,28; nótese también 1P 2:25). Más tarde comenzó a usarse el término para designar a los que supervisaban varias congregaciones en un mismo distrito.

ofensa/ofender. Véase **tropiezo.**

orgullo. Véase **jactancia.**

pacto. Promesa o acuerdo contraído entre dos partes, generalmente una superior y otra inferior, mediante una fórmula verbal o ritual, que compromete a ambas partes. En el lenguaje bíblico el pacto representa la promesa de Dios al hombre de siempre darle **vida** y **paz** y constante cuidado, y el compromiso del hombre de vivir conforme a las estipulaciones del pacto. Otros términos vinculados con el pacto son **ley** y testimonio.

paganos. (heb. *goyyim*) Término hebreo que aparece en el Antiguo Testamento para referirse a los pueblos que no conocen al Dios de Israel ni pertenecen a este pueblo. Por extensión, el mismo término designa a los pueblos y naciones en general. Para el uso de este término en el Nuevo Testamento, véase **gentiles.**

palabra. En el pensamiento bíblico, este término es más que el sonido emitido oralmente. Una vez pronunciada la palabra, tiene poder y autonomía propios, y actúa por sí misma (Gn 1; Jn 1). La palabra dicha no puede ser revocada (Gn 27:30-38; Is 55:10-11). En toda la Biblia, y especialmente en los Salmos, **palabra** aparece como sinónimo de **ley.**

palmo. Medida de longitud equivalente aproximadamente a 24 centímetros. Véase **Tabla de pesas, medidas y monedas.**

pan de la Presencia. Literalmente, «pan del rostro» (heb. *lejem happanim*), tradicionalmente traducido «pan de la proposición». Se trata del pan que cada sábado se colocaba ante la presencia de Dios, sobre una mesa en la **Tienda de reunión** (luego en el templo).

parábola. Narración con fines didácticos, que comunica su enseñanza de manera indirecta. Aunque se caracteriza por su brevedad, puede ser también un tanto extensa. En sus enseñanzas Jesús la usó con singular maestría y pertinencia.

pasiones. Véase **carne.**

pastor. Además de su sentido primario, en la literatura bíblica este término destaca la relación simbólica entre Dios y su pueblo (Sal 23), entre el rey y sus súbditos (Sal 78:70-72), entre los líderes eclesiales y la comunidad creyente (Heb 13:7), y entre Jesús y la iglesia (Jn 10:1-16).

paz. (heb. *shalom*) En el lenguaje bíblico este término no apunta hacia el estado ideal de tranquilidad y plenitud física y síquica, tanto a nivel individual como comunitario. La paz proviene de Dios y es la presencia misma de Dios entre su pueblo (Nm 6:24-26); es resultado de la **justicia** (Is 32:17) y del cumplimiento del **pacto,** y del establecimiento del reinado de Dios (Is 2:1-4; Mi 4:1-5).

pecadores. La Biblia enseña claramente que todos los seres humanos son culpables de pecado (p.ej. Ro 3:10-20). Sin embargo, en el habla de los judíos el término «pecador» se usaba también en un sentido especializado para designar a los que estaban fuera del pacto divino. Se aplicaba especialmente a los **gentiles** (p.ej. Gá 2:15), pero también a judíos cuya conducta inmoral los alejaba espiritualmente del pueblo de Dios (p.ej. Mt 11:19; Lc 15:1-2).

pecar, hacer pecar. Véase **tropiezo.**

peregrinos, cántico de los. (heb. *shir hama'aloth*) En los Salmos, título que designa a los salmos probablemente vinculados con las peregrinaciones que se hacían al templo de Jerusalén. Su etimología permite traducirlos como «cánticos de las subidas» o «cánticos graduales».

perfecto/perfección/perfeccionar. Aunque en esta vida nadie llega a estar totalmente libre de pecado, el adjetivo «perfecto» (griego *téleios*) se usa en varios pasajes con referencia a los creyentes. Es posible que se trate del concepto de madurez espiritual (véanse 1Co 2:6-7; Heb 6:1), pero el sentido es más profundo: implica un compromiso definitivo que se refleja en la conducta. En la carta a los Hebreos, el énfasis está en la idea del cumplimiento de las promesas (nótese que el verbo se aplica también a la exaltación de Jesús en 2:10; 5:9; 7:28). La ley del pacto antiguo no podía perfeccionar (7:19; 9:9; 10:1), pero los que creen en Jesús pertenecen al nuevo y perfecto pacto, de manera que ya han recibido lo que el Antiguo Testamento había prometido (10:14; 11:40).

perro. Por ser un animal común al que se consideraba ritualmente impuro (véase **puro**), el perro llegó a ser un símbolo de los que están fuera del pueblo de Dios (Ap 22:15). Se usa con referencia a los **gentiles** (Mt 15:26-27 = Mr 7:27-28) y a los adversarios del evangelio (Mt 7:6; Fil 3:2; 2P 2:22), no como insulto vulgar, sino como un comentario de índole teológica.

piedra sagrada. La palabra hebrea *matsebah* puede referirse a una columna de piedras cuyo propósito era la conmemoración de algún suceso; en ese caso se ha traducido «estela». Como en la religión cananea tales columnas se identificaron con las deidades, el Antiguo Testamento generalmente las condena.

pim. Medida de peso equivalente aproximadamente a 8 gramos. Véase **Tabla de pesas, medidas y monedas.**

portón/portones. Véase **puerta(s).**

primicias. Los primeros y más importantes frutos de la cosecha, los cuales debían ofrecerse a Dios. En el Nuevo Testamento el término se usa en varios sentidos figurados; por ejemplo, Cristo fue el primero en ser resucitado y es quien hace posible la resurrección de los demás (1Co 15:20); el Espíritu Santo es el primer fruto que reciben los creyentes, y les garantiza que recibirán toda la herencia espiritual (Ro 8:23). Nótese también el uso de «primogénito» en Col 1:15,18.

principios. Así se traduce la palabra griega *stoijeía*, que puede referirse a conceptos básicos (Heb 5:12, «verdades más elementales»), pero también a los elementos fundamentales del universo (2P 3:10). Algunos eruditos piensan que Gá 4:3,9 y Col 2:8,20 hablan de seres espirituales.

Priscila. Así se ha representado el nombre «Prisca» (en Ro 16:3; 1Co 16:19; 2Ti 4:19), del cual «Priscila» es la forma diminutiva (Hch 18:2,18,26).

propiciación. Véase **expiación.**

propiciatorio. Plancha de oro que cubría el arco del pacto y sobre la cual se rociaba la sangre una vez al año para **expiar** el pecado del pueblo (Lv 16).

proverbio. Sentencia o dicho breve e ingenioso en torno a algún hecho que encierra una enseñanza, o condensa la sabiduría popular. Aunque de origen muy antiguo, el proverbio siempre estuvo presente en la literatura sapiencial y hasta los días del Nuevo Testamento. Característico de la literatura bíblica es el proverbio antitético, en el que la segunda parte contrasta o contradice lo dicho en la primera.

prueba, poner a. Véase **tentar.**

pueblo de Dios. Véase **santos.**

puerta(s). (heb. *sha'ar*) Las antiguas ciudades eran amuralladas, y tenían puertas que se abrían al amanecer y se cerraban al caer la noche. Las puertas de la ciudad eran el centro cívico de aquellas ciudades. Allí se difundían las últimas noticias (2S 18:4), se realizaban negocios de compraventa (Rt 4:1-12), y se impartía justicia (Is 29:21; Am 5:12).

puro/impuro/purificar. En muchos pasajes (marcados con asterisco) estos términos no tienen que ver con la limpieza física o moral, sino con cuestiones de contaminación ritual, según las leyes del Antiguo Testamento.

querubines. Seres celestiales con función protectora (Gn 3:24). Dos figuras de querubines como criaturas aladas y con pies y manos cubrían el **propiciatorio.** También se usaron figuras de querubines en la decoración del templo.

quisleu. Noveno mes en el calendario hebreo (mediados de noviembre a mediados de diciembre).

Rahab. Nombre del monstruo vencido por Dios al principio de la creación. Su nombre tal vez aluda a su arrogancia. En los salmos (87:4) y en Isaías (30:9) este nombre aparece como sinónimo de Egipto.

recaudador de impuestos. Así se representa la palabra *telonēs*, que en otras versiones se ha traducido como «publicano». Se refiere a judíos que se ofrecían a cobrar los impuestos exigidos por el Imperio Romano. Como los recaudadores abusaban de sus compatriotas y colaboraban con los soldados romanos, se les consideraba traidores que no pertenecían al pueblo de Dios.

resucitar/resurrección. Véase **levantar de entre los muertos.**

retama. Arbusto típico del sur de Palestina y del desierto de Sinaí, de escasa altura pero lo bastante grande para proporcionar sombra (1R 19:4-5). Sus ramas suelen también usarse como escobas (Is 14:23) y como combustible (Job 30:4; Sal 120:4; Is 47:14).

roca. Además de su sentido primario, en el contexto desértico de Palestina este término designa de manera simbólica a Dios como fuente de protección y abrigo para su pueblo.

sábado. Día séptimo de la semana en el que, según la ley del Antiguo Testamento, los judíos debían reposar de sus trabajos. El mismo término se usa para referirse a otros días festivos.

sabiduría. Cualidad de la persona dispuesta a recibir consejo para poder discernir entre el bien y el mal, aprender a vivir, y conducirse de acuerdo con la voluntad de Dios. En la literatura sapiencial la sabiduría llega a ser personificada (Pr 8) y considerada colaboradora de Dios en su creación.

Salén. Forma abreviada de «Jerusalén» (véase Sal 76:2), ciudad conocida también como «la ciudad de David».

salvación. (heb. *yeshu'ah*) Acción de Dios en favor del hombre, que redunda en la victoria o triunfo de éste, incluyendo el poner a salvo su vida. En algunos contextos «salvación» aparece como sinónimo de «justicia». En el Nuevo Testamento la salvación divina está íntimamente relacionada con el perdón de los pecados.

sanar. En varios pasajes en los evangelios (Mt 9:21-22; Mr 5:23,28,34; 6:56; 10:52; Lc 8:36,48,50; 17:19; 18:42) este verbo es traducción de un término griego que también significa «salvar».

Santiago. Véase **Jacobo.**

santificar. Este concepto en el Antiguo Testamento indica la acción de separar algo o a alguien para un propósito sagrado. El verbo griego (*hagiádsō*) puede por lo tanto traducirse «consagrar», pero además indica una obra divina de limpieza espiritual en los creyentes. Véase también **santo.**

santo/santidad. Es principalmente un atributo de Dios, y por consiguiente de lo que está relacionado a él, por ejemplo, los profetas, los ángeles, el templo (Lc 1:70; 9:26; Hch 6:13). El Nuevo Testamento usa el término «los santos» para designar a los que forman parte de la iglesia de Cristo. Implica que los creyentes han sido santificados (véase **santificar**) y que Dios los ha constituido como su propio pueblo. En algunos pasajes donde el término castellano puede ser ambiguo, se han usado otros vocablos, por ejemplo, «creyentes» o «pueblo de Dios».

santuario. Véase **templo.**

santuarios paganos. Véase **altares paganos.**

Satanás. Nombre del príncipe del mal; la palabra hebrea *satán* significa «acusador» o «adversario».

satisfacción. Véase **jactancia.**

sátrapa. Título de quienes gobernaban las provincias (satrapías) bajo el imperio de los persas.

seah. Medida de capacidad equivalente aproximadamente a 7,3 litros. Véase **Tabla de pesas, medidas y monedas**.

sebat. Undécimo mes en el calendario hebreo (mediados de enero a mediados de febrero).

secreto. Véase **misterio**.

Selah. En los Salmos, anotación musical cuyo posible significado sea el de *pausa*. Tal sentido no ha sido aún determinado.

sencillo. Véase **inexperto**.

sentarse. Cuando los evangelios se refieren a personas sentadas a la mesa (p.ej. Mt 26:7,20; Mr 2:15; Lc 14:8), se usan varios verbos griegos que literalmente significan «recostarse», pues era costumbre en los banquetes reclinarse en divanes. También se puede traducir como «estar a la mesa» (p.ej. Lc 24:30; Jn 12:3) o aun «comer» (Mt 9:10; Mr 16:14; Lc 5:29; 1Co 8:10).

Seol. Véase **sepulcro**.

sepulcro. (heb. *she'ol*) En el pensamiento hebreo, lugar a donde iban los muertos luego de ser enterrados. Este lugar se hallaba bajo la tierra, pero sobre las aguas de abajo. Otros términos sinónimos son **abismo**, «fosa» y «tumba».

ser humano. Véase **hombre**.

siclo. Medida de peso equivalente aproximadamente a 11,5 gramos. Véase **Tabla de pesas, medidas y monedas**.

siervo. Representa en muchos pasajes el vocablo griego *doúlos*, que también puede traducirse «esclavo». Este último término en español puede tener connotaciones que confundan al lector moderno. El vocablo griego no implica necesariamente que la persona fuera maltratada, ya que en la antigüedad algunos esclavos llegaban a asumir posiciones muy importantes. La idea principal es que la persona estaba bajo el dominio de otra, de manera que se caracterizaba por su humildad y obediencia.

sigaión. Término hebreo que aparece en el título del Salmo 7. Su posible significado de «conmoción» tal vez aluda al estado de ánimo con que debía cantarse ese salmo.

Silvano. En las cartas (2Co 1:19; 1Ts 1:1; 2Ts 1:1; 1P 5:12) se usa este nombre con referencia a «Silas» (véase Hch 15:22).

Sión. Nombre de la colina fortificada de la antigua Jebús, hoy Jerusalén. Durante el reinado de David este nombre se extendió para referirse al área general del templo. Sión es considerada la morada de Dios, y en los libros poéticos aparece como sinónimo de Jerusalén.

síquico. Representa el adjetivo griego *psujikós* (sustantivo *psujē*; véase **vida**), que se ha traducido «natural» en 1Co 15:45-46 y «puramente humana» en Stg 3:15. Como contrasta con lo que es espiritual, se ha usado la frase «no tiene el Espíritu» en 1Co 2:14 y Jud 19.

Siria/sirios. Región al norte de Palestina, habitada por los arameos. En el Antiguo Testamento es traducción del nombre *Aram*.

siván. Tercer mes en el calendario hebreo (mediados de mayo a mediados de junio).

Tabernáculos, fiesta de los. Véase **Enramadas**.

talento. En el Antiguo Testamento, medida de peso equivalente aproximadamente a 34 kilogramos. En el Nuevo Testamento se usaba para cálculos monetarios; generalmente de oro, su valor (que era muy alto) variaba mucho, según el lugar y la época (Mt 18:24; 25:15-28). Véase **Tabla de pesas, medidas y monedas**.

tébet. Décimo mes en el calendario hebreo (mediados de diciembre a mediados de enero).

templo. En el Nuevo Testamento este término puede referirse justamente al «santuario» (Lc 1:9), es decir, el edificio donde se encontraban el Lugar Santo y el Lugar Santísimo, o bien al área total que incluía no sólo ese edificio sino también la plaza que lo rodeaba (el atrio de las mujeres y el atrio de los gentiles).

tentar/tentación. El verbo griego (*peirádsō*, sustantivo *peirasmós*) puede usarse en el sentido más o menos neutral de «poner a prueba», pero también en el sentido negativo de «incitar al pecado, tender una trampa». En Stg 1:2,12-14 parece haber un juego de palabras basado en este doble sentido.

Tienda de reunión. Tradicionalmente traducido «tabernáculo de reunión» (heb. *'ohel mo'ed*), esta frase se refiere a un conjunto de cortinas que, colocadas alrededor de bastidores, sirvieron como morada de Dios antes de la construcción del templo.

Todopoderoso. Cuando aparece junto con «SEÑOR», este título representa la palabra *tseba>ot*; es una frase tradicionalmente traducida como «Jehová de los ejércitos». En otros casos, **Todopoderoso** representa la palabra *shadday*, nombre con el que Dios se reveló a los patriarcas (Gn 17:1; Éx 6:3) y que se usa con frecuencia especialmente en el libro de Job.

trampa. Véanse **tentar** y **tropiezo**.

triunfo. Véase **salvación**.

tropezar/tropiezo. Es generalmente traducción del vocablo griego *skándalon* (verbo *skandalídsō*) y se refiere especialmente a lo que causa ofensa, oposición (Gá 5:11), o aun la caída moral de alguien (Mt 5:29-30; 1Co 8:13). En el uso corriente del castellano, el término *escándalo* (*escandalizar*) no corresponde justamente a este significado. En Ro 11:9 se ha traducido como «trampa». También se ha traducido el verbo con términos tales como «ofender», «hacer pecar», «hacer caer», «apartarse», «abandonar». En Jn 16:1 se ha empleado la frase «flaquear la fe».

ungido. (heb. *mashiaj*). Término hebreo para referirse al rey escogido por Dios. Después del exilio babilónico este mismo término se usó para referirse al sumo sacerdote. Véase también **Cristo**.

Unigénito. Traducción tradicional del término griego *monogenēs* («único») cuando se refiere a Jesucristo. Véanse Jn 1:14,18; 3:16,18.

urim y *tumim*. Objetos sagrados que se ponían sobre el pectoral del sumo sacerdote (Éx 28:20) y que se usaban para determinar la voluntad de Dios en algunas situaciones (1Sa 28:6; cf. 23:9-12).

Verbo. Traducción tradicional del término griego *lógos* («palabra») cuando se refiere a Jesucristo. Véanse Jn 1:1,14; 1Jn 1:1; Ap 19:13.

victoria. Véase **salvación**.

vida. Cuando esta palabra lleva asterisco, es traducción en el Antiguo Testamento de la palabra hebrea *nefesh*, y en el Nuevo, de la palabra griega *psujē*. Ambos términos tienen un amplio significado y tradicionalmente se han traducido «alma». En esta versión, la palabra hebrea también se ha traducido «aliento» y «fuerza(s)»; en algunos contextos (Sal 69:1; 105:18; Jon 2:6) se ha usado el vocablo «cuello».

zif. Segundo mes en el calendario hebreo (mediados de abril a mediados de mayo).

PLAN DE SALVACIÓN

LA BIBLIA DICE...

Que Dios te ama

«Porque tanto amó Dios al mundo, que dio a su Hijo unigénito, para que todo el que cree en él no se pierda, sino que tenga vida eterna. Dios no envió a su Hijo al mundo para condenar al mundo, sino para salvarlo por medio de él» (Juan 3.16, 17).

«Pero Dios, que es rico en misericordia, por su gran amor por nosotros, nos dio vida con Cristo, aun cuando estábamos muertos en pecados. ¡Por gracia ustedes han sido salvados!» (Efesios 2.4, 5).

«Pero Dios demuestra su amor por nosotros en esto: en que cuando todavía éramos pecadores, Cristo murió por nosotros» (Romanos 5.8).

Que el pecado te separa de Dios

El hombre está separado de Dios por su pecado. *«Pues todos han pecado y están privados de la gloria de Dios»* (Romanos 3.23).

«Así está escrito: "No hay un solo justo, ni siquiera uno"» (Romanos 3.10).

El hombre se encuentra «sin esperanza y sin Dios en el mundo» (Efesios 2.12).

«Porque la paga del pecado es muerte [separación de Dios por toda una eternidad]» (Romanos 6.23).

Muchos creen que después de esta vida todo termina, pero la Biblia nos avisa que «está establecido que los seres humanos mueran una sola vez, y después venga el juicio» (Hebreos 9.27).

Que Jesucristo murió y resucitó por ti

«Que Cristo murió por nuestros pecados según las Escrituras, que fue sepultado, que resucitó al tercer día según las Escrituras» (1 Corintios 15.3, 4).

«El mensaje de la cruz [el evangelio de Jesucristo] es una locura para los que se pierden; en cambio, para los que se salvan, es decir, para nosotros, este mensaje es el poder de Dios» (1 Corintios 1.18).

«El Hijo de Dios fue enviado precisamente para destruir las obras del diablo» (1 Juan 3.8).

«El que cree en él [Jesucristo] no es condenado, pero el que no cree ya está condenado por no haber creído en el nombre del Hijo unigénito de Dios» (Juan 3.18).

«*Las Sagradas Escrituras, que pueden darte la sabiduría necesaria para la salvación mediante la fe en Cristo Jesús*» (2 Timoteo 3.15).

La Biblia enseña que solo hay un camino que conduce a Dios. Jesús dijo: «*Yo soy el camino, la verdad y la vida [...] Nadie llega al Padre sino por mí*» (Juan 14.6).

«*Porque hay un solo Dios y un solo mediador entre Dios y los hombres, Jesucristo hombre*» (1 Timoteo 2.5).

La Biblia nos promete «*que si confiesas con tu boca que Jesús es el Señor, y crees en tu corazón que Dios lo levantó de entre los muertos, serás salvo. Porque con el corazón se cree para ser justificado, pero con la boca se confiesa para ser salvo*» (Romanos 10.9, 10).

Que recibas a Cristo como Señor y Salvador

Él está esperando que tomes la decisión más importante de tu vida. Jesucristo te invita diciendo: «*Yo soy la puerta; el que entre por esta puerta, que soy yo, será salvo*» (Juan 10.9).

Abre ahora mismo tu corazón y confiésale tus pecados. La Palabra de Dios nos dice que «*quien encubre su pecado jamás prospera; quien lo confiesa y lo*

deja, halla perdón» (Proverbios 28.13).

Jesús te invita a que recibas la nueva vida que solo él te puede ofrecer. «*Por lo tanto, si alguno está en Cristo, es una nueva creación. ¡Lo viejo ha pasado, ha llegado ya lo nuevo!*» (2 Corintios 5.17).

CRÉELO EN TU CORAZÓN Y CONFIÉSALO CON TU BOCA EN UNA ORACIÓN COMO ESTA:

Señor Jesús, creo que eres el Hijo de Dios que murió por mis pecados y resucitó. Me arrepiento de mis pecados y te pido que me perdones. Envía ahora tu Espíritu Santo a mi corazón para darme el poder de rechazar lo malo y caminar en tu voluntad. Gracias por tu amor, tu salvación y la nueva vida que me das en este día. Amén.

«El que cree [en Jesucristo] tiene vida eterna»
(Juan 6.47).